Making the MAJOR Decision

2004

Australia • Canada • Mexico • Singapore • Spain • United Kingdom • United States

About The Thomson Corporation and Peterson's

The Thomson Corporation, with 2002 revenues of US$7.8 billion, is a global leader in providing integrated information solutions to business and professional customers. The Corporation's common shares are listed on the Toronto and New York stock exchanges (TSX: TOC; NYSE: TOC). Its learning businesses and brands serve the needs of individuals, learning institutions, corporations, and government agencies with products and services for both traditional and distributed learning. Peterson's (www.petersons.com) is a leading provider of education information and advice, with books and online resources focusing on education search, test preparation, and financial aid. Its Web site offers searchable databases and interactive tools for contacting educational institutions, online practice tests and instruction, and planning tools for securing financial aid. Peterson's serves 110 million education consumers annually.

For more information, contact Peterson's, 2000 Lenox Drive, Lawrenceville, NJ 08648; 800-338-3282; or find us on the World Wide Web at www.petersons.com/about.

ISBN 0-7689-1250-4

Printed in the United States of America

10 9 8 7 6 5 4 3 2 1 05 04 03

First Edition

Contents

Making the Major Decision—The Effect on Your Future 1

Who Are You? The Questions and Answers to Set You on Your Way 4

It's the 21st Century—Do You Know the Hottest Job Trends? 9

Liberal Arts Degree or Occupation-Specific Degree—What's Right for You? 12

How to Use This Guide 15

The Undergraduate Majors Listings .. 21

The Undergraduate Majors Profiles .. 259

Making the Major Decision—The Effect on Your Future

CHOOSING A MAJOR: NOW VS. LATER

Why is choosing a major often the most gut-wrenching decision that college students have to face? Most students assume that by choosing a major they are committing themselves to a specific academic program that will lead to only one type of career. If your major is computer science, then you had better look forward to a career as a computer programmer. If the sight of blood makes you wince, you better not major in premedicine. If your major is accounting, then you had better feel comfortable calling yourself an accountant.

Nothing could be further from the truth. While some majors are required for certain careers, a major doesn't necessarily have to determine what career path you follow. The University of Virginia recently conducted a survey of 3,000 arts and sciences graduates. Seventy percent of respondents reported little connection between their college majors and their present careers. So, majoring in computer science is great if you want to become a computer programmer, but you could also get a job as a geneticist or an aerospace engineer. Premedicine is the natural major for doctors, but it's also a great major if you want to work in the pharmaceutical industry as either a research scientist or a sales representative. You see, rather than limiting your choices, choosing a major that is right for you increases your knowledge of yourself and the world and the many opportunities that are available to you!

Statistics show that students change their majors two to three times before graduation. At most colleges and universities, changing majors is no big deal—you just fill out some paperwork, meet with your new adviser, and you're all set to go. Some universities won't even let you declare a major until your sophomore year. But changing majors gets more complicated and difficult in your junior and senior years, especially if you haven't already taken the required introductory courses for that major. Incoming freshmen can avoid this problem by first identifying a few majors that they are interested in and taking the required courses. Then they can change majors at the end of their freshman or sophomore year if they are unhappy with their first choice.

Take Amy Larson, for example. Amy's favorite class in high school was English. She loved reading and could spend hours analyzing literature with her teachers, so she figured English literature would be the ideal major for her in college. By her sophomore year, she had completed all the introductory English courses and was thinking about a career as a high school English teacher. She started taking classes in education. That same year, she found a part-time job at the university-sponsored farm, and sometimes assisted a local veterinarian who treated farm animals in the area. The work gave her some extra spending money, but she also enjoyed tending to the farm animals. After graduation, Amy landed a job teaching English at a public high school. The salary was better than she expected, and everything seemed to be going according to her original plan. Except that Amy missed working with the veterinarian and still wanted to do something related to farm animals. Because she was now working full-time, she couldn't moonlight for the veterinarian anymore. A friend suggested she apply to veterinary school. But when she looked into the prerequisites, Amy discovered that she needed to take biology, chemistry, physics, and a number of other courses she hadn't even thought about while in college. It would take four more semesters to complete the credits before she could even apply to veterinary school. If only Amy had known in her junior year that she might want to work in the veterinary field, she could have taken the required courses to get her there.

With some colleges costing as much as $25,000 or more a year, few students can afford taking additional time to graduate. Choosing your major wisely, and leaving your options open to change majors at some point, will save you a considerable amount of time and money.

SO MANY MAJORS, SO LITTLE TIME!

So, how do you find a major that is right for you? Some students look at how a major translates into earning power immediately after college. Others don't think about jobs or salaries at all and pick a major that they find personally interesting. Some students decide on a major that will help them become better communicators, while others know exactly what they want to do after college and choose a major that teaches them a specific set of skills. Some students pick a major because the course load is easy, or they think demand for that major will be high by the time they graduate. Other students remain undecided for the first two years of college then pick a major after they've taken some courses in a particular area. Choosing a major is an important decision. It shouldn't be a decision that you make in an hour—or even a day. The more time you spend thinking about your interests, skills, and career goals, the greater your chance is of selecting a major that is right for you.

One great way to find your ideal major is to think about what you'd like to be doing after you graduate. Some types of careers require that you take a certain major. If you want to be a nurse, your best bet is to major in nursing. But if you want to be a lawyer, you might major in history, economics, English, political science, or even environmental sciences. Here's what one lawyer said when asked how his major helped his law career: "Taking wildlife surveys, measuring snowmelt in the Rockies, and studying forest fire issues in Yellowstone as an undergraduate provided a great foundation for the work I do now as an environmental lawyer. In fact, it provided both background and inspiration for my law practice."

What if you're not sure what you want to do after graduation? First of all, don't worry. Few 18- or 19-year-olds know what they want to do for a career. Once again, the best way to proceed is to think about a range of career options that pique your curiosity, and concentrate on the majors that will best prepare you for those careers. Seek out people whose jobs sound interesting and ask them what their major was. You might get some fascinating answers.

What do you like to do in your spare time? Are you someone who enjoys hiking and spending time outdoors, or would you rather be doing something creative like painting or taking photographs? Do you like to work in groups, or would you rather work alone? Paying attention to your personal interests and characteristics will give you some clues as to what major is right for you.

What subjects have you done well with in the past? What were your favorite classes in high school? Are you the kind of person who enjoys solving problems, or are you more interested in various forms of creative expression? Understanding your skills and talents will help you determine what major may be right for you.

How important is the salary of your first job? Students who need to repay student loans after graduation, or have other financial considerations, will certainly be looking into majors that lead to careers with higher starting salaries, like computer science, accounting/finance, or one of the engineering majors. But a high starting salary probably shouldn't be your only consideration when selecting a major. In the late 1990s, when the stock market was in the stratosphere and dot.com companies were all the rage, computer science majors could look forward to multiple job offers, signing bonuses, and some of the highest salaries for any college graduates. Today, starting salaries for computer science majors have come down a bit (but they are still much higher than average). Richard L. Wright, director of career services at Rutgers University in New Jersey, suggests that students ignore what majors are currently in demand because four years from now, there could be an oversupply of students with the same major. Instead, he advises students to pick a major that they find personally fulfilling because, if they like the subject, they are more likely to do well in it. And remember, academic performance is one way that employers evaluate prospective candidates.

It's also important to keep in mind that salaries change over time, depending on your experience, the industry you are working in, and how successful you are in your job. Social workers who earned $20,000 straight out of school may be earning $75,000 after ten years. Conversely, a salesperson starting out with the same salary may be earning hundreds of thousands of dollars after ten years if he/she is successful. (A note about salaries in this book: These starting salaries can vary tremendously, depending on where in the country you are working).

Still can't decide? You might want to try a double major or creating your own major. Some universities work with students to design their own majors.

YOUR MAJOR DECISION

Choosing a major goes hand in hand with choosing a college or university. Many colleges, universities, and community colleges offer specialized majors that lead to certain careers. It pays to find out which universities have especially strong or renowned academic departments, as often the professors in those departments have good connections within the industry.

When you graduate from college, your major is a big part of your resume but it's not the only thing. There is also your GPA, your interests, and your experiences, such as internships and summer jobs. Employers often value these things as much as your major. As you gain experience in the working world, your major not only becomes less important, it also literally gets smaller on your resume. Some career counselors and corporate recruiters even say that your major doesn't make much of a difference at all.

The key to making the major decision is knowing yourself—your passions, your talents and abilities, your likes and dislikes, and your dreams. Are you interested enough in a particular major to want to devote your college career to it? Your major is important in that it directs your field of study, but beyond your first job, the rest is up to you. Whatever you do, don't despair. Your major is somewhere in this book, waiting to be discovered, and you're sure to find it!

Who Are You? The Questions and Answers to Set You on Your Way

ARE YOU LOOKING for a formula, a tried-and-true method for choosing the right major? Unfortunately, it doesn't exist. But here's some good advice that will set you on your way, from bestselling author Chip Bell: "Effective questions bring insight, which fuels curiosity, which cultivates wisdom."

This section will help you gain insight from the person who is best equipped to answer the major decision question: You. Finding the right major is all about understanding life's possibilities, asking yourself the right questions, and listening for the answers.

Start by opening your eyes and looking at the people around you. Begin with the people you know—your parents, your family, and your friends and acquaintances. What do these people do for a living? What are their jobs? If your friends are students like yourself, what do their parents do for a living?

Once you've exhausted your personal connections, open your eyes a little wider and look at what other people are doing. Make a list of the careers that sound interesting to you—try to identify at least five—and ask yourself why these careers sound interesting, making sure to be as specific as possible. All too often we overlook our own curiosity. The simple act of putting your observations down on paper (or on a computer screen) will help you understand and identify aspects of a particular career that make you want to learn more about it.

For now, ignore the financial rewards of a particular career. You don't want to start your search for the perfect major with a search for the biggest paycheck. There will be plenty of time to think about money and salaries later. Money is an important consideration, but the search for financial reward for its own sake will lead you astray.

THE TWELVE-YEAR EXPERIMENT

By the time you finish high school you will have slogged through twelve years of facts, rules, dates, theories, methods, equations, and a host of other details that you may or may not need later on in life. Besides taking in all this information (and being asked to memorize and regurgitate it in various ways) you've also learned something about yourself. Hopefully. Whether you look back on your school career as the best time of your life or the worst, it's still *your* life. Whatever you do, don't ignore your past experiences.

The formal and informal knowledge you have gained is your own database of personal facts and figures. Start by looking at the obvious: your academic career. Those subjects that you've enjoyed up to this point are a good indication of what you will enjoy in a major. Don't just focus on the classes that you aced, although you certainly don't want to ignore them either. Perhaps you've always found mathematics to be a cakewalk; you regularly completed all your homework assignments while watching reruns of *The Osbournes*. But the class you looked forward to every day was art because you loved using your imagination to create. Chances are, you're more likely to enjoy a major in the field of art than a major in mathematics. Better yet, perhaps you should look into a major that combines the analytical skills used in math and the creative skills used in art. Architecture might be the perfect major.

A big part of figuring out what major is right for you is understanding both your abilities and your interests. In most cases, your abilities are related to your interests—if you have always done well in English, then you probably enjoy reading and writing. But there are always exceptions, so it's important that you also consider your abilities and interests separately and look for where they intersect.

What about your extracurricular activities, like the school newspaper, literary magazine, or various clubs? Were you involved in student government? Did you ever take part in volunteer activities in the community? What about organizing school events or activities? How about athletics, outings, or special events like field trips? Looking back and analyzing your extracurricular activities will give you a better idea of your interests, which will help you choose a major that is right for you.

FOUR QUESTIONS TO CONSIDER

While taking stock of yourself and those in your immediate family and social circles, you'll also want to get a feel for "what's out there" and a surefire way for doing that is by talking to people in the workplace. You'll want to begin by asking four questions.

First Question

Ask people to rank the three most important skills they need to function in their jobs. Every job requires a few crucial skills. Perhaps it's analyzing numbers, creating slogans, solving problems, greeting people, making sales pitches over the phone, fixing machines, building structures, or motivating others to do their jobs. Again, you want to know: What are three skills they use every day?

Second Question

What are the tools needed to do the job? Every job requires tangible tools, like wrenches, hammers, microscopes, and even our hands, but there are also intangible tools—creativity, the ability to prioritize, coping mechanisms for stress, and knowing how to work in a team environment. You will learn a lot about different careers by asking people what tools they use in their work.

Third Question

Where do people work? This is a good question because the physical environment of the job often affects our enjoyment of the work. Is it an office building, a factory or industrial setting, a hospital or health-care facility, a hotel, a laboratory, a classroom, a studio, a gallery or museum, a government agency or department, a retail store, a national park, or a farm? Or do they work out of their home?

Fourth Question

Finally, you should ask people what their major was in college and how they came to their present position. What path did they travel to get from their major to their current job? Even if you have no idea what kind of career you want, it's important to see connections between a major and a career. People with the same career started out with different majors, and people who had the same majors ended up in different careers. What were the steps that led them from their major to their present career? Ask people what route they took.

THE MOST IMPORTANT QUESTION: WHO ARE YOU?

Here are some questions that will help you determine what kind of person you are and what kind of major might be right for you.

Do you find yourself drawn to artistic or creative endeavors, such as art, music, film, or fields that require an artistic sensibility, such as publishing or advertising? If so, you may be interested in these majors:

- Advertising
- English language and literature
- Creative writing
- Publishing
- Journalism
- Public relations
- Computer graphics
- Furniture designer/maker
- Crafts, folk art, and artisanry
- Commercial photography
- Fashion design/illustration
- Drawing
- Ceramics
- Music
- Drama/theater arts

Are you an inquisitive person? Do you think like a scientist or a detective? Do you enjoy the physical sciences, working with numbers, equations, or theories? Do you like doing experiments or dealing with data? Do you enjoy mathematics? Are you intellectual by nature? If so, you may be interested in these majors:

- Chemical, computer, or engineering science
- Systems engineering
- Biology
- Molecular biology
- Neuroscience
- Pathology
- Mathematics
- Chemistry
- Physics
- Aerospace science
- Nuclear physics
- Fluid and thermal sciences
- Pharmacology
- Computer science

Do you see yourself as a natural salesperson, someone who is willing to stand up in front of an audience and dazzle them with your personality and convince them that they need to buy your product? If so, you may be interested in these majors:

- General sales and marketing operations
- Communications
- Advertising
- Public relations
- Speech/rhetorical studies
- Psychology
- American government/politics
- Business administration/management
- Office supervision/management
- Marketing

Do you enjoy interacting with and helping people in various capacities? Do you consider yourself a "people" person? Do you care about how people feel? If so, you might be interested in some of these majors:

- Education
- Cosmetic services
- Mortuary science
- Family/community studies
- Dietetics/human nutritional studies
- Marriage and family counseling
- Child development, care, and guidance
- Athletic training/sports medicine
- Psychology
- Social work
- Law enforcement
- Health services technician
- Physician assistant
- Premedicine or predentistry
- Nursing
- Public health
- Physical therapy

Are you someone who enjoys thinking about and discussing current events and social topics? Are you comfortable exploring different ideas as they relate to people, politics, and culture? If so, you may be interested in these majors:

- City/urban/community planning
- English literature
- Area studies
- Journalism and broadcast journalism
- Education
- Foreign languages/literatures
- Law and legal studies
- Religion and philosophy
- Psychology
- Economics
- History
- International affairs
- Organizational behavior studies

Are you good with your hands and naturally mechanical? Do you enjoy working with tools, gauges, machines, and other technological devices, either repairing, building, or servicing machines? Would you rather be working in a physical context than sitting behind a desk? If so, you may be interested in these majors:

- Farm/ranch management
- Crop production management
- Agricultural animal health
- Plant protection
- Wildlife management
- Natural resources management
- Industrial electronics installer or repairer
- Aviation systems/avionics maintenance technologist
- Maritime science
- Architecture

MORE TO PONDER

Would you rather be spending time helping children, or would you rather spend time helping adults? If you enjoy spending time with children, teaching might be an ideal career. If you would rather help adults, you might want to think about social work.

Do you enjoy working as part of a large team in a competitive environment or are you more self-motivated and work better by yourself? If you would rather work as part of a large team in a competitive environment, business, marketing, or sales might be the right kind of careers to get into. If you'd rather work alone in a noncompetitive environment, you may be interested in a more solitary career, like writing, library science, or design.

Do you consider yourself analytical, or do you consider yourself artistic? If you are more the analytical type, you might want to consider becoming a scientist, engineer, or computer technician. If you are more artistic, you could be a photographer, graphic designer, or advertising executive.

Do you want a career in which you go to work every day knowing what to expect? Or would you rather have a career in which every day brings something new and unexpected? If you prefer consistency in life, you might want to think about accounting. If you're ready and willing to take on whatever is thrown at you, journalism might be the perfect career for you.

Would you rather work with language and effective communication, or would you rather work with numbers, statistics, or measurements? If you would rather work with language and writing, then you might want to be a translator or a diplomat or a public relations executive. If you want to work with numbers, statistics, or measurements, you might want to consider actuarial science.

You've spent the last twelve years learning about the world and racking up experiences and knowledge about yourself. Making the major decision means asking the right questions, collecting the information, and analyzing your own feelings in preparation for the rest of your life. College is simply the next stage of the experiment. It is an opportunity to expand your knowledge and take everything that you've learned up to that point and figure out how to make a life out of it. The major decision is the first step.

It's the 21st Century—Do You Know the Hottest Job Trends?

IN THESE CHALLENGING economic times, when companies have scaled back their hiring practices and it's harder than ever to land that dream job directly out of college, it's important to know the hottest growth industries for the 21st century and where tomorrow's jobs will be found.

Ten years ago, many experts were predicting increases in technology and computer-related jobs. Despite the prolonged downturn of many computer companies, the technology revolution is far from over—in fact, it is only now just beginning in many industries. This trend will continue over the next decade, as businesses across a wide spectrum of industries continue to incorporate new technologies into their operations. According to the Bureau of Labor Statistics, of the ten fastest-growing occupations between now and 2010, the top five will be computer related. Occupations such as *computer engineers* and *computer systems analysts* are expected to account for increasing portions of employment in nearly every industry. Computer-related jobs that didn't exist ten—or even five—years ago are sprouting up with increasing frequency, jobs such as *computer security expert*, *information technology professional*, and *artificial intelligence and multimedia specialist*. In addition, there will be increasing demand for *computer/technical support specialists* and *data warehousing/mining administrators*. Opportunities will be best for workers who have advanced business degrees and technical knowledge, but good communication and administrative skills will also be important factors for employers considering candidates in these fields.

Of course, the flip side of technology- and computer-related jobs is that they will have a negative effect on new job creation in other industries. In mining and agriculture, for example, as overall productivity has risen, the number of jobs has declined over the past decade, and will continue to do so, as automation and technological innovations replace human labor. The need for typists, bookkeepers, tellers, and switchboard operators will decline in many industries as well. Companies that once employed whole staffs of operators and other support personnel are now employing computer systems to handle many routine tasks and business practices.

Another revolution that is beginning to transform the face of American business has to do with demographics and the increasing cost of health-care services. As the baby boomers continue to grow older (the group aged 55 to 64 will increase by 11 million persons by 2010—more than any other group), you can expect to see a dramatic rise in many health-care–related jobs. Doctors and other health-care providers are looking to experienced assistants to perform routine tasks to reduce costs. Indeed, three of the fastest-growing occupations are in the health-care field: *personal-care and home health aide*, *medical assistant,* and *physician's assistant*.

There will be an increased need for *physical and occupational therapists* as well as *medical technologists,* such as *respiratory therapists* and *cardiovascular technologists and technicians.*

> According to the U.S. Department of Labor, the fastest-growing occupations in the United States are:
>
> 1. Computer software engineers, applications
> 2. Computer support specialists
> 3. Computer software engineers, systems software
> 4. Network and computer systems administrators
> 5. Network systems and data communications analysts
> 6. Desktop publishers
> 7. Database administrators
> 8. Personal- and home-care aides
> 9. Computer systems analysts
> 10. Medical assistants

Since many labor experts say that the current crisis in nursing will continue for at least another decade, *registered nurses* will continue to be in demand.

Employment opportunities for *medical and health services managers* in hospitals and resident-care facilities should increase as well. Students who majored in biomedical engineering should see more job opportunities, as the aging population demands new and better medical equipment.

The transformations in technology, demographics, and health care, along with changes in government programs like Medicaid and health management regulations, have had a dramatic effect on new job development. One recently created occupation, *assessment specialist*, entails the testing of the mental and physical functioning of residents in assisted-living facilities. *Utilization review coordinators* and *restorative therapy coordinators* examine patient health-care records to make sure treatment is in line with an organization's standards. Employment opportunities for these careers will expand as medical costs are scrutinized and shared by health-care providers, third-party payers, consumers, regulators, and the courts.

The health care and human service fields are vast, with dozens of possible majors for students who find themselves drawn to these areas. From gerontological services and genetics to speech-language pathology and optometric services, there is no shortage of majors that will lead to lucrative positions, and these opportunities will only increase over time.

The growing importance of biotechnology will ensure that students who majored in one of the biological sciences, along with computer science, will likely secure well-paying jobs. The same applies to students majoring in pharmacology—the prospects for well-paying positions over the next decade will be much better than average.

In the areas of financial management and business operations, *management analysts and consultants* and *financial analysts* should see better-than-average increases in job availability over the next decade. In today's increasingly complex and competitive business environment, many organizations have been forced to alter their business practices, fueling the need for *management analysts and consultants*. Businesses and individuals are looking for better ways to manage financial assets, so experienced *financial analysts* should be in great demand over the next decade. Business management and administration majors with a strong background in mathematics, economics, finance, and investments will be well prepared to enter one of these fields.

Another area of significant growth will be the *customer service* and *public relations* fields, as companies vie to retain customers and improve overall customer relations and services. Students who are creative and have majored in communications, public relations, marketing, or advertising should find a good number of employment opportunities in these fields.

The 24/7 news cycle, coupled with an aggressive media environment, has created demand for *advertising* and *promotions* professionals who can serve as effective liaisons between organizations and the media. Competition for these jobs has always been stiff and will continue to be so, but students who have majored in public relations, marketing, or advertising should find good employment opportunities in these fields.

The environment will be a significant factor in job creation over the next decade. Some experts have predicted a rise in the number of *landscape architects* as interest in preservation of natural areas grows and the adoption of ecological ideals becomes more widespread. The need to address environmental laws and regulations in buildings, homes, and public spaces will spur demand for *environmental engineers*.

With the exception of *computer engineers*, *environmental engineers*, and *biomedical engineers,* many of the other engineering specialties, such as *industrial engineering*, *mechanical engineering,* and *materials engineering* will see only slow to average growth over the next decade, as these specialties depend on growth in the manufacturing industries. According to Roger Moncarz and Azure Rease of *Occupational Outlook Quarterly*, most of the growth in engineering will be in the service industries, especially research and testing. Engineering positions, however, will continue to pay relatively high salaries.

A 2002 Bureau of Labor Statistics survey indicated higher employment possibilities for *actors, producers, directors,* and *writers* over the next decade as the entertainment and media industries continue to expand. Despite the relatively low starting pay of many of these jobs, competition for new positions will continue to be intense. Creative students with good writing and communication skills will be in the best position to land jobs.

The field of education will experience average to better-than-average growth over the next decade. Enrollments in primary and secondary schools are dropping, but demand for new teachers is still strong because of increased teacher retirements. *Special education teachers* will have the greatest demand over the next ten years as more students are diagnosed with learning disabilities. Students who majored in special education and have some previous teaching experience should be able to find their dream job quite easily. Students who majored in speech pathology and therapy will also see lots of opportunities to apply their skills. *Teaching assistants* will also be in great demand over the next ten years.

Remember, for every major there are hundreds of different types of careers, each requiring unique skills and knowledge. Open your mind to all the possibilities, check out some of the hottest trends, both now and predicted for five to ten years down the line, and you are sure to find your perfect fit.

Liberal Arts Degree or Occupation-Specific Degree—What's Right for You?

WHY ARE YOU GOING TO COLLEGE?

That might seem like an obvious question but it's still worth asking. Are you going to college because your parents expect you to, or because everyone else is doing it? Are you going to college to improve your overall education and become a more well-rounded person? Are you going to college so you can be assured of a getting good job when you graduate?

When asked, most students say they are going to college because they want a good job after they graduate. But according to a Department of Education report, many college graduates are finding themselves in low-paying service jobs and other lines of work not traditionally associated with college education. From this perspective, a college degree is no longer a guarantee of a "college-level job" in an organization that provides reasonable pay, good benefits, training opportunities, and the prospect of advancement.

If college is no longer the guarantee that it once was, what role does your major play in determining your job prospects? Your major may determine how easy it is to secure that first job after graduation. For example, you should have no problem finding a well-paying job in computer science, nursing, or accounting. But if you choose to pursue a liberal arts education and major in a subject like history or philosophy or English literature, you might find it more difficult to land that first job. What are the advantages and disadvantages of a liberal arts education versus an occupation-specific degree? How do you decide what is right for you?

CHOOSING A LIBERAL ARTS EDUCATION . . .

The primary purpose of a liberal arts education is to provide you with a better understanding of the world and a broad set of skills that can be employed across a wide spectrum of careers. These skills include

The liberal arts education has traditionally encompassed a range of studies that can be grouped into five categories:

- language studies, logic, and mathematics
- music, graphic arts, and literature
- historical studies
- natural sciences
- religion and philosophy

effective writing and oral communication and the ability to think critically, solve problems, and see cause-and-effect relationships. A liberal arts education will not teach you any occupation-specific skills. Rather, its purpose is to teach you how to learn and think for yourself.

In today's world, human labor is becoming more specialized, making it more difficult for liberal arts majors to compete in today's job market. However, as students gain job experience, the liberal arts education will become more valuable because it prepares them to deal with change. In *Leading Change*, author John Kotter says, "The role of change is not going to slow down anytime soon. Competition in most industries will speed up in the next decade." Change is everywhere these days. Jobs change almost overnight, which means that the skills necessary to perform those jobs also change. Many of today's jobs didn't even exist ten years ago, and new jobs are being created every day. A liberal arts education teaches broad-based skills that are highly transferable, skills that can be used in many different types of jobs, and skills that won't become obsolete over time.

Liberal arts majors have the option of working in almost any field, from advertising to health-care management to politics. Carly Fiorina, CEO of Hewlett-Packard, majored in Medieval history and philosophy. Carol Browner, former director of the Environmental Protection Agency, majored in English. Brian Lamb, CEO of C-SPAN, majored in speech and communication. With such a wide array of choices, it's extremely important to know yourself and what you want from a career. But you shouldn't major in liberal arts because every other major sounds boring. More than anything else, a liberal arts major teaches breadth of knowledge.

Be aware, however, that liberal arts majors often have a more difficult time making the transition from academics to the work world because they do not yet have the specific skills and knowledge to jump right into a career. Liberal arts majors need to take advantage of summer internships, part-time work, and other activities to gain direct work experience to augment their education. Many liberal arts majors go on to graduate school in areas such as medicine, law, business, public policy, and education where they gain the knowledge and vocational skills to enter these professions.

. . . OR CHOOSING A VOCATIONAL OR OCCUPATION-SPECIFIC EDUCATION

Vocational or occupation-specific majors, on the other hand, prepare undergraduate students for specific careers such as nursing, medicine, law, accounting, engineering, or other technical and creative jobs. Many of the jobs available to students graduating with occupation-specific majors are support positions. For example, if you earn a baccalaureate degree in law and legal studies, you should easily be able to find a job as a paralegal. But if you want to become a lawyer, you need to attend graduate law school. The same is true for medicine; a major in one of the health sciences will prepare you for a variety of positions, including nursing, medical laboratory technician, and diagnostic medical sonography. But if your plans are to eventually become a doctor, you will need to go to graduate medical school, which means additional years of schooling.

The great advantage for students who choose an occupation-specific major is that they are then able to put their knowledge to work immediately after graduation, as they have learned the skills and concepts through the actual experience of doing the job. Some colleges and universities with departments specializing in occupation-specific majors and vocational trades often have better connections to potential employers within the industry. Since the focus of these majors is learning specific skills and landing a job, opportunities are more readily available to graduates.

As to salary, don't assume that occupation-specific degrees lead to lower-paying jobs. Some careers, like journalism, advertising, and book publishing, have always paid relatively low starting salaries. But careers in accounting, engineering and engineering technologies, and nursing pay better-than-average salaries.

Keep in mind that one of the disadvantages of occupation-specific majors is that they often don't provide the breadth of knowledge and learning that a liberal arts major provides. Students who choose an occupation-specific major or a vocational trade need to find ways to constantly update their skills and knowledge; otherwise they will find themselves out of a job.

THE CHOICE IS YOURS

As we've said before, your college major is the connection between your interests and potential careers. It is the launching pad for your life after college, so it's important to choose your major wisely. Otherwise you may go off in the wrong direction. The liberal arts major gives you a broad-based education that may not translate as easily into a career but will give you skills and knowledge that are no less important and may be crucial as you progress through your career. Occupation-specific or vocational majors will prepare you for certain types of careers immediately after college, but they may not give you the tools to handle the ever-changing landscape of work.

A liberal arts education and an occupation-specific education each have their advantages and disadvantages, but in and of themselves they may be insufficient to prepare students for careers that require continual learning. Liberal arts students should participate in internships and extracurricular activities related to their major, and they should seek to incorporate career planning in their general studies. Students who major in one of the occupation-specific majors should pay close attention to new developments in their chosen professions and constantly try to seek out ways to keep their skills up to date.

The social philosopher Eric Hoffer once said, "In times of change, learners inherit the Earth, while the learned find themselves beautifully equipped to deal with a world that no longer exists." Whether your major is computer science or cartography, philosophy or film studies, make sure you choose a major that makes you so excited that you'll want to learn about it for the rest of your life.

Occupation-specific majors span almost every category of education including

- agriculture
- marketing and merchandising
- journalism
- public relations and advertising
- engineering
- health sciences

How to Use This Guide

WELCOME TO THE first edition of Peterson's *Making the Major Decision!* Inside, you'll find descriptive information on more than 800 majors offered at nearly 2,000 four-year colleges and universities. You'll be able to hone in on the majors that most interest you by referring to the first section of the book, where the majors are listed alphabetically, and checking out an overview of that major. Following each major is a list of colleges and universities offering that major and a page reference. Turn to that page and learn all about the college's vital statistics and information.

Within this guide you'll also find useful articles on how to make YOUR major decision. "Making the Major Decision—The Effect on Your Future" explains how your chosen major impacts finding your way into the workforce and your future employment opportunities. "Who Are You? The Questions and Answers to Set You on Your Way" details the personal inventory you'll want to take to reveal how your personality matches up with a major. In "It's the 21st Century—Do You Know the Hottest Job Trends?" you'll catch up on the predictions about current and future job trends—will your major be "hot" or not? Finally, "Liberal Arts Degree or Occupation-Specific Degree—What's Right for You?" demystifies the differences between these two degree types.

The majors represented in *Making the Major Decision* are based on the National Center for Education Statistics (NCES) 2000 Classification of Instructional Programs (CIP). The CIP is a taxonomic coding scheme that contains titles and descriptions of instructional programs, primarily at the postsecondary level. CIP was originally developed to facilitate NCES' collection and reporting of postsecondary degree completions, by major field of study, using standard classifications that capture the majority of program activity. The CIP is now the accepted federal government statistical standard for classifying instructional programs. However, although the term "major" is used in this guide, some colleges may use other terms, such as "concentration," "program of study," or "field."

Peterson's publishes a full line of resources to help you and your family with any information you need to guide you through the admission process. Peterson's publications can be found at your local bookstore, library, and high school guidance office. You'll also want to visit us on the Web at www.petersons.com/majordecision to check out the top seventy-five majors viewed by visitors to Petersons.com and get even more major information!

Colleges will be pleased to know that Peterson's helped you in your selection. Admissions staff members are more than happy to answer questions, address specific problems, and help you in any way they can. The editors at Peterson's wish you great success in your college search.

THE UNDERGRADUATE MAJORS LISTINGS

Here, in alphabetical order, you'll find overview descriptions of each major, as well as course requirements; related majors or areas of study recommended for electives, minors, and/or concentrations; and related careers and their salary potential. The schools offering each major are then alphabetically listed, followed by the page of the school's profile description.

THE UNDERGRADUATE MAJORS PROFILES

The college profiles contain basic data in capsule form for quick review and comparison. The following outline of the profile format shows the section heading and the items that each section covers. Any item that does not apply to a particular college or for which no information was supplied is omitted from that college's profile.

Bulleted Highlights

The bulleted highlights feature important information for quick reference. The number of *possible* bulleted highlights that an ideal profile would have if all questions were answered in a timely manner are represented below. However, not every institution provides all of the information necessary to fill out every bulleted line. In such instances, the line will not appear.

Setting

Schools are designated as *urban* (located within a major city), *suburban* (a residential area within commuting distance of a major city), *small-town* (a small but compactly settled area not within commuting distance of a major city), or *rural* (a remote and sparsely populated area).

Institutional Control

Private institutions are designated as *independent* (nonprofit), *proprietary* (profit-making), or *independent, with a specific religious denomination or affiliation*. Nondenominational or interdenominational religious orientation is possible and would be indicated. Public institutions are designated by the source of funding. Designations include federal, state, province, commonwealth (Puerto Rico), territory (U.S. territories), county, district (an educational administrative unit often having boundaries different from units of local government), city, state and local (local may refer to county, district, or city), or state-related (funded primarily by the state but administratively autonomous).

Student Body

An institution is *coed* (coeducational—admits men and women), *primarily* (80 percent or more) *women*, *primarily men*, *women only*, or *men only*.

College Profiles

Web Site

Where you can find the school on the Web.

Contact

The name, title, and telephone number of the person to contact for application information are given. The admission office address is listed. Toll-free telephone numbers may also be included. The admission office fax number and e-mail address, if available, are listed, provided the school wanted them printed for use by prospective students.

Getting in Last Year

Percentages and/or numbers of applicants who applied, were granted admission, and actually enrolled are given here.

Financial Matters

Costs given include tuition and fees, room and board, percent of need met, and the average financial aid amount received per undergraduate.

Academics

First given are the full range of levels of certificates, diplomas, and degrees, including prebaccalaureate, graduate, and professional, that are offered by this institution.

Associate Degree Normally requires at least two but fewer than four years of full-time college work or its equivalent.

Bachelor's Degree (baccalaureate) Requires at least four years but not more than five years of full-time college-level work or its equivalent. This includes all bachelor's degrees in which the normal four years of work are completed in three years and bachelor's degrees conferred in a five-year cooperative (work-study plan) program. A cooperative plan provides for alternate class attendance and employment in business, industry, or government. This allows students to combine actual work experience with their college studies.

Master's Degree Requires the successful completion of a program of study of at least the full-time equivalent of one but not more than two years of work beyond the bachelor's degree.

Doctoral Degree (doctorate) The highest degree in graduate study. The doctoral degree classification includes Doctor of Education, Doctor of Juridical Science, Doctor of Public Health, and the Doctor of Philosophy in any nonprofessional field.

First Professional Degree The first postbaccalaureate degree in one of the following fields: chiropractic (DC, DCM), dentistry (DDS, DMD), medicine (MD), optometry (OD), osteopathic medicine (DO), rabbinical and Talmudic studies (MHL, Rav), pharmacy (BPharm, PharmD), podiatry (PodD, DP, DPM), veterinary medicine (DVM), law (JD), or divinity/ministry (BD, MDiv).

First Professional Certificate (postdegree) Requires completion of an organized program of study after completion of the first professional degree. Examples are refresher courses or additional units of study in a specialty or subspeciality.

Post-master's Certificate Requires completion of an organized program of study of 24 credit hours beyond the master's degree but does not meet the requirements of academic degrees at the doctoral level.

Details on challenging opportunities and special programs available at each college are listed next.

Accelerated Degree Program Students may earn a bachelor's degree in three academic years.

Academic Remediation for Entering Students Instructional courses designed for students deficient in the general competencies necessary for a regular postsecondary curriculum and educational setting.

Adult/Continuing Education Programs Courses offered for nontraditional students who are currently working or are returning to formal education.

Advanced Placement Credit toward a degree awarded for acceptable scores on College Board Advanced Placement tests.

Cooperative (co-op) Education Programs Formal arrangements with off-campus employers allowing students to combine work and study in order to gain degree-related experience, usually extending the time required to complete a degree.

Distance Learning For-credit courses that can be accessed off campus via cable television, the Internet, satellite, videotapes, correspondence course, or other media.

Double Major A program of study in which a student concurrently completes the requirements of two majors.

English as a Second Language (ESL) A course of study designed specifically for students whose native language is not English.

External Degree Programs A program of study in which students earn credits toward a degree through a combination of independent study, college courses, proficiency examinations, and personal experience. External degree programs require minimal or no classroom attendance.

Freshmen Honors College A separate academic program for talented freshmen.

Honors Programs Any special program for very able students, offering the opportunity for educational enrichment, independent study, acceleration, or some combination of these.

Independent Study Academic work, usually undertaken outside the regular classroom structure, chosen or designed by the student with the departmental approval and instructor supervision.

Internships Any short-term, supervised work experience, usually related to a student's major field, for which the student earns academic credit. The work can be full- or part-time, on or off campus, paid or unpaid.

Off-campus Study A formal arrangement with one or more domestic institutions under which students may take courses at the other institution(s) for credit.

Part-time Degree Program Students may earn a degree through part-time enrollment in regular session (daytime) classes or evening, weekend, or summer classes.

Self-designed Major Program of study based on individual interests, designed by the student with the assistance of an adviser.

Services for LD Students Special help for learning-disabled students with resolvable difficulties, such as dyslexia.

Study Abroad An arrangement by which a student completes part of the academic program while studying in another country. A college may operate a campus abroad or it may have a cooperative agreement with other U.S. institutions or institutions in other countries.

Summer Session for Credit Summer courses through which students may make up degree work or accelerate their program.

Tutorials Undergraduates can arrange for special, in-depth academic assignments (not for remediation), working with faculty members one-on-one or in small groups.

ROTC Army, Naval, or Air Force Reserve Officers' Training Corps programs offered either on campus or at a cooperating host institution [designated by (C)].

Unusual Degree Programs Nontraditional programs such as a 3-2 degree program, in which three years of liberal arts study is followed by two years of study in a professional field at another institution (or in a professional division of the same institution), resulting in two bachelor's degrees or a bachelor's and a master's degree.

Up to three of the most frequently chosen baccalaureate fields are then listed.

Next are the total number of faculty members, the percentage of full-time faculty members as of fall 2002, and the percentage of full-time faculty members who hold doctoral/first professional/terminal degrees.

Finally is the school's estimate of the ratio of matriculated undergraduate students to faculty members teaching undergraduate courses.

Students of

Represents the number of full-time and part-time students enrolled in undergraduate degree programs as of fall 2002. The percentage of full-time undergraduates and the percentage of men and women are given. The list provides the number of states and U.S. territories, including the District of Columbia and Puerto Rico, (or, for Canadian institutions, provinces and territories) and other countries from where undergraduates come. Percentages are given of undergraduates who are from out of state; Native American, African American, and Asian American or Pacific Islander; international students; transfer students; and living on campus. The percentage of 2001 freshman who returned for the fall 2002 term is listed last.

Applying

Application requirements are grouped into three categories; *required for all*, *required for some*, and *recommended*. They may include an essay, standardized test scores, a high school transcript, a minimum high school grade point average (expressed as a number on a scale of 0 to 4.0, where 4.0 equals A, 3.0 equals B, etc.), letters of recommendation, an interview on campus or with local alumni, and, for certain types of schools or programs, special requirements such as a musical audition or an art portfolio.

Admission application deadlines and dates for notification of acceptance or rejection are given either as specific dates or as *rolling* and *continuous*. Rolling means that applications are processed as they are received, and qualified students are accepted as long as there are openings. Continuous means that applicants are notified of acceptance or rejection as applications are processed up until the date indicated or the actual beginning of classes. The application deadline and the notification date for transfers are given if they differ from the dates for freshmen. Early decision and early action application deadlines and notification dates are also indicated when relevant.

CRITERIA FOR INCLUSION IN THIS BOOK

The term "four-year college" is the commonly used designation for institutions that grant the baccalaureate degree. Four years is the expected amount of time required to earn this degree, although some bachelor's degree programs may be completed in three years, others require five years, and part-time programs may take considerably longer. Upper-level institutions offer only the junior and senior years and accept only students with two years of college-level credit. Therefore, "four-year college" is a conventional term that accurately describes most of the institutions included in this guide, but it should not be taken literally in all cases.

To be included in this guide, an institution must have full accreditation or be a candidate for accreditation (preaccreditation) status by an institutional or specialized accrediting body recognized by the U.S. Department of Education or the Council for Higher Education Accreditation (CHEA). Institutional accrediting bodies, which review each institution as a whole, include the six regional associations of schools and colleges (Middle States, New England, North Central, Northwest, Southern, and Western), each of which is responsible for a specified portion of the United States and its territories. Other institutional accrediting bodies are national in scope and accredit specific kinds of institutions (e.g., Bible colleges, independent colleges, and rabbinical and Talmudic schools). Program registration by the New York State Board of Regents is considered to be the equivalent of institutional accreditation, since the board requires that all programs offered by an institution meet its standards before recognition is granted. A Canadian institution must be chartered and authorized to grant degrees by the provincial government, affiliated with a chartered institution, or accredited by a recognized U.S. accrediting body This guide also includes institutions outside the United States that are accredited by these U.S. accrediting bodies. There are recognized specialized or professional accrediting bodies in more than forty different fields, each of which is authorized to accredit institutions for specific programs in its particular field. For specialized institutions that offer programs in one field only, we designate this to be the equivalent of institutional accreditation. A full explanation of the accrediting process and complete information on recognized, institutional (regional and national) and specialized accrediting bodies can be found online at www.chea.org or at www.ed.gov/offices/OPE/accreditation/index.html.

RESEARCH PROCEDURES

The data contained in the college profiles were researched between fall 2002 and spring 2003 through *Peterson's Annual Survey of Undergraduate Institutions*. Questionnaires were sent to the more than 2,100 colleges that meet the criteria for inclusion in this guide. All data included in this edition have been submitted by officials (usually admission and financial aid officers, registrars, or institutional research personnel) at the colleges themselves. In addition, the great majority of institutions that submitted data were contacted directly by Peterson's research staff to verify unusual figures, resolve discrepancies, and obtain additional data. All usable information received in time for publication has been included. The omission of any particular item from a profile listing signifies that either the item is not applicable to that institution or that data were not available. Because of the comprehensive editorial review that takes place in our offices and because all material comes directly from college officials, Peterson's has every reason to believe that the information presented in this guide is accurate at the time of printing. However, students should check with a specific college or university at the time of application to verify such figures as tuition and fees, which may have changed since the publication of this volume.

THE UNDERGRADUATE MAJORS LISTINGS

ACCOUNTING

Overview: Students learn the system of recording, summarizing, analyzing, verifying and reporting business and financial transactions. *Related majors:* mathematics, statistics, computer science, finance. *Potential careers:* accountant, bookkeeper, auditor, business manager, financial analyst. *Salary potential:* $27k-$37k.

Abilene Christian U (TX) **260**
Adams State Coll (CO) **260**
Adelphi U (NY) **260**
Adrian Coll (MI) **260**
Alabama A&M U (AL) **261**
Alabama State U (AL) **261**
Alaska Pacific U (AK) **261**
Albany State U (GA) **262**
Albertson Coll of Idaho (ID) **262**
Albertus Magnus Coll (CT) **262**
Albright Coll (PA) **263**
Alcorn State U (MS) **263**
Alderson-Broaddus Coll (WV) **263**
Alfred U (NY) **263**
Alma Coll (MI) **264**
Alvernia Coll (PA) **265**
Amberton U (TX) **265**
American International Coll (MA) **267**
The American U in Cairo(Egypt) **267**
American U of Puerto Rico (PR) **268**
Anderson Coll (SC) **268**
Anderson U (IN) **268**
Andrews U (MI) **269**
Angelo State U (TX) **269**
Appalachian State U (NC) **270**
Aquinas Coll (MI) **270**
Arcadia U (PA) **271**
Arizona State U (AZ) **271**
Arizona State U West (AZ) **272**
Arkansas State U (AR) **272**
Arkansas Tech U (AR) **272**
Asbury Coll (KY) **274**
Ashland U (OH) **274**
Assumption Coll (MA) **275**
Athabasca U (AB, Canada) **275**
Athens State U (AL) **275**
Atlantic Union Coll (MA) **276**
Auburn U (AL) **276**
Auburn U Montgomery (AL) **276**
Augsburg Coll (MN) **276**
Augustana Coll (IL) **276**
Augustana Coll (SD) **276**
Augusta State U (GA) **277**
Aurora U (IL) **277**
Averett U (VA) **278**
Avila U (MO) **278**
Azusa Pacific U (CA) **278**
Babson Coll (MA) **278**
Baker Coll of Auburn Hills (MI) **279**
Baker Coll of Cadillac (MI) **279**
Baker Coll of Flint (MI) **279**
Baker Coll of Jackson (MI) **279**
Baker Coll of Muskegon (MI) **279**
Baker Coll of Owosso (MI) **279**
Baker Coll of Port Huron (MI) **280**
Baker U (KS) **280**
Baldwin-Wallace Coll (OH) **280**
Ball State U (IN) **280**
Barber-Scotia Coll (NC) **281**
Barry U (FL) **282**
Barton Coll (NC) **282**
Bayamón Central U (PR) **283**
Baylor U (TX) **283**
Becker Coll (MA) **283**
Belhaven Coll (MS) **283**
Bellarmine U (KY) **284**
Bellevue U (NE) **284**
Belmont Abbey Coll (NC) **284**
Belmont U (TN) **284**
Bemidji State U (MN) **285**
Benedict Coll (SC) **285**
Benedictine Coll (KS) **285**
Benedictine U (IL) **285**
Bennett Coll (NC) **286**
Bentley Coll (MA) **286**
Baruch Coll of the City U of NY (NY) **286**
Berry Coll (GA) **287**
Bethany Coll (KS) **287**
Bethany Coll (WV) **287**
Bethel Coll (IN) **288**
Bethel Coll (KS) **288**
Bethel Coll (MN) **288**
Bethel Coll (TN) **288**
Bethune-Cookman Coll (FL) **289**
Birmingham-Southern Coll (AL) **289**
Bishop's U (QC, Canada) **289**
Black Hills State U (SD) **290**
Bloomfield Coll (NJ) **290**
Bloomsburg U of Pennsylvania (PA) **290**
Bluefield State Coll (WV) **291**
Bluffton Coll (OH) **291**
Boston Coll (MA) **292**
Boston U (MA) **292**
Bowie State U (MD) **292**
Bowling Green State U (OH) **292**
Bradley U (IL) **293**
Brenau U (GA) **293**
Brescia U (KY) **293**
Brewton-Parker Coll (GA) **294**
Briar Cliff U (IA) **294**
Bridgewater Coll (VA) **294**
Bridgewater State Coll (MA) **294**
Briercrest Bible Coll (SK, Canada) **295**
Brigham Young U (UT) **295**
Brigham Young U–Hawaii (HI) **295**
Brock U (ON, Canada) **295**
Brooklyn Coll of the City U of NY (NY) **295**
Bryant Coll (RI) **296**
Bucknell U (PA) **297**
Buena Vista U (IA) **297**
Butler U (IN) **297**
Cabrini Coll (PA) **298**
Caldwell Coll (NJ) **298**
California Coll for Health Sciences (CA) **298**
California Lutheran U (CA) **299**
California State Polytechnic U, Pomona (CA) **300**
California State U, Dominguez Hills (CA) **300**
California State U, Fresno (CA) **301**
California State U, Fullerton (CA) **301**
California State U, Hayward (CA) **301**
California State U, Long Beach (CA) **301**
California State U, Northridge (CA) **301**
California State U, Sacramento (CA) **301**
California State U, San Bernardino (CA) **302**
California State U, San Marcos (CA) **302**
California State U, Stanislaus (CA) **302**
California U of Pennsylvania (PA) **302**
Calumet Coll of Saint Joseph (IN) **302**
Calvin Coll (MI) **303**
Cameron U (OK) **303**
Campbellsville U (KY) **303**
Campbell U (NC) **303**
Canisius Coll (NY) **304**
Capital U (OH) **304**
Cardinal Stritch U (WI) **305**
Carleton U (ON, Canada) **305**
Carlow Coll (PA) **305**
Carroll Coll (MT) **306**
Carroll Coll (WI) **306**
Carson-Newman Coll (TN) **306**
Carthage Coll (WI) **306**
Case Western Reserve U (OH) **307**
Castleton State Coll (VT) **307**
The Catholic U of America (DC) **307**
Cazenovia Coll (NY) **308**
Cedar Crest Coll (PA) **308**
Cedarville U (OH) **308**
Centenary Coll (NJ) **308**
Centenary Coll of Louisiana (LA) **308**
Central Christian Coll of Kansas (KS) **309**
Central Coll (IA) **309**
Central Connecticut State U (CT) **309**
Central Methodist Coll (MO) **309**
Central Michigan U (MI) **310**
Central Missouri State U (MO) **310**
Central Washington U (WA) **310**
Chaminade U of Honolulu (HI) **311**
Champlain Coll (VT) **311**
Chapman U (CA) **311**
Charleston Southern U (SC) **311**
Chatham Coll (PA) **312**
Chestnut Hill Coll (PA) **312**
Chowan Coll (NC) **312**
Christian Brothers U (TN) **313**
Christopher Newport U (VA) **313**
City U (WA) **314**
Claremont McKenna Coll (CA) **315**
Clarion U of Pennsylvania (PA) **315**
Clark Atlanta U (GA) **315**
Clarke Coll (IA) **315**
Clarkson U (NY) **316**
Clayton Coll & State U (GA) **316**
Clearwater Christian Coll (FL) **316**
Cleary U (MI) **317**
Clemson U (SC) **317**
Cleveland State U (OH) **317**
Coastal Carolina U (SC) **318**
Coe Coll (IA) **318**
Coker Coll (SC) **318**
Coll Misericordia (PA) **319**
Coll of Charleston (SC) **320**
Coll of Mount St. Joseph (OH) **320**
The Coll of New Jersey (NJ) **320**
Coll of Saint Benedict (MN) **321**
Coll of St. Catherine (MN) **321**
Coll of Saint Elizabeth (NJ) **321**
Coll of St. Joseph (VT) **322**
The Coll of Saint Rose (NY) **322**
The Coll of St. Scholastica (MN) **322**
Coll of Santa Fe (NM) **323**
The Coll of Southeastern Europe, The American U of Athens(Greece) **323**
Coll of Staten Island of the City U of NY (NY) **323**
Coll of the Holy Cross (MA) **323**
Coll of the Ozarks (MO) **323**
Coll of the Southwest (NM) **324**
Colorado Christian U (CO) **325**
Colorado State U (CO) **325**
Colorado State U-Pueblo (CO) **325**
Colorado Tech U Sioux Falls Campus (SD) **326**
Columbia Coll (MO) **326**
Columbia Coll (SC) **327**
Columbia Union Coll (MD) **328**
Columbus State U (GA) **328**
Concord Coll (WV) **329**
Concordia Coll (MN) **329**
Concordia U (IL) **330**
Concordia U (MN) **330**
Concordia U (NE) **330**
Concordia U (QC, Canada) **331**
Concordia U at Austin (TX) **331**
Concordia U Wisconsin (WI) **331**
Converse Coll (SC) **332**
Cornerstone U (MI) **333**
Creighton U (NE) **333**
Culver-Stockton Coll (MO) **334**
Cumberland Coll (KY) **335**
Cumberland U (TN) **335**
Daemen Coll (NY) **335**
Dakota State U (SD) **335**
Dakota Wesleyan U (SD) **336**
Dalhousie U (NS, Canada) **336**
Dallas Baptist U (TX) **336**
Davenport U, Grand Rapids (MI) **337**
Davenport U, Kalamazoo (MI) **337**
Davenport U, Lansing (MI) **337**
Davis & Elkins Coll (WV) **338**
Defiance Coll (OH) **338**
Delaware State U (DE) **338**
Delaware Valley Coll (PA) **339**
Delta State U (MS) **339**
DePaul U (IL) **339**
Deree Coll(Greece) **339**
DeSales U (PA) **340**
Dickinson State U (ND) **344**
Dillard U (LA) **344**
Doane Coll (NE) **344**
Dominican Coll (NY) **344**
Dominican U (IL) **345**
Dordt Coll (IA) **345**
Dowling Coll (NY) **345**
Drake U (IA) **345**
Drexel U (PA) **346**
Drury U (MO) **346**
Duquesne U (PA) **346**
D'Youville Coll (NY) **347**
East Carolina U (NC) **347**
East Central U (OK) **347**
Eastern Connecticut State U (CT) **347**
Eastern Illinois U (IL) **348**
Eastern Kentucky U (KY) **348**
Eastern Mennonite U (VA) **348**
Eastern Michigan U (MI) **348**
Eastern New Mexico U (NM) **349**
Eastern Oregon U (OR) **349**
Eastern U (PA) **349**
Eastern Washington U (WA) **349**
East Tennessee State U (TN) **349**
East Texas Baptist U (TX) **350**
East-West U (IL) **350**
École des hautes études commerciales de Montréal (QC, Canada) **350**
Edgewood Coll (WI) **351**
Elizabeth City State U (NC) **351**
Elizabethtown Coll (PA) **351**
Elmhurst Coll (IL) **351**
Elmira Coll (NY) **351**
Elms Coll (MA) **352**
Elon U (NC) **352**
Emmanuel Coll (MA) **353**
Emory & Henry Coll (VA) **353**
Emory U (GA) **354**
Emporia State U (KS) **354**
Eureka Coll (IL) **355**
Evangel U (MO) **355**
Excelsior Coll (NY) **356**
Fairfield U (CT) **356**
Fairleigh Dickinson U, Florham (NJ) **356**
Fairleigh Dickinson U, Teaneck-Metro Campus (NJ) **356**
Fairmont State Coll (WV) **356**
Faulkner U (AL) **357**
Fayetteville State U (NC) **357**
Felician Coll (NJ) **357**
Ferris State U (MI) **358**
Ferrum Coll (VA) **358**
Fisk U (TN) **358**
Fitchburg State Coll (MA) **358**
Flagler Coll (FL) **359**
Florida A&M U (FL) **359**
Florida Atlantic U (FL) **359**
Florida Gulf Coast U (FL) **359**
Florida International U (FL) **360**
Florida Metropolitan U-Tampa Coll, Brandon (FL) **360**
Florida Metropolitan U-Fort Lauderdale Coll (FL) **360**
Florida Metropolitan U–Jacksonville Campus (FL) **360**
Florida Metropolitan U-Melbourne (FL) **360**
Florida Metropolitan U-Orlando Coll, North (FL) **361**
Florida Metropolitan U-Tampa Coll, Pinellas (FL) **361**
Florida Metropolitan U-Orlando Coll, South (FL) **361**
Florida Southern Coll (FL) **361**
Florida State U (FL) **361**
Fontbonne U (MO) **361**
Fordham U (NY) **362**
Fort Hays State U (KS) **362**
Fort Lewis Coll (CO) **362**
Fort Valley State U (GA) **362**
Framingham State Coll (MA) **362**
The Franciscan U (IA) **363**
Franciscan U of Steubenville (OH) **363**
Francis Marion U (SC) **363**
Franklin Coll (IN) **363**
Franklin Pierce Coll (NH) **364**
Franklin U (OH) **364**
Freed-Hardeman U (TN) **364**
Fresno Pacific U (CA) **364**
Frostburg State U (MD) **365**
Furman U (SC) **365**
Gallaudet U (DC) **365**
Gannon U (PA) **365**
Gardner-Webb U (NC) **365**
Geneva Coll (PA) **366**
George Mason U (VA) **366**
Georgetown Coll (KY) **366**
Georgetown U (DC) **366**
The George Washington U (DC) **367**
Georgia Coll & State U (GA) **367**
Georgian Court Coll (NJ) **367**
Georgia Southern U (GA) **367**
Georgia Southwestern State U (GA) **368**
Georgia State U (GA) **368**
Gettysburg Coll (PA) **368**
Glenville State Coll (WV) **368**
Golden Gate U (CA) **369**
Goldey-Beacom Coll (DE) **369**
Gonzaga U (WA) **369**
Gordon Coll (MA) **370**
Goshen Coll (IN) **370**
Governors State U (IL) **370**
Grace Coll (IN) **370**
Graceland U (IA) **371**
Grace U (NE) **371**
Grambling State U (LA) **371**
Grand Canyon U (AZ) **371**
Grand Valley State U (MI) **371**
Grand View Coll (IA) **372**
Greensboro Coll (NC) **372**
Greenville Coll (IL) **373**
Grove City Coll (PA) **373**
Guilford Coll (NC) **373**
Gustavus Adolphus Coll (MN) **374**

Gwynedd-Mercy Coll (PA) **374**
Hampton U (VA) **375**
Hannibal-LaGrange Coll (MO) **375**
Harding U (AR) **375**
Hardin-Simmons U (TX) **376**
Harris-Stowe State Coll (MO) **376**
Hartwick Coll (NY) **376**
Hastings Coll (NE) **377**
Hawai'i Pacific U (HI) **377**
Heidelberg Coll (OH) **377**
Henderson State U (AR) **378**
Hendrix Coll (AR) **378**
High Point U (NC) **379**
Hilbert Coll (NY) **379**
Hillsdale Coll (MI) **379**
Hofstra U (NY) **380**
Holy Family U (PA) **380**
Hope Coll (MI) **381**
Houghton Coll (NY) **381**
Houston Baptist U (TX) **382**
Howard Payne U (TX) **382**
Howard U (DC) **382**
Humboldt State U (CA) **382**
Hunter Coll of the City U of NY (NY) **382**
Huntingdon Coll (AL) **383**
Huntington Coll (IN) **383**
Husson Coll (ME) **383**
Huston-Tillotson Coll (TX) **383**
Idaho State U (ID) **384**
Illinois Coll (IL) **384**
Illinois State U (IL) **384**
Illinois Wesleyan U (IL) **385**
Immaculata U (PA) **385**
Indiana Inst of Technology (IN) **385**
Indiana State U (IN) **385**
Indiana U Bloomington (IN) **385**
Indiana U Northwest (IN) **386**
Indiana U of Pennsylvania (PA) **386**
Indiana U–Purdue U Fort Wayne (IN) **386**
Indiana Wesleyan U (IN) **387**
Inst of Public Administration(Ireland) **387**
Insto Tecno Estudios Sups Monterrey(Mexico) **388**
Inter American U of PR, Aguadilla Campus (PR) **388**
Inter Amer U of PR, Barranquitas Campus (PR) **388**
Inter American U of PR, Guayama Campus (PR) **388**
Inter American U of PR, San Germán Campus (PR) **388**
International Coll (FL) **389**
International Coll of the Cayman Islands(Cayman Islands) **389**
Iona Coll (NY) **390**
Iowa State U of Science and Technology (IA) **390**
Iowa Wesleyan Coll (IA) **390**
Ithaca Coll (NY) **390**
Jackson State U (MS) **390**
Jacksonville State U (AL) **390**
Jacksonville U (FL) **391**
James Madison U (VA) **391**
Jamestown Coll (ND) **391**
John Brown U (AR) **392**
John Carroll U (OH) **392**
John F. Kennedy U (CA) **392**
Johnson & Wales U (RI) **393**
Johnson C. Smith U (NC) **394**
Johnson State Coll (VT) **394**
Jones Coll (FL) **394**
Judson Coll (IL) **395**
Juniata Coll (PA) **395**
Kansas State U (KS) **396**
Kean U (NJ) **396**
Kennesaw State U (GA) **397**
Kent State U (OH) **397**
Kentucky Wesleyan Coll (KY) **397**
Kettering U (MI) **398**
Keuka Coll (NY) **398**
King Coll (TN) **398**
King's Coll (PA) **398**
Kutztown U of Pennsylvania (PA) **399**
LaGrange Coll (GA) **400**
Lake Erie Coll (OH) **400**
Lakehead U (ON, Canada) **400**
Lakeland Coll (WI) **401**
Lamar U (TX) **401**
Lambuth U (TN) **401**
Lander U (SC) **401**
Langston U (OK) **402**
La Roche Coll (PA) **402**
La Salle U (PA) **402**
Lasell Coll (MA) **402**
La Sierra U (CA) **403**
Lebanon Valley Coll (PA) **403**
Lee U (TN) **404**
Lehigh U (PA) **404**
Lehman Coll of the City U of NY (NY) **404**
Le Moyne Coll (NY) **404**
Lenoir-Rhyne Coll (NC) **405**
LeTourneau U (TX) **405**
Lewis-Clark State Coll (ID) **406**
Lewis U (IL) **406**
Liberty U (VA) **406**
Limestone Coll (SC) **406**
Lincoln Memorial U (TN) **407**
Lincoln U (CA) **407**
Lincoln U (PA) **407**
Lindenwood U (MO) **407**
Lindsey Wilson Coll (KY) **407**
Linfield Coll (OR) **408**
Lipscomb U (TN) **408**
Lock Haven U of Pennsylvania (PA) **408**
Long Island U, Brentwood Campus (NY) **408**
Long Island U, Brooklyn Campus (NY) **409**
Long Island U, C.W. Post Campus (NY) **409**
Long Island U, Southampton Coll (NY) **409**
Longwood U (VA) **409**
Loras Coll (IA) **410**
Louisiana Coll (LA) **410**
Louisiana State U and A&M Coll (LA) **410**
Louisiana State U in Shreveport (LA) **410**
Louisiana Tech U (LA) **410**
Lourdes Coll (OH) **411**
Loyola Coll in Maryland (MD) **411**
Loyola Marymount U (CA) **411**
Loyola U Chicago (IL) **411**
Loyola U New Orleans (LA) **411**
Lubbock Christian U (TX) **412**
Luther Coll (IA) **412**
Lycoming Coll (PA) **412**
Lynchburg Coll (VA) **413**
Lyndon State Coll (VT) **413**
Lynn U (FL) **413**
Lyon Coll (AR) **413**
MacMurray Coll (IL) **414**
Madonna U (MI) **414**
Malone Coll (OH) **415**
Manchester Coll (IN) **415**
Manhattan Coll (NY) **416**
Mansfield U of Pennsylvania (PA) **416**
Marian Coll (IN) **417**
Marian Coll of Fond du Lac (WI) **417**
Marietta Coll (OH) **417**
Marist Coll (NY) **417**
Marquette U (WI) **418**
Marshall U (WV) **418**
Mars Hill Coll (NC) **418**
Martin U (IN) **419**
Mary Baldwin Coll (VA) **419**
Marymount Coll of Fordham U (NY) **419**
Marymount Manhattan Coll (NY) **420**
Marymount U (VA) **420**
Maryville U of Saint Louis (MO) **420**
Marywood U (PA) **421**
Massachusetts Coll of Liberal Arts (MA) **421**
The Master's Coll and Seminary (CA) **422**
McGill U (QC, Canada) **423**
McKendree Coll (IL) **423**
McMurry U (TX) **423**
McNeese State U (LA) **423**
McPherson Coll (KS) **423**
Medaille Coll (NY) **424**
Medgar Evers Coll of the City U of NY (NY) **424**
Memorial U of Newfoundland (NF, Canada) **424**
Mercer U (GA) **425**
Mercy Coll (NY) **425**
Mercyhurst Coll (PA) **425**
Meredith Coll (NC) **426**
Merrimack Coll (MA) **426**
Mesa State Coll (CO) **426**
Messiah Coll (PA) **426**
Methodist Coll (NC) **427**
Metropolitan State Coll of Denver (CO) **427**
Metropolitan State U (MN) **427**
Miami U (OH) **428**
Michigan State U (MI) **428**
Michigan Technological U (MI) **428**
MidAmerica Nazarene U (KS) **428**
Middle Tennessee State U (TN) **429**
Midland Lutheran Coll (NE) **429**
Midwestern State U (TX) **430**
Milligan Coll (TN) **430**
Millikin U (IL) **430**
Millsaps Coll (MS) **431**
Minnesota State U, Mankato (MN) **431**
Minnesota State U, Moorhead (MN) **432**
Minot State U (ND) **432**
Mississippi Coll (MS) **432**
Mississippi State U (MS) **432**
Mississippi Valley State U (MS) **432**
Missouri Southern State Coll (MO) **433**
Missouri Valley Coll (MO) **433**
Missouri Western State Coll (MO) **433**
Molloy Coll (NY) **433**
Monmouth Coll (IL) **434**
Monmouth U (NJ) **434**
Montana State U–Billings (MT) **434**
Montana Tech of The U of Montana (MT) **435**
Montclair State U (NJ) **435**
Montreat Coll (NC) **435**
Moravian Coll (PA) **436**
Morehead State U (KY) **436**
Morehouse Coll (GA) **436**
Morgan State U (MD) **436**
Morningside Coll (IA) **437**
Mount Allison U (NB, Canada) **437**
Mount Aloysius Coll (PA) **437**
Mount Marty Coll (SD) **438**
Mount Mary Coll (WI) **438**
Mount Mercy Coll (IA) **438**
Mount Olive Coll (NC) **439**
Mount Saint Mary Coll (NY) **439**
Mount St. Mary's Coll (CA) **439**
Mount Saint Mary's Coll and Seminary (MD) **439**
Mount Saint Vincent U (NS, Canada) **439**
Mount Union Coll (OH) **440**
Mount Vernon Nazarene U (OH) **440**
Muhlenberg Coll (PA) **440**
Murray State U (KY) **440**
Muskingum Coll (OH) **441**
National American U, Colorado Springs (CO) **441**
National American U, Denver (CO) **441**
National American U (NM) **441**
National American U (SD) **442**
National American U–Sioux Falls Branch (SD) **442**
National-Louis U (IL) **442**
National U (CA) **442**
Nazareth Coll of Rochester (NY) **443**
Neumann Coll (PA) **443**
Newberry Coll (SC) **444**
Newbury Coll (MA) **444**
New England Coll (NH) **444**
Newman U (KS) **445**
New Mexico Highlands U (NM) **446**
New Mexico State U (NM) **446**
New York Inst of Technology (NY) **447**
New York U (NY) **447**
Niagara U (NY) **447**
Nicholls State U (LA) **447**
Nichols Coll (MA) **448**
Norfolk State U (VA) **448**
North Carolina Ag and Tech State U (NC) **448**
North Carolina Central U (NC) **448**
North Carolina State U (NC) **449**
North Carolina Wesleyan Coll (NC) **449**
North Central Coll (IL) **449**
North Dakota State U (ND) **449**
Northeastern Illinois U (IL) **450**
Northeastern State U (OK) **450**
Northeastern U (MA) **450**
Northern Arizona U (AZ) **450**
Northern Illinois U (IL) **450**
Northern Kentucky U (KY) **451**
Northern Michigan U (MI) **451**
Northern State U (SD) **451**
North Georgia Coll & State U (GA) **451**
North Park U (IL) **452**
Northwestern Coll (IA) **453**
Northwestern Coll (MN) **453**
Northwestern Oklahoma State U (OK) **453**
Northwestern State U of Louisiana (LA) **453**
Northwest Missouri State U (MO) **454**
Northwest Nazarene U (ID) **454**
Northwood U (MI) **454**
Northwood U, Florida Campus (FL) **454**
Northwood U, Texas Campus (TX) **454**
Notre Dame Coll (OH) **455**
Notre Dame de Namur U (CA) **455**
Nova Southeastern U (FL) **455**
Nyack Coll (NY) **456**
Oakland City U (IN) **456**
Oakland U (MI) **456**
Oakwood Coll (AL) **456**
Oglethorpe U (GA) **457**
Ohio Dominican U (OH) **457**
Ohio Northern U (OH) **457**
The Ohio State U (OH) **457**
Ohio U (OH) **458**
Ohio Valley Coll (WV) **459**
Ohio Wesleyan U (OH) **459**
Oklahoma Baptist U (OK) **459**
Oklahoma Christian U (OK) **459**
Oklahoma City U (OK) **460**
Oklahoma Panhandle State U (OK) **460**
Oklahoma State U (OK) **460**
Oklahoma Wesleyan U (OK) **460**
Old Dominion U (VA) **460**
Olivet Coll (MI) **461**
Olivet Nazarene U (IL) **461**
Oral Roberts U (OK) **461**
Oregon Inst of Technology (OR) **461**
Oregon State U (OR) **462**
Otterbein Coll (OH) **462**
Ouachita Baptist U (AR) **462**
Our Lady of Holy Cross Coll (LA) **463**
Our Lady of the Lake U of San Antonio (TX) **463**
Pace U (NY) **463**
Pacific Lutheran U (WA) **463**
Pacific Union Coll (CA) **464**
Pacific U (OR) **464**
Park U (MO) **465**
Paul Quinn Coll (TX) **466**
Pennsylvania Coll of Technology (PA) **467**
Penn State U at Erie, The Behrend Coll (PA) **467**
Penn State U Harrisburg Campus of the Capital Coll (PA) **468**
Penn State U Univ Park Campus (PA) **468**
Pepperdine U, Malibu (CA) **469**
Peru State Coll (NE) **469**
Pfeiffer U (NC) **469**
Philadelphia U (PA) **469**
Pittsburg State U (KS) **470**
Plattsburgh State U of NY (NY) **471**
Plymouth State Coll (NH) **471**
Point Loma Nazarene U (CA) **471**
Point Park Coll (PA) **471**
Pontifical Catholic U of Puerto Rico (PR) **472**
Portland State U (OR) **472**
Prairie View A&M U (TX) **473**
Presbyterian Coll (SC) **473**
Prescott Coll (AZ) **474**
Providence Coll (RI) **474**
Purdue U (IN) **475**
Purdue U Calumet (IN) **475**
Queens Coll of the City U of NY (NY) **475**
Queens U of Charlotte (NC) **476**
Quincy U (IL) **476**
Quinnipiac U (CT) **476**
Radford U (VA) **476**
Ramapo Coll of New Jersey (NJ) **477**
Randolph-Macon Coll (VA) **477**
Reformed Bible Coll (MI) **477**
Regis U (CO) **478**
Rhode Island Coll (RI) **479**
Rider U (NJ) **480**
Robert Morris U (PA) **481**
Roberts Wesleyan Coll (NY) **481**
Rochester Coll (MI) **482**
Rochester Inst of Technology (NY) **482**
Rockford Coll (IL) **482**
Rockhurst U (MO) **482**
Rocky Mountain Coll (MT) **482**
Roger Williams U (RI) **483**
Roosevelt U (IL) **483**
Rosemont Coll (PA) **484**
Rowan U (NJ) **484**
Rutgers, The State U of New Jersey, Camden (NJ) **485**
Rutgers, The State U of New Jersey, Newark (NJ) **485**
Rutgers, The State U of New Jersey, New Brunswick (NJ) **485**
Ryerson U (ON, Canada) **485**
Sacred Heart U (CT) **486**
Sage Coll of Albany (NY) **486**
Saginaw Valley State U (MI) **486**
St. Ambrose U (IA) **486**
Saint Anselm Coll (NH) **487**
Saint Augustine's Coll (NC) **487**
St. Bonaventure U (NY) **487**
St. Cloud State U (MN) **488**
St. Edward's U (TX) **488**
St. Francis Coll (NY) **488**

ACCOUNTING (continued)

Saint Francis U (PA) ***488***
St. Francis Xavier U (NS, Canada) ***489***
St. John Fisher Coll (NY) ***489***
Saint John's U (MN) ***490***
St. John's U (NY) ***490***
Saint Joseph Coll (CT) ***490***
Saint Joseph's Coll (IN) ***490***
St. Joseph's Coll, New York (NY) ***491***
Saint Joseph's Coll of Maine (ME) ***491***
St. Joseph's Coll, Suffolk Campus (NY) ***491***
Saint Joseph's U (PA) ***491***
Saint Leo U (FL) ***492***
Saint Louis U (MO) ***492***
Saint Martin's Coll (WA) ***493***
Saint Mary Coll (KS) ***493***
Saint Mary-of-the-Woods Coll (IN) ***493***
Saint Mary's Coll (IN) ***493***
Saint Mary's Coll of California (CA) ***494***
Saint Mary's Coll of Madonna U (MI) ***493***
Saint Mary's U (NS, Canada) ***494***
Saint Mary's U of Minnesota (MN) ***494***
St. Mary's U of San Antonio (TX) ***494***
Saint Michael's Coll (VT) ***494***
St. Norbert Coll (WI) ***495***
Saint Peter's Coll (NJ) ***495***
St. Thomas Aquinas Coll (NY) ***495***
St. Thomas U (FL) ***496***
Saint Vincent Coll (PA) ***496***
Saint Xavier U (IL) ***496***
Salem Coll (NC) ***496***
Salem State Coll (MA) ***497***
Salisbury U (MD) ***497***
Salve Regina U (RI) ***497***
Samford U (AL) ***497***
Sam Houston State U (TX) ***497***
San Diego State U (CA) ***498***
San Francisco State U (CA) ***498***
San Jose State U (CA) ***499***
Santa Clara U (CA) ***499***
Savannah State U (GA) ***499***
Schreiner U (TX) ***501***
Seattle Pacific U (WA) ***501***
Seattle U (WA) ***501***
Seton Hall U (NJ) ***502***
Seton Hill U (PA) ***502***
Shaw U (NC) ***502***
Shepherd Coll (WV) ***503***
Shippensburg U of Pennsylvania (PA) ***503***
Shorter Coll (GA) ***504***
Siena Coll (NY) ***504***
Siena Heights U (MI) ***504***
Silver Lake Coll (WI) ***504***
Simmons Coll (MA) ***504***
Simpson Coll (IA) ***505***
Si Tanka Huron U (SD) ***505***
Slippery Rock U of Pennsylvania (PA) ***506***
South Carolina State U (SC) ***506***
Southeastern Coll of the Assemblies of God (FL) ***507***
Southeastern Louisiana U (LA) ***508***
Southeastern Oklahoma State U (OK) ***508***
Southeastern U (DC) ***508***
Southeast Missouri State U (MO) ***508***
Southern Adventist U (TN) ***508***
Southern Arkansas U–Magnolia (AR) ***509***
Southern Connecticut State U (CT) ***509***
Southern Illinois U Carbondale (IL) ***509***
Southern Illinois U Edwardsville (IL) ***509***
Southern Methodist U (TX) ***510***
Southern Nazarene U (OK) ***510***
Southern New Hampshire U (NH) ***510***
Southern Oregon U (OR) ***510***
Southern U and A&M Coll (LA) ***511***
Southern Utah U (UT) ***511***
Southern Vermont Coll (VT) ***511***
Southern Wesleyan U (SC) ***511***
Southwest Baptist U (MO) ***512***
Southwestern Assemblies of God U (TX) ***512***
Southwestern Oklahoma State U (OK) ***512***
Southwestern U (TX) ***513***
Southwest Missouri State U (MO) ***513***
Southwest State U (MN) ***513***
Southwest Texas State U (TX) ***513***
Spalding U (KY) ***513***
Spring Arbor U (MI) ***514***
Spring Hill Coll (AL) ***514***
State U of NY at Albany (NY) ***514***
State U of NY at Binghamton (NY) ***515***
State U of NY at New Paltz (NY) ***515***
State U of NY at Oswego (NY) ***515***
State U of NY Coll at Brockport (NY) ***515***
State U of NY Coll at Fredonia (NY) ***516***
State U of NY Coll at Geneseo (NY) ***516***
State U of NY Coll at Old Westbury (NY) ***516***
State U of NY Coll at Oneonta (NY) ***517***
State U of NY Inst of Tech at Utica/Rome (NY) ***518***
State U of West Georgia (GA) ***518***
Stephen F. Austin State U (TX) ***518***
Stephens Coll (MO) ***519***
Stetson U (FL) ***519***
Stonehill Coll (MA) ***520***
Strayer U (DC) ***520***
Suffolk U (MA) ***520***
Sullivan U (KY) ***521***
Sul Ross State U (TX) ***521***
Susquehanna U (PA) ***521***
Syracuse U (NY) ***521***
Tabor Coll (KS) ***522***
Talladega Coll (AL) ***522***
Tarleton State U (TX) ***522***
Taylor U (IN) ***523***
Teikyo Post U (CT) ***523***
Temple U (PA) ***523***
Tennessee State U (TN) ***523***
Tennessee Technological U (TN) ***524***
Tennessee Temple U (TN) ***524***
Tennessee Wesleyan Coll (TN) ***524***
Texas A&M International U (TX) ***524***
Texas A&M U (TX) ***524***
Texas A&M U–Commerce (TX) ***525***
Texas A&M U–Corpus Christi (TX) ***525***
Texas A&M U–Kingsville (TX) ***525***
Texas A&M U–Texarkana (TX) ***525***
Texas Christian U (TX) ***526***
Texas Lutheran U (TX) ***526***
Texas Southern U (TX) ***526***
Texas Tech U (TX) ***526***
Texas Wesleyan U (TX) ***526***
Texas Woman's U (TX) ***527***
Thiel Coll (PA) ***527***
Thomas Coll (ME) ***527***
Thomas Edison State Coll (NJ) ***527***
Thomas More Coll (KY) ***528***
Thomas U (GA) ***528***
Tiffin U (OH) ***528***
Touro Coll (NY) ***529***
Towson U (MD) ***529***
Transylvania U (KY) ***529***
Trevecca Nazarene U (TN) ***529***
Trinity Christian Coll (IL) ***530***
Trinity International U (IL) ***531***
Trinity U (TX) ***531***
Tri-State U (IN) ***532***
Troy State U (AL) ***532***
Troy State U Montgomery (AL) ***532***
Truman State U (MO) ***532***
Tulane U (LA) ***533***
Tusculum Coll (TN) ***533***
Tuskegee U (AL) ***533***
Union Coll (KY) ***533***
Union Coll (NE) ***534***
Union U (TN) ***534***
United States International U(Kenya) ***535***
Université de Sherbrooke (QC, Canada) ***536***
U du Québec à Trois-Rivières (QC, Canada) ***536***
U du Québec à Hull (QC, Canada) ***536***
U at Buffalo, The State University of New York (NY) ***536***
U Coll of the Cariboo (BC, Canada) ***537***
The U of Akron (OH) ***537***
The U of Alabama (AL) ***537***
The U of Alabama at Birmingham (AL) ***537***
The U of Alabama in Huntsville (AL) ***537***
U of Alaska Anchorage (AK) ***538***
U of Alaska Fairbanks (AK) ***538***
U of Alaska Southeast (AK) ***538***
U of Alberta (AB, Canada) ***538***
The U of Arizona (AZ) ***538***
U of Arkansas (AR) ***539***
U of Arkansas at Little Rock (AR) ***539***
U of Arkansas at Monticello (AR) ***539***
U of Baltimore (MD) ***539***
U of Bridgeport (CT) ***540***
The U of British Columbia (BC, Canada) ***540***
U of Calgary (AB, Canada) ***540***
U of Central Arkansas (AR) ***542***
U of Central Florida (FL) ***542***
U of Central Oklahoma (OK) ***542***
U of Charleston (WV) ***542***
U of Cincinnati (OH) ***543***
U of Colorado at Boulder (CO) ***543***
U of Colorado at Colorado Springs (CO) ***543***
U of Connecticut (CT) ***544***
U of Dayton (OH) ***544***
U of Delaware (DE) ***544***
U of Denver (CO) ***544***
U of Dubuque (IA) ***545***
U of Evansville (IN) ***545***
The U of Findlay (OH) ***545***
U of Florida (FL) ***545***
U of Georgia (GA) ***545***
U of Great Falls (MT) ***545***
U of Hartford (CT) ***546***
U of Hawaii at Manoa (HI) ***546***
U of Houston (TX) ***547***
U of Houston–Clear Lake (TX) ***547***
U of Houston–Downtown (TX) ***547***
U of Idaho (ID) ***547***
U of Illinois at Chicago (IL) ***547***
U of Illinois at Springfield (IL) ***548***
U of Illinois at Urbana–Champaign (IL) ***548***
U of Indianapolis (IN) ***548***
The U of Iowa (IA) ***548***
U of Kansas (KS) ***549***
U of Kentucky (KY) ***549***
U of La Verne (CA) ***549***
The U of Lethbridge (AB, Canada) ***549***
U of Louisiana at Lafayette (LA) ***550***
U of Louisville (KY) ***550***
The U of Maine at Augusta (ME) ***550***
U of Maine at Machias (ME) ***551***
U of Maine at Presque Isle (ME) ***551***
U of Manitoba (MB, Canada) ***551***
U of Mary (ND) ***551***
U of Mary Hardin-Baylor (TX) ***551***
U of Maryland, Coll Park (MD) ***552***
U of Maryland Eastern Shore (MD) ***552***
U of Maryland University Coll (MD) ***552***
U of Massachusetts Amherst (MA) ***552***
U of Massachusetts Dartmouth (MA) ***553***
U of Massachusetts Lowell (MA) ***553***
The U of Memphis (TN) ***553***
U of Miami (FL) ***553***
U of Michigan (MI) ***554***
U of Michigan–Flint (MI) ***554***
U of Minnesota, Crookston (MN) ***554***
U of Minnesota, Duluth (MN) ***554***
U of Minnesota, Twin Cities Campus (MN) ***555***
U of Mississippi (MS) ***555***
U of Missouri–Columbia (MO) ***555***
U of Missouri–Kansas City (MO) ***555***
U of Missouri–St. Louis (MO) ***556***
U of Mobile (AL) ***556***
U of Montevallo (AL) ***557***
U of Nebraska at Omaha (NE) ***557***
U of Nebraska–Lincoln (NE) ***557***
U of Nevada, Las Vegas (NV) ***558***
U of Nevada, Reno (NV) ***558***
U of New Brunswick Fredericton (NB, Canada) ***558***
U of New Brunswick Saint John (NB, Canada) ***558***
U of New Hampshire (NH) ***558***
U of New Haven (CT) ***559***
U of New Mexico (NM) ***559***
U of New Orleans (LA) ***559***
U of North Alabama (AL) ***559***
The U of North Carolina at Asheville (NC) ***559***
The U of North Carolina at Charlotte (NC) ***560***
The U of North Carolina at Greensboro (NC) ***560***
The U of North Carolina at Pembroke (NC) ***560***
The U of North Carolina at Wilmington (NC) ***561***
U of North Dakota (ND) ***561***
U of Northern Iowa (IA) ***561***
U of North Florida (FL) ***561***
U of North Texas (TX) ***562***
U of Notre Dame (IN) ***562***
U of Oklahoma (OK) ***562***
U of Oregon (OR) ***562***
U of Ottawa (ON, Canada) ***563***
U of Pennsylvania (PA) ***563***
U of Phoenix-Atlanta Campus (GA) ***563***
U of Phoenix–Colorado Campus (CO) ***563***
U of Phoenix–Fort Lauderdale Campus (FL) ***564***
U of Phoenix–Jacksonville Campus (FL) ***564***
U of Phoenix–Louisiana Campus (LA) ***565***
U of Phoenix–Maryland Campus (MD) ***565***
U of Phoenix–Metro Detroit Campus (MI) ***565***
U of Phoenix–New Mexico Campus (NM) ***565***
U of Phoenix–Northern California Campus (CA) ***565***
U of Phoenix–Orlando Campus (FL) ***566***
U of Phoenix–Phoenix Campus (AZ) ***567***
U of Phoenix–Puerto Rico Campus (PR) ***567***
U of Phoenix–Sacramento Campus (CA) ***567***
U of Phoenix–San Diego Campus (CA) ***567***
U of Phoenix–Southern Arizona Campus (AZ) ***568***
U of Phoenix–Southern California Campus (CA) ***568***
U of Phoenix–Southern Colorado Campus (CO) ***568***
U of Phoenix–Tampa Campus (FL) ***568***
U of Phoenix–Tulsa Campus (OK) ***568***
U of Phoenix–Utah Campus (UT) ***568***
U of Phoenix-Wisconsin Campus (WI) ***569***
U of Pittsburgh (PA) ***569***
U of Pittsburgh at Greensburg (PA) ***570***
U of Pittsburgh at Johnstown (PA) ***570***
U of Portland (OR) ***570***
U of Puerto Rico at Arecibo (PR) ***570***
U of Puerto Rico, Humacao U Coll (PR) ***570***
U of Puerto Rico at Ponce (PR) ***571***
U of Puerto Rico, Cayey U Coll (PR) ***571***
U of Puerto Rico, Río Piedras (PR) ***571***
U of Redlands (CA) ***572***
U of Regina (SK, Canada) ***572***
U of Rhode Island (RI) ***572***
U of Richmond (VA) ***572***
U of Rio Grande (OH) ***572***
U of St. Francis (IL) ***573***
U of Saint Francis (IN) ***573***
U of St. Thomas (MN) ***573***
U of St. Thomas (TX) ***573***
U of San Diego (CA) ***574***
U of San Francisco (CA) ***574***
U of Saskatchewan (SK, Canada) ***574***
U of Science and Arts of Oklahoma (OK) ***574***
The U of Scranton (PA) ***574***
U of Sioux Falls (SD) ***574***
U of South Alabama (AL) ***575***
U of South Carolina (SC) ***575***
The U of South Dakota (SD) ***575***
U of Southern California (CA) ***576***
U of Southern Indiana (IN) ***576***
U of Southern Maine (ME) ***576***
U of Southern Mississippi (MS) ***576***
U of South Florida (FL) ***576***
The U of Tampa (FL) ***577***
The U of Tennessee (TN) ***577***
The U of Tennessee at Chattanooga (TN) ***577***
The U of Tennessee at Martin (TN) ***577***
The U of Texas at Arlington (TX) ***577***
The U of Texas at Austin (TX) ***578***
The U of Texas at Brownsville (TX) ***578***
The U of Texas at Dallas (TX) ***578***
The U of Texas at El Paso (TX) ***578***
The U of Texas at San Antonio (TX) ***578***
The U of Texas at Tyler (TX) ***579***
The U of Texas of the Permian Basin (TX) ***579***
The U of Texas–Pan American (TX) ***579***
U of the District of Columbia (DC) ***580***
U of the Incarnate Word (TX) ***580***
U of the Ozarks (AR) ***580***
U of the Sacred Heart (PR) ***580***
U of the Virgin Islands (VI) ***581***
U of Toledo (OH) ***581***
U of Tulsa (OK) ***581***
U of Utah (UT) ***582***
The U of Virginia's Coll at Wise (VA) ***582***
U of Washington (WA) ***583***
U of Waterloo (ON, Canada) ***583***
The U of West Alabama (AL) ***583***
U of West Florida (FL) ***583***
U of Windsor (ON, Canada) ***584***
U of Wisconsin–Eau Claire (WI) ***584***
U of Wisconsin–Green Bay (WI) ***584***
U of Wisconsin–La Crosse (WI) ***584***
U of Wisconsin–Madison (WI) ***584***
U of Wisconsin–Milwaukee (WI) ***585***
U of Wisconsin–Oshkosh (WI) ***585***
U of Wisconsin–Parkside (WI) ***585***
U of Wisconsin–Platteville (WI) ***585***
U of Wisconsin–River Falls (WI) ***585***
U of Wisconsin–Stevens Point (WI) ***585***
U of Wisconsin–Superior (WI) ***586***
U of Wisconsin–Whitewater (WI) ***586***
U of Wyoming (WY) ***586***
Upper Iowa U (IA) ***587***
Urbana U (OH) ***587***

Ursinus Coll (PA) **587**
Ursuline Coll (OH) **587**
Utah State U (UT) **587**
Utica Coll (NY) **588**
Valdosta State U (GA) **588**
Valparaiso U (IN) **588**
Vanguard U of Southern California (CA) **589**
Villa Julie Coll (MD) **590**
Villanova U (PA) **590**
Virginia Commonwealth U (VA) **590**
Virginia Polytechnic Inst and State U (VA) **591**
Virginia State U (VA) **591**
Virginia Union U (VA) **591**
Viterbo U (WI) **591**
Voorhees Coll (SC) **592**
Wagner Coll (NY) **592**
Wake Forest U (NC) **592**
Walla Walla Coll (WA) **593**
Walsh Coll of Accountancy and Business Admin (MI) **593**
Walsh U (OH) **593**
Warner Southern Coll (FL) **593**
Wartburg Coll (IA) **594**
Washington & Jefferson Coll (PA) **594**
Washington and Lee U (VA) **594**
Washington State U (WA) **595**
Washington U in St. Louis (MO) **595**
Waynesburg Coll (PA) **595**
Wayne State Coll (NE) **596**
Wayne State U (MI) **596**
Webber International U (FL) **596**
Weber State U (UT) **596**
Webster U (MO) **597**
Wesleyan Coll (GA) **597**
Wesley Coll (DE) **598**
West Chester U of Pennsylvania (PA) **598**
Western Baptist Coll (OR) **598**
Western Carolina U (NC) **598**
Western Connecticut State U (CT) **598**
Western Illinois U (IL) **599**
Western International U (AZ) **599**
Western Kentucky U (KY) **599**
Western Michigan U (MI) **599**
Western New England Coll (MA) **600**
Western New Mexico U (NM) **600**
Western State Coll of Colorado (CO) **600**
Western Washington U (WA) **600**
Westfield State Coll (MA) **600**
West Liberty State Coll (WV) **601**
Westminster Coll (MO) **601**
Westminster Coll (PA) **601**
Westminster Coll (UT) **601**
West Texas A&M U (TX) **602**
West Virginia State Coll (WV) **602**
West Virginia U (WV) **602**
West Virginia U Inst of Technology (WV) **602**
West Virginia Wesleyan Coll (WV) **603**
Wheeling Jesuit U (WV) **603**
Whitworth Coll (WA) **604**
Wichita State U (KS) **604**
Widener U (PA) **604**
Wilberforce U (OH) **605**
Wilkes U (PA) **605**
William Jewell Coll (MO) **606**
William Paterson U of New Jersey (NJ) **606**
William Penn U (IA) **606**
William Woods U (MO) **607**
Wilmington Coll (DE) **607**
Wilmington Coll (OH) **607**
Wilson Coll (PA) **607**
Wingate U (NC) **607**
Winona State U (MN) **608**
Winston-Salem State U (NC) **608**
Wofford Coll (SC) **609**
Woodbury U (CA) **609**
Worcester State Coll (MA) **609**
Wright State U (OH) **609**
Xavier U (OH) **610**
Xavier U of Louisiana (LA) **610**
York Coll (NE) **610**
York Coll of Pennsylvania (PA) **610**
York Coll of the City U of New York (NY) **611**
York U (ON, Canada) **611**
Youngstown State U (OH) **611**

ACCOUNTING RELATED

Information can be found under this major's main heading.

Canisius Coll (NY) **304**
Chestnut Hill Coll (PA) **312**
Duquesne U (PA) **346**
East Carolina U (NC) **347**
Maryville U of Saint Louis (MO) **420**
Park U (MO) **465**
St. Edward's U (TX) **488**
Saint Mary-of-the-Woods Coll (IN) **493**
State U of NY at Oswego (NY) **515**
The U of Akron (OH) **537**

ACCOUNTING TECHNICIAN

Overview: Students learn how to provide technical and computer assistance to financial managers and accounting personnel. *Related majors:* accounting, computer science, management of information systems and business data processing. *Potential careers:* accountant, computer scientist, bookkeeper. *Salary potential:* $25k-$33k.

Bryant Coll (RI) **296**
Pace U (NY) **463**
Peirce Coll (PA) **466**

ACTING/DIRECTING

Overview: This major prepares students to become professional actors and professional directors for plays, film, television, or other theatrical entertainment programs. *Related majors:* technical theater/theater design/stagecraft, film/cinema studies, drama/theater literature, playwriting and screenwriting, drama/theater arts. *Potential careers:* actor, director, producer, casting director, acting coach. *Salary potential:* $10k-$25k.

Bard Coll (NY) **281**
Barry U (FL) **282**
Baylor U (TX) **283**
Boston U (MA) **292**
Carroll Coll (MT) **306**
Columbia Coll Chicago (IL) **327**
Concordia U (QC, Canada) **331**
DePaul U (IL) **339**
Emerson Coll (MA) **353**
Florida State U (FL) **361**
Greensboro Coll (NC) **372**
Ithaca Coll (NY) **390**
Johnson State Coll (VT) **394**
Maharishi U of Management (IA) **414**
Marymount Manhattan Coll (NY) **420**
Memorial U of Newfoundland (NF, Canada) **424**
Ohio U (OH) **458**
Penn State U Univ Park Campus (PA) **468**
Ryerson U (ON, Canada) **485**
St. Cloud State U (MN) **488**
Seton Hill U (PA) **502**
Simon's Rock Coll of Bard (MA) **505**
Texas Tech U (TX) **526**
Trinity U (TX) **531**
The U of Akron (OH) **537**
U of Connecticut (CT) **544**
U of Northern Iowa (IA) **561**
U of Southern California (CA) **576**
U of Windsor (ON, Canada) **584**
York U (ON, Canada) **611**
Youngstown State U (OH) **611**

ACTUARIAL SCIENCE

Overview: In this major students learn how to use mathematics and statistics to analyze different types of risk and how these principles can be applied to insurance and other business issues. *Related majors:* mathematics, statistics, computer science, insurance and risk management, finance. *Potential careers:* actuarial, insurance adjuster or agent, risk analyst, banker, corporate strategist or analyst. *Salary potential:* $35k-$50k.

Ball State U (IN) **280**
Bellarmine U (KY) **284**
Baruch Coll of the City U of NY (NY) **286**
Bradley U (IL) **293**
Bryant Coll (RI) **296**
Butler U (IN) **297**
Carroll Coll (WI) **306**
Central Connecticut State U (CT) **309**
Central Michigan U (MI) **310**
Central Missouri State U (MO) **310**
Concordia U (QC, Canada) **331**
Dominican Coll (NY) **344**
Drake U (IA) **345**
Eastern Michigan U (MI) **348**
Elmhurst Coll (IL) **351**
Florida A&M U (FL) **359**
Florida State U (FL) **361**
Frostburg State U (MD) **365**
Georgia State U (GA) **368**
Indiana U Northwest (IN) **386**
Jamestown Coll (ND) **391**
Lebanon Valley Coll (PA) **403**
Lincoln U (PA) **407**
Lycoming Coll (PA) **412**
Mansfield U of Pennsylvania (PA) **416**
Maryville U of Saint Louis (MO) **420**
The Master's Coll and Seminary (CA) **422**
Mercy Coll (NY) **425**
Mercyhurst Coll (PA) **425**
Missouri Valley Coll (MO) **433**
New Jersey Inst of Technology (NJ) **445**
New York U (NY) **447**
North Central Coll (IL) **449**
North Dakota State U (ND) **449**
The Ohio State U (OH) **457**
Ohio U (OH) **458**
Oregon State U (OR) **462**
Penn State U Univ Park Campus (PA) **468**
Quinnipiac U (CT) **476**
Rider U (NJ) **480**
Roosevelt U (IL) **483**
St. Cloud State U (MN) **488**
St. John's U (NY) **490**
Seton Hill U (PA) **502**
Simon Fraser U (BC, Canada) **505**
Southern Adventist U (TN) **508**
State U of NY at Albany (NY) **514**
Tabor Coll (KS) **522**
Temple U (PA) **523**
Thiel Coll (PA) **527**
Université Laval (QC, Canada) **536**
U of Calgary (AB, Canada) **540**
U of Central Oklahoma (OK) **542**
U of Connecticut (CT) **544**
U of Hartford (CT) **546**
U of Illinois at Urbana–Champaign (IL) **548**
The U of Iowa (IA) **548**
U of Manitoba (MB, Canada) **551**
U of Michigan–Flint (MI) **554**
U of Minnesota, Duluth (MN) **554**
U of Minnesota, Twin Cities Campus (MN) **555**
U of Nebraska–Lincoln (NE) **557**
U of Northern Iowa (IA) **561**
U of Pennsylvania (PA) **563**
U of St. Francis (IL) **573**
U of St. Thomas (MN) **573**
U of Toronto (ON, Canada) **581**
U of Waterloo (ON, Canada) **583**
The U of Western Ontario (ON, Canada) **583**
U of Wisconsin–Madison (WI) **584**
U of Wisconsin–Stevens Point (WI) **585**
Worcester Polytechnic Inst (MA) **609**
York U (ON, Canada) **611**

ADAPTED PHYSICAL EDUCATION

Overview: This major will teach students how to develop physical education activities that are designed to promote health and well being in patients who are physically, mentally, or emotionally disabled. *Related majors:* exercise sciences/movement studies, physical therapy, psychology, special education, anatomy. *Potential careers:* physical therapist, teacher. *Salary potential:* $25k-$35k.

Bridgewater State Coll (MA) **294**
Central Michigan U (MI) **310**
Eastern Michigan U (MI) **348**
Ithaca Coll (NY) **390**
Messiah Coll (PA) **426**
Ohio U (OH) **458**
St. Ambrose U (IA) **486**
St. Cloud State U (MN) **488**
San Jose State U (CA) **499**
Shaw U (NC) **502**
Southern U and A&M Coll (LA) **511**
U of Nebraska at Kearney (NE) **557**
U of Toledo (OH) **581**

ADULT/CONTINUING EDUCATION

Overview: this major prepares students to teach adult students basic and remedial education or to upgrade specific vocational skills and knowledge. *Related majors:* education, vocational rehabilitation counseling, business teacher education, technology/industrial arts teacher education, reading teacher education. *Potential careers:* teacher, trade school teacher, computer teacher. *Salary potential:* $25k-$35k.

American International Coll (MA) **267**
Andrews U (MI) **269**
Arkansas Baptist Coll (AR) **272**
Atlantic Union Coll (MA) **276**
Auburn U (AL) **276**
Bethel Coll (MN) **288**
Biola U (CA) **289**
Brock U (ON, Canada) **295**
Christian Heritage Coll (CA) **313**
Cornerstone U (MI) **333**
Dakota Wesleyan U (SD) **336**
Delaware Valley Coll (PA) **339**
DePaul U (IL) **339**
Franklin Pierce Coll (NH) **364**
Immaculata U (PA) **385**
Iona Coll (NY) **390**
Iowa Wesleyan Coll (IA) **390**
James Madison U (VA) **391**
Laurentian U (ON, Canada) **403**
Lenoir-Rhyne Coll (NC) **405**
Long Island U, Southampton Coll, Friends World Program (NY) **409**
Louisiana Coll (LA) **410**
Lynn U (FL) **413**
Mars Hill Coll (NC) **418**
Martin U (IN) **419**
Massachusetts Coll of Liberal Arts (MA) **421**
Memorial U of Newfoundland (NF, Canada) **424**
Morehouse Coll (GA) **436**
Pittsburg State U (KS) **470**
Pratt Inst (NY) **473**
St. Joseph's Coll, Suffolk Campus (NY) **491**
Tabor Coll (KS) **522**
Tennessee State U (TN) **523**
Université de Sherbrooke (QC, Canada) **536**
U du Québec à Trois-Rivières (QC, Canada) **536**
U of Alberta (AB, Canada) **538**
U of Central Oklahoma (OK) **542**
U of La Verne (CA) **549**
U of Nevada, Las Vegas (NV) **558**
U of New Brunswick Fredericton (NB, Canada) **558**
U of New Hampshire (NH) **558**
U of Regina (SK, Canada) **572**
U of San Francisco (CA) **574**
U of the Incarnate Word (TX) **580**
U of Toledo (OH) **581**
Urbana U (OH) **587**

ADULT/CONTINUING EDUCATION ADMINISTRATION

Overview: This major prepares students to plan and manage programs designed to serve as basic education needs of under-educated adults or the continuing education need of adults. *Related majors:* community relations, continuing education, educational psychology, special education. *Potential careers:* teacher, educational

ADULT/CONTINUING EDUCATION ADMINISTRATION (continued)

administrator, community services director. *Salary potential:* $23k-$30k.

Marshall U (WV) ***418***
Penn State U Univ Park Campus (PA) ***468***

ADVERTISING

Overview: Students learn to create and execute commercial messages for the purpose of promoting and selling products, services, and brands. *Related majors:* mass communications, public relations, political science, art, marketing, rhetoric. *Potential careers:* advertising executive, market researcher, media planner, copywriter. *Salary potential:* $29k-$37k.

Abilene Christian U (TX) ***260***
Academy of Art Coll (CA) ***260***
Adams State Coll (CO) ***260***
American Academy of Art (IL) ***265***
Appalachian State U (NC) ***270***
Art Center Coll of Design (CA) ***273***
The Art Inst of California–San Diego (CA) ***273***
The Art Inst of Colorado (CO) ***274***
Ball State U (IN) ***280***
Barry U (FL) ***282***
Belmont U (TN) ***284***
Baruch Coll of the City U of NY (NY) ***286***
Bradley U (IL) ***293***
California State U, Fullerton (CA) ***301***
California State U, Hayward (CA) ***301***
Campbell U (NC) ***303***
Central Michigan U (MI) ***310***
Chapman U (CA) ***311***
Clarke Coll (IA) ***315***
The Coll of Southeastern Europe, The American U of Athens(Greece) ***323***
Colorado State U-Pueblo (CO) ***325***
Columbia Coll Chicago (IL) ***327***
Columbus Coll of Art and Design (OH) ***328***
Concordia Coll (MN) ***329***
DePaul U (IL) ***339***
Drake U (IA) ***345***
Eastern Nazarene Coll (MA) ***348***
Emerson Coll (MA) ***353***
Ferris State U (MI) ***358***
Florida Southern Coll (FL) ***361***
Florida State U (FL) ***361***
Franklin Pierce Coll (NH) ***364***
Gannon U (PA) ***365***
Grand Valley State U (MI) ***371***
Hampton U (VA) ***375***
Harding U (AR) ***375***
Hastings Coll (NE) ***377***
Hawai'i Pacific U (HI) ***377***
Howard U (DC) ***382***
Iona Coll (NY) ***390***
Iowa State U of Science and Technology (IA) ***390***
Johnson & Wales U (RI) ***393***
Kent State U (OH) ***397***
Lock Haven U of Pennsylvania (PA) ***408***
Louisiana Coll (LA) ***410***
Marist Coll (NY) ***417***
Marquette U (WI) ***418***
Mary Baldwin Coll (VA) ***419***
Memphis Coll of Art (TN) ***425***
Mercyhurst Coll (PA) ***425***
Metropolitan State U (MN) ***427***
Michigan State U (MI) ***428***
Milligan Coll (TN) ***430***
Minneapolis Coll of Art and Design (MN) ***431***
Minnesota State U, Moorhead (MN) ***432***
Murray State U (KY) ***440***
New England Coll (NH) ***444***
New England School of Communications (ME) ***445***
New York Inst of Technology (NY) ***447***
Northeastern U (MA) ***450***
Northern Arizona U (AZ) ***450***
Northwest Missouri State U (MO) ***454***
Northwood U (MI) ***454***
Northwood U, Florida Campus (FL) ***454***
Northwood U, Texas Campus (TX) ***454***
Notre Dame de Namur U (CA) ***455***
Ohio U (OH) ***458***
Oklahoma Baptist U (OK) ***459***
Oklahoma Christian U (OK) ***459***
Oklahoma City U (OK) ***460***
Oklahoma State U (OK) ***460***
Pace U (NY) ***463***
Pacific Union Coll (CA) ***464***
Penn State U Univ Park Campus (PA) ***468***
Pepperdine U, Malibu (CA) ***469***
Pittsburg State U (KS) ***470***
Point Park Coll (PA) ***471***
Portland State U (OR) ***472***
Quinnipiac U (CT) ***476***
Rider U (NJ) ***480***
Rochester Inst of Technology (NY) ***482***
Rowan U (NJ) ***484***
St. Ambrose U (IA) ***486***
St. Cloud State U (MN) ***488***
Saint Joseph's Coll of Maine (ME) ***491***
Sam Houston State U (TX) ***497***
San Jose State U (CA) ***499***
School of Visual Arts (NY) ***501***
Simmons Coll (MA) ***504***
Simpson Coll (IA) ***505***
Southeast Missouri State U (MO) ***508***
Southern Methodist U (TX) ***510***
Southern New Hampshire U (NH) ***510***
Southwest Texas State U (TX) ***513***
Spring Hill Coll (AL) ***514***
Stephens Coll (MO) ***519***
Syracuse U (NY) ***521***
Temple U (PA) ***523***
Texas A&M U–Commerce (TX) ***525***
Texas Christian U (TX) ***526***
Texas Tech U (TX) ***526***
Texas Wesleyan U (TX) ***526***
Thomas Edison State Coll (NJ) ***527***
Union U (TN) ***534***
The U of Alabama (AL) ***537***
U of Arkansas at Little Rock (AR) ***539***
U of Central Florida (FL) ***542***
U of Central Oklahoma (OK) ***542***
U of Colorado at Boulder (CO) ***543***
U of Florida (FL) ***545***
U of Georgia (GA) ***545***
U of Illinois at Urbana–Champaign (IL) ***548***
U of Kansas (KS) ***549***
U of Kentucky (KY) ***549***
U of Miami (FL) ***553***
U of Mississippi (MS) ***555***
U of Missouri–Columbia (MO) ***555***
U of Nebraska at Omaha (NE) ***557***
U of Nebraska–Lincoln (NE) ***557***
U of Nevada, Reno (NV) ***558***
U of North Texas (TX) ***562***
U of Oklahoma (OK) ***562***
U of Oregon (OR) ***562***
U of Ottawa (ON, Canada) ***563***
U of St. Thomas (MN) ***573***
U of San Francisco (CA) ***574***
U of South Carolina (SC) ***575***
The U of South Dakota (SD) ***575***
U of Southern Indiana (IN) ***576***
U of Southern Mississippi (MS) ***576***
The U of Tennessee (TN) ***577***
The U of Texas at Arlington (TX) ***577***
The U of Texas at Austin (TX) ***578***
U of the Sacred Heart (PR) ***580***
U of Wisconsin–Madison (WI) ***584***
Washington State U (WA) ***595***
Washington U in St. Louis (MO) ***595***
Waynesburg Coll (PA) ***595***
Wayne State Coll (NE) ***596***
Webster U (MO) ***597***
Wesleyan Coll (GA) ***597***
Western Kentucky U (KY) ***599***
Western New England Coll (MA) ***600***
West Texas A&M U (TX) ***602***
West Virginia U (WV) ***602***
Widener U (PA) ***604***
William Woods U (MO) ***607***
Winona State U (MN) ***608***
Xavier U (OH) ***610***
Youngstown State U (OH) ***611***

AEROSPACE ENGINEERING

Overview: Undergraduates study fundamental aerodynamics, advanced propulsion, vehicle dynamics, and design optimization of fixed-wing aircraft, rotorcraft, and space vehicles. *Related majors:* engineering physics, structural engineering, materials science, Air Force ROTC/Air Science, military technologies. *Potential careers:* astronaut, aeronautical engineer, pilot, scientist, researcher, Air Force officer. *Salary potential:* $35k-$50k.

Arizona State U (AZ) ***271***
Auburn U (AL) ***276***
Boston U (MA) ***292***
California Inst of Technology (CA) ***299***
California Polytechnic State U, San Luis Obispo (CA) ***300***
California State Polytechnic U, Pomona (CA) ***300***
California State U, Long Beach (CA) ***301***
California State U, Northridge (CA) ***301***
Carleton U (ON, Canada) ***305***
Case Western Reserve U (OH) ***307***
Clarkson U (NY) ***316***
Eastern Nazarene Coll (MA) ***348***
Embry-Riddle Aeronautical U (AZ) ***352***
Embry-Riddle Aeronautical U (FL) ***352***
Florida Inst of Technology (FL) ***360***
Georgia Inst of Technology (GA) ***367***
Illinois Inst of Technology (IL) ***384***
Iowa State U of Science and Technology (IA) ***390***
Massachusetts Inst of Technology (MA) ***421***
Miami U (OH) ***428***
Mississippi State U (MS) ***432***
North Carolina State U (NC) ***449***
North Dakota State U (ND) ***449***
The Ohio State U (OH) ***457***
Oklahoma State U (OK) ***460***
Penn State U Univ Park Campus (PA) ***468***
Polytechnic U, Brooklyn Campus (NY) ***472***
Purdue U (IN) ***475***
Rensselaer Polytechnic Inst (NY) ***478***
Rochester Inst of Technology (NY) ***482***
Ryerson U (ON, Canada) ***485***
Saint Louis U (MO) ***492***
San Diego State U (CA) ***498***
San Jose State U (CA) ***499***
Syracuse U (NY) ***521***
Texas A&M U (TX) ***524***
Texas Christian U (TX) ***526***
Tuskegee U (AL) ***533***
United States Air Force Academy (CO) ***534***
United States Military Academy (NY) ***535***
United States Naval Academy (MD) ***535***
U at Buffalo, The State University of New York (NY) ***536***
The U of Alabama (AL) ***537***
The U of Arizona (AZ) ***538***
U of Calif, Davis (CA) ***540***
U of Calif, Los Angeles (CA) ***541***
U of Calif, San Diego (CA) ***541***
U of Central Florida (FL) ***542***
U of Cincinnati (OH) ***543***
U of Colorado at Boulder (CO) ***543***
U of Florida (FL) ***545***
U of Illinois at Urbana–Champaign (IL) ***548***
U of Kansas (KS) ***549***
U of Maryland, Coll Park (MD) ***552***
U of Miami (FL) ***553***
U of Michigan (MI) ***554***
U of Minnesota, Twin Cities Campus (MN) ***555***
U of Missouri–Rolla (MO) ***556***
U of North Dakota (ND) ***561***
U of Notre Dame (IN) ***562***
U of Oklahoma (OK) ***562***
U of Southern California (CA) ***576***
The U of Tennessee (TN) ***577***
The U of Texas at Arlington (TX) ***577***
The U of Texas at Austin (TX) ***578***
U of Toronto (ON, Canada) ***581***
U of Virginia (VA) ***582***
U of Washington (WA) ***583***
Utah State U (UT) ***587***
Virginia Polytechnic Inst and State U (VA) ***591***
Weber State U (UT) ***596***
Western Michigan U (MI) ***599***
West Virginia U (WV) ***602***
West Virginia U Inst of Technology (WV) ***602***
Wichita State U (KS) ***604***
Worcester Polytechnic Inst (MA) ***609***
York U (ON, Canada) ***611***

AEROSPACE ENGINEERING TECHNOLOGY

Overview: Students choosing this major learn the necessary technical skills and become familiar with some of the scientific principles to work with scientists and other engineers who are designing, manufacturing, and testing aircraft and spacecraft. *Related majors:* electrical engineering technology, instrumentation technology, computer engineering technology, air science, military technologies. *Potential careers:* Air Force technician, aerospace technician, mechanic, researcher. *Salary potential:* $23k-$35k.

Arizona State U East (AZ) ***271***
Central Missouri State U (MO) ***310***
Eastern Michigan U (MI) ***348***
Embry-Riddle Aeronautical U (FL) ***352***
New York Inst of Technology (NY) ***447***
Northeastern U (MA) ***450***
Ohio U (OH) ***458***
Purdue U (IN) ***475***
Saint Louis U (MO) ***492***
Utah State U (UT) ***587***

AEROSPACE SCIENCE

Overview: This major focuses on the science of aeronautics and aviation technology. *Related majors:* aeronautical engineering, electrical engineering, Air Force ROTC/air science, aviation management, physics. *Potential careers:* pilot, aviation or aeronautical engineer, airport or airline manager, Air Force officer, air traffic controller. *Salary potential:* $25k-$40k.

Augsburg Coll (MN) ***276***
Bishop's U (QC, Canada) ***289***
Daniel Webster Coll (NH) ***337***
Dowling Coll (NY) ***345***
U of the District of Columbia (DC) ***580***
York U (ON, Canada) ***611***

AFRICAN-AMERICAN STUDIES

Overview: Students who choose this major study the history, sociology, politics, culture, and economics of North American peoples, including those from the Caribbean who are descended from the African Diaspora. *Related Majors:* African history, American history, art history, music, literature. *Potential careers:* editor, anthropologist, art dealer, teacher. *Salary potential:* $25k-$30k.

Amherst Coll (MA) ***268***
Antioch Coll (OH) ***269***
Arizona State U (AZ) ***271***
Bowdoin Coll (ME) ***292***
Brandeis U (MA) ***293***
Brown U (RI) ***296***
California State U, Dominguez Hills (CA) ***300***
California State U, Fresno (CA) ***301***
California State U, Fullerton (CA) ***301***
California State U, Hayward (CA) ***301***
California State U, Long Beach (CA) ***301***
California State U, Northridge (CA) ***301***
California State U, San Bernardino (CA) ***302***
City Coll of the City U of NY (NY) ***314***
Claflin U (SC) ***314***
Claremont McKenna Coll (CA) ***315***
Coe Coll (IA) ***318***
Colby Coll (ME) ***318***
Colgate U (NY) ***319***
Coll of Staten Island of the City U of NY (NY) ***323***
Coll of the Holy Cross (MA) ***323***
The Coll of William and Mary (VA) ***324***
The Coll of Wooster (OH) ***324***
Columbia Coll (NY) ***326***

Columbia U, School of General Studies (NY) **328**
Cornell U (NY) **333**
Dartmouth Coll (NH) **337**
Denison U (OH) **339**
DePaul U (IL) **339**
Duke U (NC) **346**
Earlham Coll (IN) **347**
Eastern Illinois U (IL) **348**
Eastern Michigan U (MI) **348**
Emory U (GA) **354**
Florida A&M U (FL) **359**
Fordham U (NY) **362**
Georgia State U (GA) **368**
Gettysburg Coll (PA) **368**
Goddard Coll (VT) **369**
Grinnell Coll (IA) **373**
Guilford Coll (NC) **373**
Hampshire Coll (MA) **375**
Harvard U (MA) **376**
Hobart and William Smith Colls (NY) **380**
Hofstra U (NY) **380**
Howard U (DC) **382**
Hunter Coll of the City U of NY (NY) **382**
Indiana State U (IN) **385**
Indiana U Bloomington (IN) **385**
Indiana U Northwest (IN) **386**
Kent State U (OH) **397**
Kenyon Coll (OH) **398**
Knox Coll (IL) **399**
Lehman Coll of the City U of NY (NY) **404**
Lincoln U (PA) **407**
Long Island U, Southampton Coll, Friends World Program (NY) **409**
Loyola Marymount U (CA) **411**
Luther Coll (IA) **412**
Marquette U (WI) **418**
Martin U (IN) **419**
Mercer U (GA) **425**
Metropolitan State Coll of Denver (CO) **427**
Miami U (OH) **428**
Morehouse Coll (GA) **436**
Morgan State U (MD) **436**
Mount Holyoke Coll (MA) **438**
New York U (NY) **447**
Northeastern U (MA) **450**
Northwestern U (IL) **453**
Oberlin Coll (OH) **456**
The Ohio State U (OH) **457**
Ohio U (OH) **458**
Ohio Wesleyan U (OH) **459**
Penn State U Univ Park Campus (PA) **468**
Pitzer Coll (CA) **471**
Pomona Coll (CA) **472**
Purdue U (IN) **475**
Rhode Island Coll (RI) **479**
Roosevelt U (IL) **483**
Rutgers, The State U of New Jersey, Camden (NJ) **485**
Rutgers, The State U of New Jersey, Newark (NJ) **485**
Saint Augustine's Coll (NC) **487**
San Diego State U (CA) **498**
San Francisco State U (CA) **498**
San Jose State U (CA) **499**
Sarah Lawrence Coll (NY) **499**
Savannah State U (GA) **499**
Scripps Coll (CA) **501**
Seton Hall U (NJ) **502**
Simmons Coll (MA) **504**
Simon's Rock Coll of Bard (MA) **505**
Smith Coll (MA) **506**
Sonoma State U (CA) **506**
Southern Methodist U (TX) **510**
State U of NY at Albany (NY) **514**
State U of NY at Binghamton (NY) **515**
State U of NY at New Paltz (NY) **515**
State U of NY Coll at Brockport (NY) **515**
State U of NY Coll at Cortland (NY) **516**
State U of NY Coll at Geneseo (NY) **516**
State U of NY Coll at Oneonta (NY) **517**
Suffolk U (MA) **520**
Syracuse U (NY) **521**
Talladega Coll (AL) **522**
Temple U (PA) **523**
Tufts U (MA) **533**
U at Buffalo, The State University of New York (NY) **536**
The U of Alabama at Birmingham (AL) **537**
U of Calif, Berkeley (CA) **540**
U of Calif, Davis (CA) **540**
U of Calif, Los Angeles (CA) **541**
U of Calif, Riverside (CA) **541**
U of Calif, Santa Barbara (CA) **541**
U of Chicago (IL) **542**
U of Cincinnati (OH) **543**
U of Delaware (DE) **544**
U of Georgia (GA) **545**
U of Illinois at Chicago (IL) **547**
The U of Iowa (IA) **548**
U of Kansas (KS) **549**
U of Louisville (KY) **550**
U of Maryland, Baltimore County (MD) **552**
U of Maryland, Coll Park (MD) **552**
U of Massachusetts Amherst (MA) **552**
U of Massachusetts Boston (MA) **553**
U of Miami (FL) **553**
U of Michigan (MI) **554**
U of Michigan–Flint (MI) **554**
U of Minnesota, Twin Cities Campus (MN) **555**
The U of Montana–Missoula (MT) **556**
U of Nebraska at Omaha (NE) **557**
U of Nevada, Las Vegas (NV) **558**
U of New Mexico (NM) **559**
The U of North Carolina at Chapel Hill (NC) **560**
The U of North Carolina at Charlotte (NC) **560**
The U of North Carolina at Greensboro (NC) **560**
U of Northern Colorado (CO) **561**
U of Oklahoma (OK) **562**
U of Pennsylvania (PA) **563**
U of Pittsburgh (PA) **569**
U of South Carolina (SC) **575**
U of Southern California (CA) **576**
U of South Florida (FL) **576**
U of Virginia (VA) **582**
U of Washington (WA) **583**
U of Wisconsin–Madison (WI) **584**
U of Wisconsin–Milwaukee (WI) **585**
Vanderbilt U (TN) **588**
Washington U in St. Louis (MO) **595**
Wayne State U (MI) **596**
Wellesley Coll (MA) **597**
Wells Coll (NY) **597**
Wesleyan U (CT) **597**
Western Michigan U (MI) **599**
William Paterson U of New Jersey (NJ) **606**
Yale U (CT) **610**
York Coll of the City U of New York (NY) **611**
Youngstown State U (OH) **611**

AFRICAN LANGUAGES

Overview: Students learn about one or more of the major African languages, often combined with study in African literature, culture, and history. *Related majors:* international relations, development economics and international development, African studies, anthropology. *Potential careers:* anthropologist, international economist, Peace Corps, diplomatic corps, importer-exporter. *Salary potential:* $20k-$30k.

Harvard U (MA) **376**
Lincoln U (PA) **407**
Long Island U, Southampton Coll, Friends World Program (NY) **409**
Ohio U (OH) **458**
U of Calif, Los Angeles (CA) **541**
U of Wisconsin–Madison (WI) **584**

AFRICAN STUDIES

Overview: This major teaches students about the history, society, politics, culture, economics, and languages of the people of the African continent, usually emphasizing Africa south of the Sahara desert. *Related majors:* African-American studies, economics, international relations. *Potential careers:* international development officer, foreign service officer, medical researcher, archeologist, importer/exporter, art or antiques dealer. *Salary potential:* $20k-$28k.

American U (DC) **267**
Antioch Coll (OH) **269**
Bard Coll (NY) **281**
Barnard Coll (NY) **282**
Bates Coll (ME) **282**
Bowdoin Coll (ME) **292**
Bowling Green State U (OH) **292**
Brandeis U (MA) **293**
Brooklyn Coll of the City U of NY (NY) **295**
California State U, Northridge (CA) **301**
Carleton Coll (MN) **305**
Carleton U (ON, Canada) **305**
Colgate U (NY) **319**
Coll of the Holy Cross (MA) **323**
The Coll of Wooster (OH) **324**
Connecticut Coll (CT) **331**
Cornell U (NY) **333**
Dartmouth Coll (NH) **337**
DePaul U (IL) **339**
Emory U (GA) **354**
Fordham U (NY) **362**
Franklin and Marshall Coll (PA) **363**
Hamilton Coll (NY) **374**
Hampshire Coll (MA) **375**
Harvard U (MA) **376**
Haverford Coll (PA) **377**
Hobart and William Smith Colls (NY) **380**
Indiana U Bloomington (IN) **385**
Lake Forest Coll (IL) **400**
Lehigh U (PA) **404**
Long Island U, Southampton Coll, Friends World Program (NY) **409**
Luther Coll (IA) **412**
Marlboro Coll (VT) **418**
McGill U (QC, Canada) **423**
Morgan State U (MD) **436**
Oakland U (MI) **456**
The Ohio State U (OH) **457**
Ohio U (OH) **458**
Portland State U (OR) **472**
Queens Coll of the City U of NY (NY) **475**
Rutgers, The State U of New Jersey, New Brunswick (NJ) **485**
St. Lawrence U (NY) **491**
Shaw U (NC) **502**
Stanford U (CA) **514**
State U of NY at Binghamton (NY) **515**
State U of NY Coll at Brockport (NY) **515**
Stony Brook U, State University of New York (NY) **520**
Tennessee State U (TN) **523**
Tulane U (LA) **533**
U of Calif, Davis (CA) **540**
U of Chicago (IL) **542**
The U of Iowa (IA) **548**
U of Kansas (KS) **549**
U of Michigan (MI) **554**
U of Minnesota, Twin Cities Campus (MN) **555**
U of Pennsylvania (PA) **563**
U of Toronto (ON, Canada) **581**
U of Wisconsin–Madison (WI) **584**
Vanderbilt U (TN) **588**
Vassar Coll (NY) **589**
Washington U in St. Louis (MO) **595**
Wellesley Coll (MA) **597**
William Paterson U of New Jersey (NJ) **606**
Yale U (CT) **610**
York U (ON, Canada) **611**
Youngstown State U (OH) **611**

AGRIBUSINESS

Overview: This major focuses on economics with applications to agriculture, business, and environmental and resource issues. *Related majors:* environmental sciences, crop science, agronomy, agricultural business. *Potential careers:* farm manager, natural resource economist, public policy analyst. *Salary potential:* $20k-$50k.

Abilene Christian U (TX) **260**
Arkansas State U (AR) **272**
Central Missouri State U (MO) **310**
Coll of the Ozarks (MO) **323**
Colorado State U (CO) **325**
Cornell U (NY) **333**
Illinois State U (IL) **384**
McGill U (QC, Canada) **423**
Michigan State U (MI) **428**
Middle Tennessee State U (TN) **429**
Mississippi State U (MS) **432**
North Carolina State U (NC) **449**
North Dakota State U (ND) **449**
Northwestern Coll (IA) **453**
Penn State U Univ Park Campus (PA) **468**
South Dakota State U (SD) **507**
Southwest Missouri State U (MO) **513**
Southwest Texas State U (TX) **513**
Stephen F. Austin State U (TX) **518**
Texas A&M U (TX) **524**
U of Arkansas (AR) **539**
U of Delaware (DE) **544**
West Texas A&M U (TX) **602**

AGRICULTURAL ANIMAL BREEDING

Overview: This major teaches students how to apply the science of genetics and genetic engineering to the development of new breeds and the improvement of agricultural animals. *Related majors:* animal husbandry, genetics, biotechnology, animal health. *Potential careers:* ranch manager, geneticist, veterinarian. *Salary potential:* $25k-$40k.

Texas A&M U (TX) **524**

AGRICULTURAL ANIMAL HEALTH

Overview: Students who choose this major will learn about the prevention and control of diseases in agricultural animals. *Related majors:* animal sciences, biotechnology and biochemistry, microbiology. *Potential careers:* ranch manager, veterinarian, inspector, biochemist. *Salary potential:* $25k-$40k.

Sul Ross State U (TX) **521**

AGRICULTURAL ANIMAL HUSBANDRY/PRODUCTION MANAGEMENT

Overview: This major gives students the expertise to select, breed, care for, process, and market livestock and small farm animals. *Related majors:* animal sciences, genetics/breeding, dairy science, poultry science. *Potential careers:* farm/ranch manager, veterinarian, genetic scientist. *Salary potential:* $22k-$50k.

Angelo State U (TX) **269**
Dordt Coll (IA) **345**
North Dakota State U (ND) **449**
Saint Mary-of-the-Woods Coll (IN) **493**
Texas A&M U (TX) **524**
Texas Tech U (TX) **526**
U of New Hampshire (NH) **558**
The U of Tennessee at Martin (TN) **577**

AGRICULTURAL BUSINESS

Overview: Undergraduates who choose this major will learn about business and economic principles behind the organization, operation, and management of agricultural enterprises. *Related majors:* agribusiness, agricultural economics, farm/ranch management, crop production management. *Potential careers:* farm manager, natural resource economist, commodities merchandiser. *Salary potential:* $25k-$60k.

Alcorn State U (MS) **263**
Andrews U (MI) **269**
Arizona State U East (AZ) **271**
Arkansas Tech U (AR) **272**
Berea Coll (KY) **286**
California Polytechnic State U, San Luis Obispo (CA) **300**

AGRICULTURAL BUSINESS (continued)

California State Polytechnic U, Pomona (CA) ***300***
California State U, Chico (CA) ***300***
California State U, Fresno (CA) ***301***
Cameron U (OK) ***303***
Central Missouri State U (MO) ***310***
Clemson U (SC) ***317***
Concordia U Wisconsin (WI) ***331***
Cornell U (NY) ***333***
Delaware State U (DE) ***338***
Delaware Valley Coll (PA) ***339***
Dickinson State U (ND) ***344***
Dordt Coll (IA) ***345***
Eastern Kentucky U (KY) ***348***
Eastern New Mexico U (NM) ***349***
Eastern Oregon U (OR) ***349***
Florida A&M U (FL) ***359***
Florida Southern Coll (FL) ***361***
Fort Hays State U (KS) ***362***
Fort Lewis Coll (CO) ***362***
Freed-Hardeman U (TN) ***364***
Hannibal-LaGrange Coll (MO) ***375***
Insto Tecno Estudios Sups Monterrey(Mexico) ***388***
Iowa State U of Science and Technology (IA) ***390***
Kansas State U (KS) ***396***
Louisiana State U and A&M Coll (LA) ***410***
Louisiana Tech U (LA) ***410***
Lubbock Christian U (TX) ***412***
McGill U (QC, Canada) ***423***
McPherson Coll (KS) ***423***
Michigan State U (MI) ***428***
MidAmerica Nazarene U (KS) ***428***
Missouri Valley Coll (MO) ***433***
Montana State U–Bozeman (MT) ***434***
Murray State U (KY) ***440***
New Mexico State U (NM) ***446***
Nicholls State U (LA) ***447***
North Carolina Ag and Tech State U (NC) ***448***
Northwestern Oklahoma State U (OK) ***453***
Northwest Missouri State U (MO) ***454***
The Ohio State U (OH) ***457***
Oklahoma Panhandle State U (OK) ***460***
Oklahoma State U (OK) ***460***
Oregon State U (OR) ***462***
Penn State U Univ Park Campus (PA) ***468***
Rocky Mountain Coll (MT) ***482***
Sam Houston State U (TX) ***497***
San Diego State U (CA) ***498***
Simon's Rock Coll of Bard (MA) ***505***
South Carolina State U (SC) ***506***
Southeast Missouri State U (MO) ***508***
Southern Arkansas U–Magnolia (AR) ***509***
Southwest State U (MN) ***513***
State U of NY Coll of A&T at Cobleskill (NY) ***517***
Sul Ross State U (TX) ***521***
Tabor Coll (KS) ***522***
Tarleton State U (TX) ***522***
Tennessee Technological U (TN) ***524***
Texas A&M U (TX) ***524***
Texas A&M U–Kingsville (TX) ***525***
Texas Tech U (TX) ***526***
Tuskegee U (AL) ***533***
U of Alberta (AB, Canada) ***538***
U of Calif, Davis (CA) ***540***
U of Delaware (DE) ***544***
U of Georgia (GA) ***545***
U of Guelph (ON, Canada) ***546***
U of Hawaii at Hilo (HI) ***546***
U of Idaho (ID) ***547***
The U of Lethbridge (AB, Canada) ***549***
U of Maryland Eastern Shore (MD) ***552***
U of Minnesota, Crookston (MN) ***554***
U of Minnesota, Twin Cities Campus (MN) ***555***
U of Missouri–Columbia (MO) ***555***
U of Nebraska at Kearney (NE) ***557***
U of Nebraska–Lincoln (NE) ***557***
U of New Hampshire (NH) ***558***
The U of Tennessee at Martin (TN) ***577***
U of Vermont (VT) ***582***
U of Wisconsin–Madison (WI) ***584***
U of Wisconsin–Platteville (WI) ***585***
U of Wisconsin–River Falls (WI) ***585***
U of Wyoming (WY) ***586***
Utah State U (UT) ***587***
Washington State U (WA) ***595***
Wayne State Coll (NE) ***596***
West Texas A&M U (TX) ***602***
Wilmington Coll (OH) ***607***

AGRICULTURAL BUSINESS AND PRODUCTION RELATED

Information can be found under this major's main heading.

Michigan State U (MI) ***428***
U of Nebraska–Lincoln (NE) ***557***

AGRICULTURAL BUSINESS RELATED

Information can be found under this major's main heading.

U of Nebraska–Lincoln (NE) ***557***
The U of Tennessee (TN) ***577***
Utah State U (UT) ***587***

AGRICULTURAL ECONOMICS

Overview: Students who choose this major will learn how to apply economics to the analysis of resource allocation, productivity, investment, and trends as they relate to the agricultural sector. *Related majors:* agricultural business, agribusiness, economics, agricultural production. *Potential careers:* farm manager, agricultural industry manager, inspector, biochemist. *Salary potential:* $30k-$60k.

Alabama A&M U (AL) ***261***
Alcorn State U (MS) ***263***
Auburn U (AL) ***276***
Central Missouri State U (MO) ***310***
Clemson U (SC) ***317***
Colorado State U (CO) ***325***
Cornell U (NY) ***333***
Eastern Oregon U (OR) ***349***
Fort Valley State U (GA) ***362***
Kansas State U (KS) ***396***
Langston U (OK) ***402***
McGill U (QC, Canada) ***423***
McPherson Coll (KS) ***423***
Michigan State U (MI) ***428***
Mississippi State U (MS) ***432***
Murray State U (KY) ***440***
New Mexico State U (NM) ***446***
North Carolina Ag and Tech State U (NC) ***448***
North Dakota State U (ND) ***449***
Northwest Missouri State U (MO) ***454***
The Ohio State U (OH) ***457***
Oklahoma State U (OK) ***460***
Oregon State U (OR) ***462***
Purdue U (IN) ***475***
South Dakota State U (SD) ***507***
Southern Illinois U Carbondale (IL) ***509***
Southern U and A&M Coll (LA) ***511***
Tarleton State U (TX) ***522***
Texas A&M U (TX) ***524***
Texas A&M U–Commerce (TX) ***525***
Texas Tech U (TX) ***526***
Truman State U (MO) ***532***
Université Laval (QC, Canada) ***536***
U of Alberta (AB, Canada) ***538***
The U of Arizona (AZ) ***538***
U of Calif, Davis (CA) ***540***
U of Connecticut (CT) ***544***
U of Delaware (DE) ***544***
U of Florida (FL) ***545***
U of Georgia (GA) ***545***
U of Guelph (ON, Canada) ***546***
U of Hawaii at Manoa (HI) ***546***
U of Idaho (ID) ***547***
U of Illinois at Urbana–Champaign (IL) ***548***
U of Kentucky (KY) ***549***
U of Maine (ME) ***550***
U of Manitoba (MB, Canada) ***551***
U of Maryland, Coll Park (MD) ***552***
U of Missouri–Columbia (MO) ***555***
U of Nebraska–Lincoln (NE) ***557***
U of Nevada, Reno (NV) ***558***
U of Saskatchewan (SK, Canada) ***574***
The U of Tennessee (TN) ***577***
U of Vermont (VT) ***582***
U of Wisconsin–Madison (WI) ***584***
Utah State U (UT) ***587***
Virginia Polytechnic Inst and State U (VA) ***591***
Washington State U (WA) ***595***

AGRICULTURAL EDUCATION

Overview: this major prepares undergraduates to teach vocational agricultural subjects. *Related majors:* agricultural animal husbandry and agricultural production, agronomy, farm and ranch management. *Potential careers:* agricultural teacher, vocational teacher, student counselor. *Salary potential:* $24k-$35k.

Andrews U (MI) ***269***
Arkansas State U (AR) ***272***
Auburn U (AL) ***276***
California State Polytechnic U, Pomona (CA) ***300***
California State U, Chico (CA) ***300***
California State U, Fresno (CA) ***301***
Central Missouri State U (MO) ***310***
Clemson U (SC) ***317***
Coll of the Ozarks (MO) ***323***
Colorado State U (CO) ***325***
Cornell U (NY) ***333***
Delaware State U (DE) ***338***
Eastern New Mexico U (NM) ***349***
Iowa State U of Science and Technology (IA) ***390***
Langston U (OK) ***402***
Mississippi State U (MS) ***432***
Montana State U–Bozeman (MT) ***434***
Morehead State U (KY) ***436***
Murray State U (KY) ***440***
New Mexico State U (NM) ***446***
North Carolina Ag and Tech State U (NC) ***448***
North Carolina State U (NC) ***449***
North Dakota State U (ND) ***449***
Northwest Missouri State U (MO) ***454***
The Ohio State U (OH) ***457***
Oklahoma Panhandle State U (OK) ***460***
Oklahoma State U (OK) ***460***
Prairie View A&M U (TX) ***473***
Purdue U (IN) ***475***
Sam Houston State U (TX) ***497***
South Dakota State U (SD) ***507***
Southern Arkansas U–Magnolia (AR) ***509***
Southwest Missouri State U (MO) ***513***
Tarleton State U (TX) ***522***
Tennessee Technological U (TN) ***524***
Texas A&M U–Commerce (TX) ***525***
Texas A&M U–Kingsville (TX) ***525***
The U of Arizona (AZ) ***538***
U of Arkansas (AR) ***539***
U of Calif, Davis (CA) ***540***
U of Connecticut (CT) ***544***
U of Delaware (DE) ***544***
U of Florida (FL) ***545***
U of Georgia (GA) ***545***
U of Hawaii at Manoa (HI) ***546***
U of Idaho (ID) ***547***
U of Illinois at Urbana–Champaign (IL) ***548***
U of Maryland Eastern Shore (MD) ***552***
U of Minnesota, Twin Cities Campus (MN) ***555***
U of Missouri–Columbia (MO) ***555***
U of Nebraska–Lincoln (NE) ***557***
U of Nevada, Reno (NV) ***558***
The U of Tennessee (TN) ***577***
The U of Tennessee at Martin (TN) ***577***
U of Wisconsin–Madison (WI) ***584***
U of Wisconsin–River Falls (WI) ***585***
U of Wyoming (WY) ***586***
Utah State U (UT) ***587***
Virginia Polytechnic Inst and State U (VA) ***591***
Washington State U (WA) ***595***
West Virginia U (WV) ***602***
Wilmington Coll (OH) ***607***

AGRICULTURAL ENGINEERING

Overview: Undergraduates learn the mathematical and scientific principles behind the systems, equipment, and facilities used to produce, process, and store agricultural products. *Related majors:* industrial engineering, agricultural mechanization, agricultural animal husbandry and production management, crop production management, food sciences technology. *Potential careers:* industrial engineer, production manager, researcher, quality control manager. *Salary potential;* $37k-$50k.

Auburn U (AL) ***276***
California Polytechnic State U, San Luis Obispo (CA) ***300***
California State Polytechnic U, Pomona (CA) ***300***
Clemson U (SC) ***317***
Colorado State U (CO) ***325***
Cornell U (NY) ***333***
Dalhousie U (NS, Canada) ***336***
Fort Valley State U (GA) ***362***
Iowa State U of Science and Technology (IA) ***390***
Kansas State U (KS) ***396***
McGill U (QC, Canada) ***423***
Michigan State U (MI) ***428***
Mississippi State U (MS) ***432***
Murray State U (KY) ***440***
North Carolina State U (NC) ***449***
North Dakota State U (ND) ***449***
The Ohio State U (OH) ***457***
Penn State U Univ Park Campus (PA) ***468***
Purdue U (IN) ***475***
South Dakota State U (SD) ***507***
Tennessee Technological U (TN) ***524***
Texas A&M U (TX) ***524***
The U of Arizona (AZ) ***538***
U of Arkansas (AR) ***539***
U of Calif, Davis (CA) ***540***
U of Delaware (DE) ***544***
U of Florida (FL) ***545***
U of Georgia (GA) ***545***
U of Hawaii at Manoa (HI) ***546***
U of Idaho (ID) ***547***
U of Illinois at Urbana–Champaign (IL) ***548***
U of Kentucky (KY) ***549***
U of Maine (ME) ***550***
U of Manitoba (MB, Canada) ***551***
U of Minnesota, Twin Cities Campus (MN) ***555***
U of Nebraska–Lincoln (NE) ***557***
U of Saskatchewan (SK, Canada) ***574***
The U of Tennessee (TN) ***577***
U of Wisconsin–Madison (WI) ***584***
U of Wisconsin–River Falls (WI) ***585***
Utah State U (UT) ***587***
Washington State U (WA) ***595***

AGRICULTURAL EXTENSION

Overview: This major teaches students how to provide technical assistance and educational and consulting services to gardeners, farmers, ranchers, and agribusinesses. *Related majors:* plant science, plant pathology, pest management, plant breeding/genetics, agricultural supplies. *Potential careers:* agribusiness or farm consultant, customer service representative, entomologist, mechanic, soil scientist. *Salary potential:* $25k-$30k.

Colorado State U (CO) ***325***
U of Wyoming (WY) ***586***

AGRICULTURAL/FOOD PRODUCTS PROCESSING

Overview: Students who choose this major will learn how to inspect, process, and package agricultural products as human, plant, or animal food or other industrial products. *Related majors:* nutrition, chemical and mechanical operations, consumer packaging. *Potential careers:* production manager, quality control manager, packaging designer. *Salary potential:* $30k-$45k.

Kansas State U (KS) ***396***

Michigan State U (MI) ***428***
The Ohio State U (OH) ***457***
U of Illinois at Urbana–Champaign (IL) ***548***

AGRICULTURAL MECHANIZATION

Overview: Students who choose this major will learn how to market, sell, and service different kinds of technical equipment that are used in the agricultural or agribusiness industries. *Related majors:* farm/ranch management, agricultural supplies, horticulture. *Potential careers:* agricultural equipment salesperson or technician, engineer, farm manager. *Salary potential:* $25k-$45k.

Andrews U (MI) ***269***
Cameron U (OK) ***303***
Central Missouri State U (MO) ***310***
Coll of the Ozarks (MO) ***323***
Cornell U (NY) ***333***
Eastern Kentucky U (KY) ***348***
Iowa State U of Science and Technology (IA) ***390***
Kansas State U (KS) ***396***
Lewis-Clark State Coll (ID) ***406***
Montana State U–Bozeman (MT) ***434***
North Carolina Ag and Tech State U (NC) ***448***
North Dakota State U (ND) ***449***
Northwest Missouri State U (MO) ***454***
Penn State U Univ Park Campus (PA) ***468***
Purdue U (IN) ***475***
Sam Houston State U (TX) ***497***
South Dakota State U (SD) ***507***
State U of NY Coll of A&T at Cobleskill (NY) ***517***
Stephen F. Austin State U (TX) ***518***
Texas A&M U (TX) ***524***
U of Idaho (ID) ***547***
U of Illinois at Urbana–Champaign (IL) ***548***
U of Missouri–Columbia (MO) ***555***
U of Nebraska–Lincoln (NE) ***557***
Washington State U (WA) ***595***

AGRICULTURAL PLANT PATHOLOGY

Overview: Students will focus on basic sciences related to insects, plant pathogens, and weeds and their ecology, biochemistry, and management. *Related majors:* entomology, plant sciences, agronomy. *Potential careers:* entomologist, ecologist, biological control specialist, extension agent, plant pathologist. *Salary potential:* $25k-$50k.

The Ohio State U (OH) ***457***

AGRICULTURAL PRODUCTION

Overview: Students who choose this major will focus on the economics and use of facilities, natural resources, equipment, labor, and capital that are used in the production of plant and animal products. *Related majors:* farm/ranch management, agricultural production, agricultural mechanization. *Potential careers:* natural resource economist, foreign development expert, Peace Corps, farm or agribusiness manager. *Salary potential:* $25k-$50k.

North Dakota State U (ND) ***449***
Stephen F. Austin State U (TX) ***518***
Texas Tech U (TX) ***526***
U of Hawaii at Manoa (HI) ***546***
Washington State U (WA) ***595***

AGRICULTURAL SCIENCES

Overview: This major is an interdisciplinary approach designed for students interested in cellular and molecular processes or the commercial production of agriculturally related products. *Related majors:* plant sciences, agronomy, agricultural plant pathology, plant protection. *Potential careers:* entomologist, ecologist, biological control specialist, extension agent, plant pathologist. *Salary potential:* $25k-$50k.

Alcorn State U (MS) ***263***
Andrews U (MI) ***269***
Arkansas State U (AR) ***272***
Auburn U (AL) ***276***
Austin Peay State U (TN) ***278***
Berea Coll (KY) ***286***
California Polytechnic State U, San Luis Obispo (CA) ***300***
California State Polytechnic U, Pomona (CA) ***300***
Cameron U (OK) ***303***
Colorado State U (CO) ***325***
Cornell U (NY) ***333***
Delaware State U (DE) ***338***
Dordt Coll (IA) ***345***
Eastern Kentucky U (KY) ***348***
The Evergreen State Coll (WA) ***355***
Ferrum Coll (VA) ***358***
Florida A&M U (FL) ***359***
Fort Hays State U (KS) ***362***
Hampshire Coll (MA) ***375***
Hardin-Simmons U (TX) ***376***
Illinois State U (IL) ***384***
Iowa State U of Science and Technology (IA) ***390***
Lubbock Christian U (TX) ***412***
Maharishi U of Management (IA) ***414***
McNeese State U (LA) ***423***
Mississippi State U (MS) ***432***
Morehead State U (KY) ***436***
Murray State U (KY) ***440***
New Mexico State U (NM) ***446***
North Carolina Ag and Tech State U (NC) ***448***
North Dakota State U (ND) ***449***
Northwestern Oklahoma State U (OK) ***453***
Northwest Missouri State U (MO) ***454***
Oklahoma State U (OK) ***460***
Oregon State U (OR) ***462***
Penn State U Univ Park Campus (PA) ***468***
Prairie View A&M U (TX) ***473***
Purdue U (IN) ***475***
Sam Houston State U (TX) ***497***
South Dakota State U (SD) ***507***
Southeast Missouri State U (MO) ***508***
Southern Arkansas U–Magnolia (AR) ***509***
Southern Illinois U Carbondale (IL) ***509***
Southern U and A&M Coll (LA) ***511***
Southwest Missouri State U (MO) ***513***
Southwest Texas State U (TX) ***513***
Stephen F. Austin State U (TX) ***518***
Sterling Coll (VT) ***519***
Tarleton State U (TX) ***522***
Tennessee State U (TN) ***523***
Texas A&M U (TX) ***524***
Texas A&M U–Commerce (TX) ***525***
Texas A&M U–Kingsville (TX) ***525***
Texas Tech U (TX) ***526***
Truman State U (MO) ***532***
Tuskegee U (AL) ***533***
U of Alberta (AB, Canada) ***538***
The U of Arizona (AZ) ***538***
U of Arkansas at Monticello (AR) ***539***
The U of British Columbia (BC, Canada) ***540***
U of Connecticut (CT) ***544***
U of Delaware (DE) ***544***
U of Guelph (ON, Canada) ***546***
U of Hawaii at Hilo (HI) ***546***
U of Idaho (ID) ***547***
U of Illinois at Urbana–Champaign (IL) ***548***
The U of Lethbridge (AB, Canada) ***549***
U of Louisiana at Lafayette (LA) ***550***
U of Manitoba (MB, Canada) ***551***
U of Maryland, Coll Park (MD) ***552***
U of Maryland Eastern Shore (MD) ***552***
U of Minnesota, Crookston (MN) ***554***
U of Minnesota, Twin Cities Campus (MN) ***555***
U of Missouri–Columbia (MO) ***555***
U of New Hampshire (NH) ***558***
U of Saskatchewan (SK, Canada) ***574***
The U of Tennessee at Martin (TN) ***577***
U of Vermont (VT) ***582***
U of Wisconsin–Madison (WI) ***584***
U of Wisconsin–River Falls (WI) ***585***
Utah State U (UT) ***587***
Virginia State U (VA) ***591***
Warren Wilson Coll (NC) ***594***
Western Illinois U (IL) ***599***
Western Kentucky U (KY) ***599***
Wilmington Coll (OH) ***607***

AGRICULTURAL SCIENCES RELATED

Information can be found under this major's main heading.

California State U, Chico (CA) ***300***
Maharishi U of Management (IA) ***414***
U of Kentucky (KY) ***549***
U of Wyoming (WY) ***586***

AGRICULTURAL SUPPLIES

Overview: Undergraduates of this major will learn how to sell agricultural products and supplies, provide support services to agricultural enterprises, and purchase and market agricultural products. *Related majors:* business management, marketing, agribusiness, agricultural business. *Potential careers:* salesperson, buyer, manufacturing executive. *Salary potential:* $25k-$40k.

Tarleton State U (TX) ***522***

AGRONOMY/CROP SCIENCE

Overview: This major focuses on the growth and behavior of agricultural crops, the development of new plant varieties, and the management of soils and nutrients for optimum plant productivity. *Related majors:* plant sciences, soil science, farm management, agricultural production. *Potential careers:* farm manager, soil scientist, plant breeder. *Salary potential:* $25k-$35k.

Alcorn State U (MS) ***263***
Andrews U (MI) ***269***
Brigham Young U (UT) ***295***
California Polytechnic State U, San Luis Obispo (CA) ***300***
California State Polytechnic U, Pomona (CA) ***300***
California State U, Chico (CA) ***300***
California State U, Fresno (CA) ***301***
Cameron U (OK) ***303***
Coll of the Ozarks (MO) ***323***
Colorado State U (CO) ***325***
Cornell U (NY) ***333***
Delaware Valley Coll (PA) ***339***
Eastern Oregon U (OR) ***349***
Fort Hays State U (KS) ***362***
Fort Valley State U (GA) ***362***
Insto Tecno Estudios Sups Monterrey(Mexico) ***388***
Iowa State U of Science and Technology (IA) ***390***
Kansas State U (KS) ***396***
Michigan State U (MI) ***428***
Mississippi State U (MS) ***432***
Murray State U (KY) ***440***
New Mexico State U (NM) ***446***
North Carolina State U (NC) ***449***
North Dakota State U (ND) ***449***
Northwest Missouri State U (MO) ***454***
The Ohio State U (OH) ***457***
Oklahoma Panhandle State U (OK) ***460***
Oregon State U (OR) ***462***
Penn State U Univ Park Campus (PA) ***468***
Purdue U (IN) ***475***
South Dakota State U (SD) ***507***
Southeast Missouri State U (MO) ***508***
Southwest Missouri State U (MO) ***513***
Southwest State U (MN) ***513***
State U of NY Coll of A&T at Cobleskill (NY) ***517***
Stephen F. Austin State U (TX) ***518***
Tennessee Technological U (TN) ***524***
Texas A&M U (TX) ***524***
Texas A&M U–Commerce (TX) ***525***
Texas A&M U–Kingsville (TX) ***525***
Texas Tech U (TX) ***526***
Truman State U (MO) ***532***
Tuskegee U (AL) ***533***
Université Laval (QC, Canada) ***536***
U of Alberta (AB, Canada) ***538***
U of Arkansas (AR) ***539***
U of Connecticut (CT) ***544***
U of Delaware (DE) ***544***
U of Florida (FL) ***545***
U of Georgia (GA) ***545***
U of Guelph (ON, Canada) ***546***
U of Illinois at Urbana–Champaign (IL) ***548***
U of Kentucky (KY) ***549***
U of Manitoba (MB, Canada) ***551***
U of Maryland, Coll Park (MD) ***552***
U of Minnesota, Crookston (MN) ***554***
U of Minnesota, Twin Cities Campus (MN) ***555***
U of Nebraska–Lincoln (NE) ***557***
U of New Hampshire (NH) ***558***
U of Saskatchewan (SK, Canada) ***574***
The U of Tennessee at Martin (TN) ***577***
U of Wisconsin–Madison (WI) ***584***
U of Wisconsin–Platteville (WI) ***585***
U of Wisconsin–River Falls (WI) ***585***
Utah State U (UT) ***587***
Virginia Polytechnic Inst and State U (VA) ***591***
Washington State U (WA) ***595***
West Virginia U (WV) ***602***

AIRCRAFT MECHANIC/ AIRFRAME

Overview: This major will teach students the technical skills and knowledge they need to service, repair, and maintain all aircraft components other than avionics, engines, instruments, and propellers. *Related majors:* welding technology, leatherwork and upholstery. *Potential careers:* aircraft mechanic (airframe), aircraft designer. *Salary potential:* $20k-$30k.

Coll of Aeronautics (NY) ***319***
Dowling Coll (NY) ***345***
LeTourneau U (TX) ***405***
Lewis U (IL) ***406***
Utah State U (UT) ***587***
Wilmington Coll (DE) ***607***

AIRCRAFT MECHANIC/ POWERPLANT

Overview: Students will learn the technical skills and knowledge they need to repair, maintain, and service aircraft, power plant, and related systems. *Related majors:* aircraft mechanic (airframe), instrument calibration and repair. *Potential careers:* aircraft mechanic, aircraft inspector. *Salary potential:* $20k-$30k.

Thomas Edison State Coll (NJ) ***527***

AIRCRAFT PILOT (PROFESSIONAL)

Overview: In this major students learn the skills and technical knowledge necessary to fly or navigate fixed-wing aircraft for a variety of purposes. *Related majors:* communication equipment technology, operations research, aerospace science, mathematics. *Potential careers:* airline pilot, agricultural pilot, cargo pilot, aircraft navigator, Air Force officer. *Salary potential:* $20k-$35k.

Andrews U (MI) ***269***
Averett U (VA) ***278***
Baylor U (TX) ***283***
Bowling Green State U (OH) ***292***
Bridgewater State Coll (MA) ***294***
Concordia U (MI) ***330***

AIRCRAFT PILOT (PROFESSIONAL) (continued)

Concordia U Wisconsin (WI) ***331***
Cornerstone U (MI) ***333***
Daniel Webster Coll (NH) ***337***
Delaware State U (DE) ***338***
Delta State U (MS) ***339***
Eastern Kentucky U (KY) ***348***
Embry-Riddle Aeronautical U (AZ) ***352***
Embry-Riddle Aeronautical U (FL) ***352***
Embry-Riddle Aeronautical U, Extended Campus (FL) ***352***
Everglades Coll (FL) ***355***
State U of NY at Farmingdale (NY) ***357***
Florida Inst of Technology (FL) ***360***
Grace U (NE) ***371***
Henderson State U (AR) ***378***
Indiana State U (IN) ***385***
Jacksonville U (FL) ***391***
Kansas State U (KS) ***396***
LeTourneau U (TX) ***405***
Lewis U (IL) ***406***
Lynn U (FL) ***413***
Oklahoma State U (OK) ***460***
Piedmont Baptist Coll (NC) ***470***
Providence Coll and Theological Seminary (MB, Canada) ***475***
Purdue U (IN) ***475***
Rocky Mountain Coll (MT) ***482***
St. Cloud State U (MN) ***488***
Saint Louis U (MO) ***492***
Salem International U (WV) ***496***
Southeastern Oklahoma State U (OK) ***508***
Tarleton State U (TX) ***522***
Thomas Edison State Coll (NJ) ***527***
Trinity Western U (BC, Canada) ***531***
U of Dubuque (IA) ***545***
U of Illinois at Urbana–Champaign (IL) ***548***
U of Minnesota, Crookston (MN) ***554***
U of North Dakota (ND) ***561***
U of Oklahoma (OK) ***562***
Western Michigan U (MI) ***599***
Westminster Coll (UT) ***601***

AIR FORCE R.O.T.C./AIR SCIENCE

Overview: This major will teach students the theories and practices of air science and prepare them for a career as an Air Force officer. *Related majors:* air science, military studies, military technologies, aerospace engineering, professional pilot/ navigator, mathematics and computer science. *Potential careers:* Air Force officer, aerospace engineer, pilot, navigator, weapons expert, computer scientist. *Salary potential:* $25k-$35k.

La Salle U (PA) ***402***
Ohio U (OH) ***458***
Rensselaer Polytechnic Inst (NY) ***478***
The U of Iowa (IA) ***548***
U of Washington (WA) ***583***
Weber State U (UT) ***596***

AIR TRAFFIC CONTROL

Overview: Students learn the technical knowledge and skills necessary to work as air traffic controllers at the nation's airports. *Related majors:* aviation/air science, communication equipment technology, meteorology, electronics technology. *Potential career:* air traffic controller. *Salary potential:* $25k-$30k.

Averett U (VA) ***278***
Daniel Webster Coll (NH) ***337***
Hampton U (VA) ***375***
St. Cloud State U (MN) ***488***
Thomas Edison State Coll (NJ) ***527***
U of Maryland Eastern Shore (MD) ***552***
U of North Dakota (ND) ***561***

AIR TRANSPORTATION RELATED

Information can be found under this major's main heading.

Averett U (VA) ***278***
Western Michigan U (MI) ***599***

ALCOHOL/DRUG ABUSE COUNSELING

Overview: This major teach-es students the principles of counseling individuals and/or families with drug problems and give them the skills they need to perform intervention and therapeutic services for persons suffering from addiction. *Related majors:* psychology, pharmacology, law and legal studies, clinical and medical social work. *Potential careers:* substance abuse counselor, therapist, psychologist. *Salary potential:* $24k-$34k.

Alvernia Coll (PA) ***265***
Bethany Coll of the Assemblies of God (CA) ***287***
Calumet Coll of Saint Joseph (IN) ***302***
Cedar Crest Coll (PA) ***308***
Graceland U (IA) ***371***
Indiana Wesleyan U (IN) ***387***
Martin U (IN) ***419***
Metropolitan State U (MN) ***427***
Minot State U (ND) ***432***
National-Louis U (IL) ***442***
Newman U (KS) ***445***
St. Cloud State U (MN) ***488***
Sheldon Jackson Coll (AK) ***503***
State U of NY Coll at Brockport (NY) ***515***
Towson U (MD) ***529***
U of Great Falls (MT) ***545***
U of Mary (ND) ***551***
U of St. Thomas (MN) ***573***
The U of South Dakota (SD) ***575***

AMERICAN GOVERNMENT

Overview: A branch of political science that explores the political institutions of the United States and their behavior. *Related majors:* law and legal studies, economics, communications, public relations, public policy analysis. *Potential careers:* politician or political aide, journalist, lobbyist, lawyer, sociologist. *Salary potential:* $25-$35k.

Bard Coll (NY) ***281***
Bowie State U (MD) ***292***
Bridgewater State Coll (MA) ***294***
Daemen Coll (NY) ***335***
Gallaudet U (DC) ***365***
Huston-Tillotson Coll (TX) ***383***
Lipscomb U (TN) ***408***
The Master's Coll and Seminary (CA) ***422***
Northern Arizona U (AZ) ***450***
Oklahoma Christian U (OK) ***459***
Rivier Coll (NH) ***480***
The U of Montana–Missoula (MT) ***556***

AMERICAN HISTORY

Overview: Students will study the development of the culture, society, and people of the United States, from the pre-Columbian era to the present. *Related majors:* literature, humanities, museum studies, science, religion. *Potential careers:* writer, journalist, editor, history teacher, professor. *Salary potential:* $25k-$35k.

Bard Coll (NY) ***281***
Bridgewater Coll (VA) ***294***
Calvin Coll (MI) ***303***
North Central Coll (IL) ***449***
Pitzer Coll (CA) ***471***
The U of Iowa (IA) ***548***
U of Puerto Rico, Río Piedras (PR) ***571***

AMERICAN LITERATURE

Overview: This major looks at the literary traditions of the United States from colonial times to the present. *Related majors:* folklore, African-American studies, American history, English literature, ethnic and cultural studies. *Potential careers:* writer, editor, journalist, advertising executive, politician. *Salary potential:* $23k-$32k.

Castleton State Coll (VT) ***307***
The Coll of Southeastern Europe, The American U of Athens(Greece) ***323***
Michigan State U (MI) ***428***
Queens U of Charlotte (NC) ***476***
U of Calif, Los Angeles (CA) ***541***
U of Southern California (CA) ***576***
Washington U in St. Louis (MO) ***595***

AMERICAN STUDIES

Overview: This major teaches students about the history, society, politics, culture, economics, dialects, and languages of the United States and its pre-Columbian, colonial predecessors, and immigration from other societies. *Related majors:* U.S. history, political science, economics, art history, American literature. *Potential careers:* anthropologist, writer, editor, advertising executive, librarian, teacher. *Salary potential:* $20k-$30k.

Albion Coll (MI) ***262***
Albright Coll (PA) ***263***
American U (DC) ***267***
Amherst Coll (MA) ***268***
Arizona State U West (AZ) ***272***
Ashland U (OH) ***274***
Austin Coll (TX) ***277***
Bard Coll (NY) ***281***
Barnard Coll (NY) ***282***
Bates Coll (ME) ***282***
Baylor U (TX) ***283***
Boston U (MA) ***292***
Bowling Green State U (OH) ***292***
Brandeis U (MA) ***293***
Brigham Young U (UT) ***295***
Brooklyn Coll of the City U of NY (NY) ***295***
Brown U (RI) ***296***
Cabrini Coll (PA) ***298***
California State U, Chico (CA) ***300***
California State U, Fullerton (CA) ***301***
California State U, San Bernardino (CA) ***302***
Carleton Coll (MN) ***305***
Case Western Reserve U (OH) ***307***
Cedarville U (OH) ***308***
Chapman U (CA) ***311***
Claremont McKenna Coll (CA) ***315***
Coe Coll (IA) ***318***
Colby Coll (ME) ***318***
Coll of Saint Elizabeth (NJ) ***321***
Coll of St. Joseph (VT) ***322***
The Coll of Saint Rose (NY) ***322***
Coll of Staten Island of the City U of NY (NY) ***323***
The Coll of William and Mary (VA) ***324***
Colorado State U (CO) ***325***
Columbia Coll (NY) ***326***
Connecticut Coll (CT) ***331***
Cornell U (NY) ***333***
Creighton U (NE) ***333***
Cumberland U (TN) ***335***
DePaul U (IL) ***339***
Dickinson Coll (PA) ***344***
Dominican Coll (NY) ***344***
Dominican U (IL) ***345***
Eckerd Coll (FL) ***350***
Elmhurst Coll (IL) ***351***
Elmira Coll (NY) ***351***
Elms Coll (MA) ***352***
Erskine Coll (SC) ***354***
The Evergreen State Coll (WA) ***355***
Fairfield U (CT) ***356***
Florida State U (FL) ***361***
Fordham U (NY) ***362***
Franklin and Marshall Coll (PA) ***363***
Franklin Coll (IN) ***363***
Franklin Pierce Coll (NH) ***364***
Freed-Hardeman U (TN) ***364***
Georgetown Coll (KY) ***366***
Georgetown U (DC) ***366***
The George Washington U (DC) ***367***
Gettysburg Coll (PA) ***368***
Goddard Coll (VT) ***369***
Goucher Coll (MD) ***370***
Grace U (NE) ***371***
Grinnell Coll (IA) ***373***
Hamilton Coll (NY) ***374***
Hampshire Coll (MA) ***375***
Harding U (AR) ***375***
Harvard U (MA) ***376***
High Point U (NC) ***379***
Hillsdale Coll (MI) ***379***
Hobart and William Smith Colls (NY) ***380***
Hofstra U (NY) ***380***
Howard Payne U (TX) ***382***
Huntingdon Coll (AL) ***383***
Idaho State U (ID) ***384***
Iona Coll (NY) ***390***
Johns Hopkins U (MD) ***392***
Keene State Coll (NH) ***396***
Kendall Coll (IL) ***396***
Kent State U (OH) ***397***
Kenyon Coll (OH) ***398***
King Coll (TN) ***398***
Knox Coll (IL) ***399***
Lafayette Coll (PA) ***400***
Lake Forest Coll (IL) ***400***
Lehigh U (PA) ***404***
Lehman Coll of the City U of NY (NY) ***404***
Lewis U (IL) ***406***
Lindsey Wilson Coll (KY) ***407***
Lipscomb U (TN) ***408***
Long Island U, Southampton Coll, Friends World Program (NY) ***409***
Lycoming Coll (PA) ***412***
Manhattanville Coll (NY) ***416***
Marist Coll (NY) ***417***
Marlboro Coll (VT) ***418***
Marymount Coll of Fordham U (NY) ***419***
Mary Washington Coll (VA) ***420***
Massachusetts Inst of Technology (MA) ***421***
Meredith Coll (NC) ***426***
Miami U (OH) ***428***
Middlebury Coll (VT) ***429***
Millikin U (IL) ***430***
Mills Coll (CA) ***431***
Minnesota State U, Moorhead (MN) ***432***
Montreat Coll (NC) ***435***
Mount Allison U (NB, Canada) ***437***
Mount Holyoke Coll (MA) ***438***
Mount St. Mary's Coll (CA) ***439***
Mount Union Coll (OH) ***440***
Muhlenberg Coll (PA) ***440***
Muskingum Coll (OH) ***441***
Nazareth Coll of Rochester (NY) ***443***
Northwestern U (IL) ***453***
Occidental Coll (CA) ***457***
Oglethorpe U (GA) ***457***
Oklahoma City U (OK) ***460***
Oklahoma State U (OK) ***460***
Oregon State U (OR) ***462***
Our Lady of the Lake U of San Antonio (TX) ***463***
Penn State U Abington Coll (PA) ***467***
Penn State U Univ Park Campus (PA) ***468***
Pfeiffer U (NC) ***469***
Pine Manor Coll (MA) ***470***
Pitzer Coll (CA) ***471***
Pomona Coll (CA) ***472***
Providence Coll (RI) ***474***
Queens Coll of the City U of NY (NY) ***475***
Queens U of Charlotte (NC) ***476***
Ramapo Coll of New Jersey (NJ) ***477***
Randolph-Macon Woman's Coll (VA) ***477***
Reed Coll (OR) ***477***
Rider U (NJ) ***480***
Roger Williams U (RI) ***483***
Roosevelt U (IL) ***483***
Rutgers, The State U of New Jersey, Newark (NJ) ***485***
Rutgers, The State U of New Jersey, New Brunswick (NJ) ***485***
St. Cloud State U (MN) ***488***
Saint Francis U (PA) ***488***
St. John Fisher Coll (NY) ***489***
St. John's U (NY) ***490***
Saint Joseph Coll (CT) ***490***
Saint Louis U (MO) ***492***
Saint Michael's Coll (VT) ***494***

St. Olaf Coll (MN) 495
Saint Peter's Coll (NJ) 495
Salem Coll (NC) 496
Salve Regina U (RI) 497
San Diego State U (CA) 498
San Francisco State U (CA) 498
San Jose State U (CA) 499
Sarah Lawrence Coll (NY) 499
Scripps Coll (CA) 501
Shenandoah U (VA) 503
Siena Coll (NY) 504
Simon's Rock Coll of Bard (MA) 505
Skidmore Coll (NY) 506
Smith Coll (MA) 506
Sonoma State U (CA) 506
Southern Nazarene U (OK) 510
Southern New Hampshire U (NH) 510
Southwestern U (TX) 513
Southwest Texas State U (TX) 513
Stanford U (CA) 514
State U of NY at Oswego (NY) 515
State U of NY Coll at Fredonia (NY) 516
State U of NY Coll at Geneseo (NY) 516
State U of NY Coll at Old Westbury (NY) 516
Stetson U (FL) 519
Stonehill Coll (MA) 520
Stony Brook U, State University of New York (NY) 520
Syracuse U (NY) 521
Temple U (PA) 523
Texas A&M U (TX) 524
Towson U (MD) 529
Trinity Coll (CT) 530
Tufts U (MA) 533
Tulane U (LA) 533
Union Coll (NY) 534
United States Military Academy (NY) 535
U at Buffalo, The State University of New York (NY) 536
The U of Alabama (AL) 537
U of Arkansas (AR) 539
U of Calif, Berkeley (CA) 540
U of Calif, Davis (CA) 540
U of Calif, Los Angeles (CA) 541
U of Calif, Santa Cruz (CA) 542
U of Chicago (IL) 542
U of Colorado at Boulder (CO) 543
U of Dayton (OH) 544
U of Florida (FL) 545
U of Hawaii at Manoa (HI) 546
U of Hawaii–West Oahu (HI) 546
U of Idaho (ID) 547
The U of Iowa (IA) 548
U of Kansas (KS) 549
U of Maryland, Baltimore County (MD) 552
U of Maryland, Coll Park (MD) 552
U of Massachusetts Boston (MA) 553
U of Massachusetts Lowell (MA) 553
U of Miami (FL) 553
U of Michigan (MI) 554
U of Michigan–Dearborn (MI) 554
U of Minnesota, Twin Cities Campus (MN) 555
U of Mississippi (MS) 555
U of Missouri–Kansas City (MO) 555
U of New England (ME) 558
U of New Hampshire (NH) 558
U of New Mexico (NM) 559
The U of North Carolina at Chapel Hill (NC) 560
U of Northern Iowa (IA) 561
U of Notre Dame (IN) 562
U of Pennsylvania (PA) 563
U of Pittsburgh at Bradford (PA) 569
U of Pittsburgh at Greensburg (PA) 570
U of Pittsburgh at Johnstown (PA) 570
U of Richmond (VA) 572
U of Rio Grande (OH) 572
U of Saskatchewan (SK, Canada) 574
U of Southern California (CA) 576
U of Southern Mississippi (MS) 576
U of South Florida (FL) 576
The U of Texas at Austin (TX) 578
The U of Texas at Dallas (TX) 578
The U of Texas at San Antonio (TX) 578
The U of Texas–Pan American (TX) 579
U of the South (TN) 581
U of Toledo (OH) 581
U of Toronto (ON, Canada) 581
U of Wisconsin–Madison (WI) 584
U of Wyoming (WY) 586
Upper Iowa U (IA) 587
Ursuline Coll (OH) 587
Utah State U (UT) 587
Valparaiso U (IN) 588
Vanderbilt U (TN) 588
Vassar Coll (NY) 589
Virginia Wesleyan Coll (VA) 591
Warner Pacific Coll (OR) 593
Warren Wilson Coll (NC) 594
Washington Coll (MD) 594
Washington State U (WA) 595
Washington U in St. Louis (MO) 595
Wayne State U (MI) 596
Wellesley Coll (MA) 597
Wells Coll (NY) 597
Wesleyan Coll (GA) 597
Wesleyan U (CT) 597
Wesley Coll (DE) 598
West Chester U of Pennsylvania (PA) 598
Western Connecticut State U (CT) 598
Western Michigan U (MI) 599
Western State Coll of Colorado (CO) 600
Western Washington U (WA) 600
Wheaton Coll (MA) 603
Whitworth Coll (WA) 604
Willamette U (OR) 605
Williams Coll (MA) 606
Wingate U (NC) 607
Wittenberg U (OH) 608
Yale U (CT) 610
Youngstown State U (OH) 611

ANATOMY

Overview: This major is concerned with organ and tissue systems and how these function within the whole body. *Related majors:* biology, biochemistry, cell biology, neuroscience, physiology, pathology, pharmacology. *Potential careers:* physician, endocrinologist, research scientist, medical administrator. *Salary potential:* $35k-$45k.

Andrews U (MI) 269
Cornell U (NY) 333
Duke U (NC) 346
Hampshire Coll (MA) 375
Howard U (DC) 382
Minnesota State U, Mankato (MN) 431
U of Indianapolis (IN) 548
U of Saskatchewan (SK, Canada) 574
U of Toronto (ON, Canada) 581

ANIMAL SCIENCES

Overview: This major will arm students with a scientific understanding of the breeding and husbandry of agricultural animals and the production, processing, and distribution of agricultural animal products. *Related majors:* ranch management, agricultural animal husbandry and production management, agricultural animal health, dairy and poultry science, genetics. *Potential careers:* agribusiness manager, ranch manager, veterinarian. *Salary potential:* $25k-$40k.

Abilene Christian U (TX) 260
Alabama A&M U (AL) 261
Alcorn State U (MS) 263
Angelo State U (TX) 269
Arkansas State U (AR) 272
Auburn U (AL) 276
Berry Coll (GA) 287
Brigham Young U (UT) 295
California Polytechnic State U, San Luis Obispo (CA) 300
California State Polytechnic U, Pomona (CA) 300
California State U, Chico (CA) 300
California State U, Fresno (CA) 301
Cameron U (OK) 303
Clemson U (SC) 317
Coll of the Ozarks (MO) 323
Colorado State U (CO) 325
Cornell U (NY) 333
Delaware State U (DE) 338
Delaware Valley Coll (PA) 339
Dordt Coll (IA) 345
Florida A&M U (FL) 359
Fort Hays State U (KS) 362
Fort Valley State U (GA) 362
Hampshire Coll (MA) 375
Insto Tecno Estudios Sups Monterrey(Mexico) 388
Iowa State U of Science and Technology (IA) 390
Kansas State U (KS) 396
Langston U (OK) 402
Louisiana State U and A&M Coll (LA) 410
Louisiana Tech U (LA) 410
McGill U (QC, Canada) 423
Michigan State U (MI) 428
Middle Tennessee State U (TN) 429
Mississippi State U (MS) 432
Montana State U–Bozeman (MT) 434
Mount Ida Coll (MA) 438
New Mexico State U (NM) 446
North Carolina Ag and Tech State U (NC) 448
North Carolina State U (NC) 449
North Dakota State U (ND) 449
Northwest Missouri State U (MO) 454
The Ohio State U (OH) 457
Oklahoma Panhandle State U (OK) 460
Oklahoma State U (OK) 460
Oregon State U (OR) 462
Penn State U Univ Park Campus (PA) 468
Purdue U (IN) 475
Sam Houston State U (TX) 497
South Dakota State U (SD) 507
Southeast Missouri State U (MO) 508
Southern Illinois U Carbondale (IL) 509
Southwestern U (TX) 513
Southwest Missouri State U (MO) 513
Southwest Texas State U (TX) 513
Stephen F. Austin State U (TX) 518
Sul Ross State U (TX) 521
Tarleton State U (TX) 522
Tennessee State U (TN) 523
Tennessee Technological U (TN) 524
Texas A&M U (TX) 524
Texas A&M U–Commerce (TX) 525
Texas A&M U–Kingsville (TX) 525
Texas Tech U (TX) 526
Truman State U (MO) 532
Tuskegee U (AL) 533
U Coll of the Cariboo (BC, Canada) 537
U of Alberta (AB, Canada) 538
The U of Arizona (AZ) 538
U of Arkansas (AR) 539
The U of British Columbia (BC, Canada) 540
U of Calif, Davis (CA) 540
U of Connecticut (CT) 544
U of Delaware (DE) 544
U of Denver (CO) 544
U of Florida (FL) 545
U of Georgia (GA) 545
U of Guelph (ON, Canada) 546
U of Hawaii at Hilo (HI) 546
U of Hawaii at Manoa (HI) 546
U of Idaho (ID) 547
U of Illinois at Urbana–Champaign (IL) 548
U of Kentucky (KY) 549
U of Maine (ME) 550
U of Manitoba (MB, Canada) 551
U of Maryland, Coll Park (MD) 552
U of Massachusetts Amherst (MA) 552
U of Minnesota, Crookston (MN) 554
U of Minnesota, Twin Cities Campus (MN) 555
U of Missouri–Columbia (MO) 555
U of Nebraska–Lincoln (NE) 557
U of Nevada, Reno (NV) 558
U of New Hampshire (NH) 558
U of Rhode Island (RI) 572
U of Saskatchewan (SK, Canada) 574
The U of Tennessee (TN) 577
The U of Tennessee at Martin (TN) 577
U of Vermont (VT) 582
U of Wisconsin–Madison (WI) 584
U of Wisconsin–Platteville (WI) 585
U of Wisconsin–River Falls (WI) 585
Utah State U (UT) 587
Virginia Polytechnic Inst and State U (VA) 591
Washington State U (WA) 595
West Texas A&M U (TX) 602
West Virginia U (WV) 602

ANIMAL SCIENCES RELATED

Information can be found under this major's main heading.

McGill U (QC, Canada) 423
Southwest Texas State U (TX) 513
U of Wyoming (WY) 586
Wilson Coll (PA) 607

ANTHROPOLOGY

Overview: Students choosing this major study the cultural, behavioral, and institutional aspects of human beings, prehumans and related primates in a modern, historical, and comparative context. *Related majors:* archeology, history, art history, animal behavior, psychology and behavioral sciences, folklore and area studies. *Potential careers:* anthropologist, advertising or marketing executive, diplomatic corps. *Salary potential:* $20k-$30k.

Adelphi U (NY) 260
Agnes Scott Coll (GA) 261
Albertson Coll of Idaho (ID) 262
Albion Coll (MI) 262
American U (DC) 267
The American U in Cairo(Egypt) 267
Amherst Coll (MA) 268
Antioch Coll (OH) 269
Appalachian State U (NC) 270
Arizona State U (AZ) 271
Athabasca U (AB, Canada) 275
Auburn U (AL) 276
Augustana Coll (IL) 276
Ball State U (IN) 280
Bard Coll (NY) 281
Barnard Coll (NY) 282
Bates Coll (ME) 282
Baylor U (TX) 283
Beloit Coll (WI) 285
Bennington Coll (VT) 286
Berry Coll (GA) 287
Biola U (CA) 289
Bloomsburg U of Pennsylvania (PA) 290
Boston U (MA) 292
Bowdoin Coll (ME) 292
Brandeis U (MA) 293
Bridgewater State Coll (MA) 294
Brigham Young U (UT) 295
Brooklyn Coll of the City U of NY (NY) 295
Brown U (RI) 296
Bryn Mawr Coll (PA) 297
Bucknell U (PA) 297
Butler U (IN) 297
California State Polytechnic U, Pomona (CA) 300
California State U, Bakersfield (CA) 300
California State U, Chico (CA) 300
California State U, Dominguez Hills (CA) 300
California State U, Fresno (CA) 301
California State U, Fullerton (CA) 301
California State U, Hayward (CA) 301
California State U, Long Beach (CA) 301
California State U, Northridge (CA) 301
California State U, Sacramento (CA) 301
California State U, San Bernardino (CA) 302
California State U, Stanislaus (CA) 302
California U of Pennsylvania (PA) 302
Canisius Coll (NY) 304
Carleton Coll (MN) 305
Carleton U (ON, Canada) 305
Case Western Reserve U (OH) 307
The Catholic U of America (DC) 307
Central Connecticut State U (CT) 309
Central Michigan U (MI) 310
Central Washington U (WA) 310
Centre Coll (KY) 310
City Coll of the City U of NY (NY) 314
Clarion U of Pennsylvania (PA) 315
Cleveland State U (OH) 317
Colby Coll (ME) 318
Colgate U (NY) 319
Coll of Charleston (SC) 320
Coll of Staten Island of the City U of NY (NY) 323
The Coll of William and Mary (VA) 324

ANTHROPOLOGY (continued)

The Colorado Coll (CO) *325*
Colorado State U (CO) *325*
Columbia Coll (NY) *326*
Columbia U, School of General Studies (NY) *328*
Concordia U (QC, Canada) *331*
Connecticut Coll (CT) *331*
Cornell Coll (IA) *332*
Cornell U (NY) *333*
Dalhousie U (NS, Canada) *336*
Dartmouth Coll (NH) *337*
Davidson Coll (NC) *338*
Denison U (OH) *339*
DePaul U (IL) *339*
DePauw U (IN) *339*
Dickinson Coll (PA) *344*
Dowling Coll (NY) *345*
Drake U (IA) *345*
Drew U (NJ) *346*
Duke U (NC) *346*
East Carolina U (NC) *347*
Eastern Kentucky U (KY) *348*
Eastern Michigan U (MI) *348*
Eastern New Mexico U (NM) *349*
Eastern Oregon U (OR) *349*
Eastern Washington U (WA) *349*
Eckerd Coll (FL) *350*
Edinboro U of Pennsylvania (PA) *351*
Elizabethtown Coll (PA) *351*
Elmira Coll (NY) *351*
Emory U (GA) *354*
Eugene Lang Coll, New School U (NY) *355*
The Evergreen State Coll (WA) *355*
Florida Atlantic U (FL) *359*
Florida State U (FL) *361*
Fordham U (NY) *362*
Fort Lewis Coll (CO) *362*
Framingham State Coll (MA) *362*
Franciscan U of Steubenville (OH) *363*
Franklin and Marshall Coll (PA) *363*
Franklin Pierce Coll (NH) *364*
George Mason U (VA) *366*
The George Washington U (DC) *367*
Georgia Southern U (GA) *367*
Georgia State U (GA) *368*
Gettysburg Coll (PA) *368*
Goddard Coll (VT) *369*
Grand Valley State U (MI) *371*
Grinnell Coll (IA) *373*
Gustavus Adolphus Coll (MN) *374*
Hamilton Coll (NY) *374*
Hamline U (MN) *374*
Hampshire Coll (MA) *375*
Hanover Coll (IN) *375*
Hartwick Coll (NY) *376*
Harvard U (MA) *376*
Haverford Coll (PA) *377*
Hawai'i Pacific U (HI) *377*
Heidelberg Coll (OH) *377*
Hendrix Coll (AR) *378*
Hobart and William Smith Colls (NY) *380*
Hofstra U (NY) *380*
Howard U (DC) *382*
Humboldt State U (CA) *382*
Hunter Coll of the City U of NY (NY) *382*
Idaho State U (ID) *384*
Illinois State U (IL) *384*
Indiana State U (IN) *385*
Indiana U Bloomington (IN) *385*
Indiana U of Pennsylvania (PA) *386*
Indiana U–Purdue U Fort Wayne (IN) *386*
Indiana U–Purdue U Indianapolis (IN) *387*
Iowa State U of Science and Technology (IA) *390*
Ithaca Coll (NY) *390*
Jacksonville State U (AL) *390*
James Madison U (VA) *391*
Johns Hopkins U (MD) *392*
Johnson State Coll (VT) *394*
Judson Coll (IL) *395*
Juniata Coll (PA) *395*
Kalamazoo Coll (MI) *395*
Kansas State U (KS) *396*
Kent State U (OH) *397*
Kenyon Coll (OH) *398*
Knox Coll (IL) *399*
Kutztown U of Pennsylvania (PA) *399*
Lafayette Coll (PA) *400*
Lake Forest Coll (IL) *400*
Lakehead U (ON, Canada) *400*
Laurentian U (ON, Canada) *403*
Lawrence U (WI) *403*
Lehigh U (PA) *404*
Lehman Coll of the City U of NY (NY) *404*
Lewis & Clark Coll (OR) *405*
Lincoln U (PA) *407*
Linfield Coll (OR) *408*
Lock Haven U of Pennsylvania (PA) *408*
Long Island U, Brooklyn Campus (NY) *409*
Long Island U, Southampton Coll, Friends World Program (NY) *409*
Longwood U (VA) *409*
Louisiana State U and A&M Coll (LA) *410*
Loyola U Chicago (IL) *411*
Luther Coll (IA) *412*
Lycoming Coll (PA) *412*
Macalester Coll (MN) *413*
Malaspina U-Coll (BC, Canada) *415*
Mansfield U of Pennsylvania (PA) *416*
Marlboro Coll (VT) *418*
Marquette U (WI) *418*
Massachusetts Coll of Liberal Arts (MA) *421*
Massachusetts Inst of Technology (MA) *421*
McGill U (QC, Canada) *423*
McMaster U (ON, Canada) *423*
Memorial U of Newfoundland (NF, Canada) *424*
Mercyhurst Coll (PA) *425*
Mesa State Coll (CO) *426*
Metropolitan State Coll of Denver (CO) *427*
Miami U (OH) *428*
Michigan State U (MI) *428*
Middlebury Coll (VT) *429*
Middle Tennessee State U (TN) *429*
Millersville U of Pennsylvania (PA) *430*
Millsaps Coll (MS) *431*
Mills Coll (CA) *431*
Minnesota State U, Mankato (MN) *431*
Minnesota State U, Moorhead (MN) *432*
Mississippi State U (MS) *432*
Monmouth U (NJ) *434*
Montana State U–Bozeman (MT) *434*
Montclair State U (NJ) *435*
Mount Allison U (NB, Canada) *437*
Mount Holyoke Coll (MA) *438*
Mount Saint Vincent U (NS, Canada) *439*
Muhlenberg Coll (PA) *440*
National-Louis U (IL) *442*
New Coll of Florida (FL) *444*
New Mexico Highlands U (NM) *446*
New Mexico State U (NM) *446*
New York U (NY) *447*
North Carolina Wesleyan Coll (NC) *449*
North Central Coll (IL) *449*
North Dakota State U (ND) *449*
Northeastern Illinois U (IL) *450*
Northeastern U (MA) *450*
Northern Arizona U (AZ) *450*
Northern Illinois U (IL) *450*
Northern Kentucky U (KY) *451*
North Park U (IL) *452*
Northwestern State U of Louisiana (LA) *453*
Northwestern U (IL) *453*
Oakland U (MI) *456*
Oberlin Coll (OH) *456*
Occidental Coll (CA) *457*
The Ohio State U (OH) *457*
Ohio U (OH) *458*
Ohio Wesleyan U (OH) *459*
Okanagan U Coll (BC, Canada) *459*
Oregon State U (OR) *462*
Pacific Lutheran U (WA) *463*
Penn State U Univ Park Campus (PA) *468*
Pitzer Coll (CA) *471*
Plattsburgh State U of NY (NY) *471*
Pomona Coll (CA) *472*
Portland State U (OR) *472*
Prescott Coll (AZ) *474*
Princeton U (NJ) *474*
Principia Coll (IL) *474*
Purchase Coll, State U of NY (NY) *475*
Queens Coll of the City U of NY (NY) *475*
Radford U (VA) *476*
Reed Coll (OR) *477*
Rhode Island Coll (RI) *479*
Rhodes Coll (TN) *479*
Rice U (TX) *479*
Richmond, The American International U in London(United Kingdom) *480*
Ripon Coll (WI) *480*
Rockford Coll (IL) *482*
Rollins Coll (FL) *483*
Rutgers, The State U of New Jersey, Newark (NJ) *485*
Rutgers, The State U of New Jersey, New Brunswick (NJ) *485*
St. Cloud State U (MN) *488*
Saint Francis U (PA) *488*
St. Francis Xavier U (NS, Canada) *489*
St. John Fisher Coll (NY) *489*
St. John's U (NY) *490*
St. Lawrence U (NY) *491*
Saint Mary's Coll (IN) *493*
Saint Mary's Coll of California (CA) *494*
St. Mary's Coll of Maryland (MD) *494*
Saint Mary's U (NS, Canada) *494*
St. Thomas U (NB, Canada) *496*
Saint Vincent Coll (PA) *496*
Salve Regina U (RI) *497*
San Diego State U (CA) *498*
San Francisco State U (CA) *498*
San Jose State U (CA) *499*
Santa Clara U (CA) *499*
Sarah Lawrence Coll (NY) *499*
Scripps Coll (CA) *501*
Seton Hall U (NJ) *502*
Simon Fraser U (BC, Canada) *505*
Simon's Rock Coll of Bard (MA) *505*
Skidmore Coll (NY) *506*
Slippery Rock U of Pennsylvania (PA) *506*
Smith Coll (MA) *506*
Sonoma State U (CA) *506*
Southeast Missouri State U (MO) *508*
Southern Illinois U Carbondale (IL) *509*
Southern Illinois U Edwardsville (IL) *509*
Southern Methodist U (TX) *510*
Southern Oregon U (OR) *510*
Southwest Missouri State U (MO) *513*
Southwest Texas State U (TX) *513*
Stanford U (CA) *514*
State U of NY at Albany (NY) *514*
State U of NY at Binghamton (NY) *515*
State U of NY at New Paltz (NY) *515*
State U of NY at Oswego (NY) *515*
State U of NY Coll at Brockport (NY) *515*
State U of NY Coll at Buffalo (NY) *516*
State U of NY Coll at Cortland (NY) *516*
State U of NY Coll at Geneseo (NY) *516*
State U of NY Coll at Oneonta (NY) *517*
State U of NY Coll at Potsdam (NY) *517*
State U of West Georgia (GA) *518*
Stony Brook U, State University of New York (NY) *520*
Swarthmore Coll (PA) *521*
Sweet Briar Coll (VA) *521*
Syracuse U (NY) *521*
Temple U (PA) *523*
Texas A&M U (TX) *524*
Texas A&M U–Commerce (TX) *525*
Texas A&M U–Kingsville (TX) *525*
Texas Tech U (TX) *526*
Thomas Edison State Coll (NJ) *527*
Thomas U (GA) *528*
Towson U (MD) *529*
Transylvania U (KY) *529*
Trent U (ON, Canada) *529*
Trinity Coll (CT) *530*
Trinity U (TX) *531*
Tufts U (MA) *533*
Tulane U (LA) *533*
Union Coll (NY) *534*
Université Laval (QC, Canada) *536*
U at Buffalo, The State University of New York (NY) *536*
The U of Alabama (AL) *537*
The U of Alabama at Birmingham (AL) *537*
U of Alaska Anchorage (AK) *538*
U of Alaska Fairbanks (AK) *538*
U of Alberta (AB, Canada) *538*
The U of Arizona (AZ) *538*
U of Arkansas (AR) *539*
U of Arkansas at Little Rock (AR) *539*
The U of British Columbia (BC, Canada) *540*
U of Calgary (AB, Canada) *540*
U of Calif, Berkeley (CA) *540*
U of Calif, Davis (CA) *540*
U of Calif, Irvine (CA) *541*
U of Calif, Los Angeles (CA) *541*
U of Calif, Riverside (CA) *541*
U of Calif, San Diego (CA) *541*
U of Calif, Santa Barbara (CA) *541*
U of Calif, Santa Cruz (CA) *542*
U of Central Florida (FL) *542*
U of Chicago (IL) *542*
U of Cincinnati (OH) *543*
U of Colorado at Boulder (CO) *543*
U of Colorado at Colorado Springs (CO) *543*
U of Colorado at Denver (CO) *543*
U of Connecticut (CT) *544*
U of Delaware (DE) *544*
U of Denver (CO) *544*
U of Evansville (IN) *545*
U of Florida (FL) *545*
U of Georgia (GA) *545*
U of Guelph (ON, Canada) *546*
U of Hawaii at Hilo (HI) *546*
U of Hawaii at Manoa (HI) *546*
U of Hawaii–West Oahu (HI) *546*
U of Houston (TX) *547*
U of Houston–Clear Lake (TX) *547*
U of Idaho (ID) *547*
U of Illinois at Chicago (IL) *547*
U of Illinois at Springfield (IL) *548*
U of Illinois at Urbana–Champaign (IL) *548*
U of Indianapolis (IN) *548*
The U of Iowa (IA) *548*
U of Kansas (KS) *549*
U of Kentucky (KY) *549*
U of King's Coll (NS, Canada) *549*
U of La Verne (CA) *549*
The U of Lethbridge (AB, Canada) *549*
U of Louisiana at Lafayette (LA) *550*
U of Louisville (KY) *550*
U of Maine (ME) *550*
U of Maine at Farmington (ME) *550*
U of Manitoba (MB, Canada) *551*
U of Maryland, Baltimore County (MD) *552*
U of Maryland, Coll Park (MD) *552*
U of Massachusetts Amherst (MA) *552*
U of Massachusetts Boston (MA) *553*
The U of Memphis (TN) *553*
U of Miami (FL) *553*
U of Michigan (MI) *554*
U of Michigan–Dearborn (MI) *554*
U of Michigan–Flint (MI) *554*
U of Minnesota, Duluth (MN) *554*
U of Minnesota, Twin Cities Campus (MN) *555*
U of Mississippi (MS) *555*
U of Missouri–Columbia (MO) *555*
U of Missouri–St. Louis (MO) *556*
The U of Montana–Missoula (MT) *556*
U of Nebraska–Lincoln (NE) *557*
U of Nevada, Las Vegas (NV) *558*
U of Nevada, Reno (NV) *558*
U of New Brunswick Fredericton (NB, Canada) *558*
U of New Hampshire (NH) *558*
U of New Mexico (NM) *559*
U of New Orleans (LA) *559*
The U of North Carolina at Chapel Hill (NC) *560*
The U of North Carolina at Charlotte (NC) *560*
The U of North Carolina at Greensboro (NC) *560*
The U of North Carolina at Wilmington (NC) *561*
U of North Dakota (ND) *561*
U of Northern Iowa (IA) *561*
U of North Florida (FL) *561*
U of North Texas (TX) *562*
U of Notre Dame (IN) *562*
U of Oklahoma (OK) *562*
U of Oregon (OR) *562*
U of Pennsylvania (PA) *563*
U of Pittsburgh (PA) *569*
U of Pittsburgh at Greensburg (PA) *570*
U of Prince Edward Island (PE, Canada) *570*
U of Puerto Rico, Río Piedras (PR) *571*
U of Redlands (CA) *572*
U of Regina (SK, Canada) *572*
U of Rhode Island (RI) *572*
U of Rochester (NY) *573*
U of San Diego (CA) *574*
U of Saskatchewan (SK, Canada) *574*
U of South Alabama (AL) *575*
U of South Carolina (SC) *575*
The U of South Dakota (SD) *575*
U of Southern California (CA) *576*
U of Southern Maine (ME) *576*
U of Southern Mississippi (MS) *576*
U of South Florida (FL) *576*
The U of Tennessee (TN) *577*
The U of Texas at Arlington (TX) *577*
The U of Texas at Austin (TX) *578*
The U of Texas at El Paso (TX) *578*
The U of Texas at San Antonio (TX) *578*
The U of Texas–Pan American (TX) *579*
U of the District of Columbia (DC) *580*

U of the South (TN) **581**
U of Toledo (OH) **581**
U of Toronto (ON, Canada) **581**
U of Tulsa (OK) **581**
U of Utah (UT) **582**
U of Vermont (VT) **582**
U of Victoria (BC, Canada) **582**
U of Virginia (VA) **582**
U of Washington (WA) **583**
U of Waterloo (ON, Canada) **583**
The U of Western Ontario (ON, Canada) **583**
U of West Florida (FL) **583**
U of Windsor (ON, Canada) **584**
U of Wisconsin–Madison (WI) **584**
U of Wisconsin–Milwaukee (WI) **585**
U of Wisconsin–Oshkosh (WI) **585**
U of Wyoming (WY) **586**
Ursinus Coll (PA) **587**
Utah State U (UT) **587**
Valdosta State U (GA) **588**
Vanderbilt U (TN) **588**
Vanguard U of Southern California (CA) **589**
Vassar Coll (NY) **589**
Wagner Coll (NY) **592**
Wake Forest U (NC) **592**
Warren Wilson Coll (NC) **594**
Washington and Lee U (VA) **594**
Washington Coll (MD) **594**
Washington State U (WA) **595**
Washington U in St. Louis (MO) **595**
Wayne State U (MI) **596**
Webster U (MO) **597**
Wellesley Coll (MA) **597**
Wells Coll (NY) **597**
Wesleyan U (CT) **597**
West Chester U of Pennsylvania (PA) **598**
Western Carolina U (NC) **598**
Western Connecticut State U (CT) **598**
Western Kentucky U (KY) **599**
Western Michigan U (MI) **599**
Western Oregon U (OR) **600**
Western State Coll of Colorado (CO) **600**
Western Washington U (WA) **600**
Westminster Coll (MO) **601**
Westmont Coll (CA) **602**
West Virginia U (WV) **602**
Wheaton Coll (IL) **603**
Wheaton Coll (MA) **603**
Whitman Coll (WA) **604**
Wichita State U (KS) **604**
Widener U (PA) **604**
William Paterson U of New Jersey (NJ) **606**
Williams Coll (MA) **606**
Wright State U (OH) **609**
Yale U (CT) **610**
York Coll of the City U of New York (NY) **611**
York U (ON, Canada) **611**
Youngstown State U (OH) **611**

APPAREL MARKETING

Overview: This major teaches students distribution, sales, and marketing of apparel and accessories operations. *Related majors:* marketing and marketing management; marketing research; general marketing operation; clothing, apparel, and textile studies; fashion design/illustration. *Potential careers:* apparel or accessory buyer, product marketing manager, sales representative, retail store manager. *Salary potential:* $20k-$30k.

Concordia Coll (MN) **329**
Philadelphia U (PA) **469**
U of Rhode Island (RI) **572**
Youngstown State U (OH) **611**

APPLIED ART

Overview: This broad-based major focuses on at least two of the following disciplines: commercial and advertising and industrial art and design, commercial photography, illustration, and graphic design. *Related majors:* drawing, architectural drafting, photography, multimedia. *Potential careers:* Web designer, product or packaging designer, magazine or book jacket illustrator, professional photographer. *Salary potential:* $25k-$40k.

Academy of Art Coll (CA) **260**
Alfred U (NY) **263**
American Academy of Art (IL) **265**
Athabasca U (AB, Canada) **275**
Azusa Pacific U (CA) **278**
Bemidji State U (MN) **285**
Berry Coll (GA) **287**
California Coll of Arts and Crafts (CA) **299**
California Polytechnic State U, San Luis Obispo (CA) **300**
California State U, Dominguez Hills (CA) **300**
California State U, Northridge (CA) **301**
Carthage Coll (WI) **306**
Cleveland State U (OH) **317**
Col for Creative Studies (MI) **319**
The Coll of New Rochelle (NY) **321**
Coll of Staten Island of the City U of NY (NY) **323**
Colorado State U-Pueblo (CO) **325**
Columbia Coll (MO) **326**
Columbia Coll (SC) **327**
Columbia U, School of General Studies (NY) **328**
Columbus Coll of Art and Design (OH) **328**
Converse Coll (SC) **332**
Corcoran Coll of Art and Design (DC) **332**
Cornell U (NY) **333**
Daemen Coll (NY) **335**
DePaul U (IL) **339**
Dowling Coll (NY) **345**
Elizabeth City State U (NC) **351**
Elms Coll (MA) **352**
Franklin Pierce Coll (NH) **364**
Georgia Southwestern State U (GA) **368**
Goddard Coll (VT) **369**
Howard Payne U (TX) **382**
Howard U (DC) **382**
Huntingdon Coll (AL) **383**
Illinois Wesleyan U (IL) **385**
Indiana U Bloomington (IN) **385**
Inter American U of PR, San Germán Campus (PR) **388**
Iowa Wesleyan Coll (IA) **390**
Lamar U (TX) **401**
Lindenwood U (MO) **407**
Long Island U, C.W. Post Campus (NY) **409**
Long Island U, Southampton Coll, Friends World Program (NY) **409**
Lubbock Christian U (TX) **412**
Mansfield U of Pennsylvania (PA) **416**
Marygrove Coll (MI) **419**
Marywood U (PA) **421**
McNeese State U (LA) **423**
Memphis Coll of Art (TN) **425**
Mesa State Coll (CO) **426**
Midwestern State U (TX) **430**
Minnesota State U, Mankato (MN) **431**
Minnesota State U, Moorhead (MN) **432**
Mississippi Coll (MS) **432**
Mount Vernon Nazarene U (OH) **440**
Muskingum Coll (OH) **441**
National American U (NM) **441**
New World School of the Arts (FL) **447**
Northern Michigan U (MI) **451**
Oakland City U (IN) **456**
Oklahoma Baptist U (OK) **459**
Olivet Coll (MI) **461**
Oregon State U (OR) **462**
Otis Coll of Art and Design (CA) **462**
Peru State Coll (NE) **469**
Point Park Coll (PA) **471**
Portland State U (OR) **472**
Pratt Inst (NY) **473**
Rochester Inst of Technology (NY) **482**
St. Cloud State U (MN) **488**
St. Thomas Aquinas Coll (NY) **495**
Savannah Coll of Art and Design (GA) **499**
School of the Museum of Fine Arts (MA) **501**
School of Visual Arts (NY) **501**
Seton Hill U (PA) **502**
Springfield Coll (MA) **514**
State U of NY Coll at Buffalo (NY) **516**
State U of NY Coll at Fredonia (NY) **516**
Syracuse U (NY) **521**
Truman State U (MO) **532**
The U of Akron (OH) **537**
U of Calif, Los Angeles (CA) **541**
U of Dayton (OH) **544**
U of Delaware (DE) **544**
U of Houston–Clear Lake (TX) **547**
U of Michigan (MI) **554**
The U of Montana–Western (MT) **556**
U of North Texas (TX) **562**
U of Oregon (OR) **562**
U of Ottawa (ON, Canada) **563**
U of Sioux Falls (SD) **574**
The U of South Dakota (SD) **575**
The U of Texas at Brownsville (TX) **578**
U of the South (TN) **581**
U of Toledo (OH) **581**
U of Wisconsin–Madison (WI) **584**
Viterbo U (WI) **591**
Washington U in St. Louis (MO) **595**
William Carey Coll (MS) **605**
William Paterson U of New Jersey (NJ) **606**
Winona State U (MN) **608**
York U (ON, Canada) **611**

APPLIED ECONOMICS

Overview: This major involves a branch of economics in which students examine how economic principles affect particular industries and the exploitation of resources. *Related majors:* logistics and materials management, business administration management, economics, operations management. *Potential careers:* business executive or consultant, economist, finance, international economist. *Salary potential:* $30k-$40k.

Allegheny Coll (PA) **264**
Cornell U (NY) **333**
École des hautes études commerciales de Montréal (QC, Canada) **350**
Florida State U (FL) **361**
Ithaca Coll (NY) **390**
Penn State U Univ Park Campus (PA) **468**
Plymouth State Coll (NH) **471**
Saint Joseph's Coll (IN) **490**
Southern Methodist U (TX) **510**
U of Massachusetts Amherst (MA) **552**
U of Northern Iowa (IA) **561**
U of Rhode Island (RI) **572**
U of San Francisco (CA) **574**

APPLIED HISTORY

Overview: This major will teach students how to collect, record, store, and manage accounts, information, and materials and data regarding public events and related historical archives and resources for future use. *Related majors:* history, American government/ politics, museum studies, law and legal studies, publishing. *Potential careers:* librarian, researcher, museum curator, antiques and art dealer, journalist, editor. *Salary potential:* $23k-$33k.

East Carolina U (NC) **347**
Meredith Coll (NC) **426**
U of Calif, Santa Barbara (CA) **541**
U of Hawaii at Manoa (HI) **546**
Western Michigan U (MI) **599**

APPLIED MATHEMATICS

Overview: This major teaches students how to apply the principles of mathematics to a wide range of real-world problems. *Related majors:* engineering of almost any kind, especially mechanical, structural, and computer, physics and engineering physics, statistics. *Potential careers:* engineer, technology professor, statistician, physicist. *Salary potential:* $30k-$45k.

Alderson-Broaddus Coll (WV) **263**
American U (DC) **267**
Asbury Coll (KY) **274**
Auburn U (AL) **276**
Barnard Coll (NY) **282**
Baylor U (TX) **283**
Belmont U (TN) **284**
Bowie State U (MD) **292**
Brescia U (KY) **293**
Brock U (ON, Canada) **295**
Brown U (RI) **296**
California Inst of Technology (CA) **299**
California State Polytechnic U, Pomona (CA) **300**
California State U, Chico (CA) **300**
California State U, Fullerton (CA) **301**
California State U, Hayward (CA) **301**
California State U, Long Beach (CA) **301**
California State U, Northridge (CA) **301**
Carleton U (ON, Canada) **305**
Carnegie Mellon U (PA) **305**
Case Western Reserve U (OH) **307**
Chapman U (CA) **311**
Charleston Southern U (SC) **311**
Clarkson U (NY) **316**
Coastal Carolina U (SC) **318**
Colorado State U (CO) **325**
Columbia U, School of General Studies (NY) **328**
Columbia U, School of Engineering & Applied Sci (NY) **328**
Concordia U (QC, Canada) **331**
DePaul U (IL) **339**
Dowling Coll (NY) **345**
Eastern Kentucky U (KY) **348**
Elizabeth City State U (NC) **351**
Elms Coll (MA) **352**
Emory & Henry Coll (VA) **353**
State U of NY at Farmingdale (NY) **357**
Ferris State U (MI) **358**
Florida Inst of Technology (FL) **360**
Florida International U (FL) **360**
Florida State U (FL) **361**
Franklin Coll (IN) **363**
Fresno Pacific U (CA) **364**
Geneva Coll (PA) **366**
The George Washington U (DC) **367**
Grand Valley State U (MI) **371**
Grand View Coll (IA) **372**
Hampshire Coll (MA) **375**
Harvard U (MA) **376**
Hawai'i Pacific U (HI) **377**
Hofstra U (NY) **380**
Humboldt State U (CA) **382**
Illinois Inst of Technology (IL) **384**
Indiana U of Pennsylvania (PA) **386**
Indiana U South Bend (IN) **387**
Inter American U of PR, San Germán Campus (PR) **388**
Ithaca Coll (NY) **390**
Johns Hopkins U (MD) **392**
Johnson C. Smith U (NC) **394**
Kent State U (OH) **397**
Kentucky State U (KY) **397**
Kettering U (MI) **398**
Lamar U (TX) **401**
La Roche Coll (PA) **402**
La Salle U (PA) **402**
La Sierra U (CA) **403**
Le Moyne Coll (NY) **404**
Limestone Coll (SC) **406**
Long Island U, C.W. Post Campus (NY) **409**
Longwood U (VA) **409**
Loyola Coll in Maryland (MD) **411**
Marlboro Coll (VT) **418**
Mary Baldwin Coll (VA) **419**
Maryville U of Saint Louis (MO) **420**
Massachusetts Inst of Technology (MA) **421**
The Master's Coll and Seminary (CA) **422**
McGill U (QC, Canada) **423**
McMaster U (ON, Canada) **423**
Medgar Evers Coll of the City U of NY (NY) **424**
Memorial U of Newfoundland (NF, Canada) **424**
Mesa State Coll (CO) **426**
Metropolitan State U (MN) **427**
Michigan State U (MI) **428**
Michigan Technological U (MI) **428**
Montana Tech of The U of Montana (MT) **435**
Montclair State U (NJ) **435**
Mount Allison U (NB, Canada) **437**
Mount Saint Vincent U (NS, Canada) **439**
Murray State U (KY) **440**
New Jersey Inst of Technology (NJ) **445**
New Mexico Inst of Mining and Technology (NM) **446**
North Carolina Ag and Tech State U (NC) **448**
North Carolina State U (NC) **449**
North Central Coll (IL) **449**
Northland Coll (WI) **452**

APPLIED MATHEMATICS (continued)

Northwestern U (IL) **453**
Oakland City U (IN) **456**
Oakwood Coll (AL) **456**
Ohio U (OH) **458**
Oregon State U (OR) **462**
Pacific Union Coll (CA) **464**
Penn State U Harrisburg Campus of the Capital Coll (PA) **468**
Penn State U Univ Park Campus (PA) **468**
Queens Coll of the City U of NY (NY) **475**
Queens U of Charlotte (NC) **476**
Quinnipiac U (CT) **476**
Rensselaer Polytechnic Inst (NY) **478**
Rice U (TX) **479**
Robert Morris U (PA) **481**
Rochester Inst of Technology (NY) **482**
Rutgers, The State U of New Jersey, Newark (NJ) **485**
Saint Joseph's Coll (IN) **490**
Saint Louis U (MO) **492**
Saint Mary's Coll (IN) **493**
St. Thomas Aquinas Coll (NY) **495**
Salem State Coll (MA) **497**
San Diego State U (CA) **498**
San Francisco State U (CA) **498**
San Jose State U (CA) **499**
Seattle U (WA) **501**
Shawnee State U (OH) **502**
Simon Fraser U (BC, Canada) **505**
Simon's Rock Coll of Bard (MA) **505**
Sonoma State U (CA) **506**
Southeast Missouri State U (MO) **508**
State U of NY at Albany (NY) **514**
State U of NY at New Paltz (NY) **515**
State U of NY at Oswego (NY) **515**
State U of NY Inst of Tech at Utica/Rome (NY) **518**
Stony Brook U, State University of New York (NY) **520**
Texas A&M U (TX) **524**
Trent U (ON, Canada) **529**
Trinity Western U (BC, Canada) **531**
United States Military Academy (NY) **535**
Université de Sherbrooke (QC, Canada) **536**
The U of Akron (OH) **537**
U of Alberta (AB, Canada) **538**
The U of British Columbia (BC, Canada) **540**
U of Calgary (AB, Canada) **540**
U of Calif, Berkeley (CA) **540**
U of Calif, Los Angeles (CA) **541**
U of Calif, San Diego (CA) **541**
U of Calif, Santa Cruz (CA) **542**
U of Central Oklahoma (OK) **542**
U of Chicago (IL) **542**
U of Colorado at Boulder (CO) **543**
U of Colorado at Colorado Springs (CO) **543**
U of Colorado at Denver (CO) **543**
U of Connecticut (CT) **544**
U of Guelph (ON, Canada) **546**
U of Houston (TX) **547**
U of Houston–Downtown (TX) **547**
U of Idaho (ID) **547**
U of Manitoba (MB, Canada) **551**
U of Maryland, Baltimore County (MD) **552**
U of Massachusetts Boston (MA) **553**
U of Massachusetts Lowell (MA) **553**
U of Michigan (MI) **554**
U of Missouri–Rolla (MO) **556**
U of Missouri–St. Louis (MO) **556**
The U of Montana–Missoula (MT) **556**
The U of Montana–Western (MT) **556**
U of Nevada, Las Vegas (NV) **558**
U of New Brunswick Fredericton (NB, Canada) **558**
U of New Brunswick Saint John (NB, Canada) **558**
The U of North Carolina at Chapel Hill (NC) **560**
The U of North Carolina at Greensboro (NC) **560**
U of Ottawa (ON, Canada) **563**
U of Pittsburgh (PA) **569**
U of Pittsburgh at Bradford (PA) **569**
U of Pittsburgh at Greensburg (PA) **570**
U of Rochester (NY) **573**
U of Sioux Falls (SD) **574**
U of South Carolina Aiken (SC) **575**
The U of Tennessee at Chattanooga (TN) **577**
The U of Texas at Dallas (TX) **578**
The U of Texas at El Paso (TX) **578**
U of Toronto (ON, Canada) **581**
U of Tulsa (OK) **581**
U of Vermont (VT) **582**
U of Virginia (VA) **582**
U of Washington (WA) **583**
U of Waterloo (ON, Canada) **583**
The U of Western Ontario (ON, Canada) **583**
U of Windsor (ON, Canada) **584**
U of Wisconsin–Madison (WI) **584**
U of Wisconsin–Milwaukee (WI) **585**
U of Wisconsin–Stout (WI) **586**
Ursinus Coll (PA) **587**
Valdosta State U (GA) **588**
Wake Forest U (NC) **592**
Washington U in St. Louis (MO) **595**
Wayne State Coll (NE) **596**
Weber State U (UT) **596**
Western Michigan U (MI) **599**
West Virginia State Coll (WV) **602**
William Paterson U of New Jersey (NJ) **606**
Winona State U (MN) **608**
Worcester Polytechnic Inst (MA) **609**
Yale U (CT) **610**
York U (ON, Canada) **611**

APPLIED MATHEMATICS RELATED

Information can be found under this major's main heading.

Averett U (VA) **278**
Georgia Inst of Technology (GA) **367**
U of Dayton (OH) **544**

AQUACULTURE OPERATIONS/PRODUCTION MANAGEMENT

Overview: This major instructs students in the harvesting and marketing of fish, shellfish, and marine plants and the design and operation of fish farms, breeding facilities, and related enterprises. *Related majors:* marine biology, fishing and fishing sciences. *Potential careers:* aquarium researcher, fishery manager, marine biologist. *Salary potential:* $22k-$35k.

Angelo State U (TX) **269**
Clemson U (SC) **317**
Lake Erie Coll (OH) **400**
Purdue U (IN) **475**
Texas A&M U (TX) **524**

ARABIC

Overview: Students learn to read, write, and speak Arabic, the major language spoken in the Middle East. *Related majors:* history, international affairs, Islamic studies, archeology, developmental economics/international development. *Potential careers:* translator, teacher, diplomatic corps, archeologist, importer-exporter. *Salary potential:* $22k-$30k.

Dartmouth Coll (NH) **337**
Georgetown U (DC) **366**
Harvard U (MA) **376**
Long Island U, Southampton Coll, Friends World Program (NY) **409**
The Ohio State U (OH) **457**
State U of NY at Binghamton (NY) **515**
United States Military Academy (NY) **535**
U of Alberta (AB, Canada) **538**
U of Calif, Los Angeles (CA) **541**
U of Chicago (IL) **542**
U of Miami (FL) **553**
U of Michigan (MI) **554**
U of Notre Dame (IN) **562**
The U of Texas at Austin (TX) **578**
U of Toronto (ON, Canada) **581**
U of Utah (UT) **582**
Washington U in St. Louis (MO) **595**

ARCHAEOLOGY

Overview: Students who choose this major will learn to understand extinct societies through the excavation, analysis, and interpretation of artifacts, human remains, and associated items. *Related majors:* anthropology, museum studies, folklore, area studies, history, chemistry. *Potential careers:* archeologist, historian, museum curator, tour guide, researcher, professor. *Salary potential:* $18k-$30k.

The American U in Cairo(Egypt) **267**
Appalachian State U (NC) **270**
Baltimore Hebrew U (MD) **280**
Bard Coll (NY) **281**
Baylor U (TX) **283**
Boston U (MA) **292**
Bowdoin Coll (ME) **292**
Bridgewater State Coll (MA) **294**
Brock U (ON, Canada) **295**
Brown U (RI) **296**
Bryn Mawr Coll (PA) **297**
The Coll of Southeastern Europe, The American U of Athens(Greece) **323**
The Coll of Wooster (OH) **324**
Columbia Coll (NY) **326**
Concordia U (QC, Canada) **331**
Cornell U (NY) **333**
Dartmouth Coll (NH) **337**
Fort Lewis Coll (CO) **362**
Franklin Pierce Coll (NH) **364**
The George Washington U (DC) **367**
Hampshire Coll (MA) **375**
Harvard U (MA) **376**
Haverford Coll (PA) **377**
Hunter Coll of the City U of NY (NY) **382**
Kent State U (OH) **397**
Long Island U, Southampton Coll, Friends World Program (NY) **409**
Lycoming Coll (PA) **412**
Massachusetts Inst of Technology (MA) **421**
Memorial U of Newfoundland (NF, Canada) **424**
Mercyhurst Coll (PA) **425**
Minnesota State U, Moorhead (MN) **432**
New York U (NY) **447**
Oberlin Coll (OH) **456**
Oregon State U (OR) **462**
Simon Fraser U (BC, Canada) **505**
Stanford U (CA) **514**
State U of NY Coll at Potsdam (NY) **517**
Tufts U (MA) **533**
U of Calgary (AB, Canada) **540**
U of Calif, San Diego (CA) **541**
U of Evansville (IN) **545**
U of Hawaii at Manoa (HI) **546**
U of Indianapolis (IN) **548**
U of Kansas (KS) **549**
U of Michigan (MI) **554**
U of Missouri–Columbia (MO) **555**
The U of North Carolina at Greensboro (NC) **560**
U of Saskatchewan (SK, Canada) **574**
The U of Texas at Austin (TX) **578**
U of Toronto (ON, Canada) **581**
U of Wisconsin–La Crosse (WI) **584**
Washington and Lee U (VA) **594**
Washington U in St. Louis (MO) **595**
Wellesley Coll (MA) **597**
Western Washington U (WA) **600**
Wheaton Coll (IL) **603**
Yale U (CT) **610**

ARCHITECTURAL ENGINEERING

Overview: This major teaches students about various subjects such as building architecture, building system integration, and structural and computer-aided design. *Related majors:* mathematics, physics, computer science, materials science, structural engineering. *Potential careers:* architect, structural or civil engineer. *Salary potential:* $32k-$45k.

Andrews U (MI) **269**
Auburn U (AL) **276**
California Polytechnic State U, San Luis Obispo (CA) **300**
The Coll of Southeastern Europe, The American U of Athens(Greece) **323**
Drexel U (PA) **346**
Harvard U (MA) **376**
Illinois Inst of Technology (IL) **384**
Kansas State U (KS) **396**
Milwaukee School of Engineering (WI) **431**
North Carolina Ag and Tech State U (NC) **448**
Oklahoma State U (OK) **460**
Penn State U Univ Park Campus (PA) **468**
Tennessee State U (TN) **523**
Tufts U (MA) **533**
U of Cincinnati (OH) **543**
U of Colorado at Boulder (CO) **543**
U of Kansas (KS) **549**
U of Miami (FL) **553**
U of Missouri–Rolla (MO) **556**
U of Nebraska–Lincoln (NE) **557**
U of Southern California (CA) **576**
The U of Texas at Austin (TX) **578**
U of Wyoming (WY) **586**

ARCHITECTURAL ENGINEERING TECHNOLOGY

Overview: This major gives students the technical knowledge they need to support architects, engineers and planners who are engaged in developing buildings. *Related majors:* drafting and design technology, industrial/manufacturing technology, construction management, logistics and materials management, enterprise management and operation. *Potential careers:* graphic designer, architect, construction or operations manager, purchasing manager. *Salary potential:* $25k-$40k.

Abilene Christian U (TX) **260**
Andrews U (MI) **269**
Bluefield State Coll (WV) **291**
British Columbia Inst of Technology (BC, Canada) **295**
California State U, Chico (CA) **300**
Central Missouri State U (MO) **310**
Cornell U (NY) **333**
Delaware State U (DE) **338**
Fitchburg State Coll (MA) **358**
Florida A&M U (FL) **359**
Grambling State U (LA) **371**
Indiana State U (IN) **385**
Indiana U–Purdue U Indianapolis (IN) **387**
Louisiana State U and A&M Coll (LA) **410**
Purdue U (IN) **475**
Southern Polytechnic State U (GA) **511**
Texas Southern U (TX) **526**
Texas Tech U (TX) **526**
Thomas Edison State Coll (NJ) **527**
U of Cincinnati (OH) **543**
U of Hartford (CT) **546**
U of Southern Mississippi (MS) **576**
Vermont Tech Coll (VT) **589**
Washington U in St. Louis (MO) **595**
Wentworth Inst of Technology (MA) **597**

ARCHITECTURAL ENVIRONMENTAL DESIGN

Overview: Students who choose this major will learn how to design, public and private spaces for leisure recreational, commercial, and living purposes. *Related majors:* architecture, interior design, urban planning, structural engineering. *Potential careers:* architect, interior designer, city planner, environmental lawyer, landscape designer. *Salary potential:* $25k-$35k.

Art Center Coll of Design (CA) **273**
Auburn U (AL) **276**
Ball State U (IN) **280**
Bowling Green State U (OH) **292**
Col for Creative Studies (MI) **319**
The Coll of Southeastern Europe, The American U of Athens(Greece) **323**
Coll of the Atlantic (ME) **323**
Cornell U (NY) **333**
Florida International U (FL) **360**
Hampshire Coll (MA) **375**
Harvard U (MA) **376**

Miami U (OH) **428**
Montana State U–Bozeman (MT) **434**
North Dakota State U (ND) **449**
Nova Scotia Coll of Art and Design (NS, Canada) **455**
Otis Coll of Art and Design (CA) **462**
Parsons School of Design, New School U (NY) **465**
Prescott Coll (AZ) **474**
State U of NY Coll of Environ Sci and Forestry (NY) **517**
Texas A&M U (TX) **524**
U at Buffalo, The State University of New York (NY) **536**
U of Colorado at Boulder (CO) **543**
U of Hawaii at Manoa (HI) **546**
U of Houston (TX) **547**
U of Manitoba (MB, Canada) **551**
U of Massachusetts Amherst (MA) **552**
U of New Mexico (NM) **559**
U of Oklahoma (OK) **562**
U of Pennsylvania (PA) **563**
U of Puerto Rico, Río Piedras (PR) **571**

ARCHITECTURAL HISTORY

Overview: Students will study the principles and techniques of architectural design and building methods used in historical structures, and the process of preserving and restoring old structures for contemporary use. *Related majors:* structural engineering, building technology, surveying, history, interior design, architecture. *Potential careers:* historic preservationist, architect, interior designer, lawyer, construction manager. *Salary potential:* $23k-$30k.

Coll of Charleston (SC) **320**
Goucher Coll (MD) **370**
Mary Washington Coll (VA) **420**
Roger Williams U (RI) **483**
Salve Regina U (RI) **497**
Savannah Coll of Art and Design (GA) **499**
U of Delaware (DE) **544**
U of Hawaii at Manoa (HI) **546**
Ursuline Coll (OH) **587**

ARCHITECTURAL URBAN DESIGN

Overview: This major focuses on the social, cultural, economic, behavioral, and psychological effects that architectural forms have on the design, planning, and functioning of urban environments. *Related majors:* city/urban, community planning, architectural environmental design, landscape architecture. *Potential careers:* architect, civil engineer, city planner, historical preservationist, lawyer, developer. *Salary potential:* $22k-$32k.

The Coll of Southeastern Europe, The American U of Athens(Greece) **323**
U of Hawaii at Manoa (HI) **546**
U of Nevada, Las Vegas (NV) **558**
U of Washington (WA) **583**

ARCHITECTURE

Overview: This major prepares students for the professional practice of architecture by instructing them in the aesthetic and socioeconomic aspects of the built environment. *Related majors:* graphic art, industrial design, applied mathematics and physics, engineering. *Potential careers:* architect, civil engineer, landscape architect, urban planner, interior designer. *Salary potential:* $25k-$36k.

Alliant International U (CA) **264**
Andrews U (MI) **269**
Arizona State U (AZ) **271**
Auburn U (AL) **276**
Ball State U (IN) **280**
Barnard Coll (NY) **282**
Baylor U (TX) **283**
Bennington Coll (VT) **286**
Boston Architectural Center (MA) **291**
Brown U (RI) **296**
California Coll of Arts and Crafts (CA) **299**
California Polytechnic State U, San Luis Obispo (CA) **300**
California State Polytechnic U, Pomona (CA) **300**
Carleton U (ON, Canada) **305**
Carnegie Mellon U (PA) **305**
The Catholic U of America (DC) **307**
City Coll of the City U of NY (NY) **314**
Clemson U (SC) **317**
Coe Coll (IA) **318**
Columbia Coll (NY) **326**
Columbia U, School of General Studies (NY) **328**
Concordia Coll (MN) **329**
Connecticut Coll (CT) **331**
Cooper Union for the Advancement of Science & Art (NY) **332**
Cornell Coll (IA) **332**
Cornell U (NY) **333**
Dalhousie U (NS, Canada) **336**
Drexel U (PA) **346**
Drury U (MO) **346**
Eastern Michigan U (MI) **348**
Florida A&M U (FL) **359**
Florida Atlantic U (FL) **359**
Georgia Inst of Technology (GA) **367**
Hampshire Coll (MA) **375**
Hampton U (VA) **375**
Hobart and William Smith Colls (NY) **380**
Howard U (DC) **382**
Illinois Inst of Technology (IL) **384**
Insto Tecno Estudios Sups Monterrey(Mexico) **388**
Iowa State U of Science and Technology (IA) **390**
Judson Coll (IL) **395**
Kansas State U (KS) **396**
Kent State U (OH) **397**
Lawrence Technological U (MI) **403**
Lehigh U (PA) **404**
Louisiana State U and A&M Coll (LA) **410**
Louisiana Tech U (LA) **410**
Massachusetts Coll of Art (MA) **421**
Massachusetts Inst of Technology (MA) **421**
McGill U (QC, Canada) **423**
Miami U (OH) **428**
Mississippi State U (MS) **432**
New Jersey Inst of Technology (NJ) **445**
Newschool of Architecture & Design (CA) **446**
New York Inst of Technology (NY) **447**
North Carolina State U (NC) **449**
North Dakota State U (ND) **449**
Northeastern U (MA) **450**
Norwich U (VT) **455**
The Ohio State U (OH) **457**
Oklahoma State U (OK) **460**
Parsons School of Design, New School U (NY) **465**
Penn State U Univ Park Campus (PA) **468**
Philadelphia U (PA) **469**
Portland State U (OR) **472**
Prairie View A&M U (TX) **473**
Pratt Inst (NY) **473**
Princeton U (NJ) **474**
Rensselaer Polytechnic Inst (NY) **478**
Rhode Island School of Design (RI) **479**
Rice U (TX) **479**
Roger Williams U (RI) **483**
Ryerson U (ON, Canada) **485**
Savannah Coll of Art and Design (GA) **499**
Smith Coll (MA) **506**
Southern California Inst of Architecture (CA) **509**
Southern Illinois U Carbondale (IL) **509**
Southern Polytechnic State U (GA) **511**
Southern U and A&M Coll (LA) **511**
Syracuse U (NY) **521**
Temple U (PA) **523**
Texas Tech U (TX) **526**
Tulane U (LA) **533**
Tuskegee U (AL) **533**
Université Laval (QC, Canada) **536**
U at Buffalo, The State University of New York (NY) **536**
The U of Arizona (AZ) **538**
U of Arkansas (AR) **539**
U of Calif, Berkeley (CA) **540**
U of Cincinnati (OH) **543**
U of Florida (FL) **545**
U of Hawaii at Manoa (HI) **546**
U of Houston (TX) **547**
U of Idaho (ID) **547**
U of Illinois at Chicago (IL) **547**
U of Kansas (KS) **549**
U of Kentucky (KY) **549**
U of Manitoba (MB, Canada) **551**
U of Maryland, Coll Park (MD) **552**
The U of Memphis (TN) **553**
U of Miami (FL) **553**
U of Michigan (MI) **554**
U of Minnesota, Twin Cities Campus (MN) **555**
U of Nebraska–Lincoln (NE) **557**
U of Nevada, Las Vegas (NV) **558**
U of New Mexico (NM) **559**
The U of North Carolina at Charlotte (NC) **560**
U of Notre Dame (IN) **562**
U of Oklahoma (OK) **562**
U of Oregon (OR) **562**
U of Pennsylvania (PA) **563**
U of San Francisco (CA) **574**
U of Southern California (CA) **576**
The U of Tennessee (TN) **577**
The U of Texas at Arlington (TX) **577**
The U of Texas at Austin (TX) **578**
U of the District of Columbia (DC) **580**
U of Toronto (ON, Canada) **581**
U of Utah (UT) **582**
U of Virginia (VA) **582**
U of Washington (WA) **583**
U of Waterloo (ON, Canada) **583**
U of Wisconsin–Milwaukee (WI) **585**
Virginia Polytechnic Inst and State U (VA) **591**
Washington State U (WA) **595**
Washington U in St. Louis (MO) **595**
Wellesley Coll (MA) **597**
Wentworth Inst of Technology (MA) **597**
Woodbury U (CA) **609**
Yale U (CT) **610**

ARCHITECTURE RELATED

Information can be found under this major's main heading.

Clemson U (SC) **317**
Columbia Coll (NY) **326**
New York Inst of Technology (NY) **447**
U of Illinois at Urbana–Champaign (IL) **548**
U of Kansas (KS) **549**
U of Louisiana at Lafayette (LA) **550**
Washington U in St. Louis (MO) **595**

AREA, ETHNIC, AND CULTURAL STUDIES RELATED

Information can be found under this major's main heading.

Brandeis U (MA) **293**
Linfield Coll (OR) **408**
Pratt Inst (NY) **473**
Queens Coll of the City U of NY (NY) **475**
Skidmore Coll (NY) **506**
Touro Coll (NY) **529**
U of Hawaii at Manoa (HI) **546**
The U of North Carolina at Chapel Hill (NC) **560**
The U of North Carolina at Charlotte (NC) **560**
The U of Tennessee (TN) **577**
Washington U in St. Louis (MO) **595**

AREA STUDIES

Overview: This broad-based major focuses on the defined areas, regions, and countries of the world, as well as minority groups within societies and issues relevant to gender. *Related majors:* African studies, Asian studies, Middle Eastern studies, international relations. *Potential careers:* foreign service officer, political activist, foreign correspondent, anthropologist, translator. *Salary potential:* $20k-$30k.

Abilene Christian U (TX) **260**
The American U in Cairo(Egypt) **267**
Bard Coll (NY) **281**
Bucknell U (PA) **297**
Denison U (OH) **339**
Eastern Michigan U (MI) **348**
Excelsior Coll (NY) **356**
Gettysburg Coll (PA) **368**
Hawai'i Pacific U (HI) **377**
Marymount Coll of Fordham U (NY) **419**
Memorial U of Newfoundland (NF, Canada) **424**
Millersville U of Pennsylvania (PA) **430**
United States Air Force Academy (CO) **534**
The U of Montana–Missoula (MT) **556**
U of Oklahoma (OK) **562**

AREA STUDIES RELATED

Information can be found under this major's main heading.

Boston U (MA) **292**
Drexel U (PA) **346**
Holy Names Coll (CA) **381**
Lewis U (IL) **406**
Maryville Coll (TN) **420**
McGill U (QC, Canada) **423**
Swarthmore Coll (PA) **521**
U of Alaska Fairbanks (AK) **538**
U of Illinois at Urbana–Champaign (IL) **548**
Utah State U (UT) **587**

ARMY R.O.T.C./MILITARY SCIENCE

Overview: This major introduces students to the theories of military science and prepare them for a career as an army officer. *Related majors:* military history, military technologies, history, area studies, foreign affairs and diplomacy. *Potential careers:* Army officer, defense consultant. *Salary potential:* $25k-$35k.

American Public U System (WV) **267**
Campbell U (NC) **303**
Drake U (IA) **345**
Eastern Washington U (WA) **349**
Hampton U (VA) **375**
Jacksonville State U (AL) **390**
La Salle U (PA) **402**
Longwood U (VA) **409**
Minnesota State U, Mankato (MN) **431**
Monmouth Coll (IL) **434**
Northwest Missouri State U (MO) **454**
Ohio U (OH) **458**
Purdue U Calumet (IN) **475**
Rensselaer Polytechnic Inst (NY) **478**
Rhode Island Coll (RI) **479**
United States Military Academy (NY) **535**
The U of Iowa (IA) **548**
U of Puerto Rico, Cayey U Coll (PR) **571**
The U of Texas–Pan American (TX) **579**
U of Washington (WA) **583**

ART

Overview: Students choosing this broad-based major learn about and are given instruction in the visual arts, including photography, painting, and other visual art disciplines. *Related majors:* multimedia, art history, drawing, sculpture. *Potential careers:* artist, art teacher or professor, writer, art gallery owner or art dealer. *Salary potential:* $10k-$30k.

Abilene Christian U (TX) **260**
Academy of Art Coll (CA) **260**
Adams State Coll (CO) **260**
Adrian Coll (MI) **260**
Agnes Scott Coll (GA) **261**
Alabama State U (AL) **261**
Albany State U (GA) **262**
Alberta Coll of Art & Design (AB, Canada) **262**
Albertson Coll of Idaho (ID) **262**

ART (continued)

Albertus Magnus Coll (CT) ***262***
Albion Coll (MI) ***262***
Albright Coll (PA) ***263***
Alfred U (NY) ***263***
Allegheny Coll (PA) ***264***
Alma Coll (MI) ***264***
Alverno Coll (WI) ***265***
American Academy of Art (IL) ***265***
American U (DC) ***267***
The American U in Cairo(Egypt) ***267***
Amherst Coll (MA) ***268***
Anderson Coll (SC) ***268***
Andrews U (MI) ***269***
Angelo State U (TX) ***269***
Anna Maria Coll (MA) ***269***
Appalachian State U (NC) ***270***
Aquinas Coll (MI) ***270***
Arcadia U (PA) ***271***
Arizona State U (AZ) ***271***
Arkansas State U (AR) ***272***
Arkansas Tech U (AR) ***272***
Armstrong Atlantic State U (GA) ***273***
Art Academy of Cincinnati (OH) ***273***
Art Center Coll of Design (CA) ***273***
The Art Inst of Boston at Lesley U (MA) ***273***
The Art Inst of Colorado (CO) ***274***
Ashland U (OH) ***274***
Athens State U (AL) ***275***
Atlantic Union Coll (MA) ***276***
Auburn U (AL) ***276***
Auburn U Montgomery (AL) ***276***
Augsburg Coll (MN) ***276***
Augustana Coll (IL) ***276***
Augustana Coll (SD) ***276***
Austin Coll (TX) ***277***
Austin Peay State U (TN) ***278***
Averett U (VA) ***278***
Avila U (MO) ***278***
Azusa Pacific U (CA) ***278***
Baldwin-Wallace Coll (OH) ***280***
Ball State U (IN) ***280***
Bard Coll (NY) ***281***
Bates Coll (ME) ***282***
Baylor U (TX) ***283***
Belhaven Coll (MS) ***283***
Bellarmine U (KY) ***284***
Bellevue U (NE) ***284***
Belmont U (TN) ***284***
Bemidji State U (MN) ***285***
Benedict Coll (SC) ***285***
Bennett Coll (NC) ***286***
Bennington Coll (VT) ***286***
Berea Coll (KY) ***286***
Berry Coll (GA) ***287***
Bethany Coll (KS) ***287***
Bethany Coll (WV) ***287***
Bethany Lutheran Coll (MN) ***288***
Bethel Coll (IN) ***288***
Bethel Coll (KS) ***288***
Bethel Coll (MN) ***288***
Biola U (CA) ***289***
Birmingham-Southern Coll (AL) ***289***
Bishop's U (QC, Canada) ***289***
Blackburn Coll (IL) ***290***
Black Hills State U (SD) ***290***
Bloomfield Coll (NJ) ***290***
Bluefield Coll (VA) ***291***
Bluffton Coll (OH) ***291***
Bowdoin Coll (ME) ***292***
Bowie State U (MD) ***292***
Bowling Green State U (OH) ***292***
Bradley U (IL) ***293***
Brandeis U (MA) ***293***
Brescia U (KY) ***293***
Brevard Coll (NC) ***294***
Briar Cliff U (IA) ***294***
Bridgewater Coll (VA) ***294***
Bridgewater State Coll (MA) ***294***
Brigham Young U (UT) ***295***
Brigham Young U–Hawaii (HI) ***295***
Brock U (ON, Canada) ***295***
Brooklyn Coll of the City U of NY (NY) ***295***
Brown U (RI) ***296***
Bryn Mawr Coll (PA) ***297***
Bucknell U (PA) ***297***
Buena Vista U (IA) ***297***
Burlington Coll (VT) ***297***
Caldwell Coll (NJ) ***298***
California Baptist U (CA) ***298***
California Coll of Arts and Crafts (CA) ***299***
California Inst of the Arts (CA) ***299***
California Lutheran U (CA) ***299***
California Polytechnic State U, San Luis Obispo (CA) ***300***
California State Polytechnic U, Pomona (CA) ***300***
California State U, Bakersfield (CA) ***300***
California State U, Chico (CA) ***300***
California State U, Dominguez Hills (CA) ***300***
California State U, Fresno (CA) ***301***
California State U, Fullerton (CA) ***301***
California State U, Long Beach (CA) ***301***
California State U, Northridge (CA) ***301***
California State U, Sacramento (CA) ***301***
California State U, San Bernardino (CA) ***302***
California State U, Stanislaus (CA) ***302***
California U of Pennsylvania (PA) ***302***
Calvin Coll (MI) ***303***
Cameron U (OK) ***303***
Campbellsville U (KY) ***303***
Campbell U (NC) ***303***
Capital U (OH) ***304***
Cardinal Stritch U (WI) ***305***
Carlow Coll (PA) ***305***
Carnegie Mellon U (PA) ***305***
Carroll Coll (WI) ***306***
Carson-Newman Coll (TN) ***306***
Castleton State Coll (VT) ***307***
The Catholic U of America (DC) ***307***
Cedar Crest Coll (PA) ***308***
Centenary Coll of Louisiana (LA) ***308***
Central Coll (IA) ***309***
Central Connecticut State U (CT) ***309***
Central Michigan U (MI) ***310***
Central Washington U (WA) ***310***
Centre Coll (KY) ***310***
Chadron State Coll (NE) ***311***
Chapman U (CA) ***311***
Chester Coll of New England (NH) ***312***
Cheyney U of Pennsylvania (PA) ***312***
Chowan Coll (NC) ***312***
Christopher Newport U (VA) ***313***
City Coll of the City U of NY (NY) ***314***
Claflin U (SC) ***314***
Claremont McKenna Coll (CA) ***315***
Clarion U of Pennsylvania (PA) ***315***
Clark Atlanta U (GA) ***315***
Clarke Coll (IA) ***315***
Clark U (MA) ***316***
Clemson U (SC) ***317***
Cleveland State U (OH) ***317***
Coastal Carolina U (SC) ***318***
Coe Coll (IA) ***318***
Coker Coll (SC) ***318***
Colby Coll (ME) ***318***
Colby-Sawyer Coll (NH) ***319***
Colgate U (NY) ***319***
Col for Creative Studies (MI) ***319***
Coll of Mount St. Joseph (OH) ***320***
The Coll of New Jersey (NJ) ***320***
Coll of Notre Dame of Maryland (MD) ***321***
Coll of Saint Benedict (MN) ***321***
Coll of St. Catherine (MN) ***321***
Coll of Saint Elizabeth (NJ) ***321***
Coll of the Atlantic (ME) ***323***
Coll of Visual Arts (MN) ***324***
The Coll of William and Mary (VA) ***324***
The Coll of Wooster (OH) ***324***
Colorado Christian U (CO) ***325***
Colorado State U (CO) ***325***
Colorado State U-Pueblo (CO) ***325***
Columbia Coll (MO) ***326***
Columbia Coll (SC) ***327***
Columbia Coll Chicago (IL) ***327***
Columbus Coll of Art and Design (OH) ***328***
Columbus State U (GA) ***328***
Concordia Coll (MN) ***329***
Concordia U (CA) ***330***
Concordia U (IL) ***330***
Concordia U (MI) ***330***
Concordia U (NE) ***330***
Concordia U (QC, Canada) ***331***
Concordia U Wisconsin (WI) ***331***
Connecticut Coll (CT) ***331***
Converse Coll (SC) ***332***
Cooper Union for the Advancement of Science & Art (NY) ***332***
Corcoran Coll of Art and Design (DC) ***332***
Cornell Coll (IA) ***332***
Cornell U (NY) ***333***
Cornish Coll of the Arts (WA) ***333***
Creighton U (NE) ***333***
Culver-Stockton Coll (MO) ***334***
Curry Coll (MA) ***335***
Daemen Coll (NY) ***335***
Dakota Wesleyan U (SD) ***336***
Dallas Baptist U (TX) ***336***
Dana Coll (NE) ***337***
Davidson Coll (NC) ***338***
Davis & Elkins Coll (WV) ***338***
Defiance Coll (OH) ***338***
Delaware State U (DE) ***338***
Denison U (OH) ***339***
DePaul U (IL) ***339***
Dickinson State U (ND) ***344***
Dillard U (LA) ***344***
Doane Coll (NE) ***344***
Dominican U (IL) ***345***
Dominican U of California (CA) ***345***
Dordt Coll (IA) ***345***
Dowling Coll (NY) ***345***
Drake U (IA) ***345***
Drew U (NJ) ***346***
Drury U (MO) ***346***
Duke U (NC) ***346***
Earlham Coll (IN) ***347***
East Carolina U (NC) ***347***
East Central U (OK) ***347***
Eastern Connecticut State U (CT) ***347***
Eastern Illinois U (IL) ***348***
Eastern Kentucky U (KY) ***348***
Eastern Mennonite U (VA) ***348***
Eastern Michigan U (MI) ***348***
Eastern New Mexico U (NM) ***349***
Eastern Oregon U (OR) ***349***
Eastern Washington U (WA) ***349***
East Tennessee State U (TN) ***349***
Eckerd Coll (FL) ***350***
Edgewood Coll (WI) ***351***
Elizabeth City State U (NC) ***351***
Elizabethtown Coll (PA) ***351***
Elmhurst Coll (IL) ***351***
Elmira Coll (NY) ***351***
Elms Coll (MA) ***352***
Elon U (NC) ***352***
Emmanuel Coll (MA) ***353***
Emory & Henry Coll (VA) ***353***
Emporia State U (KS) ***354***
Eureka Coll (IL) ***355***
Evangel U (MO) ***355***
The Evergreen State Coll (WA) ***355***
Fairfield U (CT) ***356***
Fayetteville State U (NC) ***357***
Felician Coll (NJ) ***357***
Ferrum Coll (VA) ***358***
Finlandia U (MI) ***358***
Fisk U (TN) ***358***
Florida A&M U (FL) ***359***
Florida Atlantic U (FL) ***359***
Florida Southern Coll (FL) ***361***
Florida State U (FL) ***361***
Fontbonne U (MO) ***361***
Fordham U (NY) ***362***
Fort Hays State U (KS) ***362***
Fort Lewis Coll (CO) ***362***
Francis Marion U (SC) ***363***
Franklin and Marshall Coll (PA) ***363***
Franklin Pierce Coll (NH) ***364***
Freed-Hardeman U (TN) ***364***
Furman U (SC) ***365***
Gallaudet U (DC) ***365***
Gardner-Webb U (NC) ***365***
George Fox U (OR) ***366***
George Mason U (VA) ***366***
Georgetown Coll (KY) ***366***
Georgetown U (DC) ***366***
The George Washington U (DC) ***367***
Georgia Coll & State U (GA) ***367***
Georgian Court Coll (NJ) ***367***
Georgia Southern U (GA) ***367***
Georgia Southwestern State U (GA) ***368***
Gettysburg Coll (PA) ***368***
Goddard Coll (VT) ***369***
Gonzaga U (WA) ***369***
Gordon Coll (MA) ***370***
Goshen Coll (IN) ***370***
Goucher Coll (MD) ***370***
Governors State U (IL) ***370***
Grace Coll (IN) ***370***
Graceland U (IA) ***371***
Grambling State U (LA) ***371***
Grand Canyon U (AZ) ***371***
Grand Valley State U (MI) ***371***
Grand View Coll (IA) ***372***
Green Mountain Coll (VT) ***372***
Greensboro Coll (NC) ***372***
Greenville Coll (IL) ***373***
Grinnell Coll (IA) ***373***
Guilford Coll (NC) ***373***
Gustavus Adolphus Coll (MN) ***374***
Hamilton Coll (NY) ***374***
Hamline U (MN) ***374***
Hampshire Coll (MA) ***375***
Hampton U (VA) ***375***
Hannibal-LaGrange Coll (MO) ***375***
Hanover Coll (IN) ***375***
Harding U (AR) ***375***
Hardin-Simmons U (TX) ***376***
Hartwick Coll (NY) ***376***
Harvard U (MA) ***376***
Hastings Coll (NE) ***377***
Haverford Coll (PA) ***377***
Henderson State U (AR) ***378***
Hendrix Coll (AR) ***378***
Hillsdale Coll (MI) ***379***
Hiram Coll (OH) ***379***
Hobart and William Smith Colls (NY) ***380***
Holy Family U (PA) ***380***
Hood Coll (MD) ***381***
Houghton Coll (NY) ***381***
Houston Baptist U (TX) ***382***
Howard Payne U (TX) ***382***
Howard U (DC) ***382***
Humboldt State U (CA) ***382***
Hunter Coll of the City U of NY (NY) ***382***
Huntingdon Coll (AL) ***383***
Huntington Coll (IN) ***383***
Huron U USA in London(United Kingdom) ***383***
Idaho State U (ID) ***384***
Illinois Coll (IL) ***384***
Illinois State U (IL) ***384***
Illinois Wesleyan U (IL) ***385***
Indiana State U (IN) ***385***
Indiana U Bloomington (IN) ***385***
Indiana U Northwest (IN) ***386***
Indiana U of Pennsylvania (PA) ***386***
Indiana U South Bend (IN) ***387***
Indiana U Southeast (IN) ***387***
Indiana Wesleyan U (IN) ***387***
Inter American U of PR, San Germán Campus (PR) ***388***
Iona Coll (NY) ***390***
Iowa State U of Science and Technology (IA) ***390***
Iowa Wesleyan Coll (IA) ***390***
Ithaca Coll (NY) ***390***
Jackson State U (MS) ***390***
Jacksonville State U (AL) ***390***
Jacksonville U (FL) ***391***
James Madison U (VA) ***391***
Jamestown Coll (ND) ***391***
Johnson State Coll (VT) ***394***
Judson Coll (AL) ***395***
Judson Coll (IL) ***395***
Kalamazoo Coll (MI) ***395***
Kansas State U (KS) ***396***
Kean U (NJ) ***396***
Keene State Coll (NH) ***396***
Kennesaw State U (GA) ***397***
Kenyon Coll (OH) ***398***
Knox Coll (IL) ***399***
Lafayette Coll (PA) ***400***
LaGrange Coll (GA) ***400***
Laguna Coll of Art & Design (CA) ***400***
Lake Erie Coll (OH) ***400***
Lakehead U (ON, Canada) ***400***
Lakeland Coll (WI) ***401***
Lamar U (TX) ***401***
Lambuth U (TN) ***401***
Lander U (SC) ***401***
Langston U (OK) ***402***
La Salle U (PA) ***402***
La Sierra U (CA) ***403***
Lehigh U (PA) ***404***
Lehman Coll of the City U of NY (NY) ***404***
Lewis & Clark Coll (OR) ***405***
Lewis U (IL) ***406***
Lincoln Memorial U (TN) ***407***
Lindenwood U (MO) ***407***
Lindsey Wilson Coll (KY) ***407***
Linfield Coll (OR) ***408***
Lipscomb U (TN) ***408***
Lock Haven U of Pennsylvania (PA) ***408***
Long Island U, Brooklyn Campus (NY) ***409***
Long Island U, C.W. Post Campus (NY) ***409***
Long Island U, Southampton Coll (NY) ***409***
Long Island U, Southampton Coll, Friends World Program (NY) ***409***
Longwood U (VA) ***409***
Louisiana Coll (LA) ***410***

Louisiana State U in Shreveport (LA) ***410***
Louisiana Tech U (LA) ***410***
Lourdes Coll (OH) ***411***
Loyola Coll in Maryland (MD) ***411***
Loyola U Chicago (IL) ***411***
Loyola U New Orleans (LA) ***411***
Luther Coll (IA) ***412***
Lycoming Coll (PA) ***412***
Lyon Coll (AR) ***413***
MacMurray Coll (IL) ***414***
Madonna U (MI) ***414***
Maharishi U of Management (IA) ***414***
Malone Coll (OH) ***415***
Manchester Coll (IN) ***415***
Manhattanville Coll (NY) ***416***
Mansfield U of Pennsylvania (PA) ***416***
Marian Coll (IN) ***417***
Marian Coll of Fond du Lac (WI) ***417***
Marietta Coll (OH) ***417***
Marist Coll (NY) ***417***
Marlboro Coll (VT) ***418***
Mars Hill Coll (NC) ***418***
Mary Baldwin Coll (VA) ***419***
Marygrove Coll (MI) ***419***
Maryland Inst Coll of Art (MD) ***419***
Marymount Coll of Fordham U (NY) ***419***
Marymount Manhattan Coll (NY) ***420***
Marymount U (VA) ***420***
Maryville Coll (TN) ***420***
Mary Washington Coll (VA) ***420***
Massachusetts Coll of Liberal Arts (MA) ***421***
McDaniel Coll (MD) ***422***
McKendree Coll (IL) ***423***
McMaster U (ON, Canada) ***423***
McMurry U (TX) ***423***
McPherson Coll (KS) ***423***
Memorial U of Newfoundland (NF, Canada) ***424***
Memphis Coll of Art (TN) ***425***
Mercer U (GA) ***425***
Mercy Coll (NY) ***425***
Mercyhurst Coll (PA) ***425***
Mesa State Coll (CO) ***426***
Methodist Coll (NC) ***427***
Metropolitan State Coll of Denver (CO) ***427***
Miami U (OH) ***428***
Michigan State U (MI) ***428***
Middlebury Coll (VT) ***429***
Middle Tennessee State U (TN) ***429***
Midland Lutheran Coll (NE) ***429***
Midwestern State U (TX) ***430***
Millersville U of Pennsylvania (PA) ***430***
Milligan Coll (TN) ***430***
Millsaps Coll (MS) ***431***
Mills Coll (CA) ***431***
Milwaukee Inst of Art and Design (WI) ***431***
Minnesota State U, Mankato (MN) ***431***
Minnesota State U, Moorhead (MN) ***432***
Minot State U (ND) ***432***
Mississippi Coll (MS) ***432***
Mississippi Valley State U (MS) ***432***
Missouri Valley Coll (MO) ***433***
Missouri Western State Coll (MO) ***433***
Molloy Coll (NY) ***433***
Monmouth Coll (IL) ***434***
Monmouth U (NJ) ***434***
Montana State U–Billings (MT) ***434***
Montana State U–Bozeman (MT) ***434***
Montclair State U (NJ) ***435***
Montserrat Coll of Art (MA) ***435***
Moore Coll of Art and Design (PA) ***436***
Moravian Coll (PA) ***436***
Morehouse Coll (GA) ***436***
Morgan State U (MD) ***436***
Morningside Coll (IA) ***437***
Mount Mary Coll (WI) ***438***
Mount Mercy Coll (IA) ***438***
Mount Olive Coll (NC) ***439***
Mount St. Mary's Coll (CA) ***439***
Mount Union Coll (OH) ***440***
Mount Vernon Nazarene U (OH) ***440***
Muhlenberg Coll (PA) ***440***
Murray State U (KY) ***440***
Muskingum Coll (OH) ***441***
Naropa U (CO) ***441***
National-Louis U (IL) ***442***
Nazareth Coll of Rochester (NY) ***443***
Nebraska Wesleyan U (NE) ***443***
Newberry Coll (SC) ***444***
New Coll of Florida (FL) ***444***
New England Coll (NH) ***444***
New Jersey City U (NJ) ***445***
New Mexico Highlands U (NM) ***446***
New Mexico State U (NM) ***446***
New World School of the Arts (FL) ***447***
New York U (NY) ***447***
Nicholls State U (LA) ***447***
Norfolk State U (VA) ***448***
North Carolina Central U (NC) ***448***
North Central Coll (IL) ***449***
North Dakota State U (ND) ***449***
Northeastern Illinois U (IL) ***450***
Northeastern State U (OK) ***450***
Northeastern U (MA) ***450***
Northern Arizona U (AZ) ***450***
Northern Illinois U (IL) ***450***
Northern Kentucky U (KY) ***451***
Northern Michigan U (MI) ***451***
Northern State U (SD) ***451***
North Georgia Coll & State U (GA) ***451***
Northland Coll (WI) ***452***
North Park U (IL) ***452***
Northwest Coll of Art (WA) ***452***
Northwestern Coll (IA) ***453***
Northwestern State U of Louisiana (LA) ***453***
Northwestern U (IL) ***453***
Northwest Missouri State U (MO) ***454***
Northwest Nazarene U (ID) ***454***
Notre Dame Coll (OH) ***455***
Notre Dame de Namur U (CA) ***455***
Nova Scotia Coll of Art and Design (NS, Canada) ***455***
Oakland City U (IN) ***456***
Oberlin Coll (OH) ***456***
Oglethorpe U (GA) ***457***
Ohio Northern U (OH) ***457***
The Ohio State U (OH) ***457***
Ohio U (OH) ***458***
Oklahoma Baptist U (OK) ***459***
Oklahoma Christian U (OK) ***459***
Oklahoma City U (OK) ***460***
Oklahoma State U (OK) ***460***
Old Dominion U (VA) ***460***
Olivet Coll (MI) ***461***
Olivet Nazarene U (IL) ***461***
Oregon State U (OR) ***462***
Otis Coll of Art and Design (CA) ***462***
Ottawa U (KS) ***462***
Otterbein Coll (OH) ***462***
Ouachita Baptist U (AR) ***462***
Our Lady of the Lake U of San Antonio (TX) ***463***
Pace U (NY) ***463***
Pacific Lutheran U (WA) ***463***
Pacific Northwest Coll of Art (OR) ***464***
Pacific Union Coll (CA) ***464***
Pacific U (OR) ***464***
Paier Coll of Art, Inc. (CT) ***464***
Palm Beach Atlantic U (FL) ***465***
Parsons School of Design, New School U (NY) ***465***
Penn State U Univ Park Campus (PA) ***468***
Pepperdine U, Malibu (CA) ***469***
Peru State Coll (NE) ***469***
Pikeville Coll (KY) ***470***
Pittsburg State U (KS) ***470***
Pitzer Coll (CA) ***471***
Plymouth State Coll (NH) ***471***
Point Loma Nazarene U (CA) ***471***
Pomona Coll (CA) ***472***
Pontifical Catholic U of Puerto Rico (PR) ***472***
Portland State U (OR) ***472***
Pratt Inst (NY) ***473***
Presbyterian Coll (SC) ***473***
Prescott Coll (AZ) ***474***
Purchase Coll, State U of NY (NY) ***475***
Purdue U (IN) ***475***
Queens Coll of the City U of NY (NY) ***475***
Queens U of Charlotte (NC) ***476***
Quincy U (IL) ***476***
Radford U (VA) ***476***
Ramapo Coll of New Jersey (NJ) ***477***
Randolph-Macon Coll (VA) ***477***
Randolph-Macon Woman's Coll (VA) ***477***
Reed Coll (OR) ***477***
Regis Coll (MA) ***478***
Rhode Island Coll (RI) ***479***
Rhode Island School of Design (RI) ***479***
Rhodes Coll (TN) ***479***
Rice U (TX) ***479***
Richmond, The American International U in London(United Kingdom) ***480***
Ripon Coll (WI) ***480***
Rivier Coll (NH) ***480***
Roanoke Coll (VA) ***481***
Roberts Wesleyan Coll (NY) ***481***
Rochester Inst of Technology (NY) ***482***
Rockford Coll (IL) ***482***
Rocky Mountain Coll (MT) ***482***
Rollins Coll (FL) ***483***
Rowan U (NJ) ***484***
Rutgers, The State U of New Jersey, Camden (NJ) ***485***
Rutgers, The State U of New Jersey, Newark (NJ) ***485***
Rutgers, The State U of New Jersey, New Brunswick (NJ) ***485***
Sacred Heart U (CT) ***486***
Saginaw Valley State U (MI) ***486***
St. Ambrose U (IA) ***486***
St. Andrews Presbyterian Coll (NC) ***487***
Saint Anselm Coll (NH) ***487***
St. Cloud State U (MN) ***488***
St. Edward's U (TX) ***488***
Saint John's U (MN) ***490***
Saint Joseph's U (PA) ***491***
St. Lawrence U (NY) ***491***
Saint Mary Coll (KS) ***493***
Saint Mary-of-the-Woods Coll (IN) ***493***
Saint Mary's Coll (IN) ***493***
Saint Mary's Coll of California (CA) ***494***
St. Mary's Coll of Maryland (MD) ***494***
Saint Michael's Coll (VT) ***494***
St. Norbert Coll (WI) ***495***
St. Olaf Coll (MN) ***495***
Saint Peter's Coll (NJ) ***495***
St. Thomas Aquinas Coll (NY) ***495***
Saint Xavier U (IL) ***496***
Salem State Coll (MA) ***497***
Salisbury U (MD) ***497***
Samford U (AL) ***497***
Sam Houston State U (TX) ***497***
San Diego State U (CA) ***498***
San Francisco Art Inst (CA) ***498***
San Francisco State U (CA) ***498***
San Jose State U (CA) ***499***
Santa Clara U (CA) ***499***
Sarah Lawrence Coll (NY) ***499***
Savannah Coll of Art and Design (GA) ***499***
School of the Art Inst of Chicago (IL) ***500***
School of the Museum of Fine Arts (MA) ***501***
School of Visual Arts (NY) ***501***
Schreiner U (TX) ***501***
Scripps Coll (CA) ***501***
Seattle Pacific U (WA) ***501***
Seattle U (WA) ***501***
Seton Hill U (PA) ***502***
Shawnee State U (OH) ***502***
Shepherd Coll (WV) ***503***
Shippensburg U of Pennsylvania (PA) ***503***
Shorter Coll (GA) ***504***
Siena Heights U (MI) ***504***
Sierra Nevada Coll (NV) ***504***
Silver Lake Coll (WI) ***504***
Simmons Coll (MA) ***504***
Simon Fraser U (BC, Canada) ***505***
Simpson Coll (IA) ***505***
Slippery Rock U of Pennsylvania (PA) ***506***
Smith Coll (MA) ***506***
Sonoma State U (CA) ***506***
South Dakota State U (SD) ***507***
Southeastern Louisiana U (LA) ***508***
Southeastern Oklahoma State U (OK) ***508***
Southeast Missouri State U (MO) ***508***
Southern Adventist U (TN) ***508***
Southern Arkansas U–Magnolia (AR) ***509***
Southern Illinois U Carbondale (IL) ***509***
Southern Illinois U Edwardsville (IL) ***509***
Southern Oregon U (OR) ***510***
Southern U and A&M Coll (LA) ***511***
Southern Utah U (UT) ***511***
Southern Virginia U (VA) ***511***
Southwest Baptist U (MO) ***512***
Southwestern U (TX) ***513***
Southwest Missouri State U (MO) ***513***
Southwest State U (MN) ***513***
Southwest Texas State U (TX) ***513***
Spalding U (KY) ***513***
Spelman Coll (GA) ***514***
Spring Arbor U (MI) ***514***
Stanford U (CA) ***514***
State U of NY at Albany (NY) ***514***
State U of NY at Binghamton (NY) ***515***
State U of NY at New Paltz (NY) ***515***
State U of NY at Oswego (NY) ***515***
State U of NY Coll at Brockport (NY) ***515***
State U of NY Coll at Buffalo (NY) ***516***
State U of NY Coll at Fredonia (NY) ***516***
State U of NY Coll at Geneseo (NY) ***516***
State U of NY Coll at Old Westbury (NY) ***516***
State U of NY Coll at Oneonta (NY) ***517***
State U of NY Coll at Potsdam (NY) ***517***
State U of NY Empire State Coll (NY) ***517***
State U of West Georgia (GA) ***518***
Stephen F. Austin State U (TX) ***518***
Sterling Coll (KS) ***519***
Stetson U (FL) ***519***
Suffolk U (MA) ***520***
Sul Ross State U (TX) ***521***
Susquehanna U (PA) ***521***
Syracuse U (NY) ***521***
Tarleton State U (TX) ***522***
Taylor U (IN) ***523***
Temple U (PA) ***523***
Tennessee State U (TN) ***523***
Tennessee Technological U (TN) ***524***
Texas A&M U–Commerce (TX) ***525***
Texas A&M U–Corpus Christi (TX) ***525***
Texas A&M U–Kingsville (TX) ***525***
Texas Christian U (TX) ***526***
Texas Coll (TX) ***526***
Texas Lutheran U (TX) ***526***
Texas Southern U (TX) ***526***
Texas Tech U (TX) ***526***
Texas Wesleyan U (TX) ***526***
Texas Woman's U (TX) ***527***
Thiel Coll (PA) ***527***
Thomas Edison State Coll (NJ) ***527***
Thomas U (GA) ***528***
Towson U (MD) ***529***
Transylvania U (KY) ***529***
Trinity Christian Coll (IL) ***530***
Trinity Coll (CT) ***530***
Trinity U (TX) ***531***
Troy State U (AL) ***532***
Truman State U (MO) ***532***
Tulane U (LA) ***533***
Tusculum Coll (TN) ***533***
Union U (TN) ***534***
U du Québec à Trois-Rivières (QC, Canada) ***536***
U du Québec à Hull (QC, Canada) ***536***
U at Buffalo, The State University of New York (NY) ***536***
The U of Akron (OH) ***537***
The U of Alabama in Huntsville (AL) ***537***
U of Alaska Anchorage (AK) ***538***
U of Alaska Fairbanks (AK) ***538***
U of Alberta (AB, Canada) ***538***
U of Arkansas (AR) ***539***
U of Arkansas at Little Rock (AR) ***539***
U of Arkansas at Monticello (AR) ***539***
U of Bridgeport (CT) ***540***
U of Calgary (AB, Canada) ***540***
U of Calif, Berkeley (CA) ***540***
U of Calif, Davis (CA) ***540***
U of Calif, Irvine (CA) ***541***
U of Calif, Los Angeles (CA) ***541***
U of Calif, San Diego (CA) ***541***
U of Calif, Santa Cruz (CA) ***542***
U of Central Arkansas (AR) ***542***
U of Central Florida (FL) ***542***
U of Central Oklahoma (OK) ***542***
U of Charleston (WV) ***542***
U of Chicago (IL) ***542***
U of Cincinnati (OH) ***543***
U of Colorado at Boulder (CO) ***543***
U of Colorado at Colorado Springs (CO) ***543***
U of Dallas (TX) ***544***
U of Dayton (OH) ***544***
U of Delaware (DE) ***544***
U of Denver (CO) ***544***
U of Evansville (IN) ***545***
The U of Findlay (OH) ***545***
U of Georgia (GA) ***545***
U of Great Falls (MT) ***545***
U of Hawaii at Hilo (HI) ***546***
U of Hawaii at Manoa (HI) ***546***
U of Houston (TX) ***547***
U of Idaho (ID) ***547***
U of Illinois at Springfield (IL) ***548***
U of Indianapolis (IN) ***548***
The U of Iowa (IA) ***548***
U of Kansas (KS) ***549***
U of La Verne (CA) ***549***
The U of Lethbridge (AB, Canada) ***549***
U of Louisiana at Lafayette (LA) ***550***
U of Maine (ME) ***550***
U of Maine at Farmington (ME) ***550***
U of Maine at Presque Isle (ME) ***551***
U of Manitoba (MB, Canada) ***551***
U of Mary Hardin-Baylor (TX) ***551***

ART (continued)

U of Maryland, Baltimore County (MD) **552**
U of Massachusetts Boston (MA) **553**
U of Massachusetts Dartmouth (MA) **553**
The U of Memphis (TN) **553**
U of Miami (FL) **553**
U of Michigan–Flint (MI) **554**
U of Minnesota, Duluth (MN) **554**
U of Minnesota, Twin Cities Campus (MN) **555**
U of Mississippi (MS) **555**
U of Missouri–Columbia (MO) **555**
U of Missouri–Kansas City (MO) **555**
U of Missouri–St. Louis (MO) **556**
U of Mobile (AL) **556**
The U of Montana–Missoula (MT) **556**
The U of Montana–Western (MT) **556**
U of Montevallo (AL) **557**
U of Nebraska at Kearney (NE) **557**
U of Nebraska at Omaha (NE) **557**
U of Nevada, Las Vegas (NV) **558**
U of Nevada, Reno (NV) **558**
U of New Hampshire (NH) **558**
U of New Haven (CT) **559**
U of New Mexico (NM) **559**
The U of North Carolina at Asheville (NC) **559**
The U of North Carolina at Charlotte (NC) **560**
The U of North Carolina at Greensboro (NC) **560**
The U of North Carolina at Pembroke (NC) **560**
U of North Dakota (ND) **561**
U of Northern Colorado (CO) **561**
U of Northern Iowa (IA) **561**
U of North Florida (FL) **561**
U of North Texas (TX) **562**
U of Oklahoma (OK) **562**
U of Oregon (OR) **562**
U of Ottawa (ON, Canada) **563**
U of Pennsylvania (PA) **563**
U of Puerto Rico, Río Piedras (PR) **571**
U of Puget Sound (WA) **571**
U of Regina (SK, Canada) **572**
U of Rhode Island (RI) **572**
U of Richmond (VA) **572**
U of Rio Grande (OH) **572**
U of Saint Francis (IN) **573**
U of San Diego (CA) **574**
U of Science and Arts of Oklahoma (OK) **574**
U of South Alabama (AL) **575**
The U of South Dakota (SD) **575**
U of Southern California (CA) **576**
U of Southern Indiana (IN) **576**
U of Southern Maine (ME) **576**
U of South Florida (FL) **576**
The U of Tampa (FL) **577**
The U of Tennessee at Chattanooga (TN) **577**
The U of Texas at Arlington (TX) **577**
The U of Texas at Austin (TX) **578**
The U of Texas at Dallas (TX) **578**
The U of Texas at El Paso (TX) **578**
The U of Texas at San Antonio (TX) **578**
The U of Texas at Tyler (TX) **579**
The U of Texas of the Permian Basin (TX) **579**
The U of Texas–Pan American (TX) **579**
U of the District of Columbia (DC) **580**
U of the Incarnate Word (TX) **580**
U of the Ozarks (AR) **580**
U of the Pacific (CA) **580**
U of the Sacred Heart (PR) **580**
U of the South (TN) **581**
U of Toledo (OH) **581**
U of Toronto (ON, Canada) **581**
U of Tulsa (OK) **581**
U of Utah (UT) **582**
U of Virginia (VA) **582**
The U of Virginia's Coll at Wise (VA) **582**
U of Washington (WA) **583**
The U of Western Ontario (ON, Canada) **583**
U of West Florida (FL) **583**
U of Windsor (ON, Canada) **584**
U of Wisconsin–Eau Claire (WI) **584**
U of Wisconsin–Green Bay (WI) **584**
U of Wisconsin–La Crosse (WI) **584**
U of Wisconsin–Madison (WI) **584**
U of Wisconsin–Milwaukee (WI) **585**
U of Wisconsin–Oshkosh (WI) **585**
U of Wisconsin–Parkside (WI) **585**
U of Wisconsin–Platteville (WI) **585**
U of Wisconsin–River Falls (WI) **585**
U of Wisconsin–Stevens Point (WI) **585**
U of Wisconsin–Whitewater (WI) **586**
U of Wyoming (WY) **586**
Upper Iowa U (IA) **587**
Ursinus Coll (PA) **587**
Ursuline Coll (OH) **587**
Utah State U (UT) **587**
Valdosta State U (GA) **588**
Valley City State U (ND) **588**
Valparaiso U (IN) **588**
Vanderbilt U (TN) **588**
Virginia Intermont Coll (VA) **590**
Virginia Polytechnic Inst and State U (VA) **591**
Virginia Wesleyan Coll (VA) **591**
Viterbo U (WI) **591**
Wabash Coll (IN) **592**
Wagner Coll (NY) **592**
Wake Forest U (NC) **592**
Walla Walla Coll (WA) **593**
Warren Wilson Coll (NC) **594**
Wartburg Coll (IA) **594**
Washington & Jefferson Coll (PA) **594**
Washington Coll (MD) **594**
Washington State U (WA) **595**
Washington U in St. Louis (MO) **595**
Watkins Coll of Art and Design (TN) **595**
Wayland Baptist U (TX) **595**
Waynesburg Coll (PA) **595**
Wayne State Coll (NE) **596**
Wayne State U (MI) **596**
Weber State U (UT) **596**
Webster U (MO) **597**
Wells Coll (NY) **597**
West Chester U of Pennsylvania (PA) **598**
Western Carolina U (NC) **598**
Western Connecticut State U (CT) **598**
Western Illinois U (IL) **599**
Western Michigan U (MI) **599**
Western New Mexico U (NM) **600**
Western Oregon U (OR) **600**
Western State Coll of Colorado (CO) **600**
Western Washington U (WA) **600**
Westfield State Coll (MA) **600**
Westminster Coll (PA) **601**
Westminster Coll (UT) **601**
Westmont Coll (CA) **602**
West Texas A&M U (TX) **602**
West Virginia State Coll (WV) **602**
West Virginia U (WV) **602**
West Virginia Wesleyan Coll (WV) **603**
Wheaton Coll (IL) **603**
Wheaton Coll (MA) **603**
Whitman Coll (WA) **604**
Whittier Coll (CA) **604**
Whitworth Coll (WA) **604**
Wichita State U (KS) **604**
Willamette U (OR) **605**
William Carey Coll (MS) **605**
William Jewell Coll (MO) **606**
William Paterson U of New Jersey (NJ) **606**
Williams Baptist Coll (AR) **606**
William Woods U (MO) **607**
Wilson Coll (PA) **607**
Wingate U (NC) **607**
Winona State U (MN) **608**
Winston-Salem State U (NC) **608**
Winthrop U (SC) **608**
Wisconsin Lutheran Coll (WI) **608**
Wittenberg U (OH) **608**
Wright State U (OH) **609**
Xavier U (OH) **610**
Xavier U of Louisiana (LA) **610**
Yale U (CT) **610**
York Coll of Pennsylvania (PA) **610**
York Coll of the City U of New York (NY) **611**
York U (ON, Canada) **611**
Youngstown State U (OH) **611**

ART EDUCATION

Overview: this major prepares undergraduates to teach a variety of forms of artistic expression (drawing, painting, ceramics, photography, etc.) and art appreciation topics (such as art history) at various education levels. *Related majors:* fine/studio art, photography, film-video making, graphic design and commercial art. *Potential careers:* art teacher. *Salary potential:* $22k-$32k.

Abilene Christian U (TX) **260**
Adams State Coll (CO) **260**
Adelphi U (NY) **260**
Adrian Coll (MI) **260**
Alabama State U (AL) **261**
Albright Coll (PA) **263**
Alfred U (NY) **263**
Allen U (SC) **264**
Alma Coll (MI) **264**
Alverno Coll (WI) **265**
Anderson Coll (SC) **268**
Anderson U (IN) **268**
Andrews U (MI) **269**
Anna Maria Coll (MA) **269**
Appalachian State U (NC) **270**
Aquinas Coll (MI) **270**
Arcadia U (PA) **271**
Arkansas State U (AR) **272**
Arkansas Tech U (AR) **272**
Armstrong Atlantic State U (GA) **273**
Asbury Coll (KY) **274**
Ashland U (OH) **274**
Atlantic Union Coll (MA) **276**
Augsburg Coll (MN) **276**
Augustana Coll (IL) **276**
Augustana Coll (SD) **276**
Averett U (VA) **278**
Avila U (MO) **278**
Baker U (KS) **280**
Baldwin-Wallace Coll (OH) **280**
Ball State U (IN) **280**
Barton Coll (NC) **282**
Baylor U (TX) **283**
Belmont U (TN) **284**
Beloit Coll (WI) **285**
Bemidji State U (MN) **285**
Benedict Coll (SC) **285**
Berea Coll (KY) **286**
Berry Coll (GA) **287**
Bethany Coll (KS) **287**
Bethel Coll (MN) **288**
Birmingham-Southern Coll (AL) **289**
Bloomfield Coll (NJ) **290**
Bluffton Coll (OH) **291**
Boston U (MA) **292**
Bowling Green State U (OH) **292**
Brenau U (GA) **293**
Brescia U (KY) **293**
Briar Cliff U (IA) **294**
Bridgewater Coll (VA) **294**
Brigham Young U (UT) **295**
Brigham Young U–Hawaii (HI) **295**
Brooklyn Coll of the City U of NY (NY) **295**
California State U, Chico (CA) **300**
California State U, Fullerton (CA) **301**
California State U, Long Beach (CA) **301**
California State U, Northridge (CA) **301**
Calumet Coll of Saint Joseph (IN) **302**
Calvin Coll (MI) **303**
Cameron U (OK) **303**
Campbellsville U (KY) **303**
Capital U (OH) **304**
Cardinal Stritch U (WI) **305**
Carlow Coll (PA) **305**
Carroll Coll (WI) **306**
Carson-Newman Coll (TN) **306**
Case Western Reserve U (OH) **307**
The Catholic U of America (DC) **307**
Centenary Coll of Louisiana (LA) **308**
Central Connecticut State U (CT) **309**
Central Michigan U (MI) **310**
Central Missouri State U (MO) **310**
Central Washington U (WA) **310**
Chadron State Coll (NE) **311**
City Coll of the City U of NY (NY) **314**
Claflin U (SC) **314**
Clark Atlanta U (GA) **315**
Clarke Coll (IA) **315**
Cleveland State U (OH) **317**
Coastal Carolina U (SC) **318**
Coe Coll (IA) **318**
Coker Coll (SC) **318**
Colby-Sawyer Coll (NH) **319**
Coll of Mount St. Joseph (OH) **320**
The Coll of New Jersey (NJ) **320**
The Coll of New Rochelle (NY) **321**
Coll of Saint Benedict (MN) **321**
Coll of St. Catherine (MN) **321**
The Coll of Saint Rose (NY) **322**
Coll of the Ozarks (MO) **323**
Colorado State U (CO) **325**
Colorado State U-Pueblo (CO) **325**
Columbia Coll (MO) **326**
Columbia Coll (SC) **327**
Columbus State U (GA) **328**
Concord Coll (WV) **329**
Concordia Coll (MN) **329**
Concordia U (IL) **330**
Concordia U (NE) **330**
Concordia U (QC, Canada) **331**
Concordia U Wisconsin (WI) **331**
Converse Coll (SC) **332**
Cornell Coll (IA) **332**
Creighton U (NE) **333**
Culver-Stockton Coll (MO) **334**
Cumberland Coll (KY) **335**
Daemen Coll (NY) **335**
Dakota State U (SD) **335**
Dakota Wesleyan U (SD) **336**
Dana Coll (NE) **337**
Defiance Coll (OH) **338**
Delaware State U (DE) **338**
Delta State U (MS) **339**
Dickinson State U (ND) **344**
Dillard U (LA) **344**
Drury U (MO) **346**
East Carolina U (NC) **347**
East Central U (OK) **347**
Eastern Kentucky U (KY) **348**
Eastern Mennonite U (VA) **348**
Eastern Michigan U (MI) **348**
Eastern Washington U (WA) **349**
Edgewood Coll (WI) **351**
Edinboro U of Pennsylvania (PA) **351**
Elmhurst Coll (IL) **351**
Elmira Coll (NY) **351**
Elms Coll (MA) **352**
Emmanuel Coll (MA) **353**
Emporia State U (KS) **354**
Escuela de Artes Plasticas de Puerto Rico (PR) **354**
Evangel U (MO) **355**
Fairmont State Coll (WV) **356**
Flagler Coll (FL) **359**
Florida A&M U (FL) **359**
Florida International U (FL) **360**
Florida Southern Coll (FL) **361**
Florida State U (FL) **361**
Fontbonne U (MO) **361**
Fort Hays State U (KS) **362**
Fort Lewis Coll (CO) **362**
Framingham State Coll (MA) **362**
Francis Marion U (SC) **363**
Franklin Pierce Coll (NH) **364**
Freed-Hardeman U (TN) **364**
Frostburg State U (MD) **365**
Gallaudet U (DC) **365**
Georgian Court Coll (NJ) **367**
Georgia Southern U (GA) **367**
Georgia Southwestern State U (GA) **368**
Georgia State U (GA) **368**
Goddard Coll (VT) **369**
Goshen Coll (IN) **370**
Grace Coll (IN) **370**
Graceland U (IA) **371**
Grambling State U (LA) **371**
Grand Canyon U (AZ) **371**
Grand Valley State U (MI) **371**
Grand View Coll (IA) **372**
Greensboro Coll (NC) **372**
Greenville Coll (IL) **373**
Gustavus Adolphus Coll (MN) **374**
Hampton U (VA) **375**
Hannibal-LaGrange Coll (MO) **375**
Harding U (AR) **375**
Hardin-Simmons U (TX) **376**
Hastings Coll (NE) **377**
Henderson State U (AR) **378**
High Point U (NC) **379**
Hofstra U (NY) **380**
Houghton Coll (NY) **381**
Houston Baptist U (TX) **382**
Howard Payne U (TX) **382**
Humboldt State U (CA) **382**
Huntingdon Coll (AL) **383**
Huntington Coll (IN) **383**
Indiana State U (IN) **385**
Indiana U Bloomington (IN) **385**
Indiana U of Pennsylvania (PA) **386**
Indiana U–Purdue U Indianapolis (IN) **387**
Indiana Wesleyan U (IN) **387**
Inter American U of PR, San Germán Campus (PR) **388**
Iowa Wesleyan Coll (IA) **390**
Jackson State U (MS) **390**
Jacksonville U (FL) **391**

Johnson State Coll (VT) **394**
Kennesaw State U (GA) **397**
Kent State U (OH) **397**
Kentucky State U (KY) **397**
Kentucky Wesleyan Coll (KY) **397**
Kutztown U of Pennsylvania (PA) **399**
LaGrange Coll (GA) **400**
Lamar U (TX) **401**
Lambuth U (TN) **401**
Langston U (OK) **402**
Lenoir-Rhyne Coll (NC) **405**
Lewis U (IL) **406**
Limestone Coll (SC) **406**
Lincoln U (PA) **407**
Lindenwood U (MO) **407**
Long Island U, Brooklyn Campus (NY) **409**
Long Island U, C.W. Post Campus (NY) **409**
Long Island U, Southampton Coll (NY) **409**
Long Island U, Southampton Coll, Friends World Program (NY) **409**
Longwood U (VA) **409**
Loras Coll (IA) **410**
Louisiana Coll (LA) **410**
Louisiana State U in Shreveport (LA) **410**
Louisiana Tech U (LA) **410**
Luther Coll (IA) **412**
Lycoming Coll (PA) **412**
Madonna U (MI) **414**
Malone Coll (OH) **415**
Manchester Coll (IN) **415**
Manhattanville Coll (NY) **416**
Mansfield U of Pennsylvania (PA) **416**
Marian Coll (IN) **417**
Marian Coll of Fond du Lac (WI) **417**
Mars Hill Coll (NC) **418**
Maryland Inst Coll of Art (MD) **419**
Marymount Coll of Fordham U (NY) **419**
Maryville Coll (TN) **420**
Maryville U of Saint Louis (MO) **420**
Marywood U (PA) **421**
Massachusetts Coll of Art (MA) **421**
McKendree Coll (IL) **423**
McMurry U (TX) **423**
McPherson Coll (KS) **423**
Mercer U (GA) **425**
Mercyhurst Coll (PA) **425**
Meredith Coll (NC) **426**
Messiah Coll (PA) **426**
Methodist Coll (NC) **427**
Miami U (OH) **428**
Michigan State U (MI) **428**
Middle Tennessee State U (TN) **429**
Midland Lutheran Coll (NE) **429**
Midwestern State U (TX) **430**
Millersville U of Pennsylvania (PA) **430**
Millikin U (IL) **430**
Minnesota State U, Mankato (MN) **431**
Minnesota State U, Moorhead (MN) **432**
Minot State U (ND) **432**
Mississippi Coll (MS) **432**
Missouri Western State Coll (MO) **433**
Montana State U–Billings (MT) **434**
Montclair State U (NJ) **435**
Montserrat Coll of Art (MA) **435**
Moore Coll of Art and Design (PA) **436**
Moravian Coll (PA) **436**
Morningside Coll (IA) **437**
Mount Mary Coll (WI) **438**
Mount Mercy Coll (IA) **438**
Mount St. Mary's Coll (CA) **439**
Mount Saint Vincent U (NS, Canada) **439**
Mount Vernon Nazarene U (OH) **440**
Murray State U (KY) **440**
Muskingum Coll (OH) **441**
Nazareth Coll of Rochester (NY) **443**
New Jersey City U (NJ) **445**
New Mexico Highlands U (NM) **446**
New York Inst of Technology (NY) **447**
Nicholls State U (LA) **447**
North Carolina Ag and Tech State U (NC) **448**
North Carolina Central U (NC) **448**
North Central Coll (IL) **449**
Northeastern State U (OK) **450**
Northern Arizona U (AZ) **450**
Northern Illinois U (IL) **450**
Northern Michigan U (MI) **451**
Northern State U (SD) **451**
North Georgia Coll & State U (GA) **451**
Northland Coll (WI) **452**
North Park U (IL) **452**
Northwestern Coll (IA) **453**
Northwestern Coll (MN) **453**
Northwest Missouri State U (MO) **454**
Northwest Nazarene U (ID) **454**
Nova Scotia Coll of Art and Design (NS, Canada) **455**
Oakland City U (IN) **456**
Ohio Dominican U (OH) **457**
Ohio Northern U (OH) **457**
The Ohio State U (OH) **457**
Ohio U (OH) **458**
Ohio Wesleyan U (OH) **459**
Oklahoma Baptist U (OK) **459**
Oklahoma Christian U (OK) **459**
Oklahoma City U (OK) **460**
Olivet Coll (MI) **461**
Olivet Nazarene U (IL) **461**
Oral Roberts U (OK) **461**
Ottawa U (KS) **462**
Otterbein Coll (OH) **462**
Ouachita Baptist U (AR) **462**
Pace U (NY) **463**
Pacific Lutheran U (WA) **463**
Pacific U (OR) **464**
Palm Beach Atlantic U (FL) **465**
Parsons School of Design, New School U (NY) **465**
Penn State U Univ Park Campus (PA) **468**
Peru State Coll (NE) **469**
Pittsburg State U (KS) **470**
Plymouth State Coll (NH) **471**
Pontifical Catholic U of Puerto Rico (PR) **472**
Pratt Inst (NY) **473**
Queens Coll of the City U of NY (NY) **475**
Queen's U at Kingston (ON, Canada) **476**
Quincy U (IL) **476**
Rhode Island Coll (RI) **479**
Roberts Wesleyan Coll (NY) **481**
Rockford Coll (IL) **482**
Rocky Mountain Coll (MT) **482**
Rocky Mountain Coll of Art & Design (CO) **483**
Rowan U (NJ) **484**
St. Ambrose U (IA) **486**
St. Bonaventure U (NY) **487**
St. Cloud State U (MN) **488**
Saint John's U (MN) **490**
St. John's U (NY) **490**
Saint Joseph Coll (CT) **490**
Saint Mary-of-the-Woods Coll (IN) **493**
Saint Mary's Coll (IN) **493**
Saint Mary's Coll of California (CA) **494**
St. Mary's U of San Antonio (TX) **494**
Saint Michael's Coll (VT) **494**
St. Thomas Aquinas Coll (NY) **495**
Saint Vincent Coll (PA) **496**
Saint Xavier U (IL) **496**
Salem State Coll (MA) **497**
San Diego State U (CA) **498**
School of the Art Inst of Chicago (IL) **500**
School of the Museum of Fine Arts (MA) **501**
School of Visual Arts (NY) **501**
Seattle Pacific U (WA) **501**
Seton Hall U (NJ) **502**
Seton Hill U (PA) **502**
Shorter Coll (GA) **504**
Siena Heights U (MI) **504**
Silver Lake Coll (WI) **504**
Simpson Coll (IA) **505**
South Carolina State U (SC) **506**
South Dakota State U (SD) **507**
Southeastern Louisiana U (LA) **508**
Southeastern Oklahoma State U (OK) **508**
Southeast Missouri State U (MO) **508**
Southern Arkansas U–Magnolia (AR) **509**
Southern Connecticut State U (CT) **509**
Southern Nazarene U (OK) **510**
Southern Utah U (UT) **511**
Southwest Baptist U (MO) **512**
Southwestern Oklahoma State U (OK) **512**
Southwestern U (TX) **513**
Southwest Missouri State U (MO) **513**
Southwest State U (MN) **513**
State U of NY at New Paltz (NY) **515**
State U of NY Coll at Buffalo (NY) **516**
State U of West Georgia (GA) **518**
Syracuse U (NY) **521**
Tabor Coll (KS) **522**
Tarleton State U (TX) **522**
Taylor U (IN) **523**
Temple U (PA) **523**
Tennessee Technological U (TN) **524**
Texas A&M U–Commerce (TX) **525**
Texas Christian U (TX) **526**
Texas Lutheran U (TX) **526**
Texas Southern U (TX) **526**
Texas Wesleyan U (TX) **526**
Thomas More Coll (KY) **528**
Towson U (MD) **529**
Transylvania U (KY) **529**
Trinity Christian Coll (IL) **530**
Troy State U (AL) **532**
Tusculum Coll (TN) **533**
Union Coll (NE) **534**
Union U (TN) **534**
U du Québec à Trois-Rivières (QC, Canada) **536**
Université Laval (QC, Canada) **536**
The U of Akron (OH) **537**
U of Alberta (AB, Canada) **538**
The U of Arizona (AZ) **538**
The U of British Columbia (BC, Canada) **540**
U of Calgary (AB, Canada) **540**
U of Central Florida (FL) **542**
U of Central Oklahoma (OK) **542**
U of Cincinnati (OH) **543**
U of Dallas (TX) **544**
U of Dayton (OH) **544**
U of Denver (CO) **544**
U of Evansville (IN) **545**
The U of Findlay (OH) **545**
U of Florida (FL) **545**
U of Georgia (GA) **545**
U of Great Falls (MT) **545**
U of Hawaii at Manoa (HI) **546**
U of Idaho (ID) **547**
U of Illinois at Chicago (IL) **547**
U of Illinois at Urbana–Champaign (IL) **548**
U of Indianapolis (IN) **548**
The U of Iowa (IA) **548**
U of Kansas (KS) **549**
U of Kentucky (KY) **549**
The U of Lethbridge (AB, Canada) **549**
U of Maine (ME) **550**
U of Maine at Presque Isle (ME) **551**
U of Mary Hardin-Baylor (TX) **551**
U of Maryland, Coll Park (MD) **552**
U of Maryland Eastern Shore (MD) **552**
U of Massachusetts Dartmouth (MA) **553**
U of Michigan (MI) **554**
U of Michigan–Dearborn (MI) **554**
U of Michigan–Flint (MI) **554**
U of Minnesota, Duluth (MN) **554**
U of Minnesota, Twin Cities Campus (MN) **555**
U of Missouri–Columbia (MO) **555**
The U of Montana–Missoula (MT) **556**
The U of Montana–Western (MT) **556**
U of Montevallo (AL) **557**
U of Nebraska–Lincoln (NE) **557**
U of Nevada, Reno (NV) **558**
U of New Brunswick Fredericton (NB, Canada) **558**
U of New England (ME) **558**
U of New Hampshire (NH) **558**
U of New Mexico (NM) **559**
The U of North Carolina at Charlotte (NC) **560**
The U of North Carolina at Greensboro (NC) **560**
The U of North Carolina at Pembroke (NC) **560**
U of Northern Iowa (IA) **561**
U of North Florida (FL) **561**
U of North Texas (TX) **562**
U of Regina (SK, Canada) **572**
U of Richmond (VA) **572**
U of Rio Grande (OH) **572**
U of Saint Francis (IN) **573**
U of Sioux Falls (SD) **574**
U of South Carolina (SC) **575**
The U of South Dakota (SD) **575**
U of Southern Maine (ME) **576**
U of South Florida (FL) **576**
The U of Tennessee (TN) **577**
The U of Tennessee at Chattanooga (TN) **577**
The U of Tennessee at Martin (TN) **577**
The U of Texas at El Paso (TX) **578**
The U of Texas–Pan American (TX) **579**
U of the District of Columbia (DC) **580**
U of the Incarnate Word (TX) **580**
U of the Ozarks (AR) **580**
U of Toledo (OH) **581**
U of Toronto (ON, Canada) **581**
U of Vermont (VT) **582**
U of Victoria (BC, Canada) **582**
The U of Western Ontario (ON, Canada) **583**
U of West Florida (FL) **583**
U of Windsor (ON, Canada) **584**
U of Wisconsin–La Crosse (WI) **584**
U of Wisconsin–Madison (WI) **584**
U of Wisconsin–Milwaukee (WI) **585**
U of Wisconsin–Oshkosh (WI) **585**
U of Wisconsin–River Falls (WI) **585**
U of Wisconsin–Stout (WI) **586**
U of Wisconsin–Superior (WI) **586**
U of Wisconsin–Whitewater (WI) **586**
Upper Iowa U (IA) **587**
Ursuline Coll (OH) **587**
Valdosta State U (GA) **588**
Valley City State U (ND) **588**
Valparaiso U (IN) **588**
Virginia Commonwealth U (VA) **590**
Virginia Intermont Coll (VA) **590**
Virginia Wesleyan Coll (VA) **591**
Viterbo U (WI) **591**
Walla Walla Coll (WA) **593**
Wartburg Coll (IA) **594**
Washington & Jefferson Coll (PA) **594**
Washington U in St. Louis (MO) **595**
Wayne State U (MI) **596**
Weber State U (UT) **596**
Western Carolina U (NC) **598**
Western Kentucky U (KY) **599**
Western Michigan U (MI) **599**
Western New Mexico U (NM) **600**
Western State Coll of Colorado (CO) **600**
Western Washington U (WA) **600**
Westfield State Coll (MA) **600**
West Liberty State Coll (WV) **601**
Westmont Coll (CA) **602**
West Virginia State Coll (WV) **602**
West Virginia Wesleyan Coll (WV) **603**
Whitworth Coll (WA) **604**
Wichita State U (KS) **604**
William Carey Coll (MS) **605**
William Paterson U of New Jersey (NJ) **606**
Williams Baptist Coll (AR) **606**
William Woods U (MO) **607**
Wilmington Coll (OH) **607**
Wingate U (NC) **607**
Winona State U (MN) **608**
Winston-Salem State U (NC) **608**
Wittenberg U (OH) **608**
Wright State U (OH) **609**
Xavier U of Louisiana (LA) **610**
York U (ON, Canada) **611**
Youngstown State U (OH) **611**

ART HISTORY

Overview: In addition to studying the history and development of art in human cultures, students learn how to analyze and interpret artworks. *Related majors:* art, fine arts, history, Western Civilization/culture, philosophy. *Potential careers:* art teacher, professor, writer, art critic, museum curator. *Salary potential:* $20k-$35k.

Adams State Coll (CO) **260**
Albertus Magnus Coll (CT) **262**
Alfred U (NY) **263**
Allegheny Coll (PA) **264**
American U (DC) **267**
The American U of Paris(France) **268**
Andrews U (MI) **269**
Appalachian State U (NC) **270**
Aquinas Coll (MI) **270**
Arcadia U (PA) **271**
Arizona State U (AZ) **271**
Art Academy of Cincinnati (OH) **273**
Augsburg Coll (MN) **276**
Augustana Coll (IL) **276**
Baker U (KS) **280**
Baldwin-Wallace Coll (OH) **280**
Bard Coll (NY) **281**
Barnard Coll (NY) **282**
Baylor U (TX) **283**
Beloit Coll (WI) **285**
Berea Coll (KY) **286**
Berry Coll (GA) **287**
Bethel Coll (MN) **288**
Birmingham-Southern Coll (AL) **289**
Blackburn Coll (IL) **290**
Bloomsburg U of Pennsylvania (PA) **290**
Boston Coll (MA) **292**
Boston U (MA) **292**
Bowdoin Coll (ME) **292**
Bowling Green State U (OH) **292**
Bradley U (IL) **293**

ART HISTORY (continued)

Brigham Young U (UT) ***295***
Brooklyn Coll of the City U of NY (NY) ***295***
Brown U (RI) ***296***
Bryn Mawr Coll (PA) ***297***
Bucknell U (PA) ***297***
California State U, Chico (CA) ***300***
California State U, Dominguez Hills (CA) ***300***
California State U, Fullerton (CA) ***301***
California State U, Hayward (CA) ***301***
California State U, Long Beach (CA) ***301***
California State U, Northridge (CA) ***301***
California State U, San Bernardino (CA) ***302***
Calvin Coll (MI) ***303***
Canisius Coll (NY) ***304***
Carleton Coll (MN) ***305***
Carleton U (ON, Canada) ***305***
Carlow Coll (PA) ***305***
Case Western Reserve U (OH) ***307***
The Catholic U of America (DC) ***307***
Centre Coll (KY) ***310***
Chapman U (CA) ***311***
Chatham Coll (PA) ***312***
Chestnut Hill Coll (PA) ***312***
City Coll of the City U of NY (NY) ***314***
Clarke Coll (IA) ***315***
Clark U (MA) ***316***
Cleveland State U (OH) ***317***
Colby Coll (ME) ***318***
Colgate U (NY) ***319***
Coll of Charleston (SC) ***320***
The Coll of New Rochelle (NY) ***321***
Coll of Saint Benedict (MN) ***321***
Coll of St. Catherine (MN) ***321***
Coll of Santa Fe (NM) ***323***
The Coll of Southeastern Europe, The American U of Athens(Greece) ***323***
Coll of the Holy Cross (MA) ***323***
The Coll of William and Mary (VA) ***324***
The Coll of Wooster (OH) ***324***
The Colorado Coll (CO) ***325***
Colorado State U (CO) ***325***
Columbia Coll (NY) ***326***
Columbia Coll (SC) ***327***
Columbia U, School of General Studies (NY) ***328***
Concordia Coll (MN) ***329***
Concordia U (MN) ***330***
Concordia U (QC, Canada) ***331***
Connecticut Coll (CT) ***331***
Converse Coll (SC) ***332***
Cornell Coll (IA) ***332***
Cornell U (NY) ***333***
Creighton U (NE) ***333***
Dartmouth Coll (NH) ***337***
Denison U (OH) ***339***
DePaul U (IL) ***339***
DePauw U (IN) ***339***
Deree Coll(Greece) ***339***
Dominican U (IL) ***345***
Dominican U of California (CA) ***345***
Drake U (IA) ***345***
Drury U (MO) ***346***
Duke U (NC) ***346***
Duquesne U (PA) ***346***
East Carolina U (NC) ***347***
Eastern Michigan U (MI) ***348***
Eastern U (PA) ***349***
Eastern Washington U (WA) ***349***
Edinboro U of Pennsylvania (PA) ***351***
Emmanuel Coll (MA) ***353***
Emory U (GA) ***354***
The Evergreen State Coll (WA) ***355***
Florida International U (FL) ***360***
Florida State U (FL) ***361***
Fordham U (NY) ***362***
Framingham State Coll (MA) ***362***
Franklin Coll Switzerland(Switzerland) ***364***
Furman U (SC) ***365***
Gallaudet U (DC) ***365***
George Mason U (VA) ***366***
The George Washington U (DC) ***367***
Georgian Court Coll (NJ) ***367***
Gettysburg Coll (PA) ***368***
Goddard Coll (VT) ***369***
Governors State U (IL) ***370***
Grand Valley State U (MI) ***371***
Gustavus Adolphus Coll (MN) ***374***
Hamilton Coll (NY) ***374***
Hamline U (MN) ***374***
Hampshire Coll (MA) ***375***
Hanover Coll (IN) ***375***
Hartwick Coll (NY) ***376***
Harvard U (MA) ***376***
Hastings Coll (NE) ***377***
Haverford Coll (PA) ***377***
Hiram Coll (OH) ***379***
Hobart and William Smith Colls (NY) ***380***
Hofstra U (NY) ***380***
Hollins U (VA) ***380***
Hope Coll (MI) ***381***
Humboldt State U (CA) ***382***
Hunter Coll of the City U of NY (NY) ***382***
Huron U USA in London(United Kingdom) ***383***
Illinois Wesleyan U (IL) ***385***
Indiana State U (IN) ***385***
Indiana U Bloomington (IN) ***385***
Indiana U–Purdue U Indianapolis (IN) ***387***
Inter American U of PR, San Germán Campus (PR) ***388***
Ithaca Coll (NY) ***390***
Jacksonville U (FL) ***391***
James Madison U (VA) ***391***
John Cabot U(Italy) ***392***
John Carroll U (OH) ***392***
Johns Hopkins U (MD) ***392***
Juniata Coll (PA) ***395***
Kalamazoo Coll (MI) ***395***
Kansas City Art Inst (MO) ***395***
Kean U (NJ) ***396***
Kendall Coll of Art and Design of Ferris State U (MI) ***396***
Kent State U (OH) ***397***
Kenyon Coll (OH) ***398***
Knox Coll (IL) ***399***
Lafayette Coll (PA) ***400***
Lake Forest Coll (IL) ***400***
Lambuth U (TN) ***401***
La Salle U (PA) ***402***
Lawrence U (WI) ***403***
Lehman Coll of the City U of NY (NY) ***404***
Lindenwood U (MO) ***407***
Long Island U, C.W. Post Campus (NY) ***409***
Long Island U, Southampton Coll, Friends World Program (NY) ***409***
Longwood U (VA) ***409***
Lourdes Coll (OH) ***411***
Loyola Marymount U (CA) ***411***
Loyola U Chicago (IL) ***411***
Lycoming Coll (PA) ***412***
Macalester Coll (MN) ***413***
MacMurray Coll (IL) ***414***
Manhattanville Coll (NY) ***416***
Mansfield U of Pennsylvania (PA) ***416***
Marian Coll (IN) ***417***
Marlboro Coll (VT) ***418***
Mars Hill Coll (NC) ***418***
Mary Baldwin Coll (VA) ***419***
Marymount Coll of Fordham U (NY) ***419***
Marymount Manhattan Coll (NY) ***420***
Mary Washington Coll (VA) ***420***
Massachusetts Coll of Art (MA) ***421***
McDaniel Coll (MD) ***422***
McGill U (QC, Canada) ***423***
McMaster U (ON, Canada) ***423***
Memorial U of Newfoundland (NF, Canada) ***424***
Meredith Coll (NC) ***426***
Messiah Coll (PA) ***426***
Miami U (OH) ***428***
Michigan State U (MI) ***428***
Middlebury Coll (VT) ***429***
Mills Coll (CA) ***431***
Minnesota State U, Mankato (MN) ***431***
Minnesota State U, Moorhead (MN) ***432***
Mississippi Coll (MS) ***432***
Monmouth U (NJ) ***434***
Montclair State U (NJ) ***435***
Moore Coll of Art and Design (PA) ***436***
Moravian Coll (PA) ***436***
Morgan State U (MD) ***436***
Mount Allison U (NB, Canada) ***437***
Mount Holyoke Coll (MA) ***438***
Muhlenberg Coll (PA) ***440***
Nazareth Coll of Rochester (NY) ***443***
New England Coll (NH) ***444***
New York U (NY) ***447***
Northern Arizona U (AZ) ***450***
Northern Illinois U (IL) ***450***
Northwestern U (IL) ***453***
Notre Dame Coll (OH) ***455***
Nova Scotia Coll of Art and Design (NS, Canada) ***455***
Oakland U (MI) ***456***
Oberlin Coll (OH) ***456***
Occidental Coll (CA) ***457***
The Ohio State U (OH) ***457***
Ohio U (OH) ***458***
Ohio Wesleyan U (OH) ***459***
Oklahoma City U (OK) ***460***
Old Dominion U (VA) ***460***
Oregon State U (OR) ***462***
Pace U (NY) ***463***
Pacific Lutheran U (WA) ***463***
Pacific Union Coll (CA) ***464***
Penn State U Univ Park Campus (PA) ***468***
Pine Manor Coll (MA) ***470***
Pitzer Coll (CA) ***471***
Plattsburgh State U of NY (NY) ***471***
Pomona Coll (CA) ***472***
Portland State U (OR) ***472***
Pratt Inst (NY) ***473***
Princeton U (NJ) ***474***
Principia Coll (IL) ***474***
Providence Coll (RI) ***474***
Purchase Coll, State U of NY (NY) ***475***
Queens Coll of the City U of NY (NY) ***475***
Queen's U at Kingston (ON, Canada) ***476***
Queens U of Charlotte (NC) ***476***
Randolph-Macon Coll (VA) ***477***
Randolph-Macon Woman's Coll (VA) ***477***
Rhode Island Coll (RI) ***479***
Rhodes Coll (TN) ***479***
Rice U (TX) ***479***
Richmond, The American International U in London(United Kingdom) ***480***
Rockford Coll (IL) ***482***
Roger Williams U (RI) ***483***
Rollins Coll (FL) ***483***
Roosevelt U (IL) ***483***
Rosemont Coll (PA) ***484***
Rutgers, The State U of New Jersey, New Brunswick (NJ) ***485***
St. Cloud State U (MN) ***488***
Saint John's U (MN) ***490***
Saint Joseph Coll (CT) ***490***
St. Lawrence U (NY) ***491***
Saint Louis U (MO) ***492***
Saint Mary's Coll of California (CA) ***494***
St. Olaf Coll (MN) ***495***
Saint Vincent Coll (PA) ***496***
Salem Coll (NC) ***496***
Salve Regina U (RI) ***497***
San Diego State U (CA) ***498***
San Jose State U (CA) ***499***
Santa Clara U (CA) ***499***
Sarah Lawrence Coll (NY) ***499***
Savannah Coll of Art and Design (GA) ***499***
School of the Art Inst of Chicago (IL) ***500***
Scripps Coll (CA) ***501***
Seattle U (WA) ***501***
Seton Hall U (NJ) ***502***
Seton Hill U (PA) ***502***
Simon's Rock Coll of Bard (MA) ***505***
Skidmore Coll (NY) ***506***
Smith Coll (MA) ***506***
Sonoma State U (CA) ***506***
Southern Connecticut State U (CT) ***509***
Southern Methodist U (TX) ***510***
Southwestern U (TX) ***513***
State U of NY at Albany (NY) ***514***
State U of NY at Binghamton (NY) ***515***
State U of NY at New Paltz (NY) ***515***
State U of NY Coll at Buffalo (NY) ***516***
State U of NY Coll at Cortland (NY) ***516***
State U of NY Coll at Fredonia (NY) ***516***
State U of NY Coll at Geneseo (NY) ***516***
State U of NY Coll at Oneonta (NY) ***517***
State U of NY Coll at Potsdam (NY) ***517***
Stephen F. Austin State U (TX) ***518***
Stony Brook U, State University of New York (NY) ***520***
Susquehanna U (PA) ***521***
Swarthmore Coll (PA) ***521***
Sweet Briar Coll (VA) ***521***
Syracuse U (NY) ***521***
Temple U (PA) ***523***
Texas A&M U–Commerce (TX) ***525***
Texas Christian U (TX) ***526***
Texas Tech U (TX) ***526***
Texas Woman's U (TX) ***527***
Trinity Coll (CT) ***530***
Trinity Coll (DC) ***530***
Trinity U (TX) ***531***
Troy State U (AL) ***532***
Truman State U (MO) ***532***
Tufts U (MA) ***533***
Tulane U (LA) ***533***
Université Laval (QC, Canada) ***536***
U at Buffalo, The State University of New York (NY) ***536***
The U of Akron (OH) ***537***
The U of Alabama (AL) ***537***
U of Alberta (AB, Canada) ***538***
The U of Arizona (AZ) ***538***
U of Arkansas at Little Rock (AR) ***539***
The U of British Columbia (BC, Canada) ***540***
U of Calgary (AB, Canada) ***540***
U of Calif, Berkeley (CA) ***540***
U of Calif, Davis (CA) ***540***
U of Calif, Irvine (CA) ***541***
U of Calif, Los Angeles (CA) ***541***
U of Calif, Riverside (CA) ***541***
U of Calif, San Diego (CA) ***541***
U of Calif, Santa Barbara (CA) ***541***
U of Calif, Santa Cruz (CA) ***542***
U of Chicago (IL) ***542***
U of Cincinnati (OH) ***543***
U of Connecticut (CT) ***544***
U of Dallas (TX) ***544***
U of Dayton (OH) ***544***
U of Delaware (DE) ***544***
U of Denver (CO) ***544***
U of Evansville (IN) ***545***
U of Florida (FL) ***545***
U of Georgia (GA) ***545***
U of Guelph (ON, Canada) ***546***
U of Hartford (CT) ***546***
U of Hawaii at Manoa (HI) ***546***
U of Houston (TX) ***547***
U of Illinois at Chicago (IL) ***547***
U of Illinois at Urbana–Champaign (IL) ***548***
U of Indianapolis (IN) ***548***
The U of Iowa (IA) ***548***
U of Kansas (KS) ***549***
U of Kentucky (KY) ***549***
U of Louisville (KY) ***550***
U of Maine (ME) ***550***
U of Manitoba (MB, Canada) ***551***
U of Maryland, Baltimore County (MD) ***552***
U of Maryland, Coll Park (MD) ***552***
U of Massachusetts Amherst (MA) ***552***
U of Massachusetts Dartmouth (MA) ***553***
The U of Memphis (TN) ***553***
U of Miami (FL) ***553***
U of Michigan (MI) ***554***
U of Michigan–Dearborn (MI) ***554***
U of Minnesota, Duluth (MN) ***554***
U of Minnesota, Morris (MN) ***555***
U of Minnesota, Twin Cities Campus (MN) ***555***
U of Mississippi (MS) ***555***
U of Missouri–Kansas City (MO) ***555***
U of Missouri–St. Louis (MO) ***556***
The U of Montana–Missoula (MT) ***556***
U of Nebraska at Omaha (NE) ***557***
U of Nebraska–Lincoln (NE) ***557***
U of Nevada, Las Vegas (NV) ***558***
U of Nevada, Reno (NV) ***558***
U of New Hampshire (NH) ***558***
U of New Mexico (NM) ***559***
U of New Orleans (LA) ***559***
The U of North Carolina at Chapel Hill (NC) ***560***
The U of North Carolina at Greensboro (NC) ***560***
The U of North Carolina at Wilmington (NC) ***561***
U of Northern Iowa (IA) ***561***
U of North Texas (TX) ***562***
U of Notre Dame (IN) ***562***
U of Oklahoma (OK) ***562***
U of Oregon (OR) ***562***
U of Pennsylvania (PA) ***563***
U of Pittsburgh (PA) ***569***
U of Puerto Rico, Río Piedras (PR) ***571***
U of Redlands (CA) ***572***
U of Regina (SK, Canada) ***572***
U of Rhode Island (RI) ***572***
U of Richmond (VA) ***572***
U of Rochester (NY) ***573***
U of St. Thomas (MN) ***573***
U of Saskatchewan (SK, Canada) ***574***
U of South Alabama (AL) ***575***
U of South Carolina (SC) ***575***
U of Southern California (CA) ***576***
The U of Tennessee (TN) ***577***
The U of Texas at Arlington (TX) ***577***
The U of Texas at Austin (TX) ***578***
The U of Texas at San Antonio (TX) ***578***
The U of Texas–Pan American (TX) ***579***

U of the Pacific (CA) **580**
U of the South (TN) **581**
U of Toledo (OH) **581**
U of Toronto (ON, Canada) **581**
U of Tulsa (OK) **581**
U of Utah (UT) **582**
U of Vermont (VT) **582**
U of Victoria (BC, Canada) **582**
U of Washington (WA) **583**
U of Waterloo (ON, Canada) **583**
The U of Western Ontario (ON, Canada) **583**
U of West Florida (FL) **583**
U of Windsor (ON, Canada) **584**
U of Wisconsin–Madison (WI) **584**
U of Wisconsin–Milwaukee (WI) **585**
U of Wisconsin–Superior (WI) **586**
U of Wisconsin–Whitewater (WI) **586**
Ursuline Coll (OH) **587**
Valparaiso U (IN) **588**
Vassar Coll (NY) **589**
Villanova U (PA) **590**
Virginia Commonwealth U (VA) **590**
Wake Forest U (NC) **592**
Washington and Lee U (VA) **594**
Washington U in St. Louis (MO) **595**
Wayne State U (MI) **596**
Webster U (MO) **597**
Wellesley Coll (MA) **597**
Wells Coll (NY) **597**
Wesleyan Coll (GA) **597**
Wesleyan U (CT) **597**
Western Michigan U (MI) **599**
Western Washington U (WA) **600**
West Virginia Wesleyan Coll (WV) **603**
Wheaton Coll (MA) **603**
Whitman Coll (WA) **604**
Whitworth Coll (WA) **604**
Wichita State U (KS) **604**
Willamette U (OR) **605**
William Paterson U of New Jersey (NJ) **606**
Williams Coll (MA) **606**
Winthrop U (SC) **608**
Wittenberg U (OH) **608**
Wofford Coll (SC) **609**
Wright State U (OH) **609**
Yale U (CT) **610**
York U (ON, Canada) **611**
Youngstown State U (OH) **611**

ARTS MANAGEMENT

Overview: Students learn the skills necessary to set up and manage art associations, organizations, and related businesses and facilities such as galleries, museums, studios, and auction houses. *Related majors:* art history, criticism and conservation, office supervision and management, operations management and supervision, business administration/management. *Potential careers:* art dealer, artists representative, auction house executive, museum curator, artist's society or organization director. *Salary potential:* $20k-$30k.

Adrian Coll (MI) **260**
Appalachian State U (NC) **270**
Baldwin-Wallace Coll (OH) **280**
Bellarmine U (KY) **284**
Benedictine Coll (KS) **285**
Benedictine U (IL) **285**
Bennett Coll (NC) **286**
Baruch Coll of the City U of NY (NY) **286**
Bishop's U (QC, Canada) **289**
Brenau U (GA) **293**
Buena Vista U (IA) **297**
Butler U (IN) **297**
California State U, Hayward (CA) **301**
Centenary Coll of Louisiana (LA) **308**
Chatham Coll (PA) **312**
Coll of Charleston (SC) **320**
Coll of Santa Fe (NM) **323**
Columbia Coll (SC) **327**
Columbia Coll Chicago (IL) **327**
Concordia Coll (NY) **329**
Culver-Stockton Coll (MO) **334**
Dakota State U (SD) **335**
DePaul U (IL) **339**
Eastern Michigan U (MI) **348**
The Evergreen State Coll (WA) **355**
Fontbonne U (MO) **361**
Georgia Coll & State U (GA) **367**
Green Mountain Coll (VT) **372**
Illinois Wesleyan U (IL) **385**
Ithaca Coll (NY) **390**
Lakeland Coll (WI) **401**
Long Island U, C.W. Post Campus (NY) **409**
Long Island U, Southampton Coll, Friends World Program (NY) **409**
Luther Coll (IA) **412**
Mary Baldwin Coll (VA) **419**
Marywood U (PA) **421**
Mercyhurst Coll (PA) **425**
Millikin U (IL) **430**
Newberry Coll (SC) **444**
North Carolina State U (NC) **449**
Northern Arizona U (AZ) **450**
Ohio U (OH) **458**
Oklahoma City U (OK) **460**
Pfeiffer U (NC) **469**
Point Park Coll (PA) **471**
Quincy U (IL) **476**
Randolph-Macon Coll (VA) **477**
Salem Coll (NC) **496**
Seton Hill U (PA) **502**
Shenandoah U (VA) **503**
Simmons Coll (MA) **504**
Southeastern Louisiana U (LA) **508**
Spring Hill Coll (AL) **514**
State U of NY Coll at Brockport (NY) **515**
State U of NY Coll at Fredonia (NY) **516**
U of Evansville (IN) **545**
The U of Iowa (IA) **548**
U of Kentucky (KY) **549**
U of Michigan–Dearborn (MI) **554**
U of Ottawa (ON, Canada) **563**
U of Portland (OR) **570**
The U of South Dakota (SD) **575**
U of Toronto (ON, Canada) **581**
U of Tulsa (OK) **581**
U of Waterloo (ON, Canada) **583**
U of Windsor (ON, Canada) **584**
U of Wisconsin–Stevens Point (WI) **585**
Upper Iowa U (IA) **587**
Viterbo U (WI) **591**
Wagner Coll (NY) **592**
Wartburg Coll (IA) **594**
Waynesburg Coll (PA) **595**
Whitworth Coll (WA) **604**

ART THERAPY

Overview: This major teaches students to use art media such as drawing, painting, and collage in order to treat patients who are mentally, emotionally, or physically disabled. *Related majors:* psychology, counseling or developmental psychology, art teacher education, nursing (psychiatric/mental health), fine/studio arts. *Potential careers:* art therapist, art teacher, psychologist, therapist. *Salary potential:* $25k-$30k.

Albertus Magnus Coll (CT) **262**
Alverno Coll (WI) **265**
Anna Maria Coll (MA) **269**
Arcadia U (PA) **271**
Avila U (MO) **278**
Bowling Green State U (OH) **292**
Brescia U (KY) **293**
Capital U (OH) **304**
The Coll of New Rochelle (NY) **321**
Coll of Santa Fe (NM) **323**
Concordia U (QC, Canada) **331**
Converse Coll (SC) **332**
Edgewood Coll (WI) **351**
Elms Coll (MA) **352**
Emmanuel Coll (MA) **353**
Goshen Coll (IN) **370**
Harding U (AR) **375**
Howard U (DC) **382**
Long Island U, C.W. Post Campus (NY) **409**
Long Island U, Southampton Coll, Friends World Program (NY) **409**
Marygrove Coll (MI) **419**
Marymount Coll of Fordham U (NY) **419**
Marywood U (PA) **421**
Mercyhurst Coll (PA) **425**
Millikin U (IL) **430**
Mount Mary Coll (WI) **438**
Nazareth Coll of Rochester (NY) **443**
Ohio U (OH) **458**
Ohio Wesleyan U (OH) **459**
Pittsburg State U (KS) **470**
Prescott Coll (AZ) **474**
Russell Sage Coll (NY) **484**
St. Thomas Aquinas Coll (NY) **495**
School of the Art Inst of Chicago (IL) **500**
School of Visual Arts (NY) **501**
Seton Hill U (PA) **502**
Springfield Coll (MA) **514**
Spring Hill Coll (AL) **514**
U of Indianapolis (IN) **548**
U of Wisconsin–Superior (WI) **586**
Webster U (MO) **597**

ASIAN-AMERICAN STUDIES

Overview: Students who undertake this major study the history, sociology, politics, culture, and economics of Asian peoples who have immigrated to the United States or Canada, from the Colonial period to the present day. *Related majors:* comparative literature, economics, history, south Asian studies, east Asian studies. *Potential careers:* journalist, editor, translator, social worker, historian. *Salary potential:* $25k-$30k.

California State U, Fullerton (CA) **301**
California State U, Hayward (CA) **301**
Columbia Coll (NY) **326**
The Ohio State U (OH) **457**
Pitzer Coll (CA) **471**
Scripps Coll (CA) **501**
U of Calif, Berkeley (CA) **540**
U of Calif, Los Angeles (CA) **541**
U of Calif, Riverside (CA) **541**
U of Calif, Santa Barbara (CA) **541**
U of Denver (CO) **544**
U of Southern California (CA) **576**

ASIAN STUDIES

Overview: This major teaches students about the history, society, politics, culture, economics, and languages and dialects of people of the Asian continent. *Related majors:* Chinese, Japanese, Korean languages and histories, international politics. *Potential careers:* business consultant, foreign service officer, translator, journalist. *Salary potential:* $20k-$35k.

American U (DC) **267**
Amherst Coll (MA) **268**
Augustana Coll (IL) **276**
Bard Coll (NY) **281**
Barnard Coll (NY) **282**
Baylor U (TX) **283**
Beloit Coll (WI) **285**
Birmingham-Southern Coll (AL) **289**
Bowdoin Coll (ME) **292**
Bowling Green State U (OH) **292**
Brigham Young U (UT) **295**
California State U, Chico (CA) **300**
California State U, Long Beach (CA) **301**
California State U, Sacramento (CA) **301**
Carleton Coll (MN) **305**
Carleton U (ON, Canada) **305**
Case Western Reserve U (OH) **307**
City Coll of the City U of NY (NY) **314**
Claremont McKenna Coll (CA) **315**
Clark U (MA) **316**
Coe Coll (IA) **318**
Colgate U (NY) **319**
Coll of the Holy Cross (MA) **323**
The Coll of Wooster (OH) **324**
The Colorado Coll (CO) **325**
Colorado State U (CO) **325**
Cornell U (NY) **333**
Dartmouth Coll (NH) **337**
Duke U (NC) **346**
Earlham Coll (IN) **347**
Emory U (GA) **354**
The Evergreen State Coll (WA) **355**
Florida State U (FL) **361**
Fort Lewis Coll (CO) **362**
Furman U (SC) **365**
The George Washington U (DC) **367**
Gonzaga U (WA) **369**
Hamilton Coll (NY) **374**
Hamline U (MN) **374**
Hampshire Coll (MA) **375**
Harvard U (MA) **376**
Hobart and William Smith Colls (NY) **380**
Hofstra U (NY) **380**
Indiana U Bloomington (IN) **385**
John Carroll U (OH) **392**
Kenyon Coll (OH) **398**
Lake Forest Coll (IL) **400**
Lehigh U (PA) **404**
Long Island U, Southampton Coll, Friends World Program (NY) **409**
Macalester Coll (MN) **413**
Manhattanville Coll (NY) **416**
Marlboro Coll (VT) **418**
Mary Baldwin Coll (VA) **419**
Mount Holyoke Coll (MA) **438**
Mount Union Coll (OH) **440**
Northwestern U (IL) **453**
Occidental Coll (CA) **457**
Ohio U (OH) **458**
Pitzer Coll (CA) **471**
Pomona Coll (CA) **472**
Queens Coll of the City U of NY (NY) **475**
Rice U (TX) **479**
St. Andrews Presbyterian Coll (NC) **487**
St. John's U (NY) **490**
St. Lawrence U (NY) **491**
Saint Mary's U (NS, Canada) **494**
St. Olaf Coll (MN) **495**
Salem International U (WV) **496**
Samford U (AL) **497**
San Diego State U (CA) **498**
Sarah Lawrence Coll (NY) **499**
Scripps Coll (CA) **501**
Seton Hall U (NJ) **502**
Simon's Rock Coll of Bard (MA) **505**
Skidmore Coll (NY) **506**
Southwest Texas State U (TX) **513**
Stanford U (CA) **514**
State U of NY at Albany (NY) **514**
State U of NY Coll at Brockport (NY) **515**
Swarthmore Coll (PA) **521**
Temple U (PA) **523**
Texas Christian U (TX) **526**
Trinity U (TX) **531**
Tufts U (MA) **533**
Tulane U (LA) **533**
The U of Alabama (AL) **537**
The U of British Columbia (BC, Canada) **540**
U of Calif, Berkeley (CA) **540**
U of Calif, Riverside (CA) **541**
U of Calif, Santa Barbara (CA) **541**
U of Calif, Santa Cruz (CA) **542**
U of Chicago (IL) **542**
U of Cincinnati (OH) **543**
U of Colorado at Boulder (CO) **543**
U of Florida (FL) **545**
U of Hawaii at Manoa (HI) **546**
U of Hawaii–West Oahu (HI) **546**
U of Illinois at Urbana–Champaign (IL) **548**
The U of Iowa (IA) **548**
U of Michigan (MI) **554**
The U of Montana–Missoula (MT) **556**
U of New Mexico (NM) **559**
The U of North Carolina at Chapel Hill (NC) **560**
U of Northern Iowa (IA) **561**
U of Oregon (OR) **562**
U of Puget Sound (WA) **571**
U of Redlands (CA) **572**
The U of Texas at Austin (TX) **578**
U of the South (TN) **581**
U of Toledo (OH) **581**
U of Toronto (ON, Canada) **581**
U of Utah (UT) **582**
U of Vermont (VT) **582**
U of Victoria (BC, Canada) **582**
U of Washington (WA) **583**
U of Wisconsin–Madison (WI) **584**
Utah State U (UT) **587**
Vassar Coll (NY) **589**
Washington State U (WA) **595**
Washington U in St. Louis (MO) **595**
Wayne State U (MI) **596**
Western Michigan U (MI) **599**
Western Washington U (WA) **600**
Wheaton Coll (MA) **603**
Whitman Coll (WA) **604**
Willamette U (OR) **605**
Williams Coll (MA) **606**

ASIAN STUDIES (continued)

Wittenberg U (OH) ***608***
York U (ON, Canada) ***611***

ASTRONOMY

Overview: This major focuses on the scientific theories of planetary, galactic, and stellar phenomena that occur in outer space. *Related majors:* astrophysics, mathematics, earth and planetary science, optics, philosophy, computer science. *Potential careers:* astronomer, computer scientist, cosmologist, professor, research scientist. *Salary potential:* $30k-$37k.

Amherst Coll (MA) ***268***
Barnard Coll (NY) ***282***
Benedictine Coll (KS) ***285***
Boston U (MA) ***292***
Bryn Mawr Coll (PA) ***297***
California Inst of Technology (CA) ***299***
Case Western Reserve U (OH) ***307***
Central Michigan U (MI) ***310***
Colgate U (NY) ***319***
Columbia Coll (NY) ***326***
Columbia U, School of General Studies (NY) ***328***
Cornell U (NY) ***333***
Dartmouth Coll (NH) ***337***
Drake U (IA) ***345***
Eastern U (PA) ***349***
Hampshire Coll (MA) ***375***
Harvard U (MA) ***376***
Haverford Coll (PA) ***377***
Indiana U Bloomington (IN) ***385***
Laurentian U (ON, Canada) ***403***
Lycoming Coll (PA) ***412***
Marlboro Coll (VT) ***418***
Minnesota State U, Mankato (MN) ***431***
Mount Holyoke Coll (MA) ***438***
Mount Union Coll (OH) ***440***
Northern Arizona U (AZ) ***450***
Northwestern U (IL) ***453***
The Ohio State U (OH) ***457***
Ohio Wesleyan U (OH) ***459***
Penn State U Univ Park Campus (PA) ***468***
Pomona Coll (CA) ***472***
Rice U (TX) ***479***
Saint Mary's U (NS, Canada) ***494***
San Diego State U (CA) ***498***
San Francisco State U (CA) ***498***
Smith Coll (MA) ***506***
State U of NY Coll at Brockport (NY) ***515***
Stony Brook U, State University of New York (NY) ***520***
Swarthmore Coll (PA) ***521***
Texas Christian U (TX) ***526***
Tufts U (MA) ***533***
The U of Arizona (AZ) ***538***
The U of British Columbia (BC, Canada) ***540***
U of Colorado at Boulder (CO) ***543***
U of Delaware (DE) ***544***
U of Florida (FL) ***545***
U of Georgia (GA) ***545***
U of Hawaii at Manoa (HI) ***546***
U of Illinois at Urbana–Champaign (IL) ***548***
The U of Iowa (IA) ***548***
U of Kansas (KS) ***549***
U of Manitoba (MB, Canada) ***551***
U of Maryland, Coll Park (MD) ***552***
U of Massachusetts Amherst (MA) ***552***
U of Michigan (MI) ***554***
U of Minnesota, Twin Cities Campus (MN) ***555***
The U of Montana–Missoula (MT) ***556***
U of Oklahoma (OK) ***562***
U of Rochester (NY) ***573***
U of Southern California (CA) ***576***
The U of Texas at Austin (TX) ***578***
U of Toronto (ON, Canada) ***581***
U of Victoria (BC, Canada) ***582***
U of Virginia (VA) ***582***
U of Washington (WA) ***583***
The U of Western Ontario (ON, Canada) ***583***
U of Wisconsin–Madison (WI) ***584***
U of Wyoming (WY) ***586***
Valdosta State U (GA) ***588***
Valparaiso U (IN) ***588***
Vanderbilt U (TN) ***588***
Vassar Coll (NY) ***589***
Villanova U (PA) ***590***
Wellesley Coll (MA) ***597***
Wesleyan U (CT) ***597***
Wheaton Coll (MA) ***603***
Whitman Coll (WA) ***604***
Williams Coll (MA) ***606***
Yale U (CT) ***610***
York U (ON, Canada) ***611***
Youngstown State U (OH) ***611***

ASTROPHYSICS

Overview: This major is different than astronomy in that it focuses mostly on the science of star and star-system structure, properties and behavior, life cycles, and related phenomena. *Related majors:* astronomy, mathematics, physics and theoretical physics, computer science, optics. *Potential careers:* astronomer, astrophysicist, research scientist, professor. *Salary potential:* $30k-$40k.

Agnes Scott Coll (GA) ***261***
Augsburg Coll (MN) ***276***
Boston U (MA) ***292***
Brigham Young U (UT) ***295***
California Inst of Technology (CA) ***299***
California State U, Northridge (CA) ***301***
Colgate U (NY) ***319***
Columbia Coll (NY) ***326***
Connecticut Coll (CT) ***331***
Florida Inst of Technology (FL) ***360***
Hampshire Coll (MA) ***375***
Harvard U (MA) ***376***
Indiana U Bloomington (IN) ***385***
Marlboro Coll (VT) ***418***
McMaster U (ON, Canada) ***423***
Michigan State U (MI) ***428***
New Mexico Inst of Mining and Technology (NM) ***446***
Ohio U (OH) ***458***
Pacific Union Coll (CA) ***464***
Penn State U Univ Park Campus (PA) ***468***
Princeton U (NJ) ***474***
Queen's U at Kingston (ON, Canada) ***476***
Rice U (TX) ***479***
Saint Mary's U (NS, Canada) ***494***
San Francisco State U (CA) ***498***
Swarthmore Coll (PA) ***521***
Texas Christian U (TX) ***526***
U of Calgary (AB, Canada) ***540***
U of Calif, Berkeley (CA) ***540***
U of Calif, Los Angeles (CA) ***541***
U of Calif, Santa Cruz (CA) ***542***
U of Delaware (DE) ***544***
U of Minnesota, Twin Cities Campus (MN) ***555***
U of Missouri–St. Louis (MO) ***556***
U of New Mexico (NM) ***559***
U of Oklahoma (OK) ***562***
U of Wyoming (WY) ***586***
Villanova U (PA) ***590***
Wellesley Coll (MA) ***597***
Williams Coll (MA) ***606***
Yale U (CT) ***610***

ATHLETIC TRAINING/ SPORTS MEDICINE

Overview: This major prepares students to work with physicians to identify, prevent, and treat sports-related injuries and conditions. *Related majors:* anatomy, exercise sciences, physical therapy. *Potential careers:* athletic trainer or coach, sports medicine specialist, physician. *Salary potential:* $22k-$35k.

Adams State Coll (CO) ***260***
Alderson-Broaddus Coll (WV) ***263***
Alfred U (NY) ***263***
Alma Coll (MI) ***264***
Anderson U (IN) ***268***
Angelo State U (TX) ***269***
Appalachian State U (NC) ***270***
Aquinas Coll (MI) ***270***
Arkansas State U (AR) ***272***
Ashland U (OH) ***274***
Augsburg Coll (MN) ***276***
Augustana Coll (SD) ***276***
Averett U (VA) ***278***
Azusa Pacific U (CA) ***278***
Baldwin-Wallace Coll (OH) ***280***
Ball State U (IN) ***280***
Barton Coll (NC) ***282***
Belhaven Coll (MS) ***283***
Bethany Coll (KS) ***287***
Bethel Coll (MN) ***288***
Bluefield Coll (VA) ***291***
Boston U (MA) ***292***
Bowling Green State U (OH) ***292***
Bridgewater Coll (VA) ***294***
Bridgewater State Coll (MA) ***294***
Buena Vista U (IA) ***297***
California Lutheran U (CA) ***299***
California State U, Hayward (CA) ***301***
California State U, Long Beach (CA) ***301***
California State U, Northridge (CA) ***301***
Calvin Coll (MI) ***303***
Campbellsville U (KY) ***303***
Campbell U (NC) ***303***
Canisius Coll (NY) ***304***
Capital U (OH) ***304***
Carroll Coll (WI) ***306***
Carson-Newman Coll (TN) ***306***
Carthage Coll (WI) ***306***
Castleton State Coll (VT) ***307***
Catawba Coll (NC) ***307***
Cedarville U (OH) ***308***
Central Connecticut State U (CT) ***309***
Central Methodist Coll (MO) ***309***
Central Michigan U (MI) ***310***
Chapman U (CA) ***311***
Chowan Coll (NC) ***312***
Christian Heritage Coll (CA) ***313***
Clarke Coll (IA) ***315***
Coe Coll (IA) ***318***
Coker Coll (SC) ***318***
Colby-Sawyer Coll (NH) ***319***
Coll of the Southwest (NM) ***324***
Colorado State U (CO) ***325***
Colorado State U-Pueblo (CO) ***325***
Columbus State U (GA) ***328***
Comm Hospital Roanoke Valley–Coll of Health Scis (VA) ***328***
Concordia U (NE) ***330***
Concordia U (QC, Canada) ***331***
Concordia U Wisconsin (WI) ***331***
Culver-Stockton Coll (MO) ***334***
Cumberland U (TN) ***335***
Dakota Wesleyan U (SD) ***336***
Defiance Coll (OH) ***338***
DePauw U (IN) ***339***
Dominican Coll (NY) ***344***
Duquesne U (PA) ***346***
East Carolina U (NC) ***347***
Eastern Kentucky U (KY) ***348***
Eastern Michigan U (MI) ***348***
Eastern Washington U (WA) ***349***
East Stroudsburg U of Pennsylvania (PA) ***349***
East Texas Baptist U (TX) ***350***
Elon U (NC) ***352***
Endicott Coll (MA) ***354***
Erskine Coll (SC) ***354***
Eureka Coll (IL) ***355***
Faulkner U (AL) ***357***
Ferrum Coll (VA) ***358***
Florida Southern Coll (FL) ***361***
The Franciscan U (IA) ***363***
Franklin Coll (IN) ***363***
Free Will Baptist Bible Coll (TN) ***364***
Fresno Pacific U (CA) ***364***
Gardner-Webb U (NC) ***365***
George Fox U (OR) ***366***
Georgia Southern U (GA) ***367***
Graceland U (IA) ***371***
Grand Canyon U (AZ) ***371***
Grand Valley State U (MI) ***371***
Greensboro Coll (NC) ***372***
Guilford Coll (NC) ***373***
Gustavus Adolphus Coll (MN) ***374***
Hamline U (MN) ***374***
Heidelberg Coll (OH) ***377***
Henderson State U (AR) ***378***
High Point U (NC) ***379***
Hope Coll (MI) ***381***
Hope International U (CA) ***381***
Houghton Coll (NY) ***381***
Howard Payne U (TX) ***382***
Huntingdon Coll (AL) ***383***
Indiana State U (IN) ***385***
Indiana U Bloomington (IN) ***385***
Indiana Wesleyan U (IN) ***387***
Ithaca Coll (NY) ***390***
John Brown U (AR) ***392***
Johnson State Coll (VT) ***394***
Keene State Coll (NH) ***396***
Kent State U (OH) ***397***
King's Coll (PA) ***398***
Lakehead U (ON, Canada) ***400***
Lambuth U (TN) ***401***
Lees-McRae Coll (NC) ***404***
Lenoir-Rhyne Coll (NC) ***405***
Liberty U (VA) ***406***
Limestone Coll (SC) ***406***
Lincoln Memorial U (TN) ***407***
Lindenwood U (MO) ***407***
Linfield Coll (OR) ***408***
Lipscomb U (TN) ***408***
Lock Haven U of Pennsylvania (PA) ***408***
Long Island U, Brooklyn Campus (NY) ***409***
Longwood U (VA) ***409***
Loras Coll (IA) ***410***
Louisiana Coll (LA) ***410***
Lubbock Christian U (TX) ***412***
Lynchburg Coll (VA) ***413***
Lyndon State Coll (VT) ***413***
Manchester Coll (IN) ***415***
Marietta Coll (OH) ***417***
Marist Coll (NY) ***417***
Marquette U (WI) ***418***
Mars Hill Coll (NC) ***418***
Marywood U (PA) ***421***
Massachusetts Coll of Liberal Arts (MA) ***421***
McKendree Coll (IL) ***423***
Memorial U of Newfoundland (NF, Canada) ***424***
Mercyhurst Coll (PA) ***425***
Merrimack Coll (MA) ***426***
Messiah Coll (PA) ***426***
Methodist Coll (NC) ***427***
Miami U (OH) ***428***
MidAmerica Nazarene U (KS) ***428***
Middle Tennessee State U (TN) ***429***
Midland Lutheran Coll (NE) ***429***
Millikin U (IL) ***430***
Minnesota State U, Mankato (MN) ***431***
Mount Marty Coll (SD) ***438***
Mount Olive Coll (NC) ***439***
Mount Union Coll (OH) ***440***
Mount Vernon Nazarene U (OH) ***440***
National American U (SD) ***442***
Nebraska Wesleyan U (NE) ***443***
Newberry Coll (SC) ***444***
New England Coll (NH) ***444***
Newman U (KS) ***445***
New Mexico State U (NM) ***446***
North Carolina Central U (NC) ***448***
North Central Coll (IL) ***449***
North Dakota State U (ND) ***449***
Northeastern U (MA) ***450***
Northern Michigan U (MI) ***451***
North Park U (IL) ***452***
Northwestern Coll (MN) ***453***
Northwest Nazarene U (ID) ***454***
Norwich U (VT) ***455***
Ohio Northern U (OH) ***457***
The Ohio State U (OH) ***457***
Ohio U (OH) ***458***
Oklahoma Baptist U (OK) ***459***
Oklahoma Wesleyan U (OK) ***460***
Olivet Coll (MI) ***461***
Olivet Nazarene U (IL) ***461***
Oregon State U (OR) ***462***
Otterbein Coll (OH) ***462***
Pacific U (OR) ***464***
Park U (MO) ***465***
Pepperdine U, Malibu (CA) ***469***
Pfeiffer U (NC) ***469***
Plymouth State Coll (NH) ***471***
Point Loma Nazarene U (CA) ***471***
Quincy U (IL) ***476***
Quinnipiac U (CT) ***476***
Roanoke Coll (VA) ***481***
Rocky Mountain Coll (MT) ***482***
Russell Sage Coll (NY) ***484***
Sacred Heart U (CT) ***486***
St. Ambrose U (IA) ***486***
Salem International U (WV) ***496***
Salisbury U (MD) ***497***
Samford U (AL) ***497***
San Jose State U (CA) ***499***
Shawnee State U (OH) ***502***
Simpson Coll (IA) ***505***
Slippery Rock U of Pennsylvania (PA) ***506***

South Dakota State U (SD) **507**
Southeast Missouri State U (MO) **508**
Southern Connecticut State U (CT) **509**
Southern Nazarene U (OK) **510**
Southwest Baptist U (MO) **512**
Southwestern Coll (KS) **512**
Southwest Missouri State U (MO) **513**
Southwest Texas State U (TX) **513**
Springfield Coll (MA) **514**
State U of NY Coll at Brockport (NY) **515**
State U of NY Coll at Cortland (NY) **516**
Sterling Coll (KS) **519**
Stetson U (FL) **519**
Tabor Coll (KS) **522**
Taylor U (IN) **523**
Temple U (PA) **523**
Tennessee Wesleyan Coll (TN) **524**
Texas Lutheran U (TX) **526**
Texas Wesleyan U (TX) **526**
Towson U (MD) **529**
Trinity International U (IL) **531**
Troy State U (AL) **532**
Tusculum Coll (TN) **533**
Union U (TN) **534**
Université de Sherbrooke (QC, Canada) **536**
The U of Akron (OH) **537**
The U of Alabama (AL) **537**
U of Alberta (AB, Canada) **538**
U of Central Arkansas (AR) **542**
U of Charleston (WV) **542**
U of Delaware (DE) **544**
U of Evansville (IN) **545**
The U of Findlay (OH) **545**
U of Hawaii at Manoa (HI) **546**
U of Idaho (ID) **547**
U of Indianapolis (IN) **548**
The U of Iowa (IA) **548**
U of Maine at Presque Isle (ME) **551**
U of Mary (ND) **551**
U of Miami (FL) **553**
U of Michigan (MI) **554**
U of Mobile (AL) **556**
U of Nebraska–Lincoln (NE) **557**
U of Nevada, Las Vegas (NV) **558**
U of New Hampshire (NH) **558**
The U of North Carolina at Wilmington (NC) **561**
U of North Dakota (ND) **561**
U of Pittsburgh at Bradford (PA) **569**
U of Puerto Rico at Ponce (PR) **571**
U of San Francisco (CA) **574**
U of Southern Maine (ME) **576**
The U of Tennessee at Martin (TN) **577**
The U of Texas at Arlington (TX) **577**
U of Tulsa (OK) **581**
U of Vermont (VT) **582**
The U of West Alabama (AL) **583**
U of Windsor (ON, Canada) **584**
U of Wisconsin–La Crosse (WI) **584**
U of Wisconsin–Stevens Point (WI) **585**
Upper Iowa U (IA) **587**
Urbana U (OH) **587**
Ursinus Coll (PA) **587**
Valdosta State U (GA) **588**
Valparaiso U (IN) **588**
Vanguard U of Southern California (CA) **589**
Walsh U (OH) **593**
Washington State U (WA) **595**
Waynesburg Coll (PA) **595**
Weber State U (UT) **596**
West Chester U of Pennsylvania (PA) **598**
Western State Coll of Colorado (CO) **600**
Western Washington U (WA) **600**
Westminster Coll (MO) **601**
West Virginia Wesleyan Coll (WV) **603**
Whitworth Coll (WA) **604**
William Woods U (MO) **607**
Wilmington Coll (OH) **607**
Wingate U (NC) **607**
Winona State U (MN) **608**
Xavier U (OH) **610**
Youngstown State U (OH) **611**

ATMOSPHERIC SCIENCES

Overview: Students of this major will study the science of the earth's atmosphere, both its composition and behavior. *Related majors:* chemistry, physics, environmental sciences, environmental engineering. *Potential careers:* weather forecaster, environmental engineer, ecologist, chemist. *Salary potential:* $27k-$37k.

California State U, Chico (CA) **300**
Cornell U (NY) **333**
Creighton U (NE) **333**
Florida Inst of Technology (FL) **360**
Florida State U (FL) **361**
Harvard U (MA) **376**
Iowa State U of Science and Technology (IA) **390**
Jackson State U (MS) **390**
Lyndon State Coll (VT) **413**
McGill U (QC, Canada) **423**
Metropolitan State Coll of Denver (CO) **427**
Millersville U of Pennsylvania (PA) **430**
New Mexico Inst of Mining and Technology (NM) **446**
North Carolina State U (NC) **449**
Northern Illinois U (IL) **450**
Northland Coll (WI) **452**
Ohio U (OH) **458**
Penn State U Univ Park Campus (PA) **468**
Plymouth State Coll (NH) **471**
Rutgers, The State U of New Jersey, New Brunswick (NJ) **485**
St. Cloud State U (MN) **488**
Saint Louis U (MO) **492**
San Francisco State U (CA) **498**
San Jose State U (CA) **499**
State U of NY at Albany (NY) **514**
State U of NY at Oswego (NY) **515**
State U of NY Coll at Brockport (NY) **515**
State U of NY Coll at Oneonta (NY) **517**
State U of NY Maritime Coll (NY) **518**
Stony Brook U, State University of New York (NY) **520**
Texas A&M U (TX) **524**
United States Air Force Academy (CO) **534**
U of Alberta (AB, Canada) **538**
The U of Arizona (AZ) **538**
The U of British Columbia (BC, Canada) **540**
U of Calif, Davis (CA) **540**
U of Calif, Los Angeles (CA) **541**
U of Hawaii at Manoa (HI) **546**
U of Kansas (KS) **549**
U of Miami (FL) **553**
U of Michigan (MI) **554**
U of Missouri–Columbia (MO) **555**
U of Nebraska–Lincoln (NE) **557**
The U of North Carolina at Asheville (NC) **559**
U of North Dakota (ND) **561**
U of Oklahoma (OK) **562**
U of South Alabama (AL) **575**
U of Utah (UT) **582**
U of Victoria (BC, Canada) **582**
U of Washington (WA) **583**
U of Wisconsin–Milwaukee (WI) **585**
Valparaiso U (IN) **588**
Western Connecticut State U (CT) **598**
York U (ON, Canada) **611**

AUDIO ENGINEERING

Overview: Students study the disciplines of electronics, acoustics, and music to prepare for a career in the recording and music industries. *Related majors:* music (general, performance, and theory and composition), music business management and merchandising, musical instrument technology. *Potential careers:* recording technician, record company executive, musician. *Salary potential:* $25k-$35k.

American U (DC) **267**
Berklee Coll of Music (MA) **286**
Cleveland Inst of Music (OH) **317**
Cogswell Polytechnical Coll (CA) **318**
The Evergreen State Coll (WA) **355**
Five Towns Coll (NY) **359**
Mount Vernon Nazarene U (OH) **440**
New England School of Communications (ME) **445**
Peabody Conserv of Music of Johns Hopkins U (MD) **466**
State U of NY Coll at Fredonia (NY) **516**
U of Hartford (CT) **546**
U of Southern California (CA) **576**
Webster U (MO) **597**

AUTO MECHANIC/ TECHNICIAN

Overview: This major will teach students the technical skills and knowledge they need to repair, service, and maintain systems and machinery of all types of gas-powered automobiles. *Related majors:* small engine mechanics, auto body repair. *Potential careers:* auto mechanic, service station owner. *Salary potential:* $18k-$28k.

Andrews U (MI) **269**
Colorado State U-Pueblo (CO) **325**
Ferris State U (MI) **358**
Lewis-Clark State Coll (ID) **406**
Montana State U–Northern (MT) **434**
Pittsburg State U (KS) **470**
Walla Walla Coll (WA) **593**
Weber State U (UT) **596**

AUTOMOTIVE ENGINEERING TECHNOLOGY

Overview: This major teaches students the theory, operation, diagnosis, and overhaul of all automotive system components. *Related majors:* instrumentation technology, computer engineering technology. *Potential careers:* auto mechanic or technician, researcher, designer. *Salary potential:* $24k-$35k.

Central Michigan U (MI) **310**
Central Missouri State U (MO) **310**
Grambling State U (LA) **371**
Indiana State U (IN) **385**
Minnesota State U, Mankato (MN) **431**
Pennsylvania Coll of Technology (PA) **467**
Rochester Inst of Technology (NY) **482**
Southern Illinois U Carbondale (IL) **509**
U of Windsor (ON, Canada) **584**
Weber State U (UT) **596**
Western Michigan U (MI) **599**
Western Washington U (WA) **600**

AVIATION/AIRWAY SCIENCE

Overview: Students who enroll in this major study aviation and the aviation industry, including in-flight and ground support operations. *Related majors:* aviation management, aerospace technology, operations management and supervision, business administration, air traffic control. *Potential careers:* Air traffic controller, airport manager, airline supervisor and manager. *Salary potential:* $25k-$35k.

Central Washington U (WA) **310**
Delta State U (MS) **339**
Embry-Riddle Aeronautical U (AZ) **352**
Embry-Riddle Aeronautical U (FL) **352**
Embry-Riddle Aeronautical U, Extended Campus (FL) **352**
Florida Inst of Technology (FL) **360**
Kansas State U (KS) **396**
Kent State U (OH) **397**
Louisiana Tech U (LA) **410**
Middle Tennessee State U (TN) **429**
Ohio U (OH) **458**
Purdue U (IN) **475**
Quincy U (IL) **476**
San Jose State U (CA) **499**
U of North Dakota (ND) **561**
Western Michigan U (MI) **599**

AVIATION MANAGEMENT

Overview: This major prepares students to effectively manage airlines and other aviation and aviation-related industry operations. *Related majors:* aviation/airway science, aircraft pilot and navigator, operations management and supervision, procurement, and contracts management. *Potential careers:* airline executive, assistant airport controller, union representative, airline personal supervisor, airline food service manager. *Salary potential:* $30k-$45k.

Averett U (VA) **278**
Baker Coll of Muskegon (MI) **279**
Bowling Green State U (OH) **292**
Bridgewater State Coll (MA) **294**
Coll of Aeronautics (NY) **319**
Daniel Webster Coll (NH) **337**
Delaware State U (DE) **338**
Dowling Coll (NY) **345**
Eastern Kentucky U (KY) **348**
Embry-Riddle Aeronautical U (AZ) **352**
Embry-Riddle Aeronautical U (FL) **352**
Embry-Riddle Aeronautical U, Extended Campus (FL) **352**
Everglades Coll (FL) **355**
Fairmont State Coll (WV) **356**
State U of NY at Farmingdale (NY) **357**
Florida Inst of Technology (FL) **360**
Geneva Coll (PA) **366**
Hampton U (VA) **375**
Indiana State U (IN) **385**
Jacksonville U (FL) **391**
Lewis U (IL) **406**
Louisiana Tech U (LA) **410**
Lynn U (FL) **413**
Marywood U (PA) **421**
Metropolitan State Coll of Denver (CO) **427**
Minnesota State U, Mankato (MN) **431**
The Ohio State U (OH) **457**
Ohio U (OH) **458**
Oklahoma State U (OK) **460**
Park U (MO) **465**
Quincy U (IL) **476**
Robert Morris U (PA) **481**
Rocky Mountain Coll (MT) **482**
St. Cloud State U (MN) **488**
St. Francis Coll (NY) **488**
Saint Louis U (MO) **492**
Salem State Coll (MA) **497**
San Jose State U (CA) **499**
Southeastern Oklahoma State U (OK) **508**
Southern Illinois U Carbondale (IL) **509**
Southern Nazarene U (OK) **510**
Tarleton State U (TX) **522**
Texas Southern U (TX) **526**
U of Dubuque (IA) **545**
U of Nebraska at Kearney (NE) **557**
U of Nebraska at Omaha (NE) **557**
U of New Haven (CT) **559**
U of North Dakota (ND) **561**
Western Michigan U (MI) **599**
Westminster Coll (UT) **601**
Wheeling Jesuit U (WV) **603**
Wilmington Coll (DE) **607**
Winona State U (MN) **608**

AVIATION TECHNOLOGY

Overview: Students will learn the technical skills and knowledge they need to repair, service, and maintain the operating, control, and electronic systems of all types of aircraft. *Related majors:* air science, communication equipment technology, computer systems analysis, aeronautical engineering technology. *Potential careers:* aircraft technician, Air Force or Navy mechanic. *Salary potential:* $25k-$30k.

Andrews U (MI) **269**
Averett U (VA) **278**
Christian Heritage Coll (CA) **313**
Coll of Aeronautics (NY) **319**
Coll of the Ozarks (MO) **323**
Elizabeth City State U (NC) **351**
Fairmont State Coll (WV) **356**
Grace U (NE) **371**
Hampton U (VA) **375**
LeTourneau U (TX) **405**
Lewis U (IL) **406**
Moody Bible Inst (IL) **435**
The Ohio State U (OH) **457**
Oklahoma State U (OK) **460**
Piedmont Baptist Coll (NC) **470**

AVIATION TECHNOLOGY (continued)

Providence Coll and Theological Seminary (MB, Canada) ***475***
San Jose State U (CA) ***499***
Southern Illinois U Carbondale (IL) ***509***
Walla Walla Coll (WA) ***593***
Western Michigan U (MI) ***599***
Wilmington Coll (DE) ***607***

BAKER/PASTRY CHEF

Overview: This major prepares students to serve as professional bakers and pastry chefs in restaurants or other commercial baking establishments. *Related majors:* culinary arts, restaurant operations. *Potential careers:* commercial baking manager, restaurant owner, pastry chef. *Salary potential:* $20k-$30k.

Johnson & Wales U (RI) ***393***

BANKING

Overview: This major prepares students to work in a variety of positions at banks, insurance companies, and other financial institutions that cater to the public. *Related majors:* business communications, public relations, economics, and financial planning. *Potential careers:* customer service representative, loan officer, insurance agent. *Salary potential:* $27k-$37k.

Central Michigan U (MI) ***310***
Clearwater Christian Coll (FL) ***316***
Delaware State U (DE) ***338***
Husson Coll (ME) ***383***
National U (CA) ***442***
Southeastern U (DC) ***508***
Southeast Missouri State U (MO) ***508***
Thomas Edison State Coll (NJ) ***527***
U of Indianapolis (IN) ***548***
U of Nebraska at Omaha (NE) ***557***
U of North Florida (FL) ***561***
The U of Texas at Arlington (TX) ***577***
West Liberty State Coll (WV) ***601***
Youngstown State U (OH) ***611***

BEHAVIORAL SCIENCES

Overview: This interdisciplinary major includes studies from a number of different disciplines, including anthropology, sociology, psychology, and human ecology and gives students an understanding of human behavior, social interaction, institution building, and comparative social systems in preparation for both careers and graduate work. *Related majors:* anthropology, human ecology, psychology, sociology. *Potential careers:* human services coordinator, psychologist, teacher, politician, anthropologist. *Salary potential:* $23k-$33k.

Andrews U (MI) ***269***
Anna Maria Coll (MA) ***269***
Antioch Coll (OH) ***269***
Athens State U (AL) ***275***
Augsburg Coll (MN) ***276***
Averett U (VA) ***278***
Avila U (MO) ***278***
Belmont U (TN) ***284***
Bemidji State U (MN) ***285***
Brown U (RI) ***296***
California Baptist U (CA) ***298***
California State Polytechnic U, Pomona (CA) ***300***
California State U, Dominguez Hills (CA) ***300***
Cedar Crest Coll (PA) ***308***
Chaminade U of Honolulu (HI) ***311***
Circleville Bible Coll (OH) ***314***
Coker Coll (SC) ***318***
Columbia Coll (MO) ***326***
Concordia U (CA) ***330***
Concordia U (NE) ***330***
Concordia U (QC, Canada) ***331***
Concordia U at Austin (TX) ***331***
Cornell U (NY) ***333***
Dakota Wesleyan U (SD) ***336***
Drew U (NJ) ***346***
Drury U (MO) ***346***
East Texas Baptist U (TX) ***350***
East-West U (IL) ***350***
Erskine Coll (SC) ***354***
Evangel U (MO) ***355***
Felician Coll (NJ) ***357***
Freed-Hardeman U (TN) ***364***
Georgia Southwestern State U (GA) ***368***
Glenville State Coll (WV) ***368***
Goddard Coll (VT) ***369***
Grand Valley State U (MI) ***371***
Green Mountain Coll (VT) ***372***
Gwynedd-Mercy Coll (PA) ***374***
Hampshire Coll (MA) ***375***
Harvard U (MA) ***376***
Hawai'i Pacific U (HI) ***377***
Howard Payne U (TX) ***382***
Indiana U Kokomo (IN) ***386***
Inter American U of PR, San Germán Campus (PR) ***388***
Iona Coll (NY) ***390***
John Jay Coll of Criminal Justice, the City U of NY (NY) ***392***
Johns Hopkins U (MD) ***392***
King Coll (TN) ***398***
Lakeland Coll (WI) ***401***
Laurentian U (ON, Canada) ***403***
Lincoln U (PA) ***407***
Long Island U, Southampton Coll (NY) ***409***
Long Island U, Southampton Coll, Friends World Program (NY) ***409***
Loyola U New Orleans (LA) ***411***
Marist Coll (NY) ***417***
Marlboro Coll (VT) ***418***
Mars Hill Coll (NC) ***418***
McPherson Coll (KS) ***423***
Mercy Coll (NY) ***425***
Mesa State Coll (CO) ***426***
Methodist Coll (NC) ***427***
Metropolitan State Coll of Denver (CO) ***427***
Mid-Continent Coll (KY) ***429***
Midland Lutheran Coll (NE) ***429***
Minnesota State U, Mankato (MN) ***431***
Morgan State U (MD) ***436***
Mountain State U (WV) ***437***
Mount Aloysius Coll (PA) ***437***
Mount Marty Coll (SD) ***438***
Mount Mary Coll (WI) ***438***
National-Louis U (IL) ***442***
National U (CA) ***442***
New Mexico Inst of Mining and Technology (NM) ***446***
Northeastern U (MA) ***450***
Northwest Coll (WA) ***452***
Northwest Missouri State U (MO) ***454***
Notre Dame de Namur U (CA) ***455***
Oklahoma Wesleyan U (OK) ***460***
Our Lady of Holy Cross Coll (LA) ***463***
Pacific Union Coll (CA) ***464***
Point Park Coll (PA) ***471***
Purdue U Calumet (IN) ***475***
Rhode Island Coll (RI) ***479***
Rochester Coll (MI) ***482***
St. Cloud State U (MN) ***488***
St. Joseph's Coll, Suffolk Campus (NY) ***491***
San Jose State U (CA) ***499***
Sterling Coll (KS) ***519***
Syracuse U (NY) ***521***
Tennessee Wesleyan Coll (TN) ***524***
Texas Wesleyan U (TX) ***526***
Trevecca Nazarene U (TN) ***529***
Tufts U (MA) ***533***
United States Air Force Academy (CO) ***534***
United States Military Academy (NY) ***535***
The U of Akron (OH) ***537***
U of Chicago (IL) ***542***
U of Houston–Clear Lake (TX) ***547***
U of La Verne (CA) ***549***
U of Maine at Fort Kent (ME) ***551***
U of Maine at Machias (ME) ***551***
U of Maine at Presque Isle (ME) ***551***
U of Mary (ND) ***551***
U of Michigan–Dearborn (MI) ***554***
U of Missouri–St. Louis (MO) ***556***
U of Mobile (AL) ***556***
U of North Texas (TX) ***562***
U of Ottawa (ON, Canada) ***563***
U of St. Thomas (MN) ***573***
U of Sioux Falls (SD) ***574***
U of Utah (UT) ***582***
U System Coll for Lifelong Learning (NH) ***586***
Walsh U (OH) ***593***
Western International U (AZ) ***599***
Westminster Coll (PA) ***601***
Widener U (PA) ***604***
William Paterson U of New Jersey (NJ) ***606***
Wilmington Coll (DE) ***607***
Wilson Coll (PA) ***607***
Wittenberg U (OH) ***608***
York Coll of Pennsylvania (PA) ***610***
York U (ON, Canada) ***611***

BIBLICAL LANGUAGES/ LITERATURES

Overview: Students will learn about the original languages used in Biblical Jewish and Christian religious texts. *Related majors:* Arabic, Greek, Hebrew, Latin, religion, Bible/Biblical studies. *Potential careers:* archeologist, clergy, professor, writer, historical researcher. *Salary potential:* $23k-$33k.

American Christian Coll and Seminary (OK) ***265***
Baltimore Hebrew U (MD) ***280***
Baylor U (TX) ***283***
Belmont U (TN) ***284***
Bethany Coll of the Assemblies of God (CA) ***287***
Bethel Coll (IN) ***288***
Carson-Newman Coll (TN) ***306***
Central Bible Coll (MO) ***309***
Columbia International U (SC) ***327***
Concordia U (IL) ***330***
Concordia U (MI) ***330***
Concordia U Wisconsin (WI) ***331***
Cornerstone U (MI) ***333***
Harding U (AR) ***375***
Harvard U (MA) ***376***
Howard Payne U (TX) ***382***
Indiana Wesleyan U (IN) ***387***
Laura and Alvin Siegal Coll of Judaic Studies (OH) ***403***
Lipscomb U (TN) ***408***
Long Island U, Southampton Coll, Friends World Program (NY) ***409***
Lubbock Christian U (TX) ***412***
Luther Coll (IA) ***412***
The Master's Coll and Seminary (CA) ***422***
Mid-Continent Coll (KY) ***429***
Multnomah Bible Coll and Biblical Seminary (OR) ***440***
North Greenville Coll (SC) ***451***
Northwest Nazarene U (ID) ***454***
Oklahoma Baptist U (OK) ***459***
Ozark Christian Coll (MO) ***463***
Prairie Bible Coll (AB, Canada) ***473***
Southeastern Bible Coll (AL) ***507***
Southwestern Assemblies of God U (TX) ***512***
Taylor U (IN) ***523***
Toccoa Falls Coll (GA) ***528***
Union U (TN) ***534***
U of Chicago (IL) ***542***
U of Toronto (ON, Canada) ***581***
Walla Walla Coll (WA) ***593***
York Coll (NE) ***610***
York U (ON, Canada) ***611***

BIBLICAL STUDIES

Overview: Students will study the Jewish and/or Christian Bible and associated literatures and languages, interpreting the religious messages therein. *Related majors:* history, Biblical languages/literatures, religious studies, philosophy. *Potential careers:* clergy, writer, anthropologist, theologian, teacher. *Salary potential:* $25k-$30k.

Abilene Christian U (TX) ***260***
Alaska Bible Coll (AK) ***261***
American Baptist Coll of American Baptist Theol Sem (TN) ***265***
Anderson U (IN) ***268***
Andrews U (MI) ***269***
Appalachian Bible Coll (WV) ***270***
Arlington Baptist Coll (TX) ***272***
Asbury Coll (KY) ***274***
Atlanta Christian Coll (GA) ***275***
Atlantic Baptist U (NB, Canada) ***275***
Austin Graduate School of Theology (TX) ***277***
Azusa Pacific U (CA) ***278***
Baltimore Hebrew U (MD) ***280***
The Baptist Coll of Florida (FL) ***281***
Barclay Coll (KS) ***281***
Beacon Coll and Graduate School (GA) ***283***
Belhaven Coll (MS) ***283***
Belmont U (TN) ***284***
Bethany Bible Coll (NB, Canada) ***287***
Bethany Coll of the Assemblies of God (CA) ***287***
Bethel Coll (IN) ***288***
Bethel Coll (MN) ***288***
Bethesda Christian U (CA) ***288***
Beulah Heights Bible Coll (GA) ***289***
Biola U (CA) ***289***
Bluefield Coll (VA) ***291***
Blue Mountain Coll (MS) ***291***
Boise Bible Coll (ID) ***291***
Briercrest Bible Coll (SK, Canada) ***295***
Bryan Coll (TN) ***296***
California Christian Coll (CA) ***298***
Calvin Coll (MI) ***303***
Campbellsville U (KY) ***303***
Canadian Bible Coll (AB, Canada) ***303***
Canadian Mennonite U (MB, Canada) ***304***
Carson-Newman Coll (TN) ***306***
Cascade Coll (OR) ***307***
Cedarville U (OH) ***308***
Central Baptist Coll (AR) ***309***
Central Bible Coll (MO) ***309***
Central Christian Coll of Kansas (KS) ***309***
Christian Heritage Coll (CA) ***313***
Cincinnati Bible Coll and Seminary (OH) ***314***
Circleville Bible Coll (OH) ***314***
Clear Creek Baptist Bible Coll (KY) ***316***
Clearwater Christian Coll (FL) ***316***
Coll of Biblical Studies–Houston (TX) ***320***
Colorado Christian U (CO) ***325***
Columbia Bible Coll (BC, Canada) ***326***
Columbia International U (SC) ***327***
Concordia U at Austin (TX) ***331***
Cornerstone U (MI) ***333***
Covenant Coll (GA) ***333***
Crichton Coll (TN) ***334***
Crossroads Coll (MN) ***334***
Crown Coll (MN) ***334***
Dallas Baptist U (TX) ***336***
Dallas Christian Coll (TX) ***336***
Eastern Mennonite U (VA) ***348***
Eastern U (PA) ***349***
Emmanuel Coll (GA) ***353***
Emmaus Bible Coll (IA) ***353***
Erskine Coll (SC) ***354***
Eugene Bible Coll (OR) ***355***
Evangel U (MO) ***355***
Faith Baptist Bible Coll and Theological Seminary (IA) ***356***
Faulkner U (AL) ***357***
Florida Coll (FL) ***359***
Freed-Hardeman U (TN) ***364***
Free Will Baptist Bible Coll (TN) ***364***
Fresno Pacific U (CA) ***364***
Geneva Coll (PA) ***366***
George Fox U (OR) ***366***
Global U of the Assemblies of God (MO) ***368***
God's Bible School and Coll (OH) ***369***
Gordon Coll (MA) ***370***
Goshen Coll (IN) ***370***
Grace Bible Coll (MI) ***370***
Grace Coll (IN) ***370***
Grace U (NE) ***371***
Grand Canyon U (AZ) ***371***
Great Lakes Christian Coll (MI) ***372***
Hannibal-LaGrange Coll (MO) ***375***
Harding U (AR) ***375***
Hardin-Simmons U (TX) ***376***
Harvard U (MA) ***376***
Heritage Christian U (AL) ***379***
Holy Apostles Coll and Seminary (CT) ***380***
Hope International U (CA) ***381***
Houghton Coll (NY) ***381***
Houston Baptist U (TX) ***382***
Howard Payne U (TX) ***382***
Huntington Coll (IN) ***383***
Indiana Wesleyan U (IN) ***387***
Jewish Theological Seminary of America (NY) ***391***

John Brown U (AR) ***392***
Johnson Bible Coll (TN) ***394***
John Wesley Coll (NC) ***394***
Judson Coll (IL) ***395***
King Coll (TN) ***398***
Lancaster Bible Coll (PA) ***401***
Laura and Alvin Siegal Coll of Judaic Studies (OH) ***403***
Lee U (TN) ***404***
LeTourneau U (TX) ***405***
Life Pacific Coll (CA) ***406***
Lincoln Christian Coll (IL) ***407***
Lipscomb U (TN) ***408***
Long Island U, Southampton Coll, Friends World Program (NY) ***409***
Lubbock Christian U (TX) ***412***
Luther Rice Bible Coll and Seminary (GA) ***412***
Magnolia Bible Coll (MS) ***414***
Malone Coll (OH) ***415***
Manhattan Christian Coll (KS) ***415***
Maranatha Baptist Bible Coll (WI) ***417***
Marlboro Coll (VT) ***418***
The Master's Coll and Seminary (CA) ***422***
Messenger Coll (MO) ***426***
Messiah Coll (PA) ***426***
Methodist Coll (NC) ***427***
Mid-Continent Coll (KY) ***429***
Milligan Coll (TN) ***430***
Montreat Coll (NC) ***435***
Moody Bible Inst (IL) ***435***
Mount Vernon Nazarene U (OH) ***440***
Multnomah Bible Coll and Biblical Seminary (OR) ***440***
Nazarene Bible Coll (CO) ***442***
Ner Israel Rabbinical Coll (MD) ***443***
North Greenville Coll (SC) ***451***
North Park U (IL) ***452***
Northwest Bible Coll (AB, Canada) ***452***
Northwest Christian Coll (OR) ***452***
Northwest Coll (WA) ***452***
Northwestern Coll (MN) ***453***
Nyack Coll (NY) ***456***
Oak Hills Christian Coll (MN) ***456***
Oakland City U (IN) ***456***
Ohio Valley Coll (WV) ***459***
Oklahoma Baptist U (OK) ***459***
Oklahoma Christian U (OK) ***459***
Olivet Nazarene U (IL) ***461***
Oral Roberts U (OK) ***461***
Ouachita Baptist U (AR) ***462***
Ozark Christian Coll (MO) ***463***
Patten Coll (CA) ***466***
Philadelphia Biblical U (PA) ***469***
Piedmont Baptist Coll (NC) ***470***
Pillsbury Baptist Bible Coll (MN) ***470***
Practical Bible Coll (NY) ***473***
Providence Coll and Theological Seminary (MB, Canada) ***475***
Reformed Bible Coll (MI) ***477***
Roanoke Bible Coll (NC) ***481***
Rochester Coll (MI) ***482***
Rocky Mountain Coll (AB, Canada) ***482***
St. Louis Christian Coll (MO) ***492***
Saint Paul U (ON, Canada) ***495***
Samford U (AL) ***497***
San Jose Christian Coll (CA) ***498***
Shasta Bible Coll (CA) ***502***
Simpson Coll and Graduate School (CA) ***505***
Southeastern Baptist Coll (MS) ***507***
Southeastern Bible Coll (AL) ***507***
Southeastern Coll of the Assemblies of God (FL) ***507***
Southern Christian U (AL) ***509***
Southern Methodist Coll (SC) ***510***
Southern Nazarene U (OK) ***510***
Southwest Baptist U (MO) ***512***
Southwestern Assemblies of God U (TX) ***512***
Southwestern Christian Coll (TX) ***512***
Steinbach Bible Coll (MB, Canada) ***518***
Tabor Coll (KS) ***522***
Talmudic Coll of Florida (FL) ***522***
Taylor U (IN) ***523***
Taylor U, Fort Wayne Campus (IN) ***523***
Tennessee Temple U (TN) ***524***
Toccoa Falls Coll (GA) ***528***
Touro Coll (NY) ***529***
Trinity Baptist Coll (FL) ***530***
Trinity Bible Coll (ND) ***530***
Trinity Coll of Florida (FL) ***531***
Trinity International U (IL) ***531***
Trinity Lutheran Coll (WA) ***531***
Trinity Western U (BC, Canada) ***531***
Tyndale Coll & Seminary (ON, Canada) ***533***
Union U (TN) ***534***
Universidad Adventista de las Antillas (PR) ***536***
U of Evansville (IN) ***545***
U of Michigan (MI) ***554***
Valley Forge Christian Coll (PA) ***588***
Vanguard U of Southern California (CA) ***589***
Warner Pacific Coll (OR) ***593***
Warner Southern Coll (FL) ***593***
Washington Bible Coll (MD) ***594***
Western Baptist Coll (OR) ***598***
Wheaton Coll (IL) ***603***
William Carey Coll (MS) ***605***
York Coll (NE) ***610***

BILINGUAL/BICULTURAL EDUCATION

Overview: Students in this major will learn about teaching methods for bilingual or bicultural children or adults and the development of specific educational programs for producing bilingual/bicultural individuals. *Related majors:* French, German, and Spanish language teacher instruction; teaching English as a second language; foreign language teacher education. *Potential careers:* bilingual teacher, language teacher, school administrator. *Salary potential:* $23k-$29k.

Adrian Coll (MI) ***260***
Alfred U (NY) ***263***
Belmont U (TN) ***284***
Biola U (CA) ***289***
Boston U (MA) ***292***
Brooklyn Coll of the City U of NY (NY) ***295***
California State Polytechnic U, Pomona (CA) ***300***
California State U, Dominguez Hills (CA) ***300***
California State U, Sacramento (CA) ***301***
Calvin Coll (MI) ***303***
Coll of the Southwest (NM) ***324***
Eastern Michigan U (MI) ***348***
Elms Coll (MA) ***352***
Florida State U (FL) ***361***
Fordham U (NY) ***362***
Fresno Pacific U (CA) ***364***
Goshen Coll (IN) ***370***
Houston Baptist U (TX) ***382***
Indiana U Bloomington (IN) ***385***
Long Island U, Southampton Coll, Friends World Program (NY) ***409***
Marquette U (WI) ***418***
Mercy Coll (NY) ***425***
Mount Mary Coll (WI) ***438***
New Mexico Highlands U (NM) ***446***
Northeastern Illinois U (IL) ***450***
Prescott Coll (AZ) ***474***
Rider U (NJ) ***480***
St. Edward's U (TX) ***488***
State U of NY Coll at Old Westbury (NY) ***516***
Texas A&M International U (TX) ***524***
Texas A&M U–Kingsville (TX) ***525***
Texas Christian U (TX) ***526***
Texas Southern U (TX) ***526***
Texas Wesleyan U (TX) ***526***
U of Alberta (AB, Canada) ***538***
U of Delaware (DE) ***544***
The U of Findlay (OH) ***545***
U of Michigan–Dearborn (MI) ***554***
U of Ottawa (ON, Canada) ***563***
U of Regina (SK, Canada) ***572***
U of San Francisco (CA) ***574***
The U of Texas at Brownsville (TX) ***578***
The U of Texas at San Antonio (TX) ***578***
U of the Sacred Heart (PR) ***580***
U of Washington (WA) ***583***
U of Wisconsin–Milwaukee (WI) ***585***
Weber State U (UT) ***596***
Western Illinois U (IL) ***599***
York U (ON, Canada) ***611***

BIOCHEMICAL TECHNOLOGY

Overview: This major teaches students the basic science and technical skills that will enable them to assist in biochemical research and industrial operations. *Related majors:* chemistry, biochemistry, biotechnology, environmental/pollution control technology,. *Potential careers:* biotechnology research associate, process development assistant, quality control inspector, instrumentation technician, manufacturing research associate. *Salary potential:* $25k-$37k.

Norwich U (VT) ***455***
U at Buffalo, The State University of New York (NY) ***536***
U of Windsor (ON, Canada) ***584***

BIOCHEMISTRY

Overview: This major focuses on the chemistry of living systems, their chemical structures, and how these chemicals react. *Related majors:* chemistry, molecular biology, nutritional sciences, toxicology, biotechnology research. *Potential careers:* physician, pharmacist, research scientist, pharmaceutical company executive, salesperson. *Salary potential:* $30k-$45k.

Abilene Christian U (TX) ***260***
Adelphi U (NY) ***260***
Agnes Scott Coll (GA) ***261***
Albright Coll (PA) ***263***
Allegheny Coll (PA) ***264***
Alma Coll (MI) ***264***
Alvernia Coll (PA) ***265***
American International Coll (MA) ***267***
American U (DC) ***267***
Andrews U (MI) ***269***
Angelo State U (TX) ***269***
Arizona State U (AZ) ***271***
Asbury Coll (KY) ***274***
Atlantic Union Coll (MA) ***276***
Auburn U (AL) ***276***
Azusa Pacific U (CA) ***278***
Bard Coll (NY) ***281***
Barnard Coll (NY) ***282***
Bates Coll (ME) ***282***
Baylor U (TX) ***283***
Belmont U (TN) ***284***
Beloit Coll (WI) ***285***
Benedictine Coll (KS) ***285***
Benedictine U (IL) ***285***
Bennington Coll (VT) ***286***
Berry Coll (GA) ***287***
Bethel Coll (MN) ***288***
Biola U (CA) ***289***
Bishop's U (QC, Canada) ***289***
Bloomfield Coll (NJ) ***290***
Boston Coll (MA) ***292***
Boston U (MA) ***292***
Bowdoin Coll (ME) ***292***
Bowling Green State U (OH) ***292***
Bradley U (IL) ***293***
Brandeis U (MA) ***293***
Bridgewater State Coll (MA) ***294***
Brigham Young U (UT) ***295***
Brock U (ON, Canada) ***295***
Brown U (RI) ***296***
California Inst of Technology (CA) ***299***
California Lutheran U (CA) ***299***
California Polytechnic State U, San Luis Obispo (CA) ***300***
California State U, Chico (CA) ***300***
California State U, Dominguez Hills (CA) ***300***
California State U, Fullerton (CA) ***301***
California State U, Hayward (CA) ***301***
California State U, Long Beach (CA) ***301***
California State U, Northridge (CA) ***301***
California State U, San Bernardino (CA) ***302***
California State U, San Marcos (CA) ***302***
Calvin Coll (MI) ***303***
Campbell U (NC) ***303***
Canisius Coll (NY) ***304***
Carleton U (ON, Canada) ***305***
Carnegie Mellon U (PA) ***305***
Carroll Coll (WI) ***306***
Case Western Reserve U (OH) ***307***
The Catholic U of America (DC) ***307***
Cedar Crest Coll (PA) ***308***
Centenary Coll of Louisiana (LA) ***308***
Centre Coll (KY) ***310***
Chapman U (CA) ***311***
Charleston Southern U (SC) ***311***
Chatham Coll (PA) ***312***
Chestnut Hill Coll (PA) ***312***
City Coll of the City U of NY (NY) ***314***
Claremont McKenna Coll (CA) ***315***
Clarkson U (NY) ***316***
Clark U (MA) ***316***
Clemson U (SC) ***317***
Coe Coll (IA) ***318***
Colby Coll (ME) ***318***
Colgate U (NY) ***319***
Coll Misericordia (PA) ***319***
Coll of Charleston (SC) ***320***
Coll of Mount St. Joseph (OH) ***320***
Coll of Mount Saint Vincent (NY) ***320***
Coll of Saint Benedict (MN) ***321***
Coll of St. Catherine (MN) ***321***
Coll of Saint Elizabeth (NJ) ***321***
The Coll of Saint Rose (NY) ***322***
The Coll of St. Scholastica (MN) ***322***
The Coll of Southeastern Europe, The American U of Athens(Greece) ***323***
Coll of Staten Island of the City U of NY (NY) ***323***
Coll of the Holy Cross (MA) ***323***
The Coll of Wooster (OH) ***324***
The Colorado Coll (CO) ***325***
Colorado State U (CO) ***325***
Columbia Coll (NY) ***326***
Columbia Union Coll (MD) ***328***
Concordia U (QC, Canada) ***331***
Connecticut Coll (CT) ***331***
Converse Coll (SC) ***332***
Cornell Coll (IA) ***332***
Cornell U (NY) ***333***
Daemen Coll (NY) ***335***
Dalhousie U (NS, Canada) ***336***
Dartmouth Coll (NH) ***337***
Denison U (OH) ***339***
DePaul U (IL) ***339***
Dickinson Coll (PA) ***344***
Dominican U (IL) ***345***
Drew U (NJ) ***346***
Duquesne U (PA) ***346***
East Carolina U (NC) ***347***
Eastern Kentucky U (KY) ***348***
Eastern Mennonite U (VA) ***348***
Eastern Michigan U (MI) ***348***
Eastern U (PA) ***349***
Eastern Washington U (WA) ***349***
East Stroudsburg U of Pennsylvania (PA) ***349***
Edinboro U of Pennsylvania (PA) ***351***
Elizabethtown Coll (PA) ***351***
Elmira Coll (NY) ***351***
Emmanuel Coll (MA) ***353***
The Evergreen State Coll (WA) ***355***
Fairleigh Dickinson U, Teaneck-Metro Campus (NJ) ***356***
Felician Coll (NJ) ***357***
Florida Inst of Technology (FL) ***360***
Florida State U (FL) ***361***
Fort Lewis Coll (CO) ***362***
Franklin and Marshall Coll (PA) ***363***
Furman U (SC) ***365***
Georgetown U (DC) ***366***
Georgian Court Coll (NJ) ***367***
Gettysburg Coll (PA) ***368***
Gonzaga U (WA) ***369***
Grinnell Coll (IA) ***373***
Grove City Coll (PA) ***373***
Gustavus Adolphus Coll (MN) ***374***
Hamilton Coll (NY) ***374***
Hampden-Sydney Coll (VA) ***374***
Hampshire Coll (MA) ***375***
Harding U (AR) ***375***
Hartwick Coll (NY) ***376***
Harvard U (MA) ***376***
Haverford Coll (PA) ***377***
Hobart and William Smith Colls (NY) ***380***
Hofstra U (NY) ***380***
Holy Family U (PA) ***380***
Hood Coll (MD) ***381***
Hope Coll (MI) ***381***
Humboldt State U (CA) ***382***
Idaho State U (ID) ***384***
Immaculata U (PA) ***385***
Indiana U Bloomington (IN) ***385***
Indiana U of Pennsylvania (PA) ***386***
Insto Tecno Estudios Sups Monterrey(Mexico) ***388***
Iona Coll (NY) ***390***
Iowa State U of Science and Technology (IA) ***390***

BIOCHEMISTRY (continued)

Ithaca Coll (NY) ***390***
Jamestown Coll (ND) ***391***
John Brown U (AR) ***392***
Juniata Coll (PA) ***395***
Kansas State U (KS) ***396***
Kenyon Coll (OH) ***398***
Keuka Coll (NY) ***398***
King Coll (TN) ***398***
Knox Coll (IL) ***399***
Lafayette Coll (PA) ***400***
LaGrange Coll (GA) ***400***
La Salle U (PA) ***402***
La Sierra U (CA) ***403***
Laurentian U (ON, Canada) ***403***
Lebanon Valley Coll (PA) ***403***
Lehigh U (PA) ***404***
Lehman Coll of the City U of NY (NY) ***404***
Le Moyne Coll (NY) ***404***
Lewis & Clark Coll (OR) ***405***
Lewis U (IL) ***406***
Lipscomb U (TN) ***408***
Loras Coll (IA) ***410***
Louisiana State U and A&M Coll (LA) ***410***
Loyola Marymount U (CA) ***411***
Loyola U Chicago (IL) ***411***
Madonna U (MI) ***414***
Maharishi U of Management (IA) ***414***
Manhattan Coll (NY) ***416***
Manhattanville Coll (NY) ***416***
Mansfield U of Pennsylvania (PA) ***416***
Marietta Coll (OH) ***417***
Marist Coll (NY) ***417***
Marlboro Coll (VT) ***418***
Marquette U (WI) ***418***
Mary Baldwin Coll (VA) ***419***
Maryville Coll (TN) ***420***
McDaniel Coll (MD) ***422***
McGill U (QC, Canada) ***423***
McMaster U (ON, Canada) ***423***
McMurry U (TX) ***423***
Memorial U of Newfoundland (NF, Canada) ***424***
Merrimack Coll (MA) ***426***
Messiah Coll (PA) ***426***
Miami U (OH) ***428***
Michigan State U (MI) ***428***
Michigan Technological U (MI) ***428***
Middlebury Coll (VT) ***429***
Mills Coll (CA) ***431***
Minnesota State U, Mankato (MN) ***431***
Mississippi State U (MS) ***432***
Montclair State U (NJ) ***435***
Mount Allison U (NB, Canada) ***437***
Mount Holyoke Coll (MA) ***438***
Mount St. Mary's Coll (CA) ***439***
Mount Saint Mary's Coll and Seminary (MD) ***439***
Muhlenberg Coll (PA) ***440***
Nazareth Coll of Rochester (NY) ***443***
Nebraska Wesleyan U (NE) ***443***
New Mexico State U (NM) ***446***
New York U (NY) ***447***
Niagara U (NY) ***447***
North Carolina State U (NC) ***449***
North Central Coll (IL) ***449***
North Dakota State U (ND) ***449***
Northeastern U (MA) ***450***
Northern Michigan U (MI) ***451***
Northwestern U (IL) ***453***
Notre Dame Coll (OH) ***455***
Notre Dame de Namur U (CA) ***455***
Oakland U (MI) ***456***
Oakwood Coll (AL) ***456***
Oberlin Coll (OH) ***456***
Occidental Coll (CA) ***457***
Ohio Northern U (OH) ***457***
The Ohio State U (OH) ***457***
Ohio U (OH) ***458***
Oklahoma Christian U (OK) ***459***
Oklahoma City U (OK) ***460***
Oklahoma State U (OK) ***460***
Old Dominion U (VA) ***460***
Olivet Coll (MI) ***461***
Olivet Nazarene U (IL) ***461***
Oral Roberts U (OK) ***461***
Oregon State U (OR) ***462***
Otterbein Coll (OH) ***462***
Pace U (NY) ***463***
Pacific Lutheran U (WA) ***463***
Pacific Union Coll (CA) ***464***
Penn State U Univ Park Campus (PA) ***468***
Philadelphia U (PA) ***469***
Plattsburgh State U of NY (NY) ***471***
Point Loma Nazarene U (CA) ***471***
Pomona Coll (CA) ***472***
Portland State U (OR) ***472***
Purdue U (IN) ***475***
Queens Coll of the City U of NY (NY) ***475***
Queen's U at Kingston (ON, Canada) ***476***
Queens U of Charlotte (NC) ***476***
Quinnipiac U (CT) ***476***
Ramapo Coll of New Jersey (NJ) ***477***
Reed Coll (OR) ***477***
Regis Coll (MA) ***478***
Regis U (CO) ***478***
Rensselaer Polytechnic Inst (NY) ***478***
Rhodes Coll (TN) ***479***
Rice U (TX) ***479***
The Richard Stockton Coll of New Jersey (NJ) ***479***
Rider U (NJ) ***480***
Ripon Coll (WI) ***480***
Roanoke Coll (VA) ***481***
Roberts Wesleyan Coll (NY) ***481***
Rochester Inst of Technology (NY) ***482***
Rockford Coll (IL) ***482***
Rosemont Coll (PA) ***484***
Russell Sage Coll (NY) ***484***
Sacred Heart U (CT) ***486***
Saginaw Valley State U (MI) ***486***
Saint Anselm Coll (NH) ***487***
St. Bonaventure U (NY) ***487***
St. Edward's U (TX) ***488***
St. John Fisher Coll (NY) ***489***
Saint John's U (MN) ***490***
Saint Joseph Coll (CT) ***490***
Saint Joseph's Coll (IN) ***490***
St. Lawrence U (NY) ***491***
St. Mary's U of San Antonio (TX) ***494***
Saint Michael's Coll (VT) ***494***
Saint Peter's Coll (NJ) ***495***
Saint Vincent Coll (PA) ***496***
Samford U (AL) ***497***
San Francisco State U (CA) ***498***
San Jose State U (CA) ***499***
Schreiner U (TX) ***501***
Scripps Coll (CA) ***501***
Seattle Pacific U (WA) ***501***
Seattle U (WA) ***501***
Seton Hall U (NJ) ***502***
Seton Hill U (PA) ***502***
Simmons Coll (MA) ***504***
Simon Fraser U (BC, Canada) ***505***
Simpson Coll (IA) ***505***
Skidmore Coll (NY) ***506***
Smith Coll (MA) ***506***
South Dakota State U (SD) ***507***
Southern Adventist U (TN) ***508***
Southern Connecticut State U (CT) ***509***
Southern Methodist U (TX) ***510***
Southern Oregon U (OR) ***510***
Southwestern Coll (KS) ***512***
Spelman Coll (GA) ***514***
Spring Arbor U (MI) ***514***
State U of NY at Albany (NY) ***514***
State U of NY at Binghamton (NY) ***515***
State U of NY at New Paltz (NY) ***515***
State U of NY Coll at Brockport (NY) ***515***
State U of NY Coll at Fredonia (NY) ***516***
State U of NY Coll at Geneseo (NY) ***516***
State U of NY Coll of Environ Sci and Forestry (NY) ***517***
Stetson U (FL) ***519***
Stevens Inst of Technology (NJ) ***519***
Stonehill Coll (MA) ***520***
Stony Brook U, State University of New York (NY) ***520***
Suffolk U (MA) ***520***
Susquehanna U (PA) ***521***
Swarthmore Coll (PA) ***521***
Sweet Briar Coll (VA) ***521***
Syracuse U (NY) ***521***
Temple U (PA) ***523***
Tennessee Technological U (TN) ***524***
Texas A&M U (TX) ***524***
Texas Christian U (TX) ***526***
Texas Tech U (TX) ***526***
Texas Wesleyan U (TX) ***526***
Towson U (MD) ***529***
Trent U (ON, Canada) ***529***
Trinity Coll (CT) ***530***
Trinity Coll (DC) ***530***
Trinity U (TX) ***531***
Tulane U (LA) ***533***
Union Coll (NE) ***534***
Union Coll (NY) ***534***
United States Air Force Academy (CO) ***534***
Université de Sherbrooke (QC, Canada) ***536***
U du Québec à Trois-Rivières (QC, Canada) ***536***
Université Laval (QC, Canada) ***536***
U at Buffalo, The State University of New York (NY) ***536***
U Coll of the Cariboo (BC, Canada) ***537***
U of Alberta (AB, Canada) ***538***
The U of Arizona (AZ) ***538***
The U of British Columbia (BC, Canada) ***540***
U of Calgary (AB, Canada) ***540***
U of Calif, Davis (CA) ***540***
U of Calif, Los Angeles (CA) ***541***
U of Calif, Riverside (CA) ***541***
U of Calif, San Diego (CA) ***541***
U of Calif, Santa Barbara (CA) ***541***
U of Calif, Santa Cruz (CA) ***542***
U of Chicago (IL) ***542***
U of Cincinnati (OH) ***543***
U of Colorado at Boulder (CO) ***543***
U of Dallas (TX) ***544***
U of Dayton (OH) ***544***
U of Delaware (DE) ***544***
U of Denver (CO) ***544***
U of Evansville (IN) ***545***
U of Georgia (GA) ***545***
U of Guelph (ON, Canada) ***546***
U of Hawaii at Manoa (HI) ***546***
U of Houston (TX) ***547***
U of Illinois at Chicago (IL) ***547***
U of Illinois at Urbana–Champaign (IL) ***548***
The U of Iowa (IA) ***548***
U of Kansas (KS) ***549***
U of King's Coll (NS, Canada) ***549***
The U of Lethbridge (AB, Canada) ***549***
U of Maine (ME) ***550***
U of Maryland, Baltimore County (MD) ***552***
U of Maryland, Coll Park (MD) ***552***
U of Massachusetts Amherst (MA) ***552***
U of Massachusetts Boston (MA) ***553***
U of Miami (FL) ***553***
U of Michigan (MI) ***554***
U of Michigan–Dearborn (MI) ***554***
U of Minnesota, Duluth (MN) ***554***
U of Minnesota, Twin Cities Campus (MN) ***555***
U of Missouri–Columbia (MO) ***555***
U of Missouri–St. Louis (MO) ***556***
The U of Montana–Missoula (MT) ***556***
U of Nebraska–Lincoln (NE) ***557***
U of Nevada, Las Vegas (NV) ***558***
U of Nevada, Reno (NV) ***558***
U of New Brunswick Fredericton (NB, Canada) ***558***
U of New England (ME) ***558***
U of New Hampshire (NH) ***558***
U of New Mexico (NM) ***559***
U of Northern Iowa (IA) ***561***
U of North Texas (TX) ***562***
U of Notre Dame (IN) ***562***
U of Oklahoma (OK) ***562***
U of Oregon (OR) ***562***
U of Ottawa (ON, Canada) ***563***
U of Pennsylvania (PA) ***563***
U of Regina (SK, Canada) ***572***
U of Rochester (NY) ***573***
U of St. Thomas (MN) ***573***
U of San Francisco (CA) ***574***
U of Saskatchewan (SK, Canada) ***574***
U of Southern California (CA) ***576***
The U of Tampa (FL) ***577***
The U of Tennessee (TN) ***577***
The U of Texas at Arlington (TX) ***577***
The U of Texas at Austin (TX) ***578***
U of the Pacific (CA) ***580***
U of the Sciences in Philadelphia (PA) ***580***
U of Toronto (ON, Canada) ***581***
U of Tulsa (OK) ***581***
U of Vermont (VT) ***582***
U of Victoria (BC, Canada) ***582***
U of Washington (WA) ***583***
U of Waterloo (ON, Canada) ***583***
The U of Western Ontario (ON, Canada) ***583***
U of Windsor (ON, Canada) ***584***
U of Wisconsin–Eau Claire (WI) ***584***
U of Wisconsin–Madison (WI) ***584***
U of Wisconsin–Milwaukee (WI) ***585***
U of Wisconsin–River Falls (WI) ***585***
Ursinus Coll (PA) ***587***
Vassar Coll (NY) ***589***
Virginia Polytechnic Inst and State U (VA) ***591***
Viterbo U (WI) ***591***
Warren Wilson Coll (NC) ***594***
Wartburg Coll (IA) ***594***
Washington State U (WA) ***595***
Washington U in St. Louis (MO) ***595***
Wellesley Coll (MA) ***597***
Wells Coll (NY) ***597***
Wesleyan U (CT) ***597***
West Chester U of Pennsylvania (PA) ***598***
Western Kentucky U (KY) ***599***
Western Michigan U (MI) ***599***
Western Washington U (WA) ***600***
Wheaton Coll (MA) ***603***
Whitman Coll (WA) ***604***
Whittier Coll (CA) ***604***
Wilkes U (PA) ***605***
William Jewell Coll (MO) ***606***
Wittenberg U (OH) ***608***
Worcester Polytechnic Inst (MA) ***609***
Xavier U of Louisiana (LA) ***610***

BIOENGINEERING

Overview: Students learn to apply mathematics, chemistry, and other scientific principles to a wide range of health products and systems, such as prostheses, information systems, artificial organs, and health care delivery systems. *Related majors:* biomedical technology, biotechnology, computer engineering, electrical and electronics engineering, environmental health engineering. *Potential careers:* computer engineer, medical device designer, researcher. *Salary potential:* \$37k-\$55k.

Arizona State U (AZ) ***271***
Auburn U (AL) ***276***
Boston U (MA) ***292***
Brown U (RI) ***296***
California State U, Long Beach (CA) ***301***
Carnegie Mellon U (PA) ***305***
Case Western Reserve U (OH) ***307***
The Catholic U of America (DC) ***307***
Cedar Crest Coll (PA) ***308***
Columbia U, School of Engineering & Applied Sci (NY) ***328***
Cornell U (NY) ***333***
Drexel U (PA) ***346***
Duke U (NC) ***346***
Eastern Nazarene Coll (MA) ***348***
Florida State U (FL) ***361***
Harvard U (MA) ***376***
Illinois Inst of Technology (IL) ***384***
Indiana U–Purdue U Indianapolis (IN) ***387***
Johns Hopkins U (MD) ***392***
LeTourneau U (TX) ***405***
Louisiana State U and A&M Coll (LA) ***410***
Louisiana Tech U (LA) ***410***
Marquette U (WI) ***418***
Massachusetts Inst of Technology (MA) ***421***
Mercer U (GA) ***425***
Michigan State U (MI) ***428***
Milwaukee School of Engineering (WI) ***431***
Mississippi State U (MS) ***432***
New Jersey Inst of Technology (NJ) ***445***
North Dakota State U (ND) ***449***
Northwestern U (IL) ***453***
Oklahoma State U (OK) ***460***
Oral Roberts U (OK) ***461***
Penn State U Univ Park Campus (PA) ***468***
Rensselaer Polytechnic Inst (NY) ***478***
Rice U (TX) ***479***
Saint Louis U (MO) ***492***
Stevens Inst of Technology (NJ) ***519***
Stony Brook U, State University of New York (NY) ***520***
Syracuse U (NY) ***521***
Texas A&M U (TX) ***524***
Trinity Coll (CT) ***530***
Trinity Coll (DC) ***530***
Tulane U (LA) ***533***
The U of Akron (OH) ***537***
The U of Alabama at Birmingham (AL) ***537***
The U of British Columbia (BC, Canada) ***540***
U of Calif, Berkeley (CA) ***540***
U of Calif, Davis (CA) ***540***
U of Calif, San Diego (CA) ***541***

U of Central Oklahoma (OK) **542**
U of Connecticut (CT) **544**
U of Guelph (ON, Canada) **546**
U of Hartford (CT) **546**
U of Idaho (ID) **547**
U of Illinois at Chicago (IL) **547**
U of Illinois at Urbana–Champaign (IL) **548**
The U of Iowa (IA) **548**
U of Miami (FL) **553**
U of Missouri–Columbia (MO) **555**
U of Nebraska–Lincoln (NE) **557**
U of Pennsylvania (PA) **563**
U of Pittsburgh (PA) **569**
U of Rhode Island (RI) **572**
U of Rochester (NY) **573**
U of Southern California (CA) **576**
The U of Texas at Austin (TX) **578**
U of the Pacific (CA) **580**
U of Toledo (OH) **581**
U of Toronto (ON, Canada) **581**
U of Wisconsin–Madison (WI) **584**
Vanderbilt U (TN) **588**
Virginia Commonwealth U (VA) **590**
Walla Walla Coll (WA) **593**
Washington U in St. Louis (MO) **595**
Western New England Coll (MA) **600**
Worcester Polytechnic Inst (MA) **609**
Wright State U (OH) **609**
Yale U (CT) **610**

BIOLOGICAL/PHYSICAL SCIENCES

Overview: This major is a combination of one or more of the biological and physical sciences or an area of study that draws from the biological and physical sciences. *Related majors:* biochemistry, biophysics, biotechnology research, genetics, molecular biology. *Potential careers:* biochemist, research scientist, chemical engineer. *Salary potential:* $35k-$45k.

Adams State Coll (CO) **260**
Adelphi U (NY) **260**
Alfred U (NY) **263**
Alice Lloyd Coll (KY) **263**
Alma Coll (MI) **264**
Alvernia Coll (PA) **265**
Antioch Coll (OH) **269**
Athabasca U (AB, Canada) **275**
Atlantic Union Coll (MA) **276**
Augsburg Coll (MN) **276**
Averett U (VA) **278**
Bard Coll (NY) **281**
Bayamón Central U (PR) **283**
Belmont U (TN) **284**
Bemidji State U (MN) **285**
Benedictine Coll (KS) **285**
Bennington Coll (VT) **286**
Bishop's U (QC, Canada) **289**
Bluefield State Coll (WV) **291**
Brescia U (KY) **293**
Brock U (ON, Canada) **295**
Buena Vista U (IA) **297**
California State U, Fresno (CA) **301**
California U of Pennsylvania (PA) **302**
Calvin Coll (MI) **303**
Cameron U (OK) **303**
Carleton U (ON, Canada) **305**
Case Western Reserve U (OH) **307**
Castleton State Coll (VT) **307**
Cedar Crest Coll (PA) **308**
Cedarville U (OH) **308**
Cheyney U of Pennsylvania (PA) **312**
Chowan Coll (NC) **312**
Clarion U of Pennsylvania (PA) **315**
Coe Coll (IA) **318**
Coll of Santa Fe (NM) **323**
Coll of the Atlantic (ME) **323**
Concordia U (IL) **330**
Concordia U (MI) **330**
Concordia U (OR) **330**
Delta State U (MS) **339**
Dowling Coll (NY) **345**
Drexel U (PA) **346**
Eastern Michigan U (MI) **348**
Eastern Nazarene Coll (MA) **348**
Eastern Oregon U (OR) **349**
Eastern Washington U (WA) **349**
Edinboro U of Pennsylvania (PA) **351**
Erskine Coll (SC) **354**
Eureka Coll (IL) **355**
The Evergreen State Coll (WA) **355**
Fairleigh Dickinson U, Teaneck-Metro Campus (NJ) **356**
Fordham U (NY) **362**
Fort Hays State U (KS) **362**
Framingham State Coll (MA) **362**
Freed-Hardeman U (TN) **364**
Gannon U (PA) **365**
Georgia Southwestern State U (GA) **368**
Gettysburg Coll (PA) **368**
Goddard Coll (VT) **369**
Grand Valley State U (MI) **371**
Grand View Coll (IA) **372**
Grinnell Coll (IA) **373**
Hampshire Coll (MA) **375**
Harding U (AR) **375**
Harvard U (MA) **376**
Hofstra U (NY) **380**
Houghton Coll (NY) **381**
Huntington Coll (IN) **383**
Indiana U Kokomo (IN) **386**
Indiana U of Pennsylvania (PA) **386**
Iowa Wesleyan Coll (IA) **390**
John Carroll U (OH) **392**
Johns Hopkins U (MD) **392**
Johnson C. Smith U (NC) **394**
Judson Coll (IL) **395**
Juniata Coll (PA) **395**
King Coll (TN) **398**
King's Coll (PA) **398**
Kutztown U of Pennsylvania (PA) **399**
Lakehead U (ON, Canada) **400**
Lees-McRae Coll (NC) **404**
Lee U (TN) **404**
Le Moyne Coll (NY) **404**
Lewis-Clark State Coll (ID) **406**
Lock Haven U of Pennsylvania (PA) **408**
Long Island U, Brooklyn Campus (NY) **409**
Louisiana State U in Shreveport (LA) **410**
Lyndon State Coll (VT) **413**
Madonna U (MI) **414**
Mansfield U of Pennsylvania (PA) **416**
Marian Coll of Fond du Lac (WI) **417**
Mars Hill Coll (NC) **418**
Marygrove Coll (MI) **419**
Marymount Coll of Fordham U (NY) **419**
Maryville U of Saint Louis (MO) **420**
Massachusetts Coll of Liberal Arts (MA) **421**
The Master's Coll and Seminary (CA) **422**
McMaster U (ON, Canada) **423**
Memorial U of Newfoundland (NF, Canada) **424**
Methodist Coll (NC) **427**
Michigan State U (MI) **428**
Middlebury Coll (VT) **429**
Middle Tennessee State U (TN) **429**
Midland Lutheran Coll (NE) **429**
Milligan Coll (TN) **430**
Minnesota State U, Mankato (MN) **431**
Mississippi State U (MS) **432**
Montana State U–Northern (MT) **434**
Montana Tech of The U of Montana (MT) **435**
Mount Allison U (NB, Canada) **437**
Mount Saint Vincent U (NS, Canada) **439**
Mount Vernon Nazarene U (OH) **440**
National-Louis U (IL) **442**
Nebraska Wesleyan U (NE) **443**
New Mexico Inst of Mining and Technology (NM) **446**
Northern State U (SD) **451**
Northland Coll (WI) **452**
North Park U (IL) **452**
Northwestern U (IL) **453**
Northwest Missouri State U (MO) **454**
Oakland City U (IN) **456**
Oklahoma Baptist U (OK) **459**
Oklahoma Christian U (OK) **459**
Oklahoma City U (OK) **460**
Oklahoma Panhandle State U (OK) **460**
Oklahoma Wesleyan U (OK) **460**
Olivet Nazarene U (IL) **461**
Oregon State U (OR) **462**
Palmer Coll of Chiropractic (IA) **465**
Penn State U Abington Coll (PA) **467**
Penn State U Berks Cmps of Berks-Lehigh Valley Coll (PA) **468**
Penn State U Univ Park Campus (PA) **468**
Peru State Coll (NE) **469**
Pillsbury Baptist Bible Coll (MN) **470**
Point Park Coll (PA) **471**
Pontifical Catholic U of Puerto Rico (PR) **472**
Portland State U (OR) **472**
Purdue U (IN) **475**
Purdue U Calumet (IN) **475**
Quinnipiac U (CT) **476**
Rensselaer Polytechnic Inst (NY) **478**
Rhode Island Coll (RI) **479**
Roberts Wesleyan Coll (NY) **481**
Rochester Coll (MI) **482**
Rochester Inst of Technology (NY) **482**
Rockford Coll (IL) **482**
Rocky Mountain Coll (MT) **482**
Saginaw Valley State U (MI) **486**
Saint Anselm Coll (NH) **487**
St. Francis Xavier U (NS, Canada) **489**
Saint Mary-of-the-Woods Coll (IN) **493**
St. Norbert Coll (WI) **495**
Saint Peter's Coll (NJ) **495**
Saint Xavier U (IL) **496**
San Francisco State U (CA) **498**
Santa Clara U (CA) **499**
Sarah Lawrence Coll (NY) **499**
Seattle U (WA) **501**
Shawnee State U (OH) **502**
Sierra Nevada Coll (NV) **504**
Simon Fraser U (BC, Canada) **505**
Simpson Coll (IA) **505**
Southeast Missouri State U (MO) **508**
Southern Arkansas U–Magnolia (AR) **509**
Southern Nazarene U (OK) **510**
State U of NY Coll at Fredonia (NY) **516**
State U of NY Coll of Environ Sci and Forestry (NY) **517**
State U of NY Empire State Coll (NY) **517**
Tabor Coll (KS) **522**
Tennessee Temple U (TN) **524**
Texas A&M U (TX) **524**
Texas Tech U (TX) **526**
Towson U (MD) **529**
Trent U (ON, Canada) **529**
Trevecca Nazarene U (TN) **529**
Trinity Western U (BC, Canada) **531**
Union Coll (NY) **534**
Union U (TN) **534**
United States Air Force Academy (CO) **534**
United States Military Academy (NY) **535**
The U of Akron (OH) **537**
The U of Alabama (AL) **537**
The U of Alabama at Birmingham (AL) **537**
U of Alaska Anchorage (AK) **538**
U of Alaska Fairbanks (AK) **538**
U of Alberta (AB, Canada) **538**
U of Central Arkansas (AR) **542**
U of Charleston (WV) **542**
U of Denver (CO) **544**
U of Dubuque (IA) **545**
The U of Findlay (OH) **545**
U of Georgia (GA) **545**
U of Guelph (ON, Canada) **546**
U of Houston–Clear Lake (TX) **547**
U of Houston–Downtown (TX) **547**
U of Kansas (KS) **549**
U of La Verne (CA) **549**
The U of Lethbridge (AB, Canada) **549**
The U of Maine at Augusta (ME) **550**
U of Mary (ND) **551**
U of Massachusetts Amherst (MA) **552**
U of Michigan–Dearborn (MI) **554**
U of Mobile (AL) **556**
U of Nebraska at Omaha (NE) **557**
U of New Brunswick Fredericton (NB, Canada) **558**
U of New Hampshire (NH) **558**
U of New Orleans (LA) **559**
U of Northern Iowa (IA) **561**
U of North Florida (FL) **561**
U of Oregon (OR) **562**
U of Ottawa (ON, Canada) **563**
U of Pittsburgh (PA) **569**
U of Puerto Rico, Río Piedras (PR) **571**
U of Regina (SK, Canada) **572**
U of Rochester (NY) **573**
U of Saint Francis (IN) **573**
U of Southern Indiana (IN) **576**
U of South Florida (FL) **576**
The U of Texas at San Antonio (TX) **578**
U of Toledo (OH) **581**
U of Toronto (ON, Canada) **581**
U of Waterloo (ON, Canada) **583**
The U of Western Ontario (ON, Canada) **583**
U of West Florida (FL) **583**
U of Windsor (ON, Canada) **584**
U of Wisconsin–Platteville (WI) **585**
U of Wisconsin–Superior (WI) **586**
U of Wisconsin–Whitewater (WI) **586**
Upper Iowa U (IA) **587**
Vanguard U of Southern California (CA) **589**
Villa Julie Coll (MD) **590**
Virginia Commonwealth U (VA) **590**
Virginia Wesleyan Coll (VA) **591**
Walsh U (OH) **593**
Warner Pacific Coll (OR) **593**
Washington State U (WA) **595**
Washington U in St. Louis (MO) **595**
Wayland Baptist U (TX) **595**
West Chester U of Pennsylvania (PA) **598**
Western New Mexico U (NM) **600**
Western Washington U (WA) **600**
William Carey Coll (MS) **605**
Wilmington Coll (OH) **607**
Winona State U (MN) **608**
Wittenberg U (OH) **608**
Worcester State Coll (MA) **609**
Xavier U (OH) **610**
York Coll (NE) **610**
York U (ON, Canada) **611**
Youngstown State U (OH) **611**

BIOLOGICAL SCIENCES/LIFE SCIENCES RELATED

Information can be found under this major's main heading.

Arizona State U (AZ) **271**
Boston U (MA) **292**
Brandeis U (MA) **293**
Canisius Coll (NY) **304**
Guilford Coll (NC) **373**
Holy Names Coll (CA) **381**
Kent State U (OH) **397**
Loras Coll (IA) **410**
Louisiana State U and A&M Coll (LA) **410**
National U (CA) **442**
Park U (MO) **465**
Rochester Inst of Technology (NY) **482**
Skidmore Coll (NY) **506**
Swarthmore Coll (PA) **521**
Texas Wesleyan U (TX) **526**
U of Nebraska–Lincoln (NE) **557**
U of North Alabama (AL) **559**
U of Wisconsin–Parkside (WI) **585**
Ursuline Coll (OH) **587**
Washington U in St. Louis (MO) **595**

BIOLOGICAL SPECIALIZATIONS RELATED

Information can be found under this major's main heading.

Arizona State U (AZ) **271**
King Coll (TN) **398**
Marymount U (VA) **420**
Marywood U (PA) **421**
Okanagan U Coll (BC, Canada) **459**
Saint Mary's U of Minnesota (MN) **494**
U of Hawaii at Manoa (HI) **546**
U of Louisiana at Lafayette (LA) **550**
Utah State U (UT) **587**
Wilson Coll (PA) **607**

BIOLOGICAL TECHNOLOGY

Overview: Students who choose this major will learn the scientific principles and technical skills in order to support biotechnologists in their research. *Related majors:* biology, biochemistry, cell and molecular biology, biotechnology research. *Potential careers:* lab technician, hazardous materials safety manager, pharmaceutical company sales rep, researcher, biologist. *Salary potential:* $28k-$38k.

British Columbia Inst of Technology (BC, Canada) **295**
California State Polytechnic U, Pomona (CA) **300**
Carleton U (ON, Canada) **305**
Harvard U (MA) **376**
McMaster U (ON, Canada) **423**
Michigan Technological U (MI) **428**
Minnesota State U, Mankato (MN) **431**
Niagara U (NY) **447**

BIOLOGICAL TECHNOLOGY (continued)

Northeastern U (MA) **450**
Penn State U Univ Park Campus (PA) **468**
Purdue U Calumet (IN) **475**
St. Cloud State U (MN) **488**
Salem International U (WV) **496**
State U of NY Coll at Brockport (NY) **515**
State U of NY Coll at Fredonia (NY) **516**
State U of NY Coll at Oneonta (NY) **517**
Suffolk U (MA) **520**
Université de Sherbrooke (QC, Canada) **536**
U of Alberta (AB, Canada) **538**
U of Delaware (DE) **544**
U of Missouri–St. Louis (MO) **556**
U of Nebraska at Omaha (NE) **557**
U of New Haven (CT) **559**
U of Ottawa (ON, Canada) **563**
U of Windsor (ON, Canada) **584**
Villa Julie Coll (MD) **590**
Westminster Coll (PA) **601**
Worcester Polytechnic Inst (MA) **609**
Worcester State Coll (MA) **609**
York Coll of the City U of New York (NY) **611**

BIOLOGY

Overview: Those who choose this broad based major study the processes that are fundamental to all forms of life. *Related majors:* biochemistry, anatomy, nutritional sciences, premedicine studies, ecology. *Potential careers:* biologist, physician, research scientist, environmentalist, ecologist. *Salary potential:* $25k-$40k.

Abilene Christian U (TX) **260**
Acadia U (NS, Canada) **260**
Adams State Coll (CO) **260**
Adelphi U (NY) **260**
Adrian Coll (MI) **260**
Agnes Scott Coll (GA) **261**
Alabama A&M U (AL) **261**
Alabama State U (AL) **261**
Albany State U (GA) **262**
Albertson Coll of Idaho (ID) **262**
Albertus Magnus Coll (CT) **262**
Albion Coll (MI) **262**
Albright Coll (PA) **263**
Alcorn State U (MS) **263**
Alderson-Broaddus Coll (WV) **263**
Alfred U (NY) **263**
Alice Lloyd Coll (KY) **263**
Allegheny Coll (PA) **264**
Allen U (SC) **264**
Alma Coll (MI) **264**
Alvernia Coll (PA) **265**
Alverno Coll (WI) **265**
American International Coll (MA) **267**
American U (DC) **267**
The American U in Cairo(Egypt) **267**
Amherst Coll (MA) **268**
Anderson Coll (SC) **268**
Anderson U (IN) **268**
Andrews U (MI) **269**
Angelo State U (TX) **269**
Anna Maria Coll (MA) **269**
Antioch Coll (OH) **269**
Appalachian State U (NC) **270**
Aquinas Coll (MI) **270**
Arcadia U (PA) **271**
Arizona State U (AZ) **271**
Arizona State U West (AZ) **272**
Arkansas State U (AR) **272**
Arkansas Tech U (AR) **272**
Armstrong Atlantic State U (GA) **273**
Asbury Coll (KY) **274**
Ashland U (OH) **274**
Assumption Coll (MA) **275**
Athens State U (AL) **275**
Atlantic Baptist U (NB, Canada) **275**
Atlantic Union Coll (MA) **276**
Auburn U (AL) **276**
Auburn U Montgomery (AL) **276**
Augsburg Coll (MN) **276**
Augustana Coll (IL) **276**
Augustana Coll (SD) **276**
Augusta State U (GA) **277**
Aurora U (IL) **277**
Austin Coll (TX) **277**
Austin Peay State U (TN) **278**
Averett U (VA) **278**
Avila U (MO) **278**
Azusa Pacific U (CA) **278**
Baker U (KS) **280**
Baldwin-Wallace Coll (OH) **280**
Ball State U (IN) **280**
Barber-Scotia Coll (NC) **281**
Bard Coll (NY) **281**
Barnard Coll (NY) **282**
Barry U (FL) **282**
Barton Coll (NC) **282**
Bates Coll (ME) **282**
Bayamón Central U (PR) **283**
Baylor U (TX) **283**
Belhaven Coll (MS) **283**
Bellarmine U (KY) **284**
Belmont Abbey Coll (NC) **284**
Belmont U (TN) **284**
Beloit Coll (WI) **285**
Bemidji State U (MN) **285**
Benedict Coll (SC) **285**
Benedictine Coll (KS) **285**
Benedictine U (IL) **285**
Bennett Coll (NC) **286**
Bennington Coll (VT) **286**
Berea Coll (KY) **286**
Berry Coll (GA) **287**
Bethany Coll (KS) **287**
Bethany Coll (WV) **287**
Bethany Lutheran Coll (MN) **288**
Bethel Coll (IN) **288**
Bethel Coll (KS) **288**
Bethel Coll (MN) **288**
Bethel Coll (TN) **288**
Bethune-Cookman Coll (FL) **289**
Biola U (CA) **289**
Birmingham-Southern Coll (AL) **289**
Bishop's U (QC, Canada) **289**
Blackburn Coll (IL) **290**
Black Hills State U (SD) **290**
Bloomfield Coll (NJ) **290**
Bloomsburg U of Pennsylvania (PA) **290**
Bluefield Coll (VA) **291**
Blue Mountain Coll (MS) **291**
Bluffton Coll (OH) **291**
Boston Coll (MA) **292**
Boston U (MA) **292**
Bowdoin Coll (ME) **292**
Bowie State U (MD) **292**
Bowling Green State U (OH) **292**
Bradley U (IL) **293**
Brandeis U (MA) **293**
Brandon U (MB, Canada) **293**
Brenau U (GA) **293**
Brescia U (KY) **293**
Brewton-Parker Coll (GA) **294**
Briar Cliff U (IA) **294**
Bridgewater Coll (VA) **294**
Bridgewater State Coll (MA) **294**
Brigham Young U (UT) **295**
Brigham Young U–Hawaii (HI) **295**
Brock U (ON, Canada) **295**
Brooklyn Coll of the City U of NY (NY) **295**
Brown U (RI) **296**
Bryan Coll (TN) **296**
Bryn Athyn Coll of the New Church (PA) **297**
Bryn Mawr Coll (PA) **297**
Bucknell U (PA) **297**
Buena Vista U (IA) **297**
Butler U (IN) **297**
Cabrini Coll (PA) **298**
Caldwell Coll (NJ) **298**
California Baptist U (CA) **298**
California Inst of Technology (CA) **299**
California Lutheran U (CA) **299**
California Polytechnic State U, San Luis Obispo (CA) **300**
California State Polytechnic U, Pomona (CA) **300**
California State U, Bakersfield (CA) **300**
California State U, Chico (CA) **300**
California State U, Dominguez Hills (CA) **300**
California State U, Fresno (CA) **301**
California State U, Fullerton (CA) **301**
California State U, Hayward (CA) **301**
California State U, Long Beach (CA) **301**
California State U, Northridge (CA) **301**
California State U, Sacramento (CA) **301**
California State U, San Bernardino (CA) **302**
California State U, San Marcos (CA) **302**
California State U, Stanislaus (CA) **302**
California U of Pennsylvania (PA) **302**
Calvin Coll (MI) **303**
Cameron U (OK) **303**
Campbellsville U (KY) **303**
Campbell U (NC) **303**
Canisius Coll (NY) **304**
Capital U (OH) **304**
Cardinal Stritch U (WI) **305**
Carleton Coll (MN) **305**
Carleton U (ON, Canada) **305**
Carlow Coll (PA) **305**
Carnegie Mellon U (PA) **305**
Carroll Coll (MT) **306**
Carroll Coll (WI) **306**
Carson-Newman Coll (TN) **306**
Carthage Coll (WI) **306**
Case Western Reserve U (OH) **307**
Castleton State Coll (VT) **307**
Catawba Coll (NC) **307**
The Catholic U of America (DC) **307**
Cedar Crest Coll (PA) **308**
Cedarville U (OH) **308**
Centenary Coll (NJ) **308**
Centenary Coll of Louisiana (LA) **308**
Central Coll (IA) **309**
Central Connecticut State U (CT) **309**
Central Methodist Coll (MO) **309**
Central Michigan U (MI) **310**
Central Missouri State U (MO) **310**
Central Washington U (WA) **310**
Centre Coll (KY) **310**
Chadron State Coll (NE) **311**
Chaminade U of Honolulu (HI) **311**
Chapman U (CA) **311**
Charleston Southern U (SC) **311**
Chatham Coll (PA) **312**
Chestnut Hill Coll (PA) **312**
Cheyney U of Pennsylvania (PA) **312**
Chowan Coll (NC) **312**
Christian Brothers U (TN) **313**
Christian Heritage Coll (CA) **313**
Christopher Newport U (VA) **313**
Citadel, The Military Coll of South Carolina (SC) **314**
City Coll of the City U of NY (NY) **314**
Claflin U (SC) **314**
Claremont McKenna Coll (CA) **315**
Clarion U of Pennsylvania (PA) **315**
Clark Atlanta U (GA) **315**
Clarke Coll (IA) **315**
Clarkson U (NY) **316**
Clark U (MA) **316**
Clearwater Christian Coll (FL) **316**
Clemson U (SC) **317**
Cleveland State U (OH) **317**
Coastal Carolina U (SC) **318**
Coe Coll (IA) **318**
Coker Coll (SC) **318**
Colby Coll (ME) **318**
Colby-Sawyer Coll (NH) **319**
Colgate U (NY) **319**
Coll Misericordia (PA) **319**
Coll of Charleston (SC) **320**
Coll of Mount St. Joseph (OH) **320**
Coll of Mount Saint Vincent (NY) **320**
The Coll of New Jersey (NJ) **320**
The Coll of New Rochelle (NY) **321**
Coll of Notre Dame of Maryland (MD) **321**
Coll of Saint Benedict (MN) **321**
Coll of St. Catherine (MN) **321**
Coll of Saint Elizabeth (NJ) **321**
Coll of Saint Mary (NE) **322**
The Coll of Saint Rose (NY) **322**
The Coll of St. Scholastica (MN) **322**
Coll of Santa Fe (NM) **323**
The Coll of Southeastern Europe, The American U of Athens(Greece) **323**
Coll of Staten Island of the City U of NY (NY) **323**
Coll of the Atlantic (ME) **323**
Coll of the Holy Cross (MA) **323**
Coll of the Ozarks (MO) **323**
Coll of the Southwest (NM) **324**
The Coll of William and Mary (VA) **324**
The Coll of Wooster (OH) **324**
Colorado Christian U (CO) **325**
The Colorado Coll (CO) **325**
Colorado State U (CO) **325**
Colorado State U-Pueblo (CO) **325**
Columbia Coll (MO) **326**
Columbia Coll (NY) **326**
Columbia Coll (SC) **327**
Columbia Union Coll (MD) **328**
Columbia U, School of General Studies (NY) **328**
Columbus State U (GA) **328**
Concord Coll (WV) **329**
Concordia Coll (MN) **329**
Concordia Coll (NY) **329**
Concordia U (CA) **330**
Concordia U (IL) **330**
Concordia U (MI) **330**
Concordia U (MN) **330**
Concordia U (NE) **330**
Concordia U (OR) **330**
Concordia U (QC, Canada) **331**
Concordia U at Austin (TX) **331**
Concordia U Coll of Alberta (AB, Canada) **331**
Concordia U Wisconsin (WI) **331**
Connecticut Coll (CT) **331**
Converse Coll (SC) **332**
Cornell Coll (IA) **332**
Cornell U (NY) **333**
Cornerstone U (MI) **333**
Covenant Coll (GA) **333**
Creighton U (NE) **333**
Crichton Coll (TN) **334**
Culver-Stockton Coll (MO) **334**
Cumberland Coll (KY) **335**
Cumberland U (TN) **335**
Curry Coll (MA) **335**
Daemen Coll (NY) **335**
Dakota State U (SD) **335**
Dakota Wesleyan U (SD) **336**
Dalhousie U (NS, Canada) **336**
Dallas Baptist U (TX) **336**
Dana Coll (NE) **337**
Dartmouth Coll (NH) **337**
Davidson Coll (NC) **338**
Davis & Elkins Coll (WV) **338**
Defiance Coll (OH) **338**
Delaware State U (DE) **338**
Delaware Valley Coll (PA) **339**
Delta State U (MS) **339**
Denison U (OH) **339**
DePaul U (IL) **339**
DePauw U (IN) **339**
DeSales U (PA) **340**
Dickinson Coll (PA) **344**
Dickinson State U (ND) **344**
Dillard U (LA) **344**
Doane Coll (NE) **344**
Dominican Coll (NY) **344**
Dominican U (IL) **345**
Dominican U of California (CA) **345**
Dordt Coll (IA) **345**
Dowling Coll (NY) **345**
Drake U (IA) **345**
Drew U (NJ) **346**
Drexel U (PA) **346**
Drury U (MO) **346**
Duke U (NC) **346**
Duquesne U (PA) **346**
D'Youville Coll (NY) **347**
Earlham Coll (IN) **347**
East Carolina U (NC) **347**
East Central U (OK) **347**
Eastern Connecticut State U (CT) **347**
Eastern Illinois U (IL) **348**
Eastern Kentucky U (KY) **348**
Eastern Mennonite U (VA) **348**
Eastern Michigan U (MI) **348**
Eastern Nazarene Coll (MA) **348**
Eastern New Mexico U (NM) **349**
Eastern Oregon U (OR) **349**
Eastern U (PA) **349**
Eastern Washington U (WA) **349**
East Stroudsburg U of Pennsylvania (PA) **349**
East Tennessee State U (TN) **349**
East Texas Baptist U (TX) **350**
East-West U (IL) **350**
Eckerd Coll (FL) **350**
Edgewood Coll (WI) **351**
Edinboro U of Pennsylvania (PA) **351**
Elizabeth City State U (NC) **351**
Elizabethtown Coll (PA) **351**
Elmhurst Coll (IL) **351**
Elmira Coll (NY) **351**
Elms Coll (MA) **352**
Elon U (NC) **352**
Emmanuel Coll (MA) **353**
Emory & Henry Coll (VA) **353**
Emory U (GA) **354**
Emporia State U (KS) **354**
Erskine Coll (SC) **354**
Eureka Coll (IL) **355**
Evangel U (MO) **355**
The Evergreen State Coll (WA) **355**
Excelsior Coll (NY) **356**

Fairfield U (CT) ***356***
Fairleigh Dickinson U, Florham (NJ) ***356***
Fairleigh Dickinson U, Teaneck-Metro Campus (NJ) ***356***
Fairmont State Coll (WV) ***356***
Faulkner U (AL) ***357***
Fayetteville State U (NC) ***357***
Felician Coll (NJ) ***357***
Ferris State U (MI) ***358***
Ferrum Coll (VA) ***358***
Fisk U (TN) ***358***
Fitchburg State Coll (MA) ***358***
Florida A&M U (FL) ***359***
Florida Atlantic U (FL) ***359***
Florida Inst of Technology (FL) ***360***
Florida International U (FL) ***360***
Florida Southern Coll (FL) ***361***
Florida State U (FL) ***361***
Fontbonne U (MO) ***361***
Fordham U (NY) ***362***
Fort Hays State U (KS) ***362***
Fort Lewis Coll (CO) ***362***
Fort Valley State U (GA) ***362***
Framingham State Coll (MA) ***362***
The Franciscan U (IA) ***363***
Franciscan U of Steubenville (OH) ***363***
Francis Marion U (SC) ***363***
Franklin and Marshall Coll (PA) ***363***
Franklin Coll (IN) ***363***
Franklin Pierce Coll (NH) ***364***
Freed-Hardeman U (TN) ***364***
Fresno Pacific U (CA) ***364***
Frostburg State U (MD) ***365***
Furman U (SC) ***365***
Gallaudet U (DC) ***365***
Gannon U (PA) ***365***
Gardner-Webb U (NC) ***365***
Geneva Coll (PA) ***366***
George Fox U (OR) ***366***
George Mason U (VA) ***366***
Georgetown Coll (KY) ***366***
Georgetown U (DC) ***366***
The George Washington U (DC) ***367***
Georgia Coll & State U (GA) ***367***
Georgia Inst of Technology (GA) ***367***
Georgian Court Coll (NJ) ***367***
Georgia Southern U (GA) ***367***
Georgia Southwestern State U (GA) ***368***
Georgia State U (GA) ***368***
Gettysburg Coll (PA) ***368***
Glenville State Coll (WV) ***368***
Goddard Coll (VT) ***369***
Gonzaga U (WA) ***369***
Gordon Coll (MA) ***370***
Goshen Coll (IN) ***370***
Goucher Coll (MD) ***370***
Governors State U (IL) ***370***
Grace Coll (IN) ***370***
Graceland U (IA) ***371***
Grambling State U (LA) ***371***
Grand Canyon U (AZ) ***371***
Grand Valley State U (MI) ***371***
Grand View Coll (IA) ***372***
Green Mountain Coll (VT) ***372***
Greensboro Coll (NC) ***372***
Greenville Coll (IL) ***373***
Grinnell Coll (IA) ***373***
Grove City Coll (PA) ***373***
Guilford Coll (NC) ***373***
Gustavus Adolphus Coll (MN) ***374***
Gwynedd-Mercy Coll (PA) ***374***
Hamilton Coll (NY) ***374***
Hamline U (MN) ***374***
Hampden-Sydney Coll (VA) ***374***
Hampshire Coll (MA) ***375***
Hampton U (VA) ***375***
Hannibal-LaGrange Coll (MO) ***375***
Hanover Coll (IN) ***375***
Harding U (AR) ***375***
Hardin-Simmons U (TX) ***376***
Hartwick Coll (NY) ***376***
Harvard U (MA) ***376***
Harvey Mudd Coll (CA) ***377***
Hastings Coll (NE) ***377***
Haverford Coll (PA) ***377***
Hawai'i Pacific U (HI) ***377***
Heidelberg Coll (OH) ***377***
Henderson State U (AR) ***378***
Hendrix Coll (AR) ***378***
High Point U (NC) ***379***
Hillsdale Coll (MI) ***379***
Hiram Coll (OH) ***379***
Hobart and William Smith Colls (NY) ***380***
Hofstra U (NY) ***380***
Hollins U (VA) ***380***
Holy Family U (PA) ***380***
Hood Coll (MD) ***381***
Hope Coll (MI) ***381***
Houghton Coll (NY) ***381***
Houston Baptist U (TX) ***382***
Howard Payne U (TX) ***382***
Howard U (DC) ***382***
Humboldt State U (CA) ***382***
Hunter Coll of the City U of NY (NY) ***382***
Huntingdon Coll (AL) ***383***
Huntington Coll (IN) ***383***
Husson Coll (ME) ***383***
Huston-Tillotson Coll (TX) ***383***
Idaho State U (ID) ***384***
Illinois Coll (IL) ***384***
Illinois Inst of Technology (IL) ***384***
Illinois State U (IL) ***384***
Illinois Wesleyan U (IL) ***385***
Immaculata U (PA) ***385***
Indiana State U (IN) ***385***
Indiana U Bloomington (IN) ***385***
Indiana U East (IN) ***386***
Indiana U Kokomo (IN) ***386***
Indiana U Northwest (IN) ***386***
Indiana U of Pennsylvania (PA) ***386***
Indiana U–Purdue U Fort Wayne (IN) ***386***
Indiana U–Purdue U Indianapolis (IN) ***387***
Indiana U South Bend (IN) ***387***
Indiana U Southeast (IN) ***387***
Indiana Wesleyan U (IN) ***387***
Inter American U of PR, Aguadilla Campus (PR) ***388***
Inter American U of PR, San Germán Campus (PR) ***388***
Iona Coll (NY) ***390***
Iowa State U of Science and Technology (IA) ***390***
Iowa Wesleyan Coll (IA) ***390***
Ithaca Coll (NY) ***390***
Jackson State U (MS) ***390***
Jacksonville State U (AL) ***390***
Jacksonville U (FL) ***391***
James Madison U (VA) ***391***
Jamestown Coll (ND) ***391***
John Brown U (AR) ***392***
John Carroll U (OH) ***392***
Johns Hopkins U (MD) ***392***
Johnson C. Smith U (NC) ***394***
Johnson State Coll (VT) ***394***
Judson Coll (AL) ***395***
Judson Coll (IL) ***395***
Juniata Coll (PA) ***395***
Kalamazoo Coll (MI) ***395***
Kansas State U (KS) ***396***
Kean U (NJ) ***396***
Keene State Coll (NH) ***396***
Kennesaw State U (GA) ***397***
Kent State U (OH) ***397***
Kentucky State U (KY) ***397***
Kentucky Wesleyan Coll (KY) ***397***
Kenyon Coll (OH) ***398***
Keuka Coll (NY) ***398***
King Coll (TN) ***398***
King's Coll (PA) ***398***
The King's U Coll (AB, Canada) ***399***
Knox Coll (IL) ***399***
Kutztown U of Pennsylvania (PA) ***399***
Lafayette Coll (PA) ***400***
LaGrange Coll (GA) ***400***
Lake Erie Coll (OH) ***400***
Lake Forest Coll (IL) ***400***
Lakehead U (ON, Canada) ***400***
Lakeland Coll (WI) ***401***
Lamar U (TX) ***401***
Lambuth U (TN) ***401***
Lander U (SC) ***401***
Lane Coll (TN) ***402***
Langston U (OK) ***402***
La Roche Coll (PA) ***402***
La Salle U (PA) ***402***
La Sierra U (CA) ***403***
Laurentian U (ON, Canada) ***403***
Lawrence U (WI) ***403***
Lebanon Valley Coll (PA) ***403***
Lees-McRae Coll (NC) ***404***
Lee U (TN) ***404***
Lehigh U (PA) ***404***
Lehman Coll of the City U of NY (NY) ***404***
Le Moyne Coll (NY) ***404***
Lenoir-Rhyne Coll (NC) ***405***
LeTourneau U (TX) ***405***
Lewis & Clark Coll (OR) ***405***
Lewis-Clark State Coll (ID) ***406***
Lewis U (IL) ***406***
Liberty U (VA) ***406***
Life U (GA) ***406***
Limestone Coll (SC) ***406***
Lincoln Memorial U (TN) ***407***
Lincoln U (PA) ***407***
Lindenwood U (MO) ***407***
Lindsey Wilson Coll (KY) ***407***
Linfield Coll (OR) ***408***
Lipscomb U (TN) ***408***
Lock Haven U of Pennsylvania (PA) ***408***
Logan U-Coll of Chiropractic (MO) ***408***
Long Island U, Brooklyn Campus (NY) ***409***
Long Island U, C.W. Post Campus (NY) ***409***
Long Island U, Southampton Coll (NY) ***409***
Longwood U (VA) ***409***
Loras Coll (IA) ***410***
Louisiana Coll (LA) ***410***
Louisiana State U in Shreveport (LA) ***410***
Louisiana Tech U (LA) ***410***
Lourdes Coll (OH) ***411***
Loyola Coll in Maryland (MD) ***411***
Loyola Marymount U (CA) ***411***
Loyola U Chicago (IL) ***411***
Loyola U New Orleans (LA) ***411***
Lubbock Christian U (TX) ***412***
Luther Coll (IA) ***412***
Lycoming Coll (PA) ***412***
Lynchburg Coll (VA) ***413***
Lyon Coll (AR) ***413***
Macalester Coll (MN) ***413***
MacMurray Coll (IL) ***414***
Madonna U (MI) ***414***
Maharishi U of Management (IA) ***414***
Malaspina U-Coll (BC, Canada) ***415***
Malone Coll (OH) ***415***
Manchester Coll (IN) ***415***
Manhattan Coll (NY) ***416***
Manhattanville Coll (NY) ***416***
Mansfield U of Pennsylvania (PA) ***416***
Marian Coll (IN) ***417***
Marian Coll of Fond du Lac (WI) ***417***
Marietta Coll (OH) ***417***
Marist Coll (NY) ***417***
Marlboro Coll (VT) ***418***
Marquette U (WI) ***418***
Marshall U (WV) ***418***
Mars Hill Coll (NC) ***418***
Martin U (IN) ***419***
Mary Baldwin Coll (VA) ***419***
Marygrove Coll (MI) ***419***
Marymount Coll of Fordham U (NY) ***419***
Marymount Manhattan Coll (NY) ***420***
Marymount U (VA) ***420***
Maryville Coll (TN) ***420***
Maryville U of Saint Louis (MO) ***420***
Mary Washington Coll (VA) ***420***
Marywood U (PA) ***421***
Massachusetts Coll of Liberal Arts (MA) ***421***
Massachusetts Inst of Technology (MA) ***421***
The Master's Coll and Seminary (CA) ***422***
Mayville State U (ND) ***422***
McDaniel Coll (MD) ***422***
McGill U (QC, Canada) ***423***
McKendree Coll (IL) ***423***
McMaster U (ON, Canada) ***423***
McMurry U (TX) ***423***
McNeese State U (LA) ***423***
McPherson Coll (KS) ***423***
Medaille Coll (NY) ***424***
Medgar Evers Coll of the City U of NY (NY) ***424***
Memorial U of Newfoundland (NF, Canada) ***424***
Mercer U (GA) ***425***
Mercy Coll (NY) ***425***
Mercyhurst Coll (PA) ***425***
Meredith Coll (NC) ***426***
Merrimack Coll (MA) ***426***
Mesa State Coll (CO) ***426***
Messiah Coll (PA) ***426***
Methodist Coll (NC) ***427***
Metropolitan State Coll of Denver (CO) ***427***
Metropolitan State U (MN) ***427***
Miami U (OH) ***428***
Michigan State U (MI) ***428***
Michigan Technological U (MI) ***428***
MidAmerica Nazarene U (KS) ***428***
Middlebury Coll (VT) ***429***
Middle Tennessee State U (TN) ***429***
Midland Lutheran Coll (NE) ***429***
Midway Coll (KY) ***429***
Midwestern State U (TX) ***430***
Miles Coll (AL) ***430***
Millersville U of Pennsylvania (PA) ***430***
Milligan Coll (TN) ***430***
Millikin U (IL) ***430***
Millsaps Coll (MS) ***431***
Mills Coll (CA) ***431***
Minnesota State U, Mankato (MN) ***431***
Minnesota State U, Moorhead (MN) ***432***
Minot State U (ND) ***432***
Mississippi Coll (MS) ***432***
Mississippi State U (MS) ***432***
Mississippi Valley State U (MS) ***432***
Missouri Southern State Coll (MO) ***433***
Missouri Valley Coll (MO) ***433***
Missouri Western State Coll (MO) ***433***
Molloy Coll (NY) ***433***
Monmouth Coll (IL) ***434***
Monmouth U (NJ) ***434***
Montana State U–Billings (MT) ***434***
Montana State U–Bozeman (MT) ***434***
Montana State U–Northern (MT) ***434***
Montana Tech of The U of Montana (MT) ***435***
Montclair State U (NJ) ***435***
Moravian Coll (PA) ***436***
Morehead State U (KY) ***436***
Morehouse Coll (GA) ***436***
Morgan State U (MD) ***436***
Morningside Coll (IA) ***437***
Morris Coll (SC) ***437***
Mount Allison U (NB, Canada) ***437***
Mount Holyoke Coll (MA) ***438***
Mount Marty Coll (SD) ***438***
Mount Mary Coll (WI) ***438***
Mount Mercy Coll (IA) ***438***
Mount Olive Coll (NC) ***439***
Mount Saint Mary Coll (NY) ***439***
Mount St. Mary's Coll (CA) ***439***
Mount Saint Mary's Coll and Seminary (MD) ***439***
Mount Saint Vincent U (NS, Canada) ***439***
Mount Union Coll (OH) ***440***
Mount Vernon Nazarene U (OH) ***440***
Muhlenberg Coll (PA) ***440***
Murray State U (KY) ***440***
Muskingum Coll (OH) ***441***
National-Louis U (IL) ***442***
Nazareth Coll of Rochester (NY) ***443***
Nebraska Wesleyan U (NE) ***443***
Neumann Coll (PA) ***443***
Newberry Coll (SC) ***444***
New Coll of Florida (FL) ***444***
New England Coll (NH) ***444***
New Jersey City U (NJ) ***445***
New Jersey Inst of Technology (NJ) ***445***
Newman U (KS) ***445***
New Mexico Highlands U (NM) ***446***
New Mexico Inst of Mining and Technology (NM) ***446***
New Mexico State U (NM) ***446***
New York Inst of Technology (NY) ***447***
New York U (NY) ***447***
Niagara U (NY) ***447***
Nicholls State U (LA) ***447***
Nipissing U (ON, Canada) ***448***
Norfolk State U (VA) ***448***
North Carolina Ag and Tech State U (NC) ***448***
North Carolina Central U (NC) ***448***
North Carolina State U (NC) ***449***
North Carolina Wesleyan Coll (NC) ***449***
North Central Coll (IL) ***449***
North Dakota State U (ND) ***449***
Northeastern Illinois U (IL) ***450***
Northeastern State U (OK) ***450***
Northeastern U (MA) ***450***
Northern Arizona U (AZ) ***450***
Northern Illinois U (IL) ***450***
Northern Kentucky U (KY) ***451***
Northern Michigan U (MI) ***451***
Northern State U (SD) ***451***
North Georgia Coll & State U (GA) ***451***
Northland Coll (WI) ***452***
North Park U (IL) ***452***
Northwestern Coll (IA) ***453***
Northwestern Coll (MN) ***453***
Northwestern Oklahoma State U (OK) ***453***
Northwestern State U of Louisiana (LA) ***453***
Northwestern U (IL) ***453***
Northwest Missouri State U (MO) ***454***
Northwest Nazarene U (ID) ***454***
Norwich U (VT) ***455***
Notre Dame Coll (OH) ***455***

BIOLOGY (continued)

Notre Dame de Namur U (CA) ***455***
Nova Southeastern U (FL) ***455***
Oakland City U (IN) ***456***
Oakland U (MI) ***456***
Oakwood Coll (AL) ***456***
Oberlin Coll (OH) ***456***
Occidental Coll (CA) ***457***
Oglethorpe U (GA) ***457***
Ohio Dominican U (OH) ***457***
Ohio Northern U (OH) ***457***
The Ohio State U (OH) ***457***
Ohio Wesleyan U (OH) ***459***
Okanagan U Coll (BC, Canada) ***459***
Oklahoma Baptist U (OK) ***459***
Oklahoma Christian U (OK) ***459***
Oklahoma City U (OK) ***460***
Oklahoma Panhandle State U (OK) ***460***
Oklahoma State U (OK) ***460***
Oklahoma Wesleyan U (OK) ***460***
Old Dominion U (VA) ***460***
Olivet Coll (MI) ***461***
Olivet Nazarene U (IL) ***461***
Oral Roberts U (OK) ***461***
Oregon State U (OR) ***462***
Ottawa U (KS) ***462***
Otterbein Coll (OH) ***462***
Ouachita Baptist U (AR) ***462***
Our Lady of Holy Cross Coll (LA) ***463***
Our Lady of the Lake U of San Antonio (TX) ***463***
Pace U (NY) ***463***
Pacific Lutheran U (WA) ***463***
Pacific Union Coll (CA) ***464***
Pacific U (OR) ***464***
Paine Coll (GA) ***465***
Palm Beach Atlantic U (FL) ***465***
Park U (MO) ***465***
Paul Quinn Coll (TX) ***466***
Peace Coll (NC) ***466***
Penn State U at Erie, The Behrend Coll (PA) ***467***
Penn State U Univ Park Campus (PA) ***468***
Pepperdine U, Malibu (CA) ***469***
Peru State Coll (NE) ***469***
Pfeiffer U (NC) ***469***
Philadelphia U (PA) ***469***
Piedmont Coll (GA) ***470***
Pikeville Coll (KY) ***470***
Pine Manor Coll (MA) ***470***
Pittsburg State U (KS) ***470***
Pitzer Coll (CA) ***471***
Plattsburgh State U of NY (NY) ***471***
Plymouth State Coll (NH) ***471***
Point Loma Nazarene U (CA) ***471***
Point Park Coll (PA) ***471***
Pomona Coll (CA) ***472***
Pontifical Catholic U of Puerto Rico (PR) ***472***
Portland State U (OR) ***472***
Prairie View A&M U (TX) ***473***
Presbyterian Coll (SC) ***473***
Prescott Coll (AZ) ***474***
Principia Coll (IL) ***474***
Providence Coll (RI) ***474***
Purchase Coll, State U of NY (NY) ***475***
Purdue U (IN) ***475***
Purdue U Calumet (IN) ***475***
Purdue U North Central (IN) ***475***
Queens Coll of the City U of NY (NY) ***475***
Queen's U at Kingston (ON, Canada) ***476***
Queens U of Charlotte (NC) ***476***
Quincy U (IL) ***476***
Quinnipiac U (CT) ***476***
Radford U (VA) ***476***
Ramapo Coll of New Jersey (NJ) ***477***
Randolph-Macon Coll (VA) ***477***
Randolph-Macon Woman's Coll (VA) ***477***
Reed Coll (OR) ***477***
Regis Coll (MA) ***478***
Regis U (CO) ***478***
Reinhardt Coll (GA) ***478***
Rensselaer Polytechnic Inst (NY) ***478***
Rhode Island Coll (RI) ***479***
Rhodes Coll (TN) ***479***
Rice U (TX) ***479***
The Richard Stockton Coll of New Jersey (NJ) ***479***
Rider U (NJ) ***480***
Ripon Coll (WI) ***480***
Rivier Coll (NH) ***480***
Roanoke Coll (VA) ***481***
Roberts Wesleyan Coll (NY) ***481***
Rochester Inst of Technology (NY) ***482***
Rockford Coll (IL) ***482***
Rockhurst U (MO) ***482***
Rocky Mountain Coll (MT) ***482***
Rogers State U (OK) ***483***
Roger Williams U (RI) ***483***
Rollins Coll (FL) ***483***
Roosevelt U (IL) ***483***
Rose-Hulman Inst of Technology (IN) ***484***
Rosemont Coll (PA) ***484***
Rowan U (NJ) ***484***
Russell Sage Coll (NY) ***484***
Rust Coll (MS) ***485***
Rutgers, The State U of New Jersey, Camden (NJ) ***485***
Rutgers, The State U of New Jersey, Newark (NJ) ***485***
Rutgers, The State U of New Jersey, New Brunswick (NJ) ***485***
Ryerson U (ON, Canada) ***485***
Sacred Heart U (CT) ***486***
Saginaw Valley State U (MI) ***486***
St. Ambrose U (IA) ***486***
St. Andrews Presbyterian Coll (NC) ***487***
Saint Anselm Coll (NH) ***487***
Saint Augustine's Coll (NC) ***487***
St. Bonaventure U (NY) ***487***
St. Cloud State U (MN) ***488***
St. Edward's U (TX) ***488***
St. Francis Coll (NY) ***488***
Saint Francis U (PA) ***488***
St. Francis Xavier U (NS, Canada) ***489***
St. John Fisher Coll (NY) ***489***
Saint John's U (MN) ***490***
St. John's U (NY) ***490***
Saint Joseph Coll (CT) ***490***
Saint Joseph's Coll (IN) ***490***
St. Joseph's Coll, New York (NY) ***491***
Saint Joseph's Coll of Maine (ME) ***491***
St. Joseph's Coll, Suffolk Campus (NY) ***491***
Saint Joseph's U (PA) ***491***
St. Lawrence U (NY) ***491***
Saint Leo U (FL) ***492***
Saint Louis U (MO) ***492***
Saint Martin's Coll (WA) ***493***
Saint Mary Coll (KS) ***493***
Saint Mary-of-the-Woods Coll (IN) ***493***
Saint Mary's Coll (IN) ***493***
Saint Mary's Coll of California (CA) ***494***
Saint Mary's Coll of Madonna U (MI) ***493***
St. Mary's Coll of Maryland (MD) ***494***
Saint Mary's U (NS, Canada) ***494***
Saint Mary's U of Minnesota (MN) ***494***
St. Mary's U of San Antonio (TX) ***494***
Saint Michael's Coll (VT) ***494***
St. Norbert Coll (WI) ***495***
St. Olaf Coll (MN) ***495***
Saint Peter's Coll (NJ) ***495***
St. Thomas Aquinas Coll (NY) ***495***
St. Thomas U (FL) ***496***
Saint Vincent Coll (PA) ***496***
Saint Xavier U (IL) ***496***
Salem Coll (NC) ***496***
Salem International U (WV) ***496***
Salem State Coll (MA) ***497***
Salisbury U (MD) ***497***
Salve Regina U (RI) ***497***
Samford U (AL) ***497***
Sam Houston State U (TX) ***497***
San Diego State U (CA) ***498***
San Francisco State U (CA) ***498***
San Jose State U (CA) ***499***
Santa Clara U (CA) ***499***
Sarah Lawrence Coll (NY) ***499***
Savannah State U (GA) ***499***
Schreiner U (TX) ***501***
Scripps Coll (CA) ***501***
Seattle Pacific U (WA) ***501***
Seattle U (WA) ***501***
Seton Hall U (NJ) ***502***
Seton Hill U (PA) ***502***
Shawnee State U (OH) ***502***
Shaw U (NC) ***502***
Shenandoah U (VA) ***503***
Shepherd Coll (WV) ***503***
Shippensburg U of Pennsylvania (PA) ***503***
Shorter Coll (GA) ***504***
Siena Coll (NY) ***504***
Siena Heights U (MI) ***504***
Silver Lake Coll (WI) ***504***
Simmons Coll (MA) ***504***
Simon Fraser U (BC, Canada) ***505***
Simon's Rock Coll of Bard (MA) ***505***
Simpson Coll (IA) ***505***
Skidmore Coll (NY) ***506***
Slippery Rock U of Pennsylvania (PA) ***506***
Smith Coll (MA) ***506***
Sonoma State U (CA) ***506***
South Carolina State U (SC) ***506***
South Dakota State U (SD) ***507***
Southeastern Coll of the Assemblies of God (FL) ***507***
Southeastern Louisiana U (LA) ***508***
Southeastern Oklahoma State U (OK) ***508***
Southeast Missouri State U (MO) ***508***
Southern Adventist U (TN) ***508***
Southern Arkansas U–Magnolia (AR) ***509***
Southern Connecticut State U (CT) ***509***
Southern Illinois U Carbondale (IL) ***509***
Southern Illinois U Edwardsville (IL) ***509***
Southern Methodist U (TX) ***510***
Southern Nazarene U (OK) ***510***
Southern Oregon U (OR) ***510***
Southern U and A&M Coll (LA) ***511***
Southern Utah U (UT) ***511***
Southern Wesleyan U (SC) ***511***
Southwest Baptist U (MO) ***512***
Southwestern Coll (KS) ***512***
Southwestern Oklahoma State U (OK) ***512***
Southwestern U (TX) ***513***
Southwest Missouri State U (MO) ***513***
Southwest State U (MN) ***513***
Southwest Texas State U (TX) ***513***
Spalding U (KY) ***513***
Spelman Coll (GA) ***514***
Spring Arbor U (MI) ***514***
Springfield Coll (MA) ***514***
Spring Hill Coll (AL) ***514***
Stanford U (CA) ***514***
State U of NY at Albany (NY) ***514***
State U of NY at Binghamton (NY) ***515***
State U of NY at New Paltz (NY) ***515***
State U of NY at Oswego (NY) ***515***
State U of NY Coll at Brockport (NY) ***515***
State U of NY Coll at Buffalo (NY) ***516***
State U of NY Coll at Cortland (NY) ***516***
State U of NY Coll at Fredonia (NY) ***516***
State U of NY Coll at Geneseo (NY) ***516***
State U of NY Coll at Old Westbury (NY) ***516***
State U of NY Coll at Oneonta (NY) ***517***
State U of NY Coll at Potsdam (NY) ***517***
State U of NY Coll of Environ Sci and Forestry (NY) ***517***
State U of West Georgia (GA) ***518***
Stephen F. Austin State U (TX) ***518***
Stephens Coll (MO) ***519***
Sterling Coll (KS) ***519***
Stetson U (FL) ***519***
Stonehill Coll (MA) ***520***
Stony Brook U, State University of New York (NY) ***520***
Suffolk U (MA) ***520***
Sul Ross State U (TX) ***521***
Susquehanna U (PA) ***521***
Swarthmore Coll (PA) ***521***
Sweet Briar Coll (VA) ***521***
Syracuse U (NY) ***521***
Tabor Coll (KS) ***522***
Talladega Coll (AL) ***522***
Tarleton State U (TX) ***522***
Taylor U (IN) ***523***
Teikyo Post U (CT) ***523***
Temple U (PA) ***523***
Tennessee State U (TN) ***523***
Tennessee Technological U (TN) ***524***
Tennessee Temple U (TN) ***524***
Tennessee Wesleyan Coll (TN) ***524***
Texas A&M International U (TX) ***524***
Texas A&M U (TX) ***524***
Texas A&M U–Commerce (TX) ***525***
Texas A&M U–Corpus Christi (TX) ***525***
Texas A&M U–Kingsville (TX) ***525***
Texas A&M U–Texarkana (TX) ***525***
Texas Christian U (TX) ***526***
Texas Coll (TX) ***526***
Texas Lutheran U (TX) ***526***
Texas Southern U (TX) ***526***
Texas Tech U (TX) ***526***
Texas Wesleyan U (TX) ***526***
Texas Woman's U (TX) ***527***
Thiel Coll (PA) ***527***
Thomas Edison State Coll (NJ) ***527***
Thomas More Coll (KY) ***528***
Thomas More Coll of Liberal Arts (NH) ***528***
Thomas U (GA) ***528***
Touro Coll (NY) ***529***
Towson U (MD) ***529***
Transylvania U (KY) ***529***
Trent U (ON, Canada) ***529***
Trevecca Nazarene U (TN) ***529***
Trinity Christian Coll (IL) ***530***
Trinity Coll (CT) ***530***
Trinity Coll (DC) ***530***
Trinity International U (IL) ***531***
Trinity U (TX) ***531***
Trinity Western U (BC, Canada) ***531***
Tri-State U (IN) ***532***
Troy State U (AL) ***532***
Troy State U Dothan (AL) ***532***
Truman State U (MO) ***532***
Tufts U (MA) ***533***
Tulane U (LA) ***533***
Tusculum Coll (TN) ***533***
Tuskegee U (AL) ***533***
Union Coll (KY) ***533***
Union Coll (NE) ***534***
Union Coll (NY) ***534***
Union U (TN) ***534***
United States Air Force Academy (CO) ***534***
United States Military Academy (NY) ***535***
Universidad Adventista de las Antillas (PR) ***536***
Université de Sherbrooke (QC, Canada) ***536***
U du Québec à Trois-Rivières (QC, Canada) ***536***
Université Laval (QC, Canada) ***536***
U at Buffalo, The State University of New York (NY) ***536***
U Coll of the Cariboo (BC, Canada) ***537***
The U of Akron (OH) ***537***
The U of Alabama (AL) ***537***
The U of Alabama at Birmingham (AL) ***537***
The U of Alabama in Huntsville (AL) ***537***
U of Alaska Fairbanks (AK) ***538***
U of Alaska Southeast (AK) ***538***
U of Alberta (AB, Canada) ***538***
The U of Arizona (AZ) ***538***
U of Arkansas (AR) ***539***
U of Arkansas at Little Rock (AR) ***539***
U of Arkansas at Monticello (AR) ***539***
U of Bridgeport (CT) ***540***
The U of British Columbia (BC, Canada) ***540***
U of Calgary (AB, Canada) ***540***
U of Calif, Davis (CA) ***540***
U of Calif, Irvine (CA) ***541***
U of Calif, Los Angeles (CA) ***541***
U of Calif, Riverside (CA) ***541***
U of Calif, San Diego (CA) ***541***
U of Calif, Santa Barbara (CA) ***541***
U of Calif, Santa Cruz (CA) ***542***
U of Central Arkansas (AR) ***542***
U of Central Florida (FL) ***542***
U of Central Oklahoma (OK) ***542***
U of Charleston (WV) ***542***
U of Chicago (IL) ***542***
U of Cincinnati (OH) ***543***
U of Colorado at Boulder (CO) ***543***
U of Colorado at Colorado Springs (CO) ***543***
U of Colorado at Denver (CO) ***543***
U of Connecticut (CT) ***544***
U of Dallas (TX) ***544***
U of Dayton (OH) ***544***
U of Delaware (DE) ***544***
U of Denver (CO) ***544***
U of Dubuque (IA) ***545***
U of Evansville (IN) ***545***
The U of Findlay (OH) ***545***
U of Georgia (GA) ***545***
U of Great Falls (MT) ***545***
U of Guelph (ON, Canada) ***546***
U of Hartford (CT) ***546***
U of Hawaii at Hilo (HI) ***546***
U of Hawaii at Manoa (HI) ***546***
U of Houston (TX) ***547***
U of Houston–Clear Lake (TX) ***547***
U of Houston–Downtown (TX) ***547***
U of Idaho (ID) ***547***
U of Illinois at Chicago (IL) ***547***
U of Illinois at Springfield (IL) ***548***
U of Illinois at Urbana–Champaign (IL) ***548***
U of Indianapolis (IN) ***548***
The U of Iowa (IA) ***548***
U of Kansas (KS) ***549***
U of Kentucky (KY) ***549***
U of King's Coll (NS, Canada) ***549***
U of La Verne (CA) ***549***
The U of Lethbridge (AB, Canada) ***549***
U of Louisiana at Lafayette (LA) ***550***
U of Louisville (KY) ***550***
U of Maine (ME) ***550***

U of Maine at Farmington (ME) **550**
U of Maine at Fort Kent (ME) **551**
U of Maine at Machias (ME) **551**
U of Maine at Presque Isle (ME) **551**
U of Manitoba (MB, Canada) **551**
U of Mary (ND) **551**
U of Mary Hardin-Baylor (TX) **551**
U of Maryland, Baltimore County (MD) **552**
U of Maryland, Coll Park (MD) **552**
U of Maryland Eastern Shore (MD) **552**
U of Massachusetts Amherst (MA) **552**
U of Massachusetts Boston (MA) **553**
U of Massachusetts Dartmouth (MA) **553**
U of Massachusetts Lowell (MA) **553**
The U of Memphis (TN) **553**
U of Miami (FL) **553**
U of Michigan (MI) **554**
U of Michigan–Dearborn (MI) **554**
U of Michigan–Flint (MI) **554**
U of Minnesota, Duluth (MN) **554**
U of Minnesota, Morris (MN) **555**
U of Minnesota, Twin Cities Campus (MN) **555**
U of Mississippi (MS) **555**
U of Missouri–Columbia (MO) **555**
U of Missouri–Kansas City (MO) **555**
U of Missouri–Rolla (MO) **556**
U of Missouri–St. Louis (MO) **556**
U of Mobile (AL) **556**
The U of Montana–Missoula (MT) **556**
The U of Montana–Western (MT) **556**
U of Montevallo (AL) **557**
U of Nebraska at Kearney (NE) **557**
U of Nebraska at Omaha (NE) **557**
U of Nevada, Las Vegas (NV) **558**
U of Nevada, Reno (NV) **558**
U of New Brunswick Fredericton (NB, Canada) **558**
U of New Brunswick Saint John (NB, Canada) **558**
U of New England (ME) **558**
U of New Hampshire (NH) **558**
U of New Mexico (NM) **559**
U of New Orleans (LA) **559**
U of North Alabama (AL) **559**
The U of North Carolina at Asheville (NC) **559**
The U of North Carolina at Chapel Hill (NC) **560**
The U of North Carolina at Charlotte (NC) **560**
The U of North Carolina at Greensboro (NC) **560**
The U of North Carolina at Pembroke (NC) **560**
The U of North Carolina at Wilmington (NC) **561**
U of North Dakota (ND) **561**
U of Northern Colorado (CO) **561**
U of Northern Iowa (IA) **561**
U of North Florida (FL) **561**
U of North Texas (TX) **562**
U of Notre Dame (IN) **562**
U of Oregon (OR) **562**
U of Ottawa (ON, Canada) **563**
U of Pennsylvania (PA) **563**
U of Pittsburgh (PA) **569**
U of Pittsburgh at Bradford (PA) **569**
U of Pittsburgh at Greensburg (PA) **570**
U of Pittsburgh at Johnstown (PA) **570**
U of Portland (OR) **570**
U of Prince Edward Island (PE, Canada) **570**
U of Puerto Rico, Humacao U Coll (PR) **570**
U of Puerto Rico, Cayey U Coll (PR) **571**
U of Puerto Rico, Río Piedras (PR) **571**
U of Puget Sound (WA) **571**
U of Redlands (CA) **572**
U of Regina (SK, Canada) **572**
U of Rhode Island (RI) **572**
U of Richmond (VA) **572**
U of Rio Grande (OH) **572**
U of Rochester (NY) **573**
U of St. Francis (IL) **573**
U of Saint Francis (IN) **573**
U of St. Thomas (MN) **573**
U of St. Thomas (TX) **573**
U of San Diego (CA) **574**
U of San Francisco (CA) **574**
U of Saskatchewan (SK, Canada) **574**
U of Science and Arts of Oklahoma (OK) **574**
The U of Scranton (PA) **574**
U of Sioux Falls (SD) **574**
U of South Alabama (AL) **575**
U of South Carolina (SC) **575**
U of South Carolina Aiken (SC) **575**
U of South Carolina Spartanburg (SC) **575**
The U of South Dakota (SD) **575**
U of Southern California (CA) **576**
U of Southern Indiana (IN) **576**
U of Southern Maine (ME) **576**
U of Southern Mississippi (MS) **576**
U of South Florida (FL) **576**
The U of Tampa (FL) **577**
The U of Tennessee (TN) **577**
The U of Tennessee at Chattanooga (TN) **577**
The U of Tennessee at Martin (TN) **577**
The U of Texas at Arlington (TX) **577**
The U of Texas at Austin (TX) **578**
The U of Texas at Brownsville (TX) **578**
The U of Texas at Dallas (TX) **578**
The U of Texas at El Paso (TX) **578**
The U of Texas at San Antonio (TX) **578**
The U of Texas at Tyler (TX) **579**
The U of Texas of the Permian Basin (TX) **579**
The U of Texas–Pan American (TX) **579**
U of the District of Columbia (DC) **580**
U of the Incarnate Word (TX) **580**
U of the Ozarks (AR) **580**
U of the Pacific (CA) **580**
U of the Sacred Heart (PR) **580**
U of the Sciences in Philadelphia (PA) **580**
U of the South (TN) **581**
U of the Virgin Islands (VI) **581**
U of Toledo (OH) **581**
U of Toronto (ON, Canada) **581**
U of Tulsa (OK) **581**
U of Utah (UT) **582**
U of Vermont (VT) **582**
U of Victoria (BC, Canada) **582**
U of Virginia (VA) **582**
The U of Virginia's Coll at Wise (VA) **582**
U of Washington (WA) **583**
U of Waterloo (ON, Canada) **583**
The U of West Alabama (AL) **583**
The U of Western Ontario (ON, Canada) **583**
U of West Florida (FL) **583**
U of Windsor (ON, Canada) **584**
U of Wisconsin–Eau Claire (WI) **584**
U of Wisconsin–Green Bay (WI) **584**
U of Wisconsin–La Crosse (WI) **584**
U of Wisconsin–Madison (WI) **584**
U of Wisconsin–Milwaukee (WI) **585**
U of Wisconsin–Oshkosh (WI) **585**
U of Wisconsin–Platteville (WI) **585**
U of Wisconsin–River Falls (WI) **585**
U of Wisconsin–Stevens Point (WI) **585**
U of Wisconsin–Superior (WI) **586**
U of Wisconsin–Whitewater (WI) **586**
U of Wyoming (WY) **586**
Upper Iowa U (IA) **587**
Urbana U (OH) **587**
Ursinus Coll (PA) **587**
Ursuline Coll (OH) **587**
Utah State U (UT) **587**
Utica Coll (NY) **588**
Valdosta State U (GA) **588**
Valley City State U (ND) **588**
Valparaiso U (IN) **588**
Vanderbilt U (TN) **588**
Vanguard U of Southern California (CA) **589**
Vassar Coll (NY) **589**
Villa Julie Coll (MD) **590**
Villanova U (PA) **590**
Virginia Commonwealth U (VA) **590**
Virginia Intermont Coll (VA) **590**
Virginia Military Inst (VA) **591**
Virginia Polytechnic Inst and State U (VA) **591**
Virginia State U (VA) **591**
Virginia Union U (VA) **591**
Virginia Wesleyan Coll (VA) **591**
Viterbo U (WI) **591**
Voorhees Coll (SC) **592**
Wabash Coll (IN) **592**
Wagner Coll (NY) **592**
Wake Forest U (NC) **592**
Walla Walla Coll (WA) **593**
Walsh U (OH) **593**
Warner Pacific Coll (OR) **593**
Warner Southern Coll (FL) **593**
Warren Wilson Coll (NC) **594**
Wartburg Coll (IA) **594**
Washington & Jefferson Coll (PA) **594**
Washington and Lee U (VA) **594**
Washington Coll (MD) **594**
Washington State U (WA) **595**
Washington U in St. Louis (MO) **595**
Wayland Baptist U (TX) **595**
Waynesburg Coll (PA) **595**
Wayne State Coll (NE) **596**
Wayne State U (MI) **596**
Webster U (MO) **597**
Wellesley Coll (MA) **597**
Wells Coll (NY) **597**
Wesleyan Coll (GA) **597**
Wesleyan U (CT) **597**
Wesley Coll (DE) **598**
West Chester U of Pennsylvania (PA) **598**
Western Carolina U (NC) **598**
Western Connecticut State U (CT) **598**
Western Illinois U (IL) **599**
Western Kentucky U (KY) **599**
Western Michigan U (MI) **599**
Western New England Coll (MA) **600**
Western New Mexico U (NM) **600**
Western Oregon U (OR) **600**
Western State Coll of Colorado (CO) **600**
Western Washington U (WA) **600**
Westfield State Coll (MA) **600**
West Liberty State Coll (WV) **601**
Westminster Coll (MO) **601**
Westminster Coll (PA) **601**
Westminster Coll (UT) **601**
Westmont Coll (CA) **602**
West Texas A&M U (TX) **602**
West Virginia State Coll (WV) **602**
West Virginia U (WV) **602**
West Virginia U Inst of Technology (WV) **602**
West Virginia Wesleyan Coll (WV) **603**
Wheaton Coll (IL) **603**
Wheaton Coll (MA) **603**
Wheeling Jesuit U (WV) **603**
Whitman Coll (WA) **604**
Whittier Coll (CA) **604**
Whitworth Coll (WA) **604**
Wichita State U (KS) **604**
Widener U (PA) **604**
Wilberforce U (OH) **605**
Wiley Coll (TX) **605**
Wilkes U (PA) **605**
Willamette U (OR) **605**
William Carey Coll (MS) **605**
William Jewell Coll (MO) **606**
William Paterson U of New Jersey (NJ) **606**
William Penn U (IA) **606**
Williams Baptist Coll (AR) **606**
Williams Coll (MA) **606**
William Woods U (MO) **607**
Wilmington Coll (OH) **607**
Wilson Coll (PA) **607**
Wingate U (NC) **607**
Winona State U (MN) **608**
Winston-Salem State U (NC) **608**
Winthrop U (SC) **608**
Wisconsin Lutheran Coll (WI) **608**
Wittenberg U (OH) **608**
Wofford Coll (SC) **609**
Worcester Polytechnic Inst (MA) **609**
Worcester State Coll (MA) **609**
Wright State U (OH) **609**
Xavier U (OH) **610**
Xavier U of Louisiana (LA) **610**
Yale U (CT) **610**
York Coll (NE) **610**
York Coll of Pennsylvania (PA) **610**
York Coll of the City U of New York (NY) **611**
York U (ON, Canada) **611**
Youngstown State U (OH) **611**

BIOLOGY EDUCATION

Overview: This major prepares undergraduates to teach biology and biology-related topics such as human anatomy, botany, and ecology at the junior high and high school levels. *Related majors:* biology, ecology, anatomy, science teacher education. *Potential career:* biology teacher. *Salary potential:* $24k-$35k.

Abilene Christian U (TX) **260**
Adams State Coll (CO) **260**
Alvernia Coll (PA) **265**
Anderson Coll (SC) **268**
Arkansas State U (AR) **272**
Arkansas Tech U (AR) **272**
Averett U (VA) **278**
Baylor U (TX) **283**
Berea Coll (KY) **286**
Berry Coll (GA) **287**
Bethany Coll (KS) **287**
Bethel Coll (TN) **288**
Bethune-Cookman Coll (FL) **289**
Bloomfield Coll (NJ) **290**
Blue Mountain Coll (MS) **291**
Bowling Green State U (OH) **292**
Bridgewater Coll (VA) **294**
Brigham Young U–Hawaii (HI) **295**
Cabrini Coll (PA) **298**
Campbell U (NC) **303**
Canisius Coll (NY) **304**
Carroll Coll (MT) **306**
The Catholic U of America (DC) **307**
Cedarville U (OH) **308**
Central Methodist Coll (MO) **309**
Central Michigan U (MI) **310**
Central Missouri State U (MO) **310**
Central Washington U (WA) **310**
Chadron State Coll (NE) **311**
Christian Brothers U (TN) **313**
Citadel, The Military Coll of South Carolina (SC) **314**
Clearwater Christian Coll (FL) **316**
Colby-Sawyer Coll (NH) **319**
The Coll of New Jersey (NJ) **320**
Coll of St. Catherine (MN) **321**
Coll of the Ozarks (MO) **323**
Colorado State U (CO) **325**
Concordia Coll (MN) **329**
Concordia U (IL) **330**
Concordia U (NE) **330**
Crichton Coll (TN) **334**
Cumberland U (TN) **335**
Daemen Coll (NY) **335**
Dakota Wesleyan U (SD) **336**
Delta State U (MS) **339**
Dillard U (LA) **344**
Dominican Coll (NY) **344**
Duquesne U (PA) **346**
Eastern Mennonite U (VA) **348**
Eastern Michigan U (MI) **348**
East Texas Baptist U (TX) **350**
Elmhurst Coll (IL) **351**
Elmira Coll (NY) **351**
Florida Inst of Technology (FL) **360**
Framingham State Coll (MA) **362**
Franklin Coll (IN) **363**
Freed-Hardeman U (TN) **364**
George Fox U (OR) **366**
Georgia Southern U (GA) **367**
Greensboro Coll (NC) **372**
Greenville Coll (IL) **373**
Gustavus Adolphus Coll (MN) **374**
Hardin-Simmons U (TX) **376**
Hastings Coll (NE) **377**
Henderson State U (AR) **378**
Hofstra U (NY) **380**
Howard Payne U (TX) **382**
Husson Coll (ME) **383**
Indiana U Bloomington (IN) **385**
Indiana U Northwest (IN) **386**
Indiana U–Purdue U Fort Wayne (IN) **386**
Indiana U South Bend (IN) **387**
Indiana U Southeast (IN) **387**
Inter American U of PR, Aguadilla Campus (PR) **388**
Ithaca Coll (NY) **390**
Johnson State Coll (VT) **394**
Juniata Coll (PA) **395**
Kennesaw State U (GA) **397**
Keuka Coll (NY) **398**
King Coll (TN) **398**
La Roche Coll (PA) **402**
Liberty U (VA) **406**
Limestone Coll (SC) **406**
Lipscomb U (TN) **408**
Long Island U, C.W. Post Campus (NY) **409**
Louisiana State U in Shreveport (LA) **410**
Luther Coll (IA) **412**
Malone Coll (OH) **415**
Manhattanville Coll (NY) **416**
Mansfield U of Pennsylvania (PA) **416**
Marymount Coll of Fordham U (NY) **419**
Maryville Coll (TN) **420**
Mayville State U (ND) **422**
McGill U (QC, Canada) **423**
McKendree Coll (IL) **423**
McMurry U (TX) **423**
Messiah Coll (PA) **426**
Miami U (OH) **428**

BIOLOGY EDUCATION (continued)

Minot State U (ND) ***432***
Molloy Coll (NY) ***433***
Montana State U–Billings (MT) ***434***
Nazareth Coll of Rochester (NY) ***443***
New York Inst of Technology (NY) ***447***
New York U (NY) ***447***
Niagara U (NY) ***447***
North Carolina Central U (NC) ***448***
North Carolina State U (NC) ***449***
North Dakota State U (ND) ***449***
Northern Arizona U (AZ) ***450***
Northwest Nazarene U (ID) ***454***
Ohio U (OH) ***458***
Oklahoma Baptist U (OK) ***459***
Pace U (NY) ***463***
Pikeville Coll (KY) ***470***
Point Park Coll (PA) ***471***
Pontifical Catholic U of Puerto Rico (PR) ***472***
Rivier Coll (NH) ***480***
Rust Coll (MS) ***485***
St. Ambrose U (IA) ***486***
Saint Augustine's Coll (NC) ***487***
St. John's U (NY) ***490***
Saint Joseph's Coll of Maine (ME) ***491***
Saint Xavier U (IL) ***496***
Salve Regina U (RI) ***497***
San Diego State U (CA) ***498***
Seattle Pacific U (WA) ***501***
Seton Hill U (PA) ***502***
Shaw U (NC) ***502***
Southern Arkansas U–Magnolia (AR) ***509***
Southern Nazarene U (OK) ***510***
Southwest Missouri State U (MO) ***513***
Southwest State U (MN) ***513***
State U of NY at Albany (NY) ***514***
State U of NY Coll at Potsdam (NY) ***517***
State U of NY Coll of Environ Sci and Forestry (NY) ***517***
State U of West Georgia (GA) ***518***
Talladega Coll (AL) ***522***
Tennessee Wesleyan Coll (TN) ***524***
Texas A&M International U (TX) ***524***
Texas Wesleyan U (TX) ***526***
Trevecca Nazarene U (TN) ***529***
Trinity Christian Coll (IL) ***530***
Union Coll (NE) ***534***
The U of Arizona (AZ) ***538***
U of Delaware (DE) ***544***
U of Illinois at Chicago (IL) ***547***
U of Maine at Farmington (ME) ***550***
U of Mary (ND) ***551***
U of Nebraska–Lincoln (NE) ***557***
The U of North Carolina at Wilmington (NC) ***561***
U of North Texas (TX) ***562***
U of Puerto Rico, Cayey U Coll (PR) ***571***
U of Rio Grande (OH) ***572***
The U of Tennessee at Martin (TN) ***577***
U of Utah (UT) ***582***
U of Washington (WA) ***583***
U of Waterloo (ON, Canada) ***583***
U of Windsor (ON, Canada) ***584***
U of Wisconsin–River Falls (WI) ***585***
U of Wisconsin–Superior (WI) ***586***
Utah State U (UT) ***587***
Utica Coll (NY) ***588***
Valley City State U (ND) ***588***
Virginia Intermont Coll (VA) ***590***
Viterbo U (WI) ***591***
Washington U in St. Louis (MO) ***595***
Weber State U (UT) ***596***
Westminster Coll (UT) ***601***
Wheeling Jesuit U (WV) ***603***
Xavier U (OH) ***610***
York U (ON, Canada) ***611***
Youngstown State U (OH) ***611***

BIOMEDICAL ENGINEERING-RELATED TECHNOLOGY

Overview: This major gives students the basic engineering knowledge and skills to support those biomedical engineers who are developing biological or medical systems and products. *Related majors:* electrical engineering technology, computer programming, medical technology. *Potential careers:* researcher, medical technician, robotics engineer. *Salary potential:* $26k-$38k.

Indiana State U (IN) ***385***
New York Inst of Technology (NY) ***447***
Oral Roberts U (OK) ***461***
Thomas Edison State Coll (NJ) ***527***

BIOMEDICAL SCIENCE

Overview: This broad-based major provides students with a comprehensive background in math and the sciences and prepares them to enter professional programs for a range of disciplines, such as medical, dental, optometry, allied health, and veterinary. *Related majors:* physiology, biophysics, biochemistry, pharmacology, pathology. *Potential careers:* physician, quality control engineer, immunologist, research scientist, dentist. *Salary potential:* $35k-$48k.

Antioch Coll (OH) ***269***
Brown U (RI) ***296***
Cedar Crest Coll (PA) ***308***
City Coll of the City U of NY (NY) ***314***
Comm Hospital Roanoke Valley–Coll of Health Scis (VA) ***328***
Emory U (GA) ***354***
Framingham State Coll (MA) ***362***
Grand Valley State U (MI) ***371***
Harvard U (MA) ***376***
Howard U (DC) ***382***
Immaculata U (PA) ***385***
Inter American U of PR, San Germán Campus (PR) ***388***
Marquette U (WI) ***418***
Polytechnic U, Brooklyn Campus (NY) ***472***
Rutgers, The State U of New Jersey, New Brunswick (NJ) ***485***
St. Cloud State U (MN) ***488***
St. Francis Coll (NY) ***488***
State U of NY Coll at Fredonia (NY) ***516***
Stephens Coll (MO) ***519***
Suffolk U (MA) ***520***
U du Québec à Trois-Rivières (QC, Canada) ***536***
U of Calif, Riverside (CA) ***541***
U of Guelph (ON, Canada) ***546***
U of Michigan (MI) ***554***
U of Mississippi (MS) ***555***
The U of North Carolina at Pembroke (NC) ***560***
U of Ottawa (ON, Canada) ***563***
U of South Alabama (AL) ***575***
U of Utah (UT) ***582***
Western Michigan U (MI) ***599***
Worcester Polytechnic Inst (MA) ***609***

BIOMEDICAL TECHNOLOGY

Overview: This major teaches students basic scientific concepts and skills so they can work alongside or in support of physicians and biomedical engineers. *Related majors:* biochemistry. *Potential careers:* lab technician, X-ray technican, biochemist, pharmaceutical company research assistant. *Salary potential:* $25k-$37k.

Alfred U (NY) ***263***
Alvernia Coll (PA) ***265***
Andrews U (MI) ***269***
California State U, Hayward (CA) ***301***
Cedar Crest Coll (PA) ***308***
Cleveland State U (OH) ***317***
Colorado State U-Pueblo (CO) ***325***
Northwest Missouri State U (MO) ***454***
Suffolk U (MA) ***520***
U of New Hampshire (NH) ***558***
Walla Walla Coll (WA) ***593***

BIOMETRICS

Overview: Students who major in biometrics will learn how to apply statistics and other mathematical methods to biological, agricultural, and other natural science problems. *Related majors:* statistics, mathematics and computer science, biology, agronomy, ecology. *Potential careers:* research scientist, geneticist, ecologist, biologist. *Salary potential:* $30k-$40k.

Cornell U (NY) ***333***
Harvard U (MA) ***376***
Rutgers, The State U of New Jersey, New Brunswick (NJ) ***485***
U of Michigan (MI) ***554***

BIOPHYSICS

Overview: Undergraduates choosing this major study the physics of biological processes, usually at the cellular level. *Related majors:* molecular biology, neuroscience, biometrics, cell biology, molecular physics. *Potential careers:* research scientist, chemical engineer, professor. *Salary potential:* $32k-$42k.

Andrews U (MI) ***269***
Brandeis U (MA) ***293***
Brown U (RI) ***296***
Carnegie Mellon U (PA) ***305***
Centenary Coll of Louisiana (LA) ***308***
Claremont McKenna Coll (CA) ***315***
Clarkson U (NY) ***316***
Columbia Coll (NY) ***326***
Hampden-Sydney Coll (VA) ***374***
Hampshire Coll (MA) ***375***
Harvard U (MA) ***376***
Haverford Coll (PA) ***377***
Howard U (DC) ***382***
Illinois Inst of Technology (IL) ***384***
Iowa State U of Science and Technology (IA) ***390***
Johns Hopkins U (MD) ***392***
King Coll (TN) ***398***
La Sierra U (CA) ***403***
Longwood U (VA) ***409***
Oregon State U (OR) ***462***
Pacific Union Coll (CA) ***464***
Rensselaer Polytechnic Inst (NY) ***478***
St. Bonaventure U (NY) ***487***
St. Lawrence U (NY) ***491***
Saint Mary's U of Minnesota (MN) ***494***
Southwestern Oklahoma State U (OK) ***512***
State U of NY Coll at Geneseo (NY) ***516***
Suffolk U (MA) ***520***
U du Québec à Trois-Rivières (QC, Canada) ***536***
U at Buffalo, The State University of New York (NY) ***536***
U of Calif, San Diego (CA) ***541***
U of Connecticut (CT) ***544***
U of Guelph (ON, Canada) ***546***
U of Hawaii at Manoa (HI) ***546***
U of Illinois at Urbana–Champaign (IL) ***548***
U of Michigan (MI) ***554***
U of New Brunswick Fredericton (NB, Canada) ***558***
U of Pennsylvania (PA) ***563***
U of San Francisco (CA) ***574***
The U of Scranton (PA) ***574***
U of Southern California (CA) ***576***
U of Southern Indiana (IN) ***576***
U of Toronto (ON, Canada) ***581***
The U of Western Ontario (ON, Canada) ***583***
U of Windsor (ON, Canada) ***584***
Walla Walla Coll (WA) ***593***
Washington State U (WA) ***595***
Washington U in St. Louis (MO) ***595***
Whitman Coll (WA) ***604***

BIOPSYCHOLOGY

Overview: Students who take this major will study the connections between biology and psychology and the role that biochemical and biophysical functions have on the central nervous system. *Related majors:* biochemistry, biophysics, neuroscience, psychology, physiological psychology. *Potential careers:* physician, psychologist/psychiatrist, therapist, criminologist. *Salary potential:* $25k-$35k

Barnard Coll (NY) ***282***
Bucknell U (PA) ***297***
Coll of the Holy Cross (MA) ***323***
The Coll of William and Mary (VA) ***324***
Columbia Coll (NY) ***326***
Morningside Coll (IA) ***437***
Mount Allison U (NB, Canada) ***437***
Nebraska Wesleyan U (NE) ***443***
Philadelphia U (PA) ***469***
Rider U (NJ) ***480***
Russell Sage Coll (NY) ***484***
U of Calif, Santa Barbara (CA) ***541***
U of Denver (CO) ***544***
U of Pittsburgh at Johnstown (PA) ***570***
U of Windsor (ON, Canada) ***584***
Washington U in St. Louis (MO) ***595***

BIOSTATISTICS

Overview: Students learn how to apply descriptive and inferential statistics to biomedical research and public health and industrial issues that are related to humans. *Related majors:* public health, biotechnology research, human ecology, statistics, pathology. *Potential careers:* research scientist, public health official, biomedical researcher. *Salary potential:* $27k-$35k.

Cornell U (NY) ***333***
U of Hawaii at Manoa (HI) ***546***
U of Washington (WA) ***583***

BIOTECHNOLOGY RESEARCH

Overview: This major will teach students how to apply biology and biochemistry principles to the development of agricultural, environmental, clinical, and industrial products, including the use of plants and animals. *Related majors:* biological sciences, genetics, biochemistry, plant and animal pathology, applied mathematics. *Potential careers:* biotechnology scientist, agricultural researcher, pharmaceutical company scientist, biochemist, biological engineer. *Salary potential:* $33k-$45k.

Assumption Coll (MA) ***275***
Brock U (ON, Canada) ***295***
Cabrini Coll (PA) ***298***
Calvin Coll (MI) ***303***
Clarkson U (NY) ***316***
Cleveland State U (OH) ***317***
East Stroudsburg U of Pennsylvania (PA) ***349***
Elizabethtown Coll (PA) ***351***
Manhattan Coll (NY) ***416***
Missouri Southern State Coll (MO) ***433***
Montana State U–Bozeman (MT) ***434***
North Dakota State U (ND) ***449***
The Ohio State U (OH) ***457***
Plymouth State Coll (NH) ***471***
Rochester Inst of Technology (NY) ***482***
Rutgers, The State U of New Jersey, New Brunswick (NJ) ***485***
State U of NY Coll of Environ Sci and Forestry (NY) ***517***
Thomas Jefferson U (PA) ***527***
U at Buffalo, The State University of New York (NY) ***536***
U of Calif, San Diego (CA) ***541***
U of Delaware (DE) ***544***
U of Nebraska at Omaha (NE) ***557***
U of Southern Maine (ME) ***576***
U of Waterloo (ON, Canada) ***583***
U of Windsor (ON, Canada) ***584***
U of Wisconsin–River Falls (WI) ***585***
York U (ON, Canada) ***611***

BOTANY

Overview: This major is the scientific study of plant life (structure, growth, development and reproduction, microbial organisms, plant habitats, and ecosystems. *Related majors:* plant sciences, plant breeding and genetics, plant pathology, cell biology, plant physiology. *Potential careers:* agronomist, biologist, ecologist, research scientist, ecologist. *Salary potential:* $32k.

Andrews U (MI) ***269***
Arizona State U (AZ) ***271***
Ball State U (IN) ***280***
Brandon U (MB, Canada) ***293***
Brigham Young U (UT) ***295***
California State Polytechnic U, Pomona (CA) ***300***
Carleton U (ON, Canada) ***305***
Coll of the Atlantic (ME) ***323***
Colorado State U (CO) ***325***
Concordia U (QC, Canada) ***331***
Connecticut Coll (CT) ***331***
Cornell U (NY) ***333***
Eastern Washington U (WA) ***349***
Fort Valley State U (GA) ***362***
Hampshire Coll (MA) ***375***
Howard U (DC) ***382***
Humboldt State U (CA) ***382***
Idaho State U (ID) ***384***
Iowa State U of Science and Technology (IA) ***390***
Juniata Coll (PA) ***395***
Kent State U (OH) ***397***
Marlboro Coll (VT) ***418***
Mars Hill Coll (NC) ***418***
McGill U (QC, Canada) ***423***
Miami U (OH) ***428***
Michigan State U (MI) ***428***
Minnesota State U, Mankato (MN) ***431***
North Carolina State U (NC) ***449***
North Dakota State U (ND) ***449***
Northern Arizona U (AZ) ***450***
Northern Michigan U (MI) ***451***
Northwest Missouri State U (MO) ***454***
The Ohio State U (OH) ***457***
Ohio U (OH) ***458***
Ohio Wesleyan U (OH) ***459***
Oklahoma State U (OK) ***460***
Oregon State U (OR) ***462***
Purdue U (IN) ***475***
Purdue U Calumet (IN) ***475***
Rutgers, The State U of New Jersey, Newark (NJ) ***485***
St. Cloud State U (MN) ***488***
Saint Xavier U (IL) ***496***
San Francisco State U (CA) ***498***
Sonoma State U (CA) ***506***
Southeastern Oklahoma State U (OK) ***508***
Southern Connecticut State U (CT) ***509***
Southern Illinois U Carbondale (IL) ***509***
Southern Utah U (UT) ***511***
Southwest Texas State U (TX) ***513***
State U of NY Coll of Environ Sci and Forestry (NY) ***517***
Texas A&M U (TX) ***524***
The U of Akron (OH) ***537***
U of Alberta (AB, Canada) ***538***
U of Arkansas (AR) ***539***
U of Calgary (AB, Canada) ***540***
U of Calif, Davis (CA) ***540***
U of Calif, Riverside (CA) ***541***
U of Calif, Santa Cruz (CA) ***542***
U of Delaware (DE) ***544***
U of Florida (FL) ***545***
U of Georgia (GA) ***545***
U of Great Falls (MT) ***545***
U of Guelph (ON, Canada) ***546***
U of Hawaii at Manoa (HI) ***546***
U of Idaho (ID) ***547***
U of Illinois at Urbana–Champaign (IL) ***548***
U of Maine (ME) ***550***
U of Manitoba (MB, Canada) ***551***
U of Michigan (MI) ***554***
U of Minnesota, Twin Cities Campus (MN) ***555***
The U of Montana–Missoula (MT) ***556***
U of Nevada, Reno (NV) ***558***
U of New Brunswick Fredericton (NB, Canada) ***558***
U of New Hampshire (NH) ***558***
U of Oklahoma (OK) ***562***
The U of Tennessee (TN) ***577***
The U of Texas at Austin (TX) ***578***
The U of Texas at El Paso (TX) ***578***
U of Toronto (ON, Canada) ***581***
U of Vermont (VT) ***582***
U of Victoria (BC, Canada) ***582***
U of Washington (WA) ***583***
U of Wisconsin–Madison (WI) ***584***
U of Wyoming (WY) ***586***
Utah State U (UT) ***587***
Weber State U (UT) ***596***
Western New Mexico U (NM) ***600***
Wittenberg U (OH) ***608***

BOTANY RELATED

Information can be found under this major's main heading.

McGill U (QC, Canada) ***423***

BRITISH LITERATURE

Overview: Students focus on the literature and literary history of the English speaking people of the British Commonwealth, including Ireland. *Related majors:* English language/literature, history, Western Civilization/culture. *Potential careers:* writer, editor, historian, teacher or professor, librarian. *Salary potential:* $23k-$32k.

The Coll of Southeastern Europe, The American U of Athens(Greece) ***323***
Gannon U (PA) ***365***
Maharishi U of Management (IA) ***414***
Oral Roberts U (OK) ***461***
Point Loma Nazarene U (CA) ***471***
U of Pittsburgh (PA) ***569***
U of Southern California (CA) ***576***
Washington U in St. Louis (MO) ***595***

BROADCAST JOURNALISM

Overview: Students learn the correct techniques for reporting, producing, and delivering news programs via television, radio, and video or film media. *Related majors:* journalism, communications, radio and television engineering, multimedia, law. *Potential careers:* broadcast journalist, editor, producer, director, film or radio technician. *Salary potential:* $25k-$30k.

Adrian Coll (MI) ***260***
Alderson-Broaddus Coll (WV) ***263***
American U (DC) ***267***
Auburn U (AL) ***276***
Baldwin-Wallace Coll (OH) ***280***
Barry U (FL) ***282***
Barton Coll (NC) ***282***
Belmont U (TN) ***284***
Bemidji State U (MN) ***285***
Benedict Coll (SC) ***285***
Berry Coll (GA) ***287***
Bowie State U (MD) ***292***
Bowling Green State U (OH) ***292***
Bradley U (IL) ***293***
Brooklyn Coll of the City U of NY (NY) ***295***
California State U, Hayward (CA) ***301***
California State U, Long Beach (CA) ***301***
California State U, Northridge (CA) ***301***
Carson-Newman Coll (TN) ***306***
Cedarville U (OH) ***308***
Chapman U (CA) ***311***
The Coll of New Rochelle (NY) ***321***
The Coll of Southeastern Europe, The American U of Athens(Greece) ***323***
Coll of the Ozarks (MO) ***323***
Colorado Christian U (CO) ***325***
Colorado State U-Pueblo (CO) ***325***
Columbia Coll Chicago (IL) ***327***
Columbia Coll Hollywood (CA) ***327***
Columbia Union Coll (MD) ***328***
Concordia Coll (MN) ***329***
Drake U (IA) ***345***
East Carolina U (NC) ***347***
Eastern Kentucky U (KY) ***348***
Eastern Michigan U (MI) ***348***
Eastern Washington U (WA) ***349***
Edinboro U of Pennsylvania (PA) ***351***
Elizabeth City State U (NC) ***351***
Elon U (NC) ***352***
Emerson Coll (MA) ***353***
Evangel U (MO) ***355***
Florida International U (FL) ***360***
Florida Southern Coll (FL) ***361***
Fontbonne U (MO) ***361***
Fordham U (NY) ***362***
Franklin Coll (IN) ***363***
Gonzaga U (WA) ***369***
Goshen Coll (IN) ***370***
Grace U (NE) ***371***
Grand Valley State U (MI) ***371***
Hampton U (VA) ***375***
Hofstra U (NY) ***380***
Houston Baptist U (TX) ***382***
Howard U (DC) ***382***
Humboldt State U (CA) ***382***
Huntington Coll (IN) ***383***
Indiana U Bloomington (IN) ***385***
Iona Coll (NY) ***390***
Ithaca Coll (NY) ***390***
John Brown U (AR) ***392***
Lamar U (TX) ***401***
Langston U (OK) ***402***
La Salle U (PA) ***402***
Lewis U (IL) ***406***
Lindenwood U (MO) ***407***
Lock Haven U of Pennsylvania (PA) ***408***
Long Island U, C.W. Post Campus (NY) ***409***
Louisiana Coll (LA) ***410***
Malone Coll (OH) ***415***
Mansfield U of Pennsylvania (PA) ***416***
Marist Coll (NY) ***417***
Marquette U (WI) ***418***
Massachusetts Coll of Liberal Arts (MA) ***421***
Mercyhurst Coll (PA) ***425***
Mesa State Coll (CO) ***426***
Midland Lutheran Coll (NE) ***429***
Milligan Coll (TN) ***430***
Minnesota State U, Moorhead (MN) ***432***
Montclair State U (NJ) ***435***
Morris Coll (SC) ***437***
Mount Vernon Nazarene U (OH) ***440***
New England School of Communications (ME) ***445***
North Central Coll (IL) ***449***
Northern Michigan U (MI) ***451***
Northwest Missouri State U (MO) ***454***
Ohio Northern U (OH) ***457***
Ohio U (OH) ***458***
Ohio Wesleyan U (OH) ***459***
Oklahoma Baptist U (OK) ***459***
Oklahoma Christian U (OK) ***459***
Oklahoma City U (OK) ***460***
Oklahoma State U (OK) ***460***
Olivet Nazarene U (IL) ***461***
Pacific Lutheran U (WA) ***463***
Pacific U (OR) ***464***
Pittsburg State U (KS) ***470***
Plattsburgh State U of NY (NY) ***471***
Point Park Coll (PA) ***471***
Quinnipiac U (CT) ***476***
Reformed Bible Coll (MI) ***477***
Rust Coll (MS) ***485***
Ryerson U (ON, Canada) ***485***
St. Cloud State U (MN) ***488***
St. Francis Coll (NY) ***488***
San Jose State U (CA) ***499***
Shorter Coll (GA) ***504***
Southern Adventist U (TN) ***508***
Southern Arkansas U–Magnolia (AR) ***509***
Southern Methodist U (TX) ***510***
Southern Nazarene U (OK) ***510***
Southwest Texas State U (TX) ***513***
State U of NY at New Paltz (NY) ***515***
State U of NY Coll at Brockport (NY) ***515***
State U of NY Coll at Buffalo (NY) ***516***
State U of NY Coll at Fredonia (NY) ***516***
Stephens Coll (MO) ***519***
Suffolk U (MA) ***520***
Syracuse U (NY) ***521***
Temple U (PA) ***523***
Texas Christian U (TX) ***526***
Troy State U (AL) ***532***
Union U (TN) ***534***
The U of Akron (OH) ***537***
U of Central Oklahoma (OK) ***542***
U of Cincinnati (OH) ***543***
U of Colorado at Boulder (CO) ***543***
U of Dayton (OH) ***544***
The U of Findlay (OH) ***545***
U of Georgia (GA) ***545***
U of Illinois at Urbana–Champaign (IL) ***548***
The U of Iowa (IA) ***548***
U of Kansas (KS) ***549***
U of La Verne (CA) ***549***
U of Maryland, Coll Park (MD) ***552***
U of Miami (FL) ***553***
U of Missouri–Columbia (MO) ***555***
U of Montevallo (AL) ***557***
U of Nebraska at Omaha (NE) ***557***
U of Nebraska–Lincoln (NE) ***557***
U of Nevada, Reno (NV) ***558***
The U of North Carolina at Pembroke (NC) ***560***
U of Northern Iowa (IA) ***561***
U of North Texas (TX) ***562***
U of Oklahoma (OK) ***562***
U of Oregon (OR) ***562***
U of St. Francis (IL) ***573***
U of St. Thomas (MN) ***573***
U of San Francisco (CA) ***574***
U of South Carolina (SC) ***575***
The U of South Dakota (SD) ***575***
U of Southern California (CA) ***576***
The U of Tennessee at Chattanooga (TN) ***577***
The U of Tennessee at Martin (TN) ***577***
The U of Texas at El Paso (TX) ***578***
U of Tulsa (OK) ***581***
U of Utah (UT) ***582***
U of Windsor (ON, Canada) ***584***
U of Wisconsin–Madison (WI) ***584***
U of Wisconsin–Milwaukee (WI) ***585***
U of Wisconsin–Oshkosh (WI) ***585***
U of Wisconsin–Platteville (WI) ***585***
U of Wisconsin–River Falls (WI) ***585***
U of Wisconsin–Superior (WI) ***586***
Valdosta State U (GA) ***588***
Waldorf Coll (IA) ***592***
Wartburg Coll (IA) ***594***
Webster U (MO) ***597***
Western Washington U (WA) ***600***
Westminster Coll (PA) ***601***
West Texas A&M U (TX) ***602***
William Woods U (MO) ***607***
Winona State U (MN) ***608***

BUILDING MAINTENANCE/ MANAGEMENT

Overview: This major will teach students how to effectively manage buildings and to service a variety of residential, commercial, and industrial structures. *Related majors:* electronics installer/repairer; major appliance installer/repairer; heating, air conditioning, and refrigeration mechanics; operations management; accounting. *Potential careers:* building manager. *Salary potential:* $19k-$29k.

State U of NY at Farmingdale (NY) ***357***
Peirce Coll (PA) ***466***

BUSINESS

Overview: This major teaches students the general theories and principles of business, such as buying, selling, manufacturing and producing, business organization, and accounting and prepares students for more specialized study in the field of business. *Related majors:* mathematics, psychology, accounting, business administration and management. *Potential careers:* salesperson, accountant, entrepreneur, financial analyst, marketing and advertising executive. *Salary potential:* $30k-$40k.

Alabama A&M U (AL) ***261***
Andrew Jackson U (AL) ***269***
Arizona State U East (AZ) ***271***
Asbury Coll (KY) ***274***
Auburn U Montgomery (AL) ***276***
Aurora U (IL) ***277***
Austin Peay State U (TN) ***278***
Averett U (VA) ***278***
Baker Coll of Jackson (MI) ***279***
Bayamón Central U (PR) ***283***
Baylor U (TX) ***283***
Bay Path Coll (MA) ***283***
Benedictine U (IL) ***285***
Bentley Coll (MA) ***286***

BUSINESS (continued)

Blue Mountain Coll (MS) 291
Bowling Green State U (OH) 292
Brescia U (KY) 293
Brevard Coll (NC) 294
Briarcliffe Coll (NY) 294
Brock U (ON, Canada) 295
California Coll for Health Sciences (CA) 298
California State U, Chico (CA) 300
California State U, Stanislaus (CA) 302
Cameron U (OK) 303
Campbell U (NC) 303
Capella U (MN) 304
Carlow Coll (PA) 305
The Catholic U of America (DC) 307
Central Michigan U (MI) 310
Champlain Coll (VT) 311
Christian Brothers U (TN) 313
Circleville Bible Coll (OH) 314
The Coll of Southeastern Europe, The American U of Athens(Greece) 323
Coll of Staten Island of the City U of NY (NY) 323
Colorado Christian U (CO) 325
Concordia Coll (MN) 329
Concordia U (NE) 330
Cumberland Coll (KY) 335
Cumberland U (TN) 335
Delta State U (MS) 339
DePaul U (IL) 339
Dominican Coll (NY) 344
Drake U (IA) 345
Drexel U (PA) 346
Duquesne U (PA) 346
Eastern Connecticut State U (CT) 347
Eastern Illinois U (IL) 348
Eastern Michigan U (MI) 348
East Texas Baptist U (TX) 350
École des hautes études commerciales de Montréal (QC, Canada) 350
Florida Metropolitan U-Tampa Coll, Pinellas (FL) 361
Florida Southern Coll (FL) 361
Florida State U (FL) 361
Franklin Coll (IN) 363
Georgia Coll & State U (GA) 367
Grace Coll (IN) 370
Green Mountain Coll (VT) 372
Henderson State U (AR) 378
Hillsdale Free Will Baptist Coll (OK) 379
Hollins U (VA) 380
Howard Payne U (TX) 382
Indiana U Bloomington (IN) 385
Indiana U East (IN) 386
Indiana U Kokomo (IN) 386
Indiana U–Purdue U Indianapolis (IN) 387
Indiana U South Bend (IN) 387
Indiana U Southeast (IN) 387
Ithaca Coll (NY) 390
Jacksonville U (FL) 391
Johns Hopkins U (MD) 392
Johnson State Coll (VT) 394
Judson Coll (AL) 395
Limestone Coll (SC) 406
Linfield Coll (OR) 408
Loras Coll (IA) 410
Loyola Coll in Maryland (MD) 411
Luther Coll (IA) 412
Maharishi U of Management (IA) 414
Malaspina U-Coll (BC, Canada) 415
Manchester Coll (IN) 415
Marygrove Coll (MI) 419
Maryville U of Saint Louis (MO) 420
McMurry U (TX) 423
Mercer U (GA) 425
Miami U (OH) 428
Milwaukee School of Engineering (WI) 431
Montana State U–Billings (MT) 434
Montana State U–Bozeman (MT) 434
Montana Tech of The U of Montana (MT) 435
Mount Allison U (NB, Canada) 437
Murray State U (KY) 440
New Mexico State U (NM) 446
Nichols Coll (MA) 448
Norfolk State U (VA) 448
Northeastern Illinois U (IL) 450
Northeastern U (MA) 450
Northern Arizona U (AZ) 450
Northern Illinois U (IL) 450
Ohio U (OH) 458
Oklahoma Christian U (OK) 459
Oklahoma City U (OK) 460
Oklahoma State U (OK) 460
Peirce Coll (PA) 466
Penn State U Abington Coll (PA) 467
Penn State U Altoona Coll (PA) 467
Penn State U Berks Cmps of Berks-Lehigh Valley Coll (PA) 468
Penn State U Lehigh Valley Cmps of Berks-Lehigh Valley Coll (PA) 468
Penn State U Schuylkill Campus of the Capital Coll (PA) 468
Regis Coll (MA) 478
Rockhurst U (MO) 482
Roger Williams U (RI) 483
Saginaw Valley State U (MI) 486
St. Ambrose U (IA) 486
Saint Anselm Coll (NH) 487
Saint Mary's U of Minnesota (MN) 494
St. Norbert Coll (WI) 495
Saint Xavier U (IL) 496
Sam Houston State U (TX) 497
Schreiner U (TX) 501
Skidmore Coll (NY) 506
Southern Arkansas U–Magnolia (AR) 509
Southern Illinois U Carbondale (IL) 509
Southern Illinois U Edwardsville (IL) 509
Southwest Missouri State U (MO) 513
Stephen F. Austin State U (TX) 518
Texas A&M U–Texarkana (TX) 525
Texas Coll (TX) 526
Thomas More Coll (KY) 528
Touro U International (CA) 529
Trinity Christian Coll (IL) 530
Troy State U Montgomery (AL) 532
Tyndale Coll & Seminary (ON, Canada) 533
Union Inst & U (OH) 534
The U of Akron (OH) 537
The U of Arizona (AZ) 538
U of Arkansas (AR) 539
U of Arkansas at Little Rock (AR) 539
U of Central Arkansas (AR) 542
U of Central Florida (FL) 542
U of Central Oklahoma (OK) 542
U of Connecticut (CT) 544
U of Denver (CO) 544
U of Georgia (GA) 545
U of Hawaii at Manoa (HI) 546
U of Houston–Clear Lake (TX) 547
U of Houston–Downtown (TX) 547
U of Illinois at Urbana–Champaign (IL) 548
U of Kansas (KS) 549
U of Kentucky (KY) 549
U of Maryland, Coll Park (MD) 552
U of Mississippi (MS) 555
U of Missouri–Rolla (MO) 556
The U of Montana–Missoula (MT) 556
The U of Montana–Western (MT) 556
U of Nevada, Reno (NV) 558
U of North Dakota (ND) 561
U of North Texas (TX) 562
U of Notre Dame (IN) 562
U of Pittsburgh (PA) 569
U of Puerto Rico, Humacao U Coll (PR) 570
U of Puerto Rico, Río Piedras (PR) 571
U of Puget Sound (WA) 571
U of Redlands (CA) 572
U of San Francisco (CA) 574
U of Saskatchewan (SK, Canada) 574
U of Science and Arts of Oklahoma (OK) 574
U of South Alabama (AL) 575
U of Southern Indiana (IN) 576
U of South Florida (FL) 576
The U of Tennessee (TN) 577
The U of Texas at Austin (TX) 578
The U of Texas at Dallas (TX) 578
The U of Texas at San Antonio (TX) 578
The U of Texas–Pan American (TX) 579
U of the Incarnate Word (TX) 580
U of Victoria (BC, Canada) 582
U of Virginia (VA) 582
U of Washington (WA) 583
U of Wisconsin–Whitewater (WI) 586
Utah State U (UT) 587
Virginia Polytechnic Inst and State U (VA) 591
Wake Forest U (NC) 592
Washington U in St. Louis (MO) 595
Webber International U (FL) 596
Webster U (MO) 597
Western Governors U (UT) 599
Western Illinois U (IL) 599
Western Michigan U (MI) 599
Western Oregon U (OR) 600
Westminster Coll (UT) 601
Westmont Coll (CA) 602
West Texas A&M U (TX) 602
Xavier U (OH) 610
York U (ON, Canada) 611
Youngstown State U (OH) 611

BUSINESS ADMINISTRATION

Overview: This major prepares students to organize and manage the functions and processes of businesses or other types of organizations. *Related major:* psychology, business, accounting, operations management and supervision, financial planning. *Potential careers:* business owner, industrial manufacturer, sales or marketing manager, hospital administrator. *Salary potential:* $30k-$40k.

Abilene Christian U (TX) 260
Acadia U (NS, Canada) 260
Adams State Coll (CO) 260
Adelphi U (NY) 260
Adrian Coll (MI) 260
Alabama A&M U (AL) 261
Alabama State U (AL) 261
Alaska Pacific U (AK) 261
Albany State U (GA) 262
Albertson Coll of Idaho (ID) 262
Albion Coll (MI) 262
Albright Coll (PA) 263
Alcorn State U (MS) 263
Alderson-Broaddus Coll (WV) 263
Alfred U (NY) 263
Alice Lloyd Coll (KY) 263
Allen U (SC) 264
Alliant International U (CA) 264
Alma Coll (MI) 264
Alvernia Coll (PA) 265
Alverno Coll (WI) 265
Amberton U (TX) 265
American Christian Coll and Seminary (OK) 265
American Coll of Thessaloniki(Greece) 266
American InterContinental U (CA) 266
American InterContinental U, Atlanta (GA) 266
American InterContinental U-London(United Kingdom) 267
American International Coll (MA) 267
American U (DC) 267
The American U in Cairo(Egypt) 267
The American U in Dubai(United Arab Emirates) 267
American U of Puerto Rico (PR) 268
American U of Rome(Italy) 268
Anderson Coll (SC) 268
Anderson U (IN) 268
Andrews U (MI) 269
Angelo State U (TX) 269
Anna Maria Coll (MA) 269
Antioch Coll (OH) 269
Antioch U McGregor (OH) 270
Appalachian State U (NC) 270
Aquinas Coll (MI) 270
Arcadia U (PA) 271
Arizona State U (AZ) 271
Arizona State U West (AZ) 272
Arkansas Baptist Coll (AR) 272
Arkansas State U (AR) 272
Arkansas Tech U (AR) 272
Ashland U (OH) 274
Assumption Coll (MA) 275
Athabasca U (AB, Canada) 275
Athens State U (AL) 275
Atlanta Christian Coll (GA) 275
Atlantic Baptist U (NB, Canada) 275
Atlantic Union Coll (MA) 276
Auburn U (AL) 276
Auburn U Montgomery (AL) 276
Augsburg Coll (MN) 276
Augustana Coll (IL) 276
Augustana Coll (SD) 276
Augusta State U (GA) 277
Austin Coll (TX) 277
Averett U (VA) 278
Avila U (MO) 278
Azusa Pacific U (CA) 278
Babson Coll (MA) 278
Baker Coll of Auburn Hills (MI) 279
Baker Coll of Cadillac (MI) 279
Baker Coll of Clinton Township (MI) 279
Baker Coll of Flint (MI) 279
Baker Coll of Jackson (MI) 279
Baker Coll of Muskegon (MI) 279
Baker Coll of Owosso (MI) 279
Baker Coll of Port Huron (MI) 280
Baker U (KS) 280
Baldwin-Wallace Coll (OH) 280
Ball State U (IN) 280
Baptist Bible Coll (MO) 281
Barber-Scotia Coll (NC) 281
Barclay Coll (KS) 281
Barry U (FL) 282
Barton Coll (NC) 282
Bayamón Central U (PR) 283
Baylor U (TX) 283
Beacon Coll and Graduate School (GA) 283
Becker Coll (MA) 283
Belhaven Coll (MS) 283
Bellarmine U (KY) 284
Bellevue U (NE) 284
Belmont Abbey Coll (NC) 284
Belmont U (TN) 284
Beloit Coll (WI) 285
Bemidji State U (MN) 285
Benedict Coll (SC) 285
Benedictine Coll (KS) 285
Bennett Coll (NC) 286
Bentley Coll (MA) 286
Berea Coll (KY) 286
Baruch Coll of the City U of NY (NY) 286
Berry Coll (GA) 287
Bethany Coll (KS) 287
Bethany Coll (WV) 287
Bethany Lutheran Coll (MN) 288
Bethel Coll (IN) 288
Bethel Coll (KS) 288
Bethel Coll (MN) 288
Bethel Coll (TN) 288
Bethune-Cookman Coll (FL) 289
Biola U (CA) 289
Birmingham-Southern Coll (AL) 289
Bishop's U (QC, Canada) 289
Blackburn Coll (IL) 290
Black Hills State U (SD) 290
Bloomfield Coll (NJ) 290
Bloomsburg U of Pennsylvania (PA) 290
Bluefield Coll (VA) 291
Bluefield State Coll (WV) 291
Blue Mountain Coll (MS) 291
Bluffton Coll (OH) 291
Boston Coll (MA) 292
Boston U (MA) 292
Bowie State U (MD) 292
Bowling Green State U (OH) 292
Bradley U (IL) 293
Brandon U (MB, Canada) 293
Brenau U (GA) 293
Brewton-Parker Coll (GA) 294
Briar Cliff U (IA) 294
Bridgewater Coll (VA) 294
Bridgewater State Coll (MA) 294
Briercrest Bible Coll (SK, Canada) 295
Brigham Young U (UT) 295
Brigham Young U–Hawaii (HI) 295
British Columbia Inst of Technology (BC, Canada) 295
Brock U (ON, Canada) 295
Brooklyn Coll of the City U of NY (NY) 295
Bryan Coll (TN) 296
Bryant Coll (RI) 296
Bucknell U (PA) 297
Buena Vista U (IA) 297
Butler U (IN) 297
Cabrini Coll (PA) 298
Caldwell Coll (NJ) 298
California Baptist U (CA) 298
California Lutheran U (CA) 299
California Maritime Academy (CA) 299
California Polytechnic State U, San Luis Obispo (CA) 300
California State Polytechnic U, Pomona (CA) 300
California State U, Bakersfield (CA) 300
California State U, Chico (CA) 300
California State U, Dominguez Hills (CA) 300
California State U, Fresno (CA) 301
California State U, Fullerton (CA) 301
California State U, Hayward (CA) 301
California State U, Long Beach (CA) 301
California State U, Northridge (CA) 301
California State U, Sacramento (CA) 301

California State U, San Bernardino (CA) **302**
California State U, San Marcos (CA) **302**
California State U, Stanislaus (CA) **302**
California U of Pennsylvania (PA) **302**
Calumet Coll of Saint Joseph (IN) **302**
Calvin Coll (MI) **303**
Cameron U (OK) **303**
Campbellsville U (KY) **303**
Canisius Coll (NY) **304**
Capital U (OH) **304**
Cardinal Stritch U (WI) **305**
Carleton U (ON, Canada) **305**
Carnegie Mellon U (PA) **305**
Carroll Coll (MT) **306**
Carroll Coll (WI) **306**
Carson-Newman Coll (TN) **306**
Carthage Coll (WI) **306**
Cascade Coll (OR) **307**
Case Western Reserve U (OH) **307**
Castleton State Coll (VT) **307**
Catawba Coll (NC) **307**
The Catholic U of America (DC) **307**
Cazenovia Coll (NY) **308**
Cedar Crest Coll (PA) **308**
Cedarville U (OH) **308**
Centenary Coll (NJ) **308**
Centenary Coll of Louisiana (LA) **308**
Central Christian Coll of Kansas (KS) **309**
Central Coll (IA) **309**
Central Connecticut State U (CT) **309**
Central Methodist Coll (MO) **309**
Central Michigan U (MI) **310**
Central Missouri State U (MO) **310**
Central Washington U (WA) **310**
Chadron State Coll (NE) **311**
Chaminade U of Honolulu (HI) **311**
Champlain Coll (VT) **311**
Chapman U (CA) **311**
Charleston Southern U (SC) **311**
Chatham Coll (PA) **312**
Chestnut Hill Coll (PA) **312**
Cheyney U of Pennsylvania (PA) **312**
Chowan Coll (NC) **312**
Christian Brothers U (TN) **313**
Christian Heritage Coll (CA) **313**
Christopher Newport U (VA) **313**
Citadel, The Military Coll of South Carolina (SC) **314**
City Coll of the City U of NY (NY) **314**
City U (WA) **314**
Claflin U (SC) **314**
Clarion U of Pennsylvania (PA) **315**
Clark Atlanta U (GA) **315**
Clarke Coll (IA) **315**
Clarkson Coll (NE) **315**
Clarkson U (NY) **316**
Clark U (MA) **316**
Clayton Coll & State U (GA) **316**
Clearwater Christian Coll (FL) **316**
Cleary U (MI) **317**
Clemson U (SC) **317**
Coastal Carolina U (SC) **318**
Coe Coll (IA) **318**
Coker Coll (SC) **318**
Colby-Sawyer Coll (NH) **319**
Coll Misericordia (PA) **319**
Coll of Charleston (SC) **320**
Coll of Mount St. Joseph (OH) **320**
Coll of Mount Saint Vincent (NY) **320**
The Coll of New Jersey (NJ) **320**
The Coll of New Rochelle (NY) **321**
Coll of Notre Dame of Maryland (MD) **321**
Coll of Saint Benedict (MN) **321**
Coll of St. Catherine (MN) **321**
Coll of Saint Elizabeth (NJ) **321**
Coll of St. Joseph (VT) **322**
Coll of Saint Mary (NE) **322**
The Coll of Saint Rose (NY) **322**
Coll of Santa Fe (NM) **323**
The Coll of Southeastern Europe, The American U of Athens(Greece) **323**
Coll of the Ozarks (MO) **323**
Coll of the Southwest (NM) **324**
The Coll of William and Mary (VA) **324**
Colorado Christian U (CO) **325**
Colorado State U (CO) **325**
Colorado State U-Pueblo (CO) **325**
Colorado Tech U (CO) **326**
Colorado Tech U Denver Campus (CO) **326**
Colorado Tech U Sioux Falls Campus (SD) **326**
Columbia Coll (MO) **326**
Columbia Coll (SC) **327**
Columbia Coll Chicago (IL) **327**
Columbia Southern U (AL) **327**
Columbia Union Coll (MD) **328**
Columbus State U (GA) **328**
Concord Coll (WV) **329**
Concordia Coll (MN) **329**
Concordia Coll (NY) **329**
Concordia U (CA) **330**
Concordia U (IL) **330**
Concordia U (MI) **330**
Concordia U (MN) **330**
Concordia U (NE) **330**
Concordia U (OR) **330**
Concordia U (QC, Canada) **331**
Concordia U at Austin (TX) **331**
Concordia U Wisconsin (WI) **331**
Converse Coll (SC) **332**
Cornell U (NY) **333**
Cornerstone U (MI) **333**
Covenant Coll (GA) **333**
Crichton Coll (TN) **334**
Crown Coll (MN) **334**
Culver-Stockton Coll (MO) **334**
Curry Coll (MA) **335**
Daemen Coll (NY) **335**
Dakota State U (SD) **335**
Dakota Wesleyan U (SD) **336**
Dalhousie U (NS, Canada) **336**
Dallas Baptist U (TX) **336**
Dallas Christian Coll (TX) **336**
Dana Coll (NE) **337**
Daniel Webster Coll (NH) **337**
Davenport U, Grand Rapids (MI) **337**
Davenport U, Kalamazoo (MI) **337**
Davenport U, Lansing (MI) **337**
Davis & Elkins Coll (WV) **338**
Defiance Coll (OH) **338**
Delaware State U (DE) **338**
Delaware Valley Coll (PA) **339**
Delta State U (MS) **339**
DePaul U (IL) **339**
Deree Coll(Greece) **339**
DeSales U (PA) **340**
Dickinson State U (ND) **344**
Dillard U (LA) **344**
Doane Coll (NE) **344**
Dominican Coll (NY) **344**
Dominican U (IL) **345**
Dordt Coll (IA) **345**
Dowling Coll (NY) **345**
Drake U (IA) **345**
Drury U (MO) **346**
D'Youville Coll (NY) **347**
Earlham Coll (IN) **347**
East Carolina U (NC) **347**
East Central U (OK) **347**
Eastern Connecticut State U (CT) **347**
Eastern Kentucky U (KY) **348**
Eastern Mennonite U (VA) **348**
Eastern Michigan U (MI) **348**
Eastern Nazarene Coll (MA) **348**
Eastern New Mexico U (NM) **349**
Eastern Washington U (WA) **349**
East Stroudsburg U of Pennsylvania (PA) **349**
East Tennessee State U (TN) **349**
East Texas Baptist U (TX) **350**
East-West U (IL) **350**
Eckerd Coll (FL) **350**
École des hautes études commerciales de Montréal (QC, Canada) **350**
Edgewood Coll (WI) **351**
Edinboro U of Pennsylvania (PA) **351**
Elizabeth City State U (NC) **351**
Elizabethtown Coll (PA) **351**
Elmhurst Coll (IL) **351**
Elmira Coll (NY) **351**
Elms Coll (MA) **352**
Elon U (NC) **352**
Embry-Riddle Aeronautical U (AZ) **352**
Embry-Riddle Aeronautical U (FL) **352**
Embry-Riddle Aeronautical U, Extended Campus (FL) **352**
Emmanuel Coll (GA) **353**
Emmanuel Coll (MA) **353**
Emory & Henry Coll (VA) **353**
Emory U (GA) **354**
Emporia State U (KS) **354**
Endicott Coll (MA) **354**
Erskine Coll (SC) **354**
Eureka Coll (IL) **355**
Evangel U (MO) **355**
Everglades Coll (FL) **355**
The Evergreen State Coll (WA) **355**
Excelsior Coll (NY) **356**
Fairfield U (CT) **356**
Fairleigh Dickinson U, Florham (NJ) **356**
Fairleigh Dickinson U, Teaneck-Metro Campus (NJ) **356**
Fairmont State Coll (WV) **356**
Faulkner U (AL) **357**
Fayetteville State U (NC) **357**
Felician Coll (NJ) **357**
Ferris State U (MI) **358**
Ferrum Coll (VA) **358**
Finlandia U (MI) **358**
Fisk U (TN) **358**
Fitchburg State Coll (MA) **358**
Five Towns Coll (NY) **359**
Flagler Coll (FL) **359**
Florida A&M U (FL) **359**
Florida Atlantic U (FL) **359**
Florida Gulf Coast U (FL) **359**
Florida Inst of Technology (FL) **360**
Florida International U (FL) **360**
Florida Metropolitan U-Tampa Coll, Brandon (FL) **360**
Florida Metropolitan U-Fort Lauderdale Coll (FL) **360**
Florida Metropolitan U–Jacksonville Campus (FL) **360**
Florida Metropolitan U-Melbourne (FL) **360**
Florida Metropolitan U-Orlando Coll, North (FL) **361**
Florida Metropolitan U-Orlando Coll, South (FL) **361**
Florida Southern Coll (FL) **361**
Florida State U (FL) **361**
Fontbonne U (MO) **361**
Fordham U (NY) **362**
Fort Hays State U (KS) **362**
Fort Lewis Coll (CO) **362**
Fort Valley State U (GA) **362**
Framingham State Coll (MA) **362**
The Franciscan U (IA) **363**
Franciscan U of Steubenville (OH) **363**
Francis Marion U (SC) **363**
Franklin and Marshall Coll (PA) **363**
Franklin Coll (IN) **363**
Franklin Pierce Coll (NH) **364**
Freed-Hardeman U (TN) **364**
Free Will Baptist Bible Coll (TN) **364**
Fresno Pacific U (CA) **364**
Frostburg State U (MD) **365**
Furman U (SC) **365**
Gallaudet U (DC) **365**
Gannon U (PA) **365**
Gardner-Webb U (NC) **365**
Geneva Coll (PA) **366**
George Fox U (OR) **366**
George Mason U (VA) **366**
Georgetown Coll (KY) **366**
Georgetown U (DC) **366**
The George Washington U (DC) **367**
Georgia Coll & State U (GA) **367**
Georgia Inst of Technology (GA) **367**
Georgian Court Coll (NJ) **367**
Georgia Southern U (GA) **367**
Georgia Southwestern State U (GA) **368**
Georgia State U (GA) **368**
Gettysburg Coll (PA) **368**
Glenville State Coll (WV) **368**
Golden Gate U (CA) **369**
Goldey-Beacom Coll (DE) **369**
Gonzaga U (WA) **369**
Gordon Coll (MA) **370**
Goshen Coll (IN) **370**
Governors State U (IL) **370**
Grace Bible Coll (MI) **370**
Grace Coll (IN) **370**
Graceland U (IA) **371**
Grace U (NE) **371**
Grambling State U (LA) **371**
Grand Canyon U (AZ) **371**
Grand Valley State U (MI) **371**
Grand View Coll (IA) **372**
Green Mountain Coll (VT) **372**
Greenville Coll (IL) **373**
Griggs U (MD) **373**
Grove City Coll (PA) **373**
Guilford Coll (NC) **373**
Gustavus Adolphus Coll (MN) **374**
Gwynedd-Mercy Coll (PA) **374**
Hamline U (MN) **374**
Hampton U (VA) **375**
Hannibal-LaGrange Coll (MO) **375**
Hanover Coll (IN) **375**
Harding U (AR) **375**
Hardin-Simmons U (TX) **376**
Harris-Stowe State Coll (MO) **376**
Hartwick Coll (NY) **376**
Hastings Coll (NE) **377**
Hawai'i Pacific U (HI) **377**
Heidelberg Coll (OH) **377**
Henry Cogswell Coll (WA) **378**
High Point U (NC) **379**
Hilbert Coll (NY) **379**
Hillsdale Coll (MI) **379**
Hiram Coll (OH) **379**
Hofstra U (NY) **380**
Holy Family U (PA) **380**
Holy Names Coll (CA) **381**
Hood Coll (MD) **381**
Hope Coll (MI) **381**
Hope International U (CA) **381**
Houghton Coll (NY) **381**
Houston Baptist U (TX) **382**
Howard Payne U (TX) **382**
Howard U (DC) **382**
Humboldt State U (CA) **382**
Huntingdon Coll (AL) **383**
Huntington Coll (IN) **383**
Huron U USA in London(United Kingdom) **383**
Husson Coll (ME) **383**
Huston-Tillotson Coll (TX) **383**
Idaho State U (ID) **384**
Illinois Coll (IL) **384**
Illinois State U (IL) **384**
Illinois Wesleyan U (IL) **385**
Immaculata U (PA) **385**
Indiana Inst of Technology (IN) **385**
Indiana State U (IN) **385**
Indiana U Bloomington (IN) **385**
Indiana U Northwest (IN) **386**
Indiana U of Pennsylvania (PA) **386**
Indiana U–Purdue U Fort Wayne (IN) **386**
Indiana Wesleyan U (IN) **387**
Insto Tecno Estudios Sups Monterrey(Mexico) **388**
Inter American U of PR, Aguadilla Campus (PR) **388**
Inter Amer U of PR, Barranquitas Campus (PR) **388**
Inter American U of PR, Guayama Campus (PR) **388**
Inter American U of PR, San Germán Campus (PR) **388**
International Coll (FL) **389**
International Coll of the Cayman Islands(Cayman Islands) **389**
Iona Coll (NY) **390**
Iowa State U of Science and Technology (IA) **390**
Iowa Wesleyan Coll (IA) **390**
Ithaca Coll (NY) **390**
Jackson State U (MS) **390**
Jacksonville State U (AL) **390**
Jacksonville U (FL) **391**
James Madison U (VA) **391**
Jamestown Coll (ND) **391**
John Brown U (AR) **392**
John Cabot U(Italy) **392**
John Carroll U (OH) **392**
John F. Kennedy U (CA) **392**
Johnson & Wales U (RI) **393**
Johnson C. Smith U (NC) **394**
Johnson State Coll (VT) **394**
John Wesley Coll (NC) **394**
Jones Coll (FL) **394**
Jones International U (CO) **394**
Judson Coll (IL) **395**
Juniata Coll (PA) **395**
Kansas State U (KS) **396**
Kean U (NJ) **396**
Keene State Coll (NH) **396**
Kendall Coll (IL) **396**
Kennesaw State U (GA) **397**
Kent State U (OH) **397**
Kentucky Christian Coll (KY) **397**
Kentucky State U (KY) **397**
Kentucky Wesleyan Coll (KY) **397**
Kettering U (MI) **398**
Keuka Coll (NY) **398**
King Coll (TN) **398**
King's Coll (PA) **398**
The King's U Coll (AB, Canada) **399**
LaGrange Coll (GA) **400**
Lake Erie Coll (OH) **400**
Lakehead U (ON, Canada) **400**

BUSINESS ADMINISTRATION (continued)

Lakeland Coll (WI) ***401***
Lamar U (TX) ***401***
Lambuth U (TN) ***401***
Lander U (SC) ***401***
Lane Coll (TN) ***402***
Langston U (OK) ***402***
La Roche Coll (PA) ***402***
La Salle U (PA) ***402***
Lasell Coll (MA) ***402***
La Sierra U (CA) ***403***
Laurentian U (ON, Canada) ***403***
Lawrence Technological U (MI) ***403***
Lebanon Valley Coll (PA) ***403***
Lees-McRae Coll (NC) ***404***
Lee U (TN) ***404***
Lehigh U (PA) ***404***
Lehman Coll of the City U of NY (NY) ***404***
Le Moyne Coll (NY) ***404***
Lenoir-Rhyne Coll (NC) ***405***
Lesley U (MA) ***405***
LeTourneau U (TX) ***405***
Lewis-Clark State Coll (ID) ***406***
Lewis U (IL) ***406***
Liberty U (VA) ***406***
Life U (GA) ***406***
Limestone Coll (SC) ***406***
Lincoln Christian Coll (IL) ***407***
Lincoln Memorial U (TN) ***407***
Lincoln U (CA) ***407***
Lincoln U (PA) ***407***
Lindenwood U (MO) ***407***
Lindsey Wilson Coll (KY) ***407***
Lipscomb U (TN) ***408***
Lock Haven U of Pennsylvania (PA) ***408***
Long Island U, Brentwood Campus (NY) ***408***
Long Island U, Brooklyn Campus (NY) ***409***
Long Island U, C.W. Post Campus (NY) ***409***
Long Island U, Southampton Coll (NY) ***409***
Longwood U (VA) ***409***
Loras Coll (IA) ***410***
Louisiana Coll (LA) ***410***
Louisiana State U and A&M Coll (LA) ***410***
Louisiana State U in Shreveport (LA) ***410***
Louisiana Tech U (LA) ***410***
Lourdes Coll (OH) ***411***
Loyola Marymount U (CA) ***411***
Loyola U Chicago (IL) ***411***
Loyola U New Orleans (LA) ***411***
Lubbock Christian U (TX) ***412***
Luther Coll (IA) ***412***
Lycoming Coll (PA) ***412***
Lynchburg Coll (VA) ***413***
Lyndon State Coll (VT) ***413***
Lynn U (FL) ***413***
Lyon Coll (AR) ***413***
MacMurray Coll (IL) ***414***
Madonna U (MI) ***414***
Maharishi U of Management (IA) ***414***
Maine Maritime Academy (ME) ***415***
Malone Coll (OH) ***415***
Manchester Coll (IN) ***415***
Manhattan Christian Coll (KS) ***415***
Manhattanville Coll (NY) ***416***
Mansfield U of Pennsylvania (PA) ***416***
Maranatha Baptist Bible Coll (WI) ***417***
Marian Coll (IN) ***417***
Marian Coll of Fond du Lac (WI) ***417***
Marietta Coll (OH) ***417***
Marist Coll (NY) ***417***
Marquette U (WI) ***418***
Marshall U (WV) ***418***
Mars Hill Coll (NC) ***418***
Martin Methodist Coll (TN) ***418***
Martin U (IN) ***419***
Mary Baldwin Coll (VA) ***419***
Marygrove Coll (MI) ***419***
Marymount Coll of Fordham U (NY) ***419***
Marymount Manhattan Coll (NY) ***420***
Marymount U (VA) ***420***
Maryville Coll (TN) ***420***
Maryville U of Saint Louis (MO) ***420***
Mary Washington Coll (VA) ***420***
Marywood U (PA) ***421***
Massachusetts Coll of Liberal Arts (MA) ***421***
Massachusetts Inst of Technology (MA) ***421***
The Master's Coll and Seminary (CA) ***422***
Mayville State U (ND) ***422***
McDaniel Coll (MD) ***422***
McGill U (QC, Canada) ***423***
McKendree Coll (IL) ***423***
McMaster U (ON, Canada) ***423***
McNeese State U (LA) ***423***
McPherson Coll (KS) ***423***
Medaille Coll (NY) ***424***
Medgar Evers Coll of the City U of NY (NY) ***424***
Memorial U of Newfoundland (NF, Canada) ***424***
Menlo Coll (CA) ***425***
Mercer U (GA) ***425***
Mercy Coll (NY) ***425***
Mercyhurst Coll (PA) ***425***
Meredith Coll (NC) ***426***
Merrimack Coll (MA) ***426***
Mesa State Coll (CO) ***426***
Messiah Coll (PA) ***426***
Methodist Coll (NC) ***427***
Metropolitan Coll of New York (NY) ***427***
Metropolitan State U (MN) ***427***
Miami U (OH) ***428***
Michigan State U (MI) ***428***
Michigan Technological U (MI) ***428***
MidAmerica Nazarene U (KS) ***428***
Middle Tennessee State U (TN) ***429***
Midland Lutheran Coll (NE) ***429***
Midway Coll (KY) ***429***
Midwestern State U (TX) ***430***
Miles Coll (AL) ***430***
Millersville U of Pennsylvania (PA) ***430***
Milligan Coll (TN) ***430***
Millikin U (IL) ***430***
Millsaps Coll (MS) ***431***
Minnesota State U, Mankato (MN) ***431***
Minnesota State U, Moorhead (MN) ***432***
Minot State U (ND) ***432***
Mississippi Coll (MS) ***432***
Mississippi State U (MS) ***432***
Mississippi Valley State U (MS) ***432***
Missouri Southern State Coll (MO) ***433***
Missouri Valley Coll (MO) ***433***
Missouri Western State Coll (MO) ***433***
Mitchell Coll (CT) ***433***
Molloy Coll (NY) ***433***
Monmouth Coll (IL) ***434***
Monmouth U (NJ) ***434***
Montana State U–Billings (MT) ***434***
Montana State U–Northern (MT) ***434***
Montana Tech of The U of Montana (MT) ***435***
Montclair State U (NJ) ***435***
Montreat Coll (NC) ***435***
Moravian Coll (PA) ***436***
Morehead State U (KY) ***436***
Morehouse Coll (GA) ***436***
Morgan State U (MD) ***436***
Morningside Coll (IA) ***437***
Morris Coll (SC) ***437***
Mount Allison U (NB, Canada) ***437***
Mount Aloysius Coll (PA) ***437***
Mount Ida Coll (MA) ***438***
Mount Marty Coll (SD) ***438***
Mount Mary Coll (WI) ***438***
Mount Mercy Coll (IA) ***438***
Mount Olive Coll (NC) ***439***
Mount Saint Mary Coll (NY) ***439***
Mount St. Mary's Coll (CA) ***439***
Mount Saint Mary's Coll and Seminary (MD) ***439***
Mount Saint Vincent U (NS, Canada) ***439***
Mount Union Coll (OH) ***440***
Mount Vernon Nazarene U (OH) ***440***
Muhlenberg Coll (PA) ***440***
Murray State U (KY) ***440***
Muskingum Coll (OH) ***441***
National American U, Colorado Springs (CO) ***441***
National American U, Denver (CO) ***441***
National American U (NM) ***441***
National American U (SD) ***442***
National American U–Sioux Falls Branch (SD) ***442***
The National Hispanic U (CA) ***442***
National-Louis U (IL) ***442***
National U (CA) ***442***
Nazareth Coll of Rochester (NY) ***443***
Nebraska Wesleyan U (NE) ***443***
Neumann Coll (PA) ***443***
Newberry Coll (SC) ***444***
Newbury Coll (MA) ***444***
New England Coll (NH) ***444***
New Jersey City U (NJ) ***445***
New Jersey Inst of Technology (NJ) ***445***
Newman U (KS) ***445***
New Mexico Highlands U (NM) ***446***
New Mexico Inst of Mining and Technology (NM) ***446***
New Mexico State U (NM) ***446***
New York Inst of Technology (NY) ***447***
New York U (NY) ***447***
Niagara U (NY) ***447***
Nicholls State U (LA) ***447***
Nichols Coll (MA) ***448***
Nipissing U (ON, Canada) ***448***
North Carolina Ag and Tech State U (NC) ***448***
North Carolina Central U (NC) ***448***
North Carolina State U (NC) ***449***
North Carolina Wesleyan Coll (NC) ***449***
North Central Coll (IL) ***449***
Northcentral U (AZ) ***449***
North Dakota State U (ND) ***449***
Northeastern State U (OK) ***450***
Northern Arizona U (AZ) ***450***
Northern Illinois U (IL) ***450***
Northern Kentucky U (KY) ***451***
Northern Michigan U (MI) ***451***
Northern State U (SD) ***451***
North Georgia Coll & State U (GA) ***451***
North Greenville Coll (SC) ***451***
Northland Coll (WI) ***452***
North Park U (IL) ***452***
Northwest Christian Coll (OR) ***452***
Northwest Coll (WA) ***452***
Northwestern Coll (IA) ***453***
Northwestern Coll (MN) ***453***
Northwestern Oklahoma State U (OK) ***453***
Northwestern Polytechnic U (CA) ***453***
Northwestern State U of Louisiana (LA) ***453***
Northwest Missouri State U (MO) ***454***
Northwest Nazarene U (ID) ***454***
Northwood U (MI) ***454***
Northwood U, Florida Campus (FL) ***454***
Northwood U, Texas Campus (TX) ***454***
Norwich U (VT) ***455***
Notre Dame Coll (OH) ***455***
Notre Dame de Namur U (CA) ***455***
Nova Southeastern U (FL) ***455***
Nyack Coll (NY) ***456***
Oak Hills Christian Coll (MN) ***456***
Oakland City U (IN) ***456***
Oakland U (MI) ***456***
Oakwood Coll (AL) ***456***
Oglethorpe U (GA) ***457***
Ohio Dominican U (OH) ***457***
Ohio Northern U (OH) ***457***
The Ohio State U (OH) ***457***
Ohio U (OH) ***458***
Ohio U–Chillicothe (OH) ***458***
Ohio U–Lancaster (OH) ***458***
Ohio U–Southern Campus (OH) ***458***
Ohio Valley Coll (WV) ***459***
Ohio Wesleyan U (OH) ***459***
Okanagan U Coll (BC, Canada) ***459***
Oklahoma Baptist U (OK) ***459***
Oklahoma Christian U (OK) ***459***
Oklahoma City U (OK) ***460***
Oklahoma Panhandle State U (OK) ***460***
Oklahoma Wesleyan U (OK) ***460***
Old Dominion U (VA) ***460***
Olivet Coll (MI) ***461***
Olivet Nazarene U (IL) ***461***
Oral Roberts U (OK) ***461***
Oregon Inst of Technology (OR) ***461***
Oregon State U (OR) ***462***
Ottawa U (KS) ***462***
Otterbein Coll (OH) ***462***
Ouachita Baptist U (AR) ***462***
Our Lady of Holy Cross Coll (LA) ***463***
Our Lady of the Lake U of San Antonio (TX) ***463***
Pace U (NY) ***463***
Pacific Lutheran U (WA) ***463***
Pacific States U (CA) ***464***
Pacific Union Coll (CA) ***464***
Pacific U (OR) ***464***
Paine Coll (GA) ***465***
Palm Beach Atlantic U (FL) ***465***
Park U (MO) ***465***
Patten Coll (CA) ***466***
Paul Quinn Coll (TX) ***466***
Peace Coll (NC) ***466***
Peirce Coll (PA) ***466***
Pennsylvania Coll of Technology (PA) ***467***
Penn State U at Erie, The Behrend Coll (PA) ***467***
Penn State U Harrisburg Campus of the Capital Coll (PA) ***468***
Penn State U Univ Park Campus (PA) ***468***
Pepperdine U, Malibu (CA) ***469***
Peru State Coll (NE) ***469***
Pfeiffer U (NC) ***469***
Philadelphia Biblical U (PA) ***469***
Philadelphia U (PA) ***469***
Piedmont Coll (GA) ***470***
Pikeville Coll (KY) ***470***
Pillsbury Baptist Bible Coll (MN) ***470***
Pine Manor Coll (MA) ***470***
Pittsburg State U (KS) ***470***
Plattsburgh State U of NY (NY) ***471***
Plymouth State Coll (NH) ***471***
Point Loma Nazarene U (CA) ***471***
Point Park Coll (PA) ***471***
Pontifical Catholic U of Puerto Rico (PR) ***472***
Portland State U (OR) ***472***
Potomac Coll (DC) ***473***
Prairie View A&M U (TX) ***473***
Presbyterian Coll (SC) ***473***
Presentation Coll (SD) ***474***
Principia Coll (IL) ***474***
Providence Coll (RI) ***474***
Providence Coll and Theological Seminary (MB, Canada) ***475***
Purdue U (IN) ***475***
Purdue U Calumet (IN) ***475***
Purdue U North Central (IN) ***475***
Queen's U at Kingston (ON, Canada) ***476***
Queens U of Charlotte (NC) ***476***
Quincy U (IL) ***476***
Quinnipiac U (CT) ***476***
Radford U (VA) ***476***
Ramapo Coll of New Jersey (NJ) ***477***
Reformed Bible Coll (MI) ***477***
Regis U (CO) ***478***
Reinhardt Coll (GA) ***478***
Rensselaer Polytechnic Inst (NY) ***478***
Rhode Island Coll (RI) ***479***
Rhodes Coll (TN) ***479***
Rice U (TX) ***479***
The Richard Stockton Coll of New Jersey (NJ) ***479***
Richmond, The American International U in London(United Kingdom) ***480***
Rider U (NJ) ***480***
Ripon Coll (WI) ***480***
Rivier Coll (NH) ***480***
Roanoke Coll (VA) ***481***
Robert Morris Coll (IL) ***481***
Robert Morris U (PA) ***481***
Roberts Wesleyan Coll (NY) ***481***
Rochester Coll (MI) ***482***
Rochester Inst of Technology (NY) ***482***
Rockford Coll (IL) ***482***
Rockhurst U (MO) ***482***
Rocky Mountain Coll (MT) ***482***
Roger Williams U (RI) ***483***
Roosevelt U (IL) ***483***
Rosemont Coll (PA) ***484***
Rowan U (NJ) ***484***
Royal Roads U (BC, Canada) ***484***
Russell Sage Coll (NY) ***484***
Rust Coll (MS) ***485***
Rutgers, The State U of New Jersey, Camden (NJ) ***485***
Rutgers, The State U of New Jersey, Newark (NJ) ***485***
Rutgers, The State U of New Jersey, New Brunswick (NJ) ***485***
Ryerson U (ON, Canada) ***485***
Sacred Heart U (CT) ***486***
Sage Coll of Albany (NY) ***486***
Saginaw Valley State U (MI) ***486***
St. Ambrose U (IA) ***486***
St. Andrews Presbyterian Coll (NC) ***487***
Saint Augustine's Coll (NC) ***487***
St. Bonaventure U (NY) ***487***
St. Cloud State U (MN) ***488***
St. Edward's U (TX) ***488***
St. Francis Coll (NY) ***488***
Saint Francis U (PA) ***488***
St. Francis Xavier U (NS, Canada) ***489***
St. Gregory's U (OK) ***489***
St. John Fisher Coll (NY) ***489***
Saint John's U (MN) ***490***
St. John's U (NY) ***490***
Saint Joseph Coll (CT) ***490***
Saint Joseph's Coll (IN) ***490***
St. Joseph's Coll, New York (NY) ***491***
Saint Joseph's Coll of Maine (ME) ***491***
St. Joseph's Coll, Suffolk Campus (NY) ***491***
Saint Joseph's U (PA) ***491***
Saint Leo U (FL) ***492***
Saint Louis U (MO) ***492***
Saint Martin's Coll (WA) ***493***

Saint Mary Coll (KS) ***493***
Saint Mary-of-the-Woods Coll (IN) ***493***
Saint Mary's Coll (IN) ***493***
Saint Mary's Coll of California (CA) ***494***
Saint Mary's Coll of Madonna U (MI) ***493***
Saint Mary's U (NS, Canada) ***494***
Saint Mary's U of Minnesota (MN) ***494***
St. Mary's U of San Antonio (TX) ***494***
Saint Michael's Coll (VT) ***494***
Saint Peter's Coll (NJ) ***495***
St. Thomas Aquinas Coll (NY) ***495***
St. Thomas U (FL) ***496***
Saint Vincent Coll (PA) ***496***
Salem Coll (NC) ***496***
Salem International U (WV) ***496***
Salem State Coll (MA) ***497***
Salisbury U (MD) ***497***
Salve Regina U (RI) ***497***
Samford U (AL) ***497***
Sam Houston State U (TX) ***497***
San Diego State U (CA) ***498***
San Francisco State U (CA) ***498***
San Jose State U (CA) ***499***
Santa Clara U (CA) ***499***
Savannah State U (GA) ***499***
Schiller International U(France) ***500***
Schiller International U(Spain) ***500***
Schiller International U, American Coll of Switzerland(Switzerland) ***500***
Schreiner U (TX) ***501***
Seattle Pacific U (WA) ***501***
Seattle U (WA) ***501***
Seton Hall U (NJ) ***502***
Seton Hill U (PA) ***502***
Shawnee State U (OH) ***502***
Shaw U (NC) ***502***
Sheldon Jackson Coll (AK) ***503***
Shenandoah U (VA) ***503***
Shepherd Coll (WV) ***503***
Shippensburg U of Pennsylvania (PA) ***503***
Shorter Coll (GA) ***504***
Siena Heights U (MI) ***504***
Sierra Nevada Coll (NV) ***504***
Silver Lake Coll (WI) ***504***
Simmons Coll (MA) ***504***
Simon Fraser U (BC, Canada) ***505***
Simpson Coll (IA) ***505***
Simpson Coll and Graduate School (CA) ***505***
Si Tanka Huron U (SD) ***505***
Slippery Rock U of Pennsylvania (PA) ***506***
Sonoma State U (CA) ***506***
South Carolina State U (SC) ***506***
Southeastern Louisiana U (LA) ***508***
Southeastern Oklahoma State U (OK) ***508***
Southeastern U (DC) ***508***
Southeast Missouri State U (MO) ***508***
Southern Adventist U (TN) ***508***
Southern Connecticut State U (CT) ***509***
Southern Illinois U Carbondale (IL) ***509***
Southern Methodist U (TX) ***510***
Southern Nazarene U (OK) ***510***
Southern New Hampshire U (NH) ***510***
Southern Oregon U (OR) ***510***
Southern U and A&M Coll (LA) ***511***
Southern Utah U (UT) ***511***
Southern Vermont Coll (VT) ***511***
Southern Virginia U (VA) ***511***
Southern Wesleyan U (SC) ***511***
Southwest Baptist U (MO) ***512***
Southwestern Assemblies of God U (TX) ***512***
Southwestern Coll (KS) ***512***
Southwestern Oklahoma State U (OK) ***512***
Southwestern U (TX) ***513***
Southwest Missouri State U (MO) ***513***
Southwest State U (MN) ***513***
Southwest Texas State U (TX) ***513***
Spalding U (KY) ***513***
Spring Arbor U (MI) ***514***
Springfield Coll (MA) ***514***
Spring Hill Coll (AL) ***514***
State U of NY at Albany (NY) ***514***
State U of NY at New Paltz (NY) ***515***
State U of NY at Oswego (NY) ***515***
State U of NY Coll at Brockport (NY) ***515***
State U of NY Coll at Buffalo (NY) ***516***
State U of NY Coll at Fredonia (NY) ***516***
State U of NY Coll at Geneseo (NY) ***516***
State U of NY Coll at Old Westbury (NY) ***516***
State U of NY Coll at Potsdam (NY) ***517***
State U of NY Empire State Coll (NY) ***517***
State U of NY Inst of Tech at Utica/Rome (NY) ***518***
State U of NY Maritime Coll (NY) ***518***
State U of West Georgia (GA) ***518***
Stephen F. Austin State U (TX) ***518***
Stephens Coll (MO) ***519***
Sterling Coll (KS) ***519***
Stetson U (FL) ***519***
Stonehill Coll (MA) ***520***
Stony Brook U, State University of New York (NY) ***520***
Strayer U (DC) ***520***
Suffolk U (MA) ***520***
Sullivan U (KY) ***521***
Sul Ross State U (TX) ***521***
Susquehanna U (PA) ***521***
Syracuse U (NY) ***521***
Tabor Coll (KS) ***522***
Talladega Coll (AL) ***522***
Tarleton State U (TX) ***522***
Taylor U (IN) ***523***
Taylor U, Fort Wayne Campus (IN) ***523***
Teikyo Post U (CT) ***523***
Temple U (PA) ***523***
Tennessee State U (TN) ***523***
Tennessee Technological U (TN) ***524***
Tennessee Temple U (TN) ***524***
Tennessee Wesleyan Coll (TN) ***524***
Texas A&M International U (TX) ***524***
Texas A&M U (TX) ***524***
Texas A&M U at Galveston (TX) ***524***
Texas A&M U–Commerce (TX) ***525***
Texas A&M U–Corpus Christi (TX) ***525***
Texas A&M U–Kingsville (TX) ***525***
Texas A&M U–Texarkana (TX) ***525***
Texas Christian U (TX) ***526***
Texas Coll (TX) ***526***
Texas Lutheran U (TX) ***526***
Texas Southern U (TX) ***526***
Texas Tech U (TX) ***526***
Texas Wesleyan U (TX) ***526***
Texas Woman's U (TX) ***527***
Thiel Coll (PA) ***527***
Thomas Coll (ME) ***527***
Thomas Edison State Coll (NJ) ***527***
Thomas U (GA) ***528***
Tiffin U (OH) ***528***
Touro Coll (NY) ***529***
Towson U (MD) ***529***
Transylvania U (KY) ***529***
Trent U (ON, Canada) ***529***
Trevecca Nazarene U (TN) ***529***
Trinity Bible Coll (ND) ***530***
Trinity Christian Coll (IL) ***530***
Trinity Coll (DC) ***530***
Trinity International U (IL) ***531***
Trinity U (TX) ***531***
Trinity Western U (BC, Canada) ***531***
Tri-State U (IN) ***532***
Troy State U (AL) ***532***
Troy State U Dothan (AL) ***532***
Troy State U Montgomery (AL) ***532***
Truman State U (MO) ***532***
Tulane U (LA) ***533***
Tusculum Coll (TN) ***533***
Tuskegee U (AL) ***533***
Union Coll (KY) ***533***
Union Coll (NE) ***534***
Union U (TN) ***534***
United States Air Force Academy (CO) ***534***
United States International U(Kenya) ***535***
United States Military Academy (NY) ***535***
Universidad Adventista de las Antillas (PR) ***536***
Université de Sherbrooke (QC, Canada) ***536***
U du Québec à Trois-Rivières (QC, Canada) ***536***
U du Québec à Hull (QC, Canada) ***536***
Université Laval (QC, Canada) ***536***
U at Buffalo, The State University of New York (NY) ***536***
U Coll of the Cariboo (BC, Canada) ***537***
The U of Akron (OH) ***537***
The U of Alabama (AL) ***537***
The U of Alabama at Birmingham (AL) ***537***
The U of Alabama in Huntsville (AL) ***537***
U of Alaska Anchorage (AK) ***538***
U of Alaska Fairbanks (AK) ***538***
U of Alaska Southeast (AK) ***538***
U of Alberta (AB, Canada) ***538***
U of Arkansas (AR) ***539***
U of Arkansas at Little Rock (AR) ***539***
U of Arkansas at Monticello (AR) ***539***
U of Baltimore (MD) ***539***
U of Bridgeport (CT) ***540***
The U of British Columbia (BC, Canada) ***540***
U of Calgary (AB, Canada) ***540***
U of Calif, Berkeley (CA) ***540***
U of Calif, Riverside (CA) ***541***
U of Central Arkansas (AR) ***542***
U of Central Florida (FL) ***542***
U of Central Oklahoma (OK) ***542***
U of Charleston (WV) ***542***
U of Cincinnati (OH) ***543***
U of Colorado at Boulder (CO) ***543***
U of Colorado at Colorado Springs (CO) ***543***
U of Colorado at Denver (CO) ***543***
U of Dayton (OH) ***544***
U of Delaware (DE) ***544***
U of Denver (CO) ***544***
U of Dubuque (IA) ***545***
U of Evansville (IN) ***545***
The U of Findlay (OH) ***545***
U of Florida (FL) ***545***
U of Georgia (GA) ***545***
U of Great Falls (MT) ***545***
U of Hartford (CT) ***546***
U of Hawaii at Hilo (HI) ***546***
U of Hawaii at Manoa (HI) ***546***
U of Hawaii–West Oahu (HI) ***546***
U of Houston (TX) ***547***
U of Houston–Clear Lake (TX) ***547***
U of Houston–Downtown (TX) ***547***
U of Houston–Victoria (TX) ***547***
U of Illinois at Chicago (IL) ***547***
U of Illinois at Springfield (IL) ***548***
U of Indianapolis (IN) ***548***
The U of Iowa (IA) ***548***
U of La Verne (CA) ***549***
The U of Lethbridge (AB, Canada) ***549***
U of Louisiana at Lafayette (LA) ***550***
U of Louisville (KY) ***550***
U of Maine (ME) ***550***
The U of Maine at Augusta (ME) ***550***
U of Maine at Fort Kent (ME) ***551***
U of Maine at Machias (ME) ***551***
U of Maine at Presque Isle (ME) ***551***
U of Manitoba (MB, Canada) ***551***
U of Mary (ND) ***551***
U of Mary Hardin-Baylor (TX) ***551***
U of Maryland Eastern Shore (MD) ***552***
U of Maryland University Coll (MD) ***552***
U of Massachusetts Amherst (MA) ***552***
U of Massachusetts Boston (MA) ***553***
U of Massachusetts Dartmouth (MA) ***553***
U of Massachusetts Lowell (MA) ***553***
The U of Memphis (TN) ***553***
U of Miami (FL) ***553***
U of Michigan (MI) ***554***
U of Michigan–Dearborn (MI) ***554***
U of Michigan–Flint (MI) ***554***
U of Minnesota, Crookston (MN) ***554***
U of Minnesota, Duluth (MN) ***554***
U of Minnesota, Morris (MN) ***555***
U of Mississippi (MS) ***555***
U of Missouri–Columbia (MO) ***555***
U of Missouri–Kansas City (MO) ***555***
U of Missouri–Rolla (MO) ***556***
U of Missouri–St. Louis (MO) ***556***
U of Mobile (AL) ***556***
U of Montevallo (AL) ***557***
U of Nebraska at Kearney (NE) ***557***
U of Nebraska–Lincoln (NE) ***557***
U of Nevada, Las Vegas (NV) ***558***
U of New Brunswick Fredericton (NB, Canada) ***558***
U of New Brunswick Saint John (NB, Canada) ***558***
U of New England (ME) ***558***
U of New Hampshire (NH) ***558***
U of New Haven (CT) ***559***
U of New Mexico (NM) ***559***
U of New Orleans (LA) ***559***
U of North Alabama (AL) ***559***
The U of North Carolina at Asheville (NC) ***559***
The U of North Carolina at Chapel Hill (NC) ***560***
The U of North Carolina at Charlotte (NC) ***560***
The U of North Carolina at Greensboro (NC) ***560***
The U of North Carolina at Pembroke (NC) ***560***
The U of North Carolina at Wilmington (NC) ***561***
U of Northern Colorado (CO) ***561***
U of Northern Iowa (IA) ***561***
U of North Florida (FL) ***561***
U of Oklahoma (OK) ***562***
U of Oregon (OR) ***562***
U of Ottawa (ON, Canada) ***563***
U of Pennsylvania (PA) ***563***
U of Phoenix-Atlanta Campus (GA) ***563***
U of Phoenix–Boston Campus (MA) ***563***
U of Phoenix–Colorado Campus (CO) ***563***
U of Phoenix–Dallas Campus (TX) ***564***
U of Phoenix–Fort Lauderdale Campus (FL) ***564***
U of Phoenix–Houston Campus (TX) ***564***
U of Phoenix–Jacksonville Campus (FL) ***564***
U of Phoenix–Louisiana Campus (LA) ***565***
U of Phoenix–Maryland Campus (MD) ***565***
U of Phoenix–Metro Detroit Campus (MI) ***565***
U of Phoenix–Nevada Campus (NV) ***565***
U of Phoenix–New Mexico Campus (NM) ***565***
U of Phoenix–Northern California Campus (CA) ***565***
U of Phoenix–Ohio Campus (OH) ***566***
U of Phoenix–Oklahoma City Campus (OK) ***566***
U of Phoenix–Oregon Campus (OR) ***566***
U of Phoenix–Orlando Campus (FL) ***566***
U of Phoenix–Philadelphia Campus (PA) ***566***
U of Phoenix–Phoenix Campus (AZ) ***567***
U of Phoenix–Pittsburgh Campus (PA) ***567***
U of Phoenix–Puerto Rico Campus (PR) ***567***
U of Phoenix–Sacramento Campus (CA) ***567***
U of Phoenix–St. Louis Campus (MO) ***567***
U of Phoenix–San Diego Campus (CA) ***567***
U of Phoenix–Southern Arizona Campus (AZ) ***568***
U of Phoenix–Southern California Campus (CA) ***568***
U of Phoenix–Southern Colorado Campus (CO) ***568***
U of Phoenix–Tampa Campus (FL) ***568***
U of Phoenix–Tulsa Campus (OK) ***568***
U of Phoenix–Utah Campus (UT) ***568***
U of Phoenix–West Michigan Campus (MI) ***569***
U of Phoenix-Wisconsin Campus (WI) ***569***
U of Pittsburgh at Bradford (PA) ***569***
U of Pittsburgh at Greensburg (PA) ***570***
U of Pittsburgh at Johnstown (PA) ***570***
U of Portland (OR) ***570***
U of Prince Edward Island (PE, Canada) ***570***
U of Puerto Rico at Arecibo (PR) ***570***
U of Puerto Rico, Humacao U Coll (PR) ***570***
U of Puerto Rico at Ponce (PR) ***571***
U of Puerto Rico, Cayey U Coll (PR) ***571***
U of Puerto Rico, Río Piedras (PR) ***571***
U of Redlands (CA) ***572***
U of Regina (SK, Canada) ***572***
U of Rhode Island (RI) ***572***
U of Richmond (VA) ***572***
U of Rio Grande (OH) ***572***
U of St. Francis (IL) ***573***
U of Saint Francis (IN) ***573***
U of St. Thomas (MN) ***573***
U of St. Thomas (TX) ***573***
U of San Diego (CA) ***574***
U of San Francisco (CA) ***574***
U of Science and Arts of Oklahoma (OK) ***574***
The U of Scranton (PA) ***574***
U of Sioux Falls (SD) ***574***
U of South Alabama (AL) ***575***
U of South Carolina (SC) ***575***
U of South Carolina Aiken (SC) ***575***
U of South Carolina Spartanburg (SC) ***575***
The U of South Dakota (SD) ***575***
U of Southern California (CA) ***576***
U of Southern Indiana (IN) ***576***
U of Southern Maine (ME) ***576***
U of Southern Mississippi (MS) ***576***
U of South Florida (FL) ***576***
The U of Tampa (FL) ***577***
The U of Tennessee (TN) ***577***
The U of Tennessee at Chattanooga (TN) ***577***
The U of Tennessee at Martin (TN) ***577***
The U of Texas at Arlington (TX) ***577***
The U of Texas at Austin (TX) ***578***
The U of Texas at Brownsville (TX) ***578***
The U of Texas at El Paso (TX) ***578***
The U of Texas at San Antonio (TX) ***578***
The U of Texas at Tyler (TX) ***579***
The U of Texas of the Permian Basin (TX) ***579***
The U of Texas–Pan American (TX) ***579***
U of the District of Columbia (DC) ***580***
U of the Incarnate Word (TX) ***580***

BUSINESS ADMINISTRATION (continued)

U of the Ozarks (AR) 580
U of the Pacific (CA) 580
U of the Sacred Heart (PR) 580
U of the Virgin Islands (VI) 581
U of Toledo (OH) 581
U of Toronto (ON, Canada) 581
U of Tulsa (OK) 581
U of Utah (UT) 582
U of Vermont (VT) 582
The U of Virginia's Coll at Wise (VA) 582
U of Washington (WA) 583
U of Waterloo (ON, Canada) 583
The U of West Alabama (AL) 583
The U of Western Ontario (ON, Canada) 583
U of West Florida (FL) 583
U of Windsor (ON, Canada) 584
U of Wisconsin–Eau Claire (WI) 584
U of Wisconsin–Green Bay (WI) 584
U of Wisconsin–La Crosse (WI) 584
U of Wisconsin–Madison (WI) 584
U of Wisconsin–Milwaukee (WI) 585
U of Wisconsin–Oshkosh (WI) 585
U of Wisconsin–Parkside (WI) 585
U of Wisconsin–Platteville (WI) 585
U of Wisconsin–River Falls (WI) 585
U of Wisconsin–Stevens Point (WI) 585
U of Wisconsin–Stout (WI) 586
U of Wisconsin–Superior (WI) 586
U of Wisconsin–Whitewater (WI) 586
U of Wyoming (WY) 586
U System Coll for Lifelong Learning (NH) 586
Upper Iowa U (IA) 587
Urbana U (OH) 587
Ursinus Coll (PA) 587
Ursuline Coll (OH) 587
Utah State U (UT) 587
Utica Coll (NY) 588
Valdosta State U (GA) 588
Valley City State U (ND) 588
Valparaiso U (IN) 588
Vanguard U of Southern California (CA) 589
Villa Julie Coll (MD) 590
Villanova U (PA) 590
Virginia Coll at Birmingham (AL) 590
Virginia Commonwealth U (VA) 590
Virginia Intermont Coll (VA) 590
Virginia Polytechnic Inst and State U (VA) 591
Virginia State U (VA) 591
Virginia Union U (VA) 591
Virginia Wesleyan Coll (VA) 591
Viterbo U (WI) 591
Voorhees Coll (SC) 592
Wagner Coll (NY) 592
Waldorf Coll (IA) 592
Walla Walla Coll (WA) 593
Walsh Coll of Accountancy and Business Admin (MI) 593
Walsh U (OH) 593
Warner Pacific Coll (OR) 593
Warner Southern Coll (FL) 593
Warren Wilson Coll (NC) 594
Wartburg Coll (IA) 594
Washington & Jefferson Coll (PA) 594
Washington and Lee U (VA) 594
Washington Coll (MD) 594
Washington State U (WA) 595
Washington U in St. Louis (MO) 595
Wayland Baptist U (TX) 595
Waynesburg Coll (PA) 595
Wayne State Coll (NE) 596
Wayne State U (MI) 596
Webber International U (FL) 596
Weber State U (UT) 596
Webster U (MO) 597
Wells Coll (NY) 597
Wentworth Inst of Technology (MA) 597
Wesleyan Coll (GA) 597
Wesley Coll (DE) 598
West Chester U of Pennsylvania (PA) 598
Western Baptist Coll (OR) 598
Western Carolina U (NC) 598
Western Connecticut State U (CT) 598
Western International U (AZ) 599
Western Kentucky U (KY) 599
Western Michigan U (MI) 599
Western New England Coll (MA) 600
Western New Mexico U (NM) 600
Western State Coll of Colorado (CO) 600
Western Washington U (WA) 600
Westfield State Coll (MA) 600
West Liberty State Coll (WV) 601
Westminster Coll (MO) 601
Westminster Coll (PA) 601
Westminster Coll (UT) 601
West Texas A&M U (TX) 602
West Virginia State Coll (WV) 602
West Virginia U (WV) 602
West Virginia U Inst of Technology (WV) 602
West Virginia Wesleyan Coll (WV) 603
Wheeling Jesuit U (WV) 603
Whittier Coll (CA) 604
Whitworth Coll (WA) 604
Wichita State U (KS) 604
Widener U (PA) 604
Wilberforce U (OH) 605
Wiley Coll (TX) 605
Wilkes U (PA) 605
William Carey Coll (MS) 605
William Jewell Coll (MO) 606
William Paterson U of New Jersey (NJ) 606
William Penn U (IA) 606
Williams Baptist Coll (AR) 606
William Woods U (MO) 607
Wilmington Coll (DE) 607
Wilmington Coll (OH) 607
Wilson Coll (PA) 607
Wingate U (NC) 607
Winona State U (MN) 608
Winston-Salem State U (NC) 608
Winthrop U (SC) 608
Wittenberg U (OH) 608
Woodbury U (CA) 609
Worcester Polytechnic Inst (MA) 609
Worcester State Coll (MA) 609
Wright State U (OH) 609
Xavier U (OH) 610
Xavier U of Louisiana (LA) 610
York Coll (NE) 610
York Coll of Pennsylvania (PA) 610
York Coll of the City U of New York (NY) 611
York U (ON, Canada) 611
Youngstown State U (OH) 611

BUSINESS ADMINISTRATION/ MANAGEMENT RELATED

Information can be found under this major's main heading.

Averett U (VA) 278
Carlos Albizu Univ - Miami (FL) 305
Chestnut Hill Coll (PA) 312
Daemen Coll (NY) 335
DePaul U (IL) 339
DeVry Inst of Technology (NY) 340
DeVry U (AZ) 340
DeVry U, Fremont (CA) 340
DeVry U, Long Beach (CA) 341
DeVry U, Pomona (CA) 341
DeVry U, West Hills (CA) 341
DeVry U, Colorado Springs (CO) 341
DeVry U, Orlando (FL) 342
DeVry U, Alpharetta (GA) 342
DeVry U, Decatur (GA) 342
DeVry U, Addison (IL) 342
DeVry U, Chicago (IL) 342
DeVry U, Tinley Park (IL) 342
DeVry U (MO) 343
DeVry U (OH) 343
DeVry U (TX) 343
DeVry U (VA) 343
DeVry U (WA) 343
Marymount U (VA) 420
Pennsylvania Coll of Technology (PA) 467
Saint Mary-of-the-Woods Coll (IN) 493
Sweet Briar Coll (VA) 521
Teikyo Post U (CT) 523
Texas Tech U (TX) 526
Towson U (MD) 529
Trinity Christian Coll (IL) 530
U of Hawaii at Manoa (HI) 546
U of Maryland, Coll Park (MD) 552
U of Notre Dame (IN) 562
U of Phoenix-Idaho Campus (ID) 564
U of St. Thomas (MN) 573
The U of Scranton (PA) 574
The U of Texas at Austin (TX) 578
U of Waterloo (ON, Canada) 583
U of Wisconsin–Stout (WI) 586
Woodbury U (CA) 609

BUSINESS COMMUNICATIONS

Overview: Students learn the skills they need to communicate effectively in a business or to function as an editor, writer, or public relations specialist for an organization or firm. *Related majors:* public relations, communications, journalism. *Potential careers:* copywriter, executive secretary or assistant, speechwriter, corporate communications assistant. *Salary potential:* $27k-$37k.

Assumption Coll (MA) 275
Augustana Coll (SD) 276
Babson Coll (MA) 278
Bentley Coll (MA) 286
Brenau U (GA) 293
Brock U (ON, Canada) 295
Calvin Coll (MI) 303
Chestnut Hill Coll (PA) 312
Coll of Saint Mary (NE) 322
The Coll of St. Scholastica (MN) 322
Elon U (NC) 352
Florida State U (FL) 361
Grove City Coll (PA) 373
Jones International U (CO) 394
Marietta Coll (OH) 417
Morningside Coll (IA) 437
Northwest Christian Coll (OR) 452
Ohio Dominican U (OH) 457
Ohio Valley Coll (WV) 459
Point Loma Nazarene U (CA) 471
Point Park Coll (PA) 471
Polytechnic U, Brooklyn Campus (NY) 472
Rochester Coll (MI) 482
Rockhurst U (MO) 482
Simpson Coll (IA) 505
Southern Christian U (AL) 509
State U of NY Coll of A&T at Cobleskill (NY) 517
The U of Findlay (OH) 545
U of Houston (TX) 547
U of Mary (ND) 551
The U of Montana–Western (MT) 556
U of Rio Grande (OH) 572
U of St. Thomas (MN) 573

BUSINESS COMPUTER FACILITIES OPERATION

Overview: Students learn to operate and oversee the operation of computer hardware systems, ensuring that these machines are used as efficiently as possible. They may work with mainframes, minicomputers, or networks of personal computers. *Related majors:* computer programming, systems analysis, business systems analysis and design, business systems networking and telecommunications. *Potential careers:* computer operator, computer consultant, computer security specialist. *Salary potential:* $30k-$35k

Eastern Illinois U (IL) 348
Seattle Pacific U (WA) 501
Southwest Texas State U (TX) 513

BUSINESS COMPUTER PROGRAMMING

Overview: This major teaches students how to design computer programs for a variety of business purposes. *Related majors:* computer programming, specific applications, computer programming, computer systems analysis. *Potential careers:* computer programmer, computer consultant, systems analyst. *Salary potential:* $45k-$55k.

Averett U (VA) 278
DePaul U (IL) 339
DeVry U (AZ) 340
Husson Coll (ME) 383
Inst of Public Administration(Ireland) 387
Kent State U (OH) 397
Limestone Coll (SC) 406
Luther Coll (IA) 412
Oklahoma Baptist U (OK) 459
St. Norbert Coll (WI) 495
U of North Texas (TX) 562
U of Puget Sound (WA) 571
U of Windsor (ON, Canada) 584
Western Michigan U (MI) 599

BUSINESS ECONOMICS

Overview: Students in this major learn the economic principles of effective business operation and organization and analyze the economic environment in which an organization operates. *Related majors:* economics, logistics and materials management, accounting, business administration/management. *Potential careers:* corporate consultant, research analyst, operations manager, corporate strategist, financial analyst. *Salary potential:* $35k-$45k.

Alabama A&M U (AL) 261
Albertus Magnus Coll (CT) 262
Alfred U (NY) 263
American International Coll (MA) 267
American U (DC) 267
Anderson U (IN) 268
Andrews U (MI) 269
Arkansas State U (AR) 272
Auburn U (AL) 276
Auburn U Montgomery (AL) 276
Augsburg Coll (MN) 276
Aurora U (IL) 277
Ball State U (IN) 280
Baylor U (TX) 283
Bellarmine U (KY) 284
Belmont U (TN) 284
Beloit Coll (WI) 285
Benedictine U (IL) 285
Bentley Coll (MA) 286
Baruch Coll of the City U of NY (NY) 286
Berry Coll (GA) 287
Bethany Coll (KS) 287
Bethany Coll (WV) 287
Bishop's U (QC, Canada) 289
Bloomsburg U of Pennsylvania (PA) 290
Bluffton Coll (OH) 291
Bradley U (IL) 293
Bridgewater Coll (VA) 294
Brock U (ON, Canada) 295
Buena Vista U (IA) 297
Butler U (IN) 297
California Inst of Technology (CA) 299
California State U, Fullerton (CA) 301
California State U, Hayward (CA) 301
California State U, Long Beach (CA) 301
California State U, San Bernardino (CA) 302
Cameron U (OK) 303
Campbellsville U (KY) 303
Cardinal Stritch U (WI) 305
Carnegie Mellon U (PA) 305
Carroll Coll (MT) 306
Carson-Newman Coll (TN) 306
Catawba Coll (NC) 307
Cedar Crest Coll (PA) 308
Centenary Coll of Louisiana (LA) 308
Chapman U (CA) 311
Charleston Southern U (SC) 311
Christopher Newport U (VA) 313
Clarion U of Pennsylvania (PA) 315
Clarkson U (NY) 316
Cleveland State U (OH) 317
Coll of Mount Saint Vincent (NY) 320
The Coll of New Jersey (NJ) 320
The Coll of Southeastern Europe, The American U of Athens(Greece) 323
The Coll of Wooster (OH) 324
Columbus State U (GA) 328
Concordia U (QC, Canada) 331
Cornell Coll (IA) 332
Creighton U (NE) 333
Dallas Baptist U (TX) 336
Delaware State U (DE) 338
DePaul U (IL) 339
Dominican Coll (NY) 344
Drexel U (PA) 346

East Central U (OK) ***347***
Eastern Kentucky U (KY) ***348***
Eastern Michigan U (MI) ***348***
Eastern Oregon U (OR) ***349***
Eastern Washington U (WA) ***349***
East Tennessee State U (TN) ***349***
École des hautes études commerciales de Montréal (QC, Canada) ***350***
Elmira Coll (NY) ***351***
Emmanuel Coll (MA) ***353***
Emory U (GA) ***354***
Fairleigh Dickinson U, Florham (NJ) ***356***
Fairleigh Dickinson U, Teaneck-Metro Campus (NJ) ***356***
Ferris State U (MI) ***358***
Fordham U (NY) ***362***
Fort Hays State U (KS) ***362***
Framingham State Coll (MA) ***362***
Francis Marion U (SC) ***363***
Freed-Hardeman U (TN) ***364***
George Fox U (OR) ***366***
The George Washington U (DC) ***367***
Georgia Coll & State U (GA) ***367***
Georgia Inst of Technology (GA) ***367***
Georgia Southern U (GA) ***367***
Georgia State U (GA) ***368***
Gonzaga U (WA) ***369***
Grambling State U (LA) ***371***
Grand Canyon U (AZ) ***371***
Green Mountain Coll (VT) ***372***
Greensboro Coll (NC) ***372***
Grove City Coll (PA) ***373***
Gustavus Adolphus Coll (MN) ***374***
Hampden-Sydney Coll (VA) ***374***
Hampshire Coll (MA) ***375***
Hawai'i Pacific U (HI) ***377***
Hendrix Coll (AR) ***378***
Houston Baptist U (TX) ***382***
Huntingdon Coll (AL) ***383***
Huntington Coll (IN) ***383***
Illinois Coll (IL) ***384***
Immaculata U (PA) ***385***
Indiana U Bloomington (IN) ***385***
Indiana U–Purdue U Fort Wayne (IN) ***386***
Indiana U Southeast (IN) ***387***
Inter American U of PR, San Germán Campus (PR) ***388***
Iona Coll (NY) ***390***
Ithaca Coll (NY) ***390***
Jackson State U (MS) ***390***
James Madison U (VA) ***391***
Jamestown Coll (ND) ***391***
Kalamazoo Coll (MI) ***395***
Kennesaw State U (GA) ***397***
Kent State U (OH) ***397***
Lafayette Coll (PA) ***400***
LaGrange Coll (GA) ***400***
Lake Forest Coll (IL) ***400***
Lakeland Coll (WI) ***401***
Lander U (SC) ***401***
La Salle U (PA) ***402***
Lehigh U (PA) ***404***
Lewis U (IL) ***406***
Limestone Coll (SC) ***406***
Lincoln Memorial U (TN) ***407***
Lipscomb U (TN) ***408***
Lock Haven U of Pennsylvania (PA) ***408***
Longwood U (VA) ***409***
Louisiana State U and A&M Coll (LA) ***410***
Louisiana Tech U (LA) ***410***
Loyola U Chicago (IL) ***411***
Loyola U New Orleans (LA) ***411***
Marian Coll of Fond du Lac (WI) ***417***
Marquette U (WI) ***418***
Marshall U (WV) ***418***
Mars Hill Coll (NC) ***418***
Mary Baldwin Coll (VA) ***419***
Marymount Coll of Fordham U (NY) ***419***
McGill U (QC, Canada) ***423***
McMurry U (TX) ***423***
Mercy Coll (NY) ***425***
Meredith Coll (NC) ***426***
Merrimack Coll (MA) ***426***
Mesa State Coll (CO) ***426***
Messiah Coll (PA) ***426***
Miami U (OH) ***428***
Michigan Technological U (MI) ***428***
Middle Tennessee State U (TN) ***429***
Milligan Coll (TN) ***430***
Mills Coll (CA) ***431***
Mississippi State U (MS) ***432***
Montana State U–Billings (MT) ***434***
Montclair State U (NJ) ***435***
Montreat Coll (NC) ***435***
Morehead State U (KY) ***436***
Morgan State U (MD) ***436***
Mount Allison U (NB, Canada) ***437***
Newberry Coll (SC) ***444***
New Mexico State U (NM) ***446***
New York U (NY) ***447***
Niagara U (NY) ***447***
Northern Arizona U (AZ) ***450***
Northern State U (SD) ***451***
North Georgia Coll & State U (GA) ***451***
North Greenville Coll (SC) ***451***
Northland Coll (WI) ***452***
Northwest Missouri State U (MO) ***454***
Northwood U (MI) ***454***
Notre Dame de Namur U (CA) ***455***
Occidental Coll (CA) ***457***
Oglethorpe U (GA) ***457***
The Ohio State U (OH) ***457***
Ohio Wesleyan U (OH) ***459***
Oklahoma City U (OK) ***460***
Oklahoma State U (OK) ***460***
Old Dominion U (VA) ***460***
Olivet Nazarene U (IL) ***461***
Otterbein Coll (OH) ***462***
Pace U (NY) ***463***
Park U (MO) ***465***
Penn State U at Erie, The Behrend Coll (PA) ***467***
Penn State U Univ Park Campus (PA) ***468***
Pittsburg State U (KS) ***470***
Plattsburgh State U of NY (NY) ***471***
Providence Coll (RI) ***474***
Quinnipiac U (CT) ***476***
Randolph-Macon Coll (VA) ***477***
Rider U (NJ) ***480***
Robert Morris U (PA) ***481***
Rockford Coll (IL) ***482***
Rocky Mountain Coll (MT) ***482***
Roosevelt U (IL) ***483***
Ryerson U (ON, Canada) ***485***
Sacred Heart U (CT) ***486***
Saginaw Valley State U (MI) ***486***
St. Bonaventure U (NY) ***487***
St. John's U (NY) ***490***
Saint Louis U (MO) ***492***
Saint Mary's U (NS, Canada) ***494***
Saint Peter's Coll (NJ) ***495***
Salem State Coll (MA) ***497***
Sam Houston State U (TX) ***497***
Santa Clara U (CA) ***499***
Seattle Pacific U (WA) ***501***
Seattle U (WA) ***501***
Seton Hall U (NJ) ***502***
Seton Hill U (PA) ***502***
Siena Coll (NY) ***504***
Sonoma State U (CA) ***506***
South Carolina State U (SC) ***506***
Southeastern Oklahoma State U (OK) ***508***
Southeast Missouri State U (MO) ***508***
Southern Connecticut State U (CT) ***509***
Southern Illinois U Carbondale (IL) ***509***
Southern Illinois U Edwardsville (IL) ***509***
Southern New Hampshire U (NH) ***510***
Southern U and A&M Coll (LA) ***511***
Southwest Texas State U (TX) ***513***
State U of NY at New Paltz (NY) ***515***
State U of NY Coll at Oneonta (NY) ***517***
State U of NY Coll at Potsdam (NY) ***517***
State U of West Georgia (GA) ***518***
Stephen F. Austin State U (TX) ***518***
Stetson U (FL) ***519***
Stonehill Coll (MA) ***520***
Susquehanna U (PA) ***521***
Temple U (PA) ***523***
Tennessee State U (TN) ***523***
Texas A&M International U (TX) ***524***
Texas A&M U–Kingsville (TX) ***525***
Texas Wesleyan U (TX) ***526***
Union U (TN) ***534***
U du Québec à Trois-Rivières (QC, Canada) ***536***
The U of Alabama (AL) ***537***
The U of Alabama at Birmingham (AL) ***537***
U of Alaska Anchorage (AK) ***538***
The U of Arizona (AZ) ***538***
U of Arkansas (AR) ***539***
U of Calif, Los Angeles (CA) ***541***
U of Calif, Riverside (CA) ***541***
U of Calif, Santa Barbara (CA) ***541***
U of Calif, Santa Cruz (CA) ***542***
U of Central Florida (FL) ***542***
U of Central Oklahoma (OK) ***542***
U of Dayton (OH) ***544***
U of Delaware (DE) ***544***
U of Denver (CO) ***544***
U of Evansville (IN) ***545***
U of Georgia (GA) ***545***
U of Guelph (ON, Canada) ***546***
U of Hartford (CT) ***546***
U of Hawaii at Manoa (HI) ***546***
U of Indianapolis (IN) ***548***
The U of Iowa (IA) ***548***
U of Judaism (CA) ***548***
U of Kentucky (KY) ***549***
U of La Verne (CA) ***549***
U of Louisiana at Lafayette (LA) ***550***
U of Louisville (KY) ***550***
U of Maine at Farmington (ME) ***550***
U of Manitoba (MB, Canada) ***551***
The U of Memphis (TN) ***553***
U of Miami (FL) ***553***
U of Mississippi (MS) ***555***
U of Missouri–Columbia (MO) ***555***
U of Nebraska at Omaha (NE) ***557***
U of Nebraska–Lincoln (NE) ***557***
U of Nevada, Reno (NV) ***558***
U of New Brunswick Fredericton (NB, Canada) ***558***
U of New Haven (CT) ***559***
U of New Orleans (LA) ***559***
U of North Alabama (AL) ***559***
The U of North Carolina at Charlotte (NC) ***560***
The U of North Carolina at Wilmington (NC) ***561***
U of North Dakota (ND) ***561***
U of North Florida (FL) ***561***
U of Oklahoma (OK) ***562***
U of Ottawa (ON, Canada) ***563***
U of Pittsburgh at Johnstown (PA) ***570***
U of Puerto Rico, Río Piedras (PR) ***571***
U of Richmond (VA) ***572***
U of San Diego (CA) ***574***
U of Saskatchewan (SK, Canada) ***574***
U of South Alabama (AL) ***575***
U of South Carolina (SC) ***575***
The U of South Dakota (SD) ***575***
U of Southern Mississippi (MS) ***576***
U of South Florida (FL) ***576***
The U of Tennessee (TN) ***577***
The U of Tennessee at Martin (TN) ***577***
The U of Texas at Arlington (TX) ***577***
The U of Texas at San Antonio (TX) ***578***
U of Toledo (OH) ***581***
U of West Florida (FL) ***583***
U of Windsor (ON, Canada) ***584***
U of Wisconsin–Platteville (WI) ***585***
U of Wisconsin–Superior (WI) ***586***
U of Wisconsin–Whitewater (WI) ***586***
U of Wyoming (WY) ***586***
Urbana U (OH) ***587***
Utica Coll (NY) ***588***
Valdosta State U (GA) ***588***
Villanova U (PA) ***590***
Virginia Commonwealth U (VA) ***590***
Virginia State U (VA) ***591***
Washington U in St. Louis (MO) ***595***
Wayne State Coll (NE) ***596***
Weber State U (UT) ***596***
West Chester U of Pennsylvania (PA) ***598***
Western Illinois U (IL) ***599***
Western Kentucky U (KY) ***599***
Western Washington U (WA) ***600***
West Liberty State Coll (WV) ***601***
Westminster Coll (UT) ***601***
Westmont Coll (CA) ***602***
West Texas A&M U (TX) ***602***
West Virginia Wesleyan Coll (WV) ***603***
Wheaton Coll (IL) ***603***
Widener U (PA) ***604***
Wilberforce U (OH) ***605***
William Paterson U of New Jersey (NJ) ***606***
William Woods U (MO) ***607***
Wilmington Coll (OH) ***607***
Wingate U (NC) ***607***
Winona State U (MN) ***608***
Wisconsin Lutheran Coll (WI) ***608***
Wittenberg U (OH) ***608***
Wofford Coll (SC) ***609***
Wright State U (OH) ***609***
Xavier U (OH) ***610***
Xavier U of Louisiana (LA) ***610***
York Coll of Pennsylvania (PA) ***610***
York U (ON, Canada) ***611***
Youngstown State U (OH) ***611***

BUSINESS EDUCATION

Overview: this major prepares undergraduates to teach basic economics and vocational business programs at the junior high and high school levels. *Related majors:* economics, accounting, investments and securities, history. *Potential careers:* high school economics teacher, vocational business teacher. *Salary potential:* $24k-$34k.

Abilene Christian U (TX) ***260***
Adams State Coll (CO) ***260***
Adrian Coll (MI) ***260***
Alabama State U (AL) ***261***
Albany State U (GA) ***262***
Alfred U (NY) ***263***
Allen U (SC) ***264***
American International Coll (MA) ***267***
Appalachian State U (NC) ***270***
Arkansas State U (AR) ***272***
Arkansas Tech U (AR) ***272***
Armstrong Atlantic State U (GA) ***273***
Atlantic Union Coll (MA) ***276***
Auburn U (AL) ***276***
Avila U (MO) ***278***
Baldwin-Wallace Coll (OH) ***280***
Ball State U (IN) ***280***
Baylor U (TX) ***283***
Belmont U (TN) ***284***
Bethany Coll (KS) ***287***
Bethel Coll (IN) ***288***
Bethune-Cookman Coll (FL) ***289***
Black Hills State U (SD) ***290***
Bloomsburg U of Pennsylvania (PA) ***290***
Bluefield Coll (VA) ***291***
Blue Mountain Coll (MS) ***291***
Bluffton Coll (OH) ***291***
Bowling Green State U (OH) ***292***
Brewton-Parker Coll (GA) ***294***
Brigham Young U–Hawaii (HI) ***295***
Buena Vista U (IA) ***297***
California State U, Fresno (CA) ***301***
California State U, Northridge (CA) ***301***
California State U, Sacramento (CA) ***301***
Campbellsville U (KY) ***303***
Canisius Coll (NY) ***304***
Carson-Newman Coll (TN) ***306***
Central Michigan U (MI) ***310***
Central Missouri State U (MO) ***310***
Central Washington U (WA) ***310***
Chadron State Coll (NE) ***311***
Clark Atlanta U (GA) ***315***
Clearwater Christian Coll (FL) ***316***
Coll of Santa Fe (NM) ***323***
Coll of the Ozarks (MO) ***323***
Coll of the Southwest (NM) ***324***
Colorado State U (CO) ***325***
Columbia Coll (MO) ***326***
Concord Coll (WV) ***329***
Concordia Coll (MN) ***329***
Concordia Coll (NY) ***329***
Concordia U (NE) ***330***
Concordia U Wisconsin (WI) ***331***
Cornell Coll (IA) ***332***
Cornerstone U (MI) ***333***
Cumberland Coll (KY) ***335***
Daemen Coll (NY) ***335***
Dakota State U (SD) ***335***
Dakota Wesleyan U (SD) ***336***
Dana Coll (NE) ***337***
Davis & Elkins Coll (WV) ***338***
Defiance Coll (OH) ***338***
Delaware State U (DE) ***338***
Delta State U (MS) ***339***
Dickinson State U (ND) ***344***
Doane Coll (NE) ***344***
Dordt Coll (IA) ***345***
Drake U (IA) ***345***
D'Youville Coll (NY) ***347***
East Carolina U (NC) ***347***
East Central U (OK) ***347***
Eastern Kentucky U (KY) ***348***
Eastern Michigan U (MI) ***348***
Eastern New Mexico U (NM) ***349***
Eastern Washington U (WA) ***349***
Elizabeth City State U (NC) ***351***
Emporia State U (KS) ***354***
Evangel U (MO) ***355***
Fairmont State Coll (WV) ***356***
Fayetteville State U (NC) ***357***

BUSINESS EDUCATION (continued)

Ferris State U (MI) ***358***
Florida A&M U (FL) ***359***
Fort Hays State U (KS) ***362***
The Franciscan U (IA) ***363***
Frostburg State U (MD) ***365***
Geneva Coll (PA) ***366***
Georgia Southern U (GA) ***367***
Georgia Southwestern State U (GA) ***368***
Glenville State Coll (WV) ***368***
Goshen Coll (IN) ***370***
Grambling State U (LA) ***371***
Grand Canyon U (AZ) ***371***
Grand View Coll (IA) ***372***
Gwynedd-Mercy Coll (PA) ***374***
Hampton U (VA) ***375***
Hardin-Simmons U (TX) ***376***
Hastings Coll (NE) ***377***
Henderson State U (AR) ***378***
Howard Payne U (TX) ***382***
Huntington Coll (IN) ***383***
Husson Coll (ME) ***383***
Illinois State U (IL) ***384***
Indiana State U (IN) ***385***
Indiana U of Pennsylvania (PA) ***386***
International Coll of the Cayman Islands(Cayman Islands) ***389***
Jackson State U (MS) ***390***
James Madison U (VA) ***391***
John Brown U (AR) ***392***
Kent State U (OH) ***397***
Lakeland Coll (WI) ***401***
La Salle U (PA) ***402***
Lee U (TN) ***404***
Lehman Coll of the City U of NY (NY) ***404***
Lenoir-Rhyne Coll (NC) ***405***
Lincoln Memorial U (TN) ***407***
Lindenwood U (MO) ***407***
Louisiana Coll (LA) ***410***
Maranatha Baptist Bible Coll (WI) ***417***
Mayville State U (ND) ***422***
McGill U (QC, Canada) ***423***
McKendree Coll (IL) ***423***
McMurry U (TX) ***423***
McPherson Coll (KS) ***423***
Mercyhurst Coll (PA) ***425***
MidAmerica Nazarene U (KS) ***428***
Middle Tennessee State U (TN) ***429***
Midland Lutheran Coll (NE) ***429***
Midwestern State U (TX) ***430***
Minot State U (ND) ***432***
Mississippi Coll (MS) ***432***
Mississippi State U (MS) ***432***
Montana State U–Northern (MT) ***434***
Montclair State U (NJ) ***435***
Morehead State U (KY) ***436***
Morgan State U (MD) ***436***
Morningside Coll (IA) ***437***
Mount Mary Coll (WI) ***438***
Mount St. Mary's Coll (CA) ***439***
Mount Vernon Nazarene U (OH) ***440***
Murray State U (KY) ***440***
Muskingum Coll (OH) ***441***
Nazareth Coll of Rochester (NY) ***443***
New York Inst of Technology (NY) ***447***
Niagara U (NY) ***447***
Nicholls State U (LA) ***447***
Norfolk State U (VA) ***448***
North Carolina Ag and Tech State U (NC) ***448***
North Central Coll (IL) ***449***
Northeastern State U (OK) ***450***
Northern Kentucky U (KY) ***451***
Northern Michigan U (MI) ***451***
Northern State U (SD) ***451***
Northwestern Coll (IA) ***453***
Northwestern Oklahoma State U (OK) ***453***
Northwest Missouri State U (MO) ***454***
Oakland City U (IN) ***456***
Oakwood Coll (AL) ***456***
Ohio U–Lancaster (OH) ***458***
Oklahoma Panhandle State U (OK) ***460***
Oklahoma Wesleyan U (OK) ***460***
Ouachita Baptist U (AR) ***462***
Our Lady of Holy Cross Coll (LA) ***463***
Pace U (NY) ***463***
Pacific Union Coll (CA) ***464***
Pillsbury Baptist Bible Coll (MN) ***470***
Pontifical Catholic U of Puerto Rico (PR) ***472***
Rider U (NJ) ***480***
Robert Morris U (PA) ***481***
Rust Coll (MS) ***485***
St. Ambrose U (IA) ***486***
Saint Augustine's Coll (NC) ***487***
St. Bonaventure U (NY) ***487***
St. Francis Coll (NY) ***488***
Saint Joseph's Coll (IN) ***490***
Saint Mary's Coll (IN) ***493***
St. Mary's U of San Antonio (TX) ***494***
Saint Vincent Coll (PA) ***496***
Salem State Coll (MA) ***497***
Sam Houston State U (TX) ***497***
Shippensburg U of Pennsylvania (PA) ***503***
Siena Heights U (MI) ***504***
South Carolina State U (SC) ***506***
Southeastern Oklahoma State U (OK) ***508***
Southeast Missouri State U (MO) ***508***
Southern Arkansas U–Magnolia (AR) ***509***
Southern Nazarene U (OK) ***510***
Southern New Hampshire U (NH) ***510***
Southern Utah U (UT) ***511***
Southwest Baptist U (MO) ***512***
Southwest Missouri State U (MO) ***513***
Spalding U (KY) ***513***
State U of NY Coll at Buffalo (NY) ***516***
State U of West Georgia (GA) ***518***
Suffolk U (MA) ***520***
Tabor Coll (KS) ***522***
Tarleton State U (TX) ***522***
Temple U (PA) ***523***
Tennessee State U (TN) ***523***
Texas A&M U–Commerce (TX) ***525***
Texas Southern U (TX) ***526***
Texas Wesleyan U (TX) ***526***
Thomas Coll (ME) ***527***
Thomas More Coll (KY) ***528***
Trinity Christian Coll (IL) ***530***
Troy State U (AL) ***532***
Union Coll (KY) ***533***
Union Coll (NE) ***534***
Union U (TN) ***534***
The U of Akron (OH) ***537***
U of Alberta (AB, Canada) ***538***
U of Arkansas at Monticello (AR) ***539***
The U of British Columbia (BC, Canada) ***540***
U of Central Arkansas (AR) ***542***
U of Central Florida (FL) ***542***
U of Central Oklahoma (OK) ***542***
The U of Findlay (OH) ***545***
U of Georgia (GA) ***545***
U of Hawaii at Manoa (HI) ***546***
U of Idaho (ID) ***547***
U of Indianapolis (IN) ***548***
The U of Lethbridge (AB, Canada) ***549***
U of Maine at Machias (ME) ***551***
U of Mary Hardin-Baylor (TX) ***551***
U of Maryland Eastern Shore (MD) ***552***
U of Minnesota, Twin Cities Campus (MN) ***555***
U of Missouri–St. Louis (MO) ***556***
The U of Montana–Missoula (MT) ***556***
The U of Montana–Western (MT) ***556***
U of Nebraska at Kearney (NE) ***557***
U of Nebraska–Lincoln (NE) ***557***
U of Nevada, Reno (NV) ***558***
U of New Brunswick Fredericton (NB, Canada) ***558***
U of New Mexico (NM) ***559***
The U of North Carolina at Greensboro (NC) ***560***
U of North Dakota (ND) ***561***
U of Northern Iowa (IA) ***561***
U of North Texas (TX) ***562***
U of Regina (SK, Canada) ***572***
U of Rio Grande (OH) ***572***
U of Saint Francis (IN) ***573***
U of Southern Indiana (IN) ***576***
U of Southern Mississippi (MS) ***576***
U of South Florida (FL) ***576***
The U of Tennessee (TN) ***577***
The U of Tennessee at Martin (TN) ***577***
U of the District of Columbia (DC) ***580***
U of the Ozarks (AR) ***580***
U of Toledo (OH) ***581***
The U of Western Ontario (ON, Canada) ***583***
U of Wisconsin–Superior (WI) ***586***
U of Wisconsin–Whitewater (WI) ***586***
Upper Iowa U (IA) ***587***
Utah State U (UT) ***587***
Utica Coll (NY) ***588***
Valdosta State U (GA) ***588***
Valley City State U (ND) ***588***
Virginia Intermont Coll (VA) ***590***
Virginia Polytechnic Inst and State U (VA) ***591***
Virginia State U (VA) ***591***
Virginia Union U (VA) ***591***
Viterbo U (WI) ***591***
Walla Walla Coll (WA) ***593***
Walsh U (OH) ***593***
Warner Southern Coll (FL) ***593***
Wayne State Coll (NE) ***596***
Weber State U (UT) ***596***
Western Kentucky U (KY) ***599***
Western Michigan U (MI) ***599***
Western New Mexico U (NM) ***600***
Westfield State Coll (MA) ***600***
West Virginia State Coll (WV) ***602***
Wiley Coll (TX) ***605***
William Penn U (IA) ***606***
Wilmington Coll (OH) ***607***
Winona State U (MN) ***608***
Winthrop U (SC) ***608***
Wright State U (OH) ***609***
Youngstown State U (OH) ***611***

BUSINESS HOME ECONOMICS

Overview: Students who choose this major study the management of home-based businesses and their effect on the individual and family. *Related majors:* accounting, business services marketing, entrepreneurship. *Potential careers:* accountant, bookkeeper, entrepreneur, computer technician. *Salary potential:* $22k-$32k.

The Ohio State U (OH) ***457***
Point Loma Nazarene U (CA) ***471***
U of Houston (TX) ***547***

BUSINESS INFORMATION/ DATA PROCESSING RELATED

Information can be found under this major's main heading.

Anderson Coll (SC) ***268***
Carroll Coll (WI) ***306***
Columbia Southern U (AL) ***327***
State U of NY at Farmingdale (NY) ***357***
Lewis U (IL) ***406***
Rogers State U (OK) ***483***
Westminster Coll (UT) ***601***

BUSINESS MANAGEMENT/ ADMINISTRATIVE SERVICES RELATED

Information can be found under this major's main heading.

Adelphi U (NY) ***260***
Athens State U (AL) ***275***
Benedictine U (IL) ***285***
Clemson U (SC) ***317***
Coll of Biblical Studies–Houston (TX) ***320***
The Coll of St. Scholastica (MN) ***322***
Drexel U (PA) ***346***
Duquesne U (PA) ***346***
George Mason U (VA) ***366***
Iowa State U of Science and Technology (IA) ***390***
Malone Coll (OH) ***415***
Messiah Coll (PA) ***426***
Nebraska Wesleyan U (NE) ***443***
Ohio U (OH) ***458***
Park U (MO) ***465***
Saint Mary's U of Minnesota (MN) ***494***
Saint Vincent Coll (PA) ***496***
Skidmore Coll (NY) ***506***
Southeastern Coll of the Assemblies of God (FL) ***507***
Texas Wesleyan U (TX) ***526***
Troy State U Dothan (AL) ***532***
U of Utah (UT) ***582***
Utica Coll (NY) ***588***

BUSINESS MARKETING AND MARKETING MANAGEMENT

Overview: Students learn how to develop and identify consumer markets for products and devise methods for getting these products into the hands of consumers. *Related majors:* marketing research, advertising, retail management, general marketing operations, psychology. *Potential careers:* advertising and market executive, media planner, publicist, sales manager, market researcher. *Salary potential:* $26k-$33k.

Abilene Christian U (TX) ***260***
Adams State Coll (CO) ***260***
Alabama A&M U (AL) ***261***
Alabama State U (AL) ***261***
Albany State U (GA) ***262***
Albertus Magnus Coll (CT) ***262***
Albright Coll (PA) ***263***
Alderson-Broaddus Coll (WV) ***263***
Alfred U (NY) ***263***
Alma Coll (MI) ***264***
Alvernia Coll (PA) ***265***
Amberton U (TX) ***265***
American InterContinental U (CA) ***266***
American InterContinental U, Atlanta (GA) ***266***
American InterContinental U-London(United Kingdom) ***267***
American International Coll (MA) ***267***
American U (DC) ***267***
Anderson Coll (SC) ***268***
Anderson U (IN) ***268***
Andrews U (MI) ***269***
Angelo State U (TX) ***269***
Appalachian State U (NC) ***270***
Arcadia U (PA) ***271***
Arizona State U (AZ) ***271***
Arkansas State U (AR) ***272***
The Art Inst of California–San Francisco (CA) ***273***
Ashland U (OH) ***274***
Assumption Coll (MA) ***275***
Auburn U (AL) ***276***
Auburn U Montgomery (AL) ***276***
Augsburg Coll (MN) ***276***
Augustana Coll (IL) ***276***
Augusta State U (GA) ***277***
Aurora U (IL) ***277***
Averett U (VA) ***278***
Avila U (MO) ***278***
Azusa Pacific U (CA) ***278***
Babson Coll (MA) ***278***
Baker Coll of Auburn Hills (MI) ***279***
Baker Coll of Flint (MI) ***279***
Baker Coll of Jackson (MI) ***279***
Baker Coll of Muskegon (MI) ***279***
Baker Coll of Owosso (MI) ***279***
Baker Coll of Port Huron (MI) ***280***
Baldwin-Wallace Coll (OH) ***280***
Ball State U (IN) ***280***
Barber-Scotia Coll (NC) ***281***
Barry U (FL) ***282***
Bayamón Central U (PR) ***283***
Baylor U (TX) ***283***
Becker Coll (MA) ***283***
Bellevue U (NE) ***284***
Belmont U (TN) ***284***
Benedict Coll (SC) ***285***
Benedictine Coll (KS) ***285***
Benedictine U (IL) ***285***
Bentley Coll (MA) ***286***
Baruch Coll of the City U of NY (NY) ***286***
Berry Coll (GA) ***287***
Bishop's U (QC, Canada) ***289***
Black Hills State U (SD) ***290***
Bloomfield Coll (NJ) ***290***
Bluefield State Coll (WV) ***291***
Boston Coll (MA) ***292***
Boston U (MA) ***292***
Bowie State U (MD) ***292***
Bowling Green State U (OH) ***292***
Bradley U (IL) ***293***
Brenau U (GA) ***293***
Brescia U (KY) ***293***
Bridgewater Coll (VA) ***294***
Bridgewater State Coll (MA) ***294***
Brigham Young U (UT) ***295***
Brock U (ON, Canada) ***295***
Bryant Coll (RI) ***296***
Buena Vista U (IA) ***297***
Butler U (IN) ***297***
Cabrini Coll (PA) ***298***
Caldwell Coll (NJ) ***298***
California Lutheran U (CA) ***299***

California State Polytechnic U, Pomona (CA) ***300***
California State U, Chico (CA) ***300***
California State U, Dominguez Hills (CA) ***300***
California State U, Fresno (CA) ***301***
California State U, Fullerton (CA) ***301***
California State U, Hayward (CA) ***301***
California State U, Long Beach (CA) ***301***
California State U, Northridge (CA) ***301***
California State U, San Bernardino (CA) ***302***
California State U, Stanislaus (CA) ***302***
Cameron U (OK) ***303***
Campbellsville U (KY) ***303***
Canisius Coll (NY) ***304***
Capital U (OH) ***304***
Carleton U (ON, Canada) ***305***
Carroll Coll (WI) ***306***
Carson-Newman Coll (TN) ***306***
Castleton State Coll (VT) ***307***
Catawba Coll (NC) ***307***
Cedarville U (OH) ***308***
Centenary Coll (NJ) ***308***
Central Connecticut State U (CT) ***309***
Central Michigan U (MI) ***310***
Central Missouri State U (MO) ***310***
Chaminade U of Honolulu (HI) ***311***
Champlain Coll (VT) ***311***
Chapman U (CA) ***311***
Charleston Southern U (SC) ***311***
Chatham Coll (PA) ***312***
Chestnut Hill Coll (PA) ***312***
Chowan Coll (NC) ***312***
Christian Brothers U (TN) ***313***
Christopher Newport U (VA) ***313***
Clarion U of Pennsylvania (PA) ***315***
Clarke Coll (IA) ***315***
Clarkson U (NY) ***316***
Cleary U (MI) ***317***
Clemson U (SC) ***317***
Cleveland State U (OH) ***317***
Coastal Carolina U (SC) ***318***
Coker Coll (SC) ***318***
Coll Misericordia (PA) ***319***
Coll of St. Catherine (MN) ***321***
Coll of Saint Elizabeth (NJ) ***321***
The Coll of Southeastern Europe, The American U of Athens(Greece) ***323***
Coll of the Ozarks (MO) ***323***
Coll of the Southwest (NM) ***324***
Colorado State U (CO) ***325***
Colorado State U-Pueblo (CO) ***325***
Colorado Tech U Sioux Falls Campus (SD) ***326***
Columbia Coll (MO) ***326***
Columbia Coll (SC) ***327***
Columbia Coll Chicago (IL) ***327***
Columbia Southern U (AL) ***327***
Columbus State U (GA) ***328***
Concordia U (QC, Canada) ***331***
Concordia U Wisconsin (WI) ***331***
Converse Coll (SC) ***332***
Cornerstone U (MI) ***333***
Creighton U (NE) ***333***
Dakota State U (SD) ***335***
Dakota Wesleyan U (SD) ***336***
Dallas Baptist U (TX) ***336***
Dalton State Coll (GA) ***336***
Davenport U, Grand Rapids (MI) ***337***
Davenport U, Kalamazoo (MI) ***337***
Davis & Elkins Coll (WV) ***338***
Defiance Coll (OH) ***338***
Delaware State U (DE) ***338***
Delaware Valley Coll (PA) ***339***
Delta State U (MS) ***339***
DePaul U (IL) ***339***
Deree Coll(Greece) ***339***
DeSales U (PA) ***340***
Dickinson State U (ND) ***344***
Dowling Coll (NY) ***345***
Drake U (IA) ***345***
Drexel U (PA) ***346***
Duquesne U (PA) ***346***
D'Youville Coll (NY) ***347***
East Carolina U (NC) ***347***
East Central U (OK) ***347***
Eastern Illinois U (IL) ***348***
Eastern Kentucky U (KY) ***348***
Eastern Michigan U (MI) ***348***
Eastern New Mexico U (NM) ***349***
Eastern U (PA) ***349***
Eastern Washington U (WA) ***349***
East Tennessee State U (TN) ***349***
East Texas Baptist U (TX) ***350***
École des hautes études commerciales de Montréal (QC, Canada) ***350***
Elmhurst Coll (IL) ***351***
Elmira Coll (NY) ***351***
Elms Coll (MA) ***352***
Emerson Coll (MA) ***353***
Emory U (GA) ***354***
Emporia State U (KS) ***354***
Evangel U (MO) ***355***
Excelsior Coll (NY) ***356***
Fairfield U (CT) ***356***
Fairleigh Dickinson U, Florham (NJ) ***356***
Faulkner U (AL) ***357***
Fayetteville State U (NC) ***357***
Felician Coll (NJ) ***357***
Ferris State U (MI) ***358***
Fitchburg State Coll (MA) ***358***
Florida Atlantic U (FL) ***359***
Florida Gulf Coast U (FL) ***359***
Florida International U (FL) ***360***
Florida Metropolitan U-Tampa Coll, Brandon (FL) ***360***
Florida Metropolitan U-Fort Lauderdale Coll (FL) ***360***
Florida Metropolitan U-Orlando Coll, North (FL) ***361***
Florida Metropolitan U-Tampa Coll, Pinellas (FL) ***361***
Florida Southern Coll (FL) ***361***
Florida State U (FL) ***361***
Fontbonne U (MO) ***361***
Fordham U (NY) ***362***
Fort Hays State U (KS) ***362***
Fort Lewis Coll (CO) ***362***
Fort Valley State U (GA) ***362***
Framingham State Coll (MA) ***362***
Francis Marion U (SC) ***363***
Franklin Coll (IN) ***363***
Franklin Pierce Coll (NH) ***364***
Franklin U (OH) ***364***
Freed-Hardeman U (TN) ***364***
Fresno Pacific U (CA) ***364***
Gannon U (PA) ***365***
George Mason U (VA) ***366***
Georgetown Coll (KY) ***366***
Georgetown U (DC) ***366***
The George Washington U (DC) ***367***
Georgia Coll & State U (GA) ***367***
Georgia Southern U (GA) ***367***
Georgia Southwestern State U (GA) ***368***
Georgia State U (GA) ***368***
Glenville State Coll (WV) ***368***
Golden Gate U (CA) ***369***
Goldey-Beacom Coll (DE) ***369***
Gonzaga U (WA) ***369***
Governors State U (IL) ***370***
Grambling State U (LA) ***371***
Grand Canyon U (AZ) ***371***
Grand Valley State U (MI) ***371***
Greenville Coll (IL) ***373***
Grove City Coll (PA) ***373***
Gwynedd-Mercy Coll (PA) ***374***
Hampton U (VA) ***375***
Hannibal-LaGrange Coll (MO) ***375***
Harding U (AR) ***375***
Hardin-Simmons U (TX) ***376***
Hastings Coll (NE) ***377***
Hawai'i Pacific U (HI) ***377***
High Point U (NC) ***379***
Hillsdale Coll (MI) ***379***
Hofstra U (NY) ***380***
Holy Family U (PA) ***380***
Houston Baptist U (TX) ***382***
Howard Payne U (TX) ***382***
Howard U (DC) ***382***
Humboldt State U (CA) ***382***
Huntingdon Coll (AL) ***383***
Husson Coll (ME) ***383***
Idaho State U (ID) ***384***
Illinois State U (IL) ***384***
Immaculata U (PA) ***385***
Indiana Inst of Technology (IN) ***385***
Indiana State U (IN) ***385***
Indiana U Bloomington (IN) ***385***
Indiana U of Pennsylvania (PA) ***386***
Indiana U–Purdue U Fort Wayne (IN) ***386***
Indiana U South Bend (IN) ***387***
Indiana Wesleyan U (IN) ***387***
Inst of Public Administration(Ireland) ***387***
Insto Tecno Estudios Sups Monterrey(Mexico) ***388***
Inter American U of PR, Aguadilla Campus (PR) ***388***
Inter American U of PR, San Germán Campus (PR) ***388***
Iona Coll (NY) ***390***
Iowa State U of Science and Technology (IA) ***390***
Ithaca Coll (NY) ***390***
Jackson State U (MS) ***390***
Jacksonville State U (AL) ***390***
Jacksonville U (FL) ***391***
James Madison U (VA) ***391***
John Carroll U (OH) ***392***
Johnson & Wales U (RI) ***393***
Johnson C. Smith U (NC) ***394***
Johnson State Coll (VT) ***394***
Juniata Coll (PA) ***395***
Kansas State U (KS) ***396***
Kean U (NJ) ***396***
Kendall Coll (IL) ***396***
Kennesaw State U (GA) ***397***
Kent State U (OH) ***397***
Kettering U (MI) ***398***
Keuka Coll (NY) ***398***
King's Coll (PA) ***398***
Kutztown U of Pennsylvania (PA) ***399***
Laboratory Inst of Merchandising (NY) ***399***
Lakehead U (ON, Canada) ***400***
Lakeland Coll (WI) ***401***
Lamar U (TX) ***401***
Lambuth U (TN) ***401***
La Salle U (PA) ***402***
Lasell Coll (MA) ***402***
Lehigh U (PA) ***404***
LeTourneau U (TX) ***405***
Lewis U (IL) ***406***
Limestone Coll (SC) ***406***
Lincoln Memorial U (TN) ***407***
Lindenwood U (MO) ***407***
Lipscomb U (TN) ***408***
Long Island U, Brentwood Campus (NY) ***408***
Long Island U, Brooklyn Campus (NY) ***409***
Long Island U, C.W. Post Campus (NY) ***409***
Longwood U (VA) ***409***
Loras Coll (IA) ***410***
Louisiana Coll (LA) ***410***
Louisiana State U and A&M Coll (LA) ***410***
Louisiana State U in Shreveport (LA) ***410***
Louisiana Tech U (LA) ***410***
Loyola U Chicago (IL) ***411***
Loyola U New Orleans (LA) ***411***
Luther Coll (IA) ***412***
Lycoming Coll (PA) ***412***
Lynchburg Coll (VA) ***413***
Lynn U (FL) ***413***
MacMurray Coll (IL) ***414***
Madonna U (MI) ***414***
Manchester Coll (IN) ***415***
Manhattan Coll (NY) ***416***
Mansfield U of Pennsylvania (PA) ***416***
Marian Coll of Fond du Lac (WI) ***417***
Marietta Coll (OH) ***417***
Marquette U (WI) ***418***
Marshall U (WV) ***418***
Mars Hill Coll (NC) ***418***
Martin U (IN) ***419***
Marygrove Coll (MI) ***419***
Marymount Coll of Fordham U (NY) ***419***
Marymount U (VA) ***420***
Maryville U of Saint Louis (MO) ***420***
Marywood U (PA) ***421***
Massachusetts Coll of Liberal Arts (MA) ***421***
McKendree Coll (IL) ***423***
McMurry U (TX) ***423***
McNeese State U (LA) ***423***
Medaille Coll (NY) ***424***
Memorial U of Newfoundland (NF, Canada) ***424***
Mercer U (GA) ***425***
Mercy Coll (NY) ***425***
Mercyhurst Coll (PA) ***425***
Meredith Coll (NC) ***426***
Merrimack Coll (MA) ***426***
Mesa State Coll (CO) ***426***
Messiah Coll (PA) ***426***
Metropolitan State U (MN) ***427***
Miami U (OH) ***428***
Michigan State U (MI) ***428***
Michigan Technological U (MI) ***428***
Middle Tennessee State U (TN) ***429***
Midland Lutheran Coll (NE) ***429***
Midwestern State U (TX) ***430***
Millikin U (IL) ***430***
Minnesota State U, Mankato (MN) ***431***
Minnesota State U, Moorhead (MN) ***432***
Minot State U (ND) ***432***
Mississippi Coll (MS) ***432***
Mississippi State U (MS) ***432***
Missouri Southern State Coll (MO) ***433***
Missouri Valley Coll (MO) ***433***
Missouri Western State Coll (MO) ***433***
Monmouth U (NJ) ***434***
Montana State U–Billings (MT) ***434***
Montclair State U (NJ) ***435***
Montreat Coll (NC) ***435***
Morehead State U (KY) ***436***
Morehouse Coll (GA) ***436***
Morgan State U (MD) ***436***
Morningside Coll (IA) ***437***
Mount Ida Coll (MA) ***438***
Mount Mercy Coll (IA) ***438***
Mount St. Mary's Coll (CA) ***439***
Mount Saint Vincent U (NS, Canada) ***439***
Mount Vernon Nazarene U (OH) ***440***
Murray State U (KY) ***440***
National U (CA) ***442***
Nazareth Coll of Rochester (NY) ***443***
Neumann Coll (PA) ***443***
Newbury Coll (MA) ***444***
New England Coll (NH) ***444***
New England School of Communications (ME) ***445***
Newman U (KS) ***445***
New Mexico Highlands U (NM) ***446***
New Mexico State U (NM) ***446***
New York Inst of Technology (NY) ***447***
New York U (NY) ***447***
Niagara U (NY) ***447***
Nicholls State U (LA) ***447***
Nichols Coll (MA) ***448***
North Carolina State U (NC) ***449***
North Central Coll (IL) ***449***
Northeastern Illinois U (IL) ***450***
Northeastern State U (OK) ***450***
Northeastern U (MA) ***450***
Northern Arizona U (AZ) ***450***
Northern Illinois U (IL) ***450***
Northern Kentucky U (KY) ***451***
Northern Michigan U (MI) ***451***
Northern State U (SD) ***451***
North Georgia Coll & State U (GA) ***451***
North Park U (IL) ***452***
Northwest Christian Coll (OR) ***452***
Northwestern Coll (MN) ***453***
Northwest Missouri State U (MO) ***454***
Northwest Nazarene U (ID) ***454***
Northwood U (MI) ***454***
Northwood U, Florida Campus (FL) ***454***
Northwood U, Texas Campus (TX) ***454***
Notre Dame Coll (OH) ***455***
Notre Dame de Namur U (CA) ***455***
Oakland U (MI) ***456***
The Ohio State U (OH) ***457***
Ohio U (OH) ***458***
Oklahoma Baptist U (OK) ***459***
Oklahoma Christian U (OK) ***459***
Oklahoma City U (OK) ***460***
Oklahoma State U (OK) ***460***
Old Dominion U (VA) ***460***
Olivet Coll (MI) ***461***
Olivet Nazarene U (IL) ***461***
Oral Roberts U (OK) ***461***
Oregon State U (OR) ***462***
Otterbein Coll (OH) ***462***
Ouachita Baptist U (AR) ***462***
Our Lady of the Lake U of San Antonio (TX) ***463***
Pace U (NY) ***463***
Pacific Lutheran U (WA) ***463***
Pacific Union Coll (CA) ***464***
Pacific U (OR) ***464***
Palm Beach Atlantic U (FL) ***465***
Park U (MO) ***465***
Penn State U at Erie, The Behrend Coll (PA) ***467***
Penn State U Harrisburg Campus of the Capital Coll (PA) ***468***
Penn State U Univ Park Campus (PA) ***468***
Peru State Coll (NE) ***469***
Philadelphia U (PA) ***469***
Pittsburg State U (KS) ***470***
Plattsburgh State U of NY (NY) ***471***
Plymouth State Coll (NH) ***471***
Pontifical Catholic U of Puerto Rico (PR) ***472***
Portland State U (OR) ***472***
Prairie View A&M U (TX) ***473***
Providence Coll (RI) ***474***
Purdue U Calumet (IN) ***475***

BUSINESS MARKETING AND MARKETING MANAGEMENT (continued)

Quincy U (IL) **476**
Quinnipiac U (CT) **476**
Radford U (VA) **476**
Rhode Island Coll (RI) **479**
Rider U (NJ) **480**
Robert Morris U (PA) **481**
Roberts Wesleyan Coll (NY) **481**
Rochester Coll (MI) **482**
Rochester Inst of Technology (NY) **482**
Rockford Coll (IL) **482**
Rockhurst U (MO) **482**
Roger Williams U (RI) **483**
Roosevelt U (IL) **483**
Rowan U (NJ) **484**
Rutgers, The State U of New Jersey, Camden (NJ) **485**
Rutgers, The State U of New Jersey, Newark (NJ) **485**
Rutgers, The State U of New Jersey, New Brunswick (NJ) **485**
Ryerson U (ON, Canada) **485**
Sacred Heart U (CT) **486**
St. Ambrose U (IA) **486**
St. Bonaventure U (NY) **487**
St. Cloud State U (MN) **488**
Saint Francis U (PA) **488**
St. John Fisher Coll (NY) **489**
Saint Joseph's Coll (IN) **490**
Saint Joseph's Coll of Maine (ME) **491**
Saint Joseph's U (PA) **491**
Saint Leo U (FL) **492**
Saint Louis U (MO) **492**
Saint Martin's Coll (WA) **493**
Saint Mary-of-the-Woods Coll (IN) **493**
Saint Mary's Coll (IN) **493**
Saint Mary's Coll of Madonna U (MI) **493**
Saint Mary's U (NS, Canada) **494**
Saint Mary's U of Minnesota (MN) **494**
St. Mary's U of San Antonio (TX) **494**
Saint Peter's Coll (NJ) **495**
St. Thomas Aquinas Coll (NY) **495**
St. Thomas U (FL) **496**
Saint Vincent Coll (PA) **496**
Salem State Coll (MA) **497**
Salisbury U (MD) **497**
Sam Houston State U (TX) **497**
San Diego State U (CA) **498**
San Francisco State U (CA) **498**
San Jose State U (CA) **499**
Santa Clara U (CA) **499**
Savannah State U (GA) **499**
Schiller International U (FL) **500**
Schiller International U(Spain) **500**
Schreiner U (TX) **501**
Seattle U (WA) **501**
Seton Hall U (NJ) **502**
Seton Hill U (PA) **502**
Shippensburg U of Pennsylvania (PA) **503**
Siena Coll (NY) **504**
Siena Heights U (MI) **504**
Simmons Coll (MA) **504**
Slippery Rock U of Pennsylvania (PA) **506**
South Carolina State U (SC) **506**
Southeastern Coll of the Assemblies of God (FL) **507**
Southeastern Louisiana U (LA) **508**
Southeastern Oklahoma State U (OK) **508**
Southeastern U (DC) **508**
Southeast Missouri State U (MO) **508**
Southern Adventist U (TN) **508**
Southern Illinois U Carbondale (IL) **509**
Southern Methodist U (TX) **510**
Southern Nazarene U (OK) **510**
Southern New Hampshire U (NH) **510**
Southern Oregon U (OR) **510**
Southern U and A&M Coll (LA) **511**
Southwestern Oklahoma State U (OK) **512**
Southwest Missouri State U (MO) **513**
Southwest State U (MN) **513**
Southwest Texas State U (TX) **513**
Spring Hill Coll (AL) **514**
State U of NY at New Paltz (NY) **515**
State U of NY at Oswego (NY) **515**
State U of NY Coll at Brockport (NY) **515**
State U of NY Coll at Fredonia (NY) **516**
State U of NY Coll at Old Westbury (NY) **516**
State U of West Georgia (GA) **518**
Stephen F. Austin State U (TX) **518**
Stephens Coll (MO) **519**
Stetson U (FL) **519**
Stonehill Coll (MA) **520**
Suffolk U (MA) **520**
Sullivan U (KY) **521**
Susquehanna U (PA) **521**
Syracuse U (NY) **521**
Tabor Coll (KS) **522**
Tarleton State U (TX) **522**
Taylor U (IN) **523**
Teikyo Post U (CT) **523**
Temple U (PA) **523**
Tennessee Technological U (TN) **524**
Texas A&M International U (TX) **524**
Texas A&M U (TX) **524**
Texas A&M U–Commerce (TX) **525**
Texas A&M U–Corpus Christi (TX) **525**
Texas A&M U–Kingsville (TX) **525**
Texas A&M U–Texarkana (TX) **525**
Texas Christian U (TX) **526**
Texas Southern U (TX) **526**
Texas Tech U (TX) **526**
Texas Wesleyan U (TX) **526**
Texas Woman's U (TX) **527**
Thomas Coll (ME) **527**
Thomas Edison State Coll (NJ) **527**
Tiffin U (OH) **528**
Trevecca Nazarene U (TN) **529**
Trinity Christian Coll (IL) **530**
Trinity International U (IL) **531**
Trinity U (TX) **531**
Tri-State U (IN) **532**
Tulane U (LA) **533**
Tuskegee U (AL) **533**
Union U (TN) **534**
Université de Sherbrooke (QC, Canada) **536**
U Coll of the Cariboo (BC, Canada) **537**
The U of Akron (OH) **537**
The U of Alabama (AL) **537**
The U of Alabama at Birmingham (AL) **537**
The U of Alabama in Huntsville (AL) **537**
U of Alaska Anchorage (AK) **538**
U of Alberta (AB, Canada) **538**
The U of Arizona (AZ) **538**
U of Arkansas (AR) **539**
U of Arkansas at Little Rock (AR) **539**
U of Baltimore (MD) **539**
U of Bridgeport (CT) **540**
The U of British Columbia (BC, Canada) **540**
U of Calgary (AB, Canada) **540**
U of Central Arkansas (AR) **542**
U of Central Florida (FL) **542**
U of Central Oklahoma (OK) **542**
U of Charleston (WV) **542**
U of Cincinnati (OH) **543**
U of Colorado at Boulder (CO) **543**
U of Colorado at Colorado Springs (CO) **543**
U of Connecticut (CT) **544**
U of Dayton (OH) **544**
U of Delaware (DE) **544**
U of Denver (CO) **544**
U of Evansville (IN) **545**
The U of Findlay (OH) **545**
U of Florida (FL) **545**
U of Georgia (GA) **545**
U of Guelph (ON, Canada) **546**
U of Hartford (CT) **546**
U of Hawaii at Manoa (HI) **546**
U of Houston–Clear Lake (TX) **547**
U of Houston–Downtown (TX) **547**
U of Idaho (ID) **547**
U of Illinois at Chicago (IL) **547**
U of Indianapolis (IN) **548**
The U of Iowa (IA) **548**
U of Kentucky (KY) **549**
U of La Verne (CA) **549**
The U of Lethbridge (AB, Canada) **549**
U of Louisiana at Lafayette (LA) **550**
U of Louisville (KY) **550**
U of Maine at Machias (ME) **551**
U of Mary Hardin-Baylor (TX) **551**
U of Maryland, Coll Park (MD) **552**
U of Maryland University Coll (MD) **552**
U of Massachusetts Amherst (MA) **552**
U of Massachusetts Dartmouth (MA) **553**
The U of Memphis (TN) **553**
U of Miami (FL) **553**
U of Michigan–Dearborn (MI) **554**
U of Minnesota, Duluth (MN) **554**
U of Minnesota, Twin Cities Campus (MN) **555**
U of Mississippi (MS) **555**
U of Missouri–Columbia (MO) **555**
U of Missouri–St. Louis (MO) **556**
The U of Montana–Missoula (MT) **556**
U of Montevallo (AL) **557**
U of Nebraska at Omaha (NE) **557**
U of Nebraska–Lincoln (NE) **557**
U of Nevada, Las Vegas (NV) **558**
U of Nevada, Reno (NV) **558**
U of New Brunswick Fredericton (NB, Canada) **558**
U of New Haven (CT) **559**
U of New Orleans (LA) **559**
U of North Alabama (AL) **559**
The U of North Carolina at Charlotte (NC) **560**
The U of North Carolina at Greensboro (NC) **560**
The U of North Carolina at Wilmington (NC) **561**
U of North Dakota (ND) **561**
U of Northern Iowa (IA) **561**
U of North Florida (FL) **561**
U of North Texas (TX) **562**
U of Notre Dame (IN) **562**
U of Oklahoma (OK) **562**
U of Oregon (OR) **562**
U of Ottawa (ON, Canada) **563**
U of Pennsylvania (PA) **563**
U of Phoenix-Atlanta Campus (GA) **563**
U of Phoenix–Fort Lauderdale Campus (FL) **564**
U of Phoenix–Jacksonville Campus (FL) **564**
U of Phoenix–Metro Detroit Campus (MI) **565**
U of Phoenix–Northern California Campus (CA) **565**
U of Phoenix–Ohio Campus (OH) **566**
U of Phoenix–Oregon Campus (OR) **566**
U of Phoenix–Orlando Campus (FL) **566**
U of Phoenix–Phoenix Campus (AZ) **567**
U of Phoenix–San Diego Campus (CA) **567**
U of Phoenix–Southern Arizona Campus (AZ) **568**
U of Phoenix–Tampa Campus (FL) **568**
U of Phoenix–Utah Campus (UT) **568**
U of Pittsburgh (PA) **569**
U of Portland (OR) **570**
U of Puerto Rico, Río Piedras (PR) **571**
U of Regina (SK, Canada) **572**
U of Rhode Island (RI) **572**
U of Richmond (VA) **572**
U of Rio Grande (OH) **572**
U of St. Francis (IL) **573**
U of Saint Francis (IN) **573**
U of St. Thomas (MN) **573**
U of St. Thomas (TX) **573**
U of San Francisco (CA) **574**
U of Saskatchewan (SK, Canada) **574**
The U of Scranton (PA) **574**
U of Sioux Falls (SD) **574**
U of South Alabama (AL) **575**
U of South Carolina (SC) **575**
The U of South Dakota (SD) **575**
U of Southern Indiana (IN) **576**
U of Southern Mississippi (MS) **576**
U of South Florida (FL) **576**
The U of Tampa (FL) **577**
The U of Tennessee (TN) **577**
The U of Tennessee at Chattanooga (TN) **577**
The U of Tennessee at Martin (TN) **577**
The U of Texas at Arlington (TX) **577**
The U of Texas at Austin (TX) **578**
The U of Texas at Brownsville (TX) **578**
The U of Texas at Dallas (TX) **578**
The U of Texas at El Paso (TX) **578**
The U of Texas at San Antonio (TX) **578**
The U of Texas at Tyler (TX) **579**
The U of Texas of the Permian Basin (TX) **579**
The U of Texas–Pan American (TX) **579**
U of the District of Columbia (DC) **580**
U of the Incarnate Word (TX) **580**
U of the Ozarks (AR) **580**
U of the Sacred Heart (PR) **580**
U of Toledo (OH) **581**
U of Tulsa (OK) **581**
U of Utah (UT) **582**
U of West Florida (FL) **583**
U of Windsor (ON, Canada) **584**
U of Wisconsin–Eau Claire (WI) **584**
U of Wisconsin–La Crosse (WI) **584**
U of Wisconsin–Milwaukee (WI) **585**
U of Wisconsin–Oshkosh (WI) **585**
U of Wisconsin–River Falls (WI) **585**
U of Wisconsin–Stout (WI) **586**
U of Wisconsin–Superior (WI) **586**
U of Wisconsin–Whitewater (WI) **586**
U of Wyoming (WY) **586**
Upper Iowa U (IA) **587**
Urbana U (OH) **587**
Ursuline Coll (OH) **587**
Utah State U (UT) **587**
Valdosta State U (GA) **588**
Valparaiso U (IN) **588**
Vanguard U of Southern California (CA) **589**
Villanova U (PA) **590**
Virginia Commonwealth U (VA) **590**
Virginia Intermont Coll (VA) **590**
Virginia Polytechnic Inst and State U (VA) **591**
Virginia State U (VA) **591**
Virginia Union U (VA) **591**
Viterbo U (WI) **591**
Walla Walla Coll (WA) **593**
Walsh Coll of Accountancy and Business Admin (MI) **593**
Walsh U (OH) **593**
Warner Southern Coll (FL) **593**
Wartburg Coll (IA) **594**
Washington State U (WA) **595**
Washington U in St. Louis (MO) **595**
Waynesburg Coll (PA) **595**
Wayne State U (MI) **596**
Webber International U (FL) **596**
Weber State U (UT) **596**
Webster U (MO) **597**
Wesley Coll (DE) **598**
West Chester U of Pennsylvania (PA) **598**
Western Carolina U (NC) **598**
Western Connecticut State U (CT) **598**
Western Illinois U (IL) **599**
Western International U (AZ) **599**
Western Kentucky U (KY) **599**
Western Michigan U (MI) **599**
Western New England Coll (MA) **600**
Western New Mexico U (NM) **600**
Western State Coll of Colorado (CO) **600**
Western Washington U (WA) **600**
Westfield State Coll (MA) **600**
West Liberty State Coll (WV) **601**
Westminster Coll (MO) **601**
Westminster Coll (UT) **601**
West Texas A&M U (TX) **602**
West Virginia U (WV) **602**
West Virginia Wesleyan Coll (WV) **603**
Wheeling Jesuit U (WV) **603**
Wichita State U (KS) **604**
Wilberforce U (OH) **605**
Wilmington Coll (OH) **607**
Wingate U (NC) **607**
Winona State U (MN) **608**
Wittenberg U (OH) **608**
Woodbury U (CA) **609**
Worcester State Coll (MA) **609**
Wright State U (OH) **609**
Xavier U (OH) **610**
Xavier U of Louisiana (LA) **610**
York Coll of Pennsylvania (PA) **610**
York Coll of the City U of New York (NY) **611**
York U (ON, Canada) **611**
Youngstown State U (OH) **611**

BUSINESS QUANTITATIVE METHODS/MANAGEMENT SCIENCE RELATED

Information can be found under this major's main heading.

The Coll of Southeastern Europe, The American U of Athens(Greece) **323**
Georgia Coll & State U (GA) **367**
Indiana State U (IN) **385**
U of Nebraska–Lincoln (NE) **557**
U of Pennsylvania (PA) **563**

BUSINESS SERVICES MARKETING

Overview: Students who take this major learn the principles of marketing various products and services to a wide range of businesses and organizations. *Related majors:* accounting and taxation, business systems networking and telecommunications, business systems analysis and design, marketing research, logistics and materials management. *Potential careers:* marketing or advertising executive, account sales person, computer analyst, accountant, Web page designer. *Salary potential:* $30k-$40k.

American Public U System (WV) ***267***
Southern New Hampshire U (NH) ***510***

BUSINESS STATISTICS

Overview: Students learn how to use statistics to describe and analyze business data and other information and forecast future business activity. *Related majors:* mathematics, statistics, computer science, finance. *Potential careers:* industrial statistician, insurance statistician, business systems consultant, risk analyst. *Salary potential:* $35k-$45k.

Alabama A&M U (AL) ***261***
Baylor U (TX) ***283***
École des hautes études commerciales de Montréal (QC, Canada) ***350***
Southern Oregon U (OR) ***510***
U of Houston (TX) ***547***
U of Puerto Rico, Río Piedras (PR) ***571***
Western Michigan U (MI) ***599***
York U (ON, Canada) ***611***

BUSINESS SYSTEMS ANALYSIS/DESIGN

Overview: Students learn how to program, analyze, select, and repair customized business computer and software programs. *Related majors:* computer hardware and software, business computer programming, systems analysis, management of information systems and data management, computer engineering. *Potential careers:* systems analysis, computer engineer, business computer programmer, manager of information technology, computer consultant. *Salary potential:* $40k-$55k.

American U (DC) ***267***
Cameron U (OK) ***303***
DeVry Inst of Technology (NY) ***340***
DeVry U, Fremont (CA) ***340***
DeVry U, Long Beach (CA) ***341***
DeVry U, Pomona (CA) ***341***
DeVry U, West Hills (CA) ***341***
DeVry U, Colorado Springs (CO) ***341***
DeVry U, Orlando (FL) ***342***
DeVry U, Alpharetta (GA) ***342***
DeVry U, Decatur (GA) ***342***
DeVry U, Addison (IL) ***342***
DeVry U, Chicago (IL) ***342***
DeVry U, Tinley Park (IL) ***342***
DeVry U (MO) ***343***
DeVry U (OH) ***343***
DeVry U (TX) ***343***
DeVry U (VA) ***343***
DeVry U (WA) ***343***
École des hautes études commerciales de Montréal (QC, Canada) ***350***
Kent State U (OH) ***397***
Marshall U (WV) ***418***
Metropolitan State U (MN) ***427***
Mount Saint Vincent U (NS, Canada) ***439***
Pennsylvania Coll of Technology (PA) ***467***
Seattle Pacific U (WA) ***501***
Shippensburg U of Pennsylvania (PA) ***503***
Southern Illinois U Carbondale (IL) ***509***
U of Louisiana at Lafayette (LA) ***550***

BUSINESS SYSTEMS NETWORKING/ TELECOMMUNICATIONS

Overview: Students learn how to design and implement a linked system of computers across a single business or organization so that individual users may enter, access, and analyze business operations data. *Related majors:* business computer programming, business systems analysis and design, information resources management, data warehousing and database administration. *Potential careers:* systems analysis, computer engineer, business computer programmer, manager of information technology, computer consultant. *Salary potential:* $40k-$55k.

Aurora U (IL) ***277***
California State U, Hayward (CA) ***301***
Champlain Coll (VT) ***311***
Crown Coll (MN) ***334***
DePaul U (IL) ***339***
DeVry Inst of Technology (NY) ***340***
DeVry U (AZ) ***340***
DeVry U, Fremont (CA) ***340***
DeVry U, Long Beach (CA) ***341***
DeVry U, Pomona (CA) ***341***
DeVry U, West Hills (CA) ***341***
DeVry U, Orlando (FL) ***342***
DeVry U, Alpharetta (GA) ***342***
DeVry U, Decatur (GA) ***342***
DeVry U, Addison (IL) ***342***
DeVry U, Chicago (IL) ***342***
DeVry U, Tinley Park (IL) ***342***
DeVry U (MO) ***343***
DeVry U (TX) ***343***
DeVry U (VA) ***343***
DeVry U (WA) ***343***
Illinois State U (IL) ***384***
Northwestern Oklahoma State U (OK) ***453***
Our Lady of the Lake U of San Antonio (TX) ***463***
Peirce Coll (PA) ***466***
Pennsylvania Coll of Technology (PA) ***467***
Ryerson U (ON, Canada) ***485***
The U of Findlay (OH) ***545***
U of St. Francis (IL) ***573***
U of Wisconsin–Stout (WI) ***586***
Weber State U (UT) ***596***

BUYING OPERATIONS

Overview: Students who choose this major prepare to work as buyers of resale products and product categories for supermarkets, retail stores, and chain stores. *Related majors:* retail management, purchasing, procurement, and contracts management. *Potential careers:* buyer for a wide range of retail establishments. *Salary potential:* $25k-$35k.

Lake Erie Coll (OH) ***400***
Youngstown State U (OH) ***611***

CANADIAN STUDIES

Overview: Undergraduates who choose this major study the history, politics, culture, languages, and economics of Canada. *Related majors:* French, international relations, economics, literature, natural resources management. *Potential careers:* environmentalist, economist, foreign service officer, natural resource manager, tour guide. *Salary potential:* $22k-$35k.

Acadia U (NS, Canada) ***260***
Athabasca U (AB, Canada) ***275***
Bishop's U (QC, Canada) ***289***
Brandon U (MB, Canada) ***293***
Brock U (ON, Canada) ***295***
Carleton U (ON, Canada) ***305***
Concordia U Coll of Alberta (AB, Canada) ***331***
Dalhousie U (NS, Canada) ***336***
Franklin Coll (IN) ***363***
Hampshire Coll (MA) ***375***
Long Island U, Southampton Coll, Friends World Program (NY) ***409***
McGill U (QC, Canada) ***423***
Memorial U of Newfoundland (NF, Canada) ***424***
Mount Allison U (NB, Canada) ***437***
Plattsburgh State U of NY (NY) ***471***
Queen's U at Kingston (ON, Canada) ***476***
St. Francis Xavier U (NS, Canada) ***489***
St. Lawrence U (NY) ***491***
Saint Mary's U (NS, Canada) ***494***
Simon Fraser U (BC, Canada) ***505***
State U of NY Coll at Brockport (NY) ***515***
Trent U (ON, Canada) ***529***
U Coll of the Cariboo (BC, Canada) ***537***
U of Alberta (AB, Canada) ***538***
The U of British Columbia (BC, Canada) ***540***
U of Calgary (AB, Canada) ***540***
The U of Lethbridge (AB, Canada) ***549***
U of Manitoba (MB, Canada) ***551***
U of New Brunswick Fredericton (NB, Canada) ***558***
U of Ottawa (ON, Canada) ***563***
U of Prince Edward Island (PE, Canada) ***570***
U of Regina (SK, Canada) ***572***
U of Toronto (ON, Canada) ***581***
U of Vermont (VT) ***582***
U of Washington (WA) ***583***
U of Waterloo (ON, Canada) ***583***
Western Washington U (WA) ***600***
York U (ON, Canada) ***611***

CARDIOVASCULAR TECHNOLOGY

Overview: This major teaches students how to perform examinations of the cardiovascular system requested by physicians and how to diagnose and treat heart and blood vessel ailments. *Related majors:* premedicine studies, surgical/operating room technologies. *Potential careers:* cardiovascular technician or technologist, perfusionist. *Salary potential:* $25k-$35k.

Avila U (MO) ***278***
Nebraska Methodist Coll (NE) ***443***
State U of New York Upstate Medical University (NY) ***518***
Thomas Jefferson U (PA) ***527***

CARPENTRY

Overview: This major will teach students the specialized knowledge and technical skills they need to work as professional carpenters or in related construction positions. *Related majors:* construction technology, architecture, architectural drafting, construction/ building inspection, woodworking. *Potential careers:* carpenter, building inspector, construction manager, woodworker, building contractor. *Salary potential:* $24k-$34k.

Andrews U (MI) ***269***

CARTOGRAPHY

Overview: Students will apply mathematical, computer, and other techniques to the science of mapping geographical information. *Related majors:* surveying, mathematics, computer science, information sciences, electrical drafting. *Potential careers:* cartographer (mapmaker), research scientist, statistician, geographer, surveyor. *Salary potential:* $25k-$35k.

Appalachian State U (NC) ***270***
Ball State U (IN) ***280***
California State U, Northridge (CA) ***301***
East Central U (OK) ***347***
Frostburg State U (MD) ***365***
Memorial U of Newfoundland (NF, Canada) ***424***
Salem State Coll (MA) ***497***
Samford U (AL) ***497***
San Jose State U (CA) ***499***
Southwest Missouri State U (MO) ***513***
Southwest Texas State U (TX) ***513***
State U of NY Coll at Oneonta (NY) ***517***
Texas A&M U–Corpus Christi (TX) ***525***
The U of Akron (OH) ***537***
U of Alberta (AB, Canada) ***538***
U of Idaho (ID) ***547***
U of Maryland, Coll Park (MD) ***552***
U of Wisconsin–Madison (WI) ***584***
U of Wisconsin–Platteville (WI) ***585***
Wittenberg U (OH) ***608***

CELL AND MOLECULAR BIOLOGY RELATED

Information can be found under this major's main heading.

Brandeis U (MA) ***293***
Connecticut Coll (CT) ***331***
Florida State U (FL) ***361***
Huntingdon Coll (AL) ***383***
Marymount U (VA) ***420***
Northern Arizona U (AZ) ***450***
U of Connecticut (CT) ***544***
U of Illinois at Urbana–Champaign (IL) ***548***
U of Kentucky (KY) ***549***
Yale U (CT) ***610***

CELL BIOLOGY

Overview: This major focuses on the science of the cell structure and function, both single and as components within a larger system. *Related majors:* biochemistry, molecular biology, nutritional sciences, medical cell biology. *Potential careers:* cell biologist, biochemist, research scientist, physician, pharmaceutical sales rep. *Salary potential:* $25k-$32k.

Ball State U (IN) ***280***
Beloit Coll (WI) ***285***
Bucknell U (PA) ***297***
California Inst of Technology (CA) ***299***
California State U, Fresno (CA) ***301***
California State U, Long Beach (CA) ***301***
California State U, Northridge (CA) ***301***
California State U, San Marcos (CA) ***302***
Clarkson U (NY) ***316***
Colby Coll (ME) ***318***
Concordia U (QC, Canada) ***331***
Cornell U (NY) ***333***
Fort Lewis Coll (CO) ***362***
Hampshire Coll (MA) ***375***
Harvard U (MA) ***376***
Humboldt State U (CA) ***382***
Juniata Coll (PA) ***395***
Lindenwood U (MO) ***407***
Lock Haven U of Pennsylvania (PA) ***408***
Mansfield U of Pennsylvania (PA) ***416***
Marlboro Coll (VT) ***418***
Memorial U of Newfoundland (NF, Canada) ***424***
Northeastern State U (OK) ***450***
Northwestern U (IL) ***453***
Ohio U (OH) ***458***
Okanagan U Coll (BC, Canada) ***459***
Oklahoma State U (OK) ***460***
Oregon State U (OR) ***462***
Pomona Coll (CA) ***472***
Rutgers, The State U of New Jersey, New Brunswick (NJ) ***485***
San Francisco State U (CA) ***498***
Sonoma State U (CA) ***506***
Southwest Missouri State U (MO) ***513***
State U of NY Coll at Brockport (NY) ***515***
Texas A&M U (TX) ***524***
Texas Tech U (TX) ***526***
Tulane U (LA) ***533***
U Coll of the Cariboo (BC, Canada) ***537***
U of Alberta (AB, Canada) ***538***
The U of Arizona (AZ) ***538***
The U of British Columbia (BC, Canada) ***540***
U of Calgary (AB, Canada) ***540***
U of Calif, Davis (CA) ***540***
U of Calif, Los Angeles (CA) ***541***
U of Calif, San Diego (CA) ***541***
U of Calif, Santa Barbara (CA) ***541***
U of Calif, Santa Cruz (CA) ***542***
U of Colorado at Boulder (CO) ***543***
U of Georgia (GA) ***545***
U of Illinois at Urbana–Champaign (IL) ***548***
U of Michigan (MI) ***554***
U of Minnesota, Duluth (MN) ***554***

CELL BIOLOGY (continued)

U of Minnesota, Twin Cities Campus (MN) 555
U of New Hampshire (NH) 558
U of Rochester (NY) 573
U of Vermont (VT) 582
U of Washington (WA) 583
The U of Western Ontario (ON, Canada) 583
U of Wisconsin–Madison (WI) 584
U of Wisconsin–Superior (WI) 586
West Chester U of Pennsylvania (PA) 598
Western Washington U (WA) 600
William Jewell Coll (MO) 606
Wittenberg U (OH) 608
Worcester Polytechnic Inst (MA) 609

CERAMIC ARTS

Overview: This major teaches students the theories, artistic skills, and techniques of ceramics arts. *Related majors:* fine arts, drawing, sculpture, art history. *Potential careers:* fine artist, potter, gallery owner, ceramics teacher, sculpture. *Salary potential:* $10k-$25k.

Adams State Coll (CO) 260
Alberta Coll of Art & Design (AB, Canada) 262
Alfred U (NY) 263
Arcadia U (PA) 271
Arizona State U (AZ) 271
Ball State U (IN) 280
Barton Coll (NC) 282
Bennington Coll (VT) 286
Bethany Coll (KS) 287
Bowling Green State U (OH) 292
California Coll of Arts and Crafts (CA) 299
California State U, Fullerton (CA) 301
California State U, Hayward (CA) 301
California State U, Long Beach (CA) 301
California State U, Northridge (CA) 301
Carnegie Mellon U (PA) 305
The Cleveland Inst of Art (OH) 317
Col for Creative Studies (MI) 319
Coll of the Atlantic (ME) 323
Colorado State U (CO) 325
Columbus Coll of Art and Design (OH) 328
Concord Coll (WV) 329
Concordia U (QC, Canada) 331
Corcoran Coll of Art and Design (DC) 332
Eastern Kentucky U (KY) 348
The Evergreen State Coll (WA) 355
Finlandia U (MI) 358
Franklin Pierce Coll (NH) 364
Georgia Southwestern State U (GA) 368
Goddard Coll (VT) 369
Grand Valley State U (MI) 371
Hampton U (VA) 375
Howard U (DC) 382
Indiana U Bloomington (IN) 385
Indiana Wesleyan U (IN) 387
Inter American U of PR, San Germán Campus (PR) 388
Kansas City Art Inst (MO) 395
Long Island U, Southampton Coll, Friends World Program (NY) 409
Loyola U Chicago (IL) 411
Maharishi U of Management (IA) 414
Maine Coll of Art (ME) 415
Marlboro Coll (VT) 418
Maryland Inst Coll of Art (MD) 419
Massachusetts Coll of Art (MA) 421
McNeese State U (LA) 423
Memphis Coll of Art (TN) 425
Minnesota State U, Mankato (MN) 431
Minnesota State U, Moorhead (MN) 432
Nazareth Coll of Rochester (NY) 443
Northern Michigan U (MI) 451
Northwest Nazarene U (ID) 454
Nova Scotia Coll of Art and Design (NS, Canada) 455
Ohio Northern U (OH) 457
The Ohio State U (OH) 457
Ohio U (OH) 458
Pacific Northwest Coll of Art (OR) 464
Pratt Inst (NY) 473
Rhode Island School of Design (RI) 479
Rochester Inst of Technology (NY) 482
Rutgers, The State U of New Jersey, New Brunswick (NJ) 485
St. Cloud State U (MN) 488
San Francisco Art Inst (CA) 498
School of the Museum of Fine Arts (MA) 501
Seton Hill U (PA) 502
Simon's Rock Coll of Bard (MA) 505
State U of NY at New Paltz (NY) 515
State U of NY Coll at Brockport (NY) 515
State U of NY Coll at Potsdam (NY) 517
Syracuse U (NY) 521
Temple U (PA) 523
Texas Woman's U (TX) 527
Trinity Christian Coll (IL) 530
The U of Akron (OH) 537
U of Dallas (TX) 544
U of Evansville (IN) 545
U of Hartford (CT) 546
The U of Iowa (IA) 548
U of Massachusetts Dartmouth (MA) 553
U of Miami (FL) 553
U of Michigan (MI) 554
U of Montevallo (AL) 557
U of North Texas (TX) 562
U of Oklahoma (OK) 562
U of Oregon (OR) 562
The U of South Dakota (SD) 575
The U of Texas at El Paso (TX) 578
U of the District of Columbia (DC) 580
U of Washington (WA) 583
U of Wisconsin–Milwaukee (WI) 585
Washington U in St. Louis (MO) 595
Webster U (MO) 597
Western Washington U (WA) 600
West Virginia Wesleyan Coll (WV) 603
Wittenberg U (OH) 608

CERAMIC SCIENCES/ ENGINEERING

Overview: This major teaches students about the scientific principles behind the development and use of industrial ceramics. *Related majors:* chemical engineering, materials engineering, materials science, applied physics. *Potential careers:* chemical engineer, chemist, materials engineer, researcher. *Salary potential:* $40k-$55k.

Alfred U (NY) 263
Clemson U (SC) 317
Iowa State U of Science and Technology (IA) 390
The Ohio State U (OH) 457
U of Missouri–Rolla (MO) 556
U of Washington (WA) 583

CHEMICAL AND ATOMIC/ MOLECULAR PHYSICS

Overview: This major is a branch of physics that focuses on how matter and energy behave at the atomic and molecular level. *Related majors:* nuclear physics, physical and theoretical chemistry, mathematics, theoretical and mathematical physics. *Potential careers:* chemist, physicist, research scientist, professor. *Salary potential:* $27k-$37k.

The Catholic U of America (DC) 307
The Coll of Wooster (OH) 324
Columbia Coll (NY) 326
Maryville Coll (TN) 420
Ohio U (OH) 458
Queen's U at Kingston (ON, Canada) 476
Saint Mary's U of Minnesota (MN) 494
San Diego State U (CA) 498
Simon Fraser U (BC, Canada) 505
Swarthmore Coll (PA) 521
U of Calif, San Diego (CA) 541
U of Guelph (ON, Canada) 546
U of Waterloo (ON, Canada) 583

CHEMICAL ENGINEERING

Overview: This major explores the scientific and mathematical principles behind a wide range of topics as they apply to chemical processes, such as chemical reactions, electrochemical reactions, energy conservation, heat and mass transfer, kinetics, corrosion, pollution, and fluid mechanics. *Potential careers:* chemical engineer, environmentalist, quality control manager, researcher, chemist. *Salary potential:* $40k-$55k.

Arizona State U (AZ) 271
Auburn U (AL) 276
Brigham Young U (UT) 295
Brown U (RI) 296
Bucknell U (PA) 297
California Inst of Technology (CA) 299
California State Polytechnic U, Pomona (CA) 300
California State U, Long Beach (CA) 301
California State U, Northridge (CA) 301
Calvin Coll (MI) 303
Carlow Coll (PA) 305
Carnegie Mellon U (PA) 305
Case Western Reserve U (OH) 307
Christian Brothers U (TN) 313
City Coll of the City U of NY (NY) 314
Clarkson U (NY) 316
Clemson U (SC) 317
Cleveland State U (OH) 317
Colorado School of Mines (CO) 325
Colorado State U (CO) 325
Columbia U, School of Engineering & Applied Sci (NY) 328
Cooper Union for the Advancement of Science & Art (NY) 332
Cornell U (NY) 333
Dalhousie U (NS, Canada) 336
Drexel U (PA) 346
Florida A&M U (FL) 359
Florida Inst of Technology (FL) 360
Florida International U (FL) 360
Florida State U (FL) 361
Geneva Coll (PA) 366
Georgia Inst of Technology (GA) 367
Hampton U (VA) 375
Harvard U (MA) 376
Howard U (DC) 382
Illinois Inst of Technology (IL) 384
Insto Tecno Estudios Sups Monterrey(Mexico) 388
Iowa State U of Science and Technology (IA) 390
Johns Hopkins U (MD) 392
Kansas State U (KS) 396
Lafayette Coll (PA) 400
Lakehead U (ON, Canada) 400
Lamar U (TX) 401
Lehigh U (PA) 404
Louisiana State U and A&M Coll (LA) 410
Louisiana Tech U (LA) 410
Manhattan Coll (NY) 416
Massachusetts Inst of Technology (MA) 421
McGill U (QC, Canada) 423
McMaster U (ON, Canada) 423
Memorial U of Newfoundland (NF, Canada) 424
Michigan State U (MI) 428
Michigan Technological U (MI) 428
Mississippi State U (MS) 432
Montana State U–Bozeman (MT) 434
New Jersey Inst of Technology (NJ) 445
New Mexico Inst of Mining and Technology (NM) 446
New Mexico State U (NM) 446
New York U (NY) 447
North Carolina Ag and Tech State U (NC) 448
North Carolina State U (NC) 449
Northeastern U (MA) 450
Northwestern U (IL) 453
The Ohio State U (OH) 457
Ohio U (OH) 458
Oklahoma State U (OK) 460
Oregon State U (OR) 462
Penn State U Univ Park Campus (PA) 468
Polytechnic U, Brooklyn Campus (NY) 472
Prairie View A&M U (TX) 473
Princeton U (NJ) 474
Purdue U (IN) 475
Queen's U at Kingston (ON, Canada) 476
Rensselaer Polytechnic Inst (NY) 478
Rice U (TX) 479
Rose-Hulman Inst of Technology (IN) 484
Rowan U (NJ) 484
Ryerson U (ON, Canada) 485
San Diego State U (CA) 498
San Jose State U (CA) 499
South Dakota School of Mines and Technology (SD) 507
Stanford U (CA) 514
State U of NY Coll of Environ Sci and Forestry (NY) 517
Stevens Inst of Technology (NJ) 519
Stony Brook U, State University of New York (NY) 520
Syracuse U (NY) 521
Tennessee Technological U (TN) 524
Texas A&M U (TX) 524
Texas A&M U–Kingsville (TX) 525
Texas Tech U (TX) 526
Thiel Coll (PA) 527
Tri-State U (IN) 532
Tufts U (MA) 533
Tulane U (LA) 533
Tuskegee U (AL) 533
United States Military Academy (NY) 535
Université de Sherbrooke (QC, Canada) 536
U du Québec à Trois-Rivières (QC, Canada) 536
Université Laval (QC, Canada) 536
U at Buffalo, The State University of New York (NY) 536
The U of Akron (OH) 537
The U of Alabama (AL) 537
The U of Alabama in Huntsville (AL) 537
U of Alberta (AB, Canada) 538
The U of Arizona (AZ) 538
U of Arkansas (AR) 539
The U of British Columbia (BC, Canada) 540
U of Calgary (AB, Canada) 540
U of Calif, Berkeley (CA) 540
U of Calif, Davis (CA) 540
U of Calif, Irvine (CA) 541
U of Calif, Los Angeles (CA) 541
U of Calif, Riverside (CA) 541
U of Calif, San Diego (CA) 541
U of Calif, Santa Barbara (CA) 541
U of Cincinnati (OH) 543
U of Colorado at Boulder (CO) 543
U of Connecticut (CT) 544
U of Dayton (OH) 544
U of Delaware (DE) 544
U of Florida (FL) 545
U of Houston (TX) 547
U of Idaho (ID) 547
U of Illinois at Chicago (IL) 547
U of Illinois at Urbana–Champaign (IL) 548
The U of Iowa (IA) 548
U of Kansas (KS) 549
U of Kentucky (KY) 549
U of Louisiana at Lafayette (LA) 550
U of Louisville (KY) 550
U of Maine (ME) 550
U of Maryland, Baltimore County (MD) 552
U of Maryland, Coll Park (MD) 552
U of Massachusetts Amherst (MA) 552
U of Massachusetts Lowell (MA) 553
U of Michigan (MI) 554
U of Minnesota, Duluth (MN) 554
U of Minnesota, Twin Cities Campus (MN) 555
U of Mississippi (MS) 555
U of Missouri–Columbia (MO) 555
U of Missouri–Rolla (MO) 556
U of Nebraska–Lincoln (NE) 557
U of Nevada, Reno (NV) 558
U of New Brunswick Fredericton (NB, Canada) 558
U of New Brunswick Saint John (NB, Canada) 558
U of New Hampshire (NH) 558
U of New Haven (CT) 559
U of New Mexico (NM) 559
U of North Dakota (ND) 561
U of Notre Dame (IN) 562
U of Oklahoma (OK) 562
U of Ottawa (ON, Canada) 563
U of Pennsylvania (PA) 563
U of Pittsburgh (PA) 569
U of Rhode Island (RI) 572
U of Rochester (NY) 573
U of Saskatchewan (SK, Canada) 574
U of South Alabama (AL) 575
U of South Carolina (SC) 575
U of Southern California (CA) 576
U of South Florida (FL) 576
The U of Tennessee (TN) 577
The U of Tennessee at Chattanooga (TN) 577
The U of Texas at Austin (TX) 578
U of Toledo (OH) 581

U of Toronto (ON, Canada) **581**
U of Tulsa (OK) **581**
U of Utah (UT) **582**
U of Virginia (VA) **582**
U of Washington (WA) **583**
U of Waterloo (ON, Canada) **583**
The U of Western Ontario (ON, Canada) **583**
U of Wisconsin–Madison (WI) **584**
U of Wyoming (WY) **586**
Vanderbilt U (TN) **588**
Villanova U (PA) **590**
Virginia Commonwealth U (VA) **590**
Virginia Polytechnic Inst and State U (VA) **591**
Washington and Lee U (VA) **594**
Washington State U (WA) **595**
Washington U in St. Louis (MO) **595**
Wayne State U (MI) **596**
Western Michigan U (MI) **599**
West Virginia U (WV) **602**
West Virginia U Inst of Technology (WV) **602**
Widener U (PA) **604**
Winona State U (MN) **608**
Worcester Polytechnic Inst (MA) **609**
Xavier U (OH) **610**
Yale U (CT) **610**
Youngstown State U (OH) **611**

CHEMICAL ENGINEERING TECHNOLOGY

Overview: This major provides students with a basic understanding of chemistry, including electronic structure, intermolecular forces, states of matter, chemical reactions, organic chemistry, chemical equilibrium, and other topics. *Related majors:* chemistry, polymer chemistry, chemical technology. *Potential careers:* laboratory supervisor, research technician, chemical sales representative, chemical equipment representative. *Salary potential:* $35k-$45k.

Excelsior Coll (NY) **356**
Gallaudet U (DC) **365**
Inter American U of PR, Guayama Campus (PR) **388**
Lakehead U (ON, Canada) **400**
Midwestern State U (TX) **430**
Savannah State U (GA) **499**
The U of Akron (OH) **537**
U of Calif, Santa Barbara (CA) **541**
U of Hartford (CT) **546**

CHEMICAL TECHNOLOGY

Overview: This major prepares students to assist in chemical research and industrial operations. *Related majors:* chemistry, environmental/pollution control technology, water quality/wastewater treatment. *Potential careers:* biotechnology research associate, process development assistant, quality control inspector, instrumentation technician, manufacturing research associate. *Salary potential:* $25k-$37k.

U of Massachusetts Lowell (MA) **553**

CHEMISTRY

Overview: This major is the scientific study of the composition and behavior of matter and the processes of chemical change. *Related majors:* mathematics, theoretical and mathematical physics, cell and molecular biology, pharmaceutical sciences. *Potential careers:* chemist, biochemist, professor, chemical engineer, environmental scientist, pharmacist. *Salary potential:* $35k-$55k.

Abilene Christian U (TX) **260**
Acadia U (NS, Canada) **260**
Adams State Coll (CO) **260**
Adelphi U (NY) **260**
Adrian Coll (MI) **260**
Agnes Scott Coll (GA) **261**
Alabama A&M U (AL) **261**
Alabama State U (AL) **261**
Albany State U (GA) **262**
Albertson Coll of Idaho (ID) **262**
Albertus Magnus Coll (CT) **262**
Albion Coll (MI) **262**
Albright Coll (PA) **263**
Alcorn State U (MS) **263**
Alderson-Broaddus Coll (WV) **263**
Alfred U (NY) **263**
Allegheny Coll (PA) **264**
Alma Coll (MI) **264**
Alvernia Coll (PA) **265**
Alverno Coll (WI) **265**
American International Coll (MA) **267**
American U (DC) **267**
The American U in Cairo(Egypt) **267**
Amherst Coll (MA) **268**
Anderson U (IN) **268**
Andrews U (MI) **269**
Angelo State U (TX) **269**
Antioch Coll (OH) **269**
Appalachian State U (NC) **270**
Aquinas Coll (MI) **270**
Arcadia U (PA) **271**
Arizona State U (AZ) **271**
Arkansas State U (AR) **272**
Arkansas Tech U (AR) **272**
Armstrong Atlantic State U (GA) **273**
Asbury Coll (KY) **274**
Ashland U (OH) **274**
Assumption Coll (MA) **275**
Athens State U (AL) **275**
Atlantic Union Coll (MA) **276**
Auburn U (AL) **276**
Augsburg Coll (MN) **276**
Augustana Coll (IL) **276**
Augustana Coll (SD) **276**
Augusta State U (GA) **277**
Aurora U (IL) **277**
Austin Coll (TX) **277**
Austin Peay State U (TN) **278**
Averett U (VA) **278**
Avila U (MO) **278**
Azusa Pacific U (CA) **278**
Baker U (KS) **280**
Baldwin-Wallace Coll (OH) **280**
Ball State U (IN) **280**
Bard Coll (NY) **281**
Barnard Coll (NY) **282**
Barry U (FL) **282**
Barton Coll (NC) **282**
Bates Coll (ME) **282**
Bayamón Central U (PR) **283**
Baylor U (TX) **283**
Belhaven Coll (MS) **283**
Bellarmine U (KY) **284**
Belmont U (TN) **284**
Beloit Coll (WI) **285**
Bemidji State U (MN) **285**
Benedict Coll (SC) **285**
Benedictine Coll (KS) **285**
Benedictine U (IL) **285**
Bennett Coll (NC) **286**
Bennington Coll (VT) **286**
Berea Coll (KY) **286**
Berry Coll (GA) **287**
Bethany Coll (KS) **287**
Bethany Coll (WV) **287**
Bethany Lutheran Coll (MN) **288**
Bethel Coll (IN) **288**
Bethel Coll (KS) **288**
Bethel Coll (MN) **288**
Bethel Coll (TN) **288**
Bethune-Cookman Coll (FL) **289**
Birmingham-Southern Coll (AL) **289**
Bishop's U (QC, Canada) **289**
Blackburn Coll (IL) **290**
Black Hills State U (SD) **290**
Bloomfield Coll (NJ) **290**
Bloomsburg U of Pennsylvania (PA) **290**
Bluefield Coll (VA) **291**
Blue Mountain Coll (MS) **291**
Bluffton Coll (OH) **291**
Boston Coll (MA) **292**
Boston U (MA) **292**
Bowdoin Coll (ME) **292**
Bowling Green State U (OH) **292**
Bradley U (IL) **293**
Brandeis U (MA) **293**
Brandon U (MB, Canada) **293**
Brescia U (KY) **293**
Briar Cliff U (IA) **294**
Bridgewater Coll (VA) **294**
Bridgewater State Coll (MA) **294**
Brigham Young U (UT) **295**
Brigham Young U–Hawaii (HI) **295**
Brock U (ON, Canada) **295**
Brooklyn Coll of the City U of NY (NY) **295**
Brown U (RI) **296**
Bryn Athyn Coll of the New Church (PA) **297**
Bryn Mawr Coll (PA) **297**
Bucknell U (PA) **297**
Buena Vista U (IA) **297**
Butler U (IN) **297**
Cabrini Coll (PA) **298**
Caldwell Coll (NJ) **298**
California Inst of Technology (CA) **299**
California Lutheran U (CA) **299**
California Polytechnic State U, San Luis Obispo (CA) **300**
California State Polytechnic U, Pomona (CA) **300**
California State U, Bakersfield (CA) **300**
California State U, Chico (CA) **300**
California State U, Dominguez Hills (CA) **300**
California State U, Fresno (CA) **301**
California State U, Fullerton (CA) **301**
California State U, Hayward (CA) **301**
California State U, Long Beach (CA) **301**
California State U, Northridge (CA) **301**
California State U, Sacramento (CA) **301**
California State U, San Bernardino (CA) **302**
California State U, San Marcos (CA) **302**
California State U, Stanislaus (CA) **302**
California U of Pennsylvania (PA) **302**
Calvin Coll (MI) **303**
Cameron U (OK) **303**
Campbellsville U (KY) **303**
Campbell U (NC) **303**
Canisius Coll (NY) **304**
Cardinal Stritch U (WI) **305**
Carleton Coll (MN) **305**
Carleton U (ON, Canada) **305**
Carlow Coll (PA) **305**
Carnegie Mellon U (PA) **305**
Carroll Coll (MT) **306**
Carroll Coll (WI) **306**
Carson-Newman Coll (TN) **306**
Carthage Coll (WI) **306**
Case Western Reserve U (OH) **307**
Catawba Coll (NC) **307**
The Catholic U of America (DC) **307**
Cedar Crest Coll (PA) **308**
Cedarville U (OH) **308**
Centenary Coll of Louisiana (LA) **308**
Central Coll (IA) **309**
Central Connecticut State U (CT) **309**
Central Methodist Coll (MO) **309**
Central Michigan U (MI) **310**
Central Missouri State U (MO) **310**
Central Washington U (WA) **310**
Centre Coll (KY) **310**
Chadron State Coll (NE) **311**
Chaminade U of Honolulu (HI) **311**
Chapman U (CA) **311**
Charleston Southern U (SC) **311**
Chatham Coll (PA) **312**
Chestnut Hill Coll (PA) **312**
Cheyney U of Pennsylvania (PA) **312**
Christian Brothers U (TN) **313**
Citadel, The Military Coll of South Carolina (SC) **314**
City Coll of the City U of NY (NY) **314**
Claflin U (SC) **314**
Claremont McKenna Coll (CA) **315**
Clarion U of Pennsylvania (PA) **315**
Clark Atlanta U (GA) **315**
Clarke Coll (IA) **315**
Clarkson U (NY) **316**
Clark U (MA) **316**
Clemson U (SC) **317**
Cleveland State U (OH) **317**
Coastal Carolina U (SC) **318**
Coe Coll (IA) **318**
Coker Coll (SC) **318**
Colby Coll (ME) **318**
Colgate U (NY) **319**
Coll Misericordia (PA) **319**
Coll of Charleston (SC) **320**
Coll of Mount St. Joseph (OH) **320**
Coll of Mount Saint Vincent (NY) **320**
The Coll of New Jersey (NJ) **320**
The Coll of New Rochelle (NY) **321**
Coll of Notre Dame of Maryland (MD) **321**
Coll of Saint Benedict (MN) **321**
Coll of St. Catherine (MN) **321**
Coll of Saint Elizabeth (NJ) **321**
Coll of Saint Mary (NE) **322**
The Coll of Saint Rose (NY) **322**
The Coll of St. Scholastica (MN) **322**
The Coll of Southeastern Europe, The American U of Athens(Greece) **323**
Coll of Staten Island of the City U of NY (NY) **323**
Coll of the Holy Cross (MA) **323**
Coll of the Ozarks (MO) **323**
The Coll of William and Mary (VA) **324**
The Coll of Wooster (OH) **324**
The Colorado Coll (CO) **325**
Colorado School of Mines (CO) **325**
Colorado State U (CO) **325**
Colorado State U-Pueblo (CO) **325**
Columbia Coll (MO) **326**
Columbia Coll (NY) **326**
Columbia Coll (SC) **327**
Columbia Union Coll (MD) **328**
Columbia U, School of General Studies (NY) **328**
Columbus State U (GA) **328**
Concord Coll (WV) **329**
Concordia Coll (MN) **329**
Concordia U (IL) **330**
Concordia U (NE) **330**
Concordia U (OR) **330**
Concordia U (QC, Canada) **331**
Concordia U Coll of Alberta (AB, Canada) **331**
Connecticut Coll (CT) **331**
Converse Coll (SC) **332**
Cornell Coll (IA) **332**
Cornell U (NY) **333**
Covenant Coll (GA) **333**
Creighton U (NE) **333**
Crichton Coll (TN) **334**
Culver-Stockton Coll (MO) **334**
Cumberland Coll (KY) **335**
Curry Coll (MA) **335**
Dakota State U (SD) **335**
Dalhousie U (NS, Canada) **336**
Dana Coll (NE) **337**
Dartmouth Coll (NH) **337**
Davidson Coll (NC) **338**
Davis & Elkins Coll (WV) **338**
Defiance Coll (OH) **338**
Delaware State U (DE) **338**
Delaware Valley Coll (PA) **339**
Delta State U (MS) **339**
Denison U (OH) **339**
DePaul U (IL) **339**
DePauw U (IN) **339**
DeSales U (PA) **340**
Dickinson Coll (PA) **344**
Dickinson State U (ND) **344**
Dillard U (LA) **344**
Doane Coll (NE) **344**
Dominican U (IL) **345**
Dordt Coll (IA) **345**
Drake U (IA) **345**
Drew U (NJ) **346**
Drexel U (PA) **346**
Drury U (MO) **346**
Duke U (NC) **346**
Duquesne U (PA) **346**
Earlham Coll (IN) **347**
East Carolina U (NC) **347**
East Central U (OK) **347**
Eastern Illinois U (IL) **348**
Eastern Kentucky U (KY) **348**
Eastern Mennonite U (VA) **348**
Eastern Michigan U (MI) **348**
Eastern Nazarene Coll (MA) **348**
Eastern New Mexico U (NM) **349**
Eastern Oregon U (OR) **349**
Eastern U (PA) **349**
Eastern Washington U (WA) **349**
East Stroudsburg U of Pennsylvania (PA) **349**
East Tennessee State U (TN) **349**
East Texas Baptist U (TX) **350**
Eckerd Coll (FL) **350**
Edgewood Coll (WI) **351**
Edinboro U of Pennsylvania (PA) **351**
Elizabeth City State U (NC) **351**
Elizabethtown Coll (PA) **351**
Elmhurst Coll (IL) **351**

CHEMISTRY (continued)

Elmira Coll (NY) **351**
Elms Coll (MA) **352**
Elon U (NC) **352**
Emmanuel Coll (MA) **353**
Emory & Henry Coll (VA) **353**
Emory U (GA) **354**
Emporia State U (KS) **354**
Erskine Coll (SC) **354**
Eureka Coll (IL) **355**
Evangel U (MO) **355**
The Evergreen State Coll (WA) **355**
Excelsior Coll (NY) **356**
Fairfield U (CT) **356**
Fairleigh Dickinson U, Florham (NJ) **356**
Fairleigh Dickinson U, Teaneck-Metro Campus (NJ) **356**
Fairmont State Coll (WV) **356**
Fayetteville State U (NC) **357**
Ferrum Coll (VA) **358**
Fisk U (TN) **358**
Florida A&M U (FL) **359**
Florida Atlantic U (FL) **359**
Florida Inst of Technology (FL) **360**
Florida International U (FL) **360**
Florida Southern Coll (FL) **361**
Florida State U (FL) **361**
Fordham U (NY) **362**
Fort Hays State U (KS) **362**
Fort Lewis Coll (CO) **362**
Fort Valley State U (GA) **362**
Framingham State Coll (MA) **362**
Franciscan U of Steubenville (OH) **363**
Francis Marion U (SC) **363**
Franklin and Marshall Coll (PA) **363**
Franklin Coll (IN) **363**
Freed-Hardeman U (TN) **364**
Fresno Pacific U (CA) **364**
Frostburg State U (MD) **365**
Furman U (SC) **365**
Gallaudet U (DC) **365**
Gannon U (PA) **365**
Gardner-Webb U (NC) **365**
Geneva Coll (PA) **366**
George Fox U (OR) **366**
George Mason U (VA) **366**
Georgetown Coll (KY) **366**
Georgetown U (DC) **366**
The George Washington U (DC) **367**
Georgia Coll & State U (GA) **367**
Georgia Inst of Technology (GA) **367**
Georgian Court Coll (NJ) **367**
Georgia Southern U (GA) **367**
Georgia Southwestern State U (GA) **368**
Georgia State U (GA) **368**
Gettysburg Coll (PA) **368**
Glenville State Coll (WV) **368**
Gonzaga U (WA) **369**
Gordon Coll (MA) **370**
Goshen Coll (IN) **370**
Goucher Coll (MD) **370**
Governors State U (IL) **370**
Graceland U (IA) **371**
Grambling State U (LA) **371**
Grand Canyon U (AZ) **371**
Grand Valley State U (MI) **371**
Greensboro Coll (NC) **372**
Greenville Coll (IL) **373**
Grinnell Coll (IA) **373**
Grove City Coll (PA) **373**
Guilford Coll (NC) **373**
Gustavus Adolphus Coll (MN) **374**
Hamilton Coll (NY) **374**
Hamline U (MN) **374**
Hampden-Sydney Coll (VA) **374**
Hampshire Coll (MA) **375**
Hampton U (VA) **375**
Hanover Coll (IN) **375**
Harding U (AR) **375**
Hardin-Simmons U (TX) **376**
Hartwick Coll (NY) **376**
Harvard U (MA) **376**
Harvey Mudd Coll (CA) **377**
Hastings Coll (NE) **377**
Haverford Coll (PA) **377**
Heidelberg Coll (OH) **377**
Henderson State U (AR) **378**
Hendrix Coll (AR) **378**
High Point U (NC) **379**
Hillsdale Coll (MI) **379**
Hiram Coll (OH) **379**
Hobart and William Smith Colls (NY) **380**
Hofstra U (NY) **380**
Hollins U (VA) **380**
Holy Family U (PA) **380**
Hood Coll (MD) **381**
Hope Coll (MI) **381**
Houghton Coll (NY) **381**
Houston Baptist U (TX) **382**
Howard Payne U (TX) **382**
Howard U (DC) **382**
Humboldt State U (CA) **382**
Hunter Coll of the City U of NY (NY) **382**
Huntingdon Coll (AL) **383**
Huntington Coll (IN) **383**
Huston-Tillotson Coll (TX) **383**
Idaho State U (ID) **384**
Illinois Coll (IL) **384**
Illinois Inst of Technology (IL) **384**
Illinois State U (IL) **384**
Illinois Wesleyan U (IL) **385**
Immaculata U (PA) **385**
Indiana State U (IN) **385**
Indiana U Bloomington (IN) **385**
Indiana U Northwest (IN) **386**
Indiana U of Pennsylvania (PA) **386**
Indiana U–Purdue U Fort Wayne (IN) **386**
Indiana U–Purdue U Indianapolis (IN) **387**
Indiana U South Bend (IN) **387**
Indiana U Southeast (IN) **387**
Indiana Wesleyan U (IN) **387**
Insto Tecno Estudios Sups Monterrey(Mexico) **388**
Inter American U of PR, Guayama Campus (PR) **388**
Inter American U of PR, San Germán Campus (PR) **388**
Iona Coll (NY) **390**
Iowa State U of Science and Technology (IA) **390**
Iowa Wesleyan Coll (IA) **390**
Ithaca Coll (NY) **390**
Jackson State U (MS) **390**
Jacksonville State U (AL) **390**
Jacksonville U (FL) **391**
James Madison U (VA) **391**
Jamestown Coll (ND) **391**
John Brown U (AR) **392**
John Carroll U (OH) **392**
Johns Hopkins U (MD) **392**
Johnson C. Smith U (NC) **394**
Judson Coll (AL) **395**
Judson Coll (IL) **395**
Juniata Coll (PA) **395**
Kalamazoo Coll (MI) **395**
Kansas State U (KS) **396**
Kean U (NJ) **396**
Keene State Coll (NH) **396**
Kennesaw State U (GA) **397**
Kent State U (OH) **397**
Kentucky State U (KY) **397**
Kentucky Wesleyan Coll (KY) **397**
Kenyon Coll (OH) **398**
Kettering U (MI) **398**
King Coll (TN) **398**
King's Coll (PA) **398**
The King's U Coll (AB, Canada) **399**
Knox Coll (IL) **399**
Kutztown U of Pennsylvania (PA) **399**
Lafayette Coll (PA) **400**
LaGrange Coll (GA) **400**
Lake Erie Coll (OH) **400**
Lake Forest Coll (IL) **400**
Lakehead U (ON, Canada) **400**
Lakeland Coll (WI) **401**
Lamar U (TX) **401**
Lambuth U (TN) **401**
Lander U (SC) **401**
Lane Coll (TN) **402**
Langston U (OK) **402**
La Roche Coll (PA) **402**
La Salle U (PA) **402**
La Sierra U (CA) **403**
Laurentian U (ON, Canada) **403**
Lawrence Technological U (MI) **403**
Lawrence U (WI) **403**
Lebanon Valley Coll (PA) **403**
Lee U (TN) **404**
Lehigh U (PA) **404**
Lehman Coll of the City U of NY (NY) **404**
Le Moyne Coll (NY) **404**
Lenoir-Rhyne Coll (NC) **405**
LeTourneau U (TX) **405**
Lewis & Clark Coll (OR) **405**
Lewis-Clark State Coll (ID) **406**
Lewis U (IL) **406**
Limestone Coll (SC) **406**
Lincoln Memorial U (TN) **407**
Lincoln U (PA) **407**
Lindenwood U (MO) **407**
Linfield Coll (OR) **408**
Lipscomb U (TN) **408**
Lock Haven U of Pennsylvania (PA) **408**
Long Island U, Brooklyn Campus (NY) **409**
Long Island U, C.W. Post Campus (NY) **409**
Long Island U, Southampton Coll (NY) **409**
Longwood U (VA) **409**
Loras Coll (IA) **410**
Louisiana Coll (LA) **410**
Louisiana State U and A&M Coll (LA) **410**
Louisiana State U in Shreveport (LA) **410**
Louisiana Tech U (LA) **410**
Lourdes Coll (OH) **411**
Loyola Coll in Maryland (MD) **411**
Loyola Marymount U (CA) **411**
Loyola U Chicago (IL) **411**
Loyola U New Orleans (LA) **411**
Lubbock Christian U (TX) **412**
Luther Coll (IA) **412**
Lycoming Coll (PA) **412**
Lynchburg Coll (VA) **413**
Lyon Coll (AR) **413**
Macalester Coll (MN) **413**
MacMurray Coll (IL) **414**
Madonna U (MI) **414**
Maharishi U of Management (IA) **414**
Malone Coll (OH) **415**
Manchester Coll (IN) **415**
Manhattan Coll (NY) **416**
Manhattanville Coll (NY) **416**
Mansfield U of Pennsylvania (PA) **416**
Marian Coll (IN) **417**
Marian Coll of Fond du Lac (WI) **417**
Marietta Coll (OH) **417**
Marist Coll (NY) **417**
Marlboro Coll (VT) **418**
Marquette U (WI) **418**
Marshall U (WV) **418**
Mars Hill Coll (NC) **418**
Martin U (IN) **419**
Mary Baldwin Coll (VA) **419**
Marygrove Coll (MI) **419**
Marymount Coll of Fordham U (NY) **419**
Maryville Coll (TN) **420**
Maryville U of Saint Louis (MO) **420**
Mary Washington Coll (VA) **420**
Massachusetts Coll of Liberal Arts (MA) **421**
Mass Coll of Pharmacy and Allied Health Sciences (MA) **421**
Massachusetts Inst of Technology (MA) **421**
Mayville State U (ND) **422**
McDaniel Coll (MD) **422**
McGill U (QC, Canada) **423**
McKendree Coll (IL) **423**
McMaster U (ON, Canada) **423**
McMurry U (TX) **423**
McNeese State U (LA) **423**
McPherson Coll (KS) **423**
Memorial U of Newfoundland (NF, Canada) **424**
Mercer U (GA) **425**
Mercyhurst Coll (PA) **425**
Meredith Coll (NC) **426**
Merrimack Coll (MA) **426**
Mesa State Coll (CO) **426**
Messiah Coll (PA) **426**
Methodist Coll (NC) **427**
Metropolitan State Coll of Denver (CO) **427**
Miami U (OH) **428**
Michigan State U (MI) **428**
Michigan Technological U (MI) **428**
MidAmerica Nazarene U (KS) **428**
Middlebury Coll (VT) **429**
Middle Tennessee State U (TN) **429**
Midland Lutheran Coll (NE) **429**
Midwestern State U (TX) **430**
Miles Coll (AL) **430**
Millersville U of Pennsylvania (PA) **430**
Milligan Coll (TN) **430**
Millikin U (IL) **430**
Millsaps Coll (MS) **431**
Mills Coll (CA) **431**
Minnesota State U, Mankato (MN) **431**
Minnesota State U, Moorhead (MN) **432**
Minot State U (ND) **432**
Mississippi Coll (MS) **432**
Mississippi State U (MS) **432**
Mississippi Valley State U (MS) **432**
Missouri Southern State Coll (MO) **433**
Missouri Western State Coll (MO) **433**
Monmouth Coll (IL) **434**
Monmouth U (NJ) **434**
Montana State U–Billings (MT) **434**
Montana State U–Bozeman (MT) **434**
Montana Tech of The U of Montana (MT) **435**
Montclair State U (NJ) **435**
Moravian Coll (PA) **436**
Morehead State U (KY) **436**
Morehouse Coll (GA) **436**
Morgan State U (MD) **436**
Morningside Coll (IA) **437**
Mount Allison U (NB, Canada) **437**
Mount Holyoke Coll (MA) **438**
Mount Marty Coll (SD) **438**
Mount Mary Coll (WI) **438**
Mount Saint Mary Coll (NY) **439**
Mount St. Mary's Coll (CA) **439**
Mount Saint Mary's Coll and Seminary (MD) **439**
Mount Saint Vincent U (NS, Canada) **439**
Mount Union Coll (OH) **440**
Mount Vernon Nazarene U (OH) **440**
Muhlenberg Coll (PA) **440**
Murray State U (KY) **440**
Muskingum Coll (OH) **441**
Nazareth Coll of Rochester (NY) **443**
Nebraska Wesleyan U (NE) **443**
Newberry Coll (SC) **444**
New Coll of Florida (FL) **444**
New Jersey City U (NJ) **445**
New Jersey Inst of Technology (NJ) **445**
Newman U (KS) **445**
New Mexico Highlands U (NM) **446**
New Mexico Inst of Mining and Technology (NM) **446**
New Mexico State U (NM) **446**
New York Inst of Technology (NY) **447**
New York U (NY) **447**
Niagara U (NY) **447**
Nicholls State U (LA) **447**
Norfolk State U (VA) **448**
North Carolina Ag and Tech State U (NC) **448**
North Carolina Central U (NC) **448**
North Carolina State U (NC) **449**
North Carolina Wesleyan Coll (NC) **449**
North Central Coll (IL) **449**
North Dakota State U (ND) **449**
Northeastern Illinois U (IL) **450**
Northeastern State U (OK) **450**
Northeastern U (MA) **450**
Northern Arizona U (AZ) **450**
Northern Illinois U (IL) **450**
Northern Kentucky U (KY) **451**
Northern Michigan U (MI) **451**
Northern State U (SD) **451**
North Georgia Coll & State U (GA) **451**
Northland Coll (WI) **452**
North Park U (IL) **452**
Northwestern Coll (IA) **453**
Northwestern Oklahoma State U (OK) **453**
Northwestern State U of Louisiana (LA) **453**
Northwestern U (IL) **453**
Northwest Missouri State U (MO) **454**
Northwest Nazarene U (ID) **454**
Norwich U (VT) **455**
Notre Dame Coll (OH) **455**
Oakland City U (IN) **456**
Oakland U (MI) **456**
Oakwood Coll (AL) **456**
Oberlin Coll (OH) **456**
Occidental Coll (CA) **457**
Oglethorpe U (GA) **457**
Ohio Dominican U (OH) **457**
Ohio Northern U (OH) **457**
The Ohio State U (OH) **457**
Ohio U (OH) **458**
Ohio Wesleyan U (OH) **459**
Okanagan U Coll (BC, Canada) **459**
Oklahoma Baptist U (OK) **459**
Oklahoma Christian U (OK) **459**
Oklahoma City U (OK) **460**
Oklahoma Panhandle State U (OK) **460**
Oklahoma State U (OK) **460**
Oklahoma Wesleyan U (OK) **460**
Old Dominion U (VA) **460**
Olivet Coll (MI) **461**
Olivet Nazarene U (IL) **461**
Oral Roberts U (OK) **461**
Oregon State U (OR) **462**
Otterbein Coll (OH) **462**
Ouachita Baptist U (AR) **462**

Our Lady of the Lake U of San Antonio (TX) 463
Pace U (NY) 463
Pacific Lutheran U (WA) 463
Pacific Union Coll (CA) 464
Pacific U (OR) 464
Paine Coll (GA) 465
Park U (MO) 465
Penn State U at Erie, The Behrend Coll (PA) 467
Penn State U Univ Park Campus (PA) 468
Pepperdine U, Malibu (CA) 469
Peru State Coll (NE) 469
Pfeiffer U (NC) 469
Philadelphia U (PA) 469
Piedmont Coll (GA) 470
Pikeville Coll (KY) 470
Pittsburg State U (KS) 470
Pitzer Coll (CA) 471
Plattsburgh State U of NY (NY) 471
Plymouth State Coll (NH) 471
Point Loma Nazarene U (CA) 471
Polytechnic U, Brooklyn Campus (NY) 472
Pomona Coll (CA) 472
Pontifical Catholic U of Puerto Rico (PR) 472
Portland State U (OR) 472
Prairie View A&M U (TX) 473
Presbyterian Coll (SC) 473
Princeton U (NJ) 474
Principia Coll (IL) 474
Providence Coll (RI) 474
Purchase Coll, State U of NY (NY) 475
Purdue U (IN) 475
Purdue U Calumet (IN) 475
Queens Coll of the City U of NY (NY) 475
Queen's U at Kingston (ON, Canada) 476
Quincy U (IL) 476
Quinnipiac U (CT) 476
Radford U (VA) 476
Ramapo Coll of New Jersey (NJ) 477
Randolph-Macon Coll (VA) 477
Randolph-Macon Woman's Coll (VA) 477
Reed Coll (OR) 477
Regis Coll (MA) 478
Regis U (CO) 478
Rensselaer Polytechnic Inst (NY) 478
Rhode Island Coll (RI) 479
Rhodes Coll (TN) 479
Rice U (TX) 479
The Richard Stockton Coll of New Jersey (NJ) 479
Rider U (NJ) 480
Ripon Coll (WI) 480
Rivier Coll (NH) 480
Roanoke Coll (VA) 481
Roberts Wesleyan Coll (NY) 481
Rochester Inst of Technology (NY) 482
Rockford Coll (IL) 482
Rockhurst U (MO) 482
Rocky Mountain Coll (MT) 482
Roger Williams U (RI) 483
Rollins Coll (FL) 483
Roosevelt U (IL) 483
Rose-Hulman Inst of Technology (IN) 484
Rosemont Coll (PA) 484
Rowan U (NJ) 484
Russell Sage Coll (NY) 484
Rust Coll (MS) 485
Rutgers, The State U of New Jersey, Camden (NJ) 485
Rutgers, The State U of New Jersey, Newark (NJ) 485
Rutgers, The State U of New Jersey, New Brunswick (NJ) 485
Ryerson U (ON, Canada) 485
Sacred Heart U (CT) 486
Saginaw Valley State U (MI) 486
St. Ambrose U (IA) 486
St. Andrews Presbyterian Coll (NC) 487
Saint Augustine's Coll (NC) 487
St. Bonaventure U (NY) 487
St. Cloud State U (MN) 488
St. Edward's U (TX) 488
Saint Francis U (PA) 488
St. Francis Xavier U (NS, Canada) 489
St. John Fisher Coll (NY) 489
Saint John's U (MN) 490
St. John's U (NY) 490
Saint Joseph Coll (CT) 490
Saint Joseph's Coll (IN) 490
St. Joseph's Coll, New York (NY) 491
Saint Joseph's Coll of Maine (ME) 491
Saint Joseph's U (PA) 491
St. Lawrence U (NY) 491
Saint Louis U (MO) 492
Saint Martin's Coll (WA) 493
Saint Mary Coll (KS) 493
Saint Mary's Coll (IN) 493
Saint Mary's Coll of California (CA) 494
Saint Mary's Coll of Madonna U (MI) 493
St. Mary's Coll of Maryland (MD) 494
Saint Mary's U (NS, Canada) 494
Saint Mary's U of Minnesota (MN) 494
St. Mary's U of San Antonio (TX) 494
Saint Michael's Coll (VT) 494
St. Norbert Coll (WI) 495
St. Olaf Coll (MN) 495
Saint Peter's Coll (NJ) 495
St. Thomas U (FL) 496
Saint Vincent Coll (PA) 496
Saint Xavier U (IL) 496
Salem Coll (NC) 496
Salem State Coll (MA) 497
Salisbury U (MD) 497
Salve Regina U (RI) 497
Samford U (AL) 497
Sam Houston State U (TX) 497
San Diego State U (CA) 498
San Francisco State U (CA) 498
San Jose State U (CA) 499
Santa Clara U (CA) 499
Sarah Lawrence Coll (NY) 499
Savannah State U (GA) 499
Schreiner U (TX) 501
Scripps Coll (CA) 501
Seattle Pacific U (WA) 501
Seattle U (WA) 501
Seton Hall U (NJ) 502
Seton Hill U (PA) 502
Shawnee State U (OH) 502
Shaw U (NC) 502
Shenandoah U (VA) 503
Shepherd Coll (WV) 503
Shippensburg U of Pennsylvania (PA) 503
Shorter Coll (GA) 504
Siena Coll (NY) 504
Siena Heights U (MI) 504
Simmons Coll (MA) 504
Simon Fraser U (BC, Canada) 505
Simon's Rock Coll of Bard (MA) 505
Simpson Coll (IA) 505
Skidmore Coll (NY) 506
Slippery Rock U of Pennsylvania (PA) 506
Smith Coll (MA) 506
Sonoma State U (CA) 506
South Carolina State U (SC) 506
South Dakota School of Mines and Technology (SD) 507
South Dakota State U (SD) 507
Southeastern Louisiana U (LA) 508
Southeastern Oklahoma State U (OK) 508
Southeast Missouri State U (MO) 508
Southern Adventist U (TN) 508
Southern Arkansas U–Magnolia (AR) 509
Southern Connecticut State U (CT) 509
Southern Illinois U Carbondale (IL) 509
Southern Illinois U Edwardsville (IL) 509
Southern Methodist U (TX) 510
Southern Nazarene U (OK) 510
Southern Oregon U (OR) 510
Southern U and A&M Coll (LA) 511
Southern Utah U (UT) 511
Southern Wesleyan U (SC) 511
Southwest Baptist U (MO) 512
Southwestern Coll (KS) 512
Southwestern Oklahoma State U (OK) 512
Southwestern U (TX) 513
Southwest Missouri State U (MO) 513
Southwest State U (MN) 513
Southwest Texas State U (TX) 513
Spalding U (KY) 513
Spelman Coll (GA) 514
Spring Arbor U (MI) 514
Springfield Coll (MA) 514
Spring Hill Coll (AL) 514
Stanford U (CA) 514
State U of NY at Albany (NY) 514
State U of NY at Binghamton (NY) 515
State U of NY at New Paltz (NY) 515
State U of NY at Oswego (NY) 515
State U of NY Coll at Brockport (NY) 515
State U of NY Coll at Buffalo (NY) 516
State U of NY Coll at Cortland (NY) 516
State U of NY Coll at Fredonia (NY) 516
State U of NY Coll at Geneseo (NY) 516
State U of NY Coll at Old Westbury (NY) 516
State U of NY Coll at Oneonta (NY) 517
State U of NY Coll at Potsdam (NY) 517
State U of NY Coll of Environ Sci and Forestry (NY) 517
State U of West Georgia (GA) 518
Stephen F. Austin State U (TX) 518
Stetson U (FL) 519
Stevens Inst of Technology (NJ) 519
Stonehill Coll (MA) 520
Stony Brook U, State University of New York (NY) 520
Suffolk U (MA) 520
Sul Ross State U (TX) 521
Susquehanna U (PA) 521
Swarthmore Coll (PA) 521
Sweet Briar Coll (VA) 521
Syracuse U (NY) 521
Tabor Coll (KS) 522
Talladega Coll (AL) 522
Tarleton State U (TX) 522
Taylor U (IN) 523
Temple U (PA) 523
Tennessee State U (TN) 523
Tennessee Technological U (TN) 524
Tennessee Wesleyan Coll (TN) 524
Texas A&M International U (TX) 524
Texas A&M U (TX) 524
Texas A&M U–Commerce (TX) 525
Texas A&M U–Corpus Christi (TX) 525
Texas A&M U–Kingsville (TX) 525
Texas Christian U (TX) 526
Texas Lutheran U (TX) 526
Texas Southern U (TX) 526
Texas Tech U (TX) 526
Texas Wesleyan U (TX) 526
Texas Woman's U (TX) 527
Thiel Coll (PA) 527
Thomas Edison State Coll (NJ) 527
Thomas More Coll (KY) 528
Touro Coll (NY) 529
Towson U (MD) 529
Transylvania U (KY) 529
Trent U (ON, Canada) 529
Trevecca Nazarene U (TN) 529
Trinity Christian Coll (IL) 530
Trinity Coll (CT) 530
Trinity Coll (DC) 530
Trinity International U (IL) 531
Trinity U (TX) 531
Trinity Western U (BC, Canada) 531
Tri-State U (IN) 532
Troy State U (AL) 532
Truman State U (MO) 532
Tufts U (MA) 533
Tulane U (LA) 533
Tuskegee U (AL) 533
Union Coll (KY) 533
Union Coll (NE) 534
Union Coll (NY) 534
Union U (TN) 534
United States Air Force Academy (CO) 534
United States Military Academy (NY) 535
United States Naval Academy (MD) 535
Universidad Adventista de las Antillas (PR) 536
Université de Sherbrooke (QC, Canada) 536
U du Québec à Trois-Rivières (QC, Canada) 536
Université Laval (QC, Canada) 536
U at Buffalo, The State University of New York (NY) 536
U Coll of the Cariboo (BC, Canada) 537
The U of Akron (OH) 537
The U of Alabama (AL) 537
The U of Alabama at Birmingham (AL) 537
The U of Alabama in Huntsville (AL) 537
U of Alaska Anchorage (AK) 538
U of Alaska Fairbanks (AK) 538
U of Alberta (AB, Canada) 538
The U of Arizona (AZ) 538
U of Arkansas (AR) 539
U of Arkansas at Little Rock (AR) 539
U of Arkansas at Monticello (AR) 539
The U of British Columbia (BC, Canada) 540
U of Calgary (AB, Canada) 540
U of Calif, Berkeley (CA) 540
U of Calif, Davis (CA) 540
U of Calif, Irvine (CA) 541
U of Calif, Los Angeles (CA) 541
U of Calif, Riverside (CA) 541
U of Calif, San Diego (CA) 541
U of Calif, Santa Barbara (CA) 541
U of Calif, Santa Cruz (CA) 542
U of Central Arkansas (AR) 542
U of Central Florida (FL) 542
U of Central Oklahoma (OK) 542
U of Charleston (WV) 542
U of Chicago (IL) 542
U of Cincinnati (OH) 543
U of Colorado at Boulder (CO) 543
U of Colorado at Colorado Springs (CO) 543
U of Colorado at Denver (CO) 543
U of Connecticut (CT) 544
U of Dallas (TX) 544
U of Dayton (OH) 544
U of Delaware (DE) 544
U of Denver (CO) 544
U of Evansville (IN) 545
U of Florida (FL) 545
U of Georgia (GA) 545
U of Guelph (ON, Canada) 546
U of Hartford (CT) 546
U of Hawaii at Hilo (HI) 546
U of Hawaii at Manoa (HI) 546
U of Houston (TX) 547
U of Houston–Clear Lake (TX) 547
U of Houston–Downtown (TX) 547
U of Idaho (ID) 547
U of Illinois at Chicago (IL) 547
U of Illinois at Springfield (IL) 548
U of Illinois at Urbana–Champaign (IL) 548
U of Indianapolis (IN) 548
The U of Iowa (IA) 548
U of Kansas (KS) 549
U of Kentucky (KY) 549
U of King's Coll (NS, Canada) 549
U of La Verne (CA) 549
The U of Lethbridge (AB, Canada) 549
U of Louisiana at Lafayette (LA) 550
U of Louisville (KY) 550
U of Maine (ME) 550
U of Maine at Farmington (ME) 550
U of Manitoba (MB, Canada) 551
U of Mary Hardin-Baylor (TX) 551
U of Maryland, Baltimore County (MD) 552
U of Maryland, Coll Park (MD) 552
U of Maryland Eastern Shore (MD) 552
U of Massachusetts Amherst (MA) 552
U of Massachusetts Boston (MA) 553
U of Massachusetts Dartmouth (MA) 553
U of Massachusetts Lowell (MA) 553
The U of Memphis (TN) 553
U of Miami (FL) 553
U of Michigan (MI) 554
U of Michigan–Dearborn (MI) 554
U of Michigan–Flint (MI) 554
U of Minnesota, Duluth (MN) 554
U of Minnesota, Morris (MN) 555
U of Minnesota, Twin Cities Campus (MN) 555
U of Mississippi (MS) 555
U of Missouri–Columbia (MO) 555
U of Missouri–Kansas City (MO) 555
U of Missouri–Rolla (MO) 556
U of Missouri–St. Louis (MO) 556
U of Mobile (AL) 556
The U of Montana–Missoula (MT) 556
The U of Montana–Western (MT) 556
U of Montevallo (AL) 557
U of Nebraska at Kearney (NE) 557
U of Nebraska at Omaha (NE) 557
U of Nebraska–Lincoln (NE) 557
U of Nevada, Las Vegas (NV) 558
U of Nevada, Reno (NV) 558
U of New Brunswick Fredericton (NB, Canada) 558
U of New Hampshire (NH) 558
U of New Haven (CT) 559
U of New Mexico (NM) 559
U of New Orleans (LA) 559
U of North Alabama (AL) 559
The U of North Carolina at Asheville (NC) 559
The U of North Carolina at Chapel Hill (NC) 560
The U of North Carolina at Charlotte (NC) 560
The U of North Carolina at Greensboro (NC) 560
The U of North Carolina at Pembroke (NC) 560
The U of North Carolina at Wilmington (NC) 561
U of North Dakota (ND) 561
U of Northern Colorado (CO) 561
U of Northern Iowa (IA) 561

CHEMISTRY (continued)

U of North Florida (FL) ***561***
U of North Texas (TX) ***562***
U of Notre Dame (IN) ***562***
U of Oklahoma (OK) ***562***
U of Oregon (OR) ***562***
U of Ottawa (ON, Canada) ***563***
U of Pennsylvania (PA) ***563***
U of Pittsburgh (PA) ***569***
U of Pittsburgh at Bradford (PA) ***569***
U of Pittsburgh at Johnstown (PA) ***570***
U of Portland (OR) ***570***
U of Prince Edward Island (PE, Canada) ***570***
U of Puerto Rico, Humacao U Coll (PR) ***570***
U of Puerto Rico, Cayey U Coll (PR) ***571***
U of Puerto Rico, Río Piedras (PR) ***571***
U of Puget Sound (WA) ***571***
U of Redlands (CA) ***572***
U of Regina (SK, Canada) ***572***
U of Rhode Island (RI) ***572***
U of Richmond (VA) ***572***
U of Rio Grande (OH) ***572***
U of Rochester (NY) ***573***
U of Saint Francis (IN) ***573***
U of St. Thomas (MN) ***573***
U of St. Thomas (TX) ***573***
U of San Diego (CA) ***574***
U of San Francisco (CA) ***574***
U of Saskatchewan (SK, Canada) ***574***
U of Science and Arts of Oklahoma (OK) ***574***
The U of Scranton (PA) ***574***
U of Sioux Falls (SD) ***574***
U of South Alabama (AL) ***575***
U of South Carolina (SC) ***575***
U of South Carolina Aiken (SC) ***575***
U of South Carolina Spartanburg (SC) ***575***
The U of South Dakota (SD) ***575***
U of Southern California (CA) ***576***
U of Southern Indiana (IN) ***576***
U of Southern Maine (ME) ***576***
U of Southern Mississippi (MS) ***576***
U of South Florida (FL) ***576***
The U of Tampa (FL) ***577***
The U of Tennessee (TN) ***577***
The U of Tennessee at Chattanooga (TN) ***577***
The U of Tennessee at Martin (TN) ***577***
The U of Texas at Arlington (TX) ***577***
The U of Texas at Austin (TX) ***578***
The U of Texas at Dallas (TX) ***578***
The U of Texas at El Paso (TX) ***578***
The U of Texas at San Antonio (TX) ***578***
The U of Texas at Tyler (TX) ***579***
The U of Texas of the Permian Basin (TX) ***579***
The U of Texas–Pan American (TX) ***579***
U of the District of Columbia (DC) ***580***
U of the Incarnate Word (TX) ***580***
U of the Ozarks (AR) ***580***
U of the Pacific (CA) ***580***
U of the Sacred Heart (PR) ***580***
U of the Sciences in Philadelphia (PA) ***580***
U of the South (TN) ***581***
U of the Virgin Islands (VI) ***581***
U of Toledo (OH) ***581***
U of Toronto (ON, Canada) ***581***
U of Tulsa (OK) ***581***
U of Utah (UT) ***582***
U of Vermont (VT) ***582***
U of Victoria (BC, Canada) ***582***
U of Virginia (VA) ***582***
The U of Virginia's Coll at Wise (VA) ***582***
U of Washington (WA) ***583***
U of Waterloo (ON, Canada) ***583***
The U of West Alabama (AL) ***583***
The U of Western Ontario (ON, Canada) ***583***
U of West Florida (FL) ***583***
U of Windsor (ON, Canada) ***584***
U of Wisconsin–Eau Claire (WI) ***584***
U of Wisconsin–Green Bay (WI) ***584***
U of Wisconsin–La Crosse (WI) ***584***
U of Wisconsin–Madison (WI) ***584***
U of Wisconsin–Milwaukee (WI) ***585***
U of Wisconsin–Oshkosh (WI) ***585***
U of Wisconsin–Parkside (WI) ***585***
U of Wisconsin–River Falls (WI) ***585***
U of Wisconsin–Stevens Point (WI) ***585***
U of Wisconsin–Superior (WI) ***586***
U of Wisconsin–Whitewater (WI) ***586***
U of Wyoming (WY) ***586***
Upper Iowa U (IA) ***587***
Urbana U (OH) ***587***
Ursinus Coll (PA) ***587***
Utah State U (UT) ***587***
Utica Coll (NY) ***588***
Valdosta State U (GA) ***588***
Valley City State U (ND) ***588***
Valparaiso U (IN) ***588***
Vanderbilt U (TN) ***588***
Vanguard U of Southern California (CA) ***589***
Vassar Coll (NY) ***589***
Villa Julie Coll (MD) ***590***
Villanova U (PA) ***590***
Virginia Commonwealth U (VA) ***590***
Virginia Military Inst (VA) ***591***
Virginia Polytechnic Inst and State U (VA) ***591***
Virginia State U (VA) ***591***
Virginia Union U (VA) ***591***
Virginia Wesleyan Coll (VA) ***591***
Viterbo U (WI) ***591***
Voorhees Coll (SC) ***592***
Wabash Coll (IN) ***592***
Wagner Coll (NY) ***592***
Wake Forest U (NC) ***592***
Walla Walla Coll (WA) ***593***
Walsh U (OH) ***593***
Warren Wilson Coll (NC) ***594***
Wartburg Coll (IA) ***594***
Washington & Jefferson Coll (PA) ***594***
Washington and Lee U (VA) ***594***
Washington Coll (MD) ***594***
Washington State U (WA) ***595***
Washington U in St. Louis (MO) ***595***
Wayland Baptist U (TX) ***595***
Waynesburg Coll (PA) ***595***
Wayne State Coll (NE) ***596***
Wayne State U (MI) ***596***
Weber State U (UT) ***596***
Wellesley Coll (MA) ***597***
Wells Coll (NY) ***597***
Wesleyan Coll (GA) ***597***
Wesleyan U (CT) ***597***
West Chester U of Pennsylvania (PA) ***598***
Western Carolina U (NC) ***598***
Western Connecticut State U (CT) ***598***
Western Illinois U (IL) ***599***
Western Kentucky U (KY) ***599***
Western Michigan U (MI) ***599***
Western New England Coll (MA) ***600***
Western New Mexico U (NM) ***600***
Western Oregon U (OR) ***600***
Western State Coll of Colorado (CO) ***600***
Western Washington U (WA) ***600***
West Liberty State Coll (WV) ***601***
Westminster Coll (MO) ***601***
Westminster Coll (PA) ***601***
Westminster Coll (UT) ***601***
Westmont Coll (CA) ***602***
West Texas A&M U (TX) ***602***
West Virginia State Coll (WV) ***602***
West Virginia U (WV) ***602***
West Virginia U Inst of Technology (WV) ***602***
West Virginia Wesleyan Coll (WV) ***603***
Wheaton Coll (IL) ***603***
Wheaton Coll (MA) ***603***
Wheeling Jesuit U (WV) ***603***
Whitman Coll (WA) ***604***
Whittier Coll (CA) ***604***
Whitworth Coll (WA) ***604***
Wichita State U (KS) ***604***
Widener U (PA) ***604***
Wilberforce U (OH) ***605***
Wiley Coll (TX) ***605***
Wilkes U (PA) ***605***
Willamette U (OR) ***605***
William Carey Coll (MS) ***605***
William Jewell Coll (MO) ***606***
Williams Coll (MA) ***606***
Wilmington Coll (OH) ***607***
Wilson Coll (PA) ***607***
Wingate U (NC) ***607***
Winona State U (MN) ***608***
Winston-Salem State U (NC) ***608***
Winthrop U (SC) ***608***
Wisconsin Lutheran Coll (WI) ***608***
Wittenberg U (OH) ***608***
Wofford Coll (SC) ***609***
Worcester Polytechnic Inst (MA) ***609***
Worcester State Coll (MA) ***609***
Wright State U (OH) ***609***
Xavier U (OH) ***610***
Xavier U of Louisiana (LA) ***610***
Yale U (CT) ***610***
York Coll of Pennsylvania (PA) ***610***
York Coll of the City U of New York (NY) ***611***
York U (ON, Canada) ***611***
Youngstown State U (OH) ***611***

CHEMISTRY EDUCATION

Overview: This major teaches undergraduates the basic skills and knowledge necessary to teach chemistry at various educational levels. *Related majors:* chemistry, physical and theoretical chemistry. *Potential career:* chemistry teacher. *Salary potential:* $25k-$35k.

Abilene Christian U (TX) ***260***
Adams State Coll (CO) ***260***
Alvernia Coll (PA) ***265***
Appalachian State U (NC) ***270***
Arkansas State U (AR) ***272***
Arkansas Tech U (AR) ***272***
Averett U (VA) ***278***
Baylor U (TX) ***283***
Berry Coll (GA) ***287***
Bethany Coll (KS) ***287***
Bethune-Cookman Coll (FL) ***289***
Blue Mountain Coll (MS) ***291***
Boston U (MA) ***292***
Bowling Green State U (OH) ***292***
Bridgewater Coll (VA) ***294***
Brigham Young U (UT) ***295***
Cabrini Coll (PA) ***298***
Canisius Coll (NY) ***304***
The Catholic U of America (DC) ***307***
Central Methodist Coll (MO) ***309***
Central Michigan U (MI) ***310***
Central Missouri State U (MO) ***310***
Central Washington U (WA) ***310***
Chadron State Coll (NE) ***311***
Christian Brothers U (TN) ***313***
The Coll of New Jersey (NJ) ***320***
Coll of St. Catherine (MN) ***321***
Coll of the Ozarks (MO) ***323***
Colorado State U (CO) ***325***
Concordia Coll (MN) ***329***
Concordia U (NE) ***330***
Delta State U (MS) ***339***
Duquesne U (PA) ***346***
Eastern Mennonite U (VA) ***348***
Eastern Michigan U (MI) ***348***
East Texas Baptist U (TX) ***350***
Elmhurst Coll (IL) ***351***
Elmira Coll (NY) ***351***
Florida Inst of Technology (FL) ***360***
Framingham State Coll (MA) ***362***
Franklin Coll (IN) ***363***
George Fox U (OR) ***366***
Georgia Southern U (GA) ***367***
Greenville Coll (IL) ***373***
Gustavus Adolphus Coll (MN) ***374***
Hardin-Simmons U (TX) ***376***
Hastings Coll (NE) ***377***
Henderson State U (AR) ***378***
Hofstra U (NY) ***380***
Huntingdon Coll (AL) ***383***
Indiana U Bloomington (IN) ***385***
Indiana U Northwest (IN) ***386***
Indiana U–Purdue U Fort Wayne (IN) ***386***
Indiana U South Bend (IN) ***387***
Ithaca Coll (NY) ***390***
Juniata Coll (PA) ***395***
Kennesaw State U (GA) ***397***
King Coll (TN) ***398***
La Roche Coll (PA) ***402***
Long Island U, C.W. Post Campus (NY) ***409***
Louisiana State U in Shreveport (LA) ***410***
Luther Coll (IA) ***412***
Malone Coll (OH) ***415***
Manhattanville Coll (NY) ***416***
Mansfield U of Pennsylvania (PA) ***416***
Marymount Coll of Fordham U (NY) ***419***
Maryville Coll (TN) ***420***
Mayville State U (ND) ***422***
McGill U (QC, Canada) ***423***
Messiah Coll (PA) ***426***
Michigan State U (MI) ***428***
MidAmerica Nazarene U (KS) ***428***
Minot State U (ND) ***432***
Montana State U–Billings (MT) ***434***
Mount Marty Coll (SD) ***438***
Nazareth Coll of Rochester (NY) ***443***
New York Inst of Technology (NY) ***447***
New York U (NY) ***447***
Niagara U (NY) ***447***
North Carolina Central U (NC) ***448***
North Carolina State U (NC) ***449***
North Dakota State U (ND) ***449***
Northwest Nazarene U (ID) ***454***
Oklahoma Baptist U (OK) ***459***
Pace U (NY) ***463***
Rivier Coll (NH) ***480***
Rocky Mountain Coll (MT) ***482***
St. Ambrose U (IA) ***486***
St. John's U (NY) ***490***
Saint Joseph's Coll of Maine (ME) ***491***
Saint Mary's U of Minnesota (MN) ***494***
Salve Regina U (RI) ***497***
San Diego State U (CA) ***498***
Seton Hill U (PA) ***502***
Southern Arkansas U–Magnolia (AR) ***509***
Southern Nazarene U (OK) ***510***
Southwest Missouri State U (MO) ***513***
Southwest State U (MN) ***513***
State U of NY at Albany (NY) ***514***
State U of NY Coll at Potsdam (NY) ***517***
State U of NY Coll of Environ Sci and Forestry (NY) ***517***
State U of West Georgia (GA) ***518***
Talladega Coll (AL) ***522***
Tennessee Wesleyan Coll (TN) ***524***
Trevecca Nazarene U (TN) ***529***
Trinity Christian Coll (IL) ***530***
Union Coll (NE) ***534***
The U of Arizona (AZ) ***538***
U of Calif, San Diego (CA) ***541***
U of Delaware (DE) ***544***
U of Illinois at Chicago (IL) ***547***
The U of Iowa (IA) ***548***
U of Nebraska–Lincoln (NE) ***557***
The U of North Carolina at Charlotte (NC) ***560***
The U of North Carolina at Wilmington (NC) ***561***
U of North Texas (TX) ***562***
U of Puerto Rico, Cayey U Coll (PR) ***571***
The U of Tennessee at Martin (TN) ***577***
U of Waterloo (ON, Canada) ***583***
U of Windsor (ON, Canada) ***584***
U of Wisconsin–River Falls (WI) ***585***
U of Wisconsin–Superior (WI) ***586***
Utah State U (UT) ***587***
Utica Coll (NY) ***588***
Valley City State U (ND) ***588***
Viterbo U (WI) ***591***
Washington U in St. Louis (MO) ***595***
Weber State U (UT) ***596***
Wheeling Jesuit U (WV) ***603***
Xavier U (OH) ***610***
York U (ON, Canada) ***611***
Youngstown State U (OH) ***611***

CHEMISTRY RELATED

Information can be found under this major's main heading.

Clemson U (SC) ***317***
Connecticut Coll (CT) ***331***
Dartmouth Coll (NH) ***337***
Duquesne U (PA) ***346***
Edinboro U of Pennsylvania (PA) ***351***
Georgia Inst of Technology (GA) ***367***
McGill U (QC, Canada) ***423***
Northern Arizona U (AZ) ***450***
Okanagan U Coll (BC, Canada) ***459***
Saint Anselm Coll (NH) ***487***
San Diego State U (CA) ***498***
Spring Hill Coll (AL) ***514***
Texas Wesleyan U (TX) ***526***
U of Miami (FL) ***553***
U of Notre Dame (IN) ***562***
The U of Scranton (PA) ***574***
U of Southern Mississippi (MS) ***576***
U of the Pacific (CA) ***580***

CHILD CARE/DEVELOPMENT

Overview: Students who choose this major study the biological, emotional, intellectual, and social development of children and the design of programs to serve these needs. *Related majors:* developmental psychology, child care and guidance, early childhood teacher education, human services. *Potential careers:* psychiatrist/psychologist, child-care worker or administrator, social worker, preschool or kindergarten teacher. *Salary potential:* $18k-$25k.

Albertus Magnus Coll (CT) **262**
Alverno Coll (WI) **265**
Ashland U (OH) **274**
Auburn U (AL) **276**
Becker Coll (MA) **283**
Benedict Coll (SC) **285**
Berea Coll (KY) **286**
Bethel Coll (MN) **288**
Bluffton Coll (OH) **291**
Bowling Green State U (OH) **292**
Briercrest Bible Coll (SK, Canada) **295**
California State U, Dominguez Hills (CA) **300**
California State U, Fresno (CA) **301**
California State U, Hayward (CA) **301**
California State U, Long Beach (CA) **301**
California State U, Northridge (CA) **301**
Cameron U (OK) **303**
Carleton U (ON, Canada) **305**
Carson-Newman Coll (TN) **306**
Coll of the Ozarks (MO) **323**
Concordia Coll (MN) **329**
Cornell U (NY) **333**
Crown Coll (MN) **334**
East Carolina U (NC) **347**
Eastern Kentucky U (KY) **348**
East Tennessee State U (TN) **349**
Florida State U (FL) **361**
Freed-Hardeman U (TN) **364**
Gallaudet U (DC) **365**
Goddard Coll (VT) **369**
Goshen Coll (IN) **370**
Hampshire Coll (MA) **375**
Hampton U (VA) **375**
Harding U (AR) **375**
Hope International U (CA) **381**
Humboldt State U (CA) **382**
Indiana U Bloomington (IN) **385**
Jackson State U (MS) **390**
Kansas State U (KS) **396**
Lasell Coll (MA) **402**
Lesley U (MA) **405**
Lincoln Christian Coll (IL) **407**
Long Island U, Southampton Coll, Friends World Program (NY) **409**
Louisiana Tech U (LA) **410**
Madonna U (MI) **414**
McNeese State U (LA) **423**
Medaille Coll (NY) **424**
Meredith Coll (NC) **426**
Miami U (OH) **428**
Minnesota State U, Mankato (MN) **431**
Mitchell Coll (CT) **433**
Montclair State U (NJ) **435**
Montreat Coll (NC) **435**
Mount Ida Coll (MA) **438**
Mount Saint Vincent U (NS, Canada) **439**
North Carolina Ag and Tech State U (NC) **448**
North Dakota State U (ND) **449**
Northern Michigan U (MI) **451**
Northwest Missouri State U (MO) **454**
Ohio U (OH) **458**
Oklahoma Baptist U (OK) **459**
Oklahoma Christian U (OK) **459**
Oklahoma State U (OK) **460**
Olivet Nazarene U (IL) **461**
Oregon State U (OR) **462**
Pacific Oaks Coll (CA) **464**
Pittsburg State U (KS) **470**
Plattsburgh State U of NY (NY) **471**
Point Loma Nazarene U (CA) **471**
Portland State U (OR) **472**
Quinnipiac U (CT) **476**
Reformed Bible Coll (MI) **477**
Ryerson U (ON, Canada) **485**
St. Cloud State U (MN) **488**
Saint Joseph Coll (CT) **490**
San Diego State U (CA) **498**
San Jose State U (CA) **499**
Seton Hill U (PA) **502**
South Dakota State U (SD) **507**
Southern Vermont Coll (VT) **511**
State U of NY Coll at Oneonta (NY) **517**
Stephens Coll (MO) **519**
Syracuse U (NY) **521**
Tennessee Technological U (TN) **524**
Texas A&M U–Kingsville (TX) **525**
Texas Southern U (TX) **526**
Texas Tech U (TX) **526**
Texas Woman's U (TX) **527**
Tufts U (MA) **533**
The U of Akron (OH) **537**
U of Alberta (AB, Canada) **538**
U of Central Oklahoma (OK) **542**
U of Delaware (DE) **544**
U of Guelph (ON, Canada) **546**
U of Idaho (ID) **547**
U of Illinois at Springfield (IL) **548**
U of La Verne (CA) **549**
U of Maine (ME) **550**
U of Manitoba (MB, Canada) **551**
U of Maryland Eastern Shore (MD) **552**
U of Michigan–Dearborn (MI) **554**
U of Missouri–St. Louis (MO) **556**
U of New Hampshire (NH) **558**
U of Pittsburgh (PA) **569**
U of Puerto Rico, Río Piedras (PR) **571**
The U of Tennessee at Martin (TN) **577**
The U of Texas at Arlington (TX) **577**
U of Utah (UT) **582**
U of Vermont (VT) **582**
U of Victoria (BC, Canada) **582**
U of Wisconsin–Madison (WI) **584**
Villa Julie Coll (MD) **590**
Washington & Jefferson Coll (PA) **594**
Weber State U (UT) **596**
Western Michigan U (MI) **599**
Wheelock Coll (MA) **603**
Youngstown State U (OH) **611**

CHILD CARE/GUIDANCE

Overview: This major teaches students how to teach children in childcare centers, nursery schools, preschools, public schools, private households, family childcare homes, and before- and after-school programs. *Related majors:* childcare provider, school principal, administrator. *Potential careers:* teacher, teacher's assistant, home childcare worker, school administrator. *Salary potential:* $16k-27k.

Central Michigan U (MI) **310**
Malaspina U-Coll (BC, Canada) **415**

CHILD CARE SERVICES MANAGEMENT

Overview: This major teaches students how to manage child care services, facilities and programs to meet children's developmental needs and interests and that provide safe and healthy environments. *Related majors:* education administration and supervision, early childhood teacher education, business management, developmental psychology, family counseling. *Potential careers:* childcare worker, childcare administrator, principal. *Salary potential:* $16k-$27k.

Chestnut Hill Coll (PA) **312**
Pacific Union Coll (CA) **464**
Saint Mary-of-the-Woods Coll (IN) **493**
Seton Hill U (PA) **502**

CHILD GUIDANCE

Overview: This course is designed to prepare students to understand children's physical mental, emotional, and social growth and development and usually includes hands-on experience with children in day-care settings. *Related majors:* early childhood/kindergarten teacher education, childcare and guidance, developmental psychology. *Potential careers:* homemaker, childcare worker, psychologist. *Salary potential:* $16k-$25k.

Alcorn State U (MS) **263**
California State U, Stanislaus (CA) **302**
Coll of the Ozarks (MO) **323**
Oklahoma Baptist U (OK) **459**
Pace U (NY) **463**
Reformed Bible Coll (MI) **477**
Rochester Coll (MI) **482**
St. Joseph's Coll, New York (NY) **491**
Siena Heights U (MI) **504**
Thomas Edison State Coll (NJ) **527**
U of Central Oklahoma (OK) **542**
U of North Texas (TX) **562**

CHINESE

Overview: Students learn the Chinese language and its many different dialects and literature. *Related majors:* Chinese studies, history of philosophy. *Potential careers:* translator, foreign business consultant, teacher, journalist. *Salary potential:* $25k-$32k.

Arizona State U (AZ) **271**
Bard Coll (NY) **281**
Bates Coll (ME) **282**
Bennington Coll (VT) **286**
Brigham Young U (UT) **295**
California State U, Long Beach (CA) **301**
Claremont McKenna Coll (CA) **315**
Colgate U (NY) **319**
Connecticut Coll (CT) **331**
Cornell U (NY) **333**
Dartmouth Coll (NH) **337**
Georgetown U (DC) **366**
The George Washington U (DC) **367**
Grinnell Coll (IA) **373**
Harvard U (MA) **376**
Hobart and William Smith Colls (NY) **380**
Hunter Coll of the City U of NY (NY) **382**
Indiana U Bloomington (IN) **385**
Long Island U, Southampton Coll, Friends World Program (NY) **409**
Michigan State U (MI) **428**
Middlebury Coll (VT) **429**
The Ohio State U (OH) **457**
Pacific Lutheran U (WA) **463**
Pacific U (OR) **464**
Pomona Coll (CA) **472**
Portland State U (OR) **472**
Reed Coll (OR) **477**
Rutgers, The State U of New Jersey, New Brunswick (NJ) **485**
San Francisco State U (CA) **498**
San Jose State U (CA) **499**
Scripps Coll (CA) **501**
Stanford U (CA) **514**
State U of NY at Albany (NY) **514**
Swarthmore Coll (PA) **521**
Trinity U (TX) **531**
Tufts U (MA) **533**
United States Military Academy (NY) **535**
U of Alberta (AB, Canada) **538**
The U of British Columbia (BC, Canada) **540**
U of Calif, Berkeley (CA) **540**
U of Calif, Davis (CA) **540**
U of Calif, Los Angeles (CA) **541**
U of Calif, Riverside (CA) **541**
U of Calif, San Diego (CA) **541**
U of Calif, Santa Barbara (CA) **541**
U of Calif, Santa Cruz (CA) **542**
U of Chicago (IL) **542**
U of Colorado at Boulder (CO) **543**
U of Hawaii at Manoa (HI) **546**
The U of Iowa (IA) **548**
U of Kansas (KS) **549**
U of Maryland, Coll Park (MD) **552**
U of Massachusetts Amherst (MA) **552**
U of Michigan (MI) **554**
U of Minnesota, Twin Cities Campus (MN) **555**
The U of Montana–Missoula (MT) **556**
U of Notre Dame (IN) **562**
U of Oregon (OR) **562**
U of Pittsburgh (PA) **569**
U of Southern California (CA) **576**
U of Toronto (ON, Canada) **581**
U of Utah (UT) **582**
U of Victoria (BC, Canada) **582**
U of Washington (WA) **583**
U of Wisconsin–Madison (WI) **584**
Washington U in St. Louis (MO) **595**
Wellesley Coll (MA) **597**
Williams Coll (MA) **606**
Yale U (CT) **610**

CITY/COMMUNITY/ REGIONAL PLANNING

Overview: This major instructs individuals in the planning, analysis, improvement, development, and architecture of urban areas. *Related majors:* architecture, civil engineering, historical preservation, land use planning, economics. *Potential careers:* architect, civil engineer, city planner, historical preservationist, lawyer. *Salary potential:* $22k-$32k.

Alabama A&M U (AL) **261**
Appalachian State U (NC) **270**
Arizona State U (AZ) **271**
Ball State U (IN) **280**
Bard Coll (NY) **281**
Bridgewater State Coll (MA) **294**
California Polytechnic State U, San Luis Obispo (CA) **300**
California State Polytechnic U, Pomona (CA) **300**
California State U, Chico (CA) **300**
Carleton U (ON, Canada) **305**
Cornell U (NY) **333**
DePaul U (IL) **339**
East Carolina U (NC) **347**
Eastern Kentucky U (KY) **348**
Eastern Michigan U (MI) **348**
Eastern Oregon U (OR) **349**
Eastern Washington U (WA) **349**
Florida Atlantic U (FL) **359**
Framingham State Coll (MA) **362**
Hampshire Coll (MA) **375**
Harvard U (MA) **376**
Indiana U Bloomington (IN) **385**
Indiana U of Pennsylvania (PA) **386**
Iowa State U of Science and Technology (IA) **390**
Long Island U, Southampton Coll, Friends World Program (NY) **409**
Mansfield U of Pennsylvania (PA) **416**
Massachusetts Inst of Technology (MA) **421**
Miami U (OH) **428**
Michigan State U (MI) **428**
Minnesota State U, Mankato (MN) **431**
New Mexico State U (NM) **446**
New York U (NY) **447**
Northern Michigan U (MI) **451**
Nova Scotia Coll of Art and Design (NS, Canada) **455**
The Ohio State U (OH) **457**
Plymouth State Coll (NH) **471**
Portland State U (OR) **472**
Pratt Inst (NY) **473**
Ryerson U (ON, Canada) **485**
St. Cloud State U (MN) **488**
Salem State Coll (MA) **497**
Southwest Missouri State U (MO) **513**
Southwest Texas State U (TX) **513**
State U of NY at New Paltz (NY) **515**
State U of NY Coll at Buffalo (NY) **516**
State U of NY Coll of Environ Sci and Forestry (NY) **517**
Texas Southern U (TX) **526**
The U of Arizona (AZ) **538**
U of Cincinnati (OH) **543**
U of Hawaii at Manoa (HI) **546**
U of Illinois at Urbana–Champaign (IL) **548**
U of Michigan–Flint (MI) **554**
The U of Montana–Missoula (MT) **556**
U of New Hampshire (NH) **558**
U of Oregon (OR) **562**
U of Southern California (CA) **576**
U of Southern Mississippi (MS) **576**
U of the District of Columbia (DC) **580**
U of Virginia (VA) **582**
U of Washington (WA) **583**
U of Waterloo (ON, Canada) **583**
The U of Western Ontario (ON, Canada) **583**
U of Windsor (ON, Canada) **584**
Western Washington U (WA) **600**
Westfield State Coll (MA) **600**
West Virginia U Inst of Technology (WV) **602**
Winona State U (MN) **608**
Wright State U (OH) **609**

CIVIL ENGINEERING

Overview: This major prepares students to apply mathematics and scientific principles to design, develop, and build large structural projects such as highways, buildings, railroads, bridges, reservoirs, dams, irrigation and water systems, airports, and other structures. *Related majors:* structural engineering, construction/building technology, computer engineering, mathematics and physics. *Potential careers:* construction company executive, engineering consultant, project manager, architect. *Salary potential:* $40k-$55k.

Alabama A&M U (AL) ***261***
Arizona State U (AZ) ***271***
Auburn U (AL) ***276***
Bradley U (IL) ***293***
Brigham Young U (UT) ***295***
Brown U (RI) ***296***
Bucknell U (PA) ***297***
California Inst of Technology (CA) ***299***
California Polytechnic State U, San Luis Obispo (CA) ***300***
California State Polytechnic U, Pomona (CA) ***300***
California State U, Chico (CA) ***300***
California State U, Fresno (CA) ***301***
California State U, Fullerton (CA) ***301***
California State U, Long Beach (CA) ***301***
California State U, Northridge (CA) ***301***
Calvin Coll (MI) ***303***
Carleton U (ON, Canada) ***305***
Carnegie Mellon U (PA) ***305***
Carroll Coll (MT) ***306***
Case Western Reserve U (OH) ***307***
The Catholic U of America (DC) ***307***
Christian Brothers U (TN) ***313***
Citadel, The Military Coll of South Carolina (SC) ***314***
City Coll of the City U of NY (NY) ***314***
Clarkson U (NY) ***316***
Clemson U (SC) ***317***
Cleveland State U (OH) ***317***
The Coll of Southeastern Europe, The American U of Athens(Greece) ***323***
Colorado School of Mines (CO) ***325***
Colorado State U (CO) ***325***
Columbia U, School of Engineering & Applied Sci (NY) ***328***
Concordia U (QC, Canada) ***331***
Cooper Union for the Advancement of Science & Art (NY) ***332***
Cornell U (NY) ***333***
Dalhousie U (NS, Canada) ***336***
Delaware State U (DE) ***338***
Drexel U (PA) ***346***
Duke U (NC) ***346***
Embry-Riddle Aeronautical U (FL) ***352***
Florida A&M U (FL) ***359***
Florida Atlantic U (FL) ***359***
Florida Inst of Technology (FL) ***360***
Florida International U (FL) ***360***
Florida State U (FL) ***361***
Gallaudet U (DC) ***365***
The George Washington U (DC) ***367***
Georgia Inst of Technology (GA) ***367***
Gonzaga U (WA) ***369***
Harvard U (MA) ***376***
Howard U (DC) ***382***
Illinois Inst of Technology (IL) ***384***
Indiana Inst of Technology (IN) ***385***
Insto Tecno Estudios Sups Monterrey(Mexico) ***388***
Iowa State U of Science and Technology (IA) ***390***
Johns Hopkins U (MD) ***392***
Kansas State U (KS) ***396***
Lafayette Coll (PA) ***400***
Lakehead U (ON, Canada) ***400***
Lamar U (TX) ***401***
Lawrence Technological U (MI) ***403***
Lehigh U (PA) ***404***
Louisiana State U and A&M Coll (LA) ***410***
Louisiana Tech U (LA) ***410***
Loyola Marymount U (CA) ***411***
Manhattan Coll (NY) ***416***
Marquette U (WI) ***418***
Massachusetts Inst of Technology (MA) ***421***
McMaster U (ON, Canada) ***423***
Memorial U of Newfoundland (NF, Canada) ***424***
Merrimack Coll (MA) ***426***
Messiah Coll (PA) ***426***
Michigan State U (MI) ***428***
Michigan Technological U (MI) ***428***
Minnesota State U, Mankato (MN) ***431***
Mississippi State U (MS) ***432***
Montana State U–Bozeman (MT) ***434***
Montana Tech of The U of Montana (MT) ***435***
Morgan State U (MD) ***436***
New Jersey Inst of Technology (NJ) ***445***
New Mexico State U (NM) ***446***
New York U (NY) ***447***
North Carolina Ag and Tech State U (NC) ***448***
North Carolina State U (NC) ***449***
North Dakota State U (ND) ***449***
Northeastern U (MA) ***450***
Northern Arizona U (AZ) ***450***
Northwestern U (IL) ***453***
Norwich U (VT) ***455***
Ohio Northern U (OH) ***457***
The Ohio State U (OH) ***457***
Ohio U (OH) ***458***
Oklahoma State U (OK) ***460***
Old Dominion U (VA) ***460***
Oregon Inst of Technology (OR) ***461***
Oregon State U (OR) ***462***
Penn State U Univ Park Campus (PA) ***468***
Polytechnic U, Brooklyn Campus (NY) ***472***
Portland State U (OR) ***472***
Prairie View A&M U (TX) ***473***
Princeton U (NJ) ***474***
Purdue U (IN) ***475***
Queen's U at Kingston (ON, Canada) ***476***
Rensselaer Polytechnic Inst (NY) ***478***
Rice U (TX) ***479***
Rose-Hulman Inst of Technology (IN) ***484***
Rowan U (NJ) ***484***
Ryerson U (ON, Canada) ***485***
Saint Martin's Coll (WA) ***493***
San Diego State U (CA) ***498***
San Francisco State U (CA) ***498***
San Jose State U (CA) ***499***
Santa Clara U (CA) ***499***
Savannah State U (GA) ***499***
Seattle U (WA) ***501***
South Dakota School of Mines and Technology (SD) ***507***
South Dakota State U (SD) ***507***
Southern Illinois U Carbondale (IL) ***509***
Southern Illinois U Edwardsville (IL) ***509***
Southern U and A&M Coll (LA) ***511***
Stanford U (CA) ***514***
Stevens Inst of Technology (NJ) ***519***
Syracuse U (NY) ***521***
Temple U (PA) ***523***
Tennessee State U (TN) ***523***
Tennessee Technological U (TN) ***524***
Texas A&M U (TX) ***524***
Texas A&M U–Kingsville (TX) ***525***
Texas Tech U (TX) ***526***
Tri-State U (IN) ***532***
Tufts U (MA) ***533***
Tulane U (LA) ***533***
United States Air Force Academy (CO) ***534***
United States Coast Guard Academy (CT) ***535***
United States Military Academy (NY) ***535***
Université de Sherbrooke (QC, Canada) ***536***
Université Laval (QC, Canada) ***536***
U at Buffalo, The State University of New York (NY) ***536***
The U of Akron (OH) ***537***
The U of Alabama (AL) ***537***
The U of Alabama at Birmingham (AL) ***537***
The U of Alabama in Huntsville (AL) ***537***
U of Alaska Anchorage (AK) ***538***
U of Alaska Fairbanks (AK) ***538***
U of Alberta (AB, Canada) ***538***
The U of Arizona (AZ) ***538***
U of Arkansas (AR) ***539***
The U of British Columbia (BC, Canada) ***540***
U of Calgary (AB, Canada) ***540***
U of Calif, Berkeley (CA) ***540***
U of Calif, Davis (CA) ***540***
U of Calif, Irvine (CA) ***541***
U of Calif, Los Angeles (CA) ***541***
U of Central Florida (FL) ***542***
U of Cincinnati (OH) ***543***
U of Colorado at Boulder (CO) ***543***
U of Colorado at Denver (CO) ***543***
U of Connecticut (CT) ***544***
U of Dayton (OH) ***544***
U of Delaware (DE) ***544***
U of Evansville (IN) ***545***
U of Florida (FL) ***545***
U of Hartford (CT) ***546***
U of Hawaii at Manoa (HI) ***546***
U of Houston (TX) ***547***
U of Idaho (ID) ***547***
U of Illinois at Chicago (IL) ***547***
U of Illinois at Urbana–Champaign (IL) ***548***
The U of Iowa (IA) ***548***
U of Kansas (KS) ***549***
U of Kentucky (KY) ***549***
U of Louisiana at Lafayette (LA) ***550***
U of Louisville (KY) ***550***
U of Maine (ME) ***550***
U of Manitoba (MB, Canada) ***551***
U of Maryland, Coll Park (MD) ***552***
U of Massachusetts Amherst (MA) ***552***
U of Massachusetts Dartmouth (MA) ***553***
U of Massachusetts Lowell (MA) ***553***
The U of Memphis (TN) ***553***
U of Miami (FL) ***553***
U of Michigan (MI) ***554***
U of Minnesota, Twin Cities Campus (MN) ***555***
U of Mississippi (MS) ***555***
U of Missouri–Columbia (MO) ***555***
U of Missouri–Kansas City (MO) ***555***
U of Missouri–Rolla (MO) ***556***
U of Missouri–St. Louis (MO) ***556***
U of Nebraska–Lincoln (NE) ***557***
U of Nevada, Las Vegas (NV) ***558***
U of Nevada, Reno (NV) ***558***
U of New Brunswick Fredericton (NB, Canada) ***558***
U of New Brunswick Saint John (NB, Canada) ***558***
U of New Hampshire (NH) ***558***
U of New Haven (CT) ***559***
U of New Mexico (NM) ***559***
U of New Orleans (LA) ***559***
The U of North Carolina at Charlotte (NC) ***560***
U of North Dakota (ND) ***561***
U of North Florida (FL) ***561***
U of Notre Dame (IN) ***562***
U of Oklahoma (OK) ***562***
U of Ottawa (ON, Canada) ***563***
U of Pennsylvania (PA) ***563***
U of Pittsburgh (PA) ***569***
U of Portland (OR) ***570***
U of Rhode Island (RI) ***572***
U of Saskatchewan (SK, Canada) ***574***
U of South Alabama (AL) ***575***
U of South Carolina (SC) ***575***
U of Southern California (CA) ***576***
U of South Florida (FL) ***576***
The U of Tennessee (TN) ***577***
The U of Tennessee at Chattanooga (TN) ***577***
The U of Texas at Arlington (TX) ***577***
The U of Texas at Austin (TX) ***578***
The U of Texas at El Paso (TX) ***578***
The U of Texas at San Antonio (TX) ***578***
U of the District of Columbia (DC) ***580***
U of the Pacific (CA) ***580***
U of Toledo (OH) ***581***
U of Toronto (ON, Canada) ***581***
U of Utah (UT) ***582***
U of Vermont (VT) ***582***
U of Virginia (VA) ***582***
U of Washington (WA) ***583***
U of Waterloo (ON, Canada) ***583***
The U of Western Ontario (ON, Canada) ***583***
U of Windsor (ON, Canada) ***584***
U of Wisconsin–Madison (WI) ***584***
U of Wisconsin–Milwaukee (WI) ***585***
U of Wisconsin–Platteville (WI) ***585***
U of Wyoming (WY) ***586***
Utah State U (UT) ***587***
Valparaiso U (IN) ***588***
Vanderbilt U (TN) ***588***
Villanova U (PA) ***590***
Virginia Military Inst (VA) ***591***
Virginia Polytechnic Inst and State U (VA) ***591***
Walla Walla Coll (WA) ***593***
Washington State U (WA) ***595***
Washington U in St. Louis (MO) ***595***
Wayne State U (MI) ***596***
Western Kentucky U (KY) ***599***
West Virginia U (WV) ***602***
West Virginia U Inst of Technology (WV) ***602***
Widener U (PA) ***604***
Worcester Polytechnic Inst (MA) ***609***
Youngstown State U (OH) ***611***

CIVIL ENGINEERING RELATED

Information can be found under this major's main heading.

Bradley U (IL) ***293***
Drexel U (PA) ***346***
George Mason U (VA) ***366***

CIVIL ENGINEERING TECHNOLOGY

Overview: Students learn the basic engineering principles of civil engineering so they can work with civil engineers who are designing or building public works projects like highways, dams, bridges, or other projects. *Related majors:* drafting and design technology, construction management, logistics and materials management, enterprise management and operation. *Potential careers:* graphic designer, architect, purchasing manager. *Salary potential:* $25k-$35k.

Alabama A&M U (AL) ***261***
Bluefield State Coll (WV) ***291***
Central Connecticut State U (CT) ***309***
Colorado State U-Pueblo (CO) ***325***
Delaware State U (DE) ***338***
Fairleigh Dickinson U, Teaneck-Metro Campus (NJ) ***356***
Fairmont State Coll (WV) ***356***
Florida A&M U (FL) ***359***
Fontbonne U (MO) ***361***
Francis Marion U (SC) ***363***
Georgia Southern U (GA) ***367***
Lakehead U (ON, Canada) ***400***
Louisiana Tech U (LA) ***410***
Metropolitan State Coll of Denver (CO) ***427***
Missouri Western State Coll (MO) ***433***
Montana State U–Northern (MT) ***434***
Murray State U (KY) ***440***
Pennsylvania Coll of Technology (PA) ***467***
Point Park Coll (PA) ***471***
Purdue U Calumet (IN) ***475***
Rochester Inst of Technology (NY) ***482***
Savannah State U (GA) ***499***
South Carolina State U (SC) ***506***
Southern Polytechnic State U (GA) ***511***
State U of NY Inst of Tech at Utica/Rome (NY) ***518***
Temple U (PA) ***523***
Texas Southern U (TX) ***526***
Thomas Edison State Coll (NJ) ***527***
U of Cincinnati (OH) ***543***
U of Houston (TX) ***547***
U of Houston–Downtown (TX) ***547***
U of Massachusetts Lowell (MA) ***553***
The U of North Carolina at Charlotte (NC) ***560***
U of North Texas (TX) ***562***
U of Pittsburgh at Johnstown (PA) ***570***
U of Toledo (OH) ***581***
Washington U in St. Louis (MO) ***595***
Wentworth Inst of Technology (MA) ***597***
West Virginia U Inst of Technology (WV) ***602***
Youngstown State U (OH) ***611***

CLASSICAL AND ANCIENT NEAR EASTERN LANGUAGES RELATED

Information can be found under this major's main heading.

Austin Coll (TX) ***277***
Brandeis U (MA) ***293***
Cornell U (NY) ***333***
Université Laval (QC, Canada) ***536***

CLASSICS

Overview: Students study the literary culture and history of the

Mediterranean world of the ancient Greeks and Romans and, to a lesser extent, the societies of the Near East and Egypt. *Related majors:* Greek, Latin, archeology, ancient history, literature. *Potential careers:* archeologist, art historian, editor, teacher, historian/archivist. *Salary potential:* $21k-$27k.

Acadia U (NS, Canada) ***260***
Agnes Scott Coll (GA) ***261***
Albertus Magnus Coll (CT) ***262***
Amherst Coll (MA) ***268***
Asbury Coll (KY) ***274***
Assumption Coll (MA) ***275***
Augustana Coll (IL) ***276***
Austin Coll (TX) ***277***
Ave Maria Coll (MI) ***278***
Ball State U (IN) ***280***
Bard Coll (NY) ***281***
Barnard Coll (NY) ***282***
Bates Coll (ME) ***282***
Baylor U (TX) ***283***
Beloit Coll (WI) ***285***
Berea Coll (KY) ***286***
Bishop's U (QC, Canada) ***289***
Boston Coll (MA) ***292***
Boston U (MA) ***292***
Bowdoin Coll (ME) ***292***
Bowling Green State U (OH) ***292***
Brigham Young U (UT) ***295***
Brock U (ON, Canada) ***295***
Brooklyn Coll of the City U of NY (NY) ***295***
Brown U (RI) ***296***
Bryn Mawr Coll (PA) ***297***
Bucknell U (PA) ***297***
California State U, Northridge (CA) ***301***
Calvin Coll (MI) ***303***
Carleton Coll (MN) ***305***
Carleton U (ON, Canada) ***305***
Carthage Coll (WI) ***306***
Case Western Reserve U (OH) ***307***
The Catholic U of America (DC) ***307***
Centre Coll (KY) ***310***
Christendom Coll (VA) ***313***
Claremont McKenna Coll (CA) ***315***
Clark U (MA) ***316***
Coe Coll (IA) ***318***
Colby Coll (ME) ***318***
Colgate U (NY) ***319***
Coll of Charleston (SC) ***320***
The Coll of New Rochelle (NY) ***321***
Coll of Notre Dame of Maryland (MD) ***321***
Coll of Saint Benedict (MN) ***321***
Coll of the Holy Cross (MA) ***323***
The Coll of William and Mary (VA) ***324***
The Coll of Wooster (OH) ***324***
The Colorado Coll (CO) ***325***
Columbia Coll (NY) ***326***
Columbia U, School of General Studies (NY) ***328***
Concordia Coll (MN) ***329***
Concordia U (QC, Canada) ***331***
Connecticut Coll (CT) ***331***
Cornell Coll (IA) ***332***
Cornell U (NY) ***333***
Creighton U (NE) ***333***
Dalhousie U (NS, Canada) ***336***
Dartmouth Coll (NH) ***337***
Davidson Coll (NC) ***338***
Denison U (OH) ***339***
DePauw U (IN) ***339***
Dickinson Coll (PA) ***344***
Drew U (NJ) ***346***
Duke U (NC) ***346***
Duquesne U (PA) ***346***
Earlham Coll (IN) ***347***
Elmira Coll (NY) ***351***
Emory U (GA) ***354***
The Evergreen State Coll (WA) ***355***
Florida State U (FL) ***361***
Fordham U (NY) ***362***
Franciscan U of Steubenville (OH) ***363***
Franklin and Marshall Coll (PA) ***363***
Georgetown U (DC) ***366***
The George Washington U (DC) ***367***
Georgia State U (GA) ***368***
Gettysburg Coll (PA) ***368***
Grinnell Coll (IA) ***373***
Gustavus Adolphus Coll (MN) ***374***
Hamilton Coll (NY) ***374***
Hampden-Sydney Coll (VA) ***374***
Hanover Coll (IN) ***375***
Harvard U (MA) ***376***
Haverford Coll (PA) ***377***
Hellenic Coll (MA) ***378***
Hillsdale Coll (MI) ***379***
Hiram Coll (OH) ***379***
Hobart and William Smith Colls (NY) ***380***
Hofstra U (NY) ***380***
Hollins U (VA) ***380***
Hope Coll (MI) ***381***
Howard U (DC) ***382***
Hunter Coll of the City U of NY (NY) ***382***
Indiana U Bloomington (IN) ***385***
John Carroll U (OH) ***392***
Johns Hopkins U (MD) ***392***
Kalamazoo Coll (MI) ***395***
Kent State U (OH) ***397***
Kenyon Coll (OH) ***398***
Knox Coll (IL) ***399***
La Salle U (PA) ***402***
Laurentian U (ON, Canada) ***403***
Lawrence U (WI) ***403***
Lehigh U (PA) ***404***
Lehman Coll of the City U of NY (NY) ***404***
Lenoir-Rhyne Coll (NC) ***405***
Loras Coll (IA) ***410***
Loyola Coll in Maryland (MD) ***411***
Loyola Marymount U (CA) ***411***
Loyola U Chicago (IL) ***411***
Loyola U New Orleans (LA) ***411***
Luther Coll (IA) ***412***
Macalester Coll (MN) ***413***
Manhattan Coll (NY) ***416***
Manhattanville Coll (NY) ***416***
Marlboro Coll (VT) ***418***
Marquette U (WI) ***418***
Mary Washington Coll (VA) ***420***
McGill U (QC, Canada) ***423***
McMaster U (ON, Canada) ***423***
Memorial U of Newfoundland (NF, Canada) ***424***
Mercer U (GA) ***425***
Miami U (OH) ***428***
Middlebury Coll (VT) ***429***
Millsaps Coll (MS) ***431***
Monmouth Coll (IL) ***434***
Montclair State U (NJ) ***435***
Moravian Coll (PA) ***436***
Mount Allison U (NB, Canada) ***437***
Mount Holyoke Coll (MA) ***438***
New Coll of Florida (FL) ***444***
New York U (NY) ***447***
Nipissing U (ON, Canada) ***448***
North Central Coll (IL) ***449***
Northwestern U (IL) ***453***
Oberlin Coll (OH) ***456***
The Ohio State U (OH) ***457***
Ohio U (OH) ***458***
Ohio Wesleyan U (OH) ***459***
Pacific Lutheran U (WA) ***463***
Penn State U Univ Park Campus (PA) ***468***
Pitzer Coll (CA) ***471***
Pomona Coll (CA) ***472***
Princeton U (NJ) ***474***
Queens Coll of the City U of NY (NY) ***475***
Queen's U at Kingston (ON, Canada) ***476***
Randolph-Macon Coll (VA) ***477***
Randolph-Macon Woman's Coll (VA) ***477***
Reed Coll (OR) ***477***
Rhodes Coll (TN) ***479***
Rice U (TX) ***479***
Rockford Coll (IL) ***482***
Rollins Coll (FL) ***483***
Rutgers, The State U of New Jersey, Newark (NJ) ***485***
Rutgers, The State U of New Jersey, New Brunswick (NJ) ***485***
Saint Anselm Coll (NH) ***487***
St. Bonaventure U (NY) ***487***
St. Francis Xavier U (NS, Canada) ***489***
St. John's Coll (NM) ***490***
Saint John's U (MN) ***490***
Saint Louis U (MO) ***492***
Saint Mary's U (NS, Canada) ***494***
Saint Michael's Coll (VT) ***494***
St. Olaf Coll (MN) ***495***
Saint Peter's Coll (NJ) ***495***
Samford U (AL) ***497***
San Diego State U (CA) ***498***
San Francisco State U (CA) ***498***
Santa Clara U (CA) ***499***
Sarah Lawrence Coll (NY) ***499***
Scripps Coll (CA) ***501***
Seattle Pacific U (WA) ***501***
Seton Hall U (NJ) ***502***
Siena Coll (NY) ***504***
Skidmore Coll (NY) ***506***
Smith Coll (MA) ***506***
Southern Illinois U Carbondale (IL) ***509***
Stanford U (CA) ***514***
State U of NY at Albany (NY) ***514***
State U of NY at Binghamton (NY) ***515***
Swarthmore Coll (PA) ***521***
Sweet Briar Coll (VA) ***521***
Syracuse U (NY) ***521***
Temple U (PA) ***523***
Texas Christian U (TX) ***526***
Texas Tech U (TX) ***526***
Trent U (ON, Canada) ***529***
Trinity Coll (CT) ***530***
Trinity U (TX) ***531***
Truman State U (MO) ***532***
Tufts U (MA) ***533***
Tulane U (LA) ***533***
Union Coll (NY) ***534***
U at Buffalo, The State University of New York (NY) ***536***
The U of Akron (OH) ***537***
The U of Alabama (AL) ***537***
U of Alberta (AB, Canada) ***538***
The U of Arizona (AZ) ***538***
U of Arkansas (AR) ***539***
The U of British Columbia (BC, Canada) ***540***
U of Calgary (AB, Canada) ***540***
U of Calif, Berkeley (CA) ***540***
U of Calif, Irvine (CA) ***541***
U of Calif, Los Angeles (CA) ***541***
U of Calif, Riverside (CA) ***541***
U of Calif, San Diego (CA) ***541***
U of Calif, Santa Barbara (CA) ***541***
U of Calif, Santa Cruz (CA) ***542***
U of Chicago (IL) ***542***
U of Cincinnati (OH) ***543***
U of Colorado at Boulder (CO) ***543***
U of Connecticut (CT) ***544***
U of Dallas (TX) ***544***
U of Delaware (DE) ***544***
U of Evansville (IN) ***545***
U of Florida (FL) ***545***
U of Georgia (GA) ***545***
U of Guelph (ON, Canada) ***546***
U of Hawaii at Manoa (HI) ***546***
U of Houston (TX) ***547***
U of Idaho (ID) ***547***
U of Illinois at Chicago (IL) ***547***
U of Illinois at Urbana–Champaign (IL) ***548***
The U of Iowa (IA) ***548***
U of Kansas (KS) ***549***
U of Kentucky (KY) ***549***
U of King's Coll (NS, Canada) ***549***
U of Maine (ME) ***550***
U of Manitoba (MB, Canada) ***551***
U of Maryland, Baltimore County (MD) ***552***
U of Maryland, Coll Park (MD) ***552***
U of Massachusetts Amherst (MA) ***552***
U of Massachusetts Boston (MA) ***553***
U of Miami (FL) ***553***
U of Michigan (MI) ***554***
U of Mississippi (MS) ***555***
U of Missouri–Columbia (MO) ***555***
The U of Montana–Missoula (MT) ***556***
U of Nebraska–Lincoln (NE) ***557***
U of New Brunswick Fredericton (NB, Canada) ***558***
U of New Hampshire (NH) ***558***
U of New Mexico (NM) ***559***
The U of North Carolina at Asheville (NC) ***559***
The U of North Carolina at Chapel Hill (NC) ***560***
The U of North Carolina at Greensboro (NC) ***560***
U of Notre Dame (IN) ***562***
U of Oklahoma (OK) ***562***
U of Oregon (OR) ***562***
U of Ottawa (ON, Canada) ***563***
U of Pennsylvania (PA) ***563***
U of Pittsburgh (PA) ***569***
U of Puget Sound (WA) ***571***
U of Regina (SK, Canada) ***572***
U of Rhode Island (RI) ***572***
U of Richmond (VA) ***572***
U of Rochester (NY) ***573***
U of St. Thomas (MN) ***573***
U of Saskatchewan (SK, Canada) ***574***
U of South Carolina (SC) ***575***
The U of South Dakota (SD) ***575***
U of Southern California (CA) ***576***
U of Southern Maine (ME) ***576***
U of South Florida (FL) ***576***
The U of Tennessee (TN) ***577***
The U of Texas at Arlington (TX) ***577***
The U of Texas at Austin (TX) ***578***
The U of Texas at San Antonio (TX) ***578***
U of the Pacific (CA) ***580***
U of the South (TN) ***581***
U of Toronto (ON, Canada) ***581***
U of Utah (UT) ***582***
U of Vermont (VT) ***582***
U of Victoria (BC, Canada) ***582***
U of Virginia (VA) ***582***
U of Washington (WA) ***583***
U of Waterloo (ON, Canada) ***583***
The U of Western Ontario (ON, Canada) ***583***
U of Windsor (ON, Canada) ***584***
U of Wisconsin–Madison (WI) ***584***
U of Wisconsin–Milwaukee (WI) ***585***
Ursinus Coll (PA) ***587***
Valparaiso U (IN) ***588***
Vanderbilt U (TN) ***588***
Vassar Coll (NY) ***589***
Villanova U (PA) ***590***
Wabash Coll (IN) ***592***
Wake Forest U (NC) ***592***
Washington and Lee U (VA) ***594***
Washington State U (WA) ***595***
Washington U in St. Louis (MO) ***595***
Wayne State U (MI) ***596***
Wellesley Coll (MA) ***597***
Wesleyan U (CT) ***597***
Western Washington U (WA) ***600***
Westminster Coll (MO) ***601***
Westminster Coll (PA) ***601***
Wheaton Coll (MA) ***603***
Whitman Coll (WA) ***604***
Willamette U (OR) ***605***
Williams Coll (MA) ***606***
Wright State U (OH) ***609***
Xavier U (OH) ***610***
Yale U (CT) ***610***
York U (ON, Canada) ***611***

CLINICAL PSYCHOLOGY

Overview: A branch of psychology that prepares students for the professional practice of clinical psychology that involves analysis, diagnosis, and treatment of behavioral and psychological disorders. *Related majors:* psychology, counseling psychology, behavioral sciences, family counseling. *Potential careers:* therapist, psychologist or psychiatrist, family counselor, school counselor, alcohol or drug abuse counselor. *Salary potential:* $23k-$33k.

Alfred U (NY) ***263***
Averett U (VA) ***278***
Biola U (CA) ***289***
Bridgewater State Coll (MA) ***294***
California State U, Fullerton (CA) ***301***
The Coll of Southeastern Europe, The American U of Athens(Greece) ***323***
Colorado State U-Pueblo (CO) ***325***
Crichton Coll (TN) ***334***
Eastern Nazarene Coll (MA) ***348***
Fairfield U (CT) ***356***
Franklin Pierce Coll (NH) ***364***
George Fox U (OR) ***366***
Husson Coll (ME) ***383***
Lakehead U (ON, Canada) ***400***
Lamar U (TX) ***401***
La Sierra U (CA) ***403***
Long Island U, Brooklyn Campus (NY) ***409***
Mansfield U of Pennsylvania (PA) ***416***
Moravian Coll (PA) ***436***
Purdue U Calumet (IN) ***475***
Tennessee State U (TN) ***523***
U of Alberta (AB, Canada) ***538***
The U of British Columbia (BC, Canada) ***540***
U of Michigan–Flint (MI) ***554***
U of Missouri–St. Louis (MO) ***556***
U of New Brunswick Fredericton (NB, Canada) ***558***
U of Windsor (ON, Canada) ***584***
Western State Coll of Colorado (CO) ***600***

CLOTHING/APPAREL/ TEXTILE

Overview: This major prepares students for a professional career in the apparel industries. Emphasis is be placed on production, pricing, promotion, and distribution throughout the soft-goods chain. *Related majors:* clothing and textiles, fashion and apparel merchandising, retail operations, textile sciences. *Potential careers:* textile producer, apparel manufacturer, clothing retailer. *Salary potential:* $20k-$32k.

Concordia Coll (MN) ***329***
Wayne State U (MI) ***596***

CLOTHING/APPAREL/ TEXTILE STUDIES

Overview: Students learn about the design, development, and distribution of textile and clothing products. *Related majors:* art history, business management, clothing and textiles, fashion design/illustration, sociology. *Potential careers:* fashion or product designer, textile manufacturer, apparel sales representative, store buyer. *Salary potential:* $21k-$28k.

Albright Coll (PA) ***263***
Appalachian State U (NC) ***270***
Auburn U (AL) ***276***
Baylor U (TX) ***283***
Central Missouri State U (MO) ***310***
Coll of the Ozarks (MO) ***323***
Colorado State U (CO) ***325***
East Carolina U (NC) ***347***
Florida State U (FL) ***361***
Freed-Hardeman U (TN) ***364***
Gallaudet U (DC) ***365***
Georgia Southern U (GA) ***367***
Indiana State U (IN) ***385***
Indiana U Bloomington (IN) ***385***
Iowa State U of Science and Technology (IA) ***390***
Kansas State U (KS) ***396***
Kentucky State U (KY) ***397***
Michigan State U (MI) ***428***
Middle Tennessee State U (TN) ***429***
Murray State U (KY) ***440***
North Dakota State U (ND) ***449***
Northern Illinois U (IL) ***450***
The Ohio State U (OH) ***457***
Ohio U (OH) ***458***
Purdue U (IN) ***475***
Seattle Pacific U (WA) ***501***
Southeast Missouri State U (MO) ***508***
Southern Illinois U Carbondale (IL) ***509***
Southwest Missouri State U (MO) ***513***
Texas Tech U (TX) ***526***
Texas Woman's U (TX) ***527***
The U of Alabama (AL) ***537***
U of Arkansas (AR) ***539***
U of Calif, Davis (CA) ***540***
U of Georgia (GA) ***545***
U of Hawaii at Manoa (HI) ***546***
U of Idaho (ID) ***547***
U of Kentucky (KY) ***549***
U of Missouri–Columbia (MO) ***555***
U of Nebraska–Lincoln (NE) ***557***
U of Northern Iowa (IA) ***561***
U of Rhode Island (RI) ***572***
U of Southern Mississippi (MS) ***576***
The U of Texas at Austin (TX) ***578***
U of Wisconsin–Stout (WI) ***586***
Washington State U (WA) ***595***
Western Kentucky U (KY) ***599***
Youngstown State U (OH) ***611***

CLOTHING/TEXTILES

Overview: This major is designed to teach students how to make sound decisions related to the selection, use, and care of clothing and textile products in their daily lives. *Related majors:* clothing, apparel and textile studies, consumer and homemaking education. *Potential careers:* homemaker, social worker, consumer advocate. *Salary potential:* $0-$25k.

Appalachian State U (NC) ***270***
Bluffton Coll (OH) ***291***
Bowling Green State U (OH) ***292***
California State U, Long Beach (CA) ***301***
California State U, Northridge (CA) ***301***
Cheyney U of Pennsylvania (PA) ***312***
Concordia Coll (MN) ***329***
Cornell U (NY) ***333***
Delaware State U (DE) ***338***
Eastern Kentucky U (KY) ***348***
Framingham State Coll (MA) ***362***
Indiana U Bloomington (IN) ***385***
Jacksonville State U (AL) ***390***
Long Island U, Southampton Coll, Friends World Program (NY) ***409***
Marymount Coll of Fordham U (NY) ***419***
Mercyhurst Coll (PA) ***425***
Minnesota State U, Mankato (MN) ***431***
New Mexico State U (NM) ***446***
North Carolina Ag and Tech State U (NC) ***448***
North Dakota State U (ND) ***449***
Northwest Missouri State U (MO) ***454***
The Ohio State U (OH) ***457***
Oklahoma State U (OK) ***460***
Olivet Nazarene U (IL) ***461***
Oregon State U (OR) ***462***
Philadelphia U (PA) ***469***
Queens Coll of the City U of NY (NY) ***475***
Rhode Island School of Design (RI) ***479***
San Francisco State U (CA) ***498***
Syracuse U (NY) ***521***
Tennessee Technological U (TN) ***524***
Texas Southern U (TX) ***526***
The U of Akron (OH) ***537***
U of Alberta (AB, Canada) ***538***
U of Central Oklahoma (OK) ***542***
U of Manitoba (MB, Canada) ***551***
U of Minnesota, Twin Cities Campus (MN) ***555***
The U of North Carolina at Greensboro (NC) ***560***
U of the District of Columbia (DC) ***580***
The U of Western Ontario (ON, Canada) ***583***
U of Wisconsin–Madison (WI) ***584***
Virginia Polytechnic Inst and State U (VA) ***591***

COGNITIVE PSYCHOLOGY/ PSYCHOLINGUISTICS

Overview: Students who choose this major will learn the science behind the mechanisms and processes of learning, thinking, speaking, and related systems. *Related majors:* education, educational psychology, developmental psychology. *Potential careers:* psycholinguist, speech therapist, special education teacher, early childhood teacher, psychologist. *Salary potential:* $23k-$33k.

Averett U (VA) ***278***
Brown U (RI) ***296***
California State U, Stanislaus (CA) ***302***
Carleton U (ON, Canada) ***305***
Carnegie Mellon U (PA) ***305***
Dartmouth Coll (NH) ***337***
George Fox U (OR) ***366***
Hampshire Coll (MA) ***375***
Harvard U (MA) ***376***
Indiana U Bloomington (IN) ***385***
Johns Hopkins U (MD) ***392***
Lawrence U (WI) ***403***
Lehigh U (PA) ***404***
Massachusetts Inst of Technology (MA) ***421***
Northwestern U (IL) ***453***
Occidental Coll (CA) ***457***
Queen's U at Kingston (ON, Canada) ***476***
Simon Fraser U (BC, Canada) ***505***
Simon's Rock Coll of Bard (MA) ***505***
State U of NY at Oswego (NY) ***515***
Tulane U (LA) ***533***
U of Calif, Irvine (CA) ***541***
U of Calif, Los Angeles (CA) ***541***
U of Calif, San Diego (CA) ***541***
U of Calif, Santa Cruz (CA) ***542***
U of Georgia (GA) ***545***
U of Kansas (KS) ***549***
U of Rochester (NY) ***573***
The U of Texas at Dallas (TX) ***578***
Vanderbilt U (TN) ***588***
Vassar Coll (NY) ***589***
Washington U in St. Louis (MO) ***595***
Wellesley Coll (MA) ***597***
Yale U (CT) ***610***

COLLEGE/POSTSECONDARY STUDENT COUNSELING

Overview: this major prepares undergraduates to advise and counsel college students and provide them with appropriate assistance and administrative services or refer them to those services. *Related majors:* counseling psychology, alcohol/drug abuse counseling. *Potential careers:* professor, psychiatrist, student counselor. *Salary potential:* $25k-$37k.

Bowling Green State U (OH) ***292***

COMMERCIAL PHOTOGRAPHY

Overview: Students choosing this major study the techniques and theories of digital or film photography for a variety of commercial and industrial uses. *Related majors:* design and visual communication, photography, graphic design, commercial art, illustration. *Potential careers:* professional photographer, photo editor, designer, product designer. *Salary potential:* $23k-$35k.

Memphis Coll of Art (TN) ***425***
Minnesota State U, Moorhead (MN) ***432***
Ohio U (OH) ***458***
Rochester Inst of Technology (NY) ***482***

COMMUNICATION DISORDERS

Overview: Students taking this major study the causes and treatments of speech, language, hearing, and communication disorders that may be caused by disease, injury, or dysfunction. *Related majors:* special education, education of speech impaired, audiology, speech language pathology, speech therapy. *Potential careers:* audiologist or speech language pathologist, teacher, speech therapist, psychologist. *Salary potential:* $27k-$37k

Baylor U (TX) ***283***
Biola U (CA) ***289***
Boston U (MA) ***292***
Bowling Green State U (OH) ***292***
Bridgewater State Coll (MA) ***294***
Brock U (ON, Canada) ***295***
California State U, Chico (CA) ***300***
California State U, Fresno (CA) ***301***
California State U, Fullerton (CA) ***301***
Case Western Reserve U (OH) ***307***
The Coll of Saint Rose (NY) ***322***
Eastern Illinois U (IL) ***348***
Edinboro U of Pennsylvania (PA) ***351***
Emerson Coll (MA) ***353***
Harding U (AR) ***375***
Kansas State U (KS) ***396***
Longwood U (VA) ***409***
Marshall U (WV) ***418***
Minnesota State U, Mankato (MN) ***431***
Minot State U (ND) ***432***
Northern Illinois U (IL) ***450***
Northwestern U (IL) ***453***
Oklahoma State U (OK) ***460***
Plattsburgh State U of NY (NY) ***471***
Radford U (VA) ***476***
San Diego State U (CA) ***498***
Southern Illinois U Carbondale (IL) ***509***
State U of NY Coll at Fredonia (NY) ***516***
Syracuse U (NY) ***521***
Truman State U (MO) ***532***
U at Buffalo, The State University of New York (NY) ***536***
The U of Akron (OH) ***537***
The U of Arizona (AZ) ***538***
U of Colorado at Boulder (CO) ***543***
U of Georgia (GA) ***545***
U of Kansas (KS) ***549***
U of Maine (ME) ***550***
U of Massachusetts Amherst (MA) ***552***
U of Nebraska at Kearney (NE) ***557***
U of Rhode Island (RI) ***572***
The U of Texas at Austin (TX) ***578***
U of Vermont (VT) ***582***
U of Wisconsin–Eau Claire (WI) ***584***
U of Wisconsin–River Falls (WI) ***585***
Western Carolina U (NC) ***598***
Western Illinois U (IL) ***599***
West Texas A&M U (TX) ***602***
Winthrop U (SC) ***608***

COMMUNICATION DISORDERS SCIENCES/ SERVICES RELATED

Information can be found under this major's main heading.

Ohio U (OH) ***458***
U of Hawaii at Manoa (HI) ***546***

COMMUNICATION EQUIPMENT TECHNOLOGY

Overview: Students will learn how to operate and maintain various communication devices and equipment such as cameras (still, film, and video), sound recording and mixed-media technologies, as well as skills such as editing, dubbing, and mixing. *Related majors:* Photographic technology, radio and television broadcast technology, Web and multimedia design. *Potential careers:* film editor or director, production manager, camera operator, sound engineer. *Salary potential:* $27k-$37k.

California State U, Sacramento (CA) ***301***
Cedarville U (OH) ***308***
Cheyney U of Pennsylvania (PA) ***312***
Eastern Michigan U (MI) ***348***
State U of NY at Farmingdale (NY) ***357***
Ferris State U (MI) ***358***
Hastings Coll (NE) ***377***
Insto Tecno Estudios Sups Monterrey(Mexico) ***388***
Saint Mary-of-the-Woods Coll (IN) ***493***
U of Michigan–Dearborn (MI) ***554***
Wilmington Coll (DE) ***607***

COMMUNICATIONS

Overview: Undergraduates will study the principles of human communications in a variety of formats, media, and contexts; the techniques for effective communication; and the analysis of communication problems. *Related majors:* psychology, education, linguistics, English and creative writing, political science. *Potential careers:* advertising executive, copywriter, journalist, teacher, speechwriter, editor. *Salary potential:* $25k-$35k.

Adams State Coll (CO) ***260***
Adelphi U (NY) ***260***
Albright Coll (PA) ***263***
Allegheny Coll (PA) ***264***
Alliant International U (CA) ***264***
Alvernia Coll (PA) ***265***
Alverno Coll (WI) ***265***
American U of Rome(Italy) ***268***
Andrew Jackson U (AL) ***269***

Angelo State U (TX) **269**
Antioch Coll (OH) **269**
Aquinas Coll (MI) **270**
Arizona State U (AZ) **271**
Arizona State U West (AZ) **272**
Auburn U Montgomery (AL) **276**
Augusta State U (GA) **277**
Aurora U (IL) **277**
Austin Coll (TX) **277**
Avila U (MO) **278**
Azusa Pacific U (CA) **278**
Barry U (FL) **282**
Baylor U (TX) **283**
Bay Path Coll (MA) **283**
Belhaven Coll (MS) **283**
Bellarmine U (KY) **284**
Benedictine U (IL) **285**
Berry Coll (GA) **287**
Bethany Coll (KS) **287**
Bethany Coll (WV) **287**
Bethany Lutheran Coll (MN) **288**
Bethel Coll (IN) **288**
Bethel Coll (KS) **288**
Bloomsburg U of Pennsylvania (PA) **290**
Boston U (MA) **292**
Bowling Green State U (OH) **292**
Bradley U (IL) **293**
Brigham Young U (UT) **295**
Brock U (ON, Canada) **295**
Bryant Coll (RI) **296**
Buena Vista U (IA) **297**
Cabrini Coll (PA) **298**
Caldwell Coll (NJ) **298**
California Baptist U (CA) **298**
California State U, Chico (CA) **300**
California State U, Fullerton (CA) **301**
California State U, San Marcos (CA) **302**
California State U, Stanislaus (CA) **302**
California U of Pennsylvania (PA) **302**
Campbell U (NC) **303**
Cardinal Stritch U (WI) **305**
Carlow Coll (PA) **305**
Carroll Coll (MT) **306**
Carroll Coll (WI) **306**
Castleton State Coll (VT) **307**
The Catholic U of America (DC) **307**
Cedar Crest Coll (PA) **308**
Cedarville U (OH) **308**
Central Coll (IA) **309**
Central Connecticut State U (CT) **309**
Central Methodist Coll (MO) **309**
Champlain Coll (VT) **311**
Chatham Coll (PA) **312**
Christian Heritage Coll (CA) **313**
Christopher Newport U (VA) **313**
Clarion U of Pennsylvania (PA) **315**
Clarkson U (NY) **316**
Clearwater Christian Coll (FL) **316**
Colby-Sawyer Coll (NH) **319**
Coll Misericordia (PA) **319**
Coll of Charleston (SC) **320**
Coll of Mount St. Joseph (OH) **320**
Coll of Saint Elizabeth (NJ) **321**
Coll of St. Joseph (VT) **322**
The Coll of Saint Rose (NY) **322**
The Coll of St. Scholastica (MN) **322**
Coll of Staten Island of the City U of NY (NY) **323**
The Coll of Wooster (OH) **324**
Colorado Christian U (CO) **325**
Columbia International U (SC) **327**
Concordia Coll (MN) **329**
Concordia U (CA) **330**
Concordia U (IL) **330**
Concordia U (MI) **330**
Concordia U (NE) **330**
Concordia U (QC, Canada) **331**
Cornell U (NY) **333**
Crichton Coll (TN) **334**
Cumberland Coll (KY) **335**
Dana Coll (NE) **337**
Delaware Valley Coll (PA) **339**
DePaul U (IL) **339**
Doane Coll (NE) **344**
Dominican U of California (CA) **345**
Dowling Coll (NY) **345**
Duquesne U (PA) **346**
East Carolina U (NC) **347**
Eastern Connecticut State U (CT) **347**
Eastern Mennonite U (VA) **348**
Eastern New Mexico U (NM) **349**
Eastern U (PA) **349**
East Stroudsburg U of Pennsylvania (PA) **349**
Eckerd Coll (FL) **350**
Edinboro U of Pennsylvania (PA) **351**
Elizabethtown Coll (PA) **351**
Elmhurst Coll (IL) **351**
Elon U (NC) **352**
Embry-Riddle Aeronautical U (FL) **352**
Emerson Coll (MA) **353**
Emmanuel Coll (GA) **353**
Emporia State U (KS) **354**
Endicott Coll (MA) **354**
Fairleigh Dickinson U, Florham (NJ) **356**
Fairleigh Dickinson U, Teaneck-Metro Campus (NJ) **356**
Fitchburg State Coll (MA) **358**
Flagler Coll (FL) **359**
Florida Inst of Technology (FL) **360**
Florida International U (FL) **360**
Florida Southern Coll (FL) **361**
Florida State U (FL) **361**
Franciscan U of Steubenville (OH) **363**
Franklin Coll Switzerland(Switzerland) **364**
Freed-Hardeman U (TN) **364**
Furman U (SC) **365**
Gallaudet U (DC) **365**
Gannon U (PA) **365**
Geneva Coll (PA) **366**
George Fox U (OR) **366**
Georgia Southern U (GA) **367**
Gordon Coll (MA) **370**
Grace U (NE) **371**
Green Mountain Coll (VT) **372**
Harding U (AR) **375**
Hastings Coll (NE) **377**
Hawai'i Pacific U (HI) **377**
Hofstra U (NY) **380**
Hollins U (VA) **380**
Holy Family U (PA) **380**
Hope Coll (MI) **381**
Howard Payne U (TX) **382**
Huntingdon Coll (AL) **383**
Huron U USA in London(United Kingdom) **383**
Idaho State U (ID) **384**
Indiana State U (IN) **385**
Indiana U Bloomington (IN) **385**
Indiana U East (IN) **386**
Indiana U Kokomo (IN) **386**
Indiana U of Pennsylvania (PA) **386**
Indiana U–Purdue U Indianapolis (IN) **387**
Indiana U Southeast (IN) **387**
Indiana Wesleyan U (IN) **387**
Insto Tecno Estudios Sups Monterrey(Mexico) **388**
Jacksonville State U (AL) **390**
Jacksonville U (FL) **391**
James Madison U (VA) **391**
Jamestown Coll (ND) **391**
Juniata Coll (PA) **395**
Kansas State U (KS) **396**
Kean U (NJ) **396**
Kennesaw State U (GA) **397**
Kentucky Wesleyan Coll (KY) **397**
Keuka Coll (NY) **398**
King Coll (TN) **398**
King's Coll (PA) **398**
Lake Forest Coll (IL) **400**
La Roche Coll (PA) **402**
Lasell Coll (MA) **402**
La Sierra U (CA) **403**
Le Moyne Coll (NY) **404**
Lewis & Clark Coll (OR) **405**
Liberty U (VA) **406**
Linfield Coll (OR) **408**
Long Island U, C.W. Post Campus (NY) **409**
Longwood U (VA) **409**
Loyola Coll in Maryland (MD) **411**
Loyola U Chicago (IL) **411**
Loyola U New Orleans (LA) **411**
Macalester Coll (MN) **413**
Malone Coll (OH) **415**
Marietta Coll (OH) **417**
Marist Coll (NY) **417**
Marquette U (WI) **418**
Martin U (IN) **419**
Mary Baldwin Coll (VA) **419**
Marymount U (VA) **420**
Maryville U of Saint Louis (MO) **420**
McDaniel Coll (MD) **422**
McMurry U (TX) **423**
Mercer U (GA) **425**
Meredith Coll (NC) **426**
Merrimack Coll (MA) **426**
Messiah Coll (PA) **426**
Metropolitan State U (MN) **427**
Michigan State U (MI) **428**
Michigan Technological U (MI) **428**
Millersville U of Pennsylvania (PA) **430**
Millikin U (IL) **430**
Mississippi Coll (MS) **432**
Mississippi State U (MS) **432**
Molloy Coll (NY) **433**
Monmouth U (NJ) **434**
Montana Tech of The U of Montana (MT) **435**
Moody Bible Inst (IL) **435**
Morehead State U (KY) **436**
Mount Mary Coll (WI) **438**
Mount Mercy Coll (IA) **438**
Mount Saint Mary's Coll and Seminary (MD) **439**
Mount Union Coll (OH) **440**
Mount Vernon Nazarene U (OH) **440**
Muhlenberg Coll (PA) **440**
Multnomah Bible Coll and Biblical Seminary (OR) **440**
National U (CA) **442**
Nebraska Wesleyan U (NE) **443**
Neumann Coll (PA) **443**
New England School of Communications (ME) **445**
New Jersey City U (NJ) **445**
New York U (NY) **447**
North Carolina State U (NC) **449**
Northeastern U (MA) **450**
Northern Arizona U (AZ) **450**
Northern Illinois U (IL) **450**
Northwestern Coll (MN) **453**
Northwestern U (IL) **453**
Norwich U (VT) **455**
Notre Dame Coll (OH) **455**
Notre Dame de Namur U (CA) **455**
Nyack Coll (NY) **456**
Oakland U (MI) **456**
Ohio Dominican U (OH) **457**
The Ohio State U (OH) **457**
Ohio U (OH) **458**
Oral Roberts U (OK) **461**
Oregon Inst of Technology (OR) **461**
Our Lady of the Lake U of San Antonio (TX) **463**
Park U (MO) **465**
Peace Coll (NC) **466**
Penn State U at Erie, The Behrend Coll (PA) **467**
Penn State U Univ Park Campus (PA) **468**
Pepperdine U, Malibu (CA) **469**
Pikeville Coll (KY) **470**
Pine Manor Coll (MA) **470**
Plattsburgh State U of NY (NY) **471**
Plymouth State Coll (NH) **471**
Point Loma Nazarene U (CA) **471**
Prescott Coll (AZ) **474**
Purchase Coll, State U of NY (NY) **475**
Purdue U (IN) **475**
Queens Coll of the City U of NY (NY) **475**
Quincy U (IL) **476**
Radford U (VA) **476**
Ramapo Coll of New Jersey (NJ) **477**
Reformed Bible Coll (MI) **477**
Regis Coll (MA) **478**
Regis U (CO) **478**
The Richard Stockton Coll of New Jersey (NJ) **479**
Rivier Coll (NH) **480**
Robert Morris U (PA) **481**
Roberts Wesleyan Coll (NY) **481**
Rochester Coll (MI) **482**
Rochester Inst of Technology (NY) **482**
Rockhurst U (MO) **482**
Rocky Mountain Coll (MT) **482**
Roger Williams U (RI) **483**
Rosemont Coll (PA) **484**
Rutgers, The State U of New Jersey, New Brunswick (NJ) **485**
Saginaw Valley State U (MI) **486**
Saint Augustine's Coll (NC) **487**
St. Edward's U (TX) **488**
St. Francis Coll (NY) **488**
St. John's U (NY) **490**
Saint Joseph's Coll (IN) **490**
Saint Louis U (MO) **492**
Saint Mary's Coll (IN) **493**
St. Mary's U of San Antonio (TX) **494**
St. Norbert Coll (WI) **495**
Saint Peter's Coll (NJ) **495**
Saint Vincent Coll (PA) **496**
Saint Xavier U (IL) **496**
Salisbury U (MD) **497**
Santa Clara U (CA) **499**
Seattle Pacific U (WA) **501**
Seton Hall U (NJ) **502**
Seton Hill U (PA) **502**
Shenandoah U (VA) **503**
Shepherd Coll (WV) **503**
Simon Fraser U (BC, Canada) **505**
Simpson Coll and Graduate School (CA) **505**
Southeastern Coll of the Assemblies of God (FL) **507**
Southeastern Oklahoma State U (OK) **508**
Southern Connecticut State U (CT) **509**
Southern New Hampshire U (NH) **510**
Southern Oregon U (OR) **510**
Southern Vermont Coll (VT) **511**
Southwest Baptist U (MO) **512**
Southwestern Coll (KS) **512**
Southwest Missouri State U (MO) **513**
Southwest State U (MN) **513**
Spring Arbor U (MI) **514**
Stanford U (CA) **514**
State U of NY Coll at Cortland (NY) **516**
State U of NY Coll at Geneseo (NY) **516**
State U of NY Coll at Old Westbury (NY) **516**
Stephen F. Austin State U (TX) **518**
Stonehill Coll (MA) **520**
Susquehanna U (PA) **521**
Tabor Coll (KS) **522**
Texas A&M International U (TX) **524**
Texas A&M U–Corpus Christi (TX) **525**
Texas Lutheran U (TX) **526**
Thiel Coll (PA) **527**
Thomas Edison State Coll (NJ) **527**
Thomas More Coll (KY) **528**
Thomas U (GA) **528**
Tiffin U (OH) **528**
Towson U (MD) **529**
Trevecca Nazarene U (TN) **529**
Trinity Christian Coll (IL) **530**
Trinity U (TX) **531**
Trinity Western U (BC, Canada) **531**
Tri-State U (IN) **532**
Union Coll (KY) **533**
Union Inst & U (OH) **534**
The U of Alabama at Birmingham (AL) **537**
U of Alaska Fairbanks (AK) **538**
The U of Arizona (AZ) **538**
U of Arkansas (AR) **539**
U of Calgary (AB, Canada) **540**
U of Calif, Los Angeles (CA) **541**
U of Calif, Santa Barbara (CA) **541**
U of Central Florida (FL) **542**
U of Central Oklahoma (OK) **542**
U of Colorado at Boulder (CO) **543**
U of Colorado at Colorado Springs (CO) **543**
U of Colorado at Denver (CO) **543**
U of Connecticut (CT) **544**
U of Delaware (DE) **544**
U of Denver (CO) **544**
U of Hartford (CT) **546**
U of Hawaii at Manoa (HI) **546**
U of Houston (TX) **547**
U of Houston–Clear Lake (TX) **547**
U of Idaho (ID) **547**
U of Indianapolis (IN) **548**
U of Kentucky (KY) **549**
U of La Verne (CA) **549**
U of Louisiana at Lafayette (LA) **550**
U of Louisville (KY) **550**
U of Maine (ME) **550**
U of Maine at Presque Isle (ME) **551**
U of Mary Hardin-Baylor (TX) **551**
U of Maryland, Coll Park (MD) **552**
U of Maryland University Coll (MD) **552**
U of Massachusetts Amherst (MA) **552**
The U of Memphis (TN) **553**
U of Miami (FL) **553**
U of Missouri–Columbia (MO) **555**
U of Missouri–St. Louis (MO) **556**
U of Nebraska at Omaha (NE) **557**
U of Nebraska–Lincoln (NE) **557**
U of Nevada, Las Vegas (NV) **558**
U of Nevada, Reno (NV) **558**
U of New Brunswick Saint John (NB, Canada) **558**
U of New Haven (CT) **559**
U of New Orleans (LA) **559**
The U of North Carolina at Chapel Hill (NC) **560**
The U of North Carolina at Charlotte (NC) **560**
U of North Dakota (ND) **561**

COMMUNICATIONS (continued)

U of Northern Colorado (CO) ***561***
U of Northern Iowa (IA) ***561***
U of North Florida (FL) ***561***
U of North Texas (TX) ***562***
U of Oklahoma (OK) ***562***
U of Pennsylvania (PA) ***563***
U of Pittsburgh (PA) ***569***
U of Puget Sound (WA) ***571***
U of Rhode Island (RI) ***572***
U of Rio Grande (OH) ***572***
U of Saint Francis (IN) ***573***
U of St. Thomas (MN) ***573***
U of St. Thomas (TX) ***573***
U of San Francisco (CA) ***574***
U of Science and Arts of Oklahoma (OK) ***574***
The U of Scranton (PA) ***574***
U of South Alabama (AL) ***575***
U of South Carolina Aiken (SC) ***575***
U of South Carolina Spartanburg (SC) ***575***
U of Southern Indiana (IN) ***576***
U of Southern Maine (ME) ***576***
U of Southern Mississippi (MS) ***576***
U of South Florida (FL) ***576***
The U of Texas at Arlington (TX) ***577***
The U of Texas at Austin (TX) ***578***
The U of Texas at San Antonio (TX) ***578***
The U of Texas–Pan American (TX) ***579***
The U of the Arts (PA) ***579***
U of the Incarnate Word (TX) ***580***
U of the Ozarks (AR) ***580***
U of the Pacific (CA) ***580***
U of the Sacred Heart (PR) ***580***
U of Toledo (OH) ***581***
U of Tulsa (OK) ***581***
U of Utah (UT) ***582***
The U of Virginia's Coll at Wise (VA) ***582***
U of Washington (WA) ***583***
U of West Florida (FL) ***583***
U of Windsor (ON, Canada) ***584***
U of Wisconsin–Eau Claire (WI) ***584***
U of Wisconsin–Green Bay (WI) ***584***
U of Wisconsin–La Crosse (WI) ***584***
U of Wisconsin–Parkside (WI) ***585***
U of Wisconsin–Stevens Point (WI) ***585***
U of Wyoming (WY) ***586***
Utica Coll (NY) ***588***
Valparaiso U (IN) ***588***
Virginia Polytechnic Inst and State U (VA) ***591***
Virginia Wesleyan Coll (VA) ***591***
Wake Forest U (NC) ***592***
Warner Southern Coll (FL) ***593***
Washington U in St. Louis (MO) ***595***
Waynesburg Coll (PA) ***595***
Wayne State U (MI) ***596***
Wesleyan Coll (GA) ***597***
Western Carolina U (NC) ***598***
Western Illinois U (IL) ***599***
Western Kentucky U (KY) ***599***
Western Michigan U (MI) ***599***
Western New England Coll (MA) ***600***
Western Washington U (WA) ***600***
Westminster Coll (UT) ***601***
Westmont Coll (CA) ***602***
Wichita State U (KS) ***604***
Wilkes U (PA) ***605***
William Penn U (IA) ***606***
William Woods U (MO) ***607***
Wisconsin Lutheran Coll (WI) ***608***
Wittenberg U (OH) ***608***
Woodbury U (CA) ***609***
York U (ON, Canada) ***611***
Youngstown State U (OH) ***611***

COMMUNICATIONS RELATED

Information can be found under this major's main heading.

Arizona State U East (AZ) ***271***
The Art Inst of California–San Diego (CA) ***273***
Bradley U (IL) ***293***
Drexel U (PA) ***346***
The Franciscan U (IA) ***363***
Indiana State U (IN) ***385***
Juniata Coll (PA) ***395***
Loyola U Chicago (IL) ***411***
McMaster U (ON, Canada) ***423***
Milwaukee School of Engineering (WI) ***431***
New England School of Communications (ME) ***445***
Northern Arizona U (AZ) ***450***
Notre Dame de Namur U (CA) ***455***
The Ohio State U (OH) ***457***
Ohio U (OH) ***458***
Oklahoma State U (OK) ***460***
Quinnipiac U (CT) ***476***
Saint Louis U (MO) ***492***
San Diego State U (CA) ***498***
State U of NY Inst of Tech at Utica/Rome (NY) ***518***
Sterling Coll (KS) ***519***
Taylor U, Fort Wayne Campus (IN) ***523***
The U of Akron (OH) ***537***
U of Hawaii at Manoa (HI) ***546***
U of Miami (FL) ***553***
U of Nebraska–Lincoln (NE) ***557***
U of Southern Mississippi (MS) ***576***
The U of the Arts (PA) ***579***
Western Kentucky U (KY) ***599***
Wisconsin Lutheran Coll (WI) ***608***

COMMUNICATIONS TECHNOLOGIES RELATED

Information can be found under this major's main heading.

Alverno Coll (WI) ***265***
Chestnut Hill Coll (PA) ***312***
Columbia Coll Chicago (IL) ***327***
Hofstra U (NY) ***380***
Lebanon Valley Coll (PA) ***403***
New England School of Communications (ME) ***445***
Saint Mary-of-the-Woods Coll (IN) ***493***
Saint Mary's U of Minnesota (MN) ***494***
U of Windsor (ON, Canada) ***584***

COMMUNITY HEALTH LIAISON

Overview: This major prepares students to advocate for and refer affected communities to necessary health-care professionals. *Related majors:* human services, social work, community organization, resources and services, public health education/promotion. *Potential careers:* health-care administrator, social worker, public health advocate, community health liaison. *Salary potential:* $30k-$40k.

California State U, Chico (CA) ***300***
Central Washington U (WA) ***310***
Cumberland Coll (KY) ***335***
Florida State U (FL) ***361***
Hofstra U (NY) ***380***
Indiana State U (IN) ***385***
James Madison U (VA) ***391***
Longwood U (VA) ***409***
Marymount Coll of Fordham U (NY) ***419***
Minnesota State U, Moorhead (MN) ***432***
Northern Illinois U (IL) ***450***
Ohio U (OH) ***458***
Prairie View A&M U (TX) ***473***
Sam Houston State U (TX) ***497***
Southwest Texas State U (TX) ***513***
Stephen F. Austin State U (TX) ***518***
Texas A&M U (TX) ***524***
Texas Tech U (TX) ***526***
Texas Woman's U (TX) ***527***
U of Central Arkansas (AR) ***542***
U of Houston (TX) ***547***
U of Nebraska–Lincoln (NE) ***557***
U of Northern Iowa (IA) ***561***
The U of Texas at Austin (TX) ***578***
The U of Texas at San Antonio (TX) ***578***
The U of Texas–Pan American (TX) ***579***
U of West Florida (FL) ***583***
Western Kentucky U (KY) ***599***
Western Michigan U (MI) ***599***
Worcester State Coll (MA) ***609***
Youngstown State U (OH) ***611***

COMMUNITY PSYCHOLOGY

Overview: A branch of psychology that focuses on the analysis of social problems and the development and implementation of strategies for addressing these problems. *Related majors:* sociology, human ecology, community organization, resources and services, public policy analysis. *Potential careers:* social worker, community organizer or advocate, school psychologist, economist, outreach program coordinator. *Salary potential:* $23k-$33k.

New York Inst of Technology (NY) ***447***
Northwestern U (IL) ***453***
Saint Mary Coll (KS) ***493***

COMMUNITY SERVICES

Overview: This major teaches students the theories and principles behind human and social services as well as community organization and advocacy, preparing them for careers. *Related majors:* social work, human services, housing studies, consumer education, public relations, law and legal services, psychology. *Potential careers:* consumer advocate, social worker, public administration official, community liaison coordinator. *Salary potential:* $20k-$30k.

Alverno Coll (WI) ***265***
Aquinas Coll (MI) ***270***
Arcadia U (PA) ***271***
Bellarmine U (KY) ***284***
Bemidji State U (MN) ***285***
Brandon U (MB, Canada) ***293***
Cazenovia Coll (NY) ***308***
Central Michigan U (MI) ***310***
Cornell U (NY) ***333***
Emory & Henry Coll (VA) ***353***
The Evergreen State Coll (WA) ***355***
Framingham State Coll (MA) ***362***
Goddard Coll (VT) ***369***
Hampshire Coll (MA) ***375***
High Point U (NC) ***379***
International Coll of the Cayman Islands(Cayman Islands) ***389***
Iowa State U of Science and Technology (IA) ***390***
Long Island U, Southampton Coll, Friends World Program (NY) ***409***
Montana State U–Northern (MT) ***434***
Northern State U (SD) ***451***
North Park U (IL) ***452***
Oklahoma Christian U (OK) ***459***
Providence Coll (RI) ***474***
Rockhurst U (MO) ***482***
Roosevelt U (IL) ***483***
St. John's U (NY) ***490***
Saint Martin's Coll (WA) ***493***
Saint Mary Coll (KS) ***493***
Samford U (AL) ***497***
Siena Heights U (MI) ***504***
Southern Arkansas U–Magnolia (AR) ***509***
Southern Connecticut State U (CT) ***509***
Springfield Coll (MA) ***514***
State U of NY Empire State Coll (NY) ***517***
Thomas Edison State Coll (NJ) ***527***
Touro Coll (NY) ***529***
U of Alaska Fairbanks (AK) ***538***
U of Delaware (DE) ***544***
U of Hartford (CT) ***546***
U of Massachusetts Boston (MA) ***553***
U of Oregon (OR) ***562***
The U of Texas at El Paso (TX) ***578***
U of Toledo (OH) ***581***
Western Baptist Coll (OR) ***598***
West Virginia U Inst of Technology (WV) ***602***

COMPARATIVE LITERATURE

Overview: Students choosing this major focus on two or more literary traditions in the original language or translation. *Related majors:* English language/literature, drama/theater literature, history and criticism, foreign language/literatures, history. *Potential careers:* writer, editor, professor, lawyer, copywriter or advertising executive. *Salary potential:* $23k-$32k.

The American U in Cairo(Egypt) ***267***
The American U of Paris(France) ***268***
Antioch Coll (OH) ***269***
Bard Coll (NY) ***281***
Barnard Coll (NY) ***282***
Beloit Coll (WI) ***285***
Bennington Coll (VT) ***286***
Brandeis U (MA) ***293***
Brigham Young U (UT) ***295***
Brooklyn Coll of the City U of NY (NY) ***295***
Brown U (RI) ***296***
Bryn Mawr Coll (PA) ***297***
California State U, Fullerton (CA) ***301***
California State U, Long Beach (CA) ***301***
Carleton U (ON, Canada) ***305***
Case Western Reserve U (OH) ***307***
Cedar Crest Coll (PA) ***308***
Chapman U (CA) ***311***
Clark U (MA) ***316***
The Coll of Wooster (OH) ***324***
The Colorado Coll (CO) ***325***
Columbia Coll (NY) ***326***
Columbia U, School of General Studies (NY) ***328***
Cornell U (NY) ***333***
Dartmouth Coll (NH) ***337***
DePaul U (IL) ***339***
Eckerd Coll (FL) ***350***
Emory U (GA) ***354***
The Evergreen State Coll (WA) ***355***
Fordham U (NY) ***362***
Georgetown U (DC) ***366***
Goddard Coll (VT) ***369***
Hamilton Coll (NY) ***374***
Hampshire Coll (MA) ***375***
Harvard U (MA) ***376***
Haverford Coll (PA) ***377***
Hillsdale Coll (MI) ***379***
Hobart and William Smith Colls (NY) ***380***
Hofstra U (NY) ***380***
Hunter Coll of the City U of NY (NY) ***382***
Indiana U Bloomington (IN) ***385***
Long Island U, Southampton Coll, Friends World Program (NY) ***409***
Marlboro Coll (VT) ***418***
McMaster U (ON, Canada) ***423***
Mills Coll (CA) ***431***
New York U (NY) ***447***
Northwestern U (IL) ***453***
Oberlin Coll (OH) ***456***
Occidental Coll (CA) ***457***
The Ohio State U (OH) ***457***
Oregon State U (OR) ***462***
Penn State U Univ Park Campus (PA) ***468***
Princeton U (NJ) ***474***
Queens Coll of the City U of NY (NY) ***475***
Ramapo Coll of New Jersey (NJ) ***477***
Roosevelt U (IL) ***483***
Rutgers, The State U of New Jersey, New Brunswick (NJ) ***485***
St. Cloud State U (MN) ***488***
Salem State Coll (MA) ***497***
San Diego State U (CA) ***498***
San Francisco State U (CA) ***498***
Sarah Lawrence Coll (NY) ***499***
Simmons Coll (MA) ***504***
Smith Coll (MA) ***506***
Stanford U (CA) ***514***
State U of NY at Binghamton (NY) ***515***
State U of NY at New Paltz (NY) ***515***
State U of NY Coll at Geneseo (NY) ***516***
Stony Brook U, State University of New York (NY) ***520***
Swarthmore Coll (PA) ***521***
Trinity Coll (CT) ***530***
U of Alberta (AB, Canada) ***538***
U of Calif, Berkeley (CA) ***540***
U of Calif, Davis (CA) ***540***
U of Calif, Irvine (CA) ***541***
U of Calif, Los Angeles (CA) ***541***
U of Calif, Riverside (CA) ***541***
U of Calif, Santa Barbara (CA) ***541***
U of Calif, Santa Cruz (CA) ***542***
U of Cincinnati (OH) ***543***
U of Delaware (DE) ***544***
U of Georgia (GA) ***545***
U of Illinois at Urbana–Champaign (IL) ***548***
The U of Iowa (IA) ***548***
U of La Verne (CA) ***549***
U of Massachusetts Amherst (MA) ***552***
U of Michigan (MI) ***554***

U of Michigan–Dearborn (MI) **554**
U of Minnesota, Twin Cities Campus (MN) **555**
U of Nevada, Las Vegas (NV) **558**
U of New Brunswick Fredericton (NB, Canada) **558**
U of New Mexico (NM) **559**
The U of North Carolina at Chapel Hill (NC) **560**
U of Oregon (OR) **562**
U of Pennsylvania (PA) **563**
U of Puerto Rico, Río Piedras (PR) **571**
U of Rhode Island (RI) **572**
U of Rochester (NY) **573**
U of St. Thomas (MN) **573**
U of Southern California (CA) **576**
U of the South (TN) **581**
U of Virginia (VA) **582**
U of Washington (WA) **583**
U of Windsor (ON, Canada) **584**
U of Wisconsin–Madison (WI) **584**
U of Wisconsin–Milwaukee (WI) **585**
Washington U in St. Louis (MO) **595**
Wellesley Coll (MA) **597**
West Chester U of Pennsylvania (PA) **598**
Western Washington U (WA) **600**
Willamette U (OR) **605**
William Woods U (MO) **607**
Wittenberg U (OH) **608**

COMPUTER EDUCATION

Overview: This major prepares undergraduates to teach basic computer skills and related computer education programs at the junior high, high school, or vocational school level. *Related majors:* computer science, computer maintenance technology, computer installation or repair, computer programming. *Potential careers:* computer teacher, computer consultant. *Salary potential:* $25k-$35k.

Abilene Christian U (TX) **260**
Baylor U (TX) **283**
Bowling Green State U (OH) **292**
Bridgewater Coll (VA) **294**
Central Michigan U (MI) **310**
Concordia U (IL) **330**
Concordia U (NE) **330**
Eastern Michigan U (MI) **348**
Florida Inst of Technology (FL) **360**
Hardin-Simmons U (TX) **376**
McMurry U (TX) **423**
Pontifical Catholic U of Puerto Rico (PR) **472**
San Diego State U (CA) **498**
South Dakota State U (SD) **507**
Union Coll (NE) **534**
The U of Akron (OH) **537**
U of Illinois at Urbana–Champaign (IL) **548**
U of Nebraska–Lincoln (NE) **557**
U of North Texas (TX) **562**
U of Wisconsin–River Falls (WI) **585**
Utica Coll (NY) **588**
Viterbo U (WI) **591**
Youngstown State U (OH) **611**

COMPUTER ENGINEERING

Overview: This major gives students the math and science training to design, develop and analyze, and operate computer hardware and software and related equipment and systems. *Related majors:* electrical engineering, computer hardware engineering, mathematics, computer software engineering. *Potential careers:* computer programmer, software developer, electronics technician, systems analyst. *Salary potential:* $40k-$50k.

Arizona State U (AZ) **271**
Auburn U (AL) **276**
Bellarmine U (KY) **284**
Boston U (MA) **292**
Brigham Young U (UT) **295**
Brown U (RI) **296**
Bucknell U (PA) **297**
California Inst of Technology (CA) **299**
California Polytechnic State U, San Luis Obispo (CA) **300**
California State Polytechnic U, Pomona (CA) **300**
California State U, Chico (CA) **300**
California State U, Fresno (CA) **301**
California State U, Long Beach (CA) **301**
California State U, Northridge (CA) **301**
California State U, Sacramento (CA) **301**
Capitol Coll (MD) **304**
Carleton U (ON, Canada) **305**
Carnegie Mellon U (PA) **305**
Case Western Reserve U (OH) **307**
The Catholic U of America (DC) **307**
Christian Brothers U (TN) **313**
Christopher Newport U (VA) **313**
Clarkson U (NY) **316**
Clemson U (SC) **317**
Colorado State U (CO) **325**
Colorado Tech U (CO) **326**
Columbia U, School of Engineering & Applied Sci (NY) **328**
Concordia U (QC, Canada) **331**
Dalhousie U (NS, Canada) **336**
Dominican U (IL) **345**
Drexel U (PA) **346**
Eastern Michigan U (MI) **348**
Eastern Nazarene Coll (MA) **348**
Elizabethtown Coll (PA) **351**
Embry-Riddle Aeronautical U (AZ) **352**
Embry-Riddle Aeronautical U (FL) **352**
Florida Atlantic U (FL) **359**
Florida Inst of Technology (FL) **360**
Florida International U (FL) **360**
Florida State U (FL) **361**
Gallaudet U (DC) **365**
George Mason U (VA) **366**
The George Washington U (DC) **367**
Georgia Inst of Technology (GA) **367**
Gonzaga U (WA) **369**
Grantham U (LA) **372**
Harding U (AR) **375**
Harvard U (MA) **376**
Illinois Inst of Technology (IL) **384**
Indiana Inst of Technology (IN) **385**
Indiana U–Purdue U Indianapolis (IN) **387**
Insto Tecno Estudios Sups Monterrey(Mexico) **388**
Iona Coll (NY) **390**
Iowa State U of Science and Technology (IA) **390**
Johns Hopkins U (MD) **392**
Johnson & Wales U (RI) **393**
Johnson C. Smith U (NC) **394**
Kansas State U (KS) **396**
Kettering U (MI) **398**
Lakehead U (ON, Canada) **400**
Lehigh U (PA) **404**
LeTourneau U (TX) **405**
Louisiana State U and A&M Coll (LA) **410**
Manhattan Coll (NY) **416**
Marquette U (WI) **418**
Massachusetts Inst of Technology (MA) **421**
McGill U (QC, Canada) **423**
McMaster U (ON, Canada) **423**
Mercer U (GA) **425**
Merrimack Coll (MA) **426**
Michigan State U (MI) **428**
Michigan Technological U (MI) **428**
Milwaukee School of Engineering (WI) **431**
Minnesota State U, Mankato (MN) **431**
Mississippi State U (MS) **432**
Missouri Tech (MO) **433**
Montana State U–Bozeman (MT) **434**
Montana Tech of The U of Montana (MT) **435**
New Jersey Inst of Technology (NJ) **445**
New York U (NY) **447**
North Carolina State U (NC) **449**
North Dakota State U (ND) **449**
Northeastern U (MA) **450**
Northwestern Polytechnic U (CA) **453**
Northwestern U (IL) **453**
Oakland U (MI) **456**
Ohio Northern U (OH) **457**
The Ohio State U (OH) **457**
Oklahoma Christian U (OK) **459**
Oklahoma State U (OK) **460**
Old Dominion U (VA) **460**
Oral Roberts U (OK) **461**
Oregon State U (OR) **462**
Pacific Lutheran U (WA) **463**
Penn State U at Erie, The Behrend Coll (PA) **467**
Penn State U Univ Park Campus (PA) **468**
Polytechnic U, Brooklyn Campus (NY) **472**
Portland State U (OR) **472**
Princeton U (NJ) **474**
Purdue U (IN) **475**
Purdue U Calumet (IN) **475**
Queen's U at Kingston (ON, Canada) **476**
Rensselaer Polytechnic Inst (NY) **478**
Rice U (TX) **479**
Richmond, The American International U in London(United Kingdom) **480**
Robert Morris U (PA) **481**
Rochester Inst of Technology (NY) **482**
Rose-Hulman Inst of Technology (IN) **484**
St. Cloud State U (MN) **488**
St. Mary's U of San Antonio (TX) **494**
San Diego State U (CA) **498**
San Jose State U (CA) **499**
Santa Clara U (CA) **499**
Savannah State U (GA) **499**
South Dakota School of Mines and Technology (SD) **507**
Southern Illinois U Carbondale (IL) **509**
Southern Illinois U Edwardsville (IL) **509**
Southern Methodist U (TX) **510**
State U of NY at Binghamton (NY) **515**
State U of NY at New Paltz (NY) **515**
Stevens Inst of Technology (NJ) **519**
Stonehill Coll (MA) **520**
Stony Brook U, State University of New York (NY) **520**
Suffolk U (MA) **520**
Syracuse U (NY) **521**
Taylor U (IN) **523**
Tennessee Technological U (TN) **524**
Texas A&M U (TX) **524**
Texas Tech U (TX) **526**
Tufts U (MA) **533**
Tulane U (LA) **533**
United States Military Academy (NY) **535**
Université de Sherbrooke (QC, Canada) **536**
U du Québec à Trois-Rivières (QC, Canada) **536**
Université Laval (QC, Canada) **536**
The U of Akron (OH) **537**
The U of Alabama in Huntsville (AL) **537**
U of Alberta (AB, Canada) **538**
The U of Arizona (AZ) **538**
U of Arkansas (AR) **539**
U of Bridgeport (CT) **540**
The U of British Columbia (BC, Canada) **540**
U of Calgary (AB, Canada) **540**
U of Calif, Davis (CA) **540**
U of Calif, Irvine (CA) **541**
U of Calif, Los Angeles (CA) **541**
U of Calif, San Diego (CA) **541**
U of Calif, Santa Cruz (CA) **542**
U of Central Florida (FL) **542**
U of Cincinnati (OH) **543**
U of Colorado at Boulder (CO) **543**
U of Colorado at Colorado Springs (CO) **543**
U of Connecticut (CT) **544**
U of Dayton (OH) **544**
U of Delaware (DE) **544**
U of Denver (CO) **544**
U of Evansville (IN) **545**
U of Florida (FL) **545**
U of Hartford (CT) **546**
U of Houston–Clear Lake (TX) **547**
U of Idaho (ID) **547**
U of Illinois at Chicago (IL) **547**
U of Illinois at Urbana–Champaign (IL) **548**
The U of Iowa (IA) **548**
U of Kansas (KS) **549**
U of Louisiana at Lafayette (LA) **550**
U of Louisville (KY) **550**
U of Maine (ME) **550**
U of Manitoba (MB, Canada) **551**
U of Maryland, Baltimore County (MD) **552**
U of Maryland, Coll Park (MD) **552**
U of Massachusetts Amherst (MA) **552**
U of Massachusetts Dartmouth (MA) **553**
The U of Memphis (TN) **553**
U of Miami (FL) **553**
U of Michigan (MI) **554**
U of Minnesota, Duluth (MN) **554**
U of Missouri–Columbia (MO) **555**
U of Missouri–Rolla (MO) **556**
U of Nebraska–Lincoln (NE) **557**
U of Nevada, Las Vegas (NV) **558**
U of New Brunswick Fredericton (NB, Canada) **558**
U of New Hampshire (NH) **558**
U of New Mexico (NM) **559**
The U of North Carolina at Charlotte (NC) **560**
U of Notre Dame (IN) **562**
U of Oklahoma (OK) **562**
U of Ottawa (ON, Canada) **563**
U of Pennsylvania (PA) **563**
U of Pittsburgh (PA) **569**
U of Portland (OR) **570**
U of Rhode Island (RI) **572**
The U of Scranton (PA) **574**
U of South Alabama (AL) **575**
U of South Carolina (SC) **575**
U of Southern California (CA) **576**
U of South Florida (FL) **576**
The U of Tennessee (TN) **577**
The U of Texas at Arlington (TX) **577**
The U of Texas at Dallas (TX) **578**
U of the Pacific (CA) **580**
U of Toledo (OH) **581**
U of Toronto (ON, Canada) **581**
U of Utah (UT) **582**
U of Victoria (BC, Canada) **582**
U of Virginia (VA) **582**
U of Washington (WA) **583**
U of Waterloo (ON, Canada) **583**
U of West Florida (FL) **583**
U of Windsor (ON, Canada) **584**
U of Wisconsin–Madison (WI) **584**
U of Wyoming (WY) **586**
Utah State U (UT) **587**
Vanderbilt U (TN) **588**
Villanova U (PA) **590**
Virginia Polytechnic Inst and State U (VA) **591**
Virginia State U (VA) **591**
Washington State U (WA) **595**
Washington U in St. Louis (MO) **595**
Western Michigan U (MI) **599**
West Virginia U (WV) **602**
Wichita State U (KS) **604**
Wilberforce U (OH) **605**
Worcester Polytechnic Inst (MA) **609**
Wright State U (OH) **609**
York U (ON, Canada) **611**

COMPUTER ENGINEERING RELATED

Information can be found under this major's main heading.

Queen's U at Kingston (ON, Canada) **476**
Ryerson U (ON, Canada) **485**

COMPUTER ENGINEERING TECHNOLOGY

Overview: Students who choose this major learn the principles of basic computer engineering as well as the necessary skills to work with computer engineers who are developing computer systems. *Related majors:* computer science, computer systems analysis, electronics. *Potential careers:* computer technician, computer programmer, computer systems analyst. *Salary potential:* $28k-$40k.

Andrews U (MI) **269**
Arizona State U East (AZ) **271**
Brock U (ON, Canada) **295**
California State U, Long Beach (CA) **301**
Capitol Coll (MD) **304**
Central Michigan U (MI) **310**
Colorado State U-Pueblo (CO) **325**
DeVry Inst of Technology (NY) **340**
DeVry U (AZ) **340**
DeVry U, Fremont (CA) **340**
DeVry U, Long Beach (CA) **341**
DeVry U, Pomona (CA) **341**
DeVry U, West Hills (CA) **341**
DeVry U, Orlando (FL) **342**
DeVry U, Alpharetta (GA) **342**
DeVry U, Decatur (GA) **342**
DeVry U, Addison (IL) **342**
DeVry U, Chicago (IL) **342**
DeVry U, Tinley Park (IL) **342**
DeVry U (MO) **343**
DeVry U (OH) **343**
DeVry U (TX) **343**

COMPUTER ENGINEERING TECHNOLOGY (continued)

DeVry U (VA) ***343***
DeVry U (WA) ***343***
East Carolina U (NC) ***347***
Eastern Washington U (WA) ***349***
East-West U (IL) ***350***
Excelsior Coll (NY) ***356***
State U of NY at Farmingdale (NY) ***357***
Georgia Southwestern State U (GA) ***368***
Grantham U (LA) ***372***
Harvard U (MA) ***376***
Indiana State U (IN) ***385***
Iona Coll (NY) ***390***
LeTourneau U (TX) ***405***
Lewis-Clark State Coll (ID) ***406***
Marist Coll (NY) ***417***
Martin U (IN) ***419***
Minnesota State U, Mankato (MN) ***431***
Murray State U (KY) ***440***
Norfolk State U (VA) ***448***
Northeastern U (MA) ***450***
Oregon Inst of Technology (OR) ***461***
Peirce Coll (PA) ***466***
Prairie View A&M U (TX) ***473***
Purdue U Calumet (IN) ***475***
Purdue U North Central (IN) ***475***
Rochester Inst of Technology (NY) ***482***
Savannah State U (GA) ***499***
Shawnee State U (OH) ***502***
Southern Polytechnic State U (GA) ***511***
State U of NY Inst of Tech at Utica/Rome (NY) ***518***
Texas Southern U (TX) ***526***
U at Buffalo, The State University of New York (NY) ***536***
U of Arkansas at Little Rock (AR) ***539***
U of Dayton (OH) ***544***
U of Guelph (ON, Canada) ***546***
U of Hartford (CT) ***546***
U of Houston (TX) ***547***
U of Houston–Clear Lake (TX) ***547***
U of Houston–Downtown (TX) ***547***
The U of Memphis (TN) ***553***
U of New Brunswick Saint John (NB, Canada) ***558***
U of Rochester (NY) ***573***
U of Southern Mississippi (MS) ***576***
Utah State U (UT) ***587***
Vermont Tech Coll (VT) ***589***
Wentworth Inst of Technology (MA) ***597***

COMPUTER GRAPHICS

Overview: Students will learn about the software and hardware used to create and display two- and three-dimensional objects on a computer screen. *Related majors:* graphic art, mathematics, computer programming, computer science, multimedia. *Potential careers:* graphic artist, Web page designer, art director. *Salary potential:* $40k-$50k.

Academy of Art Coll (CA) ***260***
Alberta Coll of Art & Design (AB, Canada) ***262***
American Academy of Art (IL) ***265***
The Art Inst of California–San Francisco (CA) ***273***
The Art Inst of Colorado (CO) ***274***
The Art Inst of Portland (OR) ***274***
Atlanta Coll of Art (GA) ***275***
Baker Coll of Flint (MI) ***279***
Bloomfield Coll (NJ) ***290***
Bowie State U (MD) ***292***
California Inst of the Arts (CA) ***299***
California State U, Hayward (CA) ***301***
Capella U (MN) ***304***
Cogswell Polytechnical Coll (CA) ***318***
Col for Creative Studies (MI) ***319***
Coll of Aeronautics (NY) ***319***
The Coll of Southeastern Europe, The American U of Athens(Greece) ***323***
Coll of the Atlantic (ME) ***323***
Columbia Coll (MO) ***326***
Columbia Coll Chicago (IL) ***327***
Dakota State U (SD) ***335***
DePaul U (IL) ***339***
Dominican U (IL) ***345***
Dominican U of California (CA) ***345***
Hampshire Coll (MA) ***375***
Harvard U (MA) ***376***
Henry Cogswell Coll (WA) ***378***
Huntingdon Coll (AL) ***383***
The Illinois Inst of Art (IL) ***384***
Indiana Wesleyan U (IN) ***387***
John Brown U (AR) ***392***
Judson Coll (IL) ***395***
Long Island U, C.W. Post Campus (NY) ***409***
Maharishi U of Management (IA) ***414***
Memphis Coll of Art (TN) ***425***
New England School of Communications (ME) ***445***
Newschool of Architecture & Design (CA) ***446***
Northern Michigan U (MI) ***451***
Oakland City U (IN) ***456***
Pratt Inst (NY) ***473***
Rochester Inst of Technology (NY) ***482***
Savannah Coll of Art and Design (GA) ***499***
School of the Art Inst of Chicago (IL) ***500***
School of the Museum of Fine Arts (MA) ***501***
School of Visual Arts (NY) ***501***
Simon's Rock Coll of Bard (MA) ***505***
South Dakota State U (SD) ***507***
Southern Adventist U (TN) ***508***
Springfield Coll (MA) ***514***
State U of NY Coll at Fredonia (NY) ***516***
State U of NY Coll at Oneonta (NY) ***517***
Syracuse U (NY) ***521***
U of Advancing Technology (AZ) ***537***
U of Dubuque (IA) ***545***
U of Mary Hardin-Baylor (TX) ***551***
The U of Tampa (FL) ***577***
Villa Julie Coll (MD) ***590***
Wingate U (NC) ***607***
Wittenberg U (OH) ***608***

COMPUTER HARDWARE ENGINEERING

Overview: This major prepares students to design, develop, analyze, and operate computer hardware and other related equipment and systems such as computer circuits, chip designs, and circuitry. *Related majors:* electrical engineering, computer engineering, mathematics, industrial engineering, materials engineering. *Potential careers:* researcher, computer hardware developer, electronics technician, computer engineer, manufacturer. *Salary potential:* $32k-$47k.

Queen's U at Kingston (ON, Canada) ***476***
York U (ON, Canada) ***611***

COMPUTER/INFORMATION SCIENCES

Overview: An interdisciplinary approach to solving problems with the aid of computers, computer science, and information science and systems. *Related majors:* information science and systems, computer science, computer programming. *Potential careers:* computer engineer, software developer, system programmer, database administrator. *Salary potential:* $45k-$60k.

Abilene Christian U (TX) ***260***
Adelphi U (NY) ***260***
Alabama A&M U (AL) ***261***
Albany State U (GA) ***262***
Alcorn State U (MS) ***263***
Allegheny Coll (PA) ***264***
Amberton U (TX) ***265***
Andrews U (MI) ***269***
Arkansas State U (AR) ***272***
Asbury Coll (KY) ***274***
Athabasca U (AB, Canada) ***275***
Augusta State U (GA) ***277***
Aurora U (IL) ***277***
Austin Peay State U (TN) ***278***
Baker Coll of Muskegon (MI) ***279***
Bellarmine U (KY) ***284***
Benedict Coll (SC) ***285***
Bentley Coll (MA) ***286***
Berry Coll (GA) ***287***
Bethel Coll (IN) ***288***
Biola U (CA) ***289***
Bishop's U (QC, Canada) ***289***
Bloomsburg U of Pennsylvania (PA) ***290***
Bluefield State Coll (WV) ***291***
Bowie State U (MD) ***292***
Bowling Green State U (OH) ***292***
Bradley U (IL) ***293***
Brooklyn Coll of the City U of NY (NY) ***295***
Bryant Coll (RI) ***296***
Bucknell U (PA) ***297***
Cabrini Coll (PA) ***298***
Caldwell Coll (NJ) ***298***
California State Polytechnic U, Pomona (CA) ***300***
California State U, Chico (CA) ***300***
California State U, Sacramento (CA) ***301***
California State U, San Bernardino (CA) ***302***
California State U, Stanislaus (CA) ***302***
Cameron U (OK) ***303***
Campbell U (NC) ***303***
Carnegie Mellon U (PA) ***305***
Carroll Coll (WI) ***306***
Castleton State Coll (VT) ***307***
Cedar Crest Coll (PA) ***308***
Central Connecticut State U (CT) ***309***
Central Michigan U (MI) ***310***
Central Missouri State U (MO) ***310***
Central Washington U (WA) ***310***
Chaminade U of Honolulu (HI) ***311***
Chatham Coll (PA) ***312***
Chestnut Hill Coll (PA) ***312***
Christopher Newport U (VA) ***313***
Clarion U of Pennsylvania (PA) ***315***
Clarkson U (NY) ***316***
Clemson U (SC) ***317***
Cleveland State U (OH) ***317***
Coll of Charleston (SC) ***320***
Coll of St. Catherine (MN) ***321***
The Coll of St. Scholastica (MN) ***322***
The Coll of Southeastern Europe, The American U of Athens(Greece) ***323***
Coll of the Ozarks (MO) ***323***
Colorado Christian U (CO) ***325***
Colorado Tech U Denver Campus (CO) ***326***
Concordia U (NE) ***330***
Connecticut Coll (CT) ***331***
Cumberland Coll (KY) ***335***
Dallas Baptist U (TX) ***336***
Delaware State U (DE) ***338***
DePaul U (IL) ***339***
Deree Coll(Greece) ***339***
Doane Coll (NE) ***344***
Drury U (MO) ***346***
Eastern Connecticut State U (CT) ***347***
Eastern Michigan U (MI) ***348***
Eastern New Mexico U (NM) ***349***
Eastern Washington U (WA) ***349***
East Stroudsburg U of Pennsylvania (PA) ***349***
East Tennessee State U (TN) ***349***
East Texas Baptist U (TX) ***350***
Edinboro U of Pennsylvania (PA) ***351***
Embry-Riddle Aeronautical U (AZ) ***352***
Embry-Riddle Aeronautical U (FL) ***352***
Emmaus Bible Coll (IA) ***353***
Emporia State U (KS) ***354***
Endicott Coll (MA) ***354***
Fairleigh Dickinson U, Florham (NJ) ***356***
Fairleigh Dickinson U, Teaneck-Metro Campus (NJ) ***356***
Florida Atlantic U (FL) ***359***
Florida International U (FL) ***360***
Florida Metropolitan U-Orlando Coll, North (FL) ***361***
Florida Metropolitan U-Tampa Coll, Pinellas (FL) ***361***
Florida Metropolitan U-Orlando Coll, South (FL) ***361***
Florida State U (FL) ***361***
Fordham U (NY) ***362***
The Franciscan U (IA) ***363***
Franciscan U of Steubenville (OH) ***363***
Franklin Coll (IN) ***363***
Freed-Hardeman U (TN) ***364***
Fresno Pacific U (CA) ***364***
Frostburg State U (MD) ***365***
Gallaudet U (DC) ***365***
Gannon U (PA) ***365***
George Fox U (OR) ***366***
George Mason U (VA) ***366***
The George Washington U (DC) ***367***
Georgia Coll & State U (GA) ***367***
Georgia Inst of Technology (GA) ***367***
Georgia Southern U (GA) ***367***
Georgia State U (GA) ***368***
Grand Valley State U (MI) ***371***
Guilford Coll (NC) ***373***
Hampshire Coll (MA) ***375***
Harding U (AR) ***375***
Hartwick Coll (NY) ***376***
Harvard U (MA) ***376***
Hastings Coll (NE) ***377***
Hawai'i Pacific U (HI) ***377***
Henderson State U (AR) ***378***
High Point U (NC) ***379***
Holy Family U (PA) ***380***
Hood Coll (MD) ***381***
Idaho State U (ID) ***384***
Immaculata U (PA) ***385***
Indiana State U (IN) ***385***
Indiana U Bloomington (IN) ***385***
Indiana U of Pennsylvania (PA) ***386***
Indiana U–Purdue U Indianapolis (IN) ***387***
Indiana Wesleyan U (IN) ***387***
Insto Tecno Estudios Sups Monterrey(Mexico) ***388***
International Coll (FL) ***389***
Ithaca Coll (NY) ***390***
Jackson State U (MS) ***390***
Jacksonville State U (AL) ***390***
Jacksonville U (FL) ***391***
James Madison U (VA) ***391***
Johns Hopkins U (MD) ***392***
Johnson & Wales U (RI) ***393***
Juniata Coll (PA) ***395***
Kansas State U (KS) ***396***
Kean U (NJ) ***396***
Kentucky State U (KY) ***397***
King's Coll (PA) ***398***
Knox Coll (IL) ***399***
Kutztown U of Pennsylvania (PA) ***399***
La Roche Coll (PA) ***402***
La Salle U (PA) ***402***
Liberty U (VA) ***406***
Long Island U, Brooklyn Campus (NY) ***409***
Long Island U, C.W. Post Campus (NY) ***409***
Loyola Coll in Maryland (MD) ***411***
Loyola U New Orleans (LA) ***411***
Luther Coll (IA) ***412***
Lyndon State Coll (VT) ***413***
Malaspina U-Coll (BC, Canada) ***415***
Mansfield U of Pennsylvania (PA) ***416***
Marygrove Coll (MI) ***419***
Marymount Coll of Fordham U (NY) ***419***
Marymount U (VA) ***420***
Marywood U (PA) ***421***
Massachusetts Coll of Liberal Arts (MA) ***421***
The Master's Coll and Seminary (CA) ***422***
Mayville State U (ND) ***422***
McGill U (QC, Canada) ***423***
Medaille Coll (NY) ***424***
Mercer U (GA) ***425***
Meredith Coll (NC) ***426***
Metropolitan State Coll of Denver (CO) ***427***
Miami U (OH) ***428***
Michigan State U (MI) ***428***
Millikin U (IL) ***430***
Minnesota State U, Moorhead (MN) ***432***
Mississippi Coll (MS) ***432***
Mississippi State U (MS) ***432***
Missouri Southern State Coll (MO) ***433***
Missouri Western State Coll (MO) ***433***
Monmouth U (NJ) ***434***
Montana State U–Billings (MT) ***434***
Montana Tech of The U of Montana (MT) ***435***
Montclair State U (NJ) ***435***
Morehouse Coll (GA) ***436***
Mount Mercy Coll (IA) ***438***
Mount Saint Mary Coll (NY) ***439***
Mount Saint Vincent U (NS, Canada) ***439***
Murray State U (KY) ***440***
Neumann Coll (PA) ***443***
New Jersey City U (NJ) ***445***
New Jersey Inst of Technology (NJ) ***445***
New York Inst of Technology (NY) ***447***
New York U (NY) ***447***
Norfolk State U (VA) ***448***
Northeastern Illinois U (IL) ***450***
Northern Arizona U (AZ) ***450***
Northern Kentucky U (KY) ***451***
North Georgia Coll & State U (GA) ***451***
Northwestern U (IL) ***453***
Nova Southeastern U (FL) ***455***
Oakland U (MI) ***456***
The Ohio State U (OH) ***457***
Oklahoma Baptist U (OK) ***459***

Oklahoma State U (OK) **460**
Old Dominion U (VA) **460**
Oregon Inst of Technology (OR) **461**
Pace U (NY) **463**
Pacific Union Coll (CA) **464**
Park U (MO) **465**
Penn State U at Erie, The Behrend Coll (PA) **467**
Penn State U Harrisburg Campus of the Capital Coll (PA) **468**
Penn State U Univ Park Campus (PA) **468**
Philadelphia U (PA) **469**
Portland State U (OR) **472**
Prescott Coll (AZ) **474**
Principia Coll (IL) **474**
Purdue U (IN) **475**
Purdue U Calumet (IN) **475**
Queen's U at Kingston (ON, Canada) **476**
Ramapo Coll of New Jersey (NJ) **477**
Reformed Bible Coll (MI) **477**
Regis Coll (MA) **478**
Rensselaer Polytechnic Inst (NY) **478**
Rice U (TX) **479**
The Richard Stockton Coll of New Jersey (NJ) **479**
Robert Morris Coll (IL) **481**
Rochester Inst of Technology (NY) **482**
Rutgers, The State U of New Jersey, Camden (NJ) **485**
Rutgers, The State U of New Jersey, Newark (NJ) **485**
Sacred Heart U (CT) **486**
Sage Coll of Albany (NY) **486**
Saginaw Valley State U (MI) **486**
Saint Augustine's Coll (NC) **487**
St. Edward's U (TX) **488**
St. Francis Xavier U (NS, Canada) **489**
St. John's U (NY) **490**
Saint Joseph's Coll (IN) **490**
Saint Louis U (MO) **492**
Saint Mary-of-the-Woods Coll (IN) **493**
Saint Peter's Coll (NJ) **495**
Saint Vincent Coll (PA) **496**
Saint Xavier U (IL) **496**
Salisbury U (MD) **497**
Sam Houston State U (TX) **497**
San Diego State U (CA) **498**
Seton Hall U (NJ) **502**
Shaw U (NC) **502**
Shepherd Coll (WV) **503**
Shippensburg U of Pennsylvania (PA) **503**
Sierra Nevada Coll (NV) **504**
Silver Lake Coll (WI) **504**
Skidmore Coll (NY) **506**
South Dakota State U (SD) **507**
Southeastern Oklahoma State U (OK) **508**
Southeast Missouri State U (MO) **508**
Southern Arkansas U–Magnolia (AR) **509**
Southern Illinois U Carbondale (IL) **509**
Southern Illinois U Edwardsville (IL) **509**
Southern New Hampshire U (NH) **510**
Southern Polytechnic State U (GA) **511**
Southern Wesleyan U (SC) **511**
Southwestern Coll (KS) **512**
Southwestern Oklahoma State U (OK) **512**
Southwest Texas State U (TX) **513**
Spring Hill Coll (AL) **514**
State U of NY at Albany (NY) **514**
State U of NY Coll at Potsdam (NY) **517**
State U of NY Inst of Tech at Utica/Rome (NY) **518**
Stephen F. Austin State U (TX) **518**
Sterling Coll (KS) **519**
Suffolk U (MA) **520**
Swarthmore Coll (PA) **521**
Syracuse U (NY) **521**
Texas A&M U (TX) **524**
Texas Tech U (TX) **526**
Texas Wesleyan U (TX) **526**
Texas Woman's U (TX) **527**
Thomas Coll (ME) **527**
Thomas Edison State Coll (NJ) **527**
Thomas More Coll (KY) **528**
Towson U (MD) **529**
Trinity U (TX) **531**
Troy State U (AL) **532**
Troy State U Dothan (AL) **532**
Troy State U Montgomery (AL) **532**
Tulane U (LA) **533**
Union Coll (NY) **534**
The U of Alabama (AL) **537**
The U of Alabama at Birmingham (AL) **537**
The U of Alabama in Huntsville (AL) **537**
The U of Arizona (AZ) **538**
U of Arkansas (AR) **539**
U of Baltimore (MD) **539**
U of Calif, Berkeley (CA) **540**
U of Calif, Irvine (CA) **541**
U of Central Arkansas (AR) **542**
U of Central Florida (FL) **542**
U of Charleston (WV) **542**
U of Cincinnati (OH) **543**
U of Colorado at Boulder (CO) **543**
U of Colorado at Colorado Springs (CO) **543**
U of Delaware (DE) **544**
U of Denver (CO) **544**
U of Florida (FL) **545**
U of Georgia (GA) **545**
U of Hartford (CT) **546**
U of Hawaii at Manoa (HI) **546**
U of Houston (TX) **547**
U of Houston–Downtown (TX) **547**
U of Illinois at Chicago (IL) **547**
U of Illinois at Urbana–Champaign (IL) **548**
U of Kansas (KS) **549**
U of Kentucky (KY) **549**
U of Mary Hardin-Baylor (TX) **551**
U of Maryland, Coll Park (MD) **552**
U of Maryland University Coll (MD) **552**
U of Massachusetts Dartmouth (MA) **553**
U of Michigan–Dearborn (MI) **554**
U of Mississippi (MS) **555**
The U of Montana–Missoula (MT) **556**
U of Nebraska at Kearney (NE) **557**
U of Nebraska at Omaha (NE) **557**
U of Nevada, Reno (NV) **558**
U of New Haven (CT) **559**
U of New Mexico (NM) **559**
U of North Alabama (AL) **559**
The U of North Carolina at Greensboro (NC) **560**
The U of North Carolina at Wilmington (NC) **561**
U of North Dakota (ND) **561**
U of Northern Iowa (IA) **561**
U of North Florida (FL) **561**
U of North Texas (TX) **562**
U of Notre Dame (IN) **562**
U of Ottawa (ON, Canada) **563**
U of Pennsylvania (PA) **563**
U of Phoenix-Atlanta Campus (GA) **563**
U of Phoenix–Fort Lauderdale Campus (FL) **564**
U of Phoenix-Idaho Campus (ID) **564**
U of Phoenix–Louisiana Campus (LA) **565**
U of Phoenix–Nevada Campus (NV) **565**
U of Phoenix–Ohio Campus (OH) **566**
U of Phoenix–Orlando Campus (FL) **566**
U of Phoenix–Tampa Campus (FL) **568**
U of Phoenix–Tulsa Campus (OK) **568**
U of Phoenix–Utah Campus (UT) **568**
U of Phoenix–Vancouver Campus (BC, Canada) **569**
U of Phoenix–Washington Campus (WA) **569**
U of Phoenix-Wisconsin Campus (WI) **569**
U of Pittsburgh at Greensburg (PA) **570**
U of Puerto Rico, Río Piedras (PR) **571**
U of Rhode Island (RI) **572**
U of St. Thomas (MN) **573**
U of San Francisco (CA) **574**
U of South Alabama (AL) **575**
U of South Carolina (SC) **575**
U of South Carolina Spartanburg (SC) **575**
U of Southern Indiana (IN) **576**
U of Southern Mississippi (MS) **576**
U of South Florida (FL) **576**
The U of Texas at Austin (TX) **578**
The U of Texas at Dallas (TX) **578**
The U of Texas at San Antonio (TX) **578**
The U of Texas–Pan American (TX) **579**
U of the Sciences in Philadelphia (PA) **580**
U of Virginia (VA) **582**
The U of Virginia's Coll at Wise (VA) **582**
U of Washington (WA) **583**
The U of Western Ontario (ON, Canada) **583**
U of West Florida (FL) **583**
U of Wisconsin–Eau Claire (WI) **584**
U of Wisconsin–River Falls (WI) **585**
U of Wisconsin–Stevens Point (WI) **585**
U of Wisconsin–Superior (WI) **586**
U of Wyoming (WY) **586**
Utah State U (UT) **587**
Utica Coll (NY) **588**
Valley City State U (ND) **588**
Virginia Commonwealth U (VA) **590**
Wake Forest U (NC) **592**
Walsh Coll of Accountancy and Business Admin (MI) **593**
Washington U in St. Louis (MO) **595**
Waynesburg Coll (PA) **595**
Wayne State U (MI) **596**
Weber State U (UT) **596**
Wesleyan Coll (GA) **597**
Western Illinois U (IL) **599**
Western Kentucky U (KY) **599**
Western Michigan U (MI) **599**
West Texas A&M U (TX) **602**
Wichita State U (KS) **604**
Widener U (PA) **604**
Wiley Coll (TX) **605**
Wilkes U (PA) **605**
Williams Baptist Coll (AR) **606**
William Woods U (MO) **607**
Winona State U (MN) **608**
Worcester Polytechnic Inst (MA) **609**
Yale U (CT) **610**
York U (ON, Canada) **611**
Youngstown State U (OH) **611**

COMPUTER/INFORMATION SCIENCES RELATED

Information can be found under this major's main heading.

Anna Maria Coll (MA) **269**
California State U, Chico (CA) **300**
City U (WA) **314**
Coll of Staten Island of the City U of NY (NY) **323**
Columbia Coll Chicago (IL) **327**
East Stroudsburg U of Pennsylvania (PA) **349**
Fairleigh Dickinson U, Teaneck-Metro Campus (NJ) **356**
Georgian Court Coll (NJ) **367**
New Jersey Inst of Technology (NJ) **445**
Park U (MO) **465**
Rochester Inst of Technology (NY) **482**
Saint Louis U (MO) **492**
Saint Mary's U of Minnesota (MN) **494**
Southwestern Coll (KS) **512**
Strayer U (DC) **520**
U of Missouri–Rolla (MO) **556**
U of Notre Dame (IN) **562**
U of South Florida (FL) **576**
Utah State U (UT) **587**
Valley City State U (ND) **588**
Washington U in St. Louis (MO) **595**

COMPUTER/INFORMATION SYSTEMS SECURITY

Overview: Students learn to assess computer and network systems, recommend strategies for safeguarding against unauthorized users, and implement and manage security systems. *Related majors:* system administration, computer programming, computer systems analyst, law enforcement. *Potential careers:* computer security specialist, FBI agent, cryptographer. *Salary potential:* $30k-$45k.

Briar Cliff U (IA) **294**

COMPUTER/INFORMATION TECHNOLOGY SERVICES ADMINISTRATION AND MANAGEMENT RELATED

Information can be found under this major's main heading.

Bethel Coll (KS) **288**
Capella U (MN) **304**
Dalhousie U (NS, Canada) **336**
Golden Gate U (CA) **369**
Polytechnic U, Brooklyn Campus (NY) **472**

COMPUTER MAINTENANCE TECHNOLOGY

Overview: This major gives students the essential knowledge and skills to maintain computer and computer network systems and diagnose problems that may disable such systems. *Related majors:* computer systems analysis, computer/technical support, system administration. *Potential careers:* technical support specialist, computer network manager, Web master. *Salary potential:* $26k-$35k.

Peirce Coll (PA) **466**

COMPUTER MANAGEMENT

Overview: This major prepares students to manage a wide range of business computer systems, assess business needs for information and security systems, and oversee and regulate computer systems and performance requirements for an entire organization. *Related majors:* management information systems and business data processing, business computer programming, business systems analysis and design, business systems networking and telecommunications. *Potential careers:* systems analyst, information officer, corporate computer consultant. *Salary potential:* $40k-$55k.

American InterContinental U (CA) **266**
American InterContinental U, Atlanta (GA) **266**
American InterContinental U-London(United Kingdom) **267**
Belmont U (TN) **284**
Champlain Coll (VT) **311**
Coll of Saint Mary (NE) **322**
Columbia Southern U (AL) **327**
Columbus State U (GA) **328**
Daniel Webster Coll (NH) **337**
École des hautes études commerciales de Montréal (QC, Canada) **350**
Faulkner U (AL) **357**
Fordham U (NY) **362**
Grove City Coll (PA) **373**
Holy Family U (PA) **380**
Insto Tecno Estudios Sups Monterrey(Mexico) **388**
Lehman Coll of the City U of NY (NY) **404**
Life U (GA) **406**
Luther Coll (IA) **412**
Mary Baldwin Coll (VA) **419**
National American U (SD) **442**
National-Louis U (IL) **442**
New England Coll (NH) **444**
Northwest Missouri State U (MO) **454**
Northwood U (MI) **454**
Oakland City U (IN) **456**
Oklahoma Baptist U (OK) **459**
Oklahoma State U (OK) **460**
Pacific Union Coll (CA) **464**
Pontifical Catholic U of Puerto Rico (PR) **472**
Potomac Coll (DC) **473**
Rochester Coll (MI) **482**
St. Mary's U of San Antonio (TX) **494**
Simpson Coll (IA) **505**
Thomas Coll (ME) **527**
Tiffin U (OH) **528**
Université de Sherbrooke (QC, Canada) **536**
U of Cincinnati (OH) **543**
U of Great Falls (MT) **545**
U of the Incarnate Word (TX) **580**
Webster U (MO) **597**
West Chester U of Pennsylvania (PA) **598**
Western International U (AZ) **599**
Western Washington U (WA) **600**
West Virginia U Inst of Technology (WV) **602**
York Coll of the City U of New York (NY) **611**

COMPUTER PROGRAMMING

Overview: Students learn to write, install, and maintain computer programs (software) that run on operating systems (hardware). *Related majors:* computer programming, specific applications, computer science, data warehousing and mining, computer and information systems

COMPUTER PROGRAMMING (continued)

security, data processing. *Potential careers:* Web designer, computer programmer, systems administrator. *Salary potential:* 47-$57k.

Andrews U (MI) **269**
Arcadia U (PA) **271**
Baker Coll of Flint (MI) **279**
Baker Coll of Owosso (MI) **279**
Belmont U (TN) **284**
Brigham Young U–Hawaii (HI) **295**
Brock U (ON, Canada) **295**
Carleton U (ON, Canada) **305**
Charleston Southern U (SC) **311**
City U (WA) **314**
Colorado State U-Pueblo (CO) **325**
Columbus State U (GA) **328**
Daniel Webster Coll (NH) **337**
Davenport U, Grand Rapids (MI) **337**
Davenport U, Kalamazoo (MI) **337**
DePaul U (IL) **339**
East-West U (IL) **350**
Ferris State U (MI) **358**
Florida Metropolitan U-Tampa Coll, Brandon (FL) **360**
Florida Metropolitan U-Fort Lauderdale Coll (FL) **360**
Florida Metropolitan U-Orlando Coll, North (FL) **361**
Fontbonne U (MO) **361**
Franklin Pierce Coll (NH) **364**
Grand Valley State U (MI) **371**
Hampshire Coll (MA) **375**
Hannibal-LaGrange Coll (MO) **375**
Harvard U (MA) **376**
Husson Coll (ME) **383**
Inter American U of PR, San Germán Campus (PR) **388**
Iowa Wesleyan Coll (IA) **390**
Lamar U (TX) **401**
La Salle U (PA) **402**
Limestone Coll (SC) **406**
Luther Coll (IA) **412**
McPherson Coll (KS) **423**
Memorial U of Newfoundland (NF, Canada) **424**
Michigan Technological U (MI) **428**
Midland Lutheran Coll (NE) **429**
Miles Coll (AL) **430**
Minnesota State U, Mankato (MN) **431**
Montana Tech of The U of Montana (MT) **435**
National American U (SD) **442**
National American U–Sioux Falls Branch (SD) **442**
The National Hispanic U (CA) **442**
Newbury Coll (MA) **444**
New Mexico Highlands U (NM) **446**
New Mexico Inst of Mining and Technology (NM) **446**
Northern Michigan U (MI) **451**
Northwest Missouri State U (MO) **454**
Oregon Inst of Technology (OR) **461**
Pacific Union Coll (CA) **464**
Pittsburg State U (KS) **470**
Richmond, The American International U in London(United Kingdom) **480**
Rochester Inst of Technology (NY) **482**
Rockhurst U (MO) **482**
Saint Peter's Coll (NJ) **495**
Southeast Missouri State U (MO) **508**
Taylor U (IN) **523**
Texas Southern U (TX) **526**
Thomas Coll (ME) **527**
U du Québec à Trois-Rivières (QC, Canada) **536**
U of Advancing Technology (AZ) **537**
U of Cincinnati (OH) **543**
U of St. Francis (IL) **573**
The U of Tampa (FL) **577**
U of Toledo (OH) **581**
Villa Julie Coll (MD) **590**
West Chester U of Pennsylvania (PA) **598**
Western Washington U (WA) **600**
West Virginia U Inst of Technology (WV) **602**
Wheeling Jesuit U (WV) **603**
Winona State U (MN) **608**
York U (ON, Canada) **611**
Youngstown State U (OH) **611**

COMPUTER SCIENCE

Overview: This broad-based major will teach students many different aspects of computers, from the design of computer systems and user interfaces to analyzing problems and solutions associated with computer hardware and software. *Related majors:* computer programming, computer systems analysis, computer and information sciences, data processing technology. *Potential careers:* technical support specialist, computer programmer, computer systems analyst, computer engineer, system administrator. *Salary potential:* $40k-$50k.

Abilene Christian U (TX) **260**
Acadia U (NS, Canada) **260**
Adams State Coll (CO) **260**
Alabama State U (AL) **261**
Albertson Coll of Idaho (ID) **262**
Albion Coll (MI) **262**
Albright Coll (PA) **263**
Alderson-Broaddus Coll (WV) **263**
Alfred U (NY) **263**
Alma Coll (MI) **264**
Alverno Coll (WI) **265**
American Coll of Computer & Information Sciences (AL) **266**
American Public U System (WV) **267**
American U (DC) **267**
The American U in Cairo(Egypt) **267**
The American U of Paris(France) **268**
Amherst Coll (MA) **268**
Anderson U (IN) **268**
Andrews U (MI) **269**
Angelo State U (TX) **269**
Antioch Coll (OH) **269**
Appalachian State U (NC) **270**
Arcadia U (PA) **271**
Arizona State U (AZ) **271**
Arkansas Baptist Coll (AR) **272**
Arkansas Tech U (AR) **272**
Armstrong Atlantic State U (GA) **273**
Ashland U (OH) **274**
Assumption Coll (MA) **275**
Athens State U (AL) **275**
Atlantic Union Coll (MA) **276**
Augsburg Coll (MN) **276**
Augustana Coll (IL) **276**
Augustana Coll (SD) **276**
Austin Coll (TX) **277**
Avila U (MO) **278**
Azusa Pacific U (CA) **278**
Baker Coll of Muskegon (MI) **279**
Baker Coll of Owosso (MI) **279**
Baker U (KS) **280**
Baldwin-Wallace Coll (OH) **280**
Ball State U (IN) **280**
Barber-Scotia Coll (NC) **281**
Barnard Coll (NY) **282**
Barry U (FL) **282**
Baylor U (TX) **283**
Belhaven Coll (MS) **283**
Bellarmine U (KY) **284**
Belmont U (TN) **284**
Beloit Coll (WI) **285**
Bemidji State U (MN) **285**
Benedict Coll (SC) **285**
Benedictine Coll (KS) **285**
Benedictine U (IL) **285**
Bennett Coll (NC) **286**
Bennington Coll (VT) **286**
Berry Coll (GA) **287**
Bethany Coll (WV) **287**
Bethel Coll (IN) **288**
Bethel Coll (KS) **288**
Bethel Coll (MN) **288**
Bethune-Cookman Coll (FL) **289**
Birmingham-Southern Coll (AL) **289**
Bishop's U (QC, Canada) **289**
Blackburn Coll (IL) **290**
Bluefield Coll (VA) **291**
Bluffton Coll (OH) **291**
Boston Coll (MA) **292**
Boston U (MA) **292**
Bowdoin Coll (ME) **292**
Brandeis U (MA) **293**
Brandon U (MB, Canada) **293**
Briar Cliff U (IA) **294**
Bridgewater Coll (VA) **294**
Bridgewater State Coll (MA) **294**
Brigham Young U (UT) **295**
British Columbia Inst of Technology (BC, Canada) **295**
Brock U (ON, Canada) **295**
Brooklyn Coll of the City U of NY (NY) **295**
Brown U (RI) **296**
Bryan Coll (TN) **296**
Buena Vista U (IA) **297**
Butler U (IN) **297**
Caldwell Coll (NJ) **298**
California Inst of Technology (CA) **299**
California Lutheran U (CA) **299**
California Polytechnic State U, San Luis Obispo (CA) **300**
California State Polytechnic U, Pomona (CA) **300**
California State U, Bakersfield (CA) **300**
California State U, Dominguez Hills (CA) **300**
California State U, Fresno (CA) **301**
California State U, Fullerton (CA) **301**
California State U, Hayward (CA) **301**
California State U, Long Beach (CA) **301**
California State U, Northridge (CA) **301**
California State U, San Bernardino (CA) **302**
California State U, San Marcos (CA) **302**
California State U, Stanislaus (CA) **302**
Calvin Coll (MI) **303**
Cameron U (OK) **303**
Canisius Coll (NY) **304**
Capital U (OH) **304**
Cardinal Stritch U (WI) **305**
Carleton Coll (MN) **305**
Carleton U (ON, Canada) **305**
Carlow Coll (PA) **305**
Carnegie Mellon U (PA) **305**
Carroll Coll (MT) **306**
Carroll Coll (WI) **306**
Carson-Newman Coll (TN) **306**
Carthage Coll (WI) **306**
Case Western Reserve U (OH) **307**
Catawba Coll (NC) **307**
The Catholic U of America (DC) **307**
Cedarville U (OH) **308**
Central Coll (IA) **309**
Central Methodist Coll (MO) **309**
Centre Coll (KY) **310**
Chapman U (CA) **311**
Charleston Southern U (SC) **311**
Chestnut Hill Coll (PA) **312**
Cheyney U of Pennsylvania (PA) **312**
Christian Brothers U (TN) **313**
Christopher Newport U (VA) **313**
Citadel, The Military Coll of South Carolina (SC) **314**
City Coll of the City U of NY (NY) **314**
Claflin U (SC) **314**
Claremont McKenna Coll (CA) **315**
Clarke Coll (IA) **315**
Clarkson U (NY) **316**
Clark U (MA) **316**
Cleveland State U (OH) **317**
Coastal Carolina U (SC) **318**
Coe Coll (IA) **318**
Coker Coll (SC) **318**
Colby Coll (ME) **318**
Colgate U (NY) **319**
Coll Misericordia (PA) **319**
Coll of Mount St. Joseph (OH) **320**
Coll of Mount Saint Vincent (NY) **320**
The Coll of New Jersey (NJ) **320**
Coll of Notre Dame of Maryland (MD) **321**
Coll of Saint Benedict (MN) **321**
Coll of Saint Elizabeth (NJ) **321**
Coll of Santa Fe (NM) **323**
The Coll of Southeastern Europe, The American U of Athens(Greece) **323**
Coll of Staten Island of the City U of NY (NY) **323**
Coll of the Ozarks (MO) **323**
The Coll of William and Mary (VA) **324**
The Coll of Wooster (OH) **324**
Colorado School of Mines (CO) **325**
Colorado State U (CO) **325**
Colorado State U-Pueblo (CO) **325**
Colorado Tech U (CO) **326**
Colorado Tech U Denver Campus (CO) **326**
Colorado Tech U Sioux Falls Campus (SD) **326**
Columbia Coll (NY) **326**
Columbia Union Coll (MD) **328**
Columbia U, School of General Studies (NY) **328**
Columbia U, School of Engineering & Applied Sci (NY) **328**
Columbus State U (GA) **328**
Concord Coll (WV) **329**
Concordia Coll (MN) **329**
Concordia U (IL) **330**
Concordia U (NE) **330**
Concordia U (QC, Canada) **331**
Concordia U at Austin (TX) **331**
Concordia U Wisconsin (WI) **331**
Converse Coll (SC) **332**
Cornell Coll (IA) **332**
Cornell U (NY) **333**
Covenant Coll (GA) **333**
Creighton U (NE) **333**
Dakota State U (SD) **335**
Dalhousie U (NS, Canada) **336**
Dallas Baptist U (TX) **336**
Dana Coll (NE) **337**
Daniel Webster Coll (NH) **337**
Dartmouth Coll (NH) **337**
Davis & Elkins Coll (WV) **338**
Defiance Coll (OH) **338**
Delaware State U (DE) **338**
Denison U (OH) **339**
DePaul U (IL) **339**
DePauw U (IN) **339**
DeSales U (PA) **340**
Dickinson Coll (PA) **344**
Dickinson State U (ND) **344**
Dillard U (LA) **344**
Doane Coll (NE) **344**
Dominican U (IL) **345**
Dordt Coll (IA) **345**
Dowling Coll (NY) **345**
Drake U (IA) **345**
Drew U (NJ) **346**
Drexel U (PA) **346**
Drury U (MO) **346**
Duke U (NC) **346**
Duquesne U (PA) **346**
Earlham Coll (IN) **347**
East Carolina U (NC) **347**
East Central U (OK) **347**
Eastern Kentucky U (KY) **348**
Eastern Mennonite U (VA) **348**
Eastern Nazarene Coll (MA) **348**
Eastern Oregon U (OR) **349**
Eastern Washington U (WA) **349**
East-West U (IL) **350**
Eckerd Coll (FL) **350**
Elizabeth City State U (NC) **351**
Elizabethtown Coll (PA) **351**
Elmhurst Coll (IL) **351**
Elms Coll (MA) **352**
Elon U (NC) **352**
Emory & Henry Coll (VA) **353**
Emory U (GA) **354**
Eureka Coll (IL) **355**
Evangel U (MO) **355**
The Evergreen State Coll (WA) **355**
Excelsior Coll (NY) **356**
Fairfield U (CT) **356**
Fairmont State Coll (WV) **356**
Fayetteville State U (NC) **357**
Felician Coll (NJ) **357**
Ferrum Coll (VA) **358**
Fisk U (TN) **358**
Fitchburg State Coll (MA) **358**
Florida Inst of Technology (FL) **360**
Florida International U (FL) **360**
Florida Metropolitan U-Tampa Coll, Brandon (FL) **360**
Florida Metropolitan U–Jacksonville Campus (FL) **360**
Florida Southern Coll (FL) **361**
Florida State U (FL) **361**
Fontbonne U (MO) **361**
Fordham U (NY) **362**
Fort Lewis Coll (CO) **362**
Fort Valley State U (GA) **362**
Framingham State Coll (MA) **362**
Franciscan U of Steubenville (OH) **363**
Francis Marion U (SC) **363**
Franklin Coll (IN) **363**
Franklin Pierce Coll (NH) **364**
Freed-Hardeman U (TN) **364**
Furman U (SC) **365**
Gallaudet U (DC) **365**
Gardner-Webb U (NC) **365**
Geneva Coll (PA) **366**

Georgetown Coll (KY) **366**
Georgetown U (DC) **366**
The George Washington U (DC) **367**
Georgian Court Coll (NJ) **367**
Georgia Southwestern State U (GA) **368**
Gettysburg Coll (PA) **368**
Glenville State Coll (WV) **368**
Gonzaga U (WA) **369**
Gordon Coll (MA) **370**
Goshen Coll (IN) **370**
Goucher Coll (MD) **370**
Governors State U (IL) **370**
Graceland U (IA) **371**
Grace U (NE) **371**
Grambling State U (LA) **371**
Grand Valley State U (MI) **371**
Grand View Coll (IA) **372**
Grantham U (LA) **372**
Greenville Coll (IL) **373**
Grinnell Coll (IA) **373**
Gustavus Adolphus Coll (MN) **374**
Hamilton Coll (NY) **374**
Hampden-Sydney Coll (VA) **374**
Hampshire Coll (MA) **375**
Hampton U (VA) **375**
Hanover Coll (IN) **375**
Harding U (AR) **375**
Hardin-Simmons U (TX) **376**
Hartwick Coll (NY) **376**
Harvard U (MA) **376**
Harvey Mudd Coll (CA) **377**
Hastings Coll (NE) **377**
Haverford Coll (PA) **377**
Hawai'i Pacific U (HI) **377**
Heidelberg Coll (OH) **377**
Hendrix Coll (AR) **378**
Henry Cogswell Coll (WA) **378**
High Point U (NC) **379**
Hillsdale Coll (MI) **379**
Hiram Coll (OH) **379**
Hobart and William Smith Colls (NY) **380**
Hofstra U (NY) **380**
Hollins U (VA) **380**
Hood Coll (MD) **381**
Hope Coll (MI) **381**
Houghton Coll (NY) **381**
Houston Baptist U (TX) **382**
Hunter Coll of the City U of NY (NY) **382**
Huntingdon Coll (AL) **383**
Huntington Coll (IN) **383**
Huston-Tillotson Coll (TX) **383**
Illinois Coll (IL) **384**
Illinois Inst of Technology (IL) **384**
Illinois State U (IL) **384**
Illinois Wesleyan U (IL) **385**
Immaculata U (PA) **385**
Indiana Inst of Technology (IN) **385**
Indiana U–Purdue U Fort Wayne (IN) **386**
Indiana U South Bend (IN) **387**
Indiana U Southeast (IN) **387**
Insto Tecno Estudios Sups Monterrey(Mexico) **388**
Inter American U of PR, Aguadilla Campus (PR) **388**
Inter American U of PR, San Germán Campus (PR) **388**
Iona Coll (NY) **390**
Iowa State U of Science and Technology (IA) **390**
Iowa Wesleyan Coll (IA) **390**
Ithaca Coll (NY) **390**
Jackson State U (MS) **390**
Jamestown Coll (ND) **391**
John Carroll U (OH) **392**
Johnson & Wales U (RI) **393**
Johnson C. Smith U (NC) **394**
Judson Coll (IL) **395**
Kalamazoo Coll (MI) **395**
Keene State Coll (NH) **396**
Kendall Coll (IL) **396**
Kennesaw State U (GA) **397**
Kentucky Wesleyan Coll (KY) **397**
Kettering U (MI) **398**
King's Coll (PA) **398**
The King's U Coll (AB, Canada) **399**
Lafayette Coll (PA) **400**
LaGrange Coll (GA) **400**
Lake Forest Coll (IL) **400**
Lakehead U (ON, Canada) **400**
Lakeland Coll (WI) **401**
Lamar U (TX) **401**
Lander U (SC) **401**
Lane Coll (TN) **402**
Langston U (OK) **402**
La Salle U (PA) **402**
La Sierra U (CA) **403**
Laurentian U (ON, Canada) **403**
Lawrence Technological U (MI) **403**
Lawrence U (WI) **403**
Lebanon Valley Coll (PA) **403**
Lehigh U (PA) **404**
Lehman Coll of the City U of NY (NY) **404**
Lenoir-Rhyne Coll (NC) **405**
LeTourneau U (TX) **405**
Lewis & Clark Coll (OR) **405**
Lewis U (IL) **406**
Limestone Coll (SC) **406**
Lincoln U (CA) **407**
Lincoln U (PA) **407**
Lindenwood U (MO) **407**
Linfield Coll (OR) **408**
Lipscomb U (TN) **408**
Lock Haven U of Pennsylvania (PA) **408**
Long Island U, Brooklyn Campus (NY) **409**
Long Island U, C.W. Post Campus (NY) **409**
Longwood U (VA) **409**
Loras Coll (IA) **410**
Louisiana State U and A&M Coll (LA) **410**
Louisiana State U in Shreveport (LA) **410**
Louisiana Tech U (LA) **410**
Loyola Marymount U (CA) **411**
Loyola U Chicago (IL) **411**
Lubbock Christian U (TX) **412**
Luther Coll (IA) **412**
Lycoming Coll (PA) **412**
Lynchburg Coll (VA) **413**
Lyon Coll (AR) **413**
Macalester Coll (MN) **413**
MacMurray Coll (IL) **414**
Madonna U (MI) **414**
Maharishi U of Management (IA) **414**
Malone Coll (OH) **415**
Manchester Coll (IN) **415**
Manhattan Coll (NY) **416**
Manhattanville Coll (NY) **416**
Mansfield U of Pennsylvania (PA) **416**
Marietta Coll (OH) **417**
Marist Coll (NY) **417**
Marlboro Coll (VT) **418**
Marquette U (WI) **418**
Mars Hill Coll (NC) **418**
Marymount U (VA) **420**
Maryville Coll (TN) **420**
Maryville U of Saint Louis (MO) **420**
Mary Washington Coll (VA) **420**
Massachusetts Coll of Liberal Arts (MA) **421**
Massachusetts Inst of Technology (MA) **421**
McGill U (QC, Canada) **423**
McKendree Coll (IL) **423**
McMaster U (ON, Canada) **423**
McMurry U (TX) **423**
McNeese State U (LA) **423**
McPherson Coll (KS) **423**
Memorial U of Newfoundland (NF, Canada) **424**
Mercer U (GA) **425**
Mercy Coll (NY) **425**
Mercyhurst Coll (PA) **425**
Meredith Coll (NC) **426**
Merrimack Coll (MA) **426**
Mesa State Coll (CO) **426**
Messiah Coll (PA) **426**
Methodist Coll (NC) **427**
Metropolitan State Coll of Denver (CO) **427**
Metropolitan State U (MN) **427**
Michigan Technological U (MI) **428**
MidAmerica Nazarene U (KS) **428**
Middlebury Coll (VT) **429**
Middle Tennessee State U (TN) **429**
Midland Lutheran Coll (NE) **429**
Midwestern State U (TX) **430**
Millersville U of Pennsylvania (PA) **430**
Milligan Coll (TN) **430**
Millsaps Coll (MS) **431**
Mills Coll (CA) **431**
Minnesota State U, Mankato (MN) **431**
Minnesota State U, Moorhead (MN) **432**
Minot State U (ND) **432**
Mississippi Coll (MS) **432**
Mississippi Valley State U (MS) **432**
Missouri Southern State Coll (MO) **433**
Missouri Valley Coll (MO) **433**
Molloy Coll (NY) **433**
Monmouth Coll (IL) **434**
Montana State U–Bozeman (MT) **434**
Montana Tech of The U of Montana (MT) **435**
Montclair State U (NJ) **435**
Moravian Coll (PA) **436**
Morgan State U (MD) **436**
Morningside Coll (IA) **437**
Mountain State U (WV) **437**
Mount Allison U (NB, Canada) **437**
Mount Holyoke Coll (MA) **438**
Mount Marty Coll (SD) **438**
Mount Mary Coll (WI) **438**
Mount Mercy Coll (IA) **438**
Mount Saint Mary Coll (NY) **439**
Mount Saint Mary's Coll and Seminary (MD) **439**
Mount Union Coll (OH) **440**
Mount Vernon Nazarene U (OH) **440**
Muhlenberg Coll (PA) **440**
Muskingum Coll (OH) **441**
National U (CA) **442**
Nebraska Wesleyan U (NE) **443**
Newberry Coll (SC) **444**
Newbury Coll (MA) **444**
New Jersey Inst of Technology (NJ) **445**
New Mexico Highlands U (NM) **446**
New Mexico Inst of Mining and Technology (NM) **446**
New Mexico State U (NM) **446**
New York U (NY) **447**
Niagara U (NY) **447**
Nicholls State U (LA) **447**
Nipissing U (ON, Canada) **448**
Norfolk State U (VA) **448**
North Carolina Ag and Tech State U (NC) **448**
North Carolina Central U (NC) **448**
North Carolina State U (NC) **449**
North Central Coll (IL) **449**
North Dakota State U (ND) **449**
Northeastern State U (OK) **450**
Northeastern U (MA) **450**
Northern Illinois U (IL) **450**
Northern Kentucky U (KY) **451**
Northern Michigan U (MI) **451**
North Georgia Coll & State U (GA) **451**
Northwestern Coll (IA) **453**
Northwestern Oklahoma State U (OK) **453**
Northwestern Polytechnic U (CA) **453**
Northwestern U (IL) **453**
Northwest Missouri State U (MO) **454**
Northwest Nazarene U (ID) **454**
Norwich U (VT) **455**
Notre Dame de Namur U (CA) **455**
Nova Southeastern U (FL) **455**
Nyack Coll (NY) **456**
Oakwood Coll (AL) **456**
Oberlin Coll (OH) **456**
Oglethorpe U (GA) **457**
Ohio Dominican U (OH) **457**
Ohio Northern U (OH) **457**
The Ohio State U (OH) **457**
Ohio U (OH) **458**
Ohio Wesleyan U (OH) **459**
Oklahoma Baptist U (OK) **459**
Oklahoma Christian U (OK) **459**
Oklahoma City U (OK) **460**
Oklahoma State U (OK) **460**
Olivet Coll (MI) **461**
Olivet Nazarene U (IL) **461**
Oral Roberts U (OK) **461**
Oregon State U (OR) **462**
Otterbein Coll (OH) **462**
Ouachita Baptist U (AR) **462**
Pacific Lutheran U (WA) **463**
Pacific States U (CA) **464**
Pacific Union Coll (CA) **464**
Pacific U (OR) **464**
Park U (MO) **465**
Paul Quinn Coll (TX) **466**
Pepperdine U, Malibu (CA) **469**
Peru State Coll (NE) **469**
Philadelphia U (PA) **469**
Piedmont Coll (GA) **470**
Pikeville Coll (KY) **470**
Pittsburg State U (KS) **470**
Plattsburgh State U of NY (NY) **471**
Plymouth State Coll (NH) **471**
Point Loma Nazarene U (CA) **471**
Point Park Coll (PA) **471**
Polytechnic U, Brooklyn Campus (NY) **472**
Pomona Coll (CA) **472**
Pontifical Catholic U of Puerto Rico (PR) **472**
Portland State U (OR) **472**
Prairie View A&M U (TX) **473**
Presbyterian Coll (SC) **473**
Providence Coll (RI) **474**
Purdue U Calumet (IN) **475**
Queens Coll of the City U of NY (NY) **475**
Queen's U at Kingston (ON, Canada) **476**
Quincy U (IL) **476**
Quinnipiac U (CT) **476**
Radford U (VA) **476**
Randolph-Macon Coll (VA) **477**
Regis U (CO) **478**
Rensselaer Polytechnic Inst (NY) **478**
Rhode Island Coll (RI) **479**
Rhodes Coll (TN) **479**
The Richard Stockton Coll of New Jersey (NJ) **479**
Richmond, The American International U in London(United Kingdom) **480**
Rider U (NJ) **480**
Ripon Coll (WI) **480**
Rivier Coll (NH) **480**
Roanoke Coll (VA) **481**
Roberts Wesleyan Coll (NY) **481**
Rochester Inst of Technology (NY) **482**
Rockford Coll (IL) **482**
Rockhurst U (MO) **482**
Rocky Mountain Coll (MT) **482**
Roger Williams U (RI) **483**
Rollins Coll (FL) **483**
Roosevelt U (IL) **483**
Rose-Hulman Inst of Technology (IN) **484**
Rowan U (NJ) **484**
Russell Sage Coll (NY) **484**
Rust Coll (MS) **485**
Rutgers, The State U of New Jersey, Newark (NJ) **485**
Rutgers, The State U of New Jersey, New Brunswick (NJ) **485**
Ryerson U (ON, Canada) **485**
Sacred Heart U (CT) **486**
St. Ambrose U (IA) **486**
Saint Anselm Coll (NH) **487**
Saint Augustine's Coll (NC) **487**
St. Bonaventure U (NY) **487**
St. Cloud State U (MN) **488**
St. Edward's U (TX) **488**
Saint Francis U (PA) **488**
St. John Fisher Coll (NY) **489**
Saint John's U (MN) **490**
Saint Joseph Coll (CT) **490**
Saint Joseph's Coll (IN) **490**
St. Joseph's Coll, Suffolk Campus (NY) **491**
Saint Joseph's U (PA) **491**
St. Lawrence U (NY) **491**
Saint Martin's Coll (WA) **493**
St. Mary's Coll of Maryland (MD) **494**
Saint Mary's U (NS, Canada) **494**
Saint Mary's U of Minnesota (MN) **494**
St. Mary's U of San Antonio (TX) **494**
Saint Michael's Coll (VT) **494**
St. Thomas U (FL) **496**
Saint Xavier U (IL) **496**
Salem International U (WV) **496**
Salem State Coll (MA) **497**
Samford U (AL) **497**
San Francisco State U (CA) **498**
San Jose State U (CA) **499**
Santa Clara U (CA) **499**
Sarah Lawrence Coll (NY) **499**
Scripps Coll (CA) **501**
Seattle Pacific U (WA) **501**
Seattle U (WA) **501**
Seton Hill U (PA) **502**
Shaw U (NC) **502**
Siena Coll (NY) **504**
Simmons Coll (MA) **504**
Simon Fraser U (BC, Canada) **505**
Simon's Rock Coll of Bard (MA) **505**
Simpson Coll (IA) **505**
Si Tanka Huron U (SD) **505**
Slippery Rock U of Pennsylvania (PA) **506**
Smith Coll (MA) **506**
Sonoma State U (CA) **506**
South Carolina State U (SC) **506**
South Dakota School of Mines and Technology (SD) **507**
Southeastern Louisiana U (LA) **508**
Southeastern U (DC) **508**
Southern Adventist U (TN) **508**
Southern Connecticut State U (CT) **509**
Southern Methodist U (TX) **510**
Southern Nazarene U (OK) **510**
Southern Oregon U (OR) **510**
Southern U and A&M Coll (LA) **511**
Southern Utah U (UT) **511**
Southwest Baptist U (MO) **512**

COMPUTER SCIENCE (continued)

Southwestern Oklahoma State U (OK) ***512***
Southwestern U (TX) ***513***
Southwest Missouri State U (MO) ***513***
Southwest State U (MN) ***513***
Spalding U (KY) ***513***
Spelman Coll (GA) ***514***
Spring Arbor U (MI) ***514***
Springfield Coll (MA) ***514***
Stanford U (CA) ***514***
State U of NY at Albany (NY) ***514***
State U of NY at Binghamton (NY) ***515***
State U of NY at New Paltz (NY) ***515***
State U of NY at Oswego (NY) ***515***
State U of NY Coll at Brockport (NY) ***515***
State U of NY Coll at Fredonia (NY) ***516***
State U of NY Coll at Geneseo (NY) ***516***
State U of NY Coll at Oneonta (NY) ***517***
State U of NY Inst of Tech at Utica/Rome (NY) ***518***
State U of West Georgia (GA) ***518***
Stetson U (FL) ***519***
Stevens Inst of Technology (NJ) ***519***
Stonehill Coll (MA) ***520***
Stony Brook U, State University of New York (NY) ***520***
Suffolk U (MA) ***520***
Sullivan U (KY) ***521***
Susquehanna U (PA) ***521***
Sweet Briar Coll (VA) ***521***
Syracuse U (NY) ***521***
Tabor Coll (KS) ***522***
Talladega Coll (AL) ***522***
Taylor U (IN) ***523***
Taylor U, Fort Wayne Campus (IN) ***523***
Temple U (PA) ***523***
Tennessee State U (TN) ***523***
Tennessee Technological U (TN) ***524***
Texas A&M U–Commerce (TX) ***525***
Texas A&M U–Corpus Christi (TX) ***525***
Texas A&M U–Kingsville (TX) ***525***
Texas Christian U (TX) ***526***
Texas Coll (TX) ***526***
Texas Lutheran U (TX) ***526***
Texas Southern U (TX) ***526***
Thiel Coll (PA) ***527***
Thomas Coll (ME) ***527***
Thomas Edison State Coll (NJ) ***527***
Touro Coll (NY) ***529***
Transylvania U (KY) ***529***
Trent U (ON, Canada) ***529***
Trinity Christian Coll (IL) ***530***
Trinity Coll (CT) ***530***
Trinity International U (IL) ***531***
Trinity Western U (BC, Canada) ***531***
Tri-State U (IN) ***532***
Truman State U (MO) ***532***
Tufts U (MA) ***533***
Tulane U (LA) ***533***
Tusculum Coll (TN) ***533***
Tuskegee U (AL) ***533***
Union Coll (NE) ***534***
Union U (TN) ***534***
United States Air Force Academy (CO) ***534***
United States Military Academy (NY) ***535***
United States Naval Academy (MD) ***535***
Universidad Adventista de las Antillas (PR) ***536***
Université de Sherbrooke (QC, Canada) ***536***
U du Québec à Trois-Rivières (QC, Canada) ***536***
U du Québec à Hull (QC, Canada) ***536***
Université Laval (QC, Canada) ***536***
U at Buffalo, The State University of New York (NY) ***536***
U Coll of the Cariboo (BC, Canada) ***537***
The U of Akron (OH) ***537***
U of Alaska Anchorage (AK) ***538***
U of Alaska Fairbanks (AK) ***538***
U of Alberta (AB, Canada) ***538***
U of Arkansas at Little Rock (AR) ***539***
U of Bridgeport (CT) ***540***
The U of British Columbia (BC, Canada) ***540***
U of Calgary (AB, Canada) ***540***
U of Calif, Irvine (CA) ***541***
U of Calif, Los Angeles (CA) ***541***
U of Calif, Riverside (CA) ***541***
U of Calif, San Diego (CA) ***541***
U of Calif, Santa Barbara (CA) ***541***
U of Calif, Santa Cruz (CA) ***542***
U of Central Oklahoma (OK) ***542***
U of Chicago (IL) ***542***
U of Cincinnati (OH) ***543***
U of Colorado at Boulder (CO) ***543***
U of Colorado at Colorado Springs (CO) ***543***
U of Colorado at Denver (CO) ***543***
U of Connecticut (CT) ***544***
U of Dallas (TX) ***544***
U of Dayton (OH) ***544***
U of Delaware (DE) ***544***
U of Dubuque (IA) ***545***
U of Evansville (IN) ***545***
The U of Findlay (OH) ***545***
U of Guelph (ON, Canada) ***546***
U of Hawaii at Hilo (HI) ***546***
U of Houston–Clear Lake (TX) ***547***
U of Houston–Victoria (TX) ***547***
U of Idaho (ID) ***547***
U of Illinois at Springfield (IL) ***548***
U of Indianapolis (IN) ***548***
The U of Iowa (IA) ***548***
U of King's Coll (NS, Canada) ***549***
U of La Verne (CA) ***549***
The U of Lethbridge (AB, Canada) ***549***
U of Louisiana at Lafayette (LA) ***550***
U of Maine (ME) ***550***
U of Maine at Farmington (ME) ***550***
U of Maine at Fort Kent (ME) ***551***
U of Manitoba (MB, Canada) ***551***
U of Mary Hardin-Baylor (TX) ***551***
U of Maryland, Baltimore County (MD) ***552***
U of Maryland, Coll Park (MD) ***552***
U of Maryland Eastern Shore (MD) ***552***
U of Maryland University Coll (MD) ***552***
U of Massachusetts Amherst (MA) ***552***
U of Massachusetts Boston (MA) ***553***
U of Massachusetts Lowell (MA) ***553***
The U of Memphis (TN) ***553***
U of Miami (FL) ***553***
U of Michigan (MI) ***554***
U of Michigan–Dearborn (MI) ***554***
U of Michigan–Flint (MI) ***554***
U of Minnesota, Duluth (MN) ***554***
U of Minnesota, Morris (MN) ***555***
U of Minnesota, Twin Cities Campus (MN) ***555***
U of Missouri–Columbia (MO) ***555***
U of Missouri–Kansas City (MO) ***555***
U of Missouri–Rolla (MO) ***556***
U of Missouri–St. Louis (MO) ***556***
U of Mobile (AL) ***556***
The U of Montana–Missoula (MT) ***556***
U of Nebraska at Omaha (NE) ***557***
U of Nebraska–Lincoln (NE) ***557***
U of Nevada, Las Vegas (NV) ***558***
U of Nevada, Reno (NV) ***558***
U of New Brunswick Fredericton (NB, Canada) ***558***
U of New Brunswick Saint John (NB, Canada) ***558***
U of New Hampshire (NH) ***558***
U of New Mexico (NM) ***559***
U of New Orleans (LA) ***559***
The U of North Carolina at Asheville (NC) ***559***
The U of North Carolina at Charlotte (NC) ***560***
The U of North Carolina at Pembroke (NC) ***560***
U of Northern Iowa (IA) ***561***
U of Oklahoma (OK) ***562***
U of Oregon (OR) ***562***
U of Ottawa (ON, Canada) ***563***
U of Pittsburgh (PA) ***569***
U of Pittsburgh at Bradford (PA) ***569***
U of Pittsburgh at Johnstown (PA) ***570***
U of Portland (OR) ***570***
U of Prince Edward Island (PE, Canada) ***570***
U of Puerto Rico at Arecibo (PR) ***570***
U of Puerto Rico at Ponce (PR) ***571***
U of Puerto Rico, Río Piedras (PR) ***571***
U of Puget Sound (WA) ***571***
U of Redlands (CA) ***572***
U of Regina (SK, Canada) ***572***
U of Richmond (VA) ***572***
U of Rio Grande (OH) ***572***
U of Rochester (NY) ***573***
U of St. Francis (IL) ***573***
U of San Diego (CA) ***574***
U of San Francisco (CA) ***574***
U of Saskatchewan (SK, Canada) ***574***
U of Science and Arts of Oklahoma (OK) ***574***
The U of Scranton (PA) ***574***
U of Sioux Falls (SD) ***574***
The U of South Dakota (SD) ***575***
U of Southern California (CA) ***576***
U of Southern Maine (ME) ***576***
The U of Tennessee (TN) ***577***
The U of Tennessee at Chattanooga (TN) ***577***
The U of Tennessee at Martin (TN) ***577***
The U of Texas at Dallas (TX) ***578***
The U of Texas at El Paso (TX) ***578***
The U of Texas at Tyler (TX) ***579***
The U of Texas of the Permian Basin (TX) ***579***
The U of Texas–Pan American (TX) ***579***
U of the District of Columbia (DC) ***580***
U of the Pacific (CA) ***580***
U of the Sacred Heart (PR) ***580***
U of the Sciences in Philadelphia (PA) ***580***
U of the South (TN) ***581***
U of Toledo (OH) ***581***
U of Toronto (ON, Canada) ***581***
U of Tulsa (OK) ***581***
U of Utah (UT) ***582***
U of Vermont (VT) ***582***
U of Victoria (BC, Canada) ***582***
U of Washington (WA) ***583***
U of Waterloo (ON, Canada) ***583***
The U of Western Ontario (ON, Canada) ***583***
U of Windsor (ON, Canada) ***584***
U of Wisconsin–Green Bay (WI) ***584***
U of Wisconsin–La Crosse (WI) ***584***
U of Wisconsin–Madison (WI) ***584***
U of Wisconsin–Milwaukee (WI) ***585***
U of Wisconsin–Oshkosh (WI) ***585***
U of Wisconsin–Parkside (WI) ***585***
U of Wisconsin–Platteville (WI) ***585***
U of Wisconsin–River Falls (WI) ***585***
U of Wisconsin–Superior (WI) ***586***
U of Wisconsin–Whitewater (WI) ***586***
Ursinus Coll (PA) ***587***
Valdosta State U (GA) ***588***
Valparaiso U (IN) ***588***
Vanderbilt U (TN) ***588***
Vassar Coll (NY) ***589***
Villanova U (PA) ***590***
Virginia Military Inst (VA) ***591***
Virginia Polytechnic Inst and State U (VA) ***591***
Virginia State U (VA) ***591***
Virginia Wesleyan Coll (VA) ***591***
Voorhees Coll (SC) ***592***
Wagner Coll (NY) ***592***
Walla Walla Coll (WA) ***593***
Walsh U (OH) ***593***
Wartburg Coll (IA) ***594***
Washington and Lee U (VA) ***594***
Washington State U (WA) ***595***
Washington U in St. Louis (MO) ***595***
Waynesburg Coll (PA) ***595***
Wayne State Coll (NE) ***596***
Weber State U (UT) ***596***
Webster U (MO) ***597***
Wellesley Coll (MA) ***597***
Wells Coll (NY) ***597***
Wentworth Inst of Technology (MA) ***597***
Wesleyan U (CT) ***597***
West Chester U of Pennsylvania (PA) ***598***
Western Baptist Coll (OR) ***598***
Western Carolina U (NC) ***598***
Western Connecticut State U (CT) ***598***
Western Michigan U (MI) ***599***
Western New England Coll (MA) ***600***
Western New Mexico U (NM) ***600***
Western Oregon U (OR) ***600***
Western State Coll of Colorado (CO) ***600***
Western Washington U (WA) ***600***
Westfield State Coll (MA) ***600***
Westminster Coll (MO) ***601***
Westminster Coll (PA) ***601***
Westminster Coll (UT) ***601***
Westmont Coll (CA) ***602***
West Virginia U (WV) ***602***
West Virginia U Inst of Technology (WV) ***602***
West Virginia Wesleyan Coll (WV) ***603***
Wheaton Coll (IL) ***603***
Wheaton Coll (MA) ***603***
Wheeling Jesuit U (WV) ***603***
Whitworth Coll (WA) ***604***
Widener U (PA) ***604***
Wilberforce U (OH) ***605***
Wiley Coll (TX) ***605***
Willamette U (OR) ***605***
William Jewell Coll (MO) ***606***
William Paterson U of New Jersey (NJ) ***606***
William Penn U (IA) ***606***
Williams Coll (MA) ***606***
Wilmington Coll (OH) ***607***
Winona State U (MN) ***608***
Winston-Salem State U (NC) ***608***
Winthrop U (SC) ***608***
Wittenberg U (OH) ***608***
Wofford Coll (SC) ***609***
Worcester Polytechnic Inst (MA) ***609***
Worcester State Coll (MA) ***609***
Wright State U (OH) ***609***
Xavier U (OH) ***610***
Xavier U of Louisiana (LA) ***610***
York U (ON, Canada) ***611***
Youngstown State U (OH) ***611***

COMPUTER SCIENCE RELATED

Information can be found under this major's main heading.

Allegheny Coll (PA) ***264***
Holy Names Coll (CA) ***381***
Indiana State U (IN) ***385***
Kenyon Coll (OH) ***398***
McGill U (QC, Canada) ***423***
Queen's U at Kingston (ON, Canada) ***476***

COMPUTER SOFTWARE AND MEDIA APPLICATIONS RELATED

Information can be found under this major's main heading.

Carroll Coll (WI) ***306***
Champlain Coll (VT) ***311***
Dakota Wesleyan U (SD) ***336***
Grand View Coll (IA) ***372***
New England School of Communications (ME) ***445***
U of Windsor (ON, Canada) ***584***

COMPUTER SOFTWARE ENGINEERING

Overview: Students learn the mathematical and scientific principles behind the design, analysis, and maintenance of computer software and related programs and systems and programming languages. *Related majors:* computer science, mathematics, computer programming. *Potential careers:* computer programmer, software developer, systems analyst, Web developer, inventor. *Salary potential:* $32k-$47k.

Champlain Coll (VT) ***311***
Clarkson U (NY) ***316***
Fairfield U (CT) ***356***
Florida State U (FL) ***361***
Milwaukee School of Engineering (WI) ***431***
Mississippi State U (MS) ***432***
Notre Dame de Namur U (CA) ***455***
Queen's U at Kingston (ON, Canada) ***476***
Saint Louis U (MO) ***492***
U of Waterloo (ON, Canada) ***583***
The U of Western Ontario (ON, Canada) ***583***
York U (ON, Canada) ***611***

COMPUTER SYSTEMS ANALYSIS

Overview: This major teaches students how to analyze, select, implement, and maintain customized software and hardware systems for individuals or organizations. *Related majors:* computer programming, computer systems networking and telecommunications, networking and LAN/WAN management, computer technical support. *Potential careers:* computer systems analyst, computer programmer, system administrator, computer support specialist. *Salary potential:* $40k-$50k.

Baker Coll of Flint (MI) ***279***

British Columbia Inst of Technology (BC, Canada) **295**
Eastern Mennonite U (VA) **348**
Kent State U (OH) **397**
Miami U (OH) **428**
Montana Tech of The U of Montana (MT) **435**
Oklahoma Baptist U (OK) **459**
Rockhurst U (MO) **482**
Saginaw Valley State U (MI) **486**
St. Ambrose U (IA) **486**
U du Québec à Trois-Rivières (QC, Canada) **536**
U of Advancing Technology (AZ) **537**
U of Houston (TX) **547**
U of Louisville (KY) **550**
U of Miami (FL) **553**

COMPUTER SYSTEMS NETWORKING/ TELECOMMUNICATIONS

Overview: Students will learn how to design, implement, and manage linked systems of computers and software applications. *Related majors:* computer systems analysis, system administrator, telecommunications. *Potential careers:* system administrator, networking manager, system analyst. *Salary potential:* $35k-$45k.

Capella U (MN) **304**
The Coll of Southeastern Europe, The American U of Athens(Greece) **323**
Sage Coll of Albany (NY) **486**
Strayer U (DC) **520**

COMPUTER TYPOGRAPHY/ COMPOSITION

Overview: Students will learn the technical skills necessary to use computers to design typeset pages and create layouts and to make use of computer graphics. *Related majors:* Web page, digital/multimedia, and information resources design; computer graphics; graphic design; commercial art and illustration. *Potential careers:* book jacket designer, magazine layout designer, desktop publisher, Web page designer. *Salary potential:* $27k-$35k.

Baltimore Hebrew U (MD) **280**

CONSERVATION AND RENEWABLE NATURAL RESOURCES RELATED

Information can be found under this major's main heading.

Stephen F. Austin State U (TX) **518**
U of Alaska Fairbanks (AK) **538**
U of Louisiana at Lafayette (LA) **550**
Utah State U (UT) **587**

CONSTRUCTION/BUILDING INSPECTION

Overview: This major will prepare students for careers as construction or building inspectors or for related construction management careers. *Related majors:* construction/building technology, architectural and structural engineering, architectural drafting, construction management, law and legal studies. *Potential careers:* construction inspector, fire safety expert, construction manager. *Salary potential:* $25k-$30k.

Tuskegee U (AL) **533**

CONSTRUCTION ENGINEERING

Overview: This major teaches students a range of technical skills and knowledge, from construction materials and methods of construction to structural systems analysis and construction project management. *Related majors:* logistics and materials management, applied mathematics, operations management and supervision, surveying, structural engineering, architectural drafting. *Potential careers:* construction inspector, architectural draftsperson, project manager. *Salary potential:* $27k-$38k.

The American U in Cairo(Egypt) **267**
Andrews U (MI) **269**
Bradley U (IL) **293**
The Catholic U of America (DC) **307**
Concordia U (QC, Canada) **331**
John Brown U (AR) **392**
Lawrence Technological U (MI) **403**
Michigan Technological U (MI) **428**
North Carolina State U (NC) **449**
North Dakota State U (ND) **449**
Oregon State U (OR) **462**
State U of NY Coll of Environ Sci and Forestry (NY) **517**
Temple U (PA) **523**
Texas A&M U–Commerce (TX) **525**
U du Québec, École de technologie supérieure (QC, Canada) **536**
U of Alberta (AB, Canada) **538**
U of Cincinnati (OH) **543**
U of Nevada, Las Vegas (NV) **558**
U of New Brunswick Fredericton (NB, Canada) **558**
Western Michigan U (MI) **599**

CONSTRUCTION MANAGEMENT

Overview: Students will learn how to plan, manage, oversee, and inspect construction sites, buildings under construction or renovation, and related structures and facilities. *Related majors:* construction technology, structural engineering, logistics and materials management, architecture, architectural drafting. *Potential careers:* construction manager, contractor, building code inspector, carpenter, architect. *Salary potential:* $20k-$30k.

Andrews U (MI) **269**
Brigham Young U (UT) **295**
California State U, Long Beach (CA) **301**
State U of NY at Farmingdale (NY) **357**
Ferris State U (MI) **358**
Hampton U (VA) **375**
John Brown U (AR) **392**
Minnesota State U, Mankato (MN) **431**
Mississippi State U (MS) **432**
North Carolina Ag and Tech State U (NC) **448**
North Dakota State U (ND) **449**
Oklahoma State U (OK) **460**
Oregon State U (OR) **462**
Pittsburg State U (KS) **470**
Polytechnic U, Brooklyn Campus (NY) **472**
Pratt Inst (NY) **473**
Roger Williams U (RI) **483**
Sam Houston State U (TX) **497**
U of Cincinnati (OH) **543**
U of Denver (CO) **544**
U of Maryland Eastern Shore (MD) **552**
U of Minnesota, Twin Cities Campus (MN) **555**
U of the District of Columbia (DC) **580**
U of Washington (WA) **583**
U of Wisconsin–Madison (WI) **584**
U of Wisconsin–Platteville (WI) **585**
Utica Coll (NY) **588**
Wentworth Inst of Technology (MA) **597**
Western Michigan U (MI) **599**

CONSTRUCTION TECHNOLOGY

Overview: This major teaches students how to apply recent advances in the fields of materials, manufacturing, and thermofluid sciences to the construction of new buildings and to the efficient operation of buildings. *Related majors:* structural engineering, drafting and design technology, architecture, surveying, mathematics. *Potential careers:* project manager, construction supervisor, architect, research scientist, systems analyst. *Salary potential:* $30k-$42k.

Andrews U (MI) **269**
Arizona State U (AZ) **271**
Bemidji State U (MN) **285**
Bowling Green State U (OH) **292**
California State Polytechnic U, Pomona (CA) **300**
California State U, Fresno (CA) **301**
California State U, Long Beach (CA) **301**
California State U, Sacramento (CA) **301**
Central Connecticut State U (CT) **309**
Central Michigan U (MI) **310**
Central Missouri State U (MO) **310**
Colorado State U (CO) **325**
Colorado State U-Pueblo (CO) **325**
Eastern Kentucky U (KY) **348**
Eastern Washington U (WA) **349**
Fairleigh Dickinson U, Teaneck-Metro Campus (NJ) **356**
Fitchburg State Coll (MA) **358**
Florida A&M U (FL) **359**
Florida International U (FL) **360**
Georgia Inst of Technology (GA) **367**
Georgia Southern U (GA) **367**
Grambling State U (LA) **371**
Hampton U (VA) **375**
Indiana U–Purdue U Fort Wayne (IN) **386**
Minnesota State U, Moorhead (MN) **432**
Montana State U–Bozeman (MT) **434**
Murray State U (KY) **440**
Norfolk State U (VA) **448**
Northern Arizona U (AZ) **450**
Northern Michigan U (MI) **451**
Oklahoma State U (OK) **460**
Pittsburg State U (KS) **470**
Purdue U Calumet (IN) **475**
South Dakota State U (SD) **507**
Southern Illinois U Carbondale (IL) **509**
Southern Illinois U Edwardsville (IL) **509**
Southern Polytechnic State U (GA) **511**
Southern Utah U (UT) **511**
Southwest Missouri State U (MO) **513**
Southwest Texas State U (TX) **513**
Texas A&M U (TX) **524**
Texas Southern U (TX) **526**
Thomas Edison State Coll (NJ) **527**
Tuskegee U (AL) **533**
U of Arkansas at Little Rock (AR) **539**
U of Cincinnati (OH) **543**
U of Florida (FL) **545**
U of Houston (TX) **547**
U of Maine (ME) **550**
U of Maryland Eastern Shore (MD) **552**
U of Nebraska–Lincoln (NE) **557**
U of New Mexico (NM) **559**
U of North Florida (FL) **561**
U of Oklahoma (OK) **562**
U of Toledo (OH) **581**
U of Wisconsin–Stout (WI) **586**
Virginia Polytechnic Inst and State U (VA) **591**
Washington State U (WA) **595**
Wentworth Inst of Technology (MA) **597**

CONSUMER ECONOMICS

Overview: Students who choose this major learn how small- and large-scale economies are affected by consumer behavior and consumption of goods and services. *Related majors:* economics, sociology, market research. *Potential careers:* market researcher, sociologist, economic theorist or forecaster. *Salary potential:* $24k-$35k.

Indiana U of Pennsylvania (PA) **386**
Louisiana Tech U (LA) **410**
Southeastern Louisiana U (LA) **508**
Texas Woman's U (TX) **527**
The U of Alabama (AL) **537**
The U of Arizona (AZ) **538**
U of Delaware (DE) **544**
U of Georgia (GA) **545**
U of Illinois at Urbana–Champaign (IL) **548**
U of Rhode Island (RI) **572**
The U of Tennessee (TN) **577**

CONSUMER/HOMEMAKING EDUCATION

Overview: This major teaches undergraduate students about food and nutrition, consumer education, family living and parenthood education, child development and guidance, housing, home management (including resource management), and clothing and textiles in preparation for the occupation of homemaking. *Related majors:* consumer education, food and nutrition, family living and parenthood. *Potential careers:* homemaker, home economics teacher. *Salary potential:* $0-$27k.

Virginia Polytechnic Inst and State U (VA) **591**

CONSUMER SERVICES

Overview: Students learn to identify products and services that are unsafe, unreliable, or unhealthy and then to provide advice and other services to individuals and groups who are affected by these products. *Related majors:* law and legal studies, food and nutrition, consumer education, safety and security technology, community organization. *Potential careers:* consumer affairs director, product analyst, broadcast journalist, public relations executive. *Salary potential:* $26k-$32k.

Carson-Newman Coll (TN) **306**
Coll of the Ozarks (MO) **323**
Cornell U (NY) **333**
Iowa State U of Science and Technology (IA) **390**
Pacific Union Coll (CA) **464**
South Dakota State U (SD) **507**
State U of NY Coll at Oneonta (NY) **517**
Syracuse U (NY) **521**
Tennessee State U (TN) **523**
Université Laval (QC, Canada) **536**
The U of Memphis (TN) **553**
U of Wisconsin–Madison (WI) **584**

CORRECTIONS

Overview: Students who choose this major study the theory and principles of correctional science as well as the effective management of institutional facilities and programs to rehabilitate criminals. *Related majors:* law and legal studies, criminal justice, public administration, facilities planning and management, psychology. *Potential careers:* prison administrator, attorney, criminologist, psychologist, social worker. *Salary potential:* $25k-$35k.

Bluefield State Coll (WV) **291**
California State U, Hayward (CA) **301**
Coll of the Ozarks (MO) **323**
Colorado State U-Pueblo (CO) **325**
Eastern Kentucky U (KY) **348**
Eastern Washington U (WA) **349**
Hardin-Simmons U (TX) **376**
Jacksonville State U (AL) **390**
John Jay Coll of Criminal Justice, the City U of NY (NY) **392**
Lamar U (TX) **401**

CORRECTIONS (continued)

Langston U (OK) ***402***
Mercyhurst Coll (PA) ***425***
Minnesota State U, Mankato (MN) ***431***
Murray State U (KY) ***440***
Northeastern U (MA) ***450***
Oklahoma City U (OK) ***460***
St. Cloud State U (MN) ***488***
Saint Louis U (MO) ***492***
Sam Houston State U (TX) ***497***
Southeast Missouri State U (MO) ***508***
Southwest Texas State U (TX) ***513***
State U of NY Coll at Brockport (NY) ***515***
Stephen F. Austin State U (TX) ***518***
Tiffin U (OH) ***528***
Troy State U (AL) ***532***
The U of Akron (OH) ***537***
U of Indianapolis (IN) ***548***
U of New Mexico (NM) ***559***
U of Pittsburgh (PA) ***569***
The U of Tennessee at Chattanooga (TN) ***577***
The U of Texas at Brownsville (TX) ***578***
The U of Texas at San Antonio (TX) ***578***
The U of Texas–Pan American (TX) ***579***
Weber State U (UT) ***596***
Western Oregon U (OR) ***600***
Westfield State Coll (MA) ***600***
Winona State U (MN) ***608***
York Coll of Pennsylvania (PA) ***610***
Youngstown State U (OH) ***611***

COUNSELING PSYCHOLOGY

Overview: This major prepares students to become professional psychologists who specialize in rendering therapeutic services to people or groups of people who experience psychological problems or distress. *Related majors:* social work, alcohol/drug abuse counseling, marriage and family counseling, school psychology, psychology. *Related majors:* psychologist, marriage counselor, family therapist, grief counselor, crisis management specialist. *Salary potential:* $23k-$33k.

Atlanta Christian Coll (GA) ***275***
Central Baptist Coll (AR) ***309***
Crichton Coll (TN) ***334***
Crossroads Coll (MN) ***334***
Grace Coll (IN) ***370***
Limestone Coll (SC) ***406***
Mid-Continent Coll (KY) ***429***
Morningside Coll (IA) ***437***
Northwestern U (IL) ***453***
Oregon Inst of Technology (OR) ***461***
Rochester Coll (MI) ***482***
Saint Xavier U (IL) ***496***
Samford U (AL) ***497***
Texas Wesleyan U (TX) ***526***
Toccoa Falls Coll (GA) ***528***
U of Great Falls (MT) ***545***
U of North Alabama (AL) ***559***
U of Phoenix–Phoenix Campus (AZ) ***567***

COUNSELOR EDUCATION/ GUIDANCE

Overview: this major teachs students the theories and principles of guidance and counseling for supporting the personal, social, and educational developments of school age children. *Related majors:* developmental and counseling psychology, communication disorders, mental health rehabilitation, rehabilitation therapy. *Potential careers:* teacher, therapist, psychiatrist, school counselor. *Salary potential:* $26k-$35k.

Amberton U (TX) ***265***
Belmont U (TN) ***284***
Bowling Green State U (OH) ***292***
Brandon U (MB, Canada) ***293***
California State Polytechnic U, Pomona (CA) ***300***
Circleville Bible Coll (OH) ***314***
DePaul U (IL) ***339***
East Central U (OK) ***347***
The Evergreen State Coll (WA) ***355***
Franklin Pierce Coll (NH) ***364***
Houston Baptist U (TX) ***382***
Howard U (DC) ***382***
Lamar U (TX) ***401***
Marshall U (WV) ***418***
Martin U (IN) ***419***
Memorial U of Newfoundland (NF, Canada) ***424***
Mesa State Coll (CO) ***426***
Northern Arizona U (AZ) ***450***
Northwest Missouri State U (MO) ***454***
Ohio U (OH) ***458***
Pittsburg State U (KS) ***470***
Purdue U Calumet (IN) ***475***
St. Cloud State U (MN) ***488***
Tarleton State U (TX) ***522***
Texas A&M U–Commerce (TX) ***525***
Texas Southern U (TX) ***526***
Université de Sherbrooke (QC, Canada) ***536***
Université Laval (QC, Canada) ***536***
The U of British Columbia (BC, Canada) ***540***
U of Central Oklahoma (OK) ***542***
U of Hawaii at Manoa (HI) ***546***
U of New Brunswick Fredericton (NB, Canada) ***558***
U of North Texas (TX) ***562***
U of Toronto (ON, Canada) ***581***
U of Windsor (ON, Canada) ***584***
U of Wisconsin–Superior (WI) ***586***
Valdosta State U (GA) ***588***
Wayne State Coll (NE) ***596***
Western Washington U (WA) ***600***
Westfield State Coll (MA) ***600***

COURT REPORTING

Overview: Students learn the skills and duties of court reporters, including the recording and transcription of testimony, judicial orders, legal opinions, and other legal proceedings. *Related majors:* word processing, law and legal studies. *Potential careers:* legal secretary, court reporter. *Salary potential:* $30k-$40k.

Central Michigan U (MI) ***310***
Johnson & Wales U (RI) ***393***
Metropolitan Coll, Tulsa (OK) ***427***
Northwood U, Texas Campus (TX) ***454***
U of Mississippi (MS) ***555***

CRAFT/FOLK ART

Overview: Students study the aesthetics and techniques for designing and fashioning handicraft and folk art objects, such as ceramics, textiles, or metal arts. *Related majors:* art history, ceramics arts, fiber, textile and weaving arts, metal and jewelry arts. *Potential careers:* professional artist (weaver, potter, jewelry designer), gallery owner. *Salary potential:* $10k-$25k.

Bowling Green State U (OH) ***292***
Bridgewater State Coll (MA) ***294***
The Cleveland Inst of Art (OH) ***317***
Kent State U (OH) ***397***
Kutztown U of Pennsylvania (PA) ***399***
Oregon Coll of Art & Craft (OR) ***461***
Rochester Inst of Technology (NY) ***482***
U of Illinois at Urbana–Champaign (IL) ***548***
The U of the Arts (PA) ***579***
Virginia Commonwealth U (VA) ***590***

CREATIVE WRITING

Overview: Students learn the techniques of original composition in various literary forms such as short story, poetry, and novel. *Related majors:* English composition, journalism, English literature. *Potential careers:* writer, editor, journalist, copywriter, book or magazine publishing professional. *Salary potential:* $23k-$32k.

Agnes Scott Coll (GA) ***261***
Albertson Coll of Idaho (ID) ***262***
Alderson-Broaddus Coll (WV) ***263***
Anderson Coll (SC) ***268***
Antioch Coll (OH) ***269***
Arkansas Tech U (AR) ***272***
Ashland U (OH) ***274***
Augustana Coll (IL) ***276***
Bard Coll (NY) ***281***
Beloit Coll (WI) ***285***
Bennington Coll (VT) ***286***
Baruch Coll of the City U of NY (NY) ***286***
Bethel Coll (MN) ***288***
Bloomfield Coll (NJ) ***290***
Bowie State U (MD) ***292***
Bowling Green State U (OH) ***292***
Briar Cliff U (IA) ***294***
Bridgewater State Coll (MA) ***294***
Brooklyn Coll of the City U of NY (NY) ***295***
Brown U (RI) ***296***
California State U, Hayward (CA) ***301***
California State U, Long Beach (CA) ***301***
California State U, Northridge (CA) ***301***
California State U, San Bernardino (CA) ***302***
Cardinal Stritch U (WI) ***305***
Carlow Coll (PA) ***305***
Carnegie Mellon U (PA) ***305***
Carroll Coll (WI) ***306***
Carson-Newman Coll (TN) ***306***
Central Michigan U (MI) ***310***
Chapman U (CA) ***311***
Chester Coll of New England (NH) ***312***
City Coll of the City U of NY (NY) ***314***
Coll of St. Catherine (MN) ***321***
Coll of Santa Fe (NM) ***323***
The Colorado Coll (CO) ***325***
Colorado State U (CO) ***325***
Columbia Coll (SC) ***327***
Columbia Coll Chicago (IL) ***327***
Concordia Coll (MN) ***329***
Concordia U (QC, Canada) ***331***
Cornell U (NY) ***333***
Dartmouth Coll (NH) ***337***
Davis & Elkins Coll (WV) ***338***
Denison U (OH) ***339***
DePaul U (IL) ***339***
Dominican U of California (CA) ***345***
Eastern U (PA) ***349***
Eastern Washington U (WA) ***349***
Eckerd Coll (FL) ***350***
Emerson Coll (MA) ***353***
Emory & Henry Coll (VA) ***353***
Emory U (GA) ***354***
Eugene Lang Coll, New School U (NY) ***355***
The Evergreen State Coll (WA) ***355***
Florida State U (FL) ***361***
Fordham U (NY) ***362***
Franklin Pierce Coll (NH) ***364***
Geneva Coll (PA) ***366***
Goddard Coll (VT) ***369***
Grand Valley State U (MI) ***371***
Green Mountain Coll (VT) ***372***
Hamilton Coll (NY) ***374***
Hampshire Coll (MA) ***375***
Harvard U (MA) ***376***
Hastings Coll (NE) ***377***
High Point U (NC) ***379***
Hollins U (VA) ***380***
Houghton Coll (NY) ***381***
Huntingdon Coll (AL) ***383***
Indiana Wesleyan U (IN) ***387***
Ithaca Coll (NY) ***390***
Johns Hopkins U (MD) ***392***
Johnson State Coll (VT) ***394***
Kenyon Coll (OH) ***398***
King Coll (TN) ***398***
Knox Coll (IL) ***399***
Lakeland Coll (WI) ***401***
La Salle U (PA) ***402***
Lehman Coll of the City U of NY (NY) ***404***
Le Moyne Coll (NY) ***404***
Linfield Coll (OR) ***408***
Long Island U, Southampton Coll (NY) ***409***
Long Island U, Southampton Coll, Friends World Program (NY) ***409***
Loras Coll (IA) ***410***
Loyola Coll in Maryland (MD) ***411***
Loyola U New Orleans (LA) ***411***
Lycoming Coll (PA) ***412***
Lynchburg Coll (VA) ***413***
Malaspina U-Coll (BC, Canada) ***415***
Marlboro Coll (VT) ***418***
Marquette U (WI) ***418***
Marymount Coll of Fordham U (NY) ***419***
Massachusetts Coll of Liberal Arts (MA) ***421***
McMurry U (TX) ***423***
Mercyhurst Coll (PA) ***425***
Methodist Coll (NC) ***427***
Miami U (OH) ***428***
Millikin U (IL) ***430***
Mills Coll (CA) ***431***
Minnesota State U, Mankato (MN) ***431***
Montclair State U (NJ) ***435***
Mount Saint Mary's Coll and Seminary (MD) ***439***
Naropa U (CO) ***441***
Nazareth Coll of Rochester (NY) ***443***
North Carolina State U (NC) ***449***
Northern Michigan U (MI) ***451***
Northland Coll (WI) ***452***
Northwestern Coll (MN) ***453***
Oberlin Coll (OH) ***456***
Ohio Northern U (OH) ***457***
The Ohio State U (OH) ***457***
Ohio U (OH) ***458***
Ohio Wesleyan U (OH) ***459***
Oklahoma Christian U (OK) ***459***
Pacific U (OR) ***464***
Pine Manor Coll (MA) ***470***
Pratt Inst (NY) ***473***
Purchase Coll, State U of NY (NY) ***475***
Randolph-Macon Woman's Coll (VA) ***477***
Rockhurst U (MO) ***482***
Roger Williams U (RI) ***483***
St. Andrews Presbyterian Coll (NC) ***487***
St. Cloud State U (MN) ***488***
St. Edward's U (TX) ***488***
Saint Joseph's Coll (IN) ***490***
St. Lawrence U (NY) ***491***
Saint Leo U (FL) ***492***
Saint Mary's Coll (IN) ***493***
San Diego State U (CA) ***498***
San Francisco State U (CA) ***498***
Sarah Lawrence Coll (NY) ***499***
Seattle U (WA) ***501***
Seton Hill U (PA) ***502***
Simon's Rock Coll of Bard (MA) ***505***
Southern Connecticut State U (CT) ***509***
Southern Methodist U (TX) ***510***
Southern Vermont Coll (VT) ***511***
Southwest State U (MN) ***513***
State U of NY at New Paltz (NY) ***515***
State U of NY at Oswego (NY) ***515***
State U of NY Coll at Brockport (NY) ***515***
Stephens Coll (MO) ***519***
Susquehanna U (PA) ***521***
Sweet Briar Coll (VA) ***521***
Taylor U (IN) ***523***
Trinity Coll (CT) ***530***
The U of Arizona (AZ) ***538***
The U of British Columbia (BC, Canada) ***540***
U of Calif, Riverside (CA) ***541***
U of Calif, San Diego (CA) ***541***
U of Calif, Santa Cruz (CA) ***542***
U of Charleston (WV) ***542***
U of Chicago (IL) ***542***
U of Denver (CO) ***544***
U of Evansville (IN) ***545***
The U of Findlay (OH) ***545***
U of Houston (TX) ***547***
The U of Iowa (IA) ***548***
U of Maine at Farmington (ME) ***550***
U of Miami (FL) ***553***
U of Michigan (MI) ***554***
The U of Montana–Missoula (MT) ***556***
U of Nebraska at Omaha (NE) ***557***
U of New Mexico (NM) ***559***
The U of North Carolina at Wilmington (NC) ***561***
U of Pittsburgh (PA) ***569***
U of Pittsburgh at Bradford (PA) ***569***
U of Pittsburgh at Greensburg (PA) ***570***
U of Pittsburgh at Johnstown (PA) ***570***
U of Puget Sound (WA) ***571***
U of Redlands (CA) ***572***
U of St. Thomas (MN) ***573***
The U of South Dakota (SD) ***575***
U of Southern California (CA) ***576***
The U of Tampa (FL) ***577***
The U of Tennessee at Chattanooga (TN) ***577***
The U of Texas at El Paso (TX) ***578***
U of Victoria (BC, Canada) ***582***
U of Washington (WA) ***583***
U of Windsor (ON, Canada) ***584***
U of Wisconsin–Parkside (WI) ***585***
Ursinus Coll (PA) ***587***
Warren Wilson Coll (NC) ***594***
Washington U in St. Louis (MO) ***595***
Wayne State Coll (NE) ***596***

Webster U (MO) ***597***
Wells Coll (NY) ***597***
Western Michigan U (MI) ***599***
Western Washington U (WA) ***600***
Westminster Coll (MO) ***601***
Westminster Coll (PA) ***601***
West Virginia Wesleyan Coll (WV) ***603***
Wittenberg U (OH) ***608***
York U (ON, Canada) ***611***

CRIMINAL JUSTICE/ CORRECTIONS RELATED

Information can be found under this major's main heading.

Averett U (VA) ***278***
Chadron State Coll (NE) ***311***
Mount Mary Coll (WI) ***438***
The U of Alabama at Birmingham (AL) ***537***
U of Alaska Fairbanks (AK) ***538***
U of Phoenix–Southern Colorado Campus (CO) ***568***

CRIMINAL JUSTICE/LAW ENFORCEMENT ADMINISTRATION

Overview: This major teaches students the theories and effective management practices of criminal justice agencies. *Related majors:* public administration, criminology, office supervision/ management, law enforcement/police science. *Potential careers:* police officer, police department administrator, protective services executive. *Salary potential:* $25k-$35k.

Abilene Christian U (TX) ***260***
Adrian Coll (MI) ***260***
Alabama State U (AL) ***261***
Albertus Magnus Coll (CT) ***262***
Alvernia Coll (PA) ***265***
American International Coll (MA) ***267***
Anderson U (IN) ***268***
Anna Maria Coll (MA) ***269***
Appalachian State U (NC) ***270***
Arizona State U West (AZ) ***272***
Armstrong Atlantic State U (GA) ***273***
Ashland U (OH) ***274***
Athens State U (AL) ***275***
Aurora U (IL) ***277***
Averett U (VA) ***278***
Baldwin-Wallace Coll (OH) ***280***
Ball State U (IN) ***280***
Barber-Scotia Coll (NC) ***281***
Bay Path Coll (MA) ***283***
Becker Coll (MA) ***283***
Bellevue U (NE) ***284***
Bemidji State U (MN) ***285***
Benedict Coll (SC) ***285***
Benedictine Coll (KS) ***285***
Bethune-Cookman Coll (FL) ***289***
Blackburn Coll (IL) ***290***
Bloomfield Coll (NJ) ***290***
Bluefield Coll (VA) ***291***
Bluffton Coll (OH) ***291***
Bowie State U (MD) ***292***
Bradley U (IL) ***293***
Briar Cliff U (IA) ***294***
Buena Vista U (IA) ***297***
California Lutheran U (CA) ***299***
California State U, Bakersfield (CA) ***300***
California State U, Chico (CA) ***300***
California State U, Dominguez Hills (CA) ***300***
California State U, Fullerton (CA) ***301***
California State U, Hayward (CA) ***301***
California State U, Long Beach (CA) ***301***
California State U, Sacramento (CA) ***301***
California State U, San Bernardino (CA) ***302***
California State U, Stanislaus (CA) ***302***
Calumet Coll of Saint Joseph (IN) ***302***
Calvin Coll (MI) ***303***
Cameron U (OK) ***303***
Campbellsville U (KY) ***303***
Campbell U (NC) ***303***
Canisius Coll (NY) ***304***
Carleton U (ON, Canada) ***305***
Carroll Coll (WI) ***306***
Carthage Coll (WI) ***306***
Castleton State Coll (VT) ***307***
Cedarville U (OH) ***308***
Central Missouri State U (MO) ***310***
Central Washington U (WA) ***310***
Chaminade U of Honolulu (HI) ***311***
Champlain Coll (VT) ***311***
Chapman U (CA) ***311***
Charleston Southern U (SC) ***311***
Chestnut Hill Coll (PA) ***312***
Christopher Newport U (VA) ***313***
Citadel, The Military Coll of South Carolina (SC) ***314***
Clark Atlanta U (GA) ***315***
Coker Coll (SC) ***318***
The Coll of New Jersey (NJ) ***320***
Coll of the Ozarks (MO) ***323***
Columbia Coll (MO) ***326***
Columbus State U (GA) ***328***
Concordia U (MI) ***330***
Concordia U Wisconsin (WI) ***331***
Culver-Stockton Coll (MO) ***334***
Cumberland U (TN) ***335***
Curry Coll (MA) ***335***
Dakota Wesleyan U (SD) ***336***
Dallas Baptist U (TX) ***336***
Defiance Coll (OH) ***338***
Delaware State U (DE) ***338***
Delaware Valley Coll (PA) ***339***
DeSales U (PA) ***340***
Dordt Coll (IA) ***345***
East Central U (OK) ***347***
Eastern Kentucky U (KY) ***348***
Eastern Michigan U (MI) ***348***
Eastern Washington U (WA) ***349***
East Tennessee State U (TN) ***349***
Edgewood Coll (WI) ***351***
Elizabeth City State U (NC) ***351***
Elmira Coll (NY) ***351***
Evangel U (MO) ***355***
Faulkner U (AL) ***357***
Fayetteville State U (NC) ***357***
Ferris State U (MI) ***358***
Fitchburg State Coll (MA) ***358***
Florida A&M U (FL) ***359***
Florida Metropolitan U-Tampa Coll, Brandon (FL) ***360***
Florida Metropolitan U-Melbourne (FL) ***360***
Fordham U (NY) ***362***
Fort Valley State U (GA) ***362***
Franklin Pierce Coll (NH) ***364***
Gardner-Webb U (NC) ***365***
The George Washington U (DC) ***367***
Georgia Coll & State U (GA) ***367***
Gonzaga U (WA) ***369***
Governors State U (IL) ***370***
Grace Coll (IN) ***370***
Graceland U (IA) ***371***
Grambling State U (LA) ***371***
Grand Canyon U (AZ) ***371***
Grand Valley State U (MI) ***371***
Grand View Coll (IA) ***372***
Gustavus Adolphus Coll (MN) ***374***
Hamline U (MN) ***374***
Hampton U (VA) ***375***
Hannibal-LaGrange Coll (MO) ***375***
Harris-Stowe State Coll (MO) ***376***
Hawai'i Pacific U (HI) ***377***
Hilbert Coll (NY) ***379***
Holy Family U (PA) ***380***
Indiana U Northwest (IN) ***386***
Indiana U South Bend (IN) ***387***
Inter Amer U of PR, Barranquitas Campus (PR) ***388***
Inter American U of PR, Guayama Campus (PR) ***388***
International Coll (FL) ***389***
Iona Coll (NY) ***390***
Iowa Wesleyan Coll (IA) ***390***
Jackson State U (MS) ***390***
Jacksonville State U (AL) ***390***
John Jay Coll of Criminal Justice, the City U of NY (NY) ***392***
Johnson & Wales U (RI) ***393***
Johnson C. Smith U (NC) ***394***
Kean U (NJ) ***396***
Keuka Coll (NY) ***398***
Lamar U (TX) ***401***
Lambuth U (TN) ***401***
Lane Coll (TN) ***402***
Langston U (OK) ***402***
Lees-McRae Coll (NC) ***404***
Lewis-Clark State Coll (ID) ***406***
Lewis U (IL) ***406***
Lincoln U (PA) ***407***
Lindenwood U (MO) ***407***
Lindsey Wilson Coll (KY) ***407***
Lock Haven U of Pennsylvania (PA) ***408***
Long Island U, C.W. Post Campus (NY) ***409***
Longwood U (VA) ***409***
Louisiana Coll (LA) ***410***
Lourdes Coll (OH) ***411***
Lycoming Coll (PA) ***412***
MacMurray Coll (IL) ***414***
Madonna U (MI) ***414***
Mansfield U of Pennsylvania (PA) ***416***
Marian Coll of Fond du Lac (WI) ***417***
Marist Coll (NY) ***417***
Mars Hill Coll (NC) ***418***
Martin U (IN) ***419***
McKendree Coll (IL) ***423***
McMurry U (TX) ***423***
Mercer U (GA) ***425***
Mercy Coll (NY) ***425***
Mercyhurst Coll (PA) ***425***
Methodist Coll (NC) ***427***
Metropolitan State Coll of Denver (CO) ***427***
MidAmerica Nazarene U (KS) ***428***
Middle Tennessee State U (TN) ***429***
Midland Lutheran Coll (NE) ***429***
Midwestern State U (TX) ***430***
Mississippi Coll (MS) ***432***
Mississippi Valley State U (MS) ***432***
Missouri Southern State Coll (MO) ***433***
Missouri Valley Coll (MO) ***433***
Mitchell Coll (CT) ***433***
Moravian Coll (PA) ***436***
Morris Coll (SC) ***437***
Mount Ida Coll (MA) ***438***
Mount Mercy Coll (IA) ***438***
Mount Olive Coll (NC) ***439***
Mount Vernon Nazarene U (OH) ***440***
National U (CA) ***442***
Newbury Coll (MA) ***444***
New England Coll (NH) ***444***
New Mexico State U (NM) ***446***
New York Inst of Technology (NY) ***447***
Niagara U (NY) ***447***
North Carolina Central U (NC) ***448***
North Carolina State U (NC) ***449***
North Carolina Wesleyan Coll (NC) ***449***
North Dakota State U (ND) ***449***
Northeastern State U (OK) ***450***
Northern Arizona U (AZ) ***450***
Northern Kentucky U (KY) ***451***
Northern Michigan U (MI) ***451***
North Georgia Coll & State U (GA) ***451***
Norwich U (VT) ***455***
Oakland City U (IN) ***456***
Oakland U (MI) ***456***
Ohio Dominican U (OH) ***457***
Ohio Northern U (OH) ***457***
Ohio U (OH) ***458***
Ohio U–Chillicothe (OH) ***458***
Ohio U–Lancaster (OH) ***458***
Ohio U–Zanesville (OH) ***458***
Oklahoma City U (OK) ***460***
Olivet Nazarene U (IL) ***461***
Pace U (NY) ***463***
Park U (MO) ***465***
Paul Quinn Coll (TX) ***466***
Penn State U Univ Park Campus (PA) ***468***
Peru State Coll (NE) ***469***
Pfeiffer U (NC) ***469***
Pittsburg State U (KS) ***470***
Pontifical Catholic U of Puerto Rico (PR) ***472***
Portland State U (OR) ***472***
Purdue U Calumet (IN) ***475***
Quincy U (IL) ***476***
Radford U (VA) ***476***
Regis U (CO) ***478***
Roberts Wesleyan Coll (NY) ***481***
Rochester Inst of Technology (NY) ***482***
Rockford Coll (IL) ***482***
Roger Williams U (RI) ***483***
Russell Sage Coll (NY) ***484***
Rutgers, The State U of New Jersey, New Brunswick (NJ) ***485***
Ryerson U (ON, Canada) ***485***
Sacred Heart U (CT) ***486***
Sage Coll of Albany (NY) ***486***
St. Cloud State U (MN) ***488***
St. Edward's U (TX) ***488***
Saint Francis U (PA) ***488***
St. John's U (NY) ***490***
Saint Joseph's U (PA) ***491***
Saint Martin's Coll (WA) ***493***
Saint Mary's U of Minnesota (MN) ***494***
St. Mary's U of San Antonio (TX) ***494***
St. Thomas Aquinas Coll (NY) ***495***
St. Thomas U (FL) ***496***
Salem International U (WV) ***496***
Salem State Coll (MA) ***497***
Salve Regina U (RI) ***497***
Samford U (AL) ***497***
San Diego State U (CA) ***498***
San Francisco State U (CA) ***498***
San Jose State U (CA) ***499***
Savannah State U (GA) ***499***
Seattle U (WA) ***501***
Shenandoah U (VA) ***503***
Siena Heights U (MI) ***504***
Simpson Coll (IA) ***505***
Si Tanka Huron U (SD) ***505***
Sonoma State U (CA) ***506***
South Carolina State U (SC) ***506***
Southeast Missouri State U (MO) ***508***
Southern Illinois U Carbondale (IL) ***509***
Southern Vermont Coll (VT) ***511***
Southwest Baptist U (MO) ***512***
Southwestern Oklahoma State U (OK) ***512***
State U of NY at Albany (NY) ***514***
State U of NY at Oswego (NY) ***515***
State U of NY Coll at Brockport (NY) ***515***
State U of NY Coll at Buffalo (NY) ***516***
State U of NY Coll at Fredonia (NY) ***516***
State U of West Georgia (GA) ***518***
Suffolk U (MA) ***520***
Sul Ross State U (TX) ***521***
Tarleton State U (TX) ***522***
Taylor U, Fort Wayne Campus (IN) ***523***
Teikyo Post U (CT) ***523***
Temple U (PA) ***523***
Tennessee State U (TN) ***523***
Texas A&M U–Commerce (TX) ***525***
Texas A&M U–Corpus Christi (TX) ***525***
Texas Southern U (TX) ***526***
Thomas Coll (ME) ***527***
Thomas Edison State Coll (NJ) ***527***
Thomas More Coll (KY) ***528***
Thomas U (GA) ***528***
Tiffin U (OH) ***528***
Tri-State U (IN) ***532***
Truman State U (MO) ***532***
Union Coll (KY) ***533***
Union Inst & U (OH) ***534***
The U of Akron (OH) ***537***
U of Alaska Anchorage (AK) ***538***
U of Alberta (AB, Canada) ***538***
The U of Arizona (AZ) ***538***
U of Arkansas at Little Rock (AR) ***539***
U of Baltimore (MD) ***539***
U of Central Oklahoma (OK) ***542***
U of Cincinnati (OH) ***543***
U of Dayton (OH) ***544***
U of Delaware (DE) ***544***
U of Dubuque (IA) ***545***
U of Evansville (IN) ***545***
The U of Findlay (OH) ***545***
U of Guelph (ON, Canada) ***546***
U of Hartford (CT) ***546***
U of Hawaii–West Oahu (HI) ***546***
U of Illinois at Springfield (IL) ***548***
U of Indianapolis (IN) ***548***
U of Louisville (KY) ***550***
The U of Maine at Augusta (ME) ***550***
U of Maine at Presque Isle (ME) ***551***
U of Mary Hardin-Baylor (TX) ***551***
U of Maryland Eastern Shore (MD) ***552***
U of Maryland University Coll (MD) ***552***
U of Massachusetts Lowell (MA) ***553***
The U of Memphis (TN) ***553***
U of Michigan–Flint (MI) ***554***
U of Missouri–Kansas City (MO) ***555***
U of Missouri–St. Louis (MO) ***556***
U of Nebraska at Omaha (NE) ***557***
U of Nevada, Las Vegas (NV) ***558***
U of New Haven (CT) ***559***
U of North Alabama (AL) ***559***
The U of North Carolina at Pembroke (NC) ***560***
U of North Texas (TX) ***562***
U of Ottawa (ON, Canada) ***563***
U of Phoenix–Colorado Campus (CO) ***563***
U of Phoenix–New Mexico Campus (NM) ***565***
U of Phoenix–Phoenix Campus (AZ) ***567***
U of Phoenix–Tulsa Campus (OK) ***568***
U of Pittsburgh at Bradford (PA) ***569***
U of Pittsburgh at Greensburg (PA) ***570***
U of Regina (SK, Canada) ***572***
U of Richmond (VA) ***572***

CRIMINAL JUSTICE/LAW ENFORCEMENT ADMINISTRATION (continued)

U of South Alabama (AL) ***575***
U of South Carolina (SC) ***575***
U of South Carolina Spartanburg (SC) ***575***
The U of South Dakota (SD) ***575***
The U of Tennessee at Chattanooga (TN) ***577***
The U of Tennessee at Martin (TN) ***577***
The U of Texas at Brownsville (TX) ***578***
The U of Texas at El Paso (TX) ***578***
The U of Texas at San Antonio (TX) ***578***
The U of Texas at Tyler (TX) ***579***
The U of Texas–Pan American (TX) ***579***
U of the District of Columbia (DC) ***580***
U of Washington (WA) ***583***
U of Wisconsin–Milwaukee (WI) ***585***
U of Wisconsin–Oshkosh (WI) ***585***
U of Wisconsin–Parkside (WI) ***585***
U of Wisconsin–Platteville (WI) ***585***
U of Wyoming (WY) ***586***
U System Coll for Lifelong Learning (NH) ***586***
Urbana U (OH) ***587***
Utica Coll (NY) ***588***
Valdosta State U (GA) ***588***
Villanova U (PA) ***590***
Virginia Commonwealth U (VA) ***590***
Viterbo U (WI) ***591***
Voorhees Coll (SC) ***592***
Washington State U (WA) ***595***
Waynesburg Coll (PA) ***595***
Wayne State Coll (NE) ***596***
West Chester U of Pennsylvania (PA) ***598***
Western Illinois U (IL) ***599***
Western International U (AZ) ***599***
Western New England Coll (MA) ***600***
Western New Mexico U (NM) ***600***
Western Oregon U (OR) ***600***
Westfield State Coll (MA) ***600***
West Liberty State Coll (WV) ***601***
Westminster Coll (PA) ***601***
West Texas A&M U (TX) ***602***
West Virginia State Coll (WV) ***602***
Wheeling Jesuit U (WV) ***603***
Widener U (PA) ***604***
Wilmington Coll (DE) ***607***
Wilmington Coll (OH) ***607***
Winona State U (MN) ***608***
York Coll of Pennsylvania (PA) ***610***
Youngstown State U (OH) ***611***

CRIMINAL JUSTICE STUDIES

Overview: Students study the agencies, organization, and processes of the criminal justice system, along with its legal and public policy contexts. *Related majors:* criminal justice/law enforcement administration, police science, criminology, public policy analysis, law and legal studies. *Potential careers:* lawyer, criminologist, law enforcement administrator, professor, sociologist. *Salary potential:* $25k-$35k.

Albany State U (GA) ***262***
Alcorn State U (MS) ***263***
Alfred U (NY) ***263***
American Public U System (WV) ***267***
American U (DC) ***267***
Andrew Jackson U (AL) ***269***
Angelo State U (TX) ***269***
Appalachian State U (NC) ***270***
Arizona State U (AZ) ***271***
Auburn U Montgomery (AL) ***276***
Augsburg Coll (MN) ***276***
Augusta State U (GA) ***277***
Aurora U (IL) ***277***
Avila U (MO) ***278***
Barton Coll (NC) ***282***
Bellarmine U (KY) ***284***
Bethany Coll (KS) ***287***
Bethel Coll (IN) ***288***
Bethel Coll (KS) ***288***
Bloomsburg U of Pennsylvania (PA) ***290***
Bluefield State Coll (WV) ***291***
Bridgewater State Coll (MA) ***294***
Butler U (IN) ***297***
Caldwell Coll (NJ) ***298***
California Baptist U (CA) ***298***
Cazenovia Coll (NY) ***308***
Central Methodist Coll (MO) ***309***
Champlain Coll (VT) ***311***
Chowan Coll (NC) ***312***
Coll of Saint Elizabeth (NJ) ***321***
Coll of the Southwest (NM) ***324***
Colorado State U (CO) ***325***
Colorado Tech U Sioux Falls Campus (SD) ***326***
Columbia Southern U (AL) ***327***
Concordia Coll (MN) ***329***
Delta State U (MS) ***339***
DeSales U (PA) ***340***
East Carolina U (NC) ***347***
Eastern New Mexico U (NM) ***349***
Edinboro U of Pennsylvania (PA) ***351***
Elizabethtown Coll (PA) ***351***
Endicott Coll (MA) ***354***
Fairleigh Dickinson U, Teaneck-Metro Campus (NJ) ***356***
Ferrum Coll (VA) ***358***
Florida Atlantic U (FL) ***359***
Florida Gulf Coast U (FL) ***359***
Florida International U (FL) ***360***
Florida Metropolitan U–Jacksonville Campus (FL) ***360***
Florida Metropolitan U-Orlando Coll, North (FL) ***361***
Florida Metropolitan U-Tampa Coll, Pinellas (FL) ***361***
Florida Metropolitan U-Orlando Coll, South (FL) ***361***
Florida Southern Coll (FL) ***361***
Fort Hays State U (KS) ***362***
The Franciscan U (IA) ***363***
Frostburg State U (MD) ***365***
Gannon U (PA) ***365***
Georgia Southern U (GA) ***367***
Georgia State U (GA) ***368***
Guilford Coll (NC) ***373***
Harding U (AR) ***375***
High Point U (NC) ***379***
Illinois State U (IL) ***384***
Indiana U Bloomington (IN) ***385***
Indiana U Kokomo (IN) ***386***
Indiana U–Purdue U Fort Wayne (IN) ***386***
Indiana U–Purdue U Indianapolis (IN) ***387***
Indiana Wesleyan U (IN) ***387***
Inter American U of PR, Aguadilla Campus (PR) ***388***
International Coll (FL) ***389***
Jackson State U (MS) ***390***
Jamestown Coll (ND) ***391***
Judson Coll (AL) ***395***
Judson Coll (IL) ***395***
Juniata Coll (PA) ***395***
Kendall Coll (IL) ***396***
Kent State U (OH) ***397***
Kentucky State U (KY) ***397***
Kentucky Wesleyan Coll (KY) ***397***
King's Coll (PA) ***398***
Kutztown U of Pennsylvania (PA) ***399***
La Roche Coll (PA) ***402***
La Salle U (PA) ***402***
Lasell Coll (MA) ***402***
Limestone Coll (SC) ***406***
Long Island U, Brentwood Campus (NY) ***408***
Loras Coll (IA) ***410***
Louisiana State U in Shreveport (LA) ***410***
Loyola U Chicago (IL) ***411***
Loyola U New Orleans (LA) ***411***
Marshall U (WV) ***418***
McNeese State U (LA) ***423***
Medaille Coll (NY) ***424***
Metropolitan State U (MN) ***427***
Michigan State U (MI) ***428***
Minnesota State U, Moorhead (MN) ***432***
Minot State U (ND) ***432***
Missouri Western State Coll (MO) ***433***
Molloy Coll (NY) ***433***
Monmouth U (NJ) ***434***
Mountain State U (WV) ***437***
Mount Aloysius Coll (PA) ***437***
Mount Marty Coll (SD) ***438***
Mount Saint Mary Coll (NY) ***439***
Murray State U (KY) ***440***
National U (CA) ***442***
New Jersey City U (NJ) ***445***
New Mexico Highlands U (NM) ***446***
Northeastern Illinois U (IL) ***450***
Northeastern U (MA) ***450***
Northern Kentucky U (KY) ***451***
Northwestern Coll (MN) ***453***
Northwestern State U of Louisiana (LA) ***453***
The Ohio State U (OH) ***457***
Ohio U (OH) ***458***
Olivet Coll (MI) ***461***
Penn State U Abington Coll (PA) ***467***
Penn State U Altoona Coll (PA) ***467***
Penn State U Harrisburg Campus of the Capital Coll (PA) ***468***
Penn State U Schuylkill Campus of the Capital Coll (PA) ***468***
Penn State U Univ Park Campus (PA) ***468***
Pikeville Coll (KY) ***470***
Pittsburg State U (KS) ***470***
Point Park Coll (PA) ***471***
Prairie View A&M U (TX) ***473***
Prescott Coll (AZ) ***474***
Quinnipiac U (CT) ***476***
Rhode Island Coll (RI) ***479***
Roanoke Coll (VA) ***481***
Rochester Inst of Technology (NY) ***482***
Roosevelt U (IL) ***483***
Rutgers, The State U of New Jersey, Camden (NJ) ***485***
Rutgers, The State U of New Jersey, Newark (NJ) ***485***
Saginaw Valley State U (MI) ***486***
St. Ambrose U (IA) ***486***
Saint Anselm Coll (NH) ***487***
Saint Joseph's Coll (IN) ***490***
Saint Joseph's Coll of Maine (ME) ***491***
Saint Louis U (MO) ***492***
Saint Peter's Coll (NJ) ***495***
Saint Xavier U (IL) ***496***
Sam Houston State U (TX) ***497***
Seton Hall U (NJ) ***502***
Seton Hill U (PA) ***502***
Shaw U (NC) ***502***
Shippensburg U of Pennsylvania (PA) ***503***
Southeastern Louisiana U (LA) ***508***
Southeastern Oklahoma State U (OK) ***508***
Southeast Missouri State U (MO) ***508***
Southern Arkansas U–Magnolia (AR) ***509***
Southern Illinois U Edwardsville (IL) ***509***
Southern Nazarene U (OK) ***510***
Southern U and A&M Coll (LA) ***511***
Southwestern Coll (KS) ***512***
Southwest Missouri State U (MO) ***513***
Southwest State U (MN) ***513***
Southwest Texas State U (TX) ***513***
State U of NY Coll at Potsdam (NY) ***517***
Stephen F. Austin State U (TX) ***518***
Stonehill Coll (MA) ***520***
Taylor U, Fort Wayne Campus (IN) ***523***
Texas A&M International U (TX) ***524***
Texas A&M U–Texarkana (TX) ***525***
Texas Christian U (TX) ***526***
Texas Wesleyan U (TX) ***526***
Texas Woman's U (TX) ***527***
Thiel Coll (PA) ***527***
Troy State U Dothan (AL) ***532***
The U of Akron (OH) ***537***
The U of Alabama (AL) ***537***
U of Arkansas (AR) ***539***
U of Arkansas at Monticello (AR) ***539***
U of Central Florida (FL) ***542***
U of Central Oklahoma (OK) ***542***
U of Florida (FL) ***545***
U of Georgia (GA) ***545***
U of Houston–Downtown (TX) ***547***
U of Idaho (ID) ***547***
U of Illinois at Chicago (IL) ***547***
U of Louisiana at Lafayette (LA) ***550***
U of Massachusetts Boston (MA) ***553***
U of Nebraska at Kearney (NE) ***557***
U of Nebraska at Omaha (NE) ***557***
The U of North Carolina at Charlotte (NC) ***560***
The U of North Carolina at Wilmington (NC) ***561***
U of North Dakota (ND) ***561***
U of North Florida (FL) ***561***
U of Portland (OR) ***570***
U of Regina (SK, Canada) ***572***
The U of Scranton (PA) ***574***
U of Southern Mississippi (MS) ***576***
U of South Florida (FL) ***576***
The U of Texas at Arlington (TX) ***577***
U of the Sacred Heart (PR) ***580***
U of Toledo (OH) ***581***
The U of Virginia's Coll at Wise (VA) ***582***
U of West Florida (FL) ***583***
U of Windsor (ON, Canada) ***584***
U of Wisconsin–Eau Claire (WI) ***584***
U of Wisconsin–Superior (WI) ***586***
Virginia State U (VA) ***591***
Virginia Wesleyan Coll (VA) ***591***
Wayland Baptist U (TX) ***595***
Wayne State U (MI) ***596***
Weber State U (UT) ***596***
Western Carolina U (NC) ***598***
Western Michigan U (MI) ***599***
Wichita State U (KS) ***604***
Xavier U (OH) ***610***
Youngstown State U (OH) ***611***

CRIMINOLOGY

Overview: This major examines crime and criminal behavior from a sociopathological perspective, as well as the social institutions that have developed to respond to crime. *Related majors:* clinical psychology, criminal justice studies, philosophy, sociology, law and legal studies. *Potential careers:* criminology, police or FBI detective, researcher. *Salary potential:* $25-$30k.

Adams State Coll (CO) ***260***
Albright Coll (PA) ***263***
Arkansas State U (AR) ***272***
Auburn U (AL) ***276***
Ball State U (IN) ***280***
Barry U (FL) ***282***
Bridgewater State Coll (MA) ***294***
California State U, Fresno (CA) ***301***
Capital U (OH) ***304***
Carleton U (ON, Canada) ***305***
Castleton State Coll (VT) ***307***
Centenary Coll (NJ) ***308***
Central Connecticut State U (CT) ***309***
Central Michigan U (MI) ***310***
Coll of the Ozarks (MO) ***323***
Colorado State U-Pueblo (CO) ***325***
Dominican U (IL) ***345***
Drury U (MO) ***346***
Eastern Michigan U (MI) ***348***
Florida State U (FL) ***361***
Gallaudet U (DC) ***365***
Husson Coll (ME) ***383***
Indiana State U (IN) ***385***
Indiana U of Pennsylvania (PA) ***386***
Kent State U (OH) ***397***
Le Moyne Coll (NY) ***404***
Lindenwood U (MO) ***407***
Marquette U (WI) ***418***
Marymount U (VA) ***420***
Maryville U of Saint Louis (MO) ***420***
Memorial U of Newfoundland (NF, Canada) ***424***
Mesa State Coll (CO) ***426***
Midland Lutheran Coll (NE) ***429***
New Mexico Highlands U (NM) ***446***
Niagara U (NY) ***447***
The Ohio State U (OH) ***457***
Ohio U (OH) ***458***
Old Dominion U (VA) ***460***
Plattsburgh State U of NY (NY) ***471***
Pontifical Catholic U of Puerto Rico (PR) ***472***
The Richard Stockton Coll of New Jersey (NJ) ***479***
Saint Augustine's Coll (NC) ***487***
St. Cloud State U (MN) ***488***
Saint Leo U (FL) ***492***
Saint Mary's U (NS, Canada) ***494***
St. Mary's U of San Antonio (TX) ***494***
St. Thomas U (NB, Canada) ***496***
San Jose State U (CA) ***499***
Simon Fraser U (BC, Canada) ***505***
Southern Oregon U (OR) ***510***
State U of NY Coll at Brockport (NY) ***515***
State U of NY Coll at Old Westbury (NY) ***516***
Texas A&M U–Kingsville (TX) ***525***
U of Alberta (AB, Canada) ***538***
U of Calif, Irvine (CA) ***541***
U of La Verne (CA) ***549***
U of Maryland, Coll Park (MD) ***552***
The U of Memphis (TN) ***553***
U of Miami (FL) ***553***
U of Minnesota, Duluth (MN) ***554***
U of Missouri–St. Louis (MO) ***556***
U of Nevada, Reno (NV) ***558***
U of Northern Iowa (IA) ***561***
U of Oklahoma (OK) ***562***
U of Ottawa (ON, Canada) ***563***

U of St. Thomas (MN) **573**
U of Southern Maine (ME) **576**
The U of Tampa (FL) **577**
The U of Texas at Dallas (TX) **578**
The U of Texas of the Permian Basin (TX) **579**
U of Windsor (ON, Canada) **584**
Upper Iowa U (IA) **587**
Valparaiso U (IN) **588**
Virginia Union U (VA) **591**
Western Michigan U (MI) **599**
William Penn U (IA) **606**

CROP PRODUCTION MANAGEMENT

Overview: This major teaches students how to grow and cultivate grains, fibers, fruits, nuts, vegetables, and other domesticated plant products. *Related majors:* plant science, soil sciences, agribusiness. *Potential careers:* farmer, ecologist, entomologist, researcher. *Salary potential:* $20k-$30k.

Cornell U (NY) **333**

CULINARY ARTS

Overview: Students who choose this major will learn the skills they need to cook professionally or to work in a restaurant or commercial food establishment. *Related majors:* hospitality management, hotel/motel and restaurant management. *Potential careers:* professional chef, restaurant owner, caterer, hotel or country club manager. *Salary potential:* $20k-$30k.

The Art Inst of Colorado (CO) **274**
The Culinary Inst of America (NY) **334**
Drexel U (PA) **346**
Johnson & Wales U (FL) **393**
Johnson & Wales U (RI) **393**
Kendall Coll (IL) **396**
Mercyhurst Coll (PA) **425**
Metropolitan State U (MN) **427**
Northern Michigan U (MI) **451**
Paul Smith's Coll of Arts and Sciences (NY) **466**
Pennsylvania Coll of Technology (PA) **467**
Sullivan U (KY) **521**
U of Nevada, Las Vegas (NV) **558**

CULINARY ARTS AND SERVICES RELATED

Information can be found under this major's main heading.

Newbury Coll (MA) **444**

CULTURAL STUDIES

Overview: Undergraduates who choose this major study the history, sociology, politics, culture, language, and economics of one or a number of North American peoples including African-Americans, Native Americans, Hispanic Americans, and Asian-Americans. *Related majors:* African-American studies, Native American studies, Hispanic American studies, Asian-American Studies, American history. *Potential careers:* anthropologist, journalist, teacher, translator, lawyer. *Salary potential:* $24k-$30k.

Azusa Pacific U (CA) **278**
Baltimore Hebrew U (MD) **280**
Bard Coll (NY) **281**
Bethel Coll (MN) **288**
Bridgewater Coll (VA) **294**
Briercrest Bible Coll (SK, Canada) **295**
Brigham Young U–Hawaii (HI) **295**
California State Polytechnic U, Pomona (CA) **300**
California State U, Chico (CA) **300**
California State U, Fullerton (CA) **301**
California State U, Hayward (CA) **301**
California State U, Northridge (CA) **301**
California State U, Sacramento (CA) **301**
Clark U (MA) **316**
The Coll of William and Mary (VA) **324**
Columbia International U (SC) **327**
Concordia U (QC, Canada) **331**
Cornell Coll (IA) **332**
The Evergreen State Coll (WA) **355**
Fort Lewis Coll (CO) **362**
Goddard Coll (VT) **369**
Hampshire Coll (MA) **375**
Harvard U (MA) **376**
Houghton Coll (NY) **381**
Indiana Wesleyan U (IN) **387**
Kent State U (OH) **397**
Long Island U, Southampton Coll, Friends World Program (NY) **409**
Marlboro Coll (VT) **418**
Mills Coll (CA) **431**
Minnesota State U, Mankato (MN) **431**
The Ohio State U (OH) **457**
Ohio Wesleyan U (OH) **459**
Oregon State U (OR) **462**
Penn State U Univ Park Campus (PA) **468**
Reformed Bible Coll (MI) **477**
St. Francis Xavier U (NS, Canada) **489**
Saint Mary-of-the-Woods Coll (IN) **493**
St. Olaf Coll (MN) **495**
Simon's Rock Coll of Bard (MA) **505**
Sonoma State U (CA) **506**
The U of British Columbia (BC, Canada) **540**
U of Calif, Berkeley (CA) **540**
U of Calif, Irvine (CA) **541**
U of Calif, Riverside (CA) **541**
U of Calif, San Diego (CA) **541**
U of Colorado at Boulder (CO) **543**
U of Nevada, Las Vegas (NV) **558**
U of Oregon (OR) **562**
U of Southern California (CA) **576**
The U of Tennessee (TN) **577**
The U of Texas–Pan American (TX) **579**
U of Toronto (ON, Canada) **581**
U of Virginia (VA) **582**
U of Washington (WA) **583**
U of Wisconsin–Milwaukee (WI) **585**
Washington U in St. Louis (MO) **595**
Western Washington U (WA) **600**
Yale U (CT) **610**
York U (ON, Canada) **611**

CURRICULUM AND INSTRUCTION

Overview: This major teaches individuals how to design educational curriculums to a variety of student needs. *Related majors:* education administration, educational media design, educational psychology. *Potential careers:* teacher, principal, school administrator. *Salary potential:* $22k-$28k.

Long Island U, C.W. Post Campus (NY) **409**
Ohio U (OH) **458**
Texas A&M U (TX) **524**
Texas Southern U (TX) **526**
U of Hawaii at Manoa (HI) **546**
The U of Montana–Missoula (MT) **556**
Utah State U (UT) **587**
York U (ON, Canada) **611**

CYTOTECHNOLOGY

Overview: Students learn how to detect and diagnose malignant cells that may indicate early development of cancer and other diseases and report their findings to pathologists. *Related majors:* pathology, health/medical laboratory technology, medical laboratory technician, medical cell biology. *Potential careers:* cytotechnologist, clinical laboratory technologist and technician, medical cell biologist. *Salary potential:* $37k-$43k.

Alderson-Broaddus Coll (WV) **263**
Anderson Coll (SC) **268**
Barry U (FL) **282**
Bloomfield Coll (NJ) **290**
California State U, Dominguez Hills (CA) **300**
Coll of Saint Elizabeth (NJ) **321**
The Coll of Saint Rose (NY) **322**
Eastern Kentucky U (KY) **348**
Eastern Michigan U (MI) **348**
Edgewood Coll (WI) **351**
Elmhurst Coll (IL) **351**
Felician Coll (NJ) **357**
The Franciscan U (IA) **363**
Illinois Coll (IL) **384**
Indiana U–Purdue U Indianapolis (IN) **387**
Indiana U Southeast (IN) **387**
Jewish Hospital Coll of Nursing and Allied Health (MO) **391**
Loma Linda U (CA) **408**
Long Island U, Brooklyn Campus (NY) **409**
Long Island U, C.W. Post Campus (NY) **409**
Luther Coll (IA) **412**
Marian Coll of Fond du Lac (WI) **417**
Marshall U (WV) **418**
Mayo School of Health Sciences (MN) **422**
Minnesota State U, Moorhead (MN) **432**
Monmouth U (NJ) **434**
Northern Michigan U (MI) **451**
Oakland U (MI) **456**
Roosevelt U (IL) **483**
St. John's U (NY) **490**
Saint Mary's Coll (IN) **493**
Saint Mary's U of Minnesota (MN) **494**
Salve Regina U (RI) **497**
Slippery Rock U of Pennsylvania (PA) **506**
State U of New York Upstate Medical University (NY) **518**
Stony Brook U, State University of New York (NY) **520**
Suffolk U (MA) **520**
Thiel Coll (PA) **527**
Thomas Edison State Coll (NJ) **527**
Thomas Jefferson U (PA) **527**
The U of Akron (OH) **537**
The U of Alabama at Birmingham (AL) **537**
U of Arkansas for Medical Sciences (AR) **539**
U of Connecticut (CT) **544**
U of Kansas (KS) **549**
U of Louisville (KY) **550**
U of Mississippi Medical Center (MS) **555**
U of Missouri–St. Louis (MO) **556**
U of North Dakota (ND) **561**
U of North Texas (TX) **562**
Winona State U (MN) **608**

DAIRY SCIENCE

Overview: Undergraduates of this major will learn about the production and management of dairy animals as well as the production and handling of dairy products. *Related majors:* animal science, agricultural animal health, animal breeding, food science, feed science. *Potential careers:* dairy ranch manager, inspector, veterinarian, animal geneticist, buyer. *Salary potential:* $25k-$35k.

California Polytechnic State U, San Luis Obispo (CA) **300**
Cornell U (NY) **333**
Delaware Valley Coll (PA) **339**
Eastern Kentucky U (KY) **348**
Iowa State U of Science and Technology (IA) **390**
Oregon State U (OR) **462**
South Dakota State U (SD) **507**
State U of NY Coll of A&T at Cobleskill (NY) **517**
Texas A&M U (TX) **524**
U of Alberta (AB, Canada) **538**
U of Florida (FL) **545**
U of Georgia (GA) **545**
U of New Hampshire (NH) **558**
U of Vermont (VT) **582**
U of Wisconsin–Madison (WI) **584**
U of Wisconsin–River Falls (WI) **585**
Utah State U (UT) **587**
Virginia Polytechnic Inst and State U (VA) **591**

DANCE

Overview: Students who choose this major study the theories and techniques of a number of dance disciplines including ballet, modern dance, and folk dance as well as choreography, history, and production. *Related majors:* drama/theater arts, music, design/visual communications. *Potential careers:* dance teacher, choreographer, professional dancer. *Salary potential:* $10k-$20k.

Adelphi U (NY) **260**
Alma Coll (MI) **264**
Amherst Coll (MA) **268**
Antioch Coll (OH) **269**
Arizona State U (AZ) **271**
Baldwin-Wallace Coll (OH) **280**
Ball State U (IN) **280**
Bard Coll (NY) **281**
Barnard Coll (NY) **282**
Belhaven Coll (MS) **283**
Bennington Coll (VT) **286**
Birmingham-Southern Coll (AL) **289**
Bowling Green State U (OH) **292**
Brenau U (GA) **293**
Brigham Young U (UT) **295**
Butler U (IN) **297**
California Inst of the Arts (CA) **299**
California State U, Fresno (CA) **301**
California State U, Fullerton (CA) **301**
California State U, Hayward (CA) **301**
California State U, Long Beach (CA) **301**
California State U, Northridge (CA) **301**
Cedar Crest Coll (PA) **308**
Centenary Coll of Louisiana (LA) **308**
Chapman U (CA) **311**
Coker Coll (SC) **318**
The Colorado Coll (CO) **325**
Colorado State U (CO) **325**
Columbia Coll (NY) **326**
Columbia Coll (SC) **327**
Columbia Coll Chicago (IL) **327**
Columbia U, School of General Studies (NY) **328**
Concordia U (QC, Canada) **331**
Connecticut Coll (CT) **331**
Cornell U (NY) **333**
Cornish Coll of the Arts (WA) **333**
Denison U (OH) **339**
Deree Coll(Greece) **339**
DeSales U (PA) **340**
Dickinson Coll (PA) **344**
East Carolina U (NC) **347**
Eastern Kentucky U (KY) **348**
Eastern Michigan U (MI) **348**
Eastern Washington U (WA) **349**
Emerson Coll (MA) **353**
Emory U (GA) **354**
The Evergreen State Coll (WA) **355**
Florida International U (FL) **360**
Florida State U (FL) **361**
Fordham U (NY) **362**
Frostburg State U (MD) **365**
George Mason U (VA) **366**
The George Washington U (DC) **367**
Goucher Coll (MD) **370**
Gustavus Adolphus Coll (MN) **374**
Hamilton Coll (NY) **374**
Hampshire Coll (MA) **375**
Hobart and William Smith Colls (NY) **380**
Hofstra U (NY) **380**
Hollins U (VA) **380**
Hope Coll (MI) **381**
Hunter Coll of the City U of NY (NY) **382**
Huntingdon Coll (AL) **383**
Indiana U Bloomington (IN) **385**
Ithaca Coll (NY) **390**
Jacksonville U (FL) **391**
Johnson State Coll (VT) **394**
The Juilliard School (NY) **395**
Kent State U (OH) **397**
Kenyon Coll (OH) **398**
Lake Erie Coll (OH) **400**
Lamar U (TX) **401**
La Roche Coll (PA) **402**
Lehman Coll of the City U of NY (NY) **404**
Lindenwood U (MO) **407**
Long Island U, Brooklyn Campus (NY) **409**
Long Island U, C.W. Post Campus (NY) **409**

DANCE (continued)

Long Island U, Southampton Coll, Friends World Program (NY) ***409***
Longwood U (VA) ***409***
Loyola Marymount U (CA) ***411***
Luther Coll (IA) ***412***
Manhattanville Coll (NY) ***416***
Marlboro Coll (VT) ***418***
Marygrove Coll (MI) ***419***
Marymount Manhattan Coll (NY) ***420***
Mercyhurst Coll (PA) ***425***
Meredith Coll (NC) ***426***
Middlebury Coll (VT) ***429***
Mills Coll (CA) ***431***
Montclair State U (NJ) ***435***
Mount Holyoke Coll (MA) ***438***
Muhlenberg Coll (PA) ***440***
Naropa U (CO) ***441***
New Mexico State U (NM) ***446***
New World School of the Arts (FL) ***447***
New York U (NY) ***447***
North Carolina School of the Arts (NC) ***449***
Northwestern U (IL) ***453***
Oakland U (MI) ***456***
Oberlin Coll (OH) ***456***
The Ohio State U (OH) ***457***
Ohio U (OH) ***458***
Oklahoma City U (OK) ***460***
Otterbein Coll (OH) ***462***
Pitzer Coll (CA) ***471***
Point Park Coll (PA) ***471***
Pomona Coll (CA) ***472***
Prescott Coll (AZ) ***474***
Purchase Coll, State U of NY (NY) ***475***
Queens Coll of the City U of NY (NY) ***475***
Radford U (VA) ***476***
Randolph-Macon Woman's Coll (VA) ***477***
Reed Coll (OR) ***477***
Rhode Island Coll (RI) ***479***
Roger Williams U (RI) ***483***
Rutgers, The State U of New Jersey, New Brunswick (NJ) ***485***
Ryerson U (ON, Canada) ***485***
Saint Mary's Coll of California (CA) ***494***
St. Olaf Coll (MN) ***495***
Sam Houston State U (TX) ***497***
San Diego State U (CA) ***498***
San Francisco State U (CA) ***498***
San Jose State U (CA) ***499***
Sarah Lawrence Coll (NY) ***499***
Scripps Coll (CA) ***501***
Shenandoah U (VA) ***503***
Simon Fraser U (BC, Canada) ***505***
Simon's Rock Coll of Bard (MA) ***505***
Skidmore Coll (NY) ***506***
Slippery Rock U of Pennsylvania (PA) ***506***
Smith Coll (MA) ***506***
Southern Illinois U Edwardsville (IL) ***509***
Southern Methodist U (TX) ***510***
Southern Utah U (UT) ***511***
Southwest Missouri State U (MO) ***513***
Southwest Texas State U (TX) ***513***
State U of NY Coll at Brockport (NY) ***515***
State U of NY Coll at Fredonia (NY) ***516***
State U of NY Coll at Potsdam (NY) ***517***
Stephen F. Austin State U (TX) ***518***
Stephens Coll (MO) ***519***
Swarthmore Coll (PA) ***521***
Sweet Briar Coll (VA) ***521***
Temple U (PA) ***523***
Texas Christian U (TX) ***526***
Texas Tech U (TX) ***526***
Texas Woman's U (TX) ***527***
Thomas Edison State Coll (NJ) ***527***
Towson U (MD) ***529***
Trinity Coll (CT) ***530***
U at Buffalo, The State University of New York (NY) ***536***
The U of Akron (OH) ***537***
The U of Alabama (AL) ***537***
U of Alberta (AB, Canada) ***538***
The U of Arizona (AZ) ***538***
U of Calgary (AB, Canada) ***540***
U of Calif, Irvine (CA) ***541***
U of Calif, Riverside (CA) ***541***
U of Calif, San Diego (CA) ***541***
U of Calif, Santa Barbara (CA) ***541***
U of Calif, Santa Cruz (CA) ***542***
U of Central Oklahoma (OK) ***542***
U of Cincinnati (OH) ***543***
U of Colorado at Boulder (CO) ***543***
U of Florida (FL) ***545***
U of Hartford (CT) ***546***
U of Hawaii at Manoa (HI) ***546***
U of Idaho (ID) ***547***
U of Illinois at Urbana–Champaign (IL) ***548***
The U of Iowa (IA) ***548***
U of Kansas (KS) ***549***
U of Maryland, Baltimore County (MD) ***552***
U of Maryland, Coll Park (MD) ***552***
U of Massachusetts Amherst (MA) ***552***
U of Miami (FL) ***553***
U of Michigan (MI) ***554***
U of Minnesota, Twin Cities Campus (MN) ***555***
U of Missouri–Kansas City (MO) ***555***
The U of Montana–Missoula (MT) ***556***
U of Nebraska–Lincoln (NE) ***557***
U of Nevada, Las Vegas (NV) ***558***
U of New Mexico (NM) ***559***
The U of North Carolina at Charlotte (NC) ***560***
The U of North Carolina at Greensboro (NC) ***560***
U of North Texas (TX) ***562***
U of Oklahoma (OK) ***562***
U of Oregon (OR) ***562***
U of Southern Mississippi (MS) ***576***
U of South Florida (FL) ***576***
The U of Texas at Austin (TX) ***578***
The U of the Arts (PA) ***579***
U of Utah (UT) ***582***
U of Washington (WA) ***583***
U of Wisconsin–Milwaukee (WI) ***585***
U of Wisconsin–Stevens Point (WI) ***585***
Utah State U (UT) ***587***
Virginia Commonwealth U (VA) ***590***
Virginia Intermont Coll (VA) ***590***
Washington U in St. Louis (MO) ***595***
Wayne State U (MI) ***596***
Weber State U (UT) ***596***
Webster U (MO) ***597***
Wells Coll (NY) ***597***
Wesleyan U (CT) ***597***
Western Michigan U (MI) ***599***
Western Oregon U (OR) ***600***
Westmont Coll (CA) ***602***
West Texas A&M U (TX) ***602***
Winthrop U (SC) ***608***
Wright State U (OH) ***609***
York U (ON, Canada) ***611***

DANCE THERAPY

Overview: This major teaches students how to use dance and other creative movement techniques to treat patients who suffer from a physical, mental, or emotional disorders. *Related majors:* psychology, counseling or developmental psychology, drama and dance teacher education, nursing (psychiatric/mental health), dance. *Potential careers:* dance or movement therapist, dance teacher, psychologist, therapist. *Salary potential:* $25k-$30k.

Long Island U, Southampton Coll, Friends World Program (NY) ***409***
Mercyhurst Coll (PA) ***425***
Naropa U (CO) ***441***

DATA PROCESSING

Overview: Students learn how to use computer equipment to enter, process, and retrieve information and data for a range of business and administrative purposes. *Related majors:* word processing, administrative assistant. *Potential careers:* data entry clerk, information processing technician, accounting technician. *Salary potential:* $20k-$27k.

East Carolina U (NC) ***347***
Eastern Michigan U (MI) ***348***
Peirce Coll (PA) ***466***

DATA PROCESSING TECHNOLOGY

Overview: Students will learn how to create and use computer software programs for importing, organizing, storing, retrieving, and extracting large amounts of information. *Related majors:* information technology, computer programming, data entry, information systems security, data warehousing/mining. *Potential careers:* computer programmer, systems administrator, database administrator, researcher, data processing technician. *Salary potential:* $40k-$50k.

Arkansas State U (AR) ***272***
Bemidji State U (MN) ***285***
Central Baptist Coll (AR) ***309***
Cleary U (MI) ***317***
Florida Metropolitan U-Orlando Coll, North (FL) ***361***
Gardner-Webb U (NC) ***365***
Hannibal-LaGrange Coll (MO) ***375***
Harding U (AR) ***375***
Indiana U Kokomo (IN) ***386***
Indiana U Northwest (IN) ***386***
Minnesota State U, Mankato (MN) ***431***
Mount Vernon Nazarene U (OH) ***440***
Murray State U (KY) ***440***
Northern Michigan U (MI) ***451***
Northwest Missouri State U (MO) ***454***
Pacific Union Coll (CA) ***464***
Peirce Coll (PA) ***466***
Saint Mary's U (NS, Canada) ***494***
Stephen F. Austin State U (TX) ***518***
U of Advancing Technology (AZ) ***537***
U of Arkansas (AR) ***539***
U of New Brunswick Fredericton (NB, Canada) ***558***
U of Southern Indiana (IN) ***576***
U of Southern Mississippi (MS) ***576***
U of Washington (WA) ***583***
West Virginia U Inst of Technology (WV) ***602***

DENTAL HYGIENE

Overview: This major prepares students to assist dentists in providing basic dental care such as cleaning teeth, administering radiographs, providing education, and diagnosing oral diseases and/or oral injuries. *Related majors:* dental assistant, predentistry studies. *Potential careers:* dentist, dental hygienist. *Salary potential:* $27k-$35k.

Armstrong Atlantic State U (GA) ***273***
Dalhousie U (NS, Canada) ***336***
Eastern Washington U (WA) ***349***
East Tennessee State U (TN) ***349***
State U of NY at Farmingdale (NY) ***357***
Howard U (DC) ***382***
Idaho State U (ID) ***384***
Indiana U–Purdue U Indianapolis (IN) ***387***
Loma Linda U (CA) ***408***
Louisiana State U Health Sciences Center (LA) ***410***
Marquette U (WI) ***418***
Mars Hill Coll (NC) ***418***
Medical Coll of Georgia (GA) ***424***
Midwestern State U (TX) ***430***
Minnesota State U, Mankato (MN) ***431***
New York U (NY) ***447***
Northeastern U (MA) ***450***
Northern Arizona U (AZ) ***450***
The Ohio State U (OH) ***457***
Old Dominion U (VA) ***460***
Oregon Inst of Technology (OR) ***461***
Pennsylvania Coll of Technology (PA) ***467***
Southern Illinois U Carbondale (IL) ***509***
Tennessee State U (TN) ***523***
Texas A&M U System Health Science Center (TX) ***525***
Texas Woman's U (TX) ***527***
Thomas Edison State Coll (NJ) ***527***
U of Alberta (AB, Canada) ***538***
U of Arkansas for Medical Sciences (AR) ***539***
U of Bridgeport (CT) ***540***
The U of British Columbia (BC, Canada) ***540***
U of Colorado Health Sciences Center (CO) ***543***
U of Hawaii at Manoa (HI) ***546***
U of Louisiana at Lafayette (LA) ***550***
U of Louisville (KY) ***550***
U of Manitoba (MB, Canada) ***551***
U of Michigan (MI) ***554***
U of Minnesota, Twin Cities Campus (MN) ***555***
U of Mississippi Medical Center (MS) ***555***
U of Missouri–Kansas City (MO) ***555***
U of Nebraska Medical Center (NE) ***557***
U of New England (ME) ***558***
U of New Haven (CT) ***559***
U of New Mexico (NM) ***559***
The U of North Carolina at Chapel Hill (NC) ***560***
U of Oklahoma Health Sciences Center (OK) ***562***
U of Pittsburgh (PA) ***569***
U of Rhode Island (RI) ***572***
The U of South Dakota (SD) ***575***
U of Southern California (CA) ***576***
U of Texas-Houston Health Science Center (TX) ***579***
U of Washington (WA) ***583***
U of Wyoming (WY) ***586***
Virginia Commonwealth U (VA) ***590***
Weber State U (UT) ***596***
Western Kentucky U (KY) ***599***
West Liberty State Coll (WV) ***601***
West Virginia U (WV) ***602***
Wichita State U (KS) ***604***

DENTAL LABORATORY TECHNICIAN

Overview: Students choosing this major learn how to design and construct dental prostheses and work under the supervision of licensed dentists and orthodontists. *Related majors:* predentistry studies, oral hygiene and dental assisting. *Potential careers:* dental laboratory technician, orthodontic technician. *Salary potential:* $20k-$27k.

Boston U (MA) ***292***
Louisiana State U Health Sciences Center (LA) ***410***

DESIGN/APPLIED ARTS RELATED

Information can be found under this major's main heading.

The Art Inst of California–San Diego (CA) ***273***
Bennington Coll (VT) ***286***
Drexel U (PA) ***346***
Maine Coll of Art (ME) ***415***
New York Inst of Technology (NY) ***447***
Ohio U (OH) ***458***
Ringling School of Art and Design (FL) ***480***
Robert Morris Coll (IL) ***481***
The U of Akron (OH) ***537***
U of Saint Francis (IN) ***573***
U of Wisconsin–Stout (WI) ***586***

DESIGN/VISUAL COMMUNICATIONS

Overview: Students of this major examine techniques and principles for effective communication of concepts and information and how to package products to various audiences. *Related majors:* graphic design, commercial art, illustration, industrial design, commercial photography. *Potential careers:* book jacket designer, interior designer, Web page designer. *Salary potential:* $25k-$40k.

Adams State Coll (CO) ***260***
American Academy of Art (IL) ***265***
The American U in Dubai(United Arab Emirates) ***267***
The Art Inst of Phoenix (AZ) ***274***
Atlanta Coll of Art (GA) ***275***
Bethel Coll (IN) ***288***
Bowling Green State U (OH) ***292***
Brigham Young U (UT) ***295***
California State U, Chico (CA) ***300***
Calvin Coll (MI) ***303***

Canisius Coll (NY) ***304***
Carlow Coll (PA) ***305***
Carroll Coll (WI) ***306***
Cazenovia Coll (NY) ***308***
Central Connecticut State U (CT) ***309***
Collins Coll: A School of Design and Technology (AZ) ***324***
State U of NY at Farmingdale (NY) ***357***
The Illinois Inst of Art-Schaumburg (IL) ***384***
International Academy of Design & Technology (FL) ***388***
International Acad of Merchandising & Design, Ltd (IL) ***389***
Iowa State U of Science and Technology (IA) ***390***
Jacksonville U (FL) ***391***
Kean U (NJ) ***396***
Kendall Coll of Art and Design of Ferris State U (MI) ***396***
Laguna Coll of Art & Design (CA) ***400***
Maharishi U of Management (IA) ***414***
Marywood U (PA) ***421***
Mount Union Coll (OH) ***440***
Mount Vernon Nazarene U (OH) ***440***
North Carolina State U (NC) ***449***
Northwestern State U of Louisiana (LA) ***453***
Ohio Dominican U (OH) ***457***
The Ohio State U (OH) ***457***
Ohio U (OH) ***458***
Paier Coll of Art, Inc. (CT) ***464***
Peace Coll (NC) ***466***
Purdue U (IN) ***475***
Rochester Inst of Technology (NY) ***482***
Saginaw Valley State U (MI) ***486***
St. Ambrose U (IA) ***486***
Saint Mary-of-the-Woods Coll (IN) ***493***
San Diego State U (CA) ***498***
Southern Illinois U Carbondale (IL) ***509***
Southwest Missouri State U (MO) ***513***
Syracuse U (NY) ***521***
Texas Woman's U (TX) ***527***
U of Advancing Technology (AZ) ***537***
U of Calif, Davis (CA) ***540***
U of Calif, Los Angeles (CA) ***541***
U of Kansas (KS) ***549***
U of Massachusetts Dartmouth (MA) ***553***
U of Michigan (MI) ***554***
U of Notre Dame (IN) ***562***
The U of Texas at Austin (TX) ***578***
Ursuline Coll (OH) ***587***
Virginia Commonwealth U (VA) ***590***
Washington U in St. Louis (MO) ***595***
Weber State U (UT) ***596***
William Woods U (MO) ***607***
York U (ON, Canada) ***611***

DEVELOPMENTAL/CHILD PSYCHOLOGY

Overview: This major examines how individuals develop psychologically from infants into adults. *Related majors:* education, early childhood education, educational psychology, child, growth, social work. *Potential careers:* school psychologist or child psychologist, social worker, children's services coordinator, family law attorney, teacher. *Salary potential:* $23k-$33k.

Appalachian State U (NC) ***270***
Auburn U (AL) ***276***
Becker Coll (MA) ***283***
Belmont U (TN) ***284***
Bennington Coll (VT) ***286***
Berea Coll (KY) ***286***
Bluffton Coll (OH) ***291***
California Polytechnic State U, San Luis Obispo (CA) ***300***
California State U, Bakersfield (CA) ***300***
California State U, Hayward (CA) ***301***
California State U, Northridge (CA) ***301***
California State U, San Bernardino (CA) ***302***
Carson-Newman Coll (TN) ***306***
Castleton State Coll (VT) ***307***
Christopher Newport U (VA) ***313***
Clark Atlanta U (GA) ***315***
Colby-Sawyer Coll (NH) ***319***
Colorado State U-Pueblo (CO) ***325***
Concordia U (QC, Canada) ***331***
Cornell U (NY) ***333***
Eastern Washington U (WA) ***349***
Edgewood Coll (WI) ***351***
Fitchburg State Coll (MA) ***358***
Fort Valley State U (GA) ***362***
Framingham State Coll (MA) ***362***
Fresno Pacific U (CA) ***364***
Goddard Coll (VT) ***369***
Hampshire Coll (MA) ***375***
Hampton U (VA) ***375***
Houston Baptist U (TX) ***382***
Humboldt State U (CA) ***382***
Iowa State U of Science and Technology (IA) ***390***
Langston U (OK) ***402***
Long Island U, Southampton Coll, Friends World Program (NY) ***409***
Longwood U (VA) ***409***
Lynchburg Coll (VA) ***413***
Madonna U (MI) ***414***
Marlboro Coll (VT) ***418***
Maryville Coll (TN) ***420***
Metropolitan State U (MN) ***427***
Mills Coll (CA) ***431***
Minnesota State U, Mankato (MN) ***431***
Mount St. Mary's Coll (CA) ***439***
Mount Saint Vincent U (NS, Canada) ***439***
Northwest Missouri State U (MO) ***454***
Oklahoma Baptist U (OK) ***459***
Olivet Nazarene U (IL) ***461***
Quinnipiac U (CT) ***476***
Rockford Coll (IL) ***482***
St. Joseph's Coll, New York (NY) ***491***
St. Joseph's Coll, Suffolk Campus (NY) ***491***
San Jose State U (CA) ***499***
Sarah Lawrence Coll (NY) ***499***
Simon's Rock Coll of Bard (MA) ***505***
Sonoma State U (CA) ***506***
Spelman Coll (GA) ***514***
Suffolk U (MA) ***520***
Tufts U (MA) ***533***
The U of Akron (OH) ***537***
U of Alberta (AB, Canada) ***538***
The U of British Columbia (BC, Canada) ***540***
U of Calif, Santa Cruz (CA) ***542***
U of Delaware (DE) ***544***
U of Kansas (KS) ***549***
U of La Verne (CA) ***549***
U of Michigan–Dearborn (MI) ***554***
U of Minnesota, Twin Cities Campus (MN) ***555***
U of Missouri–Columbia (MO) ***555***
U of New Brunswick Fredericton (NB, Canada) ***558***
U of New England (ME) ***558***
U of Ottawa (ON, Canada) ***563***
U of the District of Columbia (DC) ***580***
U of the Incarnate Word (TX) ***580***
U of Toledo (OH) ***581***
U of Utah (UT) ***582***
U of Wisconsin–Green Bay (WI) ***584***
U of Wisconsin–Madison (WI) ***584***
Utica Coll (NY) ***588***
Villa Julie Coll (MD) ***590***
Western Washington U (WA) ***600***
Whittier Coll (CA) ***604***
Wittenberg U (OH) ***608***

DEVELOPMENT ECONOMICS

Overview: This branch of economics deals with the issues and applications of economic development and sustainability in specific countries and regions. *Related majors:* international economics, area studies, agricultural economics, banking and financial support services, international finance. *Potential careers:* international aid officer, investment banker, diplomatic corps, economist, currency trader. *Salary potential:* $32k-$45k.

American U (DC) ***267***
Arkansas State U (AR) ***272***
Brown U (RI) ***296***
Clark U (MA) ***316***
Eastern Mennonite U (VA) ***348***
Fitchburg State Coll (MA) ***358***
Georgia Southern U (GA) ***367***
The Ohio State U (OH) ***457***
U of Calgary (AB, Canada) ***540***
U of Guelph (ON, Canada) ***546***
U of King's Coll (NS, Canada) ***549***
U of Windsor (ON, Canada) ***584***
York U (ON, Canada) ***611***

DIAGNOSTIC MEDICAL SONOGRAPHY

Overview: This major prepares students to operate ultrasound equipment that directs high-frequency sound waves into areas of the patient's body, producing images that show the shape and position of internal organs, fluid accumulations, masses, etc. *Related majors:* sonographer (ultrasound technician), nuclear medical technology, medical radiologic technology. *Potential careers:* radiologic technologists, nuclear medicine technologists, cardiology technologists, electroencephalographic technologists. *Salary potential:* $35k-$40k.

Medical Coll of Georgia (GA) ***424***
Mountain State U (WV) ***437***
Nebraska Methodist Coll (NE) ***443***
Rochester Inst of Technology (NY) ***482***
Seattle U (WA) ***501***
U of Nebraska Medical Center (NE) ***557***
Weber State U (UT) ***596***

DIETETICS

Overview: This major gives students knowledge to apply the principles of food and nutrition sciences and human behavior in order to design and manage effective nutrition programs in a variety of settings. *Related majors:* food and nutrition sciences, dietitian assistant, counseling psychology. *Potential careers:* dietitian, nutritionist, therapist, psychologist. *Salary potential:* $20k-$30k.

Abilene Christian U (TX) ***260***
Acadia U (NS, Canada) ***260***
Andrews U (MI) ***269***
Arizona State U East (AZ) ***271***
Ashland U (OH) ***274***
Ball State U (IN) ***280***
Bastyr U (WA) ***282***
Baylor U (TX) ***283***
Bennett Coll (NC) ***286***
Berea Coll (KY) ***286***
Bluffton Coll (OH) ***291***
Bowling Green State U (OH) ***292***
Brigham Young U (UT) ***295***
California State Polytechnic U, Pomona (CA) ***300***
California State U, Fresno (CA) ***301***
California State U, Long Beach (CA) ***301***
California State U, Northridge (CA) ***301***
California State U, San Bernardino (CA) ***302***
Carson-Newman Coll (TN) ***306***
Case Western Reserve U (OH) ***307***
Central Michigan U (MI) ***310***
Central Missouri State U (MO) ***310***
Coll of Saint Benedict (MN) ***321***
Coll of St. Catherine (MN) ***321***
Coll of Saint Elizabeth (NJ) ***321***
Coll of the Ozarks (MO) ***323***
Colorado State U (CO) ***325***
Concordia Coll (MN) ***329***
Cornell U (NY) ***333***
Dominican U (IL) ***345***
D'Youville Coll (NY) ***347***
East Carolina U (NC) ***347***
Eastern Kentucky U (KY) ***348***
Eastern Michigan U (MI) ***348***
Florida International U (FL) ***360***
Florida State U (FL) ***361***
Fontbonne U (MO) ***361***
Framingham State Coll (MA) ***362***
Gannon U (PA) ***365***
Georgia State U (GA) ***368***
Harding U (AR) ***375***
Immaculata U (PA) ***385***
Indiana U Bloomington (IN) ***385***
Indiana U of Pennsylvania (PA) ***386***
Iowa State U of Science and Technology (IA) ***390***
Jacksonville State U (AL) ***390***
Kansas State U (KS) ***396***
Keene State Coll (NH) ***396***
Lamar U (TX) ***401***
Langston U (OK) ***402***
Lehman Coll of the City U of NY (NY) ***404***
Lipscomb U (TN) ***408***
Loma Linda U (CA) ***408***
Louisiana State U and A&M Coll (LA) ***410***
Louisiana Tech U (LA) ***410***
Madonna U (MI) ***414***
Mansfield U of Pennsylvania (PA) ***416***
Marshall U (WV) ***418***
Marymount Coll of Fordham U (NY) ***419***
Marywood U (PA) ***421***
McGill U (QC, Canada) ***423***
Memorial U of Newfoundland (NF, Canada) ***424***
Mercyhurst Coll (PA) ***425***
Meredith Coll (NC) ***426***
Messiah Coll (PA) ***426***
Miami U (OH) ***428***
Michigan State U (MI) ***428***
Minnesota State U, Mankato (MN) ***431***
Montclair State U (NJ) ***435***
Morgan State U (MD) ***436***
Mount Mary Coll (WI) ***438***
Mount Saint Vincent U (NS, Canada) ***439***
Nicholls State U (LA) ***447***
North Carolina Ag and Tech State U (NC) ***448***
North Dakota State U (ND) ***449***
Northern Michigan U (MI) ***451***
Northwest Missouri State U (MO) ***454***
Notre Dame Coll (OH) ***455***
Oakwood Coll (AL) ***456***
The Ohio State U (OH) ***457***
Ohio U (OH) ***458***
Olivet Nazarene U (IL) ***461***
Oregon State U (OR) ***462***
Ouachita Baptist U (AR) ***462***
Pacific Union Coll (CA) ***464***
Point Loma Nazarene U (CA) ***471***
Queens Coll of the City U of NY (NY) ***475***
Radford U (VA) ***476***
Rochester Inst of Technology (NY) ***482***
Saint John's U (MN) ***490***
Saint Joseph Coll (CT) ***490***
Saint Louis U (MO) ***492***
Samford U (AL) ***497***
San Francisco State U (CA) ***498***
San Jose State U (CA) ***499***
Seton Hill U (PA) ***502***
Simmons Coll (MA) ***504***
South Dakota State U (SD) ***507***
Southwest Missouri State U (MO) ***513***
Spalding U (KY) ***513***
State U of NY Coll at Buffalo (NY) ***516***
State U of NY Coll at Oneonta (NY) ***517***
Syracuse U (NY) ***521***
Tarleton State U (TX) ***522***
Tennessee Technological U (TN) ***524***
Texas A&M U–Kingsville (TX) ***525***
Texas Christian U (TX) ***526***
Texas Southern U (TX) ***526***
Texas Tech U (TX) ***526***
Texas Woman's U (TX) ***527***
Tuskegee U (AL) ***533***
The U of Akron (OH) ***537***
The U of British Columbia (BC, Canada) ***540***
U of Central Oklahoma (OK) ***542***
U of Connecticut (CT) ***544***
U of Dayton (OH) ***544***
U of Delaware (DE) ***544***
U of Georgia (GA) ***545***
U of Guelph (ON, Canada) ***546***
U of Louisiana at Lafayette (LA) ***550***
U of Maryland, Coll Park (MD) ***552***
U of Maryland Eastern Shore (MD) ***552***
U of Missouri–Columbia (MO) ***555***
U of Montevallo (AL) ***557***
U of Nebraska at Kearney (NE) ***557***
U of New Hampshire (NH) ***558***
U of New Haven (CT) ***559***
The U of North Carolina at Greensboro (NC) ***560***
U of North Dakota (ND) ***561***
U of Northern Colorado (CO) ***561***
U of Northern Iowa (IA) ***561***
U of Oklahoma Health Sciences Center (OK) ***562***
U of Ottawa (ON, Canada) ***563***
U of Pittsburgh (PA) ***569***
U of Puerto Rico, Río Piedras (PR) ***571***

DIETETICS (continued)

U of Rhode Island (RI) ***572***
U of Southern Mississippi (MS) ***576***
The U of Tennessee at Martin (TN) ***577***
The U of Texas–Pan American (TX) ***579***
U of Vermont (VT) ***582***
The U of Western Ontario (ON, Canada) ***583***
U of Wisconsin–Madison (WI) ***584***
U of Wisconsin–Stevens Point (WI) ***585***
U of Wisconsin–Stout (WI) ***586***
Virginia Polytechnic Inst and State U (VA) ***591***
Viterbo U (WI) ***591***
Wayne State U (MI) ***596***
Western Carolina U (NC) ***598***
Western Michigan U (MI) ***599***
Youngstown State U (OH) ***611***

DISTRIBUTION OPERATIONS

Overview: Students taking this major study the distribution operations for a variety of businesses and enterprises. *Related majors:* logistics management, general retail operations, computer management. *Potential careers:* distribution manager, inventory control manager. *Salary potential:* $30k-$40k.

McKendree Coll (IL) ***423***
U of Wisconsin–Superior (WI) ***586***
Youngstown State U (OH) ***611***

DIVINITY/MINISTRY

Overview: Students will learn church law, liturgy and ritual, theology, Christian ethics, church history in preparation to become an ordained Christian priest or minister. *Related majors:* Bible studies, religious studies, missionary studies, pastoral counseling, psychology, Biblical languages and literatures. *Potential careers:* minister, priest, or any related vocation within the Christian faith. *Salary potential:* $20k-$30k.

Arlington Baptist Coll (TX) ***272***
Atlantic Union Coll (MA) ***276***
Azusa Pacific U (CA) ***278***
Baptist Bible Coll (MO) ***281***
Barclay Coll (KS) ***281***
Belmont U (TN) ***284***
Bethany Bible Coll (NB, Canada) ***287***
Bethany Coll of the Assemblies of God (CA) ***287***
Bethel Coll (IN) ***288***
Biola U (CA) ***289***
Bluffton Coll (OH) ***291***
Boise Bible Coll (ID) ***291***
Brewton-Parker Coll (GA) ***294***
Briercrest Bible Coll (SK, Canada) ***295***
Campbellsville U (KY) ***303***
Cardinal Stritch U (WI) ***305***
Central Christian Coll of Kansas (KS) ***309***
Christian Heritage Coll (CA) ***313***
Cincinnati Bible Coll and Seminary (OH) ***314***
Clear Creek Baptist Bible Coll (KY) ***316***
Colorado Christian U (CO) ***325***
Concordia U (CA) ***330***
Cornerstone U (MI) ***333***
Emmanuel Coll (GA) ***353***
Eugene Bible Coll (OR) ***355***
Faith Baptist Bible Coll and Theological Seminary (IA) ***356***
Faulkner U (AL) ***357***
Fresno Pacific U (CA) ***364***
Global U of the Assemblies of God (MO) ***368***
Grace Coll (IN) ***370***
Grace U (NE) ***371***
Grand Canyon U (AZ) ***371***
Great Lakes Christian Coll (MI) ***372***
Greenville Coll (IL) ***373***
Grove City Coll (PA) ***373***
Hannibal-LaGrange Coll (MO) ***375***
Hardin-Simmons U (TX) ***376***
Huntington Coll (IN) ***383***
John Brown U (AR) ***392***
John Wesley Coll (NC) ***394***
Lincoln Christian Coll (IL) ***407***
Lipscomb U (TN) ***408***
Manhattan Christian Coll (KS) ***415***
Martin Methodist Coll (TN) ***418***
The Master's Coll and Seminary (CA) ***422***
Master's Coll and Seminary (ON, Canada) ***422***
Messenger Coll (MO) ***426***
Mount Olive Coll (NC) ***439***
Multnomah Bible Coll and Biblical Seminary (OR) ***440***
Nebraska Christian Coll (NE) ***443***
North Park U (IL) ***452***
Northwest Coll (WA) ***452***
Northwest Nazarene U (ID) ***454***
Oakland City U (IN) ***456***
Oklahoma Baptist U (OK) ***459***
Oklahoma Christian U (OK) ***459***
Oklahoma Wesleyan U (OK) ***460***
Patten Coll (CA) ***466***
Pillsbury Baptist Bible Coll (MN) ***470***
Providence Coll and Theological Seminary (MB, Canada) ***475***
Reformed Bible Coll (MI) ***477***
Roberts Wesleyan Coll (NY) ***481***
St. Louis Christian Coll (MO) ***492***
Saint Paul U (ON, Canada) ***495***
San Jose Christian Coll (CA) ***498***
Shorter Coll (GA) ***504***
Southeastern Bible Coll (AL) ***507***
Southern Wesleyan U (SC) ***511***
Southwestern Assemblies of God U (TX) ***512***
Tabor Coll (KS) ***522***
Taylor U, Fort Wayne Campus (IN) ***523***
Trinity International U (IL) ***531***
Trinity Western U (BC, Canada) ***531***
Tyndale Coll & Seminary (ON, Canada) ***533***
U of Mary (ND) ***551***
U of Saint Francis (IN) ***573***
Warner Pacific Coll (OR) ***593***
Western Baptist Coll (OR) ***598***
Williams Baptist Coll (AR) ***606***

DRAFTING

Overview: This general major will teach students how to create working drawings, schematics, visual plans, illustrations, or computer simulations that may be used in a variety of applications. *Related majors:* mathematics, computer science, structural engineering, drafting and design technology. *Potential careers:* draftsperson, structural engineer, architect, construction manager. *Salary potential:* $35k-$45k.

Baker Coll of Flint (MI) ***279***
Baker Coll of Owosso (MI) ***279***
Central Missouri State U (MO) ***310***
Columbus Coll of Art and Design (OH) ***328***
East Central U (OK) ***347***
Grambling State U (LA) ***371***
Keene State Coll (NH) ***396***
Lewis-Clark State Coll (ID) ***406***
Lynn U (FL) ***413***
Montana State U–Northern (MT) ***434***
Murray State U (KY) ***440***
Northern Michigan U (MI) ***451***
Northern State U (SD) ***451***
Pacific Union Coll (CA) ***464***
Prairie View A&M U (TX) ***473***
Robert Morris Coll (IL) ***481***
Sam Houston State U (TX) ***497***
Southwest Missouri State U (MO) ***513***
Texas Southern U (TX) ***526***
Thomas Edison State Coll (NJ) ***527***
Tri-State U (IN) ***532***
U of Houston (TX) ***547***
U of Nebraska at Omaha (NE) ***557***
U of Rio Grande (OH) ***572***
Western Michigan U (MI) ***599***

DRAFTING/DESIGN TECHNOLOGY

Overview: Students learn how to create technical drawings and computer simulations for a variety of industrial applications. *Related majors:* applied mathematics, mechanical drafting, computer graphics. *Potential careers:* draftsperson, architect, computer graphic designer. *Salary potential:* $25k-$33k.

Hillsdale Coll (MI) ***379***
Lewis-Clark State Coll (ID) ***406***
Norfolk State U (VA) ***448***
Texas Southern U (TX) ***526***
Tri-State U (IN) ***532***

DRAMA/DANCE EDUCATION

Overview: This major teaches undergraduates how to teach drama and dance classes at various educational levels. *Related majors:* drama/theater arts, dance, acting and directing. *Potential careers:* drama teacher, dance teacher, visual and performing arts. *Salary potential:* $22k-$30k.

Abilene Christian U (TX) ***260***
Appalachian State U (NC) ***270***
Baylor U (TX) ***283***
Boston U (MA) ***292***
Bowling Green State U (OH) ***292***
Brenau U (GA) ***293***
Bridgewater State Coll (MA) ***294***
Brigham Young U (UT) ***295***
The Catholic U of America (DC) ***307***
Central Washington U (WA) ***310***
Chadron State Coll (NE) ***311***
Coll of St. Catherine (MN) ***321***
Concordia U (QC, Canada) ***331***
Dana Coll (NE) ***337***
East Carolina U (NC) ***347***
Eastern Michigan U (MI) ***348***
East Texas Baptist U (TX) ***350***
Emerson Coll (MA) ***353***
Greensboro Coll (NC) ***372***
Greenville Coll (IL) ***373***
Hastings Coll (NE) ***377***
Howard Payne U (TX) ***382***
Huntingdon Coll (AL) ***383***
Indiana U–Purdue U Fort Wayne (IN) ***386***
Jacksonville U (FL) ***391***
Johnson State Coll (VT) ***394***
Luther Coll (IA) ***412***
Marywood U (PA) ***421***
McMurry U (TX) ***423***
Meredith Coll (NC) ***426***
Minnesota State U, Moorhead (MN) ***432***
New York U (NY) ***447***
Northern Arizona U (AZ) ***450***
The Ohio State U (OH) ***457***
Oklahoma Baptist U (OK) ***459***
Point Park Coll (PA) ***471***
Ryerson U (ON, Canada) ***485***
Salve Regina U (RI) ***497***
San Diego State U (CA) ***498***
Southwestern Coll (KS) ***512***
Southwest State U (MN) ***513***
Texas Wesleyan U (TX) ***526***
The U of Akron (OH) ***537***
The U of Arizona (AZ) ***538***
U of Calgary (AB, Canada) ***540***
U of Georgia (GA) ***545***
The U of Iowa (IA) ***548***
U of Maryland, Coll Park (MD) ***552***
The U of North Carolina at Charlotte (NC) ***560***
U of St. Thomas (MN) ***573***
U of South Florida (FL) ***576***
U of Utah (UT) ***582***
U of Windsor (ON, Canada) ***584***
Viterbo U (WI) ***591***
Washington U in St. Louis (MO) ***595***
Weber State U (UT) ***596***
William Jewell Coll (MO) ***606***
York U (ON, Canada) ***611***
Youngstown State U (OH) ***611***

DRAMA/THEATER LITERATURE

Overview: Students analyze the history and literature of written plays or scripts and study the methods and techniques of theatrical productions. *Related majors:* English literature, drama/theater arts, playwriting and scriptwriting, comparative literature. *Potential careers:* writer, theater or film critic, professor, director. *Salary potential:* $20k-$30k.

Averett U (VA) ***278***
Bard Coll (NY) ***281***
Barnard Coll (NY) ***282***
Boston U (MA) ***292***
DePaul U (IL) ***339***
Marymount Manhattan Coll (NY) ***420***
Memorial U of Newfoundland (NF, Canada) ***424***
Northwestern U (IL) ***453***
Ohio U (OH) ***458***
U of Connecticut (CT) ***544***
U of Northern Iowa (IA) ***561***
Virginia Wesleyan Coll (VA) ***591***
Washington U in St. Louis (MO) ***595***

DRAMA THERAPY

Overview: This major teaches students how to use drama, acting, and other expressive techniques to treat patients who suffer from a physical, mental, or emotional disorders. *Related majors:* psychology, counseling or developmental psychology, drama and dance teacher education, nursing (psychiatric/mental health), acting and directing. *Potential careers:* drama therapist, drama teacher, psychologist, therapist. *Salary potential:* $25k-30k.

Howard U (DC) ***382***
Long Island U, Southampton Coll, Friends World Program (NY) ***409***
Virginia Union U (VA) ***591***

DRAWING

Overview: This major teaches students the artistic skills and techniques of drawing. *Related majors:* fine arts, painting, art history. *Potential careers:* fine artist, set designer, book jacket or magazine designer, creative director, Web page designer. *Salary potential:* $10k-$35k.

Academy of Art Coll (CA) ***260***
Adams State Coll (CO) ***260***
Alberta Coll of Art & Design (AB, Canada) ***262***
Alfred U (NY) ***263***
Alma Coll (MI) ***264***
American Academy of Art (IL) ***265***
Anderson Coll (SC) ***268***
Antioch Coll (OH) ***269***
Aquinas Coll (MI) ***270***
Arcadia U (PA) ***271***
Arizona State U (AZ) ***271***
Art Academy of Cincinnati (OH) ***273***
Atlanta Coll of Art (GA) ***275***
Ball State U (IN) ***280***
Bard Coll (NY) ***281***
Bennington Coll (VT) ***286***
Bethany Coll (KS) ***287***
Biola U (CA) ***289***
Birmingham-Southern Coll (AL) ***289***
Boston U (MA) ***292***
Bowling Green State U (OH) ***292***
Brock U (ON, Canada) ***295***
California Coll of Arts and Crafts (CA) ***299***
California State U, Fullerton (CA) ***301***
California State U, Hayward (CA) ***301***
California State U, Long Beach (CA) ***301***
California State U, Northridge (CA) ***301***
Carson-Newman Coll (TN) ***306***
Centenary Coll of Louisiana (LA) ***308***
The Cleveland Inst of Art (OH) ***317***
Col for Creative Studies (MI) ***319***
Coll of the Atlantic (ME) ***323***
Coll of Visual Arts (MN) ***324***
Colorado State U (CO) ***325***
Columbia Coll (MO) ***326***
Columbus Coll of Art and Design (OH) ***328***
Concordia U (QC, Canada) ***331***
Corcoran Coll of Art and Design (DC) ***332***
Cornell U (NY) ***333***
DePaul U (IL) ***339***

Drake U (IA) **345**
Eastern Kentucky U (KY) **348**
Framingham State Coll (MA) **362**
Georgia Southwestern State U (GA) **368**
Georgia State U (GA) **368**
Goddard Coll (VT) **369**
Governors State U (IL) **370**
Grace Coll (IN) **370**
Grand Valley State U (MI) **371**
Hampshire Coll (MA) **375**
Hampton U (VA) **375**
Illinois Wesleyan U (IL) **385**
Indiana U Bloomington (IN) **385**
Inter American U of PR, San Germán Campus (PR) **388**
Judson Coll (IL) **395**
Laguna Coll of Art & Design (CA) **400**
Lewis U (IL) **406**
Lindenwood U (MO) **407**
Long Island U, Southampton Coll, Friends World Program (NY) **409**
Longwood U (VA) **409**
LymeAcademy Coll of Fine Arts (CT) **412**
Maharishi U of Management (IA) **414**
Marlboro Coll (VT) **418**
Maryland Inst Coll of Art (MD) **419**
McNeese State U (LA) **423**
Memorial U of Newfoundland (NF, Canada) **424**
Memphis Coll of Art (TN) **425**
Middlebury Coll (VT) **429**
Milwaukee Inst of Art and Design (WI) **431**
Minneapolis Coll of Art and Design (MN) **431**
Minnesota State U, Mankato (MN) **431**
Montserrat Coll of Art (MA) **435**
Mount Allison U (NB, Canada) **437**
Nazareth Coll of Rochester (NY) **443**
New England Coll (NH) **444**
New York U (NY) **447**
Northern Michigan U (MI) **451**
Northwest Missouri State U (MO) **454**
Nova Scotia Coll of Art and Design (NS, Canada) **455**
The Ohio State U (OH) **457**
Ohio U (OH) **458**
Otis Coll of Art and Design (CA) **462**
Pacific Northwest Coll of Art (OR) **464**
Parsons School of Design, New School U (NY) **465**
Portland State U (OR) **472**
Pratt Inst (NY) **473**
Rhode Island School of Design (RI) **479**
Rivier Coll (NH) **480**
Rowan U (NJ) **484**
Rutgers, The State U of New Jersey, New Brunswick (NJ) **485**
Sacred Heart U (CT) **486**
St. Cloud State U (MN) **488**
Salem State Coll (MA) **497**
San Francisco Art Inst (CA) **498**
Sarah Lawrence Coll (NY) **499**
School of the Art Inst of Chicago (IL) **500**
School of the Museum of Fine Arts (MA) **501**
School of Visual Arts (NY) **501**
Seton Hill U (PA) **502**
Shawnee State U (OH) **502**
Simon's Rock Coll of Bard (MA) **505**
Sonoma State U (CA) **506**
State U of NY at Binghamton (NY) **515**
State U of NY at New Paltz (NY) **515**
State U of NY Coll at Brockport (NY) **515**
State U of NY Coll at Buffalo (NY) **516**
State U of NY Coll at Fredonia (NY) **516**
Temple U (PA) **523**
Texas A&M U–Commerce (TX) **525**
Trinity Christian Coll (IL) **530**
The U of Akron (OH) **537**
U of Alberta (AB, Canada) **538**
U of Calif, Santa Cruz (CA) **542**
U of Evansville (IN) **545**
U of Hartford (CT) **546**
The U of Iowa (IA) **548**
U of Michigan (MI) **554**
The U of Montana–Missoula (MT) **556**
U of Montevallo (AL) **557**
U of North Texas (TX) **562**
U of Oregon (OR) **562**
U of Puerto Rico, Río Piedras (PR) **571**
U of San Francisco (CA) **574**
The U of South Dakota (SD) **575**
The U of Texas at El Paso (TX) **578**
U of the South (TN) **581**
U of Toledo (OH) **581**
U of Windsor (ON, Canada) **584**
Washington U in St. Louis (MO) **595**
Webster U (MO) **597**
West Virginia Wesleyan Coll (WV) **603**
William Carey Coll (MS) **605**
Wingate U (NC) **607**
Winona State U (MN) **608**
Wittenberg U (OH) **608**
Wright State U (OH) **609**
York U (ON, Canada) **611**

DRIVER/SAFETY EDUCATION

Overview: This major prepares undergraduates to teach driving skills and driver safety classes at the high school level. *Related majors:* law and legal studies, auto mechanic/technician. *Potential careers:* driver education teacher, driving school owner/instructor. *Salary potential:* $18k-$27k.

Bridgewater Coll (VA) **294**
William Penn U (IA) **606**

EARLY CHILDHOOD EDUCATION

Overview: Undergraduates learn the skills necessary to teach preschool or kindergarten age children (generally age 3-6). *Related majors:* elementary teacher education, developmental psychology, educational psychology, child growth, care and development studies. *Potential careers:* pre-school or kindergarten teacher, family therapist, school administrator. *Salary potential:* $18k-$30k.

Alabama A&M U (AL) **261**
Alabama State U (AL) **261**
Albany State U (GA) **262**
Albright Coll (PA) **263**
Allen U (SC) **264**
Alma Coll (MI) **264**
Alvernia Coll (PA) **265**
American International Coll (MA) **267**
Anderson Coll (SC) **268**
Anna Maria Coll (MA) **269**
Appalachian State U (NC) **270**
Arcadia U (PA) **271**
Arizona State U (AZ) **271**
Arkansas State U (AR) **272**
Arkansas Tech U (AR) **272**
Armstrong Atlantic State U (GA) **273**
Ashland U (OH) **274**
Athens State U (AL) **275**
Atlanta Christian Coll (GA) **275**
Atlantic Union Coll (MA) **276**
Auburn U (AL) **276**
Augsburg Coll (MN) **276**
Augusta State U (GA) **277**
Ball State U (IN) **280**
Barry U (FL) **282**
Bayamón Central U (PR) **283**
Baylor U (TX) **283**
Bay Path Coll (MA) **283**
Becker Coll (MA) **283**
Belmont U (TN) **284**
Benedict Coll (SC) **285**
Bennett Coll (NC) **286**
Bennington Coll (VT) **286**
Berea Coll (KY) **286**
Berry Coll (GA) **287**
Bethany Coll of the Assemblies of God (CA) **287**
Bethel Coll (MN) **288**
Bethesda Christian U (CA) **288**
Birmingham-Southern Coll (AL) **289**
Black Hills State U (SD) **290**
Bloomsburg U of Pennsylvania (PA) **290**
Bluefield Coll (VA) **291**
Bluffton Coll (OH) **291**
Boston Coll (MA) **292**
Boston U (MA) **292**
Bowie State U (MD) **292**
Bowling Green State U (OH) **292**
Bradley U (IL) **293**
Brandon U (MB, Canada) **293**
Brenau U (GA) **293**
Brewton-Parker Coll (GA) **294**
Bridgewater State Coll (MA) **294**
Brigham Young U (UT) **295**
Brooklyn Coll of the City U of NY (NY) **295**
Bryan Coll (TN) **296**
Bucknell U (PA) **297**
Cabrini Coll (PA) **298**
California Polytechnic State U, San Luis Obispo (CA) **300**
California State U, Chico (CA) **300**
California State U, Sacramento (CA) **301**
California U of Pennsylvania (PA) **302**
Cardinal Stritch U (WI) **305**
Carlow Coll (PA) **305**
Carroll Coll (WI) **306**
Carson-Newman Coll (TN) **306**
The Catholic U of America (DC) **307**
Cazenovia Coll (NY) **308**
Cedarville U (OH) **308**
Centenary Coll of Louisiana (LA) **308**
Central Connecticut State U (CT) **309**
Central Methodist Coll (MO) **309**
Central Washington U (WA) **310**
Chaminade U of Honolulu (HI) **311**
Champlain Coll (VT) **311**
Charleston Southern U (SC) **311**
Chestnut Hill Coll (PA) **312**
Cheyney U of Pennsylvania (PA) **312**
Cincinnati Bible Coll and Seminary (OH) **314**
City Coll of the City U of NY (NY) **314**
Clarion U of Pennsylvania (PA) **315**
Clark Atlanta U (GA) **315**
Clarke Coll (IA) **315**
Clemson U (SC) **317**
Cleveland State U (OH) **317**
Coastal Carolina U (SC) **318**
Coker Coll (SC) **318**
Coll Misericordia (PA) **319**
Coll of Mount St. Joseph (OH) **320**
The Coll of New Jersey (NJ) **320**
Coll of Notre Dame of Maryland (MD) **321**
Coll of St. Catherine (MN) **321**
Coll of St. Joseph (VT) **322**
Coll of Saint Mary (NE) **322**
Coll of Santa Fe (NM) **323**
Columbia Bible Coll (BC, Canada) **326**
Columbia Coll (SC) **327**
Columbia Coll Chicago (IL) **327**
Columbia International U (SC) **327**
Columbia Union Coll (MD) **328**
Columbus State U (GA) **328**
Concord Coll (WV) **329**
Concordia Coll (AL) **329**
Concordia Coll (MN) **329**
Concordia U (CA) **330**
Concordia U (IL) **330**
Concordia U (MN) **330**
Concordia U (NE) **330**
Concordia U (OR) **330**
Concordia U (QC, Canada) **331**
Concordia U at Austin (TX) **331**
Concordia U Wisconsin (WI) **331**
Converse Coll (SC) **332**
Cornerstone U (MI) **333**
Crown Coll (MN) **334**
Curry Coll (MA) **335**
Daemen Coll (NY) **335**
Dallas Baptist U (TX) **336**
Delaware State U (DE) **338**
Delta State U (MS) **339**
DePaul U (IL) **339**
Dillard U (LA) **344**
Duquesne U (PA) **346**
East Carolina U (NC) **347**
East Central U (OK) **347**
Eastern Connecticut State U (CT) **347**
Eastern Illinois U (IL) **348**
Eastern Kentucky U (KY) **348**
Eastern Mennonite U (VA) **348**
Eastern Nazarene Coll (MA) **348**
Eastern New Mexico U (NM) **349**
East Stroudsburg U of Pennsylvania (PA) **349**
East Texas Baptist U (TX) **350**
Edgewood Coll (WI) **351**
Edinboro U of Pennsylvania (PA) **351**
Elizabeth City State U (NC) **351**
Elizabethtown Coll (PA) **351**
Elmhurst Coll (IL) **351**
Elms Coll (MA) **352**
Endicott Coll (MA) **354**
Erskine Coll (SC) **354**
Evangel U (MO) **355**
Faulkner U (AL) **357**
Fayetteville State U (NC) **357**
Fitchburg State Coll (MA) **358**
Florida A&M U (FL) **359**
Florida Gulf Coast U (FL) **359**
Florida Southern Coll (FL) **361**
Florida State U (FL) **361**
Fontbonne U (MO) **361**
Fort Hays State U (KS) **362**
Fort Lewis Coll (CO) **362**
Fort Valley State U (GA) **362**
Framingham State Coll (MA) **362**
The Franciscan U (IA) **363**
Francis Marion U (SC) **363**
Franklin Pierce Coll (NH) **364**
Frostburg State U (MD) **365**
Furman U (SC) **365**
Gallaudet U (DC) **365**
Gannon U (PA) **365**
Gardner-Webb U (NC) **365**
Georgetown Coll (KY) **366**
Georgia Coll & State U (GA) **367**
Georgia Southern U (GA) **367**
Georgia Southwestern State U (GA) **368**
Georgia State U (GA) **368**
Glenville State Coll (WV) **368**
Goddard Coll (VT) **369**
Gordon Coll (MA) **370**
Goshen Coll (IN) **370**
Governors State U (IL) **370**
Grace Bible Coll (MI) **370**
Grambling State U (LA) **371**
Greensboro Coll (NC) **372**
Greenville Coll (IL) **373**
Grove City Coll (PA) **373**
Gwynedd-Mercy Coll (PA) **374**
Hampshire Coll (MA) **375**
Hampton U (VA) **375**
Hannibal-LaGrange Coll (MO) **375**
Harding U (AR) **375**
Harris-Stowe State Coll (MO) **376**
Henderson State U (AR) **378**
High Point U (NC) **379**
Hillsdale Coll (MI) **379**
Hofstra U (NY) **380**
Holy Family U (PA) **380**
Hood Coll (MD) **381**
Houston Baptist U (TX) **382**
Howard Payne U (TX) **382**
Howard U (DC) **382**
Humboldt State U (CA) **382**
Hunter Coll of the City U of NY (NY) **382**
Idaho State U (ID) **384**
Illinois State U (IL) **384**
Immaculata U (PA) **385**
Indiana State U (IN) **385**
Indiana U Bloomington (IN) **385**
Indiana U of Pennsylvania (PA) **386**
Inter American U of PR, Aguadilla Campus (PR) **388**
Inter American U of PR, Guayama Campus (PR) **388**
Inter American U of PR, San Germán Campus (PR) **388**
Iowa State U of Science and Technology (IA) **390**
Iowa Wesleyan Coll (IA) **390**
Jacksonville State U (AL) **390**
James Madison U (VA) **391**
John Brown U (AR) **392**
John Carroll U (OH) **392**
Johnson Bible Coll (TN) **394**
Johnson C. Smith U (NC) **394**
Judson Coll (IL) **395**
Juniata Coll (PA) **395**
Kean U (NJ) **396**
Keene State Coll (NH) **396**
Kendall Coll (IL) **396**
Kennesaw State U (GA) **397**
Kent State U (OH) **397**
King Coll (TN) **398**
King's Coll (PA) **398**
LaGrange Coll (GA) **400**
Lakeland Coll (WI) **401**
Lamar U (TX) **401**
Lander U (SC) **401**
Langston U (OK) **402**
La Roche Coll (PA) **402**
Lasell Coll (MA) **402**
Lenoir-Rhyne Coll (NC) **405**
Lesley U (MA) **405**
Lincoln Christian Coll (IL) **407**
Lincoln Memorial U (TN) **407**
Lincoln U (PA) **407**
Lindenwood U (MO) **407**

EARLY CHILDHOOD EDUCATION (continued)

Lock Haven U of Pennsylvania (PA) *408*
Long Island U, Brooklyn Campus (NY) *409*
Long Island U, C.W. Post Campus (NY) *409*
Long Island U, Southampton Coll, Friends World Program (NY) *409*
Longwood U (VA) *409*
Loras Coll (IA) *410*
Louisiana Coll (LA) *410*
Louisiana Tech U (LA) *410*
Lourdes Coll (OH) *411*
Loyola U Chicago (IL) *411*
Luther Coll (IA) *412*
Lynchburg Coll (VA) *413*
Lynn U (FL) *413*
Malone Coll (OH) *415*
Mansfield U of Pennsylvania (PA) *416*
Maranatha Baptist Bible Coll (WI) *417*
Marian Coll (IN) *417*
Marian Coll of Fond du Lac (WI) *417*
Mars Hill Coll (NC) *418*
Martin Luther Coll (MN) *418*
Martin U (IN) *419*
Marygrove Coll (MI) *419*
Maryville U of Saint Louis (MO) *420*
Massachusetts Coll of Liberal Arts (MA) *421*
McNeese State U (LA) *423*
McPherson Coll (KS) *423*
Medaille Coll (NY) *424*
Mercer U (GA) *425*
Mercy Coll (NY) *425*
Mercyhurst Coll (PA) *425*
Messiah Coll (PA) *426*
Methodist Coll (NC) *427*
Miami U (OH) *428*
Middle Tennessee State U (TN) *429*
Midland Lutheran Coll (NE) *429*
Midway Coll (KY) *429*
Miles Coll (AL) *430*
Millersville U of Pennsylvania (PA) *430*
Milligan Coll (TN) *430*
Mills Coll (CA) *431*
Minnesota State U, Mankato (MN) *431*
Minnesota State U, Moorhead (MN) *432*
Mississippi Valley State U (MS) *432*
Missouri Southern State Coll (MO) *433*
Mitchell Coll (CT) *433*
Montclair State U (NJ) *435*
Morehead State U (KY) *436*
Morris Coll (SC) *437*
Mount Aloysius Coll (PA) *437*
Mount Ida Coll (MA) *438*
Mount Mary Coll (WI) *438*
Mount Saint Vincent U (NS, Canada) *439*
Mount Union Coll (OH) *440*
Mount Vernon Nazarene U (OH) *440*
Muskingum Coll (OH) *441*
Naropa U (CO) *441*
National-Louis U (IL) *442*
Neumann Coll (PA) *443*
Newberry Coll (SC) *444*
New Jersey City U (NJ) *445*
New Mexico Highlands U (NM) *446*
New Mexico State U (NM) *446*
New York U (NY) *447*
Nicholls State U (LA) *447*
Norfolk State U (VA) *448*
North Carolina Ag and Tech State U (NC) *448*
North Carolina Central U (NC) *448*
North Central Coll (IL) *449*
Northeastern Illinois U (IL) *450*
Northeastern State U (OK) *450*
Northeastern U (MA) *450*
Northern Illinois U (IL) *450*
Northern Kentucky U (KY) *451*
North Georgia Coll & State U (GA) *451*
North Greenville Coll (SC) *451*
North Park U (IL) *452*
Northwestern Coll (MN) *453*
Northwestern Oklahoma State U (OK) *453*
Northwestern State U of Louisiana (LA) *453*
Northwest Missouri State U (MO) *454*
Notre Dame Coll (OH) *455*
Nova Southeastern U (FL) *455*
Oglethorpe U (GA) *457*
Ohio Northern U (OH) *457*
Ohio U (OH) *458*
Oklahoma Baptist U (OK) *459*
Oklahoma Christian U (OK) *459*
Oklahoma City U (OK) *460*
Olivet Nazarene U (IL) *461*
Oral Roberts U (OK) *461*
Oregon State U (OR) *462*
Ouachita Baptist U (AR) *462*
Our Lady of the Lake U of San Antonio (TX) *463*
Pacific Lutheran U (WA) *463*
Pacific Oaks Coll (CA) *464*
Pacific Union Coll (CA) *464*
Pacific U (OR) *464*
Paine Coll (GA) *465*
Palm Beach Atlantic U (FL) *465*
Park U (MO) *465*
Patten Coll (CA) *466*
Peru State Coll (NE) *469*
Philadelphia Biblical U (PA) *469*
Piedmont Coll (GA) *470*
Pine Manor Coll (MA) *470*
Pittsburg State U (KS) *470*
Plymouth State Coll (NH) *471*
Point Park Coll (PA) *471*
Pontifical Catholic U of Puerto Rico (PR) *472*
Presbyterian Coll (SC) *473*
Prescott Coll (AZ) *474*
Purdue U (IN) *475*
Queens Coll of the City U of NY (NY) *475*
Queens U of Charlotte (NC) *476*
Reinhardt Coll (GA) *478*
Rhode Island Coll (RI) *479*
Rider U (NJ) *480*
Ripon Coll (WI) *480*
Rivier Coll (NH) *480*
Roosevelt U (IL) *483*
Rowan U (NJ) *484*
Ryerson U (ON, Canada) *485*
Sacred Heart U (CT) *486*
St. Ambrose U (IA) *486*
St. Cloud State U (MN) *488*
Saint Joseph Coll (CT) *490*
St. Joseph's Coll, Suffolk Campus (NY) *491*
Saint Mary-of-the-Woods Coll (IN) *493*
Saint Mary's U of Minnesota (MN) *494*
St. Thomas Aquinas Coll (NY) *495*
Saint Xavier U (IL) *496*
Salem State Coll (MA) *497*
Salve Regina U (RI) *497*
Samford U (AL) *497*
Sarah Lawrence Coll (NY) *499*
Seton Hall U (NJ) *502*
Seton Hill U (PA) *502*
Siena Heights U (MI) *504*
Silver Lake Coll (WI) *504*
Simmons Coll (MA) *504*
Simpson Coll (IA) *505*
Slippery Rock U of Pennsylvania (PA) *506*
South Carolina State U (SC) *506*
South Dakota State U (SD) *507*
Southeastern Oklahoma State U (OK) *508*
Southeast Missouri State U (MO) *508*
Southern Adventist U (TN) *508*
Southern Arkansas U–Magnolia (AR) *509*
Southern Connecticut State U (CT) *509*
Southern Illinois U Carbondale (IL) *509*
Southern Illinois U Edwardsville (IL) *509*
Southern Nazarene U (OK) *510*
Southern New Hampshire U (NH) *510*
Southern Wesleyan U (SC) *511*
Southwestern Coll (KS) *512*
Southwest Missouri State U (MO) *513*
Southwest State U (MN) *513*
Spalding U (KY) *513*
Spring Arbor U (MI) *514*
Springfield Coll (MA) *514*
Spring Hill Coll (AL) *514*
State U of NY at New Paltz (NY) *515*
State U of NY Coll at Buffalo (NY) *516*
State U of NY Coll at Cortland (NY) *516*
State U of NY Coll at Fredonia (NY) *516*
State U of NY Coll at Geneseo (NY) *516*
Stephens Coll (MO) *519*
Stonehill Coll (MA) *520*
Susquehanna U (PA) *521*
Syracuse U (NY) *521*
Tabor Coll (KS) *522*
Temple U (PA) *523*
Tennessee State U (TN) *523*
Tennessee Technological U (TN) *524*
Texas A&M International U (TX) *524*
Texas A&M U–Commerce (TX) *525*
Texas A&M U–Kingsville (TX) *525*
Texas Southern U (TX) *526*
Thomas U (GA) *528*
Toccoa Falls Coll (GA) *528*
Touro Coll (NY) *529*
Towson U (MD) *529*
Trevecca Nazarene U (TN) *529*
Trinity Coll (DC) *530*
Troy State U (AL) *532*
Troy State U Dothan (AL) *532*
Tufts U (MA) *533*
Tusculum Coll (TN) *533*
Union U (TN) *534*
Université de Sherbrooke (QC, Canada) *536*
U du Québec à Trois-Rivières (QC, Canada) *536*
U du Québec à Hull (QC, Canada) *536*
Université Laval (QC, Canada) *536*
The U of Akron (OH) *537*
The U of Alabama (AL) *537*
The U of Alabama at Birmingham (AL) *537*
U of Alaska Anchorage (AK) *538*
U of Alaska Southeast (AK) *538*
U of Alberta (AB, Canada) *538*
The U of Arizona (AZ) *538*
U of Arkansas at Little Rock (AR) *539*
The U of British Columbia (BC, Canada) *540*
U of Calgary (AB, Canada) *540*
U of Central Arkansas (AR) *542*
U of Central Florida (FL) *542*
U of Central Oklahoma (OK) *542*
U of Cincinnati (OH) *543*
U of Dayton (OH) *544*
U of Delaware (DE) *544*
U of Georgia (GA) *545*
U of Great Falls (MT) *545*
U of Hartford (CT) *546*
U of Hawaii at Manoa (HI) *546*
U of Illinois at Urbana–Champaign (IL) *548*
U of Kentucky (KY) *549*
U of La Verne (CA) *549*
U of Maine (ME) *550*
U of Maine at Farmington (ME) *550*
U of Manitoba (MB, Canada) *551*
U of Mary (ND) *551*
U of Mary Hardin-Baylor (TX) *551*
U of Maryland, Coll Park (MD) *552*
U of Maryland Eastern Shore (MD) *552*
U of Michigan–Dearborn (MI) *554*
U of Michigan–Flint (MI) *554*
U of Minnesota, Crookston (MN) *554*
U of Minnesota, Duluth (MN) *554*
U of Minnesota, Twin Cities Campus (MN) *555*
U of Missouri–Columbia (MO) *555*
U of Missouri–Kansas City (MO) *555*
U of Missouri–St. Louis (MO) *556*
U of Mobile (AL) *556*
U of Montevallo (AL) *557*
U of Nevada, Las Vegas (NV) *558*
U of New Brunswick Fredericton (NB, Canada) *558*
U of New Hampshire (NH) *558*
U of New Mexico (NM) *559*
U of North Alabama (AL) *559*
The U of North Carolina at Chapel Hill (NC) *560*
The U of North Carolina at Charlotte (NC) *560*
The U of North Carolina at Pembroke (NC) *560*
The U of North Carolina at Wilmington (NC) *561*
U of North Dakota (ND) *561*
U of Northern Iowa (IA) *561*
U of North Texas (TX) *562*
U of Oklahoma (OK) *562*
U of Ottawa (ON, Canada) *563*
U of Regina (SK, Canada) *572*
U of Science and Arts of Oklahoma (OK) *574*
The U of Scranton (PA) *574*
U of South Alabama (AL) *575*
U of South Carolina Aiken (SC) *575*
U of South Carolina Spartanburg (SC) *575*
U of South Florida (FL) *576*
The U of Tennessee at Chattanooga (TN) *577*
The U of Tennessee at Martin (TN) *577*
The U of Texas at Brownsville (TX) *578*
The U of Texas–Pan American (TX) *579*
U of the District of Columbia (DC) *580*
U of the Incarnate Word (TX) *580*
U of the Ozarks (AR) *580*
U of Toledo (OH) *581*
U of Utah (UT) *582*
U of Vermont (VT) *582*
U of Victoria (BC, Canada) *582*
The U of West Alabama (AL) *583*
The U of Western Ontario (ON, Canada) *583*
U of West Florida (FL) *583*
U of Windsor (ON, Canada) *584*
U of Wisconsin–La Crosse (WI) *584*
U of Wisconsin–Madison (WI) *584*
U of Wisconsin–Milwaukee (WI) *585*
U of Wisconsin–Oshkosh (WI) *585*
U of Wisconsin–Platteville (WI) *585*
U of Wisconsin–Stevens Point (WI) *585*
U of Wisconsin–Stout (WI) *586*
U of Wisconsin–Whitewater (WI) *586*
U System Coll for Lifelong Learning (NH) *586*
Utah State U (UT) *587*
Valdosta State U (GA) *588*
Vanderbilt U (TN) *588*
Villa Julie Coll (MD) *590*
Virginia Polytechnic Inst and State U (VA) *591*
Virginia Union U (VA) *591*
Voorhees Coll (SC) *592*
Wagner Coll (NY) *592*
Waldorf Coll (IA) *592*
Walsh U (OH) *593*
Warner Pacific Coll (OR) *593*
Wartburg Coll (IA) *594*
Washington Bible Coll (MD) *594*
Wayne State Coll (NE) *596*
Weber State U (UT) *596*
Webster U (MO) *597*
Wesleyan Coll (GA) *597*
West Chester U of Pennsylvania (PA) *598*
Western Carolina U (NC) *598*
Western Kentucky U (KY) *599*
Western New Mexico U (NM) *600*
Western Washington U (WA) *600*
Westfield State Coll (MA) *600*
West Liberty State Coll (WV) *601*
Westminster Coll (MO) *601*
Westminster Coll (UT) *601*
West Virginia State Coll (WV) *602*
West Virginia Wesleyan Coll (WV) *603*
Wheelock Coll (MA) *603*
Whittier Coll (CA) *604*
Widener U (PA) *604*
Williams Baptist Coll (AR) *606*
Wingate U (NC) *607*
Winona State U (MN) *608*
Winston-Salem State U (NC) *608*
Winthrop U (SC) *608*
Worcester State Coll (MA) *609*
Wright State U (OH) *609*
Xavier U of Louisiana (LA) *610*
York U (ON, Canada) *611*
Youngstown State U (OH) *611*

EARTH SCIENCES

Overview: Students who choose this broad-based major focus on a number of areas of study having to do with the Earth and planets, including geology, atmospheric sciences, oceanography, physics, chemistry and biology, and environmental sciences. *Related majors:* geology, oceanography, atmospheric sciences, biology, chemistry, and environmental sciences. *Potential careers:* environmentalist, geologist, ecologist, research scientist, seismologist, meteorologist, biochemist, ecologist. *Salary potential:* $27k-$37k.

Adams State Coll (CO) *260*
Adelphi U (NY) *260*
Adrian Coll (MI) *260*
Alfred U (NY) *263*
Antioch Coll (OH) *269*
Augustana Coll (IL) *276*
Baylor U (TX) *283*
Bemidji State U (MN) *285*
Bloomsburg U of Pennsylvania (PA) *290*
Boston U (MA) *292*
Bridgewater State Coll (MA) *294*
Brigham Young U (UT) *295*
Brock U (ON, Canada) *295*
Brooklyn Coll of the City U of NY (NY) *295*
California Inst of Technology (CA) *299*
California State Polytechnic U, Pomona (CA) *300*
California State U, Chico (CA) *300*
California State U, Dominguez Hills (CA) *300*
California State U, Long Beach (CA) *301*
California State U, Northridge (CA) *301*

California U of Pennsylvania (PA) 302
Carleton U (ON, Canada) 305
Central Connecticut State U (CT) 309
Central Michigan U (MI) 310
Central Missouri State U (MO) 310
Central Washington U (WA) 310
City Coll of the City U of NY (NY) 314
Clarion U of Pennsylvania (PA) 315
Clark U (MA) 316
Colby Coll (ME) 318
Dalhousie U (NS, Canada) 336
Dartmouth Coll (NH) 337
DePauw U (IN) 339
Dickinson State U (ND) 344
Eastern Kentucky U (KY) 348
Eastern Michigan U (MI) 348
Eastern Washington U (WA) 349
East Stroudsburg U of Pennsylvania (PA) 349
Edinboro U of Pennsylvania (PA) 351
Emporia State U (KS) 354
The Evergreen State Coll (WA) 355
Fitchburg State Coll (MA) 358
Framingham State Coll (MA) 362
Frostburg State U (MD) 365
Gannon U (PA) 365
Georgia Inst of Technology (GA) 367
Georgia Southwestern State U (GA) 368
Grand Valley State U (MI) 371
Guilford Coll (NC) 373
Hampshire Coll (MA) 375
Harvard U (MA) 376
Indiana U of Pennsylvania (PA) 386
Iowa State U of Science and Technology (IA) 390
Johns Hopkins U (MD) 392
Kean U (NJ) 396
Kent State U (OH) 397
Kutztown U of Pennsylvania (PA) 399
Lakehead U (ON, Canada) 400
Laurentian U (ON, Canada) 403
Lewis-Clark State Coll (ID) 406
Lock Haven U of Pennsylvania (PA) 408
Long Island U, C.W. Post Campus (NY) 409
Longwood U (VA) 409
Mansfield U of Pennsylvania (PA) 416
Massachusetts Inst of Technology (MA) 421
McGill U (QC, Canada) 423
McMaster U (ON, Canada) 423
Memorial U of Newfoundland (NF, Canada) 424
Mercer U (GA) 425
Mercyhurst Coll (PA) 425
Miami U (OH) 428
Michigan State U (MI) 428
Michigan Technological U (MI) 428
Millersville U of Pennsylvania (PA) 430
Minnesota State U, Mankato (MN) 431
Montana State U–Bozeman (MT) 434
Montclair State U (NJ) 435
Murray State U (KY) 440
Muskingum Coll (OH) 441
National U (CA) 442
North Dakota State U (ND) 449
Northeastern Illinois U (IL) 450
Northern Michigan U (MI) 451
Northland Coll (WI) 452
Northwest Missouri State U (MO) 454
Ohio Wesleyan U (OH) 459
Olivet Nazarene U (IL) 461
Pacific Lutheran U (WA) 463
Penn State U Univ Park Campus (PA) 468
Queens Coll of the City U of NY (NY) 475
St. Cloud State U (MN) 488
St. Mary's U of San Antonio (TX) 494
Salem State Coll (MA) 497
Shippensburg U of Pennsylvania (PA) 503
Simon Fraser U (BC, Canada) 505
Slippery Rock U of Pennsylvania (PA) 506
Sonoma State U (CA) 506
Southeast Missouri State U (MO) 508
Southern Connecticut State U (CT) 509
Stanford U (CA) 514
State U of NY at Albany (NY) 514
State U of NY at New Paltz (NY) 515
State U of NY Coll at Brockport (NY) 515
State U of NY Coll at Buffalo (NY) 516
State U of NY Coll at Cortland (NY) 516
State U of NY Coll at Fredonia (NY) 516
State U of NY Coll at Oneonta (NY) 517
State U of West Georgia (GA) 518
Stony Brook U, State University of New York (NY) 520
Tennessee Temple U (TN) 524
Texas A&M U (TX) 524
Texas A&M U–Commerce (TX) 525
Texas Tech U (TX) 526
Tulane U (LA) 533
U of Alaska Fairbanks (AK) 538
U of Alberta (AB, Canada) 538
The U of Arizona (AZ) 538
U of Arkansas (AR) 539
The U of British Columbia (BC, Canada) 540
U of Calgary (AB, Canada) 540
U of Calif, Berkeley (CA) 540
U of Calif, Los Angeles (CA) 541
U of Calif, San Diego (CA) 541
U of Calif, Santa Cruz (CA) 542
U of Guelph (ON, Canada) 546
U of Indianapolis (IN) 548
The U of Iowa (IA) 548
U of King's Coll (NS, Canada) 549
The U of Lethbridge (AB, Canada) 549
U of Manitoba (MB, Canada) 551
U of Massachusetts Amherst (MA) 552
U of Michigan–Flint (MI) 554
U of Missouri–Kansas City (MO) 555
U of Nebraska at Omaha (NE) 557
U of Nevada, Las Vegas (NV) 558
U of New Hampshire (NH) 558
U of New Mexico (NM) 559
The U of North Carolina at Charlotte (NC) 560
U of Northern Colorado (CO) 561
U of Ottawa (ON, Canada) 563
U of Rochester (NY) 573
The U of South Dakota (SD) 575
The U of Texas of the Permian Basin (TX) 579
U of Toronto (ON, Canada) 581
U of Victoria (BC, Canada) 582
U of Waterloo (ON, Canada) 583
The U of Western Ontario (ON, Canada) 583
U of Windsor (ON, Canada) 584
U of Wisconsin–Green Bay (WI) 584
U of Wisconsin–Madison (WI) 584
U of Wisconsin–Milwaukee (WI) 585
Virginia Wesleyan Coll (VA) 591
Washington U in St. Louis (MO) 595
Wesleyan U (CT) 597
West Chester U of Pennsylvania (PA) 598
Western Connecticut State U (CT) 598
Western Michigan U (MI) 599
Western Washington U (WA) 600
Wilkes U (PA) 605
Winona State U (MN) 608
Wittenberg U (OH) 608
York U (ON, Canada) 611
Youngstown State U (OH) 611

EAST AND SOUTHEAST ASIAN LANGUAGES RELATED

Information can be found under this major's main heading.

Dartmouth Coll (NH) 337
Michigan State U (MI) 428
U of Hawaii at Manoa (HI) 546
U of Kansas (KS) 549
Washington U in St. Louis (MO) 595

EAST ASIAN STUDIES

Overview: This major teaches students about the history, society, politics, culture, economics, and languages of the people of East Asia, defined as including China, Japan, Mongolia, Taiwan, and Tibet. *Related majors:* languages and dialects of these countries, histories of these countries, political relations, comparative literature, international business. *Potential careers:* translator, language teacher, business consultant, importer/exporter, foreign service officer. *Salary potential:* $25k-$35k.

Augsburg Coll (MN) 276
Barnard Coll (NY) 282
Bates Coll (ME) 282
Boston U (MA) 292
Brown U (RI) 296
Bryn Mawr Coll (PA) 297
Bucknell U (PA) 297
Carleton U (ON, Canada) 305
Colby Coll (ME) 318
Colgate U (NY) 319
The Coll of William and Mary (VA) 324
Columbia Coll (NY) 326
Columbia U, School of General Studies (NY) 328
Connecticut Coll (CT) 331
Cornell U (NY) 333
Denison U (OH) 339
DePaul U (IL) 339
DePauw U (IN) 339
Dickinson Coll (PA) 344
Emory & Henry Coll (VA) 353
The George Washington U (DC) 367
Hamilton Coll (NY) 374
Hamline U (MN) 374
Hampshire Coll (MA) 375
Harvard U (MA) 376
Haverford Coll (PA) 377
Indiana U Bloomington (IN) 385
John Carroll U (OH) 392
Johns Hopkins U (MD) 392
Lawrence U (WI) 403
Lewis & Clark Coll (OR) 405
Long Island U, Southampton Coll, Friends World Program (NY) 409
Marlboro Coll (VT) 418
Massachusetts Inst of Technology (MA) 421
McGill U (QC, Canada) 423
Middlebury Coll (VT) 429
New York U (NY) 447
Oakland U (MI) 456
Oberlin Coll (OH) 456
The Ohio State U (OH) 457
Ohio Wesleyan U (OH) 459
Penn State U Univ Park Campus (PA) 468
Pomona Coll (CA) 472
Portland State U (OR) 472
Princeton U (NJ) 474
Queens Coll of the City U of NY (NY) 475
Rutgers, The State U of New Jersey, New Brunswick (NJ) 485
San Jose State U (CA) 499
Scripps Coll (CA) 501
Seattle U (WA) 501
Simmons Coll (MA) 504
Smith Coll (MA) 506
Stanford U (CA) 514
State U of NY at Albany (NY) 514
United States Military Academy (NY) 535
U of Alberta (AB, Canada) 538
The U of Arizona (AZ) 538
U of Calgary (AB, Canada) 540
U of Calif, Davis (CA) 540
U of Calif, Irvine (CA) 541
U of Calif, Los Angeles (CA) 541
U of Calif, Santa Cruz (CA) 542
U of Chicago (IL) 542
U of Delaware (DE) 544
U of Hawaii at Manoa (HI) 546
U of Minnesota, Twin Cities Campus (MN) 555
The U of Montana–Missoula (MT) 556
U of Oregon (OR) 562
U of Pennsylvania (PA) 563
U of St. Thomas (MN) 573
U of Southern California (CA) 576
U of Toronto (ON, Canada) 581
U of Washington (WA) 583
Ursinus Coll (PA) 587
Valparaiso U (IN) 588
Vanderbilt U (TN) 588
Washington and Lee U (VA) 594
Washington U in St. Louis (MO) 595
Wayne State U (MI) 596
Wellesley Coll (MA) 597
Wesleyan U (CT) 597
Western Washington U (WA) 600
Wittenberg U (OH) 608
Yale U (CT) 610
York U (ON, Canada) 611

EASTERN EUROPEAN AREA STUDIES

Overview: This major teaches students about the history, society, politics, culture, economics, and languages of the countries that make up Eastern Europe, defined as Austria, the Balkans, the Baltic States, Belarus, Czech Republic, Hungary, Romania, Poland, Russia, Slovakia and Ukraine. *Related majors:* any of the languages of these countries, Russian history and literature, international relations, economics, Jewish studies. *Potential careers:* Foreign service officer, business consultant, translator, entrepreneur. *Salary potential:* $25k-$32k.

Baltimore Hebrew U (MD) 280
Bard Coll (NY) 281
Barnard Coll (NY) 282
Carleton U (ON, Canada) 305
Connecticut Coll (CT) 331
Cornell U (NY) 333
Emory U (GA) 354
Florida State U (FL) 361
Fordham U (NY) 362
Hamline U (MN) 374
Hampshire Coll (MA) 375
Harvard U (MA) 376
Indiana U Bloomington (IN) 385
Kent State U (OH) 397
Long Island U, Southampton Coll, Friends World Program (NY) 409
Marlboro Coll (VT) 418
McGill U (QC, Canada) 423
Middlebury Coll (VT) 429
Portland State U (OR) 472
Rutgers, The State U of New Jersey, New Brunswick (NJ) 485
Salem State Coll (MA) 497
Sarah Lawrence Coll (NY) 499
State U of NY at Albany (NY) 514
United States Military Academy (NY) 535
U of Alberta (AB, Canada) 538
U of Chicago (IL) 542
U of Connecticut (CT) 544
The U of Iowa (IA) 548
U of Oregon (OR) 562
U of Richmond (VA) 572
U of Toronto (ON, Canada) 581
U of Vermont (VT) 582
U of Victoria (BC, Canada) 582
Wesleyan U (CT) 597

EAST EUROPEAN LANGUAGES RELATED

Information can be found under this major's main heading.

Princeton U (NJ) 474
Rutgers, The State U of New Jersey, Newark (NJ) 485
The U of North Carolina at Chapel Hill (NC) 560

ECOLOGY

Overview: The study of the relationships and interactions between plants, animals, and microorganisms. *Related majors:* biology, biochemistry, marine/aquatic biology, environmental biology, entomology. *Potential careers:* ecologist, botanist, environmental scientist, forest ranger, research scientist, marine biologist. *Salary potential:* $24k-$34k.

Adelphi U (NY) 260
Alma Coll (MI) 264
Appalachian State U (NC) 270
Averett U (VA) 278
Ball State U (IN) 280
Bard Coll (NY) 281
Barry U (FL) 282
Bemidji State U (MN) 285
Bennington Coll (VT) 286
Boston U (MA) 292
Bradley U (IL) 293
Brevard Coll (NC) 294
California State U, Fresno (CA) 301
California State U, Hayward (CA) 301
California State U, Sacramento (CA) 301
California State U, San Marcos (CA) 302
Carleton U (ON, Canada) 305
Carlow Coll (PA) 305
The Catholic U of America (DC) 307

ECOLOGY (continued)

Clark U (MA) **316**
Coll of the Atlantic (ME) **323**
Concordia Coll (NY) **329**
Concordia U (QC, Canada) **331**
Connecticut Coll (CT) **331**
Cornell U (NY) **333**
Dartmouth Coll (NH) **337**
Defiance Coll (OH) **338**
East Central U (OK) **347**
Eastern Kentucky U (KY) **348**
East Stroudsburg U of Pennsylvania (PA) **349**
The Evergreen State Coll (WA) **355**
Florida Inst of Technology (FL) **360**
Florida State U (FL) **361**
Franklin Pierce Coll (NH) **364**
Frostburg State U (MD) **365**
Georgetown Coll (KY) **366**
Goddard Coll (VT) **369**
Hampshire Coll (MA) **375**
Harvard U (MA) **376**
Huntingdon Coll (AL) **383**
Idaho State U (ID) **384**
Iona Coll (NY) **390**
Iowa State U of Science and Technology (IA) **390**
Jacksonville State U (AL) **390**
Juniata Coll (PA) **395**
Keene State Coll (NH) **396**
Lawrence U (WI) **403**
Lenoir-Rhyne Coll (NC) **405**
Lock Haven U of Pennsylvania (PA) **408**
Long Island U, Southampton Coll, Friends World Program (NY) **409**
Maharishi U of Management (IA) **414**
Manchester Coll (IN) **415**
Marlboro Coll (VT) **418**
McGill U (QC, Canada) **423**
Memorial U of Newfoundland (NF, Canada) **424**
Michigan Technological U (MI) **428**
Minnesota State U, Mankato (MN) **431**
Missouri Southern State Coll (MO) **433**
Montreat Coll (NC) **435**
Morehead State U (KY) **436**
Naropa U (CO) **441**
New England Coll (NH) **444**
Northern Arizona U (AZ) **450**
Northern Michigan U (MI) **451**
Northland Coll (WI) **452**
Northwestern U (IL) **453**
Northwest Missouri State U (MO) **454**
Oberlin Coll (OH) **456**
Okanagan U Coll (BC, Canada) **459**
Pace U (NY) **463**
Plymouth State Coll (NH) **471**
Pomona Coll (CA) **472**
Prescott Coll (AZ) **474**
Princeton U (NJ) **474**
Rice U (TX) **479**
Rutgers, The State U of New Jersey, New Brunswick (NJ) **485**
St. Bonaventure U (NY) **487**
St. Cloud State U (MN) **488**
St. John's U (NY) **490**
St. Lawrence U (NY) **491**
San Diego State U (CA) **498**
San Francisco State U (CA) **498**
San Jose State U (CA) **499**
Sarah Lawrence Coll (NY) **499**
Sierra Nevada Coll (NV) **504**
Simon's Rock Coll of Bard (MA) **505**
Slippery Rock U of Pennsylvania (PA) **506**
Sonoma State U (CA) **506**
Springfield Coll (MA) **514**
State U of NY Coll of Environ Sci and Forestry (NY) **517**
State U of West Georgia (GA) **518**
Sterling Coll (VT) **519**
Towson U (MD) **529**
Tufts U (MA) **533**
Tulane U (LA) **533**
Unity Coll (ME) **535**
Université de Sherbrooke (QC, Canada) **536**
U Coll of the Cariboo (BC, Canada) **537**
The U of Arizona (AZ) **538**
U of Calgary (AB, Canada) **540**
U of Calif, Irvine (CA) **541**
U of Calif, Los Angeles (CA) **541**
U of Calif, San Diego (CA) **541**
U of Calif, Santa Barbara (CA) **541**
U of Calif, Santa Cruz (CA) **542**
U of Colorado at Colorado Springs (CO) **543**
U of Connecticut (CT) **544**
U of Delaware (DE) **544**
U of Georgia (GA) **545**
U of Guelph (ON, Canada) **546**
U of Illinois at Urbana–Champaign (IL) **548**
U of Maine at Machias (ME) **551**
U of Manitoba (MB, Canada) **551**
U of Maryland, Coll Park (MD) **552**
U of Maryland Eastern Shore (MD) **552**
U of Miami (FL) **553**
U of Michigan (MI) **554**
U of Minnesota, Twin Cities Campus (MN) **555**
U of Missouri–St. Louis (MO) **556**
U of New Brunswick Fredericton (NB, Canada) **558**
U of New Hampshire (NH) **558**
U of Pittsburgh (PA) **569**
U of Pittsburgh at Johnstown (PA) **570**
U of Rio Grande (OH) **572**
The U of Tennessee (TN) **577**
The U of Texas at Austin (TX) **578**
U of Toronto (ON, Canada) **581**
U of Vermont (VT) **582**
U of Victoria (BC, Canada) **582**
The U of Western Ontario (ON, Canada) **583**
U of Wisconsin–Milwaukee (WI) **585**
Ursinus Coll (PA) **587**
Utah State U (UT) **587**
Vanderbilt U (TN) **588**
West Chester U of Pennsylvania (PA) **598**
Western Washington U (WA) **600**
William Paterson U of New Jersey (NJ) **606**
Winona State U (MN) **608**
Yale U (CT) **610**
York U (ON, Canada) **611**

ECONOMICS

Overview: This is the study of production and allocation of resources in conditions of scarcity. *Related majors:* business administration, accounting, finance, financial planning, logistics and materials management. *Potential careers:* economist, financial adviser, accountant, banker, professor, business executive. *Salary potential:* $30k-$40k.

Acadia U (NS, Canada) **260**
Adams State Coll (CO) **260**
Adelphi U (NY) **260**
Adrian Coll (MI) **260**
Agnes Scott Coll (GA) **261**
Alabama A&M U (AL) **261**
Alabama State U (AL) **261**
Albertson Coll of Idaho (ID) **262**
Albertus Magnus Coll (CT) **262**
Albion Coll (MI) **262**
Albright Coll (PA) **263**
Alcorn State U (MS) **263**
Alfred U (NY) **263**
Allegheny Coll (PA) **264**
Alma Coll (MI) **264**
American International Coll (MA) **267**
American U (DC) **267**
The American U in Cairo(Egypt) **267**
The American U of Paris(France) **268**
Amherst Coll (MA) **268**
Andrews U (MI) **269**
Antioch Coll (OH) **269**
Appalachian State U (NC) **270**
Aquinas Coll (MI) **270**
Arizona State U (AZ) **271**
Arkansas State U (AR) **272**
Arkansas Tech U (AR) **272**
Armstrong Atlantic State U (GA) **273**
Ashland U (OH) **274**
Assumption Coll (MA) **275**
Auburn U (AL) **276**
Augsburg Coll (MN) **276**
Augustana Coll (IL) **276**
Augustana Coll (SD) **276**
Aurora U (IL) **277**
Austin Coll (TX) **277**
Ave Maria Coll (MI) **278**
Babson Coll (MA) **278**
Baker U (KS) **280**
Baldwin-Wallace Coll (OH) **280**
Ball State U (IN) **280**
Bard Coll (NY) **281**
Barnard Coll (NY) **282**
Barry U (FL) **282**
Bates Coll (ME) **282**
Baylor U (TX) **283**
Bellarmine U (KY) **284**
Belmont Abbey Coll (NC) **284**
Belmont U (TN) **284**
Beloit Coll (WI) **285**
Bemidji State U (MN) **285**
Benedictine Coll (KS) **285**
Benedictine U (IL) **285**
Bentley Coll (MA) **286**
Berea Coll (KY) **286**
Baruch Coll of the City U of NY (NY) **286**
Berry Coll (GA) **287**
Bethany Coll (WV) **287**
Bethel Coll (MN) **288**
Birmingham-Southern Coll (AL) **289**
Bishop's U (QC, Canada) **289**
Bloomfield Coll (NJ) **290**
Bloomsburg U of Pennsylvania (PA) **290**
Bluffton Coll (OH) **291**
Boston Coll (MA) **292**
Boston U (MA) **292**
Bowdoin Coll (ME) **292**
Bowie State U (MD) **292**
Bowling Green State U (OH) **292**
Bradley U (IL) **293**
Brandeis U (MA) **293**
Brandon U (MB, Canada) **293**
Bridgewater Coll (VA) **294**
Bridgewater State Coll (MA) **294**
Brigham Young U (UT) **295**
Brock U (ON, Canada) **295**
Brooklyn Coll of the City U of NY (NY) **295**
Brown U (RI) **296**
Bryant Coll (RI) **296**
Bryn Mawr Coll (PA) **297**
Bucknell U (PA) **297**
Buena Vista U (IA) **297**
Butler U (IN) **297**
California Inst of Technology (CA) **299**
California Lutheran U (CA) **299**
California Polytechnic State U, San Luis Obispo (CA) **300**
California State Polytechnic U, Pomona (CA) **300**
California State U, Bakersfield (CA) **300**
California State U, Chico (CA) **300**
California State U, Dominguez Hills (CA) **300**
California State U, Fresno (CA) **301**
California State U, Fullerton (CA) **301**
California State U, Hayward (CA) **301**
California State U, Long Beach (CA) **301**
California State U, Northridge (CA) **301**
California State U, Sacramento (CA) **301**
California State U, San Bernardino (CA) **302**
California State U, San Marcos (CA) **302**
California State U, Stanislaus (CA) **302**
California U of Pennsylvania (PA) **302**
Calvin Coll (MI) **303**
Campbellsville U (KY) **303**
Campbell U (NC) **303**
Canisius Coll (NY) **304**
Capital U (OH) **304**
Carleton Coll (MN) **305**
Carleton U (ON, Canada) **305**
Carnegie Mellon U (PA) **305**
Carson-Newman Coll (TN) **306**
Carthage Coll (WI) **306**
Case Western Reserve U (OH) **307**
The Catholic U of America (DC) **307**
Centenary Coll of Louisiana (LA) **308**
Central Coll (IA) **309**
Central Connecticut State U (CT) **309**
Central Methodist Coll (MO) **309**
Central Michigan U (MI) **310**
Central Missouri State U (MO) **310**
Central Washington U (WA) **310**
Centre Coll (KY) **310**
Chapman U (CA) **311**
Chatham Coll (PA) **312**
Chestnut Hill Coll (PA) **312**
Cheyney U of Pennsylvania (PA) **312**
Christian Brothers U (TN) **313**
Christopher Newport U (VA) **313**
City Coll of the City U of NY (NY) **314**
Claremont McKenna Coll (CA) **315**
Clarion U of Pennsylvania (PA) **315**
Clark Atlanta U (GA) **315**
Clarke Coll (IA) **315**
Clarkson U (NY) **316**
Clark U (MA) **316**
Clemson U (SC) **317**
Cleveland State U (OH) **317**
Coe Coll (IA) **318**
Colby Coll (ME) **318**
Colgate U (NY) **319**
Coll of Charleston (SC) **320**
Coll of Mount Saint Vincent (NY) **320**
The Coll of New Jersey (NJ) **320**
The Coll of New Rochelle (NY) **321**
Coll of Notre Dame of Maryland (MD) **321**
Coll of Saint Benedict (MN) **321**
Coll of St. Catherine (MN) **321**
Coll of Saint Elizabeth (NJ) **321**
The Coll of St. Scholastica (MN) **322**
Coll of Staten Island of the City U of NY (NY) **323**
Coll of the Atlantic (ME) **323**
Coll of the Holy Cross (MA) **323**
The Coll of William and Mary (VA) **324**
The Coll of Wooster (OH) **324**
The Colorado Coll (CO) **325**
Colorado School of Mines (CO) **325**
Colorado State U (CO) **325**
Columbia Coll (NY) **326**
Columbia U, School of General Studies (NY) **328**
Concordia Coll (MN) **329**
Concordia U (MN) **330**
Concordia U (QC, Canada) **331**
Concordia U Wisconsin (WI) **331**
Connecticut Coll (CT) **331**
Converse Coll (SC) **332**
Cornell Coll (IA) **332**
Cornell U (NY) **333**
Covenant Coll (GA) **333**
Creighton U (NE) **333**
Dalhousie U (NS, Canada) **336**
Dartmouth Coll (NH) **337**
Davidson Coll (NC) **338**
Davis & Elkins Coll (WV) **338**
Delaware State U (DE) **338**
Denison U (OH) **339**
DePaul U (IL) **339**
DePauw U (IN) **339**
Deree Coll(Greece) **339**
Dickinson Coll (PA) **344**
Dillard U (LA) **344**
Doane Coll (NE) **344**
Dominican Coll (NY) **344**
Dominican U (IL) **345**
Dowling Coll (NY) **345**
Drake U (IA) **345**
Drew U (NJ) **346**
Drury U (MO) **346**
Duke U (NC) **346**
Earlham Coll (IN) **347**
East Carolina U (NC) **347**
Eastern Connecticut State U (CT) **347**
Eastern Illinois U (IL) **348**
Eastern Kentucky U (KY) **348**
Eastern Mennonite U (VA) **348**
Eastern Michigan U (MI) **348**
Eastern Oregon U (OR) **349**
Eastern Washington U (WA) **349**
East Stroudsburg U of Pennsylvania (PA) **349**
East Tennessee State U (TN) **349**
Eckerd Coll (FL) **350**
Edgewood Coll (WI) **351**
Edinboro U of Pennsylvania (PA) **351**
Elizabethtown Coll (PA) **351**
Elmhurst Coll (IL) **351**
Elmira Coll (NY) **351**
Elon U (NC) **352**
Emmanuel Coll (MA) **353**
Emory & Henry Coll (VA) **353**
Emory U (GA) **354**
Emporia State U (KS) **354**
Eugene Lang Coll, New School U (NY) **355**
Eureka Coll (IL) **355**
The Evergreen State Coll (WA) **355**
Excelsior Coll (NY) **356**
Fairfield U (CT) **356**
Fairleigh Dickinson U, Florham (NJ) **356**
Fairmont State Coll (WV) **356**
Fayetteville State U (NC) **357**
Fisk U (TN) **358**
Fitchburg State Coll (MA) **358**
Florida A&M U (FL) **359**
Florida Atlantic U (FL) **359**
Florida International U (FL) **360**
Florida Southern Coll (FL) **361**
Florida State U (FL) **361**
Fordham U (NY) **362**
Fort Hays State U (KS) **362**

Fort Lewis Coll (CO) 362
Fort Valley State U (GA) 362
Framingham State Coll (MA) 362
Franciscan U of Steubenville (OH) 363
Francis Marion U (SC) 363
Franklin and Marshall Coll (PA) 363
Franklin Coll (IN) 363
Franklin Pierce Coll (NH) 364
Frostburg State U (MD) 365
Furman U (SC) 365
Gallaudet U (DC) 365
George Mason U (VA) 366
Georgetown U (DC) 366
The George Washington U (DC) 367
Georgia Southern U (GA) 367
Georgia State U (GA) 368
Gettysburg Coll (PA) 368
Gonzaga U (WA) 369
Gordon Coll (MA) 370
Goshen Coll (IN) 370
Goucher Coll (MD) 370
Graceland U (IA) 371
Grand Canyon U (AZ) 371
Grand Valley State U (MI) 371
Grinnell Coll (IA) 373
Grove City Coll (PA) 373
Guilford Coll (NC) 373
Gustavus Adolphus Coll (MN) 374
Hamilton Coll (NY) 374
Hamline U (MN) 374
Hampden-Sydney Coll (VA) 374
Hampshire Coll (MA) 375
Hampton U (VA) 375
Hanover Coll (IN) 375
Harding U (AR) 375
Hartwick Coll (NY) 376
Harvard U (MA) 376
Hastings Coll (NE) 377
Haverford Coll (PA) 377
Hawai'i Pacific U (HI) 377
Heidelberg Coll (OH) 377
Hendrix Coll (AR) 378
Hillsdale Coll (MI) 379
Hiram Coll (OH) 379
Hobart and William Smith Colls (NY) 380
Hofstra U (NY) 380
Hollins U (VA) 380
Holy Family U (PA) 380
Hood Coll (MD) 381
Hope Coll (MI) 381
Houston Baptist U (TX) 382
Howard U (DC) 382
Humboldt State U (CA) 382
Hunter Coll of the City U of NY (NY) 382
Huntington Coll (IN) 383
Idaho State U (ID) 384
Illinois Coll (IL) 384
Illinois State U (IL) 384
Illinois Wesleyan U (IL) 385
Immaculata U (PA) 385
Indiana State U (IN) 385
Indiana U Bloomington (IN) 385
Indiana U Northwest (IN) 386
Indiana U of Pennsylvania (PA) 386
Indiana U–Purdue U Fort Wayne (IN) 386
Indiana U–Purdue U Indianapolis (IN) 387
Indiana U South Bend (IN) 387
Indiana U Southeast (IN) 387
Indiana Wesleyan U (IN) 387
Insto Tecno Estudios Sups Monterrey(Mexico) 388
Inter American U of PR, San Germán Campus (PR) 388
Iona Coll (NY) 390
Iowa State U of Science and Technology (IA) 390
Ithaca Coll (NY) 390
Jackson State U (MS) 390
Jacksonville State U (AL) 390
Jacksonville U (FL) 391
James Madison U (VA) 391
John Carroll U (OH) 392
Johns Hopkins U (MD) 392
Johnson C. Smith U (NC) 394
Juniata Coll (PA) 395
Kansas State U (KS) 396
Kean U (NJ) 396
Keene State Coll (NH) 396
Kennesaw State U (GA) 397
Kent State U (OH) 397
Kenyon Coll (OH) 398
King Coll (TN) 398
King's Coll (PA) 398
Knox Coll (IL) 399
Lafayette Coll (PA) 400
LaGrange Coll (GA) 400
Lake Forest Coll (IL) 400
Lakehead U (ON, Canada) 400
Lakeland Coll (WI) 401
Lamar U (TX) 401
Langston U (OK) 402
La Salle U (PA) 402
Laurentian U (ON, Canada) 403
Lawrence U (WI) 403
Lebanon Valley Coll (PA) 403
Lehigh U (PA) 404
Lehman Coll of the City U of NY (NY) 404
Le Moyne Coll (NY) 404
Lenoir-Rhyne Coll (NC) 405
Lewis & Clark Coll (OR) 405
Lewis U (IL) 406
Lincoln U (CA) 407
Lincoln U (PA) 407
Lindenwood U (MO) 407
Linfield Coll (OR) 408
Lock Haven U of Pennsylvania (PA) 408
Long Island U, Brooklyn Campus (NY) 409
Long Island U, C.W. Post Campus (NY) 409
Longwood U (VA) 409
Loras Coll (IA) 410
Louisiana Coll (LA) 410
Louisiana State U and A&M Coll (LA) 410
Loyola Coll in Maryland (MD) 411
Loyola Marymount U (CA) 411
Loyola U Chicago (IL) 411
Loyola U New Orleans (LA) 411
Luther Coll (IA) 412
Lycoming Coll (PA) 412
Lynchburg Coll (VA) 413
Lyon Coll (AR) 413
Macalester Coll (MN) 413
Manchester Coll (IN) 415
Manhattan Coll (NY) 416
Manhattanville Coll (NY) 416
Mansfield U of Pennsylvania (PA) 416
Marietta Coll (OH) 417
Marist Coll (NY) 417
Marlboro Coll (VT) 418
Marquette U (WI) 418
Marshall U (WV) 418
Mary Baldwin Coll (VA) 419
Marymount Coll of Fordham U (NY) 419
Marymount U (VA) 420
Maryville Coll (TN) 420
Mary Washington Coll (VA) 420
Massachusetts Coll of Liberal Arts (MA) 421
Massachusetts Inst of Technology (MA) 421
McDaniel Coll (MD) 422
McGill U (QC, Canada) 423
McKendree Coll (IL) 423
McMaster U (ON, Canada) 423
Memorial U of Newfoundland (NF, Canada) 424
Mercer U (GA) 425
Meredith Coll (NC) 426
Merrimack Coll (MA) 426
Messiah Coll (PA) 426
Methodist Coll (NC) 427
Metropolitan State Coll of Denver (CO) 427
Metropolitan State U (MN) 427
Miami U (OH) 428
Michigan State U (MI) 428
Middlebury Coll (VT) 429
Middle Tennessee State U (TN) 429
Midland Lutheran Coll (NE) 429
Midwestern State U (TX) 430
Millersville U of Pennsylvania (PA) 430
Millsaps Coll (MS) 431
Mills Coll (CA) 431
Minnesota State U, Mankato (MN) 431
Minnesota State U, Moorhead (MN) 432
Minot State U (ND) 432
Mississippi State U (MS) 432
Missouri Valley Coll (MO) 433
Missouri Western State Coll (MO) 433
Monmouth Coll (IL) 434
Monmouth U (NJ) 434
Montana State U–Bozeman (MT) 434
Montclair State U (NJ) 435
Montreat Coll (NC) 435
Moravian Coll (PA) 436
Morehouse Coll (GA) 436
Morgan State U (MD) 436
Mount Allison U (NB, Canada) 437
Mount Holyoke Coll (MA) 438
Mount Saint Mary's Coll and Seminary (MD) 439
Mount Saint Vincent U (NS, Canada) 439
Mount Union Coll (OH) 440
Muhlenberg Coll (PA) 440
Murray State U (KY) 440
Muskingum Coll (OH) 441
Nazareth Coll of Rochester (NY) 443
Nebraska Wesleyan U (NE) 443
Newberry Coll (SC) 444
New Coll of Florida (FL) 444
New Jersey City U (NJ) 445
New Mexico State U (NM) 446
New York Inst of Technology (NY) 447
New York U (NY) 447
Niagara U (NY) 447
Nichols Coll (MA) 448
Nipissing U (ON, Canada) 448
Norfolk State U (VA) 448
North Carolina Ag and Tech State U (NC) 448
North Carolina State U (NC) 449
North Central Coll (IL) 449
North Dakota State U (ND) 449
Northeastern Illinois U (IL) 450
Northeastern U (MA) 450
Northern Arizona U (AZ) 450
Northern Illinois U (IL) 450
Northern Kentucky U (KY) 451
Northern Michigan U (MI) 451
Northern State U (SD) 451
Northland Coll (WI) 452
North Park U (IL) 452
Northwestern Coll (IA) 453
Northwestern U (IL) 453
Northwest Missouri State U (MO) 454
Northwood U (MI) 454
Norwich U (VT) 455
Oakland U (MI) 456
Oakwood Coll (AL) 456
Oberlin Coll (OH) 456
Occidental Coll (CA) 457
Oglethorpe U (GA) 457
Ohio Dominican U (OH) 457
The Ohio State U (OH) 457
Ohio U (OH) 458
Ohio Wesleyan U (OH) 459
Okanagan U Coll (BC, Canada) 459
Oklahoma State U (OK) 460
Old Dominion U (VA) 460
Olivet Coll (MI) 461
Olivet Nazarene U (IL) 461
Oregon State U (OR) 462
Otterbein Coll (OH) 462
Pace U (NY) 463
Pacific Lutheran U (WA) 463
Pacific U (OR) 464
Park U (MO) 465
Penn State U at Erie, The Behrend Coll (PA) 467
Penn State U Univ Park Campus (PA) 468
Pepperdine U, Malibu (CA) 469
Pittsburg State U (KS) 470
Pitzer Coll (CA) 471
Plattsburgh State U of NY (NY) 471
Point Loma Nazarene U (CA) 471
Pomona Coll (CA) 472
Pontifical Catholic U of Puerto Rico (PR) 472
Portland State U (OR) 472
Presbyterian Coll (SC) 473
Princeton U (NJ) 474
Principia Coll (IL) 474
Providence Coll (RI) 474
Purchase Coll, State U of NY (NY) 475
Purdue U (IN) 475
Purdue U Calumet (IN) 475
Queens Coll of the City U of NY (NY) 475
Queen's U at Kingston (ON, Canada) 476
Quinnipiac U (CT) 476
Radford U (VA) 476
Ramapo Coll of New Jersey (NJ) 477
Randolph-Macon Coll (VA) 477
Randolph-Macon Woman's Coll (VA) 477
Reed Coll (OR) 477
Regis Coll (MA) 478
Regis U (CO) 478
Rensselaer Polytechnic Inst (NY) 478
Rhode Island Coll (RI) 479
Rhodes Coll (TN) 479
Rice U (TX) 479
The Richard Stockton Coll of New Jersey (NJ) 479
Richmond, The American International U in London(United Kingdom) 480
Rider U (NJ) 480
Ripon Coll (WI) 480
Roanoke Coll (VA) 481
Robert Morris U (PA) 481
Rochester Inst of Technology (NY) 482
Rockford Coll (IL) 482
Rockhurst U (MO) 482
Rocky Mountain Coll (MT) 482
Rollins Coll (FL) 483
Roosevelt U (IL) 483
Rose-Hulman Inst of Technology (IN) 484
Rosemont Coll (PA) 484
Rowan U (NJ) 484
Russell Sage Coll (NY) 484
Rutgers, The State U of New Jersey, Camden (NJ) 485
Rutgers, The State U of New Jersey, Newark (NJ) 485
Rutgers, The State U of New Jersey, New Brunswick (NJ) 485
Ryerson U (ON, Canada) 485
Sacred Heart U (CT) 486
Saginaw Valley State U (MI) 486
St. Ambrose U (IA) 486
Saint Anselm Coll (NH) 487
St. Cloud State U (MN) 488
St. Edward's U (TX) 488
St. Francis Coll (NY) 488
Saint Francis U (PA) 488
St. Francis Xavier U (NS, Canada) 489
St. John Fisher Coll (NY) 489
Saint John's U (MN) 490
St. John's U (NY) 490
Saint Joseph Coll (CT) 490
Saint Joseph's Coll (IN) 490
Saint Joseph's U (PA) 491
St. Lawrence U (NY) 491
Saint Louis U (MO) 492
Saint Martin's Coll (WA) 493
Saint Mary's Coll (IN) 493
Saint Mary's Coll of California (CA) 494
St. Mary's Coll of Maryland (MD) 494
Saint Mary's U (NS, Canada) 494
St. Mary's U of San Antonio (TX) 494
Saint Michael's Coll (VT) 494
St. Norbert Coll (WI) 495
St. Olaf Coll (MN) 495
Saint Peter's Coll (NJ) 495
St. Thomas U (NB, Canada) 496
Saint Vincent Coll (PA) 496
Salem Coll (NC) 496
Salem State Coll (MA) 497
Salisbury U (MD) 497
Salve Regina U (RI) 497
San Diego State U (CA) 498
San Francisco State U (CA) 498
San Jose State U (CA) 499
Santa Clara U (CA) 499
Sarah Lawrence Coll (NY) 499
Schiller International U(Germany) 500
Schiller International U(United Kingdom) 500
Schiller International U, American Coll of Switzerland(Switzerland) 500
Scripps Coll (CA) 501
Seattle Pacific U (WA) 501
Seattle U (WA) 501
Seton Hall U (NJ) 502
Seton Hill U (PA) 502
Shepherd Coll (WV) 503
Shippensburg U of Pennsylvania (PA) 503
Shorter Coll (GA) 504
Siena Coll (NY) 504
Simmons Coll (MA) 504
Simon Fraser U (BC, Canada) 505
Simpson Coll (IA) 505
Skidmore Coll (NY) 506
Slippery Rock U of Pennsylvania (PA) 506
Smith Coll (MA) 506
Sonoma State U (CA) 506
South Carolina State U (SC) 506
South Dakota State U (SD) 507
Southeast Missouri State U (MO) 508
Southern Connecticut State U (CT) 509
Southern Illinois U Carbondale (IL) 509
Southern Illinois U Edwardsville (IL) 509
Southern Methodist U (TX) 510
Southern New Hampshire U (NH) 510
Southern Oregon U (OR) 510
Southern Utah U (UT) 511
Southwestern U (TX) 513
Southwest Missouri State U (MO) 513
Southwest Texas State U (TX) 513
Spelman Coll (GA) 514

ECONOMICS (continued)

Stanford U (CA) **514**
State U of NY at Albany (NY) **514**
State U of NY at Binghamton (NY) **515**
State U of NY at New Paltz (NY) **515**
State U of NY at Oswego (NY) **515**
State U of NY Coll at Buffalo (NY) **516**
State U of NY Coll at Cortland (NY) **516**
State U of NY Coll at Fredonia (NY) **516**
State U of NY Coll at Geneseo (NY) **516**
State U of NY Coll at Oneonta (NY) **517**
State U of NY Coll at Potsdam (NY) **517**
State U of NY Empire State Coll (NY) **517**
State U of West Georgia (GA) **518**
Stephen F. Austin State U (TX) **518**
Stetson U (FL) **519**
Stonehill Coll (MA) **520**
Stony Brook U, State University of New York (NY) **520**
Strayer U (DC) **520**
Suffolk U (MA) **520**
Susquehanna U (PA) **521**
Swarthmore Coll (PA) **521**
Sweet Briar Coll (VA) **521**
Syracuse U (NY) **521**
Talladega Coll (AL) **522**
Tarleton State U (TX) **522**
Taylor U (IN) **523**
Temple U (PA) **523**
Tennessee Technological U (TN) **524**
Texas A&M U (TX) **524**
Texas A&M U–Commerce (TX) **525**
Texas A&M U–Kingsville (TX) **525**
Texas Christian U (TX) **526**
Texas Lutheran U (TX) **526**
Texas Southern U (TX) **526**
Texas Tech U (TX) **526**
Texas Wesleyan U (TX) **526**
Texas Woman's U (TX) **527**
Thomas Edison State Coll (NJ) **527**
Thomas More Coll (KY) **528**
Tiffin U (OH) **528**
Touro Coll (NY) **529**
Towson U (MD) **529**
Transylvania U (KY) **529**
Trent U (ON, Canada) **529**
Trinity Coll (CT) **530**
Trinity Coll (DC) **530**
Trinity International U (IL) **531**
Trinity U (TX) **531**
Truman State U (MO) **532**
Tufts U (MA) **533**
Tulane U (LA) **533**
Tuskegee U (AL) **533**
Union Coll (NY) **534**
Union U (TN) **534**
United States Air Force Academy (CO) **534**
United States Military Academy (NY) **535**
United States Naval Academy (MD) **535**
Université de Sherbrooke (QC, Canada) **536**
U du Québec à Trois-Rivières (QC, Canada) **536**
Université Laval (QC, Canada) **536**
U at Buffalo, The State University of New York (NY) **536**
U Coll of the Cariboo (BC, Canada) **537**
The U of Akron (OH) **537**
U of Alaska Anchorage (AK) **538**
U of Alaska Fairbanks (AK) **538**
U of Alberta (AB, Canada) **538**
The U of Arizona (AZ) **538**
U of Arkansas (AR) **539**
U of Arkansas at Little Rock (AR) **539**
U of Baltimore (MD) **539**
U of Bridgeport (CT) **540**
The U of British Columbia (BC, Canada) **540**
U of Calgary (AB, Canada) **540**
U of Calif, Berkeley (CA) **540**
U of Calif, Davis (CA) **540**
U of Calif, Irvine (CA) **541**
U of Calif, Los Angeles (CA) **541**
U of Calif, Riverside (CA) **541**
U of Calif, San Diego (CA) **541**
U of Calif, Santa Barbara (CA) **541**
U of Calif, Santa Cruz (CA) **542**
U of Central Arkansas (AR) **542**
U of Central Florida (FL) **542**
U of Central Oklahoma (OK) **542**
U of Chicago (IL) **542**
U of Cincinnati (OH) **543**
U of Colorado at Boulder (CO) **543**
U of Colorado at Colorado Springs (CO) **543**
U of Colorado at Denver (CO) **543**
U of Connecticut (CT) **544**
U of Dallas (TX) **544**
U of Dayton (OH) **544**
U of Delaware (DE) **544**
U of Denver (CO) **544**
U of Evansville (IN) **545**
The U of Findlay (OH) **545**
U of Florida (FL) **545**
U of Georgia (GA) **545**
U of Guelph (ON, Canada) **546**
U of Hartford (CT) **546**
U of Hawaii at Hilo (HI) **546**
U of Hawaii at Manoa (HI) **546**
U of Hawaii–West Oahu (HI) **546**
U of Houston (TX) **547**
U of Idaho (ID) **547**
U of Illinois at Chicago (IL) **547**
U of Illinois at Springfield (IL) **548**
U of Illinois at Urbana–Champaign (IL) **548**
The U of Iowa (IA) **548**
U of Kansas (KS) **549**
U of Kentucky (KY) **549**
U of King's Coll (NS, Canada) **549**
The U of Lethbridge (AB, Canada) **549**
U of Louisville (KY) **550**
U of Maine (ME) **550**
U of Maine at Farmington (ME) **550**
U of Manitoba (MB, Canada) **551**
U of Mary Hardin-Baylor (TX) **551**
U of Maryland, Baltimore County (MD) **552**
U of Maryland, Coll Park (MD) **552**
U of Massachusetts Amherst (MA) **552**
U of Massachusetts Boston (MA) **553**
U of Massachusetts Dartmouth (MA) **553**
U of Massachusetts Lowell (MA) **553**
The U of Memphis (TN) **553**
U of Michigan (MI) **554**
U of Michigan–Dearborn (MI) **554**
U of Michigan–Flint (MI) **554**
U of Minnesota, Duluth (MN) **554**
U of Minnesota, Morris (MN) **555**
U of Minnesota, Twin Cities Campus (MN) **555**
U of Mississippi (MS) **555**
U of Missouri–Columbia (MO) **555**
U of Missouri–Kansas City (MO) **555**
U of Missouri–Rolla (MO) **556**
U of Missouri–St. Louis (MO) **556**
U of Mobile (AL) **556**
The U of Montana–Missoula (MT) **556**
U of Nebraska at Kearney (NE) **557**
U of Nebraska at Omaha (NE) **557**
U of Nebraska–Lincoln (NE) **557**
U of Nevada, Las Vegas (NV) **558**
U of New Brunswick Fredericton (NB, Canada) **558**
U of New Brunswick Saint John (NB, Canada) **558**
U of New Hampshire (NH) **558**
U of New Haven (CT) **559**
U of New Mexico (NM) **559**
U of New Orleans (LA) **559**
The U of North Carolina at Asheville (NC) **559**
The U of North Carolina at Chapel Hill (NC) **560**
The U of North Carolina at Charlotte (NC) **560**
The U of North Carolina at Greensboro (NC) **560**
The U of North Carolina at Pembroke (NC) **560**
The U of North Carolina at Wilmington (NC) **561**
U of North Dakota (ND) **561**
U of Northern Colorado (CO) **561**
U of Northern Iowa (IA) **561**
U of North Florida (FL) **561**
U of North Texas (TX) **562**
U of Notre Dame (IN) **562**
U of Oklahoma (OK) **562**
U of Oregon (OR) **562**
U of Ottawa (ON, Canada) **563**
U of Pennsylvania (PA) **563**
U of Pittsburgh (PA) **569**
U of Pittsburgh at Bradford (PA) **569**
U of Pittsburgh at Johnstown (PA) **570**
U of Prince Edward Island (PE, Canada) **570**
U of Puerto Rico, Cayey U Coll (PR) **571**
U of Puerto Rico, Río Piedras (PR) **571**
U of Puget Sound (WA) **571**
U of Redlands (CA) **572**
U of Regina (SK, Canada) **572**
U of Rhode Island (RI) **572**
U of Richmond (VA) **572**
U of Rio Grande (OH) **572**
U of Rochester (NY) **573**
U of Saint Francis (IN) **573**
U of St. Thomas (MN) **573**
U of St. Thomas (TX) **573**
U of San Diego (CA) **574**
U of San Francisco (CA) **574**
U of Saskatchewan (SK, Canada) **574**
U of Science and Arts of Oklahoma (OK) **574**
The U of Scranton (PA) **574**
U of Sioux Falls (SD) **574**
U of South Carolina (SC) **575**
The U of South Dakota (SD) **575**
U of Southern California (CA) **576**
U of Southern Indiana (IN) **576**
U of Southern Maine (ME) **576**
U of South Florida (FL) **576**
The U of Tampa (FL) **577**
The U of Tennessee (TN) **577**
The U of Tennessee at Chattanooga (TN) **577**
The U of Tennessee at Martin (TN) **577**
The U of Texas at Arlington (TX) **577**
The U of Texas at Austin (TX) **578**
The U of Texas at Dallas (TX) **578**
The U of Texas at El Paso (TX) **578**
The U of Texas at Tyler (TX) **579**
The U of Texas of the Permian Basin (TX) **579**
The U of Texas–Pan American (TX) **579**
U of the District of Columbia (DC) **580**
U of the Pacific (CA) **580**
U of the South (TN) **581**
U of Toledo (OH) **581**
U of Toronto (ON, Canada) **581**
U of Tulsa (OK) **581**
U of Utah (UT) **582**
U of Vermont (VT) **582**
U of Victoria (BC, Canada) **582**
U of Virginia (VA) **582**
The U of Virginia's Coll at Wise (VA) **582**
U of Washington (WA) **583**
U of Waterloo (ON, Canada) **583**
The U of Western Ontario (ON, Canada) **583**
U of Windsor (ON, Canada) **584**
U of Wisconsin–Eau Claire (WI) **584**
U of Wisconsin–Green Bay (WI) **584**
U of Wisconsin–La Crosse (WI) **584**
U of Wisconsin–Madison (WI) **584**
U of Wisconsin–Milwaukee (WI) **585**
U of Wisconsin–Oshkosh (WI) **585**
U of Wisconsin–Parkside (WI) **585**
U of Wisconsin–Platteville (WI) **585**
U of Wisconsin–River Falls (WI) **585**
U of Wisconsin–Stevens Point (WI) **585**
U of Wisconsin–Superior (WI) **586**
U of Wisconsin–Whitewater (WI) **586**
Ursinus Coll (PA) **587**
Utah State U (UT) **587**
Utica Coll (NY) **588**
Valdosta State U (GA) **588**
Valparaiso U (IN) **588**
Vanderbilt U (TN) **588**
Vassar Coll (NY) **589**
Villanova U (PA) **590**
Virginia Military Inst (VA) **591**
Virginia Polytechnic Inst and State U (VA) **591**
Wabash Coll (IN) **592**
Wake Forest U (NC) **592**
Walla Walla Coll (WA) **593**
Warren Wilson Coll (NC) **594**
Wartburg Coll (IA) **594**
Washington & Jefferson Coll (PA) **594**
Washington and Lee U (VA) **594**
Washington Coll (MD) **594**
Washington State U (WA) **595**
Washington U in St. Louis (MO) **595**
Wayne State U (MI) **596**
Weber State U (UT) **596**
Webster U (MO) **597**
Wellesley Coll (MA) **597**
Wells Coll (NY) **597**
Wesleyan Coll (GA) **597**
Wesleyan U (CT) **597**
West Chester U of Pennsylvania (PA) **598**
Western Connecticut State U (CT) **598**
Western Illinois U (IL) **599**
Western Kentucky U (KY) **599**
Western Michigan U (MI) **599**
Western New England Coll (MA) **600**
Western Oregon U (OR) **600**
Western State Coll of Colorado (CO) **600**
Western Washington U (WA) **600**
Westfield State Coll (MA) **600**
Westminster Coll (MO) **601**
Westminster Coll (PA) **601**
Westmont Coll (CA) **602**
West Texas A&M U (TX) **602**
West Virginia State Coll (WV) **602**
West Virginia U (WV) **602**
West Virginia Wesleyan Coll (WV) **603**
Wheaton Coll (IL) **603**
Wheaton Coll (MA) **603**
Whitman Coll (WA) **604**
Whittier Coll (CA) **604**
Whitworth Coll (WA) **604**
Wichita State U (KS) **604**
Widener U (PA) **604**
Wilberforce U (OH) **605**
Willamette U (OR) **605**
William Carey Coll (MS) **605**
William Jewell Coll (MO) **606**
Williams Coll (MA) **606**
Wilmington Coll (OH) **607**
Wingate U (NC) **607**
Winona State U (MN) **608**
Winston-Salem State U (NC) **608**
Wittenberg U (OH) **608**
Wofford Coll (SC) **609**
Worcester Polytechnic Inst (MA) **609**
Worcester State Coll (MA) **609**
Wright State U (OH) **609**
Xavier U (OH) **610**
Xavier U of Louisiana (LA) **610**
Yale U (CT) **610**
York Coll of Pennsylvania (PA) **610**
York Coll of the City U of New York (NY) **611**
York U (ON, Canada) **611**
Youngstown State U (OH) **611**

ECONOMICS RELATED

Information can be found under this major's main heading.

Bloomsburg U of Pennsylvania (PA) **290**
The Colorado Coll (CO) **325**
Marymount U (VA) **420**
State U of West Georgia (GA) **518**
The U of Akron (OH) **537**
U of Dallas (TX) **544**

EDUCATION

Overview: This broad-based major will teach students the general theories and practices of learning and teaching as well as the basic principles of educational psychology. *Related majors:* education administration, social and philosophical foundations of education, curriculum and instruction, teacher education, labor studies, counseling. *Potential careers:* school principal, teacher, union representative, school guidance counselor. *Salary potential:* $20k-$27k

Acadia U (NS, Canada) **260**
Adrian Coll (MI) **260**
Alabama State U (AL) **261**
Albion Coll (MI) **262**
Alderson-Broaddus Coll (WV) **263**
Alfred U (NY) **263**
Allen U (SC) **264**
Alma Coll (MI) **264**
Alvernia Coll (PA) **265**
Alverno Coll (WI) **265**
American International Coll (MA) **267**
American U of Puerto Rico (PR) **268**
Anderson Coll (SC) **268**
Anderson U (IN) **268**
Andrews U (MI) **269**
Antioch Coll (OH) **269**
Arcadia U (PA) **271**
Arlington Baptist Coll (TX) **272**
Armstrong Atlantic State U (GA) **273**
Ashland U (OH) **274**
Assumption Coll (MA) **275**
Atlantic Baptist U (NB, Canada) **275**
Atlantic Union Coll (MA) **276**
Augsburg Coll (MN) **276**
Augustana Coll (IL) **276**
Baldwin-Wallace Coll (OH) **280**

Ball State U (IN) **280**
Baltimore Hebrew U (MD) **280**
The Baptist Coll of Florida (FL) **281**
Barry U (FL) **282**
Barton Coll (NC) **282**
Baylor U (TX) **283**
Bellarmine U (KY) **284**
Belmont Abbey Coll (NC) **284**
Belmont U (TN) **284**
Beloit Coll (WI) **285**
Bemidji State U (MN) **285**
Benedictine U (IL) **285**
Berea Coll (KY) **286**
Baruch Coll of the City U of NY (NY) **286**
Berry Coll (GA) **287**
Bethany Coll (KS) **287**
Bethany Coll (WV) **287**
Bethany Coll of the Assemblies of God (CA) **287**
Bethel Coll (IN) **288**
Bethel Coll (MN) **288**
Bethel Coll (TN) **288**
Biola U (CA) **289**
Birmingham-Southern Coll (AL) **289**
Bishop's U (QC, Canada) **289**
Bluefield Coll (VA) **291**
Bluffton Coll (OH) **291**
Boston U (MA) **292**
Bowie State U (MD) **292**
Bowling Green State U (OH) **292**
Brandon U (MB, Canada) **293**
Brenau U (GA) **293**
Brescia U (KY) **293**
Brewton-Parker Coll (GA) **294**
Briar Cliff U (IA) **294**
Bridgewater State Coll (MA) **294**
Brigham Young U–Hawaii (HI) **295**
Brock U (ON, Canada) **295**
Brooklyn Coll of the City U of NY (NY) **295**
Brown U (RI) **296**
Bryan Coll (TN) **296**
Bucknell U (PA) **297**
Buena Vista U (IA) **297**
Cabrini Coll (PA) **298**
California State U, Sacramento (CA) **301**
California U of Pennsylvania (PA) **302**
Cameron U (OK) **303**
Campbell U (NC) **303**
Canisius Coll (NY) **304**
Capital U (OH) **304**
Cardinal Stritch U (WI) **305**
Carroll Coll (MT) **306**
Carroll Coll (WI) **306**
Carson-Newman Coll (TN) **306**
Carthage Coll (WI) **306**
Catawba Coll (NC) **307**
The Catholic U of America (DC) **307**
Cedar Crest Coll (PA) **308**
Cedarville U (OH) **308**
Centenary Coll (NJ) **308**
Centenary Coll of Louisiana (LA) **308**
Central Methodist Coll (MO) **309**
Central Missouri State U (MO) **310**
Charleston Southern U (SC) **311**
Cheyney U of Pennsylvania (PA) **312**
Christian Brothers U (TN) **313**
Christian Heritage Coll (CA) **313**
Christopher Newport U (VA) **313**
Cincinnati Bible Coll and Seminary (OH) **314**
Circleville Bible Coll (OH) **314**
City Coll of the City U of NY (NY) **314**
Clarion U of Pennsylvania (PA) **315**
Clark Atlanta U (GA) **315**
Clarke Coll (IA) **315**
Clark U (MA) **316**
Clearwater Christian Coll (FL) **316**
Cleveland State U (OH) **317**
Coe Coll (IA) **318**
Coker Coll (SC) **318**
Colgate U (NY) **319**
Coll of Mount Saint Vincent (NY) **320**
The Coll of New Jersey (NJ) **320**
The Coll of New Rochelle (NY) **321**
Coll of Notre Dame of Maryland (MD) **321**
Coll of Saint Benedict (MN) **321**
Coll of St. Catherine (MN) **321**
Coll of St. Joseph (VT) **322**
Coll of Saint Mary (NE) **322**
The Coll of Saint Rose (NY) **322**
The Coll of St. Scholastica (MN) **322**
Coll of Staten Island of the City U of NY (NY) **323**
Coll of the Atlantic (ME) **323**
Coll of the Ozarks (MO) **323**
Coll of the Southwest (NM) **324**
Colorado State U-Pueblo (CO) **325**
Columbia Coll (MO) **326**
Columbia Coll (SC) **327**
Columbus State U (GA) **328**
Concord Coll (WV) **329**
Concordia Coll (MN) **329**
Concordia Coll (NY) **329**
Concordia U (IL) **330**
Concordia U (MN) **330**
Concordia U (NE) **330**
Concordia U (OR) **330**
Concordia U Coll of Alberta (AB, Canada) **331**
Concordia U Wisconsin (WI) **331**
Converse Coll (SC) **332**
Cornell Coll (IA) **332**
Cornell U (NY) **333**
Cornerstone U (MI) **333**
Creighton U (NE) **333**
Cumberland U (TN) **335**
Curry Coll (MA) **335**
Dakota State U (SD) **335**
Dallas Baptist U (TX) **336**
Dallas Christian Coll (TX) **336**
Dana Coll (NE) **337**
Davis & Elkins Coll (WV) **338**
Defiance Coll (OH) **338**
Delaware State U (DE) **338**
Delta State U (MS) **339**
DePaul U (IL) **339**
Dickinson State U (ND) **344**
Dillard U (LA) **344**
Dominican Coll (NY) **344**
Dordt Coll (IA) **345**
Dowling Coll (NY) **345**
Drury U (MO) **346**
Duquesne U (PA) **346**
D'Youville Coll (NY) **347**
Earlham Coll (IN) **347**
East Central U (OK) **347**
Eastern Kentucky U (KY) **348**
Eastern Nazarene Coll (MA) **348**
Eastern Oregon U (OR) **349**
Eastern Washington U (WA) **349**
Edgewood Coll (WI) **351**
Elizabeth City State U (NC) **351**
Elizabethtown Coll (PA) **351**
Elmhurst Coll (IL) **351**
Elmira Coll (NY) **351**
Elms Coll (MA) **352**
Elon U (NC) **352**
Emmanuel Coll (MA) **353**
Emory U (GA) **354**
Endicott Coll (MA) **354**
Eugene Lang Coll, New School U (NY) **355**
Eureka Coll (IL) **355**
Evangel U (MO) **355**
The Evergreen State Coll (WA) **355**
Fairmont State Coll (WV) **356**
Faulkner U (AL) **357**
Fayetteville State U (NC) **357**
Felician Coll (NJ) **357**
Ferris State U (MI) **358**
Ferrum Coll (VA) **358**
Finlandia U (MI) **358**
Fitchburg State Coll (MA) **358**
Florida A&M U (FL) **359**
Florida Southern Coll (FL) **361**
Fontbonne U (MO) **361**
Fordham U (NY) **362**
Fort Lewis Coll (CO) **362**
Framingham State Coll (MA) **362**
The Franciscan U (IA) **363**
Franklin Pierce Coll (NH) **364**
Freed-Hardeman U (TN) **364**
Free Will Baptist Bible Coll (TN) **364**
Fresno Pacific U (CA) **364**
Frostburg State U (MD) **365**
Furman U (SC) **365**
Gallaudet U (DC) **365**
Gardner-Webb U (NC) **365**
Georgetown Coll (KY) **366**
Georgia Southwestern State U (GA) **368**
Gettysburg Coll (PA) **368**
Glenville State Coll (WV) **368**
Goddard Coll (VT) **369**
Gordon Coll (MA) **370**
Goshen Coll (IN) **370**
Goucher Coll (MD) **370**
Graceland U (IA) **371**
Grand Valley State U (MI) **371**
Grand View Coll (IA) **372**
Great Lakes Christian Coll (MI) **372**
Greensboro Coll (NC) **372**
Greenville Coll (IL) **373**
Gustavus Adolphus Coll (MN) **374**
Gwynedd-Mercy Coll (PA) **374**
Hamline U (MN) **374**
Hampshire Coll (MA) **375**
Hampton U (VA) **375**
Hannibal-LaGrange Coll (MO) **375**
Hastings Coll (NE) **377**
Haverford Coll (PA) **377**
Heidelberg Coll (OH) **377**
High Point U (NC) **379**
Hillsdale Coll (MI) **379**
Holy Family U (PA) **380**
Houston Baptist U (TX) **382**
Howard Payne U (TX) **382**
Howard U (DC) **382**
Humboldt State U (CA) **382**
Huntingdon Coll (AL) **383**
Huntington Coll (IN) **383**
Huston-Tillotson Coll (TX) **383**
Idaho State U (ID) **384**
Illinois Coll (IL) **384**
Illinois Wesleyan U (IL) **385**
Immaculata U (PA) **385**
Indiana U Bloomington (IN) **385**
Indiana U East (IN) **386**
Indiana U Northwest (IN) **386**
Indiana U–Purdue U Fort Wayne (IN) **386**
Indiana U–Purdue U Indianapolis (IN) **387**
Indiana U South Bend (IN) **387**
Indiana U Southeast (IN) **387**
Indiana Wesleyan U (IN) **387**
Inter American U of PR, San Germán Campus (PR) **388**
Iona Coll (NY) **390**
Iowa State U of Science and Technology (IA) **390**
Iowa Wesleyan Coll (IA) **390**
Jacksonville State U (AL) **390**
Jacksonville U (FL) **391**
James Madison U (VA) **391**
John Brown U (AR) **392**
John Carroll U (OH) **392**
Johnson C. Smith U (NC) **394**
Johnson State Coll (VT) **394**
Judson Coll (AL) **395**
Judson Coll (IL) **395**
Juniata Coll (PA) **395**
Keene State Coll (NH) **396**
Kennesaw State U (GA) **397**
Kent State U (OH) **397**
King Coll (TN) **398**
Knox Coll (IL) **399**
Kutztown U of Pennsylvania (PA) **399**
LaGrange Coll (GA) **400**
Lake Forest Coll (IL) **400**
Lakehead U (ON, Canada) **400**
Lakeland Coll (WI) **401**
Lamar U (TX) **401**
Lambuth U (TN) **401**
Lancaster Bible Coll (PA) **401**
Lander U (SC) **401**
Lane Coll (TN) **402**
Langston U (OK) **402**
La Salle U (PA) **402**
Lasell Coll (MA) **402**
Laura and Alvin Siegal Coll of Judaic Studies (OH) **403**
Laurentian U (ON, Canada) **403**
Lees-McRae Coll (NC) **404**
Lee U (TN) **404**
Lenoir-Rhyne Coll (NC) **405**
Lesley U (MA) **405**
Lewis-Clark State Coll (ID) **406**
Lewis U (IL) **406**
Limestone Coll (SC) **406**
Lincoln Memorial U (TN) **407**
Lincoln U (PA) **407**
Lindenwood U (MO) **407**
Lindsey Wilson Coll (KY) **407**
Lipscomb U (TN) **408**
Lock Haven U of Pennsylvania (PA) **408**
Long Island U, Brooklyn Campus (NY) **409**
Long Island U, C.W. Post Campus (NY) **409**
Long Island U, Southampton Coll, Friends World Program (NY) **409**
Longwood U (VA) **409**
Loras Coll (IA) **410**
Loyola Coll in Maryland (MD) **411**
Loyola U New Orleans (LA) **411**
Lubbock Christian U (TX) **412**
Luther Coll (IA) **412**
Lycoming Coll (PA) **412**
Lynchburg Coll (VA) **413**
Lynn U (FL) **413**
Madonna U (MI) **414**
Maharishi U of Management (IA) **414**
Malaspina U-Coll (BC, Canada) **415**
Manchester Coll (IN) **415**
Manhattan Coll (NY) **416**
Manhattanville Coll (NY) **416**
Mansfield U of Pennsylvania (PA) **416**
Maranatha Baptist Bible Coll (WI) **417**
Marian Coll (IN) **417**
Marian Coll of Fond du Lac (WI) **417**
Marietta Coll (OH) **417**
Marquette U (WI) **418**
Marshall U (WV) **418**
Mars Hill Coll (NC) **418**
Martin U (IN) **419**
Marymount Coll of Fordham U (NY) **419**
Maryville Coll (TN) **420**
Marywood U (PA) **421**
Massachusetts Coll of Liberal Arts (MA) **421**
The Master's Coll and Seminary (CA) **422**
Mayville State U (ND) **422**
McGill U (QC, Canada) **423**
McNeese State U (LA) **423**
McPherson Coll (KS) **423**
Medaille Coll (NY) **424**
Medgar Evers Coll of the City U of NY (NY) **424**
Memorial U of Newfoundland (NF, Canada) **424**
Mercy Coll (NY) **425**
Mercyhurst Coll (PA) **425**
Mesa State Coll (CO) **426**
Methodist Coll (NC) **427**
Middlebury Coll (VT) **429**
Midland Lutheran Coll (NE) **429**
Midway Coll (KY) **429**
Milligan Coll (TN) **430**
Millsaps Coll (MS) **431**
Mills Coll (CA) **431**
Minnesota State U, Mankato (MN) **431**
Mississippi Coll (MS) **432**
Mississippi Valley State U (MS) **432**
Missouri Southern State Coll (MO) **433**
Missouri Valley Coll (MO) **433**
Molloy Coll (NY) **433**
Monmouth Coll (IL) **434**
Monmouth U (NJ) **434**
Montana State U–Billings (MT) **434**
Montana State U–Northern (MT) **434**
Montreat Coll (NC) **435**
Moravian Coll (PA) **436**
Morgan State U (MD) **436**
Morningside Coll (IA) **437**
Mount Holyoke Coll (MA) **438**
Mount Marty Coll (SD) **438**
Mount Mary Coll (WI) **438**
Mount Mercy Coll (IA) **438**
Mount Saint Mary Coll (NY) **439**
Mount St. Mary's Coll (CA) **439**
Mount Saint Vincent U (NS, Canada) **439**
Mount Vernon Nazarene U (OH) **440**
Muskingum Coll (OH) **441**
The National Hispanic U (CA) **442**
Nazareth Coll of Rochester (NY) **443**
Newberry Coll (SC) **444**
New England Coll (NH) **444**
Newman U (KS) **445**
New Mexico Highlands U (NM) **446**
New York Inst of Technology (NY) **447**
New York U (NY) **447**
Niagara U (NY) **447**
Nicholls State U (LA) **447**
Nipissing U (ON, Canada) **448**
North Carolina Ag and Tech State U (NC) **448**
North Carolina State U (NC) **449**
North Carolina Wesleyan Coll (NC) **449**
North Central Coll (IL) **449**
North Dakota State U (ND) **449**
Northeastern State U (OK) **450**
Northeastern U (MA) **450**
Northern Arizona U (AZ) **450**
Northern Illinois U (IL) **450**
Northern Kentucky U (KY) **451**
Northern Michigan U (MI) **451**
Northern State U (SD) **451**
North Georgia Coll & State U (GA) **451**
Northland Coll (WI) **452**
North Park U (IL) **452**
Northwest Coll (WA) **452**

EDUCATION (continued)

Northwestern Coll (IA) ***453***
Northwestern U (IL) ***453***
Northwest Missouri State U (MO) ***454***
Notre Dame de Namur U (CA) ***455***
Nova Scotia Coll of Art and Design (NS, Canada) ***455***
Oakland City U (IN) ***456***
Oglethorpe U (GA) ***457***
Ohio Dominican U (OH) ***457***
Ohio U (OH) ***458***
Ohio U–Lancaster (OH) ***458***
Ohio U–Southern Campus (OH) ***458***
Ohio Valley Coll (WV) ***459***
Ohio Wesleyan U (OH) ***459***
Okanagan U Coll (BC, Canada) ***459***
Oklahoma Baptist U (OK) ***459***
Oklahoma City U (OK) ***460***
Oklahoma State U (OK) ***460***
Oklahoma Wesleyan U (OK) ***460***
Olivet Coll (MI) ***461***
Olivet Nazarene U (IL) ***461***
Oral Roberts U (OK) ***461***
Otterbein Coll (OH) ***462***
Ouachita Baptist U (AR) ***462***
Our Lady of Holy Cross Coll (LA) ***463***
Pacific Lutheran U (WA) ***463***
Pacific Union Coll (CA) ***464***
Pacific U (OR) ***464***
Palm Beach Atlantic U (FL) ***465***
Paul Quinn Coll (TX) ***466***
Pepperdine U, Malibu (CA) ***469***
Peru State Coll (NE) ***469***
Pfeiffer U (NC) ***469***
Piedmont Baptist Coll (NC) ***470***
Pillsbury Baptist Bible Coll (MN) ***470***
Pittsburg State U (KS) ***470***
Plattsburgh State U of NY (NY) ***471***
Point Park Coll (PA) ***471***
Pontifical Catholic U of Puerto Rico (PR) ***472***
Presbyterian Coll (SC) ***473***
Prescott Coll (AZ) ***474***
Providence Coll and Theological Seminary (MB, Canada) ***475***
Purdue U (IN) ***475***
Purdue U Calumet (IN) ***475***
Queens Coll of the City U of NY (NY) ***475***
Queen's U at Kingston (ON, Canada) ***476***
Queens U of Charlotte (NC) ***476***
Quinnipiac U (CT) ***476***
Regis U (CO) ***478***
Rhode Island Coll (RI) ***479***
Rider U (NJ) ***480***
Ripon Coll (WI) ***480***
Rivier Coll (NH) ***480***
Roberts Wesleyan Coll (NY) ***481***
Rockford Coll (IL) ***482***
Rockhurst U (MO) ***482***
Rocky Mountain Coll (MT) ***482***
Rocky Mountain Coll (AB, Canada) ***482***
Rollins Coll (FL) ***483***
Roosevelt U (IL) ***483***
Sacred Heart U (CT) ***486***
St. Ambrose U (IA) ***486***
St. Cloud State U (MN) ***488***
Saint Francis U (PA) ***488***
St. Francis Xavier U (NS, Canada) ***489***
Saint John's U (MN) ***490***
Saint Joseph Coll (CT) ***490***
St. Joseph's Coll, New York (NY) ***491***
Saint Joseph's Coll of Maine (ME) ***491***
St. Joseph's Coll, Suffolk Campus (NY) ***491***
Saint Joseph's U (PA) ***491***
Saint Leo U (FL) ***492***
Saint Martin's Coll (WA) ***493***
Saint Mary-of-the-Woods Coll (IN) ***493***
Saint Mary's Coll (IN) ***493***
Saint Mary's Coll of California (CA) ***494***
St. Mary's U of San Antonio (TX) ***494***
Saint Michael's Coll (VT) ***494***
St. Thomas Aquinas Coll (NY) ***495***
St. Thomas U (NB, Canada) ***496***
Salem Coll (NC) ***496***
Salem International U (WV) ***496***
Salem State Coll (MA) ***497***
Salisbury U (MD) ***497***
San Jose Christian Coll (CA) ***498***
Sarah Lawrence Coll (NY) ***499***
Seton Hill U (PA) ***502***
Shasta Bible Coll (CA) ***502***
Shawnee State U (OH) ***502***
Sheldon Jackson Coll (AK) ***503***
Simmons Coll (MA) ***504***
Simon Fraser U (BC, Canada) ***505***
Simpson Coll (IA) ***505***
Simpson Coll and Graduate School (CA) ***505***
Slippery Rock U of Pennsylvania (PA) ***506***
Smith Coll (MA) ***506***
South Carolina State U (SC) ***506***
South Dakota State U (SD) ***507***
Southeastern Bible Coll (AL) ***507***
Southeastern Oklahoma State U (OK) ***508***
Southern Connecticut State U (CT) ***509***
Southern Nazarene U (OK) ***510***
Southern Utah U (UT) ***511***
Southern Wesleyan U (SC) ***511***
Southwestern Oklahoma State U (OK) ***512***
Southwest State U (MN) ***513***
Spalding U (KY) ***513***
Springfield Coll (MA) ***514***
State U of NY at New Paltz (NY) ***515***
State U of NY at Oswego (NY) ***515***
State U of NY Coll at Brockport (NY) ***515***
State U of NY Coll at Fredonia (NY) ***516***
State U of NY Coll at Geneseo (NY) ***516***
State U of NY Coll at Oneonta (NY) ***517***
State U of NY Empire State Coll (NY) ***517***
Stetson U (FL) ***519***
Stonehill Coll (MA) ***520***
Suffolk U (MA) ***520***
Syracuse U (NY) ***521***
Tabor Coll (KS) ***522***
Talladega Coll (AL) ***522***
Tarleton State U (TX) ***522***
Taylor U (IN) ***523***
Temple U (PA) ***523***
Tennessee State U (TN) ***523***
Tennessee Technological U (TN) ***524***
Tennessee Temple U (TN) ***524***
Tennessee Wesleyan Coll (TN) ***524***
Texas A&M U–Commerce (TX) ***525***
Texas A&M U–Kingsville (TX) ***525***
Texas Lutheran U (TX) ***526***
Texas Southern U (TX) ***526***
Texas Wesleyan U (TX) ***526***
Toccoa Falls Coll (GA) ***528***
Touro Coll (NY) ***529***
Trent U (ON, Canada) ***529***
Trinity Christian Coll (IL) ***530***
Trinity Coll (CT) ***530***
Trinity Coll (DC) ***530***
Trinity International U (IL) ***531***
Trinity Western U (BC, Canada) ***531***
Tri-State U (IN) ***532***
Troy State U (AL) ***532***
Tusculum Coll (TN) ***533***
Union Coll (KY) ***533***
Union Coll (NE) ***534***
Union Inst & U (OH) ***534***
Union U (TN) ***534***
Université de Sherbrooke (QC, Canada) ***536***
U du Québec à Trois-Rivières (QC, Canada) ***536***
U du Québec à Hull (QC, Canada) ***536***
The U of Akron (OH) ***537***
U of Alaska Anchorage (AK) ***538***
U of Alaska Fairbanks (AK) ***538***
U of Alaska Southeast (AK) ***538***
U of Alberta (AB, Canada) ***538***
U of Arkansas at Little Rock (AR) ***539***
U of Arkansas at Monticello (AR) ***539***
The U of British Columbia (BC, Canada) ***540***
U of Calgary (AB, Canada) ***540***
U of Charleston (WV) ***542***
U of Cincinnati (OH) ***543***
U of Dallas (TX) ***544***
U of Dayton (OH) ***544***
U of Delaware (DE) ***544***
The U of Findlay (OH) ***545***
U of Hawaii at Manoa (HI) ***546***
U of Houston–Clear Lake (TX) ***547***
U of Houston–Victoria (TX) ***547***
U of Indianapolis (IN) ***548***
The U of Iowa (IA) ***548***
U of La Verne (CA) ***549***
The U of Lethbridge (AB, Canada) ***549***
U of Maine (ME) ***550***
U of Maine at Fort Kent (ME) ***551***
U of Maine at Machias (ME) ***551***
U of Maine at Presque Isle (ME) ***551***
U of Manitoba (MB, Canada) ***551***
U of Mary (ND) ***551***
U of Mary Hardin-Baylor (TX) ***551***
U of Maryland, Coll Park (MD) ***552***
U of Maryland Eastern Shore (MD) ***552***
U of Massachusetts Amherst (MA) ***552***
U of Miami (FL) ***553***
U of Michigan (MI) ***554***
U of Michigan–Dearborn (MI) ***554***
U of Michigan–Flint (MI) ***554***
U of Minnesota, Duluth (MN) ***554***
U of Minnesota, Morris (MN) ***555***
U of Minnesota, Twin Cities Campus (MN) ***555***
U of Missouri–Columbia (MO) ***555***
U of Missouri–Kansas City (MO) ***555***
U of Missouri–St. Louis (MO) ***556***
The U of Montana–Missoula (MT) ***556***
The U of Montana–Western (MT) ***556***
U of Nebraska at Omaha (NE) ***557***
U of Nevada, Las Vegas (NV) ***558***
U of New Brunswick Fredericton (NB, Canada) ***558***
U of New Brunswick Saint John (NB, Canada) ***558***
U of New England (ME) ***558***
U of New Mexico (NM) ***559***
The U of North Carolina at Pembroke (NC) ***560***
U of Oregon (OR) ***562***
U of Ottawa (ON, Canada) ***563***
U of Pittsburgh at Greensburg (PA) ***570***
U of Pittsburgh at Johnstown (PA) ***570***
U of Portland (OR) ***570***
U of Prince Edward Island (PE, Canada) ***570***
U of Redlands (CA) ***572***
U of Regina (SK, Canada) ***572***
U of Richmond (VA) ***572***
U of Rio Grande (OH) ***572***
U of Saint Francis (IN) ***573***
U of St. Thomas (TX) ***573***
U of San Diego (CA) ***574***
U of San Francisco (CA) ***574***
U of Saskatchewan (SK, Canada) ***574***
U of Sioux Falls (SD) ***574***
The U of South Dakota (SD) ***575***
U of Southern California (CA) ***576***
U of South Florida (FL) ***576***
The U of Tennessee at Chattanooga (TN) ***577***
U of the Incarnate Word (TX) ***580***
U of the Pacific (CA) ***580***
U of the Sacred Heart (PR) ***580***
U of Toledo (OH) ***581***
U of Toronto (ON, Canada) ***581***
U of Tulsa (OK) ***581***
U of Vermont (VT) ***582***
U of Victoria (BC, Canada) ***582***
U of Washington (WA) ***583***
The U of Western Ontario (ON, Canada) ***583***
U of Windsor (ON, Canada) ***584***
U of Wisconsin–La Crosse (WI) ***584***
U of Wisconsin–Milwaukee (WI) ***585***
U of Wisconsin–Oshkosh (WI) ***585***
U of Wisconsin–Platteville (WI) ***585***
U of Wisconsin–River Falls (WI) ***585***
U of Wisconsin–Stevens Point (WI) ***585***
U of Wisconsin–Superior (WI) ***586***
U of Wisconsin–Whitewater (WI) ***586***
Upper Iowa U (IA) ***587***
Urbana U (OH) ***587***
Ursinus Coll (PA) ***587***
Ursuline Coll (OH) ***587***
Valdosta State U (GA) ***588***
Valley City State U (ND) ***588***
Valparaiso U (IN) ***588***
Vanderbilt U (TN) ***588***
Vanguard U of Southern California (CA) ***589***
Villanova U (PA) ***590***
Virginia Commonwealth U (VA) ***590***
Virginia Wesleyan Coll (VA) ***591***
Voorhees Coll (SC) ***592***
Wagner Coll (NY) ***592***
Wake Forest U (NC) ***592***
Walsh U (OH) ***593***
Warner Pacific Coll (OR) ***593***
Warren Wilson Coll (NC) ***594***
Washington State U (WA) ***595***
Washington U in St. Louis (MO) ***595***
Wayland Baptist U (TX) ***595***
Wayne State Coll (NE) ***596***
Webster U (MO) ***597***
Wells Coll (NY) ***597***
Wesleyan Coll (GA) ***597***
Wesley Coll (DE) ***598***
West Chester U of Pennsylvania (PA) ***598***
Western Baptist Coll (OR) ***598***
Western Connecticut State U (CT) ***598***
Western New Mexico U (NM) ***600***
Western State Coll of Colorado (CO) ***600***
Western Washington U (WA) ***600***
Westfield State Coll (MA) ***600***
West Liberty State Coll (WV) ***601***
Westminster Coll (MO) ***601***
Westminster Coll (PA) ***601***
Westmont Coll (CA) ***602***
West Virginia State Coll (WV) ***602***
West Virginia Wesleyan Coll (WV) ***603***
Wheeling Jesuit U (WV) ***603***
Wheelock Coll (MA) ***603***
Wilkes U (PA) ***605***
William Carey Coll (MS) ***605***
William Jewell Coll (MO) ***606***
William Paterson U of New Jersey (NJ) ***606***
William Penn U (IA) ***606***
Williams Baptist Coll (AR) ***606***
William Woods U (MO) ***607***
Wilmington Coll (OH) ***607***
Wingate U (NC) ***607***
Winona State U (MN) ***608***
Winston-Salem State U (NC) ***608***
Wittenberg U (OH) ***608***
Wright State U (OH) ***609***
Xavier U (OH) ***610***
Xavier U of Louisiana (LA) ***610***
York Coll (NE) ***610***
York Coll of Pennsylvania (PA) ***610***
York U (ON, Canada) ***611***
Youngstown State U (OH) ***611***

EDUCATION ADMINISTRATION

Overview: Students will learn the general principles, methods, and techniques for organizing and managing a variety of schools and other educational organizations. *Related majors:* education, elementary, middle and secondary education administration, labor relations, school psychology. *Potential careers:* principal, school administrator, teacher. *Salary potential:* $26k-$30k.

Campbell U (NC) ***303***
Eureka Coll (IL) ***355***
Lamar U (TX) ***401***
Laura and Alvin Siegal Coll of Judaic Studies (OH) ***403***
Lindenwood U (MO) ***407***
Long Island U, Brooklyn Campus (NY) ***409***
McNeese State U (LA) ***423***
Northern Arizona U (AZ) ***450***
Northwest Missouri State U (MO) ***454***
Ohio U (OH) ***458***
Oral Roberts U (OK) ***461***
Purdue U Calumet (IN) ***475***
St. Cloud State U (MN) ***488***
Tarleton State U (TX) ***522***
Tennessee State U (TN) ***523***
Texas Southern U (TX) ***526***
The U of British Columbia (BC, Canada) ***540***
U of Central Oklahoma (OK) ***542***
U of Hawaii at Manoa (HI) ***546***
The U of Lethbridge (AB, Canada) ***549***
U of Nebraska at Omaha (NE) ***557***
U of Oregon (OR) ***562***
U of San Francisco (CA) ***574***
U of Windsor (ON, Canada) ***584***
U of Wisconsin–Superior (WI) ***586***
Valdosta State U (GA) ***588***
Western Washington U (WA) ***600***
William Carey Coll (MS) ***605***

EDUCATION ADMINISTRATION/ SUPERVISION RELATED

Information can be found under this major's main heading.

U of Miami (FL) ***553***

EDUCATIONAL MEDIA DESIGN

Overview: Students learn the principles of developing instructional aids and other teaching products in various formats, such as film, recording, text, and CD-ROM computer software. *Related majors:* educational theory, psychology, speech-language audiology, art therapy, computer graphics. *Potential careers:* counselor, speech therapist, psychologist, educational product developer, computer programmer. *Salary potential:* $24k-$30k.

Ball State U (IN) **280**
Bayamón Central U (PR) **283**
California State U, Chico (CA) **300**
The Coll of St. Scholastica (MN) **322**
Indiana State U (IN) **385**
Ithaca Coll (NY) **390**
Jacksonville State U (AL) **390**
James Madison U (VA) **391**
Norwich U (VT) **455**
Ohio U (OH) **458**
St. Cloud State U (MN) **488**
Texas Southern U (TX) **526**
U of Central Oklahoma (OK) **542**
U of Hawaii at Manoa (HI) **546**
U of Nebraska at Omaha (NE) **557**
U of Toledo (OH) **581**
Western Illinois U (IL) **599**
Western Oregon U (OR) **600**
Widener U (PA) **604**

EDUCATIONAL MEDIA TECHNOLOGY

Overview: Students will learn the principles and techniques behind creating educational and instructional materials and products using audio, film, video, computer software, and other visual formats. *Related majors:* radio and television broadcasting technology, publishing, Web design, education, multimedia management and technology. *Potential careers:* Web site designer, editor, educational consultant, copywriter, television technician. *Salary potential:* $25k-$35k.

Duquesne U (PA) **346**
Salve Regina U (RI) **497**
Seton Hill U (PA) **502**
U of Maine (ME) **550**
U of Wisconsin–Superior (WI) **586**

EDUCATIONAL PSYCHOLOGY

Overview: Students apply the principles of psychology to the study of teachers and students, the nature of learning environments, and the psychological effects of methods, resources, organization, and educational processes. *Related majors:* educational media design, social foundation of education, school psychology. *Potential careers:* school psychologist, school administrator, teacher, professor. *Salary potential:* $25k-$36k.

Alcorn State U (MS) **263**
Christian Brothers U (TN) **313**
Jacksonville State U (AL) **390**
Marymount U (VA) **420**
Mississippi State U (MS) **432**
St. Mary's Coll of Maryland (MD) **494**
Shenandoah U (VA) **503**
U of Hawaii at Manoa (HI) **546**

EDUCATIONAL STATISTICS/ RESEARCH METHODS

Overview: Students learn how to apply statistics to the analysis of educational research problems and studies. *Related majors:* mathematical statistics, computer programming, education, social/philosophical foundations in education. *Potential careers:* school administrator, educational researcher, sociologist. *Salary potential:* $26k-$33k.

Bucknell U (PA) **297**
Ohio U (OH) **458**

EDUCATION (K-12)

Overview: a generalized program that prepares undergraduates to teach kindergarten through high school students. Undergraduates who wish to teach at the high school level may combine this major with a specific subject matter, such as math, science, English, a foreign language, etc. *Potential careers:* kindergarten-high school teacher, school administrator. *Salary potential:* $18k-$34k.

Adrian Coll (MI) **260**
Atlantic Baptist U (NB, Canada) **275**
Augustana Coll (SD) **276**
Belmont U (TN) **284**
Bethany Coll (WV) **287**
Bethel Coll (TN) **288**
Biola U (CA) **289**
Briar Cliff U (IA) **294**
Campbell U (NC) **303**
Centenary Coll of Louisiana (LA) **308**
Charleston Southern U (SC) **311**
Christian Heritage Coll (CA) **313**
Clearwater Christian Coll (FL) **316**
Coll of Saint Mary (NE) **322**
The Coll of St. Scholastica (MN) **322**
Columbia Coll (MO) **326**
Columbia Coll (NY) **326**
Columbus State U (GA) **328**
Creighton U (NE) **333**
Dickinson State U (ND) **344**
Dominican U (IL) **345**
Dordt Coll (IA) **345**
D'Youville Coll (NY) **347**
Felician Coll (NJ) **357**
Finlandia U (MI) **358**
Franklin Coll (IN) **363**
Graceland U (IA) **371**
Grace U (NE) **371**
Gwynedd-Mercy Coll (PA) **374**
Hamline U (MN) **374**
Hastings Coll (NE) **377**
Hillsdale Coll (MI) **379**
Illinois Coll (IL) **384**
Indiana Wesleyan U (IN) **387**
Ithaca Coll (NY) **390**
Jamestown Coll (ND) **391**
John Carroll U (OH) **392**
Lake Erie Coll (OH) **400**
Lambuth U (TN) **401**
Lewis-Clark State Coll (ID) **406**
Lewis U (IL) **406**
Lindenwood U (MO) **407**
McKendree Coll (IL) **423**
McPherson Coll (KS) **423**
Methodist Coll (NC) **427**
Metropolitan State Coll of Denver (CO) **427**
Midland Lutheran Coll (NE) **429**
Mount Saint Mary Coll (NY) **439**
New England Coll (NH) **444**
Northwestern Oklahoma State U (OK) **453**
Ohio Dominican U (OH) **457**
Ohio Wesleyan U (OH) **459**
Our Lady of Holy Cross Coll (LA) **463**
Pacific Union Coll (CA) **464**
Pikeville Coll (KY) **470**
Queens Coll of the City U of NY (NY) **475**
Quincy U (IL) **476**
Rocky Mountain Coll (MT) **482**
Rutgers, The State U of New Jersey, Camden (NJ) **485**
Rutgers, The State U of New Jersey, Newark (NJ) **485**
St. Ambrose U (IA) **486**
Saint Augustine's Coll (NC) **487**
Saint Mary-of-the-Woods Coll (IN) **493**
St. Norbert Coll (WI) **495**
Salem International U (WV) **496**
Southern New Hampshire U (NH) **510**
Southwest Baptist U (MO) **512**
Syracuse U (NY) **521**
Tabor Coll (KS) **522**
Tennessee Wesleyan Coll (TN) **524**
Thomas Coll (ME) **527**
Transylvania U (KY) **529**
Trevecca Nazarene U (TN) **529**
Trinity International U (IL) **531**
The U of Lethbridge (AB, Canada) **549**
U of Maine at Fort Kent (ME) **551**
U of Minnesota, Morris (MN) **555**
The U of Montana–Western (MT) **556**
U of St. Thomas (MN) **573**
U of Southern California (CA) **576**
The U of Tampa (FL) **577**
The U of Tennessee at Martin (TN) **577**
U of Windsor (ON, Canada) **584**
U of Wisconsin–Superior (WI) **586**
Walla Walla Coll (WA) **593**
Washington U in St. Louis (MO) **595**
West Virginia Wesleyan Coll (WV) **603**
York U (ON, Canada) **611**

EDUCATION (MULTIPLE LEVELS)

Overview: this general major prepares undergraduates to teach a variety of related grade levels, such as preschool to first grade, kindergarten to fourth grade, first grade to seventh grade or seventh grade through high school, depending on the particular school system. *Related majors:* early childhood; elementary, middle school, and high school education; curriculum and instruction; school administration; educational psychology. *Potential careers:* teacher, school administrator, teacher's aid, student counselor. *Salary potential:* $18k-$34k.

Averett U (VA) **278**
California State U, Sacramento (CA) **301**
Chestnut Hill Coll (PA) **312**
Coll of Saint Elizabeth (NJ) **321**
East Texas Baptist U (TX) **350**
George Fox U (OR) **366**
Howard Payne U (TX) **382**
Ithaca Coll (NY) **390**
Manhattan Coll (NY) **416**
Martin Luther Coll (MN) **418**
Ohio Valley Coll (WV) **459**
Oral Roberts U (OK) **461**
The Richard Stockton Coll of New Jersey (NJ) **479**
Saint Louis U (MO) **492**
Texas Lutheran U (TX) **526**
U of Nebraska–Lincoln (NE) **557**
U of North Alabama (AL) **559**
U of Rio Grande (OH) **572**
U of Washington (WA) **583**
Utah State U (UT) **587**
Western Washington U (WA) **600**
York Coll (NE) **610**
Youngstown State U (OH) **611**

EDUCATION OF THE EMOTIONALLY HANDICAPPED

Overview: this major prepares graduates with the knowledge and skills they need to teach children or adults who are emotionally handicapped in such a way as to adversely affect their educational performance. *Related majors:* special education, developmental psychology, counseling. *Potential careers:* teacher, therapist. *Salary potential:* $24k-$37k.

Bradley U (IL) **293**
Central Michigan U (MI) **310**
East Carolina U (NC) **347**
Eastern Mennonite U (VA) **348**
Eastern Michigan U (MI) **348**
Florida International U (FL) **360**
Florida State U (FL) **361**
Greensboro Coll (NC) **372**
Hope Coll (MI) **381**
Loras Coll (IA) **410**
Marygrove Coll (MI) **419**
Minnesota State U, Moorhead (MN) **432**
Oklahoma Baptist U (OK) **459**
Trinity Christian Coll (IL) **530**
U of Maine at Farmington (ME) **550**
U of Nebraska at Omaha (NE) **557**
The U of North Carolina at Wilmington (NC) **561**
U of South Florida (FL) **576**
Western Michigan U (MI) **599**

EDUCATION OF THE GIFTED/TALENTED

Overview: this major prepares graduates with the knowledge and skills they need to teach children or adults who exhibit exceptional intellectual or artistic talent or potential. *Related majors:* developmental psychology, counseling, educational/instructional media design. *Potential careers:* teacher, therapist. *Salary potential:* $24k-$35k.

U of Great Falls (MT) **545**

EDUCATION OF THE HEARING IMPAIRED

Overview: This major prepares graduates with the knowledge and skills they need to teach children or adults who are either deaf or who have hearing impairments. *Related majors:* education of speech impaired, special education, speech therapy, developmental psychology, speech language pathology/audiology. *Potential careers:* teacher, speech therapist. *Salary potential:* $24k-$37k.

Augustana Coll (SD) **276**
Barton Coll (NC) **282**
Boston U (MA) **292**
Bowling Green State U (OH) **292**
The Coll of New Jersey (NJ) **320**
Eastern Michigan U (MI) **348**
Flagler Coll (FL) **359**
Indiana U of Pennsylvania (PA) **386**
Lambuth U (TN) **401**
Minot State U (ND) **432**
Texas Christian U (TX) **526**
U of Arkansas at Little Rock (AR) **539**
U of Nebraska at Omaha (NE) **557**
U of Nebraska–Lincoln (NE) **557**
The U of North Carolina at Greensboro (NC) **560**
U of Science and Arts of Oklahoma (OK) **574**
U of Southern Mississippi (MS) **576**

EDUCATION OF THE MENTALLY HANDICAPPED

Overview: this major prepares graduates with the knowledge and skills they need to teach children or adults with mental handicaps that might impair their educational performance. *Related majors:* special education, speech therapy, developmental psychology, counseling. *Potential careers:* teacher, speech therapist. *Salary potential:* $24k-$37k.

Augusta State U (GA) **277**
Bowling Green State U (OH) **292**
Bradley U (IL) **293**
Central Michigan U (MI) **310**
East Carolina U (NC) **347**
Eastern Mennonite U (VA) **348**
Eastern Michigan U (MI) **348**
Flagler Coll (FL) **359**
Florida International U (FL) **360**
Florida State U (FL) **361**
Greensboro Coll (NC) **372**
Loras Coll (IA) **410**
Minnesota State U, Moorhead (MN) **432**
Minot State U (ND) **432**
Oklahoma Baptist U (OK) **459**
Shaw U (NC) **502**
Silver Lake Coll (WI) **504**

EDUCATION OF THE MENTALLY HANDICAPPED (continued)

State U of West Georgia (GA) ***518***
Trinity Christian Coll (IL) ***530***
U du Québec à Trois-Rivières (QC, Canada) ***536***
U of Maine at Farmington (ME) ***550***
The U of North Carolina at Charlotte (NC) ***560***
The U of North Carolina at Wilmington (NC) ***561***
U of Northern Iowa (IA) ***561***
U of Rio Grande (OH) ***572***
U of South Florida (FL) ***576***
Western Michigan U (MI) ***599***
York Coll (NE) ***610***

EDUCATION OF THE MULTIPLE HANDICAPPED

Overview: this major prepares graduates with the knowledge and skills they need to teach children or adults who have multiple disabilities that adversely affect their educational performance. *Related majors:* special education, speech therapy, developmental psychology, counseling, physical therapy. *Potential careers:* teacher, therapist or counselor, physical therapist. *Salary potential:* $25k-$37k.

Bowling Green State U (OH) ***292***
The U of Akron (OH) ***537***
U of Northern Iowa (IA) ***561***

EDUCATION OF THE PHYSICALLY HANDICAPPED

Overview: this major prepares graduates with the knowledge and skills they need to teach children or adults who are physically handicapped in such a way as it interferes with their educational performance. *Related majors:* special education, physical therapist, orthotics/prosthetics, movement therapy, pediatric nursing. *Potential careers:* teacher, physical therapist. *Salary potential:* $26k-$39k.

Eastern Michigan U (MI) ***348***
Indiana U of Pennsylvania (PA) ***386***

EDUCATION OF THE SPECIFIC LEARNING DISABLED

Overview: this major prepares graduates with the knowledge and skills they need to teach children or adults who have specific learning disabilities which adversely affect their educational performance. *Related majors:* special education, speech and occupational therapies, developmental psychology and psychology, communication disorders, nursing. *Potential careers:* teacher, speech therapist, nurse. *Salary potential:* $24k-$38k.

Appalachian State U (NC) ***270***
Aquinas Coll (MI) ***270***
Bethune-Cookman Coll (FL) ***289***
Bowling Green State U (OH) ***292***
Bradley U (IL) ***293***
East Carolina U (NC) ***347***
Eastern Mennonite U (VA) ***348***
Flagler Coll (FL) ***359***
Florida International U (FL) ***360***
Florida Southern Coll (FL) ***361***
Florida State U (FL) ***361***
Greensboro Coll (NC) ***372***
Harding U (AR) ***375***
Hope Coll (MI) ***381***
Malone Coll (OH) ***415***
Mercer U (GA) ***425***
Minnesota State U, Moorhead (MN) ***432***
Northwestern U (IL) ***453***
Oklahoma Baptist U (OK) ***459***
Pace U (NY) ***463***
Silver Lake Coll (WI) ***504***
Trinity Christian Coll (IL) ***530***
The U of Akron (OH) ***537***
U of Maine at Farmington (ME) ***550***
The U of North Carolina at Wilmington (NC) ***561***
U of Rio Grande (OH) ***572***
U of South Florida (FL) ***576***
Wheeling Jesuit U (WV) ***603***
Winston-Salem State U (NC) ***608***
Youngstown State U (OH) ***611***

EDUCATION OF THE SPEECH IMPAIRED

Overview: this major prepares graduates with the knowledge and skills they need to teach children or adults who have speech impairments that adversely affect their educational development. *Related majors:* special education, speech therapy, developmental psychology, speech-language pathology/audiology. *Potential careers:* teacher, speech therapist. *Salary potential:* $24k-$36k.

Alabama A&M U (AL) ***261***
Baylor U (TX) ***283***
Bloomsburg U of Pennsylvania (PA) ***290***
Eastern Michigan U (MI) ***348***
Emerson Coll (MA) ***353***
Indiana U of Pennsylvania (PA) ***386***
Ithaca Coll (NY) ***390***
Kutztown U of Pennsylvania (PA) ***399***
Louisiana Tech U (LA) ***410***
Minot State U (ND) ***432***
New York U (NY) ***447***
Northern Arizona U (AZ) ***450***
St. John's U (NY) ***490***
Southeastern Louisiana U (LA) ***508***
State U of NY Coll at Cortland (NY) ***516***
The U of Akron (OH) ***537***
U of Toledo (OH) ***581***
Wayne State U (MI) ***596***
Western Kentucky U (KY) ***599***

EDUCATION OF THE VISUALLY HANDICAPPED

Overview: this major prepares graduates with the knowledge and skills they need to teach children or adults who may be either blind or visually handicapped in such a way as to adversely affect their educational development. *Related majors:* special education, psychology, child care guidance. *Potential careers:* teacher, speech therapist. *Salary potential:* $26k-$38k.

Auburn U (AL) ***276***
Dominican Coll (NY) ***344***
Eastern Michigan U (MI) ***348***
Florida State U (FL) ***361***
Western Michigan U (MI) ***599***

EDUCATION RELATED

Information can be found under this major's main heading.

Albany State U (GA) ***262***
Arkansas State U (AR) ***272***
Eastern Illinois U (IL) ***348***
Marywood U (PA) ***421***
Park U (MO) ***465***
State U of NY Coll at Potsdam (NY) ***517***
Swarthmore Coll (PA) ***521***
U of Missouri–St. Louis (MO) ***556***
The U of the Arts (PA) ***579***

ELECTRICAL/ELECTRONIC ENGINEERING TECHNOLOGIES RELATED

Information can be found under this major's main heading.

Embry-Riddle Aeronautical U (FL) ***352***
New York Inst of Technology (NY) ***447***
Pennsylvania Coll of Technology (PA) ***467***
Southern Illinois U Carbondale (IL) ***509***

ELECTRICAL/ELECTRONIC ENGINEERING TECHNOLOGY

Overview: This major teaches the principles of basic electrical engineering and relevant technical skills. *Related majors:* communication equipment technology, electronics, computer systems networking. *Potential careers:* computer technician, computer systems analyst, electrical technician, aerospace technician, Air Force technician. *Salary potential:* $26k-$40k.

Andrews U (MI) ***269***
Appalachian State U (NC) ***270***
Arizona State U East (AZ) ***271***
Baker Coll of Muskegon (MI) ***279***
Baker Coll of Owosso (MI) ***279***
Bluefield State Coll (WV) ***291***
Bowling Green State U (OH) ***292***
Bradley U (IL) ***293***
Brigham Young U (UT) ***295***
British Columbia Inst of Technology (BC, Canada) ***295***
Bryant and Stratton Coll, Cleveland (OH) ***296***
California State Polytechnic U, Pomona (CA) ***300***
California State U, Long Beach (CA) ***301***
California U of Pennsylvania (PA) ***302***
Cameron U (OK) ***303***
Capitol Coll (MD) ***304***
Central Michigan U (MI) ***310***
Central Missouri State U (MO) ***310***
Central Washington U (WA) ***310***
Cleveland State U (OH) ***317***
Cogswell Polytechnical Coll (CA) ***318***
Colorado State U-Pueblo (CO) ***325***
Colorado Tech U (CO) ***326***
Delaware State U (DE) ***338***
DeVry Coll of Technology (NJ) ***340***
DeVry Inst of Technology (NY) ***340***
DeVry U (AZ) ***340***
DeVry U, Fremont (CA) ***340***
DeVry U, Long Beach (CA) ***341***
DeVry U, Pomona (CA) ***341***
DeVry U, West Hills (CA) ***341***
DeVry U, Colorado Springs (CO) ***341***
DeVry U, Orlando (FL) ***342***
DeVry U, Alpharetta (GA) ***342***
DeVry U, Decatur (GA) ***342***
DeVry U, Addison (IL) ***342***
DeVry U, Chicago (IL) ***342***
DeVry U, Tinley Park (IL) ***342***
DeVry U (MO) ***343***
DeVry U (OH) ***343***
DeVry U (TX) ***343***
DeVry U (VA) ***343***
DeVry U (WA) ***343***
East Central U (OK) ***347***
Eastern Washington U (WA) ***349***
East-West U (IL) ***350***
Edinboro U of Pennsylvania (PA) ***351***
Elizabeth City State U (NC) ***351***
Embry-Riddle Aeronautical U (FL) ***352***
Excelsior Coll (NY) ***356***
Fairleigh Dickinson U, Teaneck-Metro Campus (NJ) ***356***
Fairmont State Coll (WV) ***356***
State U of NY at Farmingdale (NY) ***357***
Ferris State U (MI) ***358***
Fitchburg State Coll (MA) ***358***
Florida A&M U (FL) ***359***
Fort Valley State U (GA) ***362***
Francis Marion U (SC) ***363***
Georgia Southern U (GA) ***367***
Grambling State U (LA) ***371***
Grantham U (LA) ***372***
Hamilton Tech Coll (IA) ***374***
Hampton U (VA) ***375***
Indiana State U (IN) ***385***
Indiana U–Purdue U Fort Wayne (IN) ***386***
Indiana U–Purdue U Indianapolis (IN) ***387***
Inter American U of PR, Aguadilla Campus (PR) ***388***
Inter American U of PR, San Germán Campus (PR) ***388***
Jackson State U (MS) ***390***
Jacksonville State U (AL) ***390***
Johnson & Wales U (RI) ***393***
Kansas State U (KS) ***396***
Keene State Coll (NH) ***396***
Lakehead U (ON, Canada) ***400***
LeTourneau U (TX) ***405***
Lewis-Clark State Coll (ID) ***406***
Louisiana Tech U (LA) ***410***
Maharishi U of Management (IA) ***414***
McNeese State U (LA) ***423***
Metropolitan State Coll of Denver (CO) ***427***
Michigan Technological U (MI) ***428***
Midwestern State U (TX) ***430***
Milwaukee School of Engineering (WI) ***431***
Minnesota State U, Mankato (MN) ***431***
Missouri Western State Coll (MO) ***433***
Montana State U–Bozeman (MT) ***434***
Montana State U–Northern (MT) ***434***
Murray State U (KY) ***440***
New York Inst of Technology (NY) ***447***
Norfolk State U (VA) ***448***
Northeastern State U (OK) ***450***
Northeastern U (MA) ***450***
Northern Kentucky U (KY) ***451***
Northern Michigan U (MI) ***451***
Northern State U (SD) ***451***
Northwestern State U of Louisiana (LA) ***453***
Oklahoma State U (OK) ***460***
Oregon Inst of Technology (OR) ***461***
Pacific Union Coll (CA) ***464***
Penn State U Berks Cmps of Berks-Lehigh Valley Coll (PA) ***468***
Penn State U Harrisburg Campus of the Capital Coll (PA) ***468***
Pittsburg State U (KS) ***470***
Point Park Coll (PA) ***471***
Prairie View A&M U (TX) ***473***
Purdue U (IN) ***475***
Purdue U Calumet (IN) ***475***
Rochester Inst of Technology (NY) ***482***
Roosevelt U (IL) ***483***
St. Cloud State U (MN) ***488***
Sam Houston State U (TX) ***497***
Savannah State U (GA) ***499***
South Carolina State U (SC) ***506***
South Dakota State U (SD) ***507***
Southeastern Oklahoma State U (OK) ***508***
Southeast Missouri State U (MO) ***508***
Southern Polytechnic State U (GA) ***511***
Southern U and A&M Coll (LA) ***511***
Southern Utah U (UT) ***511***
Southwest Missouri State U (MO) ***513***
State U of NY Coll at Buffalo (NY) ***516***
State U of NY Inst of Tech at Utica/Rome (NY) ***518***
Temple U (PA) ***523***
Texas Southern U (TX) ***526***
Texas Tech U (TX) ***526***
Thomas Edison State Coll (NJ) ***527***
U of Arkansas at Little Rock (AR) ***539***
U of Calif, Santa Barbara (CA) ***541***
U of Central Florida (FL) ***542***
U of Cincinnati (OH) ***543***
U of Dayton (OH) ***544***
U of Hartford (CT) ***546***
U of Maine (ME) ***550***
U of Maryland Eastern Shore (MD) ***552***
U of Massachusetts Dartmouth (MA) ***553***
U of Massachusetts Lowell (MA) ***553***
The U of Memphis (TN) ***553***
U of New Hampshire (NH) ***558***
The U of North Carolina at Charlotte (NC) ***560***
U of North Texas (TX) ***562***
U of Pittsburgh at Johnstown (PA) ***570***
U of Regina (SK, Canada) ***572***
U of Southern Mississippi (MS) ***576***
U of Toledo (OH) ***581***
Wayne State U (MI) ***596***
Weber State U (UT) ***596***
Wentworth Inst of Technology (MA) ***597***
Western Carolina U (NC) ***598***
Western Washington U (WA) ***600***
World Coll (VA) ***609***

Youngstown State U (OH) **611**

ELECTRICAL/ELECTRONICS DRAFTING

Overview: This major prepares students to create schematics, blueprints, or computer simulations for electrical engineers and computer engineers. *Related majors:* computer science, electrical and computer engineering, drafting and design technology. *Potential careers:* electrical draftsperson, computer or electrical technician, computer programmer, electrician. *Salary potential:* $32k-$45k.

Idaho State U (ID) **384**

ELECTRICAL ENGINEERING

Overview: Students learn the math and science behind developing electrical, electronic, and communications systems, including power generation plants, and topics like superconductivity and energy storage and retrieval. *Related majors:* computer engineering, computer hardware engineering, electromechanical technology, physics and mathematics, chemistry. *Potential careers:* electrical engineer, aerospace technician, power plant engineer, electrical technician. *Salary potential:* $40k-$50k.

Abilene Christian U (TX) **260**
Alabama A&M U (AL) **261**
Alfred U (NY) **263**
The American U in Cairo(Egypt) **267**
Arizona State U (AZ) **271**
Arkansas Tech U (AR) **272**
Auburn U (AL) **276**
Baylor U (TX) **283**
Bloomsburg U of Pennsylvania (PA) **290**
Boston U (MA) **292**
Bradley U (IL) **293**
Brigham Young U (UT) **295**
Brown U (RI) **296**
Bucknell U (PA) **297**
California Inst of Technology (CA) **299**
California Polytechnic State U, San Luis Obispo (CA) **300**
California State Polytechnic U, Pomona (CA) **300**
California State U, Chico (CA) **300**
California State U, Fresno (CA) **301**
California State U, Fullerton (CA) **301**
California State U, Long Beach (CA) **301**
California State U, Northridge (CA) **301**
California State U, Sacramento (CA) **301**
Calvin Coll (MI) **303**
Capitol Coll (MD) **304**
Carleton U (ON, Canada) **305**
Carnegie Mellon U (PA) **305**
Case Western Reserve U (OH) **307**
The Catholic U of America (DC) **307**
Cedarville U (OH) **308**
Christian Brothers U (TN) **313**
Citadel, The Military Coll of South Carolina (SC) **314**
City Coll of the City U of NY (NY) **314**
Clarkson U (NY) **316**
Clemson U (SC) **317**
Cleveland State U (OH) **317**
Cogswell Polytechnical Coll (CA) **318**
The Coll of Southeastern Europe, The American U of Athens(Greece) **323**
Colorado School of Mines (CO) **325**
Colorado State U (CO) **325**
Colorado Tech U (CO) **326**
Columbia U, School of Engineering & Applied Sci (NY) **328**
Concordia U (QC, Canada) **331**
Cooper Union for the Advancement of Science & Art (NY) **332**
Cornell U (NY) **333**
Dominican U (IL) **345**
Dordt Coll (IA) **345**
Drexel U (PA) **346**
Duke U (NC) **346**
Eastern Nazarene Coll (MA) **348**
East-West U (IL) **350**
Embry-Riddle Aeronautical U (AZ) **352**
Fairfield U (CT) **356**
Fairleigh Dickinson U, Teaneck-Metro Campus (NJ) **356**
Florida A&M U (FL) **359**
Florida Atlantic U (FL) **359**
Florida Inst of Technology (FL) **360**
Florida International U (FL) **360**
Florida State U (FL) **361**
Frostburg State U (MD) **365**
Gallaudet U (DC) **365**
Gannon U (PA) **365**
George Mason U (VA) **366**
The George Washington U (DC) **367**
Georgia Inst of Technology (GA) **367**
Gonzaga U (WA) **369**
Grand Valley State U (MI) **371**
Grantham U (LA) **372**
Grove City Coll (PA) **373**
Hampton U (VA) **375**
Harvard U (MA) **376**
Henry Cogswell Coll (WA) **378**
Hofstra U (NY) **380**
Howard U (DC) **382**
Illinois Inst of Technology (IL) **384**
Indiana Inst of Technology (IN) **385**
Indiana U–Purdue U Fort Wayne (IN) **386**
Indiana U–Purdue U Indianapolis (IN) **387**
Insto Tecno Estudios Sups Monterrey(Mexico) **388**
Iowa State U of Science and Technology (IA) **390**
Jacksonville U (FL) **391**
John Brown U (AR) **392**
Johns Hopkins U (MD) **392**
Johnson & Wales U (RI) **393**
Kansas State U (KS) **396**
Kettering U (MI) **398**
Lafayette Coll (PA) **400**
Lakehead U (ON, Canada) **400**
Lamar U (TX) **401**
Lawrence Technological U (MI) **403**
Lehigh U (PA) **404**
LeTourneau U (TX) **405**
Louisiana State U and A&M Coll (LA) **410**
Louisiana Tech U (LA) **410**
Loyola Coll in Maryland (MD) **411**
Loyola Marymount U (CA) **411**
Maharishi U of Management (IA) **414**
Manhattan Coll (NY) **416**
Marquette U (WI) **418**
Massachusetts Inst of Technology (MA) **421**
McGill U (QC, Canada) **423**
McMaster U (ON, Canada) **423**
McNeese State U (LA) **423**
Memorial U of Newfoundland (NF, Canada) **424**
Mercer U (GA) **425**
Merrimack Coll (MA) **426**
Michigan State U (MI) **428**
Michigan Technological U (MI) **428**
Milwaukee School of Engineering (WI) **431**
Minnesota State U, Mankato (MN) **431**
Mississippi State U (MS) **432**
Missouri Tech (MO) **433**
Montana State U–Bozeman (MT) **434**
Morgan State U (MD) **436**
New Jersey Inst of Technology (NJ) **445**
New Mexico Inst of Mining and Technology (NM) **446**
New Mexico State U (NM) **446**
New York Inst of Technology (NY) **447**
New York U (NY) **447**
Norfolk State U (VA) **448**
North Carolina Ag and Tech State U (NC) **448**
North Carolina State U (NC) **449**
North Dakota State U (ND) **449**
Northeastern U (MA) **450**
Northern Arizona U (AZ) **450**
Northern Illinois U (IL) **450**
Northwestern Polytechnic U (CA) **453**
Northwestern U (IL) **453**
Norwich U (VT) **455**
Oakland U (MI) **456**
Ohio Northern U (OH) **457**
The Ohio State U (OH) **457**
Ohio U (OH) **458**
Oklahoma Christian U (OK) **459**
Oklahoma State U (OK) **460**
Old Dominion U (VA) **460**
Oral Roberts U (OK) **461**
Oregon State U (OR) **462**
Pacific Lutheran U (WA) **463**
Pacific States U (CA) **464**
Penn State U Altoona Coll (PA) **467**
Penn State U at Erie, The Behrend Coll (PA) **467**
Penn State U Harrisburg Campus of the Capital Coll (PA) **468**
Penn State U Univ Park Campus (PA) **468**
Polytechnic U, Brooklyn Campus (NY) **472**
Portland State U (OR) **472**
Prairie View A&M U (TX) **473**
Princeton U (NJ) **474**
Purdue U (IN) **475**
Purdue U Calumet (IN) **475**
Queen's U at Kingston (ON, Canada) **476**
Rensselaer Polytechnic Inst (NY) **478**
Rice U (TX) **479**
Rochester Inst of Technology (NY) **482**
Rose-Hulman Inst of Technology (IN) **484**
Rowan U (NJ) **484**
Ryerson U (ON, Canada) **485**
Saginaw Valley State U (MI) **486**
St. Cloud State U (MN) **488**
Saint Louis U (MO) **492**
St. Mary's U of San Antonio (TX) **494**
San Diego State U (CA) **498**
San Francisco State U (CA) **498**
San Jose State U (CA) **499**
Santa Clara U (CA) **499**
Seattle Pacific U (WA) **501**
Seattle U (WA) **501**
South Dakota School of Mines and Technology (SD) **507**
South Dakota State U (SD) **507**
Southern Illinois U Carbondale (IL) **509**
Southern Illinois U Edwardsville (IL) **509**
Southern Methodist U (TX) **510**
Southern U and A&M Coll (LA) **511**
Stanford U (CA) **514**
State U of NY at Binghamton (NY) **515**
State U of NY at New Paltz (NY) **515**
State U of NY Maritime Coll (NY) **518**
Stevens Inst of Technology (NJ) **519**
Suffolk U (MA) **520**
Syracuse U (NY) **521**
Temple U (PA) **523**
Tennessee State U (TN) **523**
Tennessee Technological U (TN) **524**
Texas A&M U (TX) **524**
Texas A&M U–Kingsville (TX) **525**
Texas Tech U (TX) **526**
Tri-State U (IN) **532**
Tufts U (MA) **533**
Tulane U (LA) **533**
Tuskegee U (AL) **533**
Union Coll (NY) **534**
United States Air Force Academy (CO) **534**
United States Coast Guard Academy (CT) **535**
United States Military Academy (NY) **535**
United States Naval Academy (MD) **535**
Université de Sherbrooke (QC, Canada) **536**
U du Québec à Trois-Rivières (QC, Canada) **536**
U du Québec, École de technologie supérieure (QC, Canada) **536**
Université Laval (QC, Canada) **536**
U at Buffalo, The State University of New York (NY) **536**
The U of Akron (OH) **537**
The U of Alabama (AL) **537**
The U of Alabama at Birmingham (AL) **537**
The U of Alabama in Huntsville (AL) **537**
U of Alaska Fairbanks (AK) **538**
U of Alberta (AB, Canada) **538**
The U of Arizona (AZ) **538**
U of Arkansas (AR) **539**
The U of British Columbia (BC, Canada) **540**
U of Calgary (AB, Canada) **540**
U of Calif, Berkeley (CA) **540**
U of Calif, Davis (CA) **540**
U of Calif, Irvine (CA) **541**
U of Calif, Los Angeles (CA) **541**
U of Calif, Riverside (CA) **541**
U of Calif, San Diego (CA) **541**
U of Calif, Santa Barbara (CA) **541**
U of Calif, Santa Cruz (CA) **542**
U of Central Florida (FL) **542**
U of Cincinnati (OH) **543**
U of Colorado at Boulder (CO) **543**
U of Colorado at Colorado Springs (CO) **543**
U of Colorado at Denver (CO) **543**
U of Connecticut (CT) **544**
U of Dayton (OH) **544**
U of Delaware (DE) **544**
U of Denver (CO) **544**
U of Evansville (IN) **545**
U of Florida (FL) **545**
U of Hartford (CT) **546**
U of Hawaii at Manoa (HI) **546**
U of Houston (TX) **547**
U of Idaho (ID) **547**
U of Illinois at Chicago (IL) **547**
U of Illinois at Urbana–Champaign (IL) **548**
U of Indianapolis (IN) **548**
The U of Iowa (IA) **548**
U of Kansas (KS) **549**
U of Kentucky (KY) **549**
U of Louisiana at Lafayette (LA) **550**
U of Louisville (KY) **550**
U of Maine (ME) **550**
U of Manitoba (MB, Canada) **551**
U of Maryland, Coll Park (MD) **552**
U of Massachusetts Amherst (MA) **552**
U of Massachusetts Dartmouth (MA) **553**
U of Massachusetts Lowell (MA) **553**
The U of Memphis (TN) **553**
U of Miami (FL) **553**
U of Michigan (MI) **554**
U of Michigan–Dearborn (MI) **554**
U of Minnesota, Duluth (MN) **554**
U of Minnesota, Twin Cities Campus (MN) **555**
U of Mississippi (MS) **555**
U of Missouri–Columbia (MO) **555**
U of Missouri–Kansas City (MO) **555**
U of Missouri–Rolla (MO) **556**
U of Missouri–St. Louis (MO) **556**
U of Nebraska–Lincoln (NE) **557**
U of Nevada, Las Vegas (NV) **558**
U of Nevada, Reno (NV) **558**
U of New Brunswick Fredericton (NB, Canada) **558**
U of New Brunswick Saint John (NB, Canada) **558**
U of New Hampshire (NH) **558**
U of New Haven (CT) **559**
U of New Mexico (NM) **559**
U of New Orleans (LA) **559**
The U of North Carolina at Charlotte (NC) **560**
U of North Dakota (ND) **561**
U of North Florida (FL) **561**
U of Notre Dame (IN) **562**
U of Oklahoma (OK) **562**
U of Ottawa (ON, Canada) **563**
U of Pennsylvania (PA) **563**
U of Pittsburgh (PA) **569**
U of Portland (OR) **570**
U of Regina (SK, Canada) **572**
U of Rhode Island (RI) **572**
U of Rochester (NY) **573**
U of St. Thomas (MN) **573**
U of San Diego (CA) **574**
U of Saskatchewan (SK, Canada) **574**
The U of Scranton (PA) **574**
U of South Alabama (AL) **575**
U of South Carolina (SC) **575**
U of Southern California (CA) **576**
U of Southern Maine (ME) **576**
U of South Florida (FL) **576**
The U of Tennessee (TN) **577**
The U of Tennessee at Chattanooga (TN) **577**
The U of Texas at Arlington (TX) **577**
The U of Texas at Austin (TX) **578**
The U of Texas at Dallas (TX) **578**
The U of Texas at El Paso (TX) **578**
The U of Texas at San Antonio (TX) **578**
The U of Texas at Tyler (TX) **579**
The U of Texas–Pan American (TX) **579**
U of the District of Columbia (DC) **580**
U of the Pacific (CA) **580**
U of Toledo (OH) **581**
U of Toronto (ON, Canada) **581**
U of Tulsa (OK) **581**
U of Utah (UT) **582**
U of Vermont (VT) **582**
U of Victoria (BC, Canada) **582**
U of Virginia (VA) **582**
U of Washington (WA) **583**
U of Waterloo (ON, Canada) **583**
The U of Western Ontario (ON, Canada) **583**
U of Windsor (ON, Canada) **584**
U of Wisconsin–Madison (WI) **584**
U of Wisconsin–Milwaukee (WI) **585**
U of Wisconsin–Platteville (WI) **585**

ELECTRICAL ENGINEERING (continued)

U of Wyoming (WY) ***586***
Utah State U (UT) ***587***
Valparaiso U (IN) ***588***
Vanderbilt U (TN) ***588***
Villanova U (PA) ***590***
Virginia Commonwealth U (VA) ***590***
Virginia Military Inst (VA) ***591***
Virginia Polytechnic Inst and State U (VA) ***591***
Walla Walla Coll (WA) ***593***
Washington State U (WA) ***595***
Washington U in St. Louis (MO) ***595***
Wayne State U (MI) ***596***
Wentworth Inst of Technology (MA) ***597***
Western Kentucky U (KY) ***599***
Western Michigan U (MI) ***599***
Western New England Coll (MA) ***600***
West Virginia U (WV) ***602***
West Virginia U Inst of Technology (WV) ***602***
Wichita State U (KS) ***604***
Widener U (PA) ***604***
Wilberforce U (OH) ***605***
Wilkes U (PA) ***605***
Worcester Polytechnic Inst (MA) ***609***
Wright State U (OH) ***609***
Yale U (CT) ***610***
Youngstown State U (OH) ***611***

ELECTROENCEPHALOGRAPH TECHNOLOGY

Overview: This major teaches students how to perform diagnostic tests that record a patient's brain waves to determine brain diseases, injuries, or tumors. *Related majors:* neuroscience, psychology, diagnostic medical sonography. *Potential careers:* electroencephalograph technician, radiologic technologist, sonographer, ophthalmic technician. *Salary potential:* $23k-$33k.

Johns Hopkins U (MD) ***392***

ELECTROMECHANICAL TECHNOLOGY

Overview: Students who choose this major get a basic knowledge in developing and testing automated mechanical and other electromechanical devices and systems. *Related majors:* electronics engineering, computer science, mechanical engineering technology. *Potential careers:* machinist, robotics engineer, mechanical engineer. *Salary potential:* $25k-$40k.

Excelsior Coll (NY) ***356***
Insto Tecno Estudios Sups Monterrey(Mexico) ***388***
Penn State U Berks Cmps of Berks-Lehigh Valley Coll (PA) ***468***
U of Houston (TX) ***547***
U of the District of Columbia (DC) ***580***
U of Toledo (OH) ***581***
Vermont Tech Coll (VT) ***589***
Wayne State U (MI) ***596***

ELEMENTARY EDUCATION

Overview: undergraduates learn the skills necessary to teach elementary age children (kindergarten through grade 8). *Related majors:* education, curriculum and instruction, educational psychology, early childhood/ kindergarten education. *Potential careers:* teacher, teacher's aid, elementary school administrator. *Salary potential:* $22k-$31k.

Abilene Christian U (TX) ***260***
Acadia U (NS, Canada) ***260***
Adams State Coll (CO) ***260***
Adelphi U (NY) ***260***
Adrian Coll (MI) ***260***
Alabama A&M U (AL) ***261***
Alabama State U (AL) ***261***
Alaska Pacific U (AK) ***261***
Albion Coll (MI) ***262***
Albright Coll (PA) ***263***
Alcorn State U (MS) ***263***
Alderson-Broaddus Coll (WV) ***263***
Alfred U (NY) ***263***
Alice Lloyd Coll (KY) ***263***
Allen U (SC) ***264***
Alliant International U (CA) ***264***
Alma Coll (MI) ***264***
Alvernia Coll (PA) ***265***
Alverno Coll (WI) ***265***
American Indian Coll of the Assemblies of God, Inc (AZ) ***266***
American International Coll (MA) ***267***
American U (DC) ***267***
American U of Puerto Rico (PR) ***268***
Anderson Coll (SC) ***268***
Anderson U (IN) ***268***
Andrews U (MI) ***269***
Anna Maria Coll (MA) ***269***
Aquinas Coll (MI) ***270***
Aquinas Coll (TN) ***271***
Arcadia U (PA) ***271***
Arizona State U (AZ) ***271***
Arizona State U East (AZ) ***271***
Arizona State U West (AZ) ***272***
Arkansas Baptist Coll (AR) ***272***
Arkansas Tech U (AR) ***272***
Armstrong Atlantic State U (GA) ***273***
Asbury Coll (KY) ***274***
Ashland U (OH) ***274***
Assumption Coll (MA) ***275***
Athens State U (AL) ***275***
Atlantic Union Coll (MA) ***276***
Auburn U (AL) ***276***
Auburn U Montgomery (AL) ***276***
Augsburg Coll (MN) ***276***
Augustana Coll (IL) ***276***
Augustana Coll (SD) ***276***
Augusta State U (GA) ***277***
Aurora U (IL) ***277***
Avila U (MO) ***278***
Baker U (KS) ***280***
Baldwin-Wallace Coll (OH) ***280***
Ball State U (IN) ***280***
Baptist Bible Coll (MO) ***281***
The Baptist Coll of Florida (FL) ***281***
Barber-Scotia Coll (NC) ***281***
Barclay Coll (KS) ***281***
Barry U (FL) ***282***
Barton Coll (NC) ***282***
Bayamón Central U (PR) ***283***
Baylor U (TX) ***283***
Bay Path Coll (MA) ***283***
Becker Coll (MA) ***283***
Belhaven Coll (MS) ***283***
Bellarmine U (KY) ***284***
Belmont Abbey Coll (NC) ***284***
Belmont U (TN) ***284***
Beloit Coll (WI) ***285***
Bemidji State U (MN) ***285***
Benedict Coll (SC) ***285***
Benedictine Coll (KS) ***285***
Benedictine U (IL) ***285***
Bennett Coll (NC) ***286***
Berea Coll (KY) ***286***
Berry Coll (GA) ***287***
Bethany Bible Coll (NB, Canada) ***287***
Bethany Coll (KS) ***287***
Bethany Coll (WV) ***287***
Bethany Coll of the Assemblies of God (CA) ***287***
Bethel Coll (IN) ***288***
Bethel Coll (KS) ***288***
Bethel Coll (MN) ***288***
Bethel Coll (TN) ***288***
Bethune-Cookman Coll (FL) ***289***
Biola U (CA) ***289***
Birmingham-Southern Coll (AL) ***289***
Blackburn Coll (IL) ***290***
Black Hills State U (SD) ***290***
Bloomsburg U of Pennsylvania (PA) ***290***
Bluefield Coll (VA) ***291***
Bluefield State Coll (WV) ***291***
Blue Mountain Coll (MS) ***291***
Bluffton Coll (OH) ***291***
Boston Coll (MA) ***292***
Boston U (MA) ***292***
Bowie State U (MD) ***292***
Bowling Green State U (OH) ***292***
Bradley U (IL) ***293***
Brandon U (MB, Canada) ***293***
Brescia U (KY) ***293***
Brewton-Parker Coll (GA) ***294***
Briar Cliff U (IA) ***294***
Bridgewater Coll (VA) ***294***
Bridgewater State Coll (MA) ***294***
Brigham Young U (UT) ***295***
Brigham Young U–Hawaii (HI) ***295***
Brock U (ON, Canada) ***295***
Brooklyn Coll of the City U of NY (NY) ***295***
Bryan Coll (TN) ***296***
Bryn Athyn Coll of the New Church (PA) ***297***
Bucknell U (PA) ***297***
Buena Vista U (IA) ***297***
Butler U (IN) ***297***
Cabrini Coll (PA) ***298***
Caldwell Coll (NJ) ***298***
California State U, Fresno (CA) ***301***
California U of Pennsylvania (PA) ***302***
Calumet Coll of Saint Joseph (IN) ***302***
Calvin Coll (MI) ***303***
Cameron U (OK) ***303***
Campbellsville U (KY) ***303***
Campbell U (NC) ***303***
Canisius Coll (NY) ***304***
Capital U (OH) ***304***
Cardinal Stritch U (WI) ***305***
Carlos Albizu Univ - Miami (FL) ***305***
Carlow Coll (PA) ***305***
Carroll Coll (MT) ***306***
Carroll Coll (WI) ***306***
Carson-Newman Coll (TN) ***306***
Carthage Coll (WI) ***306***
Catawba Coll (NC) ***307***
The Catholic U of America (DC) ***307***
Cedar Crest Coll (PA) ***308***
Cedarville U (OH) ***308***
Centenary Coll (NJ) ***308***
Centenary Coll of Louisiana (LA) ***308***
Central Coll (IA) ***309***
Central Connecticut State U (CT) ***309***
Central Methodist Coll (MO) ***309***
Central Michigan U (MI) ***310***
Central Missouri State U (MO) ***310***
Central Washington U (WA) ***310***
Centre Coll (KY) ***310***
Chadron State Coll (NE) ***311***
Chaminade U of Honolulu (HI) ***311***
Champlain Coll (VT) ***311***
Charleston Southern U (SC) ***311***
Chestnut Hill Coll (PA) ***312***
Cheyney U of Pennsylvania (PA) ***312***
Chowan Coll (NC) ***312***
Christian Brothers U (TN) ***313***
Christian Heritage Coll (CA) ***313***
Christopher Newport U (VA) ***313***
Circleville Bible Coll (OH) ***314***
City Coll of the City U of NY (NY) ***314***
City U (WA) ***314***
Claflin U (SC) ***314***
Clarion U of Pennsylvania (PA) ***315***
Clark Atlanta U (GA) ***315***
Clarke Coll (IA) ***315***
Clark U (MA) ***316***
Clearwater Christian Coll (FL) ***316***
Clemson U (SC) ***317***
Cleveland State U (OH) ***317***
Coastal Carolina U (SC) ***318***
Coe Coll (IA) ***318***
Coker Coll (SC) ***318***
Colby-Sawyer Coll (NH) ***319***
Coll Misericordia (PA) ***319***
Coll of Charleston (SC) ***320***
Coll of Mount Saint Vincent (NY) ***320***
The Coll of New Jersey (NJ) ***320***
The Coll of New Rochelle (NY) ***321***
Coll of Notre Dame of Maryland (MD) ***321***
Coll of Saint Benedict (MN) ***321***
Coll of St. Catherine (MN) ***321***
Coll of St. Joseph (VT) ***322***
Coll of Saint Mary (NE) ***322***
The Coll of Saint Rose (NY) ***322***
Coll of Santa Fe (NM) ***323***
Coll of the Atlantic (ME) ***323***
Coll of the Ozarks (MO) ***323***
Coll of the Southwest (NM) ***324***
Colorado State U-Pueblo (CO) ***325***
Columbia Coll (MO) ***326***
Columbia Coll (SC) ***327***
Columbia International U (SC) ***327***
Columbia Union Coll (MD) ***328***
Columbus State U (GA) ***328***
Concord Coll (WV) ***329***
Concordia Coll (AL) ***329***
Concordia Coll (MN) ***329***
Concordia Coll (NY) ***329***
Concordia U (CA) ***330***
Concordia U (IL) ***330***
Concordia U (MI) ***330***
Concordia U (MN) ***330***
Concordia U (NE) ***330***
Concordia U (OR) ***330***
Concordia U (QC, Canada) ***331***
Concordia U at Austin (TX) ***331***
Concordia U Wisconsin (WI) ***331***
Converse Coll (SC) ***332***
Cornell Coll (IA) ***332***
Cornerstone U (MI) ***333***
Covenant Coll (GA) ***333***
Creighton U (NE) ***333***
Crichton Coll (TN) ***334***
Crown Coll (MN) ***334***
Culver-Stockton Coll (MO) ***334***
Cumberland Coll (KY) ***335***
Cumberland U (TN) ***335***
Curry Coll (MA) ***335***
Daemen Coll (NY) ***335***
Dakota State U (SD) ***335***
Dakota Wesleyan U (SD) ***336***
Dallas Baptist U (TX) ***336***
Dana Coll (NE) ***337***
Davis & Elkins Coll (WV) ***338***
Defiance Coll (OH) ***338***
Delaware State U (DE) ***338***
Delta State U (MS) ***339***
DePaul U (IL) ***339***
DePauw U (IN) ***339***
DeSales U (PA) ***340***
Dickinson State U (ND) ***344***
Dillard U (LA) ***344***
Doane Coll (NE) ***344***
Dominican Coll (NY) ***344***
Dominican U (IL) ***345***
Dordt Coll (IA) ***345***
Dowling Coll (NY) ***345***
Drake U (IA) ***345***
Drury U (MO) ***346***
Duquesne U (PA) ***346***
D'Youville Coll (NY) ***347***
East Carolina U (NC) ***347***
East Central U (OK) ***347***
Eastern Connecticut State U (CT) ***347***
Eastern Illinois U (IL) ***348***
Eastern Kentucky U (KY) ***348***
Eastern Mennonite U (VA) ***348***
Eastern Michigan U (MI) ***348***
Eastern Nazarene Coll (MA) ***348***
Eastern New Mexico U (NM) ***349***
Eastern U (PA) ***349***
Eastern Washington U (WA) ***349***
East Stroudsburg U of Pennsylvania (PA) ***349***
East Texas Baptist U (TX) ***350***
Edgewood Coll (WI) ***351***
Edinboro U of Pennsylvania (PA) ***351***
Elizabeth City State U (NC) ***351***
Elizabethtown Coll (PA) ***351***
Elmhurst Coll (IL) ***351***
Elmira Coll (NY) ***351***
Elms Coll (MA) ***352***
Elon U (NC) ***352***
Emmanuel Coll (GA) ***353***
Emmanuel Coll (MA) ***353***
Emmaus Bible Coll (IA) ***353***
Emory U (GA) ***354***
Emporia State U (KS) ***354***
Endicott Coll (MA) ***354***
Erskine Coll (SC) ***354***
Eureka Coll (IL) ***355***
Evangel U (MO) ***355***
Fairmont State Coll (WV) ***356***
Faith Baptist Bible Coll and Theological Seminary (IA) ***356***
Faulkner U (AL) ***357***
Fayetteville State U (NC) ***357***
Felician Coll (NJ) ***357***
Fitchburg State Coll (MA) ***358***
Five Towns Coll (NY) ***359***
Flagler Coll (FL) ***359***
Florida A&M U (FL) ***359***
Florida Atlantic U (FL) ***359***
Florida Coll (FL) ***359***
Florida Gulf Coast U (FL) ***359***
Florida International U (FL) ***360***
Florida Southern Coll (FL) ***361***
Florida State U (FL) ***361***

Fontbonne U (MO) 361
Fordham U (NY) 362
Fort Hays State U (KS) 362
Fort Lewis Coll (CO) 362
Framingham State Coll (MA) 362
The Franciscan U (IA) 363
Franciscan U of Steubenville (OH) 363
Francis Marion U (SC) 363
Franklin Coll (IN) 363
Franklin Pierce Coll (NH) 364
Freed-Hardeman U (TN) 364
Free Will Baptist Bible Coll (TN) 364
Fresno Pacific U (CA) 364
Frostburg State U (MD) 365
Furman U (SC) 365
Gallaudet U (DC) 365
Gannon U (PA) 365
Gardner-Webb U (NC) 365
Geneva Coll (PA) 366
George Fox U (OR) 366
Georgetown Coll (KY) 366
Georgian Court Coll (NJ) 367
Georgia Southwestern State U (GA) 368
Gettysburg Coll (PA) 368
Glenville State Coll (WV) 368
Goddard Coll (VT) 369
Gonzaga U (WA) 369
Gordon Coll (MA) 370
Goshen Coll (IN) 370
Goucher Coll (MD) 370
Governors State U (IL) 370
Grace Bible Coll (MI) 370
Grace Coll (IN) 370
Graceland U (IA) 371
Grace U (NE) 371
Grambling State U (LA) 371
Grand Canyon U (AZ) 371
Grand Valley State U (MI) 371
Grand View Coll (IA) 372
Green Mountain Coll (VT) 372
Greensboro Coll (NC) 372
Greenville Coll (IL) 373
Grove City Coll (PA) 373
Guilford Coll (NC) 373
Gustavus Adolphus Coll (MN) 374
Gwynedd-Mercy Coll (PA) 374
Hamline U (MN) 374
Hampshire Coll (MA) 375
Hampton U (VA) 375
Hannibal-LaGrange Coll (MO) 375
Hanover Coll (IN) 375
Harding U (AR) 375
Hardin-Simmons U (TX) 376
Harris-Stowe State Coll (MO) 376
Haskell Indian Nations U (KS) 377
Hastings Coll (NE) 377
Heidelberg Coll (OH) 377
Hellenic Coll (MA) 378
Henderson State U (AR) 378
Hendrix Coll (AR) 378
High Point U (NC) 379
Hillsdale Coll (MI) 379
Hiram Coll (OH) 379
Hofstra U (NY) 380
Holy Family U (PA) 380
Hope Coll (MI) 381
Hope International U (CA) 381
Houghton Coll (NY) 381
Houston Baptist U (TX) 382
Howard Payne U (TX) 382
Humboldt State U (CA) 382
Hunter Coll of the City U of NY (NY) 382
Huntington Coll (IN) 383
Husson Coll (ME) 383
Huston-Tillotson Coll (TX) 383
Idaho State U (ID) 384
Illinois Coll (IL) 384
Illinois State U (IL) 384
Illinois Wesleyan U (IL) 385
Immaculata U (PA) 385
Indiana State U (IN) 385
Indiana U Bloomington (IN) 385
Indiana U East (IN) 386
Indiana U Kokomo (IN) 386
Indiana U Northwest (IN) 386
Indiana U of Pennsylvania (PA) 386
Indiana U–Purdue U Fort Wayne (IN) 386
Indiana U–Purdue U Indianapolis (IN) 387
Indiana U South Bend (IN) 387
Indiana U Southeast (IN) 387
Indiana Wesleyan U (IN) 387
Inter American U of PR, Aguadilla Campus (PR) 388
Inter Amer U of PR, Barranquitas Campus (PR) 388
Inter American U of PR, Guayama Campus (PR) 388
Inter American U of PR, San Germán Campus (PR) 388
International Coll of the Cayman Islands(Cayman Islands) 389
Iona Coll (NY) 390
Iowa State U of Science and Technology (IA) 390
Iowa Wesleyan Coll (IA) 390
Jackson State U (MS) 390
Jacksonville State U (AL) 390
Jacksonville U (FL) 391
James Madison U (VA) 391
Jamestown Coll (ND) 391
John Brown U (AR) 392
John Carroll U (OH) 392
Johnson Bible Coll (TN) 394
Johnson C. Smith U (NC) 394
Johnson State Coll (VT) 394
John Wesley Coll (NC) 394
Judson Coll (AL) 395
Judson Coll (IL) 395
Juniata Coll (PA) 395
Kansas State U (KS) 396
Kean U (NJ) 396
Keene State Coll (NH) 396
Kennesaw State U (GA) 397
Kentucky Christian Coll (KY) 397
Kentucky State U (KY) 397
Kentucky Wesleyan Coll (KY) 397
Keuka Coll (NY) 398
King Coll (TN) 398
King's Coll (PA) 398
The King's U Coll (AB, Canada) 399
Kutztown U of Pennsylvania (PA) 399
LaGrange Coll (GA) 400
Lake Erie Coll (OH) 400
Lake Forest Coll (IL) 400
Lakehead U (ON, Canada) 400
Lakeland Coll (WI) 401
Lamar U (TX) 401
Lambuth U (TN) 401
Lander U (SC) 401
Langston U (OK) 402
La Roche Coll (PA) 402
La Salle U (PA) 402
Lasell Coll (MA) 402
La Sierra U (CA) 403
Lebanon Valley Coll (PA) 403
Lees-McRae Coll (NC) 404
Lee U (TN) 404
Le Moyne Coll (NY) 404
Lenoir-Rhyne Coll (NC) 405
Lesley U (MA) 405
LeTourneau U (TX) 405
Lewis-Clark State Coll (ID) 406
Lewis U (IL) 406
Liberty U (VA) 406
Limestone Coll (SC) 406
Lincoln Christian Coll (IL) 407
Lincoln Memorial U (TN) 407
Lincoln U (PA) 407
Lindenwood U (MO) 407
Lindsey Wilson Coll (KY) 407
Linfield Coll (OR) 408
Lipscomb U (TN) 408
Lock Haven U of Pennsylvania (PA) 408
Long Island U, Brooklyn Campus (NY) 409
Long Island U, C.W. Post Campus (NY) 409
Long Island U, Southampton Coll (NY) 409
Long Island U, Southampton Coll, Friends World Program (NY) 409
Longwood U (VA) 409
Loras Coll (IA) 410
Louisiana Coll (LA) 410
Louisiana State U and A&M Coll (LA) 410
Louisiana State U in Shreveport (LA) 410
Louisiana Tech U (LA) 410
Loyola Coll in Maryland (MD) 411
Loyola U Chicago (IL) 411
Loyola U New Orleans (LA) 411
Lubbock Christian U (TX) 412
Luther Coll (IA) 412
Lycoming Coll (PA) 412
Lynchburg Coll (VA) 413
Lyndon State Coll (VT) 413
Lynn U (FL) 413
MacMurray Coll (IL) 414
Madonna U (MI) 414
Manchester Coll (IN) 415
Manhattan Coll (NY) 416
Manhattanville Coll (NY) 416
Mansfield U of Pennsylvania (PA) 416
Maranatha Baptist Bible Coll (WI) 417
Marian Coll (IN) 417
Marian Coll of Fond du Lac (WI) 417
Marietta Coll (OH) 417
Marist Coll (NY) 417
Marquette U (WI) 418
Marshall U (WV) 418
Mars Hill Coll (NC) 418
Martin Luther Coll (MN) 418
Martin Methodist Coll (TN) 418
Martin U (IN) 419
Marymount Coll of Fordham U (NY) 419
Maryville U of Saint Louis (MO) 420
Mary Washington Coll (VA) 420
Marywood U (PA) 421
Massachusetts Coll of Liberal Arts (MA) 421
The Master's Coll and Seminary (CA) 422
Mayville State U (ND) 422
McGill U (QC, Canada) 423
McKendree Coll (IL) 423
McMurry U (TX) 423
McNeese State U (LA) 423
McPherson Coll (KS) 423
Medaille Coll (NY) 424
Memorial U of Newfoundland (NF, Canada) 424
Mercer U (GA) 425
Mercy Coll (NY) 425
Mercyhurst Coll (PA) 425
Merrimack Coll (MA) 426
Mesa State Coll (CO) 426
Messiah Coll (PA) 426
Methodist Coll (NC) 427
Miami U (OH) 428
Michigan State U (MI) 428
MidAmerica Nazarene U (KS) 428
Mid-Continent Coll (KY) 429
Midland Lutheran Coll (NE) 429
Midway Coll (KY) 429
Midwestern State U (TX) 430
Miles Coll (AL) 430
Millersville U of Pennsylvania (PA) 430
Millikin U (IL) 430
Mills Coll (CA) 431
Minnesota State U, Mankato (MN) 431
Minnesota State U, Moorhead (MN) 432
Minot State U (ND) 432
Mississippi Coll (MS) 432
Mississippi State U (MS) 432
Mississippi Valley State U (MS) 432
Missouri Southern State Coll (MO) 433
Missouri Valley Coll (MO) 433
Missouri Western State Coll (MO) 433
Molloy Coll (NY) 433
Monmouth Coll (IL) 434
Montana State U–Billings (MT) 434
Montana State U–Bozeman (MT) 434
Montana State U–Northern (MT) 434
Montreat Coll (NC) 435
Moravian Coll (PA) 436
Morehead State U (KY) 436
Morehouse Coll (GA) 436
Morgan State U (MD) 436
Morningside Coll (IA) 437
Morris Coll (SC) 437
Mount Marty Coll (SD) 438
Mount Mary Coll (WI) 438
Mount Mercy Coll (IA) 438
Mount Saint Mary Coll (NY) 439
Mount St. Mary's Coll (CA) 439
Mount Saint Mary's Coll and Seminary (MD) 439
Mount Saint Vincent U (NS, Canada) 439
Mount Vernon Nazarene U (OH) 440
Muhlenberg Coll (PA) 440
Murray State U (KY) 440
Muskingum Coll (OH) 441
National-Louis U (IL) 442
Nazareth Coll of Rochester (NY) 443
Nebraska Christian Coll (NE) 443
Nebraska Wesleyan U (NE) 443
Neumann Coll (PA) 443
Newberry Coll (SC) 444
New England Coll (NH) 444
New Jersey City U (NJ) 445
Newman U (KS) 445
New Mexico Highlands U (NM) 446
New Mexico State U (NM) 446
New York Inst of Technology (NY) 447
New York U (NY) 447
Niagara U (NY) 447
Nicholls State U (LA) 447
North Carolina Ag and Tech State U (NC) 448
North Carolina Central U (NC) 448
North Carolina Wesleyan Coll (NC) 449
North Central Coll (IL) 449
North Dakota State U (ND) 449
Northeastern Illinois U (IL) 450
Northeastern State U (OK) 450
Northeastern U (MA) 450
Northern Arizona U (AZ) 450
Northern Illinois U (IL) 450
Northern Kentucky U (KY) 451
Northern Michigan U (MI) 451
Northern State U (SD) 451
North Georgia Coll & State U (GA) 451
North Greenville Coll (SC) 451
Northland Coll (WI) 452
North Park U (IL) 452
Northwest Christian Coll (OR) 452
Northwest Coll (WA) 452
Northwestern Coll (IA) 453
Northwestern Coll (MN) 453
Northwestern Oklahoma State U (OK) 453
Northwestern State U of Louisiana (LA) 453
Northwest Missouri State U (MO) 454
Northwest Nazarene U (ID) 454
Notre Dame Coll (OH) 455
Notre Dame de Namur U (CA) 455
Nova Southeastern U (FL) 455
Nyack Coll (NY) 456
Oakland City U (IN) 456
Oakland U (MI) 456
Oakwood Coll (AL) 456
Oglethorpe U (GA) 457
Ohio Northern U (OH) 457
The Ohio State U at Lima (OH) 458
Ohio U (OH) 458
Ohio U–Chillicothe (OH) 458
Ohio U–Lancaster (OH) 458
Ohio U–Zanesville (OH) 458
Ohio Valley Coll (WV) 459
Ohio Wesleyan U (OH) 459
Oklahoma Baptist U (OK) 459
Oklahoma Christian U (OK) 459
Oklahoma City U (OK) 460
Oklahoma Panhandle State U (OK) 460
Oklahoma State U (OK) 460
Oklahoma Wesleyan U (OK) 460
Olivet Coll (MI) 461
Olivet Nazarene U (IL) 461
Oral Roberts U (OK) 461
Ottawa U (KS) 462
Otterbein Coll (OH) 462
Our Lady of Holy Cross Coll (LA) 463
Pace U (NY) 463
Pacific Lutheran U (WA) 463
Pacific Oaks Coll (CA) 464
Pacific Union Coll (CA) 464
Pacific U (OR) 464
Paine Coll (GA) 465
Palm Beach Atlantic U (FL) 465
Park U (MO) 465
Paul Quinn Coll (TX) 466
Penn State U Univ Park Campus (PA) 468
Pepperdine U, Malibu (CA) 469
Peru State Coll (NE) 469
Pfeiffer U (NC) 469
Philadelphia Biblical U (PA) 469
Piedmont Baptist Coll (NC) 470
Pikeville Coll (KY) 470
Pillsbury Baptist Bible Coll (MN) 470
Pine Manor Coll (MA) 470
Pittsburg State U (KS) 470
Plattsburgh State U of NY (NY) 471
Plymouth State Coll (NH) 471
Point Park Coll (PA) 471
Pontifical Catholic U of Puerto Rico (PR) 472
Presbyterian Coll (SC) 473
Prescott Coll (AZ) 474
Principia Coll (IL) 474
Purdue U (IN) 475
Purdue U Calumet (IN) 475
Purdue U North Central (IN) 475
Queens Coll of the City U of NY (NY) 475
Queen's U at Kingston (ON, Canada) 476
Queens U of Charlotte (NC) 476
Quincy U (IL) 476
Reformed Bible Coll (MI) 477
Regis U (CO) 478
Rhode Island Coll (RI) 479
Rider U (NJ) 480
Ripon Coll (WI) 480

ELEMENTARY EDUCATION (continued)

Rivier Coll (NH) 480
Robert Morris U (PA) 481
Roberts Wesleyan Coll (NY) 481
Rockford Coll (IL) 482
Rockhurst U (MO) 482
Rocky Mountain Coll (MT) 482
Roger Williams U (RI) 483
Rollins Coll (FL) 483
Roosevelt U (IL) 483
Rowan U (NJ) 484
Russell Sage Coll (NY) 484
Rust Coll (MS) 485
Sacred Heart U (CT) 486
Saginaw Valley State U (MI) 486
St. Ambrose U (IA) 486
Saint Augustine's Coll (NC) 487
St. Bonaventure U (NY) 487
St. Cloud State U (MN) 488
St. Edward's U (TX) 488
St. Francis Coll (NY) 488
Saint Francis U (PA) 488
St. Francis Xavier U (NS, Canada) 489
St. John Fisher Coll (NY) 489
Saint John's U (MN) 490
St. John's U (NY) 490
Saint Joseph Coll (CT) 490
Saint Joseph's Coll (IN) 490
Saint Joseph's Coll of Maine (ME) 491
St. Joseph's Coll, Suffolk Campus (NY) 491
Saint Joseph's U (PA) 491
Saint Leo U (FL) 492
Saint Martin's Coll (WA) 493
Saint Mary Coll (KS) 493
Saint Mary-of-the-Woods Coll (IN) 493
Saint Mary's Coll (IN) 493
Saint Michael's Coll (VT) 494
St. Norbert Coll (WI) 495
Saint Peter's Coll (NJ) 495
St. Thomas Aquinas Coll (NY) 495
St. Thomas U (FL) 496
Saint Xavier U (IL) 496
Salem International U (WV) 496
Salem State Coll (MA) 497
Salisbury U (MD) 497
Salve Regina U (RI) 497
Samford U (AL) 497
Seton Hall U (NJ) 502
Seton Hill U (PA) 502
Shawnee State U (OH) 502
Shaw U (NC) 502
Sheldon Jackson Coll (AK) 503
Shepherd Coll (WV) 503
Shippensburg U of Pennsylvania (PA) 503
Shorter Coll (GA) 504
Siena Heights U (MI) 504
Silver Lake Coll (WI) 504
Simmons Coll (MA) 504
Simpson Coll (IA) 505
Simpson Coll and Graduate School (CA) 505
Si Tanka Huron U (SD) 505
Skidmore Coll (NY) 506
Slippery Rock U of Pennsylvania (PA) 506
South Carolina State U (SC) 506
Southeastern Coll of the Assemblies of God (FL) 507
Southeastern Louisiana U (LA) 508
Southeastern Oklahoma State U (OK) 508
Southeast Missouri State U (MO) 508
Southern Adventist U (TN) 508
Southern Arkansas U–Magnolia (AR) 509
Southern Connecticut State U (CT) 509
Southern Illinois U Carbondale (IL) 509
Southern Illinois U Edwardsville (IL) 509
Southern Nazarene U (OK) 510
Southern U and A&M Coll (LA) 511
Southern Utah U (UT) 511
Southern Wesleyan U (SC) 511
Southwest Baptist U (MO) 512
Southwestern Assemblies of God U (TX) 512
Southwestern Coll (KS) 512
Southwestern Oklahoma State U (OK) 512
Southwest Missouri State U (MO) 513
Southwest State U (MN) 513
Spalding U (KY) 513
Spring Arbor U (MI) 514
Springfield Coll (MA) 514
Spring Hill Coll (AL) 514
State U of NY at New Paltz (NY) 515
State U of NY at Oswego (NY) 515
State U of NY Coll at Brockport (NY) 515
State U of NY Coll at Buffalo (NY) 516
State U of NY Coll at Cortland (NY) 516
State U of NY Coll at Fredonia (NY) 516
State U of NY Coll at Geneseo (NY) 516
State U of NY Coll at Old Westbury (NY) 516
State U of NY Coll at Oneonta (NY) 517
State U of NY Coll at Potsdam (NY) 517
State U of West Georgia (GA) 518
Stephens Coll (MO) 519
Sterling Coll (KS) 519
Stetson U (FL) 519
Stonehill Coll (MA) 520
Suffolk U (MA) 520
Sul Ross State U (TX) 521
Susquehanna U (PA) 521
Syracuse U (NY) 521
Tabor Coll (KS) 522
Tarleton State U (TX) 522
Taylor U (IN) 523
Taylor U, Fort Wayne Campus (IN) 523
Temple U (PA) 523
Tennessee State U (TN) 523
Tennessee Technological U (TN) 524
Tennessee Temple U (TN) 524
Tennessee Wesleyan Coll (TN) 524
Texas A&M U–Commerce (TX) 525
Texas A&M U–Kingsville (TX) 525
Texas Christian U (TX) 526
Texas Coll (TX) 526
Texas Lutheran U (TX) 526
Texas Southern U (TX) 526
Texas Wesleyan U (TX) 526
Thiel Coll (PA) 527
Thomas Coll (ME) 527
Thomas More Coll (KY) 528
Toccoa Falls Coll (GA) 528
Towson U (MD) 529
Transylvania U (KY) 529
Trent U (ON, Canada) 529
Trinity Baptist Coll (FL) 530
Trinity Bible Coll (ND) 530
Trinity Christian Coll (IL) 530
Trinity Coll (DC) 530
Trinity Coll of Florida (FL) 531
Trinity International U (IL) 531
Trinity Western U (BC, Canada) 531
Tri-State U (IN) 532
Troy State U (AL) 532
Troy State U Dothan (AL) 532
Tufts U (MA) 533
Tusculum Coll (TN) 533
Tuskegee U (AL) 533
Union Coll (KY) 533
Union Coll (NE) 534
Union U (TN) 534
Universidad Adventista de las Antillas (PR) 536
Université de Sherbrooke (QC, Canada) 536
U du Québec à Trois-Rivières (QC, Canada) 536
U du Québec à Hull (QC, Canada) 536
Université Laval (QC, Canada) 536
U Coll of the Cariboo (BC, Canada) 537
The U of Akron (OH) 537
The U of Alabama (AL) 537
The U of Alabama at Birmingham (AL) 537
The U of Alabama in Huntsville (AL) 537
U of Alaska Anchorage (AK) 538
U of Alaska Fairbanks (AK) 538
U of Alaska Southeast (AK) 538
U of Alberta (AB, Canada) 538
The U of Arizona (AZ) 538
U of Arkansas (AR) 539
U of Arkansas at Little Rock (AR) 539
U of Arkansas at Monticello (AR) 539
The U of British Columbia (BC, Canada) 540
U of Calgary (AB, Canada) 540
U of Central Arkansas (AR) 542
U of Central Florida (FL) 542
U of Central Oklahoma (OK) 542
U of Charleston (WV) 542
U of Cincinnati (OH) 543
U of Connecticut (CT) 544
U of Dallas (TX) 544
U of Dayton (OH) 544
U of Delaware (DE) 544
U of Dubuque (IA) 545
U of Evansville (IN) 545
The U of Findlay (OH) 545
U of Florida (FL) 545
U of Great Falls (MT) 545
U of Hartford (CT) 546
U of Hawaii at Hilo (HI) 546
U of Hawaii at Manoa (HI) 546
U of Idaho (ID) 547
U of Illinois at Chicago (IL) 547
U of Illinois at Springfield (IL) 548
U of Illinois at Urbana–Champaign (IL) 548
U of Indianapolis (IN) 548
The U of Iowa (IA) 548
U of Kansas (KS) 549
U of Kentucky (KY) 549
U of La Verne (CA) 549
U of Louisiana at Lafayette (LA) 550
U of Louisville (KY) 550
U of Maine (ME) 550
U of Maine at Farmington (ME) 550
U of Maine at Fort Kent (ME) 551
U of Maine at Machias (ME) 551
U of Maine at Presque Isle (ME) 551
U of Manitoba (MB, Canada) 551
U of Mary (ND) 551
U of Mary Hardin-Baylor (TX) 551
U of Maryland, Coll Park (MD) 552
U of Maryland Eastern Shore (MD) 552
U of Miami (FL) 553
U of Michigan (MI) 554
U of Michigan–Dearborn (MI) 554
U of Michigan–Flint (MI) 554
U of Minnesota, Duluth (MN) 554
U of Minnesota, Morris (MN) 555
U of Minnesota, Twin Cities Campus (MN) 555
U of Mississippi (MS) 555
U of Missouri–Columbia (MO) 555
U of Missouri–Kansas City (MO) 555
U of Missouri–St. Louis (MO) 556
U of Mobile (AL) 556
The U of Montana–Missoula (MT) 556
The U of Montana–Western (MT) 556
U of Montevallo (AL) 557
U of Nebraska at Kearney (NE) 557
U of Nebraska at Omaha (NE) 557
U of Nebraska–Lincoln (NE) 557
U of Nevada, Las Vegas (NV) 558
U of Nevada, Reno (NV) 558
U of New Brunswick Fredericton (NB, Canada) 558
U of New Brunswick Saint John (NB, Canada) 558
U of New England (ME) 558
U of New Mexico (NM) 559
U of New Orleans (LA) 559
U of North Alabama (AL) 559
The U of North Carolina at Chapel Hill (NC) 560
The U of North Carolina at Charlotte (NC) 560
The U of North Carolina at Greensboro (NC) 560
The U of North Carolina at Pembroke (NC) 560
The U of North Carolina at Wilmington (NC) 561
U of North Dakota (ND) 561
U of Northern Iowa (IA) 561
U of North Florida (FL) 561
U of Oklahoma (OK) 562
U of Ottawa (ON, Canada) 563
U of Pennsylvania (PA) 563
U of Pittsburgh at Johnstown (PA) 570
U of Portland (OR) 570
U of Prince Edward Island (PE, Canada) 570
U of Puerto Rico at Arecibo (PR) 570
U of Puerto Rico, Humacao U Coll (PR) 570
U of Puerto Rico at Ponce (PR) 571
U of Puerto Rico, Utuado (PR) 571
U of Puerto Rico, Cayey U Coll (PR) 571
U of Puerto Rico, Río Piedras (PR) 571
U of Redlands (CA) 572
U of Regina (SK, Canada) 572
U of Rhode Island (RI) 572
U of Richmond (VA) 572
U of Rio Grande (OH) 572
U of St. Francis (IL) 573
U of Saint Francis (IN) 573
U of St. Thomas (MN) 573
U of St. Thomas (TX) 573
U of San Francisco (CA) 574
U of Saskatchewan (SK, Canada) 574
U of Science and Arts of Oklahoma (OK) 574
The U of Scranton (PA) 574
U of Sioux Falls (SD) 574
U of South Alabama (AL) 575
U of South Carolina Aiken (SC) 575
U of South Carolina Spartanburg (SC) 575
The U of South Dakota (SD) 575
U of Southern Indiana (IN) 576
U of Southern Mississippi (MS) 576
U of South Florida (FL) 576
The U of Tampa (FL) 577
The U of Tennessee at Chattanooga (TN) 577
The U of Tennessee at Martin (TN) 577
The U of Texas–Pan American (TX) 579
U of the District of Columbia (DC) 580
U of the Incarnate Word (TX) 580
U of the Sacred Heart (PR) 580
U of the Virgin Islands (VI) 581
U of Toledo (OH) 581
U of Tulsa (OK) 581
U of Utah (UT) 582
U of Vermont (VT) 582
U of Victoria (BC, Canada) 582
U of Washington (WA) 583
The U of West Alabama (AL) 583
The U of Western Ontario (ON, Canada) 583
U of West Florida (FL) 583
U of Windsor (ON, Canada) 584
U of Wisconsin–Eau Claire (WI) 584
U of Wisconsin–Green Bay (WI) 584
U of Wisconsin–La Crosse (WI) 584
U of Wisconsin–Madison (WI) 584
U of Wisconsin–Milwaukee (WI) 585
U of Wisconsin–Oshkosh (WI) 585
U of Wisconsin–Platteville (WI) 585
U of Wisconsin–River Falls (WI) 585
U of Wisconsin–Stevens Point (WI) 585
U of Wisconsin–Superior (WI) 586
U of Wisconsin–Whitewater (WI) 586
U of Wyoming (WY) 586
Upper Iowa U (IA) 587
Urbana U (OH) 587
Utah State U (UT) 587
Utica Coll (NY) 588
Valdosta State U (GA) 588
Valley City State U (ND) 588
Valley Forge Christian Coll (PA) 588
Valparaiso U (IN) 588
Vanderbilt U (TN) 588
Vassar Coll (NY) 589
Villa Julie Coll (MD) 590
Villanova U (PA) 590
Virginia Intermont Coll (VA) 590
Virginia Union U (VA) 591
Virginia Wesleyan Coll (VA) 591
Viterbo U (WI) 591
Voorhees Coll (SC) 592
Wagner Coll (NY) 592
Wake Forest U (NC) 592
Walla Walla Coll (WA) 593
Walsh U (OH) 593
Warner Pacific Coll (OR) 593
Warner Southern Coll (FL) 593
Warren Wilson Coll (NC) 594
Wartburg Coll (IA) 594
Washington Bible Coll (MD) 594
Washington State U (WA) 595
Washington U in St. Louis (MO) 595
Wayland Baptist U (TX) 595
Waynesburg Coll (PA) 595
Wayne State Coll (NE) 596
Wayne State U (MI) 596
Weber State U (UT) 596
Webster U (MO) 597
Wells Coll (NY) 597
Wesley Coll (DE) 598
West Chester U of Pennsylvania (PA) 598
Western Baptist Coll (OR) 598
Western Carolina U (NC) 598
Western Connecticut State U (CT) 598
Western Illinois U (IL) 599
Western Kentucky U (KY) 599
Western Michigan U (MI) 599
Western New Mexico U (NM) 600
Western State Coll of Colorado (CO) 600
Western Washington U (WA) 600
Westfield State Coll (MA) 600
West Liberty State Coll (WV) 601
Westminster Coll (MO) 601
Westminster Coll (PA) 601
Westminster Coll (UT) 601
Westmont Coll (CA) 602
West Virginia State Coll (WV) 602
West Virginia U (WV) 602
West Virginia Wesleyan Coll (WV) 603
Wheaton Coll (IL) 603
Wheeling Jesuit U (WV) 603
Wheelock Coll (MA) 603
Whitworth Coll (WA) 604
Wichita State U (KS) 604
Widener U (PA) 604

Wiley Coll (TX) **605**
Wilkes U (PA) **605**
William Carey Coll (MS) **605**
William Jewell Coll (MO) **606**
William Paterson U of New Jersey (NJ) **606**
William Penn U (IA) **606**
Williams Baptist Coll (AR) **606**
William Woods U (MO) **607**
Wilmington Coll (DE) **607**
Wilmington Coll (OH) **607**
Wilson Coll (PA) **607**
Wingate U (NC) **607**
Winona State U (MN) **608**
Winston-Salem State U (NC) **608**
Winthrop U (SC) **608**
Wisconsin Lutheran Coll (WI) **608**
Wittenberg U (OH) **608**
Worcester State Coll (MA) **609**
Wright State U (OH) **609**
Xavier U (OH) **610**
Xavier U of Louisiana (LA) **610**
York Coll (NE) **610**
York Coll of Pennsylvania (PA) **610**
York U (ON, Canada) **611**
Youngstown State U (OH) **611**

ELEMENTARY/MIDDLE/ SECONDARY EDUCATION ADMINISTRATION

Overview: This major prepares undergraduates for elementary, middle, or secondary school administration positions. *Related majors:* developmental psychology, operations management, policy studies, counseling. *Potential careers:* teacher, principal, school administrator. *Salary potential:* $24k-$30k.

Campbell U (NC) **303**
Ohio U (OH) **458**
U of Central Arkansas (AR) **542**

EMERGENCY MEDICAL TECHNOLOGY

Overview: Students learn how to deliver, in communication with licensed physicians, emergency treatment at the site of an accident or other medical emergency. *Related majors:* anatomy, physiology, premedicine. *Potential careers:* EMT, policeman, firefighter, emergency room technician, ambulance technician. *Salary potential:* $23k-$28k.

Central Washington U (WA) **310**
Creighton U (NE) **333**
The George Washington U (DC) **367**
Loma Linda U (CA) **408**
Nebraska Methodist Coll (NE) **443**
Springfield Coll (MA) **514**
U of Maryland, Baltimore County (MD) **552**
U of Minnesota, Twin Cities Campus (MN) **555**
U of the District of Columbia (DC) **580**
Western Carolina U (NC) **598**

ENERGY MANAGEMENT TECHNOLOGY

Overview: Students choosing this major learn the technical skills and knowledge so they can work on developing energy-efficient systems or systems to monitor energy use. *Related majors:* electrical engineering technology, instrumentation technology, medical technology, business systems analysis and design. *Potential careers:* electrician, business consultant, environmental engineer, instrument technician. *Salary potential:* $24k-$34k.

Eastern Michigan U (MI) **348**
The Evergreen State Coll (WA) **355**
Ferris State U (MI) **358**
Fitchburg State Coll (MA) **358**
Lamar U (TX) **401**
Miles Coll (AL) **430**
U of Oklahoma (OK) **562**

ENGINEERING

Overview: This general major teaches undergraduates how to apply mathematical and scientific principles to a variety of practical problems in industry, organization, public works, and commerce. *Related majors:* specific engineering majors such as civil engineering, electrical engineering, environmental engineering, mechanical engineering, etc., mathematics, physics. *Potential careers:* depending upon specialization, almost any type of engineer, professor, scientist, researcher. *Salary potential:* depending on area of specialization, $35k-$60k.

Arkansas State U (AR) **272**
Arkansas Tech U (AR) **272**
Auburn U (AL) **276**
Baker U (KS) **280**
Barry U (FL) **282**
Baylor U (TX) **283**
Beloit Coll (WI) **285**
Bethel Coll (IN) **288**
Boston U (MA) **292**
Brigham Young U (UT) **295**
Brown U (RI) **296**
California Inst of Technology (CA) **299**
California State U, Fullerton (CA) **301**
California State U, Long Beach (CA) **301**
California State U, Northridge (CA) **301**
California State U, Sacramento (CA) **301**
Calvin Coll (MI) **303**
Carleton U (ON, Canada) **305**
Carnegie Mellon U (PA) **305**
Carroll Coll (MT) **306**
Carthage Coll (WI) **306**
Case Western Reserve U (OH) **307**
The Catholic U of America (DC) **307**
Chatham Coll (PA) **312**
Clark Atlanta U (GA) **315**
Clarkson U (NY) **316**
Clark U (MA) **316**
Cogswell Polytechnical Coll (CA) **318**
Coll of Staten Island of the City U of NY (NY) **323**
Colorado School of Mines (CO) **325**
Cooper Union for the Advancement of Science & Art (NY) **332**
Cornell U (NY) **333**
Dalhousie U (NS, Canada) **336**
Dartmouth Coll (NH) **337**
Dordt Coll (IA) **345**
Drexel U (PA) **346**
Elizabethtown Coll (PA) **351**
Elon U (NC) **352**
Embry-Riddle Aeronautical U (AZ) **352**
Embry-Riddle Aeronautical U (FL) **352**
Fontbonne U (MO) **361**
Gallaudet U (DC) **365**
Gannon U (PA) **365**
Geneva Coll (PA) **366**
George Fox U (OR) **366**
The George Washington U (DC) **367**
Gonzaga U (WA) **369**
Grand Valley State U (MI) **371**
Harvard U (MA) **376**
Harvey Mudd Coll (CA) **377**
Hood Coll (MD) **381**
Hope Coll (MI) **381**
Houston Baptist U (TX) **382**
Idaho State U (ID) **384**
Indiana U–Purdue U Fort Wayne (IN) **386**
Indiana U–Purdue U Indianapolis (IN) **387**
Iowa State U of Science and Technology (IA) **390**
John Brown U (AR) **392**
Johns Hopkins U (MD) **392**
Juniata Coll (PA) **395**
Lafayette Coll (PA) **400**
Lakehead U (ON, Canada) **400**
Lehigh U (PA) **404**
LeTourneau U (TX) **405**
Lock Haven U of Pennsylvania (PA) **408**
Loyola Coll in Maryland (MD) **411**
Maine Maritime Academy (ME) **415**
Manhattan Coll (NY) **416**
Marquette U (WI) **418**
Maryville Coll (TN) **420**
Massachusetts Inst of Technology (MA) **421**
Massachusetts Maritime Academy (MA) **421**
McNeese State U (LA) **423**
Memorial U of Newfoundland (NF, Canada) **424**
Messiah Coll (PA) **426**
Michigan State U (MI) **428**
Michigan Technological U (MI) **428**
Montana Tech of The U of Montana (MT) **435**
Morehouse Coll (GA) **436**
Morgan State U (MD) **436**
New Jersey Inst of Technology (NJ) **445**
New Mexico Highlands U (NM) **446**
New Mexico Inst of Mining and Technology (NM) **446**
New York U (NY) **447**
North Carolina State U (NC) **449**
North Dakota State U (ND) **449**
Northeastern U (MA) **450**
Northern Arizona U (AZ) **450**
Northwestern U (IL) **453**
Oakwood Coll (AL) **456**
Ohio U (OH) **458**
Oklahoma Christian U (OK) **459**
Oklahoma State U (OK) **460**
Olivet Nazarene U (IL) **461**
Oregon State U (OR) **462**
Pacific Union Coll (CA) **464**
Pitzer Coll (CA) **471**
Purdue U (IN) **475**
Purdue U Calumet (IN) **475**
Queen's U at Kingston (ON, Canada) **476**
Rensselaer Polytechnic Inst (NY) **478**
Rochester Inst of Technology (NY) **482**
Roger Williams U (RI) **483**
Rowan U (NJ) **484**
Russell Sage Coll (NY) **484**
Rutgers, The State U of New Jersey, New Brunswick (NJ) **485**
Saint Anselm Coll (NH) **487**
St. Cloud State U (MN) **488**
Saint Mary's Coll of California (CA) **494**
Saint Mary's U (NS, Canada) **494**
St. Mary's U of San Antonio (TX) **494**
Saint Vincent Coll (PA) **496**
San Diego State U (CA) **498**
San Jose State U (CA) **499**
Santa Clara U (CA) **499**
Schreiner U (TX) **501**
Seton Hill U (PA) **502**
Spelman Coll (GA) **514**
Stanford U (CA) **514**
State U of NY Coll at Buffalo (NY) **516**
Swarthmore Coll (PA) **521**
Tennessee State U (TN) **523**
Texas Christian U (TX) **526**
Texas Tech U (TX) **526**
Trinity Coll (CT) **530**
Tufts U (MA) **533**
United States Air Force Academy (CO) **534**
United States Military Academy (NY) **535**
United States Naval Academy (MD) **535**
Université de Sherbrooke (QC, Canada) **536**
U du Québec, École de technologie supérieure (QC, Canada) **536**
The U of Akron (OH) **537**
U of Alberta (AB, Canada) **538**
The U of Arizona (AZ) **538**
U of Calif, Berkeley (CA) **540**
U of Calif, Davis (CA) **540**
U of Calif, Irvine (CA) **541**
U of Calif, San Diego (CA) **541**
U of Cincinnati (OH) **543**
U of Delaware (DE) **544**
U of Denver (CO) **544**
U of Florida (FL) **545**
U of Hartford (CT) **546**
U of Hawaii at Manoa (HI) **546**
U of Idaho (ID) **547**
U of Illinois at Urbana–Champaign (IL) **548**
The U of Iowa (IA) **548**
U of Louisville (KY) **550**
U of Maryland, Coll Park (MD) **552**
U of Michigan (MI) **554**
U of Michigan–Dearborn (MI) **554**
U of Michigan–Flint (MI) **554**
U of Mississippi (MS) **555**
U of New Brunswick Fredericton (NB, Canada) **558**
U of New Haven (CT) **559**
U of New Mexico (NM) **559**
U of Oklahoma (OK) **562**
U of Ottawa (ON, Canada) **563**
U of Portland (OR) **570**
U of Regina (SK, Canada) **572**
U of Rochester (NY) **573**
U of South Florida (FL) **576**
The U of Tennessee at Chattanooga (TN) **577**
The U of Tennessee at Martin (TN) **577**
U of Toronto (ON, Canada) **581**
U of Tulsa (OK) **581**
U of Virginia (VA) **582**
U of Washington (WA) **583**
U of Waterloo (ON, Canada) **583**
U of Windsor (ON, Canada) **584**
U of Wisconsin–Madison (WI) **584**
U of Wisconsin–Milwaukee (WI) **585**
Valparaiso U (IN) **588**
Vanderbilt U (TN) **588**
Virginia Polytechnic Inst and State U (VA) **591**
Walla Walla Coll (WA) **593**
Wartburg Coll (IA) **594**
Washington U in St. Louis (MO) **595**
Wells Coll (NY) **597**
Western New England Coll (MA) **600**
West Virginia U Inst of Technology (WV) **602**
Wilkes U (PA) **605**
Winona State U (MN) **608**
Youngstown State U (OH) **611**

ENGINEERING DESIGN

Overview: This major focuses on applying mathematics and scientific principles to creating new designs and solving engineering-related problems. *Related majors:* mechanical engineering, mathematics, materials science, computer engineering, industrial design. *Potential careers:* inventor, product developer, engineering consultant, project manager. *Salary potential:* $40k-$55k.

Cameron U (OK) **303**
Carnegie Mellon U (PA) **305**
Lawrence Technological U (MI) **403**
Pacific Union Coll (CA) **464**
Tufts U (MA) **533**
U of Houston–Downtown (TX) **547**
Western Washington U (WA) **600**
Worcester Polytechnic Inst (MA) **609**

ENGINEERING/INDUSTRIAL MANAGEMENT

Overview: This major teaches students how to plan and manage industrial and manufacturing operations. *Related majors:* accounting, logistics and materials management, operations management and supervision, systems engineering, computer systems analysis. *Potential careers:* plant manager, management consultant, occupational safety expert, organizational psychologist. *Salary potential:* $35k-$50k.

California State U, Long Beach (CA) **301**
Claremont McKenna Coll (CA) **315**
Columbia U, School of Engineering & Applied Sci (NY) **328**
State U of NY at Farmingdale (NY) **357**
Fort Lewis Coll (CO) **362**
Grand Valley State U (MI) **371**
Idaho State U (ID) **384**
Illinois Inst of Technology (IL) **384**
Insto Tecno Estudios Sups Monterrey(Mexico) **388**
John Brown U (AR) **392**
Kettering U (MI) **398**
McMaster U (ON, Canada) **423**
Mercer U (GA) **425**
Miami U (OH) **428**
Missouri Tech (MO) **433**
North Dakota State U (ND) **449**
Pitzer Coll (CA) **471**
Princeton U (NJ) **474**
Rensselaer Polytechnic Inst (NY) **478**
Robert Morris U (PA) **481**

ENGINEERING/INDUSTRIAL MANAGEMENT (continued)

Saint Louis U (MO) ***492***
Stevens Inst of Technology (NJ) ***519***
Tri-State U (IN) ***532***
United States Merchant Marine Academy (NY) ***535***
United States Military Academy (NY) ***535***
U du Québec à Trois-Rivières (QC, Canada) ***536***
U of Evansville (IN) ***545***
U of Illinois at Chicago (IL) ***547***
The U of Iowa (IA) ***548***
U of Missouri–Rolla (MO) ***556***
U of Ottawa (ON, Canada) ***563***
U of Portland (OR) ***570***
U of Southern California (CA) ***576***
The U of Tennessee at Chattanooga (TN) ***577***
U of the Pacific (CA) ***580***
U of Vermont (VT) ***582***
U of Wisconsin–Stout (WI) ***586***
Western Michigan U (MI) ***599***
Widener U (PA) ***604***
Wilkes U (PA) ***605***
Worcester Polytechnic Inst (MA) ***609***
York Coll of Pennsylvania (PA) ***610***

ENGINEERING MECHANICS

Overview: Students learn the scientific principles behind statics, kinetics, dynamics, kinematics, stress and failure, and electromagnetism and how forces are applied to structures and materials. *Related majors:* electrical engineering, structural engineering, engineering physics, materials engineering. *Potential careers:* industrial engineer, aerospace engineer, structural engineer, scientist. *Salary potential:* $40k-$50k.

Columbia U, School of Engineering & Applied Sci (NY) ***328***
Dordt Coll (IA) ***345***
Johns Hopkins U (MD) ***392***
Lehigh U (PA) ***404***
Michigan State U (MI) ***428***
Michigan Technological U (MI) ***428***
New Mexico Inst of Mining and Technology (NM) ***446***
Oral Roberts U (OK) ***461***
United States Air Force Academy (CO) ***534***
U du Québec à Trois-Rivières (QC, Canada) ***536***
U of Cincinnati (OH) ***543***
U of Illinois at Urbana–Champaign (IL) ***548***
U of Southern California (CA) ***576***
U of Windsor (ON, Canada) ***584***
U of Wisconsin–Madison (WI) ***584***
Wentworth Inst of Technology (MA) ***597***
West Virginia Wesleyan Coll (WV) ***603***
Worcester Polytechnic Inst (MA) ***609***

ENGINEERING PHYSICS

Overview: Students learn the mathematical and scientific principles of physics in order to address engineering problems in areas such as superconductivity, thermodynamics, molecular and particle physics, space science research, and temperature. *Related majors:* electrical engineering, chemistry, physics, molecular physics mathematics. *Potential careers:* physicist, aerospace engineer, electrical engineer, structural engineer, scientist. *Salary potential:* $35k-$50k.

Abilene Christian U (TX) ***260***
Arkansas Tech U (AR) ***272***
Augustana Coll (IL) ***276***
Augustana Coll (SD) ***276***
Aurora U (IL) ***277***
Bemidji State U (MN) ***285***
Bradley U (IL) ***293***
Brandeis U (MA) ***293***
Brown U (RI) ***296***
California Inst of Technology (CA) ***299***
California State U, Northridge (CA) ***301***
Case Western Reserve U (OH) ***307***
Christian Brothers U (TN) ***313***
Colorado School of Mines (CO) ***325***
Colorado State U (CO) ***325***
Connecticut Coll (CT) ***331***
Cornell U (NY) ***333***
Dartmouth Coll (NH) ***337***
Eastern Nazarene Coll (MA) ***348***
Elizabethtown Coll (PA) ***351***
Embry-Riddle Aeronautical U (FL) ***352***
Harvard U (MA) ***376***
Hope Coll (MI) ***381***
Houston Baptist U (TX) ***382***
Insto Tecno Estudios Sups Monterrey(Mexico) ***388***
Jacksonville U (FL) ***391***
John Carroll U (OH) ***392***
Juniata Coll (PA) ***395***
Lehigh U (PA) ***404***
Loras Coll (IA) ***410***
Loyola Marymount U (CA) ***411***
McMaster U (ON, Canada) ***423***
Merrimack Coll (MA) ***426***
Miami U (OH) ***428***
Michigan Technological U (MI) ***428***
Morgan State U (MD) ***436***
Morningside Coll (IA) ***437***
Murray State U (KY) ***440***
New York U (NY) ***447***
North Carolina Ag and Tech State U (NC) ***448***
North Dakota State U (ND) ***449***
Northeastern State U (OK) ***450***
Northern Arizona U (AZ) ***450***
Northwest Nazarene U (ID) ***454***
Oakland U (MI) ***456***
The Ohio State U (OH) ***457***
Oklahoma Christian U (OK) ***459***
Oregon State U (OR) ***462***
Pacific Lutheran U (WA) ***463***
Point Loma Nazarene U (CA) ***471***
Queen's U at Kingston (ON, Canada) ***476***
Rensselaer Polytechnic Inst (NY) ***478***
Rutgers, The State U of New Jersey, New Brunswick (NJ) ***485***
St. Ambrose U (IA) ***486***
St. Bonaventure U (NY) ***487***
Saint Mary's U of Minnesota (MN) ***494***
Samford U (AL) ***497***
Santa Clara U (CA) ***499***
South Dakota State U (SD) ***507***
Southeast Missouri State U (MO) ***508***
Southern Arkansas U–Magnolia (AR) ***509***
Southwestern Oklahoma State U (OK) ***512***
Southwest Missouri State U (MO) ***513***
State U of NY at New Paltz (NY) ***515***
Syracuse U (NY) ***521***
Taylor U (IN) ***523***
Texas Tech U (TX) ***526***
Thiel Coll (PA) ***527***
Tufts U (MA) ***533***
United States Military Academy (NY) ***535***
Université Laval (QC, Canada) ***536***
U at Buffalo, The State University of New York (NY) ***536***
U of Alberta (AB, Canada) ***538***
The U of Arizona (AZ) ***538***
The U of British Columbia (BC, Canada) ***540***
U of Calif, Berkeley (CA) ***540***
U of Calif, San Diego (CA) ***541***
U of Colorado at Boulder (CO) ***543***
U of Connecticut (CT) ***544***
U of Illinois at Chicago (IL) ***547***
U of Illinois at Urbana–Champaign (IL) ***548***
U of Kansas (KS) ***549***
U of Maine (ME) ***550***
U of Massachusetts Boston (MA) ***553***
U of Michigan (MI) ***554***
U of Nevada, Reno (NV) ***558***
U of Northern Iowa (IA) ***561***
U of Oklahoma (OK) ***562***
U of Pittsburgh (PA) ***569***
U of Saskatchewan (SK, Canada) ***574***
The U of Tennessee (TN) ***577***
U of the Pacific (CA) ***580***
U of Toronto (ON, Canada) ***581***
U of Tulsa (OK) ***581***
U of Wisconsin–Madison (WI) ***584***
Washington and Lee U (VA) ***594***
Washington U in St. Louis (MO) ***595***
Westmont Coll (CA) ***602***
West Virginia U Inst of Technology (WV) ***602***
West Virginia Wesleyan Coll (WV) ***603***
Wilberforce U (OH) ***605***
Worcester Polytechnic Inst (MA) ***609***
Wright State U (OH) ***609***
Yale U (CT) ***610***
York U (ON, Canada) ***611***

ENGINEERING RELATED

Information can be found under this major's main heading.

Boston U (MA) ***292***
California State U, Chico (CA) ***300***
Cedar Crest Coll (PA) ***308***
Eastern Illinois U (IL) ***348***
Fairfield U (CT) ***356***
Iowa State U of Science and Technology (IA) ***390***
McGill U (QC, Canada) ***423***
Northwestern U (IL) ***453***
Ohio U (OH) ***458***
Ohio Wesleyan U (OH) ***459***
Park U (MO) ***465***
Principia Coll (IL) ***474***
Rochester Inst of Technology (NY) ***482***
State U of NY Maritime Coll (NY) ***518***
Texas Wesleyan U (TX) ***526***
Université Laval (QC, Canada) ***536***
The U of Arizona (AZ) ***538***
U of Connecticut (CT) ***544***
U of Hawaii at Manoa (HI) ***546***
U of Maryland, Coll Park (MD) ***552***
U of Nebraska–Lincoln (NE) ***557***
Western Michigan U (MI) ***599***
Wheaton Coll (IL) ***603***

ENGINEERING-RELATED TECHNOLOGY

Overview: This is a general program that prepares students to apply basic engineering principles and technical skills to a wide range of engineering projects. *Related majors:* computer engineering technology, industrial engineering. *Potential careers:* designer, production manager, quality assurance manager, technical services manager, sales and distribution specialist. *Salary potential:* $28k-$38k.

Arkansas State U (AR) ***272***
Charleston Southern U (SC) ***311***
Dordt Coll (IA) ***345***
Eastern New Mexico U (NM) ***349***
East Tennessee State U (TN) ***349***
Fitchburg State Coll (MA) ***358***
Lewis-Clark State Coll (ID) ***406***
Middle Tennessee State U (TN) ***429***
Missouri Tech (MO) ***433***
New Mexico State U (NM) ***446***
Quincy U (IL) ***476***
Rochester Inst of Technology (NY) ***482***
Southern Illinois U Carbondale (IL) ***509***
Southwest Texas State U (TX) ***513***
Texas A&M U (TX) ***524***
Texas Tech U (TX) ***526***
Tuskegee U (AL) ***533***
The U of Akron (OH) ***537***
Walla Walla Coll (WA) ***593***
Youngstown State U (OH) ***611***

ENGINEERING SCIENCE

Overview: In this broad-based major, students learn the scientific principles behind a wide range of engineering issues and problems in areas such as statistics, biology, chemistry, earth and planetary sciences, atmospherics, and human behavior. *Related majors:* mathematics, physics, chemistry, biological and physical sciences, system science and theory. *Potential careers:* astronomer, physics teacher, scientific researcher. *Salary potential:* $33k-$42k.

Abilene Christian U (TX) ***260***
Appalachian State U (NC) ***270***
Baldwin-Wallace Coll (OH) ***280***
Belmont U (TN) ***284***
Benedictine U (IL) ***285***
California Polytechnic State U, San Luis Obispo (CA) ***300***
California State U, Fullerton (CA) ***301***
Case Western Reserve U (OH) ***307***
The Coll of New Jersey (NJ) ***320***
Coll of Notre Dame of Maryland (MD) ***321***
Colorado School of Mines (CO) ***325***
Colorado State U (CO) ***325***
Cornell U (NY) ***333***
Franciscan U of Steubenville (OH) ***363***
Gallaudet U (DC) ***365***
Harvard U (MA) ***376***
Hofstra U (NY) ***380***
Houston Baptist U (TX) ***382***
Iowa State U of Science and Technology (IA) ***390***
Lamar U (TX) ***401***
Lipscomb U (TN) ***408***
Lock Haven U of Pennsylvania (PA) ***408***
Manchester Coll (IN) ***415***
Montana Tech of The U of Montana (MT) ***435***
New Jersey Inst of Technology (NJ) ***445***
Northwestern U (IL) ***453***
Ohio Wesleyan U (OH) ***459***
Pacific Lutheran U (WA) ***463***
Penn State U Univ Park Campus (PA) ***468***
Pfeiffer U (NC) ***469***
Queen's U at Kingston (ON, Canada) ***476***
Rensselaer Polytechnic Inst (NY) ***478***
St. Mary's U of San Antonio (TX) ***494***
St. Thomas Aquinas Coll (NY) ***495***
Seattle Pacific U (WA) ***501***
Simon Fraser U (BC, Canada) ***505***
Spring Hill Coll (AL) ***514***
State U of NY Coll at Oneonta (NY) ***517***
Stony Brook U, State University of New York (NY) ***520***
Trinity U (TX) ***531***
Tufts U (MA) ***533***
Tulane U (LA) ***533***
United States Air Force Academy (CO) ***534***
U of Calif, San Diego (CA) ***541***
U of Cincinnati (OH) ***543***
U of Manitoba (MB, Canada) ***551***
U of Maryland, Baltimore County (MD) ***552***
U of Miami (FL) ***553***
U of Michigan (MI) ***554***
U of Michigan–Flint (MI) ***554***
U of New Mexico (NM) ***559***
U of Ottawa (ON, Canada) ***563***
U of Portland (OR) ***570***
U of Rochester (NY) ***573***
The U of Tennessee (TN) ***577***
U of Toronto (ON, Canada) ***581***
Vanderbilt U (TN) ***588***
Virginia Polytechnic Inst and State U (VA) ***591***
Washington U in St. Louis (MO) ***595***
Yale U (CT) ***610***

ENGINEERING TECHNOLOGIES RELATED

Information can be found under this major's main heading.

California Maritime Academy (CA) ***299***
East Carolina U (NC) ***347***
Ohio U (OH) ***458***
Old Dominion U (VA) ***460***
Point Park Coll (PA) ***471***
Rogers State U (OK) ***483***
The U of British Columbia (BC, Canada) ***540***
Western Michigan U (MI) ***599***

ENGINEERING TECHNOLOGY

Overview: This broad-based major provides hands-on skills and teaches individuals how to apply science, math, and computer principles to real-world engineering problems. *Related majors:* applied mathematics, engineering physics, chemistry, engineering design, computer science. *Potential careers:* designer, production manager, quality assurance manager, technical services manager, sales and distribution specialist. *Salary potential:* $28k-$38k.

Andrews U (MI) ***269***
Austin Peay State U (TN) ***278***
Brigham Young U (UT) ***295***

California State Polytechnic U, Pomona (CA) **300**
California State U, Long Beach (CA) **301**
Central Connecticut State U (CT) **309**
Colorado State U-Pueblo (CO) **325**
Delaware State U (DE) **338**
Embry-Riddle Aeronautical U (AZ) **352**
Embry-Riddle Aeronautical U (FL) **352**
Fairmont State Coll (WV) **356**
Gallaudet U (DC) **365**
Grantham U (LA) **372**
Jackson State U (MS) **390**
Lawrence Technological U (MI) **403**
LeTourneau U (TX) **405**
Maine Maritime Academy (ME) **415**
Massachusetts Maritime Academy (MA) **421**
Miami U (OH) **428**
Midwestern State U (TX) **430**
New Jersey Inst of Technology (NJ) **445**
New Mexico State U (NM) **446**
Northeastern U (MA) **450**
Northern Illinois U (IL) **450**
Oklahoma State U (OK) **460**
Pacific Union Coll (CA) **464**
Pittsburg State U (KS) **470**
Prairie View A&M U (TX) **473**
Purdue U Calumet (IN) **475**
Rochester Inst of Technology (NY) **482**
St. Cloud State U (MN) **488**
Southern Illinois U Carbondale (IL) **509**
Southwestern Oklahoma State U (OK) **512**
Southwest Texas State U (TX) **513**
State U of NY Coll at Buffalo (NY) **516**
Temple U (PA) **523**
Texas A&M U–Corpus Christi (TX) **525**
Texas Tech U (TX) **526**
U of Central Florida (FL) **542**
U of Hartford (CT) **546**
U of Maine (ME) **550**
U of Maryland Eastern Shore (MD) **552**
U of New Hampshire (NH) **558**
U of North Texas (TX) **562**
U of Pittsburgh at Johnstown (PA) **570**
U of the District of Columbia (DC) **580**
The U of West Alabama (AL) **583**
U of Wisconsin–River Falls (WI) **585**
Virginia State U (VA) **591**
Wentworth Inst of Technology (MA) **597**
Western Washington U (WA) **600**
West Virginia U Inst of Technology (WV) **602**
William Penn U (IA) **606**
Youngstown State U (OH) **611**

ENGLISH

Overview: Students who choose this major study the English language through its structure, literature, and history as well as the culture of the English speaking people. *Related majors:* English composition, creative writing, American literature, history. *Potential careers:* writer, editor, teacher, professor. *Salary potential:* $23k-$32k.

Abilene Christian U (TX) **260**
Acadia U (NS, Canada) **260**
Adams State Coll (CO) **260**
Adelphi U (NY) **260**
Adrian Coll (MI) **260**
Agnes Scott Coll (GA) **261**
Alabama A&M U (AL) **261**
Alabama State U (AL) **261**
Albany State U (GA) **262**
Albertson Coll of Idaho (ID) **262**
Albertus Magnus Coll (CT) **262**
Albion Coll (MI) **262**
Albright Coll (PA) **263**
Alcorn State U (MS) **263**
Alfred U (NY) **263**
Alice Lloyd Coll (KY) **263**
Allegheny Coll (PA) **264**
Allen U (SC) **264**
Alliant International U (CA) **264**
Alma Coll (MI) **264**
Alvernia Coll (PA) **265**
Alverno Coll (WI) **265**
American Christian Coll and Seminary (OK) **265**
American Coll of Thessaloniki(Greece) **266**
American International Coll (MA) **267**
The American U in Cairo(Egypt) **267**
Amherst Coll (MA) **268**
Anderson Coll (SC) **268**
Anderson U (IN) **268**
Andrews U (MI) **269**
Angelo State U (TX) **269**
Anna Maria Coll (MA) **269**
Antioch Coll (OH) **269**
Appalachian State U (NC) **270**
Aquinas Coll (MI) **270**
Arcadia U (PA) **271**
Arizona State U (AZ) **271**
Arizona State U West (AZ) **272**
Arkansas State U (AR) **272**
Arkansas Tech U (AR) **272**
Armstrong Atlantic State U (GA) **273**
Asbury Coll (KY) **274**
Ashland U (OH) **274**
Assumption Coll (MA) **275**
Athabasca U (AB, Canada) **275**
Athens State U (AL) **275**
Atlantic Baptist U (NB, Canada) **275**
Atlantic Union Coll (MA) **276**
Auburn U (AL) **276**
Auburn U Montgomery (AL) **276**
Augsburg Coll (MN) **276**
Augustana Coll (IL) **276**
Augustana Coll (SD) **276**
Augusta State U (GA) **277**
Aurora U (IL) **277**
Austin Coll (TX) **277**
Austin Peay State U (TN) **278**
Averett U (VA) **278**
Avila U (MO) **278**
Azusa Pacific U (CA) **278**
Baker U (KS) **280**
Baldwin-Wallace Coll (OH) **280**
Ball State U (IN) **280**
Barber-Scotia Coll (NC) **281**
Bard Coll (NY) **281**
Barnard Coll (NY) **282**
Barry U (FL) **282**
Barton Coll (NC) **282**
Bates Coll (ME) **282**
Baylor U (TX) **283**
Belhaven Coll (MS) **283**
Bellarmine U (KY) **284**
Bellevue U (NE) **284**
Belmont Abbey Coll (NC) **284**
Belmont U (TN) **284**
Beloit Coll (WI) **285**
Bemidji State U (MN) **285**
Benedict Coll (SC) **285**
Benedictine Coll (KS) **285**
Benedictine U (IL) **285**
Bennett Coll (NC) **286**
Bennington Coll (VT) **286**
Bentley Coll (MA) **286**
Berea Coll (KY) **286**
Baruch Coll of the City U of NY (NY) **286**
Berry Coll (GA) **287**
Bethany Coll (KS) **287**
Bethany Coll (WV) **287**
Bethany Coll of the Assemblies of God (CA) **287**
Bethel Coll (IN) **288**
Bethel Coll (KS) **288**
Bethel Coll (MN) **288**
Bethel Coll (TN) **288**
Bethune-Cookman Coll (FL) **289**
Biola U (CA) **289**
Birmingham-Southern Coll (AL) **289**
Bishop's U (QC, Canada) **289**
Blackburn Coll (IL) **290**
Black Hills State U (SD) **290**
Bloomfield Coll (NJ) **290**
Bloomsburg U of Pennsylvania (PA) **290**
Bluefield Coll (VA) **291**
Blue Mountain Coll (MS) **291**
Bluffton Coll (OH) **291**
Boston Coll (MA) **292**
Boston U (MA) **292**
Bowdoin Coll (ME) **292**
Bowie State U (MD) **292**
Bowling Green State U (OH) **292**
Bradley U (IL) **293**
Brandeis U (MA) **293**
Brandon U (MB, Canada) **293**
Brenau U (GA) **293**
Brescia U (KY) **293**
Brevard Coll (NC) **294**
Brewton-Parker Coll (GA) **294**
Briar Cliff U (IA) **294**
Bridgewater Coll (VA) **294**
Bridgewater State Coll (MA) **294**
Brigham Young U (UT) **295**
Brigham Young U–Hawaii (HI) **295**
Brock U (ON, Canada) **295**
Brooklyn Coll of the City U of NY (NY) **295**
Brown U (RI) **296**
Bryan Coll (TN) **296**
Bryant Coll (RI) **296**
Bryn Athyn Coll of the New Church (PA) **297**
Bryn Mawr Coll (PA) **297**
Bucknell U (PA) **297**
Buena Vista U (IA) **297**
Butler U (IN) **297**
Cabrini Coll (PA) **298**
Caldwell Coll (NJ) **298**
California Baptist U (CA) **298**
California Lutheran U (CA) **299**
California Polytechnic State U, San Luis Obispo (CA) **300**
California State Polytechnic U, Pomona (CA) **300**
California State U, Bakersfield (CA) **300**
California State U, Chico (CA) **300**
California State U, Dominguez Hills (CA) **300**
California State U, Fresno (CA) **301**
California State U, Fullerton (CA) **301**
California State U, Hayward (CA) **301**
California State U, Long Beach (CA) **301**
California State U, Northridge (CA) **301**
California State U, Sacramento (CA) **301**
California State U, San Bernardino (CA) **302**
California State U, San Marcos (CA) **302**
California State U, Stanislaus (CA) **302**
California U of Pennsylvania (PA) **302**
Calumet Coll of Saint Joseph (IN) **302**
Calvin Coll (MI) **303**
Cameron U (OK) **303**
Campbellsville U (KY) **303**
Campbell U (NC) **303**
Canisius Coll (NY) **304**
Capital U (OH) **304**
Cardinal Stritch U (WI) **305**
Carleton Coll (MN) **305**
Carleton U (ON, Canada) **305**
Carlow Coll (PA) **305**
Carnegie Mellon U (PA) **305**
Carroll Coll (MT) **306**
Carroll Coll (WI) **306**
Carson-Newman Coll (TN) **306**
Carthage Coll (WI) **306**
Case Western Reserve U (OH) **307**
Catawba Coll (NC) **307**
The Catholic U of America (DC) **307**
Cazenovia Coll (NY) **308**
Cedar Crest Coll (PA) **308**
Cedarville U (OH) **308**
Centenary Coll (NJ) **308**
Centenary Coll of Louisiana (LA) **308**
Central Coll (IA) **309**
Central Connecticut State U (CT) **309**
Central Methodist Coll (MO) **309**
Central Michigan U (MI) **310**
Central Missouri State U (MO) **310**
Central Washington U (WA) **310**
Centre Coll (KY) **310**
Chadron State Coll (NE) **311**
Chaminade U of Honolulu (HI) **311**
Chapman U (CA) **311**
Charleston Southern U (SC) **311**
Chatham Coll (PA) **312**
Chestnut Hill Coll (PA) **312**
Cheyney U of Pennsylvania (PA) **312**
Chowan Coll (NC) **312**
Christian Brothers U (TN) **313**
Christian Heritage Coll (CA) **313**
Christopher Newport U (VA) **313**
Citadel, The Military Coll of South Carolina (SC) **314**
City Coll of the City U of NY (NY) **314**
Claflin U (SC) **314**
Claremont McKenna Coll (CA) **315**
Clarion U of Pennsylvania (PA) **315**
Clark Atlanta U (GA) **315**
Clarke Coll (IA) **315**
Clark U (MA) **316**
Clearwater Christian Coll (FL) **316**
Clemson U (SC) **317**
Cleveland State U (OH) **317**
Coastal Carolina U (SC) **318**
Coe Coll (IA) **318**
Coker Coll (SC) **318**
Colby Coll (ME) **318**
Colby-Sawyer Coll (NH) **319**
Colgate U (NY) **319**
Coll Misericordia (PA) **319**
Coll of Charleston (SC) **320**
Coll of Mount St. Joseph (OH) **320**
Coll of Mount Saint Vincent (NY) **320**
The Coll of New Jersey (NJ) **320**
The Coll of New Rochelle (NY) **321**
Coll of Notre Dame of Maryland (MD) **321**
Coll of Saint Benedict (MN) **321**
Coll of St. Catherine (MN) **321**
Coll of Saint Elizabeth (NJ) **321**
Coll of St. Joseph (VT) **322**
Coll of Saint Mary (NE) **322**
The Coll of Saint Rose (NY) **322**
The Coll of St. Scholastica (MN) **322**
Coll of Santa Fe (NM) **323**
Coll of Staten Island of the City U of NY (NY) **323**
Coll of the Atlantic (ME) **323**
Coll of the Holy Cross (MA) **323**
Coll of the Ozarks (MO) **323**
Coll of the Southwest (NM) **324**
The Coll of William and Mary (VA) **324**
The Coll of Wooster (OH) **324**
Colorado Christian U (CO) **325**
The Colorado Coll (CO) **325**
Colorado State U (CO) **325**
Colorado State U-Pueblo (CO) **325**
Columbia Coll (MO) **326**
Columbia Coll (NY) **326**
Columbia Coll (SC) **327**
Columbia Union Coll (MD) **328**
Columbia U, School of General Studies (NY) **328**
Columbus State U (GA) **328**
Concord Coll (WV) **329**
Concordia Coll (MN) **329**
Concordia Coll (NY) **329**
Concordia U (CA) **330**
Concordia U (IL) **330**
Concordia U (MI) **330**
Concordia U (MN) **330**
Concordia U (NE) **330**
Concordia U (OR) **330**
Concordia U (QC, Canada) **331**
Concordia U at Austin (TX) **331**
Concordia U Coll of Alberta (AB, Canada) **331**
Concordia U Wisconsin (WI) **331**
Connecticut Coll (CT) **331**
Converse Coll (SC) **332**
Cornell Coll (IA) **332**
Cornell U (NY) **333**
Cornerstone U (MI) **333**
Covenant Coll (GA) **333**
Creighton U (NE) **333**
Crichton Coll (TN) **334**
Crown Coll (MN) **334**
Culver-Stockton Coll (MO) **334**
Cumberland Coll (KY) **335**
Cumberland U (TN) **335**
Curry Coll (MA) **335**
Daemen Coll (NY) **335**
Dakota State U (SD) **335**
Dakota Wesleyan U (SD) **336**
Dalhousie U (NS, Canada) **336**
Dallas Baptist U (TX) **336**
Dana Coll (NE) **337**
Dartmouth Coll (NH) **337**
Davidson Coll (NC) **338**
Davis & Elkins Coll (WV) **338**
Defiance Coll (OH) **338**
Delaware State U (DE) **338**
Delaware Valley Coll (PA) **339**
Delta State U (MS) **339**
Denison U (OH) **339**
DePaul U (IL) **339**
DePauw U (IN) **339**
Deree Coll(Greece) **339**
DeSales U (PA) **340**
Dickinson Coll (PA) **344**
Dickinson State U (ND) **344**
Dillard U (LA) **344**
Doane Coll (NE) **344**
Dominican Coll (NY) **344**
Dominican U (IL) **345**
Dominican U of California (CA) **345**
Dordt Coll (IA) **345**
Dowling Coll (NY) **345**
Drake U (IA) **345**
Drew U (NJ) **346**
Drury U (MO) **346**
Duke U (NC) **346**
Duquesne U (PA) **346**
D'Youville Coll (NY) **347**

ENGLISH (continued)

Earlham Coll (IN) **347**
East Carolina U (NC) **347**
East Central U (OK) **347**
Eastern Connecticut State U (CT) **347**
Eastern Illinois U (IL) **348**
Eastern Kentucky U (KY) **348**
Eastern Mennonite U (VA) **348**
Eastern Michigan U (MI) **348**
Eastern Nazarene Coll (MA) **348**
Eastern New Mexico U (NM) **349**
Eastern Oregon U (OR) **349**
Eastern U (PA) **349**
Eastern Washington U (WA) **349**
East Stroudsburg U of Pennsylvania (PA) **349**
East Tennessee State U (TN) **349**
East Texas Baptist U (TX) **350**
East-West U (IL) **350**
Eckerd Coll (FL) **350**
Edgewood Coll (WI) **351**
Edinboro U of Pennsylvania (PA) **351**
Elizabeth City State U (NC) **351**
Elizabethtown Coll (PA) **351**
Elmhurst Coll (IL) **351**
Elmira Coll (NY) **351**
Elms Coll (MA) **352**
Elon U (NC) **352**
Emmanuel Coll (GA) **353**
Emmanuel Coll (MA) **353**
Emory & Henry Coll (VA) **353**
Emory U (GA) **354**
Emporia State U (KS) **354**
Erskine Coll (SC) **354**
Eugene Lang Coll, New School U (NY) **355**
Eureka Coll (IL) **355**
Evangel U (MO) **355**
The Evergreen State Coll (WA) **355**
Fairfield U (CT) **356**
Fairleigh Dickinson U, Florham (NJ) **356**
Fairleigh Dickinson U, Teaneck-Metro Campus (NJ) **356**
Fairmont State Coll (WV) **356**
Faulkner U (AL) **357**
Fayetteville State U (NC) **357**
Felician Coll (NJ) **357**
Ferrum Coll (VA) **358**
Fisk U (TN) **358**
Fitchburg State Coll (MA) **358**
Flagler Coll (FL) **359**
Florida A&M U (FL) **359**
Florida Atlantic U (FL) **359**
Florida International U (FL) **360**
Florida Southern Coll (FL) **361**
Florida State U (FL) **361**
Fontbonne U (MO) **361**
Fordham U (NY) **362**
Fort Hays State U (KS) **362**
Fort Lewis Coll (CO) **362**
Framingham State Coll (MA) **362**
The Franciscan U (IA) **363**
Franciscan U of Steubenville (OH) **363**
Francis Marion U (SC) **363**
Franklin and Marshall Coll (PA) **363**
Franklin Coll (IN) **363**
Franklin Pierce Coll (NH) **364**
Freed-Hardeman U (TN) **364**
Free Will Baptist Bible Coll (TN) **364**
Fresno Pacific U (CA) **364**
Frostburg State U (MD) **365**
Furman U (SC) **365**
Gallaudet U (DC) **365**
Gardner-Webb U (NC) **365**
Geneva Coll (PA) **366**
George Fox U (OR) **366**
George Mason U (VA) **366**
Georgetown Coll (KY) **366**
Georgetown U (DC) **366**
The George Washington U (DC) **367**
Georgia Coll & State U (GA) **367**
Georgian Court Coll (NJ) **367**
Georgia Southern U (GA) **367**
Georgia Southwestern State U (GA) **368**
Georgia State U (GA) **368**
Gettysburg Coll (PA) **368**
Glenville State Coll (WV) **368**
Goddard Coll (VT) **369**
Gonzaga U (WA) **369**
Gordon Coll (MA) **370**
Goshen Coll (IN) **370**
Goucher Coll (MD) **370**
Governors State U (IL) **370**
Grace Coll (IN) **370**
Graceland U (IA) **371**
Grambling State U (LA) **371**
Grand Canyon U (AZ) **371**
Grand Valley State U (MI) **371**
Grand View Coll (IA) **372**
Green Mountain Coll (VT) **372**
Greensboro Coll (NC) **372**
Greenville Coll (IL) **373**
Grinnell Coll (IA) **373**
Grove City Coll (PA) **373**
Guilford Coll (NC) **373**
Gustavus Adolphus Coll (MN) **374**
Gwynedd-Mercy Coll (PA) **374**
Hamilton Coll (NY) **374**
Hamline U (MN) **374**
Hampden-Sydney Coll (VA) **374**
Hampshire Coll (MA) **375**
Hampton U (VA) **375**
Hannibal-LaGrange Coll (MO) **375**
Hanover Coll (IN) **375**
Harding U (AR) **375**
Hardin-Simmons U (TX) **376**
Hartwick Coll (NY) **376**
Harvard U (MA) **376**
Hastings Coll (NE) **377**
Haverford Coll (PA) **377**
Heidelberg Coll (OH) **377**
Henderson State U (AR) **378**
Hendrix Coll (AR) **378**
High Point U (NC) **379**
Hilbert Coll (NY) **379**
Hillsdale Coll (MI) **379**
Hiram Coll (OH) **379**
Hobart and William Smith Colls (NY) **380**
Hofstra U (NY) **380**
Hollins U (VA) **380**
Holy Family U (PA) **380**
Holy Names Coll (CA) **381**
Hood Coll (MD) **381**
Hope Coll (MI) **381**
Houghton Coll (NY) **381**
Houston Baptist U (TX) **382**
Howard Payne U (TX) **382**
Howard U (DC) **382**
Humboldt State U (CA) **382**
Hunter Coll of the City U of NY (NY) **382**
Huntingdon Coll (AL) **383**
Huntington Coll (IN) **383**
Huston-Tillotson Coll (TX) **383**
Idaho State U (ID) **384**
Illinois Coll (IL) **384**
Illinois State U (IL) **384**
Illinois Wesleyan U (IL) **385**
Immaculata U (PA) **385**
Indiana State U (IN) **385**
Indiana U Bloomington (IN) **385**
Indiana U East (IN) **386**
Indiana U Kokomo (IN) **386**
Indiana U Northwest (IN) **386**
Indiana U of Pennsylvania (PA) **386**
Indiana U–Purdue U Fort Wayne (IN) **386**
Indiana U–Purdue U Indianapolis (IN) **387**
Indiana U South Bend (IN) **387**
Indiana U Southeast (IN) **387**
Indiana Wesleyan U (IN) **387**
Inter American U of PR, San Germán Campus (PR) **388**
Iona Coll (NY) **390**
Iowa State U of Science and Technology (IA) **390**
Iowa Wesleyan Coll (IA) **390**
Ithaca Coll (NY) **390**
Jackson State U (MS) **390**
Jacksonville State U (AL) **390**
Jacksonville U (FL) **391**
James Madison U (VA) **391**
Jamestown Coll (ND) **391**
John Brown U (AR) **392**
John Carroll U (OH) **392**
Johns Hopkins U (MD) **392**
Johnson C. Smith U (NC) **394**
Johnson State Coll (VT) **394**
Judson Coll (AL) **395**
Judson Coll (IL) **395**
Juniata Coll (PA) **395**
Kalamazoo Coll (MI) **395**
Kansas State U (KS) **396**
Kean U (NJ) **396**
Keene State Coll (NH) **396**
Kennesaw State U (GA) **397**
Kent State U (OH) **397**
Kentucky State U (KY) **397**
Kentucky Wesleyan Coll (KY) **397**
Kenyon Coll (OH) **398**
Keuka Coll (NY) **398**
King Coll (TN) **398**
King's Coll (PA) **398**
The King's U Coll (AB, Canada) **399**
Knox Coll (IL) **399**
Kutztown U of Pennsylvania (PA) **399**
Lafayette Coll (PA) **400**
LaGrange Coll (GA) **400**
Lake Erie Coll (OH) **400**
Lake Forest Coll (IL) **400**
Lakehead U (ON, Canada) **400**
Lakeland Coll (WI) **401**
Lamar U (TX) **401**
Lambuth U (TN) **401**
Lander U (SC) **401**
Lane Coll (TN) **402**
Langston U (OK) **402**
La Roche Coll (PA) **402**
La Salle U (PA) **402**
La Sierra U (CA) **403**
Laurentian U (ON, Canada) **403**
Lawrence U (WI) **403**
Lebanon Valley Coll (PA) **403**
Lees-McRae Coll (NC) **404**
Lee U (TN) **404**
Lehigh U (PA) **404**
Lehman Coll of the City U of NY (NY) **404**
Le Moyne Coll (NY) **404**
Lenoir-Rhyne Coll (NC) **405**
LeTourneau U (TX) **405**
Lewis & Clark Coll (OR) **405**
Lewis-Clark State Coll (ID) **406**
Lewis U (IL) **406**
Liberty U (VA) **406**
Limestone Coll (SC) **406**
Lincoln Memorial U (TN) **407**
Lincoln U (PA) **407**
Lindenwood U (MO) **407**
Lindsey Wilson Coll (KY) **407**
Linfield Coll (OR) **408**
Lipscomb U (TN) **408**
Lock Haven U of Pennsylvania (PA) **408**
Long Island U, Brooklyn Campus (NY) **409**
Long Island U, C.W. Post Campus (NY) **409**
Long Island U, Southampton Coll (NY) **409**
Long Island U, Southampton Coll, Friends World Program (NY) **409**
Longwood U (VA) **409**
Loras Coll (IA) **410**
Louisiana Coll (LA) **410**
Louisiana State U and A&M Coll (LA) **410**
Louisiana State U in Shreveport (LA) **410**
Louisiana Tech U (LA) **410**
Lourdes Coll (OH) **411**
Loyola Coll in Maryland (MD) **411**
Loyola Marymount U (CA) **411**
Loyola U Chicago (IL) **411**
Loyola U New Orleans (LA) **411**
Lubbock Christian U (TX) **412**
Luther Coll (IA) **412**
Lycoming Coll (PA) **412**
Lynchburg Coll (VA) **413**
Lyndon State Coll (VT) **413**
Lynn U (FL) **413**
Lyon Coll (AR) **413**
Macalester Coll (MN) **413**
MacMurray Coll (IL) **414**
Madonna U (MI) **414**
Maharishi U of Management (IA) **414**
Malone Coll (OH) **415**
Manchester Coll (IN) **415**
Manhattan Coll (NY) **416**
Manhattanville Coll (NY) **416**
Mansfield U of Pennsylvania (PA) **416**
Marian Coll (IN) **417**
Marian Coll of Fond du Lac (WI) **417**
Marietta Coll (OH) **417**
Marist Coll (NY) **417**
Marlboro Coll (VT) **418**
Marquette U (WI) **418**
Marshall U (WV) **418**
Mars Hill Coll (NC) **418**
Martin Methodist Coll (TN) **418**
Martin U (IN) **419**
Mary Baldwin Coll (VA) **419**
Marygrove Coll (MI) **419**
Marymount Coll of Fordham U (NY) **419**
Marymount Manhattan Coll (NY) **420**
Marymount U (VA) **420**
Maryville Coll (TN) **420**
Maryville U of Saint Louis (MO) **420**
Mary Washington Coll (VA) **420**
Marywood U (PA) **421**
Massachusetts Coll of Liberal Arts (MA) **421**
The Master's Coll and Seminary (CA) **422**
Mayville State U (ND) **422**
McDaniel Coll (MD) **422**
McGill U (QC, Canada) **423**
McKendree Coll (IL) **423**
McMaster U (ON, Canada) **423**
McMurry U (TX) **423**
McNeese State U (LA) **423**
McPherson Coll (KS) **423**
Memorial U of Newfoundland (NF, Canada) **424**
Mercer U (GA) **425**
Mercy Coll (NY) **425**
Mercyhurst Coll (PA) **425**
Meredith Coll (NC) **426**
Merrimack Coll (MA) **426**
Mesa State Coll (CO) **426**
Messiah Coll (PA) **426**
Methodist Coll (NC) **427**
Metropolitan State Coll of Denver (CO) **427**
Metropolitan State U (MN) **427**
Miami U (OH) **428**
Michigan State U (MI) **428**
Michigan Technological U (MI) **428**
MidAmerica Nazarene U (KS) **428**
Mid-Continent Coll (KY) **429**
Middlebury Coll (VT) **429**
Middle Tennessee State U (TN) **429**
Midland Lutheran Coll (NE) **429**
Midway Coll (KY) **429**
Midwestern State U (TX) **430**
Miles Coll (AL) **430**
Millersville U of Pennsylvania (PA) **430**
Milligan Coll (TN) **430**
Millikin U (IL) **430**
Millsaps Coll (MS) **431**
Mills Coll (CA) **431**
Minnesota State U, Mankato (MN) **431**
Minnesota State U, Moorhead (MN) **432**
Minot State U (ND) **432**
Mississippi Coll (MS) **432**
Mississippi State U (MS) **432**
Mississippi Valley State U (MS) **432**
Missouri Southern State Coll (MO) **433**
Missouri Valley Coll (MO) **433**
Missouri Western State Coll (MO) **433**
Molloy Coll (NY) **433**
Monmouth Coll (IL) **434**
Monmouth U (NJ) **434**
Montana State U–Billings (MT) **434**
Montana State U–Bozeman (MT) **434**
Montclair State U (NJ) **435**
Montreat Coll (NC) **435**
Moravian Coll (PA) **436**
Morehead State U (KY) **436**
Morehouse Coll (GA) **436**
Morgan State U (MD) **436**
Morningside Coll (IA) **437**
Morris Coll (SC) **437**
Mount Allison U (NB, Canada) **437**
Mount Aloysius Coll (PA) **437**
Mount Holyoke Coll (MA) **438**
Mount Marty Coll (SD) **438**
Mount Mary Coll (WI) **438**
Mount Mercy Coll (IA) **438**
Mount Olive Coll (NC) **439**
Mount Saint Mary Coll (NY) **439**
Mount St. Mary's Coll (CA) **439**
Mount Saint Mary's Coll and Seminary (MD) **439**
Mount Saint Vincent U (NS, Canada) **439**
Mount Union Coll (OH) **440**
Mount Vernon Nazarene U (OH) **440**
Muhlenberg Coll (PA) **440**
Murray State U (KY) **440**
Muskingum Coll (OH) **441**
National-Louis U (IL) **442**
Nazareth Coll of Rochester (NY) **443**
Nebraska Wesleyan U (NE) **443**
Neumann Coll (PA) **443**
Newberry Coll (SC) **444**
New England Coll (NH) **444**
New Jersey City U (NJ) **445**
Newman U (KS) **445**
New Mexico Highlands U (NM) **446**
New Mexico State U (NM) **446**
New York Inst of Technology (NY) **447**
New York U (NY) **447**
Niagara U (NY) **447**
Nicholls State U (LA) **447**
Nichols Coll (MA) **448**
Nipissing U (ON, Canada) **448**

Norfolk State U (VA) **448**
North Carolina Ag and Tech State U (NC) **448**
North Carolina Central U (NC) **448**
North Carolina State U (NC) **449**
North Carolina Wesleyan Coll (NC) **449**
North Central Coll (IL) **449**
North Dakota State U (ND) **449**
Northeastern Illinois U (IL) **450**
Northeastern State U (OK) **450**
Northeastern U (MA) **450**
Northern Arizona U (AZ) **450**
Northern Illinois U (IL) **450**
Northern Kentucky U (KY) **451**
Northern Michigan U (MI) **451**
Northern State U (SD) **451**
North Georgia Coll & State U (GA) **451**
Northland Coll (WI) **452**
North Park U (IL) **452**
Northwest Coll (WA) **452**
Northwestern Coll (IA) **453**
Northwestern Coll (MN) **453**
Northwestern Oklahoma State U (OK) **453**
Northwestern State U of Louisiana (LA) **453**
Northwestern U (IL) **453**
Northwest Missouri State U (MO) **454**
Northwest Nazarene U (ID) **454**
Norwich U (VT) **455**
Notre Dame Coll (OH) **455**
Notre Dame de Namur U (CA) **455**
Nyack Coll (NY) **456**
Oakland City U (IN) **456**
Oakland U (MI) **456**
Oakwood Coll (AL) **456**
Oberlin Coll (OH) **456**
Oglethorpe U (GA) **457**
Ohio Dominican U (OH) **457**
Ohio Northern U (OH) **457**
The Ohio State U (OH) **457**
The Ohio State U at Lima (OH) **458**
Ohio U (OH) **458**
Ohio Wesleyan U (OH) **459**
Okanagan U Coll (BC, Canada) **459**
Oklahoma Baptist U (OK) **459**
Oklahoma Christian U (OK) **459**
Oklahoma City U (OK) **460**
Oklahoma Panhandle State U (OK) **460**
Oklahoma State U (OK) **460**
Oklahoma Wesleyan U (OK) **460**
Old Dominion U (VA) **460**
Olivet Coll (MI) **461**
Olivet Nazarene U (IL) **461**
Oregon State U (OR) **462**
Ottawa U (KS) **462**
Otterbein Coll (OH) **462**
Ouachita Baptist U (AR) **462**
Our Lady of Holy Cross Coll (LA) **463**
Our Lady of the Lake U of San Antonio (TX) **463**
Pace U (NY) **463**
Pacific Lutheran U (WA) **463**
Pacific Union Coll (CA) **464**
Pacific U (OR) **464**
Paine Coll (GA) **465**
Palm Beach Atlantic U (FL) **465**
Park U (MO) **465**
Paul Quinn Coll (TX) **466**
Peace Coll (NC) **466**
Penn State U Abington Coll (PA) **467**
Penn State U Altoona Coll (PA) **467**
Penn State U at Erie, The Behrend Coll (PA) **467**
Penn State U Univ Park Campus (PA) **468**
Pepperdine U, Malibu (CA) **469**
Peru State Coll (NE) **469**
Pfeiffer U (NC) **469**
Piedmont Baptist Coll (NC) **470**
Piedmont Coll (GA) **470**
Pikeville Coll (KY) **470**
Pillsbury Baptist Bible Coll (MN) **470**
Pine Manor Coll (MA) **470**
Pittsburg State U (KS) **470**
Pitzer Coll (CA) **471**
Plattsburgh State U of NY (NY) **471**
Plymouth State Coll (NH) **471**
Point Park Coll (PA) **471**
Pomona Coll (CA) **472**
Pontifical Catholic U of Puerto Rico (PR) **472**
Pontifical Coll Josephinum (OH) **472**
Portland State U (OR) **472**
Prairie View A&M U (TX) **473**
Presbyterian Coll (SC) **473**
Princeton U (NJ) **474**
Principia Coll (IL) **474**
Providence Coll (RI) **474**
Purdue U (IN) **475**
Purdue U Calumet (IN) **475**
Purdue U North Central (IN) **475**
Queens Coll of the City U of NY (NY) **475**
Queen's U at Kingston (ON, Canada) **476**
Queens U of Charlotte (NC) **476**
Quincy U (IL) **476**
Quinnipiac U (CT) **476**
Radford U (VA) **476**
Randolph-Macon Coll (VA) **477**
Randolph-Macon Woman's Coll (VA) **477**
Reed Coll (OR) **477**
Regis Coll (MA) **478**
Regis U (CO) **478**
Rhode Island Coll (RI) **479**
Rhodes Coll (TN) **479**
Rice U (TX) **479**
The Richard Stockton Coll of New Jersey (NJ) **479**
Richmond, The American International U in London(United Kingdom) **480**
Rider U (NJ) **480**
Ripon Coll (WI) **480**
Rivier Coll (NH) **480**
Roanoke Coll (VA) **481**
Robert Morris U (PA) **481**
Roberts Wesleyan Coll (NY) **481**
Rochester Coll (MI) **482**
Rockford Coll (IL) **482**
Rockhurst U (MO) **482**
Rocky Mountain Coll (MT) **482**
Roger Williams U (RI) **483**
Rollins Coll (FL) **483**
Roosevelt U (IL) **483**
Rosemont Coll (PA) **484**
Rowan U (NJ) **484**
Russell Sage Coll (NY) **484**
Rutgers, The State U of New Jersey, Camden (NJ) **485**
Rutgers, The State U of New Jersey, Newark (NJ) **485**
Rutgers, The State U of New Jersey, New Brunswick (NJ) **485**
Sacred Heart U (CT) **486**
Saginaw Valley State U (MI) **486**
St. Ambrose U (IA) **486**
St. Andrews Presbyterian Coll (NC) **487**
Saint Anselm Coll (NH) **487**
Saint Augustine's Coll (NC) **487**
St. Bonaventure U (NY) **487**
St. Cloud State U (MN) **488**
St. Edward's U (TX) **488**
St. Francis Coll (NY) **488**
Saint Francis U (PA) **488**
St. Francis Xavier U (NS, Canada) **489**
St. John Fisher Coll (NY) **489**
Saint John's U (MN) **490**
St. John's U (NY) **490**
Saint Joseph Coll (CT) **490**
Saint Joseph's Coll (IN) **490**
St. Joseph's Coll, New York (NY) **491**
Saint Joseph's Coll of Maine (ME) **491**
St. Joseph's Coll, Suffolk Campus (NY) **491**
Saint Joseph's U (PA) **491**
St. Lawrence U (NY) **491**
Saint Leo U (FL) **492**
Saint Louis U (MO) **492**
Saint Martin's Coll (WA) **493**
Saint Mary Coll (KS) **493**
Saint Mary-of-the-Woods Coll (IN) **493**
Saint Mary's Coll (IN) **493**
Saint Mary's Coll of California (CA) **494**
Saint Mary's Coll of Madonna U (MI) **493**
St. Mary's Coll of Maryland (MD) **494**
Saint Mary's U (NS, Canada) **494**
Saint Mary's U of Minnesota (MN) **494**
St. Mary's U of San Antonio (TX) **494**
Saint Michael's Coll (VT) **494**
St. Norbert Coll (WI) **495**
St. Olaf Coll (MN) **495**
Saint Peter's Coll (NJ) **495**
St. Thomas Aquinas Coll (NY) **495**
St. Thomas U (FL) **496**
St. Thomas U (NB, Canada) **496**
Saint Vincent Coll (PA) **496**
Saint Xavier U (IL) **496**
Salem Coll (NC) **496**
Salem State Coll (MA) **497**
Salisbury U (MD) **497**
Salve Regina U (RI) **497**
Samford U (AL) **497**
Sam Houston State U (TX) **497**
San Diego State U (CA) **498**
San Francisco State U (CA) **498**
San Jose State U (CA) **499**
Santa Clara U (CA) **499**
Sarah Lawrence Coll (NY) **499**
Savannah State U (GA) **499**
Schreiner U (TX) **501**
Scripps Coll (CA) **501**
Seattle Pacific U (WA) **501**
Seattle U (WA) **501**
Seton Hall U (NJ) **502**
Seton Hill U (PA) **502**
Shawnee State U (OH) **502**
Shaw U (NC) **502**
Shenandoah U (VA) **503**
Shepherd Coll (WV) **503**
Shippensburg U of Pennsylvania (PA) **503**
Shorter Coll (GA) **504**
Siena Coll (NY) **504**
Siena Heights U (MI) **504**
Silver Lake Coll (WI) **504**
Simmons Coll (MA) **504**
Simon Fraser U (BC, Canada) **505**
Simpson Coll (IA) **505**
Simpson Coll and Graduate School (CA) **505**
Slippery Rock U of Pennsylvania (PA) **506**
Smith Coll (MA) **506**
Sonoma State U (CA) **506**
South Carolina State U (SC) **506**
South Dakota State U (SD) **507**
Southeastern Coll of the Assemblies of God (FL) **507**
Southeastern Louisiana U (LA) **508**
Southeastern Oklahoma State U (OK) **508**
Southeast Missouri State U (MO) **508**
Southern Adventist U (TN) **508**
Southern Arkansas U–Magnolia (AR) **509**
Southern Connecticut State U (CT) **509**
Southern Illinois U Carbondale (IL) **509**
Southern Illinois U Edwardsville (IL) **509**
Southern Methodist U (TX) **510**
Southern Nazarene U (OK) **510**
Southern New Hampshire U (NH) **510**
Southern Oregon U (OR) **510**
Southern U and A&M Coll (LA) **511**
Southern Utah U (UT) **511**
Southern Vermont Coll (VT) **511**
Southern Virginia U (VA) **511**
Southern Wesleyan U (SC) **511**
Southwest Baptist U (MO) **512**
Southwestern Coll (KS) **512**
Southwestern Oklahoma State U (OK) **512**
Southwestern U (TX) **513**
Southwest Missouri State U (MO) **513**
Southwest State U (MN) **513**
Southwest Texas State U (TX) **513**
Spalding U (KY) **513**
Spelman Coll (GA) **514**
Spring Arbor U (MI) **514**
Springfield Coll (MA) **514**
Spring Hill Coll (AL) **514**
Stanford U (CA) **514**
State U of NY at Albany (NY) **514**
State U of NY at Binghamton (NY) **515**
State U of NY at New Paltz (NY) **515**
State U of NY at Oswego (NY) **515**
State U of NY Coll at Brockport (NY) **515**
State U of NY Coll at Buffalo (NY) **516**
State U of NY Coll at Cortland (NY) **516**
State U of NY Coll at Fredonia (NY) **516**
State U of NY Coll at Geneseo (NY) **516**
State U of NY Coll at Oneonta (NY) **517**
State U of NY Coll at Potsdam (NY) **517**
State U of West Georgia (GA) **518**
Stephen F. Austin State U (TX) **518**
Stephens Coll (MO) **519**
Sterling Coll (KS) **519**
Stetson U (FL) **519**
Stevens Inst of Technology (NJ) **519**
Stonehill Coll (MA) **520**
Stony Brook U, State University of New York (NY) **520**
Suffolk U (MA) **520**
Sul Ross State U (TX) **521**
Susquehanna U (PA) **521**
Swarthmore Coll (PA) **521**
Sweet Briar Coll (VA) **521**
Syracuse U (NY) **521**
Tabor Coll (KS) **522**
Talladega Coll (AL) **522**
Tarleton State U (TX) **522**
Taylor U (IN) **523**
Taylor U, Fort Wayne Campus (IN) **523**
Teikyo Post U (CT) **523**
Temple U (PA) **523**
Tennessee State U (TN) **523**
Tennessee Technological U (TN) **524**
Tennessee Temple U (TN) **524**
Tennessee Wesleyan Coll (TN) **524**
Texas A&M International U (TX) **524**
Texas A&M U (TX) **524**
Texas A&M U–Commerce (TX) **525**
Texas A&M U–Corpus Christi (TX) **525**
Texas A&M U–Kingsville (TX) **525**
Texas A&M U–Texarkana (TX) **525**
Texas Christian U (TX) **526**
Texas Coll (TX) **526**
Texas Lutheran U (TX) **526**
Texas Southern U (TX) **526**
Texas Tech U (TX) **526**
Texas Wesleyan U (TX) **526**
Texas Woman's U (TX) **527**
Thiel Coll (PA) **527**
Thomas Edison State Coll (NJ) **527**
Thomas More Coll (KY) **528**
Thomas U (GA) **528**
Toccoa Falls Coll (GA) **528**
Touro Coll (NY) **529**
Towson U (MD) **529**
Transylvania U (KY) **529**
Trent U (ON, Canada) **529**
Trevecca Nazarene U (TN) **529**
Trinity Christian Coll (IL) **530**
Trinity Coll (CT) **530**
Trinity Coll (DC) **530**
Trinity International U (IL) **531**
Trinity U (TX) **531**
Trinity Western U (BC, Canada) **531**
Troy State U (AL) **532**
Troy State U Dothan (AL) **532**
Troy State U Montgomery (AL) **532**
Truman State U (MO) **532**
Tufts U (MA) **533**
Tulane U (LA) **533**
Tusculum Coll (TN) **533**
Tuskegee U (AL) **533**
Tyndale Coll & Seminary (ON, Canada) **533**
Union Coll (KY) **533**
Union Coll (NE) **534**
Union Coll (NY) **534**
Union U (TN) **534**
United States Air Force Academy (CO) **534**
United States Naval Academy (MD) **535**
Université de Sherbrooke (QC, Canada) **536**
Université Laval (QC, Canada) **536**
U at Buffalo, The State University of New York (NY) **536**
U Coll of the Cariboo (BC, Canada) **537**
The U of Akron (OH) **537**
The U of Alabama (AL) **537**
The U of Alabama at Birmingham (AL) **537**
The U of Alabama in Huntsville (AL) **537**
U of Alaska Anchorage (AK) **538**
U of Alaska Fairbanks (AK) **538**
U of Alberta (AB, Canada) **538**
The U of Arizona (AZ) **538**
U of Arkansas (AR) **539**
U of Arkansas at Little Rock (AR) **539**
U of Arkansas at Monticello (AR) **539**
U of Baltimore (MD) **539**
U of Bridgeport (CT) **540**
The U of British Columbia (BC, Canada) **540**
U of Calgary (AB, Canada) **540**
U of Calif, Berkeley (CA) **540**
U of Calif, Davis (CA) **540**
U of Calif, Irvine (CA) **541**
U of Calif, Los Angeles (CA) **541**
U of Calif, Riverside (CA) **541**
U of Calif, San Diego (CA) **541**
U of Calif, Santa Barbara (CA) **541**
U of Central Arkansas (AR) **542**
U of Central Florida (FL) **542**
U of Central Oklahoma (OK) **542**
U of Charleston (WV) **542**
U of Chicago (IL) **542**
U of Cincinnati (OH) **543**
U of Colorado at Boulder (CO) **543**
U of Colorado at Colorado Springs (CO) **543**
U of Colorado at Denver (CO) **543**
U of Connecticut (CT) **544**
U of Dallas (TX) **544**
U of Dayton (OH) **544**
U of Delaware (DE) **544**
U of Denver (CO) **544**
U of Dubuque (IA) **545**
U of Evansville (IN) **545**

ENGLISH (continued)

The U of Findlay (OH) 545
U of Florida (FL) 545
U of Georgia (GA) 545
U of Guelph (ON, Canada) 546
U of Hartford (CT) 546
U of Hawaii at Hilo (HI) 546
U of Hawaii at Manoa (HI) 546
U of Hawaii–West Oahu (HI) 546
U of Houston (TX) 547
U of Houston–Downtown (TX) 547
U of Idaho (ID) 547
U of Illinois at Chicago (IL) 547
U of Illinois at Springfield (IL) 548
U of Illinois at Urbana–Champaign (IL) 548
U of Indianapolis (IN) 548
The U of Iowa (IA) 548
U of Kansas (KS) 549
U of Kentucky (KY) 549
U of King's Coll (NS, Canada) 549
U of La Verne (CA) 549
The U of Lethbridge (AB, Canada) 549
U of Louisiana at Lafayette (LA) 550
U of Louisville (KY) 550
U of Maine (ME) 550
The U of Maine at Augusta (ME) 550
U of Maine at Farmington (ME) 550
U of Maine at Fort Kent (ME) 551
U of Maine at Machias (ME) 551
U of Maine at Presque Isle (ME) 551
U of Manitoba (MB, Canada) 551
U of Mary (ND) 551
U of Mary Hardin-Baylor (TX) 551
U of Maryland, Baltimore County (MD) 552
U of Maryland, Coll Park (MD) 552
U of Maryland Eastern Shore (MD) 552
U of Maryland University Coll (MD) 552
U of Massachusetts Amherst (MA) 552
U of Massachusetts Boston (MA) 553
U of Massachusetts Dartmouth (MA) 553
U of Massachusetts Lowell (MA) 553
The U of Memphis (TN) 553
U of Miami (FL) 553
U of Michigan (MI) 554
U of Michigan–Dearborn (MI) 554
U of Michigan–Flint (MI) 554
U of Minnesota, Duluth (MN) 554
U of Minnesota, Morris (MN) 555
U of Minnesota, Twin Cities Campus (MN) 555
U of Mississippi (MS) 555
U of Missouri–Columbia (MO) 555
U of Missouri–Kansas City (MO) 555
U of Missouri–Rolla (MO) 556
U of Missouri–St. Louis (MO) 556
U of Mobile (AL) 556
The U of Montana–Missoula (MT) 556
The U of Montana–Western (MT) 556
U of Montevallo (AL) 557
U of Nebraska at Kearney (NE) 557
U of Nebraska at Omaha (NE) 557
U of Nebraska–Lincoln (NE) 557
U of Nevada, Las Vegas (NV) 558
U of Nevada, Reno (NV) 558
U of New Brunswick Fredericton (NB, Canada) 558
U of New Brunswick Saint John (NB, Canada) 558
U of New England (ME) 558
U of New Hampshire (NH) 558
U of New Haven (CT) 559
U of New Mexico (NM) 559
U of New Orleans (LA) 559
U of North Alabama (AL) 559
The U of North Carolina at Asheville (NC) 559
The U of North Carolina at Chapel Hill (NC) 560
The U of North Carolina at Charlotte (NC) 560
The U of North Carolina at Greensboro (NC) 560
The U of North Carolina at Pembroke (NC) 560
The U of North Carolina at Wilmington (NC) 561
U of North Dakota (ND) 561
U of Northern Colorado (CO) 561
U of Northern Iowa (IA) 561
U of North Florida (FL) 561
U of North Texas (TX) 562
U of Notre Dame (IN) 562
U of Oklahoma (OK) 562
U of Oregon (OR) 562
U of Ottawa (ON, Canada) 563
U of Pennsylvania (PA) 563
U of Pittsburgh (PA) 569
U of Pittsburgh at Bradford (PA) 569
U of Pittsburgh at Greensburg (PA) 570
U of Pittsburgh at Johnstown (PA) 570
U of Portland (OR) 570
U of Prince Edward Island (PE, Canada) 570
U of Puerto Rico, Cayey U Coll (PR) 571
U of Puerto Rico, Río Piedras (PR) 571
U of Puget Sound (WA) 571
U of Redlands (CA) 572
U of Regina (SK, Canada) 572
U of Rhode Island (RI) 572
U of Richmond (VA) 572
U of Rio Grande (OH) 572
U of Rochester (NY) 573
U of St. Francis (IL) 573
U of Saint Francis (IN) 573
U of St. Thomas (MN) 573
U of St. Thomas (TX) 573
U of San Diego (CA) 574
U of San Francisco (CA) 574
U of Saskatchewan (SK, Canada) 574
U of Science and Arts of Oklahoma (OK) 574
The U of Scranton (PA) 574
U of Sioux Falls (SD) 574
U of South Alabama (AL) 575
U of South Carolina (SC) 575
U of South Carolina Aiken (SC) 575
U of South Carolina Spartanburg (SC) 575
The U of South Dakota (SD) 575
U of Southern California (CA) 576
U of Southern Indiana (IN) 576
U of Southern Maine (ME) 576
U of Southern Mississippi (MS) 576
U of South Florida (FL) 576
The U of Tampa (FL) 577
The U of Tennessee (TN) 577
The U of Tennessee at Chattanooga (TN) 577
The U of Tennessee at Martin (TN) 577
The U of Texas at Arlington (TX) 577
The U of Texas at Austin (TX) 578
The U of Texas at Brownsville (TX) 578
The U of Texas at El Paso (TX) 578
The U of Texas at San Antonio (TX) 578
The U of Texas at Tyler (TX) 579
The U of Texas of the Permian Basin (TX) 579
The U of Texas–Pan American (TX) 579
U of the District of Columbia (DC) 580
U of the Incarnate Word (TX) 580
U of the Ozarks (AR) 580
U of the Pacific (CA) 580
U of the Sacred Heart (PR) 580
U of the South (TN) 581
U of the Virgin Islands (VI) 581
U of Toledo (OH) 581
U of Toronto (ON, Canada) 581
U of Tulsa (OK) 581
U of Utah (UT) 582
U of Vermont (VT) 582
U of Victoria (BC, Canada) 582
U of Virginia (VA) 582
The U of Virginia's Coll at Wise (VA) 582
U of Washington (WA) 583
U of Waterloo (ON, Canada) 583
The U of West Alabama (AL) 583
The U of Western Ontario (ON, Canada) 583
U of West Florida (FL) 583
U of Windsor (ON, Canada) 584
U of Wisconsin–Eau Claire (WI) 584
U of Wisconsin–Green Bay (WI) 584
U of Wisconsin–La Crosse (WI) 584
U of Wisconsin–Madison (WI) 584
U of Wisconsin–Milwaukee (WI) 585
U of Wisconsin–Oshkosh (WI) 585
U of Wisconsin–Parkside (WI) 585
U of Wisconsin–Platteville (WI) 585
U of Wisconsin–River Falls (WI) 585
U of Wisconsin–Stevens Point (WI) 585
U of Wisconsin–Superior (WI) 586
U of Wisconsin–Whitewater (WI) 586
U of Wyoming (WY) 586
Upper Iowa U (IA) 587
Urbana U (OH) 587
Ursinus Coll (PA) 587
Ursuline Coll (OH) 587
Utah State U (UT) 587
Utica Coll (NY) 588
Valdosta State U (GA) 588
Valley City State U (ND) 588
Valparaiso U (IN) 588
Vanderbilt U (TN) 588
Vanguard U of Southern California (CA) 589
Vassar Coll (NY) 589
Villa Julie Coll (MD) 590
Villanova U (PA) 590
Virginia Commonwealth U (VA) 590
Virginia Intermont Coll (VA) 590
Virginia Military Inst (VA) 591
Virginia Polytechnic Inst and State U (VA) 591
Virginia State U (VA) 591
Virginia Union U (VA) 591
Virginia Wesleyan Coll (VA) 591
Viterbo U (WI) 591
Voorhees Coll (SC) 592
Wabash Coll (IN) 592
Wagner Coll (NY) 592
Wake Forest U (NC) 592
Waldorf Coll (IA) 592
Walla Walla Coll (WA) 593
Walsh U (OH) 593
Warner Pacific Coll (OR) 593
Warner Southern Coll (FL) 593
Warren Wilson Coll (NC) 594
Wartburg Coll (IA) 594
Washington & Jefferson Coll (PA) 594
Washington and Lee U (VA) 594
Washington Coll (MD) 594
Washington State U (WA) 595
Washington U in St. Louis (MO) 595
Wayland Baptist U (TX) 595
Waynesburg Coll (PA) 595
Wayne State Coll (NE) 596
Wayne State U (MI) 596
Weber State U (UT) 596
Webster U (MO) 597
Wellesley Coll (MA) 597
Wells Coll (NY) 597
Wesleyan Coll (GA) 597
Wesleyan U (CT) 597
Wesley Coll (DE) 598
West Chester U of Pennsylvania (PA) 598
Western Baptist Coll (OR) 598
Western Carolina U (NC) 598
Western Connecticut State U (CT) 598
Western Illinois U (IL) 599
Western Kentucky U (KY) 599
Western Michigan U (MI) 599
Western New England Coll (MA) 600
Western New Mexico U (NM) 600
Western Oregon U (OR) 600
Western State Coll of Colorado (CO) 600
Western Washington U (WA) 600
Westfield State Coll (MA) 600
West Liberty State Coll (WV) 601
Westminster Coll (MO) 601
Westminster Coll (PA) 601
Westminster Coll (UT) 601
Westmont Coll (CA) 602
West Texas A&M U (TX) 602
West Virginia State Coll (WV) 602
West Virginia U (WV) 602
West Virginia Wesleyan Coll (WV) 603
Wheaton Coll (IL) 603
Wheaton Coll (MA) 603
Wheeling Jesuit U (WV) 603
Whitman Coll (WA) 604
Whittier Coll (CA) 604
Whitworth Coll (WA) 604
Wichita State U (KS) 604
Widener U (PA) 604
Wiley Coll (TX) 605
Wilkes U (PA) 605
Willamette U (OR) 605
William Carey Coll (MS) 605
William Jewell Coll (MO) 606
William Paterson U of New Jersey (NJ) 606
Williams Baptist Coll (AR) 606
Williams Coll (MA) 606
William Woods U (MO) 607
Wilmington Coll (OH) 607
Wilson Coll (PA) 607
Wingate U (NC) 607
Winona State U (MN) 608
Winston-Salem State U (NC) 608
Winthrop U (SC) 608
Wisconsin Lutheran Coll (WI) 608
Wittenberg U (OH) 608
Wofford Coll (SC) 609
Worcester State Coll (MA) 609
Wright State U (OH) 609
Xavier U (OH) 610
Xavier U of Louisiana (LA) 610
Yale U (CT) 610
York Coll (NE) 610
York Coll of Pennsylvania (PA) 610
York Coll of the City U of New York (NY) 611
York U (ON, Canada) 611
Youngstown State U (OH) 611

ENGLISH COMPOSITION

Overview: Students study the principles of English grammar, semantics, syntax, and vocabulary as well as how to arrange and express ideas in written forms. *Related majors:* English language/literature, creative writing, speech/rhetorical studies, technical/business writing, journalism. *Potential careers:* writer, editor, journalist, speech writer, lawyer. *Salary potential:* $23k-$32k.

Aurora U (IL) 277
Baylor U (TX) 283
DePauw U (IN) 339
Dillard U (LA) 344
Eastern Michigan U (MI) 348
Florida Southern Coll (FL) 361
Gallaudet U (DC) 365
Graceland U (IA) 371
Luther Coll (IA) 412
Metropolitan State U (MN) 427
Mount Union Coll (OH) 440
Oklahoma Baptist U (OK) 459
Rochester Coll (MI) 482
Rust Coll (MS) 485
U of Central Arkansas (AR) 542
U of Colorado at Denver (CO) 543
U of Illinois at Urbana–Champaign (IL) 548
U of Nevada, Reno (NV) 558
U of North Texas (TX) 562
Wartburg Coll (IA) 594
William Woods U (MO) 607

ENGLISH EDUCATION

Overview: This major prepares undergraduates to teach a variety of English grammar usage rules, writing skills, and British and American literature to a range of educational levels. *Related majors:* creative writing, English or American literature, English composition. *Potential careers:* English teacher, creative writing teacher. *Salary potential:* $24k-$35k.

Abilene Christian U (TX) 260
Adams State Coll (CO) 260
Alliant International U (CA) 264
Alvernia Coll (PA) 265
Alverno Coll (WI) 265
Anderson Coll (SC) 268
Anderson U (IN) 268
Appalachian State U (NC) 270
Arkansas State U (AR) 272
Arkansas Tech U (AR) 272
Averett U (VA) 278
Barry U (FL) 282
Bayamón Central U (PR) 283
Baylor U (TX) 283
Berea Coll (KY) 286
Berry Coll (GA) 287
Bethany Coll (KS) 287
Bethel Coll (IN) 288
Bethel Coll (TN) 288
Bethune-Cookman Coll (FL) 289
Bloomfield Coll (NJ) 290
Blue Mountain Coll (MS) 291
Boston U (MA) 292
Bowling Green State U (OH) 292
Bridgewater Coll (VA) 294
Brigham Young U (UT) 295
Brigham Young U–Hawaii (HI) 295
Cabrini Coll (PA) 298
California State U, Chico (CA) 300
Canisius Coll (NY) 304
Carroll Coll (MT) 306
The Catholic U of America (DC) 307
Cedarville U (OH) 308
Central Michigan U (MI) 310
Central Missouri State U (MO) 310

Central Washington U (WA) **310**
Chadron State Coll (NE) **311**
Chowan Coll (NC) **312**
Christian Brothers U (TN) **313**
Citadel, The Military Coll of South Carolina (SC) **314**
Clearwater Christian Coll (FL) **316**
Colby-Sawyer Coll (NH) **319**
The Coll of New Jersey (NJ) **320**
Coll of St. Catherine (MN) **321**
Coll of Santa Fe (NM) **323**
Coll of the Ozarks (MO) **323**
Colorado State U (CO) **325**
Columbia Union Coll (MD) **328**
Concordia Coll (MN) **329**
Concordia U (IL) **330**
Concordia U (NE) **330**
Concordia U (OR) **330**
Crichton Coll (TN) **334**
Crown Coll (MN) **334**
Culver-Stockton Coll (MO) **334**
Daemen Coll (NY) **335**
Dakota Wesleyan U (SD) **336**
Dana Coll (NE) **337**
Delta State U (MS) **339**
Dominican Coll (NY) **344**
Duquesne U (PA) **346**
East Carolina U (NC) **347**
Eastern Mennonite U (VA) **348**
Eastern Michigan U (MI) **348**
Eastern U (PA) **349**
East Texas Baptist U (TX) **350**
Elmhurst Coll (IL) **351**
Elmira Coll (NY) **351**
Elms Coll (MA) **352**
Faith Baptist Bible Coll and Theological Seminary (IA) **356**
Florida Atlantic U (FL) **359**
Florida International U (FL) **360**
Florida State U (FL) **361**
Framingham State Coll (MA) **362**
Franklin Coll (IN) **363**
Freed-Hardeman U (TN) **364**
Gallaudet U (DC) **365**
George Fox U (OR) **366**
Georgia Southern U (GA) **367**
Grace Coll (IN) **370**
Grambling State U (LA) **371**
Greensboro Coll (NC) **372**
Greenville Coll (IL) **373**
Hardin-Simmons U (TX) **376**
Hastings Coll (NE) **377**
Henderson State U (AR) **378**
Hofstra U (NY) **380**
Hope International U (CA) **381**
Howard Payne U (TX) **382**
Huntingdon Coll (AL) **383**
Indiana U Bloomington (IN) **385**
Indiana U Northwest (IN) **386**
Indiana U of Pennsylvania (PA) **386**
Indiana U–Purdue U Indianapolis (IN) **387**
Indiana U South Bend (IN) **387**
Indiana U Southeast (IN) **387**
Indiana Wesleyan U (IN) **387**
Ithaca Coll (NY) **390**
Johnson State Coll (VT) **394**
Judson Coll (AL) **395**
Juniata Coll (PA) **395**
Kennesaw State U (GA) **397**
Keuka Coll (NY) **398**
King Coll (TN) **398**
La Roche Coll (PA) **402**
Le Moyne Coll (NY) **404**
Liberty U (VA) **406**
Limestone Coll (SC) **406**
Lincoln U (PA) **407**
Long Island U, C.W. Post Campus (NY) **409**
Louisiana State U in Shreveport (LA) **410**
Luther Coll (IA) **412**
Malone Coll (OH) **415**
Manhattanville Coll (NY) **416**
Mansfield U of Pennsylvania (PA) **416**
Maryville Coll (TN) **420**
Mayville State U (ND) **422**
McGill U (QC, Canada) **423**
McKendree Coll (IL) **423**
McMurry U (TX) **423**
Mercer U (GA) **425**
Messiah Coll (PA) **426**
Miami U (OH) **428**
MidAmerica Nazarene U (KS) **428**
Millersville U of Pennsylvania (PA) **430**
Minnesota State U, Moorhead (MN) **432**
Minot State U (ND) **432**
Mississippi Valley State U (MS) **432**
Missouri Western State Coll (MO) **433**
Molloy Coll (NY) **433**
Montana State U–Billings (MT) **434**
Mount Marty Coll (SD) **438**
Mount Vernon Nazarene U (OH) **440**
Nazareth Coll of Rochester (NY) **443**
New York Inst of Technology (NY) **447**
New York U (NY) **447**
North Carolina Central U (NC) **448**
North Carolina State U (NC) **449**
North Dakota State U (ND) **449**
Northern Arizona U (AZ) **450**
Northwest Coll (WA) **452**
Northwestern Coll (MN) **453**
Northwest Nazarene U (ID) **454**
Oakland City U (IN) **456**
Ohio Valley Coll (WV) **459**
Oklahoma Baptist U (OK) **459**
Oklahoma Christian U (OK) **459**
Oral Roberts U (OK) **461**
Pace U (NY) **463**
Philadelphia Biblical U (PA) **469**
Pikeville Coll (KY) **470**
Point Park Coll (PA) **471**
Pontifical Catholic U of Puerto Rico (PR) **472**
Prescott Coll (AZ) **474**
Queens U of Charlotte (NC) **476**
Rivier Coll (NH) **480**
Rocky Mountain Coll (MT) **482**
Rust Coll (MS) **485**
Rutgers, The State U of New Jersey, Camden (NJ) **485**
St. Ambrose U (IA) **486**
Saint Augustine's Coll (NC) **487**
St. Edward's U (TX) **488**
St. John's U (NY) **490**
Saint Joseph's Coll of Maine (ME) **491**
Saint Mary's U of Minnesota (MN) **494**
Saint Xavier U (IL) **496**
Salve Regina U (RI) **497**
San Diego State U (CA) **498**
Seattle Pacific U (WA) **501**
Seton Hill U (PA) **502**
Shaw U (NC) **502**
Simpson Coll and Graduate School (CA) **505**
Southeastern Coll of the Assemblies of God (FL) **507**
Southeastern Louisiana U (LA) **508**
Southeastern Oklahoma State U (OK) **508**
Southern Adventist U (TN) **508**
Southern Arkansas U–Magnolia (AR) **509**
Southern Nazarene U (OK) **510**
Southern New Hampshire U (NH) **510**
Southwest Baptist U (MO) **512**
Southwestern Coll (KS) **512**
Southwestern Oklahoma State U (OK) **512**
Southwest Missouri State U (MO) **513**
Southwest State U (MN) **513**
State U of NY at Albany (NY) **514**
State U of NY Coll at Potsdam (NY) **517**
State U of West Georgia (GA) **518**
Syracuse U (NY) **521**
Talladega Coll (AL) **522**
Tennessee Wesleyan Coll (TN) **524**
Texas A&M International U (TX) **524**
Texas Christian U (TX) **526**
Texas Wesleyan U (TX) **526**
Toccoa Falls Coll (GA) **528**
Trevecca Nazarene U (TN) **529**
Trinity Christian Coll (IL) **530**
Tri-State U (IN) **532**
Union Coll (NE) **534**
U du Québec à Trois-Rivières (QC, Canada) **536**
The U of Arizona (AZ) **538**
U of Central Arkansas (AR) **542**
U of Central Florida (FL) **542**
U of Central Oklahoma (OK) **542**
U of Delaware (DE) **544**
U of Georgia (GA) **545**
U of Hawaii at Manoa (HI) **546**
U of Illinois at Chicago (IL) **547**
U of Illinois at Urbana–Champaign (IL) **548**
U of Indianapolis (IN) **548**
U of Maine at Farmington (ME) **550**
U of Mary (ND) **551**
U of Maryland, Coll Park (MD) **552**
U of Minnesota, Twin Cities Campus (MN) **555**
U of Mississippi (MS) **555**
The U of Montana–Western (MT) **556**
U of Nebraska–Lincoln (NE) **557**
U of Nevada, Reno (NV) **558**
U of New Orleans (LA) **559**
The U of North Carolina at Charlotte (NC) **560**
The U of North Carolina at Wilmington (NC) **561**
U of Northern Iowa (IA) **561**
U of North Texas (TX) **562**
U of Oklahoma (OK) **562**
U of Puerto Rico, Cayey U Coll (PR) **571**
U of Rio Grande (OH) **572**
U of South Florida (FL) **576**
The U of Tennessee at Martin (TN) **577**
U of Toledo (OH) **581**
U of Vermont (VT) **582**
U of West Florida (FL) **583**
U of Windsor (ON, Canada) **584**
U of Wisconsin–River Falls (WI) **585**
U of Wisconsin–Superior (WI) **586**
Ursuline Coll (OH) **587**
Utica Coll (NY) **588**
Valley City State U (ND) **588**
Virginia Intermont Coll (VA) **590**
Viterbo U (WI) **591**
Warner Southern Coll (FL) **593**
Warren Wilson Coll (NC) **594**
Wayne State U (MI) **596**
Weber State U (UT) **596**
Western Carolina U (NC) **598**
Westmont Coll (CA) **602**
Wheeling Jesuit U (WV) **603**
William Penn U (IA) **606**
William Woods U (MO) **607**
Winston-Salem State U (NC) **608**
York U (ON, Canada) **611**
Youngstown State U (OH) **611**

ENGLISH RELATED

Information can be found under this major's main heading.

Chatham Coll (PA) **312**
Drexel U (PA) **346**
Duquesne U (PA) **346**
McGill U (QC, Canada) **423**
Moravian Coll (PA) **436**
Nebraska Wesleyan U (NE) **443**
Saint Leo U (FL) **492**
Saint Mary-of-the-Woods Coll (IN) **493**
Skidmore Coll (NY) **506**
Spring Hill Coll (AL) **514**
U of Calif, Santa Cruz (CA) **542**
Washington U in St. Louis (MO) **595**
Western Kentucky U (KY) **599**

ENTERPRISE MANAGEMENT

Overview: Students learn how to manage and operate all aspects of a business or organization. *Related majors:* business administration/ management, operations management and supervision, accounting, business/ managerial economics. *Potential careers:* entrepreneur, small business owner, product manager, franchise owner. *Salary potential:* $25k-$35k.

American U (DC) **267**
Baylor U (TX) **283**
Bridgewater State Coll (MA) **294**
Chatham Coll (PA) **312**
Concordia U (QC, Canada) **331**
École des hautes études commerciales de Montréal (QC, Canada) **350**
Gannon U (PA) **365**
Iowa State U of Science and Technology (IA) **390**
Lyndon State Coll (VT) **413**
McGill U (QC, Canada) **423**
Morris Coll (SC) **437**
Northeastern U (MA) **450**
Northwood U (MI) **454**
Northwood U, Texas Campus (TX) **454**
Southern Polytechnic State U (GA) **511**
Syracuse U (NY) **521**
Texas Christian U (TX) **526**
Tri-State U (IN) **532**
Union Coll (NE) **534**
U du Québec à Trois-Rivières (QC, Canada) **536**
The U of Arizona (AZ) **538**
U of Massachusetts Lowell (MA) **553**
U of Miami (FL) **553**
U of Nebraska at Omaha (NE) **557**
U of Nevada, Reno (NV) **558**
U of Phoenix-Atlanta Campus (GA) **563**
U of Phoenix–Fort Lauderdale Campus (FL) **564**
U of Phoenix–Jacksonville Campus (FL) **564**
U of Phoenix–Louisiana Campus (LA) **565**
U of Phoenix–Metro Detroit Campus (MI) **565**
U of Phoenix–Nevada Campus (NV) **565**
U of Phoenix–Orlando Campus (FL) **566**
U of Phoenix–Phoenix Campus (AZ) **567**
U of Phoenix–San Diego Campus (CA) **567**
U of Phoenix–Southern Arizona Campus (AZ) **568**
U of Phoenix–Tulsa Campus (OK) **568**
U of Phoenix–Washington Campus (WA) **569**
U of Puerto Rico, Río Piedras (PR) **571**
U of St. Thomas (MN) **573**
The U of Scranton (PA) **574**
U of Wyoming (WY) **586**

ENTOMOLOGY

Overview: This major focuses on the science of insects in respect to life cycles, morphology, genetics, ecology, population dynamics, environmental and economic impact. *Related majors:* toxicology, agricultural sciences, (plant protection) pest control, plant pathology. *Potential careers:* ecologist, entomologist, environmental scientist, pest control specialist. *Salary potential:* $23k-$33k.

California State U, Long Beach (CA) **301**
Colorado State U (CO) **325**
Cornell U (NY) **333**
Florida A&M U (FL) **359**
Harvard U (MA) **376**
Iowa State U of Science and Technology (IA) **390**
Memorial U of Newfoundland (NF, Canada) **424**
Michigan State U (MI) **428**
The Ohio State U (OH) **457**
Oklahoma State U (OK) **460**
Oregon State U (OR) **462**
Purdue U (IN) **475**
San Jose State U (CA) **499**
State U of NY Coll of Environ Sci and Forestry (NY) **517**
Texas A&M U (TX) **524**
U of Alberta (AB, Canada) **538**
U of Calif, Davis (CA) **540**
U of Calif, Riverside (CA) **541**
U of Delaware (DE) **544**
U of Florida (FL) **545**
U of Georgia (GA) **545**
U of Hawaii at Manoa (HI) **546**
U of Idaho (ID) **547**
U of Illinois at Urbana–Champaign (IL) **548**
U of Manitoba (MB, Canada) **551**
U of New Brunswick Fredericton (NB, Canada) **558**
The U of Scranton (PA) **574**
U of Wisconsin–Madison (WI) **584**
Utah State U (UT) **587**
Washington State U (WA) **595**

ENTREPRENEURSHIP

Overview: This major teaches students how to identify business opportunities and develop and manage new or start-up businesses. *Related majors:* business administration/management, marketing research, accounting, finance, enterprise management and operations. *Potential careers:* entrepreneur, investor, venture capitalist. *Salary potential:* varies greatly according to success of business.

Babson Coll (MA) **278**
Black Hills State U (SD) **290**
Brock U (ON, Canada) **295**

ENTREPRENEURSHIP (continued)

Canisius Coll (NY) ***304***
Central Michigan U (MI) ***310***
Clarkson U (NY) ***316***
Columbia Coll (SC) ***327***
École des hautes études commerciales de Montréal (QC, Canada) ***350***
Fairleigh Dickinson U, Florham (NJ) ***356***
Fairleigh Dickinson U, Teaneck-Metro Campus (NJ) ***356***
Florida State U (FL) ***361***
Hampton U (VA) ***375***
Hawai'i Pacific U (HI) ***377***
Husson Coll (ME) ***383***
Johnson & Wales U (RI) ***393***
Kendall Coll (IL) ***396***
McGill U (QC, Canada) ***423***
Middle Tennessee State U (TN) ***429***
New England Coll (NH) ***444***
Ohio U (OH) ***458***
Quinnipiac U (CT) ***476***
Ryerson U (ON, Canada) ***485***
St. Mary's U of San Antonio (TX) ***494***
Seton Hill U (PA) ***502***
Sierra Nevada Coll (NV) ***504***
Syracuse U (NY) ***521***
Texas Christian U (TX) ***526***
Thomas Coll (ME) ***527***
Thomas Edison State Coll (NJ) ***527***
Trinity Christian Coll (IL) ***530***
U of Baltimore (MD) ***539***
The U of Findlay (OH) ***545***
U of Hartford (CT) ***546***
U of Houston (TX) ***547***
The U of Iowa (IA) ***548***
U of North Texas (TX) ***562***
U of Pennsylvania (PA) ***563***
Western Carolina U (NC) ***598***
Wichita State U (KS) ***604***
Xavier U (OH) ***610***
York U (ON, Canada) ***611***

ENVIRONMENTAL BIOLOGY

Overview: Students who study environmental biology will study the processes of evolution, function, and interactions of communities, species, and ecosystems in a particular environment. *Related majors:* ecology and human ecology, biology, biometrics, wildlife biology, marine biology. *Potential careers:* ecologist, environmentalist, park ranger, research scientist. *Salary potential:* $24k-$30k.

Antioch Coll (OH) ***269***
Arcadia U (PA) ***271***
Bard Coll (NY) ***281***
Beloit Coll (WI) ***285***
Bennington Coll (VT) ***286***
Bethel Coll (IN) ***288***
Bloomfield Coll (NJ) ***290***
Bridgewater State Coll (MA) ***294***
California Polytechnic State U, San Luis Obispo (CA) ***300***
California State U, Northridge (CA) ***301***
Carlow Coll (PA) ***305***
Cedar Crest Coll (PA) ***308***
Cedarville U (OH) ***308***
Central Methodist Coll (MO) ***309***
Chowan Coll (NC) ***312***
Colgate U (NY) ***319***
Coll of the Atlantic (ME) ***323***
Colorado State U-Pueblo (CO) ***325***
Columbia Coll (NY) ***326***
Concordia U (QC, Canada) ***331***
Concordia U Coll of Alberta (AB, Canada) ***331***
Eastern Kentucky U (KY) ***348***
Eastern Washington U (WA) ***349***
The Evergreen State Coll (WA) ***355***
Fort Lewis Coll (CO) ***362***
Framingham State Coll (MA) ***362***
Franklin Pierce Coll (NH) ***364***
Georgia Southwestern State U (GA) ***368***
Grand Canyon U (AZ) ***371***
Greenville Coll (IL) ***373***
Hampshire Coll (MA) ***375***
Harvard U (MA) ***376***
Heidelberg Coll (OH) ***377***
Humboldt State U (CA) ***382***
Iowa Wesleyan Coll (IA) ***390***
Jacksonville State U (AL) ***390***
Lakehead U (ON, Canada) ***400***
Lewis-Clark State Coll (ID) ***406***
Lock Haven U of Pennsylvania (PA) ***408***
Long Island U, Southampton Coll (NY) ***409***
Luther Coll (IA) ***412***
Maharishi U of Management (IA) ***414***
Mansfield U of Pennsylvania (PA) ***416***
Marist Coll (NY) ***417***
Marlboro Coll (VT) ***418***
The Master's Coll and Seminary (CA) ***422***
McGill U (QC, Canada) ***423***
Memorial U of Newfoundland (NF, Canada) ***424***
Midway Coll (KY) ***429***
Minnesota State U, Mankato (MN) ***431***
Mount Union Coll (OH) ***440***
New Mexico Inst of Mining and Technology (NM) ***446***
Nipissing U (ON, Canada) ***448***
Northland Coll (WI) ***452***
Northwest Coll (WA) ***452***
Ohio U (OH) ***458***
Oregon State U (OR) ***462***
Otterbein Coll (OH) ***462***
Pittsburg State U (KS) ***470***
Queens U of Charlotte (NC) ***476***
Sacred Heart U (CT) ***486***
St. Cloud State U (MN) ***488***
Simpson Coll (IA) ***505***
State U of NY Coll at Brockport (NY) ***515***
State U of NY Coll at Cortland (NY) ***516***
State U of NY Coll of Environ Sci and Forestry (NY) ***517***
Suffolk U (MA) ***520***
Tabor Coll (KS) ***522***
Taylor U (IN) ***523***
Trinity Western U (BC, Canada) ***531***
Tulane U (LA) ***533***
Unity Coll (ME) ***535***
U Coll of the Cariboo (BC, Canada) ***537***
U of Alberta (AB, Canada) ***538***
The U of British Columbia (BC, Canada) ***540***
U of Calif, Davis (CA) ***540***
U of Charleston (WV) ***542***
U of Dayton (OH) ***544***
U of Dubuque (IA) ***545***
U of Guelph (ON, Canada) ***546***
U of La Verne (CA) ***549***
U of Nebraska at Omaha (NE) ***557***
U of New England (ME) ***558***
U of Pittsburgh at Greensburg (PA) ***570***
U of Pittsburgh at Johnstown (PA) ***570***
U of Regina (SK, Canada) ***572***
The U of Tampa (FL) ***577***
U of Vermont (VT) ***582***
U of Windsor (ON, Canada) ***584***
Ursuline Coll (OH) ***587***
Western Washington U (WA) ***600***
Westfield State Coll (MA) ***600***
William Penn U (IA) ***606***
Wingate U (NC) ***607***
Winona State U (MN) ***608***
Wittenberg U (OH) ***608***
York U (ON, Canada) ***611***

ENVIRONMENTAL CONTROL TECHNOLOGIES RELATED

Information can be found under this major's main heading.

New York Inst of Technology (NY) ***447***

ENVIRONMENTAL EDUCATION

Overview: Undergraduates study a wide range of subjects (such as pollution, ecosystems, waste and recycling, conservation, human health and water) that prepare them to teach environmental topics at a variety of educational levels. *Related majors:* ecology, environmental biology, human ecology, atmospheric sciences, natural resources conservation. *Potential careers:* science teacher, biology teacher, environmental teacher, museum curator, park ranger. *Salary potential:* $23k-$28k.

Coll of the Atlantic (ME) ***323***
Concordia U (MN) ***330***
The Evergreen State Coll (WA) ***355***
Goddard Coll (VT) ***369***
Johnson State Coll (VT) ***394***
Long Island U, Southampton Coll (NY) ***409***
Long Island U, Southampton Coll, Friends World Program (NY) ***409***
Neumann Coll (PA) ***443***
Northland Coll (WI) ***452***
The Ohio State U (OH) ***457***
Prescott Coll (AZ) ***474***
Slippery Rock U of Pennsylvania (PA) ***506***
Sonoma State U (CA) ***506***
State U of NY Coll of Environ Sci and Forestry (NY) ***517***
Unity Coll (ME) ***535***
U of Maine at Machias (ME) ***551***
The U of Montana–Missoula (MT) ***556***
Western Washington U (WA) ***600***
York U (ON, Canada) ***611***

ENVIRONMENTAL ENGINEERING

Overview: Students learn about controlling indoor living environments as well as how to control the outdoor, natural environment, including pollution, waste and hazardous material management, conservation, etc. *Related majors:* environmental science, occupational and health technologies, chemical engineering, pollution control technology. *Potential careers:* environmental scientist, quality control manager, occupational and health administrator, hazardous waste manager. *Salary potential:* $40k-$52k.

Bradley U (IL) ***293***
California Inst of Technology (CA) ***299***
California Polytechnic State U, San Luis Obispo (CA) ***300***
California State U, Northridge (CA) ***301***
Carleton U (ON, Canada) ***305***
Carnegie Mellon U (PA) ***305***
Christian Brothers U (TN) ***313***
Clarkson U (NY) ***316***
Colorado School of Mines (CO) ***325***
Colorado State U (CO) ***325***
Columbia U, School of Engineering & Applied Sci (NY) ***328***
Concordia U (QC, Canada) ***331***
Cornell U (NY) ***333***
Drexel U (PA) ***346***
Florida State U (FL) ***361***
Gannon U (PA) ***365***
The George Washington U (DC) ***367***
Harvard U (MA) ***376***
Humboldt State U (CA) ***382***
Johns Hopkins U (MD) ***392***
Lafayette Coll (PA) ***400***
Louisiana State U and A&M Coll (LA) ***410***
Manhattan Coll (NY) ***416***
Marquette U (WI) ***418***
Massachusetts Inst of Technology (MA) ***421***
Massachusetts Maritime Academy (MA) ***421***
Mercer U (GA) ***425***
Michigan Technological U (MI) ***428***
Montana Tech of The U of Montana (MT) ***435***
New Jersey Inst of Technology (NJ) ***445***
New Mexico Inst of Mining and Technology (NM) ***446***
North Carolina State U (NC) ***449***
Northern Arizona U (AZ) ***450***
Northwestern U (IL) ***453***
Old Dominion U (VA) ***460***
Oregon State U (OR) ***462***
Penn State U Berks Cmps of Berks-Lehigh Valley Coll (PA) ***468***
Penn State U Harrisburg Campus of the Capital Coll (PA) ***468***
Penn State U Univ Park Campus (PA) ***468***
Rensselaer Polytechnic Inst (NY) ***478***
Rice U (TX) ***479***
Roger Williams U (RI) ***483***
Seattle U (WA) ***501***
South Dakota School of Mines and Technology (SD) ***507***
South Dakota State U (SD) ***507***
Southern Methodist U (TX) ***510***
Stanford U (CA) ***514***
State U of NY Coll of Environ Sci and Forestry (NY) ***517***
Stevens Inst of Technology (NJ) ***519***
Syracuse U (NY) ***521***
Texas A&M U–Kingsville (TX) ***525***
Texas Tech U (TX) ***526***
Tufts U (MA) ***533***
Tulane U (LA) ***533***
United States Air Force Academy (CO) ***534***
United States Military Academy (NY) ***535***
Université Laval (QC, Canada) ***536***
U at Buffalo, The State University of New York (NY) ***536***
U of Alberta (AB, Canada) ***538***
U of Calif, Berkeley (CA) ***540***
U of Calif, Irvine (CA) ***541***
U of Calif, Riverside (CA) ***541***
U of Central Florida (FL) ***542***
U of Colorado at Boulder (CO) ***543***
U of Connecticut (CT) ***544***
U of Delaware (DE) ***544***
U of Florida (FL) ***545***
U of Guelph (ON, Canada) ***546***
U of Hartford (CT) ***546***
The U of Iowa (IA) ***548***
U of Miami (FL) ***553***
U of Michigan (MI) ***554***
U of Nevada, Reno (NV) ***558***
U of New Hampshire (NH) ***558***
U of North Dakota (ND) ***561***
U of Notre Dame (IN) ***562***
U of Oklahoma (OK) ***562***
U of Regina (SK, Canada) ***572***
U of Southern California (CA) ***576***
U of Utah (UT) ***582***
U of Waterloo (ON, Canada) ***583***
U of Windsor (ON, Canada) ***584***
U of Wisconsin–Madison (WI) ***584***
Utah State U (UT) ***587***
Wentworth Inst of Technology (MA) ***597***
Western Michigan U (MI) ***599***
Wilkes U (PA) ***605***
Worcester Polytechnic Inst (MA) ***609***
Yale U (CT) ***610***
Youngstown State U (OH) ***611***

ENVIRONMENTAL HEALTH

Overview: This major focuses on the study of environmental factors affecting human health and prepares students for a career as an environmental health specialist. *Related majors:* environmental science, public health, toxicology, ecology, biomedical sciences. *Potential careers:* environmental health officer, public health administrator, epidemiologist, waste management specialist, CDC investigator. *Salary potential:* $40k-$50k.

Benedict Coll (SC) ***285***
Bowling Green State U (OH) ***292***
British Columbia Inst of Technology (BC, Canada) ***295***
California State U, Northridge (CA) ***301***
California State U, Sacramento (CA) ***301***
Clarkson U (NY) ***316***
Colorado State U (CO) ***325***
Colorado State U-Pueblo (CO) ***325***
Delaware State U (DE) ***338***
East Carolina U (NC) ***347***
East Central U (OK) ***347***
Eastern Kentucky U (KY) ***348***
East Tennessee State U (TN) ***349***
Ferris State U (MI) ***358***
Hampshire Coll (MA) ***375***
Illinois State U (IL) ***384***
Indiana State U (IN) ***385***
Indiana U of Pennsylvania (PA) ***386***
Iowa Wesleyan Coll (IA) ***390***
Missouri Southern State Coll (MO) ***433***
New Mexico State U (NM) ***446***
Oakland U (MI) ***456***
Ohio U (OH) ***458***
Oregon State U (OR) ***462***
Ryerson U (ON, Canada) ***485***
Salisbury U (MD) ***497***
San Jose State U (CA) ***499***
Springfield Coll (MA) ***514***
Texas Southern U (TX) ***526***

U of Arkansas at Little Rock (AR) **539**
U of Georgia (GA) **545**
U of Miami (FL) **553**
U of Michigan–Flint (MI) **554**
The U of North Carolina at Chapel Hill (NC) **560**
U of Southern Maine (ME) **576**
U of Utah (UT) **582**
U of Washington (WA) **583**
U of Wisconsin–Eau Claire (WI) **584**
West Chester U of Pennsylvania (PA) **598**
Western Carolina U (NC) **598**
Wright State U (OH) **609**
York Coll of the City U of New York (NY) **611**

ENVIRONMENTAL SCIENCE

Overview: This major explores the physical environment through the application of biological, chemical, and physical principles and the solutions to environmental problems such as pollution. *Related majors:* ecology, biology, law, biochemistry, public policy. *Potential careers:* environmentalist, ecologist, hazardous waste manager, chemical engineer. *Salary potential:* $25k-$35k.

Abilene Christian U (TX) **260**
Acadia U (NS, Canada) **260**
Adams State Coll (CO) **260**
Adrian Coll (MI) **260**
Alaska Pacific U (AK) **261**
Albion Coll (MI) **262**
Albright Coll (PA) **263**
Alderson-Broaddus Coll (WV) **263**
Alfred U (NY) **263**
Allegheny Coll (PA) **264**
Alliant International U (CA) **264**
Alverno Coll (WI) **265**
American U (DC) **267**
Antioch Coll (OH) **269**
Aquinas Coll (MI) **270**
Ashland U (OH) **274**
Assumption Coll (MA) **275**
Auburn U (AL) **276**
Augustana Coll (IL) **276**
Aurora U (IL) **277**
Averett U (VA) **278**
Baldwin-Wallace Coll (OH) **280**
Ball State U (IN) **280**
Bard Coll (NY) **281**
Barnard Coll (NY) **282**
Barton Coll (NC) **282**
Bates Coll (ME) **282**
Bayamón Central U (PR) **283**
Baylor U (TX) **283**
Bellevue U (NE) **284**
Beloit Coll (WI) **285**
Bemidji State U (MN) **285**
Benedictine U (IL) **285**
Bennington Coll (VT) **286**
Berry Coll (GA) **287**
Bethany Coll (WV) **287**
Bethel Coll (MN) **288**
Black Hills State U (SD) **290**
Boston Coll (MA) **292**
Boston U (MA) **292**
Bowdoin Coll (ME) **292**
Brenau U (GA) **293**
Brevard Coll (NC) **294**
Briar Cliff U (IA) **294**
Brock U (ON, Canada) **295**
Brown U (RI) **296**
Bucknell U (PA) **297**
Cabrini Coll (PA) **298**
California State U, Chico (CA) **300**
California State U, Hayward (CA) **301**
California State U, San Bernardino (CA) **302**
California U of Pennsylvania (PA) **302**
Calvin Coll (MI) **303**
Cameron U (OK) **303**
Canisius Coll (NY) **304**
Capital U (OH) **304**
Carleton U (ON, Canada) **305**
Carroll Coll (MT) **306**
Carroll Coll (WI) **306**
Carthage Coll (WI) **306**
Case Western Reserve U (OH) **307**
Castleton State Coll (VT) **307**
Catawba Coll (NC) **307**
Cedar Crest Coll (PA) **308**
Centenary Coll of Louisiana (LA) **308**
Central Coll (IA) **309**
Central Methodist Coll (MO) **309**
Central Michigan U (MI) **310**
Chapman U (CA) **311**
Charleston Southern U (SC) **311**
Chatham Coll (PA) **312**
Chestnut Hill Coll (PA) **312**
Christopher Newport U (VA) **313**
Claremont McKenna Coll (CA) **315**
Clarion U of Pennsylvania (PA) **315**
Clarkson U (NY) **316**
Clark U (MA) **316**
Cleveland State U (OH) **317**
Coe Coll (IA) **318**
Colby Coll (ME) **318**
Colby-Sawyer Coll (NH) **319**
Colgate U (NY) **319**
The Coll of Saint Rose (NY) **322**
Coll of Santa Fe (NM) **323**
Coll of the Atlantic (ME) **323**
Coll of the Holy Cross (MA) **323**
Coll of the Southwest (NM) **324**
The Coll of William and Mary (VA) **324**
The Colorado Coll (CO) **325**
Columbia Coll (NY) **326**
Columbia Southern U (AL) **327**
Concordia Coll (MN) **329**
Concordia U (IL) **330**
Concordia U (MN) **330**
Concordia U (OR) **330**
Concordia U (QC, Canada) **331**
Concordia U at Austin (TX) **331**
Cornell Coll (IA) **332**
Cornell U (NY) **333**
Creighton U (NE) **333**
Curry Coll (MA) **335**
Dana Coll (NE) **337**
Dartmouth Coll (NH) **337**
Davis & Elkins Coll (WV) **338**
Defiance Coll (OH) **338**
Delaware Valley Coll (PA) **339**
Denison U (OH) **339**
DePaul U (IL) **339**
DeSales U (PA) **340**
Dickinson Coll (PA) **344**
Dickinson State U (ND) **344**
Doane Coll (NE) **344**
Dominican Coll (NY) **344**
Dominican U (IL) **345**
Dominican U of California (CA) **345**
Dordt Coll (IA) **345**
Drake U (IA) **345**
Drexel U (PA) **346**
Drury U (MO) **346**
Duke U (NC) **346**
Duquesne U (PA) **346**
Earlham Coll (IN) **347**
East Central U (OK) **347**
Eastern Kentucky U (KY) **348**
Eastern Mennonite U (VA) **348**
Eastern U (PA) **349**
Eckerd Coll (FL) **350**
Edinboro U of Pennsylvania (PA) **351**
Elizabethtown Coll (PA) **351**
Elmhurst Coll (IL) **351**
Elmira Coll (NY) **351**
Elon U (NC) **352**
Emory & Henry Coll (VA) **353**
The Evergreen State Coll (WA) **355**
Fairleigh Dickinson U, Teaneck-Metro Campus (NJ) **356**
Felician Coll (NJ) **357**
Ferrum Coll (VA) **358**
Fitchburg State Coll (MA) **358**
Florida Inst of Technology (FL) **360**
Florida International U (FL) **360**
Florida Southern Coll (FL) **361**
Florida State U (FL) **361**
Framingham State Coll (MA) **362**
Franklin Pierce Coll (NH) **364**
Frostburg State U (MD) **365**
Furman U (SC) **365**
Georgetown Coll (KY) **366**
The George Washington U (DC) **367**
Gettysburg Coll (PA) **368**
Goddard Coll (VT) **369**
Goshen Coll (IN) **370**
Green Mountain Coll (VT) **372**
Grinnell Coll (IA) **373**
Guilford Coll (NC) **373**
Gustavus Adolphus Coll (MN) **374**
Hamline U (MN) **374**
Hampshire Coll (MA) **375**
Hampton U (VA) **375**
Harvard U (MA) **376**
Hawai'i Pacific U (HI) **377**
Hiram Coll (OH) **379**
Hobart and William Smith Colls (NY) **380**
Hofstra U (NY) **380**
Hood Coll (MD) **381**
Hope Coll (MI) **381**
Humboldt State U (CA) **382**
Huntingdon Coll (AL) **383**
Illinois Coll (IL) **384**
Indiana U Bloomington (IN) **385**
Indiana U of Pennsylvania (PA) **386**
Inter American U of PR, San Germán Campus (PR) **388**
Iowa State U of Science and Technology (IA) **390**
Ithaca Coll (NY) **390**
Jacksonville U (FL) **391**
John Brown U (AR) **392**
John Carroll U (OH) **392**
Johns Hopkins U (MD) **392**
Johnson State Coll (VT) **394**
Juniata Coll (PA) **395**
Keene State Coll (NH) **396**
Kentucky Wesleyan Coll (KY) **397**
Kenyon Coll (OH) **398**
Kettering U (MI) **398**
King's Coll (PA) **398**
The King's U Coll (AB, Canada) **399**
Knox Coll (IL) **399**
Kutztown U of Pennsylvania (PA) **399**
Lake Erie Coll (OH) **400**
Lake Forest Coll (IL) **400**
Lakehead U (ON, Canada) **400**
Lamar U (TX) **401**
Lander U (SC) **401**
La Salle U (PA) **402**
Lawrence U (WI) **403**
Lees-McRae Coll (NC) **404**
Lehigh U (PA) **404**
Lenoir-Rhyne Coll (NC) **405**
Lewis & Clark Coll (OR) **405**
Lewis U (IL) **406**
Lincoln Memorial U (TN) **407**
Lipscomb U (TN) **408**
Long Island U, C.W. Post Campus (NY) **409**
Long Island U, Southampton Coll (NY) **409**
Long Island U, Southampton Coll, Friends World Program (NY) **409**
Longwood U (VA) **409**
Louisiana State U and A&M Coll (LA) **410**
Louisiana State U in Shreveport (LA) **410**
Louisiana Tech U (LA) **410**
Loyola U Chicago (IL) **411**
Lynchburg Coll (VA) **413**
Lynn U (FL) **413**
Lyon Coll (AR) **413**
Macalester Coll (MN) **413**
Maharishi U of Management (IA) **414**
Manchester Coll (IN) **415**
Mansfield U of Pennsylvania (PA) **416**
Marian Coll of Fond du Lac (WI) **417**
Marietta Coll (OH) **417**
Marist Coll (NY) **417**
Marlboro Coll (VT) **418**
Marshall U (WV) **418**
Marygrove Coll (MI) **419**
Marymount U (VA) **420**
Maryville Coll (TN) **420**
Maryville U of Saint Louis (MO) **420**
Mary Washington Coll (VA) **420**
Marywood U (PA) **421**
Massachusetts Coll of Liberal Arts (MA) **421**
Massachusetts Inst of Technology (MA) **421**
Massachusetts Maritime Academy (MA) **421**
McGill U (QC, Canada) **423**
McMaster U (ON, Canada) **423**
McMurry U (TX) **423**
McNeese State U (LA) **423**
McPherson Coll (KS) **423**
Medgar Evers Coll of the City U of NY (NY) **424**
Memorial U of Newfoundland (NF, Canada) **424**
Mercer U (GA) **425**
Meredith Coll (NC) **426**
Merrimack Coll (MA) **426**
Messiah Coll (PA) **426**
Metropolitan State Coll of Denver (CO) **427**
Middlebury Coll (VT) **429**
Midland Lutheran Coll (NE) **429**
Midwestern State U (TX) **430**
Mills Coll (CA) **431**
Minnesota State U, Mankato (MN) **431**
Molloy Coll (NY) **433**
Monmouth Coll (IL) **434**
Montana State U–Billings (MT) **434**
Montana State U–Bozeman (MT) **434**
Montclair State U (NJ) **435**
Montreat Coll (NC) **435**
Mount Allison U (NB, Canada) **437**
Mount Holyoke Coll (MA) **438**
Mount Marty Coll (SD) **438**
Mount Olive Coll (NC) **439**
Muhlenberg Coll (PA) **440**
Muskingum Coll (OH) **441**
Naropa U (CO) **441**
Nazareth Coll of Rochester (NY) **443**
New Coll of Florida (FL) **444**
New England Coll (NH) **444**
New Jersey Inst of Technology (NJ) **445**
New Mexico Highlands U (NM) **446**
New Mexico Inst of Mining and Technology (NM) **446**
New Mexico State U (NM) **446**
Nipissing U (ON, Canada) **448**
North Carolina Central U (NC) **448**
North Carolina State U (NC) **449**
North Carolina Wesleyan Coll (NC) **449**
Northeastern Illinois U (IL) **450**
Northeastern U (MA) **450**
Northern Arizona U (AZ) **450**
Northern Kentucky U (KY) **451**
Northern Michigan U (MI) **451**
Northern State U (SD) **451**
Northland Coll (WI) **452**
Northwestern Coll (IA) **453**
Northwestern U (IL) **453**
Norwich U (VT) **455**
Notre Dame Coll (OH) **455**
Oberlin Coll (OH) **456**
Occidental Coll (CA) **457**
Ohio Northern U (OH) **457**
The Ohio State U (OH) **457**
Ohio Wesleyan U (OH) **459**
Oklahoma State U (OK) **460**
Olivet Coll (MI) **461**
Olivet Nazarene U (IL) **461**
Oregon Inst of Technology (OR) **461**
Oregon State U (OR) **462**
Pacific Lutheran U (WA) **463**
Pacific U (OR) **464**
Paul Smith's Coll of Arts and Sciences (NY) **466**
Penn State U Altoona Coll (PA) **467**
Pfeiffer U (NC) **469**
Piedmont Coll (GA) **470**
Pittsburg State U (KS) **470**
Pitzer Coll (CA) **471**
Plattsburgh State U of NY (NY) **471**
Point Park Coll (PA) **471**
Pomona Coll (CA) **472**
Pontifical Catholic U of Puerto Rico (PR) **472**
Portland State U (OR) **472**
Prescott Coll (AZ) **474**
Principia Coll (IL) **474**
Providence Coll (RI) **474**
Purchase Coll, State U of NY (NY) **475**
Queens Coll of the City U of NY (NY) **475**
Queen's U at Kingston (ON, Canada) **476**
Quincy U (IL) **476**
Ramapo Coll of New Jersey (NJ) **477**
Randolph-Macon Coll (VA) **477**
Randolph-Macon Woman's Coll (VA) **477**
Regis U (CO) **478**
Rensselaer Polytechnic Inst (NY) **478**
The Richard Stockton Coll of New Jersey (NJ) **479**
Richmond, The American International U in London(United Kingdom) **480**
Rider U (NJ) **480**
Ripon Coll (WI) **480**
Roanoke Coll (VA) **481**
Rochester Inst of Technology (NY) **482**
Rocky Mountain Coll (MT) **482**
Roger Williams U (RI) **483**
Rollins Coll (FL) **483**
Roosevelt U (IL) **483**
Royal Roads U (BC, Canada) **484**
Rutgers, The State U of New Jersey, Newark (NJ) **485**
Rutgers, The State U of New Jersey, New Brunswick (NJ) **485**
Sacred Heart U (CT) **486**

ENVIRONMENTAL SCIENCE (continued)

Saint Anselm Coll (NH) **487**
St. Bonaventure U (NY) **487**
Saint Francis U (PA) **488**
St. Francis Xavier U (NS, Canada) **489**
Saint Joseph Coll (CT) **490**
Saint Joseph's Coll (IN) **490**
Saint Joseph's Coll of Maine (ME) **491**
Saint Joseph's U (PA) **491**
St. Lawrence U (NY) **491**
Saint Leo U (FL) **492**
Saint Louis U (MO) **492**
Saint Mary's Coll of Madonna U (MI) **493**
Saint Michael's Coll (VT) **494**
Saint Vincent Coll (PA) **496**
Salem International U (WV) **496**
Samford U (AL) **497**
Sam Houston State U (TX) **497**
San Diego State U (CA) **498**
San Jose State U (CA) **499**
Sarah Lawrence Coll (NY) **499**
Savannah State U (GA) **499**
Scripps Coll (CA) **501**
Seattle U (WA) **501**
Shaw U (NC) **502**
Shenandoah U (VA) **503**
Shepherd Coll (WV) **503**
Shippensburg U of Pennsylvania (PA) **503**
Shorter Coll (GA) **504**
Siena Coll (NY) **504**
Sierra Nevada Coll (NV) **504**
Simmons Coll (MA) **504**
Simon Fraser U (BC, Canada) **505**
Simon's Rock Coll of Bard (MA) **505**
Slippery Rock U of Pennsylvania (PA) **506**
Sonoma State U (CA) **506**
Southeastern Oklahoma State U (OK) **508**
Southeast Missouri State U (MO) **508**
Southern Methodist U (TX) **510**
Southern Nazarene U (OK) **510**
Southern Oregon U (OR) **510**
Southern Vermont Coll (VT) **511**
Southwest State U (MN) **513**
Southwest Texas State U (TX) **513**
Spelman Coll (GA) **514**
Springfield Coll (MA) **514**
Spring Hill Coll (AL) **514**
Stanford U (CA) **514**
State U of NY at Binghamton (NY) **515**
State U of NY at New Paltz (NY) **515**
State U of NY Coll at Brockport (NY) **515**
State U of NY Coll at Fredonia (NY) **516**
State U of NY Coll at Oneonta (NY) **517**
State U of NY Coll of A&T at Cobleskill (NY) **517**
State U of NY Coll of Environ Sci and Forestry (NY) **517**
State U of NY Maritime Coll (NY) **518**
State U of West Georgia (GA) **518**
Stephen F. Austin State U (TX) **518**
Stephens Coll (MO) **519**
Sterling Coll (VT) **519**
Stetson U (FL) **519**
Stony Brook U, State University of New York (NY) **520**
Suffolk U (MA) **520**
Sul Ross State U (TX) **521**
Sweet Briar Coll (VA) **521**
Syracuse U (NY) **521**
Taylor U (IN) **523**
Teikyo Post U (CT) **523**
Texas A&M U (TX) **524**
Texas A&M U–Corpus Christi (TX) **525**
Texas Christian U (TX) **526**
Thiel Coll (PA) **527**
Thomas Edison State Coll (NJ) **527**
Trent U (ON, Canada) **529**
Trinity Coll (DC) **530**
Trinity Western U (BC, Canada) **531**
Tri-State U (IN) **532**
Tufts U (MA) **533**
Tulane U (LA) **533**
Tusculum Coll (TN) **533**
Tuskegee U (AL) **533**
United States Military Academy (NY) **535**
Unity Coll (ME) **535**
Université Laval (QC, Canada) **536**
U of Alaska Southeast (AK) **538**
U of Alberta (AB, Canada) **538**
The U of Arizona (AZ) **538**
The U of British Columbia (BC, Canada) **540**
U of Calgary (AB, Canada) **540**
U of Calif, Berkeley (CA) **540**
U of Calif, Riverside (CA) **541**
U of Calif, San Diego (CA) **541**
U of Calif, Santa Barbara (CA) **541**
U of Calif, Santa Cruz (CA) **542**
U of Central Arkansas (AR) **542**
U of Charleston (WV) **542**
U of Chicago (IL) **542**
U of Colorado at Boulder (CO) **543**
U of Connecticut (CT) **544**
U of Dayton (OH) **544**
U of Delaware (DE) **544**
U of Denver (CO) **544**
U of Dubuque (IA) **545**
U of Evansville (IN) **545**
The U of Findlay (OH) **545**
U of Florida (FL) **545**
U of Guelph (ON, Canada) **546**
U of Houston–Clear Lake (TX) **547**
U of Idaho (ID) **547**
U of Illinois at Urbana–Champaign (IL) **548**
U of Indianapolis (IN) **548**
The U of Iowa (IA) **548**
The U of Lethbridge (AB, Canada) **549**
U of Maine at Farmington (ME) **550**
U of Maine at Fort Kent (ME) **551**
U of Maine at Machias (ME) **551**
U of Maine at Presque Isle (ME) **551**
U of Manitoba (MB, Canada) **551**
U of Maryland, Baltimore County (MD) **552**
U of Maryland, Coll Park (MD) **552**
U of Maryland Eastern Shore (MD) **552**
U of Maryland University Coll (MD) **552**
U of Massachusetts Amherst (MA) **552**
U of Miami (FL) **553**
U of Michigan (MI) **554**
U of Michigan–Dearborn (MI) **554**
U of Michigan–Flint (MI) **554**
U of Minnesota, Crookston (MN) **554**
U of Minnesota, Duluth (MN) **554**
U of Minnesota, Twin Cities Campus (MN) **555**
U of Mobile (AL) **556**
The U of Montana–Missoula (MT) **556**
The U of Montana–Western (MT) **556**
U of Nebraska–Lincoln (NE) **557**
U of Nevada, Las Vegas (NV) **558**
U of New England (ME) **558**
U of New Hampshire (NH) **558**
U of New Haven (CT) **559**
The U of North Carolina at Asheville (NC) **559**
The U of North Carolina at Chapel Hill (NC) **560**
The U of North Carolina at Wilmington (NC) **561**
U of Northern Iowa (IA) **561**
U of Notre Dame (IN) **562**
U of Oklahoma (OK) **562**
U of Oregon (OR) **562**
U of Ottawa (ON, Canada) **563**
U of Pittsburgh at Bradford (PA) **569**
U of Pittsburgh at Johnstown (PA) **570**
U of Portland (OR) **570**
U of Puerto Rico, Río Piedras (PR) **571**
U of Redlands (CA) **572**
U of Rhode Island (RI) **572**
U of Richmond (VA) **572**
U of Rochester (NY) **573**
U of St. Francis (IL) **573**
U of Saint Francis (IN) **573**
U of St. Thomas (MN) **573**
U of St. Thomas (TX) **573**
U of San Francisco (CA) **574**
U of Saskatchewan (SK, Canada) **574**
The U of Scranton (PA) **574**
U of Southern California (CA) **576**
U of Southern Maine (ME) **576**
U of South Florida (FL) **576**
The U of Tampa (FL) **577**
The U of Tennessee at Chattanooga (TN) **577**
The U of Tennessee at Martin (TN) **577**
The U of Texas of the Permian Basin (TX) **579**
U of the District of Columbia (DC) **580**
U of the Incarnate Word (TX) **580**
U of the Ozarks (AR) **580**
U of the Pacific (CA) **580**
U of the Sciences in Philadelphia (PA) **580**
U of the South (TN) **581**
U of Toledo (OH) **581**
U of Toronto (ON, Canada) **581**
U of Tulsa (OK) **581**
U of Utah (UT) **582**
U of Vermont (VT) **582**
U of Victoria (BC, Canada) **582**
U of Virginia (VA) **582**
The U of Virginia's Coll at Wise (VA) **582**
U of Washington (WA) **583**
U of Waterloo (ON, Canada) **583**
The U of Western Ontario (ON, Canada) **583**
U of West Florida (FL) **583**
U of Windsor (ON, Canada) **584**
U of Wisconsin–Green Bay (WI) **584**
U of Wisconsin–River Falls (WI) **585**
U of Wyoming (WY) **586**
Ursinus Coll (PA) **587**
Valdosta State U (GA) **588**
Valparaiso U (IN) **588**
Vassar Coll (NY) **589**
Villa Julie Coll (MD) **590**
Virginia Intermont Coll (VA) **590**
Virginia Polytechnic Inst and State U (VA) **591**
Virginia Wesleyan Coll (VA) **591**
Walla Walla Coll (WA) **593**
Warren Wilson Coll (NC) **594**
Washington Coll (MD) **594**
Washington State U (WA) **595**
Washington U in St. Louis (MO) **595**
Waynesburg Coll (PA) **595**
Webster U (MO) **597**
Wellesley Coll (MA) **597**
Wells Coll (NY) **597**
Wesleyan U (CT) **597**
Wesley Coll (DE) **598**
West Chester U of Pennsylvania (PA) **598**
Western Connecticut State U (CT) **598**
Western Michigan U (MI) **599**
Western New England Coll (MA) **600**
Western State Coll of Colorado (CO) **600**
Western Washington U (WA) **600**
Westminster Coll (MO) **601**
Westminster Coll (PA) **601**
West Texas A&M U (TX) **602**
West Virginia U (WV) **602**
Wheaton Coll (IL) **603**
Wheaton Coll (MA) **603**
Wheeling Jesuit U (WV) **603**
Whitman Coll (WA) **604**
Widener U (PA) **604**
Willamette U (OR) **605**
William Paterson U of New Jersey (NJ) **606**
Wilson Coll (PA) **607**
Wittenberg U (OH) **608**
Worcester Polytechnic Inst (MA) **609**
Xavier U (OH) **610**
Xavier U of Louisiana (LA) **610**
Yale U (CT) **610**
York U (ON, Canada) **611**
Youngstown State U (OH) **611**

ENVIRONMENTAL TECHNOLOGY

Overview: Students interested in working with and assisting engineers and other specialists who are engaged in indoor and outdoor environmental pollution control systems will want to consider this major. *Related majors:* industrial/manufacturing technology, occupational safety and health technology, atmospheric sciences, ecology, environmental health. *Potential careers:* ecologist, environmental researcher, pollution control analyst or inspector. *Salary potential:* $22k-$35k.

Arizona State U East (AZ) **271**
British Columbia Inst of Technology (BC, Canada) **295**
California State U, Long Beach (CA) **301**
East Carolina U (NC) **347**
Middle Tennessee State U (TN) **429**
New York Inst of Technology (NY) **447**
San Jose State U (CA) **499**
Shawnee State U (OH) **502**
Texas Southern U (TX) **526**
Unity Coll (ME) **535**
U of Delaware (DE) **544**
U of Guelph (ON, Canada) **546**
U of North Dakota (ND) **561**
Western Kentucky U (KY) **599**

EQUESTRIAN STUDIES

Overview: This major teaches students about horses, horsemanship, the care and management of horses, and horse equipment. *Related majors:* genetics, animal sciences, feed and grain science, biology. *Potential careers:* horse breeder, manager, trainer, veterinarian, paddock manager. *Salary potential:* $17k-$30k.

Averett U (VA) **278**
Cazenovia Coll (NY) **308**
Centenary Coll (NJ) **308**
Colorado State U (CO) **325**
Delaware Valley Coll (PA) **339**
Johnson & Wales U (RI) **393**
Lake Erie Coll (OH) **400**
Midway Coll (KY) **429**
Mount Ida Coll (MA) **438**
National American U (SD) **442**
North Dakota State U (ND) **449**
Oregon State U (OR) **462**
Otterbein Coll (OH) **462**
Rocky Mountain Coll (MT) **482**
St. Andrews Presbyterian Coll (NC) **487**
Saint Mary-of-the-Woods Coll (IN) **493**
Salem International U (WV) **496**
Stephens Coll (MO) **519**
Sul Ross State U (TX) **521**
Teikyo Post U (CT) **523**
Truman State U (MO) **532**
The U of Findlay (OH) **545**
U of Louisville (KY) **550**
U of Minnesota, Crookston (MN) **554**
U of New Hampshire (NH) **558**
U of Wisconsin–River Falls (WI) **585**
Virginia Intermont Coll (VA) **590**
West Texas A&M U (TX) **602**
William Woods U (MO) **607**

ETHNIC/CULTURAL STUDIES RELATED

Information can be found under this major's main heading.

Boston U (MA) **292**
The Colorado Coll (CO) **325**
Connecticut Coll (CT) **331**
Metropolitan State U (MN) **427**
St. Olaf Coll (MN) **495**
U of Hawaii at Manoa (HI) **546**
U of Pittsburgh (PA) **569**
The U of Texas at Austin (TX) **578**
The U of Texas at Dallas (TX) **578**
Washington U in St. Louis (MO) **595**
Wellesley Coll (MA) **597**
Yale U (CT) **610**

EUROPEAN HISTORY

Overview: Students will study the development of the cultures, societies, and peoples of the European continent, from its origins to the present day. *Related majors:* comparative and English literature, art history, criticism and conservation, Medieval and Renaissance studies, history and philosophy of science and technology. *Potential careers:* journalist, history teacher, attorney, anthropologist, diplomatic aide. *Salary potential:* $25k-$35k.

Bard Coll (NY) **281**
Calvin Coll (MI) **303**
Pitzer Coll (CA) **471**
U of Calif, Santa Cruz (CA) **542**
U of Puerto Rico, Río Piedras (PR) **571**

EUROPEAN STUDIES

Overview: This major teaches students about the history, society, politics, culture, and economics of the peoples of the European continent, including the study of European migration. *Related majors:* European history, art history, philosophy, political thought, economics. *Potential careers:* business consultant, economist, journalist, art historian, urban planner. *Salary potential:* $25k-$30k.

American U (DC) ***267***
The American U of Paris(France) ***268***
Amherst Coll (MA) ***268***
Antioch Coll (OH) ***269***
Bard Coll (NY) ***281***
Barnard Coll (NY) ***282***
Beloit Coll (WI) ***285***
Bennington Coll (VT) ***286***
Brandeis U (MA) ***293***
Brigham Young U (UT) ***295***
Brock U (ON, Canada) ***295***
Canisius Coll (NY) ***304***
Carleton U (ON, Canada) ***305***
Carnegie Mellon U (PA) ***305***
Case Western Reserve U (OH) ***307***
Central Michigan U (MI) ***310***
Chapman U (CA) ***311***
Claremont McKenna Coll (CA) ***315***
The Coll of William and Mary (VA) ***324***
The Coll of Wooster (OH) ***324***
Cornell U (NY) ***333***
Elmira Coll (NY) ***351***
The Evergreen State Coll (WA) ***355***
Fort Lewis Coll (CO) ***362***
Franklin Coll Switzerland(Switzerland) ***364***
Georgetown Coll (KY) ***366***
The George Washington U (DC) ***367***
Grace U (NE) ***371***
Hamline U (MN) ***374***
Hampshire Coll (MA) ***375***
Harvard U (MA) ***376***
Hillsdale Coll (MI) ***379***
Hobart and William Smith Colls (NY) ***380***
Howard Payne U (TX) ***382***
Huntingdon Coll (AL) ***383***
Illinois Wesleyan U (IL) ***385***
Lake Forest Coll (IL) ***400***
Long Island U, Southampton Coll, Friends World Program (NY) ***409***
Loyola Marymount U (CA) ***411***
Marlboro Coll (VT) ***418***
Millsaps Coll (MS) ***431***
Mount Holyoke Coll (MA) ***438***
New York U (NY) ***447***
Ohio U (OH) ***458***
Pitzer Coll (CA) ***471***
Richmond, The American International U in London(United Kingdom) ***480***
Salem State Coll (MA) ***497***
San Diego State U (CA) ***498***
San Jose State U (CA) ***499***
Sarah Lawrence Coll (NY) ***499***
Scripps Coll (CA) ***501***
Seattle Pacific U (WA) ***501***
Simon's Rock Coll of Bard (MA) ***505***
Southern Methodist U (TX) ***510***
Southwest Texas State U (TX) ***513***
State U of NY Coll at Brockport (NY) ***515***
Sweet Briar Coll (VA) ***521***
Trinity U (TX) ***531***
United States Military Academy (NY) ***535***
U of Calif, Los Angeles (CA) ***541***
U of Guelph (ON, Canada) ***546***
U of Hawaii–West Oahu (HI) ***546***
U of Kansas (KS) ***549***
U of Michigan (MI) ***554***
U of Minnesota, Morris (MN) ***555***
U of Minnesota, Twin Cities Campus (MN) ***555***
U of New Mexico (NM) ***559***
The U of North Carolina at Greensboro (NC) ***560***
U of Northern Iowa (IA) ***561***
U of Richmond (VA) ***572***
U of South Carolina (SC) ***575***
U of the South (TN) ***581***
U of Toledo (OH) ***581***
U of Toronto (ON, Canada) ***581***
U of Vermont (VT) ***582***
U of Washington (WA) ***583***
Valparaiso U (IN) ***588***
Vanderbilt U (TN) ***588***
Washington U in St. Louis (MO) ***595***
Western Michigan U (MI) ***599***

EVOLUTIONARY BIOLOGY

Overview: In this major students study the genetic and theoretical principles of how organisms mutate over time. *Related majors:* genetics, cell biology, physiology, mathematics, computer science. *Potential careers:* geneticist, veterinarian, biologist, ecologist, research scientist. *Salary potential:* $25k-$33k.

Case Western Reserve U (OH) ***307***
Coll of the Atlantic (ME) ***323***
Dartmouth Coll (NH) ***337***
Florida State U (FL) ***361***
Hampshire Coll (MA) ***375***
Harvard U (MA) ***376***
Oregon State U (OR) ***462***
Rice U (TX) ***479***
Rutgers, The State U of New Jersey, New Brunswick (NJ) ***485***
San Diego State U (CA) ***498***
Tulane U (LA) ***533***
The U of Arizona (AZ) ***538***
U of New Hampshire (NH) ***558***
U of Rochester (NY) ***573***
Yale U (CT) ***610***

EXECUTIVE ASSISTANT

Overview: Similar to the major for administrative assistant, this major teaches students additional skills they need in order to work as special assistants or secretaries for top management executives. *Related majors:* business communication, public relations, law and legal studies, accounting, word processing. *Potential careers:* executive assistant. This major enables students to enter into a wide variety of fields such as finance and accounting, non-profit, governmental, media, education. *Salary potential:* $27k-$33k.

Cumberland Coll (KY) ***335***
Eastern Michigan U (MI) ***348***
Youngstown State U (OH) ***611***

EXERCISE SCIENCES

Overview: Students will learn about the science of exercise, including the anatomy, biochemistry, and biophysics of human movement as well as applications to physical therapies. *Related majors:* anatomy, biochemistry, biophysics, physical therapy, athletic training/sports medicine. *Potential careers:* physician, sports doctor, athletic trainer, physical therapist. *Salary potential:* $25k-$37k.

Abilene Christian U (TX) ***260***
Acadia U (NS, Canada) ***260***
Adams State Coll (CO) ***260***
Adrian Coll (MI) ***260***
Albertson Coll of Idaho (ID) ***262***
Alma Coll (MI) ***264***
Andrews U (MI) ***269***
Arizona State U (AZ) ***271***
Arkansas State U (AR) ***272***
Augustana Coll (SD) ***276***
Avila U (MO) ***278***
Ball State U (IN) ***280***
Barry U (FL) ***282***
Bastyr U (WA) ***282***
Becker Coll (MA) ***283***
Bethel Coll (IN) ***288***
Biola U (CA) ***289***
Bloomsburg U of Pennsylvania (PA) ***290***
Bluefield Coll (VA) ***291***
Bluffton Coll (OH) ***291***
Boston U (MA) ***292***
Bowling Green State U (OH) ***292***
Brevard Coll (NC) ***294***
Bridgewater Coll (VA) ***294***
Bridgewater State Coll (MA) ***294***
Brock U (ON, Canada) ***295***
Cabrini Coll (PA) ***298***
California Baptist U (CA) ***298***
California State U, Chico (CA) ***300***
California State U, Hayward (CA) ***301***
California State U, Long Beach (CA) ***301***
Calvin Coll (MI) ***303***
Carroll Coll (WI) ***306***
Carson-Newman Coll (TN) ***306***
Castleton State Coll (VT) ***307***
Central Coll (IA) ***309***
Central Washington U (WA) ***310***
Chapman U (CA) ***311***
Chowan Coll (NC) ***312***
Coker Coll (SC) ***318***
Colby-Sawyer Coll (NH) ***319***
Coll of Mount Saint Vincent (NY) ***320***
The Coll of St. Scholastica (MN) ***322***
Colorado State U (CO) ***325***
Colorado State U-Pueblo (CO) ***325***
Columbia Union Coll (MD) ***328***
Columbus State U (GA) ***328***
Concordia Coll (MN) ***329***
Concordia U (CA) ***330***
Concordia U (IL) ***330***
Concordia U (NE) ***330***
Concordia U (QC, Canada) ***331***
Cornell Coll (IA) ***332***
Creighton U (NE) ***333***
Dakota State U (SD) ***335***
Dalhousie U (NS, Canada) ***336***
Davis & Elkins Coll (WV) ***338***
Defiance Coll (OH) ***338***
Dordt Coll (IA) ***345***
Drury U (MO) ***346***
East Carolina U (NC) ***347***
Eastern Kentucky U (KY) ***348***
Eastern Washington U (WA) ***349***
East Stroudsburg U of Pennsylvania (PA) ***349***
Elmhurst Coll (IL) ***351***
Emmanuel Coll (GA) ***353***
Eureka Coll (IL) ***355***
Fitchburg State Coll (MA) ***358***
Florida Atlantic U (FL) ***359***
Florida International U (FL) ***360***
Frostburg State U (MD) ***365***
Furman U (SC) ***365***
The George Washington U (DC) ***367***
Georgia Southern U (GA) ***367***
Gonzaga U (WA) ***369***
Gordon Coll (MA) ***370***
Grand Canyon U (AZ) ***371***
Guilford Coll (NC) ***373***
Hamline U (MN) ***374***
Hampshire Coll (MA) ***375***
Harding U (AR) ***375***
Hardin-Simmons U (TX) ***376***
High Point U (NC) ***379***
Hofstra U (NY) ***380***
Hope Coll (MI) ***381***
Houston Baptist U (TX) ***382***
Howard Payne U (TX) ***382***
Humboldt State U (CA) ***382***
Huntingdon Coll (AL) ***383***
Huntington Coll (IN) ***383***
Indiana Wesleyan U (IN) ***387***
Inter American U of PR, San Germán Campus (PR) ***388***
Iowa Wesleyan Coll (IA) ***390***
Ithaca Coll (NY) ***390***
Jacksonville State U (AL) ***390***
John Brown U (AR) ***392***
Johnson State Coll (VT) ***394***
Judson Coll (AL) ***395***
Kansas State U (KS) ***396***
Kennesaw State U (GA) ***397***
Kent State U (OH) ***397***
Lakeland Coll (WI) ***401***
Lander U (SC) ***401***
Lasell Coll (MA) ***402***
La Sierra U (CA) ***403***
Laurentian U (ON, Canada) ***403***
Lenoir-Rhyne Coll (NC) ***405***
Lewis-Clark State Coll (ID) ***406***
Liberty U (VA) ***406***
Linfield Coll (OR) ***408***
Lipscomb U (TN) ***408***
Longwood U (VA) ***409***
Loras Coll (IA) ***410***
Louisiana Coll (LA) ***410***
Lynchburg Coll (VA) ***413***
Malone Coll (OH) ***415***
Marquette U (WI) ***418***
McDaniel Coll (MD) ***422***
McGill U (QC, Canada) ***423***
McMaster U (ON, Canada) ***423***
Memorial U of Newfoundland (NF, Canada) ***424***
Meredith Coll (NC) ***426***
Mesa State Coll (CO) ***426***
Messiah Coll (PA) ***426***
Metropolitan State Coll of Denver (CO) ***427***
Miami U (OH) ***428***
MidAmerica Nazarene U (KS) ***428***
Midwestern State U (TX) ***430***
Milligan Coll (TN) ***430***
Missouri Southern State Coll (MO) ***433***
Missouri Western State Coll (MO) ***433***
Montclair State U (NJ) ***435***
Mount Union Coll (OH) ***440***
Mount Vernon Nazarene U (OH) ***440***
Murray State U (KY) ***440***
Nebraska Wesleyan U (NE) ***443***
Norfolk State U (VA) ***448***
North Central Coll (IL) ***449***
Northern Arizona U (AZ) ***450***
Northern Kentucky U (KY) ***451***
Northern Michigan U (MI) ***451***
North Park U (IL) ***452***
Northwestern Coll (IA) ***453***
Oakland U (MI) ***456***
Occidental Coll (CA) ***457***
The Ohio State U (OH) ***457***
Ohio U (OH) ***458***
Oklahoma Baptist U (OK) ***459***
Oklahoma Wesleyan U (OK) ***460***
Olivet Nazarene U (IL) ***461***
Oral Roberts U (OK) ***461***
Oregon State U (OR) ***462***
Pacific Union Coll (CA) ***464***
Pacific U (OR) ***464***
Rocky Mountain Coll (MT) ***482***
Rutgers, The State U of New Jersey, New Brunswick (NJ) ***485***
St. Cloud State U (MN) ***488***
St. Francis Xavier U (NS, Canada) ***489***
Saint Joseph's Coll of Maine (ME) ***491***
Saint Louis U (MO) ***492***
St. Mary's U of San Antonio (TX) ***494***
Salem State Coll (MA) ***497***
Samford U (AL) ***497***
Sam Houston State U (TX) ***497***
San Jose State U (CA) ***499***
Schreiner U (TX) ***501***
Seattle Pacific U (WA) ***501***
Simon Fraser U (BC, Canada) ***505***
Skidmore Coll (NY) ***506***
Slippery Rock U of Pennsylvania (PA) ***506***
Southern Adventist U (TN) ***508***
Southern Arkansas U–Magnolia (AR) ***509***
Southern Nazarene U (OK) ***510***
Springfield Coll (MA) ***514***
State U of NY Coll at Brockport (NY) ***515***
State U of NY Coll at Buffalo (NY) ***516***
Stetson U (FL) ***519***
Syracuse U (NY) ***521***
Tarleton State U (TX) ***522***
Tennessee Wesleyan Coll (TN) ***524***
Texas Lutheran U (TX) ***526***
Texas Tech U (TX) ***526***
Towson U (MD) ***529***
Transylvania U (KY) ***529***
Trevecca Nazarene U (TN) ***529***
Truman State U (MO) ***532***
Tulane U (LA) ***533***
Union U (TN) ***534***
Université de Sherbrooke (QC, Canada) ***536***
Université Laval (QC, Canada) ***536***
U at Buffalo, The State University of New York (NY) ***536***
U of Alberta (AB, Canada) ***538***
The U of British Columbia (BC, Canada) ***540***
U of Calgary (AB, Canada) ***540***
U of Calif, Los Angeles (CA) ***541***
U of Central Arkansas (AR) ***542***
U of Colorado at Boulder (CO) ***543***
U of Dayton (OH) ***544***
U of Delaware (DE) ***544***
U of Evansville (IN) ***545***
U of Florida (FL) ***545***
U of Guelph (ON, Canada) ***546***
U of Hawaii at Manoa (HI) ***546***
U of Houston (TX) ***547***
U of Houston–Clear Lake (TX) ***547***
The U of Iowa (IA) ***548***
U of Mary (ND) ***551***
U of Massachusetts Amherst (MA) ***552***

EXERCISE SCIENCES (continued)

U of Massachusetts Lowell (MA) **553**
The U of Memphis (TN) **553**
U of Miami (FL) **553**
U of Michigan (MI) **554**
U of Minnesota, Duluth (MN) **554**
U of Mississippi (MS) **555**
U of Nebraska–Lincoln (NE) **557**
U of Nevada, Las Vegas (NV) **558**
U of New Brunswick Fredericton (NB, Canada) **558**
U of New Brunswick Saint John (NB, Canada) **558**
U of New Hampshire (NH) **558**
U of Northern Colorado (CO) **561**
U of North Texas (TX) **562**
U of Oregon (OR) **562**
U of Puget Sound (WA) **571**
U of Regina (SK, Canada) **572**
U of San Francisco (CA) **574**
The U of Scranton (PA) **574**
U of Sioux Falls (SD) **574**
U of South Carolina (SC) **575**
U of South Carolina Aiken (SC) **575**
U of Southern California (CA) **576**
U of Southern Indiana (IN) **576**
The U of Tampa (FL) **577**
The U of Tennessee (TN) **577**
The U of Texas at Brownsville (TX) **578**
The U of Texas at Tyler (TX) **579**
The U of Texas of the Permian Basin (TX) **579**
U of the Pacific (CA) **580**
U of the Sacred Heart (PR) **580**
U of Toledo (OH) **581**
U of Tulsa (OK) **581**
U of Utah (UT) **582**
U of Victoria (BC, Canada) **582**
U of Waterloo (ON, Canada) **583**
U of Windsor (ON, Canada) **584**
U of Wisconsin–Eau Claire (WI) **584**
U of Wisconsin–La Crosse (WI) **584**
U of Wyoming (WY) **586**
Upper Iowa U (IA) **587**
Valparaiso U (IN) **588**
Vanguard U of Southern California (CA) **589**
Voorhees Coll (SC) **592**
Wake Forest U (NC) **592**
Walla Walla Coll (WA) **593**
Warner Pacific Coll (OR) **593**
Warner Southern Coll (FL) **593**
Washington State U (WA) **595**
Waynesburg Coll (PA) **595**
Wayne State Coll (NE) **596**
Weber State U (UT) **596**
Wesley Coll (DE) **598**
West Chester U of Pennsylvania (PA) **598**
Western Michigan U (MI) **599**
Western State Coll of Colorado (CO) **600**
Western Washington U (WA) **600**
West Liberty State Coll (WV) **601**
Westmont Coll (CA) **602**
West Virginia U (WV) **602**
Wheaton Coll (IL) **603**
Willamette U (OR) **605**
William Paterson U of New Jersey (NJ) **606**
Wilson Coll (PA) **607**
Winona State U (MN) **608**
Youngstown State U (OH) **611**

EXPERIMENTAL PSYCHOLOGY

Overview: This major prepares students to conduct controlled psychological experiments in order to analyze behavior and behavioral responses. *Related majors:* educational psychology, statistics, psychology, human ecology. *Potential careers:* experimental psychologist, scientific researcher, professor. *Salary potential:* $25k-$35k.

Alfred U (NY) **263**
Cedar Crest Coll (PA) **308**
Colorado State U-Pueblo (CO) **325**
Embry-Riddle Aeronautical U (FL) **352**
La Sierra U (CA) **403**
Longwood U (VA) **409**
Marlboro Coll (VT) **418**
Millikin U (IL) **430**
Moravian Coll (PA) **436**
New Mexico Inst of Mining and Technology (NM) **446**
Southwestern U (TX) **513**
Tufts U (MA) **533**
U of Alberta (AB, Canada) **538**
The U of British Columbia (BC, Canada) **540**
U of South Carolina (SC) **575**
U of Toledo (OH) **581**
U of Wisconsin–Madison (WI) **584**

FAMILY/COMMUNITY STUDIES

Overview: Students focus on the social, economic, and psychological relationships between individuals, families, and communities and learn how to develop various support systems for these groups. *Related majors:* human nutritional services, gerontology services, marriage and family counseling, resources and services, social work. *Potential careers:* social worker, cooperative services agent, nutrition educator. *Salary potential:* $20k-$25k.

Andrews U (MI) **269**
Bowling Green State U (OH) **292**
Brandon U (MB, Canada) **293**
Brigham Young U (UT) **295**
Cornell U (NY) **333**
Eastern Illinois U (IL) **348**
Eastern Kentucky U (KY) **348**
Goshen Coll (IN) **370**
Iowa State U of Science and Technology (IA) **390**
Liberty U (VA) **406**
Long Island U, Southampton Coll, Friends World Program (NY) **409**
Messiah Coll (PA) **426**
Oklahoma Christian U (OK) **459**
Oklahoma State U (OK) **460**
Olivet Nazarene U (IL) **461**
Oregon State U (OR) **462**
Our Lady of the Lake U of San Antonio (TX) **463**
Pacific Union Coll (CA) **464**
Prairie View A&M U (TX) **473**
Saint Paul U (ON, Canada) **495**
Seton Hill U (PA) **502**
Southern Utah U (UT) **511**
Syracuse U (NY) **521**
Toccoa Falls Coll (GA) **528**
Union U (TN) **534**
U of Calif, Santa Cruz (CA) **542**
U of Delaware (DE) **544**
U of Florida (FL) **545**
U of Maryland, Coll Park (MD) **552**
U of Minnesota, Twin Cities Campus (MN) **555**
The U of North Carolina at Greensboro (NC) **560**
U of Northern Iowa (IA) **561**
U of Utah (UT) **582**
U of Vermont (VT) **582**
U of Wyoming (WY) **586**
Ursuline Coll (OH) **587**
Youngstown State U (OH) **611**

FAMILY/CONSUMER RESOURCE MANAGEMENT RELATED

Information can be found under this major's main heading.

U of Hawaii at Manoa (HI) **546**
U of Nebraska–Lincoln (NE) **557**
Utah State U (UT) **587**
Virginia State U (VA) **591**

FAMILY/CONSUMER STUDIES

Overview: This major is devoted to the study of how individuals and families assess their needs and interact with their environment, including an examination of how humans seek fulfillment of their goals by identifying, developing, and managing resources available to them. *Related majors:* economics, psychology, family resource management studies, home economics. *Potential careers:* sociologist, consumer analyst, purchasing agent, market research. *Salary potential:* $23k-$33k.

Alabama A&M U (AL) **261**
Andrews U (MI) **269**
Ashland U (OH) **274**
Baldwin-Wallace Coll (OH) **280**
Ball State U (IN) **280**
Berea Coll (KY) **286**
California State U, Fresno (CA) **301**
California State U, Northridge (CA) **301**
California State U, Sacramento (CA) **301**
Carson-Newman Coll (TN) **306**
Chadron State Coll (NE) **311**
Concordia Coll (MN) **329**
Cornell U (NY) **333**
Fairmont State Coll (WV) **356**
Florida State U (FL) **361**
Framingham State Coll (MA) **362**
Hampshire Coll (MA) **375**
Harding U (AR) **375**
Howard U (DC) **382**
Illinois State U (IL) **384**
Indiana U Bloomington (IN) **385**
Iowa State U of Science and Technology (IA) **390**
Lambuth U (TN) **401**
Lipscomb U (TN) **408**
Louisiana Coll (LA) **410**
Miami U (OH) **428**
Minnesota State U, Mankato (MN) **431**
Mississippi Coll (MS) **432**
Montclair State U (NJ) **435**
Mount Saint Vincent U (NS, Canada) **439**
Murray State U (KY) **440**
New Mexico State U (NM) **446**
North Carolina Central U (NC) **448**
North Dakota State U (ND) **449**
Northern Michigan U (MI) **451**
Northwest Missouri State U (MO) **454**
Oklahoma State U (OK) **460**
Oregon State U (OR) **462**
Pacific Union Coll (CA) **464**
Ryerson U (ON, Canada) **485**
Saint Joseph Coll (CT) **490**
Seattle Pacific U (WA) **501**
Seton Hill U (PA) **502**
Southeast Missouri State U (MO) **508**
Southern Illinois U Carbondale (IL) **509**
Tennessee State U (TN) **523**
Towson U (MD) **529**
The U of Akron (OH) **537**
U of Alberta (AB, Canada) **538**
U of Delaware (DE) **544**
U of Hawaii at Manoa (HI) **546**
U of Maryland Eastern Shore (MD) **552**
U of Missouri–Columbia (MO) **555**
U of Montevallo (AL) **557**
U of Nebraska at Kearney (NE) **557**
U of New Hampshire (NH) **558**
U of Northern Iowa (IA) **561**
U of Prince Edward Island (PE, Canada) **570**
The U of Tennessee at Chattanooga (TN) **577**
U of Utah (UT) **582**
U of Vermont (VT) **582**
U of Windsor (ON, Canada) **584**
U of Wisconsin–Madison (WI) **584**
U of Wisconsin–Stevens Point (WI) **585**
Wayne State Coll (NE) **596**

FAMILY LIVING/ PARENTHOOD

Overview: Students who choose this major study the relationships between the child, family, and educators, including a study of parent education and involvement, family lifestyles, child abuse, and current family life issues. The student also examine parenting styles and effective parenting techniques and learn signs of abuse and neglect and ways to work effectively with abused and neglected children. *Related majors:* child care and guidance, child growth, care and development studies, developmental psychology. *Potential careers:* child care worker, psychologist, homemaker. *Salary potential:* $16k-$26k.

U of North Texas (TX) **562**

FAMILY RESOURCE MANAGEMENT STUDIES

Overview: Students learn how to help individuals and families manage their personal and home finances. *Related majors:* accounting, adult education, counseling psychology. *Potential careers:* accountant, financial adviser, credit counselor. *Salary potential:* $24k-$32k.

Arizona State U (AZ) **271**
Bradley U (IL) **293**
Central Michigan U (MI) **310**
Cornell U (NY) **333**
Eastern Michigan U (MI) **348**
George Fox U (OR) **366**
Iowa State U of Science and Technology (IA) **390**
Michigan State U (MI) **428**
Middle Tennessee State U (TN) **429**
New Mexico State U (NM) **446**
The Ohio State U (OH) **457**
Ohio U (OH) **458**

FAMILY STUDIES

Overview: Undergraduates who choose this major will study all aspects of the family unit and its impact on individuals as well as society. *Related majors:* individual family development studies, counseling psychology and social psychology, sociology. *Potential careers:* researcher, psychologist, professor, sociologist. *Salary potential:* $23k-$29k.

Anderson U (IN) **268**
Brigham Young U (UT) **295**
Central Michigan U (MI) **310**
Gallaudet U (DC) **365**
Michigan State U (MI) **428**
Point Loma Nazarene U (CA) **471**
Southern Adventist U (TN) **508**
Spring Arbor U (MI) **514**
Syracuse U (NY) **521**
Texas Tech U (TX) **526**
Toccoa Falls Coll (GA) **528**
The U of Akron (OH) **537**
U of Guelph (ON, Canada) **546**
U of Southern Mississippi (MS) **576**
The U of Tennessee (TN) **577**
Weber State U (UT) **596**
Western Michigan U (MI) **599**

FARM/RANCH MANAGEMENT

Overview: Students who choose this major will learn how to manage farms, ranches, and similar enterprises. *Related majors:* business management, accounting, agribusiness. *Potential careers:* farm manager, loan officer, lobbyist. *Salary potential:* $20k-$40k.

California Polytechnic State U, San Luis Obispo (CA) **300**
California State Polytechnic U, Pomona (CA) **300**
Colorado State U (CO) **325**
Cornell U (NY) **333**
Eastern Kentucky U (KY) **348**
Iowa State U of Science and Technology (IA) **390**
Johnson & Wales U (RI) **393**
North Dakota State U (ND) **449**
Northwest Missouri State U (MO) **454**
Tarleton State U (TX) **522**
U of Alberta (AB, Canada) **538**

The U of Findlay (OH) 545
U of Wisconsin–Madison (WI) 584

FASHION DESIGN/ ILLUSTRATION

Overview: Students study the theories, practices, and techniques of fashion, apparel and accessory design and related product and packaging development. *Related majors:* design and visual communications, graphic art, commercial art, illustration, textiles and weaving arts, metal and jewelry arts. *Potential careers:* fashion designer, jewelry designer, wedding consultant. *Salary potential:* $25k-$35k.

Academy of Art Coll (CA) 260
American InterContinental U (CA) 266
American InterContinental U, Atlanta (GA) 266
American InterContinental U-London(United Kingdom) 267
The Art Inst of California–San Francisco (CA) 273
The Art Inst of Portland (OR) 274
Baylor U (TX) 283
Bluffton Coll (OH) 291
Bowling Green State U (OH) 292
California Coll of Arts and Crafts (CA) 299
Centenary Coll (NJ) 308
Clark Atlanta U (GA) 315
Columbia Coll Chicago (IL) 327
Columbus Coll of Art and Design (OH) 328
Dominican U (IL) 345
Drexel U (PA) 346
Fashion Inst of Technology (NY) 357
Florida State U (FL) 361
Framingham State Coll (MA) 362
Hampton U (VA) 375
Howard U (DC) 382
The Illinois Inst of Art (IL) 384
Indiana U Bloomington (IN) 385
International Academy of Design & Technology (FL) 388
International Acad of Merchandising & Design, Ltd (IL) 389
Iowa State U of Science and Technology (IA) 390
Kent State U (OH) 397
Lamar U (TX) 401
Lasell Coll (MA) 402
Lindenwood U (MO) 407
Long Island U, Southampton Coll, Friends World Program (NY) 409
Lynn U (FL) 413
Marist Coll (NY) 417
Marymount Coll of Fordham U (NY) 419
Marymount U (VA) 420
Massachusetts Coll of Art (MA) 421
Meredith Coll (NC) 426
Minnesota State U, Mankato (MN) 431
Moore Coll of Art and Design (PA) 436
Mount Ida Coll (MA) 438
Mount Mary Coll (WI) 438
North Dakota State U (ND) 449
Northwest Missouri State U (MO) 454
O'More Coll of Design (TN) 461
Oregon State U (OR) 462
Otis Coll of Art and Design (CA) 462
Parsons School of Design, New School U (NY) 465
Philadelphia U (PA) 469
Pontifical Catholic U of Puerto Rico (PR) 472
Pratt Inst (NY) 473
Radford U (VA) 476
Rhode Island School of Design (RI) 479
Ryerson U (ON, Canada) 485
Savannah Coll of Art and Design (GA) 499
School of the Art Inst of Chicago (IL) 500
State U of NY Coll at Buffalo (NY) 516
Stephens Coll (MO) 519
Syracuse U (NY) 521
Texas Christian U (TX) 526
Texas Tech U (TX) 526
Texas Woman's U (TX) 527
U of Cincinnati (OH) 543
U of Delaware (DE) 544
U of Maryland Eastern Shore (MD) 552
U of North Texas (TX) 562
U of San Francisco (CA) 574
U of the Incarnate Word (TX) 580
Ursuline Coll (OH) 587
Virginia Commonwealth U (VA) 590
Washington U in St. Louis (MO) 595
Woodbury U (CA) 609

FASHION MERCHANDISING

Overview: This major teaches students the knowledge and skills they need to work in the fashion merchandising industry, such as promoting product lines, organizing fashion shows, advertising and public relations, and marketing to retail establishments. *Related majors:* apparel/accessories marketing, public relations, advertising, fashion design/illustration. *Potential careers:* fashion show promoter, publicist, marketing or advertising executive, fashion designer, sales manager. *Salary potential:* $20k-$30k.

Abilene Christian U (TX) 260
Academy of Art Coll (CA) 260
American InterContinental U (CA) 266
American InterContinental U, Atlanta (GA) 266
American InterContinental U-London(United Kingdom) 267
Ashland U (OH) 274
Ball State U (IN) 280
Bennett Coll (NC) 286
Bluffton Coll (OH) 291
Bowling Green State U (OH) 292
Brenau U (GA) 293
Bridgewater Coll (VA) 294
California State U, Long Beach (CA) 301
California State U, Northridge (CA) 301
Carson-Newman Coll (TN) 306
Central Michigan U (MI) 310
Central Washington U (WA) 310
Coll of St. Catherine (MN) 321
Delta State U (MS) 339
Dominican U (IL) 345
East Central U (OK) 347
Eastern Kentucky U (KY) 348
Eastern Michigan U (MI) 348
Fashion Inst of Technology (NY) 357
Florida State U (FL) 361
Fontbonne U (MO) 361
Framingham State Coll (MA) 362
Freed-Hardeman U (TN) 364
George Fox U (OR) 366
Hampton U (VA) 375
Harding U (AR) 375
The Illinois Inst of Art (IL) 384
Immaculata U (PA) 385
Indiana U Bloomington (IN) 385
Indiana U of Pennsylvania (PA) 386
International Acad of Merchandising & Design, Ltd (IL) 389
Judson Coll (AL) 395
Kent State U (OH) 397
Laboratory Inst of Merchandising (NY) 399
Lamar U (TX) 401
Lambuth U (TN) 401
Lasell Coll (MA) 402
Lindenwood U (MO) 407
Lipscomb U (TN) 408
Louisiana State U and A&M Coll (LA) 410
Lynn U (FL) 413
Madonna U (MI) 414
Marist Coll (NY) 417
Mars Hill Coll (NC) 418
Marygrove Coll (MI) 419
Marymount Coll of Fordham U (NY) 419
Marymount U (VA) 420
Mercyhurst Coll (PA) 425
Meredith Coll (NC) 426
Mississippi Coll (MS) 432
Montclair State U (NJ) 435
Mount Ida Coll (MA) 438
Mount Mary Coll (WI) 438
New Mexico State U (NM) 446
North Dakota State U (ND) 449
Northeastern State U (OK) 450
Northwest Missouri State U (MO) 454
Northwood U (MI) 454
Northwood U, Texas Campus (TX) 454
Oklahoma State U (OK) 460
Olivet Nazarene U (IL) 461
O'More Coll of Design (TN) 461
Oregon State U (OR) 462
Our Lady of the Lake U of San Antonio (TX) 463
Pacific Union Coll (CA) 464
Parsons School of Design, New School U (NY) 465
Philadelphia U (PA) 469
Pittsburg State U (KS) 470
Ryerson U (ON, Canada) 485
Sam Houston State U (TX) 497
South Carolina State U (SC) 506
South Dakota State U (SD) 507
Southeast Missouri State U (MO) 508
Southwest Texas State U (TX) 513
State U of NY Coll at Buffalo (NY) 516
State U of NY Coll at Oneonta (NY) 517
Stephen F. Austin State U (TX) 518
Stephens Coll (MO) 519
Tarleton State U (TX) 522
Tennessee Technological U (TN) 524
Texas A&M U–Kingsville (TX) 525
Texas Christian U (TX) 526
Texas Southern U (TX) 526
Texas Tech U (TX) 526
Texas Woman's U (TX) 527
The U of Akron (OH) 537
U of Bridgeport (CT) 540
U of Central Oklahoma (OK) 542
U of Delaware (DE) 544
U of Georgia (GA) 545
U of Louisiana at Lafayette (LA) 550
U of Maryland Eastern Shore (MD) 552
The U of Montana–Missoula (MT) 556
U of Montevallo (AL) 557
U of Nebraska at Omaha (NE) 557
U of North Texas (TX) 562
The U of Tennessee at Martin (TN) 577
U of the Incarnate Word (TX) 580
U of Wisconsin–Madison (WI) 584
Ursuline Coll (OH) 587
Utah State U (UT) 587
Warren Wilson Coll (NC) 594
Wayne State Coll (NE) 596
Woodbury U (CA) 609
Youngstown State U (OH) 611

FILM STUDIES

Overview: This major examines the history, theory, and criticism of film, as well as the basic techniques of filmmaking. *Related majors:* film-video making/cinematography and production, playwriting, scriptwriting, acting and directing. *Potential careers:* critic, director, producer, actor, scriptwriter. *Salary potential:* $20k-$30k.

Academy of Art Coll (CA) 260
Art Center Coll of Design (CA) 273
Bard Coll (NY) 281
Bennington Coll (VT) 286
Bowling Green State U (OH) 292
Brock U (ON, Canada) 295
Brooklyn Coll of the City U of NY (NY) 295
Brown U (RI) 296
Burlington Coll (VT) 297
California Coll of Arts and Crafts (CA) 299
California Inst of the Arts (CA) 299
California State U, Long Beach (CA) 301
California State U, Northridge (CA) 301
Calvin Coll (MI) 303
Carleton U (ON, Canada) 305
Carson-Newman Coll (TN) 306
Centenary Coll of Louisiana (LA) 308
Chapman U (CA) 311
Claremont McKenna Coll (CA) 315
Clark U (MA) 316
Coll of Santa Fe (NM) 323
The Colorado Coll (CO) 325
Columbia Coll (NY) 326
Columbia Coll Chicago (IL) 327
Columbia Coll Hollywood (CA) 327
Columbia U, School of General Studies (NY) 328
Concordia U (QC, Canada) 331
Connecticut Coll (CT) 331
Curry Coll (MA) 335
Dartmouth Coll (NH) 337
Denison U (OH) 339
Emerson Coll (MA) 353
Emory U (GA) 354
The Evergreen State Coll (WA) 355
Florida State U (FL) 361
Fordham U (NY) 362
Georgia State U (GA) 368
Grand Valley State U (MI) 371
Hampshire Coll (MA) 375
Harvard U (MA) 376
Hofstra U (NY) 380
Howard U (DC) 382
Hunter Coll of the City U of NY (NY) 382
Iona Coll (NY) 390
Ithaca Coll (NY) 390
Johns Hopkins U (MD) 392
Keene State Coll (NH) 396
La Salle U (PA) 402
Laurentian U (ON, Canada) 403
Long Island U, C.W. Post Campus (NY) 409
Long Island U, Southampton Coll, Friends World Program (NY) 409
Marlboro Coll (VT) 418
Middlebury Coll (VT) 429
Mount Holyoke Coll (MA) 438
New York U (NY) 447
North Carolina School of the Arts (NC) 449
Northern Michigan U (MI) 451
Northwestern U (IL) 453
Olivet Nazarene U (IL) 461
Penn State U Univ Park Campus (PA) 468
Pitzer Coll (CA) 471
Pomona Coll (CA) 472
Prescott Coll (AZ) 474
Purchase Coll, State U of NY (NY) 475
Queens Coll of the City U of NY (NY) 475
Queen's U at Kingston (ON, Canada) 476
Quinnipiac U (CT) 476
Rhode Island Coll (RI) 479
Rhode Island School of Design (RI) 479
Rutgers, The State U of New Jersey, New Brunswick (NJ) 485
Ryerson U (ON, Canada) 485
Sacred Heart U (CT) 486
St. Cloud State U (MN) 488
San Francisco Art Inst (CA) 498
San Francisco State U (CA) 498
San Jose State U (CA) 499
Sarah Lawrence Coll (NY) 499
School of the Art Inst of Chicago (IL) 500
School of the Museum of Fine Arts (MA) 501
School of Visual Arts (NY) 501
Simon Fraser U (BC, Canada) 505
Southern Methodist U (TX) 510
State U of NY at Binghamton (NY) 515
State U of NY Coll at Brockport (NY) 515
State U of NY Coll at Cortland (NY) 516
State U of NY Coll at Fredonia (NY) 516
Stony Brook U, State University of New York (NY) 520
Syracuse U (NY) 521
Temple U (PA) 523
U at Buffalo, The State University of New York (NY) 536
The U of British Columbia (BC, Canada) 540
U of Calif, Irvine (CA) 541
U of Calif, Los Angeles (CA) 541
U of Calif, San Diego (CA) 541
U of Calif, Santa Barbara (CA) 541
U of Calif, Santa Cruz (CA) 542
U of Chicago (IL) 542
U of Colorado at Boulder (CO) 543
U of Delaware (DE) 544
U of Hartford (CT) 546
The U of Iowa (IA) 548
U of Manitoba (MB, Canada) 551
U of Maryland, Baltimore County (MD) 552
U of Miami (FL) 553
U of Michigan (MI) 554
U of Minnesota, Twin Cities Campus (MN) 555
U of Nebraska–Lincoln (NE) 557
U of Nevada, Las Vegas (NV) 558
U of New Mexico (NM) 559
U of Pittsburgh (PA) 569
U of Regina (SK, Canada) 572
U of Rochester (NY) 573
U of Southern California (CA) 576
U of Toledo (OH) 581
U of Toronto (ON, Canada) 581
U of Utah (UT) 582
U of Waterloo (ON, Canada) 583
The U of Western Ontario (ON, Canada) 583
U of Windsor (ON, Canada) 584
U of Wisconsin–Milwaukee (WI) 585

FILM STUDIES (continued)

Vassar Coll (NY) ***589***
Washington U in St. Louis (MO) ***595***
Watkins Coll of Art and Design (TN) ***595***
Wayne State U (MI) ***596***
Webster U (MO) ***597***
Wellesley Coll (MA) ***597***
Wesleyan U (CT) ***597***
Wright State U (OH) ***609***
Yale U (CT) ***610***
York U (ON, Canada) ***611***

FILM/VIDEO AND PHOTOGRAPHIC ARTS RELATED

Information can be found under this major's main heading.

Bloomfield Coll (NJ) ***290***
Col for Creative Studies (MI) ***319***
New England School of Communications (ME) ***445***
Rocky Mountain Coll of Art & Design (CO) ***483***
Scripps Coll (CA) ***501***
Southern Illinois U Carbondale (IL) ***509***
The U of the Arts (PA) ***579***

FILM/VIDEO PRODUCTION

Overview: This major teaches students how to become a film or video camera operator, or related positions such as film editors and special effects specialists. *Related majors:* film/cinema studies, technical theater/theater design/stagecraft, acting and directing. *Potential careers:* film or video camera operator, film editor, special effects technician, film loader, first and second assistant photographer. *Salary potential:* $25k-$32k.

Academy of Art Coll (CA) ***260***
American InterContinental U (CA) ***266***
American InterContinental U, Atlanta (GA) ***266***
American InterContinental U-London(United Kingdom) ***267***
American U (DC) ***267***
Antioch Coll (OH) ***269***
The Art Inst of Phoenix (AZ) ***274***
Atlanta Coll of Art (GA) ***275***
Bard Coll (NY) ***281***
Boston U (MA) ***292***
Brooks Inst of Photography (CA) ***296***
Burlington Coll (VT) ***297***
California State U, Long Beach (CA) ***301***
California State U, Northridge (CA) ***301***
Chapman U (CA) ***311***
City Coll of the City U of NY (NY) ***314***
Coll of Santa Fe (NM) ***323***
Coll of Staten Island of the City U of NY (NY) ***323***
Colorado State U-Pueblo (CO) ***325***
Columbia Coll Chicago (IL) ***327***
Columbia Coll Hollywood (CA) ***327***
Concordia U (QC, Canada) ***331***
DeSales U (PA) ***340***
Drexel U (PA) ***346***
Emerson Coll (MA) ***353***
The Evergreen State Coll (WA) ***355***
Fairleigh Dickinson U, Florham (NJ) ***356***
Fitchburg State Coll (MA) ***358***
Five Towns Coll (NY) ***359***
Florida State U (FL) ***361***
Grand Valley State U (MI) ***371***
Hampshire Coll (MA) ***375***
Hofstra U (NY) ***380***
The Illinois Inst of Art-Schaumburg (IL) ***384***
Iowa Wesleyan Coll (IA) ***390***
Ithaca Coll (NY) ***390***
Long Island U, C.W. Post Campus (NY) ***409***
Long Island U, Southampton Coll, Friends World Program (NY) ***409***
Loyola Marymount U (CA) ***411***
Maharishi U of Management (IA) ***414***
Massachusetts Coll of Art (MA) ***421***
Minneapolis Coll of Art and Design (MN) ***431***
Montana State U–Bozeman (MT) ***434***
New England School of Communications (ME) ***445***
New York U (NY) ***447***
North Carolina School of the Arts (NC) ***449***
Northern Michigan U (MI) ***451***
Ohio U (OH) ***458***
Oklahoma City U (OK) ***460***
Point Park Coll (PA) ***471***
Pratt Inst (NY) ***473***
Purchase Coll, State U of NY (NY) ***475***
Quinnipiac U (CT) ***476***
Rochester Inst of Technology (NY) ***482***
Sacred Heart U (CT) ***486***
Sarah Lawrence Coll (NY) ***499***
Savannah Coll of Art and Design (GA) ***499***
School of the Art Inst of Chicago (IL) ***500***
School of the Museum of Fine Arts (MA) ***501***
School of Visual Arts (NY) ***501***
Southern Adventist U (TN) ***508***
Syracuse U (NY) ***521***
Temple U (PA) ***523***
U of Advancing Technology (AZ) ***537***
U of Calif, Berkeley (CA) ***540***
U of Calif, Santa Cruz (CA) ***542***
U of Central Florida (FL) ***542***
U of Hartford (CT) ***546***
U of Illinois at Chicago (IL) ***547***
The U of Iowa (IA) ***548***
U of Miami (FL) ***553***
The U of North Carolina at Greensboro (NC) ***560***
The U of North Carolina at Wilmington (NC) ***561***
U of Oklahoma (OK) ***562***
U of Regina (SK, Canada) ***572***
The U of South Dakota (SD) ***575***
U of Southern California (CA) ***576***
The U of Texas at Arlington (TX) ***577***
The U of the Arts (PA) ***579***
Vanguard U of Southern California (CA) ***589***
Villa Julie Coll (MD) ***590***
Waldorf Coll (IA) ***592***
Webster U (MO) ***597***
York U (ON, Canada) ***611***

FINANCE

Overview: Students learn how to manage and analyze all financial aspects of a business or organization, work with lending institutions, and apply principles of accounting and budgeting to a business. *Related majors:* accounting, economics, business administration/management, managerial economics, banking and financial support services. *Potential careers:* corporate financier, banker, financial analyst, accountant, venture capitalist. *Salary potential:* $38k-$48k.

Abilene Christian U (TX) ***260***
Adams State Coll (CO) ***260***
Adelphi U (NY) ***260***
Alabama A&M U (AL) ***261***
Alabama State U (AL) ***261***
Albertus Magnus Coll (CT) ***262***
Albright Coll (PA) ***263***
Alderson-Broaddus Coll (WV) ***263***
Alfred U (NY) ***263***
American International Coll (MA) ***267***
American U (DC) ***267***
Anderson Coll (SC) ***268***
Anderson U (IN) ***268***
Angelo State U (TX) ***269***
Appalachian State U (NC) ***270***
Arcadia U (PA) ***271***
Arizona State U (AZ) ***271***
Arkansas State U (AR) ***272***
Ashland U (OH) ***274***
Auburn U (AL) ***276***
Auburn U Montgomery (AL) ***276***
Augustana Coll (IL) ***276***
Augusta State U (GA) ***277***
Aurora U (IL) ***277***
Averett U (VA) ***278***
Avila U (MO) ***278***
Babson Coll (MA) ***278***
Baldwin-Wallace Coll (OH) ***280***
Ball State U (IN) ***280***
Barber-Scotia Coll (NC) ***281***
Barry U (FL) ***282***
Barton Coll (NC) ***282***
Baylor U (TX) ***283***
Belmont U (TN) ***284***
Benedict Coll (SC) ***285***
Benedictine Coll (KS) ***285***
Benedictine U (IL) ***285***
Bentley Coll (MA) ***286***
Baruch Coll of the City U of NY (NY) ***286***
Berry Coll (GA) ***287***
Bethel Coll (MN) ***288***
Bishop's U (QC, Canada) ***289***
Bloomfield Coll (NJ) ***290***
Boston Coll (MA) ***292***
Boston U (MA) ***292***
Bowling Green State U (OH) ***292***
Bradley U (IL) ***293***
Brescia U (KY) ***293***
Bridgewater Coll (VA) ***294***
Bridgewater State Coll (MA) ***294***
Brock U (ON, Canada) ***295***
Bryant Coll (RI) ***296***
Buena Vista U (IA) ***297***
Butler U (IN) ***297***
Cabrini Coll (PA) ***298***
California Coll for Health Sciences (CA) ***298***
California State Polytechnic U, Pomona (CA) ***300***
California State U, Bakersfield (CA) ***300***
California State U, Chico (CA) ***300***
California State U, Dominguez Hills (CA) ***300***
California State U, Fresno (CA) ***301***
California State U, Fullerton (CA) ***301***
California State U, Hayward (CA) ***301***
California State U, Long Beach (CA) ***301***
California State U, Northridge (CA) ***301***
California State U, San Bernardino (CA) ***302***
California State U, Stanislaus (CA) ***302***
Cameron U (OK) ***303***
Campbell U (NC) ***303***
Canisius Coll (NY) ***304***
Capital U (OH) ***304***
Carleton U (ON, Canada) ***305***
Carroll Coll (MT) ***306***
Carroll Coll (WI) ***306***
Castleton State Coll (VT) ***307***
The Catholic U of America (DC) ***307***
Cedarville U (OH) ***308***
Central Connecticut State U (CT) ***309***
Central Michigan U (MI) ***310***
Central Missouri State U (MO) ***310***
Chapman U (CA) ***311***
Christian Brothers U (TN) ***313***
Christopher Newport U (VA) ***313***
Clarion U of Pennsylvania (PA) ***315***
Clarkson U (NY) ***316***
Cleary U (MI) ***317***
Clemson U (SC) ***317***
Cleveland State U (OH) ***317***
Coastal Carolina U (SC) ***318***
Coker Coll (SC) ***318***
The Coll of New Jersey (NJ) ***320***
Coll of St. Joseph (VT) ***322***
The Coll of Southeastern Europe, The American U of Athens(Greece) ***323***
Colorado State U (CO) ***325***
Colorado State U-Pueblo (CO) ***325***
Colorado Tech U Sioux Falls Campus (SD) ***326***
Columbia Coll (MO) ***326***
Columbus State U (GA) ***328***
Concordia U (MN) ***330***
Concordia U (QC, Canada) ***331***
Creighton U (NE) ***333***
Culver-Stockton Coll (MO) ***334***
Dakota State U (SD) ***335***
Dakota Wesleyan U (SD) ***336***
Dallas Baptist U (TX) ***336***
Davenport U, Grand Rapids (MI) ***337***
Davenport U, Lansing (MI) ***337***
Defiance Coll (OH) ***338***
Delta State U (MS) ***339***
DePaul U (IL) ***339***
Deree Coll(Greece) ***339***
DeSales U (PA) ***340***
Dickinson State U (ND) ***344***
Dominican Coll (NY) ***344***
Dowling Coll (NY) ***345***
Drake U (IA) ***345***
Drexel U (PA) ***346***
Duquesne U (PA) ***346***
East Carolina U (NC) ***347***
East Central U (OK) ***347***
Eastern Illinois U (IL) ***348***
Eastern Kentucky U (KY) ***348***
Eastern Michigan U (MI) ***348***
Eastern New Mexico U (NM) ***349***
Eastern U (PA) ***349***
Eastern Washington U (WA) ***349***
East Tennessee State U (TN) ***349***
East Texas Baptist U (TX) ***350***
East-West U (IL) ***350***
École des hautes études commerciales de Montréal (QC, Canada) ***350***
Elmhurst Coll (IL) ***351***
Emory U (GA) ***354***
Eureka Coll (IL) ***355***
Excelsior Coll (NY) ***356***
Fairfield U (CT) ***356***
Fairmont State Coll (WV) ***356***
Fayetteville State U (NC) ***357***
Ferris State U (MI) ***358***
Ferrum Coll (VA) ***358***
Fisk U (TN) ***358***
Florida A&M U (FL) ***359***
Florida Atlantic U (FL) ***359***
Florida Gulf Coast U (FL) ***359***
Florida International U (FL) ***360***
Florida Southern Coll (FL) ***361***
Florida State U (FL) ***361***
Fontbonne U (MO) ***361***
Fordham U (NY) ***362***
Fort Hays State U (KS) ***362***
Fort Lewis Coll (CO) ***362***
Framingham State Coll (MA) ***362***
Francis Marion U (SC) ***363***
Franklin and Marshall Coll (PA) ***363***
Franklin Coll (IN) ***363***
Franklin Pierce Coll (NH) ***364***
Franklin U (OH) ***364***
Freed-Hardeman U (TN) ***364***
Fresno Pacific U (CA) ***364***
Gannon U (PA) ***365***
George Mason U (VA) ***366***
Georgetown Coll (KY) ***366***
Georgetown U (DC) ***366***
The George Washington U (DC) ***367***
Georgia Southern U (GA) ***367***
Georgia State U (GA) ***368***
Glenville State Coll (WV) ***368***
Golden Gate U (CA) ***369***
Goldey-Beacom Coll (DE) ***369***
Gonzaga U (WA) ***369***
Governors State U (IL) ***370***
Grand Canyon U (AZ) ***371***
Grand Valley State U (MI) ***371***
Grove City Coll (PA) ***373***
Gwynedd-Mercy Coll (PA) ***374***
Hampton U (VA) ***375***
Harding U (AR) ***375***
Hardin-Simmons U (TX) ***376***
Hawai'i Pacific U (HI) ***377***
Hillsdale Coll (MI) ***379***
Hofstra U (NY) ***380***
Houston Baptist U (TX) ***382***
Howard Payne U (TX) ***382***
Howard U (DC) ***382***
Husson Coll (ME) ***383***
Idaho State U (ID) ***384***
Illinois Coll (IL) ***384***
Illinois State U (IL) ***384***
Indiana Inst of Technology (IN) ***385***
Indiana State U (IN) ***385***
Indiana U Bloomington (IN) ***385***
Indiana U of Pennsylvania (PA) ***386***
Indiana U–Purdue U Fort Wayne (IN) ***386***
Indiana Wesleyan U (IN) ***387***
Inter American U of PR, San Germán Campus (PR) ***388***
Iona Coll (NY) ***390***
Iowa State U of Science and Technology (IA) ***390***
Ithaca Coll (NY) ***390***
Jackson State U (MS) ***390***
Jacksonville State U (AL) ***390***
Jacksonville U (FL) ***391***
James Madison U (VA) ***391***
John Carroll U (OH) ***392***
Johnson C. Smith U (NC) ***394***
Juniata Coll (PA) ***395***
Kansas State U (KS) ***396***
Kean U (NJ) ***396***
Kennesaw State U (GA) ***397***
Kent State U (OH) ***397***
Kettering U (MI) ***398***
King's Coll (PA) ***398***
Kutztown U of Pennsylvania (PA) ***399***
Lake Forest Coll (IL) ***400***

Lakehead U (ON, Canada) **400**
Lakeland Coll (WI) **401**
Lamar U (TX) **401**
La Roche Coll (PA) **402**
La Salle U (PA) **402**
Lasell Coll (MA) **402**
Lehigh U (PA) **404**
LeTourneau U (TX) **405**
Lewis U (IL) **406**
Lincoln Memorial U (TN) **407**
Lincoln U (PA) **407**
Lindenwood U (MO) **407**
Linfield Coll (OR) **408**
Lipscomb U (TN) **408**
Long Island U, Brentwood Campus (NY) **408**
Long Island U, Brooklyn Campus (NY) **409**
Long Island U, C.W. Post Campus (NY) **409**
Longwood U (VA) **409**
Loras Coll (IA) **410**
Louisiana Coll (LA) **410**
Louisiana State U and A&M Coll (LA) **410**
Louisiana State U in Shreveport (LA) **410**
Louisiana Tech U (LA) **410**
Loyola Coll in Maryland (MD) **411**
Loyola U Chicago (IL) **411**
Loyola U New Orleans (LA) **411**
Lubbock Christian U (TX) **412**
Lycoming Coll (PA) **412**
Madonna U (MI) **414**
Manchester Coll (IN) **415**
Manhattan Coll (NY) **416**
Manhattanville Coll (NY) **416**
Marian Coll (IN) **417**
Marian Coll of Fond du Lac (WI) **417**
Marquette U (WI) **418**
Marshall U (WV) **418**
Mars Hill Coll (NC) **418**
Marymount Coll of Fordham U (NY) **419**
Marymount U (VA) **420**
Massachusetts Coll of Liberal Arts (MA) **421**
The Master's Coll and Seminary (CA) **422**
McGill U (QC, Canada) **423**
McKendree Coll (IL) **423**
McMurry U (TX) **423**
McNeese State U (LA) **423**
McPherson Coll (KS) **423**
Memorial U of Newfoundland (NF, Canada) **424**
Mercer U (GA) **425**
Mercy Coll (NY) **425**
Mercyhurst Coll (PA) **425**
Meredith Coll (NC) **426**
Merrimack Coll (MA) **426**
Mesa State Coll (CO) **426**
Methodist Coll (NC) **427**
Metropolitan State Coll of Denver (CO) **427**
Metropolitan State U (MN) **427**
Miami U (OH) **428**
Michigan State U (MI) **428**
Michigan Technological U (MI) **428**
Middle Tennessee State U (TN) **429**
Midwestern State U (TX) **430**
Millikin U (IL) **430**
Minnesota State U, Mankato (MN) **431**
Minnesota State U, Moorhead (MN) **432**
Minot State U (ND) **432**
Mississippi State U (MS) **432**
Missouri Southern State Coll (MO) **433**
Missouri Western State Coll (MO) **433**
Monmouth U (NJ) **434**
Montana State U–Billings (MT) **434**
Montana Tech of The U of Montana (MT) **435**
Montclair State U (NJ) **435**
Morehead State U (KY) **436**
Morehouse Coll (GA) **436**
Morgan State U (MD) **436**
Murray State U (KY) **440**
National U (CA) **442**
Newbury Coll (MA) **444**
New Mexico State U (NM) **446**
New York Inst of Technology (NY) **447**
New York U (NY) **447**
Nicholls State U (LA) **447**
Nichols Coll (MA) **448**
North Central Coll (IL) **449**
Northeastern Illinois U (IL) **450**
Northeastern State U (OK) **450**
Northeastern U (MA) **450**
Northern Arizona U (AZ) **450**
Northern Illinois U (IL) **450**
Northern Kentucky U (KY) **451**
Northern Michigan U (MI) **451**
Northern State U (SD) **451**
North Georgia Coll & State U (GA) **451**
North Park U (IL) **452**
Northwestern Coll (MN) **453**
Northwest Missouri State U (MO) **454**
Northwest Nazarene U (ID) **454**
Northwood U (MI) **454**
Northwood U, Florida Campus (FL) **454**
Northwood U, Texas Campus (TX) **454**
Notre Dame Coll (OH) **455**
Notre Dame de Namur U (CA) **455**
Oakland U (MI) **456**
The Ohio State U (OH) **457**
Ohio U (OH) **458**
Oklahoma Baptist U (OK) **459**
Oklahoma City U (OK) **460**
Oklahoma State U (OK) **460**
Old Dominion U (VA) **460**
Olivet Coll (MI) **461**
Olivet Nazarene U (IL) **461**
Oral Roberts U (OK) **461**
Oregon State U (OR) **462**
Otterbein Coll (OH) **462**
Ouachita Baptist U (AR) **462**
Pace U (NY) **463**
Pacific Lutheran U (WA) **463**
Pacific Union Coll (CA) **464**
Pacific U (OR) **464**
Palm Beach Atlantic U (FL) **465**
Penn State U at Erie, The Behrend Coll (PA) **467**
Penn State U Harrisburg Campus of the Capital Coll (PA) **468**
Penn State U Univ Park Campus (PA) **468**
Philadelphia U (PA) **469**
Pittsburg State U (KS) **470**
Pontifical Catholic U of Puerto Rico (PR) **472**
Portland State U (OR) **472**
Prairie View A&M U (TX) **473**
Providence Coll (RI) **474**
Quincy U (IL) **476**
Quinnipiac U (CT) **476**
Radford U (VA) **476**
Rhode Island Coll (RI) **479**
Rider U (NJ) **480**
Robert Morris U (PA) **481**
Rochester Inst of Technology (NY) **482**
Rockford Coll (IL) **482**
Rockhurst U (MO) **482**
Roosevelt U (IL) **483**
Rowan U (NJ) **484**
Rutgers, The State U of New Jersey, Camden (NJ) **485**
Rutgers, The State U of New Jersey, Newark (NJ) **485**
Rutgers, The State U of New Jersey, New Brunswick (NJ) **485**
Ryerson U (ON, Canada) **485**
Sacred Heart U (CT) **486**
Saginaw Valley State U (MI) **486**
St. Ambrose U (IA) **486**
Saint Anselm Coll (NH) **487**
St. Bonaventure U (NY) **487**
St. Cloud State U (MN) **488**
St. Edward's U (TX) **488**
Saint Francis U (PA) **488**
St. John Fisher Coll (NY) **489**
St. John's U (NY) **490**
Saint Joseph's Coll (IN) **490**
Saint Joseph's Coll of Maine (ME) **491**
Saint Joseph's U (PA) **491**
Saint Louis U (MO) **492**
Saint Martin's Coll (WA) **493**
Saint Mary's Coll (IN) **493**
Saint Mary's U (NS, Canada) **494**
St. Mary's U of San Antonio (TX) **494**
St. Thomas Aquinas Coll (NY) **495**
St. Thomas U (FL) **496**
Saint Vincent Coll (PA) **496**
Salem State Coll (MA) **497**
Sam Houston State U (TX) **497**
San Diego State U (CA) **498**
San Francisco State U (CA) **498**
San Jose State U (CA) **499**
Santa Clara U (CA) **499**
Schreiner U (TX) **501**
Seattle U (WA) **501**
Seton Hall U (NJ) **502**
Seton Hill U (PA) **502**
Shippensburg U of Pennsylvania (PA) **503**
Siena Coll (NY) **504**
Simmons Coll (MA) **504**
Si Tanka Huron U (SD) **505**
Slippery Rock U of Pennsylvania (PA) **506**
Southeastern Louisiana U (LA) **508**
Southeastern Oklahoma State U (OK) **508**
Southeastern U (DC) **508**
Southeast Missouri State U (MO) **508**
Southern Connecticut State U (CT) **509**
Southern Illinois U Carbondale (IL) **509**
Southern Methodist U (TX) **510**
Southern Nazarene U (OK) **510**
Southern New Hampshire U (NH) **510**
Southwestern Oklahoma State U (OK) **512**
Southwest Missouri State U (MO) **513**
Southwest Texas State U (TX) **513**
Spring Hill Coll (AL) **514**
State U of NY at New Paltz (NY) **515**
State U of NY at Oswego (NY) **515**
State U of NY Coll at Brockport (NY) **515**
State U of NY Coll at Fredonia (NY) **516**
State U of NY Coll at Old Westbury (NY) **516**
State U of NY Inst of Tech at Utica/Rome (NY) **518**
State U of West Georgia (GA) **518**
Stephen F. Austin State U (TX) **518**
Stetson U (FL) **519**
Stonehill Coll (MA) **520**
Suffolk U (MA) **520**
Susquehanna U (PA) **521**
Syracuse U (NY) **521**
Talladega Coll (AL) **522**
Tarleton State U (TX) **522**
Taylor U (IN) **523**
Teikyo Post U (CT) **523**
Temple U (PA) **523**
Tennessee Technological U (TN) **524**
Tennessee Wesleyan Coll (TN) **524**
Texas A&M International U (TX) **524**
Texas A&M U (TX) **524**
Texas A&M U–Commerce (TX) **525**
Texas A&M U–Corpus Christi (TX) **525**
Texas A&M U–Kingsville (TX) **525**
Texas A&M U–Texarkana (TX) **525**
Texas Christian U (TX) **526**
Texas Lutheran U (TX) **526**
Texas Southern U (TX) **526**
Texas Tech U (TX) **526**
Thomas Coll (ME) **527**
Thomas Edison State Coll (NJ) **527**
Tiffin U (OH) **528**
Touro Coll (NY) **529**
Trinity U (TX) **531**
Troy State U (AL) **532**
Troy State U Montgomery (AL) **532**
Truman State U (MO) **532**
Tulane U (LA) **533**
Tuskegee U (AL) **533**
Union U (TN) **534**
Université de Sherbrooke (QC, Canada) **536**
U Coll of the Cariboo (BC, Canada) **537**
The U of Akron (OH) **537**
The U of Alabama (AL) **537**
The U of Alabama at Birmingham (AL) **537**
The U of Alabama in Huntsville (AL) **537**
U of Alaska Anchorage (AK) **538**
U of Alberta (AB, Canada) **538**
The U of Arizona (AZ) **538**
U of Arkansas (AR) **539**
U of Arkansas at Little Rock (AR) **539**
U of Baltimore (MD) **539**
U of Bridgeport (CT) **540**
The U of British Columbia (BC, Canada) **540**
U of Calgary (AB, Canada) **540**
U of Central Arkansas (AR) **542**
U of Central Florida (FL) **542**
U of Central Oklahoma (OK) **542**
U of Cincinnati (OH) **543**
U of Colorado at Boulder (CO) **543**
U of Colorado at Colorado Springs (CO) **543**
U of Connecticut (CT) **544**
U of Dayton (OH) **544**
U of Delaware (DE) **544**
U of Denver (CO) **544**
U of Evansville (IN) **545**
U of Florida (FL) **545**
U of Georgia (GA) **545**
U of Hartford (CT) **546**
U of Hawaii at Manoa (HI) **546**
U of Houston (TX) **547**
U of Houston–Clear Lake (TX) **547**
U of Houston–Downtown (TX) **547**
U of Idaho (ID) **547**
U of Illinois at Chicago (IL) **547**
U of Illinois at Urbana–Champaign (IL) **548**
The U of Iowa (IA) **548**
U of Kentucky (KY) **549**
The U of Lethbridge (AB, Canada) **549**
U of Louisiana at Lafayette (LA) **550**
U of Louisville (KY) **550**
U of Manitoba (MB, Canada) **551**
U of Mary Hardin-Baylor (TX) **551**
U of Maryland, Coll Park (MD) **552**
U of Massachusetts Amherst (MA) **552**
U of Massachusetts Dartmouth (MA) **553**
The U of Memphis (TN) **553**
U of Miami (FL) **553**
U of Michigan–Dearborn (MI) **554**
U of Michigan–Flint (MI) **554**
U of Minnesota, Duluth (MN) **554**
U of Minnesota, Twin Cities Campus (MN) **555**
U of Mississippi (MS) **555**
U of Missouri–Columbia (MO) **555**
U of Missouri–St. Louis (MO) **556**
U of Nebraska at Omaha (NE) **557**
U of Nebraska–Lincoln (NE) **557**
U of Nevada, Las Vegas (NV) **558**
U of Nevada, Reno (NV) **558**
U of New Brunswick Fredericton (NB, Canada) **558**
U of New Hampshire (NH) **558**
U of New Haven (CT) **559**
U of New Orleans (LA) **559**
U of North Alabama (AL) **559**
The U of North Carolina at Charlotte (NC) **560**
The U of North Carolina at Greensboro (NC) **560**
The U of North Carolina at Wilmington (NC) **561**
U of North Dakota (ND) **561**
U of Northern Iowa (IA) **561**
U of North Florida (FL) **561**
U of North Texas (TX) **562**
U of Notre Dame (IN) **562**
U of Oklahoma (OK) **562**
U of Oregon (OR) **562**
U of Ottawa (ON, Canada) **563**
U of Pennsylvania (PA) **563**
U of Pittsburgh (PA) **569**
U of Pittsburgh at Johnstown (PA) **570**
U of Portland (OR) **570**
U of Puerto Rico at Arecibo (PR) **570**
U of Puerto Rico, Río Piedras (PR) **571**
U of Regina (SK, Canada) **572**
U of Rhode Island (RI) **572**
U of Richmond (VA) **572**
U of St. Francis (IL) **573**
U of Saint Francis (IN) **573**
U of St. Thomas (MN) **573**
U of St. Thomas (TX) **573**
U of San Francisco (CA) **574**
U of Saskatchewan (SK, Canada) **574**
The U of Scranton (PA) **574**
U of South Alabama (AL) **575**
U of South Carolina (SC) **575**
The U of South Dakota (SD) **575**
U of Southern Indiana (IN) **576**
U of Southern Mississippi (MS) **576**
U of South Florida (FL) **576**
The U of Tampa (FL) **577**
The U of Tennessee (TN) **577**
The U of Tennessee at Chattanooga (TN) **577**
The U of Tennessee at Martin (TN) **577**
The U of Texas at Austin (TX) **578**
The U of Texas at Brownsville (TX) **578**
The U of Texas at El Paso (TX) **578**
The U of Texas at San Antonio (TX) **578**
The U of Texas at Tyler (TX) **579**
The U of Texas of the Permian Basin (TX) **579**
The U of Texas–Pan American (TX) **579**
U of the District of Columbia (DC) **580**
U of the Incarnate Word (TX) **580**
U of Toledo (OH) **581**
U of Toronto (ON, Canada) **581**
U of Tulsa (OK) **581**
U of Utah (UT) **582**
U of West Florida (FL) **583**
U of Windsor (ON, Canada) **584**
U of Wisconsin–Eau Claire (WI) **584**
U of Wisconsin–La Crosse (WI) **584**
U of Wisconsin–Madison (WI) **584**
U of Wisconsin–Milwaukee (WI) **585**
U of Wisconsin–Oshkosh (WI) **585**
U of Wisconsin–Parkside (WI) **585**
U of Wisconsin–River Falls (WI) **585**
U of Wisconsin–Whitewater (WI) **586**
U of Wyoming (WY) **586**

FINANCE (continued)

Utah State U (UT) **587**
Valdosta State U (GA) **588**
Valparaiso U (IN) **588**
Vanguard U of Southern California (CA) **589**
Villanova U (PA) **590**
Virginia Polytechnic Inst and State U (VA) **591**
Wagner Coll (NY) **592**
Wake Forest U (NC) **592**
Waldorf Coll (IA) **592**
Walsh Coll of Accountancy and Business Admin (MI) **593**
Walsh U (OH) **593**
Warner Southern Coll (FL) **593**
Wartburg Coll (IA) **594**
Washington State U (WA) **595**
Washington U in St. Louis (MO) **595**
Waynesburg Coll (PA) **595**
Wayne State Coll (NE) **596**
Wayne State U (MI) **596**
Webber International U (FL) **596**
Weber State U (UT) **596**
Western Baptist Coll (OR) **598**
Western Carolina U (NC) **598**
Western Connecticut State U (CT) **598**
Western Illinois U (IL) **599**
Western International U (AZ) **599**
Western Kentucky U (KY) **599**
Western Michigan U (MI) **599**
Western New England Coll (MA) **600**
Western Washington U (WA) **600**
Westfield State Coll (MA) **600**
Westminster Coll (MO) **601**
Westminster Coll (UT) **601**
West Texas A&M U (TX) **602**
West Virginia U (WV) **602**
Wichita State U (KS) **604**
Wilberforce U (OH) **605**
William Carey Coll (MS) **605**
Wilmington Coll (DE) **607**
Wingate U (NC) **607**
Winona State U (MN) **608**
Wittenberg U (OH) **608**
Wofford Coll (SC) **609**
Wright State U (OH) **609**
Xavier U (OH) **610**
York Coll (NE) **610**
York Coll of Pennsylvania (PA) **610**
York U (ON, Canada) **611**
Youngstown State U (OH) **611**

FINANCIAL MANAGEMENT AND SERVICES RELATED

Information can be found under this major's main heading.

Bryant Coll (RI) **296**
Park U (MO) **465**
San Diego State U (CA) **498**
The U of Akron (OH) **537**

FINANCIAL PLANNING

Overview: Students learn the skills necessary to advise individuals and companies in planning for future growth of their holdings and other matters of financial growth and management. *Related majors:* finance, economics, business communications, investments and securities. *Potential careers:* financial analyst, investment advisor, financial planner, stockbroker, estate planner. *Salary potential:* $40k-$55k.

Baylor U (TX) **283**
Bethany Coll (KS) **287**
British Columbia Inst of Technology (BC, Canada) **295**
Central Michigan U (MI) **310**
Marywood U (PA) **421**
Medaille Coll (NY) **424**
The Ohio State U at Lima (OH) **458**
Roger Williams U (RI) **483**
Trinity Christian Coll (IL) **530**

FINANCIAL SERVICES MARKETING

Overview: This major teaches students marketing principles for a range of financial services and products, from tax preparation to investment advice and insurance to individual consumers. *Related majors:* accounting and taxation, investments and securities, insurance and risk management. *Potential careers:* marketing or advertising executive; insurance agent; securities, commodities, or other financial service sales agent. *Salary potential:* $25k-$35k.

Nipissing U (ON, Canada) **448**

FINE ARTS AND ART STUDIES RELATED

Information can be found under this major's main heading.

Allegheny Coll (PA) **264**
Angelo State U (TX) **269**
The Catholic U of America (DC) **307**
Chestnut Hill Coll (PA) **312**
Coll of Staten Island of the City U of NY (NY) **323**
Indiana State U (IN) **385**
Kentucky Wesleyan Coll (KY) **397**
Loyola U Chicago (IL) **411**
Okanagan U Coll (BC, Canada) **459**
Oregon Coll of Art & Craft (OR) **461**
Our Lady of the Lake U of San Antonio (TX) **463**
San Diego State U (CA) **498**
Skidmore Coll (NY) **506**
The U of Akron (OH) **537**
U of North Alabama (AL) **559**
U of Saint Francis (IN) **573**
U of Wyoming (WY) **586**

FINE/STUDIO ARTS

Overview: In this major, students concentrate on one or more disciplines in preparation for a career as a creative artist. *Related majors:* drawing, painting, multimedia, arts management, sculpture. *Potential careers:* fine artist, set designer, book jacket or magazine designer, creative consultant. *Salary potential:* $10k-$25k.

Abilene Christian U (TX) **260**
Academy of Art Coll (CA) **260**
Adams State Coll (CO) **260**
Alberta Coll of Art & Design (AB, Canada) **262**
Albertus Magnus Coll (CT) **262**
Alfred U (NY) **263**
Allegheny Coll (PA) **264**
American Academy of Art (IL) **265**
American U (DC) **267**
Amherst Coll (MA) **268**
Anderson Coll (SC) **268**
Anderson U (IN) **268**
Angelo State U (TX) **269**
Anna Maria Coll (MA) **269**
Appalachian State U (NC) **270**
Aquinas Coll (MI) **270**
Arcadia U (PA) **271**
Arizona State U (AZ) **271**
Art Academy of Cincinnati (OH) **273**
Asbury Coll (KY) **274**
Ashland U (OH) **274**
Atlanta Coll of Art (GA) **275**
Auburn U (AL) **276**
Augsburg Coll (MN) **276**
Augustana Coll (IL) **276**
Baker U (KS) **280**
Baldwin-Wallace Coll (OH) **280**
Ball State U (IN) **280**
Bard Coll (NY) **281**
Barton Coll (NC) **282**
Baylor U (TX) **283**
Bay Path Coll (MA) **283**
Belmont U (TN) **284**
Beloit Coll (WI) **285**
Bemidji State U (MN) **285**
Benedictine U (IL) **285**
Bennington Coll (VT) **286**
Berea Coll (KY) **286**
Berry Coll (GA) **287**
Bethany Coll (WV) **287**
Bethel Coll (MN) **288**
Biola U (CA) **289**
Birmingham-Southern Coll (AL) **289**
Bloomsburg U of Pennsylvania (PA) **290**
Boston Coll (MA) **292**
Bowdoin Coll (ME) **292**
Bradley U (IL) **293**
Brandeis U (MA) **293**
Brenau U (GA) **293**
Briarcliffe Coll (NY) **294**
Bridgewater State Coll (MA) **294**
Brock U (ON, Canada) **295**
Brown U (RI) **296**
Bucknell U (PA) **297**
Cabrini Coll (PA) **298**
California Baptist U (CA) **298**
California Coll of Arts and Crafts (CA) **299**
California Inst of the Arts (CA) **299**
California State U, Chico (CA) **300**
California State U, Dominguez Hills (CA) **300**
California State U, Fullerton (CA) **301**
California State U, Hayward (CA) **301**
California State U, Long Beach (CA) **301**
California State U, Northridge (CA) **301**
Calvin Coll (MI) **303**
Campbell U (NC) **303**
Capital U (OH) **304**
Cardinal Stritch U (WI) **305**
Carleton Coll (MN) **305**
Carnegie Mellon U (PA) **305**
Carroll Coll (WI) **306**
Carthage Coll (WI) **306**
Cedar Crest Coll (PA) **308**
Centenary Coll of Louisiana (LA) **308**
Central Missouri State U (MO) **310**
Chapman U (CA) **311**
Chatham Coll (PA) **312**
Chestnut Hill Coll (PA) **312**
Chowan Coll (NC) **312**
Clarke Coll (IA) **315**
Clark U (MA) **316**
Coe Coll (IA) **318**
Coker Coll (SC) **318**
Col for Creative Studies (MI) **319**
Coll of Charleston (SC) **320**
Coll of Mount St. Joseph (OH) **320**
The Coll of New Jersey (NJ) **320**
The Coll of New Rochelle (NY) **321**
Coll of Saint Benedict (MN) **321**
Coll of St. Catherine (MN) **321**
The Coll of Saint Rose (NY) **322**
Coll of Santa Fe (NM) **323**
Coll of the Holy Cross (MA) **323**
Coll of the Ozarks (MO) **323**
The Coll of Wooster (OH) **324**
The Colorado Coll (CO) **325**
Colorado State U (CO) **325**
Columbia Coll (MO) **326**
Columbia Coll (SC) **327**
Columbia Coll Chicago (IL) **327**
Columbus Coll of Art and Design (OH) **328**
Concordia Coll (MN) **329**
Concordia U (NE) **330**
Concordia U (QC, Canada) **331**
Converse Coll (SC) **332**
Corcoran Coll of Art and Design (DC) **332**
Cornell U (NY) **333**
Cornish Coll of the Arts (WA) **333**
Cumberland Coll (KY) **335**
Cumberland U (TN) **335**
Daemen Coll (NY) **335**
Dartmouth Coll (NH) **337**
Denison U (OH) **339**
DePaul U (IL) **339**
DePauw U (IN) **339**
Dickinson Coll (PA) **344**
Dominican U (IL) **345**
Drake U (IA) **345**
Drury U (MO) **346**
Duquesne U (PA) **346**
East Carolina U (NC) **347**
Eastern Washington U (WA) **349**
Edinboro U of Pennsylvania (PA) **351**
Elmira Coll (NY) **351**
Emmanuel Coll (MA) **353**
Endicott Coll (MA) **354**
The Evergreen State Coll (WA) **355**
Felician Coll (NJ) **357**
Ferris State U (MI) **358**
Ferrum Coll (VA) **358**
Finlandia U (MI) **358**
Flagler Coll (FL) **359**
Florida International U (FL) **360**
Florida Southern Coll (FL) **361**
Florida State U (FL) **361**
Fontbonne U (MO) **361**
Fordham U (NY) **362**
Fort Lewis Coll (CO) **362**
Framingham State Coll (MA) **362**
Franklin Pierce Coll (NH) **364**
Furman U (SC) **365**
Gallaudet U (DC) **365**
George Mason U (VA) **366**
The George Washington U (DC) **367**
Georgia Southwestern State U (GA) **368**
Gettysburg Coll (PA) **368**
Goddard Coll (VT) **369**
Governors State U (IL) **370**
Graceland U (IA) **371**
Grand Canyon U (AZ) **371**
Grand Valley State U (MI) **371**
Grand View Coll (IA) **372**
Green Mountain Coll (VT) **372**
Hamilton Coll (NY) **374**
Hamline U (MN) **374**
Hampden-Sydney Coll (VA) **374**
Hampshire Coll (MA) **375**
Harvard U (MA) **376**
High Point U (NC) **379**
Hiram Coll (OH) **379**
Hobart and William Smith Colls (NY) **380**
Hofstra U (NY) **380**
Hollins U (VA) **380**
Hope Coll (MI) **381**
Howard Payne U (TX) **382**
Humboldt State U (CA) **382**
Hunter Coll of the City U of NY (NY) **382**
Illinois Wesleyan U (IL) **385**
Indiana State U (IN) **385**
Indiana U Bloomington (IN) **385**
Indiana U–Purdue U Fort Wayne (IN) **386**
Indiana U–Purdue U Indianapolis (IN) **387**
Indiana U South Bend (IN) **387**
Indiana U Southeast (IN) **387**
Iowa Wesleyan Coll (IA) **390**
Ithaca Coll (NY) **390**
Jacksonville U (FL) **391**
Johnson State Coll (VT) **394**
Judson Coll (IL) **395**
Juniata Coll (PA) **395**
Kean U (NJ) **396**
Kendall Coll of Art and Design of Ferris State U (MI) **396**
Kennesaw State U (GA) **397**
Kent State U (OH) **397**
Kentucky State U (KY) **397**
Kenyon Coll (OH) **398**
King Coll (TN) **398**
Kutztown U of Pennsylvania (PA) **399**
Lafayette Coll (PA) **400**
Lake Erie Coll (OH) **400**
Lake Forest Coll (IL) **400**
Lamar U (TX) **401**
Lambuth U (TN) **401**
La Sierra U (CA) **403**
Lawrence U (WI) **403**
Lewis U (IL) **406**
Limestone Coll (SC) **406**
Lindenwood U (MO) **407**
Lipscomb U (TN) **408**
Long Island U, C.W. Post Campus (NY) **409**
Long Island U, Southampton Coll (NY) **409**
Long Island U, Southampton Coll, Friends World Program (NY) **409**
Longwood U (VA) **409**
Loras Coll (IA) **410**
Louisiana Coll (LA) **410**
Louisiana State U and A&M Coll (LA) **410**
Loyola Marymount U (CA) **411**
Lycoming Coll (PA) **412**
Lynchburg Coll (VA) **413**
Macalester Coll (MN) **413**
MacMurray Coll (IL) **414**
Manchester Coll (IN) **415**
Manhattanville Coll (NY) **416**
Mansfield U of Pennsylvania (PA) **416**
Marian Coll (IN) **417**
Marietta Coll (OH) **417**
Marist Coll (NY) **417**

Marlboro Coll (VT) **418**
Martin U (IN) **419**
Mary Baldwin Coll (VA) **419**
Marygrove Coll (MI) **419**
Maryland Inst Coll of Art (MD) **419**
Marymount Coll of Fordham U (NY) **419**
Marymount Manhattan Coll (NY) **420**
Maryville Coll (TN) **420**
Maryville U of Saint Louis (MO) **420**
Mary Washington Coll (VA) **420**
Marywood U (PA) **421**
Massachusetts Coll of Art (MA) **421**
Memphis Coll of Art (TN) **425**
Mercyhurst Coll (PA) **425**
Meredith Coll (NC) **426**
Merrimack Coll (MA) **426**
Messiah Coll (PA) **426**
Miami U (OH) **428**
Middlebury Coll (VT) **429**
Millikin U (IL) **430**
Mills Coll (CA) **431**
Minneapolis Coll of Art and Design (MN) **431**
Minnesota State U, Mankato (MN) **431**
Minnesota State U, Moorhead (MN) **432**
Monmouth U (NJ) **434**
Montana State U–Bozeman (MT) **434**
Montclair State U (NJ) **435**
Montserrat Coll of Art (MA) **435**
Moore Coll of Art and Design (PA) **436**
Moravian Coll (PA) **436**
Morehead State U (KY) **436**
Morningside Coll (IA) **437**
Mount Allison U (NB, Canada) **437**
Mount Holyoke Coll (MA) **438**
Mount Saint Vincent U (NS, Canada) **439**
Muhlenberg Coll (PA) **440**
Murray State U (KY) **440**
Nazareth Coll of Rochester (NY) **443**
New Coll of Florida (FL) **444**
New England Coll (NH) **444**
New Hampshire Inst of Art (NH) **445**
New Mexico State U (NM) **446**
New World School of the Arts (FL) **447**
New York Inst of Technology (NY) **447**
New York U (NY) **447**
North Carolina Central U (NC) **448**
Northeastern State U (OK) **450**
Northern Illinois U (IL) **450**
Northern Kentucky U (KY) **451**
Northern Michigan U (MI) **451**
Northland Coll (WI) **452**
North Park U (IL) **452**
Northwestern Coll (MN) **453**
Northwest Missouri State U (MO) **454**
Notre Dame Coll (OH) **455**
Notre Dame de Namur U (CA) **455**
Nova Scotia Coll of Art and Design (NS, Canada) **455**
Oberlin Coll (OH) **456**
Occidental Coll (CA) **457**
Ohio Dominican U (OH) **457**
The Ohio State U (OH) **457**
Ohio U (OH) **458**
Ohio Wesleyan U (OH) **459**
Oklahoma Baptist U (OK) **459**
Oklahoma City U (OK) **460**
Oklahoma State U (OK) **460**
Olivet Coll (MI) **461**
Oral Roberts U (OK) **461**
Oregon State U (OR) **462**
Otis Coll of Art and Design (CA) **462**
Pacific Lutheran U (WA) **463**
Pacific Northwest Coll of Art (OR) **464**
Pacific Union Coll (CA) **464**
Paier Coll of Art, Inc. (CT) **464**
Park U (MO) **465**
Pennsylvania Coll of Art & Design (PA) **467**
Piedmont Coll (GA) **470**
Pine Manor Coll (MA) **470**
Pittsburg State U (KS) **470**
Pitzer Coll (CA) **471**
Plattsburgh State U of NY (NY) **471**
Plymouth State Coll (NH) **471**
Pomona Coll (CA) **472**
Pratt Inst (NY) **473**
Principia Coll (IL) **474**
Providence Coll (RI) **474**
Queens Coll of the City U of NY (NY) **475**
Queen's U at Kingston (ON, Canada) **476**
Queens U of Charlotte (NC) **476**
Quincy U (IL) **476**
Ramapo Coll of New Jersey (NJ) **477**
Randolph-Macon Coll (VA) **477**
Randolph-Macon Woman's Coll (VA) **477**
Reed Coll (OR) **477**
Rhode Island Coll (RI) **479**
Rhodes Coll (TN) **479**
Rice U (TX) **479**
Richmond, The American International U in London(United Kingdom) **480**
Ringling School of Art and Design (FL) **480**
Rivier Coll (NH) **480**
Roberts Wesleyan Coll (NY) **481**
Rochester Inst of Technology (NY) **482**
Rockford Coll (IL) **482**
Rollins Coll (FL) **483**
Rosemont Coll (PA) **484**
Rowan U (NJ) **484**
Saginaw Valley State U (MI) **486**
St. Ambrose U (IA) **486**
St. Andrews Presbyterian Coll (NC) **487**
St. Cloud State U (MN) **488**
Saint John's U (MN) **490**
St. John's U (NY) **490**
Saint Louis U (MO) **492**
Saint Mary-of-the-Woods Coll (IN) **493**
Saint Mary's U of Minnesota (MN) **494**
Saint Peter's Coll (NJ) **495**
St. Thomas Aquinas Coll (NY) **495**
Saint Vincent Coll (PA) **496**
Salem Coll (NC) **496**
Salve Regina U (RI) **497**
San Francisco Art Inst (CA) **498**
San Jose State U (CA) **499**
Sarah Lawrence Coll (NY) **499**
School of the Art Inst of Chicago (IL) **500**
School of the Museum of Fine Arts (MA) **501**
School of Visual Arts (NY) **501**
Scripps Coll (CA) **501**
Seattle U (WA) **501**
Seton Hill U (PA) **502**
Shawnee State U (OH) **502**
Shorter Coll (GA) **504**
Sierra Nevada Coll (NV) **504**
Simon's Rock Coll of Bard (MA) **505**
Smith Coll (MA) **506**
Sonoma State U (CA) **506**
Southern Connecticut State U (CT) **509**
Southern Illinois U Carbondale (IL) **509**
Southern Illinois U Edwardsville (IL) **509**
Southern Methodist U (TX) **510**
Southwestern U (TX) **513**
Southwest State U (MN) **513**
Southwest Texas State U (TX) **513**
Spring Hill Coll (AL) **514**
State U of NY at Binghamton (NY) **515**
State U of NY at New Paltz (NY) **515**
State U of NY Coll at Brockport (NY) **515**
State U of NY Coll at Buffalo (NY) **516**
State U of NY Coll at Cortland (NY) **516**
State U of NY Coll at Fredonia (NY) **516**
State U of NY Coll at Geneseo (NY) **516**
State U of NY Coll at Oneonta (NY) **517**
Stonehill Coll (MA) **520**
Stony Brook U, State University of New York (NY) **520**
Swarthmore Coll (PA) **521**
Sweet Briar Coll (VA) **521**
Syracuse U (NY) **521**
Texas A&M U–Corpus Christi (TX) **525**
Texas Christian U (TX) **526**
Texas Tech U (TX) **526**
Texas Woman's U (TX) **527**
Thomas More Coll (KY) **528**
Transylvania U (KY) **529**
Trinity Coll (CT) **530**
Troy State U (AL) **532**
Truman State U (MO) **532**
Tulane U (LA) **533**
Union Coll (NE) **534**
Union Coll (NY) **534**
Université Laval (QC, Canada) **536**
U at Buffalo, The State University of New York (NY) **536**
U Coll of the Cariboo (BC, Canada) **537**
The U of Akron (OH) **537**
The U of Alabama (AL) **537**
The U of Alabama at Birmingham (AL) **537**
U of Alberta (AB, Canada) **538**
The U of Arizona (AZ) **538**
The U of British Columbia (BC, Canada) **540**
U of Calif, Irvine (CA) **541**
U of Calif, Riverside (CA) **541**
U of Calif, San Diego (CA) **541**
U of Calif, Santa Barbara (CA) **541**
U of Central Florida (FL) **542**
U of Chicago (IL) **542**
U of Colorado at Boulder (CO) **543**
U of Colorado at Colorado Springs (CO) **543**
U of Colorado at Denver (CO) **543**
U of Connecticut (CT) **544**
U of Dallas (TX) **544**
U of Dayton (OH) **544**
U of Denver (CO) **544**
U of Florida (FL) **545**
U of Georgia (GA) **545**
U of Great Falls (MT) **545**
U of Guelph (ON, Canada) **546**
U of Houston (TX) **547**
U of Idaho (ID) **547**
U of Illinois at Chicago (IL) **547**
U of Indianapolis (IN) **548**
The U of Iowa (IA) **548**
U of Kansas (KS) **549**
U of Kentucky (KY) **549**
U of Louisville (KY) **550**
U of Maine (ME) **550**
U of Maine at Presque Isle (ME) **551**
U of Maryland, Coll Park (MD) **552**
U of Massachusetts Amherst (MA) **552**
U of Miami (FL) **553**
U of Minnesota, Duluth (MN) **554**
U of Minnesota, Morris (MN) **555**
U of Missouri–Kansas City (MO) **555**
U of Missouri–St. Louis (MO) **556**
U of Montevallo (AL) **557**
U of Nebraska at Omaha (NE) **557**
U of Nebraska–Lincoln (NE) **557**
U of New Hampshire (NH) **558**
U of North Alabama (AL) **559**
The U of North Carolina at Asheville (NC) **559**
The U of North Carolina at Chapel Hill (NC) **560**
The U of North Carolina at Charlotte (NC) **560**
The U of North Carolina at Greensboro (NC) **560**
The U of North Carolina at Wilmington (NC) **561**
U of Northern Iowa (IA) **561**
U of North Florida (FL) **561**
U of Notre Dame (IN) **562**
U of Oklahoma (OK) **562**
U of Ottawa (ON, Canada) **563**
U of Pittsburgh (PA) **569**
U of Redlands (CA) **572**
U of Richmond (VA) **572**
U of Rochester (NY) **573**
U of St. Thomas (TX) **573**
U of San Francisco (CA) **574**
U of Saskatchewan (SK, Canada) **574**
U of South Carolina (SC) **575**
U of South Carolina Aiken (SC) **575**
The U of South Dakota (SD) **575**
U of Southern California (CA) **576**
The U of Tennessee (TN) **577**
The U of Texas at Arlington (TX) **577**
The U of Texas at Austin (TX) **578**
The U of Texas at El Paso (TX) **578**
The U of Texas–Pan American (TX) **579**
U of the District of Columbia (DC) **580**
U of the Pacific (CA) **580**
U of the South (TN) **581**
U of Toledo (OH) **581**
U of Toronto (ON, Canada) **581**
U of Vermont (VT) **582**
U of Victoria (BC, Canada) **582**
U of Waterloo (ON, Canada) **583**
The U of Western Ontario (ON, Canada) **583**
U of West Florida (FL) **583**
U of Windsor (ON, Canada) **584**
U of Wisconsin–Milwaukee (WI) **585**
U of Wisconsin–Oshkosh (WI) **585**
U of Wisconsin–Stevens Point (WI) **585**
U of Wisconsin–Superior (WI) **586**
Utica Coll (NY) **588**
Valdosta State U (GA) **588**
Valparaiso U (IN) **588**
Vassar Coll (NY) **589**
Washington and Lee U (VA) **594**
Washington U in St. Louis (MO) **595**
Webster U (MO) **597**
Wellesley Coll (MA) **597**
Wells Coll (NY) **597**
Wesleyan Coll (GA) **597**
Wesleyan U (CT) **597**
West Chester U of Pennsylvania (PA) **598**
Western Carolina U (NC) **598**
Western Illinois U (IL) **599**
Western Kentucky U (KY) **599**
Western State Coll of Colorado (CO) **600**
Western Washington U (WA) **600**
West Texas A&M U (TX) **602**
West Virginia Wesleyan Coll (WV) **603**
Wheaton Coll (MA) **603**
Whitworth Coll (WA) **604**
Wilberforce U (OH) **605**
Willamette U (OR) **605**
William Carey Coll (MS) **605**
William Paterson U of New Jersey (NJ) **606**
Williams Baptist Coll (AR) **606**
Williams Coll (MA) **606**
William Woods U (MO) **607**
Wingate U (NC) **607**
Winona State U (MN) **608**
Wittenberg U (OH) **608**
Xavier U (OH) **610**
York U (ON, Canada) **611**
Youngstown State U (OH) **611**

FIRE PROTECTION RELATED

Information can be found under this major's main heading.

The U of Akron (OH) **537**

FIRE PROTECTION/SAFETY TECHNOLOGY

Overview: This major will teach students the skills and knowledge necessary to reduce fire risk, limit property loss, conduct fire investigations, and advise on safety procedures and fire prevention techniques. *Related majors:* fire science, community organization, resources and services, social work, police science. *Potential careers:* fire fighter, community safety liaison, insurance inspector, social worker, building inspector. *Salary potential:* $25k-$32k.

Columbia Southern U (AL) **327**
Eastern Kentucky U (KY) **348**
Oklahoma State U (OK) **460**
Thomas Edison State Coll (NJ) **527**
U of Cincinnati (OH) **543**
U of New Haven (CT) **559**

FIRE SCIENCE

Overview: Students will learn how to fight fires, operate fire-fighting equipment, understand fire behavior, handle hazardous materials, and rescue victims of fire. *Related majors:* fire protection and safety technology, emergency medical technology, safety and security technology. *Salary potential:* $25k-$30k.

Anna Maria Coll (MA) **269**
Cogswell Polytechnical Coll (CA) **318**
Eastern Kentucky U (KY) **348**
Eastern Oregon U (OR) **349**
Hampton U (VA) **375**
Holy Family U (PA) **380**
Jackson State U (MS) **390**
John Jay Coll of Criminal Justice, the City U of NY (NY) **392**
Madonna U (MI) **414**
Mercy Coll (NY) **425**
U of Maryland University Coll (MD) **552**
U of New Brunswick Fredericton (NB, Canada) **558**
U of the District of Columbia (DC) **580**

FIRE SERVICES ADMINISTRATION

Overview: This major will teach students how to manage fire departments, fire control services, fire inspections, and related rescue services. *Related majors:* fire protection, operations management and

FIRE SERVICES ADMINISTRATION (continued)

supervision, fire sciences, public administration. *Potential careers:* fire department administrator, fire inspection manager, ambulance company executive. *Salary potential:* $28k-$35k.

Columbia Southern U (AL) ***327***
Southern Illinois U Carbondale (IL) ***509***
Western Oregon U (OR) ***600***

FISH/GAME MANAGEMENT

Overview: This major prepares students for a career managing diverse fish, wildlife, and plant resources and the habitats on which they depend for ecological values and their use and enjoyment by the public. *Related majors:* fisheries science and management, wildlife and wildlands management, forest management, natural resources law enforcement. *Potential careers:* research scientist, fish and game warden, firearms instructor, park ranger. *Salary potential:* $25k-$30k.

Delaware State U (DE) ***338***
The Evergreen State Coll (WA) ***355***
Humboldt State U (CA) ***382***
Iowa State U of Science and Technology (IA) ***390***
Lincoln Memorial U (TN) ***407***
North Dakota State U (ND) ***449***
Northland Coll (WI) ***452***
Oregon State U (OR) ***462***
Pittsburg State U (KS) ***470***
Rutgers, The State U of New Jersey, New Brunswick (NJ) ***485***
South Dakota State U (SD) ***507***
Southeastern Oklahoma State U (OK) ***508***
State U of NY Coll of Environ Sci and Forestry (NY) ***517***
Texas A&M U at Galveston (TX) ***524***
Texas A&M U–Kingsville (TX) ***525***
The U of British Columbia (BC, Canada) ***540***
U of Idaho (ID) ***547***
U of Minnesota, Duluth (MN) ***554***
U of Minnesota, Twin Cities Campus (MN) ***555***
U of Missouri–Columbia (MO) ***555***
U of New Brunswick Fredericton (NB, Canada) ***558***
The U of South Dakota (SD) ***575***
U of Vermont (VT) ***582***
West Virginia U (WV) ***602***

FISHING SCIENCES

Overview: Students who choose this major will study the management and production of nondomesticated fish and shellfish populations for recreational and commercial purposes as well as fishing and marine/aquatic product processing to ensure adequate conservation. *Related majors:* fish and game management, marine biology, water resources, environmental science. *Potential careers:* commercial fisherman, inspector, environmental scientist, lobbyist. *Salary potential:* $20k-$27k.

Colorado State U (CO) ***325***
Malaspina U-Coll (BC, Canada) ***415***
Mansfield U of Pennsylvania (PA) ***416***
Murray State U (KY) ***440***
The Ohio State U (OH) ***457***
Penn State U Univ Park Campus (PA) ***468***
State U of NY Coll of A&T at Cobleskill (NY) ***517***
State U of NY Coll of Environ Sci and Forestry (NY) ***517***
Texas Tech U (TX) ***526***
Unity Coll (ME) ***535***
U of Alaska Fairbanks (AK) ***538***
U of Georgia (GA) ***545***
U of Nebraska–Lincoln (NE) ***557***
U of Rhode Island (RI) ***572***
U of Washington (WA) ***583***

FLUID/THERMAL SCIENCES

Overview: This major combines physics with chemical engineering and students focus on the fundamental aspects of thermodynamics, heat transfer, and fluid dynamics. *Related majors:* chemical engineering, chemistry, environmental engineering, pollution control technology. *Potential careers:* chemical engineer, petroleum engineer, environmentalist, research scientist, industrial engineer. *Salary potential:* $37k-$50k.

Harvard U (MA) ***376***
Worcester Polytechnic Inst (MA) ***609***

FOLKLORE

Overview: Students explore the dynamics of tradition and creativity in daily life as well as in times of crisis, celebration, and change. Folklorists study the ways in which human beings seek understanding and involvement through the shaping of tradition to fit new and challenging circumstances. *Related majors:* area and cultural studies, ethnomusicology, art history, comparative literature. *Potential careers:* anthropologist, archeologist, folklorist, teacher, historian. *Salary potential:* $23k-$28k.

Harvard U (MA) ***376***
Indiana U Bloomington (IN) ***385***
Laurentian U (ON, Canada) ***403***
Long Island U, Southampton Coll, Friends World Program (NY) ***409***
Marlboro Coll (VT) ***418***
Memorial U of Newfoundland (NF, Canada) ***424***
The Ohio State U (OH) ***457***
U of Alberta (AB, Canada) ***538***
U of Oregon (OR) ***562***
U of Pennsylvania (PA) ***563***

FOOD AND BEVERAGE/ RESTAURANT OPERATIONS

Overview: This major prepares students to manage food and beverage operations, restaurants, and catering services. *Related majors:* logistics, hotel/motel and restaurant management, hospitality management, event planning, business administration. *Salary potential:* $25k-$32k.

Lewis-Clark State Coll (ID) ***406***

FOOD PRODUCTS RETAILING

Overview: This major teaches students about the retail operations of supermarkets and alternative food stores, including issues of logistics and personnel management. *Related majors:* marketing, retail management, logistics. *Potential careers:* supermarket, alternative food store, or category manager; food wholesaler; market analyst; market researcher; sales manager or brand manager. *Salary potential:* $25k-$35k.

Ball State U (IN) ***280***
California State U, Northridge (CA) ***301***
Concord Coll (WV) ***329***
Delaware Valley Coll (PA) ***339***
Dominican U (IL) ***345***
Immaculata U (PA) ***385***
Iowa State U of Science and Technology (IA) ***390***
Johnson & Wales U (RI) ***393***
Lindenwood U (MO) ***407***
Lipscomb U (TN) ***408***
Lynn U (FL) ***413***
Madonna U (MI) ***414***
Montclair State U (NJ) ***435***
Mount Saint Vincent U (NS, Canada) ***439***
North Carolina Wesleyan Coll (NC) ***449***
Northern Michigan U (MI) ***451***
Oregon State U (OR) ***462***
Rochester Inst of Technology (NY) ***482***
San Francisco State U (CA) ***498***
State U of NY Coll at Buffalo (NY) ***516***
Syracuse U (NY) ***521***
U of Alberta (AB, Canada) ***538***
U of Maryland Eastern Shore (MD) ***552***
Wayne State Coll (NE) ***596***
Western New Mexico U (NM) ***600***

FOOD SALES OPERATIONS

Overview: Students who choose this major learn how to market and promote food products to the general public and learn how to function as a sales representative for a food production company. *Related majors:* food products retailing, marketing, marketing research. *Potential careers:* market researcher, marketing executive, sales representative for a food company. *Salary potential:* $20k-$30k.

Immaculata U (PA) ***385***
Johnson & Wales U (RI) ***393***
Northwest Missouri State U (MO) ***454***
Rochester Inst of Technology (NY) ***482***
Saint Joseph's U (PA) ***491***
U of Delaware (DE) ***544***

FOOD SCIENCES

Overview: Students will learn the scientific principles and applications (manufacturing, packaging, and storage) of converting raw agricultural products into processed forms suitable for human consumption. *Related majors:* agricultural sciences, agricultural and food products processing, chemistry, physiology and nutrition. *Potential careers:* nutritionist, food inspector, biochemist, agribusiness manager, quality control manager. *Salary potential:* $28k-$50k.

Acadia U (NS, Canada) ***260***
Alabama A&M U (AL) ***261***
Arizona State U East (AZ) ***271***
Auburn U (AL) ***276***
Brigham Young U (UT) ***295***
California Polytechnic State U, San Luis Obispo (CA) ***300***
California State U, Northridge (CA) ***301***
Chapman U (CA) ***311***
Clemson U (SC) ***317***
Cornell U (NY) ***333***
Dalhousie U (NS, Canada) ***336***
Delaware Valley Coll (PA) ***339***
Dominican U (IL) ***345***
Framingham State Coll (MA) ***362***
Insto Tecno Estudios Sups Monterrey(Mexico) ***388***
Kansas State U (KS) ***396***
Lamar U (TX) ***401***
Louisiana State U and A&M Coll (LA) ***410***
Marymount Coll of Fordham U (NY) ***419***
McGill U (QC, Canada) ***423***
Memorial U of Newfoundland (NF, Canada) ***424***
Michigan State U (MI) ***428***
Mississippi State U (MS) ***432***
North Carolina Ag and Tech State U (NC) ***448***
North Carolina State U (NC) ***449***
North Dakota State U (ND) ***449***
Northwest Missouri State U (MO) ***454***
The Ohio State U (OH) ***457***
Olivet Nazarene U (IL) ***461***
Oregon State U (OR) ***462***
Penn State U Univ Park Campus (PA) ***468***
Purdue U (IN) ***475***
Rutgers, The State U of New Jersey, New Brunswick (NJ) ***485***
San Jose State U (CA) ***499***
South Dakota State U (SD) ***507***
Texas A&M U (TX) ***524***
Texas A&M U–Kingsville (TX) ***525***
Texas Tech U (TX) ***526***
Tuskegee U (AL) ***533***
Université Laval (QC, Canada) ***536***
The U of Akron (OH) ***537***
U of Alberta (AB, Canada) ***538***
U of Arkansas (AR) ***539***
The U of British Columbia (BC, Canada) ***540***
U of Calif, Davis (CA) ***540***
U of Delaware (DE) ***544***
U of Florida (FL) ***545***
U of Georgia (GA) ***545***
U of Hawaii at Manoa (HI) ***546***
U of Idaho (ID) ***547***
U of Illinois at Urbana–Champaign (IL) ***548***
U of Kentucky (KY) ***549***
U of Maine (ME) ***550***
U of Manitoba (MB, Canada) ***551***
U of Maryland, Coll Park (MD) ***552***
U of Massachusetts Amherst (MA) ***552***
U of Missouri–Columbia (MO) ***555***
U of Nebraska–Lincoln (NE) ***557***
U of Saskatchewan (SK, Canada) ***574***
The U of Tennessee (TN) ***577***
U of the District of Columbia (DC) ***580***
U of Utah (UT) ***582***
U of Wisconsin–Madison (WI) ***584***
U of Wisconsin–River Falls (WI) ***585***
Virginia Polytechnic Inst and State U (VA) ***591***

FOOD SERVICES TECHNOLOGY

Overview: This major focuses on engineering principles and technology relating to packaging, preserving, storing, distributing, and serving food products. *Related majors:* food science and technology, chemistry, industrial/ manufacturing engineering, quality control technology, occupational health and industrial hygiene. *Potential careers:* food service administrator, plant manager, quality control manager, catering company scientist. *Salary potential:* $28k-$36k.

California State U, Northridge (CA) ***301***
Delaware Valley Coll (PA) ***339***
Iowa State U of Science and Technology (IA) ***390***
Johnson & Wales U (RI) ***393***
Madonna U (MI) ***414***
Mansfield U of Pennsylvania (PA) ***416***
San Jose State U (CA) ***499***
Tennessee State U (TN) ***523***

FOODS/NUTRITION STUDIES RELATED

Information can be found under this major's main heading.

U of Wisconsin–Stout (WI) ***586***
Utah State U (UT) ***587***

FOOD SYSTEMS ADMINISTRATION

Overview: This major teaches undergraduates about the administration of food service systems in institutional settings. *Related majors:* food services technology, restaurant operations, food and nutrition studies, culinary arts, operations management and supervision. *Potential careers:* chef, caterer, public or private food services administrator. *Salary potential:* $23k-$30k.

Johnson & Wales U (VA) ***393***
Western Michigan U (MI) ***599***

FOREIGN LANGUAGES EDUCATION

Overview: This major prepares undergraduates for teaching foreign languages other than French, German or Spanish at various educational levels. *Related majors:* Italian, Chinese, Japanese, Latin, Russian, and other foreign languages and literatures. *Potential careers:* language teacher, school tour guide. *Salary potential:* $25k-$35k.

Arkansas Tech U (AR) ***272***
Baylor U (TX) ***283***
Berea Coll (KY) ***286***
Bethune-Cookman Coll (FL) ***289***
Boston U (MA) ***292***
Bowling Green State U (OH) ***292***
Brigham Young U (UT) ***295***
Central Methodist Coll (MO) ***309***
Dana Coll (NE) ***337***
Delta State U (MS) ***339***
Duquesne U (PA) ***346***
Eastern Michigan U (MI) ***348***
Elmira Coll (NY) ***351***
Florida International U (FL) ***360***
Florida State U (FL) ***361***
Gannon U (PA) ***365***
Greenville Coll (IL) ***373***
Hastings Coll (NE) ***377***
Juniata Coll (PA) ***395***
Le Moyne Coll (NY) ***404***
Lincoln U (PA) ***407***
Long Island U, C.W. Post Campus (NY) ***409***
Luther Coll (IA) ***412***
McMurry U (TX) ***423***
Mercer U (GA) ***425***
Millersville U of Pennsylvania (PA) ***430***
Nazareth Coll of Rochester (NY) ***443***
New York U (NY) ***447***
Rivier Coll (NH) ***480***
St. John's U (NY) ***490***
San Diego State U (CA) ***498***
Seton Hill U (PA) ***502***
Southwestern Coll (KS) ***512***
Southwest Missouri State U (MO) ***513***
State U of NY at Albany (NY) ***514***
State U of NY Coll at Potsdam (NY) ***517***
State U of West Georgia (GA) ***518***
Texas Wesleyan U (TX) ***526***
The U of Akron (OH) ***537***
The U of Arizona (AZ) ***538***
U of Central Florida (FL) ***542***
U of Delaware (DE) ***544***
U of Georgia (GA) ***545***
U of Hawaii at Manoa (HI) ***546***
U of Illinois at Chicago (IL) ***547***
U of Illinois at Urbana–Champaign (IL) ***548***
U of Maryland, Coll Park (MD) ***552***
U of Minnesota, Twin Cities Campus (MN) ***555***
U of Nebraska–Lincoln (NE) ***557***
U of Nevada, Reno (NV) ***558***
U of New Orleans (LA) ***559***
U of Northern Iowa (IA) ***561***
U of Oklahoma (OK) ***562***
U of South Florida (FL) ***576***
U of Vermont (VT) ***582***
U of West Florida (FL) ***583***
Wheeling Jesuit U (WV) ***603***
Youngstown State U (OH) ***611***

FOREIGN LANGUAGES/ LITERATURES

Overview: This major introduces students to one or more foreign languages that are not specific as to the name of the language studied and introduces students to language studies at a basic level. *Related majors:* any specific language study, Romance languages, modern languages. *Salary potential:* $22k-$30k.

Adelphi U (NY) ***260***
Arkansas Tech U (AR) ***272***
Assumption Coll (MA) ***275***
Auburn U Montgomery (AL) ***276***
Augustana Coll (SD) ***276***
Austin Peay State U (TN) ***278***
Bethune-Cookman Coll (FL) ***289***
Boston U (MA) ***292***
Central Methodist Coll (MO) ***309***
Central Washington U (WA) ***310***
Clemson U (SC) ***317***
The Coll of Southeastern Europe, The American U of Athens(Greece) ***323***
Delta State U (MS) ***339***
Duquesne U (PA) ***346***
Eastern Illinois U (IL) ***348***
East Tennessee State U (TN) ***349***
Elmira Coll (NY) ***351***
Elon U (NC) ***352***
Emporia State U (KS) ***354***
Excelsior Coll (NY) ***356***
Frostburg State U (MD) ***365***
Gannon U (PA) ***365***
George Mason U (VA) ***366***
Gordon Coll (MA) ***370***
Graceland U (IA) ***371***
Hastings Coll (NE) ***377***
Indiana State U (IN) ***385***
James Madison U (VA) ***391***
Juniata Coll (PA) ***395***
Kansas State U (KS) ***396***
Kentucky Wesleyan Coll (KY) ***397***
Knox Coll (IL) ***399***
Marshall U (WV) ***418***
Massachusetts Inst of Technology (MA) ***421***
McGill U (QC, Canada) ***423***
Metropolitan State Coll of Denver (CO) ***427***
Middle Tennessee State U (TN) ***429***
Millikin U (IL) ***430***
Minnesota State U, Moorhead (MN) ***432***
Mississippi Coll (MS) ***432***
Mississippi State U (MS) ***432***
Monmouth U (NJ) ***434***
Montana State U–Bozeman (MT) ***434***
New Mexico State U (NM) ***446***
Oakland U (MI) ***456***
Old Dominion U (VA) ***460***
Pace U (NY) ***463***
Principia Coll (IL) ***474***
Purdue U (IN) ***475***
Radford U (VA) ***476***
The Richard Stockton Coll of New Jersey (NJ) ***479***
Roger Williams U (RI) ***483***
Rutgers, The State U of New Jersey, New Brunswick (NJ) ***485***
St. Lawrence U (NY) ***491***
Saint Peter's Coll (NJ) ***495***
Samford U (AL) ***497***
Scripps Coll (CA) ***501***
Seton Hall U (NJ) ***502***
Simon's Rock Coll of Bard (MA) ***505***
Southern Adventist U (TN) ***508***
Southern Illinois U Edwardsville (IL) ***509***
Southern Methodist U (TX) ***510***
Southwestern Coll (KS) ***512***
Stonehill Coll (MA) ***520***
Syracuse U (NY) ***521***
Texas A&M U (TX) ***524***
Thomas Edison State Coll (NJ) ***527***
Union Coll (NY) ***534***
Union U (TN) ***534***
The U of Alabama in Huntsville (AL) ***537***
U of Alaska Anchorage (AK) ***538***
U of Alaska Fairbanks (AK) ***538***
U of Calif, San Diego (CA) ***541***
U of Calif, Santa Cruz (CA) ***542***
U of Central Florida (FL) ***542***
U of Delaware (DE) ***544***
U of Georgia (GA) ***545***
U of Hartford (CT) ***546***
U of Idaho (ID) ***547***
U of Massachusetts Lowell (MA) ***553***
The U of Memphis (TN) ***553***
The U of Montana–Missoula (MT) ***556***
U of New Mexico (NM) ***559***
U of North Alabama (AL) ***559***
U of North Dakota (ND) ***561***
U of Northern Iowa (IA) ***561***
U of Puerto Rico, Río Piedras (PR) ***571***
The U of Scranton (PA) ***574***
U of South Alabama (AL) ***575***
U of Southern Mississippi (MS) ***576***
The U of Texas at Austin (TX) ***578***
The U of Virginia's Coll at Wise (VA) ***582***
Virginia Commonwealth U (VA) ***590***
Virginia Wesleyan Coll (VA) ***591***
Washington and Lee U (VA) ***594***
Wayne State U (MI) ***596***
West Virginia U (WV) ***602***
Widener U (PA) ***604***
Wilson Coll (PA) ***607***
Youngstown State U (OH) ***611***

FOREIGN LANGUAGES/ LITERATURES RELATED

Information can be found under this major's main heading.

Clemson U (SC) ***317***
Southern Illinois U Carbondale (IL) ***509***
U of Hawaii at Manoa (HI) ***546***
Yale U (CT) ***610***

FOREIGN LANGUAGE TRANSLATION

Overview: This major prepares students to work as professional translators or interpreters; it often includes intensive instruction in one or more foreign languages. *Related majors:* linguistics, any specific language. *Potential careers:* translator, diplomatic corps, business consultant, editor. *Salary potential:* $25k-$34k.

Concordia U (QC, Canada) ***331***
Laurentian U (ON, Canada) ***403***
Université Laval (QC, Canada) ***536***
York U (ON, Canada) ***611***

FORENSIC TECHNOLOGY

Overview: This major teaches students how to apply physical, biomedical, and social sciences to forensic work, including the analysis and evaluation of physical evidence, human testimony, and criminal suspects. *Related majors:* police science, psychology, criminology, computer science, biology, chemistry. *Potential careers:* forensic scientist, detective, police officer, attorney, criminologist. *Salary potential:* $25k-$35k.

Alvernia Coll (PA) ***265***
Baylor U (TX) ***283***
Carroll Coll (WI) ***306***
Chaminade U of Honolulu (HI) ***311***
Coll of the Ozarks (MO) ***323***
Columbia Coll (MO) ***326***
Eastern Kentucky U (KY) ***348***
Indiana U Bloomington (IN) ***385***
Jacksonville State U (AL) ***390***
John Jay Coll of Criminal Justice, the City U of NY (NY) ***392***
Loyola U New Orleans (LA) ***411***
State U of NY Coll at Buffalo (NY) ***516***
U of Baltimore (MD) ***539***
U of Central Florida (FL) ***542***
U of Central Oklahoma (OK) ***542***
U of Mississippi (MS) ***555***
U of New Haven (CT) ***559***
Waynesburg Coll (PA) ***595***
West Chester U of Pennsylvania (PA) ***598***
West Virginia U (WV) ***602***

FOREST ENGINEERING

Overview: This major prepares students to apply scientific, engineering, and forestry principles to the design of mechanical devices and processors for efficient forest management and timber production. *Related majors:* wood science and pulp/paper technology, forest-harvesting production technology, forest management. *Potential careers:* logger, logging company executive or technician. *Salary potential:* $28k-$40k.

Oregon State U (OR) ***462***
State U of NY Coll of Environ Sci and Forestry (NY) ***517***
U of Maine (ME) ***550***
U of New Brunswick Fredericton (NB, Canada) ***558***
U of New Brunswick Saint John (NB, Canada) ***558***
U of Washington (WA) ***583***

FOREST HARVESTING PRODUCTION TECHNOLOGY

Overview: This major teaches students about the production, harvesting, and processing of forest products and resources and prepares individuals for associated managerial functions. *Related majors:* forest engineering, wood science and pulp/paper technology, agricultural business. *Potential careers:* logging company executive or salesperson, forest manager, lobbyist. *Salary potential:* $25k-$34k.

Lakehead U (ON, Canada) ***400***

FOREST MANAGEMENT

Overview: This major combines principles of forestry and natural resources management, the administration of forestlands, and related resources. *Related majors:* forestry, natural resources management. *Potential careers:* park ranger, ecologist, environmental scientist. *Salary potential:* $20k-$27k.

Clemson U (SC) ***317***
Louisiana State U and A&M Coll (LA) ***410***
North Carolina State U (NC) ***449***
State U of NY Coll of Environ Sci and Forestry (NY) ***517***
Stephen F. Austin State U (TX) ***518***
Université Laval (QC, Canada) ***536***
U of Minnesota, Twin Cities Campus (MN) ***555***
The U of Montana–Missoula (MT) ***556***
U of Washington (WA) ***583***
Warren Wilson Coll (NC) ***594***

FOREST PRODUCTION AND PROCESSING RELATED

Information can be found under this major's main heading.

Université Laval (QC, Canada) ***536***

FOREST PRODUCTS TECHNOLOGY

Overview: This major prepares students to assist foresters in the management and production of forest resources, including instruction in tree identification, timber measurement, logging and timber harvesting, forest propagation and regeneration, and forest fire fighting. *Related majors:* environmental science, forest management, natural resources management, soil sciences. *Potential careers:* lobbyist, park ranger, fire fighter, logger. *Salary potential:* $23k-$30k.

Penn State U Univ Park Campus (PA) ***468***
Southern U and A&M Coll (LA) ***511***

FORESTRY

Overview: This major arms students with the knowledge to manage and develop forest areas for economic, recreational, and ecological purposes. *Related majors:* natural resources management, statistics, forest-harvesting production technology, soil sciences, plant

FORESTRY (continued)

protection. *Potential career:* park ranger, environmental scientist or activist, logging executive or salesperson, lobbyist. *Salary potential:* $20k-$30k.

Albright Coll (PA) ***263***
Baylor U (TX) ***283***
California Polytechnic State U, San Luis Obispo (CA) ***300***
Coll of Saint Benedict (MN) ***321***
Humboldt State U (CA) ***382***
Iowa State U of Science and Technology (IA) ***390***
Lakehead U (ON, Canada) ***400***
Lees-McRae Coll (NC) ***404***
Louisiana Tech U (LA) ***410***
Michigan State U (MI) ***428***
Michigan Technological U (MI) ***428***
Mississippi State U (MS) ***432***
North Dakota State U (ND) ***449***
Northland Coll (WI) ***452***
Northwest Missouri State U (MO) ***454***
The Ohio State U (OH) ***457***
Oklahoma State U (OK) ***460***
Oregon State U (OR) ***462***
Purdue U (IN) ***475***
Saint John's U (MN) ***490***
Southern Illinois U Carbondale (IL) ***509***
State U of NY Coll of Environ Sci and Forestry (NY) ***517***
Stephen F. Austin State U (TX) ***518***
Sterling Coll (VT) ***519***
Texas A&M U (TX) ***524***
Thomas Edison State Coll (NJ) ***527***
Unity Coll (ME) ***535***
U of Alberta (AB, Canada) ***538***
U of Arkansas at Monticello (AR) ***539***
The U of British Columbia (BC, Canada) ***540***
U of Florida (FL) ***545***
U of Georgia (GA) ***545***
U of Idaho (ID) ***547***
U of Illinois at Urbana–Champaign (IL) ***548***
U of Maine (ME) ***550***
U of Massachusetts Amherst (MA) ***552***
U of Minnesota, Twin Cities Campus (MN) ***555***
U of Missouri–Columbia (MO) ***555***
The U of Montana–Missoula (MT) ***556***
U of Nevada, Reno (NV) ***558***
U of New Brunswick Fredericton (NB, Canada) ***558***
U of New Brunswick Saint John (NB, Canada) ***558***
U of New Hampshire (NH) ***558***
The U of Tennessee (TN) ***577***
U of the District of Columbia (DC) ***580***
U of the South (TN) ***581***
U of Toronto (ON, Canada) ***581***
U of Vermont (VT) ***582***
U of Washington (WA) ***583***
U of Wisconsin–Madison (WI) ***584***
U of Wisconsin–Milwaukee (WI) ***585***
U of Wisconsin–Stevens Point (WI) ***585***
Utah State U (UT) ***587***
Virginia Polytechnic Inst and State U (VA) ***591***
Washington and Lee U (VA) ***594***
Washington State U (WA) ***595***
West Virginia U (WV) ***602***

FORESTRY SCIENCES

Overview: This major focuses on the environmental factors affecting forests and the growth and management of forest resources. *Related majors:* soil sciences, natural resource management, forestry, forest management, forest-harvesting production, plant protection. *Potential careers:* logging executive or salesperson, environmental scientist, park ranger, ecologist. *Salary potential:* $20k-$30k.

Auburn U (AL) ***276***
Colorado State U (CO) ***325***
Memorial U of Newfoundland (NF, Canada) ***424***
Northern Arizona U (AZ) ***450***
Penn State U Univ Park Campus (PA) ***468***
Rutgers, The State U of New Jersey, New Brunswick (NJ) ***485***
U of Calif, Berkeley (CA) ***540***
U of Georgia (GA) ***545***
U of Kentucky (KY) ***549***
U of Washington (WA) ***583***

FORESTRY SCIENCES RELATED

Information can be found under this major's main heading.

Utah State U (UT) ***587***

FRENCH

Overview: Students learn how to speak, read, and write the French language. *Related majors:* Western civilization, history, international relations, museum studies, art history. *Potential careers:* international banker, diplomatic corps, language teacher or tutor, art historian, advertising executive. *Salary potential:* $22k-$30k.

Abilene Christian U (TX) ***260***
Acadia U (NS, Canada) ***260***
Adelphi U (NY) ***260***
Adrian Coll (MI) ***260***
Agnes Scott Coll (GA) ***261***
Alabama State U (AL) ***261***
Albany State U (GA) ***262***
Albertus Magnus Coll (CT) ***262***
Albion Coll (MI) ***262***
Albright Coll (PA) ***263***
Alfred U (NY) ***263***
Allegheny Coll (PA) ***264***
Alma Coll (MI) ***264***
American U (DC) ***267***
The American U of Paris(France) ***268***
Amherst Coll (MA) ***268***
Anderson U (IN) ***268***
Andrews U (MI) ***269***
Angelo State U (TX) ***269***
Antioch Coll (OH) ***269***
Appalachian State U (NC) ***270***
Aquinas Coll (MI) ***270***
Arizona State U (AZ) ***271***
Arkansas State U (AR) ***272***
Arkansas Tech U (AR) ***272***
Asbury Coll (KY) ***274***
Ashland U (OH) ***274***
Assumption Coll (MA) ***275***
Athabasca U (AB, Canada) ***275***
Atlantic Union Coll (MA) ***276***
Auburn U (AL) ***276***
Augsburg Coll (MN) ***276***
Augustana Coll (IL) ***276***
Augustana Coll (SD) ***276***
Augusta State U (GA) ***277***
Austin Coll (TX) ***277***
Baker U (KS) ***280***
Baldwin-Wallace Coll (OH) ***280***
Ball State U (IN) ***280***
Bard Coll (NY) ***281***
Barnard Coll (NY) ***282***
Barry U (FL) ***282***
Bates Coll (ME) ***282***
Baylor U (TX) ***283***
Bellarmine U (KY) ***284***
Beloit Coll (WI) ***285***
Benedictine Coll (KS) ***285***
Bennington Coll (VT) ***286***
Berea Coll (KY) ***286***
Berry Coll (GA) ***287***
Bethany Coll (WV) ***287***
Birmingham-Southern Coll (AL) ***289***
Bishop's U (QC, Canada) ***289***
Bloomsburg U of Pennsylvania (PA) ***290***
Blue Mountain Coll (MS) ***291***
Boston Coll (MA) ***292***
Boston U (MA) ***292***
Bowdoin Coll (ME) ***292***
Bowling Green State U (OH) ***292***
Bradley U (IL) ***293***
Brandeis U (MA) ***293***
Brandon U (MB, Canada) ***293***
Bridgewater Coll (VA) ***294***
Brigham Young U (UT) ***295***
Brock U (ON, Canada) ***295***
Brooklyn Coll of the City U of NY (NY) ***295***
Brown U (RI) ***296***
Bryn Mawr Coll (PA) ***297***
Bucknell U (PA) ***297***
Butler U (IN) ***297***
Cabrini Coll (PA) ***298***
Caldwell Coll (NJ) ***298***
California Lutheran U (CA) ***299***
California State U, Chico (CA) ***300***
California State U, Dominguez Hills (CA) ***300***
California State U, Fresno (CA) ***301***
California State U, Fullerton (CA) ***301***
California State U, Hayward (CA) ***301***
California State U, Long Beach (CA) ***301***
California State U, Northridge (CA) ***301***
California State U, Sacramento (CA) ***301***
California State U, San Bernardino (CA) ***302***
California State U, Stanislaus (CA) ***302***
California U of Pennsylvania (PA) ***302***
Calvin Coll (MI) ***303***
Campbell U (NC) ***303***
Canisius Coll (NY) ***304***
Capital U (OH) ***304***
Cardinal Stritch U (WI) ***305***
Carleton Coll (MN) ***305***
Carleton U (ON, Canada) ***305***
Carnegie Mellon U (PA) ***305***
Carroll Coll (MT) ***306***
Carson-Newman Coll (TN) ***306***
Carthage Coll (WI) ***306***
Case Western Reserve U (OH) ***307***
Catawba Coll (NC) ***307***
The Catholic U of America (DC) ***307***
Cedar Crest Coll (PA) ***308***
Centenary Coll of Louisiana (LA) ***308***
Central Coll (IA) ***309***
Central Connecticut State U (CT) ***309***
Central Methodist Coll (MO) ***309***
Central Michigan U (MI) ***310***
Central Missouri State U (MO) ***310***
Centre Coll (KY) ***310***
Chapman U (CA) ***311***
Chatham Coll (PA) ***312***
Chestnut Hill Coll (PA) ***312***
Cheyney U of Pennsylvania (PA) ***312***
Christendom Coll (VA) ***313***
Christopher Newport U (VA) ***313***
Citadel, The Military Coll of South Carolina (SC) ***314***
City Coll of the City U of NY (NY) ***314***
Claremont McKenna Coll (CA) ***315***
Clarion U of Pennsylvania (PA) ***315***
Clark Atlanta U (GA) ***315***
Clarke Coll (IA) ***315***
Clark U (MA) ***316***
Cleveland State U (OH) ***317***
Coe Coll (IA) ***318***
Coker Coll (SC) ***318***
Colby Coll (ME) ***318***
Colgate U (NY) ***319***
Coll of Charleston (SC) ***320***
Coll of Mount Saint Vincent (NY) ***320***
The Coll of New Rochelle (NY) ***321***
Coll of Saint Benedict (MN) ***321***
Coll of St. Catherine (MN) ***321***
Coll of the Holy Cross (MA) ***323***
Coll of the Ozarks (MO) ***323***
The Coll of William and Mary (VA) ***324***
The Coll of Wooster (OH) ***324***
The Colorado Coll (CO) ***325***
Colorado State U (CO) ***325***
Columbia Coll (NY) ***326***
Columbia Coll (SC) ***327***
Columbia U, School of General Studies (NY) ***328***
Concordia Coll (MN) ***329***
Concordia U (QC, Canada) ***331***
Concordia U Coll of Alberta (AB, Canada) ***331***
Connecticut Coll (CT) ***331***
Converse Coll (SC) ***332***
Cornell Coll (IA) ***332***
Cornell U (NY) ***333***
Creighton U (NE) ***333***
Daemen Coll (NY) ***335***
Dalhousie U (NS, Canada) ***336***
Dartmouth Coll (NH) ***337***
Davidson Coll (NC) ***338***
Davis & Elkins Coll (WV) ***338***
Delaware State U (DE) ***338***
Denison U (OH) ***339***
DePaul U (IL) ***339***
DePauw U (IN) ***339***
Dickinson Coll (PA) ***344***
Dillard U (LA) ***344***
Doane Coll (NE) ***344***
Dominican U (IL) ***345***
Drew U (NJ) ***346***
Drury U (MO) ***346***
Duke U (NC) ***346***
Earlham Coll (IN) ***347***
East Carolina U (NC) ***347***
Eastern Kentucky U (KY) ***348***
Eastern Mennonite U (VA) ***348***
Eastern Michigan U (MI) ***348***
Eastern U (PA) ***349***
Eastern Washington U (WA) ***349***
East Stroudsburg U of Pennsylvania (PA) ***349***
Eckerd Coll (FL) ***350***
Edgewood Coll (WI) ***351***
Elizabethtown Coll (PA) ***351***
Elmhurst Coll (IL) ***351***
Elmira Coll (NY) ***351***
Elms Coll (MA) ***352***
Elon U (NC) ***352***
Emory & Henry Coll (VA) ***353***
Emory U (GA) ***354***
Erskine Coll (SC) ***354***
The Evergreen State Coll (WA) ***355***
Fairfield U (CT) ***356***
Fairleigh Dickinson U, Florham (NJ) ***356***
Fairleigh Dickinson U, Teaneck-Metro Campus (NJ) ***356***
Fairmont State Coll (WV) ***356***
Ferrum Coll (VA) ***358***
Fisk U (TN) ***358***
Florida A&M U (FL) ***359***
Florida Atlantic U (FL) ***359***
Florida International U (FL) ***360***
Florida State U (FL) ***361***
Fordham U (NY) ***362***
Fort Hays State U (KS) ***362***
Fort Valley State U (GA) ***362***
Framingham State Coll (MA) ***362***
Franciscan U of Steubenville (OH) ***363***
Francis Marion U (SC) ***363***
Franklin and Marshall Coll (PA) ***363***
Franklin Coll (IN) ***363***
Furman U (SC) ***365***
Gallaudet U (DC) ***365***
Gardner-Webb U (NC) ***365***
Georgetown Coll (KY) ***366***
Georgetown U (DC) ***366***
The George Washington U (DC) ***367***
Georgia Coll & State U (GA) ***367***
Georgian Court Coll (NJ) ***367***
Georgia Southern U (GA) ***367***
Georgia Southwestern State U (GA) ***368***
Georgia State U (GA) ***368***
Gettysburg Coll (PA) ***368***
Gonzaga U (WA) ***369***
Gordon Coll (MA) ***370***
Goucher Coll (MD) ***370***
Grace Coll (IN) ***370***
Grambling State U (LA) ***371***
Grand Valley State U (MI) ***371***
Greensboro Coll (NC) ***372***
Grinnell Coll (IA) ***373***
Grove City Coll (PA) ***373***
Guilford Coll (NC) ***373***
Gustavus Adolphus Coll (MN) ***374***
Hamilton Coll (NY) ***374***
Hamline U (MN) ***374***
Hampden-Sydney Coll (VA) ***374***
Hanover Coll (IN) ***375***
Harding U (AR) ***375***
Hardin-Simmons U (TX) ***376***
Hartwick Coll (NY) ***376***
Harvard U (MA) ***376***
Haverford Coll (PA) ***377***
Hendrix Coll (AR) ***378***
High Point U (NC) ***379***
Hillsdale Coll (MI) ***379***
Hiram Coll (OH) ***379***
Hobart and William Smith Colls (NY) ***380***
Hofstra U (NY) ***380***
Hollins U (VA) ***380***
Holy Family U (PA) ***380***
Hood Coll (MD) ***381***
Hope Coll (MI) ***381***
Houghton Coll (NY) ***381***
Houston Baptist U (TX) ***382***
Howard U (DC) ***382***
Humboldt State U (CA) ***382***
Hunter Coll of the City U of NY (NY) ***382***
Idaho State U (ID) ***384***

Illinois Coll (IL) ***384***
Illinois State U (IL) ***384***
Illinois Wesleyan U (IL) ***385***
Immaculata U (PA) ***385***
Indiana State U (IN) ***385***
Indiana U Bloomington (IN) ***385***
Indiana U Northwest (IN) ***386***
Indiana U of Pennsylvania (PA) ***386***
Indiana U–Purdue U Fort Wayne (IN) ***386***
Indiana U–Purdue U Indianapolis (IN) ***387***
Indiana U South Bend (IN) ***387***
Indiana U Southeast (IN) ***387***
Iona Coll (NY) ***390***
Iowa State U of Science and Technology (IA) ***390***
Ithaca Coll (NY) ***390***
Jacksonville State U (AL) ***390***
Jacksonville U (FL) ***391***
James Madison U (VA) ***391***
John Carroll U (OH) ***392***
Johns Hopkins U (MD) ***392***
Juniata Coll (PA) ***395***
Kalamazoo Coll (MI) ***395***
Keene State Coll (NH) ***396***
Kennesaw State U (GA) ***397***
Kent State U (OH) ***397***
Kenyon Coll (OH) ***398***
King Coll (TN) ***398***
King's Coll (PA) ***398***
Knox Coll (IL) ***399***
Kutztown U of Pennsylvania (PA) ***399***
Lafayette Coll (PA) ***400***
Lake Erie Coll (OH) ***400***
Lake Forest Coll (IL) ***400***
Lakehead U (ON, Canada) ***400***
Lamar U (TX) ***401***
Lane Coll (TN) ***402***
La Salle U (PA) ***402***
Laurentian U (ON, Canada) ***403***
Lawrence U (WI) ***403***
Lebanon Valley Coll (PA) ***403***
Lehigh U (PA) ***404***
Lehman Coll of the City U of NY (NY) ***404***
Le Moyne Coll (NY) ***404***
Lenoir-Rhyne Coll (NC) ***405***
Lewis & Clark Coll (OR) ***405***
Lincoln U (PA) ***407***
Lindenwood U (MO) ***407***
Linfield Coll (OR) ***408***
Lipscomb U (TN) ***408***
Lock Haven U of Pennsylvania (PA) ***408***
Long Island U, C.W. Post Campus (NY) ***409***
Long Island U, Southampton Coll, Friends World Program (NY) ***409***
Longwood U (VA) ***409***
Loras Coll (IA) ***410***
Louisiana Coll (LA) ***410***
Louisiana State U and A&M Coll (LA) ***410***
Louisiana State U in Shreveport (LA) ***410***
Louisiana Tech U (LA) ***410***
Loyola Coll in Maryland (MD) ***411***
Loyola Marymount U (CA) ***411***
Loyola U Chicago (IL) ***411***
Loyola U New Orleans (LA) ***411***
Luther Coll (IA) ***412***
Lycoming Coll (PA) ***412***
Lynchburg Coll (VA) ***413***
Macalester Coll (MN) ***413***
Madonna U (MI) ***414***
Manchester Coll (IN) ***415***
Manhattan Coll (NY) ***416***
Manhattanville Coll (NY) ***416***
Mansfield U of Pennsylvania (PA) ***416***
Marian Coll (IN) ***417***
Marist Coll (NY) ***417***
Marlboro Coll (VT) ***418***
Marquette U (WI) ***418***
Mary Baldwin Coll (VA) ***419***
Marymount Coll of Fordham U (NY) ***419***
Mary Washington Coll (VA) ***420***
Marywood U (PA) ***421***
McDaniel Coll (MD) ***422***
McGill U (QC, Canada) ***423***
McMaster U (ON, Canada) ***423***
McNeese State U (LA) ***423***
Memorial U of Newfoundland (NF, Canada) ***424***
Mercer U (GA) ***425***
Mercy Coll (NY) ***425***
Mercyhurst Coll (PA) ***425***
Meredith Coll (NC) ***426***
Merrimack Coll (MA) ***426***
Messiah Coll (PA) ***426***
Methodist Coll (NC) ***427***
Miami U (OH) ***428***
Michigan State U (MI) ***428***
Middlebury Coll (VT) ***429***
Millersville U of Pennsylvania (PA) ***430***
Millikin U (IL) ***430***
Millsaps Coll (MS) ***431***
Mills Coll (CA) ***431***
Minnesota State U, Mankato (MN) ***431***
Minot State U (ND) ***432***
Mississippi Coll (MS) ***432***
Missouri Southern State Coll (MO) ***433***
Missouri Western State Coll (MO) ***433***
Molloy Coll (NY) ***433***
Monmouth Coll (IL) ***434***
Montclair State U (NJ) ***435***
Moravian Coll (PA) ***436***
Morehead State U (KY) ***436***
Morehouse Coll (GA) ***436***
Mount Allison U (NB, Canada) ***437***
Mount Holyoke Coll (MA) ***438***
Mount Mary Coll (WI) ***438***
Mount St. Mary's Coll (CA) ***439***
Mount Saint Mary's Coll and Seminary (MD) ***439***
Mount Saint Vincent U (NS, Canada) ***439***
Mount Union Coll (OH) ***440***
Muhlenberg Coll (PA) ***440***
Murray State U (KY) ***440***
Muskingum Coll (OH) ***441***
Nazareth Coll of Rochester (NY) ***443***
Nebraska Wesleyan U (NE) ***443***
Newberry Coll (SC) ***444***
New Coll of Florida (FL) ***444***
New York U (NY) ***447***
Niagara U (NY) ***447***
Nicholls State U (LA) ***447***
North Carolina Ag and Tech State U (NC) ***448***
North Carolina Central U (NC) ***448***
North Carolina State U (NC) ***449***
North Central Coll (IL) ***449***
North Dakota State U (ND) ***449***
Northeastern Illinois U (IL) ***450***
Northeastern State U (OK) ***450***
Northeastern U (MA) ***450***
Northern Arizona U (AZ) ***450***
Northern Illinois U (IL) ***450***
Northern Kentucky U (KY) ***451***
Northern Michigan U (MI) ***451***
Northern State U (SD) ***451***
North Georgia Coll & State U (GA) ***451***
North Park U (IL) ***452***
Northwestern U (IL) ***453***
Northwest Missouri State U (MO) ***454***
Notre Dame de Namur U (CA) ***455***
Oakland U (MI) ***456***
Oakwood Coll (AL) ***456***
Oberlin Coll (OH) ***456***
Occidental Coll (CA) ***457***
Ohio Northern U (OH) ***457***
The Ohio State U (OH) ***457***
Ohio U (OH) ***458***
Ohio Wesleyan U (OH) ***459***
Oklahoma Baptist U (OK) ***459***
Oklahoma City U (OK) ***460***
Oklahoma State U (OK) ***460***
Oral Roberts U (OK) ***461***
Oregon State U (OR) ***462***
Otterbein Coll (OH) ***462***
Ouachita Baptist U (AR) ***462***
Pacific Lutheran U (WA) ***463***
Pacific Union Coll (CA) ***464***
Pacific U (OR) ***464***
Penn State U Univ Park Campus (PA) ***468***
Pepperdine U, Malibu (CA) ***469***
Pittsburg State U (KS) ***470***
Pitzer Coll (CA) ***471***
Plattsburgh State U of NY (NY) ***471***
Plymouth State Coll (NH) ***471***
Pomona Coll (CA) ***472***
Pontifical Catholic U of Puerto Rico (PR) ***472***
Portland State U (OR) ***472***
Presbyterian Coll (SC) ***473***
Principia Coll (IL) ***474***
Providence Coll (RI) ***474***
Purchase Coll, State U of NY (NY) ***475***
Purdue U Calumet (IN) ***475***
Queens Coll of the City U of NY (NY) ***475***
Queen's U at Kingston (ON, Canada) ***476***
Queens U of Charlotte (NC) ***476***
Randolph-Macon Coll (VA) ***477***
Randolph-Macon Woman's Coll (VA) ***477***
Reed Coll (OR) ***477***
Regis Coll (MA) ***478***
Regis U (CO) ***478***
Rhode Island Coll (RI) ***479***
Rhodes Coll (TN) ***479***
Rice U (TX) ***479***
Rider U (NJ) ***480***
Ripon Coll (WI) ***480***
Rivier Coll (NH) ***480***
Roanoke Coll (VA) ***481***
Rockford Coll (IL) ***482***
Rockhurst U (MO) ***482***
Rollins Coll (FL) ***483***
Rosemont Coll (PA) ***484***
Rutgers, The State U of New Jersey, Camden (NJ) ***485***
Rutgers, The State U of New Jersey, Newark (NJ) ***485***
Rutgers, The State U of New Jersey, New Brunswick (NJ) ***485***
Saginaw Valley State U (MI) ***486***
St. Ambrose U (IA) ***486***
Saint Anselm Coll (NH) ***487***
Saint Augustine's Coll (NC) ***487***
St. Bonaventure U (NY) ***487***
St. Cloud State U (MN) ***488***
Saint Francis U (PA) ***488***
St. Francis Xavier U (NS, Canada) ***489***
St. John Fisher Coll (NY) ***489***
Saint John's U (MN) ***490***
St. John's U (NY) ***490***
Saint Joseph Coll (CT) ***490***
Saint Joseph's U (PA) ***491***
St. Lawrence U (NY) ***491***
Saint Louis U (MO) ***492***
Saint Mary-of-the-Woods Coll (IN) ***493***
Saint Mary's Coll (IN) ***493***
Saint Mary's Coll of California (CA) ***494***
Saint Mary's U (NS, Canada) ***494***
Saint Mary's U of Minnesota (MN) ***494***
St. Mary's U of San Antonio (TX) ***494***
Saint Michael's Coll (VT) ***494***
St. Norbert Coll (WI) ***495***
St. Olaf Coll (MN) ***495***
St. Thomas U (NB, Canada) ***496***
Salem Coll (NC) ***496***
Salisbury U (MD) ***497***
Salve Regina U (RI) ***497***
Samford U (AL) ***497***
Sam Houston State U (TX) ***497***
San Diego State U (CA) ***498***
San Francisco State U (CA) ***498***
San Jose State U (CA) ***499***
Santa Clara U (CA) ***499***
Sarah Lawrence Coll (NY) ***499***
Scripps Coll (CA) ***501***
Seattle Pacific U (WA) ***501***
Seattle U (WA) ***501***
Seton Hall U (NJ) ***502***
Shippensburg U of Pennsylvania (PA) ***503***
Shorter Coll (GA) ***504***
Siena Coll (NY) ***504***
Simmons Coll (MA) ***504***
Simon Fraser U (BC, Canada) ***505***
Simon's Rock Coll of Bard (MA) ***505***
Simpson Coll (IA) ***505***
Skidmore Coll (NY) ***506***
Slippery Rock U of Pennsylvania (PA) ***506***
Smith Coll (MA) ***506***
Sonoma State U (CA) ***506***
South Carolina State U (SC) ***506***
South Dakota State U (SD) ***507***
Southeastern Louisiana U (LA) ***508***
Southeast Missouri State U (MO) ***508***
Southern Connecticut State U (CT) ***509***
Southern Illinois U Carbondale (IL) ***509***
Southern Methodist U (TX) ***510***
Southern U and A&M Coll (LA) ***511***
Southern Utah U (UT) ***511***
Southwestern U (TX) ***513***
Southwest Missouri State U (MO) ***513***
Southwest Texas State U (TX) ***513***
Spelman Coll (GA) ***514***
Stanford U (CA) ***514***
State U of NY at Albany (NY) ***514***
State U of NY at Binghamton (NY) ***515***
State U of NY at New Paltz (NY) ***515***
State U of NY at Oswego (NY) ***515***
State U of NY Coll at Brockport (NY) ***515***
State U of NY Coll at Buffalo (NY) ***516***
State U of NY Coll at Cortland (NY) ***516***
State U of NY Coll at Fredonia (NY) ***516***
State U of NY Coll at Geneseo (NY) ***516***
State U of NY Coll at Oneonta (NY) ***517***
State U of NY Coll at Potsdam (NY) ***517***
State U of West Georgia (GA) ***518***
Stephen F. Austin State U (TX) ***518***
Stetson U (FL) ***519***
Stony Brook U, State University of New York (NY) ***520***
Suffolk U (MA) ***520***
Susquehanna U (PA) ***521***
Swarthmore Coll (PA) ***521***
Sweet Briar Coll (VA) ***521***
Syracuse U (NY) ***521***
Talladega Coll (AL) ***522***
Taylor U (IN) ***523***
Temple U (PA) ***523***
Tennessee State U (TN) ***523***
Tennessee Technological U (TN) ***524***
Texas A&M U (TX) ***524***
Texas A&M U–Commerce (TX) ***525***
Texas Christian U (TX) ***526***
Texas Southern U (TX) ***526***
Texas Tech U (TX) ***526***
Thiel Coll (PA) ***527***
Towson U (MD) ***529***
Transylvania U (KY) ***529***
Trent U (ON, Canada) ***529***
Trinity Coll (CT) ***530***
Trinity Coll (DC) ***530***
Trinity U (TX) ***531***
Truman State U (MO) ***532***
Tufts U (MA) ***533***
Tulane U (LA) ***533***
Union Coll (NE) ***534***
Union U (TN) ***534***
United States Military Academy (NY) ***535***
Université de Sherbrooke (QC, Canada) ***536***
U du Québec à Trois-Rivières (QC, Canada) ***536***
Université Laval (QC, Canada) ***536***
U at Buffalo, The State University of New York (NY) ***536***
The U of Akron (OH) ***537***
The U of Alabama (AL) ***537***
The U of Alabama at Birmingham (AL) ***537***
U of Alberta (AB, Canada) ***538***
The U of Arizona (AZ) ***538***
U of Arkansas (AR) ***539***
U of Arkansas at Little Rock (AR) ***539***
The U of British Columbia (BC, Canada) ***540***
U of Calgary (AB, Canada) ***540***
U of Calif, Berkeley (CA) ***540***
U of Calif, Davis (CA) ***540***
U of Calif, Irvine (CA) ***541***
U of Calif, Los Angeles (CA) ***541***
U of Calif, Riverside (CA) ***541***
U of Calif, San Diego (CA) ***541***
U of Calif, Santa Barbara (CA) ***541***
U of Calif, Santa Cruz (CA) ***542***
U of Central Arkansas (AR) ***542***
U of Central Florida (FL) ***542***
U of Central Oklahoma (OK) ***542***
U of Chicago (IL) ***542***
U of Cincinnati (OH) ***543***
U of Colorado at Boulder (CO) ***543***
U of Colorado at Denver (CO) ***543***
U of Connecticut (CT) ***544***
U of Dallas (TX) ***544***
U of Dayton (OH) ***544***
U of Delaware (DE) ***544***
U of Denver (CO) ***544***
U of Evansville (IN) ***545***
U of Florida (FL) ***545***
U of Georgia (GA) ***545***
U of Guelph (ON, Canada) ***546***
U of Hawaii at Manoa (HI) ***546***
U of Houston (TX) ***547***
U of Idaho (ID) ***547***
U of Illinois at Chicago (IL) ***547***
U of Illinois at Urbana–Champaign (IL) ***548***
U of Indianapolis (IN) ***548***
The U of Iowa (IA) ***548***
U of Kansas (KS) ***549***
U of Kentucky (KY) ***549***
U of King's Coll (NS, Canada) ***549***
U of La Verne (CA) ***549***
The U of Lethbridge (AB, Canada) ***549***
U of Louisville (KY) ***550***
U of Maine (ME) ***550***
U of Maine at Fort Kent (ME) ***551***
U of Maine at Presque Isle (ME) ***551***
U of Manitoba (MB, Canada) ***551***
U of Maryland, Baltimore County (MD) ***552***
U of Maryland, Coll Park (MD) ***552***
U of Massachusetts Amherst (MA) ***552***

FRENCH (continued)

U of Massachusetts Boston (MA) 553
U of Massachusetts Dartmouth (MA) 553
U of Miami (FL) 553
U of Michigan (MI) 554
U of Michigan–Dearborn (MI) 554
U of Michigan–Flint (MI) 554
U of Minnesota, Morris (MN) 555
U of Minnesota, Twin Cities Campus (MN) 555
U of Mississippi (MS) 555
U of Missouri–Columbia (MO) 555
U of Missouri–Kansas City (MO) 555
U of Missouri–St. Louis (MO) 556
The U of Montana–Missoula (MT) 556
U of Montevallo (AL) 557
U of Nebraska at Kearney (NE) 557
U of Nebraska at Omaha (NE) 557
U of Nebraska–Lincoln (NE) 557
U of Nevada, Las Vegas (NV) 558
U of Nevada, Reno (NV) 558
U of New Brunswick Fredericton (NB, Canada) 558
U of New Brunswick Saint John (NB, Canada) 558
U of New Hampshire (NH) 558
U of New Mexico (NM) 559
U of New Orleans (LA) 559
The U of North Carolina at Asheville (NC) 559
The U of North Carolina at Charlotte (NC) 560
The U of North Carolina at Greensboro (NC) 560
The U of North Carolina at Wilmington (NC) 561
U of North Dakota (ND) 561
U of Northern Colorado (CO) 561
U of Northern Iowa (IA) 561
U of North Texas (TX) 562
U of Notre Dame (IN) 562
U of Oklahoma (OK) 562
U of Oregon (OR) 562
U of Ottawa (ON, Canada) 563
U of Pennsylvania (PA) 563
U of Pittsburgh (PA) 569
U of Prince Edward Island (PE, Canada) 570
U of Puerto Rico, Río Piedras (PR) 571
U of Puget Sound (WA) 571
U of Redlands (CA) 572
U of Rhode Island (RI) 572
U of Richmond (VA) 572
U of Rochester (NY) 573
U of St. Thomas (MN) 573
U of St. Thomas (TX) 573
U of San Diego (CA) 574
U of San Francisco (CA) 574
U of Saskatchewan (SK, Canada) 574
The U of Scranton (PA) 574
U of South Carolina (SC) 575
U of South Carolina Spartanburg (SC) 575
The U of South Dakota (SD) 575
U of Southern California (CA) 576
U of Southern Indiana (IN) 576
U of Southern Maine (ME) 576
U of South Florida (FL) 576
The U of Tennessee (TN) 577
The U of Tennessee at Chattanooga (TN) 577
The U of Tennessee at Martin (TN) 577
The U of Texas at Arlington (TX) 577
The U of Texas at Austin (TX) 578
The U of Texas at El Paso (TX) 578
The U of Texas at San Antonio (TX) 578
The U of Texas–Pan American (TX) 579
U of the District of Columbia (DC) 580
U of the Pacific (CA) 580
U of the Sacred Heart (PR) 580
U of the South (TN) 581
U of Toledo (OH) 581
U of Toronto (ON, Canada) 581
U of Tulsa (OK) 581
U of Utah (UT) 582
U of Vermont (VT) 582
U of Victoria (BC, Canada) 582
U of Virginia (VA) 582
The U of Virginia's Coll at Wise (VA) 582
U of Washington (WA) 583
U of Waterloo (ON, Canada) 583
The U of Western Ontario (ON, Canada) 583
U of Windsor (ON, Canada) 584
U of Wisconsin–Eau Claire (WI) 584
U of Wisconsin–Green Bay (WI) 584
U of Wisconsin–La Crosse (WI) 584
U of Wisconsin–Madison (WI) 584
U of Wisconsin–Milwaukee (WI) 585
U of Wisconsin–Oshkosh (WI) 585
U of Wisconsin–Parkside (WI) 585
U of Wisconsin–Platteville (WI) 585
U of Wisconsin–River Falls (WI) 585
U of Wisconsin–Stevens Point (WI) 585
U of Wisconsin–Whitewater (WI) 586
U of Wyoming (WY) 586
Ursinus Coll (PA) 587
Utah State U (UT) 587
Valdosta State U (GA) 588
Valparaiso U (IN) 588
Vanderbilt U (TN) 588
Vassar Coll (NY) 589
Villanova U (PA) 590
Virginia Polytechnic Inst and State U (VA) 591
Virginia Wesleyan Coll (VA) 591
Wabash Coll (IN) 592
Wake Forest U (NC) 592
Walla Walla Coll (WA) 593
Walsh U (OH) 593
Wartburg Coll (IA) 594
Washington & Jefferson Coll (PA) 594
Washington and Lee U (VA) 594
Washington Coll (MD) 594
Washington State U (WA) 595
Washington U in St. Louis (MO) 595
Wayne State Coll (NE) 596
Wayne State U (MI) 596
Weber State U (UT) 596
Webster U (MO) 597
Wellesley Coll (MA) 597
Wells Coll (NY) 597
Wesleyan U (CT) 597
West Chester U of Pennsylvania (PA) 598
Western Illinois U (IL) 599
Western Kentucky U (KY) 599
Western Michigan U (MI) 599
Western State Coll of Colorado (CO) 600
Western Washington U (WA) 600
Westminster Coll (MO) 601
Westminster Coll (PA) 601
Westmont Coll (CA) 602
Wheaton Coll (IL) 603
Wheaton Coll (MA) 603
Wheeling Jesuit U (WV) 603
Whitman Coll (WA) 604
Whittier Coll (CA) 604
Whitworth Coll (WA) 604
Wichita State U (KS) 604
Widener U (PA) 604
Wilkes U (PA) 605
Willamette U (OR) 605
William Jewell Coll (MO) 606
Williams Coll (MA) 606
Winona State U (MN) 608
Wittenberg U (OH) 608
Wofford Coll (SC) 609
Wright State U (OH) 609
Xavier U (OH) 610
Xavier U of Louisiana (LA) 610
Yale U (CT) 610
York Coll of the City U of New York (NY) 611
York U (ON, Canada) 611
Youngstown State U (OH) 611

FRENCH LANGUAGE EDUCATION

Overview: This major prepares individuals for a career of teaching French language at various educational levels. *Related majors:* French, comparative literature. *Potential career:* French teacher. *Salary potential:* $24k-$34k.

Abilene Christian U (TX) 260
Anderson U (IN) 268
Arkansas State U (AR) 272
Baylor U (TX) 283
Berea Coll (KY) 286
Berry Coll (GA) 287
Blue Mountain Coll (MS) 291
Bowling Green State U (OH) 292
Bridgewater Coll (VA) 294
Brigham Young U (UT) 295
Canisius Coll (NY) 304
The Catholic U of America (DC) 307
Central Michigan U (MI) 310
Central Missouri State U (MO) 310
Coll of St. Catherine (MN) 321
Colorado State U (CO) 325
Concordia Coll (MN) 329
Daemen Coll (NY) 335
Duquesne U (PA) 346
East Carolina U (NC) 347
Eastern Mennonite U (VA) 348
Eastern Michigan U (MI) 348
Elmhurst Coll (IL) 351
Elmira Coll (NY) 351
Framingham State Coll (MA) 362
Franklin Coll (IN) 363
Georgia Southern U (GA) 367
Grace Coll (IN) 370
Grambling State U (LA) 371
Hardin-Simmons U (TX) 376
Hofstra U (NY) 380
Indiana U Bloomington (IN) 385
Indiana U Northwest (IN) 386
Indiana U–Purdue U Fort Wayne (IN) 386
Indiana U–Purdue U Indianapolis (IN) 387
Indiana U South Bend (IN) 387
Ithaca Coll (NY) 390
Juniata Coll (PA) 395
Kennesaw State U (GA) 397
King Coll (TN) 398
Lipscomb U (TN) 408
Long Island U, C.W. Post Campus (NY) 409
Louisiana State U in Shreveport (LA) 410
Louisiana Tech U (LA) 410
Luther Coll (IA) 412
Manhattanville Coll (NY) 416
Mansfield U of Pennsylvania (PA) 416
Marymount Coll of Fordham U (NY) 419
McGill U (QC, Canada) 423
Messiah Coll (PA) 426
Minot State U (ND) 432
Missouri Western State Coll (MO) 433
Molloy Coll (NY) 433
New York U (NY) 447
Niagara U (NY) 447
North Carolina Central U (NC) 448
North Carolina State U (NC) 449
North Dakota State U (ND) 449
Ohio U (OH) 458
Oklahoma Baptist U (OK) 459
Oral Roberts U (OK) 461
Pace U (NY) 463
St. Ambrose U (IA) 486
St. John's U (NY) 490
Saint Mary's U of Minnesota (MN) 494
Salve Regina U (RI) 497
San Diego State U (CA) 498
Southeastern Louisiana U (LA) 508
Southwest Missouri State U (MO) 513
State U of NY at Albany (NY) 514
State U of NY Coll at Potsdam (NY) 517
Talladega Coll (AL) 522
Université Laval (QC, Canada) 536
The U of Arizona (AZ) 538
U of Illinois at Chicago (IL) 547
U of Illinois at Urbana–Champaign (IL) 548
U of Indianapolis (IN) 548
The U of Iowa (IA) 548
U of Minnesota, Duluth (MN) 554
U of Nebraska–Lincoln (NE) 557
The U of North Carolina at Charlotte (NC) 560
The U of North Carolina at Wilmington (NC) 561
U of North Texas (TX) 562
The U of Tennessee at Martin (TN) 577
U of Toledo (OH) 581
U of Utah (UT) 582
U of Waterloo (ON, Canada) 583
U of Windsor (ON, Canada) 584
U of Wisconsin–River Falls (WI) 585
Washington U in St. Louis (MO) 595
Weber State U (UT) 596
Western Carolina U (NC) 598
Wheeling Jesuit U (WV) 603
William Woods U (MO) 607
Youngstown State U (OH) 611

FURNITURE DESIGN

Overview: Students will learn how to design, assemble, finish, and repair furniture. *Related majors:* woodworking, sheet metalworking, sculpture, drawing, industrial design. *Potential careers:* furniture designer or manufacturer, furniture refinisher. *Salary potential:* $18k-$26k.

Ferris State U (MI) 358
Rochester Inst of Technology (NY) 482

GENERAL RETAILING/ WHOLESALING

Overview: This major teaches students about all aspects of direct wholesale and retail buying and selling operations. *Related majors:* general buying, retailing and selling operations, entrepreneurship, retail management, marketing. *Potential careers:* brand manager, wholesaler, retail store buyer, store manager. *Salary potential:* $25k-$35k.

U of New Haven (CT) 559
U of South Carolina (SC) 575

GENERAL RETAILING/ WHOLESALING RELATED

Information can be found under this major's main heading.

The U of Akron (OH) 537

GENERAL STUDIES

Overview: Much like the liberal arts and sciences major, students who choose this major acquire knowledge from different areas such as arts, humanities, and sciences that can be interrelated so that the major reflects varied career interests and prepares students for a specific field of study. *Related majors:* liberal arts and sciences, philosophy, history, psychology, biology. *Potential careers:* teacher, librarian, editor. *Salary potential:* $23k-$28k.

Alfred U (NY) 263
Alverno Coll (WI) 265
Angelo State U (TX) 269
Antioch U Santa Barbara (CA) 270
Arkansas State U (AR) 272
Arkansas Tech U (AR) 272
Avila U (MO) 278
Bluefield State Coll (WV) 291
Brandon U (MB, Canada) 293
Brenau U (GA) 293
Bridgewater Coll (VA) 294
Calumet Coll of Saint Joseph (IN) 302
Carroll Coll (MT) 306
The Catholic U of America (DC) 307
Central Christian Coll of Kansas (KS) 309
Central Coll (IA) 309
City U (WA) 314
Clearwater Christian Coll (FL) 316
Coll of Mount St. Joseph (OH) 320
Columbia International U (SC) 327
Crown Coll (MN) 334
Cumberland Coll (KY) 335
DePaul U (IL) 339
Drexel U (PA) 346
East Tennessee State U (TN) 349
Emporia State U (KS) 354
Fairleigh Dickinson U, Teaneck-Metro Campus (NJ) 356
Ferrum Coll (VA) 358
Fitchburg State Coll (MA) 358
The Franciscan U (IA) 363
Georgia Southern U (GA) 367
Hampton U (VA) 375
Harding U (AR) 375
Howard Payne U (TX) 382
Idaho State U (ID) 384
Indiana State U (IN) 385
Indiana U Bloomington (IN) 385
Indiana U East (IN) 386
Indiana U Kokomo (IN) 386
Indiana U Northwest (IN) 386
Indiana U of Pennsylvania (PA) 386
Indiana U–Purdue U Fort Wayne (IN) 386
Indiana U–Purdue U Indianapolis (IN) 387
Indiana U South Bend (IN) 387

Indiana U Southeast (IN) **387**
Indiana Wesleyan U (IN) **387**
Kent State U (OH) **397**
Lambuth U (TN) **401**
La Roche Coll (PA) **402**
Liberty U (VA) **406**
Louisiana State U and A&M Coll (LA) **410**
Louisiana State U in Shreveport (LA) **410**
Louisiana Tech U (LA) **410**
Loyola U New Orleans (LA) **411**
Marshall U (WV) **418**
Metropolitan State U (MN) **427**
Michigan Technological U (MI) **428**
Mid-Continent Coll (KY) **429**
Minot State U (ND) **432**
Missouri Western State Coll (MO) **433**
Morehead State U (KY) **436**
Mount Marty Coll (SD) **438**
Mount Saint Mary's Coll and Seminary (MD) **439**
Nicholls State U (LA) **447**
Northcentral U (AZ) **449**
Northern Arizona U (AZ) **450**
Northwestern State U of Louisiana (LA) **453**
Nova Southeastern U (FL) **455**
Ohio U (OH) **458**
Ohio Wesleyan U (OH) **459**
Our Lady of Holy Cross Coll (LA) **463**
Point Park Coll (PA) **471**
Rochester Inst of Technology (NY) **482**
Saginaw Valley State U (MI) **486**
St. Joseph's Coll, New York (NY) **491**
Samford U (AL) **497**
Seattle Pacific U (WA) **501**
Seton Hill U (PA) **502**
Shepherd Coll (WV) **503**
Siena Heights U (MI) **504**
Simon Fraser U (BC, Canada) **505**
Southeastern Louisiana U (LA) **508**
Southeastern U (DC) **508**
Southern Nazarene U (OK) **510**
Southwestern Assemblies of God U (TX) **512**
Southwestern Coll (KS) **512**
Springfield Coll (MA) **514**
Spring Hill Coll (AL) **514**
State U of NY Inst of Tech at Utica/Rome (NY) **518**
Sweet Briar Coll (VA) **521**
Texas A&M U–Texarkana (TX) **525**
Texas Christian U (TX) **526**
Texas Tech U (TX) **526**
Trinity Western U (BC, Canada) **531**
U of Calgary (AB, Canada) **540**
U of Connecticut (CT) **544**
U of Dayton (OH) **544**
U of Idaho (ID) **547**
U of Louisiana at Lafayette (LA) **550**
U of Maine at Farmington (ME) **550**
U of Maine at Machias (ME) **551**
U of Massachusetts Amherst (MA) **552**
U of Miami (FL) **553**
U of Michigan (MI) **554**
U of Missouri–St. Louis (MO) **556**
U of Mobile (AL) **556**
U of Nebraska at Kearney (NE) **557**
U of Nebraska at Omaha (NE) **557**
U of Nevada, Reno (NV) **558**
U of New Mexico (NM) **559**
U of New Orleans (LA) **559**
U of North Alabama (AL) **559**
U of North Texas (TX) **562**
U of Puerto Rico, Río Piedras (PR) **571**
U of St. Thomas (TX) **573**
U of South Florida (FL) **576**
U of Washington (WA) **583**
U of Windsor (ON, Canada) **584**
U of Wisconsin–Green Bay (WI) **584**
U of Wisconsin–Stevens Point (WI) **585**
U System Coll for Lifelong Learning (NH) **586**
Virginia Commonwealth U (VA) **590**
Western Kentucky U (KY) **599**
Western Washington U (WA) **600**
West Texas A&M U (TX) **602**
Winston-Salem State U (NC) **608**
York Coll (NE) **610**

GENETICS

Overview: Students taking this major will study the genetics of multicellular plants and animals from the experimental, clinical, and industrial perspectives. *Related majors:* bio-statistics, biology, molecular biology, evolutionary biology, mathematics/computer science. *Potential careers:* geneticist, physician, research scientist, veterinarian. *Salary potential:* $25k-$35k.

Ball State U (IN) **280**
Cedar Crest Coll (PA) **308**
Cornell U (NY) **333**
Dartmouth Coll (NH) **337**
The Evergreen State Coll (WA) **355**
Florida State U (FL) **361**
Hampshire Coll (MA) **375**
Harvard U (MA) **376**
Iowa State U of Science and Technology (IA) **390**
Jacksonville State U (AL) **390**
McGill U (QC, Canada) **423**
Missouri Southern State Coll (MO) **433**
North Dakota State U (ND) **449**
The Ohio State U (OH) **457**
Ohio Wesleyan U (OH) **459**
Rochester Inst of Technology (NY) **482**
Rutgers, The State U of New Jersey, New Brunswick (NJ) **485**
St. Cloud State U (MN) **488**
Sarah Lawrence Coll (NY) **499**
Texas A&M U (TX) **524**
U of Alberta (AB, Canada) **538**
The U of British Columbia (BC, Canada) **540**
U of Calif, Berkeley (CA) **540**
U of Calif, Davis (CA) **540**
U of Georgia (GA) **545**
U of Hawaii at Manoa (HI) **546**
U of Manitoba (MB, Canada) **551**
U of Minnesota, Twin Cities Campus (MN) **555**
U of Rochester (NY) **573**
U of Toronto (ON, Canada) **581**
The U of Western Ontario (ON, Canada) **583**
U of Wisconsin–Madison (WI) **584**
Washington State U (WA) **595**
Worcester Polytechnic Inst (MA) **609**

GEOCHEMISTRY

Overview: This branch of geology concerns the study of the formation, behavior, and properties of naturally forming minerals. *Related majors:* physical and theoretical chemistry, materials engineering, physics, chemical and atomic physics, mining/minerals engineering. *Potential careers:* mining, structural or chemical engineer, chemist, research scientist, geologist. *Salary potential:* $35k-$45k.

Bridgewater State Coll (MA) **294**
Brown U (RI) **296**
California Inst of Technology (CA) **299**
Columbia Coll (NY) **326**
Hampshire Coll (MA) **375**
Harvard U (MA) **376**
New Mexico Inst of Mining and Technology (NM) **446**
Northern Arizona U (AZ) **450**
Pomona Coll (CA) **472**
San Diego State U (CA) **498**
State U of NY at Oswego (NY) **515**
State U of NY Coll at Cortland (NY) **516**
State U of NY Coll at Fredonia (NY) **516**
State U of NY Coll at Geneseo (NY) **516**
U of Calif, Los Angeles (CA) **541**
U of New Brunswick Fredericton (NB, Canada) **558**
U of Waterloo (ON, Canada) **583**
West Chester U of Pennsylvania (PA) **598**

GEOGRAPHY

Overview: Students who choose this major will study the diverse physical, biologica,l and cultural features of the earth's surface. *Related majors:* geology, anthropology, environmental sciences, natural resource management, sociology. *Potential careers:* geographer, cartographer, surveyor, environmental scientist, traffic pattern researcher. *Salary potential:* $25k-$40k.

Appalachian State U (NC) **270**
Aquinas Coll (MI) **270**
Arizona State U (AZ) **271**
Arkansas State U (AR) **272**
Auburn U (AL) **276**
Augustana Coll (IL) **276**
Austin Peay State U (TN) **278**
Ball State U (IN) **280**
Baylor U (TX) **283**
Bellevue U (NE) **284**
Bemidji State U (MN) **285**
Bishop's U (QC, Canada) **289**
Bloomsburg U of Pennsylvania (PA) **290**
Boston U (MA) **292**
Bowling Green State U (OH) **292**
Brandon U (MB, Canada) **293**
Bridgewater State Coll (MA) **294**
Brigham Young U (UT) **295**
Brock U (ON, Canada) **295**
Bucknell U (PA) **297**
California State Polytechnic U, Pomona (CA) **300**
California State U, Chico (CA) **300**
California State U, Dominguez Hills (CA) **300**
California State U, Fresno (CA) **301**
California State U, Fullerton (CA) **301**
California State U, Hayward (CA) **301**
California State U, Long Beach (CA) **301**
California State U, Northridge (CA) **301**
California State U, Sacramento (CA) **301**
California State U, San Bernardino (CA) **302**
California State U, Stanislaus (CA) **302**
California U of Pennsylvania (PA) **302**
Calvin Coll (MI) **303**
Carleton U (ON, Canada) **305**
Carroll Coll (WI) **306**
Carthage Coll (WI) **306**
Central Connecticut State U (CT) **309**
Central Michigan U (MI) **310**
Central Missouri State U (MO) **310**
Central Washington U (WA) **310**
Cheyney U of Pennsylvania (PA) **312**
City Coll of the City U of NY (NY) **314**
Clarion U of Pennsylvania (PA) **315**
Clark U (MA) **316**
Colgate U (NY) **319**
Concord Coll (WV) **329**
Concordia U (IL) **330**
Concordia U (NE) **330**
Concordia U (QC, Canada) **331**
Dartmouth Coll (NH) **337**
DePaul U (IL) **339**
DePauw U (IN) **339**
Dickinson State U (ND) **344**
East Carolina U (NC) **347**
Eastern Illinois U (IL) **348**
Eastern Kentucky U (KY) **348**
Eastern Michigan U (MI) **348**
Eastern Washington U (WA) **349**
East Stroudsburg U of Pennsylvania (PA) **349**
East Tennessee State U (TN) **349**
Edinboro U of Pennsylvania (PA) **351**
Elmhurst Coll (IL) **351**
Emory & Henry Coll (VA) **353**
Excelsior Coll (NY) **356**
Fayetteville State U (NC) **357**
Fitchburg State Coll (MA) **358**
Florida Atlantic U (FL) **359**
Florida International U (FL) **360**
Florida State U (FL) **361**
Framingham State Coll (MA) **362**
Francis Marion U (SC) **363**
Frostburg State U (MD) **365**
George Mason U (VA) **366**
The George Washington U (DC) **367**
Georgia Southern U (GA) **367**
Georgia State U (GA) **368**
Grambling State U (LA) **371**
Gustavus Adolphus Coll (MN) **374**
Hampshire Coll (MA) **375**
Hofstra U (NY) **380**
Humboldt State U (CA) **382**
Hunter Coll of the City U of NY (NY) **382**
Illinois State U (IL) **384**
Indiana State U (IN) **385**
Indiana U Bloomington (IN) **385**
Indiana U of Pennsylvania (PA) **386**
Indiana U–Purdue U Indianapolis (IN) **387**
Indiana U Southeast (IN) **387**
Jacksonville State U (AL) **390**
Jacksonville U (FL) **391**
James Madison U (VA) **391**
Johns Hopkins U (MD) **392**
Kansas State U (KS) **396**
Keene State Coll (NH) **396**
Kent State U (OH) **397**
Kutztown U of Pennsylvania (PA) **399**
Lakehead U (ON, Canada) **400**
Laurentian U (ON, Canada) **403**
Lehman Coll of the City U of NY (NY) **404**
Lock Haven U of Pennsylvania (PA) **408**
Long Island U, C.W. Post Campus (NY) **409**
Long Island U, Southampton Coll, Friends World Program (NY) **409**
Longwood U (VA) **409**
Louisiana State U and A&M Coll (LA) **410**
Louisiana State U in Shreveport (LA) **410**
Louisiana Tech U (LA) **410**
Macalester Coll (MN) **413**
Mansfield U of Pennsylvania (PA) **416**
Marshall U (WV) **418**
Mary Washington Coll (VA) **420**
McGill U (QC, Canada) **423**
McMaster U (ON, Canada) **423**
Memorial U of Newfoundland (NF, Canada) **424**
Miami U (OH) **428**
Michigan State U (MI) **428**
Middlebury Coll (VT) **429**
Millersville U of Pennsylvania (PA) **430**
Minnesota State U, Mankato (MN) **431**
Montclair State U (NJ) **435**
Morehead State U (KY) **436**
Mount Allison U (NB, Canada) **437**
Mount Holyoke Coll (MA) **438**
Murray State U (KY) **440**
New Mexico State U (NM) **446**
Nipissing U (ON, Canada) **448**
North Carolina Central U (NC) **448**
Northeastern Illinois U (IL) **450**
Northeastern State U (OK) **450**
Northern Arizona U (AZ) **450**
Northern Illinois U (IL) **450**
Northern Kentucky U (KY) **451**
Northern Michigan U (MI) **451**
Northwestern U (IL) **453**
Northwest Missouri State U (MO) **454**
The Ohio State U (OH) **457**
Ohio U (OH) **458**
Ohio Wesleyan U (OH) **459**
Oklahoma State U (OK) **460**
Old Dominion U (VA) **460**
Oregon State U (OR) **462**
Penn State U Univ Park Campus (PA) **468**
Pittsburg State U (KS) **470**
Plattsburgh State U of NY (NY) **471**
Plymouth State Coll (NH) **471**
Portland State U (OR) **472**
Queen's U at Kingston (ON, Canada) **476**
Radford U (VA) **476**
Rhode Island Coll (RI) **479**
Rowan U (NJ) **484**
Rutgers, The State U of New Jersey, New Brunswick (NJ) **485**
Ryerson U (ON, Canada) **485**
St. Cloud State U (MN) **488**
Saint Mary's U (NS, Canada) **494**
Salem State Coll (MA) **497**
Salisbury U (MD) **497**
Samford U (AL) **497**
Sam Houston State U (TX) **497**
San Diego State U (CA) **498**
San Francisco State U (CA) **498**
San Jose State U (CA) **499**
Shippensburg U of Pennsylvania (PA) **503**
Simon Fraser U (BC, Canada) **505**
Simon's Rock Coll of Bard (MA) **505**
Slippery Rock U of Pennsylvania (PA) **506**
Sonoma State U (CA) **506**
South Dakota State U (SD) **507**
Southeast Missouri State U (MO) **508**
Southern Connecticut State U (CT) **509**
Southern Illinois U Carbondale (IL) **509**
Southern Illinois U Edwardsville (IL) **509**
Southern Oregon U (OR) **510**
Southwest Missouri State U (MO) **513**
Southwest Texas State U (TX) **513**
State U of NY at Albany (NY) **514**
State U of NY at Binghamton (NY) **515**
State U of NY at New Paltz (NY) **515**
State U of NY Coll at Buffalo (NY) **516**
State U of NY Coll at Cortland (NY) **516**
State U of NY Coll at Geneseo (NY) **516**

GEOGRAPHY (continued)

State U of NY Coll at Oneonta (NY) 517
State U of NY Coll at Potsdam (NY) 517
State U of West Georgia (GA) 518
Stephen F. Austin State U (TX) 518
Stetson U (FL) 519
Syracuse U (NY) 521
Temple U (PA) 523
Texas A&M U (TX) 524
Texas A&M U–Commerce (TX) 525
Texas A&M U–Kingsville (TX) 525
Texas Tech U (TX) 526
Towson U (MD) 529
Trent U (ON, Canada) 529
Trinity Western U (BC, Canada) 531
United States Air Force Academy (CO) 534
United States Military Academy (NY) 535
Université de Sherbrooke (QC, Canada) 536
U du Québec à Trois-Rivières (QC, Canada) 536
Université Laval (QC, Canada) 536
U at Buffalo, The State University of New York (NY) 536
U Coll of the Cariboo (BC, Canada) 537
The U of Akron (OH) 537
The U of Alabama (AL) 537
U of Alaska Fairbanks (AK) 538
U of Alberta (AB, Canada) 538
The U of Arizona (AZ) 538
U of Arkansas (AR) 539
The U of British Columbia (BC, Canada) 540
U of Calgary (AB, Canada) 540
U of Calif, Berkeley (CA) 540
U of Calif, Irvine (CA) 541
U of Calif, Los Angeles (CA) 541
U of Calif, Santa Barbara (CA) 541
U of Central Arkansas (AR) 542
U of Central Oklahoma (OK) 542
U of Chicago (IL) 542
U of Cincinnati (OH) 543
U of Colorado at Boulder (CO) 543
U of Colorado at Colorado Springs (CO) 543
U of Colorado at Denver (CO) 543
U of Connecticut (CT) 544
U of Delaware (DE) 544
U of Denver (CO) 544
U of Florida (FL) 545
U of Georgia (GA) 545
U of Guelph (ON, Canada) 546
U of Hawaii at Hilo (HI) 546
U of Hawaii at Manoa (HI) 546
U of Houston–Clear Lake (TX) 547
U of Idaho (ID) 547
U of Illinois at Chicago (IL) 547
U of Illinois at Urbana–Champaign (IL) 548
The U of Iowa (IA) 548
U of Kansas (KS) 549
U of Kentucky (KY) 549
The U of Lethbridge (AB, Canada) 549
U of Louisville (KY) 550
U of Maine at Farmington (ME) 550
U of Manitoba (MB, Canada) 551
U of Maryland, Baltimore County (MD) 552
U of Maryland, Coll Park (MD) 552
U of Massachusetts Amherst (MA) 552
U of Massachusetts Boston (MA) 553
The U of Memphis (TN) 553
U of Miami (FL) 553
U of Michigan (MI) 554
U of Michigan–Flint (MI) 554
U of Minnesota, Duluth (MN) 554
U of Minnesota, Twin Cities Campus (MN) 555
U of Missouri–Columbia (MO) 555
U of Missouri–Kansas City (MO) 555
The U of Montana–Missoula (MT) 556
U of Nebraska at Kearney (NE) 557
U of Nebraska at Omaha (NE) 557
U of Nebraska–Lincoln (NE) 557
U of Nevada, Reno (NV) 558
U of New Hampshire (NH) 558
U of New Mexico (NM) 559
U of New Orleans (LA) 559
U of North Alabama (AL) 559
The U of North Carolina at Chapel Hill (NC) 560
The U of North Carolina at Charlotte (NC) 560
The U of North Carolina at Greensboro (NC) 560
The U of North Carolina at Wilmington (NC) 561
U of North Dakota (ND) 561
U of Northern Colorado (CO) 561
U of Northern Iowa (IA) 561
U of North Texas (TX) 562
U of Oklahoma (OK) 562
U of Oregon (OR) 562
U of Ottawa (ON, Canada) 563
U of Pittsburgh at Johnstown (PA) 570
U of Puerto Rico, Río Piedras (PR) 571
U of Regina (SK, Canada) 572
U of St. Thomas (MN) 573
U of Saskatchewan (SK, Canada) 574
U of South Alabama (AL) 575
U of South Carolina (SC) 575
U of Southern California (CA) 576
U of Southern Maine (ME) 576
U of Southern Mississippi (MS) 576
U of South Florida (FL) 576
The U of Tennessee (TN) 577
The U of Tennessee at Martin (TN) 577
The U of Texas at Austin (TX) 578
The U of Texas at Dallas (TX) 578
The U of Texas at El Paso (TX) 578
The U of Texas at San Antonio (TX) 578
U of the District of Columbia (DC) 580
U of Toledo (OH) 581
U of Toronto (ON, Canada) 581
U of Utah (UT) 582
U of Vermont (VT) 582
U of Victoria (BC, Canada) 582
U of Washington (WA) 583
U of Waterloo (ON, Canada) 583
The U of Western Ontario (ON, Canada) 583
U of Wisconsin–Eau Claire (WI) 584
U of Wisconsin–La Crosse (WI) 584
U of Wisconsin–Madison (WI) 584
U of Wisconsin–Milwaukee (WI) 585
U of Wisconsin–Oshkosh (WI) 585
U of Wisconsin–Parkside (WI) 585
U of Wisconsin–Platteville (WI) 585
U of Wisconsin–River Falls (WI) 585
U of Wisconsin–Stevens Point (WI) 585
U of Wisconsin–Whitewater (WI) 586
U of Wyoming (WY) 586
Utah State U (UT) 587
Valparaiso U (IN) 588
Vassar Coll (NY) 589
Villanova U (PA) 590
Virginia Polytechnic Inst and State U (VA) 591
Wayne State Coll (NE) 596
Wayne State U (MI) 596
Weber State U (UT) 596
West Chester U of Pennsylvania (PA) 598
Western Illinois U (IL) 599
Western Kentucky U (KY) 599
Western Michigan U (MI) 599
Western Oregon U (OR) 600
Western Washington U (WA) 600
Westfield State Coll (MA) 600
West Texas A&M U (TX) 602
West Virginia U (WV) 602
William Paterson U of New Jersey (NJ) 606
Wittenberg U (OH) 608
Worcester State Coll (MA) 609
Wright State U (OH) 609
York U (ON, Canada) 611
Youngstown State U (OH) 611

GEOLOGICAL ENGINEERING

Overview: This major teaches students the science behind analyzing and evaluating the geological aspects (rocks and soils) of construction sites. *Related majors:* mathematics, physics, geology, chemistry, soil sciences, structural engineering. *Potential careers:* geologist, structural engineer, construction manager. *Salary potential:* $32k-$45k.

Auburn U (AL) 276
Colorado School of Mines (CO) 325
Cornell U (NY) 333
Harvard U (MA) 376
Laurentian U (ON, Canada) 403
Memorial U of Newfoundland (NF, Canada) 424
Michigan Technological U (MI) 428
Montana Tech of The U of Montana (MT) 435
New Mexico State U (NM) 446
Oregon State U (OR) 462
Queen's U at Kingston (ON, Canada) 476
South Dakota School of Mines and Technology (SD) 507
Université Laval (QC, Canada) 536
The U of Akron (OH) 537
U of Alaska Fairbanks (AK) 538
The U of Arizona (AZ) 538
The U of British Columbia (BC, Canada) 540
U of Calgary (AB, Canada) 540
U of Calif, Los Angeles (CA) 541
U of Idaho (ID) 547
U of Manitoba (MB, Canada) 551
U of Minnesota, Twin Cities Campus (MN) 555
U of Mississippi (MS) 555
U of Missouri–Rolla (MO) 556
U of Nevada, Reno (NV) 558
U of New Brunswick Fredericton (NB, Canada) 558
U of New Brunswick Saint John (NB, Canada) 558
U of North Dakota (ND) 561
U of Oklahoma (OK) 562
U of Saskatchewan (SK, Canada) 574
U of Toronto (ON, Canada) 581
U of Utah (UT) 582
U of Waterloo (ON, Canada) 583

GEOLOGICAL SCIENCES RELATED

Information can be found under this major's main heading.

Ohio U (OH) 458
San Diego State U (CA) 498
The U of Akron (OH) 537
U of Hawaii at Manoa (HI) 546
U of Miami (FL) 553
U of Nevada, Las Vegas (NV) 558
U of Pittsburgh (PA) 569
The U of Texas at Austin (TX) 578
U of Utah (UT) 582
U of Wyoming (WY) 586
Western Michigan U (MI) 599
Yale U (CT) 610

GEOLOGY

Overview: This major concerns the study of the behavior of the solids, liquids, and gasses that make up the earth and the forces acting upon these. *Related majors:* geophysics, physics, chemistry, mathematics, geophysics, petroleum or mining engineering. *Potential careers:* geologist, petroleum engineer, chemical engineer, hydrologist, seismologist, mining engineer. *Salary potential:* $32k-$47k.

Abilene Christian U (TX) 260
Acadia U (NS, Canada) 260
Adams State Coll (CO) 260
Albion Coll (MI) 262
Alfred U (NY) 263
Allegheny Coll (PA) 264
Amherst Coll (MA) 268
Antioch Coll (OH) 269
Appalachian State U (NC) 270
Arizona State U (AZ) 271
Arkansas Tech U (AR) 272
Ashland U (OH) 274
Auburn U (AL) 276
Augustana Coll (IL) 276
Austin Peay State U (TN) 278
Baldwin-Wallace Coll (OH) 280
Ball State U (IN) 280
Bates Coll (ME) 282
Baylor U (TX) 283
Beloit Coll (WI) 285
Bemidji State U (MN) 285
Bloomsburg U of Pennsylvania (PA) 290
Boston Coll (MA) 292
Boston U (MA) 292
Bowdoin Coll (ME) 292
Bowling Green State U (OH) 292
Bradley U (IL) 293
Brandon U (MB, Canada) 293
Bridgewater State Coll (MA) 294
Brigham Young U (UT) 295
Brock U (ON, Canada) 295
Brooklyn Coll of the City U of NY (NY) 295
Brown U (RI) 296
Bryn Mawr Coll (PA) 297
Bucknell U (PA) 297
California Inst of Technology (CA) 299
California Lutheran U (CA) 299
California State Polytechnic U, Pomona (CA) 300
California State U, Bakersfield (CA) 300
California State U, Chico (CA) 300
California State U, Dominguez Hills (CA) 300
California State U, Fresno (CA) 301
California State U, Fullerton (CA) 301
California State U, Hayward (CA) 301
California State U, Long Beach (CA) 301
California State U, Northridge (CA) 301
California State U, Sacramento (CA) 301
California State U, San Bernardino (CA) 302
California State U, Stanislaus (CA) 302
California U of Pennsylvania (PA) 302
Calvin Coll (MI) 303
Carleton Coll (MN) 305
Carleton U (ON, Canada) 305
Case Western Reserve U (OH) 307
Castleton State Coll (VT) 307
Centenary Coll of Louisiana (LA) 308
Central Michigan U (MI) 310
Central Missouri State U (MO) 310
Central Washington U (WA) 310
City Coll of the City U of NY (NY) 314
Clarion U of Pennsylvania (PA) 315
Clemson U (SC) 317
Cleveland State U (OH) 317
Colby Coll (ME) 318
Colgate U (NY) 319
Coll of Charleston (SC) 320
The Coll of William and Mary (VA) 324
The Coll of Wooster (OH) 324
The Colorado Coll (CO) 325
Colorado State U (CO) 325
Columbia Coll (MO) 326
Columbia Coll (NY) 326
Columbia U, School of General Studies (NY) 328
Columbus State U (GA) 328
Cornell Coll (IA) 332
Cornell U (NY) 333
Denison U (OH) 339
DePauw U (IN) 339
Dickinson Coll (PA) 344
Duke U (NC) 346
Earlham Coll (IN) 347
East Carolina U (NC) 347
Eastern Illinois U (IL) 348
Eastern Kentucky U (KY) 348
Eastern Michigan U (MI) 348
Eastern New Mexico U (NM) 349
Eastern Washington U (WA) 349
Edinboro U of Pennsylvania (PA) 351
Elizabeth City State U (NC) 351
The Evergreen State Coll (WA) 355
Excelsior Coll (NY) 356
Florida Atlantic U (FL) 359
Florida International U (FL) 360
Florida State U (FL) 361
Fort Hays State U (KS) 362
Fort Lewis Coll (CO) 362
Franklin and Marshall Coll (PA) 363
Furman U (SC) 365
George Mason U (VA) 366
The George Washington U (DC) 367
Georgia Southern U (GA) 367
Georgia Southwestern State U (GA) 368
Georgia State U (GA) 368
Grand Valley State U (MI) 371
Guilford Coll (NC) 373
Gustavus Adolphus Coll (MN) 374
Hamilton Coll (NY) 374
Hampshire Coll (MA) 375
Hanover Coll (IN) 375
Hardin-Simmons U (TX) 376
Hartwick Coll (NY) 376
Harvard U (MA) 376
Haverford Coll (PA) 377
Hobart and William Smith Colls (NY) 380
Hofstra U (NY) 380
Hope Coll (MI) 381
Howard U (DC) 382
Humboldt State U (CA) 382
Idaho State U (ID) 384
Illinois State U (IL) 384
Indiana State U (IN) 385
Indiana U Bloomington (IN) 385
Indiana U Northwest (IN) 386
Indiana U of Pennsylvania (PA) 386

Indiana U–Purdue U Fort Wayne (IN) **386**
Indiana U–Purdue U Indianapolis (IN) **387**
Iowa State U of Science and Technology (IA) **390**
Jacksonville State U (AL) **390**
James Madison U (VA) **391**
Juniata Coll (PA) **395**
Kansas State U (KS) **396**
Keene State Coll (NH) **396**
Kent State U (OH) **397**
Kutztown U of Pennsylvania (PA) **399**
Lafayette Coll (PA) **400**
Lakehead U (ON, Canada) **400**
Lamar U (TX) **401**
La Salle U (PA) **402**
Laurentian U (ON, Canada) **403**
Lawrence U (WI) **403**
Lehman Coll of the City U of NY (NY) **404**
Lewis-Clark State Coll (ID) **406**
Lock Haven U of Pennsylvania (PA) **408**
Long Island U, C.W. Post Campus (NY) **409**
Long Island U, Southampton Coll, Friends World Program (NY) **409**
Louisiana State U and A&M Coll (LA) **410**
Louisiana Tech U (LA) **410**
Macalester Coll (MN) **413**
Marietta Coll (OH) **417**
Marshall U (WV) **418**
Mary Washington Coll (VA) **420**
McMaster U (ON, Canada) **423**
Memorial U of Newfoundland (NF, Canada) **424**
Mercyhurst Coll (PA) **425**
Mesa State Coll (CO) **426**
Miami U (OH) **428**
Michigan State U (MI) **428**
Michigan Technological U (MI) **428**
Middlebury Coll (VT) **429**
Middle Tennessee State U (TN) **429**
Midwestern State U (TX) **430**
Millersville U of Pennsylvania (PA) **430**
Millsaps Coll (MS) **431**
Minot State U (ND) **432**
Mississippi State U (MS) **432**
Moravian Coll (PA) **436**
Morehead State U (KY) **436**
Mount Allison U (NB, Canada) **437**
Mount Holyoke Coll (MA) **438**
Mount Union Coll (OH) **440**
Murray State U (KY) **440**
Muskingum Coll (OH) **441**
New Jersey City U (NJ) **445**
New Mexico Inst of Mining and Technology (NM) **446**
New Mexico State U (NM) **446**
North Carolina State U (NC) **449**
North Dakota State U (ND) **449**
Northeastern U (MA) **450**
Northern Arizona U (AZ) **450**
Northern Illinois U (IL) **450**
Northern Kentucky U (KY) **451**
Northland Coll (WI) **452**
Northwestern U (IL) **453**
Northwest Missouri State U (MO) **454**
Norwich U (VT) **455**
Oberlin Coll (OH) **456**
Occidental Coll (CA) **457**
The Ohio State U (OH) **457**
Ohio U (OH) **458**
Ohio Wesleyan U (OH) **459**
Oklahoma State U (OK) **460**
Old Dominion U (VA) **460**
Olivet Nazarene U (IL) **461**
Oregon State U (OR) **462**
Pacific Lutheran U (WA) **463**
Penn State U Univ Park Campus (PA) **468**
Plattsburgh State U of NY (NY) **471**
Pomona Coll (CA) **472**
Portland State U (OR) **472**
Princeton U (NJ) **474**
Purdue U (IN) **475**
Queens Coll of the City U of NY (NY) **475**
Queen's U at Kingston (ON, Canada) **476**
Radford U (VA) **476**
Rensselaer Polytechnic Inst (NY) **478**
Rice U (TX) **479**
The Richard Stockton Coll of New Jersey (NJ) **479**
Rider U (NJ) **480**
Rocky Mountain Coll (MT) **482**
Rutgers, The State U of New Jersey, Newark (NJ) **485**
Rutgers, The State U of New Jersey, New Brunswick (NJ) **485**
St. Francis Xavier U (NS, Canada) **489**
St. Lawrence U (NY) **491**
Saint Louis U (MO) **492**
Saint Mary's U (NS, Canada) **494**
St. Mary's U of San Antonio (TX) **494**
St. Norbert Coll (WI) **495**
Salem State Coll (MA) **497**
Sam Houston State U (TX) **497**
San Diego State U (CA) **498**
San Francisco State U (CA) **498**
San Jose State U (CA) **499**
Sarah Lawrence Coll (NY) **499**
Scripps Coll (CA) **501**
Simon's Rock Coll of Bard (MA) **505**
Skidmore Coll (NY) **506**
Slippery Rock U of Pennsylvania (PA) **506**
Smith Coll (MA) **506**
Sonoma State U (CA) **506**
South Dakota School of Mines and Technology (SD) **507**
Southeast Missouri State U (MO) **508**
Southern Illinois U Carbondale (IL) **509**
Southern Methodist U (TX) **510**
Southern Oregon U (OR) **510**
Southern Utah U (UT) **511**
Southwest Missouri State U (MO) **513**
Stanford U (CA) **514**
State U of NY at Albany (NY) **514**
State U of NY at Binghamton (NY) **515**
State U of NY at New Paltz (NY) **515**
State U of NY at Oswego (NY) **515**
State U of NY Coll at Brockport (NY) **515**
State U of NY Coll at Buffalo (NY) **516**
State U of NY Coll at Cortland (NY) **516**
State U of NY Coll at Fredonia (NY) **516**
State U of NY Coll at Geneseo (NY) **516**
State U of NY Coll at Oneonta (NY) **517**
State U of NY Coll at Potsdam (NY) **517**
State U of West Georgia (GA) **518**
Stephen F. Austin State U (TX) **518**
Stony Brook U, State University of New York (NY) **520**
Sul Ross State U (TX) **521**
Susquehanna U (PA) **521**
Syracuse U (NY) **521**
Tarleton State U (TX) **522**
Temple U (PA) **523**
Tennessee Technological U (TN) **524**
Texas A&M U (TX) **524**
Texas A&M U–Commerce (TX) **525**
Texas A&M U–Corpus Christi (TX) **525**
Texas A&M U–Kingsville (TX) **525**
Texas Christian U (TX) **526**
Texas Tech U (TX) **526**
Towson U (MD) **529**
Trinity U (TX) **531**
Tufts U (MA) **533**
Tulane U (LA) **533**
Union Coll (NY) **534**
Université Laval (QC, Canada) **536**
U at Buffalo, The State University of New York (NY) **536**
The U of Akron (OH) **537**
The U of Alabama (AL) **537**
U of Alaska Fairbanks (AK) **538**
U of Alberta (AB, Canada) **538**
The U of Arizona (AZ) **538**
U of Arkansas (AR) **539**
U of Arkansas at Little Rock (AR) **539**
The U of British Columbia (BC, Canada) **540**
U of Calgary (AB, Canada) **540**
U of Calif, Berkeley (CA) **540**
U of Calif, Davis (CA) **540**
U of Calif, Los Angeles (CA) **541**
U of Calif, Riverside (CA) **541**
U of Calif, Santa Barbara (CA) **541**
U of Calif, Santa Cruz (CA) **542**
U of Cincinnati (OH) **543**
U of Colorado at Boulder (CO) **543**
U of Colorado at Denver (CO) **543**
U of Connecticut (CT) **544**
U of Dayton (OH) **544**
U of Delaware (DE) **544**
U of Florida (FL) **545**
U of Georgia (GA) **545**
U of Hawaii at Hilo (HI) **546**
U of Hawaii at Manoa (HI) **546**
U of Houston (TX) **547**
U of Idaho (ID) **547**
U of Illinois at Chicago (IL) **547**
U of Illinois at Urbana–Champaign (IL) **548**
The U of Iowa (IA) **548**
U of Kansas (KS) **549**
U of Kentucky (KY) **549**
U of Louisiana at Lafayette (LA) **550**
U of Maine (ME) **550**
U of Maine at Farmington (ME) **550**
U of Maine at Presque Isle (ME) **551**
U of Manitoba (MB, Canada) **551**
U of Maryland, Coll Park (MD) **552**
U of Massachusetts Amherst (MA) **552**
The U of Memphis (TN) **553**
U of Miami (FL) **553**
U of Michigan (MI) **554**
U of Minnesota, Duluth (MN) **554**
U of Minnesota, Morris (MN) **555**
U of Minnesota, Twin Cities Campus (MN) **555**
U of Mississippi (MS) **555**
U of Missouri–Columbia (MO) **555**
U of Missouri–Kansas City (MO) **555**
U of Missouri–Rolla (MO) **556**
The U of Montana–Missoula (MT) **556**
The U of Montana–Western (MT) **556**
U of Nebraska at Omaha (NE) **557**
U of Nebraska–Lincoln (NE) **557**
U of Nevada, Las Vegas (NV) **558**
U of Nevada, Reno (NV) **558**
U of New Brunswick Fredericton (NB, Canada) **558**
U of New Hampshire (NH) **558**
U of New Mexico (NM) **559**
U of New Orleans (LA) **559**
U of North Alabama (AL) **559**
The U of North Carolina at Chapel Hill (NC) **560**
The U of North Carolina at Charlotte (NC) **560**
The U of North Carolina at Wilmington (NC) **561**
U of North Dakota (ND) **561**
U of Northern Iowa (IA) **561**
U of Notre Dame (IN) **562**
U of Oklahoma (OK) **562**
U of Oregon (OR) **562**
U of Ottawa (ON, Canada) **563**
U of Pennsylvania (PA) **563**
U of Pittsburgh (PA) **569**
U of Pittsburgh at Bradford (PA) **569**
U of Pittsburgh at Johnstown (PA) **570**
U of Puget Sound (WA) **571**
U of Regina (SK, Canada) **572**
U of Rhode Island (RI) **572**
U of Rochester (NY) **573**
U of St. Thomas (MN) **573**
U of Saskatchewan (SK, Canada) **574**
U of South Alabama (AL) **575**
U of South Carolina (SC) **575**
U of Southern California (CA) **576**
U of Southern Indiana (IN) **576**
U of Southern Maine (ME) **576**
U of Southern Mississippi (MS) **576**
U of South Florida (FL) **576**
The U of Tennessee (TN) **577**
The U of Tennessee at Chattanooga (TN) **577**
The U of Tennessee at Martin (TN) **577**
The U of Texas at Arlington (TX) **577**
The U of Texas at Austin (TX) **578**
The U of Texas at Dallas (TX) **578**
The U of Texas at El Paso (TX) **578**
The U of Texas at San Antonio (TX) **578**
The U of Texas of the Permian Basin (TX) **579**
U of the Pacific (CA) **580**
U of the South (TN) **581**
U of Toledo (OH) **581**
U of Toronto (ON, Canada) **581**
U of Tulsa (OK) **581**
U of Utah (UT) **582**
U of Vermont (VT) **582**
U of Victoria (BC, Canada) **582**
U of Washington (WA) **583**
U of Waterloo (ON, Canada) **583**
The U of Western Ontario (ON, Canada) **583**
U of Windsor (ON, Canada) **584**
U of Wisconsin–Eau Claire (WI) **584**
U of Wisconsin–Madison (WI) **584**
U of Wisconsin–Milwaukee (WI) **585**
U of Wisconsin–Oshkosh (WI) **585**
U of Wisconsin–Parkside (WI) **585**
U of Wisconsin–Platteville (WI) **585**
U of Wisconsin–River Falls (WI) **585**
U of Wyoming (WY) **586**
Utah State U (UT) **587**
Valparaiso U (IN) **588**
Vanderbilt U (TN) **588**
Vassar Coll (NY) **589**
Virginia Polytechnic Inst and State U (VA) **591**
Washington and Lee U (VA) **594**
Washington State U (WA) **595**
Wayne State U (MI) **596**
Weber State U (UT) **596**
Wellesley Coll (MA) **597**
West Chester U of Pennsylvania (PA) **598**
Western Illinois U (IL) **599**
Western Kentucky U (KY) **599**
Western Michigan U (MI) **599**
Western New Mexico U (NM) **600**
Western State Coll of Colorado (CO) **600**
Western Washington U (WA) **600**
West Texas A&M U (TX) **602**
West Virginia U (WV) **602**
Wheaton Coll (IL) **603**
Whitman Coll (WA) **604**
Wichita State U (KS) **604**
Williams Coll (MA) **606**
Winona State U (MN) **608**
Wittenberg U (OH) **608**
Wright State U (OH) **609**
York Coll of the City U of New York (NY) **611**
Youngstown State U (OH) **611**

GEOPHYSICAL ENGINEERING

Overview: In this major, students study the exploration and appraisal of the earth's interior by collecting and analyzing physical measurements that are collected at the earth's surface. *Related majors:* mathematics, physics, geology, chemistry, hydrology, and computer science. *Potential careers:* seismologist, geologist, geohydrologist, petroleum engineer, mining engineer. *Salary potential:* $35-$50k.

Colorado School of Mines (CO) **325**
Harvard U (MA) **376**
Montana Tech of The U of Montana (MT) **435**
New Jersey Inst of Technology (NJ) **445**
Rutgers, The State U of New Jersey, Newark (NJ) **485**
Tufts U (MA) **533**
U of Calif, Los Angeles (CA) **541**
U of Saskatchewan (SK, Canada) **574**
U of Toronto (ON, Canada) **581**

GEOPHYSICS/SEISMOLOGY

Overview: Students choosing this major will study the structure and behavior of solid masses of the earth. *Related majors:* geological and geophysical engineering, physics, mathematics, surveying, mining and petroleum engineering, soil sciences, geology. *Potential careers:* geologist, seismologist, mining or petroleum engineer, research scientist. *Salary potential:* $32k-$45k.

Baylor U (TX) **283**
Boston Coll (MA) **292**
Bowling Green State U (OH) **292**
Brown U (RI) **296**
California Inst of Technology (CA) **299**
California State U, Northridge (CA) **301**
Eastern Michigan U (MI) **348**
Hampshire Coll (MA) **375**
Harvard U (MA) **376**
Hope Coll (MI) **381**
Kansas State U (KS) **396**
McGill U (QC, Canada) **423**
Memorial U of Newfoundland (NF, Canada) **424**
Michigan Technological U (MI) **428**
New Mexico Inst of Mining and Technology (NM) **446**
Oregon State U (OR) **462**
Rice U (TX) **479**
St. Lawrence U (NY) **491**
Saint Louis U (MO) **492**
San Jose State U (CA) **499**
Southern Methodist U (TX) **510**

GEOPHYSICS/SEISMOLOGY (continued)

Stanford U (CA) ***514***
State U of NY Coll at Fredonia (NY) ***516***
State U of NY Coll at Geneseo (NY) ***516***
Texas A&M U (TX) ***524***
Texas Tech U (TX) ***526***
Université de Sherbrooke (QC, Canada) ***536***
The U of Akron (OH) ***537***
U of Alberta (AB, Canada) ***538***
The U of British Columbia (BC, Canada) ***540***
U of Calgary (AB, Canada) ***540***
U of Calif, Berkeley (CA) ***540***
U of Calif, Los Angeles (CA) ***541***
U of Calif, Riverside (CA) ***541***
U of Calif, Santa Barbara (CA) ***541***
U of Calif, Santa Cruz (CA) ***542***
U of Chicago (IL) ***542***
U of Delaware (DE) ***544***
U of Houston (TX) ***547***
U of Minnesota, Twin Cities Campus (MN) ***555***
U of Missouri–Rolla (MO) ***556***
U of Nevada, Reno (NV) ***558***
U of New Brunswick Fredericton (NB, Canada) ***558***
U of New Orleans (LA) ***559***
U of Oklahoma (OK) ***562***
U of Ottawa (ON, Canada) ***563***
U of Saskatchewan (SK, Canada) ***574***
U of South Carolina (SC) ***575***
The U of Texas at Austin (TX) ***578***
The U of Texas at El Paso (TX) ***578***
U of Toronto (ON, Canada) ***581***
U of Tulsa (OK) ***581***
U of Utah (UT) ***582***
U of Victoria (BC, Canada) ***582***
U of Washington (WA) ***583***
The U of Western Ontario (ON, Canada) ***583***
U of Wisconsin–Madison (WI) ***584***
Western Michigan U (MI) ***599***
Western Washington U (WA) ***600***

GEOTECHNICAL ENGINEERING

Overview: This major teaches students how to manipulate and control surface and subsurface features such as moving and stabilizing earth and rock for structural use, land fills, underground construction, hazardous materials containment, etc. *Related majors:* soil science, structural engineering, geological engineering, mining/mineral engineering, environmental science. *Potential careers:* geotechnical engineer, civil engineer, architect, structural engineer, researcher. *Salary potential: $33k-$45k.*

Montana Tech of The U of Montana (MT) ***435***
York U (ON, Canada) ***611***

GERMAN

Overview: Students learn to read, speak, and understand the German language and related languages of Austria, Switzerland, and neighboring countries. *Related majors:* banking and international finance, history, history of science and technology, comparative literature, philosophy. *Potential careers:* diplomatic corps, journalist, translator, scientific consultant, engineering consultant. *Salary potential:* $28k-$40k.

Adrian Coll (MI) ***260***
Agnes Scott Coll (GA) ***261***
Albion Coll (MI) ***262***
Alfred U (NY) ***263***
Allegheny Coll (PA) ***264***
Alma Coll (MI) ***264***
American U (DC) ***267***
Amherst Coll (MA) ***268***
Anderson U (IN) ***268***
Angelo State U (TX) ***269***
Antioch Coll (OH) ***269***
Aquinas Coll (MI) ***270***
Arizona State U (AZ) ***271***
Arkansas Tech U (AR) ***272***
Auburn U (AL) ***276***
Augsburg Coll (MN) ***276***
Augustana Coll (IL) ***276***
Augustana Coll (SD) ***276***
Austin Coll (TX) ***277***
Baker U (KS) ***280***
Baldwin-Wallace Coll (OH) ***280***
Ball State U (IN) ***280***
Bard Coll (NY) ***281***
Barnard Coll (NY) ***282***
Bates Coll (ME) ***282***
Baylor U (TX) ***283***
Bellarmine U (KY) ***284***
Beloit Coll (WI) ***285***
Bemidji State U (MN) ***285***
Bennington Coll (VT) ***286***
Berea Coll (KY) ***286***
Berry Coll (GA) ***287***
Bethany Coll (WV) ***287***
Bethel Coll (KS) ***288***
Birmingham-Southern Coll (AL) ***289***
Bishop's U (QC, Canada) ***289***
Bloomsburg U of Pennsylvania (PA) ***290***
Boston Coll (MA) ***292***
Boston U (MA) ***292***
Bowdoin Coll (ME) ***292***
Bowling Green State U (OH) ***292***
Bradley U (IL) ***293***
Brandeis U (MA) ***293***
Brigham Young U (UT) ***295***
Brock U (ON, Canada) ***295***
Brooklyn Coll of the City U of NY (NY) ***295***
Brown U (RI) ***296***
Bryn Mawr Coll (PA) ***297***
Bucknell U (PA) ***297***
Butler U (IN) ***297***
California Lutheran U (CA) ***299***
California State U, Chico (CA) ***300***
California State U, Fullerton (CA) ***301***
California State U, Long Beach (CA) ***301***
California State U, Northridge (CA) ***301***
California State U, Sacramento (CA) ***301***
California U of Pennsylvania (PA) ***302***
Calvin Coll (MI) ***303***
Canisius Coll (NY) ***304***
Carleton Coll (MN) ***305***
Carleton U (ON, Canada) ***305***
Carnegie Mellon U (PA) ***305***
Carthage Coll (WI) ***306***
Case Western Reserve U (OH) ***307***
The Catholic U of America (DC) ***307***
Centenary Coll of Louisiana (LA) ***308***
Central Coll (IA) ***309***
Central Connecticut State U (CT) ***309***
Central Michigan U (MI) ***310***
Central Missouri State U (MO) ***310***
Centre Coll (KY) ***310***
Christopher Newport U (VA) ***313***
Citadel, The Military Coll of South Carolina (SC) ***314***
Claremont McKenna Coll (CA) ***315***
Clark Atlanta U (GA) ***315***
Cleveland State U (OH) ***317***
Coe Coll (IA) ***318***
Colby Coll (ME) ***318***
Colgate U (NY) ***319***
Coll of Charleston (SC) ***320***
Coll of Saint Benedict (MN) ***321***
Coll of the Holy Cross (MA) ***323***
Coll of the Ozarks (MO) ***323***
The Coll of William and Mary (VA) ***324***
The Coll of Wooster (OH) ***324***
The Colorado Coll (CO) ***325***
Colorado State U (CO) ***325***
Columbia Coll (NY) ***326***
Columbia U, School of General Studies (NY) ***328***
Concordia Coll (MN) ***329***
Concordia U (NE) ***330***
Concordia U (QC, Canada) ***331***
Concordia U Wisconsin (WI) ***331***
Connecticut Coll (CT) ***331***
Cornell Coll (IA) ***332***
Cornell U (NY) ***333***
Creighton U (NE) ***333***
Dalhousie U (NS, Canada) ***336***
Dana Coll (NE) ***337***
Dartmouth Coll (NH) ***337***
Davidson Coll (NC) ***338***
Denison U (OH) ***339***
DePaul U (IL) ***339***
DePauw U (IN) ***339***
Dickinson Coll (PA) ***344***
Dillard U (LA) ***344***
Doane Coll (NE) ***344***
Dordt Coll (IA) ***345***
Drew U (NJ) ***346***
Drury U (MO) ***346***
Duke U (NC) ***346***
Earlham Coll (IN) ***347***
East Carolina U (NC) ***347***
Eastern Kentucky U (KY) ***348***
Eastern Mennonite U (VA) ***348***
Eastern Michigan U (MI) ***348***
Eckerd Coll (FL) ***350***
Edinboro U of Pennsylvania (PA) ***351***
Elizabethtown Coll (PA) ***351***
Elmhurst Coll (IL) ***351***
Emory U (GA) ***354***
Fairfield U (CT) ***356***
Florida Atlantic U (FL) ***359***
Florida International U (FL) ***360***
Florida State U (FL) ***361***
Fordham U (NY) ***362***
Fort Hays State U (KS) ***362***
Francis Marion U (SC) ***363***
Franklin and Marshall Coll (PA) ***363***
Furman U (SC) ***365***
Georgetown Coll (KY) ***366***
Georgetown U (DC) ***366***
The George Washington U (DC) ***367***
Georgia Southern U (GA) ***367***
Georgia State U (GA) ***368***
Gettysburg Coll (PA) ***368***
Gonzaga U (WA) ***369***
Gordon Coll (MA) ***370***
Goshen Coll (IN) ***370***
Grace Coll (IN) ***370***
Graceland U (IA) ***371***
Grand Valley State U (MI) ***371***
Grinnell Coll (IA) ***373***
Guilford Coll (NC) ***373***
Gustavus Adolphus Coll (MN) ***374***
Hamilton Coll (NY) ***374***
Hamline U (MN) ***374***
Hampden-Sydney Coll (VA) ***374***
Hanover Coll (IN) ***375***
Hardin-Simmons U (TX) ***376***
Hartwick Coll (NY) ***376***
Harvard U (MA) ***376***
Hastings Coll (NE) ***377***
Haverford Coll (PA) ***377***
Heidelberg Coll (OH) ***377***
Hendrix Coll (AR) ***378***
Hillsdale Coll (MI) ***379***
Hiram Coll (OH) ***379***
Hofstra U (NY) ***380***
Hollins U (VA) ***380***
Hope Coll (MI) ***381***
Howard U (DC) ***382***
Humboldt State U (CA) ***382***
Hunter Coll of the City U of NY (NY) ***382***
Idaho State U (ID) ***384***
Illinois Coll (IL) ***384***
Illinois State U (IL) ***384***
Illinois Wesleyan U (IL) ***385***
Immaculata U (PA) ***385***
Indiana State U (IN) ***385***
Indiana U Bloomington (IN) ***385***
Indiana U of Pennsylvania (PA) ***386***
Indiana U–Purdue U Fort Wayne (IN) ***386***
Indiana U–Purdue U Indianapolis (IN) ***387***
Indiana U South Bend (IN) ***387***
Indiana U Southeast (IN) ***387***
Iowa State U of Science and Technology (IA) ***390***
Ithaca Coll (NY) ***390***
Jacksonville State U (AL) ***390***
James Madison U (VA) ***391***
John Carroll U (OH) ***392***
Johns Hopkins U (MD) ***392***
Juniata Coll (PA) ***395***
Kalamazoo Coll (MI) ***395***
Kent State U (OH) ***397***
Kenyon Coll (OH) ***398***
Knox Coll (IL) ***399***
Lafayette Coll (PA) ***400***
Lake Erie Coll (OH) ***400***
Lake Forest Coll (IL) ***400***
Lakeland Coll (WI) ***401***
La Salle U (PA) ***402***
Lawrence U (WI) ***403***
Lebanon Valley Coll (PA) ***403***
Lehigh U (PA) ***404***
Lenoir-Rhyne Coll (NC) ***405***
Lewis & Clark Coll (OR) ***405***
Linfield Coll (OR) ***408***
Lipscomb U (TN) ***408***
Lock Haven U of Pennsylvania (PA) ***408***
Long Island U, C.W. Post Campus (NY) ***409***
Long Island U, Southampton Coll, Friends World Program (NY) ***409***
Longwood U (VA) ***409***
Louisiana State U and A&M Coll (LA) ***410***
Loyola Coll in Maryland (MD) ***411***
Loyola U Chicago (IL) ***411***
Loyola U New Orleans (LA) ***411***
Luther Coll (IA) ***412***
Lycoming Coll (PA) ***412***
Manchester Coll (IN) ***415***
Mansfield U of Pennsylvania (PA) ***416***
Marlboro Coll (VT) ***418***
Marquette U (WI) ***418***
Mary Baldwin Coll (VA) ***419***
Mary Washington Coll (VA) ***420***
Massachusetts Inst of Technology (MA) ***421***
McDaniel Coll (MD) ***422***
McGill U (QC, Canada) ***423***
McMaster U (ON, Canada) ***423***
Memorial U of Newfoundland (NF, Canada) ***424***
Mercer U (GA) ***425***
Mercyhurst Coll (PA) ***425***
Messiah Coll (PA) ***426***
Miami U (OH) ***428***
Michigan State U (MI) ***428***
Middlebury Coll (VT) ***429***
Millersville U of Pennsylvania (PA) ***430***
Millikin U (IL) ***430***
Millsaps Coll (MS) ***431***
Mills Coll (CA) ***431***
Minnesota State U, Mankato (MN) ***431***
Minot State U (ND) ***432***
Missouri Southern State Coll (MO) ***433***
Montclair State U (NJ) ***435***
Moravian Coll (PA) ***436***
Morehouse Coll (GA) ***436***
Mount Allison U (NB, Canada) ***437***
Mount Holyoke Coll (MA) ***438***
Mount Saint Mary's Coll and Seminary (MD) ***439***
Mount Saint Vincent U (NS, Canada) ***439***
Mount Union Coll (OH) ***440***
Muhlenberg Coll (PA) ***440***
Murray State U (KY) ***440***
Muskingum Coll (OH) ***441***
Nazareth Coll of Rochester (NY) ***443***
Nebraska Wesleyan U (NE) ***443***
Newberry Coll (SC) ***444***
New Coll of Florida (FL) ***444***
New York U (NY) ***447***
North Carolina State U (NC) ***449***
North Central Coll (IL) ***449***
Northeastern State U (OK) ***450***
Northeastern U (MA) ***450***
Northern Arizona U (AZ) ***450***
Northern Illinois U (IL) ***450***
Northern State U (SD) ***451***
Northwestern U (IL) ***453***
Oakland U (MI) ***456***
Oberlin Coll (OH) ***456***
The Ohio State U (OH) ***457***
Ohio U (OH) ***458***
Ohio Wesleyan U (OH) ***459***
Oklahoma Baptist U (OK) ***459***
Oklahoma City U (OK) ***460***
Oklahoma State U (OK) ***460***
Oral Roberts U (OK) ***461***
Oregon State U (OR) ***462***
Pacific Lutheran U (WA) ***463***
Pacific U (OR) ***464***
Penn State U Univ Park Campus (PA) ***468***
Pepperdine U, Malibu (CA) ***469***
Pitzer Coll (CA) ***471***
Pomona Coll (CA) ***472***
Portland State U (OR) ***472***
Presbyterian Coll (SC) ***473***
Princeton U (NJ) ***474***
Principia Coll (IL) ***474***
Purdue U Calumet (IN) ***475***
Queens Coll of the City U of NY (NY) ***475***
Queen's U at Kingston (ON, Canada) ***476***
Randolph-Macon Coll (VA) ***477***
Randolph-Macon Woman's Coll (VA) ***477***
Reed Coll (OR) ***477***
Rensselaer Polytechnic Inst (NY) ***478***
Rhodes Coll (TN) ***479***
Rice U (TX) ***479***

Rider U (NJ) ***480***
Ripon Coll (WI) ***480***
Rockford Coll (IL) ***482***
Rollins Coll (FL) ***483***
Rosemont Coll (PA) ***484***
Rutgers, The State U of New Jersey, Camden (NJ) ***485***
Rutgers, The State U of New Jersey, Newark (NJ) ***485***
Rutgers, The State U of New Jersey, New Brunswick (NJ) ***485***
St. Ambrose U (IA) ***486***
St. Cloud State U (MN) ***488***
St. John Fisher Coll (NY) ***489***
Saint John's U (MN) ***490***
Saint Joseph's U (PA) ***491***
St. Lawrence U (NY) ***491***
Saint Louis U (MO) ***492***
Saint Mary's Coll of California (CA) ***494***
Saint Mary's U (NS, Canada) ***494***
St. Norbert Coll (WI) ***495***
St. Olaf Coll (MN) ***495***
Salem Coll (NC) ***496***
Samford U (AL) ***497***
Sam Houston State U (TX) ***497***
San Diego State U (CA) ***498***
San Francisco State U (CA) ***498***
San Jose State U (CA) ***499***
Sarah Lawrence Coll (NY) ***499***
Scripps Coll (CA) ***501***
Seattle Pacific U (WA) ***501***
Seattle U (WA) ***501***
Simon's Rock Coll of Bard (MA) ***505***
Simpson Coll (IA) ***505***
Skidmore Coll (NY) ***506***
Smith Coll (MA) ***506***
Sonoma State U (CA) ***506***
South Dakota State U (SD) ***507***
Southeast Missouri State U (MO) ***508***
Southern Connecticut State U (CT) ***509***
Southern Illinois U Carbondale (IL) ***509***
Southern Methodist U (TX) ***510***
Southern Utah U (UT) ***511***
Southwestern U (TX) ***513***
Southwest Missouri State U (MO) ***513***
Southwest Texas State U (TX) ***513***
Stanford U (CA) ***514***
State U of NY at Binghamton (NY) ***515***
State U of NY at New Paltz (NY) ***515***
State U of NY at Oswego (NY) ***515***
State U of NY Coll at Cortland (NY) ***516***
Stetson U (FL) ***519***
Stony Brook U, State University of New York (NY) ***520***
Susquehanna U (PA) ***521***
Swarthmore Coll (PA) ***521***
Sweet Briar Coll (VA) ***521***
Syracuse U (NY) ***521***
Temple U (PA) ***523***
Tennessee Technological U (TN) ***524***
Texas A&M U (TX) ***524***
Texas Southern U (TX) ***526***
Texas Tech U (TX) ***526***
Towson U (MD) ***529***
Trent U (ON, Canada) ***529***
Trinity Coll (CT) ***530***
Trinity U (TX) ***531***
Truman State U (MO) ***532***
Tufts U (MA) ***533***
Tulane U (LA) ***533***
Union Coll (NE) ***534***
United States Military Academy (NY) ***535***
U at Buffalo, The State University of New York (NY) ***536***
The U of Akron (OH) ***537***
The U of Alabama (AL) ***537***
U of Alberta (AB, Canada) ***538***
The U of Arizona (AZ) ***538***
U of Arkansas (AR) ***539***
The U of British Columbia (BC, Canada) ***540***
U of Calgary (AB, Canada) ***540***
U of Calif, Berkeley (CA) ***540***
U of Calif, Davis (CA) ***540***
U of Calif, Irvine (CA) ***541***
U of Calif, Los Angeles (CA) ***541***
U of Calif, Riverside (CA) ***541***
U of Calif, San Diego (CA) ***541***
U of Calif, Santa Barbara (CA) ***541***
U of Calif, Santa Cruz (CA) ***542***
U of Central Oklahoma (OK) ***542***
U of Chicago (IL) ***542***
U of Cincinnati (OH) ***543***
U of Colorado at Boulder (CO) ***543***
U of Colorado at Denver (CO) ***543***
U of Connecticut (CT) ***544***
U of Dallas (TX) ***544***
U of Dayton (OH) ***544***
U of Delaware (DE) ***544***
U of Denver (CO) ***544***
U of Evansville (IN) ***545***
U of Florida (FL) ***545***
U of Georgia (GA) ***545***
U of Hawaii at Manoa (HI) ***546***
U of Houston (TX) ***547***
U of Idaho (ID) ***547***
U of Illinois at Chicago (IL) ***547***
U of Illinois at Urbana–Champaign (IL) ***548***
U of Indianapolis (IN) ***548***
The U of Iowa (IA) ***548***
U of Kansas (KS) ***549***
U of Kentucky (KY) ***549***
U of King's Coll (NS, Canada) ***549***
U of La Verne (CA) ***549***
The U of Lethbridge (AB, Canada) ***549***
U of Louisville (KY) ***550***
U of Maine (ME) ***550***
U of Manitoba (MB, Canada) ***551***
U of Maryland, Baltimore County (MD) ***552***
U of Maryland, Coll Park (MD) ***552***
U of Massachusetts Amherst (MA) ***552***
U of Massachusetts Boston (MA) ***553***
U of Miami (FL) ***553***
U of Michigan (MI) ***554***
U of Michigan–Dearborn (MI) ***554***
U of Michigan–Flint (MI) ***554***
U of Minnesota, Morris (MN) ***555***
U of Minnesota, Twin Cities Campus (MN) ***555***
U of Mississippi (MS) ***555***
U of Missouri–Columbia (MO) ***555***
U of Missouri–Kansas City (MO) ***555***
U of Missouri–St. Louis (MO) ***556***
The U of Montana–Missoula (MT) ***556***
U of Nebraska at Kearney (NE) ***557***
U of Nebraska at Omaha (NE) ***557***
U of Nebraska–Lincoln (NE) ***557***
U of Nevada, Las Vegas (NV) ***558***
U of Nevada, Reno (NV) ***558***
U of New Brunswick Fredericton (NB, Canada) ***558***
U of New Hampshire (NH) ***558***
U of New Mexico (NM) ***559***
The U of North Carolina at Asheville (NC) ***559***
The U of North Carolina at Chapel Hill (NC) ***560***
The U of North Carolina at Charlotte (NC) ***560***
The U of North Carolina at Greensboro (NC) ***560***
U of North Dakota (ND) ***561***
U of Northern Colorado (CO) ***561***
U of Northern Iowa (IA) ***561***
U of North Texas (TX) ***562***
U of Notre Dame (IN) ***562***
U of Oklahoma (OK) ***562***
U of Oregon (OR) ***562***
U of Ottawa (ON, Canada) ***563***
U of Pennsylvania (PA) ***563***
U of Pittsburgh (PA) ***569***
U of Prince Edward Island (PE, Canada) ***570***
U of Puget Sound (WA) ***571***
U of Redlands (CA) ***572***
U of Regina (SK, Canada) ***572***
U of Rhode Island (RI) ***572***
U of Richmond (VA) ***572***
U of Rochester (NY) ***573***
U of St. Thomas (MN) ***573***
U of Saskatchewan (SK, Canada) ***574***
The U of Scranton (PA) ***574***
U of South Carolina (SC) ***575***
The U of South Dakota (SD) ***575***
U of Southern California (CA) ***576***
U of Southern Indiana (IN) ***576***
U of South Florida (FL) ***576***
The U of Tennessee (TN) ***577***
The U of Texas at Arlington (TX) ***577***
The U of Texas at Austin (TX) ***578***
The U of Texas at El Paso (TX) ***578***
The U of Texas at San Antonio (TX) ***578***
U of the Pacific (CA) ***580***
U of the South (TN) ***581***
U of Toledo (OH) ***581***
U of Toronto (ON, Canada) ***581***
U of Tulsa (OK) ***581***
U of Utah (UT) ***582***
U of Vermont (VT) ***582***
U of Victoria (BC, Canada) ***582***
U of Virginia (VA) ***582***
U of Washington (WA) ***583***
U of Waterloo (ON, Canada) ***583***
The U of Western Ontario (ON, Canada) ***583***
U of Windsor (ON, Canada) ***584***
U of Wisconsin–Eau Claire (WI) ***584***
U of Wisconsin–Green Bay (WI) ***584***
U of Wisconsin–La Crosse (WI) ***584***
U of Wisconsin–Madison (WI) ***584***
U of Wisconsin–Milwaukee (WI) ***585***
U of Wisconsin–Oshkosh (WI) ***585***
U of Wisconsin–Parkside (WI) ***585***
U of Wisconsin–Platteville (WI) ***585***
U of Wisconsin–River Falls (WI) ***585***
U of Wisconsin–Stevens Point (WI) ***585***
U of Wisconsin–Whitewater (WI) ***586***
U of Wyoming (WY) ***586***
Ursinus Coll (PA) ***587***
Utah State U (UT) ***587***
Valparaiso U (IN) ***588***
Vanderbilt U (TN) ***588***
Vassar Coll (NY) ***589***
Villanova U (PA) ***590***
Virginia Polytechnic Inst and State U (VA) ***591***
Virginia Wesleyan Coll (VA) ***591***
Wabash Coll (IN) ***592***
Wake Forest U (NC) ***592***
Walla Walla Coll (WA) ***593***
Wartburg Coll (IA) ***594***
Washington & Jefferson Coll (PA) ***594***
Washington and Lee U (VA) ***594***
Washington Coll (MD) ***594***
Washington State U (WA) ***595***
Washington U in St. Louis (MO) ***595***
Wayne State Coll (NE) ***596***
Wayne State U (MI) ***596***
Weber State U (UT) ***596***
Webster U (MO) ***597***
Wellesley Coll (MA) ***597***
Wells Coll (NY) ***597***
Wesleyan U (CT) ***597***
West Chester U of Pennsylvania (PA) ***598***
Western Carolina U (NC) ***598***
Western Kentucky U (KY) ***599***
Western Michigan U (MI) ***599***
Western Washington U (WA) ***600***
Westminster Coll (PA) ***601***
Wheaton Coll (IL) ***603***
Wheaton Coll (MA) ***603***
Whitman Coll (WA) ***604***
Willamette U (OR) ***605***
Williams Coll (MA) ***606***
Winona State U (MN) ***608***
Wittenberg U (OH) ***608***
Wofford Coll (SC) ***609***
Wright State U (OH) ***609***
Xavier U (OH) ***610***
Yale U (CT) ***610***
York U (ON, Canada) ***611***

GERMAN LANGUAGE EDUCATION

Overview: This major prepares individuals for a career of teaching German language at various educational levels. *Related majors:* German, comparative literature. *Potential career:* German teacher. *Salary potential:* $23k-$28k.

Anderson U (IN) ***268***
Baylor U (TX) ***283***
Berea Coll (KY) ***286***
Berry Coll (GA) ***287***
Bridgewater Coll (VA) ***294***
Brigham Young U (UT) ***295***
Canisius Coll (NY) ***304***
The Catholic U of America (DC) ***307***
Central Michigan U (MI) ***310***
Central Missouri State U (MO) ***310***
Colorado State U (CO) ***325***
Concordia Coll (MN) ***329***
Duquesne U (PA) ***346***
East Carolina U (NC) ***347***
Eastern Mennonite U (VA) ***348***
Eastern Michigan U (MI) ***348***
Elmhurst Coll (IL) ***351***
Georgia Southern U (GA) ***367***
Grace Coll (IN) ***370***
Hardin-Simmons U (TX) ***376***
Hofstra U (NY) ***380***
Indiana U Bloomington (IN) ***385***
Indiana U–Purdue U Fort Wayne (IN) ***386***
Indiana U–Purdue U Indianapolis (IN) ***387***
Indiana U South Bend (IN) ***387***
Ithaca Coll (NY) ***390***
Juniata Coll (PA) ***395***
Luther Coll (IA) ***412***
Mansfield U of Pennsylvania (PA) ***416***
Messiah Coll (PA) ***426***
Minot State U (ND) ***432***
Ohio U (OH) ***458***
Oklahoma Baptist U (OK) ***459***
Oral Roberts U (OK) ***461***
St. Ambrose U (IA) ***486***
San Diego State U (CA) ***498***
Southwest Missouri State U (MO) ***513***
The U of Akron (OH) ***537***
The U of Arizona (AZ) ***538***
U of Illinois at Chicago (IL) ***547***
U of Illinois at Urbana–Champaign (IL) ***548***
The U of Iowa (IA) ***548***
U of Minnesota, Duluth (MN) ***554***
U of Nebraska–Lincoln (NE) ***557***
The U of North Carolina at Charlotte (NC) ***560***
U of North Texas (TX) ***562***
The U of Tennessee at Martin (TN) ***577***
U of Utah (UT) ***582***
U of Windsor (ON, Canada) ***584***
U of Wisconsin–River Falls (WI) ***585***
Washington U in St. Louis (MO) ***595***
Weber State U (UT) ***596***
Western Carolina U (NC) ***598***
Youngstown State U (OH) ***611***

GERONTOLOGICAL SERVICES

Overview: This major focuses on the programs and services that serve the social, economic, medical, and psychological needs of aging adults. *Related majors:* counseling psychology, gerontology, nursing, occupational therapy, physical therapy. *Potential careers:* nursing home or assisted-living administrator, senior-citizen center manager, psychiatrist, nurse, state and local program coordinator. *Salary potential:* $18k-$25k.

Bowling Green State U (OH) ***292***
Mount Saint Vincent U (NS, Canada) ***439***
Ohio U (OH) ***458***
Saint Mary-of-the-Woods Coll (IN) ***493***
St. Thomas U (NB, Canada) ***496***
U of Northern Colorado (CO) ***561***

GERONTOLOGY

Overview: This major uses social sciences, psychology, and biological and health sciences to study the human aging process and aged human populations. *Related majors:* psychology, neuroscience, physiology, economics, sociology, health science, food and nutrition studies. *Potential careers:* physician, psychologist, social worker, adult health nurse, research scientist. *Salary potential:* $28k-$38k

Alfred U (NY) ***263***
Alma Coll (MI) ***264***
Avila U (MO) ***278***
Bethune-Cookman Coll (FL) ***289***
Bishop's U (QC, Canada) ***289***
Bowling Green State U (OH) ***292***
California State U, Dominguez Hills (CA) ***300***
California State U, Hayward (CA) ***301***
California State U, Northridge (CA) ***301***
California State U, Sacramento (CA) ***301***
California U of Pennsylvania (PA) ***302***
Case Western Reserve U (OH) ***307***
Cedar Crest Coll (PA) ***308***
Central Washington U (WA) ***310***
Chestnut Hill Coll (PA) ***312***
Coll of Mount St. Joseph (OH) ***320***

GERONTOLOGY (continued)

Coll of the Holy Cross (MA) ***323***
Coll of the Ozarks (MO) ***323***
Dominican U (IL) ***345***
Felician Coll (NJ) ***357***
Framingham State Coll (MA) ***362***
Gwynedd-Mercy Coll (PA) ***374***
Iona Coll (NY) ***390***
Ithaca Coll (NY) ***390***
John Carroll U (OH) ***392***
King's Coll (PA) ***398***
Lakehead U (ON, Canada) ***400***
Langston U (OK) ***402***
Lindenwood U (MO) ***407***
Long Island U, Southampton Coll, Friends World Program (NY) ***409***
Lourdes Coll (OH) ***411***
Lynn U (FL) ***413***
Madonna U (MI) ***414***
Mars Hill Coll (NC) ***418***
McMaster U (ON, Canada) ***423***
Mercy Coll (NY) ***425***
Mount St. Mary's Coll (CA) ***439***
Mount Saint Vincent U (NS, Canada) ***439***
National-Louis U (IL) ***442***
Nazareth Coll of Rochester (NY) ***443***
Pontifical Catholic U of Puerto Rico (PR) ***472***
Quinnipiac U (CT) ***476***
Roosevelt U (IL) ***483***
St. Cloud State U (MN) ***488***
Saint Mary-of-the-Woods Coll (IN) ***493***
St. Thomas U (NB, Canada) ***496***
San Diego State U (CA) ***498***
Shaw U (NC) ***502***
Southeastern Oklahoma State U (OK) ***508***
Southwest Missouri State U (MO) ***513***
Springfield Coll (MA) ***514***
State U of NY Coll at Brockport (NY) ***515***
State U of NY Coll at Fredonia (NY) ***516***
State U of NY Coll at Oneonta (NY) ***517***
Stephen F. Austin State U (TX) ***518***
Thomas Edison State Coll (NJ) ***527***
Towson U (MD) ***529***
The U of Akron (OH) ***537***
U of Evansville (IN) ***545***
U of Guelph (ON, Canada) ***546***
U of Hawaii at Manoa (HI) ***546***
U of Massachusetts Boston (MA) ***553***
U of Missouri–St. Louis (MO) ***556***
U of Nebraska at Omaha (NE) ***557***
U of Nevada, Las Vegas (NV) ***558***
The U of North Carolina at Greensboro (NC) ***560***
U of North Texas (TX) ***562***
The U of Scranton (PA) ***574***
U of Southern California (CA) ***576***
U of South Florida (FL) ***576***
U of Windsor (ON, Canada) ***584***
Wagner Coll (NY) ***592***
Weber State U (UT) ***596***
Western Michigan U (MI) ***599***
Wichita State U (KS) ***604***
Winston-Salem State U (NC) ***608***
York Coll of the City U of New York (NY) ***611***
York U (ON, Canada) ***611***

GRAPHIC DESIGN/ COMMERCIAL ART/ ILLUSTRATION

Overview: This major prepares students to use artistic and computer techniques to create visual presentations of commercial concepts and ideas for various audiences. *Related majors:* design and visual communication, computer graphics, fashion design/ illustration, drawing, multimedia. *Potential careers:* book jacket or magazine layout designer, Web page designer, creative director for an advertising agency, cartoonist, fashion illustrator. *Salary potential:* $25k-$40k.

Abilene Christian U (TX) ***260***
Academy of Art Coll (CA) ***260***
Alberta Coll of Art & Design (AB, Canada) ***262***
Albertus Magnus Coll (CT) ***262***
Alfred U (NY) ***263***
American Academy of Art (IL) ***265***
American InterContinental U (CA) ***266***
American InterContinental U, Atlanta (GA) ***266***
American InterContinental U-London(United Kingdom) ***267***
American U (DC) ***267***
Anderson Coll (SC) ***268***
Anderson U (IN) ***268***
Andrews U (MI) ***269***
Appalachian State U (NC) ***270***
Arcadia U (PA) ***271***
Arizona State U (AZ) ***271***
Arkansas State U (AR) ***272***
Art Academy of Cincinnati (OH) ***273***
Art Center Coll of Design (CA) ***273***
The Art Inst of Boston at Lesley U (MA) ***273***
The Art Inst of California–San Diego (CA) ***273***
The Art Inst of California–San Francisco (CA) ***273***
The Art Inst of Colorado (CO) ***274***
The Art Inst of Phoenix (AZ) ***274***
The Art Inst of Portland (OR) ***274***
The Art Inst of Washington (VA) ***274***
Ashland U (OH) ***274***
Atlanta Coll of Art (GA) ***275***
Auburn U (AL) ***276***
Avila U (MO) ***278***
Baker Coll of Flint (MI) ***279***
Baker Coll of Owosso (MI) ***279***
Ball State U (IN) ***280***
Barton Coll (NC) ***282***
Becker Coll (MA) ***283***
Bellevue U (NE) ***284***
Bemidji State U (MN) ***285***
Benedict Coll (SC) ***285***
Biola U (CA) ***289***
Black Hills State U (SD) ***290***
Bluffton Coll (OH) ***291***
Boston U (MA) ***292***
Brenau U (GA) ***293***
Brescia U (KY) ***293***
Briar Cliff U (IA) ***294***
Bridgewater State Coll (MA) ***294***
Brigham Young U (UT) ***295***
Buena Vista U (IA) ***297***
Cabrini Coll (PA) ***298***
California Coll of Arts and Crafts (CA) ***299***
California Inst of the Arts (CA) ***299***
California Polytechnic State U, San Luis Obispo (CA) ***300***
California State Polytechnic U, Pomona (CA) ***300***
California State U, Dominguez Hills (CA) ***300***
California State U, Fresno (CA) ***301***
California State U, Fullerton (CA) ***301***
California State U, Hayward (CA) ***301***
California State U, Long Beach (CA) ***301***
California State U, Northridge (CA) ***301***
California State U, San Bernardino (CA) ***302***
Campbell U (NC) ***303***
Cardinal Stritch U (WI) ***305***
Carnegie Mellon U (PA) ***305***
Carroll Coll (WI) ***306***
Carson-Newman Coll (TN) ***306***
Carthage Coll (WI) ***306***
Centenary Coll (NJ) ***308***
Central Michigan U (MI) ***310***
Central Missouri State U (MO) ***310***
Champlain Coll (VT) ***311***
Chapman U (CA) ***311***
Chatham Coll (PA) ***312***
Chester Coll of New England (NH) ***312***
Chowan Coll (NC) ***312***
Clark U (MA) ***316***
The Cleveland Inst of Art (OH) ***317***
Cogswell Polytechnical Coll (CA) ***318***
Coker Coll (SC) ***318***
Colby-Sawyer Coll (NH) ***319***
Col for Creative Studies (MI) ***319***
Coll of Mount St. Joseph (OH) ***320***
The Coll of New Jersey (NJ) ***320***
The Coll of Saint Rose (NY) ***322***
The Coll of Southeastern Europe, The American U of Athens(Greece) ***323***
Coll of Visual Arts (MN) ***324***
Colorado State U (CO) ***325***
Columbia Coll (MO) ***326***
Columbia Coll (SC) ***327***
Columbia Coll Chicago (IL) ***327***
Columbus Coll of Art and Design (OH) ***328***
Concord Coll (WV) ***329***
Concordia U (IL) ***330***
Concordia U (NE) ***330***
Concordia U (QC, Canada) ***331***
Concordia U Wisconsin (WI) ***331***
Cooper Union for the Advancement of Science & Art (NY) ***332***
Corcoran Coll of Art and Design (DC) ***332***
Cornish Coll of the Arts (WA) ***333***
Creighton U (NE) ***333***
Curry Coll (MA) ***335***
Daemen Coll (NY) ***335***
DePaul U (IL) ***339***
Dominican U (IL) ***345***
Dordt Coll (IA) ***345***
Drake U (IA) ***345***
Drexel U (PA) ***346***
Eastern Kentucky U (KY) ***348***
Edgewood Coll (WI) ***351***
Elms Coll (MA) ***352***
Emmanuel Coll (MA) ***353***
Endicott Coll (MA) ***354***
Escuela de Artes Plasticas de Puerto Rico (PR) ***354***
Fairmont State Coll (WV) ***356***
State U of NY at Farmingdale (NY) ***357***
Fashion Inst of Technology (NY) ***357***
Felician Coll (NJ) ***357***
Fitchburg State Coll (MA) ***358***
Flagler Coll (FL) ***359***
Florida A&M U (FL) ***359***
Florida Southern Coll (FL) ***361***
Florida State U (FL) ***361***
Fontbonne U (MO) ***361***
Fordham U (NY) ***362***
Fort Hays State U (KS) ***362***
Franklin Pierce Coll (NH) ***364***
Freed-Hardeman U (TN) ***364***
Gallaudet U (DC) ***365***
Georgian Court Coll (NJ) ***367***
Georgia Southwestern State U (GA) ***368***
Grace Coll (IN) ***370***
Graceland U (IA) ***371***
Grand Canyon U (AZ) ***371***
Grand Valley State U (MI) ***371***
Grand View Coll (IA) ***372***
Hampshire Coll (MA) ***375***
Hampton U (VA) ***375***
Harding U (AR) ***375***
Howard U (DC) ***382***
Huntington Coll (IN) ***383***
The Illinois Inst of Art (IL) ***384***
Illinois Wesleyan U (IL) ***385***
Indiana U Bloomington (IN) ***385***
Indiana U–Purdue U Fort Wayne (IN) ***386***
International Academy of Design & Technology (FL) ***388***
Iowa State U of Science and Technology (IA) ***390***
Iowa Wesleyan Coll (IA) ***390***
John Brown U (AR) ***392***
Judson Coll (IL) ***395***
Kansas City Art Inst (MO) ***395***
Keene State Coll (NH) ***396***
Kendall Coll of Art and Design of Ferris State U (MI) ***396***
Kent State U (OH) ***397***
Kutztown U of Pennsylvania (PA) ***399***
Laguna Coll of Art & Design (CA) ***400***
Lamar U (TX) ***401***
Lambuth U (TN) ***401***
La Roche Coll (PA) ***402***
La Salle U (PA) ***402***
Lasell Coll (MA) ***402***
La Sierra U (CA) ***403***
Lewis U (IL) ***406***
Limestone Coll (SC) ***406***
Lipscomb U (TN) ***408***
Long Island U, C.W. Post Campus (NY) ***409***
Long Island U, Southampton Coll (NY) ***409***
Longwood U (VA) ***409***
Louisiana Coll (LA) ***410***
Louisiana Tech U (LA) ***410***
Loyola U New Orleans (LA) ***411***
Lubbock Christian U (TX) ***412***
Lycoming Coll (PA) ***412***
Lyndon State Coll (VT) ***413***
Lynn U (FL) ***413***
Madonna U (MI) ***414***
Maharishi U of Management (IA) ***414***
Maine Coll of Art (ME) ***415***
Marietta Coll (OH) ***417***
Mary Baldwin Coll (VA) ***419***
Maryland Inst Coll of Art (MD) ***419***
Marymount U (VA) ***420***
Maryville U of Saint Louis (MO) ***420***
Massachusetts Coll of Art (MA) ***421***
Memphis Coll of Art (TN) ***425***
Mercy Coll (NY) ***425***
Meredith Coll (NC) ***426***
MidAmerica Nazarene U (KS) ***428***
Millikin U (IL) ***430***
Milwaukee Inst of Art and Design (WI) ***431***
Minneapolis Coll of Art and Design (MN) ***431***
Minnesota State U, Mankato (MN) ***431***
Minnesota State U, Moorhead (MN) ***432***
Mississippi Coll (MS) ***432***
Missouri Southern State Coll (MO) ***433***
Missouri Western State Coll (MO) ***433***
Monmouth U (NJ) ***434***
Montana State U–Northern (MT) ***434***
Montserrat Coll of Art (MA) ***435***
Moore Coll of Art and Design (PA) ***436***
Moravian Coll (PA) ***436***
Morningside Coll (IA) ***437***
Mount Ida Coll (MA) ***438***
Mount Mary Coll (WI) ***438***
Mount Olive Coll (NC) ***439***
Nazareth Coll of Rochester (NY) ***443***
New Mexico Highlands U (NM) ***446***
New World School of the Arts (FL) ***447***
New York Inst of Technology (NY) ***447***
New York U (NY) ***447***
North Carolina State U (NC) ***449***
Northeastern State U (OK) ***450***
Northeastern U (MA) ***450***
Northern Kentucky U (KY) ***451***
Northern Michigan U (MI) ***451***
Northwest Coll of Art (WA) ***452***
Northwestern Coll (MN) ***453***
Northwest Missouri State U (MO) ***454***
Northwest Nazarene U (ID) ***454***
Notre Dame de Namur U (CA) ***455***
Nova Scotia Coll of Art and Design (NS, Canada) ***455***
Ohio Northern U (OH) ***457***
The Ohio State U (OH) ***457***
Ohio U (OH) ***458***
Oklahoma Christian U (OK) ***459***
Oklahoma City U (OK) ***460***
Oklahoma State U (OK) ***460***
Olivet Coll (MI) ***461***
Olivet Nazarene U (IL) ***461***
O'More Coll of Design (TN) ***461***
Oral Roberts U (OK) ***461***
Otis Coll of Art and Design (CA) ***462***
Pacific Northwest Coll of Art (OR) ***464***
Paier Coll of Art, Inc. (CT) ***464***
Park U (MO) ***465***
Parsons School of Design, New School U (NY) ***465***
Pennsylvania Coll of Art & Design (PA) ***467***
Pennsylvania Coll of Technology (PA) ***467***
Penn State U Univ Park Campus (PA) ***468***
Peru State Coll (NE) ***469***
Philadelphia U (PA) ***469***
Pittsburg State U (KS) ***470***
Plymouth State Coll (NH) ***471***
Point Loma Nazarene U (CA) ***471***
Portland State U (OR) ***472***
Pratt Inst (NY) ***473***
Rhode Island School of Design (RI) ***479***
Ringling School of Art and Design (FL) ***480***
Rivier Coll (NH) ***480***
Roberts Wesleyan Coll (NY) ***481***
Rochester Inst of Technology (NY) ***482***
Rocky Mountain Coll of Art & Design (CO) ***483***
Rowan U (NJ) ***484***
Rutgers, The State U of New Jersey, New Brunswick (NJ) ***485***
Ryerson U (ON, Canada) ***485***
Sacred Heart U (CT) ***486***
St. Cloud State U (MN) ***488***
St. John's U (NY) ***490***
Saint Mary's U of Minnesota (MN) ***494***
St. Norbert Coll (WI) ***495***
St. Thomas Aquinas Coll (NY) ***495***
Salem State Coll (MA) ***497***
Samford U (AL) ***497***
Sam Houston State U (TX) ***497***
San Jose State U (CA) ***499***
Savannah Coll of Art and Design (GA) ***499***
School of the Art Inst of Chicago (IL) ***500***
School of the Museum of Fine Arts (MA) ***501***
School of Visual Arts (NY) ***501***
Schreiner U (TX) ***501***
Seton Hall U (NJ) ***502***

Seton Hill U (PA) **502**
Simmons Coll (MA) **504**
Simpson Coll (IA) **505**
Southern Connecticut State U (CT) **509**
Southwest Baptist U (MO) **512**
Southwestern Oklahoma State U (OK) **512**
Southwest Texas State U (TX) **513**
Spring Hill Coll (AL) **514**
State U of NY at New Paltz (NY) **515**
State U of NY at Oswego (NY) **515**
State U of NY Coll at Buffalo (NY) **516**
State U of NY Coll at Fredonia (NY) **516**
Suffolk U (MA) **520**
Syracuse U (NY) **521**
Taylor U (IN) **523**
Temple U (PA) **523**
Texas A&M U–Commerce (TX) **525**
Texas Christian U (TX) **526**
Texas Tech U (TX) **526**
Trinity Christian Coll (IL) **530**
Truman State U (MO) **532**
Union Coll (NE) **534**
Université Laval (QC, Canada) **536**
U of Advancing Technology (AZ) **537**
The U of Akron (OH) **537**
U of Bridgeport (CT) **540**
U of Central Oklahoma (OK) **542**
U of Cincinnati (OH) **543**
U of Dayton (OH) **544**
U of Delaware (DE) **544**
U of Denver (CO) **544**
U of Evansville (IN) **545**
U of Florida (FL) **545**
U of Hartford (CT) **546**
U of Illinois at Chicago (IL) **547**
U of Illinois at Urbana–Champaign (IL) **548**
U of Indianapolis (IN) **548**
U of Massachusetts Dartmouth (MA) **553**
U of Miami (FL) **553**
U of Michigan (MI) **554**
U of Minnesota, Duluth (MN) **554**
U of Minnesota, Twin Cities Campus (MN) **555**
U of Missouri–St. Louis (MO) **556**
U of Montevallo (AL) **557**
U of Oregon (OR) **562**
U of Saint Francis (IN) **573**
U of San Francisco (CA) **574**
U of Sioux Falls (SD) **574**
The U of South Dakota (SD) **575**
The U of Tennessee (TN) **577**
The U of Tennessee at Martin (TN) **577**
The U of Texas at El Paso (TX) **578**
The U of the Arts (PA) **579**
U of the Incarnate Word (TX) **580**
U of the Pacific (CA) **580**
U of Washington (WA) **583**
U of Wisconsin–Platteville (WI) **585**
U of Wisconsin–Stevens Point (WI) **585**
Upper Iowa U (IA) **587**
Villa Julie Coll (MD) **590**
Viterbo U (WI) **591**
Walla Walla Coll (WA) **593**
Wartburg Coll (IA) **594**
Washington U in St. Louis (MO) **595**
Watkins Coll of Art and Design (TN) **595**
Waynesburg Coll (PA) **595**
Wayne State Coll (NE) **596**
Weber State U (UT) **596**
Webster U (MO) **597**
Western Connecticut State U (CT) **598**
Western Kentucky U (KY) **599**
Western Michigan U (MI) **599**
Western State Coll of Colorado (CO) **600**
Western Washington U (WA) **600**
Westfield State Coll (MA) **600**
West Liberty State Coll (WV) **601**
West Texas A&M U (TX) **602**
West Virginia Wesleyan Coll (WV) **603**
Wichita State U (KS) **604**
William Paterson U of New Jersey (NJ) **606**
William Woods U (MO) **607**
Winona State U (MN) **608**
Wittenberg U (OH) **608**
Woodbury U (CA) **609**
York Coll of Pennsylvania (PA) **610**
York U (ON, Canada) **611**
Youngstown State U (OH) **611**

GRAPHIC/PRINTING EQUIPMENT

Overview: Students will learn how to operate and repair graphic and standard printing press equipment. *Related majors:* industrial machinery repair and maintenance, printing press operator, lithographer, platemaker. *Potential careers:* printing press operator, technician. *Salary potential:* $23k-$30k.

Andrews U (MI) **269**
Appalachian State U (NC) **270**
Arkansas State U (AR) **272**
California Polytechnic State U, San Luis Obispo (CA) **300**
Central Missouri State U (MO) **310**
Chowan Coll (NC) **312**
Fairmont State Coll (WV) **356**
Ferris State U (MI) **358**
Florida A&M U (FL) **359**
Georgia Southern U (GA) **367**
Indiana State U (IN) **385**
Kean U (NJ) **396**
Murray State U (KY) **440**
Pennsylvania Coll of Technology (PA) **467**
Pittsburg State U (KS) **470**
Rochester Inst of Technology (NY) **482**
Southwest Texas State U (TX) **513**
Texas A&M U–Commerce (TX) **525**
U of the District of Columbia (DC) **580**
West Virginia U Inst of Technology (WV) **602**

GREEK (ANCIENT AND MEDIEVAL)

Overview: Students study the language and literatures of the ancient Greeks through the fall of the Byzantine Empire. *Related majors:* classics, Western civilization and culture, history, history of philosophy, drama. *Potential careers:* archeologist, historian/archivist, professor. *Salary potential:* $21k-$27k.

Amherst Coll (MA) **268**
Asbury Coll (KY) **274**
Bard Coll (NY) **281**
Barnard Coll (NY) **282**
Baylor U (TX) **283**
Boston U (MA) **292**
Brandeis U (MA) **293**
Brock U (ON, Canada) **295**
Bryn Mawr Coll (PA) **297**
Carleton Coll (MN) **305**
Columbia Coll (NY) **326**
Dartmouth Coll (NH) **337**
Dickinson Coll (PA) **344**
Duke U (NC) **346**
Duquesne U (PA) **346**
Elmira Coll (NY) **351**
Franklin and Marshall Coll (PA) **363**
Hobart and William Smith Colls (NY) **380**
Hunter Coll of the City U of NY (NY) **382**
Indiana U Bloomington (IN) **385**
Loyola U Chicago (IL) **411**
Miami U (OH) **428**
Mount Allison U (NB, Canada) **437**
Multnomah Bible Coll and Biblical Seminary (OR) **440**
New Coll of Florida (FL) **444**
Ohio U (OH) **458**
Randolph-Macon Coll (VA) **477**
Randolph-Macon Woman's Coll (VA) **477**
Rice U (TX) **479**
Rutgers, The State U of New Jersey, New Brunswick (NJ) **485**
Saint Louis U (MO) **492**
St. Olaf Coll (MN) **495**
Samford U (AL) **497**
Santa Clara U (CA) **499**
Smith Coll (MA) **506**
Swarthmore Coll (PA) **521**
Sweet Briar Coll (VA) **521**
U of Calif, Berkeley (CA) **540**
U of Calif, Santa Cruz (CA) **542**
U of Chicago (IL) **542**
U of Georgia (GA) **545**
U of Hawaii at Manoa (HI) **546**
U of Nebraska–Lincoln (NE) **557**
U of Notre Dame (IN) **562**
U of St. Thomas (MN) **573**
The U of Scranton (PA) **574**
U of Southern California (CA) **576**
The U of Texas at Austin (TX) **578**
U of Vermont (VT) **582**
U of Victoria (BC, Canada) **582**
U of Washington (WA) **583**
The U of Western Ontario (ON, Canada) **583**
Wake Forest U (NC) **592**
Washington U in St. Louis (MO) **595**
Wellesley Coll (MA) **597**
Yale U (CT) **610**

GREEK (MODERN)

Overview: Students learn how to read, speak, and understand Modern Greek and the development of the language. *Related majors:* history, Western civilization, international economics, art history, archeology. *Potential careers:* archeologist, diplomatic corps, business consultant, international development specialist, teacher. *Salary potential:* $24k-$34k.

Ball State U (IN) **280**
Bard Coll (NY) **281**
Belmont U (TN) **284**
Boise Bible Coll (ID) **291**
Boston U (MA) **292**
Brooklyn Coll of the City U of NY (NY) **295**
Butler U (IN) **297**
Calvin Coll (MI) **303**
Carleton U (ON, Canada) **305**
Claremont McKenna Coll (CA) **315**
Colgate U (NY) **319**
The Coll of William and Mary (VA) **324**
The Coll of Wooster (OH) **324**
Columbia Coll (NY) **326**
Concordia U Wisconsin (WI) **331**
Cornell Coll (IA) **332**
Cornell U (NY) **333**
Creighton U (NE) **333**
DePauw U (IN) **339**
Emory U (GA) **354**
Florida State U (FL) **361**
Fordham U (NY) **362**
Furman U (SC) **365**
Gettysburg Coll (PA) **368**
Hamilton Coll (NY) **374**
Hampden-Sydney Coll (VA) **374**
Harvard U (MA) **376**
Haverford Coll (PA) **377**
John Carroll U (OH) **392**
Kenyon Coll (OH) **398**
La Salle U (PA) **402**
Lehman Coll of the City U of NY (NY) **404**
Long Island U, Southampton Coll, Friends World Program (NY) **409**
Loyola Marymount U (CA) **411**
Luther Coll (IA) **412**
Macalester Coll (MN) **413**
Marlboro Coll (VT) **418**
Memorial U of Newfoundland (NF, Canada) **424**
Monmouth Coll (IL) **434**
Mount Holyoke Coll (MA) **438**
New York U (NY) **447**
Oberlin Coll (OH) **456**
The Ohio State U (OH) **457**
Queens Coll of the City U of NY (NY) **475**
Queen's U at Kingston (ON, Canada) **476**
Rhodes Coll (TN) **479**
Rockford Coll (IL) **482**
Saint Mary's Coll of California (CA) **494**
Syracuse U (NY) **521**
Trent U (ON, Canada) **529**
Tufts U (MA) **533**
Tulane U (LA) **533**
U of Alberta (AB, Canada) **538**
U of Calif, Los Angeles (CA) **541**
The U of Iowa (IA) **548**
U of Manitoba (MB, Canada) **551**
U of Michigan (MI) **554**
U of Minnesota, Twin Cities Campus (MN) **555**
U of New Brunswick Fredericton (NB, Canada) **558**
U of New Hampshire (NH) **558**
U of Oregon (OR) **562**
U of Richmond (VA) **572**
U of Saskatchewan (SK, Canada) **574**
The U of Tennessee at Chattanooga (TN) **577**
U of the South (TN) **581**
U of Toronto (ON, Canada) **581**
U of Utah (UT) **582**
U of Windsor (ON, Canada) **584**
U of Wisconsin–Madison (WI) **584**
U of Wisconsin–Milwaukee (WI) **585**
Ursinus Coll (PA) **587**
Wabash Coll (IN) **592**
Wright State U (OH) **609**
York U (ON, Canada) **611**

HEALTH AIDE

Overview: This major prepares students for a career assisting health-care therapists and other rehabilitation specialists who care for elderly people, patients recovering from illness, or handicapped persons either in their homes or in health-care institutions. *Related majors:* home health aide, nurse training, nurse assistant/aide. *Potential careers:* home health aide, nurse, nurse aide. *Salary potential:* $19k-$25k.

Campbell U (NC) **303**

HEALTH EDUCATION

Overview: This program prepares undergraduates to teach various health programs, such as nutrition, sex education, exercise, and substance abuse, to students from a variety of educational levels. *Related majors:* food and nutrition; social, school, and counseling psychology; community health; alcohol/drug-abuse counseling; health science. *Potential careers:* health teacher, community health liaison, sex-education teacher, nutritionist, school psychiatrist. *Salary potential:* $25k-$37k.

Abilene Christian U (TX) **260**
Anderson U (IN) **268**
Appalachian State U (NC) **270**
Aquinas Coll (MI) **270**
Arkansas State U (AR) **272**
Armstrong Atlantic State U (GA) **273**
Ashland U (OH) **274**
Auburn U (AL) **276**
Augsburg Coll (MN) **276**
Austin Peay State U (TN) **278**
Averett U (VA) **278**
Baldwin-Wallace Coll (OH) **280**
Ball State U (IN) **280**
Baylor U (TX) **283**
Belmont U (TN) **284**
Bemidji State U (MN) **285**
Berry Coll (GA) **287**
Bethel Coll (MN) **288**
Bluffton Coll (OH) **291**
Bowling Green State U (OH) **292**
Briar Cliff U (IA) **294**
Bridgewater State Coll (MA) **294**
California State U, Chico (CA) **300**
California State U, Northridge (CA) **301**
California State U, San Bernardino (CA) **302**
Campbellsville U (KY) **303**
Capital U (OH) **304**
Carroll Coll (WI) **306**
Cedarville U (OH) **308**
Centenary Coll of Louisiana (LA) **308**
Central Michigan U (MI) **310**
Central Washington U (WA) **310**
Christopher Newport U (VA) **313**
Clark Atlanta U (GA) **315**
Coll of Mount Saint Vincent (NY) **320**
Concord Coll (WV) **329**
Concordia Coll (MN) **329**
Concordia U (MN) **330**
Concordia U (NE) **330**
Cumberland Coll (KY) **335**
Curry Coll (MA) **335**
Dalhousie U (NS, Canada) **336**
Davis & Elkins Coll (WV) **338**

HEALTH EDUCATION (continued)

Defiance Coll (OH) ***338***
Delaware State U (DE) ***338***
Dillard U (LA) ***344***
East Carolina U (NC) ***347***
Eastern Illinois U (IL) ***348***
Eastern Kentucky U (KY) ***348***
Eastern Mennonite U (VA) ***348***
Eastern Washington U (WA) ***349***
East Stroudsburg U of Pennsylvania (PA) ***349***
Elon U (NC) ***352***
Emporia State U (KS) ***354***
Fayetteville State U (NC) ***357***
Florida A&M U (FL) ***359***
Florida International U (FL) ***360***
Florida State U (FL) ***361***
Fort Valley State U (GA) ***362***
Freed-Hardeman U (TN) ***364***
Gardner-Webb U (NC) ***365***
George Fox U (OR) ***366***
George Mason U (VA) ***366***
Georgia Coll & State U (GA) ***367***
Graceland U (IA) ***371***
Gustavus Adolphus Coll (MN) ***374***
Gwynedd-Mercy Coll (PA) ***374***
Hamline U (MN) ***374***
Hampton U (VA) ***375***
Heidelberg Coll (OH) ***377***
Hofstra U (NY) ***380***
Hunter Coll of the City U of NY (NY) ***382***
Idaho State U (ID) ***384***
Illinois State U (IL) ***384***
Indiana State U (IN) ***385***
Indiana U–Purdue U Indianapolis (IN) ***387***
Iowa State U of Science and Technology (IA) ***390***
Ithaca Coll (NY) ***390***
Jackson State U (MS) ***390***
Jacksonville State U (AL) ***390***
John Brown U (AR) ***392***
Johnson C. Smith U (NC) ***394***
Keene State Coll (NH) ***396***
Kennesaw State U (GA) ***397***
Kent State U (OH) ***397***
Lamar U (TX) ***401***
Lee U (TN) ***404***
Lehman Coll of the City U of NY (NY) ***404***
Liberty U (VA) ***406***
Lincoln Memorial U (TN) ***407***
Lincoln U (PA) ***407***
Lipscomb U (TN) ***408***
Lock Haven U of Pennsylvania (PA) ***408***
Long Island U, C.W. Post Campus (NY) ***409***
Longwood U (VA) ***409***
Louisiana Coll (LA) ***410***
Luther Coll (IA) ***412***
Lynchburg Coll (VA) ***413***
Malone Coll (OH) ***415***
Manchester Coll (IN) ***415***
Marywood U (PA) ***421***
Mayville State U (ND) ***422***
Miami U (OH) ***428***
MidAmerica Nazarene U (KS) ***428***
Middle Tennessee State U (TN) ***429***
Minnesota State U, Mankato (MN) ***431***
Minnesota State U, Moorhead (MN) ***432***
Missouri Valley Coll (MO) ***433***
Montana State U–Billings (MT) ***434***
Montclair State U (NJ) ***435***
Morehead State U (KY) ***436***
Morgan State U (MD) ***436***
Mount Vernon Nazarene U (OH) ***440***
Murray State U (KY) ***440***
Muskingum Coll (OH) ***441***
New Mexico Highlands U (NM) ***446***
Nicholls State U (LA) ***447***
North Carolina Ag and Tech State U (NC) ***448***
North Carolina Central U (NC) ***448***
North Central Coll (IL) ***449***
Northeastern State U (OK) ***450***
Northern Arizona U (AZ) ***450***
Northern Illinois U (IL) ***450***
Northern Michigan U (MI) ***451***
Northern State U (SD) ***451***
Northwestern Oklahoma State U (OK) ***453***
Northwest Missouri State U (MO) ***454***
Ohio Northern U (OH) ***457***
Ohio Wesleyan U (OH) ***459***
Otterbein Coll (OH) ***462***
Peru State Coll (NE) ***469***
Pittsburg State U (KS) ***470***
Pontifical Catholic U of Puerto Rico (PR) ***472***
Portland State U (OR) ***472***
Queen's U at Kingston (ON, Canada) ***476***
Radford U (VA) ***476***
Rhode Island Coll (RI) ***479***
Rocky Mountain Coll (MT) ***482***
St. Ambrose U (IA) ***486***
St. Cloud State U (MN) ***488***
Saint Mary's Coll of California (CA) ***494***
Salem State Coll (MA) ***497***
Salisbury U (MD) ***497***
San Francisco State U (CA) ***498***
Slippery Rock U of Pennsylvania (PA) ***506***
South Carolina State U (SC) ***506***
Southeastern Oklahoma State U (OK) ***508***
Southern Illinois U Carbondale (IL) ***509***
Southern Illinois U Edwardsville (IL) ***509***
Southern Nazarene U (OK) ***510***
Southern Oregon U (OR) ***510***
Southwest State U (MN) ***513***
Springfield Coll (MA) ***514***
State U of NY Coll at Brockport (NY) ***515***
State U of NY Coll at Cortland (NY) ***516***
Syracuse U (NY) ***521***
Tabor Coll (KS) ***522***
Temple U (PA) ***523***
Tennessee State U (TN) ***523***
Tennessee Technological U (TN) ***524***
Texas A&M U (TX) ***524***
Texas A&M U–Commerce (TX) ***525***
Texas A&M U–Kingsville (TX) ***525***
Texas Southern U (TX) ***526***
Touro U International (CA) ***529***
Troy State U (AL) ***532***
Union Coll (KY) ***533***
The U of Akron (OH) ***537***
The U of Alabama at Birmingham (AL) ***537***
The U of Arizona (AZ) ***538***
U of Arkansas at Little Rock (AR) ***539***
U of Central Arkansas (AR) ***542***
U of Cincinnati (OH) ***543***
U of Dayton (OH) ***544***
U of Delaware (DE) ***544***
U of Florida (FL) ***545***
U of Georgia (GA) ***545***
U of Hawaii at Manoa (HI) ***546***
The U of Iowa (IA) ***548***
U of Kansas (KS) ***549***
U of Kentucky (KY) ***549***
The U of Lethbridge (AB, Canada) ***549***
U of Maine (ME) ***550***
U of Maine at Farmington (ME) ***550***
U of Maine at Presque Isle (ME) ***551***
U of Maryland, Coll Park (MD) ***552***
U of Massachusetts Lowell (MA) ***553***
U of Minnesota, Duluth (MN) ***554***
The U of Montana–Missoula (MT) ***556***
The U of Montana–Western (MT) ***556***
U of Nebraska at Omaha (NE) ***557***
U of Nebraska–Lincoln (NE) ***557***
U of Nevada, Las Vegas (NV) ***558***
U of Nevada, Reno (NV) ***558***
U of New Brunswick Fredericton (NB, Canada) ***558***
U of New Mexico (NM) ***559***
The U of North Carolina at Greensboro (NC) ***560***
The U of North Carolina at Pembroke (NC) ***560***
U of Northern Iowa (IA) ***561***
U of North Texas (TX) ***562***
U of Puerto Rico Medical Sciences Campus (PR) ***571***
U of Regina (SK, Canada) ***572***
U of Richmond (VA) ***572***
U of Rio Grande (OH) ***572***
U of Saint Francis (IN) ***573***
U of St. Thomas (MN) ***573***
U of Sioux Falls (SD) ***574***
The U of Tennessee (TN) ***577***
The U of Texas–Pan American (TX) ***579***
U of the District of Columbia (DC) ***580***
U of Toledo (OH) ***581***
U of Toronto (ON, Canada) ***581***
U of Utah (UT) ***582***
U of Wisconsin–La Crosse (WI) ***584***
U of Wyoming (WY) ***586***
Upper Iowa U (IA) ***587***
Urbana U (OH) ***587***
Ursinus Coll (PA) ***587***
Utah State U (UT) ***587***
Valley City State U (ND) ***588***
Virginia Commonwealth U (VA) ***590***
Virginia Polytechnic Inst and State U (VA) ***591***
Washington State U (WA) ***595***
West Chester U of Pennsylvania (PA) ***598***
Western Connecticut State U (CT) ***598***
Western Illinois U (IL) ***599***
Western Michigan U (MI) ***599***
Western Washington U (WA) ***600***
West Liberty State Coll (WV) ***601***
West Virginia State Coll (WV) ***602***
West Virginia U Inst of Technology (WV) ***602***
West Virginia Wesleyan Coll (WV) ***603***
William Carey Coll (MS) ***605***
William Paterson U of New Jersey (NJ) ***606***
William Penn U (IA) ***606***
Wilmington Coll (OH) ***607***
Winona State U (MN) ***608***
Wright State U (OH) ***609***
Xavier U of Louisiana (LA) ***610***
York Coll of the City U of New York (NY) ***611***
Youngstown State U (OH) ***611***

HEALTH FACILITIES ADMINISTRATION

Overview: This major prepares students to manage health facilities such as clinics, hospitals, and nursing homes. *Related majors:* business administration and management, finance and accounting, operations management and supervision, human resources management and labor relations. *Potential careers:* hospital or clinic administrator, nursing home director. *Salary potential:* $35k-$50k.

Carson-Newman Coll (TN) ***306***
Central Michigan U (MI) ***310***
Coll of Mount Saint Vincent (NY) ***320***
Eastern U (PA) ***349***
Ithaca Coll (NY) ***390***
Long Island U, C.W. Post Campus (NY) ***409***
Ohio U (OH) ***458***
St. John's U (NY) ***490***
Southern Illinois U Carbondale (IL) ***509***
Southwest Texas State U (TX) ***513***
The U of Alabama (AL) ***537***
U of Pennsylvania (PA) ***563***
U of Toledo (OH) ***581***
Worcester State Coll (MA) ***609***
York U (ON, Canada) ***611***

HEALTH/MEDICAL ADMINISTRATIVE SERVICES RELATED

Information can be found under this major's main heading.

Pennsylvania Coll of Technology (PA) ***467***
Robert Morris U (PA) ***481***
U of Baltimore (MD) ***539***
Ursuline Coll (OH) ***587***

HEALTH/MEDICAL ASSISTANTS RELATED

Information can be found under this major's main heading.

Wayne State U (MI) ***596***

HEALTH/MEDICAL BIOSTATISTICS

Overview: This major equips students with the knowledge to use different types of statistical analysis in areas that are related to human health, such as biomedical research and public health. *Related majors:* mathematics, statistics, computer science, genetics, pathology, human ecology. *Potential careers:* research scientist, public health official, biomedical researcher. *Salary potential:* $30k-$37k.

Insto Tecno Estudios Sups Monterrey(Mexico) ***388***
The U of North Carolina at Chapel Hill (NC) ***560***

HEALTH/MEDICAL DIAGNOSTIC AND TREATMENT SERVICES RELATED

Information can be found under this major's main heading.

Fairleigh Dickinson U, Florham (NJ) ***356***
Fairleigh Dickinson U, Teaneck-Metro Campus (NJ) ***356***
Florida Gulf Coast U (FL) ***359***
Georgian Court Coll (NJ) ***367***
Rutgers, The State U of New Jersey, Newark (NJ) ***485***
U of Connecticut (CT) ***544***
U of Toledo (OH) ***581***
Virginia Commonwealth U (VA) ***590***

HEALTH/MEDICAL LABORATORY TECHNOLOGIES RELATED

Information can be found under this major's main heading.

Saint Louis U (MO) ***492***

HEALTH/MEDICAL PREPARATORY PROGRAMS RELATED

Information can be found under this major's main heading.

Allegheny Coll (PA) ***264***
Aurora U (IL) ***277***
Chadron State Coll (NE) ***311***
Duquesne U (PA) ***346***
Guilford Coll (NC) ***373***
Ithaca Coll (NY) ***390***
Juniata Coll (PA) ***395***
Lander U (SC) ***401***
Rhode Island Coll (RI) ***479***
The U of Akron (OH) ***537***
U of Louisville (KY) ***550***
U of Miami (FL) ***553***
U of South Alabama (AL) ***575***
Utica Coll (NY) ***588***

HEALTH OCCUPATIONS EDUCATION

Overview: This major provides undergraduates with a variety of learning experiences that allow them to teach health-related subjects, such as nutrition, fitness and wellness, health promotion and disease prevention, and substance abuse. *Related majors:* foods/nutrition studies, human services, health and physical education, nursing. *Potential careers:* dietitian, high school health counselor or teacher, health educator, health unit coordinator, hospital worker. *Salary potential:* $23k-$34k.

New York Inst of Technology (NY) ***447***
North Carolina State U (NC) ***449***
U of Central Oklahoma (OK) ***542***
U of Louisville (KY) ***550***
U of Maine at Farmington (ME) ***550***

HEALTH/PHYSICAL EDUCATION

Overview: Student learn how to devise and manage activities that promote physical fitness and athletic prowess. *Related majors:* athletic training/sports medicine, exercise sciences and movement studies, health science, movement therapy. *Potential careers:* physical education teacher, sports doctor, physical therapist, athletic coach, personal trainer. *Salary potential:* $20k-$30k.

Abilene Christian U (TX) 260
Anderson U (IN) 268
Angelo State U (TX) 269
Arkansas State U (AR) 272
Asbury Coll (KY) 274
Austin Peay State U (TN) 278
Averett U (VA) 278
Baylor U (TX) 283
Bethel Coll (KS) 288
Bethel Coll (TN) 288
Black Hills State U (SD) 290
Bridgewater Coll (VA) 294
Bridgewater State Coll (MA) 294
Brigham Young U (UT) 295
Brigham Young U–Hawaii (HI) 295
California State U, Fullerton (CA) 301
California State U, Sacramento (CA) 301
Cameron U (OK) 303
Campbell U (NC) 303
Castleton State Coll (VT) 307
Cedarville U (OH) 308
Central Michigan U (MI) 310
Christopher Newport U (VA) 313
Coll of St. Catherine (MN) 321
Coll of the Ozarks (MO) 323
Concordia Coll (MN) 329
Concordia U (NE) 330
Dana Coll (NE) 337
Doane Coll (NE) 344
Eastern Michigan U (MI) 348
Eastern U (PA) 349
East Tennessee State U (TN) 349
East Texas Baptist U (TX) 350
Edinboro U of Pennsylvania (PA) 351
Elmhurst Coll (IL) 351
Emory & Henry Coll (VA) 353
Freed-Hardeman U (TN) 364
Georgia Southern U (GA) 367
Hastings Coll (NE) 377
Houghton Coll (NY) 381
Howard Payne U (TX) 382
Indiana U of Pennsylvania (PA) 386
Iowa State U of Science and Technology (IA) 390
Ithaca Coll (NY) 390
Jacksonville State U (AL) 390
James Madison U (VA) 391
Johnson State Coll (VT) 394
Kentucky State U (KY) 397
La Sierra U (CA) 403
Liberty U (VA) 406
Linfield Coll (OR) 408
Louisiana Tech U (LA) 410
Luther Coll (IA) 412
Lyndon State Coll (VT) 413
Malone Coll (OH) 415
Marywood U (PA) 421
Mayville State U (ND) 422
Miami U (OH) 428
Middle Tennessee State U (TN) 429
Minnesota State U, Moorhead (MN) 432
Montana State U–Bozeman (MT) 434
New England Coll (NH) 444
North Carolina Central U (NC) 448
North Dakota State U (ND) 449
Northwest Nazarene U (ID) 454
Ohio U (OH) 458
Oklahoma Baptist U (OK) 459
Oklahoma State U (OK) 460
Olivet Coll (MI) 461
Pillsbury Baptist Bible Coll (MN) 470
Point Loma Nazarene U (CA) 471
Queen's U at Kingston (ON, Canada) 476
Roanoke Coll (VA) 481
St. Mary's U of San Antonio (TX) 494
Salisbury U (MD) 497
Samford U (AL) 497
San Jose State U (CA) 499
Schreiner U (TX) 501
South Dakota State U (SD) 507
Southeast Missouri State U (MO) 508
Southern Illinois U Edwardsville (IL) 509
Southern Virginia U (VA) 511
Southwestern Coll (KS) 512
Southwest State U (MN) 513
Southwest Texas State U (TX) 513
Spring Arbor U (MI) 514
Stephen F. Austin State U (TX) 518
Tennessee Wesleyan Coll (TN) 524
Texas A&M International U (TX) 524
Texas A&M U (TX) 524
Texas Coll (TX) 526
Texas Southern U (TX) 526
Texas Tech U (TX) 526
Texas Wesleyan U (TX) 526
Texas Woman's U (TX) 527
Trinity Western U (BC, Canada) 531
U du Québec à Trois-Rivières (QC, Canada) 536
U of Arkansas (AR) 539
U of Delaware (DE) 544
U of Great Falls (MT) 545
U of Hawaii at Manoa (HI) 546
U of Houston (TX) 547
U of Illinois at Chicago (IL) 547
U of Illinois at Urbana–Champaign (IL) 548
U of Kansas (KS) 549
U of Louisville (KY) 550
U of Missouri–Kansas City (MO) 555
U of Montevallo (AL) 557
The U of North Carolina at Chapel Hill (NC) 560
The U of North Carolina at Charlotte (NC) 560
The U of North Carolina at Wilmington (NC) 561
U of Oklahoma (OK) 562
U of Rio Grande (OH) 572
U of St. Thomas (MN) 573
U of San Francisco (CA) 574
U of Science and Arts of Oklahoma (OK) 574
U of Southern Mississippi (MS) 576
The U of Tennessee at Martin (TN) 577
The U of Texas at Arlington (TX) 577
The U of Texas at Austin (TX) 578
The U of Texas at San Antonio (TX) 578
The U of Texas–Pan American (TX) 579
U of Utah (UT) 582
U of West Florida (FL) 583
U of Windsor (ON, Canada) 584
U of Wisconsin–Stevens Point (WI) 585
Valparaiso U (IN) 588
Vanguard U of Southern California (CA) 589
Walla Walla Coll (WA) 593
Weber State U (UT) 596
West Texas A&M U (TX) 602
William Penn U (IA) 606
York U (ON, Canada) 611
Youngstown State U (OH) 611

HEALTH/PHYSICAL EDUCATION/FITNESS RELATED

Information can be found under this major's main heading.

Arizona State U East (AZ) 271
Averett U (VA) 278
Briar Cliff U (IA) 294
Colorado Christian U (CO) 325
East Carolina U (NC) 347
Mayville State U (ND) 422
Reinhardt Coll (GA) 478
Texas Lutheran U (TX) 526
The U of Akron (OH) 537
U of Central Oklahoma (OK) 542

HEALTH PHYSICS/ RADIOLOGIC HEALTH

Overview: This major teaches students the concepts of nuclear science, radiological science, and physics that can be used to diagnose health problems, treat disease, and contribute to overall public health. *Related majors:* nuclear physics, nuclear medical technology, environmental health, radiological science. *Potential careers:* public health administrator, epidemiologist, radioactive waste management specialist, CDC investigator, health services research analyst. *Salary potential:* $37k-$45k.

Bloomsburg U of Pennsylvania (PA) 290
U of Nevada, Las Vegas (NV) 558

HEALTH PRODUCTS/ SERVICES MARKETING

Overview: This major will prepare students to perform marketing and sales operations for a variety of health products and services. *Related majors:* marketing and marketing research, personal services marketing, general selling/sales operations. *Potential careers:* health products marketer, network marketer. *Salary potential:* $18k-$25k.

Carlow Coll (PA) 305
Quinnipiac U (CT) 476

HEALTH PROFESSIONS AND RELATED SCIENCES

Information can be found under this major's main heading.

Albany State U (GA) 262
Alcorn State U (MS) 263
Bradley U (IL) 293
California State U, Fullerton (CA) 301
Clemson U (SC) 317
East Tennessee State U (TN) 349
George Mason U (VA) 366
Hofstra U (NY) 380
King Coll (TN) 398
King's Coll (PA) 398
Lebanon Valley Coll (PA) 403
Maharishi U of Management (IA) 414
Mass Coll of Pharmacy and Allied Health Sciences (MA) 421
The Ohio State U (OH) 457
Ohio U (OH) 458
Old Dominion U (VA) 460
Pennsylvania Coll of Technology (PA) 467
Randolph-Macon Woman's Coll (VA) 477
San Diego State U (CA) 498
Touro Coll (NY) 529
The U of Alabama (AL) 537
U of Arkansas (AR) 539
U of Miami (FL) 553
U of Pennsylvania (PA) 563
U of Pittsburgh (PA) 569
U of Utah (UT) 582
U of Wyoming (WY) 586
Washington U in St. Louis (MO) 595

HEALTH SCIENCE

Overview: This is a general major that helps students prepare for a wide range of health-care careers as well as specialization in other health-related fields. *Related majors:* biology, premedicine, nursing, psychology, human physiology and anatomy. *Potential careers:* health educator, health organization administrator, health-care consultant, pharmaceutical sales representative, physician assistant. *Salary potential:* $30k-$40k.

Alma Coll (MI) 264
American U (DC) 267
Armstrong Atlantic State U (GA) 273
Athens State U (AL) 275
Azusa Pacific U (CA) 278
Ball State U (IN) 280
Bastyr U (WA) 282
Benedictine U (IL) 285
Boston U (MA) 292
Bradley U (IL) 293
Brigham Young U (UT) 295
Brock U (ON, Canada) 295
Brooklyn Coll of the City U of NY (NY) 295
California State U, Chico (CA) 300
California State U, Dominguez Hills (CA) 300
California State U, Fresno (CA) 301
California State U, Hayward (CA) 301
California State U, Long Beach (CA) 301
California State U, Northridge (CA) 301
California State U, San Bernardino (CA) 302
Campbell U (NC) 303
Carlow Coll (PA) 305
Castleton State Coll (VT) 307
Cedar Crest Coll (PA) 308
Centenary Coll of Louisiana (LA) 308
Chapman U (CA) 311
Coll Misericordia (PA) 319
Coll of Mount Saint Vincent (NY) 320
The Coll of St. Scholastica (MN) 322
Coll of the Ozarks (MO) 323
Columbus State U (GA) 328
Dalhousie U (NS, Canada) 336
Delaware State U (DE) 338
Eastern Nazarene Coll (MA) 348
Erskine Coll (SC) 354
Fairmont State Coll (WV) 356
Florida Atlantic U (FL) 359
Florida International U (FL) 360
Gannon U (PA) 365
Gettysburg Coll (PA) 368
Graceland U (IA) 371
Grand Valley State U (MI) 371
Gwynedd-Mercy Coll (PA) 374
Hampshire Coll (MA) 375
Hiram Coll (OH) 379
Inter American U of PR, San Germán Campus (PR) 388
Johnson State Coll (VT) 394
Kalamazoo Coll (MI) 395
Kansas State U (KS) 396
Lamar U (TX) 401
Lock Haven U of Pennsylvania (PA) 408
Long Island U, Brooklyn Campus (NY) 409
Longwood U (VA) 409
Manchester Coll (IN) 415
Marymount U (VA) 420
Maryville U of Saint Louis (MO) 420
Medical U of South Carolina (SC) 424
Merrimack Coll (MA) 426
Milligan Coll (TN) 430
Minnesota State U, Mankato (MN) 431
Montana Tech of The U of Montana (MT) 435
Montclair State U (NJ) 435
Morris Coll (SC) 437
Mount Olive Coll (NC) 439
New Jersey City U (NJ) 445
Newman U (KS) 445
Northeastern U (MA) 450
Northern Illinois U (IL) 450
Northwest Missouri State U (MO) 454
Oakland U (MI) 456
Ohio U (OH) 458
Oklahoma State U (OK) 460
Oregon State U (OR) 462
Our Lady of Holy Cross Coll (LA) 463
Pacific U (OR) 464
Queen's U at Kingston (ON, Canada) 476
Roosevelt U (IL) 483
Samuel Merritt Coll (CA) 498
San Francisco State U (CA) 498
San Jose State U (CA) 499
Sonoma State U (CA) 506
State U of NY Coll at Brockport (NY) 515
State U of NY Coll at Cortland (NY) 516
Stony Brook U, State University of New York (NY) 520
Syracuse U (NY) 521
Tennessee Wesleyan Coll (TN) 524
Texas A&M U–Corpus Christi (TX) 525
Texas Christian U (TX) 526
Texas Southern U (TX) 526
Touro Coll (NY) 529
Towson U (MD) 529
Truman State U (MO) 532
Union Inst & U (OH) 534
U du Québec à Trois-Rivières (QC, Canada) 536
U of Alaska Anchorage (AK) 538
U of Arkansas at Little Rock (AR) 539
U of Central Florida (FL) 542
U of Colorado at Colorado Springs (CO) 543
U of Florida (FL) 545
U of Hartford (CT) 546
U of Maryland, Baltimore County (MD) 552
U of Missouri–St. Louis (MO) 556
U of Nevada, Las Vegas (NV) 558
U of New Brunswick Saint John (NB, Canada) 558
U of New England (ME) 558
U of North Florida (FL) 561
U of Puerto Rico Medical Sciences Campus (PR) 571
U of Rochester (NY) 573
U of St. Francis (IL) 573
U of Saint Francis (IN) 573
U of St. Thomas (MN) 573
U of Southern California (CA) 576
U of Southern Maine (ME) 576
The U of Texas at El Paso (TX) 578
The U of Texas at San Antonio (TX) 578
The U of Texas at Tyler (TX) 579
U of the Sciences in Philadelphia (PA) 580

HEALTH SCIENCE (continued)

U of Waterloo (ON, Canada) ***583***
The U of Western Ontario (ON, Canada) ***583***
U of Wisconsin–Milwaukee (WI) ***585***
Ursinus Coll (PA) ***587***
Ursuline Coll (OH) ***587***
Valdosta State U (GA) ***588***
Waldorf Coll (IA) ***592***
Walla Walla Coll (WA) ***593***
Warner Pacific Coll (OR) ***593***
Wayne State U (MI) ***596***
West Chester U of Pennsylvania (PA) ***598***
Western Baptist Coll (OR) ***598***
West Liberty State Coll (WV) ***601***
William Paterson U of New Jersey (NJ) ***606***
Winona State U (MN) ***608***
York U (ON, Canada) ***611***
Youngstown State U (OH) ***611***

HEALTH SERVICES ADMINISTRATION

Overview: This major prepares students to plan, organize, and manage health-care systems, operations, and services that are part of larger health-care facilities. *Related majors:* health facilities administration, business administration and management, health science, human resource management. *Potential careers:* health services administrator or manager. *Salary potential:* $27k-$37k.

Albertus Magnus Coll (CT) ***262***
Alfred U (NY) ***263***
Alvernia Coll (PA) ***265***
Appalachian State U (NC) ***270***
Arcadia U (PA) ***271***
Auburn U (AL) ***276***
Augustana Coll (SD) ***276***
Baker Coll of Auburn Hills (MI) ***279***
Baker Coll of Flint (MI) ***279***
Baker Coll of Muskegon (MI) ***279***
Baker Coll of Owosso (MI) ***279***
Baker Coll of Port Huron (MI) ***280***
Bellevue U (NE) ***284***
Belmont U (TN) ***284***
Benedictine U (IL) ***285***
Black Hills State U (SD) ***290***
Bowling Green State U (OH) ***292***
British Columbia Inst of Technology (BC, Canada) ***295***
Brock U (ON, Canada) ***295***
California Coll for Health Sciences (CA) ***298***
California State U, Chico (CA) ***300***
California State U, Dominguez Hills (CA) ***300***
California State U, Long Beach (CA) ***301***
California State U, Northridge (CA) ***301***
California State U, San Bernardino (CA) ***302***
Calumet Coll of Saint Joseph (IN) ***302***
Cedar Crest Coll (PA) ***308***
Chestnut Hill Coll (PA) ***312***
Clayton Coll & State U (GA) ***316***
Cleary U (MI) ***317***
Coll of Mount St. Joseph (OH) ***320***
The Coll of St. Scholastica (MN) ***322***
Columbia Southern U (AL) ***327***
Columbia Union Coll (MD) ***328***
Comm Hospital Roanoke Valley–Coll of Health Scis (VA) ***328***
Concordia Coll (MN) ***329***
Concordia U (MI) ***330***
Concordia U (NE) ***330***
Concordia U (OR) ***330***
Concordia U Wisconsin (WI) ***331***
Creighton U (NE) ***333***
Dallas Baptist U (TX) ***336***
Davenport U, Grand Rapids (MI) ***337***
Davenport U, Kalamazoo (MI) ***337***
Davis & Elkins Coll (WV) ***338***
Dillard U (LA) ***344***
Dominican Coll (NY) ***344***
Drexel U (PA) ***346***
Duquesne U (PA) ***346***
D'Youville Coll (NY) ***347***
Eastern Kentucky U (KY) ***348***
Eastern Michigan U (MI) ***348***
Eastern Washington U (WA) ***349***
Ferris State U (MI) ***358***
Fisk U (TN) ***358***
Florida A&M U (FL) ***359***
Florida Atlantic U (FL) ***359***
Florida International U (FL) ***360***
Florida Metropolitan U-Orlando Coll, North (FL) ***361***
Florida Metropolitan U-Orlando Coll, South (FL) ***361***
The Franciscan U (IA) ***363***
Franklin U (OH) ***364***
Frostburg State U (MD) ***365***
Governors State U (IL) ***370***
Gwynedd-Mercy Coll (PA) ***374***
Harding U (AR) ***375***
Harris-Stowe State Coll (MO) ***376***
Hastings Coll (NE) ***377***
Heidelberg Coll (OH) ***377***
Howard Payne U (TX) ***382***
Idaho State U (ID) ***384***
Indiana U Northwest (IN) ***386***
Indiana U–Purdue U Fort Wayne (IN) ***386***
Indiana U–Purdue U Indianapolis (IN) ***387***
Indiana U South Bend (IN) ***387***
Inst of Public Administration(Ireland) ***387***
Iona Coll (NY) ***390***
Ithaca Coll (NY) ***390***
John Brown U (AR) ***392***
Johnson & Wales U (RI) ***393***
King's Coll (PA) ***398***
Lander U (SC) ***401***
Langston U (OK) ***402***
Lehman Coll of the City U of NY (NY) ***404***
Lewis U (IL) ***406***
Lindenwood U (MO) ***407***
Long Island U, C.W. Post Campus (NY) ***409***
Lynn U (FL) ***413***
Macon State Coll (GA) ***414***
Martin Methodist Coll (TN) ***418***
Mary Baldwin Coll (VA) ***419***
Maryville U of Saint Louis (MO) ***420***
Marywood U (PA) ***421***
Mercy Coll (NY) ***425***
Methodist Coll (NC) ***427***
Metropolitan State Coll of Denver (CO) ***427***
Milligan Coll (TN) ***430***
Minnesota State U, Moorhead (MN) ***432***
Montana State U–Billings (MT) ***434***
Montana State U–Bozeman (MT) ***434***
Mountain State U (WV) ***437***
Mount St. Mary's Coll (CA) ***439***
National-Louis U (IL) ***442***
National U (CA) ***442***
Newbury Coll (MA) ***444***
New Mexico Highlands U (NM) ***446***
Norfolk State U (VA) ***448***
Northeastern State U (OK) ***450***
Northeastern U (MA) ***450***
Ohio U (OH) ***458***
Oregon State U (OR) ***462***
Peirce Coll (PA) ***466***
Penn State U Univ Park Campus (PA) ***468***
Point Park Coll (PA) ***471***
Presentation Coll (SD) ***474***
Providence Coll (RI) ***474***
Quinnipiac U (CT) ***476***
Robert Morris U (PA) ***481***
Roosevelt U (IL) ***483***
Ryerson U (ON, Canada) ***485***
St. Francis Coll (NY) ***488***
St. Joseph's Coll, New York (NY) ***491***
St. Joseph's Coll, Suffolk Campus (NY) ***491***
Saint Joseph's U (PA) ***491***
Saint Leo U (FL) ***492***
Saint Louis U (MO) ***492***
Saint Mary's U of Minnesota (MN) ***494***
Saint Peter's Coll (NJ) ***495***
San Jose State U (CA) ***499***
Slippery Rock U of Pennsylvania (PA) ***506***
Southeastern U (DC) ***508***
Southern Adventist U (TN) ***508***
Southwestern Oklahoma State U (OK) ***512***
Southwest Texas State U (TX) ***513***
Spring Arbor U (MI) ***514***
Springfield Coll (MA) ***514***
State U of NY Coll at Fredonia (NY) ***516***
State U of NY Inst of Tech at Utica/Rome (NY) ***518***
Stonehill Coll (MA) ***520***
Tennessee State U (TN) ***523***
Texas Southern U (TX) ***526***
Thomas Edison State Coll (NJ) ***527***
Touro U International (CA) ***529***
Towson U (MD) ***529***
The U of Arizona (AZ) ***538***
U of Central Florida (FL) ***542***
U of Cincinnati (OH) ***543***
U of Connecticut (CT) ***544***
U of Evansville (IN) ***545***
U of Great Falls (MT) ***545***
U of Hawaii–West Oahu (HI) ***546***
U of Houston–Clear Lake (TX) ***547***
U of Illinois at Springfield (IL) ***548***
U of Kentucky (KY) ***549***
U of La Verne (CA) ***549***
U of Maryland, Baltimore County (MD) ***552***
U of Michigan–Dearborn (MI) ***554***
U of Michigan–Flint (MI) ***554***
U of Nevada, Las Vegas (NV) ***558***
U of New England (ME) ***558***
U of New Hampshire (NH) ***558***
The U of North Carolina at Chapel Hill (NC) ***560***
U of Rhode Island (RI) ***572***
U of Saskatchewan (SK, Canada) ***574***
The U of Scranton (PA) ***574***
The U of South Dakota (SD) ***575***
U of Southern Indiana (IN) ***576***
The U of Texas at El Paso (TX) ***578***
U of Victoria (BC, Canada) ***582***
U of Wisconsin–Eau Claire (WI) ***584***
U of Wisconsin–Milwaukee (WI) ***585***
U System Coll for Lifelong Learning (NH) ***586***
Ursuline Coll (OH) ***587***
Viterbo U (WI) ***591***
Waynesburg Coll (PA) ***595***
Weber State U (UT) ***596***
Webster U (MO) ***597***
Western International U (AZ) ***599***
Western Kentucky U (KY) ***599***
West Virginia U Inst of Technology (WV) ***602***
Wheeling Jesuit U (WV) ***603***
Wichita State U (KS) ***604***
Wilberforce U (OH) ***605***
Winona State U (MN) ***608***
Worcester State Coll (MA) ***609***
York Coll of Pennsylvania (PA) ***610***

HEALTH UNIT MANAGEMENT

Overview: Students taking this major learn how to manage and operate one or more health-care units within a hospital or health-care facility. Ward supervisors generally work under the supervision of nursing and medical service administrators. *Related majors:* business administration, human resources management, health science, applications to specific health-care services. *Potential careers:* ward supervisor, health-care administrator or manager. *Salary potential:* $34k-$45k.

Ursuline Coll (OH) ***587***

HEARING SCIENCES

Overview: This major examines how humans hear, hearing loss, diagnosing hearing disorders and impairments, and suggesting various treatments, therapies, and devices for hearing loss. *Related majors:* audio engineering, computer science, human anatomy, acoustics, education of deaf/hearing impaired. *Potential careers:* audiologist or speech teacher, speech therapist, psychologist, researcher, hearing loss technician. *Salary potential:* $27k-$37k

Arizona State U (AZ) ***271***
Brigham Young U (UT) ***295***
Indiana U Bloomington (IN) ***385***
Northwestern U (IL) ***453***
Stephen F. Austin State U (TX) ***518***
Texas Tech U (TX) ***526***
U of Northern Colorado (CO) ***561***
The U of Tennessee (TN) ***577***

HEATING/AIR CONDITIONING/ REFRIGERATION

Overview: This major will teach students the knowledge and technical skills they need to service, install, repair, and maintain heaters, air conditioners, refrigerators and refrigeration systems, and ventilation systems for commercial, residential, or industrial uses. *Related majors:* major appliance installation and repair, electrical/electronics installation and repair, environmental/pollution control technology. *Potential careers:* electrical company technician, major appliance installer or repairperson, refrigeration technician, ventilation specialist. *Salary potential:* $20k-$25k.

Ferris State U (MI) ***358***

HEATING/AIR CONDITIONING/ REFRIGERATION TECHNOLOGY

Overview: This major arms students with the technical skills and knowledge they need to design and maintain heating, air conditioning, and refrigerator systems. *Related majors:* energy management technology, quality control technology, occupational/health technology. *Potential careers:* electrician, heating and cooling technician or installation specialist for hospital, developer, supermarket or school service technician, salesperson. *Salary potential:* $25k-$34k.

Pennsylvania Coll of Technology (PA) ***467***

HEAVY EQUIPMENT MAINTENANCE

Overview: This major gives students the technical skills and understanding they need to maintain, repair, inspect, and overhaul heavy equipment. *Related majors:* industrial machinery maintenance and repair, instrument calibration and repair, auto and diesel engine mechanic, electrical and electronics equipment installation and repair, welding technologist. *Potential career:* automobile and large vehicle repairperson, electrician, brake specialist. *Salary potential:* $15k-$25k.

Ferris State U (MI) ***358***
Pittsburg State U (KS) ***470***

HEBREW

Overview: Students who choose this major learn about the Hebrew language, culture, and thought, while developing effective communication skills in Modern Hebrew. *Related majors:* Bible and biblical studies, biblical languages, Arabic, rabbinical-Talmudic studies, Jewish/ Judaic studies. *Potential careers:* archeologist, trade specialist, translator, diplomatic corps, teacher or professor. *Salary potential:* $25k-$30k.

Baltimore Hebrew U (MD) ***280***
Bard Coll (NY) ***281***
Concordia U (QC, Canada) ***331***
Concordia U Wisconsin (WI) ***331***
Cornell U (NY) ***333***
Dartmouth Coll (NH) ***337***
Harvard U (MA) ***376***

Hofstra U (NY) **380**
Hunter Coll of the City U of NY (NY) **382**
Laura and Alvin Siegal Coll of Judaic Studies (OH) **403**
Lehman Coll of the City U of NY (NY) **404**
Long Island U, Southampton Coll, Friends World Program (NY) **409**
Luther Coll (IA) **412**
Machzikei Hadath Rabbinical Coll (NY) **413**
New York U (NY) **447**
The Ohio State U (OH) **457**
Queens Coll of the City U of NY (NY) **475**
State U of NY at Binghamton (NY) **515**
Temple U (PA) **523**
Touro Coll (NY) **529**
U of Alberta (AB, Canada) **538**
U of Calif, Los Angeles (CA) **541**
U of Michigan (MI) **554**
U of Minnesota, Twin Cities Campus (MN) **555**
U of Oregon (OR) **562**
The U of Texas at Austin (TX) **578**
U of Toronto (ON, Canada) **581**
U of Wisconsin–Madison (WI) **584**
U of Wisconsin–Milwaukee (WI) **585**
Washington U in St. Louis (MO) **595**
York U (ON, Canada) **611**

HIGHER EDUCATION ADMINISTRATION

Overview: This major teaches students about the principles and practices of administration at colleges and universities. *Related majors:* operations management, college counseling. *Potential careers:* college professor, college counselor, college administrator. *Salary potential:* $28k-$34k.

Bowling Green State U (OH) **292**

HISPANIC-AMERICAN STUDIES

Overview: Students who choose this major study the history, sociology, politics, culture, and economics of one or more of the Hispanic American immigrant populations within the U.S. and Canada. *Related majors:* anthropology, American and Latin American history, comparative literature, international business, politics. *Potential careers:* anthropologist, editor, politician, teacher. *Salary potential:* $25-$30k.

Arizona State U (AZ) **271**
Barton Coll (NC) **282**
Boston Coll (MA) **292**
Brown U (RI) **296**
California State U, Fullerton (CA) **301**
California State U, Northridge (CA) **301**
Columbia Coll (NY) **326**
Columbia U, School of General Studies (NY) **328**
Cornell U (NY) **333**
Dartmouth Coll (NH) **337**
The Evergreen State Coll (WA) **355**
Fordham U (NY) **362**
Goshen Coll (IN) **370**
Hampshire Coll (MA) **375**
Harvard U (MA) **376**
Hofstra U (NY) **380**
Hunter Coll of the City U of NY (NY) **382**
Inter American U of PR, San Germán Campus (PR) **388**
Lewis & Clark Coll (OR) **405**
Long Island U, Southampton Coll, Friends World Program (NY) **409**
McMaster U (ON, Canada) **423**
Mills Coll (CA) **431**
Mount Saint Mary Coll (NY) **439**
Pomona Coll (CA) **472**
Pontifical Catholic U of Puerto Rico (PR) **472**
Queen's U at Kingston (ON, Canada) **476**
Rutgers, The State U of New Jersey, Newark (NJ) **485**
Rutgers, The State U of New Jersey, New Brunswick (NJ) **485**
St. Francis Coll (NY) **488**
St. Olaf Coll (MN) **495**
San Diego State U (CA) **498**
Scripps Coll (CA) **501**
Sonoma State U (CA) **506**
State U of NY at Albany (NY) **514**
State U of NY Coll at Oneonta (NY) **517**
Trent U (ON, Canada) **529**
Tulane U (LA) **533**
The U of Arizona (AZ) **538**
U of Calif, Berkeley (CA) **540**
U of Calif, Santa Cruz (CA) **542**
U of Michigan (MI) **554**
U of Michigan–Dearborn (MI) **554**
U of Northern Colorado (CO) **561**
U of Ottawa (ON, Canada) **563**
U of San Diego (CA) **574**
U of Southern California (CA) **576**
U of Southern Maine (ME) **576**
The U of Texas at San Antonio (TX) **578**
U of Toronto (ON, Canada) **581**
U of Windsor (ON, Canada) **584**
U of Wisconsin–Madison (WI) **584**
Vassar Coll (NY) **589**
Wayne State U (MI) **596**
Western New Mexico U (NM) **600**
Wheaton Coll (MA) **603**
Willamette U (OR) **605**
York U (ON, Canada) **611**

HISTORY

Overview: This major focuses on studying, collecting information about, and interpreting events and people of the past. *Related majors:* area studies and cultural studies, literature, humanities, historic preservation and architectural history, museum studies. *Potential careers:* writer, journalist, editor, professor, attorney. *Salary potential:* $25k-$35k.

Abilene Christian U (TX) **260**
Acadia U (NS, Canada) **260**
Adams State Coll (CO) **260**
Adelphi U (NY) **260**
Adrian Coll (MI) **260**
Agnes Scott Coll (GA) **261**
Alabama State U (AL) **261**
Albany State U (GA) **262**
Albertson Coll of Idaho (ID) **262**
Albertus Magnus Coll (CT) **262**
Albion Coll (MI) **262**
Albright Coll (PA) **263**
Alcorn State U (MS) **263**
Alderson-Broaddus Coll (WV) **263**
Alfred U (NY) **263**
Alice Lloyd Coll (KY) **263**
Allegheny Coll (PA) **264**
Alma Coll (MI) **264**
Alvernia Coll (PA) **265**
Alverno Coll (WI) **265**
American Coll of Thessaloniki(Greece) **266**
American International Coll (MA) **267**
American Public U System (WV) **267**
American U (DC) **267**
The American U in Cairo(Egypt) **267**
The American U of Paris(France) **268**
Amherst Coll (MA) **268**
Anderson Coll (SC) **268**
Anderson U (IN) **268**
Andrews U (MI) **269**
Angelo State U (TX) **269**
Anna Maria Coll (MA) **269**
Antioch Coll (OH) **269**
Appalachian State U (NC) **270**
Aquinas Coll (MI) **270**
Arcadia U (PA) **271**
Arizona State U (AZ) **271**
Arizona State U West (AZ) **272**
Arkansas State U (AR) **272**
Arkansas Tech U (AR) **272**
Armstrong Atlantic State U (GA) **273**
Asbury Coll (KY) **274**
Ashland U (OH) **274**
Assumption Coll (MA) **275**
Athabasca U (AB, Canada) **275**
Athens State U (AL) **275**
Atlantic Baptist U (NB, Canada) **275**
Atlantic Union Coll (MA) **276**
Auburn U (AL) **276**
Auburn U Montgomery (AL) **276**
Augsburg Coll (MN) **276**
Augustana Coll (IL) **276**
Augustana Coll (SD) **276**
Augusta State U (GA) **277**
Aurora U (IL) **277**
Austin Coll (TX) **277**
Austin Peay State U (TN) **278**
Ave Maria Coll (MI) **278**
Averett U (VA) **278**
Avila U (MO) **278**
Azusa Pacific U (CA) **278**
Baker U (KS) **280**
Baldwin-Wallace Coll (OH) **280**
Ball State U (IN) **280**
Bard Coll (NY) **281**
Barnard Coll (NY) **282**
Barry U (FL) **282**
Barton Coll (NC) **282**
Bates Coll (ME) **282**
Baylor U (TX) **283**
Bay Path Coll (MA) **283**
Belhaven Coll (MS) **283**
Bellarmine U (KY) **284**
Bellevue U (NE) **284**
Belmont Abbey Coll (NC) **284**
Belmont U (TN) **284**
Beloit Coll (WI) **285**
Bemidji State U (MN) **285**
Benedict Coll (SC) **285**
Benedictine Coll (KS) **285**
Benedictine U (IL) **285**
Bennington Coll (VT) **286**
Bentley Coll (MA) **286**
Berea Coll (KY) **286**
Baruch Coll of the City U of NY (NY) **286**
Berry Coll (GA) **287**
Bethany Coll (KS) **287**
Bethany Coll (WV) **287**
Bethel Coll (IN) **288**
Bethel Coll (KS) **288**
Bethel Coll (MN) **288**
Bethel Coll (TN) **288**
Bethune-Cookman Coll (FL) **289**
Biola U (CA) **289**
Birmingham-Southern Coll (AL) **289**
Bishop's U (QC, Canada) **289**
Blackburn Coll (IL) **290**
Black Hills State U (SD) **290**
Bloomfield Coll (NJ) **290**
Bloomsburg U of Pennsylvania (PA) **290**
Bluefield Coll (VA) **291**
Blue Mountain Coll (MS) **291**
Bluffton Coll (OH) **291**
Boston Coll (MA) **292**
Boston U (MA) **292**
Bowdoin Coll (ME) **292**
Bowie State U (MD) **292**
Bowling Green State U (OH) **292**
Bradley U (IL) **293**
Brandeis U (MA) **293**
Brandon U (MB, Canada) **293**
Brenau U (GA) **293**
Brescia U (KY) **293**
Brevard Coll (NC) **294**
Brewton-Parker Coll (GA) **294**
Briar Cliff U (IA) **294**
Bridgewater Coll (VA) **294**
Bridgewater State Coll (MA) **294**
Brigham Young U (UT) **295**
Brigham Young U–Hawaii (HI) **295**
Brock U (ON, Canada) **295**
Brooklyn Coll of the City U of NY (NY) **295**
Brown U (RI) **296**
Bryan Coll (TN) **296**
Bryant Coll (RI) **296**
Bryn Athyn Coll of the New Church (PA) **297**
Bryn Mawr Coll (PA) **297**
Bucknell U (PA) **297**
Buena Vista U (IA) **297**
Butler U (IN) **297**
Cabrini Coll (PA) **298**
Caldwell Coll (NJ) **298**
California Baptist U (CA) **298**
California Inst of Technology (CA) **299**
California Lutheran U (CA) **299**
California Polytechnic State U, San Luis Obispo (CA) **300**
California State Polytechnic U, Pomona (CA) **300**
California State U, Bakersfield (CA) **300**
California State U, Chico (CA) **300**
California State U, Dominguez Hills (CA) **300**
California State U, Fresno (CA) **301**
California State U, Fullerton (CA) **301**
California State U, Hayward (CA) **301**
California State U, Long Beach (CA) **301**
California State U, Northridge (CA) **301**
California State U, Sacramento (CA) **301**
California State U, San Bernardino (CA) **302**
California State U, San Marcos (CA) **302**
California State U, Stanislaus (CA) **302**
California U of Pennsylvania (PA) **302**
Calvin Coll (MI) **303**
Cameron U (OK) **303**
Campbellsville U (KY) **303**
Campbell U (NC) **303**
Canisius Coll (NY) **304**
Capital U (OH) **304**
Cardinal Stritch U (WI) **305**
Carleton Coll (MN) **305**
Carleton U (ON, Canada) **305**
Carlow Coll (PA) **305**
Carnegie Mellon U (PA) **305**
Carroll Coll (MT) **306**
Carroll Coll (WI) **306**
Carson-Newman Coll (TN) **306**
Carthage Coll (WI) **306**
Case Western Reserve U (OH) **307**
Castleton State Coll (VT) **307**
Catawba Coll (NC) **307**
The Catholic U of America (DC) **307**
Cedar Crest Coll (PA) **308**
Cedarville U (OH) **308**
Centenary Coll (NJ) **308**
Centenary Coll of Louisiana (LA) **308**
Central Coll (IA) **309**
Central Connecticut State U (CT) **309**
Central Methodist Coll (MO) **309**
Central Michigan U (MI) **310**
Central Missouri State U (MO) **310**
Central Washington U (WA) **310**
Centre Coll (KY) **310**
Chadron State Coll (NE) **311**
Chaminade U of Honolulu (HI) **311**
Chapman U (CA) **311**
Charleston Southern U (SC) **311**
Chatham Coll (PA) **312**
Chestnut Hill Coll (PA) **312**
Chowan Coll (NC) **312**
Christendom Coll (VA) **313**
Christian Brothers U (TN) **313**
Christian Heritage Coll (CA) **313**
Christopher Newport U (VA) **313**
Citadel, The Military Coll of South Carolina (SC) **314**
City Coll of the City U of NY (NY) **314**
Claflin U (SC) **314**
Claremont McKenna Coll (CA) **315**
Clarion U of Pennsylvania (PA) **315**
Clark Atlanta U (GA) **315**
Clarke Coll (IA) **315**
Clarkson U (NY) **316**
Clark U (MA) **316**
Clearwater Christian Coll (FL) **316**
Clemson U (SC) **317**
Cleveland State U (OH) **317**
Coastal Carolina U (SC) **318**
Coe Coll (IA) **318**
Coker Coll (SC) **318**
Colby Coll (ME) **318**
Colgate U (NY) **319**
Coll Misericordia (PA) **319**
Coll of Charleston (SC) **320**
Coll of Mount St. Joseph (OH) **320**
Coll of Mount Saint Vincent (NY) **320**
The Coll of New Jersey (NJ) **320**
The Coll of New Rochelle (NY) **321**
Coll of Notre Dame of Maryland (MD) **321**
Coll of Saint Benedict (MN) **321**
Coll of St. Catherine (MN) **321**
Coll of Saint Elizabeth (NJ) **321**
Coll of St. Joseph (VT) **322**
The Coll of Saint Rose (NY) **322**
The Coll of St. Scholastica (MN) **322**
The Coll of Southeastern Europe, The American U of Athens(Greece) **323**
Coll of Staten Island of the City U of NY (NY) **323**
Coll of the Holy Cross (MA) **323**
Coll of the Ozarks (MO) **323**
Coll of the Southwest (NM) **324**
The Coll of William and Mary (VA) **324**
The Coll of Wooster (OH) **324**
Colorado Christian U (CO) **325**

HISTORY (continued)

The Colorado Coll (CO) ***325***
Colorado State U (CO) ***325***
Colorado State U-Pueblo (CO) ***325***
Columbia Coll (MO) ***326***
Columbia Coll (NY) ***326***
Columbia Coll (SC) ***327***
Columbia Union Coll (MD) ***328***
Columbia U, School of General Studies (NY) ***328***
Columbus State U (GA) ***328***
Concord Coll (WV) ***329***
Concordia Coll (MN) ***329***
Concordia Coll (NY) ***329***
Concordia U (CA) ***330***
Concordia U (IL) ***330***
Concordia U (MN) ***330***
Concordia U (NE) ***330***
Concordia U (QC, Canada) ***331***
Concordia U at Austin (TX) ***331***
Concordia U Coll of Alberta (AB, Canada) ***331***
Concordia U Wisconsin (WI) ***331***
Connecticut Coll (CT) ***331***
Converse Coll (SC) ***332***
Cornell Coll (IA) ***332***
Cornell U (NY) ***333***
Cornerstone U (MI) ***333***
Covenant Coll (GA) ***333***
Creighton U (NE) ***333***
Crichton Coll (TN) ***334***
Crown Coll (MN) ***334***
Culver-Stockton Coll (MO) ***334***
Cumberland Coll (KY) ***335***
Cumberland U (TN) ***335***
Curry Coll (MA) ***335***
Daemen Coll (NY) ***335***
Dakota Wesleyan U (SD) ***336***
Dalhousie U (NS, Canada) ***336***
Dallas Baptist U (TX) ***336***
Dana Coll (NE) ***337***
Dartmouth Coll (NH) ***337***
Davidson Coll (NC) ***338***
Davis & Elkins Coll (WV) ***338***
Defiance Coll (OH) ***338***
Delaware State U (DE) ***338***
Delta State U (MS) ***339***
Denison U (OH) ***339***
DePaul U (IL) ***339***
DePauw U (IN) ***339***
Deree Coll(Greece) ***339***
DeSales U (PA) ***340***
Dickinson Coll (PA) ***344***
Dickinson State U (ND) ***344***
Dillard U (LA) ***344***
Doane Coll (NE) ***344***
Dominican Coll (NY) ***344***
Dominican U (IL) ***345***
Dominican U of California (CA) ***345***
Dordt Coll (IA) ***345***
Dowling Coll (NY) ***345***
Drake U (IA) ***345***
Drew U (NJ) ***346***
Drexel U (PA) ***346***
Drury U (MO) ***346***
Duke U (NC) ***346***
Duquesne U (PA) ***346***
D'Youville Coll (NY) ***347***
Earlham Coll (IN) ***347***
East Carolina U (NC) ***347***
East Central U (OK) ***347***
Eastern Connecticut State U (CT) ***347***
Eastern Illinois U (IL) ***348***
Eastern Kentucky U (KY) ***348***
Eastern Mennonite U (VA) ***348***
Eastern Michigan U (MI) ***348***
Eastern Nazarene Coll (MA) ***348***
Eastern New Mexico U (NM) ***349***
Eastern Oregon U (OR) ***349***
Eastern U (PA) ***349***
Eastern Washington U (WA) ***349***
East Stroudsburg U of Pennsylvania (PA) ***349***
East Tennessee State U (TN) ***349***
East Texas Baptist U (TX) ***350***
Eckerd Coll (FL) ***350***
Edgewood Coll (WI) ***351***
Edinboro U of Pennsylvania (PA) ***351***
Elizabeth City State U (NC) ***351***
Elizabethtown Coll (PA) ***351***
Elmhurst Coll (IL) ***351***
Elmira Coll (NY) ***351***
Elms Coll (MA) ***352***
Elon U (NC) ***352***
Emmanuel Coll (GA) ***353***
Emmanuel Coll (MA) ***353***
Emory & Henry Coll (VA) ***353***
Emory U (GA) ***354***
Emporia State U (KS) ***354***
Erskine Coll (SC) ***354***
Eugene Lang Coll, New School U (NY) ***355***
Eureka Coll (IL) ***355***
Evangel U (MO) ***355***
The Evergreen State Coll (WA) ***355***
Excelsior Coll (NY) ***356***
Fairfield U (CT) ***356***
Fairleigh Dickinson U, Florham (NJ) ***356***
Fairleigh Dickinson U, Teaneck-Metro Campus (NJ) ***356***
Fairmont State Coll (WV) ***356***
Faulkner U (AL) ***357***
Fayetteville State U (NC) ***357***
Felician Coll (NJ) ***357***
Ferrum Coll (VA) ***358***
Fisk U (TN) ***358***
Fitchburg State Coll (MA) ***358***
Flagler Coll (FL) ***359***
Florida A&M U (FL) ***359***
Florida Atlantic U (FL) ***359***
Florida International U (FL) ***360***
Florida Southern Coll (FL) ***361***
Florida State U (FL) ***361***
Fontbonne U (MO) ***361***
Fordham U (NY) ***362***
Fort Hays State U (KS) ***362***
Fort Lewis Coll (CO) ***362***
Framingham State Coll (MA) ***362***
Franciscan U of Steubenville (OH) ***363***
Francis Marion U (SC) ***363***
Franklin and Marshall Coll (PA) ***363***
Franklin Coll (IN) ***363***
Franklin Coll Switzerland(Switzerland) ***364***
Franklin Pierce Coll (NH) ***364***
Freed-Hardeman U (TN) ***364***
Fresno Pacific U (CA) ***364***
Frostburg State U (MD) ***365***
Furman U (SC) ***365***
Gallaudet U (DC) ***365***
Gannon U (PA) ***365***
Gardner-Webb U (NC) ***365***
Geneva Coll (PA) ***366***
George Fox U (OR) ***366***
George Mason U (VA) ***366***
Georgetown Coll (KY) ***366***
Georgetown U (DC) ***366***
The George Washington U (DC) ***367***
Georgia Coll & State U (GA) ***367***
Georgian Court Coll (NJ) ***367***
Georgia Southern U (GA) ***367***
Georgia Southwestern State U (GA) ***368***
Georgia State U (GA) ***368***
Gettysburg Coll (PA) ***368***
Glenville State Coll (WV) ***368***
Goddard Coll (VT) ***369***
Gonzaga U (WA) ***369***
Gordon Coll (MA) ***370***
Goshen Coll (IN) ***370***
Goucher Coll (MD) ***370***
Graceland U (IA) ***371***
Grambling State U (LA) ***371***
Grand Canyon U (AZ) ***371***
Grand Valley State U (MI) ***371***
Grand View Coll (IA) ***372***
Green Mountain Coll (VT) ***372***
Greensboro Coll (NC) ***372***
Greenville Coll (IL) ***373***
Grinnell Coll (IA) ***373***
Grove City Coll (PA) ***373***
Guilford Coll (NC) ***373***
Gustavus Adolphus Coll (MN) ***374***
Gwynedd-Mercy Coll (PA) ***374***
Hamilton Coll (NY) ***374***
Hamline U (MN) ***374***
Hampden-Sydney Coll (VA) ***374***
Hampshire Coll (MA) ***375***
Hampton U (VA) ***375***
Hannibal-LaGrange Coll (MO) ***375***
Hanover Coll (IN) ***375***
Harding U (AR) ***375***
Hardin-Simmons U (TX) ***376***
Hartwick Coll (NY) ***376***
Harvard U (MA) ***376***
Hastings Coll (NE) ***377***
Haverford Coll (PA) ***377***
Hawai'i Pacific U (HI) ***377***
Heidelberg Coll (OH) ***377***
Henderson State U (AR) ***378***
Hendrix Coll (AR) ***378***
High Point U (NC) ***379***
Hillsdale Coll (MI) ***379***
Hiram Coll (OH) ***379***
Hobart and William Smith Colls (NY) ***380***
Hofstra U (NY) ***380***
Hollins U (VA) ***380***
Holy Family U (PA) ***380***
Holy Names Coll (CA) ***381***
Hood Coll (MD) ***381***
Hope Coll (MI) ***381***
Houghton Coll (NY) ***381***
Houston Baptist U (TX) ***382***
Howard Payne U (TX) ***382***
Howard U (DC) ***382***
Humboldt State U (CA) ***382***
Hunter Coll of the City U of NY (NY) ***382***
Huntingdon Coll (AL) ***383***
Huntington Coll (IN) ***383***
Idaho State U (ID) ***384***
Illinois Coll (IL) ***384***
Illinois State U (IL) ***384***
Illinois Wesleyan U (IL) ***385***
Immaculata U (PA) ***385***
Indiana State U (IN) ***385***
Indiana U Bloomington (IN) ***385***
Indiana U Northwest (IN) ***386***
Indiana U of Pennsylvania (PA) ***386***
Indiana U–Purdue U Fort Wayne (IN) ***386***
Indiana U–Purdue U Indianapolis (IN) ***387***
Indiana U South Bend (IN) ***387***
Indiana U Southeast (IN) ***387***
Indiana Wesleyan U (IN) ***387***
Iona Coll (NY) ***390***
Iowa State U of Science and Technology (IA) ***390***
Iowa Wesleyan Coll (IA) ***390***
Ithaca Coll (NY) ***390***
Jackson State U (MS) ***390***
Jacksonville State U (AL) ***390***
Jacksonville U (FL) ***391***
James Madison U (VA) ***391***
Jamestown Coll (ND) ***391***
Jewish Theological Seminary of America (NY) ***391***
John Brown U (AR) ***392***
John Carroll U (OH) ***392***
Johns Hopkins U (MD) ***392***
Johnson C. Smith U (NC) ***394***
Johnson State Coll (VT) ***394***
Judson Coll (AL) ***395***
Judson Coll (IL) ***395***
Juniata Coll (PA) ***395***
Kalamazoo Coll (MI) ***395***
Kansas State U (KS) ***396***
Kean U (NJ) ***396***
Keene State Coll (NH) ***396***
Kennesaw State U (GA) ***397***
Kent State U (OH) ***397***
Kentucky Christian Coll (KY) ***397***
Kentucky State U (KY) ***397***
Kentucky Wesleyan Coll (KY) ***397***
Kenyon Coll (OH) ***398***
Keuka Coll (NY) ***398***
King Coll (TN) ***398***
King's Coll (PA) ***398***
The King's U Coll (AB, Canada) ***399***
Knox Coll (IL) ***399***
Kutztown U of Pennsylvania (PA) ***399***
Lafayette Coll (PA) ***400***
LaGrange Coll (GA) ***400***
Lake Forest Coll (IL) ***400***
Lakehead U (ON, Canada) ***400***
Lakeland Coll (WI) ***401***
Lamar U (TX) ***401***
Lambuth U (TN) ***401***
Lander U (SC) ***401***
Lane Coll (TN) ***402***
Langston U (OK) ***402***
La Roche Coll (PA) ***402***
La Salle U (PA) ***402***
La Sierra U (CA) ***403***
Laura and Alvin Siegal Coll of Judaic Studies (OH) ***403***
Laurentian U (ON, Canada) ***403***
Lawrence U (WI) ***403***
Lebanon Valley Coll (PA) ***403***
Lees-McRae Coll (NC) ***404***
Lee U (TN) ***404***
Lehigh U (PA) ***404***
Lehman Coll of the City U of NY (NY) ***404***
Le Moyne Coll (NY) ***404***
Lenoir-Rhyne Coll (NC) ***405***
LeTourneau U (TX) ***405***
Lewis & Clark Coll (OR) ***405***
Lewis-Clark State Coll (ID) ***406***
Lewis U (IL) ***406***
Liberty U (VA) ***406***
Limestone Coll (SC) ***406***
Lincoln Memorial U (TN) ***407***
Lincoln U (PA) ***407***
Lindenwood U (MO) ***407***
Lindsey Wilson Coll (KY) ***407***
Linfield Coll (OR) ***408***
Lipscomb U (TN) ***408***
Lock Haven U of Pennsylvania (PA) ***408***
Long Island U, Brooklyn Campus (NY) ***409***
Long Island U, C.W. Post Campus (NY) ***409***
Long Island U, Southampton Coll (NY) ***409***
Long Island U, Southampton Coll, Friends World Program (NY) ***409***
Longwood U (VA) ***409***
Loras Coll (IA) ***410***
Louisiana Coll (LA) ***410***
Louisiana State U and A&M Coll (LA) ***410***
Louisiana State U in Shreveport (LA) ***410***
Louisiana Tech U (LA) ***410***
Lourdes Coll (OH) ***411***
Loyola Coll in Maryland (MD) ***411***
Loyola Marymount U (CA) ***411***
Loyola U Chicago (IL) ***411***
Loyola U New Orleans (LA) ***411***
Lubbock Christian U (TX) ***412***
Luther Coll (IA) ***412***
Lycoming Coll (PA) ***412***
Lynchburg Coll (VA) ***413***
Lynn U (FL) ***413***
Lyon Coll (AR) ***413***
Macalester Coll (MN) ***413***
MacMurray Coll (IL) ***414***
Madonna U (MI) ***414***
Malaspina U-Coll (BC, Canada) ***415***
Malone Coll (OH) ***415***
Manchester Coll (IN) ***415***
Manhattan Coll (NY) ***416***
Manhattanville Coll (NY) ***416***
Mansfield U of Pennsylvania (PA) ***416***
Marian Coll (IN) ***417***
Marian Coll of Fond du Lac (WI) ***417***
Marietta Coll (OH) ***417***
Marist Coll (NY) ***417***
Marlboro Coll (VT) ***418***
Marquette U (WI) ***418***
Marshall U (WV) ***418***
Mars Hill Coll (NC) ***418***
Martin U (IN) ***419***
Mary Baldwin Coll (VA) ***419***
Marygrove Coll (MI) ***419***
Marymount Coll of Fordham U (NY) ***419***
Marymount Manhattan Coll (NY) ***420***
Marymount U (VA) ***420***
Maryville Coll (TN) ***420***
Maryville U of Saint Louis (MO) ***420***
Mary Washington Coll (VA) ***420***
Massachusetts Coll of Liberal Arts (MA) ***421***
Massachusetts Inst of Technology (MA) ***421***
The Master's Coll and Seminary (CA) ***422***
McDaniel Coll (MD) ***422***
McGill U (QC, Canada) ***423***
McKendree Coll (IL) ***423***
McMaster U (ON, Canada) ***423***
McMurry U (TX) ***423***
McNeese State U (LA) ***423***
McPherson Coll (KS) ***423***
Memorial U of Newfoundland (NF, Canada) ***424***
Mercer U (GA) ***425***
Mercy Coll (NY) ***425***
Mercyhurst Coll (PA) ***425***
Meredith Coll (NC) ***426***
Merrimack Coll (MA) ***426***
Mesa State Coll (CO) ***426***
Messiah Coll (PA) ***426***
Methodist Coll (NC) ***427***
Metropolitan State Coll of Denver (CO) ***427***
Metropolitan State U (MN) ***427***
Miami U (OH) ***428***
Michigan State U (MI) ***428***
Michigan Technological U (MI) ***428***
MidAmerica Nazarene U (KS) ***428***
Middlebury Coll (VT) ***429***
Middle Tennessee State U (TN) ***429***
Midland Lutheran Coll (NE) ***429***
Midwestern State U (TX) ***430***
Millersville U of Pennsylvania (PA) ***430***
Milligan Coll (TN) ***430***
Millikin U (IL) ***430***

Millsaps Coll (MS) **431**
Mills Coll (CA) **431**
Minnesota State U, Mankato (MN) **431**
Minnesota State U, Moorhead (MN) **432**
Minot State U (ND) **432**
Mississippi Coll (MS) **432**
Mississippi State U (MS) **432**
Mississippi Valley State U (MS) **432**
Missouri Southern State Coll (MO) **433**
Missouri Valley Coll (MO) **433**
Missouri Western State Coll (MO) **433**
Molloy Coll (NY) **433**
Monmouth Coll (IL) **434**
Monmouth U (NJ) **434**
Montana State U–Billings (MT) **434**
Montana State U–Bozeman (MT) **434**
Montclair State U (NJ) **435**
Montreat Coll (NC) **435**
Moravian Coll (PA) **436**
Morehead State U (KY) **436**
Morehouse Coll (GA) **436**
Morgan State U (MD) **436**
Morningside Coll (IA) **437**
Morris Coll (SC) **437**
Mount Allison U (NB, Canada) **437**
Mount Holyoke Coll (MA) **438**
Mount Marty Coll (SD) **438**
Mount Mary Coll (WI) **438**
Mount Mercy Coll (IA) **438**
Mount Olive Coll (NC) **439**
Mount Saint Mary Coll (NY) **439**
Mount St. Mary's Coll (CA) **439**
Mount Saint Mary's Coll and Seminary (MD) **439**
Mount Saint Vincent U (NS, Canada) **439**
Mount Union Coll (OH) **440**
Mount Vernon Nazarene U (OH) **440**
Muhlenberg Coll (PA) **440**
Multnomah Bible Coll and Biblical Seminary (OR) **440**
Murray State U (KY) **440**
Muskingum Coll (OH) **441**
Nazareth Coll of Rochester (NY) **443**
Nebraska Wesleyan U (NE) **443**
Newberry Coll (SC) **444**
New Coll of Florida (FL) **444**
New England Coll (NH) **444**
New Jersey City U (NJ) **445**
New Jersey Inst of Technology (NJ) **445**
Newman U (KS) **445**
New Mexico Highlands U (NM) **446**
New Mexico State U (NM) **446**
New York U (NY) **447**
Niagara U (NY) **447**
Nicholls State U (LA) **447**
Nichols Coll (MA) **448**
Nipissing U (ON, Canada) **448**
Norfolk State U (VA) **448**
North Carolina Ag and Tech State U (NC) **448**
North Carolina Central U (NC) **448**
North Carolina State U (NC) **449**
North Carolina Wesleyan Coll (NC) **449**
North Central Coll (IL) **449**
North Dakota State U (ND) **449**
Northeastern Illinois U (IL) **450**
Northeastern State U (OK) **450**
Northeastern U (MA) **450**
Northern Arizona U (AZ) **450**
Northern Illinois U (IL) **450**
Northern Kentucky U (KY) **451**
Northern Michigan U (MI) **451**
Northern State U (SD) **451**
North Georgia Coll & State U (GA) **451**
Northland Coll (WI) **452**
North Park U (IL) **452**
Northwest Coll (WA) **452**
Northwestern Coll (IA) **453**
Northwestern Coll (MN) **453**
Northwestern Oklahoma State U (OK) **453**
Northwestern State U of Louisiana (LA) **453**
Northwestern U (IL) **453**
Northwest Missouri State U (MO) **454**
Northwest Nazarene U (ID) **454**
Norwich U (VT) **455**
Notre Dame Coll (OH) **455**
Notre Dame de Namur U (CA) **455**
Nyack Coll (NY) **456**
Oakland U (MI) **456**
Oakwood Coll (AL) **456**
Oberlin Coll (OH) **456**
Occidental Coll (CA) **457**
Oglethorpe U (GA) **457**
Ohio Dominican U (OH) **457**
Ohio Northern U (OH) **457**
The Ohio State U (OH) **457**
Ohio U (OH) **458**
Ohio Wesleyan U (OH) **459**
Okanagan U Coll (BC, Canada) **459**
Oklahoma Baptist U (OK) **459**
Oklahoma Christian U (OK) **459**
Oklahoma City U (OK) **460**
Oklahoma Panhandle State U (OK) **460**
Oklahoma State U (OK) **460**
Oklahoma Wesleyan U (OK) **460**
Old Dominion U (VA) **460**
Olivet Coll (MI) **461**
Olivet Nazarene U (IL) **461**
Oral Roberts U (OK) **461**
Oregon State U (OR) **462**
Ottawa U (KS) **462**
Otterbein Coll (OH) **462**
Ouachita Baptist U (AR) **462**
Our Lady of Holy Cross Coll (LA) **463**
Our Lady of the Lake U of San Antonio (TX) **463**
Pace U (NY) **463**
Pacific Lutheran U (WA) **463**
Pacific Union Coll (CA) **464**
Pacific U (OR) **464**
Paine Coll (GA) **465**
Palm Beach Atlantic U (FL) **465**
Park U (MO) **465**
Paul Quinn Coll (TX) **466**
Penn State U Abington Coll (PA) **467**
Penn State U at Erie, The Behrend Coll (PA) **467**
Penn State U Univ Park Campus (PA) **468**
Pepperdine U, Malibu (CA) **469**
Peru State Coll (NE) **469**
Pfeiffer U (NC) **469**
Piedmont Coll (GA) **470**
Pikeville Coll (KY) **470**
Pillsbury Baptist Bible Coll (MN) **470**
Pine Manor Coll (MA) **470**
Pittsburg State U (KS) **470**
Pitzer Coll (CA) **471**
Plattsburgh State U of NY (NY) **471**
Plymouth State Coll (NH) **471**
Point Loma Nazarene U (CA) **471**
Point Park Coll (PA) **471**
Pomona Coll (CA) **472**
Pontifical Catholic U of Puerto Rico (PR) **472**
Portland State U (OR) **472**
Prairie View A&M U (TX) **473**
Presbyterian Coll (SC) **473**
Prescott Coll (AZ) **474**
Princeton U (NJ) **474**
Principia Coll (IL) **474**
Providence Coll (RI) **474**
Providence Coll and Theological Seminary (MB, Canada) **475**
Purchase Coll, State U of NY (NY) **475**
Purdue U (IN) **475**
Purdue U Calumet (IN) **475**
Queens Coll of the City U of NY (NY) **475**
Queen's U at Kingston (ON, Canada) **476**
Queens U of Charlotte (NC) **476**
Quincy U (IL) **476**
Quinnipiac U (CT) **476**
Radford U (VA) **476**
Ramapo Coll of New Jersey (NJ) **477**
Randolph-Macon Coll (VA) **477**
Randolph-Macon Woman's Coll (VA) **477**
Reed Coll (OR) **477**
Regis Coll (MA) **478**
Regis U (CO) **478**
Rhode Island Coll (RI) **479**
Rhodes Coll (TN) **479**
Rice U (TX) **479**
The Richard Stockton Coll of New Jersey (NJ) **479**
Richmond, The American International U in London(United Kingdom) **480**
Rider U (NJ) **480**
Ripon Coll (WI) **480**
Rivier Coll (NH) **480**
Roanoke Coll (VA) **481**
Roberts Wesleyan Coll (NY) **481**
Rochester Coll (MI) **482**
Rockford Coll (IL) **482**
Rockhurst U (MO) **482**
Rocky Mountain Coll (MT) **482**
Roger Williams U (RI) **483**
Rollins Coll (FL) **483**
Roosevelt U (IL) **483**
Rosemont Coll (PA) **484**
Rowan U (NJ) **484**
Russell Sage Coll (NY) **484**
Rutgers, The State U of New Jersey, Camden (NJ) **485**
Rutgers, The State U of New Jersey, Newark (NJ) **485**
Rutgers, The State U of New Jersey, New Brunswick (NJ) **485**
Sacred Heart U (CT) **486**
Saginaw Valley State U (MI) **486**
St. Ambrose U (IA) **486**
St. Andrews Presbyterian Coll (NC) **487**
Saint Anselm Coll (NH) **487**
Saint Augustine's Coll (NC) **487**
St. Bonaventure U (NY) **487**
St. Cloud State U (MN) **488**
St. Edward's U (TX) **488**
St. Francis Coll (NY) **488**
Saint Francis U (PA) **488**
St. Francis Xavier U (NS, Canada) **489**
St. John Fisher Coll (NY) **489**
Saint John's U (MN) **490**
St. John's U (NY) **490**
Saint Joseph Coll (CT) **490**
Saint Joseph's Coll (IN) **490**
St. Joseph's Coll, New York (NY) **491**
St. Joseph's Coll, Suffolk Campus (NY) **491**
Saint Joseph's U (PA) **491**
St. Lawrence U (NY) **491**
Saint Leo U (FL) **492**
Saint Louis U (MO) **492**
Saint Martin's Coll (WA) **493**
Saint Mary Coll (KS) **493**
Saint Mary-of-the-Woods Coll (IN) **493**
Saint Mary's Coll (IN) **493**
Saint Mary's Coll of California (CA) **494**
St. Mary's Coll of Maryland (MD) **494**
Saint Mary's U (NS, Canada) **494**
Saint Mary's U of Minnesota (MN) **494**
St. Mary's U of San Antonio (TX) **494**
Saint Michael's Coll (VT) **494**
St. Norbert Coll (WI) **495**
St. Olaf Coll (MN) **495**
Saint Peter's Coll (NJ) **495**
St. Thomas Aquinas Coll (NY) **495**
St. Thomas U (FL) **496**
St. Thomas U (NB, Canada) **496**
Saint Vincent Coll (PA) **496**
Saint Xavier U (IL) **496**
Salem Coll (NC) **496**
Salem State Coll (MA) **497**
Salisbury U (MD) **497**
Salve Regina U (RI) **497**
Samford U (AL) **497**
Sam Houston State U (TX) **497**
San Diego State U (CA) **498**
San Francisco State U (CA) **498**
San Jose State U (CA) **499**
Santa Clara U (CA) **499**
Sarah Lawrence Coll (NY) **499**
Savannah State U (GA) **499**
Schreiner U (TX) **501**
Scripps Coll (CA) **501**
Seattle Pacific U (WA) **501**
Seattle U (WA) **501**
Seton Hall U (NJ) **502**
Seton Hill U (PA) **502**
Shawnee State U (OH) **502**
Shenandoah U (VA) **503**
Shepherd Coll (WV) **503**
Shippensburg U of Pennsylvania (PA) **503**
Shorter Coll (GA) **504**
Siena Coll (NY) **504**
Siena Heights U (MI) **504**
Silver Lake Coll (WI) **504**
Simmons Coll (MA) **504**
Simon Fraser U (BC, Canada) **505**
Simpson Coll (IA) **505**
Simpson Coll and Graduate School (CA) **505**
Skidmore Coll (NY) **506**
Slippery Rock U of Pennsylvania (PA) **506**
Smith Coll (MA) **506**
Sonoma State U (CA) **506**
South Carolina State U (SC) **506**
South Dakota State U (SD) **507**
Southeastern Louisiana U (LA) **508**
Southeastern Oklahoma State U (OK) **508**
Southeast Missouri State U (MO) **508**
Southern Adventist U (TN) **508**
Southern Arkansas U–Magnolia (AR) **509**
Southern Connecticut State U (CT) **509**
Southern Illinois U Carbondale (IL) **509**
Southern Illinois U Edwardsville (IL) **509**
Southern Methodist U (TX) **510**
Southern Nazarene U (OK) **510**
Southern Oregon U (OR) **510**
Southern U and A&M Coll (LA) **511**
Southern Utah U (UT) **511**
Southern Virginia U (VA) **511**
Southern Wesleyan U (SC) **511**
Southwest Baptist U (MO) **512**
Southwestern Coll (KS) **512**
Southwestern Oklahoma State U (OK) **512**
Southwestern U (TX) **513**
Southwest Missouri State U (MO) **513**
Southwest State U (MN) **513**
Southwest Texas State U (TX) **513**
Spalding U (KY) **513**
Spelman Coll (GA) **514**
Spring Arbor U (MI) **514**
Springfield Coll (MA) **514**
Spring Hill Coll (AL) **514**
Stanford U (CA) **514**
State U of NY at Albany (NY) **514**
State U of NY at Binghamton (NY) **515**
State U of NY at New Paltz (NY) **515**
State U of NY at Oswego (NY) **515**
State U of NY Coll at Brockport (NY) **515**
State U of NY Coll at Buffalo (NY) **516**
State U of NY Coll at Cortland (NY) **516**
State U of NY Coll at Fredonia (NY) **516**
State U of NY Coll at Geneseo (NY) **516**
State U of NY Coll at Oneonta (NY) **517**
State U of NY Coll at Potsdam (NY) **517**
State U of NY Empire State Coll (NY) **517**
State U of West Georgia (GA) **518**
Stephen F. Austin State U (TX) **518**
Stephens Coll (MO) **519**
Sterling Coll (KS) **519**
Stetson U (FL) **519**
Stevens Inst of Technology (NJ) **519**
Stonehill Coll (MA) **520**
Stony Brook U, State University of New York (NY) **520**
Suffolk U (MA) **520**
Sul Ross State U (TX) **521**
Susquehanna U (PA) **521**
Swarthmore Coll (PA) **521**
Sweet Briar Coll (VA) **521**
Syracuse U (NY) **521**
Tabor Coll (KS) **522**
Talladega Coll (AL) **522**
Tarleton State U (TX) **522**
Taylor U (IN) **523**
Teikyo Post U (CT) **523**
Temple U (PA) **523**
Tennessee State U (TN) **523**
Tennessee Technological U (TN) **524**
Tennessee Temple U (TN) **524**
Tennessee Wesleyan Coll (TN) **524**
Texas A&M International U (TX) **524**
Texas A&M U (TX) **524**
Texas A&M U–Commerce (TX) **525**
Texas A&M U–Corpus Christi (TX) **525**
Texas A&M U–Kingsville (TX) **525**
Texas A&M U–Texarkana (TX) **525**
Texas Christian U (TX) **526**
Texas Coll (TX) **526**
Texas Lutheran U (TX) **526**
Texas Southern U (TX) **526**
Texas Tech U (TX) **526**
Texas Wesleyan U (TX) **526**
Texas Woman's U (TX) **527**
Thiel Coll (PA) **527**
Thomas Edison State Coll (NJ) **527**
Thomas More Coll (KY) **528**
Thomas U (GA) **528**
Touro Coll (NY) **529**
Towson U (MD) **529**
Transylvania U (KY) **529**
Trent U (ON, Canada) **529**
Trevecca Nazarene U (TN) **529**
Trinity Christian Coll (IL) **530**
Trinity Coll (CT) **530**
Trinity Coll (DC) **530**
Trinity International U (IL) **531**
Trinity U (TX) **531**
Trinity Western U (BC, Canada) **531**
Troy State U (AL) **532**
Troy State U Dothan (AL) **532**
Troy State U Montgomery (AL) **532**
Truman State U (MO) **532**
Tufts U (MA) **533**
Tulane U (LA) **533**
Tusculum Coll (TN) **533**
Tuskegee U (AL) **533**

HISTORY (continued)
Tyndale Coll & Seminary (ON, Canada) ***533***
Union Coll (KY) ***533***
Union Coll (NE) ***534***
Union Coll (NY) ***534***
Union Inst & U (OH) ***534***
Union U (TN) ***534***
United States Air Force Academy (CO) ***534***
United States Military Academy (NY) ***535***
United States Naval Academy (MD) ***535***
Universidad Adventista de las Antillas (PR) ***536***
Université de Sherbrooke (QC, Canada) ***536***
U du Québec à Trois-Rivières (QC, Canada) ***536***
Université Laval (QC, Canada) ***536***
U at Buffalo, The State University of New York (NY) ***536***
U Coll of the Cariboo (BC, Canada) ***537***
The U of Akron (OH) ***537***
The U of Alabama (AL) ***537***
The U of Alabama at Birmingham (AL) ***537***
The U of Alabama in Huntsville (AL) ***537***
U of Alaska Anchorage (AK) ***538***
U of Alaska Fairbanks (AK) ***538***
U of Alberta (AB, Canada) ***538***
The U of Arizona (AZ) ***538***
U of Arkansas (AR) ***539***
U of Arkansas at Little Rock (AR) ***539***
U of Arkansas at Monticello (AR) ***539***
U of Baltimore (MD) ***539***
The U of British Columbia (BC, Canada) ***540***
U of Calgary (AB, Canada) ***540***
U of Calif, Berkeley (CA) ***540***
U of Calif, Davis (CA) ***540***
U of Calif, Irvine (CA) ***541***
U of Calif, Los Angeles (CA) ***541***
U of Calif, Riverside (CA) ***541***
U of Calif, San Diego (CA) ***541***
U of Calif, Santa Barbara (CA) ***541***
U of Calif, Santa Cruz (CA) ***542***
U of Central Arkansas (AR) ***542***
U of Central Florida (FL) ***542***
U of Central Oklahoma (OK) ***542***
U of Charleston (WV) ***542***
U of Chicago (IL) ***542***
U of Cincinnati (OH) ***543***
U of Colorado at Boulder (CO) ***543***
U of Colorado at Colorado Springs (CO) ***543***
U of Colorado at Denver (CO) ***543***
U of Connecticut (CT) ***544***
U of Dallas (TX) ***544***
U of Dayton (OH) ***544***
U of Delaware (DE) ***544***
U of Denver (CO) ***544***
U of Evansville (IN) ***545***
The U of Findlay (OH) ***545***
U of Florida (FL) ***545***
U of Georgia (GA) ***545***
U of Great Falls (MT) ***545***
U of Guelph (ON, Canada) ***546***
U of Hartford (CT) ***546***
U of Hawaii at Hilo (HI) ***546***
U of Hawaii at Manoa (HI) ***546***
U of Hawaii–West Oahu (HI) ***546***
U of Houston (TX) ***547***
U of Houston–Clear Lake (TX) ***547***
U of Idaho (ID) ***547***
U of Illinois at Chicago (IL) ***547***
U of Illinois at Springfield (IL) ***548***
U of Illinois at Urbana–Champaign (IL) ***548***
U of Indianapolis (IN) ***548***
The U of Iowa (IA) ***548***
U of Kansas (KS) ***549***
U of Kentucky (KY) ***549***
U of King's Coll (NS, Canada) ***549***
U of La Verne (CA) ***549***
The U of Lethbridge (AB, Canada) ***549***
U of Louisiana at Lafayette (LA) ***550***
U of Louisville (KY) ***550***
U of Maine (ME) ***550***
U of Maine at Farmington (ME) ***550***
U of Maine at Machias (ME) ***551***
U of Maine at Presque Isle (ME) ***551***
U of Manitoba (MB, Canada) ***551***
U of Mary Hardin-Baylor (TX) ***551***
U of Maryland, Baltimore County (MD) ***552***
U of Maryland, Coll Park (MD) ***552***
U of Maryland Eastern Shore (MD) ***552***
U of Maryland University Coll (MD) ***552***
U of Massachusetts Amherst (MA) ***552***
U of Massachusetts Boston (MA) ***553***
U of Massachusetts Dartmouth (MA) ***553***
U of Massachusetts Lowell (MA) ***553***
The U of Memphis (TN) ***553***
U of Miami (FL) ***553***
U of Michigan (MI) ***554***
U of Michigan–Dearborn (MI) ***554***
U of Michigan–Flint (MI) ***554***
U of Minnesota, Duluth (MN) ***554***
U of Minnesota, Morris (MN) ***555***
U of Minnesota, Twin Cities Campus (MN) ***555***
U of Mississippi (MS) ***555***
U of Missouri–Columbia (MO) ***555***
U of Missouri–Kansas City (MO) ***555***
U of Missouri–Rolla (MO) ***556***
U of Missouri–St. Louis (MO) ***556***
U of Mobile (AL) ***556***
The U of Montana–Missoula (MT) ***556***
U of Montevallo (AL) ***557***
U of Nebraska at Kearney (NE) ***557***
U of Nebraska at Omaha (NE) ***557***
U of Nebraska–Lincoln (NE) ***557***
U of Nevada, Las Vegas (NV) ***558***
U of Nevada, Reno (NV) ***558***
U of New Brunswick Fredericton (NB, Canada) ***558***
U of New Brunswick Saint John (NB, Canada) ***558***
U of New England (ME) ***558***
U of New Hampshire (NH) ***558***
U of New Haven (CT) ***559***
U of New Mexico (NM) ***559***
U of New Orleans (LA) ***559***
U of North Alabama (AL) ***559***
The U of North Carolina at Asheville (NC) ***559***
The U of North Carolina at Chapel Hill (NC) ***560***
The U of North Carolina at Charlotte (NC) ***560***
The U of North Carolina at Greensboro (NC) ***560***
The U of North Carolina at Pembroke (NC) ***560***
The U of North Carolina at Wilmington (NC) ***561***
U of North Dakota (ND) ***561***
U of Northern Colorado (CO) ***561***
U of Northern Iowa (IA) ***561***
U of North Florida (FL) ***561***
U of North Texas (TX) ***562***
U of Notre Dame (IN) ***562***
U of Oklahoma (OK) ***562***
U of Oregon (OR) ***562***
U of Ottawa (ON, Canada) ***563***
U of Pennsylvania (PA) ***563***
U of Pittsburgh (PA) ***569***
U of Pittsburgh at Bradford (PA) ***569***
U of Pittsburgh at Johnstown (PA) ***570***
U of Portland (OR) ***570***
U of Prince Edward Island (PE, Canada) ***570***
U of Puerto Rico, Cayey U Coll (PR) ***571***
U of Puget Sound (WA) ***571***
U of Redlands (CA) ***572***
U of Regina (SK, Canada) ***572***
U of Rhode Island (RI) ***572***
U of Richmond (VA) ***572***
U of Rio Grande (OH) ***572***
U of Rochester (NY) ***573***
U of St. Francis (IL) ***573***
U of Saint Francis (IN) ***573***
U of St. Thomas (MN) ***573***
U of St. Thomas (TX) ***573***
U of San Diego (CA) ***574***
U of San Francisco (CA) ***574***
U of Saskatchewan (SK, Canada) ***574***
U of Science and Arts of Oklahoma (OK) ***574***
The U of Scranton (PA) ***574***
U of Sioux Falls (SD) ***574***
U of South Alabama (AL) ***575***
U of South Carolina (SC) ***575***
U of South Carolina Aiken (SC) ***575***
U of South Carolina Spartanburg (SC) ***575***
The U of South Dakota (SD) ***575***
U of Southern California (CA) ***576***
U of Southern Indiana (IN) ***576***
U of Southern Maine (ME) ***576***
U of Southern Mississippi (MS) ***576***
U of South Florida (FL) ***576***
The U of Tampa (FL) ***577***
The U of Tennessee (TN) ***577***
The U of Tennessee at Chattanooga (TN) ***577***
The U of Tennessee at Martin (TN) ***577***
The U of Texas at Arlington (TX) ***577***
The U of Texas at Austin (TX) ***578***
The U of Texas at Brownsville (TX) ***578***
The U of Texas at Dallas (TX) ***578***
The U of Texas at El Paso (TX) ***578***
The U of Texas at San Antonio (TX) ***578***
The U of Texas at Tyler (TX) ***579***
The U of Texas of the Permian Basin (TX) ***579***
The U of Texas–Pan American (TX) ***579***
U of the District of Columbia (DC) ***580***
U of the Incarnate Word (TX) ***580***
U of the Ozarks (AR) ***580***
U of the Pacific (CA) ***580***
U of the Sacred Heart (PR) ***580***
U of the South (TN) ***581***
U of Toledo (OH) ***581***
U of Toronto (ON, Canada) ***581***
U of Tulsa (OK) ***581***
U of Utah (UT) ***582***
U of Vermont (VT) ***582***
U of Victoria (BC, Canada) ***582***
U of Virginia (VA) ***582***
The U of Virginia's Coll at Wise (VA) ***582***
U of Washington (WA) ***583***
U of Waterloo (ON, Canada) ***583***
The U of West Alabama (AL) ***583***
The U of Western Ontario (ON, Canada) ***583***
U of West Florida (FL) ***583***
U of Windsor (ON, Canada) ***584***
U of Wisconsin–Eau Claire (WI) ***584***
U of Wisconsin–Green Bay (WI) ***584***
U of Wisconsin–La Crosse (WI) ***584***
U of Wisconsin–Madison (WI) ***584***
U of Wisconsin–Milwaukee (WI) ***585***
U of Wisconsin–Oshkosh (WI) ***585***
U of Wisconsin–Parkside (WI) ***585***
U of Wisconsin–Platteville (WI) ***585***
U of Wisconsin–River Falls (WI) ***585***
U of Wisconsin–Stevens Point (WI) ***585***
U of Wisconsin–Superior (WI) ***586***
U of Wisconsin–Whitewater (WI) ***586***
U of Wyoming (WY) ***586***
Urbana U (OH) ***587***
Ursinus Coll (PA) ***587***
Ursuline Coll (OH) ***587***
Utah State U (UT) ***587***
Utica Coll (NY) ***588***
Valdosta State U (GA) ***588***
Valley City State U (ND) ***588***
Valparaiso U (IN) ***588***
Vanderbilt U (TN) ***588***
Vanguard U of Southern California (CA) ***589***
Vassar Coll (NY) ***589***
Villanova U (PA) ***590***
Virginia Commonwealth U (VA) ***590***
Virginia Intermont Coll (VA) ***590***
Virginia Military Inst (VA) ***591***
Virginia Polytechnic Inst and State U (VA) ***591***
Virginia State U (VA) ***591***
Virginia Union U (VA) ***591***
Virginia Wesleyan Coll (VA) ***591***
Wabash Coll (IN) ***592***
Wagner Coll (NY) ***592***
Wake Forest U (NC) ***592***
Waldorf Coll (IA) ***592***
Walla Walla Coll (WA) ***593***
Walsh U (OH) ***593***
Warner Pacific Coll (OR) ***593***
Warner Southern Coll (FL) ***593***
Warren Wilson Coll (NC) ***594***
Wartburg Coll (IA) ***594***
Washington & Jefferson Coll (PA) ***594***
Washington and Lee U (VA) ***594***
Washington Coll (MD) ***594***
Washington State U (WA) ***595***
Washington U in St. Louis (MO) ***595***
Wayland Baptist U (TX) ***595***
Waynesburg Coll (PA) ***595***
Wayne State Coll (NE) ***596***
Wayne State U (MI) ***596***
Weber State U (UT) ***596***
Webster U (MO) ***597***
Wellesley Coll (MA) ***597***
Wells Coll (NY) ***597***
Wesleyan Coll (GA) ***597***
Wesleyan U (CT) ***597***
Wesley Coll (DE) ***598***
West Chester U of Pennsylvania (PA) ***598***
Western Carolina U (NC) ***598***
Western Connecticut State U (CT) ***598***
Western Illinois U (IL) ***599***
Western Kentucky U (KY) ***599***
Western Michigan U (MI) ***599***
Western New England Coll (MA) ***600***
Western New Mexico U (NM) ***600***
Western Oregon U (OR) ***600***
Western State Coll of Colorado (CO) ***600***
Western Washington U (WA) ***600***
Westfield State Coll (MA) ***600***
West Liberty State Coll (WV) ***601***
Westminster Coll (MO) ***601***
Westminster Coll (PA) ***601***
Westminster Coll (UT) ***601***
Westmont Coll (CA) ***602***
West Texas A&M U (TX) ***602***
West Virginia State Coll (WV) ***602***
West Virginia U (WV) ***602***
West Virginia U Inst of Technology (WV) ***602***
West Virginia Wesleyan Coll (WV) ***603***
Wheaton Coll (IL) ***603***
Wheaton Coll (MA) ***603***
Wheeling Jesuit U (WV) ***603***
Whitman Coll (WA) ***604***
Whittier Coll (CA) ***604***
Whitworth Coll (WA) ***604***
Wichita State U (KS) ***604***
Widener U (PA) ***604***
Wiley Coll (TX) ***605***
Wilkes U (PA) ***605***
Willamette U (OR) ***605***
William Carey Coll (MS) ***605***
William Jewell Coll (MO) ***606***
William Paterson U of New Jersey (NJ) ***606***
William Penn U (IA) ***606***
Williams Baptist Coll (AR) ***606***
Williams Coll (MA) ***606***
William Woods U (MO) ***607***
Wilmington Coll (OH) ***607***
Wingate U (NC) ***607***
Winona State U (MN) ***608***
Winston-Salem State U (NC) ***608***
Winthrop U (SC) ***608***
Wisconsin Lutheran Coll (WI) ***608***
Wittenberg U (OH) ***608***
Wofford Coll (SC) ***609***
Woodbury U (CA) ***609***
Worcester Polytechnic Inst (MA) ***609***
Worcester State Coll (MA) ***609***
Wright State U (OH) ***609***
Xavier U (OH) ***610***
Xavier U of Louisiana (LA) ***610***
Yale U (CT) ***610***
York Coll (NE) ***610***
York Coll of Pennsylvania (PA) ***610***
York Coll of the City U of New York (NY) ***611***
York U (ON, Canada) ***611***
Youngstown State U (OH) ***611***

HISTORY EDUCATION

Overview: This major prepares undergraduates to teach a variety of historical subjects at various educational levels. *Related majors:* history, American history, Western civilization, American government and politics. *Potential careers:* history of government teacher, museum curator. *Salary potential:* $22k-$25k.

Abilene Christian U (TX) ***260***
Adams State Coll (CO) ***260***
Anderson Coll (SC) ***268***
Appalachian State U (NC) ***270***
Baylor U (TX) ***283***
Berry Coll (GA) ***287***
Bethel Coll (TN) ***288***
Bowling Green State U (OH) ***292***
Bridgewater Coll (VA) ***294***
Brigham Young U (UT) ***295***
Carroll Coll (MT) ***306***
The Catholic U of America (DC) ***307***
Central Michigan U (MI) ***310***
Central Washington U (WA) ***310***
Chadron State Coll (NE) ***311***
Christian Brothers U (TN) ***313***
Citadel, The Military Coll of South Carolina (SC) ***314***
Clearwater Christian Coll (FL) ***316***
The Coll of New Jersey (NJ) ***320***
Coll of the Ozarks (MO) ***323***
Concordia Coll (MN) ***329***
Concordia U (IL) ***330***
Concordia U (NE) ***330***
Crown Coll (MN) ***334***

Culver-Stockton Coll (MO) **334**
Cumberland U (TN) **335**
Dakota Wesleyan U (SD) **336**
Dana Coll (NE) **337**
Dominican Coll (NY) **344**
Eastern Michigan U (MI) **348**
East Texas Baptist U (TX) **350**
Elmhurst Coll (IL) **351**
Elmira Coll (NY) **351**
Framingham State Coll (MA) **362**
Franklin Coll (IN) **363**
Georgia Southern U (GA) **367**
Hardin-Simmons U (TX) **376**
Hastings Coll (NE) **377**
Howard Payne U (TX) **382**
Huntingdon Coll (AL) **383**
Johnson State Coll (VT) **394**
King Coll (TN) **398**
Liberty U (VA) **406**
Luther Coll (IA) **412**
Maryville Coll (TN) **420**
McGill U (QC, Canada) **423**
McKendree Coll (IL) **423**
McMurry U (TX) **423**
Mercer U (GA) **425**
Minot State U (ND) **432**
Montana State U–Billings (MT) **434**
Mount Marty Coll (SD) **438**
Nazareth Coll of Rochester (NY) **443**
North Carolina Central U (NC) **448**
North Dakota State U (ND) **449**
Northern Arizona U (AZ) **450**
Northwest Coll (WA) **452**
Northwest Nazarene U (ID) **454**
Oklahoma Baptist U (OK) **459**
Pontifical Catholic U of Puerto Rico (PR) **472**
Rocky Mountain Coll (MT) **482**
St. Ambrose U (IA) **486**
Saint Xavier U (IL) **496**
Salve Regina U (RI) **497**
Seton Hill U (PA) **502**
Si Tanka Huron U (SD) **505**
Southwestern Oklahoma State U (OK) **512**
Southwest Missouri State U (MO) **513**
Talladega Coll (AL) **522**
Tennessee Wesleyan Coll (TN) **524**
Texas A&M International U (TX) **524**
Texas Lutheran U (TX) **526**
Texas Wesleyan U (TX) **526**
Trevecca Nazarene U (TN) **529**
Trinity Christian Coll (IL) **530**
Union Coll (NE) **534**
The U of Akron (OH) **537**
The U of Arizona (AZ) **538**
U of Central Oklahoma (OK) **542**
U of Delaware (DE) **544**
U of Illinois at Chicago (IL) **547**
The U of Iowa (IA) **548**
The U of Montana–Western (MT) **556**
U of Nebraska–Lincoln (NE) **557**
The U of North Carolina at Charlotte (NC) **560**
The U of North Carolina at Wilmington (NC) **561**
U of North Texas (TX) **562**
U of Puerto Rico, Cayey U Coll (PR) **571**
U of Rio Grande (OH) **572**
The U of Tennessee at Martin (TN) **577**
U of Utah (UT) **582**
U of Windsor (ON, Canada) **584**
U of Wisconsin–River Falls (WI) **585**
U of Wisconsin–Superior (WI) **586**
Utica Coll (NY) **588**
Valley City State U (ND) **588**
Wartburg Coll (IA) **594**
Washington U in St. Louis (MO) **595**
Weber State U (UT) **596**
Wheeling Jesuit U (WV) **603**
York Coll (NE) **610**
York U (ON, Canada) **611**
Youngstown State U (OH) **611**

HISTORY OF PHILOSOPHY

Overview: This major focuses on the origin and development of critical thinking, ethics, and logic, including investigations of abstract and real phenomena. *Related majors:* philosophy, law and legal studies, history, Western civilization and culture, Bible and Biblical studies. *Potential careers:* philosopher, historian, archeologist, professor, attorney, writer. *Salary potential:* $25k-$30k.

Bard Coll (NY) **281**
Bennington Coll (VT) **286**
The Evergreen State Coll (WA) **355**
Hampshire Coll (MA) **375**
Harvard U (MA) **376**
Marlboro Coll (VT) **418**
Marquette U (WI) **418**
St. John's Coll (NM) **490**
Spring Arbor U (MI) **514**
U of Regina (SK, Canada) **572**
U of Southern California (CA) **576**
U of Toronto (ON, Canada) **581**

HISTORY OF SCIENCE AND TECHNOLOGY

Overview: Students choosing this major will study the origins, evolution, and development of scientific theories and technologies and how science and technology have affected human societies and cultures throughout history. *Related majors:* history, science, technology and society, sociology, anthropology. *Potential careers:* historian, writer, professor, historical preservationist, museum curator. *Salary potential:* $25k-$35k.

Bard Coll (NY) **281**
Case Western Reserve U (OH) **307**
Cornell U (NY) **333**
Dalhousie U (NS, Canada) **336**
Georgia Inst of Technology (GA) **367**
Hampshire Coll (MA) **375**
Harvard U (MA) **376**
Johns Hopkins U (MD) **392**
Oregon State U (OR) **462**
U of Chicago (IL) **542**
U of Pennsylvania (PA) **563**
U of Pittsburgh (PA) **569**
U of Toronto (ON, Canada) **581**
U of Washington (WA) **583**
U of Wisconsin–Madison (WI) **584**
Worcester Polytechnic Inst (MA) **609**

HISTORY RELATED

Information can be found under this major's main heading.

The Colorado Coll (CO) **325**
The Franciscan U (IA) **363**
The Ohio State U (OH) **457**
Ohio U (OH) **458**
Saint Mary's U of Minnesota (MN) **494**

HOME ECONOMICS

Overview: This interdisciplinary major focuses on the ways individuals develop and function in family and community settings and how they relate to their environment. *Related majors:* food and nutrition; family and community studies; sociology; child growth, care, and development; city/community planning. *Potential careers:* community services representative, cooperative services agent, social worker, sociologist, researcher. *Salary potential:* $20k-$25k.

Abilene Christian U (TX) **260**
Alcorn State U (MS) **263**
Appalachian State U (NC) **270**
Ashland U (OH) **274**
Auburn U (AL) **276**
Baldwin-Wallace Coll (OH) **280**
Ball State U (IN) **280**
Baylor U (TX) **283**
Bennett Coll (NC) **286**
Bluffton Coll (OH) **291**
Bridgewater Coll (VA) **294**
California State Polytechnic U, Pomona (CA) **300**
California State U, Long Beach (CA) **301**
California State U, Northridge (CA) **301**
Campbell U (NC) **303**
Carson-Newman Coll (TN) **306**
Central Michigan U (MI) **310**
Central Missouri State U (MO) **310**
Central Washington U (WA) **310**
Coll of St. Catherine (MN) **321**
Coll of the Ozarks (MO) **323**
Colorado State U (CO) **325**
Concordia U (NE) **330**
Delaware State U (DE) **338**
Delta State U (MS) **339**
East Central U (OK) **347**
Eastern Illinois U (IL) **348**
Eastern Kentucky U (KY) **348**
Eastern New Mexico U (NM) **349**
East Tennessee State U (TN) **349**
Fairmont State Coll (WV) **356**
Florida State U (FL) **361**
Fontbonne U (MO) **361**
Framingham State Coll (MA) **362**
Freed-Hardeman U (TN) **364**
George Fox U (OR) **366**
Henderson State U (AR) **378**
Idaho State U (ID) **384**
Immaculata U (PA) **385**
Indiana State U (IN) **385**
Iowa State U of Science and Technology (IA) **390**
Jacksonville State U (AL) **390**
Keene State Coll (NH) **396**
Kent State U (OH) **397**
Lamar U (TX) **401**
Langston U (OK) **402**
Lipscomb U (TN) **408**
Madonna U (MI) **414**
Marshall U (WV) **418**
Marymount Coll of Fordham U (NY) **419**
The Master's Coll and Seminary (CA) **422**
McNeese State U (LA) **423**
Mercyhurst Coll (PA) **425**
Meredith Coll (NC) **426**
Miami U (OH) **428**
Michigan State U (MI) **428**
Minnesota State U, Mankato (MN) **431**
Mississippi State U (MS) **432**
Montana State U–Bozeman (MT) **434**
Montclair State U (NJ) **435**
Morehead State U (KY) **436**
Morgan State U (MD) **436**
Mount Vernon Nazarene U (OH) **440**
Nicholls State U (LA) **447**
Norfolk State U (VA) **448**
North Carolina Ag and Tech State U (NC) **448**
North Carolina Central U (NC) **448**
Northeastern State U (OK) **450**
Northwestern State U of Louisiana (LA) **453**
Northwest Missouri State U (MO) **454**
Oakwood Coll (AL) **456**
Ohio U (OH) **458**
Oklahoma State U (OK) **460**
Olivet Nazarene U (IL) **461**
Oregon State U (OR) **462**
Ouachita Baptist U (AR) **462**
Pacific Union Coll (CA) **464**
Pittsburg State U (KS) **470**
Point Loma Nazarene U (CA) **471**
Pontifical Catholic U of Puerto Rico (PR) **472**
Purdue U (IN) **475**
Queens Coll of the City U of NY (NY) **475**
Saint Joseph Coll (CT) **490**
Sam Houston State U (TX) **497**
San Francisco State U (CA) **498**
Seton Hill U (PA) **502**
Shepherd Coll (WV) **503**
South Carolina State U (SC) **506**
Southeast Missouri State U (MO) **508**
Southern Utah U (UT) **511**
Southwest Texas State U (TX) **513**
State U of NY Coll at Oneonta (NY) **517**
Stephen F. Austin State U (TX) **518**
Tarleton State U (TX) **522**
Tennessee Technological U (TN) **524**
Texas A&M U–Kingsville (TX) **525**
Texas Southern U (TX) **526**
Texas Tech U (TX) **526**
Texas Woman's U (TX) **527**
The U of Akron (OH) **537**
The U of Alabama (AL) **537**
U of Alberta (AB, Canada) **538**
U of Arkansas (AR) **539**
The U of British Columbia (BC, Canada) **540**
U of Central Arkansas (AR) **542**
U of Central Oklahoma (OK) **542**
U of Hawaii at Manoa (HI) **546**
U of Houston (TX) **547**
U of Kentucky (KY) **549**
U of Manitoba (MB, Canada) **551**
U of Maryland Eastern Shore (MD) **552**
U of Mississippi (MS) **555**
U of Montevallo (AL) **557**
U of New Hampshire (NH) **558**
U of New Mexico (NM) **559**
U of North Alabama (AL) **559**
The U of North Carolina at Greensboro (NC) **560**
U of Puerto Rico, Río Piedras (PR) **571**
U of Southern Mississippi (MS) **576**
The U of Tennessee at Chattanooga (TN) **577**
The U of Tennessee at Martin (TN) **577**
The U of Texas at Austin (TX) **578**
U of the District of Columbia (DC) **580**
U of Utah (UT) **582**
The U of Western Ontario (ON, Canada) **583**
U of Wisconsin–Madison (WI) **584**
Washington State U (WA) **595**
Wayne State Coll (NE) **596**
Western Illinois U (IL) **599**
West Virginia U (WV) **602**
Youngstown State U (OH) **611**

HOME ECONOMICS COMMUNICATIONS

Overview: Students who choose this major focus on communication of human ecology, home economics, and related consumer information to a variety of audiences through print and nonprint media. *Related majors:* communication, journalism and broadcast journalism, educational/instructional media technology. *Potential careers:* advertising executive, cooperative services agent, nutrition educator, social worker, consumer advocate. *Salary potential:* $22k-$35k.

Framingham State Coll (MA) **362**

HOME ECONOMICS EDUCATION

Overview: This major prepares undergraduates to teach vocational home economics studies and skills, such as nutrition and cooking, child care, sewing skills, accounting, and education, to various educational levels. *Related majors:* accounting; business home economics; clothing/apparel/textile studies; education; child development, care, and guidance. *Potential careers:* homemaking teacher, child-care worker, vocational business teacher. *Salary potential:* $22k-$32k.

Abilene Christian U (TX) **260**
Appalachian State U (NC) **270**
Ashland U (OH) **274**
Auburn U (AL) **276**
Baldwin-Wallace Coll (OH) **280**
Ball State U (IN) **280**
Berea Coll (KY) **286**
Bluffton Coll (OH) **291**
Bowling Green State U (OH) **292**
Bridgewater Coll (VA) **294**
California State U, Northridge (CA) **301**
Campbell U (NC) **303**
Carson-Newman Coll (TN) **306**
Central Michigan U (MI) **310**
Central Missouri State U (MO) **310**
Chadron State Coll (NE) **311**
Cheyney U of Pennsylvania (PA) **312**
Coll of St. Catherine (MN) **321**
Coll of the Ozarks (MO) **323**
Colorado State U (CO) **325**
Concordia U (NE) **330**
Cornell U (NY) **333**
Delta State U (MS) **339**
East Carolina U (NC) **347**
Eastern Kentucky U (KY) **348**
Eastern Michigan U (MI) **348**
Fairmont State Coll (WV) **356**
Ferris State U (MI) **358**

HOME ECONOMICS EDUCATION (continued)

Florida International U (FL) ***360***
Florida State U (FL) ***361***
Fontbonne U (MO) ***361***
Fort Valley State U (GA) ***362***
Framingham State Coll (MA) ***362***
George Fox U (OR) ***366***
Georgia Southern U (GA) ***367***
Grambling State U (LA) ***371***
Hampton U (VA) ***375***
Henderson State U (AR) ***378***
Immaculata U (PA) ***385***
Indiana U of Pennsylvania (PA) ***386***
Iowa State U of Science and Technology (IA) ***390***
Jacksonville State U (AL) ***390***
Keene State Coll (NH) ***396***
Lamar U (TX) ***401***
Langston U (OK) ***402***
Madonna U (MI) ***414***
Marymount Coll of Fordham U (NY) ***419***
Marywood U (PA) ***421***
McNeese State U (LA) ***423***
Mercyhurst Coll (PA) ***425***
Miami U (OH) ***428***
Michigan State U (MI) ***428***
Minnesota State U, Mankato (MN) ***431***
Mississippi Coll (MS) ***432***
Montclair State U (NJ) ***435***
Morehead State U (KY) ***436***
Mount Vernon Nazarene U (OH) ***440***
Murray State U (KY) ***440***
New Mexico State U (NM) ***446***
North Carolina Ag and Tech State U (NC) ***448***
North Carolina Central U (NC) ***448***
North Dakota State U (ND) ***449***
Northeastern State U (OK) ***450***
Northern Illinois U (IL) ***450***
Northwest Missouri State U (MO) ***454***
Oakwood Coll (AL) ***456***
Olivet Nazarene U (IL) ***461***
Ouachita Baptist U (AR) ***462***
Pacific Union Coll (CA) ***464***
Pittsburg State U (KS) ***470***
Pontifical Catholic U of Puerto Rico (PR) ***472***
Queens Coll of the City U of NY (NY) ***475***
Saint Joseph Coll (CT) ***490***
Sam Houston State U (TX) ***497***
Seattle Pacific U (WA) ***501***
Seton Hill U (PA) ***502***
South Carolina State U (SC) ***506***
South Dakota State U (SD) ***507***
Southeast Missouri State U (MO) ***508***
Southern Utah U (UT) ***511***
Southwest Missouri State U (MO) ***513***
State U of NY Coll at Oneonta (NY) ***517***
Tennessee Technological U (TN) ***524***
Texas A&M U–Kingsville (TX) ***525***
The U of Akron (OH) ***537***
U of Alberta (AB, Canada) ***538***
The U of Arizona (AZ) ***538***
The U of British Columbia (BC, Canada) ***540***
U of Central Arkansas (AR) ***542***
U of Central Oklahoma (OK) ***542***
U of Georgia (GA) ***545***
U of Hawaii at Manoa (HI) ***546***
U of Idaho (ID) ***547***
U of Illinois at Springfield (IL) ***548***
U of Maryland Eastern Shore (MD) ***552***
U of Minnesota, Twin Cities Campus (MN) ***555***
U of Montevallo (AL) ***557***
U of Nevada, Reno (NV) ***558***
U of New Brunswick Fredericton (NB, Canada) ***558***
U of New Mexico (NM) ***559***
U of North Texas (TX) ***562***
U of Saskatchewan (SK, Canada) ***574***
The U of Tennessee (TN) ***577***
The U of Tennessee at Martin (TN) ***577***
U of the District of Columbia (DC) ***580***
U of Utah (UT) ***582***
U of Wisconsin–Madison (WI) ***584***
U of Wisconsin–Stevens Point (WI) ***585***
U of Wisconsin–Stout (WI) ***586***
Utah State U (UT) ***587***
Washington State U (WA) ***595***
Wayne State Coll (NE) ***596***
Western Kentucky U (KY) ***599***
Western Michigan U (MI) ***599***
Winthrop U (SC) ***608***
Youngstown State U (OH) ***611***

HOME ECONOMICS RELATED

Information can be found under this major's main heading.

Norfolk State U (VA) ***448***
Northwestern State U of Louisiana (LA) ***453***
The U of Alabama (AL) ***537***

HORTICULTURE SCIENCE

Overview: Students who choose this major will learn the scientific principles behind the cultivation, breeding, and management of garden and ornamental plants, including fruits, vegetables, flowers, and landscape and nursery crops. *Related majors:* plant sciences, plant breeding, agronomy, agricultural sciences. *Potential careers:* farm manager, soil scientist, agronomist, biotechnology scientist. *Salary potential:* $25k-$50k.

Auburn U (AL) ***276***
Berry Coll (GA) ***287***
Brigham Young U (UT) ***295***
California Polytechnic State U, San Luis Obispo (CA) ***300***
California State Polytechnic U, Pomona (CA) ***300***
Cameron U (OK) ***303***
Christopher Newport U (VA) ***313***
Clemson U (SC) ***317***
Coll of the Ozarks (MO) ***323***
Colorado State U (CO) ***325***
Cornell U (NY) ***333***
Delaware Valley Coll (PA) ***339***
Eastern Kentucky U (KY) ***348***
Florida A&M U (FL) ***359***
Florida Southern Coll (FL) ***361***
Iowa State U of Science and Technology (IA) ***390***
Kansas State U (KS) ***396***
Michigan State U (MI) ***428***
Mississippi State U (MS) ***432***
Montana State U–Bozeman (MT) ***434***
Murray State U (KY) ***440***
Naropa U (CO) ***441***
New Mexico State U (NM) ***446***
North Carolina State U (NC) ***449***
North Dakota State U (ND) ***449***
Northwest Missouri State U (MO) ***454***
The Ohio State U (OH) ***457***
Oklahoma State U (OK) ***460***
Oregon State U (OR) ***462***
Penn State U Univ Park Campus (PA) ***468***
Purdue U (IN) ***475***
Sam Houston State U (TX) ***497***
Southeastern Louisiana U (LA) ***508***
Southeast Missouri State U (MO) ***508***
Southwest Missouri State U (MO) ***513***
State U of NY Coll of A&T at Cobleskill (NY) ***517***
Stephen F. Austin State U (TX) ***518***
Tarleton State U (TX) ***522***
Tennessee Technological U (TN) ***524***
Texas A&M U–Kingsville (TX) ***525***
Texas Tech U (TX) ***526***
Thomas Edison State Coll (NJ) ***527***
U of Arkansas (AR) ***539***
The U of British Columbia (BC, Canada) ***540***
U of Calif, Davis (CA) ***540***
U of Connecticut (CT) ***544***
U of Delaware (DE) ***544***
U of Florida (FL) ***545***
U of Guelph (ON, Canada) ***546***
U of Hawaii at Hilo (HI) ***546***
U of Hawaii at Manoa (HI) ***546***
U of Idaho (ID) ***547***
U of Illinois at Urbana–Champaign (IL) ***548***
U of Maryland, Coll Park (MD) ***552***
U of Minnesota, Crookston (MN) ***554***
U of Nebraska–Lincoln (NE) ***557***
U of New Hampshire (NH) ***558***
U of Saskatchewan (SK, Canada) ***574***
U of Vermont (VT) ***582***
U of Wisconsin–Madison (WI) ***584***
U of Wisconsin–River Falls (WI) ***585***
Utah State U (UT) ***587***
Virginia Polytechnic Inst and State U (VA) ***591***
Washington State U (WA) ***595***
West Virginia U (WV) ***602***

HORTICULTURE SERVICES

Overview: This major instructs students in the production, management, and processing of domesticated plants, shrubs, flowers, trees, ground cover, and other plants. *Related majors:* turn management, soil sciences, entomology, farm management. *Potential careers:* farm manager, nursery manager, biologist. *Salary potential:* $22k-$30k.

Iowa State U of Science and Technology (IA) ***390***
South Dakota State U (SD) ***507***
Stephen F. Austin State U (TX) ***518***
Texas A&M U (TX) ***524***
Texas Tech U (TX) ***526***
U of Georgia (GA) ***545***
U of Hawaii at Manoa (HI) ***546***
U of Vermont (VT) ***582***

HOSPITALITY MANAGEMENT

Overview: This major prepares students for management, sales, or marketing careers with hotels and resorts, restaurants, cruise ships, conventions, private clubs, or other hospitality operations. *Related majors:* public relations, hospitality/recreation marketing, hotel/motel services marketing, tourism/travel marketing, business administration/management. *Potential careers:* convention center manager, hotel or resort manager, club manager, restaurant owner, caterer. *Salary potential:* $25k-$35k.

Arkansas Tech U (AR) ***272***
Bay Path Coll (MA) ***283***
Becker Coll (MA) ***283***
Belmont U (TN) ***284***
Boston U (MA) ***292***
Bowling Green State U (OH) ***292***
Central Michigan U (MI) ***310***
Champlain Coll (VT) ***311***
The Coll of Southeastern Europe, The American U of Athens(Greece) ***323***
Concord Coll (WV) ***329***
Davis & Elkins Coll (WV) ***338***
Delta State U (MS) ***339***
Eastern Michigan U (MI) ***348***
Endicott Coll (MA) ***354***
Ferris State U (MI) ***358***
Florida International U (FL) ***360***
Florida State U (FL) ***361***
Husson Coll (ME) ***383***
Indiana U–Purdue U Fort Wayne (IN) ***386***
Johnson & Wales U (FL) ***393***
Johnson & Wales U (RI) ***393***
Johnson & Wales U (SC) ***393***
Johnson State Coll (VT) ***394***
Kendall Coll (IL) ***396***
Lakeland Coll (WI) ***401***
Madonna U (MI) ***414***
Marywood U (PA) ***421***
Mercyhurst Coll (PA) ***425***
Metropolitan State Coll of Denver (CO) ***427***
Metropolitan State U (MN) ***427***
Morgan State U (MD) ***436***
Mount Saint Vincent U (NS, Canada) ***439***
National American U (NM) ***441***
North Carolina Central U (NC) ***448***
Nova Southeastern U (FL) ***455***
The Ohio State U (OH) ***457***
The Ohio State U at Lima (OH) ***458***
Penn State U Univ Park Campus (PA) ***468***
Robert Morris U (PA) ***481***
Rochester Inst of Technology (NY) ***482***
Roosevelt U (IL) ***483***
Rutgers, The State U of New Jersey, Camden (NJ) ***485***
Rutgers, The State U of New Jersey, Newark (NJ) ***485***
Ryerson U (ON, Canada) ***485***
San Francisco State U (CA) ***498***
San Jose State U (CA) ***499***
Siena Heights U (MI) ***504***
Southern New Hampshire U (NH) ***510***
Southern Vermont Coll (VT) ***511***
Stephen F. Austin State U (TX) ***518***
Syracuse U (NY) ***521***
Tiffin U (OH) ***528***
Touro U International (CA) ***529***
Tuskegee U (AL) ***533***
U of Central Florida (FL) ***542***
U of Denver (CO) ***544***
U of Kentucky (KY) ***549***
U of Massachusetts Amherst (MA) ***552***
The U of Memphis (TN) ***553***
U of Nevada, Las Vegas (NV) ***558***
U of Nevada, Reno (NV) ***558***
U of New Brunswick Saint John (NB, Canada) ***558***
U of New Haven (CT) ***559***
U of New Orleans (LA) ***559***
U of Prince Edward Island (PE, Canada) ***570***
U of South Carolina (SC) ***575***
Western Carolina U (NC) ***598***
Youngstown State U (OH) ***611***

HOSPITALITY/RECREATION MARKETING

Overview: Students learn how to promote and market hospitality and recreation services and facilities. *Related majors:* marketing, marketing research, advertising, public relations, tourism/travel marketing. *Potential careers:* marketing or advertising executive, copywriter, sales associate. *Salary potential:* $25k-$30k.

Rochester Inst of Technology (NY) ***482***

HOSPITALITY/RECREATION MARKETING OPERATIONS

Overview: This major teaches students how to provide a range of marketing services in the hospitality and leisure industries. *Related majors:* hospitality/recreation marketing, business administration/management, restaurant operations, enterprise management and operation, marketing. *Potential careers:* convention center manager, hotel or resort manager, club manager, restaurant owner, caterer. *Salary potential:* $25k-$30k.

Champlain Coll (VT) ***311***
Methodist Coll (NC) ***427***
Tuskegee U (AL) ***533***

HOSPITALITY SERVICES MANAGEMENT RELATED

Information can be found under this major's main heading.

Drexel U (PA) ***346***
Indiana U–Purdue U Indianapolis (IN) ***387***
San Diego State U (CA) ***498***
U of Hawaii at Manoa (HI) ***546***
U of Louisiana at Lafayette (LA) ***550***

HOTEL AND RESTAURANT MANAGEMENT

Overview: This major prepares students to work as managers of hotels, motels, resorts, or other lodging facilities. *Related majors:* public relations, hotel/motel services marketing, business administration/management, restaurant operations, enterprise management and operation. *Potential careers:* hotel or resort manager or sales associate, cruise ship booking agent. *Salary potential:* $25k-$35k.

Alliant International U (CA) ***264***
Appalachian State U (NC) ***270***

Ashland U (OH) 274
Auburn U (AL) 276
Barber-Scotia Coll (NC) 281
Becker Coll (MA) 283
Belmont U (TN) 284
Berea Coll (KY) 286
Bethune-Cookman Coll (FL) 289
Boston U (MA) 292
Brigham Young U–Hawaii (HI) 295
California State Polytechnic U, Pomona (CA) 300
Central Michigan U (MI) 310
Central Missouri State U (MO) 310
Champlain Coll (VT) 311
Cheyney U of Pennsylvania (PA) 312
The Coll of Southeastern Europe, The American U of Athens(Greece) 323
Coll of the Ozarks (MO) 323
Colorado State U (CO) 325
Concord Coll (WV) 329
Cornell U (NY) 333
Davenport U, Grand Rapids (MI) 337
Delaware State U (DE) 338
East Carolina U (NC) 347
East Stroudsburg U of Pennsylvania (PA) 349
Fairleigh Dickinson U, Florham (NJ) 356
Fairleigh Dickinson U, Teaneck-Metro Campus (NJ) 356
Florida Metropolitan U-Fort Lauderdale Coll (FL) 360
Florida Southern Coll (FL) 361
Georgia Southern U (GA) 367
Georgia State U (GA) 368
Grambling State U (LA) 371
Grand Valley State U (MI) 371
Hampton U (VA) 375
Howard U (DC) 382
Indiana U of Pennsylvania (PA) 386
Inter American U of PR, Aguadilla Campus (PR) 388
Iowa State U of Science and Technology (IA) 390
James Madison U (VA) 391
Johnson & Wales U (RI) 393
Johnson & Wales U (SC) 393
Kansas State U (KS) 396
Kendall Coll (IL) 396
Keuka Coll (NY) 398
Langston U (OK) 402
Lasell Coll (MA) 402
Lynn U (FL) 413
Mercyhurst Coll (PA) 425
Michigan State U (MI) 428
Morgan State U (MD) 436
Mount Ida Coll (MA) 438
Mount Saint Vincent U (NS, Canada) 439
National American U (NM) 441
National American U–Sioux Falls Branch (SD) 442
Newbury Coll (MA) 444
New Mexico State U (NM) 446
New York Inst of Technology (NY) 447
New York U (NY) 447
Niagara U (NY) 447
North Carolina Wesleyan Coll (NC) 449
North Dakota State U (ND) 449
Northern Arizona U (AZ) 450
Northwood U (MI) 454
Northwood U, Florida Campus (FL) 454
Northwood U, Texas Campus (TX) 454
Nova Southeastern U (FL) 455
Oklahoma State U (OK) 460
Pace U (NY) 463
Paul Smith's Coll of Arts and Sciences (NY) 466
Peirce Coll (PA) 466
Penn State U Univ Park Campus (PA) 468
Plattsburgh State U of NY (NY) 471
Purdue U (IN) 475
Purdue U Calumet (IN) 475
Rochester Inst of Technology (NY) 482
Ryerson U (ON, Canada) 485
St. John's U (NY) 490
Saint Leo U (FL) 492
St. Thomas U (FL) 496
San Diego State U (CA) 498
Schiller International U (FL) 500
Schiller International U(Spain) 500
Schiller International U(United Kingdom) 500
Schiller International U, American Coll of Switzerland(Switzerland) 500
Sierra Nevada Coll (NV) 504
South Dakota State U (SD) 507
Southern New Hampshire U (NH) 510
Southern Oregon U (OR) 510
Southern Vermont Coll (VT) 511
Southwest Missouri State U (MO) 513
State U of NY Coll at Buffalo (NY) 516
Sullivan U (KY) 521
Texas A&M U–Kingsville (TX) 525
Texas Tech U (TX) 526
Thomas Coll (ME) 527
Thomas Edison State Coll (NJ) 527
United States International U(Kenya) 535
The U of Alabama (AL) 537
U of Calgary (AB, Canada) 540
U of Central Oklahoma (OK) 542
U of Delaware (DE) 544
U of Denver (CO) 544
The U of Findlay (OH) 545
U of Guelph (ON, Canada) 546
U of Houston (TX) 547
U of Maine at Machias (ME) 551
U of Maryland Eastern Shore (MD) 552
U of Minnesota, Crookston (MN) 554
U of Missouri–Columbia (MO) 555
U of New Hampshire (NH) 558
U of New Haven (CT) 559
U of North Texas (TX) 562
U of San Francisco (CA) 574
U of Southern Mississippi (MS) 576
The U of Tennessee (TN) 577
U of the Incarnate Word (TX) 580
U of Victoria (BC, Canada) 582
U of Wisconsin–Stout (WI) 586
Virginia State U (VA) 591
Washington State U (WA) 595
Webber International U (FL) 596
Western Kentucky U (KY) 599
Widener U (PA) 604
Wiley Coll (TX) 605
Youngstown State U (OH) 611

HOTEL/MOTEL SERVICES MARKETING OPERATIONS

Overview: Students learn how to perform marketing, promotion, and sales services for hotels and motels. *Related majors:* marketing, advertising, public relations. *Potential careers:* marketing or advertising executive, hotel or motel manager, sales agent. *Salary potential:* $25k-$30k.

Champlain Coll (VT) 311
Lake Erie Coll (OH) 400
Lewis-Clark State Coll (ID) 406

HOUSING STUDIES

Overview: This major teaches students about the social, economic, technological, functional, and aesthetic aspects of human dwellings. *Related majors:* interior environments and design, building technology, home furnishings/equipment, architecture. *Potential careers:* housing inspector, housing advocate, city planner, property manager, appraiser. *Salary potential:* $24-29k.

Auburn U (AL) 276
Florida State U (FL) 361
Iowa State U of Science and Technology (IA) 390
Ohio U (OH) 458
Southeast Missouri State U (MO) 508
Southwest Missouri State U (MO) 513
U of Arkansas (AR) 539
U of Georgia (GA) 545
U of Missouri–Columbia (MO) 555
U of Northern Iowa (IA) 561
Utah State U (UT) 587
Western Kentucky U (KY) 599

HUMAN ECOLOGY

Overview: This broad-based major is the scientific study of interactions between individuals, families, and communities with their work, social, and personal environments and the impact of these interactions on their health, quality of life, and environment. *Related majors:* home economics, foods and nutrition science, interior environments, individual and family development studies, clothing and textile studies. *Potential careers:* ecologist, anthropologist, social worker, sociologist, nutritionist.

California State U, Hayward (CA) 301
Cameron U (OK) 303
Coll of the Atlantic (ME) 323
Concordia U (QC, Canada) 331
Connecticut Coll (CT) 331
Cornell U (NY) 333
Emory U (GA) 354
The Evergreen State Coll (WA) 355
Goddard Coll (VT) 369
Kansas State U (KS) 396
Lambuth U (TN) 401
Long Island U, Southampton Coll, Friends World Program (NY) 409
Marymount Coll of Fordham U (NY) 419
Mercyhurst Coll (PA) 425
Morgan State U (MD) 436
Mount Saint Vincent U (NS, Canada) 439
Prescott Coll (AZ) 474
Regis U (CO) 478
Rutgers, The State U of New Jersey, New Brunswick (NJ) 485
State U of NY Coll at Oneonta (NY) 517
Sterling Coll (VT) 519
U of Alberta (AB, Canada) 538
U of Calif, Irvine (CA) 541
U of Calif, San Diego (CA) 541
U of Manitoba (MB, Canada) 551
U of Maryland Eastern Shore (MD) 552

HUMANITIES

Overview: This major emphasizes languages, literatures, art, music, philosophy, and religion. *Related majors:* liberal arts and sciences, comparative literature, philosophy, religion, art history. *Potential careers:* art or music critic, museum curator, editor, art dealer, professor. *Salary potential:* $22k-$28k.

Adelphi U (NY) 260
Albertus Magnus Coll (CT) 262
Alma Coll (MI) 264
Angelo State U (TX) 269
Antioch Coll (OH) 269
Antioch U McGregor (OH) 270
Arizona State U (AZ) 271
Athens State U (AL) 275
Atlanta Christian Coll (GA) 275
Augsburg Coll (MN) 276
Aurora U (IL) 277
Avila U (MO) 278
Bard Coll (NY) 281
Becker Coll (MA) 283
Belhaven Coll (MS) 283
Bemidji State U (MN) 285
Bennington Coll (VT) 286
Biola U (CA) 289
Bishop's U (QC, Canada) 289
Bloomsburg U of Pennsylvania (PA) 290
Bluefield State Coll (WV) 291
Bluffton Coll (OH) 291
Bowling Green State U (OH) 292
Brigham Young U (UT) 295
Brock U (ON, Canada) 295
Bryn Athyn Coll of the New Church (PA) 297
Bucknell U (PA) 297
Burlington Coll (VT) 297
California State Polytechnic U, Pomona (CA) 300
California State U, Chico (CA) 300
California State U, Dominguez Hills (CA) 300
California State U, Northridge (CA) 301
California State U, Sacramento (CA) 301
California State U, San Bernardino (CA) 302
Canisius Coll (NY) 304
Carleton U (ON, Canada) 305
Carnegie Mellon U (PA) 305
Catawba Coll (NC) 307
Chaminade U of Honolulu (HI) 311
Charleston Southern U (SC) 311
Clarion U of Pennsylvania (PA) 315
Clarkson U (NY) 316
Clearwater Christian Coll (FL) 316
Colgate U (NY) 319
Coll of Mount St. Joseph (OH) 320
Coll of Saint Benedict (MN) 321
Coll of Saint Mary (NE) 322
The Coll of St. Scholastica (MN) 322
Coll of Santa Fe (NM) 323
Colorado Christian U (CO) 325
Colorado State U (CO) 325
Columbia Coll (MO) 326
Columbia International U (SC) 327
Concordia Coll (MN) 329
Concordia U (CA) 330
Concordia U (OR) 330
Concordia U Wisconsin (WI) 331
Daemen Coll (NY) 335
Dominican Coll (NY) 344
Dominican U of California (CA) 345
Dowling Coll (NY) 345
Drexel U (PA) 346
Eastern Washington U (WA) 349
Eckerd Coll (FL) 350
Edinboro U of Pennsylvania (PA) 351
Elmira Coll (NY) 351
Eugene Lang Coll, New School U (NY) 355
The Evergreen State Coll (WA) 355
Fairleigh Dickinson U, Florham (NJ) 356
Fairleigh Dickinson U, Teaneck-Metro Campus (NJ) 356
Faulkner U (AL) 357
Felician Coll (NJ) 357
Florida Inst of Technology (FL) 360
Florida International U (FL) 360
Florida Southern Coll (FL) 361
Florida State U (FL) 361
Fort Lewis Coll (CO) 362
Framingham State Coll (MA) 362
The Franciscan U (IA) 363
Franciscan U of Steubenville (OH) 363
Freed-Hardeman U (TN) 364
Fresno Pacific U (CA) 364
Gannon U (PA) 365
The George Washington U (DC) 367
Georgian Court Coll (NJ) 367
Goddard Coll (VT) 369
Grace U (NE) 371
Grand Valley State U (MI) 371
Hampden-Sydney Coll (VA) 374
Hampshire Coll (MA) 375
Harding U (AR) 375
Harvard U (MA) 376
Hawai'i Pacific U (HI) 377
Hofstra U (NY) 380
Holy Apostles Coll and Seminary (CT) 380
Holy Family U (PA) 380
Holy Names Coll (CA) 381
Hope Coll (MI) 381
Houghton Coll (NY) 381
Huron U USA in London(United Kingdom) 383
Indiana State U (IN) 385
Indiana U Kokomo (IN) 386
Jacksonville U (FL) 391
John Carroll U (OH) 392
John F. Kennedy U (CA) 392
Johnson State Coll (VT) 394
Juniata Coll (PA) 395
Kansas State U (KS) 396
Kenyon Coll (OH) 398
Lambuth U (TN) 401
Lawrence Technological U (MI) 403
Lees-McRae Coll (NC) 404
Lesley U (MA) 405
Lincoln Memorial U (TN) 407
Lock Haven U of Pennsylvania (PA) 408
Long Island U, Brooklyn Campus (NY) 409
Long Island U, Southampton Coll, Friends World Program (NY) 409
Loyola Marymount U (CA) 411
Loyola U Chicago (IL) 411
Loyola U New Orleans (LA) 411
Lubbock Christian U (TX) 412
Lynn U (FL) 413
Macalester Coll (MN) 413
Maranatha Baptist Bible Coll (WI) 417
Marist Coll (NY) 417
Marlboro Coll (VT) 418
Marshall U (WV) 418
Martin U (IN) 419
Maryville U of Saint Louis (MO) 420
Massachusetts Inst of Technology (MA) 421
McGill U (QC, Canada) 423

HUMANITIES (continued)

Medaille Coll (NY) 424
Memorial U of Newfoundland (NF, Canada) 424
Mercyhurst Coll (PA) 425
Mesa State Coll (CO) 426
Messiah Coll (PA) 426
Michigan State U (MI) 428
Middlebury Coll (VT) 429
Midland Lutheran Coll (NE) 429
Midwestern State U (TX) 430
Miles Coll (AL) 430
Milligan Coll (TN) 430
Minnesota State U, Mankato (MN) 431
Monmouth Coll (IL) 434
Montana State U–Northern (MT) 434
Montclair State U (NJ) 435
Mount Allison U (NB, Canada) 437
Mount Aloysius Coll (PA) 437
Mount Saint Vincent U (NS, Canada) 439
Muskingum Coll (OH) 441
New Coll of California (CA) 444
New York U (NY) 447
North Central Coll (IL) 449
North Dakota State U (ND) 449
Northern Arizona U (AZ) 450
North Greenville Coll (SC) 451
Northwest Christian Coll (OR) 452
Northwestern Coll (IA) 453
Northwestern U (IL) 453
Northwest Missouri State U (MO) 454
Notre Dame de Namur U (CA) 455
Nova Southeastern U (FL) 455
Oakland City U (IN) 456
The Ohio State U (OH) 457
Ohio Wesleyan U (OH) 459
Oklahoma Baptist U (OK) 459
Oklahoma City U (OK) 460
Oklahoma Panhandle State U (OK) 460
Our Lady of the Lake Coll (LA) 463
Pacific U (OR) 464
Pepperdine U, Malibu (CA) 469
Pfeiffer U (NC) 469
Plymouth State Coll (NH) 471
Pomona Coll (CA) 472
Portland State U (OR) 472
Prescott Coll (AZ) 474
Principia Coll (IL) 474
Providence Coll (RI) 474
Providence Coll and Theological Seminary (MB, Canada) 475
Purdue U (IN) 475
Purdue U Calumet (IN) 475
Quincy U (IL) 476
Regis U (CO) 478
Roberts Wesleyan Coll (NY) 481
Rockford Coll (IL) 482
Rosemont Coll (PA) 484
St. Gregory's U (OK) 489
Saint John's U (MN) 490
Saint Joseph Coll (CT) 490
Saint Joseph's U (PA) 491
Saint Louis U (MO) 492
Saint Martin's Coll (WA) 493
Saint Mary-of-the-Woods Coll (IN) 493
Saint Mary's Coll (IN) 493
St. Norbert Coll (WI) 495
Saint Peter's Coll (NJ) 495
St. Thomas Aquinas Coll (NY) 495
Samford U (AL) 497
Sam Houston State U (TX) 497
San Diego State U (CA) 498
San Francisco State U (CA) 498
San Jose State U (CA) 499
Sarah Lawrence Coll (NY) 499
Schreiner U (TX) 501
Seattle U (WA) 501
Seton Hall U (NJ) 502
Shawnee State U (OH) 502
Sheldon Jackson Coll (AK) 503
Shimer Coll (IL) 503
Shorter Coll (GA) 504
Siena Heights U (MI) 504
Sierra Nevada Coll (NV) 504
Simon Fraser U (BC, Canada) 505
Southeastern Louisiana U (LA) 508
Southern Methodist U (TX) 510
Southern New Hampshire U (NH) 510
Southwest Missouri State U (MO) 513
Spring Hill Coll (AL) 514
State U of NY Coll at Buffalo (NY) 516
State U of NY Coll at Old Westbury (NY) 516
State U of NY Empire State Coll (NY) 517
State U of NY Maritime Coll (NY) 518
Stephen F. Austin State U (TX) 518
Stetson U (FL) 519
Stevens Inst of Technology (NJ) 519
Stony Brook U, State University of New York (NY) 520
Suffolk U (MA) 520
Tabor Coll (KS) 522
Tennessee State U (TN) 523
Texas Wesleyan U (TX) 526
Thomas Edison State Coll (NJ) 527
Thomas U (GA) 528
Tiffin U (OH) 528
Touro Coll (NY) 529
Trent U (ON, Canada) 529
Trinity International U (IL) 531
Trinity U (TX) 531
Trinity Western U (BC, Canada) 531
Union Coll (NY) 534
Union Inst & U (OH) 534
United States Air Force Academy (CO) 534
United States Military Academy (NY) 535
The U of Akron (OH) 537
U of Alberta (AB, Canada) 538
The U of Arizona (AZ) 538
U of Bridgeport (CT) 540
U of Calgary (AB, Canada) 540
U of Calif, Irvine (CA) 541
U of Calif, Riverside (CA) 541
U of Central Florida (FL) 542
U of Charleston (WV) 542
U of Chicago (IL) 542
U of Cincinnati (OH) 543
U of Colorado at Boulder (CO) 543
U of Hawaii–West Oahu (HI) 546
U of Houston–Clear Lake (TX) 547
U of Houston–Downtown (TX) 547
U of Houston–Victoria (TX) 547
U of Illinois at Urbana–Champaign (IL) 548
U of Kansas (KS) 549
The U of Lethbridge (AB, Canada) 549
U of Maryland University Coll (MD) 552
U of Massachusetts Amherst (MA) 552
U of Michigan (MI) 554
U of Michigan–Dearborn (MI) 554
U of Missouri–St. Louis (MO) 556
U of Mobile (AL) 556
U of New England (ME) 558
U of New Hampshire (NH) 558
U of New Mexico (NM) 559
U of North Dakota (ND) 561
U of Northern Iowa (IA) 561
U of Ottawa (ON, Canada) 563
U of Pennsylvania (PA) 563
U of Pittsburgh (PA) 569
U of Pittsburgh at Greensburg (PA) 570
U of Pittsburgh at Johnstown (PA) 570
U of Puerto Rico, Cayey U Coll (PR) 571
U of Puerto Rico, Río Piedras (PR) 571
U of Regina (SK, Canada) 572
U of Rio Grande (OH) 572
U of San Diego (CA) 574
U of South Florida (FL) 576
The U of Tennessee at Chattanooga (TN) 577
The U of Texas at Austin (TX) 578
The U of Texas at Dallas (TX) 578
The U of Texas at San Antonio (TX) 578
The U of Texas of the Permian Basin (TX) 579
U of the Sacred Heart (PR) 580
U of the Virgin Islands (VI) 581
U of Toledo (OH) 581
U of Toronto (ON, Canada) 581
U of Washington (WA) 583
U of West Florida (FL) 583
U of Windsor (ON, Canada) 584
U of Wisconsin–Green Bay (WI) 584
U of Wisconsin–Parkside (WI) 585
U of Wyoming (WY) 586
Ursuline Coll (OH) 587
Villa Julie Coll (MD) 590
Virginia Wesleyan Coll (VA) 591
Viterbo U (WI) 591
Waldorf Coll (IA) 592
Walla Walla Coll (WA) 593
Warren Wilson Coll (NC) 594
Washington Coll (MD) 594
Washington State U (WA) 595
Wesleyan Coll (GA) 597
Wesleyan U (CT) 597
Western Baptist Coll (OR) 598
Western New Mexico U (NM) 600
Western Oregon U (OR) 600
Western Washington U (WA) 600
Widener U (PA) 604
Willamette U (OR) 605
William Paterson U of New Jersey (NJ) 606
Wittenberg U (OH) 608
Wofford Coll (SC) 609
Worcester Polytechnic Inst (MA) 609
Yale U (CT) 610
York Coll of Pennsylvania (PA) 610
York U (ON, Canada) 611

HUMAN RESOURCES MANAGEMENT

Overview: This major prepares students to manage human resources in businesses and organizations and to provide career management and related services to individual clients. *Related majors:* business administration/management, psychology, labor/personnel relations and studies, organizational behavior, law and legal studies. *Potential careers:* human resources manager, headhunter or recruiter, career counselor, attorney, mediator. *Salary potential:* $35k-$45k.

Abilene Christian U (TX) 260
Amberton U (TX) 265
American International Coll (MA) 267
American U (DC) 267
Anderson Coll (SC) 268
Antioch U McGregor (OH) 270
Arcadia U (PA) 271
Athens State U (AL) 275
Auburn U (AL) 276
Auburn U Montgomery (AL) 276
Baker Coll of Owosso (MI) 279
Ball State U (IN) 280
Barton Coll (NC) 282
Bayamón Central U (PR) 283
Baylor U (TX) 283
Bay Path Coll (MA) 283
Becker Coll (MA) 283
Bellarmine U (KY) 284
Baruch Coll of the City U of NY (NY) 286
Birmingham-Southern Coll (AL) 289
Bishop's U (QC, Canada) 289
Black Hills State U (SD) 290
Bloomfield Coll (NJ) 290
Bluefield Coll (VA) 291
Boston Coll (MA) 292
Bowling Green State U (OH) 292
Brescia U (KY) 293
Briar Cliff U (IA) 294
Brock U (ON, Canada) 295
Cabrini Coll (PA) 298
California Polytechnic State U, San Luis Obispo (CA) 300
California State Polytechnic U, Pomona (CA) 300
California State U, Chico (CA) 300
California State U, Dominguez Hills (CA) 300
California State U, Fresno (CA) 301
California State U, Hayward (CA) 301
California State U, Long Beach (CA) 301
Carleton U (ON, Canada) 305
The Catholic U of America (DC) 307
Central Baptist Coll (AR) 309
Central Michigan U (MI) 310
Central Missouri State U (MO) 310
Chestnut Hill Coll (PA) 312
Clarkson U (NY) 316
Cleary U (MI) 317
Coll of Saint Elizabeth (NJ) 321
The Coll of Southeastern Europe, The American U of Athens(Greece) 323
Colorado Christian U (CO) 325
Colorado Tech U (CO) 326
Colorado Tech U Sioux Falls Campus (SD) 326
Concordia U (QC, Canada) 331
Davenport U, Lansing (MI) 337
DePaul U (IL) 339
DeSales U (PA) 340
Dominican Coll (NY) 344
Dominican U of California (CA) 345
Drexel U (PA) 346
East Central U (OK) 347
Eastern Michigan U (MI) 348
Eastern New Mexico U (NM) 349
Eastern Washington U (WA) 349
Eckerd Coll (FL) 350
École des hautes études commerciales de Montréal (QC, Canada) 350
Excelsior Coll (NY) 356
Faulkner U (AL) 357
Florida Atlantic U (FL) 359
Florida International U (FL) 360
Florida Southern Coll (FL) 361
Florida State U (FL) 361
Framingham State Coll (MA) 362
Franklin U (OH) 364
Freed-Hardeman U (TN) 364
George Fox U (OR) 366
The George Washington U (DC) 367
Georgia Southwestern State U (GA) 368
Georgia State U (GA) 368
Golden Gate U (CA) 369
Governors State U (IL) 370
Grace U (NE) 371
Grand Canyon U (AZ) 371
Grand Valley State U (MI) 371
Gwynedd-Mercy Coll (PA) 374
Harding U (AR) 375
Hastings Coll (NE) 377
Hawai'i Pacific U (HI) 377
Holy Names Coll (CA) 381
Idaho State U (ID) 384
Indiana Inst of Technology (IN) 385
Indiana State U (IN) 385
Indiana U of Pennsylvania (PA) 386
Inter American U of PR, Guayama Campus (PR) 388
Inter American U of PR, San Germán Campus (PR) 388
Ithaca Coll (NY) 390
Judson Coll (IL) 395
Juniata Coll (PA) 395
King's Coll (PA) 398
Kutztown U of Pennsylvania (PA) 399
Lakehead U (ON, Canada) 400
La Salle U (PA) 402
Lewis U (IL) 406
Lincoln U (PA) 407
Lindenwood U (MO) 407
Loras Coll (IA) 410
Louisiana Tech U (LA) 410
Loyola U Chicago (IL) 411
Mansfield U of Pennsylvania (PA) 416
Marietta Coll (OH) 417
Marquette U (WI) 418
Martin U (IN) 419
Marymount U (VA) 420
McGill U (QC, Canada) 423
Medaille Coll (NY) 424
Mercyhurst Coll (PA) 425
Meredith Coll (NC) 426
Mesa State Coll (CO) 426
Messiah Coll (PA) 426
Metropolitan State U (MN) 427
Miami U (OH) 428
Michigan State U (MI) 428
MidAmerica Nazarene U (KS) 428
Millikin U (IL) 430
Muhlenberg Coll (PA) 440
National U (CA) 442
Nazareth Coll of Rochester (NY) 443
Newbury Coll (MA) 444
New York Inst of Technology (NY) 447
Niagara U (NY) 447
Nichols Coll (MA) 448
North Carolina State U (NC) 449
Northeastern Illinois U (IL) 450
Northeastern State U (OK) 450
Northeastern U (MA) 450
Notre Dame Coll (OH) 455
Oakland City U (IN) 456
Oakland U (MI) 456
The Ohio State U (OH) 457
Ohio U (OH) 458
Ohio Valley Coll (WV) 459
Oklahoma Baptist U (OK) 459
Oklahoma State U (OK) 460
Olivet Nazarene U (IL) 461
Our Lady of the Lake U of San Antonio (TX) 463
Pace U (NY) 463
Palm Beach Atlantic U (FL) 465
Peace Coll (NC) 466
Point Park Coll (PA) 471
Pontifical Catholic U of Puerto Rico (PR) 472
Portland State U (OR) 472
Purdue U Calumet (IN) 475

Quinnipiac U (CT) ***476***
Rider U (NJ) ***480***
Robert Morris U (PA) ***481***
Roberts Wesleyan Coll (NY) ***481***
Rockhurst U (MO) ***482***
Roosevelt U (IL) ***483***
Ryerson U (ON, Canada) ***485***
St. Cloud State U (MN) ***488***
Saint Francis U (PA) ***488***
St. John Fisher Coll (NY) ***489***
St. Joseph's Coll, New York (NY) ***491***
St. Joseph's Coll, Suffolk Campus (NY) ***491***
Saint Leo U (FL) ***492***
Saint Louis U (MO) ***492***
Saint Mary-of-the-Woods Coll (IN) ***493***
Saint Mary's Coll of Madonna U (MI) ***493***
Saint Mary's U (NS, Canada) ***494***
Saint Mary's U of Minnesota (MN) ***494***
St. Mary's U of San Antonio (TX) ***494***
Samford U (AL) ***497***
Sam Houston State U (TX) ***497***
San Jose State U (CA) ***499***
Seton Hill U (PA) ***502***
Silver Lake Coll (WI) ***504***
Simpson Coll and Graduate School (CA) ***505***
Southeast Missouri State U (MO) ***508***
Southern Christian U (AL) ***509***
Southwestern Coll (KS) ***512***
Spring Arbor U (MI) ***514***
Springfield Coll (MA) ***514***
State U of NY at Oswego (NY) ***515***
Susquehanna U (PA) ***521***
Tarleton State U (TX) ***522***
Taylor U (IN) ***523***
Temple U (PA) ***523***
Tennessee Wesleyan Coll (TN) ***524***
Texas A&M U–Commerce (TX) ***525***
Texas A&M U–Texarkana (TX) ***525***
Thomas Coll (ME) ***527***
Thomas Edison State Coll (NJ) ***527***
Tiffin U (OH) ***528***
Trinity Christian Coll (IL) ***530***
Trinity International U (IL) ***531***
Troy State U Montgomery (AL) ***532***
U du Québec à Trois-Rivières (QC, Canada) ***536***
U Coll of the Cariboo (BC, Canada) ***537***
The U of Akron (OH) ***537***
U of Alberta (AB, Canada) ***538***
The U of Arizona (AZ) ***538***
U of Baltimore (MD) ***539***
U of Central Oklahoma (OK) ***542***
The U of Findlay (OH) ***545***
U of Florida (FL) ***545***
U of Guelph (ON, Canada) ***546***
U of Hawaii at Manoa (HI) ***546***
U of Idaho (ID) ***547***
U of Indianapolis (IN) ***548***
The U of Iowa (IA) ***548***
The U of Lethbridge (AB, Canada) ***549***
U of Maryland, Coll Park (MD) ***552***
U of Maryland University Coll (MD) ***552***
U of Miami (FL) ***553***
U of Michigan–Flint (MI) ***554***
U of Minnesota, Duluth (MN) ***554***
U of Nebraska at Omaha (NE) ***557***
U of Nevada, Las Vegas (NV) ***558***
U of Nevada, Reno (NV) ***558***
U of New Brunswick Fredericton (NB, Canada) ***558***
U of New Brunswick Saint John (NB, Canada) ***558***
U of New Haven (CT) ***559***
The U of North Carolina at Chapel Hill (NC) ***560***
U of Ottawa (ON, Canada) ***563***
U of Pennsylvania (PA) ***563***
U of Puerto Rico, Humacao U Coll (PR) ***570***
U of Puerto Rico, Río Piedras (PR) ***571***
U of Saint Francis (IN) ***573***
U of St. Thomas (MN) ***573***
U of Saskatchewan (SK, Canada) ***574***
The U of Scranton (PA) ***574***
The U of South Dakota (SD) ***575***
The U of Texas at San Antonio (TX) ***578***
U of Toledo (OH) ***581***
U of Waterloo (ON, Canada) ***583***
U of Windsor (ON, Canada) ***584***
U of Wisconsin–Milwaukee (WI) ***585***
U of Wisconsin–Whitewater (WI) ***586***
U System Coll for Lifelong Learning (NH) ***586***
Urbana U (OH) ***587***
Ursuline Coll (OH) ***587***
Utah State U (UT) ***587***
Valley City State U (ND) ***588***
Vanderbilt U (TN) ***588***
Virginia Polytechnic Inst and State U (VA) ***591***
Viterbo U (WI) ***591***
Washington U in St. Louis (MO) ***595***
Weber State U (UT) ***596***
Webster U (MO) ***597***
Western Illinois U (IL) ***599***
Western Michigan U (MI) ***599***
Western State Coll of Colorado (CO) ***600***
Western Washington U (WA) ***600***
Westminster Coll (UT) ***601***
Wichita State U (KS) ***604***
Wilmington Coll (DE) ***607***
Winona State U (MN) ***608***
Worcester State Coll (MA) ***609***
Xavier U (OH) ***610***
York Coll (NE) ***610***
York U (ON, Canada) ***611***

HUMAN RESOURCES MANAGEMENT RELATED

Information can be found under this major's main heading.

Bloomfield Coll (NJ) ***290***
Capella U (MN) ***304***
Columbia Southern U (AL) ***327***
Limestone Coll (SC) ***406***
Park U (MO) ***465***

HUMAN SERVICES

Overview: This broad-based major gives students a strong understanding of the range of social and human services available to individuals and communities, while preparing students for a career as a social worker. *Related majors:* community organization and advocacy, public administration, public health, social work. *Potential careers:* social worker, community liaison, attorney, public health worker. *Salary potential:* $19k-$28k.

Adrian Coll (MI) ***260***
Alaska Pacific U (AK) ***261***
Albertus Magnus Coll (CT) ***262***
Albion Coll (MI) ***262***
American International Coll (MA) ***267***
Anderson Coll (SC) ***268***
Antioch U McGregor (OH) ***270***
Arcadia U (PA) ***271***
Assumption Coll (MA) ***275***
Baldwin-Wallace Coll (OH) ***280***
Becker Coll (MA) ***283***
Bethel Coll (IN) ***288***
Bethel Coll (TN) ***288***
Black Hills State U (SD) ***290***
Burlington Coll (VT) ***297***
California State U, Dominguez Hills (CA) ***300***
California State U, San Bernardino (CA) ***302***
Calumet Coll of Saint Joseph (IN) ***302***
Carson-Newman Coll (TN) ***306***
Cazenovia Coll (NY) ***308***
Champlain Coll (VT) ***311***
Coll of Notre Dame of Maryland (MD) ***321***
Coll of St. Joseph (VT) ***322***
Coll of Saint Mary (NE) ***322***
Cornell U (NY) ***333***
Dakota Wesleyan U (SD) ***336***
Delaware State U (DE) ***338***
Doane Coll (NE) ***344***
Elmira Coll (NY) ***351***
Elon U (NC) ***352***
The Evergreen State Coll (WA) ***355***
Fairmont State Coll (WV) ***356***
Finlandia U (MI) ***358***
Fitchburg State Coll (MA) ***358***
Florida Gulf Coast U (FL) ***359***
Fontbonne U (MO) ***361***
Framingham State Coll (MA) ***362***
The Franciscan U (IA) ***363***
Geneva Coll (PA) ***366***
The George Washington U (DC) ***367***
Grace Bible Coll (MI) ***370***
Graceland U (IA) ***371***
Grand View Coll (IA) ***372***
Hannibal-LaGrange Coll (MO) ***375***
Hastings Coll (NE) ***377***
Hawai'i Pacific U (HI) ***377***
High Point U (NC) ***379***
Hilbert Coll (NY) ***379***
Holy Names Coll (CA) ***381***
Indiana Inst of Technology (IN) ***385***
Inter American U of PR, Aguadilla Campus (PR) ***388***
Judson Coll (IL) ***395***
Kendall Coll (IL) ***396***
Kentucky Wesleyan Coll (KY) ***397***
LaGrange Coll (GA) ***400***
Lake Erie Coll (OH) ***400***
La Roche Coll (PA) ***402***
Lasell Coll (MA) ***402***
Lenoir-Rhyne Coll (NC) ***405***
Lesley U (MA) ***405***
Lincoln U (PA) ***407***
Lindenwood U (MO) ***407***
Lindsey Wilson Coll (KY) ***407***
Mansfield U of Pennsylvania (PA) ***416***
Marian Coll of Fond du Lac (WI) ***417***
Martin Methodist Coll (TN) ***418***
Medaille Coll (NY) ***424***
Mercer U (GA) ***425***
Merrimack Coll (MA) ***426***
Mesa State Coll (CO) ***426***
Metropolitan Coll of New York (NY) ***427***
Metropolitan State Coll of Denver (CO) ***427***
Metropolitan State U (MN) ***427***
Midland Lutheran Coll (NE) ***429***
Millikin U (IL) ***430***
Missouri Valley Coll (MO) ***433***
Montreat Coll (NC) ***435***
Mount Olive Coll (NC) ***439***
Mount Saint Mary Coll (NY) ***439***
National-Louis U (IL) ***442***
Northeastern U (MA) ***450***
Northern Kentucky U (KY) ***451***
Notre Dame de Namur U (CA) ***455***
Ottawa U (KS) ***462***
Pacific Oaks Coll (CA) ***464***
Park U (MO) ***465***
Pikeville Coll (KY) ***470***
Quincy U (IL) ***476***
Quinnipiac U (CT) ***476***
Roosevelt U (IL) ***483***
St. Joseph's Coll, New York (NY) ***491***
Saint Joseph's U (PA) ***491***
Saint Leo U (FL) ***492***
Saint Mary-of-the-Woods Coll (IN) ***493***
Salem International U (WV) ***496***
Seton Hill U (PA) ***502***
Siena Heights U (MI) ***504***
Simmons Coll (MA) ***504***
Southwest Baptist U (MO) ***512***
Springfield Coll (MA) ***514***
State U of NY Empire State Coll (NY) ***517***
Suffolk U (MA) ***520***
Tennessee Wesleyan Coll (TN) ***524***
Texas A&M U–Kingsville (TX) ***525***
Touro Coll (NY) ***529***
Trinity Western U (BC, Canada) ***531***
Tyndale Coll & Seminary (ON, Canada) ***533***
U of Baltimore (MD) ***539***
U of Bridgeport (CT) ***540***
U of Great Falls (MT) ***545***
U of Maine at Machias (ME) ***551***
U of Massachusetts Boston (MA) ***553***
U of Minnesota, Morris (MN) ***555***
U of Nevada, Las Vegas (NV) ***558***
U of New England (ME) ***558***
U of Oregon (OR) ***562***
U of Phoenix–Sacramento Campus (CA) ***567***
U of Rhode Island (RI) ***572***
The U of Scranton (PA) ***574***
The U of Tennessee at Chattanooga (TN) ***577***
The U of Texas–Pan American (TX) ***579***
U of Wisconsin–Oshkosh (WI) ***585***
Upper Iowa U (IA) ***587***
Villanova U (PA) ***590***
Virginia Polytechnic Inst and State U (VA) ***591***
Virginia Wesleyan Coll (VA) ***591***
Walsh U (OH) ***593***
Western Washington U (WA) ***600***
William Penn U (IA) ***606***
Wingate U (NC) ***607***

INDIVIDUAL/FAMILY DEVELOPMENT

Overview: This major focuses on human development and behavior within the family context. *Related majors:* marriage and family counseling, child growth, care and developmental studies, gerontology, family living/parenthood. *Potential careers:* family counselor, psychiatrist, social services worker, researcher. *Salary potential:* $21k-$27k.

Abilene Christian U (TX) ***260***
Amberton U (TX) ***265***
Antioch Coll (OH) ***269***
Antioch U McGregor (OH) ***270***
Ashland U (OH) ***274***
Auburn U (AL) ***276***
Baylor U (TX) ***283***
Boston Coll (MA) ***292***
Bowling Green State U (OH) ***292***
California State U, Hayward (CA) ***301***
California State U, Long Beach (CA) ***301***
California State U, San Bernardino (CA) ***302***
Cameron U (OK) ***303***
Christian Heritage Coll (CA) ***313***
Colorado State U (CO) ***325***
Concordia U (MI) ***330***
Cornell U (NY) ***333***
Crown Coll (MN) ***334***
East Carolina U (NC) ***347***
Eastern Michigan U (MI) ***348***
Eckerd Coll (FL) ***350***
Florida State U (FL) ***361***
Geneva Coll (PA) ***366***
Georgia Southern U (GA) ***367***
Goddard Coll (VT) ***369***
Hampshire Coll (MA) ***375***
Harvard U (MA) ***376***
Hawai'i Pacific U (HI) ***377***
Hellenic Coll (MA) ***378***
Hope International U (CA) ***381***
Indiana State U (IN) ***385***
Indiana U Bloomington (IN) ***385***
Indiana U of Pennsylvania (PA) ***386***
Kansas State U (KS) ***396***
Kent State U (OH) ***397***
Kentucky State U (KY) ***397***
Lee U (TN) ***404***
Louisiana State U and A&M Coll (LA) ***410***
Miami U (OH) ***428***
Mitchell Coll (CT) ***433***
Murray State U (KY) ***440***
National-Louis U (IL) ***442***
Northern Illinois U (IL) ***450***
The Ohio State U (OH) ***457***
Ohio U (OH) ***458***
Oregon State U (OR) ***462***
Pacific Oaks Coll (CA) ***464***
Penn State U Altoona Coll (PA) ***467***
Penn State U Univ Park Campus (PA) ***468***
Prescott Coll (AZ) ***474***
Purdue U (IN) ***475***
Radford U (VA) ***476***
St. Olaf Coll (MN) ***495***
Samford U (AL) ***497***
Sarah Lawrence Coll (NY) ***499***
Seton Hill U (PA) ***502***
South Dakota State U (SD) ***507***
Southeast Missouri State U (MO) ***508***
Southern U and A&M Coll (LA) ***511***
Southwest Missouri State U (MO) ***513***
Southwest Texas State U (TX) ***513***
State U of NY at Oswego (NY) ***515***
State U of NY Empire State Coll (NY) ***517***
Stephen F. Austin State U (TX) ***518***
Syracuse U (NY) ***521***
Texas Tech U (TX) ***526***
Texas Woman's U (TX) ***527***
Trinity Coll (DC) ***530***
The U of Alabama (AL) ***537***
The U of Arizona (AZ) ***538***
U of Arkansas (AR) ***539***
U of Calif, Davis (CA) ***540***
U of Calif, Riverside (CA) ***541***
U of Connecticut (CT) ***544***
U of Delaware (DE) ***544***
U of Georgia (GA) ***545***
U of Hawaii at Manoa (HI) ***546***
U of Houston (TX) ***547***

INDIVIDUAL/FAMILY DEVELOPMENT (continued)

U of Illinois at Urbana–Champaign (IL) ***548***
U of Maine (ME) ***550***
The U of Memphis (TN) ***553***
U of Missouri–Columbia (MO) ***555***
U of Nevada, Reno (NV) ***558***
U of New England (ME) ***558***
The U of North Carolina at Charlotte (NC) ***560***
The U of North Carolina at Greensboro (NC) ***560***
U of Rhode Island (RI) ***572***
The U of Tennessee (TN) ***577***
The U of Texas at Austin (TX) ***578***
U of Utah (UT) ***582***
U of Vermont (VT) ***582***
U of Wisconsin–Stout (WI) ***586***
Utah State U (UT) ***587***
Vanderbilt U (TN) ***588***
Warner Pacific Coll (OR) ***593***
Washington State U (WA) ***595***
Wheelock Coll (MA) ***603***
Youngstown State U (OH) ***611***

INDIVIDUAL/FAMILY DEVELOPMENT RELATED

Information can be found under this major's main heading.

Saint Mary's U of Minnesota (MN) ***494***
U of Louisiana at Lafayette (LA) ***550***

INDUSTRIAL ARTS

Overview: Students who choose this major study the organization, systems, and resources of technology and how industry is affected by technology. *Related majors:* any of the industrial arts. *Potential careers:* industrial arts, technology teacher education, industrial art education. *Salary potential:* $20k-$25k.

Andrews U (MI) ***269***
Appalachian State U (NC) ***270***
Ball State U (IN) ***280***
Bemidji State U (MN) ***285***
Berea Coll (KY) ***286***
California State U, Fresno (CA) ***301***
Coll of the Ozarks (MO) ***323***
Colorado State U (CO) ***325***
Colorado State U-Pueblo (CO) ***325***
Eastern Kentucky U (KY) ***348***
Elizabeth City State U (NC) ***351***
Fairmont State Coll (WV) ***356***
Fitchburg State Coll (MA) ***358***
Florida A&M U (FL) ***359***
Fort Hays State U (KS) ***362***
Humboldt State U (CA) ***382***
Jackson State U (MS) ***390***
Keene State Coll (NH) ***396***
Langston U (OK) ***402***
McPherson Coll (KS) ***423***
Millersville U of Pennsylvania (PA) ***430***
Minnesota State U, Mankato (MN) ***431***
Montclair State U (NJ) ***435***
Murray State U (KY) ***440***
New Mexico Highlands U (NM) ***446***
North Carolina Ag and Tech State U (NC) ***448***
Northeastern State U (OK) ***450***
Northern State U (SD) ***451***
Ohio Northern U (OH) ***457***
Oklahoma Panhandle State U (OK) ***460***
Oklahoma State U (OK) ***460***
Pacific Union Coll (CA) ***464***
Pittsburg State U (KS) ***470***
Rhode Island Coll (RI) ***479***
St. Cloud State U (MN) ***488***
St. John Fisher Coll (NY) ***489***
San Diego State U (CA) ***498***
San Francisco State U (CA) ***498***
South Carolina State U (SC) ***506***
Southern Utah U (UT) ***511***
Southwestern Oklahoma State U (OK) ***512***
State U of NY at Oswego (NY) ***515***
State U of NY Coll at Buffalo (NY) ***516***
Sul Ross State U (TX) ***521***
Tarleton State U (TX) ***522***
Tennessee State U (TN) ***523***
Texas A&M U–Commerce (TX) ***525***
U of Alberta (AB, Canada) ***538***
The U of British Columbia (BC, Canada) ***540***
U of Maryland Eastern Shore (MD) ***552***
The U of Montana–Western (MT) ***556***
U of Southern Maine (ME) ***576***
U of the District of Columbia (DC) ***580***
U of Wisconsin–Platteville (WI) ***585***
Walla Walla Coll (WA) ***593***
Western State Coll of Colorado (CO) ***600***
William Penn U (IA) ***606***

INDUSTRIAL ARTS EDUCATION

Overview: This major prepares undergraduates to teach industrial arts or technology subjects to students from a variety of educational levels. *Related majors:* drafting, computer installing and repairing, auto mechanic/technician, machine technology, fashion design and illustration. *Potential careers:* industrial arts teacher, vocational teacher. *Salary potential:* $24k-$35k.

Abilene Christian U (TX) ***260***
Alcorn State U (MS) ***263***
Black Hills State U (SD) ***290***
Brigham Young U (UT) ***295***
California State U, Stanislaus (CA) ***302***
Central Connecticut State U (CT) ***309***
Central Michigan U (MI) ***310***
Central Missouri State U (MO) ***310***
Central Washington U (WA) ***310***
Chadron State Coll (NE) ***311***
Clemson U (SC) ***317***
The Coll of New Jersey (NJ) ***320***
Coll of the Ozarks (MO) ***323***
Concordia U (NE) ***330***
Eastern Michigan U (MI) ***348***
Georgia Southern U (GA) ***367***
Grambling State U (LA) ***371***
Illinois State U (IL) ***384***
Jackson State U (MS) ***390***
Kean U (NJ) ***396***
Kent State U (OH) ***397***
Middle Tennessee State U (TN) ***429***
Millersville U of Pennsylvania (PA) ***430***
Mississippi State U (MS) ***432***
Montana State U–Bozeman (MT) ***434***
Morehead State U (KY) ***436***
New York Inst of Technology (NY) ***447***
Northern Arizona U (AZ) ***450***
Northern Illinois U (IL) ***450***
The Ohio State U (OH) ***457***
Oklahoma Panhandle State U (OK) ***460***
Purdue U (IN) ***475***
Southeast Missouri State U (MO) ***508***
Southwestern Oklahoma State U (OK) ***512***
Southwest Missouri State U (MO) ***513***
Texas Southern U (TX) ***526***
Texas Wesleyan U (TX) ***526***
U of Central Arkansas (AR) ***542***
U of Georgia (GA) ***545***
U of Hawaii at Manoa (HI) ***546***
U of Idaho (ID) ***547***
U of Nebraska–Lincoln (NE) ***557***
U of Nevada, Reno (NV) ***558***
U of New Mexico (NM) ***559***
U of Northern Iowa (IA) ***561***
U of Southern Mississippi (MS) ***576***
U of Wisconsin–Stout (WI) ***586***
U of Wyoming (WY) ***586***
Utah State U (UT) ***587***
Valley City State U (ND) ***588***
Virginia Polytechnic Inst and State U (VA) ***591***
Viterbo U (WI) ***591***

INDUSTRIAL DESIGN

Overview: This major teaches students how to create visual elements and objects, as well as packaging for manufactured products, for commercial and industrial uses. *Related majors:* design and visual communication, graphic design, commercial art and illustration, plastics technology, engineering design. *Potential careers:* packaging or product designer, digital artist, furniture designer, automobile designer, architect. *Salary potential:* $26k-$40k.

Academy of Art Coll (CA) ***260***
Appalachian State U (NC) ***270***
Arizona State U (AZ) ***271***
Art Center Coll of Design (CA) ***273***
The Art Inst of Colorado (CO) ***274***
Auburn U (AL) ***276***
Brigham Young U (UT) ***295***
California Coll of Arts and Crafts (CA) ***299***
California State U, Long Beach (CA) ***301***
California State U, Northridge (CA) ***301***
Campbell U (NC) ***303***
Carleton U (ON, Canada) ***305***
Carnegie Mellon U (PA) ***305***
Clemson U (SC) ***317***
The Cleveland Inst of Art (OH) ***317***
Col for Creative Studies (MI) ***319***
Columbus Coll of Art and Design (OH) ***328***
Fashion Inst of Technology (NY) ***357***
Finlandia U (MI) ***358***
Georgia Inst of Technology (GA) ***367***
Kansas City Art Inst (MO) ***395***
Kean U (NJ) ***396***
Kendall Coll of Art and Design of Ferris State U (MI) ***396***
Massachusetts Coll of Art (MA) ***421***
Metropolitan State Coll of Denver (CO) ***427***
Milwaukee Inst of Art and Design (WI) ***431***
North Carolina State U (NC) ***449***
Northern Michigan U (MI) ***451***
The Ohio State U (OH) ***457***
Parsons School of Design, New School U (NY) ***465***
Philadelphia U (PA) ***469***
Pittsburg State U (KS) ***470***
Pratt Inst (NY) ***473***
Rhode Island School of Design (RI) ***479***
Rochester Inst of Technology (NY) ***482***
San Francisco State U (CA) ***498***
San Jose State U (CA) ***499***
Savannah Coll of Art and Design (GA) ***499***
Syracuse U (NY) ***521***
U of Alberta (AB, Canada) ***538***
U of Bridgeport (CT) ***540***
U of Cincinnati (OH) ***543***
U of Illinois at Chicago (IL) ***547***
U of Illinois at Urbana–Champaign (IL) ***548***
U of Louisiana at Lafayette (LA) ***550***
U of Michigan (MI) ***554***
U of San Francisco (CA) ***574***
The U of the Arts (PA) ***579***
U of Washington (WA) ***583***
U of Wisconsin–Platteville (WI) ***585***
Virginia Polytechnic Inst and State U (VA) ***591***
Wentworth Inst of Technology (MA) ***597***
Western Michigan U (MI) ***599***
Western Washington U (WA) ***600***

INDUSTRIAL ELECTRONICS INSTALLATION/REPAIR

Overview: This major gives students the technical knowledge they need to plan, assemble, install, maintain, and fix electrical and electronic machines and devices that are used in either industrial or commercial settings. *Related majors:* electrical/power transmission installation; electronics equipment installation and repair; heating, air conditioning, and refrigeration mechanics. *Potential careers:* electrician, computer technician, building manager. *Salary potential:* $17k-$25k.

Lewis-Clark State Coll (ID) ***406***

INDUSTRIAL/MANUFACTURING ENGINEERING

Overview: This major teaches students the scientific principles behind incorporating systems of people, material, information, and energy into a manufacturing system. *Related majors:* mechanical engineering, structural engineering, mathematics, physics, computer engineering. *Potential careers:* industrial engineer, plant manager, construction manager, management consultant. *Salary potential:* $40k-$55k.

Arizona State U (AZ) ***271***
Auburn U (AL) ***276***
Boston U (MA) ***292***
Bradley U (IL) ***293***
California Polytechnic State U, San Luis Obispo (CA) ***300***
California State Polytechnic U, Pomona (CA) ***300***
California State U, Fresno (CA) ***301***
California State U, Hayward (CA) ***301***
California State U, Northridge (CA) ***301***
Central Michigan U (MI) ***310***
Clarkson U (NY) ***316***
Clemson U (SC) ***317***
Cleveland State U (OH) ***317***
The Coll of Southeastern Europe, The American U of Athens(Greece) ***323***
Colorado State U-Pueblo (CO) ***325***
Columbia U, School of Engineering & Applied Sci (NY) ***328***
Concordia U (QC, Canada) ***331***
Cornell U (NY) ***333***
Dalhousie U (NS, Canada) ***336***
Drexel U (PA) ***346***
Eastern Nazarene Coll (MA) ***348***
Elizabethtown Coll (PA) ***351***
State U of NY at Farmingdale (NY) ***357***
Ferris State U (MI) ***358***
Florida A&M U (FL) ***359***
Florida State U (FL) ***361***
Georgia Inst of Technology (GA) ***367***
Grand Valley State U (MI) ***371***
Hofstra U (NY) ***380***
Insto Tecno Estudios Sups Monterrey(Mexico) ***388***
Iowa State U of Science and Technology (IA) ***390***
Johns Hopkins U (MD) ***392***
Kansas State U (KS) ***396***
Kent State U (OH) ***397***
Kettering U (MI) ***398***
Lamar U (TX) ***401***
Lawrence Technological U (MI) ***403***
Lehigh U (PA) ***404***
Louisiana State U and A&M Coll (LA) ***410***
Louisiana Tech U (LA) ***410***
Marquette U (WI) ***418***
McMaster U (ON, Canada) ***423***
Memorial U of Newfoundland (NF, Canada) ***424***
Mercer U (GA) ***425***
Miami U (OH) ***428***
Michigan Technological U (MI) ***428***
Midwestern State U (TX) ***430***
Milwaukee School of Engineering (WI) ***431***
Mississippi State U (MS) ***432***
Montana State U–Bozeman (MT) ***434***
Morgan State U (MD) ***436***
New Jersey Inst of Technology (NJ) ***445***
New Mexico State U (NM) ***446***
New York Inst of Technology (NY) ***447***
North Carolina Ag and Tech State U (NC) ***448***
North Carolina State U (NC) ***449***
North Dakota State U (ND) ***449***
Northeastern U (MA) ***450***
Northern Illinois U (IL) ***450***
Northern Kentucky U (KY) ***451***
Northwestern U (IL) ***453***
The Ohio State U (OH) ***457***
Ohio U (OH) ***458***
Oklahoma State U (OK) ***460***
Oregon State U (OR) ***462***
Penn State U Univ Park Campus (PA) ***468***
Purdue U (IN) ***475***
Purdue U Calumet (IN) ***475***
Rensselaer Polytechnic Inst (NY) ***478***
Robert Morris U (PA) ***481***
Rochester Inst of Technology (NY) ***482***
Rutgers, The State U of New Jersey, New Brunswick (NJ) ***485***
Ryerson U (ON, Canada) ***485***
St. Ambrose U (IA) ***486***
St. Cloud State U (MN) ***488***

St. Mary's U of San Antonio (TX) **494**
San Jose State U (CA) **499**
Seattle U (WA) **501**
South Dakota School of Mines and Technology (SD) **507**
Southern Illinois U Edwardsville (IL) **509**
Southwest Texas State U (TX) **513**
Stanford U (CA) **514**
State U of NY at Binghamton (NY) **515**
Tennessee State U (TN) **523**
Tennessee Technological U (TN) **524**
Texas A&M U (TX) **524**
Texas A&M U–Commerce (TX) **525**
Texas A&M U–Kingsville (TX) **525**
Texas Tech U (TX) **526**
Tufts U (MA) **533**
U du Québec à Trois-Rivières (QC, Canada) **536**
U at Buffalo, The State University of New York (NY) **536**
The U of Alabama (AL) **537**
The U of Alabama in Huntsville (AL) **537**
The U of Arizona (AZ) **538**
U of Arkansas (AR) **539**
U of Calgary (AB, Canada) **540**
U of Calif, Berkeley (CA) **540**
U of Central Florida (FL) **542**
U of Cincinnati (OH) **543**
U of Connecticut (CT) **544**
U of Florida (FL) **545**
U of Hartford (CT) **546**
U of Houston (TX) **547**
U of Idaho (ID) **547**
U of Illinois at Chicago (IL) **547**
U of Illinois at Urbana–Champaign (IL) **548**
The U of Iowa (IA) **548**
U of Louisville (KY) **550**
U of Manitoba (MB, Canada) **551**
U of Massachusetts Amherst (MA) **552**
The U of Memphis (TN) **553**
U of Miami (FL) **553**
U of Michigan (MI) **554**
U of Michigan–Dearborn (MI) **554**
U of Minnesota, Duluth (MN) **554**
U of Minnesota, Twin Cities Campus (MN) **555**
U of Missouri–Columbia (MO) **555**
U of Nebraska–Lincoln (NE) **557**
U of New Haven (CT) **559**
U of New Mexico (NM) **559**
U of Oklahoma (OK) **562**
U of Pittsburgh (PA) **569**
U of Regina (SK, Canada) **572**
U of Rhode Island (RI) **572**
U of San Diego (CA) **574**
U of Southern California (CA) **576**
U of South Florida (FL) **576**
The U of Tennessee (TN) **577**
The U of Tennessee at Chattanooga (TN) **577**
The U of Texas at Arlington (TX) **577**
The U of Texas at Dallas (TX) **578**
The U of Texas at El Paso (TX) **578**
The U of Texas–Pan American (TX) **579**
U of Toledo (OH) **581**
U of Toronto (ON, Canada) **581**
U of Washington (WA) **583**
U of Windsor (ON, Canada) **584**
U of Wisconsin–Madison (WI) **584**
U of Wisconsin–Milwaukee (WI) **585**
U of Wisconsin–Platteville (WI) **585**
U of Wisconsin–Stout (WI) **586**
Virginia Polytechnic Inst and State U (VA) **591**
Virginia State U (VA) **591**
Washington State U (WA) **595**
Wayne State U (MI) **596**
Western Michigan U (MI) **599**
Western New England Coll (MA) **600**
West Virginia U (WV) **602**
Wichita State U (KS) **604**
Worcester Polytechnic Inst (MA) **609**
Youngstown State U (OH) **611**

INDUSTRIAL PRODUCTION TECHNOLOGIES RELATED

Information can be found under this major's main heading.

Chadron State Coll (NE) **311**
East Carolina U (NC) **347**
Georgia Southern U (GA) **367**
Indiana State U (IN) **385**
Pennsylvania Coll of Technology (PA) **467**
Southwestern Coll (KS) **512**
The U of Akron (OH) **537**
U of Nebraska–Lincoln (NE) **557**
U of Wisconsin–Stout (WI) **586**
Utah State U (UT) **587**
Wayne State U (MI) **596**
Western Kentucky U (KY) **599**

INDUSTRIAL RADIOLOGIC TECHNOLOGY

Overview: This major will teach students the scientific principles and technical skills to operate industrial and research testing equipment using radioisotopes. *Related majors:* physics, mathematics, materials science. *Potential careers:* X-ray technician, testing and inspection manager, quality control manager. *Salary potential:* $28k-$38k.

Alderson-Broaddus Coll (WV) **263**
Andrews U (MI) **269**
Armstrong Atlantic State U (GA) **273**
Baker Coll of Owosso (MI) **279**
Briar Cliff U (IA) **294**
California State U, Northridge (CA) **301**
Columbus State U (GA) **328**
Concordia U Wisconsin (WI) **331**
Francis Marion U (SC) **363**
Howard U (DC) **382**
Jamestown Coll (ND) **391**
Madonna U (MI) **414**
Marian Coll of Fond du Lac (WI) **417**
Mars Hill Coll (NC) **418**
National-Louis U (IL) **442**
Newman U (KS) **445**
Oregon Inst of Technology (OR) **461**
Saint Mary's Coll of Madonna U (MI) **493**
Thomas Jefferson U (PA) **527**
U of Arkansas for Medical Sciences (AR) **539**
U of Maryland Eastern Shore (MD) **552**
U of Oklahoma Health Sciences Center (OK) **562**
U of Sioux Falls (SD) **574**
William Carey Coll (MS) **605**

INDUSTRIAL TECHNOLOGY

Overview: This major prepares undergraduates to work with industrial engineers and managers and gives them the knowledge and skills they need to identify and resolve production problems in manufactured products. *Related majors:* engineering/industrial management, operations management and supervision, logistics and materials management, instrumentation technology. *Potential careers:* plant manager or technician, quality control manager, repairperson, machinist, business consultant. *Salary potential:* $28k-$40k.

Abilene Christian U (TX) **260**
Alcorn State U (MS) **263**
Andrews U (MI) **269**
Arizona State U East (AZ) **271**
Baker Coll of Flint (MI) **279**
Ball State U (IN) **280**
Bemidji State U (MN) **285**
Berea Coll (KY) **286**
Black Hills State U (SD) **290**
Bowling Green State U (OH) **292**
Bradley U (IL) **293**
California Polytechnic State U, San Luis Obispo (CA) **300**
California State U, Chico (CA) **300**
California State U, Fresno (CA) **301**
California State U, Long Beach (CA) **301**
California U of Pennsylvania (PA) **302**
Central Connecticut State U (CT) **309**
Central Missouri State U (MO) **310**
Central Washington U (WA) **310**
Cheyney U of Pennsylvania (PA) **312**
Colorado State U (CO) **325**
East Carolina U (NC) **347**
Eastern Illinois U (IL) **348**
Eastern Kentucky U (KY) **348**
Eastern Michigan U (MI) **348**
Eastern Washington U (WA) **349**
Elizabeth City State U (NC) **351**
Excelsior Coll (NY) **356**
Fairmont State Coll (WV) **356**
State U of NY at Farmingdale (NY) **357**
Ferris State U (MI) **358**
Fitchburg State Coll (MA) **358**
Georgia Southern U (GA) **367**
Grambling State U (LA) **371**
Illinois Inst of Technology (IL) **384**
Illinois State U (IL) **384**
Indiana State U (IN) **385**
Indiana U–Purdue U Fort Wayne (IN) **386**
Insto Tecno Estudios Sups Monterrey(Mexico) **388**
Jackson State U (MS) **390**
Jacksonville State U (AL) **390**
Kean U (NJ) **396**
Keene State Coll (NH) **396**
Kent State U (OH) **397**
Lamar U (TX) **401**
Langston U (OK) **402**
Metropolitan State Coll of Denver (CO) **427**
Middle Tennessee State U (TN) **429**
Millersville U of Pennsylvania (PA) **430**
Minnesota State U, Mankato (MN) **431**
Minnesota State U, Moorhead (MN) **432**
Mississippi State U (MS) **432**
Mississippi Valley State U (MS) **432**
Montana State U–Northern (MT) **434**
Montclair State U (NJ) **435**
Morehead State U (KY) **436**
Murray State U (KY) **440**
North Carolina Ag and Tech State U (NC) **448**
Northeastern State U (OK) **450**
Northeastern U (MA) **450**
Northern Illinois U (IL) **450**
Northern Kentucky U (KY) **451**
Northern Michigan U (MI) **451**
Northwestern State U of Louisiana (LA) **453**
Ohio Northern U (OH) **457**
Ohio U (OH) **458**
Oklahoma Panhandle State U (OK) **460**
Oklahoma State U (OK) **460**
Oregon Inst of Technology (OR) **461**
Pacific Union Coll (CA) **464**
Pennsylvania Coll of Technology (PA) **467**
Pittsburg State U (KS) **470**
Prairie View A&M U (TX) **473**
Purdue U (IN) **475**
Purdue U Calumet (IN) **475**
Rhode Island Coll (RI) **479**
Rochester Inst of Technology (NY) **482**
Roger Williams U (RI) **483**
Rowan U (NJ) **484**
Saginaw Valley State U (MI) **486**
Saint Mary's U of Minnesota (MN) **494**
Sam Houston State U (TX) **497**
San Jose State U (CA) **499**
South Carolina State U (SC) **506**
South Dakota State U (SD) **507**
Southeastern Louisiana U (LA) **508**
Southeastern Oklahoma State U (OK) **508**
Southeast Missouri State U (MO) **508**
Southern Arkansas U–Magnolia (AR) **509**
Southern Illinois U Carbondale (IL) **509**
Southern Polytechnic State U (GA) **511**
Southwestern Coll (KS) **512**
Southwestern Oklahoma State U (OK) **512**
Southwest Texas State U (TX) **513**
State U of NY Coll at Buffalo (NY) **516**
State U of NY Inst of Tech at Utica/Rome (NY) **518**
Tarleton State U (TX) **522**
Tennessee State U (TN) **523**
Tennessee Technological U (TN) **524**
Texas A&M U–Kingsville (TX) **525**
Texas Southern U (TX) **526**
Thomas Edison State Coll (NJ) **527**
The U of Akron (OH) **537**
U of Arkansas at Fort Smith (AR) **539**
U of Dayton (OH) **544**
U of Houston (TX) **547**
U of Idaho (ID) **547**
U of Louisiana at Lafayette (LA) **550**
U of Nebraska–Lincoln (NE) **557**
U of New Haven (CT) **559**
The U of North Carolina at Charlotte (NC) **560**
U of North Dakota (ND) **561**
U of Northern Iowa (IA) **561**
U of North Texas (TX) **562**
U of Puerto Rico at Arecibo (PR) **570**
U of Rio Grande (OH) **572**
U of Southern Mississippi (MS) **576**
U of Toledo (OH) **581**
The U of West Alabama (AL) **583**
U of West Florida (FL) **583**
U of Wisconsin–Platteville (WI) **585**
U of Wisconsin–Stout (WI) **586**
Wayne State U (MI) **596**
Weber State U (UT) **596**
Western Carolina U (NC) **598**
Western Illinois U (IL) **599**
Western Kentucky U (KY) **599**
Western Michigan U (MI) **599**
Western Washington U (WA) **600**
West Texas A&M U (TX) **602**
West Virginia U Inst of Technology (WV) **602**
William Penn U (IA) **606**

INFORMATION SCIENCES/ SYSTEMS

Overview: Students will learn how traditional and electronic information is collected, organized, processed, transmitted, and utilized. *Related majors:* computer programming, data processing technology, computer systems networking, economics, statistics, library science. *Potential careers:* computer programmer, librarian, researcher, statistician, economist, marketing researcher. *Salary potential:* $30k-$50k.

Alabama State U (AL) **261**
Albertus Magnus Coll (CT) **262**
Albright Coll (PA) **263**
Alfred U (NY) **263**
Alliant International U (CA) **264**
Alma Coll (MI) **264**
Alvernia Coll (PA) **265**
American Coll of Computer & Information Sciences (AL) **266**
American International Coll (MA) **267**
American U (DC) **267**
The American U in Dubai(United Arab Emirates) **267**
Anderson U (IN) **268**
Andrews U (MI) **269**
Aquinas Coll (MI) **270**
Armstrong Atlantic State U (GA) **273**
Ashland U (OH) **274**
Athabasca U (AB, Canada) **275**
Athens State U (AL) **275**
Atlantic Union Coll (MA) **276**
Averett U (VA) **278**
Avila U (MO) **278**
Baker Coll of Cadillac (MI) **279**
Baker Coll of Flint (MI) **279**
Baker Coll of Jackson (MI) **279**
Baker Coll of Muskegon (MI) **279**
Baker Coll of Owosso (MI) **279**
Baker Coll of Port Huron (MI) **280**
Baker U (KS) **280**
Baldwin-Wallace Coll (OH) **280**
Ball State U (IN) **280**
Barry U (FL) **282**
Belhaven Coll (MS) **283**
Belmont Abbey Coll (NC) **284**
Belmont U (TN) **284**
Bemidji State U (MN) **285**
Benedictine U (IL) **285**
Baruch Coll of the City U of NY (NY) **286**
Berry Coll (GA) **287**
Bethune-Cookman Coll (FL) **289**
Bloomfield Coll (NJ) **290**
Boston U (MA) **292**
Bradley U (IL) **293**
Brewton-Parker Coll (GA) **294**
Brigham Young U–Hawaii (HI) **295**
Brock U (ON, Canada) **295**
Bryant Coll (RI) **296**
Buena Vista U (IA) **297**
California Baptist U (CA) **298**
California Lutheran U (CA) **299**
California State Polytechnic U, Pomona (CA) **300**
California State U, Chico (CA) **300**
California State U, Dominguez Hills (CA) **300**
California State U, Fullerton (CA) **301**
California State U, Hayward (CA) **301**

INFORMATION SCIENCES/SYSTEMS (continued)

California State U, Northridge (CA) ***301***
Calumet Coll of Saint Joseph (IN) ***302***
Cameron U (OK) ***303***
Campbellsville U (KY) ***303***
Carleton U (ON, Canada) ***305***
Carlow Coll (PA) ***305***
Carnegie Mellon U (PA) ***305***
Carroll Coll (WI) ***306***
Carson-Newman Coll (TN) ***306***
Catawba Coll (NC) ***307***
Cedar Crest Coll (PA) ***308***
Cedarville U (OH) ***308***
Centenary Coll (NJ) ***308***
Central Coll (IA) ***309***
Chadron State Coll (NE) ***311***
Champlain Coll (VT) ***311***
Chapman U (CA) ***311***
Chowan Coll (NC) ***312***
Christopher Newport U (VA) ***313***
Claflin U (SC) ***314***
Clarion U of Pennsylvania (PA) ***315***
Clark Atlanta U (GA) ***315***
Clarke Coll (IA) ***315***
Clayton Coll & State U (GA) ***316***
Cleary U (MI) ***317***
Clemson U (SC) ***317***
Cleveland State U (OH) ***317***
Coll Misericordia (PA) ***319***
Coll of Charleston (SC) ***320***
Coll of Mount St. Joseph (OH) ***320***
Coll of Notre Dame of Maryland (MD) ***321***
Coll of St. Joseph (VT) ***322***
Coll of Saint Mary (NE) ***322***
The Coll of Saint Rose (NY) ***322***
Coll of Staten Island of the City U of NY (NY) ***323***
Colorado Christian U (CO) ***325***
Colorado State U (CO) ***325***
Colorado State U-Pueblo (CO) ***325***
Colorado Tech U (CO) ***326***
Colorado Tech U Denver Campus (CO) ***326***
Colorado Tech U Sioux Falls Campus (SD) ***326***
Columbia Coll (MO) ***326***
Columbia Union Coll (MD) ***328***
Columbus State U (GA) ***328***
Concord Coll (WV) ***329***
Concordia U (IL) ***330***
Concordia U (MI) ***330***
Cornell U (NY) ***333***
Cornerstone U (MI) ***333***
Culver-Stockton Coll (MO) ***334***
Dakota State U (SD) ***335***
Daniel Webster Coll (NH) ***337***
Davenport U, Grand Rapids (MI) ***337***
Davenport U, Lansing (MI) ***337***
Delaware State U (DE) ***338***
Delaware Valley Coll (PA) ***339***
DePaul U (IL) ***339***
DeVry Inst of Technology (NY) ***340***
DeVry U (AZ) ***340***
DeVry U, Fremont (CA) ***340***
DeVry U, Long Beach (CA) ***341***
DeVry U, Pomona (CA) ***341***
DeVry U, West Hills (CA) ***341***
DeVry U, Colorado Springs (CO) ***341***
DeVry U, Orlando (FL) ***342***
DeVry U, Alpharetta (GA) ***342***
DeVry U, Decatur (GA) ***342***
DeVry U, Addison (IL) ***342***
DeVry U, Chicago (IL) ***342***
DeVry U, Tinley Park (IL) ***342***
DeVry U (MO) ***343***
DeVry U (OH) ***343***
DeVry U (TX) ***343***
DeVry U (VA) ***343***
DeVry U (WA) ***343***
Dillard U (LA) ***344***
Dominican Coll (NY) ***344***
Dominican U (IL) ***345***
Dowling Coll (NY) ***345***
Drake U (IA) ***345***
Drexel U (PA) ***346***
Eastern Kentucky U (KY) ***348***
Eastern Michigan U (MI) ***348***
Eastern Washington U (WA) ***349***
École des hautes études commerciales de Montréal (QC, Canada) ***350***
Edgewood Coll (WI) ***351***
Elizabeth City State U (NC) ***351***
Elmira Coll (NY) ***351***
Emmanuel Coll (GA) ***353***
Emporia State U (KS) ***354***
Excelsior Coll (NY) ***356***
Fairfield U (CT) ***356***
Faulkner U (AL) ***357***
Ferris State U (MI) ***358***
Ferrum Coll (VA) ***358***
Fitchburg State Coll (MA) ***358***
Florida A&M U (FL) ***359***
Florida Inst of Technology (FL) ***360***
Florida International U (FL) ***360***
Florida Metropolitan U-Tampa Coll, Brandon (FL) ***360***
Florida Metropolitan U-Melbourne (FL) ***360***
Fontbonne U (MO) ***361***
Fordham U (NY) ***362***
Fort Hays State U (KS) ***362***
Fort Lewis Coll (CO) ***362***
Francis Marion U (SC) ***363***
Freed-Hardeman U (TN) ***364***
Gallaudet U (DC) ***365***
Georgetown Coll (KY) ***366***
Georgia Southwestern State U (GA) ***368***
Glenville State Coll (WV) ***368***
Golden Gate U (CA) ***369***
Goldey-Beacom Coll (DE) ***369***
Gonzaga U (WA) ***369***
Goshen Coll (IN) ***370***
Grambling State U (LA) ***371***
Grand Valley State U (MI) ***371***
Grand View Coll (IA) ***372***
Guilford Coll (NC) ***373***
Gwynedd-Mercy Coll (PA) ***374***
Hampton U (VA) ***375***
Hannibal-LaGrange Coll (MO) ***375***
Harris-Stowe State Coll (MO) ***376***
Harvard U (MA) ***376***
Hawai'i Pacific U (HI) ***377***
Heidelberg Coll (OH) ***377***
High Point U (NC) ***379***
Hollins U (VA) ***380***
Houston Baptist U (TX) ***382***
Howard Payne U (TX) ***382***
Howard U (DC) ***382***
Humboldt State U (CA) ***382***
Husson Coll (ME) ***383***
Idaho State U (ID) ***384***
Illinois Coll (IL) ***384***
Illinois Inst of Technology (IL) ***384***
Illinois State U (IL) ***384***
Indiana Inst of Technology (IN) ***385***
Indiana U–Purdue U Fort Wayne (IN) ***386***
Insto Tecno Estudios Sups Monterrey(Mexico) ***388***
Inter American U of PR, San Germán Campus (PR) ***388***
Iona Coll (NY) ***390***
Iowa Wesleyan Coll (IA) ***390***
James Madison U (VA) ***391***
John Jay Coll of Criminal Justice, the City U of NY (NY) ***392***
Johnson & Wales U (RI) ***393***
Johnson C. Smith U (NC) ***394***
Johnson State Coll (VT) ***394***
Jones Coll (FL) ***394***
Judson Coll (AL) ***395***
Judson Coll (IL) ***395***
Kansas State U (KS) ***396***
Kendall Coll (IL) ***396***
Kennesaw State U (GA) ***397***
Kettering U (MI) ***398***
King Coll (TN) ***398***
Lakehead U (ON, Canada) ***400***
Lamar U (TX) ***401***
Lambuth U (TN) ***401***
La Salle U (PA) ***402***
Lasell Coll (MA) ***402***
La Sierra U (CA) ***403***
Lawrence Technological U (MI) ***403***
Lees-McRae Coll (NC) ***404***
Lee U (TN) ***404***
Lehigh U (PA) ***404***
Le Moyne Coll (NY) ***404***
LeTourneau U (TX) ***405***
Limestone Coll (SC) ***406***
Lipscomb U (TN) ***408***
Lock Haven U of Pennsylvania (PA) ***408***
Long Island U, Brooklyn Campus (NY) ***409***
Long Island U, C.W. Post Campus (NY) ***409***
Loyola U Chicago (IL) ***411***
Loyola U New Orleans (LA) ***411***
MacMurray Coll (IL) ***414***
Macon State Coll (GA) ***414***
Madonna U (MI) ***414***
Mansfield U of Pennsylvania (PA) ***416***
Marietta Coll (OH) ***417***
Marist Coll (NY) ***417***
Marquette U (WI) ***418***
Marymount Coll of Fordham U (NY) ***419***
McGill U (QC, Canada) ***423***
McKendree Coll (IL) ***423***
Medaille Coll (NY) ***424***
Medgar Evers Coll of the City U of NY (NY) ***424***
Memorial U of Newfoundland (NF, Canada) ***424***
Mercer U (GA) ***425***
Mercy Coll (NY) ***425***
Mercyhurst Coll (PA) ***425***
Mesa State Coll (CO) ***426***
Messiah Coll (PA) ***426***
Metropolitan State U (MN) ***427***
Michigan Technological U (MI) ***428***
Midwestern State U (TX) ***430***
Minnesota State U, Mankato (MN) ***431***
Missouri Southern State Coll (MO) ***433***
Missouri Western State Coll (MO) ***433***
Montana State U–Northern (MT) ***434***
Montana Tech of The U of Montana (MT) ***435***
Morgan State U (MD) ***436***
Mountain State U (WV) ***437***
Mount Aloysius Coll (PA) ***437***
Mount Olive Coll (NC) ***439***
Mount Saint Vincent U (NS, Canada) ***439***
Mount Union Coll (OH) ***440***
Murray State U (KY) ***440***
National American U, Colorado Springs (CO) ***441***
National American U, Denver (CO) ***441***
National American U (NM) ***441***
National American U (SD) ***442***
National American U–Sioux Falls Branch (SD) ***442***
The National Hispanic U (CA) ***442***
National-Louis U (IL) ***442***
National U (CA) ***442***
Nazareth Coll of Rochester (NY) ***443***
Nebraska Wesleyan U (NE) ***443***
New Jersey Inst of Technology (NJ) ***445***
Newman U (KS) ***445***
New Mexico Highlands U (NM) ***446***
New Mexico State U (NM) ***446***
New York Inst of Technology (NY) ***447***
New York U (NY) ***447***
Niagara U (NY) ***447***
North Carolina Central U (NC) ***448***
North Carolina Wesleyan Coll (NC) ***449***
Northeastern U (MA) ***450***
Northern Kentucky U (KY) ***451***
Northern Michigan U (MI) ***451***
Northland Coll (WI) ***452***
Northwest Christian Coll (OR) ***452***
Northwestern Oklahoma State U (OK) ***453***
Northwestern State U of Louisiana (LA) ***453***
Northwest Missouri State U (MO) ***454***
Norwich U (VT) ***455***
Notre Dame Coll (OH) ***455***
Nova Southeastern U (FL) ***455***
Oakland City U (IN) ***456***
Oakwood Coll (AL) ***456***
Ohio Dominican U (OH) ***457***
The Ohio State U (OH) ***457***
Oklahoma Baptist U (OK) ***459***
Oklahoma Christian U (OK) ***459***
Oklahoma Panhandle State U (OK) ***460***
Oklahoma State U (OK) ***460***
Oklahoma Wesleyan U (OK) ***460***
Olivet Nazarene U (IL) ***461***
Oregon State U (OR) ***462***
Ottawa U (KS) ***462***
Pace U (NY) ***463***
Pacific Union Coll (CA) ***464***
Palm Beach Atlantic U (FL) ***465***
Peirce Coll (PA) ***466***
Penn State U Abington Coll (PA) ***467***
Penn State U Berks Cmps of Berks-Lehigh Valley Coll (PA) ***468***
Penn State U Univ Park Campus (PA) ***468***
Pfeiffer U (NC) ***469***
Philadelphia U (PA) ***469***
Piedmont Coll (GA) ***470***
Pittsburg State U (KS) ***470***
Plymouth State Coll (NH) ***471***
Purdue U Calumet (IN) ***475***
Queens U of Charlotte (NC) ***476***
Quincy U (IL) ***476***
Quinnipiac U (CT) ***476***
Ramapo Coll of New Jersey (NJ) ***477***
Reinhardt Coll (GA) ***478***
Rensselaer Polytechnic Inst (NY) ***478***
Rhode Island Coll (RI) ***479***
The Richard Stockton Coll of New Jersey (NJ) ***479***
Richmond, The American International U in London(United Kingdom) ***480***
Rider U (NJ) ***480***
Rivier Coll (NH) ***480***
Roanoke Coll (VA) ***481***
Robert Morris U (PA) ***481***
Roberts Wesleyan Coll (NY) ***481***
Rochester Inst of Technology (NY) ***482***
Rockhurst U (MO) ***482***
Rocky Mountain Coll (MT) ***482***
Roger Williams U (RI) ***483***
Rowan U (NJ) ***484***
Russell Sage Coll (NY) ***484***
Rutgers, The State U of New Jersey, Newark (NJ) ***485***
Ryerson U (ON, Canada) ***485***
St. Ambrose U (IA) ***486***
St. Cloud State U (MN) ***488***
St. Francis Xavier U (NS, Canada) ***489***
St. John's U (NY) ***490***
Saint Leo U (FL) ***492***
Saint Martin's Coll (WA) ***493***
Saint Mary Coll (KS) ***493***
Saint Mary-of-the-Woods Coll (IN) ***493***
Saint Mary's Coll of Madonna U (MI) ***493***
Saint Mary's U of Minnesota (MN) ***494***
St. Mary's U of San Antonio (TX) ***494***
Saint Peter's Coll (NJ) ***495***
St. Thomas Aquinas Coll (NY) ***495***
St. Thomas U (FL) ***496***
Salve Regina U (RI) ***497***
San Diego State U (CA) ***498***
San Francisco State U (CA) ***498***
Siena Heights U (MI) ***504***
Simpson Coll (IA) ***505***
Si Tanka Huron U (SD) ***505***
Slippery Rock U of Pennsylvania (PA) ***506***
South Dakota State U (SD) ***507***
Southeastern Oklahoma State U (OK) ***508***
Southeastern U (DC) ***508***
Southeast Missouri State U (MO) ***508***
Southern Nazarene U (OK) ***510***
Southern New Hampshire U (NH) ***510***
Southwest Baptist U (MO) ***512***
Springfield Coll (MA) ***514***
State U of NY at Albany (NY) ***514***
State U of NY at Binghamton (NY) ***515***
State U of NY at Oswego (NY) ***515***
State U of NY Coll at Buffalo (NY) ***516***
State U of NY Coll at Fredonia (NY) ***516***
State U of NY Coll at Old Westbury (NY) ***516***
State U of NY Inst of Tech at Utica/Rome (NY) ***518***
Stetson U (FL) ***519***
Stony Brook U, State University of New York (NY) ***520***
Strayer U (DC) ***520***
Suffolk U (MA) ***520***
Susquehanna U (PA) ***521***
Syracuse U (NY) ***521***
Tarleton State U (TX) ***522***
Taylor U (IN) ***523***
Temple U (PA) ***523***
Tennessee Technological U (TN) ***524***
Tennessee Temple U (TN) ***524***
Texas A&M International U (TX) ***524***
Texas A&M U–Commerce (TX) ***525***
Texas A&M U–Corpus Christi (TX) ***525***
Texas A&M U–Kingsville (TX) ***525***
Texas Lutheran U (TX) ***526***
Thiel Coll (PA) ***527***
Tiffin U (OH) ***528***
Towson U (MD) ***529***
Trevecca Nazarene U (TN) ***529***
Trinity Christian Coll (IL) ***530***
Tulane U (LA) ***533***
Tusculum Coll (TN) ***533***
Union Coll (NE) ***534***
Union U (TN) ***534***
United States Military Academy (NY) ***535***
Université de Sherbrooke (QC, Canada) ***536***
U du Québec à Trois-Rivières (QC, Canada) ***536***
U of Alberta (AB, Canada) ***538***
U of Arkansas at Little Rock (AR) ***539***
U of Baltimore (MD) ***539***

U of Bridgeport (CT) **540**
U of Calif, Santa Cruz (CA) **542**
U of Charleston (WV) **542**
U of Cincinnati (OH) **543**
U of Dayton (OH) **544**
U of Guelph (ON, Canada) **546**
U of Hartford (CT) **546**
U of Houston (TX) **547**
U of Houston–Clear Lake (TX) **547**
U of Indianapolis (IN) **548**
The U of Iowa (IA) **548**
U of Mary (ND) **551**
U of Mary Hardin-Baylor (TX) **551**
U of Maryland, Baltimore County (MD) **552**
U of Maryland University Coll (MD) **552**
U of Massachusetts Lowell (MA) **553**
U of Miami (FL) **553**
U of Michigan–Dearborn (MI) **554**
U of Minnesota, Crookston (MN) **554**
U of Missouri–Kansas City (MO) **555**
U of Missouri–Rolla (MO) **556**
U of Mobile (AL) **556**
The U of Montana–Missoula (MT) **556**
U of Nebraska at Omaha (NE) **557**
U of New Brunswick Fredericton (NB, Canada) **558**
U of New Mexico (NM) **559**
U of Northern Iowa (IA) **561**
U of North Texas (TX) **562**
U of Ottawa (ON, Canada) **563**
U of Phoenix–Jacksonville Campus (FL) **564**
U of Pittsburgh at Bradford (PA) **569**
U of San Francisco (CA) **574**
U of Saskatchewan (SK, Canada) **574**
The U of Scranton (PA) **574**
U of Sioux Falls (SD) **574**
The U of South Dakota (SD) **575**
U of South Florida (FL) **576**
The U of Tampa (FL) **577**
The U of Tennessee at Chattanooga (TN) **577**
The U of Texas at El Paso (TX) **578**
The U of Texas at San Antonio (TX) **578**
The U of Texas–Pan American (TX) **579**
U of the District of Columbia (DC) **580**
U of the Pacific (CA) **580**
U of the Sacred Heart (PR) **580**
U of Toledo (OH) **581**
U of Tulsa (OK) **581**
U of Vermont (VT) **582**
U of Washington (WA) **583**
U of Windsor (ON, Canada) **584**
U of Wisconsin–Green Bay (WI) **584**
U of Wisconsin–River Falls (WI) **585**
U of Wisconsin–Superior (WI) **586**
U of Wyoming (WY) **586**
Utah State U (UT) **587**
Valdosta State U (GA) **588**
Villa Julie Coll (MD) **590**
Villanova U (PA) **590**
Virginia Commonwealth U (VA) **590**
Virginia Polytechnic Inst and State U (VA) **591**
Viterbo U (WI) **591**
Waldorf Coll (IA) **592**
Wartburg Coll (IA) **594**
Washington U in St. Louis (MO) **595**
Wayne State Coll (NE) **596**
Wayne State U (MI) **596**
Weber State U (UT) **596**
Webster U (MO) **597**
West Chester U of Pennsylvania (PA) **598**
Western Governors U (UT) **599**
Western International U (AZ) **599**
Western New England Coll (MA) **600**
Westfield State Coll (MA) **600**
West Liberty State Coll (WV) **601**
Westminster Coll (PA) **601**
West Virginia Wesleyan Coll (WV) **603**
Widener U (PA) **604**
Wilberforce U (OH) **605**
Wilkes U (PA) **605**
William Jewell Coll (MO) **606**
Wingate U (NC) **607**
Winona State U (MN) **608**
Woodbury U (CA) **609**
Worcester Polytechnic Inst (MA) **609**
Xavier U of Louisiana (LA) **610**
York Coll of Pennsylvania (PA) **610**
York Coll of the City U of New York (NY) **611**
Youngstown State U (OH) **611**

INFORMATION TECHNOLOGY

Overview: Students learn how to design technical information and computer systems in order to solve business, research, and communications problems. *Related majors:* computer and information sciences, computer programming, computer systems analyst, computer systems networking, and telecommunications. *Potential careers:* computer analyst, computer programmer, telecommunication researcher. *Salary potential:* $40k-$55k.

Bay Path Coll (MA) **283**
Capella U (MN) **304**
Everglades Coll (FL) **355**
Jones International U (CO) **394**
Nazareth Coll of Rochester (NY) **443**
New Mexico Inst of Mining and Technology (NM) **446**
Ryerson U (ON, Canada) **485**
Simmons Coll (MA) **504**
United States International U(Kenya) **535**
U of Phoenix–Colorado Campus (CO) **563**
U of Phoenix–Hawaii Campus (HI) **564**
U of Phoenix–Maryland Campus (MD) **565**
U of Phoenix–Metro Detroit Campus (MI) **565**
U of Phoenix–New Mexico Campus (NM) **565**
U of Phoenix–Northern California Campus (CA) **565**
U of Phoenix–Oklahoma City Campus (OK) **566**
U of Phoenix–Oregon Campus (OR) **566**
U of Phoenix–Philadelphia Campus (PA) **566**
U of Phoenix–Phoenix Campus (AZ) **567**
U of Phoenix–Pittsburgh Campus (PA) **567**
U of Phoenix–Puerto Rico Campus (PR) **567**
U of Phoenix–Sacramento Campus (CA) **567**
U of Phoenix–San Diego Campus (CA) **567**
U of Phoenix–Southern Arizona Campus (AZ) **568**
U of Phoenix–Southern California Campus (CA) **568**
U of Phoenix–Southern Colorado Campus (CO) **568**
U of Phoenix–West Michigan Campus (MI) **569**
The U of Scranton (PA) **574**
Virginia Coll at Birmingham (AL) **590**
York U (ON, Canada) **611**

INSTITUTIONAL FOOD SERVICES

Overview: This major teaches students about the principles and practices of the administration of food service systems in institutional settings while preparing them to manage such operations. *Related majors:* food service workers, restaurant operations, culinary arts, operations management, supervision. *Potential careers:* food service manager, restaurant manager. *Salary potential:* $26k-$45k.

Dominican U (IL) **345**
Johnson & Wales U (RI) **393**
Pacific Union Coll (CA) **464**
State U of NY Coll at Oneonta (NY) **517**

INSTITUTIONAL FOOD WORKERS

Overview: This major prepares students for careers in production, service, and management used in governmental, commercial, or independently owned institutional food establishments and related food-industry occupations. *Related majors:* food systems administration, culinary arts, restaurant operations. *Potential careers:* institutional food service worker, chef, restaurant and food service manager, inspector. *Salary potential:* $20k-$45k.

Grambling State U (LA) **371**
Murray State U (KY) **440**
Nicholls State U (LA) **447**

INSTRUMENTATION TECHNOLOGY

Overview: This major teaches undergraduates the basic engineering principles and necessary skills to develop and use control and measurement devices and systems. *Related majors:* mathematics, electronic engineering and technology, robotic engineering and technology, laser and optical technology, electromechanical technology. *Potential careers:* aerospace engineer or technician, Air Force officer/engineer, naval officer/engineer, computer technician, power plant manager. *Salary potential:* $25k-$37k.

Colorado State U-Pueblo (CO) **325**
Indiana State U (IN) **385**
Providence Coll (RI) **474**

INSURANCE/RISK MANAGEMENT

Overview: Students learn how to manage risk in business situations and how to provide insurance services to individuals or businesses. *Related majors:* actuarial science, finance, economics. *Potential careers:* insurance agent or adjuster, financial analyst, lawyer, corporate strategist. *Salary potential:* $35k-$50k.

Appalachian State U (NC) **270**
Ball State U (IN) **280**
Baylor U (TX) **283**
Bradley U (IL) **293**
California State Polytechnic U, Pomona (CA) **300**
The Coll of Southeastern Europe, The American U of Athens(Greece) **323**
Delta State U (MS) **339**
Eastern Kentucky U (KY) **348**
Excelsior Coll (NY) **356**
Ferris State U (MI) **358**
Florida International U (FL) **360**
Florida State U (FL) **361**
Georgia State U (GA) **368**
Howard U (DC) **382**
Illinois State U (IL) **384**
Illinois Wesleyan U (IL) **385**
Indiana State U (IN) **385**
Martin U (IN) **419**
Mercyhurst Coll (PA) **425**
Minnesota State U, Mankato (MN) **431**
Mississippi State U (MS) **432**
The Ohio State U (OH) **457**
Olivet Coll (MI) **461**
Penn State U Univ Park Campus (PA) **468**
Roosevelt U (IL) **483**
St. Cloud State U (MN) **488**
St. John's U (NY) **490**
Seattle U (WA) **501**
Southwest Missouri State U (MO) **513**
Temple U (PA) **523**
Texas Southern U (TX) **526**
Thomas Edison State Coll (NJ) **527**
U of Calgary (AB, Canada) **540**
U of Central Arkansas (AR) **542**
U of Cincinnati (OH) **543**
U of Connecticut (CT) **544**
U of Florida (FL) **545**
U of Georgia (GA) **545**
U of Hartford (CT) **546**
U of Louisiana at Lafayette (LA) **550**
The U of Memphis (TN) **553**
U of Minnesota, Twin Cities Campus (MN) **555**
U of Mississippi (MS) **555**
U of North Texas (TX) **562**
U of Pennsylvania (PA) **563**
U of South Carolina (SC) **575**
U of Wisconsin–Madison (WI) **584**
Washington State U (WA) **595**

INTERDISCIPLINARY STUDIES

Overview: This major offers students the opportunity to develop an individualized crossdisciplinary major that utilizes courses from a wide range of fields, including the social sciences, the humanities, technologies, and business and professional studies. *Related majors, potential careers,* and *salary potential* depend upon the focus of the major.

Abilene Christian U (TX) **260**
Agnes Scott Coll (GA) **261**
Alaska Bible Coll (AK) **261**
Albertus Magnus Coll (CT) **262**
Albright Coll (PA) **263**
Alfred U (NY) **263**
Alice Lloyd Coll (KY) **263**
Amberton U (TX) **265**
American U (DC) **267**
American U of Rome(Italy) **268**
Amherst Coll (MA) **268**
Angelo State U (TX) **269**
Anna Maria Coll (MA) **269**
Antioch Coll (OH) **269**
Arizona State U (AZ) **271**
Arizona State U East (AZ) **271**
Arizona State U West (AZ) **272**
Asbury Coll (KY) **274**
Atlantic Baptist U (NB, Canada) **275**
Augsburg Coll (MN) **276**
Austin Peay State U (TN) **278**
Baldwin-Wallace Coll (OH) **280**
Bard Coll (NY) **281**
Bates Coll (ME) **282**
Baylor U (TX) **283**
Beloit Coll (WI) **285**
Bennett Coll (NC) **286**
Bennington Coll (VT) **286**
Bentley Coll (MA) **286**
Baruch Coll of the City U of NY (NY) **286**
Berry Coll (GA) **287**
Bethany Coll (WV) **287**
Bethany Coll of the Assemblies of God (CA) **287**
Bethel Coll (TN) **288**
Birmingham-Southern Coll (AL) **289**
Blackburn Coll (IL) **290**
Bloomsburg U of Pennsylvania (PA) **290**
Bluefield Coll (VA) **291**
Boston Coll (MA) **292**
Boston U (MA) **292**
Bowdoin Coll (ME) **292**
Brevard Coll (NC) **294**
Briar Cliff U (IA) **294**
Brigham Young U–Hawaii (HI) **295**
Brock U (ON, Canada) **295**
Brooklyn Coll of the City U of NY (NY) **295**
Bryn Athyn Coll of the New Church (PA) **297**
Bucknell U (PA) **297**
Burlington Coll (VT) **297**
California Lutheran U (CA) **299**
California State U, Bakersfield (CA) **300**
California State U, Chico (CA) **300**
California State U, Dominguez Hills (CA) **300**
California State U, Hayward (CA) **301**
California State U, Long Beach (CA) **301**
California State U, San Bernardino (CA) **302**
Calvin Coll (MI) **303**
Cameron U (OK) **303**
Capital U (OH) **304**
Carleton Coll (MN) **305**
Carleton U (ON, Canada) **305**
Carnegie Mellon U (PA) **305**
Carson-Newman Coll (TN) **306**
Catawba Coll (NC) **307**
The Catholic U of America (DC) **307**
Centenary Coll of Louisiana (LA) **308**
Central Coll (IA) **309**
Central Connecticut State U (CT) **309**
Central Methodist Coll (MO) **309**
Central Michigan U (MI) **310**
Chadron State Coll (NE) **311**
Christian Heritage Coll (CA) **313**
Christopher Newport U (VA) **313**

INTERDISCIPLINARY STUDIES (continued)

Clark Atlanta U (GA) ***315***
Clarkson U (NY) ***316***
Clark U (MA) ***316***
Cleveland State U (OH) ***317***
Coe Coll (IA) ***318***
Coll Misericordia (PA) ***319***
Coll of Mount Saint Vincent (NY) ***320***
The Coll of New Rochelle (NY) ***321***
Coll of Notre Dame of Maryland (MD) ***321***
The Coll of Saint Rose (NY) ***322***
Coll of the Atlantic (ME) ***323***
Coll of the Ozarks (MO) ***323***
The Coll of William and Mary (VA) ***324***
The Coll of Wooster (OH) ***324***
Columbia Coll Chicago (IL) ***327***
Concordia U (MN) ***330***
Concordia U (OR) ***330***
Concordia U (QC, Canada) ***331***
Connecticut Coll (CT) ***331***
Cornell Coll (IA) ***332***
Cornell U (NY) ***333***
Cornerstone U (MI) ***333***
Covenant Coll (GA) ***333***
Dallas Baptist U (TX) ***336***
Dana Coll (NE) ***337***
DePaul U (IL) ***339***
DePauw U (IN) ***339***
Dominican U of California (CA) ***345***
Dowling Coll (NY) ***345***
Drew U (NJ) ***346***
D'Youville Coll (NY) ***347***
Earlham Coll (IN) ***347***
Eastern Kentucky U (KY) ***348***
Eastern Michigan U (MI) ***348***
Eastern Washington U (WA) ***349***
Eckerd Coll (FL) ***350***
Elmhurst Coll (IL) ***351***
Elmira Coll (NY) ***351***
Elms Coll (MA) ***352***
Emerson Coll (MA) ***353***
Emmanuel Coll (MA) ***353***
Emory & Henry Coll (VA) ***353***
Eugene Lang Coll, New School U (NY) ***355***
The Evergreen State Coll (WA) ***355***
Felician Coll (NJ) ***357***
Florida Inst of Technology (FL) ***360***
Fordham U (NY) ***362***
Framingham State Coll (MA) ***362***
Franklin U (OH) ***364***
Freed-Hardeman U (TN) ***364***
George Fox U (OR) ***366***
George Mason U (VA) ***366***
Georgetown U (DC) ***366***
The George Washington U (DC) ***367***
Georgia State U (GA) ***368***
Gettysburg Coll (PA) ***368***
Goddard Coll (VT) ***369***
Goucher Coll (MD) ***370***
Grand Valley State U (MI) ***371***
Grand View Coll (IA) ***372***
Greensboro Coll (NC) ***372***
Grinnell Coll (IA) ***373***
Guilford Coll (NC) ***373***
Gustavus Adolphus Coll (MN) ***374***
Hampshire Coll (MA) ***375***
Hardin-Simmons U (TX) ***376***
Harris-Stowe State Coll (MO) ***376***
Harvard U (MA) ***376***
Hastings Coll (NE) ***377***
Hawai'i Pacific U (HI) ***377***
Hendrix Coll (AR) ***378***
Hillsdale Coll (MI) ***379***
Hillsdale Free Will Baptist Coll (OK) ***379***
Hobart and William Smith Colls (NY) ***380***
Hofstra U (NY) ***380***
Hollins U (VA) ***380***
Hope Coll (MI) ***381***
Hope International U (CA) ***381***
Houston Baptist U (TX) ***382***
Huntingdon Coll (AL) ***383***
Idaho State U (ID) ***384***
Illinois Coll (IL) ***384***
Illinois Wesleyan U (IL) ***385***
Iona Coll (NY) ***390***
Iowa State U of Science and Technology (IA) ***390***
Ithaca Coll (NY) ***390***
Jacksonville U (FL) ***391***
John Brown U (AR) ***392***
John Carroll U (OH) ***392***
Johns Hopkins U (MD) ***392***
Johnson & Wales U (RI) ***393***
Jones Coll (FL) ***394***
Judson Coll (AL) ***395***
Juniata Coll (PA) ***395***
Kalamazoo Coll (MI) ***395***
Keene State Coll (NH) ***396***
Kendall Coll (IL) ***396***
Kentucky Christian Coll (KY) ***397***
Kentucky Wesleyan Coll (KY) ***397***
Kenyon Coll (OH) ***398***
Keuka Coll (NY) ***398***
Lamar U (TX) ***401***
Lambuth U (TN) ***401***
Lander U (SC) ***401***
Lane Coll (TN) ***402***
Lasell Coll (MA) ***402***
Lees-McRae Coll (NC) ***404***
Lehman Coll of the City U of NY (NY) ***404***
LeTourneau U (TX) ***405***
Lewis-Clark State Coll (ID) ***406***
Liberty U (VA) ***406***
Long Island U, Brooklyn Campus (NY) ***409***
Long Island U, C.W. Post Campus (NY) ***409***
Long Island U, Southampton Coll, Friends World Program (NY) ***409***
Louisiana Coll (LA) ***410***
Loyola Coll in Maryland (MD) ***411***
Luther Coll (IA) ***412***
Lycoming Coll (PA) ***412***
Macalester Coll (MN) ***413***
Maharishi U of Management (IA) ***414***
Manchester Coll (IN) ***415***
Marlboro Coll (VT) ***418***
Marquette U (WI) ***418***
Mars Hill Coll (NC) ***418***
Martin Luther Coll (MN) ***418***
Mary Baldwin Coll (VA) ***419***
Marymount Coll of Fordham U (NY) ***419***
Maryville U of Saint Louis (MO) ***420***
Mary Washington Coll (VA) ***420***
Marywood U (PA) ***421***
Massachusetts Coll of Liberal Arts (MA) ***421***
Massachusetts Inst of Technology (MA) ***421***
McPherson Coll (KS) ***423***
Mercy Coll (NY) ***425***
Merrimack Coll (MA) ***426***
Miami U (OH) ***428***
Middle Tennessee State U (TN) ***429***
Midwestern State U (TX) ***430***
Millikin U (IL) ***430***
Mills Coll (CA) ***431***
Minneapolis Coll of Art and Design (MN) ***431***
Minnesota State U, Moorhead (MN) ***432***
Molloy Coll (NY) ***433***
Monmouth U (NJ) ***434***
Montana State U–Northern (MT) ***434***
Morehouse Coll (GA) ***436***
Morningside Coll (IA) ***437***
Mountain State U (WV) ***437***
Mount Allison U (NB, Canada) ***437***
Mount Holyoke Coll (MA) ***438***
Mount Saint Mary Coll (NY) ***439***
Mount Saint Mary's Coll and Seminary (MD) ***439***
Mount Saint Vincent U (NS, Canada) ***439***
Mount Union Coll (OH) ***440***
Muskingum Coll (OH) ***441***
Naropa U (CO) ***441***
National U (CA) ***442***
Nazareth Coll of Rochester (NY) ***443***
Nebraska Wesleyan U (NE) ***443***
New Mexico Inst of Mining and Technology (NM) ***446***
New Mexico State U (NM) ***446***
New York U (NY) ***447***
Norfolk State U (VA) ***448***
North Greenville Coll (SC) ***451***
Northland Coll (WI) ***452***
Northwest Christian Coll (OR) ***452***
Northwest Coll (WA) ***452***
Northwestern U (IL) ***453***
Nova Southeastern U (FL) ***455***
Nyack Coll (NY) ***456***
Oakland City U (IN) ***456***
Oakland U (MI) ***456***
Oakwood Coll (AL) ***456***
Oberlin Coll (OH) ***456***
Oglethorpe U (GA) ***457***
Ohio Dominican U (OH) ***457***
Ohio U (OH) ***458***
Oklahoma Baptist U (OK) ***459***
Olivet Nazarene U (IL) ***461***
Oregon State U (OR) ***462***
Pace U (NY) ***463***
Pacific Union Coll (CA) ***464***
Penn State U Univ Park Campus (PA) ***468***
Pepperdine U, Malibu (CA) ***469***
Piedmont Coll (GA) ***470***
Pitzer Coll (CA) ***471***
Plattsburgh State U of NY (NY) ***471***
Pomona Coll (CA) ***472***
Prairie View A&M U (TX) ***473***
Prescott Coll (AZ) ***474***
Purdue U (IN) ***475***
Queens Coll of the City U of NY (NY) ***475***
Queen's U at Kingston (ON, Canada) ***476***
Quincy U (IL) ***476***
Radford U (VA) ***476***
Ramapo Coll of New Jersey (NJ) ***477***
Reformed Bible Coll (MI) ***477***
Regis Coll (MA) ***478***
Rensselaer Polytechnic Inst (NY) ***478***
Rhodes Coll (TN) ***479***
The Richard Stockton Coll of New Jersey (NJ) ***479***
Ripon Coll (WI) ***480***
Rochester Coll (MI) ***482***
Rochester Inst of Technology (NY) ***482***
Rocky Mountain Coll (MT) ***482***
Rollins Coll (FL) ***483***
Russell Sage Coll (NY) ***484***
Rutgers, The State U of New Jersey, New Brunswick (NJ) ***485***
Saginaw Valley State U (MI) ***486***
St. Andrews Presbyterian Coll (NC) ***487***
St. Bonaventure U (NY) ***487***
St. Cloud State U (MN) ***488***
St. Francis Coll (NY) ***488***
St. John Fisher Coll (NY) ***489***
St. John's Coll (MD) ***489***
Saint Joseph's U (PA) ***491***
Saint Mary Coll (KS) ***493***
Saint Mary's Coll (IN) ***493***
Saint Mary's Coll of California (CA) ***494***
St. Mary's Coll of Maryland (MD) ***494***
Saint Mary's U (NS, Canada) ***494***
St. Norbert Coll (WI) ***495***
Salem Coll (NC) ***496***
Santa Clara U (CA) ***499***
Sarah Lawrence Coll (NY) ***499***
Schiller International U (FL) ***500***
Schiller International U(France) ***500***
Schiller International U(Germany) ***500***
Schiller International U(Spain) ***500***
Schiller International U(United Kingdom) ***500***
Schiller International U, American Coll of Switzerland(Switzerland) ***500***
Seton Hill U (PA) ***502***
Sheldon Jackson Coll (AK) ***503***
Silver Lake Coll (WI) ***504***
Simon's Rock Coll of Bard (MA) ***505***
Smith Coll (MA) ***506***
Sonoma State U (CA) ***506***
South Dakota School of Mines and Technology (SD) ***507***
Southeastern Coll of the Assemblies of God (FL) ***507***
Southeast Missouri State U (MO) ***508***
Southern Nazarene U (OK) ***510***
Southern Oregon U (OR) ***510***
Southwest State U (MN) ***513***
Stanford U (CA) ***514***
State U of NY at Albany (NY) ***514***
State U of NY at Binghamton (NY) ***515***
State U of NY Coll at Brockport (NY) ***515***
State U of NY Coll at Fredonia (NY) ***516***
State U of NY Coll at Oneonta (NY) ***517***
State U of NY Empire State Coll (NY) ***517***
Stephen F. Austin State U (TX) ***518***
Stephens Coll (MO) ***519***
Sterling Coll (KS) ***519***
Stony Brook U, State University of New York (NY) ***520***
Suffolk U (MA) ***520***
Sweet Briar Coll (VA) ***521***
Syracuse U (NY) ***521***
Tabor Coll (KS) ***522***
Tarleton State U (TX) ***522***
Taylor U, Fort Wayne Campus (IN) ***523***
Temple U (PA) ***523***
Tennessee Temple U (TN) ***524***
Tennessee Wesleyan Coll (TN) ***524***
Texas A&M U (TX) ***524***
Texas A&M U–Commerce (TX) ***525***
Texas A&M U–Corpus Christi (TX) ***525***
Texas A&M U–Texarkana (TX) ***525***
Texas Southern U (TX) ***526***
Texas Tech U (TX) ***526***
Texas Woman's U (TX) ***527***
Thomas Aquinas Coll (CA) ***527***
Touro Coll (NY) ***529***
Towson U (MD) ***529***
Trent U (ON, Canada) ***529***
Trinity Coll (CT) ***530***
Trinity Coll (DC) ***530***
United States Air Force Academy (CO) ***534***
United States Military Academy (NY) ***535***
Unity Coll (ME) ***535***
Université de Sherbrooke (QC, Canada) ***536***
Université Laval (QC, Canada) ***536***
The U of Akron (OH) ***537***
The U of Alabama (AL) ***537***
U of Alaska Anchorage (AK) ***538***
U of Baltimore (MD) ***539***
U of Bridgeport (CT) ***540***
The U of British Columbia (BC, Canada) ***540***
U of Calif, Berkeley (CA) ***540***
U of Calif, San Diego (CA) ***541***
U of Calif, Santa Barbara (CA) ***541***
U of Chicago (IL) ***542***
U of Florida (FL) ***545***
U of Hartford (CT) ***546***
U of Hawaii at Hilo (HI) ***546***
U of Houston (TX) ***547***
U of Houston–Clear Lake (TX) ***547***
U of Houston–Downtown (TX) ***547***
U of Illinois at Springfield (IL) ***548***
The U of Iowa (IA) ***548***
U of Judaism (CA) ***548***
U of Kentucky (KY) ***549***
U of Maine at Farmington (ME) ***550***
U of Mary (ND) ***551***
U of Maryland, Baltimore County (MD) ***552***
U of Massachusetts Amherst (MA) ***552***
U of Massachusetts Boston (MA) ***553***
U of Massachusetts Dartmouth (MA) ***553***
The U of Memphis (TN) ***553***
U of Michigan (MI) ***554***
U of Michigan–Dearborn (MI) ***554***
U of Minnesota, Crookston (MN) ***554***
U of Minnesota, Duluth (MN) ***554***
U of Missouri–Columbia (MO) ***555***
U of Missouri–Kansas City (MO) ***555***
U of Missouri–St. Louis (MO) ***556***
The U of Montana–Missoula (MT) ***556***
U of Nebraska at Omaha (NE) ***557***
U of Nevada, Las Vegas (NV) ***558***
U of New Hampshire (NH) ***558***
The U of North Carolina at Greensboro (NC) ***560***
U of Northern Colorado (CO) ***561***
U of North Texas (TX) ***562***
U of Ottawa (ON, Canada) ***563***
U of Pennsylvania (PA) ***563***
U of Pittsburgh (PA) ***569***
U of Portland (OR) ***570***
U of Puerto Rico, Río Piedras (PR) ***571***
U of Puget Sound (WA) ***571***
U of Redlands (CA) ***572***
U of Rhode Island (RI) ***572***
U of Richmond (VA) ***572***
U of Rochester (NY) ***573***
U of St. Thomas (MN) ***573***
U of San Francisco (CA) ***574***
U of Sioux Falls (SD) ***574***
U of South Carolina Spartanburg (SC) ***575***
U of Southern California (CA) ***576***
U of Southern Mississippi (MS) ***576***
The U of Tennessee at Chattanooga (TN) ***577***
The U of Tennessee at Martin (TN) ***577***
The U of Texas at Arlington (TX) ***577***
The U of Texas at Dallas (TX) ***578***
The U of Texas at El Paso (TX) ***578***
The U of Texas at San Antonio (TX) ***578***
The U of Texas at Tyler (TX) ***579***
The U of Texas of the Permian Basin (TX) ***579***
The U of Texas–Pan American (TX) ***579***
U of the Incarnate Word (TX) ***580***
U of the Pacific (CA) ***580***
U of the Sacred Heart (PR) ***580***
U of Vermont (VT) ***582***
The U of Virginia's Coll at Wise (VA) ***582***
U of Washington (WA) ***583***
U of Waterloo (ON, Canada) ***583***
U of Wisconsin–Green Bay (WI) ***584***
U of Wisconsin–Milwaukee (WI) ***585***
U of Wisconsin–Parkside (WI) ***585***
Valparaiso U (IN) ***588***
Vanderbilt U (TN) ***588***

Vanguard U of Southern California (CA) **589**
Vassar Coll (NY) **589**
Villa Julie Coll (MD) **590**
Virginia Intermont Coll (VA) **590**
Virginia Polytechnic Inst and State U (VA) **591**
Virginia State U (VA) **591**
Virginia Wesleyan Coll (VA) **591**
Warren Wilson Coll (NC) **594**
Washington and Lee U (VA) **594**
Washington U in St. Louis (MO) **595**
Wayne State Coll (NE) **596**
Wayne State U (MI) **596**
Webster U (MO) **597**
Wesleyan Coll (GA) **597**
Wesleyan U (CT) **597**
Western Baptist Coll (OR) **598**
Western New Mexico U (NM) **600**
Western Oregon U (OR) **600**
Western Washington U (WA) **600**
West Liberty State Coll (WV) **601**
Westminster Coll (PA) **601**
West Texas A&M U (TX) **602**
West Virginia U (WV) **602**
Wheaton Coll (MA) **603**
William Jewell Coll (MO) **606**
William Woods U (MO) **607**
Wingate U (NC) **607**
Wisconsin Lutheran Coll (WI) **608**
Wittenberg U (OH) **608**
Woodbury U (CA) **609**
Worcester Polytechnic Inst (MA) **609**
York U (ON, Canada) **611**

INTERIOR ARCHITECTURE

Overview: This major teaches students how to apply the principles of architecture to the design of structural interiors for living, recreational and business purposes. *Related majors:* architecture, structural engineering, interior design. *Potential careers:* interior designer, structural engineer, architect, construction manager. *Salary potential:* $25k-$35k.

Arizona State U (AZ) **271**
Auburn U (AL) **276**
California Coll of Arts and Crafts (CA) **299**
Central Michigan U (MI) **310**
Central Missouri State U (MO) **310**
The Coll of Southeastern Europe, The American U of Athens(Greece) **323**
Cornell U (NY) **333**
Indiana State U (IN) **385**
Indiana U of Pennsylvania (PA) **386**
Kansas State U (KS) **396**
Lawrence Technological U (MI) **403**
Louisiana State U and A&M Coll (LA) **410**
Louisiana Tech U (LA) **410**
Michigan State U (MI) **428**
Minneapolis Coll of Art and Design (MN) **431**
Ohio U (OH) **458**
Philadelphia U (PA) **469**
Southwest Texas State U (TX) **513**
Stephen F. Austin State U (TX) **518**
Texas Tech U (TX) **526**
U of Bridgeport (CT) **540**
U of Hawaii at Manoa (HI) **546**
U of Houston (TX) **547**
U of Idaho (ID) **547**
U of Louisiana at Lafayette (LA) **550**
U of Nevada, Las Vegas (NV) **558**
U of New Haven (CT) **559**
U of Oklahoma (OK) **562**
U of Southern Mississippi (MS) **576**
The U of Texas at Arlington (TX) **577**
The U of Texas at San Antonio (TX) **578**
U of Washington (WA) **583**
Washington State U (WA) **595**
Woodbury U (CA) **609**

INTERIOR DESIGN

Overview: This major teaches students how to design and plan residential and commercial interior spaces. *Related majors:* visual and performing arts, architecture, housing studies, interior environments, architectural drafting, drawing. *Potential careers:* interior designer or consultant, architect, set designer. *Salary potential:* $20k-$30k.

Abilene Christian U (TX) **260**
Academy of Art Coll (CA) **260**
Adrian Coll (MI) **260**
American InterContinental U (CA) **266**
American InterContinental U, Atlanta (GA) **266**
American InterContinental U-London(United Kingdom) **267**
The American U in Dubai(United Arab Emirates) **267**
Anderson Coll (SC) **268**
Appalachian State U (NC) **270**
Arcadia U (PA) **271**
The Art Inst of Colorado (CO) **274**
The Art Inst of Portland (OR) **274**
Atlanta Coll of Art (GA) **275**
Atlantic Union Coll (MA) **276**
Baker Coll of Flint (MI) **279**
Baylor U (TX) **283**
Becker Coll (MA) **283**
Bethel Coll (IN) **288**
Boston Architectural Center (MA) **291**
Brenau U (GA) **293**
Bridgewater Coll (VA) **294**
Brigham Young U (UT) **295**
California State U, Chico (CA) **300**
California State U, Fresno (CA) **301**
California State U, Long Beach (CA) **301**
California State U, Northridge (CA) **301**
California State U, Sacramento (CA) **301**
Carson-Newman Coll (TN) **306**
Cazenovia Coll (NY) **308**
Central Missouri State U (MO) **310**
Chaminade U of Honolulu (HI) **311**
The Cleveland Inst of Art (OH) **317**
Col for Creative Studies (MI) **319**
Coll of Mount St. Joseph (OH) **320**
Colorado State U (CO) **325**
Columbia Coll Chicago (IL) **327**
Columbus Coll of Art and Design (OH) **328**
Concordia U Wisconsin (WI) **331**
Converse Coll (SC) **332**
Cornish Coll of the Arts (WA) **333**
Design Inst of San Diego (CA) **340**
Drexel U (PA) **346**
East Carolina U (NC) **347**
Eastern Kentucky U (KY) **348**
Eastern Michigan U (MI) **348**
Endicott Coll (MA) **354**
Ferris State U (MI) **358**
Florida International U (FL) **360**
Florida State U (FL) **361**
Georgia Southern U (GA) **367**
Hampton U (VA) **375**
Harding U (AR) **375**
Harrington Inst of Interior Design (IL) **376**
High Point U (NC) **379**
Howard U (DC) **382**
The Illinois Inst of Art (IL) **384**
The Illinois Inst of Art-Schaumburg (IL) **384**
Indiana U Bloomington (IN) **385**
Indiana U–Purdue U Indianapolis (IN) **387**
International Academy of Design & Technology (FL) **388**
International Acad of Merchandising & Design, Ltd (IL) **389**
Iowa State U of Science and Technology (IA) **390**
Kansas State U (KS) **396**
Kean U (NJ) **396**
Kendall Coll of Art and Design of Ferris State U (MI) **396**
Kent State U (OH) **397**
Lamar U (TX) **401**
Lambuth U (TN) **401**
La Roche Coll (PA) **402**
Longwood U (VA) **409**
Maryland Inst Coll of Art (MD) **419**
Marymount Coll of Fordham U (NY) **419**
Marymount U (VA) **420**
Maryville U of Saint Louis (MO) **420**
Mercyhurst Coll (PA) **425**
Meredith Coll (NC) **426**
Miami U (OH) **428**
Middle Tennessee State U (TN) **429**
Milwaukee Inst of Art and Design (WI) **431**
Minnesota State U, Mankato (MN) **431**
Mississippi Coll (MS) **432**
Moore Coll of Art and Design (PA) **436**
Mount Ida Coll (MA) **438**
Mount Mary Coll (WI) **438**
Newbury Coll (MA) **444**
New York Inst of Technology (NY) **447**
New York School of Interior Design (NY) **447**
North Dakota State U (ND) **449**
Northern Arizona U (AZ) **450**
Northwest Missouri State U (MO) **454**
The Ohio State U (OH) **457**
Oklahoma Christian U (OK) **459**
Oklahoma State U (OK) **460**
O'More Coll of Design (TN) **461**
Oregon State U (OR) **462**
Otis Coll of Art and Design (CA) **462**
Pacific Union Coll (CA) **464**
Paier Coll of Art, Inc. (CT) **464**
Park U (MO) **465**
Parsons School of Design, New School U (NY) **465**
Philadelphia U (PA) **469**
Pittsburg State U (KS) **470**
Pratt Inst (NY) **473**
Radford U (VA) **476**
Rhode Island School of Design (RI) **479**
Ringling School of Art and Design (FL) **480**
Rochester Inst of Technology (NY) **482**
Rocky Mountain Coll of Art & Design (CO) **483**
Ryerson U (ON, Canada) **485**
Salem Coll (NC) **496**
Samford U (AL) **497**
Sam Houston State U (TX) **497**
San Diego State U (CA) **498**
San Francisco State U (CA) **498**
San Jose State U (CA) **499**
Savannah Coll of Art and Design (GA) **499**
School of Visual Arts (NY) **501**
South Dakota State U (SD) **507**
Southern Illinois U Carbondale (IL) **509**
Suffolk U (MA) **520**
Syracuse U (NY) **521**
Texas A&M U–Kingsville (TX) **525**
Texas Christian U (TX) **526**
The U of Akron (OH) **537**
The U of Alabama (AL) **537**
U of Central Oklahoma (OK) **542**
U of Charleston (WV) **542**
U of Cincinnati (OH) **543**
U of Florida (FL) **545**
U of Houston (TX) **547**
U of Idaho (ID) **547**
U of Kentucky (KY) **549**
U of Louisville (KY) **550**
U of Manitoba (MB, Canada) **551**
U of Massachusetts Amherst (MA) **552**
U of Michigan (MI) **554**
U of Minnesota, Twin Cities Campus (MN) **555**
U of Montevallo (AL) **557**
U of Nebraska at Omaha (NE) **557**
U of Nevada, Reno (NV) **558**
The U of North Carolina at Greensboro (NC) **560**
U of Northern Iowa (IA) **561**
U of North Texas (TX) **562**
U of Oregon (OR) **562**
U of San Francisco (CA) **574**
The U of Tennessee (TN) **577**
The U of Tennessee at Martin (TN) **577**
The U of Texas at Austin (TX) **578**
The U of Texas at San Antonio (TX) **578**
U of the Incarnate Word (TX) **580**
U of Wisconsin–Madison (WI) **584**
U of Wisconsin–Stevens Point (WI) **585**
Ursuline Coll (OH) **587**
Utah State U (UT) **587**
Valdosta State U (GA) **588**
Virginia Coll at Birmingham (AL) **590**
Virginia Commonwealth U (VA) **590**
Watkins Coll of Art and Design (TN) **595**
Wayne State Coll (NE) **596**
Wentworth Inst of Technology (MA) **597**
Western Carolina U (NC) **598**
Western Michigan U (MI) **599**
William Woods U (MO) **607**

INTERIOR ENVIRONMENTS

Overview: This major is a category of housing studies that focuses on the aspects of the interior environment and how people relate to their interior environments. *Related majors:* interior architecture, interior design, psychology, environmental health. *Potential careers:* interior designer, architect, environmental health consultant. *Salary potential:* $24k-$30k.

Lambuth U (TN) **401**
Murray State U (KY) **440**
Ohio U (OH) **458**
Syracuse U (NY) **521**
The U of Akron (OH) **537**
U of the Incarnate Word (TX) **580**

INTERNATIONAL AGRICULTURE

Overview: Undergraduates of this major study the agricultural systems of other countries and agricultural management of global food production and distribution. *Related majors:* international studies, agricultural economics, soil conservation, agricultural and animal husbandry and production management. *Potential careers:* farmer, ecologist, foreign development specialist, agribusiness manager or salesperson. *Salary potential:* $25k-$37k.

Arizona State U East (AZ) **271**
Cornell U (NY) **333**
Eastern Mennonite U (VA) **348**
Insto Tecno Estudios Sups Monterrey(Mexico) **388**
Iowa State U of Science and Technology (IA) **390**
McGill U (QC, Canada) **423**
MidAmerica Nazarene U (KS) **428**
Tarleton State U (TX) **522**
U of Calif, Davis (CA) **540**
Utah State U (UT) **587**

INTERNATIONAL BUSINESS

Overview: In this major students learn the principles necessary to manage and operate international businesses. *Related major:* international affairs, area studies, language studies, business administration/management, taxation. *Potential careers:* importer-exporter, overseas product manager, business development specialist, trade representative. *Salary potential:* $33k-$40k.

Adams State Coll (CO) **260**
Adrian Coll (MI) **260**
Albertson Coll of Idaho (ID) **262**
Albertus Magnus Coll (CT) **262**
Albright Coll (PA) **263**
Alfred U (NY) **263**
Alliant International U (CA) **264**
Alma Coll (MI) **264**
Alverno Coll (WI) **265**
American International Coll (MA) **267**
American U (DC) **267**
The American U of Paris(France) **268**
American U of Rome(Italy) **268**
Appalachian State U (NC) **270**
Aquinas Coll (MI) **270**
Arcadia U (PA) **271**
Arizona State U West (AZ) **272**
Arkansas State U (AR) **272**
Assumption Coll (MA) **275**
Auburn U (AL) **276**
Augsburg Coll (MN) **276**
Avila U (MO) **278**
Babson Coll (MA) **278**
Baker U (KS) **280**
Barry U (FL) **282**
Baylor U (TX) **283**
Bay Path Coll (MA) **283**
Bellarmine U (KY) **284**
Belmont Abbey Coll (NC) **284**
Belmont U (TN) **284**
Benedictine U (IL) **285**
Baruch Coll of the City U of NY (NY) **286**
Bethany Coll (KS) **287**
Bethel Coll (IN) **288**
Bethune-Cookman Coll (FL) **289**
Birmingham-Southern Coll (AL) **289**

INTERNATIONAL BUSINESS (continued)

Bishop's U (QC, Canada) ***289***
Boston U (MA) ***292***
Bowling Green State U (OH) ***292***
Bradley U (IL) ***293***
Bridgewater Coll (VA) ***294***
Bridgewater State Coll (MA) ***294***
Brigham Young U–Hawaii (HI) ***295***
Brock U (ON, Canada) ***295***
Buena Vista U (IA) ***297***
Butler U (IN) ***297***
Caldwell Coll (NJ) ***298***
California State Polytechnic U, Pomona (CA) ***300***
California State U, Dominguez Hills (CA) ***300***
California State U, Fresno (CA) ***301***
California State U, Fullerton (CA) ***301***
California State U, Long Beach (CA) ***301***
California State U, Northridge (CA) ***301***
Campbell U (NC) ***303***
Cardinal Stritch U (WI) ***305***
Carleton U (ON, Canada) ***305***
Cedarville U (OH) ***308***
Central Coll (IA) ***309***
Central Connecticut State U (CT) ***309***
Central Michigan U (MI) ***310***
Champlain Coll (VT) ***311***
Chapman U (CA) ***311***
Chatham Coll (PA) ***312***
Christopher Newport U (VA) ***313***
City U (WA) ***314***
Claremont McKenna Coll (CA) ***315***
Clarion U of Pennsylvania (PA) ***315***
Clarke Coll (IA) ***315***
Coll of Charleston (SC) ***320***
The Coll of New Jersey (NJ) ***320***
Coll of Notre Dame of Maryland (MD) ***321***
Coll of St. Catherine (MN) ***321***
The Coll of St. Scholastica (MN) ***322***
Coll of Santa Fe (NM) ***323***
The Coll of Southeastern Europe, The American U of Athens(Greece) ***323***
Coll of the Ozarks (MO) ***323***
Columbia Coll (MO) ***326***
Columbia Southern U (AL) ***327***
Concordia Coll (MN) ***329***
Concordia U (QC, Canada) ***331***
Converse Coll (SC) ***332***
Cornell Coll (IA) ***332***
Creighton U (NE) ***333***
Davenport U, Grand Rapids (MI) ***337***
Davis & Elkins Coll (WV) ***338***
DePaul U (IL) ***339***
Dickinson Coll (PA) ***344***
Dickinson State U (ND) ***344***
Dillard U (LA) ***344***
Dominican Coll (NY) ***344***
Dominican U (IL) ***345***
Dominican U of California (CA) ***345***
Dowling Coll (NY) ***345***
Drake U (IA) ***345***
Drexel U (PA) ***346***
Drury U (MO) ***346***
Duquesne U (PA) ***346***
D'Youville Coll (NY) ***347***
Eastern Mennonite U (VA) ***348***
Eastern Michigan U (MI) ***348***
Eckerd Coll (FL) ***350***
École des hautes études commerciales de Montréal (QC, Canada) ***350***
Elizabethtown Coll (PA) ***351***
Elmhurst Coll (IL) ***351***
Elmira Coll (NY) ***351***
Excelsior Coll (NY) ***356***
Ferris State U (MI) ***358***
Ferrum Coll (VA) ***358***
Finlandia U (MI) ***358***
Florida Atlantic U (FL) ***359***
Florida International U (FL) ***360***
Florida Metropolitan U-Fort Lauderdale Coll (FL) ***360***
Florida Southern Coll (FL) ***361***
Florida State U (FL) ***361***
Fordham U (NY) ***362***
Fort Lewis Coll (CO) ***362***
Framingham State Coll (MA) ***362***
Franklin Coll (IN) ***363***
Franklin Coll Switzerland(Switzerland) ***364***
Fresno Pacific U (CA) ***364***
Gannon U (PA) ***365***
Georgetown Coll (KY) ***366***
Georgetown U (DC) ***366***
The George Washington U (DC) ***367***
Georgia Southern U (GA) ***367***
Gettysburg Coll (PA) ***368***
Golden Gate U (CA) ***369***
Goldey-Beacom Coll (DE) ***369***
Gonzaga U (WA) ***369***
Grace Coll (IN) ***370***
Graceland U (IA) ***371***
Grand Canyon U (AZ) ***371***
Grand Valley State U (MI) ***371***
Green Mountain Coll (VT) ***372***
Grove City Coll (PA) ***373***
Gustavus Adolphus Coll (MN) ***374***
Hamline U (MN) ***374***
Hampshire Coll (MA) ***375***
Harding U (AR) ***375***
Hawai'i Pacific U (HI) ***377***
High Point U (NC) ***379***
Hiram Coll (OH) ***379***
Hofstra U (NY) ***380***
Holy Family U (PA) ***380***
Howard U (DC) ***382***
Huntingdon Coll (AL) ***383***
Husson Coll (ME) ***383***
Illinois State U (IL) ***384***
Illinois Wesleyan U (IL) ***385***
Immaculata U (PA) ***385***
Indiana U of Pennsylvania (PA) ***386***
Insto Tecno Estudios Sups Monterrey(Mexico) ***388***
Iona Coll (NY) ***390***
Iowa State U of Science and Technology (IA) ***390***
Ithaca Coll (NY) ***390***
Jacksonville U (FL) ***391***
James Madison U (VA) ***391***
John Brown U (AR) ***392***
Johnson & Wales U (FL) ***393***
Johnson & Wales U (RI) ***393***
Judson Coll (IL) ***395***
Juniata Coll (PA) ***395***
King Coll (TN) ***398***
King's Coll (PA) ***398***
Kutztown U of Pennsylvania (PA) ***399***
LaGrange Coll (GA) ***400***
Lake Erie Coll (OH) ***400***
Lakeland Coll (WI) ***401***
La Roche Coll (PA) ***402***
Lasell Coll (MA) ***402***
Lebanon Valley Coll (PA) ***403***
Lehigh U (PA) ***404***
Lenoir-Rhyne Coll (NC) ***405***
LeTourneau U (TX) ***405***
Lincoln U (CA) ***407***
Linfield Coll (OR) ***408***
Long Island U, C.W. Post Campus (NY) ***409***
Long Island U, Southampton Coll, Friends World Program (NY) ***409***
Loras Coll (IA) ***410***
Louisiana State U and A&M Coll (LA) ***410***
Loyola Coll in Maryland (MD) ***411***
Loyola U New Orleans (LA) ***411***
Luther Coll (IA) ***412***
Lycoming Coll (PA) ***412***
Lynn U (FL) ***413***
Madonna U (MI) ***414***
Maine Maritime Academy (ME) ***415***
Manhattanville Coll (NY) ***416***
Mansfield U of Pennsylvania (PA) ***416***
Marietta Coll (OH) ***417***
Marquette U (WI) ***418***
Mars Hill Coll (NC) ***418***
Marygrove Coll (MI) ***419***
Marymount Coll of Fordham U (NY) ***419***
Marymount U (VA) ***420***
Maryville Coll (TN) ***420***
Massachusetts Maritime Academy (MA) ***421***
McGill U (QC, Canada) ***423***
McPherson Coll (KS) ***423***
Mercer U (GA) ***425***
Meredith Coll (NC) ***426***
Merrimack Coll (MA) ***426***
Messiah Coll (PA) ***426***
Metropolitan State U (MN) ***427***
Millikin U (IL) ***430***
Milwaukee School of Engineering (WI) ***431***
Minnesota State U, Mankato (MN) ***431***
Minnesota State U, Moorhead (MN) ***432***
Minot State U (ND) ***432***
Missouri Southern State Coll (MO) ***433***
Montclair State U (NJ) ***435***
Moravian Coll (PA) ***436***
Mount Allison U (NB, Canada) ***437***
Mount Saint Mary Coll (NY) ***439***
Mount St. Mary's Coll (CA) ***439***
Mount Union Coll (OH) ***440***
Murray State U (KY) ***440***
Muskingum Coll (OH) ***441***
National-Louis U (IL) ***442***
Nebraska Wesleyan U (NE) ***443***
Neumann Coll (PA) ***443***
Newbury Coll (MA) ***444***
New Mexico State U (NM) ***446***
New York Inst of Technology (NY) ***447***
New York U (NY) ***447***
Niagara U (NY) ***447***
North Central Coll (IL) ***449***
Northeastern U (MA) ***450***
Northern State U (SD) ***451***
North Park U (IL) ***452***
Northwestern Coll (MN) ***453***
Northwest Missouri State U (MO) ***454***
Northwest Nazarene U (ID) ***454***
Northwood U (MI) ***454***
Northwood U, Florida Campus (FL) ***454***
Northwood U, Texas Campus (TX) ***454***
Notre Dame Coll (OH) ***455***
Notre Dame de Namur U (CA) ***455***
Ohio Dominican U (OH) ***457***
Ohio Northern U (OH) ***457***
The Ohio State U (OH) ***457***
Ohio U (OH) ***458***
Ohio Wesleyan U (OH) ***459***
Oklahoma Baptist U (OK) ***459***
Oklahoma City U (OK) ***460***
Oklahoma State U (OK) ***460***
Oregon State U (OR) ***462***
Otterbein Coll (OH) ***462***
Pace U (NY) ***463***
Pacific Lutheran U (WA) ***463***
Pacific Union Coll (CA) ***464***
Palm Beach Atlantic U (FL) ***465***
Penn State U at Erie, The Behrend Coll (PA) ***467***
Penn State U Univ Park Campus (PA) ***468***
Pepperdine U, Malibu (CA) ***469***
Philadelphia U (PA) ***469***
Plattsburgh State U of NY (NY) ***471***
Pontifical Catholic U of Puerto Rico (PR) ***472***
Quinnipiac U (CT) ***476***
Ramapo Coll of New Jersey (NJ) ***477***
Rhodes Coll (TN) ***479***
Richmond, The American International U in London(United Kingdom) ***480***
Rider U (NJ) ***480***
Rochester Inst of Technology (NY) ***482***
Roger Williams U (RI) ***483***
Rollins Coll (FL) ***483***
Roosevelt U (IL) ***483***
Ryerson U (ON, Canada) ***485***
Sacred Heart U (CT) ***486***
St. Ambrose U (IA) ***486***
St. Andrews Presbyterian Coll (NC) ***487***
St. Bonaventure U (NY) ***487***
St. Cloud State U (MN) ***488***
St. Edward's U (TX) ***488***
Saint Francis U (PA) ***488***
St. John Fisher Coll (NY) ***489***
Saint Joseph's Coll (IN) ***490***
Saint Joseph's Coll of Maine (ME) ***491***
Saint Leo U (FL) ***492***
Saint Louis U (MO) ***492***
Saint Mary's Coll (IN) ***493***
Saint Mary's Coll of California (CA) ***494***
Saint Mary's U of Minnesota (MN) ***494***
St. Mary's U of San Antonio (TX) ***494***
St. Norbert Coll (WI) ***495***
Saint Peter's Coll (NJ) ***495***
St. Thomas U (FL) ***496***
Saint Vincent Coll (PA) ***496***
Saint Xavier U (IL) ***496***
Salem Coll (NC) ***496***
Salem International U (WV) ***496***
Samford U (AL) ***497***
Sam Houston State U (TX) ***497***
San Diego State U (CA) ***498***
San Francisco State U (CA) ***498***
San Jose State U (CA) ***499***
Savannah State U (GA) ***499***
Schiller International U (FL) ***500***
Schiller International U(France) ***500***
Schiller International U(Germany) ***500***
Schiller International U(Spain) ***500***
Schiller International U(United Kingdom) ***500***
Schiller International U, American Coll of Switzerland(Switzerland) ***500***
Seattle U (WA) ***501***
Seton Hill U (PA) ***502***
Shaw U (NC) ***502***
Simpson Coll (IA) ***505***
Slippery Rock U of Pennsylvania (PA) ***506***
Southern Adventist U (TN) ***508***
Southern New Hampshire U (NH) ***510***
Spring Hill Coll (AL) ***514***
State U of NY at New Paltz (NY) ***515***
State U of NY Coll at Brockport (NY) ***515***
Stephen F. Austin State U (TX) ***518***
Stetson U (FL) ***519***
Strayer U (DC) ***520***
Tarleton State U (TX) ***522***
Taylor U (IN) ***523***
Taylor U, Fort Wayne Campus (IN) ***523***
Teikyo Post U (CT) ***523***
Temple U (PA) ***523***
Tennessee Technological U (TN) ***524***
Texas A&M U–Kingsville (TX) ***525***
Texas A&M U–Texarkana (TX) ***525***
Texas Christian U (TX) ***526***
Texas Tech U (TX) ***526***
Texas Wesleyan U (TX) ***526***
Thiel Coll (PA) ***527***
Thomas Coll (ME) ***527***
Thomas Edison State Coll (NJ) ***527***
Tiffin U (OH) ***528***
Touro Coll (NY) ***529***
Trinity U (TX) ***531***
United States International U(Kenya) ***535***
The U of Akron (OH) ***537***
U of Alberta (AB, Canada) ***538***
U of Arkansas (AR) ***539***
U of Arkansas at Little Rock (AR) ***539***
U of Baltimore (MD) ***539***
U of Bridgeport (CT) ***540***
The U of British Columbia (BC, Canada) ***540***
U of Dayton (OH) ***544***
U of Denver (CO) ***544***
U of Evansville (IN) ***545***
The U of Findlay (OH) ***545***
U of Georgia (GA) ***545***
U of Hawaii at Manoa (HI) ***546***
U of Hawaii–West Oahu (HI) ***546***
U of Indianapolis (IN) ***548***
The U of Iowa (IA) ***548***
U of La Verne (CA) ***549***
The U of Lethbridge (AB, Canada) ***549***
The U of Memphis (TN) ***553***
U of Miami (FL) ***553***
U of Minnesota, Twin Cities Campus (MN) ***555***
U of Mississippi (MS) ***555***
U of Missouri–Columbia (MO) ***555***
The U of Montana–Missoula (MT) ***556***
U of Nebraska–Lincoln (NE) ***557***
U of Nevada, Las Vegas (NV) ***558***
U of Nevada, Reno (NV) ***558***
U of New Brunswick Fredericton (NB, Canada) ***558***
U of New Haven (CT) ***559***
The U of North Carolina at Charlotte (NC) ***560***
U of North Florida (FL) ***561***
U of Oklahoma (OK) ***562***
U of Oregon (OR) ***562***
U of Ottawa (ON, Canada) ***563***
U of Portland (OR) ***570***
U of Puget Sound (WA) ***571***
U of Rhode Island (RI) ***572***
U of Richmond (VA) ***572***
U of Rio Grande (OH) ***572***
U of Saint Francis (IN) ***573***
U of St. Thomas (MN) ***573***
U of San Francisco (CA) ***574***
The U of Scranton (PA) ***574***
U of Southern Mississippi (MS) ***576***
U of South Florida (FL) ***576***
The U of Tampa (FL) ***577***
The U of Tennessee at Martin (TN) ***577***
The U of Texas at Arlington (TX) ***577***
The U of Texas at Dallas (TX) ***578***
The U of Texas at San Antonio (TX) ***578***
The U of Texas–Pan American (TX) ***579***
U of the Incarnate Word (TX) ***580***
U of Toledo (OH) ***581***
U of Tulsa (OK) ***581***
U of Victoria (BC, Canada) ***582***
U of Washington (WA) ***583***
U of Wisconsin–La Crosse (WI) ***584***
Utica Coll (NY) ***588***
Valparaiso U (IN) ***588***
Vanguard U of Southern California (CA) ***589***

Villanova U (PA) **590**
Warren Wilson Coll (NC) **594**
Wartburg Coll (IA) **594**
Washington & Jefferson Coll (PA) **594**
Washington State U (WA) **595**
Washington U in St. Louis (MO) **595**
Waynesburg Coll (PA) **595**
Wayne State Coll (NE) **596**
Webber International U (FL) **596**
Webster U (MO) **597**
Wesleyan Coll (GA) **597**
Western Carolina U (NC) **598**
Western International U (AZ) **599**
Western New England Coll (MA) **600**
Western New Mexico U (NM) **600**
Western State Coll of Colorado (CO) **600**
Western Washington U (WA) **600**
Westminster Coll (MO) **601**
Westminster Coll (PA) **601**
Westminster Coll (UT) **601**
Wheeling Jesuit U (WV) **603**
Whitworth Coll (WA) **604**
Wichita State U (KS) **604**
Widener U (PA) **604**
William Jewell Coll (MO) **606**
William Paterson U of New Jersey (NJ) **606**
William Woods U (MO) **607**
Wittenberg U (OH) **608**
Wofford Coll (SC) **609**
York Coll of Pennsylvania (PA) **610**
York U (ON, Canada) **611**

INTERNATIONAL BUSINESS MARKETING

Overview: Students apply marketing and marketing research principles to enterprises that are engaged in foreign business, such as importing or exporting goods and services. *Related majors:* marketing research, advertising, retail management, general marketing operations, psychology. *Potential careers:* marketing executive, importer-exporter, sales manager, distribution manager. *Salary potential:* $25k-$35k, depending on location.

American U (DC) **267**
Eastern Michigan U (MI) **348**
Oklahoma Baptist U (OK) **459**
Pace U (NY) **463**
York U (ON, Canada) **611**

INTERNATIONAL ECONOMICS

Overview: This branch of economics examines international economic behavior and trade policy. *Related majors:* international finance, international relations, foreign affairs, economics, international business. *Potential careers:* financial analyst, international economist, currency trader. *Salary potential:* $40k-$50k.

Albertson Coll of Idaho (ID) **262**
Albertus Magnus Coll (CT) **262**
American U (DC) **267**
The American U of Paris(France) **268**
Assumption Coll (MA) **275**
Austin Coll (TX) **277**
Bard Coll (NY) **281**
Bentley Coll (MA) **286**
Brock U (ON, Canada) **295**
Carson-Newman Coll (TN) **306**
Carthage Coll (WI) **306**
The Catholic U of America (DC) **307**
Claremont McKenna Coll (CA) **315**
Coll of St. Catherine (MN) **321**
École des hautes études commerciales de Montréal (QC, Canada) **350**
Framingham State Coll (MA) **362**
Franklin Coll Switzerland(Switzerland) **364**
Georgetown U (DC) **366**
Gettysburg Coll (PA) **368**
Hamline U (MN) **374**
Hampshire Coll (MA) **375**
Harvard U (MA) **376**
Hastings Coll (NE) **377**
Hiram Coll (OH) **379**
Howard U (DC) **382**
John Carroll U (OH) **392**
Lawrence U (WI) **403**
Long Island U, Southampton Coll, Friends World Program (NY) **409**
Longwood U (VA) **409**
Marlboro Coll (VT) **418**
Middlebury Coll (VT) **429**
Muhlenberg Coll (PA) **440**
Ohio U (OH) **458**
Rhodes Coll (TN) **479**
Rockford Coll (IL) **482**
Ryerson U (ON, Canada) **485**
San Diego State U (CA) **498**
Schiller International U, American Coll of Switzerland(Switzerland) **500**
Seattle U (WA) **501**
State U of NY at New Paltz (NY) **515**
State U of NY at Oswego (NY) **515**
State U of West Georgia (GA) **518**
Suffolk U (MA) **520**
Taylor U (IN) **523**
Université Laval (QC, Canada) **536**
U of Calif, Los Angeles (CA) **541**
U of Calif, Santa Cruz (CA) **542**
U of Central Arkansas (AR) **542**
U of Puget Sound (WA) **571**
U of Richmond (VA) **572**
Valparaiso U (IN) **588**
Washington U in St. Louis (MO) **595**
Westminster Coll (PA) **601**
Youngstown State U (OH) **611**

INTERNATIONAL FINANCE

Overview: Students focus on international finance in the areas of monetary policy, lending practices, currency trading, and management of financial institutions that operate across national boarders. *Related majors:* finance, business/managerial economics, international economics, development economics and international development, international relations/foreign affairs. *Potential careers:* international banker, corporate consultant, international financial analyst, venture capitalist, hedge fund manager. *Salary potential:* $45k-$60k.

American U (DC) **267**
Boston U (MA) **292**
The Catholic U of America (DC) **307**
École des hautes études commerciales de Montréal (QC, Canada) **350**
Franklin Coll Switzerland(Switzerland) **364**
International Coll of the Cayman Islands(Cayman Islands) **389**
Rochester Inst of Technology (NY) **482**
Ryerson U (ON, Canada) **485**
Washington U in St. Louis (MO) **595**
York U (ON, Canada) **611**

INTERNATIONAL RELATIONS

Overview: Students taking this major will explore international politics and institutions as well as diplomacy and foreign policy. *Related majors:* history, peace and conflict studies, military studies, economics, foreign language study. *Potential careers:* diplomatic corps, international banker, lobbyist, professor, economist. *Salary potential:* $30k-$40k.

Abilene Christian U (TX) **260**
Adrian Coll (MI) **260**
Agnes Scott Coll (GA) **261**
Albion Coll (MI) **262**
Allegheny Coll (PA) **264**
Alliant International U (CA) **264**
Alverno Coll (WI) **265**
American Coll of Thessaloniki(Greece) **266**
American International Coll (MA) **267**
American U (DC) **267**
The American U of Paris(France) **268**
American U of Rome(Italy) **268**
Antioch Coll (OH) **269**
Aquinas Coll (MI) **270**
Arkansas Tech U (AR) **272**
Ashland U (OH) **274**
Assumption Coll (MA) **275**
Augsburg Coll (MN) **276**
Augustana Coll (SD) **276**
Austin Coll (TX) **277**
Azusa Pacific U (CA) **278**
Baldwin-Wallace Coll (OH) **280**
Bard Coll (NY) **281**
Barry U (FL) **282**
Baylor U (TX) **283**
Bellarmine U (KY) **284**
Beloit Coll (WI) **285**
Benedictine U (IL) **285**
Bennington Coll (VT) **286**
Berry Coll (GA) **287**
Bethany Coll (WV) **287**
Bethany Coll of the Assemblies of God (CA) **287**
Bethel Coll (MN) **288**
Bethune-Cookman Coll (FL) **289**
Boston U (MA) **292**
Bowling Green State U (OH) **292**
Bradley U (IL) **293**
Brenau U (GA) **293**
Bridgewater Coll (VA) **294**
Bridgewater State Coll (MA) **294**
Brigham Young U (UT) **295**
Brown U (RI) **296**
Bryant Coll (RI) **296**
Bucknell U (PA) **297**
Butler U (IN) **297**
California Lutheran U (CA) **299**
California State U, Chico (CA) **300**
California State U, Hayward (CA) **301**
California State U, Long Beach (CA) **301**
Calvin Coll (MI) **303**
Campbell U (NC) **303**
Canisius Coll (NY) **304**
Capital U (OH) **304**
Carleton Coll (MN) **305**
Carleton U (ON, Canada) **305**
Carroll Coll (MT) **306**
Carroll Coll (WI) **306**
Case Western Reserve U (OH) **307**
Catawba Coll (NC) **307**
Cedar Crest Coll (PA) **308**
Cedarville U (OH) **308**
Centenary Coll (NJ) **308**
Central Michigan U (MI) **310**
Centre Coll (KY) **310**
Chaminade U of Honolulu (HI) **311**
Chatham Coll (PA) **312**
Christopher Newport U (VA) **313**
City Coll of the City U of NY (NY) **314**
Claremont McKenna Coll (CA) **315**
Clark U (MA) **316**
Cleveland State U (OH) **317**
Colby Coll (ME) **318**
Colgate U (NY) **319**
The Coll of New Jersey (NJ) **320**
Coll of Notre Dame of Maryland (MD) **321**
Coll of St. Catherine (MN) **321**
Coll of Saint Elizabeth (NJ) **321**
The Coll of St. Scholastica (MN) **322**
Coll of Staten Island of the City U of NY (NY) **323**
The Coll of William and Mary (VA) **324**
The Coll of Wooster (OH) **324**
Concordia Coll (MN) **329**
Concordia Coll (NY) **329**
Connecticut Coll (CT) **331**
Cornell Coll (IA) **332**
Cornell U (NY) **333**
Creighton U (NE) **333**
Dalhousie U (NS, Canada) **336**
Denison U (OH) **339**
DePaul U (IL) **339**
Dickinson Coll (PA) **344**
Doane Coll (NE) **344**
Dominican U of California (CA) **345**
Drake U (IA) **345**
Duke U (NC) **346**
Duquesne U (PA) **346**
Earlham Coll (IN) **347**
Eastern Washington U (WA) **349**
Eckerd Coll (FL) **350**
Edgewood Coll (WI) **351**
Elmira Coll (NY) **351**
Elms Coll (MA) **352**
Elon U (NC) **352**
Emory & Henry Coll (VA) **353**
Emory U (GA) **354**
Eugene Lang Coll, New School U (NY) **355**
Fairfield U (CT) **356**
Fairleigh Dickinson U, Teaneck-Metro Campus (NJ) **356**
Ferrum Coll (VA) **358**
Florida International U (FL) **360**
Florida State U (FL) **361**
Fordham U (NY) **362**
Francis Marion U (SC) **363**
Franklin Coll Switzerland(Switzerland) **364**
Frostburg State U (MD) **365**
Gallaudet U (DC) **365**
Gannon U (PA) **365**
George Fox U (OR) **366**
George Mason U (VA) **366**
Georgetown U (DC) **366**
The George Washington U (DC) **367**
Georgia Inst of Technology (GA) **367**
Georgia Southern U (GA) **367**
Gettysburg Coll (PA) **368**
Gonzaga U (WA) **369**
Gordon Coll (MA) **370**
Goucher Coll (MD) **370**
Graceland U (IA) **371**
Grand Canyon U (AZ) **371**
Grand Valley State U (MI) **371**
Guilford Coll (NC) **373**
Hamilton Coll (NY) **374**
Hamline U (MN) **374**
Hampshire Coll (MA) **375**
Hanover Coll (IN) **375**
Harding U (AR) **375**
Harvard U (MA) **376**
Hastings Coll (NE) **377**
Hawai'i Pacific U (HI) **377**
Heidelberg Coll (OH) **377**
Hendrix Coll (AR) **378**
High Point U (NC) **379**
Hillsdale Coll (MI) **379**
Hobart and William Smith Colls (NY) **380**
Hollins U (VA) **380**
Holy Names Coll (CA) **381**
Houghton Coll (NY) **381**
Huntingdon Coll (AL) **383**
Huron U USA in London(United Kingdom) **383**
Idaho State U (ID) **384**
Illinois Coll (IL) **384**
Illinois Wesleyan U (IL) **385**
Immaculata U (PA) **385**
Indiana U of Pennsylvania (PA) **386**
Insto Tecno Estudios Sups Monterrey(Mexico) **388**
Iona Coll (NY) **390**
Iowa State U of Science and Technology (IA) **390**
Jacksonville U (FL) **391**
James Madison U (VA) **391**
John Brown U (AR) **392**
John Cabot U(Italy) **392**
John Carroll U (OH) **392**
Johns Hopkins U (MD) **392**
Juniata Coll (PA) **395**
Kennesaw State U (GA) **397**
Kent State U (OH) **397**
Kenyon Coll (OH) **398**
Knox Coll (IL) **399**
Lafayette Coll (PA) **400**
Lambuth U (TN) **401**
Lane Coll (TN) **402**
La Roche Coll (PA) **402**
Lawrence U (WI) **403**
Lees-McRae Coll (NC) **404**
Lee U (TN) **404**
Lehigh U (PA) **404**
Le Moyne Coll (NY) **404**
Lenoir-Rhyne Coll (NC) **405**
Lewis & Clark Coll (OR) **405**
Lincoln U (PA) **407**
Lindenwood U (MO) **407**
Lock Haven U of Pennsylvania (PA) **408**
Long Island U, C.W. Post Campus (NY) **409**
Long Island U, Southampton Coll, Friends World Program (NY) **409**
Longwood U (VA) **409**
Loras Coll (IA) **410**
Loyola U Chicago (IL) **411**
Luther Coll (IA) **412**
Lycoming Coll (PA) **412**
Lynchburg Coll (VA) **413**
Macalester Coll (MN) **413**
Manhattan Coll (NY) **416**
Manhattanville Coll (NY) **416**

INTERNATIONAL RELATIONS (continued)

Mansfield U of Pennsylvania (PA) ***416***
Marian Coll of Fond du Lac (WI) ***417***
Marlboro Coll (VT) ***418***
Marquette U (WI) ***418***
Marshall U (WV) ***418***
Mars Hill Coll (NC) ***418***
Mary Baldwin Coll (VA) ***419***
Marymount Coll of Fordham U (NY) ***419***
Marymount Manhattan Coll (NY) ***420***
Maryville Coll (TN) ***420***
Mary Washington Coll (VA) ***420***
McKendree Coll (IL) ***423***
Meredith Coll (NC) ***426***
Methodist Coll (NC) ***427***
Miami U (OH) ***428***
Michigan State U (MI) ***428***
Middlebury Coll (VT) ***429***
Middle Tennessee State U (TN) ***429***
Midwestern State U (TX) ***430***
Millikin U (IL) ***430***
Mills Coll (CA) ***431***
Minnesota State U, Mankato (MN) ***431***
Missouri Southern State Coll (MO) ***433***
Morehouse Coll (GA) ***436***
Mount Allison U (NB, Canada) ***437***
Mount Holyoke Coll (MA) ***438***
Mount Mary Coll (WI) ***438***
Mount Mercy Coll (IA) ***438***
Mount Saint Mary Coll (NY) ***439***
Mount Saint Mary's Coll and Seminary (MD) ***439***
Muhlenberg Coll (PA) ***440***
Murray State U (KY) ***440***
Muskingum Coll (OH) ***441***
Nazareth Coll of Rochester (NY) ***443***
Nebraska Wesleyan U (NE) ***443***
New Coll of Florida (FL) ***444***
New York U (NY) ***447***
Niagara U (NY) ***447***
North Central Coll (IL) ***449***
North Dakota State U (ND) ***449***
Northeastern U (MA) ***450***
Northern Arizona U (AZ) ***450***
Northern Kentucky U (KY) ***451***
Northern Michigan U (MI) ***451***
North Park U (IL) ***452***
Northwestern U (IL) ***453***
Northwest Nazarene U (ID) ***454***
Norwich U (VT) ***455***
Oakland U (MI) ***456***
Occidental Coll (CA) ***457***
Oglethorpe U (GA) ***457***
Ohio Northern U (OH) ***457***
The Ohio State U (OH) ***457***
Ohio U (OH) ***458***
Ohio Wesleyan U (OH) ***459***
Okanagan U Coll (BC, Canada) ***459***
Old Dominion U (VA) ***460***
Olivet Coll (MI) ***461***
Oral Roberts U (OK) ***461***
Oregon State U (OR) ***462***
Otterbein Coll (OH) ***462***
Pacific Lutheran U (WA) ***463***
Pacific U (OR) ***464***
Penn State U Univ Park Campus (PA) ***468***
Pepperdine U, Malibu (CA) ***469***
Pitzer Coll (CA) ***471***
Point Park Coll (PA) ***471***
Pomona Coll (CA) ***472***
Portland State U (OR) ***472***
Prairie Bible Coll (AB, Canada) ***473***
Queens U of Charlotte (NC) ***476***
Quinnipiac U (CT) ***476***
Ramapo Coll of New Jersey (NJ) ***477***
Randolph-Macon Coll (VA) ***477***
Randolph-Macon Woman's Coll (VA) ***477***
Reed Coll (OR) ***477***
Rhodes Coll (TN) ***479***
Richmond, The American International U in London(United Kingdom) ***480***
Roanoke Coll (VA) ***481***
Rockford Coll (IL) ***482***
Rockhurst U (MO) ***482***
Rocky Mountain Coll (MT) ***482***
Rollins Coll (FL) ***483***
Roosevelt U (IL) ***483***
Russell Sage Coll (NY) ***484***
Sacred Heart U (CT) ***486***
Saginaw Valley State U (MI) ***486***
Saint Augustine's Coll (NC) ***487***
St. Cloud State U (MN) ***488***
St. Edward's U (TX) ***488***
Saint Francis U (PA) ***488***
St. John Fisher Coll (NY) ***489***
Saint Joseph's Coll (IN) ***490***
Saint Joseph's U (PA) ***491***
Saint Leo U (FL) ***492***
Saint Louis U (MO) ***492***
Saint Mary's Coll of California (CA) ***494***
Saint Mary's U (NS, Canada) ***494***
St. Norbert Coll (WI) ***495***
Saint Xavier U (IL) ***496***
Salem Coll (NC) ***496***
Samford U (AL) ***497***
San Diego State U (CA) ***498***
San Francisco State U (CA) ***498***
Sarah Lawrence Coll (NY) ***499***
Schiller International U (FL) ***500***
Schiller International U(France) ***500***
Schiller International U(Germany) ***500***
Schiller International U(Spain) ***500***
Schiller International U(United Kingdom) ***500***
Schiller International U, American Coll of Switzerland(Switzerland) ***500***
Scripps Coll (CA) ***501***
Seattle U (WA) ***501***
Seton Hall U (NJ) ***502***
Seton Hill U (PA) ***502***
Shawnee State U (OH) ***502***
Shaw U (NC) ***502***
Simmons Coll (MA) ***504***
Simpson Coll (IA) ***505***
Southern Methodist U (TX) ***510***
Southern Nazarene U (OK) ***510***
Southern Oregon U (OR) ***510***
Southwestern U (TX) ***513***
Southwest Texas State U (TX) ***513***
Spring Hill Coll (AL) ***514***
Stanford U (CA) ***514***
State U of NY at New Paltz (NY) ***515***
State U of NY at Oswego (NY) ***515***
State U of NY Coll at Brockport (NY) ***515***
State U of NY Coll at Cortland (NY) ***516***
State U of NY Coll at Geneseo (NY) ***516***
State U of NY Coll at Oneonta (NY) ***517***
State U of West Georgia (GA) ***518***
Stephens Coll (MO) ***519***
Stetson U (FL) ***519***
Stonehill Coll (MA) ***520***
Susquehanna U (PA) ***521***
Sweet Briar Coll (VA) ***521***
Syracuse U (NY) ***521***
Tabor Coll (KS) ***522***
Taylor U (IN) ***523***
Texas Christian U (TX) ***526***
Texas Lutheran U (TX) ***526***
Texas Wesleyan U (TX) ***526***
Thomas More Coll (KY) ***528***
Tiffin U (OH) ***528***
Towson U (MD) ***529***
Trent U (ON, Canada) ***529***
Trinity Coll (CT) ***530***
Trinity Coll (DC) ***530***
Trinity Western U (BC, Canada) ***531***
Tufts U (MA) ***533***
Tulane U (LA) ***533***
Union Coll (NE) ***534***
United States International U(Kenya) ***535***
Université Laval (QC, Canada) ***536***
The U of Alabama (AL) ***537***
U of Alberta (AB, Canada) ***538***
U of Arkansas (AR) ***539***
U of Arkansas at Little Rock (AR) ***539***
U of Bridgeport (CT) ***540***
The U of British Columbia (BC, Canada) ***540***
U of Calgary (AB, Canada) ***540***
U of Calif, Davis (CA) ***540***
U of Calif, Irvine (CA) ***541***
U of Calif, Los Angeles (CA) ***541***
U of Cincinnati (OH) ***543***
U of Colorado at Boulder (CO) ***543***
U of Dayton (OH) ***544***
U of Delaware (DE) ***544***
U of Denver (CO) ***544***
U of Evansville (IN) ***545***
U of Hartford (CT) ***546***
U of Idaho (ID) ***547***
U of Indianapolis (IN) ***548***
The U of Iowa (IA) ***548***
U of Kansas (KS) ***549***
U of La Verne (CA) ***549***
U of Maine (ME) ***550***
U of Maine at Farmington (ME) ***550***
U of Maine at Presque Isle (ME) ***551***
The U of Memphis (TN) ***553***
U of Miami (FL) ***553***
U of Michigan (MI) ***554***
U of Michigan–Dearborn (MI) ***554***
U of Minnesota, Duluth (MN) ***554***
U of Minnesota, Twin Cities Campus (MN) ***555***
U of Mississippi (MS) ***555***
U of Missouri–St. Louis (MO) ***556***
U of Montevallo (AL) ***557***
U of Nebraska at Kearney (NE) ***557***
U of Nebraska at Omaha (NE) ***557***
U of Nebraska–Lincoln (NE) ***557***
U of Nevada, Reno (NV) ***558***
U of New Brunswick Fredericton (NB, Canada) ***558***
U of New Brunswick Saint John (NB, Canada) ***558***
U of New Hampshire (NH) ***558***
U of North Florida (FL) ***561***
U of Oregon (OR) ***562***
U of Ottawa (ON, Canada) ***563***
U of Pennsylvania (PA) ***563***
U of Puget Sound (WA) ***571***
U of Redlands (CA) ***572***
U of Richmond (VA) ***572***
U of St. Thomas (MN) ***573***
U of St. Thomas (TX) ***573***
U of San Diego (CA) ***574***
U of Saskatchewan (SK, Canada) ***574***
The U of Scranton (PA) ***574***
U of South Carolina (SC) ***575***
U of Southern California (CA) ***576***
U of Southern Maine (ME) ***576***
U of Southern Mississippi (MS) ***576***
U of South Florida (FL) ***576***
The U of Tampa (FL) ***577***
The U of Tennessee at Martin (TN) ***577***
U of the Pacific (CA) ***580***
U of the South (TN) ***581***
U of Toledo (OH) ***581***
U of Toronto (ON, Canada) ***581***
U of Vermont (VT) ***582***
U of Virginia (VA) ***582***
U of Washington (WA) ***583***
U of Waterloo (ON, Canada) ***583***
U of West Florida (FL) ***583***
U of Windsor (ON, Canada) ***584***
U of Wisconsin–Madison (WI) ***584***
U of Wisconsin–Milwaukee (WI) ***585***
U of Wisconsin–Oshkosh (WI) ***585***
U of Wisconsin–Parkside (WI) ***585***
U of Wisconsin–Platteville (WI) ***585***
U of Wisconsin–Stevens Point (WI) ***585***
U of Wisconsin–Whitewater (WI) ***586***
U of Wyoming (WY) ***586***
Ursinus Coll (PA) ***587***
Utica Coll (NY) ***588***
Valparaiso U (IN) ***588***
Vassar Coll (NY) ***589***
Virginia Military Inst (VA) ***591***
Virginia Polytechnic Inst and State U (VA) ***591***
Virginia Wesleyan Coll (VA) ***591***
Walsh U (OH) ***593***
Wartburg Coll (IA) ***594***
Washington Coll (MD) ***594***
Washington U in St. Louis (MO) ***595***
Wayne State U (MI) ***596***
Webster U (MO) ***597***
Wellesley Coll (MA) ***597***
Wells Coll (NY) ***597***
Wesleyan Coll (GA) ***597***
West Chester U of Pennsylvania (PA) ***598***
Western International U (AZ) ***599***
Western New England Coll (MA) ***600***
Western Oregon U (OR) ***600***
Westminster Coll (MO) ***601***
Westminster Coll (PA) ***601***
West Virginia U (WV) ***602***
West Virginia Wesleyan Coll (WV) ***603***
Wheaton Coll (IL) ***603***
Wheaton Coll (MA) ***603***
Wheeling Jesuit U (WV) ***603***
Whittier Coll (CA) ***604***
Whitworth Coll (WA) ***604***
Widener U (PA) ***604***
Wilkes U (PA) ***605***
Willamette U (OR) ***605***
William Jewell Coll (MO) ***606***
William Woods U (MO) ***607***
Wilson Coll (PA) ***607***
Winona State U (MN) ***608***
Wittenberg U (OH) ***608***
Wofford Coll (SC) ***609***
Wright State U (OH) ***609***
Xavier U (OH) ***610***
York Coll of Pennsylvania (PA) ***610***
York U (ON, Canada) ***611***

INTERNET

Overview: This broad-based major will teach students about the origins and the various functions of the World Wide Web, including Internet theory, user interfaces, search engines, navigation, e-commerce. *Related majors:* computer science, information systems, data mining, science, technology and society, communications. *Potential careers:* researcher, Web page designer, Webmaster. *Salary potential:* $25k-$40k.

Bloomfield Coll (NJ) ***290***
Drexel U (PA) ***346***
Franklin U (OH) ***364***
Strayer U (DC) ***520***

INVESTMENTS AND SECURITIES

Overview: In this major students learn how to analyze capital markets and manage assets such as stocks, bonds and treasuries. *Related majors:* financial planning, fincance, taxation, economics. *Potential careers:* stockbroker, investment advisor, financial analyst, tax attorney, financial planner. *Salary potential:* $35k-$50k.

Babson Coll (MA) ***278***
Duquesne U (PA) ***346***

ISLAMIC STUDIES

Overview: Students who choose this major study the religion of Islam-its history, sociology, and culture-through various periods, localities, and branches. This major includes instruction in Islamic scripture and related writings. *Related majors:* history, comparative religion, Middle Eastern studies, art history, archeology. *Potential careers:* foreign service officer, anthropologist, archeologist, historian. *Salary potential:* $25k-$30k.

American U (DC) ***267***
Brandeis U (MA) ***293***
East-West U (IL) ***350***
Hampshire Coll (MA) ***375***
Harvard U (MA) ***376***
Long Island U, Southampton Coll, Friends World Program (NY) ***409***
The Ohio State U (OH) ***457***
U of Calif, Santa Barbara (CA) ***541***
U of Michigan (MI) ***554***
The U of Texas at Austin (TX) ***578***
U of Toronto (ON, Canada) ***581***
Washington U in St. Louis (MO) ***595***
Wellesley Coll (MA) ***597***

ITALIAN

Overview: Students learn how to read, write, and understand the Italian language. *Related majors:* art history, historic preservation, conservation and architectural history, museum studies, history. *Potential careers:* journalist, translator, diplomatic corps, art historian, writer. *Salary potential:* $23k-$30k.

Albertus Magnus Coll (CT) ***262***
American U of Rome(Italy) ***268***
Arizona State U (AZ) ***271***
Bard Coll (NY) ***281***
Barnard Coll (NY) ***282***

Bishop's U (QC, Canada) **289**
Boston Coll (MA) **292**
Boston U (MA) **292**
Brigham Young U (UT) **295**
Brock U (ON, Canada) **295**
Brooklyn Coll of the City U of NY (NY) **295**
Brown U (RI) **296**
Bryn Mawr Coll (PA) **297**
California State U, Northridge (CA) **301**
Carleton U (ON, Canada) **305**
Central Connecticut State U (CT) **309**
City Coll of the City U of NY (NY) **314**
Claremont McKenna Coll (CA) **315**
Coll of the Holy Cross (MA) **323**
Columbia Coll (NY) **326**
Columbia U, School of General Studies (NY) **328**
Concordia U (QC, Canada) **331**
Connecticut Coll (CT) **331**
Cornell U (NY) **333**
Dartmouth Coll (NH) **337**
DePaul U (IL) **339**
Dickinson Coll (PA) **344**
Dominican U (IL) **345**
Drew U (NJ) **346**
Duke U (NC) **346**
Emory U (GA) **354**
Florida International U (FL) **360**
Florida State U (FL) **361**
Fordham U (NY) **362**
Georgetown U (DC) **366**
Gonzaga U (WA) **369**
Harvard U (MA) **376**
Haverford Coll (PA) **377**
Hofstra U (NY) **380**
Hunter Coll of the City U of NY (NY) **382**
Indiana U Bloomington (IN) **385**
Iona Coll (NY) **390**
Johns Hopkins U (MD) **392**
Lake Erie Coll (OH) **400**
La Salle U (PA) **402**
Laurentian U (ON, Canada) **403**
Lehman Coll of the City U of NY (NY) **404**
Long Island U, C.W. Post Campus (NY) **409**
Long Island U, Southampton Coll, Friends World Program (NY) **409**
Loyola U Chicago (IL) **411**
Marlboro Coll (VT) **418**
McGill U (QC, Canada) **423**
Mercy Coll (NY) **425**
Middlebury Coll (VT) **429**
Montclair State U (NJ) **435**
Mount Holyoke Coll (MA) **438**
Nazareth Coll of Rochester (NY) **443**
New York U (NY) **447**
Northeastern U (MA) **450**
Northwestern U (IL) **453**
The Ohio State U (OH) **457**
Penn State U Univ Park Campus (PA) **468**
Providence Coll (RI) **474**
Queens Coll of the City U of NY (NY) **475**
Queen's U at Kingston (ON, Canada) **476**
Rosemont Coll (PA) **484**
Rutgers, The State U of New Jersey, Newark (NJ) **485**
Rutgers, The State U of New Jersey, New Brunswick (NJ) **485**
St. John Fisher Coll (NY) **489**
St. John's U (NY) **490**
San Francisco State U (CA) **498**
Santa Clara U (CA) **499**
Sarah Lawrence Coll (NY) **499**
Scripps Coll (CA) **501**
Seton Hall U (NJ) **502**
Smith Coll (MA) **506**
Southern Connecticut State U (CT) **509**
Stanford U (CA) **514**
State U of NY at Albany (NY) **514**
State U of NY at Binghamton (NY) **515**
Stony Brook U, State University of New York (NY) **520**
Sweet Briar Coll (VA) **521**
Syracuse U (NY) **521**
Temple U (PA) **523**
Trinity Coll (CT) **530**
Tulane U (LA) **533**
U at Buffalo, The State University of New York (NY) **536**
U of Alberta (AB, Canada) **538**
The U of Arizona (AZ) **538**
The U of British Columbia (BC, Canada) **540**
U of Calif, Berkeley (CA) **540**
U of Calif, Davis (CA) **540**
U of Calif, Los Angeles (CA) **541**
U of Calif, San Diego (CA) **541**
U of Calif, Santa Barbara (CA) **541**
U of Calif, Santa Cruz (CA) **542**
U of Chicago (IL) **542**
U of Colorado at Boulder (CO) **543**
U of Connecticut (CT) **544**
U of Delaware (DE) **544**
U of Denver (CO) **544**
U of Georgia (GA) **545**
U of Houston (TX) **547**
U of Illinois at Chicago (IL) **547**
U of Illinois at Urbana–Champaign (IL) **548**
The U of Iowa (IA) **548**
U of Maryland, Coll Park (MD) **552**
U of Massachusetts Amherst (MA) **552**
U of Massachusetts Boston (MA) **553**
U of Miami (FL) **553**
U of Michigan (MI) **554**
U of Minnesota, Twin Cities Campus (MN) **555**
U of Notre Dame (IN) **562**
U of Oregon (OR) **562**
U of Ottawa (ON, Canada) **563**
U of Pennsylvania (PA) **563**
U of Pittsburgh (PA) **569**
U of Rhode Island (RI) **572**
The U of Scranton (PA) **574**
U of South Carolina (SC) **575**
U of Southern California (CA) **576**
U of South Florida (FL) **576**
The U of Tennessee (TN) **577**
The U of Texas at Austin (TX) **578**
U of Toronto (ON, Canada) **581**
U of Victoria (BC, Canada) **582**
U of Virginia (VA) **582**
U of Washington (WA) **583**
U of Windsor (ON, Canada) **584**
U of Wisconsin–Madison (WI) **584**
U of Wisconsin–Milwaukee (WI) **585**
Vassar Coll (NY) **589**
Washington U in St. Louis (MO) **595**
Wayne State U (MI) **596**
Wellesley Coll (MA) **597**
Wesleyan U (CT) **597**
Yale U (CT) **610**
York Coll of the City U of New York (NY) **611**
York U (ON, Canada) **611**
Youngstown State U (OH) **611**

ITALIAN STUDIES

Overview: Students learn about the history, society, politics, culture, and economics of Italy. *Related majors:* archeology, art history, Italian, economics, history. *Potential careers:* museum curator, archeologist, importer, translator, tour guide. *Salary potential:* $25k-$30k.

Bennington Coll (VT) **286**
Brown U (RI) **296**
Columbia Coll (NY) **326**
Dominican U (IL) **345**
Lake Erie Coll (OH) **400**
Sweet Briar Coll (VA) **521**
U of Calif, Santa Cruz (CA) **542**
U of Windsor (ON, Canada) **584**
Wellesley Coll (MA) **597**
York U (ON, Canada) **611**

JAPANESE

Overview: Students learn to read, speak, and understand the Japanese language and study the culture and literature of Japan. *Related majors:* East Asian studies, Japanese studies, international economics, business management. *Potential careers:* specialist in international banking or finance, journalist, editor, teacher, diplomatic corps. *Salary potential:* $28k-$35k.

Antioch Coll (OH) **269**
Arizona State U (AZ) **271**
Ball State U (IN) **280**
Bates Coll (ME) **282**
Bennington Coll (VT) **286**
Brigham Young U (UT) **295**
California State U, Fullerton (CA) **301**
California State U, Long Beach (CA) **301**
Carnegie Mellon U (PA) **305**
Claremont McKenna Coll (CA) **315**
Colgate U (NY) **319**
Connecticut Coll (CT) **331**
Cornell U (NY) **333**
Dartmouth Coll (NH) **337**
DePaul U (IL) **339**
Dillard U (LA) **344**
Eastern Michigan U (MI) **348**
The Evergreen State Coll (WA) **355**
Georgetown U (DC) **366**
Gustavus Adolphus Coll (MN) **374**
Harvard U (MA) **376**
Hobart and William Smith Colls (NY) **380**
Indiana U Bloomington (IN) **385**
Long Island U, Southampton Coll, Friends World Program (NY) **409**
McMaster U (ON, Canada) **423**
Middlebury Coll (VT) **429**
Mount Union Coll (OH) **440**
North Central Coll (IL) **449**
The Ohio State U (OH) **457**
Pacific U (OR) **464**
Penn State U Univ Park Campus (PA) **468**
Pomona Coll (CA) **472**
Portland State U (OR) **472**
Salem International U (WV) **496**
San Diego State U (CA) **498**
San Francisco State U (CA) **498**
San Jose State U (CA) **499**
Scripps Coll (CA) **501**
Stanford U (CA) **514**
U of Alaska Fairbanks (AK) **538**
U of Alberta (AB, Canada) **538**
The U of British Columbia (BC, Canada) **540**
U of Calif, Berkeley (CA) **540**
U of Calif, Davis (CA) **540**
U of Calif, Los Angeles (CA) **541**
U of Calif, San Diego (CA) **541**
U of Calif, Santa Barbara (CA) **541**
U of Calif, Santa Cruz (CA) **542**
U of Chicago (IL) **542**
U of Colorado at Boulder (CO) **543**
The U of Findlay (OH) **545**
U of Georgia (GA) **545**
U of Hawaii at Hilo (HI) **546**
U of Hawaii at Manoa (HI) **546**
The U of Iowa (IA) **548**
U of Kansas (KS) **549**
U of Maryland, Coll Park (MD) **552**
U of Massachusetts Amherst (MA) **552**
U of Michigan (MI) **554**
U of Minnesota, Twin Cities Campus (MN) **555**
The U of Montana–Missoula (MT) **556**
U of Notre Dame (IN) **562**
U of Oregon (OR) **562**
U of Pittsburgh (PA) **569**
U of Rochester (NY) **573**
The U of Scranton (PA) **574**
U of Southern California (CA) **576**
U of the Pacific (CA) **580**
U of Toronto (ON, Canada) **581**
U of Utah (UT) **582**
U of Victoria (BC, Canada) **582**
U of Washington (WA) **583**
U of Windsor (ON, Canada) **584**
U of Wisconsin–Madison (WI) **584**
Ursinus Coll (PA) **587**
Washington U in St. Louis (MO) **595**
Wellesley Coll (MA) **597**
Williams Coll (MA) **606**
Yale U (CT) **610**
York U (ON, Canada) **611**

JAZZ

Overview: Students study both the principles of jazz as well as the performance and composition of jazz. *Related majors:* music performance, musicology/ethnomusicology. *Potential careers:* musician, vocalist, bandleader, professor. *Salary potential:* varies according to performance schedule.

Aquinas Coll (MI) **270**
Augustana Coll (IL) **276**
Bard Coll (NY) **281**
Bennington Coll (VT) **286**
Berklee Coll of Music (MA) **286**
Bowling Green State U (OH) **292**
California Inst of the Arts (CA) **299**
Capital U (OH) **304**
Concordia U (QC, Canada) **331**
DePaul U (IL) **339**
Five Towns Coll (NY) **359**
Florida State U (FL) **361**
Goddard Coll (VT) **369**
Hampshire Coll (MA) **375**
Hampton U (VA) **375**
Indiana U Bloomington (IN) **385**
Ithaca Coll (NY) **390**
Johnson State Coll (VT) **394**
Lamar U (TX) **401**
Long Island U, Brooklyn Campus (NY) **409**
Long Island U, Southampton Coll, Friends World Program (NY) **409**
Loyola U New Orleans (LA) **411**
Manhattan School of Music (NY) **416**
McGill U (QC, Canada) **423**
New England Conservatory of Music (MA) **445**
New York U (NY) **447**
North Carolina Central U (NC) **448**
North Central Coll (IL) **449**
Northwestern U (IL) **453**
Oberlin Coll (OH) **456**
The Ohio State U (OH) **457**
Roosevelt U (IL) **483**
Rowan U (NJ) **484**
Rutgers, The State U of New Jersey, New Brunswick (NJ) **485**
St. Francis Xavier U (NS, Canada) **489**
Simon's Rock Coll of Bard (MA) **505**
Southwest Texas State U (TX) **513**
State U of NY at New Paltz (NY) **515**
Temple U (PA) **523**
Texas Southern U (TX) **526**
U of Cincinnati (OH) **543**
U of Hartford (CT) **546**
The U of Iowa (IA) **548**
The U of Maine at Augusta (ME) **550**
U of Miami (FL) **553**
U of Michigan (MI) **554**
U of Minnesota, Duluth (MN) **554**
U of Nevada, Las Vegas (NV) **558**
U of North Florida (FL) **561**
U of North Texas (TX) **562**
U of Rochester (NY) **573**
U of Southern California (CA) **576**
Virginia Union U (VA) **591**
Webster U (MO) **597**
Western Washington U (WA) **600**
Westfield State Coll (MA) **600**
William Paterson U of New Jersey (NJ) **606**
York U (ON, Canada) **611**

JOURNALISM

Overview: Students learn the correct methods for gathering, processing, and delivering news. *Related majors:* English, creative writing, law, political science, rhetoric, history. *Potential careers:* journalist, editor, lawyer, teacher, court reporter, technical writer, publicist. *Salary potential:* $23k-$30k.

Abilene Christian U (TX) **260**
Adams State Coll (CO) **260**
Alabama State U (AL) **261**
Alliant International U (CA) **264**
American U (DC) **267**
The American U in Cairo(Egypt) **267**
Anderson Coll (SC) **268**
Andrews U (MI) **269**
Angelo State U (TX) **269**
Appalachian State U (NC) **270**
Arizona State U (AZ) **271**
Arkansas State U (AR) **272**
Arkansas Tech U (AR) **272**
Asbury Coll (KY) **274**
Ashland U (OH) **274**
Auburn U (AL) **276**
Augustana Coll (SD) **276**
Averett U (VA) **278**
Ball State U (IN) **280**
Barry U (FL) **282**
Bayamón Central U (PR) **283**
Baylor U (TX) **283**
Belmont U (TN) **284**
Bemidji State U (MN) **285**
Benedict Coll (SC) **285**
Benedictine Coll (KS) **285**

JOURNALISM (continued)

Baruch Coll of the City U of NY (NY) ***286***
Berry Coll (GA) ***287***
Boston U (MA) ***292***
Bowling Green State U (OH) ***292***
Bradley U (IL) ***293***
Brooklyn Coll of the City U of NY (NY) ***295***
Butler U (IN) ***297***
California Polytechnic State U, San Luis Obispo (CA) ***300***
California State Polytechnic U, Pomona (CA) ***300***
California State U, Chico (CA) ***300***
California State U, Fresno (CA) ***301***
California State U, Fullerton (CA) ***301***
California State U, Hayward (CA) ***301***
California State U, Long Beach (CA) ***301***
California State U, Northridge (CA) ***301***
California State U, Sacramento (CA) ***301***
Cameron U (OK) ***303***
Campbellsville U (KY) ***303***
Campbell U (NC) ***303***
Carleton U (ON, Canada) ***305***
Carroll Coll (WI) ***306***
Carson-Newman Coll (TN) ***306***
Castleton State Coll (VT) ***307***
Central Michigan U (MI) ***310***
Central Missouri State U (MO) ***310***
Central Washington U (WA) ***310***
Chapman U (CA) ***311***
Cincinnati Bible Coll and Seminary (OH) ***314***
Coll of St. Catherine (MN) ***321***
Coll of St. Joseph (VT) ***322***
The Coll of Southeastern Europe, The American U of Athens(Greece) ***323***
Coll of the Ozarks (MO) ***323***
Colorado State U (CO) ***325***
Colorado State U-Pueblo (CO) ***325***
Columbia Coll Chicago (IL) ***327***
Columbia Union Coll (MD) ***328***
Concordia Coll (MN) ***329***
Concordia U (QC, Canada) ***331***
Creighton U (NE) ***333***
Curry Coll (MA) ***335***
Davis & Elkins Coll (WV) ***338***
Delaware State U (DE) ***338***
Delta State U (MS) ***339***
Dordt Coll (IA) ***345***
Drake U (IA) ***345***
Duquesne U (PA) ***346***
Eastern Illinois U (IL) ***348***
Eastern Kentucky U (KY) ***348***
Eastern Michigan U (MI) ***348***
Eastern Nazarene Coll (MA) ***348***
Eastern Washington U (WA) ***349***
Edinboro U of Pennsylvania (PA) ***351***
Elon U (NC) ***352***
Emerson Coll (MA) ***353***
Evangel U (MO) ***355***
Florida A&M U (FL) ***359***
Florida Southern Coll (FL) ***361***
Fordham U (NY) ***362***
Fort Hays State U (KS) ***362***
Framingham State Coll (MA) ***362***
The Franciscan U (IA) ***363***
Franklin Coll (IN) ***363***
Franklin Pierce Coll (NH) ***364***
The George Washington U (DC) ***367***
Georgia Coll & State U (GA) ***367***
Georgia Southern U (GA) ***367***
Georgia State U (GA) ***368***
Goddard Coll (VT) ***369***
Gonzaga U (WA) ***369***
Goshen Coll (IN) ***370***
Grace U (NE) ***371***
Grand Valley State U (MI) ***371***
Grand View Coll (IA) ***372***
Hampshire Coll (MA) ***375***
Hampton U (VA) ***375***
Harding U (AR) ***375***
Hastings Coll (NE) ***377***
Hawai'i Pacific U (HI) ***377***
Henderson State U (AR) ***378***
Hofstra U (NY) ***380***
Houston Baptist U (TX) ***382***
Howard U (DC) ***382***
Humboldt State U (CA) ***382***
Indiana State U (IN) ***385***
Indiana U Bloomington (IN) ***385***
Indiana U of Pennsylvania (PA) ***386***
Indiana U–Purdue U Indianapolis (IN) ***387***
Iona Coll (NY) ***390***
Iowa State U of Science and Technology (IA) ***390***
Ithaca Coll (NY) ***390***
Jackson State U (MS) ***390***
John Brown U (AR) ***392***
Johnson State Coll (VT) ***394***
Judson Coll (IL) ***395***
Kansas State U (KS) ***396***
Keene State Coll (NH) ***396***
Lamar U (TX) ***401***
Langston U (OK) ***402***
La Salle U (PA) ***402***
Lehigh U (PA) ***404***
Lewis U (IL) ***406***
Lincoln U (PA) ***407***
Lindenwood U (MO) ***407***
Lock Haven U of Pennsylvania (PA) ***408***
Long Island U, Brooklyn Campus (NY) ***409***
Long Island U, C.W. Post Campus (NY) ***409***
Long Island U, Southampton Coll, Friends World Program (NY) ***409***
Longwood U (VA) ***409***
Loras Coll (IA) ***410***
Louisiana Coll (LA) ***410***
Louisiana Tech U (LA) ***410***
Loyola U Chicago (IL) ***411***
Lubbock Christian U (TX) ***412***
Lynchburg Coll (VA) ***413***
Lyndon State Coll (VT) ***413***
MacMurray Coll (IL) ***414***
Madonna U (MI) ***414***
Malone Coll (OH) ***415***
Mansfield U of Pennsylvania (PA) ***416***
Marietta Coll (OH) ***417***
Marist Coll (NY) ***417***
Marquette U (WI) ***418***
Marshall U (WV) ***418***
Mars Hill Coll (NC) ***418***
Mary Baldwin Coll (VA) ***419***
Marymount Coll of Fordham U (NY) ***419***
Massachusetts Coll of Liberal Arts (MA) ***421***
Mercy Coll (NY) ***425***
Mercyhurst Coll (PA) ***425***
Messiah Coll (PA) ***426***
Metropolitan State Coll of Denver (CO) ***427***
Miami U (OH) ***428***
Michigan State U (MI) ***428***
Midland Lutheran Coll (NE) ***429***
Milligan Coll (TN) ***430***
Minnesota State U, Mankato (MN) ***431***
Minnesota State U, Moorhead (MN) ***432***
Moravian Coll (PA) ***436***
Morris Coll (SC) ***437***
Mount Vernon Nazarene U (OH) ***440***
Multnomah Bible Coll and Biblical Seminary (OR) ***440***
Murray State U (KY) ***440***
Muskingum Coll (OH) ***441***
National U (CA) ***442***
New England Coll (NH) ***444***
New Mexico Highlands U (NM) ***446***
New Mexico State U (NM) ***446***
New York U (NY) ***447***
Norfolk State U (VA) ***448***
Northeastern State U (OK) ***450***
Northeastern U (MA) ***450***
Northern Arizona U (AZ) ***450***
Northern Illinois U (IL) ***450***
Northern Kentucky U (KY) ***451***
North Greenville Coll (SC) ***451***
Northwestern Coll (MN) ***453***
Northwestern State U of Louisiana (LA) ***453***
Northwestern U (IL) ***453***
Northwest Missouri State U (MO) ***454***
Oakland U (MI) ***456***
The Ohio State U (OH) ***457***
Ohio U (OH) ***458***
Ohio Wesleyan U (OH) ***459***
Oklahoma Baptist U (OK) ***459***
Oklahoma Christian U (OK) ***459***
Oklahoma City U (OK) ***460***
Oklahoma State U (OK) ***460***
Olivet Coll (MI) ***461***
Olivet Nazarene U (IL) ***461***
Oral Roberts U (OK) ***461***
Otterbein Coll (OH) ***462***
Pace U (NY) ***463***
Pacific Lutheran U (WA) ***463***
Pacific Union Coll (CA) ***464***
Pacific U (OR) ***464***
Penn State U Univ Park Campus (PA) ***468***
Pepperdine U, Malibu (CA) ***469***
Piedmont Coll (GA) ***470***
Pittsburg State U (KS) ***470***
Point Loma Nazarene U (CA) ***471***
Point Park Coll (PA) ***471***
Purchase Coll, State U of NY (NY) ***475***
Purdue U Calumet (IN) ***475***
Queens U of Charlotte (NC) ***476***
Quincy U (IL) ***476***
Quinnipiac U (CT) ***476***
Radford U (VA) ***476***
Rider U (NJ) ***480***
Roosevelt U (IL) ***483***
Rowan U (NJ) ***484***
Rust Coll (MS) ***485***
Rutgers, The State U of New Jersey, Newark (NJ) ***485***
Rutgers, The State U of New Jersey, New Brunswick (NJ) ***485***
Ryerson U (ON, Canada) ***485***
Sacred Heart U (CT) ***486***
St. Ambrose U (IA) ***486***
St. Bonaventure U (NY) ***487***
St. Cloud State U (MN) ***488***
Saint Francis U (PA) ***488***
St. John's U (NY) ***490***
Saint Joseph's Coll of Maine (ME) ***491***
Saint Mary-of-the-Woods Coll (IN) ***493***
Saint Mary's U of Minnesota (MN) ***494***
Saint Michael's Coll (VT) ***494***
St. Thomas Aquinas Coll (NY) ***495***
St. Thomas U (NB, Canada) ***496***
Salem State Coll (MA) ***497***
Samford U (AL) ***497***
Sam Houston State U (TX) ***497***
San Diego State U (CA) ***498***
San Francisco State U (CA) ***498***
San Jose State U (CA) ***499***
Seattle U (WA) ***501***
Seton Hill U (PA) ***502***
Shippensburg U of Pennsylvania (PA) ***503***
Shorter Coll (GA) ***504***
Slippery Rock U of Pennsylvania (PA) ***506***
South Dakota State U (SD) ***507***
Southeast Missouri State U (MO) ***508***
Southern Adventist U (TN) ***508***
Southern Arkansas U–Magnolia (AR) ***509***
Southern Connecticut State U (CT) ***509***
Southern Illinois U Carbondale (IL) ***509***
Southern Methodist U (TX) ***510***
Southern Nazarene U (OK) ***510***
Southwest Missouri State U (MO) ***513***
Southwest Texas State U (TX) ***513***
Spring Arbor U (MI) ***514***
Spring Hill Coll (AL) ***514***
State U of NY at New Paltz (NY) ***515***
State U of NY at Oswego (NY) ***515***
State U of NY Coll at Brockport (NY) ***515***
State U of NY Coll at Buffalo (NY) ***516***
Stephen F. Austin State U (TX) ***518***
Suffolk U (MA) ***520***
Susquehanna U (PA) ***521***
Syracuse U (NY) ***521***
Tabor Coll (KS) ***522***
Temple U (PA) ***523***
Tennessee Technological U (TN) ***524***
Texas A&M U (TX) ***524***
Texas A&M U–Commerce (TX) ***525***
Texas A&M U–Kingsville (TX) ***525***
Texas Christian U (TX) ***526***
Texas Southern U (TX) ***526***
Texas Tech U (TX) ***526***
Texas Wesleyan U (TX) ***526***
Thomas Edison State Coll (NJ) ***527***
Toccoa Falls Coll (GA) ***528***
Troy State U (AL) ***532***
Truman State U (MO) ***532***
Union Coll (NE) ***534***
Union U (TN) ***534***
United States International U(Kenya) ***535***
U Coll of the Cariboo (BC, Canada) ***537***
The U of Alabama (AL) ***537***
U of Alaska Anchorage (AK) ***538***
U of Alaska Fairbanks (AK) ***538***
The U of Arizona (AZ) ***538***
U of Arkansas (AR) ***539***
U of Arkansas at Little Rock (AR) ***539***
U of Baltimore (MD) ***539***
U of Bridgeport (CT) ***540***
U of Central Arkansas (AR) ***542***
U of Central Florida (FL) ***542***
U of Central Oklahoma (OK) ***542***
U of Colorado at Boulder (CO) ***543***
U of Connecticut (CT) ***544***
U of Dayton (OH) ***544***
U of Delaware (DE) ***544***
U of Denver (CO) ***544***
The U of Findlay (OH) ***545***
U of Florida (FL) ***545***
U of Georgia (GA) ***545***
U of Hawaii at Manoa (HI) ***546***
U of Houston (TX) ***547***
U of Idaho (ID) ***547***
U of Illinois at Urbana–Champaign (IL) ***548***
The U of Iowa (IA) ***548***
U of Kansas (KS) ***549***
U of Kentucky (KY) ***549***
U of King's Coll (NS, Canada) ***549***
U of La Verne (CA) ***549***
U of Maine (ME) ***550***
U of Maryland, Coll Park (MD) ***552***
U of Massachusetts Amherst (MA) ***552***
The U of Memphis (TN) ***553***
U of Miami (FL) ***553***
U of Michigan (MI) ***554***
U of Minnesota, Twin Cities Campus (MN) ***555***
U of Mississippi (MS) ***555***
U of Missouri–Columbia (MO) ***555***
The U of Montana–Missoula (MT) ***556***
U of Nebraska at Kearney (NE) ***557***
U of Nebraska at Omaha (NE) ***557***
U of Nevada, Reno (NV) ***558***
U of New Hampshire (NH) ***558***
U of New Mexico (NM) ***559***
The U of North Carolina at Pembroke (NC) ***560***
U of Northern Colorado (CO) ***561***
U of North Texas (TX) ***562***
U of Oklahoma (OK) ***562***
U of Oregon (OR) ***562***
U of Pittsburgh at Greensburg (PA) ***570***
U of Pittsburgh at Johnstown (PA) ***570***
U of Portland (OR) ***570***
U of Regina (SK, Canada) ***572***
U of Rhode Island (RI) ***572***
U of Richmond (VA) ***572***
U of St. Thomas (MN) ***573***
U of San Francisco (CA) ***574***
U of South Carolina (SC) ***575***
The U of South Dakota (SD) ***575***
U of Southern California (CA) ***576***
U of Southern Indiana (IN) ***576***
U of Southern Mississippi (MS) ***576***
The U of Tennessee (TN) ***577***
The U of Tennessee at Martin (TN) ***577***
The U of Texas at Arlington (TX) ***577***
The U of Texas at Austin (TX) ***578***
The U of Texas at El Paso (TX) ***578***
The U of Texas at San Antonio (TX) ***578***
The U of Texas at Tyler (TX) ***579***
The U of Texas–Pan American (TX) ***579***
U of Toledo (OH) ***581***
U of Utah (UT) ***582***
U of Windsor (ON, Canada) ***584***
U of Wisconsin–Eau Claire (WI) ***584***
U of Wisconsin–Madison (WI) ***584***
U of Wisconsin–Milwaukee (WI) ***585***
U of Wisconsin–Oshkosh (WI) ***585***
U of Wisconsin–River Falls (WI) ***585***
U of Wisconsin–Superior (WI) ***586***
U of Wisconsin–Whitewater (WI) ***586***
U of Wyoming (WY) ***586***
Utah State U (UT) ***587***
Utica Coll (NY) ***588***
Virginia Union U (VA) ***591***
Waldorf Coll (IA) ***592***
Walla Walla Coll (WA) ***593***
Wartburg Coll (IA) ***594***
Washington and Lee U (VA) ***594***
Washington State U (WA) ***595***
Waynesburg Coll (PA) ***595***
Wayne State Coll (NE) ***596***
Wayne State U (MI) ***596***
Weber State U (UT) ***596***
Webster U (MO) ***597***
Western Illinois U (IL) ***599***
Western Kentucky U (KY) ***599***
Western Michigan U (MI) ***599***
Western State Coll of Colorado (CO) ***600***
Western Washington U (WA) ***600***
West Texas A&M U (TX) ***602***
West Virginia U (WV) ***602***
Whitworth Coll (WA) ***604***
Wingate U (NC) ***607***
Winona State U (MN) ***608***
Youngstown State U (OH) ***611***

JOURNALISM AND MASS COMMUNICATION RELATED

Information can be found under this major's main heading.

Averett U (VA) ***278***
Boston U (MA) ***292***
City U (WA) ***314***
Duquesne U (PA) ***346***
Kent State U (OH) ***397***
Ohio U (OH) ***458***
Saint Mary's U of Minnesota (MN) ***494***
San Diego State U (CA) ***498***
U of Nebraska–Lincoln (NE) ***557***
The U of North Carolina at Asheville (NC) ***559***
U of St. Thomas (MN) ***573***
The U of Western Ontario (ON, Canada) ***583***

JUDAIC STUDIES

Overview: This major teaches students about the history, culture, and religion of the Jewish people both in Israel and the Jewish Diaspora throughout history. *Related majors:* religion or Biblical studies, Hebrew, Islamic studies, philosophy, anthropology. *Potential careers:* anthropologist, foreign service officer, professor, writer, rabbi. *Salary potential:* $22k-$27k.

American U (DC) ***267***
Baltimore Hebrew U (MD) ***280***
Bard Coll (NY) ***281***
Brandeis U (MA) ***293***
Brooklyn Coll of the City U of NY (NY) ***295***
Brown U (RI) ***296***
City Coll of the City U of NY (NY) ***314***
Clark U (MA) ***316***
Cornell U (NY) ***333***
DePaul U (IL) ***339***
Dickinson Coll (PA) ***344***
Emory U (GA) ***354***
Florida Atlantic U (FL) ***359***
The George Washington U (DC) ***367***
Gratz Coll (PA) ***372***
Hamline U (MN) ***374***
Hampshire Coll (MA) ***375***
Harvard U (MA) ***376***
Hofstra U (NY) ***380***
Hunter Coll of the City U of NY (NY) ***382***
Indiana U Bloomington (IN) ***385***
Jewish Theological Seminary of America (NY) ***391***
Laura and Alvin Siegal Coll of Judaic Studies (OH) ***403***
Lehman Coll of the City U of NY (NY) ***404***
Machzikei Hadath Rabbinical Coll (NY) ***413***
McGill U (QC, Canada) ***423***
Mount Holyoke Coll (MA) ***438***
Ner Israel Rabbinical Coll (MD) ***443***
New York U (NY) ***447***
Oberlin Coll (OH) ***456***
The Ohio State U (OH) ***457***
Penn State U Univ Park Campus (PA) ***468***
Queens Coll of the City U of NY (NY) ***475***
Queen's U at Kingston (ON, Canada) ***476***
Rutgers, The State U of New Jersey, New Brunswick (NJ) ***485***
Scripps Coll (CA) ***501***
State U of NY at Albany (NY) ***514***
State U of NY at Binghamton (NY) ***515***
State U of NY at New Paltz (NY) ***515***
State U of NY Coll at Brockport (NY) ***515***
Talmudic Coll of Florida (FL) ***522***
Temple U (PA) ***523***
Touro Coll (NY) ***529***
Trinity Coll (CT) ***530***
Tufts U (MA) ***533***
Tulane U (LA) ***533***
The U of Arizona (AZ) ***538***
U of Calif, Los Angeles (CA) ***541***
U of Calif, San Diego (CA) ***541***
U of Chicago (IL) ***542***
U of Cincinnati (OH) ***543***
U of Florida (FL) ***545***
U of Hartford (CT) ***546***
U of Judaism (CA) ***548***
U of Manitoba (MB, Canada) ***551***
U of Maryland, Coll Park (MD) ***552***
U of Massachusetts Amherst (MA) ***552***
U of Miami (FL) ***553***
U of Michigan (MI) ***554***
U of Minnesota, Twin Cities Campus (MN) ***555***
U of Missouri–Kansas City (MO) ***555***
U of Oregon (OR) ***562***
U of Pennsylvania (PA) ***563***
U of Southern California (CA) ***576***
U of Toronto (ON, Canada) ***581***
U of Washington (WA) ***583***
Vassar Coll (NY) ***589***
Washington U in St. Louis (MO) ***595***
Wellesley Coll (MA) ***597***
Yale U (CT) ***610***
York U (ON, Canada) ***611***

LABORATORY ANIMAL MEDICINE

Overview: This major teaches students the practice of veterinary medicine involving the prevention, diagnosis, and treatment of injuries and illnesses and the general well-being of laboratory animals. *Related majors:* veterinary science, preveterinary studies, zoology, animal sciences, agricultural animal breeding/genetics. *Potential careers:* veterinarian, animal lab technician, researcher. *Salary potential:* $29k-$36k.

North Carolina Ag and Tech State U (NC) ***448***
Quinnipiac U (CT) ***476***
Thomas Edison State Coll (NJ) ***527***

LABOR/PERSONNEL RELATIONS

Overview: Students study various aspects of employee-management issues, including disputes regarding employee working conditions and benefit packages, as well as labor organization and policy from a historical perspective. *Related majors:* history, sociology, political science, law and legal studies, economics. *Potential careers:* professor, labor or personnel relations specialist, labor-management mediator, attorney, economist. *Salary potential:* $30k-$40k.

Athabasca U (AB, Canada) ***275***
Bowling Green State U (OH) ***292***
Brock U (ON, Canada) ***295***
California State U, Dominguez Hills (CA) ***300***
Carleton U (ON, Canada) ***305***
Clarion U of Pennsylvania (PA) ***315***
Cleveland State U (OH) ***317***
Cornell U (NY) ***333***
Ferris State U (MI) ***358***
Governors State U (IL) ***370***
Grand Valley State U (MI) ***371***
Hampshire Coll (MA) ***375***
Hofstra U (NY) ***380***
Indiana U Bloomington (IN) ***385***
Indiana U Kokomo (IN) ***386***
Indiana U Northwest (IN) ***386***
Indiana U–Purdue U Fort Wayne (IN) ***386***
Indiana U–Purdue U Indianapolis (IN) ***387***
Indiana U South Bend (IN) ***387***
Indiana U Southeast (IN) ***387***
Ithaca Coll (NY) ***390***
Lakehead U (ON, Canada) ***400***
Le Moyne Coll (NY) ***404***
McGill U (QC, Canada) ***423***
McMaster U (ON, Canada) ***423***
Memorial U of Newfoundland (NF, Canada) ***424***
Norfolk State U (VA) ***448***
Northern Kentucky U (KY) ***451***
Pace U (NY) ***463***
Penn State U Univ Park Campus (PA) ***468***
Queens Coll of the City U of NY (NY) ***475***
Rhode Island Coll (RI) ***479***
Rockhurst U (MO) ***482***
Rowan U (NJ) ***484***
Rutgers, The State U of New Jersey, New Brunswick (NJ) ***485***
Saint Francis U (PA) ***488***
Saint Joseph's U (PA) ***491***
San Francisco State U (CA) ***498***
Seton Hall U (NJ) ***502***
State U of NY Coll at Fredonia (NY) ***516***
State U of NY Coll at Old Westbury (NY) ***516***
State U of NY Coll at Potsdam (NY) ***517***
State U of NY Empire State Coll (NY) ***517***
Tennessee Technological U (TN) ***524***
Texas A&M U–Commerce (TX) ***525***
Thomas Edison State Coll (NJ) ***527***
U du Québec à Hull (QC, Canada) ***536***
Université Laval (QC, Canada) ***536***
U of Alberta (AB, Canada) ***538***
The U of British Columbia (BC, Canada) ***540***
The U of Iowa (IA) ***548***
U of Manitoba (MB, Canada) ***551***
U of Massachusetts Boston (MA) ***553***
U of Puerto Rico, Río Piedras (PR) ***571***
U of Toronto (ON, Canada) ***581***
U of Windsor (ON, Canada) ***584***
U of Wisconsin–Madison (WI) ***584***
U of Wisconsin–Milwaukee (WI) ***585***
Wayne State U (MI) ***596***
Westminster Coll (PA) ***601***
West Virginia U Inst of Technology (WV) ***602***
Winona State U (MN) ***608***
York U (ON, Canada) ***611***

LANDSCAPE ARCHITECTURE

Overview: This major prepares students to apply the principles of architecture to the design of outdoor/open spaces for recreational, living, or business purposes. *Related majors:* interior architecture, architecture, horticulture, plant science, structural engineering. *Potential careers:* landscape architect, architect, interior designer. *Salary potential:* $25k-$30k.

Arizona State U (AZ) ***271***
Auburn U (AL) ***276***
Ball State U (IN) ***280***
California Polytechnic State U, San Luis Obispo (CA) ***300***
California State Polytechnic U, Pomona (CA) ***300***
City Coll of the City U of NY (NY) ***314***
Clemson U (SC) ***317***
Coll of the Atlantic (ME) ***323***
Colorado State U (CO) ***325***
Cornell U (NY) ***333***
Delaware Valley Coll (PA) ***339***
Eastern Kentucky U (KY) ***348***
Florida A&M U (FL) ***359***
Iowa State U of Science and Technology (IA) ***390***
Kansas State U (KS) ***396***
Louisiana State U and A&M Coll (LA) ***410***
Michigan State U (MI) ***428***
Mississippi State U (MS) ***432***
North Carolina Ag and Tech State U (NC) ***448***
North Carolina State U (NC) ***449***
North Dakota State U (ND) ***449***
Northwest Missouri State U (MO) ***454***
The Ohio State U (OH) ***457***
Oklahoma State U (OK) ***460***
Penn State U Univ Park Campus (PA) ***468***
Purdue U (IN) ***475***
Ryerson U (ON, Canada) ***485***
State U of NY Coll of Environ Sci and Forestry (NY) ***517***
Temple U (PA) ***523***
Texas A&M U (TX) ***524***
Texas Tech U (TX) ***526***
The U of Arizona (AZ) ***538***
U of Arkansas (AR) ***539***
The U of British Columbia (BC, Canada) ***540***
U of Calif, Berkeley (CA) ***540***
U of Calif, Davis (CA) ***540***
U of Connecticut (CT) ***544***
U of Florida (FL) ***545***
U of Georgia (GA) ***545***
U of Guelph (ON, Canada) ***546***
U of Hawaii at Manoa (HI) ***546***
U of Idaho (ID) ***547***
U of Illinois at Urbana–Champaign (IL) ***548***
U of Kentucky (KY) ***549***
U of Maryland, Coll Park (MD) ***552***
U of Massachusetts Amherst (MA) ***552***
U of Michigan (MI) ***554***
U of Minnesota, Twin Cities Campus (MN) ***555***
U of Nevada, Las Vegas (NV) ***558***
U of Oregon (OR) ***562***
U of Rhode Island (RI) ***572***
U of Southern California (CA) ***576***
U of Toronto (ON, Canada) ***581***
U of Washington (WA) ***583***
U of Wisconsin–Madison (WI) ***584***
Utah State U (UT) ***587***
Virginia Polytechnic Inst and State U (VA) ***591***
West Virginia U (WV) ***602***

LANDSCAPING MANAGEMENT

Overview: Students learn to manage and maintain both ground covers and indoor or outdoor plants. *Related majors:* horticulture, plant science, soil irrigation and nutrition, turf management, agricultural mechanization. *Potential careers:* landscape designer, gardener, lawn service owner. *Salary potential:* $20k-$25k.

Andrews U (MI) ***269***
Colorado State U (CO) ***325***
Eastern Kentucky U (KY) ***348***
Mississippi State U (MS) ***432***
Oklahoma State U (OK) ***460***
Oregon State U (OR) ***462***
Penn State U Univ Park Campus (PA) ***468***
South Dakota State U (SD) ***507***
Tennessee Technological U (TN) ***524***
U of Georgia (GA) ***545***
U of Maine (ME) ***550***
The U of Tennessee at Martin (TN) ***577***
U of Vermont (VT) ***582***

LAND USE MANAGEMENT

Overview: This major teaches students how public and/or private land and resources can be preserved, developed, and used for maximum social, economic, and environmental benefit. *Related majors:* environmental science, natural resources management and conservation, range science and management, water resources, forest management. *Potential careers:* park ranger, lobbyist, environmental scientist, ecologist. *Salary potential:* $20k-$30k.

California State U, Bakersfield (CA) ***300***
The Evergreen State Coll (WA) ***355***
Frostburg State U (MD) ***365***
Grand Valley State U (MI) ***371***
Metropolitan State Coll of Denver (CO) ***427***
Northern Michigan U (MI) ***451***
Northland Coll (WI) ***452***
State U of NY Coll of Environ Sci and Forestry (NY) ***517***
U of Alberta (AB, Canada) ***538***
U of Saskatchewan (SK, Canada) ***574***
U of Wisconsin–Platteville (WI) ***585***
U of Wisconsin–River Falls (WI) ***585***

LASER/OPTICAL TECHNOLOGY

Overview: This major gives undergraduates the skills and knowledge necessary to work alongside engineers and professionals who are developing and/or using lasers and other sophisticated optical instruments in either the commercial or industrial sectors. *Related majors:* applied mathematics, optics, biomedical engineering technology. *Potential careers:* biomedical engineer, Air Force officer, research scientist. *Salary potential:* $26k-$40k.

Excelsior Coll (NY) ***356***
Oregon Inst of Technology (OR) ***461***

LATIN AMERICAN STUDIES

Overview: This major teaches students about the history, society, politics, culture, economics, and languages of the Hispanic people of North and South America outside of Canada and the United States. *Related majors:* history, comparative literature, international relations, Spanish, Portuguese. *Potential careers:* importer/exporter, anthropologist, archeologist, teacher, translator. *Salary potential:* $23k-$29k.

Adelphi U (NY) ***260***
Albright Coll (PA) ***263***
American U (DC) ***267***
Assumption Coll (MA) ***275***
Austin Coll (TX) ***277***
Ball State U (IN) ***280***
Bard Coll (NY) ***281***
Barnard Coll (NY) ***282***
Baylor U (TX) ***283***
Beloit Coll (WI) ***285***
Boston U (MA) ***292***
Bowdoin Coll (ME) ***292***
Brandeis U (MA) ***293***
Brigham Young U (UT) ***295***
Brown U (RI) ***296***
Bucknell U (PA) ***297***
California State U, Chico (CA) ***300***
California State U, Fullerton (CA) ***301***
California State U, Hayward (CA) ***301***
Carleton Coll (MN) ***305***
Carleton U (ON, Canada) ***305***
Central Coll (IA) ***309***
Chapman U (CA) ***311***
City Coll of the City U of NY (NY) ***314***
Claremont McKenna Coll (CA) ***315***
Colby Coll (ME) ***318***
Colgate U (NY) ***319***
Coll of the Holy Cross (MA) ***323***
The Coll of William and Mary (VA) ***324***
The Coll of Wooster (OH) ***324***
Colorado State U (CO) ***325***
Columbia Coll (NY) ***326***
Connecticut Coll (CT) ***331***
Cornell Coll (IA) ***332***
Cornell U (NY) ***333***
Dartmouth Coll (NH) ***337***
Denison U (OH) ***339***
DePaul U (IL) ***339***
Earlham Coll (IN) ***347***
Emory U (GA) ***354***
The Evergreen State Coll (WA) ***355***
Flagler Coll (FL) ***359***
Florida State U (FL) ***361***
Fordham U (NY) ***362***
Fort Lewis Coll (CO) ***362***
The George Washington U (DC) ***367***
Gettysburg Coll (PA) ***368***
Grinnell Coll (IA) ***373***
Gustavus Adolphus Coll (MN) ***374***
Hamline U (MN) ***374***
Hampshire Coll (MA) ***375***
Hanover Coll (IN) ***375***
Harvard U (MA) ***376***
Haverford Coll (PA) ***377***
Hobart and William Smith Colls (NY) ***380***
Hofstra U (NY) ***380***
Hood Coll (MD) ***381***
Hunter Coll of the City U of NY (NY) ***382***
Illinois Wesleyan U (IL) ***385***
Indiana U Bloomington (IN) ***385***
Johns Hopkins U (MD) ***392***
Kent State U (OH) ***397***
Lake Forest Coll (IL) ***400***
Lehman Coll of the City U of NY (NY) ***404***
Lock Haven U of Pennsylvania (PA) ***408***
Long Island U, Southampton Coll, Friends World Program (NY) ***409***
Luther Coll (IA) ***412***
Macalester Coll (MN) ***413***
Marlboro Coll (VT) ***418***
Massachusetts Inst of Technology (MA) ***421***
McGill U (QC, Canada) ***423***
McMaster U (ON, Canada) ***423***
Mount Holyoke Coll (MA) ***438***
New York U (NY) ***447***
Oakland U (MI) ***456***
Oberlin Coll (OH) ***456***
The Ohio State U (OH) ***457***
Ohio U (OH) ***458***
Penn State U Univ Park Campus (PA) ***468***
Pitzer Coll (CA) ***471***
Plattsburgh State U of NY (NY) ***471***
Pontifical Coll Josephinum (OH) ***472***
Portland State U (OR) ***472***
Prescott Coll (AZ) ***474***
Queens Coll of the City U of NY (NY) ***475***
Queen's U at Kingston (ON, Canada) ***476***
Rice U (TX) ***479***
Ripon Coll (WI) ***480***
Rollins Coll (FL) ***483***
Rutgers, The State U of New Jersey, New Brunswick (NJ) ***485***
St. Cloud State U (MN) ***488***
Samford U (AL) ***497***
San Diego State U (CA) ***498***
Sarah Lawrence Coll (NY) ***499***
Scripps Coll (CA) ***501***
Seattle Pacific U (WA) ***501***
Simon Fraser U (BC, Canada) ***505***
Simon's Rock Coll of Bard (MA) ***505***
Smith Coll (MA) ***506***
Southern Methodist U (TX) ***510***
State U of NY at Albany (NY) ***514***
State U of NY at Binghamton (NY) ***515***
State U of NY at New Paltz (NY) ***515***
State U of NY Coll at Brockport (NY) ***515***
Stetson U (FL) ***519***
Syracuse U (NY) ***521***
Temple U (PA) ***523***
Texas Christian U (TX) ***526***
Texas Tech U (TX) ***526***
Trinity U (TX) ***531***
Tulane U (LA) ***533***
United States Military Academy (NY) ***535***
The U of Alabama (AL) ***537***
U of Alberta (AB, Canada) ***538***
The U of Arizona (AZ) ***538***
The U of British Columbia (BC, Canada) ***540***
U of Calgary (AB, Canada) ***540***
U of Calif, Berkeley (CA) ***540***
U of Calif, Los Angeles (CA) ***541***
U of Calif, Riverside (CA) ***541***
U of Calif, San Diego (CA) ***541***
U of Calif, Santa Barbara (CA) ***541***
U of Calif, Santa Cruz (CA) ***542***
U of Chicago (IL) ***542***
U of Cincinnati (OH) ***543***
U of Connecticut (CT) ***544***
U of Delaware (DE) ***544***
U of Denver (CO) ***544***
U of Idaho (ID) ***547***
U of Illinois at Chicago (IL) ***547***
U of Illinois at Urbana–Champaign (IL) ***548***
The U of Iowa (IA) ***548***
U of Kansas (KS) ***549***
U of Kentucky (KY) ***549***
U of Miami (FL) ***553***
U of Michigan (MI) ***554***
U of Minnesota, Morris (MN) ***555***
U of Minnesota, Twin Cities Campus (MN) ***555***
U of Nebraska–Lincoln (NE) ***557***
U of New Mexico (NM) ***559***
The U of North Carolina at Chapel Hill (NC) ***560***
The U of North Carolina at Greensboro (NC) ***560***
U of Northern Iowa (IA) ***561***
U of Pennsylvania (PA) ***563***
U of Rhode Island (RI) ***572***
U of Richmond (VA) ***572***
U of South Carolina (SC) ***575***
The U of Texas at Austin (TX) ***578***
The U of Texas at El Paso (TX) ***578***
U of Toledo (OH) ***581***
U of Toronto (ON, Canada) ***581***
U of Vermont (VT) ***582***
U of Washington (WA) ***583***
U of Wisconsin–Eau Claire (WI) ***584***
U of Wisconsin–Madison (WI) ***584***
U of Wisconsin–Milwaukee (WI) ***585***
Vanderbilt U (TN) ***588***
Vassar Coll (NY) ***589***
Walsh U (OH) ***593***
Warren Wilson Coll (NC) ***594***
Washington Coll (MD) ***594***
Washington U in St. Louis (MO) ***595***
Wellesley Coll (MA) ***597***
Wesleyan U (CT) ***597***
Western Washington U (WA) ***600***
Yale U (CT) ***610***
York U (ON, Canada) ***611***

LATIN (ANCIENT AND MEDIEVAL)

Overview: Students learn about the Latin language and literature from its origin through its decline, as well as current ecclesiastical/theological usage. *Related majors:* classics, linguistics, history, theology, Western civilization and culture. *Potential careers:* teacher, editor, archeologist, professor. *Salary potential:* $20k-$28k.

Acadia U (NS, Canada) ***260***
Amherst Coll (MA) ***268***
Asbury Coll (KY) ***274***
Augustana Coll (IL) ***276***
Austin Coll (TX) ***277***
Ball State U (IN) ***280***
Bard Coll (NY) ***281***
Barnard Coll (NY) ***282***
Baylor U (TX) ***283***
Boston U (MA) ***292***
Bowling Green State U (OH) ***292***
Brandeis U (MA) ***293***
Brigham Young U (UT) ***295***
Brooklyn Coll of the City U of NY (NY) ***295***
Bryn Mawr Coll (PA) ***297***
Butler U (IN) ***297***
Calvin Coll (MI) ***303***
Carleton Coll (MN) ***305***
Carleton U (ON, Canada) ***305***
Carroll Coll (MT) ***306***
The Catholic U of America (DC) ***307***
Centenary Coll of Louisiana (LA) ***308***
Claremont McKenna Coll (CA) ***315***
Colgate U (NY) ***319***
The Coll of New Rochelle (NY) ***321***
The Coll of William and Mary (VA) ***324***
The Coll of Wooster (OH) ***324***
Concordia Coll (MN) ***329***
Concordia U (QC, Canada) ***331***
Cornell Coll (IA) ***332***
Cornell U (NY) ***333***
Creighton U (NE) ***333***
Dartmouth Coll (NH) ***337***
DePauw U (IN) ***339***
Dickinson Coll (PA) ***344***
Duke U (NC) ***346***
Duquesne U (PA) ***346***
Elmira Coll (NY) ***351***
Emory U (GA) ***354***
Florida State U (FL) ***361***
Fordham U (NY) ***362***
Franklin and Marshall Coll (PA) ***363***
Furman U (SC) ***365***
Gettysburg Coll (PA) ***368***
Hamilton Coll (NY) ***374***
Hampden-Sydney Coll (VA) ***374***
Harvard U (MA) ***376***
Haverford Coll (PA) ***377***
Hobart and William Smith Colls (NY) ***380***
Hope Coll (MI) ***381***
Hunter Coll of the City U of NY (NY) ***382***
Indiana U Bloomington (IN) ***385***
John Carroll U (OH) ***392***
Kent State U (OH) ***397***
Kenyon Coll (OH) ***398***
La Salle U (PA) ***402***
Lehman Coll of the City U of NY (NY) ***404***
Lenoir-Rhyne Coll (NC) ***405***
Louisiana State U and A&M Coll (LA) ***410***
Loyola Marymount U (CA) ***411***
Loyola U Chicago (IL) ***411***
Luther Coll (IA) ***412***
Macalester Coll (MN) ***413***
Marlboro Coll (VT) ***418***
Mary Washington Coll (VA) ***420***
Memorial U of Newfoundland (NF, Canada) ***424***
Mercer U (GA) ***425***
Miami U (OH) ***428***
Michigan State U (MI) ***428***
Monmouth Coll (IL) ***434***
Montclair State U (NJ) ***435***
Mount Allison U (NB, Canada) ***437***
Mount Holyoke Coll (MA) ***438***
New Coll of Florida (FL) ***444***
New York U (NY) ***447***
Oberlin Coll (OH) ***456***
Ohio U (OH) ***458***
Queens Coll of the City U of NY (NY) ***475***
Queen's U at Kingston (ON, Canada) ***476***
Randolph-Macon Coll (VA) ***477***
Randolph-Macon Woman's Coll (VA) ***477***
Rhodes Coll (TN) ***479***
Rice U (TX) ***479***
Rockford Coll (IL) ***482***
Rutgers, The State U of New Jersey, New Brunswick (NJ) ***485***
St. Bonaventure U (NY) ***487***
Saint Mary's Coll of California (CA) ***494***
St. Olaf Coll (MN) ***495***
Samford U (AL) ***497***
Santa Clara U (CA) ***499***
Sarah Lawrence Coll (NY) ***499***
Scripps Coll (CA) ***501***
Seattle Pacific U (WA) ***501***
Smith Coll (MA) ***506***
Southwest Missouri State U (MO) ***513***
State U of NY at Albany (NY) ***514***
Swarthmore Coll (PA) ***521***
Sweet Briar Coll (VA) ***521***
Syracuse U (NY) ***521***
Trent U (ON, Canada) ***529***
Tufts U (MA) ***533***
Tulane U (LA) ***533***
U of Alberta (AB, Canada) ***538***
The U of British Columbia (BC, Canada) ***540***
U of Calif, Berkeley (CA) ***540***
U of Calif, Los Angeles (CA) ***541***
U of Calif, Santa Cruz (CA) ***542***
U of Chicago (IL) ***542***
U of Delaware (DE) ***544***
U of Georgia (GA) ***545***
U of Hawaii at Manoa (HI) ***546***
U of Houston (TX) ***547***
U of Idaho (ID) ***547***
The U of Iowa (IA) ***548***
U of Maine (ME) ***550***
U of Manitoba (MB, Canada) ***551***
U of Massachusetts Boston (MA) ***553***
U of Michigan (MI) ***554***
U of Minnesota, Twin Cities Campus (MN) ***555***
The U of Montana–Missoula (MT) ***556***
U of Nebraska–Lincoln (NE) ***557***
U of New Brunswick Fredericton (NB, Canada) ***558***
U of New Hampshire (NH) ***558***
The U of North Carolina at Greensboro (NC) ***560***
U of Notre Dame (IN) ***562***
U of Oregon (OR) ***562***
U of Ottawa (ON, Canada) ***563***
U of Richmond (VA) ***572***
U of St. Thomas (MN) ***573***
U of Saskatchewan (SK, Canada) ***574***
The U of Scranton (PA) ***574***
The U of South Dakota (SD) ***575***
U of Southern California (CA) ***576***
The U of Tennessee at Chattanooga (TN) ***577***
The U of Texas at Austin (TX) ***578***
U of the South (TN) ***581***
U of Toronto (ON, Canada) ***581***
U of Vermont (VT) ***582***
U of Victoria (BC, Canada) ***582***
U of Washington (WA) ***583***
The U of Western Ontario (ON, Canada) ***583***
U of Windsor (ON, Canada) ***584***
U of Wisconsin–Madison (WI) ***584***
U of Wisconsin–Milwaukee (WI) ***585***
Ursinus Coll (PA) ***587***
Vassar Coll (NY) ***589***
Wabash Coll (IN) ***592***
Wake Forest U (NC) ***592***
Washington U in St. Louis (MO) ***595***
Wellesley Coll (MA) ***597***
West Chester U of Pennsylvania (PA) ***598***
Western Michigan U (MI) ***599***
Westminster Coll (PA) ***601***
Wichita State U (KS) ***604***
Yale U (CT) ***610***
York U (ON, Canada) ***611***

LAW AND LEGAL STUDIES RELATED

Information can be found under this major's main heading.

Bethany Coll (KS) ***287***
Pennsylvania Coll of Technology (PA) ***467***
Texas Wesleyan U (TX) ***526***
U of Hawaii at Manoa (HI) ***546***
U of Miami (FL) ***553***

U of Nebraska–Lincoln (NE) ***557***
Wilson Coll (PA) ***607***

LAW ENFORCEMENT/POLICE SCIENCE

Overview: Students who take this major will learn how to perform the duties of police officers and other public security officers, including crowd control, public relations, and basic crime investigation and prevention methods. *Related majors:* security and loss prevention, forensic technology, law enforcement administration, psychology, criminology. *Potential careers:* police officer, FBI detective, private security officer, forensic scientist. *Salary potential:* $25k-$35k.

American International Coll (MA) ***267***
Becker Coll (MA) ***283***
Bemidji State U (MN) ***285***
California State U, Hayward (CA) ***301***
Carleton U (ON, Canada) ***305***
Coll of the Ozarks (MO) ***323***
Defiance Coll (OH) ***338***
East Central U (OK) ***347***
Eastern Kentucky U (KY) ***348***
Fairmont State Coll (WV) ***356***
Ferris State U (MI) ***358***
George Mason U (VA) ***366***
Grambling State U (LA) ***371***
Grand Valley State U (MI) ***371***
Hannibal-LaGrange Coll (MO) ***375***
Hardin-Simmons U (TX) ***376***
Hilbert Coll (NY) ***379***
Howard U (DC) ***382***
Jackson State U (MS) ***390***
Jacksonville State U (AL) ***390***
John Jay Coll of Criminal Justice, the City U of NY (NY) ***392***
Lamar U (TX) ***401***
Langston U (OK) ***402***
Lewis-Clark State Coll (ID) ***406***
Louisiana Coll (LA) ***410***
MacMurray Coll (IL) ***414***
Madonna U (MI) ***414***
Memorial U of Newfoundland (NF, Canada) ***424***
Mercyhurst Coll (PA) ***425***
Metropolitan State U (MN) ***427***
Michigan State U (MI) ***428***
Minnesota State U, Mankato (MN) ***431***
Mississippi Coll (MS) ***432***
Northeastern State U (OK) ***450***
Northeastern U (MA) ***450***
Northern Michigan U (MI) ***451***
Northern State U (SD) ***451***
Northwestern Oklahoma State U (OK) ***453***
Oklahoma City U (OK) ***460***
Purdue U Calumet (IN) ***475***
Rowan U (NJ) ***484***
Saint Mary's U of Minnesota (MN) ***494***
Sam Houston State U (TX) ***497***
Southeast Missouri State U (MO) ***508***
Southwest Texas State U (TX) ***513***
Stephen F. Austin State U (TX) ***518***
Texas A&M U–Commerce (TX) ***525***
Texas Southern U (TX) ***526***
Tiffin U (OH) ***528***
Truman State U (MO) ***532***
U of Cincinnati (OH) ***543***
U of Great Falls (MT) ***545***
U of Pittsburgh at Greensburg (PA) ***570***
U of Regina (SK, Canada) ***572***
The U of Tennessee at Chattanooga (TN) ***577***
The U of Texas at Brownsville (TX) ***578***
The U of Texas–Pan American (TX) ***579***
U of Toronto (ON, Canada) ***581***
U of Wisconsin–Milwaukee (WI) ***585***
Wayne State Coll (NE) ***596***
Weber State U (UT) ***596***
West Chester U of Pennsylvania (PA) ***598***
Western Connecticut State U (CT) ***598***
Western New Mexico U (NM) ***600***
Western Oregon U (OR) ***600***
Western State Coll of Colorado (CO) ***600***
Winona State U (MN) ***608***
Wright State U (OH) ***609***
York Coll of Pennsylvania (PA) ***610***
Youngstown State U (OH) ***611***

LEGAL ADMINISTRATIVE ASSISTANT

Overview: Students learn the skills necessary to become a legal secretary or assistant, paralegal, or an office manager of a law firm or legal department. *Related majors:* administrative assistant, executive assistant, clerical, law and legal studies, word processing. *Potential careers:* legal secretary, paralegal, office manager. *Salary potential:* $25k-$35k.

Ball State U (IN) ***280***
Davenport U, Kalamazoo (MI) ***337***
Eastern Michigan U (MI) ***348***
Northwest Missouri State U (MO) ***454***
Peirce Coll (PA) ***466***
Tabor Coll (KS) ***522***
Texas A&M U–Commerce (TX) ***525***
U of West Los Angeles (CA) ***583***

LEGAL STUDIES

Overview: This major focuses on legal issues from the perspective of the social sciences and humanities. *Related majors:* prelaw studies, speech/rhetorical studies, American government/politics, law enforcement administration, philosophy. *Potential careers:* lawyer, politician, writer, teacher. *Salary potential:* for those who go on to attend law school, the average salary for lawyers is $40k-$70k.

American U (DC) ***267***
Amherst Coll (MA) ***268***
Bay Path Coll (MA) ***283***
Becker Coll (MA) ***283***
California State U, Chico (CA) ***300***
Chapman U (CA) ***311***
Christopher Newport U (VA) ***313***
Claremont McKenna Coll (CA) ***315***
Coll of the Atlantic (ME) ***323***
Concordia U (IL) ***330***
East Central U (OK) ***347***
Elms Coll (MA) ***352***
Franciscan U of Steubenville (OH) ***363***
Gannon U (PA) ***365***
Grand Valley State U (MI) ***371***
Hamline U (MN) ***374***
Hampshire Coll (MA) ***375***
Hartford Coll for Women (CT) ***376***
Hilbert Coll (NY) ***379***
Hood Coll (MD) ***381***
Inst of Public Administration(Ireland) ***387***
Insto Tecno Estudios Sups Monterrey(Mexico) ***388***
John Jay Coll of Criminal Justice, the City U of NY (NY) ***392***
Kenyon Coll (OH) ***398***
Laurentian U (ON, Canada) ***403***
Manhattanville Coll (NY) ***416***
Marymount Coll of Fordham U (NY) ***419***
Methodist Coll (NC) ***427***
Mountain State U (WV) ***437***
National U (CA) ***442***
Newbury Coll (MA) ***444***
North Carolina Wesleyan Coll (NC) ***449***
Northeastern U (MA) ***450***
Nova Southeastern U (FL) ***455***
Oberlin Coll (OH) ***456***
Park U (MO) ***465***
Pennsylvania Coll of Technology (PA) ***467***
Point Park Coll (PA) ***471***
Quinnipiac U (CT) ***476***
Ramapo Coll of New Jersey (NJ) ***477***
Rivier Coll (NH) ***480***
Roosevelt U (IL) ***483***
Sage Coll of Albany (NY) ***486***
Schreiner U (TX) ***501***
Scripps Coll (CA) ***501***
State U of NY Coll at Fredonia (NY) ***516***
Suffolk U (MA) ***520***
United States Air Force Academy (CO) ***534***
Université de Sherbrooke (QC, Canada) ***536***
Université Laval (QC, Canada) ***536***
U of Alberta (AB, Canada) ***538***
U of Baltimore (MD) ***539***
U of Calgary (AB, Canada) ***540***
U of Calif, Berkeley (CA) ***540***
U of Calif, Santa Barbara (CA) ***541***
U of Calif, Santa Cruz (CA) ***542***
U of Evansville (IN) ***545***
U of Hartford (CT) ***546***
U of Houston–Clear Lake (TX) ***547***
U of Illinois at Springfield (IL) ***548***
U of Massachusetts Amherst (MA) ***552***
U of Massachusetts Boston (MA) ***553***
The U of Montana–Missoula (MT) ***556***
U of New Brunswick Fredericton (NB, Canada) ***558***
U of Pennsylvania (PA) ***563***
U of Pittsburgh (PA) ***569***
The U of Tennessee at Chattanooga (TN) ***577***
U of Tulsa (OK) ***581***
U of West Los Angeles (CA) ***583***
U of Windsor (ON, Canada) ***584***
U of Wisconsin–Superior (WI) ***586***
Valdosta State U (GA) ***588***
Villa Julie Coll (MD) ***590***
Webster U (MO) ***597***
Winona State U (MN) ***608***
York U (ON, Canada) ***611***

LIBERAL ARTS AND SCIENCES/LIBERAL STUDIES

Overview: Students study a wide range of subjects from the arts; biological, physical, and social sciences; and humanities, emphasizing a breadth of study. *Related majors:* English literature/language, history, biology, ecology. *Potential careers:* writer, editor, journalist, advertising executive, lawyer. *Salary potential:* $23k-$32k.

Abilene Christian U (TX) ***260***
Adams State Coll (CO) ***260***
Alabama State U (AL) ***261***
Alaska Pacific U (AK) ***261***
Albertus Magnus Coll (CT) ***262***
Alcorn State U (MS) ***263***
Alderson-Broaddus Coll (WV) ***263***
Alliant International U (CA) ***264***
Alma Coll (MI) ***264***
Alvernia Coll (PA) ***265***
American Coll of Thessaloniki(Greece) ***266***
American International Coll (MA) ***267***
American U (DC) ***267***
Anderson Coll (SC) ***268***
Andrews U (MI) ***269***
Angelo State U (TX) ***269***
Antioch U Los Angeles (CA) ***269***
Antioch U McGregor (OH) ***270***
Antioch U Seattle (WA) ***270***
Appalachian State U (NC) ***270***
Aquinas Coll (MI) ***270***
Arcadia U (PA) ***271***
Arkansas Baptist Coll (AR) ***272***
Armstrong Atlantic State U (GA) ***273***
Ashland U (OH) ***274***
Athabasca U (AB, Canada) ***275***
Auburn U Montgomery (AL) ***276***
Augsburg Coll (MN) ***276***
Augustana Coll (IL) ***276***
Augustana Coll (SD) ***276***
Averett U (VA) ***278***
Azusa Pacific U (CA) ***278***
Ball State U (IN) ***280***
Barry U (FL) ***282***
Bay Path Coll (MA) ***283***
Becker Coll (MA) ***283***
Bellarmine U (KY) ***284***
Bemidji State U (MN) ***285***
Benedictine Coll (KS) ***285***
Bennington Coll (VT) ***286***
Bentley Coll (MA) ***286***
Bethany Coll (WV) ***287***
Bethany Coll of the Assemblies of God (CA) ***287***
Bethany Lutheran Coll (MN) ***288***
Bethel Coll (IN) ***288***
Bethel Coll (TN) ***288***
Bethune-Cookman Coll (FL) ***289***
Bishop's U (QC, Canada) ***289***
Blackburn Coll (IL) ***290***
Bluefield Coll (VA) ***291***
Bluffton Coll (OH) ***291***
Bowling Green State U (OH) ***292***
Bradley U (IL) ***293***
Brandon U (MB, Canada) ***293***
Brescia U (KY) ***293***
Brevard Coll (NC) ***294***
Brewton-Parker Coll (GA) ***294***
Brock U (ON, Canada) ***295***
Bryan Coll (TN) ***296***
Buena Vista U (IA) ***297***
Burlington Coll (VT) ***297***
Cabrini Coll (PA) ***298***
California Baptist U (CA) ***298***
California Lutheran U (CA) ***299***
California Polytechnic State U, San Luis Obispo (CA) ***300***
California State Polytechnic U, Pomona (CA) ***300***
California State U, Bakersfield (CA) ***300***
California State U, Chico (CA) ***300***
California State U, Dominguez Hills (CA) ***300***
California State U, Fresno (CA) ***301***
California State U, Fullerton (CA) ***301***
California State U, Hayward (CA) ***301***
California State U, Long Beach (CA) ***301***
California State U, Northridge (CA) ***301***
California State U, Sacramento (CA) ***301***
California State U, San Bernardino (CA) ***302***
California State U, San Marcos (CA) ***302***
California State U, Stanislaus (CA) ***302***
California U of Pennsylvania (PA) ***302***
Calumet Coll of Saint Joseph (IN) ***302***
Capital U (OH) ***304***
Cardinal Stritch U (WI) ***305***
Carlow Coll (PA) ***305***
Carnegie Mellon U (PA) ***305***
Carson-Newman Coll (TN) ***306***
Cascade Coll (OR) ***307***
Cazenovia Coll (NY) ***308***
Cedar Crest Coll (PA) ***308***
Centenary Coll of Louisiana (LA) ***308***
Central Christian Coll of Kansas (KS) ***309***
Chapman U (CA) ***311***
Charter Oak State Coll (CT) ***312***
Chowan Coll (NC) ***312***
Christian Heritage Coll (CA) ***313***
Clarion U of Pennsylvania (PA) ***315***
Clarkson U (NY) ***316***
Cleveland State U (OH) ***317***
Coastal Carolina U (SC) ***318***
Coe Coll (IA) ***318***
Coll Misericordia (PA) ***319***
Coll of Mount St. Joseph (OH) ***320***
Coll of Mount Saint Vincent (NY) ***320***
The Coll of New Rochelle (NY) ***321***
Coll of Notre Dame of Maryland (MD) ***321***
Coll of Saint Benedict (MN) ***321***
Coll of St. Joseph (VT) ***322***
Coll of Saint Mary (NE) ***322***
The Coll of St. Scholastica (MN) ***322***
The Coll of Saint Thomas More (TX) ***322***
Coll of the Atlantic (ME) ***323***
Colorado Christian U (CO) ***325***
Colorado State U (CO) ***325***
Columbia Coll (MO) ***326***
Columbia Coll Chicago (IL) ***327***
Columbia Union Coll (MD) ***328***
Columbus State U (GA) ***328***
Conception Seminary Coll (MO) ***329***
Concordia Coll (NY) ***329***
Concordia U (CA) ***330***
Concordia U (MN) ***330***
Concordia U (OR) ***330***
Concordia U at Austin (TX) ***331***
Concordia U Wisconsin (WI) ***331***
Cornell Coll (IA) ***332***
Cornell U (NY) ***333***
Crichton Coll (TN) ***334***
Crossroads Coll (MN) ***334***
Crown Coll (MN) ***334***
Dallas Baptist U (TX) ***336***
Defiance Coll (OH) ***338***
DeSales U (PA) ***340***
Dickinson State U (ND) ***344***
Dominican U of California (CA) ***345***
Dowling Coll (NY) ***345***
D'Youville Coll (NY) ***347***
East Carolina U (NC) ***347***
Eastern Illinois U (IL) ***348***
Eastern Kentucky U (KY) ***348***

LIBERAL ARTS AND SCIENCES/LIBERAL STUDIES (continued)

Eastern Mennonite U (VA) ***348***
Eastern Nazarene Coll (MA) ***348***
Eastern New Mexico U (NM) ***349***
Eastern Oregon U (OR) ***349***
Eastern Washington U (WA) ***349***
Edgewood Coll (WI) ***351***
Edinboro U of Pennsylvania (PA) ***351***
Elmira Coll (NY) ***351***
Elms Coll (MA) ***352***
Emmanuel Coll (MA) ***353***
Emory U (GA) ***354***
Eugene Lang Coll, New School U (NY) ***355***
Eureka Coll (IL) ***355***
The Evergreen State Coll (WA) ***355***
Excelsior Coll (NY) ***356***
Fairleigh Dickinson U, Teaneck-Metro Campus (NJ) ***356***
Faulkner U (AL) ***357***
Ferrum Coll (VA) ***358***
Finlandia U (MI) ***358***
Florida Atlantic U (FL) ***359***
Florida Coll (FL) ***359***
Florida Gulf Coast U (FL) ***359***
Florida International U (FL) ***360***
Fontbonne U (MO) ***361***
Fordham U (NY) ***362***
Fort Hays State U (KS) ***362***
Fort Lewis Coll (CO) ***362***
Framingham State Coll (MA) ***362***
The Franciscan U (IA) ***363***
Francis Marion U (SC) ***363***
Franklin Pierce Coll (NH) ***364***
Freed-Hardeman U (TN) ***364***
Fresno Pacific U (CA) ***364***
Frostburg State U (MD) ***365***
Gannon U (PA) ***365***
Gardner-Webb U (NC) ***365***
George Mason U (VA) ***366***
Georgetown U (DC) ***366***
The George Washington U (DC) ***367***
Georgia Coll & State U (GA) ***367***
Georgia State U (GA) ***368***
Gettysburg Coll (PA) ***368***
Glenville State Coll (WV) ***368***
Goddard Coll (VT) ***369***
Gonzaga U (WA) ***369***
Goshen Coll (IN) ***370***
Governors State U (IL) ***370***
Graceland U (IA) ***371***
Grace U (NE) ***371***
Grand Canyon U (AZ) ***371***
Grand Valley State U (MI) ***371***
Grand View Coll (IA) ***372***
Green Mountain Coll (VT) ***372***
Greenville Coll (IL) ***373***
Hampshire Coll (MA) ***375***
Hannibal-LaGrange Coll (MO) ***375***
Harvard U (MA) ***376***
Hastings Coll (NE) ***377***
Hawai'i Pacific U (HI) ***377***
Hobart and William Smith Colls (NY) ***380***
Hofstra U (NY) ***380***
Hollins U (VA) ***380***
Holy Family U (PA) ***380***
Holy Names Coll (CA) ***381***
Houghton Coll (NY) ***381***
Houston Baptist U (TX) ***382***
Howard Payne U (TX) ***382***
Humboldt State U (CA) ***382***
Huntingdon Coll (AL) ***383***
Husson Coll (ME) ***383***
Illinois Coll (IL) ***384***
Illinois State U (IL) ***384***
Illinois Wesleyan U (IL) ***385***
International Coll of the Cayman Islands(Cayman Islands) ***389***
Iona Coll (NY) ***390***
Iowa State U of Science and Technology (IA) ***390***
Iowa Wesleyan Coll (IA) ***390***
Ithaca Coll (NY) ***390***
Jacksonville U (FL) ***391***
James Madison U (VA) ***391***
John F. Kennedy U (CA) ***392***
Johns Hopkins U (MD) ***392***
Johnson State Coll (VT) ***394***
Juniata Coll (PA) ***395***
Keene State Coll (NH) ***396***
Kendall Coll (IL) ***396***
Kent State U (OH) ***397***
Kentucky State U (KY) ***397***
Keuka Coll (NY) ***398***
Kutztown U of Pennsylvania (PA) ***399***
Lakehead U (ON, Canada) ***400***
Lamar U (TX) ***401***
Langston U (OK) ***402***
La Roche Coll (PA) ***402***
La Salle U (PA) ***402***
Lasell Coll (MA) ***402***
La Sierra U (CA) ***403***
Laurentian U (ON, Canada) ***403***
Lebanon Valley Coll (PA) ***403***
Lees-McRae Coll (NC) ***404***
Lesley U (MA) ***405***
Lewis-Clark State Coll (ID) ***406***
Lewis U (IL) ***406***
Limestone Coll (SC) ***406***
Lincoln Memorial U (TN) ***407***
Lindenwood U (MO) ***407***
Lindsey Wilson Coll (KY) ***407***
Lipscomb U (TN) ***408***
Lock Haven U of Pennsylvania (PA) ***408***
Long Island U, Brooklyn Campus (NY) ***409***
Long Island U, Southampton Coll (NY) ***409***
Long Island U, Southampton Coll, Friends World Program (NY) ***409***
Longwood U (VA) ***409***
Loras Coll (IA) ***410***
Louisiana Coll (LA) ***410***
Louisiana State U and A&M Coll (LA) ***410***
Lourdes Coll (OH) ***411***
Loyola Marymount U (CA) ***411***
Lubbock Christian U (TX) ***412***
Lyndon State Coll (VT) ***413***
Lynn U (FL) ***413***
MacMurray Coll (IL) ***414***
Magdalen Coll (NH) ***414***
Malaspina U-Coll (BC, Canada) ***415***
Malone Coll (OH) ***415***
Manhattan Coll (NY) ***416***
Mansfield U of Pennsylvania (PA) ***416***
Maranatha Baptist Bible Coll (WI) ***417***
Marian Coll of Fond du Lac (WI) ***417***
Marietta Coll (OH) ***417***
Mars Hill Coll (NC) ***418***
Marymount Coll of Fordham U (NY) ***419***
Marymount Manhattan Coll (NY) ***420***
Marymount U (VA) ***420***
Maryville U of Saint Louis (MO) ***420***
Mary Washington Coll (VA) ***420***
Marywood U (PA) ***421***
Massachusetts Inst of Technology (MA) ***421***
The Master's Coll and Seminary (CA) ***422***
Mayville State U (ND) ***422***
McNeese State U (LA) ***423***
Medaille Coll (NY) ***424***
Menlo Coll (CA) ***425***
Mercyhurst Coll (PA) ***425***
Mesa State Coll (CO) ***426***
Methodist Coll (NC) ***427***
Metropolitan State U (MN) ***427***
Michigan State U (MI) ***428***
Middlebury Coll (VT) ***429***
Midland Lutheran Coll (NE) ***429***
Midway Coll (KY) ***429***
Millersville U of Pennsylvania (PA) ***430***
Mills Coll (CA) ***431***
Minnesota State U, Mankato (MN) ***431***
Mississippi Coll (MS) ***432***
Mississippi State U (MS) ***432***
Missouri Valley Coll (MO) ***433***
Mitchell Coll (CT) ***433***
Monmouth Coll (IL) ***434***
Montana State U–Billings (MT) ***434***
Montana Tech of The U of Montana (MT) ***435***
Montreat Coll (NC) ***435***
Morris Coll (SC) ***437***
Mount Allison U (NB, Canada) ***437***
Mount Aloysius Coll (PA) ***437***
Mount Ida Coll (MA) ***438***
Mount Marty Coll (SD) ***438***
Mount Mercy Coll (IA) ***438***
Mount Olive Coll (NC) ***439***
Mount Saint Mary Coll (NY) ***439***
Mount Saint Vincent U (NS, Canada) ***439***
The National Hispanic U (CA) ***442***
National-Louis U (IL) ***442***
National U (CA) ***442***
Neumann Coll (PA) ***443***
New Coll of Florida (FL) ***444***
Newman U (KS) ***445***
New Mexico Inst of Mining and Technology (NM) ***446***
New Sch Bach of Arts, New Sch for Social Research (NY) ***446***
New York U (NY) ***447***
Nipissing U (ON, Canada) ***448***
North Carolina State U (NC) ***449***
North Central Coll (IL) ***449***
Northeastern Illinois U (IL) ***450***
Northeastern U (MA) ***450***
Northern Arizona U (AZ) ***450***
Northern Illinois U (IL) ***450***
Northern Michigan U (MI) ***451***
Northwest Coll (WA) ***452***
Northwestern State U of Louisiana (LA) ***453***
Northwestern U (IL) ***453***
Northwest Nazarene U (ID) ***454***
Notre Dame de Namur U (CA) ***455***
Nova Southeastern U (FL) ***455***
Nyack Coll (NY) ***456***
Oakland U (MI) ***456***
Ohio U (OH) ***458***
Ohio U–Chillicothe (OH) ***458***
Ohio U–Lancaster (OH) ***458***
Ohio U–Zanesville (OH) ***458***
Ohio Valley Coll (WV) ***459***
Okanagan U Coll (BC, Canada) ***459***
Oklahoma Christian U (OK) ***459***
Oklahoma City U (OK) ***460***
Olivet Coll (MI) ***461***
Olivet Nazarene U (IL) ***461***
Oral Roberts U (OK) ***461***
Oregon State U (OR) ***462***
Our Lady of the Lake U of San Antonio (TX) ***463***
Pace U (NY) ***463***
Pacific Union Coll (CA) ***464***
Pacific U (OR) ***464***
Park U (MO) ***465***
Patten Coll (CA) ***466***
Peace Coll (NC) ***466***
Penn State U Abington Coll (PA) ***467***
Penn State U Altoona Coll (PA) ***467***
Penn State U at Erie, The Behrend Coll (PA) ***467***
Penn State U Lehigh Valley Cmps of Berks-Lehigh Valley Coll (PA) ***468***
Penn State U Univ Park Campus (PA) ***468***
Pepperdine U, Malibu (CA) ***469***
Pittsburg State U (KS) ***470***
Point Loma Nazarene U (CA) ***471***
Point Park Coll (PA) ***471***
Polytechnic U, Brooklyn Campus (NY) ***472***
Pomona Coll (CA) ***472***
Pontifical Catholic U of Puerto Rico (PR) ***472***
Portland State U (OR) ***472***
Prescott Coll (AZ) ***474***
Principia Coll (IL) ***474***
Providence Coll (RI) ***474***
Providence Coll and Theological Seminary (MB, Canada) ***475***
Purchase Coll, State U of NY (NY) ***475***
Purdue U Calumet (IN) ***475***
Purdue U North Central (IN) ***475***
Quinnipiac U (CT) ***476***
Radford U (VA) ***476***
Randolph-Macon Woman's Coll (VA) ***477***
Regis U (CO) ***478***
Reinhardt Coll (GA) ***478***
Rhode Island Coll (RI) ***479***
The Richard Stockton Coll of New Jersey (NJ) ***479***
Richmond, The American International U in London(United Kingdom) ***480***
Rivier Coll (NH) ***480***
Rocky Mountain Coll (MT) ***482***
Rogers State U (OK) ***483***
Roger Williams U (RI) ***483***
Roosevelt U (IL) ***483***
Rowan U (NJ) ***484***
Rutgers, The State U of New Jersey, Camden (NJ) ***485***
Sage Coll of Albany (NY) ***486***
St. Andrews Presbyterian Coll (NC) ***487***
St. Cloud State U (MN) ***488***
St. Edward's U (TX) ***488***
St. Francis Xavier U (NS, Canada) ***489***
St. Gregory's U (OK) ***489***
St. John's Coll (MD) ***489***
St. John's Coll (NM) ***490***
St. John's U (NY) ***490***
Saint Joseph Coll (CT) ***490***
Saint Joseph's Coll of Maine (ME) ***491***
St. Joseph's Coll, Suffolk Campus (NY) ***491***
Saint Joseph Seminary Coll (LA) ***491***
Saint Mary Coll (KS) ***493***
Saint Mary-of-the-Woods Coll (IN) ***493***
Saint Mary's Coll of California (CA) ***494***
St. Olaf Coll (MN) ***495***
Saint Peter's Coll (NJ) ***495***
St. Thomas U (FL) ***496***
Saint Vincent Coll (PA) ***496***
Saint Xavier U (IL) ***496***
Salem International U (WV) ***496***
Salem State Coll (MA) ***497***
Salisbury U (MD) ***497***
Salve Regina U (RI) ***497***
San Diego State U (CA) ***498***
San Francisco State U (CA) ***498***
San Jose State U (CA) ***499***
Santa Clara U (CA) ***499***
Sarah Lawrence Coll (NY) ***499***
Schreiner U (TX) ***501***
Seattle U (WA) ***501***
Seton Hall U (NJ) ***502***
Seton Hill U (PA) ***502***
Shaw U (NC) ***502***
Sheldon Jackson Coll (AK) ***503***
Shenandoah U (VA) ***503***
Shimer Coll (IL) ***503***
Shorter Coll (GA) ***504***
Simon Fraser U (BC, Canada) ***505***
Simpson Coll and Graduate School (CA) ***505***
Skidmore Coll (NY) ***506***
Sonoma State U (CA) ***506***
Southeast Missouri State U (MO) ***508***
Southern Christian U (AL) ***509***
Southern Connecticut State U (CT) ***509***
Southern Illinois U Carbondale (IL) ***509***
Southern Illinois U Edwardsville (IL) ***509***
Southern Oregon U (OR) ***510***
Southern Vermont Coll (VT) ***511***
Southern Virginia U (VA) ***511***
Southwestern Coll (KS) ***512***
Spalding U (KY) ***513***
State U of NY Coll at Cortland (NY) ***516***
State U of NY Coll at Fredonia (NY) ***516***
State U of NY Coll at Oneonta (NY) ***517***
State U of West Georgia (GA) ***518***
Stephens Coll (MO) ***519***
Suffolk U (MA) ***520***
Tarleton State U (TX) ***522***
Teikyo Post U (CT) ***523***
Tennessee State U (TN) ***523***
Texas A&M U–Commerce (TX) ***525***
Texas Christian U (TX) ***526***
Texas Tech U (TX) ***526***
Thomas Aquinas Coll (CA) ***527***
Thomas Edison State Coll (NJ) ***527***
Thomas More Coll (KY) ***528***
Thomas U (GA) ***528***
Tiffin U (OH) ***528***
Touro Coll (NY) ***529***
Trent U (ON, Canada) ***529***
Trinity Coll (DC) ***530***
Trinity International U (IL) ***531***
Trinity Western U (BC, Canada) ***531***
Tulane U (LA) ***533***
Tyndale Coll & Seminary (ON, Canada) ***533***
Union Coll (NY) ***534***
Union Inst & U (OH) ***534***
Université de Sherbrooke (QC, Canada) ***536***
The U of Akron (OH) ***537***
U of Alaska Southeast (AK) ***538***
U of Alberta (AB, Canada) ***538***
The U of Arizona (AZ) ***538***
U of Arkansas at Little Rock (AR) ***539***
U of Baltimore (MD) ***539***
U of Bridgeport (CT) ***540***
The U of British Columbia (BC, Canada) ***540***
U of Calgary (AB, Canada) ***540***
U of Calif, Riverside (CA) ***541***
U of Central Florida (FL) ***542***
U of Central Oklahoma (OK) ***542***
U of Charleston (WV) ***542***
U of Chicago (IL) ***542***
U of Cincinnati (OH) ***543***
U of Delaware (DE) ***544***
U of Evansville (IN) ***545***
U of Georgia (GA) ***545***
U of Hawaii at Manoa (HI) ***546***
U of Houston–Downtown (TX) ***547***
U of Idaho (ID) ***547***
U of Illinois at Springfield (IL) ***548***
U of Illinois at Urbana–Champaign (IL) ***548***
U of Indianapolis (IN) ***548***
U of Judaism (CA) ***548***
U of Kansas (KS) ***549***

U of La Verne (CA) ***549***
U of Louisville (KY) ***550***
U of Maine at Farmington (ME) ***550***
U of Maine at Fort Kent (ME) ***551***
U of Maine at Presque Isle (ME) ***551***
U of Mary (ND) ***551***
U of Maryland Eastern Shore (MD) ***552***
U of Massachusetts Dartmouth (MA) ***553***
U of Massachusetts Lowell (MA) ***553***
U of Miami (FL) ***553***
U of Michigan (MI) ***554***
U of Michigan–Dearborn (MI) ***554***
U of Michigan–Flint (MI) ***554***
U of Minnesota, Morris (MN) ***555***
U of Mississippi (MS) ***555***
U of Missouri–Columbia (MO) ***555***
U of Missouri–Kansas City (MO) ***555***
U of Missouri–St. Louis (MO) ***556***
The U of Montana–Missoula (MT) ***556***
The U of Montana–Western (MT) ***556***
U of Nebraska–Lincoln (NE) ***557***
U of New Brunswick Fredericton (NB, Canada) ***558***
U of New England (ME) ***558***
U of New Haven (CT) ***559***
U of New Mexico (NM) ***559***
The U of North Carolina at Asheville (NC) ***559***
The U of North Carolina at Chapel Hill (NC) ***560***
The U of North Carolina at Greensboro (NC) ***560***
U of Northern Iowa (IA) ***561***
U of North Florida (FL) ***561***
U of Notre Dame (IN) ***562***
U of Oregon (OR) ***562***
U of Ottawa (ON, Canada) ***563***
U of Pennsylvania (PA) ***563***
U of Pittsburgh (PA) ***569***
U of Redlands (CA) ***572***
U of Regina (SK, Canada) ***572***
U of Rhode Island (RI) ***572***
U of St. Francis (IL) ***573***
U of Saint Francis (IN) ***573***
U of St. Thomas (TX) ***573***
U of San Diego (CA) ***574***
U of San Francisco (CA) ***574***
U of Sioux Falls (SD) ***574***
U of South Carolina (SC) ***575***
U of South Carolina Aiken (SC) ***575***
The U of South Dakota (SD) ***575***
U of Southern Indiana (IN) ***576***
U of South Florida (FL) ***576***
The U of Tampa (FL) ***577***
The U of Texas at Austin (TX) ***578***
The U of Texas at Brownsville (TX) ***578***
The U of Texas at Tyler (TX) ***579***
U of the Incarnate Word (TX) ***580***
U of Toledo (OH) ***581***
U of Utah (UT) ***582***
U of Victoria (BC, Canada) ***582***
U of Virginia (VA) ***582***
The U of Virginia's Coll at Wise (VA) ***582***
U of Washington (WA) ***583***
U of Waterloo (ON, Canada) ***583***
U of Wisconsin–Oshkosh (WI) ***585***
U of Wisconsin–Platteville (WI) ***585***
U of Wisconsin–River Falls (WI) ***585***
U System Coll for Lifelong Learning (NH) ***586***
Urbana U (OH) ***587***
Ursinus Coll (PA) ***587***
Utah State U (UT) ***587***
Utica Coll (NY) ***588***
Valdosta State U (GA) ***588***
Valparaiso U (IN) ***588***
Villa Julie Coll (MD) ***590***
Villanova U (PA) ***590***
Virginia Intermont Coll (VA) ***590***
Virginia Wesleyan Coll (VA) ***591***
Viterbo U (WI) ***591***
Walsh U (OH) ***593***
Warner Pacific Coll (OR) ***593***
Washington Coll (MD) ***594***
Washington State U (WA) ***595***
Washington U in St. Louis (MO) ***595***
Weber State U (UT) ***596***
Webster U (MO) ***597***
Wesley Coll (DE) ***598***
West Chester U of Pennsylvania (PA) ***598***
Western Baptist Coll (OR) ***598***
Western Carolina U (NC) ***598***
Western Connecticut State U (CT) ***598***
Western Illinois U (IL) ***599***
Western International U (AZ) ***599***
Western New England Coll (MA) ***600***
Western Washington U (WA) ***600***
Westfield State Coll (MA) ***600***
Westminster Choir Coll of Rider U (NJ) ***601***
Westmont Coll (CA) ***602***
West Texas A&M U (TX) ***602***
West Virginia U (WV) ***602***
Wheeling Jesuit U (WV) ***603***
Whittier Coll (CA) ***604***
Wichita State U (KS) ***604***
Wilberforce U (OH) ***605***
Wilkes U (PA) ***605***
William Carey Coll (MS) ***605***
Williams Baptist Coll (AR) ***606***
Wilmington Coll (OH) ***607***
Wingate U (NC) ***607***
Winona State U (MN) ***608***
Wittenberg U (OH) ***608***
Xavier U (OH) ***610***
York Coll (NE) ***610***
York Coll of the City U of New York (NY) ***611***
York U (ON, Canada) ***611***

LIBERAL ARTS AND STUDIES RELATED

Information can be found under this major's main heading.

The Colorado Coll (CO) ***325***
Duquesne U (PA) ***346***
Johns Hopkins U (MD) ***392***
Northern Arizona U (AZ) ***450***
Ohio U (OH) ***458***
Saint Anselm Coll (NH) ***487***
Troy State U Montgomery (AL) ***532***
The U of Akron (OH) ***537***
U of Louisville (KY) ***550***
U of Nebraska–Lincoln (NE) ***557***
U of Oklahoma (OK) ***562***
U of Pennsylvania (PA) ***563***
U of South Alabama (AL) ***575***
U of Utah (UT) ***582***

LIBRARY SCIENCE

Overview: This major teaches students the knowledge and skills they will need to work in libraries and administer and facilitate the use of information in print, audiovisual, and electronic formats. *Related majors:* information sciences and systems, data warehousing and mining, education, professional studies, English literature. *Potential careers:* librarian, researcher, writer, information consultant, teacher. *Salary potential:* $23k-$30k.

Appalachian State U (NC) ***270***
Chadron State Coll (NE) ***311***
Clarion U of Pennsylvania (PA) ***315***
Concord Coll (WV) ***329***
Florida State U (FL) ***361***
Kutztown U of Pennsylvania (PA) ***399***
Lakehead U (ON, Canada) ***400***
Longwood U (VA) ***409***
Murray State U (KY) ***440***
Northeastern State U (OK) ***450***
Ohio Dominican U (OH) ***457***
St. Cloud State U (MN) ***488***
Southern Connecticut State U (CT) ***509***
Spalding U (KY) ***513***
Texas Woman's U (TX) ***527***
U of Hawaii at Manoa (HI) ***546***
The U of Maine at Augusta (ME) ***550***
U of Nebraska at Omaha (NE) ***557***
U of Oklahoma (OK) ***562***
U of Southern Mississippi (MS) ***576***
U of the District of Columbia (DC) ***580***

LINGUISTICS

Overview: Students study the rules and laws that govern the structure of particular languages and the general laws and principles governing all natural languages. *Related majors:* rhetorical studies, philosophy, cognitive psychology, speech, artificial intelligence. *Potential careers:* editor, translator, speech therapist. *Salary potential:* $24k-$35k.

Baylor U (TX) ***283***
Boston U (MA) ***292***
Brandeis U (MA) ***293***
Brigham Young U (UT) ***295***
Brock U (ON, Canada) ***295***
Brooklyn Coll of the City U of NY (NY) ***295***
Brown U (RI) ***296***
California State U, Dominguez Hills (CA) ***300***
California State U, Fresno (CA) ***301***
California State U, Fullerton (CA) ***301***
California State U, Northridge (CA) ***301***
Carleton U (ON, Canada) ***305***
Central Coll (IA) ***309***
City Coll of the City U of NY (NY) ***314***
Cleveland State U (OH) ***317***
The Coll of William and Mary (VA) ***324***
Columbia Coll (NY) ***326***
Concordia U (QC, Canada) ***331***
Cornell U (NY) ***333***
Crown Coll (MN) ***334***
Dalhousie U (NS, Canada) ***336***
Dartmouth Coll (NH) ***337***
Duke U (NC) ***346***
Eastern Michigan U (MI) ***348***
Florida Atlantic U (FL) ***359***
Florida State U (FL) ***361***
Georgetown U (DC) ***366***
Grinnell Coll (IA) ***373***
Hampshire Coll (MA) ***375***
Harvard U (MA) ***376***
Indiana U Bloomington (IN) ***385***
Inter American U of PR, San Germán Campus (PR) ***388***
Iowa State U of Science and Technology (IA) ***390***
Judson Coll (IL) ***395***
Lawrence U (WI) ***403***
Lehman Coll of the City U of NY (NY) ***404***
Long Island U, Southampton Coll, Friends World Program (NY) ***409***
Macalester Coll (MN) ***413***
Marlboro Coll (VT) ***418***
Massachusetts Inst of Technology (MA) ***421***
McGill U (QC, Canada) ***423***
McMaster U (ON, Canada) ***423***
Memorial U of Newfoundland (NF, Canada) ***424***
Miami U (OH) ***428***
Michigan State U (MI) ***428***
Miles Coll (AL) ***430***
Montclair State U (NJ) ***435***
Moody Bible Inst (IL) ***435***
Mount Saint Vincent U (NS, Canada) ***439***
New York U (NY) ***447***
Northeastern Illinois U (IL) ***450***
Northeastern U (MA) ***450***
Northwestern U (IL) ***453***
Oakland U (MI) ***456***
The Ohio State U (OH) ***457***
Ohio U (OH) ***458***
Oklahoma Wesleyan U (OK) ***460***
Pitzer Coll (CA) ***471***
Pomona Coll (CA) ***472***
Portland State U (OR) ***472***
Queens Coll of the City U of NY (NY) ***475***
Queen's U at Kingston (ON, Canada) ***476***
Reed Coll (OR) ***477***
Rice U (TX) ***479***
Rutgers, The State U of New Jersey, New Brunswick (NJ) ***485***
St. Cloud State U (MN) ***488***
San Diego State U (CA) ***498***
San Jose State U (CA) ***499***
Scripps Coll (CA) ***501***
Simon Fraser U (BC, Canada) ***505***
Southern Illinois U Carbondale (IL) ***509***
Stanford U (CA) ***514***
State U of NY at Albany (NY) ***514***
State U of NY at Binghamton (NY) ***515***
State U of NY at Oswego (NY) ***515***
Stony Brook U, State University of New York (NY) ***520***
Swarthmore Coll (PA) ***521***
Syracuse U (NY) ***521***
Temple U (PA) ***523***
Trinity Western U (BC, Canada) ***531***
Tulane U (LA) ***533***
Université Laval (QC, Canada) ***536***
U at Buffalo, The State University of New York (NY) ***536***
U of Alaska Fairbanks (AK) ***538***
U of Alberta (AB, Canada) ***538***
The U of Arizona (AZ) ***538***
The U of British Columbia (BC, Canada) ***540***
U of Calgary (AB, Canada) ***540***
U of Calif, Berkeley (CA) ***540***
U of Calif, Davis (CA) ***540***
U of Calif, Irvine (CA) ***541***
U of Calif, Los Angeles (CA) ***541***
U of Calif, Riverside (CA) ***541***
U of Calif, San Diego (CA) ***541***
U of Calif, Santa Barbara (CA) ***541***
U of Calif, Santa Cruz (CA) ***542***
U of Chicago (IL) ***542***
U of Cincinnati (OH) ***543***
U of Colorado at Boulder (CO) ***543***
U of Connecticut (CT) ***544***
U of Delaware (DE) ***544***
U of Florida (FL) ***545***
U of Georgia (GA) ***545***
U of Hawaii at Hilo (HI) ***546***
U of Hawaii at Manoa (HI) ***546***
U of Illinois at Urbana–Champaign (IL) ***548***
The U of Iowa (IA) ***548***
U of Kansas (KS) ***549***
U of Kentucky (KY) ***549***
U of King's Coll (NS, Canada) ***549***
U of Maryland, Baltimore County (MD) ***552***
U of Maryland, Coll Park (MD) ***552***
U of Massachusetts Amherst (MA) ***552***
U of Michigan (MI) ***554***
U of Minnesota, Twin Cities Campus (MN) ***555***
U of Mississippi (MS) ***555***
U of Missouri–Columbia (MO) ***555***
U of Missouri–St. Louis (MO) ***556***
The U of Montana–Missoula (MT) ***556***
U of New Brunswick Fredericton (NB, Canada) ***558***
U of New Hampshire (NH) ***558***
U of New Mexico (NM) ***559***
The U of North Carolina at Chapel Hill (NC) ***560***
The U of North Carolina at Greensboro (NC) ***560***
U of Northern Iowa (IA) ***561***
U of Oklahoma (OK) ***562***
U of Oregon (OR) ***562***
U of Ottawa (ON, Canada) ***563***
U of Pennsylvania (PA) ***563***
U of Pittsburgh (PA) ***569***
U of Regina (SK, Canada) ***572***
U of Rochester (NY) ***573***
U of Saskatchewan (SK, Canada) ***574***
U of Southern California (CA) ***576***
U of Southern Maine (ME) ***576***
The U of Texas at Austin (TX) ***578***
The U of Texas at El Paso (TX) ***578***
U of Toledo (OH) ***581***
U of Toronto (ON, Canada) ***581***
U of Utah (UT) ***582***
U of Victoria (BC, Canada) ***582***
U of Washington (WA) ***583***
The U of Western Ontario (ON, Canada) ***583***
U of Windsor (ON, Canada) ***584***
U of Wisconsin–Madison (WI) ***584***
U of Wisconsin–Milwaukee (WI) ***585***
Washington State U (WA) ***595***
Wayne State U (MI) ***596***
Wellesley Coll (MA) ***597***
Western Washington U (WA) ***600***
Yale U (CT) ***610***
York U (ON, Canada) ***611***

LITERATURE

Overview: A general major that may focus on one on or more specialized majors such as English literature, American literature, comparative literature, or British literature. *Related majors:* English literature, American literature, comparative literature. *Potential careers:* writer, editor, teacher, professor. *Salary potential:* $23k-$32k.

Agnes Scott Coll (GA) ***261***
Alderson-Broaddus Coll (WV) ***263***
Alfred U (NY) ***263***
Alma Coll (MI) ***264***
American U (DC) ***267***
Antioch Coll (OH) ***269***
Arcadia U (PA) ***271***

LITERATURE (continued)

Augustana Coll (IL) ***276***
Ave Maria Coll (MI) ***278***
Bard Coll (NY) ***281***
Barry U (FL) ***282***
Beloit Coll (WI) ***285***
Bennington Coll (VT) ***286***
Baruch Coll of the City U of NY (NY) ***286***
Bethel Coll (MN) ***288***
Bishop's U (QC, Canada) ***289***
Blackburn Coll (IL) ***290***
Brock U (ON, Canada) ***295***
Brown U (RI) ***296***
Bryan Coll (TN) ***296***
Burlington Coll (VT) ***297***
California Inst of Technology (CA) ***299***
California State U, Dominguez Hills (CA) ***300***
California State U, Long Beach (CA) ***301***
California State U, Northridge (CA) ***301***
Capital U (OH) ***304***
Carnegie Mellon U (PA) ***305***
Carson-Newman Coll (TN) ***306***
Castleton State Coll (VT) ***307***
Cazenovia Coll (NY) ***308***
Centenary Coll of Louisiana (LA) ***308***
Chapman U (CA) ***311***
Christendom Coll (VA) ***313***
Christopher Newport U (VA) ***313***
City Coll of the City U of NY (NY) ***314***
Claremont McKenna Coll (CA) ***315***
Clark U (MA) ***316***
Coe Coll (IA) ***318***
The Coll of New Rochelle (NY) ***321***
Coll of St. Catherine (MN) ***321***
Coll of the Atlantic (ME) ***323***
Coll of the Holy Cross (MA) ***323***
Columbia Coll (SC) ***327***
Columbia U, School of General Studies (NY) ***328***
Columbus State U (GA) ***328***
Concordia U (MN) ***330***
Concordia U (NE) ***330***
Concordia U (QC, Canada) ***331***
Dalhousie U (NS, Canada) ***336***
Davis & Elkins Coll (WV) ***338***
Defiance Coll (OH) ***338***
DePaul U (IL) ***339***
Duke U (NC) ***346***
East Central U (OK) ***347***
Eastern Kentucky U (KY) ***348***
Eastern Washington U (WA) ***349***
Eckerd Coll (FL) ***350***
Elmira Coll (NY) ***351***
Emmanuel Coll (MA) ***353***
Emory U (GA) ***354***
Eugene Lang Coll, New School U (NY) ***355***
Eureka Coll (IL) ***355***
The Evergreen State Coll (WA) ***355***
Excelsior Coll (NY) ***356***
Fayetteville State U (NC) ***357***
Fitchburg State Coll (MA) ***358***
Florida State U (FL) ***361***
Fordham U (NY) ***362***
Fort Lewis Coll (CO) ***362***
Framingham State Coll (MA) ***362***
Franklin Coll Switzerland(Switzerland) ***364***
Franklin Pierce Coll (NH) ***364***
Fresno Pacific U (CA) ***364***
Gettysburg Coll (PA) ***368***
Goddard Coll (VT) ***369***
Gonzaga U (WA) ***369***
Graceland U (IA) ***371***
Grand Canyon U (AZ) ***371***
Grand Valley State U (MI) ***371***
Grove City Coll (PA) ***373***
Hamilton Coll (NY) ***374***
Hampshire Coll (MA) ***375***
Harvard U (MA) ***376***
Hastings Coll (NE) ***377***
Hawai'i Pacific U (HI) ***377***
High Point U (NC) ***379***
Holy Family U (PA) ***380***
Houghton Coll (NY) ***381***
Hunter Coll of the City U of NY (NY) ***382***
Immaculata U (PA) ***385***
Indiana U Bloomington (IN) ***385***
Insto Tecno Estudios Sups Monterrey(Mexico) ***388***
Inter American U of PR, San Germán Campus (PR) ***388***
Jewish Theological Seminary of America (NY) ***391***
John Cabot U(Italy) ***392***
John Carroll U (OH) ***392***
Johns Hopkins U (MD) ***392***
Johnson State Coll (VT) ***394***
Judson Coll (IL) ***395***
Kenyon Coll (OH) ***398***
La Salle U (PA) ***402***
Long Island U, Southampton Coll (NY) ***409***
Long Island U, Southampton Coll, Friends World Program (NY) ***409***
Lycoming Coll (PA) ***412***
Maharishi U of Management (IA) ***414***
Marist Coll (NY) ***417***
Marlboro Coll (VT) ***418***
Marymount Coll of Fordham U (NY) ***419***
Massachusetts Coll of Liberal Arts (MA) ***421***
Massachusetts Inst of Technology (MA) ***421***
Memorial U of Newfoundland (NF, Canada) ***424***
Middlebury Coll (VT) ***429***
Minnesota State U, Mankato (MN) ***431***
Montreat Coll (NC) ***435***
Morningside Coll (IA) ***437***
Mount Allison U (NB, Canada) ***437***
Mount Saint Vincent U (NS, Canada) ***439***
Mount Vernon Nazarene U (OH) ***440***
Naropa U (CO) ***441***
Nazareth Coll of Rochester (NY) ***443***
New Coll of Florida (FL) ***444***
North Central Coll (IL) ***449***
North Park U (IL) ***452***
Northwest Missouri State U (MO) ***454***
Ohio Wesleyan U (OH) ***459***
Olivet Nazarene U (IL) ***461***
Oregon State U (OR) ***462***
Otterbein Coll (OH) ***462***
Pace U (NY) ***463***
Pacific Lutheran U (WA) ***463***
Pacific U (OR) ***464***
Pitzer Coll (CA) ***471***
Prescott Coll (AZ) ***474***
Purchase Coll, State U of NY (NY) ***475***
Purdue U Calumet (IN) ***475***
Quinnipiac U (CT) ***476***
Ramapo Coll of New Jersey (NJ) ***477***
Reed Coll (OR) ***477***
Richmond, The American International U in London(United Kingdom) ***480***
Rochester Coll (MI) ***482***
Rockford Coll (IL) ***482***
Roosevelt U (IL) ***483***
Sacred Heart U (CT) ***486***
St. Edward's U (TX) ***488***
Saint Francis U (PA) ***488***
St. John's Coll (NM) ***490***
Saint Leo U (FL) ***492***
Saint Mary's Coll of California (CA) ***494***
Salem State Coll (MA) ***497***
San Francisco State U (CA) ***498***
Sarah Lawrence Coll (NY) ***499***
Schreiner U (TX) ***501***
Seton Hill U (PA) ***502***
Shimer Coll (IL) ***503***
Simon's Rock Coll of Bard (MA) ***505***
Skidmore Coll (NY) ***506***
Sonoma State U (CA) ***506***
Southern Connecticut State U (CT) ***509***
Southern Nazarene U (OK) ***510***
Southern Vermont Coll (VT) ***511***
Southwestern U (TX) ***513***
Southwest State U (MN) ***513***
State U of NY at Binghamton (NY) ***515***
State U of NY Coll at Brockport (NY) ***515***
State U of NY Coll at Old Westbury (NY) ***516***
Syracuse U (NY) ***521***
Taylor U (IN) ***523***
Thomas More Coll of Liberal Arts (NH) ***528***
Touro Coll (NY) ***529***
Trent U (ON, Canada) ***529***
United States Military Academy (NY) ***535***
Université Laval (QC, Canada) ***536***
The U of Akron (OH) ***537***
U of Alberta (AB, Canada) ***538***
U of Baltimore (MD) ***539***
U of Calif, Irvine (CA) ***541***
U of Calif, San Diego (CA) ***541***
U of Calif, Santa Cruz (CA) ***542***
U of Cincinnati (OH) ***543***
U of Evansville (IN) ***545***
U of Houston–Clear Lake (TX) ***547***
The U of Iowa (IA) ***548***
U of Judaism (CA) ***548***
U of Michigan (MI) ***554***
U of Missouri–St. Louis (MO) ***556***
The U of Montana–Western (MT) ***556***
U of New Brunswick Fredericton (NB, Canada) ***558***
U of New Hampshire (NH) ***558***
The U of North Carolina at Pembroke (NC) ***560***
U of North Texas (TX) ***562***
U of Ottawa (ON, Canada) ***563***
U of Pittsburgh at Greensburg (PA) ***570***
U of Pittsburgh at Johnstown (PA) ***570***
U of Redlands (CA) ***572***
The U of Texas at Dallas (TX) ***578***
U of the Sacred Heart (PR) ***580***
U of the South (TN) ***581***
U of Toledo (OH) ***581***
U of Toronto (ON, Canada) ***581***
U of Victoria (BC, Canada) ***582***
U of Windsor (ON, Canada) ***584***
U of Wisconsin–Milwaukee (WI) ***585***
Washington U in St. Louis (MO) ***595***
Wayne State Coll (NE) ***596***
Webster U (MO) ***597***
West Chester U of Pennsylvania (PA) ***598***
Western Washington U (WA) ***600***
Westfield State Coll (MA) ***600***
Westminster Coll (MO) ***601***
West Virginia Wesleyan Coll (WV) ***603***
Wheaton Coll (MA) ***603***
Wilberforce U (OH) ***605***
William Paterson U of New Jersey (NJ) ***606***
Williams Coll (MA) ***606***
Wittenberg U (OH) ***608***
Yale U (CT) ***610***
York U (ON, Canada) ***611***

LOGISTICS/MATERIALS MANAGEMENT

Overview: Students taking this major learn how to manage a variety of enterprise functions from acquisitions and receiving to resource allocation and delivery of goods and services produced. *Related majors:* mathematics, quality control technology, finance, organizational behavior, operations management and supervision. *Potential careers:* acquisitions and purchasing agent, consultant, inventory manager, contracts manager, sales manager. *Salary potential:* $38k-$45k.

Auburn U (AL) ***276***
Bowling Green State U (OH) ***292***
Central Michigan U (MI) ***310***
Duquesne U (PA) ***346***
Elmhurst Coll (IL) ***351***
Georgia Coll & State U (GA) ***367***
Georgia Southern U (GA) ***367***
Iowa State U of Science and Technology (IA) ***390***
Maine Maritime Academy (ME) ***415***
Michigan State U (MI) ***428***
Northeastern U (MA) ***450***
The Ohio State U (OH) ***457***
Park U (MO) ***465***
Penn State U Univ Park Campus (PA) ***468***
Portland State U (OR) ***472***
Robert Morris U (PA) ***481***
St. John's U (NY) ***490***
Texas A&M U (TX) ***524***
Thomas Edison State Coll (NJ) ***527***
U of Arkansas (AR) ***539***
The U of Findlay (OH) ***545***
U of Nevada, Reno (NV) ***558***
U of North Texas (TX) ***562***
The U of Tennessee (TN) ***577***
Wayne State U (MI) ***596***
Weber State U (UT) ***596***
Western Michigan U (MI) ***599***

MAJOR APPLIANCE INSTALLATION/REPAIR

Overview: Students will learn how to repair, install, and service consumer and commercial appliances, such as dishwashers, dryers, ice makers, refrigerators, stoves, washers, and water heaters. *Related majors:* electrical/electronics installation and repair; instrument calibration and repair; heating, air conditioning, and refrigeration mechanics. *Potential careers:* appliance salesperson, installer or repairperson. *Salary potential:* $15k-$25k.

Lewis-Clark State Coll (ID) ***406***

MANAGEMENT INFORMATION SYSTEMS/ BUSINESS DATA PROCESSING

Overview: Students learn how to manage computer systems that are designed to store and process business information and data for internal use. *Related majors:* information technology, computer science, data warehousing, data processing technology. *Potential careers:* systems analyst, system developer, telecommunications specialist, database administrator, systems security and crime prevention specialist. *Salary potential:* $40k-$50k.

Alderson-Broaddus Coll (WV) ***263***
Amberton U (TX) ***265***
American Coll of Thessaloniki(Greece) ***266***
American InterContinental U (CA) ***266***
American InterContinental U, Atlanta (GA) ***266***
American InterContinental U-London(United Kingdom) ***267***
American International Coll (MA) ***267***
American U (DC) ***267***
Angelo State U (TX) ***269***
Arcadia U (PA) ***271***
Arizona State U (AZ) ***271***
Auburn U (AL) ***276***
Auburn U Montgomery (AL) ***276***
Augsburg Coll (MN) ***276***
Augustana Coll (SD) ***276***
Aurora U (IL) ***277***
Azusa Pacific U (CA) ***278***
Babson Coll (MA) ***278***
Baker Coll of Flint (MI) ***279***
Ball State U (IN) ***280***
Barry U (FL) ***282***
Bayamón Central U (PR) ***283***
Baylor U (TX) ***283***
Bellevue U (NE) ***284***
Baruch Coll of the City U of NY (NY) ***286***
Bethel Coll (MN) ***288***
Bishop's U (QC, Canada) ***289***
Boston Coll (MA) ***292***
Boston U (MA) ***292***
Bowling Green State U (OH) ***292***
Bradley U (IL) ***293***
Brewton-Parker Coll (GA) ***294***
Briar Cliff U (IA) ***294***
Bridgewater Coll (VA) ***294***
Bridgewater State Coll (MA) ***294***
Buena Vista U (IA) ***297***
Cabrini Coll (PA) ***298***
California Polytechnic State U, San Luis Obispo (CA) ***300***
California State U, Chico (CA) ***300***
California State U, Dominguez Hills (CA) ***300***
California State U, Fresno (CA) ***301***
California State U, Hayward (CA) ***301***
California State U, Northridge (CA) ***301***
California State U, San Bernardino (CA) ***302***
Canisius Coll (NY) ***304***
Capitol Coll (MD) ***304***
Carleton U (ON, Canada) ***305***
Carson-Newman Coll (TN) ***306***
Central Connecticut State U (CT) ***309***
Central Michigan U (MI) ***310***
Central Missouri State U (MO) ***310***
Charleston Southern U (SC) ***311***
Chatham Coll (PA) ***312***
Christian Brothers U (TN) ***313***
Clarke Coll (IA) ***315***
Clarkson U (NY) ***316***
Clayton Coll & State U (GA) ***316***
Cleary U (MI) ***317***

Coll Misericordia (PA) 319
The Coll of New Jersey (NJ) 320
Coll of St. Catherine (MN) 321
Coll of Santa Fe (NM) 323
Colorado Christian U (CO) 325
Colorado Tech U (CO) 326
Colorado Tech U Sioux Falls Campus (SD) 326
Concordia U (MN) 330
Concordia U (NE) 330
Concordia U (QC, Canada) 331
Creighton U (NE) 333
Dallas Baptist U (TX) 336
Dalton State Coll (GA) 336
Daniel Webster Coll (NH) 337
Delta State U (MS) 339
DePaul U (IL) 339
DeSales U (PA) 340
Dominican Coll (NY) 344
Dordt Coll (IA) 345
Drexel U (PA) 346
Duquesne U (PA) 346
East Carolina U (NC) 347
Eastern Illinois U (IL) 348
Eastern Michigan U (MI) 348
Eastern New Mexico U (NM) 349
Eastern U (PA) 349
Eastern Washington U (WA) 349
École des hautes études commerciales de Montréal (QC, Canada) 350
Elmhurst Coll (IL) 351
Eureka Coll (IL) 355
Excelsior Coll (NY) 356
Fairfield U (CT) 356
Ferris State U (MI) 358
Florida Atlantic U (FL) 359
Florida Gulf Coast U (FL) 359
Florida Metropolitan U-Fort Lauderdale Coll (FL) 360
Florida Southern Coll (FL) 361
Florida State U (FL) 361
Fontbonne U (MO) 361
Fordham U (NY) 362
Francis Marion U (SC) 363
Franklin U (OH) 364
Gannon U (PA) 365
Gardner-Webb U (NC) 365
George Fox U (OR) 366
Georgetown Coll (KY) 366
Georgia Southern U (GA) 367
Goldey-Beacom Coll (DE) 369
Governors State U (IL) 370
Grace Coll (IN) 370
Graceland U (IA) 371
Grand Valley State U (MI) 371
Grand View Coll (IA) 372
Greenville Coll (IL) 373
Hawai'i Pacific U (HI) 377
Henderson State U (AR) 378
Hilbert Coll (NY) 379
Husson Coll (ME) 383
Illinois Coll (IL) 384
Indiana State U (IN) 385
Indiana U Bloomington (IN) 385
Indiana U of Pennsylvania (PA) 386
Insto Tecno Estudios Sups Monterrey(Mexico) 388
Iona Coll (NY) 390
Iowa State U of Science and Technology (IA) 390
Jacksonville U (FL) 391
Jamestown Coll (ND) 391
Johnson State Coll (VT) 394
Judson Coll (IL) 395
Juniata Coll (PA) 395
Lakehead U (ON, Canada) 400
La Salle U (PA) 402
LeTourneau U (TX) 405
Lewis U (IL) 406
Lincoln U (CA) 407
Lindenwood U (MO) 407
Long Island U, C.W. Post Campus (NY) 409
Longwood U (VA) 409
Loras Coll (IA) 410
Louisiana State U and A&M Coll (LA) 410
Louisiana Tech U (LA) 410
Loyola U Chicago (IL) 411
Luther Coll (IA) 412
MacMurray Coll (IL) 414
Marquette U (WI) 418
Maryville U of Saint Louis (MO) 420
The Master's Coll and Seminary (CA) 422
Metropolitan State U (MN) 427
Miami U (OH) 428
Michigan Technological U (MI) 428
Middle Tennessee State U (TN) 429
Midland Lutheran Coll (NE) 429
Millikin U (IL) 430
Milwaukee School of Engineering (WI) 431
Minnesota State U, Moorhead (MN) 432
Minot State U (ND) 432
Mississippi State U (MS) 432
Montclair State U (NJ) 435
Montreat Coll (NC) 435
Morgan State U (MD) 436
Morningside Coll (IA) 437
Mount Saint Vincent U (NS, Canada) 439
Murray State U (KY) 440
National American U, Denver (CO) 441
National American U (NM) 441
National American U (SD) 442
National American U–Sioux Falls Branch (SD) 442
Nazareth Coll of Rochester (NY) 443
New Mexico Highlands U (NM) 446
New York Inst of Technology (NY) 447
New York U (NY) 447
Nicholls State U (LA) 447
Nichols Coll (MA) 448
North Central Coll (IL) 449
North Dakota State U (ND) 449
Northeastern U (MA) 450
Northern Arizona U (AZ) 450
Northern Kentucky U (KY) 451
Northern Michigan U (MI) 451
Northern State U (SD) 451
Northwestern Coll (MN) 453
Northwest Missouri State U (MO) 454
Northwood U, Florida Campus (FL) 454
Northwood U, Texas Campus (TX) 454
Oakland U (MI) 456
The Ohio State U (OH) 457
Ohio U (OH) 458
Oklahoma Baptist U (OK) 459
Oklahoma City U (OK) 460
Oklahoma State U (OK) 460
Old Dominion U (VA) 460
Oral Roberts U (OK) 461
Oregon Inst of Technology (OR) 461
Oregon State U (OR) 462
Pace U (NY) 463
Pacific Lutheran U (WA) 463
Pacific Union Coll (CA) 464
Park U (MO) 465
Penn State U at Erie, The Behrend Coll (PA) 467
Penn State U Harrisburg Campus of the Capital Coll (PA) 468
Penn State U Univ Park Campus (PA) 468
Peru State Coll (NE) 469
Philadelphia U (PA) 469
Point Loma Nazarene U (CA) 471
Radford U (VA) 476
Rensselaer Polytechnic Inst (NY) 478
Rhode Island Coll (RI) 479
Robert Morris U (PA) 481
Roberts Wesleyan Coll (NY) 481
Rochester Inst of Technology (NY) 482
Rockford Coll (IL) 482
Rocky Mountain Coll (MT) 482
Rowan U (NJ) 484
Saint Francis U (PA) 488
St. Francis Xavier U (NS, Canada) 489
St. John Fisher Coll (NY) 489
Saint Joseph's Coll (IN) 490
Saint Joseph's U (PA) 491
Saint Louis U (MO) 492
Saint Martin's Coll (WA) 493
Saint Mary's Coll (IN) 493
St. Norbert Coll (WI) 495
Salem State Coll (MA) 497
Salisbury U (MD) 497
San Jose State U (CA) 499
Santa Clara U (CA) 499
Savannah State U (GA) 499
Seattle U (WA) 501
Seton Hall U (NJ) 502
Seton Hill U (PA) 502
Shawnee State U (OH) 502
Simmons Coll (MA) 504
Southeastern U (DC) 508
Southeast Missouri State U (MO) 508
Southern Adventist U (TN) 508
Southern Illinois U Edwardsville (IL) 509
Southern Methodist U (TX) 510
Southern Nazarene U (OK) 510
Southern New Hampshire U (NH) 510
Southwestern Coll (KS) 512
Southwest Missouri State U (MO) 513
Southwest Texas State U (TX) 513
Spring Arbor U (MI) 514
Springfield Coll (MA) 514
State U of West Georgia (GA) 518
Suffolk U (MA) 520
Tarleton State U (TX) 522
Teikyo Post U (CT) 523
Texas A&M U–Commerce (TX) 525
Texas A&M U–Texarkana (TX) 525
Texas Tech U (TX) 526
Texas Wesleyan U (TX) 526
Thiel Coll (PA) 527
Thomas Coll (ME) 527
Tiffin U (OH) 528
Touro U International (CA) 529
Trinity Christian Coll (IL) 530
Tri-State U (IN) 532
United States International U(Kenya) 535
Université de Sherbrooke (QC, Canada) 536
U du Québec à Hull (QC, Canada) 536
The U of Alabama (AL) 537
The U of Alabama in Huntsville (AL) 537
U of Alaska Anchorage (AK) 538
U of Alberta (AB, Canada) 538
The U of Arizona (AZ) 538
U of Arkansas at Monticello (AR) 539
The U of British Columbia (BC, Canada) 540
U of Calgary (AB, Canada) 540
U of Central Arkansas (AR) 542
U of Central Florida (FL) 542
U of Cincinnati (OH) 543
U of Colorado at Boulder (CO) 543
U of Connecticut (CT) 544
U of Dayton (OH) 544
U of Georgia (GA) 545
U of Hartford (CT) 546
U of Hawaii at Manoa (HI) 546
U of Houston (TX) 547
U of Houston–Downtown (TX) 547
U of Idaho (ID) 547
U of Illinois at Chicago (IL) 547
The U of Iowa (IA) 548
The U of Lethbridge (AB, Canada) 549
U of Louisville (KY) 550
U of Massachusetts Dartmouth (MA) 553
The U of Memphis (TN) 553
U of Minnesota, Twin Cities Campus (MN) 555
U of Mississippi (MS) 555
U of Missouri–St. Louis (MO) 556
U of Montevallo (AL) 557
U of Nebraska at Omaha (NE) 557
U of Nevada, Las Vegas (NV) 558
U of New Orleans (LA) 559
U of North Alabama (AL) 559
The U of North Carolina at Charlotte (NC) 560
The U of North Carolina at Greensboro (NC) 560
The U of North Carolina at Wilmington (NC) 561
U of Northern Iowa (IA) 561
U of Notre Dame (IN) 562
U of Oklahoma (OK) 562
U of Ottawa (ON, Canada) 563
U of Pennsylvania (PA) 563
U of Phoenix-Atlanta Campus (GA) 563
U of Phoenix–Boston Campus (MA) 563
U of Phoenix–Colorado Campus (CO) 563
U of Phoenix–Dallas Campus (TX) 564
U of Phoenix–Fort Lauderdale Campus (FL) 564
U of Phoenix–Hawaii Campus (HI) 564
U of Phoenix–Houston Campus (TX) 564
U of Phoenix–Jacksonville Campus (FL) 564
U of Phoenix–Louisiana Campus (LA) 565
U of Phoenix–Maryland Campus (MD) 565
U of Phoenix–Metro Detroit Campus (MI) 565
U of Phoenix–New Mexico Campus (NM) 565
U of Phoenix–Northern California Campus (CA) 565
U of Phoenix–Ohio Campus (OH) 566
U of Phoenix–Oklahoma City Campus (OK) 566
U of Phoenix–Oregon Campus (OR) 566
U of Phoenix–Orlando Campus (FL) 566
U of Phoenix–Phoenix Campus (AZ) 567
U of Phoenix–Sacramento Campus (CA) 567
U of Phoenix–St. Louis Campus (MO) 567
U of Phoenix–San Diego Campus (CA) 567
U of Phoenix–Southern Arizona Campus (AZ) 568
U of Phoenix–Southern Colorado Campus (CO) 568
U of Phoenix–Tampa Campus (FL) 568
U of Phoenix–Tulsa Campus (OK) 568
U of Phoenix–Utah Campus (UT) 568
U of Phoenix–Vancouver Campus (BC, Canada) 569
U of Phoenix–Washington Campus (WA) 569
U of Phoenix–West Michigan Campus (MI) 569
U of Redlands (CA) 572
U of Rhode Island (RI) 572
U of Richmond (VA) 572
U of St. Thomas (TX) 573
U of San Francisco (CA) 574
U of Sioux Falls (SD) 574
U of Southern Mississippi (MS) 576
The U of Tennessee at Martin (TN) 577
The U of Texas at Arlington (TX) 577
The U of Texas at Austin (TX) 578
The U of Texas at Dallas (TX) 578
The U of Texas at San Antonio (TX) 578
The U of Texas–Pan American (TX) 579
U of the Incarnate Word (TX) 580
U of Tulsa (OK) 581
U of Washington (WA) 583
The U of West Alabama (AL) 583
U of West Florida (FL) 583
U of Wisconsin–Eau Claire (WI) 584
U of Wisconsin–La Crosse (WI) 584
U of Wisconsin–Milwaukee (WI) 585
U of Wisconsin–Oshkosh (WI) 585
U of Wisconsin–River Falls (WI) 585
U of Wisconsin–Whitewater (WI) 586
Upper Iowa U (IA) 587
Ursuline Coll (OH) 587
Vanguard U of Southern California (CA) 589
Villa Julie Coll (MD) 590
Villanova U (PA) 590
Virginia Polytechnic Inst and State U (VA) 591
Virginia State U (VA) 591
Virginia Union U (VA) 591
Walla Walla Coll (WA) 593
Washington State U (WA) 595
Wayne State U (MI) 596
Weber State U (UT) 596
Webster U (MO) 597
Western Carolina U (NC) 598
Western Connecticut State U (CT) 598
Western Illinois U (IL) 599
Western Kentucky U (KY) 599
Western Michigan U (MI) 599
Western State Coll of Colorado (CO) 600
Western Washington U (WA) 600
Westfield State Coll (MA) 600
Westminster Coll (MO) 601
West Texas A&M U (TX) 602
Wichita State U (KS) 604
William Woods U (MO) 607
Wingate U (NC) 607
Winona State U (MN) 608
Winston-Salem State U (NC) 608
Worcester Polytechnic Inst (MA) 609
Wright State U (OH) 609
Xavier U (OH) 610
York U (ON, Canada) 611
Youngstown State U (OH) 611

MANAGEMENT SCIENCE

Overview: This major teaches students how to apply mathematics, statistics, and operations research to solve problems associated with business operations. *Related majors:* mathematics, statistics, operations research, business administration/ management. *Potential careers:* corporate consultant, professor, researcher. *Salary potential:* $40k-$50k

Abilene Christian U (TX) 260
American Public U System (WV) 267
Arkansas Tech U (AR) 272
Caldwell Coll (NJ) 298
Capella U (MN) 304
Central Methodist Coll (MO) 309
Clarion U of Pennsylvania (PA) 315
The Coll of St. Scholastica (MN) 322

MANAGEMENT SCIENCE (continued)

The Coll of Southeastern Europe, The American U of Athens(Greece) ***323***
Dalhousie U (NS, Canada) ***336***
Duquesne U (PA) ***346***
Eastern U (PA) ***349***
École des hautes études commerciales de Montréal (QC, Canada) ***350***
Everglades Coll (FL) ***355***
Franklin U (OH) ***364***
Georgia Inst of Technology (GA) ***367***
Goucher Coll (MD) ***370***
Inst of Public Administration(Ireland) ***387***
Louisiana Tech U (LA) ***410***
Lourdes Coll (OH) ***411***
Maharishi U of Management (IA) ***414***
Manhattan Coll (NY) ***416***
Marymount U (VA) ***420***
McGill U (QC, Canada) ***423***
Metropolitan State Coll of Denver (CO) ***427***
Miami U (OH) ***428***
Minnesota State U, Mankato (MN) ***431***
Northeastern U (MA) ***450***
Northwest Coll (WA) ***452***
Oakland City U (IN) ***456***
Oklahoma State U (OK) ***460***
Oral Roberts U (OK) ***461***
Prescott Coll (AZ) ***474***
Rider U (NJ) ***480***
Rockhurst U (MO) ***482***
Rutgers, The State U of New Jersey, New Brunswick (NJ) ***485***
Saint Louis U (MO) ***492***
Shippensburg U of Pennsylvania (PA) ***503***
Simon Fraser U (BC, Canada) ***505***
Southeastern Oklahoma State U (OK) ***508***
Southern Adventist U (TN) ***508***
Southern Methodist U (TX) ***510***
Southern Nazarene U (OK) ***510***
Southwestern Coll (KS) ***512***
State U of NY at Binghamton (NY) ***515***
State U of NY at Oswego (NY) ***515***
Trinity U (TX) ***531***
Tuskegee U (AL) ***533***
United States Coast Guard Academy (CT) ***535***
The U of Alabama (AL) ***537***
U of Calif, San Diego (CA) ***541***
U of Connecticut (CT) ***544***
U of Florida (FL) ***545***
U of Great Falls (MT) ***545***
The U of Iowa (IA) ***548***
U of Kentucky (KY) ***549***
U of Maryland University Coll (MD) ***552***
The U of Memphis (TN) ***553***
U of Minnesota, Morris (MN) ***555***
U of North Dakota (ND) ***561***
U of Pennsylvania (PA) ***563***
U of Phoenix-Atlanta Campus (GA) ***563***
U of Phoenix–Colorado Campus (CO) ***563***
U of Phoenix–Dallas Campus (TX) ***564***
U of Phoenix–Fort Lauderdale Campus (FL) ***564***
U of Phoenix–Hawaii Campus (HI) ***564***
U of Phoenix–Houston Campus (TX) ***564***
U of Phoenix–Jacksonville Campus (FL) ***564***
U of Phoenix–Maryland Campus (MD) ***565***
U of Phoenix–Metro Detroit Campus (MI) ***565***
U of Phoenix–New Mexico Campus (NM) ***565***
U of Phoenix–Northern California Campus (CA) ***565***
U of Phoenix–Oklahoma City Campus (OK) ***566***
U of Phoenix–Oregon Campus (OR) ***566***
U of Phoenix–Orlando Campus (FL) ***566***
U of Phoenix–Philadelphia Campus (PA) ***566***
U of Phoenix–Phoenix Campus (AZ) ***567***
U of Phoenix–Puerto Rico Campus (PR) ***567***
U of Phoenix–Sacramento Campus (CA) ***567***
U of Phoenix–Southern Colorado Campus (CO) ***568***
U of Phoenix–Tampa Campus (FL) ***568***
U of Phoenix–Tulsa Campus (OK) ***568***
U of Phoenix–Utah Campus (UT) ***568***
U of Phoenix–Washington Campus (WA) ***569***
The U of Scranton (PA) ***574***
U of South Carolina (SC) ***575***
U of South Florida (FL) ***576***
The U of Texas at San Antonio (TX) ***578***
U of the Incarnate Word (TX) ***580***
U of Washington (WA) ***583***
U of Windsor (ON, Canada) ***584***
U of Wyoming (WY) ***586***
Wake Forest U (NC) ***592***
Wheeling Jesuit U (WV) ***603***
York U (ON, Canada) ***611***

MARINE BIOLOGY

Overview: This major encompasses the ecology and biology of plants, animals, and microorganisms that inhabit either the oceans, freshwater, or fresh or saltwater marshes. *Related majors:* ecology, biology, fishing and fisheries science and management, biochemistry, cell biology. *Potential careers:* marine biologist, ecologist, environmentalist, research scientist. *Salary potential:* $23k-$30k.

Alabama State U (AL) ***261***
Auburn U (AL) ***276***
Ball State U (IN) ***280***
Barry U (FL) ***282***
Bemidji State U (MN) ***285***
Boston U (MA) ***292***
Brown U (RI) ***296***
California State U, Long Beach (CA) ***301***
Coastal Carolina U (SC) ***318***
Coll of Charleston (SC) ***320***
Coll of the Atlantic (ME) ***323***
Dalhousie U (NS, Canada) ***336***
East Stroudsburg U of Pennsylvania (PA) ***349***
Eckerd Coll (FL) ***350***
The Evergreen State Coll (WA) ***355***
Fairleigh Dickinson U, Florham (NJ) ***356***
Fairleigh Dickinson U, Teaneck-Metro Campus (NJ) ***356***
Florida Inst of Technology (FL) ***360***
Florida State U (FL) ***361***
Gettysburg Coll (PA) ***368***
Hampshire Coll (MA) ***375***
Hampton U (VA) ***375***
Harvard U (MA) ***376***
Hawai'i Pacific U (HI) ***377***
Hofstra U (NY) ***380***
Humboldt State U (CA) ***382***
Jacksonville State U (AL) ***390***
Juniata Coll (PA) ***395***
Long Island U, Southampton Coll (NY) ***409***
Maine Maritime Academy (ME) ***415***
McGill U (QC, Canada) ***423***
Memorial U of Newfoundland (NF, Canada) ***424***
Mississippi State U (MS) ***432***
Missouri Southern State Coll (MO) ***433***
Nicholls State U (LA) ***447***
Northeastern U (MA) ***450***
Northern Arizona U (AZ) ***450***
Nova Southeastern U (FL) ***455***
The Richard Stockton Coll of New Jersey (NJ) ***479***
Roger Williams U (RI) ***483***
Rutgers, The State U of New Jersey, New Brunswick (NJ) ***485***
Saint Francis U (PA) ***488***
Saint Joseph's Coll of Maine (ME) ***491***
Salem State Coll (MA) ***497***
Samford U (AL) ***497***
San Diego State U (CA) ***498***
San Francisco State U (CA) ***498***
San Jose State U (CA) ***499***
Sarah Lawrence Coll (NY) ***499***
Savannah State U (GA) ***499***
Sheldon Jackson Coll (AK) ***503***
Sonoma State U (CA) ***506***
Southern Connecticut State U (CT) ***509***
Southwestern Coll (KS) ***512***
Southwest Texas State U (TX) ***513***
Spring Hill Coll (AL) ***514***
Stetson U (FL) ***519***
Suffolk U (MA) ***520***
Texas A&M U at Galveston (TX) ***524***
Troy State U (AL) ***532***
Unity Coll (ME) ***535***
The U of Alabama (AL) ***537***
U of Alaska Southeast (AK) ***538***
The U of British Columbia (BC, Canada) ***540***
U of Calif, Los Angeles (CA) ***541***
U of Calif, Santa Barbara (CA) ***541***
U of Calif, Santa Cruz (CA) ***542***
U of Connecticut (CT) ***544***
U of Guelph (ON, Canada) ***546***
U of King's Coll (NS, Canada) ***549***
U of Maine (ME) ***550***
U of Maine at Machias (ME) ***551***
U of Maryland Eastern Shore (MD) ***552***
U of Miami (FL) ***553***
U of New Brunswick Saint John (NB, Canada) ***558***
U of New England (ME) ***558***
U of New Hampshire (NH) ***558***
U of New Haven (CT) ***559***
U of North Alabama (AL) ***559***
The U of North Carolina at Wilmington (NC) ***561***
U of Puerto Rico, Humacao U Coll (PR) ***570***
U of Rhode Island (RI) ***572***
U of South Carolina (SC) ***575***
U of Southern California (CA) ***576***
U of Southern Mississippi (MS) ***576***
U of the Virgin Islands (VI) ***581***
U of Victoria (BC, Canada) ***582***
The U of West Alabama (AL) ***583***
U of West Florida (FL) ***583***
U of Wisconsin–Superior (WI) ***586***
Waynesburg Coll (PA) ***595***
Western Washington U (WA) ***600***
Wittenberg U (OH) ***608***

MARINE SCIENCE

Overview: This major prepares students to serve as captains, executive officers, engineers, or supervising officers on all oceangoing, inland, and coastal water vessels. *Related majors:* marine maintenance, atmospheric science/ meteorology, maritime science, communication equipment technology. *Potential careers:* ship captain, commercial fisherman, ship's officer, ship engineer, tugboat operator. *Salary potential:* $25k-$40k.

Cornell U (NY) ***333***
Dowling Coll (NY) ***345***
The Evergreen State Coll (WA) ***355***
Hampton U (VA) ***375***
Jacksonville U (FL) ***391***
Maine Maritime Academy (ME) ***415***
Massachusetts Maritime Academy (MA) ***421***
Memorial U of Newfoundland (NF, Canada) ***424***
Oregon State U (OR) ***462***
Prescott Coll (AZ) ***474***
Rider U (NJ) ***480***
Salem State Coll (MA) ***497***
State U of NY Maritime Coll (NY) ***518***
Suffolk U (MA) ***520***
Texas A&M U at Galveston (TX) ***524***
United States Coast Guard Academy (CT) ***535***
U of New Hampshire (NH) ***558***
U of San Diego (CA) ***574***
The U of Tampa (FL) ***577***

MARINE TECHNOLOGY

Overview: Students learn the basic science and technical skills that enable them to work with marine scientists, researchers, and engineers and those involved with exploring, preserving, and exploiting the oceans. *Related majors:* chemistry, environmental sciences, ocean engineering, oceanography, maritime science. *Potential careers:* ocean research associate, environmental scientist, merchant marine officer, manufacturing, marine biologist. *Salary potential:* $25k-$37k.

California Maritime Academy (CA) ***299***
Lamar U (TX) ***401***
Thomas Edison State Coll (NJ) ***527***

MARITIME SCIENCE

Overview: This major focuses on the general study of the maritime industry, including maritime traditions and law, economics and management of commercial maritime operations, basic naval architecture and administrative aspects. *Related majors:* marine science/merchant marine officer, law and legal studies, atmospheric science/meteorology, naval engineering, marine maintenance/ship repairer. *Potential careers:* captain, tugboat operator, commercial shipping executive, fisherman. *Salary potential:* $25k-$35k.

Coll of the Atlantic (ME) ***323***
Maine Maritime Academy (ME) ***415***
Massachusetts Maritime Academy (MA) ***421***
State U of NY Maritime Coll (NY) ***518***
Texas A&M U at Galveston (TX) ***524***
United States Merchant Marine Academy (NY) ***535***

MARKETING/DISTRIBUTION EDUCATION

Overview: This major prepares undergraduates to teach sales and marketing distribution courses at various educational levels. *Related majors:* business marketing, marketing management and research marketing, enterprise management and operation. *Potential careers:* vocational business teacher, sales coach. *Salary potential:* $24k-$35k.

Appalachian State U (NC) ***270***
Bowling Green State U (OH) ***292***
Central Michigan U (MI) ***310***
Colorado State U (CO) ***325***
East Carolina U (NC) ***347***
Eastern Michigan U (MI) ***348***
Eastern New Mexico U (NM) ***349***
Kent State U (OH) ***397***
Middle Tennessee State U (TN) ***429***
New York Inst of Technology (NY) ***447***
North Carolina State U (NC) ***449***
San Diego State U (CA) ***498***
Southern New Hampshire U (NH) ***510***
U of Georgia (GA) ***545***
U of Hawaii at Manoa (HI) ***546***
U of Nebraska–Lincoln (NE) ***557***
U of North Dakota (ND) ***561***
U of Wisconsin–Stout (WI) ***586***
Utah State U (UT) ***587***
Virginia Polytechnic Inst and State U (VA) ***591***
Western Michigan U (MI) ***599***

MARKETING MANAGEMENT AND RESEARCH RELATED

Information can be found under this major's main heading.

Capella U (MN) ***304***
Duquesne U (PA) ***346***
Inter American U of PR, San Germán Campus (PR) ***388***
La Roche Coll (PA) ***402***
Maryville U of Saint Louis (MO) ***420***
Rutgers, The State U of New Jersey, Camden (NJ) ***485***
St. Edward's U (TX) ***488***
U of Utah (UT) ***582***
Washington U in St. Louis (MO) ***595***
Western Michigan U (MI) ***599***
Wilmington Coll (DE) ***607***

MARKETING OPERATIONS

Overview: Students learn how to perform general marketing, sales, and operational tasks for a variety of products/services and settings. *Related majors:* marketing management, marketing research, general selling operations, advertising. *Potential careers:* marketing manager, brand product manager. *Salary potential:* depends mostly on product or service, but generally $25k-$30k can be expected.

Avila U (MO) ***278***
Champlain Coll (VT) ***311***

Colorado Tech U Sioux Falls Campus (SD) **326**
Dalton State Coll (GA) **336**
Lake Erie Coll (OH) **400**
Lambuth U (TN) **401**
McKendree Coll (IL) **423**
New England School of Communications (ME) **445**
New York U (NY) **447**
Our Lady of Holy Cross Coll (LA) **463**
Purdue U North Central (IN) **475**
Rochester Inst of Technology (NY) **482**
Tuskegee U (AL) **533**
U of Illinois at Urbana–Champaign (IL) **548**
U of Wisconsin–Superior (WI) **586**
York U (ON, Canada) **611**
Youngstown State U (OH) **611**

MARKETING OPERATIONS/ MARKETING AND DISTRIBUTION RELATED

Information can be found under this major's main heading.

Southeast Missouri State U (MO) **508**
Washington U in St. Louis (MO) **595**

MARKETING RESEARCH

Overview: Students learn how to gather and analyze data about consumer behavior and communicate this information to marketing managers and organizational decision makers. *Related majors:* general retailing/wholesaling, advertising, psychology, family/ consumer studies, consumer economics/science. *Potential careers:* market researcher, marketing executive, market analyst, survey researcher. *Salary potential:* $25k-$30k.

Ashland U (OH) **274**
Baker Coll of Jackson (MI) **279**
Boston U (MA) **292**
Bowling Green State U (OH) **292**
Carthage Coll (WI) **306**
Concordia U (QC, Canada) **331**
Fairleigh Dickinson U, Teaneck-Metro Campus (NJ) **356**
Ithaca Coll (NY) **390**
McGill U (QC, Canada) **423**
Methodist Coll (NC) **427**
Metropolitan State Coll of Denver (CO) **427**
Mount Saint Vincent U (NS, Canada) **439**
Newbury Coll (MA) **444**
Rochester Inst of Technology (NY) **482**
Saginaw Valley State U (MI) **486**
Southern New Hampshire U (NH) **510**
Talladega Coll (AL) **522**
Texas Christian U (TX) **526**
Troy State U Montgomery (AL) **532**
U of Great Falls (MT) **545**
U of Houston–Clear Lake (TX) **547**
U of Nebraska at Omaha (NE) **557**
U of Windsor (ON, Canada) **584**
York U (ON, Canada) **611**

MARRIAGE/FAMILY COUNSELING

Overview: Students learn the theories and skills necessary to provide marriage counseling and family therapy services to couples and families. *Related majors:* psychology and counseling psychology, family life/ relation studies, individual/family development studies. *Potential careers:* psychologist, marriage counselor, family therapist, child welfare agent, women's advocate. *Salary potential:* $20k-$30k.

Grace U (NE) **371**
Oklahoma Baptist U (OK) **459**
Saint Paul U (ON, Canada) **495**
Southern Christian U (AL) **509**
U of Nevada, Las Vegas (NV) **558**
The U of North Carolina at Greensboro (NC) **560**

MASS COMMUNICATIONS

Overview: Undergraduates learn to analyze the media, how people experience and understand the media, and how the media can influence and transform culture. *Related majors:* law, advertising, communication, journalism, psychology. *Potential careers:* advertising executive, lawyer, public policy advocate, writer. *Salary potential:* $23k-$30k.

Adrian Coll (MI) **260**
Alabama State U (AL) **261**
Albertus Magnus Coll (CT) **262**
Albion Coll (MI) **262**
Alcorn State U (MS) **263**
Alderson-Broaddus Coll (WV) **263**
Alfred U (NY) **263**
Alma Coll (MI) **264**
American International Coll (MA) **267**
The American U in Cairo(Egypt) **267**
The American U of Paris(France) **268**
Anderson Coll (SC) **268**
Anderson U (IN) **268**
Andrews U (MI) **269**
Antioch Coll (OH) **269**
Arcadia U (PA) **271**
Ashland U (OH) **274**
Atlantic Baptist U (NB, Canada) **275**
Auburn U (AL) **276**
Augsburg Coll (MN) **276**
Augustana Coll (IL) **276**
Augustana Coll (SD) **276**
Austin Peay State U (TN) **278**
Baker U (KS) **280**
Baldwin-Wallace Coll (OH) **280**
Barber-Scotia Coll (NC) **281**
Barry U (FL) **282**
Barton Coll (NC) **282**
Becker Coll (MA) **283**
Belmont U (TN) **284**
Beloit Coll (WI) **285**
Bemidji State U (MN) **285**
Bennett Coll (NC) **286**
Berry Coll (GA) **287**
Bethel Coll (MN) **288**
Bethune-Cookman Coll (FL) **289**
Black Hills State U (SD) **290**
Bloomsburg U of Pennsylvania (PA) **290**
Bluefield Coll (VA) **291**
Bluffton Coll (OH) **291**
Boston Coll (MA) **292**
Boston U (MA) **292**
Bowie State U (MD) **292**
Bowling Green State U (OH) **292**
Brenau U (GA) **293**
Briar Cliff U (IA) **294**
Brock U (ON, Canada) **295**
Bryan Coll (TN) **296**
Buena Vista U (IA) **297**
California Lutheran U (CA) **299**
California State Polytechnic U, Pomona (CA) **300**
California State U, Bakersfield (CA) **300**
California State U, Dominguez Hills (CA) **300**
California State U, Fresno (CA) **301**
California State U, Hayward (CA) **301**
California State U, Long Beach (CA) **301**
California State U, Sacramento (CA) **301**
California State U, San Bernardino (CA) **302**
Calvin Coll (MI) **303**
Cameron U (OK) **303**
Campbellsville U (KY) **303**
Canisius Coll (NY) **304**
Carleton U (ON, Canada) **305**
Carnegie Mellon U (PA) **305**
Carson-Newman Coll (TN) **306**
Catawba Coll (NC) **307**
Centenary Coll (NJ) **308**
Centenary Coll of Louisiana (LA) **308**
Central Missouri State U (MO) **310**
Central Washington U (WA) **310**
Chaminade U of Honolulu (HI) **311**
Champlain Coll (VT) **311**
Chapman U (CA) **311**
Cheyney U of Pennsylvania (PA) **312**
City Coll of the City U of NY (NY) **314**
City U (WA) **314**
Claflin U (SC) **314**
Clark Atlanta U (GA) **315**
Clarke Coll (IA) **315**
Clark U (MA) **316**
Cleveland State U (OH) **317**
Coker Coll (SC) **318**
Coll of Mount Saint Vincent (NY) **320**
The Coll of New Rochelle (NY) **321**
Coll of Notre Dame of Maryland (MD) **321**
Coll of St. Catherine (MN) **321**
Coll of the Ozarks (MO) **323**
The Coll of Wooster (OH) **324**
Colorado Christian U (CO) **325**
Colorado State U-Pueblo (CO) **325**
Columbia Union Coll (MD) **328**
Columbus State U (GA) **328**
Concord Coll (WV) **329**
Concordia Coll (MN) **329**
Concordia U (MN) **330**
Concordia U (NE) **330**
Concordia U (QC, Canada) **331**
Concordia U at Austin (TX) **331**
Concordia U Wisconsin (WI) **331**
Cornell U (NY) **333**
Cornerstone U (MI) **333**
Creighton U (NE) **333**
Culver-Stockton Coll (MO) **334**
Curry Coll (MA) **335**
Davis & Elkins Coll (WV) **338**
Defiance Coll (OH) **338**
Delaware State U (DE) **338**
Denison U (OH) **339**
DePaul U (IL) **339**
DePauw U (IN) **339**
DeSales U (PA) **340**
Dillard U (LA) **344**
Doane Coll (NE) **344**
Dominican U (IL) **345**
Dordt Coll (IA) **345**
Drake U (IA) **345**
Drury U (MO) **346**
East Central U (OK) **347**
Eastern Kentucky U (KY) **348**
Eastern Nazarene Coll (MA) **348**
Eastern Washington U (WA) **349**
East Tennessee State U (TN) **349**
Edgewood Coll (WI) **351**
Emerson Coll (MA) **353**
Emmanuel Coll (MA) **353**
Emory & Henry Coll (VA) **353**
Eureka Coll (IL) **355**
Evangel U (MO) **355**
The Evergreen State Coll (WA) **355**
Excelsior Coll (NY) **356**
Fairfield U (CT) **356**
Felician Coll (NJ) **357**
Ferris State U (MI) **358**
Florida A&M U (FL) **359**
Florida State U (FL) **361**
Fordham U (NY) **362**
Fort Hays State U (KS) **362**
Fort Lewis Coll (CO) **362**
Fort Valley State U (GA) **362**
Framingham State Coll (MA) **362**
Francis Marion U (SC) **363**
Franklin Pierce Coll (NH) **364**
Freed-Hardeman U (TN) **364**
Fresno Pacific U (CA) **364**
Frostburg State U (MD) **365**
Gallaudet U (DC) **365**
Gardner-Webb U (NC) **365**
Georgetown Coll (KY) **366**
The George Washington U (DC) **367**
Gonzaga U (WA) **369**
Gordon Coll (MA) **370**
Goshen Coll (IN) **370**
Goucher Coll (MD) **370**
Governors State U (IL) **370**
Grace Coll (IN) **370**
Grace U (NE) **371**
Grambling State U (LA) **371**
Grand Canyon U (AZ) **371**
Grand Valley State U (MI) **371**
Grand View Coll (IA) **372**
Greenville Coll (IL) **373**
Grove City Coll (PA) **373**
Gustavus Adolphus Coll (MN) **374**
Hamilton Coll (NY) **374**
Hamline U (MN) **374**
Hampshire Coll (MA) **375**
Hampton U (VA) **375**
Hannibal-LaGrange Coll (MO) **375**
Hanover Coll (IN) **375**
Harding U (AR) **375**
Hardin-Simmons U (TX) **376**
Hastings Coll (NE) **377**
Hawai'i Pacific U (HI) **377**
Heidelberg Coll (OH) **377**
High Point U (NC) **379**
Hiram Coll (OH) **379**
Hobart and William Smith Colls (NY) **380**
Hofstra U (NY) **380**
Hood Coll (MD) **381**
Houston Baptist U (TX) **382**
Howard U (DC) **382**
Huntington Coll (IN) **383**
Idaho State U (ID) **384**
Illinois Coll (IL) **384**
Illinois State U (IL) **384**
Indiana U Bloomington (IN) **385**
Indiana U Northwest (IN) **386**
Indiana U South Bend (IN) **387**
Insto Tecno Estudios Sups Monterrey(Mexico) **388**
Iona Coll (NY) **390**
Iowa State U of Science and Technology (IA) **390**
Iowa Wesleyan Coll (IA) **390**
Ithaca Coll (NY) **390**
Jackson State U (MS) **390**
John Brown U (AR) **392**
John Carroll U (OH) **392**
Johnson & Wales U (RI) **393**
Johnson C. Smith U (NC) **394**
Judson Coll (IL) **395**
Keene State Coll (NH) **396**
Kentucky Mountain Bible Coll (KY) **397**
Lake Erie Coll (OH) **400**
Lamar U (TX) **401**
Lambuth U (TN) **401**
Lander U (SC) **401**
Lane Coll (TN) **402**
Langston U (OK) **402**
La Salle U (PA) **402**
Lees-McRae Coll (NC) **404**
Lee U (TN) **404**
Lehman Coll of the City U of NY (NY) **404**
Lenoir-Rhyne Coll (NC) **405**
Lewis-Clark State Coll (ID) **406**
Lewis U (IL) **406**
Lincoln Memorial U (TN) **407**
Lindenwood U (MO) **407**
Lindsey Wilson Coll (KY) **407**
Lipscomb U (TN) **408**
Lock Haven U of Pennsylvania (PA) **408**
Long Island U, Brooklyn Campus (NY) **409**
Long Island U, Southampton Coll (NY) **409**
Long Island U, Southampton Coll, Friends World Program (NY) **409**
Loras Coll (IA) **410**
Louisiana Coll (LA) **410**
Louisiana State U and A&M Coll (LA) **410**
Louisiana State U in Shreveport (LA) **410**
Loyola Marymount U (CA) **411**
Lubbock Christian U (TX) **412**
Luther Coll (IA) **412**
Lycoming Coll (PA) **412**
Lynchburg Coll (VA) **413**
Lynn U (FL) **413**
Madonna U (MI) **414**
Manchester Coll (IN) **415**
Mansfield U of Pennsylvania (PA) **416**
Marian Coll (IN) **417**
Marian Coll of Fond du Lac (WI) **417**
Marist Coll (NY) **417**
Marquette U (WI) **418**
Mars Hill Coll (NC) **418**
Mary Baldwin Coll (VA) **419**
Marymount Coll of Fordham U (NY) **419**
Marymount Manhattan Coll (NY) **420**
Massachusetts Coll of Liberal Arts (MA) **421**
The Master's Coll and Seminary (CA) **422**
McKendree Coll (IL) **423**
McNeese State U (LA) **423**
Medaille Coll (NY) **424**
Menlo Coll (CA) **425**
Mercyhurst Coll (PA) **425**
Meredith Coll (NC) **426**
Mesa State Coll (CO) **426**
Methodist Coll (NC) **427**
Miami U (OH) **428**
MidAmerica Nazarene U (KS) **428**
Middle Tennessee State U (TN) **429**
Midland Lutheran Coll (NE) **429**
Midwestern State U (TX) **430**
Miles Coll (AL) **430**

MASS COMMUNICATIONS (continued)

Minnesota State U, Mankato (MN) 431
Minnesota State U, Moorhead (MN) 432
Mississippi Valley State U (MS) 432
Missouri Southern State Coll (MO) 433
Missouri Valley Coll (MO) 433
Monmouth Coll (IL) 434
Montana State U–Billings (MT) 434
Montana State U–Northern (MT) 434
Montclair State U (NJ) 435
Montreat Coll (NC) 435
Morgan State U (MD) 436
Morningside Coll (IA) 437
Mount Ida Coll (MA) 438
Mount Saint Mary Coll (NY) 439
Mount Union Coll (OH) 440
Mount Vernon Nazarene U (OH) 440
Muskingum Coll (OH) 441
Newberry Coll (SC) 444
Newbury Coll (MA) 444
New England Coll (NH) 444
Newman U (KS) 445
New Mexico Highlands U (NM) 446
New Mexico State U (NM) 446
New York U (NY) 447
Niagara U (NY) 447
Nicholls State U (LA) 447
Norfolk State U (VA) 448
North Carolina Ag and Tech State U (NC) 448
North Central Coll (IL) 449
North Dakota State U (ND) 449
Northeastern U (MA) 450
Northern Michigan U (MI) 451
North Greenville Coll (SC) 451
North Park U (IL) 452
Northwestern Coll (IA) 453
Northwestern Oklahoma State U (OK) 453
Northwest Missouri State U (MO) 454
Northwest Nazarene U (ID) 454
Oakwood Coll (AL) 456
Oglethorpe U (GA) 457
Ohio Northern U (OH) 457
Oklahoma Baptist U (OK) 459
Oklahoma Christian U (OK) 459
Oklahoma City U (OK) 460
Oklahoma Wesleyan U (OK) 460
Olivet Coll (MI) 461
Olivet Nazarene U (IL) 461
Oregon State U (OR) 462
Ottawa U (KS) 462
Ouachita Baptist U (AR) 462
Pacific Lutheran U (WA) 463
Pacific Union Coll (CA) 464
Pacific U (OR) 464
Paine Coll (GA) 465
Paul Quinn Coll (TX) 466
Pfeiffer U (NC) 469
Piedmont Coll (GA) 470
Pine Manor Coll (MA) 470
Pittsburg State U (KS) 470
Plattsburgh State U of NY (NY) 471
Point Loma Nazarene U (CA) 471
Point Park Coll (PA) 471
Pontifical Catholic U of Puerto Rico (PR) 472
Presentation Coll (SD) 474
Principia Coll (IL) 474
Purdue U Calumet (IN) 475
Queens U of Charlotte (NC) 476
Quinnipiac U (CT) 476
Randolph-Macon Woman's Coll (VA) 477
Reinhardt Coll (GA) 478
Rensselaer Polytechnic Inst (NY) 478
Rhode Island Coll (RI) 479
Richmond, The American International U in London(United Kingdom) 480
Robert Morris U (PA) 481
Roosevelt U (IL) 483
Rowan U (NJ) 484
Russell Sage Coll (NY) 484
Rutgers, The State U of New Jersey, New Brunswick (NJ) 485
Sacred Heart U (CT) 486
St. Ambrose U (IA) 486
St. Andrews Presbyterian Coll (NC) 487
St. Bonaventure U (NY) 487
St. Cloud State U (MN) 488
Saint Francis U (PA) 488
St. John Fisher Coll (NY) 489
Saint Joseph's Coll (IN) 490
Saint Mary Coll (KS) 493
Saint Mary-of-the-Woods Coll (IN) 493
Saint Mary's Coll of California (CA) 494
Saint Mary's Coll of Madonna U (MI) 493
St. Mary's U of San Antonio (TX) 494
St. Thomas Aquinas Coll (NY) 495
St. Thomas U (FL) 496
Salem Coll (NC) 496
Salem International U (WV) 496
Salem State Coll (MA) 497
San Diego State U (CA) 498
Savannah State U (GA) 499
Seattle U (WA) 501
Seton Hill U (PA) 502
Shaw U (NC) 502
Simmons Coll (MA) 504
Simpson Coll (IA) 505
Slippery Rock U of Pennsylvania (PA) 506
Sonoma State U (CA) 506
South Dakota State U (SD) 507
Southeast Missouri State U (MO) 508
Southern Adventist U (TN) 508
Southern Arkansas U–Magnolia (AR) 509
Southern Illinois U Edwardsville (IL) 509
Southern Nazarene U (OK) 510
Southern U and A&M Coll (LA) 511
Southern Utah U (UT) 511
Southern Vermont Coll (VT) 511
Southwestern Oklahoma State U (OK) 512
Southwestern U (TX) 513
Southwest Missouri State U (MO) 513
Southwest Texas State U (TX) 513
Spalding U (KY) 513
State U of NY at Albany (NY) 514
State U of NY at New Paltz (NY) 515
State U of NY at Oswego (NY) 515
State U of NY Coll at Brockport (NY) 515
State U of NY Coll at Buffalo (NY) 516
State U of NY Coll at Fredonia (NY) 516
State U of NY Coll at Oneonta (NY) 517
State U of West Georgia (GA) 518
Stephens Coll (MO) 519
Stetson U (FL) 519
Suffolk U (MA) 520
Sul Ross State U (TX) 521
Susquehanna U (PA) 521
Tabor Coll (KS) 522
Taylor U (IN) 523
Temple U (PA) 523
Tennessee State U (TN) 523
Texas A&M U–Kingsville (TX) 525
Texas Christian U (TX) 526
Texas Southern U (TX) 526
Texas Woman's U (TX) 527
Towson U (MD) 529
Trevecca Nazarene U (TN) 529
Trinity Coll (DC) 530
Truman State U (MO) 532
Tulane U (LA) 533
Union U (TN) 534
Université de Sherbrooke (QC, Canada) 536
U du Québec à Trois-Rivières (QC, Canada) 536
Université Laval (QC, Canada) 536
U at Buffalo, The State University of New York (NY) 536
The U of Akron (OH) 537
U of Alaska Anchorage (AK) 538
U of Baltimore (MD) 539
U of Bridgeport (CT) 540
U of Calif, Berkeley (CA) 540
U of Calif, San Diego (CA) 541
U of Charleston (WV) 542
U of Cincinnati (OH) 543
U of Colorado at Boulder (CO) 543
U of Dayton (OH) 544
U of Delaware (DE) 544
U of Dubuque (IA) 545
U of Evansville (IN) 545
U of Georgia (GA) 545
U of Illinois at Springfield (IL) 548
U of Illinois at Urbana–Champaign (IL) 548
The U of Iowa (IA) 548
U of Louisiana at Lafayette (LA) 550
U of Maine (ME) 550
U of Mary (ND) 551
U of Mary Hardin-Baylor (TX) 551
U of Maryland, Coll Park (MD) 552
U of Maryland Eastern Shore (MD) 552
U of Miami (FL) 553
U of Michigan (MI) 554
U of Michigan–Flint (MI) 554
U of Minnesota, Morris (MN) 555
U of Minnesota, Twin Cities Campus (MN) 555
U of Missouri–Columbia (MO) 555
U of Missouri–Kansas City (MO) 555
U of Missouri–St. Louis (MO) 556
U of Mobile (AL) 556
U of Montevallo (AL) 557
U of Nebraska at Kearney (NE) 557
U of Nebraska at Omaha (NE) 557
U of New Hampshire (NH) 558
U of New Mexico (NM) 559
The U of North Carolina at Chapel Hill (NC) 560
The U of North Carolina at Greensboro (NC) 560
The U of North Carolina at Pembroke (NC) 560
U of North Texas (TX) 562
U of Oregon (OR) 562
U of Ottawa (ON, Canada) 563
U of Pittsburgh at Bradford (PA) 569
U of Pittsburgh at Greensburg (PA) 570
U of Pittsburgh at Johnstown (PA) 570
U of Portland (OR) 570
U of Puerto Rico, Río Piedras (PR) 571
U of Rio Grande (OH) 572
U of St. Francis (IL) 573
U of Saint Francis (IN) 573
U of St. Thomas (MN) 573
U of San Diego (CA) 574
U of San Francisco (CA) 574
U of Sioux Falls (SD) 574
The U of South Dakota (SD) 575
U of Southern California (CA) 576
U of Southern Maine (ME) 576
The U of Tampa (FL) 577
The U of Tennessee at Chattanooga (TN) 577
The U of Texas at El Paso (TX) 578
The U of Texas at San Antonio (TX) 578
The U of Texas of the Permian Basin (TX) 579
The U of Texas–Pan American (TX) 579
U of the District of Columbia (DC) 580
U of the Incarnate Word (TX) 580
U of the Sacred Heart (PR) 580
U of Toledo (OH) 581
U of Toronto (ON, Canada) 581
U of Utah (UT) 582
U of Windsor (ON, Canada) 584
U of Wisconsin–Eau Claire (WI) 584
U of Wisconsin–Madison (WI) 584
U of Wisconsin–Milwaukee (WI) 585
U of Wisconsin–Oshkosh (WI) 585
U of Wisconsin–Platteville (WI) 585
U of Wisconsin–Superior (WI) 586
U of Wisconsin–Whitewater (WI) 586
Upper Iowa U (IA) 587
Urbana U (OH) 587
Ursinus Coll (PA) 587
Valdosta State U (GA) 588
Vanderbilt U (TN) 588
Vanguard U of Southern California (CA) 589
Villa Julie Coll (MD) 590
Villanova U (PA) 590
Virginia Commonwealth U (VA) 590
Virginia State U (VA) 591
Waldorf Coll (IA) 592
Walla Walla Coll (WA) 593
Walsh U (OH) 593
Wartburg Coll (IA) 594
Washington State U (WA) 595
Wayland Baptist U (TX) 595
Wayne State Coll (NE) 596
Wesley Coll (DE) 598
West Chester U of Pennsylvania (PA) 598
Western Connecticut State U (CT) 598
Western State Coll of Colorado (CO) 600
Western Washington U (WA) 600
Westfield State Coll (MA) 600
West Liberty State Coll (WV) 601
Westminster Coll (PA) 601
West Texas A&M U (TX) 602
West Virginia State Coll (WV) 602
West Virginia U (WV) 602
Whitworth Coll (WA) 604
Widener U (PA) 604
Wilberforce U (OH) 605
Wiley Coll (TX) 605
William Carey Coll (MS) 605
William Paterson U of New Jersey (NJ) 606
Wilmington Coll (OH) 607
Wilson Coll (PA) 607
Wingate U (NC) 607
Winona State U (MN) 608
Winston-Salem State U (NC) 608
Winthrop U (SC) 608
Worcester State Coll (MA) 609
Wright State U (OH) 609
Xavier U of Louisiana (LA) 610
York Coll of Pennsylvania (PA) 610
York U (ON, Canada) 611

MATERIALS ENGINEERING

Overview: Students learn the science of creating and using materials in a variety of industrial settings. *Related majors:* chemistry, ceramic engineering, chemical engineering, materials science, polymer/plastics engineering. *Potential careers:* research scientist, inventor, textile engineer. *Salary potential:* $40k-$55k.

Arizona State U (AZ) 271
Auburn U (AL) 276
Brown U (RI) 296
California Polytechnic State U, San Luis Obispo (CA) 300
California State Polytechnic U, Pomona (CA) 300
California State U, Long Beach (CA) 301
California State U, Northridge (CA) 301
Carnegie Mellon U (PA) 305
Case Western Reserve U (OH) 307
Clarkson U (NY) 316
Cornell U (NY) 333
Drexel U (PA) 346
Florida State U (FL) 361
Georgia Inst of Technology (GA) 367
Harvard U (MA) 376
Illinois Inst of Technology (IL) 384
Johns Hopkins U (MD) 392
Lehigh U (PA) 404
Massachusetts Inst of Technology (MA) 421
McMaster U (ON, Canada) 423
Mercyhurst Coll (PA) 425
Michigan Technological U (MI) 428
Montana Tech of The U of Montana (MT) 435
New Mexico Inst of Mining and Technology (NM) 446
New York U (NY) 447
North Carolina State U (NC) 449
Northwestern U (IL) 453
The Ohio State U (OH) 457
Purdue U (IN) 475
Rensselaer Polytechnic Inst (NY) 478
Rice U (TX) 479
San Jose State U (CA) 499
Stanford U (CA) 514
The U of Alabama at Birmingham (AL) 537
The U of British Columbia (BC, Canada) 540
U of Calif, Berkeley (CA) 540
U of Calif, Davis (CA) 540
U of Calif, Los Angeles (CA) 541
U of Connecticut (CT) 544
U of Florida (FL) 545
The U of Iowa (IA) 548
U of Kentucky (KY) 549
U of Maryland, Coll Park (MD) 552
U of Michigan (MI) 554
U of Minnesota, Twin Cities Campus (MN) 555
U of New Haven (CT) 559
U of Pennsylvania (PA) 563
U of Pittsburgh (PA) 569
The U of Tennessee (TN) 577
U of Toronto (ON, Canada) 581
U of Utah (UT) 582
U of Washington (WA) 583
The U of Western Ontario (ON, Canada) 583
U of Windsor (ON, Canada) 584
U of Wisconsin–Milwaukee (WI) 585
Virginia Polytechnic Inst and State U (VA) 591
Washington State U (WA) 595
Western Michigan U (MI) 599
Winona State U (MN) 608
Worcester Polytechnic Inst (MA) 609
Wright State U (OH) 609

MATERIALS SCIENCE

Overview: Students choosing this major learn how to analyze and evaluate the behavior and chemical properties of solids for such things as thermodynamics, stress, chemical transformation, etc. *Related majors:* metallurgy, engineering mechanics, chemistry, structural engineering. *Potential careers:* industrial manufacturing manager, industrial engineer, chemist, quality control manager. *Salary potential:* $40k-$50k.

Alfred U (NY) **263**
California Inst of Technology (CA) **299**
Carnegie Mellon U (PA) **305**
Case Western Reserve U (OH) **307**
Clarkson U (NY) **316**
Columbia U, School of Engineering & Applied Sci (NY) **328**
Cornell U (NY) **333**
Duke U (NC) **346**
Harvard U (MA) **376**
Johns Hopkins U (MD) **392**
Massachusetts Inst of Technology (MA) **421**
McMaster U (ON, Canada) **423**
Michigan State U (MI) **428**
Montana Tech of The U of Montana (MT) **435**
Northwestern U (IL) **453**
The Ohio State U (OH) **457**
Oregon State U (OR) **462**
Rice U (TX) **479**
Stanford U (CA) **514**
United States Air Force Academy (CO) **534**
The U of Arizona (AZ) **538**
U of Calif, Los Angeles (CA) **541**
U of Illinois at Urbana–Champaign (IL) **548**
U of Michigan (MI) **554**
U of Minnesota, Twin Cities Campus (MN) **555**
U of Toronto (ON, Canada) **581**
U of Utah (UT) **582**
Worcester Polytechnic Inst (MA) **609**

MATHEMATICAL STATISTICS

Overview: This major will teach students the mathematical principles that underlie statistical methods and uses. *Related majors:* mathematics, statistics. *Potential careers:* statistician, mathematician, professor, analyst. *Salary potential:* $35k-$45k.

American U (DC) **267**
Appalachian State U (NC) **270**
Barnard Coll (NY) **282**
Baruch Coll of the City U of NY (NY) **286**
Bowling Green State U (OH) **292**
Brigham Young U (UT) **295**
Brock U (ON, Canada) **295**
California Polytechnic State U, San Luis Obispo (CA) **300**
California State Polytechnic U, Pomona (CA) **300**
California State U, Chico (CA) **300**
California State U, Fullerton (CA) **301**
California State U, Hayward (CA) **301**
California State U, Long Beach (CA) **301**
California State U, Northridge (CA) **301**
Carleton U (ON, Canada) **305**
Carnegie Mellon U (PA) **305**
Case Western Reserve U (OH) **307**
Central Michigan U (MI) **310**
Cleveland State U (OH) **317**
The Coll of New Jersey (NJ) **320**
Colorado State U (CO) **325**
Columbia Coll (NY) **326**
Columbia U, School of General Studies (NY) **328**
Concordia U (QC, Canada) **331**
Cornell U (NY) **333**
Dalhousie U (NS, Canada) **336**
DePaul U (IL) **339**
Eastern Kentucky U (KY) **348**
Eastern Michigan U (MI) **348**
Eastern New Mexico U (NM) **349**
Florida International U (FL) **360**
Florida State U (FL) **361**
Fort Lewis Coll (CO) **362**
Framingham State Coll (MA) **362**
The George Washington U (DC) **367**
Grand Valley State U (MI) **371**
Hampshire Coll (MA) **375**
Harvard U (MA) **376**
Hunter Coll of the City U of NY (NY) **382**
Iowa State U of Science and Technology (IA) **390**
Kansas State U (KS) **396**
Kettering U (MI) **398**
Lehigh U (PA) **404**
Loyola U Chicago (IL) **411**
Luther Coll (IA) **412**
Marquette U (WI) **418**
McGill U (QC, Canada) **423**
McMaster U (ON, Canada) **423**
Memorial U of Newfoundland (NF, Canada) **424**
Mercyhurst Coll (PA) **425**
Mesa State Coll (CO) **426**
Miami U (OH) **428**
Michigan State U (MI) **428**
Michigan Technological U (MI) **428**
Mills Coll (CA) **431**
Mount Holyoke Coll (MA) **438**
Mount Saint Vincent U (NS, Canada) **439**
New Jersey Inst of Technology (NJ) **445**
New York U (NY) **447**
North Carolina State U (NC) **449**
Northwestern U (IL) **453**
Oakland U (MI) **456**
Ohio Northern U (OH) **457**
Ohio Wesleyan U (OH) **459**
Oklahoma State U (OK) **460**
Penn State U Univ Park Campus (PA) **468**
Purdue U (IN) **475**
Queen's U at Kingston (ON, Canada) **476**
Rice U (TX) **479**
Rochester Inst of Technology (NY) **482**
Rutgers, The State U of New Jersey, New Brunswick (NJ) **485**
St. Cloud State U (MN) **488**
St. Mary's U of San Antonio (TX) **494**
San Diego State U (CA) **498**
San Francisco State U (CA) **498**
San Jose State U (CA) **499**
Sonoma State U (CA) **506**
Southern Methodist U (TX) **510**
State U of NY Coll at Oneonta (NY) **517**
Stevens Inst of Technology (NJ) **519**
Temple U (PA) **523**
Université de Sherbrooke (QC, Canada) **536**
Université Laval (QC, Canada) **536**
The U of Akron (OH) **537**
U of Alaska Fairbanks (AK) **538**
U of Alberta (AB, Canada) **538**
The U of British Columbia (BC, Canada) **540**
U of Calgary (AB, Canada) **540**
U of Calif, Berkeley (CA) **540**
U of Calif, Davis (CA) **540**
U of Calif, Riverside (CA) **541**
U of Calif, Santa Barbara (CA) **541**
U of Central Florida (FL) **542**
U of Chicago (IL) **542**
U of Connecticut (CT) **544**
U of Denver (CO) **544**
U of Florida (FL) **545**
U of Georgia (GA) **545**
U of Guelph (ON, Canada) **546**
U of Houston (TX) **547**
U of Illinois at Chicago (IL) **547**
U of Illinois at Urbana–Champaign (IL) **548**
The U of Iowa (IA) **548**
U of King's Coll (NS, Canada) **549**
U of Manitoba (MB, Canada) **551**
U of Maryland, Baltimore County (MD) **552**
U of Michigan (MI) **554**
U of Minnesota, Morris (MN) **555**
U of Missouri–Columbia (MO) **555**
U of Missouri–Kansas City (MO) **555**
The U of Montana–Missoula (MT) **556**
U of Nebraska at Kearney (NE) **557**
U of Nevada, Las Vegas (NV) **558**
U of New Brunswick Fredericton (NB, Canada) **558**
U of New Brunswick Saint John (NB, Canada) **558**
U of New Hampshire (NH) **558**
The U of North Carolina at Greensboro (NC) **560**
U of North Florida (FL) **561**
U of Oregon (OR) **562**
U of Ottawa (ON, Canada) **563**
U of Pennsylvania (PA) **563**
U of Pittsburgh (PA) **569**
U of Regina (SK, Canada) **572**
U of Rochester (NY) **573**
U of Saskatchewan (SK, Canada) **574**
U of South Alabama (AL) **575**
U of South Carolina (SC) **575**
The U of South Dakota (SD) **575**
The U of Tennessee (TN) **577**
The U of Texas at Dallas (TX) **578**
The U of Texas at El Paso (TX) **578**
The U of Texas at San Antonio (TX) **578**
U of Toronto (ON, Canada) **581**
U of Vermont (VT) **582**
U of Victoria (BC, Canada) **582**
U of Washington (WA) **583**
U of Waterloo (ON, Canada) **583**
The U of Western Ontario (ON, Canada) **583**
U of Windsor (ON, Canada) **584**
U of Wisconsin–Madison (WI) **584**
U of Wisconsin–Milwaukee (WI) **585**
U of Wyoming (WY) **586**
Utah State U (UT) **587**
Virginia Polytechnic Inst and State U (VA) **591**
Washington U in St. Louis (MO) **595**
Western Michigan U (MI) **599**
West Virginia U (WV) **602**
Winona State U (MN) **608**
Xavier U of Louisiana (LA) **610**
York U (ON, Canada) **611**

MATHEMATICS

Overview: In this general major, students use symbols, logic, and language to describe relationships between numbers and forms. *Related majors:* mathematics/computer science, statistics. *Potential careers:* professor or high school math teacher, engineer, research scientist, analyst, statistician. *Salary potential:* $27k-$45k.

Abilene Christian U (TX) **260**
Acadia U (NS, Canada) **260**
Adams State Coll (CO) **260**
Adelphi U (NY) **260**
Adrian Coll (MI) **260**
Agnes Scott Coll (GA) **261**
Alabama A&M U (AL) **261**
Alabama State U (AL) **261**
Albany State U (GA) **262**
Albertson Coll of Idaho (ID) **262**
Albertus Magnus Coll (CT) **262**
Albion Coll (MI) **262**
Albright Coll (PA) **263**
Alcorn State U (MS) **263**
Alderson-Broaddus Coll (WV) **263**
Alfred U (NY) **263**
Allegheny Coll (PA) **264**
Allen U (SC) **264**
Alma Coll (MI) **264**
Alvernia Coll (PA) **265**
Alverno Coll (WI) **265**
American International Coll (MA) **267**
American U (DC) **267**
The American U in Cairo(Egypt) **267**
Amherst Coll (MA) **268**
Anderson Coll (SC) **268**
Anderson U (IN) **268**
Andrews U (MI) **269**
Angelo State U (TX) **269**
Antioch Coll (OH) **269**
Appalachian State U (NC) **270**
Aquinas Coll (MI) **270**
Arcadia U (PA) **271**
Arizona State U (AZ) **271**
Arkansas State U (AR) **272**
Arkansas Tech U (AR) **272**
Armstrong Atlantic State U (GA) **273**
Asbury Coll (KY) **274**
Ashland U (OH) **274**
Assumption Coll (MA) **275**
Athens State U (AL) **275**
Atlantic Union Coll (MA) **276**
Auburn U (AL) **276**
Auburn U Montgomery (AL) **276**
Augsburg Coll (MN) **276**
Augustana Coll (IL) **276**
Augustana Coll (SD) **276**
Augusta State U (GA) **277**
Aurora U (IL) **277**
Austin Coll (TX) **277**
Austin Peay State U (TN) **278**
Ave Maria Coll (MI) **278**
Averett U (VA) **278**
Avila U (MO) **278**
Azusa Pacific U (CA) **278**
Baker U (KS) **280**
Baldwin-Wallace Coll (OH) **280**
Ball State U (IN) **280**
Barber-Scotia Coll (NC) **281**
Bard Coll (NY) **281**
Barnard Coll (NY) **282**
Barry U (FL) **282**
Barton Coll (NC) **282**
Bates Coll (ME) **282**
Baylor U (TX) **283**
Belhaven Coll (MS) **283**
Bellarmine U (KY) **284**
Bellevue U (NE) **284**
Belmont U (TN) **284**
Beloit Coll (WI) **285**
Bemidji State U (MN) **285**
Benedict Coll (SC) **285**
Benedictine Coll (KS) **285**
Benedictine U (IL) **285**
Bennett Coll (NC) **286**
Bennington Coll (VT) **286**
Bentley Coll (MA) **286**
Berea Coll (KY) **286**
Baruch Coll of the City U of NY (NY) **286**
Berry Coll (GA) **287**
Bethany Coll (KS) **287**
Bethany Coll (WV) **287**
Bethel Coll (IN) **288**
Bethel Coll (KS) **288**
Bethel Coll (MN) **288**
Bethel Coll (TN) **288**
Bethune-Cookman Coll (FL) **289**
Biola U (CA) **289**
Birmingham-Southern Coll (AL) **289**
Bishop's U (QC, Canada) **289**
Blackburn Coll (IL) **290**
Black Hills State U (SD) **290**
Bloomsburg U of Pennsylvania (PA) **290**
Bluefield Coll (VA) **291**
Blue Mountain Coll (MS) **291**
Bluffton Coll (OH) **291**
Boston Coll (MA) **292**
Boston U (MA) **292**
Bowdoin Coll (ME) **292**
Bowie State U (MD) **292**
Bowling Green State U (OH) **292**
Bradley U (IL) **293**
Brandeis U (MA) **293**
Brandon U (MB, Canada) **293**
Brevard Coll (NC) **294**
Brewton-Parker Coll (GA) **294**
Briar Cliff U (IA) **294**
Bridgewater Coll (VA) **294**
Bridgewater State Coll (MA) **294**
Brigham Young U (UT) **295**
Brigham Young U–Hawaii (HI) **295**
Brock U (ON, Canada) **295**
Brooklyn Coll of the City U of NY (NY) **295**
Brown U (RI) **296**
Bryan Coll (TN) **296**
Bryn Mawr Coll (PA) **297**
Bucknell U (PA) **297**
Buena Vista U (IA) **297**
Butler U (IN) **297**
Cabrini Coll (PA) **298**
Caldwell Coll (NJ) **298**
California Baptist U (CA) **298**
California Inst of Technology (CA) **299**
California Lutheran U (CA) **299**
California Polytechnic State U, San Luis Obispo (CA) **300**
California State Polytechnic U, Pomona (CA) **300**
California State U, Bakersfield (CA) **300**
California State U, Chico (CA) **300**
California State U, Dominguez Hills (CA) **300**
California State U, Fresno (CA) **301**
California State U, Fullerton (CA) **301**
California State U, Hayward (CA) **301**
California State U, Long Beach (CA) **301**
California State U, Northridge (CA) **301**
California State U, Sacramento (CA) **301**
California State U, San Bernardino (CA) **302**
California State U, San Marcos (CA) **302**
California State U, Stanislaus (CA) **302**
California U of Pennsylvania (PA) **302**
Calvin Coll (MI) **303**
Cameron U (OK) **303**
Campbellsville U (KY) **303**
Campbell U (NC) **303**
Canisius Coll (NY) **304**
Capital U (OH) **304**
Cardinal Stritch U (WI) **305**
Carleton Coll (MN) **305**
Carleton U (ON, Canada) **305**
Carlow Coll (PA) **305**

MATHEMATICS (continued)

Carnegie Mellon U (PA) **305**
Carroll Coll (MT) **306**
Carroll Coll (WI) **306**
Carson-Newman Coll (TN) **306**
Carthage Coll (WI) **306**
Case Western Reserve U (OH) **307**
Castleton State Coll (VT) **307**
Catawba Coll (NC) **307**
The Catholic U of America (DC) **307**
Cedar Crest Coll (PA) **308**
Cedarville U (OH) **308**
Centenary Coll (NJ) **308**
Centenary Coll of Louisiana (LA) **308**
Central Coll (IA) **309**
Central Connecticut State U (CT) **309**
Central Methodist Coll (MO) **309**
Central Michigan U (MI) **310**
Central Missouri State U (MO) **310**
Central Washington U (WA) **310**
Centre Coll (KY) **310**
Chadron State Coll (NE) **311**
Charleston Southern U (SC) **311**
Chatham Coll (PA) **312**
Cheyney U of Pennsylvania (PA) **312**
Chowan Coll (NC) **312**
Christian Brothers U (TN) **313**
Christian Heritage Coll (CA) **313**
Christopher Newport U (VA) **313**
Citadel, The Military Coll of South Carolina (SC) **314**
City Coll of the City U of NY (NY) **314**
Claflin U (SC) **314**
Claremont McKenna Coll (CA) **315**
Clarion U of Pennsylvania (PA) **315**
Clark Atlanta U (GA) **315**
Clarke Coll (IA) **315**
Clarkson U (NY) **316**
Clark U (MA) **316**
Clearwater Christian Coll (FL) **316**
Clemson U (SC) **317**
Cleveland State U (OH) **317**
Coe Coll (IA) **318**
Coker Coll (SC) **318**
Colby Coll (ME) **318**
Colgate U (NY) **319**
Coll Misericordia (PA) **319**
Coll of Charleston (SC) **320**
Coll of Mount St. Joseph (OH) **320**
Coll of Mount Saint Vincent (NY) **320**
The Coll of New Jersey (NJ) **320**
The Coll of New Rochelle (NY) **321**
Coll of Notre Dame of Maryland (MD) **321**
Coll of Saint Benedict (MN) **321**
Coll of St. Catherine (MN) **321**
Coll of Saint Elizabeth (NJ) **321**
Coll of Saint Mary (NE) **322**
The Coll of Saint Rose (NY) **322**
The Coll of St. Scholastica (MN) **322**
Coll of Santa Fe (NM) **323**
The Coll of Southeastern Europe, The American U of Athens(Greece) **323**
Coll of Staten Island of the City U of NY (NY) **323**
Coll of the Holy Cross (MA) **323**
Coll of the Ozarks (MO) **323**
Coll of the Southwest (NM) **324**
The Coll of William and Mary (VA) **324**
The Coll of Wooster (OH) **324**
Colorado Christian U (CO) **325**
The Colorado Coll (CO) **325**
Colorado School of Mines (CO) **325**
Colorado State U (CO) **325**
Colorado State U-Pueblo (CO) **325**
Columbia Coll (MO) **326**
Columbia Coll (NY) **326**
Columbia Coll (SC) **327**
Columbia Union Coll (MD) **328**
Columbia U, School of General Studies (NY) **328**
Columbus State U (GA) **328**
Concord Coll (WV) **329**
Concordia Coll (MN) **329**
Concordia Coll (NY) **329**
Concordia U (CA) **330**
Concordia U (IL) **330**
Concordia U (MI) **330**
Concordia U (NE) **330**
Concordia U (QC, Canada) **331**
Concordia U Coll of Alberta (AB, Canada) **331**
Concordia U Wisconsin (WI) **331**
Connecticut Coll (CT) **331**
Converse Coll (SC) **332**
Cornell Coll (IA) **332**
Cornell U (NY) **333**
Cornerstone U (MI) **333**
Covenant Coll (GA) **333**
Creighton U (NE) **333**
Culver-Stockton Coll (MO) **334**
Cumberland Coll (KY) **335**
Cumberland U (TN) **335**
Daemen Coll (NY) **335**
Dakota State U (SD) **335**
Dakota Wesleyan U (SD) **336**
Dalhousie U (NS, Canada) **336**
Dallas Baptist U (TX) **336**
Dana Coll (NE) **337**
Dartmouth Coll (NH) **337**
Davidson Coll (NC) **338**
Davis & Elkins Coll (WV) **338**
Defiance Coll (OH) **338**
Delaware State U (DE) **338**
Delta State U (MS) **339**
Denison U (OH) **339**
DePaul U (IL) **339**
DePauw U (IN) **339**
DeSales U (PA) **340**
Dickinson Coll (PA) **344**
Dickinson State U (ND) **344**
Dillard U (LA) **344**
Doane Coll (NE) **344**
Dominican Coll (NY) **344**
Dominican U (IL) **345**
Dordt Coll (IA) **345**
Dowling Coll (NY) **345**
Drake U (IA) **345**
Drew U (NJ) **346**
Drexel U (PA) **346**
Drury U (MO) **346**
Duke U (NC) **346**
Duquesne U (PA) **346**
Earlham Coll (IN) **347**
East Carolina U (NC) **347**
East Central U (OK) **347**
Eastern Connecticut State U (CT) **347**
Eastern Illinois U (IL) **348**
Eastern Kentucky U (KY) **348**
Eastern Mennonite U (VA) **348**
Eastern Michigan U (MI) **348**
Eastern Nazarene Coll (MA) **348**
Eastern Oregon U (OR) **349**
Eastern U (PA) **349**
Eastern Washington U (WA) **349**
East Stroudsburg U of Pennsylvania (PA) **349**
East Tennessee State U (TN) **349**
East Texas Baptist U (TX) **350**
East-West U (IL) **350**
Eckerd Coll (FL) **350**
Edgewood Coll (WI) **351**
Edinboro U of Pennsylvania (PA) **351**
Elizabeth City State U (NC) **351**
Elizabethtown Coll (PA) **351**
Elmhurst Coll (IL) **351**
Elmira Coll (NY) **351**
Elms Coll (MA) **352**
Elon U (NC) **352**
Emmanuel Coll (MA) **353**
Emory & Henry Coll (VA) **353**
Emory U (GA) **354**
Emporia State U (KS) **354**
Erskine Coll (SC) **354**
Eureka Coll (IL) **355**
Evangel U (MO) **355**
The Evergreen State Coll (WA) **355**
Excelsior Coll (NY) **356**
Fairfield U (CT) **356**
Fairleigh Dickinson U, Florham (NJ) **356**
Fairleigh Dickinson U, Teaneck-Metro Campus (NJ) **356**
Fairmont State Coll (WV) **356**
Fayetteville State U (NC) **357**
Felician Coll (NJ) **357**
Ferris State U (MI) **358**
Ferrum Coll (VA) **358**
Fisk U (TN) **358**
Fitchburg State Coll (MA) **358**
Florida A&M U (FL) **359**
Florida Atlantic U (FL) **359**
Florida International U (FL) **360**
Florida Southern Coll (FL) **361**
Florida State U (FL) **361**
Fontbonne U (MO) **361**
Fordham U (NY) **362**
Fort Hays State U (KS) **362**
Fort Lewis Coll (CO) **362**
Fort Valley State U (GA) **362**
Framingham State Coll (MA) **362**
Franciscan U of Steubenville (OH) **363**
Francis Marion U (SC) **363**
Franklin and Marshall Coll (PA) **363**
Franklin Coll (IN) **363**
Franklin Pierce Coll (NH) **364**
Freed-Hardeman U (TN) **364**
Fresno Pacific U (CA) **364**
Frostburg State U (MD) **365**
Furman U (SC) **365**
Gallaudet U (DC) **365**
Gannon U (PA) **365**
Gardner-Webb U (NC) **365**
George Fox U (OR) **366**
George Mason U (VA) **366**
Georgetown Coll (KY) **366**
Georgetown U (DC) **366**
The George Washington U (DC) **367**
Georgia Coll & State U (GA) **367**
Georgia Inst of Technology (GA) **367**
Georgian Court Coll (NJ) **367**
Georgia Southern U (GA) **367**
Georgia Southwestern State U (GA) **368**
Georgia State U (GA) **368**
Gettysburg Coll (PA) **368**
Gonzaga U (WA) **369**
Gordon Coll (MA) **370**
Goshen Coll (IN) **370**
Goucher Coll (MD) **370**
Grace Coll (IN) **370**
Graceland U (IA) **371**
Grace U (NE) **371**
Grambling State U (LA) **371**
Grand Canyon U (AZ) **371**
Grand Valley State U (MI) **371**
Greensboro Coll (NC) **372**
Greenville Coll (IL) **373**
Grinnell Coll (IA) **373**
Grove City Coll (PA) **373**
Guilford Coll (NC) **373**
Gustavus Adolphus Coll (MN) **374**
Gwynedd-Mercy Coll (PA) **374**
Hamilton Coll (NY) **374**
Hamline U (MN) **374**
Hampden-Sydney Coll (VA) **374**
Hampshire Coll (MA) **375**
Hampton U (VA) **375**
Hannibal-LaGrange Coll (MO) **375**
Hanover Coll (IN) **375**
Harding U (AR) **375**
Hardin-Simmons U (TX) **376**
Hartwick Coll (NY) **376**
Harvard U (MA) **376**
Harvey Mudd Coll (CA) **377**
Hastings Coll (NE) **377**
Haverford Coll (PA) **377**
Heidelberg Coll (OH) **377**
Henderson State U (AR) **378**
Hendrix Coll (AR) **378**
High Point U (NC) **379**
Hillsdale Coll (MI) **379**
Hiram Coll (OH) **379**
Hobart and William Smith Colls (NY) **380**
Hofstra U (NY) **380**
Hollins U (VA) **380**
Holy Family U (PA) **380**
Hood Coll (MD) **381**
Hope Coll (MI) **381**
Houghton Coll (NY) **381**
Houston Baptist U (TX) **382**
Howard Payne U (TX) **382**
Howard U (DC) **382**
Humboldt State U (CA) **382**
Hunter Coll of the City U of NY (NY) **382**
Huntingdon Coll (AL) **383**
Huntington Coll (IN) **383**
Huston-Tillotson Coll (TX) **383**
Idaho State U (ID) **384**
Illinois Coll (IL) **384**
Illinois State U (IL) **384**
Illinois Wesleyan U (IL) **385**
Immaculata U (PA) **385**
Indiana State U (IN) **385**
Indiana U Bloomington (IN) **385**
Indiana U Kokomo (IN) **386**
Indiana U Northwest (IN) **386**
Indiana U of Pennsylvania (PA) **386**
Indiana U–Purdue U Fort Wayne (IN) **386**
Indiana U–Purdue U Indianapolis (IN) **387**
Indiana U South Bend (IN) **387**
Indiana U Southeast (IN) **387**
Indiana Wesleyan U (IN) **387**
Inter American U of PR, San Germán Campus (PR) **388**
Iona Coll (NY) **390**
Iowa State U of Science and Technology (IA) **390**
Iowa Wesleyan Coll (IA) **390**
Ithaca Coll (NY) **390**
Jackson State U (MS) **390**
Jacksonville State U (AL) **390**
Jacksonville U (FL) **391**
James Madison U (VA) **391**
Jamestown Coll (ND) **391**
John Brown U (AR) **392**
John Carroll U (OH) **392**
Johns Hopkins U (MD) **392**
Johnson C. Smith U (NC) **394**
Johnson State Coll (VT) **394**
Judson Coll (AL) **395**
Judson Coll (IL) **395**
Juniata Coll (PA) **395**
Kalamazoo Coll (MI) **395**
Kansas State U (KS) **396**
Kean U (NJ) **396**
Keene State Coll (NH) **396**
Kennesaw State U (GA) **397**
Kent State U (OH) **397**
Kentucky State U (KY) **397**
Kentucky Wesleyan Coll (KY) **397**
Kenyon Coll (OH) **398**
Keuka Coll (NY) **398**
King Coll (TN) **398**
King's Coll (PA) **398**
Knox Coll (IL) **399**
Kutztown U of Pennsylvania (PA) **399**
Lafayette Coll (PA) **400**
LaGrange Coll (GA) **400**
Lake Erie Coll (OH) **400**
Lake Forest Coll (IL) **400**
Lakehead U (ON, Canada) **400**
Lakeland Coll (WI) **401**
Lamar U (TX) **401**
Lambuth U (TN) **401**
Lander U (SC) **401**
Lane Coll (TN) **402**
Langston U (OK) **402**
La Salle U (PA) **402**
La Sierra U (CA) **403**
Laurentian U (ON, Canada) **403**
Lawrence Technological U (MI) **403**
Lawrence U (WI) **403**
Lebanon Valley Coll (PA) **403**
Lees-McRae Coll (NC) **404**
Lee U (TN) **404**
Lehigh U (PA) **404**
Lehman Coll of the City U of NY (NY) **404**
Le Moyne Coll (NY) **404**
Lenoir-Rhyne Coll (NC) **405**
LeTourneau U (TX) **405**
Lewis & Clark Coll (OR) **405**
Lewis-Clark State Coll (ID) **406**
Lewis U (IL) **406**
Liberty U (VA) **406**
Lincoln Memorial U (TN) **407**
Lincoln U (PA) **407**
Lindenwood U (MO) **407**
Linfield Coll (OR) **408**
Lipscomb U (TN) **408**
Lock Haven U of Pennsylvania (PA) **408**
Long Island U, Brooklyn Campus (NY) **409**
Long Island U, C.W. Post Campus (NY) **409**
Longwood U (VA) **409**
Loras Coll (IA) **410**
Louisiana Coll (LA) **410**
Louisiana State U and A&M Coll (LA) **410**
Louisiana State U in Shreveport (LA) **410**
Louisiana Tech U (LA) **410**
Loyola Coll in Maryland (MD) **411**
Loyola Marymount U (CA) **411**
Loyola U Chicago (IL) **411**
Loyola U New Orleans (LA) **411**
Lubbock Christian U (TX) **412**
Luther Coll (IA) **412**
Lycoming Coll (PA) **412**
Lynchburg Coll (VA) **413**
Lyndon State Coll (VT) **413**
Lyon Coll (AR) **413**
Macalester Coll (MN) **413**
MacMurray Coll (IL) **414**
Madonna U (MI) **414**
Maharishi U of Management (IA) **414**
Malone Coll (OH) **415**
Manchester Coll (IN) **415**
Manhattan Coll (NY) **416**

Manhattanville Coll (NY) **416**
Mansfield U of Pennsylvania (PA) **416**
Marian Coll (IN) **417**
Marian Coll of Fond du Lac (WI) **417**
Marietta Coll (OH) **417**
Marist Coll (NY) **417**
Marlboro Coll (VT) **418**
Marquette U (WI) **418**
Marshall U (WV) **418**
Mars Hill Coll (NC) **418**
Martin U (IN) **419**
Mary Baldwin Coll (VA) **419**
Marygrove Coll (MI) **419**
Marymount Coll of Fordham U (NY) **419**
Marymount U (VA) **420**
Maryville Coll (TN) **420**
Maryville U of Saint Louis (MO) **420**
Mary Washington Coll (VA) **420**
Marywood U (PA) **421**
Massachusetts Coll of Liberal Arts (MA) **421**
Massachusetts Inst of Technology (MA) **421**
The Master's Coll and Seminary (CA) **422**
Mayville State U (ND) **422**
McDaniel Coll (MD) **422**
McGill U (QC, Canada) **423**
McKendree Coll (IL) **423**
McMaster U (ON, Canada) **423**
McMurry U (TX) **423**
McNeese State U (LA) **423**
McPherson Coll (KS) **423**
Memorial U of Newfoundland (NF, Canada) **424**
Mercer U (GA) **425**
Mercy Coll (NY) **425**
Mercyhurst Coll (PA) **425**
Meredith Coll (NC) **426**
Merrimack Coll (MA) **426**
Mesa State Coll (CO) **426**
Messiah Coll (PA) **426**
Methodist Coll (NC) **427**
Metropolitan State Coll of Denver (CO) **427**
Miami U (OH) **428**
Michigan State U (MI) **428**
Michigan Technological U (MI) **428**
MidAmerica Nazarene U (KS) **428**
Middlebury Coll (VT) **429**
Middle Tennessee State U (TN) **429**
Midland Lutheran Coll (NE) **429**
Midwestern State U (TX) **430**
Miles Coll (AL) **430**
Millersville U of Pennsylvania (PA) **430**
Milligan Coll (TN) **430**
Millikin U (IL) **430**
Millsaps Coll (MS) **431**
Mills Coll (CA) **431**
Minnesota State U, Mankato (MN) **431**
Minnesota State U, Moorhead (MN) **432**
Minot State U (ND) **432**
Mississippi Coll (MS) **432**
Mississippi State U (MS) **432**
Mississippi Valley State U (MS) **432**
Missouri Southern State Coll (MO) **433**
Missouri Valley Coll (MO) **433**
Missouri Western State Coll (MO) **433**
Molloy Coll (NY) **433**
Monmouth Coll (IL) **434**
Monmouth U (NJ) **434**
Montana State U–Billings (MT) **434**
Montana State U–Bozeman (MT) **434**
Montana Tech of The U of Montana (MT) **435**
Montclair State U (NJ) **435**
Montreat Coll (NC) **435**
Moravian Coll (PA) **436**
Morehead State U (KY) **436**
Morehouse Coll (GA) **436**
Morgan State U (MD) **436**
Morningside Coll (IA) **437**
Morris Coll (SC) **437**
Mount Allison U (NB, Canada) **437**
Mount Holyoke Coll (MA) **438**
Mount Marty Coll (SD) **438**
Mount Mary Coll (WI) **438**
Mount Mercy Coll (IA) **438**
Mount Olive Coll (NC) **439**
Mount Saint Mary Coll (NY) **439**
Mount St. Mary's Coll (CA) **439**
Mount Saint Mary's Coll and Seminary (MD) **439**
Mount Saint Vincent U (NS, Canada) **439**
Mount Union Coll (OH) **440**
Mount Vernon Nazarene U (OH) **440**
Muhlenberg Coll (PA) **440**
Murray State U (KY) **440**
Muskingum Coll (OH) **441**
National-Louis U (IL) **442**
National U (CA) **442**
Nazareth Coll of Rochester (NY) **443**
Nebraska Wesleyan U (NE) **443**
Newberry Coll (SC) **444**
New Coll of Florida (FL) **444**
New Jersey City U (NJ) **445**
Newman U (KS) **445**
New Mexico Highlands U (NM) **446**
New Mexico Inst of Mining and Technology (NM) **446**
New Mexico State U (NM) **446**
New York U (NY) **447**
Niagara U (NY) **447**
Nicholls State U (LA) **447**
Nichols Coll (MA) **448**
Nipissing U (ON, Canada) **448**
Norfolk State U (VA) **448**
North Carolina Ag and Tech State U (NC) **448**
North Carolina Central U (NC) **448**
North Carolina State U (NC) **449**
North Carolina Wesleyan Coll (NC) **449**
North Central Coll (IL) **449**
North Dakota State U (ND) **449**
Northeastern Illinois U (IL) **450**
Northeastern State U (OK) **450**
Northeastern U (MA) **450**
Northern Arizona U (AZ) **450**
Northern Illinois U (IL) **450**
Northern Kentucky U (KY) **451**
Northern Michigan U (MI) **451**
Northern State U (SD) **451**
North Georgia Coll & State U (GA) **451**
Northland Coll (WI) **452**
North Park U (IL) **452**
Northwestern Coll (IA) **453**
Northwestern Coll (MN) **453**
Northwestern Oklahoma State U (OK) **453**
Northwestern State U of Louisiana (LA) **453**
Northwestern U (IL) **453**
Northwest Missouri State U (MO) **454**
Northwest Nazarene U (ID) **454**
Norwich U (VT) **455**
Notre Dame Coll (OH) **455**
Nyack Coll (NY) **456**
Oakland City U (IN) **456**
Oakland U (MI) **456**
Oakwood Coll (AL) **456**
Oberlin Coll (OH) **456**
Occidental Coll (CA) **457**
Oglethorpe U (GA) **457**
Ohio Dominican U (OH) **457**
Ohio Northern U (OH) **457**
The Ohio State U (OH) **457**
Ohio U (OH) **458**
Ohio Wesleyan U (OH) **459**
Okanagan U Coll (BC, Canada) **459**
Oklahoma Baptist U (OK) **459**
Oklahoma Christian U (OK) **459**
Oklahoma City U (OK) **460**
Oklahoma Panhandle State U (OK) **460**
Oklahoma State U (OK) **460**
Oklahoma Wesleyan U (OK) **460**
Old Dominion U (VA) **460**
Olivet Coll (MI) **461**
Olivet Nazarene U (IL) **461**
Oral Roberts U (OK) **461**
Oregon State U (OR) **462**
Ottawa U (KS) **462**
Otterbein Coll (OH) **462**
Ouachita Baptist U (AR) **462**
Our Lady of Holy Cross Coll (LA) **463**
Our Lady of the Lake U of San Antonio (TX) **463**
Pace U (NY) **463**
Pacific Lutheran U (WA) **463**
Pacific Union Coll (CA) **464**
Pacific U (OR) **464**
Paine Coll (GA) **465**
Palm Beach Atlantic U (FL) **465**
Park U (MO) **465**
Paul Quinn Coll (TX) **466**
Penn State U at Erie, The Behrend Coll (PA) **467**
Penn State U Univ Park Campus (PA) **468**
Pepperdine U, Malibu (CA) **469**
Peru State Coll (NE) **469**
Pfeiffer U (NC) **469**
Piedmont Coll (GA) **470**
Pikeville Coll (KY) **470**
Pittsburg State U (KS) **470**
Pitzer Coll (CA) **471**
Plattsburgh State U of NY (NY) **471**
Plymouth State Coll (NH) **471**
Point Loma Nazarene U (CA) **471**
Polytechnic U, Brooklyn Campus (NY) **472**
Pomona Coll (CA) **472**
Pontifical Catholic U of Puerto Rico (PR) **472**
Portland State U (OR) **472**
Prairie View A&M U (TX) **473**
Presbyterian Coll (SC) **473**
Princeton U (NJ) **474**
Principia Coll (IL) **474**
Providence Coll (RI) **474**
Purchase Coll, State U of NY (NY) **475**
Purdue U (IN) **475**
Purdue U Calumet (IN) **475**
Queens Coll of the City U of NY (NY) **475**
Queen's U at Kingston (ON, Canada) **476**
Queens U of Charlotte (NC) **476**
Quincy U (IL) **476**
Quinnipiac U (CT) **476**
Radford U (VA) **476**
Ramapo Coll of New Jersey (NJ) **477**
Randolph-Macon Coll (VA) **477**
Randolph-Macon Woman's Coll (VA) **477**
Reed Coll (OR) **477**
Regis Coll (MA) **478**
Regis U (CO) **478**
Rensselaer Polytechnic Inst (NY) **478**
Rhode Island Coll (RI) **479**
Rhodes Coll (TN) **479**
Rice U (TX) **479**
The Richard Stockton Coll of New Jersey (NJ) **479**
Richmond, The American International U in London(United Kingdom) **480**
Rider U (NJ) **480**
Ripon Coll (WI) **480**
Rivier Coll (NH) **480**
Roanoke Coll (VA) **481**
Roberts Wesleyan Coll (NY) **481**
Rochester Coll (MI) **482**
Rochester Inst of Technology (NY) **482**
Rockford Coll (IL) **482**
Rockhurst U (MO) **482**
Rocky Mountain Coll (MT) **482**
Roger Williams U (RI) **483**
Rollins Coll (FL) **483**
Roosevelt U (IL) **483**
Rose-Hulman Inst of Technology (IN) **484**
Rosemont Coll (PA) **484**
Rowan U (NJ) **484**
Russell Sage Coll (NY) **484**
Rust Coll (MS) **485**
Rutgers, The State U of New Jersey, Camden (NJ) **485**
Rutgers, The State U of New Jersey, Newark (NJ) **485**
Rutgers, The State U of New Jersey, New Brunswick (NJ) **485**
Sacred Heart U (CT) **486**
Saginaw Valley State U (MI) **486**
St. Ambrose U (IA) **486**
St. Andrews Presbyterian Coll (NC) **487**
Saint Anselm Coll (NH) **487**
Saint Augustine's Coll (NC) **487**
St. Bonaventure U (NY) **487**
St. Cloud State U (MN) **488**
St. Edward's U (TX) **488**
St. Francis Coll (NY) **488**
Saint Francis U (PA) **488**
St. Francis Xavier U (NS, Canada) **489**
St. John Fisher Coll (NY) **489**
Saint John's U (MN) **490**
St. John's U (NY) **490**
Saint Joseph Coll (CT) **490**
Saint Joseph's Coll (IN) **490**
St. Joseph's Coll, New York (NY) **491**
Saint Joseph's Coll of Maine (ME) **491**
St. Joseph's Coll, Suffolk Campus (NY) **491**
Saint Joseph's U (PA) **491**
St. Lawrence U (NY) **491**
Saint Louis U (MO) **492**
Saint Martin's Coll (WA) **493**
Saint Mary Coll (KS) **493**
Saint Mary-of-the-Woods Coll (IN) **493**
Saint Mary's Coll (IN) **493**
Saint Mary's Coll of California (CA) **494**
St. Mary's Coll of Maryland (MD) **494**
Saint Mary's U (NS, Canada) **494**
Saint Mary's U of Minnesota (MN) **494**
St. Mary's U of San Antonio (TX) **494**
Saint Michael's Coll (VT) **494**
St. Norbert Coll (WI) **495**
St. Olaf Coll (MN) **495**
Saint Peter's Coll (NJ) **495**
St. Thomas Aquinas Coll (NY) **495**
St. Thomas U (NB, Canada) **496**
Saint Vincent Coll (PA) **496**
Saint Xavier U (IL) **496**
Salem Coll (NC) **496**
Salem International U (WV) **496**
Salem State Coll (MA) **497**
Salisbury U (MD) **497**
Salve Regina U (RI) **497**
Samford U (AL) **497**
Sam Houston State U (TX) **497**
San Diego State U (CA) **498**
San Francisco State U (CA) **498**
San Jose State U (CA) **499**
Santa Clara U (CA) **499**
Sarah Lawrence Coll (NY) **499**
Savannah State U (GA) **499**
Schreiner U (TX) **501**
Scripps Coll (CA) **501**
Seattle Pacific U (WA) **501**
Seattle U (WA) **501**
Seton Hall U (NJ) **502**
Seton Hill U (PA) **502**
Shawnee State U (OH) **502**
Shaw U (NC) **502**
Shenandoah U (VA) **503**
Shepherd Coll (WV) **503**
Shippensburg U of Pennsylvania (PA) **503**
Shorter Coll (GA) **504**
Siena Coll (NY) **504**
Siena Heights U (MI) **504**
Silver Lake Coll (WI) **504**
Simmons Coll (MA) **504**
Simon Fraser U (BC, Canada) **505**
Simon's Rock Coll of Bard (MA) **505**
Simpson Coll (IA) **505**
Simpson Coll and Graduate School (CA) **505**
Skidmore Coll (NY) **506**
Slippery Rock U of Pennsylvania (PA) **506**
Smith Coll (MA) **506**
Sonoma State U (CA) **506**
South Carolina State U (SC) **506**
South Dakota School of Mines and Technology (SD) **507**
South Dakota State U (SD) **507**
Southeastern Louisiana U (LA) **508**
Southeastern Oklahoma State U (OK) **508**
Southeast Missouri State U (MO) **508**
Southern Adventist U (TN) **508**
Southern Arkansas U–Magnolia (AR) **509**
Southern Connecticut State U (CT) **509**
Southern Illinois U Carbondale (IL) **509**
Southern Illinois U Edwardsville (IL) **509**
Southern Methodist U (TX) **510**
Southern Nazarene U (OK) **510**
Southern Oregon U (OR) **510**
Southern Polytechnic State U (GA) **511**
Southern U and A&M Coll (LA) **511**
Southern Utah U (UT) **511**
Southern Wesleyan U (SC) **511**
Southwest Baptist U (MO) **512**
Southwestern Coll (KS) **512**
Southwestern Oklahoma State U (OK) **512**
Southwestern U (TX) **513**
Southwest Missouri State U (MO) **513**
Southwest State U (MN) **513**
Southwest Texas State U (TX) **513**
Spalding U (KY) **513**
Spelman Coll (GA) **514**
Spring Arbor U (MI) **514**
Springfield Coll (MA) **514**
Spring Hill Coll (AL) **514**
Stanford U (CA) **514**
State U of NY at Albany (NY) **514**
State U of NY at Binghamton (NY) **515**
State U of NY at New Paltz (NY) **515**
State U of NY at Oswego (NY) **515**
State U of NY Coll at Brockport (NY) **515**
State U of NY Coll at Buffalo (NY) **516**
State U of NY Coll at Cortland (NY) **516**
State U of NY Coll at Fredonia (NY) **516**
State U of NY Coll at Geneseo (NY) **516**
State U of NY Coll at Old Westbury (NY) **516**
State U of NY Coll at Oneonta (NY) **517**
State U of NY Coll at Potsdam (NY) **517**
State U of NY Empire State Coll (NY) **517**
State U of West Georgia (GA) **518**
Stephen F. Austin State U (TX) **518**
Stephens Coll (MO) **519**
Sterling Coll (KS) **519**
Stetson U (FL) **519**

MATHEMATICS (continued)

Stonehill Coll (MA) **520**
Stony Brook U, State University of New York (NY) **520**
Suffolk U (MA) **520**
Sul Ross State U (TX) **521**
Susquehanna U (PA) **521**
Swarthmore Coll (PA) **521**
Sweet Briar Coll (VA) **521**
Syracuse U (NY) **521**
Tabor Coll (KS) **522**
Talladega Coll (AL) **522**
Tarleton State U (TX) **522**
Taylor U (IN) **523**
Temple U (PA) **523**
Tennessee State U (TN) **523**
Tennessee Technological U (TN) **524**
Tennessee Wesleyan Coll (TN) **524**
Texas A&M International U (TX) **524**
Texas A&M U (TX) **524**
Texas A&M U–Commerce (TX) **525**
Texas A&M U–Corpus Christi (TX) **525**
Texas A&M U–Kingsville (TX) **525**
Texas A&M U–Texarkana (TX) **525**
Texas Christian U (TX) **526**
Texas Coll (TX) **526**
Texas Lutheran U (TX) **526**
Texas Southern U (TX) **526**
Texas Tech U (TX) **526**
Texas Wesleyan U (TX) **526**
Texas Woman's U (TX) **527**
Thiel Coll (PA) **527**
Thomas Edison State Coll (NJ) **527**
Thomas More Coll (KY) **528**
Touro Coll (NY) **529**
Towson U (MD) **529**
Transylvania U (KY) **529**
Trent U (ON, Canada) **529**
Trevecca Nazarene U (TN) **529**
Trinity Christian Coll (IL) **530**
Trinity Coll (CT) **530**
Trinity Coll (DC) **530**
Trinity International U (IL) **531**
Trinity U (TX) **531**
Trinity Western U (BC, Canada) **531**
Tri-State U (IN) **532**
Troy State U (AL) **532**
Troy State U Dothan (AL) **532**
Troy State U Montgomery (AL) **532**
Truman State U (MO) **532**
Tufts U (MA) **533**
Tulane U (LA) **533**
Tusculum Coll (TN) **533**
Tuskegee U (AL) **533**
Union Coll (KY) **533**
Union Coll (NE) **534**
Union Coll (NY) **534**
Union U (TN) **534**
United States Air Force Academy (CO) **534**
United States Military Academy (NY) **535**
United States Naval Academy (MD) **535**
Université de Sherbrooke (QC, Canada) **536**
U du Québec à Trois-Rivières (QC, Canada) **536**
Université Laval (QC, Canada) **536**
U at Buffalo, The State University of New York (NY) **536**
U Coll of the Cariboo (BC, Canada) **537**
The U of Akron (OH) **537**
The U of Alabama (AL) **537**
The U of Alabama at Birmingham (AL) **537**
The U of Alabama in Huntsville (AL) **537**
U of Alaska Anchorage (AK) **538**
U of Alaska Fairbanks (AK) **538**
U of Alberta (AB, Canada) **538**
The U of Arizona (AZ) **538**
U of Arkansas (AR) **539**
U of Arkansas at Little Rock (AR) **539**
U of Arkansas at Monticello (AR) **539**
U of Bridgeport (CT) **540**
The U of British Columbia (BC, Canada) **540**
U of Calgary (AB, Canada) **540**
U of Calif, Berkeley (CA) **540**
U of Calif, Davis (CA) **540**
U of Calif, Irvine (CA) **541**
U of Calif, Los Angeles (CA) **541**
U of Calif, Riverside (CA) **541**
U of Calif, San Diego (CA) **541**
U of Calif, Santa Barbara (CA) **541**
U of Calif, Santa Cruz (CA) **542**
U of Central Arkansas (AR) **542**
U of Central Florida (FL) **542**
U of Central Oklahoma (OK) **542**
U of Chicago (IL) **542**
U of Cincinnati (OH) **543**
U of Colorado at Boulder (CO) **543**
U of Colorado at Colorado Springs (CO) **543**
U of Colorado at Denver (CO) **543**
U of Connecticut (CT) **544**
U of Dallas (TX) **544**
U of Dayton (OH) **544**
U of Delaware (DE) **544**
U of Denver (CO) **544**
U of Evansville (IN) **545**
The U of Findlay (OH) **545**
U of Florida (FL) **545**
U of Georgia (GA) **545**
U of Great Falls (MT) **545**
U of Guelph (ON, Canada) **546**
U of Hartford (CT) **546**
U of Hawaii at Hilo (HI) **546**
U of Hawaii at Manoa (HI) **546**
U of Houston (TX) **547**
U of Houston–Victoria (TX) **547**
U of Idaho (ID) **547**
U of Illinois at Chicago (IL) **547**
U of Illinois at Springfield (IL) **548**
U of Illinois at Urbana–Champaign (IL) **548**
U of Indianapolis (IN) **548**
The U of Iowa (IA) **548**
U of Kansas (KS) **549**
U of Kentucky (KY) **549**
U of King's Coll (NS, Canada) **549**
U of La Verne (CA) **549**
The U of Lethbridge (AB, Canada) **549**
U of Louisiana at Lafayette (LA) **550**
U of Louisville (KY) **550**
U of Maine (ME) **550**
The U of Maine at Augusta (ME) **550**
U of Maine at Farmington (ME) **550**
U of Maine at Presque Isle (ME) **551**
U of Manitoba (MB, Canada) **551**
U of Mary (ND) **551**
U of Mary Hardin-Baylor (TX) **551**
U of Maryland, Baltimore County (MD) **552**
U of Maryland, Coll Park (MD) **552**
U of Maryland Eastern Shore (MD) **552**
U of Massachusetts Amherst (MA) **552**
U of Massachusetts Boston (MA) **553**
U of Massachusetts Dartmouth (MA) **553**
U of Massachusetts Lowell (MA) **553**
The U of Memphis (TN) **553**
U of Miami (FL) **553**
U of Michigan (MI) **554**
U of Michigan–Dearborn (MI) **554**
U of Michigan–Flint (MI) **554**
U of Minnesota, Duluth (MN) **554**
U of Minnesota, Morris (MN) **555**
U of Minnesota, Twin Cities Campus (MN) **555**
U of Mississippi (MS) **555**
U of Missouri–Columbia (MO) **555**
U of Missouri–Kansas City (MO) **555**
U of Missouri–St. Louis (MO) **556**
U of Mobile (AL) **556**
The U of Montana–Missoula (MT) **556**
The U of Montana–Western (MT) **556**
U of Montevallo (AL) **557**
U of Nebraska at Kearney (NE) **557**
U of Nebraska at Omaha (NE) **557**
U of Nebraska–Lincoln (NE) **557**
U of Nevada, Las Vegas (NV) **558**
U of Nevada, Reno (NV) **558**
U of New Brunswick Fredericton (NB, Canada) **558**
U of New Hampshire (NH) **558**
U of New Haven (CT) **559**
U of New Mexico (NM) **559**
U of New Orleans (LA) **559**
U of North Alabama (AL) **559**
The U of North Carolina at Asheville (NC) **559**
The U of North Carolina at Chapel Hill (NC) **560**
The U of North Carolina at Charlotte (NC) **560**
The U of North Carolina at Greensboro (NC) **560**
The U of North Carolina at Pembroke (NC) **560**
The U of North Carolina at Wilmington (NC) **561**
U of North Dakota (ND) **561**
U of Northern Colorado (CO) **561**
U of Northern Iowa (IA) **561**
U of North Florida (FL) **561**
U of North Texas (TX) **562**
U of Notre Dame (IN) **562**
U of Oklahoma (OK) **562**
U of Oregon (OR) **562**
U of Ottawa (ON, Canada) **563**
U of Pennsylvania (PA) **563**
U of Pittsburgh (PA) **569**
U of Pittsburgh at Johnstown (PA) **570**
U of Portland (OR) **570**
U of Prince Edward Island (PE, Canada) **570**
U of Puerto Rico, Cayey U Coll (PR) **571**
U of Puerto Rico, Río Piedras (PR) **571**
U of Puget Sound (WA) **571**
U of Redlands (CA) **572**
U of Regina (SK, Canada) **572**
U of Rhode Island (RI) **572**
U of Richmond (VA) **572**
U of Rio Grande (OH) **572**
U of Rochester (NY) **573**
U of St. Francis (IL) **573**
U of St. Thomas (MN) **573**
U of St. Thomas (TX) **573**
U of San Diego (CA) **574**
U of San Francisco (CA) **574**
U of Saskatchewan (SK, Canada) **574**
U of Science and Arts of Oklahoma (OK) **574**
The U of Scranton (PA) **574**
U of Sioux Falls (SD) **574**
U of South Alabama (AL) **575**
U of South Carolina (SC) **575**
U of South Carolina Spartanburg (SC) **575**
The U of South Dakota (SD) **575**
U of Southern California (CA) **576**
U of Southern Indiana (IN) **576**
U of Southern Maine (ME) **576**
U of Southern Mississippi (MS) **576**
U of South Florida (FL) **576**
The U of Tampa (FL) **577**
The U of Tennessee (TN) **577**
The U of Tennessee at Chattanooga (TN) **577**
The U of Tennessee at Martin (TN) **577**
The U of Texas at Arlington (TX) **577**
The U of Texas at Austin (TX) **578**
The U of Texas at Brownsville (TX) **578**
The U of Texas at Dallas (TX) **578**
The U of Texas at El Paso (TX) **578**
The U of Texas at San Antonio (TX) **578**
The U of Texas at Tyler (TX) **579**
The U of Texas of the Permian Basin (TX) **579**
The U of Texas–Pan American (TX) **579**
U of the District of Columbia (DC) **580**
U of the Incarnate Word (TX) **580**
U of the Ozarks (AR) **580**
U of the Pacific (CA) **580**
U of the Sacred Heart (PR) **580**
U of the South (TN) **581**
U of the Virgin Islands (VI) **581**
U of Toledo (OH) **581**
U of Toronto (ON, Canada) **581**
U of Tulsa (OK) **581**
U of Utah (UT) **582**
U of Vermont (VT) **582**
U of Victoria (BC, Canada) **582**
U of Virginia (VA) **582**
The U of Virginia's Coll at Wise (VA) **582**
U of Washington (WA) **583**
U of Waterloo (ON, Canada) **583**
The U of West Alabama (AL) **583**
The U of Western Ontario (ON, Canada) **583**
U of West Florida (FL) **583**
U of Windsor (ON, Canada) **584**
U of Wisconsin–Eau Claire (WI) **584**
U of Wisconsin–Green Bay (WI) **584**
U of Wisconsin–La Crosse (WI) **584**
U of Wisconsin–Madison (WI) **584**
U of Wisconsin–Milwaukee (WI) **585**
U of Wisconsin–Oshkosh (WI) **585**
U of Wisconsin–Parkside (WI) **585**
U of Wisconsin–Platteville (WI) **585**
U of Wisconsin–River Falls (WI) **585**
U of Wisconsin–Stevens Point (WI) **585**
U of Wisconsin–Superior (WI) **586**
U of Wisconsin–Whitewater (WI) **586**
U of Wyoming (WY) **586**
Upper Iowa U (IA) **587**
Ursinus Coll (PA) **587**
Ursuline Coll (OH) **587**
Utah State U (UT) **587**
Utica Coll (NY) **588**
Valdosta State U (GA) **588**
Valley City State U (ND) **588**
Valparaiso U (IN) **588**
Vanderbilt U (TN) **588**
Vanguard U of Southern California (CA) **589**
Vassar Coll (NY) **589**
Villanova U (PA) **590**
Virginia Commonwealth U (VA) **590**
Virginia Intermont Coll (VA) **590**
Virginia Military Inst (VA) **591**
Virginia Polytechnic Inst and State U (VA) **591**
Virginia State U (VA) **591**
Virginia Union U (VA) **591**
Virginia Wesleyan Coll (VA) **591**
Viterbo U (WI) **591**
Voorhees Coll (SC) **592**
Wabash Coll (IN) **592**
Wagner Coll (NY) **592**
Wake Forest U (NC) **592**
Walla Walla Coll (WA) **593**
Walsh U (OH) **593**
Warren Wilson Coll (NC) **594**
Wartburg Coll (IA) **594**
Washington & Jefferson Coll (PA) **594**
Washington and Lee U (VA) **594**
Washington Coll (MD) **594**
Washington State U (WA) **595**
Washington U in St. Louis (MO) **595**
Wayland Baptist U (TX) **595**
Waynesburg Coll (PA) **595**
Wayne State Coll (NE) **596**
Wayne State U (MI) **596**
Weber State U (UT) **596**
Webster U (MO) **597**
Wellesley Coll (MA) **597**
Wells Coll (NY) **597**
Wesleyan Coll (GA) **597**
Wesleyan U (CT) **597**
West Chester U of Pennsylvania (PA) **598**
Western Baptist Coll (OR) **598**
Western Carolina U (NC) **598**
Western Connecticut State U (CT) **598**
Western Illinois U (IL) **599**
Western Kentucky U (KY) **599**
Western Michigan U (MI) **599**
Western New England Coll (MA) **600**
Western New Mexico U (NM) **600**
Western Oregon U (OR) **600**
Western State Coll of Colorado (CO) **600**
Western Washington U (WA) **600**
Westfield State Coll (MA) **600**
West Liberty State Coll (WV) **601**
Westminster Coll (MO) **601**
Westminster Coll (PA) **601**
Westminster Coll (UT) **601**
Westmont Coll (CA) **602**
West Texas A&M U (TX) **602**
West Virginia State Coll (WV) **602**
West Virginia U (WV) **602**
West Virginia U Inst of Technology (WV) **602**
West Virginia Wesleyan Coll (WV) **603**
Wheaton Coll (IL) **603**
Wheaton Coll (MA) **603**
Wheeling Jesuit U (WV) **603**
Whitman Coll (WA) **604**
Whittier Coll (CA) **604**
Whitworth Coll (WA) **604**
Wichita State U (KS) **604**
Widener U (PA) **604**
Wilberforce U (OH) **605**
Wiley Coll (TX) **605**
Wilkes U (PA) **605**
Willamette U (OR) **605**
William Carey Coll (MS) **605**
William Jewell Coll (MO) **606**
William Paterson U of New Jersey (NJ) **606**
Williams Coll (MA) **606**
William Woods U (MO) **607**
Wilmington Coll (OH) **607**
Wilson Coll (PA) **607**
Wingate U (NC) **607**
Winona State U (MN) **608**
Winston-Salem State U (NC) **608**
Winthrop U (SC) **608**
Wisconsin Lutheran Coll (WI) **608**
Wittenberg U (OH) **608**
Wofford Coll (SC) **609**
Worcester Polytechnic Inst (MA) **609**
Worcester State Coll (MA) **609**
Wright State U (OH) **609**
Xavier U (OH) **610**
Xavier U of Louisiana (LA) **610**
Yale U (CT) **610**
York Coll of Pennsylvania (PA) **610**
York Coll of the City U of New York (NY) **611**

York U (ON, Canada) **611**
Youngstown State U (OH) **611**

MATHEMATICS/COMPUTER SCIENCE

Overview: This major is a combination of mathematics and computer science. *Related majors:* mathematics, computer science, statistics, computer engineering. *Potential careers:* analyst, computer engineer/programmer, economist, aerospace engineer, mathematician. *Salary potential:* $34k-$50k.

Alfred U (NY) **263**
Anderson U (IN) **268**
Angelo State U (TX) **269**
Averett U (VA) **278**
Bethel Coll (IN) **288**
Boston U (MA) **292**
Brandon U (MB, Canada) **293**
Brescia U (KY) **293**
Brown U (RI) **296**
Cardinal Stritch U (WI) **305**
Carlow Coll (PA) **305**
Central Coll (IA) **309**
Chestnut Hill Coll (PA) **312**
Coll of Saint Benedict (MN) **321**
Coll of Santa Fe (NM) **323**
The Colorado Coll (CO) **325**
Drew U (NJ) **346**
Eastern Illinois U (IL) **348**
Hofstra U (NY) **380**
Ithaca Coll (NY) **390**
King Coll (TN) **398**
Long Island U, C.W. Post Campus (NY) **409**
Loyola U Chicago (IL) **411**
Maryville Coll (TN) **420**
McGill U (QC, Canada) **423**
McMurry U (TX) **423**
Morehead State U (KY) **436**
Mount Allison U (NB, Canada) **437**
Mount Saint Vincent U (NS, Canada) **439**
Rochester Inst of Technology (NY) **482**
Saginaw Valley State U (MI) **486**
Saint John's U (MN) **490**
Saint Joseph's Coll (IN) **490**
St. Joseph's Coll, New York (NY) **491**
Saint Mary's Coll (IN) **493**
Saint Mary's U of Minnesota (MN) **494**
St. Norbert Coll (WI) **495**
San Diego State U (CA) **498**
Southern Oregon U (OR) **510**
Stanford U (CA) **514**
State U of NY at Albany (NY) **514**
State U of NY at Binghamton (NY) **515**
Trinity Western U (BC, Canada) **531**
The U of Akron (OH) **537**
U of Houston–Clear Lake (TX) **547**
U of Illinois at Chicago (IL) **547**
U of Illinois at Urbana–Champaign (IL) **548**
U of Oregon (OR) **562**
U of Puerto Rico, Humacao U Coll (PR) **570**
U of Waterloo (ON, Canada) **583**
U of Windsor (ON, Canada) **584**
Washington State U (WA) **595**
Washington U in St. Louis (MO) **595**
Yale U (CT) **610**
York U (ON, Canada) **611**

MATHEMATICS EDUCATION

Overview: This major prepares undergraduates to teach the subject of mathematics and statistics at the secondary and high school levels. *Related majors:* mathematics, applied mathematics, statistics. *Potential careers:* mathematics or statistics teacher, mathematics coach. *Salary potential:* $24k-$35k.

Abilene Christian U (TX) **260**
Adams State Coll (CO) **260**
Alvernia Coll (PA) **265**
Anderson Coll (SC) **268**
Anderson U (IN) **268**
Appalachian State U (NC) **270**
Arkansas State U (AR) **272**
Arkansas Tech U (AR) **272**
Averett U (VA) **278**
Bayamón Central U (PR) **283**
Baylor U (TX) **283**
Berea Coll (KY) **286**
Berry Coll (GA) **287**
Bethany Coll (KS) **287**
Bethel Coll (IN) **288**
Bethune-Cookman Coll (FL) **289**
Bloomfield Coll (NJ) **290**
Blue Mountain Coll (MS) **291**
Boston U (MA) **292**
Bowie State U (MD) **292**
Bridgewater Coll (VA) **294**
Brigham Young U (UT) **295**
Brigham Young U–Hawaii (HI) **295**
Brock U (ON, Canada) **295**
Cabrini Coll (PA) **298**
California State U, Chico (CA) **300**
Canisius Coll (NY) **304**
Carroll Coll (MT) **306**
Castleton State Coll (VT) **307**
The Catholic U of America (DC) **307**
Cedarville U (OH) **308**
Central Michigan U (MI) **310**
Central Missouri State U (MO) **310**
Central Washington U (WA) **310**
Chadron State Coll (NE) **311**
Chowan Coll (NC) **312**
Christian Brothers U (TN) **313**
Citadel, The Military Coll of South Carolina (SC) **314**
Clearwater Christian Coll (FL) **316**
Clemson U (SC) **317**
The Coll of New Jersey (NJ) **320**
Coll of St. Catherine (MN) **321**
Coll of the Ozarks (MO) **323**
Colorado State U (CO) **325**
Colorado State U-Pueblo (CO) **325**
Columbia Union Coll (MD) **328**
Concordia Coll (MN) **329**
Concordia U (IL) **330**
Concordia U (NE) **330**
Concordia U (OR) **330**
Culver-Stockton Coll (MO) **334**
Cumberland U (TN) **335**
Daemen Coll (NY) **335**
Dakota Wesleyan U (SD) **336**
Dana Coll (NE) **337**
Delta State U (MS) **339**
Dominican Coll (NY) **344**
Duquesne U (PA) **346**
East Carolina U (NC) **347**
Eastern Mennonite U (VA) **348**
Eastern Michigan U (MI) **348**
East Texas Baptist U (TX) **350**
Elmhurst Coll (IL) **351**
Elmira Coll (NY) **351**
Elms Coll (MA) **352**
Felician Coll (NJ) **357**
Florida Atlantic U (FL) **359**
Florida Inst of Technology (FL) **360**
Florida International U (FL) **360**
Florida State U (FL) **361**
Franklin Coll (IN) **363**
Freed-Hardeman U (TN) **364**
Geneva Coll (PA) **366**
George Fox U (OR) **366**
Georgia Southern U (GA) **367**
Grace Coll (IN) **370**
Greensboro Coll (NC) **372**
Greenville Coll (IL) **373**
Gustavus Adolphus Coll (MN) **374**
Harding U (AR) **375**
Hardin-Simmons U (TX) **376**
Hastings Coll (NE) **377**
Henderson State U (AR) **378**
Hofstra U (NY) **380**
Huntingdon Coll (AL) **383**
Indiana U Bloomington (IN) **385**
Indiana U Northwest (IN) **386**
Indiana U of Pennsylvania (PA) **386**
Indiana U–Purdue U Fort Wayne (IN) **386**
Indiana U South Bend (IN) **387**
Indiana U Southeast (IN) **387**
Indiana Wesleyan U (IN) **387**
Ithaca Coll (NY) **390**
Jackson State U (MS) **390**
Johnson State Coll (VT) **394**
Judson Coll (AL) **395**
Juniata Coll (PA) **395**
Kennesaw State U (GA) **397**
Keuka Coll (NY) **398**
King Coll (TN) **398**
La Roche Coll (PA) **402**
Le Moyne Coll (NY) **404**
Liberty U (VA) **406**
Limestone Coll (SC) **406**
Lincoln U (PA) **407**
Long Island U, C.W. Post Campus (NY) **409**
Louisiana State U in Shreveport (LA) **410**
Luther Coll (IA) **412**
Lyndon State Coll (VT) **413**
Manhattanville Coll (NY) **416**
Mansfield U of Pennsylvania (PA) **416**
Marymount Coll of Fordham U (NY) **419**
Maryville Coll (TN) **420**
Mayville State U (ND) **422**
McGill U (QC, Canada) **423**
McKendree Coll (IL) **423**
McMurry U (TX) **423**
Mercer U (GA) **425**
Messiah Coll (PA) **426**
MidAmerica Nazarene U (KS) **428**
Millersville U of Pennsylvania (PA) **430**
Minnesota State U, Moorhead (MN) **432**
Minot State U (ND) **432**
Mississippi Valley State U (MS) **432**
Molloy Coll (NY) **433**
Montana State U–Billings (MT) **434**
Morehead State U (KY) **436**
Mount Marty Coll (SD) **438**
Mount Vernon Nazarene U (OH) **440**
Nazareth Coll of Rochester (NY) **443**
New York Inst of Technology (NY) **447**
New York U (NY) **447**
Niagara U (NY) **447**
North Carolina Central U (NC) **448**
North Carolina State U (NC) **449**
North Dakota State U (ND) **449**
Northern Arizona U (AZ) **450**
Northern Kentucky U (KY) **451**
Northwestern Coll (MN) **453**
Northwestern U (IL) **453**
Northwest Nazarene U (ID) **454**
Nova Southeastern U (FL) **455**
Oakland City U (IN) **456**
Ohio U (OH) **458**
Ohio Valley Coll (WV) **459**
Oklahoma Baptist U (OK) **459**
Oklahoma Christian U (OK) **459**
Oral Roberts U (OK) **461**
Pace U (NY) **463**
Philadelphia Biblical U (PA) **469**
Pikeville Coll (KY) **470**
Plymouth State Coll (NH) **471**
Point Park Coll (PA) **471**
Pontifical Catholic U of Puerto Rico (PR) **472**
Prescott Coll (AZ) **474**
Queens U of Charlotte (NC) **476**
Rivier Coll (NH) **480**
Rocky Mountain Coll (MT) **482**
Rust Coll (MS) **485**
St. Ambrose U (IA) **486**
Saint Augustine's Coll (NC) **487**
St. John Fisher Coll (NY) **489**
St. John's U (NY) **490**
Saint Joseph's Coll of Maine (ME) **491**
Saint Mary's U of Minnesota (MN) **494**
Saint Xavier U (IL) **496**
Salve Regina U (RI) **497**
San Diego State U (CA) **498**
Seattle Pacific U (WA) **501**
Seton Hill U (PA) **502**
Shaw U (NC) **502**
Simpson Coll and Graduate School (CA) **505**
Southeastern Coll of the Assemblies of God (FL) **507**
Southeastern Louisiana U (LA) **508**
Southeastern Oklahoma State U (OK) **508**
Southeast Missouri State U (MO) **508**
Southern Arkansas U–Magnolia (AR) **509**
Southern Nazarene U (OK) **510**
Southern Wesleyan U (SC) **511**
Southwestern Coll (KS) **512**
Southwest Missouri State U (MO) **513**
Southwest State U (MN) **513**
State U of NY at Albany (NY) **514**
State U of NY Coll at Potsdam (NY) **517**
State U of West Georgia (GA) **518**
Syracuse U (NY) **521**
Talladega Coll (AL) **522**
Tennessee Wesleyan Coll (TN) **524**
Texas A&M International U (TX) **524**
Texas Christian U (TX) **526**
Texas Lutheran U (TX) **526**
Texas Wesleyan U (TX) **526**
Thomas Coll (ME) **527**
Toccoa Falls Coll (GA) **528**
Trevecca Nazarene U (TN) **529**
Trinity Christian Coll (IL) **530**
Tri-State U (IN) **532**
Union Coll (NE) **534**
U du Québec à Trois-Rivières (QC, Canada) **536**
The U of Arizona (AZ) **538**
U of Calif, San Diego (CA) **541**
U of Calif, Santa Cruz (CA) **542**
U of Central Arkansas (AR) **542**
U of Central Florida (FL) **542**
U of Central Oklahoma (OK) **542**
U of Delaware (DE) **544**
U of Georgia (GA) **545**
U of Great Falls (MT) **545**
U of Hawaii at Manoa (HI) **546**
U of Illinois at Chicago (IL) **547**
U of Indianapolis (IN) **548**
The U of Iowa (IA) **548**
U of Maine at Farmington (ME) **550**
U of Mary (ND) **551**
U of Maryland, Coll Park (MD) **552**
U of Minnesota, Duluth (MN) **554**
U of Minnesota, Twin Cities Campus (MN) **555**
U of Mississippi (MS) **555**
The U of Montana–Missoula (MT) **556**
The U of Montana–Western (MT) **556**
U of Nebraska–Lincoln (NE) **557**
U of Nevada, Reno (NV) **558**
U of New Orleans (LA) **559**
The U of North Carolina at Charlotte (NC) **560**
The U of North Carolina at Wilmington (NC) **561**
U of Northern Iowa (IA) **561**
U of North Florida (FL) **561**
U of North Texas (TX) **562**
U of Oklahoma (OK) **562**
U of Puerto Rico, Cayey U Coll (PR) **571**
U of Rio Grande (OH) **572**
U of St. Thomas (MN) **573**
U of South Florida (FL) **576**
The U of Tennessee at Martin (TN) **577**
U of Toledo (OH) **581**
U of Utah (UT) **582**
U of Vermont (VT) **582**
U of Waterloo (ON, Canada) **583**
U of West Florida (FL) **583**
U of Windsor (ON, Canada) **584**
U of Wisconsin–River Falls (WI) **585**
U of Wisconsin–Superior (WI) **586**
Ursuline Coll (OH) **587**
Utah State U (UT) **587**
Utica Coll (NY) **588**
Valley City State U (ND) **588**
Viterbo U (WI) **591**
Wartburg Coll (IA) **594**
Washington U in St. Louis (MO) **595**
Wayne State U (MI) **596**
Western Carolina U (NC) **598**
Westmont Coll (CA) **602**
Wheeling Jesuit U (WV) **603**
William Penn U (IA) **606**
William Woods U (MO) **607**
Winston-Salem State U (NC) **608**
York Coll (NE) **610**
York U (ON, Canada) **611**
Youngstown State U (OH) **611**

MATHEMATICS RELATED

Information can be found under this major's main heading.

Anderson U (IN) **268**
Bradley U (IL) **293**
Chestnut Hill Coll (PA) **312**
Hofstra U (NY) **380**
The Ohio State U (OH) **457**
Ohio U (OH) **458**
Seattle Pacific U (WA) **501**
Sweet Briar Coll (VA) **521**
The U of Akron (OH) **537**
U of Pittsburgh (PA) **569**
The U of Scranton (PA) **574**
U of Wyoming (WY) **586**

MECHANICAL DESIGN TECHNOLOGY

Overview: This major provides undergraduates with the technical knowledge and skills to design and create drawings and computer simulations of industrial and manufacturing systems. *Related majors:* industrial design, mechanical drafting, logistics and materials management. *Potential careers:* industrial designer, mechanical engineer, plant manager, machinist. *Salary potential:* $30k-$40k.

Bowling Green State U (OH) **292**
Pittsburg State U (KS) **470**

MECHANICAL DRAFTING

Overview: This general major will teach students how to create working drawings, schematics, visual plans, blueprints, or computer simulations that may be used by industrial or mechanical engineers. *Related majors:* mathematics, computer science, mechanical or industrial engineering, engineering mechanics, metallurgy. *Potential careers:* draftsperson, industrial or mechanical engineer, architect, production line manager. *Salary potential:* $35k-$45k.

Pennsylvania Coll of Technology (PA) **467**
Purdue U (IN) **475**

MECHANICAL ENGINEERING

Overview: Students who choose this major study the science behind the development and operation of manufacturing equipment, stationary power units, and various systems for controlling movement in an industrial setting. *Related majors:* computer engineering, industrial engineering, physics, engineering mechanics. *Potential careers:* computer engineer, industrial engineer, inventor, robotics technician, quality assurance manager. *Salary potential:* $40k-$50k.

Alabama A&M U (AL) **261**
Alfred U (NY) **263**
The American U in Cairo(Egypt) **267**
Andrews U (MI) **269**
Arizona State U (AZ) **271**
Arkansas Tech U (AR) **272**
Auburn U (AL) **276**
Baker Coll of Flint (MI) **279**
Baylor U (TX) **283**
Boston U (MA) **292**
Bradley U (IL) **293**
Brigham Young U (UT) **295**
Brown U (RI) **296**
Bucknell U (PA) **297**
California Inst of Technology (CA) **299**
California Maritime Academy (CA) **299**
California Polytechnic State U, San Luis Obispo (CA) **300**
California State Polytechnic U, Pomona (CA) **300**
California State U, Chico (CA) **300**
California State U, Fresno (CA) **301**
California State U, Fullerton (CA) **301**
California State U, Long Beach (CA) **301**
California State U, Northridge (CA) **301**
California State U, Sacramento (CA) **301**
Calvin Coll (MI) **303**
Carleton U (ON, Canada) **305**
Carnegie Mellon U (PA) **305**
Case Western Reserve U (OH) **307**
The Catholic U of America (DC) **307**
Cedarville U (OH) **308**
Christian Brothers U (TN) **313**
City Coll of the City U of NY (NY) **314**
Clarkson U (NY) **316**
Clemson U (SC) **317**
Cleveland State U (OH) **317**
The Coll of Southeastern Europe, The American U of Athens(Greece) **323**
Colorado School of Mines (CO) **325**
Colorado State U (CO) **325**
Columbia U, School of Engineering & Applied Sci (NY) **328**
Concordia U (QC, Canada) **331**
Cooper Union for the Advancement of Science & Art (NY) **332**
Cornell U (NY) **333**
Dalhousie U (NS, Canada) **336**
Delaware State U (DE) **338**
Drexel U (PA) **346**
Duke U (NC) **346**
Eastern Nazarene Coll (MA) **348**
Florida A&M U (FL) **359**
Florida Atlantic U (FL) **359**
Florida Inst of Technology (FL) **360**
Florida International U (FL) **360**
Florida State U (FL) **361**
Frostburg State U (MD) **365**
Gallaudet U (DC) **365**
Gannon U (PA) **365**
The George Washington U (DC) **367**
Georgia Inst of Technology (GA) **367**
Gonzaga U (WA) **369**
Grand Valley State U (MI) **371**
Grove City Coll (PA) **373**
Harvard U (MA) **376**
Henry Cogswell Coll (WA) **378**
Hofstra U (NY) **380**
Howard U (DC) **382**
Illinois Inst of Technology (IL) **384**
Indiana Inst of Technology (IN) **385**
Indiana U–Purdue U Fort Wayne (IN) **386**
Indiana U–Purdue U Indianapolis (IN) **387**
Insto Tecno Estudios Sups Monterrey(Mexico) **388**
Iowa State U of Science and Technology (IA) **390**
Jacksonville U (FL) **391**
John Brown U (AR) **392**
Johns Hopkins U (MD) **392**
Johnson & Wales U (RI) **393**
Kansas State U (KS) **396**
Kettering U (MI) **398**
Lafayette Coll (PA) **400**
Lakehead U (ON, Canada) **400**
Lamar U (TX) **401**
Lawrence Technological U (MI) **403**
Lehigh U (PA) **404**
LeTourneau U (TX) **405**
Louisiana State U and A&M Coll (LA) **410**
Louisiana Tech U (LA) **410**
Loyola Marymount U (CA) **411**
Manhattan Coll (NY) **416**
Marquette U (WI) **418**
Massachusetts Inst of Technology (MA) **421**
McGill U (QC, Canada) **423**
McMaster U (ON, Canada) **423**
Memorial U of Newfoundland (NF, Canada) **424**
Mercer U (GA) **425**
Miami U (OH) **428**
Michigan State U (MI) **428**
Michigan Technological U (MI) **428**
Milwaukee School of Engineering (WI) **431**
Minnesota State U, Mankato (MN) **431**
Mississippi State U (MS) **432**
Montana State U–Bozeman (MT) **434**
Montana Tech of The U of Montana (MT) **435**
New Jersey Inst of Technology (NJ) **445**
New Mexico Inst of Mining and Technology (NM) **446**
New Mexico State U (NM) **446**
New York Inst of Technology (NY) **447**
New York U (NY) **447**
North Carolina Ag and Tech State U (NC) **448**
North Carolina State U (NC) **449**
North Dakota State U (ND) **449**
Northeastern U (MA) **450**
Northern Arizona U (AZ) **450**
Northern Illinois U (IL) **450**
Northwestern U (IL) **453**
Norwich U (VT) **455**
Oakland U (MI) **456**
Ohio Northern U (OH) **457**
The Ohio State U (OH) **457**
Ohio U (OH) **458**
Oklahoma Christian U (OK) **459**
Oklahoma State U (OK) **460**
Old Dominion U (VA) **460**
Oral Roberts U (OK) **461**
Oregon State U (OR) **462**
Penn State U at Erie, The Behrend Coll (PA) **467**
Penn State U Univ Park Campus (PA) **468**
Polytechnic U, Brooklyn Campus (NY) **472**
Portland State U (OR) **472**
Prairie View A&M U (TX) **473**
Princeton U (NJ) **474**
Purdue U (IN) **475**
Purdue U Calumet (IN) **475**
Queen's U at Kingston (ON, Canada) **476**
Rensselaer Polytechnic Inst (NY) **478**
Rice U (TX) **479**
Rochester Inst of Technology (NY) **482**
Rose-Hulman Inst of Technology (IN) **484**
Rowan U (NJ) **484**
Ryerson U (ON, Canada) **485**
Saginaw Valley State U (MI) **486**
St. Cloud State U (MN) **488**
Saint Louis U (MO) **492**
Saint Martin's Coll (WA) **493**
San Diego State U (CA) **498**
San Francisco State U (CA) **498**
San Jose State U (CA) **499**
Santa Clara U (CA) **499**
Seattle U (WA) **501**
South Dakota School of Mines and Technology (SD) **507**
South Dakota State U (SD) **507**
Southern Illinois U Carbondale (IL) **509**
Southern Illinois U Edwardsville (IL) **509**
Southern Methodist U (TX) **510**
Southern U and A&M Coll (LA) **511**
Stanford U (CA) **514**
State U of NY at Binghamton (NY) **515**
State U of NY Maritime Coll (NY) **518**
Stevens Inst of Technology (NJ) **519**
Stony Brook U, State University of New York (NY) **520**
Syracuse U (NY) **521**
Temple U (PA) **523**
Tennessee State U (TN) **523**
Tennessee Technological U (TN) **524**
Texas A&M U (TX) **524**
Texas A&M U–Kingsville (TX) **525**
Texas Tech U (TX) **526**
Trinity Coll (CT) **530**
Tri-State U (IN) **532**
Tufts U (MA) **533**
Tulane U (LA) **533**
Tuskegee U (AL) **533**
Union Coll (NY) **534**
United States Air Force Academy (CO) **534**
United States Coast Guard Academy (CT) **535**
United States Military Academy (NY) **535**
United States Naval Academy (MD) **535**
Université de Sherbrooke (QC, Canada) **536**
U du Québec à Trois-Rivières (QC, Canada) **536**
U du Québec, École de technologie supérieure (QC, Canada) **536**
Université Laval (QC, Canada) **536**
U at Buffalo, The State University of New York (NY) **536**
The U of Akron (OH) **537**
The U of Alabama (AL) **537**
The U of Alabama at Birmingham (AL) **537**
The U of Alabama in Huntsville (AL) **537**
U of Alaska Fairbanks (AK) **538**
U of Alberta (AB, Canada) **538**
The U of Arizona (AZ) **538**
U of Arkansas (AR) **539**
The U of British Columbia (BC, Canada) **540**
U of Calgary (AB, Canada) **540**
U of Calif, Berkeley (CA) **540**
U of Calif, Davis (CA) **540**
U of Calif, Irvine (CA) **541**
U of Calif, Los Angeles (CA) **541**
U of Calif, Riverside (CA) **541**
U of Calif, San Diego (CA) **541**
U of Calif, Santa Barbara (CA) **541**
U of Central Florida (FL) **542**
U of Cincinnati (OH) **543**
U of Colorado at Boulder (CO) **543**
U of Colorado at Colorado Springs (CO) **543**
U of Colorado at Denver (CO) **543**
U of Connecticut (CT) **544**
U of Dayton (OH) **544**
U of Delaware (DE) **544**
U of Denver (CO) **544**
U of Evansville (IN) **545**
U of Florida (FL) **545**
U of Hartford (CT) **546**
U of Hawaii at Manoa (HI) **546**
U of Houston (TX) **547**
U of Idaho (ID) **547**
U of Illinois at Chicago (IL) **547**
U of Illinois at Urbana–Champaign (IL) **548**
The U of Iowa (IA) **548**
U of Kansas (KS) **549**
U of Kentucky (KY) **549**
U of Louisiana at Lafayette (LA) **550**
U of Louisville (KY) **550**
U of Maine (ME) **550**
U of Manitoba (MB, Canada) **551**
U of Maryland, Baltimore County (MD) **552**
U of Maryland, Coll Park (MD) **552**
U of Massachusetts Amherst (MA) **552**
U of Massachusetts Dartmouth (MA) **553**
U of Massachusetts Lowell (MA) **553**
The U of Memphis (TN) **553**
U of Miami (FL) **553**
U of Michigan (MI) **554**
U of Michigan–Dearborn (MI) **554**
U of Minnesota, Twin Cities Campus (MN) **555**
U of Mississippi (MS) **555**
U of Missouri–Columbia (MO) **555**
U of Missouri–Kansas City (MO) **555**
U of Missouri–Rolla (MO) **556**
U of Missouri–St. Louis (MO) **556**
U of Nebraska–Lincoln (NE) **557**
U of Nevada, Las Vegas (NV) **558**
U of Nevada, Reno (NV) **558**
U of New Brunswick Fredericton (NB, Canada) **558**
U of New Brunswick Saint John (NB, Canada) **558**
U of New Hampshire (NH) **558**
U of New Haven (CT) **559**
U of New Mexico (NM) **559**
U of New Orleans (LA) **559**
The U of North Carolina at Charlotte (NC) **560**
U of North Dakota (ND) **561**
U of North Florida (FL) **561**
U of Notre Dame (IN) **562**
U of Oklahoma (OK) **562**
U of Ottawa (ON, Canada) **563**
U of Pennsylvania (PA) **563**
U of Pittsburgh (PA) **569**
U of Portland (OR) **570**
U of Rhode Island (RI) **572**
U of Rochester (NY) **573**
U of St. Thomas (MN) **573**
U of Saskatchewan (SK, Canada) **574**
U of South Alabama (AL) **575**
U of South Carolina (SC) **575**
U of Southern California (CA) **576**
U of South Florida (FL) **576**
The U of Tennessee (TN) **577**
The U of Tennessee at Chattanooga (TN) **577**
The U of Texas at Arlington (TX) **577**
The U of Texas at Austin (TX) **578**
The U of Texas at El Paso (TX) **578**
The U of Texas at San Antonio (TX) **578**
The U of Texas at Tyler (TX) **579**
The U of Texas–Pan American (TX) **579**
U of the District of Columbia (DC) **580**
U of the Pacific (CA) **580**
U of Toledo (OH) **581**
U of Toronto (ON, Canada) **581**
U of Tulsa (OK) **581**
U of Utah (UT) **582**
U of Vermont (VT) **582**
U of Victoria (BC, Canada) **582**
U of Virginia (VA) **582**
U of Washington (WA) **583**
U of Waterloo (ON, Canada) **583**
The U of Western Ontario (ON, Canada) **583**
U of Windsor (ON, Canada) **584**
U of Wisconsin–Madison (WI) **584**
U of Wisconsin–Milwaukee (WI) **585**
U of Wisconsin–Platteville (WI) **585**
U of Wyoming (WY) **586**
Utah State U (UT) **587**
Valparaiso U (IN) **588**
Vanderbilt U (TN) **588**
Villanova U (PA) **590**
Virginia Commonwealth U (VA) **590**
Virginia Military Inst (VA) **591**
Virginia Polytechnic Inst and State U (VA) **591**
Walla Walla Coll (WA) **593**
Washington State U (WA) **595**

Washington U in St. Louis (MO) ***595***
Wayne State U (MI) ***596***
Western Kentucky U (KY) ***599***
Western Michigan U (MI) ***599***
Western New England Coll (MA) ***600***
West Virginia U (WV) ***602***
West Virginia U Inst of Technology (WV) ***602***
Wichita State U (KS) ***604***
Widener U (PA) ***604***
Wilkes U (PA) ***605***
William Penn U (IA) ***606***
Winona State U (MN) ***608***
Worcester Polytechnic Inst (MA) ***609***
Wright State U (OH) ***609***
Yale U (CT) ***610***
York Coll of Pennsylvania (PA) ***610***
Youngstown State U (OH) ***611***

MECHANICAL ENGINEERING TECHNOLOGIES RELATED

Information can be found under this major's main heading.

Indiana State U (IN) ***385***
New York Inst of Technology (NY) ***447***

MECHANICAL ENGINEERING TECHNOLOGY

Overview: This major provides students with a background in mathematics, physics, and related technology subjects so they may perform a wide variety of tasks, ranging from the design of a system or element to its production, installation, and performance. *Related majors:* industrial design, engineering technology, industrial/manufacturing engineering technology. *Potential careers:* industrial designer, plant manager, quality control specialist, machinist. *Salary potential:* $30k-$40k.

Alabama A&M U (AL) ***261***
Andrews U (MI) ***269***
Arizona State U East (AZ) ***271***
Bluefield State Coll (WV) ***291***
British Columbia Inst of Technology (BC, Canada) ***295***
California Polytechnic State U, San Luis Obispo (CA) ***300***
California State Polytechnic U, Pomona (CA) ***300***
California State U, Sacramento (CA) ***301***
Central Connecticut State U (CT) ***309***
Central Michigan U (MI) ***310***
Central Washington U (WA) ***310***
Cleveland State U (OH) ***317***
Colorado State U-Pueblo (CO) ***325***
Delaware State U (DE) ***338***
Eastern Washington U (WA) ***349***
Excelsior Coll (NY) ***356***
Fairleigh Dickinson U, Teaneck-Metro Campus (NJ) ***356***
Fairmont State Coll (WV) ***356***
Georgia Southern U (GA) ***367***
Indiana U–Purdue U Fort Wayne (IN) ***386***
Indiana U–Purdue U Indianapolis (IN) ***387***
Johnson & Wales U (RI) ***393***
Kansas State U (KS) ***396***
Lakehead U (ON, Canada) ***400***
LeTourneau U (TX) ***405***
Metropolitan State Coll of Denver (CO) ***427***
Michigan Technological U (MI) ***428***
Milwaukee School of Engineering (WI) ***431***
Montana State U–Bozeman (MT) ***434***
Murray State U (KY) ***440***
New York Inst of Technology (NY) ***447***
Northeastern U (MA) ***450***
Oklahoma State U (OK) ***460***
Oregon Inst of Technology (OR) ***461***
Penn State U Berks Cmps of Berks-Lehigh Valley Coll (PA) ***468***
Penn State U Harrisburg Campus of the Capital Coll (PA) ***468***
Pittsburg State U (KS) ***470***
Point Park Coll (PA) ***471***
Purdue U Calumet (IN) ***475***
Purdue U North Central (IN) ***475***
Rochester Inst of Technology (NY) ***482***
Savannah State U (GA) ***499***
South Carolina State U (SC) ***506***
Southern Polytechnic State U (GA) ***511***
Southwest Missouri State U (MO) ***513***
State U of NY Coll at Buffalo (NY) ***516***
State U of NY Inst of Tech at Utica/Rome (NY) ***518***
Temple U (PA) ***523***
Texas Tech U (TX) ***526***
Thomas Edison State Coll (NJ) ***527***
The U of Akron (OH) ***537***
U of Arkansas at Little Rock (AR) ***539***
U of Cincinnati (OH) ***543***
U of Dayton (OH) ***544***
U of Hartford (CT) ***546***
U of Houston–Downtown (TX) ***547***
U of Maine (ME) ***550***
U of Massachusetts Dartmouth (MA) ***553***
U of New Hampshire (NH) ***558***
The U of North Carolina at Charlotte (NC) ***560***
U of North Texas (TX) ***562***
U of Pittsburgh at Johnstown (PA) ***570***
U of Rio Grande (OH) ***572***
U of Southern Mississippi (MS) ***576***
U of Toledo (OH) ***581***
Wayne State U (MI) ***596***
Weber State U (UT) ***596***
Wentworth Inst of Technology (MA) ***597***
Youngstown State U (OH) ***611***

MEDICAL ADMINISTRATIVE ASSISTANT

Overview: Students learn the skills necessary to provide administrative assistance to physicians, nurses, healthcare administrators, and other healthcare professionals. *Related majors:* word processing, business communication, technical writing, general office/clerical, medical transcription. *Potential careers:* medical administrative assistant or secretary, executive assistant, medical transcriber. *Salary potential:* $22k-$27k.

Baker Coll of Auburn Hills (MI) ***279***
Ohio U (OH) ***458***
Peirce Coll (PA) ***466***
Tabor Coll (KS) ***522***

MEDICAL ASSISTANT

Overview: Students choosing this major learn how to perform administrative duties in a medical or health facility, as well as certain clinical procedures and duties, including patient intake, routine diagnostic tests, examination assistance, and administration of medications. *Related majors:* medical office management, nursing, premedicine studies, nurse aid/assistant. *Potential careers:* medical assistant, nurse assistant/aid. *Salary potential:* $24k-$34k.

California State U, Dominguez Hills (CA) ***300***
Florida Metropolitan U–Jacksonville Campus (FL) ***360***
Jones Coll (FL) ***394***

MEDICAL BASIC SCIENCES RELATED

Information can be found under this major's main heading.

Fairleigh Dickinson U, Florham (NJ) ***356***
Fairleigh Dickinson U, Teaneck-Metro Campus (NJ) ***356***
Rutgers, The State U of New Jersey, Newark (NJ) ***485***
U of Hawaii at Manoa (HI) ***546***

MEDICAL CELL BIOLOGY

Overview: Students who take this major study the human cell's biochemical reactions under various types of conditions. *Related majors:* medical anatomy, medical molecular biology, medical toxicology, medical microbiology. *Potential careers:* immunologist, research scientist. *Salary potential:* $33k-$43k.

U of Utah (UT) ***582***

MEDICAL DIETICIAN

Overview: Students learn to design and manage nutritional programs as part of clinical and therapy treatment programs. *Related majors:* nutrition science, dietitian, human physiology. *Potential careers:* medical dietician, hospital food service director, nutritional scientist. *Salary potential:* $30k-$40k.

The Ohio State U (OH) ***457***
U of Illinois at Chicago (IL) ***547***

MEDICAL ILLUSTRATING

Overview: Students learn how to use computer graphics and artistic techniques to visually communicate human anatomy and other biomedical knowledge for educational, research, or clinical purposes. *Related majors:* human anatomy and physiology, pathology, computer graphics, drawing, photography. *Potential careers:* medical illustrator, graphic designer, photographer. *Salary potential:* $27k-$35k.

Alma Coll (MI) ***264***
Anna Maria Coll (MA) ***269***
Arcadia U (PA) ***271***
Clark Atlanta U (GA) ***315***
The Cleveland Inst of Art (OH) ***317***
Iowa State U of Science and Technology (IA) ***390***
Olivet Coll (MI) ***461***
Rochester Inst of Technology (NY) ***482***
Texas Woman's U (TX) ***527***
Tulane U (LA) ***533***
U of Toronto (ON, Canada) ***581***

MEDICAL LABORATORY ASSISTANT

Overview: This major prepares students to perform laboratory testing procedures on human blood, tissues, and fluids and other duties in support of laboratory technicians. *Related majors:* hematology technology, medical laboratory technology, computer technology. *Potential career:* laboratory assistant. *Salary potential:* $20k-$30k.

California State U, Chico (CA) ***300***
U of Vermont (VT) ***582***

MEDICAL LABORATORY TECHNICIAN

Overview: This major prepares students to work in a laboratory, under the supervision of clinical laboratory scientists, to conduct medical laboratory procedures and tests as well as to organize and analyze data from those tests. *Related majors:* health/medical clinical technology, medical technology, cytotechnology, hematology technology. *Potential careers:* medical laboratory technician, forensic science technician, cytotechnologist, food tester, veterinary laboratory technician. *Salary potential:* $22k-$27k.

Alabama State U (AL) ***261***
Alfred U (NY) ***263***
Andrews U (MI) ***269***
Auburn U (AL) ***276***
Barry U (FL) ***282***
Bloomsburg U of Pennsylvania (PA) ***290***
California State U, Dominguez Hills (CA) ***300***
California State U, Hayward (CA) ***301***
California State U, Northridge (CA) ***301***
California U of Pennsylvania (PA) ***302***
Columbus State U (GA) ***328***
Concordia U (NE) ***330***
DePaul U (IL) ***339***
East Central U (OK) ***347***
East Stroudsburg U of Pennsylvania (PA) ***349***
Edinboro U of Pennsylvania (PA) ***351***
Ferris State U (MI) ***358***
Gardner-Webb U (NC) ***365***
Holy Family U (PA) ***380***
Hunter Coll of the City U of NY (NY) ***382***
Long Island U, C.W. Post Campus (NY) ***409***
Longwood U (VA) ***409***
Marquette U (WI) ***418***
Massachusetts Coll of Liberal Arts (MA) ***421***
Morgan State U (MD) ***436***
Mount Saint Mary Coll (NY) ***439***
Northeastern U (MA) ***450***
Northern Michigan U (MI) ***451***
Northern State U (SD) ***451***
Northwestern Oklahoma State U (OK) ***453***
Northwest Missouri State U (MO) ***454***
Purdue U Calumet (IN) ***475***
St. Thomas Aquinas Coll (NY) ***495***
Shawnee State U (OH) ***502***
Sonoma State U (CA) ***506***
U of Alberta (AB, Canada) ***538***
The U of British Columbia (BC, Canada) ***540***
U of Mary (ND) ***551***
U of Maryland Eastern Shore (MD) ***552***
U of Missouri–Kansas City (MO) ***555***
The U of Montana–Missoula (MT) ***556***
U of New England (ME) ***558***
U of New Hampshire (NH) ***558***
The U of North Carolina at Pembroke (NC) ***560***
U of Science and Arts of Oklahoma (OK) ***574***
U of Utah (UT) ***582***
Weber State U (UT) ***596***
Winona State U (MN) ***608***

MEDICAL LABORATORY TECHNOLOGY

Overview: Students who choose this major learn how to use complex precision instruments and computers to conduct laboratory tests, clinical trials, and research experiments that play a vital role in the detection and diagnosis of disease. *Related majors:* medical laboratory technician, medical technology, medical cell biology, microbiology and molecular biology, medical toxicology. *Potential careers:* clinical laboratory scientist, medical technologist. *Salary potential:* $30k-$36k.

Auburn U (AL) ***276***
The Coll of St. Scholastica (MN) ***322***
Concordia Coll (MN) ***329***
Felician Coll (NJ) ***357***
The George Washington U (DC) ***367***
Oakland U (MI) ***456***
Quinnipiac U (CT) ***476***
Rockhurst U (MO) ***482***
Roosevelt U (IL) ***483***
Southeastern Oklahoma State U (OK) ***508***
Springfield Coll (MA) ***514***
Stony Brook U, State University of New York (NY) ***520***
U of Cincinnati (OH) ***543***
U of Illinois at Springfield (IL) ***548***
U of Nevada, Las Vegas (NV) ***558***
U of New England (ME) ***558***
U of Oklahoma (OK) ***562***
U of Puerto Rico Medical Sciences Campus (PR) ***571***
U of Windsor (ON, Canada) ***584***

MEDICAL MICROBIOLOGY

Overview: Students study pathogenic bacteria and how they may cause

MEDICAL MICROBIOLOGY (continued)

disease in humans. *Related majors:* bacteriology, medical toxicology, medical cell biology. *Potential careers:* bacteriologist, microbiologist, research scientist specializing in emerging disease, physician. *Salary potential:* $35k-$45k.

Fitchburg State Coll (MA) ***358***
U of Miami (FL) ***553***
U of Wisconsin–La Crosse (WI) ***584***

MEDICAL MOLECULAR BIOLOGY

Overview: Students study human biological functions and mechanisms at the molecular level. *Related majors:* biophysics, chemistry, molecular physics, premedicine. *Potential careers:* molecular biologist, research scientist, physician. *Salary potential:* $37k-$48k.

U of Hawaii at Manoa (HI) ***546***

MEDICAL NUTRITION

Overview: Students focus on the scientific study of how the human body utilizes food for human growth and metabolism from a biomedical perspective. *Related majors:* nutrition science, premedicine studies. *Potential careers:* physician, biomedical researcher, food scientist, nutritionist. *Salary potential:* $35k-$45k.

Edinboro U of Pennsylvania (PA) ***351***
Elmhurst Coll (IL) ***351***

MEDICAL PHARMACOLOGY AND PHARMACEUTICAL SCIENCES

Overview: This major teaches students the science of drug development, how certain chemical substances interact with the body, and the clinical trial procedures used to bring a drug to market. *Related majors:* pharmacy, pharmacy administration and pharmaceutics, chemistry, biology, biochemistry. *Potential careers:* research scientist, pharmaceutical researcher. *Salary potential:* $40k-$50k.

Campbell U (NC) ***303***
Duquesne U (PA) ***346***
The U of Montana–Missoula (MT) ***556***
U of the Sciences in Philadelphia (PA) ***580***

MEDICAL PHYSICS/ BIOPHYSICS

Overview: Medical physics is primarily concerned with the use of ionizing and nonionizing radiation and the application of physical and mathematical techniques in the diagnosis and treatment of disease. *Related majors:* medical cell biology, medical molecular biology, physics, premedicine studies, hematology technology. *Potential careers:* medical biophysicist, hematologist, medical cell biologist, research scientist. *Salary potential:* $40k-$50k.

Laurentian U (ON, Canada) ***403***

MEDICAL RADIOLOGIC TECHNOLOGY

Overview: This major teaches students how to assist radiologists in the use of X-ray and fluoroscopic equipment for the diagnosis and treatment of disease or injury. *Related majors:* nuclear medical technology, anatomy, diagnostic medical sonography, radiological science. *Potential careers:* nuclear medicine technologist, cardiovascular technologist and technician, electroencephalographic technologist. *Salary potential:* $30k-$35k.

Arkansas State U (AR) ***272***
Averett U (VA) ***278***
Avila U (MO) ***278***
Bloomsburg U of Pennsylvania (PA) ***290***
British Columbia Inst of Technology (BC, Canada) ***295***
Coll Misericordia (PA) ***319***
Fairleigh Dickinson U, Florham (NJ) ***356***
Fairleigh Dickinson U, Teaneck-Metro Campus (NJ) ***356***
Gannon U (PA) ***365***
Idaho State U (ID) ***384***
Indiana U Northwest (IN) ***386***
Indiana U–Purdue U Indianapolis (IN) ***387***
La Roche Coll (PA) ***402***
Loma Linda U (CA) ***408***
Long Island U, C.W. Post Campus (NY) ***409***
Marygrove Coll (MI) ***419***
McNeese State U (LA) ***423***
Minot State U (ND) ***432***
Mount Marty Coll (SD) ***438***
Northwestern State U of Louisiana (LA) ***453***
The Ohio State U (OH) ***457***
Presentation Coll (SD) ***474***
Saint Joseph's Coll of Maine (ME) ***491***
Southern Illinois U Carbondale (IL) ***509***
Southwest Missouri State U (MO) ***513***
Southwest Texas State U (TX) ***513***
State U of New York Upstate Medical University (NY) ***518***
Thomas Edison State Coll (NJ) ***527***
The U of Alabama at Birmingham (AL) ***537***
U of Central Arkansas (AR) ***542***
U of Central Florida (FL) ***542***
U of Hartford (CT) ***546***
U of Nebraska Medical Center (NE) ***557***
U of Nevada, Las Vegas (NV) ***558***
The U of North Carolina at Chapel Hill (NC) ***560***
U of Prince Edward Island (PE, Canada) ***570***
U of St. Francis (IL) ***573***
U of Vermont (VT) ***582***
Wayne State U (MI) ***596***
Weber State U (UT) ***596***

MEDICAL RECORDS ADMINISTRATION

Overview: Students learn how to plan, develop, and coordinate systems for managing health information in health services facilities, health financing organizations, and other related agencies. *Related majors:* information sciences/systems, data warehousing/ mining and database administration, computer programming, medical records technology, medical administrative assistant. *Potential careers:* medical records administrator, insurance records administrator, transcriptionist, medical record coder. *Salary potential:* $27k-$37k.

Alabama State U (AL) ***261***
Arkansas Tech U (AR) ***272***
Baker Coll of Auburn Hills (MI) ***279***
Baker Coll of Flint (MI) ***279***
Carroll Coll (MT) ***306***
Clark Atlanta U (GA) ***315***
Coll of Saint Mary (NE) ***322***
Dakota State U (SD) ***335***
East Carolina U (NC) ***347***
East Central U (OK) ***347***
Eastern Kentucky U (KY) ***348***
Ferris State U (MI) ***358***
Florida A&M U (FL) ***359***
Florida International U (FL) ***360***
Georgia State U (GA) ***368***
Gwynedd-Mercy Coll (PA) ***374***
Illinois State U (IL) ***384***
Indiana U Northwest (IN) ***386***
Indiana U–Purdue U Indianapolis (IN) ***387***
Jackson State U (MS) ***390***
Kean U (NJ) ***396***
Loma Linda U (CA) ***408***
Long Island U, C.W. Post Campus (NY) ***409***
Louisiana Tech U (LA) ***410***
Macon State Coll (GA) ***414***
Medical Coll of Georgia (GA) ***424***
Norfolk State U (VA) ***448***
The Ohio State U (OH) ***457***
Pace U (NY) ***463***
Regis U (CO) ***478***
Southwestern Oklahoma State U (OK) ***512***
Southwest Texas State U (TX) ***513***
Springfield Coll (MA) ***514***
State U of NY Inst of Tech at Utica/Rome (NY) ***518***
Temple U (PA) ***523***
Tennessee State U (TN) ***523***
Texas Southern U (TX) ***526***
Touro Coll (NY) ***529***
The U of Alabama at Birmingham (AL) ***537***
U of Central Florida (FL) ***542***
U of Illinois at Chicago (IL) ***547***
U of Kansas (KS) ***549***
U of Louisiana at Lafayette (LA) ***550***
U of Mississippi Medical Center (MS) ***555***
U of Pittsburgh (PA) ***569***
U of Wisconsin–Milwaukee (WI) ***585***
Western Carolina U (NC) ***598***

MEDICAL RECORDS TECHNOLOGY

Overview: This major teaches students how to organize, analyze, and evaluate medical records and compile medical-care and census data for reports on diseases, surgeries, etc. that may be used by law firms, insurance companies, and government agencies. *Related majors:* health services and facilities administration, medical records administration, information sciences/systems, data warehousing, database administration. *Potential careers:* medical record technician, health information technician, insurance information manager. *Salary potential:* $25k-$35k.

Robert Morris Coll (IL) ***481***

MEDICAL TECHNOLOGY

Overview: A general major that prepares students to work in a medical laboratory. *Related majors:* chemistry, microbiology, health/medical laboratory technology, hematology, cytotechnology. *Potential careers:* medical laboratory technician, forensic science technician, cytotechnologist, food tester, veterinary laboratory technician. *Salary potential:* $25k-$35k.

Adams State Coll (CO) ***260***
Alcorn State U (MS) ***263***
Alderson-Broaddus Coll (WV) ***263***
Alvernia Coll (PA) ***265***
American International Coll (MA) ***267***
Anderson U (IN) ***268***
Andrews U (MI) ***269***
Angelo State U (TX) ***269***
Appalachian State U (NC) ***270***
Aquinas Coll (MI) ***270***
Arizona State U (AZ) ***271***
Arkansas State U (AR) ***272***
Arkansas Tech U (AR) ***272***
Armstrong Atlantic State U (GA) ***273***
Atlantic Union Coll (MA) ***276***
Auburn U (AL) ***276***
Augustana Coll (SD) ***276***
Augusta State U (GA) ***277***
Aurora U (IL) ***277***
Austin Peay State U (TN) ***278***
Averett U (VA) ***278***
Avila U (MO) ***278***
Baldwin-Wallace Coll (OH) ***280***
Ball State U (IN) ***280***
Barry U (FL) ***282***
Belmont Abbey Coll (NC) ***284***
Belmont U (TN) ***284***
Bemidji State U (MN) ***285***
Benedictine U (IL) ***285***
Bethune-Cookman Coll (FL) ***289***
Blackburn Coll (IL) ***290***
Bloomfield Coll (NJ) ***290***
Bloomsburg U of Pennsylvania (PA) ***290***
Blue Mountain Coll (MS) ***291***
Bluffton Coll (OH) ***291***
Boston U (MA) ***292***
Bowling Green State U (OH) ***292***
Bradley U (IL) ***293***
Brescia U (KY) ***293***
Briar Cliff U (IA) ***294***
Bridgewater Coll (VA) ***294***
Cabrini Coll (PA) ***298***
Caldwell Coll (NJ) ***298***
California State U, Dominguez Hills (CA) ***300***
California State U, Northridge (CA) ***301***
Cameron U (OK) ***303***
Campbellsville U (KY) ***303***
Canisius Coll (NY) ***304***
Carroll Coll (MT) ***306***
Carroll Coll (WI) ***306***
Carson-Newman Coll (TN) ***306***
Catawba Coll (NC) ***307***
The Catholic U of America (DC) ***307***
Cedar Crest Coll (PA) ***308***
Cedarville U (OH) ***308***
Central Connecticut State U (CT) ***309***
Central Michigan U (MI) ***310***
Central Missouri State U (MO) ***310***
Cheyney U of Pennsylvania (PA) ***312***
Clarion U of Pennsylvania (PA) ***315***
Clemson U (SC) ***317***
Coker Coll (SC) ***318***
Coll Misericordia (PA) ***319***
Coll of Mount St. Joseph (OH) ***320***
Coll of St. Catherine (MN) ***321***
Coll of Saint Elizabeth (NJ) ***321***
Coll of Saint Mary (NE) ***322***
The Coll of Saint Rose (NY) ***322***
Coll of Staten Island of the City U of NY (NY) ***323***
Coll of the Ozarks (MO) ***323***
Columbia Coll (SC) ***327***
Concord Coll (WV) ***329***
Concordia Coll (MN) ***329***
Culver-Stockton Coll (MO) ***334***
Cumberland Coll (KY) ***335***
Defiance Coll (OH) ***338***
Delta State U (MS) ***339***
DePaul U (IL) ***339***
DePauw U (IN) ***339***
DeSales U (PA) ***340***
Dominican U (IL) ***345***
Dordt Coll (IA) ***345***
East Carolina U (NC) ***347***
Eastern Illinois U (IL) ***348***
Eastern Kentucky U (KY) ***348***
Eastern Mennonite U (VA) ***348***
Eastern Michigan U (MI) ***348***
Eastern New Mexico U (NM) ***349***
Eastern Washington U (WA) ***349***
East Texas Baptist U (TX) ***350***
Eckerd Coll (FL) ***350***
Edgewood Coll (WI) ***351***
Elmhurst Coll (IL) ***351***
Elmira Coll (NY) ***351***
Elms Coll (MA) ***352***
Elon U (NC) ***352***
Emory & Henry Coll (VA) ***353***
Erskine Coll (SC) ***354***
Eureka Coll (IL) ***355***
Evangel U (MO) ***355***
Fairleigh Dickinson U, Florham (NJ) ***356***
Fairleigh Dickinson U, Teaneck-Metro Campus (NJ) ***356***
Felician Coll (NJ) ***357***
Ferris State U (MI) ***358***
Ferrum Coll (VA) ***358***
Fitchburg State Coll (MA) ***358***
Florida Atlantic U (FL) ***359***
Florida Gulf Coast U (FL) ***359***
Fort Hays State U (KS) ***362***
Framingham State Coll (MA) ***362***
Francis Marion U (SC) ***363***
Gannon U (PA) ***365***
Gardner-Webb U (NC) ***365***
George Mason U (VA) ***366***

Georgetown Coll (KY) 366
The George Washington U (DC) 367
Georgia Southern U (GA) 367
Georgia State U (GA) 368
Graceland U (IA) 371
Grand Valley State U (MI) 371
Greensboro Coll (NC) 372
Gwynedd-Mercy Coll (PA) 374
Harding U (AR) 375
Hardin-Simmons U (TX) 376
Hartwick Coll (NY) 376
Henderson State U (AR) 378
High Point U (NC) 379
Houghton Coll (NY) 381
Houston Baptist U (TX) 382
Howard U (DC) 382
Humboldt State U (CA) 382
Idaho State U (ID) 384
Illinois Coll (IL) 384
Illinois State U (IL) 384
Illinois Wesleyan U (IL) 385
Indiana State U (IN) 385
Indiana U East (IN) 386
Indiana U Kokomo (IN) 386
Indiana U of Pennsylvania (PA) 386
Indiana U–Purdue U Fort Wayne (IN) 386
Indiana U–Purdue U Indianapolis (IN) 387
Indiana U Southeast (IN) 387
Indiana Wesleyan U (IN) 387
Inter American U of PR, San Germán Campus (PR) 388
Iona Coll (NY) 390
Jackson State U (MS) 390
Jacksonville U (FL) 391
Jamestown Coll (ND) 391
Jewish Hospital Coll of Nursing and Allied Health (MO) 391
John Brown U (AR) 392
Kansas State U (KS) 396
Kean U (NJ) 396
Kent State U (OH) 397
Kentucky State U (KY) 397
Kentucky Wesleyan Coll (KY) 397
Keuka Coll (NY) 398
King Coll (TN) 398
King's Coll (PA) 398
Kutztown U of Pennsylvania (PA) 399
Lamar U (TX) 401
Lander U (SC) 401
Langston U (OK) 402
Lebanon Valley Coll (PA) 403
Lee U (TN) 404
Lenoir-Rhyne Coll (NC) 405
Lewis U (IL) 406
Lincoln Memorial U (TN) 407
Lindenwood U (MO) 407
Lock Haven U of Pennsylvania (PA) 408
Loma Linda U (CA) 408
Long Island U, Brooklyn Campus (NY) 409
Long Island U, C.W. Post Campus (NY) 409
Longwood U (VA) 409
Louisiana Coll (LA) 410
Louisiana State U Health Sciences Center (LA) 410
Louisiana Tech U (LA) 410
Luther Coll (IA) 412
Lycoming Coll (PA) 412
Madonna U (MI) 414
Malone Coll (OH) 415
Manchester Coll (IN) 415
Mansfield U of Pennsylvania (PA) 416
Marian Coll of Fond du Lac (WI) 417
Marist Coll (NY) 417
Marshall U (WV) 418
Mary Baldwin Coll (VA) 419
Marymount Coll of Fordham U (NY) 419
Maryville U of Saint Louis (MO) 420
Marywood U (PA) 421
Massachusetts Coll of Liberal Arts (MA) 421
McKendree Coll (IL) 423
McNeese State U (LA) 423
Medical Coll of Georgia (GA) 424
Mercy Coll (NY) 425
Mercyhurst Coll (PA) 425
Miami U (OH) 428
Michigan State U (MI) 428
Michigan Technological U (MI) 428
Midwestern State U (TX) 430
Minnesota State U, Mankato (MN) 431
Minnesota State U, Moorhead (MN) 432
Minot State U (ND) 432
Mississippi State U (MS) 432
Missouri Southern State Coll (MO) 433
Missouri Western State Coll (MO) 433
Monmouth U (NJ) 434
Moravian Coll (PA) 436
Morehead State U (KY) 436
Morgan State U (MD) 436
Morningside Coll (IA) 437
Mount Marty Coll (SD) 438
Mount Mercy Coll (IA) 438
Mount Saint Mary Coll (NY) 439
Mount Vernon Nazarene U (OH) 440
Murray State U (KY) 440
Muskingum Coll (OH) 441
National-Louis U (IL) 442
New Mexico Inst of Mining and Technology (NM) 446
Norfolk State U (VA) 448
North Dakota State U (ND) 449
Northeastern State U (OK) 450
Northern Illinois U (IL) 450
Northern Michigan U (MI) 451
Northern State U (SD) 451
North Park U (IL) 452
Northwestern Coll (IA) 453
Northwestern State U of Louisiana (LA) 453
Northwest Missouri State U (MO) 454
Notre Dame Coll (OH) 455
Oakland U (MI) 456
Oakwood Coll (AL) 456
Ohio Northern U (OH) 457
The Ohio State U (OH) 457
Oklahoma Christian U (OK) 459
Oklahoma Panhandle State U (OK) 460
Oklahoma State U (OK) 460
Old Dominion U (VA) 460
Olivet Nazarene U (IL) 461
Oregon State U (OR) 462
Our Lady of Holy Cross Coll (LA) 463
Pace U (NY) 463
Pacific Union Coll (CA) 464
Peru State Coll (NE) 469
Pikeville Coll (KY) 470
Pittsburg State U (KS) 470
Plattsburgh State U of NY (NY) 471
Pontifical Catholic U of Puerto Rico (PR) 472
Prairie View A&M U (TX) 473
Purdue U (IN) 475
Purdue U Calumet (IN) 475
Quincy U (IL) 476
Radford U (VA) 476
Rhode Island Coll (RI) 479
Roanoke Coll (VA) 481
Roberts Wesleyan Coll (NY) 481
Rochester Inst of Technology (NY) 482
Roosevelt U (IL) 483
Rush U (IL) 484
Rutgers, The State U of New Jersey, Camden (NJ) 485
Rutgers, The State U of New Jersey, Newark (NJ) 485
Rutgers, The State U of New Jersey, New Brunswick (NJ) 485
Saginaw Valley State U (MI) 486
Saint Augustine's Coll (NC) 487
St. Bonaventure U (NY) 487
St. Cloud State U (MN) 488
St. Francis Coll (NY) 488
Saint Francis U (PA) 488
St. John's U (NY) 490
Saint Joseph Coll (CT) 490
Saint Joseph's Coll (IN) 490
Saint Leo U (FL) 492
Saint Mary-of-the-Woods Coll (IN) 493
Saint Mary's Coll (IN) 493
Saint Mary's U of Minnesota (MN) 494
St. Norbert Coll (WI) 495
St. Thomas Aquinas Coll (NY) 495
Salem Coll (NC) 496
Salem State Coll (MA) 497
Salisbury U (MD) 497
Salve Regina U (RI) 497
Sam Houston State U (TX) 497
Seattle U (WA) 501
Seton Hill U (PA) 502
Simpson Coll (IA) 505
Slippery Rock U of Pennsylvania (PA) 506
South Dakota State U (SD) 507
Southeastern Oklahoma State U (OK) 508
Southeast Missouri State U (MO) 508
Southern Adventist U (TN) 508
Southern Arkansas U–Magnolia (AR) 509
Southern Wesleyan U (SC) 511
Southwest Baptist U (MO) 512
Southwestern Oklahoma State U (OK) 512
Southwest Missouri State U (MO) 513
Southwest Texas State U (TX) 513
Spalding U (KY) 513
Springfield Coll (MA) 514
State U of NY at Albany (NY) 514
State U of NY Coll at Brockport (NY) 515
State U of NY Coll at Fredonia (NY) 516
State U of New York Upstate Medical University (NY) 518
Stephen F. Austin State U (TX) 518
Stetson U (FL) 519
Stonehill Coll (MA) 520
Suffolk U (MA) 520
Tabor Coll (KS) 522
Tarleton State U (TX) 522
Taylor U (IN) 523
Tennessee State U (TN) 523
Texas A&M U–Corpus Christi (TX) 525
Texas Southern U (TX) 526
Texas Woman's U (TX) 527
Thiel Coll (PA) 527
Thomas Jefferson U (PA) 527
Thomas More Coll (KY) 528
Trevecca Nazarene U (TN) 529
Tusculum Coll (TN) 533
Tuskegee U (AL) 533
Union Coll (NE) 534
Union U (TN) 534
U at Buffalo, The State University of New York (NY) 536
The U of Akron (OH) 537
The U of Alabama at Birmingham (AL) 537
The U of Arizona (AZ) 538
U of Arkansas for Medical Sciences (AR) 539
U of Bridgeport (CT) 540
U of Central Arkansas (AR) 542
U of Central Florida (FL) 542
U of Central Oklahoma (OK) 542
U of Cincinnati (OH) 543
U of Connecticut (CT) 544
U of Delaware (DE) 544
U of Evansville (IN) 545
The U of Findlay (OH) 545
U of Hartford (CT) 546
U of Hawaii at Manoa (HI) 546
U of Houston (TX) 547
U of Idaho (ID) 547
U of Illinois at Chicago (IL) 547
U of Indianapolis (IN) 548
The U of Iowa (IA) 548
U of Kansas (KS) 549
U of Kentucky (KY) 549
U of Louisville (KY) 550
U of Maine (ME) 550
U of Mary (ND) 551
U of Mary Hardin-Baylor (TX) 551
U of Maryland Eastern Shore (MD) 552
U of Massachusetts Amherst (MA) 552
U of Massachusetts Boston (MA) 553
U of Massachusetts Dartmouth (MA) 553
U of Massachusetts Lowell (MA) 553
U of Michigan (MI) 554
U of Michigan–Flint (MI) 554
U of Minnesota, Twin Cities Campus (MN) 555
U of Mississippi (MS) 555
U of Mississippi Medical Center (MS) 555
U of Missouri–St. Louis (MO) 556
The U of Montana–Missoula (MT) 556
U of Nebraska Medical Center (NE) 557
U of Nevada, Las Vegas (NV) 558
U of Nevada, Reno (NV) 558
U of New England (ME) 558
U of New Haven (CT) 559
U of New Orleans (LA) 559
The U of North Carolina at Chapel Hill (NC) 560
The U of North Carolina at Charlotte (NC) 560
The U of North Carolina at Greensboro (NC) 560
The U of North Carolina at Pembroke (NC) 560
The U of North Carolina at Wilmington (NC) 561
U of North Dakota (ND) 561
U of Northern Colorado (CO) 561
U of North Texas (TX) 562
U of Pittsburgh (PA) 569
U of Pittsburgh at Johnstown (PA) 570
U of Rhode Island (RI) 572
U of Rio Grande (OH) 572
U of St. Francis (IL) 573
U of Saint Francis (IN) 573
The U of Scranton (PA) 574
U of Sioux Falls (SD) 574
U of South Alabama (AL) 575
The U of South Dakota (SD) 575
U of Southern Mississippi (MS) 576
U of South Florida (FL) 576
The U of Tennessee (TN) 577
The U of Tennessee at Chattanooga (TN) 577
The U of Texas at Arlington (TX) 577
The U of Texas at Austin (TX) 578
The U of Texas at El Paso (TX) 578
The U of Texas at San Antonio (TX) 578
The U of Texas at Tyler (TX) 579
U of Texas Medical Branch at Galveston (TX) 579
The U of Texas–Pan American (TX) 579
U of the District of Columbia (DC) 580
U of the Incarnate Word (TX) 580
U of the Sciences in Philadelphia (PA) 580
U of Toledo (OH) 581
U of Utah (UT) 582
U of Vermont (VT) 582
The U of Virginia's Coll at Wise (VA) 582
U of Washington (WA) 583
U of West Florida (FL) 583
U of Wisconsin–La Crosse (WI) 584
U of Wisconsin–Madison (WI) 584
U of Wisconsin–Milwaukee (WI) 585
U of Wisconsin–Oshkosh (WI) 585
U of Wisconsin–Stevens Point (WI) 585
Utah State U (UT) 587
Virginia Commonwealth U (VA) 590
Walla Walla Coll (WA) 593
Wartburg Coll (IA) 594
Waynesburg Coll (PA) 595
Wayne State Coll (NE) 596
Weber State U (UT) 596
Wesley Coll (DE) 598
Western Carolina U (NC) 598
Western Connecticut State U (CT) 598
Western Illinois U (IL) 599
Western Kentucky U (KY) 599
Western New Mexico U (NM) 600
Westfield State Coll (MA) 600
West Liberty State Coll (WV) 601
West Texas A&M U (TX) 602
West Virginia U (WV) 602
Wichita State U (KS) 604
Wilkes U (PA) 605
William Carey Coll (MS) 605
William Jewell Coll (MO) 606
Winona State U (MN) 608
Winston-Salem State U (NC) 608
Winthrop U (SC) 608
Wright State U (OH) 609
Xavier U (OH) 610
York Coll of Pennsylvania (PA) 610
York Coll of the City U of New York (NY) 611
Youngstown State U (OH) 611

MEDICAL TOXICOLOGY

Overview: Students study how poisons and other harmful biological agents interact with the human body, as well as how to detect, prevent, and counteract them. *Related majors:* medical microbiology, toxicology, premedicine, health/medical laboratory technologies. *Potential careers:* physician, laboratory scientist, emerging pathogen investigator, forensic scientist. *Salary potential:* $35k-$45k.

Northeastern U (MA) 450

MEDICINAL/ PHARMACEUTICAL CHEMISTRY

Overview: This branch of chemistry focuses on the scientific study of creating medical substances for therapeutic purposes. *Related majors:* chemistry, chemical engineering, biochemistry and biophysics, cell biology, toxicology, pharmacology. *Potential careers:* physician, research scientist, pharmacist, biochemist,

MEDICINAL/PHARMACEUTICAL CHEMISTRY (continued)

professor, lab technician. *Salary potential:* $35k-$55k.

Butler U (IN) **297**
Ohio Northern U (OH) **457**
U at Buffalo, The State University of New York (NY) **536**
U of Calif, San Diego (CA) **541**
Worcester Polytechnic Inst (MA) **609**

MEDIEVAL/RENAISSANCE STUDIES

Overview: Students will study the Medieval and Renaissance periods of Europe and the areas surrounding the Mediterranean. *Related majors:* history, archeology, art history, music history and literature, history of philosophy. *Potential careers:* art historian, professor, historian, archeologist, anthropologist, museum curator. *Salary potential:* $24k-$30k.

Bard Coll (NY) **281**
Barnard Coll (NY) **282**
Bates Coll (ME) **282**
Brown U (RI) **296**
Carleton U (ON, Canada) **305**
Cleveland State U (OH) **317**
The Coll of William and Mary (VA) **324**
Columbia Coll (NY) **326**
Connecticut Coll (CT) **331**
Cornell Coll (IA) **332**
Cornell U (NY) **333**
Dickinson Coll (PA) **344**
Duke U (NC) **346**
Emory U (GA) **354**
Fordham U (NY) **362**
Goddard Coll (VT) **369**
Hampshire Coll (MA) **375**
Hanover Coll (IN) **375**
Harvard U (MA) **376**
Hobart and William Smith Colls (NY) **380**
Long Island U, Southampton Coll, Friends World Program (NY) **409**
Marlboro Coll (VT) **418**
Memorial U of Newfoundland (NF, Canada) **424**
Mount Allison U (NB, Canada) **437**
Mount Holyoke Coll (MA) **438**
New Coll of Florida (FL) **444**
New York U (NY) **447**
Ohio Wesleyan U (OH) **459**
Penn State U Univ Park Campus (PA) **468**
Plymouth State Coll (NH) **471**
Queen's U at Kingston (ON, Canada) **476**
Rutgers, The State U of New Jersey, New Brunswick (NJ) **485**
Smith Coll (MA) **506**
Southern Methodist U (TX) **510**
State U of NY at Albany (NY) **514**
State U of NY at Binghamton (NY) **515**
Swarthmore Coll (PA) **521**
Syracuse U (NY) **521**
Tulane U (LA) **533**
U of Calgary (AB, Canada) **540**
U of Calif, Santa Barbara (CA) **541**
U of Chicago (IL) **542**
The U of Iowa (IA) **548**
U of Manitoba (MB, Canada) **551**
U of Michigan (MI) **554**
U of Michigan–Dearborn (MI) **554**
U of Nebraska–Lincoln (NE) **557**
U of Notre Dame (IN) **562**
U of Ottawa (ON, Canada) **563**
U of the South (TN) **581**
U of Toledo (OH) **581**
U of Toronto (ON, Canada) **581**
U of Victoria (BC, Canada) **582**
U of Waterloo (ON, Canada) **583**
Vassar Coll (NY) **589**
Washington and Lee U (VA) **594**
Washington U in St. Louis (MO) **595**
Wellesley Coll (MA) **597**
Wesleyan U (CT) **597**

MENTAL HEALTH/ REHABILITATION

Overview: This major prepares students to help patients with mental or behavioral disorders to improve and maintain or restore functional skills, daily living skills, social and leisure skills, grooming and personal hygiene skills, meal-preparation skills, and support resources and/or medication education. *Related majors:* nursing (psychiatric/mental health), psychiatric/ mental health services technician, occupational therapy, psychology. *Potential careers:* mental health/ rehabilitation therapist or counselor, psychiatric/mental health services technician, psychologist. *Salary potential:* $25k-$35k.

Brandon U (MB, Canada) **293**
Elmira Coll (NY) **351**
Evangel U (MO) **355**
Governors State U (IL) **370**
Louisiana State U Health Sciences Center (LA) **410**
Morgan State U (MD) **436**
Newman U (KS) **445**
Northern Kentucky U (KY) **451**
Pittsburg State U (KS) **470**
Prescott Coll (AZ) **474**
St. Cloud State U (MN) **488**
Springfield Coll (MA) **514**
Thomas Edison State Coll (NJ) **527**
Tufts U (MA) **533**
U of Maine at Farmington (ME) **550**
U of Puerto Rico, Cayey U Coll (PR) **571**
Wright State U (OH) **609**

MENTAL HEALTH SERVICES RELATED

Information can be found under this major's main heading.

Marymount U (VA) **420**
Old Dominion U (VA) **460**
Pennsylvania Coll of Technology (PA) **467**

METAL/JEWELRY ARTS

Overview: This major teaches students the principles, artistic skills, and techniques for working with metal and designing and creating jewelry. *Related majors:* fine arts, drawing, fashion design/illustration, metallurgy, welding technology, sheet metal worker. *Potential careers:* jewelry designer, costume designer, fine artist, sculpture, product designer. *Salary potential:* $15k-$25k.

Adams State Coll (CO) **260**
Alberta Coll of Art & Design (AB, Canada) **262**
Arcadia U (PA) **271**
Arizona State U (AZ) **271**
Bowling Green State U (OH) **292**
California Coll of Arts and Crafts (CA) **299**
California State U, Long Beach (CA) **301**
The Cleveland Inst of Art (OH) **317**
Col for Creative Studies (MI) **319**
Colorado State U (CO) **325**
Eastern Kentucky U (KY) **348**
Grand Valley State U (MI) **371**
Indiana U Bloomington (IN) **385**
Long Island U, Southampton Coll, Friends World Program (NY) **409**
Loyola U Chicago (IL) **411**
Maine Coll of Art (ME) **415**
Massachusetts Coll of Art (MA) **421**
Memphis Coll of Art (TN) **425**
Northern Michigan U (MI) **451**
Northwest Missouri State U (MO) **454**
Nova Scotia Coll of Art and Design (NS, Canada) **455**
Pratt Inst (NY) **473**
Rhode Island School of Design (RI) **479**
Rochester Inst of Technology (NY) **482**
Savannah Coll of Art and Design (GA) **499**
School of the Museum of Fine Arts (MA) **501**
Seton Hill U (PA) **502**
Simon's Rock Coll of Bard (MA) **505**
State U of NY at New Paltz (NY) **515**
State U of NY Coll at Brockport (NY) **515**
Syracuse U (NY) **521**
Temple U (PA) **523**
Texas Woman's U (TX) **527**
The U of Akron (OH) **537**
The U of Iowa (IA) **548**
U of Massachusetts Dartmouth (MA) **553**
U of Michigan (MI) **554**
U of North Texas (TX) **562**
U of Oregon (OR) **562**
U of Washington (WA) **583**
U of Wisconsin–Milwaukee (WI) **585**

METALLURGICAL ENGINEERING

Overview: Students learn the science behind the physical structure of metal components that are used in various load-bearing, power, transmission and moving functions. *Related majors:* structural engineering, electrical engineering, metallurgy, chemistry. *Potential careers:* structural engineer, quality assurance manager, manufacturing specialist, Naval or Air Force officer. *Salary potential:* $35k-$50k.

Colorado School of Mines (CO) **325**
Dalhousie U (NS, Canada) **336**
Harvard U (MA) **376**
Illinois Inst of Technology (IL) **384**
Iowa State U of Science and Technology (IA) **390**
Laurentian U (ON, Canada) **403**
McGill U (QC, Canada) **423**
Michigan Technological U (MI) **428**
Montana Tech of The U of Montana (MT) **435**
New Mexico Inst of Mining and Technology (NM) **446**
The Ohio State U (OH) **457**
Oregon State U (OR) **462**
Penn State U Univ Park Campus (PA) **468**
South Dakota School of Mines and Technology (SD) **507**
Université Laval (QC, Canada) **536**
The U of Alabama (AL) **537**
U of Alberta (AB, Canada) **538**
The U of British Columbia (BC, Canada) **540**
U of Cincinnati (OH) **543**
U of Idaho (ID) **547**
U of Michigan (MI) **554**
U of Missouri–Rolla (MO) **556**
U of Nevada, Reno (NV) **558**
U of Pittsburgh (PA) **569**
The U of Texas at El Paso (TX) **578**
U of Toronto (ON, Canada) **581**
U of Utah (UT) **582**
U of Washington (WA) **583**
U of Wisconsin–Madison (WI) **584**

METALLURGICAL TECHNOLOGY

Overview: Students learn the different ways that metals and metallurgy are applied to industrial and manufacturing processes. *Related majors:* industrial and manufacturing technology, engineering design, metallurgy, welding technology. *Potential careers:* tool and die technologist, metallurgist, logistics and materials management. *Salary potential:* $25k-$34k.

U of Cincinnati (OH) **543**

METALLURGY

Overview: Students who choose this major will study the formation, structure, behavior (including chemical), and technology of metals. *Related majors:* physics, chemistry, geology, mining and mineral engineering, materials engineering. *Potential careers:* metallurgist, mining engineer, research scientist, industrial and structural engineer. *Salary potential:* $35k-$45k.

Eastern Michigan U (MI) **348**
U of Toronto (ON, Canada) **581**
Worcester Polytechnic Inst (MA) **609**

MEXICAN-AMERICAN STUDIES

Overview: Undergraduates study the history, sociology, politics, culture, and economics of people of Mexican origin who are living either in the United States or Canada. *Related majors:* Spanish, economics, political science, immigration. *Potential careers:* lawyer, editor, social worker, immigration specialist, economist. *Salary potential:* $25k-$30k.

California State U, Dominguez Hills (CA) **300**
California State U, Fresno (CA) **301**
California State U, Hayward (CA) **301**
California State U, Long Beach (CA) **301**
California State U, Northridge (CA) **301**
California State U, San Bernardino (CA) **302**
Claremont McKenna Coll (CA) **315**
Concordia U at Austin (TX) **331**
The Evergreen State Coll (WA) **355**
Hampshire Coll (MA) **375**
Long Island U, Southampton Coll, Friends World Program (NY) **409**
Loyola Marymount U (CA) **411**
Metropolitan State Coll of Denver (CO) **427**
Our Lady of the Lake U of San Antonio (TX) **463**
Pitzer Coll (CA) **471**
Pomona Coll (CA) **472**
San Francisco State U (CA) **498**
Scripps Coll (CA) **501**
Southern Methodist U (TX) **510**
Stanford U (CA) **514**
Sul Ross State U (TX) **521**
U of Calif, Davis (CA) **540**
U of Calif, Los Angeles (CA) **541**
U of Calif, Riverside (CA) **541**
U of Calif, Santa Barbara (CA) **541**
U of Michigan (MI) **554**
U of Minnesota, Twin Cities Campus (MN) **555**
U of Southern California (CA) **576**
The U of Texas at El Paso (TX) **578**
The U of Texas–Pan American (TX) **579**
U of Washington (WA) **583**

MICROBIOLOGY/ BACTERIOLOGY

Overview: Students who choose this major will study microbes and bacteria that are the cause of most illness in humans. *Related majors:* toxicology, pathology, medicinal chemistry, bioengineering, environmental biology. *Potential careers:* research scientist, physician, biochemist, virologist. *Salary potential:* $25k-$35k.

Arizona State U (AZ) **271**
Auburn U (AL) **276**
Ball State U (IN) **280**
Bowling Green State U (OH) **292**
Brigham Young U (UT) **295**
California Polytechnic State U, San Luis Obispo (CA) **300**
California State Polytechnic U, Pomona (CA) **300**
California State U, Chico (CA) **300**
California State U, Dominguez Hills (CA) **300**
California State U, Fresno (CA) **301**
California State U, Long Beach (CA) **301**
California State U, Northridge (CA) **301**
Central Michigan U (MI) **310**
Colorado State U (CO) **325**
Cornell U (NY) **333**
Dalhousie U (NS, Canada) **336**
Duquesne U (PA) **346**

Eastern Kentucky U (KY) ***348***
Eastern Washington U (WA) ***349***
The Evergreen State Coll (WA) ***355***
Framingham State Coll (MA) ***362***
Hampshire Coll (MA) ***375***
Harvard U (MA) ***376***
Humboldt State U (CA) ***382***
Idaho State U (ID) ***384***
Indiana U Bloomington (IN) ***385***
Inter American U of PR, San Germán Campus (PR) ***388***
Iowa State U of Science and Technology (IA) ***390***
Juniata Coll (PA) ***395***
Kansas State U (KS) ***396***
McGill U (QC, Canada) ***423***
Memorial U of Newfoundland (NF, Canada) ***424***
Miami U (OH) ***428***
Michigan State U (MI) ***428***
Michigan Technological U (MI) ***428***
Minnesota State U, Mankato (MN) ***431***
Mississippi State U (MS) ***432***
Missouri Southern State Coll (MO) ***433***
Montana State U–Bozeman (MT) ***434***
New Mexico State U (NM) ***446***
North Carolina State U (NC) ***449***
North Dakota State U (ND) ***449***
Northeastern State U (OK) ***450***
Northern Arizona U (AZ) ***450***
Northern Michigan U (MI) ***451***
The Ohio State U (OH) ***457***
Ohio U (OH) ***458***
Ohio Wesleyan U (OH) ***459***
Oklahoma State U (OK) ***460***
Oregon State U (OR) ***462***
Penn State U Univ Park Campus (PA) ***468***
Pomona Coll (CA) ***472***
Purdue U Calumet (IN) ***475***
Quinnipiac U (CT) ***476***
Rutgers, The State U of New Jersey, New Brunswick (NJ) ***485***
St. Cloud State U (MN) ***488***
San Diego State U (CA) ***498***
San Francisco State U (CA) ***498***
San Jose State U (CA) ***499***
Sonoma State U (CA) ***506***
South Dakota State U (SD) ***507***
Southern Connecticut State U (CT) ***509***
Southern Illinois U Carbondale (IL) ***509***
Southwest Texas State U (TX) ***513***
Texas A&M U (TX) ***524***
Texas Tech U (TX) ***526***
Université de Sherbrooke (QC, Canada) ***536***
Université Laval (QC, Canada) ***536***
The U of Akron (OH) ***537***
The U of Alabama (AL) ***537***
U of Alberta (AB, Canada) ***538***
The U of Arizona (AZ) ***538***
U of Arkansas (AR) ***539***
The U of British Columbia (BC, Canada) ***540***
U of Calif, Davis (CA) ***540***
U of Calif, Los Angeles (CA) ***541***
U of Calif, San Diego (CA) ***541***
U of Calif, Santa Barbara (CA) ***541***
U of Central Florida (FL) ***542***
U of Cincinnati (OH) ***543***
U of Florida (FL) ***545***
U of Georgia (GA) ***545***
U of Great Falls (MT) ***545***
U of Guelph (ON, Canada) ***546***
U of Hawaii at Manoa (HI) ***546***
U of Houston–Downtown (TX) ***547***
U of Idaho (ID) ***547***
U of Illinois at Urbana–Champaign (IL) ***548***
The U of Iowa (IA) ***548***
U of Kansas (KS) ***549***
U of King's Coll (NS, Canada) ***549***
U of Louisiana at Lafayette (LA) ***550***
U of Maine (ME) ***550***
U of Manitoba (MB, Canada) ***551***
U of Maryland, Coll Park (MD) ***552***
U of Massachusetts Amherst (MA) ***552***
The U of Memphis (TN) ***553***
U of Michigan (MI) ***554***
U of Michigan–Dearborn (MI) ***554***
U of Minnesota, Twin Cities Campus (MN) ***555***
U of Missouri–Columbia (MO) ***555***
The U of Montana–Missoula (MT) ***556***
U of New Brunswick Fredericton (NB, Canada) ***558***
U of New Hampshire (NH) ***558***
U of Oklahoma (OK) ***562***
U of Ottawa (ON, Canada) ***563***
U of Pittsburgh (PA) ***569***
U of Puerto Rico at Arecibo (PR) ***570***
U of Puerto Rico, Humacao U Coll (PR) ***570***
U of Rhode Island (RI) ***572***
U of Rochester (NY) ***573***
U of Saskatchewan (SK, Canada) ***574***
U of South Florida (FL) ***576***
The U of Tennessee (TN) ***577***
The U of Texas at Arlington (TX) ***577***
The U of Texas at Austin (TX) ***578***
The U of Texas at El Paso (TX) ***578***
U of the Sciences in Philadelphia (PA) ***580***
U of Toronto (ON, Canada) ***581***
U of Vermont (VT) ***582***
U of Victoria (BC, Canada) ***582***
U of Washington (WA) ***583***
The U of Western Ontario (ON, Canada) ***583***
U of Windsor (ON, Canada) ***584***
U of Wisconsin–La Crosse (WI) ***584***
U of Wisconsin–Madison (WI) ***584***
U of Wisconsin–Oshkosh (WI) ***585***
U of Wyoming (WY) ***586***
Utah State U (UT) ***587***
Wagner Coll (NY) ***592***
Washington State U (WA) ***595***
Weber State U (UT) ***596***
West Chester U of Pennsylvania (PA) ***598***
Wittenberg U (OH) ***608***
Worcester Polytechnic Inst (MA) ***609***
Xavier U of Louisiana (LA) ***610***

MIDDLE EASTERN STUDIES

Overview: This major teaches students about the history, society, politics, culture, economics, and languages of the people of what is commonly referred to the Middle East (North Africa, Southwestern Asia, Asia Minor, and the Arabian peninsula). *Related majors:* Islamic studies, Arabic, Semitic languages, history, Judaic studies. *Potential careers:* anthropologist, archeologist, translator, diplomat, business consultant. *Salary potential:* $22k-$28k.

American U (DC) ***267***
The American U in Cairo(Egypt) ***267***
Baltimore Hebrew U (MD) ***280***
Barnard Coll (NY) ***282***
Brandeis U (MA) ***293***
Brigham Young U (UT) ***295***
Brown U (RI) ***296***
Carleton U (ON, Canada) ***305***
Coll of the Holy Cross (MA) ***323***
Columbia Coll (NY) ***326***
Columbia International U (SC) ***327***
Columbia U, School of General Studies (NY) ***328***
Cornell U (NY) ***333***
Dartmouth Coll (NH) ***337***
Emory & Henry Coll (VA) ***353***
Fordham U (NY) ***362***
The George Washington U (DC) ***367***
Hampshire Coll (MA) ***375***
Harvard U (MA) ***376***
Indiana U Bloomington (IN) ***385***
Johns Hopkins U (MD) ***392***
Long Island U, Southampton Coll, Friends World Program (NY) ***409***
McGill U (QC, Canada) ***423***
New York U (NY) ***447***
Oberlin Coll (OH) ***456***
The Ohio State U (OH) ***457***
Portland State U (OR) ***472***
Princeton U (NJ) ***474***
Queens Coll of the City U of NY (NY) ***475***
Rutgers, The State U of New Jersey, New Brunswick (NJ) ***485***
Smith Coll (MA) ***506***
Southwest Texas State U (TX) ***513***
United States Military Academy (NY) ***535***
The U of Arizona (AZ) ***538***
U of Arkansas (AR) ***539***
U of Calif, Berkeley (CA) ***540***
U of Calif, Los Angeles (CA) ***541***
U of Calif, Santa Barbara (CA) ***541***
U of Chicago (IL) ***542***
U of Connecticut (CT) ***544***
U of Massachusetts Amherst (MA) ***552***
U of Michigan (MI) ***554***
U of Minnesota, Twin Cities Campus (MN) ***555***
The U of Texas at Austin (TX) ***578***
U of Toledo (OH) ***581***
U of Toronto (ON, Canada) ***581***
U of Utah (UT) ***582***
U of Washington (WA) ***583***
Washington U in St. Louis (MO) ***595***

MIDDLE SCHOOL EDUCATION

Overview: Undergraduates learn the skills necessary to teach students in the middle, intermediate, or junior high grade levels (grades 4-9). *Related majors:* education, educational psychology, counselor education and guidance, school psychology. *Potential careers:* middle school teacher, private teaching aid, middle school administrator. *Salary potential:* $25k-$34k.

Albany State U (GA) ***262***
Alverno Coll (WI) ***265***
American International Coll (MA) ***267***
Antioch Coll (OH) ***269***
Appalachian State U (NC) ***270***
Arkansas State U (AR) ***272***
Arkansas Tech U (AR) ***272***
Asbury Coll (KY) ***274***
Ashland U (OH) ***274***
Augusta State U (GA) ***277***
Avila U (MO) ***278***
Baldwin-Wallace Coll (OH) ***280***
Barton Coll (NC) ***282***
Bellarmine U (KY) ***284***
Bennett Coll (NC) ***286***
Berea Coll (KY) ***286***
Berry Coll (GA) ***287***
Bethel Coll (IN) ***288***
Black Hills State U (SD) ***290***
Bluefield Coll (VA) ***291***
Bowling Green State U (OH) ***292***
Brandon U (MB, Canada) ***293***
Brenau U (GA) ***293***
Brescia U (KY) ***293***
Brewton-Parker Coll (GA) ***294***
Bridgewater State Coll (MA) ***294***
Bryan Coll (TN) ***296***
Campbell U (NC) ***303***
Canisius Coll (NY) ***304***
Carthage Coll (WI) ***306***
Catawba Coll (NC) ***307***
Cedar Crest Coll (PA) ***308***
Centenary Coll of Louisiana (LA) ***308***
Central Methodist Coll (MO) ***309***
Central Missouri State U (MO) ***310***
Chadron State Coll (NE) ***311***
Christopher Newport U (VA) ***313***
Clark Atlanta U (GA) ***315***
Clarke Coll (IA) ***315***
Clark U (MA) ***316***
Clayton Coll & State U (GA) ***316***
Coastal Carolina U (SC) ***318***
Coker Coll (SC) ***318***
Coll of Mount St. Joseph (OH) ***320***
Coll of Mount Saint Vincent (NY) ***320***
Coll of the Atlantic (ME) ***323***
Coll of the Ozarks (MO) ***323***
Coll of the Southwest (NM) ***324***
Colorado State U-Pueblo (CO) ***325***
Columbia Coll (MO) ***326***
Columbus State U (GA) ***328***
Concordia Coll (NY) ***329***
Concordia U (MN) ***330***
Concordia U (NE) ***330***
Concordia U Wisconsin (WI) ***331***
Cumberland Coll (KY) ***335***
East Carolina U (NC) ***347***
Eastern Illinois U (IL) ***348***
Eastern Kentucky U (KY) ***348***
Eastern Mennonite U (VA) ***348***
Eastern Nazarene Coll (MA) ***348***
Elmira Coll (NY) ***351***
Elon U (NC) ***352***
Emmanuel Coll (GA) ***353***
Fitchburg State Coll (MA) ***358***
Fontbonne U (MO) ***361***
The Franciscan U (IA) ***363***
Georgia Coll & State U (GA) ***367***
Georgia Southern U (GA) ***367***
Georgia Southwestern State U (GA) ***368***
Georgia State U (GA) ***368***
Goddard Coll (VT) ***369***
Governors State U (IL) ***370***
Grace U (NE) ***371***
Grand View Coll (IA) ***372***
Greensboro Coll (NC) ***372***
Hampton U (VA) ***375***
Harris-Stowe State Coll (MO) ***376***
Henderson State U (AR) ***378***
High Point U (NC) ***379***
Idaho State U (ID) ***384***
Illinois State U (IL) ***384***
Indiana Wesleyan U (IN) ***387***
Ithaca Coll (NY) ***390***
Jacksonville State U (AL) ***390***
John Brown U (AR) ***392***
Johnson Bible Coll (TN) ***394***
Johnson State Coll (VT) ***394***
Judson Coll (AL) ***395***
Kennesaw State U (GA) ***397***
Kent State U (OH) ***397***
Kentucky Christian Coll (KY) ***397***
Kentucky Wesleyan Coll (KY) ***397***
King Coll (TN) ***398***
LaGrange Coll (GA) ***400***
Lakeland Coll (WI) ***401***
Lambuth U (TN) ***401***
Lesley U (MA) ***405***
Lindenwood U (MO) ***407***
Lipscomb U (TN) ***408***
Long Island U, Southampton Coll, Friends World Program (NY) ***409***
Lourdes Coll (OH) ***411***
Luther Coll (IA) ***412***
Lynn U (FL) ***413***
Malone Coll (OH) ***415***
Manhattan Coll (NY) ***416***
Marian Coll of Fond du Lac (WI) ***417***
Marquette U (WI) ***418***
Marymount Coll of Fordham U (NY) ***419***
Maryville U of Saint Louis (MO) ***420***
Massachusetts Coll of Liberal Arts (MA) ***421***
The Master's Coll and Seminary (CA) ***422***
Medaille Coll (NY) ***424***
Memorial U of Newfoundland (NF, Canada) ***424***
Mercer U (GA) ***425***
Merrimack Coll (MA) ***426***
Mesa State Coll (CO) ***426***
Miami U (OH) ***428***
MidAmerica Nazarene U (KS) ***428***
Midland Lutheran Coll (NE) ***429***
Midway Coll (KY) ***429***
Minnesota State U, Moorhead (MN) ***432***
Missouri Southern State Coll (MO) ***433***
Morehead State U (KY) ***436***
Morehouse Coll (GA) ***436***
Mount Mercy Coll (IA) ***438***
Mount Olive Coll (NC) ***439***
Mount Union Coll (OH) ***440***
Mount Vernon Nazarene U (OH) ***440***
Murray State U (KY) ***440***
Nebraska Wesleyan U (NE) ***443***
New York U (NY) ***447***
Nicholls State U (LA) ***447***
North Carolina Central U (NC) ***448***
North Carolina Wesleyan Coll (NC) ***449***
Northern Kentucky U (KY) ***451***
North Georgia Coll & State U (GA) ***451***
Northland Coll (WI) ***452***
Northwest Coll (WA) ***452***
Northwest Missouri State U (MO) ***454***
Oakland City U (IN) ***456***
Oglethorpe U (GA) ***457***
Ohio Dominican U (OH) ***457***
Ohio Northern U (OH) ***457***
Otterbein Coll (OH) ***462***
Ouachita Baptist U (AR) ***462***
Peru State Coll (NE) ***469***
Piedmont Coll (GA) ***470***
Pikeville Coll (KY) ***470***
Prescott Coll (AZ) ***474***
Reinhardt Coll (GA) ***478***
Rhode Island Coll (RI) ***479***
Sacred Heart U (CT) ***486***
St. Cloud State U (MN) ***488***
St. John's U (NY) ***490***
Southwest Baptist U (MO) ***512***
Southwest Missouri State U (MO) ***513***
Springfield Coll (MA) ***514***

MIDDLE SCHOOL EDUCATION (continued)

State U of NY Coll at Cortland (NY) **516**
State U of NY Coll at Old Westbury (NY) **516**
State U of West Georgia (GA) **518**
Syracuse U (NY) **521**
Taylor U (IN) **523**
Texas Christian U (TX) **526**
Texas Lutheran U (TX) **526**
Thomas More Coll (KY) **528**
Thomas U (GA) **528**
Transylvania U (KY) **529**
Trinity Christian Coll (IL) **530**
Tusculum Coll (TN) **533**
Union Coll (KY) **533**
The U of Akron (OH) **537**
U of Arkansas (AR) **539**
U of Central Arkansas (AR) **542**
U of Delaware (DE) **544**
U of Georgia (GA) **545**
U of Great Falls (MT) **545**
U of Kansas (KS) **549**
U of Kentucky (KY) **549**
U of Louisville (KY) **550**
U of Maine at Machias (ME) **551**
U of Michigan–Dearborn (MI) **554**
U of Minnesota, Duluth (MN) **554**
U of Missouri–Columbia (MO) **555**
U of Missouri–St. Louis (MO) **556**
U of Nebraska–Lincoln (NE) **557**
The U of North Carolina at Chapel Hill (NC) **560**
The U of North Carolina at Charlotte (NC) **560**
The U of North Carolina at Greensboro (NC) **560**
The U of North Carolina at Wilmington (NC) **561**
U of North Dakota (ND) **561**
U of Northern Iowa (IA) **561**
U of North Florida (FL) **561**
U of Regina (SK, Canada) **572**
U of Richmond (VA) **572**
U of Sioux Falls (SD) **574**
The U of South Dakota (SD) **575**
U of the Ozarks (AR) **580**
U of Vermont (VT) **582**
U of West Florida (FL) **583**
U of Wisconsin–Platteville (WI) **585**
Upper Iowa U (IA) **587**
Urbana U (OH) **587**
Ursuline Coll (OH) **587**
Valdosta State U (GA) **588**
Villa Julie Coll (MD) **590**
Virginia Wesleyan Coll (VA) **591**
Viterbo U (WI) **591**
Wagner Coll (NY) **592**
Warner Pacific Coll (OR) **593**
Washington U in St. Louis (MO) **595**
Webster U (MO) **597**
Wesleyan Coll (GA) **597**
Western Carolina U (NC) **598**
Western Kentucky U (KY) **599**
Westminster Coll (MO) **601**
West Virginia Wesleyan Coll (WV) **603**
Wheeling Jesuit U (WV) **603**
William Woods U (MO) **607**
Wingate U (NC) **607**
Winona State U (MN) **608**
Winston-Salem State U (NC) **608**
Wittenberg U (OH) **608**
Xavier U (OH) **610**
Xavier U of Louisiana (LA) **610**
York Coll (NE) **610**
York U (ON, Canada) **611**
Youngstown State U (OH) **611**

MILITARY STUDIES

Overview: This major focuses on the history of the armed services and the science and theory of military conflict and related politics and technologies. *Related majors:* Air Force ROTC, Army ROTC, Navy ROTC, military technologies, peace and conflict studies. *Potential careers:* armed service officer, military contractor, historian. *Salary potential:* $25k-$30k.

Hawai'i Pacific U (HI) **377**
Texas Christian U (TX) **526**
United States Air Force Academy (CO) **534**

MILITARY TECHNOLOGY

Overview: Students will learn specialized management skills and technology responsibilities for use in the armed services and other national security organizations. *Potential careers:* officer in the arms services, military analyst, operations research, CIA operative, military planner, national security agent. *Salary potential:* $28k-$35k.

U of Idaho (ID) **547**

MINING/MINERAL ENGINEERING

Overview: This major teaches students the science behind mineral extraction, processing, and refining. *Related majors:* structural engineering, geophysical and geological engineering, metallurgy, geophysics, and seismology. *Potential careers:* construction manager, mining company executive, geological engineer, petroleum engineer. *Salary potential:* $40k-$45k.

Colorado School of Mines (CO) **325**
Dalhousie U (NS, Canada) **336**
Laurentian U (ON, Canada) **403**
McGill U (QC, Canada) **423**
Michigan Technological U (MI) **428**
Montana Tech of The U of Montana (MT) **435**
New Mexico Inst of Mining and Technology (NM) **446**
Oregon State U (OR) **462**
Penn State U Univ Park Campus (PA) **468**
Queen's U at Kingston (ON, Canada) **476**
South Dakota School of Mines and Technology (SD) **507**
Southern Illinois U Carbondale (IL) **509**
Université Laval (QC, Canada) **536**
U of Alberta (AB, Canada) **538**
The U of Arizona (AZ) **538**
The U of British Columbia (BC, Canada) **540**
U of Idaho (ID) **547**
U of Kentucky (KY) **549**
U of Missouri–Rolla (MO) **556**
U of Nevada, Reno (NV) **558**
U of Utah (UT) **582**
U of Wisconsin–Madison (WI) **584**
Virginia Polytechnic Inst and State U (VA) **591**
West Virginia U (WV) **602**

MINING/PETROLEUM TECHNOLOGIES RELATED

Information can be found under this major's main heading.

U of Alaska Fairbanks (AK) **538**

MINING TECHNOLOGY

Overview: This major gives students the technical knowledge and skills necessary to work in the development and operation of mines and related processing facilities. *Related majors:* geology, surveying, mineral engineering, metallurgy, cartography. *Potential careers:* mining site analyst, research scientist, environmentalist, safety inspector, geologist. *Salary potential:* $25k-$35k.

Bluefield State Coll (WV) **291**

MISSIONARY STUDIES

Overview: Students will learn the theory and practice of religious outreach, social service and proselytization, preparing them for possible careers as missionaries or related vocations. *Related majors:* psychology, religious education, divinity/ministry, pastoral counseling, cultural and area studies. *Potential careers:* missionary, clergy, social worker. *Salary potential:* $18k-$30k.

Abilene Christian U (TX) **260**
Alaska Bible Coll (AK) **261**
Asbury Coll (KY) **274**
Bethel Coll (IN) **288**
Bethesda Christian U (CA) **288**
Biola U (CA) **289**
Briercrest Bible Coll (SK, Canada) **295**
Canadian Bible Coll (AB, Canada) **303**
Cascade Coll (OR) **307**
Cedarville U (OH) **308**
Central Christian Coll of Kansas (KS) **309**
Circleville Bible Coll (OH) **314**
Columbia Bible Coll (BC, Canada) **326**
Crown Coll (MN) **334**
Eastern U (PA) **349**
Emmaus Bible Coll (IA) **353**
Eugene Bible Coll (OR) **355**
Faith Baptist Bible Coll and Theological Seminary (IA) **356**
Freed-Hardeman U (TN) **364**
George Fox U (OR) **366**
Global U of the Assemblies of God (MO) **368**
God's Bible School and Coll (OH) **369**
Grace U (NE) **371**
Harding U (AR) **375**
Hillsdale Free Will Baptist Coll (OK) **379**
Hope International U (CA) **381**
John Brown U (AR) **392**
Kentucky Mountain Bible Coll (KY) **397**
LeTourneau U (TX) **405**
Manhattan Christian Coll (KS) **415**
Master's Coll and Seminary (ON, Canada) **422**
MidAmerica Nazarene U (KS) **428**
Mid-Continent Coll (KY) **429**
Moody Bible Inst (IL) **435**
Multnomah Bible Coll and Biblical Seminary (OR) **440**
Northwest Christian Coll (OR) **452**
Northwestern Coll (MN) **453**
Northwest Nazarene U (ID) **454**
Nyack Coll (NY) **456**
Oak Hills Christian Coll (MN) **456**
Oklahoma Baptist U (OK) **459**
Oklahoma Christian U (OK) **459**
Oral Roberts U (OK) **461**
Reformed Bible Coll (MI) **477**
Simpson Coll and Graduate School (CA) **505**
Southeastern Coll of the Assemblies of God (FL) **507**
Southern Methodist Coll (SC) **510**
Southern Nazarene U (OK) **510**
Southwestern Assemblies of God U (TX) **512**
Toccoa Falls Coll (GA) **528**
Trinity Baptist Coll (FL) **530**
Trinity Western U (BC, Canada) **531**

MODERN LANGUAGES

Overview: Students who choose this major study two or more languages, often in conjunction with courses in linguistics. *Related majors:* specific language studies, linguistics. *Potential careers:* editor, diplomatic corps, interpreter, teacher, advertising executive. *Salary potential:* $20k-$28k.

Albion Coll (MI) **262**
Alfred U (NY) **263**
Alma Coll (MI) **264**
Atlantic Union Coll (MA) **276**
Ball State U (IN) **280**
Bard Coll (NY) **281**
Beloit Coll (WI) **285**
Bemidji State U (MN) **285**
Benedictine Coll (KS) **285**
Bennington Coll (VT) **286**
Bishop's U (QC, Canada) **289**
Blue Mountain Coll (MS) **291**
Brooklyn Coll of the City U of NY (NY) **295**
Buena Vista U (IA) **297**
Carleton U (ON, Canada) **305**
Carnegie Mellon U (PA) **305**
Carthage Coll (WI) **306**
Claremont McKenna Coll (CA) **315**
Clark U (MA) **316**
Coll of Mount Saint Vincent (NY) **320**
The Coll of New Rochelle (NY) **321**
Coll of Notre Dame of Maryland (MD) **321**
The Coll of William and Mary (VA) **324**
Concordia U (QC, Canada) **331**
Converse Coll (SC) **332**
Cornell Coll (IA) **332**
Cornell U (NY) **333**
Creighton U (NE) **333**
DePaul U (IL) **339**
Dillard U (LA) **344**
Eastern Washington U (WA) **349**
Eckerd Coll (FL) **350**
Elizabethtown Coll (PA) **351**
Elmira Coll (NY) **351**
Fairfield U (CT) **356**
Fordham U (NY) **362**
Fort Lewis Coll (CO) **362**
Framingham State Coll (MA) **362**
Franklin Coll Switzerland(Switzerland) **364**
Gannon U (PA) **365**
Georgia Inst of Technology (GA) **367**
Gettysburg Coll (PA) **368**
Gordon Coll (MA) **370**
Greenville Coll (IL) **373**
Grove City Coll (PA) **373**
Hamilton Coll (NY) **374**
Hampton U (VA) **375**
Harvard U (MA) **376**
Hastings Coll (NE) **377**
Hobart and William Smith Colls (NY) **380**
Howard Payne U (TX) **382**
Immaculata U (PA) **385**
Iona Coll (NY) **390**
Judson Coll (AL) **395**
Kenyon Coll (OH) **398**
King Coll (TN) **398**
Lake Erie Coll (OH) **400**
Lambuth U (TN) **401**
La Salle U (PA) **402**
Laurentian U (ON, Canada) **403**
Lee U (TN) **404**
Lenoir-Rhyne Coll (NC) **405**
Lewis & Clark Coll (OR) **405**
Long Island U, Brooklyn Campus (NY) **409**
Long Island U, Southampton Coll, Friends World Program (NY) **409**
Longwood U (VA) **409**
Louisiana Coll (LA) **410**
Luther Coll (IA) **412**
Marian Coll of Fond du Lac (WI) **417**
Marlboro Coll (VT) **418**
Marymount Coll of Fordham U (NY) **419**
Mary Washington Coll (VA) **420**
McMaster U (ON, Canada) **423**
Merrimack Coll (MA) **426**
MidAmerica Nazarene U (KS) **428**
Middlebury Coll (VT) **429**
Minnesota State U, Mankato (MN) **431**
Mississippi Coll (MS) **432**
Monmouth Coll (IL) **434**
Mount Allison U (NB, Canada) **437**
Mount Saint Vincent U (NS, Canada) **439**
Nazareth Coll of Rochester (NY) **443**
North Central Coll (IL) **449**
Northeastern U (MA) **450**
North Park U (IL) **452**
Oakland U (MI) **456**
Olivet Nazarene U (IL) **461**
Pace U (NY) **463**
Pacific Lutheran U (WA) **463**
Pacific U (OR) **464**
Pomona Coll (CA) **472**
Presbyterian Coll (SC) **473**
Purchase Coll, State U of NY (NY) **475**
Queens Coll of the City U of NY (NY) **475**
Rivier Coll (NH) **480**
St. Bonaventure U (NY) **487**
Saint Francis U (PA) **488**
St. Francis Xavier U (NS, Canada) **489**
Saint Joseph Coll (CT) **490**
St. Lawrence U (NY) **491**
Saint Mary's Coll of California (CA) **494**
St. Mary's Coll of Maryland (MD) **494**
Saint Mary's U (NS, Canada) **494**
Saint Michael's Coll (VT) **494**
St. Thomas Aquinas Coll (NY) **495**
Sarah Lawrence Coll (NY) **499**
Scripps Coll (CA) **501**
Seton Hill U (PA) **502**
Slippery Rock U of Pennsylvania (PA) **506**
Southwestern U (TX) **513**
Stephens Coll (MO) **519**

Suffolk U (MA) **520**
Sweet Briar Coll (VA) **521**
Syracuse U (NY) **521**
Trent U (ON, Canada) **529**
Trinity Coll (CT) **530**
United States Military Academy (NY) **535**
Université Laval (QC, Canada) **536**
U of Alberta (AB, Canada) **538**
U of Chicago (IL) **542**
The U of Lethbridge (AB, Canada) **549**
U of Louisiana at Lafayette (LA) **550**
U of Maine (ME) **550**
U of Maryland, Baltimore County (MD) **552**
U of Missouri–St. Louis (MO) **556**
U of New Brunswick Fredericton (NB, Canada) **558**
U of New Hampshire (NH) **558**
U of Ottawa (ON, Canada) **563**
U of Southern Maine (ME) **576**
U of South Florida (FL) **576**
U of Toronto (ON, Canada) **581**
U of Victoria (BC, Canada) **582**
U of Windsor (ON, Canada) **584**
Ursinus Coll (PA) **587**
Virginia Military Inst (VA) **591**
Walla Walla Coll (WA) **593**
Walsh U (OH) **593**
Washington U in St. Louis (MO) **595**
Wayne State Coll (NE) **596**
West Chester U of Pennsylvania (PA) **598**
Westminster Coll (PA) **601**
Westmont Coll (CA) **602**
Widener U (PA) **604**
William Carey Coll (MS) **605**
Wilmington Coll (OH) **607**
Winthrop U (SC) **608**
Wittenberg U (OH) **608**
Wright State U (OH) **609**
York U (ON, Canada) **611**

MOLECULAR BIOLOGY

Overview: This major includes the study of biological functions and mechanisms at the molecular level. *Related majors:* biophysics, genetics, chemistry, molecular physics. *Potential careers:* geneticist, molecular biologist, research scientist, professor. *Salary potential:* $25k-$32k.

Arizona State U (AZ) **271**
Assumption Coll (MA) **275**
Auburn U (AL) **276**
Ball State U (IN) **280**
Bard Coll (NY) **281**
Beloit Coll (WI) **285**
Benedictine U (IL) **285**
Bethel Coll (MN) **288**
Boston U (MA) **292**
Bradley U (IL) **293**
Bridgewater State Coll (MA) **294**
Brigham Young U (UT) **295**
Brown U (RI) **296**
California Inst of Technology (CA) **299**
California Lutheran U (CA) **299**
California State U, Fresno (CA) **301**
California State U, Northridge (CA) **301**
California State U, San Marcos (CA) **302**
Cedar Crest Coll (PA) **308**
Centre Coll (KY) **310**
Chestnut Hill Coll (PA) **312**
Clarion U of Pennsylvania (PA) **315**
Clarkson U (NY) **316**
Clark U (MA) **316**
Coe Coll (IA) **318**
Colby Coll (ME) **318**
Colgate U (NY) **319**
The Coll of Southeastern Europe, The American U of Athens(Greece) **323**
Concordia U (QC, Canada) **331**
Cornell U (NY) **333**
Dartmouth Coll (NH) **337**
Dickinson Coll (PA) **344**
Elms Coll (MA) **352**
The Evergreen State Coll (WA) **355**
Florida A&M U (FL) **359**
Florida Inst of Technology (FL) **360**
Fort Lewis Coll (CO) **362**
Grove City Coll (PA) **373**
Hamilton Coll (NY) **374**
Hampshire Coll (MA) **375**
Hampton U (VA) **375**
Harvard U (MA) **376**
Humboldt State U (CA) **382**
Juniata Coll (PA) **395**
Kenyon Coll (OH) **398**
Lehigh U (PA) **404**
Long Island U, Brooklyn Campus (NY) **409**
Long Island U, C.W. Post Campus (NY) **409**
Marlboro Coll (VT) **418**
Marquette U (WI) **418**
McGill U (QC, Canada) **423**
McMaster U (ON, Canada) **423**
Meredith Coll (NC) **426**
Middlebury Coll (VT) **429**
Montclair State U (NJ) **435**
Muskingum Coll (OH) **441**
Northwestern U (IL) **453**
Ohio Northern U (OH) **457**
Otterbein Coll (OH) **462**
Penn State U Univ Park Campus (PA) **468**
Pomona Coll (CA) **472**
Princeton U (NJ) **474**
Rutgers, The State U of New Jersey, New Brunswick (NJ) **485**
Salem International U (WV) **496**
San Francisco State U (CA) **498**
San Jose State U (CA) **499**
Scripps Coll (CA) **501**
Southwest Missouri State U (MO) **513**
State U of NY at Albany (NY) **514**
State U of NY Coll at Brockport (NY) **515**
Stetson U (FL) **519**
Texas A&M U (TX) **524**
Texas Lutheran U (TX) **526**
Texas Tech U (TX) **526**
Towson U (MD) **529**
Tulane U (LA) **533**
U Coll of the Cariboo (BC, Canada) **537**
U of Alberta (AB, Canada) **538**
U of Calgary (AB, Canada) **540**
U of Calif, Berkeley (CA) **540**
U of Calif, Los Angeles (CA) **541**
U of Calif, San Diego (CA) **541**
U of Calif, Santa Barbara (CA) **541**
U of Calif, Santa Cruz (CA) **542**
U of Colorado at Boulder (CO) **543**
U of Denver (CO) **544**
U of Guelph (ON, Canada) **546**
U of Idaho (ID) **547**
U of Maine (ME) **550**
The U of Memphis (TN) **553**
U of Michigan (MI) **554**
U of Minnesota, Duluth (MN) **554**
U of New Brunswick Fredericton (NB, Canada) **558**
U of New Hampshire (NH) **558**
U of Pittsburgh (PA) **569**
U of Richmond (VA) **572**
U of Southern California (CA) **576**
The U of Texas at Austin (TX) **578**
U of Toronto (ON, Canada) **581**
U of Vermont (VT) **582**
U of Washington (WA) **583**
U of Wisconsin–Madison (WI) **584**
U of Wisconsin–Parkside (WI) **585**
U of Wisconsin–Superior (WI) **586**
U of Wyoming (WY) **586**
Vanderbilt U (TN) **588**
Wells Coll (NY) **597**
Wesleyan U (CT) **597**
West Chester U of Pennsylvania (PA) **598**
Western State Coll of Colorado (CO) **600**
Western Washington U (WA) **600**
Westminster Coll (PA) **601**
Whitman Coll (WA) **604**
William Jewell Coll (MO) **606**
Winston-Salem State U (NC) **608**
Worcester Polytechnic Inst (MA) **609**
Yale U (CT) **610**
York U (ON, Canada) **611**

MORTUARY SCIENCE

Overview: Undergraduates who choose this major will learn the basic elements of the funeral business, including mortuary science. *Related majors:* anatomy, pathogenic microbiology, family counseling, business administration, pastoral counseling. *Potential careers:* mortician, funeral service director, cemetery director. *Salary potential:* $25k-$30k.

Gannon U (PA) **365**
Lindenwood U (MO) **407**
Mount Ida Coll (MA) **438**
Point Park Coll (PA) **471**
St. John's U (NY) **490**
Southern Illinois U Carbondale (IL) **509**
Thiel Coll (PA) **527**
U of Central Oklahoma (OK) **542**
U of Minnesota, Twin Cities Campus (MN) **555**
U of the District of Columbia (DC) **580**
Wayne State U (MI) **596**

MOVEMENT THERAPY

Overview: This major teaches students how to use functional and expressive integration strategies and techniques to help promote physical and psychophysical awareness in clients. *Related majors:* psychology, counseling, physical therapy, exercise sciences/physiology and movement studies. *Potential careers:* movement therapist, psychologist, therapist. *Salary potential:* $25k-$30k.

Brock U (ON, Canada) **295**

MULTI/INTERDISCIPLINARY STUDIES RELATED

Information can be found under this major's main heading.

Allegheny Coll (PA) **264**
Austin Coll (TX) **277**
Brandeis U (MA) **293**
Caldwell Coll (NJ) **298**
Coll of Saint Elizabeth (NJ) **321**
Dartmouth Coll (NH) **337**
Davidson Coll (NC) **338**
Eastern Illinois U (IL) **348**
Eastern Mennonite U (VA) **348**
Eastern New Mexico U (NM) **349**
East Tennessee State U (TN) **349**
Fairleigh Dickinson U, Teaneck-Metro Campus (NJ) **356**
The Franciscan U (IA) **363**
Grace Bible Coll (MI) **370**
Huntingdon Coll (AL) **383**
Kent State U (OH) **397**
Louisiana State U and A&M Coll (LA) **410**
Marshall U (WV) **418**
Massachusetts Coll of Liberal Arts (MA) **421**
Mercer U (GA) **425**
Mississippi State U (MS) **432**
New York Inst of Technology (NY) **447**
Norfolk State U (VA) **448**
Nova Southeastern U (FL) **455**
Ohio Wesleyan U (OH) **459**
Old Dominion U (VA) **460**
Otterbein Coll (OH) **462**
Penn State U at Erie, The Behrend Coll (PA) **467**
Penn State U Berks Cmps of Berks-Lehigh Valley Coll (PA) **468**
Plymouth State Coll (NH) **471**
Princeton U (NJ) **474**
Rice U (TX) **479**
Rutgers, The State U of New Jersey, Camden (NJ) **485**
Rutgers, The State U of New Jersey, Newark (NJ) **485**
St. Olaf Coll (MN) **495**
San Diego State U (CA) **498**
Shippensburg U of Pennsylvania (PA) **503**
Sonoma State U (CA) **506**
Southwest Texas State U (TX) **513**
State U of NY Coll at Potsdam (NY) **517**
Stephen F. Austin State U (TX) **518**
Stonehill Coll (MA) **520**
Texas Wesleyan U (TX) **526**
U of Alaska Fairbanks (AK) **538**
The U of Arizona (AZ) **538**
U of Arkansas (AR) **539**
U of Colorado at Boulder (CO) **543**
U of Connecticut (CT) **544**
U of Hawaii at Manoa (HI) **546**
U of Idaho (ID) **547**
U of Kentucky (KY) **549**
U of Maryland University Coll (MD) **552**
U of Pennsylvania (PA) **563**
The U of Tennessee (TN) **577**
The U of the Arts (PA) **579**
U of Toledo (OH) **581**
U of Wyoming (WY) **586**
Ursuline Coll (OH) **587**
Utah State U (UT) **587**
Washington U in St. Louis (MO) **595**
Western Kentucky U (KY) **599**
West Texas A&M U (TX) **602**
West Virginia U Inst of Technology (WV) **602**
Wheaton Coll (IL) **603**
Wilkes U (PA) **605**
Yale U (CT) **610**

MULTIMEDIA

Overview: This major teaches students the techniques for creating works of art using a variety of materials and media, including computers, film and video. *Related majors:* fine arts, painting, drawing, sculpture, print making. *Potential careers:* multimedia artist, animator, set designer, creative director, graphic designer. *Salary potential:* $15k-$35k.

American U (DC) **267**
The Art Inst of Portland (OR) **274**
The Art Inst of Washington (VA) **274**
Augusta State U (GA) **277**
Calumet Coll of Saint Joseph (IN) **302**
Champlain Coll (VT) **311**
Columbia Coll Chicago (IL) **327**
Columbus Coll of Art and Design (OH) **328**
Eastern U (PA) **349**
Emerson Coll (MA) **353**
Indiana U of Pennsylvania (PA) **386**
Long Island U, C.W. Post Campus (NY) **409**
Maharishi U of Management (IA) **414**
Maryland Inst Coll of Art (MD) **419**
Massachusetts Coll of Art (MA) **421**
McMaster U (ON, Canada) **423**
Minneapolis Coll of Art and Design (MN) **431**
State U of NY Coll at Fredonia (NY) **516**
U of Calif, San Diego (CA) **541**
U of Central Florida (FL) **542**
U of Massachusetts Dartmouth (MA) **553**
U of Michigan (MI) **554**
U of Puerto Rico, Río Piedras (PR) **571**
U of Windsor (ON, Canada) **584**

MUSEUM STUDIES

Overview: This major will teach students the skills necessary to work in museums or galleries as a curator or other technical/managerial positions. *Related majors:* art history, history, archeology, crafts, folk art and artisanry, design/visual communications, arts management. *Potential careers:* museum curator, art dealer, librarian, professor. *Salary potential:* $20k-$25k.

Baylor U (TX) **283**
Beloit Coll (WI) **285**
Coll of the Atlantic (ME) **323**
Framingham State Coll (MA) **362**
Jewish Theological Seminary of America (NY) **391**
Juniata Coll (PA) **395**
Long Island U, Southampton Coll, Friends World Program (NY) **409**
Luther Coll (IA) **412**
Oklahoma Baptist U (OK) **459**
Randolph-Macon Woman's Coll (VA) **477**
Regis Coll (MA) **478**
Tusculum Coll (TN) **533**
The U of Iowa (IA) **548**
The U of North Carolina at Greensboro (NC) **560**
U of Southern Mississippi (MS) **576**

MUSIC

Overview: Students choosing this general major study a variety of music types, methods, and forms as well as other related performing arts, such as dance. *Related majors:* music

MUSIC (continued)

education teacher, religious/sacred music, music therapy, music history, music theory and composition. *Potential careers:* musician, record company executive, agent, professor or music teacher. *Salary potential:* $10k-$32k.

Abilene Christian U (TX) **260**
Acadia U (NS, Canada) **260**
Adams State Coll (CO) **260**
Adelphi U (NY) **260**
Adrian Coll (MI) **260**
Agnes Scott Coll (GA) **261**
Alabama State U (AL) **261**
Albany State U (GA) **262**
Albertson Coll of Idaho (ID) **262**
Albion Coll (MI) **262**
Albright Coll (PA) **263**
Alderson-Broaddus Coll (WV) **263**
Allegheny Coll (PA) **264**
Allen U (SC) **264**
Alma Coll (MI) **264**
Alverno Coll (WI) **265**
American U (DC) **267**
Amherst Coll (MA) **268**
Anderson Coll (SC) **268**
Andrews U (MI) **269**
Angelo State U (TX) **269**
Anna Maria Coll (MA) **269**
Antioch Coll (OH) **269**
Appalachian State U (NC) **270**
Aquinas Coll (MI) **270**
Arizona State U (AZ) **271**
Arkansas State U (AR) **272**
Arkansas Tech U (AR) **272**
Arlington Baptist Coll (TX) **272**
Armstrong Atlantic State U (GA) **273**
Asbury Coll (KY) **274**
Ashland U (OH) **274**
Atlanta Christian Coll (GA) **275**
Atlantic Union Coll (MA) **276**
Augsburg Coll (MN) **276**
Augustana Coll (IL) **276**
Augustana Coll (SD) **276**
Augusta State U (GA) **277**
Austin Coll (TX) **277**
Austin Peay State U (TN) **278**
Averett U (VA) **278**
Avila U (MO) **278**
Azusa Pacific U (CA) **278**
Baker U (KS) **280**
Baldwin-Wallace Coll (OH) **280**
Ball State U (IN) **280**
Baptist Bible Coll (MO) **281**
Bard Coll (NY) **281**
Barnard Coll (NY) **282**
Bates Coll (ME) **282**
Baylor U (TX) **283**
Belhaven Coll (MS) **283**
Bellarmine U (KY) **284**
Belmont U (TN) **284**
Beloit Coll (WI) **285**
Bemidji State U (MN) **285**
Benedict Coll (SC) **285**
Benedictine Coll (KS) **285**
Benedictine U (IL) **285**
Bennett Coll (NC) **286**
Bennington Coll (VT) **286**
Berea Coll (KY) **286**
Berklee Coll of Music (MA) **286**
Baruch Coll of the City U of NY (NY) **286**
Berry Coll (GA) **287**
Bethany Bible Coll (NB, Canada) **287**
Bethany Coll (KS) **287**
Bethany Coll (WV) **287**
Bethany Lutheran Coll (MN) **288**
Bethel Coll (IN) **288**
Bethel Coll (KS) **288**
Bethel Coll (MN) **288**
Bethune-Cookman Coll (FL) **289**
Biola U (CA) **289**
Birmingham-Southern Coll (AL) **289**
Bishop's U (QC, Canada) **289**
Blackburn Coll (IL) **290**
Black Hills State U (SD) **290**
Bloomsburg U of Pennsylvania (PA) **290**
Bluefield Coll (VA) **291**
Blue Mountain Coll (MS) **291**
Bluffton Coll (OH) **291**
Boston Coll (MA) **292**
Bowdoin Coll (ME) **292**
Bowling Green State U (OH) **292**
Bradley U (IL) **293**
Brandeis U (MA) **293**
Brandon U (MB, Canada) **293**
Brenau U (GA) **293**
Brevard Coll (NC) **294**
Brewton-Parker Coll (GA) **294**
Briar Cliff U (IA) **294**
Bridgewater Coll (VA) **294**
Bridgewater State Coll (MA) **294**
Briercrest Bible Coll (SK, Canada) **295**
Brigham Young U (UT) **295**
Brigham Young U–Hawaii (HI) **295**
Brock U (ON, Canada) **295**
Brooklyn Coll of the City U of NY (NY) **295**
Brown U (RI) **296**
Bryan Coll (TN) **296**
Bryn Mawr Coll (PA) **297**
Bucknell U (PA) **297**
Buena Vista U (IA) **297**
Butler U (IN) **297**
Caldwell Coll (NJ) **298**
California Baptist U (CA) **298**
California Inst of the Arts (CA) **299**
California Lutheran U (CA) **299**
California Polytechnic State U, San Luis Obispo (CA) **300**
California State Polytechnic U, Pomona (CA) **300**
California State U, Bakersfield (CA) **300**
California State U, Chico (CA) **300**
California State U, Dominguez Hills (CA) **300**
California State U, Fresno (CA) **301**
California State U, Fullerton (CA) **301**
California State U, Hayward (CA) **301**
California State U, Long Beach (CA) **301**
California State U, Northridge (CA) **301**
California State U, Sacramento (CA) **301**
California State U, San Bernardino (CA) **302**
California State U, Stanislaus (CA) **302**
Calvin Coll (MI) **303**
Cameron U (OK) **303**
Campbellsville U (KY) **303**
Campbell U (NC) **303**
Canadian Mennonite U (MB, Canada) **304**
Capital U (OH) **304**
Cardinal Stritch U (WI) **305**
Carleton Coll (MN) **305**
Carleton U (ON, Canada) **305**
Carnegie Mellon U (PA) **305**
Carroll Coll (WI) **306**
Carson-Newman Coll (TN) **306**
Carthage Coll (WI) **306**
Case Western Reserve U (OH) **307**
Castleton State Coll (VT) **307**
Catawba Coll (NC) **307**
The Catholic U of America (DC) **307**
Cedar Crest Coll (PA) **308**
Cedarville U (OH) **308**
Centenary Coll of Louisiana (LA) **308**
Central Coll (IA) **309**
Central Connecticut State U (CT) **309**
Central Methodist Coll (MO) **309**
Central Michigan U (MI) **310**
Central Missouri State U (MO) **310**
Central Washington U (WA) **310**
Centre Coll (KY) **310**
Chadron State Coll (NE) **311**
Chapman U (CA) **311**
Charleston Southern U (SC) **311**
Chatham Coll (PA) **312**
Chestnut Hill Coll (PA) **312**
Cheyney U of Pennsylvania (PA) **312**
Chowan Coll (NC) **312**
Christian Heritage Coll (CA) **313**
Christopher Newport U (VA) **313**
City Coll of the City U of NY (NY) **314**
Claflin U (SC) **314**
Claremont McKenna Coll (CA) **315**
Clark Atlanta U (GA) **315**
Clarke Coll (IA) **315**
Clark U (MA) **316**
Clayton Coll & State U (GA) **316**
Clearwater Christian Coll (FL) **316**
Cleveland Inst of Music (OH) **317**
Cleveland State U (OH) **317**
Coastal Carolina U (SC) **318**
Coe Coll (IA) **318**
Coker Coll (SC) **318**
Colby Coll (ME) **318**
Colgate U (NY) **319**
Coll of Charleston (SC) **320**
Coll of Mount St. Joseph (OH) **320**
The Coll of New Jersey (NJ) **320**
Coll of Notre Dame of Maryland (MD) **321**
Coll of Saint Benedict (MN) **321**
Coll of St. Catherine (MN) **321**
Coll of Saint Elizabeth (NJ) **321**
The Coll of Saint Rose (NY) **322**
The Coll of St. Scholastica (MN) **322**
Coll of Santa Fe (NM) **323**
Coll of Staten Island of the City U of NY (NY) **323**
Coll of the Atlantic (ME) **323**
Coll of the Holy Cross (MA) **323**
Coll of the Ozarks (MO) **323**
The Coll of William and Mary (VA) **324**
The Coll of Wooster (OH) **324**
Colorado Christian U (CO) **325**
The Colorado Coll (CO) **325**
Colorado State U (CO) **325**
Colorado State U-Pueblo (CO) **325**
Columbia Coll (NY) **326**
Columbia Coll (SC) **327**
Columbia Coll Chicago (IL) **327**
Columbia International U (SC) **327**
Columbia Union Coll (MD) **328**
Columbia U, School of General Studies (NY) **328**
Columbus State U (GA) **328**
Concordia Coll (MN) **329**
Concordia Coll (NY) **329**
Concordia U (CA) **330**
Concordia U (IL) **330**
Concordia U (MI) **330**
Concordia U (MN) **330**
Concordia U (NE) **330**
Concordia U (QC, Canada) **331**
Concordia U at Austin (TX) **331**
Concordia U Coll of Alberta (AB, Canada) **331**
Concordia U Wisconsin (WI) **331**
Connecticut Coll (CT) **331**
Conservatory of Music of Puerto Rico (PR) **332**
Converse Coll (SC) **332**
Cornell Coll (IA) **332**
Cornell U (NY) **333**
Cornerstone U (MI) **333**
Cornish Coll of the Arts (WA) **333**
Covenant Coll (GA) **333**
Creighton U (NE) **333**
Crown Coll (MN) **334**
Culver-Stockton Coll (MO) **334**
Cumberland Coll (KY) **335**
Cumberland U (TN) **335**
The Curtis Inst of Music (PA) **335**
Dalhousie U (NS, Canada) **336**
Dallas Baptist U (TX) **336**
Dana Coll (NE) **337**
Dartmouth Coll (NH) **337**
Davidson Coll (NC) **338**
Davis & Elkins Coll (WV) **338**
Delaware State U (DE) **338**
Delta State U (MS) **339**
Denison U (OH) **339**
DePaul U (IL) **339**
DePauw U (IN) **339**
Deree Coll(Greece) **339**
Dickinson Coll (PA) **344**
Dickinson State U (ND) **344**
Dillard U (LA) **344**
Doane Coll (NE) **344**
Dominican U of California (CA) **345**
Dordt Coll (IA) **345**
Dowling Coll (NY) **345**
Drake U (IA) **345**
Drew U (NJ) **346**
Drexel U (PA) **346**
Drury U (MO) **346**
Duke U (NC) **346**
Earlham Coll (IN) **347**
East Central U (OK) **347**
Eastern Illinois U (IL) **348**
Eastern Kentucky U (KY) **348**
Eastern Mennonite U (VA) **348**
Eastern Michigan U (MI) **348**
Eastern Nazarene Coll (MA) **348**
Eastern New Mexico U (NM) **349**
Eastern Oregon U (OR) **349**
Eastern U (PA) **349**
Eastern Washington U (WA) **349**
East Tennessee State U (TN) **349**
East Texas Baptist U (TX) **350**
Eckerd Coll (FL) **350**
Edgewood Coll (WI) **351**
Edinboro U of Pennsylvania (PA) **351**
Elizabeth City State U (NC) **351**
Elizabethtown Coll (PA) **351**
Elmhurst Coll (IL) **351**
Elmira Coll (NY) **351**
Elon U (NC) **352**
Emmanuel Coll (GA) **353**
Emory & Henry Coll (VA) **353**
Emory U (GA) **354**
Emporia State U (KS) **354**
Erskine Coll (SC) **354**
Eureka Coll (IL) **355**
Evangel U (MO) **355**
The Evergreen State Coll (WA) **355**
Excelsior Coll (NY) **356**
Fayetteville State U (NC) **357**
Fisk U (TN) **358**
Five Towns Coll (NY) **359**
Florida A&M U (FL) **359**
Florida Atlantic U (FL) **359**
Florida International U (FL) **360**
Florida Southern Coll (FL) **361**
Florida State U (FL) **361**
Fordham U (NY) **362**
Fort Hays State U (KS) **362**
Fort Lewis Coll (CO) **362**
The Franciscan U (IA) **363**
Franklin and Marshall Coll (PA) **363**
Franklin Pierce Coll (NH) **364**
Freed-Hardeman U (TN) **364**
Free Will Baptist Bible Coll (TN) **364**
Fresno Pacific U (CA) **364**
Frostburg State U (MD) **365**
Furman U (SC) **365**
Gardner-Webb U (NC) **365**
Geneva Coll (PA) **366**
George Fox U (OR) **366**
Georgetown Coll (KY) **366**
The George Washington U (DC) **367**
Georgia Coll & State U (GA) **367**
Georgian Court Coll (NJ) **367**
Georgia Southern U (GA) **367**
Georgia Southwestern State U (GA) **368**
Gettysburg Coll (PA) **368**
Goddard Coll (VT) **369**
Gonzaga U (WA) **369**
Gordon Coll (MA) **370**
Goshen Coll (IN) **370**
Goucher Coll (MD) **370**
Grace Bible Coll (MI) **370**
Graceland U (IA) **371**
Grace U (NE) **371**
Grand Canyon U (AZ) **371**
Grand Valley State U (MI) **371**
Great Lakes Christian Coll (MI) **372**
Greensboro Coll (NC) **372**
Greenville Coll (IL) **373**
Grinnell Coll (IA) **373**
Guilford Coll (NC) **373**
Gustavus Adolphus Coll (MN) **374**
Hamilton Coll (NY) **374**
Hamline U (MN) **374**
Hampshire Coll (MA) **375**
Hampton U (VA) **375**
Hannibal-LaGrange Coll (MO) **375**
Hanover Coll (IN) **375**
Harding U (AR) **375**
Hardin-Simmons U (TX) **376**
Hartwick Coll (NY) **376**
Harvard U (MA) **376**
Hastings Coll (NE) **377**
Haverford Coll (PA) **377**
Heidelberg Coll (OH) **377**
Henderson State U (AR) **378**
Hendrix Coll (AR) **378**
Hillsdale Coll (MI) **379**
Hiram Coll (OH) **379**
Hobart and William Smith Colls (NY) **380**
Hofstra U (NY) **380**
Hollins U (VA) **380**
Holy Names Coll (CA) **381**
Hood Coll (MD) **381**
Hope Coll (MI) **381**
Houghton Coll (NY) **381**
Houston Baptist U (TX) **382**
Howard Payne U (TX) **382**
Howard U (DC) **382**
Humboldt State U (CA) **382**
Hunter Coll of the City U of NY (NY) **382**
Huntingdon Coll (AL) **383**
Huntington Coll (IN) **383**
Huston-Tillotson Coll (TX) **383**
Idaho State U (ID) **384**

Illinois Coll (IL) **384**
Illinois State U (IL) **384**
Illinois Wesleyan U (IL) **385**
Immaculata U (PA) **385**
Indiana State U (IN) **385**
Indiana U Bloomington (IN) **385**
Indiana U of Pennsylvania (PA) **386**
Indiana U–Purdue U Fort Wayne (IN) **386**
Indiana U Southeast (IN) **387**
Indiana Wesleyan U (IN) **387**
Inter American U of PR, San Germán Campus (PR) **388**
Iowa State U of Science and Technology (IA) **390**
Iowa Wesleyan Coll (IA) **390**
Ithaca Coll (NY) **390**
Jacksonville State U (AL) **390**
Jacksonville U (FL) **391**
Jamestown Coll (ND) **391**
Jewish Theological Seminary of America (NY) **391**
John Brown U (AR) **392**
Johns Hopkins U (MD) **392**
Johnson State Coll (VT) **394**
Judson Coll (AL) **395**
Judson Coll (IL) **395**
The Juilliard School (NY) **395**
Kalamazoo Coll (MI) **395**
Kansas State U (KS) **396**
Kean U (NJ) **396**
Keene State Coll (NH) **396**
Kennesaw State U (GA) **397**
Kent State U (OH) **397**
Kentucky Christian Coll (KY) **397**
Kenyon Coll (OH) **398**
King Coll (TN) **398**
The King's U Coll (AB, Canada) **399**
Knox Coll (IL) **399**
Kutztown U of Pennsylvania (PA) **399**
Lafayette Coll (PA) **400**
LaGrange Coll (GA) **400**
Lake Erie Coll (OH) **400**
Lake Forest Coll (IL) **400**
Lakehead U (ON, Canada) **400**
Lakeland Coll (WI) **401**
Lamar U (TX) **401**
Lambuth U (TN) **401**
Lander U (SC) **401**
Lane Coll (TN) **402**
Langston U (OK) **402**
La Salle U (PA) **402**
La Sierra U (CA) **403**
Laurentian U (ON, Canada) **403**
Lawrence U (WI) **403**
Lebanon Valley Coll (PA) **403**
Lee U (TN) **404**
Lehigh U (PA) **404**
Lehman Coll of the City U of NY (NY) **404**
Lenoir-Rhyne Coll (NC) **405**
Lewis & Clark Coll (OR) **405**
Lewis U (IL) **406**
Liberty U (VA) **406**
Limestone Coll (SC) **406**
Lincoln U (PA) **407**
Lindenwood U (MO) **407**
Linfield Coll (OR) **408**
Lipscomb U (TN) **408**
Lock Haven U of Pennsylvania (PA) **408**
Long Island U, Brooklyn Campus (NY) **409**
Long Island U, C.W. Post Campus (NY) **409**
Long Island U, Southampton Coll, Friends World Program (NY) **409**
Longwood U (VA) **409**
Loras Coll (IA) **410**
Louisiana Coll (LA) **410**
Louisiana State U and A&M Coll (LA) **410**
Louisiana Tech U (LA) **410**
Loyola Marymount U (CA) **411**
Loyola U Chicago (IL) **411**
Loyola U New Orleans (LA) **411**
Lubbock Christian U (TX) **412**
Luther Coll (IA) **412**
Lycoming Coll (PA) **412**
Lynchburg Coll (VA) **413**
Lynn U (FL) **413**
Lyon Coll (AR) **413**
Macalester Coll (MN) **413**
MacMurray Coll (IL) **414**
Madonna U (MI) **414**
Malone Coll (OH) **415**
Manchester Coll (IN) **415**
Manhattan School of Music (NY) **416**
Manhattanville Coll (NY) **416**
Mannes Coll of Music, New School U (NY) **416**
Mansfield U of Pennsylvania (PA) **416**
Maranatha Baptist Bible Coll (WI) **417**
Marian Coll (IN) **417**
Marian Coll of Fond du Lac (WI) **417**
Marietta Coll (OH) **417**
Marlboro Coll (VT) **418**
Mars Hill Coll (NC) **418**
Martin U (IN) **419**
Mary Baldwin Coll (VA) **419**
Marygrove Coll (MI) **419**
Maryville Coll (TN) **420**
Maryville U of Saint Louis (MO) **420**
Mary Washington Coll (VA) **420**
Marywood U (PA) **421**
Massachusetts Coll of Liberal Arts (MA) **421**
Massachusetts Inst of Technology (MA) **421**
The Master's Coll and Seminary (CA) **422**
McDaniel Coll (MD) **422**
McGill U (QC, Canada) **423**
McKendree Coll (IL) **423**
McMaster U (ON, Canada) **423**
McMurry U (TX) **423**
McNeese State U (LA) **423**
McPherson Coll (KS) **423**
Memorial U of Newfoundland (NF, Canada) **424**
Mercer U (GA) **425**
Mercy Coll (NY) **425**
Mercyhurst Coll (PA) **425**
Meredith Coll (NC) **426**
Mesa State Coll (CO) **426**
Messenger Coll (MO) **426**
Messiah Coll (PA) **426**
Methodist Coll (NC) **427**
Miami U (OH) **428**
MidAmerica Nazarene U (KS) **428**
Middlebury Coll (VT) **429**
Middle Tennessee State U (TN) **429**
Midland Lutheran Coll (NE) **429**
Midwestern State U (TX) **430**
Miles Coll (AL) **430**
Millersville U of Pennsylvania (PA) **430**
Milligan Coll (TN) **430**
Millikin U (IL) **430**
Millsaps Coll (MS) **431**
Mills Coll (CA) **431**
Minnesota State U, Mankato (MN) **431**
Minnesota State U, Moorhead (MN) **432**
Minot State U (ND) **432**
Mississippi Coll (MS) **432**
Mississippi Valley State U (MS) **432**
Missouri Southern State Coll (MO) **433**
Missouri Western State Coll (MO) **433**
Molloy Coll (NY) **433**
Monmouth Coll (IL) **434**
Monmouth U (NJ) **434**
Montana State U–Billings (MT) **434**
Montana State U–Bozeman (MT) **434**
Montclair State U (NJ) **435**
Montreat Coll (NC) **435**
Moravian Coll (PA) **436**
Morehead State U (KY) **436**
Morehouse Coll (GA) **436**
Morgan State U (MD) **436**
Morningside Coll (IA) **437**
Mount Allison U (NB, Canada) **437**
Mount Holyoke Coll (MA) **438**
Mount Marty Coll (SD) **438**
Mount Mary Coll (WI) **438**
Mount Mercy Coll (IA) **438**
Mount St. Mary's Coll (CA) **439**
Mount Union Coll (OH) **440**
Mount Vernon Nazarene U (OH) **440**
Muhlenberg Coll (PA) **440**
Multnomah Bible Coll and Biblical Seminary (OR) **440**
Murray State U (KY) **440**
Musicians Inst (CA) **441**
Muskingum Coll (OH) **441**
Naropa U (CO) **441**
Nazareth Coll of Rochester (NY) **443**
Nebraska Wesleyan U (NE) **443**
Newberry Coll (SC) **444**
New Coll of Florida (FL) **444**
New Jersey City U (NJ) **445**
New Mexico Highlands U (NM) **446**
New Mexico State U (NM) **446**
New World School of the Arts (FL) **447**
New York U (NY) **447**
Nicholls State U (LA) **447**
Norfolk State U (VA) **448**
North Carolina Central U (NC) **448**
North Carolina School of the Arts (NC) **449**
North Central Coll (IL) **449**
North Dakota State U (ND) **449**
Northeastern Illinois U (IL) **450**
Northeastern State U (OK) **450**
Northeastern U (MA) **450**
Northern Arizona U (AZ) **450**
Northern Illinois U (IL) **450**
Northern Kentucky U (KY) **451**
Northern Michigan U (MI) **451**
Northern State U (SD) **451**
North Georgia Coll & State U (GA) **451**
North Greenville Coll (SC) **451**
Northland Coll (WI) **452**
North Park U (IL) **452**
Northwest Christian Coll (OR) **452**
Northwest Coll (WA) **452**
Northwestern Coll (IA) **453**
Northwestern Coll (MN) **453**
Northwestern Oklahoma State U (OK) **453**
Northwestern State U of Louisiana (LA) **453**
Northwestern U (IL) **453**
Northwest Missouri State U (MO) **454**
Northwest Nazarene U (ID) **454**
Notre Dame de Namur U (CA) **455**
Nyack Coll (NY) **456**
Oak Hills Christian Coll (MN) **456**
Oakland City U (IN) **456**
Oakland U (MI) **456**
Oakwood Coll (AL) **456**
Oberlin Coll (OH) **456**
Occidental Coll (CA) **457**
Ohio Northern U (OH) **457**
The Ohio State U (OH) **457**
Ohio U (OH) **458**
Ohio Wesleyan U (OH) **459**
Oklahoma Baptist U (OK) **459**
Oklahoma Christian U (OK) **459**
Oklahoma City U (OK) **460**
Oklahoma State U (OK) **460**
Oklahoma Wesleyan U (OK) **460**
Olivet Nazarene U (IL) **461**
Oral Roberts U (OK) **461**
Oregon State U (OR) **462**
Ottawa U (KS) **462**
Otterbein Coll (OH) **462**
Ouachita Baptist U (AR) **462**
Pacific Lutheran U (WA) **463**
Pacific Union Coll (CA) **464**
Pacific U (OR) **464**
Palm Beach Atlantic U (FL) **465**
Peabody Conserv of Music of Johns Hopkins U (MD) **466**
Penn State U Univ Park Campus (PA) **468**
Pepperdine U, Malibu (CA) **469**
Peru State Coll (NE) **469**
Pfeiffer U (NC) **469**
Philadelphia Biblical U (PA) **469**
Piedmont Baptist Coll (NC) **470**
Piedmont Coll (GA) **470**
Pillsbury Baptist Bible Coll (MN) **470**
Pittsburg State U (KS) **470**
Plattsburgh State U of NY (NY) **471**
Plymouth State Coll (NH) **471**
Point Loma Nazarene U (CA) **471**
Pomona Coll (CA) **472**
Pontifical Catholic U of Puerto Rico (PR) **472**
Portland State U (OR) **472**
Prairie Bible Coll (AB, Canada) **473**
Prairie View A&M U (TX) **473**
Presbyterian Coll (SC) **473**
Princeton U (NJ) **474**
Principia Coll (IL) **474**
Providence Coll (RI) **474**
Providence Coll and Theological Seminary (MB, Canada) **475**
Purchase Coll, State U of NY (NY) **475**
Queens Coll of the City U of NY (NY) **475**
Queen's U at Kingston (ON, Canada) **476**
Queens U of Charlotte (NC) **476**
Quincy U (IL) **476**
Radford U (VA) **476**
Randolph-Macon Coll (VA) **477**
Randolph-Macon Woman's Coll (VA) **477**
Reed Coll (OR) **477**
Rhode Island Coll (RI) **479**
Rhodes Coll (TN) **479**
Rice U (TX) **479**
Rider U (NJ) **480**
Ripon Coll (WI) **480**
Roanoke Coll (VA) **481**
Roberts Wesleyan Coll (NY) **481**
Rochester Coll (MI) **482**
Rocky Mountain Coll (MT) **482**
Rocky Mountain Coll (AB, Canada) **482**
Rollins Coll (FL) **483**
Roosevelt U (IL) **483**
Rowan U (NJ) **484**
Rust Coll (MS) **485**
Rutgers, The State U of New Jersey, Camden (NJ) **485**
Rutgers, The State U of New Jersey, Newark (NJ) **485**
Rutgers, The State U of New Jersey, New Brunswick (NJ) **485**
Saginaw Valley State U (MI) **486**
St. Ambrose U (IA) **486**
St. Cloud State U (MN) **488**
St. Francis Xavier U (NS, Canada) **489**
Saint John's U (MN) **490**
Saint Joseph's Coll (IN) **490**
St. Lawrence U (NY) **491**
Saint Louis U (MO) **492**
Saint Mary-of-the-Woods Coll (IN) **493**
Saint Mary's Coll (IN) **493**
Saint Mary's Coll of California (CA) **494**
St. Mary's Coll of Maryland (MD) **494**
Saint Mary's U of Minnesota (MN) **494**
St. Mary's U of San Antonio (TX) **494**
Saint Michael's Coll (VT) **494**
St. Norbert Coll (WI) **495**
St. Olaf Coll (MN) **495**
Saint Vincent Coll (PA) **496**
Saint Xavier U (IL) **496**
Salem Coll (NC) **496**
Salisbury U (MD) **497**
Salve Regina U (RI) **497**
Sam Houston State U (TX) **497**
San Diego State U (CA) **498**
San Francisco Conservatory of Music (CA) **498**
San Francisco State U (CA) **498**
San Jose Christian Coll (CA) **498**
San Jose State U (CA) **499**
Santa Clara U (CA) **499**
Sarah Lawrence Coll (NY) **499**
Savannah State U (GA) **499**
Scripps Coll (CA) **501**
Seattle Pacific U (WA) **501**
Seton Hall U (NJ) **502**
Seton Hill U (PA) **502**
Shaw U (NC) **502**
Shenandoah U (VA) **503**
Shepherd Coll (WV) **503**
Shorter Coll (GA) **504**
Siena Heights U (MI) **504**
Sierra Nevada Coll (NV) **504**
Silver Lake Coll (WI) **504**
Simmons Coll (MA) **504**
Simon Fraser U (BC, Canada) **505**
Simon's Rock Coll of Bard (MA) **505**
Simpson Coll (IA) **505**
Simpson Coll and Graduate School (CA) **505**
Slippery Rock U of Pennsylvania (PA) **506**
Smith Coll (MA) **506**
Sonoma State U (CA) **506**
South Dakota State U (SD) **507**
Southeastern Bible Coll (AL) **507**
Southeastern Oklahoma State U (OK) **508**
Southeast Missouri State U (MO) **508**
Southern Adventist U (TN) **508**
Southern Illinois U Carbondale (IL) **509**
Southern Illinois U Edwardsville (IL) **509**
Southern Methodist U (TX) **510**
Southern Oregon U (OR) **510**
Southern Utah U (UT) **511**
Southern Virginia U (VA) **511**
Southern Wesleyan U (SC) **511**
Southwest Baptist U (MO) **512**
Southwestern Assemblies of God U (TX) **512**
Southwestern Coll (KS) **512**
Southwestern Oklahoma State U (OK) **512**
Southwestern U (TX) **513**
Southwest Missouri State U (MO) **513**
Southwest State U (MN) **513**
Southwest Texas State U (TX) **513**
Spelman Coll (GA) **514**
Spring Arbor U (MI) **514**
Stanford U (CA) **514**
State U of NY at Albany (NY) **514**
State U of NY at Binghamton (NY) **515**
State U of NY at New Paltz (NY) **515**
State U of NY at Oswego (NY) **515**
State U of NY Coll at Buffalo (NY) **516**
State U of NY Coll at Fredonia (NY) **516**

MUSIC (continued)

State U of NY Coll at Geneseo (NY) 516
State U of NY Coll at Oneonta (NY) 517
State U of NY Coll at Potsdam (NY) 517
Steinbach Bible Coll (MB, Canada) 518
Stephen F. Austin State U (TX) 518
Sterling Coll (KS) 519
Stetson U (FL) 519
Stony Brook U, State University of New York (NY) 520
Sul Ross State U (TX) 521
Susquehanna U (PA) 521
Swarthmore Coll (PA) 521
Sweet Briar Coll (VA) 521
Syracuse U (NY) 521
Tabor Coll (KS) 522
Talladega Coll (AL) 522
Tarleton State U (TX) 522
Taylor U (IN) 523
Taylor U, Fort Wayne Campus (IN) 523
Temple U (PA) 523
Tennessee State U (TN) 523
Tennessee Technological U (TN) 524
Tennessee Temple U (TN) 524
Tennessee Wesleyan Coll (TN) 524
Texas A&M U (TX) 524
Texas A&M U–Commerce (TX) 525
Texas A&M U–Corpus Christi (TX) 525
Texas A&M U–Kingsville (TX) 525
Texas Christian U (TX) 526
Texas Coll (TX) 526
Texas Lutheran U (TX) 526
Texas Southern U (TX) 526
Texas Tech U (TX) 526
Texas Wesleyan U (TX) 526
Texas Woman's U (TX) 527
Thomas Edison State Coll (NJ) 527
Thomas U (GA) 528
Toccoa Falls Coll (GA) 528
Towson U (MD) 529
Trevecca Nazarene U (TN) 529
Trinity Bible Coll (ND) 530
Trinity Christian Coll (IL) 530
Trinity Coll (CT) 530
Trinity Coll of Florida (FL) 531
Trinity International U (IL) 531
Trinity U (TX) 531
Trinity Western U (BC, Canada) 531
Truman State U (MO) 532
Tufts U (MA) 533
Tulane U (LA) 533
Union Coll (KY) 533
Union Coll (NE) 534
Union U (TN) 534
Universidad Adventista de las Antillas (PR) 536
Université de Sherbrooke (QC, Canada) 536
Université Laval (QC, Canada) 536
U at Buffalo, The State University of New York (NY) 536
The U of Akron (OH) 537
The U of Alabama (AL) 537
The U of Alabama at Birmingham (AL) 537
The U of Alabama in Huntsville (AL) 537
U of Alaska Anchorage (AK) 538
U of Alaska Fairbanks (AK) 538
U of Alberta (AB, Canada) 538
The U of Arizona (AZ) 538
U of Arkansas at Little Rock (AR) 539
U of Arkansas at Monticello (AR) 539
U of Bridgeport (CT) 540
The U of British Columbia (BC, Canada) 540
U of Calgary (AB, Canada) 540
U of Calif, Berkeley (CA) 540
U of Calif, Davis (CA) 540
U of Calif, Irvine (CA) 541
U of Calif, Los Angeles (CA) 541
U of Calif, Riverside (CA) 541
U of Calif, San Diego (CA) 541
U of Calif, Santa Barbara (CA) 541
U of Calif, Santa Cruz (CA) 542
U of Central Arkansas (AR) 542
U of Central Oklahoma (OK) 542
U of Charleston (WV) 542
U of Chicago (IL) 542
U of Cincinnati (OH) 543
U of Colorado at Boulder (CO) 543
U of Colorado at Denver (CO) 543
U of Connecticut (CT) 544
U of Dayton (OH) 544
U of Delaware (DE) 544
U of Denver (CO) 544
U of Evansville (IN) 545
U of Florida (FL) 545
U of Georgia (GA) 545
U of Guelph (ON, Canada) 546
U of Hartford (CT) 546
U of Hawaii at Hilo (HI) 546
U of Hawaii at Manoa (HI) 546
U of Houston (TX) 547
U of Illinois at Chicago (IL) 547
U of Illinois at Urbana–Champaign (IL) 548
U of Indianapolis (IN) 548
The U of Iowa (IA) 548
U of Kansas (KS) 549
U of La Verne (CA) 549
The U of Lethbridge (AB, Canada) 549
U of Louisville (KY) 550
U of Maine (ME) 550
U of Maine at Farmington (ME) 550
U of Manitoba (MB, Canada) 551
U of Mary (ND) 551
U of Maryland, Baltimore County (MD) 552
U of Maryland, Coll Park (MD) 552
U of Massachusetts Amherst (MA) 552
U of Massachusetts Boston (MA) 553
U of Massachusetts Dartmouth (MA) 553
The U of Memphis (TN) 553
U of Miami (FL) 553
U of Michigan (MI) 554
U of Michigan–Dearborn (MI) 554
U of Michigan–Flint (MI) 554
U of Minnesota, Duluth (MN) 554
U of Minnesota, Morris (MN) 555
U of Minnesota, Twin Cities Campus (MN) 555
U of Mississippi (MS) 555
U of Missouri–Columbia (MO) 555
U of Missouri–Kansas City (MO) 555
U of Missouri–St. Louis (MO) 556
U of Mobile (AL) 556
The U of Montana–Missoula (MT) 556
The U of Montana–Western (MT) 556
U of Montevallo (AL) 557
U of Nebraska at Kearney (NE) 557
U of Nebraska at Omaha (NE) 557
U of Nebraska–Lincoln (NE) 557
U of Nevada, Las Vegas (NV) 558
U of Nevada, Reno (NV) 558
U of New Hampshire (NH) 558
U of New Haven (CT) 559
U of New Orleans (LA) 559
U of North Alabama (AL) 559
The U of North Carolina at Asheville (NC) 559
The U of North Carolina at Chapel Hill (NC) 560
The U of North Carolina at Pembroke (NC) 560
The U of North Carolina at Wilmington (NC) 561
U of North Dakota (ND) 561
U of Northern Colorado (CO) 561
U of Northern Iowa (IA) 561
U of North Florida (FL) 561
U of North Texas (TX) 562
U of Notre Dame (IN) 562
U of Oklahoma (OK) 562
U of Oregon (OR) 562
U of Ottawa (ON, Canada) 563
U of Pennsylvania (PA) 563
U of Pittsburgh (PA) 569
U of Portland (OR) 570
U of Prince Edward Island (PE, Canada) 570
U of Puerto Rico, Río Piedras (PR) 571
U of Puget Sound (WA) 571
U of Redlands (CA) 572
U of Regina (SK, Canada) 572
U of Rhode Island (RI) 572
U of Richmond (VA) 572
U of Rio Grande (OH) 572
U of Rochester (NY) 573
U of St. Thomas (MN) 573
U of St. Thomas (TX) 573
U of San Diego (CA) 574
U of Saskatchewan (SK, Canada) 574
U of Science and Arts of Oklahoma (OK) 574
U of Sioux Falls (SD) 574
U of South Alabama (AL) 575
U of South Carolina (SC) 575
The U of South Dakota (SD) 575
U of Southern California (CA) 576
U of Southern Maine (ME) 576
U of Southern Mississippi (MS) 576
The U of Tampa (FL) 577
The U of Tennessee (TN) 577
The U of Tennessee at Chattanooga (TN) 577
The U of Tennessee at Martin (TN) 577
The U of Texas at Arlington (TX) 577
The U of Texas at Austin (TX) 578
The U of Texas at El Paso (TX) 578
The U of Texas at San Antonio (TX) 578
The U of Texas at Tyler (TX) 579
The U of Texas–Pan American (TX) 579
U of the District of Columbia (DC) 580
U of the Incarnate Word (TX) 580
U of the Ozarks (AR) 580
U of the Pacific (CA) 580
U of the South (TN) 581
U of Toledo (OH) 581
U of Toronto (ON, Canada) 581
U of Tulsa (OK) 581
U of Utah (UT) 582
U of Vermont (VT) 582
U of Victoria (BC, Canada) 582
U of Virginia (VA) 582
U of Washington (WA) 583
U of Waterloo (ON, Canada) 583
The U of Western Ontario (ON, Canada) 583
U of Windsor (ON, Canada) 584
U of Wisconsin–Eau Claire (WI) 584
U of Wisconsin–Green Bay (WI) 584
U of Wisconsin–La Crosse (WI) 584
U of Wisconsin–Madison (WI) 584
U of Wisconsin–Milwaukee (WI) 585
U of Wisconsin–Oshkosh (WI) 585
U of Wisconsin–Parkside (WI) 585
U of Wisconsin–Platteville (WI) 585
U of Wisconsin–River Falls (WI) 585
U of Wisconsin–Stevens Point (WI) 585
U of Wisconsin–Superior (WI) 586
U of Wisconsin–Whitewater (WI) 586
U of Wyoming (WY) 586
Upper Iowa U (IA) 587
Ursinus Coll (PA) 587
Utah State U (UT) 587
Valdosta State U (GA) 588
Valley City State U (ND) 588
Valparaiso U (IN) 588
Vanderbilt U (TN) 588
Vanguard U of Southern California (CA) 589
Vassar Coll (NY) 589
Virginia Polytechnic Inst and State U (VA) 591
Virginia Union U (VA) 591
Virginia Wesleyan Coll (VA) 591
Viterbo U (WI) 591
Wabash Coll (IN) 592
Wagner Coll (NY) 592
Wake Forest U (NC) 592
Walla Walla Coll (WA) 593
Warner Pacific Coll (OR) 593
Wartburg Coll (IA) 594
Washington & Jefferson Coll (PA) 594
Washington and Lee U (VA) 594
Washington Bible Coll (MD) 594
Washington Coll (MD) 594
Washington State U (WA) 595
Washington U in St. Louis (MO) 595
Wayland Baptist U (TX) 595
Wayne State Coll (NE) 596
Wayne State U (MI) 596
Weber State U (UT) 596
Webster U (MO) 597
Wellesley Coll (MA) 597
Wells Coll (NY) 597
Wesleyan Coll (GA) 597
Wesleyan U (CT) 597
West Chester U of Pennsylvania (PA) 598
Western Baptist Coll (OR) 598
Western Carolina U (NC) 598
Western Connecticut State U (CT) 598
Western Illinois U (IL) 599
Western Kentucky U (KY) 599
Western Michigan U (MI) 599
Western New Mexico U (NM) 600
Western Oregon U (OR) 600
Western State Coll of Colorado (CO) 600
Western Washington U (WA) 600
Westfield State Coll (MA) 600
Westminster Choir Coll of Rider U (NJ) 601
Westminster Coll (PA) 601
Westmont Coll (CA) 602
West Texas A&M U (TX) 602
West Virginia U (WV) 602
West Virginia Wesleyan Coll (WV) 603
Wheaton Coll (IL) 603
Wheaton Coll (MA) 603
Whitman Coll (WA) 604
Whittier Coll (CA) 604
Whitworth Coll (WA) 604
Wichita State U (KS) 604
Wiley Coll (TX) 605
Willamette U (OR) 605
William Carey Coll (MS) 605
William Jewell Coll (MO) 606
William Paterson U of New Jersey (NJ) 606
Williams Baptist Coll (AR) 606
Williams Coll (MA) 606
Wingate U (NC) 607
Winona State U (MN) 608
Winthrop U (SC) 608
Wisconsin Lutheran Coll (WI) 608
Wittenberg U (OH) 608
Worcester Polytechnic Inst (MA) 609
Wright State U (OH) 609
Xavier U (OH) 610
Xavier U of Louisiana (LA) 610
Yale U (CT) 610
York Coll (NE) 610
York Coll of Pennsylvania (PA) 610
York Coll of the City U of New York (NY) 611
York U (ON, Canada) 611
Youngstown State U (OH) 611

MUSICAL INSTRUMENT TECHNOLOGY

Overview: Students who choose this major study the principles of sound creation in various types of musical instruments; learn how to design, build, and repair musical instruments; and work with computers in creating musical sound. *Related majors:* music theory and composition, music history, literature and theory, musicology, audio engineering. *Potential careers:* musical instrument designer, repairer, or tuner; computer scientist; audio engineer. *Salary potential:* $20k-$35k.

Ball State U (IN) 280
Barton Coll (NC) 282
Bellarmine U (KY) 284
Bloomfield Coll (NJ) 290
Bowie State U (MD) 292
LaGrange Coll (GA) 400
Malone Coll (OH) 415
New York U (NY) 447
The U of Texas at San Antonio (TX) 578
U of Washington (WA) 583

MUSIC BUSINESS MANAGEMENT/ MERCHANDISING

Overview: Students learn how to plan, organize, and manage musical groups, organization personnel, or facilities. *Related majors:* conducting, music performance, management and business administration, personnel management and labor relations, event promotion, law and legal studies. *Potential careers:* music or performing arts director, conductor, record executive, concert promoter, agent, theater or recording studio manager. *Salary potential:* $25k-$35k.

Anderson U (IN) 268
Appalachian State U (NC) 270
Baldwin-Wallace Coll (OH) 280
Bellarmine U (KY) 284
Belmont U (TN) 284
Benedictine Coll (KS) 285
Berklee Coll of Music (MA) 286
Berry Coll (GA) 287
Bryan Coll (TN) 296
Butler U (IN) 297
Capital U (OH) 304
Central Baptist Coll (AR) 309
Central Washington U (WA) 310
Clarion U of Pennsylvania (PA) 315
Coker Coll (SC) 318
Coll of the Ozarks (MO) 323
Columbia Coll Chicago (IL) 327
Davis & Elkins Coll (WV) 338

DePaul U (IL) **339**
DePauw U (IN) **339**
Drake U (IA) **345**
Elizabeth City State U (NC) **351**
Elmhurst Coll (IL) **351**
Erskine Coll (SC) **354**
Ferris State U (MI) **358**
Five Towns Coll (NY) **359**
Florida Southern Coll (FL) **361**
Geneva Coll (PA) **366**
Grace Bible Coll (MI) **370**
Grand Canyon U (AZ) **371**
Grove City Coll (PA) **373**
Hardin-Simmons U (TX) **376**
Heidelberg Coll (OH) **377**
Illinois Wesleyan U (IL) **385**
Jacksonville U (FL) **391**
Johnson State Coll (VT) **394**
Lebanon Valley Coll (PA) **403**
Lewis U (IL) **406**
Loyola U New Orleans (LA) **411**
Luther Coll (IA) **412**
Madonna U (MI) **414**
Manhattanville Coll (NY) **416**
Mansfield U of Pennsylvania (PA) **416**
Marian Coll of Fond du Lac (WI) **417**
The Master's Coll and Seminary (CA) **422**
Methodist Coll (NC) **427**
Middle Tennessee State U (TN) **429**
Millikin U (IL) **430**
Minnesota State U, Mankato (MN) **431**
Minnesota State U, Moorhead (MN) **432**
Monmouth U (NJ) **434**
Montreat Coll (NC) **435**
New York U (NY) **447**
Northeastern U (MA) **450**
North Park U (IL) **452**
Northwest Missouri State U (MO) **454**
Ohio Northern U (OH) **457**
Ohio U (OH) **458**
Oklahoma City U (OK) **460**
Oklahoma State U (OK) **460**
Otterbein Coll (OH) **462**
Peru State Coll (NE) **469**
Point Loma Nazarene U (CA) **471**
Quincy U (IL) **476**
Saint Augustine's Coll (NC) **487**
Saint Mary's U of Minnesota (MN) **494**
South Carolina State U (SC) **506**
South Dakota State U (SD) **507**
Southern Nazarene U (OK) **510**
Southern Oregon U (OR) **510**
Southwestern Oklahoma State U (OK) **512**
State U of NY Coll at Fredonia (NY) **516**
State U of NY Coll at Oneonta (NY) **517**
State U of NY Coll at Potsdam (NY) **517**
Syracuse U (NY) **521**
Tabor Coll (KS) **522**
Taylor U (IN) **523**
Trevecca Nazarene U (TN) **529**
Union Coll (KY) **533**
Union U (TN) **534**
U of Charleston (WV) **542**
U of Evansville (IN) **545**
U of Hartford (CT) **546**
U of Idaho (ID) **547**
The U of Memphis (TN) **553**
U of Miami (FL) **553**
U of New Haven (CT) **559**
U of Puget Sound (WA) **571**
U of St. Thomas (MN) **573**
U of Sioux Falls (SD) **574**
U of Southern California (CA) **576**
U of the Incarnate Word (TX) **580**
U of the Pacific (CA) **580**
Valparaiso U (IN) **588**
Warner Pacific Coll (OR) **593**
Westfield State Coll (MA) **600**
Wheaton Coll (IL) **603**
William Paterson U of New Jersey (NJ) **606**
Wingate U (NC) **607**
Winona State U (MN) **608**

MUSIC CONDUCTING

Overview: This major teaches students how to organize, manage, and lead groups of musicians in performance. *Related majors:* music performance, music theory and composition. *Potential careers:* musical conductor, bandleader, choral director, concert organizer, performing arts director. *Salary potential:* varies according to work schedule but full-time conductors and directors at the beginning of their careers can expect $25k-$30k.

Bowling Green State U (OH) **292**
Calvin Coll (MI) **303**
Luther Coll (IA) **412**
Mannes Coll of Music, New School U (NY) **416**
Ohio U (OH) **458**
Westminster Choir Coll of Rider U (NJ) **601**

MUSIC (GENERAL PERFORMANCE)

Overview: Students taking this major master at least one musical instrument and learn how to play that instrument in a performance role. *Related majors:* music, music theory and composition. *Potential careers:* musician, band leader. *Salary potential:* varies widely depending on location and time worked but starting musicians who belong to a union can expect $10k-$25k if working 40 hours per week.

Adams State Coll (CO) **260**
Adelphi U (NY) **260**
Alcorn State U (MS) **263**
Anderson U (IN) **268**
Appalachian State U (NC) **270**
Arizona State U (AZ) **271**
Arkansas State U (AR) **272**
Augusta State U (GA) **277**
Averett U (VA) **278**
Bard Coll (NY) **281**
Baylor U (TX) **283**
Berklee Coll of Music (MA) **286**
Bethel Coll (IN) **288**
Black Hills State U (SD) **290**
Boston U (MA) **292**
Bowling Green State U (OH) **292**
Bradley U (IL) **293**
Brandon U (MB, Canada) **293**
Brigham Young U (UT) **295**
Brigham Young U–Hawaii (HI) **295**
Bucknell U (PA) **297**
California State U, Chico (CA) **300**
California State U, Fullerton (CA) **301**
Calvin Coll (MI) **303**
Cameron U (OK) **303**
Capital U (OH) **304**
Carnegie Mellon U (PA) **305**
The Catholic U of America (DC) **307**
Central Methodist Coll (MO) **309**
Clarion U of Pennsylvania (PA) **315**
Colorado Christian U (CO) **325**
Colorado State U (CO) **325**
Columbia Coll Chicago (IL) **327**
Columbia Union Coll (MD) **328**
Concordia Coll (MN) **329**
Concordia U (QC, Canada) **331**
DePaul U (IL) **339**
DePauw U (IN) **339**
Dillard U (LA) **344**
Duquesne U (PA) **346**
East Carolina U (NC) **347**
Eastern Michigan U (MI) **348**
Eastern Nazarene Coll (MA) **348**
Elon U (NC) **352**
Florida State U (FL) **361**
Geneva Coll (PA) **366**
George Mason U (VA) **366**
Georgia Southern U (GA) **367**
Georgia State U (GA) **368**
Gordon Coll (MA) **370**
Grambling State U (LA) **371**
Henderson State U (AR) **378**
Hope Coll (MI) **381**
Howard Payne U (TX) **382**
Idaho State U (ID) **384**
Illinois State U (IL) **384**
Indiana U of Pennsylvania (PA) **386**
Indiana U South Bend (IN) **387**
Ithaca Coll (NY) **390**
Jackson State U (MS) **390**
Jacksonville U (FL) **391**
James Madison U (VA) **391**
Johns Hopkins U (MD) **392**
Johnson State Coll (VT) **394**
Kentucky State U (KY) **397**
Long Island U, C.W. Post Campus (NY) **409**
Louisiana State U and A&M Coll (LA) **410**
Louisiana Tech U (LA) **410**
Loyola U New Orleans (LA) **411**
Luther Coll (IA) **412**
Mansfield U of Pennsylvania (PA) **416**
Marygrove Coll (MI) **419**
McGill U (QC, Canada) **423**
Mercer U (GA) **425**
Metropolitan State Coll of Denver (CO) **427**
Miami U (OH) **428**
Millikin U (IL) **430**
Mississippi Coll (MS) **432**
Mount Allison U (NB, Canada) **437**
Mount Union Coll (OH) **440**
Nebraska Wesleyan U (NE) **443**
New York U (NY) **447**
Northern Arizona U (AZ) **450**
Northwestern Coll (MN) **453**
Northwestern U (IL) **453**
Northwest Nazarene U (ID) **454**
Notre Dame de Namur U (CA) **455**
The Ohio State U (OH) **457**
Ohio U (OH) **458**
Oklahoma Wesleyan U (OK) **460**
Old Dominion U (VA) **460**
Oral Roberts U (OK) **461**
Otterbein Coll (OH) **462**
Peace Coll (NC) **466**
Penn State U Univ Park Campus (PA) **468**
Piedmont Coll (GA) **470**
Rice U (TX) **479**
Saint Augustine's Coll (NC) **487**
Saint Mary's U of Minnesota (MN) **494**
St. Olaf Coll (MN) **495**
Saint Vincent Coll (PA) **496**
Saint Xavier U (IL) **496**
Salem Coll (NC) **496**
Samford U (AL) **497**
San Francisco Conservatory of Music (CA) **498**
San Jose State U (CA) **499**
Seton Hall U (NJ) **502**
Seton Hill U (PA) **502**
Shenandoah U (VA) **503**
Simpson Coll (IA) **505**
Slippery Rock U of Pennsylvania (PA) **506**
Southeastern Coll of the Assemblies of God (FL) **507**
Southeastern Louisiana U (LA) **508**
Southeastern Oklahoma State U (OK) **508**
Southeast Missouri State U (MO) **508**
Southern Adventist U (TN) **508**
Southern Methodist U (TX) **510**
Southern Nazarene U (OK) **510**
Southern U and A&M Coll (LA) **511**
Southwest Missouri State U (MO) **513**
Southwest Texas State U (TX) **513**
State U of NY at Binghamton (NY) **515**
State U of NY Coll at Potsdam (NY) **517**
State U of West Georgia (GA) **518**
Stephen F. Austin State U (TX) **518**
Stetson U (FL) **519**
Syracuse U (NY) **521**
Texas Christian U (TX) **526**
Texas Tech U (TX) **526**
Texas Woman's U (TX) **527**
Toccoa Falls Coll (GA) **528**
Transylvania U (KY) **529**
Trinity Christian Coll (IL) **530**
Trinity U (TX) **531**
Union Coll (NE) **534**
Union U (TN) **534**
U at Buffalo, The State University of New York (NY) **536**
The U of Akron (OH) **537**
U of Alaska Anchorage (AK) **538**
The U of Arizona (AZ) **538**
U of Arkansas (AR) **539**
U of Central Arkansas (AR) **542**
U of Central Florida (FL) **542**
U of Denver (CO) **544**
U of Georgia (GA) **545**
U of Hartford (CT) **546**
U of Hawaii at Manoa (HI) **546**
U of Houston (TX) **547**
U of Idaho (ID) **547**
U of Illinois at Urbana–Champaign (IL) **548**
U of Indianapolis (IN) **548**
U of Kentucky (KY) **549**
U of Louisiana at Lafayette (LA) **550**
U of Louisville (KY) **550**
U of Mary Hardin-Baylor (TX) **551**
U of Maryland, Coll Park (MD) **552**
U of Massachusetts Amherst (MA) **552**
U of Massachusetts Lowell (MA) **553**
U of Miami (FL) **553**
The U of Montana–Missoula (MT) **556**
U of Nevada, Reno (NV) **558**
U of New Mexico (NM) **559**
The U of North Carolina at Chapel Hill (NC) **560**
The U of North Carolina at Charlotte (NC) **560**
The U of North Carolina at Wilmington (NC) **561**
U of North Dakota (ND) **561**
U of Northern Iowa (IA) **561**
U of North Florida (FL) **561**
U of North Texas (TX) **562**
U of Puget Sound (WA) **571**
U of Redlands (CA) **572**
U of Rhode Island (RI) **572**
U of South Alabama (AL) **575**
U of Southern California (CA) **576**
U of Southern Maine (ME) **576**
U of South Florida (FL) **576**
The U of Texas at Austin (TX) **578**
The U of the Arts (PA) **579**
U of Vermont (VT) **582**
U of Washington (WA) **583**
U of West Florida (FL) **583**
U of Windsor (ON, Canada) **584**
U of Wyoming (WY) **586**
Valparaiso U (IN) **588**
Virginia Commonwealth U (VA) **590**
Virginia State U (VA) **591**
Viterbo U (WI) **591**
Wartburg Coll (IA) **594**
Washington State U (WA) **595**
Weber State U (UT) **596**
Webster U (MO) **597**
Western Michigan U (MI) **599**
West Texas A&M U (TX) **602**
Wheaton Coll (IL) **603**
Wheeling Jesuit U (WV) **603**
Wilkes U (PA) **605**
William Jewell Coll (MO) **606**
York U (ON, Canada) **611**
Youngstown State U (OH) **611**

MUSIC HISTORY

Overview: Students study the historical development of music and its role in human culture as well as musical instruments and techniques and musical literature. *Related majors:* music, art history, history, musicology and ethnomusicology, medieval and Renaissance studies. *Potential careers:* writer, editor, radio producer, college professor. *Salary potential:* $25k-$33k.

Appalachian State U (NC) **270**
Aquinas Coll (MI) **270**
Baldwin-Wallace Coll (OH) **280**
Bard Coll (NY) **281**
Baylor U (TX) **283**
Belmont U (TN) **284**
Bennington Coll (VT) **286**
Birmingham-Southern Coll (AL) **289**
Boston U (MA) **292**
Bowling Green State U (OH) **292**
Brandon U (MB, Canada) **293**
Bucknell U (PA) **297**
Butler U (IN) **297**
California State U, Fresno (CA) **301**
California State U, Fullerton (CA) **301**
California State U, Long Beach (CA) **301**
California State U, Northridge (CA) **301**
Calvin Coll (MI) **303**
The Catholic U of America (DC) **307**
Central Michigan U (MI) **310**
Christopher Newport U (VA) **313**
The Coll of Wooster (OH) **324**
Converse Coll (SC) **332**
Eugene Lang Coll, New School U (NY) **355**
Fairfield U (CT) **356**
Florida State U (FL) **361**
Fordham U (NY) **362**
Goddard Coll (VT) **369**
Hampshire Coll (MA) **375**
Harvard U (MA) **376**
Hastings Coll (NE) **377**

MUSIC HISTORY (continued)

Hope Coll (MI) ***381***
Indiana U Bloomington (IN) ***385***
Keene State Coll (NH) ***396***
Lafayette Coll (PA) ***400***
La Salle U (PA) ***402***
Long Island U, Southampton Coll, Friends World Program (NY) ***409***
Luther Coll (IA) ***412***
Marlboro Coll (VT) ***418***
McGill U (QC, Canada) ***423***
McMaster U (ON, Canada) ***423***
Memorial U of Newfoundland (NF, Canada) ***424***
Mount Allison U (NB, Canada) ***437***
Nazareth Coll of Rochester (NY) ***443***
New England Conservatory of Music (MA) ***445***
Northeastern U (MA) ***450***
North Greenville Coll (SC) ***451***
Northwestern U (IL) ***453***
Oberlin Coll (OH) ***456***
The Ohio State U (OH) ***457***
Ohio U (OH) ***458***
Otterbein Coll (OH) ***462***
Randolph-Macon Woman's Coll (VA) ***477***
Rice U (TX) ***479***
Rockford Coll (IL) ***482***
Rollins Coll (FL) ***483***
Roosevelt U (IL) ***483***
St. Cloud State U (MN) ***488***
Saint Joseph's Coll (IN) ***490***
Sarah Lawrence Coll (NY) ***499***
Seton Hall U (NJ) ***502***
Simmons Coll (MA) ***504***
Skidmore Coll (NY) ***506***
Southwestern U (TX) ***513***
State U of NY at New Paltz (NY) ***515***
State U of NY Coll at Fredonia (NY) ***516***
State U of NY Coll at Potsdam (NY) ***517***
Temple U (PA) ***523***
Texas Christian U (TX) ***526***
The U of Akron (OH) ***537***
U of Alberta (AB, Canada) ***538***
The U of British Columbia (BC, Canada) ***540***
U of Calif, San Diego (CA) ***541***
U of Chicago (IL) ***542***
U of Cincinnati (OH) ***543***
U of Hartford (CT) ***546***
U of Hawaii at Manoa (HI) ***546***
U of Idaho (ID) ***547***
U of Illinois at Urbana–Champaign (IL) ***548***
The U of Iowa (IA) ***548***
U of Kansas (KS) ***549***
U of Kentucky (KY) ***549***
U of Louisville (KY) ***550***
U of Michigan (MI) ***554***
U of Michigan–Dearborn (MI) ***554***
U of Missouri–St. Louis (MO) ***556***
U of New Hampshire (NH) ***558***
The U of North Carolina at Greensboro (NC) ***560***
U of North Texas (TX) ***562***
U of Ottawa (ON, Canada) ***563***
U of Redlands (CA) ***572***
U of Richmond (VA) ***572***
U of Rochester (NY) ***573***
The U of Texas at Austin (TX) ***578***
U of the Incarnate Word (TX) ***580***
U of the Pacific (CA) ***580***
U of the South (TN) ***581***
U of Toronto (ON, Canada) ***581***
U of Vermont (VT) ***582***
U of Victoria (BC, Canada) ***582***
U of Washington (WA) ***583***
The U of Western Ontario (ON, Canada) ***583***
U of Windsor (ON, Canada) ***584***
U of Wisconsin–Milwaukee (WI) ***585***
Washington U in St. Louis (MO) ***595***
West Chester U of Pennsylvania (PA) ***598***
Western Connecticut State U (CT) ***598***
Western Michigan U (MI) ***599***
Western Washington U (WA) ***600***
Westfield State Coll (MA) ***600***
Wheaton Coll (IL) ***603***
Wright State U (OH) ***609***
York U (ON, Canada) ***611***
Youngstown State U (OH) ***611***

MUSICOLOGY

Overview: Students taking this major study the role of music in Western and non-Western cultures and examine the various forms and methods for creating music. *Related studies:* area studies, folklore, history, music theory and composition, music history. *Potential careers:* anthropologist, music theorist, musician, writer, professor. *Salary potential:* $10k-$30k.

Brown U (RI) ***296***
St. Olaf Coll (MN) ***495***
Texas Christian U (TX) ***526***
The U of Akron (OH) ***537***
U of Calif, Los Angeles (CA) ***541***
U of Denver (CO) ***544***
U of Miami (FL) ***553***
U of Oregon (OR) ***562***
U of Washington (WA) ***583***
York U (ON, Canada) ***611***

MUSIC (PIANO AND ORGAN PERFORMANCE)

Overview: This major teaches students how to play the piano, organ, and other keyboard instruments. *Related majors:* music performance. *Potential careers:* musician, choral church music director, music teacher. *Salary potential:* $10k-$25k

Abilene Christian U (TX) ***260***
Acadia U (NS, Canada) ***260***
Andrews U (MI) ***269***
Anna Maria Coll (MA) ***269***
Appalachian State U (NC) ***270***
Aquinas Coll (MI) ***270***
Auburn U (AL) ***276***
Augustana Coll (IL) ***276***
Baldwin-Wallace Coll (OH) ***280***
Ball State U (IN) ***280***
Barry U (FL) ***282***
Belmont U (TN) ***284***
Benedictine Coll (KS) ***285***
Berklee Coll of Music (MA) ***286***
Berry Coll (GA) ***287***
Bethel Coll (IN) ***288***
Birmingham-Southern Coll (AL) ***289***
Blue Mountain Coll (MS) ***291***
Boston U (MA) ***292***
Bowling Green State U (OH) ***292***
Brandon U (MB, Canada) ***293***
Brenau U (GA) ***293***
Brigham Young U–Hawaii (HI) ***295***
Bryan Coll (TN) ***296***
Butler U (IN) ***297***
California Inst of the Arts (CA) ***299***
California State U, Fullerton (CA) ***301***
California State U, Northridge (CA) ***301***
Calvin Coll (MI) ***303***
Cameron U (OK) ***303***
Campbellsville U (KY) ***303***
Campbell U (NC) ***303***
Canadian Mennonite U (MB, Canada) ***304***
Capital U (OH) ***304***
Carson-Newman Coll (TN) ***306***
Catawba Coll (NC) ***307***
The Catholic U of America (DC) ***307***
Cedarville U (OH) ***308***
Centenary Coll of Louisiana (LA) ***308***
Central Washington U (WA) ***310***
Chapman U (CA) ***311***
Cincinnati Bible Coll and Seminary (OH) ***314***
Cleveland Inst of Music (OH) ***317***
Coker Coll (SC) ***318***
Columbia Coll (SC) ***327***
Columbus State U (GA) ***328***
Concordia Coll (MN) ***329***
Concordia U (IL) ***330***
Concordia U (MI) ***330***
Concordia U (NE) ***330***
Conservatory of Music of Puerto Rico (PR) ***332***
Converse Coll (SC) ***332***
Cornish Coll of the Arts (WA) ***333***
The Curtis Inst of Music (PA) ***335***
Dallas Baptist U (TX) ***336***
DePaul U (IL) ***339***
Dillard U (LA) ***344***
Drake U (IA) ***345***
Eastern Washington U (WA) ***349***
East Texas Baptist U (TX) ***350***
Erskine Coll (SC) ***354***
Five Towns Coll (NY) ***359***
Florida State U (FL) ***361***
Furman U (SC) ***365***
Georgetown Coll (KY) ***366***
Grace Coll (IN) ***370***
Grand Canyon U (AZ) ***371***
Grand Valley State U (MI) ***371***
Hannibal-LaGrange Coll (MO) ***375***
Harding U (AR) ***375***
Hardin-Simmons U (TX) ***376***
Hastings Coll (NE) ***377***
Heidelberg Coll (OH) ***377***
Houghton Coll (NY) ***381***
Howard Payne U (TX) ***382***
Huntingdon Coll (AL) ***383***
Huntington Coll (IN) ***383***
Illinois Wesleyan U (IL) ***385***
Indiana U Bloomington (IN) ***385***
Indiana U–Purdue U Fort Wayne (IN) ***386***
Inter American U of PR, San Germán Campus (PR) ***388***
Ithaca Coll (NY) ***390***
Jackson State U (MS) ***390***
The Juilliard School (NY) ***395***
Lamar U (TX) ***401***
Lambuth U (TN) ***401***
Lawrence U (WI) ***403***
Lee U (TN) ***404***
Lincoln Christian Coll (IL) ***407***
Lipscomb U (TN) ***408***
Louisiana Coll (LA) ***410***
Loyola U New Orleans (LA) ***411***
Luther Coll (IA) ***412***
Manhattan School of Music (NY) ***416***
Mannes Coll of Music, New School U (NY) ***416***
Mansfield U of Pennsylvania (PA) ***416***
Maryville Coll (TN) ***420***
The Master's Coll and Seminary (CA) ***422***
McGill U (QC, Canada) ***423***
Memorial U of Newfoundland (NF, Canada) ***424***
Meredith Coll (NC) ***426***
Milligan Coll (TN) ***430***
Minnesota State U, Mankato (MN) ***431***
Minnesota State U, Moorhead (MN) ***432***
Mississippi Coll (MS) ***432***
Montclair State U (NJ) ***435***
Montreat Coll (NC) ***435***
Mount Allison U (NB, Canada) ***437***
Mount Vernon Nazarene U (OH) ***440***
Newberry Coll (SC) ***444***
New England Conservatory of Music (MA) ***445***
New World School of the Arts (FL) ***447***
New York U (NY) ***447***
North Carolina School of the Arts (NC) ***449***
North Central Coll (IL) ***449***
Northeastern State U (OK) ***450***
Northern Michigan U (MI) ***451***
North Greenville Coll (SC) ***451***
Northwest Coll (WA) ***452***
Northwestern Coll (MN) ***453***
Northwestern U (IL) ***453***
Northwest Missouri State U (MO) ***454***
Notre Dame de Namur U (CA) ***455***
Nyack Coll (NY) ***456***
Oakland U (MI) ***456***
Oberlin Coll (OH) ***456***
The Ohio State U (OH) ***457***
Ohio U (OH) ***458***
Oklahoma Baptist U (OK) ***459***
Oklahoma City U (OK) ***460***
Olivet Nazarene U (IL) ***461***
Otterbein Coll (OH) ***462***
Ouachita Baptist U (AR) ***462***
Pacific Lutheran U (WA) ***463***
Pacific Union Coll (CA) ***464***
Peabody Conserv of Music of Johns Hopkins U (MD) ***466***
Pittsburg State U (KS) ***470***
Prairie View A&M U (TX) ***473***
Queens U of Charlotte (NC) ***476***
Rider U (NJ) ***480***
Roberts Wesleyan Coll (NY) ***481***
Roosevelt U (IL) ***483***
Saint Mary-of-the-Woods Coll (IN) ***493***
Saint Mary's Coll (IN) ***493***
Samford U (AL) ***497***
San Francisco Conservatory of Music (CA) ***498***
Sarah Lawrence Coll (NY) ***499***
Seton Hill U (PA) ***502***
Shenandoah U (VA) ***503***
Shorter Coll (GA) ***504***
Southern Methodist U (TX) ***510***
Southern Nazarene U (OK) ***510***
Southwestern Oklahoma State U (OK) ***512***
Southwestern U (TX) ***513***
Spring Arbor U (MI) ***514***
State U of NY Coll at Fredonia (NY) ***516***
Stetson U (FL) ***519***
Susquehanna U (PA) ***521***
Syracuse U (NY) ***521***
Tabor Coll (KS) ***522***
Taylor U (IN) ***523***
Temple U (PA) ***523***
Tennessee Temple U (TN) ***524***
Texas A&M U–Commerce (TX) ***525***
Texas Christian U (TX) ***526***
Texas Southern U (TX) ***526***
Toccoa Falls Coll (GA) ***528***
Trinity Christian Coll (IL) ***530***
Truman State U (MO) ***532***
Union U (TN) ***534***
The U of Akron (OH) ***537***
U of Alberta (AB, Canada) ***538***
The U of British Columbia (BC, Canada) ***540***
U of Central Oklahoma (OK) ***542***
U of Cincinnati (OH) ***543***
U of Delaware (DE) ***544***
The U of Iowa (IA) ***548***
U of Kansas (KS) ***549***
U of Miami (FL) ***553***
U of Michigan (MI) ***554***
U of Minnesota, Duluth (MN) ***554***
U of Missouri–Kansas City (MO) ***555***
U of Montevallo (AL) ***557***
U of New Hampshire (NH) ***558***
The U of North Carolina at Greensboro (NC) ***560***
U of North Texas (TX) ***562***
U of Oklahoma (OK) ***562***
U of Redlands (CA) ***572***
U of Sioux Falls (SD) ***574***
The U of South Dakota (SD) ***575***
U of Southern California (CA) ***576***
The U of Tennessee at Chattanooga (TN) ***577***
The U of Tennessee at Martin (TN) ***577***
U of the Pacific (CA) ***580***
U of Tulsa (OK) ***581***
U of Victoria (BC, Canada) ***582***
U of Washington (WA) ***583***
The U of Western Ontario (ON, Canada) ***583***
Valdosta State U (GA) ***588***
Vanderbilt U (TN) ***588***
Viterbo U (WI) ***591***
Walla Walla Coll (WA) ***593***
Weber State U (UT) ***596***
Webster U (MO) ***597***
West Chester U of Pennsylvania (PA) ***598***
Westminster Choir Coll of Rider U (NJ) ***601***
Whitworth Coll (WA) ***604***
Wingate U (NC) ***607***
Wittenberg U (OH) ***608***
Xavier U of Louisiana (LA) ***610***
York U (ON, Canada) ***611***
Youngstown State U (OH) ***611***

MUSIC RELATED

Information can be found under this major's main heading.

Brenau U (GA) ***293***
Brown U (RI) ***296***
Central Baptist Coll (AR) ***309***
Chestnut Hill Coll (PA) ***312***
Connecticut Coll (CT) ***331***
Duquesne U (PA) ***346***
Hampton U (VA) ***375***
Indiana State U (IN) ***385***
Lebanon Valley Coll (PA) ***403***
McGill U (QC, Canada) ***423***
Northwestern U (IL) ***453***
Saint Mary's U of Minnesota (MN) ***494***
St. Olaf Coll (MN) ***495***
San Diego State U (CA) ***498***
Shenandoah U (VA) ***503***
Southwest Texas State U (TX) ***513***
State U of NY Coll at Potsdam (NY) ***517***
The U of Arizona (AZ) ***538***
The U of North Carolina at Asheville (NC) ***559***
U of St. Thomas (MN) ***573***
Western Kentucky U (KY) ***599***

Wheaton Coll (IL) **603**

MUSIC TEACHER EDUCATION

Overview: This major prepares undergraduates to teach music and music appreciation courses at various educational levels. Those candidates who wish to teach a particular instrument are usually required to be proficient at that instrument. *Related majors:* music, music-general performance, music-voice and choral/opera performance, jazz. *Potential careers:* music teacher, choral director, band director. *Salary potential:* $23k-$33k.

Abilene Christian U (TX) **260**
Acadia U (NS, Canada) **260**
Adams State Coll (CO) **260**
Adelphi U (NY) **260**
Adrian Coll (MI) **260**
Alabama A&M U (AL) **261**
Alabama State U (AL) **261**
Alcorn State U (MS) **263**
Alderson-Broaddus Coll (WV) **263**
Allen U (SC) **264**
Alma Coll (MI) **264**
Alverno Coll (WI) **265**
Anderson Coll (SC) **268**
Anderson U (IN) **268**
Andrews U (MI) **269**
Anna Maria Coll (MA) **269**
Appalachian State U (NC) **270**
Aquinas Coll (MI) **270**
Arizona State U (AZ) **271**
Arkansas State U (AR) **272**
Arkansas Tech U (AR) **272**
Arlington Baptist Coll (TX) **272**
Armstrong Atlantic State U (GA) **273**
Asbury Coll (KY) **274**
Ashland U (OH) **274**
Atlantic Union Coll (MA) **276**
Auburn U (AL) **276**
Augsburg Coll (MN) **276**
Augustana Coll (IL) **276**
Augustana Coll (SD) **276**
Augusta State U (GA) **277**
Baker U (KS) **280**
Baldwin-Wallace Coll (OH) **280**
Ball State U (IN) **280**
Baptist Bible Coll (MO) **281**
Baylor U (TX) **283**
Belmont U (TN) **284**
Beloit Coll (WI) **285**
Bemidji State U (MN) **285**
Benedictine Coll (KS) **285**
Benedictine U (IL) **285**
Bennett Coll (NC) **286**
Berea Coll (KY) **286**
Berklee Coll of Music (MA) **286**
Berry Coll (GA) **287**
Bethany Coll (KS) **287**
Bethany Coll of the Assemblies of God (CA) **287**
Bethel Coll (IN) **288**
Bethel Coll (MN) **288**
Bethune-Cookman Coll (FL) **289**
Birmingham-Southern Coll (AL) **289**
Bluefield Coll (VA) **291**
Blue Mountain Coll (MS) **291**
Bluffton Coll (OH) **291**
Boston U (MA) **292**
Bowling Green State U (OH) **292**
Bradley U (IL) **293**
Brandon U (MB, Canada) **293**
Brenau U (GA) **293**
Brewton-Parker Coll (GA) **294**
Bridgewater Coll (VA) **294**
Brigham Young U (UT) **295**
Brock U (ON, Canada) **295**
Brooklyn Coll of the City U of NY (NY) **295**
Bryan Coll (TN) **296**
Bucknell U (PA) **297**
Buena Vista U (IA) **297**
Butler U (IN) **297**
California State U, Chico (CA) **300**
California State U, Dominguez Hills (CA) **300**
California State U, Fresno (CA) **301**
California State U, Fullerton (CA) **301**
California State U, Northridge (CA) **301**
Calvin Coll (MI) **303**
Cameron U (OK) **303**
Campbellsville U (KY) **303**
Campbell U (NC) **303**
Capital U (OH) **304**
Carroll Coll (WI) **306**
Carson-Newman Coll (TN) **306**
Carthage Coll (WI) **306**
Case Western Reserve U (OH) **307**
Castleton State Coll (VT) **307**
Catawba Coll (NC) **307**
The Catholic U of America (DC) **307**
Cedarville U (OH) **308**
Centenary Coll of Louisiana (LA) **308**
Central Coll (IA) **309**
Central Connecticut State U (CT) **309**
Central Methodist Coll (MO) **309**
Central Michigan U (MI) **310**
Central Missouri State U (MO) **310**
Central Washington U (WA) **310**
Chadron State Coll (NE) **311**
Chapman U (CA) **311**
Charleston Southern U (SC) **311**
Chestnut Hill Coll (PA) **312**
Chowan Coll (NC) **312**
Christian Heritage Coll (CA) **313**
Christopher Newport U (VA) **313**
City Coll of the City U of NY (NY) **314**
Claflin U (SC) **314**
Clarion U of Pennsylvania (PA) **315**
Clark Atlanta U (GA) **315**
Clarke Coll (IA) **315**
Clearwater Christian Coll (FL) **316**
Cleveland Inst of Music (OH) **317**
Coe Coll (IA) **318**
Coker Coll (SC) **318**
The Coll of New Jersey (NJ) **320**
Coll of Saint Benedict (MN) **321**
Coll of St. Catherine (MN) **321**
The Coll of Saint Rose (NY) **322**
Coll of the Ozarks (MO) **323**
The Coll of Wooster (OH) **324**
Colorado State U (CO) **325**
Colorado State U-Pueblo (CO) **325**
Columbia Coll (SC) **327**
Columbia Union Coll (MD) **328**
Columbus State U (GA) **328**
Concord Coll (WV) **329**
Concordia Coll (MN) **329**
Concordia Coll (NY) **329**
Concordia U (IL) **330**
Concordia U (MN) **330**
Concordia U (NE) **330**
Concordia U Wisconsin (WI) **331**
Connecticut Coll (CT) **331**
Conservatory of Music of Puerto Rico (PR) **332**
Converse Coll (SC) **332**
Cornell Coll (IA) **332**
Cornerstone U (MI) **333**
Crown Coll (MN) **334**
Culver-Stockton Coll (MO) **334**
Cumberland Coll (KY) **335**
Cumberland U (TN) **335**
Dakota State U (SD) **335**
Dakota Wesleyan U (SD) **336**
Dallas Baptist U (TX) **336**
Dana Coll (NE) **337**
Davis & Elkins Coll (WV) **338**
Delaware State U (DE) **338**
Delta State U (MS) **339**
DePaul U (IL) **339**
DePauw U (IN) **339**
Dickinson State U (ND) **344**
Dillard U (LA) **344**
Dordt Coll (IA) **345**
Dowling Coll (NY) **345**
Drake U (IA) **345**
Drury U (MO) **346**
Duquesne U (PA) **346**
East Carolina U (NC) **347**
East Central U (OK) **347**
Eastern Kentucky U (KY) **348**
Eastern Mennonite U (VA) **348**
Eastern Michigan U (MI) **348**
Eastern Nazarene Coll (MA) **348**
Eastern New Mexico U (NM) **349**
Eastern Washington U (WA) **349**
East Texas Baptist U (TX) **350**
Elizabeth City State U (NC) **351**
Elizabethtown Coll (PA) **351**
Elmhurst Coll (IL) **351**
Elon U (NC) **352**
Emporia State U (KS) **354**
Erskine Coll (SC) **354**
Eureka Coll (IL) **355**
Evangel U (MO) **355**
Fairmont State Coll (WV) **356**
Faith Baptist Bible Coll and Theological Seminary (IA) **356**
Fayetteville State U (NC) **357**
Fisk U (TN) **358**
Five Towns Coll (NY) **359**
Florida A&M U (FL) **359**
Florida Atlantic U (FL) **359**
Florida International U (FL) **360**
Florida Southern Coll (FL) **361**
Florida State U (FL) **361**
Fort Hays State U (KS) **362**
Fort Lewis Coll (CO) **362**
The Franciscan U (IA) **363**
Freed-Hardeman U (TN) **364**
Free Will Baptist Bible Coll (TN) **364**
Fresno Pacific U (CA) **364**
Furman U (SC) **365**
Gardner-Webb U (NC) **365**
Geneva Coll (PA) **366**
George Fox U (OR) **366**
Georgetown Coll (KY) **366**
Georgia Coll & State U (GA) **367**
Georgian Court Coll (NJ) **367**
Georgia Southern U (GA) **367**
Georgia Southwestern State U (GA) **368**
Gettysburg Coll (PA) **368**
Glenville State Coll (WV) **368**
God's Bible School and Coll (OH) **369**
Gonzaga U (WA) **369**
Gordon Coll (MA) **370**
Goshen Coll (IN) **370**
Grace Bible Coll (MI) **370**
Grace Coll (IN) **370**
Graceland U (IA) **371**
Grace U (NE) **371**
Grambling State U (LA) **371**
Grand Canyon U (AZ) **371**
Grand Valley State U (MI) **371**
Greensboro Coll (NC) **372**
Greenville Coll (IL) **373**
Grove City Coll (PA) **373**
Gustavus Adolphus Coll (MN) **374**
Hamline U (MN) **374**
Hampton U (VA) **375**
Hannibal-LaGrange Coll (MO) **375**
Harding U (AR) **375**
Hardin-Simmons U (TX) **376**
Hartwick Coll (NY) **376**
Hastings Coll (NE) **377**
Heidelberg Coll (OH) **377**
Henderson State U (AR) **378**
Hofstra U (NY) **380**
Hope Coll (MI) **381**
Hope International U (CA) **381**
Houghton Coll (NY) **381**
Houston Baptist U (TX) **382**
Howard Payne U (TX) **382**
Humboldt State U (CA) **382**
Huntingdon Coll (AL) **383**
Huntington Coll (IN) **383**
Idaho State U (ID) **384**
Illinois State U (IL) **384**
Illinois Wesleyan U (IL) **385**
Immaculata U (PA) **385**
Indiana U Bloomington (IN) **385**
Indiana U of Pennsylvania (PA) **386**
Indiana U–Purdue U Fort Wayne (IN) **386**
Indiana U South Bend (IN) **387**
Indiana Wesleyan U (IN) **387**
Inter American U of PR, San Germán Campus (PR) **388**
Iowa State U of Science and Technology (IA) **390**
Iowa Wesleyan Coll (IA) **390**
Ithaca Coll (NY) **390**
Jackson State U (MS) **390**
Jacksonville State U (AL) **390**
Jacksonville U (FL) **391**
John Brown U (AR) **392**
Johns Hopkins U (MD) **392**
Johnson State Coll (VT) **394**
Judson Coll (AL) **395**
Judson Coll (IL) **395**
Kansas State U (KS) **396**
Kean U (NJ) **396**
Keene State Coll (NH) **396**
Kennesaw State U (GA) **397**
Kent State U (OH) **397**
Kentucky Christian Coll (KY) **397**
Kentucky State U (KY) **397**
Kentucky Wesleyan Coll (KY) **397**
Lakeland Coll (WI) **401**
Lamar U (TX) **401**
Lambuth U (TN) **401**
Lander U (SC) **401**
Langston U (OK) **402**
La Sierra U (CA) **403**
Lawrence U (WI) **403**
Lebanon Valley Coll (PA) **403**
Lee U (TN) **404**
Lenoir-Rhyne Coll (NC) **405**
Liberty U (VA) **406**
Limestone Coll (SC) **406**
Lindenwood U (MO) **407**
Lipscomb U (TN) **408**
Long Island U, C.W. Post Campus (NY) **409**
Long Island U, Southampton Coll, Friends World Program (NY) **409**
Longwood U (VA) **409**
Louisiana Coll (LA) **410**
Louisiana State U and A&M Coll (LA) **410**
Louisiana Tech U (LA) **410**
Loyola U New Orleans (LA) **411**
Lubbock Christian U (TX) **412**
Luther Coll (IA) **412**
Lycoming Coll (PA) **412**
MacMurray Coll (IL) **414**
Madonna U (MI) **414**
Malone Coll (OH) **415**
Manchester Coll (IN) **415**
Manhattanville Coll (NY) **416**
Mansfield U of Pennsylvania (PA) **416**
Maranatha Baptist Bible Coll (WI) **417**
Marian Coll (IN) **417**
Marian Coll of Fond du Lac (WI) **417**
Mars Hill Coll (NC) **418**
Maryville Coll (TN) **420**
Mary Washington Coll (VA) **420**
Marywood U (PA) **421**
The Master's Coll and Seminary (CA) **422**
McGill U (QC, Canada) **423**
McMaster U (ON, Canada) **423**
McMurry U (TX) **423**
McNeese State U (LA) **423**
McPherson Coll (KS) **423**
Memorial U of Newfoundland (NF, Canada) **424**
Mercer U (GA) **425**
Mercy Coll (NY) **425**
Mercyhurst Coll (PA) **425**
Meredith Coll (NC) **426**
Mesa State Coll (CO) **426**
Messiah Coll (PA) **426**
Methodist Coll (NC) **427**
Metropolitan State Coll of Denver (CO) **427**
Miami U (OH) **428**
Michigan State U (MI) **428**
MidAmerica Nazarene U (KS) **428**
Midland Lutheran Coll (NE) **429**
Midwestern State U (TX) **430**
Millersville U of Pennsylvania (PA) **430**
Milligan Coll (TN) **430**
Millikin U (IL) **430**
Minnesota State U, Mankato (MN) **431**
Minnesota State U, Moorhead (MN) **432**
Minot State U (ND) **432**
Mississippi Coll (MS) **432**
Mississippi State U (MS) **432**
Mississippi Valley State U (MS) **432**
Missouri Southern State Coll (MO) **433**
Missouri Western State Coll (MO) **433**
Montana State U–Billings (MT) **434**
Montana State U–Bozeman (MT) **434**
Montclair State U (NJ) **435**
Moravian Coll (PA) **436**
Morehead State U (KY) **436**
Morningside Coll (IA) **437**
Mount Marty Coll (SD) **438**
Mount Mary Coll (WI) **438**
Mount Mercy Coll (IA) **438**
Mount St. Mary's Coll (CA) **439**
Mount Union Coll (OH) **440**
Mount Vernon Nazarene U (OH) **440**
Murray State U (KY) **440**
Muskingum Coll (OH) **441**
Nazareth Coll of Rochester (NY) **443**
Nebraska Wesleyan U (NE) **443**
Newberry Coll (SC) **444**
New Jersey City U (NJ) **445**
New Mexico Highlands U (NM) **446**

MUSIC TEACHER EDUCATION (continued)

New Mexico State U (NM) ***446***
New York U (NY) ***447***
Nicholls State U (LA) ***447***
North Carolina Ag and Tech State U (NC) ***448***
North Carolina Central U (NC) ***448***
North Dakota State U (ND) ***449***
Northeastern State U (OK) ***450***
Northern Arizona U (AZ) ***450***
Northern Illinois U (IL) ***450***
Northern Michigan U (MI) ***451***
Northern State U (SD) ***451***
North Georgia Coll & State U (GA) ***451***
North Greenville Coll (SC) ***451***
Northland Coll (WI) ***452***
North Park U (IL) ***452***
Northwest Coll (WA) ***452***
Northwestern Coll (IA) ***453***
Northwestern Coll (MN) ***453***
Northwestern Oklahoma State U (OK) ***453***
Northwestern State U of Louisiana (LA) ***453***
Northwestern U (IL) ***453***
Northwest Missouri State U (MO) ***454***
Northwest Nazarene U (ID) ***454***
Nyack Coll (NY) ***456***
Oakland City U (IN) ***456***
Oakland U (MI) ***456***
Oakwood Coll (AL) ***456***
Oberlin Coll (OH) ***456***
Ohio Northern U (OH) ***457***
The Ohio State U (OH) ***457***
Ohio U (OH) ***458***
Ohio Wesleyan U (OH) ***459***
Oklahoma Baptist U (OK) ***459***
Oklahoma Christian U (OK) ***459***
Oklahoma City U (OK) ***460***
Oklahoma State U (OK) ***460***
Olivet Nazarene U (IL) ***461***
Oral Roberts U (OK) ***461***
Ottawa U (KS) ***462***
Otterbein Coll (OH) ***462***
Ouachita Baptist U (AR) ***462***
Pacific Lutheran U (WA) ***463***
Pacific Union Coll (CA) ***464***
Pacific U (OR) ***464***
Paine Coll (GA) ***465***
Palm Beach Atlantic U (FL) ***465***
Peabody Conserv of Music of Johns Hopkins U (MD) ***466***
Penn State U Univ Park Campus (PA) ***468***
Pepperdine U, Malibu (CA) ***469***
Peru State Coll (NE) ***469***
Pfeiffer U (NC) ***469***
Piedmont Baptist Coll (NC) ***470***
Pillsbury Baptist Bible Coll (MN) ***470***
Pittsburg State U (KS) ***470***
Plymouth State Coll (NH) ***471***
Pontifical Catholic U of Puerto Rico (PR) ***472***
Presbyterian Coll (SC) ***473***
Prescott Coll (AZ) ***474***
Queens Coll of the City U of NY (NY) ***475***
Queen's U at Kingston (ON, Canada) ***476***
Quincy U (IL) ***476***
Reformed Bible Coll (MI) ***477***
Rhode Island Coll (RI) ***479***
Rider U (NJ) ***480***
Ripon Coll (WI) ***480***
Roberts Wesleyan Coll (NY) ***481***
Rochester Coll (MI) ***482***
Rocky Mountain Coll (MT) ***482***
Roosevelt U (IL) ***483***
Rowan U (NJ) ***484***
Rutgers, The State U of New Jersey, New Brunswick (NJ) ***485***
St. Ambrose U (IA) ***486***
Saint Augustine's Coll (NC) ***487***
St. Cloud State U (MN) ***488***
Saint John's U (MN) ***490***
Saint Joseph Coll (CT) ***490***
Saint Joseph's Coll (IN) ***490***
Saint Mary-of-the-Woods Coll (IN) ***493***
Saint Mary's Coll (IN) ***493***
Saint Mary's U of Minnesota (MN) ***494***
Saint Michael's Coll (VT) ***494***
St. Norbert Coll (WI) ***495***
St. Olaf Coll (MN) ***495***
Saint Vincent Coll (PA) ***496***
Saint Xavier U (IL) ***496***
Samford U (AL) ***497***
Sam Houston State U (TX) ***497***
San Jose State U (CA) ***499***
Seattle Pacific U (WA) ***501***
Seton Hill U (PA) ***502***
Shenandoah U (VA) ***503***
Shorter Coll (GA) ***504***
Siena Heights U (MI) ***504***
Silver Lake Coll (WI) ***504***
Simpson Coll (IA) ***505***
Simpson Coll and Graduate School (CA) ***505***
Slippery Rock U of Pennsylvania (PA) ***506***
Sonoma State U (CA) ***506***
South Carolina State U (SC) ***506***
South Dakota State U (SD) ***507***
Southeastern Coll of the Assemblies of God (FL) ***507***
Southeastern Louisiana U (LA) ***508***
Southeastern Oklahoma State U (OK) ***508***
Southeast Missouri State U (MO) ***508***
Southern Adventist U (TN) ***508***
Southern Arkansas U–Magnolia (AR) ***509***
Southern Methodist U (TX) ***510***
Southern Nazarene U (OK) ***510***
Southern U and A&M Coll (LA) ***511***
Southern Utah U (UT) ***511***
Southern Wesleyan U (SC) ***511***
Southwest Baptist U (MO) ***512***
Southwestern Coll (KS) ***512***
Southwestern Oklahoma State U (OK) ***512***
Southwestern U (TX) ***513***
Southwest Missouri State U (MO) ***513***
Southwest State U (MN) ***513***
Spring Arbor U (MI) ***514***
State U of NY Coll at Fredonia (NY) ***516***
State U of NY Coll at Potsdam (NY) ***517***
State U of West Georgia (GA) ***518***
Stephen F. Austin State U (TX) ***518***
Sterling Coll (KS) ***519***
Stetson U (FL) ***519***
Susquehanna U (PA) ***521***
Syracuse U (NY) ***521***
Tabor Coll (KS) ***522***
Talladega Coll (AL) ***522***
Tarleton State U (TX) ***522***
Taylor U (IN) ***523***
Temple U (PA) ***523***
Tennessee Technological U (TN) ***524***
Tennessee Temple U (TN) ***524***
Tennessee Wesleyan Coll (TN) ***524***
Texas A&M U–Commerce (TX) ***525***
Texas A&M U–Kingsville (TX) ***525***
Texas Christian U (TX) ***526***
Texas Lutheran U (TX) ***526***
Texas Southern U (TX) ***526***
Texas Wesleyan U (TX) ***526***
Thomas U (GA) ***528***
Toccoa Falls Coll (GA) ***528***
Towson U (MD) ***529***
Transylvania U (KY) ***529***
Trevecca Nazarene U (TN) ***529***
Trinity Christian Coll (IL) ***530***
Trinity International U (IL) ***531***
Troy State U (AL) ***532***
Union Coll (KY) ***533***
Union Coll (NE) ***534***
Union U (TN) ***534***
Universidad Adventista de las Antillas (PR) ***536***
Université Laval (QC, Canada) ***536***
The U of Akron (OH) ***537***
The U of Alabama (AL) ***537***
U of Alaska Anchorage (AK) ***538***
U of Alberta (AB, Canada) ***538***
The U of Arizona (AZ) ***538***
U of Arkansas at Monticello (AR) ***539***
The U of British Columbia (BC, Canada) ***540***
U of Central Arkansas (AR) ***542***
U of Central Florida (FL) ***542***
U of Central Oklahoma (OK) ***542***
U of Charleston (WV) ***542***
U of Cincinnati (OH) ***543***
U of Colorado at Boulder (CO) ***543***
U of Connecticut (CT) ***544***
U of Dayton (OH) ***544***
U of Delaware (DE) ***544***
U of Evansville (IN) ***545***
U of Florida (FL) ***545***
U of Georgia (GA) ***545***
U of Hartford (CT) ***546***
U of Hawaii at Manoa (HI) ***546***
U of Idaho (ID) ***547***
U of Illinois at Urbana–Champaign (IL) ***548***
U of Indianapolis (IN) ***548***
The U of Iowa (IA) ***548***
U of Kansas (KS) ***549***
U of Kentucky (KY) ***549***
U of La Verne (CA) ***549***
The U of Lethbridge (AB, Canada) ***549***
U of Louisiana at Lafayette (LA) ***550***
U of Louisville (KY) ***550***
U of Maine (ME) ***550***
U of Mary (ND) ***551***
U of Mary Hardin-Baylor (TX) ***551***
U of Maryland, Coll Park (MD) ***552***
U of Maryland Eastern Shore (MD) ***552***
U of Miami (FL) ***553***
U of Michigan (MI) ***554***
U of Michigan–Flint (MI) ***554***
U of Minnesota, Duluth (MN) ***554***
U of Minnesota, Twin Cities Campus (MN) ***555***
U of Missouri–Columbia (MO) ***555***
U of Missouri–Kansas City (MO) ***555***
U of Missouri–St. Louis (MO) ***556***
The U of Montana–Missoula (MT) ***556***
The U of Montana–Western (MT) ***556***
U of Montevallo (AL) ***557***
U of Nebraska at Omaha (NE) ***557***
U of Nebraska–Lincoln (NE) ***557***
U of Nevada, Reno (NV) ***558***
U of New Brunswick Fredericton (NB, Canada) ***558***
U of New Hampshire (NH) ***558***
U of New Mexico (NM) ***559***
U of New Orleans (LA) ***559***
The U of North Carolina at Charlotte (NC) ***560***
The U of North Carolina at Greensboro (NC) ***560***
The U of North Carolina at Pembroke (NC) ***560***
The U of North Carolina at Wilmington (NC) ***561***
U of North Dakota (ND) ***561***
U of Northern Colorado (CO) ***561***
U of Northern Iowa (IA) ***561***
U of North Florida (FL) ***561***
U of North Texas (TX) ***562***
U of Oklahoma (OK) ***562***
U of Oregon (OR) ***562***
U of Ottawa (ON, Canada) ***563***
U of Portland (OR) ***570***
U of Prince Edward Island (PE, Canada) ***570***
U of Puget Sound (WA) ***571***
U of Redlands (CA) ***572***
U of Regina (SK, Canada) ***572***
U of Rhode Island (RI) ***572***
U of Rio Grande (OH) ***572***
U of Rochester (NY) ***573***
U of St. Thomas (MN) ***573***
U of St. Thomas (TX) ***573***
U of Saskatchewan (SK, Canada) ***574***
U of Sioux Falls (SD) ***574***
U of South Carolina (SC) ***575***
The U of South Dakota (SD) ***575***
U of Southern Maine (ME) ***576***
U of Southern Mississippi (MS) ***576***
U of South Florida (FL) ***576***
The U of Tennessee (TN) ***577***
The U of Tennessee at Chattanooga (TN) ***577***
The U of Tennessee at Martin (TN) ***577***
U of the District of Columbia (DC) ***580***
U of the Incarnate Word (TX) ***580***
U of the Ozarks (AR) ***580***
U of the Pacific (CA) ***580***
U of the Virgin Islands (VI) ***581***
U of Toledo (OH) ***581***
U of Toronto (ON, Canada) ***581***
U of Tulsa (OK) ***581***
U of Utah (UT) ***582***
U of Vermont (VT) ***582***
U of Victoria (BC, Canada) ***582***
U of Washington (WA) ***583***
The U of Western Ontario (ON, Canada) ***583***
U of West Florida (FL) ***583***
U of Windsor (ON, Canada) ***584***
U of Wisconsin–La Crosse (WI) ***584***
U of Wisconsin–Madison (WI) ***584***
U of Wisconsin–Milwaukee (WI) ***585***
U of Wisconsin–Oshkosh (WI) ***585***
U of Wisconsin–River Falls (WI) ***585***
U of Wisconsin–Stevens Point (WI) ***585***
U of Wisconsin–Superior (WI) ***586***
U of Wisconsin–Whitewater (WI) ***586***
U of Wyoming (WY) ***586***
Upper Iowa U (IA) ***587***
Utah State U (UT) ***587***
Valdosta State U (GA) ***588***
Valley City State U (ND) ***588***
Valparaiso U (IN) ***588***
VanderCook Coll of Music (IL) ***589***
Virginia Wesleyan Coll (VA) ***591***
Viterbo U (WI) ***591***
Walla Walla Coll (WA) ***593***
Warner Pacific Coll (OR) ***593***
Warner Southern Coll (FL) ***593***
Wartburg Coll (IA) ***594***
Washington Bible Coll (MD) ***594***
Wayland Baptist U (TX) ***595***
Wayne State Coll (NE) ***596***
Weber State U (UT) ***596***
Webster U (MO) ***597***
West Chester U of Pennsylvania (PA) ***598***
Western Baptist Coll (OR) ***598***
Western Carolina U (NC) ***598***
Western Connecticut State U (CT) ***598***
Western Kentucky U (KY) ***599***
Western Michigan U (MI) ***599***
Western New Mexico U (NM) ***600***
Western State Coll of Colorado (CO) ***600***
Western Washington U (WA) ***600***
Westfield State Coll (MA) ***600***
West Liberty State Coll (WV) ***601***
Westminster Choir Coll of Rider U (NJ) ***601***
Westminster Coll (PA) ***601***
West Virginia State Coll (WV) ***602***
West Virginia Wesleyan Coll (WV) ***603***
Wheaton Coll (IL) ***603***
Whitworth Coll (WA) ***604***
Wichita State U (KS) ***604***
Wiley Coll (TX) ***605***
Wilkes U (PA) ***605***
Willamette U (OR) ***605***
William Carey Coll (MS) ***605***
William Jewell Coll (MO) ***606***
William Paterson U of New Jersey (NJ) ***606***
Williams Baptist Coll (AR) ***606***
Wilmington Coll (OH) ***607***
Wingate U (NC) ***607***
Winona State U (MN) ***608***
Winston-Salem State U (NC) ***608***
Winthrop U (SC) ***608***
Wittenberg U (OH) ***608***
Wright State U (OH) ***609***
Xavier U (OH) ***610***
Xavier U of Louisiana (LA) ***610***
York Coll (NE) ***610***
York Coll of Pennsylvania (PA) ***610***
York U (ON, Canada) ***611***
Youngstown State U (OH) ***611***

MUSIC THEORY AND COMPOSITION

Overview: Students study the theories and principles of making music and the various techniques for arranging sounds into musical forms. *Related majors:* music history, literature and theory, computer science, music performance. *Potential careers:* composer, musician, music producer, recording technician. *Salary potential:* $20k-$35k.

Appalachian State U (NC) ***270***
Arizona State U (AZ) ***271***
Bard Coll (NY) ***281***
Baylor U (TX) ***283***
Berklee Coll of Music (MA) ***286***
Boston U (MA) ***292***
Bowling Green State U (OH) ***292***
Bradley U (IL) ***293***
Brandon U (MB, Canada) ***293***
Brigham Young U (UT) ***295***
Bucknell U (PA) ***297***
Calvin Coll (MI) ***303***
Cameron U (OK) ***303***
Campbell U (NC) ***303***
Carnegie Mellon U (PA) ***305***
Carson-Newman Coll (TN) ***306***
The Catholic U of America (DC) ***307***
Central Michigan U (MI) ***310***
Central Missouri State U (MO) ***310***
Central Washington U (WA) ***310***
Christopher Newport U (VA) ***313***
Concordia Coll (MN) ***329***
Dallas Baptist U (TX) ***336***
DePaul U (IL) ***339***
DePauw U (IN) ***339***
East Carolina U (NC) ***347***
Florida State U (FL) ***361***

Georgia Southern U (GA) **367**
Hope Coll (MI) **381**
Houghton Coll (NY) **381**
Indiana Wesleyan U (IN) **387**
Ithaca Coll (NY) **390**
Jacksonville U (FL) **391**
Johns Hopkins U (MD) **392**
Loyola U New Orleans (LA) **411**
Luther Coll (IA) **412**
Mannes Coll of Music, New School U (NY) **416**
McGill U (QC, Canada) **423**
Memorial U of Newfoundland (NF, Canada) **424**
Meredith Coll (NC) **426**
Michigan State U (MI) **428**
Minnesota State U, Moorhead (MN) **432**
New England Conservatory of Music (MA) **445**
New York U (NY) **447**
Northwestern U (IL) **453**
Northwest Nazarene U (ID) **454**
Nyack Coll (NY) **456**
Oakland U (MI) **456**
The Ohio State U (OH) **457**
Ohio U (OH) **458**
Oklahoma Baptist U (OK) **459**
Oklahoma City U (OK) **460**
Oral Roberts U (OK) **461**
Ouachita Baptist U (AR) **462**
Rice U (TX) **479**
Rider U (NJ) **480**
Samford U (AL) **497**
San Francisco Conservatory of Music (CA) **498**
San Jose State U (CA) **499**
Seton Hill U (PA) **502**
Shenandoah U (VA) **503**
Simon's Rock Coll of Bard (MA) **505**
Southeast Missouri State U (MO) **508**
Southern Adventist U (TN) **508**
Southern Methodist U (TX) **510**
State U of NY Coll at Potsdam (NY) **517**
State U of West Georgia (GA) **518**
Stetson U (FL) **519**
Syracuse U (NY) **521**
Texas Christian U (TX) **526**
Texas Tech U (TX) **526**
Trinity U (TX) **531**
The U of Akron (OH) **537**
The U of British Columbia (BC, Canada) **540**
U of Delaware (DE) **544**
U of Georgia (GA) **545**
U of Hartford (CT) **546**
U of Houston (TX) **547**
U of Idaho (ID) **547**
U of Illinois at Urbana–Champaign (IL) **548**
U of Kansas (KS) **549**
U of Louisville (KY) **550**
U of Miami (FL) **553**
U of Michigan (MI) **554**
U of Nevada, Las Vegas (NV) **558**
U of Northern Iowa (IA) **561**
U of North Texas (TX) **562**
U of Oklahoma (OK) **562**
U of Redlands (CA) **572**
U of Rhode Island (RI) **572**
U of Rochester (NY) **573**
U of South Alabama (AL) **575**
U of Southern California (CA) **576**
The U of Texas at Austin (TX) **578**
The U of the Arts (PA) **579**
U of the Pacific (CA) **580**
U of Victoria (BC, Canada) **582**
U of Washington (WA) **583**
U of Windsor (ON, Canada) **584**
U of Wyoming (WY) **586**
Valparaiso U (IN) **588**
Viterbo U (WI) **591**
Wartburg Coll (IA) **594**
Washington State U (WA) **595**
Washington U in St. Louis (MO) **595**
Webster U (MO) **597**
Western Michigan U (MI) **599**
Westminster Choir Coll of Rider U (NJ) **601**
West Texas A&M U (TX) **602**
Wheaton Coll (IL) **603**
Wilberforce U (OH) **605**
William Jewell Coll (MO) **606**
York U (ON, Canada) **611**
Youngstown State U (OH) **611**

MUSIC THERAPY

Overview: This major teaches students how to use music, in consultation with rehabilitation experts, to address physical, mental, cognition, emotional, or social need disorders of individuals of all ages. *Related majors:* psychology, counseling or developmental psychology, music teacher education, nursing (mental health), music. *Potential careers:* music therapist, music teacher, psychologist, therapist. *Salary potential:* $25k-$30k.

Alverno Coll (WI) **265**
Anna Maria Coll (MA) **269**
Appalachian State U (NC) **270**
Arizona State U (AZ) **271**
Augsburg Coll (MN) **276**
Baldwin-Wallace Coll (OH) **280**
Berklee Coll of Music (MA) **286**
Chapman U (CA) **311**
Charleston Southern U (SC) **311**
The Coll of Wooster (OH) **324**
Colorado State U (CO) **325**
Dillard U (LA) **344**
Duquesne U (PA) **346**
East Carolina U (NC) **347**
Eastern Michigan U (MI) **348**
Elizabethtown Coll (PA) **351**
Florida State U (FL) **361**
Georgia Coll & State U (GA) **367**
Immaculata U (PA) **385**
Indiana U–Purdue U Fort Wayne (IN) **386**
Long Island U, Southampton Coll, Friends World Program (NY) **409**
Loyola U New Orleans (LA) **411**
Mansfield U of Pennsylvania (PA) **416**
Maryville U of Saint Louis (MO) **420**
Marywood U (PA) **421**
Mercyhurst Coll (PA) **425**
Michigan State U (MI) **428**
Molloy Coll (NY) **433**
Montclair State U (NJ) **435**
Nazareth Coll of Rochester (NY) **443**
Queens U of Charlotte (NC) **476**
Radford U (VA) **476**
Saint Mary-of-the-Woods Coll (IN) **493**
Sam Houston State U (TX) **497**
Shenandoah U (VA) **503**
Slippery Rock U of Pennsylvania (PA) **506**
Southern Methodist U (TX) **510**
Southwestern Oklahoma State U (OK) **512**
State U of NY at New Paltz (NY) **515**
State U of NY Coll at Fredonia (NY) **516**
Temple U (PA) **523**
Tennessee Technological U (TN) **524**
Texas Woman's U (TX) **527**
U of Dayton (OH) **544**
U of Evansville (IN) **545**
U of Georgia (GA) **545**
The U of Iowa (IA) **548**
U of Kansas (KS) **549**
U of Louisville (KY) **550**
U of Miami (FL) **553**
U of Minnesota, Twin Cities Campus (MN) **555**
U of Missouri–Kansas City (MO) **555**
U of the Incarnate Word (TX) **580**
U of the Pacific (CA) **580**
U of Windsor (ON, Canada) **584**
U of Wisconsin–Eau Claire (WI) **584**
U of Wisconsin–Milwaukee (WI) **585**
U of Wisconsin–Oshkosh (WI) **585**
Utah State U (UT) **587**
Wartburg Coll (IA) **594**
Western Michigan U (MI) **599**
West Texas A&M U (TX) **602**
Willamette U (OR) **605**
William Carey Coll (MS) **605**

MUSIC (VOICE AND CHORAL/OPERA PERFORMANCE)

Overview: Students learn the principles and skills of voice and singing for a variety of performances such as choir, opera, and solo. *Related majors:* music performance, music theory and composition. *Potential careers:* vocalist, opera performer, ensemble member, choir member, singer. *Salary potential:* varies according to position but full-time employees can expect $15k-$25k.

Abilene Christian U (TX) **260**
Acadia U (NS, Canada) **260**
Adams State Coll (CO) **260**
Alma Coll (MI) **264**
Andrews U (MI) **269**
Anna Maria Coll (MA) **269**
Appalachian State U (NC) **270**
Aquinas Coll (MI) **270**
Augustana Coll (IL) **276**
Baldwin-Wallace Coll (OH) **280**
Ball State U (IN) **280**
Bard Coll (NY) **281**
Barry U (FL) **282**
Bellarmine U (KY) **284**
Belmont U (TN) **284**
Benedictine Coll (KS) **285**
Bennington Coll (VT) **286**
Berklee Coll of Music (MA) **286**
Berry Coll (GA) **287**
Bethel Coll (IN) **288**
Birmingham-Southern Coll (AL) **289**
Black Hills State U (SD) **290**
Blue Mountain Coll (MS) **291**
Boston U (MA) **292**
Bowling Green State U (OH) **292**
Brandon U (MB, Canada) **293**
Brenau U (GA) **293**
Brigham Young U–Hawaii (HI) **295**
Bryan Coll (TN) **296**
Butler U (IN) **297**
California Inst of the Arts (CA) **299**
California State U, Fullerton (CA) **301**
California State U, Long Beach (CA) **301**
California State U, Northridge (CA) **301**
Calvin Coll (MI) **303**
Cameron U (OK) **303**
Campbellsville U (KY) **303**
Canadian Mennonite U (MB, Canada) **304**
Capital U (OH) **304**
Carroll Coll (WI) **306**
Carson-Newman Coll (TN) **306**
Catawba Coll (NC) **307**
The Catholic U of America (DC) **307**
Cedarville U (OH) **308**
Centenary Coll of Louisiana (LA) **308**
Central Washington U (WA) **310**
Chapman U (CA) **311**
Charleston Southern U (SC) **311**
Christian Heritage Coll (CA) **313**
Cincinnati Bible Coll and Seminary (OH) **314**
Clarke Coll (IA) **315**
Cleveland Inst of Music (OH) **317**
Coker Coll (SC) **318**
The Coll of Wooster (OH) **324**
Colorado Christian U (CO) **325**
Columbia Coll (SC) **327**
Columbus State U (GA) **328**
Concordia Coll (MN) **329**
Concordia U (IL) **330**
Concordia U (NE) **330**
Conservatory of Music of Puerto Rico (PR) **332**
Converse Coll (SC) **332**
Cornish Coll of the Arts (WA) **333**
The Curtis Inst of Music (PA) **335**
Dallas Baptist U (TX) **336**
DePaul U (IL) **339**
Drake U (IA) **345**
Eastern Washington U (WA) **349**
East Texas Baptist U (TX) **350**
Erskine Coll (SC) **354**
Eureka Coll (IL) **355**
Five Towns Coll (NY) **359**
Florida State U (FL) **361**
Furman U (SC) **365**
Georgetown Coll (KY) **366**
Georgia Coll & State U (GA) **367**
God's Bible School and Coll (OH) **369**
Grand Canyon U (AZ) **371**
Grand Valley State U (MI) **371**
Hannibal-LaGrange Coll (MO) **375**
Harding U (AR) **375**
Hardin-Simmons U (TX) **376**
Hastings Coll (NE) **377**
Heidelberg Coll (OH) **377**
Houghton Coll (NY) **381**
Howard Payne U (TX) **382**
Huntingdon Coll (AL) **383**
Huntington Coll (IN) **383**
Illinois Wesleyan U (IL) **385**
Immaculata U (PA) **385**
Indiana U Bloomington (IN) **385**
Indiana U–Purdue U Fort Wayne (IN) **386**
Inter American U of PR, San Germán Campus (PR) **388**
Ithaca Coll (NY) **390**
Jacksonville U (FL) **391**
John Brown U (AR) **392**
Judson Coll (IL) **395**
The Juilliard School (NY) **395**
Kennesaw State U (GA) **397**
Lamar U (TX) **401**
Lambuth U (TN) **401**
Langston U (OK) **402**
Lawrence U (WI) **403**
Lee U (TN) **404**
Lincoln Christian Coll (IL) **407**
Lindenwood U (MO) **407**
Lipscomb U (TN) **408**
Louisiana Coll (LA) **410**
Luther Coll (IA) **412**
Manhattan School of Music (NY) **416**
Mannes Coll of Music, New School U (NY) **416**
Mansfield U of Pennsylvania (PA) **416**
Mars Hill Coll (NC) **418**
Maryville Coll (TN) **420**
The Master's Coll and Seminary (CA) **422**
McGill U (QC, Canada) **423**
Memorial U of Newfoundland (NF, Canada) **424**
Mercyhurst Coll (PA) **425**
Meredith Coll (NC) **426**
MidAmerica Nazarene U (KS) **428**
Milligan Coll (TN) **430**
Millikin U (IL) **430**
Minnesota State U, Mankato (MN) **431**
Minnesota State U, Moorhead (MN) **432**
Mississippi Coll (MS) **432**
Montclair State U (NJ) **435**
Montreat Coll (NC) **435**
Mount Allison U (NB, Canada) **437**
Mount Mercy Coll (IA) **438**
Mount St. Mary's Coll (CA) **439**
Mount Vernon Nazarene U (OH) **440**
Newberry Coll (SC) **444**
New England Conservatory of Music (MA) **445**
New World School of the Arts (FL) **447**
New York U (NY) **447**
North Carolina School of the Arts (NC) **449**
North Central Coll (IL) **449**
Northeastern State U (OK) **450**
Northern Michigan U (MI) **451**
Northern State U (SD) **451**
North Greenville Coll (SC) **451**
North Park U (IL) **452**
Northwest Coll (WA) **452**
Northwestern Coll (MN) **453**
Northwestern U (IL) **453**
Northwest Missouri State U (MO) **454**
Notre Dame de Namur U (CA) **455**
Nyack Coll (NY) **456**
Oakland U (MI) **456**
Oberlin Coll (OH) **456**
The Ohio State U (OH) **457**
Ohio U (OH) **458**
Oklahoma Baptist U (OK) **459**
Oklahoma Christian U (OK) **459**
Oklahoma City U (OK) **460**
Olivet Nazarene U (IL) **461**
Otterbein Coll (OH) **462**
Ouachita Baptist U (AR) **462**
Pacific Lutheran U (WA) **463**
Palm Beach Atlantic U (FL) **465**
Peabody Conserv of Music of Johns Hopkins U (MD) **466**
Peru State Coll (NE) **469**
Pittsburg State U (KS) **470**
Prairie View A&M U (TX) **473**
Queens U of Charlotte (NC) **476**
Randolph-Macon Woman's Coll (VA) **477**
Rider U (NJ) **480**
Roberts Wesleyan Coll (NY) **481**
Rochester Coll (MI) **482**
Roosevelt U (IL) **483**
Rowan U (NJ) **484**
St. Cloud State U (MN) **488**
Saint Mary-of-the-Woods Coll (IN) **493**

MUSIC (VOICE AND CHORAL/OPERA PERFORMANCE) (continued)

Saint Mary's Coll (IN) ***493***
Samford U (AL) ***497***
San Francisco Conservatory of Music (CA) ***498***
San Jose State U (CA) ***499***
Sarah Lawrence Coll (NY) ***499***
Seton Hill U (PA) ***502***
Shorter Coll (GA) ***504***
Southern Nazarene U (OK) ***510***
Southwestern Oklahoma State U (OK) ***512***
State U of NY Coll at Fredonia (NY) ***516***
Stetson U (FL) ***519***
Susquehanna U (PA) ***521***
Syracuse U (NY) ***521***
Tabor Coll (KS) ***522***
Talladega Coll (AL) ***522***
Taylor U (IN) ***523***
Temple U (PA) ***523***
Tennessee Temple U (TN) ***524***
Texas A&M U–Commerce (TX) ***525***
Texas Christian U (TX) ***526***
Texas Southern U (TX) ***526***
Texas Wesleyan U (TX) ***526***
Toccoa Falls Coll (GA) ***528***
Trinity Christian Coll (IL) ***530***
Trinity U (TX) ***531***
Truman State U (MO) ***532***
Union Coll (KY) ***533***
Union U (TN) ***534***
The U of Akron (OH) ***537***
U of Alberta (AB, Canada) ***538***
The U of British Columbia (BC, Canada) ***540***
U of Central Oklahoma (OK) ***542***
U of Charleston (WV) ***542***
U of Cincinnati (OH) ***543***
U of Delaware (DE) ***544***
U of Idaho (ID) ***547***
U of Illinois at Urbana–Champaign (IL) ***548***
The U of Iowa (IA) ***548***
U of Kansas (KS) ***549***
U of Miami (FL) ***553***
U of Michigan (MI) ***554***
U of Missouri–Kansas City (MO) ***555***
U of Montevallo (AL) ***557***
U of Nebraska at Omaha (NE) ***557***
U of New Hampshire (NH) ***558***
The U of North Carolina at Greensboro (NC) ***560***
U of North Texas (TX) ***562***
U of Oklahoma (OK) ***562***
U of Oregon (OR) ***562***
U of Ottawa (ON, Canada) ***563***
U of Redlands (CA) ***572***
U of Sioux Falls (SD) ***574***
The U of South Dakota (SD) ***575***
U of Southern California (CA) ***576***
The U of Tennessee at Chattanooga (TN) ***577***
The U of Tennessee at Martin (TN) ***577***
U of the Pacific (CA) ***580***
U of Tulsa (OK) ***581***
U of Victoria (BC, Canada) ***582***
U of Washington (WA) ***583***
The U of Western Ontario (ON, Canada) ***583***
U of Wisconsin–Milwaukee (WI) ***585***
Valdosta State U (GA) ***588***
Vanderbilt U (TN) ***588***
Viterbo U (WI) ***591***
Walla Walla Coll (WA) ***593***
Washington U in St. Louis (MO) ***595***
Webster U (MO) ***597***
West Chester U of Pennsylvania (PA) ***598***
Western Michigan U (MI) ***599***
Westfield State Coll (MA) ***600***
Westminster Choir Coll of Rider U (NJ) ***601***
Westminster Coll (PA) ***601***
Whitworth Coll (WA) ***604***
Wilberforce U (OH) ***605***
William Carey Coll (MS) ***605***
William Paterson U of New Jersey (NJ) ***606***
Wingate U (NC) ***607***
Winona State U (MN) ***608***
Wittenberg U (OH) ***608***
York U (ON, Canada) ***611***
Youngstown State U (OH) ***611***

NATIVE AMERICAN LANGUAGES

Overview: Students focus on one or more of the languages of Native Americans, usually concentrating on one of languages of the American Indians. *Related majors:* anthropology, archeology, U.S. history, sociology, American Indian/Native American studies. *Potential careers:* anthropologist, archeologist, teacher. *Salary potential:* $20k-$24k.

Bemidji State U (MN) ***285***
The U of Lethbridge (AB, Canada) ***549***

NATIVE AMERICAN STUDIES

Overview: Students who choose this major study the history, sociology, politics, culture, and economics of one or more of the native peoples of the Americas from the earliest times to the present. *Related majors:* Latin American history, American history, art history, government, archeology. *Potential careers:* anthropologist, archeologist, art dealer. *Salary potential:* $25-$30k.

Arizona State U (AZ) ***271***
Bemidji State U (MN) ***285***
Black Hills State U (SD) ***290***
Brandon U (MB, Canada) ***293***
California State U, Hayward (CA) ***301***
Colgate U (NY) ***319***
Cornell U (NY) ***333***
Dartmouth Coll (NH) ***337***
The Evergreen State Coll (WA) ***355***
Hampshire Coll (MA) ***375***
Humboldt State U (CA) ***382***
Laurentian U (ON, Canada) ***403***
Long Island U, Southampton Coll, Friends World Program (NY) ***409***
Naropa U (CO) ***441***
Northeastern State U (OK) ***450***
Northern Arizona U (AZ) ***450***
Northland Coll (WI) ***452***
St. Thomas U (NB, Canada) ***496***
Sonoma State U (CA) ***506***
Stanford U (CA) ***514***
Trent U (ON, Canada) ***529***
U at Buffalo, The State University of New York (NY) ***536***
U of Alaska Fairbanks (AK) ***538***
U of Alberta (AB, Canada) ***538***
U of Calif, Berkeley (CA) ***540***
U of Calif, Davis (CA) ***540***
U of Calif, Riverside (CA) ***541***
The U of Iowa (IA) ***548***
The U of Lethbridge (AB, Canada) ***549***
U of Minnesota, Duluth (MN) ***554***
U of Minnesota, Twin Cities Campus (MN) ***555***
The U of Montana–Missoula (MT) ***556***
The U of North Carolina at Pembroke (NC) ***560***
U of North Dakota (ND) ***561***
U of Oklahoma (OK) ***562***
U of Regina (SK, Canada) ***572***
U of Saskatchewan (SK, Canada) ***574***
U of Science and Arts of Oklahoma (OK) ***574***
U of the Incarnate Word (TX) ***580***
U of Toronto (ON, Canada) ***581***
U of Washington (WA) ***583***
U of Wisconsin–Eau Claire (WI) ***584***
U of Wisconsin–Milwaukee (WI) ***585***

NATURAL RESOURCES CONSERVATION

Overview: This major teaches students how to apply concepts of environmental science and natural resources management to the conservation, use, and improvement of the natural environment. *Related majors:* soil sciences, plant sciences, water resources, environmental sciences. *Potential careers:* ecologist, environmentalist, park ranger, conservationist, lobbyist. *Salary potential:* $25k-$35k.

Central Michigan U (MI) ***310***
Coll of Santa Fe (NM) ***323***
The Evergreen State Coll (WA) ***355***
Harvard U (MA) ***376***
Humboldt State U (CA) ***382***
Iowa Wesleyan Coll (IA) ***390***
Kent State U (OH) ***397***
Long Island U, Southampton Coll, Friends World Program (NY) ***409***
Louisiana Tech U (LA) ***410***
Marlboro Coll (VT) ***418***
McGill U (QC, Canada) ***423***
Michigan State U (MI) ***428***
Montana State U–Bozeman (MT) ***434***
Mount Vernon Nazarene U (OH) ***440***
Muskingum Coll (OH) ***441***
North Carolina State U (NC) ***449***
Northern Michigan U (MI) ***451***
Northland Coll (WI) ***452***
Northwest Missouri State U (MO) ***454***
Penn State U Univ Park Campus (PA) ***468***
Peru State Coll (NE) ***469***
Prescott Coll (AZ) ***474***
Purdue U (IN) ***475***
Southeastern Oklahoma State U (OK) ***508***
Springfield Coll (MA) ***514***
State U of NY Coll of Environ Sci and Forestry (NY) ***517***
Sterling Coll (VT) ***519***
Texas A&M U (TX) ***524***
Texas Tech U (TX) ***526***
Unity Coll (ME) ***535***
U Coll of the Cariboo (BC, Canada) ***537***
U of Alberta (AB, Canada) ***538***
The U of British Columbia (BC, Canada) ***540***
U of Calif, Berkeley (CA) ***540***
U of Calif, Davis (CA) ***540***
U of Connecticut (CT) ***544***
U of Kentucky (KY) ***549***
U of Maryland, Coll Park (MD) ***552***
The U of Montana–Missoula (MT) ***556***
U of Nebraska–Lincoln (NE) ***557***
U of Nevada, Reno (NV) ***558***
U of New Hampshire (NH) ***558***
U of Rhode Island (RI) ***572***
U of Vermont (VT) ***582***
U of Wisconsin–Milwaukee (WI) ***585***
U of Wisconsin–River Falls (WI) ***585***
U of Wisconsin–Stevens Point (WI) ***585***
Upper Iowa U (IA) ***587***
Washington State U (WA) ***595***
Washington U in St. Louis (MO) ***595***
Winona State U (MN) ***608***

NATURAL RESOURCES MANAGEMENT

Overview: This major will teach students how to plan, develop, manage, and evaluate programs to protect and regulate natural habitats and renewable natural resources. *Related majors:* environmental science, natural resources conservation, law and public policy, wildlife and wildlands management, forest management. *Potential careers:* park ranger, environmental scientist, lobbyist, environmental lawyer. *Salary potential:* $20k-$27k.

Alaska Pacific U (AK) ***261***
Albright Coll (PA) ***263***
Arizona State U East (AZ) ***271***
Ball State U (IN) ***280***
Bowling Green State U (OH) ***292***
California State U, Chico (CA) ***300***
Clark U (MA) ***316***
Colorado State U (CO) ***325***
Cornell U (NY) ***333***
Delaware State U (DE) ***338***
Eastern Oregon U (OR) ***349***
The Evergreen State Coll (WA) ***355***
Fort Hays State U (KS) ***362***
Grand Valley State U (MI) ***371***
Green Mountain Coll (VT) ***372***
Humboldt State U (CA) ***382***
Huntington Coll (IN) ***383***
Iowa State U of Science and Technology (IA) ***390***
Johnson State Coll (VT) ***394***
Long Island U, Southampton Coll, Friends World Program (NY) ***409***
McGill U (QC, Canada) ***423***
New Mexico Highlands U (NM) ***446***
North Carolina State U (NC) ***449***
North Dakota State U (ND) ***449***
Northland Coll (WI) ***452***
The Ohio State U (OH) ***457***
Oregon State U (OR) ***462***
Paul Smith's Coll of Arts and Sciences (NY) ***466***
Prescott Coll (AZ) ***474***
Rochester Inst of Technology (NY) ***482***
State U of NY Coll of Environ Sci and Forestry (NY) ***517***
Sterling Coll (VT) ***519***
Tuskegee U (AL) ***533***
Unity Coll (ME) ***535***
U of Alberta (AB, Canada) ***538***
The U of British Columbia (BC, Canada) ***540***
U of Calif, Berkeley (CA) ***540***
U of Calif, San Diego (CA) ***541***
U of Delaware (DE) ***544***
U of Guelph (ON, Canada) ***546***
U of Houston–Clear Lake (TX) ***547***
U of Idaho (ID) ***547***
U of La Verne (CA) ***549***
U of Maine (ME) ***550***
U of Massachusetts Amherst (MA) ***552***
U of Miami (FL) ***553***
U of Michigan (MI) ***554***
U of Michigan–Flint (MI) ***554***
U of Minnesota, Crookston (MN) ***554***
U of Minnesota, Twin Cities Campus (MN) ***555***
The U of Montana–Missoula (MT) ***556***
U of Nebraska–Lincoln (NE) ***557***
U of Nevada, Reno (NV) ***558***
U of New Hampshire (NH) ***558***
U of Rhode Island (RI) ***572***
U of Southern California (CA) ***576***
U of the South (TN) ***581***
U of Vermont (VT) ***582***
U of Washington (WA) ***583***
The U of Western Ontario (ON, Canada) ***583***
U of Windsor (ON, Canada) ***584***
U of Wisconsin–Madison (WI) ***584***
U of Wisconsin–Stevens Point (WI) ***585***
Warren Wilson Coll (NC) ***594***
Washington State U (WA) ***595***
Western Carolina U (NC) ***598***
Western Washington U (WA) ***600***
West Virginia U (WV) ***602***

NATURAL RESOURCES MANAGEMENT/PROTECTIVE SERVICES RELATED

Information can be found under this major's main heading.

McGill U (QC, Canada) ***423***
The U of British Columbia (BC, Canada) ***540***

NATURAL RESOURCES PROTECTIVE SERVICES

Overview: This major focuses on enforcing the fish and game laws and rules as well as laws relating to littering, forestry, state parks, environmental and solid waste, pleasure boating, and whitewater rafting. *Related majors:* fish and game management, law enforcement. *Potential careers:* fish and game warden, park ranger. *Salary potential:* $24k-$30k.

Arkansas Tech U (AR) ***272***
The Ohio State U (OH) ***457***
Unity Coll (ME) ***535***

NATURAL SCIENCES

Overview: A broad-based major that examines biology, chemistry, earth sciences, physics, and mathematics. *Related majors:* biology, chemistry, earth sciences, physics, mathematics. *Potential careers:* teacher, science journalist, lawyer, physician, public relations specialist. *Salary potential:* $25k-$35k.

Alderson-Broaddus Coll (WV) ***263***
Antioch Coll (OH) ***269***
Appalachian State U (NC) ***270***
Arcadia U (PA) ***271***
Arkansas Tech U (AR) ***272***
Atlantic Union Coll (MA) ***276***
Augsburg Coll (MN) ***276***
Avila U (MO) ***278***
Azusa Pacific U (CA) ***278***
Bard Coll (NY) ***281***
Bemidji State U (MN) ***285***
Benedictine Coll (KS) ***285***
Bennington Coll (VT) ***286***
Baruch Coll of the City U of NY (NY) ***286***
Bethel Coll (KS) ***288***
Bishop's U (QC, Canada) ***289***
Blue Mountain Coll (MS) ***291***
Buena Vista U (IA) ***297***
California State U, Fresno (CA) ***301***
California State U, San Bernardino (CA) ***302***
Calvin Coll (MI) ***303***
Cameron U (OK) ***303***
Carthage Coll (WI) ***306***
Castleton State Coll (VT) ***307***
Cedar Crest Coll (PA) ***308***
Charleston Southern U (SC) ***311***
Christian Brothers U (TN) ***313***
Colgate U (NY) ***319***
Coll of Mount St. Joseph (OH) ***320***
Coll of Saint Benedict (MN) ***321***
Coll of Saint Mary (NE) ***322***
The Coll of St. Scholastica (MN) ***322***
Coll of the Atlantic (ME) ***323***
Coll of the Southwest (NM) ***324***
Concordia U (IL) ***330***
Concordia U (MN) ***330***
Concordia U (NE) ***330***
Concordia U (OR) ***330***
Covenant Coll (GA) ***333***
Daemen Coll (NY) ***335***
Davis & Elkins Coll (WV) ***338***
Defiance Coll (OH) ***338***
Doane Coll (NE) ***344***
Dordt Coll (IA) ***345***
Dowling Coll (NY) ***345***
Eastern Kentucky U (KY) ***348***
Eastern Washington U (WA) ***349***
Edgewood Coll (WI) ***351***
Elms Coll (MA) ***352***
Erskine Coll (SC) ***354***
Eureka Coll (IL) ***355***
The Evergreen State Coll (WA) ***355***
Felician Coll (NJ) ***357***
Florida Southern Coll (FL) ***361***
Fordham U (NY) ***362***
Framingham State Coll (MA) ***362***
Fresno Pacific U (CA) ***364***
Goddard Coll (VT) ***369***
Goshen Coll (IN) ***370***
Grand Valley State U (MI) ***371***
Hampshire Coll (MA) ***375***
Hofstra U (NY) ***380***
Humboldt State U (CA) ***382***
Inter American U of PR, San Germán Campus (PR) ***388***
Iona Coll (NY) ***390***
Iowa Wesleyan Coll (IA) ***390***
Johns Hopkins U (MD) ***392***
Juniata Coll (PA) ***395***
Kenyon Coll (OH) ***398***
Lakehead U (ON, Canada) ***400***
Lees-McRae Coll (NC) ***404***
Lee U (TN) ***404***
Lehigh U (PA) ***404***
Lesley U (MA) ***405***
LeTourneau U (TX) ***405***
Lewis-Clark State Coll (ID) ***406***
Lock Haven U of Pennsylvania (PA) ***408***
Long Island U, Southampton Coll (NY) ***409***
Long Island U, Southampton Coll, Friends World Program (NY) ***409***
Longwood U (VA) ***409***
Loyola Marymount U (CA) ***411***
Loyola U Chicago (IL) ***411***
Lynn U (FL) ***413***
Madonna U (MI) ***414***
Marlboro Coll (VT) ***418***
The Master's Coll and Seminary (CA) ***422***
Middlebury Coll (VT) ***429***
Midland Lutheran Coll (NE) ***429***
Minnesota State U, Mankato (MN) ***431***
Monmouth Coll (IL) ***434***
Mount Allison U (NB, Canada) ***437***
Muhlenberg Coll (PA) ***440***
New Coll of Florida (FL) ***444***
North Central Coll (IL) ***449***
Northland Coll (WI) ***452***
North Park U (IL) ***452***
Oakwood Coll (AL) ***456***
Oklahoma Baptist U (OK) ***459***
Oklahoma Panhandle State U (OK) ***460***
Oklahoma Wesleyan U (OK) ***460***
Olivet Nazarene U (IL) ***461***
Our Lady of the Lake U of San Antonio (TX) ***463***
Park U (MO) ***465***
Pepperdine U, Malibu (CA) ***469***
Peru State Coll (NE) ***469***
Rensselaer Polytechnic Inst (NY) ***478***
Rocky Mountain Coll (MT) ***482***
St. Cloud State U (MN) ***488***
St. Gregory's U (OK) ***489***
Saint John's U (MN) ***490***
Saint Joseph Coll (CT) ***490***
St. Mary's Coll of Maryland (MD) ***494***
St. Thomas Aquinas Coll (NY) ***495***
San Jose State U (CA) ***499***
Sarah Lawrence Coll (NY) ***499***
Shawnee State U (OH) ***502***
Shimer Coll (IL) ***503***
Shorter Coll (GA) ***504***
Siena Heights U (MI) ***504***
Simon's Rock Coll of Bard (MA) ***505***
Southern Nazarene U (OK) ***510***
Spelman Coll (GA) ***514***
State U of NY Coll at Geneseo (NY) ***516***
Stephens Coll (MO) ***519***
Syracuse U (NY) ***521***
Tabor Coll (KS) ***522***
Taylor U (IN) ***523***
Thomas Edison State Coll (NJ) ***527***
Trent U (ON, Canada) ***529***
Trinity Western U (BC, Canada) ***531***
The U of Akron (OH) ***537***
U of Alaska Anchorage (AK) ***538***
U of Cincinnati (OH) ***543***
The U of Findlay (OH) ***545***
U of Hawaii at Hilo (HI) ***546***
U of La Verne (CA) ***549***
U of Mary (ND) ***551***
U of Michigan–Dearborn (MI) ***554***
U of New Hampshire (NH) ***558***
U of Ottawa (ON, Canada) ***563***
U of Pittsburgh at Greensburg (PA) ***570***
U of Pittsburgh at Johnstown (PA) ***570***
U of Puerto Rico, Cayey U Coll (PR) ***571***
U of Puerto Rico, Río Piedras (PR) ***571***
U of Puget Sound (WA) ***571***
U of Rochester (NY) ***573***
U of Science and Arts of Oklahoma (OK) ***574***
U of Toledo (OH) ***581***
U of Wisconsin–River Falls (WI) ***585***
U of Wisconsin–Stevens Point (WI) ***585***
Villanova U (PA) ***590***
Virginia Wesleyan Coll (VA) ***591***
Walsh U (OH) ***593***
Washington U in St. Louis (MO) ***595***
Wayne State Coll (NE) ***596***
West Chester U of Pennsylvania (PA) ***598***
Western Oregon U (OR) ***600***
Winona State U (MN) ***608***
Wittenberg U (OH) ***608***
Worcester State Coll (MA) ***609***
York Coll (NE) ***610***
York U (ON, Canada) ***611***

NAVAL ARCHITECTURE/ MARINE ENGINEERING

Overview: Students learn the science behind designing and developing a variety of vessels that operate either on or underneath the water. *Related majors:* structural engineering, chemistry, electrical engineering, mechanical engineering and design, energy management/systems. *Potential careers:* naval officer, ship builder, mechanical engineer. *Salary potential:* $30k-$45k.

Maine Maritime Academy (ME) ***415***
Massachusetts Inst of Technology (MA) ***421***
Massachusetts Maritime Academy (MA) ***421***
Memorial U of Newfoundland (NF, Canada) ***424***
State U of NY Maritime Coll (NY) ***518***
Texas A&M U at Galveston (TX) ***524***
United States Coast Guard Academy (CT) ***535***
United States Merchant Marine Academy (NY) ***535***
United States Naval Academy (MD) ***535***
U of Michigan (MI) ***554***
U of New Brunswick Saint John (NB, Canada) ***558***
U of New Orleans (LA) ***559***
Webb Inst (NY) ***596***

NAVY/MARINE CORPS R.O.T.C./NAVAL SCIENCE

Overview: This major introduces students to the theories of military science and prepare them for a career as a naval or marine officer. *Related majors:* military history, military technologies, history, naval architecture, marine engineering. *Potential careers:* naval officer, marine corps. *Salary potential:* $25k-$35k.

Hampton U (VA) ***375***
Massachusetts Inst of Technology (MA) ***421***
Rensselaer Polytechnic Inst (NY) ***478***
State U of NY Maritime Coll (NY) ***518***
U of Washington (WA) ***583***

NEUROSCIENCE

Overview: Students taking this major will study the molecular, structural, and other aspects of the brain and nervous system. *Related majors:* cell biology, molecular biology, pharmacology, psychology, psychobiology. *Potential careers:* physician, neuroscientist, psychologist/psychiatrist. *Salary potential:* $26k-$32k.

Allegheny Coll (PA) ***264***
Amherst Coll (MA) ***268***
Baldwin-Wallace Coll (OH) ***280***
Bates Coll (ME) ***282***
Bishop's U (QC, Canada) ***289***
Boston U (MA) ***292***
Bowdoin Coll (ME) ***292***
Bowling Green State U (OH) ***292***
Brandeis U (MA) ***293***
Brock U (ON, Canada) ***295***
Brown U (RI) ***296***
California Inst of Technology (CA) ***299***
Carthage Coll (WI) ***306***
Cedar Crest Coll (PA) ***308***
Central Michigan U (MI) ***310***
Chatham Coll (PA) ***312***
Clark U (MA) ***316***
Colgate U (NY) ***319***
The Colorado Coll (CO) ***325***
Concordia U (QC, Canada) ***331***
Connecticut Coll (CT) ***331***
Cornell U (NY) ***333***
Dalhousie U (NS, Canada) ***336***
Drew U (NJ) ***346***
Emory U (GA) ***354***
Fairfield U (CT) ***356***
Franklin and Marshall Coll (PA) ***363***
Hamilton Coll (NY) ***374***
Hampshire Coll (MA) ***375***
Harvard U (MA) ***376***
Haverford Coll (PA) ***377***
John Carroll U (OH) ***392***
Johns Hopkins U (MD) ***392***
Kenyon Coll (OH) ***398***
King's Coll (PA) ***398***
Lawrence U (WI) ***403***
Lehigh U (PA) ***404***
Macalester Coll (MN) ***413***
Manhattanville Coll (NY) ***416***
Memorial U of Newfoundland (NF, Canada) ***424***
Muskingum Coll (OH) ***441***
New York U (NY) ***447***
Northwestern U (IL) ***453***
Oberlin Coll (OH) ***456***
Ohio Wesleyan U (OH) ***459***
Pitzer Coll (CA) ***471***
Pomona Coll (CA) ***472***
Regis U (CO) ***478***
Rice U (TX) ***479***
St. Lawrence U (NY) ***491***
Scripps Coll (CA) ***501***
Smith Coll (MA) ***506***
Texas Christian U (TX) ***526***
Trinity Coll (CT) ***530***
U of Calif, Los Angeles (CA) ***541***
U of Calif, Riverside (CA) ***541***
U of Delaware (DE) ***544***
U of King's Coll (NS, Canada) ***549***
The U of Lethbridge (AB, Canada) ***549***
U of Minnesota, Twin Cities Campus (MN) ***555***
U of Pittsburgh (PA) ***569***
U of Rochester (NY) ***573***
The U of Scranton (PA) ***574***
U of Southern California (CA) ***576***
The U of Texas at Dallas (TX) ***578***
U of Toronto (ON, Canada) ***581***
U of Windsor (ON, Canada) ***584***
Washington and Lee U (VA) ***594***
Washington State U (WA) ***595***
Washington U in St. Louis (MO) ***595***
Wellesley Coll (MA) ***597***
Wesleyan U (CT) ***597***
Westmont Coll (CA) ***602***

NONPROFIT/PUBLIC MANAGEMENT

Overview: Students learn how to use core business and accounting skills to manage nonprofit organizations, foundations, associations, public agencies, and governmental organizations. *Related majors:* accounting, financial planning, human resources management, and business law. *Potential careers:* hospital or health care service administrator, university administrator, charitable organizational administrator, planned giving officer, program director. *Salary potential:* $20k-$30k.

Austin Peay State U (TN) ***278***
Fresno Pacific U (CA) ***364***
Manchester Coll (IN) ***415***
Saint Mary-of-the-Woods Coll (IN) ***493***
Southern Adventist U (TN) ***508***
U of Guelph (ON, Canada) ***546***
Warren Wilson Coll (NC) ***594***
Worcester State Coll (MA) ***609***

NUCLEAR ENGINEERING

Overview: Students who choose this major learn the science behind generating and controlling energy that is created by either nuclear fission or fusion. *Related majors:* structural and mechanical engineering, nuclear physics, environmental engineering, energy management systems technology. *Potential careers:* nuclear physicist, nuclear engineer, naval engineer, hazardous waste material technician. *Salary potential:* $40k-$65k.

California State U, Northridge (CA) ***301***
Georgia Inst of Technology (GA) ***367***
Kansas State U (KS) ***396***
Massachusetts Inst of Technology (MA) ***421***
North Carolina State U (NC) ***449***
Oregon State U (OR) ***462***
Penn State U Univ Park Campus (PA) ***468***
Purdue U (IN) ***475***
Rensselaer Polytechnic Inst (NY) ***478***
Texas A&M U (TX) ***524***
United States Military Academy (NY) ***535***
The U of Arizona (AZ) ***538***
U of Calif, Berkeley (CA) ***540***
U of Cincinnati (OH) ***543***
U of Florida (FL) ***545***
U of Illinois at Urbana–Champaign (IL) ***548***
U of Maryland, Coll Park (MD) ***552***
U of Michigan (MI) ***554***

NUCLEAR ENGINEERING (continued)

U of Missouri–Rolla (MO) **556**
U of New Mexico (NM) **559**
The U of Tennessee (TN) **577**
U of Toronto (ON, Canada) **581**
U of Wisconsin–Madison (WI) **584**
Worcester Polytechnic Inst (MA) **609**

NUCLEAR MEDICAL TECHNOLOGY

Overview: This major prepares students to perform nuclear imaging scans and administer radioactive drugs under the supervision of a physician. *Related majors:* electrocardiograph technology, medical radiologic technology, medical technology. *Potential careers:* nuclear medicine technician, radiologic technologist, diagnostic medical sonographer, technologist, clinical laboratory technologist. *Salary potential:* $33k-$40k.

Alverno Coll (WI) **265**
Aquinas Coll (MI) **270**
Barry U (FL) **282**
Benedictine U (IL) **285**
California State U, Dominguez Hills (CA) **300**
Cedar Crest Coll (PA) **308**
Ferris State U (MI) **358**
Houston Baptist U (TX) **382**
Indiana U of Pennsylvania (PA) **386**
Indiana U–Purdue U Indianapolis (IN) **387**
Lebanon Valley Coll (PA) **403**
Long Island U, Brooklyn Campus (NY) **409**
Long Island U, C.W. Post Campus (NY) **409**
Manhattan Coll (NY) **416**
Mass Coll of Pharmacy and Allied Health Sciences (MA) **421**
Medical Coll of Georgia (GA) **424**
Oakland U (MI) **456**
Old Dominion U (VA) **460**
Peru State Coll (NE) **469**
Rochester Inst of Technology (NY) **482**
St. Cloud State U (MN) **488**
Saint Louis U (MO) **492**
Saint Mary's U of Minnesota (MN) **494**
Salem State Coll (MA) **497**
Thomas Edison State Coll (NJ) **527**
U at Buffalo, The State University of New York (NY) **536**
The U of Alabama at Birmingham (AL) **537**
U of Arkansas for Medical Sciences (AR) **539**
U of Central Arkansas (AR) **542**
U of Cincinnati (OH) **543**
The U of Findlay (OH) **545**
The U of Iowa (IA) **548**
U of Louisville (KY) **550**
U of Missouri–Columbia (MO) **555**
U of Nebraska Medical Center (NE) **557**
U of Nevada, Las Vegas (NV) **558**
U of Oklahoma Health Sciences Center (OK) **562**
U of Puerto Rico Medical Sciences Campus (PR) **571**
U of St. Francis (IL) **573**
U of the Incarnate Word (TX) **580**
U of Wisconsin–La Crosse (WI) **584**
Weber State U (UT) **596**
Wheeling Jesuit U (WV) **603**
York Coll of Pennsylvania (PA) **610**

NUCLEAR PHYSICS

Overview: Students who major in this branch of physics will study the properties and behavior of atomic nuclei and fission and fusion reactions. *Related majors:* physics, chemistry, theoretical and mathematical physics, nuclear engineering, nuclear power technology. *Potential careers:* nuclear engineer, research scientist, physicist, professor. *Salary potential:* $35k-$45k.

California Inst of Technology (CA) **299**
Harvard U (MA) **376**

NUCLEAR TECHNOLOGY

Overview: This major will teach students the science and skills necessary to work with engineers and research scientists at nuclear reactors or other nuclear process and disposal facilities. *Related majors:* nuclear physics, instrumentation technology, robotics technology, computer science. *Potential careers:* shift supervisor, instrument and control technician, health physics technician, safety technician. *Salary potential:* $27k-$35k.

Excelsior Coll (NY) **356**
San Jose State U (CA) **499**
Thomas Edison State Coll (NJ) **527**

NURSERY MANAGEMENT

Overview: This major prepares students to operate and manage outdoor plant farms- tree and shrub nurseries for the purpose of propagation, harvesting, and transplantation. *Related majors:* plant science, horticulture, farm management, agricultural mechanization. *Potential careers:* farmer, nursery manager, landscape designer. *Salary potential:* $22k-$30k.

Colorado State U (CO) **325**

NURSING

Overview: Students learn the skills necessary to become a medical nurse, providing care for sick and disabled individuals. *Related majors:* physicians assistant, social work, clinical and medical social work, health-unit coordinator. *Potential careers:* nurse, social worker, physician assistant, ward clerk. *Salary potential:* $30k-$40k.

Abilene Christian U (TX) **260**
Adelphi U (NY) **260**
Albany State U (GA) **262**
Alcorn State U (MS) **263**
Alderson-Broaddus Coll (WV) **263**
Allen Coll (IA) **264**
Alvernia Coll (PA) **265**
Alverno Coll (WI) **265**
American International Coll (MA) **267**
Anderson U (IN) **268**
Andrews U (MI) **269**
Angelo State U (TX) **269**
Anna Maria Coll (MA) **269**
Aquinas Coll (TN) **271**
Arizona State U (AZ) **271**
Arkansas State U (AR) **272**
Arkansas Tech U (AR) **272**
Armstrong Atlantic State U (GA) **273**
Athabasca U (AB, Canada) **275**
Atlantic Union Coll (MA) **276**
Auburn U (AL) **276**
Auburn U Montgomery (AL) **276**
Augsburg Coll (MN) **276**
Augustana Coll (SD) **276**
Aurora U (IL) **277**
Austin Peay State U (TN) **278**
Avila U (MO) **278**
Azusa Pacific U (CA) **278**
Baker U (KS) **280**
Ball State U (IN) **280**
Barry U (FL) **282**
Barton Coll (NC) **282**
Bayamón Central U (PR) **283**
Baylor U (TX) **283**
Bellarmine U (KY) **284**
Bellin Coll of Nursing (WI) **284**
Belmont U (TN) **284**
Bemidji State U (MN) **285**
Berea Coll (KY) **286**
Bethel Coll (IN) **288**
Bethel Coll (KS) **288**
Bethel Coll (MN) **288**
Bethune-Cookman Coll (FL) **289**
Biola U (CA) **289**
Blessing-Rieman Coll of Nursing (IL) **290**
Bloomfield Coll (NJ) **290**
Bloomsburg U of Pennsylvania (PA) **290**
Boston Coll (MA) **292**
Bowie State U (MD) **292**
Bowling Green State U (OH) **292**
Bradley U (IL) **293**
Brenau U (GA) **293**
Briar Cliff U (IA) **294**
Brigham Young U (UT) **295**
California State U, Bakersfield (CA) **300**
California State U, Chico (CA) **300**
California State U, Dominguez Hills (CA) **300**
California State U, Fresno (CA) **301**
California State U, Fullerton (CA) **301**
California State U, Hayward (CA) **301**
California State U, Long Beach (CA) **301**
California State U, Northridge (CA) **301**
California State U, Sacramento (CA) **301**
California State U, San Bernardino (CA) **302**
California State U, Stanislaus (CA) **302**
California U of Pennsylvania (PA) **302**
Calvin Coll (MI) **303**
Capital U (OH) **304**
Cardinal Stritch U (WI) **305**
Carlow Coll (PA) **305**
Carroll Coll (MT) **306**
Carroll Coll (WI) **306**
Carson-Newman Coll (TN) **306**
Case Western Reserve U (OH) **307**
The Catholic U of America (DC) **307**
Cedarville U (OH) **308**
Central Connecticut State U (CT) **309**
Central Methodist Coll (MO) **309**
Central Missouri State U (MO) **310**
Charleston Southern U (SC) **311**
Christopher Newport U (VA) **313**
Clarion U of Pennsylvania (PA) **315**
Clarkson Coll (NE) **315**
Clayton Coll & State U (GA) **316**
Clemson U (SC) **317**
Cleveland State U (OH) **317**
Coe Coll (IA) **318**
Colby-Sawyer Coll (NH) **319**
Coll Misericordia (PA) **319**
Coll of Mount St. Joseph (OH) **320**
Coll of Mount Saint Vincent (NY) **320**
The Coll of New Jersey (NJ) **320**
The Coll of New Rochelle (NY) **321**
Coll of Notre Dame of Maryland (MD) **321**
Coll of Saint Benedict (MN) **321**
Coll of St. Catherine (MN) **321**
Coll of Saint Mary (NE) **322**
The Coll of St. Scholastica (MN) **322**
Coll of Staten Island of the City U of NY (NY) **323**
Colorado State U-Pueblo (CO) **325**
Columbia Coll of Nursing (WI) **327**
Columbia Union Coll (MD) **328**
Columbus State U (GA) **328**
Comm Hospital Roanoke Valley–Coll of Health Scis (VA) **328**
Concordia Coll (MN) **329**
Concordia U (IL) **330**
Concordia U Wisconsin (WI) **331**
Creighton U (NE) **333**
Culver-Stockton Coll (MO) **334**
Cumberland U (TN) **335**
Curry Coll (MA) **335**
Dalhousie U (NS, Canada) **336**
Deaconess Coll of Nursing (MO) **338**
Delaware State U (DE) **338**
Delta State U (MS) **339**
DePaul U (IL) **339**
DeSales U (PA) **340**
Dickinson State U (ND) **344**
Dillard U (LA) **344**
Dominican Coll (NY) **344**
Dominican U of California (CA) **345**
Dordt Coll (IA) **345**
Drury U (MO) **346**
Duquesne U (PA) **346**
D'Youville Coll (NY) **347**
East Carolina U (NC) **347**
East Central U (OK) **347**
Eastern Kentucky U (KY) **348**
Eastern Mennonite U (VA) **348**
Eastern Michigan U (MI) **348**
Eastern New Mexico U (NM) **349**
Eastern U (PA) **349**
Eastern Washington U (WA) **349**
East Stroudsburg U of Pennsylvania (PA) **349**
East Tennessee State U (TN) **349**
East Texas Baptist U (TX) **350**
Edgewood Coll (WI) **351**
Edinboro U of Pennsylvania (PA) **351**
Elmhurst Coll (IL) **351**
Elmira Coll (NY) **351**
Elms Coll (MA) **352**
Emory U (GA) **354**
Endicott Coll (MA) **354**
Eureka Coll (IL) **355**
Excelsior Coll (NY) **356**
Fairfield U (CT) **356**
Fairmont State Coll (WV) **356**
Fayetteville State U (NC) **357**
Felician Coll (NJ) **357**
Ferris State U (MI) **358**
Fitchburg State Coll (MA) **358**
Florida A&M U (FL) **359**
Florida Atlantic U (FL) **359**
Florida Gulf Coast U (FL) **359**
Florida International U (FL) **360**
Florida State U (FL) **361**
Fort Hays State U (KS) **362**
Franciscan U of Steubenville (OH) **363**
Gannon U (PA) **365**
Gardner-Webb U (NC) **365**
George Mason U (VA) **366**
Georgetown U (DC) **366**
Georgia Coll & State U (GA) **367**
Georgia Southern U (GA) **367**
Georgia Southwestern State U (GA) **368**
Georgia State U (GA) **368**
Glenville State Coll (WV) **368**
Gonzaga U (WA) **369**
Goshen Coll (IN) **370**
Governors State U (IL) **370**
Graceland U (IA) **371**
Grace U (NE) **371**
Grambling State U (LA) **371**
Grand Canyon U (AZ) **371**
Grand Valley State U (MI) **371**
Grand View Coll (IA) **372**
Gustavus Adolphus Coll (MN) **374**
Gwynedd-Mercy Coll (PA) **374**
Hampton U (VA) **375**
Hannibal-LaGrange Coll (MO) **375**
Harding U (AR) **375**
Hardin-Simmons U (TX) **376**
Hartwick Coll (NY) **376**
Hawai'i Pacific U (HI) **377**
Henderson State U (AR) **378**
Hope Coll (MI) **381**
Houston Baptist U (TX) **382**
Howard U (DC) **382**
Humboldt State U (CA) **382**
Hunter Coll of the City U of NY (NY) **382**
Husson Coll (ME) **383**
Idaho State U (ID) **384**
Illinois State U (IL) **384**
Illinois Wesleyan U (IL) **385**
Indiana State U (IN) **385**
Indiana U East (IN) **386**
Indiana U Kokomo (IN) **386**
Indiana U Northwest (IN) **386**
Indiana U of Pennsylvania (PA) **386**
Indiana U–Purdue U Fort Wayne (IN) **386**
Indiana U–Purdue U Indianapolis (IN) **387**
Indiana U South Bend (IN) **387**
Indiana U Southeast (IN) **387**
Indiana Wesleyan U (IN) **387**
Inter American U of PR, Guayama Campus (PR) **388**
Inter American U of PR, San Germán Campus (PR) **388**
Iowa Wesleyan Coll (IA) **390**
Jacksonville State U (AL) **390**
Jacksonville U (FL) **391**
James Madison U (VA) **391**
Jamestown Coll (ND) **391**
Jewish Hospital Coll of Nursing and Allied Health (MO) **391**
Johns Hopkins U (MD) **392**
Judson Coll (IL) **395**
Kennesaw State U (GA) **397**
Kent State U (OH) **397**
Kentucky Christian Coll (KY) **397**
Keuka Coll (NY) **398**
King Coll (TN) **398**
LaGrange Coll (GA) **400**
Lakehead U (ON, Canada) **400**
Lakeview Coll of Nursing (IL) **401**
Lamar U (TX) **401**
Lander U (SC) **401**
Langston U (OK) **402**
La Salle U (PA) **402**
Laurentian U (ON, Canada) **403**

Lehman Coll of the City U of NY (NY) **404**
Lenoir-Rhyne Coll (NC) **405**
Lester L. Cox Coll of Nursing and Health Sciences (MO) **405**
Lewis-Clark State Coll (ID) **406**
Lewis U (IL) **406**
Liberty U (VA) **406**
Lincoln Memorial U (TN) **407**
Lipscomb U (TN) **408**
Loma Linda U (CA) **408**
Long Island U, Brooklyn Campus (NY) **409**
Louisiana Coll (LA) **410**
Louisiana State U Health Sciences Center (LA) **410**
Lourdes Coll (OH) **411**
Loyola U Chicago (IL) **411**
Loyola U New Orleans (LA) **411**
Luther Coll (IA) **412**
Lynchburg Coll (VA) **413**
Lynn U (FL) **413**
MacMurray Coll (IL) **414**
Madonna U (MI) **414**
Mansfield U of Pennsylvania (PA) **416**
Maranatha Baptist Bible Coll (WI) **417**
Marian Coll (IN) **417**
Marian Coll of Fond du Lac (WI) **417**
Marquette U (WI) **418**
Marshall U (WV) **418**
Mars Hill Coll (NC) **418**
Marymount U (VA) **420**
Maryville Coll (TN) **420**
Maryville U of Saint Louis (MO) **420**
Marywood U (PA) **421**
McGill U (QC, Canada) **423**
McKendree Coll (IL) **423**
McMaster U (ON, Canada) **423**
McNeese State U (LA) **423**
Medcenter One Coll of Nursing (ND) **424**
Medgar Evers Coll of the City U of NY (NY) **424**
Medical Coll of Georgia (GA) **424**
Medical U of South Carolina (SC) **424**
Memorial U of Newfoundland (NF, Canada) **424**
Mercer U (GA) **425**
Mercy Coll (NY) **425**
Mercyhurst Coll (PA) **425**
Mesa State Coll (CO) **426**
Messiah Coll (PA) **426**
Metropolitan State Coll of Denver (CO) **427**
Miami U (OH) **428**
Michigan State U (MI) **428**
MidAmerica Nazarene U (KS) **428**
Middle Tennessee State U (TN) **429**
Midland Lutheran Coll (NE) **429**
Midway Coll (KY) **429**
Midwestern State U (TX) **430**
Milligan Coll (TN) **430**
Millikin U (IL) **430**
Milwaukee School of Engineering (WI) **431**
Minnesota State U, Mankato (MN) **431**
Minnesota State U, Moorhead (MN) **432**
Minot State U (ND) **432**
Mississippi Coll (MS) **432**
Missouri Southern State Coll (MO) **433**
Missouri Western State Coll (MO) **433**
Molloy Coll (NY) **433**
Montana State U–Bozeman (MT) **434**
Montana State U–Northern (MT) **434**
Moravian Coll (PA) **436**
Morehead State U (KY) **436**
Morningside Coll (IA) **437**
Mountain State U (WV) **437**
Mount Marty Coll (SD) **438**
Mount Mercy Coll (IA) **438**
Mount Saint Mary Coll (NY) **439**
Mount St. Mary's Coll (CA) **439**
Murray State U (KY) **440**
Nazareth Coll of Rochester (NY) **443**
Nebraska Methodist Coll (NE) **443**
Neumann Coll (PA) **443**
Newman U (KS) **445**
New Mexico State U (NM) **446**
New York Inst of Technology (NY) **447**
New York U (NY) **447**
Niagara U (NY) **447**
Nicholls State U (LA) **447**
Nipissing U (ON, Canada) **448**
Norfolk State U (VA) **448**
North Carolina Ag and Tech State U (NC) **448**
North Carolina Central U (NC) **448**
North Dakota State U (ND) **449**
Northeastern State U (OK) **450**
Northern Arizona U (AZ) **450**
Northern Illinois U (IL) **450**
Northern Kentucky U (KY) **451**
Northern Michigan U (MI) **451**
North Georgia Coll & State U (GA) **451**
North Park U (IL) **452**
Northwestern Oklahoma State U (OK) **453**
Northwestern State U of Louisiana (LA) **453**
Northwest Nazarene U (ID) **454**
Norwich U (VT) **455**
Oakland U (MI) **456**
Oakwood Coll (AL) **456**
The Ohio State U (OH) **457**
Ohio U (OH) **458**
Ohio U–Chillicothe (OH) **458**
Ohio U–Zanesville (OH) **458**
Oklahoma Baptist U (OK) **459**
Oklahoma City U (OK) **460**
Oklahoma Panhandle State U (OK) **460**
Oklahoma Wesleyan U (OK) **460**
Old Dominion U (VA) **460**
Olivet Nazarene U (IL) **461**
Oral Roberts U (OK) **461**
Otterbein Coll (OH) **462**
Our Lady of Holy Cross Coll (LA) **463**
Our Lady of the Lake Coll (LA) **463**
Pace U (NY) **463**
Pacific Lutheran U (WA) **463**
Pacific Union Coll (CA) **464**
Penn State U Altoona Coll (PA) **467**
Penn State U Univ Park Campus (PA) **468**
Piedmont Coll (GA) **470**
Pittsburg State U (KS) **470**
Plattsburgh State U of NY (NY) **471**
Point Loma Nazarene U (CA) **471**
Pontifical Catholic U of Puerto Rico (PR) **472**
Prairie View A&M U (TX) **473**
Presentation Coll (SD) **474**
Purdue U (IN) **475**
Purdue U Calumet (IN) **475**
Purdue U North Central (IN) **475**
Queen's U at Kingston (ON, Canada) **476**
Queens U of Charlotte (NC) **476**
Quincy U (IL) **476**
Quinnipiac U (CT) **476**
Radford U (VA) **476**
Ramapo Coll of New Jersey (NJ) **477**
Regis Coll (MA) **478**
Regis U (CO) **478**
Research Coll of Nursing (MO) **479**
Rhode Island Coll (RI) **479**
The Richard Stockton Coll of New Jersey (NJ) **479**
Rivier Coll (NH) **480**
Roberts Wesleyan Coll (NY) **481**
Rockford Coll (IL) **482**
Rockhurst U (MO) **482**
Rush U (IL) **484**
Russell Sage Coll (NY) **484**
Rutgers, The State U of New Jersey, Camden (NJ) **485**
Rutgers, The State U of New Jersey, Newark (NJ) **485**
Ryerson U (ON, Canada) **485**
Sacred Heart U (CT) **486**
Saginaw Valley State U (MI) **486**
St. Ambrose U (IA) **486**
Saint Anthony Coll of Nursing (IL) **487**
St. Cloud State U (MN) **488**
Saint Francis Medical Center Coll of Nursing (IL) **488**
Saint Francis U (PA) **488**
St. Francis Xavier U (NS, Canada) **489**
St. John Fisher Coll (NY) **489**
St. John's Coll (IL) **489**
Saint John's U (MN) **490**
Saint Joseph Coll (CT) **490**
St. Joseph's Coll, New York (NY) **491**
Saint Joseph's Coll of Maine (ME) **491**
St. Joseph's Coll, Suffolk Campus (NY) **491**
Saint Louis U (MO) **492**
Saint Luke's Coll (MO) **492**
Saint Mary's Coll (IN) **493**
Saint Mary's Coll of California (CA) **494**
St. Olaf Coll (MN) **495**
Saint Xavier U (IL) **496**
Salem State Coll (MA) **497**
Salisbury U (MD) **497**
Salve Regina U (RI) **497**
Samford U (AL) **497**
Samuel Merritt Coll (CA) **498**
San Diego State U (CA) **498**
San Francisco State U (CA) **498**
San Jose State U (CA) **499**
Seattle Pacific U (WA) **501**
Seattle U (WA) **501**
Seton Hall U (NJ) **502**
Seton Hill U (PA) **502**
Shenandoah U (VA) **503**
Shepherd Coll (WV) **503**
Simmons Coll (MA) **504**
Si Tanka Huron U (SD) **505**
Slippery Rock U of Pennsylvania (PA) **506**
Sonoma State U (CA) **506**
South Carolina State U (SC) **506**
South Dakota State U (SD) **507**
Southeastern Louisiana U (LA) **508**
Southeast Missouri State U (MO) **508**
Southern Connecticut State U (CT) **509**
Southern Illinois U Edwardsville (IL) **509**
Southern Nazarene U (OK) **510**
Southern Oregon U (OR) **510**
Southern U and A&M Coll (LA) **511**
Southern Vermont Coll (VT) **511**
Southwest Baptist U (MO) **512**
Southwestern Christian Coll (TX) **512**
Southwestern Coll (KS) **512**
Southwestern Oklahoma State U (OK) **512**
Southwest Missouri State U (MO) **513**
Spalding U (KY) **513**
Spring Hill Coll (AL) **514**
State U of NY at Binghamton (NY) **515**
State U of NY at New Paltz (NY) **515**
State U of NY Coll at Brockport (NY) **515**
State U of NY Health Science Center at Brooklyn (NY) **517**
State U of NY Inst of Tech at Utica/Rome (NY) **518**
State U of West Georgia (GA) **518**
Stephen F. Austin State U (TX) **518**
Stony Brook U, State University of New York (NY) **520**
Syracuse U (NY) **521**
Tarleton State U (TX) **522**
Temple U (PA) **523**
Tennessee State U (TN) **523**
Tennessee Technological U (TN) **524**
Tennessee Wesleyan Coll (TN) **524**
Texas A&M International U (TX) **524**
Texas A&M U–Corpus Christi (TX) **525**
Texas Christian U (TX) **526**
Texas Southern U (TX) **526**
Texas Woman's U (TX) **527**
Thomas Jefferson U (PA) **527**
Thomas More Coll (KY) **528**
Thomas U (GA) **528**
Towson U (MD) **529**
Trent U (ON, Canada) **529**
Trinity Christian Coll (IL) **530**
Trinity Coll of Nursing and Health Sciences Schools (IL) **531**
Trinity Western U (BC, Canada) **531**
Troy State U (AL) **532**
Truman State U (MO) **532**
Tuskegee U (AL) **533**
Union Coll (NE) **534**
Union U (TN) **534**
Universidad Adventista de las Antillas (PR) **536**
Université de Sherbrooke (QC, Canada) **536**
U du Québec à Trois-Rivières (QC, Canada) **536**
U du Québec à Hull (QC, Canada) **536**
Université Laval (QC, Canada) **536**
U at Buffalo, The State University of New York (NY) **536**
The U of Akron (OH) **537**
The U of Alabama (AL) **537**
The U of Alabama at Birmingham (AL) **537**
The U of Alabama in Huntsville (AL) **537**
U of Alaska Anchorage (AK) **538**
U of Alberta (AB, Canada) **538**
The U of Arizona (AZ) **538**
U of Arkansas (AR) **539**
U of Arkansas at Monticello (AR) **539**
U of Arkansas for Medical Sciences (AR) **539**
The U of British Columbia (BC, Canada) **540**
U of Calgary (AB, Canada) **540**
U of Calif, Los Angeles (CA) **541**
U of Central Arkansas (AR) **542**
U of Central Florida (FL) **542**
U of Central Oklahoma (OK) **542**
U of Charleston (WV) **542**
U of Cincinnati (OH) **543**
U of Colorado at Colorado Springs (CO) **543**
U of Colorado Health Sciences Center (CO) **543**
U of Connecticut (CT) **544**
U of Delaware (DE) **544**
U of Evansville (IN) **545**
U of Florida (FL) **545**
U of Hartford (CT) **546**
U of Hawaii at Hilo (HI) **546**
U of Hawaii at Manoa (HI) **546**
U of Illinois at Chicago (IL) **547**
U of Illinois at Springfield (IL) **548**
U of Indianapolis (IN) **548**
The U of Iowa (IA) **548**
U of Kentucky (KY) **549**
The U of Lethbridge (AB, Canada) **549**
U of Louisiana at Lafayette (LA) **550**
U of Louisville (KY) **550**
U of Maine (ME) **550**
U of Maine at Fort Kent (ME) **551**
U of Manitoba (MB, Canada) **551**
U of Mary (ND) **551**
U of Mary Hardin-Baylor (TX) **551**
U of Massachusetts Amherst (MA) **552**
U of Massachusetts Boston (MA) **553**
U of Massachusetts Dartmouth (MA) **553**
U of Massachusetts Lowell (MA) **553**
The U of Memphis (TN) **553**
U of Miami (FL) **553**
U of Michigan (MI) **554**
U of Michigan–Flint (MI) **554**
U of Minnesota, Twin Cities Campus (MN) **555**
U of Mississippi Medical Center (MS) **555**
U of Missouri–Columbia (MO) **555**
U of Missouri–Kansas City (MO) **555**
U of Missouri–St. Louis (MO) **556**
U of Mobile (AL) **556**
U of Nebraska Medical Center (NE) **557**
U of Nevada, Las Vegas (NV) **558**
U of Nevada, Reno (NV) **558**
U of New Brunswick Fredericton (NB, Canada) **558**
U of New Brunswick Saint John (NB, Canada) **558**
U of New England (ME) **558**
U of New Hampshire (NH) **558**
U of New Mexico (NM) **559**
U of North Alabama (AL) **559**
The U of North Carolina at Chapel Hill (NC) **560**
The U of North Carolina at Charlotte (NC) **560**
The U of North Carolina at Greensboro (NC) **560**
The U of North Carolina at Pembroke (NC) **560**
The U of North Carolina at Wilmington (NC) **561**
U of North Dakota (ND) **561**
U of Northern Colorado (CO) **561**
U of North Florida (FL) **561**
U of Oklahoma Health Sciences Center (OK) **562**
U of Ottawa (ON, Canada) **563**
U of Pennsylvania (PA) **563**
U of Phoenix–Hawaii Campus (HI) **564**
U of Phoenix–New Mexico Campus (NM) **565**
U of Phoenix–Southern Arizona Campus (AZ) **568**
U of Phoenix–Tulsa Campus (OK) **568**
U of Phoenix–Utah Campus (UT) **568**
U of Pittsburgh (PA) **569**
U of Pittsburgh at Bradford (PA) **569**
U of Portland (OR) **570**
U of Prince Edward Island (PE, Canada) **570**
U of Puerto Rico, Humacao U Coll (PR) **570**
U of Puerto Rico Medical Sciences Campus (PR) **571**
U of Rhode Island (RI) **572**
U of St. Francis (IL) **573**
U of Saint Francis (IN) **573**
U of San Francisco (CA) **574**
U of Saskatchewan (SK, Canada) **574**
The U of Scranton (PA) **574**
U of South Alabama (AL) **575**
U of South Carolina (SC) **575**
U of South Carolina Aiken (SC) **575**
U of South Carolina Spartanburg (SC) **575**
U of Southern California (CA) **576**
U of Southern Indiana (IN) **576**
U of Southern Maine (ME) **576**
U of Southern Mississippi (MS) **576**
U of South Florida (FL) **576**

NURSING (continued)

The U of Tampa (FL) **577**
The U of Tennessee (TN) **577**
The U of Tennessee at Chattanooga (TN) **577**
The U of Tennessee at Martin (TN) **577**
The U of Texas at Arlington (TX) **577**
The U of Texas at Austin (TX) **578**
The U of Texas at Brownsville (TX) **578**
The U of Texas at El Paso (TX) **578**
The U of Texas at Tyler (TX) **579**
U of Texas-Houston Health Science Center (TX) **579**
U of Texas Medical Branch at Galveston (TX) **579**
The U of Texas–Pan American (TX) **579**
U of the District of Columbia (DC) **580**
U of the Incarnate Word (TX) **580**
U of the Sacred Heart (PR) **580**
U of the Virgin Islands (VI) **581**
U of Toledo (OH) **581**
U of Toronto (ON, Canada) **581**
U of Tulsa (OK) **581**
U of Utah (UT) **582**
U of Vermont (VT) **582**
U of Virginia (VA) **582**
U of Washington (WA) **583**
The U of Western Ontario (ON, Canada) **583**
U of West Florida (FL) **583**
U of Windsor (ON, Canada) **584**
U of Wisconsin–Eau Claire (WI) **584**
U of Wisconsin–Madison (WI) **584**
U of Wisconsin–Milwaukee (WI) **585**
U of Wisconsin–Oshkosh (WI) **585**
U of Wisconsin–Parkside (WI) **585**
U of Wyoming (WY) **586**
Ursuline Coll (OH) **587**
Utica Coll (NY) **588**
Valdosta State U (GA) **588**
Valparaiso U (IN) **588**
Villa Julie Coll (MD) **590**
Villanova U (PA) **590**
Virginia Commonwealth U (VA) **590**
Viterbo U (WI) **591**
Wagner Coll (NY) **592**
Walla Walla Coll (WA) **593**
Walsh U (OH) **593**
Washington State U (WA) **595**
Waynesburg Coll (PA) **595**
Wayne State U (MI) **596**
Weber State U (UT) **596**
Webster U (MO) **597**
West Chester U of Pennsylvania (PA) **598**
Western Carolina U (NC) **598**
Western Connecticut State U (CT) **598**
Western Kentucky U (KY) **599**
Western Michigan U (MI) **599**
West Liberty State Coll (WV) **601**
Westminster Coll (UT) **601**
West Suburban Coll of Nursing (IL) **602**
West Texas A&M U (TX) **602**
West Virginia U (WV) **602**
West Virginia U Inst of Technology (WV) **602**
West Virginia Wesleyan Coll (WV) **603**
Wheeling Jesuit U (WV) **603**
Whitworth Coll (WA) **604**
Widener U (PA) **604**
Wilkes U (PA) **605**
William Carey Coll (MS) **605**
William Jewell Coll (MO) **606**
William Paterson U of New Jersey (NJ) **606**
Wilmington Coll (DE) **607**
Winona State U (MN) **608**
Winston-Salem State U (NC) **608**
Worcester State Coll (MA) **609**
Wright State U (OH) **609**
York Coll of Pennsylvania (PA) **610**
York Coll of the City U of New York (NY) **611**
Youngstown State U (OH) **611**

NURSING ADMINISTRATION

Overview: This major teaches students who are already registered nurses how to manage hospital or health care nursing personnel. *Related majors:* nursing, labor/personnel relations and studies, office supervision and management. *Potential careers:* nurse, ward supervisor, health-care facility manager. *Salary potential:* $37k-$47k.

Central Methodist Coll (MO) **309**
Clarkson Coll (NE) **315**
Emmanuel Coll (MA) **353**
Framingham State Coll (MA) **362**
Nebraska Wesleyan U (NE) **443**
Ryerson U (ON, Canada) **485**
U of San Francisco (CA) **574**
U of Saskatchewan (SK, Canada) **574**
The U of Western Ontario (ON, Canada) **583**
U of Windsor (ON, Canada) **584**
Wheeling Jesuit U (WV) **603**

NURSING (ADULT HEALTH)

Overview: This major prepares students who are already registered nurses how to provide primary and general care for adult patients. *Related majors:* nursing. *Potential careers:* nurse. *Salary potential:* $30k-$40k.

Northern Kentucky U (KY) **451**
Okanagan U Coll (BC, Canada) **459**
Pennsylvania Coll of Technology (PA) **467**
U du Québec à Trois-Rivières (QC, Canada) **536**

NURSING (ANESTHETIST)

Overview: Registered nurses who enroll in this major learn how to work with anesthesiologists, administer anesthetics to patients under the direction of attending physicians, and care for patients after anesthesia. *Related majors:* biochemistry, anesthesiology, medical anatomy and physiology, clinical pharmacology. *Potential careers:* nurse anesthetist. $45k-$60k.

Webster U (MO) **597**

NURSING (FAMILY PRACTICE)

Overview: Registered nurses who enroll in this major learn how to provide primary and general medical care to family groups and individuals in the context of family living. *Related majors:* individual/family development studies; marriage and family counseling; child growth, care, and development studies; psychology; nursing. *Potential careers:* family health services counselor, family therapist, family practice nurse, nurse practitioner. *Salary potential:* $34k-$45k.

U du Québec à Trois-Rivières (QC, Canada) **536**
The U of Virginia's Coll at Wise (VA) **582**

NURSING (MATERNAL/ CHILD HEALTH)

Overview: Registered nurses who enroll in this major learn how to provide basic medical care for pregnant women, mothers and their newborn babies. *Related majors:* nursing midwifery, pediatric nursing. *Potential careers:* maternal nurse, neonatal nurse, educator, midwife. *Salary potential:* $35k-$45k.

U of Washington (WA) **583**

NURSING (MIDWIFERY)

Overview: Registered nurses who enroll in this major learn the skills necessary to independently deliver babies and treat mothers, usually in the patient's home, without the assistance of physicians. *Related majors:* neonatal nursing, maternal nursing. *Potential careers:* midwife, nurse. *Salary potential:* $35k-$45k.

Marquette U (WI) **418**
McMaster U (ON, Canada) **423**
Ryerson U (ON, Canada) **485**
U du Québec à Trois-Rivières (QC, Canada) **536**

NURSING (PSYCHIATRIC/ MENTAL HEALTH)

Overview: Registered nurses who take this major learn how to care for patients with mental, emotional, or behavioral problems. *Related majors:* clinical psychology, behavioral sciences, mental-health services technician. *Potential careers:* mental-health facility supervisor, psychiatric nurse, therapist. *Salary potential:* $33k-$43k.

Brandon U (MB, Canada) **293**

NURSING (PUBLIC HEALTH)

Overview: Registered nurses who take this major learn how to educate individuals and communities about health issues and disease-prevention strategies under the supervision of a public health agency. *Related majors:* public health education/promotion, public health, nursing, social work, human services. *Potential careers:* public health advocate, nurse, health educator, community health assessor, family therapist. *Salary potential:* $33k-$43k.

Ryerson U (ON, Canada) **485**
U du Québec à Trois-Rivières (QC, Canada) **536**
U of San Francisco (CA) **574**
U of Washington (WA) **583**

NURSING RELATED

Information can be found under this major's main heading.

Adelphi U (NY) **260**
Alverno Coll (WI) **265**
British Columbia Inst of Technology (BC, Canada) **295**
California State U, Fullerton (CA) **301**
Coll of Staten Island of the City U of NY (NY) **323**
Malaspina U-Coll (BC, Canada) **415**
Malone Coll (OH) **415**
Metropolitan State U (MN) **427**
New York Inst of Technology (NY) **447**
Northeastern U (MA) **450**
Thomas More Coll (KY) **528**
The U of Akron (OH) **537**
U of Hawaii at Manoa (HI) **546**
U of Kentucky (KY) **549**
U of Pennsylvania (PA) **563**
Western Kentucky U (KY) **599**
Wheaton Coll (IL) **603**

NURSING SCIENCE

Overview: Registered nurses who enroll in this major focus on advanced nursing practices and managing complex services and facilities. *Related majors:* nursing, health-facilities administration, enterprise management and operation, premedicine studies, information and computer science. *Potential careers:* nurse supervisor, hospital administrator, medical laboratory technologist, research scientist, professor. *Salary potential:* $40k-$55k.

Benedictine U (IL) **285**
Brandon U (MB, Canada) **293**
Brock U (ON, Canada) **295**
Cedar Crest Coll (PA) **308**
Clarke Coll (IA) **315**
Clarkson Coll (NE) **315**
Coll of Saint Elizabeth (NJ) **321**
Daemen Coll (NY) **335**
Dominican Coll (NY) **344**
Elmira Coll (NY) **351**
Emporia State U (KS) **354**
Fairleigh Dickinson U, Teaneck-Metro Campus (NJ) **356**
Holy Family U (PA) **380**
Holy Names Coll (CA) **381**
Immaculata U (PA) **385**
Inter American U of PR, Aguadilla Campus (PR) **388**
Kean U (NJ) **396**
Kutztown U of Pennsylvania (PA) **399**
La Roche Coll (PA) **402**
Long Island U, C.W. Post Campus (NY) **409**
Millersville U of Pennsylvania (PA) **430**
Monmouth U (NJ) **434**
Mount Aloysius Coll (PA) **437**
National U (CA) **442**
New Jersey City U (NJ) **445**
New Jersey Inst of Technology (NJ) **445**
The Ohio State U (OH) **457**
Penn State U Harrisburg Campus of the Capital Coll (PA) **468**
Queens U of Charlotte (NC) **476**
The Richard Stockton Coll of New Jersey (NJ) **479**
St. Francis Xavier U (NS, Canada) **489**
Saint Joseph's Coll (IN) **490**
Saint Peter's Coll (NJ) **495**
Southern Adventist U (TN) **508**
State U of New York Upstate Medical University (NY) **518**
Thomas Edison State Coll (NJ) **527**
Trinity Coll of Nursing and Health Sciences Schools (IL) **531**
U Coll of the Cariboo (BC, Canada) **537**
The U of Akron (OH) **537**
U of Delaware (DE) **544**
U of Hawaii at Manoa (HI) **546**
U of Kansas (KS) **549**
U of Phoenix-Atlanta Campus (GA) **563**
U of Phoenix–Colorado Campus (CO) **563**
U of Phoenix–Fort Lauderdale Campus (FL) **564**
U of Phoenix–Hawaii Campus (HI) **564**
U of Phoenix–Jacksonville Campus (FL) **564**
U of Phoenix–Louisiana Campus (LA) **565**
U of Phoenix–Metro Detroit Campus (MI) **565**
U of Phoenix–New Mexico Campus (NM) **565**
U of Phoenix–Northern California Campus (CA) **565**
U of Phoenix–Orlando Campus (FL) **566**
U of Phoenix–Phoenix Campus (AZ) **567**
U of Phoenix–Sacramento Campus (CA) **567**
U of Phoenix–San Diego Campus (CA) **567**
U of Phoenix–Southern Arizona Campus (AZ) **568**
U of Phoenix–Southern California Campus (CA) **568**
U of Phoenix–Southern Colorado Campus (CO) **568**
U of Phoenix–Tampa Campus (FL) **568**
U of Phoenix–Tulsa Campus (OK) **568**
U of Phoenix–Utah Campus (UT) **568**
U of Phoenix–West Michigan Campus (MI) **569**
U of Victoria (BC, Canada) **582**
U of Wisconsin–Green Bay (WI) **584**
Wichita State U (KS) **604**
Xavier U (OH) **610**
York U (ON, Canada) **611**

NURSING (SURGICAL)

Overview: Registered nurses who take this major learn how to assist operating room surgeons and provide care for pre and postsurgery patients. *Related majors:* nursing, physicians assistant, surgical/operating room technology, respiratory therapy technology, anesthesiology. *Potential careers:* operating room nurse, operating room technician, respiratory technician, nurse anesthetist. *Salary potential:* $40k-$55k.

Texas A&M International U (TX) **524**
Wheeling Jesuit U (WV) **603**

NUTRITIONAL SCIENCES

Overview: Students who take this major study how the body utilizes and metabolizes the nutrients in food, from agricultural, human, biological, and biomedical science perspectives. *Related majors:* biology, toxicology, anatomy, biochemistry, food sciences/ technology. *Potential careers:* nutritionist, nutritional scientist, biochemical engineer. *Salary potential:* $25k-$40k.

Benedictine U (IL) ***285***
Boston U (MA) ***292***
Brigham Young U (UT) ***295***
Cornell U (NY) ***333***
Drexel U (PA) ***346***
La Salle U (PA) ***402***
McGill U (QC, Canada) ***423***
Mount Saint Vincent U (NS, Canada) ***439***
New York Inst of Technology (NY) ***447***
Russell Sage Coll (NY) ***484***
Rutgers, The State U of New Jersey, New Brunswick (NJ) ***485***
Texas Woman's U (TX) ***527***
Université Laval (QC, Canada) ***536***
The U of Arizona (AZ) ***538***
U of Calif, Berkeley (CA) ***540***
U of Connecticut (CT) ***544***
U of Delaware (DE) ***544***
U of Guelph (ON, Canada) ***546***
U of Hawaii at Manoa (HI) ***546***
U of Nevada, Las Vegas (NV) ***558***
U of Saskatchewan (SK, Canada) ***574***
U of the District of Columbia (DC) ***580***
U of Vermont (VT) ***582***
U of Wisconsin–Green Bay (WI) ***584***

NUTRITION SCIENCE

Overview: Students learn about the development of food products and the principles of nutrition assessment, food safety, and food composition. *Related majors:* food sciences and technology, agricultural and food products processing, chemical engineering, food and nutrition. *Potential careers:* nutritionist, food inspector, biochemist, new-product researcher. *Salary potential:* $25k-$36k.

Acadia U (NS, Canada) ***260***
Andrews U (MI) ***269***
Appalachian State U (NC) ***270***
Ashland U (OH) ***274***
Bastyr U (WA) ***282***
Bluffton Coll (OH) ***291***
Bowling Green State U (OH) ***292***
Brooklyn Coll of the City U of NY (NY) ***295***
California Polytechnic State U, San Luis Obispo (CA) ***300***
California State Polytechnic U, Pomona (CA) ***300***
California State U, Fresno (CA) ***301***
California State U, Northridge (CA) ***301***
California State U, San Bernardino (CA) ***302***
Carson-Newman Coll (TN) ***306***
Case Western Reserve U (OH) ***307***
Cedar Crest Coll (PA) ***308***
Coll of Saint Benedict (MN) ***321***
Coll of St. Catherine (MN) ***321***
Coll of the Ozarks (MO) ***323***
Colorado State U (CO) ***325***
Concordia Coll (MN) ***329***
Cornell U (NY) ***333***
Delaware State U (DE) ***338***
Dominican U (IL) ***345***
Florida State U (FL) ***361***
Fort Valley State U (GA) ***362***
Framingham State Coll (MA) ***362***
Gallaudet U (DC) ***365***
Hampshire Coll (MA) ***375***
Howard U (DC) ***382***
Hunter Coll of the City U of NY (NY) ***382***
Immaculata U (PA) ***385***
Indiana U Bloomington (IN) ***385***
Iowa State U of Science and Technology (IA) ***390***
Ithaca Coll (NY) ***390***
Jacksonville State U (AL) ***390***
Keene State Coll (NH) ***396***
Langston U (OK) ***402***
Lehman Coll of the City U of NY (NY) ***404***
Long Island U, C.W. Post Campus (NY) ***409***
Long Island U, Southampton Coll, Friends World Program (NY) ***409***
Madonna U (MI) ***414***
Marymount Coll of Fordham U (NY) ***419***
The Master's Coll and Seminary (CA) ***422***
McGill U (QC, Canada) ***423***
McNeese State U (LA) ***423***
Memorial U of Newfoundland (NF, Canada) ***424***
Michigan State U (MI) ***428***
Middle Tennessee State U (TN) ***429***
Minnesota State U, Mankato (MN) ***431***
Montclair State U (NJ) ***435***
Morgan State U (MD) ***436***
Mount Marty Coll (SD) ***438***
Mount Saint Vincent U (NS, Canada) ***439***
New Mexico State U (NM) ***446***
New York U (NY) ***447***
North Carolina Ag and Tech State U (NC) ***448***
North Dakota State U (ND) ***449***
Northeastern State U (OK) ***450***
Northwest Missouri State U (MO) ***454***
Notre Dame Coll (OH) ***455***
Oklahoma State U (OK) ***460***
Oregon State U (OR) ***462***
Pacific Union Coll (CA) ***464***
Pepperdine U, Malibu (CA) ***469***
Plattsburgh State U of NY (NY) ***471***
Prairie View A&M U (TX) ***473***
Queens Coll of the City U of NY (NY) ***475***
Ryerson U (ON, Canada) ***485***
St. Francis Xavier U (NS, Canada) ***489***
Saint John's U (MN) ***490***
Saint Joseph Coll (CT) ***490***
Sam Houston State U (TX) ***497***
San Diego State U (CA) ***498***
San Jose State U (CA) ***499***
Seattle Pacific U (WA) ***501***
Seton Hill U (PA) ***502***
Simmons Coll (MA) ***504***
South Carolina State U (SC) ***506***
South Dakota State U (SD) ***507***
Southeast Missouri State U (MO) ***508***
Syracuse U (NY) ***521***
Tennessee Technological U (TN) ***524***
Texas A&M U–Kingsville (TX) ***525***
Tuskegee U (AL) ***533***
Université Laval (QC, Canada) ***536***
U of Alberta (AB, Canada) ***538***
The U of British Columbia (BC, Canada) ***540***
U of Calif, Davis (CA) ***540***
U of Central Oklahoma (OK) ***542***
U of Cincinnati (OH) ***543***
U of Dayton (OH) ***544***
U of Delaware (DE) ***544***
U of Guelph (ON, Canada) ***546***
U of Kentucky (KY) ***549***
U of Maine (ME) ***550***
U of Manitoba (MB, Canada) ***551***
U of Maryland, Coll Park (MD) ***552***
U of Michigan (MI) ***554***
U of Minnesota, Twin Cities Campus (MN) ***555***
U of Missouri–Columbia (MO) ***555***
U of New Hampshire (NH) ***558***
U of Northern Iowa (IA) ***561***
U of Oklahoma Health Sciences Center (OK) ***562***
U of Ottawa (ON, Canada) ***563***
U of Prince Edward Island (PE, Canada) ***570***
The U of Tennessee (TN) ***577***
U of the Incarnate Word (TX) ***580***
U of Toronto (ON, Canada) ***581***
U of Vermont (VT) ***582***
The U of Western Ontario (ON, Canada) ***583***
U of Wisconsin–Madison (WI) ***584***
Virginia Polytechnic Inst and State U (VA) ***591***
Winthrop U (SC) ***608***

NUTRITION STUDIES

Overview: This major focuses on the role of food and nutrition in human health. *Related majors:* foods and nutrition science, human nutritional services, health teacher education. *Potential careers:* food-service administrator, dietician or nutritionist, health teacher, home economics teacher. *Salary potential:* $20k-$26k.

Alcorn State U (MS) ***263***
Appalachian State U (NC) ***270***
Arizona State U East (AZ) ***271***
Auburn U (AL) ***276***
California State U, Chico (CA) ***300***
Central Washington U (WA) ***310***
Eastern Michigan U (MI) ***348***
Florida State U (FL) ***361***
Framingham State Coll (MA) ***362***
Georgia Southern U (GA) ***367***
Idaho State U (ID) ***384***
Indiana State U (IN) ***385***
Indiana U of Pennsylvania (PA) ***386***
Ithaca Coll (NY) ***390***
James Madison U (VA) ***391***
Kansas State U (KS) ***396***
Kent State U (OH) ***397***
Lambuth U (TN) ***401***
Loyola U Chicago (IL) ***411***
Marygrove Coll (MI) ***419***
Murray State U (KY) ***440***
Northern Illinois U (IL) ***450***
The Ohio State U (OH) ***457***
Ohio U (OH) ***458***
Penn State U Univ Park Campus (PA) ***468***
Purdue U (IN) ***475***
San Diego State U (CA) ***498***
Southern Illinois U Carbondale (IL) ***509***
Southwest Texas State U (TX) ***513***
Stephen F. Austin State U (TX) ***518***
Syracuse U (NY) ***521***
Texas A&M U (TX) ***524***
Texas Christian U (TX) ***526***
Texas Southern U (TX) ***526***
Texas Tech U (TX) ***526***
Texas Woman's U (TX) ***527***
The U of Akron (OH) ***537***
The U of Alabama (AL) ***537***
U of Arkansas (AR) ***539***
U of Delaware (DE) ***544***
U of Georgia (GA) ***545***
U of Houston (TX) ***547***
U of Idaho (ID) ***547***
U of Kentucky (KY) ***549***
U of Massachusetts Amherst (MA) ***552***
U of Nebraska–Lincoln (NE) ***557***
U of Nevada, Reno (NV) ***558***
U of New Mexico (NM) ***559***
The U of North Carolina at Chapel Hill (NC) ***560***
The U of North Carolina at Greensboro (NC) ***560***
U of Northern Iowa (IA) ***561***
U of Puerto Rico, Río Piedras (PR) ***571***
U of Rhode Island (RI) ***572***
The U of Texas at Austin (TX) ***578***
U of Vermont (VT) ***582***
U of Wisconsin–Stout (WI) ***586***
Washington State U (WA) ***595***
Wayne State U (MI) ***596***
Western Kentucky U (KY) ***599***
Western Michigan U (MI) ***599***
Youngstown State U (OH) ***611***

OCCUPATIONAL HEALTH/ INDUSTRIAL HYGIENE

Overview: This major prepares students for public health careers that focus on monitoring and determining health and safety standards of industrial and commercial workplaces. *Related majors:* occupation safety/health technology, interior environments, building/property management. *Potential careers:* occupational therapist, public health administrator, epidemiologist, health-services research analyst, EPA researcher/ analyst. *Salary potential:* $37k-$47k.

California State U, Fresno (CA) ***301***
Illinois State U (IL) ***384***
Montana Tech of The U of Montana (MT) ***435***
Oakland U (MI) ***456***
Ryerson U (ON, Canada) ***485***
Saint Augustine's Coll (NC) ***487***

OCCUPATIONAL SAFETY/ HEALTH TECHNOLOGY

Overview: This major teaches students the basic science and technical skills to analyze and maintain job-related health and safety standards. *Related majors:* occupational health, environmental pollution control technology, interior environments. *Potential careers:* OSHA inspector, consultant, heating and air-conditioning technician, mechanical engineering. *Salary potential:* $28k-$36k.

Ball State U (IN) ***280***
Bayamón Central U (PR) ***283***
California State U, Fresno (CA) ***301***
California State U, Northridge (CA) ***301***
Central Missouri State U (MO) ***310***
Central Washington U (WA) ***310***
Columbia Southern U (AL) ***327***
Fairmont State Coll (WV) ***356***
Ferris State U (MI) ***358***
Grand Valley State U (MI) ***371***
Indiana State U (IN) ***385***
Indiana U of Pennsylvania (PA) ***386***
Jacksonville State U (AL) ***390***
Keene State Coll (NH) ***396***
Madonna U (MI) ***414***
Marshall U (WV) ***418***
Mercy Coll (NY) ***425***
Millersville U of Pennsylvania (PA) ***430***
Montana Tech of The U of Montana (MT) ***435***
Murray State U (KY) ***440***
National U (CA) ***442***
North Carolina Ag and Tech State U (NC) ***448***
Oregon State U (OR) ***462***
Rochester Inst of Technology (NY) ***482***
Saint Augustine's Coll (NC) ***487***
Southeastern Oklahoma State U (OK) ***508***
Southwest Baptist U (MO) ***512***
Texas Southern U (TX) ***526***
U of Central Oklahoma (OK) ***542***
U of New Haven (CT) ***559***
U of North Dakota (ND) ***561***
Utah State U (UT) ***587***

OCCUPATIONAL THERAPY

Overview: Students taking this major learn how to teach a variety of techniques, skills, and technologies and personalized strategies to patients who are limited by physical, mental, emotional, or learning disabilities so that they may establish and maintain their personal independence and health. *Related majors:* cognitive psychology, nursing (psychiatric/mental health), mental health/rehabilitation, environmental health, counseling psychology. *Potential careers:* occupational therapist, rehabilitation center or nursing home manager, home-health therapist. *Salary potential:* $40k-$45k.

Alabama State U (AL) ***261***
Alma Coll (MI) ***264***
Alvernia Coll (PA) ***265***
American International Coll (MA) ***267***
Augustana Coll (IL) ***276***
Avila U (MO) ***278***
Baker Coll of Flint (MI) ***279***
Bay Path Coll (MA) ***283***
Boston U (MA) ***292***
Brenau U (GA) ***293***
Calvin Coll (MI) ***303***
Carthage Coll (WI) ***306***
Centenary Coll of Louisiana (LA) ***308***
Cleveland State U (OH) ***317***
Coll of Saint Benedict (MN) ***321***
Coll of St. Catherine (MN) ***321***
Coll of Saint Mary (NE) ***322***
The Coll of St. Scholastica (MN) ***322***
Concordia Coll (MN) ***329***
Concordia U Wisconsin (WI) ***331***
Dalhousie U (NS, Canada) ***336***
Davis & Elkins Coll (WV) ***338***
Dominican Coll (NY) ***344***

OCCUPATIONAL THERAPY (continued)

Dominican U of California (CA) ***345***
Duquesne U (PA) ***346***
D'Youville Coll (NY) ***347***
East Carolina U (NC) ***347***
Eastern Kentucky U (KY) ***348***
Eastern Michigan U (MI) ***348***
Eastern Washington U (WA) ***349***
Elizabethtown Coll (PA) ***351***
Elmhurst Coll (IL) ***351***
Florida A&M U (FL) ***359***
Florida Gulf Coast U (FL) ***359***
Florida International U (FL) ***360***
Gannon U (PA) ***365***
Gustavus Adolphus Coll (MN) ***374***
Hamline U (MN) ***374***
Howard U (DC) ***382***
Husson Coll (ME) ***383***
Illinois Coll (IL) ***384***
Indiana U–Purdue U Indianapolis (IN) ***387***
Ithaca Coll (NY) ***390***
Kean U (NJ) ***396***
Keuka Coll (NY) ***398***
La Salle U (PA) ***402***
Lenoir-Rhyne Coll (NC) ***405***
Loma Linda U (CA) ***408***
McGill U (QC, Canada) ***423***
Medical Coll of Georgia (GA) ***424***
Mount Aloysius Coll (PA) ***437***
Mount Mary Coll (WI) ***438***
Newman U (KS) ***445***
New York Inst of Technology (NY) ***447***
The Ohio State U (OH) ***457***
Queen's U at Kingston (ON, Canada) ***476***
Quinnipiac U (CT) ***476***
Russell Sage Coll (NY) ***484***
Sacred Heart U (CT) ***486***
Saginaw Valley State U (MI) ***486***
Saint Francis U (PA) ***488***
Saint John's U (MN) ***490***
Saint Louis U (MO) ***492***
Saint Vincent Coll (PA) ***496***
San Jose State U (CA) ***499***
Shawnee State U (OH) ***502***
Spalding U (KY) ***513***
State U of NY Health Science Center at Brooklyn (NY) ***517***
Stephens Coll (MO) ***519***
Temple U (PA) ***523***
Texas Woman's U (TX) ***527***
Thomas Jefferson U (PA) ***527***
Towson U (MD) ***529***
Tuskegee U (AL) ***533***
Université Laval (QC, Canada) ***536***
U at Buffalo, The State University of New York (NY) ***536***
U of Alberta (AB, Canada) ***538***
The U of British Columbia (BC, Canada) ***540***
U of Central Arkansas (AR) ***542***
The U of Findlay (OH) ***545***
U of Florida (FL) ***545***
U of Hartford (CT) ***546***
U of Manitoba (MB, Canada) ***551***
U of Minnesota, Twin Cities Campus (MN) ***555***
U of Mississippi Medical Center (MS) ***555***
U of Missouri–Columbia (MO) ***555***
U of New England (ME) ***558***
U of New Hampshire (NH) ***558***
U of New Mexico (NM) ***559***
U of North Dakota (ND) ***561***
U of Ottawa (ON, Canada) ***563***
U of Pittsburgh (PA) ***569***
U of Puerto Rico Medical Sciences Campus (PR) ***571***
U of Puget Sound (WA) ***571***
The U of Scranton (PA) ***574***
U of Southern Indiana (IN) ***576***
The U of Tennessee at Chattanooga (TN) ***577***
The U of Texas at San Antonio (TX) ***578***
U of Texas Medical Branch at Galveston (TX) ***579***
U of the Sciences in Philadelphia (PA) ***580***
U of Toronto (ON, Canada) ***581***
U of Washington (WA) ***583***
The U of Western Ontario (ON, Canada) ***583***
U of Wisconsin–La Crosse (WI) ***584***
U of Wisconsin–Madison (WI) ***584***
U of Wisconsin–Milwaukee (WI) ***585***
Utica Coll (NY) ***588***
Wartburg Coll (IA) ***594***
Wayne State U (MI) ***596***
Western Michigan U (MI) ***599***
West Virginia U (WV) ***602***
Winston-Salem State U (NC) ***608***
Worcester State Coll (MA) ***609***
Xavier U (OH) ***610***
York Coll of the City U of New York (NY) ***611***

OCCUPATIONAL THERAPY ASSISTANT

Overview: This major prepares students to provide rehabilitative services under the supervision of an occupational therapist to restore and maintain function in persons with mental, physical, emotional, or developmental disabilities. *Related major:* occupational therapy. *Potential careers:* occupational therapist aid or assistant. *Salary potential:* $17k-$25k.

Grand Valley State U (MI) ***371***
U of Puerto Rico, Humacao U Coll (PR) ***570***

OCEAN ENGINEERING

Overview: Students learn the science behind the design and use of a variety of systems that function in or around the ocean, such as underwater platforms, dykes, and tide and current control systems as well as how seawater affects the operation and behavior of physical systems. *Related majors:* structural engineering, chemical engineering, naval engineering, marine biology, oceanography. *Potential careers:* naval engineer, marine biologist, oceanographer, quality assurance manager, construction manager. *Salary potential:* $30-$50k.

California State U, Long Beach (CA) ***301***
Florida Atlantic U (FL) ***359***
Florida Inst of Technology (FL) ***360***
Massachusetts Inst of Technology (MA) ***421***
Memorial U of Newfoundland (NF, Canada) ***424***
Texas A&M U (TX) ***524***
Texas A&M U at Galveston (TX) ***524***
United States Naval Academy (MD) ***535***
U of Hawaii at Manoa (HI) ***546***
U of New Hampshire (NH) ***558***
U of Rhode Island (RI) ***572***
Virginia Polytechnic Inst and State U (VA) ***591***

OCEANOGRAPHY

Overview: Students will study the chemistry, structure, and movements of ocean waters as well as their interaction with the land and atmosphere. *Related majors:* chemistry, atmospheric sciences, geology, ocean engineering, environmental engineering. *Potential careers:* oceanographer, environmentalist, meteorologist, marine biologist, fisheries specialist. *Salary potential:* $25k-$35k.

Central Michigan U (MI) ***310***
Florida Inst of Technology (FL) ***360***
Hampshire Coll (MA) ***375***
Hawai'i Pacific U (HI) ***377***
Humboldt State U (CA) ***382***
Kutztown U of Pennsylvania (PA) ***399***
Lamar U (TX) ***401***
Maine Maritime Academy (ME) ***415***
Memorial U of Newfoundland (NF, Canada) ***424***
Millersville U of Pennsylvania (PA) ***430***
North Carolina State U (NC) ***449***
Nova Southeastern U (FL) ***455***
Rider U (NJ) ***480***
San Jose State U (CA) ***499***
Sheldon Jackson Coll (AK) ***503***
State U of NY Maritime Coll (NY) ***518***
Texas A&M U at Galveston (TX) ***524***
United States Naval Academy (MD) ***535***
The U of British Columbia (BC, Canada) ***540***
U of Hawaii at Manoa (HI) ***546***
U of Miami (FL) ***553***
U of Michigan (MI) ***554***
U of New Hampshire (NH) ***558***
U of San Diego (CA) ***574***
U of Victoria (BC, Canada) ***582***
U of Washington (WA) ***583***

OFFICE MANAGEMENT

Overview: This major teaches students how to manage and supervise operations and employees of business enterprises and management divisions. *Related majors:* human resource management, labor/personnel relations and studies, enterprise management, business administration and management. *Potential careers:* office manager, divisional manager. *Salary potential:* $36k-$46k.

Arkansas Tech U (AR) ***272***
Baker Coll of Flint (MI) ***279***
Bowling Green State U (OH) ***292***
Central Michigan U (MI) ***310***
Central Missouri State U (MO) ***310***
Central Washington U (WA) ***310***
Concordia Coll (MN) ***329***
Delta State U (MS) ***339***
Georgia Coll & State U (GA) ***367***
Indiana State U (IN) ***385***
Indiana U of Pennsylvania (PA) ***386***
International Coll of the Cayman Islands(Cayman Islands) ***389***
Jackson State U (MS) ***390***
Mayville State U (ND) ***422***
Middle Tennessee State U (TN) ***429***
Mississippi Valley State U (MS) ***432***
Norfolk State U (VA) ***448***
Peirce Coll (PA) ***466***
Radford U (VA) ***476***
Southeastern Oklahoma State U (OK) ***508***
Southeast Missouri State U (MO) ***508***
State U of West Georgia (GA) ***518***
Stephen F. Austin State U (TX) ***518***
Tarleton State U (TX) ***522***
Texas Southern U (TX) ***526***
Texas Woman's U (TX) ***527***
U of Houston–Downtown (TX) ***547***
U of Nebraska–Lincoln (NE) ***557***
U of North Dakota (ND) ***561***
U of Puerto Rico at Arecibo (PR) ***570***
U of Puerto Rico, Utuado (PR) ***571***
U of South Carolina (SC) ***575***
U of the Sacred Heart (PR) ***580***
Valley City State U (ND) ***588***
Weber State U (UT) ***596***
Youngstown State U (OH) ***611***

OPERATIONS MANAGEMENT

Overview: Students who take this major learn how to manage and direct the technical aspects of a business, such as manufacturing, research, or development. *Related majors:* industrial engineering, systems analysis, labor/personnel relations studies, industrial machinery maintenance, manufacturing technology. *Potential careers:* production manager, manufacturer, product fulfillment manager, operations director. *Salary potential:* $45k-$60k.

Appalachian State U (NC) ***270***
Auburn U (AL) ***276***
Aurora U (IL) ***277***
Baker Coll of Flint (MI) ***279***
Baylor U (TX) ***283***
Boston U (MA) ***292***
Bowling Green State U (OH) ***292***
California State U, Chico (CA) ***300***
California State U, Stanislaus (CA) ***302***
Central Michigan U (MI) ***310***
Central Washington U (WA) ***310***
Clarkson U (NY) ***316***
Clemson U (SC) ***317***
Concordia U (NE) ***330***
Dalton State Coll (GA) ***336***
DeVry U (AZ) ***340***
DeVry U, Fremont (CA) ***340***
DeVry U, Long Beach (CA) ***341***
DeVry U, Pomona (CA) ***341***
DeVry U, West Hills (CA) ***341***
DeVry U, Alpharetta (GA) ***342***
DeVry U, Decatur (GA) ***342***
DeVry U, Addison (IL) ***342***
DeVry U, Chicago (IL) ***342***
DeVry U, Tinley Park (IL) ***342***
DeVry U (MO) ***343***
DeVry U (OH) ***343***
DeVry U (TX) ***343***
Edinboro U of Pennsylvania (PA) ***351***
Excelsior Coll (NY) ***356***
State U of NY at Farmingdale (NY) ***357***
Florida Southern Coll (FL) ***361***
Franklin U (OH) ***364***
Georgia Inst of Technology (GA) ***367***
Golden Gate U (CA) ***369***
Indiana U–Purdue U Fort Wayne (IN) ***386***
Indiana U–Purdue U Indianapolis (IN) ***387***
Kennesaw State U (GA) ***397***
Kettering U (MI) ***398***
Louisiana Tech U (LA) ***410***
Loyola U Chicago (IL) ***411***
Metropolitan State U (MN) ***427***
Miami U (OH) ***428***
Michigan State U (MI) ***428***
Michigan Technological U (MI) ***428***
National U (CA) ***442***
Northern Illinois U (IL) ***450***
The Ohio State U (OH) ***457***
Purdue U (IN) ***475***
Robert Morris U (PA) ***481***
Saginaw Valley State U (MI) ***486***
Sam Houston State U (TX) ***497***
San Jose State U (CA) ***499***
Seattle U (WA) ***501***
Southeast Missouri State U (MO) ***508***
Tennessee Technological U (TN) ***524***
Texas Southern U (TX) ***526***
Thomas Edison State Coll (NJ) ***527***
Tri-State U (IN) ***532***
The U of Arizona (AZ) ***538***
U of Delaware (DE) ***544***
U of Houston (TX) ***547***
U of Idaho (ID) ***547***
U of Indianapolis (IN) ***548***
U of Maryland, Coll Park (MD) ***552***
U of Nebraska at Kearney (NE) ***557***
U of Nebraska at Omaha (NE) ***557***
The U of North Carolina at Asheville (NC) ***559***
The U of North Carolina at Charlotte (NC) ***560***
U of North Texas (TX) ***562***
U of Pennsylvania (PA) ***563***
U of St. Francis (IL) ***573***
U of St. Thomas (MN) ***573***
U of Saskatchewan (SK, Canada) ***574***
The U of Scranton (PA) ***574***
The U of Texas at San Antonio (TX) ***578***
Utah State U (UT) ***587***
Washington U in St. Louis (MO) ***595***
Western Washington U (WA) ***600***
Worcester State Coll (MA) ***609***
Youngstown State U (OH) ***611***

OPERATIONS RESEARCH

Overview: Students will learn how to use complex mathematical and simulation models to solve problems involving operational systems. *Related majors:* statistics, applied mathematics, logistics and materials management, engineering and industrial management, aerospace science and engineering. *Potential careers:* management consultant, statistical analysts, industrial engineer, aerospace engineer. *Salary potential:* $35k-$45k.

Babson Coll (MA) ***278***
Baruch Coll of the City U of NY (NY) ***286***
Boston Coll (MA) ***292***
California State U, Fullerton (CA) ***301***
California State U, Northridge (CA) ***301***
Carleton U (ON, Canada) ***305***
Columbia U, School of Engineering & Applied Sci (NY) ***328***
Concordia U (QC, Canada) ***331***

Cornell U (NY) ***333***
DePaul U (IL) ***339***
Georgia State U (GA) ***368***
Iona Coll (NY) ***390***
Mercy Coll (NY) ***425***
Miami U (OH) ***428***
New York U (NY) ***447***
Texas A&M U (TX) ***524***
United States Air Force Academy (CO) ***534***
United States Coast Guard Academy (CT) ***535***
United States Military Academy (NY) ***535***
Université de Sherbrooke (QC, Canada) ***536***
U du Québec à Trois-Rivières (QC, Canada) ***536***
U of Cincinnati (OH) ***543***
U of Denver (CO) ***544***
U of Michigan–Flint (MI) ***554***
U of New Brunswick Fredericton (NB, Canada) ***558***
U of Waterloo (ON, Canada) ***583***
York U (ON, Canada) ***611***

OPHTHALMIC/OPTOMETRIC SERVICES

Overview: This major provides students with the knowledge and skills they need to examine, diagnose, and treat conditions of the eye. *Related majors:* optics, ophthalmic medical technology. *Potential careers:* optometrist, opticianry. *Salary potential:* $40k-$50k.

Ferris State U (MI) ***358***
Gannon U (PA) ***365***
Indiana U Bloomington (IN) ***385***
Northeastern State U (OK) ***450***
Nova Southeastern U (FL) ***455***
State U of NY at New Paltz (NY) ***515***
State U of NY Coll at Oneonta (NY) ***517***
U of Waterloo (ON, Canada) ***583***

OPHTHALMIC/OPTOMETRIC SERVICES RELATED

Information can be found under this major's main heading.

Concordia Coll (MN) ***329***
Tennessee Wesleyan Coll (TN) ***524***

OPTICS

Overview: Students who choose this major study the behavior and properties of light energy under various conditions. *Related majors:* laser/optical technology, aerospace engineering, theoretical physics, mathematics, astrophysics. *Potential careers:* research scientist, laser engineer, Air Force officer, astrophysicist, aerospace engineer. *Salary potential:* $35k-$45k.

Albright Coll (PA) ***263***
Rose-Hulman Inst of Technology (IN) ***484***
Saginaw Valley State U (MI) ***486***
The U of Arizona (AZ) ***538***
U of Rochester (NY) ***573***

OPTOMETRIC/OPHTHALMIC LABORATORY TECHNICIAN

Overview: Students learn how to cut and grind lenses for corrective eyewear and to work with ophthalmologists and optometrists. *Related majors:* optics, optical technician, opticianry, optometric services. *Potential careers:* ophthalmic laboratory technician, manufacturing optician, optical mechanic, optical goods worker. *Salary potential:* $20k-$25k.

Louisiana State U Health Sciences Center (LA) ***410***
Viterbo U (WI) ***591***

ORGANIZATIONAL BEHAVIOR

Overview: This major combines psychology and business administration and management, focusing on individual and group behavior within an organization or business. *Related majors:* psychology, business administration/management, labor/personnel relations and studies, office supervision and management. *Potential careers:* industrial psychologist, human resources specialist, corporate consultant, professor or industrial researcher. *Salary potential:* $40-$50k.

Anderson U (IN) ***268***
Benedictine U (IL) ***285***
Boston U (MA) ***292***
Bridgewater Coll (VA) ***294***
Brown U (RI) ***296***
California Baptist U (CA) ***298***
Carroll Coll (WI) ***306***
Denison U (OH) ***339***
Manhattan Coll (NY) ***416***
McGill U (QC, Canada) ***423***
Memorial U of Newfoundland (NF, Canada) ***424***
Miami U (OH) ***428***
Mid-Continent Coll (KY) ***429***
Northern Kentucky U (KY) ***451***
Northwestern Coll (MN) ***453***
Northwestern U (IL) ***453***
Oakland City U (IN) ***456***
Penn State U Harrisburg Campus of the Capital Coll (PA) ***468***
St. Ambrose U (IA) ***486***
Seattle Pacific U (WA) ***501***
Southern Methodist U (TX) ***510***
Thomas Edison State Coll (NJ) ***527***
U of Houston (TX) ***547***
U of La Verne (CA) ***549***
U of New England (ME) ***558***
U of North Texas (TX) ***562***
U of Pennsylvania (PA) ***563***
The U of Texas at Dallas (TX) ***578***
U of the Incarnate Word (TX) ***580***
Wayne State U (MI) ***596***
York U (ON, Canada) ***611***

ORGANIZATIONAL PSYCHOLOGY

Overview: In this branch of psychology, students focus on human well-being and the improvement of human performance in organizational and work settings. *Related majors:* psychology, business administration and management, organizational behavior studies, human resources management. *Potential careers:* organizational development specialist, human resources researcher manager, employee relations director, training and development manager, headhunter. *Salary potential:* $30k-$40k.

Abilene Christian U (TX) ***260***
Albright Coll (PA) ***263***
Averett U (VA) ***278***
Bridgewater State Coll (MA) ***294***
California State U, Hayward (CA) ***301***
Clarkson U (NY) ***316***
Fitchburg State Coll (MA) ***358***
Georgia Inst of Technology (GA) ***367***
Holy Family U (PA) ***380***
Husson Coll (ME) ***383***
Ithaca Coll (NY) ***390***
Lincoln U (PA) ***407***
Marymount U (VA) ***420***
Maryville U of Saint Louis (MO) ***420***
Middle Tennessee State U (TN) ***429***
Moravian Coll (PA) ***436***
Nebraska Wesleyan U (NE) ***443***
Point Loma Nazarene U (CA) ***471***
Saint Xavier U (IL) ***496***
Texas Wesleyan U (TX) ***526***

ORNAMENTAL HORTICULTURE

Overview: This major teaches students how to breed, grow, and use plant varieties for different kinds of commercial and aesthetic purposes. *Related majors:* environmental design, landscape design, plant science, plant protection and pathology, plant genetics. *Potential careers:* landscape designer, greenhouse or nursery manager. *Salary potential:* $22k-$27k.

Auburn U (AL) ***276***
California Polytechnic State U, San Luis Obispo (CA) ***300***
California State Polytechnic U, Pomona (CA) ***300***
California State U, Fresno (CA) ***301***
Cornell U (NY) ***333***
Delaware Valley Coll (PA) ***339***
Eastern Kentucky U (KY) ***348***
Florida A&M U (FL) ***359***
Florida Southern Coll (FL) ***361***
Fort Valley State U (GA) ***362***
Iowa State U of Science and Technology (IA) ***390***
Long Island U, Southampton Coll, Friends World Program (NY) ***409***
Texas A&M U (TX) ***524***
U of Arkansas (AR) ***539***
U of Delaware (DE) ***544***
U of Illinois at Urbana–Champaign (IL) ***548***
The U of Tennessee (TN) ***577***
U of the District of Columbia (DC) ***580***
Utah State U (UT) ***587***

ORTHOTICS/PROSTHETICS

Overview: Students taking this major learn how to design, make, and fit devices and appliances for body deformities or disabling conditions of the body, following the prescription of a doctor. *Related majors:* biomechanics, mechanics engineering, materials science, rehabilitation therapy, physical therapy. *Potential careers:* orthotist, prosthetist, physical therapist. *Salary potential:* $25k-$30k.

Florida International U (FL) ***360***
U of Washington (WA) ***583***

PACIFIC AREA STUDIES

Overview: This major teaches students about the history, society, politics, culture, economics, and languages of the people of Pacific Region, including Australasia and related island groups. *Related majors:* history, American history, anthropology, oceanography, marine biology, environmental conservation. *Potential careers:* importer/exporter, tour guide, anthropologist, conservationist. *Salary potential:* $23k-$29k.

Brigham Young U–Hawaii (HI) ***295***
U of Hawaii at Manoa (HI) ***546***

PAINTING

Overview: This major teaches students the theories and artistic skills and techniques of painting. *Related majors:* fine arts, drawing, art history. *Potential careers:* fine artist, set designer, book jacket or magazine designer, creative director, Web page designer. *Salary potential:* $10k-$35k.

Adams State Coll (CO) ***260***
American Academy of Art (IL) ***265***
Atlanta Coll of Art (GA) ***275***
Bard Coll (NY) ***281***
Barton Coll (NC) ***282***
Bellarmine U (KY) ***284***
Bethany Coll (KS) ***287***
Birmingham-Southern Coll (AL) ***289***
Boston U (MA) ***292***
Bowling Green State U (OH) ***292***
California Coll of Arts and Crafts (CA) ***299***
California State U, Hayward (CA) ***301***
California State U, Stanislaus (CA) ***302***
The Catholic U of America (DC) ***307***
The Cleveland Inst of Art (OH) ***317***
Coll of Santa Fe (NM) ***323***
Coll of Visual Arts (MN) ***324***
Colorado State U (CO) ***325***
Columbus Coll of Art and Design (OH) ***328***
Concordia U (QC, Canada) ***331***
Escuela de Artes Plasticas de Puerto Rico (PR) ***354***
Grace Coll (IN) ***370***
Harding U (AR) ***375***
Henderson State U (AR) ***378***
Indiana Wesleyan U (IN) ***387***
Kansas City Art Inst (MO) ***395***
Lewis U (IL) ***406***
LymeAcademy Coll of Fine Arts (CT) ***412***
Maharishi U of Management (IA) ***414***
Maine Coll of Art (ME) ***415***
Maryland Inst Coll of Art (MD) ***419***
Massachusetts Coll of Art (MA) ***421***
Memorial U of Newfoundland (NF, Canada) ***424***
Memphis Coll of Art (TN) ***425***
Milwaukee Inst of Art and Design (WI) ***431***
Minneapolis Coll of Art and Design (MN) ***431***
Minnesota State U, Moorhead (MN) ***432***
Northwest Nazarene U (ID) ***454***
Nova Scotia Coll of Art and Design (NS, Canada) ***455***
The Ohio State U (OH) ***457***
Ohio U (OH) ***458***
Pacific Northwest Coll of Art (OR) ***464***
Paier Coll of Art, Inc. (CT) ***464***
Rivier Coll (NH) ***480***
Rocky Mountain Coll of Art & Design (CO) ***483***
Rutgers, The State U of New Jersey, New Brunswick (NJ) ***485***
Sam Houston State U (TX) ***497***
San Diego State U (CA) ***498***
San Francisco Art Inst (CA) ***498***
Savannah Coll of Art and Design (GA) ***499***
School of Visual Arts (NY) ***501***
Seton Hill U (PA) ***502***
Shawnee State U (OH) ***502***
Simon's Rock Coll of Bard (MA) ***505***
State U of NY Coll at Brockport (NY) ***515***
State U of NY Coll at Potsdam (NY) ***517***
Syracuse U (NY) ***521***
Texas Woman's U (TX) ***527***
Trinity Christian Coll (IL) ***530***
U of Dallas (TX) ***544***
U of Hartford (CT) ***546***
U of Houston (TX) ***547***
U of Illinois at Urbana–Champaign (IL) ***548***
The U of Iowa (IA) ***548***
U of Kansas (KS) ***549***
U of Massachusetts Dartmouth (MA) ***553***
U of Miami (FL) ***553***
U of Michigan (MI) ***554***
U of North Texas (TX) ***562***
U of Puerto Rico, Río Piedras (PR) ***571***
U of San Francisco (CA) ***574***
The U of the Arts (PA) ***579***
U of Washington (WA) ***583***
U of Windsor (ON, Canada) ***584***
Virginia Commonwealth U (VA) ***590***
Washington U in St. Louis (MO) ***595***
Webster U (MO) ***597***
York U (ON, Canada) ***611***
Youngstown State U (OH) ***611***

PALEONTOLOGY

Overview: This major is the study of extinct life forms from their fossil remains and reconstruction of these ancient life forms. *Related majors:* geology, ecology, earth and planetary sciences, soil sciences, oceanography. *Potential careers:* paleontologist, professor or teacher, museum curator. *Salary potential:* $25k-$35k.

Bowling Green State U (OH) ***292***

PALEONTOLOGY (continued)

Long Island U, Southampton Coll, Friends World Program (NY) **409**
Mercyhurst Coll (PA) **425**
San Diego State U (CA) **498**
Southeast Missouri State U (MO) **508**
U of Alberta (AB, Canada) **538**
U of Delaware (DE) **544**
U of Toronto (ON, Canada) **581**

PARALEGAL/LEGAL ASSISTANT

Overview: This major teaches students skills they need to work as a paralegal or legal assistant, such as legal research and drafting of legal documents. *Related majors:* English composition, law and legal studies, American government/politics, criminal justice/law enforcement administration, public administration. *Potential careers:* paralegal or legal assistant, court reporter, court administrator. *Salary potential:* $30k-$40k.

Anna Maria Coll (MA) **269**
Avila U (MO) **278**
Ball State U (IN) **280**
Boston U (MA) **292**
Brenau U (GA) **293**
Calumet Coll of Saint Joseph (IN) **302**
Cedar Crest Coll (PA) **308**
Champlain Coll (VT) **311**
Coll of Mount St. Joseph (OH) **320**
Coll of Saint Mary (NE) **322**
Concordia U Wisconsin (WI) **331**
Davenport U, Grand Rapids (MI) **337**
Davenport U, Kalamazoo (MI) **337**
Eastern Kentucky U (KY) **348**
Elms Coll (MA) **352**
Florida Metropolitan U-Orlando Coll, North (FL) **361**
Florida Metropolitan U-Orlando Coll, South (FL) **361**
Gannon U (PA) **365**
Grand Valley State U (MI) **371**
Hamline U (MN) **374**
Hampton U (VA) **375**
Hartford Coll for Women (CT) **376**
Hilbert Coll (NY) **379**
Howard Payne U (TX) **382**
Husson Coll (ME) **383**
International Coll (FL) **389**
Johnson & Wales U (RI) **393**
Jones Coll (FL) **394**
Lake Erie Coll (OH) **400**
Lasell Coll (MA) **402**
Madonna U (MI) **414**
Marist Coll (NY) **417**
Marymount U (VA) **420**
Maryville U of Saint Louis (MO) **420**
Marywood U (PA) **421**
McMurry U (TX) **423**
Mercy Coll (NY) **425**
Midway Coll (KY) **429**
Minnesota State U, Moorhead (MN) **432**
Mississippi Coll (MS) **432**
Morehead State U (KY) **436**
National American U (SD) **442**
National American U–Sioux Falls Branch (SD) **442**
Notre Dame Coll (OH) **455**
Nova Southeastern U (FL) **455**
Peirce Coll (PA) **466**
Quinnipiac U (CT) **476**
Robert Morris Coll (IL) **481**
Roger Williams U (RI) **483**
Roosevelt U (IL) **483**
St. John's U (NY) **490**
Saint Mary-of-the-Woods Coll (IN) **493**
Southern Illinois U Carbondale (IL) **509**
Stephen F. Austin State U (TX) **518**
Suffolk U (MA) **520**
Sullivan U (KY) **521**
Teikyo Post U (CT) **523**
Texas Woman's U (TX) **527**
Thomas Edison State Coll (NJ) **527**
U of Central Florida (FL) **542**
U of Great Falls (MT) **545**
U of La Verne (CA) **549**
U of Maryland University Coll (MD) **552**
U of Nebraska at Omaha (NE) **557**
U of Southern Mississippi (MS) **576**
The U of Tennessee at Chattanooga (TN) **577**
U of West Florida (FL) **583**
U of West Los Angeles (CA) **583**
U of Wisconsin–Superior (WI) **586**
Valdosta State U (GA) **588**
Villa Julie Coll (MD) **590**
Virginia Intermont Coll (VA) **590**
Wesley Coll (DE) **598**
William Woods U (MO) **607**
Winona State U (MN) **608**

PARKS, RECREATION, LEISURE AND FITNESS STUDIES RELATED

Information can be found under this major's main heading.

Chadron State Coll (NE) **311**
Culver-Stockton Coll (MO) **334**
U of North Alabama (AL) **559**
Utah State U (UT) **587**

PASTORAL COUNSELING

Overview: Students of this major will study the theory and practice of pastoral care in preparation for a career in pastoral counseling to individuals and groups. *Related majors:* divinity/ministry, missionary studies, psychology. *Potential careers:* missionary, pastor, or other religious clergy vocation. *Salary potential:* $15k-$25k.

Abilene Christian U (TX) **260**
Alaska Bible Coll (AK) **261**
American Christian Coll and Seminary (OK) **265**
American Indian Coll of the Assemblies of God, Inc (AZ) **266**
Baptist Bible Coll (MO) **281**
The Baptist Coll of Florida (FL) **281**
Barclay Coll (KS) **281**
Belhaven Coll (MS) **283**
Bellarmine U (KY) **284**
Belmont U (TN) **284**
Bethany Coll of the Assemblies of God (CA) **287**
Bethesda Christian U (CA) **288**
Biola U (CA) **289**
Boise Bible Coll (ID) **291**
Briercrest Bible Coll (SK, Canada) **295**
Campbellsville U (KY) **303**
Cedarville U (OH) **308**
Central Bible Coll (MO) **309**
Central Christian Coll of Kansas (KS) **309**
Christian Heritage Coll (CA) **313**
Clearwater Christian Coll (FL) **316**
Coll Dominicain de Philosophie et de Théologie (ON, Canada) **319**
Coll of Mount St. Joseph (OH) **320**
Colorado Christian U (CO) **325**
Columbia Bible Coll (BC, Canada) **326**
Columbia International U (SC) **327**
Concordia U (IL) **330**
Concordia U (MN) **330**
Concordia U (NE) **330**
Concordia U Wisconsin (WI) **331**
Cornerstone U (MI) **333**
Crown Coll (MN) **334**
Dallas Baptist U (TX) **336**
Dordt Coll (IA) **345**
East Texas Baptist U (TX) **350**
Emmanuel Coll (GA) **353**
Eugene Bible Coll (OR) **355**
Faith Baptist Bible Coll and Theological Seminary (IA) **356**
Faulkner U (AL) **357**
Fresno Pacific U (CA) **364**
George Fox U (OR) **366**
Global U of the Assemblies of God (MO) **368**
God's Bible School and Coll (OH) **369**
Grace Bible Coll (MI) **370**
Grace Coll (IN) **370**
Grace U (NE) **371**
Greenville Coll (IL) **373**
Hannibal-LaGrange Coll (MO) **375**
Harding U (AR) **375**
Hardin-Simmons U (TX) **376**
Houghton Coll (NY) **381**
Indiana Wesleyan U (IN) **387**
John Brown U (AR) **392**
John Wesley Coll (NC) **394**
Kentucky Christian Coll (KY) **397**
LaGrange Coll (GA) **400**
Lee U (TN) **404**
Lenoir-Rhyne Coll (NC) **405**
Life Pacific Coll (CA) **406**
Luther Rice Bible Coll and Seminary (GA) **412**
Madonna U (MI) **414**
Malone Coll (OH) **415**
Manhattan Christian Coll (KS) **415**
The Master's Coll and Seminary (CA) **422**
Mercyhurst Coll (PA) **425**
Milligan Coll (TN) **430**
Multnomah Bible Coll and Biblical Seminary (OR) **440**
Nazarene Bible Coll (CO) **442**
Nebraska Christian Coll (NE) **443**
Newman U (KS) **445**
North Greenville Coll (SC) **451**
Northwest Coll (WA) **452**
Northwestern Coll (MN) **453**
Northwest Nazarene U (ID) **454**
Notre Dame Coll (OH) **455**
Nyack Coll (NY) **456**
Oklahoma Baptist U (OK) **459**
Oklahoma Christian U (OK) **459**
Olivet Nazarene U (IL) **461**
Oral Roberts U (OK) **461**
Ouachita Baptist U (AR) **462**
Pacific Union Coll (CA) **464**
Patten Coll (CA) **466**
Pillsbury Baptist Bible Coll (MN) **470**
Providence Coll (RI) **474**
Providence Coll and Theological Seminary (MB, Canada) **475**
Reformed Bible Coll (MI) **477**
Roberts Wesleyan Coll (NY) **481**
Rochester Coll (MI) **482**
Rocky Mountain Coll (AB, Canada) **482**
Saint Francis U (PA) **488**
Saint Mary-of-the-Woods Coll (IN) **493**
Saint Mary's Coll of Madonna U (MI) **493**
Saint Mary's U of Minnesota (MN) **494**
St. Thomas U (FL) **496**
San Jose Christian Coll (CA) **498**
Simpson Coll and Graduate School (CA) **505**
Southeastern Baptist Coll (MS) **507**
Southeastern Bible Coll (AL) **507**
Southeastern Coll of the Assemblies of God (FL) **507**
Southern Christian U (AL) **509**
Southwestern Assemblies of God U (TX) **512**
Spalding U (KY) **513**
Tabor Coll (KS) **522**
Taylor U, Fort Wayne Campus (IN) **523**
Tennessee Temple U (TN) **524**
Toccoa Falls Coll (GA) **528**
Trinity Baptist Coll (FL) **530**
Trinity Bible Coll (ND) **530**
Trinity Coll of Florida (FL) **531**
Trinity Lutheran Coll (WA) **531**
Tyndale Coll & Seminary (ON, Canada) **533**
Union Coll (NE) **534**
Universidad Adventista de las Antillas (PR) **536**
U of Ottawa (ON, Canada) **563**
U of St. Thomas (TX) **573**
U of Sioux Falls (SD) **574**
Vanguard U of Southern California (CA) **589**
Walsh U (OH) **593**
Warner Pacific Coll (OR) **593**
Western Baptist Coll (OR) **598**
Williams Baptist Coll (AR) **606**

PATHOLOGY

Overview: This major is the study of tissue injury and disease in animals and humans and how pathogens affect molecular, cellular and system mechanisms. *Related majors:* toxicology, microbiology or bacteriology, anatomy, cell biology, pharmacology, physiology. *Potential careers:* physician, research scientist, lab technician (pathologist), public health worker, immunologist. *Salary potential:* $35k-$45k.

U of Connecticut (CT) **544**

PEACE/CONFLICT STUDIES

Overview: In this major, students study the origins, resolution, and prevention of international and intergroup conflicts. *Related majors:* history, psychology, international relations, area studies, economics, anthropology. *Potential careers:* lawyer, politician, diplomatic corps, journalist, historian, mediator. *Salary potential:* $22k-$28k.

American U (DC) **267**
Antioch Coll (OH) **269**
Bethel Coll (KS) **288**
Bluffton Coll (OH) **291**
Chapman U (CA) **311**
Clark U (MA) **316**
Colgate U (NY) **319**
Coll of Saint Benedict (MN) **321**
Coll of the Holy Cross (MA) **323**
DePauw U (IN) **339**
Earlham Coll (IN) **347**
Eastern Mennonite U (VA) **348**
Elizabethtown Coll (PA) **351**
Fordham U (NY) **362**
Goddard Coll (VT) **369**
Goshen Coll (IN) **370**
Guilford Coll (NC) **373**
Hampshire Coll (MA) **375**
Haverford Coll (PA) **377**
Juniata Coll (PA) **395**
Kent State U (OH) **397**
Long Island U, Southampton Coll, Friends World Program (NY) **409**
Manchester Coll (IN) **415**
Molloy Coll (NY) **433**
Mount Saint Vincent U (NS, Canada) **439**
Nebraska Wesleyan U (NE) **443**
Northland Coll (WI) **452**
Norwich U (VT) **455**
Ohio Dominican U (OH) **457**
The Ohio State U (OH) **457**
Rocky Mountain Coll (MT) **482**
Saint John's U (MN) **490**
Salisbury U (MD) **497**
U of Calif, Berkeley (CA) **540**
U of Calif, Santa Cruz (CA) **542**
The U of North Carolina at Chapel Hill (NC) **560**
U of St. Thomas (MN) **573**
U of Wisconsin–Milwaukee (WI) **585**
Wayne State U (MI) **596**
Wellesley Coll (MA) **597**
Whitworth Coll (WA) **604**

PERFUSION TECHNOLOGY

Overview: This major teaches students how to operate the heart/lung machine that regulates a patient's oxygen, carbon dioxide, and blood chemistry and circulation when physicians are performing cardiac surgery. *Related majors:* biochemistry, toxicology, physiology, premedicine studies. *Potential careers:* perfusionist, dialysis technician, nurse anesthetist, nuclear medicine technologist, respiratory therapist. *Salary potential:* $45k-$60k.

Medical U of South Carolina (SC) **424**
Rush U (IL) **484**
State U of New York Upstate Medical University (NY) **518**
Thomas Edison State Coll (NJ) **527**

PERSONAL SERVICES MARKETING OPERATIONS

Overview: This major concerns the marketing/promotion and operational aspects of personal service businesses, such as childcare, funeral services, cosmetology, cleaning services, home care specialists, and fitness and health.

Related majors: marketing management, marketing research, personal services, advertising, public relations. *Potential careers:* corporate marketing manager, publicist, advertising executive, market researcher, retail management. *Salary potential:* $20k-$30k.

Lake Erie Coll (OH) ***400***

PETROLEUM ENGINEERING

Overview: This major prepares students for a career in the petroleum industry, either designing or operating systems for extracting, processing, and refining oil and gas. *Related majors:* mining and mineral engineering, chemical engineering, industrial engineering, logistics, and materials management. *Potential careers:* construction manager, petroleum company executive, geologist, chemical engineer. *Salary potential:* $35k-$60k.

California State Polytechnic U, Pomona (CA) ***300***
Colorado School of Mines (CO) ***325***
Louisiana State U and A&M Coll (LA) ***410***
Marietta Coll (OH) ***417***
Montana Tech of The U of Montana (MT) ***435***
New Mexico Inst of Mining and Technology (NM) ***446***
Penn State U Univ Park Campus (PA) ***468***
Stanford U (CA) ***514***
Texas A&M U (TX) ***524***
Texas A&M U–Kingsville (TX) ***525***
Texas Tech U (TX) ***526***
U of Alaska Fairbanks (AK) ***538***
U of Alberta (AB, Canada) ***538***
U of Calif, Berkeley (CA) ***540***
U of Kansas (KS) ***549***
U of Louisiana at Lafayette (LA) ***550***
U of Missouri–Rolla (MO) ***556***
U of Oklahoma (OK) ***562***
U of Regina (SK, Canada) ***572***
U of Southern California (CA) ***576***
The U of Texas at Austin (TX) ***578***
U of Toronto (ON, Canada) ***581***
U of Tulsa (OK) ***581***
West Virginia U (WV) ***602***

PETROLEUM TECHNOLOGY

Overview: This major teaches students the technical knowledge necessary to work in the petroleum industry developing and operating oil and natural gas extraction operations. *Related majors:* petroleum engineering, geology, geophysics and seismology, geochemistry, chemical engineering and technology. *Potential careers:* geologist, environmentalist, petroleum engineer, plant manager, oil company technician. *Salary potential:* $30k-$45k.

Mercyhurst Coll (PA) ***425***
Montana State U–Billings (MT) ***434***
Nicholls State U (LA) ***447***

PHARMACOLOGY

Overview: This major concerns the study of how drugs interact with biological systems and organisms and the origins and chemical properties of drugs. *Related majors:* toxicology, chemical engineering, biochemistry, cell and molecular biology, medical pharmacology. *Potential careers:* pharmaceutical sales representative or research scientist, pharmacist, physician. *Salary potential:* $35k-$45k.

Belmont U (TN) ***284***
McMaster U (ON, Canada) ***423***
Stony Brook U, State University of New York (NY) ***520***
U of Alberta (AB, Canada) ***538***
The U of British Columbia (BC, Canada) ***540***
U of Calif, Santa Barbara (CA) ***541***
U of Cincinnati (OH) ***543***
U of Hawaii at Manoa (HI) ***546***
U of the Sciences in Philadelphia (PA) ***580***
U of Toronto (ON, Canada) ***581***
The U of Western Ontario (ON, Canada) ***583***
U of Wisconsin–Madison (WI) ***584***

PHARMACY

Overview: This major gives students the knowledge and technical skills they need to prepare and dispense drugs and medications that physicians have prescribed to patients and to council patients on a drug's side effects. *Related majors:* biochemistry, chemistry, medical anatomy and toxicology and human physiology. *Potential careers:* physician, pharmacist, pharmaceutical representative. *Salary potential:* depends on size and location but generally ranges from $35k-$55k.

Albany Coll of Pharmacy of Union U (NY) ***262***
Briar Cliff U (IA) ***294***
Butler U (IN) ***297***
Campbell U (NC) ***303***
Dalhousie U (NS, Canada) ***336***
Drake U (IA) ***345***
Eastern Nazarene Coll (MA) ***348***
Ferris State U (MI) ***358***
Florida A&M U (FL) ***359***
Howard U (DC) ***382***
Idaho State U (ID) ***384***
Long Island U, Brooklyn Campus (NY) ***409***
Longwood U (VA) ***409***
Mass Coll of Pharmacy and Allied Health Sciences (MA) ***421***
Memorial U of Newfoundland (NF, Canada) ***424***
North Dakota State U (ND) ***449***
Northeastern U (MA) ***450***
Ohio Northern U (OH) ***457***
The Ohio State U (OH) ***457***
Oregon State U (OR) ***462***
Purdue U (IN) ***475***
Rutgers, The State U of New Jersey, New Brunswick (NJ) ***485***
St. John's U (NY) ***490***
St. Louis Coll of Pharmacy (MO) ***492***
Saint Vincent Coll (PA) ***496***
Simmons Coll (MA) ***504***
South Dakota State U (SD) ***507***
Southwestern Oklahoma State U (OK) ***512***
Texas Southern U (TX) ***526***
Université Laval (QC, Canada) ***536***
U of Alberta (AB, Canada) ***538***
The U of British Columbia (BC, Canada) ***540***
U of Cincinnati (OH) ***543***
U of Connecticut (CT) ***544***
U of Florida (FL) ***545***
U of Georgia (GA) ***545***
U of Houston (TX) ***547***
The U of Iowa (IA) ***548***
U of Manitoba (MB, Canada) ***551***
U of Michigan (MI) ***554***
U of Mississippi (MS) ***555***
U of Missouri–Kansas City (MO) ***555***
The U of Montana–Missoula (MT) ***556***
U of New Mexico (NM) ***559***
U of Pittsburgh (PA) ***569***
U of Puerto Rico Medical Sciences Campus (PR) ***571***
U of Rhode Island (RI) ***572***
U of Saskatchewan (SK, Canada) ***574***
The U of Texas at Austin (TX) ***578***
U of the Pacific (CA) ***580***
U of the Sciences in Philadelphia (PA) ***580***
U of Toledo (OH) ***581***
U of Toronto (ON, Canada) ***581***
U of Utah (UT) ***582***
U of Washington (WA) ***583***
U of Wisconsin–Madison (WI) ***584***
Virginia Commonwealth U (VA) ***590***
Wayne State U (MI) ***596***
West Virginia U (WV) ***602***

PHARMACY ADMINISTRATION/ PHARMACEUTICS

Overview: This major focuses on the management and economic aspects of drug and medicine distribution and use as well as the formation of medicinal chemicals into effective pharmaceutical products. *Related majors:* economics, finance, organizational behavior studies, logistics and materials management, management info systems and business data processing. *Potential career:* pharmaceutical executive, either drug development or sales/marketing/distribution, pharmacy manager. *Salary potential:* $40k-$65k.

DeSales U (PA) ***340***
Drake U (IA) ***345***
U at Buffalo, The State University of New York (NY) ***536***
U of the Sciences in Philadelphia (PA) ***580***

PHARMACY RELATED

Information can be found under this major's main heading.

Mass Coll of Pharmacy and Allied Health Sciences (MA) ***421***
U of the Sciences in Philadelphia (PA) ***580***

PHARMACY TECHNICIAN/ ASSISTANT

Overview: This major prepares students to assist licensed pharmacists in the preparation of medications, advising of patients, and management of pharmacy operations. *Related majors:* pharmacy, general office/clerical, medical assistant, accounting, information processing. *Potential careers:* pharmacy technician, pharmacist, ward clerk. *Salary potential:* $20k-$25k.

The U of Montana–Missoula (MT) ***556***

PHILOSOPHY

Overview: Students who choose this major will study ideas and their logical structure, including debates about abstract and real phenomena. *Related majors:* history, political science, ethics, mathematics, law and legal studies. *Potential careers:* philosopher, attorney, professor, teacher, writer, editor, ethicist. *Salary potential:* $25k-$30k.

Acadia U (NS, Canada) ***260***
Adelphi U (NY) ***260***
Agnes Scott Coll (GA) ***261***
Albertson Coll of Idaho (ID) ***262***
Albion Coll (MI) ***262***
Albright Coll (PA) ***263***
Alfred U (NY) ***263***
Allegheny Coll (PA) ***264***
Alma Coll (MI) ***264***
Alvernia Coll (PA) ***265***
Alverno Coll (WI) ***265***
American International Coll (MA) ***267***
American U (DC) ***267***
The American U in Cairo(Egypt) ***267***
Amherst Coll (MA) ***268***
Anderson U (IN) ***268***
Anna Maria Coll (MA) ***269***
Antioch Coll (OH) ***269***
Aquinas Coll (MI) ***270***
Arcadia U (PA) ***271***
Arizona State U (AZ) ***271***
Arkansas State U (AR) ***272***
Asbury Coll (KY) ***274***
Ashland U (OH) ***274***
Assumption Coll (MA) ***275***
Auburn U (AL) ***276***
Augsburg Coll (MN) ***276***
Augustana Coll (IL) ***276***
Augustana Coll (SD) ***276***
Aurora U (IL) ***277***
Austin Coll (TX) ***277***
Austin Peay State U (TN) ***278***
Ave Maria Coll (MI) ***278***
Azusa Pacific U (CA) ***278***
Baker U (KS) ***280***
Baldwin-Wallace Coll (OH) ***280***
Ball State U (IN) ***280***
Baltimore Hebrew U (MD) ***280***
Bard Coll (NY) ***281***
Barnard Coll (NY) ***282***
Barry U (FL) ***282***
Barton Coll (NC) ***282***
Bates Coll (ME) ***282***
Bayamón Central U (PR) ***283***
Baylor U (TX) ***283***
Belhaven Coll (MS) ***283***
Bellarmine U (KY) ***284***
Bellevue U (NE) ***284***
Belmont Abbey Coll (NC) ***284***
Belmont U (TN) ***284***
Beloit Coll (WI) ***285***
Bemidji State U (MN) ***285***
Benedict Coll (SC) ***285***
Benedictine Coll (KS) ***285***
Benedictine U (IL) ***285***
Bennington Coll (VT) ***286***
Bentley Coll (MA) ***286***
Berea Coll (KY) ***286***
Baruch Coll of the City U of NY (NY) ***286***
Berry Coll (GA) ***287***
Bethany Coll (KS) ***287***
Bethany Coll (WV) ***287***
Bethel Coll (IN) ***288***
Bethel Coll (MN) ***288***
Biola U (CA) ***289***
Birmingham-Southern Coll (AL) ***289***
Bishop's U (QC, Canada) ***289***
Bloomfield Coll (NJ) ***290***
Bloomsburg U of Pennsylvania (PA) ***290***
Bluefield Coll (VA) ***291***
Bluffton Coll (OH) ***291***
Boston Coll (MA) ***292***
Boston U (MA) ***292***
Bowdoin Coll (ME) ***292***
Bowling Green State U (OH) ***292***
Bradley U (IL) ***293***
Brandeis U (MA) ***293***
Brandon U (MB, Canada) ***293***
Bridgewater State Coll (MA) ***294***
Brigham Young U (UT) ***295***
Brock U (ON, Canada) ***295***
Brooklyn Coll of the City U of NY (NY) ***295***
Brown U (RI) ***296***
Bryn Mawr Coll (PA) ***297***
Bucknell U (PA) ***297***
Buena Vista U (IA) ***297***
Butler U (IN) ***297***
Cabrini Coll (PA) ***298***
California Baptist U (CA) ***298***
California Lutheran U (CA) ***299***
California Polytechnic State U, San Luis Obispo (CA) ***300***
California State Polytechnic U, Pomona (CA) ***300***
California State U, Bakersfield (CA) ***300***
California State U, Chico (CA) ***300***
California State U, Dominguez Hills (CA) ***300***
California State U, Fresno (CA) ***301***
California State U, Fullerton (CA) ***301***
California State U, Hayward (CA) ***301***
California State U, Long Beach (CA) ***301***
California State U, Northridge (CA) ***301***
California State U, Sacramento (CA) ***301***
California State U, San Bernardino (CA) ***302***
California State U, Stanislaus (CA) ***302***
California U of Pennsylvania (PA) ***302***
Calvin Coll (MI) ***303***
Canisius Coll (NY) ***304***
Capital U (OH) ***304***
Carleton Coll (MN) ***305***
Carleton U (ON, Canada) ***305***
Carlow Coll (PA) ***305***
Carnegie Mellon U (PA) ***305***
Carroll Coll (MT) ***306***
Carson-Newman Coll (TN) ***306***
Carthage Coll (WI) ***306***
Case Western Reserve U (OH) ***307***
Catawba Coll (NC) ***307***
The Catholic U of America (DC) ***307***
Cedar Crest Coll (PA) ***308***

PHILOSOPHY (continued)

Cedarville U (OH) **308**
Centenary Coll of Louisiana (LA) **308**
Central Coll (IA) **309**
Central Connecticut State U (CT) **309**
Central Methodist Coll (MO) **309**
Central Michigan U (MI) **310**
Central Washington U (WA) **310**
Centre Coll (KY) **310**
Chaminade U of Honolulu (HI) **311**
Chapman U (CA) **311**
Chatham Coll (PA) **312**
Christendom Coll (VA) **313**
Christopher Newport U (VA) **313**
City Coll of the City U of NY (NY) **314**
Claremont McKenna Coll (CA) **315**
Clarion U of Pennsylvania (PA) **315**
Clark Atlanta U (GA) **315**
Clarke Coll (IA) **315**
Clark U (MA) **316**
Clemson U (SC) **317**
Cleveland State U (OH) **317**
Coastal Carolina U (SC) **318**
Coe Coll (IA) **318**
Colby Coll (ME) **318**
Colgate U (NY) **319**
Coll Dominicain de Philosophie et de Théologie (ON, Canada) **319**
Coll Misericordia (PA) **319**
Coll of Charleston (SC) **320**
Coll of Mount Saint Vincent (NY) **320**
The Coll of New Jersey (NJ) **320**
The Coll of New Rochelle (NY) **321**
Coll of Saint Benedict (MN) **321**
Coll of St. Catherine (MN) **321**
Coll of Saint Elizabeth (NJ) **321**
The Coll of Southeastern Europe, The American U of Athens(Greece) **323**
Coll of Staten Island of the City U of NY (NY) **323**
Coll of the Atlantic (ME) **323**
Coll of the Holy Cross (MA) **323**
Coll of the Ozarks (MO) **323**
The Coll of William and Mary (VA) **324**
The Coll of Wooster (OH) **324**
The Colorado Coll (CO) **325**
Colorado State U (CO) **325**
Columbia Coll (NY) **326**
Columbia U, School of General Studies (NY) **328**
Concordia Coll (MN) **329**
Concordia U (IL) **330**
Concordia U (QC, Canada) **331**
Concordia U Coll of Alberta (AB, Canada) **331**
Connecticut Coll (CT) **331**
Cornell Coll (IA) **332**
Cornell U (NY) **333**
Covenant Coll (GA) **333**
Creighton U (NE) **333**
Curry Coll (MA) **335**
Dakota Wesleyan U (SD) **336**
Dalhousie U (NS, Canada) **336**
Dallas Baptist U (TX) **336**
Dartmouth Coll (NH) **337**
Davidson Coll (NC) **338**
Denison U (OH) **339**
DePaul U (IL) **339**
DePauw U (IN) **339**
Deree Coll(Greece) **339**
Dickinson Coll (PA) **344**
Doane Coll (NE) **344**
Dominican School of Philosophy and Theology (CA) **345**
Dominican U (IL) **345**
Dordt Coll (IA) **345**
Drake U (IA) **345**
Drew U (NJ) **346**
Drury U (MO) **346**
Duke U (NC) **346**
Duquesne U (PA) **346**
D'Youville Coll (NY) **347**
Earlham Coll (IN) **347**
East Carolina U (NC) **347**
Eastern Illinois U (IL) **348**
Eastern Kentucky U (KY) **348**
Eastern Michigan U (MI) **348**
Eastern U (PA) **349**
Eastern Washington U (WA) **349**
East Stroudsburg U of Pennsylvania (PA) **349**
East Tennessee State U (TN) **349**
Eckerd Coll (FL) **350**
Edinboro U of Pennsylvania (PA) **351**
Elizabethtown Coll (PA) **351**
Elmhurst Coll (IL) **351**
Elmira Coll (NY) **351**
Elon U (NC) **352**
Emory & Henry Coll (VA) **353**
Emory U (GA) **354**
Erskine Coll (SC) **354**
Eugene Lang Coll, New School U (NY) **355**
Eureka Coll (IL) **355**
The Evergreen State Coll (WA) **355**
Excelsior Coll (NY) **356**
Fairfield U (CT) **356**
Fairleigh Dickinson U, Florham (NJ) **356**
Fairleigh Dickinson U, Teaneck-Metro Campus (NJ) **356**
Felician Coll (NJ) **357**
Ferrum Coll (VA) **358**
Fisk U (TN) **358**
Flagler Coll (FL) **359**
Florida A&M U (FL) **359**
Florida Atlantic U (FL) **359**
Florida International U (FL) **360**
Florida State U (FL) **361**
Fordham U (NY) **362**
Fort Hays State U (KS) **362**
Fort Lewis Coll (CO) **362**
Franciscan U of Steubenville (OH) **363**
Franklin and Marshall Coll (PA) **363**
Franklin Coll (IN) **363**
Freed-Hardeman U (TN) **364**
Frostburg State U (MD) **365**
Furman U (SC) **365**
Gallaudet U (DC) **365**
Gannon U (PA) **365**
Geneva Coll (PA) **366**
George Mason U (VA) **366**
Georgetown Coll (KY) **366**
Georgetown U (DC) **366**
The George Washington U (DC) **367**
Georgia Southern U (GA) **367**
Georgia State U (GA) **368**
Gettysburg Coll (PA) **368**
Goddard Coll (VT) **369**
Gonzaga U (WA) **369**
Gordon Coll (MA) **370**
Goucher Coll (MD) **370**
Grand Valley State U (MI) **371**
Greenville Coll (IL) **373**
Grinnell Coll (IA) **373**
Grove City Coll (PA) **373**
Guilford Coll (NC) **373**
Gustavus Adolphus Coll (MN) **374**
Hamilton Coll (NY) **374**
Hamline U (MN) **374**
Hampden-Sydney Coll (VA) **374**
Hampshire Coll (MA) **375**
Hanover Coll (IN) **375**
Hardin-Simmons U (TX) **376**
Hartwick Coll (NY) **376**
Harvard U (MA) **376**
Hastings Coll (NE) **377**
Haverford Coll (PA) **377**
Heidelberg Coll (OH) **377**
Hendrix Coll (AR) **378**
High Point U (NC) **379**
Hillsdale Coll (MI) **379**
Hiram Coll (OH) **379**
Hobart and William Smith Colls (NY) **380**
Hofstra U (NY) **380**
Hollins U (VA) **380**
Holy Apostles Coll and Seminary (CT) **380**
Holy Names Coll (CA) **381**
Hood Coll (MD) **381**
Hope Coll (MI) **381**
Houghton Coll (NY) **381**
Howard Payne U (TX) **382**
Howard U (DC) **382**
Humboldt State U (CA) **382**
Hunter Coll of the City U of NY (NY) **382**
Huntington Coll (IN) **383**
Idaho State U (ID) **384**
Illinois Coll (IL) **384**
Illinois State U (IL) **384**
Illinois Wesleyan U (IL) **385**
Indiana State U (IN) **385**
Indiana U Bloomington (IN) **385**
Indiana U Northwest (IN) **386**
Indiana U of Pennsylvania (PA) **386**
Indiana U–Purdue U Fort Wayne (IN) **386**
Indiana U–Purdue U Indianapolis (IN) **387**
Indiana U South Bend (IN) **387**
Indiana U Southeast (IN) **387**
Indiana Wesleyan U (IN) **387**
Iona Coll (NY) **390**
Iowa State U of Science and Technology (IA) **390**
Ithaca Coll (NY) **390**
Jacksonville U (FL) **391**
James Madison U (VA) **391**
Jamestown Coll (ND) **391**
Jewish Theological Seminary of America (NY) **391**
John Carroll U (OH) **392**
Johns Hopkins U (MD) **392**
Judson Coll (IL) **395**
Kalamazoo Coll (MI) **395**
Kansas State U (KS) **396**
Kent State U (OH) **397**
Kentucky Wesleyan Coll (KY) **397**
Kenyon Coll (OH) **398**
King's Coll (PA) **398**
The King's U Coll (AB, Canada) **399**
Knox Coll (IL) **399**
Kutztown U of Pennsylvania (PA) **399**
Lafayette Coll (PA) **400**
Lake Forest Coll (IL) **400**
Lakehead U (ON, Canada) **400**
Lakeland Coll (WI) **401**
La Salle U (PA) **402**
Laurentian U (ON, Canada) **403**
Lawrence U (WI) **403**
Lebanon Valley Coll (PA) **403**
Lehigh U (PA) **404**
Lehman Coll of the City U of NY (NY) **404**
Le Moyne Coll (NY) **404**
Lenoir-Rhyne Coll (NC) **405**
Lewis & Clark Coll (OR) **405**
Lewis U (IL) **406**
Lincoln U (PA) **407**
Linfield Coll (OR) **408**
Lipscomb U (TN) **408**
Lock Haven U of Pennsylvania (PA) **408**
Long Island U, Brooklyn Campus (NY) **409**
Long Island U, C.W. Post Campus (NY) **409**
Long Island U, Southampton Coll, Friends World Program (NY) **409**
Loras Coll (IA) **410**
Louisiana Coll (LA) **410**
Louisiana State U and A&M Coll (LA) **410**
Loyola Coll in Maryland (MD) **411**
Loyola Marymount U (CA) **411**
Loyola U Chicago (IL) **411**
Loyola U New Orleans (LA) **411**
Luther Coll (IA) **412**
Lycoming Coll (PA) **412**
Lynchburg Coll (VA) **413**
Macalester Coll (MN) **413**
MacMurray Coll (IL) **414**
Manchester Coll (IN) **415**
Manhattan Coll (NY) **416**
Manhattanville Coll (NY) **416**
Mansfield U of Pennsylvania (PA) **416**
Marian Coll (IN) **417**
Marietta Coll (OH) **417**
Marlboro Coll (VT) **418**
Marquette U (WI) **418**
Mary Baldwin Coll (VA) **419**
Marymount U (VA) **420**
Maryville U of Saint Louis (MO) **420**
Mary Washington Coll (VA) **420**
Massachusetts Coll of Liberal Arts (MA) **421**
Massachusetts Inst of Technology (MA) **421**
McDaniel Coll (MD) **422**
McGill U (QC, Canada) **423**
McKendree Coll (IL) **423**
McMaster U (ON, Canada) **423**
McMurry U (TX) **423**
McPherson Coll (KS) **423**
Memorial U of Newfoundland (NF, Canada) **424**
Mercer U (GA) **425**
Mercyhurst Coll (PA) **425**
Merrimack Coll (MA) **426**
Messiah Coll (PA) **426**
Metropolitan State Coll of Denver (CO) **427**
Metropolitan State U (MN) **427**
Miami U (OH) **428**
Michigan State U (MI) **428**
Middlebury Coll (VT) **429**
Middle Tennessee State U (TN) **429**
Millersville U of Pennsylvania (PA) **430**
Millikin U (IL) **430**
Millsaps Coll (MS) **431**
Mills Coll (CA) **431**
Minnesota State U, Mankato (MN) **431**
Minnesota State U, Moorhead (MN) **432**
Mississippi State U (MS) **432**
Missouri Valley Coll (MO) **433**
Molloy Coll (NY) **433**
Monmouth Coll (IL) **434**
Montana State U–Bozeman (MT) **434**
Montclair State U (NJ) **435**
Moravian Coll (PA) **436**
Morehead State U (KY) **436**
Morehouse Coll (GA) **436**
Morgan State U (MD) **436**
Morningside Coll (IA) **437**
Mount Allison U (NB, Canada) **437**
Mount Holyoke Coll (MA) **438**
Mount Mary Coll (WI) **438**
Mount St. Mary's Coll (CA) **439**
Mount Saint Mary's Coll and Seminary (MD) **439**
Mount Saint Vincent U (NS, Canada) **439**
Mount Union Coll (OH) **440**
Mount Vernon Nazarene U (OH) **440**
Muhlenberg Coll (PA) **440**
Murray State U (KY) **440**
Muskingum Coll (OH) **441**
Nazareth Coll of Rochester (NY) **443**
Nebraska Wesleyan U (NE) **443**
Newberry Coll (SC) **444**
New Coll of Florida (FL) **444**
New England Coll (NH) **444**
New Jersey City U (NJ) **445**
New Mexico State U (NM) **446**
New York U (NY) **447**
Niagara U (NY) **447**
Nipissing U (ON, Canada) **448**
North Carolina State U (NC) **449**
North Carolina Wesleyan Coll (NC) **449**
North Central Coll (IL) **449**
Northeastern Illinois U (IL) **450**
Northeastern U (MA) **450**
Northern Arizona U (AZ) **450**
Northern Illinois U (IL) **450**
Northern Kentucky U (KY) **451**
Northern Michigan U (MI) **451**
Northland Coll (WI) **452**
North Park U (IL) **452**
Northwest Coll (WA) **452**
Northwestern Coll (IA) **453**
Northwestern U (IL) **453**
Northwest Missouri State U (MO) **454**
Northwest Nazarene U (ID) **454**
Notre Dame de Namur U (CA) **455**
Nyack Coll (NY) **456**
Oakland U (MI) **456**
Oberlin Coll (OH) **456**
Occidental Coll (CA) **457**
Oglethorpe U (GA) **457**
Ohio Dominican U (OH) **457**
Ohio Northern U (OH) **457**
The Ohio State U (OH) **457**
Ohio U (OH) **458**
Ohio Wesleyan U (OH) **459**
Okanagan U Coll (BC, Canada) **459**
Oklahoma Baptist U (OK) **459**
Oklahoma City U (OK) **460**
Oklahoma State U (OK) **460**
Old Dominion U (VA) **460**
Olivet Nazarene U (IL) **461**
Oral Roberts U (OK) **461**
Oregon State U (OR) **462**
Otterbein Coll (OH) **462**
Ouachita Baptist U (AR) **462**
Our Lady of the Lake U of San Antonio (TX) **463**
Pacific Lutheran U (WA) **463**
Pacific U (OR) **464**
Paine Coll (GA) **465**
Palm Beach Atlantic U (FL) **465**
Penn State U Univ Park Campus (PA) **468**
Pepperdine U, Malibu (CA) **469**
Piedmont Coll (GA) **470**
Pitzer Coll (CA) **471**
Plattsburgh State U of NY (NY) **471**
Plymouth State Coll (NH) **471**
Point Loma Nazarene U (CA) **471**
Pomona Coll (CA) **472**
Pontifical Catholic U of Puerto Rico (PR) **472**
Pontifical Coll Josephinum (OH) **472**
Portland State U (OR) **472**
Presbyterian Coll (SC) **473**
Prescott Coll (AZ) **474**
Princeton U (NJ) **474**
Principia Coll (IL) **474**
Providence Coll (RI) **474**
Purchase Coll, State U of NY (NY) **475**
Purdue U (IN) **475**

Purdue U Calumet (IN) ***475***
Queens Coll of the City U of NY (NY) ***475***
Queen's U at Kingston (ON, Canada) ***476***
Queens U of Charlotte (NC) ***476***
Quincy U (IL) ***476***
Radford U (VA) ***476***
Randolph-Macon Coll (VA) ***477***
Randolph-Macon Woman's Coll (VA) ***477***
Reed Coll (OR) ***477***
Regis U (CO) ***478***
Rensselaer Polytechnic Inst (NY) ***478***
Rhode Island Coll (RI) ***479***
Rhodes Coll (TN) ***479***
Rice U (TX) ***479***
The Richard Stockton Coll of New Jersey (NJ) ***479***
Rider U (NJ) ***480***
Ripon Coll (WI) ***480***
Roanoke Coll (VA) ***481***
Roberts Wesleyan Coll (NY) ***481***
Rockford Coll (IL) ***482***
Rockhurst U (MO) ***482***
Rocky Mountain Coll (MT) ***482***
Roger Williams U (RI) ***483***
Rollins Coll (FL) ***483***
Roosevelt U (IL) ***483***
Rosemont Coll (PA) ***484***
Rutgers, The State U of New Jersey, Camden (NJ) ***485***
Rutgers, The State U of New Jersey, Newark (NJ) ***485***
Rutgers, The State U of New Jersey, New Brunswick (NJ) ***485***
Sacred Heart Major Seminary (MI) ***486***
Sacred Heart U (CT) ***486***
St. Ambrose U (IA) ***486***
St. Andrews Presbyterian Coll (NC) ***487***
Saint Anselm Coll (NH) ***487***
St. Bonaventure U (NY) ***487***
St. Charles Borromeo Seminary, Overbrook (PA) ***488***
St. Cloud State U (MN) ***488***
St. Edward's U (TX) ***488***
St. Francis Coll (NY) ***488***
Saint Francis U (PA) ***488***
St. Francis Xavier U (NS, Canada) ***489***
St. John Fisher Coll (NY) ***489***
Saint John's U (MN) ***490***
St. John's U (NY) ***490***
Saint Joseph Coll (CT) ***490***
Saint Joseph's Coll (IN) ***490***
Saint Joseph's Coll of Maine (ME) ***491***
Saint Joseph's U (PA) ***491***
St. Lawrence U (NY) ***491***
Saint Louis U (MO) ***492***
Saint Mary's Coll (IN) ***493***
Saint Mary's Coll of California (CA) ***494***
Saint Mary's Coll of Madonna U (MI) ***493***
St. Mary's Coll of Maryland (MD) ***494***
Saint Mary's U (NS, Canada) ***494***
Saint Mary's U of Minnesota (MN) ***494***
St. Mary's U of San Antonio (TX) ***494***
Saint Michael's Coll (VT) ***494***
St. Norbert Coll (WI) ***495***
St. Olaf Coll (MN) ***495***
Saint Paul U (ON, Canada) ***495***
Saint Peter's Coll (NJ) ***495***
St. Thomas Aquinas Coll (NY) ***495***
St. Thomas U (NB, Canada) ***496***
Saint Vincent Coll (PA) ***496***
Saint Xavier U (IL) ***496***
Salem Coll (NC) ***496***
Salisbury U (MD) ***497***
Salve Regina U (RI) ***497***
Samford U (AL) ***497***
Sam Houston State U (TX) ***497***
San Diego State U (CA) ***498***
San Francisco State U (CA) ***498***
San Jose State U (CA) ***499***
Santa Clara U (CA) ***499***
Sarah Lawrence Coll (NY) ***499***
Schreiner U (TX) ***501***
Scripps Coll (CA) ***501***
Seattle Pacific U (WA) ***501***
Seattle U (WA) ***501***
Seton Hall U (NJ) ***502***
Shaw U (NC) ***502***
Siena Coll (NY) ***504***
Siena Heights U (MI) ***504***
Simmons Coll (MA) ***504***
Simon Fraser U (BC, Canada) ***505***
Simon's Rock Coll of Bard (MA) ***505***
Simpson Coll (IA) ***505***
Skidmore Coll (NY) ***506***
Slippery Rock U of Pennsylvania (PA) ***506***
Smith Coll (MA) ***506***
Sonoma State U (CA) ***506***
Southeast Missouri State U (MO) ***508***
Southern Connecticut State U (CT) ***509***
Southern Illinois U Carbondale (IL) ***509***
Southern Illinois U Edwardsville (IL) ***509***
Southern Methodist U (TX) ***510***
Southern Nazarene U (OK) ***510***
Southern Virginia U (VA) ***511***
Southwestern U (TX) ***513***
Southwest Missouri State U (MO) ***513***
Southwest State U (MN) ***513***
Southwest Texas State U (TX) ***513***
Spalding U (KY) ***513***
Spelman Coll (GA) ***514***
Spring Arbor U (MI) ***514***
Spring Hill Coll (AL) ***514***
Stanford U (CA) ***514***
State U of NY at Albany (NY) ***514***
State U of NY at Binghamton (NY) ***515***
State U of NY at New Paltz (NY) ***515***
State U of NY at Oswego (NY) ***515***
State U of NY Coll at Brockport (NY) ***515***
State U of NY Coll at Buffalo (NY) ***516***
State U of NY Coll at Cortland (NY) ***516***
State U of NY Coll at Fredonia (NY) ***516***
State U of NY Coll at Geneseo (NY) ***516***
State U of NY Coll at Old Westbury (NY) ***516***
State U of NY Coll at Oneonta (NY) ***517***
State U of NY Coll at Potsdam (NY) ***517***
State U of West Georgia (GA) ***518***
Stephens Coll (MO) ***519***
Stetson U (FL) ***519***
Stevens Inst of Technology (NJ) ***519***
Stonehill Coll (MA) ***520***
Stony Brook U, State University of New York (NY) ***520***
Suffolk U (MA) ***520***
Susquehanna U (PA) ***521***
Swarthmore Coll (PA) ***521***
Sweet Briar Coll (VA) ***521***
Syracuse U (NY) ***521***
Tabor Coll (KS) ***522***
Taylor U (IN) ***523***
Temple U (PA) ***523***
Texas A&M U (TX) ***524***
Texas Christian U (TX) ***526***
Texas Lutheran U (TX) ***526***
Texas Tech U (TX) ***526***
Thiel Coll (PA) ***527***
Thomas Edison State Coll (NJ) ***527***
Thomas More Coll (KY) ***528***
Thomas More Coll of Liberal Arts (NH) ***528***
Toccoa Falls Coll (GA) ***528***
Touro Coll (NY) ***529***
Towson U (MD) ***529***
Transylvania U (KY) ***529***
Trent U (ON, Canada) ***529***
Trinity Christian Coll (IL) ***530***
Trinity Coll (CT) ***530***
Trinity International U (IL) ***531***
Trinity U (TX) ***531***
Trinity Western U (BC, Canada) ***531***
Truman State U (MO) ***532***
Tufts U (MA) ***533***
Tulane U (LA) ***533***
Tyndale Coll & Seminary (ON, Canada) ***533***
Union Coll (NY) ***534***
Union U (TN) ***534***
United States Military Academy (NY) ***535***
Université de Sherbrooke (QC, Canada) ***536***
U du Québec à Trois-Rivières (QC, Canada) ***536***
Université Laval (QC, Canada) ***536***
U at Buffalo, The State University of New York (NY) ***536***
The U of Akron (OH) ***537***
The U of Alabama (AL) ***537***
The U of Alabama at Birmingham (AL) ***537***
The U of Alabama in Huntsville (AL) ***537***
U of Alaska Fairbanks (AK) ***538***
U of Alberta (AB, Canada) ***538***
The U of Arizona (AZ) ***538***
U of Arkansas (AR) ***539***
U of Arkansas at Little Rock (AR) ***539***
The U of British Columbia (BC, Canada) ***540***
U of Calgary (AB, Canada) ***540***
U of Calif, Berkeley (CA) ***540***
U of Calif, Davis (CA) ***540***
U of Calif, Irvine (CA) ***541***
U of Calif, Los Angeles (CA) ***541***
U of Calif, Riverside (CA) ***541***
U of Calif, San Diego (CA) ***541***
U of Calif, Santa Barbara (CA) ***541***
U of Calif, Santa Cruz (CA) ***542***
U of Central Arkansas (AR) ***542***
U of Central Florida (FL) ***542***
U of Central Oklahoma (OK) ***542***
U of Charleston (WV) ***542***
U of Chicago (IL) ***542***
U of Cincinnati (OH) ***543***
U of Colorado at Boulder (CO) ***543***
U of Colorado at Colorado Springs (CO) ***543***
U of Colorado at Denver (CO) ***543***
U of Connecticut (CT) ***544***
U of Dallas (TX) ***544***
U of Dayton (OH) ***544***
U of Delaware (DE) ***544***
U of Denver (CO) ***544***
U of Dubuque (IA) ***545***
U of Evansville (IN) ***545***
The U of Findlay (OH) ***545***
U of Florida (FL) ***545***
U of Georgia (GA) ***545***
U of Guelph (ON, Canada) ***546***
U of Hartford (CT) ***546***
U of Hawaii at Hilo (HI) ***546***
U of Hawaii at Manoa (HI) ***546***
U of Hawaii–West Oahu (HI) ***546***
U of Houston (TX) ***547***
U of Idaho (ID) ***547***
U of Illinois at Chicago (IL) ***547***
U of Illinois at Urbana–Champaign (IL) ***548***
U of Indianapolis (IN) ***548***
The U of Iowa (IA) ***548***
U of Kansas (KS) ***549***
U of Kentucky (KY) ***549***
U of King's Coll (NS, Canada) ***549***
U of La Verne (CA) ***549***
The U of Lethbridge (AB, Canada) ***549***
U of Louisiana at Lafayette (LA) ***550***
U of Louisville (KY) ***550***
U of Maine (ME) ***550***
U of Maine at Farmington (ME) ***550***
U of Manitoba (MB, Canada) ***551***
U of Maryland, Baltimore County (MD) ***552***
U of Maryland, Coll Park (MD) ***552***
U of Massachusetts Amherst (MA) ***552***
U of Massachusetts Boston (MA) ***553***
U of Massachusetts Dartmouth (MA) ***553***
U of Massachusetts Lowell (MA) ***553***
The U of Memphis (TN) ***553***
U of Miami (FL) ***553***
U of Michigan (MI) ***554***
U of Michigan–Dearborn (MI) ***554***
U of Michigan–Flint (MI) ***554***
U of Minnesota, Duluth (MN) ***554***
U of Minnesota, Morris (MN) ***555***
U of Minnesota, Twin Cities Campus (MN) ***555***
U of Mississippi (MS) ***555***
U of Missouri–Columbia (MO) ***555***
U of Missouri–Kansas City (MO) ***555***
U of Missouri–Rolla (MO) ***556***
U of Missouri–St. Louis (MO) ***556***
The U of Montana–Missoula (MT) ***556***
U of Nebraska at Omaha (NE) ***557***
U of Nebraska–Lincoln (NE) ***557***
U of Nevada, Las Vegas (NV) ***558***
U of Nevada, Reno (NV) ***558***
U of New Brunswick Fredericton (NB, Canada) ***558***
U of New Brunswick Saint John (NB, Canada) ***558***
U of New Hampshire (NH) ***558***
U of New Mexico (NM) ***559***
U of New Orleans (LA) ***559***
The U of North Carolina at Asheville (NC) ***559***
The U of North Carolina at Chapel Hill (NC) ***560***
The U of North Carolina at Charlotte (NC) ***560***
The U of North Carolina at Greensboro (NC) ***560***
The U of North Carolina at Pembroke (NC) ***560***
U of North Dakota (ND) ***561***
U of Northern Colorado (CO) ***561***
U of Northern Iowa (IA) ***561***
U of North Florida (FL) ***561***
U of North Texas (TX) ***562***
U of Notre Dame (IN) ***562***
U of Oklahoma (OK) ***562***
U of Oregon (OR) ***562***
U of Ottawa (ON, Canada) ***563***
U of Pennsylvania (PA) ***563***
U of Pittsburgh (PA) ***569***
U of Portland (OR) ***570***
U of Prince Edward Island (PE, Canada) ***570***
U of Puerto Rico, Río Piedras (PR) ***571***
U of Puget Sound (WA) ***571***
U of Redlands (CA) ***572***
U of Regina (SK, Canada) ***572***
U of Rhode Island (RI) ***572***
U of Richmond (VA) ***572***
U of Rochester (NY) ***573***
U of St. Thomas (MN) ***573***
U of St. Thomas (TX) ***573***
U of San Diego (CA) ***574***
U of San Francisco (CA) ***574***
U of Saskatchewan (SK, Canada) ***574***
The U of Scranton (PA) ***574***
U of Sioux Falls (SD) ***574***
U of South Alabama (AL) ***575***
U of South Carolina (SC) ***575***
The U of South Dakota (SD) ***575***
U of Southern California (CA) ***576***
U of Southern Indiana (IN) ***576***
U of Southern Maine (ME) ***576***
U of Southern Mississippi (MS) ***576***
U of South Florida (FL) ***576***
The U of Tennessee (TN) ***577***
The U of Tennessee at Chattanooga (TN) ***577***
The U of Tennessee at Martin (TN) ***577***
The U of Texas at Arlington (TX) ***577***
The U of Texas at Austin (TX) ***578***
The U of Texas at El Paso (TX) ***578***
The U of Texas at San Antonio (TX) ***578***
The U of Texas–Pan American (TX) ***579***
U of the District of Columbia (DC) ***580***
U of the Incarnate Word (TX) ***580***
U of the Pacific (CA) ***580***
U of the South (TN) ***581***
U of Toledo (OH) ***581***
U of Toronto (ON, Canada) ***581***
U of Tulsa (OK) ***581***
U of Utah (UT) ***582***
U of Vermont (VT) ***582***
U of Victoria (BC, Canada) ***582***
U of Virginia (VA) ***582***
U of Washington (WA) ***583***
U of Waterloo (ON, Canada) ***583***
The U of Western Ontario (ON, Canada) ***583***
U of West Florida (FL) ***583***
U of Windsor (ON, Canada) ***584***
U of Wisconsin–Eau Claire (WI) ***584***
U of Wisconsin–Green Bay (WI) ***584***
U of Wisconsin–La Crosse (WI) ***584***
U of Wisconsin–Madison (WI) ***584***
U of Wisconsin–Milwaukee (WI) ***585***
U of Wisconsin–Oshkosh (WI) ***585***
U of Wisconsin–Parkside (WI) ***585***
U of Wisconsin–Platteville (WI) ***585***
U of Wisconsin–Stevens Point (WI) ***585***
U of Wyoming (WY) ***586***
Urbana U (OH) ***587***
Ursinus Coll (PA) ***587***
Ursuline Coll (OH) ***587***
Utah State U (UT) ***587***
Utica Coll (NY) ***588***
Valdosta State U (GA) ***588***
Valparaiso U (IN) ***588***
Vanderbilt U (TN) ***588***
Vassar Coll (NY) ***589***
Villanova U (PA) ***590***
Virginia Commonwealth U (VA) ***590***
Virginia Polytechnic Inst and State U (VA) ***591***
Virginia Wesleyan Coll (VA) ***591***
Wabash Coll (IN) ***592***
Wake Forest U (NC) ***592***
Walla Walla Coll (WA) ***593***
Walsh U (OH) ***593***
Wartburg Coll (IA) ***594***
Washington & Jefferson Coll (PA) ***594***
Washington and Lee U (VA) ***594***
Washington Coll (MD) ***594***
Washington State U (WA) ***595***
Washington U in St. Louis (MO) ***595***
Wayne State U (MI) ***596***
Webster U (MO) ***597***
Wellesley Coll (MA) ***597***
Wells Coll (NY) ***597***
Wesleyan Coll (GA) ***597***
Wesleyan U (CT) ***597***
West Chester U of Pennsylvania (PA) ***598***

PHILOSOPHY (continued)

Western Carolina U (NC) **598**
Western Illinois U (IL) **599**
Western Kentucky U (KY) **599**
Western Michigan U (MI) **599**
Western Oregon U (OR) **600**
Western Washington U (WA) **600**
Westminster Coll (MO) **601**
Westminster Coll (PA) **601**
Westminster Coll (UT) **601**
Westmont Coll (CA) **602**
West Virginia U (WV) **602**
West Virginia Wesleyan Coll (WV) **603**
Wheaton Coll (IL) **603**
Wheaton Coll (MA) **603**
Wheeling Jesuit U (WV) **603**
Whitman Coll (WA) **604**
Whittier Coll (CA) **604**
Whitworth Coll (WA) **604**
Wichita State U (KS) **604**
Wiley Coll (TX) **605**
Wilkes U (PA) **605**
Willamette U (OR) **605**
William Jewell Coll (MO) **606**
William Paterson U of New Jersey (NJ) **606**
Williams Coll (MA) **606**
Wilmington Coll (OH) **607**
Wingate U (NC) **607**
Winthrop U (SC) **608**
Wittenberg U (OH) **608**
Wofford Coll (SC) **609**
Worcester Polytechnic Inst (MA) **609**
Wright State U (OH) **609**
Xavier U (OH) **610**
Xavier U of Louisiana (LA) **610**
Yale U (CT) **610**
York Coll of the City U of New York (NY) **611**
York U (ON, Canada) **611**
Youngstown State U (OH) **611**

PHILOSOPHY AND RELIGION RELATED

Information can be found under this major's main heading.

Bethune-Cookman Coll (FL) **289**
Bridgewater Coll (VA) **294**
Eastern Mennonite U (VA) **348**
Graceland U (IA) **371**
Kean U (NJ) **396**
Kentucky Wesleyan Coll (KY) **397**
Lyon Coll (AR) **413**
McGill U (QC, Canada) **423**
Point Loma Nazarene U (CA) **471**
Southwestern Coll (KS) **512**
State U of NY at Oswego (NY) **515**
Sterling Coll (KS) **519**
Union U (TN) **534**
The U of North Carolina at Wilmington (NC) **561**
U of Notre Dame (IN) **562**
U of Oklahoma (OK) **562**
Washington U in St. Louis (MO) **595**

PHOTOGRAPHIC TECHNOLOGY

Overview: This major gives students the technical knowledge to operate photographic, video, film, or lighting equipment. *Related majors:* broadcast journalism, television broadcasting technology, multimedia design, theater. *Potential careers:* professional photographer, lab technician, film or video editor, Web designer, camera person, set and lighting designer. *Salary potential:* $27k-$35k.

Kent State U (OH) **397**
Ohio U (OH) **458**
Rochester Inst of Technology (NY) **482**
Ryerson U (ON, Canada) **485**

PHOTOGRAPHY

Overview: This major teaches students the principles and techniques creating film or digital images and prepares them for careers as professional photographers. *Related majors:* commercial photography, drawing and painting, visual communications. *Potential careers:* professional photographer, photo editor, film developer, lighting specialist. *Salary potential:* $17k-$27k.

Academy of Art Coll (CA) **260**
Adams State Coll (CO) **260**
Alberta Coll of Art & Design (AB, Canada) **262**
Albertus Magnus Coll (CT) **262**
Alfred U (NY) **263**
American InterContinental U (CA) **266**
American InterContinental U, Atlanta (GA) **266**
American InterContinental U-London(United Kingdom) **267**
Andrews U (MI) **269**
Arcadia U (PA) **271**
Arizona State U (AZ) **271**
Art Academy of Cincinnati (OH) **273**
Art Center Coll of Design (CA) **273**
The Art Inst of Boston at Lesley U (MA) **273**
Atlanta Coll of Art (GA) **275**
Ball State U (IN) **280**
Bard Coll (NY) **281**
Barry U (FL) **282**
Barton Coll (NC) **282**
Bennington Coll (VT) **286**
Bowling Green State U (OH) **292**
Brigham Young U (UT) **295**
Brooks Inst of Photography (CA) **296**
California Coll of Arts and Crafts (CA) **299**
California Inst of the Arts (CA) **299**
California State U, Fullerton (CA) **301**
California State U, Hayward (CA) **301**
California State U, Long Beach (CA) **301**
California State U, Northridge (CA) **301**
Carson-Newman Coll (TN) **306**
Cazenovia Coll (NY) **308**
Central Missouri State U (MO) **310**
Chester Coll of New England (NH) **312**
The Cleveland Inst of Art (OH) **317**
Coker Coll (SC) **318**
Col for Creative Studies (MI) **319**
Coll of Santa Fe (NM) **323**
Coll of Staten Island of the City U of NY (NY) **323**
Coll of Visual Arts (MN) **324**
Colorado State U (CO) **325**
Columbia Coll (MO) **326**
Columbia Coll Chicago (IL) **327**
Columbus Coll of Art and Design (OH) **328**
Concordia U (QC, Canada) **331**
Corcoran Coll of Art and Design (DC) **332**
Cornell U (NY) **333**
Dominican U (IL) **345**
Drexel U (PA) **346**
The Evergreen State Coll (WA) **355**
Fitchburg State Coll (MA) **358**
Fordham U (NY) **362**
Gallaudet U (DC) **365**
Goddard Coll (VT) **369**
Governors State U (IL) **370**
Grand Valley State U (MI) **371**
Hampshire Coll (MA) **375**
Hampton U (VA) **375**
Indiana U Bloomington (IN) **385**
Indiana Wesleyan U (IN) **387**
Inter American U of PR, San Germán Campus (PR) **388**
Ithaca Coll (NY) **390**
Kansas City Art Inst (MO) **395**
Long Island U, C.W. Post Campus (NY) **409**
Long Island U, Southampton Coll, Friends World Program (NY) **409**
Louisiana Tech U (LA) **410**
Loyola U Chicago (IL) **411**
Maine Coll of Art (ME) **415**
Marlboro Coll (VT) **418**
Maryland Inst Coll of Art (MD) **419**
Massachusetts Coll of Art (MA) **421**
McNeese State U (LA) **423**
Memorial U of Newfoundland (NF, Canada) **424**
Memphis Coll of Art (TN) **425**
Milwaukee Inst of Art and Design (WI) **431**
Minneapolis Coll of Art and Design (MN) **431**
Montserrat Coll of Art (MA) **435**
Morningside Coll (IA) **437**
Mount Allison U (NB, Canada) **437**
Nazareth Coll of Rochester (NY) **443**
New England Coll (NH) **444**
New World School of the Arts (FL) **447**
New York U (NY) **447**
Northern Arizona U (AZ) **450**
Northern Michigan U (MI) **451**
Nova Scotia Coll of Art and Design (NS, Canada) **455**
Ohio U (OH) **458**
Otis Coll of Art and Design (CA) **462**
Pacific Northwest Coll of Art (OR) **464**
Parsons School of Design, New School U (NY) **465**
Point Park Coll (PA) **471**
Pratt Inst (NY) **473**
Prescott Coll (AZ) **474**
Rhode Island School of Design (RI) **479**
Ringling School of Art and Design (FL) **480**
Rivier Coll (NH) **480**
Rochester Inst of Technology (NY) **482**
Rutgers, The State U of New Jersey, New Brunswick (NJ) **485**
Ryerson U (ON, Canada) **485**
St. Edward's U (TX) **488**
St. John's U (NY) **490**
Saint Mary-of-the-Woods Coll (IN) **493**
Salem State Coll (MA) **497**
Sam Houston State U (TX) **497**
San Francisco Art Inst (CA) **498**
San Jose State U (CA) **499**
Sarah Lawrence Coll (NY) **499**
Savannah Coll of Art and Design (GA) **499**
School of the Museum of Fine Arts (MA) **501**
School of Visual Arts (NY) **501**
Seattle U (WA) **501**
Simon's Rock Coll of Bard (MA) **505**
State U of NY at New Paltz (NY) **515**
State U of NY Coll at Buffalo (NY) **516**
State U of NY Coll at Potsdam (NY) **517**
Syracuse U (NY) **521**
Temple U (PA) **523**
Texas A&M U–Commerce (TX) **525**
Texas Christian U (TX) **526**
Texas Southern U (TX) **526**
Texas Woman's U (TX) **527**
Thomas Edison State Coll (NJ) **527**
Trinity Christian Coll (IL) **530**
The U of Akron (OH) **537**
U of Calif, Santa Cruz (CA) **542**
U of Central Oklahoma (OK) **542**
U of Dayton (OH) **544**
U of Hartford (CT) **546**
U of Houston (TX) **547**
U of Idaho (ID) **547**
U of Illinois at Chicago (IL) **547**
U of Illinois at Urbana–Champaign (IL) **548**
The U of Iowa (IA) **548**
U of Maryland, Baltimore County (MD) **552**
U of Massachusetts Dartmouth (MA) **553**
U of Miami (FL) **553**
U of Michigan (MI) **554**
U of Missouri–St. Louis (MO) **556**
U of Montevallo (AL) **557**
U of North Texas (TX) **562**
U of Ottawa (ON, Canada) **563**
U of San Francisco (CA) **574**
The U of South Dakota (SD) **575**
The U of Texas at Arlington (TX) **577**
The U of the Arts (PA) **579**
U of Washington (WA) **583**
Virginia Commonwealth U (VA) **590**
Virginia Intermont Coll (VA) **590**
Washington U in St. Louis (MO) **595**
Watkins Coll of Art and Design (TN) **595**
Weber State U (UT) **596**
Webster U (MO) **597**
Wright State U (OH) **609**
York U (ON, Canada) **611**
Youngstown State U (OH) **611**

PHYSICAL EDUCATION

Overview: This major prepares undergraduates to teach general physical education courses as well as coach sports at various educational levels. *Related majors:* health and physical education, athletic training and sports medicine, sport and fitness administration, physical therapy. *Potential careers:* physical education teacher, coach, sports trainer. *Salary potential:* $24k-$35k.

Abilene Christian U (TX) **260**
Adams State Coll (CO) **260**
Adelphi U (NY) **260**
Adrian Coll (MI) **260**
Alabama A&M U (AL) **261**
Alabama State U (AL) **261**
Albany State U (GA) **262**
Albertson Coll of Idaho (ID) **262**
Albion Coll (MI) **262**
Alcorn State U (MS) **263**
Alderson-Broaddus Coll (WV) **263**
Alice Lloyd Coll (KY) **263**
Allen U (SC) **264**
American U of Puerto Rico (PR) **268**
Anderson Coll (SC) **268**
Anderson U (IN) **268**
Andrews U (MI) **269**
Appalachian State U (NC) **270**
Aquinas Coll (MI) **270**
Arkansas State U (AR) **272**
Arkansas Tech U (AR) **272**
Armstrong Atlantic State U (GA) **273**
Asbury Coll (KY) **274**
Ashland U (OH) **274**
Athens State U (AL) **275**
Atlantic Union Coll (MA) **276**
Auburn U (AL) **276**
Augsburg Coll (MN) **276**
Augustana Coll (IL) **276**
Augustana Coll (SD) **276**
Augusta State U (GA) **277**
Aurora U (IL) **277**
Austin Coll (TX) **277**
Averett U (VA) **278**
Azusa Pacific U (CA) **278**
Baker U (KS) **280**
Baldwin-Wallace Coll (OH) **280**
Ball State U (IN) **280**
Barry U (FL) **282**
Barton Coll (NC) **282**
Bayamón Central U (PR) **283**
Baylor U (TX) **283**
Bellevue U (NE) **284**
Belmont U (TN) **284**
Bemidji State U (MN) **285**
Benedictine Coll (KS) **285**
Berea Coll (KY) **286**
Berry Coll (GA) **287**
Bethany Coll (KS) **287**
Bethany Coll (WV) **287**
Bethel Coll (IN) **288**
Bethel Coll (MN) **288**
Bethel Coll (TN) **288**
Bethune-Cookman Coll (FL) **289**
Biola U (CA) **289**
Blackburn Coll (IL) **290**
Bluefield Coll (VA) **291**
Blue Mountain Coll (MS) **291**
Bluffton Coll (OH) **291**
Boston U (MA) **292**
Bowling Green State U (OH) **292**
Brewton-Parker Coll (GA) **294**
Briar Cliff U (IA) **294**
Bridgewater State Coll (MA) **294**
Brigham Young U (UT) **295**
Brigham Young U–Hawaii (HI) **295**
Brock U (ON, Canada) **295**
Brooklyn Coll of the City U of NY (NY) **295**
Bryan Coll (TN) **296**
Buena Vista U (IA) **297**
California Lutheran U (CA) **299**
California Polytechnic State U, San Luis Obispo (CA) **300**
California State Polytechnic U, Pomona (CA) **300**
California State U, Bakersfield (CA) **300**
California State U, Chico (CA) **300**
California State U, Dominguez Hills (CA) **300**
California State U, Fresno (CA) **301**
California State U, Fullerton (CA) **301**
California State U, Hayward (CA) **301**
California State U, Long Beach (CA) **301**
California State U, Northridge (CA) **301**
California State U, San Bernardino (CA) **302**
California State U, Stanislaus (CA) **302**
Calvin Coll (MI) **303**
Cameron U (OK) **303**
Campbellsville U (KY) **303**
Campbell U (NC) **303**
Canisius Coll (NY) **304**
Capital U (OH) **304**

Carroll Coll (MT) **306**
Carroll Coll (WI) **306**
Carson-Newman Coll (TN) **306**
Carthage Coll (WI) **306**
Castleton State Coll (VT) **307**
Catawba Coll (NC) **307**
Cedarville U (OH) **308**
Centenary Coll of Louisiana (LA) **308**
Central Connecticut State U (CT) **309**
Central Methodist Coll (MO) **309**
Central Michigan U (MI) **310**
Central Missouri State U (MO) **310**
Central Washington U (WA) **310**
Chadron State Coll (NE) **311**
Chapman U (CA) **311**
Charleston Southern U (SC) **311**
Chowan Coll (NC) **312**
Christian Heritage Coll (CA) **313**
Christopher Newport U (VA) **313**
Citadel, The Military Coll of South Carolina (SC) **314**
Claflin U (SC) **314**
Clark Atlanta U (GA) **315**
Clarke Coll (IA) **315**
Clearwater Christian Coll (FL) **316**
Cleveland State U (OH) **317**
Coastal Carolina U (SC) **318**
Coe Coll (IA) **318**
Coker Coll (SC) **318**
Coll of Charleston (SC) **320**
Coll of Mount St. Joseph (OH) **320**
Coll of Mount Saint Vincent (NY) **320**
The Coll of New Jersey (NJ) **320**
Coll of St. Catherine (MN) **321**
Coll of the Ozarks (MO) **323**
Coll of the Southwest (NM) **324**
The Coll of William and Mary (VA) **324**
Colorado State U (CO) **325**
Colorado State U-Pueblo (CO) **325**
Columbus State U (GA) **328**
Concord Coll (WV) **329**
Concordia Coll (MN) **329**
Concordia U (IL) **330**
Concordia U (MI) **330**
Concordia U (MN) **330**
Concordia U (NE) **330**
Concordia U (OR) **330**
Concordia U Wisconsin (WI) **331**
Cornell Coll (IA) **332**
Cornerstone U (MI) **333**
Crown Coll (MN) **334**
Culver-Stockton Coll (MO) **334**
Cumberland Coll (KY) **335**
Cumberland U (TN) **335**
Dakota State U (SD) **335**
Dakota Wesleyan U (SD) **336**
Dallas Baptist U (TX) **336**
Dana Coll (NE) **337**
Davis & Elkins Coll (WV) **338**
Defiance Coll (OH) **338**
Delaware State U (DE) **338**
Delta State U (MS) **339**
Denison U (OH) **339**
DePaul U (IL) **339**
Dickinson State U (ND) **344**
Dillard U (LA) **344**
Doane Coll (NE) **344**
Dordt Coll (IA) **345**
Drury U (MO) **346**
East Carolina U (NC) **347**
East Central U (OK) **347**
Eastern Connecticut State U (CT) **347**
Eastern Illinois U (IL) **348**
Eastern Kentucky U (KY) **348**
Eastern Mennonite U (VA) **348**
Eastern Michigan U (MI) **348**
Eastern Nazarene Coll (MA) **348**
Eastern New Mexico U (NM) **349**
Eastern Oregon U (OR) **349**
Eastern Washington U (WA) **349**
East Stroudsburg U of Pennsylvania (PA) **349**
East Texas Baptist U (TX) **350**
Edinboro U of Pennsylvania (PA) **351**
Elizabeth City State U (NC) **351**
Elmhurst Coll (IL) **351**
Elon U (NC) **352**
Emporia State U (KS) **354**
Erskine Coll (SC) **354**
Eureka Coll (IL) **355**
Evangel U (MO) **355**
Fairmont State Coll (WV) **356**
Faulkner U (AL) **357**
Fayetteville State U (NC) **357**
Ferrum Coll (VA) **358**
Florida A&M U (FL) **359**
Florida International U (FL) **360**
Florida Southern Coll (FL) **361**
Florida State U (FL) **361**
Fort Hays State U (KS) **362**
Fort Lewis Coll (CO) **362**
Fort Valley State U (GA) **362**
Franklin Coll (IN) **363**
Freed-Hardeman U (TN) **364**
Free Will Baptist Bible Coll (TN) **364**
Fresno Pacific U (CA) **364**
Frostburg State U (MD) **365**
Gallaudet U (DC) **365**
Gardner-Webb U (NC) **365**
George Fox U (OR) **366**
George Mason U (VA) **366**
Georgetown Coll (KY) **366**
Georgia Coll & State U (GA) **367**
Georgia Southern U (GA) **367**
Georgia Southwestern State U (GA) **368**
Georgia State U (GA) **368**
Gettysburg Coll (PA) **368**
Glenville State Coll (WV) **368**
Gonzaga U (WA) **369**
Goshen Coll (IN) **370**
Grace Coll (IN) **370**
Graceland U (IA) **371**
Grambling State U (LA) **371**
Grand Canyon U (AZ) **371**
Grand Valley State U (MI) **371**
Greensboro Coll (NC) **372**
Greenville Coll (IL) **373**
Gustavus Adolphus Coll (MN) **374**
Hamline U (MN) **374**
Hampton U (VA) **375**
Hannibal-LaGrange Coll (MO) **375**
Hanover Coll (IN) **375**
Harding U (AR) **375**
Hardin-Simmons U (TX) **376**
Hastings Coll (NE) **377**
Heidelberg Coll (OH) **377**
Henderson State U (AR) **378**
Hendrix Coll (AR) **378**
High Point U (NC) **379**
Hillsdale Coll (MI) **379**
Hofstra U (NY) **380**
Hope Coll (MI) **381**
Houghton Coll (NY) **381**
Howard Payne U (TX) **382**
Howard U (DC) **382**
Humboldt State U (CA) **382**
Hunter Coll of the City U of NY (NY) **382**
Huntingdon Coll (AL) **383**
Huntington Coll (IN) **383**
Husson Coll (ME) **383**
Huston-Tillotson Coll (TX) **383**
Idaho State U (ID) **384**
Illinois Coll (IL) **384**
Illinois State U (IL) **384**
Indiana State U (IN) **385**
Indiana U Bloomington (IN) **385**
Indiana U of Pennsylvania (PA) **386**
Indiana U–Purdue U Indianapolis (IN) **387**
Indiana Wesleyan U (IN) **387**
Inter American U of PR, Guayama Campus (PR) **388**
Inter American U of PR, San Germán Campus (PR) **388**
Iowa Wesleyan Coll (IA) **390**
Ithaca Coll (NY) **390**
Jackson State U (MS) **390**
Jacksonville State U (AL) **390**
Jacksonville U (FL) **391**
Jamestown Coll (ND) **391**
John Brown U (AR) **392**
John Carroll U (OH) **392**
Johnson C. Smith U (NC) **394**
Johnson State Coll (VT) **394**
Judson Coll (IL) **395**
Kean U (NJ) **396**
Keene State Coll (NH) **396**
Kennesaw State U (GA) **397**
Kent State U (OH) **397**
Kentucky State U (KY) **397**
Kentucky Wesleyan Coll (KY) **397**
Lakehead U (ON, Canada) **400**
Lamar U (TX) **401**
Lambuth U (TN) **401**
Lander U (SC) **401**
Lane Coll (TN) **402**
Langston U (OK) **402**
Laurentian U (ON, Canada) **403**
Lees-McRae Coll (NC) **404**
Lee U (TN) **404**
Lenoir-Rhyne Coll (NC) **405**
LeTourneau U (TX) **405**
Lewis-Clark State Coll (ID) **406**
Lewis U (IL) **406**
Liberty U (VA) **406**
Limestone Coll (SC) **406**
Lincoln Memorial U (TN) **407**
Lincoln U (PA) **407**
Lindenwood U (MO) **407**
Lindsey Wilson Coll (KY) **407**
Lipscomb U (TN) **408**
Lock Haven U of Pennsylvania (PA) **408**
Long Island U, Brooklyn Campus (NY) **409**
Long Island U, C.W. Post Campus (NY) **409**
Longwood U (VA) **409**
Loras Coll (IA) **410**
Louisiana Coll (LA) **410**
Louisiana State U and A&M Coll (LA) **410**
Louisiana State U in Shreveport (LA) **410**
Louisiana Tech U (LA) **410**
Lubbock Christian U (TX) **412**
Luther Coll (IA) **412**
Lynchburg Coll (VA) **413**
Lyndon State Coll (VT) **413**
MacMurray Coll (IL) **414**
Malone Coll (OH) **415**
Manchester Coll (IN) **415**
Manhattan Coll (NY) **416**
Maranatha Baptist Bible Coll (WI) **417**
Marian Coll (IN) **417**
Marshall U (WV) **418**
Mars Hill Coll (NC) **418**
Maryville Coll (TN) **420**
Marywood U (PA) **421**
The Master's Coll and Seminary (CA) **422**
Mayville State U (ND) **422**
McGill U (QC, Canada) **423**
McKendree Coll (IL) **423**
McMurry U (TX) **423**
McNeese State U (LA) **423**
McPherson Coll (KS) **423**
Memorial U of Newfoundland (NF, Canada) **424**
Meredith Coll (NC) **426**
Mesa State Coll (CO) **426**
Messiah Coll (PA) **426**
Methodist Coll (NC) **427**
Miami U (OH) **428**
Michigan State U (MI) **428**
MidAmerica Nazarene U (KS) **428**
Midland Lutheran Coll (NE) **429**
Milligan Coll (TN) **430**
Millikin U (IL) **430**
Minnesota State U, Mankato (MN) **431**
Minnesota State U, Moorhead (MN) **432**
Minot State U (ND) **432**
Mississippi State U (MS) **432**
Mississippi Valley State U (MS) **432**
Missouri Southern State Coll (MO) **433**
Missouri Valley Coll (MO) **433**
Monmouth Coll (IL) **434**
Montana State U–Billings (MT) **434**
Montana State U–Northern (MT) **434**
Montclair State U (NJ) **435**
Morehead State U (KY) **436**
Morehouse Coll (GA) **436**
Morgan State U (MD) **436**
Mount Marty Coll (SD) **438**
Mount Union Coll (OH) **440**
Mount Vernon Nazarene U (OH) **440**
Murray State U (KY) **440**
Muskingum Coll (OH) **441**
Nebraska Wesleyan U (NE) **443**
Newberry Coll (SC) **444**
New England Coll (NH) **444**
New Mexico Highlands U (NM) **446**
New Mexico State U (NM) **446**
Nicholls State U (LA) **447**
North Carolina Ag and Tech State U (NC) **448**
North Carolina Central U (NC) **448**
North Carolina Wesleyan Coll (NC) **449**
North Central Coll (IL) **449**
North Dakota State U (ND) **449**
Northeastern Illinois U (IL) **450**
Northeastern State U (OK) **450**
Northeastern U (MA) **450**
Northern Arizona U (AZ) **450**
Northern Illinois U (IL) **450**
Northern Kentucky U (KY) **451**
Northern Michigan U (MI) **451**
Northern State U (SD) **451**
North Georgia Coll & State U (GA) **451**
North Park U (IL) **452**
Northwest Coll (WA) **452**
Northwestern Coll (IA) **453**
Northwestern Coll (MN) **453**
Northwestern Oklahoma State U (OK) **453**
Northwestern State U of Louisiana (LA) **453**
Northwest Missouri State U (MO) **454**
Northwest Nazarene U (ID) **454**
Norwich U (VT) **455**
Oakland City U (IN) **456**
Oakwood Coll (AL) **456**
Ohio Northern U (OH) **457**
The Ohio State U (OH) **457**
Ohio U (OH) **458**
Ohio Valley Coll (WV) **459**
Ohio Wesleyan U (OH) **459**
Oklahoma Baptist U (OK) **459**
Oklahoma Christian U (OK) **459**
Oklahoma City U (OK) **460**
Oklahoma Panhandle State U (OK) **460**
Oklahoma State U (OK) **460**
Oklahoma Wesleyan U (OK) **460**
Old Dominion U (VA) **460**
Olivet Coll (MI) **461**
Olivet Nazarene U (IL) **461**
Oral Roberts U (OK) **461**
Oregon State U (OR) **462**
Ottawa U (KS) **462**
Otterbein Coll (OH) **462**
Ouachita Baptist U (AR) **462**
Pacific Lutheran U (WA) **463**
Pacific Union Coll (CA) **464**
Palm Beach Atlantic U (FL) **465**
Paul Quinn Coll (TX) **466**
Pepperdine U, Malibu (CA) **469**
Peru State Coll (NE) **469**
Pfeiffer U (NC) **469**
Philadelphia Biblical U (PA) **469**
Piedmont Baptist Coll (NC) **470**
Pittsburg State U (KS) **470**
Plymouth State Coll (NH) **471**
Pontifical Catholic U of Puerto Rico (PR) **472**
Prescott Coll (AZ) **474**
Purdue U (IN) **475**
Queens Coll of the City U of NY (NY) **475**
Queen's U at Kingston (ON, Canada) **476**
Quincy U (IL) **476**
Radford U (VA) **476**
Reinhardt Coll (GA) **478**
Rhode Island Coll (RI) **479**
Rice U (TX) **479**
Ripon Coll (WI) **480**
Rockford Coll (IL) **482**
Rocky Mountain Coll (MT) **482**
Rowan U (NJ) **484**
Saginaw Valley State U (MI) **486**
St. Ambrose U (IA) **486**
St. Andrews Presbyterian Coll (NC) **487**
Saint Augustine's Coll (NC) **487**
St. Bonaventure U (NY) **487**
St. Cloud State U (MN) **488**
St. Edward's U (TX) **488**
St. Francis Coll (NY) **488**
St. Francis Xavier U (NS, Canada) **489**
Saint Joseph's Coll (IN) **490**
Saint Joseph's Coll of Maine (ME) **491**
Saint Leo U (FL) **492**
Saint Mary's Coll of California (CA) **494**
Salem International U (WV) **496**
Salem State Coll (MA) **497**
Salisbury U (MD) **497**
Samford U (AL) **497**
San Diego State U (CA) **498**
San Francisco State U (CA) **498**
San Jose State U (CA) **499**
Seattle Pacific U (WA) **501**
Shenandoah U (VA) **503**
Simpson Coll (IA) **505**
Si Tanka Huron U (SD) **505**
Slippery Rock U of Pennsylvania (PA) **506**
Sonoma State U (CA) **506**
South Carolina State U (SC) **506**
South Dakota State U (SD) **507**
Southeastern Bible Coll (AL) **507**
Southeastern Louisiana U (LA) **508**
Southeastern Oklahoma State U (OK) **508**
Southeast Missouri State U (MO) **508**
Southern Adventist U (TN) **508**
Southern Arkansas U–Magnolia (AR) **509**
Southern Connecticut State U (CT) **509**
Southern Illinois U Carbondale (IL) **509**
Southern Nazarene U (OK) **510**

PHYSICAL EDUCATION (continued)

Southern Oregon U (OR) ***510***
Southern Utah U (UT) ***511***
Southern Wesleyan U (SC) ***511***
Southwest Baptist U (MO) ***512***
Southwestern Coll (KS) ***512***
Southwestern Oklahoma State U (OK) ***512***
Southwestern U (TX) ***513***
Southwest Missouri State U (MO) ***513***
Southwest State U (MN) ***513***
Spring Arbor U (MI) ***514***
Springfield Coll (MA) ***514***
State U of NY Coll at Brockport (NY) ***515***
State U of NY Coll at Cortland (NY) ***516***
State U of NY Coll at Potsdam (NY) ***517***
State U of West Georgia (GA) ***518***
Sterling Coll (KS) ***519***
Sul Ross State U (TX) ***521***
Syracuse U (NY) ***521***
Tabor Coll (KS) ***522***
Tarleton State U (TX) ***522***
Taylor U (IN) ***523***
Temple U (PA) ***523***
Tennessee State U (TN) ***523***
Tennessee Technological U (TN) ***524***
Tennessee Wesleyan Coll (TN) ***524***
Texas A&M International U (TX) ***524***
Texas A&M U–Commerce (TX) ***525***
Texas A&M U–Corpus Christi (TX) ***525***
Texas A&M U–Kingsville (TX) ***525***
Texas Christian U (TX) ***526***
Texas Lutheran U (TX) ***526***
Texas Southern U (TX) ***526***
Texas Wesleyan U (TX) ***526***
Towson U (MD) ***529***
Transylvania U (KY) ***529***
Trevecca Nazarene U (TN) ***529***
Trinity Christian Coll (IL) ***530***
Trinity International U (IL) ***531***
Trinity Western U (BC, Canada) ***531***
Tri-State U (IN) ***532***
Troy State U (AL) ***532***
Tusculum Coll (TN) ***533***
Union Coll (KY) ***533***
Union Coll (NE) ***534***
Union U (TN) ***534***
Université de Sherbrooke (QC, Canada) ***536***
Université Laval (QC, Canada) ***536***
The U of Akron (OH) ***537***
The U of Alabama (AL) ***537***
The U of Alabama at Birmingham (AL) ***537***
U of Alaska Anchorage (AK) ***538***
U of Alberta (AB, Canada) ***538***
The U of Arizona (AZ) ***538***
U of Arkansas at Monticello (AR) ***539***
U of Calif, Davis (CA) ***540***
U of Central Arkansas (AR) ***542***
U of Central Florida (FL) ***542***
U of Central Oklahoma (OK) ***542***
U of Cincinnati (OH) ***543***
U of Connecticut (CT) ***544***
U of Dayton (OH) ***544***
U of Delaware (DE) ***544***
U of Evansville (IN) ***545***
The U of Findlay (OH) ***545***
U of Florida (FL) ***545***
U of Georgia (GA) ***545***
U of Hawaii at Manoa (HI) ***546***
U of Idaho (ID) ***547***
U of Indianapolis (IN) ***548***
U of Kansas (KS) ***549***
U of Kentucky (KY) ***549***
U of La Verne (CA) ***549***
The U of Lethbridge (AB, Canada) ***549***
U of Louisiana at Lafayette (LA) ***550***
U of Maine (ME) ***550***
U of Maine at Presque Isle (ME) ***551***
U of Manitoba (MB, Canada) ***551***
U of Mary (ND) ***551***
U of Mary Hardin-Baylor (TX) ***551***
U of Maryland, Coll Park (MD) ***552***
U of Maryland Eastern Shore (MD) ***552***
U of Massachusetts Boston (MA) ***553***
U of Miami (FL) ***553***
U of Michigan (MI) ***554***
U of Minnesota, Duluth (MN) ***554***
U of Minnesota, Twin Cities Campus (MN) ***555***
U of Missouri–Kansas City (MO) ***555***
U of Missouri–St. Louis (MO) ***556***
U of Mobile (AL) ***556***
The U of Montana–Missoula (MT) ***556***
The U of Montana–Western (MT) ***556***
U of Nebraska at Kearney (NE) ***557***
U of Nebraska at Omaha (NE) ***557***
U of Nebraska–Lincoln (NE) ***557***
U of Nevada, Las Vegas (NV) ***558***
U of Nevada, Reno (NV) ***558***
U of New Brunswick Fredericton (NB, Canada) ***558***
U of New Hampshire (NH) ***558***
U of New Mexico (NM) ***559***
U of New Orleans (LA) ***559***
The U of North Carolina at Greensboro (NC) ***560***
The U of North Carolina at Pembroke (NC) ***560***
The U of North Carolina at Wilmington (NC) ***561***
U of North Dakota (ND) ***561***
U of Northern Iowa (IA) ***561***
U of North Florida (FL) ***561***
U of North Texas (TX) ***562***
U of Ottawa (ON, Canada) ***563***
U of Pittsburgh (PA) ***569***
U of Puerto Rico, Cayey U Coll (PR) ***571***
U of Regina (SK, Canada) ***572***
U of Rhode Island (RI) ***572***
U of Richmond (VA) ***572***
U of Rio Grande (OH) ***572***
U of St. Thomas (MN) ***573***
U of San Francisco (CA) ***574***
U of Saskatchewan (SK, Canada) ***574***
U of Sioux Falls (SD) ***574***
U of South Alabama (AL) ***575***
U of South Carolina (SC) ***575***
U of South Carolina Spartanburg (SC) ***575***
The U of South Dakota (SD) ***575***
U of Southern Indiana (IN) ***576***
U of Southern Mississippi (MS) ***576***
U of South Florida (FL) ***576***
The U of Tampa (FL) ***577***
The U of Tennessee at Chattanooga (TN) ***577***
The U of Texas–Pan American (TX) ***579***
U of the District of Columbia (DC) ***580***
U of the Incarnate Word (TX) ***580***
U of the Ozarks (AR) ***580***
U of Toledo (OH) ***581***
U of Toronto (ON, Canada) ***581***
U of Utah (UT) ***582***
U of Vermont (VT) ***582***
U of Victoria (BC, Canada) ***582***
U of Virginia (VA) ***582***
The U of West Alabama (AL) ***583***
The U of Western Ontario (ON, Canada) ***583***
U of West Florida (FL) ***583***
U of Windsor (ON, Canada) ***584***
U of Wisconsin–La Crosse (WI) ***584***
U of Wisconsin–Madison (WI) ***584***
U of Wisconsin–Oshkosh (WI) ***585***
U of Wisconsin–River Falls (WI) ***585***
U of Wisconsin–Stevens Point (WI) ***585***
U of Wisconsin–Superior (WI) ***586***
U of Wisconsin–Whitewater (WI) ***586***
U of Wyoming (WY) ***586***
Upper Iowa U (IA) ***587***
Ursinus Coll (PA) ***587***
Utah State U (UT) ***587***
Valdosta State U (GA) ***588***
Valley City State U (ND) ***588***
Valparaiso U (IN) ***588***
Vanguard U of Southern California (CA) ***589***
Virginia Intermont Coll (VA) ***590***
Virginia State U (VA) ***591***
Voorhees Coll (SC) ***592***
Walla Walla Coll (WA) ***593***
Walsh U (OH) ***593***
Warner Pacific Coll (OR) ***593***
Warner Southern Coll (FL) ***593***
Wartburg Coll (IA) ***594***
Washington State U (WA) ***595***
Wayland Baptist U (TX) ***595***
Wayne State Coll (NE) ***596***
Wayne State U (MI) ***596***
Weber State U (UT) ***596***
Wesley Coll (DE) ***598***
West Chester U of Pennsylvania (PA) ***598***
Western Carolina U (NC) ***598***
Western Illinois U (IL) ***599***
Western Kentucky U (KY) ***599***
Western Michigan U (MI) ***599***
Western New Mexico U (NM) ***600***
Western State Coll of Colorado (CO) ***600***
Western Washington U (WA) ***600***
Westfield State Coll (MA) ***600***
West Liberty State Coll (WV) ***601***
Westminster Coll (MO) ***601***
Westmont Coll (CA) ***602***
West Virginia State Coll (WV) ***602***
West Virginia U (WV) ***602***
West Virginia U Inst of Technology (WV) ***602***
West Virginia Wesleyan Coll (WV) ***603***
Whittier Coll (CA) ***604***
Whitworth Coll (WA) ***604***
Wichita State U (KS) ***604***
Wiley Coll (TX) ***605***
Willamette U (OR) ***605***
William Carey Coll (MS) ***605***
William Paterson U of New Jersey (NJ) ***606***
William Penn U (IA) ***606***
Williams Baptist Coll (AR) ***606***
William Woods U (MO) ***607***
Wilmington Coll (OH) ***607***
Wingate U (NC) ***607***
Winona State U (MN) ***608***
Winston-Salem State U (NC) ***608***
Winthrop U (SC) ***608***
Wright State U (OH) ***609***
Xavier U of Louisiana (LA) ***610***
York Coll (NE) ***610***
York Coll of the City U of New York (NY) ***611***
York U (ON, Canada) ***611***
Youngstown State U (OH) ***611***

PHYSICAL SCIENCES

Overview: Students who choose this major will study a broad range of topics and concepts that relate to inanimate objects, matter, energy and related phenomena. *Related majors:* astronomy, chemistry, physics, geology, earth and planetary sciences. *Potential careers:* geophysicist, chemical engineer, astronomer, physicist, hydrologist, research scientist, professor. *Salary potential:* \$30k-\$40k.

Antioch Coll (OH) ***269***
Arkansas Tech U (AR) ***272***
Armstrong Atlantic State U (GA) ***273***
Asbury Coll (KY) ***274***
Auburn U Montgomery (AL) ***276***
Augusta State U (GA) ***277***
Bard Coll (NY) ***281***
Bemidji State U (MN) ***285***
Biola U (CA) ***289***
Black Hills State U (SD) ***290***
Bridgewater Coll (VA) ***294***
Brigham Young U–Hawaii (HI) ***295***
Brock U (ON, Canada) ***295***
California Inst of Technology (CA) ***299***
California Polytechnic State U, San Luis Obispo (CA) ***300***
California State U, Chico (CA) ***300***
California State U, Hayward (CA) ***301***
California State U, Sacramento (CA) ***301***
California State U, Stanislaus (CA) ***302***
Calvin Coll (MI) ***303***
Centenary Coll of Louisiana (LA) ***308***
Central Connecticut State U (CT) ***309***
Central Michigan U (MI) ***310***
Chowan Coll (NC) ***312***
Coe Coll (IA) ***318***
Colgate U (NY) ***319***
Colorado State U (CO) ***325***
Columbia Coll (SC) ***327***
Concordia U (IL) ***330***
Concordia U (MN) ***330***
Concordia U (NE) ***330***
Concordia U (OR) ***330***
Defiance Coll (OH) ***338***
Doane Coll (NE) ***344***
Eastern Michigan U (MI) ***348***
Eastern Washington U (WA) ***349***
East Stroudsburg U of Pennsylvania (PA) ***349***
Emporia State U (KS) ***354***
Eureka Coll (IL) ***355***
The Evergreen State Coll (WA) ***355***
Florida State U (FL) ***361***
Fordham U (NY) ***362***
Fort Hays State U (KS) ***362***
Framingham State Coll (MA) ***362***
Freed-Hardeman U (TN) ***364***
Georgia Southwestern State U (GA) ***368***
Goddard Coll (VT) ***369***
Goshen Coll (IN) ***370***
Graceland U (IA) ***371***
Grand Canyon U (AZ) ***371***
Grand Valley State U (MI) ***371***
Hampshire Coll (MA) ***375***
Hampton U (VA) ***375***
Hardin-Simmons U (TX) ***376***
Harvard U (MA) ***376***
Humboldt State U (CA) ***382***
Judson Coll (IL) ***395***
Juniata Coll (PA) ***395***
Kansas State U (KS) ***396***
Kutztown U of Pennsylvania (PA) ***399***
La Sierra U (CA) ***403***
Lenoir-Rhyne Coll (NC) ***405***
Lincoln U (PA) ***407***
Linfield Coll (OR) ***408***
Lock Haven U of Pennsylvania (PA) ***408***
Loras Coll (IA) ***410***
Lyndon State Coll (VT) ***413***
Mansfield U of Pennsylvania (PA) ***416***
The Master's Coll and Seminary (CA) ***422***
Mayville State U (ND) ***422***
McMaster U (ON, Canada) ***423***
McPherson Coll (KS) ***423***
Mesa State Coll (CO) ***426***
Michigan State U (MI) ***428***
Michigan Technological U (MI) ***428***
Middlebury Coll (VT) ***429***
Midland Lutheran Coll (NE) ***429***
Midwestern State U (TX) ***430***
Minnesota State U, Mankato (MN) ***431***
Minot State U (ND) ***432***
Muhlenberg Coll (PA) ***440***
Northern Arizona U (AZ) ***450***
Northwest Missouri State U (MO) ***454***
Oklahoma Baptist U (OK) ***459***
Olivet Nazarene U (IL) ***461***
Oregon State U (OR) ***462***
Otterbein Coll (OH) ***462***
Pacific Union Coll (CA) ***464***
Penn State U at Erie, The Behrend Coll (PA) ***467***
Peru State Coll (NE) ***469***
Pittsburg State U (KS) ***470***
Radford U (VA) ***476***
Rensselaer Polytechnic Inst (NY) ***478***
Rhode Island Coll (RI) ***479***
Rowan U (NJ) ***484***
St. Cloud State U (MN) ***488***
St. Francis Xavier U (NS, Canada) ***489***
St. John's U (NY) ***490***
Saint Michael's Coll (VT) ***494***
San Diego State U (CA) ***498***
San Francisco State U (CA) ***498***
San Jose State U (CA) ***499***
Shawnee State U (OH) ***502***
Slippery Rock U of Pennsylvania (PA) ***506***
Southern Utah U (UT) ***511***
Southwest State U (MN) ***513***
Texas A&M International U (TX) ***524***
Trent U (ON, Canada) ***529***
Tri-State U (IN) ***532***
Troy State U (AL) ***532***
Troy State U Dothan (AL) ***532***
U of Alberta (AB, Canada) ***538***
U of Arkansas at Monticello (AR) ***539***
U of Calif, Berkeley (CA) ***540***
U of Calif, Riverside (CA) ***541***
U of Central Arkansas (AR) ***542***
U of Dayton (OH) ***544***
U of Guelph (ON, Canada) ***546***
U of Houston–Clear Lake (TX) ***547***
U of Maryland, Coll Park (MD) ***552***
U of Michigan–Dearborn (MI) ***554***
U of Michigan–Flint (MI) ***554***
U of Missouri–St. Louis (MO) ***556***
The U of Montana–Western (MT) ***556***
U of North Alabama (AL) ***559***
U of Ottawa (ON, Canada) ***563***
U of Pittsburgh (PA) ***569***
U of Pittsburgh at Bradford (PA) ***569***
U of Rio Grande (OH) ***572***
U of Southern California (CA) ***576***
U of the Pacific (CA) ***580***
U of Toledo (OH) ***581***
U of Wisconsin–River Falls (WI) ***585***
U of Wisconsin–Superior (WI) ***586***
Walsh U (OH) ***593***
Warner Pacific Coll (OR) ***593***
Washington U in St. Louis (MO) ***595***
Wayland Baptist U (TX) ***595***
Wayne State Coll (NE) ***596***
Wesleyan Coll (GA) ***597***
Western New Mexico U (NM) ***600***

Westfield State Coll (MA) ***600***
Wheaton Coll (IL) ***603***
Wiley Coll (TX) ***605***
William Paterson U of New Jersey (NJ) ***606***
Winona State U (MN) ***608***
Wittenberg U (OH) ***608***
York Coll of Pennsylvania (PA) ***610***
York U (ON, Canada) ***611***

PHYSICAL SCIENCES RELATED

Information can be found under this major's main heading.

Florida State U (FL) ***361***
Grand View Coll (IA) ***372***
Ohio U (OH) ***458***
The U of Texas at Austin (TX) ***578***

PHYSICAL SCIENCE TECHNOLOGIES RELATED

Information can be found under this major's main heading.

Millersville U of Pennsylvania (PA) ***430***

PHYSICAL/THEORETICAL CHEMISTRY

Overview: Students study the theoretical properties of matter and how the chemical structure and physical forces of matter influence the behavior of molecules and other compounds. *Related majors:* chemical and atomic/molecular physics, chemistry, fluid and thermal sciences, mathematics, metallurgy, materials science. *Potential careers:* chemical engineer, chemist, research scientist, professor. *Salary potential:* $35k-$55k.

Michigan State U (MI) ***428***
Rice U (TX) ***479***

PHYSICAL THERAPY

Overview: Students learn how to design and implement therapeutic strategies and techniques for patients who are suffering from physical impairments caused by injury or disease. *Related majors:* anatomy and physiology, neuroscience, rehabilitation therapy, exercise sciences/physiology and movement studies. *Potential careers:* physical therapist. *Salary potential:* $40k-$50k.

Alcorn State U (MS) ***263***
Andrews U (MI) ***269***
Armstrong Atlantic State U (GA) ***273***
Avila U (MO) ***278***
Baldwin-Wallace Coll (OH) ***280***
Boston U (MA) ***292***
Bowling Green State U (OH) ***292***
Bradley U (IL) ***293***
California State U, Fresno (CA) ***301***
California State U, Northridge (CA) ***301***
Centenary Coll of Louisiana (LA) ***308***
Clarke Coll (IA) ***315***
Cleveland State U (OH) ***317***
Coll of Mount St. Joseph (OH) ***320***
Coll of Saint Benedict (MN) ***321***
The Coll of St. Scholastica (MN) ***322***
Coll of Staten Island of the City U of NY (NY) ***323***
Concordia Coll (MN) ***329***
Concordia U (CA) ***330***
Concordia U Wisconsin (WI) ***331***
Daemen Coll (NY) ***335***
Dalhousie U (NS, Canada) ***336***
Duquesne U (PA) ***346***
D'Youville Coll (NY) ***347***
Eastern Nazarene Coll (MA) ***348***
Eastern Washington U (WA) ***349***
Elmhurst Coll (IL) ***351***
Florida A&M U (FL) ***359***
Florida Gulf Coast U (FL) ***359***
Georgia State U (GA) ***368***
Grand Valley State U (MI) ***371***
Gustavus Adolphus Coll (MN) ***374***
Hamline U (MN) ***374***
Hampton U (VA) ***375***
Hope International U (CA) ***381***
Howard U (DC) ***382***
Hunter Coll of the City U of NY (NY) ***382***
Huntingdon Coll (AL) ***383***
Husson Coll (ME) ***383***
Indiana U–Purdue U Indianapolis (IN) ***387***
Ithaca Coll (NY) ***390***
Kean U (NJ) ***396***
Langston U (OK) ***402***
La Salle U (PA) ***402***
Long Island U, Brooklyn Campus (NY) ***409***
Marquette U (WI) ***418***
McGill U (QC, Canada) ***423***
Merrimack Coll (MA) ***426***
Mount Saint Mary Coll (NY) ***439***
Mount Vernon Nazarene U (OH) ***440***
Nazareth Coll of Rochester (NY) ***443***
New York Inst of Technology (NY) ***447***
Northeastern U (MA) ***450***
Northern Illinois U (IL) ***450***
Northwest Nazarene U (ID) ***454***
Oakland U (MI) ***456***
The Ohio State U (OH) ***457***
Oklahoma Wesleyan U (OK) ***460***
Pittsburg State U (KS) ***470***
Queen's U at Kingston (ON, Canada) ***476***
Quinnipiac U (CT) ***476***
Russell Sage Coll (NY) ***484***
Sacred Heart U (CT) ***486***
St. Cloud State U (MN) ***488***
Saint Francis U (PA) ***488***
Saint John's U (MN) ***490***
Saint Mary's U of Minnesota (MN) ***494***
Saint Vincent Coll (PA) ***496***
Simmons Coll (MA) ***504***
Simpson Coll (IA) ***505***
Springfield Coll (MA) ***514***
State U of NY Health Science Center at Brooklyn (NY) ***517***
State U of New York Upstate Medical University (NY) ***518***
Tennessee State U (TN) ***523***
Texas Southern U (TX) ***526***
Thomas Jefferson U (PA) ***527***
Université Laval (QC, Canada) ***536***
U of Alberta (AB, Canada) ***538***
The U of British Columbia (BC, Canada) ***540***
U of Central Arkansas (AR) ***542***
U of Connecticut (CT) ***544***
U of Evansville (IN) ***545***
The U of Findlay (OH) ***545***
U of Florida (FL) ***545***
U of Hartford (CT) ***546***
U of Illinois at Chicago (IL) ***547***
U of Kentucky (KY) ***549***
U of Louisville (KY) ***550***
U of Manitoba (MB, Canada) ***551***
U of Maryland Eastern Shore (MD) ***552***
U of Minnesota, Morris (MN) ***555***
U of Minnesota, Twin Cities Campus (MN) ***555***
U of Missouri–Columbia (MO) ***555***
The U of Montana–Missoula (MT) ***556***
U of Nevada, Reno (NV) ***558***
U of New England (ME) ***558***
U of New Mexico (NM) ***559***
U of North Dakota (ND) ***561***
U of Ottawa (ON, Canada) ***563***
U of Puerto Rico Medical Sciences Campus (PR) ***571***
U of Saskatchewan (SK, Canada) ***574***
The U of Scranton (PA) ***574***
U of South Alabama (AL) ***575***
The U of Tennessee at Chattanooga (TN) ***577***
The U of Texas at San Antonio (TX) ***578***
The U of Texas–Pan American (TX) ***579***
U of the Sciences in Philadelphia (PA) ***580***
U of Toledo (OH) ***581***
U of Toronto (ON, Canada) ***581***
U of Utah (UT) ***582***
U of Washington (WA) ***583***
The U of Western Ontario (ON, Canada) ***583***
U of Wisconsin–Milwaukee (WI) ***585***
Ursinus Coll (PA) ***587***
Utica Coll (NY) ***588***
Vanguard U of Southern California (CA) ***589***
Villa Julie Coll (MD) ***590***
West Virginia U (WV) ***602***
Wheeling Jesuit U (WV) ***603***
William Carey Coll (MS) ***605***
Winona State U (MN) ***608***

PHYSICAL THERAPY ASSISTANT

Overview: This major prepares students to administer various treatments under the direction of physical therapists. Typical duties include giving heat, light, and sound treatments and massages and exercises that help heal muscles, nerves, bones, and joints. *Related majors:* physical therapy, medical assistant, health/physical education, athletic training, sports medicine. *Potential careers:* physical therapy assistant, massage therapist. *Salary potential:* $20k-$25k.

U of Central Arkansas (AR) ***542***

PHYSICIAN ASSISTANT

Overview: This major prepares students to work under the supervision of a medical doctor, assisting in the diagnosis and treatment of diseases and injuries. Physician assistants may interview patients, take medical histories, give physical examinations, order laboratory tests, make diagnoses, and prescribe appropriate treatment. *Related majors:* premedicine studies, medical physiology, nursing. *Potential careers:* physician assistant, MEDEX, physician associate, community health medic. *Salary potential:* $40k-$50k.

Alderson-Broaddus Coll (WV) ***263***
Augsburg Coll (MN) ***276***
Bethel Coll (TN) ***288***
Butler U (IN) ***297***
California State U, Dominguez Hills (CA) ***300***
Catawba Coll (NC) ***307***
City Coll of the City U of NY (NY) ***314***
Coll of Staten Island of the City U of NY (NY) ***323***
Comm Hospital Roanoke Valley–Coll of Health Scis (VA) ***328***
Daemen Coll (NY) ***335***
Duquesne U (PA) ***346***
D'Youville Coll (NY) ***347***
East Carolina U (NC) ***347***
Elmhurst Coll (IL) ***351***
Gannon U (PA) ***365***
Gardner-Webb U (NC) ***365***
The George Washington U (DC) ***367***
Grand Valley State U (MI) ***371***
High Point U (NC) ***379***
Howard U (DC) ***382***
Idaho State U (ID) ***384***
Le Moyne Coll (NY) ***404***
Lenoir-Rhyne Coll (NC) ***405***
Long Island U, Brooklyn Campus (NY) ***409***
Louisiana State U Health Sciences Center (LA) ***410***
Marquette U (WI) ***418***
Mars Hill Coll (NC) ***418***
Marywood U (PA) ***421***
Medical Coll of Georgia (GA) ***424***
Medical U of South Carolina (SC) ***424***
Methodist Coll (NC) ***427***
Mountain State U (WV) ***437***
New York Inst of Technology (NY) ***447***
Nova Southeastern U (FL) ***455***
Pace U (NY) ***463***
Peru State Coll (NE) ***469***
Philadelphia U (PA) ***469***
Quinnipiac U (CT) ***476***
Rochester Inst of Technology (NY) ***482***
Rocky Mountain Coll (MT) ***482***
Saint Francis U (PA) ***488***
St. John's U (NY) ***490***
Saint Louis U (MO) ***492***
Saint Vincent Coll (PA) ***496***
Salem Coll (NC) ***496***
Seton Hill U (PA) ***502***
Southern Illinois U Carbondale (IL) ***509***
Springfield Coll (MA) ***514***
State U of NY Health Science Center at Brooklyn (NY) ***517***
Stony Brook U, State University of New York (NY) ***520***
Touro Coll (NY) ***529***
Union Coll (NE) ***534***
The U of Alabama at Birmingham (AL) ***537***
The U of Findlay (OH) ***545***
U of New England (ME) ***558***
U of New Mexico (NM) ***559***
The U of South Dakota (SD) ***575***
U of the Sciences in Philadelphia (PA) ***580***
U of Washington (WA) ***583***
U of Wisconsin–La Crosse (WI) ***584***
U of Wisconsin–Madison (WI) ***584***
Wagner Coll (NY) ***592***
Wake Forest U (NC) ***592***
Wichita State U (KS) ***604***

PHYSICS

Overview: Physics is the scientific study of matter and energy and the scientific laws that govern them. *Related majors:* mathematics, chemistry, many of the engineering majors. *Potential careers:* astronomer, structural or mechanical engineer, physicist, research scientist, nuclear physicist, professor or teacher. *Salary potential:* $32k-$45k.

Abilene Christian U (TX) ***260***
Acadia U (NS, Canada) ***260***
Adams State Coll (CO) ***260***
Adelphi U (NY) ***260***
Adrian Coll (MI) ***260***
Agnes Scott Coll (GA) ***261***
Alabama A&M U (AL) ***261***
Albertson Coll of Idaho (ID) ***262***
Albion Coll (MI) ***262***
Albright Coll (PA) ***263***
Alfred U (NY) ***263***
Allegheny Coll (PA) ***264***
Alma Coll (MI) ***264***
American U (DC) ***267***
The American U in Cairo(Egypt) ***267***
Amherst Coll (MA) ***268***
Anderson U (IN) ***268***
Andrews U (MI) ***269***
Angelo State U (TX) ***269***
Antioch Coll (OH) ***269***
Appalachian State U (NC) ***270***
Arizona State U (AZ) ***271***
Arkansas State U (AR) ***272***
Ashland U (OH) ***274***
Athens State U (AL) ***275***
Auburn U (AL) ***276***
Augsburg Coll (MN) ***276***
Augustana Coll (IL) ***276***
Augustana Coll (SD) ***276***
Augusta State U (GA) ***277***
Austin Coll (TX) ***277***
Austin Peay State U (TN) ***278***
Azusa Pacific U (CA) ***278***
Baker U (KS) ***280***
Baldwin-Wallace Coll (OH) ***280***
Ball State U (IN) ***280***
Bard Coll (NY) ***281***
Barnard Coll (NY) ***282***
Bates Coll (ME) ***282***
Baylor U (TX) ***283***
Belmont U (TN) ***284***
Beloit Coll (WI) ***285***
Bemidji State U (MN) ***285***
Benedict Coll (SC) ***285***
Benedictine Coll (KS) ***285***
Benedictine U (IL) ***285***
Bennington Coll (VT) ***286***
Berea Coll (KY) ***286***
Berry Coll (GA) ***287***
Bethany Coll (WV) ***287***
Bethel Coll (IN) ***288***
Bethel Coll (KS) ***288***
Bethel Coll (MN) ***288***
Bethune-Cookman Coll (FL) ***289***
Birmingham-Southern Coll (AL) ***289***
Bishop's U (QC, Canada) ***289***
Bloomsburg U of Pennsylvania (PA) ***290***
Bluffton Coll (OH) ***291***
Boston Coll (MA) ***292***
Boston U (MA) ***292***
Bowdoin Coll (ME) ***292***

PHYSICS (continued)

Bowling Green State U (OH) ***292***
Bradley U (IL) ***293***
Brandeis U (MA) ***293***
Brandon U (MB, Canada) ***293***
Bridgewater Coll (VA) ***294***
Bridgewater State Coll (MA) ***294***
Brigham Young U (UT) ***295***
Brock U (ON, Canada) ***295***
Brooklyn Coll of the City U of NY (NY) ***295***
Brown U (RI) ***296***
Bryn Mawr Coll (PA) ***297***
Bucknell U (PA) ***297***
Buena Vista U (IA) ***297***
Butler U (IN) ***297***
California Inst of Technology (CA) ***299***
California Lutheran U (CA) ***299***
California Polytechnic State U, San Luis Obispo (CA) ***300***
California State Polytechnic U, Pomona (CA) ***300***
California State U, Bakersfield (CA) ***300***
California State U, Chico (CA) ***300***
California State U, Dominguez Hills (CA) ***300***
California State U, Fresno (CA) ***301***
California State U, Fullerton (CA) ***301***
California State U, Hayward (CA) ***301***
California State U, Long Beach (CA) ***301***
California State U, Northridge (CA) ***301***
California State U, Sacramento (CA) ***301***
California State U, San Bernardino (CA) ***302***
California State U, Stanislaus (CA) ***302***
California U of Pennsylvania (PA) ***302***
Calvin Coll (MI) ***303***
Cameron U (OK) ***303***
Canisius Coll (NY) ***304***
Carleton Coll (MN) ***305***
Carleton U (ON, Canada) ***305***
Carnegie Mellon U (PA) ***305***
Carthage Coll (WI) ***306***
Case Western Reserve U (OH) ***307***
The Catholic U of America (DC) ***307***
Centenary Coll of Louisiana (LA) ***308***
Central Coll (IA) ***309***
Central Connecticut State U (CT) ***309***
Central Methodist Coll (MO) ***309***
Central Michigan U (MI) ***310***
Central Missouri State U (MO) ***310***
Central Washington U (WA) ***310***
Centre Coll (KY) ***310***
Chadron State Coll (NE) ***311***
Chatham Coll (PA) ***312***
Christian Brothers U (TN) ***313***
Christopher Newport U (VA) ***313***
Citadel, The Military Coll of South Carolina (SC) ***314***
City Coll of the City U of NY (NY) ***314***
Claremont McKenna Coll (CA) ***315***
Clarion U of Pennsylvania (PA) ***315***
Clark Atlanta U (GA) ***315***
Clarkson U (NY) ***316***
Clark U (MA) ***316***
Clemson U (SC) ***317***
Cleveland State U (OH) ***317***
Coe Coll (IA) ***318***
Colby Coll (ME) ***318***
Colgate U (NY) ***319***
Coll of Charleston (SC) ***320***
Coll of Mount Saint Vincent (NY) ***320***
The Coll of New Jersey (NJ) ***320***
The Coll of New Rochelle (NY) ***321***
Coll of Notre Dame of Maryland (MD) ***321***
Coll of Saint Benedict (MN) ***321***
Coll of St. Catherine (MN) ***321***
The Coll of Southeastern Europe, The American U of Athens(Greece) ***323***
Coll of Staten Island of the City U of NY (NY) ***323***
Coll of the Holy Cross (MA) ***323***
The Coll of William and Mary (VA) ***324***
The Coll of Wooster (OH) ***324***
The Colorado Coll (CO) ***325***
Colorado State U (CO) ***325***
Colorado State U-Pueblo (CO) ***325***
Columbia Coll (MO) ***326***
Columbia Coll (NY) ***326***
Columbia U, School of General Studies (NY) ***328***
Columbia U, School of Engineering & Applied Sci (NY) ***328***
Concordia Coll (MN) ***329***
Concordia U (QC, Canada) ***331***
Connecticut Coll (CT) ***331***
Cornell Coll (IA) ***332***
Cornell U (NY) ***333***
Covenant Coll (GA) ***333***
Creighton U (NE) ***333***
Cumberland Coll (KY) ***335***
Cumberland U (TN) ***335***
Curry Coll (MA) ***335***
Dakota State U (SD) ***335***
Dalhousie U (NS, Canada) ***336***
Dartmouth Coll (NH) ***337***
Davidson Coll (NC) ***338***
Delaware State U (DE) ***338***
Denison U (OH) ***339***
DePaul U (IL) ***339***
DePauw U (IN) ***339***
Dickinson Coll (PA) ***344***
Dillard U (LA) ***344***
Doane Coll (NE) ***344***
Dordt Coll (IA) ***345***
Drake U (IA) ***345***
Drew U (NJ) ***346***
Drury U (MO) ***346***
Duke U (NC) ***346***
Duquesne U (PA) ***346***
Earlham Coll (IN) ***347***
East Carolina U (NC) ***347***
East Central U (OK) ***347***
Eastern Illinois U (IL) ***348***
Eastern Kentucky U (KY) ***348***
Eastern Michigan U (MI) ***348***
Eastern Nazarene Coll (MA) ***348***
Eastern New Mexico U (NM) ***349***
Eastern Oregon U (OR) ***349***
Eastern Washington U (WA) ***349***
East Stroudsburg U of Pennsylvania (PA) ***349***
East Tennessee State U (TN) ***349***
Eckerd Coll (FL) ***350***
Edinboro U of Pennsylvania (PA) ***351***
Elizabeth City State U (NC) ***351***
Elizabethtown Coll (PA) ***351***
Elmhurst Coll (IL) ***351***
Elon U (NC) ***352***
Emmanuel Coll (MA) ***353***
Emory & Henry Coll (VA) ***353***
Emory U (GA) ***354***
Emporia State U (KS) ***354***
Erskine Coll (SC) ***354***
The Evergreen State Coll (WA) ***355***
Excelsior Coll (NY) ***356***
Fairfield U (CT) ***356***
Fisk U (TN) ***358***
Florida A&M U (FL) ***359***
Florida Atlantic U (FL) ***359***
Florida Inst of Technology (FL) ***360***
Florida International U (FL) ***360***
Florida Southern Coll (FL) ***361***
Florida State U (FL) ***361***
Fordham U (NY) ***362***
Fort Hays State U (KS) ***362***
Fort Lewis Coll (CO) ***362***
Francis Marion U (SC) ***363***
Franklin and Marshall Coll (PA) ***363***
Franklin Coll (IN) ***363***
Frostburg State U (MD) ***365***
Furman U (SC) ***365***
Gallaudet U (DC) ***365***
Geneva Coll (PA) ***366***
George Mason U (VA) ***366***
Georgetown Coll (KY) ***366***
Georgetown U (DC) ***366***
The George Washington U (DC) ***367***
Georgia Inst of Technology (GA) ***367***
Georgian Court Coll (NJ) ***367***
Georgia Southern U (GA) ***367***
Georgia State U (GA) ***368***
Gettysburg Coll (PA) ***368***
Gonzaga U (WA) ***369***
Gordon Coll (MA) ***370***
Goshen Coll (IN) ***370***
Goucher Coll (MD) ***370***
Grambling State U (LA) ***371***
Grand Valley State U (MI) ***371***
Greenville Coll (IL) ***373***
Grinnell Coll (IA) ***373***
Grove City Coll (PA) ***373***
Guilford Coll (NC) ***373***
Gustavus Adolphus Coll (MN) ***374***
Hamilton Coll (NY) ***374***
Hamline U (MN) ***374***
Hampden-Sydney Coll (VA) ***374***
Hampshire Coll (MA) ***375***
Hampton U (VA) ***375***
Hanover Coll (IN) ***375***
Harding U (AR) ***375***
Hardin-Simmons U (TX) ***376***
Hartwick Coll (NY) ***376***
Harvard U (MA) ***376***
Harvey Mudd Coll (CA) ***377***
Hastings Coll (NE) ***377***
Haverford Coll (PA) ***377***
Heidelberg Coll (OH) ***377***
Henderson State U (AR) ***378***
Hendrix Coll (AR) ***378***
Hillsdale Coll (MI) ***379***
Hiram Coll (OH) ***379***
Hobart and William Smith Colls (NY) ***380***
Hofstra U (NY) ***380***
Hollins U (VA) ***380***
Hope Coll (MI) ***381***
Houghton Coll (NY) ***381***
Houston Baptist U (TX) ***382***
Howard U (DC) ***382***
Humboldt State U (CA) ***382***
Hunter Coll of the City U of NY (NY) ***382***
Idaho State U (ID) ***384***
Illinois Coll (IL) ***384***
Illinois Inst of Technology (IL) ***384***
Illinois State U (IL) ***384***
Illinois Wesleyan U (IL) ***385***
Immaculata U (PA) ***385***
Indiana State U (IN) ***385***
Indiana U Bloomington (IN) ***385***
Indiana U of Pennsylvania (PA) ***386***
Indiana U–Purdue U Fort Wayne (IN) ***386***
Indiana U–Purdue U Indianapolis (IN) ***387***
Indiana U South Bend (IN) ***387***
Insto Tecno Estudios Sups Monterrey(Mexico) ***388***
Iona Coll (NY) ***390***
Iowa State U of Science and Technology (IA) ***390***
Ithaca Coll (NY) ***390***
Jackson State U (MS) ***390***
Jacksonville State U (AL) ***390***
Jacksonville U (FL) ***391***
James Madison U (VA) ***391***
John Carroll U (OH) ***392***
Johns Hopkins U (MD) ***392***
Juniata Coll (PA) ***395***
Kalamazoo Coll (MI) ***395***
Kansas State U (KS) ***396***
Keene State Coll (NH) ***396***
Kent State U (OH) ***397***
Kentucky Wesleyan Coll (KY) ***397***
Kenyon Coll (OH) ***398***
Kettering U (MI) ***398***
King Coll (TN) ***398***
Knox Coll (IL) ***399***
Kutztown U of Pennsylvania (PA) ***399***
Lafayette Coll (PA) ***400***
Lake Forest Coll (IL) ***400***
Lakehead U (ON, Canada) ***400***
Lamar U (TX) ***401***
Lane Coll (TN) ***402***
Laurentian U (ON, Canada) ***403***
Lawrence Technological U (MI) ***403***
Lawrence U (WI) ***403***
Lebanon Valley Coll (PA) ***403***
Lehigh U (PA) ***404***
Lehman Coll of the City U of NY (NY) ***404***
Le Moyne Coll (NY) ***404***
Lenoir-Rhyne Coll (NC) ***405***
Lewis & Clark Coll (OR) ***405***
Lewis U (IL) ***406***
Lincoln U (PA) ***407***
Linfield Coll (OR) ***408***
Lipscomb U (TN) ***408***
Lock Haven U of Pennsylvania (PA) ***408***
Long Island U, Brooklyn Campus (NY) ***409***
Long Island U, C.W. Post Campus (NY) ***409***
Longwood U (VA) ***409***
Loras Coll (IA) ***410***
Louisiana Coll (LA) ***410***
Louisiana State U and A&M Coll (LA) ***410***
Louisiana State U in Shreveport (LA) ***410***
Louisiana Tech U (LA) ***410***
Loyola Coll in Maryland (MD) ***411***
Loyola Marymount U (CA) ***411***
Loyola U Chicago (IL) ***411***
Loyola U New Orleans (LA) ***411***
Luther Coll (IA) ***412***
Lycoming Coll (PA) ***412***
Lynchburg Coll (VA) ***413***
Macalester Coll (MN) ***413***
MacMurray Coll (IL) ***414***
Manchester Coll (IN) ***415***
Manhattan Coll (NY) ***416***
Mansfield U of Pennsylvania (PA) ***416***
Marietta Coll (OH) ***417***
Marlboro Coll (VT) ***418***
Marquette U (WI) ***418***
Marshall U (WV) ***418***
Mary Baldwin Coll (VA) ***419***
Mary Washington Coll (VA) ***420***
Massachusetts Coll of Liberal Arts (MA) ***421***
Massachusetts Inst of Technology (MA) ***421***
McDaniel Coll (MD) ***422***
McGill U (QC, Canada) ***423***
McMaster U (ON, Canada) ***423***
McMurry U (TX) ***423***
McNeese State U (LA) ***423***
Memorial U of Newfoundland (NF, Canada) ***424***
Mercer U (GA) ***425***
Mercyhurst Coll (PA) ***425***
Merrimack Coll (MA) ***426***
Mesa State Coll (CO) ***426***
Messiah Coll (PA) ***426***
Metropolitan State Coll of Denver (CO) ***427***
Miami U (OH) ***428***
Michigan State U (MI) ***428***
Michigan Technological U (MI) ***428***
MidAmerica Nazarene U (KS) ***428***
Middlebury Coll (VT) ***429***
Middle Tennessee State U (TN) ***429***
Midwestern State U (TX) ***430***
Millersville U of Pennsylvania (PA) ***430***
Millikin U (IL) ***430***
Millsaps Coll (MS) ***431***
Minnesota State U, Mankato (MN) ***431***
Minnesota State U, Moorhead (MN) ***432***
Minot State U (ND) ***432***
Mississippi Coll (MS) ***432***
Mississippi State U (MS) ***432***
Missouri Southern State Coll (MO) ***433***
Monmouth Coll (IL) ***434***
Montana State U–Bozeman (MT) ***434***
Montclair State U (NJ) ***435***
Moravian Coll (PA) ***436***
Morehead State U (KY) ***436***
Morehouse Coll (GA) ***436***
Morgan State U (MD) ***436***
Morningside Coll (IA) ***437***
Mount Allison U (NB, Canada) ***437***
Mount Holyoke Coll (MA) ***438***
Mount Union Coll (OH) ***440***
Muhlenberg Coll (PA) ***440***
Murray State U (KY) ***440***
Muskingum Coll (OH) ***441***
Nebraska Wesleyan U (NE) ***443***
New Coll of Florida (FL) ***444***
New Jersey City U (NJ) ***445***
New Jersey Inst of Technology (NJ) ***445***
New Mexico Inst of Mining and Technology (NM) ***446***
New Mexico State U (NM) ***446***
New York Inst of Technology (NY) ***447***
New York U (NY) ***447***
Norfolk State U (VA) ***448***
North Carolina Ag and Tech State U (NC) ***448***
North Carolina Central U (NC) ***448***
North Carolina State U (NC) ***449***
North Central Coll (IL) ***449***
North Dakota State U (ND) ***449***
Northeastern Illinois U (IL) ***450***
Northeastern State U (OK) ***450***
Northeastern U (MA) ***450***
Northern Arizona U (AZ) ***450***
Northern Illinois U (IL) ***450***
Northern Kentucky U (KY) ***451***
Northern Michigan U (MI) ***451***
North Georgia Coll & State U (GA) ***451***
North Park U (IL) ***452***
Northwestern State U of Louisiana (LA) ***453***
Northwestern U (IL) ***453***
Northwest Missouri State U (MO) ***454***
Northwest Nazarene U (ID) ***454***
Norwich U (VT) ***455***
Oakland U (MI) ***456***
Oberlin Coll (OH) ***456***
Occidental Coll (CA) ***457***
Oglethorpe U (GA) ***457***
Ohio Northern U (OH) ***457***
The Ohio State U (OH) ***457***
Ohio U (OH) ***458***
Ohio Wesleyan U (OH) ***459***
Okanagan U Coll (BC, Canada) ***459***
Oklahoma Baptist U (OK) ***459***
Oklahoma City U (OK) ***460***

Oklahoma State U (OK) **460**
Old Dominion U (VA) **460**
Oral Roberts U (OK) **461**
Oregon State U (OR) **462**
Otterbein Coll (OH) **462**
Ouachita Baptist U (AR) **462**
Pace U (NY) **463**
Pacific Lutheran U (WA) **463**
Pacific Union Coll (CA) **464**
Pacific U (OR) **464**
Penn State U at Erie, The Behrend Coll (PA) **467**
Penn State U Univ Park Campus (PA) **468**
Pittsburg State U (KS) **470**
Pitzer Coll (CA) **471**
Plattsburgh State U of NY (NY) **471**
Point Loma Nazarene U (CA) **471**
Polytechnic U, Brooklyn Campus (NY) **472**
Pomona Coll (CA) **472**
Pontifical Catholic U of Puerto Rico (PR) **472**
Portland State U (OR) **472**
Prairie View A&M U (TX) **473**
Presbyterian Coll (SC) **473**
Princeton U (NJ) **474**
Principia Coll (IL) **474**
Purdue U (IN) **475**
Purdue U Calumet (IN) **475**
Queens Coll of the City U of NY (NY) **475**
Queen's U at Kingston (ON, Canada) **476**
Ramapo Coll of New Jersey (NJ) **477**
Randolph-Macon Coll (VA) **477**
Randolph-Macon Woman's Coll (VA) **477**
Reed Coll (OR) **477**
Rensselaer Polytechnic Inst (NY) **478**
Rhode Island Coll (RI) **479**
Rhodes Coll (TN) **479**
Rice U (TX) **479**
The Richard Stockton Coll of New Jersey (NJ) **479**
Rider U (NJ) **480**
Ripon Coll (WI) **480**
Roanoke Coll (VA) **481**
Roberts Wesleyan Coll (NY) **481**
Rochester Inst of Technology (NY) **482**
Rockhurst U (MO) **482**
Rollins Coll (FL) **483**
Rose-Hulman Inst of Technology (IN) **484**
Rutgers, The State U of New Jersey, Camden (NJ) **485**
Rutgers, The State U of New Jersey, Newark (NJ) **485**
Rutgers, The State U of New Jersey, New Brunswick (NJ) **485**
Saginaw Valley State U (MI) **486**
St. Ambrose U (IA) **486**
St. Bonaventure U (NY) **487**
St. Cloud State U (MN) **488**
St. Francis Xavier U (NS, Canada) **489**
St. John Fisher Coll (NY) **489**
Saint John's U (MN) **490**
St. John's U (NY) **490**
Saint Joseph's U (PA) **491**
St. Lawrence U (NY) **491**
Saint Louis U (MO) **492**
Saint Mary's Coll of California (CA) **494**
St. Mary's Coll of Maryland (MD) **494**
Saint Mary's U (NS, Canada) **494**
St. Mary's U of San Antonio (TX) **494**
Saint Michael's Coll (VT) **494**
St. Norbert Coll (WI) **495**
St. Olaf Coll (MN) **495**
Saint Peter's Coll (NJ) **495**
Saint Vincent Coll (PA) **496**
Salisbury U (MD) **497**
Samford U (AL) **497**
Sam Houston State U (TX) **497**
San Diego State U (CA) **498**
San Francisco State U (CA) **498**
San Jose State U (CA) **499**
Santa Clara U (CA) **499**
Sarah Lawrence Coll (NY) **499**
Scripps Coll (CA) **501**
Seattle Pacific U (WA) **501**
Seattle U (WA) **501**
Seton Hall U (NJ) **502**
Seton Hill U (PA) **502**
Shaw U (NC) **502**
Shippensburg U of Pennsylvania (PA) **503**
Siena Coll (NY) **504**
Simon Fraser U (BC, Canada) **505**
Simon's Rock Coll of Bard (MA) **505**
Skidmore Coll (NY) **506**
Slippery Rock U of Pennsylvania (PA) **506**
Smith Coll (MA) **506**
Sonoma State U (CA) **506**
South Carolina State U (SC) **506**
South Dakota School of Mines and Technology (SD) **507**
South Dakota State U (SD) **507**
Southeastern Louisiana U (LA) **508**
Southeastern Oklahoma State U (OK) **508**
Southeast Missouri State U (MO) **508**
Southern Adventist U (TN) **508**
Southern Connecticut State U (CT) **509**
Southern Illinois U Carbondale (IL) **509**
Southern Illinois U Edwardsville (IL) **509**
Southern Methodist U (TX) **510**
Southern Nazarene U (OK) **510**
Southern Oregon U (OR) **510**
Southern Polytechnic State U (GA) **511**
Southern U and A&M Coll (LA) **511**
Southwestern Coll (KS) **512**
Southwestern Oklahoma State U (OK) **512**
Southwestern U (TX) **513**
Southwest Missouri State U (MO) **513**
Southwest Texas State U (TX) **513**
Spelman Coll (GA) **514**
Stanford U (CA) **514**
State U of NY at Albany (NY) **514**
State U of NY at Binghamton (NY) **515**
State U of NY at New Paltz (NY) **515**
State U of NY at Oswego (NY) **515**
State U of NY Coll at Brockport (NY) **515**
State U of NY Coll at Buffalo (NY) **516**
State U of NY Coll at Cortland (NY) **516**
State U of NY Coll at Fredonia (NY) **516**
State U of NY Coll at Geneseo (NY) **516**
State U of NY Coll at Oneonta (NY) **517**
State U of NY Coll at Potsdam (NY) **517**
State U of West Georgia (GA) **518**
Stephen F. Austin State U (TX) **518**
Stetson U (FL) **519**
Stevens Inst of Technology (NJ) **519**
Stony Brook U, State University of New York (NY) **520**
Suffolk U (MA) **520**
Susquehanna U (PA) **521**
Swarthmore Coll (PA) **521**
Sweet Briar Coll (VA) **521**
Syracuse U (NY) **521**
Talladega Coll (AL) **522**
Tarleton State U (TX) **522**
Taylor U (IN) **523**
Temple U (PA) **523**
Tennessee State U (TN) **523**
Tennessee Technological U (TN) **524**
Texas A&M U (TX) **524**
Texas A&M U–Commerce (TX) **525**
Texas A&M U–Kingsville (TX) **525**
Texas Christian U (TX) **526**
Texas Lutheran U (TX) **526**
Texas Southern U (TX) **526**
Texas Tech U (TX) **526**
Thiel Coll (PA) **527**
Thomas Edison State Coll (NJ) **527**
Thomas More Coll (KY) **528**
Towson U (MD) **529**
Transylvania U (KY) **529**
Trent U (ON, Canada) **529**
Trevecca Nazarene U (TN) **529**
Trinity Coll (CT) **530**
Trinity U (TX) **531**
Truman State U (MO) **532**
Tufts U (MA) **533**
Tulane U (LA) **533**
Tuskegee U (AL) **533**
Union Coll (KY) **533**
Union Coll (NE) **534**
Union Coll (NY) **534**
Union U (TN) **534**
United States Air Force Academy (CO) **534**
United States Military Academy (NY) **535**
United States Naval Academy (MD) **535**
Université de Sherbrooke (QC, Canada) **536**
U du Québec à Trois-Rivières (QC, Canada) **536**
Université Laval (QC, Canada) **536**
U at Buffalo, The State University of New York (NY) **536**
U Coll of the Cariboo (BC, Canada) **537**
The U of Akron (OH) **537**
The U of Alabama (AL) **537**
The U of Alabama at Birmingham (AL) **537**
The U of Alabama in Huntsville (AL) **537**
U of Alaska Fairbanks (AK) **538**
U of Alberta (AB, Canada) **538**
The U of Arizona (AZ) **538**
U of Arkansas (AR) **539**
U of Arkansas at Little Rock (AR) **539**
The U of British Columbia (BC, Canada) **540**
U of Calgary (AB, Canada) **540**
U of Calif, Berkeley (CA) **540**
U of Calif, Davis (CA) **540**
U of Calif, Irvine (CA) **541**
U of Calif, Los Angeles (CA) **541**
U of Calif, Riverside (CA) **541**
U of Calif, San Diego (CA) **541**
U of Calif, Santa Barbara (CA) **541**
U of Calif, Santa Cruz (CA) **542**
U of Central Arkansas (AR) **542**
U of Central Florida (FL) **542**
U of Central Oklahoma (OK) **542**
U of Chicago (IL) **542**
U of Cincinnati (OH) **543**
U of Colorado at Boulder (CO) **543**
U of Colorado at Colorado Springs (CO) **543**
U of Colorado at Denver (CO) **543**
U of Connecticut (CT) **544**
U of Dallas (TX) **544**
U of Dayton (OH) **544**
U of Delaware (DE) **544**
U of Denver (CO) **544**
U of Evansville (IN) **545**
U of Florida (FL) **545**
U of Georgia (GA) **545**
U of Guelph (ON, Canada) **546**
U of Hartford (CT) **546**
U of Hawaii at Hilo (HI) **546**
U of Hawaii at Manoa (HI) **546**
U of Houston (TX) **547**
U of Houston–Downtown (TX) **547**
U of Idaho (ID) **547**
U of Illinois at Chicago (IL) **547**
U of Illinois at Urbana–Champaign (IL) **548**
U of Indianapolis (IN) **548**
The U of Iowa (IA) **548**
U of Kansas (KS) **549**
U of Kentucky (KY) **549**
U of King's Coll (NS, Canada) **549**
U of La Verne (CA) **549**
The U of Lethbridge (AB, Canada) **549**
U of Louisiana at Lafayette (LA) **550**
U of Louisville (KY) **550**
U of Maine (ME) **550**
U of Manitoba (MB, Canada) **551**
U of Maryland, Baltimore County (MD) **552**
U of Maryland, Coll Park (MD) **552**
U of Massachusetts Amherst (MA) **552**
U of Massachusetts Boston (MA) **553**
U of Massachusetts Dartmouth (MA) **553**
U of Massachusetts Lowell (MA) **553**
The U of Memphis (TN) **553**
U of Miami (FL) **553**
U of Michigan (MI) **554**
U of Michigan–Dearborn (MI) **554**
U of Michigan–Flint (MI) **554**
U of Minnesota, Duluth (MN) **554**
U of Minnesota, Morris (MN) **555**
U of Minnesota, Twin Cities Campus (MN) **555**
U of Mississippi (MS) **555**
U of Missouri–Columbia (MO) **555**
U of Missouri–Kansas City (MO) **555**
U of Missouri–Rolla (MO) **556**
U of Missouri–St. Louis (MO) **556**
The U of Montana–Missoula (MT) **556**
U of Nebraska at Kearney (NE) **557**
U of Nebraska at Omaha (NE) **557**
U of Nebraska–Lincoln (NE) **557**
U of Nevada, Las Vegas (NV) **558**
U of Nevada, Reno (NV) **558**
U of New Brunswick Fredericton (NB, Canada) **558**
U of New Hampshire (NH) **558**
U of New Mexico (NM) **559**
U of New Orleans (LA) **559**
U of North Alabama (AL) **559**
The U of North Carolina at Asheville (NC) **559**
The U of North Carolina at Chapel Hill (NC) **560**
The U of North Carolina at Charlotte (NC) **560**
The U of North Carolina at Greensboro (NC) **560**
The U of North Carolina at Wilmington (NC) **561**
U of North Dakota (ND) **561**
U of Northern Colorado (CO) **561**
U of Northern Iowa (IA) **561**
U of North Florida (FL) **561**
U of North Texas (TX) **562**
U of Notre Dame (IN) **562**
U of Oklahoma (OK) **562**
U of Oregon (OR) **562**
U of Ottawa (ON, Canada) **563**
U of Pennsylvania (PA) **563**
U of Pittsburgh (PA) **569**
U of Portland (OR) **570**
U of Prince Edward Island (PE, Canada) **570**
U of Puerto Rico, Humacao U Coll (PR) **570**
U of Puget Sound (WA) **571**
U of Redlands (CA) **572**
U of Regina (SK, Canada) **572**
U of Rhode Island (RI) **572**
U of Richmond (VA) **572**
U of Rochester (NY) **573**
U of St. Thomas (MN) **573**
U of San Diego (CA) **574**
U of San Francisco (CA) **574**
U of Saskatchewan (SK, Canada) **574**
U of Science and Arts of Oklahoma (OK) **574**
The U of Scranton (PA) **574**
U of South Alabama (AL) **575**
U of South Carolina (SC) **575**
The U of South Dakota (SD) **575**
U of Southern California (CA) **576**
U of Southern Maine (ME) **576**
U of Southern Mississippi (MS) **576**
U of South Florida (FL) **576**
The U of Tennessee (TN) **577**
The U of Tennessee at Chattanooga (TN) **577**
The U of Texas at Arlington (TX) **577**
The U of Texas at Austin (TX) **578**
The U of Texas at Dallas (TX) **578**
The U of Texas at El Paso (TX) **578**
The U of Texas at San Antonio (TX) **578**
The U of Texas–Pan American (TX) **579**
U of the District of Columbia (DC) **580**
U of the Ozarks (AR) **580**
U of the Pacific (CA) **580**
U of the South (TN) **581**
U of Toledo (OH) **581**
U of Toronto (ON, Canada) **581**
U of Tulsa (OK) **581**
U of Utah (UT) **582**
U of Vermont (VT) **582**
U of Victoria (BC, Canada) **582**
U of Virginia (VA) **582**
U of Washington (WA) **583**
U of Waterloo (ON, Canada) **583**
The U of Western Ontario (ON, Canada) **583**
U of West Florida (FL) **583**
U of Windsor (ON, Canada) **584**
U of Wisconsin–Eau Claire (WI) **584**
U of Wisconsin–La Crosse (WI) **584**
U of Wisconsin–Madison (WI) **584**
U of Wisconsin–Milwaukee (WI) **585**
U of Wisconsin–Oshkosh (WI) **585**
U of Wisconsin–Parkside (WI) **585**
U of Wisconsin–River Falls (WI) **585**
U of Wisconsin–Stevens Point (WI) **585**
U of Wisconsin–Whitewater (WI) **586**
U of Wyoming (WY) **586**
Ursinus Coll (PA) **587**
Utah State U (UT) **587**
Utica Coll (NY) **588**
Valdosta State U (GA) **588**
Valparaiso U (IN) **588**
Vanderbilt U (TN) **588**
Vassar Coll (NY) **589**
Villanova U (PA) **590**
Virginia Commonwealth U (VA) **590**
Virginia Military Inst (VA) **591**
Virginia Polytechnic Inst and State U (VA) **591**
Virginia State U (VA) **591**
Wabash Coll (IN) **592**
Wagner Coll (NY) **592**
Wake Forest U (NC) **592**
Walla Walla Coll (WA) **593**
Wartburg Coll (IA) **594**
Washington & Jefferson Coll (PA) **594**
Washington and Lee U (VA) **594**
Washington Coll (MD) **594**
Washington State U (WA) **595**
Washington U in St. Louis (MO) **595**
Wayne State U (MI) **596**
Weber State U (UT) **596**
Wellesley Coll (MA) **597**
Wells Coll (NY) **597**
Wesleyan Coll (GA) **597**

PHYSICS (continued)

Wesleyan U (CT) ***597***
West Chester U of Pennsylvania (PA) ***598***
Western Illinois U (IL) ***599***
Western Kentucky U (KY) ***599***
Western Michigan U (MI) ***599***
Western State Coll of Colorado (CO) ***600***
Western Washington U (WA) ***600***
Westminster Coll (MO) ***601***
Westminster Coll (PA) ***601***
Westminster Coll (UT) ***601***
Westmont Coll (CA) ***602***
West Texas A&M U (TX) ***602***
West Virginia U (WV) ***602***
West Virginia Wesleyan Coll (WV) ***603***
Wheaton Coll (IL) ***603***
Wheaton Coll (MA) ***603***
Wheeling Jesuit U (WV) ***603***
Whitman Coll (WA) ***604***
Whittier Coll (CA) ***604***
Whitworth Coll (WA) ***604***
Wichita State U (KS) ***604***
Widener U (PA) ***604***
Wiley Coll (TX) ***605***
Willamette U (OR) ***605***
William Jewell Coll (MO) ***606***
Williams Coll (MA) ***606***
Winona State U (MN) ***608***
Wittenberg U (OH) ***608***
Wofford Coll (SC) ***609***
Worcester Polytechnic Inst (MA) ***609***
Wright State U (OH) ***609***
Xavier U (OH) ***610***
Xavier U of Louisiana (LA) ***610***
Yale U (CT) ***610***
York Coll of the City U of New York (NY) ***611***
York U (ON, Canada) ***611***
Youngstown State U (OH) ***611***

PHYSICS EDUCATION

Overview: This major prepares undergraduates to teach physics and physics-related courses at various educational levels. *Related majors:* physics, nuclear physics, mathematics, fluid and thermal sciences. *Potential careers:* physics teacher, science museum curator. *Salary potential:* $23k-$28k.

Abilene Christian U (TX) ***260***
Appalachian State U (NC) ***270***
Arkansas State U (AR) ***272***
Baylor U (TX) ***283***
Berry Coll (GA) ***287***
Bethune-Cookman Coll (FL) ***289***
Bowling Green State U (OH) ***292***
Bridgewater Coll (VA) ***294***
Brigham Young U (UT) ***295***
Canisius Coll (NY) ***304***
Central Methodist Coll (MO) ***309***
Central Michigan U (MI) ***310***
Central Missouri State U (MO) ***310***
Chadron State Coll (NE) ***311***
Christian Brothers U (TN) ***313***
The Coll of New Jersey (NJ) ***320***
Colorado State U (CO) ***325***
Concordia Coll (MN) ***329***
Concordia U (NE) ***330***
Connecticut Coll (CT) ***331***
Duquesne U (PA) ***346***
Eastern Michigan U (MI) ***348***
Elmhurst Coll (IL) ***351***
Florida Inst of Technology (FL) ***360***
Georgia Southern U (GA) ***367***
Greenville Coll (IL) ***373***
Gustavus Adolphus Coll (MN) ***374***
Hardin-Simmons U (TX) ***376***
Hastings Coll (NE) ***377***
Henderson State U (AR) ***378***
Hofstra U (NY) ***380***
Indiana U Bloomington (IN) ***385***
Indiana U–Purdue U Fort Wayne (IN) ***386***
Indiana U South Bend (IN) ***387***
Ithaca Coll (NY) ***390***
Juniata Coll (PA) ***395***
King Coll (TN) ***398***
Louisiana State U in Shreveport (LA) ***410***
Luther Coll (IA) ***412***
Malone Coll (OH) ***415***
Mansfield U of Pennsylvania (PA) ***416***
Maryville Coll (TN) ***420***
McGill U (QC, Canada) ***423***
Minot State U (ND) ***432***
New York Inst of Technology (NY) ***447***
New York U (NY) ***447***
North Carolina Central U (NC) ***448***
North Dakota State U (ND) ***449***
Northern Arizona U (AZ) ***450***
Pace U (NY) ***463***
St. Ambrose U (IA) ***486***
St. John's U (NY) ***490***
Saint Mary's U of Minnesota (MN) ***494***
Saint Vincent Coll (PA) ***496***
Seton Hill U (PA) ***502***
Southern Arkansas U–Magnolia (AR) ***509***
Southwest Missouri State U (MO) ***513***
State U of NY Coll at Potsdam (NY) ***517***
State U of West Georgia (GA) ***518***
Union Coll (NE) ***534***
The U of Arizona (AZ) ***538***
U of Calif, San Diego (CA) ***541***
U of Delaware (DE) ***544***
U of Illinois at Chicago (IL) ***547***
U of Nebraska–Lincoln (NE) ***557***
The U of North Carolina at Wilmington (NC) ***561***
U of North Texas (TX) ***562***
U of Puerto Rico, Cayey U Coll (PR) ***571***
U of Rio Grande (OH) ***572***
U of Utah (UT) ***582***
U of Waterloo (ON, Canada) ***583***
U of Windsor (ON, Canada) ***584***
U of Wisconsin–River Falls (WI) ***585***
Utah State U (UT) ***587***
Utica Coll (NY) ***588***
Washington U in St. Louis (MO) ***595***
Weber State U (UT) ***596***
Wheeling Jesuit U (WV) ***603***
Xavier U (OH) ***610***
York U (ON, Canada) ***611***
Youngstown State U (OH) ***611***

PHYSICS RELATED

Information can be found under this major's main heading.

Angelo State U (TX) ***269***
Drexel U (PA) ***346***
Northern Arizona U (AZ) ***450***
Ohio U (OH) ***458***
Rutgers, The State U of New Jersey, Newark (NJ) ***485***
U of Alaska Fairbanks (AK) ***538***
U of Miami (FL) ***553***
U of Nevada, Las Vegas (NV) ***558***
U of Notre Dame (IN) ***562***

PHYSIOLOGICAL PSYCHOLOGY/ PSYCHOBIOLOGY

Overview: This branch of psychology examines the biological bases for certain psychological behaviors and functioning and their applications to experimental and therapeutic issues. *Related majors:* neuroscience, biochemistry, biophysics, physiology, pharmacology. *Potential careers:* psychologist or psychiatrist, pharmaceutical scientist, physician, drug and alcohol counselor, professor. *Salary potential:* $25k-$40k.

Albright Coll (PA) ***263***
Arcadia U (PA) ***271***
Averett U (VA) ***278***
Barnard Coll (NY) ***282***
Baylor U (TX) ***283***
Centre Coll (KY) ***310***
Chatham Coll (PA) ***312***
Claremont McKenna Coll (CA) ***315***
Coll of Notre Dame of Maryland (MD) ***321***
Fayetteville State U (NC) ***357***
Florida Atlantic U (FL) ***359***
Grand Valley State U (MI) ***371***
Hamilton Coll (NY) ***374***
Hampshire Coll (MA) ***375***
Harvard U (MA) ***376***
Hiram Coll (OH) ***379***
Holy Family U (PA) ***380***
Hope International U (CA) ***381***
Johns Hopkins U (MD) ***392***
La Sierra U (CA) ***403***
Lebanon Valley Coll (PA) ***403***
Lincoln U (PA) ***407***
Long Island U, Southampton Coll (NY) ***409***
Long Island U, Southampton Coll, Friends World Program (NY) ***409***
Luther Coll (IA) ***412***
Lynchburg Coll (VA) ***413***
McGill U (QC, Canada) ***423***
Mount Allison U (NB, Canada) ***437***
Oberlin Coll (OH) ***456***
Occidental Coll (CA) ***457***
Quinnipiac U (CT) ***476***
Ripon Coll (WI) ***480***
Scripps Coll (CA) ***501***
Simmons Coll (MA) ***504***
State U of NY at Binghamton (NY) ***515***
State U of NY at New Paltz (NY) ***515***
Swarthmore Coll (PA) ***521***
U of Calif, Los Angeles (CA) ***541***
U of Calif, Riverside (CA) ***541***
U of Calif, Santa Cruz (CA) ***542***
U of Evansville (IN) ***545***
U of Miami (FL) ***553***
U of New Brunswick Fredericton (NB, Canada) ***558***
U of New England (ME) ***558***
U of Pennsylvania (PA) ***563***
U of Southern California (CA) ***576***
Vassar Coll (NY) ***589***
Wagner Coll (NY) ***592***
Washington Coll (MD) ***594***
Westminster Coll (PA) ***601***
Wheaton Coll (MA) ***603***
Wilson Coll (PA) ***607***
Wittenberg U (OH) ***608***
York Coll (NE) ***610***

PHYSIOLOGY

Overview: Students who choose this major will study the science of cell-to-cell communication and dynamics (including function, morphology, and regulation) in vertebrate and invertabrate animals. *Related majors:* cell biology, anatomy, biochemistry, medical physiology. *Potential careers:* physician, research scientist, pathologist, physical therapist. *Salary potential:* $30k-$45k.

Boston U (MA) ***292***
California State U, Fresno (CA) ***301***
California State U, Long Beach (CA) ***301***
Cornell U (NY) ***333***
Florida State U (FL) ***361***
Hampshire Coll (MA) ***375***
McGill U (QC, Canada) ***423***
Michigan State U (MI) ***428***
Minnesota State U, Mankato (MN) ***431***
Northern Michigan U (MI) ***451***
Okanagan U Coll (BC, Canada) ***459***
Queen's U at Kingston (ON, Canada) ***476***
Rutgers, The State U of New Jersey, New Brunswick (NJ) ***485***
St. Cloud State U (MN) ***488***
San Francisco State U (CA) ***498***
San Jose State U (CA) ***499***
Sonoma State U (CA) ***506***
Southern Illinois U Carbondale (IL) ***509***
Southwest Texas State U (TX) ***513***
The U of Akron (OH) ***537***
U of Alberta (AB, Canada) ***538***
The U of Arizona (AZ) ***538***
U of Calif, Davis (CA) ***540***
U of Calif, San Diego (CA) ***541***
U of Calif, Santa Barbara (CA) ***541***
U of Connecticut (CT) ***544***
U of Great Falls (MT) ***545***
U of Hawaii at Manoa (HI) ***546***
U of Illinois at Urbana–Champaign (IL) ***548***
U of Minnesota, Twin Cities Campus (MN) ***555***
U of New Brunswick Fredericton (NB, Canada) ***558***
U of Ottawa (ON, Canada) ***563***
U of Saskatchewan (SK, Canada) ***574***
U of Toronto (ON, Canada) ***581***
The U of Western Ontario (ON, Canada) ***583***
Utah State U (UT) ***587***

PLANT BREEDING

Overview: Students who choose this major will learn about the application of genetics and genetic engineering for development of new plant varieties and the improvement of agricultural plant populations. *Related majors:* agronomy, genetics and genetic engineering, biotechnology, plant sciences. *Potential careers:* geneticist, agronomist, ecologist, biotechnology researcher. *Salary potential:* $25k-$50k.

Brigham Young U (UT) ***295***
Cornell U (NY) ***333***
North Dakota State U (ND) ***449***

PLANT PATHOLOGY

Overview: This major teaches students about the science of plant health and disease and includes instruction on controlling plant diseases. *Related majors:* botany, cell biology, plant sciences, plant breeding/genetics, plant protection. *Potential careers:* research scientist, botanist, agricultural company representative, environmental biologist, ecologist. *Salary potential:* $28k-$40k.

Cornell U (NY) ***333***
Michigan State U (MI) ***428***
State U of NY Coll of Environ Sci and Forestry (NY) ***517***
U of Florida (FL) ***545***
U of Hawaii at Manoa (HI) ***546***

PLANT PHYSIOLOGY

Overview: Students learn about plant internal dynamics and systems, plant-environment interactions, and the life cycles and processes of plants. *Related majors:* plant science, plant genetics, botany, cell biology, ecology. *Potential careers:* research scientist, botanist, ecologist, farm manager. *Salary potential:* $25k-$35k.

Florida State U (FL) ***361***
State U of NY Coll of Environ Sci and Forestry (NY) ***517***
U of Hawaii at Manoa (HI) ***546***

PLANT PROTECTION

Overview: Students will learn the principles behind the control of animal, pest, and weed infestations on domesticated plant populations and agricultural crops. *Related majors:* entomology, plant science, animal sciences, environmental toxicology. *Potential career:* exterminator, biochemist, environmental scientist, ecologist. *Salary potential:* $25k-$35k.

California State Polytechnic U, Pomona (CA) ***300***
Colorado State U (CO) ***325***
Florida A&M U (FL) ***359***
Iowa State U of Science and Technology (IA) ***390***
Mississippi State U (MS) ***432***
North Dakota State U (ND) ***449***
State U of NY Coll of Environ Sci and Forestry (NY) ***517***
Texas Tech U (TX) ***526***
U of Arkansas (AR) ***539***
U of Delaware (DE) ***544***
U of Georgia (GA) ***545***
U of Nebraska–Lincoln (NE) ***557***
The U of Tennessee (TN) ***577***
West Texas A&M U (TX) ***602***

PLANT SCIENCES

Overview: Undergraduates of this major will study the science behind cultivation, breeding, and production of agricultural plants and the production, processing, and distribution of agricultural plant products. *Related majors:* agricultural and food products processing, farm management, agricultural production, crop production. *Potential careers:* farm manager, food product engineer, biochemist, nutritionist. *Salary potential:* $25k-$50k.

Arkansas State U (AR) ***272***
California State U, Fresno (CA) ***301***
Cornell U (NY) ***333***
Louisiana State U and A&M Coll (LA) ***410***
Louisiana Tech U (LA) ***410***
McGill U (QC, Canada) ***423***
Middle Tennessee State U (TN) ***429***
Montana State U–Bozeman (MT) ***434***
The Ohio State U (OH) ***457***
Oklahoma State U (OK) ***460***
Southern Illinois U Carbondale (IL) ***509***
State U of NY Coll of A&T at Cobleskill (NY) ***517***
State U of NY Coll of Environ Sci and Forestry (NY) ***517***
Texas A&M U (TX) ***524***
Tuskegee U (AL) ***533***
The U of Arizona (AZ) ***538***
U of Calif, Los Angeles (CA) ***541***
U of Calif, Santa Cruz (CA) ***542***
U of Florida (FL) ***545***
U of Idaho (ID) ***547***
U of Maryland, Coll Park (MD) ***552***
U of Massachusetts Amherst (MA) ***552***
U of Minnesota, Twin Cities Campus (MN) ***555***
U of Missouri–Columbia (MO) ***555***
U of Saskatchewan (SK, Canada) ***574***
The U of Tennessee (TN) ***577***
U of Vermont (VT) ***582***
The U of Western Ontario (ON, Canada) ***583***
Utah State U (UT) ***587***
Washington State U (WA) ***595***
West Virginia U (WV) ***602***

PLANT SCIENCES RELATED

Information can be found under this major's main heading.

Utah State U (UT) ***587***
West Texas A&M U (TX) ***602***

PLASTICS ENGINEERING

Overview: Students who choose this major learn the science behind creating synthetic molecular compounds such as plastic and nylon and their various industrial uses. *Related majors:* polymer chemistry, fluid and thermal sciences, chemical engineering, textile sciences engineering. *Potential careers:* chemical engineer or chemist, manufacturer, research scientist. *Salary potential:* $40-$55k.

Ball State U (IN) ***280***
Case Western Reserve U (OH) ***307***
Eastern Michigan U (MI) ***348***
Ferris State U (MI) ***358***
Kettering U (MI) ***398***
North Dakota State U (ND) ***449***
Penn State U at Erie, The Behrend Coll (PA) ***467***
The U of Akron (OH) ***537***
U of Massachusetts Lowell (MA) ***553***
U of Toronto (ON, Canada) ***581***
Winona State U (MN) ***608***

PLASTICS TECHNOLOGY

Overview: This major teaches students the scientific knowledge and skills necessary to work on the development and use of industrial plastics. *Related majors:* polymer/plastics engineering, polymer chemistry, purchasing, procurement and contracts management, general distribution operations, industrial design. *Potential careers:* chemical engineer, salesperson, research scientist, machinist. *Salary potential:* $25k-$38k.

Ball State U (IN) ***280***
Central Connecticut State U (CT) ***309***
Eastern Michigan U (MI) ***348***
Ferris State U (MI) ***358***
Pennsylvania Coll of Technology (PA) ***467***
Pittsburg State U (KS) ***470***
Shawnee State U (OH) ***502***
Western Washington U (WA) ***600***

PLAY/SCREENWRITING

Overview: This major teaches students the principles and techniques for writing creative plays and scripts for either the theater or film. *Related majors:* acting and directing, drama/theater arts, drama/theater literature, history and criticism, creative writing. *Potential careers:* playwright, scriptwriter, writer, editor, agent. *Salary potential:* $18k-$28k.

Bard Coll (NY) ***281***
Columbia Coll Chicago (IL) ***327***
Concordia U (QC, Canada) ***331***
DePaul U (IL) ***339***
Drexel U (PA) ***346***
Emerson Coll (MA) ***353***
Metropolitan State U (MN) ***427***
New York U (NY) ***447***
Ohio U (OH) ***458***
Purchase Coll, State U of NY (NY) ***475***
Simon's Rock Coll of Bard (MA) ***505***
U of Michigan (MI) ***554***
U of Southern California (CA) ***576***
York U (ON, Canada) ***611***

POLITICAL SCIENCE

Overview: This general major examines a wide range of political institutions and organizations and their behavior. *Related majors:* law and legal studies, philosophy, history, economics, sociology. *Potential careers:* politician or political aide, diplomatic corps, lobbyist, journalist, professor. *Salary potential:* $25k-$35k.

Abilene Christian U (TX) ***260***
Acadia U (NS, Canada) ***260***
Adams State Coll (CO) ***260***
Adelphi U (NY) ***260***
Adrian Coll (MI) ***260***
Agnes Scott Coll (GA) ***261***
Alabama A&M U (AL) ***261***
Alabama State U (AL) ***261***
Albany State U (GA) ***262***
Albertson Coll of Idaho (ID) ***262***
Albertus Magnus Coll (CT) ***262***
Albion Coll (MI) ***262***
Albright Coll (PA) ***263***
Alcorn State U (MS) ***263***
Alderson-Broaddus Coll (WV) ***263***
Alfred U (NY) ***263***
Allegheny Coll (PA) ***264***
Alliant International U (CA) ***264***
Alma Coll (MI) ***264***
Alvernia Coll (PA) ***265***
American International Coll (MA) ***267***
American U (DC) ***267***
The American U in Cairo(Egypt) ***267***
Amherst Coll (MA) ***268***
Anderson U (IN) ***268***
Andrews U (MI) ***269***
Angelo State U (TX) ***269***
Anna Maria Coll (MA) ***269***
Antioch Coll (OH) ***269***
Appalachian State U (NC) ***270***
Aquinas Coll (MI) ***270***
Arcadia U (PA) ***271***
Arizona State U (AZ) ***271***
Arizona State U West (AZ) ***272***
Arkansas State U (AR) ***272***
Armstrong Atlantic State U (GA) ***273***
Ashland U (OH) ***274***
Assumption Coll (MA) ***275***
Athens State U (AL) ***275***
Auburn U (AL) ***276***
Auburn U Montgomery (AL) ***276***
Augsburg Coll (MN) ***276***
Augustana Coll (IL) ***276***
Augustana Coll (SD) ***276***
Augusta State U (GA) ***277***
Aurora U (IL) ***277***
Austin Coll (TX) ***277***
Austin Peay State U (TN) ***278***
Ave Maria Coll (MI) ***278***
Averett U (VA) ***278***
Avila U (MO) ***278***
Azusa Pacific U (CA) ***278***
Baker U (KS) ***280***
Baldwin-Wallace Coll (OH) ***280***
Ball State U (IN) ***280***
Barber-Scotia Coll (NC) ***281***
Bard Coll (NY) ***281***
Barnard Coll (NY) ***282***
Barry U (FL) ***282***
Barton Coll (NC) ***282***
Bates Coll (ME) ***282***
Baylor U (TX) ***283***
Bellarmine U (KY) ***284***
Bellevue U (NE) ***284***
Belmont Abbey Coll (NC) ***284***
Belmont U (TN) ***284***
Beloit Coll (WI) ***285***
Bemidji State U (MN) ***285***
Benedict Coll (SC) ***285***
Benedictine Coll (KS) ***285***
Benedictine U (IL) ***285***
Bennett Coll (NC) ***286***
Berea Coll (KY) ***286***
Baruch Coll of the City U of NY (NY) ***286***
Berry Coll (GA) ***287***
Bethany Coll (KS) ***287***
Bethany Coll (WV) ***287***
Bethel Coll (MN) ***288***
Bethune-Cookman Coll (FL) ***289***
Birmingham-Southern Coll (AL) ***289***
Bishop's U (QC, Canada) ***289***
Blackburn Coll (IL) ***290***
Black Hills State U (SD) ***290***
Bloomfield Coll (NJ) ***290***
Bloomsburg U of Pennsylvania (PA) ***290***
Bluffton Coll (OH) ***291***
Boston Coll (MA) ***292***
Boston U (MA) ***292***
Bowdoin Coll (ME) ***292***
Bowie State U (MD) ***292***
Bowling Green State U (OH) ***292***
Bradley U (IL) ***293***
Brandeis U (MA) ***293***
Brandon U (MB, Canada) ***293***
Brenau U (GA) ***293***
Briar Cliff U (IA) ***294***
Bridgewater Coll (VA) ***294***
Bridgewater State Coll (MA) ***294***
Brigham Young U (UT) ***295***
Brigham Young U–Hawaii (HI) ***295***
Brock U (ON, Canada) ***295***
Brooklyn Coll of the City U of NY (NY) ***295***
Brown U (RI) ***296***
Bryn Mawr Coll (PA) ***297***
Bucknell U (PA) ***297***
Buena Vista U (IA) ***297***
Butler U (IN) ***297***
Cabrini Coll (PA) ***298***
Caldwell Coll (NJ) ***298***
California Baptist U (CA) ***298***
California Lutheran U (CA) ***299***
California Polytechnic State U, San Luis Obispo (CA) ***300***
California State Polytechnic U, Pomona (CA) ***300***
California State U, Bakersfield (CA) ***300***
California State U, Chico (CA) ***300***
California State U, Dominguez Hills (CA) ***300***
California State U, Fresno (CA) ***301***
California State U, Fullerton (CA) ***301***
California State U, Hayward (CA) ***301***
California State U, Long Beach (CA) ***301***
California State U, Northridge (CA) ***301***
California State U, Sacramento (CA) ***301***
California State U, San Bernardino (CA) ***302***
California State U, San Marcos (CA) ***302***
California State U, Stanislaus (CA) ***302***
California U of Pennsylvania (PA) ***302***
Calumet Coll of Saint Joseph (IN) ***302***
Calvin Coll (MI) ***303***
Cameron U (OK) ***303***
Campbellsville U (KY) ***303***
Campbell U (NC) ***303***
Canisius Coll (NY) ***304***
Capital U (OH) ***304***
Cardinal Stritch U (WI) ***305***
Carleton Coll (MN) ***305***
Carleton U (ON, Canada) ***305***
Carnegie Mellon U (PA) ***305***
Carroll Coll (MT) ***306***
Carroll Coll (WI) ***306***
Carson-Newman Coll (TN) ***306***
Carthage Coll (WI) ***306***
Case Western Reserve U (OH) ***307***
Catawba Coll (NC) ***307***
The Catholic U of America (DC) ***307***
Cedar Crest Coll (PA) ***308***
Cedarville U (OH) ***308***
Centenary Coll (NJ) ***308***
Centenary Coll of Louisiana (LA) ***308***
Central Coll (IA) ***309***
Central Connecticut State U (CT) ***309***
Central Methodist Coll (MO) ***309***
Central Michigan U (MI) ***310***
Central Missouri State U (MO) ***310***
Central Washington U (WA) ***310***
Centre Coll (KY) ***310***
Chaminade U of Honolulu (HI) ***311***
Chapman U (CA) ***311***
Charleston Southern U (SC) ***311***
Chatham Coll (PA) ***312***
Chestnut Hill Coll (PA) ***312***
Cheyney U of Pennsylvania (PA) ***312***
Christendom Coll (VA) ***313***
Christopher Newport U (VA) ***313***
Citadel, The Military Coll of South Carolina (SC) ***314***
City Coll of the City U of NY (NY) ***314***
Claremont McKenna Coll (CA) ***315***
Clarion U of Pennsylvania (PA) ***315***
Clark Atlanta U (GA) ***315***
Clarkson U (NY) ***316***
Clark U (MA) ***316***
Clemson U (SC) ***317***
Cleveland State U (OH) ***317***
Coastal Carolina U (SC) ***318***
Coe Coll (IA) ***318***
Coker Coll (SC) ***318***
Colby Coll (ME) ***318***
Colgate U (NY) ***319***
Coll of Charleston (SC) ***320***
The Coll of New Jersey (NJ) ***320***
The Coll of New Rochelle (NY) ***321***
Coll of Notre Dame of Maryland (MD) ***321***
Coll of Saint Benedict (MN) ***321***
Coll of St. Catherine (MN) ***321***
Coll of St. Joseph (VT) ***322***
Coll of Santa Fe (NM) ***323***
The Coll of Southeastern Europe, The American U of Athens(Greece) ***323***
Coll of Staten Island of the City U of NY (NY) ***323***
Coll of the Holy Cross (MA) ***323***
Coll of the Ozarks (MO) ***323***
The Coll of William and Mary (VA) ***324***
The Coll of Wooster (OH) ***324***
Colorado Christian U (CO) ***325***
The Colorado Coll (CO) ***325***
Colorado State U (CO) ***325***
Colorado State U-Pueblo (CO) ***325***
Columbia Coll (MO) ***326***
Columbia Coll (NY) ***326***
Columbia Coll (SC) ***327***
Columbia Union Coll (MD) ***328***
Columbia U, School of General Studies (NY) ***328***
Columbus State U (GA) ***328***
Concord Coll (WV) ***329***
Concordia Coll (MN) ***329***
Concordia U (CA) ***330***
Concordia U (IL) ***330***
Concordia U (QC, Canada) ***331***
Concordia U Coll of Alberta (AB, Canada) ***331***
Connecticut Coll (CT) ***331***
Converse Coll (SC) ***332***
Cornell Coll (IA) ***332***
Cornell U (NY) ***333***
Creighton U (NE) ***333***
Cumberland Coll (KY) ***335***
Cumberland U (TN) ***335***
Curry Coll (MA) ***335***
Daemen Coll (NY) ***335***
Dalhousie U (NS, Canada) ***336***
Dallas Baptist U (TX) ***336***
Dartmouth Coll (NH) ***337***
Davidson Coll (NC) ***338***

POLITICAL SCIENCE (continued)

Davis & Elkins Coll (WV) **338**
Delaware State U (DE) **338**
Delta State U (MS) **339**
Denison U (OH) **339**
DePaul U (IL) **339**
DePauw U (IN) **339**
DeSales U (PA) **340**
Dickinson Coll (PA) **344**
Dickinson State U (ND) **344**
Dillard U (LA) **344**
Doane Coll (NE) **344**
Dominican Coll (NY) **344**
Dominican U (IL) **345**
Dominican U of California (CA) **345**
Dordt Coll (IA) **345**
Dowling Coll (NY) **345**
Drake U (IA) **345**
Drew U (NJ) **346**
Drury U (MO) **346**
Duke U (NC) **346**
Duquesne U (PA) **346**
Earlham Coll (IN) **347**
East Carolina U (NC) **347**
East Central U (OK) **347**
Eastern Connecticut State U (CT) **347**
Eastern Illinois U (IL) **348**
Eastern Kentucky U (KY) **348**
Eastern Michigan U (MI) **348**
Eastern New Mexico U (NM) **349**
Eastern U (PA) **349**
Eastern Washington U (WA) **349**
East Stroudsburg U of Pennsylvania (PA) **349**
East Tennessee State U (TN) **349**
Eckerd Coll (FL) **350**
Edgewood Coll (WI) **351**
Edinboro U of Pennsylvania (PA) **351**
Elizabeth City State U (NC) **351**
Elizabethtown Coll (PA) **351**
Elmhurst Coll (IL) **351**
Elmira Coll (NY) **351**
Elon U (NC) **352**
Emmanuel Coll (MA) **353**
Emory & Henry Coll (VA) **353**
Emory U (GA) **354**
Emporia State U (KS) **354**
Eugene Lang Coll, New School U (NY) **355**
Eureka Coll (IL) **355**
Evangel U (MO) **355**
The Evergreen State Coll (WA) **355**
Excelsior Coll (NY) **356**
Fairfield U (CT) **356**
Fairleigh Dickinson U, Florham (NJ) **356**
Fairleigh Dickinson U, Teaneck-Metro Campus (NJ) **356**
Fairmont State Coll (WV) **356**
Faulkner U (AL) **357**
Fayetteville State U (NC) **357**
Felician Coll (NJ) **357**
Ferrum Coll (VA) **358**
Fisk U (TN) **358**
Fitchburg State Coll (MA) **358**
Flagler Coll (FL) **359**
Florida A&M U (FL) **359**
Florida Atlantic U (FL) **359**
Florida International U (FL) **360**
Florida Southern Coll (FL) **361**
Florida State U (FL) **361**
Fordham U (NY) **362**
Fort Hays State U (KS) **362**
Fort Lewis Coll (CO) **362**
Fort Valley State U (GA) **362**
Framingham State Coll (MA) **362**
Franciscan U of Steubenville (OH) **363**
Francis Marion U (SC) **363**
Franklin and Marshall Coll (PA) **363**
Franklin Coll (IN) **363**
Franklin Pierce Coll (NH) **364**
Fresno Pacific U (CA) **364**
Frostburg State U (MD) **365**
Furman U (SC) **365**
Gannon U (PA) **365**
Gardner-Webb U (NC) **365**
Geneva Coll (PA) **366**
George Mason U (VA) **366**
Georgetown Coll (KY) **366**
Georgetown U (DC) **366**
The George Washington U (DC) **367**
Georgia Coll & State U (GA) **367**
Georgia Southern U (GA) **367**
Georgia Southwestern State U (GA) **368**
Georgia State U (GA) **368**
Gettysburg Coll (PA) **368**
Goddard Coll (VT) **369**
Gonzaga U (WA) **369**
Gordon Coll (MA) **370**
Goshen Coll (IN) **370**
Goucher Coll (MD) **370**
Grambling State U (LA) **371**
Grand Canyon U (AZ) **371**
Grand Valley State U (MI) **371**
Grand View Coll (IA) **372**
Greensboro Coll (NC) **372**
Greenville Coll (IL) **373**
Grinnell Coll (IA) **373**
Grove City Coll (PA) **373**
Guilford Coll (NC) **373**
Gustavus Adolphus Coll (MN) **374**
Hamilton Coll (NY) **374**
Hamline U (MN) **374**
Hampden-Sydney Coll (VA) **374**
Hampshire Coll (MA) **375**
Hampton U (VA) **375**
Hanover Coll (IN) **375**
Harding U (AR) **375**
Hardin-Simmons U (TX) **376**
Hartwick Coll (NY) **376**
Harvard U (MA) **376**
Hastings Coll (NE) **377**
Haverford Coll (PA) **377**
Hawai'i Pacific U (HI) **377**
Heidelberg Coll (OH) **377**
Henderson State U (AR) **378**
Hendrix Coll (AR) **378**
High Point U (NC) **379**
Hillsdale Coll (MI) **379**
Hiram Coll (OH) **379**
Hobart and William Smith Colls (NY) **380**
Hofstra U (NY) **380**
Hollins U (VA) **380**
Hood Coll (MD) **381**
Hope Coll (MI) **381**
Houghton Coll (NY) **381**
Houston Baptist U (TX) **382**
Howard Payne U (TX) **382**
Howard U (DC) **382**
Humboldt State U (CA) **382**
Hunter Coll of the City U of NY (NY) **382**
Huntingdon Coll (AL) **383**
Huston-Tillotson Coll (TX) **383**
Idaho State U (ID) **384**
Illinois Coll (IL) **384**
Illinois Inst of Technology (IL) **384**
Illinois State U (IL) **384**
Illinois Wesleyan U (IL) **385**
Indiana State U (IN) **385**
Indiana U Bloomington (IN) **385**
Indiana U Northwest (IN) **386**
Indiana U of Pennsylvania (PA) **386**
Indiana U–Purdue U Fort Wayne (IN) **386**
Indiana U–Purdue U Indianapolis (IN) **387**
Indiana U South Bend (IN) **387**
Indiana U Southeast (IN) **387**
Indiana Wesleyan U (IN) **387**
Inter American U of PR, San Germán Campus (PR) **388**
Iona Coll (NY) **390**
Iowa State U of Science and Technology (IA) **390**
Ithaca Coll (NY) **390**
Jackson State U (MS) **390**
Jacksonville State U (AL) **390**
Jacksonville U (FL) **391**
James Madison U (VA) **391**
Jamestown Coll (ND) **391**
John Cabot U(Italy) **392**
John Carroll U (OH) **392**
Johns Hopkins U (MD) **392**
Johnson C. Smith U (NC) **394**
Johnson State Coll (VT) **394**
Juniata Coll (PA) **395**
Kalamazoo Coll (MI) **395**
Kansas State U (KS) **396**
Kean U (NJ) **396**
Keene State Coll (NH) **396**
Kennesaw State U (GA) **397**
Kent State U (OH) **397**
Kentucky State U (KY) **397**
Kentucky Wesleyan Coll (KY) **397**
Kenyon Coll (OH) **398**
King Coll (TN) **398**
King's Coll (PA) **398**
Knox Coll (IL) **399**
Kutztown U of Pennsylvania (PA) **399**
Lafayette Coll (PA) **400**
LaGrange Coll (GA) **400**
Lake Forest Coll (IL) **400**
Lakehead U (ON, Canada) **400**
Lamar U (TX) **401**
Lambuth U (TN) **401**
Lander U (SC) **401**
La Salle U (PA) **402**
La Sierra U (CA) **403**
Laurentian U (ON, Canada) **403**
Lawrence U (WI) **403**
Lebanon Valley Coll (PA) **403**
Lehigh U (PA) **404**
Lehman Coll of the City U of NY (NY) **404**
Le Moyne Coll (NY) **404**
Lenoir-Rhyne Coll (NC) **405**
Lewis & Clark Coll (OR) **405**
Lewis U (IL) **406**
Liberty U (VA) **406**
Lincoln U (PA) **407**
Lindenwood U (MO) **407**
Linfield Coll (OR) **408**
Lipscomb U (TN) **408**
Lock Haven U of Pennsylvania (PA) **408**
Long Island U, Brooklyn Campus (NY) **409**
Long Island U, C.W. Post Campus (NY) **409**
Long Island U, Southampton Coll (NY) **409**
Long Island U, Southampton Coll, Friends World Program (NY) **409**
Longwood U (VA) **409**
Loras Coll (IA) **410**
Louisiana State U and A&M Coll (LA) **410**
Louisiana State U in Shreveport (LA) **410**
Louisiana Tech U (LA) **410**
Loyola Coll in Maryland (MD) **411**
Loyola Marymount U (CA) **411**
Loyola U Chicago (IL) **411**
Loyola U New Orleans (LA) **411**
Luther Coll (IA) **412**
Lycoming Coll (PA) **412**
Lynchburg Coll (VA) **413**
Lynn U (FL) **413**
Lyon Coll (AR) **413**
Macalester Coll (MN) **413**
MacMurray Coll (IL) **414**
Malone Coll (OH) **415**
Manchester Coll (IN) **415**
Manhattan Coll (NY) **416**
Manhattanville Coll (NY) **416**
Mansfield U of Pennsylvania (PA) **416**
Marian Coll of Fond du Lac (WI) **417**
Marietta Coll (OH) **417**
Marist Coll (NY) **417**
Marlboro Coll (VT) **418**
Marquette U (WI) **418**
Marshall U (WV) **418**
Mars Hill Coll (NC) **418**
Martin U (IN) **419**
Mary Baldwin Coll (VA) **419**
Marygrove Coll (MI) **419**
Marymount Coll of Fordham U (NY) **419**
Marymount Manhattan Coll (NY) **420**
Marymount U (VA) **420**
Maryville Coll (TN) **420**
Maryville U of Saint Louis (MO) **420**
Mary Washington Coll (VA) **420**
Massachusetts Inst of Technology (MA) **421**
The Master's Coll and Seminary (CA) **422**
McDaniel Coll (MD) **422**
McGill U (QC, Canada) **423**
McKendree Coll (IL) **423**
McMaster U (ON, Canada) **423**
McMurry U (TX) **423**
McNeese State U (LA) **423**
Medaille Coll (NY) **424**
Memorial U of Newfoundland (NF, Canada) **424**
Mercer U (GA) **425**
Mercy Coll (NY) **425**
Mercyhurst Coll (PA) **425**
Meredith Coll (NC) **426**
Merrimack Coll (MA) **426**
Mesa State Coll (CO) **426**
Messiah Coll (PA) **426**
Methodist Coll (NC) **427**
Metropolitan State Coll of Denver (CO) **427**
Miami U (OH) **428**
Michigan State U (MI) **428**
Middlebury Coll (VT) **429**
Middle Tennessee State U (TN) **429**
Midwestern State U (TX) **430**
Miles Coll (AL) **430**
Millersville U of Pennsylvania (PA) **430**
Millikin U (IL) **430**
Millsaps Coll (MS) **431**
Minnesota State U, Mankato (MN) **431**
Minnesota State U, Moorhead (MN) **432**
Mississippi Coll (MS) **432**
Mississippi State U (MS) **432**
Mississippi Valley State U (MS) **432**
Missouri Southern State Coll (MO) **433**
Missouri Valley Coll (MO) **433**
Missouri Western State Coll (MO) **433**
Molloy Coll (NY) **433**
Monmouth Coll (IL) **434**
Monmouth U (NJ) **434**
Montana State U–Bozeman (MT) **434**
Montclair State U (NJ) **435**
Moravian Coll (PA) **436**
Morehead State U (KY) **436**
Morehouse Coll (GA) **436**
Morgan State U (MD) **436**
Morningside Coll (IA) **437**
Morris Coll (SC) **437**
Mount Allison U (NB, Canada) **437**
Mount Holyoke Coll (MA) **438**
Mount Mercy Coll (IA) **438**
Mount Saint Mary Coll (NY) **439**
Mount St. Mary's Coll (CA) **439**
Mount Saint Mary's Coll and Seminary (MD) **439**
Mount Saint Vincent U (NS, Canada) **439**
Mount Union Coll (OH) **440**
Muhlenberg Coll (PA) **440**
Murray State U (KY) **440**
Muskingum Coll (OH) **441**
Nazareth Coll of Rochester (NY) **443**
Nebraska Wesleyan U (NE) **443**
Neumann Coll (PA) **443**
Newberry Coll (SC) **444**
New Coll of Florida (FL) **444**
New England Coll (NH) **444**
New Jersey City U (NJ) **445**
New Mexico Highlands U (NM) **446**
New Mexico State U (NM) **446**
New York Inst of Technology (NY) **447**
New York U (NY) **447**
Niagara U (NY) **447**
Nicholls State U (LA) **447**
Norfolk State U (VA) **448**
North Carolina Ag and Tech State U (NC) **448**
North Carolina Central U (NC) **448**
North Carolina State U (NC) **449**
North Carolina Wesleyan Coll (NC) **449**
North Central Coll (IL) **449**
North Dakota State U (ND) **449**
Northeastern Illinois U (IL) **450**
Northeastern State U (OK) **450**
Northeastern U (MA) **450**
Northern Arizona U (AZ) **450**
Northern Illinois U (IL) **450**
Northern Kentucky U (KY) **451**
Northern Michigan U (MI) **451**
Northern State U (SD) **451**
North Georgia Coll & State U (GA) **451**
North Park U (IL) **452**
Northwestern Coll (IA) **453**
Northwestern Oklahoma State U (OK) **453**
Northwestern State U of Louisiana (LA) **453**
Northwestern U (IL) **453**
Northwest Missouri State U (MO) **454**
Northwest Nazarene U (ID) **454**
Norwich U (VT) **455**
Notre Dame Coll (OH) **455**
Notre Dame de Namur U (CA) **455**
Oakland U (MI) **456**
Oberlin Coll (OH) **456**
Occidental Coll (CA) **457**
Oglethorpe U (GA) **457**
Ohio Dominican U (OH) **457**
Ohio Northern U (OH) **457**
The Ohio State U (OH) **457**
Ohio U (OH) **458**
Ohio Wesleyan U (OH) **459**
Okanagan U Coll (BC, Canada) **459**
Oklahoma Baptist U (OK) **459**
Oklahoma City U (OK) **460**
Oklahoma State U (OK) **460**
Oklahoma Wesleyan U (OK) **460**
Old Dominion U (VA) **460**
Oral Roberts U (OK) **461**
Oregon State U (OR) **462**
Ottawa U (KS) **462**
Otterbein Coll (OH) **462**
Ouachita Baptist U (AR) **462**
Our Lady of the Lake U of San Antonio (TX) **463**
Pace U (NY) **463**

Pacific Lutheran U (WA) **463**
Pacific Union Coll (CA) **464**
Pacific U (OR) **464**
Palm Beach Atlantic U (FL) **465**
Park U (MO) **465**
Penn State U at Erie, The Behrend Coll (PA) **467**
Penn State U Univ Park Campus (PA) **468**
Pepperdine U, Malibu (CA) **469**
Pfeiffer U (NC) **469**
Pine Manor Coll (MA) **470**
Pittsburg State U (KS) **470**
Pitzer Coll (CA) **471**
Plattsburgh State U of NY (NY) **471**
Plymouth State Coll (NH) **471**
Point Loma Nazarene U (CA) **471**
Point Park Coll (PA) **471**
Pomona Coll (CA) **472**
Pontifical Catholic U of Puerto Rico (PR) **472**
Portland State U (OR) **472**
Prairie View A&M U (TX) **473**
Presbyterian Coll (SC) **473**
Prescott Coll (AZ) **474**
Princeton U (NJ) **474**
Principia Coll (IL) **474**
Providence Coll (RI) **474**
Purchase Coll, State U of NY (NY) **475**
Purdue U (IN) **475**
Purdue U Calumet (IN) **475**
Queens Coll of the City U of NY (NY) **475**
Queen's U at Kingston (ON, Canada) **476**
Queens U of Charlotte (NC) **476**
Quincy U (IL) **476**
Quinnipiac U (CT) **476**
Radford U (VA) **476**
Ramapo Coll of New Jersey (NJ) **477**
Randolph-Macon Coll (VA) **477**
Randolph-Macon Woman's Coll (VA) **477**
Reed Coll (OR) **477**
Regis Coll (MA) **478**
Regis U (CO) **478**
Rhode Island Coll (RI) **479**
Rhodes Coll (TN) **479**
Rice U (TX) **479**
The Richard Stockton Coll of New Jersey (NJ) **479**
Richmond, The American International U in London(United Kingdom) **480**
Rider U (NJ) **480**
Ripon Coll (WI) **480**
Roanoke Coll (VA) **481**
Rockford Coll (IL) **482**
Rockhurst U (MO) **482**
Rocky Mountain Coll (MT) **482**
Roger Williams U (RI) **483**
Rollins Coll (FL) **483**
Roosevelt U (IL) **483**
Rosemont Coll (PA) **484**
Rowan U (NJ) **484**
Russell Sage Coll (NY) **484**
Rust Coll (MS) **485**
Rutgers, The State U of New Jersey, Camden (NJ) **485**
Rutgers, The State U of New Jersey, Newark (NJ) **485**
Rutgers, The State U of New Jersey, New Brunswick (NJ) **485**
Sacred Heart U (CT) **486**
Saginaw Valley State U (MI) **486**
St. Ambrose U (IA) **486**
St. Andrews Presbyterian Coll (NC) **487**
Saint Anselm Coll (NH) **487**
Saint Augustine's Coll (NC) **487**
St. Bonaventure U (NY) **487**
St. Cloud State U (MN) **488**
St. Edward's U (TX) **488**
St. Francis Coll (NY) **488**
Saint Francis U (PA) **488**
St. Francis Xavier U (NS, Canada) **489**
St. John Fisher Coll (NY) **489**
Saint John's U (MN) **490**
St. John's U (NY) **490**
Saint Joseph Coll (CT) **490**
Saint Joseph's Coll (IN) **490**
Saint Joseph's U (PA) **491**
St. Lawrence U (NY) **491**
Saint Leo U (FL) **492**
Saint Louis U (MO) **492**
Saint Martin's Coll (WA) **493**
Saint Mary Coll (KS) **493**
Saint Mary's Coll (IN) **493**
Saint Mary's Coll of California (CA) **494**
St. Mary's Coll of Maryland (MD) **494**
Saint Mary's U (NS, Canada) **494**
Saint Mary's U of Minnesota (MN) **494**
St. Mary's U of San Antonio (TX) **494**
Saint Michael's Coll (VT) **494**
St. Norbert Coll (WI) **495**
St. Olaf Coll (MN) **495**
Saint Peter's Coll (NJ) **495**
St. Thomas U (FL) **496**
St. Thomas U (NB, Canada) **496**
Saint Vincent Coll (PA) **496**
Saint Xavier U (IL) **496**
Salem State Coll (MA) **497**
Salisbury U (MD) **497**
Salve Regina U (RI) **497**
Samford U (AL) **497**
Sam Houston State U (TX) **497**
San Diego State U (CA) **498**
San Francisco State U (CA) **498**
San Jose State U (CA) **499**
Santa Clara U (CA) **499**
Sarah Lawrence Coll (NY) **499**
Savannah State U (GA) **499**
Scripps Coll (CA) **501**
Seattle Pacific U (WA) **501**
Seattle U (WA) **501**
Seton Hall U (NJ) **502**
Seton Hill U (PA) **502**
Shaw U (NC) **502**
Shepherd Coll (WV) **503**
Shippensburg U of Pennsylvania (PA) **503**
Siena Coll (NY) **504**
Simmons Coll (MA) **504**
Simon Fraser U (BC, Canada) **505**
Simon's Rock Coll of Bard (MA) **505**
Simpson Coll (IA) **505**
Skidmore Coll (NY) **506**
Slippery Rock U of Pennsylvania (PA) **506**
Smith Coll (MA) **506**
Sonoma State U (CA) **506**
South Carolina State U (SC) **506**
South Dakota State U (SD) **507**
Southeastern Louisiana U (LA) **508**
Southeastern Oklahoma State U (OK) **508**
Southeast Missouri State U (MO) **508**
Southern Arkansas U–Magnolia (AR) **509**
Southern Connecticut State U (CT) **509**
Southern Illinois U Carbondale (IL) **509**
Southern Illinois U Edwardsville (IL) **509**
Southern Methodist U (TX) **510**
Southern Nazarene U (OK) **510**
Southern New Hampshire U (NH) **510**
Southern Oregon U (OR) **510**
Southern U and A&M Coll (LA) **511**
Southern Utah U (UT) **511**
Southwest Baptist U (MO) **512**
Southwestern Oklahoma State U (OK) **512**
Southwestern U (TX) **513**
Southwest Missouri State U (MO) **513**
Southwest State U (MN) **513**
Southwest Texas State U (TX) **513**
Spelman Coll (GA) **514**
Springfield Coll (MA) **514**
Spring Hill Coll (AL) **514**
Stanford U (CA) **514**
State U of NY at Albany (NY) **514**
State U of NY at Binghamton (NY) **515**
State U of NY at New Paltz (NY) **515**
State U of NY at Oswego (NY) **515**
State U of NY Coll at Brockport (NY) **515**
State U of NY Coll at Buffalo (NY) **516**
State U of NY Coll at Cortland (NY) **516**
State U of NY Coll at Fredonia (NY) **516**
State U of NY Coll at Geneseo (NY) **516**
State U of NY Coll at Oneonta (NY) **517**
State U of NY Coll at Potsdam (NY) **517**
State U of West Georgia (GA) **518**
Stephen F. Austin State U (TX) **518**
Stephens Coll (MO) **519**
Stetson U (FL) **519**
Stonehill Coll (MA) **520**
Stony Brook U, State University of New York (NY) **520**
Suffolk U (MA) **520**
Sul Ross State U (TX) **521**
Susquehanna U (PA) **521**
Swarthmore Coll (PA) **521**
Sweet Briar Coll (VA) **521**
Syracuse U (NY) **521**
Tarleton State U (TX) **522**
Taylor U (IN) **523**
Temple U (PA) **523**
Tennessee State U (TN) **523**
Tennessee Technological U (TN) **524**
Texas A&M International U (TX) **524**
Texas A&M U (TX) **524**
Texas A&M U–Commerce (TX) **525**
Texas A&M U–Corpus Christi (TX) **525**
Texas A&M U–Kingsville (TX) **525**
Texas Christian U (TX) **526**
Texas Coll (TX) **526**
Texas Lutheran U (TX) **526**
Texas Southern U (TX) **526**
Texas Tech U (TX) **526**
Texas Wesleyan U (TX) **526**
Texas Woman's U (TX) **527**
Thiel Coll (PA) **527**
Thomas Edison State Coll (NJ) **527**
Thomas More Coll of Liberal Arts (NH) **528**
Thomas U (GA) **528**
Touro Coll (NY) **529**
Towson U (MD) **529**
Transylvania U (KY) **529**
Trent U (ON, Canada) **529**
Trinity Coll (CT) **530**
Trinity Coll (DC) **530**
Trinity U (TX) **531**
Trinity Western U (BC, Canada) **531**
Troy State U (AL) **532**
Troy State U Montgomery (AL) **532**
Truman State U (MO) **532**
Tufts U (MA) **533**
Tulane U (LA) **533**
Tuskegee U (AL) **533**
Union Coll (NY) **534**
Union U (TN) **534**
United States Air Force Academy (CO) **534**
United States Coast Guard Academy (CT) **535**
United States Military Academy (NY) **535**
United States Naval Academy (MD) **535**
Université Laval (QC, Canada) **536**
U at Buffalo, The State University of New York (NY) **536**
The U of Akron (OH) **537**
The U of Alabama (AL) **537**
The U of Alabama at Birmingham (AL) **537**
The U of Alabama in Huntsville (AL) **537**
U of Alaska Anchorage (AK) **538**
U of Alaska Fairbanks (AK) **538**
U of Alaska Southeast (AK) **538**
U of Alberta (AB, Canada) **538**
The U of Arizona (AZ) **538**
U of Arkansas (AR) **539**
U of Arkansas at Little Rock (AR) **539**
U of Arkansas at Monticello (AR) **539**
U of Baltimore (MD) **539**
The U of British Columbia (BC, Canada) **540**
U of Calgary (AB, Canada) **540**
U of Calif, Berkeley (CA) **540**
U of Calif, Davis (CA) **540**
U of Calif, Irvine (CA) **541**
U of Calif, Los Angeles (CA) **541**
U of Calif, Riverside (CA) **541**
U of Calif, San Diego (CA) **541**
U of Calif, Santa Barbara (CA) **541**
U of Calif, Santa Cruz (CA) **542**
U of Central Arkansas (AR) **542**
U of Central Florida (FL) **542**
U of Central Oklahoma (OK) **542**
U of Charleston (WV) **542**
U of Chicago (IL) **542**
U of Cincinnati (OH) **543**
U of Colorado at Boulder (CO) **543**
U of Colorado at Colorado Springs (CO) **543**
U of Colorado at Denver (CO) **543**
U of Connecticut (CT) **544**
U of Dallas (TX) **544**
U of Dayton (OH) **544**
U of Delaware (DE) **544**
U of Denver (CO) **544**
U of Evansville (IN) **545**
The U of Findlay (OH) **545**
U of Florida (FL) **545**
U of Georgia (GA) **545**
U of Great Falls (MT) **545**
U of Guelph (ON, Canada) **546**
U of Hartford (CT) **546**
U of Hawaii at Hilo (HI) **546**
U of Hawaii at Manoa (HI) **546**
U of Hawaii–West Oahu (HI) **546**
U of Houston (TX) **547**
U of Idaho (ID) **547**
U of Illinois at Chicago (IL) **547**
U of Illinois at Springfield (IL) **548**
U of Illinois at Urbana–Champaign (IL) **548**
U of Indianapolis (IN) **548**
The U of Iowa (IA) **548**
U of Judaism (CA) **548**
U of Kansas (KS) **549**
U of Kentucky (KY) **549**
U of King's Coll (NS, Canada) **549**
U of La Verne (CA) **549**
The U of Lethbridge (AB, Canada) **549**
U of Louisiana at Lafayette (LA) **550**
U of Louisville (KY) **550**
U of Maine (ME) **550**
U of Maine at Farmington (ME) **550**
U of Maine at Presque Isle (ME) **551**
U of Manitoba (MB, Canada) **551**
U of Mary Hardin-Baylor (TX) **551**
U of Maryland, Baltimore County (MD) **552**
U of Maryland, Coll Park (MD) **552**
U of Massachusetts Amherst (MA) **552**
U of Massachusetts Boston (MA) **553**
U of Massachusetts Dartmouth (MA) **553**
U of Massachusetts Lowell (MA) **553**
The U of Memphis (TN) **553**
U of Miami (FL) **553**
U of Michigan (MI) **554**
U of Michigan–Dearborn (MI) **554**
U of Michigan–Flint (MI) **554**
U of Minnesota, Duluth (MN) **554**
U of Minnesota, Morris (MN) **555**
U of Minnesota, Twin Cities Campus (MN) **555**
U of Mississippi (MS) **555**
U of Missouri–Columbia (MO) **555**
U of Missouri–Kansas City (MO) **555**
U of Missouri–St. Louis (MO) **556**
U of Mobile (AL) **556**
U of Montevallo (AL) **557**
U of Nebraska at Kearney (NE) **557**
U of Nebraska at Omaha (NE) **557**
U of Nebraska–Lincoln (NE) **557**
U of Nevada, Las Vegas (NV) **558**
U of Nevada, Reno (NV) **558**
U of New Brunswick Fredericton (NB, Canada) **558**
U of New Brunswick Saint John (NB, Canada) **558**
U of New Hampshire (NH) **558**
U of New Haven (CT) **559**
U of New Mexico (NM) **559**
U of New Orleans (LA) **559**
U of North Alabama (AL) **559**
The U of North Carolina at Asheville (NC) **559**
The U of North Carolina at Chapel Hill (NC) **560**
The U of North Carolina at Charlotte (NC) **560**
The U of North Carolina at Greensboro (NC) **560**
The U of North Carolina at Pembroke (NC) **560**
The U of North Carolina at Wilmington (NC) **561**
U of North Dakota (ND) **561**
U of Northern Colorado (CO) **561**
U of Northern Iowa (IA) **561**
U of North Florida (FL) **561**
U of North Texas (TX) **562**
U of Notre Dame (IN) **562**
U of Oklahoma (OK) **562**
U of Oregon (OR) **562**
U of Ottawa (ON, Canada) **563**
U of Pennsylvania (PA) **563**
U of Pittsburgh (PA) **569**
U of Pittsburgh at Bradford (PA) **569**
U of Pittsburgh at Greensburg (PA) **570**
U of Pittsburgh at Johnstown (PA) **570**
U of Portland (OR) **570**
U of Prince Edward Island (PE, Canada) **570**
U of Puerto Rico, Río Piedras (PR) **571**
U of Puget Sound (WA) **571**
U of Redlands (CA) **572**
U of Regina (SK, Canada) **572**
U of Rhode Island (RI) **572**
U of Richmond (VA) **572**
U of Rio Grande (OH) **572**
U of Rochester (NY) **573**
U of St. Francis (IL) **573**
U of St. Thomas (MN) **573**
U of St. Thomas (TX) **573**
U of San Diego (CA) **574**
U of San Francisco (CA) **574**
U of Saskatchewan (SK, Canada) **574**
U of Science and Arts of Oklahoma (OK) **574**
The U of Scranton (PA) **574**
U of Sioux Falls (SD) **574**

POLITICAL SCIENCE (continued)

U of South Alabama (AL) ***575***
U of South Carolina (SC) ***575***
U of South Carolina Aiken (SC) ***575***
U of South Carolina Spartanburg (SC) ***575***
The U of South Dakota (SD) ***575***
U of Southern California (CA) ***576***
U of Southern Indiana (IN) ***576***
U of Southern Maine (ME) ***576***
U of Southern Mississippi (MS) ***576***
U of South Florida (FL) ***576***
The U of Tampa (FL) ***577***
The U of Tennessee (TN) ***577***
The U of Tennessee at Chattanooga (TN) ***577***
The U of Tennessee at Martin (TN) ***577***
The U of Texas at Arlington (TX) ***577***
The U of Texas at Austin (TX) ***578***
The U of Texas at Brownsville (TX) ***578***
The U of Texas at Dallas (TX) ***578***
The U of Texas at El Paso (TX) ***578***
The U of Texas at San Antonio (TX) ***578***
The U of Texas at Tyler (TX) ***579***
The U of Texas of the Permian Basin (TX) ***579***
The U of Texas–Pan American (TX) ***579***
U of the District of Columbia (DC) ***580***
U of the Incarnate Word (TX) ***580***
U of the Ozarks (AR) ***580***
U of the Pacific (CA) ***580***
U of the South (TN) ***581***
U of Toledo (OH) ***581***
U of Toronto (ON, Canada) ***581***
U of Tulsa (OK) ***581***
U of Utah (UT) ***582***
U of Vermont (VT) ***582***
U of Victoria (BC, Canada) ***582***
U of Virginia (VA) ***582***
The U of Virginia's Coll at Wise (VA) ***582***
U of Washington (WA) ***583***
U of Waterloo (ON, Canada) ***583***
The U of Western Ontario (ON, Canada) ***583***
U of West Florida (FL) ***583***
U of Windsor (ON, Canada) ***584***
U of Wisconsin–Eau Claire (WI) ***584***
U of Wisconsin–Green Bay (WI) ***584***
U of Wisconsin–La Crosse (WI) ***584***
U of Wisconsin–Madison (WI) ***584***
U of Wisconsin–Milwaukee (WI) ***585***
U of Wisconsin–Oshkosh (WI) ***585***
U of Wisconsin–Parkside (WI) ***585***
U of Wisconsin–Platteville (WI) ***585***
U of Wisconsin–River Falls (WI) ***585***
U of Wisconsin–Stevens Point (WI) ***585***
U of Wisconsin–Superior (WI) ***586***
U of Wisconsin–Whitewater (WI) ***586***
U of Wyoming (WY) ***586***
Ursinus Coll (PA) ***587***
Utah State U (UT) ***587***
Utica Coll (NY) ***588***
Valdosta State U (GA) ***588***
Valparaiso U (IN) ***588***
Vanderbilt U (TN) ***588***
Vanguard U of Southern California (CA) ***589***
Vassar Coll (NY) ***589***
Villanova U (PA) ***590***
Virginia Commonwealth U (VA) ***590***
Virginia Intermont Coll (VA) ***590***
Virginia Polytechnic Inst and State U (VA) ***591***
Virginia State U (VA) ***591***
Virginia Union U (VA) ***591***
Virginia Wesleyan Coll (VA) ***591***
Voorhees Coll (SC) ***592***
Wabash Coll (IN) ***592***
Wagner Coll (NY) ***592***
Wake Forest U (NC) ***592***
Walsh U (OH) ***593***
Warren Wilson Coll (NC) ***594***
Wartburg Coll (IA) ***594***
Washington & Jefferson Coll (PA) ***594***
Washington and Lee U (VA) ***594***
Washington Coll (MD) ***594***
Washington State U (WA) ***595***
Washington U in St. Louis (MO) ***595***
Wayland Baptist U (TX) ***595***
Waynesburg Coll (PA) ***595***
Wayne State Coll (NE) ***596***
Wayne State U (MI) ***596***
Weber State U (UT) ***596***
Webster U (MO) ***597***
Wellesley Coll (MA) ***597***
Wells Coll (NY) ***597***
Wesleyan Coll (GA) ***597***
Wesleyan U (CT) ***597***
West Chester U of Pennsylvania (PA) ***598***
Western Carolina U (NC) ***598***
Western Connecticut State U (CT) ***598***
Western Illinois U (IL) ***599***
Western Kentucky U (KY) ***599***
Western Michigan U (MI) ***599***
Western New England Coll (MA) ***600***
Western Oregon U (OR) ***600***
Western State Coll of Colorado (CO) ***600***
Western Washington U (WA) ***600***
Westfield State Coll (MA) ***600***
West Liberty State Coll (WV) ***601***
Westminster Coll (MO) ***601***
Westminster Coll (PA) ***601***
Westminster Coll (UT) ***601***
Westmont Coll (CA) ***602***
West Texas A&M U (TX) ***602***
West Virginia State Coll (WV) ***602***
West Virginia U (WV) ***602***
West Virginia Wesleyan Coll (WV) ***603***
Wheaton Coll (IL) ***603***
Wheaton Coll (MA) ***603***
Wheeling Jesuit U (WV) ***603***
Whitman Coll (WA) ***604***
Whittier Coll (CA) ***604***
Whitworth Coll (WA) ***604***
Wichita State U (KS) ***604***
Widener U (PA) ***604***
Wilberforce U (OH) ***605***
Wilkes U (PA) ***605***
Willamette U (OR) ***605***
William Jewell Coll (MO) ***606***
William Paterson U of New Jersey (NJ) ***606***
William Penn U (IA) ***606***
Williams Coll (MA) ***606***
William Woods U (MO) ***607***
Wilmington Coll (OH) ***607***
Winona State U (MN) ***608***
Winston-Salem State U (NC) ***608***
Winthrop U (SC) ***608***
Wisconsin Lutheran Coll (WI) ***608***
Wittenberg U (OH) ***608***
Wofford Coll (SC) ***609***
Woodbury U (CA) ***609***
Wright State U (OH) ***609***
Xavier U (OH) ***610***
Xavier U of Louisiana (LA) ***610***
Yale U (CT) ***610***
York Coll of Pennsylvania (PA) ***610***
York Coll of the City U of New York (NY) ***611***
York U (ON, Canada) ***611***
Youngstown State U (OH) ***611***

POLITICAL SCIENCE/ GOVERNMENT RELATED

Information can be found under this major's main heading.

Nebraska Wesleyan U (NE) ***443***
Rochester Inst of Technology (NY) ***482***
The U of Akron (OH) ***537***
Western New England Coll (MA) ***600***

POLYMER CHEMISTRY

Overview: This branch of chemistry is concerned with manmade chemical substances and their properties and behavior. *Related majors:* polymer/ plastics engineering or technology, chemical engineering or technology, chemistry, chemical and atomic physics. *Potential careers:* chemical engineer or technologist, chemist, research scientist, inventor, textile manufacturer. *Salary potential:* $35k-$55k.

Carnegie Mellon U (PA) ***305***
Clemson U (SC) ***317***
Georgia Inst of Technology (GA) ***367***
Harvard U (MA) ***376***
Loras Coll (IA) ***410***
North Dakota State U (ND) ***449***
Rochester Inst of Technology (NY) ***482***
State U of NY Coll of Environ Sci and Forestry (NY) ***517***
The U of Akron (OH) ***537***
U of Wisconsin–Stevens Point (WI) ***585***
Winona State U (MN) ***608***

PORTUGUESE

Overview: Students learn to read, write, and understand the Portuguese language as it is used in Portugal and in other parts of the world, such as Brazil. *Related majors:* anthropology, Latin American studies, international economics, international relations, natural resources conservation. *Potential careers:* international banker, diplomatic corps, anthropologist, environmentalist, journalist. *Salary potential:* $23k-$30k.

Brigham Young U (UT) ***295***
Florida International U (FL) ***360***
Georgetown U (DC) ***366***
Harvard U (MA) ***376***
Indiana U Bloomington (IN) ***385***
Long Island U, Southampton Coll, Friends World Program (NY) ***409***
Marlboro Coll (VT) ***418***
New York U (NY) ***447***
The Ohio State U (OH) ***457***
Rutgers, The State U of New Jersey, New Brunswick (NJ) ***485***
Smith Coll (MA) ***506***
Tulane U (LA) ***533***
United States Military Academy (NY) ***535***
U of Calif, Los Angeles (CA) ***541***
U of Calif, Santa Barbara (CA) ***541***
U of Connecticut (CT) ***544***
U of Florida (FL) ***545***
U of Illinois at Urbana–Champaign (IL) ***548***
The U of Iowa (IA) ***548***
U of Massachusetts Amherst (MA) ***552***
U of Massachusetts Dartmouth (MA) ***553***
U of Miami (FL) ***553***
U of Minnesota, Twin Cities Campus (MN) ***555***
U of New Mexico (NM) ***559***
The U of Scranton (PA) ***574***
The U of Texas at Austin (TX) ***578***
U of Toronto (ON, Canada) ***581***
U of Wisconsin–Madison (WI) ***584***
Vanderbilt U (TN) ***588***
Yale U (CT) ***610***

POULTRY SCIENCE

Overview: This major teaches students about the production and management of poultry animals as well as the proper handling of poultry products. *Related majors:* animal science, agricultural animal health, animal breeding, avian sciences, feed science. *Potential careers:* ranch manager, inspector, veterinarian, animal geneticist, buyer. *Salary potential:* $25K-$35K.

Auburn U (AL) ***276***
Coll of the Ozarks (MO) ***323***
Cornell U (NY) ***333***
Mississippi State U (MS) ***432***
North Carolina State U (NC) ***449***
Stephen F. Austin State U (TX) ***518***
Texas A&M U (TX) ***524***
Tuskegee U (AL) ***533***
U of Arkansas (AR) ***539***
U of Calif, Davis (CA) ***540***
U of Florida (FL) ***545***
U of Georgia (GA) ***545***
U of Maryland Eastern Shore (MD) ***552***
U of Wisconsin–Madison (WI) ***584***
Virginia Polytechnic Inst and State U (VA) ***591***

PRACTICAL NURSE

Overview: Students who enroll in this major learn the skills necessary to assist nurses and doctors and provide patients with basic nursing care. *Related majors:* nursing, physician assistant, clinical and medical social work. *Potential careers:* nurse practitioner, nurse, clinical social worker. *Salary potential:* $25k-$35k.

Comm Hospital Roanoke Valley–Coll of Health Scis (VA) ***328***

PRE-DENTISTRY

Overview: This major prepares students to enroll in a postgraduate-level program in dentistry so they may become professional dentists. *Related majors:* dental hygienist, dental laboratory technician. *Potential careers:* dentist, orthodontist, maxillofacial surgeon, endodontist, periodontist. *Salary potential:* $35k-$45k.

Abilene Christian U (TX) ***260***
Acadia U (NS, Canada) ***260***
Adams State Coll (CO) ***260***
Albertus Magnus Coll (CT) ***262***
Albright Coll (PA) ***263***
Alderson-Broaddus Coll (WV) ***263***
Alfred U (NY) ***263***
Alice Lloyd Coll (KY) ***263***
Allegheny Coll (PA) ***264***
Alma Coll (MI) ***264***
American International Coll (MA) ***267***
American U (DC) ***267***
Anderson U (IN) ***268***
Aquinas Coll (MI) ***270***
Arcadia U (PA) ***271***
Ashland U (OH) ***274***
Atlantic Union Coll (MA) ***276***
Auburn U (AL) ***276***
Augsburg Coll (MN) ***276***
Augustana Coll (IL) ***276***
Augustana Coll (SD) ***276***
Baker U (KS) ***280***
Baldwin-Wallace Coll (OH) ***280***
Ball State U (IN) ***280***
Bard Coll (NY) ***281***
Barry U (FL) ***282***
Barton Coll (NC) ***282***
Baylor U (TX) ***283***
Bellarmine U (KY) ***284***
Belmont Abbey Coll (NC) ***284***
Beloit Coll (WI) ***285***
Benedict Coll (SC) ***285***
Benedictine U (IL) ***285***
Berea Coll (KY) ***286***
Berry Coll (GA) ***287***
Bethany Coll (WV) ***287***
Bethel Coll (IN) ***288***
Bethel Coll (MN) ***288***
Bethel Coll (TN) ***288***
Birmingham-Southern Coll (AL) ***289***
Blackburn Coll (IL) ***290***
Bloomfield Coll (NJ) ***290***
Blue Mountain Coll (MS) ***291***
Boston U (MA) ***292***
Brandon U (MB, Canada) ***293***
Brevard Coll (NC) ***294***
Briar Cliff U (IA) ***294***
Buena Vista U (IA) ***297***
California State U, Chico (CA) ***300***
California State U, Dominguez Hills (CA) ***300***
California State U, Fullerton (CA) ***301***
California State U, Hayward (CA) ***301***
California State U, Northridge (CA) ***301***
Calvin Coll (MI) ***303***
Campbellsville U (KY) ***303***
Campbell U (NC) ***303***
Capital U (OH) ***304***
Cardinal Stritch U (WI) ***305***
Carroll Coll (MT) ***306***
Carthage Coll (WI) ***306***
Catawba Coll (NC) ***307***
Cedar Crest Coll (PA) ***308***
Cedarville U (OH) ***308***
Centenary Coll of Louisiana (LA) ***308***
Central Missouri State U (MO) ***310***
Centre Coll (KY) ***310***
Chapman U (CA) ***311***
Charleston Southern U (SC) ***311***
Chowan Coll (NC) ***312***
Christian Brothers U (TN) ***313***
City Coll of the City U of NY (NY) ***314***
Claremont McKenna Coll (CA) ***315***
Clark U (MA) ***316***
Coe Coll (IA) ***318***
Coll Misericordia (PA) ***319***
Coll of Charleston (SC) ***320***
Coll of Mount Saint Vincent (NY) ***320***
Coll of Saint Benedict (MN) ***321***

Coll of St. Catherine (MN) **321**
Coll of Saint Elizabeth (NJ) **321**
Coll of Saint Mary (NE) **322**
Coll of Santa Fe (NM) **323**
Coll of the Holy Cross (MA) **323**
The Coll of Wooster (OH) **324**
Colorado State U (CO) **325**
Colorado State U-Pueblo (CO) **325**
Columbia Coll (MO) **326**
Columbia Coll (SC) **327**
Columbia Union Coll (MD) **328**
Columbus State U (GA) **328**
Concordia Coll (MN) **329**
Concordia U (IL) **330**
Concordia U at Austin (TX) **331**
Concordia U Wisconsin (WI) **331**
Converse Coll (SC) **332**
Cornerstone U (MI) **333**
Cumberland U (TN) **335**
Dakota State U (SD) **335**
Dalhousie U (NS, Canada) **336**
Davis & Elkins Coll (WV) **338**
Defiance Coll (OH) **338**
DeSales U (PA) **340**
Dickinson Coll (PA) **344**
Dickinson State U (ND) **344**
Dillard U (LA) **344**
Dominican U (IL) **345**
Dordt Coll (IA) **345**
Drake U (IA) **345**
Drury U (MO) **346**
D'Youville Coll (NY) **347**
East Central U (OK) **347**
Eastern Kentucky U (KY) **348**
Eastern Mennonite U (VA) **348**
Eastern Oregon U (OR) **349**
Eastern Washington U (WA) **349**
Eckerd Coll (FL) **350**
Edgewood Coll (WI) **351**
Elizabethtown Coll (PA) **351**
Elmhurst Coll (IL) **351**
Elmira Coll (NY) **351**
Elms Coll (MA) **352**
Elon U (NC) **352**
Emmanuel Coll (MA) **353**
Emory & Henry Coll (VA) **353**
Eureka Coll (IL) **355**
Evangel U (MO) **355**
The Evergreen State Coll (WA) **355**
Florida A&M U (FL) **359**
Florida Southern Coll (FL) **361**
Florida State U (FL) **361**
Fordham U (NY) **362**
Fort Lewis Coll (CO) **362**
Framingham State Coll (MA) **362**
Francis Marion U (SC) **363**
Franklin Pierce Coll (NH) **364**
Freed-Hardeman U (TN) **364**
Furman U (SC) **365**
Gannon U (PA) **365**
Georgetown Coll (KY) **366**
The George Washington U (DC) **367**
Georgian Court Coll (NJ) **367**
Georgia Southwestern State U (GA) **368**
Gettysburg Coll (PA) **368**
Goshen Coll (IN) **370**
Graceland U (IA) **371**
Grand Canyon U (AZ) **371**
Grand Valley State U (MI) **371**
Greenville Coll (IL) **373**
Grove City Coll (PA) **373**
Gustavus Adolphus Coll (MN) **374**
Gwynedd-Mercy Coll (PA) **374**
Hamline U (MN) **374**
Hampton U (VA) **375**
Harding U (AR) **375**
Hardin-Simmons U (TX) **376**
Harvard U (MA) **376**
Hastings Coll (NE) **377**
Heidelberg Coll (OH) **377**
High Point U (NC) **379**
Hillsdale Coll (MI) **379**
Hiram Coll (OH) **379**
Hobart and William Smith Colls (NY) **380**
Holy Family U (PA) **380**
Hood Coll (MD) **381**
Houghton Coll (NY) **381**
Houston Baptist U (TX) **382**
Humboldt State U (CA) **382**
Huntingdon Coll (AL) **383**
Huntington Coll (IN) **383**
Illinois Coll (IL) **384**
Illinois Wesleyan U (IL) **385**
Immaculata U (PA) **385**
Indiana U Bloomington (IN) **385**
Indiana U–Purdue U Fort Wayne (IN) **386**
Indiana U–Purdue U Indianapolis (IN) **387**
Indiana Wesleyan U (IN) **387**
Iowa State U of Science and Technology (IA) **390**
Iowa Wesleyan Coll (IA) **390**
Jackson State U (MS) **390**
Jacksonville U (FL) **391**
John Carroll U (OH) **392**
Juniata Coll (PA) **395**
Kansas State U (KS) **396**
Kent State U (OH) **397**
Kentucky Wesleyan Coll (KY) **397**
King's Coll (PA) **398**
LaGrange Coll (GA) **400**
Lake Erie Coll (OH) **400**
Lake Forest Coll (IL) **400**
Lamar U (TX) **401**
Lambuth U (TN) **401**
Lander U (SC) **401**
Langston U (OK) **402**
La Salle U (PA) **402**
La Sierra U (CA) **403**
Lawrence U (WI) **403**
Lebanon Valley Coll (PA) **403**
Lehigh U (PA) **404**
Le Moyne Coll (NY) **404**
Lenoir-Rhyne Coll (NC) **405**
LeTourneau U (TX) **405**
Lewis & Clark Coll (OR) **405**
Lewis U (IL) **406**
Lindenwood U (MO) **407**
Lindsey Wilson Coll (KY) **407**
Lipscomb U (TN) **408**
Lock Haven U of Pennsylvania (PA) **408**
Long Island U, C.W. Post Campus (NY) **409**
Longwood U (VA) **409**
Loyola U Chicago (IL) **411**
Lubbock Christian U (TX) **412**
Luther Coll (IA) **412**
Lycoming Coll (PA) **412**
Lynchburg Coll (VA) **413**
MacMurray Coll (IL) **414**
Manchester Coll (IN) **415**
Manhattanville Coll (NY) **416**
Marian Coll (IN) **417**
Marian Coll of Fond du Lac (WI) **417**
Marist Coll (NY) **417**
Marquette U (WI) **418**
Mars Hill Coll (NC) **418**
Mary Washington Coll (VA) **420**
Massachusetts Inst of Technology (MA) **421**
Mayville State U (ND) **422**
McKendree Coll (IL) **423**
McPherson Coll (KS) **423**
Mercy Coll (NY) **425**
Mercyhurst Coll (PA) **425**
Meredith Coll (NC) **426**
Merrimack Coll (MA) **426**
Methodist Coll (NC) **427**
Miami U (OH) **428**
Michigan Technological U (MI) **428**
Middlebury Coll (VT) **429**
Midland Lutheran Coll (NE) **429**
Midwestern State U (TX) **430**
Milligan Coll (TN) **430**
Millikin U (IL) **430**
Minnesota State U, Mankato (MN) **431**
Minnesota State U, Moorhead (MN) **432**
Mississippi Coll (MS) **432**
Missouri Southern State Coll (MO) **433**
Molloy Coll (NY) **433**
Montclair State U (NJ) **435**
Montreat Coll (NC) **435**
Morgan State U (MD) **436**
Morningside Coll (IA) **437**
Mount Allison U (NB, Canada) **437**
Mount Mary Coll (WI) **438**
Mount Mercy Coll (IA) **438**
Mount St. Mary's Coll (CA) **439**
Mount Vernon Nazarene U (OH) **440**
Muhlenberg Coll (PA) **440**
Muskingum Coll (OH) **441**
Nazareth Coll of Rochester (NY) **443**
Newberry Coll (SC) **444**
Newman U (KS) **445**
New Mexico Inst of Mining and Technology (NM) **446**
New York U (NY) **447**
Niagara U (NY) **447**
Nicholls State U (LA) **447**
North Central Coll (IL) **449**
North Dakota State U (ND) **449**
Northeastern State U (OK) **450**
Northern Kentucky U (KY) **451**
Northern Michigan U (MI) **451**
Northern State U (SD) **451**
North Georgia Coll & State U (GA) **451**
Northland Coll (WI) **452**
North Park U (IL) **452**
Northwestern Oklahoma State U (OK) **453**
Northwest Missouri State U (MO) **454**
Notre Dame Coll (OH) **455**
Notre Dame de Namur U (CA) **455**
Nova Southeastern U (FL) **455**
Oakland U (MI) **456**
Oglethorpe U (GA) **457**
Ohio U (OH) **458**
Ohio Wesleyan U (OH) **459**
Oklahoma Baptist U (OK) **459**
Oklahoma City U (OK) **460**
Oklahoma State U (OK) **460**
Oklahoma Wesleyan U (OK) **460**
Olivet Coll (MI) **461**
Olivet Nazarene U (IL) **461**
Oral Roberts U (OK) **461**
Oregon State U (OR) **462**
Otterbein Coll (OH) **462**
Ouachita Baptist U (AR) **462**
Pacific Union Coll (CA) **464**
Pacific U (OR) **464**
Paine Coll (GA) **465**
Pepperdine U, Malibu (CA) **469**
Peru State Coll (NE) **469**
Pittsburg State U (KS) **470**
Presbyterian Coll (SC) **473**
Purdue U Calumet (IN) **475**
Queens Coll of the City U of NY (NY) **475**
Quincy U (IL) **476**
Quinnipiac U (CT) **476**
Regis U (CO) **478**
Rensselaer Polytechnic Inst (NY) **478**
Rhode Island Coll (RI) **479**
Ripon Coll (WI) **480**
Rivier Coll (NH) **480**
Roberts Wesleyan Coll (NY) **481**
Rochester Inst of Technology (NY) **482**
Rockford Coll (IL) **482**
Roger Williams U (RI) **483**
Rollins Coll (FL) **483**
Roosevelt U (IL) **483**
Rutgers, The State U of New Jersey, New Brunswick (NJ) **485**
Sacred Heart U (CT) **486**
Saint Anselm Coll (NH) **487**
St. Bonaventure U (NY) **487**
St. Francis Coll (NY) **488**
Saint Francis U (PA) **488**
St. Francis Xavier U (NS, Canada) **489**
Saint John's U (MN) **490**
St. Joseph's Coll, Suffolk Campus (NY) **491**
Saint Leo U (FL) **492**
Saint Martin's Coll (WA) **493**
Saint Mary-of-the-Woods Coll (IN) **493**
Saint Mary's Coll of California (CA) **494**
St. Mary's U of San Antonio (TX) **494**
Saint Michael's Coll (VT) **494**
St. Norbert Coll (WI) **495**
St. Thomas U (FL) **496**
Salem State Coll (MA) **497**
Sarah Lawrence Coll (NY) **499**
Schreiner U (TX) **501**
Seattle Pacific U (WA) **501**
Seton Hill U (PA) **502**
Siena Coll (NY) **504**
Simmons Coll (MA) **504**
Simpson Coll (IA) **505**
Slippery Rock U of Pennsylvania (PA) **506**
Sonoma State U (CA) **506**
South Carolina State U (SC) **506**
South Dakota State U (SD) **507**
Southern Connecticut State U (CT) **509**
Southern Nazarene U (OK) **510**
Southwestern Oklahoma State U (OK) **512**
Southwest State U (MN) **513**
Springfield Coll (MA) **514**
Spring Hill Coll (AL) **514**
State U of NY at New Paltz (NY) **515**
State U of NY at Oswego (NY) **515**
State U of NY Coll at Brockport (NY) **515**
State U of NY Coll at Buffalo (NY) **516**
State U of NY Coll at Cortland (NY) **516**
State U of NY Coll at Geneseo (NY) **516**
State U of NY Coll at Oneonta (NY) **517**
State U of NY Coll of Environ Sci and Forestry (NY) **517**
Stetson U (FL) **519**
Stevens Inst of Technology (NJ) **519**
Stonehill Coll (MA) **520**
Suffolk U (MA) **520**
Sul Ross State U (TX) **521**
Susquehanna U (PA) **521**
Syracuse U (NY) **521**
Tabor Coll (KS) **522**
Talladega Coll (AL) **522**
Taylor U (IN) **523**
Tennessee Technological U (TN) **524**
Tennessee Wesleyan Coll (TN) **524**
Texas A&M U–Kingsville (TX) **525**
Texas Lutheran U (TX) **526**
Texas Southern U (TX) **526**
Texas Wesleyan U (TX) **526**
Thiel Coll (PA) **527**
Touro Coll (NY) **529**
Trinity Christian Coll (IL) **530**
Trinity U (TX) **531**
Trinity Western U (BC, Canada) **531**
Troy State U (AL) **532**
Truman State U (MO) **532**
Union Coll (KY) **533**
Union U (TN) **534**
Université Laval (QC, Canada) **536**
The U of Akron (OH) **537**
U of Alberta (AB, Canada) **538**
U of Arkansas at Monticello (AR) **539**
U of Bridgeport (CT) **540**
The U of British Columbia (BC, Canada) **540**
U of Colorado at Colorado Springs (CO) **543**
U of Dallas (TX) **544**
U of Dayton (OH) **544**
U of Evansville (IN) **545**
U of Hartford (CT) **546**
U of Hawaii at Manoa (HI) **546**
U of Houston (TX) **547**
U of Illinois at Chicago (IL) **547**
U of Indianapolis (IN) **548**
The U of Iowa (IA) **548**
U of La Verne (CA) **549**
U of Manitoba (MB, Canada) **551**
U of Mary Hardin-Baylor (TX) **551**
U of Maryland, Baltimore County (MD) **552**
U of Maryland Eastern Shore (MD) **552**
U of Massachusetts Amherst (MA) **552**
U of Miami (FL) **553**
U of Minnesota, Duluth (MN) **554**
U of Minnesota, Morris (MN) **555**
U of Minnesota, Twin Cities Campus (MN) **555**
U of Missouri–Rolla (MO) **556**
U of Missouri–St. Louis (MO) **556**
The U of Montana–Western (MT) **556**
U of Montevallo (AL) **557**
U of Nebraska–Lincoln (NE) **557**
U of Nevada, Reno (NV) **558**
U of New Brunswick Fredericton (NB, Canada) **558**
U of New England (ME) **558**
U of New Orleans (LA) **559**
The U of North Carolina at Greensboro (NC) **560**
U of North Texas (TX) **562**
U of Oklahoma (OK) **562**
U of Oregon (OR) **562**
U of Pennsylvania (PA) **563**
U of Pittsburgh at Johnstown (PA) **570**
U of Portland (OR) **570**
U of Prince Edward Island (PE, Canada) **570**
U of Puget Sound (WA) **571**
U of Regina (SK, Canada) **572**
U of Rio Grande (OH) **572**
U of St. Francis (IL) **573**
U of Saint Francis (IN) **573**
U of St. Thomas (TX) **573**
U of San Francisco (CA) **574**
U of Saskatchewan (SK, Canada) **574**
U of Sioux Falls (SD) **574**
The U of South Dakota (SD) **575**
The U of Tampa (FL) **577**
The U of Tennessee at Martin (TN) **577**
The U of Texas–Pan American (TX) **579**
U of the Incarnate Word (TX) **580**
U of the Ozarks (AR) **580**
U of the Sciences in Philadelphia (PA) **580**
U of Toledo (OH) **581**
U of Toronto (ON, Canada) **581**
U of Victoria (BC, Canada) **582**
U of Windsor (ON, Canada) **584**

PRE-DENTISTRY (continued)

U of Wisconsin–Green Bay (WI) ***584***
U of Wisconsin–Milwaukee (WI) ***585***
U of Wisconsin–Oshkosh (WI) ***585***
U of Wisconsin–Parkside (WI) ***585***
U of Wisconsin–River Falls (WI) ***585***
Upper Iowa U (IA) ***587***
Urbana U (OH) ***587***
Ursinus Coll (PA) ***587***
Utah State U (UT) ***587***
Utica Coll (NY) ***588***
Valdosta State U (GA) ***588***
Valley City State U (ND) ***588***
Villa Julie Coll (MD) ***590***
Villanova U (PA) ***590***
Virginia Wesleyan Coll (VA) ***591***
Viterbo U (WI) ***591***
Wagner Coll (NY) ***592***
Walla Walla Coll (WA) ***593***
Walsh U (OH) ***593***
Washington Coll (MD) ***594***
Washington State U (WA) ***595***
Washington U in St. Louis (MO) ***595***
Waynesburg Coll (PA) ***595***
Wells Coll (NY) ***597***
West Chester U of Pennsylvania (PA) ***598***
Western Connecticut State U (CT) ***598***
Western State Coll of Colorado (CO) ***600***
West Liberty State Coll (WV) ***601***
Westminster Coll (MO) ***601***
Westminster Coll (PA) ***601***
Westmont Coll (CA) ***602***
West Virginia State Coll (WV) ***602***
West Virginia Wesleyan Coll (WV) ***603***
Whitworth Coll (WA) ***604***
Wiley Coll (TX) ***605***
Wilkes U (PA) ***605***
Willamette U (OR) ***605***
William Carey Coll (MS) ***605***
William Jewell Coll (MO) ***606***
William Paterson U of New Jersey (NJ) ***606***
William Penn U (IA) ***606***
Williams Baptist Coll (AR) ***606***
Wilmington Coll (OH) ***607***
Winona State U (MN) ***608***
Wittenberg U (OH) ***608***
Wofford Coll (SC) ***609***
Xavier U of Louisiana (LA) ***610***
York Coll of Pennsylvania (PA) ***610***
York U (ON, Canada) ***611***
Youngstown State U (OH) ***611***

PRE-ENGINEERING

Overview: This major is offered by colleges that don't have dedicated engineering schools or departments. Students who choose this major focus on a wide range of math, physics, and other science-related courses to prepare them for applying to an engineering or technology school for post-doctoral work in a specific area. *Related majors:* mathematics, physics, chemistry, computer science. *Potential careers:* civil engineer, electrical engineer or technician, computer engineer or technician, chemical engineer or technician. *Salary potential:* $30k-$50k, after postdoctoral studies in engineering or technology.

Azusa Pacific U (CA) ***278***
Columbia Coll (MO) ***326***
Concordia Coll (MN) ***329***
Grand View Coll (IA) ***372***
Lewis & Clark Coll (OR) ***405***
McPherson Coll (KS) ***423***
Rutgers, The State U of New Jersey, Camden (NJ) ***485***
St. Norbert Coll (WI) ***495***
The U of Montana–Missoula (MT) ***556***
Valley City State U (ND) ***588***
Waynesburg Coll (PA) ***595***

PRE-LAW

Overview: This major prepares students to attend law school. *Related majors:* law and legal studies, speech/rhetorical studies, American government/politics, law enforcement administration, philosophy. *Potential careers:* lawyer, politician, writer, teacher. *Salary potential:* for those who go on to attend law school, the average salary for lawyers is $40k-$70k.

Abilene Christian U (TX) ***260***
Acadia U (NS, Canada) ***260***
Adams State Coll (CO) ***260***
Albertus Magnus Coll (CT) ***262***
Albion Coll (MI) ***262***
Albright Coll (PA) ***263***
Alderson-Broaddus Coll (WV) ***263***
Alfred U (NY) ***263***
Alice Lloyd Coll (KY) ***263***
Allegheny Coll (PA) ***264***
Alma Coll (MI) ***264***
Alvernia Coll (PA) ***265***
American International Coll (MA) ***267***
American U (DC) ***267***
Anderson U (IN) ***268***
Andrews U (MI) ***269***
Antioch Coll (OH) ***269***
Aquinas Coll (MI) ***270***
Arcadia U (PA) ***271***
Arizona State U (AZ) ***271***
Ashland U (OH) ***274***
Atlantic Union Coll (MA) ***276***
Auburn U (AL) ***276***
Augsburg Coll (MN) ***276***
Augustana Coll (IL) ***276***
Augustana Coll (SD) ***276***
Azusa Pacific U (CA) ***278***
Baker U (KS) ***280***
Baldwin-Wallace Coll (OH) ***280***
Ball State U (IN) ***280***
Barber-Scotia Coll (NC) ***281***
Bard Coll (NY) ***281***
Barry U (FL) ***282***
Barton Coll (NC) ***282***
Baylor U (TX) ***283***
Bellarmine U (KY) ***284***
Belmont Abbey Coll (NC) ***284***
Beloit Coll (WI) ***285***
Bemidji State U (MN) ***285***
Benedict Coll (SC) ***285***
Benedictine Coll (KS) ***285***
Benedictine U (IL) ***285***
Berry Coll (GA) ***287***
Bethany Coll (WV) ***287***
Bethel Coll (IN) ***288***
Bethel Coll (MN) ***288***
Biola U (CA) ***289***
Birmingham-Southern Coll (AL) ***289***
Blackburn Coll (IL) ***290***
Blue Mountain Coll (MS) ***291***
Bluffton Coll (OH) ***291***
Bowling Green State U (OH) ***292***
Brandon U (MB, Canada) ***293***
Brewton-Parker Coll (GA) ***294***
Briar Cliff U (IA) ***294***
Bridgewater State Coll (MA) ***294***
Buena Vista U (IA) ***297***
California State Polytechnic U, Pomona (CA) ***300***
California State U, Dominguez Hills (CA) ***300***
California State U, Fresno (CA) ***301***
California State U, Northridge (CA) ***301***
Calumet Coll of Saint Joseph (IN) ***302***
Calvin Coll (MI) ***303***
Campbellsville U (KY) ***303***
Campbell U (NC) ***303***
Cardinal Stritch U (WI) ***305***
Carleton U (ON, Canada) ***305***
Carroll Coll (MT) ***306***
Carthage Coll (WI) ***306***
Catawba Coll (NC) ***307***
Cedar Crest Coll (PA) ***308***
Cedarville U (OH) ***308***
Centenary Coll of Louisiana (LA) ***308***
Central Christian Coll of Kansas (KS) ***309***
Centre Coll (KY) ***310***
Chapman U (CA) ***311***
Charleston Southern U (SC) ***311***
Chowan Coll (NC) ***312***
Christian Brothers U (TN) ***313***
Christopher Newport U (VA) ***313***
City Coll of the City U of NY (NY) ***314***
Claremont McKenna Coll (CA) ***315***
Clarkson U (NY) ***316***
Clark U (MA) ***316***
Clearwater Christian Coll (FL) ***316***
Coe Coll (IA) ***318***
Coll Misericordia (PA) ***319***
Coll of Mount Saint Vincent (NY) ***320***
The Coll of New Jersey (NJ) ***320***
The Coll of New Rochelle (NY) ***321***
Coll of Notre Dame of Maryland (MD) ***321***
Coll of Saint Benedict (MN) ***321***
Coll of St. Catherine (MN) ***321***
Coll of Saint Elizabeth (NJ) ***321***
Coll of St. Joseph (VT) ***322***
Coll of Saint Mary (NE) ***322***
Coll of Santa Fe (NM) ***323***
Coll of the Holy Cross (MA) ***323***
The Coll of Wooster (OH) ***324***
Colorado State U (CO) ***325***
Colorado State U-Pueblo (CO) ***325***
Columbia Coll (MO) ***326***
Columbia Coll (SC) ***327***
Columbia Union Coll (MD) ***328***
Columbus State U (GA) ***328***
Concordia Coll (MN) ***329***
Concordia Coll (NY) ***329***
Concordia U (CA) ***330***
Concordia U (IL) ***330***
Concordia U (MI) ***330***
Concordia U at Austin (TX) ***331***
Concordia U Wisconsin (WI) ***331***
Converse Coll (SC) ***332***
Cornell U (NY) ***333***
Cornerstone U (MI) ***333***
Covenant Coll (GA) ***333***
Crichton Coll (TN) ***334***
Curry Coll (MA) ***335***
Dakota State U (SD) ***335***
Dalhousie U (NS, Canada) ***336***
Davis & Elkins Coll (WV) ***338***
Defiance Coll (OH) ***338***
DePaul U (IL) ***339***
Dickinson Coll (PA) ***344***
Dickinson State U (ND) ***344***
Dillard U (LA) ***344***
Dominican Coll (NY) ***344***
Dominican U (IL) ***345***
Drake U (IA) ***345***
Drury U (MO) ***346***
D'Youville Coll (NY) ***347***
Earlham Coll (IN) ***347***
East Central U (OK) ***347***
Eastern Kentucky U (KY) ***348***
Eastern Nazarene Coll (MA) ***348***
Eastern Oregon U (OR) ***349***
Eastern Washington U (WA) ***349***
Eckerd Coll (FL) ***350***
Edgewood Coll (WI) ***351***
Elizabethtown Coll (PA) ***351***
Elmhurst Coll (IL) ***351***
Elmira Coll (NY) ***351***
Elms Coll (MA) ***352***
Elon U (NC) ***352***
Emmanuel Coll (GA) ***353***
Emmanuel Coll (MA) ***353***
Emory & Henry Coll (VA) ***353***
Eureka Coll (IL) ***355***
Evangel U (MO) ***355***
The Evergreen State Coll (WA) ***355***
Faulkner U (AL) ***357***
Felician Coll (NJ) ***357***
Florida State U (FL) ***361***
Fontbonne U (MO) ***361***
Fordham U (NY) ***362***
Fort Hays State U (KS) ***362***
Fort Lewis Coll (CO) ***362***
Framingham State Coll (MA) ***362***
The Franciscan U (IA) ***363***
Francis Marion U (SC) ***363***
Franklin Pierce Coll (NH) ***364***
Freed-Hardeman U (TN) ***364***
Fresno Pacific U (CA) ***364***
Frostburg State U (MD) ***365***
Furman U (SC) ***365***
Gannon U (PA) ***365***
Gardner-Webb U (NC) ***365***
Georgetown Coll (KY) ***366***
The George Washington U (DC) ***367***
Georgian Court Coll (NJ) ***367***
Georgia Southwestern State U (GA) ***368***
Gettysburg Coll (PA) ***368***
Goshen Coll (IN) ***370***
Graceland U (IA) ***371***
Grambling State U (LA) ***371***
Grand Canyon U (AZ) ***371***
Grand Valley State U (MI) ***371***
Grand View Coll (IA) ***372***
Greenville Coll (IL) ***373***
Grove City Coll (PA) ***373***
Gustavus Adolphus Coll (MN) ***374***
Gwynedd-Mercy Coll (PA) ***374***
Hamline U (MN) ***374***
Hampton U (VA) ***375***
Harding U (AR) ***375***
Hardin-Simmons U (TX) ***376***
Hartwick Coll (NY) ***376***
Harvard U (MA) ***376***
Hastings Coll (NE) ***377***
Haverford Coll (PA) ***377***
Heidelberg Coll (OH) ***377***
High Point U (NC) ***379***
Hiram Coll (OH) ***379***
Hobart and William Smith Colls (NY) ***380***
Holy Family U (PA) ***380***
Hood Coll (MD) ***381***
Houghton Coll (NY) ***381***
Houston Baptist U (TX) ***382***
Howard Payne U (TX) ***382***
Humboldt State U (CA) ***382***
Huntingdon Coll (AL) ***383***
Huntington Coll (IN) ***383***
Illinois Coll (IL) ***384***
Illinois Wesleyan U (IL) ***385***
Immaculata U (PA) ***385***
Indiana U Bloomington (IN) ***385***
Indiana U–Purdue U Indianapolis (IN) ***387***
Indiana Wesleyan U (IN) ***387***
Iowa State U of Science and Technology (IA) ***390***
Iowa Wesleyan Coll (IA) ***390***
Ithaca Coll (NY) ***390***
Jackson State U (MS) ***390***
Jacksonville U (FL) ***391***
John Brown U (AR) ***392***
John Carroll U (OH) ***392***
John Jay Coll of Criminal Justice, the City U of NY (NY) ***392***
Johnson C. Smith U (NC) ***394***
Judson Coll (IL) ***395***
Juniata Coll (PA) ***395***
Kentucky Wesleyan Coll (KY) ***397***
King Coll (TN) ***398***
King's Coll (PA) ***398***
LaGrange Coll (GA) ***400***
Lake Erie Coll (OH) ***400***
Lake Forest Coll (IL) ***400***
Lakeland Coll (WI) ***401***
Lambuth U (TN) ***401***
Lander U (SC) ***401***
Langston U (OK) ***402***
La Sierra U (CA) ***403***
Lawrence U (WI) ***403***
Lebanon Valley Coll (PA) ***403***
Lees-McRae Coll (NC) ***404***
Le Moyne Coll (NY) ***404***
Lenoir-Rhyne Coll (NC) ***405***
LeTourneau U (TX) ***405***
Lewis & Clark Coll (OR) ***405***
Lewis-Clark State Coll (ID) ***406***
Lewis U (IL) ***406***
Limestone Coll (SC) ***406***
Lincoln Memorial U (TN) ***407***
Lindenwood U (MO) ***407***
Lindsey Wilson Coll (KY) ***407***
Lipscomb U (TN) ***408***
Lock Haven U of Pennsylvania (PA) ***408***
Long Island U, Brooklyn Campus (NY) ***409***
Long Island U, C.W. Post Campus (NY) ***409***
Long Island U, Southampton Coll (NY) ***409***
Longwood U (VA) ***409***
Louisiana Coll (LA) ***410***
Loyola U Chicago (IL) ***411***
Lubbock Christian U (TX) ***412***
Luther Coll (IA) ***412***
Lycoming Coll (PA) ***412***
Lynchburg Coll (VA) ***413***
Lynn U (FL) ***413***
MacMurray Coll (IL) ***414***
Madonna U (MI) ***414***
Maharishi U of Management (IA) ***414***
Manchester Coll (IN) ***415***
Manhattanville Coll (NY) ***416***
Mansfield U of Pennsylvania (PA) ***416***
Marian Coll (IN) ***417***
Marian Coll of Fond du Lac (WI) ***417***
Marist Coll (NY) ***417***
Marlboro Coll (VT) ***418***
Marquette U (WI) ***418***
Mars Hill Coll (NC) ***418***
Marymount Coll of Fordham U (NY) ***419***

Mary Washington Coll (VA) **420**
Massachusetts Coll of Liberal Arts (MA) **421**
Massachusetts Inst of Technology (MA) **421**
Mayville State U (ND) **422**
McKendree Coll (IL) **423**
Medaille Coll (NY) **424**
Mercy Coll (NY) **425**
Mercyhurst Coll (PA) **425**
Merrimack Coll (MA) **426**
Methodist Coll (NC) **427**
Miami U (OH) **428**
Middlebury Coll (VT) **429**
Midland Lutheran Coll (NE) **429**
Midwestern State U (TX) **430**
Millikin U (IL) **430**
Minnesota State U, Mankato (MN) **431**
Minnesota State U, Moorhead (MN) **432**
Mississippi Coll (MS) **432**
Missouri Valley Coll (MO) **433**
Molloy Coll (NY) **433**
Montclair State U (NJ) **435**
Montreat Coll (NC) **435**
Morgan State U (MD) **436**
Morningside Coll (IA) **437**
Mount Allison U (NB, Canada) **437**
Mount Aloysius Coll (PA) **437**
Mount Mary Coll (WI) **438**
Mount Mercy Coll (IA) **438**
Mount Saint Mary Coll (NY) **439**
Mount St. Mary's Coll (CA) **439**
Mount Vernon Nazarene U (OH) **440**
Muhlenberg Coll (PA) **440**
Muskingum Coll (OH) **441**
Nazareth Coll of Rochester (NY) **443**
Newberry Coll (SC) **444**
Newbury Coll (MA) **444**
New England Coll (NH) **444**
Newman U (KS) **445**
New Mexico Highlands U (NM) **446**
New York U (NY) **447**
Niagara U (NY) **447**
North Central Coll (IL) **449**
North Dakota State U (ND) **449**
Northeastern State U (OK) **450**
Northeastern U (MA) **450**
Northern Arizona U (AZ) **450**
Northern Kentucky U (KY) **451**
Northern Michigan U (MI) **451**
Northern State U (SD) **451**
Northland Coll (WI) **452**
North Park U (IL) **452**
Northwest Coll (WA) **452**
Northwestern Oklahoma State U (OK) **453**
Northwest Missouri State U (MO) **454**
Northwest Nazarene U (ID) **454**
Notre Dame Coll (OH) **455**
Notre Dame de Namur U (CA) **455**
Nova Southeastern U (FL) **455**
Oakland City U (IN) **456**
Oakland U (MI) **456**
Oglethorpe U (GA) **457**
Ohio U (OH) **458**
Ohio Wesleyan U (OH) **459**
Oklahoma Baptist U (OK) **459**
Oklahoma Christian U (OK) **459**
Oklahoma City U (OK) **460**
Oklahoma State U (OK) **460**
Oklahoma Wesleyan U (OK) **460**
Olivet Coll (MI) **461**
Olivet Nazarene U (IL) **461**
Otterbein Coll (OH) **462**
Pacific Union Coll (CA) **464**
Palm Beach Atlantic U (FL) **465**
Pepperdine U, Malibu (CA) **469**
Peru State Coll (NE) **469**
Pfeiffer U (NC) **469**
Pittsburg State U (KS) **470**
Point Park Coll (PA) **471**
Pontifical Catholic U of Puerto Rico (PR) **472**
Presbyterian Coll (SC) **473**
Purdue U Calumet (IN) **475**
Queens U of Charlotte (NC) **476**
Quinnipiac U (CT) **476**
Regis U (CO) **478**
Rensselaer Polytechnic Inst (NY) **478**
Rhode Island Coll (RI) **479**
Ripon Coll (WI) **480**
Rivier Coll (NH) **480**
Roberts Wesleyan Coll (NY) **481**
Rochester Inst of Technology (NY) **482**
Rockford Coll (IL) **482**
Rocky Mountain Coll (MT) **482**
Rollins Coll (FL) **483**
Roosevelt U (IL) **483**
Rowan U (NJ) **484**
Rutgers, The State U of New Jersey, New Brunswick (NJ) **485**
St. Andrews Presbyterian Coll (NC) **487**
Saint Anselm Coll (NH) **487**
St. Bonaventure U (NY) **487**
St. Cloud State U (MN) **488**
St. Francis Coll (NY) **488**
Saint Francis U (PA) **488**
St. Francis Xavier U (NS, Canada) **489**
Saint John's U (MN) **490**
Saint Joseph Coll (CT) **490**
St. Joseph's Coll, New York (NY) **491**
St. Joseph's Coll, Suffolk Campus (NY) **491**
Saint Leo U (FL) **492**
Saint Martin's Coll (WA) **493**
Saint Mary-of-the-Woods Coll (IN) **493**
Saint Mary's Coll of California (CA) **494**
Saint Michael's Coll (VT) **494**
St. Norbert Coll (WI) **495**
St. Thomas U (FL) **496**
Salem State Coll (MA) **497**
San Diego State U (CA) **498**
Sarah Lawrence Coll (NY) **499**
Schreiner U (TX) **501**
Seattle Pacific U (WA) **501**
Seton Hill U (PA) **502**
Shawnee State U (OH) **502**
Siena Coll (NY) **504**
Siena Heights U (MI) **504**
Simmons Coll (MA) **504**
Simon's Rock Coll of Bard (MA) **505**
Simpson Coll (IA) **505**
Sonoma State U (CA) **506**
South Carolina State U (SC) **506**
South Dakota State U (SD) **507**
Southern Connecticut State U (CT) **509**
Southern Nazarene U (OK) **510**
Southern Oregon U (OR) **510**
Southwestern Oklahoma State U (OK) **512**
Southwest State U (MN) **513**
Spalding U (KY) **513**
Springfield Coll (MA) **514**
State U of NY at Binghamton (NY) **515**
State U of NY at New Paltz (NY) **515**
State U of NY at Oswego (NY) **515**
State U of NY Coll at Brockport (NY) **515**
State U of NY Coll at Buffalo (NY) **516**
State U of NY Coll at Cortland (NY) **516**
State U of NY Coll at Fredonia (NY) **516**
State U of NY Coll at Geneseo (NY) **516**
State U of NY Coll at Oneonta (NY) **517**
State U of NY Coll of Environ Sci and Forestry (NY) **517**
State U of West Georgia (GA) **518**
Stephens Coll (MO) **519**
Stetson U (FL) **519**
Stevens Inst of Technology (NJ) **519**
Stonehill Coll (MA) **520**
Suffolk U (MA) **520**
Sul Ross State U (TX) **521**
Susquehanna U (PA) **521**
Syracuse U (NY) **521**
Talladega Coll (AL) **522**
Taylor U (IN) **523**
Taylor U, Fort Wayne Campus (IN) **523**
Tennessee Technological U (TN) **524**
Tennessee Wesleyan Coll (TN) **524**
Texas A&M U–Kingsville (TX) **525**
Texas Lutheran U (TX) **526**
Texas Wesleyan U (TX) **526**
Thiel Coll (PA) **527**
Thomas More Coll (KY) **528**
Touro Coll (NY) **529**
Trinity Coll (DC) **530**
Trinity U (TX) **531**
Trinity Western U (BC, Canada) **531**
Tri-State U (IN) **532**
Truman State U (MO) **532**
Tusculum Coll (TN) **533**
Union Coll (KY) **533**
Union U (TN) **534**
United States Military Academy (NY) **535**
The U of Akron (OH) **537**
U of Alberta (AB, Canada) **538**
U of Arkansas at Monticello (AR) **539**
U of Bridgeport (CT) **540**
The U of British Columbia (BC, Canada) **540**
U of Calif, Riverside (CA) **541**
U of Cincinnati (OH) **543**
U of Colorado at Colorado Springs (CO) **543**
U of Dallas (TX) **544**
U of Dayton (OH) **544**
U of Evansville (IN) **545**
The U of Findlay (OH) **545**
U of Hawaii at Manoa (HI) **546**
U of Houston (TX) **547**
U of Illinois at Chicago (IL) **547**
U of Indianapolis (IN) **548**
The U of Iowa (IA) **548**
U of La Verne (CA) **549**
U of Louisiana at Lafayette (LA) **550**
U of Manitoba (MB, Canada) **551**
U of Mary Hardin-Baylor (TX) **551**
U of Maryland, Baltimore County (MD) **552**
U of Maryland Eastern Shore (MD) **552**
U of Miami (FL) **553**
U of Minnesota, Duluth (MN) **554**
U of Minnesota, Morris (MN) **555**
U of Minnesota, Twin Cities Campus (MN) **555**
U of Missouri–Rolla (MO) **556**
U of Missouri–St. Louis (MO) **556**
The U of Montana–Missoula (MT) **556**
The U of Montana–Western (MT) **556**
U of Montevallo (AL) **557**
U of Nebraska at Omaha (NE) **557**
U of New Brunswick Fredericton (NB, Canada) **558**
U of New England (ME) **558**
The U of North Carolina at Greensboro (NC) **560**
The U of North Carolina at Pembroke (NC) **560**
U of Ottawa (ON, Canada) **563**
U of Pittsburgh at Greensburg (PA) **570**
U of Pittsburgh at Johnstown (PA) **570**
U of Portland (OR) **570**
U of Puget Sound (WA) **571**
U of Regina (SK, Canada) **572**
U of Rio Grande (OH) **572**
U of Saint Francis (IN) **573**
U of St. Thomas (TX) **573**
U of San Francisco (CA) **574**
U of Saskatchewan (SK, Canada) **574**
U of Sioux Falls (SD) **574**
The U of South Dakota (SD) **575**
The U of Tampa (FL) **577**
U of the Incarnate Word (TX) **580**
U of Toledo (OH) **581**
U of Toronto (ON, Canada) **581**
U of Victoria (BC, Canada) **582**
U of West Los Angeles (CA) **583**
U of Windsor (ON, Canada) **584**
U of Wisconsin–Milwaukee (WI) **585**
U of Wisconsin–Oshkosh (WI) **585**
U of Wisconsin–Parkside (WI) **585**
U of Wisconsin–River Falls (WI) **585**
U of Wisconsin–Superior (WI) **586**
U of Wisconsin–Whitewater (WI) **586**
Urbana U (OH) **587**
Ursinus Coll (PA) **587**
Ursuline Coll (OH) **587**
Utah State U (UT) **587**
Utica Coll (NY) **588**
Valdosta State U (GA) **588**
Valley City State U (ND) **588**
Vanguard U of Southern California (CA) **589**
Villa Julie Coll (MD) **590**
Villanova U (PA) **590**
Virginia Intermont Coll (VA) **590**
Virginia Wesleyan Coll (VA) **591**
Viterbo U (WI) **591**
Wabash Coll (IN) **592**
Wagner Coll (NY) **592**
Walla Walla Coll (WA) **593**
Walsh U (OH) **593**
Warner Pacific Coll (OR) **593**
Warner Southern Coll (FL) **593**
Washington Coll (MD) **594**
Washington State U (WA) **595**
Waynesburg Coll (PA) **595**
Webber International U (FL) **596**
Wells Coll (NY) **597**
West Chester U of Pennsylvania (PA) **598**
Western Baptist Coll (OR) **598**
Western New Mexico U (NM) **600**
Western State Coll of Colorado (CO) **600**
Western Washington U (WA) **600**
Westfield State Coll (MA) **600**
West Liberty State Coll (WV) **601**
Westminster Coll (MO) **601**
Westminster Coll (PA) **601**
Westmont Coll (CA) **602**
West Virginia Wesleyan Coll (WV) **603**
Whitworth Coll (WA) **604**
Wiley Coll (TX) **605**
Wilkes U (PA) **605**
Willamette U (OR) **605**
William Carey Coll (MS) **605**
William Jewell Coll (MO) **606**
William Paterson U of New Jersey (NJ) **606**
William Penn U (IA) **606**
Williams Baptist Coll (AR) **606**
Wilmington Coll (OH) **607**
Wingate U (NC) **607**
Winona State U (MN) **608**
Wittenberg U (OH) **608**
Wofford Coll (SC) **609**
Xavier U of Louisiana (LA) **610**
York Coll of Pennsylvania (PA) **610**
York U (ON, Canada) **611**
Youngstown State U (OH) **611**

PRE-MEDICINE

Overview: This major prepares students to enroll in a postgraduate-level program in medicine so they may become professional, licensed physicians. *Related majors:* medical anatomy, medical physiology, biology. *Potential careers:* physician (pediatrics, obstetrics, gynecological, cardiovascular, pathologist). *Salary potential:* $38k-$48k.

Abilene Christian U (TX) **260**
Acadia U (NS, Canada) **260**
Adams State Coll (CO) **260**
Adrian Coll (MI) **260**
Alabama State U (AL) **261**
Albertson Coll of Idaho (ID) **262**
Albertus Magnus Coll (CT) **262**
Albion Coll (MI) **262**
Albright Coll (PA) **263**
Alderson-Broaddus Coll (WV) **263**
Alfred U (NY) **263**
Alice Lloyd Coll (KY) **263**
Allegheny Coll (PA) **264**
Alma Coll (MI) **264**
Alvernia Coll (PA) **265**
American International Coll (MA) **267**
American U (DC) **267**
Anderson U (IN) **268**
Andrews U (MI) **269**
Antioch Coll (OH) **269**
Appalachian State U (NC) **270**
Aquinas Coll (MI) **270**
Arcadia U (PA) **271**
Ashland U (OH) **274**
Atlantic Union Coll (MA) **276**
Auburn U (AL) **276**
Augsburg Coll (MN) **276**
Augustana Coll (IL) **276**
Augustana Coll (SD) **276**
Averett U (VA) **278**
Avila U (MO) **278**
Baker U (KS) **280**
Baldwin-Wallace Coll (OH) **280**
Ball State U (IN) **280**
Bard Coll (NY) **281**
Barnard Coll (NY) **282**
Barry U (FL) **282**
Barton Coll (NC) **282**
Baylor U (TX) **283**
Bellarmine U (KY) **284**
Belmont Abbey Coll (NC) **284**
Beloit Coll (WI) **285**
Bemidji State U (MN) **285**
Benedict Coll (SC) **285**
Benedictine U (IL) **285**
Bennington Coll (VT) **286**
Berea Coll (KY) **286**
Berry Coll (GA) **287**
Bethany Coll (WV) **287**
Bethel Coll (IN) **288**
Bethel Coll (MN) **288**
Bethel Coll (TN) **288**
Birmingham-Southern Coll (AL) **289**
Blackburn Coll (IL) **290**
Bloomfield Coll (NJ) **290**
Blue Mountain Coll (MS) **291**
Bluffton Coll (OH) **291**
Boston Coll (MA) **292**
Bowdoin Coll (ME) **292**
Brandon U (MB, Canada) **293**
Brevard Coll (NC) **294**

PRE-MEDICINE (continued)
Briar Cliff U (IA) ***294***
Bryan Coll (TN) ***296***
Buena Vista U (IA) ***297***
California Polytechnic State U, San Luis Obispo (CA) ***300***
California State Polytechnic U, Pomona (CA) ***300***
California State U, Chico (CA) ***300***
California State U, Dominguez Hills (CA) ***300***
California State U, Fullerton (CA) ***301***
California State U, Hayward (CA) ***301***
California State U, Northridge (CA) ***301***
Calvin Coll (MI) ***303***
Campbellsville U (KY) ***303***
Campbell U (NC) ***303***
Capital U (OH) ***304***
Cardinal Stritch U (WI) ***305***
Carroll Coll (MT) ***306***
Carroll Coll (WI) ***306***
Carthage Coll (WI) ***306***
Catawba Coll (NC) ***307***
Cedar Crest Coll (PA) ***308***
Cedarville U (OH) ***308***
Centenary Coll of Louisiana (LA) ***308***
Central Missouri State U (MO) ***310***
Centre Coll (KY) ***310***
Chapman U (CA) ***311***
Charleston Southern U (SC) ***311***
Chowan Coll (NC) ***312***
Christian Brothers U (TN) ***313***
City Coll of the City U of NY (NY) ***314***
Claflin U (SC) ***314***
Claremont McKenna Coll (CA) ***315***
Clarkson U (NY) ***316***
Clark U (MA) ***316***
Clearwater Christian Coll (FL) ***316***
Clemson U (SC) ***317***
Cleveland State U (OH) ***317***
Coe Coll (IA) ***318***
Coll Misericordia (PA) ***319***
Coll of Charleston (SC) ***320***
Coll of Mount Saint Vincent (NY) ***320***
The Coll of New Jersey (NJ) ***320***
The Coll of New Rochelle (NY) ***321***
Coll of Notre Dame of Maryland (MD) ***321***
Coll of Saint Benedict (MN) ***321***
Coll of St. Catherine (MN) ***321***
Coll of Saint Elizabeth (NJ) ***321***
Coll of Saint Mary (NE) ***322***
Coll of Santa Fe (NM) ***323***
Coll of the Holy Cross (MA) ***323***
Coll of the Ozarks (MO) ***323***
The Coll of Wooster (OH) ***324***
Colorado State U (CO) ***325***
Colorado State U-Pueblo (CO) ***325***
Columbia Coll (MO) ***326***
Columbia Coll (SC) ***327***
Columbia Union Coll (MD) ***328***
Columbus State U (GA) ***328***
Concord Coll (WV) ***329***
Concordia Coll (MN) ***329***
Concordia U (CA) ***330***
Concordia U (IL) ***330***
Concordia U (MI) ***330***
Concordia U (OR) ***330***
Concordia U at Austin (TX) ***331***
Concordia U Wisconsin (WI) ***331***
Converse Coll (SC) ***332***
Cornell U (NY) ***333***
Cornerstone U (MI) ***333***
Covenant Coll (GA) ***333***
Cumberland U (TN) ***335***
Dakota State U (SD) ***335***
Dalhousie U (NS, Canada) ***336***
Davis & Elkins Coll (WV) ***338***
Defiance Coll (OH) ***338***
DeSales U (PA) ***340***
Dickinson Coll (PA) ***344***
Dickinson State U (ND) ***344***
Dillard U (LA) ***344***
Dominican U (IL) ***345***
Dordt Coll (IA) ***345***
Drake U (IA) ***345***
Drury U (MO) ***346***
D'Youville Coll (NY) ***347***
Earlham Coll (IN) ***347***
East Central U (OK) ***347***
Eastern Kentucky U (KY) ***348***
Eastern Mennonite U (VA) ***348***
Eastern Michigan U (MI) ***348***
Eastern Nazarene Coll (MA) ***348***
Eastern Oregon U (OR) ***349***
Eastern Washington U (WA) ***349***
Eckerd Coll (FL) ***350***
Edgewood Coll (WI) ***351***
Elizabethtown Coll (PA) ***351***
Elmhurst Coll (IL) ***351***
Elmira Coll (NY) ***351***
Elms Coll (MA) ***352***
Elon U (NC) ***352***
Emmanuel Coll (MA) ***353***
Emory & Henry Coll (VA) ***353***
Eureka Coll (IL) ***355***
Evangel U (MO) ***355***
The Evergreen State Coll (WA) ***355***
Felician Coll (NJ) ***357***
Florida Southern Coll (FL) ***361***
Florida State U (FL) ***361***
Fontbonne U (MO) ***361***
Fordham U (NY) ***362***
Fort Lewis Coll (CO) ***362***
Framingham State Coll (MA) ***362***
The Franciscan U (IA) ***363***
Francis Marion U (SC) ***363***
Franklin Pierce Coll (NH) ***364***
Freed-Hardeman U (TN) ***364***
Fresno Pacific U (CA) ***364***
Furman U (SC) ***365***
Gannon U (PA) ***365***
Gardner-Webb U (NC) ***365***
Georgetown Coll (KY) ***366***
The George Washington U (DC) ***367***
Georgian Court Coll (NJ) ***367***
Georgia Southwestern State U (GA) ***368***
Gettysburg Coll (PA) ***368***
Goshen Coll (IN) ***370***
Graceland U (IA) ***371***
Grand Canyon U (AZ) ***371***
Grand Valley State U (MI) ***371***
Greenville Coll (IL) ***373***
Grove City Coll (PA) ***373***
Gustavus Adolphus Coll (MN) ***374***
Gwynedd-Mercy Coll (PA) ***374***
Hamline U (MN) ***374***
Hampshire Coll (MA) ***375***
Hampton U (VA) ***375***
Harding U (AR) ***375***
Hardin-Simmons U (TX) ***376***
Hartwick Coll (NY) ***376***
Harvard U (MA) ***376***
Hastings Coll (NE) ***377***
Haverford Coll (PA) ***377***
Hawai'i Pacific U (HI) ***377***
Heidelberg Coll (OH) ***377***
High Point U (NC) ***379***
Hillsdale Coll (MI) ***379***
Hiram Coll (OH) ***379***
Hobart and William Smith Colls (NY) ***380***
Holy Family U (PA) ***380***
Holy Names Coll (CA) ***381***
Hood Coll (MD) ***381***
Houghton Coll (NY) ***381***
Houston Baptist U (TX) ***382***
Howard Payne U (TX) ***382***
Humboldt State U (CA) ***382***
Huntingdon Coll (AL) ***383***
Huntington Coll (IN) ***383***
Huston-Tillotson Coll (TX) ***383***
Illinois Coll (IL) ***384***
Illinois Wesleyan U (IL) ***385***
Immaculata U (PA) ***385***
Indiana U Bloomington (IN) ***385***
Indiana U–Purdue U Fort Wayne (IN) ***386***
Indiana U–Purdue U Indianapolis (IN) ***387***
Indiana Wesleyan U (IN) ***387***
Iowa State U of Science and Technology (IA) ***390***
Iowa Wesleyan Coll (IA) ***390***
Ithaca Coll (NY) ***390***
Jackson State U (MS) ***390***
Jacksonville U (FL) ***391***
John Brown U (AR) ***392***
John Carroll U (OH) ***392***
Johnson C. Smith U (NC) ***394***
Johnson State Coll (VT) ***394***
Judson Coll (IL) ***395***
Juniata Coll (PA) ***395***
Kansas State U (KS) ***396***
Kentucky Wesleyan Coll (KY) ***397***
King Coll (TN) ***398***
King's Coll (PA) ***398***
LaGrange Coll (GA) ***400***
Lake Erie Coll (OH) ***400***
Lake Forest Coll (IL) ***400***
Lambuth U (TN) ***401***
Lander U (SC) ***401***
Langston U (OK) ***402***
La Salle U (PA) ***402***
La Sierra U (CA) ***403***
Lawrence U (WI) ***403***
Lebanon Valley Coll (PA) ***403***
Lees-McRae Coll (NC) ***404***
Lehigh U (PA) ***404***
Le Moyne Coll (NY) ***404***
Lenoir-Rhyne Coll (NC) ***405***
LeTourneau U (TX) ***405***
Lewis & Clark Coll (OR) ***405***
Lewis U (IL) ***406***
Lincoln Memorial U (TN) ***407***
Lindenwood U (MO) ***407***
Lindsey Wilson Coll (KY) ***407***
Lipscomb U (TN) ***408***
Lock Haven U of Pennsylvania (PA) ***408***
Long Island U, Brooklyn Campus (NY) ***409***
Long Island U, C.W. Post Campus (NY) ***409***
Longwood U (VA) ***409***
Lourdes Coll (OH) ***411***
Loyola U Chicago (IL) ***411***
Luther Coll (IA) ***412***
Lycoming Coll (PA) ***412***
Lynchburg Coll (VA) ***413***
Lynn U (FL) ***413***
MacMurray Coll (IL) ***414***
Madonna U (MI) ***414***
Maharishi U of Management (IA) ***414***
Manchester Coll (IN) ***415***
Manhattanville Coll (NY) ***416***
Mansfield U of Pennsylvania (PA) ***416***
Marian Coll (IN) ***417***
Marian Coll of Fond du Lac (WI) ***417***
Marist Coll (NY) ***417***
Marlboro Coll (VT) ***418***
Marquette U (WI) ***418***
Mars Hill Coll (NC) ***418***
Marymount Coll of Fordham U (NY) ***419***
Mary Washington Coll (VA) ***420***
Mass Coll of Pharmacy and Allied Health Sciences (MA) ***421***
Massachusetts Inst of Technology (MA) ***421***
The Master's Coll and Seminary (CA) ***422***
Mayville State U (ND) ***422***
McKendree Coll (IL) ***423***
McPherson Coll (KS) ***423***
Medgar Evers Coll of the City U of NY (NY) ***424***
Memorial U of Newfoundland (NF, Canada) ***424***
Mercy Coll (NY) ***425***
Mercyhurst Coll (PA) ***425***
Meredith Coll (NC) ***426***
Merrimack Coll (MA) ***426***
Methodist Coll (NC) ***427***
Miami U (OH) ***428***
Michigan Technological U (MI) ***428***
Middlebury Coll (VT) ***429***
Midland Lutheran Coll (NE) ***429***
Midwestern State U (TX) ***430***
Milligan Coll (TN) ***430***
Millikin U (IL) ***430***
Mills Coll (CA) ***431***
Minnesota State U, Mankato (MN) ***431***
Minnesota State U, Moorhead (MN) ***432***
Mississippi Coll (MS) ***432***
Missouri Southern State Coll (MO) ***433***
Missouri Valley Coll (MO) ***433***
Molloy Coll (NY) ***433***
Montclair State U (NJ) ***435***
Montreat Coll (NC) ***435***
Morgan State U (MD) ***436***
Morningside Coll (IA) ***437***
Mount Allison U (NB, Canada) ***437***
Mount Mary Coll (WI) ***438***
Mount Mercy Coll (IA) ***438***
Mount St. Mary's Coll (CA) ***439***
Mount Vernon Nazarene U (OH) ***440***
Muhlenberg Coll (PA) ***440***
Muskingum Coll (OH) ***441***
Nazareth Coll of Rochester (NY) ***443***
Newberry Coll (SC) ***444***
Newman U (KS) ***445***
New Mexico Highlands U (NM) ***446***
New Mexico Inst of Mining and Technology (NM) ***446***
New York Inst of Technology (NY) ***447***
New York U (NY) ***447***
Niagara U (NY) ***447***
Nicholls State U (LA) ***447***
North Carolina Wesleyan Coll (NC) ***449***
North Central Coll (IL) ***449***
North Dakota State U (ND) ***449***
Northeastern State U (OK) ***450***
Northern Arizona U (AZ) ***450***
Northern Kentucky U (KY) ***451***
Northern Michigan U (MI) ***451***
Northern State U (SD) ***451***
North Georgia Coll & State U (GA) ***451***
Northland Coll (WI) ***452***
North Park U (IL) ***452***
Northwestern Oklahoma State U (OK) ***453***
Northwestern U (IL) ***453***
Northwest Missouri State U (MO) ***454***
Northwest Nazarene U (ID) ***454***
Notre Dame Coll (OH) ***455***
Notre Dame de Namur U (CA) ***455***
Nova Southeastern U (FL) ***455***
Oakland City U (IN) ***456***
Oakland U (MI) ***456***
Oglethorpe U (GA) ***457***
Ohio U (OH) ***458***
Ohio Wesleyan U (OH) ***459***
Oklahoma Baptist U (OK) ***459***
Oklahoma City U (OK) ***460***
Oklahoma State U (OK) ***460***
Oklahoma Wesleyan U (OK) ***460***
Olivet Coll (MI) ***461***
Olivet Nazarene U (IL) ***461***
Oral Roberts U (OK) ***461***
Oregon Inst of Technology (OR) ***461***
Oregon State U (OR) ***462***
Otterbein Coll (OH) ***462***
Pacific Union Coll (CA) ***464***
Pacific U (OR) ***464***
Paine Coll (GA) ***465***
Palm Beach Atlantic U (FL) ***465***
Paul Quinn Coll (TX) ***466***
Penn State U Univ Park Campus (PA) ***468***
Pepperdine U, Malibu (CA) ***469***
Peru State Coll (NE) ***469***
Pfeiffer U (NC) ***469***
Philadelphia U (PA) ***469***
Pittsburg State U (KS) ***470***
Pitzer Coll (CA) ***471***
Polytechnic U, Brooklyn Campus (NY) ***472***
Pomona Coll (CA) ***472***
Pontifical Catholic U of Puerto Rico (PR) ***472***
Presbyterian Coll (SC) ***473***
Purdue U (IN) ***475***
Purdue U Calumet (IN) ***475***
Queens Coll of the City U of NY (NY) ***475***
Queens U of Charlotte (NC) ***476***
Quincy U (IL) ***476***
Quinnipiac U (CT) ***476***
Regis U (CO) ***478***
Rensselaer Polytechnic Inst (NY) ***478***
Rhode Island Coll (RI) ***479***
Ripon Coll (WI) ***480***
Rivier Coll (NH) ***480***
Roberts Wesleyan Coll (NY) ***481***
Rochester Inst of Technology (NY) ***482***
Rockford Coll (IL) ***482***
Rocky Mountain Coll (MT) ***482***
Roger Williams U (RI) ***483***
Rollins Coll (FL) ***483***
Roosevelt U (IL) ***483***
Rowan U (NJ) ***484***
Rutgers, The State U of New Jersey, New Brunswick (NJ) ***485***
Sacred Heart U (CT) ***486***
St. Andrews Presbyterian Coll (NC) ***487***
Saint Anselm Coll (NH) ***487***
Saint Augustine's Coll (NC) ***487***
St. Bonaventure U (NY) ***487***
St. Cloud State U (MN) ***488***
St. Francis Coll (NY) ***488***
Saint Francis U (PA) ***488***
St. Francis Xavier U (NS, Canada) ***489***
Saint John's U (MN) ***490***
Saint Joseph Coll (CT) ***490***
St. Joseph's Coll, Suffolk Campus (NY) ***491***
Saint Leo U (FL) ***492***
Saint Martin's Coll (WA) ***493***
Saint Mary-of-the-Woods Coll (IN) ***493***
Saint Mary's Coll of California (CA) ***494***
Saint Michael's Coll (VT) ***494***
St. Norbert Coll (WI) ***495***
St. Thomas Aquinas Coll (NY) ***495***
St. Thomas U (FL) ***496***
Salem State Coll (MA) ***497***
Sarah Lawrence Coll (NY) ***499***
Schreiner U (TX) ***501***
Seattle Pacific U (WA) ***501***

Seton Hill U (PA) 502
Shawnee State U (OH) 502
Siena Coll (NY) 504
Simmons Coll (MA) 504
Simon's Rock Coll of Bard (MA) 505
Simpson Coll (IA) 505
Slippery Rock U of Pennsylvania (PA) 506
Sonoma State U (CA) 506
South Carolina State U (SC) 506
South Dakota State U (SD) 507
Southeastern Coll of the Assemblies of God (FL) 507
Southern Connecticut State U (CT) 509
Southern Nazarene U (OK) 510
Southern Oregon U (OR) 510
Southwestern Oklahoma State U (OK) 512
Southwest State U (MN) 513
Spalding U (KY) 513
Springfield Coll (MA) 514
Spring Hill Coll (AL) 514
State U of NY at New Paltz (NY) 515
State U of NY at Oswego (NY) 515
State U of NY Coll at Brockport (NY) 515
State U of NY Coll at Buffalo (NY) 516
State U of NY Coll at Cortland (NY) 516
State U of NY Coll at Fredonia (NY) 516
State U of NY Coll at Geneseo (NY) 516
State U of NY Coll at Oneonta (NY) 517
State U of NY Coll of Environ Sci and Forestry (NY) 517
State U of West Georgia (GA) 518
Stephens Coll (MO) 519
Stetson U (FL) 519
Stevens Inst of Technology (NJ) 519
Stonehill Coll (MA) 520
Suffolk U (MA) 520
Sul Ross State U (TX) 521
Susquehanna U (PA) 521
Syracuse U (NY) 521
Tabor Coll (KS) 522
Talladega Coll (AL) 522
Taylor U (IN) 523
Tennessee Technological U (TN) 524
Tennessee Wesleyan Coll (TN) 524
Texas A&M U–Kingsville (TX) 525
Texas Lutheran U (TX) 526
Texas Southern U (TX) 526
Texas Wesleyan U (TX) 526
Thiel Coll (PA) 527
Touro Coll (NY) 529
Trinity Christian Coll (IL) 530
Trinity Coll (DC) 530
Trinity International U (IL) 531
Trinity U (TX) 531
Trinity Western U (BC, Canada) 531
Tri-State U (IN) 532
Troy State U (AL) 532
Truman State U (MO) 532
Tusculum Coll (TN) 533
Union Coll (KY) 533
Union U (TN) 534
United States Military Academy (NY) 535
Université de Sherbrooke (QC, Canada) 536
Université Laval (QC, Canada) 536
The U of Akron (OH) 537
U of Alberta (AB, Canada) 538
U of Arkansas (AR) 539
U of Arkansas at Monticello (AR) 539
U of Bridgeport (CT) 540
The U of British Columbia (BC, Canada) 540
U of Cincinnati (OH) 543
U of Colorado at Colorado Springs (CO) 543
U of Dallas (TX) 544
U of Dayton (OH) 544
U of Evansville (IN) 545
The U of Findlay (OH) 545
U of Hawaii at Manoa (HI) 546
U of Houston (TX) 547
U of Idaho (ID) 547
U of Indianapolis (IN) 548
The U of Iowa (IA) 548
U of Judaism (CA) 548
U of La Verne (CA) 549
U of Maine (ME) 550
U of Manitoba (MB, Canada) 551
U of Mary Hardin-Baylor (TX) 551
U of Maryland, Baltimore County (MD) 552
U of Maryland Eastern Shore (MD) 552
U of Massachusetts Amherst (MA) 552
U of Miami (FL) 553
U of Minnesota, Duluth (MN) 554
U of Minnesota, Morris (MN) 555
U of Minnesota, Twin Cities Campus (MN) 555
U of Missouri–Rolla (MO) 556
U of Missouri–St. Louis (MO) 556
The U of Montana–Missoula (MT) 556
The U of Montana–Western (MT) 556
U of Montevallo (AL) 557
U of Nebraska at Omaha (NE) 557
U of Nebraska–Lincoln (NE) 557
U of Nevada, Reno (NV) 558
U of New Brunswick Fredericton (NB, Canada) 558
U of New England (ME) 558
U of New Hampshire (NH) 558
U of New Orleans (LA) 559
The U of North Carolina at Greensboro (NC) 560
U of North Texas (TX) 562
U of Notre Dame (IN) 562
U of Oklahoma (OK) 562
U of Oregon (OR) 562
U of Ottawa (ON, Canada) 563
U of Pittsburgh at Johnstown (PA) 570
U of Portland (OR) 570
U of Prince Edward Island (PE, Canada) 570
U of Puget Sound (WA) 571
U of Regina (SK, Canada) 572
U of Rio Grande (OH) 572
U of St. Francis (IL) 573
U of Saint Francis (IN) 573
U of St. Thomas (TX) 573
U of San Diego (CA) 574
U of San Francisco (CA) 574
U of Saskatchewan (SK, Canada) 574
U of Sioux Falls (SD) 574
The U of South Dakota (SD) 575
The U of Tampa (FL) 577
The U of Tennessee at Chattanooga (TN) 577
The U of Tennessee at Martin (TN) 577
The U of Texas–Pan American (TX) 579
U of the Incarnate Word (TX) 580
U of the Ozarks (AR) 580
U of the Sciences in Philadelphia (PA) 580
U of Toledo (OH) 581
U of Toronto (ON, Canada) 581
U of Victoria (BC, Canada) 582
U of Windsor (ON, Canada) 584
U of Wisconsin–Milwaukee (WI) 585
U of Wisconsin–Oshkosh (WI) 585
U of Wisconsin–Parkside (WI) 585
U of Wisconsin–River Falls (WI) 585
Upper Iowa U (IA) 587
Urbana U (OH) 587
Ursinus Coll (PA) 587
Ursuline Coll (OH) 587
Utah State U (UT) 587
Utica Coll (NY) 588
Valdosta State U (GA) 588
Valley City State U (ND) 588
Villa Julie Coll (MD) 590
Villanova U (PA) 590
Virginia Intermont Coll (VA) 590
Virginia Wesleyan Coll (VA) 591
Viterbo U (WI) 591
Wabash Coll (IN) 592
Wagner Coll (NY) 592
Walla Walla Coll (WA) 593
Walsh U (OH) 593
Warner Pacific Coll (OR) 593
Warren Wilson Coll (NC) 594
Washington Coll (MD) 594
Washington State U (WA) 595
Washington U in St. Louis (MO) 595
Waynesburg Coll (PA) 595
Wayne State Coll (NE) 596
Wells Coll (NY) 597
West Chester U of Pennsylvania (PA) 598
Western Connecticut State U (CT) 598
Western State Coll of Colorado (CO) 600
Westfield State Coll (MA) 600
West Liberty State Coll (WV) 601
Westminster Coll (MO) 601
Westminster Coll (PA) 601
Westmont Coll (CA) 602
West Virginia State Coll (WV) 602
West Virginia Wesleyan Coll (WV) 603
Wheaton Coll (MA) 603
Whitworth Coll (WA) 604
Widener U (PA) 604
Wiley Coll (TX) 605
Wilkes U (PA) 605
Willamette U (OR) 605
William Carey Coll (MS) 605
William Jewell Coll (MO) 606
William Paterson U of New Jersey (NJ) 606
William Penn U (IA) 606
Williams Baptist Coll (AR) 606
Wilmington Coll (OH) 607
Wingate U (NC) 607
Winona State U (MN) 608
Wittenberg U (OH) 608
Wofford Coll (SC) 609
Xavier U of Louisiana (LA) 610
York Coll of Pennsylvania (PA) 610
York U (ON, Canada) 611
Youngstown State U (OH) 611

PRE-PHARMACY STUDIES

Overview: This major prepares students to enroll in a postgraduate-level program in pharmacy so they may become licensed pharmacists. *Related majors:* medical physiology, medical toxicology, cell biology, pharmacy, medical pharmacology/pharmaceutical sciences. *Potential careers:* professional pharmacist. *Salary potential:* $30k-$40k.

Abilene Christian U (TX) 260
Adams State Coll (CO) 260
Allegheny Coll (PA) 264
American U (DC) 267
Ashland U (OH) 274
Barry U (FL) 282
Barton Coll (NC) 282
Bellarmine U (KY) 284
Belmont Abbey Coll (NC) 284
Blue Mountain Coll (MS) 291
Brevard Coll (NC) 294
Carroll Coll (MT) 306
Central Missouri State U (MO) 310
Christian Brothers U (TN) 313
Clemson U (SC) 317
Coll of Saint Benedict (MN) 321
Coll of the Ozarks (MO) 323
Elmhurst Coll (IL) 351
Florida State U (FL) 361
Freed-Hardeman U (TN) 364
Holy Family U (PA) 380
Juniata Coll (PA) 395
King Coll (TN) 398
King's Coll (PA) 398
Lander U (SC) 401
Le Moyne Coll (NY) 404
Long Island U, C.W. Post Campus (NY) 409
Mayville State U (ND) 422
McPherson Coll (KS) 423
Meredith Coll (NC) 426
Missouri Southern State Coll (MO) 433
Mount Allison U (NB, Canada) 437
Mount Vernon Nazarene U (OH) 440
Ohio U (OH) 458
Oklahoma Baptist U (OK) 459
Roberts Wesleyan Coll (NY) 481
Saint John's U (MN) 490
Saint Martin's Coll (WA) 493
Saint Mary-of-the-Woods Coll (IN) 493
Southern Nazarene U (OK) 510
Tennessee Wesleyan Coll (TN) 524
Union U (TN) 534
The U of Akron (OH) 537
U of Connecticut (CT) 544
U of Hawaii at Manoa (HI) 546
The U of Iowa (IA) 548
U of Mary Hardin-Baylor (TX) 551
U of Miami (FL) 553
U of Minnesota, Duluth (MN) 554
U of Minnesota, Morris (MN) 555
The U of Montana–Missoula (MT) 556
U of Nebraska–Lincoln (NE) 557
U of Nevada, Reno (NV) 558
U of Saskatchewan (SK, Canada) 574
The U of Tennessee at Martin (TN) 577
U of Windsor (ON, Canada) 584
U of Wisconsin–Parkside (WI) 585
U of Wisconsin–River Falls (WI) 585
Valley City State U (ND) 588
Viterbo U (WI) 591
Washington U in St. Louis (MO) 595
Westmont Coll (CA) 602
York U (ON, Canada) 611
Youngstown State U (OH) 611

PRE-THEOLOGY

Overview: This major prepares students for programs that will lead to religious ordination. *Related majors:* Biblical studies, divinity/ministry, religious studies, philosophy. *Potential careers:* priest, deacon or other Christian religious vocation. *Salary potential:* $15k-$25k.

Alma Coll (MI) 264
Ashland U (OH) 274
Atlanta Christian Coll (GA) 275
Blue Mountain Coll (MS) 291
California Christian Coll (CA) 298
Central Christian Coll of Kansas (KS) 309
Christian Brothers U (TN) 313
Circleville Bible Coll (OH) 314
Coll of Saint Benedict (MN) 321
Coll of Santa Fe (NM) 323
Columbia Bible Coll (BC, Canada) 326
Columbia International U (SC) 327
Concordia Coll (MN) 329
Concordia U (IL) 330
Concordia U (OR) 330
Emmaus Bible Coll (IA) 353
Florida State U (FL) 361
Geneva Coll (PA) 366
Grace U (NE) 371
Juniata Coll (PA) 395
Kentucky Mountain Bible Coll (KY) 397
Loras Coll (IA) 410
Loyola U Chicago (IL) 411
Luther Coll (IA) 412
Martin Luther Coll (MN) 418
Minnesota State U, Mankato (MN) 431
Moody Bible Inst (IL) 435
Mount Allison U (NB, Canada) 437
Northwest Christian Coll (OR) 452
Northwestern Coll (MN) 453
Ohio Wesleyan U (OH) 459
Reformed Bible Coll (MI) 477
Saint John's U (MN) 490
Southwestern Coll (KS) 512
Tennessee Wesleyan Coll (TN) 524
Toccoa Falls Coll (GA) 528
Trinity Christian Coll (IL) 530
U of Dallas (TX) 544
U of Indianapolis (IN) 548
U of North Texas (TX) 562
U of Rio Grande (OH) 572
Valparaiso U (IN) 588
Warner Southern Coll (FL) 593
Waynesburg Coll (PA) 595
Westmont Coll (CA) 602

PRE-VETERINARY STUDIES

Overview: This major prepares students to enroll in postgraduate-level programs in veterinary medicine so they may become licensed veterinarians. *Related majors:* veterinary sciences, zoology, animal sciences, pathology, physiology. *Potential careers:* veterinarian, zoologist, animal-care specialist. *Salary potential:* $33k-$40k.

Abilene Christian U (TX) 260
Acadia U (NS, Canada) 260
Adams State Coll (CO) 260
Adrian Coll (MI) 260
Albertus Magnus Coll (CT) 262
Albion Coll (MI) 262
Albright Coll (PA) 263
Alderson-Broaddus Coll (WV) 263
Alfred U (NY) 263
Alice Lloyd Coll (KY) 263
Allegheny Coll (PA) 264
Alma Coll (MI) 264
American International Coll (MA) 267
American U (DC) 267
Anderson U (IN) 268
Andrews U (MI) 269
Antioch Coll (OH) 269
Aquinas Coll (MI) 270
Arcadia U (PA) 271
Arizona State U East (AZ) 271
Ashland U (OH) 274
Atlantic Union Coll (MA) 276

PRE-VETERINARY STUDIES (continued)

Auburn U (AL) ***276***
Augsburg Coll (MN) ***276***
Augustana Coll (IL) ***276***
Augustana Coll (SD) ***276***
Baker U (KS) ***280***
Baldwin-Wallace Coll (OH) ***280***
Bard Coll (NY) ***281***
Barry U (FL) ***282***
Barton Coll (NC) ***282***
Bellarmine U (KY) ***284***
Belmont Abbey Coll (NC) ***284***
Bemidji State U (MN) ***285***
Benedictine U (IL) ***285***
Bennington Coll (VT) ***286***
Berea Coll (KY) ***286***
Berry Coll (GA) ***287***
Bethany Coll (WV) ***287***
Bethel Coll (MN) ***288***
Blackburn Coll (IL) ***290***
Bloomfield Coll (NJ) ***290***
Blue Mountain Coll (MS) ***291***
Brandon U (MB, Canada) ***293***
Brevard Coll (NC) ***294***
Briar Cliff U (IA) ***294***
Buena Vista U (IA) ***297***
California State Polytechnic U, Pomona (CA) ***300***
California State U, Chico (CA) ***300***
California State U, Dominguez Hills (CA) ***300***
California State U, Fullerton (CA) ***301***
California State U, Hayward (CA) ***301***
California State U, Northridge (CA) ***301***
Calvin Coll (MI) ***303***
Campbellsville U (KY) ***303***
Campbell U (NC) ***303***
Capital U (OH) ***304***
Cardinal Stritch U (WI) ***305***
Carroll Coll (MT) ***306***
Carthage Coll (WI) ***306***
Catawba Coll (NC) ***307***
Cedar Crest Coll (PA) ***308***
Cedarville U (OH) ***308***
Centenary Coll of Louisiana (LA) ***308***
Central Missouri State U (MO) ***310***
Chapman U (CA) ***311***
Chowan Coll (NC) ***312***
City Coll of the City U of NY (NY) ***314***
Clarkson U (NY) ***316***
Clark U (MA) ***316***
Clemson U (SC) ***317***
Cleveland State U (OH) ***317***
Coe Coll (IA) ***318***
Coll Misericordia (PA) ***319***
Coll of Notre Dame of Maryland (MD) ***321***
Coll of Saint Benedict (MN) ***321***
Coll of St. Catherine (MN) ***321***
Coll of Saint Elizabeth (NJ) ***321***
Coll of Saint Mary (NE) ***322***
Coll of Santa Fe (NM) ***323***
Coll of the Atlantic (ME) ***323***
Coll of the Ozarks (MO) ***323***
The Coll of Wooster (OH) ***324***
Colorado State U (CO) ***325***
Colorado State U-Pueblo (CO) ***325***
Columbia Coll (MO) ***326***
Columbia Coll (SC) ***327***
Columbia Union Coll (MD) ***328***
Columbus State U (GA) ***328***
Concord Coll (WV) ***329***
Concordia Coll (MN) ***329***
Converse Coll (SC) ***332***
Cornell U (NY) ***333***
Cornerstone U (MI) ***333***
Cumberland U (TN) ***335***
Dakota State U (SD) ***335***
Dalhousie U (NS, Canada) ***336***
Davis & Elkins Coll (WV) ***338***
Defiance Coll (OH) ***338***
Delaware State U (DE) ***338***
Delaware Valley Coll (PA) ***339***
DeSales U (PA) ***340***
Dickinson State U (ND) ***344***
Dillard U (LA) ***344***
Dominican U (IL) ***345***
Dordt Coll (IA) ***345***
Drake U (IA) ***345***
Drury U (MO) ***346***
D'Youville Coll (NY) ***347***
East Central U (OK) ***347***
Eastern Kentucky U (KY) ***348***
Eastern Mennonite U (VA) ***348***
Eastern Oregon U (OR) ***349***
Eastern Washington U (WA) ***349***
Eckerd Coll (FL) ***350***
Edgewood Coll (WI) ***351***
Elizabethtown Coll (PA) ***351***
Elmhurst Coll (IL) ***351***
Elmira Coll (NY) ***351***
Elms Coll (MA) ***352***
Elon U (NC) ***352***
Emory & Henry Coll (VA) ***353***
Eureka Coll (IL) ***355***
Evangel U (MO) ***355***
The Evergreen State Coll (WA) ***355***
Florida Southern Coll (FL) ***361***
Florida State U (FL) ***361***
Fordham U (NY) ***362***
Fort Lewis Coll (CO) ***362***
Framingham State Coll (MA) ***362***
Francis Marion U (SC) ***363***
Franklin Pierce Coll (NH) ***364***
Freed-Hardeman U (TN) ***364***
Furman U (SC) ***365***
Gannon U (PA) ***365***
Gardner-Webb U (NC) ***365***
Georgia Southwestern State U (GA) ***368***
Gettysburg Coll (PA) ***368***
Goshen Coll (IN) ***370***
Grand Canyon U (AZ) ***371***
Grand Valley State U (MI) ***371***
Greenville Coll (IL) ***373***
Grove City Coll (PA) ***373***
Gustavus Adolphus Coll (MN) ***374***
Gwynedd-Mercy Coll (PA) ***374***
Hamline U (MN) ***374***
Hampshire Coll (MA) ***375***
Hampton U (VA) ***375***
Harding U (AR) ***375***
Hartwick Coll (NY) ***376***
Harvard U (MA) ***376***
Hastings Coll (NE) ***377***
Haverford Coll (PA) ***377***
Heidelberg Coll (OH) ***377***
High Point U (NC) ***379***
Hillsdale Coll (MI) ***379***
Hiram Coll (OH) ***379***
Hobart and William Smith Colls (NY) ***380***
Holy Family U (PA) ***380***
Hood Coll (MD) ***381***
Houghton Coll (NY) ***381***
Houston Baptist U (TX) ***382***
Humboldt State U (CA) ***382***
Huntingdon Coll (AL) ***383***
Huntington Coll (IN) ***383***
Illinois Coll (IL) ***384***
Illinois Wesleyan U (IL) ***385***
Immaculata U (PA) ***385***
Indiana U–Purdue U Indianapolis (IN) ***387***
Indiana Wesleyan U (IN) ***387***
Iowa State U of Science and Technology (IA) ***390***
Iowa Wesleyan Coll (IA) ***390***
Jackson State U (MS) ***390***
Jacksonville U (FL) ***391***
John Brown U (AR) ***392***
John Carroll U (OH) ***392***
Juniata Coll (PA) ***395***
Kansas State U (KS) ***396***
Kentucky Wesleyan Coll (KY) ***397***
King Coll (TN) ***398***
King's Coll (PA) ***398***
LaGrange Coll (GA) ***400***
Lake Erie Coll (OH) ***400***
Lake Forest Coll (IL) ***400***
Lander U (SC) ***401***
Langston U (OK) ***402***
La Salle U (PA) ***402***
Lawrence U (WI) ***403***
Lebanon Valley Coll (PA) ***403***
Lees-McRae Coll (NC) ***404***
Le Moyne Coll (NY) ***404***
Lenoir-Rhyne Coll (NC) ***405***
LeTourneau U (TX) ***405***
Lewis & Clark Coll (OR) ***405***
Lewis U (IL) ***406***
Lincoln Memorial U (TN) ***407***
Lindenwood U (MO) ***407***
Lipscomb U (TN) ***408***
Lock Haven U of Pennsylvania (PA) ***408***
Long Island U, C.W. Post Campus (NY) ***409***
Longwood U (VA) ***409***
Loyola U Chicago (IL) ***411***
Lubbock Christian U (TX) ***412***
Luther Coll (IA) ***412***
Lycoming Coll (PA) ***412***
Lynchburg Coll (VA) ***413***
MacMurray Coll (IL) ***414***
Madonna U (MI) ***414***
Manchester Coll (IN) ***415***
Marian Coll (IN) ***417***
Marian Coll of Fond du Lac (WI) ***417***
Marist Coll (NY) ***417***
Marlboro Coll (VT) ***418***
Mars Hill Coll (NC) ***418***
Mary Washington Coll (VA) ***420***
Massachusetts Inst of Technology (MA) ***421***
Mayville State U (ND) ***422***
McKendree Coll (IL) ***423***
McPherson Coll (KS) ***423***
Mercyhurst Coll (PA) ***425***
Meredith Coll (NC) ***426***
Mesa State Coll (CO) ***426***
Methodist Coll (NC) ***427***
Miami U (OH) ***428***
Michigan Technological U (MI) ***428***
Middlebury Coll (VT) ***429***
Midland Lutheran Coll (NE) ***429***
Midwestern State U (TX) ***430***
Milligan Coll (TN) ***430***
Millikin U (IL) ***430***
Minnesota State U, Mankato (MN) ***431***
Minnesota State U, Moorhead (MN) ***432***
Missouri Southern State Coll (MO) ***433***
Missouri Valley Coll (MO) ***433***
Molloy Coll (NY) ***433***
Morningside Coll (IA) ***437***
Mount Allison U (NB, Canada) ***437***
Mount Mary Coll (WI) ***438***
Mount Mercy Coll (IA) ***438***
Mount Vernon Nazarene U (OH) ***440***
Muhlenberg Coll (PA) ***440***
Muskingum Coll (OH) ***441***
Nazareth Coll of Rochester (NY) ***443***
Newberry Coll (SC) ***444***
Newman U (KS) ***445***
New Mexico Inst of Mining and Technology (NM) ***446***
Niagara U (NY) ***447***
North Central Coll (IL) ***449***
North Dakota State U (ND) ***449***
Northeastern State U (OK) ***450***
Northern Arizona U (AZ) ***450***
Northern Kentucky U (KY) ***451***
Northern Michigan U (MI) ***451***
North Georgia Coll & State U (GA) ***451***
Northland Coll (WI) ***452***
North Park U (IL) ***452***
Northwest Missouri State U (MO) ***454***
Nova Southeastern U (FL) ***455***
Oakland City U (IN) ***456***
Oakland U (MI) ***456***
Oglethorpe U (GA) ***457***
Ohio U (OH) ***458***
Ohio Wesleyan U (OH) ***459***
Oklahoma Baptist U (OK) ***459***
Oklahoma City U (OK) ***460***
Oklahoma State U (OK) ***460***
Oklahoma Wesleyan U (OK) ***460***
Olivet Coll (MI) ***461***
Olivet Nazarene U (IL) ***461***
Oregon State U (OR) ***462***
Otterbein Coll (OH) ***462***
Pacific Union Coll (CA) ***464***
Paine Coll (GA) ***465***
Peru State Coll (NE) ***469***
Pittsburg State U (KS) ***470***
Presbyterian Coll (SC) ***473***
Purdue U (IN) ***475***
Purdue U Calumet (IN) ***475***
Queens U of Charlotte (NC) ***476***
Quincy U (IL) ***476***
Quinnipiac U (CT) ***476***
Regis U (CO) ***478***
Rhode Island Coll (RI) ***479***
Ripon Coll (WI) ***480***
Rivier Coll (NH) ***480***
Roberts Wesleyan Coll (NY) ***481***
Rochester Inst of Technology (NY) ***482***
Rockford Coll (IL) ***482***
Rocky Mountain Coll (MT) ***482***
Roger Williams U (RI) ***483***
Rollins Coll (FL) ***483***
Sacred Heart U (CT) ***486***
St. Andrews Presbyterian Coll (NC) ***487***
St. Bonaventure U (NY) ***487***
St. Cloud State U (MN) ***488***
Saint Francis U (PA) ***488***
St. Francis Xavier U (NS, Canada) ***489***
Saint John's U (MN) ***490***
St. Joseph's Coll, Suffolk Campus (NY) ***491***
Saint Leo U (FL) ***492***
Saint Martin's Coll (WA) ***493***
Saint Mary-of-the-Woods Coll (IN) ***493***
Saint Mary's Coll of California (CA) ***494***
Saint Michael's Coll (VT) ***494***
St. Norbert Coll (WI) ***495***
Salem State Coll (MA) ***497***
Seton Hill U (PA) ***502***
Shawnee State U (OH) ***502***
Simpson Coll (IA) ***505***
Slippery Rock U of Pennsylvania (PA) ***506***
Sonoma State U (CA) ***506***
South Carolina State U (SC) ***506***
South Dakota State U (SD) ***507***
Southern Connecticut State U (CT) ***509***
Southwestern Oklahoma State U (OK) ***512***
Southwest State U (MN) ***513***
Spring Hill Coll (AL) ***514***
State U of NY at Oswego (NY) ***515***
State U of NY Coll at Brockport (NY) ***515***
State U of NY Coll at Buffalo (NY) ***516***
State U of NY Coll at Fredonia (NY) ***516***
State U of NY Coll at Geneseo (NY) ***516***
State U of NY Coll at Oneonta (NY) ***517***
State U of NY Coll of Environ Sci and Forestry (NY) ***517***
State U of West Georgia (GA) ***518***
Stephens Coll (MO) ***519***
Stetson U (FL) ***519***
Stonehill Coll (MA) ***520***
Suffolk U (MA) ***520***
Sul Ross State U (TX) ***521***
Susquehanna U (PA) ***521***
Syracuse U (NY) ***521***
Taylor U (IN) ***523***
Tennessee Technological U (TN) ***524***
Tennessee Wesleyan Coll (TN) ***524***
Texas A&M U–Kingsville (TX) ***525***
Texas Lutheran U (TX) ***526***
Thiel Coll (PA) ***527***
Trinity Christian Coll (IL) ***530***
Trinity U (TX) ***531***
Trinity Western U (BC, Canada) ***531***
Tri-State U (IN) ***532***
Troy State U (AL) ***532***
Truman State U (MO) ***532***
Tusculum Coll (TN) ***533***
Union Coll (KY) ***533***
The U of Akron (OH) ***537***
U of Alberta (AB, Canada) ***538***
The U of Arizona (AZ) ***538***
U of Arkansas at Monticello (AR) ***539***
U of Bridgeport (CT) ***540***
The U of British Columbia (BC, Canada) ***540***
U of Cincinnati (OH) ***543***
U of Colorado at Colorado Springs (CO) ***543***
U of Delaware (DE) ***544***
U of Evansville (IN) ***545***
The U of Findlay (OH) ***545***
U of Houston (TX) ***547***
U of Illinois at Urbana–Champaign (IL) ***548***
U of Indianapolis (IN) ***548***
The U of Iowa (IA) ***548***
U of Maine (ME) ***550***
U of Manitoba (MB, Canada) ***551***
U of Mary Hardin-Baylor (TX) ***551***
U of Maryland, Baltimore County (MD) ***552***
U of Maryland, Coll Park (MD) ***552***
U of Massachusetts Amherst (MA) ***552***
U of Miami (FL) ***553***
U of Minnesota, Duluth (MN) ***554***
U of Minnesota, Morris (MN) ***555***
U of Minnesota, Twin Cities Campus (MN) ***555***
U of Missouri–St. Louis (MO) ***556***
The U of Montana–Western (MT) ***556***
U of Montevallo (AL) ***557***
U of Nebraska–Lincoln (NE) ***557***
U of Nevada, Reno (NV) ***558***
U of New Brunswick Fredericton (NB, Canada) ***558***
U of New England (ME) ***558***
U of New Hampshire (NH) ***558***
U of New Orleans (LA) ***559***
The U of North Carolina at Greensboro (NC) ***560***
U of Oklahoma (OK) ***562***
U of Pittsburgh at Johnstown (PA) ***570***
U of Prince Edward Island (PE, Canada) ***570***
U of Puget Sound (WA) ***571***
U of Regina (SK, Canada) ***572***

U of Rio Grande (OH) **572**
U of St. Francis (IL) **573**
U of Saint Francis (IN) **573**
U of San Francisco (CA) **574**
U of Saskatchewan (SK, Canada) **574**
U of Sioux Falls (SD) **574**
The U of South Dakota (SD) **575**
The U of Tampa (FL) **577**
The U of Tennessee at Chattanooga (TN) **577**
The U of Tennessee at Martin (TN) **577**
U of the Ozarks (AR) **580**
U of the Sciences in Philadelphia (PA) **580**
U of Vermont (VT) **582**
U of Victoria (BC, Canada) **582**
U of Wisconsin–Oshkosh (WI) **585**
U of Wisconsin–Parkside (WI) **585**
U of Wisconsin–River Falls (WI) **585**
Upper Iowa U (IA) **587**
Urbana U (OH) **587**
Ursinus Coll (PA) **587**
Utah State U (UT) **587**
Utica Coll (NY) **588**
Valley City State U (ND) **588**
Villa Julie Coll (MD) **590**
Villanova U (PA) **590**
Virginia Intermont Coll (VA) **590**
Virginia Wesleyan Coll (VA) **591**
Viterbo U (WI) **591**
Wabash Coll (IN) **592**
Walla Walla Coll (WA) **593**
Walsh U (OH) **593**
Warner Pacific Coll (OR) **593**
Warren Wilson Coll (NC) **594**
Washington Coll (MD) **594**
Washington U in St. Louis (MO) **595**
Waynesburg Coll (PA) **595**
Wayne State Coll (NE) **596**
Wells Coll (NY) **597**
West Chester U of Pennsylvania (PA) **598**
Western New Mexico U (NM) **600**
Western State Coll of Colorado (CO) **600**
Westminster Coll (MO) **601**
Westminster Coll (PA) **601**
Westmont Coll (CA) **602**
West Virginia State Coll (WV) **602**
West Virginia Wesleyan Coll (WV) **603**
Whitworth Coll (WA) **604**
Wilkes U (PA) **605**
Willamette U (OR) **605**
William Carey Coll (MS) **605**
William Jewell Coll (MO) **606**
Wilmington Coll (OH) **607**
Wingate U (NC) **607**
Winona State U (MN) **608**
Wittenberg U (OH) **608**
Wofford Coll (SC) **609**
Xavier U of Louisiana (LA) **610**
York Coll of Pennsylvania (PA) **610**
York U (ON, Canada) **611**
Youngstown State U (OH) **611**

PRINTMAKING

Overview: This major teaches students the theories, artistic skills, and techniques of printmaking. *Related majors:* fine arts, painting, drawing, art history, printing press operator, lithography/platemaking. *Potential careers:* fine artist, printing press operator, publisher, book jacket or magazine designer, lithographer. *Salary potential:* $15k-$25k.

Academy of Art Coll (CA) **260**
Adams State Coll (CO) **260**
Alberta Coll of Art & Design (AB, Canada) **262**
Alfred U (NY) **263**
Arizona State U (AZ) **271**
Atlanta Coll of Art (GA) **275**
Ball State U (IN) **280**
Bennington Coll (VT) **286**
Birmingham-Southern Coll (AL) **289**
Bowling Green State U (OH) **292**
California Coll of Arts and Crafts (CA) **299**
California State U, Fullerton (CA) **301**
California State U, Hayward (CA) **301**
California State U, Long Beach (CA) **301**
California State U, Stanislaus (CA) **302**
The Cleveland Inst of Art (OH) **317**
Coll of Santa Fe (NM) **323**
Coll of Visual Arts (MN) **324**
Colorado State U (CO) **325**
Columbus Coll of Art and Design (OH) **328**
Concordia U (QC, Canada) **331**
Corcoran Coll of Art and Design (DC) **332**
Emmanuel Coll (MA) **353**
Escuela de Artes Plasticas de Puerto Rico (PR) **354**
Framingham State Coll (MA) **362**
Grand Valley State U (MI) **371**
Indiana Wesleyan U (IN) **387**
Kansas City Art Inst (MO) **395**
Long Island U, Southampton Coll, Friends World Program (NY) **409**
Longwood U (VA) **409**
Maine Coll of Art (ME) **415**
Maryland Inst Coll of Art (MD) **419**
Massachusetts Coll of Art (MA) **421**
McNeese State U (LA) **423**
Memorial U of Newfoundland (NF, Canada) **424**
Memphis Coll of Art (TN) **425**
Milwaukee Inst of Art and Design (WI) **431**
Minneapolis Coll of Art and Design (MN) **431**
Minnesota State U, Moorhead (MN) **432**
Montserrat Coll of Art (MA) **435**
Mount Allison U (NB, Canada) **437**
New World School of the Arts (FL) **447**
Northern Michigan U (MI) **451**
Nova Scotia Coll of Art and Design (NS, Canada) **455**
The Ohio State U (OH) **457**
Ohio U (OH) **458**
Pacific Northwest Coll of Art (OR) **464**
Pratt Inst (NY) **473**
Rhode Island School of Design (RI) **479**
Rutgers, The State U of New Jersey, New Brunswick (NJ) **485**
School of the Art Inst of Chicago (IL) **500**
School of the Museum of Fine Arts (MA) **501**
Seton Hill U (PA) **502**
Simon's Rock Coll of Bard (MA) **505**
Sonoma State U (CA) **506**
State U of NY Coll at Buffalo (NY) **516**
State U of NY Coll at Potsdam (NY) **517**
Syracuse U (NY) **521**
Texas Christian U (TX) **526**
Trinity Christian Coll (IL) **530**
The U of Akron (OH) **537**
U of Alberta (AB, Canada) **538**
U of Calif, Santa Cruz (CA) **542**
U of Dallas (TX) **544**
U of Houston (TX) **547**
The U of Iowa (IA) **548**
U of Kansas (KS) **549**
U of Massachusetts Dartmouth (MA) **553**
U of Miami (FL) **553**
U of Michigan (MI) **554**
U of Missouri–St. Louis (MO) **556**
U of Montevallo (AL) **557**
U of North Texas (TX) **562**
U of Oklahoma (OK) **562**
U of Oregon (OR) **562**
U of San Francisco (CA) **574**
The U of South Dakota (SD) **575**
The U of Texas at El Paso (TX) **578**
The U of the Arts (PA) **579**
U of Washington (WA) **583**
Washington U in St. Louis (MO) **595**
Webster U (MO) **597**
York U (ON, Canada) **611**
Youngstown State U (OH) **611**

PROFESSIONAL STUDIES

Overview: This major is offered mainly to people who are already working in a particular industry and wish to expand their education and knowledge as it applies to that industry. Professional studies may encompass a number of different fields, including business management, foreign language, computers or information technology, and liberal arts. *Related majors:* business management, computers, liberal arts, technology. *Potential careers:* N/A. *Salary potential:* N/A.

Bemidji State U (MN) **285**
Briar Cliff U (IA) **294**
Champlain Coll (VT) **311**
Grand View Coll (IA) **372**
Juniata Coll (PA) **395**
Kent State U (OH) **397**
Lake Erie Coll (OH) **400**
Missouri Southern State Coll (MO) **433**
Mount Aloysius Coll (PA) **437**
Saint Mary-of-the-Woods Coll (IN) **493**
Thomas Coll (ME) **527**
U of Dubuque (IA) **545**
The U of Memphis (TN) **553**
U of Oklahoma (OK) **562**
The U of Tennessee at Martin (TN) **577**

PROTECTIVE SERVICES RELATED

Information can be found under this major's main heading.

Franklin U (OH) **364**
Lewis U (IL) **406**
Northwestern Oklahoma State U (OK) **453**
Ohio U (OH) **458**

PSYCHIATRIC/MENTAL HEALTH SERVICES

Overview: This major teaches students how to work with mental health teams, doctors, psychologists, and rehabilitation therapists to treat institutionalized patients who are mentally ill, emotionally disturbed, or developmentally disabled and return them to the community. *Related majors:* psychology, clinical and medical social work, nursing, psychiatric/mental health. *Potential careers:* psychologist, social worker, nurse specializing in mental health, ward supervisor. *Salary potential:* $23k-$29k.

Franciscan U of Steubenville (OH) **363**
Pennsylvania Coll of Technology (PA) **467**

PSYCHOLOGY

Overview: This general major examines the science behind individual and collective behavior and the analysis and treatment of behavior problems and disorders. *Related majors:* biology, neuroscience, physiology, pharmacology, marriage and family counseling. *Potential careers:* therapist, psychiatrist or psychologist, advertising or marketing executive, criminologist, career counselor. *Salary potential:* $23k-$33k.

Abilene Christian U (TX) **260**
Acadia U (NS, Canada) **260**
Adams State Coll (CO) **260**
Adelphi U (NY) **260**
Adrian Coll (MI) **260**
Agnes Scott Coll (GA) **261**
Alabama A&M U (AL) **261**
Alabama State U (AL) **261**
Alaska Pacific U (AK) **261**
Albany State U (GA) **262**
Albertson Coll of Idaho (ID) **262**
Albertus Magnus Coll (CT) **262**
Albion Coll (MI) **262**
Albright Coll (PA) **263**
Alderson-Broaddus Coll (WV) **263**
Alfred U (NY) **263**
Allegheny Coll (PA) **264**
Alliant International U (CA) **264**
Alma Coll (MI) **264**
Alvernia Coll (PA) **265**
Alverno Coll (WI) **265**
American Coll of Thessaloniki(Greece) **266**
American International Coll (MA) **267**
American U (DC) **267**
The American U in Cairo(Egypt) **267**
Amherst Coll (MA) **268**
Anderson Coll (SC) **268**
Anderson U (IN) **268**
Andrews U (MI) **269**
Angelo State U (TX) **269**
Anna Maria Coll (MA) **269**
Antioch Coll (OH) **269**
Appalachian State U (NC) **270**
Aquinas Coll (MI) **270**
Arcadia U (PA) **271**
Arizona State U (AZ) **271**
Arizona State U East (AZ) **271**
Arizona State U West (AZ) **272**
Arkansas State U (AR) **272**
Arkansas Tech U (AR) **272**
Armstrong Atlantic State U (GA) **273**
Asbury Coll (KY) **274**
Ashland U (OH) **274**
Assumption Coll (MA) **275**
Athabasca U (AB, Canada) **275**
Athens State U (AL) **275**
Atlantic Baptist U (NB, Canada) **275**
Atlantic Union Coll (MA) **276**
Auburn U (AL) **276**
Auburn U Montgomery (AL) **276**
Augsburg Coll (MN) **276**
Augustana Coll (IL) **276**
Augustana Coll (SD) **276**
Augusta State U (GA) **277**
Aurora U (IL) **277**
Austin Coll (TX) **277**
Austin Peay State U (TN) **278**
Avila U (MO) **278**
Azusa Pacific U (CA) **278**
Baker U (KS) **280**
Baldwin-Wallace Coll (OH) **280**
Ball State U (IN) **280**
Barclay Coll (KS) **281**
Bard Coll (NY) **281**
Barnard Coll (NY) **282**
Barry U (FL) **282**
Barton Coll (NC) **282**
Bastyr U (WA) **282**
Bates Coll (ME) **282**
Bayamón Central U (PR) **283**
Baylor U (TX) **283**
Bay Path Coll (MA) **283**
Beacon Coll and Graduate School (GA) **283**
Becker Coll (MA) **283**
Belhaven Coll (MS) **283**
Bellarmine U (KY) **284**
Bellevue U (NE) **284**
Belmont Abbey Coll (NC) **284**
Belmont U (TN) **284**
Beloit Coll (WI) **285**
Bemidji State U (MN) **285**
Benedictine Coll (KS) **285**
Benedictine U (IL) **285**
Bennett Coll (NC) **286**
Bennington Coll (VT) **286**
Berea Coll (KY) **286**
Baruch Coll of the City U of NY (NY) **286**
Berry Coll (GA) **287**
Bethany Coll (KS) **287**
Bethany Coll (WV) **287**
Bethany Coll of the Assemblies of God (CA) **287**
Bethel Coll (IN) **288**
Bethel Coll (KS) **288**
Bethel Coll (MN) **288**
Bethel Coll (TN) **288**
Bethune-Cookman Coll (FL) **289**
Biola U (CA) **289**
Birmingham-Southern Coll (AL) **289**
Bishop's U (QC, Canada) **289**
Blackburn Coll (IL) **290**
Black Hills State U (SD) **290**
Bloomfield Coll (NJ) **290**
Bloomsburg U of Pennsylvania (PA) **290**
Bluefield Coll (VA) **291**
Blue Mountain Coll (MS) **291**
Bluffton Coll (OH) **291**
Boston Coll (MA) **292**
Boston U (MA) **292**
Bowdoin Coll (ME) **292**
Bowie State U (MD) **292**
Bowling Green State U (OH) **292**
Bradley U (IL) **293**
Brandeis U (MA) **293**
Brandon U (MB, Canada) **293**
Brenau U (GA) **293**
Brescia U (KY) **293**
Brewton-Parker Coll (GA) **294**
Briar Cliff U (IA) **294**
Bridgewater Coll (VA) **294**
Bridgewater State Coll (MA) **294**
Brigham Young U (UT) **295**
Brigham Young U–Hawaii (HI) **295**
Brock U (ON, Canada) **295**
Brooklyn Coll of the City U of NY (NY) **295**

PSYCHOLOGY (continued)
Brown U (RI) ***296***
Bryan Coll (TN) ***296***
Bryant Coll (RI) ***296***
Bryn Mawr Coll (PA) ***297***
Bucknell U (PA) ***297***
Buena Vista U (IA) ***297***
Burlington Coll (VT) ***297***
Butler U (IN) ***297***
Cabrini Coll (PA) ***298***
Caldwell Coll (NJ) ***298***
California Baptist U (CA) ***298***
California Lutheran U (CA) ***299***
California Polytechnic State U, San Luis Obispo (CA) ***300***
California State Polytechnic U, Pomona (CA) ***300***
California State U, Bakersfield (CA) ***300***
California State U, Chico (CA) ***300***
California State U, Dominguez Hills (CA) ***300***
California State U, Fresno (CA) ***301***
California State U, Fullerton (CA) ***301***
California State U, Hayward (CA) ***301***
California State U, Long Beach (CA) ***301***
California State U, Northridge (CA) ***301***
California State U, Sacramento (CA) ***301***
California State U, San Bernardino (CA) ***302***
California State U, San Marcos (CA) ***302***
California State U, Stanislaus (CA) ***302***
California U of Pennsylvania (PA) ***302***
Calumet Coll of Saint Joseph (IN) ***302***
Calvin Coll (MI) ***303***
Cambridge Coll (MA) ***303***
Cameron U (OK) ***303***
Campbellsville U (KY) ***303***
Campbell U (NC) ***303***
Canisius Coll (NY) ***304***
Cardinal Stritch U (WI) ***305***
Carleton Coll (MN) ***305***
Carleton U (ON, Canada) ***305***
Carlos Albizu Univ - Miami (FL) ***305***
Carlow Coll (PA) ***305***
Carnegie Mellon U (PA) ***305***
Carroll Coll (MT) ***306***
Carroll Coll (WI) ***306***
Carson-Newman Coll (TN) ***306***
Carthage Coll (WI) ***306***
Cascade Coll (OR) ***307***
Case Western Reserve U (OH) ***307***
Castleton State Coll (VT) ***307***
Catawba Coll (NC) ***307***
The Catholic U of America (DC) ***307***
Cazenovia Coll (NY) ***308***
Cedar Crest Coll (PA) ***308***
Cedarville U (OH) ***308***
Centenary Coll (NJ) ***308***
Centenary Coll of Louisiana (LA) ***308***
Central Coll (IA) ***309***
Central Connecticut State U (CT) ***309***
Central Methodist Coll (MO) ***309***
Central Michigan U (MI) ***310***
Central Missouri State U (MO) ***310***
Central Washington U (WA) ***310***
Centre Coll (KY) ***310***
Chadron State Coll (NE) ***311***
Chaminade U of Honolulu (HI) ***311***
Chapman U (CA) ***311***
Charleston Southern U (SC) ***311***
Chatham Coll (PA) ***312***
Chestnut Hill Coll (PA) ***312***
Cheyney U of Pennsylvania (PA) ***312***
Chowan Coll (NC) ***312***
Christian Brothers U (TN) ***313***
Christian Heritage Coll (CA) ***313***
Christopher Newport U (VA) ***313***
Cincinnati Bible Coll and Seminary (OH) ***314***
Citadel, The Military Coll of South Carolina (SC) ***314***
City Coll of the City U of NY (NY) ***314***
City U (WA) ***314***
Claremont McKenna Coll (CA) ***315***
Clarion U of Pennsylvania (PA) ***315***
Clark Atlanta U (GA) ***315***
Clarke Coll (IA) ***315***
Clarkson U (NY) ***316***
Clark U (MA) ***316***
Clearwater Christian Coll (FL) ***316***
Clemson U (SC) ***317***
Cleveland State U (OH) ***317***
Coastal Carolina U (SC) ***318***
Coe Coll (IA) ***318***
Coker Coll (SC) ***318***
Colby Coll (ME) ***318***
Colby-Sawyer Coll (NH) ***319***
Colgate U (NY) ***319***
Coll Misericordia (PA) ***319***
Coll of Charleston (SC) ***320***
Coll of Mount St. Joseph (OH) ***320***
Coll of Mount Saint Vincent (NY) ***320***
The Coll of New Jersey (NJ) ***320***
The Coll of New Rochelle (NY) ***321***
Coll of Notre Dame of Maryland (MD) ***321***
Coll of Saint Benedict (MN) ***321***
Coll of St. Catherine (MN) ***321***
Coll of Saint Elizabeth (NJ) ***321***
Coll of St. Joseph (VT) ***322***
Coll of Saint Mary (NE) ***322***
The Coll of Saint Rose (NY) ***322***
The Coll of St. Scholastica (MN) ***322***
Coll of Santa Fe (NM) ***323***
The Coll of Southeastern Europe, The American U of Athens(Greece) ***323***
Coll of Staten Island of the City U of NY (NY) ***323***
Coll of the Atlantic (ME) ***323***
Coll of the Holy Cross (MA) ***323***
Coll of the Ozarks (MO) ***323***
Coll of the Southwest (NM) ***324***
The Coll of William and Mary (VA) ***324***
The Coll of Wooster (OH) ***324***
Colorado Christian U (CO) ***325***
The Colorado Coll (CO) ***325***
Colorado State U (CO) ***325***
Colorado State U-Pueblo (CO) ***325***
Columbia Coll (MO) ***326***
Columbia Coll (NY) ***326***
Columbia Coll (SC) ***327***
Columbia International U (SC) ***327***
Columbia Union Coll (MD) ***328***
Columbia U, School of General Studies (NY) ***328***
Columbus State U (GA) ***328***
Concord Coll (WV) ***329***
Concordia Coll (MN) ***329***
Concordia U (CA) ***330***
Concordia U (IL) ***330***
Concordia U (MI) ***330***
Concordia U (MN) ***330***
Concordia U (NE) ***330***
Concordia U (OR) ***330***
Concordia U (QC, Canada) ***331***
Concordia U Coll of Alberta (AB, Canada) ***331***
Concordia U Wisconsin (WI) ***331***
Connecticut Coll (CT) ***331***
Converse Coll (SC) ***332***
Cornell Coll (IA) ***332***
Cornell U (NY) ***333***
Cornerstone U (MI) ***333***
Covenant Coll (GA) ***333***
Creighton U (NE) ***333***
Crichton Coll (TN) ***334***
Crown Coll (MN) ***334***
Culver-Stockton Coll (MO) ***334***
Cumberland Coll (KY) ***335***
Cumberland U (TN) ***335***
Curry Coll (MA) ***335***
Daemen Coll (NY) ***335***
Dakota Wesleyan U (SD) ***336***
Dalhousie U (NS, Canada) ***336***
Dallas Baptist U (TX) ***336***
Dana Coll (NE) ***337***
Dartmouth Coll (NH) ***337***
Davidson Coll (NC) ***338***
Davis & Elkins Coll (WV) ***338***
Defiance Coll (OH) ***338***
Delaware State U (DE) ***338***
Delta State U (MS) ***339***
Denison U (OH) ***339***
DePaul U (IL) ***339***
DePauw U (IN) ***339***
Deree Coll(Greece) ***339***
DeSales U (PA) ***340***
Dickinson Coll (PA) ***344***
Dickinson State U (ND) ***344***
Dillard U (LA) ***344***
Doane Coll (NE) ***344***
Dominican Coll (NY) ***344***
Dominican U (IL) ***345***
Dominican U of California (CA) ***345***
Dordt Coll (IA) ***345***
Dowling Coll (NY) ***345***
Drake U (IA) ***345***
Drew U (NJ) ***346***
Drexel U (PA) ***346***
Drury U (MO) ***346***
Duke U (NC) ***346***
Duquesne U (PA) ***346***
Earlham Coll (IN) ***347***
East Carolina U (NC) ***347***
East Central U (OK) ***347***
Eastern Connecticut State U (CT) ***347***
Eastern Illinois U (IL) ***348***
Eastern Kentucky U (KY) ***348***
Eastern Mennonite U (VA) ***348***
Eastern Michigan U (MI) ***348***
Eastern Nazarene Coll (MA) ***348***
Eastern New Mexico U (NM) ***349***
Eastern Oregon U (OR) ***349***
Eastern U (PA) ***349***
Eastern Washington U (WA) ***349***
East Stroudsburg U of Pennsylvania (PA) ***349***
East Tennessee State U (TN) ***349***
East Texas Baptist U (TX) ***350***
Eckerd Coll (FL) ***350***
Edgewood Coll (WI) ***351***
Edinboro U of Pennsylvania (PA) ***351***
Elizabeth City State U (NC) ***351***
Elizabethtown Coll (PA) ***351***
Elmhurst Coll (IL) ***351***
Elmira Coll (NY) ***351***
Elms Coll (MA) ***352***
Elon U (NC) ***352***
Emmanuel Coll (GA) ***353***
Emmanuel Coll (MA) ***353***
Emory & Henry Coll (VA) ***353***
Emory U (GA) ***354***
Emporia State U (KS) ***354***
Endicott Coll (MA) ***354***
Erskine Coll (SC) ***354***
Eugene Lang Coll, New School U (NY) ***355***
Eureka Coll (IL) ***355***
Evangel U (MO) ***355***
The Evergreen State Coll (WA) ***355***
Excelsior Coll (NY) ***356***
Fairfield U (CT) ***356***
Fairleigh Dickinson U, Florham (NJ) ***356***
Fairleigh Dickinson U, Teaneck-Metro Campus (NJ) ***356***
Fairmont State Coll (WV) ***356***
Faulkner U (AL) ***357***
Fayetteville State U (NC) ***357***
Felician Coll (NJ) ***357***
Ferrum Coll (VA) ***358***
Fisk U (TN) ***358***
Fitchburg State Coll (MA) ***358***
Flagler Coll (FL) ***359***
Florida A&M U (FL) ***359***
Florida Atlantic U (FL) ***359***
Florida Inst of Technology (FL) ***360***
Florida International U (FL) ***360***
Florida Southern Coll (FL) ***361***
Florida State U (FL) ***361***
Fontbonne U (MO) ***361***
Fordham U (NY) ***362***
Fort Hays State U (KS) ***362***
Fort Lewis Coll (CO) ***362***
Fort Valley State U (GA) ***362***
Framingham State Coll (MA) ***362***
The Franciscan U (IA) ***363***
Franciscan U of Steubenville (OH) ***363***
Francis Marion U (SC) ***363***
Franklin and Marshall Coll (PA) ***363***
Franklin Coll (IN) ***363***
Franklin Pierce Coll (NH) ***364***
Freed-Hardeman U (TN) ***364***
Fresno Pacific U (CA) ***364***
Frostburg State U (MD) ***365***
Furman U (SC) ***365***
Gallaudet U (DC) ***365***
Gannon U (PA) ***365***
Gardner-Webb U (NC) ***365***
Geneva Coll (PA) ***366***
George Fox U (OR) ***366***
George Mason U (VA) ***366***
Georgetown Coll (KY) ***366***
Georgetown U (DC) ***366***
The George Washington U (DC) ***367***
Georgia Coll & State U (GA) ***367***
Georgian Court Coll (NJ) ***367***
Georgia Southern U (GA) ***367***
Georgia Southwestern State U (GA) ***368***
Georgia State U (GA) ***368***
Gettysburg Coll (PA) ***368***
Goddard Coll (VT) ***369***
Gonzaga U (WA) ***369***
Gordon Coll (MA) ***370***
Goshen Coll (IN) ***370***
Goucher Coll (MD) ***370***
Governors State U (IL) ***370***
Grace Coll (IN) ***370***
Graceland U (IA) ***371***
Grace U (NE) ***371***
Grambling State U (LA) ***371***
Grand Canyon U (AZ) ***371***
Grand Valley State U (MI) ***371***
Grand View Coll (IA) ***372***
Greensboro Coll (NC) ***372***
Greenville Coll (IL) ***373***
Grinnell Coll (IA) ***373***
Grove City Coll (PA) ***373***
Guilford Coll (NC) ***373***
Gustavus Adolphus Coll (MN) ***374***
Gwynedd-Mercy Coll (PA) ***374***
Hamilton Coll (NY) ***374***
Hamline U (MN) ***374***
Hampden-Sydney Coll (VA) ***374***
Hampshire Coll (MA) ***375***
Hampton U (VA) ***375***
Hannibal-LaGrange Coll (MO) ***375***
Hanover Coll (IN) ***375***
Harding U (AR) ***375***
Hardin-Simmons U (TX) ***376***
Hartwick Coll (NY) ***376***
Harvard U (MA) ***376***
Hastings Coll (NE) ***377***
Haverford Coll (PA) ***377***
Hawai'i Pacific U (HI) ***377***
Heidelberg Coll (OH) ***377***
Henderson State U (AR) ***378***
Hendrix Coll (AR) ***378***
High Point U (NC) ***379***
Hilbert Coll (NY) ***379***
Hillsdale Coll (MI) ***379***
Hiram Coll (OH) ***379***
Hobart and William Smith Colls (NY) ***380***
Hofstra U (NY) ***380***
Hollins U (VA) ***380***
Holy Family U (PA) ***380***
Holy Names Coll (CA) ***381***
Hood Coll (MD) ***381***
Hope Coll (MI) ***381***
Hope International U (CA) ***381***
Houghton Coll (NY) ***381***
Houston Baptist U (TX) ***382***
Howard Payne U (TX) ***382***
Howard U (DC) ***382***
Humboldt State U (CA) ***382***
Hunter Coll of the City U of NY (NY) ***382***
Huntingdon Coll (AL) ***383***
Huntington Coll (IN) ***383***
Huston-Tillotson Coll (TX) ***383***
Idaho State U (ID) ***384***
Illinois Coll (IL) ***384***
Illinois Inst of Technology (IL) ***384***
Illinois State U (IL) ***384***
Illinois Wesleyan U (IL) ***385***
Immaculata U (PA) ***385***
Indiana State U (IN) ***385***
Indiana U Bloomington (IN) ***385***
Indiana U East (IN) ***386***
Indiana U Kokomo (IN) ***386***
Indiana U Northwest (IN) ***386***
Indiana U of Pennsylvania (PA) ***386***
Indiana U–Purdue U Fort Wayne (IN) ***386***
Indiana U–Purdue U Indianapolis (IN) ***387***
Indiana U South Bend (IN) ***387***
Indiana U Southeast (IN) ***387***
Indiana Wesleyan U (IN) ***387***
Inter American U of PR, San Germán Campus (PR) ***388***
Iona Coll (NY) ***390***
Iowa State U of Science and Technology (IA) ***390***
Iowa Wesleyan Coll (IA) ***390***
Ithaca Coll (NY) ***390***
Jackson State U (MS) ***390***
Jacksonville State U (AL) ***390***
Jacksonville U (FL) ***391***
James Madison U (VA) ***391***
Jamestown Coll (ND) ***391***
John Brown U (AR) ***392***
John Carroll U (OH) ***392***
John F. Kennedy U (CA) ***392***
John Jay Coll of Criminal Justice, the City U of NY (NY) ***392***
Johns Hopkins U (MD) ***392***
Johnson C. Smith U (NC) ***394***
Johnson State Coll (VT) ***394***
John Wesley Coll (NC) ***394***
Judson Coll (AL) ***395***
Judson Coll (IL) ***395***
Juniata Coll (PA) ***395***

Kalamazoo Coll (MI) ***395***
Kansas State U (KS) ***396***
Kean U (NJ) ***396***
Keene State Coll (NH) ***396***
Kendall Coll (IL) ***396***
Kennesaw State U (GA) ***397***
Kent State U (OH) ***397***
Kentucky Christian Coll (KY) ***397***
Kentucky State U (KY) ***397***
Kentucky Wesleyan Coll (KY) ***397***
Kenyon Coll (OH) ***398***
Keuka Coll (NY) ***398***
King Coll (TN) ***398***
King's Coll (PA) ***398***
The King's U Coll (AB, Canada) ***399***
Knox Coll (IL) ***399***
Kutztown U of Pennsylvania (PA) ***399***
Lafayette Coll (PA) ***400***
LaGrange Coll (GA) ***400***
Lake Erie Coll (OH) ***400***
Lake Forest Coll (IL) ***400***
Lakehead U (ON, Canada) ***400***
Lakeland Coll (WI) ***401***
Lamar U (TX) ***401***
Lambuth U (TN) ***401***
Lander U (SC) ***401***
Langston U (OK) ***402***
La Roche Coll (PA) ***402***
La Salle U (PA) ***402***
Lasell Coll (MA) ***402***
La Sierra U (CA) ***403***
Laurentian U (ON, Canada) ***403***
Lawrence U (WI) ***403***
Lebanon Valley Coll (PA) ***403***
Lees-McRae Coll (NC) ***404***
Lee U (TN) ***404***
Lehigh U (PA) ***404***
Lehman Coll of the City U of NY (NY) ***404***
Le Moyne Coll (NY) ***404***
Lenoir-Rhyne Coll (NC) ***405***
LeTourneau U (TX) ***405***
Lewis & Clark Coll (OR) ***405***
Lewis-Clark State Coll (ID) ***406***
Lewis U (IL) ***406***
Liberty U (VA) ***406***
Limestone Coll (SC) ***406***
Lincoln Memorial U (TN) ***407***
Lincoln U (PA) ***407***
Lindenwood U (MO) ***407***
Linfield Coll (OR) ***408***
Lipscomb U (TN) ***408***
Lock Haven U of Pennsylvania (PA) ***408***
Long Island U, Brooklyn Campus (NY) ***409***
Long Island U, C.W. Post Campus (NY) ***409***
Long Island U, Southampton Coll (NY) ***409***
Long Island U, Southampton Coll, Friends World Program (NY) ***409***
Longwood U (VA) ***409***
Loras Coll (IA) ***410***
Louisiana Coll (LA) ***410***
Louisiana State U and A&M Coll (LA) ***410***
Louisiana State U in Shreveport (LA) ***410***
Louisiana Tech U (LA) ***410***
Lourdes Coll (OH) ***411***
Loyola Coll in Maryland (MD) ***411***
Loyola Marymount U (CA) ***411***
Loyola U Chicago (IL) ***411***
Loyola U New Orleans (LA) ***411***
Lubbock Christian U (TX) ***412***
Luther Coll (IA) ***412***
Lycoming Coll (PA) ***412***
Lynchburg Coll (VA) ***413***
Lyndon State Coll (VT) ***413***
Lynn U (FL) ***413***
Lyon Coll (AR) ***413***
Macalester Coll (MN) ***413***
MacMurray Coll (IL) ***414***
Madonna U (MI) ***414***
Maharishi U of Management (IA) ***414***
Malaspina U-Coll (BC, Canada) ***415***
Malone Coll (OH) ***415***
Manchester Coll (IN) ***415***
Manhattan Coll (NY) ***416***
Manhattanville Coll (NY) ***416***
Mansfield U of Pennsylvania (PA) ***416***
Marian Coll (IN) ***417***
Marian Coll of Fond du Lac (WI) ***417***
Marietta Coll (OH) ***417***
Marist Coll (NY) ***417***
Marlboro Coll (VT) ***418***
Marquette U (WI) ***418***
Marshall U (WV) ***418***
Mars Hill Coll (NC) ***418***
Martin U (IN) ***419***
Mary Baldwin Coll (VA) ***419***
Marygrove Coll (MI) ***419***
Marymount Coll of Fordham U (NY) ***419***
Marymount Manhattan Coll (NY) ***420***
Marymount U (VA) ***420***
Maryville Coll (TN) ***420***
Maryville U of Saint Louis (MO) ***420***
Mary Washington Coll (VA) ***420***
Marywood U (PA) ***421***
Massachusetts Coll of Liberal Arts (MA) ***421***
McDaniel Coll (MD) ***422***
McGill U (QC, Canada) ***423***
McKendree Coll (IL) ***423***
McMaster U (ON, Canada) ***423***
McMurry U (TX) ***423***
McNeese State U (LA) ***423***
McPherson Coll (KS) ***423***
Medaille Coll (NY) ***424***
Medgar Evers Coll of the City U of NY (NY) ***424***
Memorial U of Newfoundland (NF, Canada) ***424***
Mercer U (GA) ***425***
Mercy Coll (NY) ***425***
Mercyhurst Coll (PA) ***425***
Meredith Coll (NC) ***426***
Merrimack Coll (MA) ***426***
Mesa State Coll (CO) ***426***
Messiah Coll (PA) ***426***
Methodist Coll (NC) ***427***
Metropolitan State Coll of Denver (CO) ***427***
Metropolitan State U (MN) ***427***
Miami U (OH) ***428***
Michigan State U (MI) ***428***
MidAmerica Nazarene U (KS) ***428***
Middlebury Coll (VT) ***429***
Middle Tennessee State U (TN) ***429***
Midland Lutheran Coll (NE) ***429***
Midway Coll (KY) ***429***
Midwestern State U (TX) ***430***
Millersville U of Pennsylvania (PA) ***430***
Milligan Coll (TN) ***430***
Millikin U (IL) ***430***
Millsaps Coll (MS) ***431***
Mills Coll (CA) ***431***
Minnesota State U, Mankato (MN) ***431***
Minnesota State U, Moorhead (MN) ***432***
Minot State U (ND) ***432***
Mississippi Coll (MS) ***432***
Mississippi State U (MS) ***432***
Missouri Southern State Coll (MO) ***433***
Missouri Valley Coll (MO) ***433***
Missouri Western State Coll (MO) ***433***
Molloy Coll (NY) ***433***
Monmouth Coll (IL) ***434***
Monmouth U (NJ) ***434***
Montana State U–Billings (MT) ***434***
Montana State U–Bozeman (MT) ***434***
Montclair State U (NJ) ***435***
Moravian Coll (PA) ***436***
Morehead State U (KY) ***436***
Morehouse Coll (GA) ***436***
Morgan State U (MD) ***436***
Morningside Coll (IA) ***437***
Mount Allison U (NB, Canada) ***437***
Mount Aloysius Coll (PA) ***437***
Mount Holyoke Coll (MA) ***438***
Mount Mercy Coll (IA) ***438***
Mount Olive Coll (NC) ***439***
Mount Saint Mary Coll (NY) ***439***
Mount St. Mary's Coll (CA) ***439***
Mount Saint Mary's Coll and Seminary (MD) ***439***
Mount Saint Vincent U (NS, Canada) ***439***
Mount Union Coll (OH) ***440***
Mount Vernon Nazarene U (OH) ***440***
Muhlenberg Coll (PA) ***440***
Murray State U (KY) ***440***
Muskingum Coll (OH) ***441***
Naropa U (CO) ***441***
National-Louis U (IL) ***442***
National U (CA) ***442***
Nazareth Coll of Rochester (NY) ***443***
Nebraska Wesleyan U (NE) ***443***
Neumann Coll (PA) ***443***
Newberry Coll (SC) ***444***
Newbury Coll (MA) ***444***
New Coll of Florida (FL) ***444***
New England Coll (NH) ***444***
New Jersey City U (NJ) ***445***
Newman U (KS) ***445***
New Mexico Highlands U (NM) ***446***
New Mexico Inst of Mining and Technology (NM) ***446***
New Mexico State U (NM) ***446***
New York Inst of Technology (NY) ***447***
New York U (NY) ***447***
Niagara U (NY) ***447***
Nicholls State U (LA) ***447***
Nichols Coll (MA) ***448***
Nipissing U (ON, Canada) ***448***
Norfolk State U (VA) ***448***
North Carolina Ag and Tech State U (NC) ***448***
North Carolina Central U (NC) ***448***
North Carolina State U (NC) ***449***
North Carolina Wesleyan Coll (NC) ***449***
North Central Coll (IL) ***449***
Northcentral U (AZ) ***449***
North Dakota State U (ND) ***449***
Northeastern Illinois U (IL) ***450***
Northeastern State U (OK) ***450***
Northeastern U (MA) ***450***
Northern Arizona U (AZ) ***450***
Northern Illinois U (IL) ***450***
Northern Kentucky U (KY) ***451***
Northern Michigan U (MI) ***451***
Northern State U (SD) ***451***
North Georgia Coll & State U (GA) ***451***
Northland Coll (WI) ***452***
North Park U (IL) ***452***
Northwest Christian Coll (OR) ***452***
Northwest Coll (WA) ***452***
Northwestern Coll (IA) ***453***
Northwestern Coll (MN) ***453***
Northwestern Oklahoma State U (OK) ***453***
Northwestern State U of Louisiana (LA) ***453***
Northwestern U (IL) ***453***
Northwest Missouri State U (MO) ***454***
Northwest Nazarene U (ID) ***454***
Norwich U (VT) ***455***
Notre Dame Coll (OH) ***455***
Notre Dame de Namur U (CA) ***455***
Nova Southeastern U (FL) ***455***
Nyack Coll (NY) ***456***
Oak Hills Christian Coll (MN) ***456***
Oakland U (MI) ***456***
Oakwood Coll (AL) ***456***
Oberlin Coll (OH) ***456***
Occidental Coll (CA) ***457***
Oglethorpe U (GA) ***457***
Ohio Dominican U (OH) ***457***
Ohio Northern U (OH) ***457***
The Ohio State U (OH) ***457***
The Ohio State U at Lima (OH) ***458***
Ohio U (OH) ***458***
Ohio Valley Coll (WV) ***459***
Ohio Wesleyan U (OH) ***459***
Okanagan U Coll (BC, Canada) ***459***
Oklahoma Baptist U (OK) ***459***
Oklahoma Christian U (OK) ***459***
Oklahoma City U (OK) ***460***
Oklahoma Panhandle State U (OK) ***460***
Oklahoma State U (OK) ***460***
Old Dominion U (VA) ***460***
Olivet Coll (MI) ***461***
Olivet Nazarene U (IL) ***461***
Oral Roberts U (OK) ***461***
Oregon State U (OR) ***462***
Ottawa U (KS) ***462***
Otterbein Coll (OH) ***462***
Ouachita Baptist U (AR) ***462***
Our Lady of the Lake U of San Antonio (TX) ***463***
Pace U (NY) ***463***
Pacific Lutheran U (WA) ***463***
Pacific Union Coll (CA) ***464***
Pacific U (OR) ***464***
Paine Coll (GA) ***465***
Palm Beach Atlantic U (FL) ***465***
Park U (MO) ***465***
Peace Coll (NC) ***466***
Penn State U at Erie, The Behrend Coll (PA) ***467***
Penn State U Harrisburg Campus of the Capital Coll (PA) ***468***
Penn State U Lehigh Valley Cmps of Berks-Lehigh Valley Coll (PA) ***468***
Penn State U Schuylkill Campus of the Capital Coll (PA) ***468***
Penn State U Univ Park Campus (PA) ***468***
Pepperdine U, Malibu (CA) ***469***
Peru State Coll (NE) ***469***
Pfeiffer U (NC) ***469***
Philadelphia U (PA) ***469***
Piedmont Coll (GA) ***470***
Pikeville Coll (KY) ***470***
Pine Manor Coll (MA) ***470***
Pittsburg State U (KS) ***470***
Pitzer Coll (CA) ***471***
Plattsburgh State U of NY (NY) ***471***
Plymouth State Coll (NH) ***471***
Point Loma Nazarene U (CA) ***471***
Point Park Coll (PA) ***471***
Pomona Coll (CA) ***472***
Pontifical Catholic U of Puerto Rico (PR) ***472***
Portland State U (OR) ***472***
Prairie View A&M U (TX) ***473***
Presbyterian Coll (SC) ***473***
Prescott Coll (AZ) ***474***
Princeton U (NJ) ***474***
Providence Coll (RI) ***474***
Purchase Coll, State U of NY (NY) ***475***
Purdue U (IN) ***475***
Purdue U Calumet (IN) ***475***
Queens Coll of the City U of NY (NY) ***475***
Queen's U at Kingston (ON, Canada) ***476***
Queens U of Charlotte (NC) ***476***
Quincy U (IL) ***476***
Quinnipiac U (CT) ***476***
Radford U (VA) ***476***
Ramapo Coll of New Jersey (NJ) ***477***
Randolph-Macon Coll (VA) ***477***
Randolph-Macon Woman's Coll (VA) ***477***
Reed Coll (OR) ***477***
Regis Coll (MA) ***478***
Regis U (CO) ***478***
Reinhardt Coll (GA) ***478***
Rensselaer Polytechnic Inst (NY) ***478***
Rhode Island Coll (RI) ***479***
Rhodes Coll (TN) ***479***
Rice U (TX) ***479***
The Richard Stockton Coll of New Jersey (NJ) ***479***
Richmond, The American International U in London(United Kingdom) ***480***
Rider U (NJ) ***480***
Ripon Coll (WI) ***480***
Rivier Coll (NH) ***480***
Roanoke Coll (VA) ***481***
Roberts Wesleyan Coll (NY) ***481***
Rochester Coll (MI) ***482***
Rochester Inst of Technology (NY) ***482***
Rockford Coll (IL) ***482***
Rockhurst U (MO) ***482***
Rocky Mountain Coll (MT) ***482***
Roger Williams U (RI) ***483***
Rollins Coll (FL) ***483***
Roosevelt U (IL) ***483***
Rosemont Coll (PA) ***484***
Rowan U (NJ) ***484***
Russell Sage Coll (NY) ***484***
Rutgers, The State U of New Jersey, Camden (NJ) ***485***
Rutgers, The State U of New Jersey, Newark (NJ) ***485***
Rutgers, The State U of New Jersey, New Brunswick (NJ) ***485***
Sacred Heart U (CT) ***486***
Sage Coll of Albany (NY) ***486***
Saginaw Valley State U (MI) ***486***
St. Ambrose U (IA) ***486***
St. Andrews Presbyterian Coll (NC) ***487***
Saint Anselm Coll (NH) ***487***
Saint Augustine's Coll (NC) ***487***
St. Bonaventure U (NY) ***487***
St. Cloud State U (MN) ***488***
St. Edward's U (TX) ***488***
St. Francis Coll (NY) ***488***
Saint Francis U (PA) ***488***
St. Francis Xavier U (NS, Canada) ***489***
St. John Fisher Coll (NY) ***489***
Saint John's U (MN) ***490***
St. John's U (NY) ***490***
Saint Joseph Coll (CT) ***490***
Saint Joseph's Coll (IN) ***490***
St. Joseph's Coll, New York (NY) ***491***
Saint Joseph's Coll of Maine (ME) ***491***
St. Joseph's Coll, Suffolk Campus (NY) ***491***
Saint Joseph's U (PA) ***491***
St. Lawrence U (NY) ***491***
Saint Leo U (FL) ***492***
Saint Louis U (MO) ***492***
Saint Martin's Coll (WA) ***493***
Saint Mary Coll (KS) ***493***
Saint Mary-of-the-Woods Coll (IN) ***493***
Saint Mary's Coll (IN) ***493***
Saint Mary's Coll of California (CA) ***494***
Saint Mary's Coll of Madonna U (MI) ***493***

PSYCHOLOGY (continued)

St. Mary's Coll of Maryland (MD) ***494***
Saint Mary's U (NS, Canada) ***494***
Saint Mary's U of Minnesota (MN) ***494***
St. Mary's U of San Antonio (TX) ***494***
Saint Michael's Coll (VT) ***494***
St. Norbert Coll (WI) ***495***
St. Olaf Coll (MN) ***495***
Saint Peter's Coll (NJ) ***495***
St. Thomas Aquinas Coll (NY) ***495***
St. Thomas U (FL) ***496***
St. Thomas U (NB, Canada) ***496***
Saint Vincent Coll (PA) ***496***
Saint Xavier U (IL) ***496***
Salem Coll (NC) ***496***
Salem State Coll (MA) ***497***
Salisbury U (MD) ***497***
Salve Regina U (RI) ***497***
Samford U (AL) ***497***
Sam Houston State U (TX) ***497***
San Diego State U (CA) ***498***
San Francisco State U (CA) ***498***
San Jose State U (CA) ***499***
Santa Clara U (CA) ***499***
Sarah Lawrence Coll (NY) ***499***
Schiller International U(United Kingdom) ***500***
Schreiner U (TX) ***501***
Scripps Coll (CA) ***501***
Seattle Pacific U (WA) ***501***
Seattle U (WA) ***501***
Seton Hall U (NJ) ***502***
Seton Hill U (PA) ***502***
Shaw U (NC) ***502***
Shenandoah U (VA) ***503***
Shepherd Coll (WV) ***503***
Shippensburg U of Pennsylvania (PA) ***503***
Shorter Coll (GA) ***504***
Siena Coll (NY) ***504***
Siena Heights U (MI) ***504***
Silver Lake Coll (WI) ***504***
Simmons Coll (MA) ***504***
Simon Fraser U (BC, Canada) ***505***
Simon's Rock Coll of Bard (MA) ***505***
Simpson Coll (IA) ***505***
Simpson Coll and Graduate School (CA) ***505***
Skidmore Coll (NY) ***506***
Slippery Rock U of Pennsylvania (PA) ***506***
Smith Coll (MA) ***506***
Sonoma State U (CA) ***506***
South Carolina State U (SC) ***506***
South Dakota State U (SD) ***507***
Southeastern Coll of the Assemblies of God (FL) ***507***
Southeastern Louisiana U (LA) ***508***
Southeastern Oklahoma State U (OK) ***508***
Southeast Missouri State U (MO) ***508***
Southern Adventist U (TN) ***508***
Southern Arkansas U–Magnolia (AR) ***509***
Southern Connecticut State U (CT) ***509***
Southern Illinois U Carbondale (IL) ***509***
Southern Illinois U Edwardsville (IL) ***509***
Southern Methodist U (TX) ***510***
Southern Nazarene U (OK) ***510***
Southern New Hampshire U (NH) ***510***
Southern Oregon U (OR) ***510***
Southern U and A&M Coll (LA) ***511***
Southern Utah U (UT) ***511***
Southern Vermont Coll (VT) ***511***
Southern Wesleyan U (SC) ***511***
Southwest Baptist U (MO) ***512***
Southwestern Coll (KS) ***512***
Southwestern Oklahoma State U (OK) ***512***
Southwestern U (TX) ***513***
Southwest Missouri State U (MO) ***513***
Southwest State U (MN) ***513***
Southwest Texas State U (TX) ***513***
Spalding U (KY) ***513***
Spelman Coll (GA) ***514***
Spring Arbor U (MI) ***514***
Springfield Coll (MA) ***514***
Spring Hill Coll (AL) ***514***
Stanford U (CA) ***514***
State U of NY at Albany (NY) ***514***
State U of NY at Binghamton (NY) ***515***
State U of NY at New Paltz (NY) ***515***
State U of NY at Oswego (NY) ***515***
State U of NY Coll at Brockport (NY) ***515***
State U of NY Coll at Buffalo (NY) ***516***
State U of NY Coll at Cortland (NY) ***516***
State U of NY Coll at Fredonia (NY) ***516***
State U of NY Coll at Geneseo (NY) ***516***
State U of NY Coll at Old Westbury (NY) ***516***
State U of NY Coll at Oneonta (NY) ***517***
State U of NY Coll at Potsdam (NY) ***517***
State U of NY Inst of Tech at Utica/Rome (NY) ***518***
State U of West Georgia (GA) ***518***
Stephen F. Austin State U (TX) ***518***
Stephens Coll (MO) ***519***
Stetson U (FL) ***519***
Stonehill Coll (MA) ***520***
Stony Brook U, State University of New York (NY) ***520***
Suffolk U (MA) ***520***
Sul Ross State U (TX) ***521***
Susquehanna U (PA) ***521***
Swarthmore Coll (PA) ***521***
Sweet Briar Coll (VA) ***521***
Syracuse U (NY) ***521***
Tabor Coll (KS) ***522***
Talladega Coll (AL) ***522***
Tarleton State U (TX) ***522***
Taylor U (IN) ***523***
Taylor U, Fort Wayne Campus (IN) ***523***
Teikyo Post U (CT) ***523***
Temple U (PA) ***523***
Tennessee State U (TN) ***523***
Tennessee Technological U (TN) ***524***
Tennessee Temple U (TN) ***524***
Tennessee Wesleyan Coll (TN) ***524***
Texas A&M International U (TX) ***524***
Texas A&M U (TX) ***524***
Texas A&M U–Commerce (TX) ***525***
Texas A&M U–Corpus Christi (TX) ***525***
Texas A&M U–Kingsville (TX) ***525***
Texas A&M U–Texarkana (TX) ***525***
Texas Christian U (TX) ***526***
Texas Lutheran U (TX) ***526***
Texas Southern U (TX) ***526***
Texas Tech U (TX) ***526***
Texas Wesleyan U (TX) ***526***
Texas Woman's U (TX) ***527***
Thiel Coll (PA) ***527***
Thomas Coll (ME) ***527***
Thomas Edison State Coll (NJ) ***527***
Thomas More Coll (KY) ***528***
Thomas U (GA) ***528***
Tiffin U (OH) ***528***
Toccoa Falls Coll (GA) ***528***
Touro Coll (NY) ***529***
Towson U (MD) ***529***
Transylvania U (KY) ***529***
Trent U (ON, Canada) ***529***
Trevecca Nazarene U (TN) ***529***
Trinity Bible Coll (ND) ***530***
Trinity Christian Coll (IL) ***530***
Trinity Coll (CT) ***530***
Trinity Coll (DC) ***530***
Trinity International U (IL) ***531***
Trinity U (TX) ***531***
Trinity Western U (BC, Canada) ***531***
Tri-State U (IN) ***532***
Troy State U (AL) ***532***
Troy State U Dothan (AL) ***532***
Troy State U Montgomery (AL) ***532***
Truman State U (MO) ***532***
Tufts U (MA) ***533***
Tulane U (LA) ***533***
Tusculum Coll (TN) ***533***
Tuskegee U (AL) ***533***
Tyndale Coll & Seminary (ON, Canada) ***533***
Union Coll (KY) ***533***
Union Coll (NE) ***534***
Union Coll (NY) ***534***
Union Inst & U (OH) ***534***
Union U (TN) ***534***
United States International U(Kenya) ***535***
United States Military Academy (NY) ***535***
Université de Sherbrooke (QC, Canada) ***536***
U du Québec à Trois-Rivières (QC, Canada) ***536***
Université Laval (QC, Canada) ***536***
U at Buffalo, The State University of New York (NY) ***536***
U Coll of the Cariboo (BC, Canada) ***537***
The U of Akron (OH) ***537***
The U of Alabama (AL) ***537***
The U of Alabama at Birmingham (AL) ***537***
The U of Alabama in Huntsville (AL) ***537***
U of Alaska Anchorage (AK) ***538***
U of Alaska Fairbanks (AK) ***538***
U of Alberta (AB, Canada) ***538***
The U of Arizona (AZ) ***538***
U of Arkansas (AR) ***539***
U of Arkansas at Little Rock (AR) ***539***
U of Arkansas at Monticello (AR) ***539***
U of Baltimore (MD) ***539***
The U of British Columbia (BC, Canada) ***540***
U of Calgary (AB, Canada) ***540***
U of Calif, Berkeley (CA) ***540***
U of Calif, Davis (CA) ***540***
U of Calif, Irvine (CA) ***541***
U of Calif, Los Angeles (CA) ***541***
U of Calif, Riverside (CA) ***541***
U of Calif, San Diego (CA) ***541***
U of Calif, Santa Barbara (CA) ***541***
U of Calif, Santa Cruz (CA) ***542***
U of Central Arkansas (AR) ***542***
U of Central Florida (FL) ***542***
U of Central Oklahoma (OK) ***542***
U of Charleston (WV) ***542***
U of Chicago (IL) ***542***
U of Cincinnati (OH) ***543***
U of Colorado at Boulder (CO) ***543***
U of Colorado at Colorado Springs (CO) ***543***
U of Colorado at Denver (CO) ***543***
U of Connecticut (CT) ***544***
U of Dallas (TX) ***544***
U of Dayton (OH) ***544***
U of Delaware (DE) ***544***
U of Denver (CO) ***544***
U of Dubuque (IA) ***545***
U of Evansville (IN) ***545***
The U of Findlay (OH) ***545***
U of Florida (FL) ***545***
U of Georgia (GA) ***545***
U of Great Falls (MT) ***545***
U of Guelph (ON, Canada) ***546***
U of Hartford (CT) ***546***
U of Hawaii at Hilo (HI) ***546***
U of Hawaii at Manoa (HI) ***546***
U of Hawaii–West Oahu (HI) ***546***
U of Houston (TX) ***547***
U of Houston–Clear Lake (TX) ***547***
U of Houston–Downtown (TX) ***547***
U of Idaho (ID) ***547***
U of Illinois at Chicago (IL) ***547***
U of Illinois at Springfield (IL) ***548***
U of Illinois at Urbana–Champaign (IL) ***548***
U of Indianapolis (IN) ***548***
The U of Iowa (IA) ***548***
U of Judaism (CA) ***548***
U of Kansas (KS) ***549***
U of Kentucky (KY) ***549***
U of King's Coll (NS, Canada) ***549***
U of La Verne (CA) ***549***
The U of Lethbridge (AB, Canada) ***549***
U of Louisiana at Lafayette (LA) ***550***
U of Louisville (KY) ***550***
U of Maine (ME) ***550***
U of Maine at Farmington (ME) ***550***
U of Maine at Machias (ME) ***551***
U of Manitoba (MB, Canada) ***551***
U of Mary (ND) ***551***
U of Mary Hardin-Baylor (TX) ***551***
U of Maryland, Baltimore County (MD) ***552***
U of Maryland, Coll Park (MD) ***552***
U of Maryland University Coll (MD) ***552***
U of Massachusetts Amherst (MA) ***552***
U of Massachusetts Boston (MA) ***553***
U of Massachusetts Dartmouth (MA) ***553***
U of Massachusetts Lowell (MA) ***553***
The U of Memphis (TN) ***553***
U of Miami (FL) ***553***
U of Michigan (MI) ***554***
U of Michigan–Dearborn (MI) ***554***
U of Michigan–Flint (MI) ***554***
U of Minnesota, Duluth (MN) ***554***
U of Minnesota, Morris (MN) ***555***
U of Minnesota, Twin Cities Campus (MN) ***555***
U of Mississippi (MS) ***555***
U of Missouri–Columbia (MO) ***555***
U of Missouri–Kansas City (MO) ***555***
U of Missouri–Rolla (MO) ***556***
U of Missouri–St. Louis (MO) ***556***
U of Mobile (AL) ***556***
The U of Montana–Missoula (MT) ***556***
U of Montevallo (AL) ***557***
U of Nebraska at Kearney (NE) ***557***
U of Nebraska at Omaha (NE) ***557***
U of Nebraska–Lincoln (NE) ***557***
U of Nevada, Las Vegas (NV) ***558***
U of Nevada, Reno (NV) ***558***
U of New Brunswick Fredericton (NB, Canada) ***558***
U of New Brunswick Saint John (NB, Canada) ***558***
U of New England (ME) ***558***
U of New Hampshire (NH) ***558***
U of New Haven (CT) ***559***
U of New Mexico (NM) ***559***
U of New Orleans (LA) ***559***
U of North Alabama (AL) ***559***
The U of North Carolina at Asheville (NC) ***559***
The U of North Carolina at Chapel Hill (NC) ***560***
The U of North Carolina at Charlotte (NC) ***560***
The U of North Carolina at Greensboro (NC) ***560***
The U of North Carolina at Pembroke (NC) ***560***
The U of North Carolina at Wilmington (NC) ***561***
U of North Dakota (ND) ***561***
U of Northern Colorado (CO) ***561***
U of Northern Iowa (IA) ***561***
U of North Florida (FL) ***561***
U of North Texas (TX) ***562***
U of Notre Dame (IN) ***562***
U of Oklahoma (OK) ***562***
U of Oregon (OR) ***562***
U of Ottawa (ON, Canada) ***563***
U of Pennsylvania (PA) ***563***
U of Pittsburgh (PA) ***569***
U of Pittsburgh at Bradford (PA) ***569***
U of Pittsburgh at Greensburg (PA) ***570***
U of Pittsburgh at Johnstown (PA) ***570***
U of Portland (OR) ***570***
U of Prince Edward Island (PE, Canada) ***570***
U of Puerto Rico, Cayey U Coll (PR) ***571***
U of Puerto Rico, Río Piedras (PR) ***571***
U of Puget Sound (WA) ***571***
U of Redlands (CA) ***572***
U of Regina (SK, Canada) ***572***
U of Rhode Island (RI) ***572***
U of Richmond (VA) ***572***
U of Rochester (NY) ***573***
U of St. Francis (IL) ***573***
U of Saint Francis (IN) ***573***
U of St. Thomas (MN) ***573***
U of St. Thomas (TX) ***573***
U of San Diego (CA) ***574***
U of San Francisco (CA) ***574***
U of Saskatchewan (SK, Canada) ***574***
U of Science and Arts of Oklahoma (OK) ***574***
The U of Scranton (PA) ***574***
U of Sioux Falls (SD) ***574***
U of South Alabama (AL) ***575***
U of South Carolina Aiken (SC) ***575***
U of South Carolina Spartanburg (SC) ***575***
The U of South Dakota (SD) ***575***
U of Southern California (CA) ***576***
U of Southern Indiana (IN) ***576***
U of Southern Maine (ME) ***576***
U of Southern Mississippi (MS) ***576***
U of South Florida (FL) ***576***
The U of Tampa (FL) ***577***
The U of Tennessee (TN) ***577***
The U of Tennessee at Chattanooga (TN) ***577***
The U of Tennessee at Martin (TN) ***577***
The U of Texas at Arlington (TX) ***577***
The U of Texas at Austin (TX) ***578***
The U of Texas at Dallas (TX) ***578***
The U of Texas at El Paso (TX) ***578***
The U of Texas at San Antonio (TX) ***578***
The U of Texas at Tyler (TX) ***579***
The U of Texas of the Permian Basin (TX) ***579***
The U of Texas–Pan American (TX) ***579***
U of the District of Columbia (DC) ***580***
U of the Incarnate Word (TX) ***580***
U of the Ozarks (AR) ***580***
U of the Pacific (CA) ***580***
U of the Sacred Heart (PR) ***580***
U of the Sciences in Philadelphia (PA) ***580***
U of the South (TN) ***581***
U of the Virgin Islands (VI) ***581***
U of Toledo (OH) ***581***
U of Toronto (ON, Canada) ***581***
U of Tulsa (OK) ***581***
U of Utah (UT) ***582***
U of Vermont (VT) ***582***
U of Victoria (BC, Canada) ***582***
U of Virginia (VA) ***582***
The U of Virginia's Coll at Wise (VA) ***582***
U of Washington (WA) ***583***
U of Waterloo (ON, Canada) ***583***
The U of West Alabama (AL) ***583***
The U of Western Ontario (ON, Canada) ***583***

U of West Florida (FL) 583
U of Windsor (ON, Canada) 584
U of Wisconsin–Eau Claire (WI) 584
U of Wisconsin–Green Bay (WI) 584
U of Wisconsin–La Crosse (WI) 584
U of Wisconsin–Madison (WI) 584
U of Wisconsin–Milwaukee (WI) 585
U of Wisconsin–Oshkosh (WI) 585
U of Wisconsin–Parkside (WI) 585
U of Wisconsin–Platteville (WI) 585
U of Wisconsin–River Falls (WI) 585
U of Wisconsin–Stevens Point (WI) 585
U of Wisconsin–Stout (WI) 586
U of Wisconsin–Superior (WI) 586
U of Wisconsin–Whitewater (WI) 586
U of Wyoming (WY) 586
Upper Iowa U (IA) 587
Urbana U (OH) 587
Ursinus Coll (PA) 587
Ursuline Coll (OH) 587
Utah State U (UT) 587
Utica Coll (NY) 588
Valdosta State U (GA) 588
Valparaiso U (IN) 588
Vanderbilt U (TN) 588
Vanguard U of Southern California (CA) 589
Vassar Coll (NY) 589
Villa Julie Coll (MD) 590
Villanova U (PA) 590
Virginia Commonwealth U (VA) 590
Virginia Intermont Coll (VA) 590
Virginia Military Inst (VA) 591
Virginia Polytechnic Inst and State U (VA) 591
Virginia State U (VA) 591
Virginia Union U (VA) 591
Virginia Wesleyan Coll (VA) 591
Viterbo U (WI) 591
Wabash Coll (IN) 592
Wagner Coll (NY) 592
Wake Forest U (NC) 592
Walla Walla Coll (WA) 593
Walsh U (OH) 593
Warner Pacific Coll (OR) 593
Warner Southern Coll (FL) 593
Warren Wilson Coll (NC) 594
Wartburg Coll (IA) 594
Washington & Jefferson Coll (PA) 594
Washington and Lee U (VA) 594
Washington Coll (MD) 594
Washington State U (WA) 595
Washington U in St. Louis (MO) 595
Wayland Baptist U (TX) 595
Waynesburg Coll (PA) 595
Wayne State Coll (NE) 596
Wayne State U (MI) 596
Weber State U (UT) 596
Webster U (MO) 597
Wellesley Coll (MA) 597
Wells Coll (NY) 597
Wesleyan Coll (GA) 597
Wesleyan U (CT) 597
Wesley Coll (DE) 598
West Chester U of Pennsylvania (PA) 598
Western Baptist Coll (OR) 598
Western Carolina U (NC) 598
Western Connecticut State U (CT) 598
Western Illinois U (IL) 599
Western Kentucky U (KY) 599
Western Michigan U (MI) 599
Western New England Coll (MA) 600
Western New Mexico U (NM) 600
Western Oregon U (OR) 600
Western State Coll of Colorado (CO) 600
Western Washington U (WA) 600
Westfield State Coll (MA) 600
West Liberty State Coll (WV) 601
Westminster Coll (MO) 601
Westminster Coll (PA) 601
Westminster Coll (UT) 601
Westmont Coll (CA) 602
West Texas A&M U (TX) 602
West Virginia State Coll (WV) 602
West Virginia U (WV) 602
West Virginia Wesleyan Coll (WV) 603
Wheaton Coll (IL) 603
Wheaton Coll (MA) 603
Wheeling Jesuit U (WV) 603
Whitman Coll (WA) 604
Whittier Coll (CA) 604
Whitworth Coll (WA) 604
Wichita State U (KS) 604
Widener U (PA) 604
Wilberforce U (OH) 605
Wilkes U (PA) 605
Willamette U (OR) 605
William Carey Coll (MS) 605
William Jewell Coll (MO) 606
William Paterson U of New Jersey (NJ) 606
William Penn U (IA) 606
Williams Baptist Coll (AR) 606
Williams Coll (MA) 606
William Woods U (MO) 607
Wilmington Coll (OH) 607
Wingate U (NC) 607
Winona State U (MN) 608
Winston-Salem State U (NC) 608
Winthrop U (SC) 608
Wisconsin Lutheran Coll (WI) 608
Wittenberg U (OH) 608
Wofford Coll (SC) 609
Woodbury U (CA) 609
Worcester State Coll (MA) 609
Wright State U (OH) 609
Xavier U (OH) 610
Xavier U of Louisiana (LA) 610
Yale U (CT) 610
York Coll (NE) 610
York Coll of Pennsylvania (PA) 610
York Coll of the City U of New York (NY) 611
York U (ON, Canada) 611
Youngstown State U (OH) 611

PSYCHOLOGY RELATED

Information can be found under this major's main heading.

Averett U (VA) 278
Kean U (NJ) 396
Loyola U Chicago (IL) 411
Point Park Coll (PA) 471
Skidmore Coll (NY) 506
State U of NY at Oswego (NY) 515
Wilmington Coll (DE) 607

PUBLIC ADMINISTRATION

Overview: This major will prepare students to become administrators or managers in local, state, and federal government agencies. *Related majors:* business administration, public policy analysis, law and legal studies, American government/politics, urban affairs/studies. *Potential careers:* governmental agency administrator, hospital executive, school administrator. *Salary potential:* $27k-$35k.

Abilene Christian U (TX) 260
Alfred U (NY) 263
American International Coll (MA) 267
Athabasca U (AB, Canada) 275
Auburn U (AL) 276
Augustana Coll (IL) 276
Bayamón Central U (PR) 283
Baylor U (TX) 283
Baruch Coll of the City U of NY (NY) 286
Blackburn Coll (IL) 290
Bloomfield Coll (NJ) 290
Bowling Green State U (OH) 292
Brock U (ON, Canada) 295
Buena Vista U (IA) 297
California State Polytechnic U, Pomona (CA) 300
California State U, Bakersfield (CA) 300
California State U, Chico (CA) 300
California State U, Dominguez Hills (CA) 300
California State U, Fresno (CA) 301
California State U, Fullerton (CA) 301
California State U, Hayward (CA) 301
California State U, Sacramento (CA) 301
California State U, San Bernardino (CA) 302
Calvin Coll (MI) 303
Campbell U (NC) 303
Canisius Coll (NY) 304
Carleton U (ON, Canada) 305
Carroll Coll (MT) 306
Cedarville U (OH) 308
Central Methodist Coll (MO) 309
Christopher Newport U (VA) 313
Concordia U (QC, Canada) 331
Doane Coll (NE) 344
Dominican Coll (NY) 344
Eastern Michigan U (MI) 348
Eastern Washington U (WA) 349
Edgewood Coll (WI) 351
Elon U (NC) 352
Evangel U (MO) 355
The Evergreen State Coll (WA) 355
Ferris State U (MI) 358
Fisk U (TN) 358
Florida A&M U (FL) 359
Florida Atlantic U (FL) 359
Florida International U (FL) 360
Fordham U (NY) 362
Framingham State Coll (MA) 362
George Mason U (VA) 366
Governors State U (IL) 370
Grambling State U (LA) 371
Grand Valley State U (MI) 371
Hamline U (MN) 374
Harding U (AR) 375
Hawai'i Pacific U (HI) 377
Heidelberg Coll (OH) 377
Henderson State U (AR) 378
Huntingdon Coll (AL) 383
Indiana U Bloomington (IN) 385
Indiana U Northwest (IN) 386
Indiana U–Purdue U Fort Wayne (IN) 386
Indiana U–Purdue U Indianapolis (IN) 387
Indiana U South Bend (IN) 387
Inst of Public Administration(Ireland) 387
Inter American U of PR, San Germán Campus (PR) 388
Iowa State U of Science and Technology (IA) 390
James Madison U (VA) 391
John Carroll U (OH) 392
John Jay Coll of Criminal Justice, the City U of NY (NY) 392
Johns Hopkins U (MD) 392
Juniata Coll (PA) 395
Kean U (NJ) 396
Kentucky State U (KY) 397
Kutztown U of Pennsylvania (PA) 399
Lakeland Coll (WI) 401
La Salle U (PA) 402
Lewis U (IL) 406
Lindenwood U (MO) 407
Lipscomb U (TN) 408
Long Island U, Brooklyn Campus (NY) 409
Long Island U, C.W. Post Campus (NY) 409
Louisiana Coll (LA) 410
Madonna U (MI) 414
Marist Coll (NY) 417
Medgar Evers Coll of the City U of NY (NY) 424
Mercyhurst Coll (PA) 425
Metropolitan State U (MN) 427
Miami U (OH) 428
Michigan State U (MI) 428
Minnesota State U, Mankato (MN) 431
Mississippi Valley State U (MS) 432
Missouri Valley Coll (MO) 433
Northeastern U (MA) 450
Northern Kentucky U (KY) 451
Northern Michigan U (MI) 451
Northern State U (SD) 451
Northwest Missouri State U (MO) 454
Oakland U (MI) 456
Ohio Wesleyan U (OH) 459
Park U (MO) 465
Plymouth State Coll (NH) 471
Point Park Coll (PA) 471
Pontifical Catholic U of Puerto Rico (PR) 472
Princeton U (NJ) 474
Rhode Island Coll (RI) 479
Roger Williams U (RI) 483
Roosevelt U (IL) 483
Ryerson U (ON, Canada) 485
Saginaw Valley State U (MI) 486
St. Ambrose U (IA) 486
St. Cloud State U (MN) 488
Saint Francis U (PA) 488
St. John's U (NY) 490
Saint Joseph's U (PA) 491
Saint Leo U (FL) 492
Saint Mary's U of Minnesota (MN) 494
St. Thomas U (FL) 496
Samford U (AL) 497
San Diego State U (CA) 498
San Jose State U (CA) 499
Seattle U (WA) 501
Seton Hill U (PA) 502
Shaw U (NC) 502
Shenandoah U (VA) 503
Shippensburg U of Pennsylvania (PA) 503
Siena Heights U (MI) 504
Slippery Rock U of Pennsylvania (PA) 506
Southeastern U (DC) 508
Southwest Missouri State U (MO) 513
Southwest State U (MN) 513
Southwest Texas State U (TX) 513
State U of NY at Albany (NY) 514
Stephen F. Austin State U (TX) 518
Stonehill Coll (MA) 520
Suffolk U (MA) 520
Talladega Coll (AL) 522
Tennessee State U (TN) 523
Texas A&M U–Kingsville (TX) 525
Texas Southern U (TX) 526
Texas Woman's U (TX) 527
Thomas Edison State Coll (NJ) 527
Union Inst & U (OH) 534
The U of Arizona (AZ) 538
U of Arkansas (AR) 539
U of Calif, Riverside (CA) 541
U of Central Arkansas (AR) 542
U of Central Florida (FL) 542
U of Denver (CO) 544
U of Hartford (CT) 546
U of Hawaii at Manoa (HI) 546
U of Hawaii–West Oahu (HI) 546
U of La Verne (CA) 549
The U of Lethbridge (AB, Canada) 549
U of Maine (ME) 550
The U of Maine at Augusta (ME) 550
U of Maine at Fort Kent (ME) 551
U of Manitoba (MB, Canada) 551
U of Massachusetts Boston (MA) 553
U of Michigan–Dearborn (MI) 554
U of Michigan–Flint (MI) 554
U of Mississippi (MS) 555
U of Missouri–St. Louis (MO) 556
U of Nebraska at Omaha (NE) 557
U of New Haven (CT) 559
The U of North Carolina at Pembroke (NC) 560
U of North Dakota (ND) 561
U of Northern Iowa (IA) 561
U of Oklahoma (OK) 562
U of Oregon (OR) 562
U of Ottawa (ON, Canada) 563
U of Pittsburgh (PA) 569
U of Regina (SK, Canada) 572
U of San Francisco (CA) 574
U of Saskatchewan (SK, Canada) 574
U of Southern California (CA) 576
The U of Tennessee (TN) 577
The U of Tennessee at Martin (TN) 577
The U of Texas at Dallas (TX) 578
The U of Texas–Pan American (TX) 579
U of the District of Columbia (DC) 580
U of Toronto (ON, Canada) 581
U of Victoria (BC, Canada) 582
U of Washington (WA) 583
The U of Western Ontario (ON, Canada) 583
U of Wisconsin–Green Bay (WI) 584
U of Wisconsin–La Crosse (WI) 584
U of Wisconsin–Stevens Point (WI) 585
U of Wisconsin–Whitewater (WI) 586
Upper Iowa U (IA) 587
Virginia State U (VA) 591
Wagner Coll (NY) 592
Washington State U (WA) 595
Waynesburg Coll (PA) 595
Wayne State Coll (NE) 596
Wayne State U (MI) 596
West Chester U of Pennsylvania (PA) 598
Western Michigan U (MI) 599
Western New Mexico U (NM) 600
Western Oregon U (OR) 600
Westminster Coll (MO) 601
West Texas A&M U (TX) 602
West Virginia U Inst of Technology (WV) 602
Winona State U (MN) 608
York Coll of Pennsylvania (PA) 610
York U (ON, Canada) 611
Youngstown State U (OH) 611

PUBLIC ADMINISTRATION AND SERVICES RELATED

Information can be found under this major's main heading.

Kentucky Wesleyan Coll (KY) 397
Ohio U (OH) 458
Southern Christian U (AL) 509
U of Phoenix–Colorado Campus (CO) 563

PUBLIC ADMINISTRATION AND SERVICES RELATED (continued)

U of Phoenix–Hawaii Campus (HI) ***564***
U of Phoenix–Nevada Campus (NV) ***565***
U of Phoenix–New Mexico Campus (NM) ***565***
U of Phoenix–Northern California Campus (CA) ***565***
U of Phoenix–Phoenix Campus (AZ) ***567***
U of Phoenix–San Diego Campus (CA) ***567***
U of Phoenix–Southern Arizona Campus (AZ) ***568***
U of Phoenix–Southern California Campus (CA) ***568***
U of Phoenix–Southern Colorado Campus (CO) ***568***
U of Phoenix–Tampa Campus (FL) ***568***
U of Phoenix–Utah Campus (UT) ***568***
U of Phoenix–West Michigan Campus (MI) ***569***

PUBLIC HEALTH

Overview: This major prepares students for a career as a public health officer, either managing, planning, or evaluating public health-care services and facilities. *Related majors:* public policy analysis, public administration, health/medical biostatistics, health science, public health education/promotion. *Potential careers:* health and human services officer, public health administrator, epidemiologist, waste management specialist, CDC investigator. *Salary potential:* $35k-$45k.

Alma Coll (MI) ***264***
Brock U (ON, Canada) ***295***
California State U, Dominguez Hills (CA) ***300***
California State U, Long Beach (CA) ***301***
Central Michigan U (MI) ***310***
Dillard U (LA) ***344***
Eastern Kentucky U (KY) ***348***
Eastern Washington U (WA) ***349***
East Tennessee State U (TN) ***349***
Grand Valley State U (MI) ***371***
Hampshire Coll (MA) ***375***
Hunter Coll of the City U of NY (NY) ***382***
Indiana U Bloomington (IN) ***385***
Indiana U–Purdue U Indianapolis (IN) ***387***
Johns Hopkins U (MD) ***392***
Maryville U of Saint Louis (MO) ***420***
Minnesota State U, Mankato (MN) ***431***
New Mexico State U (NM) ***446***
Oregon State U (OR) ***462***
The Richard Stockton Coll of New Jersey (NJ) ***479***
Rutgers, The State U of New Jersey, New Brunswick (NJ) ***485***
Ryerson U (ON, Canada) ***485***
St. Joseph's Coll, New York (NY) ***491***
Salem International U (WV) ***496***
Slippery Rock U of Pennsylvania (PA) ***506***
Southern Connecticut State U (CT) ***509***
Springfield Coll (MA) ***514***
Touro U International (CA) ***529***
Truman State U (MO) ***532***
Tufts U (MA) ***533***
U of Cincinnati (OH) ***543***
U of Hawaii at Manoa (HI) ***546***
U of Minnesota, Twin Cities Campus (MN) ***555***
U of Southern Mississippi (MS) ***576***
U of Washington (WA) ***583***
U of Wisconsin–Eau Claire (WI) ***584***
West Chester U of Pennsylvania (PA) ***598***
William Paterson U of New Jersey (NJ) ***606***
Winona State U (MN) ***608***
York U (ON, Canada) ***611***

PUBLIC HEALTH EDUCATION/PROMOTION

Overview: This major prepares students to become public health educators and health-promotion specialists. *Related majors:* public health, nursing (public health), communications and public relations, health education teaching, human services. *Potential careers:* health education teacher, public health administrator, state health-care administrator, nutritionist. *Salary potential:* $33k-43k.

Appalachian State U (NC) ***270***
Coastal Carolina U (SC) ***318***
Dillard U (LA) ***344***
East Carolina U (NC) ***347***
Georgia Southern U (GA) ***367***
Ithaca Coll (NY) ***390***
Laurentian U (ON, Canada) ***403***
Malone Coll (OH) ***415***
North Carolina Central U (NC) ***448***
Plymouth State Coll (NH) ***471***
St. Francis Coll (NY) ***488***
U of Northern Colorado (CO) ***561***
U of North Texas (TX) ***562***
U of St. Thomas (MN) ***573***
U of Toledo (OH) ***581***
U of Wisconsin–La Crosse (WI) ***584***
Walla Walla Coll (WA) ***593***
Western Washington U (WA) ***600***
Worcester State Coll (MA) ***609***

PUBLIC HEALTH RELATED

Information can be found under this major's main heading.

Florida Gulf Coast U (FL) ***359***
U of Hawaii at Manoa (HI) ***546***
U of Illinois at Urbana–Champaign (IL) ***548***
Utah State U (UT) ***587***

PUBLIC POLICY ANALYSIS

Overview: This major teaches students about the processes of how public policy is formulated and put into practice. *Related majors:* American government/politics, economics, history, political science, statistics. *Potential careers:* lobbyist, political manager or aide, journalist, economist, government administrator. *Salary potential:* $25k-$30k.

Albion Coll (MI) ***262***
Baruch Coll of the City U of NY (NY) ***286***
Bloomfield Coll (NJ) ***290***
Central Washington U (WA) ***310***
Chatham Coll (PA) ***312***
Coll of the Atlantic (ME) ***323***
The Coll of William and Mary (VA) ***324***
Columbia Coll (SC) ***327***
Concordia U (QC, Canada) ***331***
Cornell U (NY) ***333***
DePaul U (IL) ***339***
Dickinson Coll (PA) ***344***
Duke U (NC) ***346***
Eastern Washington U (WA) ***349***
Edgewood Coll (WI) ***351***
The Evergreen State Coll (WA) ***355***
The George Washington U (DC) ***367***
Georgia Inst of Technology (GA) ***367***
Grand Valley State U (MI) ***371***
Hamilton Coll (NY) ***374***
Hampden-Sydney Coll (VA) ***374***
Hampshire Coll (MA) ***375***
Harvard U (MA) ***376***
Hobart and William Smith Colls (NY) ***380***
Indiana U Bloomington (IN) ***385***
Kenyon Coll (OH) ***398***
Lincoln U (PA) ***407***
Long Island U, Southampton Coll, Friends World Program (NY) ***409***
Marymount U (VA) ***420***
Mills Coll (CA) ***431***
Muskingum Coll (OH) ***441***
New Coll of Florida (FL) ***444***
North Carolina State U (NC) ***449***
Northern Arizona U (AZ) ***450***
Northwestern U (IL) ***453***
Occidental Coll (CA) ***457***
Penn State U Harrisburg Campus of the Capital Coll (PA) ***468***
Pomona Coll (CA) ***472***
Rice U (TX) ***479***
Rochester Inst of Technology (NY) ***482***
St. Cloud State U (MN) ***488***
St. Mary's Coll of Maryland (MD) ***494***
Saint Peter's Coll (NJ) ***495***
Saint Vincent Coll (PA) ***496***
San Jose State U (CA) ***499***
Sarah Lawrence Coll (NY) ***499***
Simmons Coll (MA) ***504***
Southern Methodist U (TX) ***510***
Stanford U (CA) ***514***
State U of NY at Albany (NY) ***514***
Suffolk U (MA) ***520***
Syracuse U (NY) ***521***
Texas Southern U (TX) ***526***
Trinity Coll (CT) ***530***
United States Military Academy (NY) ***535***
U of Chicago (IL) ***542***
U of Cincinnati (OH) ***543***
U of Massachusetts Boston (MA) ***553***
U of Miami (FL) ***553***
U of Missouri–St. Louis (MO) ***556***
The U of North Carolina at Chapel Hill (NC) ***560***
U of Oregon (OR) ***562***
U of Ottawa (ON, Canada) ***563***
U of Pennsylvania (PA) ***563***
U of Rhode Island (RI) ***572***
U of Toledo (OH) ***581***
U of Wisconsin–Whitewater (WI) ***586***
Washington and Lee U (VA) ***594***
Wells Coll (NY) ***597***
Western State Coll of Colorado (CO) ***600***
York U (ON, Canada) ***611***

PUBLIC RELATIONS

Overview: Students will learn how to manage the media image of a business, an organization, or an individual, as well as the communication processes, such as mission statements and group relations, within organizations. *Related majors:* communication, journalism, advertising, psychology, organizational management. *Potential careers:* advertising executive, public relations executive, publicist, personal manager, journalist, editor. *Salary potential:* $25k-$37k.

Alabama State U (AL) ***261***
American U (DC) ***267***
Andrews U (MI) ***269***
Appalachian State U (NC) ***270***
Assumption Coll (MA) ***275***
Auburn U (AL) ***276***
Ball State U (IN) ***280***
Barry U (FL) ***282***
Berry Coll (GA) ***287***
Boston U (MA) ***292***
Bowling Green State U (OH) ***292***
Bradley U (IL) ***293***
Buena Vista U (IA) ***297***
Butler U (IN) ***297***
California State Polytechnic U, Pomona (CA) ***300***
California State U, Chico (CA) ***300***
California State U, Dominguez Hills (CA) ***300***
California State U, Fresno (CA) ***301***
California State U, Fullerton (CA) ***301***
California State U, Hayward (CA) ***301***
California State U, Long Beach (CA) ***301***
Cameron U (OK) ***303***
Campbell U (NC) ***303***
Capital U (OH) ***304***
Cardinal Stritch U (WI) ***305***
Carroll Coll (MT) ***306***
Carroll Coll (WI) ***306***
Central Michigan U (MI) ***310***
Central Missouri State U (MO) ***310***
Central Washington U (WA) ***310***
Champlain Coll (VT) ***311***
Chapman U (CA) ***311***
Clarke Coll (IA) ***315***
Cleveland State U (OH) ***317***
Coe Coll (IA) ***318***
The Coll of Southeastern Europe, The American U of Athens(Greece) ***323***
Coll of the Ozarks (MO) ***323***
Colorado State U (CO) ***325***
Colorado State U-Pueblo (CO) ***325***
Columbia Coll Chicago (IL) ***327***
Columbus State U (GA) ***328***
Concordia Coll (MN) ***329***
Curry Coll (MA) ***335***
Defiance Coll (OH) ***338***
Doane Coll (NE) ***344***
Drake U (IA) ***345***
Eastern Kentucky U (KY) ***348***
Eastern Michigan U (MI) ***348***
Eastern Washington U (WA) ***349***
Emerson Coll (MA) ***353***
Ferris State U (MI) ***358***
Florida A&M U (FL) ***359***
Florida Southern Coll (FL) ***361***
Florida State U (FL) ***361***
Fontbonne U (MO) ***361***
Fort Hays State U (KS) ***362***
Framingham State Coll (MA) ***362***
Freed-Hardeman U (TN) ***364***
George Fox U (OR) ***366***
Georgia Southern U (GA) ***367***
Gonzaga U (WA) ***369***
Grand Valley State U (MI) ***371***
Greenville Coll (IL) ***373***
Gwynedd-Mercy Coll (PA) ***374***
Hampton U (VA) ***375***
Harding U (AR) ***375***
Hastings Coll (NE) ***377***
Hawai'i Pacific U (HI) ***377***
Heidelberg Coll (OH) ***377***
Hofstra U (NY) ***380***
Howard Payne U (TX) ***382***
Illinois State U (IL) ***384***
Indiana U Northwest (IN) ***386***
Indiana U–Purdue U Fort Wayne (IN) ***386***
Iona Coll (NY) ***390***
Ithaca Coll (NY) ***390***
John Brown U (AR) ***392***
Kent State U (OH) ***397***
Lambuth U (TN) ***401***
La Salle U (PA) ***402***
Lewis U (IL) ***406***
Lindenwood U (MO) ***407***
Lipscomb U (TN) ***408***
Lock Haven U of Pennsylvania (PA) ***408***
Long Island U, C.W. Post Campus (NY) ***409***
Long Island U, Southampton Coll, Friends World Program (NY) ***409***
Loras Coll (IA) ***410***
Madonna U (MI) ***414***
Malone Coll (OH) ***415***
Mansfield U of Pennsylvania (PA) ***416***
Marietta Coll (OH) ***417***
Marist Coll (NY) ***417***
Marquette U (WI) ***418***
Mary Baldwin Coll (VA) ***419***
Marywood U (PA) ***421***
The Master's Coll and Seminary (CA) ***422***
McKendree Coll (IL) ***423***
Mercyhurst Coll (PA) ***425***
Mesa State Coll (CO) ***426***
Metropolitan State Coll of Denver (CO) ***427***
MidAmerica Nazarene U (KS) ***428***
Middle Tennessee State U (TN) ***429***
Milligan Coll (TN) ***430***
Minnesota State U, Mankato (MN) ***431***
Minnesota State U, Moorhead (MN) ***432***
Monmouth Coll (IL) ***434***
Montana State U–Billings (MT) ***434***
Mount Mary Coll (WI) ***438***
Mount Saint Mary Coll (NY) ***439***
Mount Saint Vincent U (NS, Canada) ***439***
Murray State U (KY) ***440***
New England Coll (NH) ***444***
North Central Coll (IL) ***449***
Northeastern U (MA) ***450***
Northern Arizona U (AZ) ***450***
Northern Michigan U (MI) ***451***
Northwestern Coll (MN) ***453***
Northwestern Oklahoma State U (OK) ***453***
Northwest Missouri State U (MO) ***454***
Northwest Nazarene U (ID) ***454***
Ohio Dominican U (OH) ***457***
Ohio Northern U (OH) ***457***
Ohio U (OH) ***458***
Ohio U–Zanesville (OH) ***458***
Oklahoma Baptist U (OK) ***459***
Oklahoma Christian U (OK) ***459***
Oklahoma City U (OK) ***460***
Oral Roberts U (OK) ***461***
Otterbein Coll (OH) ***462***
Pacific Union Coll (CA) ***464***
Pepperdine U, Malibu (CA) ***469***
Pittsburg State U (KS) ***470***
Point Park Coll (PA) ***471***
Pontifical Catholic U of Puerto Rico (PR) ***472***
Purdue U Calumet (IN) ***475***

Queens U of Charlotte (NC) ***476***
Quincy U (IL) ***476***
Quinnipiac U (CT) ***476***
Rider U (NJ) ***480***
Rockhurst U (MO) ***482***
Roosevelt U (IL) ***483***
Rowan U (NJ) ***484***
St. Ambrose U (IA) ***486***
St. Cloud State U (MN) ***488***
Saint Francis U (PA) ***488***
Saint Louis U (MO) ***492***
Saint Mary-of-the-Woods Coll (IN) ***493***
Saint Mary's U of Minnesota (MN) ***494***
Salem State Coll (MA) ***497***
Sam Houston State U (TX) ***497***
San Diego State U (CA) ***498***
San Jose State U (CA) ***499***
Seattle U (WA) ***501***
Seton Hill U (PA) ***502***
Shorter Coll (GA) ***504***
Simmons Coll (MA) ***504***
Southeast Missouri State U (MO) ***508***
Southern Adventist U (TN) ***508***
Southern Methodist U (TX) ***510***
Southwest Texas State U (TX) ***513***
Spring Hill Coll (AL) ***514***
State U of NY at Oswego (NY) ***515***
State U of NY Coll at Brockport (NY) ***515***
State U of NY Coll at Buffalo (NY) ***516***
Stephens Coll (MO) ***519***
Suffolk U (MA) ***520***
Susquehanna U (PA) ***521***
Syracuse U (NY) ***521***
Tabor Coll (KS) ***522***
Taylor U, Fort Wayne Campus (IN) ***523***
Temple U (PA) ***523***
Texas Tech U (TX) ***526***
Toccoa Falls Coll (GA) ***528***
Trinity Christian Coll (IL) ***530***
Union Coll (NE) ***534***
Union U (TN) ***534***
The U of Alabama (AL) ***537***
U of Central Oklahoma (OK) ***542***
U of Dayton (OH) ***544***
U of Delaware (DE) ***544***
The U of Findlay (OH) ***545***
U of Florida (FL) ***545***
U of Georgia (GA) ***545***
U of Houston (TX) ***547***
U of Idaho (ID) ***547***
The U of Iowa (IA) ***548***
U of Louisiana at Lafayette (LA) ***550***
U of Miami (FL) ***553***
U of Nebraska at Omaha (NE) ***557***
U of Nevada, Reno (NV) ***558***
The U of North Carolina at Pembroke (NC) ***560***
U of Northern Iowa (IA) ***561***
U of North Texas (TX) ***562***
U of Oklahoma (OK) ***562***
U of Oregon (OR) ***562***
U of Ottawa (ON, Canada) ***563***
U of Pittsburgh at Bradford (PA) ***569***
U of Rio Grande (OH) ***572***
U of St. Thomas (MN) ***573***
U of Sioux Falls (SD) ***574***
U of South Carolina (SC) ***575***
The U of South Dakota (SD) ***575***
U of Southern California (CA) ***576***
U of Southern Indiana (IN) ***576***
The U of Tennessee at Martin (TN) ***577***
The U of Texas at Arlington (TX) ***577***
The U of Texas at Austin (TX) ***578***
U of Utah (UT) ***582***
U of Wisconsin–Madison (WI) ***584***
U of Wisconsin–River Falls (WI) ***585***
Ursuline Coll (OH) ***587***
Utica Coll (NY) ***588***
Valdosta State U (GA) ***588***
Walla Walla Coll (WA) ***593***
Wartburg Coll (IA) ***594***
Washington State U (WA) ***595***
Wayne State U (MI) ***596***
Weber State U (UT) ***596***
Webster U (MO) ***597***
Western Kentucky U (KY) ***599***
Western Michigan U (MI) ***599***
Westminster Coll (PA) ***601***
West Virginia Wesleyan Coll (WV) ***603***
William Woods U (MO) ***607***
Wingate U (NC) ***607***
Winona State U (MN) ***608***
Xavier U (OH) ***610***
York Coll of Pennsylvania (PA) ***610***
Youngstown State U (OH) ***611***

PUBLISHING

Overview: Students who choose this major will learn about all aspects of book (print and electronic) publishing, including editing, copyright, production, distribution, marketing, and sales. *Related majors:* advertising, English, journalism, law, retailing. *Potential careers:* editor, journalist, writer/author, agent or book packager, copyright lawyer. *Salary potential:* $24k-$30k.

Benedictine U (IL) ***285***
Emerson Coll (MA) ***353***
Graceland U (IA) ***371***
Pontifical Catholic U of Puerto Rico (PR) ***472***
Rochester Inst of Technology (NY) ***482***
U of Missouri–Columbia (MO) ***555***
U of St. Thomas (MN) ***573***

PURCHASING/CONTRACTS MANAGEMENT

Overview: This major teaches students how to contract for and manage the raw materials, goods, and/or services that a business uses in its own operations. *Related majors:* logistics and materials management, law and legal studies, economics, finance, accounting. *Potential careers:* production manager, buyer, contracts manager, state procurement manager, purchasing agent. *Salary potential:* $35k-$45k.

American U of Puerto Rico (PR) ***268***
Arizona State U (AZ) ***271***
Bloomfield Coll (NJ) ***290***
California State U, Hayward (CA) ***301***
Eastern Michigan U (MI) ***348***
Miami U (OH) ***428***
Michigan State U (MI) ***428***
Thomas Edison State Coll (NJ) ***527***
U of Houston–Downtown (TX) ***547***
U of the District of Columbia (DC) ***580***

QUALITY CONTROL TECHNOLOGY

Overview: This major teaches undergraduates the technical knowledge and the basic engineering principles to analyze and maintain consistent standards for manufacturing and construction. *Related majors:* construction technology, industrial engineering technology, logistics and material management, operations management and supervision. *Potential careers:* building inspector, quality control specialist, business consultant, mechanical engineer: *Salary potential:* $26k-$38k.

California State U, Long Beach (CA) ***301***
Ferris State U (MI) ***358***
Winona State U (MN) ***608***

QUANTITATIVE ECONOMICS

Overview: Students will study economic phenomena and problems and their mathematical and statistical underpinnings. *Related majors:* finance, statistics, mathematics, computer science, economics. *Potential careers:* investment banker, bond trader, financial analyst, professor, economist. *Salary potential:* $35k-$45k.

The Colorado Coll (CO) ***325***
Haverford Coll (PA) ***377***
San Diego State U (CA) ***498***
Southern Methodist U (TX) ***510***
State U of NY at Oswego (NY) ***515***
United States Naval Academy (MD) ***535***
Université Laval (QC, Canada) ***536***
U of Calif, San Diego (CA) ***541***
U of Guelph (ON, Canada) ***546***
U of Northern Iowa (IA) ***561***
U of Rhode Island (RI) ***572***
Youngstown State U (OH) ***611***

RABBINICAL/TALMUDIC STUDIES

Overview: Students of this major will study the Talmud, Jewish law, philosophy, and ethics in preparation for entry into a program leading to ordination as Rabbis. *Related majors:* Arabic, Hebrew, Biblical languages, history, history of philosophy. *Potential careers:* Rabbi, scholar specializing in Jewish history and culture. *Salary potential:* $18k-$35k.

Baltimore Hebrew U (MD) ***280***
Ner Israel Rabbinical Coll (MD) ***443***
Talmudical Yeshiva of Philadelphia (PA) ***522***
Talmudic Coll of Florida (FL) ***522***
Université Laval (QC, Canada) ***536***

RADIOLOGICAL SCIENCE

Overview: Radiological science is the field of study concerned with science and engineering practices that form the basis for the efficacious and safe use of radiation in industry, research, and medicine. *Related majors:* nuclear engineering or technology, medical physics or biophysics, medical radiologic technology. *Potential careers:* physician, researcher, nuclear medicine specialist. *Salary potential:* $40k-$50k.

Austin Peay State U (TN) ***278***
Champlain Coll (VT) ***311***
Clarion U of Pennsylvania (PA) ***315***
Clarkson Coll (NE) ***315***
Comm Hospital Roanoke Valley–Coll of Health Scis (VA) ***328***
The George Washington U (DC) ***367***
Holy Family U (PA) ***380***
Indiana U Northwest (IN) ***386***
Manhattan Coll (NY) ***416***
Mass Coll of Pharmacy and Allied Health Sciences (MA) ***421***
Medical Coll of Georgia (GA) ***424***
Midwestern State U (TX) ***430***
Mount Aloysius Coll (PA) ***437***
The Ohio State U (OH) ***457***
Oregon Inst of Technology (OR) ***461***
Quinnipiac U (CT) ***476***
St. Francis Coll (NY) ***488***
State U of New York Upstate Medical University (NY) ***518***
Suffolk U (MA) ***520***
U of Charleston (WV) ***542***
The U of Findlay (OH) ***545***
U of Mary (ND) ***551***
U of Michigan (MI) ***554***
U of Missouri–Columbia (MO) ***555***
U of Pittsburgh at Bradford (PA) ***569***
U of St. Francis (IL) ***573***
U of South Alabama (AL) ***575***
U of Southern Indiana (IN) ***576***

RADIO/TELEVISION BROADCASTING

Overview: Students will learn how to plan, produce, and distribute audio and visual programming for either radio or television. *Related majors:* advertising; broadcast journalism; and journalism, radio, and television broadcast technology. *Potential careers:* disk jockey or radio station manager, television producer, broadcast journalist, editor, technician. *Salary potential:* $20k-$27k.

Alabama State U (AL) ***261***
Appalachian State U (NC) ***270***
Arizona State U (AZ) ***271***
Arkansas State U (AR) ***272***
Ashland U (OH) ***274***
Auburn U (AL) ***276***
Barry U (FL) ***282***
Belmont U (TN) ***284***
Bemidji State U (MN) ***285***
Biola U (CA) ***289***
Boston U (MA) ***292***
Bowling Green State U (OH) ***292***
Bradley U (IL) ***293***
Brooklyn Coll of the City U of NY (NY) ***295***
Buena Vista U (IA) ***297***
California State U, Chico (CA) ***300***
California State U, Fresno (CA) ***301***
California State U, Fullerton (CA) ***301***
California State U, Long Beach (CA) ***301***
California State U, Northridge (CA) ***301***
Cameron U (OK) ***303***
Campbell U (NC) ***303***
Castleton State Coll (VT) ***307***
Cedarville U (OH) ***308***
Central Michigan U (MI) ***310***
Central Missouri State U (MO) ***310***
Central Washington U (WA) ***310***
Colorado State U (CO) ***325***
Colorado State U-Pueblo (CO) ***325***
Columbia Coll Chicago (IL) ***327***
Columbia Coll Hollywood (CA) ***327***
Concordia Coll (MN) ***329***
Curry Coll (MA) ***335***
Drake U (IA) ***345***
East Central U (OK) ***347***
Eastern Kentucky U (KY) ***348***
Eastern Nazarene Coll (MA) ***348***
Eastern Washington U (WA) ***349***
Emerson Coll (MA) ***353***
Evangel U (MO) ***355***
Florida State U (FL) ***361***
Fordham U (NY) ***362***
Fort Hays State U (KS) ***362***
Franklin Pierce Coll (NH) ***364***
Freed-Hardeman U (TN) ***364***
Gallaudet U (DC) ***365***
Gannon U (PA) ***365***
Geneva Coll (PA) ***366***
George Fox U (OR) ***366***
The George Washington U (DC) ***367***
Georgia Southern U (GA) ***367***
Grace U (NE) ***371***
Grand Valley State U (MI) ***371***
Grand View Coll (IA) ***372***
Hampshire Coll (MA) ***375***
Harding U (AR) ***375***
Hastings Coll (NE) ***377***
Howard U (DC) ***382***
Indiana State U (IN) ***385***
Indiana U Bloomington (IN) ***385***
Ithaca Coll (NY) ***390***
John Brown U (AR) ***392***
Kent State U (OH) ***397***
Lamar U (TX) ***401***
Langston U (OK) ***402***
La Salle U (PA) ***402***
Lindenwood U (MO) ***407***
Lock Haven U of Pennsylvania (PA) ***408***
Long Island U, Brooklyn Campus (NY) ***409***
Long Island U, C.W. Post Campus (NY) ***409***
Lyndon State Coll (VT) ***413***
Mansfield U of Pennsylvania (PA) ***416***
Marietta Coll (OH) ***417***
Marist Coll (NY) ***417***
Marywood U (PA) ***421***
The Master's Coll and Seminary (CA) ***422***
Mercy Coll (NY) ***425***
Mercyhurst Coll (PA) ***425***
Mesa State Coll (CO) ***426***
Messiah Coll (PA) ***426***
Milligan Coll (TN) ***430***
Minot State U (ND) ***432***
Murray State U (KY) ***440***
Muskingum Coll (OH) ***441***
New York Inst of Technology (NY) ***447***
New York U (NY) ***447***
Northeastern U (MA) ***450***
Northern Arizona U (AZ) ***450***
Northern Kentucky U (KY) ***451***
Northwestern Coll (MN) ***453***
Northwestern U (IL) ***453***
Northwest Missouri State U (MO) ***454***
Ohio U (OH) ***458***

RADIO/TELEVISION BROADCASTING (continued)

Oklahoma Baptist U (OK) ***459***
Oklahoma Christian U (OK) ***459***
Oklahoma City U (OK) ***460***
Olivet Coll (MI) ***461***
Olivet Nazarene U (IL) ***461***
Oral Roberts U (OK) ***461***
Otterbein Coll (OH) ***462***
Pacific Lutheran U (WA) ***463***
Pacific U (OR) ***464***
Pittsburg State U (KS) ***470***
Point Park Coll (PA) ***471***
Pontifical Catholic U of Puerto Rico (PR) ***472***
Purdue U Calumet (IN) ***475***
Quincy U (IL) ***476***
Rider U (NJ) ***480***
Rowan U (NJ) ***484***
Ryerson U (ON, Canada) ***485***
Sacred Heart U (CT) ***486***
St. Ambrose U (IA) ***486***
St. Cloud State U (MN) ***488***
Salem International U (WV) ***496***
Sam Houston State U (TX) ***497***
San Diego State U (CA) ***498***
San Francisco State U (CA) ***498***
San Jose State U (CA) ***499***
Southeast Missouri State U (MO) ***508***
Southern Illinois U Carbondale (IL) ***509***
Southern Methodist U (TX) ***510***
Southwest State U (MN) ***513***
Spring Arbor U (MI) ***514***
Spring Hill Coll (AL) ***514***
State U of NY at New Paltz (NY) ***515***
State U of NY Coll at Brockport (NY) ***515***
State U of NY Coll at Buffalo (NY) ***516***
State U of NY Coll at Fredonia (NY) ***516***
Stephen F. Austin State U (TX) ***518***
Stephens Coll (MO) ***519***
Susquehanna U (PA) ***521***
Syracuse U (NY) ***521***
Temple U (PA) ***523***
Texas A&M U–Commerce (TX) ***525***
Texas Christian U (TX) ***526***
Texas Southern U (TX) ***526***
Texas Tech U (TX) ***526***
Texas Wesleyan U (TX) ***526***
Toccoa Falls Coll (GA) ***528***
Union U (TN) ***534***
The U of Alabama (AL) ***537***
The U of Arizona (AZ) ***538***
U of Arkansas at Little Rock (AR) ***539***
U of Calif, Los Angeles (CA) ***541***
U of Central Florida (FL) ***542***
U of Central Oklahoma (OK) ***542***
U of Cincinnati (OH) ***543***
U of Dayton (OH) ***544***
U of Florida (FL) ***545***
U of Houston (TX) ***547***
U of Idaho (ID) ***547***
The U of Iowa (IA) ***548***
U of Kansas (KS) ***549***
U of Kentucky (KY) ***549***
U of La Verne (CA) ***549***
U of Miami (FL) ***553***
U of Mississippi (MS) ***555***
U of Missouri–Columbia (MO) ***555***
The U of Montana–Missoula (MT) ***556***
U of Montevallo (AL) ***557***
U of Nebraska at Omaha (NE) ***557***
The U of North Carolina at Greensboro (NC) ***560***
U of Northern Iowa (IA) ***561***
U of North Texas (TX) ***562***
U of Oklahoma (OK) ***562***
U of Oregon (OR) ***562***
U of San Francisco (CA) ***574***
U of Sioux Falls (SD) ***574***
The U of South Dakota (SD) ***575***
U of Southern California (CA) ***576***
U of Southern Indiana (IN) ***576***
U of Southern Mississippi (MS) ***576***
The U of Tennessee (TN) ***577***
The U of Texas at Arlington (TX) ***577***
The U of Texas at Austin (TX) ***578***
U of Utah (UT) ***582***
U of Windsor (ON, Canada) ***584***
U of Wisconsin–Madison (WI) ***584***
U of Wisconsin–Oshkosh (WI) ***585***
U of Wisconsin–River Falls (WI) ***585***
U of Wisconsin–Superior (WI) ***586***
Valdosta State U (GA) ***588***
Vanguard U of Southern California (CA) ***589***
Walla Walla Coll (WA) ***593***
Washington State U (WA) ***595***
Waynesburg Coll (PA) ***595***
Wayne State U (MI) ***596***
Weber State U (UT) ***596***
Webster U (MO) ***597***
Western Kentucky U (KY) ***599***
Western Michigan U (MI) ***599***
Western State Coll of Colorado (CO) ***600***
Westfield State Coll (MA) ***600***
Westminster Coll (PA) ***601***
William Woods U (MO) ***607***
Winona State U (MN) ***608***
Xavier U (OH) ***610***
York Coll of Pennsylvania (PA) ***610***
Youngstown State U (OH) ***611***

RADIO/TELEVISION BROADCASTING TECHNOLOGY

Overview: This major gives students the technical knowledge and skills for the production of radio and television programs, including camera operation, lighting, sound, and studio operations. *Related majors:* photographic technology, radio and television broadcasting, multimedia management, graphic communications. *Potential careers:* camera operator, disk jockey, radio station manager, film director, producer. *Salary potential:* $25k-$40k.

Alabama A&M U (AL) ***261***
Asbury Coll (KY) ***274***
Eastern Michigan U (MI) ***348***
East Stroudsburg U of Pennsylvania (PA) ***349***
Emerson Coll (MA) ***353***
Hofstra U (NY) ***380***
Lewis U (IL) ***406***
New England School of Communications (ME) ***445***
Ohio U (OH) ***458***
Texas Tech U (TX) ***526***
Towson U (MD) ***529***
Trevecca Nazarene U (TN) ***529***
U of Georgia (GA) ***545***
U of Puerto Rico at Arecibo (PR) ***570***
U of Southern California (CA) ***576***

RANGE MANAGEMENT

Overview: Undergraduates of this major will study the effective resource and environmental management of rangelands, arid regions, grasslands, and other areas. *Related majors:* plant sciences, ecology, wildlife management, soil science. *Potential careers:* ecologist, natural resources scientist, conservationist, teacher, ranch manager. *Salary potential:* $25k-$30k.

Abilene Christian U (TX) ***260***
Angelo State U (TX) ***269***
Brigham Young U (UT) ***295***
California State U, Chico (CA) ***300***
Chadron State Coll (NE) ***311***
Colorado State U (CO) ***325***
Fort Hays State U (KS) ***362***
Humboldt State U (CA) ***382***
Montana State U–Bozeman (MT) ***434***
New Mexico State U (NM) ***446***
North Dakota State U (ND) ***449***
Oregon State U (OR) ***462***
South Dakota State U (SD) ***507***
Sul Ross State U (TX) ***521***
Tarleton State U (TX) ***522***
Texas A&M U (TX) ***524***
Texas A&M U–Kingsville (TX) ***525***
Texas Tech U (TX) ***526***
U of Alberta (AB, Canada) ***538***
U of Calif, Davis (CA) ***540***
U of Idaho (ID) ***547***
U of Nebraska–Lincoln (NE) ***557***
U of Nevada, Reno (NV) ***558***
U of Saskatchewan (SK, Canada) ***574***
U of Wyoming (WY) ***586***
Utah State U (UT) ***587***
Washington State U (WA) ***595***

READING EDUCATION

Overview: This program teaches undergraduates how to design reading programs and materials for students at various levels. It also teaches undergraduates how to diagnose reading problems in particular students. *Related majors:* educational/instructional media design, curriculum and instruction, education of specific learning disabled, developmental psychology, communication disorders. *Potential careers:* teacher, reading coach. *Salary potential:* $25k-$36k.

Abilene Christian U (TX) ***260***
Aquinas Coll (MI) ***270***
Baylor U (TX) ***283***
Belmont U (TN) ***284***
Bowling Green State U (OH) ***292***
Catawba Coll (NC) ***307***
Central Missouri State U (MO) ***310***
City Coll of the City U of NY (NY) ***314***
Clarion U of Pennsylvania (PA) ***315***
Eastern Washington U (WA) ***349***
Grand Valley State U (MI) ***371***
Hardin-Simmons U (TX) ***376***
Longwood U (VA) ***409***
Luther Coll (IA) ***412***
Lyndon State Coll (VT) ***413***
Millersville U of Pennsylvania (PA) ***430***
Mount Saint Vincent U (NS, Canada) ***439***
Northeastern State U (OK) ***450***
Northwest Missouri State U (MO) ***454***
Ohio U (OH) ***458***
Our Lady of Holy Cross Coll (LA) ***463***
Pacific Lutheran U (WA) ***463***
St. Cloud State U (MN) ***488***
St. Mary's U of San Antonio (TX) ***494***
State U of NY Coll at Cortland (NY) ***516***
Tennessee State U (TN) ***523***
Texas A&M International U (TX) ***524***
Texas A&M U–Commerce (TX) ***525***
Texas Southern U (TX) ***526***
Texas Wesleyan U (TX) ***526***
U of Alberta (AB, Canada) ***538***
The U of British Columbia (BC, Canada) ***540***
U of Central Arkansas (AR) ***542***
U of Central Oklahoma (OK) ***542***
U of Georgia (GA) ***545***
U of Great Falls (MT) ***545***
U of Mary Hardin-Baylor (TX) ***551***
U of Missouri–St. Louis (MO) ***556***
The U of Montana–Missoula (MT) ***556***
U of New Orleans (LA) ***559***
U of Northern Iowa (IA) ***561***
U of North Texas (TX) ***562***
The U of Texas–Pan American (TX) ***579***
U of the Incarnate Word (TX) ***580***
U of Wisconsin–Superior (WI) ***586***
Upper Iowa U (IA) ***587***
Walsh U (OH) ***593***
Westfield State Coll (MA) ***600***
Wingate U (NC) ***607***
Winona State U (MN) ***608***
Wright State U (OH) ***609***
York Coll (NE) ***610***

REAL ESTATE

Overview: Students who major in this subject learn the skills necessary to buy, sell, develop, and manage real property. *Related majors:* building/property maintenance and management, law and legal studies, investments and securities, construction management, architecture. *Potential careers:* real estate developer, real estate broker or agent, architect, building or site manager. *Salary potential:* $24k-$33k.

Angelo State U (TX) ***269***
Appalachian State U (NC) ***270***
Arizona State U (AZ) ***271***
Ball State U (IN) ***280***
Baylor U (TX) ***283***
California State Polytechnic U, Pomona (CA) ***300***
California State U, Dominguez Hills (CA) ***300***
California State U, Fresno (CA) ***301***
California State U, Hayward (CA) ***301***
California State U, Northridge (CA) ***301***
Christopher Newport U (VA) ***313***
Clarion U of Pennsylvania (PA) ***315***
Colorado State U (CO) ***325***
Eastern Kentucky U (KY) ***348***
Eastern Michigan U (MI) ***348***
Florida Atlantic U (FL) ***359***
Florida International U (FL) ***360***
Florida State U (FL) ***361***
Georgia State U (GA) ***368***
Indiana U Bloomington (IN) ***385***
Minnesota State U, Mankato (MN) ***431***
Mississippi State U (MS) ***432***
Morehead State U (KY) ***436***
New York U (NY) ***447***
The Ohio State U (OH) ***457***
Penn State U Univ Park Campus (PA) ***468***
St. Cloud State U (MN) ***488***
St. John's U (NY) ***490***
San Diego State U (CA) ***498***
San Francisco State U (CA) ***498***
Schreiner U (TX) ***501***
Southern Methodist U (TX) ***510***
State U of West Georgia (GA) ***518***
Temple U (PA) ***523***
Texas A&M U–Kingsville (TX) ***525***
Texas Christian U (TX) ***526***
Thomas Edison State Coll (NJ) ***527***
U of Central Oklahoma (OK) ***542***
U of Cincinnati (OH) ***543***
U of Connecticut (CT) ***544***
U of Denver (CO) ***544***
U of Florida (FL) ***545***
U of Georgia (GA) ***545***
U of Guelph (ON, Canada) ***546***
U of Hawaii at Manoa (HI) ***546***
U of Houston–Downtown (TX) ***547***
The U of Memphis (TN) ***553***
U of Miami (FL) ***553***
U of Mississippi (MS) ***555***
U of Missouri–Columbia (MO) ***555***
U of Nebraska at Omaha (NE) ***557***
U of Nevada, Las Vegas (NV) ***558***
U of New Orleans (LA) ***559***
U of Northern Iowa (IA) ***561***
U of North Texas (TX) ***562***
U of Oklahoma (OK) ***562***
U of Pennsylvania (PA) ***563***
U of St. Thomas (MN) ***573***
U of South Carolina (SC) ***575***
The U of Texas at Arlington (TX) ***577***
The U of Texas at El Paso (TX) ***578***
U of Wisconsin–Madison (WI) ***584***
U of Wisconsin–Milwaukee (WI) ***585***
Washington State U (WA) ***595***
Webster U (MO) ***597***

RECREATIONAL THERAPY

Overview: This major teaches students how to organize recreational activities for patients who are physically, mentally, or emotionally disabled. *Related majors:* mental health/rehabilitation, psychology, parks, recreation, leisure studies, special education. *Potential careers:* recreational therapist, special education teacher. *Salary potential:* $20k-$25k.

Alderson-Broaddus Coll (WV) ***263***
Ashland U (OH) ***274***
Belmont Abbey Coll (NC) ***284***
California State U, Chico (CA) ***300***
California State U, Hayward (CA) ***301***
California State U, Northridge (CA) ***301***
Catawba Coll (NC) ***307***
Coll of Mount St. Joseph (OH) ***320***
Columbus State U (GA) ***328***
Concordia U (QC, Canada) ***331***
East Carolina U (NC) ***347***
Eastern Kentucky U (KY) ***348***
Eastern Washington U (WA) ***349***
Gallaudet U (DC) ***365***
Grand Valley State U (MI) ***371***
Green Mountain Coll (VT) ***372***
Hampton U (VA) ***375***
Indiana Inst of Technology (IN) ***385***

Indiana U Bloomington (IN) ***385***
Ithaca Coll (NY) ***390***
Jackson State U (MS) ***390***
Lock Haven U of Pennsylvania (PA) ***408***
Long Island U, Southampton Coll, Friends World Program (NY) ***409***
Longwood U (VA) ***409***
Mars Hill Coll (NC) ***418***
Minnesota State U, Mankato (MN) ***431***
Montclair State U (NJ) ***435***
Northeastern U (MA) ***450***
Northland Coll (WI) ***452***
Northwest Missouri State U (MO) ***454***
Ohio U (OH) ***458***
Pacific Lutheran U (WA) ***463***
Pittsburg State U (KS) ***470***
St. Joseph's Coll, Suffolk Campus (NY) ***491***
San Jose State U (CA) ***499***
Shorter Coll (GA) ***504***
Slippery Rock U of Pennsylvania (PA) ***506***
Southwestern Oklahoma State U (OK) ***512***
Springfield Coll (MA) ***514***
State U of NY Coll at Cortland (NY) ***516***
The U of Findlay (OH) ***545***
The U of Iowa (IA) ***548***
U of New Hampshire (NH) ***558***
U of St. Francis (IL) ***573***
U of Southern Maine (ME) ***576***
U of Toledo (OH) ***581***
U of Wisconsin–La Crosse (WI) ***584***
U of Wisconsin–Milwaukee (WI) ***585***
Utica Coll (NY) ***588***
Voorhees Coll (SC) ***592***
Western Carolina U (NC) ***598***
West Virginia State Coll (WV) ***602***
Winona State U (MN) ***608***
Winston-Salem State U (NC) ***608***
York Coll of Pennsylvania (PA) ***610***

RECREATION/LEISURE FACILITIES MANAGEMENT

Overview: This major will teach students how to create and run park facilities and other indoor and outdoor recreation facilities. *Related majors:* parks recreation, leisure studies, supervision management, generosity management, safety and security technology. *Potential careers:* building manager, park manager, recreation services coordinator, school administrator. *Salary potential:* $25k-$33k.

Appalachian State U (NC) ***270***
Arkansas Tech U (AR) ***272***
Asbury Coll (KY) ***274***
Ball State U (IN) ***280***
Brigham Young U (UT) ***295***
California State U, Chico (CA) ***300***
California State U, Sacramento (CA) ***301***
California U of Pennsylvania (PA) ***302***
Central Michigan U (MI) ***310***
Clemson U (SC) ***317***
Coll of St. Joseph (VT) ***322***
Coll of the Ozarks (MO) ***323***
Colorado State U (CO) ***325***
Columbus State U (GA) ***328***
Concord Coll (WV) ***329***
Delaware State U (DE) ***338***
East Carolina U (NC) ***347***
Eastern Illinois U (IL) ***348***
Eastern Kentucky U (KY) ***348***
Eastern Michigan U (MI) ***348***
Eastern Washington U (WA) ***349***
Florida International U (FL) ***360***
Florida State U (FL) ***361***
Franklin Pierce Coll (NH) ***364***
Georgia State U (GA) ***368***
Grand Valley State U (MI) ***371***
Green Mountain Coll (VT) ***372***
Hannibal-LaGrange Coll (MO) ***375***
Henderson State U (AR) ***378***
High Point U (NC) ***379***
Humboldt State U (CA) ***382***
Huntingdon Coll (AL) ***383***
Illinois State U (IL) ***384***
Indiana Inst of Technology (IN) ***385***
Indiana State U (IN) ***385***
Indiana U Bloomington (IN) ***385***
Indiana U Southeast (IN) ***387***
Indiana Wesleyan U (IN) ***387***
John Brown U (AR) ***392***
Johnson & Wales U (RI) ***393***
Kansas State U (KS) ***396***
Kean U (NJ) ***396***
Kent State U (OH) ***397***
Lock Haven U of Pennsylvania (PA) ***408***
Long Island U, Southampton Coll, Friends World Program (NY) ***409***
Lyndon State Coll (VT) ***413***
Lynn U (FL) ***413***
Marshall U (WV) ***418***
Mercyhurst Coll (PA) ***425***
Methodist Coll (NC) ***427***
Michigan State U (MI) ***428***
Middle Tennessee State U (TN) ***429***
Minnesota State U, Mankato (MN) ***431***
Missouri Valley Coll (MO) ***433***
Missouri Western State Coll (MO) ***433***
Montclair State U (NJ) ***435***
Morehead State U (KY) ***436***
Mount Marty Coll (SD) ***438***
Murray State U (KY) ***440***
New England Coll (NH) ***444***
North Carolina Central U (NC) ***448***
North Carolina State U (NC) ***449***
Northland Coll (WI) ***452***
Oak Hills Christian Coll (MN) ***456***
Ohio U (OH) ***458***
Old Dominion U (VA) ***460***
Oregon State U (OR) ***462***
Penn State U Univ Park Campus (PA) ***468***
Rust Coll (MS) ***485***
Saint Leo U (FL) ***492***
San Jose State U (CA) ***499***
Savannah State U (GA) ***499***
Slippery Rock U of Pennsylvania (PA) ***506***
South Dakota State U (SD) ***507***
Southeast Missouri State U (MO) ***508***
Southwest Texas State U (TX) ***513***
Springfield Coll (MA) ***514***
State U of NY Coll at Cortland (NY) ***516***
State U of West Georgia (GA) ***518***
Sterling Coll (VT) ***519***
Texas A&M U (TX) ***524***
Thomas U (GA) ***528***
Tri-State U (IN) ***532***
Union Coll (KY) ***533***
Union U (TN) ***534***
Unity Coll (ME) ***535***
U of Alberta (AB, Canada) ***538***
The U of British Columbia (BC, Canada) ***540***
U of Connecticut (CT) ***544***
U of Delaware (DE) ***544***
U of Florida (FL) ***545***
U of Maine (ME) ***550***
U of Maine at Machias (ME) ***551***
U of Minnesota, Twin Cities Campus (MN) ***555***
The U of North Carolina at Chapel Hill (NC) ***560***
The U of North Carolina at Greensboro (NC) ***560***
The U of North Carolina at Wilmington (NC) ***561***
U of Northern Colorado (CO) ***561***
The U of Tennessee (TN) ***577***
The U of Tennessee at Martin (TN) ***577***
U of Utah (UT) ***582***
U of Vermont (VT) ***582***
U of Wisconsin–La Crosse (WI) ***584***
U of Wyoming (WY) ***586***
Virginia Commonwealth U (VA) ***590***
Washington State U (WA) ***595***
Webber International U (FL) ***596***
Western Carolina U (NC) ***598***
Western Illinois U (IL) ***599***
Western Kentucky U (KY) ***599***
Western State Coll of Colorado (CO) ***600***
West Virginia U (WV) ***602***
Winona State U (MN) ***608***

RECREATION/LEISURE STUDIES

Overview: Students who choose this major will study recreational and leisure activities, providing indoor and outdoor recreational facilities and services. *Related majors:* health and physical education, community organization, resources and services, social work, forest management. *Potential careers:* park manager or park ranger, recreation services coordinator, wilderness field instructor, instructor. *Salary potential:* $20k-$30k.

Alabama State U (AL) ***261***
Alaska Pacific U (AK) ***261***
Alcorn State U (MS) ***263***
Alderson-Broaddus Coll (WV) ***263***
Appalachian State U (NC) ***270***
Arizona State U (AZ) ***271***
Arizona State U West (AZ) ***272***
Armstrong Atlantic State U (GA) ***273***
Ashland U (OH) ***274***
Auburn U (AL) ***276***
Belmont U (TN) ***284***
Bemidji State U (MN) ***285***
Benedict Coll (SC) ***285***
Bethany Coll (KS) ***287***
Bethune-Cookman Coll (FL) ***289***
Black Hills State U (SD) ***290***
Bluffton Coll (OH) ***291***
Boston U (MA) ***292***
Bowling Green State U (OH) ***292***
Brevard Coll (NC) ***294***
Brewton-Parker Coll (GA) ***294***
Bridgewater State Coll (MA) ***294***
Brock U (ON, Canada) ***295***
California Polytechnic State U, San Luis Obispo (CA) ***300***
California State U, Chico (CA) ***300***
California State U, Dominguez Hills (CA) ***300***
California State U, Fresno (CA) ***301***
California State U, Hayward (CA) ***301***
California State U, Long Beach (CA) ***301***
California State U, Northridge (CA) ***301***
California State U, Sacramento (CA) ***301***
Calvin Coll (MI) ***303***
Campbellsville U (KY) ***303***
Carson-Newman Coll (TN) ***306***
Carthage Coll (WI) ***306***
Catawba Coll (NC) ***307***
Central Christian Coll of Kansas (KS) ***309***
Central Michigan U (MI) ***310***
Central Missouri State U (MO) ***310***
Central Washington U (WA) ***310***
Cheyney U of Pennsylvania (PA) ***312***
Christopher Newport U (VA) ***313***
Colorado Christian U (CO) ***325***
Colorado State U-Pueblo (CO) ***325***
Columbia Bible Coll (BC, Canada) ***326***
Concordia U (QC, Canada) ***331***
Dalhousie U (NS, Canada) ***336***
Davis & Elkins Coll (WV) ***338***
Delaware State U (DE) ***338***
Dordt Coll (IA) ***345***
Eastern Kentucky U (KY) ***348***
Eastern Washington U (WA) ***349***
East Stroudsburg U of Pennsylvania (PA) ***349***
Elon U (NC) ***352***
Emporia State U (KS) ***354***
Evangel U (MO) ***355***
Ferris State U (MI) ***358***
Ferrum Coll (VA) ***358***
Franklin Coll (IN) ***363***
Frostburg State U (MD) ***365***
Georgetown Coll (KY) ***366***
Georgia Coll & State U (GA) ***367***
Georgia Southern U (GA) ***367***
Georgia Southwestern State U (GA) ***368***
Gordon Coll (MA) ***370***
Graceland U (IA) ***371***
Green Mountain Coll (VT) ***372***
Greenville Coll (IL) ***373***
Hannibal-LaGrange Coll (MO) ***375***
High Point U (NC) ***379***
Houghton Coll (NY) ***381***
Houston Baptist U (TX) ***382***
Howard Payne U (TX) ***382***
Humboldt State U (CA) ***382***
Huntingdon Coll (AL) ***383***
Huntington Coll (IN) ***383***
Indiana U Bloomington (IN) ***385***
Ithaca Coll (NY) ***390***
Jacksonville State U (AL) ***390***
Johnson State Coll (VT) ***394***
Kansas State U (KS) ***396***
Lakehead U (ON, Canada) ***400***
Lehman Coll of the City U of NY (NY) ***404***
Lincoln U (PA) ***407***
Lock Haven U of Pennsylvania (PA) ***408***
Long Island U, Southampton Coll, Friends World Program (NY) ***409***
Lynchburg Coll (VA) ***413***
Lyndon State Coll (VT) ***413***
Malone Coll (OH) ***415***
Mars Hill Coll (NC) ***418***
Marymount U (VA) ***420***
Maryville Coll (TN) ***420***
Memorial U of Newfoundland (NF, Canada) ***424***
Mercyhurst Coll (PA) ***425***
Messiah Coll (PA) ***426***
Metropolitan State Coll of Denver (CO) ***427***
Midland Lutheran Coll (NE) ***429***
Minnesota State U, Mankato (MN) ***431***
Missouri Valley Coll (MO) ***433***
Montclair State U (NJ) ***435***
Morgan State U (MD) ***436***
Morris Coll (SC) ***437***
Mount Olive Coll (NC) ***439***
New England Coll (NH) ***444***
North Carolina Ag and Tech State U (NC) ***448***
North Dakota State U (ND) ***449***
Northern Arizona U (AZ) ***450***
Northern Michigan U (MI) ***451***
Northland Coll (WI) ***452***
Northwest Missouri State U (MO) ***454***
Northwest Nazarene U (ID) ***454***
Ohio U (OH) ***458***
Oklahoma Baptist U (OK) ***459***
Oklahoma Panhandle State U (OK) ***460***
Oregon State U (OR) ***462***
Pacific Union Coll (CA) ***464***
Pittsburg State U (KS) ***470***
Plymouth State Coll (NH) ***471***
Prescott Coll (AZ) ***474***
Radford U (VA) ***476***
St. Joseph's Coll, Suffolk Campus (NY) ***491***
St. Thomas Aquinas Coll (NY) ***495***
Salem State Coll (MA) ***497***
San Diego State U (CA) ***498***
San Francisco State U (CA) ***498***
San Jose State U (CA) ***499***
Shaw U (NC) ***502***
Shepherd Coll (WV) ***503***
Shorter Coll (GA) ***504***
Slippery Rock U of Pennsylvania (PA) ***506***
South Dakota State U (SD) ***507***
Southeastern Oklahoma State U (OK) ***508***
Southeast Missouri State U (MO) ***508***
Southern Connecticut State U (CT) ***509***
Southern Illinois U Carbondale (IL) ***509***
Southern Wesleyan U (SC) ***511***
Southwest Baptist U (MO) ***512***
Southwestern Oklahoma State U (OK) ***512***
Southwest Missouri State U (MO) ***513***
Springfield Coll (MA) ***514***
State U of NY Coll at Brockport (NY) ***515***
State U of NY Coll at Cortland (NY) ***516***
State U of NY Coll of Environ Sci and Forestry (NY) ***517***
Sterling Coll (VT) ***519***
Taylor U (IN) ***523***
Temple U (PA) ***523***
Tennessee State U (TN) ***523***
Tennessee Wesleyan Coll (TN) ***524***
Texas Tech U (TX) ***526***
Thomas Edison State Coll (NJ) ***527***
Troy State U (AL) ***532***
Tyndale Coll & Seminary (ON, Canada) ***533***
U du Québec à Trois-Rivières (QC, Canada) ***536***
U of Alberta (AB, Canada) ***538***
U of Arkansas (AR) ***539***
U of Calgary (AB, Canada) ***540***
U of Hawaii at Manoa (HI) ***546***
U of Idaho (ID) ***547***
U of Illinois at Urbana–Champaign (IL) ***548***
The U of Iowa (IA) ***548***
U of Maine at Machias (ME) ***551***
U of Maine at Presque Isle (ME) ***551***
U of Mary Hardin-Baylor (TX) ***551***
The U of Memphis (TN) ***553***
U of Michigan (MI) ***554***
U of Minnesota, Duluth (MN) ***554***
U of Mississippi (MS) ***555***
U of Missouri–Columbia (MO) ***555***
The U of Montana–Missoula (MT) ***556***
U of Nebraska at Kearney (NE) ***557***
U of Nebraska at Omaha (NE) ***557***
U of Nevada, Las Vegas (NV) ***558***
U of Nevada, Reno (NV) ***558***

RECREATION/LEISURE STUDIES (continued)

U of New Brunswick Fredericton (NB, Canada) 558
U of New Hampshire (NH) 558
U of New Mexico (NM) 559
The U of North Carolina at Pembroke (NC) 560
U of North Dakota (ND) 561
U of Northern Iowa (IA) 561
U of North Texas (TX) 562
U of Ottawa (ON, Canada) 563
U of St. Francis (IL) 573
U of Saskatchewan (SK, Canada) 574
The U of South Dakota (SD) 575
U of Southern Mississippi (MS) 576
The U of Tennessee at Chattanooga (TN) 577
The U of Texas–Pan American (TX) 579
U of the District of Columbia (DC) 580
U of Toledo (OH) 581
U of Utah (UT) 582
U of Vermont (VT) 582
U of Waterloo (ON, Canada) 583
U of Windsor (ON, Canada) 584
U of Wisconsin–Madison (WI) 584
U of Wisconsin–Milwaukee (WI) 585
Upper Iowa U (IA) 587
Utah State U (UT) 587
Virginia Wesleyan Coll (VA) 591
Warner Southern Coll (FL) 593
Warren Wilson Coll (NC) 594
Washington State U (WA) 595
Wayne State Coll (NE) 596
Wayne State U (MI) 596
Western Michigan U (MI) 599
Western State Coll of Colorado (CO) 600
Western Washington U (WA) 600
Westfield State Coll (MA) 600
West Texas A&M U (TX) 602
West Virginia State Coll (WV) 602
West Virginia U (WV) 602
William Paterson U of New Jersey (NJ) 606
William Penn U (IA) 606
Wingate U (NC) 607
Winona State U (MN) 608
York Coll of Pennsylvania (PA) 610

RECREATION PRODUCTS/ SERVICES MARKETING OPERATIONS

Overview: This major prepares students to provide marketing, sales, and promotional services to a wide range of recreation equipment and services, such as playgrounds, specialty parks, and swimming pools. *Related majors:* marketing and marketing research; advertising; child growth, care, and development; construction technology. *Potential careers:* marketing executive, equipment salesperson. *Salary potential:* $20k-$25k.

Tyndale Coll & Seminary (ON, Canada) 533

REHABILITATION/ THERAPEUTIC SERVICES RELATED

Information can be found under this major's main heading.

Central Michigan U (MI) 310
Southern Illinois U Carbondale (IL) 509
U of Pittsburgh (PA) 569

REHABILITATION THERAPY

Overview: This major teaches students how to help individuals whose ability to cope with daily activities has been impaired by illness or injury to regain their independence and good health. *Related majors:* occupational therapy, physical therapy. *Potential careers:* occupational therapist, rehabilitation therapist. *Salary potential:* $35k-$45k.

Arkansas Tech U (AR) 272
Baker Coll of Muskegon (MI) 279
Boston U (MA) 292
East Stroudsburg U of Pennsylvania (PA) 349
Ithaca Coll (NY) 390
Montana State U–Billings (MT) 434
Northeastern U (MA) 450
Queen's U at Kingston (ON, Canada) 476
Southern U and A&M Coll (LA) 511
Springfield Coll (MA) 514
Stephen F. Austin State U (TX) 518
Thomas U (GA) 528
The U of British Columbia (BC, Canada) 540
U of Calgary (AB, Canada) 540
U of Florida (FL) 545
U of Maine at Farmington (ME) 550
U of Manitoba (MB, Canada) 551
U of Maryland Eastern Shore (MD) 552
U of North Texas (TX) 562
U of Ottawa (ON, Canada) 563
The U of Texas–Pan American (TX) 579
U of Toronto (ON, Canada) 581
Wilberforce U (OH) 605
York U (ON, Canada) 611

RELIGIOUS EDUCATION

Overview: Students will learn how to become educators or administrators who specialize in teaching a specific religious philosophy. *Related majors:* religious studies, divinity/ministry, education, pastoral counseling. *Potential careers:* teacher, clergy, religious school administrator. *Salary potential:* $20k-$27k.

Alaska Bible Coll (AK) 261
Andrews U (MI) 269
Aquinas Coll (MI) 270
Asbury Coll (KY) 274
Ashland U (OH) 274
Baltimore Hebrew U (MD) 280
Baptist Bible Coll (MO) 281
The Baptist Coll of Florida (FL) 281
Barclay Coll (KS) 281
Bethany Bible Coll (NB, Canada) 287
Biola U (CA) 289
Boise Bible Coll (ID) 291
Bryan Coll (TN) 296
Campbellsville U (KY) 303
Canadian Bible Coll (AB, Canada) 303
Cardinal Stritch U (WI) 305
Carroll Coll (MT) 306
The Catholic U of America (DC) 307
Central Bible Coll (MO) 309
Cincinnati Bible Coll and Seminary (OH) 314
Circleville Bible Coll (OH) 314
Coll of Mount St. Joseph (OH) 320
Coll of Saint Benedict (MN) 321
Columbia Coll (SC) 327
Columbia International U (SC) 327
Concordia U (CA) 330
Concordia U (IL) 330
Concordia U (MN) 330
Concordia U (NE) 330
Concordia U (OR) 330
Cornerstone U (MI) 333
Crossroads Coll (MN) 334
Crown Coll (MN) 334
Cumberland Coll (KY) 335
Dallas Baptist U (TX) 336
Davis & Elkins Coll (WV) 338
Defiance Coll (OH) 338
Eastern Nazarene Coll (MA) 348
East Texas Baptist U (TX) 350
Erskine Coll (SC) 354
Eugene Bible Coll (OR) 355
Faith Baptist Bible Coll and Theological Seminary (IA) 356
Faulkner U (AL) 357
Florida Southern Coll (FL) 361
Free Will Baptist Bible Coll (TN) 364
Gardner-Webb U (NC) 365
George Fox U (OR) 366
Global U of the Assemblies of God (MO) 368
God's Bible School and Coll (OH) 369
Gordon Coll (MA) 370
Grace Bible Coll (MI) 370
Grace U (NE) 371
Griggs U (MD) 373
Hannibal-LaGrange Coll (MO) 375
Hillsdale Free Will Baptist Coll (OK) 379
Holy Family U (PA) 380
Houghton Coll (NY) 381
Howard Payne U (TX) 382
Huntingdon Coll (AL) 383
Indiana Wesleyan U (IN) 387
John Brown U (AR) 392
John Carroll U (OH) 392
John Wesley Coll (NC) 394
Kentucky Christian Coll (KY) 397
Kentucky Mountain Bible Coll (KY) 397
LaGrange Coll (GA) 400
La Roche Coll (PA) 402
La Salle U (PA) 402
Laura and Alvin Siegal Coll of Judaic Studies (OH) 403
Lee U (TN) 404
Lenoir-Rhyne Coll (NC) 405
Lincoln Christian Coll (IL) 407
Louisiana Coll (LA) 410
Loyola U New Orleans (LA) 411
Manhattan Christian Coll (KS) 415
Maranatha Baptist Bible Coll (WI) 417
Marian Coll (IN) 417
Mars Hill Coll (NC) 418
Marywood U (PA) 421
The Master's Coll and Seminary (CA) 422
Master's Coll and Seminary (ON, Canada) 422
McGill U (QC, Canada) 423
McMaster U (ON, Canada) 423
McMurry U (TX) 423
Mercyhurst Coll (PA) 425
Messiah Coll (PA) 426
MidAmerica Nazarene U (KS) 428
Mid-Continent Coll (KY) 429
Milligan Coll (TN) 430
Moody Bible Inst (IL) 435
Morris Coll (SC) 437
Mount Mary Coll (WI) 438
Mount Vernon Nazarene U (OH) 440
Multnomah Bible Coll and Biblical Seminary (OR) 440
Nazarene Bible Coll (CO) 442
Nebraska Christian Coll (NE) 443
Ner Israel Rabbinical Coll (MD) 443
North Greenville Coll (SC) 451
Northwest Coll (WA) 452
Northwestern Coll (IA) 453
Northwestern Coll (MN) 453
Northwest Nazarene U (ID) 454
Nyack Coll (NY) 456
Oakland City U (IN) 456
Oakwood Coll (AL) 456
Oklahoma Baptist U (OK) 459
Oklahoma Christian U (OK) 459
Oklahoma City U (OK) 460
Olivet Nazarene U (IL) 461
Ozark Christian Coll (MO) 463
Pepperdine U, Malibu (CA) 469
Pfeiffer U (NC) 469
Pillsbury Baptist Bible Coll (MN) 470
Prairie Bible Coll (AB, Canada) 473
Providence Coll and Theological Seminary (MB, Canada) 475
Reformed Bible Coll (MI) 477
St. Bonaventure U (NY) 487
Saint John's U (MN) 490
St. Louis Christian Coll (MO) 492
Saint Mary-of-the-Woods Coll (IN) 493
Saint Vincent Coll (PA) 496
Seattle Pacific U (WA) 501
Seton Hall U (NJ) 502
Simpson Coll and Graduate School (CA) 505
Southeastern Bible Coll (AL) 507
Southern Adventist U (TN) 508
Southern Nazarene U (OK) 510
Southwestern Assemblies of God U (TX) 512
Sterling Coll (KS) 519
Talmudic Coll of Florida (FL) 522
Taylor U (IN) 523
Taylor U, Fort Wayne Campus (IN) 523
Tennessee Temple U (TN) 524
Texas Wesleyan U (TX) 526
Thiel Coll (PA) 527
Toccoa Falls Coll (GA) 528
Trinity Bible Coll (ND) 530
Trinity Christian Coll (IL) 530
Trinity Lutheran Coll (WA) 531
Tyndale Coll & Seminary (ON, Canada) 533
Union Coll (KY) 533
Union Coll (NE) 534
Universidad Adventista de las Antillas (PR) 536
U of Dayton (OH) 544
U of Mobile (AL) 556
U of the Ozarks (AR) 580
Valley Forge Christian Coll (PA) 588
Vanguard U of Southern California (CA) 589
Viterbo U (WI) 591
Warner Pacific Coll (OR) 593
Washington Bible Coll (MD) 594
Wayland Baptist U (TX) 595
Western Baptist Coll (OR) 598
Westminster Coll (PA) 601
West Virginia Wesleyan Coll (WV) 603
Wheaton Coll (IL) 603
Williams Baptist Coll (AR) 606
York Coll (NE) 610

RELIGIOUS MUSIC

Overview: Students who choose this major will study the history and theory of religious and sacred music. *Related majors:* music history and literature, music, theory and composition, voice and choral performance, piano and organ performance. *Potential careers:* organist, Cantor, choir director. *Salary potential:* $15k-$25k.

Alderson-Broaddus Coll (WV) 263
Anderson U (IN) 268
Appalachian State U (NC) 270
Aquinas Coll (MI) 270
Atlantic Union Coll (MA) 276
Augustana Coll (IL) 276
Averett U (VA) 278
The Baptist Coll of Florida (FL) 281
Barclay Coll (KS) 281
Baylor U (TX) 283
Belmont U (TN) 284
Bethany Coll of the Assemblies of God (CA) 287
Bethany Lutheran Coll (MN) 288
Bethel Coll (IN) 288
Bethel Coll (MN) 288
Bethesda Christian U (CA) 288
Bluefield Coll (VA) 291
Boise Bible Coll (ID) 291
Briercrest Bible Coll (SK, Canada) 295
Bryan Coll (TN) 296
Calvin Coll (MI) 303
Campbellsville U (KY) 303
Canadian Bible Coll (AB, Canada) 303
Cedarville U (OH) 308
Centenary Coll of Louisiana (LA) 308
Central Baptist Coll (AR) 309
Central Bible Coll (MO) 309
Charleston Southern U (SC) 311
Christian Heritage Coll (CA) 313
Cincinnati Bible Coll and Seminary (OH) 314
Circleville Bible Coll (OH) 314
Clearwater Christian Coll (FL) 316
Coll of the Ozarks (MO) 323
Colorado Christian U (CO) 325
Columbia Coll (SC) 327
Concordia Coll (NY) 329
Concordia U (IL) 330
Concordia U (MI) 330
Concordia U (MN) 330
Concordia U (NE) 330
Crossroads Coll (MN) 334
Dallas Baptist U (TX) 336
Drake U (IA) 345
Eastern Nazarene Coll (MA) 348
East Texas Baptist U (TX) 350
Erskine Coll (SC) 354
Eugene Bible Coll (OR) 355
Evangel U (MO) 355
Faith Baptist Bible Coll and Theological Seminary (IA) 356
Florida Southern Coll (FL) 361
Free Will Baptist Bible Coll (TN) 364
Fresno Pacific U (CA) 364
Furman U (SC) 365
Gardner-Webb U (NC) 365
God's Bible School and Coll (OH) 369
Grace U (NE) 371
Grand Canyon U (AZ) 371
Greenville Coll (IL) 373
Gustavus Adolphus Coll (MN) 374
Hannibal-LaGrange Coll (MO) 375
Hardin-Simmons U (TX) 376
Hillsdale Free Will Baptist Coll (OK) 379
Hope International U (CA) 381
Houston Baptist U (TX) 382
Howard Payne U (TX) 382

Indiana Wesleyan U (IN) ***387***
Johnson Bible Coll (TN) ***394***
Lambuth U (TN) ***401***
Lenoir-Rhyne Coll (NC) ***405***
Lincoln Christian Coll (IL) ***407***
Louisiana Coll (LA) ***410***
Loyola U New Orleans (LA) ***411***
Malone Coll (OH) ***415***
Manhattan Christian Coll (KS) ***415***
Maranatha Baptist Bible Coll (WI) ***417***
Mars Hill Coll (NC) ***418***
Marywood U (PA) ***421***
The Master's Coll and Seminary (CA) ***422***
MidAmerica Nazarene U (KS) ***428***
Milligan Coll (TN) ***430***
Millikin U (IL) ***430***
Mississippi Coll (MS) ***432***
Moody Bible Inst (IL) ***435***
Mount Vernon Nazarene U (OH) ***440***
Nazarene Bible Coll (CO) ***442***
Nebraska Christian Coll (NE) ***443***
Newberry Coll (SC) ***444***
North Carolina Central U (NC) ***448***
Northeastern State U (OK) ***450***
North Greenville Coll (SC) ***451***
North Park U (IL) ***452***
Northwest Bible Coll (AB, Canada) ***452***
Northwest Coll (WA) ***452***
Northwest Nazarene U (ID) ***454***
Nyack Coll (NY) ***456***
Oak Hills Christian Coll (MN) ***456***
Oklahoma Baptist U (OK) ***459***
Oklahoma City U (OK) ***460***
Olivet Nazarene U (IL) ***461***
Oral Roberts U (OK) ***461***
Ouachita Baptist U (AR) ***462***
Ozark Christian Coll (MO) ***463***
Pacific Lutheran U (WA) ***463***
Palm Beach Atlantic U (FL) ***465***
Patten Coll (CA) ***466***
Pfeiffer U (NC) ***469***
Piedmont Coll (GA) ***470***
Pillsbury Baptist Bible Coll (MN) ***470***
Point Loma Nazarene U (CA) ***471***
Rider U (NJ) ***480***
Saint Joseph's Coll (IN) ***490***
St. Louis Christian Coll (MO) ***492***
Samford U (AL) ***497***
Seton Hill U (PA) ***502***
Shorter Coll (GA) ***504***
Simpson Coll and Graduate School (CA) ***505***
Southeastern Bible Coll (AL) ***507***
Southeastern Coll of the Assemblies of God (FL) ***507***
Southern Nazarene U (OK) ***510***
Southwestern Assemblies of God U (TX) ***512***
Southwestern Oklahoma State U (OK) ***512***
Southwestern U (TX) ***513***
Stetson U (FL) ***519***
Susquehanna U (PA) ***521***
Taylor U (IN) ***523***
Tennessee Temple U (TN) ***524***
Toccoa Falls Coll (GA) ***528***
Trevecca Nazarene U (TN) ***529***
Trinity International U (IL) ***531***
Union U (TN) ***534***
U of Mary Hardin-Baylor (TX) ***551***
Valley Forge Christian Coll (PA) ***588***
Valparaiso U (IN) ***588***
Warner Southern Coll (FL) ***593***
Wartburg Coll (IA) ***594***
Wayland Baptist U (TX) ***595***
Westminster Choir Coll of Rider U (NJ) ***601***
Westminster Coll (PA) ***601***
William Carey Coll (MS) ***605***
William Jewell Coll (MO) ***606***
Williams Baptist Coll (AR) ***606***

RELIGIOUS STUDIES

Overview: Students will study the nature of religious belief and specific religions. *Related majors:* philosophy, Biblical studies, anthropology, history, folklore and mythology, political science. *Potential careers:* clergy, writer, philosopher, archeologist or researcher, professor. *Salary potential:* $25k-$33k.

Adrian Coll (MI) ***260***
Agnes Scott Coll (GA) ***261***
Albertson Coll of Idaho (ID) ***262***
Albertus Magnus Coll (CT) ***262***
Albion Coll (MI) ***262***
Albright Coll (PA) ***263***
Alderson-Broaddus Coll (WV) ***263***
Allegheny Coll (PA) ***264***
Alma Coll (MI) ***264***
Alvernia Coll (PA) ***265***
Alverno Coll (WI) ***265***
Amherst Coll (MA) ***268***
Anderson Coll (SC) ***268***
Anderson U (IN) ***268***
Andrews U (MI) ***269***
Anna Maria Coll (MA) ***269***
Antioch Coll (OH) ***269***
Appalachian State U (NC) ***270***
Aquinas Coll (MI) ***270***
Arizona State U (AZ) ***271***
Arkansas Baptist Coll (AR) ***272***
Arlington Baptist Coll (TX) ***272***
Ashland U (OH) ***274***
Athens State U (AL) ***275***
Atlantic Baptist U (NB, Canada) ***275***
Atlantic Union Coll (MA) ***276***
Augsburg Coll (MN) ***276***
Augustana Coll (IL) ***276***
Augustana Coll (SD) ***276***
Austin Coll (TX) ***277***
Averett U (VA) ***278***
Azusa Pacific U (CA) ***278***
Baldwin-Wallace Coll (OH) ***280***
Ball State U (IN) ***280***
Baltimore Hebrew U (MD) ***280***
Bard Coll (NY) ***281***
Barnard Coll (NY) ***282***
Barton Coll (NC) ***282***
Bates Coll (ME) ***282***
Bayamón Central U (PR) ***283***
Baylor U (TX) ***283***
Beloit Coll (WI) ***285***
Bemidji State U (MN) ***285***
Benedict Coll (SC) ***285***
Benedictine Coll (KS) ***285***
Berea Coll (KY) ***286***
Berry Coll (GA) ***287***
Bethany Bible Coll (NB, Canada) ***287***
Bethany Coll (KS) ***287***
Bethany Coll (WV) ***287***
Bethel Coll (KS) ***288***
Biola U (CA) ***289***
Birmingham-Southern Coll (AL) ***289***
Bishop's U (QC, Canada) ***289***
Bloomfield Coll (NJ) ***290***
Bluefield Coll (VA) ***291***
Bluffton Coll (OH) ***291***
Boise Bible Coll (ID) ***291***
Boston U (MA) ***292***
Bowdoin Coll (ME) ***292***
Bradley U (IL) ***293***
Brandon U (MB, Canada) ***293***
Brescia U (KY) ***293***
Brevard Coll (NC) ***294***
Brewton-Parker Coll (GA) ***294***
Briercrest Bible Coll (SK, Canada) ***295***
Brooklyn Coll of the City U of NY (NY) ***295***
Brown U (RI) ***296***
Bryn Athyn Coll of the New Church (PA) ***297***
Bryn Mawr Coll (PA) ***297***
Bucknell U (PA) ***297***
Buena Vista U (IA) ***297***
Butler U (IN) ***297***
Cabrini Coll (PA) ***298***
California Baptist U (CA) ***298***
California Lutheran U (CA) ***299***
California State U, Bakersfield (CA) ***300***
California State U, Chico (CA) ***300***
California State U, Dominguez Hills (CA) ***300***
California State U, Fresno (CA) ***301***
California State U, Fullerton (CA) ***301***
California State U, Hayward (CA) ***301***
California State U, Long Beach (CA) ***301***
California State U, Northridge (CA) ***301***
Calumet Coll of Saint Joseph (IN) ***302***
Calvin Coll (MI) ***303***
Campbellsville U (KY) ***303***
Campbell U (NC) ***303***
Canadian Mennonite U (MB, Canada) ***304***
Canisius Coll (NY) ***304***
Capital U (OH) ***304***
Cardinal Stritch U (WI) ***305***
Carleton Coll (MN) ***305***
Carleton U (ON, Canada) ***305***
Carroll Coll (MT) ***306***
Carroll Coll (WI) ***306***
Carson-Newman Coll (TN) ***306***
Carthage Coll (WI) ***306***
Case Western Reserve U (OH) ***307***
Catawba Coll (NC) ***307***
The Catholic U of America (DC) ***307***
Centenary Coll of Louisiana (LA) ***308***
Central Bible Coll (MO) ***309***
Central Christian Coll of Kansas (KS) ***309***
Central Coll (IA) ***309***
Central Methodist Coll (MO) ***309***
Central Michigan U (MI) ***310***
Central Pentecostal Coll (SK, Canada) ***310***
Centre Coll (KY) ***310***
Chaminade U of Honolulu (HI) ***311***
Chapman U (CA) ***311***
Charleston Southern U (SC) ***311***
Chowan Coll (NC) ***312***
Christian Brothers U (TN) ***313***
Christopher Newport U (VA) ***313***
Circleville Bible Coll (OH) ***314***
Claflin U (SC) ***314***
Claremont McKenna Coll (CA) ***315***
Clark Atlanta U (GA) ***315***
Clarke Coll (IA) ***315***
Cleveland State U (OH) ***317***
Coe Coll (IA) ***318***
Coker Coll (SC) ***318***
Colby Coll (ME) ***318***
Colgate U (NY) ***319***
Coll of Charleston (SC) ***320***
Coll of Mount St. Joseph (OH) ***320***
Coll of Mount Saint Vincent (NY) ***320***
The Coll of New Rochelle (NY) ***321***
Coll of Notre Dame of Maryland (MD) ***321***
The Coll of Saint Rose (NY) ***322***
The Coll of St. Scholastica (MN) ***322***
Coll of Santa Fe (NM) ***323***
Coll of the Holy Cross (MA) ***323***
Coll of the Ozarks (MO) ***323***
The Coll of William and Mary (VA) ***324***
The Coll of Wooster (OH) ***324***
The Colorado Coll (CO) ***325***
Columbia Bible Coll (BC, Canada) ***326***
Columbia Coll (NY) ***326***
Columbia Coll (SC) ***327***
Columbia Union Coll (MD) ***328***
Columbia U, School of General Studies (NY) ***328***
Concordia Coll (MN) ***329***
Concordia Coll (NY) ***329***
Concordia U (MI) ***330***
Concordia U (MN) ***330***
Concordia U (OR) ***330***
Concordia U (QC, Canada) ***331***
Concordia U at Austin (TX) ***331***
Concordia U Coll of Alberta (AB, Canada) ***331***
Concordia U Wisconsin (WI) ***331***
Connecticut Coll (CT) ***331***
Converse Coll (SC) ***332***
Cornell Coll (IA) ***332***
Cornell U (NY) ***333***
Cornerstone U (MI) ***333***
Culver-Stockton Coll (MO) ***334***
Daemen Coll (NY) ***335***
Dakota Wesleyan U (SD) ***336***
Dalhousie U (NS, Canada) ***336***
Dana Coll (NE) ***337***
Dartmouth Coll (NH) ***337***
Davidson Coll (NC) ***338***
Defiance Coll (OH) ***338***
Denison U (OH) ***339***
DePaul U (IL) ***339***
DePauw U (IN) ***339***
Dickinson Coll (PA) ***344***
Dillard U (LA) ***344***
Doane Coll (NE) ***344***
Dominican U (IL) ***345***
Dominican U of California (CA) ***345***
Dordt Coll (IA) ***345***
Drake U (IA) ***345***
Drew U (NJ) ***346***
Drury U (MO) ***346***
Duke U (NC) ***346***
Earlham Coll (IN) ***347***
Eastern Michigan U (MI) ***348***
Eastern Nazarene Coll (MA) ***348***
Eastern New Mexico U (NM) ***349***
East Texas Baptist U (TX) ***350***
Eckerd Coll (FL) ***350***
Edgewood Coll (WI) ***351***
Elizabethtown Coll (PA) ***351***
Elmira Coll (NY) ***351***
Elms Coll (MA) ***352***
Elon U (NC) ***352***
Emory & Henry Coll (VA) ***353***
Emory U (GA) ***354***
Erskine Coll (SC) ***354***
Eugene Lang Coll, New School U (NY) ***355***
Eureka Coll (IL) ***355***
Fairfield U (CT) ***356***
Faulkner U (AL) ***357***
Felician Coll (NJ) ***357***
Ferrum Coll (VA) ***358***
Fisk U (TN) ***358***
Flagler Coll (FL) ***359***
Florida A&M U (FL) ***359***
Florida International U (FL) ***360***
Florida Southern Coll (FL) ***361***
Florida State U (FL) ***361***
Fordham U (NY) ***362***
The Franciscan U (IA) ***363***
Franklin and Marshall Coll (PA) ***363***
Franklin Coll (IN) ***363***
Fresno Pacific U (CA) ***364***
Furman U (SC) ***365***
Gardner-Webb U (NC) ***365***
George Fox U (OR) ***366***
George Mason U (VA) ***366***
Georgetown Coll (KY) ***366***
Georgetown U (DC) ***366***
The George Washington U (DC) ***367***
Georgian Court Coll (NJ) ***367***
Georgia State U (GA) ***368***
Gettysburg Coll (PA) ***368***
Gonzaga U (WA) ***369***
Goshen Coll (IN) ***370***
Goucher Coll (MD) ***370***
Graceland U (IA) ***371***
Grand Canyon U (AZ) ***371***
Grand View Coll (IA) ***372***
Greensboro Coll (NC) ***372***
Greenville Coll (IL) ***373***
Griggs U (MD) ***373***
Grinnell Coll (IA) ***373***
Grove City Coll (PA) ***373***
Guilford Coll (NC) ***373***
Gustavus Adolphus Coll (MN) ***374***
Hamilton Coll (NY) ***374***
Hamline U (MN) ***374***
Hampden-Sydney Coll (VA) ***374***
Hampshire Coll (MA) ***375***
Hampton U (VA) ***375***
Hannibal-LaGrange Coll (MO) ***375***
Harding U (AR) ***375***
Hartwick Coll (NY) ***376***
Harvard U (MA) ***376***
Hastings Coll (NE) ***377***
Haverford Coll (PA) ***377***
Heidelberg Coll (OH) ***377***
Hellenic Coll (MA) ***378***
Hendrix Coll (AR) ***378***
High Point U (NC) ***379***
Hillsdale Coll (MI) ***379***
Hiram Coll (OH) ***379***
Hobart and William Smith Colls (NY) ***380***
Hollins U (VA) ***380***
Holy Apostles Coll and Seminary (CT) ***380***
Holy Family U (PA) ***380***
Holy Names Coll (CA) ***381***
Hood Coll (MD) ***381***
Hope Coll (MI) ***381***
Houghton Coll (NY) ***381***
Houston Baptist U (TX) ***382***
Howard Payne U (TX) ***382***
Humboldt State U (CA) ***382***
Hunter Coll of the City U of NY (NY) ***382***
Huntingdon Coll (AL) ***383***
Huntington Coll (IN) ***383***
Illinois Coll (IL) ***384***
Illinois Wesleyan U (IL) ***385***
Indiana U Bloomington (IN) ***385***
Indiana U of Pennsylvania (PA) ***386***
Indiana U–Purdue U Indianapolis (IN) ***387***
Iona Coll (NY) ***390***
Iowa State U of Science and Technology (IA) ***390***
James Madison U (VA) ***391***
Jamestown Coll (ND) ***391***
Jewish Theological Seminary of America (NY) ***391***
John Brown U (AR) ***392***
John Carroll U (OH) ***392***
John Wesley Coll (NC) ***394***
Judson Coll (AL) ***395***
Judson Coll (IL) ***395***
Kalamazoo Coll (MI) ***395***

RELIGIOUS STUDIES (continued)

Kentucky Mountain Bible Coll (KY) **397**
Kenyon Coll (OH) **398**
King Coll (TN) **398**
Lafayette Coll (PA) **400**
LaGrange Coll (GA) **400**
Lakeland Coll (WI) **401**
Lambuth U (TN) **401**
Lane Coll (TN) **402**
La Roche Coll (PA) **402**
La Salle U (PA) **402**
La Sierra U (CA) **403**
Laura and Alvin Siegal Coll of Judaic Studies (OH) **403**
Laurentian U (ON, Canada) **403**
Lawrence U (WI) **403**
Lebanon Valley Coll (PA) **403**
Lees-McRae Coll (NC) **404**
Lehigh U (PA) **404**
Le Moyne Coll (NY) **404**
Lenoir-Rhyne Coll (NC) **405**
LeTourneau U (TX) **405**
Lewis & Clark Coll (OR) **405**
Lewis U (IL) **406**
Liberty U (VA) **406**
Lincoln U (PA) **407**
Lindenwood U (MO) **407**
Linfield Coll (OR) **408**
Long Island U, Southampton Coll, Friends World Program (NY) **409**
Loras Coll (IA) **410**
Louisiana Coll (LA) **410**
Lourdes Coll (OH) **411**
Loyola Coll in Maryland (MD) **411**
Loyola U New Orleans (LA) **411**
Luther Coll (IA) **412**
Lycoming Coll (PA) **412**
Lynchburg Coll (VA) **413**
Macalester Coll (MN) **413**
MacMurray Coll (IL) **414**
Madonna U (MI) **414**
Manchester Coll (IN) **415**
Manhattan Christian Coll (KS) **415**
Manhattan Coll (NY) **416**
Manhattanville Coll (NY) **416**
Maranatha Baptist Bible Coll (WI) **417**
Marlboro Coll (VT) **418**
Mars Hill Coll (NC) **418**
Martin Methodist Coll (TN) **418**
Martin U (IN) **419**
Mary Baldwin Coll (VA) **419**
Marygrove Coll (MI) **419**
Marymount U (VA) **420**
Maryville Coll (TN) **420**
Maryville U of Saint Louis (MO) **420**
Mary Washington Coll (VA) **420**
Marywood U (PA) **421**
The Master's Coll and Seminary (CA) **422**
McDaniel Coll (MD) **422**
McGill U (QC, Canada) **423**
McKendree Coll (IL) **423**
McMaster U (ON, Canada) **423**
McMurry U (TX) **423**
McPherson Coll (KS) **423**
Memorial U of Newfoundland (NF, Canada) **424**
Mercer U (GA) **425**
Mercyhurst Coll (PA) **425**
Meredith Coll (NC) **426**
Merrimack Coll (MA) **426**
Messiah Coll (PA) **426**
Methodist Coll (NC) **427**
Miami U (OH) **428**
Michigan State U (MI) **428**
MidAmerica Nazarene U (KS) **428**
Middlebury Coll (VT) **429**
Midland Lutheran Coll (NE) **429**
Millsaps Coll (MS) **431**
Mississippi Coll (MS) **432**
Missouri Valley Coll (MO) **433**
Molloy Coll (NY) **433**
Monmouth Coll (IL) **434**
Montclair State U (NJ) **435**
Montreat Coll (NC) **435**
Moravian Coll (PA) **436**
Morehouse Coll (GA) **436**
Morgan State U (MD) **436**
Morningside Coll (IA) **437**
Mount Allison U (NB, Canada) **437**
Mount Holyoke Coll (MA) **438**
Mount Marty Coll (SD) **438**
Mount Mary Coll (WI) **438**
Mount Mercy Coll (IA) **438**
Mount Olive Coll (NC) **439**
Mount St. Mary's Coll (CA) **439**
Mount Saint Vincent U (NS, Canada) **439**
Mount Union Coll (OH) **440**
Mount Vernon Nazarene U (OH) **440**
Muhlenberg Coll (PA) **440**
Muskingum Coll (OH) **441**
Naropa U (CO) **441**
Nazareth Coll of Rochester (NY) **443**
Nebraska Christian Coll (NE) **443**
Nebraska Wesleyan U (NE) **443**
Newberry Coll (SC) **444**
New Coll of Florida (FL) **444**
New York U (NY) **447**
Niagara U (NY) **447**
North Carolina State U (NC) **449**
North Carolina Wesleyan Coll (NC) **449**
North Central Coll (IL) **449**
Northern Arizona U (AZ) **450**
North Greenville Coll (SC) **451**
Northland Coll (WI) **452**
North Park U (IL) **452**
Northwest Coll (WA) **452**
Northwestern Coll (IA) **453**
Northwestern U (IL) **453**
Northwest Nazarene U (ID) **454**
Notre Dame de Namur U (CA) **455**
Nyack Coll (NY) **456**
Oakland City U (IN) **456**
Oberlin Coll (OH) **456**
Occidental Coll (CA) **457**
Ohio Northern U (OH) **457**
The Ohio State U (OH) **457**
Ohio Valley Coll (WV) **459**
Ohio Wesleyan U (OH) **459**
Oklahoma Baptist U (OK) **459**
Oklahoma Christian U (OK) **459**
Oklahoma City U (OK) **460**
Oklahoma Wesleyan U (OK) **460**
Olivet Nazarene U (IL) **461**
Oral Roberts U (OK) **461**
Ottawa U (KS) **462**
Otterbein Coll (OH) **462**
Our Lady of the Lake U of San Antonio (TX) **463**
Pacific Lutheran U (WA) **463**
Pacific Union Coll (CA) **464**
Paine Coll (GA) **465**
Palm Beach Atlantic U (FL) **465**
Paul Quinn Coll (TX) **466**
Penn State U Univ Park Campus (PA) **468**
Pepperdine U, Malibu (CA) **469**
Pfeiffer U (NC) **469**
Philadelphia Biblical U (PA) **469**
Piedmont Baptist Coll (NC) **470**
Piedmont Coll (GA) **470**
Pikeville Coll (KY) **470**
Pitzer Coll (CA) **471**
Point Loma Nazarene U (CA) **471**
Pomona Coll (CA) **472**
Presbyterian Coll (SC) **473**
Princeton U (NJ) **474**
Principia Coll (IL) **474**
Providence Coll and Theological Seminary (MB, Canada) **475**
Queens Coll of the City U of NY (NY) **475**
Queen's U at Kingston (ON, Canada) **476**
Queens U of Charlotte (NC) **476**
Radford U (VA) **476**
Randolph-Macon Coll (VA) **477**
Randolph-Macon Woman's Coll (VA) **477**
Reed Coll (OR) **477**
Regis U (CO) **478**
Rhodes Coll (TN) **479**
Rice U (TX) **479**
Ripon Coll (WI) **480**
Roanoke Bible Coll (NC) **481**
Roanoke Coll (VA) **481**
Roberts Wesleyan Coll (NY) **481**
Rocky Mountain Coll (MT) **482**
Rollins Coll (FL) **483**
Rosemont Coll (PA) **484**
Rutgers, The State U of New Jersey, New Brunswick (NJ) **485**
Sacred Heart U (CT) **486**
St. Andrews Presbyterian Coll (NC) **487**
St. Edward's U (TX) **488**
Saint Francis U (PA) **488**
St. Francis Xavier U (NS, Canada) **489**
St. John Fisher Coll (NY) **489**
Saint Joseph Coll (CT) **490**
Saint Joseph's Coll (IN) **490**
Saint Joseph's Coll of Maine (ME) **491**
St. Lawrence U (NY) **491**
Saint Leo U (FL) **492**
Saint Martin's Coll (WA) **493**
Saint Mary-of-the-Woods Coll (IN) **493**
Saint Mary's Coll (IN) **493**
Saint Mary's Coll of California (CA) **494**
St. Mary's Coll of Maryland (MD) **494**
Saint Mary's U (NS, Canada) **494**
Saint Michael's Coll (VT) **494**
St. Norbert Coll (WI) **495**
St. Olaf Coll (MN) **495**
Saint Paul U (ON, Canada) **495**
Saint Peter's Coll (NJ) **495**
St. Thomas Aquinas Coll (NY) **495**
St. Thomas U (FL) **496**
St. Thomas U (NB, Canada) **496**
Saint Xavier U (IL) **496**
Salem Coll (NC) **496**
Salve Regina U (RI) **497**
Samford U (AL) **497**
San Diego State U (CA) **498**
San Francisco State U (CA) **498**
San Jose Christian Coll (CA) **498**
San Jose State U (CA) **499**
Santa Clara U (CA) **499**
Sarah Lawrence Coll (NY) **499**
Schreiner U (TX) **501**
Scripps Coll (CA) **501**
Seattle Pacific U (WA) **501**
Seattle U (WA) **501**
Seton Hall U (NJ) **502**
Seton Hill U (PA) **502**
Shaw U (NC) **502**
Shenandoah U (VA) **503**
Shorter Coll (GA) **504**
Siena Coll (NY) **504**
Siena Heights U (MI) **504**
Simon's Rock Coll of Bard (MA) **505**
Simpson Coll (IA) **505**
Skidmore Coll (NY) **506**
Smith Coll (MA) **506**
Southeastern Bible Coll (AL) **507**
Southern Adventist U (TN) **508**
Southern Methodist U (TX) **510**
Southern Nazarene U (OK) **510**
Southern Wesleyan U (SC) **511**
Southwest Baptist U (MO) **512**
Southwestern Assemblies of God U (TX) **512**
Southwestern Christian Coll (TX) **512**
Southwestern U (TX) **513**
Southwest Missouri State U (MO) **513**
Spalding U (KY) **513**
Spelman Coll (GA) **514**
Spring Arbor U (MI) **514**
Stanford U (CA) **514**
State U of NY at Albany (NY) **514**
State U of NY Coll at Old Westbury (NY) **516**
Steinbach Bible Coll (MB, Canada) **518**
Stetson U (FL) **519**
Stonehill Coll (MA) **520**
Stony Brook U, State University of New York (NY) **520**
Susquehanna U (PA) **521**
Swarthmore Coll (PA) **521**
Sweet Briar Coll (VA) **521**
Syracuse U (NY) **521**
Tabor Coll (KS) **522**
Taylor U (IN) **523**
Temple U (PA) **523**
Tennessee Wesleyan Coll (TN) **524**
Texas Christian U (TX) **526**
Texas Wesleyan U (TX) **526**
Thiel Coll (PA) **527**
Thomas Edison State Coll (NJ) **527**
Thomas More Coll (KY) **528**
Toccoa Falls Coll (GA) **528**
Towson U (MD) **529**
Transylvania U (KY) **529**
Trevecca Nazarene U (TN) **529**
Trinity Christian Coll (IL) **530**
Trinity Coll (CT) **530**
Trinity U (TX) **531**
Trinity Western U (BC, Canada) **531**
Truman State U (MO) **532**
Tulane U (LA) **533**
Union Coll (KY) **533**
Union Coll (NE) **534**
Union U (TN) **534**
The U of Alabama (AL) **537**
U of Alberta (AB, Canada) **538**
The U of Arizona (AZ) **538**
U of Bridgeport (CT) **540**
The U of British Columbia (BC, Canada) **540**
U of Calgary (AB, Canada) **540**
U of Calif, Berkeley (CA) **540**
U of Calif, Davis (CA) **540**
U of Calif, Los Angeles (CA) **541**
U of Calif, Riverside (CA) **541**
U of Calif, San Diego (CA) **541**
U of Calif, Santa Barbara (CA) **541**
U of Calif, Santa Cruz (CA) **542**
U of Central Arkansas (AR) **542**
U of Charleston (WV) **542**
U of Chicago (IL) **542**
U of Colorado at Boulder (CO) **543**
U of Dayton (OH) **544**
U of Denver (CO) **544**
U of Dubuque (IA) **545**
U of Evansville (IN) **545**
The U of Findlay (OH) **545**
U of Florida (FL) **545**
U of Georgia (GA) **545**
U of Great Falls (MT) **545**
U of Hawaii at Manoa (HI) **546**
U of Illinois at Urbana–Champaign (IL) **548**
U of Indianapolis (IN) **548**
The U of Iowa (IA) **548**
U of Kansas (KS) **549**
U of King's Coll (NS, Canada) **549**
U of La Verne (CA) **549**
The U of Lethbridge (AB, Canada) **549**
U of Maine at Farmington (ME) **550**
U of Manitoba (MB, Canada) **551**
U of Mary (ND) **551**
U of Mary Hardin-Baylor (TX) **551**
U of Miami (FL) **553**
U of Michigan (MI) **554**
U of Minnesota, Twin Cities Campus (MN) **555**
U of Missouri–Columbia (MO) **555**
U of Mobile (AL) **556**
U of Nebraska at Omaha (NE) **557**
U of New Mexico (NM) **559**
The U of North Carolina at Chapel Hill (NC) **560**
The U of North Carolina at Charlotte (NC) **560**
The U of North Carolina at Greensboro (NC) **560**
The U of North Carolina at Pembroke (NC) **560**
U of North Dakota (ND) **561**
U of Northern Iowa (IA) **561**
U of Notre Dame (IN) **562**
U of Oklahoma (OK) **562**
U of Oregon (OR) **562**
U of Ottawa (ON, Canada) **563**
U of Pennsylvania (PA) **563**
U of Pittsburgh (PA) **569**
U of Prince Edward Island (PE, Canada) **570**
U of Puget Sound (WA) **571**
U of Redlands (CA) **572**
U of Regina (SK, Canada) **572**
U of Richmond (VA) **572**
U of Rochester (NY) **573**
U of Saint Francis (IN) **573**
U of St. Thomas (MN) **573**
U of San Diego (CA) **574**
U of San Francisco (CA) **574**
U of Saskatchewan (SK, Canada) **574**
The U of Scranton (PA) **574**
U of Sioux Falls (SD) **574**
U of South Carolina (SC) **575**
U of Southern California (CA) **576**
U of South Florida (FL) **576**
The U of Tennessee (TN) **577**
The U of Texas at Austin (TX) **578**
U of the Incarnate Word (TX) **580**
U of the Pacific (CA) **580**
U of the South (TN) **581**
U of Toronto (ON, Canada) **581**
U of Tulsa (OK) **581**
U of Vermont (VT) **582**
U of Virginia (VA) **582**
U of Washington (WA) **583**
U of Waterloo (ON, Canada) **583**
The U of Western Ontario (ON, Canada) **583**
U of West Florida (FL) **583**
U of Wisconsin–Eau Claire (WI) **584**
U of Wisconsin–Milwaukee (WI) **585**
U of Wisconsin–Oshkosh (WI) **585**
Urbana U (OH) **587**
Ursinus Coll (PA) **587**
Ursuline Coll (OH) **587**
Vanderbilt U (TN) **588**
Vanguard U of Southern California (CA) **589**

Vassar Coll (NY) **589**
Villanova U (PA) **590**
Virginia Commonwealth U (VA) **590**
Virginia Intermont Coll (VA) **590**
Virginia Wesleyan Coll (VA) **591**
Viterbo U (WI) **591**
Wabash Coll (IN) **592**
Wake Forest U (NC) **592**
Walla Walla Coll (WA) **593**
Walsh U (OH) **593**
Warner Pacific Coll (OR) **593**
Wartburg Coll (IA) **594**
Washington and Lee U (VA) **594**
Washington Bible Coll (MD) **594**
Washington State U (WA) **595**
Washington U in St. Louis (MO) **595**
Wayland Baptist U (TX) **595**
Webster U (MO) **597**
Wellesley Coll (MA) **597**
Wells Coll (NY) **597**
Wesleyan Coll (GA) **597**
Wesleyan U (CT) **597**
West Chester U of Pennsylvania (PA) **598**
Western Baptist Coll (OR) **598**
Western Kentucky U (KY) **599**
Western Michigan U (MI) **599**
Westminster Coll (MO) **601**
Westminster Coll (PA) **601**
Westmont Coll (CA) **602**
West Virginia Wesleyan Coll (WV) **603**
Wheaton Coll (IL) **603**
Wheaton Coll (MA) **603**
Wheeling Jesuit U (WV) **603**
Whittier Coll (CA) **604**
Whitworth Coll (WA) **604**
Wiley Coll (TX) **605**
Willamette U (OR) **605**
William Carey Coll (MS) **605**
William Jewell Coll (MO) **606**
Williams Baptist Coll (AR) **606**
Williams Coll (MA) **606**
Wilmington Coll (OH) **607**
Wingate U (NC) **607**
Winthrop U (SC) **608**
Wittenberg U (OH) **608**
Wofford Coll (SC) **609**
Wright State U (OH) **609**
Yale U (CT) **610**
York Coll (NE) **610**
York U (ON, Canada) **611**
Youngstown State U (OH) **611**

RESPIRATORY THERAPY

Overview: Students learn how to treat patients with heart, lung, or breathing problems in hospital emergency rooms, intensive care units, and medical and other health facilities. *Related majors:* perfusion technology, emergency medical technology, electrocardiograph technology. *Potential careers:* respiratory therapist, EMT, perfusionist. *Salary potential:* $30k-$35k.

Armstrong Atlantic State U (GA) **273**
California Coll for Health Sciences (CA) **298**
Champlain Coll (VT) **311**
Columbia Union Coll (MD) **328**
Comm Hospital Roanoke Valley–Coll of Health Scis (VA) **328**
Concordia Coll (MN) **329**
Dakota State U (SD) **335**
Florida A&M U (FL) **359**
Gannon U (PA) **365**
Georgia State U (GA) **368**
Indiana U of Pennsylvania (PA) **386**
Indiana U–Purdue U Indianapolis (IN) **387**
La Roche Coll (PA) **402**
Lee U (TN) **404**
Loma Linda U (CA) **408**
Long Island U, Brooklyn Campus (NY) **409**
Louisiana State U Health Sciences Center (LA) **410**
Marygrove Coll (MI) **419**
Medical Coll of Georgia (GA) **424**
Midland Lutheran Coll (NE) **429**
Midwestern State U (TX) **430**
Mountain State U (WV) **437**
National-Louis U (IL) **442**
Nebraska Methodist Coll (NE) **443**
North Dakota State U (ND) **449**
The Ohio State U (OH) **457**
Our Lady of Holy Cross Coll (LA) **463**
Pace U (NY) **463**
Point Park Coll (PA) **471**
Quinnipiac U (CT) **476**
Salisbury U (MD) **497**
Shenandoah U (VA) **503**
Southwest Missouri State U (MO) **513**
Southwest Texas State U (TX) **513**
State U of New York Upstate Medical University (NY) **518**
Stony Brook U, State University of New York (NY) **520**
Tennessee State U (TN) **523**
Texas Southern U (TX) **526**
Thomas Edison State Coll (NJ) **527**
U Coll of the Cariboo (BC, Canada) **537**
The U of Alabama at Birmingham (AL) **537**
U of Bridgeport (CT) **540**
U of Central Arkansas (AR) **542**
U of Central Florida (FL) **542**
U of Charleston (WV) **542**
U of Hartford (CT) **546**
U of Kansas (KS) **549**
U of Louisville (KY) **550**
U of Mary (ND) **551**
U of Missouri–Columbia (MO) **555**
U of South Alabama (AL) **575**
U of Texas Medical Branch at Galveston (TX) **579**
U of the Ozarks (AR) **580**
U of Toledo (OH) **581**
Weber State U (UT) **596**
Wheeling Jesuit U (WV) **603**
York Coll of Pennsylvania (PA) **610**
Youngstown State U (OH) **611**

RETAILING OPERATIONS

Overview: Students that choose this major learn the processes of retail sales for a wide variety of products and establishments. *Related majors:* food products retailing, apparel/accessories marketing, general sales operations, marketing. *Potential careers:* retail store manager, chain store manager, supermarket manager. *Salary potential:* $20k-$30k.

Johnson & Wales U (RI) **393**
Lake Erie Coll (OH) **400**
Pace U (NY) **463**
The U of Akron (OH) **537**
Youngstown State U (OH) **611**

RETAIL MANAGEMENT

Overview: Students taking this major learn how to manage and supervise all aspects of retail operations. *Related majors:* general retailing operations, advertising, marketing management, general retailing/wholesaling. *Potential careers:* store manager or territory manager, retail analyst, buyer. *Salary potential:* $25k-$35k.

Belmont U (TN) **284**
Bluffton Coll (OH) **291**
California State U, Northridge (CA) **301**
Eastern Kentucky U (KY) **348**
École des hautes études commerciales de Montréal (QC, Canada) **350**
Ferris State U (MI) **358**
Fontbonne U (MO) **361**
Governors State U (IL) **370**
Indiana U Bloomington (IN) **385**
John F. Kennedy U (CA) **392**
Johnson & Wales U (RI) **393**
Lasell Coll (MA) **402**
Lewis-Clark State Coll (ID) **406**
Lindenwood U (MO) **407**
Marymount U (VA) **420**
Marywood U (PA) **421**
Montclair State U (NJ) **435**
Mount Ida Coll (MA) **438**
Northern Michigan U (MI) **451**
Northwest Missouri State U (MO) **454**
Rowan U (NJ) **484**
Ryerson U (ON, Canada) **485**
Salem State Coll (MA) **497**
San Francisco State U (CA) **498**
Simmons Coll (MA) **504**
Southern New Hampshire U (NH) **510**
Syracuse U (NY) **521**
Thomas Coll (ME) **527**
Thomas Edison State Coll (NJ) **527**
U of Central Oklahoma (OK) **542**
The U of Memphis (TN) **553**
U of Montevallo (AL) **557**
U of Nebraska at Omaha (NE) **557**
Winona State U (MN) **608**
Youngstown State U (OH) **611**

ROBOTICS

Overview: Students learn the engineering, programming, and technical skills to develop and use robots. *Related majors:* artificial intelligence and robotics, electromechanical technology, computer science, industrial and mechanical engineering, applied physics. *Potential careers:* computer scientist, mechanical engineer, research scientist. *Salary potential:* $40k-$50k.

Harvard U (MA) **376**
Montana Tech of The U of Montana (MT) **435**
Pacific Union Coll (CA) **464**
Queen's U at Kingston (ON, Canada) **476**
U du Québec à Trois-Rivières (QC, Canada) **536**
U du Québec, École de technologie supérieure (QC, Canada) **536**
U of New Mexico (NM) **559**

ROBOTICS TECHNOLOGY

Overview: Students learn specific skills and the basic scientific principles so they can work with and help develop robots or robot systems. *Related majors:* engineering design, electromechanical technology, artificial intelligence and robotics. *Potential careers:* computer technician, robotic technician, mechanical engineer, power plant technician, research scientist. *Salary potential:* $30k-$40k.

Indiana State U (IN) **385**
Indiana U–Purdue U Indianapolis (IN) **387**
Purdue U (IN) **475**
U of Rio Grande (OH) **572**

ROMANCE LANGUAGES

Overview: Students who choose this major often concentrate on at least two of the Romance languages and their cultures. The Romance languages include French, Spanish, Italian, and Portuguese. *Related majors:* Western civilization and culture, history, medieval/Renaissance studies, advertising. *Potential careers:* teacher, curator, writer, advertising executive. *Salary potential:* $23k-$30k.

Albertus Magnus Coll (CT) **262**
Bard Coll (NY) **281**
Beloit Coll (WI) **285**
Baruch Coll of the City U of NY (NY) **286**
Bowdoin Coll (ME) **292**
Bryn Mawr Coll (PA) **297**
Cameron U (OK) **303**
Carleton Coll (MN) **305**
The Catholic U of America (DC) **307**
City Coll of the City U of NY (NY) **314**
Colgate U (NY) **319**
Cornell U (NY) **333**
Dartmouth Coll (NH) **337**
DePauw U (IN) **339**
Dowling Coll (NY) **345**
Elmira Coll (NY) **351**
Fordham U (NY) **362**
Franklin Coll Switzerland(Switzerland) **364**
Gettysburg Coll (PA) **368**
Harvard U (MA) **376**
Haverford Coll (PA) **377**
Hunter Coll of the City U of NY (NY) **382**
Kenyon Coll (OH) **398**
Long Island U, Southampton Coll, Friends World Program (NY) **409**
Manhattanville Coll (NY) **416**
Marlboro Coll (VT) **418**
Middlebury Coll (VT) **429**
Mount Allison U (NB, Canada) **437**
Mount Holyoke Coll (MA) **438**
New York U (NY) **447**
Northwest Missouri State U (MO) **454**
Oberlin Coll (OH) **456**
Olivet Nazarene U (IL) **461**
Pitzer Coll (CA) **471**
Point Loma Nazarene U (CA) **471**
Pomona Coll (CA) **472**
Princeton U (NJ) **474**
Queens Coll of the City U of NY (NY) **475**
Ripon Coll (WI) **480**
St. Thomas Aquinas Coll (NY) **495**
Sarah Lawrence Coll (NY) **499**
State U of NY at Albany (NY) **514**
Tufts U (MA) **533**
U of Alberta (AB, Canada) **538**
The U of British Columbia (BC, Canada) **540**
U of Chicago (IL) **542**
U of Cincinnati (OH) **543**
U of Maine (ME) **550**
U of Michigan (MI) **554**
U of Nevada, Las Vegas (NV) **558**
U of New Brunswick Fredericton (NB, Canada) **558**
U of New Hampshire (NH) **558**
The U of North Carolina at Chapel Hill (NC) **560**
U of Oregon (OR) **562**
U of Pennsylvania (PA) **563**
U of Toronto (ON, Canada) **581**
U of Vermont (VT) **582**
U of Victoria (BC, Canada) **582**
U of Washington (WA) **583**
U of Windsor (ON, Canada) **584**
Ursinus Coll (PA) **587**
Walsh U (OH) **593**
Washington U in St. Louis (MO) **595**
Wesleyan U (CT) **597**
West Chester U of Pennsylvania (PA) **598**
Wheeling Jesuit U (WV) **603**
York U (ON, Canada) **611**

ROMANCE LANGUAGES RELATED

Information can be found under this major's main heading.

The Colorado Coll (CO) **325**

RUSSIAN

Overview: Students focus on learning to speak, read, and understand the Russian language and its various dialects and gain an understanding of Russian culture and literature. *Related majors:* international economics, history, history of science and technology, comparative literature. *Potential careers:* diplomatic corps, entrepreneur, translator. *Salary potential:* $30k-$35k.

American U (DC) **267**
Amherst Coll (MA) **268**
Arizona State U (AZ) **271**
Bard Coll (NY) **281**
Barnard Coll (NY) **282**
Bates Coll (ME) **282**
Baylor U (TX) **283**
Beloit Coll (WI) **285**
Boston Coll (MA) **292**
Boston U (MA) **292**
Bowdoin Coll (ME) **292**
Bowling Green State U (OH) **292**
Brandeis U (MA) **293**
Brigham Young U (UT) **295**
Brooklyn Coll of the City U of NY (NY) **295**
Bryn Mawr Coll (PA) **297**
Bucknell U (PA) **297**
California State U, Northridge (CA) **301**
Carleton Coll (MN) **305**
Carleton U (ON, Canada) **305**
Carnegie Mellon U (PA) **305**
Claremont McKenna Coll (CA) **315**

RUSSIAN (continued)

Colgate U (NY) ***319***
Coll of the Holy Cross (MA) ***323***
The Coll of Wooster (OH) ***324***
Columbia Coll (NY) ***326***
Columbia U, School of General Studies (NY) ***328***
Connecticut Coll (CT) ***331***
Cornell Coll (IA) ***332***
Cornell U (NY) ***333***
Dalhousie U (NS, Canada) ***336***
Dartmouth Coll (NH) ***337***
Dickinson Coll (PA) ***344***
Drew U (NJ) ***346***
Duke U (NC) ***346***
Eckerd Coll (FL) ***350***
Emory U (GA) ***354***
The Evergreen State Coll (WA) ***355***
Ferrum Coll (VA) ***358***
Florida State U (FL) ***361***
Fordham U (NY) ***362***
Georgetown U (DC) ***366***
The George Washington U (DC) ***367***
Goucher Coll (MD) ***370***
Grinnell Coll (IA) ***373***
Gustavus Adolphus Coll (MN) ***374***
Harvard U (MA) ***376***
Haverford Coll (PA) ***377***
Hobart and William Smith Colls (NY) ***380***
Hofstra U (NY) ***380***
Howard U (DC) ***382***
Hunter Coll of the City U of NY (NY) ***382***
Indiana U Bloomington (IN) ***385***
Indiana U of Pennsylvania (PA) ***386***
Iowa State U of Science and Technology (IA) ***390***
James Madison U (VA) ***391***
Juniata Coll (PA) ***395***
Kent State U (OH) ***397***
Knox Coll (IL) ***399***
La Salle U (PA) ***402***
Lawrence U (WI) ***403***
Lehman Coll of the City U of NY (NY) ***404***
Lincoln U (PA) ***407***
Long Island U, Southampton Coll, Friends World Program (NY) ***409***
Loyola U New Orleans (LA) ***411***
Macalester Coll (MN) ***413***
Massachusetts Inst of Technology (MA) ***421***
McGill U (QC, Canada) ***423***
McMaster U (ON, Canada) ***423***
Memorial U of Newfoundland (NF, Canada) ***424***
Miami U (OH) ***428***
Michigan State U (MI) ***428***
Middlebury Coll (VT) ***429***
Mount Holyoke Coll (MA) ***438***
New Coll of Florida (FL) ***444***
New York U (NY) ***447***
Northeastern U (MA) ***450***
Northern Illinois U (IL) ***450***
Oakland U (MI) ***456***
Oberlin Coll (OH) ***456***
The Ohio State U (OH) ***457***
Ohio U (OH) ***458***
Oklahoma State U (OK) ***460***
Ouachita Baptist U (AR) ***462***
Penn State U Univ Park Campus (PA) ***468***
Pitzer Coll (CA) ***471***
Pomona Coll (CA) ***472***
Portland State U (OR) ***472***
Principia Coll (IL) ***474***
Queens Coll of the City U of NY (NY) ***475***
Reed Coll (OR) ***477***
Rice U (TX) ***479***
Rider U (NJ) ***480***
Rutgers, The State U of New Jersey, New Brunswick (NJ) ***485***
Saint Louis U (MO) ***492***
St. Olaf Coll (MN) ***495***
St. Thomas U (NB, Canada) ***496***
San Diego State U (CA) ***498***
San Francisco State U (CA) ***498***
Sarah Lawrence Coll (NY) ***499***
Scripps Coll (CA) ***501***
Seattle Pacific U (WA) ***501***
Smith Coll (MA) ***506***
Southern Illinois U Carbondale (IL) ***509***
Southern Methodist U (TX) ***510***
State U of NY at Albany (NY) ***514***
Stony Brook U, State University of New York (NY) ***520***
Swarthmore Coll (PA) ***521***
Syracuse U (NY) ***521***
Temple U (PA) ***523***
Texas A&M U (TX) ***524***
Trinity Coll (CT) ***530***
Trinity U (TX) ***531***
Truman State U (MO) ***532***
Tufts U (MA) ***533***
Tulane U (LA) ***533***
United States Military Academy (NY) ***535***
The U of Alabama (AL) ***537***
U of Alberta (AB, Canada) ***538***
The U of Arizona (AZ) ***538***
The U of British Columbia (BC, Canada) ***540***
U of Calgary (AB, Canada) ***540***
U of Calif, Davis (CA) ***540***
U of Calif, Irvine (CA) ***541***
U of Calif, Los Angeles (CA) ***541***
U of Calif, Riverside (CA) ***541***
U of Calif, San Diego (CA) ***541***
U of Chicago (IL) ***542***
U of Delaware (DE) ***544***
U of Denver (CO) ***544***
U of Florida (FL) ***545***
U of Georgia (GA) ***545***
U of Hawaii at Manoa (HI) ***546***
U of Illinois at Chicago (IL) ***547***
U of Illinois at Urbana–Champaign (IL) ***548***
The U of Iowa (IA) ***548***
U of Kansas (KS) ***549***
U of Kentucky (KY) ***549***
U of King's Coll (NS, Canada) ***549***
U of Louisville (KY) ***550***
U of Manitoba (MB, Canada) ***551***
U of Maryland, Baltimore County (MD) ***552***
U of Maryland, Coll Park (MD) ***552***
U of Massachusetts Boston (MA) ***553***
U of Miami (FL) ***553***
U of Michigan (MI) ***554***
U of Minnesota, Twin Cities Campus (MN) ***555***
U of Missouri–Columbia (MO) ***555***
The U of Montana–Missoula (MT) ***556***
U of Nebraska–Lincoln (NE) ***557***
U of New Brunswick Fredericton (NB, Canada) ***558***
U of New Hampshire (NH) ***558***
U of New Mexico (NM) ***559***
The U of North Carolina at Chapel Hill (NC) ***560***
The U of North Carolina at Greensboro (NC) ***560***
U of Northern Iowa (IA) ***561***
U of Notre Dame (IN) ***562***
U of Oklahoma (OK) ***562***
U of Oregon (OR) ***562***
U of Ottawa (ON, Canada) ***563***
U of Pennsylvania (PA) ***563***
U of Pittsburgh (PA) ***569***
U of Rochester (NY) ***573***
U of St. Thomas (MN) ***573***
U of Saskatchewan (SK, Canada) ***574***
The U of Scranton (PA) ***574***
U of Southern California (CA) ***576***
U of South Florida (FL) ***576***
The U of Tennessee (TN) ***577***
The U of Texas at Arlington (TX) ***577***
The U of Texas at Austin (TX) ***578***
U of the South (TN) ***581***
U of Toronto (ON, Canada) ***581***
U of Utah (UT) ***582***
U of Vermont (VT) ***582***
U of Victoria (BC, Canada) ***582***
U of Washington (WA) ***583***
U of Waterloo (ON, Canada) ***583***
The U of Western Ontario (ON, Canada) ***583***
U of Windsor (ON, Canada) ***584***
U of Wisconsin–Madison (WI) ***584***
U of Wisconsin–Milwaukee (WI) ***585***
U of Wyoming (WY) ***586***
Vanderbilt U (TN) ***588***
Vassar Coll (NY) ***589***
Wake Forest U (NC) ***592***
Washington State U (WA) ***595***
Washington U in St. Louis (MO) ***595***
Wayne State U (MI) ***596***
Wellesley Coll (MA) ***597***
Wesleyan U (CT) ***597***
West Chester U of Pennsylvania (PA) ***598***
Wheaton Coll (MA) ***603***
Williams Coll (MA) ***606***
Yale U (CT) ***610***
York U (ON, Canada) ***611***

RUSSIAN/SLAVIC STUDIES

Overview: Undergraduates who choose this major will study the history, politics, culture, languages, and economics of one or more of the peoples of the Russian Federation (including its Soviet and Czarist periods) and the Slavic peoples inhabiting Europe and Asia, including the study of migration patterns. *Related majors:* Russian, Russian literature, Russian history, Polish, Czech. *Potential careers:* translator, foreign service officer, business consultant/entrepreneur. *Salary potential:* $25k-$30k.

American U (DC) ***267***
Bard Coll (NY) ***281***
Barnard Coll (NY) ***282***
Baylor U (TX) ***283***
Beloit Coll (WI) ***285***
Boston Coll (MA) ***292***
Boston U (MA) ***292***
Brandeis U (MA) ***293***
Brock U (ON, Canada) ***295***
Brown U (RI) ***296***
California State U, Fullerton (CA) ***301***
Carleton U (ON, Canada) ***305***
Colby Coll (ME) ***318***
Colgate U (NY) ***319***
The Coll of William and Mary (VA) ***324***
The Colorado Coll (CO) ***325***
Columbia Coll (NY) ***326***
Concordia Coll (MN) ***329***
Cornell Coll (IA) ***332***
Cornell U (NY) ***333***
Dartmouth Coll (NH) ***337***
DePauw U (IN) ***339***
Dickinson Coll (PA) ***344***
Duke U (NC) ***346***
The Evergreen State Coll (WA) ***355***
Florida State U (FL) ***361***
Fordham U (NY) ***362***
George Mason U (VA) ***366***
The George Washington U (DC) ***367***
Grand Valley State U (MI) ***371***
Gustavus Adolphus Coll (MN) ***374***
Hamilton Coll (NY) ***374***
Hamline U (MN) ***374***
Hampshire Coll (MA) ***375***
Harvard U (MA) ***376***
Hobart and William Smith Colls (NY) ***380***
Indiana U Bloomington (IN) ***385***
Kent State U (OH) ***397***
Knox Coll (IL) ***399***
Lafayette Coll (PA) ***400***
La Salle U (PA) ***402***
Lawrence U (WI) ***403***
Lehigh U (PA) ***404***
Long Island U, Southampton Coll, Friends World Program (NY) ***409***
Louisiana State U and A&M Coll (LA) ***410***
Macalester Coll (MN) ***413***
Marlboro Coll (VT) ***418***
Massachusetts Inst of Technology (MA) ***421***
McGill U (QC, Canada) ***423***
McMaster U (ON, Canada) ***423***
Middlebury Coll (VT) ***429***
Mount Holyoke Coll (MA) ***438***
Muhlenberg Coll (PA) ***440***
Oakland U (MI) ***456***
Oberlin Coll (OH) ***456***
The Ohio State U (OH) ***457***
Randolph-Macon Woman's Coll (VA) ***477***
Rhodes Coll (TN) ***479***
Rice U (TX) ***479***
Rutgers, The State U of New Jersey, New Brunswick (NJ) ***485***
St. Olaf Coll (MN) ***495***
San Diego State U (CA) ***498***
Smith Coll (MA) ***506***
Southern Methodist U (TX) ***510***
Southwest Texas State U (TX) ***513***
State U of NY at Albany (NY) ***514***
Stetson U (FL) ***519***
Syracuse U (NY) ***521***
Texas Tech U (TX) ***526***
Tufts U (MA) ***533***
Tulane U (LA) ***533***
U of Alaska Fairbanks (AK) ***538***
U of Alberta (AB, Canada) ***538***
The U of British Columbia (BC, Canada) ***540***
U of Calif, Los Angeles (CA) ***541***
U of Calif, Riverside (CA) ***541***
U of Calif, San Diego (CA) ***541***
U of Calif, Santa Cruz (CA) ***542***
U of Chicago (IL) ***542***
U of Colorado at Boulder (CO) ***543***
U of Connecticut (CT) ***544***
U of Houston (TX) ***547***
U of Illinois at Urbana–Champaign (IL) ***548***
U of Kansas (KS) ***549***
U of Louisville (KY) ***550***
U of Manitoba (MB, Canada) ***551***
U of Maryland, Coll Park (MD) ***552***
U of Massachusetts Amherst (MA) ***552***
U of Michigan (MI) ***554***
U of Minnesota, Twin Cities Campus (MN) ***555***
U of Missouri–Columbia (MO) ***555***
The U of Montana–Missoula (MT) ***556***
U of New Mexico (NM) ***559***
The U of North Carolina at Chapel Hill (NC) ***560***
U of Northern Iowa (IA) ***561***
U of Ottawa (ON, Canada) ***563***
U of Rochester (NY) ***573***
U of St. Thomas (MN) ***573***
U of Southern Maine (ME) ***576***
The U of Texas at Austin (TX) ***578***
U of the South (TN) ***581***
U of Toronto (ON, Canada) ***581***
U of Vermont (VT) ***582***
U of Victoria (BC, Canada) ***582***
U of Washington (WA) ***583***
U of Waterloo (ON, Canada) ***583***
U of Wisconsin–Milwaukee (WI) ***585***
Washington and Lee U (VA) ***594***
Washington U in St. Louis (MO) ***595***
Wellesley Coll (MA) ***597***
Wesleyan U (CT) ***597***
Western Michigan U (MI) ***599***
Wheaton Coll (MA) ***603***
Wittenberg U (OH) ***608***
Yale U (CT) ***610***
York U (ON, Canada) ***611***

SAFETY/SECURITY TECHNOLOGY

Overview: This major focuses on the technological aspects of loss prevention and safety procedures. *Related majors:* electrical and electronics installation, computer installation, communication system installation, instrument calibration, fire protection and safety technology. *Potential careers:* burglar/fire alarm executive/installer, locksmith. *Salary potential:* $23k-$33k.

Eastern Kentucky U (KY) ***348***
State U of NY at Farmingdale (NY) ***357***
John Jay Coll of Criminal Justice, the City U of NY (NY) ***392***
Keene State Coll (NH) ***396***
Madonna U (MI) ***414***
Mercy Coll (NY) ***425***
U of Central Oklahoma (OK) ***542***
U of Wisconsin–Whitewater (WI) ***586***
York Coll of Pennsylvania (PA) ***610***

SALES OPERATIONS

Overview: This major prepares students to become direct sellers of products or services, and to function as a sales representative or sales manager. *Related majors:* psychology, marketing, business communications, accounting. *Potential careers:* product or service sales representative. *Salary potential:* $30k-$40k, depending on industry and products.

Harding U (AR) ***375***
Lake Erie Coll (OH) ***400***
Texas A&M U (TX) ***524***
The U of Akron (OH) ***537***
Youngstown State U (OH) ***611***

SANITATION TECHNOLOGY

Overview: This major teaches students the fundamental aspects of food hygiene and sanitation technology. *Related majors:* food science technology, restaurant operations, quality control technology, environmental health engineering, microbiology/bacteriology. *Potential careers:* quality control manager, research scientist, food systems administrator, food inspector. *Salary potential:* $30k-40k.

Grand Valley State U (MI) ***371***

SCANDINAVIAN LANGUAGES

Overview: Students learn the languages, literature, history, politics, and cultures of one or more of the Scandinavian countries (Denmark, Finland, Iceland, Norway, Sweden) and the Baltic States (Estonia, Latvia, Lithuania). *Related majors:* banking and international finance, history, history of science and technology, comparative literature, philosophy. *Potential careers:* diplomatic corps, journalist, translator, scientific consultant, engineering consultant. *Salary potential:* $27k-$34k.

Augsburg Coll (MN) ***276***
Augustana Coll (IL) ***276***
Concordia Coll (MN) ***329***
Gustavus Adolphus Coll (MN) ***374***
Harvard U (MA) ***376***
Long Island U, Southampton Coll, Friends World Program (NY) ***409***
Luther Coll (IA) ***412***
North Park U (IL) ***452***
Pacific Lutheran U (WA) ***463***
St. Olaf Coll (MN) ***495***
U of Alberta (AB, Canada) ***538***
U of Calif, Berkeley (CA) ***540***
U of Calif, Los Angeles (CA) ***541***
U of Minnesota, Twin Cities Campus (MN) ***555***
U of North Dakota (ND) ***561***
The U of Texas at Austin (TX) ***578***
U of Washington (WA) ***583***
U of Wisconsin–Madison (WI) ***584***

SCANDINAVIAN STUDIES

Overview: Undergraduates study the history, politics, culture, languages, and economics of one or more of the peoples of Scandinavia (Denmark, Finland, Iceland, Norway, Sweden, and Greenland). *Related majors:* Scandinavian language and history, economics, comparative literature. *Potential careers:* translator, foreign service officer, business consultant/ entrepreneur. *Potential salary:* $25k-$35k.

Luther Coll (IA) ***412***
U of Michigan (MI) ***554***
U of Washington (WA) ***583***

SCHOOL PSYCHOLOGY

Overview: This branch of psychology examines the clinical and counseling issues related to the diagnosis and treatment of students' behavioral problems. *Related majors:* social psychology, counseling psychology, educational psychology, social work, developmental psychology. *Potential careers:* school psychologist, or therapist, family therapist, teacher, school administrator, research scientist, professor. *Salary potential:* $23k-$33k.

Bowling Green State U (OH) ***292***
Crichton Coll (TN) ***334***
Fort Hays State U (KS) ***362***
Texas Wesleyan U (TX) ***526***

SCIENCE EDUCATION

Overview: This major prepares undergraduates to teach various science subjects, including basic biology, chemistry, physics, ecology, and astronomy, to students from various educational levels below the college level. *Related majors:* biology, chemistry, physics, ecology, astronomy. *Potential careers:* secondary or high school science teacher, aquarium or science museum curator. *Salary potential:* $24k-$35k.

Abilene Christian U (TX) ***260***
Adams State Coll (CO) ***260***
Adrian Coll (MI) ***260***
Alabama State U (AL) ***261***
Albany State U (GA) ***262***
Alderson-Broaddus Coll (WV) ***263***
Alfred U (NY) ***263***
Alice Lloyd Coll (KY) ***263***
Alvernia Coll (PA) ***265***
Alverno Coll (WI) ***265***
Anderson U (IN) ***268***
Andrews U (MI) ***269***
Antioch Coll (OH) ***269***
Appalachian State U (NC) ***270***
Armstrong Atlantic State U (GA) ***273***
Ashland U (OH) ***274***
Athens State U (AL) ***275***
Auburn U (AL) ***276***
Baldwin-Wallace Coll (OH) ***280***
Ball State U (IN) ***280***
Barton Coll (NC) ***282***
Bayamón Central U (PR) ***283***
Baylor U (TX) ***283***
Beloit Coll (WI) ***285***
Bemidji State U (MN) ***285***
Benedictine Coll (KS) ***285***
Benedictine U (IL) ***285***
Bennett Coll (NC) ***286***
Berry Coll (GA) ***287***
Bethel Coll (IN) ***288***
Bethel Coll (MN) ***288***
Bloomfield Coll (NJ) ***290***
Bloomsburg U of Pennsylvania (PA) ***290***
Bluefield Coll (VA) ***291***
Blue Mountain Coll (MS) ***291***
Boston U (MA) ***292***
Bowie State U (MD) ***292***
Bowling Green State U (OH) ***292***
Brewton-Parker Coll (GA) ***294***
Brigham Young U–Hawaii (HI) ***295***
Brock U (ON, Canada) ***295***
Bryan Coll (TN) ***296***
Buena Vista U (IA) ***297***
California State U, Chico (CA) ***300***
California State U, San Marcos (CA) ***302***
Calvin Coll (MI) ***303***
Campbellsville U (KY) ***303***
Canisius Coll (NY) ***304***
Capital U (OH) ***304***
Cardinal Stritch U (WI) ***305***
Carroll Coll (WI) ***306***
Carthage Coll (WI) ***306***
Castleton State Coll (VT) ***307***
Cedar Crest Coll (PA) ***308***
Cedarville U (OH) ***308***
Centenary Coll of Louisiana (LA) ***308***
Central Methodist Coll (MO) ***309***
Central Michigan U (MI) ***310***
Central Missouri State U (MO) ***310***
Central Washington U (WA) ***310***
Chadron State Coll (NE) ***311***
Charleston Southern U (SC) ***311***
Christopher Newport U (VA) ***313***
Citadel, The Military Coll of South Carolina (SC) ***314***
Clarion U of Pennsylvania (PA) ***315***
Clark Atlanta U (GA) ***315***
Clearwater Christian Coll (FL) ***316***
Clemson U (SC) ***317***
Coe Coll (IA) ***318***
Coll of Mount Saint Vincent (NY) ***320***
Coll of Saint Mary (NE) ***322***
Coll of Santa Fe (NM) ***323***
Coll of the Atlantic (ME) ***323***
Coll of the Ozarks (MO) ***323***
Coll of the Southwest (NM) ***324***
Colorado State U (CO) ***325***
Colorado State U-Pueblo (CO) ***325***
Columbia Coll (MO) ***326***
Columbia Coll (SC) ***327***
Columbus State U (GA) ***328***
Concordia Coll (MN) ***329***
Concordia Coll (NY) ***329***
Concordia U (IL) ***330***
Concordia U (MN) ***330***
Concordia U (NE) ***330***
Concordia U (OR) ***330***
Concordia U Wisconsin (WI) ***331***
Cornerstone U (MI) ***333***
Culver-Stockton Coll (MO) ***334***
Daemen Coll (NY) ***335***
Dallas Baptist U (TX) ***336***
Dana Coll (NE) ***337***
Defiance Coll (OH) ***338***
Delaware State U (DE) ***338***
Delta State U (MS) ***339***
Dickinson State U (ND) ***344***
Dillard U (LA) ***344***
Dominican Coll (NY) ***344***
Drake U (IA) ***345***
Duquesne U (PA) ***346***
D'Youville Coll (NY) ***347***
East Carolina U (NC) ***347***
Eastern Kentucky U (KY) ***348***
Eastern Michigan U (MI) ***348***
Eastern Washington U (WA) ***349***
East Texas Baptist U (TX) ***350***
Elizabethtown Coll (PA) ***351***
Elmira Coll (NY) ***351***
Elms Coll (MA) ***352***
Elon U (NC) ***352***
Emporia State U (KS) ***354***
Eureka Coll (IL) ***355***
Evangel U (MO) ***355***
Fairmont State Coll (WV) ***356***
Ferris State U (MI) ***358***
Florida Atlantic U (FL) ***359***
Florida Inst of Technology (FL) ***360***
Florida International U (FL) ***360***
Florida State U (FL) ***361***
Fort Hays State U (KS) ***362***
Framingham State Coll (MA) ***362***
The Franciscan U (IA) ***363***
Freed-Hardeman U (TN) ***364***
Fresno Pacific U (CA) ***364***
Georgia Southwestern State U (GA) ***368***
Gettysburg Coll (PA) ***368***
Glenville State Coll (WV) ***368***
Goshen Coll (IN) ***370***
Governors State U (IL) ***370***
Grace Coll (IN) ***370***
Graceland U (IA) ***371***
Grambling State U (LA) ***371***
Grand Canyon U (AZ) ***371***
Grand Valley State U (MI) ***371***
Grand View Coll (IA) ***372***
Greensboro Coll (NC) ***372***
Greenville Coll (IL) ***373***
Grove City Coll (PA) ***373***
Gwynedd-Mercy Coll (PA) ***374***
Hamline U (MN) ***374***
Harding U (AR) ***375***
Hardin-Simmons U (TX) ***376***
Hastings Coll (NE) ***377***
Heidelberg Coll (OH) ***377***
Henderson State U (AR) ***378***
Howard Payne U (TX) ***382***
Huntington Coll (IN) ***383***
Illinois Wesleyan U (IL) ***385***
Indiana State U (IN) ***385***
Indiana U Bloomington (IN) ***385***
Indiana U of Pennsylvania (PA) ***386***
Indiana U–Purdue U Fort Wayne (IN) ***386***
Indiana U South Bend (IN) ***387***
Indiana U Southeast (IN) ***387***
Indiana Wesleyan U (IN) ***387***
Inter American U of PR, San Germán Campus (PR) ***388***
Iona Coll (NY) ***390***
Ithaca Coll (NY) ***390***
Jackson State U (MS) ***390***
Johnson C. Smith U (NC) ***394***
Judson Coll (AL) ***395***
Judson Coll (IL) ***395***
Juniata Coll (PA) ***395***
Kent State U (OH) ***397***
LaGrange Coll (GA) ***400***
Lakehead U (ON, Canada) ***400***
Lakeland Coll (WI) ***401***
La Salle U (PA) ***402***
Le Moyne Coll (NY) ***404***
Lenoir-Rhyne Coll (NC) ***405***
Lewis-Clark State Coll (ID) ***406***
Liberty U (VA) ***406***
Lincoln Memorial U (TN) ***407***
Lincoln U (PA) ***407***
Lock Haven U of Pennsylvania (PA) ***408***
Longwood U (VA) ***409***
Louisiana Coll (LA) ***410***
Luther Coll (IA) ***412***
Lyndon State Coll (VT) ***413***
Malone Coll (OH) ***415***
Manchester Coll (IN) ***415***
Mansfield U of Pennsylvania (PA) ***416***
Maranatha Baptist Bible Coll (WI) ***417***
Marian Coll of Fond du Lac (WI) ***417***
Mars Hill Coll (NC) ***418***
Marymount Coll of Fordham U (NY) ***419***
Marywood U (PA) ***421***
The Master's Coll and Seminary (CA) ***422***
Mayville State U (ND) ***422***
McGill U (QC, Canada) ***423***
McMurry U (TX) ***423***
Memorial U of Newfoundland (NF, Canada) ***424***
Mercer U (GA) ***425***
Mercyhurst Coll (PA) ***425***
Mesa State Coll (CO) ***426***
Methodist Coll (NC) ***427***
Miami U (OH) ***428***
Michigan Technological U (MI) ***428***
MidAmerica Nazarene U (KS) ***428***
Midland Lutheran Coll (NE) ***429***
Millersville U of Pennsylvania (PA) ***430***
Milligan Coll (TN) ***430***
Minnesota State U, Mankato (MN) ***431***
Minnesota State U, Moorhead (MN) ***432***
Minot State U (ND) ***432***
Mississippi Coll (MS) ***432***
Mississippi Valley State U (MS) ***432***
Missouri Valley Coll (MO) ***433***
Montana State U–Billings (MT) ***434***
Montana State U–Northern (MT) ***434***
Moravian Coll (PA) ***436***
Morehead State U (KY) ***436***
Morningside Coll (IA) ***437***
Mount Mercy Coll (IA) ***438***
Mount Vernon Nazarene U (OH) ***440***
Muskingum Coll (OH) ***441***
Nazareth Coll of Rochester (NY) ***443***
Nebraska Wesleyan U (NE) ***443***
New Mexico Highlands U (NM) ***446***
New Mexico Inst of Mining and Technology (NM) ***446***
New York U (NY) ***447***
Niagara U (NY) ***447***
Nicholls State U (LA) ***447***
North Carolina State U (NC) ***449***
North Central Coll (IL) ***449***
North Dakota State U (ND) ***449***
Northern Arizona U (AZ) ***450***
Northern Kentucky U (KY) ***451***
Northern Michigan U (MI) ***451***
Northland Coll (WI) ***452***
Northwestern Oklahoma State U (OK) ***453***
Northwest Missouri State U (MO) ***454***
Oakland City U (IN) ***456***
Oakwood Coll (AL) ***456***
Ohio Dominican U (OH) ***457***
Ohio U (OH) ***458***
Ohio Valley Coll (WV) ***459***
Oklahoma Baptist U (OK) ***459***
Oklahoma Christian U (OK) ***459***
Oklahoma City U (OK) ***460***
Oklahoma Panhandle State U (OK) ***460***
Oklahoma Wesleyan U (OK) ***460***
Olivet Nazarene U (IL) ***461***
Oral Roberts U (OK) ***461***
Otterbein Coll (OH) ***462***
Ouachita Baptist U (AR) ***462***
Our Lady of Holy Cross Coll (LA) ***463***
Pace U (NY) ***463***
Pacific Lutheran U (WA) ***463***
Peru State Coll (NE) ***469***
Pikeville Coll (KY) ***470***
Pillsbury Baptist Bible Coll (MN) ***470***
Pittsburg State U (KS) ***470***
Pontifical Catholic U of Puerto Rico (PR) ***472***
Prescott Coll (AZ) ***474***
Purdue U Calumet (IN) ***475***
Queen's U at Kingston (ON, Canada) ***476***

SCIENCE EDUCATION (continued)

Rensselaer Polytechnic Inst (NY) 478
Rhode Island Coll (RI) 479
Rider U (NJ) 480
Rockford Coll (IL) 482
Rocky Mountain Coll (MT) 482
Rowan U (NJ) 484
Saginaw Valley State U (MI) 486
St. Ambrose U (IA) 486
St. Cloud State U (MN) 488
Saint Francis U (PA) 488
St. John Fisher Coll (NY) 489
St. John's U (NY) 490
Saint Joseph's Coll of Maine (ME) 491
Saint Mary's U of Minnesota (MN) 494
Samford U (AL) 497
San Diego State U (CA) 498
Seattle Pacific U (WA) 501
Seton Hill U (PA) 502
Shawnee State U (OH) 502
Shorter Coll (GA) 504
Si Tanka Huron U (SD) 505
Slippery Rock U of Pennsylvania (PA) 506
Southeastern Coll of the Assemblies of God (FL) 507
Southeastern Louisiana U (LA) 508
Southeastern Oklahoma State U (OK) 508
Southeast Missouri State U (MO) 508
Southern Arkansas U–Magnolia (AR) 509
Southern Connecticut State U (CT) 509
Southern Illinois U Edwardsville (IL) 509
Southwestern Coll (KS) 512
Southwestern Oklahoma State U (OK) 512
Southwest Missouri State U (MO) 513
Springfield Coll (MA) 514
State U of NY at Albany (NY) 514
State U of NY at New Paltz (NY) 515
State U of NY at Oswego (NY) 515
State U of NY Coll at Buffalo (NY) 516
State U of NY Coll at Cortland (NY) 516
State U of NY Coll at Fredonia (NY) 516
State U of NY Coll at Old Westbury (NY) 516
State U of NY Coll at Oneonta (NY) 517
State U of NY Coll at Potsdam (NY) 517
State U of NY Coll of Environ Sci and Forestry (NY) 517
State U of West Georgia (GA) 518
Syracuse U (NY) 521
Tabor Coll (KS) 522
Talladega Coll (AL) 522
Tarleton State U (TX) 522
Taylor U (IN) 523
Temple U (PA) 523
Tennessee Temple U (TN) 524
Texas A&M International U (TX) 524
Texas Christian U (TX) 526
Texas Wesleyan U (TX) 526
Toccoa Falls Coll (GA) 528
Trinity Christian Coll (IL) 530
Tri-State U (IN) 532
Troy State U (AL) 532
Troy State U Dothan (AL) 532
Union U (TN) 534
The U of Akron (OH) 537
U of Alberta (AB, Canada) 538
The U of Arizona (AZ) 538
The U of British Columbia (BC, Canada) 540
U of Central Arkansas (AR) 542
U of Central Florida (FL) 542
U of Central Oklahoma (OK) 542
U of Charleston (WV) 542
U of Dayton (OH) 544
U of Delaware (DE) 544
U of Evansville (IN) 545
The U of Findlay (OH) 545
U of Georgia (GA) 545
U of Great Falls (MT) 545
U of Hawaii at Manoa (HI) 546
U of Illinois at Chicago (IL) 547
U of Indianapolis (IN) 548
The U of Iowa (IA) 548
U of Kentucky (KY) 549
The U of Lethbridge (AB, Canada) 549
U of Maine at Farmington (ME) 550
U of Maine at Presque Isle (ME) 551
U of Manitoba (MB, Canada) 551
U of Maryland, Coll Park (MD) 552
U of Michigan–Dearborn (MI) 554
U of Minnesota, Duluth (MN) 554
U of Minnesota, Twin Cities Campus (MN) 555
U of Mississippi (MS) 555
U of Missouri–Columbia (MO) 555
U of Missouri–St. Louis (MO) 556
The U of Montana–Missoula (MT) 556
The U of Montana–Western (MT) 556
U of Nebraska–Lincoln (NE) 557
U of Nevada, Reno (NV) 558
U of New Brunswick Fredericton (NB, Canada) 558
U of New England (ME) 558
U of New Hampshire (NH) 558
U of New Orleans (LA) 559
The U of North Carolina at Pembroke (NC) 560
U of North Dakota (ND) 561
U of Northern Iowa (IA) 561
U of North Florida (FL) 561
U of North Texas (TX) 562
U of Notre Dame (IN) 562
U of Oklahoma (OK) 562
U of Pittsburgh at Johnstown (PA) 570
U of Puerto Rico, Cayey U Coll (PR) 571
U of Regina (SK, Canada) 572
U of Rio Grande (OH) 572
U of Saint Francis (IN) 573
U of St. Thomas (MN) 573
U of Sioux Falls (SD) 574
The U of South Dakota (SD) 575
U of South Florida (FL) 576
The U of Tennessee at Chattanooga (TN) 577
The U of Tennessee at Martin (TN) 577
U of the Ozarks (AR) 580
U of the Sciences in Philadelphia (PA) 580
U of Toledo (OH) 581
U of Utah (UT) 582
U of Vermont (VT) 582
U of Washington (WA) 583
U of West Florida (FL) 583
U of Windsor (ON, Canada) 584
U of Wisconsin–Eau Claire (WI) 584
U of Wisconsin–La Crosse (WI) 584
U of Wisconsin–Madison (WI) 584
U of Wisconsin–Platteville (WI) 585
U of Wisconsin–River Falls (WI) 585
U of Wisconsin–Superior (WI) 586
Upper Iowa U (IA) 587
Urbana U (OH) 587
Ursuline Coll (OH) 587
Utah State U (UT) 587
Valley City State U (ND) 588
Villa Julie Coll (MD) 590
Virginia Wesleyan Coll (VA) 591
Viterbo U (WI) 591
Walsh U (OH) 593
Warner Pacific Coll (OR) 593
Warner Southern Coll (FL) 593
Washington U in St. Louis (MO) 595
Wayne State Coll (NE) 596
Wayne State U (MI) 596
Weber State U (UT) 596
West Chester U of Pennsylvania (PA) 598
Western Carolina U (NC) 598
Western Kentucky U (KY) 599
Western New Mexico U (NM) 600
Western State Coll of Colorado (CO) 600
Western Washington U (WA) 600
Westfield State Coll (MA) 600
West Virginia State Coll (WV) 602
Wheeling Jesuit U (WV) 603
Wichita State U (KS) 604
Widener U (PA) 604
William Penn U (IA) 606
William Woods U (MO) 607
Wilmington Coll (OH) 607
Wingate U (NC) 607
Winona State U (MN) 608
Wittenberg U (OH) 608
Wright State U (OH) 609
Xavier U (OH) 610
Xavier U of Louisiana (LA) 610
York Coll (NE) 610
York Coll of Pennsylvania (PA) 610
York U (ON, Canada) 611
Youngstown State U (OH) 611

SCIENCE TECHNOLOGIES RELATED

Information can be found under this major's main heading.

Arizona State U East (AZ) 271
Athens State U (AL) 275
Clemson U (SC) 317
Northern Arizona U (AZ) 450
U of Wisconsin–Stout (WI) 586

SCIENCE/TECHNOLOGY AND SOCIETY

Overview: Students will study the effects of science and technology on contemporary, social, and ethical issues, and how science, technology, and engineering affect public policy. *Related majors:* philosophy, history and philosophy of science and technology, law and legal studies, American government and politics, sociology. *Potential careers:* journalist/writer, editor, ethicist, lawyer, environmentalist, ecologist. *Salary potential:* $25k-$30k.

Columbia Coll (SC) 327
Cornell U (NY) 333
Georgetown U (DC) 366
Georgia Inst of Technology (GA) 367
Grinnell Coll (IA) 373
James Madison U (VA) 391
Lehigh U (PA) 404
Massachusetts Inst of Technology (MA) 421
New Jersey Inst of Technology (NJ) 445
Pitzer Coll (CA) 471
Rensselaer Polytechnic Inst (NY) 478
Rutgers, The State U of New Jersey, Newark (NJ) 485
Samford U (AL) 497
Scripps Coll (CA) 501
Slippery Rock U of Pennsylvania (PA) 506
Stanford U (CA) 514
Texas Southern U (TX) 526
U of Alaska Anchorage (AK) 538
U of Nevada, Reno (NV) 558
U of Windsor (ON, Canada) 584
Vassar Coll (NY) 589
Virginia Wesleyan Coll (VA) 591
Washington U in St. Louis (MO) 595
Wesleyan U (CT) 597
Worcester Polytechnic Inst (MA) 609
York U (ON, Canada) 611

SCULPTURE

Overview: This major teaches students the theories and artistic skills and techniques of sculpture. *Related majors:* fine arts, drawing, ceramics arts, metal and jewelry arts, art history. *Potential careers:* fine artist, set designer, product or product packaging designer, furniture designer, welder. *Salary potential:* $15k-$30k.

Academy of Art Coll (CA) 260
Adams State Coll (CO) 260
Alberta Coll of Art & Design (AB, Canada) 262
Alfred U (NY) 263
Antioch Coll (OH) 269
Aquinas Coll (MI) 270
Arizona State U (AZ) 271
Art Academy of Cincinnati (OH) 273
Atlanta Coll of Art (GA) 275
Ball State U (IN) 280
Bard Coll (NY) 281
Bellarmine U (KY) 284
Bennington Coll (VT) 286
Bethany Coll (KS) 287
Birmingham-Southern Coll (AL) 289
Boston U (MA) 292
Bowling Green State U (OH) 292
California Coll of Arts and Crafts (CA) 299
California Inst of the Arts (CA) 299
California State U, Fullerton (CA) 301
California State U, Hayward (CA) 301
California State U, Long Beach (CA) 301
California State U, Northridge (CA) 301
California State U, Stanislaus (CA) 302
Carnegie Mellon U (PA) 305
The Catholic U of America (DC) 307
The Cleveland Inst of Art (OH) 317
Col for Creative Studies (MI) 319
Coll of Santa Fe (NM) 323
Coll of Visual Arts (MN) 324
Colorado State U (CO) 325
Columbus Coll of Art and Design (OH) 328
Concordia U (QC, Canada) 331
Corcoran Coll of Art and Design (DC) 332
Cornell U (NY) 333
DePaul U (IL) 339
Drake U (IA) 345
Eastern Kentucky U (KY) 348
Escuela de Artes Plasticas de Puerto Rico (PR) 354
Framingham State Coll (MA) 362
Goddard Coll (VT) 369
Grand Valley State U (MI) 371
Hampshire Coll (MA) 375
Indiana U Bloomington (IN) 385
Inter American U of PR, San Germán Campus (PR) 388
Kansas City Art Inst (MO) 395
Long Island U, Southampton Coll, Friends World Program (NY) 409
Longwood U (VA) 409
LymeAcademy Coll of Fine Arts (CT) 412
Maharishi U of Management (IA) 414
Maine Coll of Art (ME) 415
Marlboro Coll (VT) 418
Maryland Inst Coll of Art (MD) 419
Massachusetts Coll of Art (MA) 421
Memorial U of Newfoundland (NF, Canada) 424
Memphis Coll of Art (TN) 425
Mercyhurst Coll (PA) 425
Milwaukee Inst of Art and Design (WI) 431
Minneapolis Coll of Art and Design (MN) 431
Minnesota State U, Mankato (MN) 431
Minnesota State U, Moorhead (MN) 432
Montserrat Coll of Art (MA) 435
Moore Coll of Art and Design (PA) 436
Mount Allison U (NB, Canada) 437
New World School of the Arts (FL) 447
New York U (NY) 447
Northern Michigan U (MI) 451
Northwest Missouri State U (MO) 454
Nova Scotia Coll of Art and Design (NS, Canada) 455
The Ohio State U (OH) 457
Ohio U (OH) 458
Otis Coll of Art and Design (CA) 462
Pacific Northwest Coll of Art (OR) 464
Parsons School of Design, New School U (NY) 465
Portland State U (OR) 472
Pratt Inst (NY) 473
Rhode Island School of Design (RI) 479
Rochester Inst of Technology (NY) 482
Rocky Mountain Coll of Art & Design (CO) 483
Rutgers, The State U of New Jersey, New Brunswick (NJ) 485
San Diego State U (CA) 498
San Francisco Art Inst (CA) 498
Sarah Lawrence Coll (NY) 499
School of the Art Inst of Chicago (IL) 500
School of the Museum of Fine Arts (MA) 501
School of Visual Arts (NY) 501
Seton Hill U (PA) 502
Simon's Rock Coll of Bard (MA) 505
Sonoma State U (CA) 506
State U of NY at New Paltz (NY) 515
State U of NY Coll at Brockport (NY) 515
State U of NY Coll at Buffalo (NY) 516
State U of NY Coll at Potsdam (NY) 517
Syracuse U (NY) 521
Temple U (PA) 523
Texas A&M U–Commerce (TX) 525
Texas Christian U (TX) 526
Texas Woman's U (TX) 527
Trinity Christian Coll (IL) 530
The U of Akron (OH) 537
U of Alberta (AB, Canada) 538
U of Calif, Santa Cruz (CA) 542
U of Dallas (TX) 544
U of Evansville (IN) 545
U of Hartford (CT) 546
U of Houston (TX) 547
U of Illinois at Urbana–Champaign (IL) 548
The U of Iowa (IA) 548
U of Kansas (KS) 549
U of Massachusetts Dartmouth (MA) 553
U of Miami (FL) 553
U of Michigan (MI) 554
U of Montevallo (AL) 557
The U of North Carolina at Greensboro (NC) 560
U of North Texas (TX) 562
U of Oklahoma (OK) 562
U of Oregon (OR) 562

U of Puerto Rico, Río Piedras (PR) **571**
The U of South Dakota (SD) **575**
The U of Tennessee at Chattanooga (TN) **577**
The U of Texas at El Paso (TX) **578**
The U of the Arts (PA) **579**
U of Washington (WA) **583**
U of Windsor (ON, Canada) **584**
U of Wisconsin–Milwaukee (WI) **585**
Virginia Commonwealth U (VA) **590**
Washington U in St. Louis (MO) **595**
Webster U (MO) **597**
Western Michigan U (MI) **599**
Wittenberg U (OH) **608**
York U (ON, Canada) **611**

SECONDARY EDUCATION

Overview: undergraduates learn the skills necessary to teach secondary school students (usually grades 7-12, depending on the school system). This major may require candidates to teach a generalized curriculum or a specific subject, such as math, English, science, history, or a particular foreign language. *Related majors:* education, math, science, English or foreign language teacher education. *Potential careers:* junior high or high school teacher, school administrator, student counselor. *Salary potential:* $24k-$34k.

Abilene Christian U (TX) **260**
Acadia U (NS, Canada) **260**
Adams State Coll (CO) **260**
Adrian Coll (MI) **260**
Alabama A&M U (AL) **261**
Alabama State U (AL) **261**
Albion Coll (MI) **262**
Albright Coll (PA) **263**
Alcorn State U (MS) **263**
Alderson-Broaddus Coll (WV) **263**
Alfred U (NY) **263**
Alice Lloyd Coll (KY) **263**
Alma Coll (MI) **264**
Alverno Coll (WI) **265**
American International Coll (MA) **267**
American U (DC) **267**
Anderson Coll (SC) **268**
Andrews U (MI) **269**
Antioch Coll (OH) **269**
Aquinas Coll (MI) **270**
Arcadia U (PA) **271**
Arizona State U (AZ) **271**
Arizona State U West (AZ) **272**
Arkansas Baptist Coll (AR) **272**
Armstrong Atlantic State U (GA) **273**
Ashland U (OH) **274**
Assumption Coll (MA) **275**
Athens State U (AL) **275**
Atlantic Union Coll (MA) **276**
Auburn U (AL) **276**
Auburn U Montgomery (AL) **276**
Augsburg Coll (MN) **276**
Augustana Coll (IL) **276**
Augustana Coll (SD) **276**
Baldwin-Wallace Coll (OH) **280**
Ball State U (IN) **280**
Barton Coll (NC) **282**
Baylor U (TX) **283**
Bellarmine U (KY) **284**
Belmont Abbey Coll (NC) **284**
Beloit Coll (WI) **285**
Bemidji State U (MN) **285**
Benedictine Coll (KS) **285**
Benedictine U (IL) **285**
Berea Coll (KY) **286**
Berry Coll (GA) **287**
Bethel Coll (MN) **288**
Biola U (CA) **289**
Birmingham-Southern Coll (AL) **289**
Blackburn Coll (IL) **290**
Bloomsburg U of Pennsylvania (PA) **290**
Bluefield Coll (VA) **291**
Bluffton Coll (OH) **291**
Boston Coll (MA) **292**
Bowie State U (MD) **292**
Bowling Green State U (OH) **292**
Brandon U (MB, Canada) **293**
Brescia U (KY) **293**
Brewton-Parker Coll (GA) **294**
Briar Cliff U (IA) **294**
Bridgewater Coll (VA) **294**
Brigham Young U–Hawaii (HI) **295**
Brock U (ON, Canada) **295**
Brooklyn Coll of the City U of NY (NY) **295**
Bryan Coll (TN) **296**
Bucknell U (PA) **297**
Buena Vista U (IA) **297**
Butler U (IN) **297**
Calumet Coll of Saint Joseph (IN) **302**
Calvin Coll (MI) **303**
Campbellsville U (KY) **303**
Campbell U (NC) **303**
Canisius Coll (NY) **304**
Capital U (OH) **304**
Cardinal Stritch U (WI) **305**
Carroll Coll (MT) **306**
Carson-Newman Coll (TN) **306**
Carthage Coll (WI) **306**
Catawba Coll (NC) **307**
The Catholic U of America (DC) **307**
Cedar Crest Coll (PA) **308**
Cedarville U (OH) **308**
Centenary Coll (NJ) **308**
Centenary Coll of Louisiana (LA) **308**
Central Coll (IA) **309**
Central Methodist Coll (MO) **309**
Central Missouri State U (MO) **310**
Centre Coll (KY) **310**
Chadron State Coll (NE) **311**
Charleston Southern U (SC) **311**
Cheyney U of Pennsylvania (PA) **312**
Christian Heritage Coll (CA) **313**
Christopher Newport U (VA) **313**
City Coll of the City U of NY (NY) **314**
Clark Atlanta U (GA) **315**
Clarke Coll (IA) **315**
Clark U (MA) **316**
Clearwater Christian Coll (FL) **316**
Clemson U (SC) **317**
Coastal Carolina U (SC) **318**
Coe Coll (IA) **318**
Coker Coll (SC) **318**
Coll Misericordia (PA) **319**
Coll of Mount Saint Vincent (NY) **320**
The Coll of New Jersey (NJ) **320**
The Coll of New Rochelle (NY) **321**
Coll of Saint Benedict (MN) **321**
Coll of St. Catherine (MN) **321**
Coll of St. Joseph (VT) **322**
Coll of Saint Mary (NE) **322**
Coll of Santa Fe (NM) **323**
Coll of the Atlantic (ME) **323**
Coll of the Ozarks (MO) **323**
Coll of the Southwest (NM) **324**
Colorado State U-Pueblo (CO) **325**
Columbia Coll (MO) **326**
Columbia Coll (SC) **327**
Columbus State U (GA) **328**
Concord Coll (WV) **329**
Concordia Coll (MN) **329**
Concordia Coll (NY) **329**
Concordia U (CA) **330**
Concordia U (IL) **330**
Concordia U (MI) **330**
Concordia U (MN) **330**
Concordia U (NE) **330**
Concordia U (OR) **330**
Concordia U at Austin (TX) **331**
Concordia U Wisconsin (WI) **331**
Converse Coll (SC) **332**
Cornell Coll (IA) **332**
Cornerstone U (MI) **333**
Crichton Coll (TN) **334**
Cumberland U (TN) **335**
Dakota State U (SD) **335**
Dallas Baptist U (TX) **336**
Dana Coll (NE) **337**
Davis & Elkins Coll (WV) **338**
Defiance Coll (OH) **338**
Delaware Valley Coll (PA) **339**
Delta State U (MS) **339**
DePaul U (IL) **339**
DeSales U (PA) **340**
Dickinson State U (ND) **344**
Dillard U (LA) **344**
Doane Coll (NE) **344**
Dominican Coll (NY) **344**
Dordt Coll (IA) **345**
Dowling Coll (NY) **345**
Drake U (IA) **345**
Drury U (MO) **346**
Duquesne U (PA) **346**
D'Youville Coll (NY) **347**
East Central U (OK) **347**
Eastern Kentucky U (KY) **348**
Eastern Mennonite U (VA) **348**
Eastern Michigan U (MI) **348**
Eastern Nazarene Coll (MA) **348**
Eastern U (PA) **349**
Eastern Washington U (WA) **349**
East Stroudsburg U of Pennsylvania (PA) **349**
East Texas Baptist U (TX) **350**
Elizabeth City State U (NC) **351**
Elizabethtown Coll (PA) **351**
Elmhurst Coll (IL) **351**
Elmira Coll (NY) **351**
Elms Coll (MA) **352**
Elon U (NC) **352**
Emmanuel Coll (MA) **353**
Emory U (GA) **354**
Emporia State U (KS) **354**
Eureka Coll (IL) **355**
Evangel U (MO) **355**
Fairfield U (CT) **356**
Fairmont State Coll (WV) **356**
Faulkner U (AL) **357**
Ferris State U (MI) **358**
Fitchburg State Coll (MA) **358**
Flagler Coll (FL) **359**
Florida Southern Coll (FL) **361**
Florida State U (FL) **361**
Fontbonne U (MO) **361**
Fordham U (NY) **362**
Fort Lewis Coll (CO) **362**
Framingham State Coll (MA) **362**
The Franciscan U (IA) **363**
Franklin Pierce Coll (NH) **364**
Freed-Hardeman U (TN) **364**
Free Will Baptist Bible Coll (TN) **364**
Fresno Pacific U (CA) **364**
Frostburg State U (MD) **365**
Furman U (SC) **365**
Gallaudet U (DC) **365**
Gannon U (PA) **365**
Gardner-Webb U (NC) **365**
Geneva Coll (PA) **366**
Georgetown Coll (KY) **366**
Georgia Southwestern State U (GA) **368**
Gettysburg Coll (PA) **368**
Glenville State Coll (WV) **368**
Goddard Coll (VT) **369**
Gonzaga U (WA) **369**
Goshen Coll (IN) **370**
Grace Bible Coll (MI) **370**
Graceland U (IA) **371**
Grace U (NE) **371**
Grambling State U (LA) **371**
Grand Canyon U (AZ) **371**
Grand Valley State U (MI) **371**
Grand View Coll (IA) **372**
Green Mountain Coll (VT) **372**
Greensboro Coll (NC) **372**
Greenville Coll (IL) **373**
Grove City Coll (PA) **373**
Guilford Coll (NC) **373**
Gustavus Adolphus Coll (MN) **374**
Gwynedd-Mercy Coll (PA) **374**
Hamline U (MN) **374**
Hampshire Coll (MA) **375**
Hampton U (VA) **375**
Hannibal-LaGrange Coll (MO) **375**
Hardin-Simmons U (TX) **376**
Harris-Stowe State Coll (MO) **376**
Hastings Coll (NE) **377**
Heidelberg Coll (OH) **377**
High Point U (NC) **379**
Hillsdale Coll (MI) **379**
Hiram Coll (OH) **379**
Hofstra U (NY) **380**
Holy Family U (PA) **380**
Hope Coll (MI) **381**
Houghton Coll (NY) **381**
Houston Baptist U (TX) **382**
Howard Payne U (TX) **382**
Humboldt State U (CA) **382**
Hunter Coll of the City U of NY (NY) **382**
Huntingdon Coll (AL) **383**
Huntington Coll (IN) **383**
Huston-Tillotson Coll (TX) **383**
Idaho State U (ID) **384**
Illinois Coll (IL) **384**
Illinois Wesleyan U (IL) **385**
Immaculata U (PA) **385**
Indiana U Bloomington (IN) **385**
Indiana U East (IN) **386**
Indiana U Northwest (IN) **386**
Indiana U of Pennsylvania (PA) **386**
Indiana U–Purdue U Fort Wayne (IN) **386**
Indiana U–Purdue U Indianapolis (IN) **387**
Indiana U South Bend (IN) **387**
Indiana U Southeast (IN) **387**
Indiana Wesleyan U (IN) **387**
Inter Amer U of PR, Barranquitas Campus (PR) **388**
Inter American U of PR, San Germán Campus (PR) **388**
Iona Coll (NY) **390**
Iowa State U of Science and Technology (IA) **390**
Iowa Wesleyan Coll (IA) **390**
Ithaca Coll (NY) **390**
Jackson State U (MS) **390**
Jacksonville State U (AL) **390**
Jacksonville U (FL) **391**
John Brown U (AR) **392**
John Carroll U (OH) **392**
Johnson C. Smith U (NC) **394**
Johnson State Coll (VT) **394**
Judson Coll (AL) **395**
Judson Coll (IL) **395**
Juniata Coll (PA) **395**
Kansas State U (KS) **396**
Keene State Coll (NH) **396**
Kennesaw State U (GA) **397**
Kentucky State U (KY) **397**
Kentucky Wesleyan Coll (KY) **397**
King Coll (TN) **398**
King's Coll (PA) **398**
Kutztown U of Pennsylvania (PA) **399**
LaGrange Coll (GA) **400**
Lake Forest Coll (IL) **400**
Lakehead U (ON, Canada) **400**
Lakeland Coll (WI) **401**
Lamar U (TX) **401**
Lambuth U (TN) **401**
Langston U (OK) **402**
La Salle U (PA) **402**
La Sierra U (CA) **403**
Lawrence U (WI) **403**
Lebanon Valley Coll (PA) **403**
Lee U (TN) **404**
Le Moyne Coll (NY) **404**
Lenoir-Rhyne Coll (NC) **405**
LeTourneau U (TX) **405**
Lewis U (IL) **406**
Liberty U (VA) **406**
Lincoln Christian Coll (IL) **407**
Lincoln Memorial U (TN) **407**
Lindenwood U (MO) **407**
Lipscomb U (TN) **408**
Lock Haven U of Pennsylvania (PA) **408**
Long Island U, Brooklyn Campus (NY) **409**
Long Island U, C.W. Post Campus (NY) **409**
Long Island U, Southampton Coll, Friends World Program (NY) **409**
Longwood U (VA) **409**
Loras Coll (IA) **410**
Louisiana Coll (LA) **410**
Louisiana State U and A&M Coll (LA) **410**
Louisiana Tech U (LA) **410**
Lubbock Christian U (TX) **412**
Luther Coll (IA) **412**
Lycoming Coll (PA) **412**
Lynchburg Coll (VA) **413**
Lynn U (FL) **413**
MacMurray Coll (IL) **414**
Madonna U (MI) **414**
Manchester Coll (IN) **415**
Manhattanville Coll (NY) **416**
Mansfield U of Pennsylvania (PA) **416**
Maranatha Baptist Bible Coll (WI) **417**
Marian Coll (IN) **417**
Marian Coll of Fond du Lac (WI) **417**
Marietta Coll (OH) **417**
Marist Coll (NY) **417**
Marquette U (WI) **418**
Marshall U (WV) **418**
Mars Hill Coll (NC) **418**
Martin U (IN) **419**
Marymount Coll of Fordham U (NY) **419**
Maryville U of Saint Louis (MO) **420**
Mary Washington Coll (VA) **420**
Marywood U (PA) **421**
Massachusetts Coll of Liberal Arts (MA) **421**
The Master's Coll and Seminary (CA) **422**
McGill U (QC, Canada) **423**
McKendree Coll (IL) **423**
McNeese State U (LA) **423**
McPherson Coll (KS) **423**

SECONDARY EDUCATION (continued)

Memorial U of Newfoundland (NF, Canada) ***424***
Mercy Coll (NY) ***425***
Mercyhurst Coll (PA) ***425***
Merrimack Coll (MA) ***426***
Mesa State Coll (CO) ***426***
Methodist Coll (NC) ***427***
Miami U (OH) ***428***
Michigan Technological U (MI) ***428***
MidAmerica Nazarene U (KS) ***428***
Middlebury Coll (VT) ***429***
Midland Lutheran Coll (NE) ***429***
Midwestern State U (TX) ***430***
Milligan Coll (TN) ***430***
Minnesota State U, Mankato (MN) ***431***
Minnesota State U, Moorhead (MN) ***432***
Mississippi State U (MS) ***432***
Missouri Southern State Coll (MO) ***433***
Missouri Valley Coll (MO) ***433***
Molloy Coll (NY) ***433***
Monmouth Coll (IL) ***434***
Monmouth U (NJ) ***434***
Montana State U–Billings (MT) ***434***
Montana State U–Bozeman (MT) ***434***
Montana State U–Northern (MT) ***434***
Montreat Coll (NC) ***435***
Moravian Coll (PA) ***436***
Morehouse Coll (GA) ***436***
Morgan State U (MD) ***436***
Morningside Coll (IA) ***437***
Morris Coll (SC) ***437***
Mount Marty Coll (SD) ***438***
Mount Mary Coll (WI) ***438***
Mount Mercy Coll (IA) ***438***
Mount Saint Mary Coll (NY) ***439***
Mount St. Mary's Coll (CA) ***439***
Mount Saint Mary's Coll and Seminary (MD) ***439***
Mount Saint Vincent U (NS, Canada) ***439***
Mount Vernon Nazarene U (OH) ***440***
Muhlenberg Coll (PA) ***440***
Muskingum Coll (OH) ***441***
Nazareth Coll of Rochester (NY) ***443***
Nebraska Christian Coll (NE) ***443***
Newberry Coll (SC) ***444***
New England Coll (NH) ***444***
Newman U (KS) ***445***
New Mexico Highlands U (NM) ***446***
New Mexico State U (NM) ***446***
New York U (NY) ***447***
Niagara U (NY) ***447***
Nicholls State U (LA) ***447***
Nichols Coll (MA) ***448***
North Carolina State U (NC) ***449***
North Carolina Wesleyan Coll (NC) ***449***
North Central Coll (IL) ***449***
North Dakota State U (ND) ***449***
Northeastern State U (OK) ***450***
Northern Michigan U (MI) ***451***
Northern State U (SD) ***451***
North Georgia Coll & State U (GA) ***451***
Northland Coll (WI) ***452***
North Park U (IL) ***452***
Northwest Coll (WA) ***452***
Northwestern Coll (IA) ***453***
Northwestern Oklahoma State U (OK) ***453***
Northwestern State U of Louisiana (LA) ***453***
Northwestern U (IL) ***453***
Northwest Missouri State U (MO) ***454***
Northwest Nazarene U (ID) ***454***
Notre Dame Coll (OH) ***455***
Notre Dame de Namur U (CA) ***455***
Nova Southeastern U (FL) ***455***
Nyack Coll (NY) ***456***
Oakland City U (IN) ***456***
Oakland U (MI) ***456***
Oglethorpe U (GA) ***457***
Ohio Dominican U (OH) ***457***
Ohio U (OH) ***458***
Ohio Valley Coll (WV) ***459***
Ohio Wesleyan U (OH) ***459***
Oklahoma Baptist U (OK) ***459***
Oklahoma Christian U (OK) ***459***
Oklahoma City U (OK) ***460***
Oklahoma Panhandle State U (OK) ***460***
Oklahoma State U (OK) ***460***
Oklahoma Wesleyan U (OK) ***460***
Olivet Coll (MI) ***461***
Olivet Nazarene U (IL) ***461***
Otterbein Coll (OH) ***462***
Ouachita Baptist U (AR) ***462***
Our Lady of Holy Cross Coll (LA) ***463***
Pacific Lutheran U (WA) ***463***
Pacific U (OR) ***464***
Paine Coll (GA) ***465***
Palm Beach Atlantic U (FL) ***465***
Paul Quinn Coll (TX) ***466***
Penn State U Univ Park Campus (PA) ***468***
Pepperdine U, Malibu (CA) ***469***
Peru State Coll (NE) ***469***
Piedmont Baptist Coll (NC) ***470***
Piedmont Coll (GA) ***470***
Pillsbury Baptist Bible Coll (MN) ***470***
Pine Manor Coll (MA) ***470***
Pittsburg State U (KS) ***470***
Plattsburgh State U of NY (NY) ***471***
Point Park Coll (PA) ***471***
Pontifical Catholic U of Puerto Rico (PR) ***472***
Prescott Coll (AZ) ***474***
Principia Coll (IL) ***474***
Providence Coll (RI) ***474***
Purdue U Calumet (IN) ***475***
Queens Coll of the City U of NY (NY) ***475***
Queen's U at Kingston (ON, Canada) ***476***
Queens U of Charlotte (NC) ***476***
Reformed Bible Coll (MI) ***477***
Rhode Island Coll (RI) ***479***
Rider U (NJ) ***480***
Ripon Coll (WI) ***480***
Rivier Coll (NH) ***480***
Roberts Wesleyan Coll (NY) ***481***
Rockhurst U (MO) ***482***
Rocky Mountain Coll (MT) ***482***
Roger Williams U (RI) ***483***
Roosevelt U (IL) ***483***
Rowan U (NJ) ***484***
Sacred Heart U (CT) ***486***
St. Ambrose U (IA) ***486***
Saint Anselm Coll (NH) ***487***
St. Bonaventure U (NY) ***487***
St. Cloud State U (MN) ***488***
St. Francis Coll (NY) ***488***
Saint Francis U (PA) ***488***
St. Francis Xavier U (NS, Canada) ***489***
Saint John's U (MN) ***490***
St. John's U (NY) ***490***
Saint Joseph Coll (CT) ***490***
Saint Joseph's Coll (IN) ***490***
St. Joseph's Coll, Suffolk Campus (NY) ***491***
Saint Joseph's U (PA) ***491***
Saint Leo U (FL) ***492***
Saint Martin's Coll (WA) ***493***
Saint Mary-of-the-Woods Coll (IN) ***493***
Saint Mary's Coll of California (CA) ***494***
Saint Michael's Coll (VT) ***494***
St. Thomas Aquinas Coll (NY) ***495***
St. Thomas U (FL) ***496***
Salem International U (WV) ***496***
Salisbury U (MD) ***497***
Salve Regina U (RI) ***497***
Seton Hall U (NJ) ***502***
Seton Hill U (PA) ***502***
Shawnee State U (OH) ***502***
Sheldon Jackson Coll (AK) ***503***
Shepherd Coll (WV) ***503***
Shorter Coll (GA) ***504***
Siena Coll (NY) ***504***
Siena Heights U (MI) ***504***
Simmons Coll (MA) ***504***
Simpson Coll (IA) ***505***
Simpson Coll and Graduate School (CA) ***505***
Si Tanka Huron U (SD) ***505***
Slippery Rock U of Pennsylvania (PA) ***506***
South Dakota State U (SD) ***507***
Southeastern Bible Coll (AL) ***507***
Southeastern Oklahoma State U (OK) ***508***
Southeast Missouri State U (MO) ***508***
Southern Connecticut State U (CT) ***509***
Southern Nazarene U (OK) ***510***
Southern New Hampshire U (NH) ***510***
Southern U and A&M Coll (LA) ***511***
Southern Utah U (UT) ***511***
Southwest Baptist U (MO) ***512***
Southwestern Assemblies of God U (TX) ***512***
Southwestern Oklahoma State U (OK) ***512***
Southwest State U (MN) ***513***
Spalding U (KY) ***513***
Spring Arbor U (MI) ***514***
Springfield Coll (MA) ***514***
Spring Hill Coll (AL) ***514***
State U of NY at New Paltz (NY) ***515***
State U of NY at Oswego (NY) ***515***
State U of NY Coll at Brockport (NY) ***515***
State U of NY Coll at Buffalo (NY) ***516***
State U of NY Coll at Cortland (NY) ***516***
State U of NY Coll at Fredonia (NY) ***516***
State U of NY Coll at Old Westbury (NY) ***516***
State U of NY Coll at Oneonta (NY) ***517***
State U of West Georgia (GA) ***518***
Stony Brook U, State University of New York (NY) ***520***
Suffolk U (MA) ***520***
Susquehanna U (PA) ***521***
Syracuse U (NY) ***521***
Tabor Coll (KS) ***522***
Taylor U (IN) ***523***
Temple U (PA) ***523***
Tennessee Technological U (TN) ***524***
Tennessee Temple U (TN) ***524***
Tennessee Wesleyan Coll (TN) ***524***
Texas A&M U–Commerce (TX) ***525***
Texas A&M U–Kingsville (TX) ***525***
Texas Christian U (TX) ***526***
Texas Southern U (TX) ***526***
Thiel Coll (PA) ***527***
Toccoa Falls Coll (GA) ***528***
Trent U (ON, Canada) ***529***
Trevecca Nazarene U (TN) ***529***
Trinity Baptist Coll (FL) ***530***
Trinity Christian Coll (IL) ***530***
Trinity Coll (DC) ***530***
Trinity International U (IL) ***531***
Trinity Western U (BC, Canada) ***531***
Tri-State U (IN) ***532***
Troy State U (AL) ***532***
Troy State U Dothan (AL) ***532***
Tufts U (MA) ***533***
Tusculum Coll (TN) ***533***
Union Coll (KY) ***533***
Union Coll (NE) ***534***
Union U (TN) ***534***
Universidad Adventista de las Antillas (PR) ***536***
Université de Sherbrooke (QC, Canada) ***536***
U du Québec à Trois-Rivières (QC, Canada) ***536***
U du Québec à Hull (QC, Canada) ***536***
Université Laval (QC, Canada) ***536***
The U of Akron (OH) ***537***
The U of Alabama (AL) ***537***
The U of Alabama at Birmingham (AL) ***537***
U of Alaska Anchorage (AK) ***538***
U of Alberta (AB, Canada) ***538***
The U of Arizona (AZ) ***538***
The U of British Columbia (BC, Canada) ***540***
U of Calgary (AB, Canada) ***540***
U of Central Oklahoma (OK) ***542***
U of Cincinnati (OH) ***543***
U of Dallas (TX) ***544***
U of Dayton (OH) ***544***
U of Delaware (DE) ***544***
U of Evansville (IN) ***545***
The U of Findlay (OH) ***545***
U of Great Falls (MT) ***545***
U of Hartford (CT) ***546***
U of Hawaii at Hilo (HI) ***546***
U of Hawaii at Manoa (HI) ***546***
U of Idaho (ID) ***547***
U of Illinois at Chicago (IL) ***547***
U of Illinois at Springfield (IL) ***548***
U of Indianapolis (IN) ***548***
The U of Iowa (IA) ***548***
U of Kansas (KS) ***549***
U of La Verne (CA) ***549***
U of Louisiana at Lafayette (LA) ***550***
U of Maine (ME) ***550***
U of Maine at Farmington (ME) ***550***
U of Maine at Presque Isle (ME) ***551***
U of Manitoba (MB, Canada) ***551***
U of Mary Hardin-Baylor (TX) ***551***
U of Maryland, Coll Park (MD) ***552***
U of Miami (FL) ***553***
U of Michigan (MI) ***554***
U of Michigan–Dearborn (MI) ***554***
U of Michigan–Flint (MI) ***554***
U of Minnesota, Morris (MN) ***555***
U of Mississippi (MS) ***555***
U of Missouri–Kansas City (MO) ***555***
U of Missouri–Rolla (MO) ***556***
U of Missouri–St. Louis (MO) ***556***
U of Mobile (AL) ***556***
The U of Montana–Missoula (MT) ***556***
The U of Montana–Western (MT) ***556***
U of Nebraska at Omaha (NE) ***557***
U of Nevada, Las Vegas (NV) ***558***
U of New Brunswick Fredericton (NB, Canada) ***558***
U of New England (ME) ***558***
U of New Mexico (NM) ***559***
U of New Orleans (LA) ***559***
U of North Alabama (AL) ***559***
The U of North Carolina at Pembroke (NC) ***560***
U of North Florida (FL) ***561***
U of North Texas (TX) ***562***
U of Ottawa (ON, Canada) ***563***
U of Pittsburgh at Johnstown (PA) ***570***
U of Portland (OR) ***570***
U of Prince Edward Island (PE, Canada) ***570***
U of Puerto Rico, Cayey U Coll (PR) ***571***
U of Puerto Rico, Río Piedras (PR) ***571***
U of Redlands (CA) ***572***
U of Regina (SK, Canada) ***572***
U of Rhode Island (RI) ***572***
U of Richmond (VA) ***572***
U of Rio Grande (OH) ***572***
U of Saint Francis (IN) ***573***
U of St. Thomas (MN) ***573***
U of St. Thomas (TX) ***573***
U of San Francisco (CA) ***574***
U of Saskatchewan (SK, Canada) ***574***
The U of Scranton (PA) ***574***
U of Sioux Falls (SD) ***574***
U of South Alabama (AL) ***575***
U of South Carolina Aiken (SC) ***575***
U of South Carolina Spartanburg (SC) ***575***
The U of South Dakota (SD) ***575***
The U of Tampa (FL) ***577***
The U of Tennessee at Chattanooga (TN) ***577***
The U of Texas–Pan American (TX) ***579***
U of the Incarnate Word (TX) ***580***
U of the Sacred Heart (PR) ***580***
U of Toledo (OH) ***581***
U of Utah (UT) ***582***
U of Vermont (VT) ***582***
U of Victoria (BC, Canada) ***582***
U of Washington (WA) ***583***
The U of Western Ontario (ON, Canada) ***583***
U of Windsor (ON, Canada) ***584***
U of Wisconsin–La Crosse (WI) ***584***
U of Wisconsin–Madison (WI) ***584***
U of Wisconsin–Milwaukee (WI) ***585***
U of Wisconsin–Oshkosh (WI) ***585***
U of Wisconsin–Platteville (WI) ***585***
U of Wisconsin–River Falls (WI) ***585***
U of Wisconsin–Stevens Point (WI) ***585***
U of Wisconsin–Whitewater (WI) ***586***
U of Wyoming (WY) ***586***
Upper Iowa U (IA) ***587***
Urbana U (OH) ***587***
Ursinus Coll (PA) ***587***
Utah State U (UT) ***587***
Utica Coll (NY) ***588***
Valdosta State U (GA) ***588***
Valley City State U (ND) ***588***
Valparaiso U (IN) ***588***
Vanderbilt U (TN) ***588***
Vanguard U of Southern California (CA) ***589***
Villanova U (PA) ***590***
Virginia Intermont Coll (VA) ***590***
Virginia Wesleyan Coll (VA) ***591***
Wagner Coll (NY) ***592***
Walsh U (OH) ***593***
Warner Pacific Coll (OR) ***593***
Warren Wilson Coll (NC) ***594***
Wartburg Coll (IA) ***594***
Washington State U (WA) ***595***
Washington U in St. Louis (MO) ***595***
Waynesburg Coll (PA) ***595***
Weber State U (UT) ***596***
Webster U (MO) ***597***
Wells Coll (NY) ***597***
Wesley Coll (DE) ***598***
West Chester U of Pennsylvania (PA) ***598***
Western Baptist Coll (OR) ***598***
Western Connecticut State U (CT) ***598***
Western New Mexico U (NM) ***600***
Western Oregon U (OR) ***600***
Western State Coll of Colorado (CO) ***600***
Western Washington U (WA) ***600***
Westfield State Coll (MA) ***600***
West Liberty State Coll (WV) ***601***
Westminster Coll (MO) ***601***
Westmont Coll (CA) ***602***
West Virginia State Coll (WV) ***602***
West Virginia U (WV) ***602***
West Virginia Wesleyan Coll (WV) ***603***
Wheeling Jesuit U (WV) ***603***
Whitworth Coll (WA) ***604***
Wichita State U (KS) ***604***
William Carey Coll (MS) ***605***

William Jewell Coll (MO) ***606***
William Paterson U of New Jersey (NJ) ***606***
William Penn U (IA) ***606***
William Woods U (MO) ***607***
Wilmington Coll (OH) ***607***
Wingate U (NC) ***607***
Winona State U (MN) ***608***
Wittenberg U (OH) ***608***
Wright State U (OH) ***609***
Xavier U of Louisiana (LA) ***610***
York Coll (NE) ***610***
York Coll of Pennsylvania (PA) ***610***
York U (ON, Canada) ***611***
Youngstown State U (OH) ***611***

SECRETARIAL SCIENCE

Overview: This major teaches students the skills and duties necessary to work as an administrative assistant, secretary, or stenographer. *Related majors:* business communication, general office/clerical, executive assistant/secretary, word processing. *Potential careers:* administrative or executive assistant, secretary, receptionist in a wide range of businesses. *Salary potential:* $23k-$27k.

Alabama State U (AL) ***261***
Albany State U (GA) ***262***
Alcorn State U (MS) ***263***
Allen U (SC) ***264***
American U of Puerto Rico (PR) ***268***
Appalachian State U (NC) ***270***
Arkansas State U (AR) ***272***
Baker Coll of Flint (MI) ***279***
Baker Coll of Muskegon (MI) ***279***
Baker Coll of Owosso (MI) ***279***
Baker Coll of Port Huron (MI) ***280***
Baptist Bible Coll (MO) ***281***
Bayamón Central U (PR) ***283***
Belmont U (TN) ***284***
Benedict Coll (SC) ***285***
Bluefield State Coll (WV) ***291***
California State U, Northridge (CA) ***301***
Campbellsville U (KY) ***303***
Cedarville U (OH) ***308***
Clearwater Christian Coll (FL) ***316***
Davenport U, Kalamazoo (MI) ***337***
Davenport U, Lansing (MI) ***337***
Davis & Elkins Coll (WV) ***338***
East Central U (OK) ***347***
Eastern Kentucky U (KY) ***348***
East-West U (IL) ***350***
Elizabeth City State U (NC) ***351***
Evangel U (MO) ***355***
Florida A&M U (FL) ***359***
Fort Hays State U (KS) ***362***
Fort Valley State U (GA) ***362***
Husson Coll (ME) ***383***
Inter American U of PR, Aguadilla Campus (PR) ***388***
Inter Amer U of PR, Barranquitas Campus (PR) ***388***
Inter American U of PR, Guayama Campus (PR) ***388***
Inter American U of PR, San Germán Campus (PR) ***388***
Jackson State U (MS) ***390***
Jones Coll (FL) ***394***
Lamar U (TX) ***401***
Langston U (OK) ***402***
Lee U (TN) ***404***
Lincoln Christian Coll (IL) ***407***
Maranatha Baptist Bible Coll (WI) ***417***
Mayville State U (ND) ***422***
Mercyhurst Coll (PA) ***425***
Mesa State Coll (CO) ***426***
Midland Lutheran Coll (NE) ***429***
Montclair State U (NJ) ***435***
Morehead State U (KY) ***436***
Mount Vernon Nazarene U (OH) ***440***
Murray State U (KY) ***440***
North Carolina Ag and Tech State U (NC) ***448***
Northern State U (SD) ***451***
Northwest Missouri State U (MO) ***454***
Oakwood Coll (AL) ***456***
Pacific Union Coll (CA) ***464***
Paul Quinn Coll (TX) ***466***
Peirce Coll (PA) ***466***
Pillsbury Baptist Bible Coll (MN) ***470***
Pontifical Catholic U of Puerto Rico (PR) ***472***
Ryerson U (ON, Canada) ***485***
Salem State Coll (MA) ***497***
South Carolina State U (SC) ***506***
Southeast Missouri State U (MO) ***508***
Southern Adventist U (TN) ***508***
Suffolk U (MA) ***520***
Sul Ross State U (TX) ***521***
Tabor Coll (KS) ***522***
Tennessee State U (TN) ***523***
Tennessee Temple U (TN) ***524***
Texas A&M U–Commerce (TX) ***525***
Texas Woman's U (TX) ***527***
Trinity Bible Coll (ND) ***530***
Universidad Adventista de las Antillas (PR) ***536***
U of Idaho (ID) ***547***
U of Maine at Machias (ME) ***551***
The U of Montana–Missoula (MT) ***556***
The U of North Carolina at Pembroke (NC) ***560***
U of Puerto Rico, Humacao U Coll (PR) ***570***
U of Puerto Rico at Ponce (PR) ***571***
U of Puerto Rico, Río Piedras (PR) ***571***
U of Sioux Falls (SD) ***574***
The U of Texas–Pan American (TX) ***579***
U of the Sacred Heart (PR) ***580***
U of Wisconsin–Superior (WI) ***586***
Utah State U (UT) ***587***
Valdosta State U (GA) ***588***
Weber State U (UT) ***596***
Wiley Coll (TX) ***605***
Winona State U (MN) ***608***
Youngstown State U (OH) ***611***

SECURITY

Overview: This major will teach students crime prevention, personal protection services, and inspection practices for private clients. *Related majors:* psychology, police science. *Potential careers:* private detective, security guard, bodyguard, security company executive. *Salary potential:* 25-$30k.

Ohio U (OH) ***458***
Youngstown State U (OH) ***611***

SIGN LANGUAGE INTERPRETATION

Overview: In this major, students learn to communicate using American Sign Language and other sign language systems that are used by the hearing impaired. *Related majors:* audiology/hearing sciences, education of individuals with hearing impairments, adult education. *Potential careers:* sign language interpreter or instructor, psychologist, therapist. *Salary potential:* $20k-$25k.

Bethel Coll (IN) ***288***
Bloomsburg U of Pennsylvania (PA) ***290***
California State U, Northridge (CA) ***301***
Columbia Coll Chicago (IL) ***327***
Converse Coll (SC) ***332***
Gallaudet U (DC) ***365***
Gardner-Webb U (NC) ***365***
Goshen Coll (IN) ***370***
Indiana U–Purdue U Indianapolis (IN) ***387***
Long Island U, Southampton Coll, Friends World Program (NY) ***409***
MacMurray Coll (IL) ***414***
Madonna U (MI) ***414***
Maryville Coll (TN) ***420***
Mount Aloysius Coll (PA) ***437***
Northeastern U (MA) ***450***
Ozark Christian Coll (MO) ***463***
Rochester Inst of Technology (NY) ***482***
U of Arkansas at Little Rock (AR) ***539***
U of New Mexico (NM) ***559***
The U of North Carolina at Greensboro (NC) ***560***
U of Rochester (NY) ***573***
Western Oregon U (OR) ***600***
William Woods U (MO) ***607***
York U (ON, Canada) ***611***

SLAVIC LANGUAGES

Overview: Students learn to read, speak, and understand one or more of the Slavic languages of Central and Eastern Europe (excluding Russian), as well as the international economics, history, and comparative literature. *Potential careers:* diplomatic corps, entrepreneur, translator, teacher, business consultant. *Salary potential:* $30k-$35k.

Barnard Coll (NY) ***282***
Boston Coll (MA) ***292***
Columbia Coll (NY) ***326***
Columbia U, School of General Studies (NY) ***328***
Cornell U (NY) ***333***
Duke U (NC) ***346***
Harvard U (MA) ***376***
Indiana U Bloomington (IN) ***385***
Long Island U, Southampton Coll, Friends World Program (NY) ***409***
Northwestern U (IL) ***453***
Saint Mary's Coll of Madonna U (MI) ***493***
Stanford U (CA) ***514***
State U of NY at Albany (NY) ***514***
U of Alberta (AB, Canada) ***538***
The U of British Columbia (BC, Canada) ***540***
U of Calif, Berkeley (CA) ***540***
U of Calif, Los Angeles (CA) ***541***
U of Calif, Santa Barbara (CA) ***541***
U of Chicago (IL) ***542***
U of Georgia (GA) ***545***
U of Illinois at Chicago (IL) ***547***
U of Manitoba (MB, Canada) ***551***
U of Ottawa (ON, Canada) ***563***
U of Pittsburgh (PA) ***569***
U of Saskatchewan (SK, Canada) ***574***
The U of Scranton (PA) ***574***
The U of Texas at Austin (TX) ***578***
U of Toronto (ON, Canada) ***581***
U of Victoria (BC, Canada) ***582***
U of Virginia (VA) ***582***
U of Washington (WA) ***583***
U of Windsor (ON, Canada) ***584***
U of Wisconsin–Madison (WI) ***584***
U of Wisconsin–Milwaukee (WI) ***585***
Wayne State U (MI) ***596***

SOCIAL/PHILOSOPHICAL FOUNDATIONS OF EDUCATION

Overview: Students who choose this major study the social and cultural aspects of education and the philosophy of education. *Related majors:* philosophy, history, Western civilization and culture, sociology. *Potential careers:* professor, writer, philosopher, teacher, anthropologist. *Salary potential:* $22k-$35k.

Northwestern U (IL) ***453***
Ohio U (OH) ***458***
Texas Southern U (TX) ***526***
U of Hawaii at Manoa (HI) ***546***
Washington U in St. Louis (MO) ***595***

SOCIAL PSYCHOLOGY

Overview: In this major, students study individual behavior in group contexts and group behavior. *Related majors:* psychology, education, organizational behavior, anthropology, anthropology. *Potential careers:* research scientist, professor, advertising or marketing executive, criminologist, teacher. *Salary potential:* $25k-$35k.

Clarion U of Pennsylvania (PA) ***315***
Florida Atlantic U (FL) ***359***
Loyola U Chicago (IL) ***411***
Marymount U (VA) ***420***
Maryville U of Saint Louis (MO) ***420***
Park U (MO) ***465***
U of Calif, Santa Cruz (CA) ***542***
U of Nevada, Reno (NV) ***558***
U of Wisconsin–Superior (WI) ***586***

SOCIAL SCIENCE EDUCATION

Overview: This major prepares undergraduates to teach one social science subject (history, government, economics, civics, geography, sociology, or anthropology) at either the junior high or high school level. *Related majors:* history, American government and politics, sociology, anthropology, geography. *Potential career:* teacher. *Salary potential:* $25k-$35k.

Abilene Christian U (TX) ***260***
Alverno Coll (WI) ***265***
Arkansas State U (AR) ***272***
Baylor U (TX) ***283***
Bethune-Cookman Coll (FL) ***289***
Blue Mountain Coll (MS) ***291***
Bowling Green State U (OH) ***292***
Bridgewater Coll (VA) ***294***
California State U, Chico (CA) ***300***
Carroll Coll (MT) ***306***
Central Methodist Coll (MO) ***309***
Central Michigan U (MI) ***310***
Central Washington U (WA) ***310***
Chadron State Coll (NE) ***311***
The Coll of St. Scholastica (MN) ***322***
Coll of Santa Fe (NM) ***323***
Concordia U (IL) ***330***
Concordia U (NE) ***330***
Dana Coll (NE) ***337***
Delta State U (MS) ***339***
Eastern Illinois U (IL) ***348***
Eastern Mennonite U (VA) ***348***
Eastern Michigan U (MI) ***348***
East Stroudsburg U of Pennsylvania (PA) ***349***
Elmira Coll (NY) ***351***
Elon U (NC) ***352***
Florida Atlantic U (FL) ***359***
Florida International U (FL) ***360***
Florida State U (FL) ***361***
Grambling State U (LA) ***371***
Hastings Coll (NE) ***377***
Hope International U (CA) ***381***
Howard Payne U (TX) ***382***
Jackson State U (MS) ***390***
Johnson State Coll (VT) ***394***
Judson Coll (AL) ***395***
Kennesaw State U (GA) ***397***
Liberty U (VA) ***406***
Luther Coll (IA) ***412***
Lyndon State Coll (VT) ***413***
Mansfield U of Pennsylvania (PA) ***416***
Maryville Coll (TN) ***420***
Mayville State U (ND) ***422***
McGill U (QC, Canada) ***423***
McKendree Coll (IL) ***423***
McMurry U (TX) ***423***
Michigan State U (MI) ***428***
Millikin U (IL) ***430***
Minot State U (ND) ***432***
Mississippi Coll (MS) ***432***
Mississippi Valley State U (MS) ***432***
Montana State U–Billings (MT) ***434***
North Dakota State U (ND) ***449***
Northern Arizona U (AZ) ***450***
Northwest Nazarene U (ID) ***454***
Oklahoma Baptist U (OK) ***459***
Pace U (NY) ***463***
Plymouth State Coll (NH) ***471***
Point Park Coll (PA) ***471***
Prescott Coll (AZ) ***474***
Rivier Coll (NH) ***480***
Rocky Mountain Coll (MT) ***482***
Rust Coll (MS) ***485***
St. Ambrose U (IA) ***486***
Saint Mary's U of Minnesota (MN) ***494***
Samford U (AL) ***497***
San Diego State U (CA) ***498***
Seattle Pacific U (WA) ***501***
Simpson Coll and Graduate School (CA) ***505***
Southern Nazarene U (OK) ***510***
Southwestern Oklahoma State U (OK) ***512***
State U of NY at Albany (NY) ***514***
Union Coll (NE) ***534***
The U of Akron (OH) ***537***
The U of Arizona (AZ) ***538***

SOCIAL SCIENCE EDUCATION (continued)

U of Central Florida (FL) **542**
U of Georgia (GA) **545**
U of Great Falls (MT) **545**
U of Hawaii at Manoa (HI) **546**
U of Illinois at Chicago (IL) **547**
U of Maine at Farmington (ME) **550**
U of Mary (ND) **551**
U of Minnesota, Twin Cities Campus (MN) **555**
The U of Montana–Missoula (MT) **556**
U of Nebraska–Lincoln (NE) **557**
U of Nevada, Reno (NV) **558**
U of Northern Iowa (IA) **561**
U of Puerto Rico, Cayey U Coll (PR) **571**
U of Rio Grande (OH) **572**
U of South Florida (FL) **576**
U of Utah (UT) **582**
U of Vermont (VT) **582**
U of West Florida (FL) **583**
U of Wisconsin–River Falls (WI) **585**
U of Wisconsin–Superior (WI) **586**
Utica Coll (NY) **588**
Valley City State U (ND) **588**
Warner Southern Coll (FL) **593**
Wartburg Coll (IA) **594**
Washington U in St. Louis (MO) **595**
Weber State U (UT) **596**
Westminster Coll (UT) **601**
Westmont Coll (CA) **602**
William Penn U (IA) **606**
York U (ON, Canada) **611**
Youngstown State U (OH) **611**

SOCIAL SCIENCES

Overview: This general major focuses on the study of social systems, institutions, and behavior. *Related majors:* anthropology, archeology, economics, history, sociology, urban affairs. *Potential careers:* teacher, political scientist, economist, journalist, editor. *Salary potential:* $23k-$30k.

Adams State Coll (CO) **260**
Adelphi U (NY) **260**
Adrian Coll (MI) **260**
Alabama State U (AL) **261**
Albertus Magnus Coll (CT) **262**
Alma Coll (MI) **264**
Alvernia Coll (PA) **265**
Alverno Coll (WI) **265**
American International Coll (MA) **267**
Andrews U (MI) **269**
Angelo State U (TX) **269**
Anna Maria Coll (MA) **269**
Antioch Coll (OH) **269**
Appalachian State U (NC) **270**
Aquinas Coll (MI) **270**
Arizona State U West (AZ) **272**
Asbury Coll (KY) **274**
Ashland U (OH) **274**
Augsburg Coll (MN) **276**
Averett U (VA) **278**
Azusa Pacific U (CA) **278**
Ball State U (IN) **280**
Bard Coll (NY) **281**
Barton Coll (NC) **282**
Bellevue U (NE) **284**
Bemidji State U (MN) **285**
Benedictine Coll (KS) **285**
Benedictine U (IL) **285**
Bennington Coll (VT) **286**
Berry Coll (GA) **287**
Bethany Coll of the Assemblies of God (CA) **287**
Bethel Coll (IN) **288**
Bethel Coll (KS) **288**
Biola U (CA) **289**
Bishop's U (QC, Canada) **289**
Black Hills State U (SD) **290**
Bloomsburg U of Pennsylvania (PA) **290**
Bluefield Coll (VA) **291**
Bluefield State Coll (WV) **291**
Blue Mountain Coll (MS) **291**
Bluffton Coll (OH) **291**
Bowling Green State U (OH) **292**
Brescia U (KY) **293**
Brock U (ON, Canada) **295**
Buena Vista U (IA) **297**
Caldwell Coll (NJ) **298**
California Baptist U (CA) **298**
California Inst of Technology (CA) **299**
California Lutheran U (CA) **299**
California Polytechnic State U, San Luis Obispo (CA) **300**
California State Polytechnic U, Pomona (CA) **300**
California State U, Chico (CA) **300**
California State U, Sacramento (CA) **301**
California State U, San Bernardino (CA) **302**
California State U, San Marcos (CA) **302**
California State U, Stanislaus (CA) **302**
California U of Pennsylvania (PA) **302**
Calvin Coll (MI) **303**
Campbellsville U (KY) **303**
Campbell U (NC) **303**
Cardinal Stritch U (WI) **305**
Carnegie Mellon U (PA) **305**
Carroll Coll (MT) **306**
Carthage Coll (WI) **306**
Castleton State Coll (VT) **307**
Cazenovia Coll (NY) **308**
Cedarville U (OH) **308**
Centenary Coll of Louisiana (LA) **308**
Central Coll (IA) **309**
Central Connecticut State U (CT) **309**
Central Michigan U (MI) **310**
Chaminade U of Honolulu (HI) **311**
Chapman U (CA) **311**
Charleston Southern U (SC) **311**
Chestnut Hill Coll (PA) **312**
Cheyney U of Pennsylvania (PA) **312**
Christian Heritage Coll (CA) **313**
Clarion U of Pennsylvania (PA) **315**
Clark Atlanta U (GA) **315**
Clarkson U (NY) **316**
Cleveland State U (OH) **317**
Colgate U (NY) **319**
Coll of Mount Saint Vincent (NY) **320**
Coll of Saint Benedict (MN) **321**
Coll of St. Catherine (MN) **321**
Coll of Saint Mary (NE) **322**
Coll of the Southwest (NM) **324**
Colorado State U (CO) **325**
Colorado State U-Pueblo (CO) **325**
Concordia Coll (NY) **329**
Concordia U (MI) **330**
Concordia U (MN) **330**
Concordia U (NE) **330**
Concordia U (OR) **330**
Concordia U (QC, Canada) **331**
Cumberland U (TN) **335**
Dana Coll (NE) **337**
Daniel Webster Coll (NH) **337**
Davis & Elkins Coll (WV) **338**
Defiance Coll (OH) **338**
Delta State U (MS) **339**
DePaul U (IL) **339**
Dickinson State U (ND) **344**
Doane Coll (NE) **344**
Dominican Coll (NY) **344**
Dominican U (IL) **345**
Dordt Coll (IA) **345**
Dowling Coll (NY) **345**
Drexel U (PA) **346**
Duquesne U (PA) **346**
Eastern Mennonite U (VA) **348**
Eastern Michigan U (MI) **348**
Eastern New Mexico U (NM) **349**
Eastern Washington U (WA) **349**
East-West U (IL) **350**
Edgewood Coll (WI) **351**
Edinboro U of Pennsylvania (PA) **351**
Elizabeth City State U (NC) **351**
Elizabethtown Coll (PA) **351**
Elmira Coll (NY) **351**
Emporia State U (KS) **354**
Eugene Lang Coll, New School U (NY) **355**
Eureka Coll (IL) **355**
Evangel U (MO) **355**
The Evergreen State Coll (WA) **355**
Faulkner U (AL) **357**
Fayetteville State U (NC) **357**
Felician Coll (NJ) **357**
Ferrum Coll (VA) **358**
Flagler Coll (FL) **359**
Florida A&M U (FL) **359**
Florida Atlantic U (FL) **359**
Florida Southern Coll (FL) **361**
Florida State U (FL) **361**
Fontbonne U (MO) **361**
Fordham U (NY) **362**
Fort Valley State U (GA) **362**
Framingham State Coll (MA) **362**
The Franciscan U (IA) **363**
Freed-Hardeman U (TN) **364**
Fresno Pacific U (CA) **364**
Frostburg State U (MD) **365**
Gardner-Webb U (NC) **365**
Georgia Southwestern State U (GA) **368**
Gettysburg Coll (PA) **368**
Goddard Coll (VT) **369**
Governors State U (IL) **370**
Graceland U (IA) **371**
Grand Canyon U (AZ) **371**
Grand Valley State U (MI) **371**
Gustavus Adolphus Coll (MN) **374**
Hamline U (MN) **374**
Hampshire Coll (MA) **375**
Hampton U (VA) **375**
Harding U (AR) **375**
Harvard U (MA) **376**
Hawai'i Pacific U (HI) **377**
Hofstra U (NY) **380**
Holy Apostles Coll and Seminary (CT) **380**
Holy Family U (PA) **380**
Hope International U (CA) **381**
Howard Payne U (TX) **382**
Humboldt State U (CA) **382**
Indiana Wesleyan U (IN) **387**
Inter American U of PR, San Germán Campus (PR) **388**
Iona Coll (NY) **390**
Ithaca Coll (NY) **390**
Jackson State U (MS) **390**
James Madison U (VA) **391**
John Brown U (AR) **392**
Johns Hopkins U (MD) **392**
Johnson C. Smith U (NC) **394**
Judson Coll (IL) **395**
Juniata Coll (PA) **395**
Kansas State U (KS) **396**
Keene State Coll (NH) **396**
Kendall Coll (IL) **396**
Kent State U (OH) **397**
Keuka Coll (NY) **398**
The King's U Coll (AB, Canada) **399**
Lake Erie Coll (OH) **400**
Lakeland Coll (WI) **401**
Lane Coll (TN) **402**
La Salle U (PA) **402**
Lebanon Valley Coll (PA) **403**
Lees-McRae Coll (NC) **404**
Lee U (TN) **404**
Lesley U (MA) **405**
Lewis-Clark State Coll (ID) **406**
Liberty U (VA) **406**
Lock Haven U of Pennsylvania (PA) **408**
Long Island U, Brooklyn Campus (NY) **409**
Long Island U, Southampton Coll (NY) **409**
Long Island U, Southampton Coll, Friends World Program (NY) **409**
Loyola U New Orleans (LA) **411**
Lynchburg Coll (VA) **413**
Lyndon State Coll (VT) **413**
Lynn U (FL) **413**
Madonna U (MI) **414**
Mansfield U of Pennsylvania (PA) **416**
Marlboro Coll (VT) **418**
Mars Hill Coll (NC) **418**
Marygrove Coll (MI) **419**
Marywood U (PA) **421**
Mayville State U (ND) **422**
McKendree Coll (IL) **423**
McPherson Coll (KS) **423**
Medaille Coll (NY) **424**
Memorial U of Newfoundland (NF, Canada) **424**
Mercer U (GA) **425**
Mercyhurst Coll (PA) **425**
Mesa State Coll (CO) **426**
Metropolitan State U (MN) **427**
Michigan State U (MI) **428**
Michigan Technological U (MI) **428**
Middlebury Coll (VT) **429**
Midland Lutheran Coll (NE) **429**
Miles Coll (AL) **430**
Mills Coll (CA) **431**
Minnesota State U, Mankato (MN) **431**
Minot State U (ND) **432**
Mississippi Coll (MS) **432**
Montana State U–Northern (MT) **434**
Montreat Coll (NC) **435**
Moravian Coll (PA) **436**
Morehead State U (KY) **436**
Morris Coll (SC) **437**
Mount Holyoke Coll (MA) **438**
Mount Saint Mary Coll (NY) **439**
Mount St. Mary's Coll (CA) **439**
Mount Saint Vincent U (NS, Canada) **439**
Mount Vernon Nazarene U (OH) **440**
Muhlenberg Coll (PA) **440**
Muskingum Coll (OH) **441**
National-Louis U (IL) **442**
Nazareth Coll of Rochester (NY) **443**
New Coll of Florida (FL) **444**
New York Inst of Technology (NY) **447**
New York U (NY) **447**
Niagara U (NY) **447**
North Carolina Ag and Tech State U (NC) **448**
North Central Coll (IL) **449**
North Dakota State U (ND) **449**
Northern Arizona U (AZ) **450**
Northern Illinois U (IL) **450**
Northern Kentucky U (KY) **451**
Northern Michigan U (MI) **451**
North Georgia Coll & State U (GA) **451**
Northland Coll (WI) **452**
North Park U (IL) **452**
Northwest Christian Coll (OR) **452**
Northwest Coll (WA) **452**
Northwestern Coll (MN) **453**
Northwestern Oklahoma State U (OK) **453**
Northwestern State U of Louisiana (LA) **453**
Northwest Missouri State U (MO) **454**
Northwest Nazarene U (ID) **454**
Notre Dame de Namur U (CA) **455**
Nyack Coll (NY) **456**
Oakland City U (IN) **456**
Oakwood Coll (AL) **456**
Ohio Dominican U (OH) **457**
The Ohio State U (OH) **457**
Ohio U (OH) **458**
Oklahoma Baptist U (OK) **459**
Oklahoma Panhandle State U (OK) **460**
Oklahoma Wesleyan U (OK) **460**
Olivet Coll (MI) **461**
Olivet Nazarene U (IL) **461**
Ouachita Baptist U (AR) **462**
Our Lady of Holy Cross Coll (LA) **463**
Our Lady of the Lake U of San Antonio (TX) **463**
Pace U (NY) **463**
Pacific Union Coll (CA) **464**
Peru State Coll (NE) **469**
Pfeiffer U (NC) **469**
Piedmont Coll (GA) **470**
Pikeville Coll (KY) **470**
Pittsburg State U (KS) **470**
Point Loma Nazarene U (CA) **471**
Point Park Coll (PA) **471**
Portland State U (OR) **472**
Presbyterian Coll (SC) **473**
Providence Coll (RI) **474**
Providence Coll and Theological Seminary (MB, Canada) **475**
Purdue U (IN) **475**
Quinnipiac U (CT) **476**
Radford U (VA) **476**
Ramapo Coll of New Jersey (NJ) **477**
Rhode Island Coll (RI) **479**
Richmond, The American International U in London(United Kingdom) **480**
Robert Morris U (PA) **481**
Roberts Wesleyan Coll (NY) **481**
Rockford Coll (IL) **482**
Rockhurst U (MO) **482**
Rocky Mountain Coll (AB, Canada) **482**
Rogers State U (OK) **483**
Roger Williams U (RI) **483**
Roosevelt U (IL) **483**
Rosemont Coll (PA) **484**
Rutgers, The State U of New Jersey, Newark (NJ) **485**
St. Bonaventure U (NY) **487**
St. Cloud State U (MN) **488**
St. Edward's U (TX) **488**
St. Francis Coll (NY) **488**
St. Gregory's U (OK) **489**
Saint John's U (MN) **490**
St. John's U (NY) **490**
Saint Joseph Coll (CT) **490**
Saint Joseph's Coll (IN) **490**
St. Joseph's Coll, New York (NY) **491**
St. Joseph's Coll, Suffolk Campus (NY) **491**
Saint Joseph's U (PA) **491**
Saint Louis U (MO) **492**
Saint Mary-of-the-Woods Coll (IN) **493**
Saint Mary's Coll of Madonna U (MI) **493**

Saint Mary's U of Minnesota (MN) **494**
Saint Peter's Coll (NJ) **495**
St. Thomas Aquinas Coll (NY) **495**
Saint Xavier U (IL) **496**
Salem State Coll (MA) **497**
Samford U (AL) **497**
San Diego State U (CA) **498**
San Francisco State U (CA) **498**
San Jose State U (CA) **499**
Sarah Lawrence Coll (NY) **499**
Shawnee State U (OH) **502**
Sheldon Jackson Coll (AK) **503**
Shimer Coll (IL) **503**
Shorter Coll (GA) **504**
Siena Heights U (MI) **504**
Silver Lake Coll (WI) **504**
Simpson Coll (IA) **505**
Simpson Coll and Graduate School (CA) **505**
Southern Connecticut State U (CT) **509**
Southern Illinois U Carbondale (IL) **509**
Southern Methodist U (TX) **510**
Southern New Hampshire U (NH) **510**
Southern Oregon U (OR) **510**
Southern Utah U (UT) **511**
Southern Wesleyan U (SC) **511**
Southwest Baptist U (MO) **512**
Southwestern U (TX) **513**
Spalding U (KY) **513**
Spring Arbor U (MI) **514**
Spring Hill Coll (AL) **514**
State U of NY Coll at Old Westbury (NY) **516**
State U of NY Empire State Coll (NY) **517**
Stephen F. Austin State U (TX) **518**
Stephens Coll (MO) **519**
Stetson U (FL) **519**
Stony Brook U, State University of New York (NY) **520**
Suffolk U (MA) **520**
Sul Ross State U (TX) **521**
Syracuse U (NY) **521**
Tabor Coll (KS) **522**
Taylor U (IN) **523**
Texas A&M International U (TX) **524**
Texas A&M U–Commerce (TX) **525**
Texas Wesleyan U (TX) **526**
Thomas Edison State Coll (NJ) **527**
Thomas U (GA) **528**
Tiffin U (OH) **528**
Towson U (MD) **529**
Trent U (ON, Canada) **529**
Trevecca Nazarene U (TN) **529**
Trinity International U (IL) **531**
Trinity Western U (BC, Canada) **531**
Tri-State U (IN) **532**
Troy State U (AL) **532**
Troy State U Dothan (AL) **532**
Troy State U Montgomery (AL) **532**
Union Coll (NE) **534**
Union Coll (NY) **534**
Union Inst & U (OH) **534**
United States Air Force Academy (CO) **534**
U du Québec à Hull (QC, Canada) **536**
U at Buffalo, The State University of New York (NY) **536**
The U of Akron (OH) **537**
U of Bridgeport (CT) **540**
The U of British Columbia (BC, Canada) **540**
U of Calif, Berkeley (CA) **540**
U of Calif, Irvine (CA) **541**
U of Calif, Riverside (CA) **541**
U of Central Florida (FL) **542**
U of Chicago (IL) **542**
U of Cincinnati (OH) **543**
U of Denver (CO) **544**
The U of Findlay (OH) **545**
U of Great Falls (MT) **545**
U of Hawaii–West Oahu (HI) **546**
U of Houston–Downtown (TX) **547**
U of Houston–Victoria (TX) **547**
The U of Iowa (IA) **548**
U of Kentucky (KY) **549**
U of La Verne (CA) **549**
The U of Lethbridge (AB, Canada) **549**
The U of Maine at Augusta (ME) **550**
U of Maine at Fort Kent (ME) **551**
U of Mary (ND) **551**
U of Maryland Eastern Shore (MD) **552**
U of Maryland University Coll (MD) **552**
U of Michigan (MI) **554**
U of Michigan–Dearborn (MI) **554**
U of Michigan–Flint (MI) **554**
U of Minnesota, Morris (MN) **555**
U of Missouri–St. Louis (MO) **556**
U of Mobile (AL) **556**
The U of Montana–Missoula (MT) **556**
The U of Montana–Western (MT) **556**
U of Montevallo (AL) **557**
U of Nevada, Las Vegas (NV) **558**
U of New England (ME) **558**
U of North Dakota (ND) **561**
U of Northern Colorado (CO) **561**
U of North Texas (TX) **562**
U of Ottawa (ON, Canada) **563**
U of Pittsburgh (PA) **569**
U of Pittsburgh at Bradford (PA) **569**
U of Pittsburgh at Greensburg (PA) **570**
U of Pittsburgh at Johnstown (PA) **570**
U of Puerto Rico, Cayey U Coll (PR) **571**
U of Puerto Rico, Río Piedras (PR) **571**
U of Regina (SK, Canada) **572**
U of Rio Grande (OH) **572**
U of St. Thomas (MN) **573**
U of Sioux Falls (SD) **574**
U of Southern Indiana (IN) **576**
U of Southern Maine (ME) **576**
U of South Florida (FL) **576**
The U of Tampa (FL) **577**
U of the Ozarks (AR) **580**
U of the Pacific (CA) **580**
U of the Sacred Heart (PR) **580**
U of the South (TN) **581**
U of the Virgin Islands (VI) **581**
U of Utah (UT) **582**
U of Washington (WA) **583**
U of West Florida (FL) **583**
U of Windsor (ON, Canada) **584**
U of Wisconsin–Madison (WI) **584**
U of Wisconsin–Platteville (WI) **585**
U of Wisconsin–River Falls (WI) **585**
U of Wisconsin–Stevens Point (WI) **585**
U of Wisconsin–Superior (WI) **586**
U of Wyoming (WY) **586**
Upper Iowa U (IA) **587**
Utica Coll (NY) **588**
Valley City State U (ND) **588**
Vanguard U of Southern California (CA) **589**
Virginia Wesleyan Coll (VA) **591**
Warner Pacific Coll (OR) **593**
Warner Southern Coll (FL) **593**
Washington State U (WA) **595**
Washington U in St. Louis (MO) **595**
Wayland Baptist U (TX) **595**
Waynesburg Coll (PA) **595**
Wayne State Coll (NE) **596**
Webster U (MO) **597**
Wesleyan Coll (GA) **597**
Wesleyan U (CT) **597**
West Chester U of Pennsylvania (PA) **598**
Western Baptist Coll (OR) **598**
Western Carolina U (NC) **598**
Western Connecticut State U (CT) **598**
Western Kentucky U (KY) **599**
Western New Mexico U (NM) **600**
Western Oregon U (OR) **600**
Western State Coll of Colorado (CO) **600**
Westfield State Coll (MA) **600**
West Liberty State Coll (WV) **601**
Westminster Coll (UT) **601**
Westmont Coll (CA) **602**
West Texas A&M U (TX) **602**
Widener U (PA) **604**
Wiley Coll (TX) **605**
William Carey Coll (MS) **605**
William Paterson U of New Jersey (NJ) **606**
Wilmington Coll (OH) **607**
Wilson Coll (PA) **607**
Wingate U (NC) **607**
Winona State U (MN) **608**
Winston-Salem State U (NC) **608**
Wisconsin Lutheran Coll (WI) **608**
Wittenberg U (OH) **608**
Worcester Polytechnic Inst (MA) **609**
York U (ON, Canada) **611**
Youngstown State U (OH) **611**

SOCIAL SCIENCES AND HISTORY RELATED

Information can be found under this major's main heading.

Bethel Coll (KS) **288**
Boston U (MA) **292**
Colby-Sawyer Coll (NH) **319**
The Colorado Coll (CO) **325**
Georgetown U (DC) **366**
Marywood U (PA) **421**
Mid-Continent Coll (KY) **429**
Nebraska Wesleyan U (NE) **443**
Northwestern U (IL) **453**
Plymouth State Coll (NH) **471**
Queens Coll of the City U of NY (NY) **475**
Saint Mary's U of Minnesota (MN) **494**
San Diego State U (CA) **498**
Skidmore Coll (NY) **506**
Towson U (MD) **529**
The U of Alabama at Birmingham (AL) **537**
U of Hawaii at Manoa (HI) **546**
U of Massachusetts Amherst (MA) **552**
U of Miami (FL) **553**
U of Pittsburgh at Bradford (PA) **569**

SOCIAL STUDIES EDUCATION

Overview: This major prepares students to teach a variety of social studies subjects (history, government, economics, civics, geography, sociology, or anthropology) at either the junior high or high school level. *Related majors:* history, American government and politics, sociology, anthropology, geography. *Potential career:* teacher. *Salary potential:* $23k-$32k.

Abilene Christian U (TX) **260**
Adams State Coll (CO) **260**
Alverno Coll (WI) **265**
Anderson U (IN) **268**
Appalachian State U (NC) **270**
Arkansas Tech U (AR) **272**
Augustana Coll (SD) **276**
Averett U (VA) **278**
Baylor U (TX) **283**
Bethany Coll (KS) **287**
Bethel Coll (IN) **288**
Bloomfield Coll (NJ) **290**
Bloomsburg U of Pennsylvania (PA) **290**
Boston U (MA) **292**
Bowling Green State U (OH) **292**
Brescia U (KY) **293**
Bridgewater Coll (VA) **294**
Brigham Young U (UT) **295**
Cabrini Coll (PA) **298**
Canisius Coll (NY) **304**
Carlow Coll (PA) **305**
Castleton State Coll (VT) **307**
Cedarville U (OH) **308**
Central Michigan U (MI) **310**
Central Missouri State U (MO) **310**
Citadel, The Military Coll of South Carolina (SC) **314**
Clarion U of Pennsylvania (PA) **315**
Clearwater Christian Coll (FL) **316**
Colby-Sawyer Coll (NH) **319**
Coll of St. Catherine (MN) **321**
Colorado State U (CO) **325**
Colorado State U-Pueblo (CO) **325**
Concordia Coll (MN) **329**
Concordia U (OR) **330**
Crown Coll (MN) **334**
Cumberland Coll (KY) **335**
Daemen Coll (NY) **335**
Dakota Wesleyan U (SD) **336**
Duquesne U (PA) **346**
East Carolina U (NC) **347**
Eastern Michigan U (MI) **348**
East Texas Baptist U (TX) **350**
Edinboro U of Pennsylvania (PA) **351**
Elmira Coll (NY) **351**
Elon U (NC) **352**
Erskine Coll (SC) **354**
Franklin Coll (IN) **363**
George Fox U (OR) **366**
Greensboro Coll (NC) **372**
Greenville Coll (IL) **373**
Gustavus Adolphus Coll (MN) **374**
Hardin-Simmons U (TX) **376**
Hastings Coll (NE) **377**
Hofstra U (NY) **380**
Holy Family U (PA) **380**
Huston-Tillotson Coll (TX) **383**
Illinois State U (IL) **384**
Indiana State U (IN) **385**
Indiana U Bloomington (IN) **385**
Indiana U Northwest (IN) **386**
Indiana U of Pennsylvania (PA) **386**
Indiana U–Purdue U Fort Wayne (IN) **386**
Indiana U–Purdue U Indianapolis (IN) **387**
Indiana U South Bend (IN) **387**
Indiana U Southeast (IN) **387**
Indiana Wesleyan U (IN) **387**
Ithaca Coll (NY) **390**
Johnson State Coll (VT) **394**
Juniata Coll (PA) **395**
Kent State U (OH) **397**
Kentucky State U (KY) **397**
Keuka Coll (NY) **398**
Le Moyne Coll (NY) **404**
Limestone Coll (SC) **406**
Lincoln U (PA) **407**
Long Island U, C.W. Post Campus (NY) **409**
Louisiana State U in Shreveport (LA) **410**
Malone Coll (OH) **415**
Manhattanville Coll (NY) **416**
Mansfield U of Pennsylvania (PA) **416**
Marymount Coll of Fordham U (NY) **419**
McGill U (QC, Canada) **423**
McMurry U (TX) **423**
Mercer U (GA) **425**
Messiah Coll (PA) **426**
Miami U (OH) **428**
MidAmerica Nazarene U (KS) **428**
Millersville U of Pennsylvania (PA) **430**
Minnesota State U, Mankato (MN) **431**
Minnesota State U, Moorhead (MN) **432**
Mississippi Coll (MS) **432**
Molloy Coll (NY) **433**
Mount Vernon Nazarene U (OH) **440**
Nazareth Coll of Rochester (NY) **443**
New York Inst of Technology (NY) **447**
New York U (NY) **447**
Niagara U (NY) **447**
North Carolina State U (NC) **449**
Northwestern Coll (MN) **453**
Nova Southeastern U (FL) **455**
Oakland City U (IN) **456**
Ohio U (OH) **458**
Ohio Valley Coll (WV) **459**
Oklahoma Baptist U (OK) **459**
Oklahoma Christian U (OK) **459**
Oral Roberts U (OK) **461**
Pace U (NY) **463**
Philadelphia Biblical U (PA) **469**
Pikeville Coll (KY) **470**
Pontifical Catholic U of Puerto Rico (PR) **472**
Rocky Mountain Coll (MT) **482**
Saint Augustine's Coll (NC) **487**
St. John's U (NY) **490**
Saint Joseph's Coll of Maine (ME) **491**
St. Mary's U of San Antonio (TX) **494**
St. Olaf Coll (MN) **495**
Seton Hill U (PA) **502**
Shaw U (NC) **502**
Southeastern Coll of the Assemblies of God (FL) **507**
Southeastern Louisiana U (LA) **508**
Southeastern Oklahoma State U (OK) **508**
Southeast Missouri State U (MO) **508**
Southern Arkansas U–Magnolia (AR) **509**
State U of NY Coll at Potsdam (NY) **517**
State U of West Georgia (GA) **518**
Syracuse U (NY) **521**
Texas A&M International U (TX) **524**
Texas Christian U (TX) **526**
Texas Lutheran U (TX) **526**
Texas Wesleyan U (TX) **526**
Thomas More Coll (KY) **528**
Toccoa Falls Coll (GA) **528**
Tri-State U (IN) **532**
The U of Akron (OH) **537**
The U of Arizona (AZ) **538**
U of Central Arkansas (AR) **542**
U of Central Oklahoma (OK) **542**
U of Charleston (WV) **542**
U of Hawaii at Manoa (HI) **546**
U of Indianapolis (IN) **548**
The U of Iowa (IA) **548**
U of Maryland, Coll Park (MD) **552**
U of Minnesota, Duluth (MN) **554**
U of Mississippi (MS) **555**
U of Nevada, Reno (NV) **558**
U of New Orleans (LA) **559**
U of Oklahoma (OK) **562**
U of Pittsburgh at Johnstown (PA) **570**
U of Puerto Rico, Cayey U Coll (PR) **571**
U of St. Francis (IL) **573**
U of St. Thomas (MN) **573**
U of Toledo (OH) **581**
U of Utah (UT) **582**

SOCIAL STUDIES EDUCATION (continued)

U of Wisconsin–Eau Claire (WI) ***584***
U of Wisconsin–La Crosse (WI) ***584***
U of Wisconsin–River Falls (WI) ***585***
U of Wisconsin–Superior (WI) ***586***
Ursuline Coll (OH) ***587***
Utah State U (UT) ***587***
Utica Coll (NY) ***588***
Virginia Intermont Coll (VA) ***590***
Viterbo U (WI) ***591***
Washington U in St. Louis (MO) ***595***
Wayne State U (MI) ***596***
Weber State U (UT) ***596***
Western Carolina U (NC) ***598***
Wheaton Coll (IL) ***603***
Wheeling Jesuit U (WV) ***603***
Winston-Salem State U (NC) ***608***
York U (ON, Canada) ***611***
Youngstown State U (OH) ***611***

SOCIAL WORK

Overview: This major will teach students how to provide essential support services to at-risk individuals and groups, preparing them for a career in social welfare administration and counseling. *Related majors:* community organization, resources and services, public administration, economics, human services, psychology. *Potential careers:* social worker, governmental agency administrator, school administrator, community liaison, hospital representative. *Salary potential:* $25k-$30k.

Abilene Christian U (TX) ***260***
Adams State Coll (CO) ***260***
Adelphi U (NY) ***260***
Adrian Coll (MI) ***260***
Alabama A&M U (AL) ***261***
Alabama State U (AL) ***261***
Albany State U (GA) ***262***
Allen U (SC) ***264***
Alvernia Coll (PA) ***265***
Anderson U (IN) ***268***
Andrews U (MI) ***269***
Anna Maria Coll (MA) ***269***
Appalachian State U (NC) ***270***
Arizona State U (AZ) ***271***
Arizona State U West (AZ) ***272***
Arkansas Baptist Coll (AR) ***272***
Arkansas State U (AR) ***272***
Asbury Coll (KY) ***274***
Ashland U (OH) ***274***
Atlantic Union Coll (MA) ***276***
Auburn U (AL) ***276***
Augsburg Coll (MN) ***276***
Augustana Coll (SD) ***276***
Aurora U (IL) ***277***
Austin Peay State U (TN) ***278***
Avila U (MO) ***278***
Azusa Pacific U (CA) ***278***
Baldwin-Wallace Coll (OH) ***280***
Ball State U (IN) ***280***
Barton Coll (NC) ***282***
Bayamón Central U (PR) ***283***
Baylor U (TX) ***283***
Belmont U (TN) ***284***
Bemidji State U (MN) ***285***
Benedict Coll (SC) ***285***
Bennett Coll (NC) ***286***
Bethany Coll (KS) ***287***
Bethany Coll (WV) ***287***
Bethel Coll (KS) ***288***
Bethel Coll (MN) ***288***
Bloomsburg U of Pennsylvania (PA) ***290***
Bluffton Coll (OH) ***291***
Bowie State U (MD) ***292***
Bowling Green State U (OH) ***292***
Bradley U (IL) ***293***
Brescia U (KY) ***293***
Briar Cliff U (IA) ***294***
Bridgewater State Coll (MA) ***294***
Brigham Young U (UT) ***295***
Brigham Young U–Hawaii (HI) ***295***
Buena Vista U (IA) ***297***
Cabrini Coll (PA) ***298***
California State U, Chico (CA) ***300***
California State U, Fresno (CA) ***301***
California State U, Hayward (CA) ***301***
California State U, Long Beach (CA) ***301***
California State U, Northridge (CA) ***301***
California State U, Sacramento (CA) ***301***
California State U, San Bernardino (CA) ***302***
California U of Pennsylvania (PA) ***302***
Calvin Coll (MI) ***303***
Campbellsville U (KY) ***303***
Campbell U (NC) ***303***
Capital U (OH) ***304***
Carleton U (ON, Canada) ***305***
Carlow Coll (PA) ***305***
Carroll Coll (MT) ***306***
Carroll Coll (WI) ***306***
Carthage Coll (WI) ***306***
Castleton State Coll (VT) ***307***
The Catholic U of America (DC) ***307***
Cedar Crest Coll (PA) ***308***
Cedarville U (OH) ***308***
Central Connecticut State U (CT) ***309***
Central Michigan U (MI) ***310***
Central Missouri State U (MO) ***310***
Chadron State Coll (NE) ***311***
Champlain Coll (VT) ***311***
Chapman U (CA) ***311***
Chatham Coll (PA) ***312***
Christopher Newport U (VA) ***313***
Clark Atlanta U (GA) ***315***
Clarke Coll (IA) ***315***
Cleveland State U (OH) ***317***
Coker Coll (SC) ***318***
Coll Misericordia (PA) ***319***
Coll of Mount St. Joseph (OH) ***320***
The Coll of New Rochelle (NY) ***321***
Coll of Saint Benedict (MN) ***321***
Coll of St. Catherine (MN) ***321***
The Coll of Saint Rose (NY) ***322***
The Coll of St. Scholastica (MN) ***322***
The Coll of Staten Island of the City U of NY (NY) ***323***
Coll of the Ozarks (MO) ***323***
Colorado State U (CO) ***325***
Colorado State U-Pueblo (CO) ***325***
Columbia Coll (MO) ***326***
Columbia Coll (SC) ***327***
Concord Coll (WV) ***329***
Concordia Coll (MN) ***329***
Concordia Coll (NY) ***329***
Concordia U (CA) ***330***
Concordia U (IL) ***330***
Concordia U (OR) ***330***
Concordia U Wisconsin (WI) ***331***
Cornerstone U (MI) ***333***
Creighton U (NE) ***333***
Cumberland Coll (KY) ***335***
Daemen Coll (NY) ***335***
Dalhousie U (NS, Canada) ***336***
Dalton State Coll (GA) ***336***
Dana Coll (NE) ***337***
Defiance Coll (OH) ***338***
Delaware State U (DE) ***338***
Delta State U (MS) ***339***
DeSales U (PA) ***340***
Dickinson State U (ND) ***344***
Dillard U (LA) ***344***
Dominican Coll (NY) ***344***
Dordt Coll (IA) ***345***
D'Youville Coll (NY) ***347***
East Carolina U (NC) ***347***
East Central U (OK) ***347***
Eastern Connecticut State U (CT) ***347***
Eastern Kentucky U (KY) ***348***
Eastern Mennonite U (VA) ***348***
Eastern Michigan U (MI) ***348***
Eastern Nazarene Coll (MA) ***348***
Eastern U (PA) ***349***
Eastern Washington U (WA) ***349***
East Tennessee State U (TN) ***349***
Edinboro U of Pennsylvania (PA) ***351***
Elizabeth City State U (NC) ***351***
Elizabethtown Coll (PA) ***351***
Elmira Coll (NY) ***351***
Elms Coll (MA) ***352***
Evangel U (MO) ***355***
Ferris State U (MI) ***358***
Ferrum Coll (VA) ***358***
Florida A&M U (FL) ***359***
Florida Atlantic U (FL) ***359***
Florida International U (FL) ***360***
Florida State U (FL) ***361***
Fordham U (NY) ***362***
Fort Hays State U (KS) ***362***
Fort Valley State U (GA) ***362***
Franciscan U of Steubenville (OH) ***363***
Franklin Pierce Coll (NH) ***364***
Freed-Hardeman U (TN) ***364***
Fresno Pacific U (CA) ***364***
Frostburg State U (MD) ***365***
Gallaudet U (DC) ***365***
Gannon U (PA) ***365***
George Fox U (OR) ***366***
George Mason U (VA) ***366***
Georgian Court Coll (NJ) ***367***
Georgia State U (GA) ***368***
Gordon Coll (MA) ***370***
Goshen Coll (IN) ***370***
Governors State U (IL) ***370***
Grace Coll (IN) ***370***
Graceland U (IA) ***371***
Grambling State U (LA) ***371***
Grand Valley State U (MI) ***371***
Greenville Coll (IL) ***373***
Gwynedd-Mercy Coll (PA) ***374***
Hampton U (VA) ***375***
Harding U (AR) ***375***
Hardin-Simmons U (TX) ***376***
Hawai'i Pacific U (HI) ***377***
Henderson State U (AR) ***378***
Holy Family U (PA) ***380***
Hood Coll (MD) ***381***
Hope Coll (MI) ***381***
Hope International U (CA) ***381***
Howard Payne U (TX) ***382***
Howard U (DC) ***382***
Humboldt State U (CA) ***382***
Idaho State U (ID) ***384***
Illinois State U (IL) ***384***
Immaculata U (PA) ***385***
Indiana State U (IN) ***385***
Indiana U Bloomington (IN) ***385***
Indiana U East (IN) ***386***
Indiana U–Purdue U Indianapolis (IN) ***387***
Indiana Wesleyan U (IN) ***387***
Iona Coll (NY) ***390***
Iowa Wesleyan Coll (IA) ***390***
Jackson State U (MS) ***390***
Jacksonville State U (AL) ***390***
James Madison U (VA) ***391***
Johnson C. Smith U (NC) ***394***
Juniata Coll (PA) ***395***
Kansas State U (KS) ***396***
Kean U (NJ) ***396***
Kennesaw State U (GA) ***397***
Kentucky Christian Coll (KY) ***397***
Kentucky State U (KY) ***397***
Keuka Coll (NY) ***398***
Kutztown U of Pennsylvania (PA) ***399***
LaGrange Coll (GA) ***400***
Lakehead U (ON, Canada) ***400***
Lamar U (TX) ***401***
La Salle U (PA) ***402***
La Sierra U (CA) ***403***
Laurentian U (ON, Canada) ***403***
Lehman Coll of the City U of NY (NY) ***404***
Lewis-Clark State Coll (ID) ***406***
Lewis U (IL) ***406***
Limestone Coll (SC) ***406***
Lincoln Memorial U (TN) ***407***
Lincoln U (PA) ***407***
Lindenwood U (MO) ***407***
Lindsey Wilson Coll (KY) ***407***
Lipscomb U (TN) ***408***
Lock Haven U of Pennsylvania (PA) ***408***
Long Island U, Brooklyn Campus (NY) ***409***
Long Island U, C.W. Post Campus (NY) ***409***
Long Island U, Southampton Coll, Friends World Program (NY) ***409***
Longwood U (VA) ***409***
Loras Coll (IA) ***410***
Louisiana Coll (LA) ***410***
Lourdes Coll (OH) ***411***
Loyola U Chicago (IL) ***411***
Lubbock Christian U (TX) ***412***
Luther Coll (IA) ***412***
MacMurray Coll (IL) ***414***
Madonna U (MI) ***414***
Malone Coll (OH) ***415***
Manchester Coll (IN) ***415***
Mansfield U of Pennsylvania (PA) ***416***
Marian Coll of Fond du Lac (WI) ***417***
Marist Coll (NY) ***417***
Marquette U (WI) ***418***
Marshall U (WV) ***418***
Mars Hill Coll (NC) ***418***
Mary Baldwin Coll (VA) ***419***
Marygrove Coll (MI) ***419***
Marymount Coll of Fordham U (NY) ***419***
Marywood U (PA) ***421***
Massachusetts Coll of Liberal Arts (MA) ***421***
McDaniel Coll (MD) ***422***
McGill U (QC, Canada) ***423***
McKendree Coll (IL) ***423***
McMaster U (ON, Canada) ***423***
Memorial U of Newfoundland (NF, Canada) ***424***
Mercy Coll (NY) ***425***
Mercyhurst Coll (PA) ***425***
Meredith Coll (NC) ***426***
Messiah Coll (PA) ***426***
Methodist Coll (NC) ***427***
Metropolitan State Coll of Denver (CO) ***427***
Metropolitan State U (MN) ***427***
Miami U (OH) ***428***
Michigan State U (MI) ***428***
Middle Tennessee State U (TN) ***429***
Midwestern State U (TX) ***430***
Millersville U of Pennsylvania (PA) ***430***
Minnesota State U, Mankato (MN) ***431***
Minnesota State U, Moorhead (MN) ***432***
Minot State U (ND) ***432***
Mississippi Coll (MS) ***432***
Mississippi State U (MS) ***432***
Mississippi Valley State U (MS) ***432***
Missouri Western State Coll (MO) ***433***
Molloy Coll (NY) ***433***
Monmouth U (NJ) ***434***
Morehead State U (KY) ***436***
Morgan State U (MD) ***436***
Mountain State U (WV) ***437***
Mount Mary Coll (WI) ***438***
Mount Mercy Coll (IA) ***438***
Mount Vernon Nazarene U (OH) ***440***
Murray State U (KY) ***440***
Nazareth Coll of Rochester (NY) ***443***
Nebraska Wesleyan U (NE) ***443***
New Mexico Highlands U (NM) ***446***
New Mexico State U (NM) ***446***
New York U (NY) ***447***
Niagara U (NY) ***447***
Norfolk State U (VA) ***448***
North Carolina Ag and Tech State U (NC) ***448***
North Carolina Central U (NC) ***448***
North Carolina State U (NC) ***449***
Northeastern Illinois U (IL) ***450***
Northeastern State U (OK) ***450***
Northern Arizona U (AZ) ***450***
Northern Kentucky U (KY) ***451***
Northern Michigan U (MI) ***451***
Northwestern Coll (IA) ***453***
Northwestern Oklahoma State U (OK) ***453***
Northwestern State U of Louisiana (LA) ***453***
Northwest Nazarene U (ID) ***454***
Nyack Coll (NY) ***456***
Oakwood Coll (AL) ***456***
Oglethorpe U (GA) ***457***
Ohio Dominican U (OH) ***457***
The Ohio State U (OH) ***457***
Ohio U (OH) ***458***
Okanagan U Coll (BC, Canada) ***459***
Oklahoma Baptist U (OK) ***459***
Oral Roberts U (OK) ***461***
Our Lady of the Lake U of San Antonio (TX) ***463***
Pacific Lutheran U (WA) ***463***
Pacific Union Coll (CA) ***464***
Pacific U (OR) ***464***
Paul Quinn Coll (TX) ***466***
Philadelphia Biblical U (PA) ***469***
Pittsburg State U (KS) ***470***
Plattsburgh State U of NY (NY) ***471***
Plymouth State Coll (NH) ***471***
Point Loma Nazarene U (CA) ***471***
Pontifical Catholic U of Puerto Rico (PR) ***472***
Prairie View A&M U (TX) ***473***
Presentation Coll (SD) ***474***
Providence Coll (RI) ***474***
Purdue U Calumet (IN) ***475***
Quincy U (IL) ***476***
Radford U (VA) ***476***
Ramapo Coll of New Jersey (NJ) ***477***
Reformed Bible Coll (MI) ***477***
Regis Coll (MA) ***478***
Rhode Island Coll (RI) ***479***
The Richard Stockton Coll of New Jersey (NJ) ***479***
Roberts Wesleyan Coll (NY) ***481***
Rochester Inst of Technology (NY) ***482***
Rockford Coll (IL) ***482***
Rust Coll (MS) ***485***

Rutgers, The State U of New Jersey, Camden (NJ) 485
Rutgers, The State U of New Jersey, Newark (NJ) 485
Ryerson U (ON, Canada) 485
Sacred Heart U (CT) 486
Saginaw Valley State U (MI) 486
St. Augustine Coll (IL) 487
St. Cloud State U (MN) 488
St. Edward's U (TX) 488
St. Francis Coll (NY) 488
Saint Francis U (PA) 488
Saint John's U (MN) 490
Saint Joseph Coll (CT) 490
Saint Joseph's Coll of Maine (ME) 491
Saint Leo U (FL) 492
Saint Louis U (MO) 492
Saint Mary's Coll (IN) 493
St. Olaf Coll (MN) 495
St. Thomas U (NB, Canada) 496
Salem State Coll (MA) 497
Salisbury U (MD) 497
Salve Regina U (RI) 497
San Diego State U (CA) 498
San Francisco State U (CA) 498
San Jose State U (CA) 499
Savannah State U (GA) 499
Seattle U (WA) 501
Seton Hall U (NJ) 502
Seton Hill U (PA) 502
Shaw U (NC) 502
Shepherd Coll (WV) 503
Shippensburg U of Pennsylvania (PA) 503
Siena Coll (NY) 504
Siena Heights U (MI) 504
Skidmore Coll (NY) 506
Slippery Rock U of Pennsylvania (PA) 506
South Carolina State U (SC) 506
Southeastern Coll of the Assemblies of God (FL) 507
Southeastern Louisiana U (LA) 508
Southeast Missouri State U (MO) 508
Southern Adventist U (TN) 508
Southern Arkansas U–Magnolia (AR) 509
Southern Connecticut State U (CT) 509
Southern Illinois U Carbondale (IL) 509
Southern Illinois U Edwardsville (IL) 509
Southern Nazarene U (OK) 510
Southern U and A&M Coll (LA) 511
Southern Vermont Coll (VT) 511
Southwestern Oklahoma State U (OK) 512
Southwest Missouri State U (MO) 513
Southwest State U (MN) 513
Southwest Texas State U (TX) 513
Spalding U (KY) 513
Spring Arbor U (MI) 514
State U of NY at Albany (NY) 514
State U of NY at New Paltz (NY) 515
State U of NY Coll at Brockport (NY) 515
State U of NY Coll at Buffalo (NY) 516
State U of NY Coll at Cortland (NY) 516
State U of NY Coll at Fredonia (NY) 516
Stephen F. Austin State U (TX) 518
Stony Brook U, State University of New York (NY) 520
Suffolk U (MA) 520
Syracuse U (NY) 521
Talladega Coll (AL) 522
Tarleton State U (TX) 522
Taylor U (IN) 523
Taylor U, Fort Wayne Campus (IN) 523
Temple U (PA) 523
Tennessee State U (TN) 523
Tennessee Technological U (TN) 524
Texas A&M U–Commerce (TX) 525
Texas A&M U–Kingsville (TX) 525
Texas Christian U (TX) 526
Texas Coll (TX) 526
Texas Southern U (TX) 526
Texas Tech U (TX) 526
Thomas U (GA) 528
Troy State U (AL) 532
Tuskegee U (AL) 533
Union Coll (NE) 534
Union Inst & U (OH) 534
Union U (TN) 534
Université de Sherbrooke (QC, Canada) 536
U du Québec à Hull (QC, Canada) 536
Université Laval (QC, Canada) 536
U Coll of the Cariboo (BC, Canada) 537
The U of Akron (OH) 537
The U of Alabama (AL) 537
The U of Alabama at Birmingham (AL) 537
U of Alaska Anchorage (AK) 538
U of Alaska Fairbanks (AK) 538
U of Arkansas (AR) 539
U of Arkansas at Little Rock (AR) 539
U of Arkansas at Monticello (AR) 539
The U of British Columbia (BC, Canada) 540
U of Calgary (AB, Canada) 540
U of Calif, Berkeley (CA) 540
U of Central Florida (FL) 542
U of Cincinnati (OH) 543
The U of Findlay (OH) 545
U of Georgia (GA) 545
U of Hawaii at Manoa (HI) 546
U of Houston–Clear Lake (TX) 547
U of Illinois at Chicago (IL) 547
U of Illinois at Springfield (IL) 548
U of Indianapolis (IN) 548
The U of Iowa (IA) 548
U of Kansas (KS) 549
U of Kentucky (KY) 549
U of Maine (ME) 550
U of Maine at Presque Isle (ME) 551
U of Manitoba (MB, Canada) 551
U of Mary (ND) 551
U of Mary Hardin-Baylor (TX) 551
U of Maryland, Baltimore County (MD) 552
U of Maryland Eastern Shore (MD) 552
U of Massachusetts Boston (MA) 553
The U of Memphis (TN) 553
U of Michigan–Flint (MI) 554
U of Mississippi (MS) 555
U of Missouri–Columbia (MO) 555
U of Missouri–St. Louis (MO) 556
The U of Montana–Missoula (MT) 556
U of Montevallo (AL) 557
U of Nebraska at Kearney (NE) 557
U of Nebraska at Omaha (NE) 557
U of Nevada, Las Vegas (NV) 558
U of Nevada, Reno (NV) 558
U of New Hampshire (NH) 558
U of North Alabama (AL) 559
The U of North Carolina at Charlotte (NC) 560
The U of North Carolina at Greensboro (NC) 560
The U of North Carolina at Pembroke (NC) 560
The U of North Carolina at Wilmington (NC) 561
U of North Dakota (ND) 561
U of Northern Iowa (IA) 561
U of North Texas (TX) 562
U of Oklahoma (OK) 562
U of Pittsburgh (PA) 569
U of Portland (OR) 570
U of Puerto Rico, Humacao U Coll (PR) 570
U of Puerto Rico, Río Piedras (PR) 571
U of Regina (SK, Canada) 572
U of Rio Grande (OH) 572
U of St. Francis (IL) 573
U of Saint Francis (IN) 573
U of St. Thomas (MN) 573
U of Sioux Falls (SD) 574
The U of South Dakota (SD) 575
U of Southern Indiana (IN) 576
U of Southern Maine (ME) 576
U of Southern Mississippi (MS) 576
U of South Florida (FL) 576
The U of Tennessee (TN) 577
The U of Tennessee at Chattanooga (TN) 577
The U of Tennessee at Martin (TN) 577
The U of Texas at Arlington (TX) 577
The U of Texas at Austin (TX) 578
The U of Texas at El Paso (TX) 578
The U of Texas–Pan American (TX) 579
U of the District of Columbia (DC) 580
U of the Sacred Heart (PR) 580
U of the Virgin Islands (VI) 581
U of Toledo (OH) 581
U of Utah (UT) 582
U of Vermont (VT) 582
U of Victoria (BC, Canada) 582
U of Washington (WA) 583
U of Waterloo (ON, Canada) 583
The U of Western Ontario (ON, Canada) 583
U of West Florida (FL) 583
U of Windsor (ON, Canada) 584
U of Wisconsin–Eau Claire (WI) 584
U of Wisconsin–Green Bay (WI) 584
U of Wisconsin–Madison (WI) 584
U of Wisconsin–Milwaukee (WI) 585
U of Wisconsin–Oshkosh (WI) 585
U of Wisconsin–River Falls (WI) 585
U of Wisconsin–Superior (WI) 586
U of Wisconsin–Whitewater (WI) 586
U of Wyoming (WY) 586
Ursuline Coll (OH) 587
Utah State U (UT) 587
Valparaiso U (IN) 588
Virginia Commonwealth U (VA) 590
Virginia Intermont Coll (VA) 590
Virginia State U (VA) 591
Virginia Union U (VA) 591
Viterbo U (WI) 591
Walla Walla Coll (WA) 593
Warner Pacific Coll (OR) 593
Warner Southern Coll (FL) 593
Warren Wilson Coll (NC) 594
Wartburg Coll (IA) 594
Washington State U (WA) 595
Wayne State U (MI) 596
Weber State U (UT) 596
West Chester U of Pennsylvania (PA) 598
Western Carolina U (NC) 598
Western Connecticut State U (CT) 598
Western Illinois U (IL) 599
Western Kentucky U (KY) 599
Western Michigan U (MI) 599
Western New England Coll (MA) 600
Western New Mexico U (NM) 600
West Texas A&M U (TX) 602
West Virginia State Coll (WV) 602
West Virginia U (WV) 602
Wheelock Coll (MA) 603
Whittier Coll (CA) 604
Wichita State U (KS) 604
Widener U (PA) 604
Wiley Coll (TX) 605
William Woods U (MO) 607
Wilmington Coll (OH) 607
Winona State U (MN) 608
Winthrop U (SC) 608
Wright State U (OH) 609
Xavier U (OH) 610
York Coll of the City U of New York (NY) 611
York U (ON, Canada) 611
Youngstown State U (OH) 611

SOCIOBIOLOGY

Overview: This major weaves together many biological subdisciplines, such as population biology, ecology, evolution, and animal behavior and applies them to the fields of psychology and sociology. *Related majors:* biology, ecology, evolution, psychology, and sociology. *Potential careers:* professor, research scientist. *Salary potential:* $25k-$35k.

Beloit Coll (WI) 285
Cornell U (NY) 333
Hampshire Coll (MA) 375
Harvard U (MA) 376
Long Island U, Southampton Coll, Friends World Program (NY) 409
Tufts U (MA) 533

SOCIOLOGY

Overview: Sociology is the study of human social institutions and social relationships and behavior. *Related majors:* history, political science, urban affairs/studies, anthropology, gerontology. *Potential careers:* sociologist, politician or political aide, professor, lawyer, human services counselor. *Salary potential:* $27k-$35k.

Abilene Christian U (TX) 260
Acadia U (NS, Canada) 260
Adams State Coll (CO) 260
Adelphi U (NY) 260
Adrian Coll (MI) 260
Agnes Scott Coll (GA) 261
Alabama A&M U (AL) 261
Alabama State U (AL) 261
Albany State U (GA) 262
Albertson Coll of Idaho (ID) 262
Albertus Magnus Coll (CT) 262
Albion Coll (MI) 262
Albright Coll (PA) 263
Alcorn State U (MS) 263
Alderson-Broaddus Coll (WV) 263
Alfred U (NY) 263
Allen U (SC) 264
Alliant International U (CA) 264
Alma Coll (MI) 264
American International Coll (MA) 267
American U (DC) 267
The American U in Cairo(Egypt) 267
Amherst Coll (MA) 268
Anderson U (IN) 268
Andrews U (MI) 269
Angelo State U (TX) 269
Antioch Coll (OH) 269
Appalachian State U (NC) 270
Aquinas Coll (MI) 270
Arcadia U (PA) 271
Arizona State U (AZ) 271
Arizona State U West (AZ) 272
Arkansas State U (AR) 272
Arkansas Tech U (AR) 272
Asbury Coll (KY) 274
Ashland U (OH) 274
Assumption Coll (MA) 275
Athabasca U (AB, Canada) 275
Athens State U (AL) 275
Atlantic Baptist U (NB, Canada) 275
Atlantic Union Coll (MA) 276
Auburn U (AL) 276
Auburn U Montgomery (AL) 276
Augsburg Coll (MN) 276
Augustana Coll (IL) 276
Augustana Coll (SD) 276
Augusta State U (GA) 277
Aurora U (IL) 277
Austin Coll (TX) 277
Austin Peay State U (TN) 278
Averett U (VA) 278
Avila U (MO) 278
Azusa Pacific U (CA) 278
Baker U (KS) 280
Baldwin-Wallace Coll (OH) 280
Ball State U (IN) 280
Barber-Scotia Coll (NC) 281
Bard Coll (NY) 281
Barnard Coll (NY) 282
Barry U (FL) 282
Bates Coll (ME) 282
Baylor U (TX) 283
Bellarmine U (KY) 284
Bellevue U (NE) 284
Belmont Abbey Coll (NC) 284
Belmont U (TN) 284
Beloit Coll (WI) 285
Bemidji State U (MN) 285
Benedict Coll (SC) 285
Benedictine Coll (KS) 285
Benedictine U (IL) 285
Bennett Coll (NC) 286
Bennington Coll (VT) 286
Berea Coll (KY) 286
Baruch Coll of the City U of NY (NY) 286
Berry Coll (GA) 287
Bethany Coll (KS) 287
Bethel Coll (IN) 288
Bethune-Cookman Coll (FL) 289
Biola U (CA) 289
Birmingham-Southern Coll (AL) 289
Bishop's U (QC, Canada) 289
Black Hills State U (SD) 290
Bloomfield Coll (NJ) 290
Bloomsburg U of Pennsylvania (PA) 290
Bluefield Coll (VA) 291
Bluffton Coll (OH) 291
Boston Coll (MA) 292
Boston U (MA) 292
Bowdoin Coll (ME) 292
Bowie State U (MD) 292
Bowling Green State U (OH) 292
Bradley U (IL) 293
Brandeis U (MA) 293
Brandon U (MB, Canada) 293
Brewton-Parker Coll (GA) 294
Briar Cliff U (IA) 294
Bridgewater Coll (VA) 294
Bridgewater State Coll (MA) 294
Brigham Young U (UT) 295
Brock U (ON, Canada) 295
Brooklyn Coll of the City U of NY (NY) 295
Brown U (RI) 296
Bryn Mawr Coll (PA) 297
Bucknell U (PA) 297
Butler U (IN) 297
Cabrini Coll (PA) 298
Caldwell Coll (NJ) 298

SOCIOLOGY (continued)

California Lutheran U (CA) **299**
California State Polytechnic U, Pomona (CA) **300**
California State U, Bakersfield (CA) **300**
California State U, Chico (CA) **300**
California State U, Dominguez Hills (CA) **300**
California State U, Fresno (CA) **301**
California State U, Fullerton (CA) **301**
California State U, Hayward (CA) **301**
California State U, Long Beach (CA) **301**
California State U, Northridge (CA) **301**
California State U, Sacramento (CA) **301**
California State U, San Bernardino (CA) **302**
California State U, San Marcos (CA) **302**
California State U, Stanislaus (CA) **302**
California U of Pennsylvania (PA) **302**
Calumet Coll of Saint Joseph (IN) **302**
Calvin Coll (MI) **303**
Cameron U (OK) **303**
Campbellsville U (KY) **303**
Canisius Coll (NY) **304**
Capital U (OH) **304**
Cardinal Stritch U (WI) **305**
Carleton Coll (MN) **305**
Carleton U (ON, Canada) **305**
Carlow Coll (PA) **305**
Carroll Coll (MT) **306**
Carroll Coll (WI) **306**
Carson-Newman Coll (TN) **306**
Carthage Coll (WI) **306**
Case Western Reserve U (OH) **307**
Castleton State Coll (VT) **307**
Catawba Coll (NC) **307**
The Catholic U of America (DC) **307**
Cedar Crest Coll (PA) **308**
Cedarville U (OH) **308**
Centenary Coll (NJ) **308**
Centenary Coll of Louisiana (LA) **308**
Central Coll (IA) **309**
Central Connecticut State U (CT) **309**
Central Methodist Coll (MO) **309**
Central Michigan U (MI) **310**
Central Missouri State U (MO) **310**
Central Washington U (WA) **310**
Centre Coll (KY) **310**
Chadron State Coll (NE) **311**
Chapman U (CA) **311**
Charleston Southern U (SC) **311**
Chestnut Hill Coll (PA) **312**
Cheyney U of Pennsylvania (PA) **312**
Christopher Newport U (VA) **313**
City Coll of the City U of NY (NY) **314**
Claflin U (SC) **314**
Clarion U of Pennsylvania (PA) **315**
Clark Atlanta U (GA) **315**
Clarke Coll (IA) **315**
Clarkson U (NY) **316**
Clark U (MA) **316**
Clemson U (SC) **317**
Cleveland State U (OH) **317**
Coastal Carolina U (SC) **318**
Coe Coll (IA) **318**
Coker Coll (SC) **318**
Colby Coll (ME) **318**
Colgate U (NY) **319**
Coll of Charleston (SC) **320**
Coll of Mount St. Joseph (OH) **320**
Coll of Mount Saint Vincent (NY) **320**
The Coll of New Jersey (NJ) **320**
The Coll of New Rochelle (NY) **321**
Coll of Saint Benedict (MN) **321**
Coll of St. Catherine (MN) **321**
Coll of Saint Elizabeth (NJ) **321**
The Coll of Saint Rose (NY) **322**
The Coll of Southeastern Europe, The American U of Athens(Greece) **323**
Coll of Staten Island of the City U of NY (NY) **323**
Coll of the Holy Cross (MA) **323**
Coll of the Ozarks (MO) **323**
The Coll of William and Mary (VA) **324**
The Coll of Wooster (OH) **324**
The Colorado Coll (CO) **325**
Colorado State U (CO) **325**
Colorado State U-Pueblo (CO) **325**
Columbia Coll (MO) **326**
Columbia Coll (NY) **326**
Columbia Coll (SC) **327**
Columbia U, School of General Studies (NY) **328**
Columbus State U (GA) **328**
Concord Coll (WV) **329**
Concordia Coll (MN) **329**
Concordia U (IL) **330**
Concordia U (MI) **330**
Concordia U (MN) **330**
Concordia U (NE) **330**
Concordia U (QC, Canada) **331**
Concordia U Coll of Alberta (AB, Canada) **331**
Connecticut Coll (CT) **331**
Converse Coll (SC) **332**
Cornell Coll (IA) **332**
Cornell U (NY) **333**
Cornerstone U (MI) **333**
Covenant Coll (GA) **333**
Creighton U (NE) **333**
Culver-Stockton Coll (MO) **334**
Cumberland U (TN) **335**
Curry Coll (MA) **335**
Dakota Wesleyan U (SD) **336**
Dalhousie U (NS, Canada) **336**
Dallas Baptist U (TX) **336**
Dana Coll (NE) **337**
Dartmouth Coll (NH) **337**
Davidson Coll (NC) **338**
Davis & Elkins Coll (WV) **338**
Delaware State U (DE) **338**
Denison U (OH) **339**
DePaul U (IL) **339**
DePauw U (IN) **339**
Deree Coll(Greece) **339**
Dickinson Coll (PA) **344**
Dillard U (LA) **344**
Doane Coll (NE) **344**
Dominican U (IL) **345**
Dordt Coll (IA) **345**
Dowling Coll (NY) **345**
Drake U (IA) **345**
Drew U (NJ) **346**
Drexel U (PA) **346**
Drury U (MO) **346**
Duke U (NC) **346**
Duquesne U (PA) **346**
D'Youville Coll (NY) **347**
Earlham Coll (IN) **347**
East Carolina U (NC) **347**
East Central U (OK) **347**
Eastern Connecticut State U (CT) **347**
Eastern Illinois U (IL) **348**
Eastern Kentucky U (KY) **348**
Eastern Mennonite U (VA) **348**
Eastern Michigan U (MI) **348**
Eastern Nazarene Coll (MA) **348**
Eastern New Mexico U (NM) **349**
Eastern Oregon U (OR) **349**
Eastern U (PA) **349**
Eastern Washington U (WA) **349**
East Stroudsburg U of Pennsylvania (PA) **349**
East Tennessee State U (TN) **349**
East Texas Baptist U (TX) **350**
East-West U (IL) **350**
Eckerd Coll (FL) **350**
Edgewood Coll (WI) **351**
Edinboro U of Pennsylvania (PA) **351**
Elizabeth City State U (NC) **351**
Elizabethtown Coll (PA) **351**
Elmhurst Coll (IL) **351**
Elmira Coll (NY) **351**
Elms Coll (MA) **352**
Elon U (NC) **352**
Emmanuel Coll (MA) **353**
Emory & Henry Coll (VA) **353**
Emory U (GA) **354**
Emporia State U (KS) **354**
Eugene Lang Coll, New School U (NY) **355**
Eureka Coll (IL) **355**
Evangel U (MO) **355**
The Evergreen State Coll (WA) **355**
Excelsior Coll (NY) **356**
Fairfield U (CT) **356**
Fairleigh Dickinson U, Florham (NJ) **356**
Fairleigh Dickinson U, Teaneck-Metro Campus (NJ) **356**
Fairmont State Coll (WV) **356**
Fayetteville State U (NC) **357**
Felician Coll (NJ) **357**
Fisk U (TN) **358**
Fitchburg State Coll (MA) **358**
Flagler Coll (FL) **359**
Florida A&M U (FL) **359**
Florida Atlantic U (FL) **359**
Florida International U (FL) **360**
Florida Southern Coll (FL) **361**
Florida State U (FL) **361**
Fordham U (NY) **362**
Fort Hays State U (KS) **362**
Fort Lewis Coll (CO) **362**
Fort Valley State U (GA) **362**
Framingham State Coll (MA) **362**
Franciscan U of Steubenville (OH) **363**
Francis Marion U (SC) **363**
Franklin and Marshall Coll (PA) **363**
Franklin Coll (IN) **363**
Franklin Pierce Coll (NH) **364**
Frostburg State U (MD) **365**
Furman U (SC) **365**
Gallaudet U (DC) **365**
Gardner-Webb U (NC) **365**
Geneva Coll (PA) **366**
George Fox U (OR) **366**
George Mason U (VA) **366**
Georgetown Coll (KY) **366**
Georgetown U (DC) **366**
The George Washington U (DC) **367**
Georgia Coll & State U (GA) **367**
Georgian Court Coll (NJ) **367**
Georgia Southern U (GA) **367**
Georgia Southwestern State U (GA) **368**
Georgia State U (GA) **368**
Gettysburg Coll (PA) **368**
Goddard Coll (VT) **369**
Gonzaga U (WA) **369**
Gordon Coll (MA) **370**
Goshen Coll (IN) **370**
Goucher Coll (MD) **370**
Grace Coll (IN) **370**
Graceland U (IA) **371**
Grambling State U (LA) **371**
Grand Canyon U (AZ) **371**
Grand Valley State U (MI) **371**
Greensboro Coll (NC) **372**
Greenville Coll (IL) **373**
Grinnell Coll (IA) **373**
Grove City Coll (PA) **373**
Guilford Coll (NC) **373**
Gustavus Adolphus Coll (MN) **374**
Gwynedd-Mercy Coll (PA) **374**
Hamilton Coll (NY) **374**
Hamline U (MN) **374**
Hampshire Coll (MA) **375**
Hampton U (VA) **375**
Hanover Coll (IN) **375**
Hardin-Simmons U (TX) **376**
Hartwick Coll (NY) **376**
Harvard U (MA) **376**
Hastings Coll (NE) **377**
Haverford Coll (PA) **377**
Hawai'i Pacific U (HI) **377**
Henderson State U (AR) **378**
Hendrix Coll (AR) **378**
High Point U (NC) **379**
Hillsdale Coll (MI) **379**
Hiram Coll (OH) **379**
Hobart and William Smith Colls (NY) **380**
Hofstra U (NY) **380**
Hollins U (VA) **380**
Holy Family U (PA) **380**
Holy Names Coll (CA) **381**
Hood Coll (MD) **381**
Hope Coll (MI) **381**
Houghton Coll (NY) **381**
Houston Baptist U (TX) **382**
Howard Payne U (TX) **382**
Howard U (DC) **382**
Humboldt State U (CA) **382**
Hunter Coll of the City U of NY (NY) **382**
Huntington Coll (IN) **383**
Huston-Tillotson Coll (TX) **383**
Idaho State U (ID) **384**
Illinois Coll (IL) **384**
Illinois State U (IL) **384**
Illinois Wesleyan U (IL) **385**
Immaculata U (PA) **385**
Indiana State U (IN) **385**
Indiana U Bloomington (IN) **385**
Indiana U East (IN) **386**
Indiana U Kokomo (IN) **386**
Indiana U Northwest (IN) **386**
Indiana U of Pennsylvania (PA) **386**
Indiana U–Purdue U Fort Wayne (IN) **386**
Indiana U–Purdue U Indianapolis (IN) **387**
Indiana U South Bend (IN) **387**
Indiana U Southeast (IN) **387**
Indiana Wesleyan U (IN) **387**
Inter American U of PR, San Germán Campus (PR) **388**
Iona Coll (NY) **390**
Iowa State U of Science and Technology (IA) **390**
Ithaca Coll (NY) **390**
Jackson State U (MS) **390**
Jacksonville State U (AL) **390**
Jacksonville U (FL) **391**
James Madison U (VA) **391**
John Carroll U (OH) **392**
Johns Hopkins U (MD) **392**
Johnson C. Smith U (NC) **394**
Johnson State Coll (VT) **394**
Judson Coll (IL) **395**
Juniata Coll (PA) **395**
Kalamazoo Coll (MI) **395**
Kansas State U (KS) **396**
Kean U (NJ) **396**
Keene State Coll (NH) **396**
Kennesaw State U (GA) **397**
Kent State U (OH) **397**
Kentucky State U (KY) **397**
Kentucky Wesleyan Coll (KY) **397**
Kenyon Coll (OH) **398**
Keuka Coll (NY) **398**
King's Coll (PA) **398**
The King's U Coll (AB, Canada) **399**
Knox Coll (IL) **399**
Kutztown U of Pennsylvania (PA) **399**
Lafayette Coll (PA) **400**
Lake Erie Coll (OH) **400**
Lake Forest Coll (IL) **400**
Lakehead U (ON, Canada) **400**
Lakeland Coll (WI) **401**
Lamar U (TX) **401**
Lambuth U (TN) **401**
Lander U (SC) **401**
Lane Coll (TN) **402**
Langston U (OK) **402**
La Roche Coll (PA) **402**
La Salle U (PA) **402**
Lasell Coll (MA) **402**
La Sierra U (CA) **403**
Laurentian U (ON, Canada) **403**
Lees-McRae Coll (NC) **404**
Lee U (TN) **404**
Lehigh U (PA) **404**
Lehman Coll of the City U of NY (NY) **404**
Le Moyne Coll (NY) **404**
Lenoir-Rhyne Coll (NC) **405**
Lewis & Clark Coll (OR) **405**
Lewis U (IL) **406**
Lincoln U (PA) **407**
Lindenwood U (MO) **407**
Linfield Coll (OR) **408**
Lock Haven U of Pennsylvania (PA) **408**
Long Island U, Brooklyn Campus (NY) **409**
Long Island U, C.W. Post Campus (NY) **409**
Long Island U, Southampton Coll (NY) **409**
Long Island U, Southampton Coll, Friends World Program (NY) **409**
Longwood U (VA) **409**
Loras Coll (IA) **410**
Louisiana Coll (LA) **410**
Louisiana State U and A&M Coll (LA) **410**
Louisiana State U in Shreveport (LA) **410**
Louisiana Tech U (LA) **410**
Lourdes Coll (OH) **411**
Loyola Coll in Maryland (MD) **411**
Loyola Marymount U (CA) **411**
Loyola U Chicago (IL) **411**
Loyola U New Orleans (LA) **411**
Luther Coll (IA) **412**
Lycoming Coll (PA) **412**
Lynchburg Coll (VA) **413**
Macalester Coll (MN) **413**
Madonna U (MI) **414**
Malaspina U-Coll (BC, Canada) **415**
Manchester Coll (IN) **415**
Manhattan Coll (NY) **416**
Manhattanville Coll (NY) **416**
Mansfield U of Pennsylvania (PA) **416**
Marian Coll (IN) **417**
Marlboro Coll (VT) **418**
Marquette U (WI) **418**
Marshall U (WV) **418**
Mars Hill Coll (NC) **418**
Martin U (IN) **419**
Mary Baldwin Coll (VA) **419**
Marymount Coll of Fordham U (NY) **419**
Marymount Manhattan Coll (NY) **420**
Marymount U (VA) **420**
Maryville Coll (TN) **420**
Maryville U of Saint Louis (MO) **420**
Mary Washington Coll (VA) **420**

Massachusetts Coll of Liberal Arts (MA) ***421***
McDaniel Coll (MD) ***422***
McGill U (QC, Canada) ***423***
McKendree Coll (IL) ***423***
McMaster U (ON, Canada) ***423***
McMurry U (TX) ***423***
McNeese State U (LA) ***423***
McPherson Coll (KS) ***423***
Memorial U of Newfoundland (NF, Canada) ***424***
Mercer U (GA) ***425***
Mercy Coll (NY) ***425***
Mercyhurst Coll (PA) ***425***
Meredith Coll (NC) ***426***
Merrimack Coll (MA) ***426***
Mesa State Coll (CO) ***426***
Messiah Coll (PA) ***426***
Methodist Coll (NC) ***427***
Metropolitan State Coll of Denver (CO) ***427***
Miami U (OH) ***428***
Michigan State U (MI) ***428***
MidAmerica Nazarene U (KS) ***428***
Middlebury Coll (VT) ***429***
Middle Tennessee State U (TN) ***429***
Midland Lutheran Coll (NE) ***429***
Midwestern State U (TX) ***430***
Millersville U of Pennsylvania (PA) ***430***
Milligan Coll (TN) ***430***
Millikin U (IL) ***430***
Millsaps Coll (MS) ***431***
Mills Coll (CA) ***431***
Minnesota State U, Mankato (MN) ***431***
Minnesota State U, Moorhead (MN) ***432***
Minot State U (ND) ***432***
Mississippi Coll (MS) ***432***
Mississippi State U (MS) ***432***
Mississippi Valley State U (MS) ***432***
Missouri Southern State Coll (MO) ***433***
Missouri Valley Coll (MO) ***433***
Molloy Coll (NY) ***433***
Monmouth Coll (IL) ***434***
Montana State U–Billings (MT) ***434***
Montana State U–Bozeman (MT) ***434***
Montclair State U (NJ) ***435***
Moravian Coll (PA) ***436***
Morehead State U (KY) ***436***
Morehouse Coll (GA) ***436***
Morgan State U (MD) ***436***
Morris Coll (SC) ***437***
Mount Allison U (NB, Canada) ***437***
Mount Holyoke Coll (MA) ***438***
Mount Mercy Coll (IA) ***438***
Mount Saint Mary Coll (NY) ***439***
Mount St. Mary's Coll (CA) ***439***
Mount Saint Mary's Coll and Seminary (MD) ***439***
Mount Saint Vincent U (NS, Canada) ***439***
Mount Union Coll (OH) ***440***
Mount Vernon Nazarene U (OH) ***440***
Muhlenberg Coll (PA) ***440***
Murray State U (KY) ***440***
Muskingum Coll (OH) ***441***
Nazareth Coll of Rochester (NY) ***443***
Nebraska Wesleyan U (NE) ***443***
Newberry Coll (SC) ***444***
New Coll of Florida (FL) ***444***
New England Coll (NH) ***444***
New Jersey City U (NJ) ***445***
Newman U (KS) ***445***
New Mexico Highlands U (NM) ***446***
New Mexico State U (NM) ***446***
New York Inst of Technology (NY) ***447***
New York U (NY) ***447***
Niagara U (NY) ***447***
Nicholls State U (LA) ***447***
Nipissing U (ON, Canada) ***448***
Norfolk State U (VA) ***448***
North Carolina Ag and Tech State U (NC) ***448***
North Carolina Central U (NC) ***448***
North Carolina State U (NC) ***449***
North Carolina Wesleyan Coll (NC) ***449***
North Central Coll (IL) ***449***
North Dakota State U (ND) ***449***
Northeastern Illinois U (IL) ***450***
Northeastern State U (OK) ***450***
Northeastern U (MA) ***450***
Northern Arizona U (AZ) ***450***
Northern Illinois U (IL) ***450***
Northern Kentucky U (KY) ***451***
Northern Michigan U (MI) ***451***
Northern State U (SD) ***451***
North Georgia Coll & State U (GA) ***451***
Northland Coll (WI) ***452***
North Park U (IL) ***452***
Northwestern Coll (IA) ***453***
Northwestern Oklahoma State U (OK) ***453***
Northwestern State U of Louisiana (LA) ***453***
Northwestern U (IL) ***453***
Northwest Missouri State U (MO) ***454***
Notre Dame de Namur U (CA) ***455***
Oakland U (MI) ***456***
Oberlin Coll (OH) ***456***
Occidental Coll (CA) ***457***
Oglethorpe U (GA) ***457***
Ohio Dominican U (OH) ***457***
Ohio Northern U (OH) ***457***
The Ohio State U (OH) ***457***
Ohio U (OH) ***458***
Ohio Wesleyan U (OH) ***459***
Oklahoma Baptist U (OK) ***459***
Oklahoma City U (OK) ***460***
Oklahoma State U (OK) ***460***
Old Dominion U (VA) ***460***
Olivet Coll (MI) ***461***
Oregon State U (OR) ***462***
Ottawa U (KS) ***462***
Otterbein Coll (OH) ***462***
Ouachita Baptist U (AR) ***462***
Our Lady of the Lake U of San Antonio (TX) ***463***
Pacific Lutheran U (WA) ***463***
Pacific Union Coll (CA) ***464***
Pacific U (OR) ***464***
Paine Coll (GA) ***465***
Park U (MO) ***465***
Paul Quinn Coll (TX) ***466***
Penn State U Harrisburg Campus of the Capital Coll (PA) ***468***
Penn State U Univ Park Campus (PA) ***468***
Pepperdine U, Malibu (CA) ***469***
Peru State Coll (NE) ***469***
Pfeiffer U (NC) ***469***
Piedmont Coll (GA) ***470***
Pikeville Coll (KY) ***470***
Pittsburg State U (KS) ***470***
Pitzer Coll (CA) ***471***
Plattsburgh State U of NY (NY) ***471***
Point Loma Nazarene U (CA) ***471***
Pomona Coll (CA) ***472***
Pontifical Catholic U of Puerto Rico (PR) ***472***
Portland State U (OR) ***472***
Prairie View A&M U (TX) ***473***
Presbyterian Coll (SC) ***473***
Prescott Coll (AZ) ***474***
Princeton U (NJ) ***474***
Principia Coll (IL) ***474***
Providence Coll (RI) ***474***
Purchase Coll, State U of NY (NY) ***475***
Purdue U (IN) ***475***
Purdue U Calumet (IN) ***475***
Queens Coll of the City U of NY (NY) ***475***
Queen's U at Kingston (ON, Canada) ***476***
Quincy U (IL) ***476***
Quinnipiac U (CT) ***476***
Radford U (VA) ***476***
Ramapo Coll of New Jersey (NJ) ***477***
Randolph-Macon Coll (VA) ***477***
Randolph-Macon Woman's Coll (VA) ***477***
Reed Coll (OR) ***477***
Regis Coll (MA) ***478***
Regis U (CO) ***478***
Reinhardt Coll (GA) ***478***
Rhode Island Coll (RI) ***479***
Rhodes Coll (TN) ***479***
Rice U (TX) ***479***
The Richard Stockton Coll of New Jersey (NJ) ***479***
Richmond, The American International U in London(United Kingdom) ***480***
Rider U (NJ) ***480***
Ripon Coll (WI) ***480***
Rivier Coll (NH) ***480***
Roanoke Coll (VA) ***481***
Roberts Wesleyan Coll (NY) ***481***
Rockford Coll (IL) ***482***
Rockhurst U (MO) ***482***
Rocky Mountain Coll (MT) ***482***
Rollins Coll (FL) ***483***
Roosevelt U (IL) ***483***
Rosemont Coll (PA) ***484***
Rowan U (NJ) ***484***
Russell Sage Coll (NY) ***484***
Rust Coll (MS) ***485***
Rutgers, The State U of New Jersey, Camden (NJ) ***485***
Rutgers, The State U of New Jersey, Newark (NJ) ***485***
Rutgers, The State U of New Jersey, New Brunswick (NJ) ***485***
Sacred Heart U (CT) ***486***
Saginaw Valley State U (MI) ***486***
St. Ambrose U (IA) ***486***
Saint Anselm Coll (NH) ***487***
Saint Augustine's Coll (NC) ***487***
St. Bonaventure U (NY) ***487***
St. Cloud State U (MN) ***488***
St. Edward's U (TX) ***488***
St. Francis Coll (NY) ***488***
Saint Francis U (PA) ***488***
St. Francis Xavier U (NS, Canada) ***489***
St. John Fisher Coll (NY) ***489***
Saint John's U (MN) ***490***
St. John's U (NY) ***490***
Saint Joseph Coll (CT) ***490***
Saint Joseph's Coll (IN) ***490***
Saint Joseph's Coll of Maine (ME) ***491***
St. Joseph's Coll, Suffolk Campus (NY) ***491***
Saint Joseph's U (PA) ***491***
St. Lawrence U (NY) ***491***
Saint Leo U (FL) ***492***
Saint Louis U (MO) ***492***
Saint Mary Coll (KS) ***493***
Saint Mary's Coll (IN) ***493***
Saint Mary's Coll of California (CA) ***494***
Saint Mary's Coll of Madonna U (MI) ***493***
St. Mary's Coll of Maryland (MD) ***494***
Saint Mary's U (NS, Canada) ***494***
Saint Mary's U of Minnesota (MN) ***494***
St. Mary's U of San Antonio (TX) ***494***
Saint Michael's Coll (VT) ***494***
St. Norbert Coll (WI) ***495***
St. Olaf Coll (MN) ***495***
Saint Peter's Coll (NJ) ***495***
St. Thomas U (FL) ***496***
St. Thomas U (NB, Canada) ***496***
Saint Vincent Coll (PA) ***496***
Saint Xavier U (IL) ***496***
Salem Coll (NC) ***496***
Salem State Coll (MA) ***497***
Salisbury U (MD) ***497***
Salve Regina U (RI) ***497***
Samford U (AL) ***497***
Sam Houston State U (TX) ***497***
San Diego State U (CA) ***498***
San Francisco State U (CA) ***498***
San Jose State U (CA) ***499***
Santa Clara U (CA) ***499***
Sarah Lawrence Coll (NY) ***499***
Savannah State U (GA) ***499***
Scripps Coll (CA) ***501***
Seattle Pacific U (WA) ***501***
Seattle U (WA) ***501***
Seton Hall U (NJ) ***502***
Seton Hill U (PA) ***502***
Shaw U (NC) ***502***
Shenandoah U (VA) ***503***
Shepherd Coll (WV) ***503***
Shippensburg U of Pennsylvania (PA) ***503***
Shorter Coll (GA) ***504***
Siena Coll (NY) ***504***
Simmons Coll (MA) ***504***
Simon Fraser U (BC, Canada) ***505***
Simpson Coll (IA) ***505***
Skidmore Coll (NY) ***506***
Slippery Rock U of Pennsylvania (PA) ***506***
Smith Coll (MA) ***506***
Sonoma State U (CA) ***506***
South Carolina State U (SC) ***506***
South Dakota State U (SD) ***507***
Southeastern Louisiana U (LA) ***508***
Southeastern Oklahoma State U (OK) ***508***
Southeast Missouri State U (MO) ***508***
Southern Arkansas U–Magnolia (AR) ***509***
Southern Connecticut State U (CT) ***509***
Southern Illinois U Carbondale (IL) ***509***
Southern Illinois U Edwardsville (IL) ***509***
Southern Methodist U (TX) ***510***
Southern Nazarene U (OK) ***510***
Southern Oregon U (OR) ***510***
Southern U and A&M Coll (LA) ***511***
Southern Utah U (UT) ***511***
Southwest Baptist U (MO) ***512***
Southwestern U (TX) ***513***
Southwest Missouri State U (MO) ***513***
Southwest State U (MN) ***513***
Southwest Texas State U (TX) ***513***
Spalding U (KY) ***513***
Spelman Coll (GA) ***514***
Spring Arbor U (MI) ***514***
Springfield Coll (MA) ***514***
Stanford U (CA) ***514***
State U of NY at Albany (NY) ***514***
State U of NY at Binghamton (NY) ***515***
State U of NY at New Paltz (NY) ***515***
State U of NY at Oswego (NY) ***515***
State U of NY Coll at Brockport (NY) ***515***
State U of NY Coll at Buffalo (NY) ***516***
State U of NY Coll at Cortland (NY) ***516***
State U of NY Coll at Fredonia (NY) ***516***
State U of NY Coll at Geneseo (NY) ***516***
State U of NY Coll at Old Westbury (NY) ***516***
State U of NY Coll at Oneonta (NY) ***517***
State U of NY Coll at Potsdam (NY) ***517***
State U of NY Inst of Tech at Utica/Rome (NY) ***518***
State U of West Georgia (GA) ***518***
Stephen F. Austin State U (TX) ***518***
Stetson U (FL) ***519***
Stonehill Coll (MA) ***520***
Stony Brook U, State University of New York (NY) ***520***
Suffolk U (MA) ***520***
Susquehanna U (PA) ***521***
Swarthmore Coll (PA) ***521***
Sweet Briar Coll (VA) ***521***
Syracuse U (NY) ***521***
Tabor Coll (KS) ***522***
Talladega Coll (AL) ***522***
Tarleton State U (TX) ***522***
Taylor U (IN) ***523***
Teikyo Post U (CT) ***523***
Temple U (PA) ***523***
Tennessee State U (TN) ***523***
Tennessee Technological U (TN) ***524***
Texas A&M International U (TX) ***524***
Texas A&M U (TX) ***524***
Texas A&M U–Commerce (TX) ***525***
Texas A&M U–Corpus Christi (TX) ***525***
Texas A&M U–Kingsville (TX) ***525***
Texas Christian U (TX) ***526***
Texas Coll (TX) ***526***
Texas Lutheran U (TX) ***526***
Texas Southern U (TX) ***526***
Texas Tech U (TX) ***526***
Texas Wesleyan U (TX) ***526***
Texas Woman's U (TX) ***527***
Thiel Coll (PA) ***527***
Thomas Edison State Coll (NJ) ***527***
Thomas More Coll (KY) ***528***
Thomas U (GA) ***528***
Touro Coll (NY) ***529***
Towson U (MD) ***529***
Transylvania U (KY) ***529***
Trent U (ON, Canada) ***529***
Trinity Christian Coll (IL) ***530***
Trinity Coll (CT) ***530***
Trinity International U (IL) ***531***
Trinity U (TX) ***531***
Troy State U (AL) ***532***
Troy State U Dothan (AL) ***532***
Truman State U (MO) ***532***
Tufts U (MA) ***533***
Tulane U (LA) ***533***
Tuskegee U (AL) ***533***
Union Coll (NY) ***534***
Union U (TN) ***534***
Université Laval (QC, Canada) ***536***
U at Buffalo, The State University of New York (NY) ***536***
U Coll of the Cariboo (BC, Canada) ***537***
The U of Akron (OH) ***537***
The U of Alabama (AL) ***537***
The U of Alabama at Birmingham (AL) ***537***
The U of Alabama in Huntsville (AL) ***537***
U of Alaska Anchorage (AK) ***538***
U of Alaska Fairbanks (AK) ***538***
U of Alberta (AB, Canada) ***538***
The U of Arizona (AZ) ***538***
U of Arkansas (AR) ***539***
U of Arkansas at Little Rock (AR) ***539***
The U of British Columbia (BC, Canada) ***540***
U of Calgary (AB, Canada) ***540***
U of Calif, Berkeley (CA) ***540***
U of Calif, Davis (CA) ***540***
U of Calif, Irvine (CA) ***541***
U of Calif, Los Angeles (CA) ***541***
U of Calif, Riverside (CA) ***541***
U of Calif, San Diego (CA) ***541***
U of Calif, Santa Barbara (CA) ***541***
U of Calif, Santa Cruz (CA) ***542***
U of Central Arkansas (AR) ***542***

SOCIOLOGY (continued)

U of Central Florida (FL) ***542***
U of Central Oklahoma (OK) ***542***
U of Chicago (IL) ***542***
U of Cincinnati (OH) ***543***
U of Colorado at Boulder (CO) ***543***
U of Colorado at Colorado Springs (CO) ***543***
U of Colorado at Denver (CO) ***543***
U of Connecticut (CT) ***544***
U of Dayton (OH) ***544***
U of Delaware (DE) ***544***
U of Denver (CO) ***544***
U of Dubuque (IA) ***545***
U of Evansville (IN) ***545***
The U of Findlay (OH) ***545***
U of Florida (FL) ***545***
U of Georgia (GA) ***545***
U of Great Falls (MT) ***545***
U of Guelph (ON, Canada) ***546***
U of Hartford (CT) ***546***
U of Hawaii at Hilo (HI) ***546***
U of Hawaii at Manoa (HI) ***546***
U of Hawaii–West Oahu (HI) ***546***
U of Houston (TX) ***547***
U of Houston–Clear Lake (TX) ***547***
U of Idaho (ID) ***547***
U of Illinois at Chicago (IL) ***547***
U of Illinois at Springfield (IL) ***548***
U of Illinois at Urbana–Champaign (IL) ***548***
U of Indianapolis (IN) ***548***
The U of Iowa (IA) ***548***
U of Kansas (KS) ***549***
U of Kentucky (KY) ***549***
U of King's Coll (NS, Canada) ***549***
U of La Verne (CA) ***549***
The U of Lethbridge (AB, Canada) ***549***
U of Louisiana at Lafayette (LA) ***550***
U of Louisville (KY) ***550***
U of Maine (ME) ***550***
U of Maine at Farmington (ME) ***550***
U of Maine at Presque Isle (ME) ***551***
U of Manitoba (MB, Canada) ***551***
U of Mary Hardin-Baylor (TX) ***551***
U of Maryland, Baltimore County (MD) ***552***
U of Maryland, Coll Park (MD) ***552***
U of Maryland Eastern Shore (MD) ***552***
U of Massachusetts Amherst (MA) ***552***
U of Massachusetts Boston (MA) ***553***
U of Massachusetts Dartmouth (MA) ***553***
U of Massachusetts Lowell (MA) ***553***
The U of Memphis (TN) ***553***
U of Miami (FL) ***553***
U of Michigan (MI) ***554***
U of Michigan–Dearborn (MI) ***554***
U of Michigan–Flint (MI) ***554***
U of Minnesota, Duluth (MN) ***554***
U of Minnesota, Morris (MN) ***555***
U of Minnesota, Twin Cities Campus (MN) ***555***
U of Mississippi (MS) ***555***
U of Missouri–Columbia (MO) ***555***
U of Missouri–Kansas City (MO) ***555***
U of Missouri–St. Louis (MO) ***556***
U of Mobile (AL) ***556***
The U of Montana–Missoula (MT) ***556***
U of Montevallo (AL) ***557***
U of Nebraska at Kearney (NE) ***557***
U of Nebraska at Omaha (NE) ***557***
U of Nebraska–Lincoln (NE) ***557***
U of Nevada, Las Vegas (NV) ***558***
U of Nevada, Reno (NV) ***558***
U of New Brunswick Fredericton (NB, Canada) ***558***
U of New Brunswick Saint John (NB, Canada) ***558***
U of New Hampshire (NH) ***558***
U of New Mexico (NM) ***559***
U of New Orleans (LA) ***559***
U of North Alabama (AL) ***559***
The U of North Carolina at Asheville (NC) ***559***
The U of North Carolina at Chapel Hill (NC) ***560***
The U of North Carolina at Charlotte (NC) ***560***
The U of North Carolina at Greensboro (NC) ***560***
The U of North Carolina at Pembroke (NC) ***560***
The U of North Carolina at Wilmington (NC) ***561***
U of North Dakota (ND) ***561***
U of Northern Colorado (CO) ***561***
U of Northern Iowa (IA) ***561***
U of North Florida (FL) ***561***
U of North Texas (TX) ***562***
U of Notre Dame (IN) ***562***
U of Oklahoma (OK) ***562***
U of Oregon (OR) ***562***
U of Ottawa (ON, Canada) ***563***
U of Pennsylvania (PA) ***563***
U of Pittsburgh (PA) ***569***
U of Pittsburgh at Bradford (PA) ***569***
U of Pittsburgh at Johnstown (PA) ***570***
U of Portland (OR) ***570***
U of Prince Edward Island (PE, Canada) ***570***
U of Puerto Rico, Cayey U Coll (PR) ***571***
U of Puerto Rico, Río Piedras (PR) ***571***
U of Puget Sound (WA) ***571***
U of Redlands (CA) ***572***
U of Regina (SK, Canada) ***572***
U of Rhode Island (RI) ***572***
U of Richmond (VA) ***572***
U of Rio Grande (OH) ***572***
U of St. Thomas (MN) ***573***
U of San Diego (CA) ***574***
U of San Francisco (CA) ***574***
U of Saskatchewan (SK, Canada) ***574***
U of Science and Arts of Oklahoma (OK) ***574***
The U of Scranton (PA) ***574***
U of Sioux Falls (SD) ***574***
U of South Alabama (AL) ***575***
U of South Carolina (SC) ***575***
U of South Carolina Aiken (SC) ***575***
U of South Carolina Spartanburg (SC) ***575***
The U of South Dakota (SD) ***575***
U of Southern California (CA) ***576***
U of Southern Indiana (IN) ***576***
U of Southern Maine (ME) ***576***
U of South Florida (FL) ***576***
The U of Tampa (FL) ***577***
The U of Tennessee (TN) ***577***
The U of Tennessee at Chattanooga (TN) ***577***
The U of Tennessee at Martin (TN) ***577***
The U of Texas at Arlington (TX) ***577***
The U of Texas at Austin (TX) ***578***
The U of Texas at Brownsville (TX) ***578***
The U of Texas at Dallas (TX) ***578***
The U of Texas at El Paso (TX) ***578***
The U of Texas at San Antonio (TX) ***578***
The U of Texas at Tyler (TX) ***579***
The U of Texas of the Permian Basin (TX) ***579***
The U of Texas–Pan American (TX) ***579***
U of the District of Columbia (DC) ***580***
U of the Incarnate Word (TX) ***580***
U of the Ozarks (AR) ***580***
U of the Pacific (CA) ***580***
U of Toledo (OH) ***581***
U of Toronto (ON, Canada) ***581***
U of Tulsa (OK) ***581***
U of Utah (UT) ***582***
U of Vermont (VT) ***582***
U of Victoria (BC, Canada) ***582***
U of Virginia (VA) ***582***
The U of Virginia's Coll at Wise (VA) ***582***
U of Washington (WA) ***583***
U of Waterloo (ON, Canada) ***583***
The U of West Alabama (AL) ***583***
The U of Western Ontario (ON, Canada) ***583***
U of West Florida (FL) ***583***
U of Windsor (ON, Canada) ***584***
U of Wisconsin–Eau Claire (WI) ***584***
U of Wisconsin–La Crosse (WI) ***584***
U of Wisconsin–Madison (WI) ***584***
U of Wisconsin–Milwaukee (WI) ***585***
U of Wisconsin–Oshkosh (WI) ***585***
U of Wisconsin–Parkside (WI) ***585***
U of Wisconsin–River Falls (WI) ***585***
U of Wisconsin–Stevens Point (WI) ***585***
U of Wisconsin–Superior (WI) ***586***
U of Wisconsin–Whitewater (WI) ***586***
U of Wyoming (WY) ***586***
Upper Iowa U (IA) ***587***
Urbana U (OH) ***587***
Ursinus Coll (PA) ***587***
Ursuline Coll (OH) ***587***
Utah State U (UT) ***587***
Utica Coll (NY) ***588***
Valdosta State U (GA) ***588***
Valparaiso U (IN) ***588***
Vanderbilt U (TN) ***588***
Vanguard U of Southern California (CA) ***589***
Vassar Coll (NY) ***589***
Villanova U (PA) ***590***
Virginia Commonwealth U (VA) ***590***
Virginia Polytechnic Inst and State U (VA) ***591***
Virginia State U (VA) ***591***
Virginia Union U (VA) ***591***
Virginia Wesleyan Coll (VA) ***591***
Viterbo U (WI) ***591***
Voorhees Coll (SC) ***592***
Wagner Coll (NY) ***592***
Wake Forest U (NC) ***592***
Walla Walla Coll (WA) ***593***
Walsh U (OH) ***593***
Warren Wilson Coll (NC) ***594***
Wartburg Coll (IA) ***594***
Washington & Jefferson Coll (PA) ***594***
Washington and Lee U (VA) ***594***
Washington Coll (MD) ***594***
Washington State U (WA) ***595***
Waynesburg Coll (PA) ***595***
Wayne State Coll (NE) ***596***
Wayne State U (MI) ***596***
Weber State U (UT) ***596***
Webster U (MO) ***597***
Wellesley Coll (MA) ***597***
Wells Coll (NY) ***597***
Wesleyan Coll (GA) ***597***
Wesleyan U (CT) ***597***
West Chester U of Pennsylvania (PA) ***598***
Western Carolina U (NC) ***598***
Western Connecticut State U (CT) ***598***
Western Illinois U (IL) ***599***
Western Kentucky U (KY) ***599***
Western Michigan U (MI) ***599***
Western New England Coll (MA) ***600***
Western New Mexico U (NM) ***600***
Western Oregon U (OR) ***600***
Western State Coll of Colorado (CO) ***600***
Western Washington U (WA) ***600***
Westfield State Coll (MA) ***600***
West Liberty State Coll (WV) ***601***
Westminster Coll (MO) ***601***
Westminster Coll (PA) ***601***
Westminster Coll (UT) ***601***
Westmont Coll (CA) ***602***
West Texas A&M U (TX) ***602***
West Virginia State Coll (WV) ***602***
West Virginia U (WV) ***602***
West Virginia Wesleyan Coll (WV) ***603***
Wheaton Coll (IL) ***603***
Wheaton Coll (MA) ***603***
Whitman Coll (WA) ***604***
Whittier Coll (CA) ***604***
Whitworth Coll (WA) ***604***
Wichita State U (KS) ***604***
Widener U (PA) ***604***
Wilberforce U (OH) ***605***
Wiley Coll (TX) ***605***
Wilkes U (PA) ***605***
Willamette U (OR) ***605***
William Paterson U of New Jersey (NJ) ***606***
William Penn U (IA) ***606***
Williams Coll (MA) ***606***
Wingate U (NC) ***607***
Winona State U (MN) ***608***
Winston-Salem State U (NC) ***608***
Winthrop U (SC) ***608***
Wittenberg U (OH) ***608***
Wofford Coll (SC) ***609***
Worcester State Coll (MA) ***609***
Wright State U (OH) ***609***
Xavier U (OH) ***610***
Xavier U of Louisiana (LA) ***610***
Yale U (CT) ***610***
York Coll of Pennsylvania (PA) ***610***
York Coll of the City U of New York (NY) ***611***
York U (ON, Canada) ***611***
Youngstown State U (OH) ***611***

SOCIO-PSYCHOLOGICAL SPORTS STUDIES

Overview: Students who choose this major will study the social environment related to sports and physical activity; personality, motivation, attitude, and group behavior viewed in physical activity contexts. *Related majors:* health and physical education, social psychology, sociology, cultural and area studies, health science. *Potential careers:* sociologist, physical therapist, exercise and leadership coach, professor. *Salary potential:* $25k-$35k.

Greensboro Coll (NC) ***372***
Ithaca Coll (NY) ***390***
St. John Fisher Coll (NY) ***489***
U of Minnesota, Twin Cities Campus (MN) ***555***

SOIL CONSERVATION

Overview: Students study planning, conservation, and management of soil and water resources by focusing on the application of basic science with technical crop and soil science to soil and water resource management. *Related majors:* soil science, water resource management, geology, mineralogy, chemistry. *Potential careers:* soil scientist, biochemist, agronomist, conservationist. *Salary potential:* $25k-$35k.

Ball State U (IN) ***280***
California State Polytechnic U, Pomona (CA) ***300***
Colorado State U (CO) ***325***
The Ohio State U (OH) ***457***
U of Delaware (DE) ***544***
U of New Hampshire (NH) ***558***
The U of Tennessee at Martin (TN) ***577***
U of Wisconsin–Stevens Point (WI) ***585***

SOIL SCIENCES

Overview: Students who choose this major will learn about different soils and their properties and how these may affect certain plants and agricultural crops. *Related majors:* mineralogy, geology, chemistry, hydrology, agronomy. *Potential careers:* soil scientist, ecologist, biochemist, agronomist. *Salary potential:* $25k-$35k.

Colorado State U (CO) ***325***
Cornell U (NY) ***333***
McGill U (QC, Canada) ***423***
Michigan State U (MI) ***428***
New Mexico State U (NM) ***446***
North Dakota State U (ND) ***449***
Penn State U Univ Park Campus (PA) ***468***
The U of Arizona (AZ) ***538***
The U of British Columbia (BC, Canada) ***540***
U of Delaware (DE) ***544***
U of Florida (FL) ***545***
U of Georgia (GA) ***545***
U of Hawaii at Manoa (HI) ***546***
U of Idaho (ID) ***547***
U of Maine (ME) ***550***
U of Minnesota, Twin Cities Campus (MN) ***555***
U of Nebraska–Lincoln (NE) ***557***
U of Saskatchewan (SK, Canada) ***574***
U of Vermont (VT) ***582***
U of Wisconsin–River Falls (WI) ***585***
Utah State U (UT) ***587***
Washington State U (WA) ***595***

SOLAR TECHNOLOGY

Overview: This major prepares undergraduates for a career in developing or maintaining solar-powered energy systems. *Related majors:* energy management and systems technology, instrumentation technology, optics. *Potential careers:* solar-power systems installer, maintenance, energy consultant, research scientist. *Salary potential:* $23k-$30k.

Hampshire Coll (MA) ***375***

SOLID STATE AND LOW-TEMPERATURE PHYSICS

Overview: A branch of physics that concentrates on the behavior and properties of solid matter, liquids, and dense gases. *Related majors:* physical and theoretical chemistry, materials science, mathematics. *Potential careers:* research scientist, physicist, chemical engineer, aerospace or industrial engineer, professor. *Salary potential:* $35k-$45k.

George Mason U (VA) **366**

SOUTH ASIAN LANGUAGES

Overview: Students learn one or more of the languages and literatures of the people of the Indian subcontinent. *Related majors:* history, South Asian studies, development economics, international relations, religious studies. *Potential careers:* archeologist, diplomatic corps, importer-exporter, journalist, tour guide. *Salary potential:* $22k-$30k.

Northwestern U (IL) **453**
Yale U (CT) **610**

SOUTH ASIAN STUDIES

Overview: Undergraduates who choose this major study the history, politics, culture, languages, and economics of one or more of the peoples of Afghanistan, India, Pakistan, or surrounding areas. *Related majors:* comparative religion and philosophy, archeology, anthropology, international relations, Islamic Studies. *Potential careers:* anthropologist, archeologist, foreign service officer, translator, professor. *Salary potential:* $25k-$30k.

Barnard Coll (NY) **282**
Brown U (RI) **296**
The Coll of Wooster (OH) **324**
Concordia U (QC, Canada) **331**
Gettysburg Coll (PA) **368**
Hampshire Coll (MA) **375**
Harvard U (MA) **376**
Long Island U, Southampton Coll, Friends World Program (NY) **409**
Oakland U (MI) **456**
U of Calif, Santa Cruz (CA) **542**
U of Chicago (IL) **542**
U of Hawaii at Manoa (HI) **546**
U of Manitoba (MB, Canada) **551**
U of Michigan (MI) **554**
U of Minnesota, Twin Cities Campus (MN) **555**
U of Missouri–Columbia (MO) **555**
U of Pennsylvania (PA) **563**
U of Toronto (ON, Canada) **581**
U of Washington (WA) **583**
Ursinus Coll (PA) **587**

SOUTHEAST ASIAN STUDIES

Overview: Undergraduates who choose this major will study the history, politics, culture, languages, and economics of Brunei, Cambodia, Indonesia, Laos, Malaysia, the Philippines, Singapore, Thailand, Vietnam, and surrounding areas. *Related majors:* comparative religion and philosophy, archeology, anthropology, international relations, southeast Asian languages. *Potential careers:* anthropologist, archeologist, foreign service officer, translator, tour guide. *Salary potential:* $24k-$29k.

Cornell U (NY) **333**
Hampshire Coll (MA) **375**
Harvard U (MA) **376**
Long Island U, Southampton Coll, Friends World Program (NY) **409**
Middlebury Coll (VT) **429**
Tufts U (MA) **533**
U of Calif, Berkeley (CA) **540**
U of Calif, Los Angeles (CA) **541**
U of Calif, Santa Cruz (CA) **542**
U of Chicago (IL) **542**
U of Hawaii at Manoa (HI) **546**
U of Michigan (MI) **554**
U of Washington (WA) **583**
U of Wisconsin–Madison (WI) **584**

SPANISH

Overview: Students learn to read, write, and understand the Spanish language. *Related majors:* Latin American studies, archeology, anthropology, history, international relations. *Potential careers:* archeologist, anthropologist, diplomatic corps, importer-exporter, international banker. *Salary potential:* $22k-$30k.

Abilene Christian U (TX) **260**
Adams State Coll (CO) **260**
Adelphi U (NY) **260**
Adrian Coll (MI) **260**
Agnes Scott Coll (GA) **261**
Alabama State U (AL) **261**
Albany State U (GA) **262**
Albertson Coll of Idaho (ID) **262**
Albertus Magnus Coll (CT) **262**
Albion Coll (MI) **262**
Albright Coll (PA) **263**
Alfred U (NY) **263**
Allegheny Coll (PA) **264**
Alma Coll (MI) **264**
American International Coll (MA) **267**
American U (DC) **267**
Amherst Coll (MA) **268**
Anderson Coll (SC) **268**
Anderson U (IN) **268**
Andrews U (MI) **269**
Angelo State U (TX) **269**
Antioch Coll (OH) **269**
Appalachian State U (NC) **270**
Aquinas Coll (MI) **270**
Arcadia U (PA) **271**
Arizona State U (AZ) **271**
Arizona State U West (AZ) **272**
Arkansas State U (AR) **272**
Arkansas Tech U (AR) **272**
Asbury Coll (KY) **274**
Ashland U (OH) **274**
Assumption Coll (MA) **275**
Atlantic Union Coll (MA) **276**
Auburn U (AL) **276**
Augsburg Coll (MN) **276**
Augustana Coll (IL) **276**
Augustana Coll (SD) **276**
Augusta State U (GA) **277**
Austin Coll (TX) **277**
Austin Peay State U (TN) **278**
Azusa Pacific U (CA) **278**
Baker U (KS) **280**
Baldwin-Wallace Coll (OH) **280**
Ball State U (IN) **280**
Bard Coll (NY) **281**
Barnard Coll (NY) **282**
Barry U (FL) **282**
Bates Coll (ME) **282**
Baylor U (TX) **283**
Bellarmine U (KY) **284**
Bellevue U (NE) **284**
Belmont U (TN) **284**
Beloit Coll (WI) **285**
Bemidji State U (MN) **285**
Benedictine Coll (KS) **285**
Benedictine U (IL) **285**
Bennington Coll (VT) **286**
Berea Coll (KY) **286**
Baruch Coll of the City U of NY (NY) **286**
Berry Coll (GA) **287**
Bethany Coll (WV) **287**
Bethel Coll (KS) **288**
Bethel Coll (MN) **288**
Biola U (CA) **289**
Birmingham-Southern Coll (AL) **289**
Bishop's U (QC, Canada) **289**
Blackburn Coll (IL) **290**
Black Hills State U (SD) **290**
Bloomsburg U of Pennsylvania (PA) **290**
Blue Mountain Coll (MS) **291**
Bluffton Coll (OH) **291**
Boston U (MA) **292**
Bowdoin Coll (ME) **292**
Bowling Green State U (OH) **292**
Bradley U (IL) **293**
Brandeis U (MA) **293**
Brescia U (KY) **293**
Briar Cliff U (IA) **294**
Bridgewater Coll (VA) **294**
Bridgewater State Coll (MA) **294**
Brigham Young U (UT) **295**
Brock U (ON, Canada) **295**
Brooklyn Coll of the City U of NY (NY) **295**
Brown U (RI) **296**
Bryn Mawr Coll (PA) **297**
Bucknell U (PA) **297**
Buena Vista U (IA) **297**
Butler U (IN) **297**
Cabrini Coll (PA) **298**
Caldwell Coll (NJ) **298**
California Lutheran U (CA) **299**
California State Polytechnic U, Pomona (CA) **300**
California State U, Bakersfield (CA) **300**
California State U, Chico (CA) **300**
California State U, Dominguez Hills (CA) **300**
California State U, Fresno (CA) **301**
California State U, Fullerton (CA) **301**
California State U, Hayward (CA) **301**
California State U, Long Beach (CA) **301**
California State U, Northridge (CA) **301**
California State U, Sacramento (CA) **301**
California State U, San Bernardino (CA) **302**
California State U, San Marcos (CA) **302**
California State U, Stanislaus (CA) **302**
California U of Pennsylvania (PA) **302**
Calvin Coll (MI) **303**
Campbell U (NC) **303**
Canisius Coll (NY) **304**
Capital U (OH) **304**
Cardinal Stritch U (WI) **305**
Carleton Coll (MN) **305**
Carleton U (ON, Canada) **305**
Carnegie Mellon U (PA) **305**
Carroll Coll (MT) **306**
Carroll Coll (WI) **306**
Carson-Newman Coll (TN) **306**
Carthage Coll (WI) **306**
Case Western Reserve U (OH) **307**
Castleton State Coll (VT) **307**
Catawba Coll (NC) **307**
The Catholic U of America (DC) **307**
Cedar Crest Coll (PA) **308**
Cedarville U (OH) **308**
Centenary Coll of Louisiana (LA) **308**
Central Coll (IA) **309**
Central Connecticut State U (CT) **309**
Central Methodist Coll (MO) **309**
Central Michigan U (MI) **310**
Central Missouri State U (MO) **310**
Centre Coll (KY) **310**
Chadron State Coll (NE) **311**
Chapman U (CA) **311**
Charleston Southern U (SC) **311**
Chatham Coll (PA) **312**
Chestnut Hill Coll (PA) **312**
Cheyney U of Pennsylvania (PA) **312**
Christopher Newport U (VA) **313**
Citadel, The Military Coll of South Carolina (SC) **314**
City Coll of the City U of NY (NY) **314**
Claremont McKenna Coll (CA) **315**
Clarion U of Pennsylvania (PA) **315**
Clark Atlanta U (GA) **315**
Clarke Coll (IA) **315**
Clark U (MA) **316**
Cleveland State U (OH) **317**
Coastal Carolina U (SC) **318**
Coe Coll (IA) **318**
Coker Coll (SC) **318**
Colby Coll (ME) **318**
Colgate U (NY) **319**
Coll of Charleston (SC) **320**
Coll of Mount Saint Vincent (NY) **320**
The Coll of New Jersey (NJ) **320**
The Coll of New Rochelle (NY) **321**
Coll of Saint Benedict (MN) **321**
Coll of St. Catherine (MN) **321**
Coll of Saint Elizabeth (NJ) **321**
The Coll of Saint Rose (NY) **322**
Coll of Staten Island of the City U of NY (NY) **323**
Coll of the Holy Cross (MA) **323**
Coll of the Ozarks (MO) **323**
The Coll of William and Mary (VA) **324**
The Coll of Wooster (OH) **324**
The Colorado Coll (CO) **325**
Colorado State U (CO) **325**
Colorado State U-Pueblo (CO) **325**
Columbia Coll (NY) **326**
Columbia Coll (SC) **327**
Columbia U, School of General Studies (NY) **328**
Concordia Coll (MN) **329**
Concordia U (NE) **330**
Concordia U (QC, Canada) **331**
Concordia U at Austin (TX) **331**
Concordia U Wisconsin (WI) **331**
Connecticut Coll (CT) **331**
Converse Coll (SC) **332**
Cornell Coll (IA) **332**
Cornell U (NY) **333**
Cornerstone U (MI) **333**
Creighton U (NE) **333**
Daemen Coll (NY) **335**
Dalhousie U (NS, Canada) **336**
Dana Coll (NE) **337**
Dartmouth Coll (NH) **337**
Davidson Coll (NC) **338**
Davis & Elkins Coll (WV) **338**
Delaware State U (DE) **338**
Denison U (OH) **339**
DePaul U (IL) **339**
DePauw U (IN) **339**
DeSales U (PA) **340**
Dickinson Coll (PA) **344**
Dickinson State U (ND) **344**
Dillard U (LA) **344**
Doane Coll (NE) **344**
Dominican Coll (NY) **344**
Dominican U (IL) **345**
Dordt Coll (IA) **345**
Drew U (NJ) **346**
Drury U (MO) **346**
Duke U (NC) **346**
Duquesne U (PA) **346**
Earlham Coll (IN) **347**
East Carolina U (NC) **347**
Eastern Connecticut State U (CT) **347**
Eastern Kentucky U (KY) **348**
Eastern Mennonite U (VA) **348**
Eastern Michigan U (MI) **348**
Eastern New Mexico U (NM) **349**
Eastern U (PA) **349**
Eastern Washington U (WA) **349**
East Stroudsburg U of Pennsylvania (PA) **349**
East Texas Baptist U (TX) **350**
Eckerd Coll (FL) **350**
Edgewood Coll (WI) **351**
Edinboro U of Pennsylvania (PA) **351**
Elizabethtown Coll (PA) **351**
Elmhurst Coll (IL) **351**
Elmira Coll (NY) **351**
Elms Coll (MA) **352**
Elon U (NC) **352**
Emmanuel Coll (MA) **353**
Emory & Henry Coll (VA) **353**
Emory U (GA) **354**
Erskine Coll (SC) **354**
Evangel U (MO) **355**
The Evergreen State Coll (WA) **355**
Fairfield U (CT) **356**
Fairleigh Dickinson U, Florham (NJ) **356**
Fairleigh Dickinson U, Teaneck-Metro Campus (NJ) **356**
Fayetteville State U (NC) **357**
Ferrum Coll (VA) **358**
Fisk U (TN) **358**
Flagler Coll (FL) **359**
Florida A&M U (FL) **359**
Florida Atlantic U (FL) **359**
Florida International U (FL) **360**
Florida Southern Coll (FL) **361**
Florida State U (FL) **361**
Fordham U (NY) **362**
Fort Hays State U (KS) **362**
Fort Lewis Coll (CO) **362**
Framingham State Coll (MA) **362**
Franciscan U of Steubenville (OH) **363**
Francis Marion U (SC) **363**
Franklin and Marshall Coll (PA) **363**
Franklin Coll (IN) **363**
Fresno Pacific U (CA) **364**
Furman U (SC) **365**
Gallaudet U (DC) **365**
Gardner-Webb U (NC) **365**
Geneva Coll (PA) **366**
George Fox U (OR) **366**

SPANISH (continued)

Georgetown Coll (KY) ***366***
Georgetown U (DC) ***366***
The George Washington U (DC) ***367***
Georgia Coll & State U (GA) ***367***
Georgian Court Coll (NJ) ***367***
Georgia Southern U (GA) ***367***
Georgia Southwestern State U (GA) ***368***
Georgia State U (GA) ***368***
Gettysburg Coll (PA) ***368***
Gonzaga U (WA) ***369***
Gordon Coll (MA) ***370***
Goshen Coll (IN) ***370***
Goucher Coll (MD) ***370***
Grace Coll (IN) ***370***
Graceland U (IA) ***371***
Grambling State U (LA) ***371***
Grand Valley State U (MI) ***371***
Greensboro Coll (NC) ***372***
Greenville Coll (IL) ***373***
Grinnell Coll (IA) ***373***
Grove City Coll (PA) ***373***
Guilford Coll (NC) ***373***
Gustavus Adolphus Coll (MN) ***374***
Hamilton Coll (NY) ***374***
Hamline U (MN) ***374***
Hampden-Sydney Coll (VA) ***374***
Hanover Coll (IN) ***375***
Harding U (AR) ***375***
Hardin-Simmons U (TX) ***376***
Hartwick Coll (NY) ***376***
Harvard U (MA) ***376***
Hastings Coll (NE) ***377***
Haverford Coll (PA) ***377***
Heidelberg Coll (OH) ***377***
Henderson State U (AR) ***378***
Hendrix Coll (AR) ***378***
High Point U (NC) ***379***
Hillsdale Coll (MI) ***379***
Hiram Coll (OH) ***379***
Hobart and William Smith Colls (NY) ***380***
Hofstra U (NY) ***380***
Hollins U (VA) ***380***
Holy Family U (PA) ***380***
Hood Coll (MD) ***381***
Hope Coll (MI) ***381***
Houghton Coll (NY) ***381***
Houston Baptist U (TX) ***382***
Howard Payne U (TX) ***382***
Howard U (DC) ***382***
Humboldt State U (CA) ***382***
Hunter Coll of the City U of NY (NY) ***382***
Huntingdon Coll (AL) ***383***
Idaho State U (ID) ***384***
Illinois Coll (IL) ***384***
Illinois State U (IL) ***384***
Illinois Wesleyan U (IL) ***385***
Immaculata U (PA) ***385***
Indiana State U (IN) ***385***
Indiana U Bloomington (IN) ***385***
Indiana U Northwest (IN) ***386***
Indiana U of Pennsylvania (PA) ***386***
Indiana U–Purdue U Fort Wayne (IN) ***386***
Indiana U–Purdue U Indianapolis (IN) ***387***
Indiana U South Bend (IN) ***387***
Indiana U Southeast (IN) ***387***
Indiana Wesleyan U (IN) ***387***
Iona Coll (NY) ***390***
Iowa State U of Science and Technology (IA) ***390***
Ithaca Coll (NY) ***390***
Jackson State U (MS) ***390***
Jacksonville State U (AL) ***390***
Jacksonville U (FL) ***391***
James Madison U (VA) ***391***
John Carroll U (OH) ***392***
Johns Hopkins U (MD) ***392***
Juniata Coll (PA) ***395***
Kalamazoo Coll (MI) ***395***
Kean U (NJ) ***396***
Keene State Coll (NH) ***396***
Kennesaw State U (GA) ***397***
Kent State U (OH) ***397***
Kenyon Coll (OH) ***398***
King Coll (TN) ***398***
King's Coll (PA) ***398***
Knox Coll (IL) ***399***
Kutztown U of Pennsylvania (PA) ***399***
Lafayette Coll (PA) ***400***
Lake Erie Coll (OH) ***400***
Lake Forest Coll (IL) ***400***
Lakeland Coll (WI) ***401***
Lamar U (TX) ***401***
Lander U (SC) ***401***
La Salle U (PA) ***402***
La Sierra U (CA) ***403***
Laurentian U (ON, Canada) ***403***
Lawrence U (WI) ***403***
Lebanon Valley Coll (PA) ***403***
Lehigh U (PA) ***404***
Lehman Coll of the City U of NY (NY) ***404***
Le Moyne Coll (NY) ***404***
Lenoir-Rhyne Coll (NC) ***405***
Lewis & Clark Coll (OR) ***405***
Liberty U (VA) ***406***
Lincoln U (PA) ***407***
Lindenwood U (MO) ***407***
Linfield Coll (OR) ***408***
Lipscomb U (TN) ***408***
Lock Haven U of Pennsylvania (PA) ***408***
Long Island U, C.W. Post Campus (NY) ***409***
Long Island U, Southampton Coll, Friends World Program (NY) ***409***
Longwood U (VA) ***409***
Loras Coll (IA) ***410***
Louisiana Coll (LA) ***410***
Louisiana State U and A&M Coll (LA) ***410***
Louisiana State U in Shreveport (LA) ***410***
Louisiana Tech U (LA) ***410***
Loyola Coll in Maryland (MD) ***411***
Loyola Marymount U (CA) ***411***
Loyola U Chicago (IL) ***411***
Loyola U New Orleans (LA) ***411***
Lubbock Christian U (TX) ***412***
Luther Coll (IA) ***412***
Lycoming Coll (PA) ***412***
Lynchburg Coll (VA) ***413***
Lyon Coll (AR) ***413***
Macalester Coll (MN) ***413***
MacMurray Coll (IL) ***414***
Madonna U (MI) ***414***
Malone Coll (OH) ***415***
Manchester Coll (IN) ***415***
Manhattan Coll (NY) ***416***
Manhattanville Coll (NY) ***416***
Mansfield U of Pennsylvania (PA) ***416***
Marian Coll (IN) ***417***
Marian Coll of Fond du Lac (WI) ***417***
Marietta Coll (OH) ***417***
Marist Coll (NY) ***417***
Marlboro Coll (VT) ***418***
Marquette U (WI) ***418***
Mars Hill Coll (NC) ***418***
Mary Baldwin Coll (VA) ***419***
Marymount Coll of Fordham U (NY) ***419***
Maryville Coll (TN) ***420***
Mary Washington Coll (VA) ***420***
Marywood U (PA) ***421***
Massachusetts Inst of Technology (MA) ***421***
McDaniel Coll (MD) ***422***
McGill U (QC, Canada) ***423***
McMurry U (TX) ***423***
McNeese State U (LA) ***423***
McPherson Coll (KS) ***423***
Memorial U of Newfoundland (NF, Canada) ***424***
Mercer U (GA) ***425***
Mercy Coll (NY) ***425***
Mercyhurst Coll (PA) ***425***
Meredith Coll (NC) ***426***
Merrimack Coll (MA) ***426***
Messiah Coll (PA) ***426***
Methodist Coll (NC) ***427***
Metropolitan State Coll of Denver (CO) ***427***
Miami U (OH) ***428***
Michigan State U (MI) ***428***
MidAmerica Nazarene U (KS) ***428***
Middlebury Coll (VT) ***429***
Midwestern State U (TX) ***430***
Millersville U of Pennsylvania (PA) ***430***
Millikin U (IL) ***430***
Millsaps Coll (MS) ***431***
Minnesota State U, Mankato (MN) ***431***
Minnesota State U, Moorhead (MN) ***432***
Minot State U (ND) ***432***
Mississippi Coll (MS) ***432***
Missouri Southern State Coll (MO) ***433***
Missouri Western State Coll (MO) ***433***
Molloy Coll (NY) ***433***
Monmouth Coll (IL) ***434***
Montana State U–Billings (MT) ***434***
Montclair State U (NJ) ***435***
Moravian Coll (PA) ***436***
Morehead State U (KY) ***436***
Morehouse Coll (GA) ***436***
Morningside Coll (IA) ***437***
Mount Allison U (NB, Canada) ***437***
Mount Holyoke Coll (MA) ***438***
Mount Mary Coll (WI) ***438***
Mount St. Mary's Coll (CA) ***439***
Mount Saint Mary's Coll and Seminary (MD) ***439***
Mount Saint Vincent U (NS, Canada) ***439***
Mount Union Coll (OH) ***440***
Mount Vernon Nazarene U (OH) ***440***
Muhlenberg Coll (PA) ***440***
Murray State U (KY) ***440***
Muskingum Coll (OH) ***441***
Nazareth Coll of Rochester (NY) ***443***
Nebraska Wesleyan U (NE) ***443***
Newberry Coll (SC) ***444***
New Coll of Florida (FL) ***444***
New Jersey City U (NJ) ***445***
New Mexico Highlands U (NM) ***446***
New York U (NY) ***447***
Niagara U (NY) ***447***
North Carolina Central U (NC) ***448***
North Carolina State U (NC) ***449***
North Central Coll (IL) ***449***
North Dakota State U (ND) ***449***
Northeastern Illinois U (IL) ***450***
Northeastern State U (OK) ***450***
Northeastern U (MA) ***450***
Northern Arizona U (AZ) ***450***
Northern Illinois U (IL) ***450***
Northern Kentucky U (KY) ***451***
Northern Michigan U (MI) ***451***
Northern State U (SD) ***451***
North Georgia Coll & State U (GA) ***451***
North Park U (IL) ***452***
Northwestern Coll (IA) ***453***
Northwestern Coll (MN) ***453***
Northwestern Oklahoma State U (OK) ***453***
Northwestern U (IL) ***453***
Northwest Missouri State U (MO) ***454***
Northwest Nazarene U (ID) ***454***
Notre Dame Coll (OH) ***455***
Oakland U (MI) ***456***
Oakwood Coll (AL) ***456***
Oberlin Coll (OH) ***456***
Occidental Coll (CA) ***457***
Ohio Northern U (OH) ***457***
The Ohio State U (OH) ***457***
Ohio U (OH) ***458***
Ohio Wesleyan U (OH) ***459***
Oklahoma Baptist U (OK) ***459***
Oklahoma Christian U (OK) ***459***
Oklahoma City U (OK) ***460***
Oklahoma State U (OK) ***460***
Olivet Nazarene U (IL) ***461***
Oral Roberts U (OK) ***461***
Oregon State U (OR) ***462***
Otterbein Coll (OH) ***462***
Ouachita Baptist U (AR) ***462***
Our Lady of the Lake U of San Antonio (TX) ***463***
Pace U (NY) ***463***
Pacific Lutheran U (WA) ***463***
Pacific Union Coll (CA) ***464***
Pacific U (OR) ***464***
Park U (MO) ***465***
Peace Coll (NC) ***466***
Penn State U Univ Park Campus (PA) ***468***
Pepperdine U, Malibu (CA) ***469***
Piedmont Coll (GA) ***470***
Pittsburg State U (KS) ***470***
Pitzer Coll (CA) ***471***
Plattsburgh State U of NY (NY) ***471***
Plymouth State Coll (NH) ***471***
Point Loma Nazarene U (CA) ***471***
Pomona Coll (CA) ***472***
Pontifical Catholic U of Puerto Rico (PR) ***472***
Portland State U (OR) ***472***
Prairie View A&M U (TX) ***473***
Presbyterian Coll (SC) ***473***
Prescott Coll (AZ) ***474***
Principia Coll (IL) ***474***
Providence Coll (RI) ***474***
Purchase Coll, State U of NY (NY) ***475***
Purdue U Calumet (IN) ***475***
Queens Coll of the City U of NY (NY) ***475***
Queen's U at Kingston (ON, Canada) ***476***
Queens U of Charlotte (NC) ***476***
Quinnipiac U (CT) ***476***
Randolph-Macon Coll (VA) ***477***
Randolph-Macon Woman's Coll (VA) ***477***
Reed Coll (OR) ***477***
Regis Coll (MA) ***478***
Regis U (CO) ***478***
Rhode Island Coll (RI) ***479***
Rhodes Coll (TN) ***479***
Rice U (TX) ***479***
Rider U (NJ) ***480***
Ripon Coll (WI) ***480***
Rivier Coll (NH) ***480***
Roanoke Coll (VA) ***481***
Rockford Coll (IL) ***482***
Rockhurst U (MO) ***482***
Rollins Coll (FL) ***483***
Roosevelt U (IL) ***483***
Rosemont Coll (PA) ***484***
Rowan U (NJ) ***484***
Russell Sage Coll (NY) ***484***
Rutgers, The State U of New Jersey, Camden (NJ) ***485***
Rutgers, The State U of New Jersey, Newark (NJ) ***485***
Rutgers, The State U of New Jersey, New Brunswick (NJ) ***485***
Sacred Heart U (CT) ***486***
Saginaw Valley State U (MI) ***486***
St. Ambrose U (IA) ***486***
Saint Anselm Coll (NH) ***487***
Saint Augustine's Coll (NC) ***487***
St. Bonaventure U (NY) ***487***
St. Cloud State U (MN) ***488***
St. Edward's U (TX) ***488***
Saint Francis U (PA) ***488***
St. John Fisher Coll (NY) ***489***
Saint John's U (MN) ***490***
St. John's U (NY) ***490***
Saint Joseph Coll (CT) ***490***
St. Joseph's Coll, New York (NY) ***491***
Saint Joseph's U (PA) ***491***
St. Lawrence U (NY) ***491***
Saint Louis U (MO) ***492***
Saint Mary Coll (KS) ***493***
Saint Mary-of-the-Woods Coll (IN) ***493***
Saint Mary's Coll (IN) ***493***
Saint Mary's Coll of California (CA) ***494***
Saint Mary's U of Minnesota (MN) ***494***
St. Mary's U of San Antonio (TX) ***494***
Saint Michael's Coll (VT) ***494***
St. Norbert Coll (WI) ***495***
St. Olaf Coll (MN) ***495***
Saint Peter's Coll (NJ) ***495***
St. Thomas Aquinas Coll (NY) ***495***
St. Thomas U (NB, Canada) ***496***
Saint Vincent Coll (PA) ***496***
Saint Xavier U (IL) ***496***
Salem Coll (NC) ***496***
Salisbury U (MD) ***497***
Salve Regina U (RI) ***497***
Samford U (AL) ***497***
Sam Houston State U (TX) ***497***
San Diego State U (CA) ***498***
San Francisco State U (CA) ***498***
San Jose State U (CA) ***499***
Santa Clara U (CA) ***499***
Sarah Lawrence Coll (NY) ***499***
Scripps Coll (CA) ***501***
Seattle Pacific U (WA) ***501***
Seattle U (WA) ***501***
Seton Hall U (NJ) ***502***
Seton Hill U (PA) ***502***
Shippensburg U of Pennsylvania (PA) ***503***
Shorter Coll (GA) ***504***
Siena Coll (NY) ***504***
Siena Heights U (MI) ***504***
Simmons Coll (MA) ***504***
Simon Fraser U (BC, Canada) ***505***
Simon's Rock Coll of Bard (MA) ***505***
Simpson Coll (IA) ***505***
Skidmore Coll (NY) ***506***
Slippery Rock U of Pennsylvania (PA) ***506***
Smith Coll (MA) ***506***
Sonoma State U (CA) ***506***
South Carolina State U (SC) ***506***
South Dakota State U (SD) ***507***
Southeastern Louisiana U (LA) ***508***
Southeast Missouri State U (MO) ***508***
Southern Arkansas U–Magnolia (AR) ***509***
Southern Connecticut State U (CT) ***509***
Southern Illinois U Carbondale (IL) ***509***
Southern Methodist U (TX) ***510***
Southern Nazarene U (OK) ***510***
Southern Oregon U (OR) ***510***
Southern U and A&M Coll (LA) ***511***
Southern Utah U (UT) ***511***
Southern Virginia U (VA) ***511***
Southwest Baptist U (MO) ***512***
Southwestern U (TX) ***513***

Southwest Missouri State U (MO) 513
Southwest State U (MN) 513
Southwest Texas State U (TX) 513
Spelman Coll (GA) 514
Spring Arbor U (MI) 514
Spring Hill Coll (AL) 514
Stanford U (CA) 514
State U of NY at Albany (NY) 514
State U of NY at Binghamton (NY) 515
State U of NY at New Paltz (NY) 515
State U of NY at Oswego (NY) 515
State U of NY Coll at Brockport (NY) 515
State U of NY Coll at Buffalo (NY) 516
State U of NY Coll at Cortland (NY) 516
State U of NY Coll at Fredonia (NY) 516
State U of NY Coll at Geneseo (NY) 516
State U of NY Coll at Old Westbury (NY) 516
State U of NY Coll at Oneonta (NY) 517
State U of NY Coll at Potsdam (NY) 517
State U of West Georgia (GA) 518
Stephen F. Austin State U (TX) 518
Stetson U (FL) 519
Stony Brook U, State University of New York (NY) 520
Suffolk U (MA) 520
Sul Ross State U (TX) 521
Susquehanna U (PA) 521
Swarthmore Coll (PA) 521
Sweet Briar Coll (VA) 521
Syracuse U (NY) 521
Talladega Coll (AL) 522
Tarleton State U (TX) 522
Taylor U (IN) 523
Temple U (PA) 523
Tennessee State U (TN) 523
Tennessee Technological U (TN) 524
Texas A&M International U (TX) 524
Texas A&M U (TX) 524
Texas A&M U–Commerce (TX) 525
Texas A&M U–Corpus Christi (TX) 525
Texas A&M U–Kingsville (TX) 525
Texas Christian U (TX) 526
Texas Lutheran U (TX) 526
Texas Southern U (TX) 526
Texas Tech U (TX) 526
Texas Wesleyan U (TX) 526
Texas Woman's U (TX) 527
Thiel Coll (PA) 527
Towson U (MD) 529
Transylvania U (KY) 529
Trent U (ON, Canada) 529
Trinity Christian Coll (IL) 530
Trinity Coll (CT) 530
Trinity Coll (DC) 530
Trinity U (TX) 531
Truman State U (MO) 532
Tufts U (MA) 533
Tulane U (LA) 533
Union Coll (NE) 534
Union U (TN) 534
United States Military Academy (NY) 535
Universidad Adventista de las Antillas (PR) 536
Université Laval (QC, Canada) 536
U at Buffalo, The State University of New York (NY) 536
The U of Akron (OH) 537
The U of Alabama (AL) 537
The U of Alabama at Birmingham (AL) 537
U of Alberta (AB, Canada) 538
The U of Arizona (AZ) 538
U of Arkansas (AR) 539
U of Arkansas at Little Rock (AR) 539
The U of British Columbia (BC, Canada) 540
U of Calgary (AB, Canada) 540
U of Calif, Berkeley (CA) 540
U of Calif, Davis (CA) 540
U of Calif, Irvine (CA) 541
U of Calif, Los Angeles (CA) 541
U of Calif, Riverside (CA) 541
U of Calif, San Diego (CA) 541
U of Calif, Santa Barbara (CA) 541
U of Calif, Santa Cruz (CA) 542
U of Central Arkansas (AR) 542
U of Central Florida (FL) 542
U of Central Oklahoma (OK) 542
U of Chicago (IL) 542
U of Cincinnati (OH) 543
U of Colorado at Boulder (CO) 543
U of Colorado at Colorado Springs (CO) 543
U of Colorado at Denver (CO) 543
U of Connecticut (CT) 544
U of Dallas (TX) 544
U of Dayton (OH) 544
U of Delaware (DE) 544
U of Denver (CO) 544
U of Evansville (IN) 545
The U of Findlay (OH) 545
U of Florida (FL) 545
U of Georgia (GA) 545
U of Guelph (ON, Canada) 546
U of Hawaii at Manoa (HI) 546
U of Houston (TX) 547
U of Idaho (ID) 547
U of Illinois at Chicago (IL) 547
U of Illinois at Urbana–Champaign (IL) 548
U of Indianapolis (IN) 548
The U of Iowa (IA) 548
U of Kansas (KS) 549
U of Kentucky (KY) 549
U of King's Coll (NS, Canada) 549
U of La Verne (CA) 549
U of Louisville (KY) 550
U of Maine (ME) 550
U of Manitoba (MB, Canada) 551
U of Mary Hardin-Baylor (TX) 551
U of Maryland, Baltimore County (MD) 552
U of Maryland, Coll Park (MD) 552
U of Massachusetts Amherst (MA) 552
U of Massachusetts Boston (MA) 553
U of Massachusetts Dartmouth (MA) 553
U of Miami (FL) 553
U of Michigan (MI) 554
U of Michigan–Dearborn (MI) 554
U of Michigan–Flint (MI) 554
U of Minnesota, Duluth (MN) 554
U of Minnesota, Morris (MN) 555
U of Minnesota, Twin Cities Campus (MN) 555
U of Mississippi (MS) 555
U of Missouri–Columbia (MO) 555
U of Missouri–Kansas City (MO) 555
U of Missouri–St. Louis (MO) 556
The U of Montana–Missoula (MT) 556
U of Montevallo (AL) 557
U of Nebraska at Kearney (NE) 557
U of Nebraska at Omaha (NE) 557
U of Nebraska–Lincoln (NE) 557
U of Nevada, Las Vegas (NV) 558
U of Nevada, Reno (NV) 558
U of New Brunswick Fredericton (NB, Canada) 558
U of New Hampshire (NH) 558
U of New Mexico (NM) 559
U of New Orleans (LA) 559
The U of North Carolina at Asheville (NC) 559
The U of North Carolina at Charlotte (NC) 560
The U of North Carolina at Greensboro (NC) 560
The U of North Carolina at Wilmington (NC) 561
U of North Dakota (ND) 561
U of Northern Colorado (CO) 561
U of Northern Iowa (IA) 561
U of North Florida (FL) 561
U of North Texas (TX) 562
U of Notre Dame (IN) 562
U of Oklahoma (OK) 562
U of Oregon (OR) 562
U of Ottawa (ON, Canada) 563
U of Pennsylvania (PA) 563
U of Pittsburgh (PA) 569
U of Portland (OR) 570
U of Prince Edward Island (PE, Canada) 570
U of Puerto Rico, Cayey U Coll (PR) 571
U of Puerto Rico, Río Piedras (PR) 571
U of Puget Sound (WA) 571
U of Redlands (CA) 572
U of Rhode Island (RI) 572
U of Richmond (VA) 572
U of Rochester (NY) 573
U of St. Thomas (MN) 573
U of St. Thomas (TX) 573
U of San Diego (CA) 574
U of San Francisco (CA) 574
U of Saskatchewan (SK, Canada) 574
The U of Scranton (PA) 574
U of South Carolina (SC) 575
U of South Carolina Spartanburg (SC) 575
The U of South Dakota (SD) 575
U of Southern California (CA) 576
U of Southern Indiana (IN) 576
U of South Florida (FL) 576
The U of Tampa (FL) 577
The U of Tennessee (TN) 577
The U of Tennessee at Chattanooga (TN) 577
The U of Tennessee at Martin (TN) 577
The U of Texas at Arlington (TX) 577
The U of Texas at Austin (TX) 578
The U of Texas at Brownsville (TX) 578
The U of Texas at El Paso (TX) 578
The U of Texas at San Antonio (TX) 578
The U of Texas at Tyler (TX) 579
The U of Texas of the Permian Basin (TX) 579
The U of Texas–Pan American (TX) 579
U of the District of Columbia (DC) 580
U of the Incarnate Word (TX) 580
U of the Pacific (CA) 580
U of the Sacred Heart (PR) 580
U of the South (TN) 581
U of Toledo (OH) 581
U of Toronto (ON, Canada) 581
U of Tulsa (OK) 581
U of Utah (UT) 582
U of Vermont (VT) 582
U of Victoria (BC, Canada) 582
U of Virginia (VA) 582
The U of Virginia's Coll at Wise (VA) 582
U of Washington (WA) 583
U of Waterloo (ON, Canada) 583
The U of Western Ontario (ON, Canada) 583
U of Windsor (ON, Canada) 584
U of Wisconsin–Eau Claire (WI) 584
U of Wisconsin–Green Bay (WI) 584
U of Wisconsin–La Crosse (WI) 584
U of Wisconsin–Madison (WI) 584
U of Wisconsin–Milwaukee (WI) 585
U of Wisconsin–Oshkosh (WI) 585
U of Wisconsin–Parkside (WI) 585
U of Wisconsin–Platteville (WI) 585
U of Wisconsin–River Falls (WI) 585
U of Wisconsin–Stevens Point (WI) 585
U of Wisconsin–Whitewater (WI) 586
U of Wyoming (WY) 586
Ursinus Coll (PA) 587
Utah State U (UT) 587
Valdosta State U (GA) 588
Valley City State U (ND) 588
Valparaiso U (IN) 588
Vanderbilt U (TN) 588
Vanguard U of Southern California (CA) 589
Villanova U (PA) 590
Virginia Polytechnic Inst and State U (VA) 591
Virginia Wesleyan Coll (VA) 591
Viterbo U (WI) 591
Wabash Coll (IN) 592
Wagner Coll (NY) 592
Wake Forest U (NC) 592
Walla Walla Coll (WA) 593
Walsh U (OH) 593
Wartburg Coll (IA) 594
Washington & Jefferson Coll (PA) 594
Washington and Lee U (VA) 594
Washington Coll (MD) 594
Washington State U (WA) 595
Washington U in St. Louis (MO) 595
Wayland Baptist U (TX) 595
Wayne State Coll (NE) 596
Wayne State U (MI) 596
Weber State U (UT) 596
Webster U (MO) 597
Wellesley Coll (MA) 597
Wells Coll (NY) 597
Wesleyan Coll (GA) 597
Wesleyan U (CT) 597
West Chester U of Pennsylvania (PA) 598
Western Carolina U (NC) 598
Western Connecticut State U (CT) 598
Western Illinois U (IL) 599
Western Kentucky U (KY) 599
Western Michigan U (MI) 599
Western New Mexico U (NM) 600
Western Oregon U (OR) 600
Western State Coll of Colorado (CO) 600
Western Washington U (WA) 600
Westminster Coll (MO) 601
Westminster Coll (PA) 601
Westmont Coll (CA) 602
West Texas A&M U (TX) 602
Wheaton Coll (IL) 603
Wheeling Jesuit U (WV) 603
Whitman Coll (WA) 604
Whittier Coll (CA) 604
Whitworth Coll (WA) 604
Wichita State U (KS) 604
Widener U (PA) 604
Wilkes U (PA) 605
Willamette U (OR) 605
William Carey Coll (MS) 605
William Jewell Coll (MO) 606
William Paterson U of New Jersey (NJ) 606
Williams Coll (MA) 606
William Woods U (MO) 607
Wilmington Coll (OH) 607
Wingate U (NC) 607
Winona State U (MN) 608
Winston-Salem State U (NC) 608
Wisconsin Lutheran Coll (WI) 608
Wittenberg U (OH) 608
Wofford Coll (SC) 609
Worcester State Coll (MA) 609
Wright State U (OH) 609
Xavier U (OH) 610
Xavier U of Louisiana (LA) 610
Yale U (CT) 610
York Coll of Pennsylvania (PA) 610
York Coll of the City U of New York (NY) 611
York U (ON, Canada) 611
Youngstown State U (OH) 611

SPANISH LANGUAGE EDUCATION

Overview: This major prepares individuals to teach the Spanish language to nonnative speakers at various educational levels. *Related majors:* Spanish, Latin American studies. *Potential career:* Spanish teacher. *Salary potential:* $23k-$26k.

Abilene Christian U (TX) 260
Adams State Coll (CO) 260
Anderson Coll (SC) 268
Anderson U (IN) 268
Arkansas State U (AR) 272
Bayamón Central U (PR) 283
Baylor U (TX) 283
Berea Coll (KY) 286
Berry Coll (GA) 287
Blue Mountain Coll (MS) 291
Bowling Green State U (OH) 292
Bridgewater Coll (VA) 294
Brigham Young U (UT) 295
Canisius Coll (NY) 304
Carroll Coll (MT) 306
The Catholic U of America (DC) 307
Cedarville U (OH) 308
Central Michigan U (MI) 310
Central Missouri State U (MO) 310
Chadron State Coll (NE) 311
The Coll of New Jersey (NJ) 320
Coll of St. Catherine (MN) 321
Colorado State U (CO) 325
Colorado State U-Pueblo (CO) 325
Concordia Coll (MN) 329
Concordia U (NE) 330
Daemen Coll (NY) 335
Duquesne U (PA) 346
East Carolina U (NC) 347
Eastern Mennonite U (VA) 348
Eastern Michigan U (MI) 348
East Texas Baptist U (TX) 350
Elmhurst Coll (IL) 351
Elmira Coll (NY) 351
Flagler Coll (FL) 359
Framingham State Coll (MA) 362
Franklin Coll (IN) 363
Georgia Southern U (GA) 367
Grace Coll (IN) 370
Greensboro Coll (NC) 372
Greenville Coll (IL) 373
Hardin-Simmons U (TX) 376
Henderson State U (AR) 378
Indiana U Bloomington (IN) 385
Indiana U Northwest (IN) 386
Indiana U–Purdue U Fort Wayne (IN) 386
Indiana U–Purdue U Indianapolis (IN) 387
Indiana U South Bend (IN) 387
Inter American U of PR, Aguadilla Campus (PR) 388
Ithaca Coll (NY) 390
Juniata Coll (PA) 395
Kennesaw State U (GA) 397
King Coll (TN) 398
La Roche Coll (PA) 402
Long Island U, C.W. Post Campus (NY) 409
Luther Coll (IA) 412

SPANISH LANGUAGE EDUCATION (continued)

Malone Coll (OH) ***415***
Manhattanville Coll (NY) ***416***
Mansfield U of Pennsylvania (PA) ***416***
Marymount Coll of Fordham U (NY) ***419***
Maryville Coll (TN) ***420***
Messiah Coll (PA) ***426***
MidAmerica Nazarene U (KS) ***428***
Minnesota State U, Moorhead (MN) ***432***
Minot State U (ND) ***432***
Missouri Western State Coll (MO) ***433***
Molloy Coll (NY) ***433***
Montana State U–Billings (MT) ***434***
Niagara U (NY) ***447***
North Carolina Central U (NC) ***448***
North Carolina State U (NC) ***449***
North Dakota State U (ND) ***449***
Northern Arizona U (AZ) ***450***
Northwest Nazarene U (ID) ***454***
Ohio U (OH) ***458***
Oklahoma Baptist U (OK) ***459***
Oral Roberts U (OK) ***461***
Pace U (NY) ***463***
St. Ambrose U (IA) ***486***
St. John's U (NY) ***490***
Saint Mary's U of Minnesota (MN) ***494***
Saint Xavier U (IL) ***496***
Salve Regina U (RI) ***497***
San Diego State U (CA) ***498***
Seton Hill U (PA) ***502***
Southeastern Louisiana U (LA) ***508***
Southeastern Oklahoma State U (OK) ***508***
Southern Arkansas U–Magnolia (AR) ***509***
Southern Nazarene U (OK) ***510***
Southwest Missouri State U (MO) ***513***
State U of NY at Albany (NY) ***514***
State U of NY Coll at Potsdam (NY) ***517***
Texas A&M International U (TX) ***524***
The U of Arizona (AZ) ***538***
U of Illinois at Chicago (IL) ***547***
U of Illinois at Urbana–Champaign (IL) ***548***
U of Indianapolis (IN) ***548***
The U of Iowa (IA) ***548***
U of Minnesota, Duluth (MN) ***554***
U of Nebraska–Lincoln (NE) ***557***
The U of North Carolina at Charlotte (NC) ***560***
The U of North Carolina at Wilmington (NC) ***561***
U of North Texas (TX) ***562***
U of Puerto Rico, Cayey U Coll (PR) ***571***
The U of Tennessee at Martin (TN) ***577***
U of Toledo (OH) ***581***
U of Utah (UT) ***582***
U of Wisconsin–River Falls (WI) ***585***
Valley City State U (ND) ***588***
Viterbo U (WI) ***591***
Washington U in St. Louis (MO) ***595***
Weber State U (UT) ***596***
Western Carolina U (NC) ***598***
Wheeling Jesuit U (WV) ***603***
Winston-Salem State U (NC) ***608***
Youngstown State U (OH) ***611***

SPECIAL EDUCATION

Overview: This major prepares undergraduates to become teachers who specialize in teaching children or adults with special needs or disabilities. *Related majors:* developmental psychology, family counseling. *Potential careers:* special education teacher. *Salary potential:* $23k-$34k.

Abilene Christian U (TX) ***260***
Alabama A&M U (AL) ***261***
Alabama State U (AL) ***261***
Albany State U (GA) ***262***
Albright Coll (PA) ***263***
Alcorn State U (MS) ***263***
Alderson-Broaddus Coll (WV) ***263***
American International Coll (MA) ***267***
American U of Puerto Rico (PR) ***268***
Anderson Coll (SC) ***268***
Aquinas Coll (MI) ***270***
Arcadia U (PA) ***271***
Arizona State U (AZ) ***271***
Arizona State U West (AZ) ***272***
Arkansas State U (AR) ***272***
Armstrong Atlantic State U (GA) ***273***
Ashland U (OH) ***274***
Athens State U (AL) ***275***
Augustana Coll (SD) ***276***
Augusta State U (GA) ***277***
Austin Peay State U (TN) ***278***
Avila U (MO) ***278***
Baldwin-Wallace Coll (OH) ***280***
Ball State U (IN) ***280***
Barry U (FL) ***282***
Barton Coll (NC) ***282***
Bayamón Central U (PR) ***283***
Baylor U (TX) ***283***
Bellarmine U (KY) ***284***
Belmont U (TN) ***284***
Benedictine Coll (KS) ***285***
Benedictine U (IL) ***285***
Bennett Coll (NC) ***286***
Bethel Coll (TN) ***288***
Bethune-Cookman Coll (FL) ***289***
Black Hills State U (SD) ***290***
Bloomsburg U of Pennsylvania (PA) ***290***
Bluffton Coll (OH) ***291***
Boston Coll (MA) ***292***
Boston U (MA) ***292***
Bowie State U (MD) ***292***
Bowling Green State U (OH) ***292***
Brenau U (GA) ***293***
Brescia U (KY) ***293***
Bridgewater Coll (VA) ***294***
Bridgewater State Coll (MA) ***294***
Brigham Young U–Hawaii (HI) ***295***
Buena Vista U (IA) ***297***
Cabrini Coll (PA) ***298***
California State U, Northridge (CA) ***301***
California U of Pennsylvania (PA) ***302***
Calvin Coll (MI) ***303***
Canisius Coll (NY) ***304***
Cardinal Stritch U (WI) ***305***
Carlow Coll (PA) ***305***
Carson-Newman Coll (TN) ***306***
Carthage Coll (WI) ***306***
Cedarville U (OH) ***308***
Centenary Coll (NJ) ***308***
Central Connecticut State U (CT) ***309***
Central Missouri State U (MO) ***310***
Central Washington U (WA) ***310***
Chadron State Coll (NE) ***311***
Cheyney U of Pennsylvania (PA) ***312***
City Coll of the City U of NY (NY) ***314***
City U (WA) ***314***
Clarion U of Pennsylvania (PA) ***315***
Clarke Coll (IA) ***315***
Clearwater Christian Coll (FL) ***316***
Clemson U (SC) ***317***
Cleveland State U (OH) ***317***
Coastal Carolina U (SC) ***318***
Coll Misericordia (PA) ***319***
Coll of Charleston (SC) ***320***
Coll of Mount St. Joseph (OH) ***320***
Coll of Mount Saint Vincent (NY) ***320***
The Coll of New Jersey (NJ) ***320***
The Coll of New Rochelle (NY) ***321***
Coll of Notre Dame of Maryland (MD) ***321***
Coll of Saint Elizabeth (NJ) ***321***
Coll of St. Joseph (VT) ***322***
Coll of Saint Mary (NE) ***322***
The Coll of Saint Rose (NY) ***322***
Coll of the Southwest (NM) ***324***
Columbia Coll (SC) ***327***
Columbus State U (GA) ***328***
Concord Coll (WV) ***329***
Concordia U (NE) ***330***
Converse Coll (SC) ***332***
Creighton U (NE) ***333***
Culver-Stockton Coll (MO) ***334***
Cumberland Coll (KY) ***335***
Cumberland U (TN) ***335***
Curry Coll (MA) ***335***
Daemen Coll (NY) ***335***
Dakota State U (SD) ***335***
Dakota Wesleyan U (SD) ***336***
Dana Coll (NE) ***337***
Defiance Coll (OH) ***338***
Delaware State U (DE) ***338***
Delta State U (MS) ***339***
Dillard U (LA) ***344***
Doane Coll (NE) ***344***
Dominican Coll (NY) ***344***
Dowling Coll (NY) ***345***
D'Youville Coll (NY) ***347***
East Central U (OK) ***347***
Eastern Illinois U (IL) ***348***
Eastern Kentucky U (KY) ***348***
Eastern Michigan U (MI) ***348***
Eastern Nazarene Coll (MA) ***348***
Eastern New Mexico U (NM) ***349***
Eastern Oregon U (OR) ***349***
Eastern Washington U (WA) ***349***
East Stroudsburg U of Pennsylvania (PA) ***349***
East Tennessee State U (TN) ***349***
Edinboro U of Pennsylvania (PA) ***351***
Elizabeth City State U (NC) ***351***
Elmhurst Coll (IL) ***351***
Elms Coll (MA) ***352***
Elon U (NC) ***352***
Erskine Coll (SC) ***354***
Evangel U (MO) ***355***
Fairmont State Coll (WV) ***356***
Felician Coll (NJ) ***357***
Fitchburg State Coll (MA) ***358***
Florida Atlantic U (FL) ***359***
Florida Gulf Coast U (FL) ***359***
Fontbonne U (MO) ***361***
Freed-Hardeman U (TN) ***364***
Furman U (SC) ***365***
Gannon U (PA) ***365***
Geneva Coll (PA) ***366***
Georgia Coll & State U (GA) ***367***
Georgian Court Coll (NJ) ***367***
Georgia Southern U (GA) ***367***
Georgia Southwestern State U (GA) ***368***
Glenville State Coll (WV) ***368***
Gonzaga U (WA) ***369***
Gordon Coll (MA) ***370***
Grambling State U (LA) ***371***
Grand Canyon U (AZ) ***371***
Grand Valley State U (MI) ***371***
Grand View Coll (IA) ***372***
Green Mountain Coll (VT) ***372***
Greensboro Coll (NC) ***372***
Greenville Coll (IL) ***373***
Gwynedd-Mercy Coll (PA) ***374***
Hampton U (VA) ***375***
Hastings Coll (NE) ***377***
Heidelberg Coll (OH) ***377***
High Point U (NC) ***379***
Holy Family U (PA) ***380***
Hood Coll (MD) ***381***
Houston Baptist U (TX) ***382***
Huntington Coll (IN) ***383***
Idaho State U (ID) ***384***
Illinois State U (IL) ***384***
Indiana State U (IN) ***385***
Indiana U Bloomington (IN) ***385***
Indiana U of Pennsylvania (PA) ***386***
Indiana U South Bend (IN) ***387***
Indiana U Southeast (IN) ***387***
Indiana Wesleyan U (IN) ***387***
Inter American U of PR, Guayama Campus (PR) ***388***
Iona Coll (NY) ***390***
Jackson State U (MS) ***390***
Jacksonville State U (AL) ***390***
Jacksonville U (FL) ***391***
James Madison U (VA) ***391***
John Brown U (AR) ***392***
John Carroll U (OH) ***392***
Juniata Coll (PA) ***395***
Kean U (NJ) ***396***
Keene State Coll (NH) ***396***
Kent State U (OH) ***397***
Keuka Coll (NY) ***398***
King's Coll (PA) ***398***
Kutztown U of Pennsylvania (PA) ***399***
Lamar U (TX) ***401***
Lambuth U (TN) ***401***
Lander U (SC) ***401***
Langston U (OK) ***402***
La Salle U (PA) ***402***
Lasell Coll (MA) ***402***
La Sierra U (CA) ***403***
Lee U (TN) ***404***
Lesley U (MA) ***405***
Lewis-Clark State Coll (ID) ***406***
Lewis U (IL) ***406***
Liberty U (VA) ***406***
Lindenwood U (MO) ***407***
Lock Haven U of Pennsylvania (PA) ***408***
Long Island U, Brooklyn Campus (NY) ***409***
Long Island U, Southampton Coll, Friends World Program (NY) ***409***
Longwood U (VA) ***409***
Louisiana Coll (LA) ***410***
Louisiana State U in Shreveport (LA) ***410***
Louisiana Tech U (LA) ***410***
Loyola Coll in Maryland (MD) ***411***
Loyola U Chicago (IL) ***411***
Luther Coll (IA) ***412***
Lynchburg Coll (VA) ***413***
Lyndon State Coll (VT) ***413***
MacMurray Coll (IL) ***414***
Madonna U (MI) ***414***
Manchester Coll (IN) ***415***
Manhattan Coll (NY) ***416***
Mansfield U of Pennsylvania (PA) ***416***
Marian Coll (IN) ***417***
Marist Coll (NY) ***417***
Marymount Coll of Fordham U (NY) ***419***
Marywood U (PA) ***421***
McGill U (QC, Canada) ***423***
McNeese State U (LA) ***423***
McPherson Coll (KS) ***423***
Medgar Evers Coll of the City U of NY (NY) ***424***
Memorial U of Newfoundland (NF, Canada) ***424***
Mercy Coll (NY) ***425***
Mercyhurst Coll (PA) ***425***
Methodist Coll (NC) ***427***
Miami U (OH) ***428***
Michigan State U (MI) ***428***
Middle Tennessee State U (TN) ***429***
Millersville U of Pennsylvania (PA) ***430***
Minnesota State U, Moorhead (MN) ***432***
Mississippi Coll (MS) ***432***
Mississippi State U (MS) ***432***
Missouri Southern State Coll (MO) ***433***
Missouri Valley Coll (MO) ***433***
Molloy Coll (NY) ***433***
Monmouth Coll (IL) ***434***
Monmouth U (NJ) ***434***
Montana State U–Billings (MT) ***434***
Morehead State U (KY) ***436***
Morningside Coll (IA) ***437***
Mount Marty Coll (SD) ***438***
Mount Saint Mary Coll (NY) ***439***
Mount Vernon Nazarene U (OH) ***440***
Murray State U (KY) ***440***
Muskingum Coll (OH) ***441***
Nazareth Coll of Rochester (NY) ***443***
Nebraska Wesleyan U (NE) ***443***
Newberry Coll (SC) ***444***
New England Coll (NH) ***444***
New Jersey City U (NJ) ***445***
New Mexico Highlands U (NM) ***446***
New Mexico State U (NM) ***446***
New York U (NY) ***447***
Niagara U (NY) ***447***
Nicholls State U (LA) ***447***
Norfolk State U (VA) ***448***
North Carolina Ag and Tech State U (NC) ***448***
Northeastern Illinois U (IL) ***450***
Northeastern State U (OK) ***450***
Northern Arizona U (AZ) ***450***
Northern Illinois U (IL) ***450***
Northern Kentucky U (KY) ***451***
Northern Michigan U (MI) ***451***
Northern State U (SD) ***451***
North Georgia Coll & State U (GA) ***451***
Northwest Coll (WA) ***452***
Northwestern Oklahoma State U (OK) ***453***
Northwestern State U of Louisiana (LA) ***453***
Northwest Missouri State U (MO) ***454***
Nova Southeastern U (FL) ***455***
Ohio Dominican U (OH) ***457***
The Ohio State U (OH) ***457***
Ohio U (OH) ***458***
Ohio Valley Coll (WV) ***459***
Oklahoma Baptist U (OK) ***459***
Oklahoma Christian U (OK) ***459***
Oral Roberts U (OK) ***461***
Ouachita Baptist U (AR) ***462***
Our Lady of the Lake U of San Antonio (TX) ***463***
Pace U (NY) ***463***
Pacific Lutheran U (WA) ***463***
Pacific Oaks Coll (CA) ***464***
Penn State U Univ Park Campus (PA) ***468***
Peru State Coll (NE) ***469***
Pfeiffer U (NC) ***469***
Piedmont Coll (GA) ***470***
Plattsburgh State U of NY (NY) ***471***
Pontifical Catholic U of Puerto Rico (PR) ***472***
Presbyterian Coll (SC) ***473***
Prescott Coll (AZ) ***474***
Providence Coll (RI) ***474***
Purdue U Calumet (IN) ***475***
Quincy U (IL) ***476***

Rhode Island Coll (RI) 479
Rivier Coll (NH) 480
Rowan U (NJ) 484
Russell Sage Coll (NY) 484
Saginaw Valley State U (MI) 486
Saint Augustine's Coll (NC) 487
St. Cloud State U (MN) 488
St. John Fisher Coll (NY) 489
St. John's U (NY) 490
Saint Joseph Coll (CT) 490
St. Joseph's Coll, Suffolk Campus (NY) 491
Saint Leo U (FL) 492
Saint Martin's Coll (WA) 493
Saint Mary-of-the-Woods Coll (IN) 493
St. Thomas Aquinas Coll (NY) 495
Salve Regina U (RI) 497
Seattle Pacific U (WA) 501
Seton Hall U (NJ) 502
Seton Hill U (PA) 502
Simmons Coll (MA) 504
Slippery Rock U of Pennsylvania (PA) 506
South Carolina State U (SC) 506
Southeastern Louisiana U (LA) 508
Southeastern Oklahoma State U (OK) 508
Southeast Missouri State U (MO) 508
Southern Connecticut State U (CT) 509
Southern Illinois U Carbondale (IL) 509
Southern Illinois U Edwardsville (IL) 509
Southern New Hampshire U (NH) 510
Southern U and A&M Coll (LA) 511
Southern Utah U (UT) 511
Southern Wesleyan U (SC) 511
Southwestern Oklahoma State U (OK) 512
Southwest Missouri State U (MO) 513
Spalding U (KY) 513
Springfield Coll (MA) 514
State U of NY at New Paltz (NY) 515
State U of NY Coll at Buffalo (NY) 516
State U of NY Coll at Geneseo (NY) 516
State U of NY Coll at Old Westbury (NY) 516
State U of West Georgia (GA) 518
Syracuse U (NY) 521
Tabor Coll (KS) 522
Temple U (PA) 523
Tennessee State U (TN) 523
Tennessee Technological U (TN) 524
Texas A&M International U (TX) 524
Texas A&M U–Commerce (TX) 525
Texas Christian U (TX) 526
Texas Southern U (TX) 526
Touro Coll (NY) 529
Towson U (MD) 529
Trinity Christian Coll (IL) 530
Trinity Coll (DC) 530
Troy State U (AL) 532
Tufts U (MA) 533
Tusculum Coll (TN) 533
Union Coll (KY) 533
Union U (TN) 534
Université de Sherbrooke (QC, Canada) 536
U du Québec à Hull (QC, Canada) 536
The U of Alabama (AL) 537
The U of Alabama at Birmingham (AL) 537
U of Alberta (AB, Canada) 538
The U of Arizona (AZ) 538
U of Arkansas (AR) 539
U of Arkansas at Monticello (AR) 539
The U of British Columbia (BC, Canada) 540
U of Central Arkansas (AR) 542
U of Central Florida (FL) 542
U of Central Oklahoma (OK) 542
U of Cincinnati (OH) 543
U of Connecticut (CT) 544
U of Dayton (OH) 544
U of Delaware (DE) 544
U of Evansville (IN) 545
The U of Findlay (OH) 545
U of Florida (FL) 545
U of Georgia (GA) 545
U of Great Falls (MT) 545
U of Hartford (CT) 546
U of Hawaii at Manoa (HI) 546
U of Idaho (ID) 547
U of Illinois at Urbana–Champaign (IL) 548
U of Kentucky (KY) 549
The U of Lethbridge (AB, Canada) 549
U of Louisiana at Lafayette (LA) 550
U of Maine at Farmington (ME) 550
U of Mary (ND) 551
U of Mary Hardin-Baylor (TX) 551
U of Maryland, Coll Park (MD) 552
U of Maryland Eastern Shore (MD) 552
The U of Memphis (TN) 553
U of Miami (FL) 553
U of Minnesota, Duluth (MN) 554
U of Mississippi (MS) 555
U of Missouri–St. Louis (MO) 556
The U of Montana–Western (MT) 556
U of Nebraska at Kearney (NE) 557
U of Nebraska at Omaha (NE) 557
U of Nevada, Las Vegas (NV) 558
U of Nevada, Reno (NV) 558
U of New Brunswick Fredericton (NB, Canada) 558
U of New Mexico (NM) 559
U of North Alabama (AL) 559
The U of North Carolina at Pembroke (NC) 560
U of Northern Iowa (IA) 561
U of North Florida (FL) 561
U of North Texas (TX) 562
U of Oklahoma (OK) 562
U of Ottawa (ON, Canada) 563
U of St. Francis (IL) 573
U of Saint Francis (IN) 573
The U of Scranton (PA) 574
U of South Alabama (AL) 575
The U of South Dakota (SD) 575
The U of Southern Mississippi (MS) 576
U of South Florida (FL) 576
The U of Tennessee (TN) 577
The U of Tennessee at Chattanooga (TN) 577
The U of Tennessee at Martin (TN) 577
The U of Texas at Brownsville (TX) 578
The U of Texas–Pan American (TX) 579
U of the District of Columbia (DC) 580
U of the Incarnate Word (TX) 580
U of the Pacific (CA) 580
U of Toledo (OH) 581
U of Tulsa (OK) 581
U of Victoria (BC, Canada) 582
The U of West Alabama (AL) 583
The U of Western Ontario (ON, Canada) 583
U of West Florida (FL) 583
U of Windsor (ON, Canada) 584
U of Wisconsin–Eau Claire (WI) 584
U of Wisconsin–Madison (WI) 584
U of Wisconsin–Milwaukee (WI) 585
U of Wisconsin–Oshkosh (WI) 585
U of Wisconsin–Superior (WI) 586
U of Wisconsin–Whitewater (WI) 586
U of Wyoming (WY) 586
Upper Iowa U (IA) 587
Ursuline Coll (OH) 587
Utah State U (UT) 587
Valdosta State U (GA) 588
Vanderbilt U (TN) 588
Virginia Union U (VA) 591
Walsh U (OH) 593
Warner Southern Coll (FL) 593
Washington State U (WA) 595
Waynesburg Coll (PA) 595
Wayne State Coll (NE) 596
Wayne State U (MI) 596
Webster U (MO) 597
West Chester U of Pennsylvania (PA) 598
Western Carolina U (NC) 598
Western Illinois U (IL) 599
Western Kentucky U (KY) 599
Western New Mexico U (NM) 600
Western State Coll of Colorado (CO) 600
Western Washington U (WA) 600
Westfield State Coll (MA) 600
Westminster Coll (UT) 601
Wheelock Coll (MA) 603
Whitworth Coll (WA) 604
Widener U (PA) 604
Wiley Coll (TX) 605
William Paterson U of New Jersey (NJ) 606
William Penn U (IA) 606
William Woods U (MO) 607
Winona State U (MN) 608
Winston-Salem State U (NC) 608
Winthrop U (SC) 608
Wittenberg U (OH) 608
Xavier U (OH) 610
Xavier U of Louisiana (LA) 610
York Coll of Pennsylvania (PA) 610
York U (ON, Canada) 611
Youngstown State U (OH) 611

SPECIAL EDUCATION RELATED

Information can be found under this major's main heading.

Briar Cliff U (IA) 294
Minot State U (ND) 432
The U of Akron (OH) 537
U of Nebraska–Lincoln (NE) 557
U of Wyoming (WY) 586

SPEECH EDUCATION

Overview: undergraduates who choose this major take a variety of courses that prepare them to teach speech and language arts at various educational levels. *Related majors:* communications and communication disorders, public relations, drama, speech therapy, creative writing and English composition. *Potential careers:* speech teacher, creative writing teacher, speech therapist, debate coach. *Salary potential:* $22k-$32k.

Abilene Christian U (TX) 260
Anderson U (IN) 268
Arkansas Tech U (AR) 272
Baylor U (TX) 283
Bowling Green State U (OH) 292
Cedarville U (OH) 308
Central Michigan U (MI) 310
Central Missouri State U (MO) 310
Chadron State Coll (NE) 311
Coll of St. Catherine (MN) 321
Concordia U (IL) 330
Concordia U (NE) 330
Dana Coll (NE) 337
East Texas Baptist U (TX) 350
Elmira Coll (NY) 351
Emporia State U (KS) 354
Greenville Coll (IL) 373
Hastings Coll (NE) 377
Henderson State U (AR) 378
Howard Payne U (TX) 382
Indiana U Bloomington (IN) 385
Indiana U–Purdue U Fort Wayne (IN) 386
Indiana U–Purdue U Indianapolis (IN) 387
Kean U (NJ) 396
Louisiana Tech U (LA) 410
Malone Coll (OH) 415
McMurry U (TX) 423
Minnesota State U, Moorhead (MN) 432
North Dakota State U (ND) 449
Oklahoma Baptist U (OK) 459
Pace U (NY) 463
Samford U (AL) 497
Southeastern Louisiana U (LA) 508
Southeastern Oklahoma State U (OK) 508
Southeast Missouri State U (MO) 508
Southern Nazarene U (OK) 510
Southwest Missouri State U (MO) 513
Southwest State U (MN) 513
Texas Wesleyan U (TX) 526
The U of Akron (OH) 537
The U of Arizona (AZ) 538
U of Central Arkansas (AR) 542
U of Indianapolis (IN) 548
The U of Iowa (IA) 548
U of North Texas (TX) 562
U of Rio Grande (OH) 572
William Jewell Coll (MO) 606
Youngstown State U (OH) 611

SPEECH-LANGUAGE PATHOLOGY

Overview: This major prepares students to diagnose and treat such speech disorders as stuttering, delayed or impaired language, and voice and speaking problems, as well as observe and test speech, language, hearing, and perception. *Related majors:* special education, education of speech impaired, audiology, speech-language pathology, speech therapy. *Potential careers:* audiologist or speech-language pathologist, teacher, speech therapist, psychologist. *Salary potential:* $27k-$37k.

Brigham Young U (UT) 295
Central Missouri State U (MO) 310
Duquesne U (PA) 346
Emerson Coll (MA) 353
Grambling State U (LA) 371
James Madison U (VA) 391
Loyola Coll in Maryland (MD) 411
Miami U (OH) 428
Northwestern U (IL) 453
Pace U (NY) 463
Rockhurst U (MO) 482
Saint Xavier U (IL) 496
Southeast Missouri State U (MO) 508
State U of West Georgia (GA) 518
Towson U (MD) 529
U of Maryland, Coll Park (MD) 552
U of Nebraska at Omaha (NE) 557
U of Nebraska–Lincoln (NE) 557
U of Nevada, Reno (NV) 558
U of Northern Colorado (CO) 561
U of Northern Iowa (IA) 561
U of Science and Arts of Oklahoma (OK) 574
The U of Tennessee (TN) 577
U of Toledo (OH) 581
Wayne State U (MI) 596

SPEECH-LANGUAGE PATHOLOGY/AUDIOLOGY

Overview: This major prepares students to diagnose and treat both speech- and hearing-related diseases and disorders as well as test speech, language, hearing, and perception in patients. *Related majors:* special education, education of speech impaired, education of hearing impaired, audiology, speech-language pathology. *Potential careers:* audiologist or speech-language pathologist, teacher, speech therapist, psychologist, researcher. *Salary potential:* $27k-$37k.

Abilene Christian U (TX) 260
Adelphi U (NY) 260
Andrews U (MI) 269
Appalachian State U (NC) 270
Arkansas State U (AR) 272
Auburn U (AL) 276
Augustana Coll (IL) 276
Augustana Coll (SD) 276
Baldwin-Wallace Coll (OH) 280
Ball State U (IN) 280
Brescia U (KY) 293
Brooklyn Coll of the City U of NY (NY) 295
Butler U (IN) 297
California State U, Fresno (CA) 301
California State U, Fullerton (CA) 301
California State U, Hayward (CA) 301
California State U, Long Beach (CA) 301
California State U, Northridge (CA) 301
California State U, Sacramento (CA) 301
Calvin Coll (MI) 303
Centenary Coll of Louisiana (LA) 308
Central Michigan U (MI) 310
Clarion U of Pennsylvania (PA) 315
Cleveland State U (OH) 317
The Coll of Wooster (OH) 324
Columbia Coll (SC) 327
Delta State U (MS) 339
East Carolina U (NC) 347
Eastern Kentucky U (KY) 348
Eastern New Mexico U (NM) 349
Eastern Washington U (WA) 349
East Stroudsburg U of Pennsylvania (PA) 349
Elmhurst Coll (IL) 351
Elmira Coll (NY) 351
Elms Coll (MA) 352
Emerson Coll (MA) 353
Florida Atlantic U (FL) 359
Florida State U (FL) 361
Fontbonne U (MO) 361
Fort Hays State U (KS) 362
Geneva Coll (PA) 366
The George Washington U (DC) 367
Governors State U (IL) 370
Hampton U (VA) 375
Hardin-Simmons U (TX) 376
Hofstra U (NY) 380
Idaho State U (ID) 384
Illinois State U (IL) 384
Indiana State U (IN) 385
Indiana U Bloomington (IN) 385
Indiana U–Purdue U Fort Wayne (IN) 386
Iona Coll (NY) 390

SPEECH-LANGUAGE PATHOLOGY/ AUDIOLOGY (continued)

Ithaca Coll (NY) ***390***
Jackson State U (MS) ***390***
Kean U (NJ) ***396***
Kent State U (OH) ***397***
Lamar U (TX) ***401***
Lambuth U (TN) ***401***
La Salle U (PA) ***402***
Lehman Coll of the City U of NY (NY) ***404***
Loma Linda U (CA) ***408***
Long Island U, C.W. Post Campus (NY) ***409***
Louisiana State U and A&M Coll (LA) ***410***
Louisiana State U in Shreveport (LA) ***410***
Louisiana Tech U (LA) ***410***
Marquette U (WI) ***418***
Marymount Manhattan Coll (NY) ***420***
Marywood U (PA) ***421***
Mercy Coll (NY) ***425***
Miami U (OH) ***428***
Michigan State U (MI) ***428***
Minnesota State U, Mankato (MN) ***431***
Minnesota State U, Moorhead (MN) ***432***
Molloy Coll (NY) ***433***
Murray State U (KY) ***440***
Nazareth Coll of Rochester (NY) ***443***
New Mexico State U (NM) ***446***
Nicholls State U (LA) ***447***
Northeastern State U (OK) ***450***
Northeastern U (MA) ***450***
Northern Michigan U (MI) ***451***
Northern State U (SD) ***451***
Northwestern U (IL) ***453***
Northwest Nazarene U (ID) ***454***
The Ohio State U (OH) ***457***
Ohio U (OH) ***458***
Old Dominion U (VA) ***460***
Otterbein Coll (OH) ***462***
Ouachita Baptist U (AR) ***462***
Our Lady of the Lake U of San Antonio (TX) ***463***
Pacific Union Coll (CA) ***464***
Penn State U Univ Park Campus (PA) ***468***
Plattsburgh State U of NY (NY) ***471***
Purdue U (IN) ***475***
Queens Coll of the City U of NY (NY) ***475***
The Richard Stockton Coll of New Jersey (NJ) ***479***
St. Cloud State U (MN) ***488***
St. John's U (NY) ***490***
San Francisco State U (CA) ***498***
San Jose State U (CA) ***499***
Shaw U (NC) ***502***
South Carolina State U (SC) ***506***
Southern Illinois U Edwardsville (IL) ***509***
Southern U and A&M Coll (LA) ***511***
Southwest Missouri State U (MO) ***513***
Southwest Texas State U (TX) ***513***
State U of NY at New Paltz (NY) ***515***
State U of NY Coll at Buffalo (NY) ***516***
State U of NY Coll at Cortland (NY) ***516***
State U of NY Coll at Fredonia (NY) ***516***
State U of NY Coll at Geneseo (NY) ***516***
Stephen F. Austin State U (TX) ***518***
Syracuse U (NY) ***521***
Temple U (PA) ***523***
Tennessee State U (TN) ***523***
Texas Christian U (TX) ***526***
Texas Woman's U (TX) ***527***
Thiel Coll (PA) ***527***
Touro Coll (NY) ***529***
Towson U (MD) ***529***
U at Buffalo, The State University of New York (NY) ***536***
The U of Akron (OH) ***537***
The U of Alabama (AL) ***537***
U of Arkansas (AR) ***539***
U of Arkansas at Little Rock (AR) ***539***
U of Central Arkansas (AR) ***542***
U of Central Florida (FL) ***542***
U of Central Oklahoma (OK) ***542***
U of Cincinnati (OH) ***543***
U of Florida (FL) ***545***
U of Hawaii at Manoa (HI) ***546***
U of Houston (TX) ***547***
U of Illinois at Urbana–Champaign (IL) ***548***
The U of Iowa (IA) ***548***
U of Kentucky (KY) ***549***
U of Louisiana at Lafayette (LA) ***550***
U of Minnesota, Duluth (MN) ***554***
U of Minnesota, Twin Cities Campus (MN) ***555***
U of Mississippi (MS) ***555***
The U of Montana–Missoula (MT) ***556***
U of Montevallo (AL) ***557***
U of Nebraska at Omaha (NE) ***557***
U of Nevada, Reno (NV) ***558***
U of New Hampshire (NH) ***558***
U of New Mexico (NM) ***559***
The U of North Carolina at Greensboro (NC) ***560***
U of North Dakota (ND) ***561***
U of North Texas (TX) ***562***
U of Oklahoma Health Sciences Center (OK) ***562***
U of Oregon (OR) ***562***
U of Pittsburgh (PA) ***569***
U of Puerto Rico Medical Sciences Campus (PR) ***571***
U of Redlands (CA) ***572***
U of South Alabama (AL) ***575***
The U of South Dakota (SD) ***575***
U of Southern Mississippi (MS) ***576***
U of South Florida (FL) ***576***
The U of Texas at Dallas (TX) ***578***
The U of Texas at El Paso (TX) ***578***
The U of Texas–Pan American (TX) ***579***
U of the District of Columbia (DC) ***580***
U of the Pacific (CA) ***580***
U of Tulsa (OK) ***581***
U of Utah (UT) ***582***
U of Vermont (VT) ***582***
U of Virginia (VA) ***582***
U of Washington (WA) ***583***
U of Wisconsin–Milwaukee (WI) ***585***
U of Wisconsin–Oshkosh (WI) ***585***
U of Wisconsin–Stevens Point (WI) ***585***
U of Wyoming (WY) ***586***
Utah State U (UT) ***587***
Valdosta State U (GA) ***588***
Washington State U (WA) ***595***
West Chester U of Pennsylvania (PA) ***598***
Western Michigan U (MI) ***599***
Western Washington U (WA) ***600***
West Virginia U (WV) ***602***
Wichita State U (KS) ***604***
Worcester State Coll (MA) ***609***
Xavier U of Louisiana (LA) ***610***

SPEECH/RHETORICAL STUDIES

Overview: Students study the theory, structure, and history of human communication and discourse. *Related majors:* law and legal studies, English language/literature, drama/theater literature, history and criticism, philosophy. *Potential careers:* writer, editor, speech writer, journalist, copywriter. *Salary potential:* $23k-$32k.

Abilene Christian U (TX) ***260***
Adams State Coll (CO) ***260***
Alabama State U (AL) ***261***
Albany State U (GA) ***262***
Alderson-Broaddus Coll (WV) ***263***
Anderson Coll (SC) ***268***
Appalachian State U (NC) ***270***
Arkansas State U (AR) ***272***
Arkansas Tech U (AR) ***272***
Asbury Coll (KY) ***274***
Ashland U (OH) ***274***
Auburn U (AL) ***276***
Augsburg Coll (MN) ***276***
Augustana Coll (IL) ***276***
Baker U (KS) ***280***
Ball State U (IN) ***280***
Bates Coll (ME) ***282***
Baylor U (TX) ***283***
Belmont U (TN) ***284***
Bemidji State U (MN) ***285***
Berry Coll (GA) ***287***
Bethel Coll (MN) ***288***
Blackburn Coll (IL) ***290***
Black Hills State U (SD) ***290***
Bloomsburg U of Pennsylvania (PA) ***290***
Blue Mountain Coll (MS) ***291***
Bluffton Coll (OH) ***291***
Bowling Green State U (OH) ***292***
Bradley U (IL) ***293***
Brooklyn Coll of the City U of NY (NY) ***295***
Buena Vista U (IA) ***297***
Butler U (IN) ***297***
California Polytechnic State U, San Luis Obispo (CA) ***300***
California State U, Chico (CA) ***300***
California State U, Fresno (CA) ***301***
California State U, Fullerton (CA) ***301***
California State U, Hayward (CA) ***301***
California State U, Long Beach (CA) ***301***
California State U, Northridge (CA) ***301***
Calvin Coll (MI) ***303***
Cameron U (OK) ***303***
Capital U (OH) ***304***
Carson-Newman Coll (TN) ***306***
Carthage Coll (WI) ***306***
Cedarville U (OH) ***308***
Centenary Coll of Louisiana (LA) ***308***
Central Michigan U (MI) ***310***
Central Missouri State U (MO) ***310***
Chadron State Coll (NE) ***311***
Chapman U (CA) ***311***
Charleston Southern U (SC) ***311***
Clarion U of Pennsylvania (PA) ***315***
Clark Atlanta U (GA) ***315***
Clemson U (SC) ***317***
Coe Coll (IA) ***318***
The Coll of New Jersey (NJ) ***320***
Coll of Saint Benedict (MN) ***321***
Coll of St. Catherine (MN) ***321***
Coll of the Ozarks (MO) ***323***
The Coll of Wooster (OH) ***324***
Colorado State U (CO) ***325***
Colorado State U-Pueblo (CO) ***325***
Concordia Coll (MN) ***329***
Concordia U (NE) ***330***
Cornell Coll (IA) ***332***
Cornerstone U (MI) ***333***
Creighton U (NE) ***333***
Cumberland Coll (KY) ***335***
Defiance Coll (OH) ***338***
Denison U (OH) ***339***
Dickinson State U (ND) ***344***
Dillard U (LA) ***344***
Doane Coll (NE) ***344***
Dowling Coll (NY) ***345***
Drake U (IA) ***345***
East Central U (OK) ***347***
Eastern Illinois U (IL) ***348***
Eastern Kentucky U (KY) ***348***
Eastern Michigan U (MI) ***348***
Eastern Washington U (WA) ***349***
East Stroudsburg U of Pennsylvania (PA) ***349***
East Tennessee State U (TN) ***349***
East Texas Baptist U (TX) ***350***
Emerson Coll (MA) ***353***
Evangel U (MO) ***355***
Fairmont State Coll (WV) ***356***
Fisk U (TN) ***358***
Florida Atlantic U (FL) ***359***
Frostburg State U (MD) ***365***
Geneva Coll (PA) ***366***
George Mason U (VA) ***366***
Georgetown Coll (KY) ***366***
The George Washington U (DC) ***367***
Georgia Southern U (GA) ***367***
Georgia State U (GA) ***368***
Gonzaga U (WA) ***369***
Governors State U (IL) ***370***
Graceland U (IA) ***371***
Grand Canyon U (AZ) ***371***
Greenville Coll (IL) ***373***
Gustavus Adolphus Coll (MN) ***374***
Hannibal-LaGrange Coll (MO) ***375***
Hardin-Simmons U (TX) ***376***
Hastings Coll (NE) ***377***
Henderson State U (AR) ***378***
Hillsdale Coll (MI) ***379***
Houston Baptist U (TX) ***382***
Howard Payne U (TX) ***382***
Humboldt State U (CA) ***382***
Huntingdon Coll (AL) ***383***
Illinois Coll (IL) ***384***
Illinois State U (IL) ***384***
Indiana U Bloomington (IN) ***385***
Indiana U South Bend (IN) ***387***
Iona Coll (NY) ***390***
Iowa State U of Science and Technology (IA) ***390***
Ithaca Coll (NY) ***390***
Jackson State U (MS) ***390***
Judson Coll (IL) ***395***
Kent State U (OH) ***397***
Kutztown U of Pennsylvania (PA) ***399***
La Salle U (PA) ***402***
Lehman Coll of the City U of NY (NY) ***404***
Lewis-Clark State Coll (ID) ***406***
Lewis U (IL) ***406***
Lipscomb U (TN) ***408***
Lock Haven U of Pennsylvania (PA) ***408***
Long Island U, Brooklyn Campus (NY) ***409***
Louisiana Coll (LA) ***410***
Louisiana State U and A&M Coll (LA) ***410***
Louisiana State U in Shreveport (LA) ***410***
Louisiana Tech U (LA) ***410***
Lynchburg Coll (VA) ***413***
Manchester Coll (IN) ***415***
Mansfield U of Pennsylvania (PA) ***416***
Maranatha Baptist Bible Coll (WI) ***417***
Marietta Coll (OH) ***417***
Marquette U (WI) ***418***
Marshall U (WV) ***418***
Marymount Coll of Fordham U (NY) ***419***
The Master's Coll and Seminary (CA) ***422***
McKendree Coll (IL) ***423***
McNeese State U (LA) ***423***
Mercy Coll (NY) ***425***
Metropolitan State Coll of Denver (CO) ***427***
Miami U (OH) ***428***
Minnesota State U, Mankato (MN) ***431***
Minnesota State U, Moorhead (MN) ***432***
Minot State U (ND) ***432***
Mississippi Valley State U (MS) ***432***
Missouri Valley Coll (MO) ***433***
Missouri Western State Coll (MO) ***433***
Monmouth Coll (IL) ***434***
Morehead State U (KY) ***436***
Morgan State U (MD) ***436***
Mount Mercy Coll (IA) ***438***
Mount Saint Mary's Coll and Seminary (MD) ***439***
Murray State U (KY) ***440***
Nebraska Wesleyan U (NE) ***443***
Newberry Coll (SC) ***444***
New England School of Communications (ME) ***445***
New Mexico State U (NM) ***446***
North Carolina Ag and Tech State U (NC) ***448***
North Central Coll (IL) ***449***
North Dakota State U (ND) ***449***
Northeastern Illinois U (IL) ***450***
Northern Arizona U (AZ) ***450***
Northern Kentucky U (KY) ***451***
Northern Michigan U (MI) ***451***
Northern State U (SD) ***451***
North Park U (IL) ***452***
Northwest Christian Coll (OR) ***452***
Northwestern Coll (IA) ***453***
Northwestern Oklahoma State U (OK) ***453***
Northwestern U (IL) ***453***
Northwest Missouri State U (MO) ***454***
Ohio Northern U (OH) ***457***
Ohio U (OH) ***458***
Oklahoma Baptist U (OK) ***459***
Oklahoma Christian U (OK) ***459***
Oklahoma City U (OK) ***460***
Oklahoma State U (OK) ***460***
Old Dominion U (VA) ***460***
Olivet Nazarene U (IL) ***461***
Oregon State U (OR) ***462***
Ouachita Baptist U (AR) ***462***
Pace U (NY) ***463***
Penn State U Univ Park Campus (PA) ***468***
Pepperdine U, Malibu (CA) ***469***
Pillsbury Baptist Bible Coll (MN) ***470***
Pittsburg State U (KS) ***470***
Point Loma Nazarene U (CA) ***471***
Portland State U (OR) ***472***
Rensselaer Polytechnic Inst (NY) ***478***
Rhode Island Coll (RI) ***479***
Rider U (NJ) ***480***
Ripon Coll (WI) ***480***
Rowan U (NJ) ***484***
St. Cloud State U (MN) ***488***
Saint John's U (MN) ***490***
St. John's U (NY) ***490***
St. Joseph's Coll, New York (NY) ***491***
St. Joseph's Coll, Suffolk Campus (NY) ***491***
St. Mary's U of San Antonio (TX) ***494***
Samford U (AL) ***497***
Sam Houston State U (TX) ***497***
San Diego State U (CA) ***498***
San Francisco State U (CA) ***498***
San Jose State U (CA) ***499***
Shippensburg U of Pennsylvania (PA) ***503***
Simpson Coll (IA) ***505***
South Dakota State U (SD) ***507***
Southeast Missouri State U (MO) ***508***
Southern Illinois U Carbondale (IL) ***509***
Southern Illinois U Edwardsville (IL) ***509***
Southern Nazarene U (OK) ***510***

Southern U and A&M Coll (LA) 511
Southern Utah U (UT) 511
Southwest Texas State U (TX) 513
State U of NY at Albany (NY) 514
State U of NY at New Paltz (NY) 515
State U of NY Coll at Brockport (NY) 515
State U of NY Coll at Cortland (NY) 516
State U of NY Coll at Oneonta (NY) 517
State U of NY Coll at Potsdam (NY) 517
Stephen F. Austin State U (TX) 518
Stetson U (FL) 519
Suffolk U (MA) 520
Susquehanna U (PA) 521
Syracuse U (NY) 521
Tarleton State U (TX) 522
Temple U (PA) 523
Texas A&M U (TX) 524
Texas A&M U–Kingsville (TX) 525
Texas Christian U (TX) 526
Texas Southern U (TX) 526
Texas Tech U (TX) 526
Texas Wesleyan U (TX) 526
Thomas More Coll (KY) 528
Trevecca Nazarene U (TN) 529
Trinity U (TX) 531
Troy State U (AL) 532
Truman State U (MO) 532
Union U (TN) 534
The U of Akron (OH) 537
The U of Alabama (AL) 537
The U of Alabama in Huntsville (AL) 537
U of Arkansas at Little Rock (AR) 539
U of Arkansas at Monticello (AR) 539
U of Calif, Berkeley (CA) 540
U of Calif, Davis (CA) 540
U of Central Arkansas (AR) 542
U of Central Florida (FL) 542
U of Dubuque (IA) 545
U of Georgia (GA) 545
U of Hawaii at Manoa (HI) 546
U of Houston (TX) 547
U of Illinois at Chicago (IL) 547
U of Illinois at Urbana–Champaign (IL) 548
The U of Iowa (IA) 548
U of Kansas (KS) 549
U of Michigan (MI) 554
U of Michigan–Dearborn (MI) 554
U of Minnesota, Morris (MN) 555
The U of Montana–Missoula (MT) 556
U of Montevallo (AL) 557
U of Nebraska at Kearney (NE) 557
U of Nebraska at Omaha (NE) 557
U of New Mexico (NM) 559
U of North Alabama (AL) 559
The U of North Carolina at Greensboro (NC) 560
The U of North Carolina at Wilmington (NC) 561
U of Pittsburgh (PA) 569
U of Richmond (VA) 572
U of Sioux Falls (SD) 574
The U of South Dakota (SD) 575
U of South Florida (FL) 576
The U of Tennessee (TN) 577
The U of Texas at Arlington (TX) 577
The U of Texas at El Paso (TX) 578
The U of Texas at Tyler (TX) 579
The U of Texas of the Permian Basin (TX) 579
The U of Texas–Pan American (TX) 579
U of the Incarnate Word (TX) 580
U of the Virgin Islands (VI) 581
U of Utah (UT) 582
U of Washington (WA) 583
U of Waterloo (ON, Canada) 583
U of Wisconsin–La Crosse (WI) 584
U of Wisconsin–Platteville (WI) 585
U of Wisconsin–River Falls (WI) 585
U of Wisconsin–Superior (WI) 586
U of Wisconsin–Whitewater (WI) 586
Utah State U (UT) 587
Valdosta State U (GA) 588
Vanguard U of Southern California (CA) 589
Wabash Coll (IN) 592
Walla Walla Coll (WA) 593
Wayne State Coll (NE) 596
West Chester U of Pennsylvania (PA) 598
Western Kentucky U (KY) 599
West Texas A&M U (TX) 602
West Virginia Wesleyan Coll (WV) 603
Wheaton Coll (IL) 603
Whitworth Coll (WA) 604
Willamette U (OR) 605
William Jewell Coll (MO) 606
Wingate U (NC) 607
Winona State U (MN) 608
York Coll of Pennsylvania (PA) 610
York Coll of the City U of New York (NY) 611
Youngstown State U (OH) 611

SPEECH/THEATER EDUCATION

Overview: undergraduates who choose this major learn how to teach various speech skills used either in debate or theatre settings. *Related majors:* speech teacher education, speech and rhetorical studies, drama and theater arts. *Potential careers:* drama teacher, debate coach, English teacher. *Salary potential:* $24k-$32k.

Augustana Coll (SD) 276
Bemidji State U (MN) 285
Boston U (MA) 292
Briar Cliff U (IA) 294
Columbus State U (GA) 328
Culver-Stockton Coll (MO) 334
Dickinson State U (ND) 344
Graceland U (IA) 371
Grambling State U (LA) 371
Hamline U (MN) 374
Hastings Coll (NE) 377
Idaho State U (ID) 384
King Coll (TN) 398
Lewis-Clark State Coll (ID) 406
Lewis U (IL) 406
McKendree Coll (IL) 423
McPherson Coll (KS) 423
Midland Lutheran Coll (NE) 429
Missouri Western State Coll (MO) 433
Northwestern Oklahoma State U (OK) 453
Oklahoma City U (OK) 460
St. Ambrose U (IA) 486
Southwest Baptist U (MO) 512
Southwest State U (MN) 513
Tennessee Temple U (TN) 524
U of Minnesota, Morris (MN) 555
U of St. Thomas (MN) 573
U of Windsor (ON, Canada) 584
Viterbo U (WI) 591
Wartburg Coll (IA) 594
William Woods U (MO) 607
York Coll (NE) 610
York U (ON, Canada) 611

SPEECH THERAPY

Overview: This major teaches students how to help patients of all ages with speech and language communication disorders or impairments to speak better. *Related majors:* speech-language pathology, speech-language pathology/audiology, communication disorders. *Potential careers:* speech pathologist, teacher, speech therapist. *Salary potential:* $30k-$40k.

Adelphi U (NY) 260
Auburn U (AL) 276
Augustana Coll (IL) 276
Columbia Coll (SC) 327
Eastern Kentucky U (KY) 348
Eastern Washington U (WA) 349
Elms Coll (MA) 352
Emerson Coll (MA) 353
Fontbonne U (MO) 361
Hampton U (VA) 375
Indiana U Bloomington (IN) 385
Iona Coll (NY) 390
Lamar U (TX) 401
Lambuth U (TN) 401
Murray State U (KY) 440
Northeastern State U (OK) 450
Northwestern U (IL) 453
Ohio U (OH) 458
Queens Coll of the City U of NY (NY) 475
St. Cloud State U (MN) 488
Southeast Missouri State U (MO) 508
State U of NY at New Paltz (NY) 515
State U of NY Coll at Fredonia (NY) 516
State U of NY Coll at Geneseo (NY) 516
Temple U (PA) 523
Texas A&M U–Kingsville (TX) 525
Texas Southern U (TX) 526
The U of British Columbia (BC, Canada) 540
The U of Iowa (IA) 548
U of New Hampshire (NH) 558
U of Oklahoma Health Sciences Center (OK) 562
U of Redlands (CA) 572
The U of Texas–Pan American (TX) 579
U of Toledo (OH) 581
U of Wisconsin–Madison (WI) 584
U of Wisconsin–River Falls (WI) 585
West Chester U of Pennsylvania (PA) 598
Xavier U of Louisiana (LA) 610

SPORT/FITNESS ADMINISTRATION

Overview: Students choosing this major will learn how to apply the principles of business, coaching, and physical education to the management of athletic programs and teams, rehabilitation facilities, health clubs, and recreation services. *Related majors:* business administration, health/physical education, operations management and supervision, financial management. *Salary potential:* $25k-$35k.

Albertson Coll of Idaho (ID) 262
Alvernia Coll (PA) 265
American U (DC) 267
Anderson Coll (SC) 268
Arkansas Tech U (AR) 272
Augustana Coll (SD) 276
Averett U (VA) 278
Baldwin-Wallace Coll (OH) 280
Ball State U (IN) 280
Barber-Scotia Coll (NC) 281
Barry U (FL) 282
Barton Coll (NC) 282
Baylor U (TX) 283
Becker Coll (MA) 283
Belhaven Coll (MS) 283
Bemidji State U (MN) 285
Benedictine Coll (KS) 285
Bethany Coll (WV) 287
Bethel Coll (IN) 288
Black Hills State U (SD) 290
Bluffton Coll (OH) 291
Bowling Green State U (OH) 292
Brock U (ON, Canada) 295
Campbell U (NC) 303
Carroll Coll (MT) 306
Cazenovia Coll (NY) 308
Centenary Coll (NJ) 308
Central Methodist Coll (MO) 309
Central Washington U (WA) 310
Champlain Coll (VT) 311
Chowan Coll (NC) 312
Christopher Newport U (VA) 313
Colby-Sawyer Coll (NH) 319
Coll Misericordia (PA) 319
Columbia Southern U (AL) 327
Concordia U (MI) 330
Concordia U (NE) 330
Concordia U (OR) 330
Cornerstone U (MI) 333
Crown Coll (MN) 334
Daniel Webster Coll (NH) 337
Davis & Elkins Coll (WV) 338
Defiance Coll (OH) 338
Delaware State U (DE) 338
Delaware Valley Coll (PA) 339
DeSales U (PA) 340
Eastern Connecticut State U (CT) 347
Eastern Mennonite U (VA) 348
Edinboro U of Pennsylvania (PA) 351
Elmhurst Coll (IL) 351
Elon U (NC) 352
Endicott Coll (MA) 354
Erskine Coll (SC) 354
Faulkner U (AL) 357
Flagler Coll (FL) 359
Franklin Pierce Coll (NH) 364
Fresno Pacific U (CA) 364
Gardner-Webb U (NC) 365
George Fox U (OR) 366
Georgia Southern U (GA) 367
Gonzaga U (WA) 369
Graceland U (IA) 371
Greensboro Coll (NC) 372
Guilford Coll (NC) 373
Hampton U (VA) 375
Harding U (AR) 375
Hastings Coll (NE) 377
High Point U (NC) 379
Holy Family U (PA) 380
Howard Payne U (TX) 382
Huntingdon Coll (AL) 383
Husson Coll (ME) 383
Indiana U Bloomington (IN) 385
Indiana Wesleyan U (IN) 387
Iowa Wesleyan Coll (IA) 390
Ithaca Coll (NY) 390
Johnson State Coll (VT) 394
Judson Coll (IL) 395
Keene State Coll (NH) 396
Kennesaw State U (GA) 397
Kentucky Wesleyan Coll (KY) 397
Laurentian U (ON, Canada) 403
LeTourneau U (TX) 405
Liberty U (VA) 406
Limestone Coll (SC) 406
Lock Haven U of Pennsylvania (PA) 408
Longwood U (VA) 409
Loras Coll (IA) 410
Luther Coll (IA) 412
Lynchburg Coll (VA) 413
Lyndon State Coll (VT) 413
Lynn U (FL) 413
MacMurray Coll (IL) 414
Malone Coll (OH) 415
Marian Coll of Fond du Lac (WI) 417
Mars Hill Coll (NC) 418
Marymount U (VA) 420
Medaille Coll (NY) 424
Mercyhurst Coll (PA) 425
Meredith Coll (NC) 426
Methodist Coll (NC) 427
Miami U (OH) 428
MidAmerica Nazarene U (KS) 428
Millikin U (IL) 430
Minnesota State U, Mankato (MN) 431
Minnesota State U, Moorhead (MN) 432
Minot State U (ND) 432
Montana State U–Billings (MT) 434
Montana State U–Bozeman (MT) 434
Montreat Coll (NC) 435
Morgan State U (MD) 436
Mount Union Coll (OH) 440
Mount Vernon Nazarene U (OH) 440
National American U (SD) 442
National U (CA) 442
Nebraska Wesleyan U (NE) 443
Neumann Coll (PA) 443
New England Coll (NH) 444
New York U (NY) 447
Nichols Coll (MA) 448
North Greenville Coll (SC) 451
Northwestern Coll (MN) 453
Northwest Missouri State U (MO) 454
Nova Southeastern U (FL) 455
Ohio Northern U (OH) 457
Ohio U (OH) 458
Olivet Coll (MI) 461
Olivet Nazarene U (IL) 461
Otterbein Coll (OH) 462
Pfeiffer U (NC) 469
Principia Coll (IL) 474
Quincy U (IL) 476
Reinhardt Coll (GA) 478
Robert Morris U (PA) 481
Rochester Coll (MI) 482
Sacred Heart U (CT) 486
St. Ambrose U (IA) 486
St. Andrews Presbyterian Coll (NC) 487
St. John's U (NY) 490
Saint Joseph's Coll of Maine (ME) 491
Saint Leo U (FL) 492
St. Thomas U (FL) 496
Salem International U (WV) 496
Salem State Coll (MA) 497
Seton Hall U (NJ) 502
Shawnee State U (OH) 502
Simpson Coll (IA) 505
Slippery Rock U of Pennsylvania (PA) 506
Southeast Missouri State U (MO) 508
Southern Adventist U (TN) 508
Southern Nazarene U (OK) 510
Southern New Hampshire U (NH) 510
Southern Virginia U (VA) 511

SPORT/FITNESS ADMINISTRATION (continued)

Southwest Baptist U (MO) ***512***
Southwestern Coll (KS) ***512***
Spring Arbor U (MI) ***514***
Springfield Coll (MA) ***514***
State U of NY Coll at Brockport (NY) ***515***
Stetson U (FL) ***519***
Taylor U (IN) ***523***
Temple U (PA) ***523***
Tennessee Wesleyan Coll (TN) ***524***
Texas Lutheran U (TX) ***526***
Texas Wesleyan U (TX) ***526***
Thomas Coll (ME) ***527***
Tiffin U (OH) ***528***
Towson U (MD) ***529***
Tri-State U (IN) ***532***
Tulane U (LA) ***533***
Tusculum Coll (TN) ***533***
Union Coll (KY) ***533***
Union Coll (NE) ***534***
Union U (TN) ***534***
U of Alberta (AB, Canada) ***538***
U of Dayton (OH) ***544***
U of Georgia (GA) ***545***
The U of Iowa (IA) ***548***
U of Louisville (KY) ***550***
U of Massachusetts Amherst (MA) ***552***
U of Michigan (MI) ***554***
U of Nebraska at Kearney (NE) ***557***
U of Nevada, Las Vegas (NV) ***558***
U of New England (ME) ***558***
U of New Haven (CT) ***559***
U of Pittsburgh at Bradford (PA) ***569***
U of Regina (SK, Canada) ***572***
U of San Francisco (CA) ***574***
U of South Carolina (SC) ***575***
The U of Tennessee (TN) ***577***
The U of Tennessee at Martin (TN) ***577***
U of the Incarnate Word (TX) ***580***
U of Tulsa (OK) ***581***
U of Victoria (BC, Canada) ***582***
U of Windsor (ON, Canada) ***584***
U of Wisconsin–La Crosse (WI) ***584***
U of Wisconsin–Parkside (WI) ***585***
Valparaiso U (IN) ***588***
Virginia Intermont Coll (VA) ***590***
Warner Southern Coll (FL) ***593***
Wartburg Coll (IA) ***594***
Washington State U (WA) ***595***
Wayne State Coll (NE) ***596***
Webber International U (FL) ***596***
Western Baptist Coll (OR) ***598***
Western Carolina U (NC) ***598***
Western New England Coll (MA) ***600***
West Virginia U (WV) ***602***
Wheeling Jesuit U (WV) ***603***
Widener U (PA) ***604***
William Penn U (IA) ***606***
Wilmington Coll (DE) ***607***
Wilmington Coll (OH) ***607***
Wingate U (NC) ***607***
Winona State U (MN) ***608***
Winston-Salem State U (NC) ***608***
Winthrop U (SC) ***608***
Xavier U (OH) ***610***
York Coll of Pennsylvania (PA) ***610***
York U (ON, Canada) ***611***
Youngstown State U (OH) ***611***

STRINGED INSTRUMENTS

Overview: This major teaches students to master a stringed instrument for performance purposes. *Related majors:* music performance. *Potential careers:* professional musician. *Salary potential:* varies according to performance schedule, full-time musicians starting out can expect $20k-$25k.

Acadia U (NS, Canada) ***260***
Alma Coll (MI) ***264***
Appalachian State U (NC) ***270***
Aquinas Coll (MI) ***270***
Augustana Coll (IL) ***276***
Baldwin-Wallace Coll (OH) ***280***
Ball State U (IN) ***280***
Benedictine Coll (KS) ***285***
Bennington Coll (VT) ***286***
Berklee Coll of Music (MA) ***286***
Butler U (IN) ***297***
California Inst of the Arts (CA) ***299***
California State U, Fullerton (CA) ***301***
California State U, Northridge (CA) ***301***
Capital U (OH) ***304***
Centenary Coll of Louisiana (LA) ***308***
Chapman U (CA) ***311***
Cleveland Inst of Music (OH) ***317***
Columbus State U (GA) ***328***
Conservatory of Music of Puerto Rico (PR) ***332***
Converse Coll (SC) ***332***
Cornish Coll of the Arts (WA) ***333***
The Curtis Inst of Music (PA) ***335***
DePaul U (IL) ***339***
Eastern Washington U (WA) ***349***
Five Towns Coll (NY) ***359***
Florida State U (FL) ***361***
Grand Valley State U (MI) ***371***
Harding U (AR) ***375***
Hardin-Simmons U (TX) ***376***
Hastings Coll (NE) ***377***
Heidelberg Coll (OH) ***377***
Houghton Coll (NY) ***381***
Howard Payne U (TX) ***382***
Illinois Wesleyan U (IL) ***385***
Inter American U of PR, San Germán Campus (PR) ***388***
The Juilliard School (NY) ***395***
Lamar U (TX) ***401***
Lawrence U (WI) ***403***
Lindenwood U (MO) ***407***
Lipscomb U (TN) ***408***
Luther Coll (IA) ***412***
Manhattan School of Music (NY) ***416***
Mannes Coll of Music, New School U (NY) ***416***
Mars Hill Coll (NC) ***418***
Memorial U of Newfoundland (NF, Canada) ***424***
Meredith Coll (NC) ***426***
Montclair State U (NJ) ***435***
Mount Allison U (NB, Canada) ***437***
New England Conservatory of Music (MA) ***445***
New World School of the Arts (FL) ***447***
Northern Michigan U (MI) ***451***
Northwest Missouri State U (MO) ***454***
Notre Dame de Namur U (CA) ***455***
Oberlin Coll (OH) ***456***
Oklahoma City U (OK) ***460***
Olivet Nazarene U (IL) ***461***
Otterbein Coll (OH) ***462***
Palm Beach Atlantic U (FL) ***465***
Peabody Conserv of Music of Johns Hopkins U (MD) ***466***
Pittsburg State U (KS) ***470***
Queen's U at Kingston (ON, Canada) ***476***
Roosevelt U (IL) ***483***
San Francisco Conservatory of Music (CA) ***498***
Sarah Lawrence Coll (NY) ***499***
Seton Hill U (PA) ***502***
State U of NY Coll at Fredonia (NY) ***516***
Susquehanna U (PA) ***521***
Syracuse U (NY) ***521***
Temple U (PA) ***523***
The U of Akron (OH) ***537***
U of Alberta (AB, Canada) ***538***
The U of British Columbia (BC, Canada) ***540***
U of Central Oklahoma (OK) ***542***
U of Cincinnati (OH) ***543***
The U of Iowa (IA) ***548***
U of Kansas (KS) ***549***
U of Miami (FL) ***553***
U of Michigan (MI) ***554***
U of Missouri–Kansas City (MO) ***555***
U of New Hampshire (NH) ***558***
U of North Texas (TX) ***562***
U of Oklahoma (OK) ***562***
The U of South Dakota (SD) ***575***
U of Southern California (CA) ***576***
The U of Tennessee at Martin (TN) ***577***
U of Washington (WA) ***583***
The U of Western Ontario (ON, Canada) ***583***
U of West Florida (FL) ***583***
U of Wisconsin–Milwaukee (WI) ***585***
Vanderbilt U (TN) ***588***
West Chester U of Pennsylvania (PA) ***598***
Xavier U of Louisiana (LA) ***610***
Youngstown State U (OH) ***611***

STRUCTURAL ENGINEERING

Overview: Students learn the science and mathematics of the design and construction of load bearing structures, roads, rail lines, bridges, dams, etc. *Related majors:* engineering mechanics, architectural engineering, civil engineering, applied physics, mathematics. *Potential careers:* structural engineer, construction manager, architectural engineer. *Salary potential:* $40k-$50k.

Clarkson U (NY) ***316***
The Coll of Southeastern Europe, The American U of Athens(Greece) ***323***
Johnson & Wales U (RI) ***393***
Penn State U Berks Cmps of Berks-Lehigh Valley Coll (PA) ***468***
Penn State U Harrisburg Campus of the Capital Coll (PA) ***468***
U of Calif, San Diego (CA) ***541***
U of Southern California (CA) ***576***

SURVEYING

Overview: This major provides the basic knowledge and technical skills necessary to make precise measurements for land, route, construction, geodetic, photogrammetric, and topographic surveys. *Related majors:* mathematics, construction/building technology, geography, cartography, geophysics and seismology. *Potential careers:* survey party chief, instrument person, surveying technician, highway surveyor, mapper. *Salary potential:* $22k-$30k.

British Columbia Inst of Technology (BC, Canada) ***295***
California State Polytechnic U, Pomona (CA) ***300***
California State U, Fresno (CA) ***301***
East Tennessee State U (TN) ***349***
Ferris State U (MI) ***358***
Metropolitan State Coll of Denver (CO) ***427***
Michigan Technological U (MI) ***428***
New Mexico State U (NM) ***446***
The Ohio State U (OH) ***457***
Oregon Inst of Technology (OR) ***461***
Purdue U (IN) ***475***
Southern Polytechnic State U (GA) ***511***
Texas A&M U–Corpus Christi (TX) ***525***
Thomas Edison State Coll (NJ) ***527***
Université Laval (QC, Canada) ***536***
The U of Akron (OH) ***537***
U of Alaska Anchorage (AK) ***538***
U of Arkansas at Little Rock (AR) ***539***
U of Florida (FL) ***545***
U of Maine (ME) ***550***
U of New Brunswick Fredericton (NB, Canada) ***558***
U of New Brunswick Saint John (NB, Canada) ***558***
U of Toronto (ON, Canada) ***581***
U of Wisconsin–Madison (WI) ***584***

SYSTEM ADMINISTRATION

Overview: This major teaches students how to manage computer systems that emanate from a specific site or network hub. *Related majors:* computer and information systems security, system networking and LAN/WAN management, data processing technology. *Potential careers:* data processing manager, computer systems analyst, system administrator. *Salary potential:* $35k-$45k.

American Coll of Computer & Information Sciences (AL) ***266***

SYSTEM/NETWORKING/LAN/WAN MANAGEMENT

Overview: This major teaches students how to manage the computer network system of an entire organization or a group of satellite users in either a local area (LAN) or wide area (WAN) network. *Related majors:* computer systems analysis, computer system networking, system administration. *Potential careers:* systems analyst, system administrator, networking manager, technical support specialist. *Salary potential:* $35k-$50k.

Champlain Coll (VT) ***311***

SYSTEMS ENGINEERING

Overview: Students choosing this major learn the mathematical and scientific principles behind implementing solutions to engineering problems involving various human, physical, energy, communications, and management systems. *Related majors:* statistics, industrial engineering, computer systems analysis, electrical engineering. *Potential careers:* management consultant, logistics and materials manager, industrial engineer, plant manager, systems analyst. *Salary potential:* $37k-$55k.

Boston U (MA) ***292***
California State U, Northridge (CA) ***301***
Carleton U (ON, Canada) ***305***
Case Western Reserve U (OH) ***307***
Eastern Nazarene Coll (MA) ***348***
Florida International U (FL) ***360***
George Mason U (VA) ***366***
The George Washington U (DC) ***367***
Harvard U (MA) ***376***
Insto Tecno Estudios Sups Monterrey(Mexico) ***388***
Maine Maritime Academy (ME) ***415***
Missouri Tech (MO) ***433***
Montana Tech of The U of Montana (MT) ***435***
Oakland U (MI) ***456***
The Ohio State U (OH) ***457***
Ohio U (OH) ***458***
Rensselaer Polytechnic Inst (NY) ***478***
Richmond, The American International U in London(United Kingdom) ***480***
United States Military Academy (NY) ***535***
United States Naval Academy (MD) ***535***
The U of Arizona (AZ) ***538***
U of Calif, San Diego (CA) ***541***
U of Florida (FL) ***545***
The U of Memphis (TN) ***553***
U of Pennsylvania (PA) ***563***
U of Regina (SK, Canada) ***572***
U of Southern California (CA) ***576***
U of Virginia (VA) ***582***
U of Waterloo (ON, Canada) ***583***
Washington U in St. Louis (MO) ***595***

SYSTEMS SCIENCE/THEORY

Overview: Students who choose this major will learn how to analyze and propose solutions for complex problems using a variety of data and models from the natural, social, technological, behavioral, and life sciences. *Related majors:* biology, history, economics, psychology, systems analysis, information science. *Potential careers:* mathematician, systems engineer, industrial engineer, business or scientific consultant, economist, professor. *Salary potential:* $35k-$45k.

Indiana U Bloomington (IN) ***385***
Marshall U (WV) ***418***
Miami U (OH) ***428***
Providence Coll (RI) ***474***
Stanford U (CA) ***514***

U of Kansas (KS) ***549***
U of Ottawa (ON, Canada) ***563***
Washington U in St. Louis (MO) ***595***
Yale U (CT) ***610***

TAXATION

Overview: Students learn how to provide tax advice and tax preparation services to a wide range of clients. *Related majors:* law and legal studies, investments and securities, accounting, financial planning. *Potential careers:* tax attorney, tax preparation specialist, accountant, investment advisor or stockbroker, financial planner. *Salary potential:* $25-$35k.

California State U, Fullerton (CA) ***301***
Drexel U (PA) ***346***

TEACHER ASSISTANT/AIDE

Overview: This major prepares undergraduates to assist teachers in the classroom or to provide special instruction and supervision to a variety of students and student needs. *Related majors:* special education, curriculum and instruction, teaching English as a second language, early childhood education, adult education. *Potential careers:* teacher's aid, teacher, educational coach. *Salary potential:* $20k-$25k.

Long Island U, Southampton Coll, Friends World Program (NY) ***409***

TEACHER EDUCATION RELATED

Information can be found under this major's main heading.

Boston U (MA) ***292***
U of Hawaii at Manoa (HI) ***546***
Xavier U (OH) ***610***

TEACHER EDUCATION, SPECIFIC PROGRAMS RELATED

Information can be found under this major's main heading.

Averett U (VA) ***278***
Bradley U (IL) ***293***
Chadron State Coll (NE) ***311***
Drexel U (PA) ***346***
Duquesne U (PA) ***346***
Franklin Coll (IN) ***363***
Henderson State U (AR) ***378***
Hofstra U (NY) ***380***
Juniata Coll (PA) ***395***
Louisiana State U and A&M Coll (LA) ***410***
Minot State U (ND) ***432***
Northern Arizona U (AZ) ***450***
Ohio U (OH) ***458***
Old Dominion U (VA) ***460***
Plymouth State Coll (NH) ***471***
San Diego State U (CA) ***498***
Thomas More Coll (KY) ***528***
The U of Akron (OH) ***537***
The U of Arizona (AZ) ***538***
U of Central Oklahoma (OK) ***542***
U of Hawaii at Manoa (HI) ***546***
U of Kentucky (KY) ***549***
U of Louisiana at Lafayette (LA) ***550***
U of Nebraska–Lincoln (NE) ***557***
The U of North Carolina at Wilmington (NC) ***561***
U of St. Thomas (MN) ***573***
U of Toledo (OH) ***581***
Utah State U (UT) ***587***

TEACHING ENGLISH AS A SECOND LANGUAGE

Overview: This major prepares graduates to instruct others that do not classify English as their primary language. *Related majors:* education, English. *Potential careers:* teacher. *Salary potential:* $25k-$35k.

Alaska Bible Coll (AK) ***261***
Bethel Coll (MN) ***288***
Bridgewater Coll (VA) ***294***
Brigham Young U–Hawaii (HI) ***295***
California State U, Northridge (CA) ***301***
Calvin Coll (MI) ***303***
Carleton U (ON, Canada) ***305***
Carroll Coll (MT) ***306***
Concordia U (QC, Canada) ***331***
Concordia U Wisconsin (WI) ***331***
Doane Coll (NE) ***344***
Elms Coll (MA) ***352***
Goshen Coll (IN) ***370***
Hawai'i Pacific U (HI) ***377***
Howard Payne U (TX) ***382***
Inter American U of PR, Aguadilla Campus (PR) ***388***
Inter American U of PR, Guayama Campus (PR) ***388***
Inter American U of PR, San Germán Campus (PR) ***388***
John Brown U (AR) ***392***
Langston U (OK) ***402***
Liberty U (VA) ***406***
Long Island U, Southampton Coll, Friends World Program (NY) ***409***
Maryville Coll (TN) ***420***
McGill U (QC, Canada) ***423***
Mercy Coll (NY) ***425***
Moody Bible Inst (IL) ***435***
Murray State U (KY) ***440***
Northern Arizona U (AZ) ***450***
Northwest Coll (WA) ***452***
Northwestern Coll (MN) ***453***
Nyack Coll (NY) ***456***
Ohio Dominican U (OH) ***457***
Ohio U (OH) ***458***
Oklahoma Christian U (OK) ***459***
Oklahoma Wesleyan U (OK) ***460***
Oral Roberts U (OK) ***461***
Providence Coll and Theological Seminary (MB, Canada) ***475***
Queens Coll of the City U of NY (NY) ***475***
Simmons Coll (MA) ***504***
Texas Christian U (TX) ***526***
Texas Wesleyan U (TX) ***526***
Union U (TN) ***534***
Université Laval (QC, Canada) ***536***
U of Alberta (AB, Canada) ***538***
The U of British Columbia (BC, Canada) ***540***
U of Delaware (DE) ***544***
The U of Findlay (OH) ***545***
U of Hawaii at Manoa (HI) ***546***
The U of Montana–Missoula (MT) ***556***
U of Nebraska–Lincoln (NE) ***557***
U of New Brunswick Fredericton (NB, Canada) ***558***
U of Northern Iowa (IA) ***561***
U of Ottawa (ON, Canada) ***563***
U of Puerto Rico, Humacao U Coll (PR) ***570***
U of Victoria (BC, Canada) ***582***
U of Washington (WA) ***583***
U of Wisconsin–Oshkosh (WI) ***585***
U of Wisconsin–River Falls (WI) ***585***
York U (ON, Canada) ***611***

TECHNICAL/BUSINESS WRITING

Overview: Students learn the skills and methods necessary for writing and editing technical, business, or scientific papers or documents. *Related majors:* creative writing, journalism, history and philosophy of science and technology, applied history, and archival administration. *Potential careers:* technical writer, scientific or trade journal editor, copywriter, lawyer, business consultant. *Salary potential:* $25k-$35k.

Alderson-Broaddus Coll (WV) ***263***
Bowling Green State U (OH) ***292***
Carlow Coll (PA) ***305***
Carnegie Mellon U (PA) ***305***
Carroll Coll (MT) ***306***
Cedarville U (OH) ***308***
Central Michigan U (MI) ***310***
Chester Coll of New England (NH) ***312***
Christian Brothers U (TN) ***313***
Clarkson U (NY) ***316***
Coll of Santa Fe (NM) ***323***
Drexel U (PA) ***346***
State U of NY at Farmingdale (NY) ***357***
Ferris State U (MI) ***358***
Fitchburg State Coll (MA) ***358***
Gannon U (PA) ***365***
Grand Valley State U (MI) ***371***
Iowa State U of Science and Technology (IA) ***390***
James Madison U (VA) ***391***
La Roche Coll (PA) ***402***
Lawrence Technological U (MI) ***403***
Madonna U (MI) ***414***
Maryville Coll (TN) ***420***
Mercyhurst Coll (PA) ***425***
Metropolitan State U (MN) ***427***
Miami U (OH) ***428***
Michigan Technological U (MI) ***428***
Montana Tech of The U of Montana (MT) ***435***
Mount Mary Coll (WI) ***438***
New Jersey Inst of Technology (NJ) ***445***
New Mexico Inst of Mining and Technology (NM) ***446***
New York Inst of Technology (NY) ***447***
Northeastern U (MA) ***450***
Northwestern Coll (MN) ***453***
Oklahoma State U (OK) ***460***
Oregon State U (OR) ***462***
Pennsylvania Coll of Technology (PA) ***467***
Rensselaer Polytechnic Inst (NY) ***478***
San Francisco State U (CA) ***498***
San Jose State U (CA) ***499***
Southern Polytechnic State U (GA) ***511***
Southwest Missouri State U (MO) ***513***
Tennessee Technological U (TN) ***524***
U of Arkansas at Little Rock (AR) ***539***
U of Baltimore (MD) ***539***
U of Delaware (DE) ***544***
U of Hartford (CT) ***546***
U of Houston–Downtown (TX) ***547***
The U of Montana–Missoula (MT) ***556***
U of Victoria (BC, Canada) ***582***
U of Washington (WA) ***583***
U of Wisconsin–Stout (WI) ***586***
Weber State U (UT) ***596***
Winthrop U (SC) ***608***
Wittenberg U (OH) ***608***
Worcester Polytechnic Inst (MA) ***609***
York U (ON, Canada) ***611***
Youngstown State U (OH) ***611***

TECHNICAL EDUCATION

Overview: This major prepares undergraduates to teach specific vocational and technical educational programs to a variety of students. *Related majors:* drafting and design technology; electrical and electronic technology; computer maintenance technology; heating, air conditioning, and refrigeration technology. *Potential career:* industrial arts teacher. *Salary potential:* $25k-$34k.

Bowling Green State U (OH) ***292***
Colorado State U (CO) ***325***
Idaho State U (ID) ***384***
Mississippi State U (MS) ***432***
New York Inst of Technology (NY) ***447***
The Ohio State U (OH) ***457***
San Diego State U (CA) ***498***
Texas Christian U (TX) ***526***
Université Laval (QC, Canada) ***536***
The U of Akron (OH) ***537***
U of Idaho (ID) ***547***
U of Nebraska at Kearney (NE) ***557***
U of Saskatchewan (SK, Canada) ***574***
The U of Tennessee (TN) ***577***
U of Wisconsin–Stout (WI) ***586***
Utah State U (UT) ***587***
Valley City State U (ND) ***588***
Wayne State U (MI) ***596***

TELECOMMUNICATIONS

Overview: This major will prepare students for careers in broadcast, cable and satellite television, and radio, including distribution and programming companies, the Internet industry, and wired and wireless telecommunications providers. *Related majors:* broadcast journalism, radio and television broadcast technology, telecommunications technology. *Potential careers:* programming manager, advertising sales, market analyst, producer, Internet provider, telecommunications technician. *Salary potential:* $30k-$40k.

Ball State U (IN) ***280***
Baylor U (TX) ***283***
Bowling Green State U (OH) ***292***
Butler U (IN) ***297***
California State Polytechnic U, Pomona (CA) ***300***
California State U, Hayward (CA) ***301***
Cameron U (OK) ***303***
Capitol Coll (MD) ***304***
Champlain Coll (VT) ***311***
Colorado State U-Pueblo (CO) ***325***
Colorado Tech U (CO) ***326***
Columbia Coll Hollywood (CA) ***327***
Ferris State U (MI) ***358***
Golden Gate U (CA) ***369***
Grand Valley State U (MI) ***371***
Hampshire Coll (MA) ***375***
Howard Payne U (TX) ***382***
Indiana U Bloomington (IN) ***385***
Ithaca Coll (NY) ***390***
Kean U (NJ) ***396***
Kutztown U of Pennsylvania (PA) ***399***
Marywood U (PA) ***421***
Michigan State U (MI) ***428***
Morgan State U (MD) ***436***
Murray State U (KY) ***440***
New York Inst of Technology (NY) ***447***
Ohio U (OH) ***458***
Oklahoma Baptist U (OK) ***459***
Pacific U (OR) ***464***
Penn State U Univ Park Campus (PA) ***468***
Pepperdine U, Malibu (CA) ***469***
Rochester Inst of Technology (NY) ***482***
Roosevelt U (IL) ***483***
St. John's U (NY) ***490***
Salem International U (WV) ***496***
Southern Polytechnic State U (GA) ***511***
Syracuse U (NY) ***521***
Texas Southern U (TX) ***526***
Tusculum Coll (TN) ***533***
U of Florida (FL) ***545***
U of the Sacred Heart (PR) ***580***
U of Wisconsin–Platteville (WI) ***585***
Western Michigan U (MI) ***599***
Westminster Coll (PA) ***601***
Wingate U (NC) ***607***
Winona State U (MN) ***608***
Youngstown State U (OH) ***611***

TEXTILE ARTS

Overview: This major teaches students the theories, artistic skills, and techniques for working with fiber, textiles, and other woven materials. *Related majors:* fine arts, drawing, fashion design/illustration, crafts, folk art, artisanry. *Potential careers:* fashion designer or fashion illustrator, costume designer, weaver, fine artist, clothing manufacturer. *Salary potential:* $15k-$25k.

Academy of Art Coll (CA) ***260***
Adams State Coll (CO) ***260***
Alberta Coll of Art & Design (AB, Canada) ***262***
Bowling Green State U (OH) ***292***
California Coll of Arts and Crafts (CA) ***299***
California State U, Long Beach (CA) ***301***
California State U, Northridge (CA) ***301***
The Cleveland Inst of Art (OH) ***317***
Col for Creative Studies (MI) ***319***
Colorado State U (CO) ***325***
Concordia U (QC, Canada) ***331***
Cornell U (NY) ***333***
Finlandia U (MI) ***358***

TEXTILE ARTS (continued)

Kansas City Art Inst (MO) ***395***
Long Island U, Southampton Coll, Friends World Program (NY) ***409***
Maryland Inst Coll of Art (MD) ***419***
Massachusetts Coll of Art (MA) ***421***
Memphis Coll of Art (TN) ***425***
Mercyhurst Coll (PA) ***425***
Moore Coll of Art and Design (PA) ***436***
Northern Michigan U (MI) ***451***
Northwest Missouri State U (MO) ***454***
Nova Scotia Coll of Art and Design (NS, Canada) ***455***
Oregon State U (OR) ***462***
Philadelphia U (PA) ***469***
Rhode Island School of Design (RI) ***479***
Savannah Coll of Art and Design (GA) ***499***
School of the Art Inst of Chicago (IL) ***500***
Syracuse U (NY) ***521***
Texas Woman's U (TX) ***527***
U of Massachusetts Dartmouth (MA) ***553***
U of Michigan (MI) ***554***
U of North Texas (TX) ***562***
U of Oregon (OR) ***562***
U of Washington (WA) ***583***
U of Wisconsin–Milwaukee (WI) ***585***

TEXTILE SCIENCES/ ENGINEERING

Overview: Students in this major learn how to create, evaluate, and produce synthetic and natural fibers and fiber products that will be employed in a wide variety of products or industrial uses. *Related majors:* chemical technology, materials science, polymer/ plastics engineering, agronomy, mechanical engineering. *Potential careers:* textile manufacturer, research scientist, inventor, product designer. *Salary potential:* $28k-$40k.

Auburn U (AL) ***276***
Georgia Inst of Technology (GA) ***367***
North Carolina State U (NC) ***449***
Philadelphia U (PA) ***469***
Texas Tech U (TX) ***526***
Université de Sherbrooke (QC, Canada) ***536***
U of Massachusetts Dartmouth (MA) ***553***

THEATER ARTS/DRAMA

Overview: Students study the different types of dramatic works as well as the principles and techniques for performing and producing live dramatic works. *Related majors:* technical theater, theater design and stagecraft, acting and directing, playwriting and screen writing, drama/theater literature history and criticism. *Potential careers:* actor, director, set designer, critic, playwright or scriptwriter. *Salary potential:* $15k-$25k.

Abilene Christian U (TX) ***260***
Acadia U (NS, Canada) ***260***
Adams State Coll (CO) ***260***
Adelphi U (NY) ***260***
Adrian Coll (MI) ***260***
Agnes Scott Coll (GA) ***261***
Alabama State U (AL) ***261***
Albertson Coll of Idaho (ID) ***262***
Albertus Magnus Coll (CT) ***262***
Albion Coll (MI) ***262***
Albright Coll (PA) ***263***
Alderson-Broaddus Coll (WV) ***263***
Alfred U (NY) ***263***
Allegheny Coll (PA) ***264***
Alma Coll (MI) ***264***
American U (DC) ***267***
The American U in Cairo(Egypt) ***267***
Amherst Coll (MA) ***268***
Anderson Coll (SC) ***268***
Anderson U (IN) ***268***
Angelo State U (TX) ***269***
Antioch Coll (OH) ***269***
Appalachian State U (NC) ***270***
Arcadia U (PA) ***271***
Arizona State U (AZ) ***271***
Arkansas State U (AR) ***272***
Armstrong Atlantic State U (GA) ***273***
Ashland U (OH) ***274***
Auburn U (AL) ***276***
Augsburg Coll (MN) ***276***
Augustana Coll (IL) ***276***
Augustana Coll (SD) ***276***
Averett U (VA) ***278***
Avila U (MO) ***278***
Baker U (KS) ***280***
Baldwin-Wallace Coll (OH) ***280***
Ball State U (IN) ***280***
Bard Coll (NY) ***281***
Barnard Coll (NY) ***282***
Barry U (FL) ***282***
Barton Coll (NC) ***282***
Bates Coll (ME) ***282***
Baylor U (TX) ***283***
Belhaven Coll (MS) ***283***
Belmont U (TN) ***284***
Beloit Coll (WI) ***285***
Bemidji State U (MN) ***285***
Benedictine Coll (KS) ***285***
Bennington Coll (VT) ***286***
Berea Coll (KY) ***286***
Berry Coll (GA) ***287***
Bethany Coll (WV) ***287***
Bethany Coll of the Assemblies of God (CA) ***287***
Bethel Coll (IN) ***288***
Bethel Coll (MN) ***288***
Bethel Coll (TN) ***288***
Birmingham-Southern Coll (AL) ***289***
Bishop's U (QC, Canada) ***289***
Bloomfield Coll (NJ) ***290***
Bloomsburg U of Pennsylvania (PA) ***290***
Bluefield Coll (VA) ***291***
Blue Mountain Coll (MS) ***291***
Boston Coll (MA) ***292***
Bowling Green State U (OH) ***292***
Bradley U (IL) ***293***
Brandeis U (MA) ***293***
Brenau U (GA) ***293***
Briar Cliff U (IA) ***294***
Bridgewater State Coll (MA) ***294***
Brigham Young U (UT) ***295***
Brock U (ON, Canada) ***295***
Brooklyn Coll of the City U of NY (NY) ***295***
Brown U (RI) ***296***
Bucknell U (PA) ***297***
Buena Vista U (IA) ***297***
Butler U (IN) ***297***
California Inst of the Arts (CA) ***299***
California Lutheran U (CA) ***299***
California State Polytechnic U, Pomona (CA) ***300***
California State U, Bakersfield (CA) ***300***
California State U, Chico (CA) ***300***
California State U, Dominguez Hills (CA) ***300***
California State U, Fresno (CA) ***301***
California State U, Fullerton (CA) ***301***
California State U, Hayward (CA) ***301***
California State U, Long Beach (CA) ***301***
California State U, Northridge (CA) ***301***
California State U, Sacramento (CA) ***301***
California State U, San Bernardino (CA) ***302***
California State U, Stanislaus (CA) ***302***
California U of Pennsylvania (PA) ***302***
Calvin Coll (MI) ***303***
Cameron U (OK) ***303***
Campbell U (NC) ***303***
Cardinal Stritch U (WI) ***305***
Carleton U (ON, Canada) ***305***
Carnegie Mellon U (PA) ***305***
Carroll Coll (MT) ***306***
Carroll Coll (WI) ***306***
Carson-Newman Coll (TN) ***306***
Carthage Coll (WI) ***306***
Case Western Reserve U (OH) ***307***
Castleton State Coll (VT) ***307***
Catawba Coll (NC) ***307***
The Catholic U of America (DC) ***307***
Cedar Crest Coll (PA) ***308***
Cedarville U (OH) ***308***
Centenary Coll of Louisiana (LA) ***308***
Central Coll (IA) ***309***
Central Connecticut State U (CT) ***309***
Central Methodist Coll (MO) ***309***
Central Michigan U (MI) ***310***
Central Missouri State U (MO) ***310***
Central Washington U (WA) ***310***
Centre Coll (KY) ***310***
Chadron State Coll (NE) ***311***
Chapman U (CA) ***311***
Chatham Coll (PA) ***312***
Cheyney U of Pennsylvania (PA) ***312***
Christopher Newport U (VA) ***313***
City Coll of the City U of NY (NY) ***314***
Claremont McKenna Coll (CA) ***315***
Clarion U of Pennsylvania (PA) ***315***
Clark Atlanta U (GA) ***315***
Clarke Coll (IA) ***315***
Clark U (MA) ***316***
Cleveland State U (OH) ***317***
Coastal Carolina U (SC) ***318***
Coe Coll (IA) ***318***
Coker Coll (SC) ***318***
Colby Coll (ME) ***318***
Colgate U (NY) ***319***
Coll of Charleston (SC) ***320***
Coll of Saint Benedict (MN) ***321***
Coll of St. Catherine (MN) ***321***
Coll of Santa Fe (NM) ***323***
Coll of Staten Island of the City U of NY (NY) ***323***
Coll of the Holy Cross (MA) ***323***
Coll of the Ozarks (MO) ***323***
The Coll of William and Mary (VA) ***324***
The Coll of Wooster (OH) ***324***
Colorado Christian U (CO) ***325***
The Colorado Coll (CO) ***325***
Colorado State U (CO) ***325***
Columbia Coll (NY) ***326***
Columbia Coll Chicago (IL) ***327***
Columbia U, School of General Studies (NY) ***328***
Columbus State U (GA) ***328***
Concordia Coll (MN) ***329***
Concordia U (CA) ***330***
Concordia U (IL) ***330***
Concordia U (MN) ***330***
Concordia U (NE) ***330***
Concordia U (OR) ***330***
Concordia U (QC, Canada) ***331***
Concordia U Wisconsin (WI) ***331***
Connecticut Coll (CT) ***331***
Converse Coll (SC) ***332***
Cornell Coll (IA) ***332***
Cornell U (NY) ***333***
Cornish Coll of the Arts (WA) ***333***
Creighton U (NE) ***333***
Culver-Stockton Coll (MO) ***334***
Cumberland Coll (KY) ***335***
Cumberland U (TN) ***335***
Dakota Wesleyan U (SD) ***336***
Dalhousie U (NS, Canada) ***336***
Dartmouth Coll (NH) ***337***
Davidson Coll (NC) ***338***
Davis & Elkins Coll (WV) ***338***
Delaware State U (DE) ***338***
Denison U (OH) ***339***
DePaul U (IL) ***339***
DeSales U (PA) ***340***
Dickinson Coll (PA) ***344***
Dickinson State U (ND) ***344***
Dillard U (LA) ***344***
Doane Coll (NE) ***344***
Dominican U (IL) ***345***
Dordt Coll (IA) ***345***
Dowling Coll (NY) ***345***
Drake U (IA) ***345***
Drew U (NJ) ***346***
Drury U (MO) ***346***
Duke U (NC) ***346***
Duquesne U (PA) ***346***
Earlham Coll (IN) ***347***
East Carolina U (NC) ***347***
Eastern Illinois U (IL) ***348***
Eastern Kentucky U (KY) ***348***
Eastern Mennonite U (VA) ***348***
Eastern Michigan U (MI) ***348***
Eastern Nazarene Coll (MA) ***348***
Eastern New Mexico U (NM) ***349***
Eastern Oregon U (OR) ***349***
Eastern Washington U (WA) ***349***
East Stroudsburg U of Pennsylvania (PA) ***349***
East Texas Baptist U (TX) ***350***
Eckerd Coll (FL) ***350***
Edgewood Coll (WI) ***351***
Edinboro U of Pennsylvania (PA) ***351***
Elmhurst Coll (IL) ***351***
Elmira Coll (NY) ***351***
Elon U (NC) ***352***
Emerson Coll (MA) ***353***
Emory & Henry Coll (VA) ***353***
Emory U (GA) ***354***
Emporia State U (KS) ***354***
Eugene Lang Coll, New School U (NY) ***355***
Eureka Coll (IL) ***355***
The Evergreen State Coll (WA) ***355***
Fairleigh Dickinson U, Florham (NJ) ***356***
Fairleigh Dickinson U, Teaneck-Metro Campus (NJ) ***356***
Fairmont State Coll (WV) ***356***
Fayetteville State U (NC) ***357***
Ferrum Coll (VA) ***358***
Fisk U (TN) ***358***
Fitchburg State Coll (MA) ***358***
Five Towns Coll (NY) ***359***
Flagler Coll (FL) ***359***
Florida A&M U (FL) ***359***
Florida Atlantic U (FL) ***359***
Florida International U (FL) ***360***
Florida Southern Coll (FL) ***361***
Florida State U (FL) ***361***
Fontbonne U (MO) ***361***
Fordham U (NY) ***362***
Fort Lewis Coll (CO) ***362***
Francis Marion U (SC) ***363***
Franklin and Marshall Coll (PA) ***363***
Franklin Coll (IN) ***363***
Franklin Pierce Coll (NH) ***364***
Freed-Hardeman U (TN) ***364***
Frostburg State U (MD) ***365***
Furman U (SC) ***365***
Gallaudet U (DC) ***365***
Gannon U (PA) ***365***
George Mason U (VA) ***366***
Georgetown Coll (KY) ***366***
The George Washington U (DC) ***367***
Georgia Coll & State U (GA) ***367***
Georgia Southern U (GA) ***367***
Georgia State U (GA) ***368***
Gettysburg Coll (PA) ***368***
Goddard Coll (VT) ***369***
Gonzaga U (WA) ***369***
Goshen Coll (IN) ***370***
Goucher Coll (MD) ***370***
Graceland U (IA) ***371***
Grambling State U (LA) ***371***
Grand Canyon U (AZ) ***371***
Grand Valley State U (MI) ***371***
Grand View Coll (IA) ***372***
Green Mountain Coll (VT) ***372***
Greensboro Coll (NC) ***372***
Greenville Coll (IL) ***373***
Grinnell Coll (IA) ***373***
Guilford Coll (NC) ***373***
Gustavus Adolphus Coll (MN) ***374***
Hamilton Coll (NY) ***374***
Hamline U (MN) ***374***
Hampshire Coll (MA) ***375***
Hampton U (VA) ***375***
Hannibal-LaGrange Coll (MO) ***375***
Hanover Coll (IN) ***375***
Harding U (AR) ***375***
Hardin-Simmons U (TX) ***376***
Hartwick Coll (NY) ***376***
Harvard U (MA) ***376***
Hastings Coll (NE) ***377***
Heidelberg Coll (OH) ***377***
Henderson State U (AR) ***378***
Hendrix Coll (AR) ***378***
High Point U (NC) ***379***
Hillsdale Coll (MI) ***379***
Hiram Coll (OH) ***379***
Hobart and William Smith Colls (NY) ***380***
Hofstra U (NY) ***380***
Hollins U (VA) ***380***
Hope Coll (MI) ***381***
Howard Payne U (TX) ***382***
Howard U (DC) ***382***
Humboldt State U (CA) ***382***
Hunter Coll of the City U of NY (NY) ***382***
Huntingdon Coll (AL) ***383***
Huntington Coll (IN) ***383***
Idaho State U (ID) ***384***
Illinois Coll (IL) ***384***
Illinois State U (IL) ***384***
Illinois Wesleyan U (IL) ***385***
Indiana State U (IN) ***385***
Indiana U Bloomington (IN) ***385***
Indiana U Northwest (IN) ***386***
Indiana U of Pennsylvania (PA) ***386***
Indiana U–Purdue U Fort Wayne (IN) ***386***
Indiana U South Bend (IN) ***387***
Iona Coll (NY) ***390***
Iowa State U of Science and Technology (IA) ***390***

Ithaca Coll (NY) **390**
Jacksonville State U (AL) **390**
Jacksonville U (FL) **391**
James Madison U (VA) **391**
Jamestown Coll (ND) **391**
Johnson State Coll (VT) **394**
Judson Coll (IL) **395**
The Juilliard School (NY) **395**
Kalamazoo Coll (MI) **395**
Kansas State U (KS) **396**
Kean U (NJ) **396**
Keene State Coll (NH) **396**
Kennesaw State U (GA) **397**
Kent State U (OH) **397**
Kenyon Coll (OH) **398**
King's Coll (PA) **398**
Knox Coll (IL) **399**
Kutztown U of Pennsylvania (PA) **399**
LaGrange Coll (GA) **400**
Lake Erie Coll (OH) **400**
Lakeland Coll (WI) **401**
Lamar U (TX) **401**
Lambuth U (TN) **401**
Lander U (SC) **401**
Langston U (OK) **402**
Laurentian U (ON, Canada) **403**
Lawrence U (WI) **403**
Lees-McRae Coll (NC) **404**
Lehigh U (PA) **404**
Lehman Coll of the City U of NY (NY) **404**
Le Moyne Coll (NY) **404**
Lenoir-Rhyne Coll (NC) **405**
Lewis & Clark Coll (OR) **405**
Lewis-Clark State Coll (ID) **406**
Lewis U (IL) **406**
Lindenwood U (MO) **407**
Linfield Coll (OR) **408**
Lock Haven U of Pennsylvania (PA) **408**
Long Island U, C.W. Post Campus (NY) **409**
Long Island U, Southampton Coll, Friends World Program (NY) **409**
Longwood U (VA) **409**
Louisiana Coll (LA) **410**
Louisiana State U and A&M Coll (LA) **410**
Loyola Marymount U (CA) **411**
Loyola U Chicago (IL) **411**
Loyola U New Orleans (LA) **411**
Luther Coll (IA) **412**
Lycoming Coll (PA) **412**
Lynchburg Coll (VA) **413**
Lyon Coll (AR) **413**
Macalester Coll (MN) **413**
MacMurray Coll (IL) **414**
Maharishi U of Management (IA) **414**
Malone Coll (OH) **415**
Manchester Coll (IN) **415**
Manhattanville Coll (NY) **416**
Mansfield U of Pennsylvania (PA) **416**
Marietta Coll (OH) **417**
Marist Coll (NY) **417**
Marlboro Coll (VT) **418**
Marquette U (WI) **418**
Mars Hill Coll (NC) **418**
Mary Baldwin Coll (VA) **419**
Marymount Coll of Fordham U (NY) **419**
Marymount Manhattan Coll (NY) **420**
Maryville Coll (TN) **420**
Mary Washington Coll (VA) **420**
Marywood U (PA) **421**
Massachusetts Coll of Liberal Arts (MA) **421**
Massachusetts Inst of Technology (MA) **421**
McDaniel Coll (MD) **422**
McGill U (QC, Canada) **423**
McMaster U (ON, Canada) **423**
McMurry U (TX) **423**
McNeese State U (LA) **423**
McPherson Coll (KS) **423**
Memorial U of Newfoundland (NF, Canada) **424**
Mercer U (GA) **425**
Meredith Coll (NC) **426**
Mesa State Coll (CO) **426**
Messiah Coll (PA) **426**
Methodist Coll (NC) **427**
Metropolitan State U (MN) **427**
Miami U (OH) **428**
Michigan State U (MI) **428**
Middlebury Coll (VT) **429**
Middle Tennessee State U (TN) **429**
Midland Lutheran Coll (NE) **429**
Midwestern State U (TX) **430**
Milligan Coll (TN) **430**
Millikin U (IL) **430**
Millsaps Coll (MS) **431**
Mills Coll (CA) **431**
Minnesota State U, Mankato (MN) **431**
Minnesota State U, Moorhead (MN) **432**
Missouri Southern State Coll (MO) **433**
Missouri Valley Coll (MO) **433**
Monmouth Coll (IL) **434**
Montana State U–Billings (MT) **434**
Montclair State U (NJ) **435**
Morehead State U (KY) **436**
Morehouse Coll (GA) **436**
Morgan State U (MD) **436**
Morningside Coll (IA) **437**
Mount Allison U (NB, Canada) **437**
Mount Holyoke Coll (MA) **438**
Mount Mercy Coll (IA) **438**
Mount Union Coll (OH) **440**
Mount Vernon Nazarene U (OH) **440**
Muhlenberg Coll (PA) **440**
Murray State U (KY) **440**
Muskingum Coll (OH) **441**
Naropa U (CO) **441**
National-Louis U (IL) **442**
Nazareth Coll of Rochester (NY) **443**
Nebraska Wesleyan U (NE) **443**
Newberry Coll (SC) **444**
New England Coll (NH) **444**
New Mexico State U (NM) **446**
New World School of the Arts (FL) **447**
New York U (NY) **447**
Niagara U (NY) **447**
North Carolina Ag and Tech State U (NC) **448**
North Carolina Central U (NC) **448**
North Carolina School of the Arts (NC) **449**
North Carolina Wesleyan Coll (NC) **449**
North Central Coll (IL) **449**
North Dakota State U (ND) **449**
Northeastern State U (OK) **450**
Northeastern U (MA) **450**
Northern Arizona U (AZ) **450**
Northern Illinois U (IL) **450**
Northern Kentucky U (KY) **451**
Northern Michigan U (MI) **451**
Northern State U (SD) **451**
North Park U (IL) **452**
Northwest Coll (WA) **452**
Northwestern Coll (IA) **453**
Northwestern Coll (MN) **453**
Northwestern State U of Louisiana (LA) **453**
Northwestern U (IL) **453**
Northwest Missouri State U (MO) **454**
Notre Dame de Namur U (CA) **455**
Oakland U (MI) **456**
Oberlin Coll (OH) **456**
Occidental Coll (CA) **457**
Ohio Northern U (OH) **457**
The Ohio State U (OH) **457**
Ohio U (OH) **458**
Ohio Wesleyan U (OH) **459**
Oklahoma Baptist U (OK) **459**
Oklahoma Christian U (OK) **459**
Oklahoma City U (OK) **460**
Oklahoma State U (OK) **460**
Old Dominion U (VA) **460**
Oral Roberts U (OK) **461**
Oregon State U (OR) **462**
Ottawa U (KS) **462**
Otterbein Coll (OH) **462**
Ouachita Baptist U (AR) **462**
Our Lady of the Lake U of San Antonio (TX) **463**
Pacific Lutheran U (WA) **463**
Pacific U (OR) **464**
Palm Beach Atlantic U (FL) **465**
Pepperdine U, Malibu (CA) **469**
Pfeiffer U (NC) **469**
Piedmont Coll (GA) **470**
Pitzer Coll (CA) **471**
Plattsburgh State U of NY (NY) **471**
Plymouth State Coll (NH) **471**
Point Loma Nazarene U (CA) **471**
Point Park Coll (PA) **471**
Pomona Coll (CA) **472**
Portland State U (OR) **472**
Prairie View A&M U (TX) **473**
Presbyterian Coll (SC) **473**
Prescott Coll (AZ) **474**
Principia Coll (IL) **474**
Providence Coll and Theological Seminary (MB, Canada) **475**
Purchase Coll, State U of NY (NY) **475**
Purdue U (IN) **475**
Queens Coll of the City U of NY (NY) **475**
Queen's U at Kingston (ON, Canada) **476**
Queens U of Charlotte (NC) **476**
Radford U (VA) **476**
Randolph-Macon Coll (VA) **477**
Randolph-Macon Woman's Coll (VA) **477**
Reed Coll (OR) **477**
Regis Coll (MA) **478**
Rhode Island Coll (RI) **479**
Rhode Island School of Design (RI) **479**
Rhodes Coll (TN) **479**
Richmond, The American International U in London(United Kingdom) **480**
Ripon Coll (WI) **480**
Roanoke Coll (VA) **481**
Rockford Coll (IL) **482**
Rockhurst U (MO) **482**
Rocky Mountain Coll (MT) **482**
Roger Williams U (RI) **483**
Rollins Coll (FL) **483**
Roosevelt U (IL) **483**
Rowan U (NJ) **484**
Russell Sage Coll (NY) **484**
Rutgers, The State U of New Jersey, Camden (NJ) **485**
Rutgers, The State U of New Jersey, Newark (NJ) **485**
Rutgers, The State U of New Jersey, New Brunswick (NJ) **485**
Ryerson U (ON, Canada) **485**
Sacred Heart U (CT) **486**
Saginaw Valley State U (MI) **486**
St. Ambrose U (IA) **486**
St. Cloud State U (MN) **488**
St. Edward's U (TX) **488**
Saint John's U (MN) **490**
St. Lawrence U (NY) **491**
Saint Louis U (MO) **492**
Saint Martin's Coll (WA) **493**
Saint Mary Coll (KS) **493**
Saint Mary-of-the-Woods Coll (IN) **493**
Saint Mary's Coll (IN) **493**
Saint Mary's Coll of California (CA) **494**
St. Mary's Coll of Maryland (MD) **494**
Saint Mary's U of Minnesota (MN) **494**
Saint Michael's Coll (VT) **494**
St. Olaf Coll (MN) **495**
Saint Vincent Coll (PA) **496**
Salem State Coll (MA) **497**
Salisbury U (MD) **497**
Salve Regina U (RI) **497**
Samford U (AL) **497**
Sam Houston State U (TX) **497**
San Diego State U (CA) **498**
San Francisco State U (CA) **498**
San Jose State U (CA) **499**
Santa Clara U (CA) **499**
Sarah Lawrence Coll (NY) **499**
Scripps Coll (CA) **501**
Seattle Pacific U (WA) **501**
Seattle U (WA) **501**
Seton Hill U (PA) **502**
Shaw U (NC) **502**
Shenandoah U (VA) **503**
Shorter Coll (GA) **504**
Siena Heights U (MI) **504**
Simon Fraser U (BC, Canada) **505**
Simon's Rock Coll of Bard (MA) **505**
Simpson Coll (IA) **505**
Skidmore Coll (NY) **506**
Slippery Rock U of Pennsylvania (PA) **506**
Smith Coll (MA) **506**
Sonoma State U (CA) **506**
South Carolina State U (SC) **506**
South Dakota State U (SD) **507**
Southeastern Coll of the Assemblies of God (FL) **507**
Southeastern Oklahoma State U (OK) **508**
Southeast Missouri State U (MO) **508**
Southern Arkansas U–Magnolia (AR) **509**
Southern Connecticut State U (CT) **509**
Southern Illinois U Carbondale (IL) **509**
Southern Illinois U Edwardsville (IL) **509**
Southern Methodist U (TX) **510**
Southern Oregon U (OR) **510**
Southern U and A&M Coll (LA) **511**
Southern Utah U (UT) **511**
Southern Virginia U (VA) **511**
Southwest Baptist U (MO) **512**
Southwestern Coll (KS) **512**
Southwestern U (TX) **513**
Southwest Missouri State U (MO) **513**
Southwest State U (MN) **513**
Southwest Texas State U (TX) **513**
Spalding U (KY) **513**
Spelman Coll (GA) **514**
Spring Hill Coll (AL) **514**
Stanford U (CA) **514**
State U of NY at Albany (NY) **514**
State U of NY at Binghamton (NY) **515**
State U of NY at New Paltz (NY) **515**
State U of NY at Oswego (NY) **515**
State U of NY Coll at Brockport (NY) **515**
State U of NY Coll at Buffalo (NY) **516**
State U of NY Coll at Fredonia (NY) **516**
State U of NY Coll at Geneseo (NY) **516**
State U of NY Coll at Oneonta (NY) **517**
State U of NY Coll at Potsdam (NY) **517**
State U of West Georgia (GA) **518**
Stephen F. Austin State U (TX) **518**
Stephens Coll (MO) **519**
Sterling Coll (KS) **519**
Stetson U (FL) **519**
Stony Brook U, State University of New York (NY) **520**
Suffolk U (MA) **520**
Sul Ross State U (TX) **521**
Susquehanna U (PA) **521**
Swarthmore Coll (PA) **521**
Sweet Briar Coll (VA) **521**
Syracuse U (NY) **521**
Tarleton State U (TX) **522**
Taylor U (IN) **523**
Temple U (PA) **523**
Texas A&M U (TX) **524**
Texas A&M U–Commerce (TX) **525**
Texas A&M U–Kingsville (TX) **525**
Texas Christian U (TX) **526**
Texas Lutheran U (TX) **526**
Texas Southern U (TX) **526**
Texas Tech U (TX) **526**
Texas Wesleyan U (TX) **526**
Texas Woman's U (TX) **527**
Thomas Edison State Coll (NJ) **527**
Thomas More Coll (KY) **528**
Towson U (MD) **529**
Transylvania U (KY) **529**
Trevecca Nazarene U (TN) **529**
Trinity Bible Coll (ND) **530**
Trinity Coll (CT) **530**
Trinity U (TX) **531**
Trinity Western U (BC, Canada) **531**
Troy State U (AL) **532**
Truman State U (MO) **532**
Tufts U (MA) **533**
Tulane U (LA) **533**
Union Coll (KY) **533**
Union U (TN) **534**
Université Laval (QC, Canada) **536**
U at Buffalo, The State University of New York (NY) **536**
The U of Akron (OH) **537**
The U of Alabama (AL) **537**
U of Alaska Anchorage (AK) **538**
U of Alaska Fairbanks (AK) **538**
U of Alberta (AB, Canada) **538**
The U of Arizona (AZ) **538**
U of Arkansas (AR) **539**
U of Arkansas at Little Rock (AR) **539**
The U of British Columbia (BC, Canada) **540**
U of Calgary (AB, Canada) **540**
U of Calif, Berkeley (CA) **540**
U of Calif, Davis (CA) **540**
U of Calif, Irvine (CA) **541**
U of Calif, Los Angeles (CA) **541**
U of Calif, Riverside (CA) **541**
U of Calif, San Diego (CA) **541**
U of Calif, Santa Barbara (CA) **541**
U of Calif, Santa Cruz (CA) **542**
U of Central Florida (FL) **542**
U of Central Oklahoma (OK) **542**
U of Cincinnati (OH) **543**
U of Colorado at Boulder (CO) **543**
U of Colorado at Denver (CO) **543**
U of Connecticut (CT) **544**
U of Dallas (TX) **544**
U of Dayton (OH) **544**
U of Denver (CO) **544**
U of Evansville (IN) **545**
The U of Findlay (OH) **545**
U of Florida (FL) **545**
U of Georgia (GA) **545**
U of Guelph (ON, Canada) **546**
U of Hartford (CT) **546**
U of Hawaii at Manoa (HI) **546**
U of Houston (TX) **547**
U of Idaho (ID) **547**

THEATER ARTS/DRAMA (continued)

U of Illinois at Chicago (IL) ***547***
U of Illinois at Urbana–Champaign (IL) ***548***
U of Indianapolis (IN) ***548***
The U of Iowa (IA) ***548***
U of Kansas (KS) ***549***
U of Kentucky (KY) ***549***
U of King's Coll (NS, Canada) ***549***
U of La Verne (CA) ***549***
The U of Lethbridge (AB, Canada) ***549***
U of Louisville (KY) ***550***
U of Maine (ME) ***550***
U of Maine at Farmington (ME) ***550***
U of Manitoba (MB, Canada) ***551***
U of Maryland, Baltimore County (MD) ***552***
U of Maryland, Coll Park (MD) ***552***
U of Massachusetts Amherst (MA) ***552***
U of Massachusetts Boston (MA) ***553***
The U of Memphis (TN) ***553***
U of Miami (FL) ***553***
U of Michigan (MI) ***554***
U of Michigan–Flint (MI) ***554***
U of Minnesota, Duluth (MN) ***554***
U of Minnesota, Morris (MN) ***555***
U of Minnesota, Twin Cities Campus (MN) ***555***
U of Mississippi (MS) ***555***
U of Missouri–Columbia (MO) ***555***
U of Missouri–Kansas City (MO) ***555***
U of Mobile (AL) ***556***
The U of Montana–Missoula (MT) ***556***
The U of Montana–Western (MT) ***556***
U of Montevallo (AL) ***557***
U of Nebraska at Kearney (NE) ***557***
U of Nebraska at Omaha (NE) ***557***
U of Nebraska–Lincoln (NE) ***557***
U of Nevada, Las Vegas (NV) ***558***
U of Nevada, Reno (NV) ***558***
U of New Brunswick Fredericton (NB, Canada) ***558***
U of New Hampshire (NH) ***558***
U of New Mexico (NM) ***559***
U of New Orleans (LA) ***559***
The U of North Carolina at Asheville (NC) ***559***
The U of North Carolina at Chapel Hill (NC) ***560***
The U of North Carolina at Charlotte (NC) ***560***
The U of North Carolina at Greensboro (NC) ***560***
The U of North Carolina at Pembroke (NC) ***560***
The U of North Carolina at Wilmington (NC) ***561***
U of North Dakota (ND) ***561***
U of Northern Colorado (CO) ***561***
U of Northern Iowa (IA) ***561***
U of North Texas (TX) ***562***
U of Notre Dame (IN) ***562***
U of Oklahoma (OK) ***562***
U of Oregon (OR) ***562***
U of Ottawa (ON, Canada) ***563***
U of Pennsylvania (PA) ***563***
U of Pittsburgh (PA) ***569***
U of Pittsburgh at Johnstown (PA) ***570***
U of Portland (OR) ***570***
U of Puerto Rico, Río Piedras (PR) ***571***
U of Puget Sound (WA) ***571***
U of Regina (SK, Canada) ***572***
U of Richmond (VA) ***572***
U of St. Thomas (MN) ***573***
U of St. Thomas (TX) ***573***
U of Saskatchewan (SK, Canada) ***574***
U of Science and Arts of Oklahoma (OK) ***574***
The U of Scranton (PA) ***574***
U of Sioux Falls (SD) ***574***
U of South Alabama (AL) ***575***
U of South Carolina (SC) ***575***
The U of South Dakota (SD) ***575***
U of Southern California (CA) ***576***
U of Southern Indiana (IN) ***576***
U of Southern Maine (ME) ***576***
U of Southern Mississippi (MS) ***576***
U of South Florida (FL) ***576***
The U of Tampa (FL) ***577***
The U of Tennessee (TN) ***577***
The U of Tennessee at Chattanooga (TN) ***577***
The U of Texas at Arlington (TX) ***577***
The U of Texas at Austin (TX) ***578***
The U of Texas at El Paso (TX) ***578***
The U of Texas at Tyler (TX) ***579***
The U of Texas–Pan American (TX) ***579***
The U of the Arts (PA) ***579***
U of the District of Columbia (DC) ***580***
U of the Incarnate Word (TX) ***580***
U of the Ozarks (AR) ***580***
U of the Pacific (CA) ***580***
U of the Sacred Heart (PR) ***580***
U of the South (TN) ***581***
U of the Virgin Islands (VI) ***581***
U of Toledo (OH) ***581***
U of Toronto (ON, Canada) ***581***
U of Utah (UT) ***582***
U of Vermont (VT) ***582***
U of Victoria (BC, Canada) ***582***
U of Virginia (VA) ***582***
The U of Virginia's Coll at Wise (VA) ***582***
U of Washington (WA) ***583***
U of Waterloo (ON, Canada) ***583***
U of West Florida (FL) ***583***
U of Windsor (ON, Canada) ***584***
U of Wisconsin–Eau Claire (WI) ***584***
U of Wisconsin–Green Bay (WI) ***584***
U of Wisconsin–La Crosse (WI) ***584***
U of Wisconsin–Madison (WI) ***584***
U of Wisconsin–Milwaukee (WI) ***585***
U of Wisconsin–Oshkosh (WI) ***585***
U of Wisconsin–Parkside (WI) ***585***
U of Wisconsin–River Falls (WI) ***585***
U of Wisconsin–Stevens Point (WI) ***585***
U of Wisconsin–Superior (WI) ***586***
U of Wisconsin–Whitewater (WI) ***586***
U of Wyoming (WY) ***586***
Utah State U (UT) ***587***
Utica Coll (NY) ***588***
Valdosta State U (GA) ***588***
Valparaiso U (IN) ***588***
Vanderbilt U (TN) ***588***
Vanguard U of Southern California (CA) ***589***
Vassar Coll (NY) ***589***
Virginia Commonwealth U (VA) ***590***
Virginia Intermont Coll (VA) ***590***
Virginia Polytechnic Inst and State U (VA) ***591***
Virginia Wesleyan Coll (VA) ***591***
Viterbo U (WI) ***591***
Wabash Coll (IN) ***592***
Wagner Coll (NY) ***592***
Wake Forest U (NC) ***592***
Waldorf Coll (IA) ***592***
Warren Wilson Coll (NC) ***594***
Washington & Jefferson Coll (PA) ***594***
Washington and Lee U (VA) ***594***
Washington Coll (MD) ***594***
Washington State U (WA) ***595***
Washington U in St. Louis (MO) ***595***
Wayland Baptist U (TX) ***595***
Wayne State Coll (NE) ***596***
Wayne State U (MI) ***596***
Weber State U (UT) ***596***
Webster U (MO) ***597***
Wellesley Coll (MA) ***597***
Wells Coll (NY) ***597***
Wesleyan U (CT) ***597***
West Chester U of Pennsylvania (PA) ***598***
Western Carolina U (NC) ***598***
Western Connecticut State U (CT) ***598***
Western Illinois U (IL) ***599***
Western Kentucky U (KY) ***599***
Western Michigan U (MI) ***599***
Western Oregon U (OR) ***600***
Western State Coll of Colorado (CO) ***600***
Western Washington U (WA) ***600***
Westminster Coll (PA) ***601***
Westmont Coll (CA) ***602***
West Texas A&M U (TX) ***602***
West Virginia U (WV) ***602***
West Virginia Wesleyan Coll (WV) ***603***
Wheaton Coll (MA) ***603***
Whitman Coll (WA) ***604***
Whittier Coll (CA) ***604***
Whitworth Coll (WA) ***604***
Wichita State U (KS) ***604***
Wilkes U (PA) ***605***
Willamette U (OR) ***605***
William Carey Coll (MS) ***605***
William Jewell Coll (MO) ***606***
William Paterson U of New Jersey (NJ) ***606***
Williams Coll (MA) ***606***
William Woods U (MO) ***607***
Wilmington Coll (OH) ***607***
Winona State U (MN) ***608***
Winthrop U (SC) ***608***
Wittenberg U (OH) ***608***
Wright State U (OH) ***609***
Yale U (CT) ***610***
York Coll of the City U of New York (NY) ***611***
York U (ON, Canada) ***611***
Youngstown State U (OH) ***611***

THEATER ARTS/DRAMA AND STAGECRAFT RELATED

Information can be found under this major's main heading.

California State U, Chico (CA) ***300***
Coastal Carolina U (SC) ***318***
DePaul U (IL) ***339***
Nebraska Wesleyan U (NE) ***443***
Ohio U (OH) ***458***
Seton Hill U (PA) ***502***
Shenandoah U (VA) ***503***
The U of Akron (OH) ***537***
U of Connecticut (CT) ***544***
U of Nevada, Las Vegas (NV) ***558***

THEATER DESIGN

Overview: Students study technical aspects of theatrical production and set design, including lighting, sound effects, acoustics, property management, costume design, and other topics related to theater production. *Related majors:* drama/theater arts, acting and directing, fiber, textiles and weaving arts. *Potential careers:* set or stage designer, lighting designer, costume designer, sound technician, producer. *Salary potential:* $20k-$30k.

Baylor U (TX) ***283***
Boston U (MA) ***292***
Carroll Coll (MT) ***306***
Centenary Coll (NJ) ***308***
Coll of Santa Fe (NM) ***323***
Columbia Coll Chicago (IL) ***327***
Concordia U (QC, Canada) ***331***
DePaul U (IL) ***339***
Dickinson Coll (PA) ***344***
Emerson Coll (MA) ***353***
Five Towns Coll (NY) ***359***
Florida State U (FL) ***361***
Greensboro Coll (NC) ***372***
Ithaca Coll (NY) ***390***
Maharishi U of Management (IA) ***414***
Memorial U of Newfoundland (NF, Canada) ***424***
New York U (NY) ***447***
Ohio U (OH) ***458***
Oklahoma City U (OK) ***460***
Penn State U Univ Park Campus (PA) ***468***
Purchase Coll, State U of NY (NY) ***475***
Ryerson U (ON, Canada) ***485***
Seton Hill U (PA) ***502***
Syracuse U (NY) ***521***
Texas Tech U (TX) ***526***
Trinity U (TX) ***531***
The U of Arizona (AZ) ***538***
U of Calif, Santa Cruz (CA) ***542***
U of Connecticut (CT) ***544***
U of Delaware (DE) ***544***
U of Kansas (KS) ***549***
U of Michigan (MI) ***554***
U of Northern Iowa (IA) ***561***
U of Southern California (CA) ***576***
Webster U (MO) ***597***
Western Michigan U (MI) ***599***
William Woods U (MO) ***607***
York U (ON, Canada) ***611***
Youngstown State U (OH) ***611***

THEOLOGICAL STUDIES/ RELIGIOUS VOCATIONS RELATED

Information can be found under this major's main heading.

Central Baptist Coll (AR) ***309***
Union U (TN) ***534***
Wilson Coll (PA) ***607***

THEOLOGY

Overview: Students who are of a particular religious faith will study the beliefs and doctrine of that faith. *Related majors:* religious studies. *Potential careers:* clergy, writer. *Salary potential:* $20-$30k.

Alaska Bible Coll (AK) ***261***
Alvernia Coll (PA) ***265***
American Baptist Coll of American Baptist Theol Sem (TN) ***265***
Anderson U (IN) ***268***
Andrews U (MI) ***269***
Appalachian Bible Coll (WV) ***270***
Assumption Coll (MA) ***275***
Atlanta Christian Coll (GA) ***275***
Atlantic Union Coll (MA) ***276***
Augsburg Coll (MN) ***276***
Ave Maria Coll (MI) ***278***
Avila U (MO) ***278***
Azusa Pacific U (CA) ***278***
Baker U (KS) ***280***
The Baptist Coll of Florida (FL) ***281***
Baptist Missionary Assoc Theol Sem (TX) ***281***
Barry U (FL) ***282***
Bellarmine U (KY) ***284***
Belmont Abbey Coll (NC) ***284***
Benedictine Coll (KS) ***285***
Bethany Coll of the Assemblies of God (CA) ***287***
Biola U (CA) ***289***
Boston Coll (MA) ***292***
Briar Cliff U (IA) ***294***
Briercrest Bible Coll (SK, Canada) ***295***
Caldwell Coll (NJ) ***298***
California State U, Sacramento (CA) ***301***
Calumet Coll of Saint Joseph (IN) ***302***
Calvin Coll (MI) ***303***
Canadian Bible Coll (AB, Canada) ***303***
Carlow Coll (PA) ***305***
Carroll Coll (MT) ***306***
Cedarville U (OH) ***308***
Central Bible Coll (MO) ***309***
Central Christian Coll of Kansas (KS) ***309***
Christendom Coll (VA) ***313***
Christian Heritage Coll (CA) ***313***
Circleville Bible Coll (OH) ***314***
Coll Dominicain de Philosophie et de Théologie (ON, Canada) ***319***
Coll of Emmanuel and St. Chad (SK, Canada) ***320***
Coll of Saint Benedict (MN) ***321***
Coll of St. Catherine (MN) ***321***
Coll of Saint Elizabeth (NJ) ***321***
Colorado Christian U (CO) ***325***
Columbia Union Coll (MD) ***328***
Concordia U (CA) ***330***
Concordia U (IL) ***330***
Concordia U (MN) ***330***
Concordia U (NE) ***330***
Concordia U (OR) ***330***
Concordia U (QC, Canada) ***331***
Concordia U Wisconsin (WI) ***331***
Creighton U (NE) ***333***
Crossroads Coll (MN) ***334***
Crown Coll (MN) ***334***
Dakota Wesleyan U (SD) ***336***
DeSales U (PA) ***340***
Dordt Coll (IA) ***345***
Duquesne U (PA) ***346***
Eastern Mennonite U (VA) ***348***
Eastern U (PA) ***349***
East Texas Baptist U (TX) ***350***
Elmhurst Coll (IL) ***351***
Faulkner U (AL) ***357***
Fordham U (NY) ***362***
Franciscan U of Steubenville (OH) ***363***
Gannon U (PA) ***365***
Global U of the Assemblies of God (MO) ***368***
Grace Bible Coll (MI) ***370***
Grand Canyon U (AZ) ***371***
Great Lakes Christian Coll (MI) ***372***
Greenville Coll (IL) ***373***
Griggs U (MD) ***373***
Hannibal-LaGrange Coll (MO) ***375***
Hanover Coll (IN) ***375***
Hardin-Simmons U (TX) ***376***
Hellenic Coll (MA) ***378***
Heritage Bible Coll (NC) ***378***
Hillsdale Free Will Baptist Coll (OK) ***379***

Holy Apostles Coll and Seminary (CT) **380**
Holy Trinity Orthodox Seminary (NY) **381**
Houghton Coll (NY) **381**
Howard Payne U (TX) **382**
Huntington Coll (IN) **383**
Immaculata U (PA) **385**
Indiana Wesleyan U (IN) **387**
International Coll and Graduate School (HI) **389**
John Brown U (AR) **392**
John Wesley Coll (NC) **394**
King's Coll (PA) **398**
Laura and Alvin Siegal Coll of Judaic Studies (OH) **403**
Lee U (TN) **404**
Lenoir-Rhyne Coll (NC) **405**
Life Pacific Coll (CA) **406**
Lincoln Christian Coll (IL) **407**
Lipscomb U (TN) **408**
Louisiana Coll (LA) **410**
Loyola Marymount U (CA) **411**
Loyola U Chicago (IL) **411**
Luther Coll (IA) **412**
Manhattan Christian Coll (KS) **415**
Marian Coll (IN) **417**
Marquette U (WI) **418**
Martin Luther Coll (MN) **418**
The Master's Coll and Seminary (CA) **422**
Master's Coll and Seminary (ON, Canada) **422**
Morris Coll (SC) **437**
Mount Saint Mary's Coll and Seminary (MD) **439**
Mount Vernon Nazarene U (OH) **440**
Multnomah Bible Coll and Biblical Seminary (OR) **440**
Nebraska Christian Coll (NE) **443**
Newman U (KS) **445**
North Greenville Coll (SC) **451**
North Park U (IL) **452**
Northwest Bible Coll (AB, Canada) **452**
Northwest Coll (WA) **452**
Northwestern Coll (IA) **453**
Northwest Nazarene U (ID) **454**
Notre Dame Coll (OH) **455**
Nyack Coll (NY) **456**
Oakland City U (IN) **456**
Oakwood Coll (AL) **456**
Ohio Dominican U (OH) **457**
Oklahoma Baptist U (OK) **459**
Oklahoma Wesleyan U (OK) **460**
Olivet Nazarene U (IL) **461**
Oral Roberts U (OK) **461**
Ouachita Baptist U (AR) **462**
Ozark Christian Coll (MO) **463**
Pacific Union Coll (CA) **464**
Piedmont Baptist Coll (NC) **470**
Pontifical Catholic U of Puerto Rico (PR) **472**
Prairie Bible Coll (AB, Canada) **473**
Providence Coll (RI) **474**
Providence Coll and Theological Seminary (MB, Canada) **475**
Quincy U (IL) **476**
Reformed Bible Coll (MI) **477**
Roanoke Bible Coll (NC) **481**
Roanoke Coll (VA) **481**
Rockhurst U (MO) **482**
St. Ambrose U (IA) **486**
Saint Anselm Coll (NH) **487**
St. Gregory's U (OK) **489**
Saint John's U (MN) **490**
St. John's U (NY) **490**
Saint Joseph's U (PA) **491**
St. Louis Christian Coll (MO) **492**
Saint Louis U (MO) **492**
Saint Mary Coll (KS) **493**
Saint Mary-of-the-Woods Coll (IN) **493**
Saint Mary's Coll of California (CA) **494**
Saint Mary's Coll of Madonna U (MI) **493**
Saint Mary's U of Minnesota (MN) **494**
St. Mary's U of San Antonio (TX) **494**
Saint Paul U (ON, Canada) **495**
Saint Vincent Coll (PA) **496**
San Jose Christian Coll (CA) **498**
Seattle Pacific U (WA) **501**
Seton Hill U (PA) **502**
Silver Lake Coll (WI) **504**
Southeastern Bible Coll (AL) **507**
Southern Adventist U (TN) **508**
Spring Hill Coll (AL) **514**
Talmudical Yeshiva of Philadelphia (PA) **522**
Taylor U (IN) **523**
Texas Lutheran U (TX) **526**
Trinity Bible Coll (ND) **530**
Trinity Christian Coll (IL) **530**
Union Coll (NE) **534**
Union U (TN) **534**
Universidad Adventista de las Antillas (PR) **536**
Université de Sherbrooke (QC, Canada) **536**
U du Québec à Trois-Rivières (QC, Canada) **536**
Université Laval (QC, Canada) **536**
U of Dallas (TX) **544**
U of Dubuque (IA) **545**
U of Great Falls (MT) **545**
U of Notre Dame (IN) **562**
U of Ottawa (ON, Canada) **563**
U of Portland (OR) **570**
U of St. Francis (IL) **573**
U of St. Thomas (MN) **573**
U of St. Thomas (TX) **573**
U of San Francisco (CA) **574**
U of Toronto (ON, Canada) **581**
Valley Forge Christian Coll (PA) **588**
Valparaiso U (IN) **588**
Viterbo U (WI) **591**
Walla Walla Coll (WA) **593**
Walsh U (OH) **593**
Warner Pacific Coll (OR) **593**
Washington Bible Coll (MD) **594**
Western Baptist Coll (OR) **598**
Williams Baptist Coll (AR) **606**
Wisconsin Lutheran Coll (WI) **608**
Wittenberg U (OH) **608**
Xavier U (OH) **610**
Xavier U of Louisiana (LA) **610**

THEOLOGY/MINISTRY RELATED

Information can be found under this major's main heading.

Brescia U (KY) **293**
California Baptist U (CA) **298**
Malone Coll (OH) **415**
Northwestern Coll (MN) **453**
Southeastern Coll of the Assemblies of God (FL) **507**
Wheaton Coll (IL) **603**

THEORETICAL/ MATHEMATICAL PHYSICS

Overview: This branch of physics focuses on understanding and describing the scientific and mathematical laws that govern the relationships between matter and energy. *Related majors:* astronomy, astrophysics, mathematics. *Potential careers:* theoretical physicist, research scientist, cosmologist, astronomer, philosopher, professor. *Salary potential:* $35k-$45k.

San Diego State U (CA) **498**
U of Guelph (ON, Canada) **546**
U of Saskatchewan (SK, Canada) **574**

TOOL/DIE MAKING

Overview: Students learn how to operate machine tools used in the forming of metal components as well as the fabrication of special dies, jigs, fixtures, and tools used in cutting, working, and finishing metal components. *Related majors:* machinist, machine shop assistance, sheet metalworking, computer programming, robotics. *Potential careers:* tool and die maker, machinist, sheet metal technician, machine repairperson, machine programmer. *Salary potential:* $15k-$25k.

Utah State U (UT) **587**

TOURISM PROMOTION OPERATIONS

Overview: Students who take this major learn how to provide marketing and sales operations connected with the promotion of the tourism industry. *Related majors:* tourism/travel marketing, marketing, marketing research, advertising, public relations. *Potential careers:* travel agent, hotel chain sales agent, marketing executive. *Salary potential:* $20k-$30k.

Central Connecticut State U (CT) **309**
Champlain Coll (VT) **311**
Eastern Michigan U (MI) **348**
New Mexico State U (NM) **446**
Our Lady of Holy Cross Coll (LA) **463**

TOURISM/TRAVEL MARKETING

Overview: This major teaches students how to develop and identify consumer markets for tourism- and travel-related services and devise methods for getting consumers to purchase these services. *Related majors:* marketing research, advertising. *Potential careers:* market executive, hotel or cruise ship sales representative, hotel manager. *Salary potential:* $23k-$33k.

Central Missouri State U (MO) **310**
Eastern Michigan U (MI) **348**
Johnson & Wales U (RI) **393**
Mount Saint Vincent U (NS, Canada) **439**
Ohio U (OH) **458**
Rochester Inst of Technology (NY) **482**
U Coll of the Cariboo (BC, Canada) **537**
U of Guelph (ON, Canada) **546**
The U of Montana–Western (MT) **556**
U of the Sacred Heart (PR) **580**

TOXICOLOGY

Overview: This major concerns the study of poisons and other biohazards and how these interact with organisms, as well as their prevention and management. *Related majors:* biochemistry, cell and molecular biology, pathology, medicinal and pharmaceutical chemistry. *Potential careers:* physician, military research scientist, chemical engineer, ecologist. *Salary potential:* $35k-$45k.

Ashland U (OH) **274**
Bloomfield Coll (NJ) **290**
Clarkson U (NY) **316**
Coll of Saint Elizabeth (NJ) **321**
Eastern Michigan U (MI) **348**
Felician Coll (NJ) **357**
Humboldt State U (CA) **382**
Minnesota State U, Mankato (MN) **431**
Monmouth U (NJ) **434**
St. John's U (NY) **490**
Texas Southern U (TX) **526**
U of Guelph (ON, Canada) **546**
U of Miami (FL) **553**
U of the Sciences in Philadelphia (PA) **580**
U of Toronto (ON, Canada) **581**
The U of Western Ontario (ON, Canada) **583**
U of Wisconsin–Madison (WI) **584**

TRADE/INDUSTRIAL EDUCATION

Overview: This major prepares undergraduates to teach specific trade and industry programs to students from a variety of educational levels. *Related majors:* carpentry and woodworking, drafting and printing, welding, drafting and design technology, electrical and electronic technology. *Potential careers:* teacher for any of the industrial trades, such as carpenter and construction, auto technician, machinist or repairperson, plumber, or electrician. *Salary potential:* $25k-$35k.

Athens State U (AL) **275**
Auburn U (AL) **276**
Ball State U (IN) **280**
Bemidji State U (MN) **285**
California Polytechnic State U, San Luis Obispo (CA) **300**
California State U, Fresno (CA) **301**
California State U, Long Beach (CA) **301**
California State U, San Bernardino (CA) **302**
Central Connecticut State U (CT) **309**
Central Washington U (WA) **310**
Colorado State U (CO) **325**
Dakota State U (SD) **335**
Delaware State U (DE) **338**
Eastern Kentucky U (KY) **348**
Florida A&M U (FL) **359**
Florida International U (FL) **360**
Gustavus Adolphus Coll (MN) **374**
Indiana State U (IN) **385**
Indiana U of Pennsylvania (PA) **386**
Iowa State U of Science and Technology (IA) **390**
Keene State Coll (NH) **396**
Kent State U (OH) **397**
Madonna U (MI) **414**
Memorial U of Newfoundland (NF, Canada) **424**
Morehead State U (KY) **436**
Murray State U (KY) **440**
New York Inst of Technology (NY) **447**
Norfolk State U (VA) **448**
North Carolina Ag and Tech State U (NC) **448**
Northeastern State U (OK) **450**
Northern Kentucky U (KY) **451**
Oklahoma State U (OK) **460**
Pittsburg State U (KS) **470**
Prairie View A&M U (TX) **473**
San Francisco State U (CA) **498**
South Carolina State U (SC) **506**
Southern Illinois U Carbondale (IL) **509**
State U of NY at Oswego (NY) **515**
State U of NY Coll at Buffalo (NY) **516**
Temple U (PA) **523**
Texas A&M U–Commerce (TX) **525**
Texas A&M U–Corpus Christi (TX) **525**
U of Alberta (AB, Canada) **538**
U of Arkansas (AR) **539**
U of Central Florida (FL) **542**
U of Central Oklahoma (OK) **542**
U of Hawaii at Manoa (HI) **546**
U of Idaho (ID) **547**
U of Louisville (KY) **550**
U of Nebraska at Omaha (NE) **557**
U of Nebraska–Lincoln (NE) **557**
U of Nevada, Reno (NV) **558**
U of New Hampshire (NH) **558**
U of North Dakota (ND) **561**
U of Northern Iowa (IA) **561**
U of North Florida (FL) **561**
U of Regina (SK, Canada) **572**
U of Saskatchewan (SK, Canada) **574**
U of Southern Maine (ME) **576**
U of South Florida (FL) **576**
U of the District of Columbia (DC) **580**
U of the Virgin Islands (VI) **581**
U of Toledo (OH) **581**
U of West Florida (FL) **583**
U of Wyoming (WY) **586**
Valdosta State U (GA) **588**
Virginia Polytechnic Inst and State U (VA) **591**
Virginia State U (VA) **591**
Wayland Baptist U (TX) **595**
Western Illinois U (IL) **599**
Western Kentucky U (KY) **599**
Western New Mexico U (NM) **600**

TRANSPORTATION AND MATERIALS MOVING RELATED

Information can be found under this major's main heading.

Averett U (VA) **278**

TRANSPORTATION ENGINEERING

Overview: This major concerns the planning, analysis, management, design, and development of a wide range of transportation systems for humans and materials. *Related majors:* civil engineering, structural engineering, mechanical engineering, construction engineering. *Potential careers:* city or state highway planner, construction manager, civil engineer, construction manager, researcher. *Salary potential:* $35k-$45k.

Dowling Coll (NY) ***345***
Rensselaer Polytechnic Inst (NY) ***478***
U of Pennsylvania (PA) ***563***

TRANSPORTATION TECHNOLOGY

Overview: This major provides students with the scientific knowledge to analyze and manage a variety of transportation systems, such as airports, highways, railways, and waterways. *Related majors:* applied mathematics, statistics, systems science and theory, computer science, safety and security technology. *Potential careers:* traffic researcher, systems analyst, logistics specialist, statistician, airport manager. *Salary potential:* $25k-$37k.

Auburn U (AL) ***276***
Dowling Coll (NY) ***345***
Eastern Kentucky U (KY) ***348***
Iowa State U of Science and Technology (IA) ***390***
Maine Maritime Academy (ME) ***415***
Niagara U (NY) ***447***
North Carolina Ag and Tech State U (NC) ***448***
Pacific Union Coll (CA) ***464***
San Francisco State U (CA) ***498***
Tennessee State U (TN) ***523***
Texas A&M U at Galveston (TX) ***524***
Texas Southern U (TX) ***526***
The U of British Columbia (BC, Canada) ***540***
U of Cincinnati (OH) ***543***

TRAVEL SERVICES MARKETING OPERATIONS

Overview: This major teaches students how to provide direct retail services to hotel and motel customers. *Related majors:* hotel/motel operations. *Potential careers:* hotel, motel, or cruise ship manager. *Salary potential:* $20k-$30k.

Champlain Coll (VT) ***311***

TRAVEL/TOURISM MANAGEMENT

Overview: Students learn how to manage travel and/or tourism operations and related services. *Related majors:* travel/tourism marketing, business administration/ management, office supervision and management, tourism promotion operations. *Potential careers:* travel agent, travel agency manager, tour operator or tour guide. *Salary potential:* $23k-$29k

Alliant International U (CA) ***264***
American InterContinental U (CA) ***266***
American InterContinental U, Atlanta (GA) ***266***
Arkansas State U (AR) ***272***
Ball State U (IN) ***280***
Black Hills State U (SD) ***290***
Brigham Young U–Hawaii (HI) ***295***
Brock U (ON, Canada) ***295***
Champlain Coll (VT) ***311***
Coastal Carolina U (SC) ***318***
The Coll of Southeastern Europe, The American U of Athens(Greece) ***323***
Concord Coll (WV) ***329***
Davis & Elkins Coll (WV) ***338***
Dowling Coll (NY) ***345***
Eastern Kentucky U (KY) ***348***
Fort Lewis Coll (CO) ***362***
Grand Valley State U (MI) ***371***
Hawai'i Pacific U (HI) ***377***
Johnson & Wales U (FL) ***393***
Johnson & Wales U (RI) ***393***
Johnson State Coll (VT) ***394***
Lasell Coll (MA) ***402***
Long Island U, Southampton Coll, Friends World Program (NY) ***409***
Lynn U (FL) ***413***
Malaspina U-Coll (BC, Canada) ***415***
Mansfield U of Pennsylvania (PA) ***416***
Montclair State U (NJ) ***435***
Mount Saint Vincent U (NS, Canada) ***439***
New Mexico Highlands U (NM) ***446***
New Mexico State U (NM) ***446***
New York U (NY) ***447***
Niagara U (NY) ***447***
North Carolina State U (NC) ***449***
Northeastern State U (OK) ***450***
Our Lady of Holy Cross Coll (LA) ***463***
Pontifical Catholic U of Puerto Rico (PR) ***472***
Robert Morris U (PA) ***481***
Rochester Inst of Technology (NY) ***482***
Ryerson U (ON, Canada) ***485***
St. Cloud State U (MN) ***488***
St. Thomas U (FL) ***496***
Salem State Coll (MA) ***497***
San Diego State U (CA) ***498***
Schiller International U (FL) ***500***
Schiller International U, American Coll of Switzerland(Switzerland) ***500***
Slippery Rock U of Pennsylvania (PA) ***506***
Southern New Hampshire U (NH) ***510***
Sullivan U (KY) ***521***
United States International U(Kenya) ***535***
U of Calgary (AB, Canada) ***540***
U of Maine at Machias (ME) ***551***
U of Nevada, Las Vegas (NV) ***558***
U of New Hampshire (NH) ***558***
U of New Haven (CT) ***559***
The U of Texas at San Antonio (TX) ***578***
U of the Sacred Heart (PR) ***580***
Virginia Polytechnic Inst and State U (VA) ***591***
Webber International U (FL) ***596***
Western Michigan U (MI) ***599***
Youngstown State U (OH) ***611***

TURF MANAGEMENT

Overview: Students who choose this major will learn about the science and management of turf grasses and other ground covers. *Related majors:* soil sciences, plant sciences, plant breeding, water resources. *Potential careers:* farm manager, agricultural mechanization, soil scientist, gardener or lawn service owner. *Salary potential:* $22k-$30k.

Colorado State U (CO) ***325***
The Ohio State U (OH) ***457***
Penn State U Univ Park Campus (PA) ***468***
State U of NY Coll of A&T at Cobleskill (NY) ***517***
U of Georgia (GA) ***545***
U of Maryland, Coll Park (MD) ***552***
U of Rhode Island (RI) ***572***

URBAN STUDIES

Overview: Students taking this major will study urban environments and institutions and the factors that influence social and political life in urban settings. *Related majors:* sociology, African-American studies, community organization, resources and services, housing studies. *Potential careers:* city/urban planner, human services counselor, journalist, community advocate, mediator or lawyer. *Salary potential:* $25k-$32k

Albertus Magnus Coll (CT) ***262***
Aquinas Coll (MI) ***270***
Augsburg Coll (MN) ***276***
Barnard Coll (NY) ***282***
Baylor U (TX) ***283***
Bellevue U (NE) ***284***
Beulah Heights Bible Coll (GA) ***289***
Boston U (MA) ***292***
Brown U (RI) ***296***
Bryn Mawr Coll (PA) ***297***
California State Polytechnic U, Pomona (CA) ***300***
California State U, Northridge (CA) ***301***
Canisius Coll (NY) ***304***
Carleton U (ON, Canada) ***305***
Cleveland State U (OH) ***317***
Coll of Charleston (SC) ***320***
Coll of Mount Saint Vincent (NY) ***320***
The Coll of Wooster (OH) ***324***
Columbia Coll (NY) ***326***
Columbia U, School of General Studies (NY) ***328***
Concordia U (QC, Canada) ***331***
Connecticut Coll (CT) ***331***
Cornell U (NY) ***333***
DePaul U (IL) ***339***
Dillard U (LA) ***344***
Eastern U (PA) ***349***
Eastern Washington U (WA) ***349***
Elmhurst Coll (IL) ***351***
Eugene Lang Coll, New School U (NY) ***355***
The Evergreen State Coll (WA) ***355***
Florida International U (FL) ***360***
Fordham U (NY) ***362***
Framingham State Coll (MA) ***362***
Furman U (SC) ***365***
Georgia State U (GA) ***368***
Hamline U (MN) ***374***
Hampshire Coll (MA) ***375***
Harris-Stowe State Coll (MO) ***376***
Harvard U (MA) ***376***
Haverford Coll (PA) ***377***
Hobart and William Smith Colls (NY) ***380***
Hunter Coll of the City U of NY (NY) ***382***
Indiana U Bloomington (IN) ***385***
Iona Coll (NY) ***390***
Jackson State U (MS) ***390***
Langston U (OK) ***402***
Lehigh U (PA) ***404***
Lipscomb U (TN) ***408***
Long Island U, Southampton Coll, Friends World Program (NY) ***409***
Loyola Marymount U (CA) ***411***
Macalester Coll (MN) ***413***
Manhattan Coll (NY) ***416***
McGill U (QC, Canada) ***423***
Metropolitan State Coll of Denver (CO) ***427***
Minnesota State U, Mankato (MN) ***431***
Montclair State U (NJ) ***435***
Morehouse Coll (GA) ***436***
Mount Mercy Coll (IA) ***438***
New Coll of Florida (FL) ***444***
New Jersey City U (NJ) ***445***
New York U (NY) ***447***
Northeastern Illinois U (IL) ***450***
North Park U (IL) ***452***
Northwestern U (IL) ***453***
Oglethorpe U (GA) ***457***
Ohio Wesleyan U (OH) ***459***
Portland State U (OR) ***472***
Queens Coll of the City U of NY (NY) ***475***
Rhodes Coll (TN) ***479***
Rockford Coll (IL) ***482***
Roosevelt U (IL) ***483***
Rutgers, The State U of New Jersey, Camden (NJ) ***485***
Rutgers, The State U of New Jersey, New Brunswick (NJ) ***485***
Ryerson U (ON, Canada) ***485***
St. Cloud State U (MN) ***488***
Saint Louis U (MO) ***492***
Saint Peter's Coll (NJ) ***495***
San Diego State U (CA) ***498***
San Francisco State U (CA) ***498***
Sarah Lawrence Coll (NY) ***499***
Stanford U (CA) ***514***
State U of NY at Albany (NY) ***514***
State U of NY Coll at Buffalo (NY) ***516***
Taylor U, Fort Wayne Campus (IN) ***523***
Temple U (PA) ***523***
Towson U (MD) ***529***
Trinity U (TX) ***531***
Tufts U (MA) ***533***
U of Alberta (AB, Canada) ***538***
The U of British Columbia (BC, Canada) ***540***
U of Calgary (AB, Canada) ***540***
U of Calif, San Diego (CA) ***541***
U of Cincinnati (OH) ***543***
U of Connecticut (CT) ***544***
The U of Lethbridge (AB, Canada) ***549***
U of Michigan–Flint (MI) ***554***
U of Minnesota, Duluth (MN) ***554***
U of Minnesota, Twin Cities Campus (MN) ***555***
U of Missouri–Kansas City (MO) ***555***
U of Missouri–St. Louis (MO) ***556***
U of Nebraska at Omaha (NE) ***557***
The U of North Carolina at Greensboro (NC) ***560***
U of Pennsylvania (PA) ***563***
U of Pittsburgh (PA) ***569***
U of Richmond (VA) ***572***
U of San Diego (CA) ***574***
U of Saskatchewan (SK, Canada) ***574***
U of Southern California (CA) ***576***
The U of Tampa (FL) ***577***
The U of Tennessee at Chattanooga (TN) ***577***
U of the District of Columbia (DC) ***580***
U of the Sacred Heart (PR) ***580***
U of Toledo (OH) ***581***
U of Toronto (ON, Canada) ***581***
U of Utah (UT) ***582***
The U of Western Ontario (ON, Canada) ***583***
U of Wisconsin–Green Bay (WI) ***584***
U of Wisconsin–Madison (WI) ***584***
U of Wisconsin–Milwaukee (WI) ***585***
U of Wisconsin–Oshkosh (WI) ***585***
Vanderbilt U (TN) ***588***
Vassar Coll (NY) ***589***
Virginia Commonwealth U (VA) ***590***
Virginia Polytechnic Inst and State U (VA) ***591***
Washington U in St. Louis (MO) ***595***
Wayne State U (MI) ***596***
Wittenberg U (OH) ***608***
Worcester State Coll (MA) ***609***
Wright State U (OH) ***609***
York U (ON, Canada) ***611***

VEHICLE MARKETING OPERATIONS

Overview: This major will prepare students to market and provide direct sales services for new cars, boats, or airplanes to a variety of customer clients from individuals to organizations and corporations. *Related majors:* general selling/sales operations, marketing, advertising. *Potential careers:* sales representative for car, boat, or airplane manufacturer; sales manager; sales agent; marketing manager. *Salary potential:* $18k-$27k.

Northwood U, Florida Campus (FL) ***454***
Northwood U, Texas Campus (TX) ***454***

VEHICLE PARTS/ ACCESSORIES MARKETING OPERATIONS

Overview: Students will study the distribution, marketing, sales, and retail and wholesale operations for car, boat, and airplane parts and accessories. *Related majors:* retail management, marketing, vehicle/petroleum products marketing, marketing research, advertising, vehicle engine technology, general distribution marketing. *Potential careers:* mechanic, sales representative (auto, marine, or aviation industry), retail manager, marketing executive. *Salary potential:* $23k-$35k.

Northwood U, Florida Campus (FL) ***454***
Northwood U, Texas Campus (TX) ***454***

VETERINARIAN ASSISTANT

Overview: This major prepares students to work under the supervision of a veterinarian or animal-care specialist, assisting in treating animals, managing patient care, and interviewing owners. *Related majors:* preveterinary studies, agriculture, animal health, equestrian/equine studies, animal sciences. *Potential careers:* veterinary assistant, laboratory animal technician, zoologist assistant. *Salary potential:* $20k-$30k.

Michigan State U (MI) ***428***
Morehead State U (KY) ***436***
Murray State U (KY) ***440***
U of Nebraska–Lincoln (NE) ***557***

VETERINARY SCIENCES

Overview: This major is designed to provide students with a broad biological training as well as a thorough understanding of the anatomy, breeding, diseases, genetics, management, nutrition, and physiology of farm animals, avian species, and laboratory and companion animals. *Related majors:* preveterinary studies, laboratory animal medicine, animal sciences, agricultural animal health. *Potential careers:* veterinarian, animal geneticist or breeder, researcher, agricultural animal health expert. *Salary potential:* $30k-$38k.

Becker Coll (MA) ***283***
Lincoln Memorial U (TN) ***407***
Mercy Coll (NY) ***425***
Northland Coll (WI) ***452***
Pontifical Catholic U of Puerto Rico (PR) ***472***
U of Guelph (ON, Canada) ***546***
Wagner Coll (NY) ***592***
Washington State U (WA) ***595***

VETERINARY TECHNOLOGY

Overview: This major teaches students how to work with veterinarians and animal health specialists and how to conduct medical procedures and tests and administer drugs to patients under the supervision of a veterinarian or zoologist. *Related majors:* veterinarian assistant, veterinarian, animal sciences, biology, pathology. *Potential careers:* veterinary or animal health technician, veterinary assistant, zoologist. *Salary potential:* $23k-$29k.

Mercy Coll (NY) ***425***
Michigan State U (MI) ***428***
Mount Ida Coll (MA) ***438***
Newberry Coll (SC) ***444***
North Dakota State U (ND) ***449***
Quinnipiac U (CT) ***476***
U of Puerto Rico Medical Sciences Campus (PR) ***571***

VISUAL AND PERFORMING ARTS RELATED

Information can be found under this major's main heading.

Clemson U (SC) ***317***
Illinois State U (IL) ***384***
Long Island U, C.W. Post Campus (NY) ***409***
Rice U (TX) ***479***
Scripps Coll (CA) ***501***
Simon Fraser U (BC, Canada) ***505***
State U of NY Coll at Geneseo (NY) ***516***
Swarthmore Coll (PA) ***521***
The U of Akron (OH) ***537***
U of Colorado at Boulder (CO) ***543***
U of Oklahoma (OK) ***562***
The U of the Arts (PA) ***579***

VISUAL/PERFORMING ARTS

Overview: Students choosing this broad-based major study a range of disciplines within the visual and performing arts, such as dance, drama/theater arts, photography, cinematography, crafts, and painting. *Related majors:* dance, crafts, design and applied arts, fine and studio art, music. *Potential careers:* art teacher, professional artist, professional dancer, musician, Web page designer. *Salary potential:* $15k-$30k.

American Academy of Art (IL) ***265***
Antioch Coll (OH) ***269***
Arizona State U West (AZ) ***272***
Art Center Coll of Design (CA) ***273***
Assumption Coll (MA) ***275***
Bard Coll (NY) ***281***
Bennington Coll (VT) ***286***
Bethel Coll (KS) ***288***
Brigham Young U (UT) ***295***
Brown U (RI) ***296***
California State U, San Marcos (CA) ***302***
Cazenovia Coll (NY) ***308***
Christopher Newport U (VA) ***313***
Columbia Coll (NY) ***326***
Delta State U (MS) ***339***
East Stroudsburg U of Pennsylvania (PA) ***349***
Emerson Coll (MA) ***353***
Fairleigh Dickinson U, Florham (NJ) ***356***
Fairleigh Dickinson U, Teaneck-Metro Campus (NJ) ***356***
The Franciscan U (IA) ***363***
Frostburg State U (MD) ***365***
George Mason U (VA) ***366***
Green Mountain Coll (VT) ***372***
Iowa State U of Science and Technology (IA) ***390***
Ithaca Coll (NY) ***390***
Jackson State U (MS) ***390***
Jacksonville U (FL) ***391***
Johnson State Coll (VT) ***394***
Kutztown U of Pennsylvania (PA) ***399***
Long Island U, C.W. Post Campus (NY) ***409***
Loyola U New Orleans (LA) ***411***
Maharishi U of Management (IA) ***414***
Maryland Inst Coll of Art (MD) ***419***
Marywood U (PA) ***421***
Massachusetts Coll of Liberal Arts (MA) ***421***
Miami International U of Art & Design (FL) ***428***
Mississippi State U (MS) ***432***
Mount Saint Mary's Coll and Seminary (MD) ***439***
Northwestern U (IL) ***453***
Oakland U (MI) ***456***
Ohio U (OH) ***458***
Penn State U Abington Coll (PA) ***467***
Penn State U Altoona Coll (PA) ***467***
Penn State U Univ Park Campus (PA) ***468***
Providence Coll (RI) ***474***
Regis U (CO) ***478***
The Richard Stockton Coll of New Jersey (NJ) ***479***
Roger Williams U (RI) ***483***
Saint Augustine's Coll (NC) ***487***
St. Bonaventure U (NY) ***487***
Saint Mary Coll (KS) ***493***
St. Olaf Coll (MN) ***495***
Saint Peter's Coll (NJ) ***495***
Samford U (AL) ***497***
San Jose State U (CA) ***499***
Savannah Coll of Art and Design (GA) ***499***
Seton Hall U (NJ) ***502***
Seton Hill U (PA) ***502***
Shenandoah U (VA) ***503***
Simon's Rock Coll of Bard (MA) ***505***
South Dakota State U (SD) ***507***
Southwest Missouri State U (MO) ***513***
Texas Wesleyan U (TX) ***526***
Thomas More Coll (KY) ***528***
U Coll of the Cariboo (BC, Canada) ***537***
The U of Alabama at Birmingham (AL) ***537***
The U of Arizona (AZ) ***538***
U of Louisiana at Lafayette (LA) ***550***
U of Maine at Machias (ME) ***551***
U of Maryland, Baltimore County (MD) ***552***
U of Miami (FL) ***553***
U of Michigan (MI) ***554***
U of North Texas (TX) ***562***
U of Rio Grande (OH) ***572***
U of St. Francis (IL) ***573***
U of San Francisco (CA) ***574***
U of Southern Mississippi (MS) ***576***
The U of Tampa (FL) ***577***
The U of Tennessee at Martin (TN) ***577***
The U of Texas at Austin (TX) ***578***
The U of Texas at Dallas (TX) ***578***
U of Windsor (ON, Canada) ***584***
Virginia State U (VA) ***591***
Western Kentucky U (KY) ***599***
West Virginia U (WV) ***602***
Wichita State U (KS) ***604***
York U (ON, Canada) ***611***

VOCATIONAL REHABILITATION COUNSELING

Overview: Students learn how to provide counseling to individuals who are disabled or are recovering from a disease or injury, so that they may return to work and enjoy a more productive and fulfilling life. *Related majors:* occupational therapy, counseling psychology, physical therapy, orthotics/prosthetics. *Potential careers:* vocational rehabilitation therapist or counselor, rehabilitation teacher for the blind, job development and placement specialist, work adjustment specialist, rehabilitation psychologist. *Salary potential:* $25k-$35k.

East Carolina U (NC) ***347***
Emporia State U (KS) ***354***
Florida State U (FL) ***361***
U of Wisconsin–Stout (WI) ***586***

WATER RESOURCES

Overview: This major arms students with the knowledge to understand the circulation, distribution, chemical and physical properties, and environmental interaction of surface and subsurface waters, including groundwater. *Related majors:* geophysics, thermodynamics, environmental science, natural resources management. *Potential careers:* geologist, hydrologist, environmental scientist, park ranger, lobbyist. *Salary potential:* $25k-$35k.

Colorado State U (CO) ***325***
East Central U (OK) ***347***
The Evergreen State Coll (WA) ***355***
Grand Valley State U (MI) ***371***
Heidelberg Coll (OH) ***377***
Humboldt State U (CA) ***382***
Lakehead U (ON, Canada) ***400***
Montana State U–Northern (MT) ***434***
Northern Michigan U (MI) ***451***
Northland Coll (WI) ***452***
Rensselaer Polytechnic Inst (NY) ***478***
St. Francis Xavier U (NS, Canada) ***489***
State U of NY Coll at Brockport (NY) ***515***
State U of NY Coll at Oneonta (NY) ***517***
State U of NY Coll of Environ Sci and Forestry (NY) ***517***
Tarleton State U (TX) ***522***
U of New Hampshire (NH) ***558***
U of Southern California (CA) ***576***
U of Vermont (VT) ***582***
U of Wisconsin–Madison (WI) ***584***
U of Wisconsin–Stevens Point (WI) ***585***
Wright State U (OH) ***609***

WATER RESOURCES ENGINEERING

Overview: This major teaches students about various systems for collecting, storing, moving, and conserving surfacewater and groundwater, including water quality control. *Related majors:* water resource management, environmental sciences, quality control technology, hydraulic technology. *Potential careers:* environmental scientist, city planner, ecologist, civil engineer. *Salary potential:* $30k-$45k.

State U of NY Coll of Environ Sci and Forestry (NY) ***517***
The U of Arizona (AZ) ***538***
U of Guelph (ON, Canada) ***546***
U of Nevada, Reno (NV) ***558***
U of Southern California (CA) ***576***

WATER TREATMENT TECHNOLOGY

Overview: This major offers students the skills and knowledge to work with engineers and other specialists who are developing, maintaining, and monitoring waterpower, water storage, and wastewater treatment systems. *Related majors:* water resources, environmental health, chemical engineering technology, hydraulic technology. *Potential careers:* water-treatment plant operator, wastewater analyst, environmental scientist, mechanical engineer, agricultural engineer. *Salary potential:* $27k-$38k.

Mississippi Valley State U (MS) ***432***
Murray State U (KY) ***440***

WEB/MULTIMEDIA MANAGEMENT/WEBMASTER

Overview: Students will learn how to create and manage Web servers and the hosted Web pages at one or a group of Web sites. *Related majors:* system administration, networking management, Internet, computer system security. *Potential careers:* Web master, system administrator, computer security specialist, computer systems analyst. *Salary potential:* $35k-$45k.

Champlain Coll (VT) ***311***
Nebraska Wesleyan U (NE) ***443***
New England School of Communications (ME) ***445***

WEB PAGE, DIGITAL/MULTIMEDIA AND INFORMATION RESOURCES DESIGN

Overview: Students who choose this major will learn how to create images, graphics, sound, and other multimedia for use on the World Wide Web. *Related majors:* advertising, graphic design, studio art, computer programming, Internet, computer graphics. *Potential careers:* Web page designer, art director, video editor. *Salary potential:* $28k-$45k.

Capella U (MN) ***304***
The Cleveland Inst of Art (OH) ***317***
Dakota State U (SD) ***335***
Florida Metropolitan U-Orlando Coll, North (FL) ***361***
Greenville Coll (IL) ***373***
Maharishi U of Management (IA) ***414***
New England School of Communications (ME) ***445***
Quinnipiac U (CT) ***476***
Ryerson U (ON, Canada) ***485***
Southern Virginia U (VA) ***511***

WELDING TECHNOLOGY

Overview: Students will learn the skills of welding, arc welding, soldering,

WELDING TECHNOLOGY (continued)

cutting, high-energy beam welding, and solid-state welding to join metal and will acquire a working knowledge of metallurgy and structural design. *Related majors:* metallurgical technology, sheet metal technology. *Potential careers:* welder, arc welder, machinist, mechanic, metal parts technician. *Salary potential:* $15k-$25k.

Excelsior Coll (NY) ***356***
Ferris State U (MI) ***358***
LeTourneau U (TX) ***405***
Montana Tech of The U of Montana (MT) ***435***

WESTERN CIVILIZATION

Overview: In this major students examine the major developments that have shaped Western civilization from its beginnings in Mesopotamia, Egypt, Israel, and Greece to the current trends and developments that are marking the contemporary Western world. *Related majors:* history, history of philosophy, art history, criticism and conservation, humanities. *Potential careers:* teacher, professor, writer, editor, art critic. *Salary potential:* $23k-$33k.

Bard Coll (NY) ***281***
Belmont U (TN) ***284***
Carnegie Mellon U (PA) ***305***
The Coll of Southeastern Europe, The American U of Athens(Greece) ***323***
Concordia U (QC, Canada) ***331***
The Evergreen State Coll (WA) ***355***
Gettysburg Coll (PA) ***368***
Grand Valley State U (MI) ***371***
Harvard U (MA) ***376***
Long Island U, Southampton Coll, Friends World Program (NY) ***409***
St. John's Coll (MD) ***489***
St. John's Coll (NM) ***490***
Sarah Lawrence Coll (NY) ***499***
Thomas Aquinas Coll (CA) ***527***
U of King's Coll (NS, Canada) ***549***
The U of Western Ontario (ON, Canada) ***583***
Western Washington U (WA) ***600***

WESTERN EUROPEAN STUDIES

Overview: Undergraduates who choose this major study the history, politics, culture, languages and economics of one or more of these countries: Belgium, Ireland, France, Spain, Portugal, Italy, and the United Kingdom. *Related majors:* European history, comparative literature, English literature, international relations, any of the languages associated with these countries. *Potential careers:* foreign service officer, translator, tour guide, business executive, entrepreneur. *Salary potential:* $25k-$35k.

Central Coll (IA) ***309***
Grinnell Coll (IA) ***373***
Knox Coll (IL) ***399***
The Ohio State U (OH) ***457***
St. Francis Coll (NY) ***488***
Seattle U (WA) ***501***
U of Houston (TX) ***547***
U of Nebraska–Lincoln (NE) ***557***

WILDLIFE BIOLOGY

Overview: Students choosing this major will apply biological principles to the study of animal wildlife, wildlife habitats, and related ecosystems. *Related majors:* biology, animal pathology, ecology, environmental sciences, wildlife and wildlands management, zoology. *Potential careers:* veterinarian, park ranger, zoologist, wildlife manager. *Salary potential:* $23-$30k.

Adams State Coll (CO) ***260***
Arkansas Tech U (AR) ***272***
Baker U (KS) ***280***
Ball State U (IN) ***280***
Brigham Young U (UT) ***295***
Coll of the Atlantic (ME) ***323***
The Evergreen State Coll (WA) ***355***
Framingham State Coll (MA) ***362***
Grand Canyon U (AZ) ***371***
Grand Valley State U (MI) ***371***
Iowa State U of Science and Technology (IA) ***390***
Kansas State U (KS) ***396***
McGill U (QC, Canada) ***423***
Midwestern State U (TX) ***430***
New Mexico State U (NM) ***446***
Northeastern State U (OK) ***450***
Northern Michigan U (MI) ***451***
Northland Coll (WI) ***452***
Northwest Missouri State U (MO) ***454***
Ohio U (OH) ***458***
Penn State U Univ Park Campus (PA) ***468***
St. Cloud State U (MN) ***488***
State U of NY Coll of Environ Sci and Forestry (NY) ***517***
Unity Coll (ME) ***535***
U of Guelph (ON, Canada) ***546***
U of Michigan (MI) ***554***
U of New Brunswick Fredericton (NB, Canada) ***558***
U of New Hampshire (NH) ***558***
U of Vermont (VT) ***582***
Washington State U (WA) ***595***
West Texas A&M U (TX) ***602***
Winona State U (MN) ***608***

WILDLIFE MANAGEMENT

Overview: This major arms students with the expertise and knowledge to conserve and manage wilderness areas and manage wildlife reservations and zoological facilities for recreational, commercial, and ecological purposes. *Related majors:* natural resources management, biology, forest management, range science, land use management. *Potential careers:* park ranger, biologist, ecologist, environmentalist, lobbyist. *Salary potential:* $20k-$27k.

Arkansas State U (AR) ***272***
Auburn U (AL) ***276***
Brigham Young U (UT) ***295***
Colorado State U (CO) ***325***
Delaware State U (DE) ***338***
Eastern Kentucky U (KY) ***348***
Eastern New Mexico U (NM) ***349***
Fort Hays State U (KS) ***362***
Framingham State Coll (MA) ***362***
Frostburg State U (MD) ***365***
Grand Valley State U (MI) ***371***
Humboldt State U (CA) ***382***
Lincoln Memorial U (TN) ***407***
Long Island U, Southampton Coll, Friends World Program (NY) ***409***
Louisiana State U and A&M Coll (LA) ***410***
McGill U (QC, Canada) ***423***
McNeese State U (LA) ***423***
Michigan State U (MI) ***428***
Mississippi State U (MS) ***432***
Murray State U (KY) ***440***
New Mexico State U (NM) ***446***
Northern Arizona U (AZ) ***450***
Northland Coll (WI) ***452***
Northwest Missouri State U (MO) ***454***
The Ohio State U (OH) ***457***
Oklahoma State U (OK) ***460***
Oregon State U (OR) ***462***
Peru State Coll (NE) ***469***
Pittsburg State U (KS) ***470***
Prescott Coll (AZ) ***474***
Purdue U (IN) ***475***
Purdue U Calumet (IN) ***475***
South Dakota State U (SD) ***507***
Southeastern Oklahoma State U (OK) ***508***
Southwest Missouri State U (MO) ***513***
State U of NY Coll of A&T at Cobleskill (NY) ***517***
State U of NY Coll of Environ Sci and Forestry (NY) ***517***
Stephen F. Austin State U (TX) ***518***
Sterling Coll (VT) ***519***
Sul Ross State U (TX) ***521***
Tennessee Technological U (TN) ***524***
Texas A&M U–Kingsville (TX) ***525***
Texas Tech U (TX) ***526***
U of Alaska Fairbanks (AK) ***538***
U of Alberta (AB, Canada) ***538***
The U of Arizona (AZ) ***538***
U of Arkansas at Monticello (AR) ***539***
The U of British Columbia (BC, Canada) ***540***
U of Delaware (DE) ***544***
U of Georgia (GA) ***545***
U of Idaho (ID) ***547***
U of Maine (ME) ***550***
U of Massachusetts Amherst (MA) ***552***
U of Miami (FL) ***553***
The U of Montana–Missoula (MT) ***556***
The U of Montana–Western (MT) ***556***
U of Nevada, Reno (NV) ***558***
U of New Brunswick Fredericton (NB, Canada) ***558***
U of New Hampshire (NH) ***558***
U of Puerto Rico, Humacao U Coll (PR) ***570***
U of Rhode Island (RI) ***572***
The U of Tennessee (TN) ***577***
The U of Tennessee at Martin (TN) ***577***
U of Vermont (VT) ***582***
U of Washington (WA) ***583***
U of Wisconsin–Madison (WI) ***584***
U of Wisconsin–Stevens Point (WI) ***585***
U of Wyoming (WY) ***586***
Utah State U (UT) ***587***
Warren Wilson Coll (NC) ***594***
Washington State U (WA) ***595***
Western New Mexico U (NM) ***600***
West Virginia U (WV) ***602***
Winona State U (MN) ***608***

WIND/PERCUSSION INSTRUMENTS

Overview: This major prepares students to play wind and percussion instruments for performance. *Related majors:* music performance. *Potential careers:* musician, music teacher. *Salary potential:* varies according to number of performances.

Acadia U (NS, Canada) ***260***
Alma Coll (MI) ***264***
Appalachian State U (NC) ***270***
Augustana Coll (IL) ***276***
Baldwin-Wallace Coll (OH) ***280***
Ball State U (IN) ***280***
Berklee Coll of Music (MA) ***286***
Bowling Green State U (OH) ***292***
Bryan Coll (TN) ***296***
Butler U (IN) ***297***
California State U, Fullerton (CA) ***301***
California State U, Northridge (CA) ***301***
Capital U (OH) ***304***
Centenary Coll of Louisiana (LA) ***308***
Chapman U (CA) ***311***
Cleveland Inst of Music (OH) ***317***
Columbus State U (GA) ***328***
Concordia U (IL) ***330***
Conservatory of Music of Puerto Rico (PR) ***332***
The Curtis Inst of Music (PA) ***335***
DePaul U (IL) ***339***
Eastern Washington U (WA) ***349***
Five Towns Coll (NY) ***359***
Florida State U (FL) ***361***
Georgia Southwestern State U (GA) ***368***
Grand Canyon U (AZ) ***371***
Grand Valley State U (MI) ***371***
Hardin-Simmons U (TX) ***376***
Houghton Coll (NY) ***381***
Howard Payne U (TX) ***382***
Illinois Wesleyan U (IL) ***385***
Indiana U Bloomington (IN) ***385***
Inter American U of PR, San Germán Campus (PR) ***388***
The Juilliard School (NY) ***395***
Lambuth U (TN) ***401***
Lawrence U (WI) ***403***
Lipscomb U (TN) ***408***
Luther Coll (IA) ***412***
Manhattan School of Music (NY) ***416***
Mannes Coll of Music, New School U (NY) ***416***
Mars Hill Coll (NC) ***418***
Maryville Coll (TN) ***420***
Memorial U of Newfoundland (NF, Canada) ***424***
Mercyhurst Coll (PA) ***425***
Meredith Coll (NC) ***426***
Minnesota State U, Mankato (MN) ***431***
Minnesota State U, Moorhead (MN) ***432***
Montclair State U (NJ) ***435***
Mount Allison U (NB, Canada) ***437***
Mount Vernon Nazarene U (OH) ***440***
New England Conservatory of Music (MA) ***445***
New World School of the Arts (FL) ***447***
Northern Michigan U (MI) ***451***
Northwestern U (IL) ***453***
Northwest Missouri State U (MO) ***454***
Oberlin Coll (OH) ***456***
Oklahoma Baptist U (OK) ***459***
Oklahoma Christian U (OK) ***459***
Oklahoma City U (OK) ***460***
Olivet Nazarene U (IL) ***461***
Otterbein Coll (OH) ***462***
Palm Beach Atlantic U (FL) ***465***
Peabody Conserv of Music of Johns Hopkins U (MD) ***466***
Peru State Coll (NE) ***469***
Pittsburg State U (KS) ***470***
Prairie View A&M U (TX) ***473***
Roosevelt U (IL) ***483***
San Francisco Conservatory of Music (CA) ***498***
Sarah Lawrence Coll (NY) ***499***
Seton Hill U (PA) ***502***
Southwestern Oklahoma State U (OK) ***512***
State U of NY Coll at Fredonia (NY) ***516***
Susquehanna U (PA) ***521***
Syracuse U (NY) ***521***
Temple U (PA) ***523***
Texas Southern U (TX) ***526***
Texas Wesleyan U (TX) ***526***
The U of Akron (OH) ***537***
U of Alberta (AB, Canada) ***538***
U of Central Oklahoma (OK) ***542***
U of Cincinnati (OH) ***543***
The U of Iowa (IA) ***548***
U of Kansas (KS) ***549***
U of Miami (FL) ***553***
U of Michigan (MI) ***554***
U of Missouri–Kansas City (MO) ***555***
U of New Hampshire (NH) ***558***
U of North Texas (TX) ***562***
U of Oklahoma (OK) ***562***
U of Sioux Falls (SD) ***574***
The U of South Dakota (SD) ***575***
U of Southern California (CA) ***576***
The U of Tennessee at Martin (TN) ***577***
The U of Western Ontario (ON, Canada) ***583***
U of Wisconsin–Milwaukee (WI) ***585***
Vanderbilt U (TN) ***588***
Xavier U of Louisiana (LA) ***610***

WOMEN'S STUDIES

Overview: Students who choose this major study the history, politics, and development of modern feminism in the United States and throughout the world as well as the sociology, culture, and economics of women. *Related majors:* American history, psychology, literature, art history, political science. *Potential careers:* anthropologist, lawyer, social worker, writer. *Salary potential:* $23k-$30k.

Agnes Scott Coll (GA) ***261***
Albion Coll (MI) ***262***
Albright Coll (PA) ***263***
Allegheny Coll (PA) ***264***
American U (DC) ***267***
Amherst Coll (MA) ***268***
Antioch Coll (OH) ***269***
Arizona State U (AZ) ***271***
Arizona State U West (AZ) ***272***
Athabasca U (AB, Canada) ***275***
Augsburg Coll (MN) ***276***
Augustana Coll (IL) ***276***
Barnard Coll (NY) ***282***

Bates Coll (ME) 282
Beloit Coll (WI) 285
Berea Coll (KY) 286
Bishop's U (QC, Canada) 289
Bowdoin Coll (ME) 292
Bowling Green State U (OH) 292
Brock U (ON, Canada) 295
Brooklyn Coll of the City U of NY (NY) 295
Brown U (RI) 296
Bucknell U (PA) 297
Burlington Coll (VT) 297
California State U, Fresno (CA) 301
California State U, Fullerton (CA) 301
California State U, Long Beach (CA) 301
California State U, Northridge (CA) 301
California State U, Sacramento (CA) 301
California State U, San Marcos (CA) 302
Carleton Coll (MN) 305
Carleton U (ON, Canada) 305
Case Western Reserve U (OH) 307
Chapman U (CA) 311
Chatham Coll (PA) 312
City Coll of the City U of NY (NY) 314
Claremont McKenna Coll (CA) 315
Colby Coll (ME) 318
Colgate U (NY) 319
The Coll of New Jersey (NJ) 320
The Coll of New Rochelle (NY) 321
Coll of St. Catherine (MN) 321
Coll of Staten Island of the City U of NY (NY) 323
Coll of the Holy Cross (MA) 323
The Coll of William and Mary (VA) 324
The Coll of Wooster (OH) 324
The Colorado Coll (CO) 325
Columbia Coll (NY) 326
Columbia U, School of General Studies (NY) 328
Concordia U (QC, Canada) 331
Connecticut Coll (CT) 331
Cornell Coll (IA) 332
Cornell U (NY) 333
Curry Coll (MA) 335
Dalhousie U (NS, Canada) 336
Dartmouth Coll (NH) 337
Denison U (OH) 339
DePaul U (IL) 339
DePauw U (IN) 339
Dickinson Coll (PA) 344
Drew U (NJ) 346
Duke U (NC) 346
Earlham Coll (IN) 347
East Carolina U (NC) 347
Eastern Michigan U (MI) 348
Eckerd Coll (FL) 350
Emory U (GA) 354
Eugene Lang Coll, New School U (NY) 355
The Evergreen State Coll (WA) 355
Florida International U (FL) 360
Florida State U (FL) 361
Fordham U (NY) 362
Georgetown U (DC) 366
Gettysburg Coll (PA) 368
Goddard Coll (VT) 369
Goucher Coll (MD) 370
Grand Valley State U (MI) 371
Grinnell Coll (IA) 373
Guilford Coll (NC) 373
Hamilton Coll (NY) 374
Hamline U (MN) 374
Hampshire Coll (MA) 375
Hartford Coll for Women (CT) 376
Harvard U (MA) 376
Haverford Coll (PA) 377
Hobart and William Smith Colls (NY) 380
Hollins U (VA) 380
Hunter Coll of the City U of NY (NY) 382
Indiana U Bloomington (IN) 385
Indiana U–Purdue U Fort Wayne (IN) 386
Indiana U South Bend (IN) 387
Iowa State U of Science and Technology (IA) 390
Kansas State U (KS) 396
Kenyon Coll (OH) 398
Knox Coll (IL) 399
Lake Forest Coll (IL) 400
Lakehead U (ON, Canada) 400
Laurentian U (ON, Canada) 403
Long Island U, Southampton Coll, Friends World Program (NY) 409
Longwood U (VA) 409
Macalester Coll (MN) 413
Marlboro Coll (VT) 418
Marquette U (WI) 418
Massachusetts Inst of Technology (MA) 421
McGill U (QC, Canada) 423
McMaster U (ON, Canada) 423
Memorial U of Newfoundland (NF, Canada) 424
Metropolitan State U (MN) 427
Michigan State U (MI) 428
Middlebury Coll (VT) 429
Mills Coll (CA) 431
Minnesota State U, Mankato (MN) 431
Mount Holyoke Coll (MA) 438
Mount Saint Vincent U (NS, Canada) 439
Nazareth Coll of Rochester (NY) 443
Nebraska Wesleyan U (NE) 443
New York U (NY) 447
Nipissing U (ON, Canada) 448
Northeastern Illinois U (IL) 450
Northern Arizona U (AZ) 450
Northwestern U (IL) 453
Oakland U (MI) 456
Oberlin Coll (OH) 456
Occidental Coll (CA) 457
The Ohio State U (OH) 457
Ohio U (OH) 458
Ohio Wesleyan U (OH) 459
Old Dominion U (VA) 460
Pacific Lutheran U (WA) 463
Penn State U Univ Park Campus (PA) 468
Pitzer Coll (CA) 471
Pomona Coll (CA) 472
Portland State U (OR) 472
Purchase Coll, State U of NY (NY) 475
Purdue U Calumet (IN) 475
Queens Coll of the City U of NY (NY) 475
Queen's U at Kingston (ON, Canada) 476
Randolph-Macon Coll (VA) 477
Rice U (TX) 479
Roosevelt U (IL) 483
Rosemont Coll (PA) 484
Rutgers, The State U of New Jersey, Newark (NJ) 485
Rutgers, The State U of New Jersey, New Brunswick (NJ) 485
Sacred Heart U (CT) 486
St. Francis Xavier U (NS, Canada) 489
Saint Mary's Coll of California (CA) 494
Saint Mary's U (NS, Canada) 494
St. Olaf Coll (MN) 495
San Diego State U (CA) 498
San Francisco State U (CA) 498
Sarah Lawrence Coll (NY) 499
Scripps Coll (CA) 501
Simmons Coll (MA) 504
Simon Fraser U (BC, Canada) 505
Simon's Rock Coll of Bard (MA) 505
Skidmore Coll (NY) 506
Smith Coll (MA) 506
Sonoma State U (CA) 506
Southwestern U (TX) 513
Spelman Coll (GA) 514
Stanford U (CA) 514
State U of NY at Albany (NY) 514
State U of NY at New Paltz (NY) 515
State U of NY at Oswego (NY) 515
State U of NY Coll at Brockport (NY) 515
State U of NY Coll at Fredonia (NY) 516
Stony Brook U, State University of New York (NY) 520
Suffolk U (MA) 520
Syracuse U (NY) 521
Temple U (PA) 523
Texas Christian U (TX) 526
Towson U (MD) 529
Trent U (ON, Canada) 529
Trinity Coll (CT) 530
Tufts U (MA) 533
Tulane U (LA) 533
U at Buffalo, The State University of New York (NY) 536
U of Alberta (AB, Canada) 538
The U of Arizona (AZ) 538
The U of British Columbia (BC, Canada) 540
U of Calgary (AB, Canada) 540
U of Calif, Berkeley (CA) 540
U of Calif, Davis (CA) 540
U of Calif, Irvine (CA) 541
U of Calif, Los Angeles (CA) 541
U of Calif, Riverside (CA) 541
U of Calif, San Diego (CA) 541
U of Calif, Santa Barbara (CA) 541
U of Calif, Santa Cruz (CA) 542
U of Colorado at Boulder (CO) 543
U of Connecticut (CT) 544
U of Delaware (DE) 544
U of Denver (CO) 544
U of Georgia (GA) 545
U of Guelph (ON, Canada) 546
U of Hartford (CT) 546
U of Hawaii at Manoa (HI) 546
The U of Iowa (IA) 548
U of Kansas (KS) 549
U of King's Coll (NS, Canada) 549
U of Louisville (KY) 550
U of Maine (ME) 550
U of Maine at Farmington (ME) 550
U of Manitoba (MB, Canada) 551
U of Maryland, Coll Park (MD) 552
U of Massachusetts Amherst (MA) 552
U of Massachusetts Boston (MA) 553
U of Miami (FL) 553
U of Michigan (MI) 554
U of Michigan–Dearborn (MI) 554
U of Minnesota, Duluth (MN) 554
U of Minnesota, Morris (MN) 555
U of Minnesota, Twin Cities Campus (MN) 555
The U of Montana–Missoula (MT) 556
U of Nebraska–Lincoln (NE) 557
U of Nevada, Las Vegas (NV) 558
U of Nevada, Reno (NV) 558
U of New Hampshire (NH) 558
U of New Mexico (NM) 559
The U of North Carolina at Chapel Hill (NC) 560
The U of North Carolina at Greensboro (NC) 560
U of Oklahoma (OK) 562
U of Oregon (OR) 562
U of Ottawa (ON, Canada) 563
U of Pennsylvania (PA) 563
U of Regina (SK, Canada) 572
U of Rhode Island (RI) 572
U of Richmond (VA) 572
U of Rochester (NY) 573
U of St. Thomas (MN) 573
U of Saskatchewan (SK, Canada) 574
U of South Carolina (SC) 575
U of Southern California (CA) 576
U of Southern Maine (ME) 576
U of South Florida (FL) 576
U of Toledo (OH) 581
U of Toronto (ON, Canada) 581
U of Utah (UT) 582
U of Vermont (VT) 582
U of Victoria (BC, Canada) 582
U of Washington (WA) 583
U of Waterloo (ON, Canada) 583
The U of Western Ontario (ON, Canada) 583
U of Windsor (ON, Canada) 584
U of Wisconsin–Madison (WI) 584
U of Wisconsin–Milwaukee (WI) 585
U of Wisconsin–Whitewater (WI) 586
U of Wyoming (WY) 586
Vassar Coll (NY) 589
Warren Wilson Coll (NC) 594
Washington State U (WA) 595
Washington U in St. Louis (MO) 595
Wayne State U (MI) 596
Wellesley Coll (MA) 597
Wells Coll (NY) 597
Wesleyan U (CT) 597
Western Illinois U (IL) 599
Western Michigan U (MI) 599
Western Washington U (WA) 600
Wheaton Coll (MA) 603
Wichita State U (KS) 604
Yale U (CT) 610
York U (ON, Canada) 611

WOOD SCIENCE/PAPER TECHNOLOGY

Overview: This major teaches students the chemical, physical, and engineering principles behind the properties of wood and wood-based products as well as the processes for converting wood into paper. *Related majors:* chemistry and chemical engineering, industrial and mechanical engineering, forest-harvesting production, forest management, agricultural production. *Potential careers:* logging executive or salesperson, lobbyist, paper company executive, biochemist, chemical engineer. *Salary potential:* $25-$35k.

Memphis Coll of Art (TN) 425
Miami U (OH) 428
Mississippi State U (MS) 432
North Carolina State U (NC) 449
Oregon State U (OR) 462
Pittsburg State U (KS) 470
State U of NY Coll of Environ Sci and Forestry (NY) 517
Université Laval (QC, Canada) 536
The U of British Columbia (BC, Canada) 540
U of Idaho (ID) 547
U of Maine (ME) 550
U of Massachusetts Amherst (MA) 552
U of Minnesota, Twin Cities Campus (MN) 555
U of Toronto (ON, Canada) 581
U of Washington (WA) 583
U of Wisconsin–Stevens Point (WI) 585
West Virginia U (WV) 602

ZOOLOGY

Overview: A broad-based major in which students study the cellular systems, anatomy, physiology and behavior of all animal species, including single-cell organisms. *Related majors:* biology, cell biology, wildlife biology, physiology, ecology, animal sciences. *Potential careers:* veterinarian, conservationist, biologist, zoologist, ecologist, biological supply company representative. *Salary potential:* $22k-$32k.

Andrews U (MI) 269
Auburn U (AL) 276
Ball State U (IN) 280
Brandon U (MB, Canada) 293
Brigham Young U (UT) 295
California State Polytechnic U, Pomona (CA) 300
California State U, Fresno (CA) 301
California State U, Long Beach (CA) 301
Coll of the Atlantic (ME) 323
Colorado State U (CO) 325
Concordia U (QC, Canada) 331
Connecticut Coll (CT) 331
Cornell U (NY) 333
Eastern Washington U (WA) 349
The Evergreen State Coll (WA) 355
Florida State U (FL) 361
Fort Valley State U (GA) 362
Howard U (DC) 382
Humboldt State U (CA) 382
Idaho State U (ID) 384
Iowa State U of Science and Technology (IA) 390
Juniata Coll (PA) 395
Kent State U (OH) 397
Mars Hill Coll (NC) 418
McGill U (QC, Canada) 423
Memorial U of Newfoundland (NF, Canada) 424
Miami U (OH) 428
Michigan State U (MI) 428
North Carolina State U (NC) 449
North Dakota State U (ND) 449
Northeastern State U (OK) 450
Northern Arizona U (AZ) 450
Northern Michigan U (MI) 451
Northland Coll (WI) 452
Northwest Missouri State U (MO) 454
The Ohio State U (OH) 457
Ohio U (OH) 458
Ohio Wesleyan U (OH) 459
Oklahoma State U (OK) 460
Olivet Nazarene U (IL) 461
Oregon State U (OR) 462
Quinnipiac U (CT) 476
Rutgers, The State U of New Jersey, Newark (NJ) 485
St. Cloud State U (MN) 488
San Diego State U (CA) 498
San Francisco State U (CA) 498
Sonoma State U (CA) 506
Southeastern Oklahoma State U (OK) 508
Southern Connecticut State U (CT) 509
Southern Illinois U Carbondale (IL) 509
Southern Utah U (UT) 511

ZOOLOGY (continued)

Southwest Texas State U (TX) ***513***
State U of NY at Oswego (NY) ***515***
State U of NY Coll of Environ Sci and Forestry (NY) ***517***
Tarleton State U (TX) ***522***
Texas A&M U (TX) ***524***
Texas Tech U (TX) ***526***
The U of Akron (OH) ***537***
U of Alberta (AB, Canada) ***538***
U of Arkansas (AR) ***539***
U of Calgary (AB, Canada) ***540***
U of Calif, Davis (CA) ***540***
U of Calif, Santa Barbara (CA) ***541***
U of Florida (FL) ***545***
U of Guelph (ON, Canada) ***546***
U of Hawaii at Manoa (HI) ***546***
U of Idaho (ID) ***547***
U of Louisville (KY) ***550***
U of Maine (ME) ***550***
U of Manitoba (MB, Canada) ***551***
U of Michigan (MI) ***554***
The U of Montana–Missoula (MT) ***556***
U of Nevada, Reno (NV) ***558***
U of New Brunswick Fredericton (NB, Canada) ***558***
U of New Hampshire (NH) ***558***
U of Oklahoma (OK) ***562***
U of Rhode Island (RI) ***572***
The U of South Dakota (SD) ***575***
The U of Tennessee (TN) ***577***
The U of Texas at Austin (TX) ***578***
The U of Texas at El Paso (TX) ***578***
U of Toronto (ON, Canada) ***581***
U of Vermont (VT) ***582***
U of Victoria (BC, Canada) ***582***
U of Washington (WA) ***583***
The U of Western Ontario (ON, Canada) ***583***
U of Wisconsin–Madison (WI) ***584***
U of Wisconsin–Milwaukee (WI) ***585***
U of Wyoming (WY) ***586***
Utah State U (UT) ***587***
Washington State U (WA) ***595***
Weber State U (UT) ***596***
Western New Mexico U (NM) ***600***
Winona State U (MN) ***608***

ZOOLOGY RELATED

Information can be found under this major's main heading.

McGill U (QC, Canada) ***423***

THE UNDERGRADUATE MAJORS PROFILES

ABILENE CHRISTIAN UNIVERSITY

Abilene, TX

Urban setting ■ Private ■ Independent Religious ■ Coed

Web site: www.acu.edu
Contact: Mr. Tim Johnston, Chief Strategic Enrollment Officer, ACU Box 29000, Zellner Hall Room 2006, Abilene, TX 79699-9000
Telephone: 915-674-2650 or toll-free 800-460-6228 ext. 2650
Fax: 915-674-2130
E-mail: info@admissions.acu.edu

Getting in Last Year 3,029 applied; 61% were accepted; 936 enrolled (50%).

Financial Matters $12,430 tuition and fees (2002–03); $4830 room and board; 81% average percent of need met; $10,633 average financial aid amount received per undergraduate (2001–02).

Academics ACU awards associate, bachelor's, master's, doctoral, and first-professional degrees and post-bachelor's certificates. Challenging opportunities include advanced placement credit, student-designed majors, an honors program, double majors, independent study, and a senior project. Special programs include internships, summer session for credit, off-campus study, and study-abroad. The most frequently chosen baccalaureate fields are business/marketing, education, and interdisciplinary studies. The faculty at ACU has 217 full-time members, 74% with terminal degrees. The student-faculty ratio is 18:1.

Students of ACU The student body totals 4,668, of whom 4,186 are undergraduates. 56.2% are women and 43.8% are men. Students come from 48 states and territories and 52 other countries. 80% are from Texas. 3.3% are international students. 76% returned for their sophomore year.

Applying ACU requires SAT I or ACT, a high school transcript, and 2 recommendations. The school recommends an interview and a minimum high school GPA of 2.0. Application deadline: 8/1; 3/1 priority date for financial aid.

ACADEMY OF ART COLLEGE

San Francisco, CA

Urban setting ■ Private ■ Proprietary ■ Coed

Web site: www.academyart.edu
Contact: Ms. Eliza Alden, Vice President-Admissions, 79 New Montgomery Street, San Francisco, CA 94105
Telephone: 415-263-7757 ext. 7757 or toll-free 800-544-ARTS
Fax: 415-263-4130
E-mail: info@academyart.edu

Getting in Last Year 854 applied; 63% were accepted; 460 enrolled (86%).

Financial Matters $12,060 tuition and fees (2002–03); $8400 room only; 33% average percent of need met; $6319 average financial aid amount received per undergraduate (2001–02).

Academics Academy of Art College awards associate, bachelor's, and master's degrees. Challenging opportunities include independent study and a senior project. Special programs include internships and summer session for credit. The most frequently chosen baccalaureate field is visual/performing arts. The faculty at Academy of Art College has 98 full-time members, 8% with terminal degrees. The student-faculty ratio is 15:1.

Students of Academy of Art College The student body totals 6,282, of whom 5,535 are undergraduates. 43.3% are women and 56.7% are men. Students come from 41 states and territories and 52 other countries. 61% are from California. 28.5% are international students. 58% returned for their sophomore year.

Applying Academy of Art College requires a high school transcript. The school recommends an interview, portfolio, and a minimum high school GPA of 2.0. Application deadline: rolling admissions; 3/2 priority date for financial aid. Early and deferred admission are possible.

ACADIA UNIVERSITY

Wolfville, NS Canada

Small-town setting ■ Public ■ Coed

Web site: www.acadiau.ca
Contact: Ms. Anne Scott, Manager of Admissions, Wolfville, NS B0P 1X0 Canada
Telephone: 902-585-1222 **Fax:** 902-585-1081
E-mail: admissions@acadiau.ca

Getting in Last Year 1,071 enrolled.

Financial Matters $6731 nonresident tuition and fees (2002–03); $5832 room and board.

Academics Acadia awards bachelor's and master's degrees. Challenging opportunities include advanced placement credit, an honors program, double majors, and a senior project. Special programs include cooperative education, internships, summer session for credit, off-campus study, and study-abroad. The most frequently chosen baccalaureate fields are education, business/marketing, and social sciences and history. The faculty at Acadia has 243 full-time members. The student-faculty ratio is 17:1.

Students of Acadia The student body totals 4,147, of whom 3,889 are undergraduates. 55.9% are women and 44.1% are men. Students come from 12 states and territories and 70 other countries. 63% are from Nova Scotia. 89% returned for their sophomore year.

Applying Acadia requires SAT I, a high school transcript, and a minimum high school GPA of 2.5, and in some cases an essay, SAT II Subject Tests, an interview, and recommendations. Application deadline: 7/1, 5/31 for nonresidents; 3/1 priority date for financial aid. Deferred admission is possible.

ADAMS STATE COLLEGE

Alamosa, CO

Small-town setting ■ Public ■ State-supported ■ Coed

Web site: www.adams.edu
Contact: Mr. Matt Gallegas, Director of Admissions, 208 Edgemont Boulevard, Alamosa, CO 81102
Telephone: 719-587-7712 or toll-free 800-824-6494 **Fax:** 719-587-7522
E-mail: ascadmit@adams.edu

Getting in Last Year 1,999 applied; 71% were accepted; 568 enrolled (40%).

Financial Matters $2367 resident tuition and fees (2002–03); $7185 nonresident tuition and fees (2002–03); $5607 room and board; $7184 average financial aid amount received per undergraduate (2001–02).

Academics ASC awards associate, bachelor's, and master's degrees. Challenging opportunities include advanced placement credit, accelerated degree programs, student-designed majors, double majors, independent study, and a senior project. Special programs include internships, summer session for credit, and off-campus study. The most frequently chosen baccalaureate fields are business/marketing, liberal arts/general studies, and biological/life sciences. The faculty at ASC has 98 full-time members, 78% with terminal degrees. The student-faculty ratio is 15:1.

Students of ASC The student body totals 2,417, of whom 2,034 are undergraduates. 54.3% are women and 45.7% are men. Students come from 46 states and territories and 5 other countries. 81% are from Colorado. 0.4% are international students. 59% returned for their sophomore year.

Applying ASC requires SAT I or ACT, a high school transcript, and a minimum high school GPA of 2.0, and in some cases an essay, an interview, and recommendations. Application deadline: 8/1. Early and deferred admission are possible.

ADELPHI UNIVERSITY

Garden City, NY

Suburban setting ■ Private ■ Independent ■ Coed

Web site: www.adelphi.edu
Contact: Mr. Victor Carrillo, Director of Admissions, Levermore Hall 114, 1 South Avenue, Garden City, NY 11530
Telephone: 516-877-3056 or toll-free 800-ADELPHI **Fax:** 516-877-3039
E-mail: admissions@adelphi.edu

Getting in Last Year 4,027 applied; 70% were accepted; 686 enrolled (24%).

Financial Matters $16,980 tuition and fees (2002–03); $8200 room and board; $13,200 average financial aid amount received per undergraduate.

Academics Adelphi awards associate, bachelor's, master's, and doctoral degrees and post-bachelor's and post-master's certificates. Challenging opportunities include advanced placement credit, accelerated degree programs, student-designed majors, freshman honors college, an honors program, double majors, independent study, and a senior project. Special programs include internships, summer session for credit, study-abroad, and Army and Air Force ROTC. The most frequently chosen baccalaureate fields are business/marketing, social sciences and history, and education. The faculty at Adelphi has 215 full-time members, 76% with terminal degrees. The student-faculty ratio is 15:1.

Students of Adelphi The student body totals 6,993, of whom 3,746 are undergraduates. 71.9% are women and 28.1% are men. Students come from 40 states and territories and 63 other countries. 91% are from New York. 3.3% are international students. 76% returned for their sophomore year.

Applying Adelphi requires an essay, SAT I or ACT, and a high school transcript, and in some cases an interview and auditions/portfolios for performing and fine arts. The school recommends an interview, 1 recommendation, and a minimum high school GPA of 3.0. Application deadline: rolling admissions; 3/1 priority date for financial aid. Early and deferred admission are possible.

ADRIAN COLLEGE

Adrian, MI

Small-town setting ■ Private ■ Independent Religious ■ Coed

Web site: www.adrian.edu
Contact: Ms. Janel Sutkus, Director of Admissions, 110 South Madison Street, Adrian, MI 49221
Telephone: 517-265-5161 ext. 4326 or toll-free 800-877-2246
Fax: 517-264-3331
E-mail: admissions@adrian.edu

Getting in Last Year 1,456 applied; 88% were accepted; 299 enrolled (23%).

Financial Matters $15,660 tuition and fees (2002–03); $5440 room and board; 98% average percent of need met; $14,697 average financial aid amount received per undergraduate.

Academics Adrian awards associate and bachelor's degrees. Challenging opportunities include student-designed majors, an honors program, double majors, independent study, and a senior project. Special programs include cooperative education, internships, summer session for credit, off-campus study, and study-abroad. The most frequently chosen baccalaureate fields are business/marketing, social sciences and history, and English. The faculty at Adrian has 66 full-time members, 92% with terminal degrees. The student-faculty ratio is 13:1.

Students of Adrian The student body is made up of 1,021 undergraduates. 58.4% are women and 41.6% are men. Students come from 18 states and territories and 8 other countries. 79% are from Michigan. 1.6% are international students. 86% returned for their sophomore year.

Applying Adrian requires SAT I or ACT and a high school transcript, and in some cases an essay. The school recommends ACT and an interview. Application deadline: 8/1; 3/1 priority date for financial aid. Deferred admission is possible.

AGNES SCOTT COLLEGE

Decatur, GA

Urban setting ■ *Private* ■ *Independent Religious* ■ *Women Only*

Web site: www.agnesscott.edu

Contact: Ms. Stephanie Balmer, Dean of Admission, 141 East College Avenue, Decatur, GA 30030-3797

Telephone: 404-471-6285 or toll-free 800-868-8602 **Fax:** 404-471-6414

E-mail: admission@agnesscott.edu

Getting in Last Year 743 applied; 73% were accepted; 234 enrolled (43%).

Financial Matters $19,000 tuition and fees (2002–03); $7500 room and board; 89% average percent of need met; $16,520 average financial aid amount received per undergraduate.

Academics Agnes Scott awards bachelor's and master's degrees and post-bachelor's certificates. Challenging opportunities include advanced placement credit, accelerated degree programs, student-designed majors, double majors, independent study, and a senior project. Special programs include internships, summer session for credit, off-campus study, study-abroad, and Navy and Air Force ROTC. The most frequently chosen baccalaureate fields are social sciences and history, psychology, and English. The faculty at Agnes Scott has 80 full-time members, 95% with terminal degrees. The student-faculty ratio is 10:1.

Students of Agnes Scott The student body totals 886, of whom 869 are undergraduates. Students come from 41 states and territories and 29 other countries. 50% are from Georgia. 5.3% are international students. 75% returned for their sophomore year.

Applying Agnes Scott requires an essay, SAT I or ACT, a high school transcript, and 2 recommendations, and in some cases SAT II Subject Tests. The school recommends an interview and a minimum high school GPA of 3.0. Application deadline: 3/1; 2/15 priority date for financial aid. Early and deferred admission are possible.

ALABAMA AGRICULTURAL AND MECHANICAL UNIVERSITY

Huntsville, AL

Suburban setting ■ *Public* ■ *State-supported* ■ *Coed*

Web site: www.aamu.edu

Contact: Mr. Antonio Boyle, Director of Admissions, PO Box 908, Normal, AL 35762

Telephone: 256-372-5245 or toll-free 800-553-0816 **Fax:** 256-851-9747

E-mail: aboyle@asnaam.aamu.edu

Getting in Last Year 4,676 applied; 56% were accepted; 1,126 enrolled (43%).

Financial Matters $2620 resident tuition and fees (2002–03); $4720 nonresident tuition and fees (2002–03); $4500 room and board; 61% average percent of need met; $7862 average financial aid amount received per undergraduate.

Academics Alabama A&M awards bachelor's, master's, and doctoral degrees. Challenging opportunities include advanced placement credit, an honors program, double majors, and a senior project. Special programs include cooperative education, summer session for credit, off-campus study, and Army ROTC. The most frequently chosen baccalaureate fields are business/marketing, education, and biological/life sciences. The faculty at Alabama A&M has 294 full-time members, 55% with terminal degrees. The student-faculty ratio is 16:1.

Students of Alabama A&M The student body totals 5,914, of whom 4,744 are undergraduates. 51.9% are women and 48.1% are men. Students come from 42 states and territories and 40 other countries. 87% are from Alabama. 4% are international students. 67% returned for their sophomore year.

Applying Alabama A&M requires a high school transcript and a minimum high school GPA of 2.0. The school recommends ACT and 1 recommendation. Application deadline: rolling admissions; 3/1 priority date for financial aid. Deferred admission is possible.

ALABAMA STATE UNIVERSITY

Montgomery, AL

Urban setting ■ *Public* ■ *State-supported* ■ *Coed*

Web site: www.alasu.edu

Contact: Mrs. Danielle Kennedy-Lamar, Director of Admissions and Recruitment, PO Box 271, Montgomery, AL 36101-0271

Telephone: 334-229-4291 or toll-free 800-253-5037 **Fax:** 334-229-4984

E-mail: dlamar@asunet.alasu.edu

Getting in Last Year 8,148 applied; 72% were accepted; 1,426 enrolled (24%).

Financial Matters $2904 resident tuition and fees (2002–03); $5808 nonresident tuition and fees (2002–03); $3500 room and board; 74% average percent of need met; $9148 average financial aid amount received per undergraduate (2001–02).

Academics Alabama State awards associate, bachelor's, and master's degrees. Challenging opportunities include advanced placement credit, an honors program, double majors, and a senior project. Special programs include cooperative education, internships, summer session for credit, off-campus study, study-abroad, and Army and Navy ROTC. The most frequently chosen baccalaureate fields are education, protective services/public administration, and business/marketing. The faculty at Alabama State has 233 full-time members, 58% with terminal degrees. The student-faculty ratio is 15:1.

Students of Alabama State The student body totals 6,038, of whom 5,125 are undergraduates. 58.8% are women and 41.2% are men. Students come from 39 states and territories and 5 other countries. 69% are from Alabama. 0.3% are international students.

Applying Alabama State requires a high school transcript and a minimum high school GPA of 2.0. The school recommends SAT I or ACT. Application deadline: 7/30; 5/1 priority date for financial aid. Early and deferred admission are possible.

ALASKA BIBLE COLLEGE

Glennallen, AK

Rural setting ■ *Private* ■ *Independent Religious* ■ *Coed*

Web site: www.akbible.edu

Contact: Ms. Jackie Colwell, Admissions Officer, Box 289, Glennallen, AK 99588-0289

Telephone: 907-822-3201 or toll-free 800-478-7884 **Fax:** 907-822-5027

E-mail: info@akbible.edu

Getting in Last Year 9 applied; 67% were accepted; 6 enrolled (100%).

Financial Matters $5175 tuition and fees (2002–03); $4100 room and board.

Academics ABC awards associate and bachelor's degrees. Challenging opportunities include advanced placement credit, student-designed majors, and double majors. Internships is a special program. The faculty at ABC has 2 full-time members. The student-faculty ratio is 8:1.

Students of ABC The student body is made up of 51 undergraduates. 45.1% are women and 54.9% are men. Students come from 19 states and territories. 33% are from Alaska. 50% returned for their sophomore year.

Applying ABC requires an essay, SAT I or ACT, a high school transcript, an interview, 2 recommendations, health form, and a minimum high school GPA of 2.0. Application deadline: 7/1; 7/5 for financial aid, with a 5/31 priority date. Deferred admission is possible.

ALASKA PACIFIC UNIVERSITY

Anchorage, AK

Suburban setting ■ *Private* ■ *Independent* ■ *Coed*

Web site: www.alaskapacific.edu

Contact: Mr. Michael Worner, Co-Director of Admissions, 4101 University Drive, Anchorage, AK 99508-4672

Telephone: 907-564-8248 or toll-free 800-252-7528 **Fax:** 907-564-8317

E-mail: admissions@alaskapacific.edu

Getting in Last Year 109 applied; 94% were accepted; 24 enrolled (23%).

Financial Matters $18,380 tuition and fees (2002–03); $6000 room and board; 57% average percent of need met; $8803 average financial aid amount received per undergraduate.

Academics Alaska Pacific awards associate, bachelor's, and master's degrees. Challenging opportunities include advanced placement credit, accelerated degree programs, student-designed majors, double majors, independent study, and a senior project. Special programs include internships, summer session for credit, and study-abroad. The most frequently chosen baccalaureate fields are business/marketing, natural resources/environmental science, and liberal arts/general studies. The faculty at Alaska Pacific has 28 full-time members, 86% with terminal degrees. The student-faculty ratio is 8:1.

Alaska Pacific University (continued)

Students of Alaska Pacific The student body totals 679, of whom 482 are undergraduates. 69.7% are women and 30.3% are men. Students come from 34 states and territories and 5 other countries. 75% are from Alaska. 1.2% are international students. 56% returned for their sophomore year.

Applying Alaska Pacific requires an essay, SAT I or ACT, a high school transcript, 2 recommendations, and a minimum high school GPA of 2.0, and in some cases an interview. Application deadline: 2/1; 4/15 priority date for financial aid. Deferred admission is possible.

ALBANY COLLEGE OF PHARMACY OF UNION UNIVERSITY

Albany, NY

Urban setting ■ Private ■ Independent ■ Coed

Web site: www.acp.edu

Contact: Mr. Robert Gould, Director of Admissions, 106 New Scotland Avenue, Albany, NY 12208-3425

Telephone: 518-445-7221 or toll-free 888-203-8010 **Fax:** 518-445-7202

E-mail: admissions@acp.edu

Getting in Last Year 498 applied; 61% were accepted; 170 enrolled (56%).

Financial Matters $15,523 tuition and fees (2002–03); $5100 room and board; 78% average percent of need met; $12,320 average financial aid amount received per undergraduate.

Academics Albany College of Pharmacy awards bachelor's and first-professional degrees. Challenging opportunities include advanced placement credit and accelerated degree programs. Special programs include internships, summer session for credit, off-campus study, and Army and Air Force ROTC. The most frequently chosen baccalaureate field is health professions and related sciences. The faculty at Albany College of Pharmacy has 57 full-time members, 72% with terminal degrees. The student-faculty ratio is 14:1.

Students of Albany College of Pharmacy The student body totals 768, of whom 618 are undergraduates. 63.8% are women and 36.2% are men. Students come from 10 states and territories and 7 other countries. 90% are from New York. 3.2% are international students. 72% returned for their sophomore year.

Applying Albany College of Pharmacy requires an essay, SAT I or ACT, a high school transcript, and 2 recommendations, and in some cases an interview. The school recommends a minimum high school GPA of 2.0. Application deadline: 2/1; 2/1 priority date for financial aid.

ALBANY STATE UNIVERSITY

Albany, GA

Urban setting ■ Public ■ State-supported ■ Coed

Web site: asuweb.asurams.edu/asu

Contact: Mrs. Patricia Price, Assistant Director of Recruitment and Admissions, 504 College Drive, Albany, GA 31705

Telephone: 229-430-4645 or toll-free 800-822-RAMS (in-state) **Fax:** 229-430-3936

E-mail: fsuttles@asurams.edu

Getting in Last Year 2,663 applied; 36% were accepted; 417 enrolled (44%).

Financial Matters $2554 resident tuition and fees (2002–03); $8584 nonresident tuition and fees (2002–03); $3570 room and board; 72% average percent of need met; $6759 average financial aid amount received per undergraduate.

Academics ASU awards bachelor's and master's degrees. Challenging opportunities include advanced placement credit, an honors program, double majors, independent study, and a senior project. Special programs include cooperative education, internships, summer session for credit, off-campus study, study-abroad, and Army ROTC. The most frequently chosen baccalaureate fields are education, business/marketing, and protective services/public administration. The faculty at ASU has 128 full-time members, 69% with terminal degrees. The student-faculty ratio is 20:1.

Students of ASU The student body totals 3,456, of whom 3,015 are undergraduates. 66.8% are women and 33.2% are men.

Applying ASU requires SAT I or ACT, a high school transcript, and a minimum high school GPA of 2.0, and in some cases an interview. Application deadline: 7/1; 4/15 priority date for financial aid. Early and deferred admission are possible.

ALBERTA COLLEGE OF ART & DESIGN

Calgary, AB Canada

Urban setting ■ Public ■ Coed

Web site: www.acad.ab.ca

Contact: Ms. Joy Borman, Associate Director of Admissions, 1407-14 Avenue NW, Calgary, AB T2N 4R3 Canada

Telephone: 403-284-7689 or toll-free 800-251-8290 (out-of-state) **Fax:** 403-284-7644

E-mail: admissions@acad.ab.ca

Getting in Last Year 601 applied; 45% were accepted.

Financial Matters $4196 nonresident tuition and fees (2002–03).

Academics ACAD awards bachelor's degrees. Challenging opportunities include advanced placement credit, independent study, and a senior project. Special programs include internships, summer session for credit, and study-abroad. The faculty at ACAD has 44 full-time members.

Students of ACAD The student body is made up of 1,004 undergraduates. Students come from 7 states and territories and 10 other countries. 92% returned for their sophomore year.

Applying ACAD requires an essay, a high school transcript, and portfolio of artwork. The school recommends a minimum high school GPA of 2.0. Application deadline: 4/1. Early admission is possible.

ALBERTSON COLLEGE OF IDAHO

Caldwell, ID

Small-town setting ■ Private ■ Independent ■ Coed

Web site: www.albertson.edu

Contact: Brandie Allemand, Associate Dean of Admission, 2112 Cleveland Boulevard, Caldwell, ID 83605-4494

Telephone: 208-459-5305 or toll-free 800-224-3246 **Fax:** 208-459-5757

E-mail: admission@albertson.edu

Getting in Last Year 950 applied; 77% were accepted; 252 enrolled (35%).

Financial Matters $19,800 tuition and fees (2002–03); $4640 room and board; 83% average percent of need met; $14,738 average financial aid amount received per undergraduate.

Academics Albertson awards bachelor's and master's degrees. Challenging opportunities include advanced placement credit, student-designed majors, an honors program, double majors, independent study, and a senior project. Special programs include internships, off-campus study, and study-abroad. The most frequently chosen baccalaureate fields are social sciences and history, biological/life sciences, and business/marketing. The faculty at Albertson has 71 full-time members, 93% with terminal degrees. The student-faculty ratio is 10:1.

Students of Albertson The student body totals 853, of whom 841 are undergraduates. 55.2% are women and 44.8% are men. Students come from 21 states and territories. 75% are from Idaho. 1.9% are international students. 73% returned for their sophomore year.

Applying Albertson requires an essay, SAT I or ACT, a high school transcript, and 1 recommendation. The school recommends an interview. Application deadline: 6/1; 2/15 priority date for financial aid. Early and deferred admission are possible.

ALBERTUS MAGNUS COLLEGE

New Haven, CT

Suburban setting ■ Private ■ Independent Religious ■ Coed

Web site: www.albertus.edu

Contact: Ms. Rebecca George, Associate Dean of Admissions, 700 Prospect Street, New Haven, CT 06511-1189

Telephone: 203-773-8501 or toll-free 800-578-9160 **Fax:** 203-773-5248

E-mail: admissions@albertus.edu

Getting in Last Year 406 applied; 94% were accepted; 126 enrolled (33%).

Financial Matters $15,344 tuition and fees (2002–03); $7110 room and board; 87% average percent of need met; $8000 average financial aid amount received per undergraduate (2001–02).

Academics Albertus awards associate, bachelor's, and master's degrees. Challenging opportunities include advanced placement credit, accelerated degree programs, student-designed majors, freshman honors college, an honors program, double majors, independent study, and a senior project. Special programs include internships and summer session for credit. The most frequently chosen baccalaureate fields are business/marketing, social sciences and history, and psychology. The faculty at Albertus has 35 full-time members, 57% with terminal degrees. The student-faculty ratio is 18:1.

Students of Albertus The student body totals 2,325, of whom 1,837 are undergraduates. 67% are women and 33% are men. Students come from 12 states and territories and 5 other countries. 96% are from Connecticut. 0.4% are international students. 84% returned for their sophomore year.

Applying Albertus requires SAT I or ACT, a high school transcript, and 1 recommendation, and in some cases a minimum high school GPA of 2.5. The school recommends SAT II Subject Tests, SAT II: Writing Test, an interview, and a minimum high school GPA of 2.5. Application deadline: rolling admissions; 3/15 priority date for financial aid. Deferred admission is possible.

ALBION COLLEGE

Albion, MI

Small-town setting ■ Private ■ Independent Religious ■ Coed

Web site: www.albion.edu

Contact: Mr. Doug Kellar, Associate Vice President for Enrollment, 611 East Porter Street, Albion, MI 49224

Telephone: 517-629-0600 or toll-free 800-858-6770
E-mail: admissions@albion.edu

Getting in Last Year 1,491 applied; 85% were accepted; 526 enrolled (41%).

Financial Matters $20,700 tuition and fees (2002–03); $5912 room and board; 96% average percent of need met; $17,700 average financial aid amount received per undergraduate.

Academics Albion awards bachelor's degrees. Challenging opportunities include advanced placement credit, student-designed majors, an honors program, double majors, independent study, and a senior project. Special programs include internships, summer session for credit, off-campus study, and study-abroad. The most frequently chosen baccalaureate fields are business/marketing, social sciences and history, and biological/life sciences. The faculty at Albion has 118 full-time members, 95% with terminal degrees. The student-faculty ratio is 12:1.

Students of Albion The student body is made up of 1,658 undergraduates. 57% are women and 43% are men. Students come from 27 states and territories and 14 other countries. 92% are from Michigan. 1.1% are international students. 86% returned for their sophomore year.

Applying Albion requires an essay, SAT I or ACT, a high school transcript, and 1 recommendation, and in some cases an interview. The school recommends SAT II Subject Tests, SAT II: Writing Test, and a minimum high school GPA of 3.0. Application deadline: 5/1; 2/15 priority date for financial aid. Early and deferred admission are possible.

ALBRIGHT COLLEGE

Reading, PA

Suburban setting ■ Private ■ Independent Religious ■ Coed

Web site: www.albright.edu
Contact: Mr. Gregory E. Eichhorn, Vice President for Enrollment Management, P.O. Box 15234, 13th and Bern Streets, Reading, PA 19612-5234
Telephone: 610-921-7260 or toll-free 800-252-1856 **Fax:** 610-921-7294
E-mail: admission@alb.edu

Getting in Last Year 2,589 applied; 73% were accepted; 453 enrolled (24%).

Financial Matters $22,340 tuition and fees (2002–03); $6809 room and board; 79% average percent of need met; $16,381 average financial aid amount received per undergraduate.

Academics Albright awards bachelor's and master's degrees. Challenging opportunities include advanced placement credit, accelerated degree programs, student-designed majors, an honors program, double majors, independent study, and a senior project. Special programs include internships, summer session for credit, off-campus study, and study-abroad. The most frequently chosen baccalaureate fields are business/marketing, psychology, and social sciences and history. The faculty at Albright has 95 full-time members, 81% with terminal degrees. The student-faculty ratio is 13:1.

Students of Albright The student body totals 2,087, of whom 2,076 are undergraduates. 56.3% are women and 43.7% are men. Students come from 20 states and territories and 26 other countries. 71% are from Pennsylvania. 3.9% are international students. 74% returned for their sophomore year.

Applying Albright requires an essay, SAT I or ACT, a high school transcript, 1 recommendation, and secondary school report (guidance department). The school recommends an interview. Application deadline: rolling admissions; 3/1 priority date for financial aid. Early and deferred admission are possible.

ALCORN STATE UNIVERSITY

Alcorn State, MS

Rural setting ■ Public ■ State-supported ■ Coed

Web site: www.alcorn.edu
Contact: Mr. Emanuel Barnes, Director of Admissions, 1000 ASU Drive #300, Alcorn State, MS 39096-7500
Telephone: 601-877-6147 or toll-free 800-222-6790 **Fax:** 601-877-6347
E-mail: ebarnes@loman.alcorn.edu

Getting in Last Year 3,887 applied; 21% were accepted; 433 enrolled (53%).

Financial Matters $4440 resident tuition and fees (2002–03); $8946 nonresident tuition and fees (2002–03); $3538 room and board; 76% average percent of need met; $9500 average financial aid amount received per undergraduate.

Academics ASU awards associate, bachelor's, and master's degrees and post-master's certificates. Challenging opportunities include advanced placement credit, an honors program, double majors, independent study, and a senior project. Special programs include cooperative education, internships, and Army ROTC. The most frequently chosen baccalaureate fields are liberal arts/general studies, business/marketing, and biological/life sciences. The faculty at ASU has 172 full-time members, 62% with terminal degrees. The student-faculty ratio is 16:1.

Students of ASU The student body totals 3,150, of whom 2,522 are undergraduates. 60.4% are women and 39.6% are men. Students come from 27 states and territories and 14 other countries. 85% are from Mississippi. 2% are international students.

Applying ASU requires SAT I or ACT, a high school transcript, and a minimum high school GPA of 2.0. Application deadline: rolling admissions; 4/1 priority date for financial aid. Early and deferred admission are possible.

ALDERSON-BROADDUS COLLEGE

Philippi, WV

Rural setting ■ Private ■ Independent Religious ■ Coed

Web site: www.ab.edu
Contact: Ms. Kimberly N. Klaus, Associate Director of Admissions, PO Box 2003, Philippi, WV 26416
Telephone: 304-457-1700 ext. 6255 or toll-free 800-263-1549 **Fax:** 304-457-6239
E-mail: admissions@ab.edu

Getting in Last Year 980 applied; 65% were accepted; 163 enrolled (25%).

Financial Matters $14,840 tuition and fees (2002–03); $5200 room and board; 77% average percent of need met; $15,059 average financial aid amount received per undergraduate.

Academics A-B awards associate, bachelor's, and master's degrees. Challenging opportunities include advanced placement credit, student-designed majors, an honors program, double majors, independent study, and a senior project. Special programs include internships, summer session for credit, off-campus study, study-abroad, and Army ROTC. The most frequently chosen baccalaureate fields are health professions and related sciences, biological/life sciences, and parks and recreation. The faculty at A-B has 59 full-time members, 44% with terminal degrees. The student-faculty ratio is 13:1.

Students of A-B The student body is made up of 702 undergraduates. 65.1% are women and 34.9% are men. Students come from 26 states and territories and 5 other countries. 75% are from West Virginia. 1.1% are international students. 69% returned for their sophomore year.

Applying A-B requires SAT I or ACT, a high school transcript, and a minimum high school GPA of 2.0, and in some cases an interview and 3 recommendations. Application deadline: rolling admissions; 3/1 priority date for financial aid. Deferred admission is possible.

ALFRED UNIVERSITY

Alfred, NY

Rural setting ■ Private ■ Independent ■ Coed

Web site: www.alfred.edu
Contact: Mr. Scott Hooker, Director of Admissions, Alumni Hall, Alfred, NY 14802-1205
Telephone: 607-871-2115 or toll-free 800-541-9229 **Fax:** 607-871-2198
E-mail: admwww@alfred.edu

Getting in Last Year 1,951 applied; 73% were accepted; 473 enrolled (33%).

Financial Matters $19,236 tuition and fees (2002–03); $8478 room and board; 92% average percent of need met; $18,740 average financial aid amount received per undergraduate.

Academics Alfred awards bachelor's, master's, and doctoral degrees and post-master's certificates. Challenging opportunities include advanced placement credit, accelerated degree programs, student-designed majors, an honors program, double majors, independent study, and a senior project. Special programs include cooperative education, internships, summer session for credit, off-campus study, study-abroad, and Army ROTC. The most frequently chosen baccalaureate fields are visual/performing arts, engineering/engineering technologies, and business/marketing. The faculty at Alfred has 186 full-time members. The student-faculty ratio is 12:1.

Students of Alfred The student body totals 2,419, of whom 2,080 are undergraduates. 51.8% are women and 48.2% are men. Students come from 37 states and territories and 10 other countries. 72% are from New York. 1.9% are international students. 77% returned for their sophomore year.

Applying Alfred requires SAT I or ACT, a high school transcript, and 1 recommendation, and in some cases an essay, an interview, and portfolio. The school recommends SAT II: Writing Test and an interview. Application deadline: 2/1. Early and deferred admission are possible.

ALICE LLOYD COLLEGE

Pippa Passes, KY

Rural setting ■ Private ■ Independent ■ Coed

Web site: www.alc.edu
Contact: Sean Damron, Director of Admissions, 100 Purpose Road, Pippa Passes, KY 41844
Telephone: 606-368-2101 ext. 6134 **Fax:** 606-368-6215
E-mail: admissions@alc.edu

Getting in Last Year 880 applied; 58% were accepted; 188 enrolled (37%).

Financial Matters $790 tuition and fees (2002–03); $3180 room and board; 70% average percent of need met; $7871 average financial aid amount received per undergraduate.

Alice Lloyd College (continued)

Academics ALC awards bachelor's degrees. Challenging opportunities include advanced placement credit, double majors, independent study, and a senior project. The most frequently chosen baccalaureate fields are education, biological/life sciences, and business/marketing. The faculty at ALC has 27 full-time members, 56% with terminal degrees. The student-faculty ratio is 19:1.

Students of ALC The student body is made up of 577 undergraduates. 55.1% are women and 44.9% are men. Students come from 6 states and territories and 4 other countries. 81% are from Kentucky. 0.7% are international students. 62% returned for their sophomore year.

Applying ALC requires SAT I or ACT, a high school transcript, and a minimum high school GPA of 2.25, and in some cases an essay, an interview, and 1 recommendation. Application deadline: 7/1; 3/15 priority date for financial aid. Deferred admission is possible.

ALLEGHENY COLLEGE

Meadville, PA

Small-town setting ■ Private ■ Independent Religious ■ Coed

Web site: www.allegheny.edu
Contact: Dr. W. Scott Friedhoff, Vice President for Enrollment, 520 North Main Street, Box 5, Meadville, PA 16335
Telephone: 814-332-4351 or toll-free 800-521-5293 **Fax:** 814-337-0431
E-mail: admiss@allegheny.edu

Getting in Last Year 2,612 applied; 80% were accepted; 539 enrolled (26%).

Financial Matters $23,380 tuition and fees (2002–03); $5600 room and board; 94% average percent of need met; $19,120 average financial aid amount received per undergraduate.

Academics Allegheny awards bachelor's degrees. Challenging opportunities include advanced placement credit, student-designed majors, double majors, independent study, and a senior project. Special programs include internships, off-campus study, and study-abroad. The most frequently chosen baccalaureate fields are social sciences and history, biological/life sciences, and psychology. The faculty at Allegheny has 133 full-time members, 91% with terminal degrees. The student-faculty ratio is 14:1.

Students of Allegheny The student body is made up of 1,924 undergraduates. 52.3% are women and 47.7% are men. Students come from 35 states and territories. 68% are from Pennsylvania. 0.8% are international students. 88% returned for their sophomore year.

Applying Allegheny requires an essay, SAT I or ACT, a high school transcript, and 2 recommendations. The school recommends SAT II Subject Tests, SAT II: Writing Test, and an interview. Application deadline: 2/15; 2/15 priority date for financial aid. Early and deferred admission are possible.

ALLEGHENY WESLEYAN COLLEGE

Salem, OH

Private ■ Independent Religious ■ Coed

Web site: www.awc.edu
Contact: Admissions Office, 2161 Woodsdale Road, Salem, OH 44460
Telephone: 330-337-6403 or toll-free 800-292-3153 **Fax:** 330-337-6255 ext.

Financial Matters $6050 tuition and fees (2002–03).

Academics Allegheny Wesleyan College awards bachelor's degrees.

Students of Allegheny Wesleyan College The student body is made up of 70 undergraduates.

ALLEN COLLEGE

Waterloo, IA

Suburban setting ■ Private ■ Independent ■ Coed, Primarily Women

Web site: www.allencollege.edu
Contact: Ms. Lois Hagedorn, Student Services Assistant, Barrett Forum, 1825 Logan Avenue, Waterloo, IA 50703
Telephone: 319-226-2000 **Fax:** 319-226-2051
E-mail: hagedole@ihs.org

Getting in Last Year 67 applied; 40% were accepted; 27 enrolled (100%).

Financial Matters $9287 tuition and fees (2002–03); $4606 room and board; 78% average percent of need met; $8246 average financial aid amount received per undergraduate (2001–02).

Academics Allen College awards associate, bachelor's, and master's degrees (liberal arts and general education courses are taken at either University of North Iowa or Wartburg College). Challenging opportunities include advanced placement credit, independent study, and a senior project. Special programs include internships, off-campus study, and Army ROTC. The most frequently chosen baccalaureate field is health professions and related sciences. The faculty at Allen College has 10 full-time members, 30% with terminal degrees. The student-faculty ratio is 22:1.

Students of Allen College The student body totals 273, of whom 238 are undergraduates. 97.1% are women and 2.9% are men. Students come from 2 states and territories. 99% are from Iowa. 80% returned for their sophomore year.

Applying Allen College requires an essay, SAT I and SAT II or ACT, a high school transcript, and 1 recommendation, and in some cases an interview. The school recommends a minimum high school GPA of 2.3. Application deadline: 8/1.

ALLEN UNIVERSITY

Columbia, SC

Suburban setting ■ Private ■ Independent Religious ■ Coed

Web site: www.allenuniversity.edu
Contact: Ms. Constants Adams, Admissions Representative, 1530 Harden Street, Columbia, SC 29204-1085
Telephone: 803-376-5735 or toll-free 877-625-5368 (in-state)
Fax: 803-376-5731
E-mail: admissions@aleenuniversity.edu

Getting in Last Year 321 applied; 82% were accepted; 197 enrolled (75%).

Financial Matters $7393 tuition and fees (2002–03); $4210 room and board; 65% average percent of need met; $10,800 average financial aid amount received per undergraduate (2001–02).

Academics Allen University awards bachelor's degrees. Challenging opportunities include an honors program, independent study, and a senior project. Special programs include cooperative education, internships, summer session for credit, study-abroad, and Army ROTC. The most frequently chosen baccalaureate fields are social sciences and history, business/marketing, and liberal arts/general studies. The faculty at Allen University has 22 full-time members, 41% with terminal degrees. The student-faculty ratio is 10:1.

Students of Allen University The student body is made up of 507 undergraduates. Students come from 10 states and territories and 3 other countries. 94% are from South Carolina. 1.4% are international students. 68% returned for their sophomore year.

Applying Allen University requires an essay, SAT I or ACT, a high school transcript, 1 recommendation, and a minimum high school GPA of 2.0. Application deadline: 7/31; 6/30 priority date for financial aid.

ALLIANT INTERNATIONAL UNIVERSITY

San Diego, CA

Suburban setting ■ Private ■ Independent ■ Coed

Web site: www.alliant.edu
Contact: Ms. Susan Topham, Director of Admissions, 10455 Pomerado Road, San Diego, CA 92131-1799
Telephone: 858-635-4772 **Fax:** 858-635-4739
E-mail: admissions@alliant.edu

Getting in Last Year 565 applied; 48% were accepted; 84 enrolled (31%).

Financial Matters $14,820 tuition and fees (2002–03); $6365 room and board; 100% average percent of need met; $21,250 average financial aid amount received per undergraduate.

Academics Alliant International University awards bachelor's, master's, and doctoral degrees and post-bachelor's certificates. Challenging opportunities include advanced placement credit, an honors program, independent study, and a senior project. Special programs include internships, summer session for credit, study-abroad, and Army ROTC. The most frequently chosen baccalaureate fields are business/marketing, psychology, and social sciences and history. The faculty at Alliant International University has 75 full-time members. The student-faculty ratio is 13:1.

Students of Alliant International University The student body totals 1,946, of whom 500 are undergraduates. 56.6% are women and 43.4% are men. Students come from 23 states and territories and 68 other countries. 83% are from California. 26.3% are international students. 58% returned for their sophomore year.

Applying Alliant International University requires a high school transcript and a minimum high school GPA of 2.0. The school recommends a minimum high school GPA of 3.0. Application deadline: rolling admissions; 3/2 priority date for financial aid. Deferred admission is possible.

ALMA COLLEGE

Alma, MI

Small-town setting ■ Private ■ Independent Religious ■ Coed

Web site: www.alma.edu
Contact: Mr. Paul Pollatz, Director of Admissions, Admissions Office, Alma, MI 48801-1599
Telephone: 989-463-7139 or toll-free 800-321-ALMA **Fax:** 989-463-7057
E-mail: admissions@alma.edu

Getting in Last Year 1,502 applied; 79% were accepted; 333 enrolled (28%).

Financial Matters $17,582 tuition and fees (2002–03); $6336 room and board; 90% average percent of need met; $15,914 average financial aid amount received per undergraduate.

Academics Alma awards bachelor's degrees. Challenging opportunities include advanced placement credit, student-designed majors, double majors, independent study, and a senior project. Special programs include internships, summer session for credit, off-campus study, study-abroad, and Army ROTC. The most frequently chosen baccalaureate fields are business/marketing, education, and social sciences and history. The faculty at Alma has 92 full-time members, 85% with terminal degrees. The student-faculty ratio is 12:1.

Students of Alma The student body is made up of 1,317 undergraduates. 57.1% are women and 42.9% are men. Students come from 22 states and territories. 96% are from Michigan. 0.9% are international students. 85% returned for their sophomore year.

Applying Alma requires SAT I or ACT, a high school transcript, minimum SAT score of 1030 or ACT score of 22, and a minimum high school GPA of 3.0. The school recommends an essay and an interview. Application deadline: rolling admissions; 2/21 priority date for financial aid. Early and deferred admission are possible.

ALVERNIA COLLEGE
Reading, PA

Suburban setting ■ *Private* ■ *Independent Religious* ■ *Coed*

Web site: www.alvernia.edu
Contact: Betsy Stiles, Assistant Dean of Enrollment Management, 400 Saint Bernardine Street, Reading, PA 19607
Telephone: 610-796-8220 or toll-free 888-ALVERNIA (in-state)
Fax: 610-796-8336

Getting in Last Year 692 applied; 80% were accepted; 253 enrolled (46%).

Financial Matters $15,150 tuition and fees (2002–03); $6500 room and board.

Academics Alvernia awards associate, bachelor's, and master's degrees and post-bachelor's and post-master's certificates. Challenging opportunities include advanced placement credit, accelerated degree programs, an honors program, double majors, independent study, and a senior project. Special programs include internships, summer session for credit, off-campus study, and Army ROTC. The most frequently chosen baccalaureate fields are health professions and related sciences, protective services/public administration, and business/marketing. The faculty at Alvernia has 59 full-time members, 51% with terminal degrees. The student-faculty ratio is 14:1.

Students of Alvernia The student body totals 2,187, of whom 1,781 are undergraduates. 66.3% are women and 33.7% are men. Students come from 12 states and territories and 4 other countries. 92% are from Pennsylvania. 0.4% are international students. 69% returned for their sophomore year.

Applying Alvernia requires an essay, SAT I or ACT, and a high school transcript, and in some cases an interview and 2 recommendations. The school recommends 1 recommendation and a minimum high school GPA of 2.0. Application deadline: rolling admissions; 4/1 priority date for financial aid. Deferred admission is possible.

ALVERNO COLLEGE
Milwaukee, WI

Suburban setting ■ *Private* ■ *Independent Religious* ■ *Women Only*

Web site: www.alverno.edu
Contact: Ms. Mary Kay Farrell, Director of Admissions, 3400 South 43 Street, PO Box 343922, Milwaukee, WI 53234-3922
Telephone: 414-382-6113 or toll-free 800-933-3401 **Fax:** 414-382-6354
E-mail: admissions@alverno.edu

Getting in Last Year 667 applied; 82% were accepted; 196 enrolled (36%).

Financial Matters $12,750 tuition and fees (2002–03); $4960 room and board.

Academics Alverno awards associate, bachelor's, and master's degrees (also offers weekend program with significant enrollment not reflected in profile). Challenging opportunities include advanced placement credit, double majors, and a senior project. Special programs include internships, summer session for credit, study-abroad, and Army and Air Force ROTC. The most frequently chosen baccalaureate fields are business/marketing, health professions and related sciences, and communications/communication technologies. The faculty at Alverno has 100 full-time members, 90% with terminal degrees. The student-faculty ratio is 14:1.

Students of Alverno The student body totals 1,999, of whom 1,800 are undergraduates. Students come from 13 states and territories. 98% are from Wisconsin. 0.6% are international students. 71% returned for their sophomore year.

Applying Alverno requires an essay and a high school transcript, and in some cases recommendations. The school recommends ACT and an interview. Application deadline: rolling admissions; 4/1 priority date for financial aid. Deferred admission is possible.

AMBERTON UNIVERSITY
Garland, TX

Suburban setting ■ *Private* ■ *Independent Religious* ■ *Coed*

Web site: www.amberton.edu
Contact: Dr. Algia Allen, Vice President for Academic Services, 1700 Eastgate Drive, Garland, TX 75041-5595
Telephone: 972-279-6511 ext. 135
E-mail: webteam@amberu.edu

Financial Matters $4975 tuition and fees (2002–03).

Academics Amberton University awards bachelor's and master's degrees. Student-designed majors are a challenging opportunity. Special programs include internships and summer session for credit. The most frequently chosen baccalaureate field is interdisciplinary studies. The faculty at Amberton University has 14 full-time members, 86% with terminal degrees. The student-faculty ratio is 25:1.

Students of Amberton University The student body totals 1,648, of whom 633 are undergraduates. 67% are women and 33% are men. Students come from 1 state or territory.

Applying Deferred admission is possible.

AMERICAN ACADEMY OF ART
Chicago, IL

Urban setting ■ *Private* ■ *Proprietary* ■ *Coed*

Web site: www.aaart.edu
Contact: Stuart Rosenblom, Director of Admissions, 332 South Michigan Ave, Suite 300, Chicago, IL 60604-4302
Telephone: 312-461-0600 ext. 143

Getting in Last Year 87 applied; 100% were accepted; 87 enrolled (100%).

Financial Matters $17,780 tuition and fees (2002–03); 70% average percent of need met.

Academics American Academy of Art awards bachelor's and master's degrees. Challenging opportunities include accelerated degree programs, independent study, and a senior project. Special programs include internships, summer session for credit, and study-abroad. The most frequently chosen baccalaureate field is visual/performing arts. The faculty at American Academy of Art has 26 full-time members, 77% with terminal degrees. The student-faculty ratio is 13:1.

Students of American Academy of Art The student body is made up of 360 undergraduates. 33.9% are women and 66.1% are men. Students come from 8 states and territories. 98% are from Illinois. 0.6% are international students. 82% returned for their sophomore year.

Applying Application deadline: rolling admissions.

AMERICAN BAPTIST COLLEGE OF AMERICAN BAPTIST THEOLOGICAL SEMINARY
Nashville, TN

Urban setting ■ *Private* ■ *Independent Religious* ■ *Coed*

Contact: Ms. Marcella Lockhart, Director of Enrollment Management, 1800 Baptist World Center Drive, Nashville, TN 37207
Telephone: 615-256-1463 ext. 2227 **Fax:** 615-226-7855

Getting in Last Year 148 applied; 100% were accepted; 54 enrolled (36%).

Financial Matters $4430 tuition and fees (2002–03); $1600 room only; 20% average percent of need met; $2000 average financial aid amount received per undergraduate (2001–02).

Academics American Baptist College awards associate and bachelor's degrees. Challenging opportunities include advanced placement credit and double majors. Special programs include summer session for credit and off-campus study. The faculty at American Baptist College has 1 full-time members, 100% with terminal degrees. The student-faculty ratio is 17:1.

Students of American Baptist College The student body is made up of 148 undergraduates. 31.1% are women and 68.9% are men. Students come from 10 states and territories and 2 other countries. 80% are from Tennessee. 4.1% are international students. 85% returned for their sophomore year.

Applying American Baptist College requires an essay, a high school transcript, an interview, 3 recommendations, and a minimum high school GPA of 2.0. Application deadline: 7/12; 7/23 for financial aid, with a 1/1 priority date. Deferred admission is possible.

AMERICAN CHRISTIAN COLLEGE AND SEMINARY
Oklahoma City, OK

Small-town setting ■ *Private* ■ *Independent Religious* ■ *Coed*

Web site: www.accs.edu
Contact: Dr. Mitchel Beville, Vice President of Business Affairs/Admissions, 4300 Highline Boulevard #202, Oklahoma City, OK 73108
Telephone: 405-945-0100 ext. 120 or toll-free 800-488-2528 **Fax:** 405-945-0311

American Christian College and Seminary (continued)

E-mail: info@accs.edu

Financial Matters $3576 tuition and fees (2002–03).

Academics American Christian College and Seminary awards associate, bachelor's, master's, doctoral, and first-professional degrees. Challenging opportunities include advanced placement credit and independent study. Special programs include cooperative education, internships, and summer session for credit. The faculty at American Christian College and Seminary has 17 full-time members, 71% with terminal degrees. The student-faculty ratio is 8:1.

Students of American Christian College and Seminary The student body totals 484, of whom 292 are undergraduates. 45.2% are women and 54.8% are men.

Applying American Christian College and Seminary requires a high school transcript. Application deadline: 9/9; 7/15 priority date for financial aid.

AMERICAN COLLEGE OF COMPUTER & INFORMATION SCIENCES

Birmingham, AL

Private ■ Proprietary ■ Coed, Primarily Men

Web site: www.accis.edu

Contact: Ms. Natalie Nixon, Director of Admissions, 2101 Magnolia Avenue, Birmingham, AL 35205

Telephone: 205-323-6191 or toll-free 800-767-2427 **Fax:** 205-328-2229

E-mail: admiss@accis.edu

Academics American College of Computer & Information Sciences awards bachelor's and master's degrees (offers only distance learning degree programs). Challenging opportunities include advanced placement credit, accelerated degree programs, an honors program, and a senior project. The most frequently chosen baccalaureate field is computer/information sciences. The faculty at American College of Computer & Information Sciences has 4 full-time members, 100% with terminal degrees.

Students of American College of Computer & Information Sciences The student body totals 10,696, of whom 934 are undergraduates.

Applying American College of Computer & Information Sciences requires a high school transcript. Application deadline: rolling admissions.

AMERICAN COLLEGE OF THESSALONIKI

Thessaloniki Greece

Suburban setting ■ Private ■ Independent ■ Coed

Web site: www.act.edu/act

Contact: Ms. Roula Lebetli, Admissions Officer, PO Box 21021, 555 10 Pylea, Thessaloniki Greece

E-mail: rleb@ac.anatolia.edu.gr

Getting in Last Year 123 enrolled.

Financial Matters $5875 tuition and fees (2002–03); $3400 room only.

Academics ACT awards bachelor's and master's degrees. Challenging opportunities include advanced placement credit, double majors, and independent study. Special programs include internships, summer session for credit, and study-abroad. The most frequently chosen baccalaureate fields are business/marketing, English, and psychology. The faculty at ACT has 26 full-time members, 58% with terminal degrees. The student-faculty ratio is 10:1.

Students of ACT The student body totals 658, of whom 620 are undergraduates. 55.2% are women and 44.8% are men. 90% returned for their sophomore year.

Applying ACT requires a high school transcript and proficiency in English, and in some cases an essay and an interview. The school recommends a minimum high school GPA of 2.0. Application deadline: 9/1; 8/30 priority date for financial aid. Deferred admission is possible.

AMERICAN INDIAN COLLEGE OF THE ASSEMBLIES OF GOD, INC.

Phoenix, AZ

Urban setting ■ Private ■ Independent Religious ■ Coed

Web site: www.aicag.edu

Contact: Rev. Steve Clindaniel, Admissions Director, 10020 North 15th Avenue, Phoenix, AZ 85021

Telephone: 602-944-3335 ext. 235 or toll-free 800-933-3828 **Fax:** 602-943-8299

E-mail: aicadm@aicag.com

Getting in Last Year 20 applied; 65% were accepted; 13 enrolled (100%).

Financial Matters $4975 tuition and fees (2002–03); $3500 room and board; 80% average percent of need met.

Academics American Indian College of the Assemblies of God, Inc. awards associate and bachelor's degrees. Challenging opportunities include double majors and independent study. Internships is a special program. The most frequently chosen baccalaureate fields are business/marketing and education. The faculty at American Indian College of the Assemblies of God, Inc. has 6 full-time members, 33% with terminal degrees. The student-faculty ratio is 9:1.

Students of American Indian College of the Assemblies of God, Inc. The student body is made up of 80 undergraduates. 58.8% are women and 41.2% are men. Students come from 14 states and territories and 1 other country. 60% are from Arizona. 88% returned for their sophomore year.

Applying American Indian College of the Assemblies of God, Inc. requires an essay, SAT I or ACT, a high school transcript, and 1 recommendation. Application deadline: 8/15; 4/1 priority date for financial aid.

AMERICAN INTERCONTINENTAL UNIVERSITY

Los Angeles, CA

Urban setting ■ Private ■ Proprietary ■ Coed

Web site: www.aiula.com

Contact: Berhan Bayleyegn, Associate Director of High School, 12655 West Jefferson Boulevard, Los Angeles, CA 90066

Telephone: 310-302-2000 ext. 2616 or toll-free 800-333-2652 (out-of-state) **Fax:** 310-302-2001

Getting in Last Year 629 applied; 29% were accepted.

Financial Matters $15,210 tuition and fees (2002–03).

Academics AMLA awards associate, bachelor's, and master's degrees. Challenging opportunities include accelerated degree programs, double majors, and a senior project. Special programs include internships, summer session for credit, and study-abroad. The faculty at AMLA has 19 full-time members, 42% with terminal degrees. The student-faculty ratio is 24:1.

Students of AMLA The student body totals 1,293, of whom 1,201 are undergraduates. 40.7% are women and 59.3% are men. Students come from 50 states and territories and 42 other countries. 73% are from California. 7.2% are international students.

Applying AMLA requires an essay, a high school transcript, an interview, and 2 recommendations. Application deadline: rolling admissions. Early and deferred admission are possible.

AMERICAN INTERCONTINENTAL UNIVERSITY

Plantation, FL

Suburban setting ■ Private ■ Proprietary ■ Coed

Web site: www.aiufl.edu

Contact: Ms. Lisa Bixler, Director of High School Admissions, American Inter Continental University, Admissions Office, 8151 West Peters Road, Plantation, FL 33324

Telephone: 954-233-7421 or toll-free 866-248-4723 (out-of-state) **Fax:** 954-233-8127

Getting in Last Year 646 applied; 100% were accepted.

Academics American InterContinental University awards associate, bachelor's, and master's degrees. Challenging opportunities include advanced placement credit and independent study. Special programs include internships and off-campus study. The faculty at American InterContinental University has 32 full-time members, 13% with terminal degrees. The student-faculty ratio is 24:1.

Students of American InterContinental University The student body totals 1,076, of whom 971 are undergraduates.

Applying Application deadline: rolling admissions, rolling admissions for nonresidents.

AMERICAN INTERCONTINENTAL UNIVERSITY

Atlanta, GA

Urban setting ■ Private ■ Proprietary ■ Coed

Web site: www.aiuniv.edu

Contact: Mr. William Loflin, Vice President of Academic Affairs, 3330 Peachtree Road, NE, Atlanta, GA 30326-1016

Telephone: 404-965-5786 or toll-free 888-999-4248 (out-of-state) **Fax:** 404-965-5701

E-mail: acatl@ix.netcom.com

Getting in Last Year 786 applied; 53% were accepted.

Financial Matters $13,950 tuition and fees (2002–03); $4500 room only; $6850 average financial aid amount received per undergraduate (2001–02 estimated).

Academics American InterContinental University awards associate and bachelor's degrees. Challenging opportunities include accelerated degree programs, double majors, independent study, and a senior project. Special programs include cooperative education, internships, summer session for credit, and study-abroad. The most frequently chosen baccalaureate fields are visual/performing arts and business/marketing. The faculty at American InterContinental University has 14 full-time members, 7% with terminal degrees. The student-faculty ratio is 14:1.

Students of American InterContinental University The student body is made up of 1,292 undergraduates. 63.6% are women and 36.4% are men. Students come from 31 states and territories and 39 other countries. 61% are from Georgia. 8% are international students. 55% returned for their sophomore year.

Applying American InterContinental University recommends an essay, SAT II Subject Tests, SAT I or ACT, a high school transcript, an interview, 2 recommendations, and a minimum high school GPA of 2.0. Application deadline: 10/15. Early and deferred admission are possible.

AMERICAN INTERCONTINENTAL UNIVERSITY-LONDON

London United Kingdom

Urban setting ■ Private ■ Proprietary ■ Coed

Web site: www.aiulondon.ac.uk

Contact: Mr. Jonathan Besser, Director of Admissions and Marketing, 110 Marylebone High Street, London W1U 4RY United Kingdom

E-mail: admissions@aiulondon.ac.uk

Getting in Last Year 787 applied; 71% were accepted; 132 enrolled (24%).

Financial Matters $11,010 tuition and fees (2002–03); $5625 room only.

Academics AIU-London awards associate, bachelor's, and master's degrees. Challenging opportunities include accelerated degree programs, double majors, independent study, and a senior project. Special programs include internships, summer session for credit, and study-abroad. The most frequently chosen baccalaureate fields are business/marketing and communications/communication technologies. The faculty at AIU-London has 20 full-time members. The student-faculty ratio is 12:1.

Students of AIU-London The student body totals 624, of whom 561 are undergraduates. Students come from 37 states and territories and 83 other countries.

Applying AIU-London requires an essay, a high school transcript, an interview, and 2 recommendations. Application deadline: rolling admissions. Early and deferred admission are possible.

AMERICAN INTERNATIONAL COLLEGE

Springfield, MA

Urban setting ■ Private ■ Independent ■ Coed

Web site: www.aic.edu

Contact: Dean of Admissions, 1000 State Street, Springfield, MA 01109-3189

Telephone: 413-205-3201 or toll-free 800-242-3142 **Fax:** 413-205-3051

E-mail: inquiry@acad.aic.edu

Getting in Last Year 1,354 applied; 70% were accepted; 254 enrolled (27%).

Financial Matters $15,700 tuition and fees (2002–03); $7692 room and board; 84% average percent of need met; $17,643 average financial aid amount received per undergraduate (2001–02).

Academics AIC awards associate, bachelor's, master's, and doctoral degrees and post-master's certificates. Challenging opportunities include advanced placement credit, accelerated degree programs, freshman honors college, an honors program, double majors, independent study, and a senior project. Special programs include internships, summer session for credit, off-campus study, study-abroad, and Army and Air Force ROTC. The faculty at AIC has 75 full-time members. The student-faculty ratio is 12:1.

Students of AIC The student body totals 1,565, of whom 1,095 are undergraduates. 53% are women and 47% are men. Students come from 28 states and territories and 48 other countries. 59% are from Massachusetts. 5% are international students. 62% returned for their sophomore year.

Applying AIC requires SAT I or ACT, a high school transcript, and 1 recommendation, and in some cases an interview. The school recommends an essay and an interview. Application deadline: rolling admissions; 5/1 priority date for financial aid. Early and deferred admission are possible.

AMERICAN PUBLIC UNIVERSITY SYSTEM

Charles Town, WV

Private ■ Proprietary ■ Coed

Web site: www.apus.edu

Contact: Ms. Mary Ann Heubusch, Student Service Director, 322-C West Washington Street, Charles Town, WV 25414

Telephone: 703-330-5398 or toll-free 877-468-6268

E-mail: admissions@amunet.edu

Financial Matters $9000 tuition and fees (2002–03).

Academics AMU awards associate, bachelor's, and master's degrees (profile includes American Public University, American Military University and American Community College). Independent study is a challenging opportunity. The faculty at AMU has 23 full-time members, 35% with terminal degrees. The student-faculty ratio is 11:1.

Students of AMU The student body totals 6,828. Students come from 52 states and territories. 10% are from West Virginia. 68% returned for their sophomore year.

Applying AMU requires a high school transcript. Application deadline: rolling admissions. Deferred admission is possible.

AMERICAN UNIVERSITY

Washington, DC

Suburban setting ■ Private ■ Independent Religious ■ Coed

Web site: www.american.edu

Contact: Dr. Sharon Alston, Director of Admissions, 4400 Massachusetts Avenue, NW, Washington, DC 20016-8001

Telephone: 202-885-6000 **Fax:** 202-885-1025

E-mail: afa@american.edu

Getting in Last Year 9,590 applied; 65% were accepted; 1,312 enrolled (21%).

Financial Matters $23,455 tuition and fees (2002–03); $9488 room and board; 79% average percent of need met; $21,266 average financial aid amount received per undergraduate.

Academics AU awards associate, bachelor's, master's, doctoral, and first-professional degrees and post-bachelor's certificates. Challenging opportunities include advanced placement credit, accelerated degree programs, student-designed majors, an honors program, double majors, independent study, and a senior project. Special programs include cooperative education, internships, summer session for credit, off-campus study, study-abroad, and Army and Air Force ROTC. The most frequently chosen baccalaureate fields are social sciences and history, business/marketing, and communications/communication technologies. The faculty at AU has 476 full-time members, 96% with terminal degrees. The student-faculty ratio is 15:1.

Students of AU The student body totals 11,052, of whom 5,872 are undergraduates. 61.2% are women and 38.8% are men. Students come from 54 states and territories and 148 other countries. 7% are from District of Columbia. 8.7% are international students. 85% returned for their sophomore year.

Applying AU requires an essay, SAT I or ACT, a high school transcript, 2 recommendations, and a minimum high school GPA of 2.0. The school recommends SAT II Subject Tests, SAT II: Writing Test, an interview, and a minimum high school GPA of 3.0. Application deadline: 2/1; 3/1 for financial aid. Early and deferred admission are possible.

THE AMERICAN UNIVERSITY IN CAIRO

Cairo Egypt

Urban setting ■ Private ■ Independent ■ Coed

Web site: www.aucegypt.edu

Contact: Randa Kamel, Associate Director of Admissions, The Office of Student Affairs, 420 Fifth Avenue, 3rd Floor, New York, NY 10018-2728

Telephone: 202-357-5199 **Fax:** 212-730-1600

E-mail: davidson@aucnyu.edu

Getting in Last Year 1,639 applied; 64% were accepted; 715 enrolled (68%).

Financial Matters $11,810 tuition and fees (2002–03); $2900 room only.

Academics AUC awards bachelor's and master's degrees (majority of students are Egyptians; enrollment open to all nationalities). Challenging opportunities include advanced placement credit, double majors, and independent study. Special programs include summer session for credit, off-campus study, and study-abroad. The most frequently chosen baccalaureate fields are social sciences and history, engineering/engineering technologies, and business/marketing. The faculty at AUC has 295 full-time members. The student-faculty ratio is 13:1.

Students of AUC The student body totals 5,260, of whom 4,432 are undergraduates. 51.6% are women and 48.4% are men. 95% returned for their sophomore year.

Applying AUC requires an essay, a high school transcript, and a minimum high school GPA of 2.00, and in some cases SAT I or ACT. Application deadline: 6/15.

THE AMERICAN UNIVERSITY IN DUBAI

Dubai United Arab Emirates

Private ■ Proprietary ■ Coed

Web site: www.aud.edu

Contact: Ms. Sarah McConnell, Admissions Coordinator, PO Box 28282, Dubai United Arab Emirates

Telephone: (4)-3999000 ext. 172 **Fax:** 971-4-3998899

E-mail: info@aud.edu

Financial Matters $13,500 tuition and fees (2002–03); $4725 room only.

Academics The American University in Dubai awards associate, bachelor's, and master's degrees. Challenging opportunities include advanced placement credit, accelerated degree programs, an honors program, double majors, and independent study. Special programs include internships, summer session for credit, and study-abroad. The most frequently chosen baccalaureate fields are business/marketing and visual/performing arts. The faculty at The American University in Dubai has 18 full-time members, 100% with terminal degrees. The student-faculty ratio is 21:1.

Students of The American University in Dubai The student body totals 1,272, of whom 1,213 are undergraduates.

Applying The American University in Dubai requires a high school transcript, an interview, 2 recommendations, and a minimum high school GPA of 2.0, and in

The American University in Dubai (continued)

some cases SAT I. The school recommends an essay and SAT I. Application deadline: 10/1. Early admission is possible.

THE AMERICAN UNIVERSITY OF PARIS

Paris France

Urban setting ■ Private ■ Independent ■ Coed

Web site: www.aup.edu
Contact: Ms. Candace McLaughlin, US Office, 820 South Monaco Parkway #304, Denver, CO 80224
Telephone: 303-355-1946
E-mail: usoffice@aup.edu

Getting in Last Year 580 applied; 74% were accepted; 174 enrolled (41%).

Financial Matters $19,000 tuition and fees (2002–03).

Academics AUP awards bachelor's degrees. Challenging opportunities include advanced placement credit, an honors program, double majors, independent study, and a senior project. Special programs include cooperative education, internships, summer session for credit, off-campus study, and study-abroad. The faculty at AUP has 66 full-time members, 74% with terminal degrees. The student-faculty ratio is 12:1.

Students of AUP The student body is made up of 893 undergraduates. 64.5% are women and 35.5% are men. Students come from 44 states and territories and 86 other countries.

Applying AUP requires an essay, a high school transcript, and 2 recommendations, and in some cases SAT I or ACT. The school recommends an interview and a minimum high school GPA of 3.0. Application deadline: 5/1. Deferred admission is possible.

AMERICAN UNIVERSITY OF PUERTO RICO

Bayamón, PR

Private ■ Independent ■ Coed

Contact: Ms. Margarita Cruz, Director of Admissions, PO Box 2037, Bayamón, PR 00960-2037
Telephone: 787-740-6410 **Fax:** 787-785-7377

Getting in Last Year 937 applied; 100% were accepted.

Financial Matters $4640 tuition and fees (2002–03).

Academics American awards associate and bachelor's degrees. Challenging opportunities include advanced placement credit, freshman honors college, and an honors program. Special programs include cooperative education, internships, summer session for credit, and Army ROTC. The faculty at American has 105 full-time members.

Students of American The student body is made up of 4,537 undergraduates. 54.6% are women and 45.4% are men. Students come from 1 state or territory and 1 other country.

Applying American requires SAT I, CEEB, and a high school transcript. Application deadline: 7/1; 5/30 for financial aid, with a 4/15 priority date. Deferred admission is possible.

AMERICAN UNIVERSITY OF ROME

Rome Italy

Urban setting ■ Private ■ Independent ■ Coed

Web site: www.aur.edu
Contact: Ms. Mara Nisdeo, Assistant Director for Admissions, Via Pietro Roselli 4, Rome Italy
Telephone: 39-06-58330919 or toll-free 888-791-8327 (in-state) **Fax:** 202-296-9577
E-mail: aurinfo@aur.edu

Getting in Last Year 351 applied; 48% were accepted.

Financial Matters $10,052 tuition and fees (2002–03); $5660 room only.

Academics AUR awards associate and bachelor's degrees. Challenging opportunities include advanced placement credit, student-designed majors, double majors, and independent study. Special programs include internships and summer session for credit. The most frequently chosen baccalaureate fields are business/marketing, communications/communication technologies, and liberal arts/general studies. The faculty at AUR has 6 full-time members, 50% with terminal degrees. The student-faculty ratio is 16:1.

Students of AUR The student body is made up of 490 undergraduates. 52% returned for their sophomore year.

Applying AUR requires an essay, a high school transcript, recommendations, and a minimum high school GPA of 2.5, and in some cases SAT I, ACT, and SAT I or ACT. The school recommends an interview and a minimum high school GPA of 2.5. Application deadline: 5/15. Deferred admission is possible.

AMHERST COLLEGE

Amherst, MA

Small-town setting ■ Private ■ Independent ■ Coed

Web site: www.amherst.edu
Contact: Mr. Thomas Parker, Dean of Admission and Financial Aid, PO Box 5000, Amherst, MA 01002
Telephone: 413-542-2328 **Fax:** 413-542-2040
E-mail: admission@amherst.edu

Getting in Last Year 5,238 applied; 18% were accepted; 408 enrolled (43%).

Financial Matters $28,310 tuition and fees (2002–03); $7380 room and board; 100% average percent of need met; $26,080 average financial aid amount received per undergraduate.

Academics Amherst College awards bachelor's degrees. Challenging opportunities include student-designed majors, an honors program, double majors, independent study, and a senior project. Special programs include off-campus study and study-abroad. The most frequently chosen baccalaureate fields are social sciences and history, English, and biological/life sciences. The faculty at Amherst College has 177 full-time members, 91% with terminal degrees. The student-faculty ratio is 9:1.

Students of Amherst College The student body is made up of 1,618 undergraduates. 48.5% are women and 51.5% are men. Students come from 56 states and territories and 29 other countries. 15% are from Massachusetts. 4.5% are international students. 97% returned for their sophomore year.

Applying Amherst College requires an essay, SAT I and SAT II or ACT, a high school transcript, and 3 recommendations. Application deadline: 12/31; 2/15 priority date for financial aid. Early and deferred admission are possible.

ANDERSON COLLEGE

Anderson, SC

Suburban setting ■ Private ■ Independent Religious ■ Coed

Web site: www.ac.edu
Contact: Ms. Pam Bryant, Director of Admissions, 316 Boulevard, Anderson, SC 29621
Telephone: 864-231-5607 or toll-free 800-542-3594 **Fax:** 864-231-3033
E-mail: admissions@ac.edu

Getting in Last Year 1,012 applied; 70% were accepted; 375 enrolled (53%).

Financial Matters $12,250 tuition and fees (2002–03); $5040 room and board; 82% average percent of need met; $7843 average financial aid amount received per undergraduate (2001–02).

Academics Anderson College awards bachelor's degrees. Challenging opportunities include advanced placement credit, freshman honors college, an honors program, independent study, and a senior project. Special programs include internships, summer session for credit, study-abroad, and Army and Air Force ROTC. The most frequently chosen baccalaureate fields are education, business/marketing, and visual/performing arts. The faculty at Anderson College has 66 full-time members, 65% with terminal degrees. The student-faculty ratio is 14:1.

Students of Anderson College The student body is made up of 1,639 undergraduates. 64.7% are women and 35.3% are men. Students come from 27 states and territories and 9 other countries. 90% are from South Carolina. 0.6% are international students. 62% returned for their sophomore year.

Applying Anderson College requires SAT I or ACT and a high school transcript, and in some cases an essay, an interview, and 2 recommendations. The school recommends a minimum high school GPA of 2.5. Application deadline: 6/30; 7/1 for financial aid. Early and deferred admission are possible.

ANDERSON UNIVERSITY

Anderson, IN

Suburban setting ■ Private ■ Independent Religious ■ Coed

Web site: www.anderson.edu
Contact: Mr. Jim King, Director of Admissions, 1100 East 5th Street, Anderson, IN 46012-3495
Telephone: 765-641-4080 or toll-free 800-421-3014 (in-state), 800-428-6414 (out-of-state) **Fax:** 765-641-3851
E-mail: info@anderson.edu

Getting in Last Year 2,083 applied; 72% were accepted; 598 enrolled (40%).

Financial Matters $16,140 tuition and fees (2002–03); $5620 room and board; 93% average percent of need met; $15,736 average financial aid amount received per undergraduate (2001–02).

Academics Anderson University awards associate, bachelor's, master's, doctoral, and first-professional degrees. Challenging opportunities include advanced placement credit, accelerated degree programs, student-designed majors, an honors program, double majors, independent study, and a senior project. Special programs include internships, summer session for credit, and study-abroad. The most frequently chosen baccalaureate fields are education, business/marketing, and health professions and related sciences. The faculty at Anderson University has 130 full-time members, 61% with terminal degrees. The student-faculty ratio is 13:1.

Students of Anderson University The student body totals 2,506, of whom 2,121 are undergraduates. 58.2% are women and 41.8% are men. Students come from 46 states and territories and 16 other countries. 65% are from Indiana. 1.1% are international students. 73% returned for their sophomore year.

Applying Anderson University requires SAT I or ACT, a high school transcript, 2 recommendations, lifestyle statement, and a minimum high school GPA of 2.0, and in some cases an interview. The school recommends an essay. Application deadline: 7/1; 3/1 priority date for financial aid. Deferred admission is possible.

ANDREW JACKSON UNIVERSITY

Birmingham, AL

Private ■ Coed

Web site: www.aju.edu

Contact: Ms. Bell Woods, Director of Admissions, 10 Old Montgomery Highway, Birmingham, AL 35209

Telephone: 205-871-9288 **Fax:** 800-321-9694

E-mail: info@aju.edu

Financial Matters $3350 tuition and fees (2002–03).

Academics Andrew Jackson University awards bachelor's and master's degrees (offers primarily external degree programs). Challenging opportunities include accelerated degree programs and independent study. Special programs include summer session for credit and off-campus study. The most frequently chosen baccalaureate fields are business/marketing and communications/communication technologies. The faculty at Andrew Jackson University has 50 members, 90% with terminal degrees. The student-faculty ratio is 10:1.

Students of Andrew Jackson University The student body totals 463, of whom 134 are undergraduates.

ANDREWS UNIVERSITY

Berrien Springs, MI

Small-town setting ■ Private ■ Independent Religious ■ Coed

Web site: www.andrews.edu

Contact: Ms. Charlotte Coy, Admissions Supervisor, Berrien Springs, MI 49104

Telephone: 269-471-7771 or toll-free 800-253-2874 **Fax:** 616-471-3228

E-mail: enroll@andrews.edu

Getting in Last Year 974 applied; 56% were accepted; 319 enrolled (58%).

Financial Matters $13,746 tuition and fees (2002–03); $4840 room and board; 81% average percent of need met; $16,236 average financial aid amount received per undergraduate (2001–02).

Academics Andrews awards associate, bachelor's, master's, doctoral, and first-professional degrees. Challenging opportunities include advanced placement credit, accelerated degree programs, student-designed majors, freshman honors college, an honors program, double majors, and a senior project. Special programs include cooperative education, internships, summer session for credit, off-campus study, and study-abroad. The most frequently chosen baccalaureate fields are biological/life sciences, health professions and related sciences, and business/marketing. The faculty at Andrews has 227 full-time members, 68% with terminal degrees. The student-faculty ratio is 12:1.

Students of Andrews The student body totals 2,779, of whom 1,657 are undergraduates. 54.3% are women and 45.7% are men. Students come from 46 states and territories and 50 other countries. 48% are from Michigan. 13.7% are international students. 74% returned for their sophomore year.

Applying Andrews requires an essay, SAT I or ACT, a high school transcript, 2 recommendations, and a minimum high school GPA of 2.25. The school recommends ACT. Application deadline: rolling admissions. Deferred admission is possible.

ANGELO STATE UNIVERSITY

San Angelo, TX

Urban setting ■ Public ■ State-supported ■ Coed

Web site: www.angelo.edu

Contact: Mrs. Monique Cossich, Director of Admissions, Box 11014, ASU Station, San Angelo, TX 76909

Telephone: 325-942-2185 ext. 231 or toll-free 800-946-8627 (in-state) **Fax:** 325-942-2078

E-mail: admissions@angelo.edu

Getting in Last Year 3,782 applied; 64% were accepted; 1,214 enrolled (50%).

Financial Matters $2506 resident tuition and fees (2002–03); $7738 nonresident tuition and fees (2002–03); $4256 room and board; 59% average percent of need met; $3735 average financial aid amount received per undergraduate (2001–02).

Academics ASU awards associate, bachelor's, and master's degrees. Challenging opportunities include advanced placement credit, accelerated degree programs, double majors, independent study, and a senior project. Special programs include internships, summer session for credit, off-campus study, study-abroad, and Air Force ROTC. The most frequently chosen baccalaureate fields are business/marketing, psychology, and interdisciplinary studies. The faculty at ASU has 221 full-time members, 76% with terminal degrees. The student-faculty ratio is 20:1.

Students of ASU The student body totals 6,268, of whom 5,792 are undergraduates. 55.9% are women and 44.1% are men. Students come from 37 states and territories and 22 other countries. 98% are from Texas. 1.1% are international students. 58% returned for their sophomore year.

Applying ASU requires SAT I or ACT and a high school transcript. Application deadline: 8/1; 5/1 priority date for financial aid. Early and deferred admission are possible.

ANNA MARIA COLLEGE

Paxton, MA

Rural setting ■ Private ■ Independent Religious ■ Coed

Web site: www.annamaria.edu

Contact: Ms. Jane Fidler, Director of Admissions, Box O, Sunset Lane, Paxton, MA 01612

Telephone: 508-849-3360 or toll-free 800-344-4586 ext. 360 **Fax:** 508-849-3362

E-mail: admission@annamaria.edu

Getting in Last Year 574 applied; 83% were accepted; 167 enrolled (35%).

Financial Matters $17,710 tuition and fees (2002–03); $6550 room and board; 83% average percent of need met; $13,565 average financial aid amount received per undergraduate.

Academics AMC awards associate, bachelor's, and master's degrees and post-bachelor's and post-master's certificates. Challenging opportunities include advanced placement credit, accelerated degree programs, student-designed majors, double majors, and a senior project. Special programs include cooperative education, internships, summer session for credit, off-campus study, study-abroad, and Air Force ROTC. The most frequently chosen baccalaureate fields are protective services/public administration, business/marketing, and health professions and related sciences. The faculty at AMC has 37 full-time members, 41% with terminal degrees. The student-faculty ratio is 10:1.

Students of AMC The student body totals 1,235, of whom 803 are undergraduates. 64.1% are women and 35.9% are men. Students come from 13 states and territories and 5 other countries. 84% are from Massachusetts. 0.9% are international students. 75% returned for their sophomore year.

Applying AMC requires an essay, SAT I or ACT, a high school transcript, and 2 recommendations, and in some cases audition for music programs, portfolio for art programs. The school recommends an interview and a minimum high school GPA of 2.0. Application deadline: rolling admissions. Deferred admission is possible.

ANTIOCH COLLEGE

Yellow Springs, OH

Small-town setting ■ Private ■ Independent ■ Coed

Web site: www.antioch-college.edu

Contact: Ms. Cathy Paige, Information Manager, 795 Livermore Street, Yellow Springs, OH 45387-1697

Telephone: 937-769-1100 ext. 1119 or toll-free 800-543-9436 **Fax:** 937-769-1111

E-mail: admissions@antioch-college.edu

Getting in Last Year 504 applied; 75% were accepted; 155 enrolled (41%).

Financial Matters $22,103 tuition and fees (2002–03); $5602 room and board; 78% average percent of need met; $16,692 average financial aid amount received per undergraduate (2001–02).

Academics Antioch awards bachelor's degrees. Challenging opportunities include advanced placement credit, student-designed majors, double majors, independent study, and a senior project. Special programs include cooperative education, internships, summer session for credit, off-campus study, and study-abroad. The faculty at Antioch has 57 full-time members, 100% with terminal degrees. The student-faculty ratio is 10:1.

Students of Antioch The student body totals 597, of whom 581 are undergraduates. 61.3% are women and 38.7% are men. Students come from 42 states and territories and 2 other countries. 24% are from Ohio. 0.3% are international students. 75% returned for their sophomore year.

Applying Antioch requires an essay, a high school transcript, 2 recommendations, and a minimum high school GPA of 2.5. The school recommends an interview. Application deadline: 2/1; 3/1 priority date for financial aid. Deferred admission is possible.

ANTIOCH UNIVERSITY LOS ANGELES

Marina del Rey, CA

Urban setting ■ Private ■ Independent ■ Coed

Web site: www.antiochla.edu

Antioch University Los Angeles (continued)

Contact: Ms. Kathie Rawding, Director of Admissions and Financial Aid, 13274 Fiji Way, Marina del Rey, CA 90292-7090
Telephone: 310-578-1080 ext. 217 or toll-free 800-7ANTIOCH
Fax: 310-822-4824
E-mail: admissions@antiochla.edu

Getting in Last Year 65 applied; 88% were accepted.

Financial Matters $15,445 tuition and fees (2002–03).

Academics Antioch Los Angeles awards bachelor's and master's degrees and post-bachelor's and post-master's certificates. Challenging opportunities include advanced placement credit, accelerated degree programs, student-designed majors, double majors, and independent study. Special programs include cooperative education, internships, and summer session for credit. The faculty at Antioch Los Angeles has 21 full-time members, 81% with terminal degrees. The student-faculty ratio is 14:1.

Students of Antioch Los Angeles The student body totals 650, of whom 188 are undergraduates. 75% are women and 25% are men. Students come from 1 state or territory.

Applying Antioch Los Angeles requires an essay and minimum of 20 semester/30 quarter units to transfer, and in some cases a high school transcript and an interview. Deferred admission is possible.

ANTIOCH UNIVERSITY MCGREGOR

Yellow Springs, OH

Small-town setting ■ Private ■ Independent ■ Coed

Web site: www.mcgregor.edu
Contact: Mr. Oscar Robinson, Enrollment Services Manager, Student and Alumni Services Division, Enrollment Services, 800 Livermore Street, Yellow Springs, OH 45387
Telephone: 937-769-1823 or toll-free 937-769-1818 **Fax:** 937-769-1805
E-mail: sas@mcgregor.edu

Financial Matters $10,665 tuition and fees (2002–03); 30% average percent of need met; $10,500 average financial aid amount received per undergraduate (2001–02).

Academics Antioch University McGregor awards bachelor's and master's degrees. Challenging opportunities include advanced placement credit, accelerated degree programs, double majors, independent study, and a senior project. Special programs include cooperative education, internships, and summer session for credit. The most frequently chosen baccalaureate fields are business/marketing, liberal arts/general studies, and psychology. The faculty at Antioch University McGregor has 20 full-time members, 85% with terminal degrees. The student-faculty ratio is 7:1.

Students of Antioch University McGregor The student body totals 703, of whom 163 are undergraduates. 77.3% are women and 22.7% are men. Students come from 1 state or territory. 92% returned for their sophomore year.

Applying Antioch University McGregor requires an interview, 2 recommendations, age 21 or older, and a minimum high school GPA of 2.0. Deferred admission is possible.

ANTIOCH UNIVERSITY SANTA BARBARA

Santa Barbara, CA

Small-town setting ■ Private ■ Independent ■ Coed

Web site: www.antiochsb.edu
Contact: Mr. Richard Grisel, Director of Admissions, 801 Garden Street, Santa Barbara, CA 93101-1580
Telephone: 805-962-8179 ext. 113 **Fax:** 805-962-4786
E-mail: admissions@antiochsb.edu

Financial Matters $11,400 tuition and fees (2002–03).

Academics Antioch University Santa Barbara awards bachelor's and master's degrees. Challenging opportunities include accelerated degree programs, student-designed majors, and independent study. Special programs include internships and summer session for credit. The most frequently chosen baccalaureate field is liberal arts/general studies. The faculty at Antioch University Santa Barbara has 14 full-time members. The student-faculty ratio is 15:1.

Students of Antioch University Santa Barbara The student body totals 317, of whom 134 are undergraduates. 76.1% are women and 23.9% are men. 1.5% are international students.

Applying Deferred admission is possible.

ANTIOCH UNIVERSITY SEATTLE

Seattle, WA

Urban setting ■ Private ■ Independent ■ Coed

Web site: www.antiochsea.edu
Contact: Ms. Vickie Lopez, Admissions Associate, 2326 Sixth Avenue, Seattle, WA 98121-1814
Telephone: 206-441-5352 ext. 5205
E-mail: admissions@antiochsea.edu

Financial Matters $16,740 tuition and fees (2002–03); 75% average percent of need met; $12,500 average financial aid amount received per undergraduate.

Academics Antioch University Seattle awards bachelor's and master's degrees. Challenging opportunities include advanced placement credit, accelerated degree programs, student-designed majors, and a senior project. Special programs include summer session for credit and study-abroad. The faculty at Antioch University Seattle has 8 full-time members, 50% with terminal degrees. The student-faculty ratio is 10:1.

Students of Antioch University Seattle The student body totals 770, of whom 190 are undergraduates. 75.3% are women and 24.7% are men. Students come from 5 states and territories. 98% are from Washington.

Applying Deferred admission is possible.

APPALACHIAN BIBLE COLLEGE

Bradley, WV

Small-town setting ■ Private ■ Independent Religious ■ Coed

Web site: www.abc.edu
Contact: Miss Karen Nelson, Admissions Counselor, PO Box ABC, Bradley, WV 25818
Telephone: 800-678-9ABC ext. 3213 or toll-free 800-678-9ABC ext. 3213
Fax: 304-877-5082
E-mail: admissions@abc.edu

Getting in Last Year 127 applied; 68% were accepted.

Financial Matters $7390 tuition and fees (2002–03); $3540 room and board; 87% average percent of need met; $3250 average financial aid amount received per undergraduate (2001–02).

Academics ABC awards associate and bachelor's degrees. Challenging opportunities include advanced placement credit, an honors program, and independent study. Special programs include internships and summer session for credit. The faculty at ABC has 10 full-time members, 40% with terminal degrees. The student-faculty ratio is 17:1.

Students of ABC The student body is made up of 264 undergraduates. Students come from 31 states and territories and 8 other countries. 2.3% are international students.

Applying ABC requires an essay, SAT I or ACT, a high school transcript, and 3 recommendations. The school recommends an interview and a minimum high school GPA of 2.5. Application deadline: rolling admissions; 6/30 for financial aid, with a 3/1 priority date.

APPALACHIAN STATE UNIVERSITY

Boone, NC

Small-town setting ■ Public ■ State-supported ■ Coed

Web site: www.appstate.edu
Contact: Mr. Joe Watts, Associate Vice Chancellor, Boone, NC 28608
Telephone: 828-262-2120 **Fax:** 828-262-3296
E-mail: admissions@appstate.edu

Getting in Last Year 8,874 applied; 64% were accepted; 2,419 enrolled (42%).

Financial Matters $2795 resident tuition and fees (2002–03); $11,716 nonresident tuition and fees (2002–03); $4333 room and board; 79% average percent of need met; $5566 average financial aid amount received per undergraduate.

Academics Appalachian awards bachelor's, master's, and doctoral degrees and post-master's certificates. Challenging opportunities include advanced placement credit, accelerated degree programs, student-designed majors, an honors program, double majors, independent study, and a senior project. Special programs include internships, summer session for credit, off-campus study, study-abroad, and Army ROTC. The most frequently chosen baccalaureate fields are business/marketing, education, and communications/communication technologies. The faculty at Appalachian has 619 full-time members, 80% with terminal degrees. The student-faculty ratio is 19:1.

Students of Appalachian The student body totals 14,178, of whom 12,852 are undergraduates. 51.3% are women and 48.7% are men. Students come from 44 states and territories. 88% are from North Carolina. 0.4% are international students.

Applying Appalachian requires SAT I or ACT and a high school transcript. Application deadline: rolling admissions; 3/15 priority date for financial aid. Early and deferred admission are possible.

AQUINAS COLLEGE

Grand Rapids, MI

Suburban setting ■ Private ■ Independent Religious ■ Coed

Web site: www.aquinas.edu
Contact: Ms. Amy Sprouse, Applications Specialist, 1607 Robinson Road, SE, Grand Rapids, MI 49506-1799

Telephone: 616-732-4460 ext. 5150 or toll-free 800-678-9593
Fax: 616-732-4469
E-mail: admissions@aquinas.edu

Getting in Last Year 1,300 applied; 79% were accepted; 346 enrolled (33%).

Financial Matters $15,620 tuition and fees (2002–03); $5436 room and board; 96% average percent of need met; $14,634 average financial aid amount received per undergraduate.

Academics Aquinas College awards associate, bachelor's, and master's degrees. Challenging opportunities include advanced placement credit, accelerated degree programs, student-designed majors, an honors program, double majors, and independent study. Special programs include cooperative education, internships, summer session for credit, off-campus study, and study-abroad. The most frequently chosen baccalaureate fields are business/marketing, psychology, and education. The faculty at Aquinas College has 98 full-time members, 68% with terminal degrees. The student-faculty ratio is 16:1.

Students of Aquinas College The student body totals 2,579, of whom 1,991 are undergraduates. 65.9% are women and 34.1% are men. Students come from 20 states and territories and 11 other countries. 94% are from Michigan. 0.7% are international students. 75% returned for their sophomore year.

Applying Aquinas College requires ACT, a high school transcript, and a minimum high school GPA of 2.5, and in some cases an essay and an interview. Application deadline: rolling admissions; 2/15 priority date for financial aid. Early and deferred admission are possible.

AQUINAS COLLEGE

Nashville, TN

Urban setting ■ Private ■ Independent Religious ■ Coed

Web site: www.aquinas-tn.edu
Contact: Mr. Neil J. Devine, Director of Career Planning and Admission, 4210 Harding Road, Nashville, TN 37205-2005
Telephone: 615-297-7545 ext. 426 **Fax:** 615-297-7970

Getting in Last Year 1,900 applied; 12% were accepted; 139 enrolled (62%).

Financial Matters $8830 tuition and fees (2002–03); 76% average percent of need met; $8560 average financial aid amount received per undergraduate (2001–02).

Academics Aquinas awards associate and bachelor's degrees. Challenging opportunities include advanced placement credit and independent study. Special programs include internships, summer session for credit, and Army and Air Force ROTC. The faculty at Aquinas has 60 members, 22% with terminal degrees. The student-faculty ratio is 19:1.

Students of Aquinas The student body is made up of 846 undergraduates. 78.8% are women and 21.2% are men. Students come from 5 states and territories. 97% are from Tennessee. 70% returned for their sophomore year.

Applying Aquinas requires SAT I or ACT, a high school transcript, an interview, and a minimum high school GPA of 2.0. Application deadline: rolling admissions; 3/15 priority date for financial aid. Deferred admission is possible.

ARCADIA UNIVERSITY

Glenside, PA

Suburban setting ■ Private ■ Independent Religious ■ Coed

Web site: www.arcadia.edu
Contact: Mr. Dennis L. Nostrand, Director of Enrollment Management, 450 South Easton Road, Glenside, PA 19038
Telephone: 215-572-2910 or toll-free 877-ARCADIA **Fax:** 215-572-4049
E-mail: admiss@arcadia.edu

Getting in Last Year 2,239 applied; 80% were accepted; 409 enrolled (23%).

Financial Matters $19,940 tuition and fees (2002–03); $8290 room and board; 100% average percent of need met; $16,449 average financial aid amount received per undergraduate.

Academics Arcadia University awards bachelor's, master's, and doctoral degrees. Challenging opportunities include advanced placement credit, student-designed majors, an honors program, double majors, independent study, and a senior project. Special programs include cooperative education, internships, summer session for credit, off-campus study, study-abroad, and Army ROTC. The faculty at Arcadia University has 105 full-time members, 85% with terminal degrees. The student-faculty ratio is 13:1.

Students of Arcadia University The student body totals 3,002, of whom 1,673 are undergraduates. 74.5% are women and 25.5% are men. Students come from 22 states and territories and 10 other countries. 73% are from Pennsylvania. 1.7% are international students. 82% returned for their sophomore year.

Applying Arcadia University requires an essay, SAT I or ACT, a high school transcript, and 2 recommendations, and in some cases portfolio. The school recommends an interview. Application deadline: rolling admissions; 3/1 priority date for financial aid. Early and deferred admission are possible.

ARGOSY UNIVERSITY-DALLAS

Dallas, TX

Private ■ Proprietary ■ Coed

Web site: www.argosyu.edu
Contact: Mr. Dee Pinkston, Chief Admissions Officer, 8950 North Central Expressway, Dallas, TX 75231
Telephone: 214-890-9900 or toll-free 866-954-9900
E-mail: dallasadmissions@argosyu.edu

Financial Matters $8330 tuition and fees (2002–03).

Academics Argosy University-Dallas awards bachelor's, master's, and doctoral degrees. Challenging opportunities include accelerated degree programs and a senior project. Summer session for credit is a special program. The faculty at Argosy University-Dallas has 5 full-time members, 100% with terminal degrees. The student-faculty ratio is 7:1.

Students of Argosy University-Dallas The student body totals 46, of whom 10 are undergraduates. 60% are women and 40% are men. Students come from 1 state or territory.

Applying Early and deferred admission are possible.

ARGOSY UNIVERSITY-ORANGE COUNTY

Orange, CA

Private ■ Proprietary ■ Coed

Web site: www.argosyu.edu
Contact: Mark Betz, Director, Admissions, 3745 West Chapman Avenue, Suite 100, Orange, CA 92868
Telephone: 714-940-0025 ext. 115 or toll-free 800-716-9598

Financial Matters $8280 tuition and fees (2002–03).

Academics Argosy University-Orange County awards associate, bachelor's, master's, and doctoral degrees. The faculty at Argosy University-Orange County has 7 full-time members, 86% with terminal degrees. The student-faculty ratio is 10:1.

Students of Argosy University-Orange County The student body totals 446, of whom 54 are undergraduates. 55.6% are women and 44.4% are men.

Applying Argosy University-Orange County requires (in some cases) an essay, a high school transcript, and an interview. Early and deferred admission are possible.

ARIZONA STATE UNIVERSITY

Tempe, AZ

Suburban setting ■ Public ■ State-supported ■ Coed

Web site: www.asu.edu
Contact: Mr. Timothy J. Desch, Director of Undergraduate Admissions, Box 870112, Tempe, AZ 85287-0112
Telephone: 480-965-7788 **Fax:** 480-965-3610
E-mail: ugradinq@asu.edu

Getting in Last Year 18,155 applied; 85% were accepted; 6,206 enrolled (40%).

Financial Matters $2585 resident tuition and fees (2002–03); $11,105 nonresident tuition and fees (2002–03); $5866 room and board; 70% average percent of need met; $7309 average financial aid amount received per undergraduate (2001–02).

Academics ASU Main awards bachelor's, master's, doctoral, and first-professional degrees and post-bachelor's and post-master's certificates. Challenging opportunities include advanced placement credit, accelerated degree programs, an honors program, double majors, independent study, and a senior project. Special programs include cooperative education, internships, summer session for credit, off-campus study, study-abroad, and Army and Air Force ROTC. The most frequently chosen baccalaureate fields are business/marketing, communications/communication technologies, and social sciences and history. The faculty at ASU Main has 1,730 full-time members, 85% with terminal degrees. The student-faculty ratio is 22:1.

Students of ASU Main The student body totals 47,359, of whom 36,802 are undergraduates. 51.9% are women and 48.1% are men. Students come from 53 states and territories and 105 other countries. 77% are from Arizona. 3.4% are international students. 76% returned for their sophomore year.

Applying ASU Main requires SAT I or ACT, a high school transcript, and a minimum high school GPA of 3.0. Application deadline: rolling admissions; 3/1 priority date for financial aid.

ARIZONA STATE UNIVERSITY EAST

Mesa, AZ

Suburban setting ■ Public ■ State-supported ■ Coed

Web site: www.east.asu.edu
Contact: Ms. Sarah Gerkin, Student Recruitment/Retention Specialist, 7001 East Williams Field Road #20, Mesa, AZ 85212
Telephone: 480-727-1866 **Fax:** 480-727-1008
E-mail: sarah.gerkin@asu.edu

Getting in Last Year 461 applied; 73% were accepted; 143 enrolled (43%).

Arizona State University East (continued)

Financial Matters $2534 resident tuition and fees (2002–03); $11,054 nonresident tuition and fees (2002–03); $4544 room and board; 66% average percent of need met; $7511 average financial aid amount received per undergraduate (2001–02).

Academics ASU East awards bachelor's and master's degrees. Challenging opportunities include advanced placement credit, accelerated degree programs, student-designed majors, an honors program, double majors, and independent study. Special programs include internships, summer session for credit, study-abroad, and Army and Air Force ROTC. The most frequently chosen baccalaureate fields are engineering/engineering technologies, home economics/vocational home economics, and agriculture. The faculty at ASU East has 81 full-time members, 80% with terminal degrees. The student-faculty ratio is 14:1.

Students of ASU East The student body totals 3,126, of whom 2,526 are undergraduates. 49.1% are women and 50.9% are men. Students come from 41 states and territories. 90% are from Arizona. 2% are international students.

Applying ASU East requires a high school transcript. The school recommends SAT I or ACT and a minimum high school GPA of 3.0. Application deadline: rolling admissions; 3/1 priority date for financial aid.

ARIZONA STATE UNIVERSITY WEST

Phoenix, AZ

Urban setting ■ Public ■ State-supported ■ Coed

Web site: www.west.asu.edu
Contact: Ms. Deborah Moore, Program Coordinator, 4701 West Thunderbird Road, PO Box 37100, Phoenix, AZ 85069-7100
Telephone: 602-543-8217 **Fax:** 602-543-8312

Getting in Last Year 636 applied; 85% were accepted; 321 enrolled (59%).

Financial Matters $2585 resident tuition and fees (2002–03); $11,105 nonresident tuition and fees (2002–03); 100% average percent of need met; $7223 average financial aid amount received per undergraduate (2001–02).

Academics ASU West awards bachelor's and master's degrees and post-bachelor's certificates. Challenging opportunities include student-designed majors, an honors program, double majors, independent study, and a senior project. Special programs include internships and summer session for credit. The most frequently chosen baccalaureate fields are education, business/marketing, and protective services/public administration. The faculty at ASU West has 181 full-time members, 89% with terminal degrees. The student-faculty ratio is 18:1.

Students of ASU West The student body totals 6,630, of whom 5,035 are undergraduates. 68.8% are women and 31.2% are men. Students come from 19 states and territories and 26 other countries. 98% are from Arizona. 1.1% are international students.

Applying ASU West requires SAT I or ACT and a high school transcript, and in some cases SAT I and ACT. The school recommends a minimum high school GPA of 3.0.

ARKANSAS BAPTIST COLLEGE

Little Rock, AR

Urban setting ■ Private ■ Independent Religious ■ Coed

Web site: www.arbaptcol.edu
Contact: Mrs. Terri Oates, Registrar, 1600 Bishop Street, Little Rock, AR 72202-6067
Telephone: 501-374-7856 ext. 5124

Getting in Last Year 215 enrolled.

Financial Matters $2950 tuition and fees (2002–03); $4200 room and board.

Academics Arkansas Baptist College awards associate and bachelor's degrees. Accelerated degree programs are a challenging opportunity. Summer session for credit is a special program. The most frequently chosen baccalaureate fields are business/marketing and education. The faculty at Arkansas Baptist College has 17 full-time members, 29% with terminal degrees. The student-faculty ratio is 9:1.

Students of Arkansas Baptist College The student body is made up of 375 undergraduates. 55.7% are women and 44.3% are men.

Applying Arkansas Baptist College requires a high school transcript. Application deadline: rolling admissions; 4/15 priority date for financial aid. Deferred admission is possible.

ARKANSAS STATE UNIVERSITY

State University, AR

Small-town setting ■ Public ■ State-supported ■ Coed

Web site: www.astate.edu
Contact: Ms. Paula James Lynn, Director of Admissions, PO Box 1630, State University, AR 72467
Telephone: 870-972-3024 or toll-free 800-382-3030 (in-state)
Fax: 870-910-8094
E-mail: admissions@astate.edu

Getting in Last Year 2,822 applied; 73% were accepted; 1,632 enrolled (80%).

Financial Matters $4480 resident tuition and fees (2002–03); $10,090 nonresident tuition and fees (2002–03); $3410 room and board; 65% average percent of need met; $2900 average financial aid amount received per undergraduate.

Academics ASU awards associate, bachelor's, master's, and doctoral degrees and post-bachelor's and post-master's certificates. Challenging opportunities include advanced placement credit, accelerated degree programs, an honors program, double majors, independent study, and a senior project. Special programs include cooperative education, internships, summer session for credit, off-campus study, study-abroad, and Army ROTC. The most frequently chosen baccalaureate fields are business/marketing, education, and health professions and related sciences. The faculty at ASU has 432 full-time members. The student-faculty ratio is 19:1.

Students of ASU The student body totals 10,435, of whom 9,275 are undergraduates. 58.4% are women and 41.6% are men. Students come from 43 states and territories and 37 other countries. 90% are from Arkansas. 1.1% are international students. 71% returned for their sophomore year.

Applying ASU requires SAT I, ACT, or ACT ASSET, ACT preferred, a high school transcript, proof of immunization, proof of enrollment in selective service for men over 18, and a minimum high school GPA of 2.0. Application deadline: rolling admissions; 7/1 for financial aid, with a 2/15 priority date. Early and deferred admission are possible.

ARKANSAS TECH UNIVERSITY

Russellville, AR

Small-town setting ■ Public ■ State-supported ■ Coed

Web site: www.atu.edu
Contact: Ms. Shauna Donnell, Director of Enrollment Management, L.L. "DOC" Bryan Student Services Building, Suite 141, Russellville, AR 72801-2222
Telephone: 479-968-0343 or toll-free 800-582-6953 (in-state)
Fax: 479-964-0522
E-mail: tech.enroll@mail.atu.edu

Getting in Last Year 2,691 applied; 52% were accepted; 1,197 enrolled (86%).

Financial Matters $3256 resident tuition and fees (2002–03); $6332 nonresident tuition and fees (2002–03); $3576 room and board; 53% average percent of need met; $4593 average financial aid amount received per undergraduate (2001–02).

Academics Arkansas Tech awards associate, bachelor's, and master's degrees. Challenging opportunities include advanced placement credit, an honors program, double majors, independent study, and a senior project. Special programs include internships, summer session for credit, off-campus study, and Army ROTC. The most frequently chosen baccalaureate fields are education, business/marketing, and computer/information sciences. The faculty at Arkansas Tech has 209 full-time members, 68% with terminal degrees. The student-faculty ratio is 19:1.

Students of Arkansas Tech The student body totals 5,855, of whom 5,457 are undergraduates. 52.8% are women and 47.2% are men. Students come from 34 states and territories and 38 other countries. 96% are from Arkansas. 1.4% are international students. 64% returned for their sophomore year.

Applying Arkansas Tech requires SAT I or ACT, a high school transcript, and a minimum high school GPA of 2.0. The school recommends ACT. Deferred admission is possible.

ARLINGTON BAPTIST COLLEGE

Arlington, TX

Urban setting ■ Private ■ Independent Religious ■ Coed

Web site: www.abconline.edu
Contact: Ms. Janie Hall, Registrar/Admissions, 3001 West Division, Arlington, TX 76012-3425
Telephone: 817-461-8741 ext. 105 **Fax:** 817-274-1138
E-mail: jhall@abconline.edu

Getting in Last Year 45 applied; 100% were accepted; 42 enrolled (93%).

Financial Matters $4640 tuition and fees (2002–03); $3600 room and board; $5113 average financial aid amount received per undergraduate (2001–02).

Academics ABC awards bachelor's degrees. Challenging opportunities include advanced placement credit, double majors, independent study, and a senior project. Special programs include internships and summer session for credit. The most frequently chosen baccalaureate field is education. The faculty at ABC has 5 full-time members. The student-faculty ratio is 14:1.

Students of ABC The student body is made up of 199 undergraduates. 41.7% are women and 58.3% are men. Students come from 11 states and territories and 8 other countries. 64% are from Texas. 12.2% are international students. 71% returned for their sophomore year.

Applying ABC requires an essay, a high school transcript, 1 recommendation, and pastoral recommendation, medical examination, and in some cases an interview. The school recommends SAT I and SAT II or ACT. Application deadline: rolling admissions; 8/1 priority date for financial aid. Early and deferred admission are possible.

ARMSTRONG ATLANTIC STATE UNIVERSITY

Savannah, GA

Suburban setting ■ *Public* ■ *State-supported* ■ *Coed*

Web site: www.armstrong.edu

Contact: Ms. Melanie Mirande, Assistant Director of Recruitment, 11935 Abercorn Street, Savannah, GA 31419-1997

Telephone: 912-925-5275 or toll-free 800-633-2349 **Fax:** 912-921-5462

Getting in Last Year 1,407 applied; 66% were accepted; 673 enrolled (73%).

Financial Matters $2392 resident tuition and fees (2002–03); $8422 nonresident tuition and fees (2002–03); $4608 room only; 90% average percent of need met; $6625 average financial aid amount received per undergraduate (2001–02).

Academics Armstrong awards associate, bachelor's, and master's degrees. Challenging opportunities include advanced placement credit, an honors program, double majors, independent study, and a senior project. Special programs include cooperative education, internships, summer session for credit, off-campus study, study-abroad, and Army and Navy ROTC. The most frequently chosen baccalaureate fields are health professions and related sciences, education, and liberal arts/general studies. The faculty at Armstrong has 229 full-time members, 67% with terminal degrees. The student-faculty ratio is 16:1.

Students of Armstrong The student body totals 6,026, of whom 5,213 are undergraduates. 67.9% are women and 32.1% are men. Students come from 48 states and territories and 66 other countries. 92% are from Georgia. 1.8% are international students. 61% returned for their sophomore year.

Applying Armstrong requires SAT I or ACT, a high school transcript, and proof of immunization, and in some cases SAT II Subject Tests. Application deadline: 7/1; 3/15 priority date for financial aid. Early and deferred admission are possible.

ART ACADEMY OF CINCINNATI

Cincinnati, OH

Urban setting ■ *Private* ■ *Independent* ■ *Coed*

Web site: www.artacademy.edu

Contact: Ms. Mary Jane Zumwalde, Director of Admissions, 1125 Saint Gregory Street, Cincinnati, OH 45202

Telephone: 513-562-8744 or toll-free 800-323-5692 (in-state) **Fax:** 513-562-8778

E-mail: admissions@artacademy.edu

Getting in Last Year 99 applied; 73% were accepted; 38 enrolled (53%).

Financial Matters $16,550 tuition and fees (2002–03); 67% average percent of need met; $10,735 average financial aid amount received per undergraduate.

Academics Art Academy of Cincinnati awards associate, bachelor's, and master's degrees. Challenging opportunities include advanced placement credit, student-designed majors, double majors, independent study, and a senior project. Special programs include internships, summer session for credit, off-campus study, and study-abroad. The most frequently chosen baccalaureate field is visual/performing arts. The faculty at Art Academy of Cincinnati has 17 full-time members, 88% with terminal degrees. The student-faculty ratio is 12:1.

Students of Art Academy of Cincinnati The student body totals 207, of whom 188 are undergraduates. 49.5% are women and 50.5% are men. Students come from 14 states and territories and 3 other countries. 79% are from Ohio. 1.6% are international students. 84% returned for their sophomore year.

Applying Art Academy of Cincinnati requires an essay, SAT I or ACT, a high school transcript, an interview, 1 recommendation, portfolio, and a minimum high school GPA of 2.5. Application deadline: 6/30; 3/1 priority date for financial aid. Deferred admission is possible.

ART CENTER COLLEGE OF DESIGN

Pasadena, CA

Suburban setting ■ *Private* ■ *Independent* ■ *Coed*

Web site: www.artcenter.edu

Contact: Ms. Kit Baron, Vice President of Student Services, 1700 Lida Street, Pasadena, CA 91103-1999

Telephone: 626-396-2373 **Fax:** 626-795-0578

E-mail: admissions@artcenter.edu

Getting in Last Year 1,120 applied; 66% were accepted; 31 enrolled (4%).

Financial Matters $22,148 tuition and fees (2002–03); $18,675 average financial aid amount received per undergraduate.

Academics Art Center awards bachelor's and master's degrees. Challenging opportunities include advanced placement credit, accelerated degree programs, and independent study. Special programs include internships and summer session for credit. The most frequently chosen baccalaureate field is visual/performing arts. The faculty at Art Center has 66 full-time members. The student-faculty ratio is 12:1.

Students of Art Center The student body totals 1,505, of whom 1,406 are undergraduates. 41.3% are women and 58.7% are men. Students come from 43 states and territories and 36 other countries. 80% are from California. 17% are international students. 94% returned for their sophomore year.

Applying Art Center requires an essay, a high school transcript, and portfolio, and in some cases SAT I or ACT. The school recommends an interview and a minimum high school GPA of 3.0. Application deadline: rolling admissions; 3/1 priority date for financial aid. Deferred admission is possible.

THE ART INSTITUTE OF BOSTON AT LESLEY UNIVERSITY

Boston, MA

Urban setting ■ *Private* ■ *Independent* ■ *Coed*

Web site: www.aiboston.edu

Contact: Mr. Bradford White, Director of Admissions, 700 Beacon Street, Boston, MA 02215-2598

Telephone: 617-585-6700 or toll-free 800-773-0494 (in-state) **Fax:** 617-437-1226

E-mail: admissions@aiboston.edu

Getting in Last Year 480 applied; 60% were accepted; 116 enrolled (41%).

Financial Matters $15,710 tuition and fees (2002–03); $9200 room and board.

Academics AIB awards bachelor's and master's degrees and post-bachelor's certificates. Challenging opportunities include advanced placement credit, accelerated degree programs, an honors program, double majors, independent study, and a senior project. Special programs include internships, summer session for credit, off-campus study, and study-abroad. The most frequently chosen baccalaureate field is visual/performing arts. The faculty at AIB has 24 full-time members, 83% with terminal degrees. The student-faculty ratio is 9:1.

Students of AIB The student body totals 542, of whom 519 are undergraduates. 56.1% are women and 43.9% are men. Students come from 26 states and territories and 28 other countries. 61% are from Massachusetts. 11.1% are international students. 85% returned for their sophomore year.

Applying AIB requires an essay, a high school transcript, an interview, and portfolio, and in some cases SAT I or ACT. The school recommends recommendations and a minimum high school GPA of 2.0. Application deadline: rolling admissions; 3/12 priority date for financial aid. Deferred admission is possible.

THE ART INSTITUTE OF CALIFORNIA–SAN DIEGO

San Diego, CA

Urban setting ■ *Private* ■ *Proprietary* ■ *Coed*

Web site: www.aica.artinstitutes.edu

Contact: Ms. Sandy Park, Director of Admissions, 7650 Mission Valley Road, San Diego, CA 92108

Telephone: 858-598-1399 ext. 1208 or toll-free 800-279-2422 ext. 3117 (in-state) **Fax:** 619-291-3206

E-mail: info@aii.edu

Getting in Last Year 172 enrolled.

Financial Matters $16,464 tuition and fees (2002–03); $5850 room only.

Academics The Art Institute of California–San Diego awards associate and bachelor's degrees. Challenging opportunities include double majors and a senior project. Special programs include cooperative education, internships, and summer session for credit. The most frequently chosen baccalaureate fields are communications/communication technologies and visual/performing arts. The faculty at The Art Institute of California–San Diego has 17 full-time members. The student-faculty ratio is 22:1.

Students of The Art Institute of California–San Diego The student body is made up of 800 undergraduates. 38.8% are women and 61.2% are men. Students come from 13 states and territories and 39 other countries. 91% are from California. 5.8% are international students. 85% returned for their sophomore year.

Applying The Art Institute of California–San Diego requires an essay, a high school transcript, and an interview. Application deadline: rolling admissions. Deferred admission is possible.

THE ART INSTITUTE OF CALIFORNIA–SAN FRANCISCO

San Francisco, CA

Urban setting ■ *Private* ■ *Independent* ■ *Coed*

Web site: www.aicasf.aii.edu

Contact: Admissions Department, 1170 Market Street, San Francisco, CA 94102-4908

Telephone: 415-865-0198 or toll-free 888-493-3261

Financial Matters $16,614 tuition and fees (2002–03).

Academics The Art Institute of California–San Francisco awards associate and bachelor's degrees. Challenging opportunities include accelerated degree programs and a senior project. Special programs include internships and summer session for credit. The faculty at The Art Institute of California–San Francisco has 5 full-time members. The student-faculty ratio is 16:1.

The Art Institute of California–San Francisco (continued)

Students of The Art Institute of California–San Francisco The student body is made up of 507 undergraduates.

Applying The Art Institute of California–San Francisco requires an essay and a high school transcript. The school recommends an interview, 2 recommendations, and a minimum high school GPA of 2.0. Application deadline: rolling admissions; 3/2 priority date for financial aid. Deferred admission is possible.

THE ART INSTITUTE OF COLORADO

Denver, CO

Urban setting ■ Private ■ Proprietary ■ Coed

Web site: www.aic.artinstitutes.edu
Contact: Ms. Barbara Browning, Vice President and Director of Admissions, 1200 Lincoln Street, Denver, CO 80203
Telephone: 303-837-0825 ext. 4729 or toll-free 800-275-2420
Fax: 303-860-8520
E-mail: aicinfo@aii.edu

Getting in Last Year 1,146 enrolled.

Financial Matters $15,840 tuition and fees (2002–03); $5760 room and board.

Academics The Art Institute of Colorado awards associate and bachelor's degrees. Challenging opportunities include advanced placement credit, independent study, and a senior project. Special programs include internships and study-abroad. The faculty at The Art Institute of Colorado has 65 full-time members, 22% with terminal degrees. The student-faculty ratio is 20:1.

Students of The Art Institute of Colorado The student body is made up of 2,219 undergraduates. 43.8% are women and 56.2% are men. Students come from 49 states and territories and 22 other countries. 50% are from Colorado. 65% returned for their sophomore year.

Applying The Art Institute of Colorado requires an essay, a high school transcript, and an interview. Application deadline: rolling admissions. Early and deferred admission are possible.

THE ART INSTITUTE OF PHOENIX

Phoenix, AZ

Suburban setting ■ Private ■ Proprietary ■ Coed

Web site: www.aipx.edu
Contact: Ms. Valerie Chaparro, Director of Admissions, 2233 West Dunlap Avenue, Phoenix, AZ 85021-2859
Telephone: 602-678-4300 ext. 102 or toll-free 800-474-2479 **Fax:** 602-216-0439
E-mail: smithda@aii.edu

Getting in Last Year 432 enrolled (100%).

Financial Matters $14,640 tuition and fees (2002–03); $5595 room only.

Academics AIPX awards associate and bachelor's degrees. Challenging opportunities include advanced placement credit, an honors program, independent study, and a senior project. Special programs include cooperative education and internships. The faculty at AIPX has 31 full-time members. The student-faculty ratio is 20:1.

Students of AIPX The student body is made up of 1,218 undergraduates. 37.5% are women and 62.5% are men. Students come from 41 states and territories and 12 other countries. 56% are from Arizona. 0.2% are international students.

Applying AIPX requires an essay, a high school transcript, and an interview. The school recommends SAT I or ACT and a minimum high school GPA of 2.0. Application deadline: rolling admissions.

THE ART INSTITUTE OF PORTLAND

Portland, OR

Urban setting ■ Private ■ Proprietary ■ Coed

Web site: www.aipd.artinstitutes.edu
Contact: Ms. Kelly Alston, Director of Admissions, 1122 NW Davis Street, Portland, OR 97209
Telephone: 503-228-6528 ext. 139 or toll-free 888-228-6528 **Fax:** 503-525-8331
E-mail: aipdadm@aii.edu

Getting in Last Year 163 enrolled.

Financial Matters $14,445 tuition and fees (2002–03); $5250 room only; 2% average percent of need met; $3578 average financial aid amount received per undergraduate.

Academics AIPD awards associate and bachelor's degrees. Challenging opportunities include advanced placement credit, independent study, and a senior project. Special programs include internships, summer session for credit, and study-abroad. The most frequently chosen baccalaureate fields are visual/performing arts and business/marketing. The faculty at AIPD has 19 full-time members. The student-faculty ratio is 16:1.

Students of AIPD The student body is made up of 1,108 undergraduates. 51.3% are women and 48.7% are men. 3.1% are international students. 56% returned for their sophomore year.

Applying AIPD requires an essay, a high school transcript, and an interview, and in some cases portfolio. The school recommends recommendations. Application deadline: rolling admissions. Deferred admission is possible.

THE ART INSTITUTE OF WASHINGTON

Arlington, VA

Private ■ Proprietary ■ Coed

Web site: www.aiw.artinstitute.edu
Contact: Ms. Ann Marie Drucker, Director of Admissions, 1820 North Fort Myer Drive, Arlington, VA 22209
Telephone: 703-358-9550 or toll-free 877-303-3771

Financial Matters $16,548 tuition and fees (2002–03).

Academics The Art Institute of Washington awards associate and bachelor's degrees. The student-faculty ratio is 20:1.

Applying The Art Institute of Washington requires an essay, a high school transcript, and an interview.

ASBURY COLLEGE

Wilmore, KY

Small-town setting ■ Private ■ Independent Religious ■ Coed

Web site: www.asbury.edu
Contact: Mr. Stan F. Wiggam, Dean of Admissions, 1 Macklem Drive, Wilmore, KY 40390
Telephone: 859-858-3511 ext. 2142 or toll-free 800-888-1818
Fax: 859-858-3921
E-mail: admissions@asbury.edu

Getting in Last Year 838 applied; 81% were accepted; 323 enrolled (48%).

Financial Matters $15,716 tuition and fees (2002–03); $4078 room and board; 76% average percent of need met; $10,317 average financial aid amount received per undergraduate (2001–02).

Academics Asbury College awards bachelor's and master's degrees. Challenging opportunities include advanced placement credit, double majors, independent study, and a senior project. Special programs include internships, summer session for credit, study-abroad, and Army and Air Force ROTC. The most frequently chosen baccalaureate fields are English, education, and psychology. The faculty at Asbury College has 92 full-time members, 75% with terminal degrees. The student-faculty ratio is 11:1.

Students of Asbury College The student body totals 1,314, of whom 1,271 are undergraduates. 59.7% are women and 40.3% are men. Students come from 41 states and territories and 10 other countries. 29% are from Kentucky. 1.1% are international students. 81% returned for their sophomore year.

Applying Asbury College requires an essay, SAT I or ACT, a high school transcript, 3 recommendations, and a minimum high school GPA of 2.5, and in some cases an interview. Application deadline: rolling admissions; 7/30 for financial aid, with a 3/1 priority date. Early and deferred admission are possible.

ASHLAND UNIVERSITY

Ashland, OH

Small-town setting ■ Private ■ Independent Religious ■ Coed

Web site: www.ashland.edu
Contact: Mr. Thomas Mansperger, Director of Admission, 401 College Avenue, Ashland, OH 44805
Telephone: 419-289-5052 or toll-free 800-882-1548 **Fax:** 419-289-5999
E-mail: auadmsn@ashland.edu

Getting in Last Year 1,820 applied; 88% were accepted; 560 enrolled (35%).

Financial Matters $17,270 tuition and fees (2002–03); $6212 room and board; 90% average percent of need met; $15,818 average financial aid amount received per undergraduate.

Academics AU awards associate, bachelor's, master's, doctoral, and first-professional degrees. Challenging opportunities include advanced placement credit, student-designed majors, an honors program, double majors, independent study, and a senior project. Special programs include internships, summer session for credit, off-campus study, and study-abroad. The most frequently chosen baccalaureate fields are education, business/marketing, and communications/communication technologies. The faculty at AU has 213 full-time members, 83% with terminal degrees. The student-faculty ratio is 16:1.

Students of AU The student body totals 6,430, of whom 2,748 are undergraduates. 58.3% are women and 41.7% are men. Students come from 27 states and territories and 14 other countries. 95% are from Ohio. 1.5% are international students. 74% returned for their sophomore year.

Applying AU requires an essay, SAT I or ACT, a high school transcript, and a minimum high school GPA of 2.5, and in some cases an interview and recommendations. The school recommends an interview. Application deadline: rolling admissions; 3/15 for financial aid. Deferred admission is possible.

ASSUMPTION COLLEGE
Worcester, MA

Urban setting ■ Private ■ Independent Religious ■ Coed

Web site: www.assumption.edu
Contact: Ms. Mary Bresnahan, Dean of Admission, 500 Salisbury Street, Worcester, MA 01609-1296
Telephone: 508-767-7362 or toll-free 888-882-7786 **Fax:** 508-799-4412
E-mail: admiss@assumption.edu

Getting in Last Year 2,764 applied; 77% were accepted; 621 enrolled (29%).

Financial Matters $19,980 tuition and fees (2002–03); $4850 room and board; 78% average percent of need met; $13,958 average financial aid amount received per undergraduate.

Academics Assumption awards bachelor's and master's degrees and post-master's certificates. Challenging opportunities include advanced placement credit, student-designed majors, an honors program, double majors, independent study, and a senior project. Special programs include internships, summer session for credit, off-campus study, and Air Force ROTC. The most frequently chosen baccalaureate fields are business/marketing, health professions and related sciences, and social sciences and history. The faculty at Assumption has 140 full-time members, 94% with terminal degrees. The student-faculty ratio is 13:1.

Students of Assumption The student body totals 2,380, of whom 2,067 are undergraduates. 61% are women and 39% are men. Students come from 23 states and territories. 68% are from Massachusetts. 0.3% are international students. 82% returned for their sophomore year.

Applying Assumption requires an essay, SAT I or ACT, a high school transcript, and 1 recommendation. The school recommends an interview. Application deadline: 3/1; 2/28 priority date for financial aid. Deferred admission is possible.

ATHABASCA UNIVERSITY
Athabasca, AB Canada

Small-town setting ■ Public ■ Coed

Web site: www.athabascau.ca
Contact: Ms. Teresa Wylie, Assistant Registrar, Admissions, 1 University Drive, Athabasca, AB T9S 3A3
Telephone: 780-675-6377 or toll-free 800-788-9041 **Fax:** 780-675-6437
E-mail: inquire@athabascau.ca

Getting in Last Year 4,228 enrolled.

Financial Matters $4960 resident tuition and fees (2002–03); $5660 nonresident tuition and fees (2002–03).

Academics AU awards bachelor's and master's degrees (offers only external degree programs). Challenging opportunities include advanced placement credit, accelerated degree programs, student-designed majors, and a senior project. Special programs include cooperative education, summer session for credit, off-campus study, and study-abroad. The most frequently chosen baccalaureate fields are business/marketing, health professions and related sciences, and psychology. The faculty at AU has 104 full-time members.

Students of AU The student body totals 26,350, of whom 23,955 are undergraduates. Students come from 13 states and territories and 54 other countries. 51% are from Alberta.

Applying AU requires a high school transcript. Application deadline: rolling admissions.

ATHENS STATE UNIVERSITY
Athens, AL

Small-town setting ■ Public ■ State-supported ■ Coed

Web site: www.athens.edu
Contact: Ms. Necedah Henderson, Coordinator of Admissions, 300 North Beaty Street, Athens, AL 35611-1902
Telephone: 256-233-8217 or toll-free 800-522-0272 **Fax:** 256-233-6565
E-mail: henden@athens.edu

Getting in Last Year 530 applied; 80% were accepted.

Financial Matters $3090 resident tuition and fees (2002–03); $5940 nonresident tuition and fees (2002–03); $900 room only.

Academics Athens State University awards bachelor's degrees. Challenging opportunities include advanced placement credit, double majors, independent study, and a senior project. Special programs include cooperative education, internships, summer session for credit, off-campus study, and study-abroad. The most frequently chosen baccalaureate fields are education, computer/information sciences, and protective services/public administration. The faculty at Athens State University has 66 full-time members, 71% with terminal degrees. The student-faculty ratio is 23:1.

Students of Athens State University The student body is made up of 2,528 undergraduates. 66.3% are women and 33.7% are men. Students come from 4 states and territories and 9 other countries. 95% are from Alabama. 0.5% are international students.

Applying Deferred admission is possible.

ATLANTA CHRISTIAN COLLEGE
East Point, GA

Suburban setting ■ Private ■ Independent Religious ■ Coed

Web site: www.acc.edu
Contact: Mr. Keith Wagner, Director of Admissions, 2605 Ben Hill Road, East Point, GA 30344-1999
Telephone: 404-761-8861 or toll-free 800-776-1ACC **Fax:** 404-669-2024
E-mail: admissions@acc.edu

Getting in Last Year 286 applied; 76% were accepted; 69 enrolled (32%).

Financial Matters $10,450 tuition and fees (2002–03); $3950 room and board.

Academics ACC awards associate and bachelor's degrees. Challenging opportunities include advanced placement credit, double majors, and independent study. Special programs include internships and summer session for credit. The faculty at ACC has 23 full-time members, 52% with terminal degrees. The student-faculty ratio is 16:1.

Students of ACC The student body is made up of 390 undergraduates. 53.3% are women and 46.7% are men. Students come from 13 states and territories. 88% are from Georgia.

Applying ACC requires SAT I or ACT, a high school transcript, 2 recommendations, medical history, and a minimum high school GPA of 2.0. Application deadline: 8/1; 3/15 priority date for financial aid. Early and deferred admission are possible.

ATLANTA COLLEGE OF ART
Atlanta, GA

Urban setting ■ Private ■ Independent ■ Coed

Web site: www.aca.edu
Contact: Ms. Lucy Leusch, Vice President of Enrollment Management, 1280 Peachtree Street, NE, Atlanta, GA 30309
Telephone: 404-733-5101 or toll-free 800-832-2104 **Fax:** 404-733-5107
E-mail: acainfo@woodruffcenter.org

Getting in Last Year 240 applied; 63% were accepted; 59 enrolled (39%).

Financial Matters $15,900 tuition and fees (2002–03); $4700 room only; 63% average percent of need met; $11,701 average financial aid amount received per undergraduate.

Academics ACA awards bachelor's degrees. Challenging opportunities include advanced placement credit, student-designed majors, independent study, and a senior project. Special programs include internships, summer session for credit, off-campus study, and study-abroad. The most frequently chosen baccalaureate field is visual/performing arts. The faculty at ACA has 24 full-time members. The student-faculty ratio is 12:1.

Students of ACA The student body is made up of 339 undergraduates. 52.5% are women and 47.5% are men. Students come from 30 states and territories and 17 other countries. 50% are from Georgia. 5.6% are international students. 66% returned for their sophomore year.

Applying ACA requires an essay, SAT I or ACT, a high school transcript, portfolio, and a minimum high school GPA of 2.0, and in some cases recommendations. The school recommends an interview and recommendations. Application deadline: rolling admissions; 3/15 priority date for financial aid. Deferred admission is possible.

ATLANTIC BAPTIST UNIVERSITY
Moncton, NB Canada

Urban setting ■ Private ■ Independent Religious ■ Coed

Web site: www.abu.nb.ca
Contact: Ms. Jennifer Clarke, Assistant for Student Recruitment, Box 6004, Moncton, NB E1C 9L7 Canada
Telephone: 506-858-8970 ext. 6434 or toll-free 888-YOU-N-ABU **Fax:** 506-858-9694
E-mail: admissions@abu.nb.ca

Getting in Last Year 270 enrolled.

Financial Matters $5330 tuition and fees (2002–03); $4500 room and board.

Academics ABU awards bachelor's degrees. Challenging opportunities include accelerated degree programs, an honors program, double majors, and a senior project. Special programs include cooperative education, internships, summer session for credit, and study-abroad. The most frequently chosen baccalaureate fields are communications/communication technologies, social sciences and history, and psychology. The faculty at ABU has 24 full-time members, 63% with terminal degrees. The student-faculty ratio is 17:1.

Students of ABU The student body is made up of 574 undergraduates. 71.1% are women and 28.9% are men. Students come from 11 states and territories and 3 other countries. 24% are from New Brunswick. 91% returned for their sophomore year.

Applying ABU requires an essay, a high school transcript, and 3 recommendations, and in some cases an interview. Application deadline: rolling admissions; 5/15 for financial aid. Deferred admission is possible.

ATLANTIC UNION COLLEGE

South Lancaster, MA

Small-town setting ■ Private ■ Independent Religious ■ Coed

Web site: www.atlanticuc.edu
Contact: Mrs. Rosita Lashley, Associate Director for Admissions, PO Box 1000, South Lancaster, MA 01561
Telephone: 978-368-2239 or toll-free 800-282-2030 **Fax:** 978-368-2015
E-mail: enroll@math.atlanticuc.edu

Getting in Last Year 621 applied; 19% were accepted; 83 enrolled (70%).

Financial Matters $13,960 tuition and fees (2002–03); $4788 room and board; 83% average percent of need met; $12,500 average financial aid amount received per undergraduate.

Academics AUC awards associate, bachelor's, and master's degrees. Challenging opportunities include advanced placement credit, freshman honors college, an honors program, and a senior project. Special programs include cooperative education, internships, summer session for credit, and study-abroad. The most frequently chosen baccalaureate fields are business/marketing, health professions and related sciences, and psychology. The faculty at AUC has 45 full-time members, 56% with terminal degrees. The student-faculty ratio is 13:1.

Students of AUC The student body totals 671, of whom 638 are undergraduates. 62.2% are women and 37.8% are men. Students come from 15 states and territories and 18 other countries. 55% are from Massachusetts. 8.7% are international students. 75% returned for their sophomore year.

Applying AUC requires ACT, a high school transcript, 2 recommendations, and a minimum high school GPA of 2.0, and in some cases an essay and an interview. The school recommends SAT I. Application deadline: 8/1; 4/15 priority date for financial aid.

AUBURN UNIVERSITY

Auburn University, AL

Small-town setting ■ Public ■ State-supported ■ Coed

Web site: www.auburn.edu
Contact: Dr. John Fletcher, Acting Assistant Vice President of Enrollment Management, 202 Mary Martin Hall, Auburn University, AL 36849-0001
Telephone: 334-844-4080 or toll-free 800-AUBURN9
E-mail: admissions@mail.auburn.edu

Getting in Last Year 13,264 applied; 83% were accepted; 4,184 enrolled (38%).

Financial Matters $3784 resident tuition and fees (2002–03); $11,084 nonresident tuition and fees (2002–03); $2216 room only; 51% average percent of need met; $6400 average financial aid amount received per undergraduate (2001–02).

Academics Auburn awards bachelor's, master's, doctoral, and first-professional degrees and post-master's certificates. Challenging opportunities include advanced placement credit, accelerated degree programs, an honors program, double majors, independent study, and a senior project. Special programs include cooperative education, internships, summer session for credit, study-abroad, and Army, Navy and Air Force ROTC. The most frequently chosen baccalaureate fields are business/marketing, engineering/engineering technologies, and education. The faculty at Auburn has 1,142 full-time members, 92% with terminal degrees. The student-faculty ratio is 16:1.

Students of Auburn The student body totals 23,276, of whom 19,603 are undergraduates. 47.9% are women and 52.1% are men. Students come from 54 states and territories and 61 other countries. 69% are from Alabama. 0.8% are international students. 81% returned for their sophomore year.

Applying Auburn requires SAT I or ACT, a high school transcript, and a minimum high school GPA of 2.0, and in some cases a minimum high school GPA of 3.0. Application deadline: 8/1; 3/1 priority date for financial aid. Early and deferred admission are possible.

AUBURN UNIVERSITY MONTGOMERY

Montgomery, AL

Suburban setting ■ Public ■ State-supported ■ Coed

Web site: www.aum.edu
Contact: Ms. Valerie Samuel, Assistant Director, Enrollment Services, PO Box 244023, Montgomery, AL 36124-4023
Telephone: 334-244-3667 or toll-free 800-227-2649 (in-state) **Fax:** 334-244-3795
E-mail: auminfo@mickey.aum.edu

Getting in Last Year 708 enrolled.

Financial Matters $3620 resident tuition and fees (2002–03); $10,400 nonresident tuition and fees (2002–03); $4610 room and board.

Academics AUM awards bachelor's, master's, and doctoral degrees. Challenging opportunities include advanced placement credit, accelerated degree programs, student-designed majors, an honors program, double majors, independent study, and a senior project. Special programs include cooperative education, internships, summer session for credit, off-campus study, study-abroad, and Army and Air Force ROTC. The most frequently chosen baccalaureate fields are business/marketing, education, and protective services/public administration. The faculty at AUM has 179 full-time members, 82% with terminal degrees. The student-faculty ratio is 16:1.

Students of AUM The student body totals 5,104, of whom 4,329 are undergraduates. 62.7% are women and 37.3% are men. Students come from 35 states and territories and 20 other countries. 97% are from Alabama. 0.9% are international students.

Applying AUM requires SAT I or ACT and a high school transcript. Application deadline: rolling admissions; 3/1 priority date for financial aid. Deferred admission is possible.

AUGSBURG COLLEGE

Minneapolis, MN

Urban setting ■ Private ■ Independent Religious ■ Coed

Web site: www.augsburg.edu
Contact: Ms. Sally Daniels, Director of Undergraduate Day Admissions, 2211 Riverside Avenue, Minneapolis, MN 55454-1351
Telephone: 612-330-1001 or toll-free 800-788-5678 **Fax:** 612-330-1590
E-mail: admissions@augsburg.edu

Getting in Last Year 856 applied; 80% were accepted; 352 enrolled (51%).

Financial Matters $18,193 tuition and fees (2002–03); $5690 room and board; 77% average percent of need met; $12,808 average financial aid amount received per undergraduate (2001–02).

Academics Augsburg awards bachelor's and master's degrees and post-bachelor's certificates. Challenging opportunities include advanced placement credit, student-designed majors, freshman honors college, an honors program, double majors, independent study, and a senior project. Special programs include cooperative education, internships, summer session for credit, off-campus study, study-abroad, and Army, Navy and Air Force ROTC. The most frequently chosen baccalaureate fields are business/marketing, education, and social sciences and history. The faculty at Augsburg has 147 full-time members, 80% with terminal degrees. The student-faculty ratio is 14:1.

Students of Augsburg The student body totals 2,994, of whom 2,763 are undergraduates. 57.7% are women and 42.3% are men. Students come from 42 states and territories and 35 other countries. 90% are from Minnesota. 1.5% are international students. 76% returned for their sophomore year.

Applying Augsburg requires an essay, SAT I or ACT, a high school transcript, an interview, and a minimum high school GPA of 2.5, and in some cases 2 recommendations. Application deadline: 8/15; 4/15 for financial aid. Deferred admission is possible.

AUGUSTANA COLLEGE

Rock Island, IL

Suburban setting ■ Private ■ Independent Religious ■ Coed

Web site: www.augustana.edu
Contact: Mr. Martin Sauer, Director of Admissions, 639 38th Street, Rock Island, IL 61201-2296
Telephone: 309-794-7341 or toll-free 800-798-8100 **Fax:** 309-794-7422
E-mail: admissions@augustana.edu

Getting in Last Year 2,744 applied; 74% were accepted; 602 enrolled (30%).

Financial Matters $19,608 tuition and fees (2002–03); $5586 room and board; 88% average percent of need met; $15,068 average financial aid amount received per undergraduate.

Academics Augie awards bachelor's degrees. Challenging opportunities include advanced placement credit, accelerated degree programs, an honors program, double majors, independent study, and a senior project. Special programs include internships, summer session for credit, and study-abroad. The most frequently chosen baccalaureate fields are biological/life sciences, business/marketing, and health professions and related sciences. The faculty at Augie has 142 full-time members, 90% with terminal degrees. The student-faculty ratio is 12:1.

Students of Augie The student body is made up of 2,261 undergraduates. 56.7% are women and 43.3% are men. Students come from 26 states and territories and 19 other countries. 87% are from Illinois. 1.1% are international students. 87% returned for their sophomore year.

Applying Augie requires SAT I or ACT and a high school transcript, and in some cases an essay, an interview, and 2 recommendations. Application deadline: rolling admissions; 4/1 priority date for financial aid. Deferred admission is possible.

AUGUSTANA COLLEGE

Sioux Falls, SD

Urban setting ■ Private ■ Independent Religious ■ Coed

Web site: www.augie.edu
Contact: Mr. Robert Preloger, Vice President for Enrollment, 2001 South Summit Avenue, Sioux Falls, SD 57197
Telephone: 605-274-5516 ext. 5504 or toll-free 800-727-2844 ext. 5516 (in-state), 800-727-2844 (out-of-state) **Fax:** 605-274-5518

E-mail: info@augie.edu

Getting in Last Year 1,534 applied; 79% were accepted; 455 enrolled (38%).

Financial Matters $16,088 tuition and fees (2002–03); $4668 room and board; 91% average percent of need met; $13,811 average financial aid amount received per undergraduate.

Academics Augustana awards bachelor's and master's degrees. Challenging opportunities include advanced placement credit, accelerated degree programs, student-designed majors, an honors program, double majors, independent study, and a senior project. Special programs include cooperative education, internships, summer session for credit, off-campus study, and study-abroad. The most frequently chosen baccalaureate fields are business/marketing, education, and health professions and related sciences. The faculty at Augustana has 108 full-time members, 92% with terminal degrees. The student-faculty ratio is 12:1.

Students of Augustana The student body totals 1,834, of whom 1,804 are undergraduates. 64% are women and 36% are men. Students come from 30 states and territories. 50% are from South Dakota. 1.8% are international students. 76% returned for their sophomore year.

Applying Augustana requires SAT I or ACT, a high school transcript, 1 recommendation, minimum ACT score of 20, and a minimum high school GPA of 2.5, and in some cases an essay. The school recommends an interview. Application deadline: 8/1; 3/1 priority date for financial aid. Deferred admission is possible.

AUGUSTANA UNIVERSITY COLLEGE

Camrose, AB Canada

Small-town setting ■ Public ■ Coed

Web site: www.augustana.ab.ca

Contact: Mr. Tim Hanson, Director of Admissions, 4901-46 Ave, Camrose, AB T4V 2R3

Telephone: 780-649-1135 ext. 1135 or toll-free 800-661-8714

E-mail: admissions@augustana.ab.ca

Getting in Last Year 888 applied; 80% were accepted; 369 enrolled (52%).

Financial Matters $5460 tuition and fees (2002–03).

Academics Augustana University College awards bachelor's degrees. Challenging opportunities include advanced placement credit, double majors, and independent study. The faculty at Augustana University College has 55 full-time members, 76% with terminal degrees. The student-faculty ratio is 15:1.

Students of Augustana University College The student body is made up of 1,018 undergraduates. 57.4% are women and 42.6% are men. Students come from 11 states and territories and 23 other countries. 76% are from Alberta. 40% returned for their sophomore year.

Applying Augustana University College requires a high school transcript and a minimum high school GPA of 2.0, and in some cases SAT II Subject Tests, SAT II: Writing Test, and SAT I and SAT II or ACT. Application deadline: 8/1; 7/15 for financial aid. Early and deferred admission are possible.

AUGUSTA STATE UNIVERSITY

Augusta, GA

Urban setting ■ Public ■ State-supported ■ Coed

Web site: www.aug.edu

Contact: Catherine R. Tuthill, 2500 Walton Way, Augusta, GA 30904-2200

Telephone: 706-737-1400 or toll-free 800-341-4373 **Fax:** 706-667-4355

E-mail: admissions@ac.edu

Getting in Last Year 1,680 applied; 66% were accepted; 843 enrolled (76%).

Financial Matters $2384 resident tuition and fees (2002–03); $8414 nonresident tuition and fees (2002–03); $6986 room and board; 70% average percent of need met; $7073 average financial aid amount received per undergraduate (2001–02).

Academics Augusta State University awards associate, bachelor's, and master's degrees and post-master's certificates. Challenging opportunities include advanced placement credit, an honors program, double majors, and independent study. Special programs include cooperative education, internships, summer session for credit, off-campus study, study-abroad, and Army ROTC. The most frequently chosen baccalaureate fields are business/marketing, education, and social sciences and history. The faculty at Augusta State University has 194 full-time members, 70% with terminal degrees. The student-faculty ratio is 19:1.

Students of Augusta State University The student body totals 5,884, of whom 5,041 are undergraduates. 65.1% are women and 34.9% are men. Students come from 34 states and territories and 59 other countries. 89% are from Georgia. 1.1% are international students. 49% returned for their sophomore year.

Applying Augusta State University requires SAT I or ACT, a high school transcript, and a minimum high school GPA of 2.0. Application deadline: 7/21; 5/1 for financial aid, with a 4/15 priority date. Early and deferred admission are possible.

AURORA UNIVERSITY

Aurora, IL

Suburban setting ■ Private ■ Independent ■ Coed

Web site: www.aurora.edu

Contact: Mr. James Lancaster, Freshman Recruitment Coordinator, 347 South Gladstone Avenue, Aurora, IL 60506-4892

Telephone: 630-844-5533 or toll-free 800-742-5281 **Fax:** 630-844-5535

E-mail: admissions@aurora.edu

Getting in Last Year 1,140 applied; 57% were accepted; 294 enrolled (45%).

Financial Matters $13,767 tuition and fees (2002–03); $5133 room and board; 83% average percent of need met; $14,551 average financial aid amount received per undergraduate.

Academics AU awards bachelor's, master's, and doctoral degrees and post-bachelor's and post-master's certificates. Challenging opportunities include advanced placement credit, student-designed majors, double majors, independent study, and a senior project. Special programs include internships, summer session for credit, off-campus study, study-abroad, and Army ROTC. The most frequently chosen baccalaureate fields are business/marketing, education, and protective services/public administration. The faculty at AU has 83 full-time members, 83% with terminal degrees. The student-faculty ratio is 17:1.

Students of AU The student body totals 3,316, of whom 1,446 are undergraduates. 64.9% are women and 35.1% are men. Students come from 14 states and territories. 98% are from Illinois. 76% returned for their sophomore year.

Applying AU requires a high school transcript and a minimum high school GPA of 2.0, and in some cases an essay, an interview, and 2 recommendations. The school recommends an essay, SAT I and SAT II or ACT, and an interview. Application deadline: rolling admissions; 4/15 priority date for financial aid. Early and deferred admission are possible.

AUSTIN COLLEGE

Sherman, TX

Suburban setting ■ Private ■ Independent Religious ■ Coed

Web site: www.austincollege.edu

Contact: Ms. Nan Massingill, Vice President for Institutional Enrollment, 900 North Grand Avenue, Suite 6N, Sherman, TX 75090-4400

Telephone: 903-813-3000 or toll-free 800-442-5363 **Fax:** 903-813-3198

E-mail: admission@austincollege.edu

Getting in Last Year 1,140 applied; 78% were accepted; 348 enrolled (39%).

Financial Matters $16,537 tuition and fees (2002–03); $6234 room and board; 95% average percent of need met; $16,704 average financial aid amount received per undergraduate.

Academics AC awards bachelor's and master's degrees. Challenging opportunities include advanced placement credit, student-designed majors, an honors program, double majors, independent study, and a senior project. Special programs include internships, summer session for credit, off-campus study, and study-abroad. The most frequently chosen baccalaureate fields are business/marketing, social sciences and history, and biological/life sciences. The faculty at AC has 88 full-time members, 99% with terminal degrees. The student-faculty ratio is 13:1.

Students of AC The student body totals 1,281, of whom 1,241 are undergraduates. 56.2% are women and 43.8% are men. Students come from 28 states and territories and 21 other countries. 90% are from Texas. 2.2% are international students. 83% returned for their sophomore year.

Applying AC requires an essay, SAT I or ACT, a high school transcript, and 2 recommendations, and in some cases an interview. The school recommends an interview and a minimum high school GPA of 3.0. Application deadline: 8/15; 4/1 priority date for financial aid. Early and deferred admission are possible.

AUSTIN GRADUATE SCHOOL OF THEOLOGY

Austin, TX

Urban setting ■ Private ■ Independent Religious ■ Coed

Web site: www.austingrad.edu

Contact: Ms. Laura Najera, Director of Admissions, 1909 University Avenue, Austin, TX 78705

Telephone: 512-476-2772 ext. 200 or toll-free 866-AUS-GRAD (in-state) **Fax:** 512-476-3919

E-mail: registrar@austingrad.edu

Financial Matters $3600 tuition and fees (2002–03).

Academics Austin Graduate School of Theology awards bachelor's and master's degrees. Advanced placement credit is a challenging opportunity. Summer session for credit is a special program. The faculty at Austin Graduate School of Theology has 5 full-time members, 100% with terminal degrees. The student-faculty ratio is 8:1.

Students of Austin Graduate School of Theology The student body totals 78, of whom 41 are undergraduates. 29.3% are women and 70.7% are men. Students come from 2 states and territories and 1 other country. 68% are from Texas.

Applying Austin Graduate School of Theology requires (in some cases) SAT I or ACT.

AUSTIN PEAY STATE UNIVERSITY

Clarksville, TN

Suburban setting ■ Public ■ State-supported ■ Coed

Contact: Mr. Scott McDonald, Director of Admissions, PO Box 4548, Clarksville, TN 37044-4548

Telephone: 931-221-7661 or toll-free 800-844-2778 (out-of-state)
Fax: 931-221-6168

E-mail: admissions@apsu01.apsu.edu

Getting in Last Year 2,912 applied; 45% were accepted; 1,198 enrolled (91%).

Financial Matters $3446 resident tuition and fees (2002–03); $10,404 nonresident tuition and fees (2002–03); $3820 room and board; 74% average percent of need met; $3882 average financial aid amount received per undergraduate.

Academics Austin Peay awards associate, bachelor's, and master's degrees and post-master's certificates. Challenging opportunities include advanced placement credit, an honors program, double majors, and independent study. Special programs include internships, summer session for credit, study-abroad, and Army ROTC. The most frequently chosen baccalaureate fields are business/marketing, interdisciplinary studies, and health professions and related sciences. The faculty at Austin Peay has 266 full-time members, 89% with terminal degrees. The student-faculty ratio is 18:1.

Students of Austin Peay The student body totals 7,482, of whom 7,057 are undergraduates. 61.4% are women and 38.6% are men. Students come from 36 states and territories. 0.2% are international students. 64% returned for their sophomore year.

Applying Austin Peay requires SAT I or ACT, a high school transcript, and 2.75 high school GPA, minimum ACT composite score of 19. Application deadline: 8/15; 4/1 priority date for financial aid. Early and deferred admission are possible.

AVE MARIA COLLEGE

Ypsilanti, MI

Private ■ Independent Religious ■ Coed

Web site: www.avemaria.edu

Contact: Admissions Office Manager, 300 West Forest Avenue, Ypsilanti, MI 48197

Telephone: 734-337-4545 or toll-free 866-866-3030 **Fax:** 734-337-4140

E-mail: admissions@avemaria.edu

Getting in Last Year 125 applied; 83% were accepted.

Financial Matters $8570 tuition and fees (2002–03); $5000 room and board; 72% average percent of need met; $6992 average financial aid amount received per undergraduate.

Academics Ave Maria College awards bachelor's degrees. Study-abroad is a special program. The faculty at Ave Maria College has 17 full-time members. The student-faculty ratio is 13:1.

Students of Ave Maria College The student body is made up of 234 undergraduates. Students come from 34 states and territories and 13 other countries. 38% are from Michigan. 21% are international students.

Applying Ave Maria College requires an essay, SAT I or ACT, a high school transcript, 2 recommendations, and a minimum high school GPA of 2.4. The school recommends an interview. Application deadline: 4/15 priority date for financial aid.

AVERETT UNIVERSITY

Danville, VA

Suburban setting ■ Private ■ Independent Religious ■ Coed

Web site: www.averett.edu

Contact: Mr. Gary Sherman, Vice President of Enrollment Management, English Hall, Danville, VA 24541

Telephone: 434-791-5660 or toll-free 800-AVERETT **Fax:** 434-797-2784

E-mail: admit@averett.edu

Getting in Last Year 687 applied; 90% were accepted; 223 enrolled (36%).

Financial Matters $16,800 tuition and fees (2002–03); $5150 room and board; 75% average percent of need met; $13,002 average financial aid amount received per undergraduate.

Academics Averett awards associate, bachelor's, and master's degrees. Challenging opportunities include advanced placement credit, accelerated degree programs, student-designed majors, an honors program, double majors, independent study, and a senior project. Special programs include internships, summer session for credit, off-campus study, and study-abroad. The most frequently chosen baccalaureate fields are business/marketing, education, and social sciences and history. The faculty at Averett has 61 full-time members, 79% with terminal degrees. The student-faculty ratio is 14:1.

Students of Averett The student body totals 2,739, of whom 1,987 are undergraduates. 60.1% are women and 39.9% are men. Students come from 24 states and territories and 17 other countries. 88% are from Virginia. 1.3% are international students. 57% returned for their sophomore year.

Applying Averett requires an essay, SAT I or ACT, a high school transcript, 1 recommendation, and a minimum high school GPA of 2.0. The school recommends an interview. Application deadline: rolling admissions. Early and deferred admission are possible.

AVILA UNIVERSITY

Kansas City, MO

Suburban setting ■ Private ■ Independent Religious ■ Coed

Web site: www.avila.edu

Contact: Ms. Paige Illum, Director of Admissions, 11901 Wornall Rd, Kansas City, MO 64145

Telephone: 816-501-3773 or toll-free 800-GO-AVILA **Fax:** 816-501-2453

E-mail: admissions@mail.avila.edu

Getting in Last Year 743 applied; 48% were accepted; 131 enrolled (36%).

Financial Matters $14,160 tuition and fees (2002–03); $5300 room and board.

Academics Avila awards bachelor's and master's degrees. Challenging opportunities include advanced placement credit, accelerated degree programs, double majors, independent study, and a senior project. Special programs include cooperative education, internships, summer session for credit, off-campus study, study-abroad, and Army ROTC. The most frequently chosen baccalaureate fields are business/marketing, health professions and related sciences, and education. The faculty at Avila has 62 full-time members, 73% with terminal degrees. The student-faculty ratio is 13:1.

Students of Avila The student body totals 1,746, of whom 1,236 are undergraduates. 65.4% are women and 34.6% are men. Students come from 17 states and territories and 24 other countries. 77% are from Missouri. 2.7% are international students. 80% returned for their sophomore year.

Applying Avila requires SAT I or ACT, a high school transcript, and a minimum high school GPA of 2.5, and in some cases an essay and recommendations. The school recommends an interview. Application deadline: rolling admissions. Early admission is possible.

AZUSA PACIFIC UNIVERSITY

Azusa, CA

Small-town setting ■ Private ■ Independent Religious ■ Coed

Web site: www.apu.edu

Contact: Mrs. Deana Porterfield, Dean of Enrollment, 901 East Alosta Avenue, PO Box 7000, Azusa, CA 91702-7000

Telephone: 626-812-3016 or toll-free 800-TALK-APU

E-mail: admissions@apu.edu

Getting in Last Year 2,267 applied; 81% were accepted; 857 enrolled (47%).

Financial Matters $17,594 tuition and fees (2002–03); $5314 room and board; 74% average percent of need met; $8008 average financial aid amount received per undergraduate (2001–02).

Academics APU awards bachelor's, master's, doctoral, and first-professional degrees. Challenging opportunities include advanced placement credit, accelerated degree programs, freshman honors college, an honors program, double majors, and a senior project. Special programs include cooperative education, internships, summer session for credit, off-campus study, study-abroad, and Army ROTC. The most frequently chosen baccalaureate fields are business/marketing, liberal arts/general studies, and education. The faculty at APU has 234 full-time members, 74% with terminal degrees. The student-faculty ratio is 14:1.

Students of APU The student body totals 7,693, of whom 4,059 are undergraduates. 64.6% are women and 35.4% are men. Students come from 45 states and territories and 54 other countries. 81% are from California. 2.3% are international students. 79% returned for their sophomore year.

Applying APU requires an essay, SAT I or ACT, a high school transcript, 2 recommendations, and a minimum high school GPA of 2.5, and in some cases an interview. Application deadline: 7/1; 7/1 for financial aid, with a 3/2 priority date. Early and deferred admission are possible.

BABSON COLLEGE

Babson Park, MA

Suburban setting ■ Private ■ Independent ■ Coed

Web site: www.babson.edu

Contact: Mrs. Monica Inzer, Dean of Undergraduate Admission and Student Financial Services, Mustard Hall, Babson Park, MA 02457-0310

Telephone: 800-488-3696 or toll-free 800-488-3696 **Fax:** 781-239-4006

E-mail: ugradadmission@babson.edu

Getting in Last Year 2,402 applied; 48% were accepted; 402 enrolled (35%).

Financial Matters $26,000 tuition and fees (2002–03); $9676 room and board; 98% average percent of need met; $22,004 average financial aid amount received per undergraduate.

Academics Babson awards bachelor's and master's degrees and post-master's certificates. Challenging opportunities include advanced placement credit, accelerated degree programs, student-designed majors, freshman honors college, an honors program, independent study, and a senior project. Special programs include internships, summer session for credit, off-campus study, and study-abroad. The faculty at Babson has 169 full-time members, 90% with terminal degrees. The student-faculty ratio is 13:1.

Students of Babson The student body totals 3,407, of whom 1,735 are undergraduates. 38.7% are women and 61.3% are men. Students come from 42 states and territories and 64 other countries. 56% are from Massachusetts. 18.8% are international students. 89% returned for their sophomore year.

Applying Babson requires an essay, SAT I or ACT, a high school transcript, and 2 recommendations. The school recommends SAT II: Writing Test and SAT II Subject Test in math. Application deadline: 2/1; 2/15 for financial aid. Deferred admission is possible.

BAKER COLLEGE OF AUBURN HILLS

Auburn Hills, MI

Urban setting ■ Private ■ Independent ■ Coed

Web site: www.baker.edu

Contact: Ms. Jan Bohlen, Vice President for Admissions, 1500 University Drive, Auburn Hills, MI 48326-1586

Telephone: 248-340-0600 or toll-free 888-429-0410 (in-state) **Fax:** 248-340-0608

E-mail: bohlen_j@auburnhills.baker.edu

Getting in Last Year 1,206 applied; 100% were accepted.

Financial Matters $5760 tuition and fees (2002–03).

Academics Baker awards associate and bachelor's degrees and post-bachelor's certificates. Challenging opportunities include advanced placement credit, accelerated degree programs, double majors, and independent study. Special programs include cooperative education, internships, and summer session for credit. The faculty at Baker has 9 full-time members. The student-faculty ratio is 22:1.

Students of Baker The student body is made up of 2,596 undergraduates. 68% are women and 32% are men. Students come from 1 state or territory.

Applying Baker requires a high school transcript. The school recommends SAT I or ACT. Application deadline: rolling admissions. Early and deferred admission are possible.

BAKER COLLEGE OF CADILLAC

Cadillac, MI

Small-town setting ■ Private ■ Independent ■ Coed

Web site: www.baker.edu

Contact: Mr. Mike Tisdale, Director of Admissions, 9600 East 13th Street, Cadillac, MI 49601

Telephone: 616-775-8458 or toll-free 888-313-3463 (in-state), 231-876-3100 (out-of-state) **Fax:** 231-775-8505

E-mail: runstr_e@cadillac.baker.edu

Getting in Last Year 565 applied; 100% were accepted.

Financial Matters $5760 tuition and fees (2002–03).

Academics Baker awards associate and bachelor's degrees. Challenging opportunities include advanced placement credit, double majors, and independent study. Special programs include cooperative education, internships, and summer session for credit. The faculty at Baker has 4 full-time members. The student-faculty ratio is 16:1.

Students of Baker The student body is made up of 1,174 undergraduates. 73% are women and 27% are men. Students come from 4 states and territories. 69% returned for their sophomore year.

Applying Baker requires a high school transcript. The school recommends SAT I or ACT and an interview. Application deadline: rolling admissions. Early and deferred admission are possible.

BAKER COLLEGE OF CLINTON TOWNSHIP

Clinton Township, MI

Urban setting ■ Private ■ Independent ■ Coed

Web site: www.baker.edu

Contact: Ms. Annette M. Looser, Vice President for Admissions, 34950 Little Mack Avenue, Clinton Township, MI 48035

Telephone: 810-791-6610 or toll-free 888-272-2842 **Fax:** 810-791-6611

E-mail: looser_a@mtclemens.baker.edu

Getting in Last Year 2,059 applied; 100% were accepted.

Financial Matters $5760 tuition and fees (2002–03).

Academics Baker awards associate and bachelor's degrees. Advanced placement credit is a challenging opportunity. Special programs include cooperative education, internships, and summer session for credit. The faculty at Baker has 8 full-time members. The student-faculty ratio is 19:1.

Students of Baker The student body is made up of 3,929 undergraduates. 77% are women and 23% are men.

Applying Baker requires a high school transcript. The school recommends SAT I or ACT. Application deadline: rolling admissions. Early and deferred admission are possible.

BAKER COLLEGE OF FLINT

Flint, MI

Urban setting ■ Private ■ Independent ■ Coed

Web site: www.baker.edu

Contact: Mr. Troy Crowe, Vice President for Admissions, 1050 West Bristol Road, Flint, MI 48507-5508

Telephone: 810-766-4015 or toll-free 800-964-4299 **Fax:** 810-766-4049

E-mail: heaton_m@fafl.baker.edu

Getting in Last Year 2,694 applied; 100% were accepted.

Financial Matters $5760 tuition and fees (2002–03); $2175 room only.

Academics Baker awards associate and bachelor's degrees. Challenging opportunities include advanced placement credit, accelerated degree programs, double majors, and independent study. Special programs include cooperative education, internships, and summer session for credit. The faculty at Baker has 26 full-time members. The student-faculty ratio is 37:1.

Students of Baker The student body is made up of 5,291 undergraduates. 69% are women and 31% are men. Students come from 5 states and territories. 99% are from Michigan.

Applying Baker requires a high school transcript. The school recommends SAT I or ACT. Application deadline: 9/20. Early and deferred admission are possible.

BAKER COLLEGE OF JACKSON

Jackson, MI

Urban setting ■ Private ■ Independent ■ Coed

Web site: www.baker.edu

Contact: Ms. Kelli Stepka, Director of Admissions, 2800 Springport Road, Jackson, MI 49202

Telephone: 517-788-7800 or toll-free 888-343-3683 **Fax:** 517-789-7331

E-mail: hoban_k@jackson.baker.edu

Getting in Last Year 620 applied; 100% were accepted.

Financial Matters $5760 tuition and fees (2002–03).

Academics Baker awards associate and bachelor's degrees. Challenging opportunities include advanced placement credit, accelerated degree programs, double majors, and independent study. Special programs include cooperative education, internships, and summer session for credit. The faculty at Baker has 9 full-time members, 11% with terminal degrees. The student-faculty ratio is 13:1.

Students of Baker The student body is made up of 1,392 undergraduates. 75% are women and 25% are men. Students come from 2 states and territories. 99% are from Michigan.

Applying Baker requires a high school transcript. The school recommends SAT I or ACT. Application deadline: 9/19. Early and deferred admission are possible.

BAKER COLLEGE OF MUSKEGON

Muskegon, MI

Suburban setting ■ Private ■ Independent ■ Coed

Web site: www.baker.edu

Contact: Ms. Kathy Jacobson, Vice President of Admissions, 1903 Marquette Avenue, Muskegon, MI 49442-3497

Telephone: 231-777-5207 or toll-free 800-937-0337 (in-state) **Fax:** 231-777-5201

E-mail: jacobs_k@muskegon.baker.edu

Getting in Last Year 1,446 applied; 100% were accepted.

Financial Matters $5760 tuition and fees (2002–03); $2100 room only.

Academics Baker awards associate and bachelor's degrees. Challenging opportunities include advanced placement credit, accelerated degree programs, double majors, and independent study. Special programs include cooperative education, internships, and summer session for credit. The faculty at Baker has 14 full-time members. The student-faculty ratio is 30:1.

Students of Baker The student body is made up of 3,422 undergraduates. 69% are women and 31% are men. Students come from 13 states and territories. 99% are from Michigan.

Applying Baker requires a high school transcript. The school recommends SAT I or ACT. Application deadline: 9/24. Early and deferred admission are possible.

BAKER COLLEGE OF OWOSSO

Owosso, MI

Small-town setting ■ Private ■ Independent ■ Coed

Web site: www.baker.edu

Contact: Mr. Michael Konopacke, Vice President for Admissions, 1020 South Washington Street, Owosso, MI 48867-4400

Baker College of Owosso (continued)

Telephone: 517-729-3353 or toll-free 800-879-3797 **Fax:** 517-729-3359
E-mail: konopa-_m@owosso.baker.edu

Getting in Last Year 1,160 applied; 100% were accepted.

Financial Matters $5760 tuition and fees (2002–03); $2100 room only.

Academics Baker awards associate and bachelor's degrees. Challenging opportunities include advanced placement credit and accelerated degree programs. Special programs include cooperative education, internships, and summer session for credit. The faculty at Baker has 5 full-time members, 20% with terminal degrees. The student-faculty ratio is 38:1.

Students of Baker The student body is made up of 2,361 undergraduates. 69% are women and 31% are men. Students come from 4 states and territories. 100% are from Michigan.

Applying Baker requires a high school transcript. The school recommends SAT I or ACT. Application deadline: rolling admissions. Early and deferred admission are possible.

BAKER COLLEGE OF PORT HURON

Port Huron, MI

Urban setting ■ Private ■ Independent ■ Coed

Web site: www.baker.edu
Contact: Mr. Daniel Kenny, Director of Admissions, 3403 Lapeer Road, Port Huron, MI 48060-2597
Telephone: 810-985-7000 or toll-free 888-262-2442 **Fax:** 810-985-7066
E-mail: kenny_d@porthuron.baker.edu

Getting in Last Year 477 applied; 100% were accepted.

Financial Matters $5760 tuition and fees (2002–03).

Academics Baker awards associate and bachelor's degrees. Challenging opportunities include advanced placement credit, accelerated degree programs, double majors, and independent study. Special programs include cooperative education, internships, and summer session for credit. The faculty at Baker has 10 full-time members, 10% with terminal degrees. The student-faculty ratio is 13:1.

Students of Baker The student body is made up of 1,363 undergraduates. 76% are women and 24% are men. 90% are from Michigan.

Applying Baker requires a high school transcript and an interview. Application deadline: 9/24. Early and deferred admission are possible.

BAKER UNIVERSITY

Baldwin City, KS

Small-town setting ■ Private ■ Independent Religious ■ Coed

Web site: www.bakeru.edu
Contact: Director of Admission, PO Box 65, Baldwin City, KS 66006-0065
Telephone: 785-594-6451 ext. 458 or toll-free 800-873-4282 **Fax:** 785-594-8372
E-mail: admission@bakeru.edu

Getting in Last Year 844 applied; 95% were accepted; 231 enrolled (29%).

Financial Matters $13,750 tuition and fees (2002–03); $5170 room and board; $10,900 average financial aid amount received per undergraduate.

Academics Baker awards bachelor's degrees. Challenging opportunities include advanced placement credit, student-designed majors, an honors program, double majors, independent study, and a senior project. Special programs include internships, summer session for credit, study-abroad, and Army and Air Force ROTC. The most frequently chosen baccalaureate fields are business/marketing, health professions and related sciences, and education. The faculty at Baker has 69 full-time members, 71% with terminal degrees. The student-faculty ratio is 12:1.

Students of Baker The student body is made up of 988 undergraduates. 59.7% are women and 40.3% are men. Students come from 18 states and territories and 4 other countries. 75% are from Kansas. 0.8% are international students. 81% returned for their sophomore year.

Applying Baker requires SAT I or ACT, a high school transcript, 1 recommendation, and a minimum high school GPA of 3.0, and in some cases an essay and an interview. Application deadline: rolling admissions; 3/1 priority date for financial aid. Deferred admission is possible.

BALDWIN-WALLACE COLLEGE

Berea, OH

Suburban setting ■ Private ■ Independent Religious ■ Coed

Web site: www.bw.edu
Contact: Ms. Grace B. Chalker, Interim Associate Director of Admissions, 275 Eastland Road, Berea, OH 44017-2088
Telephone: 440-826-2222 or toll-free 877-BWAPPLY (in-state) **Fax:** 440-826-3830
E-mail: admit@bw.edu

Getting in Last Year 2,193 applied; 84% were accepted; 735 enrolled (40%).

Financial Matters $17,432 tuition and fees (2002–03); $6022 room and board; 85% average percent of need met; $14,893 average financial aid amount received per undergraduate.

Academics B-W awards bachelor's and master's degrees. Challenging opportunities include advanced placement credit, accelerated degree programs, student-designed majors, an honors program, double majors, independent study, and a senior project. Special programs include internships, summer session for credit, off-campus study, study-abroad, and Army and Air Force ROTC. The most frequently chosen baccalaureate fields are business/marketing, education, and social sciences and history. The faculty at B-W has 162 full-time members, 77% with terminal degrees. The student-faculty ratio is 15:1.

Students of B-W The student body totals 4,719, of whom 3,910 are undergraduates. 62.3% are women and 37.7% are men. Students come from 31 states and territories and 29 other countries. 91% are from Ohio. 0.9% are international students. 84% returned for their sophomore year.

Applying B-W requires an essay, SAT I or ACT, a high school transcript, 1 recommendation, and a minimum high school GPA of 2.6. The school recommends an interview and a minimum high school GPA of 3.2. Application deadline: rolling admissions; 9/1 for financial aid, with a 5/1 priority date. Deferred admission is possible.

BALL STATE UNIVERSITY

Muncie, IN

Suburban setting ■ Public ■ State-supported ■ Coed

Web site: www.bsu.edu
Contact: Dr. Lawrence Waters, Dean of Admissions and Financial Aid, 2000 University Avenue, Muncie, IN 47306
Telephone: 765-285-8300 or toll-free 800-482-4BSU **Fax:** 765-285-1632
E-mail: askus@wp.bsu.edu

Getting in Last Year 10,771 applied; 76% were accepted; 4,032 enrolled (49%).

Financial Matters $4700 resident tuition and fees (2002–03); $12,480 nonresident tuition and fees (2002–03); $5546 room and board; 70% average percent of need met; $6368 average financial aid amount received per undergraduate.

Academics Ball State awards associate, bachelor's, master's, and doctoral degrees and post-bachelor's and post-master's certificates. Challenging opportunities include advanced placement credit, freshman honors college, an honors program, double majors, independent study, and a senior project. Special programs include cooperative education, internships, summer session for credit, study-abroad, and Army ROTC. The most frequently chosen baccalaureate fields are education, business/marketing, and liberal arts/general studies. The faculty at Ball State has 896 full-time members, 75% with terminal degrees. The student-faculty ratio is 16:1.

Students of Ball State The student body totals 20,113, of whom 17,061 are undergraduates. 53.1% are women and 46.9% are men. Students come from 49 states and territories. 92% are from Indiana. 77% returned for their sophomore year.

Applying Ball State requires a high school transcript, and in some cases an essay, SAT I or ACT, an interview, and recommendations. Application deadline: rolling admissions; 3/1 priority date for financial aid. Deferred admission is possible.

BALTIMORE HEBREW UNIVERSITY

Baltimore, MD

Urban setting ■ Private ■ Independent ■ Coed

Web site: www.bhu.edu
Contact: Ms. Essie Keyser, Director of Admissions, 5800 Park Heights Avenue, Baltimore, MD 21209
Telephone: 410-578-6967 or toll-free 888-248-7420 (out-of-state) **Fax:** 410-578-6940
E-mail: bhu@bhu.edu

Getting in Last Year 4 enrolled.

Financial Matters $7230 tuition and fees (2002–03); 100% average percent of need met; $8000 average financial aid amount received per undergraduate (2001–02).

Academics BHU awards associate, bachelor's, master's, and doctoral degrees. Challenging opportunities include advanced placement credit, double majors, and independent study. Special programs include summer session for credit and off-campus study. The most frequently chosen baccalaureate field is area/ethnic studies. The faculty at BHU has 10 full-time members, 90% with terminal degrees. The student-faculty ratio is 4:1.

Students of BHU The student body totals 161, of whom 96 are undergraduates. 65.6% are women and 34.4% are men. 5% are international students.

Applying BHU requires an essay, a high school transcript, and an interview, and in some cases 3 recommendations. Application deadline: rolling admissions. Early and deferred admission are possible.

BAPTIST BIBLE COLLEGE

Springfield, MO

Suburban setting ■ Private ■ Independent Religious ■ Coed

Web site: www.bbcnet.edu/bbgst.html

Contact: Dr. Joseph Gleason, Director of Admissions, 628 East Kearney, Springfield, MO 65803-3498

Telephone: 417-268-6000 ext. 6013 **Fax:** 417-268-6694

Getting in Last Year 264 applied; 76% were accepted.

Financial Matters $3760 tuition and fees (2002–03); $4590 room and board.

Academics Baptist Bible College awards associate, bachelor's, and master's degrees. Special programs include internships, summer session for credit, and Army ROTC. The faculty at Baptist Bible College has 32 full-time members.

Students of Baptist Bible College The student body is made up of 653 undergraduates. Students come from 46 states and territories and 5 other countries. 20% are from Missouri.

Applying Baptist Bible College requires ACT, a high school transcript, and 1 recommendation. Application deadline: rolling admissions. Early and deferred admission are possible.

THE BAPTIST COLLEGE OF FLORIDA

Graceville, FL

Small-town setting ■ Private ■ Independent Religious ■ Coed

Web site: www.baptistcollege.edu

Contact: Mr. Christopher Bishop, Director of Admissions, 5400 College Drive, Graceville, FL 32440-1898

Telephone: 850-263-3261 ext. 460 or toll-free 800-328-2660 ext. 460 **Fax:** 850-263-7506

E-mail: admissions@baptistcollege.edu

Getting in Last Year 75 applied; 87% were accepted; 55 enrolled (85%).

Financial Matters $5450 tuition and fees (2002–03); $3150 room and board; 59% average percent of need met; $3500 average financial aid amount received per undergraduate.

Academics The Baptist College of Florida awards associate and bachelor's degrees. Challenging opportunities include advanced placement credit, double majors, independent study, and a senior project. Special programs include internships and summer session for credit. The most frequently chosen baccalaureate field is education. The faculty at The Baptist College of Florida has 22 full-time members, 68% with terminal degrees. The student-faculty ratio is 15:1.

Students of The Baptist College of Florida The student body is made up of 581 undergraduates. 36.8% are women and 63.2% are men. Students come from 19 states and territories. 76% are from Florida. 0.2% are international students. 73% returned for their sophomore year.

Applying The Baptist College of Florida requires an essay, SAT I or ACT, a high school transcript, and 3 recommendations, and in some cases an interview. Application deadline: rolling admissions; 4/1 priority date for financial aid. Deferred admission is possible.

BAPTIST COLLEGE OF HEALTH SCIENCES

Memphis, TN

Private ■ Independent ■ Coed, Primarily Women

Web site: www.bchs.edu

Contact: Ms. Cynthia Davis, Manager of Admissions/Retention, 1003 Monroe Avenue, Memphis, TN 38104

Telephone: 901-572-2465 or toll-free 866-575-2247 **Fax:** 901-572-2461

Getting in Last Year 260 applied.

Academics Baptist College of Health Sciences awards bachelor's degrees. Challenging opportunities include advanced placement credit and a senior project. Cooperative education is a special program. The faculty at Baptist College of Health Sciences has 45 full-time members.

Students of Baptist College of Health Sciences The student body is made up of 661 undergraduates. Students come from 9 states and territories.

Applying Baptist College of Health Sciences requires ACT, a high school transcript, 3 recommendations, and a minimum high school GPA of 2.75, and in some cases an essay and an interview. Early admission is possible.

BAPTIST MISSIONARY ASSOCIATION THEOLOGICAL SEMINARY

Jacksonville, TX

Small-town setting ■ Private ■ Independent Religious ■ Coed, Primarily Men

Contact: Dr. Philip Attebery, Dean and Registrar, 1530 East Pine Street, Jacksonville, TX 75766-5407

Telephone: 903-586-2501 ext. 229 **Fax:** 903-586-0378

E-mail: bmatsem@fbmats.edu

Getting in Last Year 20 applied; 90% were accepted; 7 enrolled (39%).

Financial Matters $2330 tuition and fees (2002–03); $2400 room only; 50% average percent of need met; $1098 average financial aid amount received per undergraduate (2001–02).

Academics BMA Seminary awards associate, bachelor's, master's, and first-professional degrees. Independent study is a challenging opportunity. Special programs include internships and summer session for credit. The faculty at BMA Seminary has 7 full-time members, 86% with terminal degrees. The student-faculty ratio is 10:1.

Students of BMA Seminary The student body totals 94, of whom 48 are undergraduates. 8.3% are women and 91.7% are men. Students come from 7 states and territories. 71% are from Texas. 6.3% are international students. 100% returned for their sophomore year.

Applying BMA Seminary requires an interview and 3 recommendations. Application deadline: 7/25; 8/1 priority date for financial aid.

BARBER-SCOTIA COLLEGE

Concord, NC

Small-town setting ■ Private ■ Independent Religious ■ Coed

Web site: www.b-sc.edu

Contact: Dr. Alexander Erwin, Academic Dean, 145 Cabarrus Avenue, West, Concord, NC 28025-5187

Telephone: 704-789-2948 or toll-free 800-610-0778 **Fax:** 704-784-3817

Getting in Last Year 1,132 applied; 51% were accepted; 152 enrolled (26%).

Financial Matters $9048 tuition and fees (2002–03); $3952 room and board.

Academics BSC awards bachelor's degrees. Challenging opportunities include advanced placement credit, an honors program, and double majors. Special programs include cooperative education, internships, summer session for credit, off-campus study, and Army and Air Force ROTC. The most frequently chosen baccalaureate fields are social sciences and history, business/marketing, and parks and recreation. The faculty at BSC has 26 full-time members, 54% with terminal degrees. The student-faculty ratio is 14:1.

Students of BSC The student body is made up of 613 undergraduates. 51.4% are women and 48.6% are men. Students come from 20 states and territories. 68% are from North Carolina. 77% returned for their sophomore year.

Applying BSC requires SAT I or ACT, a high school transcript, and recommendations, and in some cases a minimum high school GPA of 2.0. The school recommends an essay, an interview, and a minimum high school GPA of 3.0. Application deadline: rolling admissions; 8/1 priority date for financial aid. Early admission is possible.

BARCLAY COLLEGE

Haviland, KS

Rural setting ■ Private ■ Independent Religious ■ Coed

Web site: www.barclaycollege.edu

Contact: Ryan Haase, Director of Admissions, 607 North Kingman, Haviland, KS 67059

Telephone: 620-862-5252 ext. 41 or toll-free 800-862-0226 **Fax:** 620-862-5242

E-mail: admissions@barclaycollege.edu

Getting in Last Year 38 applied; 100% were accepted; 20 enrolled (53%).

Financial Matters $8200 tuition and fees (2002–03); $4000 room and board; 85% average percent of need met; $6700 average financial aid amount received per undergraduate.

Academics Barclay awards associate and bachelor's degrees. Challenging opportunities include advanced placement credit, accelerated degree programs, student-designed majors, double majors, and independent study. Internships is a special program. The most frequently chosen baccalaureate fields are business/marketing, psychology, and education. The faculty at Barclay has 8 full-time members. The student-faculty ratio is 7:1.

Students of Barclay The student body is made up of 194 undergraduates. 55.2% are women and 44.8% are men. Students come from 18 states and territories and 1 other country. 59% are from Kansas. 1.5% are international students. 41% returned for their sophomore year.

Applying Barclay requires an essay, SAT I or ACT, a high school transcript, 2 recommendations, and a minimum high school GPA of 2.3. Application deadline: 9/1; 3/15 priority date for financial aid. Early and deferred admission are possible.

BARD COLLEGE

Annandale-on-Hudson, NY

Rural setting ■ Private ■ Independent ■ Coed

Web site: www.bard.edu

Contact: Ms. Mary Inga Backlund, Director of Admissions, Ravine Road, PO Box 5000, Annandale-on-Hudson, NY 12504

Telephone: 845-758-7472 **Fax:** 845-758-5208

E-mail: admission@bard.edu

Getting in Last Year 3,118 applied; 36% were accepted; 343 enrolled (31%).

Bard College (continued)

Financial Matters $27,450 tuition and fees (2002–03); $8134 room and board; 87% average percent of need met; $21,466 average financial aid amount received per undergraduate.

Academics Bard awards bachelor's, master's, and doctoral degrees. Challenging opportunities include advanced placement credit, accelerated degree programs, student-designed majors, double majors, independent study, and a senior project. Special programs include internships, off-campus study, and study-abroad. The faculty at Bard has 127 full-time members. The student-faculty ratio is 9:1.

Students of Bard The student body totals 1,653, of whom 1,454 are undergraduates. 55.3% are women and 44.7% are men. Students come from 46 states and territories and 47 other countries. 30% are from New York. 6.5% are international students. 86% returned for their sophomore year.

Applying Bard requires an essay, a high school transcript, and 3 recommendations, and in some cases an interview. The school recommends SAT II Subject Tests, SAT I or ACT, an interview, and a minimum high school GPA of 3.0. Application deadline: 1/15; 3/15 for financial aid, with a 2/15 priority date. Early and deferred admission are possible.

BARNARD COLLEGE

New York, NY

Urban setting ■ Private ■ Independent ■ Women Only

Web site: www.barnard.edu
Contact: Ms. Jennifer Gill Fondiller, Dean of Admissions, 3009 Broadway, New York, NY 10027
Telephone: 212-854-2014 **Fax:** 212-854-6220
E-mail: admissions@barnard.edu

Getting in Last Year 3,686 applied; 34% were accepted; 543 enrolled (43%).

Financial Matters $25,270 tuition and fees (2002–03); $10,140 room and board; 100% average percent of need met; $24,416 average financial aid amount received per undergraduate.

Academics Barnard awards bachelor's degrees. Challenging opportunities include advanced placement credit, accelerated degree programs, student-designed majors, an honors program, double majors, independent study, and a senior project. Special programs include internships, off-campus study, and study-abroad. The most frequently chosen baccalaureate fields are social sciences and history, English, and psychology. The faculty at Barnard has 185 full-time members, 88% with terminal degrees. The student-faculty ratio is 10:1.

Students of Barnard The student body is made up of 2,297 undergraduates. Students come from 48 states and territories and 35 other countries. 36% are from New York. 3% are international students. 93% returned for their sophomore year.

Applying Barnard requires an essay, SAT II: Writing Test, SAT I and SAT II or ACT, a high school transcript, and 3 recommendations. The school recommends an interview. Application deadline: 1/1; 2/1 for financial aid. Early and deferred admission are possible.

BARRY UNIVERSITY

Miami Shores, FL

Suburban setting ■ Private ■ Independent Religious ■ Coed

Web site: www.barry.edu
Contact: Director of Admissions, Kelly House, 11300 Northeast Second Avenue, Miami Shores, FL 33161
Telephone: 305-899-3127 or toll-free 800-695-2279 **Fax:** 305-899-2971
E-mail: admissions@mail.barry.edu

Getting in Last Year 2,407 applied; 74% were accepted; 450 enrolled (25%).

Financial Matters $18,900 tuition and fees (2002–03); $6800 room and board; 72% average percent of need met; $16,391 average financial aid amount received per undergraduate.

Academics Barry awards bachelor's, master's, doctoral, and first-professional degrees and post-bachelor's, post-master's, and first-professional certificates. Challenging opportunities include advanced placement credit, accelerated degree programs, an honors program, double majors, independent study, and a senior project. Special programs include internships, summer session for credit, off-campus study, study-abroad, and Air Force ROTC. The most frequently chosen baccalaureate fields are business/marketing, education, and liberal arts/general studies. The faculty at Barry has 334 full-time members, 82% with terminal degrees. The student-faculty ratio is 12:1.

Students of Barry The student body totals 8,469, of whom 5,622 are undergraduates. 67.1% are women and 32.9% are men. Students come from 49 states and territories and 67 other countries. 88% are from Florida. 5.4% are international students. 71% returned for their sophomore year.

Applying Barry requires SAT I or ACT, a high school transcript, and a minimum high school GPA of 2.0, and in some cases an essay. The school recommends an interview. Application deadline: rolling admissions. Early and deferred admission are possible.

BARTON COLLEGE

Wilson, NC

Small-town setting ■ Private ■ Independent Religious ■ Coed

Web site: www.barton.edu
Contact: Ms. Amy Denton, Director of Admissions, Box 5000, College Station, Wilson, NC 27893
Telephone: 252-399-6314 or toll-free 800-345-4973 **Fax:** 252-399-6572
E-mail: enroll@barton.edu

Getting in Last Year 945 applied; 82% were accepted; 299 enrolled (39%).

Financial Matters $13,084 tuition and fees (2002–03); $4754 room and board; 79% average percent of need met; $12,473 average financial aid amount received per undergraduate.

Academics Barton awards bachelor's degrees. Challenging opportunities include advanced placement credit, double majors, independent study, and a senior project. Special programs include cooperative education, internships, summer session for credit, and study-abroad. The most frequently chosen baccalaureate fields are business/marketing, health professions and related sciences, and social sciences and history. The faculty at Barton has 77 full-time members, 53% with terminal degrees. The student-faculty ratio is 14:1.

Students of Barton The student body is made up of 1,245 undergraduates. 69.3% are women and 30.7% are men. Students come from 28 states and territories and 12 other countries. 77% are from North Carolina. 2% are international students. 59% returned for their sophomore year.

Applying Barton requires SAT I or ACT and a high school transcript. The school recommends an interview and a minimum high school GPA of 2.5. Application deadline: rolling admissions; 4/1 priority date for financial aid. Deferred admission is possible.

BASTYR UNIVERSITY

Kenmore, WA

Suburban setting ■ Private ■ Independent ■ Coed

Web site: www.bastyr.edu
Contact: Mr. Richard Dent, Director of Student Enrollment, 14500 Juanita Drive NE, Kenmore, WA 98028-4966
Telephone: 425-602-3080 **Fax:** 425-602-3090
E-mail: admiss@bastyr.edu

Getting in Last Year 162 applied; 82% were accepted.

Financial Matters $12,018 tuition and fees (2002–03); $4050 room only; 50% average percent of need met; $15,766 average financial aid amount received per undergraduate.

Academics Bastyr awards bachelor's, master's, and first-professional degrees and first-professional certificates. Challenging opportunities include double majors, independent study, and a senior project. Special programs include cooperative education, internships, and summer session for credit. The faculty at Bastyr has 30 full-time members, 100% with terminal degrees. The student-faculty ratio is 15:1.

Students of Bastyr The student body totals 993, of whom 200 are undergraduates. 77.5% are women and 22.5% are men. 4% are international students.

Applying Application deadline: 5/1 priority date for financial aid. Deferred admission is possible.

BATES COLLEGE

Lewiston, ME

Suburban setting ■ Private ■ Independent ■ Coed

Web site: www.bates.edu
Contact: Mr. Wylie L. Mitchell, Dean of Admissions, 23 Campus Avenue, Lewiston, ME 04240-6028
Telephone: 207-786-6000 **Fax:** 207-786-6025
E-mail: admissions@bates.edu

Getting in Last Year 4,012 applied; 28% were accepted; 415 enrolled (37%).

Financial Matters $35,750 comprehensive fee (2002–03); 100% average percent of need met; $24,193 average financial aid amount received per undergraduate.

Academics Bates awards bachelor's degrees. Challenging opportunities include advanced placement credit, accelerated degree programs, student-designed majors, an honors program, double majors, independent study, and a senior project. Special programs include internships, off-campus study, and study-abroad. The most frequently chosen baccalaureate fields are social sciences and history, English, and physical sciences. The faculty at Bates has 163 full-time members, 96% with terminal degrees. The student-faculty ratio is 10:1.

Students of Bates The student body is made up of 1,738 undergraduates. 50.6% are women and 49.4% are men. Students come from 48 states and territories and 63 other countries. 11% are from Maine. 6.4% are international students. 93% returned for their sophomore year.

Applying Bates requires an essay, a high school transcript, and 3 recommendations. The school recommends an interview. Application deadline: 1/15; 2/1 for financial aid. Early and deferred admission are possible.

BAYAMÓN CENTRAL UNIVERSITY

Bayamón, PR

Suburban setting ■ Private ■ Independent Religious ■ Coed

Web site: www.ucb.edu.pr
Contact: Sra. Christine M. Hernandez, Director of Admissions, PO Box 1725, Bayamón, PR 00960-1725
Telephone: 787-786-3030 ext. 2102 **Fax:** 787-740-2200
E-mail: chernandez@ucb.edu.pr

Getting in Last Year 902 applied; 62% were accepted.

Financial Matters $4015 tuition and fees (2002–03).

Academics BCU awards associate, bachelor's, and master's degrees. Challenging opportunities include advanced placement credit, accelerated degree programs, student-designed majors, an honors program, independent study, and a senior project. Special programs include internships, summer session for credit, and Army and Air Force ROTC. The most frequently chosen baccalaureate fields are business/marketing, education, and health professions and related sciences. The faculty at BCU has 58 full-time members, 26% with terminal degrees. The student-faculty ratio is 23:1.

Students of BCU The student body totals 3,334, of whom 2,955 are undergraduates. Students come from 1 state or territory and 2 other countries. 0.4% are international students. 70% returned for their sophomore year.

Applying BCU requires College Examination Entrance Board Test, a high school transcript, and medical history, and in some cases an interview and recommendations. The school recommends a minimum high school GPA of 2.0. Application deadline: 8/15; 4/15 priority date for financial aid.

BAYLOR UNIVERSITY

Waco, TX

Urban setting ■ Private ■ Independent Religious ■ Coed

Web site: www.baylor.edu
Contact: Mr. James Steen, Director of Admission Services, PO Box 97056, Waco, TX 76798-7056
Telephone: 254-710-3435 or toll-free 800-BAYLOR U **Fax:** 254-710-3436
E-mail: admissions_office@baylor.edu

Getting in Last Year 7,431 applied; 81% were accepted; 2,620 enrolled (43%).

Financial Matters $17,214 tuition and fees (2002–03); $5714 room and board; 69% average percent of need met; $11,518 average financial aid amount received per undergraduate.

Academics Baylor awards bachelor's, master's, doctoral, and first-professional degrees and post-master's certificates. Challenging opportunities include advanced placement credit, accelerated degree programs, student-designed majors, an honors program, double majors, and a senior project. Special programs include internships, summer session for credit, study-abroad, and Air Force ROTC. The most frequently chosen baccalaureate fields are business/marketing, education, and health professions and related sciences. The faculty at Baylor has 756 full-time members, 77% with terminal degrees. The student-faculty ratio is 17:1.

Students of Baylor The student body totals 14,159, of whom 11,987 are undergraduates. 57.7% are women and 42.3% are men. Students come from 50 states and territories and 90 other countries. 84% are from Texas. 1.7% are international students. 85% returned for their sophomore year.

Applying Baylor requires an essay, SAT I or ACT, and a high school transcript. The school recommends an interview. Application deadline: rolling admissions; 3/1 priority date for financial aid. Early admission is possible.

BAY PATH COLLEGE

Longmeadow, MA

Suburban setting ■ Private ■ Independent ■ Women Only

Web site: www.baypath.edu
Contact: Ms. Brenda Wishart, Director of Admissions, 588 Longmeadow Street, Longmeadow, MA 01106-2292
Telephone: 413-565-1000 ext. 229 or toll-free 800-782-7284 ext. 331 **Fax:** 413-565-1105
E-mail: admiss@baypath.edu

Getting in Last Year 639 applied; 67% were accepted; 160 enrolled (37%).

Financial Matters $15,934 tuition and fees (2002–03); $7566 room and board; 74% average percent of need met; $9958 average financial aid amount received per undergraduate.

Academics Bay Path awards associate, bachelor's, and master's degrees and post-bachelor's certificates. Challenging opportunities include advanced placement credit, student-designed majors, freshman honors college, an honors program, independent study, and a senior project. Special programs include internships, summer session for credit, off-campus study, study-abroad, and Army and Air Force ROTC. The most frequently chosen baccalaureate fields are business/marketing, computer/information sciences, and liberal arts/general studies. The faculty at Bay Path has 29 full-time members, 62% with terminal degrees. The student-faculty ratio is 15:1.

Students of Bay Path The student body totals 1,103, of whom 1,055 are undergraduates. Students come from 15 states and territories and 13 other countries. 60% are from Massachusetts. 2.3% are international students. 79% returned for their sophomore year.

Applying Bay Path requires an essay, SAT I or ACT, a high school transcript, and 2 recommendations, and in some cases an interview and a minimum high school GPA of 3.0. The school recommends an interview and a minimum high school GPA of 2.0. Application deadline: rolling admissions; 3/15 priority date for financial aid. Early and deferred admission are possible.

BEACON COLLEGE AND GRADUATE SCHOOL

Columbus, GA

Urban setting ■ Private ■ Independent Religious ■ Coed

Web site: www.beacon.edu
Contact: Dr. Robert Thomas, Dean of Student Services, 6003 Veterans Parkway, Columbus, GA 31909
Telephone: 706-323-5364 ext. 259 **Fax:** 706-323-5891
E-mail: beacon@beacon.edu

Getting in Last Year 49 applied; 88% were accepted; 17 enrolled (40%).

Financial Matters $4000 tuition and fees (2002–03); 100% average percent of need met; $1500 average financial aid amount received per undergraduate.

Academics Beacon College and Graduate School awards associate, bachelor's, and master's degrees. Challenging opportunities include advanced placement credit, accelerated degree programs, double majors, and independent study. Special programs include summer session for credit and off-campus study. The faculty at Beacon College and Graduate School has 8 full-time members, 88% with terminal degrees. The student-faculty ratio is 5:1.

Students of Beacon College and Graduate School The student body totals 119, of whom 94 are undergraduates. 40.4% are women and 59.6% are men. Students come from 4 states and territories and 2 other countries. 73% are from Georgia. 2.1% are international students. 95% returned for their sophomore year.

Applying Beacon College and Graduate School requires a high school transcript, an interview, 3 recommendations, and a minimum high school GPA of 2.0, and in some cases ACT COMPASS. The school recommends SAT I or ACT. Application deadline: rolling admissions; 6/1 priority date for financial aid. Early admission is possible.

BECKER COLLEGE

Worcester, MA

Urban setting ■ Private ■ Independent ■ Coed

Web site: www.beckercollege.edu
Contact: Admissions Receptionist, 61 Sever Street, Worcester, MA 01609
Telephone: 508-791-9241 ext. 245 or toll-free 877-5BECKER ext. 245 **Fax:** 508-890-1500
E-mail: admissions@beckercollege.edu

Getting in Last Year 1,438 applied; 93% were accepted; 373 enrolled (28%).

Financial Matters $14,520 tuition and fees (2002–03); $7750 room and board; 67% average percent of need met; $10,111 average financial aid amount received per undergraduate (2001–02).

Academics Becker awards associate and bachelor's degrees (also includes Leicester, MA small town campus). Challenging opportunities include advanced placement credit, accelerated degree programs, and a senior project. Special programs include cooperative education, internships, summer session for credit, off-campus study, study-abroad, and Army and Air Force ROTC. The most frequently chosen baccalaureate field is law/legal studies. The faculty at Becker has 39 full-time members, 21% with terminal degrees. The student-faculty ratio is 15:1.

Students of Becker The student body is made up of 1,577 undergraduates. 73.4% are women and 26.6% are men. Students come from 17 states and territories. 68% are from Massachusetts. 87% returned for their sophomore year.

Applying Becker requires SAT I or ACT, a high school transcript, and a minimum high school GPA of 2.0, and in some cases an interview and a minimum high school GPA of 2.5. The school recommends an essay and recommendations. Application deadline: rolling admissions; 3/1 priority date for financial aid. Deferred admission is possible.

BELHAVEN COLLEGE

Jackson, MS

Urban setting ■ Private ■ Independent Religious ■ Coed

Web site: www.belhaven.edu
Contact: Ms. Suzanne T. Sullivan, Director of Admissions, 150 Peachtree Street, Jackson, MS 39202
Telephone: 601-968-5940 or toll-free 800-960-5940 **Fax:** 601-968-8946
E-mail: admissions@belhaven.edu

Getting in Last Year 552 applied; 63% were accepted; 232 enrolled (67%).

Belhaven College (continued)

Financial Matters $12,190 tuition and fees (2002–03); $4770 room and board; 58% average percent of need met; $9300 average financial aid amount received per undergraduate (2001–02).

Academics Belhaven awards associate, bachelor's, and master's degrees. Challenging opportunities include advanced placement credit, accelerated degree programs, an honors program, double majors, independent study, and a senior project. Special programs include internships, summer session for credit, off-campus study, and study-abroad. The most frequently chosen baccalaureate fields are business/marketing, psychology, and parks and recreation. The faculty at Belhaven has 52 full-time members, 77% with terminal degrees. The student-faculty ratio is 18:1.

Students of Belhaven The student body totals 2,021, of whom 1,748 are undergraduates. 62.2% are women and 37.8% are men. Students come from 35 states and territories and 11 other countries. 36% are from Mississippi. 1.9% are international students. 58% returned for their sophomore year.

Applying Belhaven requires SAT I or ACT, a high school transcript, 1 recommendation, 1 academic reference, and a minimum high school GPA of 2.0, and in some cases an essay and an interview. Application deadline: rolling admissions; 3/1 priority date for financial aid. Early and deferred admission are possible.

BELLARMINE UNIVERSITY

Louisville, KY

Suburban setting ■ Private ■ Independent Religious ■ Coed

Web site: www.bellarmine.edu

Contact: Mr. Timothy A. Sturgeon, Dean of Admission, 2001 Newburg Road, Louisville, KY 40205-0671

Telephone: 502-452-8131 or toll-free 800-274-4723 ext. 8131 **Fax:** 502-452-8002

E-mail: admissions@bellarmine.edu

Getting in Last Year 1,285 applied; 80% were accepted.

Financial Matters $17,010 tuition and fees (2002–03); $5300 room and board; 89% average percent of need met; $13,762 average financial aid amount received per undergraduate.

Academics Bellarmine awards bachelor's and master's degrees and post-bachelor's certificates. Challenging opportunities include advanced placement credit, accelerated degree programs, student-designed majors, an honors program, double majors, independent study, and a senior project. Special programs include internships, summer session for credit, off-campus study, study-abroad, and Army and Air Force ROTC. The most frequently chosen baccalaureate fields are business/marketing, health professions and related sciences, and education. The faculty at Bellarmine has 109 full-time members, 76% with terminal degrees. The student-faculty ratio is 12:1.

Students of Bellarmine The student body totals 2,332, of whom 1,788 are undergraduates. Students come from 19 states and territories and 12 other countries. 69% are from Kentucky. 0.7% are international students. 81% returned for their sophomore year.

Applying Bellarmine requires an essay, SAT I or ACT, a high school transcript, recommendations, and a minimum high school GPA of 2.5. The school recommends an interview. Application deadline: 8/15; 3/1 priority date for financial aid. Early and deferred admission are possible.

BELLEVUE UNIVERSITY

Bellevue, NE

Suburban setting ■ Private ■ Independent ■ Coed

Web site: www.bellevue.edu

Contact: Ms. Kelley Dengel, Information Center Manager, 1000 Galvin Road South, Bellevue, NE 68005-3098

Telephone: 402-293-3769 or toll-free 800-756-7920 **Fax:** 402-293-2020

E-mail: set@scholars.bellevue.edu

Getting in Last Year 226 enrolled.

Financial Matters $4270 tuition and fees (2002–03).

Academics Bellevue University awards bachelor's and master's degrees. Challenging opportunities include advanced placement credit, accelerated degree programs, double majors, independent study, and a senior project. Special programs include cooperative education, internships, summer session for credit, and Army and Air Force ROTC. The faculty at Bellevue University has 63 full-time members, 48% with terminal degrees. The student-faculty ratio is 17:1.

Students of Bellevue University The student body totals 4,057, of whom 3,321 are undergraduates. 51.3% are women and 48.7% are men. Students come from 40 states and territories and 67 other countries. 80% are from Nebraska. 9.5% are international students.

Applying Bellevue University requires a high school transcript and an interview, and in some cases SAT I or ACT and 3 recommendations. Application deadline: rolling admissions. Deferred admission is possible.

BELLIN COLLEGE OF NURSING

Green Bay, WI

Urban setting ■ Private ■ Independent ■ Coed, Primarily Women

Web site: www.bcon.edu

Contact: Dr. Penny Croghan, Admissions Director, 725 South Webster Avenue, Green Bay, WI 54301

Telephone: 920-433-5803 or toll-free 800-236-8707 (in-state) **Fax:** 920-433-7416

E-mail: admissio@bcon.edu

Getting in Last Year 30 enrolled.

Financial Matters $11,543 tuition and fees (2002–03); 81% average percent of need met; $12,091 average financial aid amount received per undergraduate.

Academics Bellin College awards bachelor's degrees. Challenging opportunities include advanced placement credit, accelerated degree programs, and independent study. Special programs include summer session for credit, off-campus study, and Army ROTC. The most frequently chosen baccalaureate field is health professions and related sciences. The faculty at Bellin College has 15 full-time members, 13% with terminal degrees. The student-faculty ratio is 10:1.

Students of Bellin College The student body is made up of 176 undergraduates. 94.3% are women and 5.7% are men. Students come from 3 states and territories and 1 other country. 97% are from Wisconsin. 0.6% are international students. 92% returned for their sophomore year.

Applying Bellin College requires ACT, a high school transcript, an interview, and 3 recommendations. The school recommends a minimum high school GPA of 3.0. Application deadline: rolling admissions; 3/1 priority date for financial aid.

BELMONT ABBEY COLLEGE

Belmont, NC

Small-town setting ■ Private ■ Independent Religious ■ Coed

Web site: www.belmontabbeycollege.edu

Contact: Mr. Michael Poll, Director of Admission, 100 Belmont-Mt. Holly Road, Belmont, NC 28012-1802

Telephone: 704-825-6884 or toll-free 888-BAC-0110 **Fax:** 704-825-6220

E-mail: admissions@bac.edu

Getting in Last Year 1,112 applied; 70% were accepted; 225 enrolled (29%).

Financial Matters $13,974 tuition and fees (2002–03); $6856 room and board; 73% average percent of need met; $14,500 average financial aid amount received per undergraduate.

Academics The Abbey awards bachelor's degrees. Challenging opportunities include advanced placement credit, accelerated degree programs, freshman honors college, an honors program, double majors, independent study, and a senior project. Special programs include cooperative education, internships, summer session for credit, off-campus study, study-abroad, and Army and Air Force ROTC. The most frequently chosen baccalaureate fields are business/marketing, education, and biological/life sciences. The faculty at The Abbey has 43 full-time members, 88% with terminal degrees. The student-faculty ratio is 15:1.

Students of The Abbey The student body is made up of 883 undergraduates. 58.8% are women and 41.2% are men. Students come from 40 states and territories and 15 other countries. 66% are from North Carolina. 3.2% are international students. 68% returned for their sophomore year.

Applying The Abbey requires SAT I or ACT, a high school transcript, and a minimum high school GPA of 2.0, and in some cases an essay and 2 recommendations. The school recommends an interview. Application deadline: 8/1; 4/1 priority date for financial aid. Deferred admission is possible.

BELMONT UNIVERSITY

Nashville, TN

Urban setting ■ Private ■ Independent Religious ■ Coed

Web site: www.belmont.edu

Contact: Dr. Kathryn Baugher, Dean of Enrollment Services, 1900 Belmont Boulevard, Nashville, TN 37212-3757

Telephone: 615-460-6785 or toll-free 800-56E-NROL **Fax:** 615-460-5434

E-mail: buadmission@mail.belmont.edu

Getting in Last Year 1,346 applied; 78% were accepted; 528 enrolled (50%).

Financial Matters $14,450 tuition and fees (2002–03); $5825 room and board; 36% average percent of need met; $2649 average financial aid amount received per undergraduate (2001–02).

Academics Belmont awards bachelor's, master's, and doctoral degrees and post-bachelor's certificates. Challenging opportunities include advanced placement credit, accelerated degree programs, student-designed majors, an honors program, double majors, independent study, and a senior project. Special programs include cooperative education, internships, summer session for credit, study-abroad, and Army ROTC. The most frequently chosen baccalaureate fields are visual/performing arts, business/marketing, and liberal arts/general studies. The faculty at Belmont has 196 full-time members, 67% with terminal degrees. The student-faculty ratio is 12:1.

Students of Belmont The student body totals 3,344, of whom 2,800 are undergraduates. 60.1% are women and 39.9% are men. Students come from 50 states and territories and 28 other countries. 46% are from Tennessee. 2.5% are international students. 73% returned for their sophomore year.

Applying Belmont requires an essay, SAT I or ACT, a high school transcript, recommendations, resume of activities, and a minimum high school GPA of 3.0, and in some cases an interview. Application deadline: 5/1. Early and deferred admission are possible.

BELOIT COLLEGE

Beloit, WI

Small-town setting ■ *Private* ■ *Independent* ■ *Coed*

Web site: www.beloit.edu

Contact: Mr. James S. Zielinski, Director of Admissions, 700 College Street, Beloit, WI 53511-5596

Telephone: 608-363-2500 or toll-free 800-356-0751 **Fax:** 608-363-2075

E-mail: admiss@beloit.edu

Getting in Last Year 1,677 applied; 70% were accepted; 304 enrolled (26%).

Financial Matters $23,236 tuition and fees (2002–03); $5268 room and board; 100% average percent of need met; $17,839 average financial aid amount received per undergraduate (2001–02).

Academics Beloit awards bachelor's degrees. Challenging opportunities include advanced placement credit, student-designed majors, double majors, independent study, and a senior project. Special programs include internships, summer session for credit, off-campus study, and study-abroad. The most frequently chosen baccalaureate fields are social sciences and history, visual/performing arts, and biological/life sciences. The faculty at Beloit has 99 full-time members, 99% with terminal degrees. The student-faculty ratio is 11:1.

Students of Beloit The student body is made up of 1,281 undergraduates. 61.5% are women and 38.5% are men. Students come from 49 states and territories and 59 other countries. 20% are from Wisconsin. 7.6% are international students. 89% returned for their sophomore year.

Applying Beloit requires an essay, SAT I or ACT, a high school transcript, and 1 recommendation, and in some cases an interview. The school recommends an interview. Application deadline: 2/1; 3/1 priority date for financial aid. Early and deferred admission are possible.

BEMIDJI STATE UNIVERSITY

Bemidji, MN

Small-town setting ■ *Public* ■ *State-supported* ■ *Coed*

Web site: www.bemidjistate.edu

Contact: Mr. Kevin Drexel, Director of Admissions, Deputy-102, Bemidji, MN 56601

Telephone: 218-755-2040 or toll-free 800-475-2001 (in-state), 800-652-9747 (out-of-state) **Fax:** 218-755-2074

E-mail: admissions@bemidjistate.edu

Getting in Last Year 1,338 applied; 70% were accepted; 603 enrolled (65%).

Financial Matters $4475 resident tuition and fees (2002–03); $8715 nonresident tuition and fees (2002–03); $4597 room and board; 85% average percent of need met; $7189 average financial aid amount received per undergraduate.

Academics Bemidji State University awards associate, bachelor's, and master's degrees. Challenging opportunities include advanced placement credit, an honors program, double majors, independent study, and a senior project. Special programs include cooperative education, internships, summer session for credit, off-campus study, and study-abroad. The most frequently chosen baccalaureate fields are education, business/marketing, and protective services/public administration. The faculty at Bemidji State University has 212 full-time members, 83% with terminal degrees. The student-faculty ratio is 19:1.

Students of Bemidji State University The student body totals 4,941, of whom 4,614 are undergraduates. 54.2% are women and 45.8% are men. Students come from 28 states and territories and 47 other countries. 95% are from Minnesota. 5.8% are international students. 72% returned for their sophomore year.

Applying Bemidji State University requires ACT and a high school transcript, and in some cases an essay, an interview, and recommendations. Application deadline: rolling admissions; 5/15 priority date for financial aid. Deferred admission is possible.

BENEDICT COLLEGE

Columbia, SC

Urban setting ■ *Private* ■ *Independent Religious* ■ *Coed*

Web site: www.benedict.edu

Contact: Mr. Gary Knight, Interim Vice President, Institutional Effectiveness, PO Box 98, Columbia, SC 29204

Telephone: 803-253-5275 or toll-free 800-868-6598 (in-state) **Fax:** 803-253-5167

Getting in Last Year 4,039 applied; 71% were accepted; 643 enrolled (22%).

Financial Matters $10,546 tuition and fees (2002–03); $5434 room and board; 100% average percent of need met.

Academics Benedict College awards bachelor's degrees. Challenging opportunities include advanced placement credit, an honors program, and a senior project. Special programs include internships, summer session for credit, and Army and Air Force ROTC. The most frequently chosen baccalaureate fields are business/marketing, education, and law/legal studies. The faculty at Benedict College has 127 full-time members, 60% with terminal degrees. The student-faculty ratio is 19:1.

Students of Benedict College The student body is made up of 3,005 undergraduates. 50.3% are women and 49.7% are men. Students come from 32 states and territories. 80% are from South Carolina.

Applying Benedict College requires a high school transcript. The school recommends SAT I or ACT. Application deadline: rolling admissions; 4/15 priority date for financial aid. Early and deferred admission are possible.

BENEDICTINE COLLEGE

Atchison, KS

Small-town setting ■ *Private* ■ *Independent Religious* ■ *Coed*

Web site: www.benedictine.edu

Contact: Ms. Kelly Vowels, Dean of Enrollment Management, 1020 North 2nd Street, Atchison, KS 66002

Telephone: 913-367-5340 ext. 2476 or toll-free 800-467-5340 **Fax:** 913-367-5462

E-mail: bcadmiss@benedictine.edu

Getting in Last Year 675 applied; 89% were accepted; 300 enrolled (50%).

Financial Matters $14,200 tuition and fees (2002–03); $5630 room and board; 81% average percent of need met; $13,523 average financial aid amount received per undergraduate (2001–02).

Academics Benedictine College awards associate, bachelor's, and master's degrees. Challenging opportunities include advanced placement credit, student-designed majors, and independent study. Special programs include cooperative education, internships, summer session for credit, off-campus study, study-abroad, and Army ROTC. The most frequently chosen baccalaureate fields are business/marketing, education, and social sciences and history. The faculty at Benedictine College has 56 full-time members, 79% with terminal degrees. The student-faculty ratio is 15:1.

Students of Benedictine College The student body totals 1,375, of whom 1,296 are undergraduates. 51.9% are women and 48.1% are men. Students come from 34 states and territories and 14 other countries. 47% are from Kansas. 2.7% are international students. 71% returned for their sophomore year.

Applying Benedictine College requires SAT I or ACT, a high school transcript, and a minimum high school GPA of 2.0, and in some cases an interview. Deferred admission is possible.

BENEDICTINE UNIVERSITY

Lisle, IL

Suburban setting ■ *Private* ■ *Independent Religious* ■ *Coed*

Web site: www.ben.edu

Contact: Ms. Kari Cranmer, Dean of Undergraduate Admissions, 5700 College Road, Lisle, IL 60532-0900

Telephone: 630-829-6306 or toll-free 888-829-6363 (out-of-state) **Fax:** 630-960-1126

E-mail: admissions@ben.edu

Getting in Last Year 952 applied; 74% were accepted; 303 enrolled (43%).

Financial Matters $16,660 tuition and fees (2002–03); $5800 room and board; 100% average percent of need met; $10,984 average financial aid amount received per undergraduate (2001–02).

Academics Benedictine University awards associate, bachelor's, master's, and doctoral degrees. Challenging opportunities include advanced placement credit, accelerated degree programs, an honors program, double majors, independent study, and a senior project. Special programs include internships, summer session for credit, off-campus study, study-abroad, and Army ROTC. The most frequently chosen baccalaureate fields are business/marketing, biological/life sciences, and education. The faculty at Benedictine University has 92 full-time members, 80% with terminal degrees. The student-faculty ratio is 13:1.

Students of Benedictine University The student body totals 2,809, of whom 2,044 are undergraduates. 60.4% are women and 39.6% are men. Students come from 23 states and territories and 30 other countries. 97% are from Illinois. 2.3% are international students. 75% returned for their sophomore year.

Applying Benedictine University requires an essay, SAT I or ACT, a high school transcript, and recommendations, and in some cases an interview. Application deadline: rolling admissions; 6/30 for financial aid, with a 4/15 priority date. Deferred admission is possible.

BENNETT COLLEGE

Greensboro, NC

Urban setting ■ *Private* ■ *Independent Religious* ■ *Women Only*

Web site: www.bennett.edu
Contact: Ms. Ulisa Bowles, Director of Admissions, Campus Box H, Greensboro, NC 27401
Telephone: 336-517-8624
E-mail: admiss@bennett.edu

Getting in Last Year 1,554 applied; 10% were accepted; 142 enrolled (92%).

Financial Matters $10,666 tuition and fees (2002–03); $4550 room and board.

Academics Bennett College awards bachelor's degrees. Challenging opportunities include student-designed majors, freshman honors college, an honors program, and a senior project. Special programs include cooperative education, internships, summer session for credit, off-campus study, and Army and Air Force ROTC. The most frequently chosen baccalaureate fields are biological/life sciences, business/marketing, and psychology. The faculty at Bennett College has 50 full-time members, 70% with terminal degrees. The student-faculty ratio is 9:1.

Students of Bennett College The student body is made up of 486 undergraduates. Students come from 30 states and territories and 5 other countries. 28% are from North Carolina. 0.6% are international students. 98% returned for their sophomore year.

Applying Bennett College requires an essay, SAT I or ACT, a high school transcript, recommendations, and a minimum high school GPA of 2.0, and in some cases an interview. Application deadline: rolling admissions. Deferred admission is possible.

BENNINGTON COLLEGE

Bennington, VT

Small-town setting ■ *Private* ■ *Independent* ■ *Coed*

Web site: www.bennington.edu
Contact: Mr. Ben Jones, Dean of Admissions and Financial Aid, One College Drive, Bennington, VT 05201
Telephone: 802-440-4312 or toll-free 800-833-6845 **Fax:** 802-440-4320
E-mail: admissions@bennington.edu

Getting in Last Year 701 applied; 70% were accepted; 172 enrolled (35%).

Financial Matters $26,540 tuition and fees (2002–03); $6700 room and board; 75% average percent of need met; $20,119 average financial aid amount received per undergraduate.

Academics Bennington awards bachelor's and master's degrees and post-bachelor's certificates. Challenging opportunities include accelerated degree programs, student-designed majors, double majors, independent study, and a senior project. Special programs include cooperative education, internships, off-campus study, and study-abroad. The most frequently chosen baccalaureate fields are visual/performing arts, interdisciplinary studies, and social sciences and history. The faculty at Bennington has 61 full-time members, 69% with terminal degrees. The student-faculty ratio is 9:1.

Students of Bennington The student body totals 787, of whom 627 are undergraduates. 67.6% are women and 32.4% are men. Students come from 44 states and territories and 19 other countries. 5% are from Vermont. 8.3% are international students. 79% returned for their sophomore year.

Applying Bennington requires an essay, SAT I or ACT, a high school transcript, an interview, and 2 recommendations. Application deadline: 1/1; 3/1 priority date for financial aid. Early and deferred admission are possible.

BENTLEY COLLEGE

Waltham, MA

Suburban setting ■ *Private* ■ *Independent* ■ *Coed*

Web site: www.bentley.edu
Contact: Director of Admission, 175 Forest Street, Waltham, MA 02452-4705
Telephone: 781-891-2244 or toll-free 800-523-2354 (out-of-state) **Fax:** 781-891-3414
E-mail: ugadmission@bentley.edu

Getting in Last Year 5,082 applied; 46% were accepted; 912 enrolled (39%).

Financial Matters $21,075 tuition and fees (2002–03); $9350 room and board; 96% average percent of need met; $21,514 average financial aid amount received per undergraduate.

Academics Bentley awards associate, bachelor's, and master's degrees and post-bachelor's and post-master's certificates. Challenging opportunities include advanced placement credit, accelerated degree programs, student-designed majors, an honors program, and a senior project. Special programs include internships, summer session for credit, off-campus study, study-abroad, and Army ROTC. The most frequently chosen baccalaureate fields are business/marketing, computer/information sciences, and interdisciplinary studies. The faculty at Bentley has 250 full-time members, 83% with terminal degrees. The student-faculty ratio is 14:1.

Students of Bentley The student body totals 5,648, of whom 4,325 are undergraduates. 43.3% are women and 56.7% are men. Students come from 40 states and territories and 62 other countries. 59% are from Massachusetts. 7.9% are international students. 93% returned for their sophomore year.

Applying Bentley requires an essay, SAT I or ACT, a high school transcript, and 2 recommendations. The school recommends an interview. Application deadline: 2/1; 2/1 for financial aid. Early and deferred admission are possible.

BEREA COLLEGE

Berea, KY

Small-town setting ■ *Private* ■ *Independent* ■ *Coed*

Web site: www.berea.edu
Contact: Mr. Joseph Bagnoli, Director of Admissions, CPO 2220, Berea, KY 40404
Telephone: 859-985-3500 or toll-free 800-326-5948 **Fax:** 859-985-3512
E-mail: admissions@berea.edu

Getting in Last Year 1,974 applied; 24% were accepted; 356 enrolled (74%).

Financial Matters $507 tuition and fees (2002–03); $4303 room and board; 80% average percent of need met; $21,438 average financial aid amount received per undergraduate.

Academics Berea awards bachelor's degrees. Challenging opportunities include advanced placement credit, student-designed majors, an honors program, double majors, independent study, and a senior project. Special programs include internships, summer session for credit, off-campus study, and study-abroad. The most frequently chosen baccalaureate fields are business/marketing, home economics/vocational home economics, and engineering/engineering technologies. The faculty at Berea has 134 full-time members, 86% with terminal degrees. The student-faculty ratio is 10:1.

Students of Berea The student body is made up of 1,578 undergraduates. 58.8% are women and 41.2% are men. Students come from 44 states and territories and 65 other countries. 42% are from Kentucky. 6.6% are international students. 83% returned for their sophomore year.

Applying Berea requires an essay, SAT I or ACT, a high school transcript, an interview, and financial aid application. The school recommends 2 recommendations. Application deadline: 4/15 priority date for financial aid.

BERKLEE COLLEGE OF MUSIC

Boston, MA

Urban setting ■ *Private* ■ *Independent* ■ *Coed*

Web site: www.berklee.edu
Contact: Ms. Marsha Ginn, Director of Admissions, 1140 Boyleston Street, Boston, MA 02215-3693
Telephone: 617-747-2222 or toll-free 800-BERKLEE **Fax:** 617-747-2047
E-mail: admissions@berklee.edu

Getting in Last Year 1,779 applied; 81% were accepted.

Financial Matters $18,781 tuition and fees (2002–03); $9790 room and board; 81% average percent of need met; $15,500 average financial aid amount received per undergraduate (2001–02).

Academics Berklee awards bachelor's degrees. Challenging opportunities include advanced placement credit, accelerated degree programs, student-designed majors, double majors, and a senior project. Special programs include internships, summer session for credit, and off-campus study. The most frequently chosen baccalaureate field is visual/performing arts. The faculty at Berklee has 229 full-time members. The student-faculty ratio is 15:1.

Students of Berklee The student body is made up of 3,519 undergraduates. Students come from 54 states and territories and 78 other countries. 18% are from Massachusetts. 28.6% are international students.

Applying Berklee requires an essay, a high school transcript, 2 recommendations, and 2 years of formal music study, and in some cases SAT I or ACT and an interview. The school recommends an interview. Application deadline: rolling admissions, rolling admissions for nonresidents; 3/1 priority date for financial aid. Deferred admission is possible.

BERNARD M. BARUCH COLLEGE OF THE CITY UNIVERSITY OF NEW YORK

New York, NY

Urban setting ■ *Public* ■ *State and locally supported* ■ *Coed*

Web site: www.baruch.cuny.edu
Contact: Mr. James F. Murphy, Director of Undergraduate Admissions and Financial Aid, Box H-0720, New York, NY 10010-5585
Telephone: 212-312-1400
E-mail: admissions@baruch.cuny.edu

Getting in Last Year 9,039 applied; 34% were accepted; 1,674 enrolled (54%).

Financial Matters $4100 resident tuition and fees (2002–03); $7700 nonresident tuition and fees (2002–03); 68% average percent of need met; $4705 average financial aid amount received per undergraduate.

Academics Baruch College awards bachelor's, master's, and doctoral degrees and post-master's certificates. Challenging opportunities include advanced placement credit, accelerated degree programs, student-designed majors, an honors program, double majors, independent study, and a senior project. Special programs include internships, summer session for credit, and study-abroad. The most frequently chosen baccalaureate fields are business/marketing, psychology, and social sciences and history. The faculty at Baruch College has 408 full-time members, 94% with terminal degrees. The student-faculty ratio is 19:1.

Students of Baruch College The student body totals 15,361, of whom 12,653 are undergraduates. 57.5% are women and 42.5% are men. Students come from 7 states and territories and 120 other countries. 96% are from New York. 8.8% are international students. 92% returned for their sophomore year.

Applying Baruch College requires SAT I or ACT, a high school transcript, 16 academic units, and a minimum high school GPA of 2.5, and in some cases recommendations. Application deadline: 4/1; 4/30 for financial aid, with a 3/15 priority date. Early admission is possible.

BERRY COLLEGE

Mount Berry, GA

Small-town setting ■ *Private* ■ *Independent Religious* ■ *Coed*

Web site: www.berry.edu

Contact: Mr. George Gaddie, Dean of Admissions, PO Box 490159, 2277 Martha Berry Highway, Mount Berry, GA 30149-0159

Telephone: 706-236-2215 or toll-free 800-237-7942 **Fax:** 706-290-2178

E-mail: admissions@berry.edu

Getting in Last Year 1,904 applied; 86% were accepted; 570 enrolled (35%).

Financial Matters $14,260 tuition and fees (2002–03); $5624 room and board; 84% average percent of need met; $11,684 average financial aid amount received per undergraduate (2001–02).

Academics Berry awards bachelor's and master's degrees. Challenging opportunities include advanced placement credit, accelerated degree programs, student-designed majors, an honors program, double majors, independent study, and a senior project. Special programs include cooperative education, internships, summer session for credit, and study-abroad. The most frequently chosen baccalaureate fields are business/marketing, education, and social sciences and history. The faculty at Berry has 147 full-time members, 84% with terminal degrees. The student-faculty ratio is 12:1.

Students of Berry The student body totals 2,053, of whom 1,898 are undergraduates. 62.1% are women and 37.9% are men. Students come from 32 states and territories and 26 other countries. 84% are from Georgia. 1.9% are international students. 75% returned for their sophomore year.

Applying Berry requires SAT I or ACT and a high school transcript. Application deadline: 7/28; 4/1 priority date for financial aid. Early and deferred admission are possible.

BETHANY BIBLE COLLEGE

Sussex, NB Canada

Small-town setting ■ *Private* ■ *Independent Religious* ■ *Coed*

Contact: Mr. D. Scott Rhyno, Executive Director of Admissions, 26 Western Street, Sussex, NB E4E 1E6 Canada

Telephone: 506-432-4422 or toll-free 888-432-4422 **Fax:** 506-432-4425

E-mail: steppej@bethany-ca.edu

Getting in Last Year 229 applied; 48% were accepted; 55 enrolled (50%).

Financial Matters $5376 tuition and fees (2002–03); $4300 room and board.

Academics Bethany awards bachelor's degrees. Challenging opportunities include double majors, independent study, and a senior project. Special programs include internships and summer session for credit. The faculty at Bethany has 10 full-time members, 10% with terminal degrees.

Students of Bethany The student body is made up of 274 undergraduates. 50.4% are women and 49.6% are men. Students come from 5 states and territories. 79% are from New Brunswick. 99% returned for their sophomore year.

Applying Bethany requires a high school transcript and 2 recommendations, and in some cases SAT I or ACT. The school recommends an interview. Application deadline: rolling admissions; 10/15 for financial aid.

BETHANY COLLEGE

Lindsborg, KS

Small-town setting ■ *Private* ■ *Independent Religious* ■ *Coed*

Web site: www.bethanylb.edu

Contact: Ms. Brenda Meagher, Interim Dean of Admissions and Financial Aid, 421 North First Street, Lindsborg, KS 67456

Telephone: 785-227-3311 ext. 3248 or toll-free 800-826-2281
Fax: 785-227-2004

E-mail: admissions@bethanylb.edu

Getting in Last Year 561 applied; 69% were accepted; 142 enrolled (37%).

Financial Matters $13,590 tuition and fees (2002–03); $3700 room and board; 96% average percent of need met; $14,465 average financial aid amount received per undergraduate.

Academics Bethany awards bachelor's degrees. Challenging opportunities include advanced placement credit, accelerated degree programs, student-designed majors, double majors, independent study, and a senior project. Special programs include internships, summer session for credit, and off-campus study. The most frequently chosen baccalaureate fields are business/marketing, social sciences and history, and education. The faculty at Bethany has 44 full-time members, 61% with terminal degrees. The student-faculty ratio is 10:1.

Students of Bethany The student body is made up of 623 undergraduates. 49% are women and 51% are men. Students come from 28 states and territories. 61% are from Kansas. 0.3% are international students. 73% returned for their sophomore year.

Applying Bethany requires SAT I or ACT, a high school transcript, and a minimum high school GPA of 2.5, and in some cases an essay, an interview, and recommendations. Application deadline: 7/1. Deferred admission is possible.

BETHANY COLLEGE

Bethany, WV

Rural setting ■ *Private* ■ *Independent Religious* ■ *Coed*

Web site: www.bethanywv.edu

Contact: Ms. Penny Cunningham, Dean of Admission, Office of Admission, Bethany, WV 26032

Telephone: 304-829-7591 or toll-free 800-922-7611 (out-of-state)
Fax: 304-829-7142

E-mail: admission@bethanywv.edu

Getting in Last Year 977 applied; 83% were accepted; 292 enrolled (36%).

Financial Matters $12,766 tuition and fees (2002–03); $6000 room and board; 91% average percent of need met; $16,750 average financial aid amount received per undergraduate.

Academics Bethany awards bachelor's degrees. Challenging opportunities include advanced placement credit, student-designed majors, double majors, independent study, and a senior project. Special programs include internships, off-campus study, and study-abroad. The most frequently chosen baccalaureate fields are education, communications/communication technologies, and psychology. The faculty at Bethany has 57 full-time members, 75% with terminal degrees. The student-faculty ratio is 12:1.

Students of Bethany The student body is made up of 887 undergraduates. 49% are women and 51% are men. Students come from 26 states and territories and 20 other countries. 27% are from West Virginia. 4.3% are international students. 84% returned for their sophomore year.

Applying Bethany requires an essay, SAT I or ACT, a high school transcript, 1 recommendation, documentation of student involvement, and a minimum high school GPA of 2.0, and in some cases an interview. The school recommends an interview. Application deadline: 8/15; 3/1 priority date for financial aid. Deferred admission is possible.

BETHANY COLLEGE OF THE ASSEMBLIES OF GOD

Scotts Valley, CA

Small-town setting ■ *Private* ■ *Independent Religious* ■ *Coed*

Web site: www.bethany.edu

Contact: Ms. Pam Smallwood, Director of Admissions, 800 Bethany Drive, Scotts Valley, CA 95066-2820

Telephone: 831-438-3800 ext. 1400 or toll-free 800-843-9410
Fax: 831-438-4517

E-mail: info@bethany.edu

Getting in Last Year 208 applied; 74% were accepted; 84 enrolled (55%).

Financial Matters $11,960 tuition and fees (2002–03); $5162 room and board; 41% average percent of need met; $11,025 average financial aid amount received per undergraduate.

Academics Bethany College awards associate, bachelor's, and master's degrees. Challenging opportunities include advanced placement credit, accelerated degree programs, independent study, and a senior project. Special programs include internships and summer session for credit. The most frequently chosen baccalaureate fields are psychology, interdisciplinary studies, and business/marketing. The faculty at Bethany College has 27 full-time members, 59% with terminal degrees. The student-faculty ratio is 11:1.

Students of Bethany College The student body totals 568, of whom 504 are undergraduates. 38.1% are women and 61.9% are men. Students come from 21 states and territories. 1.1% are international students. 97% returned for their sophomore year.

Applying Bethany College requires an essay, SAT I or ACT, a high school transcript, 2 recommendations, Christian commitment, and a minimum high school GPA of 2.0. Application deadline: 7/1; 3/2 priority date for financial aid. Early and deferred admission are possible.

BETHANY LUTHERAN COLLEGE

Mankato, MN

Small-town setting ■ Private ■ Independent Religious ■ Coed

Web site: www.blc.edu
Contact: Mr. Donald Westphal, Dean of Admissions, 700 Luther Drive, Mankato, MN 56001
Telephone: 507-344-7320 or toll-free 800-944-3066 **Fax:** 507-344-7376
E-mail: admiss@blc.edu

Getting in Last Year 319 applied; 90% were accepted; 218 enrolled (76%).

Financial Matters $12,520 tuition and fees (2002–03); $4688 room and board.

Academics Bethany awards associate and bachelor's degrees. Challenging opportunities include advanced placement credit, an honors program, and a senior project. Army ROTC is a special program. The most frequently chosen baccalaureate fields are liberal arts/general studies and communications/communication technologies. The faculty at Bethany has 33 full-time members, 39% with terminal degrees. The student-faculty ratio is 8:1.

Students of Bethany The student body is made up of 470 undergraduates. 57% are women and 43% are men. Students come from 20 states and territories and 13 other countries. 70% are from Minnesota. 4.3% are international students. 83% returned for their sophomore year.

Applying Bethany requires an essay, SAT I or ACT, a high school transcript, and a minimum high school GPA of 2.4, and in some cases an interview. The school recommends an interview and a minimum high school GPA of 3.2. Application deadline: 7/15; 7/15 for financial aid, with a 5/1 priority date.

BETHEL COLLEGE

Mishawaka, IN

Suburban setting ■ Private ■ Independent Religious ■ Coed

Web site: www.bethelcollege.edu
Contact: Ms. Andrea M. Helmuth, Director of Admissions, 1001 West McKinley Avenue, Mishawaka, IN 46545-5591
Telephone: 574-257-3319 or toll-free 800-422-4101 **Fax:** 574-257-3335
E-mail: admissions@bethelcollege.edu

Getting in Last Year 520 applied; 90% were accepted; 427 enrolled (91%).

Financial Matters $14,120 tuition and fees (2002–03); $4380 room and board; 90% average percent of need met; $12,041 average financial aid amount received per undergraduate.

Academics Bethel awards associate, bachelor's, and master's degrees. Challenging opportunities include advanced placement credit, accelerated degree programs, an honors program, double majors, independent study, and a senior project. Special programs include internships, summer session for credit, off-campus study, study-abroad, and Army and Air Force ROTC. The most frequently chosen baccalaureate fields are business/marketing, education, and health professions and related sciences. The faculty at Bethel has 66 full-time members, 65% with terminal degrees. The student-faculty ratio is 17:1.

Students of Bethel The student body totals 1,746, of whom 1,634 are undergraduates. 64% are women and 36% are men. Students come from 33 states and territories and 11 other countries. 72% are from Indiana. 86% returned for their sophomore year.

Applying Bethel requires an essay, SAT I or ACT, a high school transcript, 1 recommendation, and a minimum high school GPA of 2.0. The school recommends an interview and a minimum high school GPA of 2.5. Application deadline: 8/1; 3/1 priority date for financial aid. Early and deferred admission are possible.

BETHEL COLLEGE

North Newton, KS

Small-town setting ■ Private ■ Independent Religious ■ Coed

Web site: www.bethelks.edu
Contact: Ms. Pauline Buller, Associate Director of Admissions, 300 East 27th Street, North Newton, KS 67117-0531
Telephone: 316-284-5230 or toll-free 800-522-1887 ext. 230 **Fax:** 316-284-5870
E-mail: admissions@bethelks.edu

Getting in Last Year 488 applied; 68% were accepted; 99 enrolled (30%).

Financial Matters $13,000 tuition and fees (2002–03); $5500 room and board; 88% average percent of need met; $13,599 average financial aid amount received per undergraduate (2001–02).

Academics Bethel awards bachelor's degrees. Challenging opportunities include advanced placement credit, double majors, independent study, and a senior project. Special programs include cooperative education, internships, summer session for credit, off-campus study, and study-abroad. The most frequently chosen baccalaureate fields are education, health professions and related sciences, and business/marketing. The faculty at Bethel has 44 full-time members, 57% with terminal degrees. The student-faculty ratio is 9:1.

Students of Bethel The student body is made up of 471 undergraduates. 48.4% are women and 51.6% are men. Students come from 27 states and territories and 12 other countries. 62% are from Kansas. 3.2% are international students. 72% returned for their sophomore year.

Applying Bethel requires SAT I or ACT, a high school transcript, and a minimum high school GPA of 2.5, and in some cases an essay and 2 recommendations. The school recommends an interview. Application deadline: 8/1; 3/15 priority date for financial aid. Deferred admission is possible.

BETHEL COLLEGE

St. Paul, MN

Suburban setting ■ Private ■ Independent Religious ■ Coed

Web site: www.bethel.edu
Contact: Mr. Jay Fedje, Director of Admissions, 3900 Bethel Drive, St. Paul, MN 55112
Telephone: 651-638-6242 or toll-free 800-255-8706 ext. 6242 **Fax:** 651-635-1490
E-mail: bcoll-admit@bethel.edu

Getting in Last Year 1,460 applied; 89% were accepted; 579 enrolled (45%).

Financial Matters $17,735 tuition and fees (2002–03); $6200 room and board; 85% average percent of need met; $14,097 average financial aid amount received per undergraduate.

Academics Bethel awards associate, bachelor's, and master's degrees. Challenging opportunities include advanced placement credit, accelerated degree programs, student-designed majors, freshman honors college, an honors program, double majors, independent study, and a senior project. Special programs include internships, summer session for credit, off-campus study, study-abroad, and Army and Air Force ROTC. The most frequently chosen baccalaureate fields are education, business/marketing, and health professions and related sciences. The faculty at Bethel has 155 full-time members, 74% with terminal degrees. The student-faculty ratio is 9:1.

Students of Bethel The student body totals 3,091, of whom 2,772 are undergraduates. 61.1% are women and 38.9% are men. Students come from 41 states and territories. 74% are from Minnesota. 0.1% are international students. 86% returned for their sophomore year.

Applying Bethel requires an essay, SAT I, ACT, or PSAT, a high school transcript, and 2 recommendations, and in some cases an interview. The school recommends an interview. Application deadline: 3/1; 4/15 priority date for financial aid. Early admission is possible.

BETHEL COLLEGE

McKenzie, TN

Small-town setting ■ Private ■ Independent Religious ■ Coed

Web site: www.bethel-college.edu
Contact: Mrs. Tina Hodges, Director of Admissions and Marketing, 325 Cherry Avenue, McKenzie, TN 38201
Telephone: 731-352-4030 **Fax:** 731-352-4069
E-mail: admissions@bethel-college.edu

Getting in Last Year 614 applied; 63% were accepted; 140 enrolled (36%).

Financial Matters $9030 tuition and fees (2002–03); $4550 room and board; 79% average percent of need met; $9023 average financial aid amount received per undergraduate.

Academics Bethel awards bachelor's, master's, and first-professional degrees. Challenging opportunities include advanced placement credit, accelerated degree programs, student-designed majors, double majors, and a senior project. Special programs include internships, summer session for credit, and off-campus study. The most frequently chosen baccalaureate fields are business/marketing, education, and biological/life sciences. The faculty at Bethel has 35 full-time members, 51% with terminal degrees. The student-faculty ratio is 14:1.

Students of Bethel The student body totals 1,059, of whom 941 are undergraduates. 54% are women and 46% are men. Students come from 28 states and territories and 2 other countries. 88% are from Tennessee. 1.6% are international students. 54% returned for their sophomore year.

Applying Bethel requires SAT I or ACT, a high school transcript, and a minimum high school GPA of 2.5, and in some cases an essay, an interview, and 1 recommendation. Application deadline: rolling admissions; 3/1 priority date for financial aid. Early and deferred admission are possible.

BETHESDA CHRISTIAN UNIVERSITY

Anaheim, CA

Private ■ Independent Religious ■ Coed

Web site: www.bcu.edu
Contact: Mr. Samuel C. Jung, Admissions Coordinator, 730 N. Euclid Street, Anaheim, CA 92801
Telephone: 714-517-1945 **Fax:** 714-517-1948
E-mail: admission@bcu.edu

Getting in Last Year 32 enrolled.

Financial Matters $4120 tuition and fees (2002–03); 60% average percent of need met; $3337 average financial aid amount received per undergraduate (1999–2000).

Academics Bethesda Christian University awards bachelor's, master's, and first-professional degrees. Challenging opportunities include accelerated degree programs, double majors, independent study, and a senior project. Special programs include internships, summer session for credit, and study-abroad. The most frequently chosen baccalaureate field is education. The faculty at Bethesda Christian University has 6 full-time members, 100% with terminal degrees. The student-faculty ratio is 15:1.

Students of Bethesda Christian University The student body totals 206, of whom 164 are undergraduates. 54.3% are women and 45.7% are men. Students come from 3 states and territories and 3 other countries. 100% are from California. 70.1% are international students. 36% returned for their sophomore year.

Applying Bethesda Christian University requires an essay, a high school transcript, an interview, 2 recommendations, 2 photographs, and a minimum high school GPA of 2.0. Application deadline: 8/11. Early admission is possible.

BETHUNE-COOKMAN COLLEGE

Daytona Beach, FL

Urban setting ■ Private ■ Independent Religious ■ Coed

Web site: www.bethune.cookman.edu

Contact: Mr. Les Ferrier, Director of Admissions, 640 Dr. Mary McLeod Bethune Boulevard, Daytona Beach, FL 32114-3099

Telephone: 386-481-2600 or toll-free 800-448-0228 **Fax:** 386-481-2601

E-mail: admissions@cookman.edu

Getting in Last Year 2,523 applied; 72% were accepted; 620 enrolled (34%).

Financial Matters $9810 tuition and fees (2002–03); $6130 room and board; 73% average percent of need met; $13,612 average financial aid amount received per undergraduate.

Academics Bethune-Cookman awards bachelor's degrees. Challenging opportunities include advanced placement credit, accelerated degree programs, an honors program, double majors, independent study, and a senior project. Special programs include cooperative education, internships, summer session for credit, study-abroad, and Army and Air Force ROTC. The most frequently chosen baccalaureate fields are education, business/marketing, and protective services/public administration. The faculty at Bethune-Cookman has 136 full-time members, 56% with terminal degrees. The student-faculty ratio is 17:1.

Students of Bethune-Cookman The student body is made up of 2,584 undergraduates. 59.2% are women and 40.8% are men. Students come from 42 states and territories and 36 other countries. 72% are from Florida. 6.7% are international students. 76% returned for their sophomore year.

Applying Bethune-Cookman requires SAT I or ACT, a high school transcript, medical history, and a minimum high school GPA of 2.25, and in some cases an interview. Application deadline: 6/30; 4/1 priority date for financial aid. Early and deferred admission are possible.

BEULAH HEIGHTS BIBLE COLLEGE

Atlanta, GA

Urban setting ■ Private ■ Independent Religious ■ Coed

Web site: www.beulah.org

Contact: Mr. John Dreher, Associate Director of Admissions, 892 Berne Street, SE, PO Box 18145, Atlanta, GA 30316

Telephone: 404-627-2681 ext. 114 or toll-free 888-777-BHBC **Fax:** 404-627-0702

E-mail: admissions@beulah.org

Getting in Last Year 155 enrolled.

Financial Matters $3990 tuition and fees (2002–03); $4400 room only; 70% average percent of need met; $1701 average financial aid amount received per undergraduate.

Academics Beulah Heights Bible College awards associate and bachelor's degrees. Challenging opportunities include advanced placement credit, accelerated degree programs, and double majors. Special programs include cooperative education, internships, and summer session for credit. The faculty at Beulah Heights Bible College has 18 full-time members, 39% with terminal degrees. The student-faculty ratio is 17:1.

Students of Beulah Heights Bible College The student body is made up of 620 undergraduates. 57.3% are women and 42.7% are men. Students come from 22 states and territories and 12 other countries. 70% are from Georgia. 14.2% are international students. 42% returned for their sophomore year.

Applying Beulah Heights Bible College requires a high school transcript, 2 recommendations, and a minimum high school GPA of 2.0. The school recommends SAT II: Writing Test, SAT I or ACT, and an interview. Application deadline: rolling admissions; 6/30 priority date for financial aid. Early admission is possible.

BIOLA UNIVERSITY

La Mirada, CA

Suburban setting ■ Private ■ Independent Religious ■ Coed

Web site: www.biola.edu

Contact: Mr. Greg Vaughan, Director of Enrollment Management, 13800 Biola Avenue, La Mirada, CA 90639

Telephone: 562-903-4752 or toll-free 800-652-4652 **Fax:** 562-903-4709

E-mail: admissions@biola.edu

Getting in Last Year 2,293 applied; 57% were accepted; 679 enrolled (52%).

Financial Matters $18,454 tuition and fees (2002–03); $5930 room and board; 77% average percent of need met; $13,701 average financial aid amount received per undergraduate.

Academics Biola awards bachelor's, master's, doctoral, and first-professional degrees. Challenging opportunities include advanced placement credit, accelerated degree programs, freshman honors college, an honors program, double majors, independent study, and a senior project. Special programs include cooperative education, internships, summer session for credit, off-campus study, study-abroad, and Army and Air Force ROTC. The most frequently chosen baccalaureate fields are business/marketing, communications/communication technologies, and education. The faculty at Biola has 172 full-time members. The student-faculty ratio is 18:1.

Students of Biola The student body totals 4,593, of whom 3,159 are undergraduates. 61% are women and 39% are men. Students come from 47 states and territories and 40 other countries. 71% are from California. 4.3% are international students. 83% returned for their sophomore year.

Applying Biola requires an essay, SAT I or ACT, a high school transcript, an interview, and 2 recommendations. The school recommends a minimum high school GPA of 3.0. Application deadline: 3/1; 3/2 priority date for financial aid. Early and deferred admission are possible.

BIRMINGHAM-SOUTHERN COLLEGE

Birmingham, AL

Urban setting ■ Private ■ Independent Religious ■ Coed

Web site: www.bsc.edu

Contact: Ms. DeeDee Barnes Bruns, Vice President for Admission and Financial Aid, Box 549008, Birmingham, AL 35254

Telephone: 205-226-4696 or toll-free 800-523-5793 **Fax:** 205-226-3074

E-mail: admissions@bsc.edu

Getting in Last Year 1,040 applied; 90% were accepted; 341 enrolled (37%).

Financial Matters $18,050 tuition and fees (2002–03); $5940 room and board; 82% average percent of need met; $15,639 average financial aid amount received per undergraduate.

Academics Birmingham-Southern awards bachelor's and master's degrees. Challenging opportunities include advanced placement credit, student-designed majors, an honors program, double majors, independent study, and a senior project. Special programs include internships, summer session for credit, off-campus study, study-abroad, and Army and Air Force ROTC. The most frequently chosen baccalaureate fields are business/marketing, visual/performing arts, and biological/life sciences. The faculty at Birmingham-Southern has 99 full-time members, 98% with terminal degrees. The student-faculty ratio is 12:1.

Students of Birmingham-Southern The student body totals 1,407, of whom 1,316 are undergraduates. 58.1% are women and 41.9% are men. Students come from 28 states and territories. 74% are from Alabama. 0.2% are international students. 84% returned for their sophomore year.

Applying Birmingham-Southern requires an essay, SAT I or ACT, a high school transcript, 1 recommendation, and a minimum high school GPA of 2.0, and in some cases an interview. The school recommends an interview. Application deadline: rolling admissions; 3/1 priority date for financial aid. Early and deferred admission are possible.

BISHOP'S UNIVERSITY

Lennoxville, QC Canada

Small-town setting ■ Public ■ Coed

Web site: www.ubishops.ca

Contact: Mr. Hans Rouleau, Coordinator of Liaison, Lennoxville, QC J1M 1Z7 Canada

Telephone: 819-822-9600 ext. 2217 or toll-free 800-567-2792 ext. 2681 **Fax:** 819-822-9661

E-mail: liaison@ubishops.ca

Getting in Last Year 1,768 applied; 79% were accepted; 578 enrolled (41%).

Financial Matters $2455 resident tuition and fees (2002–03); $4799 nonresident tuition and fees (2002–03); $5400 room and board.

Academics Bishop's awards bachelor's and master's degrees. Challenging opportunities include advanced placement credit, accelerated degree programs, student-designed majors, an honors program, double majors, independent study, and a senior project. Special programs include cooperative education, internships,

Bishop's University (continued)

summer session for credit, off-campus study, and study-abroad. The most frequently chosen baccalaureate fields are business/marketing, social sciences and history, and education. The faculty at Bishop's has 117 full-time members, 74% with terminal degrees. The student-faculty ratio is 14:1.

Students of Bishop's The student body totals 2,430, of whom 2,423 are undergraduates. 56.5% are women and 43.5% are men. Students come from 12 states and territories and 38 other countries. 56% are from Quebec. 85% returned for their sophomore year.

Applying Bishop's requires a high school transcript, birth certificate, copy of student visa, and a minimum high school GPA of 3.0, and in some cases ACT and 1 recommendation. The school recommends SAT II Subject Tests. Application deadline: 3/1.

BLACKBURN COLLEGE

Carlinville, IL

Small-town setting ■ Private ■ Independent Religious ■ Coed

Contact: Mr. John Malin, Dean of Enrollment Management, 700 College Avenue, Carlinville, IL 62626-1498
Telephone: 217-854-3231 ext. 4252 or toll-free 800-233-3550
Fax: 217-854-3713
E-mail: admit@mail.blackburn.edu

Getting in Last Year 913 applied; 52% were accepted; 147 enrolled (31%).

Financial Matters $9420 tuition and fees (2002–03); $4270 room and board; 85% average percent of need met.

Academics Blackburn College awards bachelor's degrees. Challenging opportunities include advanced placement credit, student-designed majors, an honors program, double majors, independent study, and a senior project. Special programs include cooperative education, internships, off-campus study, and study-abroad. The most frequently chosen baccalaureate fields are business/marketing, education, and biological/life sciences. The faculty at Blackburn College has 31 full-time members, 74% with terminal degrees. The student-faculty ratio is 15:1.

Students of Blackburn College The student body is made up of 579 undergraduates. 56% are women and 44% are men. Students come from 12 states and territories and 8 other countries. 3.1% are international students. 65% returned for their sophomore year.

Applying Blackburn College requires an essay, SAT I or ACT, a high school transcript, and a minimum high school GPA of 2.0, and in some cases an interview and 1 recommendation. Application deadline: rolling admissions; 4/1 priority date for financial aid. Deferred admission is possible.

BLACK HILLS STATE UNIVERSITY

Spearfish, SD

Small-town setting ■ Public ■ State-supported ■ Coed

Web site: www.bhsu.edu
Contact: Mr. Steve Ochsner, Dean of Admissions, University Street Box 9502, Spearfish, SD 57799-9502
Telephone: 605-642-6343 or toll-free 800-255-2478
E-mail: admissions@bhsu.edu

Getting in Last Year 1,288 applied; 94% were accepted; 592 enrolled (49%).

Financial Matters $4193 resident tuition and fees (2002–03); $8726 nonresident tuition and fees (2002–03); $3127 room and board; $5463 average financial aid amount received per undergraduate (2001–02).

Academics Black Hills State University awards associate, bachelor's, and master's degrees and post-bachelor's and post-master's certificates. Challenging opportunities include advanced placement credit, accelerated degree programs, double majors, independent study, and a senior project. Special programs include cooperative education, internships, summer session for credit, off-campus study, and Army ROTC. The most frequently chosen baccalaureate fields are education, business/marketing, and psychology. The faculty at Black Hills State University has 108 full-time members, 76% with terminal degrees. The student-faculty ratio is 24:1.

Students of Black Hills State University The student body totals 3,747, of whom 3,542 are undergraduates. 62.6% are women and 37.4% are men. Students come from 36 states and territories and 6 other countries. 80% are from South Dakota. 0.2% are international students. 54% returned for their sophomore year.

Applying Black Hills State University requires SAT I or ACT, a high school transcript, and minimum 2.0 high school GPA in core curriculum. Application deadline: rolling admissions; 3/1 priority date for financial aid.

BLESSING-RIEMAN COLLEGE OF NURSING

Quincy, IL

Small-town setting ■ Private ■ Independent ■ Coed, Primarily Women

Web site: www.brcn.edu
Contact: Heather Mutter or Kelli Collins, Admissions Counselor, PO Box 7005, Quincy, IL 62305-7005
Telephone: 800-897-9140 ext. 6961 or toll-free 800-877-9140 ext. 6964
Fax: 217-223-4661
E-mail: brenadmissions@blessinghospital.com

Getting in Last Year 99 applied; 62% were accepted; 23 enrolled (38%).

Financial Matters $12,100 tuition and fees (2002–03); $5000 room and board; 75% average percent of need met.

Academics Blessing-Rieman awards bachelor's degrees. Challenging opportunities include advanced placement credit, an honors program, double majors, and a senior project. Special programs include internships and summer session for credit. The most frequently chosen baccalaureate field is health professions and related sciences. The faculty at Blessing-Rieman has 13 full-time members, 31% with terminal degrees. The student-faculty ratio is 10:1.

Students of Blessing-Rieman The student body is made up of 165 undergraduates. 95.2% are women and 4.8% are men. Students come from 8 states and territories. 66% are from Illinois. 67% returned for their sophomore year.

Applying Blessing-Rieman requires SAT I or ACT, a high school transcript, and a minimum high school GPA of 3.0. The school recommends an essay and an interview. Application deadline: rolling admissions. Deferred admission is possible.

BLOOMFIELD COLLEGE

Bloomfield, NJ

Suburban setting ■ Private ■ Independent Religious ■ Coed

Web site: www.bloomfield.edu
Contact: Mr. Ray Sheenan, Associate Dean of Admission, Office of Enrollment Management and Admission, Bloomfield, NJ 07003-9981
Telephone: 973-748-9000 ext. 390 or toll-free 800-848-4555 **Fax:** 973-748-0916
E-mail: admission@bloomfield.edu

Getting in Last Year 1,140 applied; 79% were accepted; 383 enrolled (43%).

Financial Matters $12,300 tuition and fees (2002–03); $5850 room and board; 73% average percent of need met; $10,609 average financial aid amount received per undergraduate.

Academics Bloomfield awards bachelor's degrees. Challenging opportunities include advanced placement credit, accelerated degree programs, student-designed majors, an honors program, double majors, independent study, and a senior project. Special programs include cooperative education, internships, summer session for credit, study-abroad, and Army ROTC. The most frequently chosen baccalaureate fields are business/marketing, social sciences and history, and health professions and related sciences. The faculty at Bloomfield has 62 full-time members, 77% with terminal degrees. The student-faculty ratio is 15:1.

Students of Bloomfield The student body is made up of 1,887 undergraduates. 67.6% are women and 32.4% are men. Students come from 17 states and territories and 3 other countries. 97% are from New Jersey. 2% are international students. 70% returned for their sophomore year.

Applying Bloomfield requires an essay, SAT I or ACT, a high school transcript, 2 recommendations, and a minimum high school GPA of 2.30. The school recommends an interview and sample of work. Application deadline: 8/1; 6/1 priority date for financial aid. Deferred admission is possible.

BLOOMSBURG UNIVERSITY OF PENNSYLVANIA

Bloomsburg, PA

Small-town setting ■ Public ■ State-supported ■ Coed

Web site: www.bloomu.edu
Contact: Mr. Christopher Keller, Director of Admissions, 104 Student Services Center, Bloomsburg, PA 17815-1905
Telephone: 570-389-4316
E-mail: buadmiss@bloomu.edu

Getting in Last Year 6,888 applied; 69% were accepted; 1,487 enrolled (31%).

Financial Matters $5550 resident tuition and fees (2002–03); $12,118 nonresident tuition and fees (2002–03); $4776 room and board; 65% average percent of need met; $11,492 average financial aid amount received per undergraduate.

Academics BU awards associate, bachelor's, and master's degrees and post-bachelor's certificates. Challenging opportunities include advanced placement credit, freshman honors college, an honors program, double majors, and independent study. Special programs include cooperative education, internships, summer session for credit, off-campus study, study-abroad, and Army and Air Force ROTC. The most frequently chosen baccalaureate fields are education, business/marketing, and English. The faculty at BU has 350 full-time members, 81% with terminal degrees. The student-faculty ratio is 20:1.

Students of BU The student body totals 8,039, of whom 7,298 are undergraduates. 60.5% are women and 39.5% are men. Students come from 26 states and territories and 28 other countries. 90% are from Pennsylvania. 0.5% are international students. 80% returned for their sophomore year.

Applying BU requires SAT I or ACT, a high school transcript, and recommendations. Application deadline: rolling admissions; 3/15 priority date for financial aid. Early and deferred admission are possible.

BLUEFIELD COLLEGE

Bluefield, VA

Small-town setting ■ *Private* ■ *Independent Religious* ■ *Coed*

Web site: www.bluefield.edu

Contact: Office of Admissions, 3000 College Drive, Bluefield, VA 24605-1799

Telephone: 276-326-4214 or toll-free 800-872-0175 **Fax:** 276-326-4288

E-mail: admissions@mail.bluefield.edu

Getting in Last Year 514 applied; 74% were accepted; 135 enrolled (36%).

Financial Matters $9795 tuition and fees (2002–03); $5205 room and board.

Academics BC awards bachelor's degrees. Challenging opportunities include advanced placement credit, accelerated degree programs, student-designed majors, freshman honors college, an honors program, double majors, and a senior project. Special programs include internships, summer session for credit, and study-abroad. The most frequently chosen baccalaureate fields are business/marketing, protective services/public administration, and psychology. The faculty at BC has 34 full-time members, 62% with terminal degrees. The student-faculty ratio is 15:1.

Students of BC The student body is made up of 858 undergraduates. 54.4% are women and 45.6% are men. Students come from 14 states and territories and 3 other countries. 63% are from Virginia. 0.5% are international students. 71% returned for their sophomore year.

Applying BC requires SAT I or ACT, a high school transcript, and a minimum high school GPA of 2.0, and in some cases an interview and recommendations. The school recommends an interview. Application deadline: rolling admissions; 3/10 priority date for financial aid. Deferred admission is possible.

BLUEFIELD STATE COLLEGE

Bluefield, WV

Small-town setting ■ *Public* ■ *State-supported* ■ *Coed*

Web site: www.bluefield.wvnet.edu

Contact: Mr. Kenneth Mandeville, Director of Student Recruitment, 219 Rock Street, Bluefield, WV 24701-2198

Telephone: 304-327-4067 or toll-free 800-344-8892 ext. 4065 (in-state), 800-654-7798 ext. 4065 (out-of-state) **Fax:** 304-325-7747

E-mail: bscadmit@bluefield.wvnet.edu

Getting in Last Year 1,191 applied; 99% were accepted; 603 enrolled (51%).

Financial Matters $2398 resident tuition and fees (2002–03); $6296 nonresident tuition and fees (2002–03); 70% average percent of need met; $4700 average financial aid amount received per undergraduate (2001–02).

Academics Bluefield State awards associate and bachelor's degrees. Challenging opportunities include advanced placement credit, student-designed majors, an honors program, double majors, and a senior project. Special programs include internships and summer session for credit. The most frequently chosen baccalaureate fields are engineering/engineering technologies, business/marketing, and liberal arts/general studies. The faculty at Bluefield State has 79 full-time members, 42% with terminal degrees. The student-faculty ratio is 17:1.

Students of Bluefield State The student body is made up of 2,831 undergraduates. 60.6% are women and 39.4% are men. Students come from 12 states and territories and 15 other countries. 95% are from West Virginia. 1.5% are international students. 53% returned for their sophomore year.

Applying Bluefield State requires a high school transcript and a minimum high school GPA of 2.0. The school recommends SAT I or ACT. Application deadline: rolling admissions; 3/1 priority date for financial aid. Deferred admission is possible.

BLUE MOUNTAIN COLLEGE

Blue Mountain, MS

Rural setting ■ *Private* ■ *Independent Religious* ■ *Women Only*

Web site: www.bmc.edu

Contact: Ms. Tina Barkley, Director of Admissions, PO Box 160, Blue Mountain, MS 38610-0160

Telephone: 662-685-4161 ext. 176 or toll-free 800-235-0136

E-mail: tbarkley@bmc.edu

Getting in Last Year 101 applied; 90% were accepted; 50 enrolled (55%).

Financial Matters $6570 tuition and fees (2002–03); $3400 room and board; 15% average percent of need met.

Academics Blue Mountain College awards bachelor's degrees (also offers a coordinate academic program for men preparing for church-related vocations). Challenging opportunities include advanced placement credit, accelerated degree programs, an honors program, double majors, and a senior project. Special programs include internships and summer session for credit. The most frequently chosen baccalaureate fields are education, psychology, and biological/life sciences. The faculty at Blue Mountain College has 21 full-time members, 57% with terminal degrees. The student-faculty ratio is 14:1.

Students of Blue Mountain College The student body is made up of 389 undergraduates. Students come from 10 states and territories and 1 other country. 89% are from Mississippi. 0.3% are international students. 74% returned for their sophomore year.

Applying Blue Mountain College requires SAT I or ACT and a high school transcript, and in some cases an essay, an interview, and 2 recommendations. The school recommends a minimum high school GPA of 2.0. Application deadline: rolling admissions; 3/1 priority date for financial aid. Early admission is possible.

BLUFFTON COLLEGE

Bluffton, OH

Small-town setting ■ *Private* ■ *Independent Religious* ■ *Coed*

Web site: www.bluffton.edu

Contact: Mr. Eric Fulcomer, Director of Admissions, Associate Dean for Enrollment Management, 280 West College Avenue, Suite 1, Bluffton, OH 45817-1196

Telephone: 419-358-3254 or toll-free 800-488-3257 **Fax:** 419-358-3232

E-mail: admissions@bluffton.edu

Getting in Last Year 929 applied; 78% were accepted; 263 enrolled (36%).

Financial Matters $16,430 tuition and fees (2002–03); $5636 room and board; 92% average percent of need met; $15,795 average financial aid amount received per undergraduate.

Academics Bluffton College awards bachelor's and master's degrees. Challenging opportunities include advanced placement credit, student-designed majors, an honors program, independent study, and a senior project. Special programs include internships, summer session for credit, off-campus study, and study-abroad. The most frequently chosen baccalaureate fields are business/marketing, education, and protective services/public administration. The faculty at Bluffton College has 74 full-time members, 70% with terminal degrees. The student-faculty ratio is 14:1.

Students of Bluffton College The student body totals 1,110, of whom 1,053 are undergraduates. 58.8% are women and 41.2% are men. Students come from 14 states and territories and 11 other countries. 89% are from Ohio. 2% are international students. 79% returned for their sophomore year.

Applying Bluffton College requires SAT I or ACT, a high school transcript, 2 recommendations, and rank in upper 50% of high school class or 2.3 high school GPA, and in some cases an essay. The school recommends an interview. Application deadline: 5/31; 10/1 for financial aid, with a 5/1 priority date. Deferred admission is possible.

BOISE BIBLE COLLEGE

Boise, ID

Suburban setting ■ *Private* ■ *Independent Religious* ■ *Coed*

Web site: www.boisebible.edu

Contact: Mr. Ross Knudsen, Director of Admissions, 8695 Marigold Street, Boise, ID 83704

Telephone: 208-376-7731 or toll-free 800-893-7755 **Fax:** 208-376-7743

E-mail: boibible@micron.net

Getting in Last Year 71 applied; 94% were accepted.

Financial Matters $5689 tuition and fees (2002–03); $4200 room and board; 47% average percent of need met; $5919 average financial aid amount received per undergraduate.

Academics BBC awards associate and bachelor's degrees. Challenging opportunities include advanced placement credit, double majors, independent study, and a senior project. Special programs include cooperative education and internships. The faculty at BBC has 6 full-time members. The student-faculty ratio is 13:1.

Students of BBC The student body is made up of 134 undergraduates. Students come from 9 states and territories. 56% returned for their sophomore year.

Applying BBC requires an essay, a high school transcript, 3 recommendations, and a minimum high school GPA of 2.0. The school recommends an interview. Application deadline: rolling admissions; 5/1 priority date for financial aid. Deferred admission is possible.

BOSTON ARCHITECTURAL CENTER

Boston, MA

Urban setting ■ *Private* ■ *Independent* ■ *Coed*

Web site: www.the-bac.edu

Contact: Mr. Will Dunfey, Director of Admission, 320 Newbury Street, Boston, MA 02115-2795

Telephone: 617-585-0256 or toll-free 877-585-0100 **Fax:** 617-585-0121

E-mail: admissions@the-bac.edu

Getting in Last Year 90 applied; 91% were accepted; 64 enrolled (78%).

Financial Matters $7448 tuition and fees (2002–03); 29% average percent of need met; $3661 average financial aid amount received per undergraduate.

Boston Architectural Center (continued)

Academics BAC awards bachelor's and master's degrees. Challenging opportunities include advanced placement credit, independent study, and a senior project. Special programs include internships, summer session for credit, and off-campus study. The most frequently chosen baccalaureate field is architecture. The faculty at BAC has 250 members, 28% with terminal degrees. The student-faculty ratio is 10:1.

Students of BAC The student body totals 698, of whom 431 are undergraduates. 33.9% are women and 66.1% are men. Students come from 43 states and territories. 53% are from Massachusetts. 53% returned for their sophomore year.

Applying BAC requires a high school transcript. Application deadline: rolling admissions; 4/15 priority date for financial aid.

BOSTON COLLEGE

Chestnut Hill, MA

Suburban setting ■ Private ■ Independent Religious ■ Coed

Web site: www.bc.edu
Contact: Mr. John L. Mahoney Jr., Director of Undergraduate Admission, 140 Commonwealth Avenue, Devlin Hall 208, Chestnut Hill, MA 02467-3809
Telephone: 617-552-3100 or toll-free 800-360-2522 **Fax:** 617-552-0798
E-mail: ugadmis@bc.edu

Getting in Last Year 19,059 applied; 34% were accepted; 2,103 enrolled (33%).

Financial Matters $25,862 tuition and fees (2002–03); $8990 room and board; 100% average percent of need met; $18,830 average financial aid amount received per undergraduate (2000–01).

Academics BC awards bachelor's, master's, doctoral, and first-professional degrees and post-master's certificates (also offers continuing education program with significant enrollment not reflected in profile). Challenging opportunities include advanced placement credit, accelerated degree programs, student-designed majors, freshman honors college, an honors program, double majors, and independent study. Special programs include internships, summer session for credit, off-campus study, study-abroad, and Army and Air Force ROTC. The most frequently chosen baccalaureate fields are business/marketing, social sciences and history, and communications/communication technologies. The faculty at BC has 660 full-time members. The student-faculty ratio is 13:1.

Students of BC The student body totals 13,510, of whom 9,000 are undergraduates. 52.7% are women and 47.3% are men. Students come from 50 states and territories and 100 other countries. 28% are from Massachusetts. 1.3% are international students. 95% returned for their sophomore year.

Applying BC requires an essay, SAT II: Writing Test, SAT I and SAT II or ACT, a high school transcript, and 2 recommendations. Application deadline: 1/2; 2/1 priority date for financial aid. Early and deferred admission are possible.

BOSTON UNIVERSITY

Boston, MA

Urban setting ■ Private ■ Independent ■ Coed

Web site: www.bu.edu
Contact: Ms. Kelly A. Walter, Director of Undergraduate Admissions, 121 Bay State Road, Boston, MA 02215
Telephone: 617-353-2300 **Fax:** 617-353-9695
E-mail: admissions@bu.edu

Getting in Last Year 27,038 applied; 58% were accepted; 4,560 enrolled (29%).

Financial Matters $27,414 tuition and fees (2002–03); $8978 room and board; 91% average percent of need met; $24,309 average financial aid amount received per undergraduate.

Academics Boston University awards bachelor's, master's, doctoral, and first-professional degrees and post-master's certificates. Challenging opportunities include advanced placement credit, accelerated degree programs, student-designed majors, an honors program, double majors, independent study, and a senior project. Special programs include cooperative education, internships, summer session for credit, off-campus study, study-abroad, and Army, Navy and Air Force ROTC. The most frequently chosen baccalaureate fields are communications/communication technologies, social sciences and history, and business/marketing. The faculty at Boston University has 2,500 full-time members. The student-faculty ratio is 14:1.

Students of Boston University The student body totals 28,982, of whom 17,860 are undergraduates. 59.6% are women and 40.4% are men. Students come from 52 states and territories and 101 other countries. 24% are from Massachusetts. 7% are international students. 85% returned for their sophomore year.

Applying Boston University requires an essay, SAT I or ACT, a high school transcript, and 2 recommendations, and in some cases SAT II Subject Tests, SAT II: Writing Test, an interview, and audition, portfolio. The school recommends SAT II: Writing Test and a minimum high school GPA of 3.0. Application deadline: 1/1; 2/15 priority date for financial aid. Early and deferred admission are possible.

BOWDOIN COLLEGE

Brunswick, ME

Small-town setting ■ Private ■ Independent ■ Coed

Web site: www.bowdoin.edu
Contact: Ms. Rose Woodd, Receptionist, 5000 College Station, Brunswick, ME 04011-8441
Telephone: 207-725-3958 **Fax:** 207-725-3101
E-mail: admissions@bowdoin.edu

Getting in Last Year 4,505 applied; 25% were accepted; 458 enrolled (41%).

Financial Matters $28,685 tuition and fees (2002–03); $7305 room and board; 100% average percent of need met; $24,675 average financial aid amount received per undergraduate.

Academics Bowdoin awards bachelor's degrees. Challenging opportunities include advanced placement credit, accelerated degree programs, student-designed majors, double majors, and independent study. Special programs include off-campus study and study-abroad. The most frequently chosen baccalaureate fields are social sciences and history, business/marketing, and foreign language/literature. The faculty at Bowdoin has 151 full-time members, 94% with terminal degrees. The student-faculty ratio is 10:1.

Students of Bowdoin The student body is made up of 1,657 undergraduates. 50.9% are women and 49.1% are men. Students come from 57 states and territories and 27 other countries. 15% are from Maine. 3.3% are international students. 94% returned for their sophomore year.

Applying Bowdoin requires an essay, a high school transcript, and 3 recommendations. The school recommends an interview. Application deadline: 1/1; 2/15 for financial aid. Deferred admission is possible.

BOWIE STATE UNIVERSITY

Bowie, MD

Small-town setting ■ Public ■ State-supported ■ Coed

Web site: www.bowiestate.edu
Contact: Shingiral Chanaiwa, Coordinator of Undergraduate Enrollment, 14000 Jericho Park Road, Henry Building, Bowie, MD 20715-9465
Telephone: 301-860-3425 or toll-free 877-772-6943 **Fax:** 301-860-3438
E-mail: dkiah@bowiestate.edu

Getting in Last Year 2,609 applied; 52% were accepted; 584 enrolled (43%).

Financial Matters $5025 resident tuition and fees (2002–03); $11,441 nonresident tuition and fees (2002–03); $5673 room and board; 64% average percent of need met; $6829 average financial aid amount received per undergraduate (2001–02).

Academics BSU awards bachelor's, master's, and doctoral degrees. Challenging opportunities include advanced placement credit, an honors program, double majors, independent study, and a senior project. Special programs include cooperative education, internships, summer session for credit, off-campus study, study-abroad, and Army ROTC. The most frequently chosen baccalaureate fields are business/marketing, interdisciplinary studies, and social sciences and history. The faculty at BSU has 149 full-time members, 66% with terminal degrees. The student-faculty ratio is 18:1.

Students of BSU The student body totals 5,257, of whom 3,673 are undergraduates. 61.7% are women and 38.3% are men. Students come from 39 states and territories and 47 other countries. 91% are from Maryland. 1.3% are international students. 73% returned for their sophomore year.

Applying BSU requires SAT I or ACT, a high school transcript, and a minimum high school GPA of 2.2, and in some cases recommendations. The school recommends recommendations. Application deadline: 4/1; 3/1 priority date for financial aid.

BOWLING GREEN STATE UNIVERSITY

Bowling Green, OH

Small-town setting ■ Public ■ State-supported ■ Coed

Web site: www.bgsu.edu
Contact: Mr. Gary Swegan, Director of Admissions, 110 McFall, Bowling Green, OH 43403
Telephone: 419-372-2086 **Fax:** 419-372-6955
E-mail: admissions@bgnet.bgsu.edu

Getting in Last Year 10,128 applied; 91% were accepted; 3,605 enrolled (39%).

Financial Matters $6502 resident tuition and fees (2002–03); $13,130 nonresident tuition and fees (2002–03); $6490 room and board; 69% average percent of need met; $6122 average financial aid amount received per undergraduate (2001–02).

Academics BGSU awards bachelor's, master's, and doctoral degrees and post-master's certificates. Challenging opportunities include advanced placement credit, accelerated degree programs, student-designed majors, an honors program, double majors, independent study, and a senior project. Special programs include cooperative education, internships, summer session for credit, off-campus study, study-abroad, and Army and Air Force ROTC. The most frequently chosen baccalaureate fields are education, business/marketing, and English. The faculty at BGSU has 802 full-time members, 80% with terminal degrees. The student-faculty ratio is 19:1.

Students of BGSU The student body totals 18,773, of whom 15,703 are undergraduates. 56.1% are women and 43.9% are men. Students come from 52 states and territories and 86 other countries. 94% are from Ohio. 0.7% are international students. 78% returned for their sophomore year.

Applying BGSU requires SAT I or ACT, a high school transcript, and a minimum high school GPA of 2.5. The school recommends an interview. Application deadline: 7/15. Deferred admission is possible.

BRADLEY UNIVERSITY

Peoria, IL

Urban setting ■ *Private* ■ *Independent* ■ *Coed*

Web site: www.bradley.edu

Contact: Ms. Nickie Roberson, Director of Admissions, 1501 West Bradley Avenue, 100 Swords Hall, Peoria, IL 61625-0002

Telephone: 309-677-1000 or toll-free 800-447-6460

E-mail: admissions@bradley.edu

Getting in Last Year 5,506 applied; 67% were accepted; 1,112 enrolled (30%).

Financial Matters $16,110 tuition and fees (2002–03); $5800 room and board; 83% average percent of need met; $11,997 average financial aid amount received per undergraduate (2001–02).

Academics Bradley awards bachelor's and master's degrees. Challenging opportunities include advanced placement credit, accelerated degree programs, student-designed majors, an honors program, double majors, independent study, and a senior project. Special programs include cooperative education, internships, summer session for credit, off-campus study, study-abroad, and Army ROTC. The most frequently chosen baccalaureate fields are business/marketing, engineering/engineering technologies, and communications/communication technologies. The faculty at Bradley has 330 full-time members, 82% with terminal degrees. The student-faculty ratio is 14:1.

Students of Bradley The student body totals 6,098, of whom 5,190 are undergraduates. 54.6% are women and 45.4% are men. Students come from 42 states and territories and 26 other countries. 86% are from Illinois. 1.6% are international students. 86% returned for their sophomore year.

Applying Bradley requires SAT I or ACT and a high school transcript. The school recommends an essay, an interview, recommendations, and a minimum high school GPA of 3.0. Application deadline: rolling admissions; 3/1 priority date for financial aid. Early and deferred admission are possible.

BRANDEIS UNIVERSITY

Waltham, MA

Suburban setting ■ *Private* ■ *Independent* ■ *Coed*

Web site: www.brandeis.edu

Contact: Ms. Deena Whitfield, Director of Enrollment, 415 South Street, Waltham, MA 02254-9110

Telephone: 781-736-3500 or toll-free 800-622-0622 (out-of-state) **Fax:** 781-736-3536

E-mail: sendinfo@brandeis.edu

Getting in Last Year 6,080 applied; 42% were accepted; 837 enrolled (33%).

Financial Matters $28,165 tuition and fees (2002–03); $7849 room and board; 84% average percent of need met; $21,053 average financial aid amount received per undergraduate.

Academics Brandeis awards bachelor's, master's, and doctoral degrees and post-bachelor's certificates. Challenging opportunities include advanced placement credit, student-designed majors, an honors program, double majors, independent study, and a senior project. Special programs include internships, summer session for credit, off-campus study, study-abroad, and Army and Air Force ROTC. The most frequently chosen baccalaureate fields are social sciences and history, biological/life sciences, and psychology. The faculty at Brandeis has 333 full-time members, 98% with terminal degrees. The student-faculty ratio is 8:1.

Students of Brandeis The student body totals 4,852, of whom 3,057 are undergraduates. 56.3% are women and 43.7% are men. Students come from 46 states and territories and 57 other countries. 25% are from Massachusetts. 6.1% are international students. 93% returned for their sophomore year.

Applying Brandeis requires an essay, SAT I and SAT II or ACT, a high school transcript, and 2 recommendations. The school recommends an interview and a minimum high school GPA of 3.0. Application deadline: 1/31; 1/31 priority date for financial aid. Deferred admission is possible.

BRANDON UNIVERSITY

Brandon, MB Canada

Small-town setting ■ *Public* ■ *Coed*

Web site: www.brandonu.ca

Contact: Ms. Faye Douglas, Director of Admissions, 270 18th Street, Brandon, MB R7A 6A9 Canada

Telephone: 204-727-7352 or toll-free 800-644-7644 (in-state) **Fax:** 204-728-3221

E-mail: douglas@brandonu.ca

Getting in Last Year 2,025 applied; 66% were accepted; 931 enrolled (70%).

Financial Matters $3348 nonresident tuition and fees (2002–03); $5706 room and board.

Academics BU awards bachelor's and master's degrees. Challenging opportunities include accelerated degree programs, student-designed majors, an honors program, double majors, and a senior project. Special programs include summer session for credit, off-campus study, and study-abroad. The faculty at BU has 197 full-time members, 66% with terminal degrees. The student-faculty ratio is 11:1.

Students of BU The student body totals 3,224, of whom 3,140 are undergraduates. 67.3% are women and 32.7% are men. 95% are from Manitoba. 47% returned for their sophomore year.

Applying BU requires a high school transcript, and in some cases recommendations and criminal and child abuse registry checks. Application deadline: rolling admissions; 6/30 priority date for financial aid. Deferred admission is possible.

BRENAU UNIVERSITY

Gainesville, GA

Small-town setting ■ *Private* ■ *Independent* ■ *Women Only*

Web site: www.brenau.edu

Contact: Ms. Christina Cochran, Coordinator of Women's College Admission, Admissions, 1 Centennial Circle, Gainesville, GA 30501

Telephone: 770-718-5320 or toll-free 800-252-5119 **Fax:** 770-538-4306

E-mail: wcadmissions@lib.brenau.edu

Getting in Last Year 293 applied; 75% were accepted; 112 enrolled (51%).

Financial Matters $13,440 tuition and fees (2002–03); $7320 room and board; 81% average percent of need met; $13,057 average financial aid amount received per undergraduate.

Academics Brenau awards bachelor's and master's degrees (also offers coed evening and weekend programs with significant enrollment not reflected in profile). Challenging opportunities include advanced placement credit, an honors program, double majors, independent study, and a senior project. Special programs include cooperative education, internships, summer session for credit, and study-abroad. The most frequently chosen baccalaureate fields are health professions and related sciences, education, and visual/performing arts. The faculty at Brenau has 79 full-time members, 94% with terminal degrees. The student-faculty ratio is 8:1.

Students of Brenau The student body totals 616, of whom 603 are undergraduates. Students come from 22 states and territories and 22 other countries. 88% are from Georgia. 5% are international students. 61% returned for their sophomore year.

Applying Brenau requires an essay, SAT I or ACT, a high school transcript, minimum SAT I score of 900 or ACT score of 19, and a minimum high school GPA of 2.5, and in some cases an interview. The school recommends recommendations. Application deadline: rolling admissions; 5/1 priority date for financial aid. Early and deferred admission are possible.

BRESCIA UNIVERSITY

Owensboro, KY

Urban setting ■ *Private* ■ *Independent Religious* ■ *Coed*

Web site: www.brescia.edu

Contact: Sr. Mary Austin Blank, Director of Admissions, 717 Frederica Street, Owensboro, KY 42301-3023

Telephone: 270-686-4241 ext. 241 or toll-free 877-BRESCIA **Fax:** 270-686-4201

E-mail: admissions@brescia.edu

Getting in Last Year 264 applied; 80% were accepted.

Financial Matters $10,820 tuition and fees (2002–03); $4600 room and board; 53% average percent of need met; $6494 average financial aid amount received per undergraduate.

Academics Brescia awards associate, bachelor's, and master's degrees. Challenging opportunities include advanced placement credit, student-designed majors, an honors program, double majors, independent study, and a senior project. Special programs include internships, summer session for credit, off-campus study, and study-abroad. The most frequently chosen baccalaureate fields are business/marketing, protective services/public administration, and education. The faculty at Brescia has 72 members. The student-faculty ratio is 14:1.

Students of Brescia The student body totals 837. Students come from 18 states and territories and 19 other countries. 84% are from Kentucky. 5.4% are international students. 67% returned for their sophomore year.

Applying Brescia requires an essay, SAT I or ACT, a high school transcript, and a minimum high school GPA of 2.5, and in some cases an interview and 1 recommendation. Application deadline: rolling admissions; 3/1 priority date for financial aid. Deferred admission is possible.

BREVARD COLLEGE

Brevard, NC

Small-town setting ■ Private ■ Independent Religious ■ Coed

Web site: www.brevard.edu
Contact: Ms. Bridgett N. Golman, Dean of Admissions and Financial Aid, 400 North Broad Street, Brevard, NC 28712-3306
Telephone: 828-884-8300 or toll-free 800-527-9090 **Fax:** 828-884-3790
E-mail: admissions@brevard.edu

Getting in Last Year 518 applied; 87% were accepted; 152 enrolled (34%).

Financial Matters $12,930 tuition and fees (2002–03); $5400 room and board; 80% average percent of need met; $12,240 average financial aid amount received per undergraduate.

Academics Brevard awards associate and bachelor's degrees. Challenging opportunities include advanced placement credit, student-designed majors, an honors program, double majors, independent study, and a senior project. Special programs include internships and study-abroad. The most frequently chosen baccalaureate fields are parks and recreation, business/marketing, and visual/performing arts. The faculty at Brevard has 61 full-time members, 57% with terminal degrees. The student-faculty ratio is 9:1.

Students of Brevard The student body is made up of 664 undergraduates. 47.4% are women and 52.6% are men. Students come from 37 states and territories. 47% are from North Carolina. 2.4% are international students. 52% returned for their sophomore year.

Applying Brevard requires an essay, SAT I or ACT, a high school transcript, and a minimum high school GPA of 2.0, and in some cases an interview, 3 recommendations, and students in music-auditions, music tests; students in art-portfolio. Application deadline: rolling admissions; 4/15 priority date for financial aid. Deferred admission is possible.

BREWTON-PARKER COLLEGE

Mt. Vernon, GA

Rural setting ■ Private ■ Independent Religious ■ Coed

Web site: www.bpc.edu
Contact: Mr. James E. Beall, Director of Admissions, Highway 280, Mt. Vernon, GA 30445-0197
Telephone: 912-583-3268 ext. 268 or toll-free 800-342-1087 **Fax:** 912-583-4498

Getting in Last Year 377 applied; 89% were accepted; 304 enrolled (90%).

Financial Matters $8950 tuition and fees (2002–03); $4600 room and board; 61% average percent of need met; $7757 average financial aid amount received per undergraduate (2001–02).

Academics Brewton-Parker awards associate and bachelor's degrees. Challenging opportunities include advanced placement credit, an honors program, and a senior project. Special programs include cooperative education, internships, and summer session for credit. The faculty at Brewton-Parker has 51 full-time members, 69% with terminal degrees. The student-faculty ratio is 10:1.

Students of Brewton-Parker The student body is made up of 1,269 undergraduates. 61.2% are women and 38.8% are men. Students come from 16 states and territories and 12 other countries. 94% are from Georgia. 2.8% are international students. 49% returned for their sophomore year.

Applying Brewton-Parker requires SAT I or ACT, a high school transcript, and a minimum high school GPA of 2.0. The school recommends an interview. Application deadline: rolling admissions; 4/1 priority date for financial aid. Early admission is possible.

BRIARCLIFFE COLLEGE

Bethpage, NY

Suburban setting ■ Private ■ Proprietary ■ Coed

Web site: www.briarcliffe.edu
Contact: Ms. Theresa Donohue, Vice President of Marketing and Admissions, 1055 Stewart Avenue, Bethpage, NY 11714
Telephone: 516-918-3705 or toll-free 888-333-1150 (in-state) **Fax:** 516-470-6020
E-mail: info@bcl.edu

Getting in Last Year 1,334 applied; 65% were accepted; 639 enrolled (74%).

Financial Matters $13,180 tuition and fees (2002–03).

Academics Briarcliffe awards associate and bachelor's degrees. Challenging opportunities include advanced placement credit, accelerated degree programs, and independent study. Special programs include cooperative education, internships, and summer session for credit. The most frequently chosen baccalaureate field is business/marketing. The faculty at Briarcliffe has 48 full-time members, 8% with terminal degrees. The student-faculty ratio is 16:1.

Students of Briarcliffe The student body is made up of 2,742 undergraduates. 49.8% are women and 50.2% are men. Students come from 10 states and territories and 7 other countries. 100% are from New York. 0.7% are international students. 75% returned for their sophomore year.

Applying Briarcliffe requires a high school transcript and an interview. The school recommends SAT I and SAT II or ACT. Application deadline: rolling admissions. Deferred admission is possible.

BRIAR CLIFF UNIVERSITY

Sioux City, IA

Suburban setting ■ Private ■ Independent Religious ■ Coed

Web site: www.briarcliff.edu
Contact: Ms. Tammy Namminga, Applications Specialist, 3303 Rebecca Street, Sioux City, IA 51106
Telephone: 712-279-5200 ext. 5460 or toll-free 800-662-3303 ext. 5200 **Fax:** 712-279-1632
E-mail: admissions@briarcliff.edu

Getting in Last Year 1,080 applied; 81% were accepted; 248 enrolled (28%).

Financial Matters $14,580 tuition and fees (2002–03); $4911 room and board; 91% average percent of need met; $15,950 average financial aid amount received per undergraduate (2001–02).

Academics Briar Cliff awards associate, bachelor's, and master's degrees. Challenging opportunities include advanced placement credit, accelerated degree programs, student-designed majors, double majors, independent study, and a senior project. Special programs include internships, summer session for credit, and off-campus study. The most frequently chosen baccalaureate fields are business/marketing, health professions and related sciences, and protective services/public administration. The faculty at Briar Cliff has 52 full-time members, 79% with terminal degrees. The student-faculty ratio is 12:1.

Students of Briar Cliff The student body is made up of 973 undergraduates. 58.8% are women and 41.2% are men. Students come from 27 states and territories and 3 other countries. 70% are from Iowa. 0.4% are international students. 70% returned for their sophomore year.

Applying Briar Cliff requires SAT I or ACT, a high school transcript, minimum ACT score of 18, and a minimum high school GPA of 2.0, and in some cases an interview and 3 recommendations. The school recommends an essay. Application deadline: rolling admissions; 3/15 for financial aid. Early and deferred admission are possible.

BRIDGEWATER COLLEGE

Bridgewater, VA

Small-town setting ■ Private ■ Independent Religious ■ Coed

Web site: www.bridgewater.edu
Contact: Ms. Linda F. Stout, Director of Enrollment Operations, 402 East College Street, Bridgewater, VA 22812-1599
Telephone: 540-828-5375 or toll-free 800-759-8328 **Fax:** 540-828-5481
E-mail: admissions@bridgewater.edu

Getting in Last Year 1,332 applied; 88% were accepted; 406 enrolled (35%).

Financial Matters $16,090 tuition and fees (2002–03); $7860 room and board; 90% average percent of need met; $15,822 average financial aid amount received per undergraduate.

Academics Bridgewater awards bachelor's degrees. Challenging opportunities include advanced placement credit, an honors program, double majors, independent study, and a senior project. Special programs include internships, summer session for credit, and study-abroad. The most frequently chosen baccalaureate fields are business/marketing, psychology, and education. The faculty at Bridgewater has 82 full-time members, 78% with terminal degrees. The student-faculty ratio is 15:1.

Students of Bridgewater The student body is made up of 1,363 undergraduates. 55% are women and 45% are men. Students come from 24 states and territories and 8 other countries. 78% are from Virginia. 0.6% are international students. 75% returned for their sophomore year.

Applying Bridgewater requires an essay, SAT I or ACT, a high school transcript, 2 recommendations, and a minimum high school GPA of 2.0, and in some cases an interview. The school recommends SAT I, an interview, and a minimum high school GPA of 3.0. Application deadline: rolling admissions; 3/1 priority date for financial aid. Deferred admission is possible.

BRIDGEWATER STATE COLLEGE

Bridgewater, MA

Suburban setting ■ Public ■ State-supported ■ Coed

Web site: www.bridgew.edu
Contact: Dr. Marian Spencer, Acting Director of Admissions, Gates House, Bridgewater, MA 02325
Telephone: 508-531-1237 **Fax:** 508-531-1746
E-mail: admission@bridgew.edu

Getting in Last Year 5,252 applied; 68% were accepted; 1,297 enrolled (36%).

Financial Matters $3735 resident tuition and fees (2002–03); $9875 nonresident tuition and fees (2002–03); $5366 room and board; 75% average percent of need met; $6470 average financial aid amount received per undergraduate (2001–02).

Academics Bridgewater awards bachelor's and master's degrees and post-bachelor's, post-master's, and first-professional certificates. Challenging opportunities include advanced placement credit, accelerated degree programs, an honors program, double majors, independent study, and a senior project. Special programs include internships, summer session for credit, off-campus study, study-abroad, and Army and Air Force ROTC. The most frequently chosen baccalaureate fields are social sciences and history, education, and psychology. The faculty at Bridgewater has 252 full-time members, 90% with terminal degrees. The student-faculty ratio is 19:1.

Students of Bridgewater The student body totals 9,561, of whom 7,434 are undergraduates. 61.9% are women and 38.1% are men. Students come from 23 states and territories and 33 other countries. 97% are from Massachusetts. 1.9% are international students. 74% returned for their sophomore year.

Applying Bridgewater requires an essay, SAT I or ACT, a high school transcript, and a minimum high school GPA of 2.7. The school recommends recommendations. Application deadline: 2/15; 3/1 priority date for financial aid. Early and deferred admission are possible.

BRIERCREST BIBLE COLLEGE

Caronport, SK Canada

Rural setting ■ Private ■ Independent Religious ■ Coed

Web site: www.briercrest.ca

Contact: Mr. Mike Benallick, Director of Enrollment Management, 510 College Drive, Caronport, SK S0H 0S0 Canada

Telephone: 306-756-3200 ext. 257 or toll-free 800-667-5199 (in-state)

E-mail: enrollment@briercrest.ca

Getting in Last Year 599 applied; 73% were accepted.

Financial Matters $5824 tuition and fees (2002–03); $4000 room and board.

Academics Briercrest awards associate and bachelor's degrees. Challenging opportunities include accelerated degree programs, double majors, and independent study. Special programs include internships, summer session for credit, and off-campus study. The faculty at Briercrest has 21 full-time members, 57% with terminal degrees. The student-faculty ratio is 22:1.

Students of Briercrest The student body is made up of 805 undergraduates. 48.4% are women and 51.6% are men. Students come from 11 states and territories and 4 other countries. 20% are from Saskatchewan. 77% returned for their sophomore year.

Applying Briercrest requires an essay, a high school transcript, and 2 recommendations, and in some cases an interview. Application deadline: 8/15; 1/5 priority date for financial aid. Early and deferred admission are possible.

BRIGHAM YOUNG UNIVERSITY

Provo, UT

Suburban setting ■ Private ■ Independent Religious ■ Coed

Web site: www.byu.edu

Contact: Mr. Tom Gourley, Dean of Admissions and Records, A-153 Abraham Smoot Building, Provo, UT 84602

Telephone: 801-422-2507 **Fax:** 801-422-0005

E-mail: admissions@byu.edu

Getting in Last Year 7,329 applied; 73% were accepted; 4,264 enrolled (80%).

Financial Matters $3060 tuition and fees (2002–03); $4780 room and board; 40% average percent of need met; $3853 average financial aid amount received per undergraduate (2001–02).

Academics BYU awards bachelor's, master's, doctoral, and first-professional degrees. Challenging opportunities include advanced placement credit, accelerated degree programs, freshman honors college, an honors program, double majors, independent study, and a senior project. Special programs include cooperative education, internships, summer session for credit, off-campus study, study-abroad, and Army and Air Force ROTC. The most frequently chosen baccalaureate fields are education, business/marketing, and social sciences and history. The faculty at BYU has 1,562 full-time members, 66% with terminal degrees. The student-faculty ratio is 18:1.

Students of BYU The student body totals 32,408, of whom 29,379 are undergraduates. 49.8% are women and 50.2% are men. Students come from 55 states and territories and 127 other countries. 30% are from Utah. 3.5% are international students. 91% returned for their sophomore year.

Applying BYU requires an essay, ACT, a high school transcript, an interview, and 1 recommendation. Application deadline: 2/15; 4/2 priority date for financial aid. Early and deferred admission are possible.

BRIGHAM YOUNG UNIVERSITY–HAWAII

Laie, HI

Small-town setting ■ Private ■ Independent Religious ■ Coed

Web site: www.byuh.edu

Contact: Mr. Jeffrey N. Bunker, Dean for Admissions and Records, 55-220 Kulanui Street, Laie, Oahu, HI 96762

Telephone: 808-293-7010

Getting in Last Year 2,843 applied; 30% were accepted; 270 enrolled (32%).

Financial Matters $2490 tuition and fees (2002–03); $4520 room and board; 80% average percent of need met; $2850 average financial aid amount received per undergraduate.

Academics BYU-Hawaii awards associate and bachelor's degrees and post-bachelor's certificates. Challenging opportunities include advanced placement credit, accelerated degree programs, freshman honors college, an honors program, double majors, and a senior project. Special programs include cooperative education, internships, summer session for credit, off-campus study, and Army, Navy and Air Force ROTC. The most frequently chosen baccalaureate fields are business/marketing, computer/information sciences, and education. The faculty at BYU-Hawaii has 118 full-time members, 60% with terminal degrees. The student-faculty ratio is 16:1.

Students of BYU-Hawaii The student body is made up of 2,529 undergraduates. 55.1% are women and 44.9% are men. Students come from 45 states and territories and 70 other countries. 60% are from Hawaii. 47.7% are international students.

Applying BYU-Hawaii requires an essay, ACT, a high school transcript, resume of activities, ecclesiastical endorsement, and a minimum high school GPA of 3.0, and in some cases recommendations. The school recommends SAT I. Application deadline: 2/15; 4/30 priority date for financial aid. Early and deferred admission are possible.

BRITISH COLUMBIA INSTITUTE OF TECHNOLOGY

Burnaby, BC Canada

Urban setting ■ Public ■ Coed

Web site: www.bcit.ca

Contact: Ms. Anna Dosen, Supervisor of Admissions, 3700 Willingdon Avenue, Burnaby, BC V5G 3H2 Canada

Telephone: 604-432-8576 **Fax:** 604-431-6917

Getting in Last Year 7,212 applied; 35% were accepted.

Financial Matters $3323 resident tuition and fees (2002–03); $4560 room only.

Academics British Columbia Institute of Technology awards bachelor's degrees. The most frequently chosen baccalaureate fields are health professions and related sciences, business/marketing, and computer/information sciences. The faculty at British Columbia Institute of Technology has 645 full-time members.

Students of British Columbia Institute of Technology The student body is made up of 25,485 undergraduates. 100% are from British Columbia.

BROCK UNIVERSITY

St. Catharines, ON Canada

Urban setting ■ Public ■ Coed

Web site: www.brocku.ca

Contact: Ms. Jeanette Davis, Undergraduate Admissions Officer, 500 Glenridge Avenue, St. Catharines, ON L2S 3A1 Canada

Telephone: 905-688-5550 ext. 3434

E-mail: mlea@spartan.ac.brockv.ca

Getting in Last Year 15,822 applied; 17% were accepted.

Financial Matters $4522 nonresident tuition and fees (2002–03); $5960 room and board.

Academics Brock awards bachelor's, master's, and doctoral degrees. Challenging opportunities include advanced placement credit, accelerated degree programs, student-designed majors, an honors program, double majors, and a senior project. Special programs include cooperative education, internships, summer session for credit, and study-abroad. The faculty at Brock has 385 full-time members. The student-faculty ratio is 23:1.

Students of Brock The student body totals 11,916, of whom 11,269 are undergraduates. Students come from 8 states and territories and 66 other countries.

Applying Brock requires a high school transcript and a minimum high school GPA of 3.0, and in some cases an essay, an interview, audition, portfolio, and a minimum high school GPA of 3.0. The school recommends SAT I and SAT II or ACT. Application deadline: 6/1.

BROOKLYN COLLEGE OF THE CITY UNIVERSITY OF NEW YORK

Brooklyn, NY

Urban setting ■ Public ■ State and locally supported ■ Coed

Web site: www.brooklyn.cuny.edu

Contact: Ms. Marianne Booufall-Tynan, Director of Admissions, 2900 Bedford Avenue, 1203 Plaza, Brooklyn, NY 11210-2889

Telephone: 718-951-5001 **Fax:** 718-951-4506

E-mail: admingry@brooklyn.cuny.edu

Getting in Last Year 6,184 applied; 36% were accepted; 1,224 enrolled (55%).

Brooklyn College of the City University of New York (continued)

Financial Matters $3553 resident tuition and fees (2002–03); $7153 nonresident tuition and fees (2002–03); 99% average percent of need met; $4615 average financial aid amount received per undergraduate.

Academics Brooklyn College awards bachelor's and master's degrees and post-master's certificates. Challenging opportunities include advanced placement credit, freshman honors college, an honors program, double majors, independent study, and a senior project. Special programs include internships, summer session for credit, off-campus study, and study-abroad. The most frequently chosen baccalaureate fields are business/marketing, education, and psychology. The faculty at Brooklyn College has 485 full-time members, 91% with terminal degrees. The student-faculty ratio is 16:1.

Students of Brooklyn College The student body totals 15,635, of whom 10,767 are undergraduates. 60.8% are women and 39.2% are men. Students come from 22 states and territories and 69 other countries. 98% are from New York. 4.9% are international students. 82% returned for their sophomore year.

Applying Brooklyn College requires SAT I or ACT, a high school transcript, and a minimum high school GPA of 3.0, and in some cases an essay, an interview, and recommendations. The school recommends SAT II Subject Tests. Application deadline: rolling admissions; 4/1 priority date for financial aid. Early and deferred admission are possible.

BROOKS INSTITUTE OF PHOTOGRAPHY

Santa Barbara, CA

Suburban setting ■ Private ■ Proprietary ■ Coed

Web site: www.brooks.edu

Contact: Ms. Inge B. Kautzmann, Director of Admissions, 801 Alston Road, Santa Barbara, CA 93108

Telephone: 805-966-3888 ext. 4601 or toll-free 888-304-3456 (out-of-state) **Fax:** 805-564-1475

E-mail: admissions@brooks.edu

Getting in Last Year 203 enrolled.

Financial Matters $20,250 tuition and fees (2002–03).

Academics Brooks Institute awards bachelor's and master's degrees. Challenging opportunities include advanced placement credit, accelerated degree programs, and a senior project. Special programs include internships, off-campus study, and study-abroad. The faculty at Brooks Institute has 19 full-time members. The student-faculty ratio is 12:1.

Students of Brooks Institute The student body totals 1,507, of whom 1,425 are undergraduates. 47.5% are women and 52.5% are men. Students come from 27 states and territories and 22 other countries. 2.4% are international students. 97% returned for their sophomore year.

Applying Brooks Institute requires an essay, a high school transcript, 15 semester hours of college credit, and a minimum high school GPA of 3.0. The school recommends an interview. Application deadline: rolling admissions; 3/2 priority date for financial aid. Deferred admission is possible.

BROWN UNIVERSITY

Providence, RI

Urban setting ■ Private ■ Independent ■ Coed

Web site: www.brown.edu

Contact: Mr. Michael Goldberger, Director of Admission, Box 1876, Providence, RI 02912

Telephone: 401-863-2378 **Fax:** 401-863-9300

E-mail: admission_undergraduate@brown.edu

Getting in Last Year 14,612 applied; 17% were accepted; 1,456 enrolled (59%).

Financial Matters $28,480 tuition and fees (2002–03); $7876 room and board; 100% average percent of need met; $23,249 average financial aid amount received per undergraduate.

Academics Brown awards bachelor's, master's, doctoral, and first-professional degrees. Challenging opportunities include advanced placement credit, accelerated degree programs, student-designed majors, an honors program, double majors, independent study, and a senior project. Special programs include internships, summer session for credit, off-campus study, study-abroad, and Army ROTC. The most frequently chosen baccalaureate fields are social sciences and history, liberal arts/general studies, and biological/life sciences. The faculty at Brown has 785 full-time members, 98% with terminal degrees. The student-faculty ratio is 8:1.

Students of Brown The student body totals 7,892, of whom 6,030 are undergraduates. 54.6% are women and 45.4% are men. Students come from 52 states and territories and 72 other countries. 4% are from Rhode Island. 6% are international students. 97% returned for their sophomore year.

Applying Brown requires an essay, SAT I and SAT II or ACT, a high school transcript, and 2 recommendations, and in some cases 3 recommendations. The school recommends SAT II: Writing Test. Application deadline: 1/1; 2/1 for financial aid. Early and deferred admission are possible.

BRYAN COLLEGE

Dayton, TN

Small-town setting ■ Private ■ Independent Religious ■ Coed

Web site: www.bryan.edu

Contact: Mr. Mark A. Cruver, Director of Admissions and Enrollment Management, PO Box 7000, Dayton, TN 37321-7000

Telephone: 423-775-2041 ext. 207 or toll-free 800-277-9522 **Fax:** 423-775-7199

E-mail: admiss@bryan.edu

Getting in Last Year 539 applied; 35% were accepted.

Financial Matters $12,700 tuition and fees (2002–03); $4400 room and board; 79% average percent of need met; $10,949 average financial aid amount received per undergraduate (2001–02).

Academics Bryan awards associate and bachelor's degrees. Challenging opportunities include advanced placement credit, an honors program, double majors, independent study, and a senior project. Special programs include internships, summer session for credit, and study-abroad. The most frequently chosen baccalaureate fields are business/marketing, psychology, and education. The faculty at Bryan has 35 full-time members, 80% with terminal degrees. The student-faculty ratio is 14:1.

Students of Bryan The student body totals 615, of whom 557 are undergraduates. Students come from 33 states and territories and 7 other countries. 77% returned for their sophomore year.

Applying Bryan requires an essay, ACT, a high school transcript, 3 recommendations, and a minimum high school GPA of 2.0, and in some cases an interview. Application deadline: rolling admissions; 5/1 priority date for financial aid. Early and deferred admission are possible.

BRYANT AND STRATTON COLLEGE

Cleveland, OH

Urban setting ■ Private ■ Proprietary ■ Coed

Web site: www.bryantstratton.edu

Contact: Ms. Marilyn Scheaffer, Director of Admissions, 1700 East 13th Street, Cleveland, OH 44114-3203

Telephone: 216-771-1700 **Fax:** 216-771-7787

Getting in Last Year 81 applied; 93% were accepted.

Financial Matters $10,100 tuition and fees (2002–03); $3200 room only; 89% average percent of need met; $6200 average financial aid amount received per undergraduate (2001–02).

Academics Bryant and Stratton awards associate and bachelor's degrees. Challenging opportunities include double majors, independent study, and a senior project. Special programs include cooperative education, internships, and summer session for credit. The most frequently chosen baccalaureate field is engineering/engineering technologies. The faculty at Bryant and Stratton has 5 full-time members. The student-faculty ratio is 10:1.

Students of Bryant and Stratton The student body is made up of 203 undergraduates. Students come from 2 states and territories. 75% returned for their sophomore year.

Applying Bryant and Stratton requires an essay, TABE, a high school transcript, and an interview. The school recommends SAT I or ACT. Application deadline: rolling admissions. Deferred admission is possible.

BRYANT COLLEGE

Smithfield, RI

Suburban setting ■ Private ■ Independent ■ Coed

Web site: www.bryant.edu

Contact: Ms. Cynthia Bonn, Director of Admission, 1150 Douglas Pike, Smithfield, RI 02917

Telephone: 401-232-6100 or toll-free 800-622-7001 **Fax:** 401-232-6741

E-mail: admission@bryant.edu

Getting in Last Year 2,811 applied; 74% were accepted; 744 enrolled (36%).

Financial Matters $19,776 tuition and fees (2002–03); $7950 room and board; 69% average percent of need met; $13,740 average financial aid amount received per undergraduate.

Academics Bryant awards bachelor's and master's degrees and post-master's certificates. Challenging opportunities include advanced placement credit, an honors program, double majors, independent study, and a senior project. Special programs include internships, summer session for credit, study-abroad, and Army ROTC. The most frequently chosen baccalaureate fields are business/marketing, computer/information sciences, and English. The faculty at Bryant has 132 full-time members, 86% with terminal degrees. The student-faculty ratio is 16:1.

Students of Bryant The student body totals 3,390, of whom 2,912 are undergraduates. 40% are women and 60% are men. Students come from 32 states and territories and 37 other countries. 26% are from Rhode Island. 3.9% are international students. 86% returned for their sophomore year.

Applying Bryant requires an essay, SAT I or ACT, a high school transcript, 1 recommendation, and senior year first-quarter grades. The school recommends an interview and a minimum high school GPA of 3.0. Application deadline: 2/15; 2/15 priority date for financial aid. Early and deferred admission are possible.

BRYN ATHYN COLLEGE OF THE NEW CHURCH

Bryn Athyn, PA

Small-town setting ■ Private ■ Independent Religious ■ Coed

Web site: www.newchurch.edu
Contact: Ms. Dee Smith-Johns, Admissions Coordinator, Box 717, 2895 College Drive, Bryn Athyn, PA 19009
Telephone: 215-938-2511 **Fax:** 215-938-2658
E-mail: dsjohns@newchurch.edu

Getting in Last Year 50 applied; 98% were accepted; 36 enrolled (73%).

Financial Matters $6657 tuition and fees (2002–03); $4764 room and board; 100% average percent of need met; $6470 average financial aid amount received per undergraduate.

Academics Bryn Athyn College awards associate, bachelor's, master's, and first-professional degrees and first-professional certificates. Challenging opportunities include advanced placement credit, student-designed majors, independent study, and a senior project. Special programs include cooperative education, internships, and study-abroad. The most frequently chosen baccalaureate fields are interdisciplinary studies, biological/life sciences, and education. The faculty at Bryn Athyn College has 18 full-time members, 78% with terminal degrees. The student-faculty ratio is 6:1.

Students of Bryn Athyn College The student body totals 151, of whom 132 are undergraduates. 53% are women and 47% are men. Students come from 16 states and territories and 12 other countries. 79% are from Pennsylvania. 17.1% are international students. 71% returned for their sophomore year.

Applying Bryn Athyn College requires SAT I or ACT, a high school transcript, and 2 recommendations, and in some cases an interview and 3 recommendations. Application deadline: 2/1; 6/1 priority date for financial aid. Deferred admission is possible.

BRYN MAWR COLLEGE

Bryn Mawr, PA

Suburban setting ■ Private ■ Independent ■ Women Only

Web site: www.brynmawr.edu
Contact: Ms. Jennifer Rickard, Director of Admissions and Financial Aid, 101 North Merion Avenue, Bryn Mawr, PA 19010
Telephone: 610-526-5152 or toll-free 800-BMC-1885 (out-of-state)
E-mail: admissions@brynmawr.edu

Getting in Last Year 1,743 applied; 50% were accepted; 305 enrolled (35%).

Financial Matters $26,220 tuition and fees (2002–03); $8970 room and board; 96% average percent of need met; $22,516 average financial aid amount received per undergraduate.

Academics Bryn Mawr awards bachelor's, master's, and doctoral degrees. Challenging opportunities include advanced placement credit, accelerated degree programs, student-designed majors, an honors program, double majors, independent study, and a senior project. Special programs include summer session for credit, off-campus study, study-abroad, and Air Force ROTC. The most frequently chosen baccalaureate fields are social sciences and history, foreign language/literature, and English. The faculty at Bryn Mawr has 150 full-time members, 97% with terminal degrees. The student-faculty ratio is 9:1.

Students of Bryn Mawr The student body totals 1,744, of whom 1,321 are undergraduates. Students come from 48 states and territories and 44 other countries. 20% are from Pennsylvania. 8.1% are international students. 89% returned for their sophomore year.

Applying Bryn Mawr requires an essay, SAT I and SAT II or ACT, a high school transcript, and 3 recommendations. The school recommends an interview. Application deadline: 1/15; 2/7 for financial aid. Early and deferred admission are possible.

BUCKNELL UNIVERSITY

Lewisburg, PA

Small-town setting ■ Private ■ Independent ■ Coed

Web site: www.bucknell.edu
Contact: Mr. Mark D. Davies, Dean of Admissions, Lewisburg, PA 17837
Telephone: 570-577-1101 **Fax:** 570-577-3538
E-mail: admissions@bucknell.edu

Getting in Last Year 7,760 applied; 39% were accepted; 914 enrolled (30%).

Financial Matters $27,531 tuition and fees (2002–03); $6052 room and board; 100% average percent of need met; $18,072 average financial aid amount received per undergraduate.

Academics Bucknell awards bachelor's and master's degrees. Challenging opportunities include advanced placement credit, student-designed majors, an honors program, double majors, independent study, and a senior project. Special programs include internships, summer session for credit, off-campus study, study-abroad, and Army ROTC. The most frequently chosen baccalaureate fields are social sciences and history, engineering/engineering technologies, and business/marketing. The faculty at Bucknell has 293 full-time members, 95% with terminal degrees. The student-faculty ratio is 12:1.

Students of Bucknell The student body totals 3,587, of whom 3,440 are undergraduates. 48.8% are women and 51.2% are men. Students come from 46 states and territories and 41 other countries. 32% are from Pennsylvania. 2% are international students. 94% returned for their sophomore year.

Applying Bucknell requires an essay, SAT I or ACT, a high school transcript, and 2 recommendations. The school recommends an interview. Application deadline: 1/1; 1/1 for financial aid.

BUENA VISTA UNIVERSITY

Storm Lake, IA

Small-town setting ■ Private ■ Independent Religious ■ Coed

Web site: www.bvu.edu
Contact: Ms. Louise Cummings-Simmons, Director of Admissions, 610 West Fourth Street, Storm Lake, IA 50588
Telephone: 712-749-2235 or toll-free 800-383-9600
E-mail: admissions@bvu.edu

Getting in Last Year 1,233 applied; 84% were accepted; 358 enrolled (35%).

Financial Matters $18,738 tuition and fees (2002–03); $5230 room and board; 92% average percent of need met; $18,074 average financial aid amount received per undergraduate.

Academics BVU awards bachelor's and master's degrees. Challenging opportunities include advanced placement credit, student-designed majors, freshman honors college, an honors program, double majors, independent study, and a senior project. Special programs include internships, summer session for credit, off-campus study, and study-abroad. The most frequently chosen baccalaureate fields are education, social sciences and history, and communications/communication technologies. The faculty at BVU has 79 full-time members, 67% with terminal degrees. The student-faculty ratio is 16:1.

Students of BVU The student body totals 1,345, of whom 1,267 are undergraduates. 52.4% are women and 47.6% are men. Students come from 22 states and territories and 4 other countries. 84% are from Iowa. 0.8% are international students. 72% returned for their sophomore year.

Applying BVU requires SAT I or ACT, a high school transcript, and recommendations, and in some cases an essay and an interview. The school recommends a minimum high school GPA of 3.0. Application deadline: 6/1; 6/1 priority date for financial aid. Early and deferred admission are possible.

BURLINGTON COLLEGE

Burlington, VT

Urban setting ■ Private ■ Independent ■ Coed

Web site: www.burlcol.edu
Contact: Ms. Cathleen Sullivan, Associate Director of Admissions, 95 North Avenue, Burlington, VT 05401-2998
Telephone: 802-862-9616 ext. 124 or toll-free 800-862-9616 **Fax:** 802-660-4331
E-mail: admissions@burlcol.edu

Getting in Last Year 43 applied; 95% were accepted; 28 enrolled (68%).

Financial Matters $12,150 tuition and fees (2002–03); $5750 room only; 55% average percent of need met; $9600 average financial aid amount received per undergraduate.

Academics BC awards associate and bachelor's degrees. Challenging opportunities include accelerated degree programs, student-designed majors, double majors, independent study, and a senior project. Special programs include cooperative education, internships, summer session for credit, off-campus study, and study-abroad. The most frequently chosen baccalaureate fields are psychology, English, and education. The faculty at BC has 68 members. The student-faculty ratio is 8:1.

Students of BC The student body is made up of 280 undergraduates. 62.9% are women and 37.1% are men. Students come from 20 states and territories. 60% are from Vermont. 0.8% are international students. 60% returned for their sophomore year.

Applying BC requires an essay, a high school transcript, an interview, and 2 recommendations. Application deadline: 8/1. Deferred admission is possible.

BUTLER UNIVERSITY

Indianapolis, IN

Urban setting ■ Private ■ Independent ■ Coed

Web site: www.butler.edu
Contact: Mr. William Preble, Dean of Admissions, 4600 Sunset Avenue, Indianapolis, IN 46208-3485
Telephone: 317-940-8100 ext. 8124 or toll-free 888-940-8100 **Fax:** 317-940-8150
E-mail: admission@butler.edu

Butler University (continued)

Getting in Last Year 3,817 applied; 80% were accepted; 940 enrolled (31%).

Financial Matters $20,190 tuition and fees (2002–03); $6710 room and board; $14,900 average financial aid amount received per undergraduate (2001–02).

Academics Butler awards associate, bachelor's, master's, and first-professional degrees and post-bachelor's certificates. Challenging opportunities include advanced placement credit, student-designed majors, an honors program, double majors, independent study, and a senior project. Special programs include cooperative education, internships, summer session for credit, off-campus study, study-abroad, and Army and Air Force ROTC. The most frequently chosen baccalaureate fields are business/marketing, education, and health professions and related sciences. The faculty at Butler has 255 full-time members, 84% with terminal degrees. The student-faculty ratio is 12:1.

Students of Butler The student body totals 4,326, of whom 3,512 are undergraduates. 62.6% are women and 37.4% are men. Students come from 42 states and territories and 48 other countries. 60% are from Indiana. 1.9% are international students. 81% returned for their sophomore year.

Applying Butler requires an essay, SAT I or ACT, and a high school transcript, and in some cases an interview and audition. The school recommends SAT II Subject Tests. Application deadline: 8/15; 3/1 priority date for financial aid. Deferred admission is possible.

CABRINI COLLEGE

Radnor, PA

Suburban setting ■ *Private* ■ *Independent Religious* ■ *Coed*

Web site: www.cabrini.edu

Contact: Mr. Gary E. Johnson, Dean for Enrollment, 610 King of Prussia Road, Radnor, PA 19087-3698

Telephone: 610-902-8552 or toll-free 800-848-1003 **Fax:** 610-902-8508

E-mail: admit@cabrini.edu

Getting in Last Year 1,832 applied; 85% were accepted; 427 enrolled (27%).

Financial Matters $19,220 tuition and fees (2002–03); $8180 room and board; 48% average percent of need met; $14,044 average financial aid amount received per undergraduate.

Academics Cabrini awards bachelor's and master's degrees. Challenging opportunities include advanced placement credit, accelerated degree programs, student-designed majors, an honors program, double majors, independent study, and a senior project. Special programs include cooperative education, internships, summer session for credit, off-campus study, study-abroad, and Army ROTC. The most frequently chosen baccalaureate fields are education, business/marketing, and communications/communication technologies. The faculty at Cabrini has 59 full-time members, 76% with terminal degrees. The student-faculty ratio is 15:1.

Students of Cabrini The student body totals 2,182, of whom 1,678 are undergraduates. 64.7% are women and 35.3% are men. Students come from 22 states and territories. 70% are from Pennsylvania. 1.3% are international students. 68% returned for their sophomore year.

Applying Cabrini requires SAT I or ACT, a high school transcript, and a minimum high school GPA of 2.0. The school recommends an essay, SAT I, an interview, 3 recommendations, and a minimum high school GPA of 3.0. Application deadline: rolling admissions. Early and deferred admission are possible.

CALDWELL COLLEGE

Caldwell, NJ

Suburban setting ■ *Private* ■ *Independent Religious* ■ *Coed*

Web site: www.caldwell.edu

Contact: Mr. Richard Ott, Vice President for Enrollment Management, 9 Ryerson Avenue, Caldwell, NJ 07006

Telephone: 973-618-3224 or toll-free 888-864-9516 (out-of-state) **Fax:** 973-618-3600

E-mail: admissions@caldwell.edu

Getting in Last Year 1,240 applied; 78% were accepted; 322 enrolled (33%).

Financial Matters $16,100 tuition and fees (2002–03); $6800 room and board; 71% average percent of need met; $9735 average financial aid amount received per undergraduate (2001–02).

Academics Caldwell awards bachelor's and master's degrees and post-bachelor's and post-master's certificates. Challenging opportunities include advanced placement credit, accelerated degree programs, student-designed majors, an honors program, double majors, independent study, and a senior project. Special programs include cooperative education, internships, summer session for credit, off-campus study, study-abroad, and Army ROTC. The most frequently chosen baccalaureate fields are business/marketing, psychology, and education. The faculty at Caldwell has 76 full-time members, 80% with terminal degrees. The student-faculty ratio is 13:1.

Students of Caldwell The student body totals 2,218, of whom 1,861 are undergraduates. 70% are women and 30% are men. Students come from 14 states and territories and 26 other countries. 96% are from New Jersey. 4% are international students. 73% returned for their sophomore year.

Applying Caldwell requires an essay, SAT I or ACT, a high school transcript, 1 recommendation, and a minimum high school GPA of 2.0, and in some cases an interview. Early and deferred admission are possible.

CALIFORNIA BAPTIST UNIVERSITY

Riverside, CA

Suburban setting ■ *Private* ■ *Independent Religious* ■ *Coed*

Web site: www.calbaptist.edu

Contact: Mr. Allen Johnson, Director, Undergraduate Admissions, 8432 Magnolia Avenue, Riverside, CA 92504-3297

Telephone: 909-343-4212 or toll-free 877-228-8866 **Fax:** 909-343-4525

E-mail: admissions@calbaptist.edu

Getting in Last Year 571 applied; 83% were accepted; 192 enrolled (41%).

Financial Matters $12,790 tuition and fees (2002–03); $5360 room and board; 83% average percent of need met; $10,700 average financial aid amount received per undergraduate (2001–02).

Academics Cal Baptist awards bachelor's and master's degrees. Challenging opportunities include advanced placement credit, accelerated degree programs, double majors, independent study, and a senior project. Special programs include internships, summer session for credit, off-campus study, and study-abroad. The most frequently chosen baccalaureate fields are liberal arts/general studies, business/marketing, and psychology. The faculty at Cal Baptist has 75 full-time members, 63% with terminal degrees. The student-faculty ratio is 19:1.

Students of Cal Baptist The student body totals 2,165, of whom 1,618 are undergraduates. 64.4% are women and 35.6% are men. Students come from 23 states and territories and 16 other countries. 97% are from California. 1.3% are international students. 81% returned for their sophomore year.

Applying Cal Baptist requires an essay, SAT I or ACT, a high school transcript, 2 recommendations, and a minimum high school GPA of 2.5. The school recommends an interview. Application deadline: 8/18; 3/2 priority date for financial aid. Early and deferred admission are possible.

CALIFORNIA CHRISTIAN COLLEGE

Fresno, CA

Private ■ *Independent Religious* ■ *Coed*

Web site: www.calchristiancollege.org

Contact: Mr. Brian Henderer, Director of Admissions, 4881 East University Avenue, Fresno, CA 93703

Telephone: 559-251-4215 ext. 5571 **Fax:** 559-251-4231

E-mail: cccfresno@aol.com

Getting in Last Year 21 enrolled.

Financial Matters $5230 tuition and fees (2002–03); $3350 room and board; 43% average percent of need met; $8650 average financial aid amount received per undergraduate.

Academics California Christian College awards associate and bachelor's degrees. Challenging opportunities include accelerated degree programs and independent study. Special programs include cooperative education and summer session for credit. The faculty at California Christian College has 7 full-time members, 100% with terminal degrees. The student-faculty ratio is 8:1.

Students of California Christian College The student body is made up of 83 undergraduates. 26.5% are women and 73.5% are men. Students come from 3 states and territories and 5 other countries. 98% are from California. 8.4% are international students. 23% returned for their sophomore year.

Applying California Christian College requires an essay, standardized Bible content tests; college tests for English and math placement, a high school transcript, 3 recommendations, statement of faith, moral/ethical statement, and a minimum high school GPA of 2.0. The school recommends SAT I or ACT and an interview. Application deadline: rolling admissions; 3/2 priority date for financial aid.

CALIFORNIA COLLEGE FOR HEALTH SCIENCES

National City, CA

Urban setting ■ *Private* ■ *Proprietary* ■ *Coed*

Web site: www.cchs.edu

Contact: Ms. Loreli L. Relova, Student Services Manager, 2423 Hoover Avenue, National City, CA 91950

Telephone: 619-477-4800 ext. 313 or toll-free 800-221-7374 (out-of-state) **Fax:** 619-477-4360

E-mail: admissions@cchs.edu

Financial Matters $8025 tuition and fees (2002–03); 60% average percent of need met; $5082 average financial aid amount received per undergraduate (2001–02).

Academics California College awards associate, bachelor's, and master's degrees (offers primarily external degree programs). The faculty at California College has 4 full-time members.

Students of California College The student body totals 5,458, of whom 3,578 are undergraduates. Students come from 52 states and territories and 15 other countries. 10% are from California. 85% returned for their sophomore year.

Applying California College requires a high school transcript, and in some cases employment in a health science field. The school recommends employment in a health science field. Application deadline: rolling admissions; 9/1 priority date for financial aid. Deferred admission is possible.

CALIFORNIA COLLEGE OF ARTS AND CRAFTS

San Francisco, CA

Urban setting ■ Private ■ Independent ■ Coed

Web site: www.ccac-art.edu
Contact: Ms. Molly Ryan, Director of Admissions, 1111 Eighth Street at 16th and Wisconsin, San Francisco, CA 94107
Telephone: 415-703-9523 ext. 9532 or toll-free 800-447-1ART **Fax:** 415-703-9539
E-mail: enroll@ccac-art.edu

Getting in Last Year 554 applied; 73% were accepted; 154 enrolled (38%).

Financial Matters $21,920 tuition and fees (2002–03); $7576 room and board; 61% average percent of need met; $16,062 average financial aid amount received per undergraduate.

Academics CCAC awards bachelor's and master's degrees. Challenging opportunities include advanced placement credit, student-designed majors, double majors, independent study, and a senior project. Special programs include internships, summer session for credit, off-campus study, and study-abroad. The most frequently chosen baccalaureate fields are visual/performing arts, architecture, and trade and industry. The faculty at CCAC has 34 full-time members, 71% with terminal degrees. The student-faculty ratio is 9:1.

Students of CCAC The student body totals 1,427, of whom 1,261 are undergraduates. 60.2% are women and 39.8% are men. Students come from 31 states and territories and 21 other countries. 70% are from California. 6.5% are international students. 80% returned for their sophomore year.

Applying CCAC requires an essay, a high school transcript, 2 recommendations, portfolio, and a minimum high school GPA of 2.0, and in some cases an interview. The school recommends SAT I or ACT and an interview. Application deadline: rolling admissions; 2/15 priority date for financial aid. Deferred admission is possible.

CALIFORNIA INSTITUTE OF TECHNOLOGY

Pasadena, CA

Suburban setting ■ Private ■ Independent ■ Coed

Web site: www.caltech.edu
Contact: Ms. Charlene Liebau, Director of Admissions, 1200 East California Boulevard, Pasadena, CA 91125-0001
Telephone: 626-395-6341 or toll-free 800-568-8324 **Fax:** 626-683-3026
E-mail: ugadmissions@caltech.edu

Getting in Last Year 2,615 applied; 21% were accepted; 252 enrolled (45%).

Financial Matters $22,119 tuition and fees (2002–03); $6999 room and board; 100% average percent of need met; $23,427 average financial aid amount received per undergraduate.

Academics Caltech awards bachelor's, master's, and doctoral degrees. Challenging opportunities include student-designed majors, double majors, and independent study. Special programs include internships, off-campus study, study-abroad, and Army and Air Force ROTC. The most frequently chosen baccalaureate fields are engineering/engineering technologies, physical sciences, and biological/life sciences. The faculty at Caltech has 292 full-time members, 97% with terminal degrees. The student-faculty ratio is 3:1.

Students of Caltech The student body totals 2,120, of whom 939 are undergraduates. 33.2% are women and 66.8% are men. Students come from 46 states and territories and 28 other countries. 37% are from California. 7.7% are international students. 97% returned for their sophomore year.

Applying Caltech requires an essay, SAT I, SAT II: Writing Test, SAT II Subject Test in math and either physics, chemistry, or biology, a high school transcript, and 3 recommendations. Application deadline: 1/1; 1/15 priority date for financial aid. Early and deferred admission are possible.

CALIFORNIA INSTITUTE OF THE ARTS

Valencia, CA

Suburban setting ■ Private ■ Independent ■ Coed

Web site: www.calarts.edu
Contact: Ms. Carol Kim, Director of Enrollment Services, 24700 McBean Parkway, Valencia, CA 91355
Telephone: 661-255-1050 or toll-free 800-292-2787 (in-state), 800-545-2787 (out-of-state) **Fax:** 661-253-7710
E-mail: admiss@calarts.edu

Getting in Last Year 2,608 applied; 33% were accepted; 116 enrolled (14%).

Financial Matters $22,955 tuition and fees (2002–03); $6850 room and board; 82% average percent of need met; $20,966 average financial aid amount received per undergraduate.

Academics Cal Arts awards bachelor's and master's degrees and post-bachelor's certificates. Challenging opportunities include advanced placement credit, student-designed majors, independent study, and a senior project. Special programs include internships and study-abroad. The most frequently chosen baccalaureate field is visual/performing arts. The faculty at Cal Arts has 147 full-time members. The student-faculty ratio is 6:1.

Students of Cal Arts The student body totals 1,237, of whom 787 are undergraduates. 40.7% are women and 59.3% are men. Students come from 48 states and territories and 41 other countries. 45% are from California. 8.9% are international students. 92% returned for their sophomore year.

Applying Cal Arts requires an essay, a high school transcript, 2 recommendations, and portfolio or audition, and in some cases an interview. Application deadline: rolling admissions; 3/2 priority date for financial aid. Deferred admission is possible.

CALIFORNIA LUTHERAN UNIVERSITY

Thousand Oaks, CA

Suburban setting ■ Private ■ Independent Religious ■ Coed

Web site: www.callutheran.edu
Contact: Mr. Darryl Calkins, Dean of Undergraduate Enrollment, Office of Admission, #1350, Thousand Oaks, CA 91360
Telephone: 805-493-3135 or toll-free 877-258-3678 **Fax:** 805-493-3114
E-mail: cluadm@clunet.edu

Getting in Last Year 1,051 applied; 73% were accepted; 333 enrolled (43%).

Financial Matters $19,260 tuition and fees (2002–03); $6920 room and board; 82% average percent of need met; $14,864 average financial aid amount received per undergraduate (2001–02).

Academics CLU awards bachelor's and master's degrees. Challenging opportunities include advanced placement credit, accelerated degree programs, student-designed majors, an honors program, double majors, independent study, and a senior project. Special programs include cooperative education, internships, summer session for credit, off-campus study, study-abroad, and Army and Air Force ROTC. The most frequently chosen baccalaureate fields are business/marketing, liberal arts/general studies, and communications/communication technologies. The faculty at CLU has 119 full-time members, 90% with terminal degrees. The student-faculty ratio is 15:1.

Students of CLU The student body totals 2,949, of whom 1,891 are undergraduates. 57.8% are women and 42.2% are men. Students come from 33 states and territories and 33 other countries. 79% are from California. 2.2% are international students. 79% returned for their sophomore year.

Applying CLU requires an essay, SAT I or ACT, a high school transcript, 1 recommendation, and a minimum high school GPA of 2.75. The school recommends an interview and a minimum high school GPA of 3.0. Application deadline: 6/1; 3/1 priority date for financial aid. Deferred admission is possible.

CALIFORNIA MARITIME ACADEMY

Vallejo, CA

Suburban setting ■ Public ■ State-supported ■ Coed, Primarily Men

Web site: www.csum.edu
Contact: Mr. Chris Krzak, Enrollment Services Director, PO Box 1392, Vallejo, CA 94590-0644
Telephone: 707-654-1331 or toll-free 800-561-1945 **Fax:** 707-654-1336
E-mail: admission@csum.edu

Getting in Last Year 436 applied; 76% were accepted; 159 enrolled (48%).

Financial Matters $1050 resident tuition and fees (2002–03); $9510 nonresident tuition and fees (2002–03); $6750 room and board; 50% average percent of need met; $15,329 average financial aid amount received per undergraduate.

Academics Cal Maritime awards bachelor's degrees. Challenging opportunities include advanced placement credit and a senior project. Special programs include internships and summer session for credit. The most frequently chosen baccalaureate fields are engineering/engineering technologies and business/marketing. The faculty at Cal Maritime has 49 full-time members. The student-faculty ratio is 15:1.

Students of Cal Maritime The student body is made up of 606 undergraduates. 16.8% are women and 83.2% are men. Students come from 18 states and territories and 16 other countries. 87% are from California. 5.6% are international students. 93% returned for their sophomore year.

Applying Cal Maritime requires SAT I or ACT, a high school transcript, health form, and a minimum high school GPA of 2.0. Application deadline: 4/1; 3/3 priority date for financial aid.

CALIFORNIA NATIONAL UNIVERSITY FOR ADVANCED STUDIES

Northridge, CA

Urban setting ■ Private ■ Proprietary ■ Coed

Web site: www.cnuas.edu

California National University for Advanced Studies (continued)

Contact: Ms. Stephanie M. Smith, Registrar, California National University Admissions, 8550 Balboa Boulevard, Suite 210, Northridge, CA 91325
Telephone: 818-830-2411 or toll-free 800-744-2822 (in-state), 800-782-2422 (out-of-state) **Fax:** 818-830-2418
E-mail: cnuadms@mail.cnuas.edu

Financial Matters $4280 tuition and fees (2002–03).

Academics California National University for Advanced Studies awards bachelor's and master's degrees and post-bachelor's certificates. Challenging opportunities include advanced placement credit, accelerated degree programs, double majors, independent study, and a senior project. Special programs include internships and off-campus study. The faculty at California National University for Advanced Studies has 98 members. The student-faculty ratio is 10:1.

Students of California National University for Advanced Studies The student body totals 400, of whom 250 are undergraduates.

Applying California National University for Advanced Studies requires an essay and a high school transcript, and in some cases an interview. Application deadline: rolling admissions. Deferred admission is possible.

CALIFORNIA POLYTECHNIC STATE UNIVERSITY, SAN LUIS OBISPO

San Luis Obispo, CA

Small-town setting ■ Public ■ State-supported ■ Coed

Web site: www.calpoly.edu
Contact: Mr. James Maraviglia, Director of Admissions and Evaluations, San Luis Obispo, CA 93407
Telephone: 805-756-2311 **Fax:** 805-756-5400
E-mail: admprosp@calpoly.edu

Getting in Last Year 19,739 applied; 39% were accepted; 2,601 enrolled (34%).

Financial Matters $2877 resident tuition and fees (2002–03); $9645 nonresident tuition and fees (2002–03); $7119 room and board; 76% average percent of need met; $6847 average financial aid amount received per undergraduate (2001–02).

Academics Cal Poly State University awards bachelor's and master's degrees. Challenging opportunities include advanced placement credit, an honors program, double majors, independent study, and a senior project. Special programs include cooperative education, internships, summer session for credit, off-campus study, study-abroad, and Army ROTC. The most frequently chosen baccalaureate fields are engineering/engineering technologies, business/marketing, and agriculture. The faculty at Cal Poly State University has 791 full-time members, 67% with terminal degrees. The student-faculty ratio is 19:1.

Students of Cal Poly State University The student body totals 18,453, of whom 17,401 are undergraduates. 44.3% are women and 55.7% are men. Students come from 48 states and territories and 41 other countries. 94% are from California. 0.7% are international students. 89% returned for their sophomore year.

Applying Cal Poly State University requires SAT I or ACT and a high school transcript. Application deadline: 11/30; 3/2 priority date for financial aid. Early admission is possible.

CALIFORNIA STATE POLYTECHNIC UNIVERSITY, POMONA

Pomona, CA

Urban setting ■ Public ■ State-supported ■ Coed

Web site: www.csupomona.edu
Contact: Dr. George R. Bradshaw, Director, Admissions and Outreach, 3801 West Temple Avenue, Pomona, CA 91768-2557
Telephone: 909-869-3427 **Fax:** 909-869-4529
E-mail: cppadmit@csupomona.edu

Getting in Last Year 12,021 applied; 35% were accepted; 2,267 enrolled (53%).

Financial Matters $1772 resident tuition and fees (2002–03); $9152 nonresident tuition and fees (2002–03); $6626 room and board; 85% average percent of need met; $7276 average financial aid amount received per undergraduate.

Academics Cal Poly Pomona awards bachelor's and master's degrees. Challenging opportunities include advanced placement credit, double majors, and a senior project. Special programs include cooperative education, internships, summer session for credit, off-campus study, study-abroad, and Army and Air Force ROTC. The most frequently chosen baccalaureate fields are business/marketing, engineering/engineering technologies, and liberal arts/general studies. The faculty at Cal Poly Pomona has 689 full-time members, 64% with terminal degrees. The student-faculty ratio is 20:1.

Students of Cal Poly Pomona The student body totals 19,821, of whom 17,580 are undergraduates. 43.4% are women and 56.6% are men. Students come from 52 states and territories and 116 other countries. 99% are from California. 4.5% are international students. 78% returned for their sophomore year.

Applying Cal Poly Pomona requires SAT I or ACT, a high school transcript, and a minimum high school GPA of 2.0. Application deadline: 4/1.

CALIFORNIA STATE UNIVERSITY, BAKERSFIELD

Bakersfield, CA

Urban setting ■ Public ■ State-supported ■ Coed

Web site: www.csubak.edu
Contact: Dr. Homer S. Montalvo, Associate Dean of Admissions and Records, 9001 Stockdale Highway, Balersfield, CA 93311-1099
Telephone: 805-664-2160 or toll-free 800-788-2782 (in-state)
E-mail: admissions@csub.edu

Getting in Last Year 1,935 applied; 63% were accepted; 701 enrolled (57%).

Financial Matters $1941 resident tuition and fees (2002–03); $7581 nonresident tuition and fees (2002–03); $4711 room and board; 86% average percent of need met; $5897 average financial aid amount received per undergraduate (2001–02).

Academics CSUB awards bachelor's and master's degrees. Challenging opportunities include advanced placement credit, accelerated degree programs, student-designed majors, freshman honors college, an honors program, double majors, independent study, and a senior project. Special programs include cooperative education, internships, summer session for credit, off-campus study, and study-abroad. The most frequently chosen baccalaureate fields are liberal arts/general studies, business/marketing, and social sciences and history. The faculty at CSUB has 311 full-time members.

Students of CSUB The student body totals 7,741, of whom 5,578 are undergraduates. 64.8% are women and 35.2% are men. Students come from 16 states and territories and 48 other countries. 3% are from California. 2.1% are international students.

Applying CSUB requires SAT I or ACT and a high school transcript. The school recommends SAT II Subject Tests. Application deadline: 9/23; 3/2 priority date for financial aid. Early and deferred admission are possible.

CALIFORNIA STATE UNIVERSITY, CHICO

Chico, CA

Small-town setting ■ Public ■ State-supported ■ Coed

Web site: www.csuchico.edu
Contact: Dr. John F. Swiney, Director of Admissions, Office of Admission, Chico, CA 95929-0722
Telephone: 530-898-4879 or toll-free 800-542-4426 **Fax:** 530-898-6456
E-mail: info@csuchico.edu

Getting in Last Year 8,502 applied; 78% were accepted; 2,037 enrolled (31%).

Financial Matters $703 resident tuition and fees (2002–03); $10,735 nonresident tuition and fees (2002–03); $6973 room and board.

Academics CSU, Chico awards bachelor's and master's degrees and post-bachelor's and post-master's certificates. Challenging opportunities include advanced placement credit, student-designed majors, an honors program, double majors, independent study, and a senior project. Special programs include cooperative education, internships, summer session for credit, off-campus study, and study-abroad. The most frequently chosen baccalaureate fields are business/marketing, liberal arts/general studies, and social sciences and history. The faculty at CSU, Chico has 615 full-time members, 85% with terminal degrees. The student-faculty ratio is 20:1.

Students of CSU, Chico The student body totals 16,246, of whom 14,356 are undergraduates. 52.9% are women and 47.1% are men. Students come from 47 states and territories and 53 other countries. 98% are from California. 2.5% are international students. 81% returned for their sophomore year.

Applying CSU, Chico requires SAT I or ACT, a high school transcript, and GPA of 10th and 11th grade college prep courses only. Application deadline: 11/30; 3/2 priority date for financial aid. Deferred admission is possible.

CALIFORNIA STATE UNIVERSITY, DOMINGUEZ HILLS

Carson, CA

Urban setting ■ Public ■ State-supported ■ Coed

Web site: www.csudh.edu
Contact: Information Center, 1000 East Victoria Street, Carson, CA 90747-0001
Telephone: 310-243-3696

Getting in Last Year 1,715 applied; 55% were accepted; 672 enrolled (71%).

Financial Matters $1840 resident tuition and fees (2002–03); $10,300 nonresident tuition and fees (2002–03); $7340 room and board; 64% average percent of need met; $7807 average financial aid amount received per undergraduate.

Academics CSU Dominguez Hills awards bachelor's and master's degrees. Challenging opportunities include advanced placement credit, student-designed majors, an honors program, and a senior project. Special programs include cooperative education, internships, summer session for credit, off-campus study, study-abroad, and Army and Air Force ROTC. The faculty at CSU Dominguez Hills has 318 full-time members, 75% with terminal degrees.

Students of CSU Dominguez Hills The student body totals 13,504, of whom 8,041 are undergraduates. 69.7% are women and 30.3% are men. Students come from 29 states and territories and 42 other countries. 98% are from California. 1.8% are international students. 61% returned for their sophomore year.

Applying CSU Dominguez Hills requires a high school transcript, and in some cases SAT I or ACT. Application deadline: rolling admissions; 4/15 for financial aid, with a 3/2 priority date. Early admission is possible.

CALIFORNIA STATE UNIVERSITY, FRESNO

Fresno, CA

Urban setting ■ Public ■ State-supported ■ Coed

Web site: www.csufresno.edu

Contact: Ms. Vivian Franco, Director, 5150 North Maple Avenue, M/S JA 57, Fresno, CA 93740-8026

Telephone: 559-278-2261 **Fax:** 559-278-4812

E-mail: donna_mills@csufresno.edu

Getting in Last Year 9,013 applied; 66% were accepted; 2,308 enrolled (39%).

Financial Matters $1796 resident tuition and fees (2002–03); $10,360 nonresident tuition and fees (2002–03); $8949 room and board; 54% average percent of need met; $6184 average financial aid amount received per undergraduate (2001–02).

Academics Fresno State awards bachelor's, master's, and doctoral degrees. Challenging opportunities include advanced placement credit, accelerated degree programs, student-designed majors, freshman honors college, an honors program, double majors, independent study, and a senior project. Special programs include cooperative education, internships, summer session for credit, off-campus study, study-abroad, and Army and Air Force ROTC. The most frequently chosen baccalaureate fields are education, health professions and related sciences, and social sciences and history. The faculty at Fresno State has 703 full-time members. The student-faculty ratio is 18:1.

Students of Fresno State The student body totals 21,209, of whom 17,309 are undergraduates. 57.4% are women and 42.6% are men. Students come from 43 states and territories and 61 other countries. 99% are from California. 3% are international students. 64% returned for their sophomore year.

Applying Fresno State requires SAT I or ACT and a high school transcript. Application deadline: 7/28; 3/1 priority date for financial aid.

CALIFORNIA STATE UNIVERSITY, FULLERTON

Fullerton, CA

Suburban setting ■ Public ■ State-supported ■ Coed

Web site: www.fullerton.edu

Contact: Ms. Nancy J. Dority, Admissions Director, Office of Admissions and Records, PO Box 6900, 800 North State College Boulevard, Fullerton, CA 92834-6900

Telephone: 714-278-2370

Getting in Last Year 16,636 applied; 69% were accepted; 3,430 enrolled (30%).

Financial Matters $1881 resident tuition and fees (2002–03); $10,341 nonresident tuition and fees (2002–03); $4027 room only; 68% average percent of need met; $6171 average financial aid amount received per undergraduate.

Academics Cal State Fullerton awards bachelor's and master's degrees. Challenging opportunities include advanced placement credit, student-designed majors, an honors program, double majors, independent study, and a senior project. Special programs include cooperative education, internships, summer session for credit, off-campus study, study-abroad, and Army ROTC. The most frequently chosen baccalaureate fields are business/marketing, communications/communication technologies, and education. The faculty at Cal State Fullerton has 754 full-time members, 84% with terminal degrees. The student-faculty ratio is 21:1.

Students of Cal State Fullerton The student body totals 32,143, of whom 26,434 are undergraduates. 60.3% are women and 39.7% are men. Students come from 45 states and territories and 81 other countries. 99% are from California. 3.7% are international students. 79% returned for their sophomore year.

Applying Cal State Fullerton requires SAT I or ACT, a high school transcript, and a minimum high school GPA of 2.0. Application deadline: rolling admissions; 3/2 priority date for financial aid.

CALIFORNIA STATE UNIVERSITY, HAYWARD

Hayward, CA

Suburban setting ■ Public ■ State-supported ■ Coed

Web site: www.csuhayward.edu

Contact: Ms. Susan Lakis, Associate Director of Admissions, 25800 Carlos Bee Boulevard, Hayward, CA 94542-3035

Telephone: 510-885-3248 **Fax:** 510-885-3816

E-mail: adminfo@csuhayward.edu

Getting in Last Year 3,628 applied; 89% were accepted; 716 enrolled (22%).

Financial Matters $1944 resident tuition and fees (2002–03); $10,404 nonresident tuition and fees (2002–03); $3705 room only; 62% average percent of need met; $6961 average financial aid amount received per undergraduate.

Academics Cal State, Hayward awards bachelor's and master's degrees and post-bachelor's and post-master's certificates. Challenging opportunities include advanced placement credit, accelerated degree programs, student-designed majors, an honors program, double majors, independent study, and a senior project. Special programs include cooperative education, internships, summer session for credit, off-campus study, and study-abroad. The most frequently chosen baccalaureate fields are business/marketing, liberal arts/general studies, and social sciences and history. The faculty at Cal State, Hayward has 359 full-time members, 82% with terminal degrees. The student-faculty ratio is 21:1.

Students of Cal State, Hayward The student body totals 13,240, of whom 9,528 are undergraduates. 63.5% are women and 36.5% are men. Students come from 50 states and territories and 86 other countries. 5% are international students. 80% returned for their sophomore year.

Applying Cal State, Hayward requires a high school transcript, and in some cases SAT I or ACT. Application deadline: 9/7; 3/2 priority date for financial aid. Deferred admission is possible.

CALIFORNIA STATE UNIVERSITY, LONG BEACH

Long Beach, CA

Suburban setting ■ Public ■ State-supported ■ Coed

Web site: www.csulb.edu

Contact: Mr. Thomas Enders, Director of Enrollment Services, Brotman Hall, 1250 Bellflower Boulevard, Long Beach, CA 90840

Telephone: 562-985-4641

Getting in Last Year 21,953 applied; 52% were accepted; 3,037 enrolled (26%).

Financial Matters $1744 resident tuition and fees (2002–03); $9124 nonresident tuition and fees (2002–03); $5800 room and board; 83% average percent of need met; $6692 average financial aid amount received per undergraduate.

Academics CSULB awards bachelor's and master's degrees and post-bachelor's certificates. Challenging opportunities include advanced placement credit, accelerated degree programs, student-designed majors, an honors program, double majors, independent study, and a senior project. Special programs include internships, summer session for credit, off-campus study, study-abroad, and Army ROTC. The most frequently chosen baccalaureate fields are business/marketing, visual/performing arts, and social sciences and history. The faculty at CSULB has 1,051 full-time members, 81% with terminal degrees. The student-faculty ratio is 20:1.

Students of CSULB The student body totals 34,566, of whom 27,863 are undergraduates. 58.9% are women and 41.1% are men. Students come from 43 states and territories and 101 other countries. 98% are from California. 5.2% are international students. 81% returned for their sophomore year.

Applying CSULB requires SAT I or ACT and a high school transcript, and in some cases minimum GPA of 2.4 for nonresidents and a minimum high school GPA of 2.0. Application deadline: 11/30; 3/2 priority date for financial aid.

CALIFORNIA STATE UNIVERSITY, NORTHRIDGE

Northridge, CA

Urban setting ■ Public ■ State-supported ■ Coed

Web site: www.csun.edu

Contact: Ms. Mary Baxton, Associate Director of Admissions and Records, 18111 Nordhoff Street, Northridge, CA 91330-8207

Telephone: 818-677-3777 **Fax:** 818-677-3766

E-mail: admissions.records@csun.edu

Getting in Last Year 10,600 applied; 83% were accepted; 3,298 enrolled (38%).

Financial Matters $1814 resident tuition and fees (2002–03); $9532 nonresident tuition and fees (2002–03); $6400 room and board; 86% average percent of need met; $8615 average financial aid amount received per undergraduate.

Academics CSUN awards bachelor's and master's degrees. Challenging opportunities include advanced placement credit, accelerated degree programs, student-designed majors, and an honors program. Special programs include summer session for credit, off-campus study, study-abroad, and Army and Air Force ROTC. The faculty at CSUN has 841 full-time members.

Students of CSUN The student body totals 31,448, of whom 24,462 are undergraduates. 58.9% are women and 41.1% are men. Students come from 40 states and territories and 7 other countries. 99% are from California. 3.6% are international students. 73% returned for their sophomore year.

Applying CSUN requires a high school transcript. The school recommends SAT I or ACT. Application deadline: 11/30; 3/2 priority date for financial aid. Early admission is possible.

CALIFORNIA STATE UNIVERSITY, SACRAMENTO

Sacramento, CA

Urban setting ■ Public ■ State-supported ■ Coed

Web site: www.csus.edu

Contact: Mr. Emiliano Diaz, Director of University Outreach Services, 6000 J Street, Lassen Hall, Sacramento, CA 95819-6048

Telephone: 916-278-7362 **Fax:** 916-278-5603

E-mail: admissions@csus.edu

Getting in Last Year 10,400 applied; 51% were accepted; 2,503 enrolled (47%).

California State University, Sacramento (continued)

Financial Matters $1891 resident tuition and fees (2002–03); $11,779 nonresident tuition and fees (2002–03); $6163 room and board; 73% average percent of need met; $7540 average financial aid amount received per undergraduate (2001–02).

Academics CSUS awards bachelor's, master's, and doctoral degrees. Challenging opportunities include advanced placement credit, accelerated degree programs, student-designed majors, double majors, independent study, and a senior project. Special programs include cooperative education, internships, summer session for credit, off-campus study, study-abroad, and Army and Air Force ROTC. The most frequently chosen baccalaureate fields are business/marketing, protective services/public administration, and social sciences and history. The faculty at CSUS has 874 full-time members, 76% with terminal degrees. The student-faculty ratio is 21:1.

Students of CSUS The student body totals 28,558, of whom 22,564 are undergraduates. 56.9% are women and 43.1% are men. Students come from 45 states and territories and 53 other countries. 99% are from California. 1.7% are international students. 75% returned for their sophomore year.

Applying CSUS requires a high school transcript and a minimum high school GPA of 2.0, and in some cases SAT I or ACT. Application deadline: 5/1; 3/2 priority date for financial aid. Deferred admission is possible.

CALIFORNIA STATE UNIVERSITY, SAN BERNARDINO

San Bernardino, CA

Suburban setting ■ Public ■ State-supported ■ Coed

Web site: www.csusb.edu
Contact: Ms. Cynthia Shum, Admissions Counselor, 5500 University Parkway, University Hall, Room 107, San Bernardino, CA 92407-2397
Telephone: 909-880-5212 or toll-free 909-880-5188 **Fax:** 909-880-7034
E-mail: moreinfo@mail.csusb.edu

Getting in Last Year 5,155 applied; 70% were accepted; 1,201 enrolled (33%).

Financial Matters $1931 resident tuition and fees (2002–03); $9766 nonresident tuition and fees (2002–03); $4956 room and board.

Academics CSUSB awards bachelor's and master's degrees. Challenging opportunities include advanced placement credit, student-designed majors, an honors program, double majors, independent study, and a senior project. Special programs include cooperative education, internships, summer session for credit, off-campus study, study-abroad, and Army and Air Force ROTC. The most frequently chosen baccalaureate fields are business/marketing, liberal arts/general studies, and social sciences and history. The faculty at CSUSB has 466 full-time members. The student-faculty ratio is 20:1.

Students of CSUSB The student body totals 16,341, of whom 11,256 are undergraduates. 63.5% are women and 36.5% are men. Students come from 31 states and territories and 84 other countries. 2.8% are international students. 44% returned for their sophomore year.

Applying CSUSB requires a high school transcript and a minimum high school GPA of 2.0, and in some cases SAT I or ACT. Application deadline: rolling admissions; 3/2 priority date for financial aid. Early admission is possible.

CALIFORNIA STATE UNIVERSITY, SAN MARCOS

San Marcos, CA

Suburban setting ■ Public ■ State-supported ■ Coed

Web site: www.csusm.edu
Contact: Ms. Cherine Heckman, Director of Admissions, San Marcos, CA 92096-0001
Telephone: 760-750-4848 **Fax:** 760-750-3248
E-mail: apply@csusm.edu

Getting in Last Year 4,314 applied; 67% were accepted; 837 enrolled (29%).

Financial Matters $2048 resident tuition and fees (2002–03); $9521 nonresident tuition and fees (2002–03); 33% average percent of need met; $6199 average financial aid amount received per undergraduate (2001–02).

Academics CSU San Marcos awards bachelor's and master's degrees. Challenging opportunities include advanced placement credit, student-designed majors, double majors, independent study, and a senior project. Special programs include internships, summer session for credit, off-campus study, study-abroad, and Army, Navy and Air Force ROTC. The most frequently chosen baccalaureate fields are liberal arts/general studies, social sciences and history, and business/marketing. The faculty at CSU San Marcos has 188 full-time members, 96% with terminal degrees. The student-faculty ratio is 19:1.

Students of CSU San Marcos The student body totals 6,703, of whom 6,149 are undergraduates. 60.2% are women and 39.8% are men. 100% are from California. 2% are international students. 60% returned for their sophomore year.

Applying CSU San Marcos requires SAT I or ACT, a high school transcript, and a minimum high school GPA of 3.0. Application deadline: 11/30; 3/2 priority date for financial aid.

CALIFORNIA STATE UNIVERSITY, STANISLAUS

Turlock, CA

Small-town setting ■ Public ■ State-supported ■ Coed

Web site: www.csustan.edu
Contact: Admissions Office, Enrollment Services, 801 West Monte Vista Avenue, Mary Stuart Rogers Gateway Center, Room 120, Turlock, CA 95382
Telephone: 209-667-3070 or toll-free 800-300-7420 (in-state)
Fax: 209-667-3788
E-mail: outreach_help_desk@stan.csustan.edu

Getting in Last Year 2,243 applied; 67% were accepted; 615 enrolled (41%).

Financial Matters $1879 resident tuition and fees (2002–03); $10,339 nonresident tuition and fees (2002–03); $7371 room and board; 61% average percent of need met; $6503 average financial aid amount received per undergraduate.

Academics CSU, Stanislaus awards bachelor's and master's degrees. Challenging opportunities include advanced placement credit, accelerated degree programs, student-designed majors, an honors program, double majors, independent study, and a senior project. Special programs include cooperative education, internships, summer session for credit, off-campus study, and study-abroad. The most frequently chosen baccalaureate fields are liberal arts/general studies, business/marketing, and social sciences and history. The faculty at CSU, Stanislaus has 292 full-time members, 80% with terminal degrees. The student-faculty ratio is 17:1.

Students of CSU, Stanislaus The student body totals 7,850, of whom 5,867 are undergraduates. 66.6% are women and 33.4% are men. Students come from 31 states and territories and 59 other countries. 99% are from California. 1.4% are international students. 81% returned for their sophomore year.

Applying CSU, Stanislaus requires SAT I or ACT and a high school transcript. The school recommends a minimum high school GPA of 3.0. Application deadline: 5/31; 3/2 priority date for financial aid. Deferred admission is possible.

CALIFORNIA UNIVERSITY OF PENNSYLVANIA

California, PA

Small-town setting ■ Public ■ State-supported ■ Coed

Web site: www.cup.edu
Contact: Mr. William A. Edmonds, Dean of Enrollment Management and Academic Services, 250 University Avenue, California, PA 15419
Telephone: 724-938-4404 **Fax:** 724-938-4564
E-mail: inquiry@cup.edu

Getting in Last Year 2,804 applied; 76% were accepted; 902 enrolled (42%).

Financial Matters $5742 resident tuition and fees (2002–03); $12,310 nonresident tuition and fees (2002–03); $5176 room and board; $7025 average financial aid amount received per undergraduate (2001–02).

Academics California University awards associate, bachelor's, and master's degrees. Challenging opportunities include advanced placement credit, accelerated degree programs, an honors program, double majors, and a senior project. Special programs include cooperative education, internships, summer session for credit, off-campus study, study-abroad, and Army ROTC. The most frequently chosen baccalaureate fields are education, business/marketing, and social sciences and history. The faculty at California University has 282 full-time members, 60% with terminal degrees. The student-faculty ratio is 19:1.

Students of California University The student body totals 6,082, of whom 5,127 are undergraduates. 53.1% are women and 46.9% are men. Students come from 28 states and territories and 14 other countries. 97% are from Pennsylvania. 0.7% are international students. 73% returned for their sophomore year.

Applying California University requires SAT I, a high school transcript, and a minimum high school GPA of 2.0, and in some cases an interview and recommendations. The school recommends an essay, SAT II Subject Tests, and a minimum high school GPA of 3.0. Application deadline: 7/30. Early and deferred admission are possible.

CALUMET COLLEGE OF SAINT JOSEPH

Whiting, IN

Suburban setting ■ Private ■ Independent Religious ■ Coed

Web site: www.ccsj.edu
Contact: Mr. Chuck Walz, Director of Admissions, 2400 New York Avenue, Whiting, IN 46394
Telephone: 219-473-4215 ext. 379 or toll-free 877-700-9100 **Fax:** 219-473-4259
E-mail: admissions@ccsj.edu

Getting in Last Year 391 applied; 55% were accepted; 85 enrolled (39%).

Financial Matters $7800 tuition and fees (2002–03); 90% average percent of need met.

Academics Calumet College awards associate, bachelor's, and master's degrees. Challenging opportunities include advanced placement credit, accelerated degree programs, student-designed majors, double majors, independent study, and a senior project. Special programs include cooperative education, internships, and summer session for credit. The faculty at Calumet College has 23 full-time members. The student-faculty ratio is 13:1.

Students of Calumet College The student body totals 1,143, of whom 1,079 are undergraduates. 59% are women and 41% are men. Students come from 2 states and territories. 71% are from Indiana. 0.1% are international students.

Applying Calumet College requires a high school transcript, and in some cases an essay and ACT COMPASS. The school recommends SAT I or ACT, an interview, and a minimum high school GPA of 2.0. Application deadline: rolling admissions; 3/1 priority date for financial aid. Deferred admission is possible.

CALVIN COLLEGE

Grand Rapids, MI

Suburban setting ■ Private ■ Independent Religious ■ Coed

Web site: www.calvin.edu

Contact: Mr. Dale D. Kuiper, Director of Admissions, 3201 Burton Street, SE, Grand Rapids, MI 49546-4388

Telephone: 616-957-6106 or toll-free 800-688-0122 **Fax:** 616-957-8513

E-mail: admissions@calvin.edu

Getting in Last Year 1,862 applied; 98% were accepted; 1,049 enrolled (57%).

Financial Matters $15,750 tuition and fees (2002–03); $5485 room and board; 91% average percent of need met; $12,252 average financial aid amount received per undergraduate.

Academics Calvin awards bachelor's and master's degrees and post-bachelor's certificates. Challenging opportunities include advanced placement credit, accelerated degree programs, student-designed majors, an honors program, double majors, independent study, and a senior project. Special programs include internships, summer session for credit, off-campus study, study-abroad, and Army ROTC. The most frequently chosen baccalaureate fields are business/marketing, social sciences and history, and education. The faculty at Calvin has 291 full-time members, 82% with terminal degrees. The student-faculty ratio is 15:1.

Students of Calvin The student body totals 4,324, of whom 4,286 are undergraduates. 56.3% are women and 43.7% are men. Students come from 48 states and territories and 38 other countries. 61% are from Michigan. 7.7% are international students. 86% returned for their sophomore year.

Applying Calvin requires an essay, SAT I or ACT, a high school transcript, 1 recommendation, and a minimum high school GPA of 2.5. The school recommends an interview. Application deadline: 8/15; 2/15 priority date for financial aid. Deferred admission is possible.

CAMBRIDGE COLLEGE

Cambridge, MA

Urban setting ■ Private ■ Independent ■ Coed

Web site: www.cambridgecollege.edu

Contact: Ms. Joy King, Undergraduate Enrollment Manager, 1000 Massachusetts Avenue, Cambridge, MA 02138-5304

Telephone: 617-868-1000 or toll-free 800-877-4723 **Fax:** 617-349-3545

E-mail: enroll@idea.cambridge.edu

Financial Matters $9075 tuition and fees (2002–03); $8695 average financial aid amount received per undergraduate.

Academics Cambridge College awards bachelor's and master's degrees. Challenging opportunities include accelerated degree programs, independent study, and a senior project. Special programs include internships, summer session for credit, and study-abroad. The faculty at Cambridge College has 31 full-time members, 100% with terminal degrees. The student-faculty ratio is 17:1.

Students of Cambridge College The student body totals 2,700, of whom 450 are undergraduates. Students come from 6 states and territories and 5 other countries. 98% are from Massachusetts.

Applying Cambridge College requires an essay, ACCUPLACER, a high school transcript, an interview, and recommendations. Application deadline: rolling admissions. Deferred admission is possible.

CAMERON UNIVERSITY

Lawton, OK

Suburban setting ■ Public ■ State-supported ■ Coed

Web site: www.cameron.edu

Contact: Ms. Brenda Dally, Coordinator of Student Recruitment, Cameron University, Attention: Admissions, 2800 West Gore Boulevard, Lawton, OK 73505

Telephone: 580-581-2837 or toll-free 888-454-7600 **Fax:** 580-581-5514

E-mail: admiss@cua.cameron.edu

Getting in Last Year 1,527 applied; 95% were accepted; 899 enrolled (62%).

Financial Matters $2520 resident tuition and fees (2002–03); $5850 nonresident tuition and fees (2002–03); $2830 room and board; 95% average percent of need met; $3825 average financial aid amount received per undergraduate.

Academics Cameron awards associate, bachelor's, and master's degrees. Challenging opportunities include advanced placement credit, accelerated degree programs, an honors program, double majors, and independent study. Special programs include summer session for credit, off-campus study, and Army ROTC. The most frequently chosen baccalaureate fields are business/marketing, social sciences and history, and protective services/public administration. The faculty at Cameron has 186 full-time members, 50% with terminal degrees. The student-faculty ratio is 19:1.

Students of Cameron The student body totals 5,298, of whom 4,811 are undergraduates. 57.6% are women and 42.4% are men. Students come from 22 states and territories and 21 other countries. 98% are from Oklahoma. 2.4% are international students. 37% returned for their sophomore year.

Applying Cameron requires SAT I or ACT and a high school transcript. Application deadline: rolling admissions. Early and deferred admission are possible.

CAMPBELLSVILLE UNIVERSITY

Campbellsville, KY

Small-town setting ■ Private ■ Independent Religious ■ Coed

Web site: www.campbellsville.edu

Contact: Mr. R. Trent Argo, Director of Admissions, 1 University Drive, Campbellsville, KY 42718-2799

Telephone: 270-789-5552 or toll-free 800-264-6014 **Fax:** 270-789-5071

E-mail: admissions@campbellsville.edu

Getting in Last Year 973 applied; 78% were accepted; 304 enrolled (40%).

Financial Matters $11,460 tuition and fees (2002–03); $4740 room and board; 67% average percent of need met; $8798 average financial aid amount received per undergraduate (2001–02).

Academics Campbellsville University awards associate, bachelor's, and master's degrees and post-bachelor's certificates. Challenging opportunities include advanced placement credit, accelerated degree programs, an honors program, double majors, independent study, and a senior project. Special programs include internships, summer session for credit, off-campus study, and study-abroad. The most frequently chosen baccalaureate fields are business/marketing, education, and social sciences and history. The faculty at Campbellsville University has 70 full-time members, 60% with terminal degrees. The student-faculty ratio is 17:1.

Students of Campbellsville University The student body totals 1,811, of whom 1,655 are undergraduates. 57.1% are women and 42.9% are men. Students come from 25 states and territories and 23 other countries. 92% are from Kentucky. 4.2% are international students. 67% returned for their sophomore year.

Applying Campbellsville University requires SAT I or ACT, a high school transcript, and a minimum high school GPA of 2.0. The school recommends an essay, an interview, recommendations, and a minimum high school GPA of 3.0. Application deadline: rolling admissions; 3/1 priority date for financial aid. Deferred admission is possible.

CAMPBELL UNIVERSITY

Buies Creek, NC

Rural setting ■ Private ■ Independent Religious ■ Coed

Web site: www.campbell.edu

Contact: Ms. Peggy Mason, Director of Admissions, PO Box 546, Buies Creek, NC 27506

Telephone: 910-893-1290 or toll-free 800-334-4111 ext. 1290 **Fax:** 910-893-1288

E-mail: adm@mailcenter.campbell.edu

Getting in Last Year 2,884 applied; 74% were accepted; 834 enrolled (39%).

Financial Matters $12,849 tuition and fees (2002–03); $4550 room and board; 100% average percent of need met; $19,893 average financial aid amount received per undergraduate.

Academics Campbell awards associate, bachelor's, master's, doctoral, and first-professional degrees. Challenging opportunities include advanced placement credit, accelerated degree programs, freshman honors college, an honors program, double majors, independent study, and a senior project. Special programs include cooperative education, internships, summer session for credit, study-abroad, and Army ROTC. The most frequently chosen baccalaureate fields are business/marketing, health professions and related sciences, and social sciences and history. The faculty at Campbell has 202 full-time members, 75% with terminal degrees. The student-faculty ratio is 13:1.

Students of Campbell The student body totals 4,098, of whom 2,543 are undergraduates. 55.1% are women and 44.9% are men. Students come from 50 states and territories and 56 other countries. 76% are from North Carolina. 2.7% are international students. 87% returned for their sophomore year.

Applying Campbell requires SAT I or ACT, a high school transcript, and a minimum high school GPA of 2.5, and in some cases 3 recommendations. The school recommends an essay and an interview. Application deadline: rolling admissions; 3/15 priority date for financial aid. Early and deferred admission are possible.

CANADIAN BIBLE COLLEGE

Calgary, AB Canada

Urban setting ■ Private ■ Independent Religious ■ Coed

Web site: www.cbccts.ca

Canadian Bible College (continued)

Contact: Mrs. Heather Russell-Maclean, Admissions Officer, 630, 833-4th Avenue SW, Calgary, AB T2P 3T5 Canada
Telephone: 306-545-1515 ext. 305 or toll-free 800-461-1222 **Fax:** 306-545-0210
E-mail: enrollment@cbccts.sk.ca

Getting in Last Year 129 applied; 100% were accepted; 129 enrolled (100%).

Financial Matters $5310 tuition and fees (2002–03); $4110 room and board.

Academics CBC awards bachelor's degrees (graduate and professional degrees are offered by Canadian Theological Seminary). Challenging opportunities include advanced placement credit, accelerated degree programs, an honors program, double majors, independent study, and a senior project. Special programs include cooperative education, internships, summer session for credit, off-campus study, and study-abroad. The faculty at CBC has 49 members, 76% with terminal degrees.

Students of CBC The student body is made up of 329 undergraduates. 47.4% are women and 52.6% are men. Students come from 11 states and territories. 64% are from Alberta. 1.8% are international students. 64% returned for their sophomore year.

Applying CBC requires an essay, a high school transcript, and 2 recommendations, and in some cases an interview. The school recommends medical history. Application deadline: rolling admissions; 7/31 priority date for financial aid. Early and deferred admission are possible.

CANADIAN MENNONITE UNIVERSITY

Winnipeg, MB Canada

Urban setting ■ Private ■ Independent Religious ■ Coed

Web site: www.cmu.ca
Contact: Abe Bergen, Director of Enrollment Services, 500 Shaftesbury Boulevard, Winnipeg, MB R3P 2N2 Canada
Telephone: 204-487-3300 ext. 652 or toll-free 877-231-4570 **Fax:** 204-487-3858
E-mail: cu@cmu.ca

Getting in Last Year 238 applied; 75% were accepted; 159 enrolled (89%).

Financial Matters $4060 tuition and fees (2002–03); $4145 room and board.

Academics Canadian Mennonite University awards bachelor's degrees. Challenging opportunities include double majors and a senior project. Special programs include internships, off-campus study, and study-abroad. The faculty at Canadian Mennonite University has 28 members, 79% with terminal degrees. The student-faculty ratio is 7:1.

Students of Canadian Mennonite University The student body totals 411, of whom 383 are undergraduates. 53.8% are women and 46.2% are men. Students come from 6 states and territories and 7 other countries. 40% are from Manitoba. 3.9% are international students.

Applying Canadian Mennonite University requires a high school transcript, recommendations, and a minimum high school GPA of 2.0, and in some cases an essay. Application deadline: 8/31; 9/30 for financial aid. Deferred admission is possible.

CANISIUS COLLEGE

Buffalo, NY

Urban setting ■ Private ■ Independent Religious ■ Coed

Web site: www.canisius.edu
Contact: Miss Penelope H. Lips, Director of Admissions, 2001 Main Street, Buffalo, NY 14208-1098
Telephone: 716-888-2200 or toll-free 800-843-1517 **Fax:** 716-888-3230
E-mail: inquiry@canisius.edu

Getting in Last Year 3,614 applied; 80% were accepted; 849 enrolled (29%).

Financial Matters $18,840 tuition and fees (2002–03); $7540 room and board; 81% average percent of need met; $16,403 average financial aid amount received per undergraduate.

Academics Canisius awards associate, bachelor's, and master's degrees. Challenging opportunities include advanced placement credit, student-designed majors, an honors program, independent study, and a senior project. Special programs include internships, summer session for credit, off-campus study, study-abroad, and Army ROTC. The most frequently chosen baccalaureate fields are education, social sciences and history, and business/marketing. The faculty at Canisius has 209 full-time members, 95% with terminal degrees. The student-faculty ratio is 16:1.

Students of Canisius The student body totals 5,041, of whom 3,440 are undergraduates. 53% are women and 47% are men. Students come from 29 states and territories and 35 other countries. 92% are from New York. 2.8% are international students. 81% returned for their sophomore year.

Applying Canisius requires SAT I or ACT and a high school transcript, and in some cases an interview. The school recommends an essay, an interview, and recommendations. Application deadline: rolling admissions; 2/15 priority date for financial aid. Early and deferred admission are possible.

CAPELLA UNIVERSITY

Minneapolis, MN

Private ■ Proprietary ■ Coed

Web site: www.capellauniversity.edu
Contact: Ms. Liz Hinz, Associate Director, Enrollment Services, 222 South 9th Street, 20th Floor, Minneapolis, MN 55402
Telephone: 612-659-5286 or toll-free 888-CAPELLA **Fax:** 612-339-8022
E-mail: info@capella.edu

Financial Matters $14,250 tuition and fees (2002–03); 90% average percent of need met; $10,500 average financial aid amount received per undergraduate.

Academics Capella University awards bachelor's, master's, doctoral, and first-professional degrees and first-professional certificates (offers only distance learning degree programs). Challenging opportunities include student-designed majors, double majors, independent study, and a senior project. Special programs include internships, summer session for credit, and off-campus study. The most frequently chosen baccalaureate field is computer/information sciences. The faculty at Capella University has 45 full-time members, 100% with terminal degrees. The student-faculty ratio is 12:1.

Students of Capella University The student body totals 6,500, of whom 600 are undergraduates. 15% are from Minnesota.

CAPITAL UNIVERSITY

Columbus, OH

Suburban setting ■ Private ■ Independent Religious ■ Coed

Web site: www.capital.edu
Contact: Mrs. Kimberly V. Ebbrecht, Director of Admission, 2199 East Main Street, Columbus, OH 43209
Telephone: 614-236-6101 or toll-free 800-289-6289 **Fax:** 614-236-6926
E-mail: admissions@capital.edu

Getting in Last Year 2,151 applied; 83% were accepted.

Financial Matters $18,990 tuition and fees (2002–03); $5950 room and board; 87% average percent of need met; $14,904 average financial aid amount received per undergraduate (2001–02).

Academics Capital awards bachelor's, master's, and first-professional degrees. Challenging opportunities include advanced placement credit, student-designed majors, freshman honors college, double majors, and independent study. Special programs include internships, summer session for credit, off-campus study, study-abroad, and Army and Air Force ROTC. The most frequently chosen baccalaureate fields are business/marketing, interdisciplinary studies, and social sciences and history. The faculty at Capital has 182 full-time members, 71% with terminal degrees. The student-faculty ratio is 11:1.

Students of Capital The student body totals 3,947, of whom 2,785 are undergraduates. 63.6% are women and 36.4% are men. Students come from 24 states and territories and 14 other countries. 92% are from Ohio. 0.7% are international students. 73% returned for their sophomore year.

Applying Capital requires SAT I or ACT, a high school transcript, and a minimum high school GPA of 2.6, and in some cases an essay, 1 recommendation, and audition. The school recommends an interview. Application deadline: 4/15; 2/28 priority date for financial aid. Deferred admission is possible.

CAPITOL COLLEGE

Laurel, MD

Suburban setting ■ Private ■ Independent ■ Coed

Web site: www.capitol-college.edu
Contact: Mr. John Sumpter, Director of Admissions, 11301 Springfield Road, Laurel, MD 20708
Telephone: 301-953-3200 ext. 3033 or toll-free 800-950-1992
E-mail: admissions@capitol-college.edu

Getting in Last Year 213 applied; 90% were accepted; 61 enrolled (32%).

Financial Matters $16,390 tuition and fees (2002–03); $3700 room only; 38% average percent of need met.

Academics Capitol College awards associate, bachelor's, and master's degrees and post-bachelor's certificates. Challenging opportunities include advanced placement credit, accelerated degree programs, and a senior project. Special programs include cooperative education, summer session for credit, and Army ROTC. The most frequently chosen baccalaureate fields are engineering/engineering technologies, computer/information sciences, and business/marketing. The faculty at Capitol College has 15 full-time members, 33% with terminal degrees. The student-faculty ratio is 12:1.

Students of Capitol College The student body totals 801, of whom 630 are undergraduates. 23.3% are women and 76.7% are men. Students come from 15 states and territories and 21 other countries. 86% are from Maryland. 4% are international students.

Applying Capitol College requires SAT I or ACT and a high school transcript, and in some cases an essay, an interview, and 2 recommendations. The school recommends an interview and a minimum high school GPA of 2.2. Application deadline: rolling admissions. Deferred admission is possible.

CARDINAL STRITCH UNIVERSITY

Milwaukee, WI

Suburban setting ■ Private ■ Independent Religious ■ Coed

Web site: www.stritch.edu
Contact: Mr. David Wegener, Director of Admissions, 6801 North Yates Road, Milwaukee, WI 53217-3985
Telephone: 414-410-4040 or toll-free 800-347-8822 ext. 4040
Fax: 414-410-4058
E-mail: admityou@stritch.edu

Getting in Last Year 262 enrolled.

Financial Matters $13,580 tuition and fees (2002–03); $4990 room and board; 61% average percent of need met; $7115 average financial aid amount received per undergraduate (2000–01).

Academics Stritch awards associate, bachelor's, master's, and doctoral degrees and post-bachelor's certificates. Challenging opportunities include advanced placement credit, accelerated degree programs, student-designed majors, an honors program, double majors, independent study, and a senior project. Special programs include cooperative education, internships, summer session for credit, and off-campus study. The most frequently chosen baccalaureate fields are business/marketing, education, and health professions and related sciences. The student-faculty ratio is 18:1.

Students of Stritch The student body totals 6,854, of whom 3,146 are undergraduates. 68.7% are women and 31.3% are men. Students come from 16 states and territories and 27 other countries. 1.9% are international students. 73% returned for their sophomore year.

Applying Stritch requires an essay, SAT I or ACT, a high school transcript, and a minimum high school GPA of 2.0, and in some cases recommendations. The school recommends ACT and an interview. Application deadline: rolling admissions. Deferred admission is possible.

CARLETON COLLEGE

Northfield, MN

Small-town setting ■ Private ■ Independent ■ Coed

Contact: Mr. Paul Thiboutot, Dean of Admissions, 100 South College Street, Northfield, MN 55057
Telephone: 507-646-4190 or toll-free 800-995-2275 **Fax:** 507-646-4526
E-mail: admissions@acs.carleton.edu

Getting in Last Year 4,170 applied; 35% were accepted; 502 enrolled (35%).

Financial Matters $26,910 tuition and fees (2002–03); $5535 room and board; 100% average percent of need met; $18,832 average financial aid amount received per undergraduate (2001–02).

Academics Carleton awards bachelor's degrees. Challenging opportunities include advanced placement credit, accelerated degree programs, student-designed majors, double majors, independent study, and a senior project. Special programs include internships, off-campus study, and study-abroad. The most frequently chosen baccalaureate fields are social sciences and history, physical sciences, and biological/life sciences. The faculty at Carleton has 195 full-time members, 92% with terminal degrees. The student-faculty ratio is 9:1.

Students of Carleton The student body is made up of 1,932 undergraduates. 52.1% are women and 47.9% are men. Students come from 50 states and territories and 37 other countries. 23% are from Minnesota. 3.4% are international students. 96% returned for their sophomore year.

Applying Carleton requires an essay, SAT I or ACT, a high school transcript, and 2 recommendations. The school recommends SAT II Subject Tests, SAT II: Writing Test, and an interview. Application deadline: 1/15; 2/15 priority date for financial aid. Early and deferred admission are possible.

CARLETON UNIVERSITY

Ottawa, ON Canada

Urban setting ■ Public ■ Coed

Web site: www.carleton.ca
Contact: Douglas Huckvale, Manager, Undergraduate Recruitment Office, 1125 Colonel By Drive, Ottawa, ON K1S 5B6 Canada
Telephone: 613-520-3663 or toll-free 888-354-4414 (in-state)
Fax: 613-520-3847
E-mail: liaison@admissions.carleton.ca

Getting in Last Year 14,095 applied; 72% were accepted.

Academics Carleton awards bachelor's, master's, and doctoral degrees. Challenging opportunities include accelerated degree programs, student-designed majors, an honors program, double majors, and a senior project. Special programs include cooperative education, internships, summer session for credit, off-campus study, and study-abroad. The most frequently chosen baccalaureate fields are liberal arts/general studies, engineering/engineering technologies, and law/legal studies. The faculty at Carleton has 716 members. The student-faculty ratio is 24:1.

Students of Carleton The student body totals 20,453, of whom 17,661 are undergraduates. Students come from 13 states and territories and 116 other countries. 89% are from Ontario. 85% returned for their sophomore year.

Applying Carleton requires a high school transcript and a minimum high school GPA of 2.0, and in some cases SAT I and SAT II or ACT, an interview, recommendations, and a minimum high school GPA of 3.0. Application deadline: 6/1, 4/1 for nonresidents. Deferred admission is possible.

CARLOS ALBIZU UNIVERSITY, MIAMI CAMPUS

Miami, FL

Urban setting ■ Private ■ Independent ■ Coed, Primarily Women

Web site: www.albizu.edu
Contact: Ms. Miriam E. Matos, Admissions Officer, 2173 N.W. 99th Avenue, Miami, FL 33172
Telephone: 305-593-1223 ext. 134 or toll-free 800-672-3246 **Fax:** 305-593-1854
E-mail: llozano@albizu.edu

Getting in Last Year 53 enrolled.

Financial Matters $7869 tuition and fees (2002–03); 50% average percent of need met; $7925 average financial aid amount received per undergraduate.

Academics Carlos Albizu University, Miami Campus awards bachelor's, master's, and doctoral degrees. Challenging opportunities include advanced placement credit, accelerated degree programs, and independent study. Special programs include cooperative education, internships, and summer session for credit. The most frequently chosen baccalaureate field is psychology. The faculty at Carlos Albizu University, Miami Campus has 4 full-time members, 100% with terminal degrees. The student-faculty ratio is 15:1.

Students of Carlos Albizu University, Miami Campus The student body totals 715, of whom 269 are undergraduates. 76.6% are women and 23.4% are men. Students come from 1 state or territory. 0.7% are international students. 67% returned for their sophomore year.

Applying Carlos Albizu University, Miami Campus requires a high school transcript and a minimum high school GPA of 2.0. Application deadline: 6/1 priority date for financial aid.

CARLOW COLLEGE

Pittsburgh, PA

Urban setting ■ Private ■ Independent Religious ■ Coed, Primarily Women

Web site: www.carlow.edu
Contact: Ms. Susan Winstel, Assistant Director of Admissions, 3333 Fifth Avenue, Pittsburgh, PA 15213-3165
Telephone: 412-578-6330 or toll-free 800-333-CARLOW **Fax:** 412-578-6668
E-mail: admissions@carlow.edu

Getting in Last Year 1,356 applied; 68% were accepted; 250 enrolled (27%).

Financial Matters $14,430 tuition and fees (2002–03); $5710 room and board; 87% average percent of need met; $12,363 average financial aid amount received per undergraduate.

Academics Carlow awards bachelor's and master's degrees and post-master's certificates. Challenging opportunities include advanced placement credit, accelerated degree programs, student-designed majors, an honors program, double majors, independent study, and a senior project. Special programs include cooperative education, internships, summer session for credit, off-campus study, and Army, Navy and Air Force ROTC. The most frequently chosen baccalaureate fields are health professions and related sciences, business/marketing, and education. The faculty at Carlow has 69 full-time members, 77% with terminal degrees. The student-faculty ratio is 14:1.

Students of Carlow The student body totals 2,070, of whom 1,745 are undergraduates. 94.6% are women and 5.4% are men. Students come from 12 states and territories. 96% are from Pennsylvania. 0.9% are international students. 78% returned for their sophomore year.

Applying Carlow requires SAT I or ACT and a high school transcript, and in some cases 3 recommendations. The school recommends an essay, an interview, rank in upper two-fifths of high school class, and a minimum high school GPA of 3.0. Application deadline: rolling admissions; 4/1 priority date for financial aid. Early and deferred admission are possible.

CARNEGIE MELLON UNIVERSITY

Pittsburgh, PA

Urban setting ■ Private ■ Independent ■ Coed

Web site: www.cmu.edu
Contact: Mr. Michael Steidel, Director of Admissions, 5000 Forbes Avenue, Warner Hall, Room 101, Pittsburgh, PA 15213
Telephone: 412-268-2082 **Fax:** 412-268-7838
E-mail: undergraduate-admissions@andrew.cmu.edu

Getting in Last Year 14,271 applied; 38% were accepted; 1,365 enrolled (25%).

Carnegie Mellon University (continued)

Financial Matters $27,116 tuition and fees (2002–03); $7534 room and board; 83% average percent of need met; $19,732 average financial aid amount received per undergraduate.

Academics CMU awards bachelor's, master's, and doctoral degrees and post-master's certificates. Challenging opportunities include advanced placement credit, accelerated degree programs, student-designed majors, freshman honors college, an honors program, double majors, independent study, and a senior project. Special programs include cooperative education, internships, summer session for credit, off-campus study, study-abroad, and Army, Navy and Air Force ROTC. The most frequently chosen baccalaureate fields are engineering/engineering technologies, social sciences and history, and computer/information sciences. The faculty at CMU has 747 full-time members. The student-faculty ratio is 11:1.

Students of CMU The student body totals 9,501, of whom 5,475 are undergraduates. 38.9% are women and 61.1% are men. Students come from 52 states and territories and 61 other countries. 24% are from Pennsylvania. 93% returned for their sophomore year.

Applying CMU requires an essay, SAT II Subject Tests, SAT I or ACT, a high school transcript, and 1 recommendation, and in some cases SAT II: Writing Test and portfolio, audition. The school recommends an interview. Application deadline: 1/1; 2/15 priority date for financial aid. Early and deferred admission are possible.

CARROLL COLLEGE

Helena, MT

Small-town setting ■ *Private* ■ *Independent Religious* ■ *Coed*

Web site: www.carroll.edu

Contact: Ms. Candace A. Cain, Director of Admission, 1601 North Benton Avenue, Helena, MT 59625-0002

Telephone: 406-447-4384 or toll-free 800-992-3648 **Fax:** 406-447-4533

E-mail: enroll@carroll.edu

Getting in Last Year 800 applied; 88% were accepted; 281 enrolled (40%).

Financial Matters $13,668 tuition and fees (2002–03); $5372 room and board; 86% average percent of need met; $13,047 average financial aid amount received per undergraduate.

Academics Carroll awards associate and bachelor's degrees. Challenging opportunities include advanced placement credit, accelerated degree programs, student-designed majors, freshman honors college, an honors program, double majors, independent study, and a senior project. Special programs include cooperative education, internships, summer session for credit, study-abroad, and Army ROTC. The most frequently chosen baccalaureate fields are business/marketing, biological/life sciences, and education. The faculty at Carroll has 80 full-time members, 66% with terminal degrees. The student-faculty ratio is 13:1.

Students of Carroll The student body is made up of 1,341 undergraduates. 60% are women and 40% are men. Students come from 28 states and territories and 7 other countries. 66% are from Montana. 1.2% are international students. 81% returned for their sophomore year.

Applying Carroll requires an essay, SAT I or ACT, a high school transcript, 1 recommendation, and a minimum high school GPA of 2.0, and in some cases SAT II Subject Tests, SAT II: Writing Test, and an interview. The school recommends an interview and a minimum high school GPA of 3.0. Application deadline: 6/1. Deferred admission is possible.

CARROLL COLLEGE

Waukesha, WI

Suburban setting ■ *Private* ■ *Independent Religious* ■ *Coed*

Web site: www.cc.edu

Contact: Mr. James V. Wiseman III, Vice President of Enrollment, 100 North East Avenue, Waukesha, WI 53186-5593

Telephone: 262-524-7221 or toll-free 800-CARROLL **Fax:** 262-524-7139

E-mail: cc.info@ccadmin.cc.edu

Getting in Last Year 1,773 applied; 84% were accepted; 538 enrolled (36%).

Financial Matters $16,750 tuition and fees (2002–03); $5170 room and board; 100% average percent of need met; $12,532 average financial aid amount received per undergraduate (2001–02).

Academics Carroll awards bachelor's and master's degrees (master's degrees in education and physical therapy). Challenging opportunities include advanced placement credit, student-designed majors, an honors program, double majors, independent study, and a senior project. Special programs include internships, summer session for credit, study-abroad, and Air Force ROTC. The most frequently chosen baccalaureate fields are business/marketing, health professions and related sciences, and education. The faculty at Carroll has 100 full-time members, 78% with terminal degrees. The student-faculty ratio is 16:1.

Students of Carroll The student body totals 2,968, of whom 2,705 are undergraduates. 66.1% are women and 33.9% are men. Students come from 29 states and territories and 24 other countries. 78% are from Wisconsin. 2.2% are international students. 78% returned for their sophomore year.

Applying Carroll requires SAT I and SAT II or ACT, a high school transcript, 1 recommendation, and a minimum high school GPA of 2.0, and in some cases an essay. The school recommends an interview. Application deadline: rolling admissions. Early and deferred admission are possible.

CARSON-NEWMAN COLLEGE

Jefferson City, TN

Small-town setting ■ *Private* ■ *Independent Religious* ■ *Coed*

Web site: www.cn.edu

Contact: Mrs. Sheryl M. Gray, Director of Undergraduate Admissions, PO Box 72025, Jefferson City, TN 37760

Telephone: 865-471-3223 or toll-free 800-678-9061 **Fax:** 865-471-3502

E-mail: cnadmiss@cn.edu

Getting in Last Year 1,168 applied; 86% were accepted; 431 enrolled (43%).

Financial Matters $12,890 tuition and fees (2002–03); $4350 room and board; 79% average percent of need met; $11,722 average financial aid amount received per undergraduate (2001–02).

Academics Carson-Newman awards associate, bachelor's, and master's degrees. Challenging opportunities include advanced placement credit, accelerated degree programs, student-designed majors, an honors program, and a senior project. Special programs include internships, summer session for credit, off-campus study, study-abroad, and Army and Air Force ROTC. The most frequently chosen baccalaureate fields are education, business/marketing, and psychology. The faculty at Carson-Newman has 127 full-time members, 52% with terminal degrees. The student-faculty ratio is 13:1.

Students of Carson-Newman The student body totals 2,205, of whom 2,019 are undergraduates. 56.9% are women and 43.1% are men. Students come from 42 states and territories and 15 other countries. 68% are from Tennessee. 2.8% are international students. 77% returned for their sophomore year.

Applying Carson-Newman requires SAT I or ACT, a high school transcript, medical history, and a minimum high school GPA of 2.25, and in some cases an essay, an interview, and recommendations. The school recommends an interview. Application deadline: 8/1; 4/1 priority date for financial aid. Deferred admission is possible.

CARTHAGE COLLEGE

Kenosha, WI

Suburban setting ■ *Private* ■ *Independent Religious* ■ *Coed*

Web site: www.carthage.edu

Contact: Mr. Tom Augustine, Director of Admission, 2001 Alford Park Drive, Kenosha, WI 53140-1994

Telephone: 262-551-6000 or toll-free 800-351-4058 **Fax:** 262-551-5762

E-mail: admissions@carthage.edu

Getting in Last Year 2,847 applied; 83% were accepted; 615 enrolled (26%).

Financial Matters $19,150 tuition and fees (2002–03); $5750 room and board; 95% average percent of need met; $16,277 average financial aid amount received per undergraduate.

Academics Carthage awards bachelor's and master's degrees. Challenging opportunities include advanced placement credit, accelerated degree programs, student-designed majors, an honors program, double majors, independent study, and a senior project. Special programs include cooperative education, internships, summer session for credit, off-campus study, study-abroad, and Army and Air Force ROTC. The most frequently chosen baccalaureate fields are business/marketing, education, and social sciences and history. The faculty at Carthage has 113 full-time members, 82% with terminal degrees. The student-faculty ratio is 16:1.

Students of Carthage The student body totals 2,520, of whom 2,388 are undergraduates. 58.7% are women and 41.3% are men. Students come from 27 states and territories and 12 other countries. 49% are from Wisconsin. 0.8% are international students. 72% returned for their sophomore year.

Applying Carthage requires SAT I or ACT, a high school transcript, and a minimum high school GPA of 2.0, and in some cases an essay and 2 recommendations. The school recommends an essay, an interview, and a minimum high school GPA of 3.0. Application deadline: rolling admissions; 2/15 priority date for financial aid. Deferred admission is possible.

CARVER BIBLE COLLEGE

Atlanta, GA

Private ■ *Independent Religious* ■ *Coed*

Web site: www.carverbiblecollege.edu

Contact: Ms. Patsy S. Singh, Director of Admissions, 437 Nelson Street, Atlanta, GA 30313

Telephone: 404-527-4520 ext. 4537

Getting in Last Year 61 applied; 16% were accepted.

Financial Matters $5760 tuition and fees (2002–03); $1760 room and board.

Academics Carver Bible College awards bachelor's degrees. Independent study is a challenging opportunity. Special programs include internships, summer session for credit, and off-campus study. The faculty at Carver Bible College has 3 full-time members. The student-faculty ratio is 10:1.

Students of Carver Bible College The student body is made up of 150 undergraduates. 36% are women and 64% are men. Students come from 4 states and territories and 7 other countries. 90% are from Georgia. 7.3% are international students.

Applying Carver Bible College requires an essay, a high school transcript, 4 recommendations, and a minimum high school GPA of 2.0, and in some cases an interview.

CASCADE COLLEGE

Portland, OR

Urban setting ■ Private ■ Independent Religious ■ Coed

Web site: www.cascade.edu

Contact: Mr. Clint La Rue, Director of Admissions, 9101 East Burnside, Portland, OR 97216-1515

Telephone: 503-257-1202 or toll-free 800-550-7678

E-mail: admissions@cascade.edu

Getting in Last Year 247 applied; 100% were accepted; 73 enrolled (30%).

Financial Matters $10,260 tuition and fees (2002–03); $5530 room and board; 48% average percent of need met; $13,296 average financial aid amount received per undergraduate.

Academics Cascade awards bachelor's degrees. Challenging opportunities include advanced placement credit, accelerated degree programs, double majors, independent study, and a senior project. Special programs include internships, summer session for credit, off-campus study, study-abroad, and Army and Air Force ROTC. The most frequently chosen baccalaureate fields are liberal arts/general studies, business/marketing, and psychology. The faculty at Cascade has 15 full-time members, 47% with terminal degrees. The student-faculty ratio is 17:1.

Students of Cascade The student body is made up of 341 undergraduates. 53.1% are women and 46.9% are men. Students come from 20 states and territories and 5 other countries. 41% are from Oregon. 3.3% are international students. 60% returned for their sophomore year.

Applying Cascade requires SAT I or ACT and a high school transcript. The school recommends an essay and 1 recommendation. Application deadline: rolling admissions; 8/1 for financial aid, with a 4/30 priority date. Early and deferred admission are possible.

CASE WESTERN RESERVE UNIVERSITY

Cleveland, OH

Urban setting ■ Private ■ Independent ■ Coed

Web site: www.cwru.edu

Contact: Ms. Elizabeth H. Woyczynski, Acting Dean of Undergraduate Admission, 10900 Euclid Avenue, Cleveland, OH 44106

Telephone: 216-368-4450 **Fax:** 216-368-5111

E-mail: admission@po.cwru.edu

Getting in Last Year 4,428 applied; 78% were accepted; 836 enrolled (24%).

Financial Matters $22,730 tuition and fees (2002–03); $7150 room and board; 96% average percent of need met; $21,815 average financial aid amount received per undergraduate.

Academics CWRU awards bachelor's, master's, doctoral, and first-professional degrees and post-bachelor's certificates. Challenging opportunities include advanced placement credit, accelerated degree programs, student-designed majors, an honors program, double majors, independent study, and a senior project. Special programs include cooperative education, internships, summer session for credit, off-campus study, study-abroad, and Army and Air Force ROTC. The most frequently chosen baccalaureate fields are engineering/engineering technologies, biological/life sciences, and business/marketing. The faculty at CWRU has 594 full-time members, 95% with terminal degrees. The student-faculty ratio is 8:1.

Students of CWRU The student body totals 9,097, of whom 3,457 are undergraduates. 39.4% are women and 60.6% are men. Students come from 50 states and territories and 26 other countries. 60% are from Ohio. 3.7% are international students. 90% returned for their sophomore year.

Applying CWRU requires an essay, SAT I or ACT, a high school transcript, and 1 recommendation. The school recommends SAT II Subject Tests and an interview. Application deadline: 2/1; 2/1 priority date for financial aid. Early and deferred admission are possible.

CASTLETON STATE COLLEGE

Castleton, VT

Rural setting ■ Public ■ State-supported ■ Coed

Web site: www.castleton.edu

Contact: Ms. Heather Atwell, Director of Undergraduate Admissions, Seminary Street, Castleton, VT 05735

Telephone: 802-468-1351 or toll-free 800-639-8521 **Fax:** 802-468-1476

E-mail: info@castleton.edu

Getting in Last Year 1,196 applied; 85% were accepted; 401 enrolled (39%).

Financial Matters $5654 resident tuition and fees (2002–03); $11,866 nonresident tuition and fees (2002–03); $5782 room and board; 80% average percent of need met; $7600 average financial aid amount received per undergraduate (2001–02).

Academics Castleton awards associate, bachelor's, and master's degrees and post-master's certificates. Challenging opportunities include advanced placement credit, student-designed majors, an honors program, double majors, independent study, and a senior project. Special programs include cooperative education, internships, summer session for credit, off-campus study, study-abroad, and Army ROTC. The most frequently chosen baccalaureate fields are social sciences and history, protective services/public administration, and business/marketing. The faculty at Castleton has 86 full-time members, 94% with terminal degrees. The student-faculty ratio is 13:1.

Students of Castleton The student body totals 1,725, of whom 1,643 are undergraduates. 60.5% are women and 39.5% are men. Students come from 29 states and territories. 65% are from Vermont. 0.2% are international students. 70% returned for their sophomore year.

Applying Castleton requires an essay, SAT I or ACT, a high school transcript, recommendations, and a minimum high school GPA of 2.5. The school recommends an interview. Application deadline: rolling admissions; 3/15 priority date for financial aid. Deferred admission is possible.

CATAWBA COLLEGE

Salisbury, NC

Small-town setting ■ Private ■ Independent Religious ■ Coed

Web site: www.catawba.edu

Contact: Mr. Brian Best, Chief Enrollment Officer, 2300 West Innes Street, Salisbury, NC 28144-2488

Telephone: 800-CATAWBA or toll-free 800-CATAWBA **Fax:** 704-637-4222

E-mail: bdbest@catawba.edu

Getting in Last Year 1,031 applied; 80% were accepted; 317 enrolled (38%).

Financial Matters $15,300 tuition and fees (2002–03); $5200 room and board; 51% average percent of need met; $13,766 average financial aid amount received per undergraduate (2001–02).

Academics Catawba awards bachelor's and master's degrees. Challenging opportunities include advanced placement credit, student-designed majors, an honors program, double majors, independent study, and a senior project. Special programs include internships, summer session for credit, study-abroad, and Army ROTC. The most frequently chosen baccalaureate fields are business/marketing, communications/communication technologies, and computer/information sciences. The faculty at Catawba has 78 full-time members, 72% with terminal degrees. The student-faculty ratio is 16:1.

Students of Catawba The student body totals 1,557, of whom 1,538 are undergraduates. 52.8% are women and 47.2% are men. Students come from 31 states and territories and 14 other countries. 71% are from North Carolina. 1.8% are international students. 57% returned for their sophomore year.

Applying Catawba requires SAT I or ACT, a high school transcript, and a minimum high school GPA of 2.0. The school recommends an essay, an interview, and recommendations. Application deadline: rolling admissions; 3/1 priority date for financial aid. Early and deferred admission are possible.

THE CATHOLIC UNIVERSITY OF AMERICA

Washington, DC

Urban setting ■ Private ■ Independent Religious ■ Coed

Web site: www.cua.edu

Contact: Ms. Michelle D. Petro-Siraj, Executive Director of Undergraduate Admission, 102 McMahon Hall, Washington, DC 20064

Telephone: 202-319-5305 or toll-free 202-319-5305 (in-state), 800-673-2772 (out-of-state) **Fax:** 202-319-6533

E-mail: cua-admissions@cua.edu

Getting in Last Year 2,708 applied; 82% were accepted; 712 enrolled (32%).

Financial Matters $22,000 tuition and fees (2002–03); $8632 room and board; 44% average percent of need met; $19,390 average financial aid amount received per undergraduate.

Academics CUA awards bachelor's, master's, doctoral, and first-professional degrees and post-master's certificates. Challenging opportunities include advanced placement credit, accelerated degree programs, freshman honors college, an honors program, double majors, independent study, and a senior project. Special programs include internships, summer session for credit, off-campus study, study-abroad, and Army, Navy and Air Force ROTC. The most frequently chosen baccalaureate fields are social sciences and history, architecture, and visual/performing arts. The faculty at CUA has 359 full-time members, 92% with terminal degrees. The student-faculty ratio is 7:1.

The Catholic University of America (continued)

Students of CUA The student body totals 5,527, of whom 2,668 are undergraduates. 55.4% are women and 44.6% are men. Students come from 51 states and territories and 34 other countries. 4% are from District of Columbia. 2.3% are international students. 82% returned for their sophomore year.

Applying CUA requires an essay, SAT I or ACT, a high school transcript, and 1 recommendation. The school recommends SAT II Subject Tests, SAT II: Writing Test, and a minimum high school GPA of 2.8. Application deadline: 2/15; 2/1 for financial aid, with a 1/15 priority date. Early and deferred admission are possible.

CAZENOVIA COLLEGE

Cazenovia, NY

Small-town setting ■ Private ■ Independent ■ Coed

Web site: www.cazenovia.edu

Contact: Mr. Robert A. Croot, Dean for Enrollment Management, 22 Sullivan Street, Cazenovia, NY 13035-1084

Telephone: 315-655-7208 or toll-free 800-654-3210 **Fax:** 315-655-4860

E-mail: admission@cazenovia.edu

Getting in Last Year 964 applied; 82% were accepted; 265 enrolled (33%).

Financial Matters $15,860 tuition and fees (2002–03); $6700 room and board; 80% average percent of need met; $13,827 average financial aid amount received per undergraduate.

Academics Cazenovia awards associate and bachelor's degrees. Challenging opportunities include advanced placement credit, student-designed majors, an honors program, independent study, and a senior project. Special programs include cooperative education, internships, summer session for credit, off-campus study, study-abroad, and Army and Air Force ROTC. The most frequently chosen baccalaureate fields are visual/performing arts, business/marketing, and protective services/public administration. The faculty at Cazenovia has 56 full-time members, 52% with terminal degrees. The student-faculty ratio is 11:1.

Students of Cazenovia The student body is made up of 1,005 undergraduates. 73.6% are women and 26.4% are men. Students come from 19 states and territories and 2 other countries. 87% are from New York. 0.7% are international students. 67% returned for their sophomore year.

Applying Cazenovia requires a high school transcript. The school recommends SAT I and SAT II or ACT. Application deadline: rolling admissions; 3/15 priority date for financial aid. Early and deferred admission are possible.

CEDAR CREST COLLEGE

Allentown, PA

Suburban setting ■ Private ■ Independent Religious ■ Women Only

Web site: www.cedarcrest.edu

Contact: Ms. Judith A. Neyhart, Vice President for Enrollment and Advancement, 100 College Drive, Allentown, PA 18104-6196

Telephone: 610-740-3780 or toll-free 800-360-1222 **Fax:** 610-606-4647

E-mail: cccadmis@cedarcrest.edu

Getting in Last Year 1,036 applied; 73% were accepted; 180 enrolled (24%).

Financial Matters $19,915 tuition and fees (2002–03); $6994 room and board; 79% average percent of need met; $15,319 average financial aid amount received per undergraduate.

Academics Cedar Crest awards associate, bachelor's, and master's degrees and post-bachelor's certificates. Challenging opportunities include advanced placement credit, accelerated degree programs, student-designed majors, freshman honors college, an honors program, double majors, independent study, and a senior project. Special programs include internships, summer session for credit, off-campus study, study-abroad, and Army ROTC. The most frequently chosen baccalaureate fields are psychology, health professions and related sciences, and business/marketing. The faculty at Cedar Crest has 72 full-time members, 74% with terminal degrees. The student-faculty ratio is 11:1.

Students of Cedar Crest The student body is made up of 1,590 undergraduates. Students come from 31 states and territories and 10 other countries. 82% are from Pennsylvania. 0.9% are international students. 83% returned for their sophomore year.

Applying Cedar Crest requires an essay, SAT I or ACT, and a high school transcript, and in some cases 2 recommendations. The school recommends an interview and a minimum high school GPA of 2.0. Application deadline: rolling admissions. Early and deferred admission are possible.

CEDARVILLE UNIVERSITY

Cedarville, OH

Rural setting ■ Private ■ Independent Religious ■ Coed

Web site: www.cedarville.edu

Contact: Mr. Roscoe Smith, Director of Admissions, 251 North Main Street, Cedarville, OH 45314-0601

Telephone: 937-766-7700 or toll-free 800-CEDARVILLE **Fax:** 937-766-7575

E-mail: admiss@cedarville.edu

Getting in Last Year 2,031 applied; 82% were accepted; 774 enrolled (47%).

Financial Matters $13,696 tuition and fees (2002–03); $5010 room and board; 41% average percent of need met; $10,749 average financial aid amount received per undergraduate (2001–02).

Academics Cedarville awards associate, bachelor's, and master's degrees. Challenging opportunities include advanced placement credit, accelerated degree programs, an honors program, double majors, independent study, and a senior project. Special programs include internships, summer session for credit, off-campus study, study-abroad, and Army and Air Force ROTC. The most frequently chosen baccalaureate fields are education, business/marketing, and communications/communication technologies. The faculty at Cedarville has 194 full-time members, 55% with terminal degrees. The student-faculty ratio is 16:1.

Students of Cedarville The student body totals 3,005, of whom 2,986 are undergraduates. 54.5% are women and 45.5% are men. Students come from 49 states and territories. 33% are from Ohio. 0.5% are international students. 86% returned for their sophomore year.

Applying Cedarville requires an essay, SAT I or ACT, a high school transcript, 2 recommendations, and a minimum high school GPA of 3.0, and in some cases an interview. Application deadline: rolling admissions; 3/1 priority date for financial aid. Early and deferred admission are possible.

CENTENARY COLLEGE

Hackettstown, NJ

Suburban setting ■ Private ■ Independent Religious ■ Coed

Web site: www.centenarycollege.edu

Contact: Ms. Diane Finnan, Vice President for Enrollment Management, 400 Jefferson Street, Hackettstown, NJ 07840-2100

Telephone: 908-852-1400 ext. 2217 or toll-free 800-236-8679 **Fax:** 908-852-3454

E-mail: admissions@centenarycollege.edu

Getting in Last Year 737 applied; 73% were accepted; 256 enrolled (47%).

Financial Matters $16,400 tuition and fees (2002–03); $6850 room and board; 75% average percent of need met; $11,164 average financial aid amount received per undergraduate (2001–02).

Academics Centenary awards associate, bachelor's, and master's degrees and post-bachelor's certificates. Challenging opportunities include advanced placement credit, accelerated degree programs, student-designed majors, an honors program, double majors, independent study, and a senior project. Special programs include internships, summer session for credit, off-campus study, and study-abroad. The most frequently chosen baccalaureate fields are business/marketing, social sciences and history, and psychology. The faculty at Centenary has 47 full-time members, 57% with terminal degrees. The student-faculty ratio is 15:1.

Students of Centenary The student body totals 1,857, of whom 1,549 are undergraduates. 68.4% are women and 31.6% are men. Students come from 21 states and territories and 16 other countries. 85% are from New Jersey. 4% are international students. 61% returned for their sophomore year.

Applying Centenary requires an essay, SAT I or ACT, and a high school transcript, and in some cases an interview and portfolio. The school recommends an interview, recommendations, and a minimum high school GPA of 2.0. Application deadline: rolling admissions; 4/15 priority date for financial aid. Deferred admission is possible.

CENTENARY COLLEGE OF LOUISIANA

Shreveport, LA

Suburban setting ■ Private ■ Independent Religious ■ Coed

Web site: www.centenary.edu

Contact: Dr. Eugene Gregory, Vice President of College Relations, 2911 Centenary Blvd, PO Box 41188, Shreveport, LA 71134-1188

Telephone: 318-869-5131 or toll-free 800-234-4448 **Fax:** 318-869-5005

E-mail: egregory@centenary.edu

Getting in Last Year 936 applied; 65% were accepted; 273 enrolled (45%).

Financial Matters $16,450 tuition and fees (2002–03); $5550 room and board; 79% average percent of need met; $12,815 average financial aid amount received per undergraduate.

Academics Centenary awards bachelor's and master's degrees. Challenging opportunities include advanced placement credit, student-designed majors, an honors program, double majors, independent study, and a senior project. Special programs include internships, summer session for credit, off-campus study, study-abroad, and Army ROTC. The most frequently chosen baccalaureate fields are business/marketing, visual/performing arts, and biological/life sciences. The faculty at Centenary has 73 full-time members, 92% with terminal degrees. The student-faculty ratio is 12:1.

Students of Centenary The student body totals 1,038, of whom 897 are undergraduates. 60.8% are women and 39.2% are men. Students come from 38 states and territories and 11 other countries. 3.3% are international students. 74% returned for their sophomore year.

Applying Centenary requires an essay, SAT I or ACT, a high school transcript, 1 recommendation, and a minimum high school GPA of 2.0, and in some cases SAT II Subject Tests. The school recommends an interview and class rank. Application deadline: 2/15; 2/15 priority date for financial aid. Early and deferred admission are possible.

CENTRAL BAPTIST COLLEGE

Conway, AR

Small-town setting ■ Private ■ Independent Religious ■ Coed

Web site: www.cbc.edu

Contact: Mr. Cory Calhoun, Admissions Counselor, 1501 College Avenue, Conway, AR 72034

Telephone: 501-329-6872 ext. 167 or toll-free 800-205-6872 **Fax:** 501-329-2941

E-mail: cjackson@cbc.edu

Getting in Last Year 150 applied; 81% were accepted; 92 enrolled (75%).

Financial Matters $6984 tuition and fees (2002–03); $4398 room and board.

Academics CBC awards associate and bachelor's degrees. Advanced placement credit is a challenging opportunity. Special programs include internships, summer session for credit, and Army ROTC. The faculty at CBC has 16 full-time members, 44% with terminal degrees. The student-faculty ratio is 16:1.

Students of CBC The student body is made up of 393 undergraduates. 44.5% are women and 55.5% are men. Students come from 11 states and territories and 4 other countries. 88% are from Arkansas. 1% are international students.

Applying CBC requires an essay, ACT, a high school transcript, 2 recommendations, and a minimum high school GPA of 2.5. Application deadline: 8/15; 7/1 priority date for financial aid. Early admission is possible.

CENTRAL BIBLE COLLEGE

Springfield, MO

Suburban setting ■ Private ■ Independent Religious ■ Coed

Web site: www.cbcag.edu

Contact: Mrs. Eunice A. Bruegman, Director of Admissions and Records, 3000 North Grant Avenue, Springfield, MO 65803-1096

Telephone: 417-833-2551 ext. 1184 or toll-free 800-831-4222 ext. 1184 **Fax:** 417-833-5141

E-mail: info@cbcag.edu

Getting in Last Year 265 applied; 71% were accepted; 189 enrolled (100%).

Financial Matters $7016 tuition and fees (2002–03); $3677 room and board; 53% average percent of need met; $6469 average financial aid amount received per undergraduate.

Academics CBC awards associate and bachelor's degrees. Challenging opportunities include advanced placement credit, double majors, and independent study. Special programs include internships and summer session for credit. The faculty at CBC has 40 full-time members, 13% with terminal degrees. The student-faculty ratio is 18:1.

Students of CBC The student body is made up of 817 undergraduates. 39.8% are women and 60.2% are men. Students come from 48 states and territories. 26% are from Missouri. 0.9% are international students. 75% returned for their sophomore year.

Applying CBC requires an essay, SAT I or ACT, a high school transcript, and 3 recommendations, and in some cases an interview. The school recommends a minimum high school GPA of 2.0. Application deadline: rolling admissions; 4/1 priority date for financial aid. Early and deferred admission are possible.

CENTRAL CHRISTIAN COLLEGE OF KANSAS

McPherson, KS

Small-town setting ■ Private ■ Independent Religious ■ Coed

Web site: www.centralchristian.edu

Contact: Dr. David Ferrell, Dean of Admissions, PO Box 1403, McPherson, KS 67460

Telephone: 620-241-0723 ext. 380 or toll-free 800-835-0078 **Fax:** 620-241-6032

E-mail: admissions@centralchristian.edu

Getting in Last Year 350 applied; 99% were accepted.

Financial Matters $11,700 tuition and fees (2002–03); $4000 room and board; 88% average percent of need met; $10,414 average financial aid amount received per undergraduate.

Academics Central awards associate and bachelor's degrees. Challenging opportunities include advanced placement credit, student-designed majors, double majors, and independent study. Special programs include cooperative education, internships, off-campus study, and study-abroad. The most frequently chosen baccalaureate fields are liberal arts/general studies and business/marketing. The faculty at Central has 18 full-time members, 17% with terminal degrees. The student-faculty ratio is 14:1.

Students of Central The student body is made up of 337 undergraduates. 53.7% are women and 46.3% are men. Students come from 30 states and territories and 2 other countries. 49% are from Kansas. 2.4% are international students. 67% returned for their sophomore year.

Applying Central requires SAT I or ACT, a high school transcript, 2 recommendations, and a minimum high school GPA of 2.5. The school recommends an essay and an interview. Application deadline: rolling admissions; 3/1 priority date for financial aid. Deferred admission is possible.

CENTRAL COLLEGE

Pella, IA

Small-town setting ■ Private ■ Independent Religious ■ Coed

Web site: www.central.edu

Contact: Mr. John Olsen, Vice President for Admission and Student Enrollment Services, 812 University Street, Pella, IA 50219-1999

Telephone: 641-628-7600 or toll-free 800-458-5503 **Fax:** 641-628-5316

E-mail: admissions@central.edu

Getting in Last Year 1,598 applied; 86% were accepted; 425 enrolled (31%).

Financial Matters $16,756 tuition and fees (2002–03); $5796 room and board; 82% average percent of need met; $15,658 average financial aid amount received per undergraduate.

Academics Central awards bachelor's degrees. Challenging opportunities include student-designed majors, an honors program, double majors, independent study, and a senior project. Special programs include internships, summer session for credit, off-campus study, and study-abroad. The most frequently chosen baccalaureate fields are business/marketing, education, and parks and recreation. The faculty at Central has 92 full-time members, 80% with terminal degrees. The student-faculty ratio is 13:1.

Students of Central The student body is made up of 1,659 undergraduates. 57.3% are women and 42.7% are men. Students come from 36 states and territories and 14 other countries. 83% are from Iowa. 1% are international students. 80% returned for their sophomore year.

Applying Central requires SAT I or ACT and a high school transcript, and in some cases an essay, an interview, and 3 recommendations. The school recommends an interview and a minimum high school GPA of 2.0. Application deadline: rolling admissions; 3/1 priority date for financial aid. Deferred admission is possible.

CENTRAL CONNECTICUT STATE UNIVERSITY

New Britain, CT

Suburban setting ■ Public ■ State-supported ■ Coed

Web site: www.ccsu.edu

Contact: Ms. Myrna Garcia-Bowen, Director of Admissions, 1615 Stanley Street, New Britain, CT 06050-4010

Telephone: 860-832-2285 or toll-free 800-755-2278 (out-of-state) **Fax:** 860-832-2522

E-mail: admissions@ccsu.edu

Getting in Last Year 5,123 applied; 61% were accepted; 1,534 enrolled (49%).

Financial Matters $4770 resident tuition and fees (2002–03); $9942 nonresident tuition and fees (2002–03); $6280 room and board; 74% average percent of need met; $5838 average financial aid amount received per undergraduate (2001–02).

Academics CCSU awards bachelor's and master's degrees. Challenging opportunities include advanced placement credit, student-designed majors, and an honors program. Special programs include cooperative education, internships, summer session for credit, off-campus study, study-abroad, and Army and Air Force ROTC. The most frequently chosen baccalaureate fields are business/marketing, social sciences and history, and psychology. The faculty at CCSU has 400 full-time members, 75% with terminal degrees. The student-faculty ratio is 17:1.

Students of CCSU The student body totals 12,642, of whom 9,794 are undergraduates. 50.7% are women and 49.3% are men. Students come from 26 states and territories and 50 other countries. 89% are from Connecticut. 1.7% are international students. 72% returned for their sophomore year.

Applying CCSU requires SAT I, a high school transcript, and a minimum high school GPA of 2.0, and in some cases an interview. The school recommends 1 recommendation and a minimum high school GPA of 3.0. Application deadline: 5/1; 4/18 priority date for financial aid.

CENTRAL METHODIST COLLEGE

Fayette, MO

Small-town setting ■ Private ■ Independent Religious ■ Coed

Web site: www.cmc.edu

Contact: Mr. Don Hapward, Dean of Admissions and Financial Assistance, 411 Central Methodist Square, Fayette, MO 65248-1198

Telephone: 660-248-6247 or toll-free 888-CMC-1854 (in-state) **Fax:** 660-248-1872

E-mail: admissions@cmc.edu

Central Methodist College (continued)

Getting in Last Year 1,059 applied; 76% were accepted; 236 enrolled (29%).

Financial Matters $12,840 tuition and fees (2002–03); $4820 room and board; 65% average percent of need met; $9801 average financial aid amount received per undergraduate (2001–02).

Academics CMC awards associate, bachelor's, and master's degrees. Challenging opportunities include advanced placement credit, accelerated degree programs, student-designed majors, an honors program, double majors, independent study, and a senior project. Special programs include internships, summer session for credit, off-campus study, study-abroad, and Army and Air Force ROTC. The most frequently chosen baccalaureate fields are education, business/marketing, and health professions and related sciences. The faculty at CMC has 52 full-time members, 67% with terminal degrees. The student-faculty ratio is 14:1.

Students of CMC The student body totals 1,361, of whom 1,288 are undergraduates. 57.7% are women and 42.3% are men. Students come from 20 states and territories. 97% are from Missouri. 0.9% are international students. 61% returned for their sophomore year.

Applying CMC requires SAT I or ACT, a high school transcript, and a minimum high school GPA of 2.0, and in some cases 2 recommendations. The school recommends ACT. Application deadline: 8/1; 3/15 priority date for financial aid. Early and deferred admission are possible.

CENTRAL MICHIGAN UNIVERSITY

Mount Pleasant, MI

Small-town setting ■ Public ■ State-supported ■ Coed

Web site: www.cmich.edu

Contact: Mrs. Betty J. Wagner, Director of Admissions, Office of Admissions, 105 Warriner Hall, Mt. Pleasant, MI 48859

Telephone: 989-774-3076 **Fax:** 989-774-7267

E-mail: cmuadmit@cmich.edu

Getting in Last Year 12,717 applied; 71% were accepted; 3,626 enrolled (40%).

Financial Matters $4747 resident tuition and fees (2002–03); $11,119 nonresident tuition and fees (2002–03); $5524 room and board; 100% average percent of need met; $8495 average financial aid amount received per undergraduate.

Academics Central Michigan awards bachelor's, master's, and doctoral degrees and post-bachelor's and post-master's certificates. Challenging opportunities include advanced placement credit, accelerated degree programs, student-designed majors, freshman honors college, an honors program, double majors, and a senior project. Special programs include internships, summer session for credit, study-abroad, and Army ROTC. The most frequently chosen baccalaureate fields are business/marketing, education, and social sciences and history. The faculty at Central Michigan has 719 full-time members, 78% with terminal degrees. The student-faculty ratio is 22:1.

Students of Central Michigan The student body totals 28,159, of whom 19,696 are undergraduates. 59.3% are women and 40.7% are men. Students come from 45 states and territories and 51 other countries. 98% are from Michigan. 1% are international students. 79% returned for their sophomore year.

Applying Central Michigan requires ACT and a high school transcript, and in some cases an essay, an interview, and recommendations. The school recommends a minimum high school GPA of 3.0. Application deadline: rolling admissions; 2/21 priority date for financial aid. Early and deferred admission are possible.

CENTRAL MISSOURI STATE UNIVERSITY

Warrensburg, MO

Small-town setting ■ Public ■ State-supported ■ Coed

Web site: www.cmsu.edu

Contact: Mr. Matt Melvin, Director of Admissions, 1401 Ward Edwards, Warrensburg, MO 64093

Telephone: 660-543-4290 or toll-free 800-729-2678 (in-state) **Fax:** 660-543-8517

E-mail: admit@cmsuvmb.cmsu.edu

Getting in Last Year 3,154 applied; 79% were accepted; 1,327 enrolled (54%).

Financial Matters $4410 resident tuition and fees (2002–03); $8760 nonresident tuition and fees (2002–03); $4630 room and board; 90% average percent of need met; $5929 average financial aid amount received per undergraduate (2001–02).

Academics Central awards associate, bachelor's, and master's degrees and post-bachelor's and post-master's certificates. Challenging opportunities include advanced placement credit, student-designed majors, an honors program, double majors, and a senior project. Special programs include cooperative education, internships, summer session for credit, off-campus study, study-abroad, and Army and Air Force ROTC. The most frequently chosen baccalaureate fields are education, business/marketing, and protective services/public administration. The faculty at Central has 425 full-time members, 76% with terminal degrees. The student-faculty ratio is 17:1.

Students of Central The student body totals 10,313, of whom 8,732 are undergraduates. 53.6% are women and 46.4% are men. Students come from 43 states and territories and 65 other countries. 94% are from Missouri. 3.9% are international students. 74% returned for their sophomore year.

Applying Central requires ACT, a high school transcript, and rank in upper two-thirds of high school class, minimum ACT score of 20, and in some cases recommendations. Application deadline: rolling admissions. Deferred admission is possible.

CENTRAL PENTECOSTAL COLLEGE

Saskatoon, SK Canada

Urban setting ■ Private ■ Independent Religious ■ Coed

Web site: www.cpc-paoc.edu

Contact: Ms. Angie Hume, Registrar, 1303 Jackson Avenue, Saskatoon, SK S7H 2M9 Canada

Telephone: 306-374-6655 **Fax:** 306-373-6968

E-mail: admissions@cpc-paoc.edu

Getting in Last Year 21 enrolled.

Financial Matters $4536 tuition and fees (2002–03); $3400 room and board.

Academics Central Pentecostal College awards bachelor's degrees. Challenging opportunities include student-designed majors and independent study. Special programs include internships and study-abroad. The faculty at Central Pentecostal College has 3 full-time members, 100% with terminal degrees. The student-faculty ratio is 12:1.

Students of Central Pentecostal College The student body is made up of 77 undergraduates. 45.5% are women and 54.5% are men. Students come from 6 states and territories and 1 other country. 64% are from Saskatchewan. 76% returned for their sophomore year.

Applying Central Pentecostal College requires an essay, a high school transcript, and 3 recommendations, and in some cases an interview. Application deadline: 8/15. Deferred admission is possible.

CENTRAL WASHINGTON UNIVERSITY

Ellensburg, WA

Small-town setting ■ Public ■ State-supported ■ Coed

Web site: www.cwu.edu

Contact: Mr. Mike Reilly, Director of Admissions, 400 East 8th Avenue, Ellensburg, WA 98926-7463

Telephone: 509-963-1211 or toll-free 866-298-4968 **Fax:** 509-963-3022

E-mail: cwuadmis@cwu.edu

Getting in Last Year 3,575 applied; 85% were accepted; 1,354 enrolled (44%).

Financial Matters $3792 resident tuition and fees (2002–03); $11,781 nonresident tuition and fees (2002–03); $5410 room and board; 82% average percent of need met; $4092 average financial aid amount received per undergraduate (2001–02).

Academics CWU awards bachelor's and master's degrees and post-bachelor's certificates. Challenging opportunities include advanced placement credit, student-designed majors, an honors program, double majors, independent study, and a senior project. Special programs include cooperative education, internships, summer session for credit, off-campus study, study-abroad, and Army and Air Force ROTC. The most frequently chosen baccalaureate fields are business/marketing, education, and social sciences and history. The faculty at CWU has 335 full-time members, 86% with terminal degrees. The student-faculty ratio is 21:1.

Students of CWU The student body totals 9,202, of whom 8,683 are undergraduates. 52.6% are women and 47.4% are men. Students come from 36 states and territories and 24 other countries. 97% are from Washington. 1.5% are international students. 73% returned for their sophomore year.

Applying CWU requires SAT I or ACT, a high school transcript, and a minimum high school GPA of 2.0, and in some cases an essay, an interview, and recommendations. Application deadline: rolling admissions; 3/1 priority date for financial aid.

CENTRE COLLEGE

Danville, KY

Small-town setting ■ Private ■ Independent Religious ■ Coed

Web site: www.centre.edu

Contact: Mr. J. Carey Thompson, Dean of Admission and Financial Aid, 600 West Walnut Street, Danville, KY 40422-1394

Telephone: 859-238-5350 or toll-free 800-423-6236 **Fax:** 859-238-5373

E-mail: admission@centre.edu

Getting in Last Year 1,354 applied; 78% were accepted; 298 enrolled (28%).

Financial Matters $19,125 tuition and fees (2002–03); $6475 room and board; 100% average percent of need met; $19,585 average financial aid amount received per undergraduate.

Academics Centre awards bachelor's degrees. Challenging opportunities include advanced placement credit, student-designed majors, double majors, independent study, and a senior project. Special programs include internships, off-campus study, study-abroad, and Army and Air Force ROTC. The most frequently chosen baccalaureate fields are social sciences and history, biological/life sciences, and

English. The faculty at Centre has 89 full-time members, 97% with terminal degrees. The student-faculty ratio is 11:1.

Students of Centre The student body is made up of 1,055 undergraduates. 53.2% are women and 46.8% are men. Students come from 38 states and territories and 7 other countries. 71% are from Kentucky. 1.1% are international students. 89% returned for their sophomore year.

Applying Centre requires an essay, SAT I or ACT, a high school transcript, and 1 recommendation. The school recommends an interview. Application deadline: 2/1; 3/1 for financial aid. Early and deferred admission are possible.

CHADRON STATE COLLEGE

Chadron, NE

Small-town setting ■ *Public* ■ *State-supported* ■ *Coed*

Web site: www.csc.edu

Contact: Ms. Tena Cook Gould, Director of Admissions, 1000 Main Street, Chadron, NE 69337-2690

Telephone: 308-432-6263 or toll-free 800-242-3766 (in-state)
Fax: 308-432-6229

E-mail: inquire@csc1.csc.edu

Getting in Last Year 417 applied; 100% were accepted; 417 enrolled (100%).

Financial Matters $3290 resident tuition and fees (2002–03); $5930 nonresident tuition and fees (2002–03); $3655 room and board; $2375 average financial aid amount received per undergraduate (2001–02).

Academics Chadron State awards bachelor's and master's degrees and post-master's certificates. Challenging opportunities include advanced placement credit, student-designed majors, freshman honors college, an honors program, double majors, independent study, and a senior project. Special programs include cooperative education, internships, summer session for credit, and study-abroad. The most frequently chosen baccalaureate fields are education, business/marketing, and protective services/public administration. The faculty at Chadron State has 99 full-time members, 61% with terminal degrees. The student-faculty ratio is 22:1.

Students of Chadron State The student body totals 2,712, of whom 2,392 are undergraduates. 57.7% are women and 42.3% are men. Students come from 31 states and territories and 10 other countries. 74% are from Nebraska. 1% are international students. 78% returned for their sophomore year.

Applying Chadron State requires a high school transcript and health forms. The school recommends SAT I or ACT. Application deadline: rolling admissions; 6/1 priority date for financial aid. Early admission is possible.

CHAMINADE UNIVERSITY OF HONOLULU

Honolulu, HI

Urban setting ■ *Private* ■ *Independent Religious* ■ *Coed*

Web site: www.chaminade.edu

Contact: Office of Admissions, 3140 Waialae Avenue, Honolulu, HI 96816-1578

Telephone: 808-735-4735 or toll-free 800-735-3733 (out-of-state)
Fax: 808-739-4647

E-mail: admissions@chaminade.edu

Getting in Last Year 1,140 applied; 65% were accepted; 212 enrolled (29%).

Financial Matters $13,165 tuition and fees (2002–03); $7060 room and board; 57% average percent of need met; $9918 average financial aid amount received per undergraduate (2001–02).

Academics Chaminade University awards associate, bachelor's, and master's degrees and post-bachelor's certificates. Challenging opportunities include advanced placement credit, accelerated degree programs, student-designed majors, double majors, independent study, and a senior project. Special programs include internships, summer session for credit, off-campus study, and Army and Air Force ROTC. The faculty at Chaminade University has 57 full-time members, 68% with terminal degrees. The student-faculty ratio is 16:1.

Students of Chaminade University The student body totals 2,801, of whom 2,213 are undergraduates. 60.6% are women and 39.4% are men. Students come from 52 states and territories and 16 other countries. 41% are from Hawaii. 1.6% are international students. 69% returned for their sophomore year.

Applying Chaminade University requires an essay, SAT I or ACT, and a high school transcript, and in some cases an interview and 3 recommendations. The school recommends a minimum high school GPA of 2.0. Application deadline: rolling admissions; 3/1 priority date for financial aid. Deferred admission is possible.

CHAMPLAIN COLLEGE

Burlington, VT

Suburban setting ■ *Private* ■ *Independent* ■ *Coed*

Web site: www.champlain.edu

Contact: Ms. Josephine H. Churchill, Director of Admissions, 163 South Willard Street, Burlington, VT 05401

Telephone: 802-860-2727 or toll-free 800-570-5858 **Fax:** 802-860-2767

E-mail: admission@champlain.edu

Getting in Last Year 1,330 applied; 68% were accepted; 404 enrolled (45%).

Financial Matters $12,295 tuition and fees (2002–03); $8400 room and board; 65% average percent of need met; $8239 average financial aid amount received per undergraduate.

Academics Champlain awards associate, bachelor's, and master's degrees and post-bachelor's certificates (baccalaureate programs are part of the 2+2 curriculum). Challenging opportunities include advanced placement credit, freshman honors college, an honors program, double majors, and a senior project. Special programs include cooperative education, internships, summer session for credit, off-campus study, study-abroad, and Army ROTC. The most frequently chosen baccalaureate fields are business/marketing, liberal arts/general studies, and education. The faculty at Champlain has 78 full-time members, 32% with terminal degrees. The student-faculty ratio is 15:1.

Students of Champlain The student body totals 2,508, of whom 2,466 are undergraduates. 53% are women and 47% are men. Students come from 31 states and territories and 29 other countries. 55% are from Vermont. 1.7% are international students. 71% returned for their sophomore year.

Applying Champlain requires an essay, SAT I or ACT, and a high school transcript, and in some cases SAT II Subject Tests. The school recommends an interview, 1 recommendation, and a minimum high school GPA of 2.0. Application deadline: rolling admissions; 5/1 priority date for financial aid. Deferred admission is possible.

CHAPMAN UNIVERSITY

Orange, CA

Suburban setting ■ *Private* ■ *Independent Religious* ■ *Coed*

Web site: www.chapman.edu

Contact: Mr. Michael O. Drummy, Associate Dean for Enrollment Services and Chief Admission Officer, One University Drive, Orange, CA 92866

Telephone: 714-997-6711 or toll-free 888-CUAPPLY **Fax:** 714-997-6713

E-mail: admit@chapman.edu

Getting in Last Year 2,728 applied; 60% were accepted; 740 enrolled (46%).

Financial Matters $23,316 tuition and fees (2002–03); $8082 room and board; 100% average percent of need met; $17,066 average financial aid amount received per undergraduate (2001–02).

Academics Chapman awards bachelor's, master's, and first-professional degrees. Challenging opportunities include advanced placement credit, accelerated degree programs, an honors program, double majors, independent study, and a senior project. Special programs include cooperative education, internships, summer session for credit, study-abroad, and Army and Air Force ROTC. The most frequently chosen baccalaureate fields are visual/performing arts, business/marketing, and social sciences and history. The faculty at Chapman has 222 full-time members, 82% with terminal degrees. The student-faculty ratio is 13:1.

Students of Chapman The student body totals 4,836, of whom 3,274 are undergraduates. 56.4% are women and 43.6% are men. Students come from 43 states and territories and 37 other countries. 85% are from California. 3.3% are international students. 86% returned for their sophomore year.

Applying Chapman requires an essay, SAT I or ACT, a high school transcript, 1 recommendation, and a minimum high school GPA of 2.75. The school recommends SAT II Subject Tests, an interview, and a minimum high school GPA of 3.5. Application deadline: 1/31; 3/2 priority date for financial aid. Early admission is possible.

CHARLESTON SOUTHERN UNIVERSITY

Charleston, SC

Suburban setting ■ *Private* ■ *Independent Religious* ■ *Coed*

Web site: www.charlestonsouthern.edu

Contact: Ms. Cheryl Burton, Director of Enrollment Management, PO Box 118087, 9200 University Boulevard, Charleston, SC 19423-8087

Telephone: 843-863-7050 or toll-free 800-947-7474

E-mail: enroll@csuniv.edu

Getting in Last Year 2,028 applied; 77% were accepted; 507 enrolled (32%).

Financial Matters $13,512 tuition and fees (2002–03); $5182 room and board; 72% average percent of need met; $10,613 average financial aid amount received per undergraduate (2001–02).

Academics Charleston Southern awards associate, bachelor's, and master's degrees. Challenging opportunities include advanced placement credit, accelerated degree programs, an honors program, double majors, and a senior project. Special programs include internships, summer session for credit, off-campus study, and Air Force ROTC. The most frequently chosen baccalaureate fields are biological/life sciences, business/marketing, and education. The faculty at Charleston Southern has 98 full-time members, 64% with terminal degrees. The student-faculty ratio is 18:1.

Students of Charleston Southern The student body totals 2,849, of whom 2,481 are undergraduates. 61.7% are women and 38.3% are men. Students come from 45 states and territories and 31 other countries. 82% are from South Carolina. 2.6% are international students. 72% returned for their sophomore year.

Charleston Southern University (continued)

Applying Charleston Southern requires SAT I or ACT and a high school transcript, and in some cases an essay, an interview, and 1 recommendation. The school recommends SAT II Subject Tests. Application deadline: rolling admissions; 4/15 priority date for financial aid.

CHARTER OAK STATE COLLEGE

New Britain, CT

Small-town setting ■ Public ■ State-supported ■ Coed

Web site: www.charteroak.edu
Contact: Ms. Lori Pendleton, Director of Admissions, 55 Paul Manafort Drive, New Britain, CT 06053-2142
Telephone: 860-832-3858 **Fax:** 860-832-3855
E-mail: info@charteroak.edu

Academics Charter Oak awards associate and bachelor's degrees (offers only external degree programs). Challenging opportunities include advanced placement credit, accelerated degree programs, student-designed majors, and independent study. Summer session for credit is a special program. The most frequently chosen baccalaureate field is liberal arts/general studies. The faculty at Charter Oak has 100 members, 75% with terminal degrees.

Students of Charter Oak The student body is made up of 1,561 undergraduates. Students come from 51 states and territories. 66% are from Connecticut.

Applying Application deadline: 6/1 priority date for financial aid. Deferred admission is possible.

CHATHAM COLLEGE

Pittsburgh, PA

Urban setting ■ Private ■ Independent ■ Women Only

Web site: www.chatham.edu
Contact: Mr. Alan G. McIvor, Vice President for Enrollment Management, Woodland Road, Pittsburgh, PA 15232
Telephone: 412-365-1290 or toll-free 800-837-1290 **Fax:** 412-365-1609
E-mail: admissions@chatham.edu

Getting in Last Year 376 applied; 73% were accepted; 109 enrolled (40%).

Financial Matters $19,742 tuition and fees (2002–03); $6688 room and board; 77% average percent of need met; $22,535 average financial aid amount received per undergraduate.

Academics Chatham awards bachelor's, master's, and doctoral degrees and post-bachelor's certificates. Challenging opportunities include advanced placement credit, accelerated degree programs, student-designed majors, double majors, independent study, and a senior project. Special programs include cooperative education, internships, summer session for credit, off-campus study, study-abroad, and Army, Navy and Air Force ROTC. The most frequently chosen baccalaureate fields are biological/life sciences, visual/performing arts, and social sciences and history. The faculty at Chatham has 71 full-time members, 90% with terminal degrees. The student-faculty ratio is 12:1.

Students of Chatham The student body totals 1,058, of whom 639 are undergraduates. Students come from 41 states and territories and 22 other countries. 67% are from Pennsylvania. 5.4% are international students. 71% returned for their sophomore year.

Applying Chatham requires an essay, SAT I or ACT, a high school transcript, 1 recommendation, and a minimum high school GPA of 2.5. The school recommends an interview, 3 recommendations, and a minimum high school GPA of 3.0. Application deadline: rolling admissions; 5/1 for financial aid. Early and deferred admission are possible.

CHESTER COLLEGE OF NEW ENGLAND

Chester, NH

Rural setting ■ Private ■ Independent ■ Coed

Web site: www.chestercollege.edu
Contact: Mrs. Debora Yost, Assistant Director of Admissions, 40 Chester Street, Chester, NH 03036
Telephone: 603-887-7402 or toll-free 800-974-6372 **Fax:** 603-887-1777
E-mail: admissions@chestercollege.edu

Getting in Last Year 179 applied; 71% were accepted; 54 enrolled (43%).

Financial Matters $12,630 tuition and fees (2002–03); $7000 room and board; 36% average percent of need met; $6837 average financial aid amount received per undergraduate.

Academics Chester College of New England awards associate and bachelor's degrees. Challenging opportunities include advanced placement credit, student-designed majors, an honors program, double majors, independent study, and a senior project. Special programs include cooperative education, internships, summer session for credit, and study-abroad. The most frequently chosen baccalaureate field is visual/performing arts. The faculty at Chester College of New England has 15 full-time members, 60% with terminal degrees. The student-faculty ratio is 10:1.

Students of Chester College of New England The student body is made up of 168 undergraduates. 67.3% are women and 32.7% are men. Students come from 11 states and territories and 2 other countries. 70% are from New Hampshire. 1.2% are international students.

Applying Chester College of New England requires an essay, a high school transcript, an interview, and 3 recommendations. The school recommends SAT I and SAT II or ACT, portfolio, and a minimum high school GPA of 2.0. Application deadline: rolling admissions; 3/15 priority date for financial aid. Deferred admission is possible.

CHESTNUT HILL COLLEGE

Philadelphia, PA

Suburban setting ■ Private ■ Independent Religious ■ Coed, Primarily Women

Web site: www.chc.edu
Contact: Ms. Jodie King, Director of Admissions, 9601 Germantown Avenue, Philadelphia, PA 19118-2693
Telephone: 215-248-7004 or toll-free 800-248-0052 (out-of-state) **Fax:** 215-248-7082
E-mail: chcapply@chc.edu

Getting in Last Year 536 applied; 69% were accepted; 106 enrolled (28%).

Financial Matters $18,150 tuition and fees (2002–03); $7270 room and board; 74% average percent of need met; $12,410 average financial aid amount received per undergraduate.

Academics Chestnut Hill awards associate, bachelor's, master's, and doctoral degrees and post-bachelor's and post-master's certificates (profile includes figures from both traditional and accelerated (part-time) programs). Challenging opportunities include advanced placement credit, student-designed majors, an honors program, double majors, independent study, and a senior project. Special programs include cooperative education, internships, summer session for credit, off-campus study, study-abroad, and Army ROTC. The most frequently chosen baccalaureate fields are business/marketing, social sciences and history, and education. The faculty at Chestnut Hill has 56 full-time members, 80% with terminal degrees. The student-faculty ratio is 8:1.

Students of Chestnut Hill The student body totals 1,535, of whom 846 are undergraduates. 89% are women and 11% are men. Students come from 11 states and territories and 4 other countries. 90% are from Pennsylvania. 0.7% are international students. 66% returned for their sophomore year.

Applying Chestnut Hill requires an essay, SAT I or ACT, and a high school transcript, and in some cases an interview. The school recommends an interview, 1 recommendation, and a minimum high school GPA of 2.0. Application deadline: rolling admissions; 4/15 priority date for financial aid. Early and deferred admission are possible.

CHEYNEY UNIVERSITY OF PENNSYLVANIA

Cheyney, PA

Suburban setting ■ Public ■ State-supported ■ Coed

Web site: www.cheyney.edu
Contact: Ms. Gemma Stemley, Director of Admissions, 1837 University Circle, Cheyney, PA 19319
Telephone: 610-399-2275 or toll-free 800-CHEYNEY **Fax:** 610-399-2099

Getting in Last Year 1,263 applied; 65% were accepted; 250 enrolled (31%).

Financial Matters $5033 resident tuition and fees (2002–03); $11,601 nonresident tuition and fees (2002–03); $5390 room and board; 87% average percent of need met.

Academics Cheyney awards bachelor's and master's degrees. Special programs include cooperative education, internships, summer session for credit, off-campus study, and Army and Air Force ROTC. The most frequently chosen baccalaureate fields are business/marketing, social sciences and history, and communications/communication technologies. The faculty at Cheyney has 95 full-time members, 49% with terminal degrees. The student-faculty ratio is 13:1.

Students of Cheyney The student body totals 1,523, of whom 1,138 are undergraduates. 54.1% are women and 45.9% are men. Students come from 14 states and territories and 5 other countries. 84% are from Pennsylvania. 1.3% are international students.

Applying Cheyney requires an essay, SAT I or ACT, and a high school transcript, and in some cases 3 recommendations. The school recommends SAT II Subject Tests and an interview. Application deadline: rolling admissions; 4/15 priority date for financial aid.

CHOWAN COLLEGE

Murfreesboro, NC

Rural setting ■ Private ■ Independent Religious ■ Coed

Web site: www.chowan.edu
Contact: Associate Vice President for Enrollment Management, 200 Jones Drive, Murfreesboro, NC 27855

Telephone: 252-398-6314 or toll-free 800-488-4101 **Fax:** 252-398-1190
E-mail: admissions@chowan.edu

Getting in Last Year 1,300 applied; 76% were accepted; 306 enrolled (31%).

Financial Matters $13,000 tuition and fees (2002–03); $5400 room and board; 76% average percent of need met; $10,258 average financial aid amount received per undergraduate (2001–02).

Academics Chowan awards associate and bachelor's degrees. Challenging opportunities include advanced placement credit, student-designed majors, double majors, independent study, and a senior project. Special programs include internships, summer session for credit, and study-abroad. The most frequently chosen baccalaureate fields are business/marketing, education, and computer/information sciences. The faculty at Chowan has 56 full-time members, 59% with terminal degrees. The student-faculty ratio is 11:1.

Students of Chowan The student body is made up of 776 undergraduates. 46.6% are women and 53.4% are men. Students come from 23 states and territories and 4 other countries. 43% are from North Carolina. 0.7% are international students. 58% returned for their sophomore year.

Applying Chowan requires SAT I or ACT and a high school transcript, and in some cases an essay and an interview. The school recommends 2 recommendations and a minimum high school GPA of 2.0. Application deadline: rolling admissions; 5/1 priority date for financial aid. Early and deferred admission are possible.

CHRISTENDOM COLLEGE

Front Royal, VA

Rural setting ■ Private ■ Independent Religious ■ Coed

Web site: www.christendom.edu

Contact: Mr. Paul Heisler, Director of Admissions, 134 Christendom Drive, Front Royal, VA 22630-5103

Telephone: 540-636-2900 ext. 290 or toll-free 800-877-5456 ext. 290 **Fax:** 540-636-1655

E-mail: admissions@christendom.edu

Getting in Last Year 220 applied; 77% were accepted; 94 enrolled (55%).

Financial Matters $12,650 tuition and fees (2002–03); $4800 room and board; 90% average percent of need met; $9630 average financial aid amount received per undergraduate.

Academics Christendom awards associate, bachelor's, and master's degrees. Challenging opportunities include advanced placement credit, accelerated degree programs, double majors, independent study, and a senior project. Special programs include cooperative education, internships, summer session for credit, and study-abroad. The most frequently chosen baccalaureate fields are social sciences and history, English, and foreign language/literature. The faculty at Christendom has 23 full-time members, 78% with terminal degrees. The student-faculty ratio is 12:1.

Students of Christendom The student body totals 430, of whom 352 are undergraduates. 58.5% are women and 41.5% are men. Students come from 44 states and territories and 4 other countries. 22% are from Virginia. 3.1% are international students. 83% returned for their sophomore year.

Applying Christendom requires an essay, SAT I or ACT, a high school transcript, and 2 recommendations. The school recommends an interview and a minimum high school GPA of 3.0. Application deadline: 3/1; 4/1 priority date for financial aid. Early admission is possible.

CHRISTIAN BROTHERS UNIVERSITY

Memphis, TN

Urban setting ■ Private ■ Independent Religious ■ Coed

Web site: www.cbu.edu

Contact: Ms. Courtney Fee, Dean of Admission, 650 East Parkway South, Memphis, TN 38104

Telephone: 901-321-3205 or toll-free 800-288-7576 **Fax:** 901-321-3202
E-mail: admissions@cbu.edu

Getting in Last Year 1,847 applied; 41% were accepted; 235 enrolled (31%).

Financial Matters $16,240 tuition and fees (2002–03); $4770 room and board; 75% average percent of need met; $12,522 average financial aid amount received per undergraduate.

Academics CBU awards bachelor's and master's degrees. Challenging opportunities include advanced placement credit, accelerated degree programs, an honors program, double majors, and a senior project. Special programs include internships, summer session for credit, off-campus study, study-abroad, and Army, Navy and Air Force ROTC. The most frequently chosen baccalaureate fields are business/marketing, psychology, and engineering/engineering technologies. The faculty at CBU has 109 full-time members, 84% with terminal degrees. The student-faculty ratio is 14:1.

Students of CBU The student body totals 1,989, of whom 1,585 are undergraduates. 56.1% are women and 43.9% are men. Students come from 31 states and territories and 25 other countries. 83% are from Tennessee. 3.5% are international students. 73% returned for their sophomore year.

Applying CBU requires an essay, SAT I or ACT, a high school transcript, and a minimum high school GPA of 2.5, and in some cases recommendations. The school recommends an interview. Application deadline: 8/23; 2/15 priority date for financial aid. Early and deferred admission are possible.

CHRISTIAN HERITAGE COLLEGE

El Cajon, CA

Suburban setting ■ Private ■ Independent Religious ■ Coed

Web site: www.christianheritage.edu

Contact: Ms. Misty Blount, Director of Admissions, 2100 Greenfield Drive, El Cajon, CA 92019-1157

Telephone: 619-588-7747 or toll-free 800-676-2242 **Fax:** 619-440-0209
E-mail: chcadm@adm.christianheritage.edu

Getting in Last Year 195 applied; 77% were accepted; 77 enrolled (51%).

Financial Matters $13,560 tuition and fees (2002–03); $5760 room and board; 49% average percent of need met; $9194 average financial aid amount received per undergraduate (2001–02).

Academics Christian Heritage awards bachelor's degrees. Challenging opportunities include advanced placement credit, student-designed majors, double majors, independent study, and a senior project. Special programs include internships, summer session for credit, study-abroad, and Army and Air Force ROTC. The most frequently chosen baccalaureate fields are interdisciplinary studies, business/marketing, and psychology. The faculty at Christian Heritage has 36 full-time members, 39% with terminal degrees. The student-faculty ratio is 12:1.

Students of Christian Heritage The student body is made up of 615 undergraduates. 62.3% are women and 37.7% are men. Students come from 26 states and territories and 7 other countries. 87% are from California. 1.3% are international students. 61% returned for their sophomore year.

Applying Christian Heritage requires an essay, SAT I or ACT, a high school transcript, and 2 recommendations. The school recommends an interview and a minimum high school GPA of 2.75. Application deadline: 8/1; 3/2 priority date for financial aid. Deferred admission is possible.

CHRISTIAN LIFE COLLEGE

Mount Prospect, IL

Private ■ Independent Religious ■ Coed

Web site: www.christianlifecollege.edu

Contact: Mr. Jim Spenner, Director of Admissions, 400 East Gregory Street, Mount Prospect, IL 60056

Telephone: 847-259-1840 ext. 17 **Fax:** - ext.

Getting in Last Year 14 applied; 57% were accepted; 8 enrolled (100%).

Financial Matters $6000 tuition and fees (2002–03); $3300 room only; 75% average percent of need met; $5600 average financial aid amount received per undergraduate.

Academics Christian Life College awards associate and bachelor's degrees. The faculty at Christian Life College has 6 full-time members, 33% with terminal degrees. The student-faculty ratio is 10:1.

Students of Christian Life College The student body is made up of 80 undergraduates. 43.8% are women and 56.2% are men. 9.4% are international students. 62% returned for their sophomore year.

Applying Application deadline: 6/1 priority date for financial aid.

CHRISTOPHER NEWPORT UNIVERSITY

Newport News, VA

Suburban setting ■ Public ■ State-supported ■ Coed

Web site: www.cnu.edu

Contact: Ms. Rebecca Ducknuall, Assistant Director of Admissions, 1 University Place, Newport News, VA 23606-2998

Telephone: 757-594-7205 or toll-free 800-333-4268 **Fax:** 757-594-7333
E-mail: admit@cnu.edu

Getting in Last Year 5,097 applied; 48% were accepted; 1,180 enrolled (48%).

Financial Matters $3546 resident tuition and fees (2002–03); $10,128 nonresident tuition and fees (2002–03); $6350 room and board; 62% average percent of need met; $4827 average financial aid amount received per undergraduate (2001–02).

Academics CNU awards bachelor's and master's degrees. Challenging opportunities include advanced placement credit, accelerated degree programs, student-designed majors, an honors program, double majors, independent study, and a senior project. Special programs include cooperative education, internships, summer session for credit, off-campus study, study-abroad, and Army ROTC. The most frequently chosen baccalaureate fields are business/marketing, psychology, and social sciences and history. The faculty at CNU has 185 full-time members, 84% with terminal degrees. The student-faculty ratio is 23:1.

Students of CNU The student body totals 5,391, of whom 5,192 are undergraduates. 60.1% are women and 39.9% are men. Students come from 28 states and territories and 10 other countries. 97% are from Virginia. 0.2% are international students. 81% returned for their sophomore year.

Christopher Newport University (continued)

Applying CNU requires SAT I or ACT, a high school transcript, and a minimum high school GPA of 3.0, and in some cases an essay, an interview, and 3 recommendations. Application deadline: 3/1; 3/1 priority date for financial aid. Early and deferred admission are possible.

CINCINNATI BIBLE COLLEGE AND SEMINARY

Cincinnati, OH

Urban setting ■ Private ■ Independent Religious ■ Coed

Web site: www.cincybible.edu
Contact: Mr. Alex Eady, Director of Undergraduate Admissions, 2700 Glenway Avenue, Cincinnati, OH 45204-1799
Telephone: 800-949-4222 ext. 8610 or toll-free 800-949-4CBC **Fax:** 513-244-8140
E-mail: admissions@cincybible.edu

Getting in Last Year 227 applied; 99% were accepted; 135 enrolled (60%).

Financial Matters $8890 tuition and fees (2002–03); $4840 room and board; 66% average percent of need met; $6714 average financial aid amount received per undergraduate (2001–02).

Academics Cincinnati Bible College awards associate, bachelor's, master's, and first-professional degrees. Challenging opportunities include advanced placement credit, double majors, and independent study. Special programs include internships, summer session for credit, and off-campus study. The faculty at Cincinnati Bible College has 30 full-time members. The student-faculty ratio is 16:1.

Students of Cincinnati Bible College The student body totals 922, of whom 626 are undergraduates. 43.8% are women and 56.2% are men. Students come from 33 states and territories and 6 other countries. 67% are from Ohio. 62% returned for their sophomore year.

Applying Cincinnati Bible College requires an essay, SAT I or ACT, a high school transcript, and 3 recommendations. The school recommends an interview and a minimum high school GPA of 2.0. Application deadline: 8/10; 3/15 priority date for financial aid. Early and deferred admission are possible.

CIRCLEVILLE BIBLE COLLEGE

Circleville, OH

Small-town setting ■ Private ■ Independent Religious ■ Coed

Web site: www.biblecollege.edu
Contact: Rev. James Schroeder, Acting Director of Enrollment, PO Box 458, Circleville, OH 43113-9487
Telephone: 740-477-7741 or toll-free 800-701-0222 **Fax:** 740-477-7755
E-mail: enroll@biblecollege.edu

Getting in Last Year 135 applied; 61% were accepted; 45 enrolled (54%).

Financial Matters $8736 tuition and fees (2002–03); $5090 room and board; 85% average percent of need met; $10,000 average financial aid amount received per undergraduate.

Academics CBC awards associate and bachelor's degrees. Challenging opportunities include advanced placement credit, student-designed majors, an honors program, double majors, independent study, and a senior project. Special programs include internships, summer session for credit, and off-campus study. The faculty at CBC has 10 full-time members. The student-faculty ratio is 13:1.

Students of CBC The student body is made up of 317 undergraduates. 47% are women and 53% are men. Students come from 11 states and territories. 74% are from Ohio. 71% returned for their sophomore year.

Applying CBC requires an essay, a high school transcript, 4 recommendations, and medical form, and in some cases ACT and an interview. The school recommends SAT I. Application deadline: rolling admissions; 4/1 priority date for financial aid. Early admission is possible.

THE CITADEL, THE MILITARY COLLEGE OF SOUTH CAROLINA

Charleston, SC

Urban setting ■ Public ■ State-supported ■ Coed, Primarily Men

Web site: www.citadel.edu
Contact: Lt. Col. John Powell, Director of Admissions, 171 Moultrie Street, Charleston, SC 29409
Telephone: 843-953-5230 or toll-free 800-868-1842 **Fax:** 843-953-7036
E-mail: admissions@citadel.edu

Getting in Last Year 1,922 applied; 68% were accepted; 520 enrolled (40%).

Financial Matters $4946 resident tuition and fees (2002–03); $12,417 nonresident tuition and fees (2002–03); $4575 room and board; 84% average percent of need met; $6048 average financial aid amount received per undergraduate.

Academics The Citadel awards bachelor's and master's degrees and post-master's certificates. Challenging opportunities include advanced placement credit, an honors program, double majors, independent study, and a senior project. Special programs include internships, summer session for credit, off-campus study, study-abroad, and Army, Navy and Air Force ROTC. The most frequently chosen baccalaureate fields are business/marketing, social sciences and history, and engineering/engineering technologies. The faculty at The Citadel has 148 full-time members, 96% with terminal degrees. The student-faculty ratio is 15:1.

Students of The Citadel The student body totals 4,058, of whom 2,099 are undergraduates. 8.1% are women and 91.9% are men. Students come from 48 states and territories and 27 other countries. 48% are from South Carolina. 2.9% are international students. 81% returned for their sophomore year.

Applying The Citadel requires SAT I or ACT, a high school transcript, and a minimum high school GPA of 2.0. The school recommends an interview. Application deadline: rolling admissions; 2/28 priority date for financial aid.

CITY COLLEGE OF THE CITY UNIVERSITY OF NEW YORK

New York, NY

Urban setting ■ Public ■ State and locally supported ■ Coed

Web site: www.ccny.cuny.edu
Contact: Ms. Karen Callender, Acting Director of Admissions, Convent Avenue at 138th Street, New York, NY 10031-9198
Telephone: 212-650-6977 **Fax:** 212-650-6417
E-mail: admissions@ccny.cuny.edu

Getting in Last Year 5,537 applied; 27% were accepted; 1,011 enrolled (68%).

Financial Matters $3309 resident tuition and fees (2002–03); $6909 nonresident tuition and fees (2002–03); 65% average percent of need met; $5300 average financial aid amount received per undergraduate.

Academics CCNY awards bachelor's, master's, and first-professional degrees and post-master's certificates. Challenging opportunities include advanced placement credit, accelerated degree programs, student-designed majors, freshman honors college, an honors program, independent study, and a senior project. Special programs include cooperative education, internships, summer session for credit, off-campus study, study-abroad, and Army and Air Force ROTC. The faculty at CCNY has 483 full-time members, 90% with terminal degrees. The student-faculty ratio is 15:1.

Students of CCNY The student body totals 10,119, of whom 8,638 are undergraduates. 51.3% are women and 48.7% are men. 96% are from New York. 7.5% are international students. 80% returned for their sophomore year.

Applying CCNY requires SAT I or ACT and a high school transcript, and in some cases SAT I or ACT. Application deadline: rolling admissions; 4/1 priority date for financial aid. Early and deferred admission are possible.

CITY UNIVERSITY

Bellevue, WA

Suburban setting ■ Private ■ Independent ■ Coed

Web site: www.cityu.edu
Contact: Mr. Kent Gibson, Executive Vice President, Admissions and Administration, 11900 NE First Street, Bellevue, WA 98005
Telephone: 800-426-5596 ext. 4661 or toll-free 800-426-5596 **Fax:** 425-709-5361
E-mail: info@cityu.edu

Getting in Last Year 1,460 applied; 100% were accepted.

Financial Matters $7960 tuition and fees (2002–03); 20% average percent of need met; $4361 average financial aid amount received per undergraduate (2001–02).

Academics City U awards associate, bachelor's, and master's degrees and post-bachelor's certificates. Challenging opportunities include advanced placement credit, accelerated degree programs, an honors program, double majors, and independent study. Special programs include internships and summer session for credit. The most frequently chosen baccalaureate fields are business/marketing, computer/information sciences, and liberal arts/general studies. The faculty at City U has 52 full-time members, 100% with terminal degrees.

Students of City U The student body totals 7,124, of whom 2,877 are undergraduates. 45.5% are women and 54.5% are men. Students come from 47 states and territories and 33 other countries. 65% are from Washington. 4.7% are international students.

Applying City U recommends a high school transcript. Application deadline: rolling admissions. Deferred admission is possible.

CLAFLIN UNIVERSITY

Orangeburg, SC

Small-town setting ■ Private ■ Independent Religious ■ Coed

Contact: Mr. Michael Zeigler, Director of Admissions, 400 Magnolia Street, Orangeburg, SC 29115
Telephone: 803-535-5340 or toll-free 800-922-1276 (in-state) **Fax:** 803-535-5387
E-mail: zeiglerm@claf1.claflin.edu

Getting in Last Year 1,714 applied; 51% were accepted; 350 enrolled (40%).

Financial Matters $8940 tuition and fees (2002–03); $5000 room and board; 70% average percent of need met; $9000 average financial aid amount received per undergraduate.

Academics Claflin awards bachelor's degrees. Challenging opportunities include advanced placement credit, freshman honors college, an honors program, independent study, and a senior project. Special programs include cooperative education, internships, summer session for credit, off-campus study, study-abroad, and Army ROTC. The most frequently chosen baccalaureate fields are social sciences and history, education, and business/marketing. The faculty at Claflin has 80 full-time members, 70% with terminal degrees. The student-faculty ratio is 14:1.

Students of Claflin The student body is made up of 1,546 undergraduates. 68.3% are women and 31.7% are men. Students come from 3 states and territories. 85% are from South Carolina. 5.1% are international students. 79% returned for their sophomore year.

Applying Claflin requires an essay, SAT I or ACT, a high school transcript, an interview, and a minimum high school GPA of 2.00. The school recommends SAT II Subject Tests and recommendations. Application deadline: rolling admissions. Deferred admission is possible.

CLAREMONT MCKENNA COLLEGE

Claremont, CA

Small-town setting ■ *Private* ■ *Independent* ■ *Coed*

Web site: www.claremontmckenna.edu
Contact: Mr. Richard C. Vos, Vice President/Dean of Admission and Financial Aid, 890 Columbia Avenue, Claremont, CA 91711
Telephone: 909-621-8088
E-mail: admission@mckenna.edu

Getting in Last Year 2,918 applied; 28% were accepted; 250 enrolled (31%).

Financial Matters $26,350 tuition and fees (2002–03); $8740 room and board; 100% average percent of need met; $23,059 average financial aid amount received per undergraduate.

Academics CMC awards bachelor's degrees. Challenging opportunities include advanced placement credit, accelerated degree programs, student-designed majors, an honors program, double majors, independent study, and a senior project. Special programs include internships, off-campus study, study-abroad, and Army and Air Force ROTC. The faculty at CMC has 129 full-time members, 84% with terminal degrees. The student-faculty ratio is 7:1.

Students of CMC The student body is made up of 1,024 undergraduates. 46.6% are women and 53.4% are men. Students come from 47 states and territories and 22 other countries. 49% are from California. 3.2% are international students. 94% returned for their sophomore year.

Applying CMC requires an essay, SAT I or ACT, a high school transcript, 3 recommendations, and a minimum high school GPA of 3.0. The school recommends SAT II Subject Tests and an interview. Application deadline: 1/2; 2/1 for financial aid. Early and deferred admission are possible.

CLARION UNIVERSITY OF PENNSYLVANIA

Clarion, PA

Rural setting ■ *Public* ■ *State-supported* ■ *Coed*

Web site: www.clarion.edu
Contact: Ms. Sue McMillen, Interim Director of Admissions, 890 Wood Street, Clarion, PA 16214
Telephone: 814-393-2306 or toll-free 800-672-7171 **Fax:** 814-393-2030
E-mail: smcmille@clarion.edu

Getting in Last Year 3,424 applied; 81% were accepted; 1,346 enrolled (49%).

Financial Matters $5740 resident tuition and fees (2002–03); $7930 nonresident tuition and fees (2002–03); $4344 room and board; 87% average percent of need met; $6025 average financial aid amount received per undergraduate (2001–02).

Academics Clarion University awards associate, bachelor's, and master's degrees and post-master's certificates. Challenging opportunities include advanced placement credit, accelerated degree programs, an honors program, and double majors. Special programs include internships, summer session for credit, and study-abroad. The most frequently chosen baccalaureate fields are education, business/marketing, and health professions and related sciences. The faculty at Clarion University has 298 full-time members. The student-faculty ratio is 18:1.

Students of Clarion University The student body totals 6,541, of whom 6,003 are undergraduates. 61.5% are women and 38.5% are men. Students come from 29 states and territories and 40 other countries. 95% are from Pennsylvania. 1.4% are international students. 72% returned for their sophomore year.

Applying Clarion University requires SAT I or ACT and a high school transcript, and in some cases an essay and an interview. The school recommends an essay, an interview, and recommendations. Application deadline: rolling admissions; 5/1 priority date for financial aid. Deferred admission is possible.

CLARK ATLANTA UNIVERSITY

Atlanta, GA

Urban setting ■ *Private* ■ *Independent Religious* ■ *Coed*

Web site: www.cau.edu
Contact: Office of Admissions, 223 James P. Brawley Drive, SW, 101 Trevor Arnett Hall, Atlanta, GA 30314
Telephone: 404-880-8784 ext. 6650 or toll-free 800-688-3228
Fax: 404-880-6174

Getting in Last Year 6,910 applied; 48% were accepted; 930 enrolled (28%).

Financial Matters $12,862 tuition and fees (2002–03); $6438 room and board; 23% average percent of need met; $3206 average financial aid amount received per undergraduate (2001–02).

Academics Clark Atlanta awards bachelor's, master's, and doctoral degrees and post-bachelor's and post-master's certificates. Challenging opportunities include advanced placement credit, accelerated degree programs, freshman honors college, an honors program, and a senior project. Special programs include cooperative education, internships, summer session for credit, off-campus study, study-abroad, and Army and Air Force ROTC. The most frequently chosen baccalaureate fields are business/marketing, education, and communications/communication technologies. The faculty at Clark Atlanta has 319 full-time members, 77% with terminal degrees. The student-faculty ratio is 15:1.

Students of Clark Atlanta The student body totals 4,813, of whom 3,864 are undergraduates. 70.9% are women and 29.1% are men. Students come from 43 states and territories. 40% are from Georgia. 66% returned for their sophomore year.

Applying Clark Atlanta requires an essay, SAT I or ACT, a high school transcript, 2 recommendations, and a minimum high school GPA of 2.0. The school recommends an interview and a minimum high school GPA of 2.5. Application deadline: 7/1; 4/1 priority date for financial aid. Early and deferred admission are possible.

CLARKE COLLEGE

Dubuque, IA

Urban setting ■ *Private* ■ *Independent Religious* ■ *Coed*

Web site: www.clarke.edu
Contact: Mr. Omar G. Correa, Executive Director of Admissions and Financial Aid, 1550 Clarke Drive, Dubuque, IA 52001-3198
Telephone: 563-588-6316 or toll-free 800-383-2345 **Fax:** 319-588-6789
E-mail: admissions@clarke.edu

Getting in Last Year 712 applied; 66% were accepted; 180 enrolled (38%).

Financial Matters $16,190 tuition and fees (2002–03); $5765 room and board; 100% average percent of need met; $13,913 average financial aid amount received per undergraduate.

Academics Clarke awards associate, bachelor's, and master's degrees. Challenging opportunities include advanced placement credit, student-designed majors, an honors program, double majors, independent study, and a senior project. Special programs include cooperative education, internships, summer session for credit, off-campus study, and study-abroad. The most frequently chosen baccalaureate fields are health professions and related sciences, business/marketing, and computer/information sciences. The faculty at Clarke has 77 full-time members, 55% with terminal degrees. The student-faculty ratio is 10:1.

Students of Clarke The student body totals 1,126, of whom 998 are undergraduates. 68.9% are women and 31.1% are men. Students come from 10 states and territories and 10 other countries. 62% are from Iowa. 2.4% are international students. 83% returned for their sophomore year.

Applying Clarke requires SAT I or ACT, a high school transcript, rank in upper 50% of high school class, minimum ACT score of 21 or SAT score of 1000, and a minimum high school GPA of 2.0, and in some cases an interview. Application deadline: rolling admissions; 4/15 priority date for financial aid. Deferred admission is possible.

CLARKSON COLLEGE

Omaha, NE

Urban setting ■ *Private* ■ *Independent* ■ *Coed, Primarily Women*

Web site: www.clarksoncollege.edu
Contact: Ms. Nicole Wegenast, Dean of Enrollment Services, 101 South 42nd Street, Omaha, NE 68131-2739
Telephone: 402-552-3100 or toll-free 800-647-5500 **Fax:** 402-552-6057
E-mail: admiss@clarksoncollege.edu

Getting in Last Year 142 enrolled.

Financial Matters $9378 tuition and fees (2002–03); $2900 room only; 71% average percent of need met; $8291 average financial aid amount received per undergraduate (2001–02).

Academics Clarkson awards associate, bachelor's, and master's degrees. Challenging opportunities include advanced placement credit, accelerated degree programs, double majors, independent study, and a senior project. Special

Clarkson College (continued)

programs include cooperative education, internships, summer session for credit, study-abroad, and Army and Air Force ROTC. The most frequently chosen baccalaureate fields are health professions and related sciences and business/marketing. The faculty at Clarkson has 62 full-time members, 11% with terminal degrees. The student-faculty ratio is 12:1.

Students of Clarkson The student body totals 507, of whom 421 are undergraduates. 91.2% are women and 8.8% are men. Students come from 35 states and territories. 67% are from Nebraska. 85% returned for their sophomore year.

Applying Clarkson requires an essay, a high school transcript, and a minimum high school GPA of 2.5, and in some cases SAT I or ACT and 2 recommendations. The school recommends a minimum high school GPA of 3.0. Application deadline: rolling admissions; 4/1 priority date for financial aid. Deferred admission is possible.

CLARKSON UNIVERSITY

Potsdam, NY

Small-town setting ■ Private ■ Independent ■ Coed

Web site: www.clarkson.edu
Contact: Mr. Brian T. Grant, Director of Enrollment Operations, Holcroft House, Potsdam, NY 13699
Telephone: 315-268-6479 or toll-free 800-527-6577 **Fax:** 315-268-7647
E-mail: admission@clarkson.edu

Getting in Last Year 2,556 applied; 82% were accepted; 725 enrolled (35%).

Financial Matters $22,635 tuition and fees (2002–03); $8398 room and board; 88% average percent of need met; $15,500 average financial aid amount received per undergraduate.

Academics Clarkson awards bachelor's, master's, and doctoral degrees. Challenging opportunities include advanced placement credit, accelerated degree programs, student-designed majors, an honors program, double majors, independent study, and a senior project. Special programs include cooperative education, internships, summer session for credit, off-campus study, study-abroad, and Army and Air Force ROTC. The most frequently chosen baccalaureate fields are engineering/engineering technologies, interdisciplinary studies, and business/marketing. The faculty at Clarkson has 168 full-time members, 89% with terminal degrees. The student-faculty ratio is 17:1.

Students of Clarkson The student body totals 3,107, of whom 2,756 are undergraduates. 24.5% are women and 75.5% are men. Students come from 40 states and territories and 33 other countries. 77% are from New York. 3.3% are international students. 87% returned for their sophomore year.

Applying Clarkson requires SAT I or ACT, a high school transcript, and 1 recommendation. The school recommends SAT II Subject Tests and an interview. Application deadline: 3/15; 3/1 priority date for financial aid. Early and deferred admission are possible.

CLARK UNIVERSITY

Worcester, MA

Urban setting ■ Private ■ Independent ■ Coed

Web site: www.clarku.edu
Contact: Mr. Harold M. Wingood, Dean of Admissions, 950 Main Street, Worcester, MA 01610-1477
Telephone: 508-793-7431 or toll-free 800-GO-CLARK (out-of-state)
E-mail: admissions@clarku.edu

Getting in Last Year 3,694 applied; 68% were accepted; 580 enrolled (23%).

Financial Matters $25,865 tuition and fees (2002–03); $4950 room and board; 95% average percent of need met; $20,515 average financial aid amount received per undergraduate.

Academics Clark awards bachelor's, master's, and doctoral degrees and post-bachelor's and post-master's certificates. Challenging opportunities include advanced placement credit, accelerated degree programs, student-designed majors, an honors program, double majors, independent study, and a senior project. Special programs include internships, summer session for credit, off-campus study, study-abroad, and Army, Navy and Air Force ROTC. The most frequently chosen baccalaureate fields are social sciences and history, psychology, and biological/life sciences. The faculty at Clark has 164 full-time members, 96% with terminal degrees. The student-faculty ratio is 10:1.

Students of Clark The student body totals 3,035, of whom 2,167 are undergraduates. 60.7% are women and 39.3% are men. Students come from 46 states and territories and 57 other countries. 40% are from Massachusetts. 7.5% are international students. 84% returned for their sophomore year.

Applying Clark requires an essay, SAT I or ACT, a high school transcript, and 2 recommendations. The school recommends an interview. Application deadline: 2/1; 2/1 priority date for financial aid. Early and deferred admission are possible.

CLAYTON COLLEGE & STATE UNIVERSITY

Morrow, GA

Suburban setting ■ Public ■ State-supported ■ Coed

Web site: www.clayton.edu
Contact: Ms. Carol S. Montgomery, Admissions, 5900 North Lee Street, Morrow, GA 30260-0285
Telephone: 770-961-3500 **Fax:** 770-961-3752
E-mail: csc-info@ce.clayton.peachnet.edu

Financial Matters $2436 resident tuition and fees (2002–03); $8466 nonresident tuition and fees (2002–03).

Academics Clayton State awards associate and bachelor's degrees. Challenging opportunities include advanced placement credit, student-designed majors, freshman honors college, an honors program, double majors, independent study, and a senior project. Special programs include cooperative education, internships, summer session for credit, off-campus study, study-abroad, and Army ROTC. The most frequently chosen baccalaureate fields are business/marketing, health professions and related sciences, and computer/information sciences. The faculty at Clayton State has 140 full-time members, 56% with terminal degrees. The student-faculty ratio is 16:1.

Students of Clayton State The student body is made up of 5,214 undergraduates. 66.8% are women and 33.2% are men. 98% are from Georgia. 1.9% are international students.

Applying Clayton State requires SAT I or ACT, a high school transcript, and proof of immunization, and in some cases SAT II Subject Tests. Application deadline: 7/17; 4/1 priority date for financial aid. Early and deferred admission are possible.

CLEAR CREEK BAPTIST BIBLE COLLEGE

Pineville, KY

Rural setting ■ Private ■ Independent Religious ■ Coed, Primarily Men

Web site: www.ccbbc.edu
Contact: Mr. Billy Howell, Director of Admissions, 300 Clear Creek Road, Pineville, KY 40977-9754
Telephone: 606-337-3196 ext. 103 **Fax:** 606-337-2372
E-mail: ccbbc@ccbbc.edu

Financial Matters $4340 tuition and fees (2002–03); $3380 room and board; 44% average percent of need met; $4309 average financial aid amount received per undergraduate (2001–02).

Academics Clear Creek College awards associate and bachelor's degrees. A senior project is a challenging opportunity. Summer session for credit is a special program. The faculty at Clear Creek College has 7 full-time members.

Students of Clear Creek College The student body is made up of 192 undergraduates. 16.7% are women and 83.3% are men. 83% returned for their sophomore year.

Applying Clear Creek College requires an essay and 4 recommendations. The school recommends a high school transcript and an interview. Application deadline: 7/15; 6/30 priority date for financial aid. Deferred admission is possible.

CLEARWATER CHRISTIAN COLLEGE

Clearwater, FL

Suburban setting ■ Private ■ Independent Religious ■ Coed

Web site: www.clearwater.edu
Contact: Mr. Benjamin J. Puckett, Dean of Enrollment Services, 3400 Gulf-to-Bay Boulevard, Clearwater, FL 33759-4595
Telephone: 727-726-1153 or toll-free 800-348-4463 **Fax:** 813-726-8597
E-mail: admissions@clearwater.edu

Getting in Last Year 503 applied; 86% were accepted.

Financial Matters $9710 tuition and fees (2002–03); $4290 room and board; 54% average percent of need met; $5903 average financial aid amount received per undergraduate.

Academics Clearwater Christian College awards associate and bachelor's degrees. Challenging opportunities include advanced placement credit and double majors. Special programs include internships, summer session for credit, and Army and Air Force ROTC. The faculty at Clearwater Christian College has 36 full-time members. The student-faculty ratio is 15:1.

Students of Clearwater Christian College The student body is made up of 652 undergraduates. Students come from 40 states and territories and 15 other countries. 59% returned for their sophomore year.

Applying Clearwater Christian College requires an essay, SAT I or ACT, a high school transcript, 2 recommendations, Christian testimony, and a minimum high school GPA of 2.0. The school recommends an interview. Application deadline: rolling admissions; 4/1 priority date for financial aid. Early and deferred admission are possible.

CLEARY UNIVERSITY

Ann Arbor, MI

Small-town setting ■ Private ■ Independent ■ Coed

Web site: www.cleary.edu
Contact: Ms. Colleen Murphy, Admissions Representative, 3750 Cleary Drive, Howell, MI 48843
Telephone: 517-548-3670 ext. 2252 or toll-free 888-5-CLEARY (in-state), 888-5-CLEARY ext. 2249 (out-of-state) **Fax:** 517-552-7805
E-mail: admissions@cleary.edu

Financial Matters $10,032 tuition and fees (2002–03); 60% average percent of need met; $4598 average financial aid amount received per undergraduate (2001–02).

Academics Cleary awards associate, bachelor's, and master's degrees. Challenging opportunities include advanced placement credit, accelerated degree programs, and independent study. Special programs include cooperative education, internships, and summer session for credit. The faculty at Cleary has 11 full-time members, 55% with terminal degrees. The student-faculty ratio is 10:1.

Students of Cleary The student body totals 626, of whom 594 are undergraduates. Students come from 2 states and territories. 99% are from Michigan.

Applying Cleary requires SAT I or ACT, a high school transcript, complete the Technology Skills Inventory (TSI), and a minimum high school GPA of 2.5, and in some cases an essay and 2 recommendations. The school recommends an interview. Application deadline: 8/5; 3/15 priority date for financial aid. Early and deferred admission are possible.

CLEMSON UNIVERSITY

Clemson, SC

Small-town setting ■ Public ■ State-supported ■ Coed

Web site: www.clemson.edu
Contact: Mr. Robert S. Barkley, Director of Admissions, 105 Sikes Hall, PO Box 345124, Clemson, SC 29634
Telephone: 864-656-2287 **Fax:** 864-656-2464
E-mail: cuadmissions@clemson.edu

Getting in Last Year 11,315 applied; 52% were accepted; 2,474 enrolled (42%).

Financial Matters $6034 resident tuition and fees (2002–03); $13,132 nonresident tuition and fees (2002–03); $4454 room and board; 75% average percent of need met; $8518 average financial aid amount received per undergraduate.

Academics Clemson awards bachelor's, master's, and doctoral degrees. Challenging opportunities include advanced placement credit, accelerated degree programs, an honors program, double majors, and a senior project. Special programs include cooperative education, internships, summer session for credit, study-abroad, and Army and Air Force ROTC. The most frequently chosen baccalaureate fields are business/marketing, engineering/engineering technologies, and education. The faculty at Clemson has 964 full-time members, 87% with terminal degrees. The student-faculty ratio is 16:1.

Students of Clemson The student body totals 16,876, of whom 13,734 are undergraduates. 45.3% are women and 54.7% are men. Students come from 52 states and territories and 62 other countries. 70% are from South Carolina. 0.6% are international students. 88% returned for their sophomore year.

Applying Clemson requires SAT I or ACT and a high school transcript. The school recommends an essay, an interview, and recommendations. Application deadline: 5/1; 4/1 priority date for financial aid.

CLEVELAND CHIROPRACTIC COLLEGE-KANSAS CITY CAMPUS

Kansas City, MO

Private ■ Independent ■ Coed

Web site: www.cleveland.edu
Contact: Ms. Melissa Denton, Director of Admissions, 6401 Rockhill Road, Kansas City, MO 64131
Telephone: 816-501-0100 or toll-free 800-467-2252 **Fax:** 816-501-0205
E-mail: kc.admissions@cleveland.edu

Financial Matters $3670 tuition and fees (2002–03).

Academics Cleveland Chiropractic College-Kansas City Campus awards bachelor's and first-professional degrees. Challenging opportunities include accelerated degree programs and a senior project. Special programs include cooperative education, internships, and summer session for credit. The faculty at Cleveland Chiropractic College-Kansas City Campus has 45 full-time members. The student-faculty ratio is 15:1.

Students of Cleveland Chiropractic College-Kansas City Campus The student body totals 467, of whom 61 are undergraduates. 39.3% are women and 60.7% are men. Students come from 18 states and territories. 20% are from Missouri. 41% are international students.

Applying Deferred admission is possible.

THE CLEVELAND INSTITUTE OF ART

Cleveland, OH

Urban setting ■ Private ■ Independent ■ Coed

Web site: www.cia.edu
Contact: Office of Admissions, 11141 East Boulevard, Cleveland, OH 44106
Telephone: 216-421-7418 or toll-free 800-223-4700 **Fax:** 216-754-3634
E-mail: admiss@gate.cia.edu

Getting in Last Year 423 applied; 65% were accepted; 107 enrolled (39%).

Financial Matters $21,024 tuition and fees (2002–03); $6426 room and board; 66% average percent of need met; $13,424 average financial aid amount received per undergraduate.

Academics CIA awards bachelor's and master's degrees. Challenging opportunities include advanced placement credit, an honors program, independent study, and a senior project. Special programs include internships, off-campus study, and study-abroad. The most frequently chosen baccalaureate field is visual/performing arts. The faculty at CIA has 43 full-time members, 53% with terminal degrees. The student-faculty ratio is 10:1.

Students of CIA The student body totals 641, of whom 636 are undergraduates. 52.7% are women and 47.3% are men. Students come from 28 states and territories and 10 other countries. 68% are from Ohio. 3.3% are international students. 82% returned for their sophomore year.

Applying CIA requires an essay, SAT I or ACT, a high school transcript, 2 recommendations, portfolio, and a minimum high school GPA of 2.0. The school recommends an interview. Application deadline: rolling admissions; 3/15 priority date for financial aid. Deferred admission is possible.

CLEVELAND INSTITUTE OF MUSIC

Cleveland, OH

Urban setting ■ Private ■ Independent ■ Coed

Web site: www.cim.edu
Contact: Mr. William Fay, Director of Admission, 11021 East Boulevard, Cleveland, OH 44106-1776
Telephone: 216-795-3107 **Fax:** 216-791-1530
E-mail: cimadmission@po.cwru.edu

Getting in Last Year 363 applied; 39% were accepted; 63 enrolled (44%).

Financial Matters $21,505 tuition and fees (2002–03); $6675 room and board; 83% average percent of need met; $13,980 average financial aid amount received per undergraduate (2001–02).

Academics Cleveland Institute of Music awards bachelor's, master's, and doctoral degrees. Challenging opportunities include advanced placement credit, accelerated degree programs, and a senior project. Special programs include internships, summer session for credit, off-campus study, and Army and Air Force ROTC. The faculty at Cleveland Institute of Music has 32 full-time members, 6% with terminal degrees. The student-faculty ratio is 7:1.

Students of Cleveland Institute of Music The student body totals 387, of whom 226 are undergraduates. 55.3% are women and 44.7% are men. Students come from 38 states and territories and 11 other countries. 11% are from Ohio. 10.6% are international students. 86% returned for their sophomore year.

Applying Cleveland Institute of Music requires an essay, SAT I or ACT, a high school transcript, 2 recommendations, and audition. The school recommends an interview. Application deadline: 12/1; 2/15 for financial aid. Early and deferred admission are possible.

CLEVELAND STATE UNIVERSITY

Cleveland, OH

Urban setting ■ Public ■ State-supported ■ Coed

Web site: www.csuohio.edu
Contact: Mr. Tom Steffen, Office of Admissions, 2121 Euclid Avenue, Box A, Cleveland, OH 44115
Telephone: 216-523-7244 or toll-free 888-CSU-OHIO **Fax:** 216-687-9210
E-mail: registrar@csuohio.edu

Getting in Last Year 2,561 applied; 82% were accepted; 1,011 enrolled (48%).

Financial Matters $5184 resident tuition and fees (2002–03); $10,219 nonresident tuition and fees (2002–03); $5880 room and board; 55% average percent of need met; $6557 average financial aid amount received per undergraduate.

Academics Cleveland State awards bachelor's, master's, doctoral, and first-professional degrees and post-bachelor's, post-master's, and first-professional certificates. Challenging opportunities include advanced placement credit, accelerated degree programs, student-designed majors, freshman honors college, an honors program, and independent study. Special programs include cooperative education, internships, summer session for credit, off-campus study, study-abroad, and Army and Air Force ROTC. The most frequently chosen baccalaureate fields are business/marketing, social sciences and history, and education. The faculty at Cleveland State has 486 full-time members, 94% with terminal degrees. The student-faculty ratio is 17:1.

Cleveland State University (continued)

Students of Cleveland State The student body totals 15,974, of whom 10,356 are undergraduates. 54.8% are women and 45.2% are men. Students come from 38 states and territories and 22 other countries. 98% are from Ohio. 2.4% are international students. 68% returned for their sophomore year.

Applying Cleveland State requires SAT I or ACT and a high school transcript. Application deadline: rolling admissions; 2/15 priority date for financial aid. Deferred admission is possible.

COASTAL CAROLINA UNIVERSITY

Conway, SC

Suburban setting ■ Public ■ State-supported ■ Coed

Web site: www.coastal.edu
Contact: Dr. Judy Vogt, Associate Vice President, Enrollment Services, PO Box 261954, Kingston Hall, Room 119, Conway, SC 29528
Telephone: 843-349-2037 or toll-free 800-277-7000 **Fax:** 843-349-2127
E-mail: admissions@coastal.edu

Getting in Last Year 3,599 applied; 72% were accepted; 1,078 enrolled (42%).

Financial Matters $4430 resident tuition and fees (2002–03); $11,840 nonresident tuition and fees (2002–03); $5610 room and board; 59% average percent of need met; $6717 average financial aid amount received per undergraduate (2001–02).

Academics Coastal Carolina awards bachelor's and master's degrees and post-bachelor's certificates. Challenging opportunities include advanced placement credit, accelerated degree programs, student-designed majors, an honors program, double majors, independent study, and a senior project. Special programs include cooperative education, internships, summer session for credit, and study-abroad. The most frequently chosen baccalaureate fields are business/marketing, education, and biological/life sciences. The faculty at Coastal Carolina has 200 full-time members, 81% with terminal degrees. The student-faculty ratio is 19:1.

Students of Coastal Carolina The student body totals 5,980, of whom 5,058 are undergraduates. 53.4% are women and 46.6% are men. Students come from 49 states and territories and 48 other countries. 59% are from South Carolina. 3% are international students. 68% returned for their sophomore year.

Applying Coastal Carolina requires SAT I or ACT, a high school transcript, and a minimum high school GPA of 2.0. The school recommends an essay, an interview, and 1 recommendation. Application deadline: 8/15; 4/1 priority date for financial aid. Deferred admission is possible.

COE COLLEGE

Cedar Rapids, IA

Urban setting ■ Private ■ Independent Religious ■ Coed

Web site: www.coe.edu
Contact: Mr. Dennis Trotter, Vice President of Admission and Financial Aid, 1220 1st Avenue, NE, Cedar Rapids, IA 52402-5070
Telephone: 319-399-8500 or toll-free 877-225-5263 **Fax:** 319-399-8816
E-mail: admission@coe.edu

Getting in Last Year 1,285 applied; 77% were accepted; 302 enrolled (30%).

Financial Matters $20,540 tuition and fees (2002–03); $5610 room and board; 94% average percent of need met; $18,365 average financial aid amount received per undergraduate.

Academics Coe awards bachelor's and master's degrees. Challenging opportunities include advanced placement credit, accelerated degree programs, student-designed majors, an honors program, double majors, independent study, and a senior project. Special programs include internships, summer session for credit, off-campus study, study-abroad, and Army and Air Force ROTC. The most frequently chosen baccalaureate fields are business/marketing, social sciences and history, and psychology. The faculty at Coe has 74 full-time members, 91% with terminal degrees. The student-faculty ratio is 12:1.

Students of Coe The student body totals 1,325, of whom 1,300 are undergraduates. 57% are women and 43% are men. Students come from 40 states and territories and 15 other countries. 66% are from Iowa. 3.3% are international students. 79% returned for their sophomore year.

Applying Coe requires an essay, SAT I or ACT, a high school transcript, and 1 recommendation. The school recommends an interview and a minimum high school GPA of 3.0. Application deadline: 3/1; 4/30 for financial aid, with a 3/1 priority date. Early and deferred admission are possible.

COGSWELL POLYTECHNICAL COLLEGE

Sunnyvale, CA

Suburban setting ■ Private ■ Independent ■ Coed, Primarily Men

Web site: www.cogswell.edu
Contact: Mr. Matt Clemons, Enrollment Manager, 1175 Bordeaux Drive, Sunnyvale, CA 94089
Telephone: 408-541-0100 or toll-free 800-264-7955 **Fax:** 408-747-0764
E-mail: info@cogswell.edu

Getting in Last Year 30 applied; 90% were accepted; 25 enrolled (93%).

Financial Matters $10,240 tuition and fees (2002–03); $6300 room only; 37% average percent of need met; $5064 average financial aid amount received per undergraduate.

Academics Cogswell College awards bachelor's degrees. Challenging opportunities include advanced placement credit and a senior project. Special programs include internships and summer session for credit. The most frequently chosen baccalaureate fields are visual/performing arts and engineering/engineering technologies. The faculty at Cogswell College has 14 full-time members, 43% with terminal degrees. The student-faculty ratio is 15:1.

Students of Cogswell College The student body is made up of 376 undergraduates. 14.1% are women and 85.9% are men. Students come from 20 states and territories and 5 other countries. 89% are from California. 1.3% are international students. 87% returned for their sophomore year.

Applying Cogswell College requires an essay, a high school transcript, and a minimum high school GPA of 2.5, and in some cases an interview, recommendations, and portfolio. The school recommends SAT I and SAT II or ACT. Application deadline: 6/1. Deferred admission is possible.

COKER COLLEGE

Hartsville, SC

Small-town setting ■ Private ■ Independent ■ Coed

Web site: www.coker.edu
Contact: Ms. Perry Kirven, Director of Admissions and Student Financial Planning, 300 East College Avenue, Hartsville, SC 29550
Telephone: 843-383-8050 or toll-free 800-950-1908 **Fax:** 843-383-8056
E-mail: admissions@coker.edu

Getting in Last Year 511 applied; 25% were accepted; 129 enrolled (100%).

Financial Matters $15,495 tuition and fees (2002–03); $5196 room and board; 91% average percent of need met; $14,514 average financial aid amount received per undergraduate (2001–02).

Academics Coker College awards bachelor's degrees (also offers evening program with significant enrollment not reflected in profile). Challenging opportunities include advanced placement credit, student-designed majors, an honors program, double majors, independent study, and a senior project. Special programs include cooperative education, internships, summer session for credit, and study-abroad. The most frequently chosen baccalaureate fields are education, business/marketing, and visual/performing arts. The faculty at Coker College has 57 full-time members, 81% with terminal degrees. The student-faculty ratio is 7:1.

Students of Coker College The student body is made up of 468 undergraduates. 60.3% are women and 39.7% are men. 81% are from South Carolina. 1.7% are international students. 63% returned for their sophomore year.

Applying Coker College requires SAT I or ACT, a high school transcript, and 1 recommendation, and in some cases an essay, 2 recommendations, minimum SAT score of 830 or ACT score of 17, and a minimum high school GPA of 2.2. The school recommends an interview, minimum SAT score of 830 or ACT score of 17, and a minimum high school GPA of 2.2. Application deadline: rolling admissions; 4/30 priority date for financial aid. Deferred admission is possible.

COLBY COLLEGE

Waterville, ME

Small-town setting ■ Private ■ Independent ■ Coed

Web site: www.colby.edu
Contact: Mr. Steve Thomas, Director of Admissions, Office of Admissions and Financial Aid, 4800 Mayflower Hill, Waterville, ME 04901-8848
Telephone: 207-872-3471 or toll-free 800-723-3032 **Fax:** 207-872-3474
E-mail: admissions@colby.edu

Getting in Last Year 3,873 applied; 33% were accepted; 471 enrolled (37%).

Financial Matters $35,800 comprehensive fee (2002–03); 100% average percent of need met; $22,055 average financial aid amount received per undergraduate.

Academics Colby awards bachelor's degrees. Challenging opportunities include advanced placement credit, student-designed majors, an honors program, double majors, independent study, and a senior project. Special programs include internships, off-campus study, study-abroad, and Army ROTC. The most frequently chosen baccalaureate fields are social sciences and history, biological/life sciences, and area/ethnic studies. The faculty at Colby has 158 full-time members, 95% with terminal degrees. The student-faculty ratio is 11:1.

Students of Colby The student body is made up of 1,830 undergraduates. 53.5% are women and 46.5% are men. Students come from 50 states and territories and 63 other countries. 16% are from Maine. 5.9% are international students. 94% returned for their sophomore year.

Applying Colby requires an essay, SAT I or ACT, a high school transcript, and 2 recommendations. The school recommends an interview. Application deadline: 1/1; 2/1 for financial aid. Early and deferred admission are possible.

COLBY-SAWYER COLLEGE

New London, NH

Small-town setting ■ Private ■ Independent ■ Coed

Web site: www.colby-sawyer.edu
Contact: Ms. Wendy Beckemeyer, Vice President for Enrollment Management and Dean of Admissions, 541 Main Street, New London, NH 03257
Telephone: 603-526-3700 or toll-free 800-272-1015 **Fax:** 603-526-3452
E-mail: csadmiss@colby-sawyer.edu

Getting in Last Year 1,251 applied; 86% were accepted; 270 enrolled (25%).

Financial Matters $21,140 tuition and fees (2002–03); $8110 room and board; 64% average percent of need met; $14,690 average financial aid amount received per undergraduate (2001–02).

Academics Colby-Sawyer awards associate and bachelor's degrees. Challenging opportunities include advanced placement credit, accelerated degree programs, student-designed majors, an honors program, double majors, independent study, and a senior project. Special programs include internships, off-campus study, study-abroad, and Army and Air Force ROTC. The most frequently chosen baccalaureate fields are psychology, parks and recreation, and visual/performing arts. The faculty at Colby-Sawyer has 49 full-time members, 78% with terminal degrees. The student-faculty ratio is 12:1.

Students of Colby-Sawyer The student body is made up of 940 undergraduates. 63.1% are women and 36.9% are men. Students come from 25 states and territories and 5 other countries. 30% are from New Hampshire. 1.8% are international students. 81% returned for their sophomore year.

Applying Colby-Sawyer requires SAT I or ACT, a high school transcript, 2 recommendations, and a minimum high school GPA of 2.0. The school recommends an interview. Application deadline: rolling admissions; 3/1 priority date for financial aid. Early and deferred admission are possible.

COLGATE UNIVERSITY

Hamilton, NY

Rural setting ■ Private ■ Independent ■ Coed

Web site: www.colgate.edu
Contact: Mr. Gary L. Ross, Dean of Admission, 13 Oak Drive, Hamilton, NY 13346-1383
Telephone: 315-228-7401 **Fax:** 315-228-7544
E-mail: admission@mail.colgate.edu

Getting in Last Year 6,268 applied; 34% were accepted; 727 enrolled (34%).

Financial Matters $28,355 tuition and fees (2002–03); $6775 room and board; 100% average percent of need met; $23,490 average financial aid amount received per undergraduate.

Academics Colgate awards bachelor's and master's degrees. Challenging opportunities include advanced placement credit, student-designed majors, an honors program, double majors, independent study, and a senior project. Special programs include internships, off-campus study, and study-abroad. The faculty at Colgate has 242 full-time members, 95% with terminal degrees. The student-faculty ratio is 10:1.

Students of Colgate The student body totals 2,837, of whom 2,827 are undergraduates. 51% are women and 49% are men. Students come from 48 states and territories and 32 other countries. 33% are from New York. 4.9% are international students. 97% returned for their sophomore year.

Applying Colgate requires an essay, SAT I and SAT II or ACT, a high school transcript, and 3 recommendations. Application deadline: 1/15; 2/1 for financial aid. Deferred admission is possible.

COLLÈGE DOMINICAIN DE PHILOSOPHIE ET DE THÉOLOGIE

Ottawa, ON Canada

Urban setting ■ Private ■ Independent Religious ■ Coed

Web site: www.collegedominicain.ca
Contact: Fr. Maxime Allard, OP, Registrar, 96 Empress Avenue, Ottawa, ON Canada
Telephone: 613-233-5696 **Fax:** 613-233-6064
E-mail: registraire@collegedominicain.ca

Getting in Last Year 19 enrolled.

Financial Matters $2700 tuition and fees (2002–03); $4800 room and board.

Academics Collège Dominicain de Philosophie et de Théologie awards bachelor's, master's, and doctoral degrees. Accelerated degree programs are a challenging opportunity. Summer session for credit is a special program. The faculty at Collège Dominicain de Philosophie et de Théologie has 23 full-time members, 87% with terminal degrees.

Students of Collège Dominicain de Philosophie et de Théologie The student body totals 215, of whom 159 are undergraduates. 44.7% are women and 55.3% are men. Students come from 6 states and territories and 8 other countries. 0.6% are international students. 72% returned for their sophomore year.

Applying Collège Dominicain de Philosophie et de Théologie requires a high school transcript. The school recommends an interview. Application deadline: 7/15.

COLLEGE FOR CREATIVE STUDIES

Detroit, MI

Urban setting ■ Private ■ Independent ■ Coed

Web site: www.ccscad.edu
Contact: Office of Admissions, 201 East Kirby, Detroit, MI 48202-4034
Telephone: 313-664-7425 or toll-free 800-952-ARTS **Fax:** 313-872-2739
E-mail: admissions@ccscad.edu

Getting in Last Year 429 applied; 78% were accepted; 194 enrolled (58%).

Financial Matters $18,598 tuition and fees (2002–03); $3300 room only.

Academics CCS awards bachelor's degrees. Challenging opportunities include advanced placement credit, double majors, independent study, and a senior project. Special programs include cooperative education, internships, summer session for credit, and off-campus study. The most frequently chosen baccalaureate field is visual/performing arts. The faculty at CCS has 43 full-time members. The student-faculty ratio is 10:1.

Students of CCS The student body is made up of 1,204 undergraduates. 40.9% are women and 59.1% are men. Students come from 31 states and territories and 15 other countries. 83% are from Michigan. 5.5% are international students. 79% returned for their sophomore year.

Applying CCS requires an essay, SAT I or ACT, a high school transcript, and portfolio, and in some cases an interview and recommendations. The school recommends a minimum high school GPA of 2.5. Application deadline: rolling admissions; 2/21 priority date for financial aid. Deferred admission is possible.

COLLEGE MISERICORDIA

Dallas, PA

Small-town setting ■ Private ■ Independent Religious ■ Coed

Web site: www.misericordia.edu
Contact: Ms. Jane Dessoye, Executive Director of Admissions and Financial Aid, 301 Lake Street, Dallas, PA 18612-1098
Telephone: 570-675-4449 ext. 6168 or toll-free 866-262-6363 (in-state), 866-2626363 (out-of-state) **Fax:** 570-674-6232
E-mail: admiss@misericordia.edu

Getting in Last Year 923 applied; 84% were accepted; 286 enrolled (37%).

Financial Matters $17,300 tuition and fees (2002–03); $7130 room and board; 77% average percent of need met; $12,798 average financial aid amount received per undergraduate.

Academics Misericordia awards bachelor's and master's degrees. Challenging opportunities include advanced placement credit, accelerated degree programs, student-designed majors, an honors program, double majors, independent study, and a senior project. Special programs include cooperative education, internships, summer session for credit, off-campus study, study-abroad, and Army and Air Force ROTC. The most frequently chosen baccalaureate fields are health professions and related sciences, education, and business/marketing. The faculty at Misericordia has 89 full-time members. The student-faculty ratio is 14:1.

Students of Misericordia The student body totals 1,765, of whom 1,640 are undergraduates. 73.2% are women and 26.8% are men. Students come from 17 states and territories. 80% are from Pennsylvania. 93% returned for their sophomore year.

Applying Misericordia requires SAT I or ACT and a high school transcript, and in some cases an essay, an interview, and 2 recommendations. The school recommends an interview. Application deadline: rolling admissions; 3/1 priority date for financial aid. Early and deferred admission are possible.

COLLEGE OF AERONAUTICS

Flushing, NY

Urban setting ■ Private ■ Independent ■ Coed, Primarily Men

Web site: www.aero.edu
Contact: Thomas Bracken, Associate Director, Admissions, La Guardia Airport, 86-01 23rd Avenue, Flushing, NY 11369
Telephone: 718-429-6600 ext. 167 or toll-free 800-776-2376 ext. 145 (in-state) **Fax:** 718-779-2231
E-mail: admissions@aero.edu

Getting in Last Year 539 applied; 78% were accepted; 270 enrolled (64%).

Financial Matters $9250 tuition and fees (2002–03); 50% average percent of need met; $1950 average financial aid amount received per undergraduate (2001–02).

Academics COA awards associate and bachelor's degrees. Challenging opportunities include advanced placement credit, independent study, and a senior project. Special programs include cooperative education, internships, summer session for credit, and Army and Air Force ROTC. The faculty at COA has 52 full-time members, 19% with terminal degrees. The student-faculty ratio is 11:1.

College of Aeronautics (continued)

Students of COA The student body is made up of 1,316 undergraduates. 9.3% are women and 90.7% are men. Students come from 10 states and territories and 15 other countries. 94% are from New York. 4.7% are international students. 67% returned for their sophomore year.

Applying COA requires a high school transcript, and in some cases SAT I and an interview. The school recommends an interview. Application deadline: rolling admissions. Deferred admission is possible.

COLLEGE OF BIBLICAL STUDIES–HOUSTON

Houston, TX

Private ■ Independent Religious ■ Coed

Web site: www.cbshouston.edu

Contact: Mrs. Marilynn C. Square, Registrar, 6000 Dale Carnegie Drive, Houston, TX 77036

Telephone: 713-785-5995

E-mail: cbs@cbshouston.edu

Getting in Last Year 55 applied; 100% were accepted; 55 enrolled (100%).

Financial Matters $3800 tuition and fees (2002–03).

Academics College of Biblical Studies–Houston awards associate and bachelor's degrees. Challenging opportunities include accelerated degree programs, double majors, independent study, and a senior project. The faculty at College of Biblical Studies–Houston has 10 full-time members, 50% with terminal degrees. The student-faculty ratio is 26:1.

Students of College of Biblical Studies–Houston The student body is made up of 1,433 undergraduates. 44.4% are women and 55.6% are men. Students come from 1 state or territory.

Applying College of Biblical Studies–Houston requires an essay and a high school transcript, and in some cases an interview. The school recommends SAT II: Writing Test, SAT I and SAT II or ACT, and TAAS. TASP. Application deadline: rolling admissions.

COLLEGE OF CHARLESTON

Charleston, SC

Urban setting ■ Public ■ State-supported ■ Coed

Web site: www.cofc.edu

Contact: Mr. Donald Burkard, Dean of Admissions, 66 George Street, Charleston, SC 29424-0001

Telephone: 843-953-5670 **Fax:** 843-953-6322

E-mail: admissions@cofc.edu

Getting in Last Year 8,635 applied; 60% were accepted; 2,003 enrolled (39%).

Financial Matters $4556 resident tuition and fees (2002–03); $10,290 nonresident tuition and fees (2002–03); $5661 room and board; 67% average percent of need met; $8324 average financial aid amount received per undergraduate.

Academics C of C awards bachelor's and master's degrees (also offers graduate degree programs through University of Charleston, South Carolina). Challenging opportunities include advanced placement credit, accelerated degree programs, an honors program, double majors, independent study, and a senior project. Special programs include cooperative education, internships, summer session for credit, off-campus study, study-abroad, and Air Force ROTC. The most frequently chosen baccalaureate fields are business/marketing, education, and communications/communication technologies. The faculty at C of C has 463 full-time members, 85% with terminal degrees. The student-faculty ratio is 14:1.

Students of C of C The student body totals 11,716, of whom 10,044 are undergraduates. 63.4% are women and 36.6% are men. Students come from 50 states and territories and 72 other countries. 65% are from South Carolina. 2.6% are international students. 80% returned for their sophomore year.

Applying C of C requires an essay, SAT I or ACT, and a high school transcript. The school recommends an interview and recommendations. Application deadline: 4/1, 4/1 for nonresidents; 3/15 priority date for financial aid. Early and deferred admission are possible.

COLLEGE OF EMMANUEL AND ST. CHAD

Saskatoon, SK Canada

Urban setting ■ Private ■ Independent Religious ■ Coed

Web site: www.usask.ca/stu/emmanuel

Contact: Ms. Colleen Walker, Registrar's Assistant, 1337 College Drive, Saskatoon, SK S7N 0W6 Canada

Telephone: 306-975-1558

Getting in Last Year 6 applied; 100% were accepted.

Financial Matters $4100 tuition and fees (2002–03).

Academics Emm & St C awards bachelor's and master's degrees. A senior project is a challenging opportunity. Special programs include cooperative education, internships, summer session for credit, and off-campus study. The faculty at Emm & St C has 4 full-time members.

Students of Emm & St C The student body totals 22, of whom 19 are undergraduates. Students come from 8 states and territories and 1 other country. 100% returned for their sophomore year.

Applying Emm & St C requires an essay, a high school transcript, and 3 recommendations. Application deadline: 6/30.

COLLEGE OF MOUNT ST. JOSEPH

Cincinnati, OH

Suburban setting ■ Private ■ Independent Religious ■ Coed

Web site: www.msj.edu

Contact: Ms. Peggy Minnich, Director of Admission, 5701 Delhi Road, Cincinnati, OH 45233-1672

Telephone: 513-244-4814 or toll-free 800-654-9314 **Fax:** 513-244-4629

E-mail: peggy_minnich@mail.msj.edu

Getting in Last Year 932 applied; 75% were accepted; 348 enrolled (50%).

Financial Matters $15,840 tuition and fees (2002–03); $6020 room and board; 90% average percent of need met; $11,400 average financial aid amount received per undergraduate.

Academics The Mount awards associate, bachelor's, and master's degrees and post-bachelor's certificates. Challenging opportunities include advanced placement credit, accelerated degree programs, freshman honors college, an honors program, double majors, independent study, and a senior project. Special programs include cooperative education, internships, summer session for credit, off-campus study, study-abroad, and Army and Air Force ROTC. The most frequently chosen baccalaureate fields are business/marketing, health professions and related sciences, and education. The faculty at The Mount has 119 full-time members, 57% with terminal degrees. The student-faculty ratio is 14:1.

Students of The Mount The student body totals 2,067, of whom 1,842 are undergraduates. 68.6% are women and 31.4% are men. Students come from 16 states and territories and 13 other countries. 88% are from Ohio. 1.5% are international students. 86% returned for their sophomore year.

Applying The Mount requires SAT I or ACT, a high school transcript, minimum SAT score of 960 or ACT score of 19, and a minimum high school GPA of 2.25, and in some cases an essay, an interview, and 1 recommendation. The school recommends a minimum high school GPA of 3.0. Application deadline: 8/15; 3/1 priority date for financial aid.

COLLEGE OF MOUNT SAINT VINCENT

Riverdale, NY

Suburban setting ■ Private ■ Independent ■ Coed

Web site: www.mountsaintvincent.edu

Contact: Mr. Timothy Nash, Dean of Admissions and Financial Aid, 6301 Riverdale Avenue, Riverdale, NY 10471-1093

Telephone: 718-405-3268 or toll-free 800-665-CMSV **Fax:** 718-549-7945

E-mail: admissns@mountsaintvincent.edu

Getting in Last Year 1,292 applied; 76% were accepted; 327 enrolled (33%).

Financial Matters $18,180 tuition and fees (2002–03); $7550 room and board; 74% average percent of need met; $15,000 average financial aid amount received per undergraduate.

Academics Mount Saint Vincent awards associate, bachelor's, and master's degrees and post-master's certificates. Challenging opportunities include advanced placement credit, accelerated degree programs, student-designed majors, freshman honors college, an honors program, double majors, independent study, and a senior project. Special programs include internships, summer session for credit, off-campus study, study-abroad, and Army and Air Force ROTC. The most frequently chosen baccalaureate fields are health professions and related sciences, business/marketing, and education. The faculty at Mount Saint Vincent has 69 full-time members, 90% with terminal degrees. The student-faculty ratio is 12:1.

Students of Mount Saint Vincent The student body totals 1,568, of whom 1,205 are undergraduates. 77.2% are women and 22.8% are men. Students come from 13 states and territories and 5 other countries. 93% are from New York. 1.4% are international students. 82% returned for their sophomore year.

Applying Mount Saint Vincent requires an essay, SAT I or ACT, a high school transcript, 1 recommendation, and a minimum high school GPA of 2.0, and in some cases an interview. The school recommends an interview and 2 recommendations. Application deadline: rolling admissions; 3/1 priority date for financial aid. Early and deferred admission are possible.

THE COLLEGE OF NEW JERSEY

Ewing, NJ

Suburban setting ■ Public ■ State-supported ■ Coed

Web site: www.tcnj.edu

Contact: Ms. Lisa Angeloni, Dean of Admissions, PO Box 7718, Ewing, NJ 08628

Telephone: 609-771-2131 or toll-free 800-624-0967 **Fax:** 609-637-5174

E-mail: admiss@tcnj.edu

Getting in Last Year 6,323 applied; 48% were accepted; 1,232 enrolled (41%).

Financial Matters $7516 resident tuition and fees (2002–03); $11,713 nonresident tuition and fees (2002–03); $7416 room and board; 76% average percent of need met; $2449 average financial aid amount received per undergraduate (2001–02).

Academics TCNJ awards bachelor's and master's degrees. Challenging opportunities include advanced placement credit, an honors program, double majors, independent study, and a senior project. Special programs include internships, summer session for credit, off-campus study, study-abroad, and Army and Air Force ROTC. The most frequently chosen baccalaureate fields are business/marketing, education, and social sciences and history. The faculty at TCNJ has 324 full-time members, 89% with terminal degrees. The student-faculty ratio is 12:1.

Students of TCNJ The student body totals 6,938, of whom 5,961 are undergraduates. 59.4% are women and 40.6% are men. Students come from 22 states and territories. 95% are from New Jersey. 0.2% are international students. 96% returned for their sophomore year.

Applying TCNJ requires an essay, SAT I or ACT, a high school transcript, and a minimum high school GPA of 2.0, and in some cases an interview and art portfolio or music audition. Application deadline: 2/15; 3/1 priority date for financial aid. Early and deferred admission are possible.

THE COLLEGE OF NEW ROCHELLE

New Rochelle, NY

Suburban setting ■ *Private* ■ *Independent* ■ *Women Only*

Web site: cnr.edu

Contact: Ms. Stephanie Decker, Director of Admission, 29 Castle Place, New Rochelle, NY 10805-2339

Telephone: 914-654-5452 or toll-free 800-933-5923 **Fax:** 914-654-5464

E-mail: admission@cnr.edu

Getting in Last Year 861 applied; 57% were accepted; 107 enrolled (22%).

Financial Matters $13,250 tuition and fees (2002–03); $6850 room and board; 100% average percent of need met; $15,071 average financial aid amount received per undergraduate (2001–02).

Academics CNR awards bachelor's and master's degrees and post-bachelor's and post-master's certificates (also offers a non-traditional adult program with significant enrollment not reflected in profile). Challenging opportunities include advanced placement credit, accelerated degree programs, student-designed majors, an honors program, double majors, independent study, and a senior project. Special programs include cooperative education, internships, summer session for credit, off-campus study, and study-abroad. The most frequently chosen baccalaureate fields are health professions and related sciences, psychology, and communications/communication technologies. The faculty at CNR has 88 full-time members, 73% with terminal degrees. The student-faculty ratio is 10:1.

Students of CNR The student body totals 2,853, of whom 951 are undergraduates. Students come from 18 states and territories and 5 other countries. 89% are from New York. 0.5% are international students. 73% returned for their sophomore year.

Applying CNR requires SAT I or ACT and a high school transcript. The school recommends an essay, an interview, and 2 recommendations. Application deadline: rolling admissions. Early and deferred admission are possible.

COLLEGE OF NOTRE DAME OF MARYLAND

Baltimore, MD

Suburban setting ■ *Private* ■ *Independent Religious* ■ *Women Only*

Web site: www.ndm.edu

Contact: Ms. Sharon Bogdan, Associate Vice President for Enrollment Management, 4701 North Charles Street, Baltimore, MD 21210

Telephone: 410-532-5330 or toll-free 800-435-0200 (in-state), 800-435-0300 (out-of-state) **Fax:** 410-532-6287

E-mail: admiss@ndm.edu

Getting in Last Year 400 applied; 75% were accepted; 158 enrolled (53%).

Financial Matters $17,925 tuition and fees (2002–03); $7400 room and board; 100% average percent of need met; $18,851 average financial aid amount received per undergraduate.

Academics Notre Dame awards bachelor's and master's degrees and post-bachelor's and post-master's certificates. Challenging opportunities include advanced placement credit, accelerated degree programs, student-designed majors, an honors program, double majors, independent study, and a senior project. Special programs include internships, summer session for credit, off-campus study, study-abroad, and Army ROTC. The faculty at Notre Dame has 83 full-time members, 78% with terminal degrees. The student-faculty ratio is 13:1.

Students of Notre Dame The student body totals 3,148, of whom 1,691 are undergraduates. Students come from 26 states and territories and 15 other countries. 92% are from Maryland. 1.9% are international students. 82% returned for their sophomore year.

Applying Notre Dame requires an essay, SAT I or ACT, a high school transcript, 2 recommendations, and a minimum high school GPA of 2.0. The school recommends an interview, resume, and a minimum high school GPA of 3.0. Application deadline: 2/15; 2/15 priority date for financial aid. Early and deferred admission are possible.

COLLEGE OF SAINT BENEDICT

Saint Joseph, MN

Small-town setting ■ *Private* ■ *Independent Religious* ■ *Coed, Primarily Women*

Web site: www.csbsju.edu

Contact: Karen Backes, Associate Dean of Admissions, 37 South College Avenue, St. Joseph, MN 56374

Telephone: 320-363-5308 or toll-free 800-544-1489 **Fax:** 320-363-5010

E-mail: admissions@csbsju.edu

Getting in Last Year 1,274 applied; 85% were accepted; 516 enrolled (48%).

Financial Matters $19,226 tuition and fees (2002–03); $5789 room and board; 92% average percent of need met; $16,190 average financial aid amount received per undergraduate.

Academics St. Ben's awards bachelor's degrees (coordinate with Saint John's University for men). Challenging opportunities include advanced placement credit, accelerated degree programs, student-designed majors, an honors program, double majors, independent study, and a senior project. Special programs include internships, off-campus study, study-abroad, and Army ROTC. The most frequently chosen baccalaureate fields are business/marketing, English, and health professions and related sciences. The faculty at St. Ben's has 139 full-time members, 81% with terminal degrees. The student-faculty ratio is 13:1.

Students of St. Ben's The student body is made up of 2,072 undergraduates. 100% are women. Students come from 31 states and territories and 20 other countries. 86% are from Minnesota. 3.6% are international students. 88% returned for their sophomore year.

Applying St. Ben's requires an essay, SAT I or ACT, a high school transcript, and 1 recommendation. The school recommends an interview and a minimum high school GPA of 3.0. Application deadline: rolling admissions; 3/15 priority date for financial aid. Early and deferred admission are possible.

COLLEGE OF ST. CATHERINE

St. Paul, MN

Urban setting ■ *Private* ■ *Independent Religious* ■ *Women Only*

Web site: www.stkate.edu

Contact: Ms. Cory Piper-Hauswirth, Associate Director of Admission and Financial Aid, 2004 Randolph Avenue, St. Paul, MN 55105-1789

Telephone: 651-690-6047 or toll-free 800-945-4599 (in-state) **Fax:** 651-690-8824

E-mail: admissions@stkate.edu

Getting in Last Year 856 applied; 78% were accepted; 402 enrolled (60%).

Financial Matters $18,362 tuition and fees (2002–03); $5170 room and board; 93% average percent of need met; $18,319 average financial aid amount received per undergraduate.

Academics CSC awards associate, bachelor's, master's, and doctoral degrees and post-bachelor's certificates. Challenging opportunities include advanced placement credit, student-designed majors, an honors program, double majors, independent study, and a senior project. Special programs include internships, summer session for credit, off-campus study, study-abroad, and Air Force ROTC. The most frequently chosen baccalaureate fields are health professions and related sciences, education, and business/marketing. The faculty at CSC has 169 full-time members, 70% with terminal degrees. The student-faculty ratio is 12:1.

Students of CSC The student body totals 4,704, of whom 3,569 are undergraduates. Students come from 31 states and territories and 30 other countries. 90% are from Minnesota. 2% are international students. 76% returned for their sophomore year.

Applying CSC requires SAT I or ACT, a high school transcript, and 1 recommendation, and in some cases an essay and an interview. The school recommends an interview. Application deadline: 8/15; 4/1 priority date for financial aid. Deferred admission is possible.

COLLEGE OF SAINT ELIZABETH

Morristown, NJ

Suburban setting ■ *Private* ■ *Independent Religious* ■ *Women Only*

Web site: www.cse.edu

Contact: Ms. Donna Tatarka, Dean of Admissions, 2 Convent Road, Morristown, NJ 07960-6989

Telephone: 973-290-4700 or toll-free 800-210-7900 **Fax:** 973-290-4710

E-mail: apply@cse.edu

Getting in Last Year 431 applied; 82% were accepted; 151 enrolled (43%).

Financial Matters $16,375 tuition and fees (2002–03); $7750 room and board; 85% average percent of need met; $15,328 average financial aid amount received per undergraduate (2001–02).

College of Saint Elizabeth (continued)

Academics CSE awards bachelor's and master's degrees and post-bachelor's certificates (also offers co-ed adult undergraduate degree program and co-ed graduate programs). Challenging opportunities include advanced placement credit, accelerated degree programs, student-designed majors, an honors program, double majors, independent study, and a senior project. Special programs include internships, summer session for credit, off-campus study, and study-abroad. The most frequently chosen baccalaureate fields are business/marketing, education, and psychology. The faculty at CSE has 58 full-time members, 79% with terminal degrees. The student-faculty ratio is 11:1.

Students of CSE The student body totals 1,772, of whom 1,238 are undergraduates. Students come from 8 states and territories and 22 other countries. 97% are from New Jersey. 4.2% are international students. 88% returned for their sophomore year.

Applying CSE requires an essay, SAT I or ACT, a high school transcript, 2 recommendations, and a minimum high school GPA of 2.0. The school recommends an interview. Application deadline: 8/15; 3/1 priority date for financial aid. Early and deferred admission are possible.

COLLEGE OF ST. JOSEPH

Rutland, VT

Small-town setting ■ Private ■ Independent Religious ■ Coed

Web site: www.csj.edu
Contact: Pat Ryan, Director of Admissions and Marketing, 71 Clement Road, Rutland, VT 05701-3899
Telephone: 802-773-5900 ext. 3206 or toll-free 877-270-9998 (in-state) **Fax:** 802-773-5900 ext. 4
E-mail: admissions@csj.edu

Getting in Last Year 184 applied; 88% were accepted; 4 enrolled (2%).

Financial Matters $12,200 tuition and fees (2002–03); $6400 room and board; 80% average percent of need met; $12,458 average financial aid amount received per undergraduate.

Academics CSJ awards associate, bachelor's, and master's degrees and post-bachelor's certificates. Challenging opportunities include advanced placement credit, accelerated degree programs, double majors, and a senior project. Special programs include internships, summer session for credit, and study-abroad. The most frequently chosen baccalaureate fields are business/marketing, psychology, and liberal arts/general studies. The faculty at CSJ has 14 full-time members, 57% with terminal degrees. The student-faculty ratio is 11:1.

Students of CSJ The student body totals 656, of whom 291 are undergraduates. Students come from 15 states and territories and 2 other countries. 63% are from Vermont. 71% returned for their sophomore year.

Applying CSJ requires an essay, SAT I or ACT, a high school transcript, 2 recommendations, and a minimum high school GPA of 2.0. The school recommends an interview. Application deadline: rolling admissions. Early and deferred admission are possible.

COLLEGE OF SAINT MARY

Omaha, NE

Suburban setting ■ Private ■ Independent Religious ■ Women Only

Web site: www.csm.edu
Contact: Ms. Natalie Vrbka, Senior Admissions Counselor, 1901 South 72nd Street, Omaha, NE 68124-2377
Telephone: 402-399-2405 or toll-free 800-926-5534 **Fax:** 402-399-2412
E-mail: enroll@csm.edu

Getting in Last Year 291 applied; 66% were accepted; 97 enrolled (51%).

Financial Matters $14,940 tuition and fees (2002–03); $5200 room and board; 62% average percent of need met; $10,109 average financial aid amount received per undergraduate.

Academics CSM awards associate and bachelor's degrees. Challenging opportunities include advanced placement credit, accelerated degree programs, double majors, independent study, and a senior project. Special programs include internships, summer session for credit, study-abroad, and Army and Air Force ROTC. The most frequently chosen baccalaureate fields are business/marketing, health professions and related sciences, and education. The faculty at CSM has 42 full-time members, 43% with terminal degrees. The student-faculty ratio is 10:1.

Students of CSM The student body is made up of 852 undergraduates. Students come from 18 states and territories and 6 other countries. 88% are from Nebraska. 0.8% are international students. 68% returned for their sophomore year.

Applying CSM requires SAT I or ACT, a high school transcript, and a minimum high school GPA of 2.0, and in some cases an interview, 2 recommendations, and a minimum high school GPA of 3.0. The school recommends an essay. Application deadline: rolling admissions; 4/1 priority date for financial aid.

THE COLLEGE OF SAINT ROSE

Albany, NY

Urban setting ■ Private ■ Independent ■ Coed

Web site: www.strose.edu
Contact: Ms. Mary Elizabeth Amico, Director of Undergraduate Admissions, 432 Western Avenue, Albany, NY 12203-1419
Telephone: 518-454-5150 or toll-free 800-637-8556 **Fax:** 518-454-2013
E-mail: admit@mail.strose.edu

Getting in Last Year 1,825 applied; 73% were accepted; 526 enrolled (39%).

Financial Matters $14,640 tuition and fees (2002–03); $7016 room and board; 73% average percent of need met; $10,698 average financial aid amount received per undergraduate (2001–02).

Academics CSR awards bachelor's and master's degrees and post-bachelor's and post-master's certificates. Challenging opportunities include advanced placement credit, accelerated degree programs, student-designed majors, double majors, independent study, and a senior project. Special programs include internships, summer session for credit, off-campus study, and study-abroad. The most frequently chosen baccalaureate fields are education, business/marketing, and social sciences and history. The faculty at CSR has 163 full-time members, 75% with terminal degrees. The student-faculty ratio is 15:1.

Students of CSR The student body totals 4,624, of whom 2,924 are undergraduates. 72.6% are women and 27.4% are men. Students come from 20 states and territories and 6 other countries. 94% are from New York. 0.2% are international students. 85% returned for their sophomore year.

Applying CSR requires an essay, SAT I or ACT, a high school transcript, and 1 recommendation, and in some cases an interview. The school recommends an interview and a minimum high school GPA of 3.0. Application deadline: 5/1; 3/1 priority date for financial aid. Deferred admission is possible.

THE COLLEGE OF ST. SCHOLASTICA

Duluth, MN

Suburban setting ■ Private ■ Independent Religious ■ Coed

Web site: www.css.edu
Contact: Mr. Brian Dalton, Vice President for Enrollment Management, 1200 Kenwood Avenue, Duluth, MN 55811-4199
Telephone: 218-723-6053 or toll-free 800-249-6412 **Fax:** 218-723-5991
E-mail: admissions@css.edu

Getting in Last Year 1,055 applied; 88% were accepted; 402 enrolled (43%).

Financial Matters $18,216 tuition and fees (2002–03); $5406 room and board; 82% average percent of need met; $15,908 average financial aid amount received per undergraduate.

Academics St. Scholastica awards bachelor's and master's degrees and post-bachelor's and post-master's certificates. Challenging opportunities include advanced placement credit, accelerated degree programs, student-designed majors, an honors program, double majors, independent study, and a senior project. Special programs include internships, summer session for credit, off-campus study, study-abroad, and Air Force ROTC. The most frequently chosen baccalaureate fields are health professions and related sciences, business/marketing, and biological/life sciences. The faculty at St. Scholastica has 117 full-time members, 78% with terminal degrees. The student-faculty ratio is 13:1.

Students of St. Scholastica The student body totals 2,512, of whom 1,981 are undergraduates. 70.2% are women and 29.8% are men. Students come from 23 states and territories and 11 other countries. 89% are from Minnesota. 1.1% are international students. 76% returned for their sophomore year.

Applying St. Scholastica requires SAT I or ACT and a high school transcript, and in some cases an interview and a minimum high school GPA of 2.0. The school recommends an essay, PSAT, an interview, and recommendations. Application deadline: rolling admissions; 3/15 priority date for financial aid. Early and deferred admission are possible.

THE COLLEGE OF SAINT THOMAS MORE

Fort Worth, TX

Urban setting ■ Private ■ Independent Religious ■ Coed

Web site: www.cstm.edu
Contact: Mrs. Bethany Konlande, Assistant to the Provost, 3020 Lubbock Avenue, Fort Worth, TX 76109-2323
Telephone: 817-923-8459 or toll-free 800-583-6489 (out-of-state) **Fax:** 817-924-3206
E-mail: more-info@cstm.edu

Getting in Last Year 7 enrolled.

Financial Matters $9366 tuition and fees (2002–03); $2300 room only.

Academics CSTM awards associate and bachelor's degrees. Special programs include cooperative education, summer session for credit, and study-abroad. The most frequently chosen baccalaureate field is liberal arts/general studies. The faculty at CSTM has 4 full-time members, 100% with terminal degrees. The student-faculty ratio is 4:1.

Students of CSTM The student body is made up of 30 undergraduates. 46.7% are women and 53.3% are men. Students come from 2 states and territories. 96% are from Texas.

Applying CSTM requires an essay, SAT I or ACT, a high school transcript, 1 recommendation, and a minimum high school GPA of 2.0. The school recommends an interview. Application deadline: rolling admissions. Early and deferred admission are possible.

COLLEGE OF SANTA FE

Santa Fe, NM

Suburban setting ■ *Private* ■ *Independent* ■ *Coed*

Web site: www.csf.edu

Contact: Mr. Dale H. Reinhart, Director of Admissions and Enrollment Management, Admissions Office, 1600 St. Michael's Drive, Santa Fe, NM 87505-7634

Telephone: 505-473-6133 or toll-free 800-456-2673 **Fax:** 505-473-6129

E-mail: admissions@csf.edu

Getting in Last Year 489 applied; 83% were accepted; 364 enrolled (89%).

Financial Matters $18,284 tuition and fees (2002–03); $5484 room and board; 78% average percent of need met; $16,429 average financial aid amount received per undergraduate.

Academics CSF awards associate, bachelor's, and master's degrees. Challenging opportunities include advanced placement credit, accelerated degree programs, student-designed majors, double majors, independent study, and a senior project. Special programs include internships, summer session for credit, off-campus study, study-abroad, and Air Force ROTC. The most frequently chosen baccalaureate fields are business/marketing, visual/performing arts, and education. The faculty at CSF has 70 full-time members, 81% with terminal degrees. The student-faculty ratio is 8:1.

Students of CSF The student body totals 1,722, of whom 1,403 are undergraduates. 62% are women and 38% are men. Students come from 37 states and territories and 3 other countries. 34% are from New Mexico. 0.2% are international students. 60% returned for their sophomore year.

Applying CSF requires an essay, SAT I or ACT, a high school transcript, an interview, 2 recommendations, and portfolio or audition for visual and performing arts programs. The school recommends a minimum high school GPA of 3.0. Application deadline: rolling admissions; 3/15 priority date for financial aid. Early and deferred admission are possible.

THE COLLEGE OF SOUTHEASTERN EUROPE, THE AMERICAN UNIVERSITY OF ATHENS

Athens Greece

Urban setting ■ *Private* ■ *Independent* ■ *Coed*

Web site: www.southeastern.edu.gr

Contact: Ms. Thalia Poulos, Director of Admissions, 17 Patriarchou Ieremiou Street and 117 Alexandras Avenue, Athens Greece

Telephone: 301-725-9301 **Fax:** 30-210-725-9304

E-mail: admissions@southeastern.edu.gr

Getting in Last Year 165 applied; 80% were accepted; 132 enrolled (100%).

Financial Matters $5245 tuition and fees (2002–03); $2900 room only.

Academics CSE awards bachelor's degrees. Challenging opportunities include accelerated degree programs, double majors, independent study, and a senior project. Special programs include cooperative education, internships, summer session for credit, and study-abroad. The most frequently chosen baccalaureate fields are business/marketing, engineering/engineering technologies, and computer/information sciences. The faculty at CSE has 41 full-time members, 59% with terminal degrees. The student-faculty ratio is 9:1.

Students of CSE The student body is made up of 454 undergraduates. 39% are women and 61% are men. 90% returned for their sophomore year.

Applying CSE requires an essay, a high school transcript, an interview, and 2 recommendations. Application deadline: rolling admissions.

COLLEGE OF STATEN ISLAND OF THE CITY UNIVERSITY OF NEW YORK

Staten Island, NY

Urban setting ■ *Public* ■ *State and locally supported* ■ *Coed*

Web site: www.csi.cuny.edu

Contact: Ms. Mary-Beth Riley, Director of Admissions and Recruitment, 2800 Victory Boulevard, Building 2A Room 404, Staten Island, NY 10314

Telephone: 718-982-2011 **Fax:** 718-982-2500

E-mail: recruitment@postbox.csi.cuny.edu

Getting in Last Year 6,521 applied; 100% were accepted; 1,971 enrolled (30%).

Financial Matters $3358 resident tuition and fees (2002–03); $6958 nonresident tuition and fees (2002–03); 53% average percent of need met; $4804 average financial aid amount received per undergraduate.

Academics CSI awards associate, bachelor's, and master's degrees and post-master's certificates. Challenging opportunities include advanced placement credit, accelerated degree programs, freshman honors college, an honors program, double majors, and independent study. Special programs include cooperative education, internships, summer session for credit, off-campus study, and study-abroad. The most frequently chosen baccalaureate fields are business/marketing, liberal arts/general studies, and social sciences and history. The faculty at CSI has 317 full-time members, 81% with terminal degrees. The student-faculty ratio is 21:1.

Students of CSI The student body totals 12,087, of whom 10,615 are undergraduates. 59% are women and 41% are men. Students come from 12 states and territories. 99% are from New York. 2.4% are international students. 83% returned for their sophomore year.

Applying CSI requires SAT I, a high school transcript, and a minimum high school GPA of 2.0. Application deadline: rolling admissions. Deferred admission is possible.

COLLEGE OF THE ATLANTIC

Bar Harbor, ME

Small-town setting ■ *Private* ■ *Independent* ■ *Coed*

Web site: www.coa.edu

Contact: Ms. Sarah G. Baker, Director of Admission, 105 Eden Street, Bar Harbor, ME 04609-1198

Telephone: 207-288-5015 ext. 233 or toll-free 800-528-0025 **Fax:** 207-288-4126

E-mail: inquiry@ecology.coa.edu

Getting in Last Year 282 applied; 71% were accepted; 70 enrolled (35%).

Financial Matters $22,536 tuition and fees (2002–03); $6087 room and board; 89% average percent of need met; $19,800 average financial aid amount received per undergraduate.

Academics COA awards bachelor's and master's degrees. Challenging opportunities include advanced placement credit, accelerated degree programs, student-designed majors, independent study, and a senior project. Special programs include cooperative education, internships, off-campus study, and study-abroad. The faculty at COA has 20 full-time members, 100% with terminal degrees. The student-faculty ratio is 10:1.

Students of COA The student body totals 266, of whom 262 are undergraduates. 60.3% are women and 39.7% are men. Students come from 36 states and territories and 20 other countries. 22% are from Maine. 11.9% are international students. 90% returned for their sophomore year.

Applying COA requires an essay, a high school transcript, and 3 recommendations, and in some cases an interview. The school recommends SAT I and SAT II or ACT, an interview, and a minimum high school GPA of 3.0. Application deadline: 3/1; 2/15 priority date for financial aid. Early and deferred admission are possible.

COLLEGE OF THE HOLY CROSS

Worcester, MA

Suburban setting ■ *Private* ■ *Independent Religious* ■ *Coed*

Web site: www.holycross.edu

Contact: Ms. Ann Bowe McDermott, Director of Admissions, 1 College Street, Worcester, MA 01610-2395

Telephone: 508-793-2443 or toll-free 800-442-2421 **Fax:** 508-793-3888

E-mail: admissions@holycross.edu

Getting in Last Year 4,884 applied; 43% were accepted; 700 enrolled (34%).

Financial Matters $26,440 tuition and fees (2002–03); $8000 room and board; 100% average percent of need met; $18,427 average financial aid amount received per undergraduate (2001–02).

Academics Holy Cross awards bachelor's degrees. Challenging opportunities include advanced placement credit, accelerated degree programs, student-designed majors, an honors program, double majors, independent study, and a senior project. Special programs include internships, off-campus study, study-abroad, and Army, Navy and Air Force ROTC. The most frequently chosen baccalaureate fields are social sciences and history, English, and psychology. The faculty at Holy Cross has 236 full-time members, 94% with terminal degrees. The student-faculty ratio is 11:1.

Students of Holy Cross The student body is made up of 2,801 undergraduates. 52.8% are women and 47.2% are men. Students come from 48 states and territories and 17 other countries. 34% are from Massachusetts. 1.2% are international students. 95% returned for their sophomore year.

Applying Holy Cross requires an essay, SAT II: Writing Test, SAT I and SAT II or ACT, a high school transcript, and 2 recommendations. The school recommends an interview. Application deadline: 1/15; 2/1 for financial aid. Early and deferred admission are possible.

COLLEGE OF THE OZARKS

Point Lookout, MO

Small-town setting ■ *Private* ■ *Independent Religious* ■ *Coed*

College of the Ozarks (continued)

Web site: www.cofo.edu
Contact: Mrs. Gayle Groves, Admissions Secretary, PO Box 17, Point Lookout, MO 65726
Telephone: 417-334-6411 ext. 4217 or toll-free 800-222-0525
Fax: 417-335-2618
E-mail: admiss4@cofo.edu

Getting in Last Year 2,417 applied; 12% were accepted; 269 enrolled (89%).

Financial Matters $200 tuition and fees (2002–03); $2840 room and board; 90% average percent of need met; $12,484 average financial aid amount received per undergraduate (2001–02).

Academics C of O awards bachelor's degrees. Challenging opportunities include advanced placement credit, accelerated degree programs, student-designed majors, an honors program, and a senior project. Special programs include cooperative education, internships, summer session for credit, study-abroad, and Army ROTC. The most frequently chosen baccalaureate fields are education, business/marketing, and protective services/public administration. The faculty at C of O has 73 full-time members, 63% with terminal degrees. The student-faculty ratio is 14:1.

Students of C of O The student body is made up of 1,348 undergraduates. 56.8% are women and 43.2% are men. Students come from 26 states and territories and 22 other countries. 67% are from Missouri. 1.6% are international students. 81% returned for their sophomore year.

Applying C of O requires SAT I or ACT, a high school transcript, an interview, 2 recommendations, and medical history, financial statement. The school recommends an essay and a minimum high school GPA of 2.0. Application deadline: 2/15; 3/15 priority date for financial aid. Early admission is possible.

COLLEGE OF THE SOUTHWEST

Hobbs, NM

Small-town setting ■ Private ■ Independent ■ Coed

Web site: www.csw.edu
Contact: Director of Admissions, 6610 Lovington Highway, Hobbs, NM 88240
Telephone: 505-392-6561 or toll-free 800-530-4400 ext. 1004
Fax: 505-392-6006

Getting in Last Year 102 applied; 49% were accepted; 42 enrolled (84%).

Financial Matters $5800 tuition and fees (2002–03); $3666 room and board; 40% average percent of need met; $7217 average financial aid amount received per undergraduate (2001–02).

Academics CSW awards bachelor's and master's degrees. Challenging opportunities include advanced placement credit, accelerated degree programs, and a senior project. Special programs include internships and summer session for credit. The most frequently chosen baccalaureate fields are education, business/marketing, and psychology. The faculty at CSW has 27 full-time members, 37% with terminal degrees. The student-faculty ratio is 11:1.

Students of CSW The student body totals 886, of whom 637 are undergraduates. 62.6% are women and 37.4% are men. Students come from 10 states and territories and 4 other countries. 79% are from New Mexico. 1.6% are international students. 55% returned for their sophomore year.

Applying CSW requires SAT I or ACT, a high school transcript, 2 recommendations, and medical history. Application deadline: rolling admissions; 4/1 priority date for financial aid. Early and deferred admission are possible.

COLLEGE OF VISUAL ARTS

St. Paul, MN

Urban setting ■ Private ■ Independent ■ Coed

Web site: www.cva.edu
Contact: Ms. Elizabeth Catron, Associate Director of Admissions, 344 Summit Avenue, St. Paul, MN 55102-2124
Telephone: 651-224-3416 or toll-free 800-224-1536 **Fax:** 651-224-8854
E-mail: info@cva.edu

Getting in Last Year 61 applied; 44% were accepted; 27 enrolled (100%).

Financial Matters $14,418 tuition and fees (2002–03); $8625 average financial aid amount received per undergraduate (2001–02).

Academics CVA awards bachelor's degrees. Challenging opportunities include advanced placement credit, an honors program, double majors, independent study, and a senior project. Special programs include internships, summer session for credit, and study-abroad. The most frequently chosen baccalaureate field is visual/performing arts. The faculty at CVA has 10 full-time members, 100% with terminal degrees. The student-faculty ratio is 8:1.

Students of CVA The student body is made up of 228 undergraduates. 53.1% are women and 46.9% are men. Students come from 13 states and territories. 90% are from Minnesota. 0.4% are international students. 77% returned for their sophomore year.

Applying CVA requires an essay, SAT I or ACT, a high school transcript, an interview, portfolio, and a minimum high school GPA of 2.7. The school recommends recommendations and a minimum high school GPA of 3.0. Application deadline: rolling admissions. Deferred admission is possible.

THE COLLEGE OF WILLIAM AND MARY

Williamsburg, VA

Small-town setting ■ Public ■ State-supported ■ Coed

Web site: www.wm.edu
Contact: Ms. Karen R. Cottrell, Associate Provost for Enrollment, PO Box 8795, Williamsburg, VA 23187-8795
Telephone: 757-221-4223 **Fax:** 757-221-1242
E-mail: admiss@facstaff.wm.edu

Getting in Last Year 8,917 applied; 35% were accepted; 1,320 enrolled (43%).

Financial Matters $5484 resident tuition and fees (2002–03); $19,652 nonresident tuition and fees (2002–03); $5489 room and board; 83% average percent of need met; $8154 average financial aid amount received per undergraduate (2001–02).

Academics William and Mary awards bachelor's, master's, doctoral, and first-professional degrees and post-master's certificates. Challenging opportunities include advanced placement credit, accelerated degree programs, student-designed majors, an honors program, double majors, independent study, and a senior project. Special programs include summer session for credit, study-abroad, and Army ROTC. The most frequently chosen baccalaureate fields are social sciences and history, business/marketing, and English. The faculty at William and Mary has 567 full-time members, 92% with terminal degrees. The student-faculty ratio is 12:1.

Students of William and Mary The student body totals 7,645, of whom 5,694 are undergraduates. 56.5% are women and 43.5% are men. Students come from 50 states and territories and 52 other countries. 64% are from Virginia. 1.3% are international students. 95% returned for their sophomore year.

Applying William and Mary requires an essay, SAT I or ACT, and a high school transcript. The school recommends SAT II Subject Tests, SAT II: Writing Test, and 1 recommendation. Application deadline: 1/7; 3/15 for financial aid, with a 2/15 priority date. Early and deferred admission are possible.

THE COLLEGE OF WOOSTER

Wooster, OH

Small-town setting ■ Private ■ Independent Religious ■ Coed

Web site: www.wooster.edu
Contact: Ms. Ruth Vedvik, Director of Admissions, 1189 Beall Avenue, Wooster, OH 44691
Telephone: 330-263-2270 ext. 2118 or toll-free 800-877-9905
Fax: 330-263-2621
E-mail: admissions@wooster.edu

Getting in Last Year 2,392 applied; 72% were accepted; 512 enrolled (30%).

Financial Matters $23,840 tuition and fees (2002–03); $5960 room and board; 98% average percent of need met; $20,629 average financial aid amount received per undergraduate.

Academics Wooster awards bachelor's degrees. Challenging opportunities include advanced placement credit, student-designed majors, double majors, independent study, and a senior project. Special programs include internships, summer session for credit, off-campus study, and study-abroad. The most frequently chosen baccalaureate fields are social sciences and history, English, and biological/life sciences. The faculty at Wooster has 133 full-time members, 95% with terminal degrees. The student-faculty ratio is 13:1.

Students of Wooster The student body is made up of 1,856 undergraduates. 53.2% are women and 46.8% are men. Students come from 39 states and territories and 21 other countries. 56% are from Ohio. 7.3% are international students. 88% returned for their sophomore year.

Applying Wooster requires an essay, SAT I or ACT, a high school transcript, and 2 recommendations. The school recommends an interview. Application deadline: 2/15; 2/15 priority date for financial aid. Early and deferred admission are possible.

COLLINS COLLEGE: A SCHOOL OF DESIGN AND TECHNOLOGY

Tempe, AZ

Urban setting ■ Private ■ Proprietary ■ Coed

Web site: www.collinscollege.edu
Contact: 1140 South Priest, Tempe, AZ 85281
Telephone: 480-966-3000 or toll-free 800-876-7070 (out-of-state)
Fax: 480-966-2599
E-mail: info@collinscollege.edu

Getting in Last Year 2,553 applied; 65% were accepted.

Financial Matters 58% average percent of need met; $10,500 average financial aid amount received per undergraduate (2001–02).

Academics Collins College: A School of Design and Technology awards associate and bachelor's degrees. The most frequently chosen baccalaureate field is visual/performing arts. The faculty at Collins College: A School of Design and Technology has 73 full-time members, 5% with terminal degrees.

Students of Collins College: A School of Design and Technology The student body is made up of 2,142 undergraduates. 33.3% are women and 66.7% are men. Students come from 49 states and territories.

Applying Collins College: A School of Design and Technology requires an essay, a high school transcript, and an interview. The school recommends SAT I or ACT. Application deadline: rolling admissions. Early and deferred admission are possible.

COLORADO CHRISTIAN UNIVERSITY

Lakewood, CO

Suburban setting ■ Private ■ Independent Religious ■ Coed

Web site: www.ccu.edu

Contact: Ms. Kim Myrick, Vice President for Enrollment Management, 180 South Garrison Street, Lakewood, CO 80226

Telephone: 303-963-3403 or toll-free 800-44-FAITH **Fax:** 303-963-3201

E-mail: admission@ccu.edu

Getting in Last Year 896 applied; 58% were accepted; 201 enrolled (39%).

Financial Matters $14,320 tuition and fees (2002–03); $5950 room and board; 95% average percent of need met; $8850 average financial aid amount received per undergraduate.

Academics CCU awards associate, bachelor's, and master's degrees. Challenging opportunities include advanced placement credit, accelerated degree programs, student-designed majors, an honors program, double majors, independent study, and a senior project. Special programs include cooperative education, internships, summer session for credit, off-campus study, study-abroad, and Army ROTC. The most frequently chosen baccalaureate fields are business/marketing, computer/information sciences, and liberal arts/general studies. The faculty at CCU has 56 full-time members. The student-faculty ratio is 12:1.

Students of CCU The student body totals 1,801, of whom 1,691 are undergraduates. 56.8% are women and 43.2% are men. Students come from 48 states and territories and 16 other countries. 48% are from Colorado. 0.7% are international students. 68% returned for their sophomore year.

Applying CCU requires an essay, SAT I or ACT, a high school transcript, and 2 recommendations, and in some cases an interview and 3 recommendations. Application deadline: 8/1. Deferred admission is possible.

THE COLORADO COLLEGE

Colorado Springs, CO

Urban setting ■ Private ■ Independent ■ Coed

Web site: www.coloradocollege.edu

Contact: Mr. Mark Hatch, Dean of Admission and Financial Aid, 900 Block North Cascade, West, Colorado Springs, CO 80903-3294

Telephone: 719-389-6344 or toll-free 800-542-7214 **Fax:** 719-389-6816

E-mail: admission@coloradocollege.edu

Getting in Last Year 3,411 applied; 53% were accepted; 482 enrolled (26%).

Financial Matters $26,333 tuition and fees (2002–03); $6480 room and board; 95% average percent of need met; $21,385 average financial aid amount received per undergraduate.

Academics CC awards bachelor's and master's degrees (master's degree in education only). Challenging opportunities include advanced placement credit, student-designed majors, double majors, independent study, and a senior project. Special programs include internships, summer session for credit, off-campus study, study-abroad, and Army ROTC. The most frequently chosen baccalaureate fields are social sciences and history, biological/life sciences, and English. The faculty at CC has 163 full-time members, 97% with terminal degrees. The student-faculty ratio is 9:1.

Students of CC The student body totals 1,930, of whom 1,902 are undergraduates. 55.8% are women and 44.2% are men. Students come from 52 states and territories and 26 other countries. 33% are from Colorado. 3.3% are international students. 98% returned for their sophomore year.

Applying CC requires an essay, SAT I or ACT, a high school transcript, and 3 recommendations. Application deadline: 1/15; 2/15 for financial aid. Deferred admission is possible.

COLORADO SCHOOL OF MINES

Golden, CO

Small-town setting ■ Public ■ State-supported ■ Coed

Web site: www.mines.edu

Contact: Ms. Tricia Douthit, Associate Director of Admissions, Student Center, 1600 Maple Street, Golden, CO 80401

Telephone: 303-273-3224 or toll-free 800-446-9488 (out-of-state) **Fax:** 303-273-3509

E-mail: admit@mines.edu

Getting in Last Year 2,720 applied; 67% were accepted; 564 enrolled (31%).

Financial Matters $6380 resident tuition and fees (2002–03); $19,570 nonresident tuition and fees (2002–03); $5860 room and board; 100% average percent of need met; $5200 average financial aid amount received per undergraduate.

Academics CSM awards bachelor's, master's, and doctoral degrees. Challenging opportunities include advanced placement credit, accelerated degree programs, an honors program, double majors, independent study, and a senior project. Special programs include cooperative education, internships, summer session for credit, study-abroad, and Army ROTC. The most frequently chosen baccalaureate fields are engineering/engineering technologies, mathematics, and physical sciences. The faculty at CSM has 196 full-time members, 92% with terminal degrees. The student-faculty ratio is 12:1.

Students of CSM The student body totals 3,261, of whom 2,504 are undergraduates. 24.2% are women and 75.8% are men. Students come from 51 states and territories and 62 other countries. 79% are from Colorado. 4.5% are international students. 83% returned for their sophomore year.

Applying CSM requires SAT I or ACT and a high school transcript, and in some cases an essay, an interview, and recommendations. The school recommends rank in upper one-third of high school class. Application deadline: 6/1; 3/1 priority date for financial aid. Deferred admission is possible.

COLORADO STATE UNIVERSITY

Fort Collins, CO

Urban setting ■ Public ■ State-supported ■ Coed

Web site: www.colostate.edu

Contact: Ms. Mary Ontiveros, Director of Admissions, Spruce Hall, Fort Collins, CO 80523-0015

Telephone: 970-491-6909 **Fax:** 970-491-7799

E-mail: admissions@vines.colostate.edu

Getting in Last Year 12,249 applied; 77% were accepted; 3,829 enrolled (40%).

Financial Matters $3435 resident tuition and fees (2002–03); $12,705 nonresident tuition and fees (2002–03); $5780 room and board; 82% average percent of need met; $7522 average financial aid amount received per undergraduate (2001–02).

Academics Colorado State awards bachelor's, master's, doctoral, and first-professional degrees. Challenging opportunities include advanced placement credit, accelerated degree programs, student-designed majors, an honors program, double majors, independent study, and a senior project. Special programs include cooperative education, internships, summer session for credit, off-campus study, study-abroad, and Army and Air Force ROTC. The most frequently chosen baccalaureate fields are business/marketing, agriculture, and engineering/engineering technologies. The faculty at Colorado State has 860 full-time members, 99% with terminal degrees. The student-faculty ratio is 17:1.

Students of Colorado State The student body totals 27,290, of whom 21,677 are undergraduates. 51.3% are women and 48.7% are men. Students come from 59 states and territories and 48 other countries. 80% are from Colorado. 1.1% are international students. 81% returned for their sophomore year.

Applying Colorado State requires SAT I or ACT and a high school transcript. The school recommends an essay and recommendations. Application deadline: 7/1; 3/1 priority date for financial aid. Deferred admission is possible.

COLORADO STATE UNIVERSITY-PUEBLO

Pueblo, CO

Suburban setting ■ Public ■ State-supported ■ Coed

Web site: www.colostate-pueblo.edu

Contact: Ms. Pamela L. Anastassiou, Director of Admissions and Records, 2200 Bonforte Boulevard, Pueblo, CO 81001

Telephone: 719-549-2461 or toll-free 877-872-9653 **Fax:** 719-549-2419

E-mail: info@uscolo.edu

Getting in Last Year 1,634 applied; 83% were accepted; 667 enrolled (49%).

Financial Matters $2681 resident tuition and fees (2002–03); $10,597 nonresident tuition and fees (2002–03); $5624 room and board; 59% average percent of need met; $6560 average financial aid amount received per undergraduate.

Academics Colorado State University-Pueblo awards bachelor's and master's degrees. Challenging opportunities include advanced placement credit, accelerated degree programs, an honors program, double majors, independent study, and a senior project. Special programs include cooperative education, internships, summer session for credit, off-campus study, study-abroad, and Army ROTC. The faculty at Colorado State University-Pueblo has 159 full-time members, 71% with terminal degrees. The student-faculty ratio is 17:1.

Students of Colorado State University-Pueblo The student body totals 5,531, of whom 5,324 are undergraduates. 57.3% are women and 42.7% are men. Students come from 44 states and territories and 37 other countries. 92% are from Colorado. 3.7% are international students. 66% returned for their sophomore year.

Applying Colorado State University-Pueblo requires SAT I or ACT and a high school transcript, and in some cases an essay and recommendations. Application deadline: rolling admissions; 3/1 priority date for financial aid. Deferred admission is possible.

COLORADO TECHNICAL UNIVERSITY

Colorado Springs, CO

Suburban setting ■ Private ■ Proprietary ■ Coed

Web site: www.coloradotech.edu
Contact: Mr. Ron Begora, Director of Admissions, 4435 North Chestnut Street, Colorado Springs, CO 80907-3896
Telephone: 719-598-0200 **Fax:** 719-598-3740
E-mail: rbegora@coloradotech.edu

Getting in Last Year 180 applied; 93% were accepted; 167 enrolled (100%).

Financial Matters $8982 tuition and fees (2002–03).

Academics Colorado Tech awards associate, bachelor's, master's, and doctoral degrees and post-bachelor's certificates. Challenging opportunities include advanced placement credit, accelerated degree programs, double majors, independent study, and a senior project. Special programs include cooperative education, internships, summer session for credit, and Army ROTC. The most frequently chosen baccalaureate fields are engineering/engineering technologies and computer/information sciences. The faculty at Colorado Tech has 35 full-time members, 54% with terminal degrees. The student-faculty ratio is 20:1.

Students of Colorado Tech The student body totals 1,684, of whom 1,215 are undergraduates. 26.1% are women and 73.9% are men. Students come from 10 states and territories. 98% are from Colorado. 0.5% are international students.

Applying Colorado Tech requires (in some cases) an essay and ACT COMPASS. The school recommends SAT I or ACT, a high school transcript, an interview, and a minimum high school GPA of 3.0. Application deadline: rolling admissions. Deferred admission is possible.

COLORADO TECHNICAL UNIVERSITY DENVER CAMPUS

Greenwood Village, CO

Urban setting ■ Private ■ Proprietary ■ Coed

Web site: www.coloradotech.edu
Contact: Ms. Suzanne Hyman, Director of Admissions, 5775 DTC Boulevard, Suite 100, Greenwood Village, CO 80111
Telephone: 303-694-6600 **Fax:** 303-694-6673
E-mail: ctudenver@coloradotech.edu

Getting in Last Year 23 applied; 65% were accepted; 15 enrolled (100%).

Financial Matters $8982 tuition and fees (2002–03).

Academics Colorado Tech awards associate, bachelor's, and master's degrees and post-bachelor's certificates. Challenging opportunities include advanced placement credit, double majors, independent study, and a senior project. Special programs include cooperative education and summer session for credit. The most frequently chosen baccalaureate fields are computer/information sciences and engineering/engineering technologies. The faculty at Colorado Tech has 5 full-time members, 60% with terminal degrees. The student-faculty ratio is 14:1.

Students of Colorado Tech The student body totals 298, of whom 192 are undergraduates. 19.8% are women and 80.2% are men. Students come from 12 states and territories and 7 other countries. 98% are from Colorado. 5.1% are international students.

Applying Colorado Tech requires (in some cases) an essay and ACT COMPASS. The school recommends SAT I or ACT, a high school transcript, an interview, and a minimum high school GPA of 3.0. Application deadline: rolling admissions. Deferred admission is possible.

COLORADO TECHNICAL UNIVERSITY SIOUX FALLS CAMPUS

Sioux Falls, SD

Urban setting ■ Private ■ Proprietary ■ Coed

Web site: www.colotechu.edu
Contact: Ms. Angela Haley, Admissions Advisor/Mentor, 3901 West 59th Street, Sioux Falls, SD 57108
Telephone: 605-361-0200 ext. 113 **Fax:** 605-361-5954
E-mail: callen@sf.coloradotech.edu

Getting in Last Year 133 enrolled.

Financial Matters $9288 tuition and fees (2002–03); 45% average percent of need met; $3500 average financial aid amount received per undergraduate (2000–01).

Academics Colorado Technical University Sioux Falls Campus awards associate, bachelor's, and master's degrees. Challenging opportunities include accelerated degree programs, double majors, and a senior project. Special programs include cooperative education, internships, summer session for credit, and Army ROTC. The most frequently chosen baccalaureate fields are business/marketing, protective services/public administration, and computer/information sciences. The faculty at Colorado Technical University Sioux Falls Campus has 9 full-time members, 33% with terminal degrees. The student-faculty ratio is 18:1.

Students of Colorado Technical University Sioux Falls Campus The student body totals 923, of whom 837 are undergraduates. 56.3% are women and 43.7% are men. Students come from 3 states and territories. 95% are from South Dakota.

Applying Colorado Technical University Sioux Falls Campus requires a high school transcript and an interview. The school recommends ACT. Application deadline: rolling admissions. Early and deferred admission are possible.

COLUMBIA BIBLE COLLEGE

Abbotsford, BC Canada

Urban setting ■ Private ■ Independent Religious ■ Coed

Web site: www.columbiabc.edu
Contact: Ms. Esther Martens, Academic Assistant, 2940 Clearbrook Road, Abbotsford, BC V2T 2Z8
Telephone: 604-853-3358 ext. 306 or toll-free 800-283-0881 **Fax:** 604-853-3063
E-mail: ron.penner@columbiabc.edu

Getting in Last Year 262 applied; 81% were accepted; 88 enrolled (41%).

Financial Matters $4600 tuition and fees (2002–03); $4400 room and board.

Academics CBC awards bachelor's degrees. Challenging opportunities include advanced placement credit, double majors, and independent study. Special programs include cooperative education and internships. The faculty at CBC has 13 full-time members. The student-faculty ratio is 18:1.

Students of CBC The student body is made up of 510 undergraduates. 50% are women and 50% are men. Students come from 5 states and territories and 11 other countries. 60% are from British Columbia. 84% returned for their sophomore year.

Applying CBC requires an essay, a high school transcript, and recommendations, and in some cases an interview. Application deadline: 8/15.

COLUMBIA COLLEGE

Columbia, MO

Small-town setting ■ Private ■ Independent Religious ■ Coed

Web site: www.ccis.edu
Contact: Ms. Regina Morin, Director of Admissions, 1001 Rogers Street, Columbia, MO 65216
Telephone: 573-875-7352 or toll-free 800-231-2391 ext. 7366 **Fax:** 573-875-7506
E-mail: admissions@ccis.edu

Getting in Last Year 666 applied; 63% were accepted; 160 enrolled (38%).

Financial Matters $10,926 tuition and fees (2002–03); $4666 room and board; 61% average percent of need met; $12,167 average financial aid amount received per undergraduate.

Academics Columbia College awards associate, bachelor's, and master's degrees (offers continuing education program with significant enrollment not reflected in profile). Challenging opportunities include advanced placement credit, accelerated degree programs, student-designed majors, an honors program, double majors, independent study, and a senior project. Special programs include cooperative education, internships, summer session for credit, off-campus study, study-abroad, and Army, Navy and Air Force ROTC. The most frequently chosen baccalaureate fields are business/marketing, liberal arts/general studies, and education. The faculty at Columbia College has 51 full-time members, 76% with terminal degrees. The student-faculty ratio is 12:1.

Students of Columbia College The student body totals 1,038, of whom 886 are undergraduates. 56.5% are women and 43.5% are men. Students come from 19 states and territories and 32 other countries. 94% are from Missouri. 6.6% are international students. 61% returned for their sophomore year.

Applying Columbia College requires ACT, a high school transcript, and a minimum high school GPA of 2.0, and in some cases an essay, an interview, and recommendations. The school recommends SAT I and rank in upper 50% of high school class. Application deadline: rolling admissions; 3/1 priority date for financial aid. Early and deferred admission are possible.

COLUMBIA COLLEGE

New York, NY

Urban setting ■ Private ■ Independent ■ Coed

Web site: www.college.columbia.edu
Contact: Mr. Eric Furda, Director of Undergraduate Admissions, 1130 Amsterdam Avenue MC 2807, New York, NY 10027
Telephone: 212-854-2522 **Fax:** 212-854-1209

Getting in Last Year 14,129 applied; 12% were accepted; 1,038 enrolled (63%).

Financial Matters $28,206 tuition and fees (2002–03); $9736 room and board; 100% average percent of need met; $25,327 average financial aid amount received per undergraduate.

Academics Columbia awards bachelor's degrees. Challenging opportunities include advanced placement credit, accelerated degree programs, student-designed majors, double majors, and a senior project. Special programs include internships, summer session for credit, off-campus study, study-abroad, and

Army, Navy and Air Force ROTC. The faculty at Columbia has 659 full-time members. The student-faculty ratio is 7:1.

Students of Columbia The student body is made up of 4,109 undergraduates. 50.5% are women and 49.5% are men. Students come from 54 states and territories and 72 other countries. 25% are from New York. 4.9% are international students. 98% returned for their sophomore year.

Applying Columbia requires an essay, SAT II Subject Tests, SAT II: Writing Test, SAT I or ACT, a high school transcript, and 3 recommendations. Application deadline: 1/2; 2/10 for financial aid. Early and deferred admission are possible.

COLUMBIA COLLEGE

Columbia, SC

Suburban setting ■ Private ■ Independent Religious ■ Women Only

Web site: www.columbiacollegesc.edu

Contact: Ms. Julie King, Director of Freshman Admissions, 1301 Columbia College Drive, Columbia, SC 29203

Telephone: 803-786-3871 or toll-free 800-277-1301 **Fax:** 803-786-3674

E-mail: admissions@colacoll.edu

Getting in Last Year 994 applied; 26% were accepted; 251 enrolled (96%).

Financial Matters $16,970 tuition and fees (2002–03); $5240 room and board; 89% average percent of need met; $15,305 average financial aid amount received per undergraduate.

Academics Columbia College awards bachelor's and master's degrees. Challenging opportunities include advanced placement credit, accelerated degree programs, student-designed majors, freshman honors college, an honors program, double majors, independent study, and a senior project. Special programs include internships, summer session for credit, study-abroad, and Army ROTC. The most frequently chosen baccalaureate fields are education, business/marketing, and protective services/public administration. The faculty at Columbia College has 96 full-time members, 81% with terminal degrees. The student-faculty ratio is 10:1.

Students of Columbia College The student body totals 1,474, of whom 1,203 are undergraduates. Students come from 17 states and territories and 9 other countries. 96% are from South Carolina. 0.8% are international students. 67% returned for their sophomore year.

Applying Columbia College requires SAT I or ACT, a high school transcript, and 1 recommendation, and in some cases an interview. The school recommends a minimum high school GPA of 3.0. Application deadline: rolling admissions; 4/1 priority date for financial aid. Early and deferred admission are possible.

COLUMBIA COLLEGE CHICAGO

Chicago, IL

Urban setting ■ Private ■ Independent ■ Coed

Web site: www.colum.edu

Contact: Mr. Murphy Monroe, Director of Admissions and Recruitment, 600 South Michigan Avenue, Chicago, IL 60605-1996

Telephone: 312-663-1600 ext. 7133

E-mail: admissions@mail.colum.edu

Getting in Last Year 3,199 applied; 90% were accepted; 1,699 enrolled (59%).

Financial Matters $14,104 tuition and fees (2002–03); $6305 room and board.

Academics Columbia awards bachelor's and master's degrees and post-bachelor's certificates. Challenging opportunities include advanced placement credit, student-designed majors, and independent study. Special programs include internships, summer session for credit, off-campus study, and study-abroad. The most frequently chosen baccalaureate fields are communications/communication technologies, liberal arts/general studies, and visual/performing arts. The faculty at Columbia has 288 full-time members. The student-faculty ratio is 13:1.

Students of Columbia The student body totals 9,803, of whom 9,257 are undergraduates. 51.2% are women and 48.8% are men. Students come from 50 states and territories and 73 other countries. 78% are from Illinois. 2.6% are international students.

Applying Columbia requires an essay, a high school transcript, and recommendations, and in some cases an interview. The school recommends SAT I or ACT, an interview, and a minimum high school GPA of 2.0. Application deadline: 8/15; 8/15 priority date for financial aid. Deferred admission is possible.

COLUMBIA COLLEGE HOLLYWOOD

Tarzana, CA

Urban setting ■ Private ■ Independent ■ Coed

Web site: www.columbiacollege.edu

Contact: Ms. Amanda Kraus, Admissions Director, 18618 Oxnard Street, Tarzana, CA 91356

Telephone: 818-345-8414 **Fax:** 818-345-9053

E-mail: cchadfin@columbiacollege.edu

Getting in Last Year 56 applied; 93% were accepted; 32 enrolled (62%).

Financial Matters $10,725 tuition and fees (2002–03); $3827 average financial aid amount received per undergraduate (2001–02).

Academics CCH awards associate and bachelor's degrees. Accelerated degree programs are a challenging opportunity. Summer session for credit is a special program. The most frequently chosen baccalaureate field is communications/communication technologies. The faculty at CCH has 27 full-time members, 7% with terminal degrees. The student-faculty ratio is 5:1.

Students of CCH The student body is made up of 133 undergraduates. 33.8% are women and 66.2% are men. Students come from 23 states and territories. 53% are from California. 83% returned for their sophomore year.

Applying CCH requires an essay, a high school transcript, an interview, 2 recommendations, and a minimum high school GPA of 2.0. The school recommends SAT I. Application deadline: rolling admissions; 2/24 priority date for financial aid. Deferred admission is possible.

COLUMBIA COLLEGE OF NURSING

Milwaukee, WI

Urban setting ■ Private ■ Independent ■ Coed, Primarily Women

Web site: www.ccon.edu

Contact: Ms. Amy Dobson, Dean of Admissions, Carroll College, 100 North East Avenue, Milwaukee, WI 53186

Telephone: 414-256-1219 **Fax:** 262-524-7646

E-mail: jwiseman@ccadmin.cc.edu

Financial Matters $14,615 tuition and fees (2002–03); $3750 room and board; 100% average percent of need met; $13,219 average financial aid amount received per undergraduate (2000–01 estimated).

Academics Columbia College of Nursing awards bachelor's degrees. Challenging opportunities include advanced placement credit, an honors program, double majors, independent study, and a senior project. Special programs include summer session for credit and off-campus study. The most frequently chosen baccalaureate field is health professions and related sciences. The faculty at Columbia College of Nursing has 10 full-time members, 50% with terminal degrees. The student-faculty ratio is 18:1.

Students of Columbia College of Nursing The student body is made up of 175 undergraduates. 87% are from Wisconsin. 63% returned for their sophomore year.

Applying Columbia College of Nursing requires SAT I or ACT and a high school transcript, and in some cases an essay. The school recommends an essay, an interview, and 1 recommendation. Application deadline: rolling admissions.

COLUMBIA INTERNATIONAL UNIVERSITY

Columbia, SC

Suburban setting ■ Private ■ Independent Religious ■ Coed

Web site: www.ciu.edu

Contact: Miss Kandi A. Mulligan, Director of College Admissions, PO Box 3122, Columbia, SC 29230-3122

Telephone: 803-754-4100 ext. 3024 or toll-free 800-777-2227 ext. 3024 **Fax:** 803-786-4041

E-mail: yesciu@ciu.edu

Getting in Last Year 310 applied; 65% were accepted; 116 enrolled (57%).

Financial Matters $10,688 tuition and fees (2002–03); $4940 room and board; 53% average percent of need met; $8397 average financial aid amount received per undergraduate.

Academics CIU awards associate, bachelor's, master's, doctoral, and first-professional degrees and post-bachelor's certificates. Challenging opportunities include advanced placement credit, accelerated degree programs, double majors, and independent study. Special programs include cooperative education, internships, summer session for credit, off-campus study, and study-abroad. The faculty at CIU has 27 full-time members. The student-faculty ratio is 17:1.

Students of CIU The student body totals 1,022, of whom 634 are undergraduates. 56.5% are women and 43.5% are men. Students come from 39 states and territories. 43% are from South Carolina. 2.7% are international students. 78% returned for their sophomore year.

Applying CIU requires an essay, SAT I or ACT, 4 recommendations, and a minimum high school GPA of 2.0, and in some cases a high school transcript and an interview. Application deadline: rolling admissions; 3/17 for financial aid. Deferred admission is possible.

COLUMBIA SOUTHERN UNIVERSITY

Orange Beach, AL

Private ■ Proprietary ■ Coed

Web site: www.columbiasouthern.edu

Contact: Mr. Poche Waguespack, Dean of Students, 24847 Commercial Avenue, Orange Beach, AL 36561

Telephone: 251-981-3771 ext. 110 or toll-free 800-977-8449

E-mail: tommy@columbiasouthern.edu

Financial Matters $3000 tuition and fees (2002–03).

Academics Columbia Southern University awards associate, bachelor's, and master's degrees (offers only distance learning degree programs). A senior project

Columbia Southern University (continued)

is a challenging opportunity. The most frequently chosen baccalaureate fields are business/marketing, natural resources/environmental science, and health professions and related sciences. The faculty at Columbia Southern University has 1 full-time members, 100% with terminal degrees.

Students of Columbia Southern University The student body totals 2,200, of whom 1,600 are undergraduates. Students come from 54 states and territories and 42 other countries.

Applying Application deadline: rolling admissions.

COLUMBIA UNION COLLEGE

Takoma Park, MD

Suburban setting ■ Private ■ Independent Religious ■ Coed

Web site: www.cuc.edu
Contact: Mr. Emil John, Director of Admissions, 7600 Flower Avenue, Takoma Park, MD 20912-7796
Telephone: 301-891-4502 or toll-free 800-835-4212 **Fax:** 301-891-4230
E-mail: enroll@cuc.edu

Getting in Last Year 739 applied; 63% were accepted; 178 enrolled (38%).

Financial Matters $14,548 tuition and fees (2002–03); $5043 room and board.

Academics CUC awards associate, bachelor's, and master's degrees. Challenging opportunities include advanced placement credit, accelerated degree programs, student-designed majors, double majors, independent study, and a senior project. Special programs include cooperative education, internships, summer session for credit, off-campus study, and study-abroad. The most frequently chosen baccalaureate fields are business/marketing, psychology, and computer/information sciences. The faculty at CUC has 54 full-time members, 41% with terminal degrees. The student-faculty ratio is 13:1.

Students of CUC The student body totals 1,162, of whom 1,154 are undergraduates. 62.7% are women and 37.3% are men. Students come from 37 states and territories and 38 other countries. 57% are from Maryland. 1.6% are international students. 52% returned for their sophomore year.

Applying CUC requires SAT I or ACT, a high school transcript, 2 recommendations, and a minimum high school GPA of 2.50, and in some cases an essay and an interview. Application deadline: rolling admissions; 3/1 priority date for financial aid. Early and deferred admission are possible.

COLUMBIA UNIVERSITY, SCHOOL OF GENERAL STUDIES

New York, NY

Urban setting ■ Private ■ Independent ■ Coed

Web site: www.gs.columbia.edu
Contact: Mr. Carlos A. Porro, Director of Admissions, Mail Code 4101, Lewisohn Hall, 2970 Broadway, New York, NY 10027-9829
Telephone: 212-854-2772 or toll-free 800-895-1169 (out-of-state)
Fax: 212-854-6316
E-mail: gsdegree@columbia.edu

Getting in Last Year 752 applied; 47% were accepted.

Financial Matters $27,267 tuition and fees (2002–03); $6240 room only.

Academics School of General Studies awards bachelor's degrees and post-bachelor's certificates. Challenging opportunities include advanced placement credit, accelerated degree programs, student-designed majors, an honors program, double majors, and a senior project. Special programs include internships, summer session for credit, off-campus study, and study-abroad. The faculty at School of General Studies has 632 full-time members, 100% with terminal degrees. The student-faculty ratio is 7:1.

Students of School of General Studies The student body is made up of 1,167 undergraduates. Students come from 36 states and territories. 62% are from New York. 90% returned for their sophomore year.

Applying School of General Studies requires an essay, a high school transcript, recommendations, and General Studies Admissions Exam, and in some cases SAT I or ACT and an interview. Application deadline: 7/1; 7/1 priority date for financial aid. Deferred admission is possible.

COLUMBIA UNIVERSITY, THE FU FOUNDATION SCHOOL OF ENGINEERING AND APPLIED SCIENCE

New York, NY

Urban setting ■ Private ■ Independent ■ Coed

Web site: www.engineering.columbia.edu
Contact: Mr. Eric J. Furda, Director of Undergraduate Admissions, 1130 Amsterdam Avenue MC 2807, New York, NY 10027
Telephone: 212-854-2522 **Fax:** 212-854-1209

Getting in Last Year 2,025 applied; 31% were accepted; 333 enrolled (53%).

Financial Matters $28,206 tuition and fees (2002–03); $9736 room and board; 100% average percent of need met; $25,613 average financial aid amount received per undergraduate.

Academics Columbia SEAS awards bachelor's, master's, and doctoral degrees. Advanced placement credit is a challenging opportunity. Special programs include internships, summer session for credit, study-abroad, and Army, Navy and Air Force ROTC. The most frequently chosen baccalaureate fields are engineering/engineering technologies, social sciences and history, and computer/information sciences. The faculty at Columbia SEAS has 121 full-time members. The student-faculty ratio is 7:1.

Students of Columbia SEAS The student body is made up of 1,301 undergraduates. 26.1% are women and 73.9% are men. Students come from 44 states and territories and 59 other countries. 30% are from New York. 10.3% are international students. 97% returned for their sophomore year.

Applying Columbia SEAS requires an essay, SAT II Subject Tests, SAT II: Writing Test, SAT I or ACT, a high school transcript, and 3 recommendations. The school recommends an interview. Application deadline: 1/2; 2/10 for financial aid. Early and deferred admission are possible.

COLUMBUS COLLEGE OF ART AND DESIGN

Columbus, OH

Urban setting ■ Private ■ Independent ■ Coed

Web site: www.ccad.edu
Contact: Mr. Thomas E. Green, Director of Admissions, 107 North Ninth Street, Columbus, OH 43215-1758
Telephone: 614-224-9101 **Fax:** 614-232-8344
E-mail: brooke@ccad.edu

Getting in Last Year 801 applied; 71% were accepted; 188 enrolled (33%).

Financial Matters $17,660 tuition and fees (2002–03); $6300 room and board; 65% average percent of need met; $11,226 average financial aid amount received per undergraduate (2001–02).

Academics CCAD awards bachelor's degrees. Challenging opportunities include advanced placement credit, double majors, independent study, and a senior project. Special programs include internships, summer session for credit, and off-campus study. The faculty at CCAD has 80 full-time members, 64% with terminal degrees. The student-faculty ratio is 11:1.

Students of CCAD The student body is made up of 1,681 undergraduates. 52.5% are women and 47.5% are men. Students come from 30 states and territories and 11 other countries. 76% are from Ohio. 4.6% are international students. 85% returned for their sophomore year.

Applying CCAD requires an essay, SAT I or ACT, a high school transcript, portfolio, and a minimum high school GPA of 2.0, and in some cases recommendations. The school recommends an interview. Application deadline: rolling admissions; 3/3 priority date for financial aid. Deferred admission is possible.

COLUMBUS STATE UNIVERSITY

Columbus, GA

Suburban setting ■ Public ■ State-supported ■ Coed

Web site: www.colstate.edu
Contact: Ms. Susan Lovell, Associate Director of Admissions, 4225 University Avenue, Columbus, GA 31907-5645
Telephone: 706-568-2035 ext. 1681 or toll-free 866-264-2035
Fax: 706-568-2462

Financial Matters $2466 resident tuition and fees (2002–03); $8476 nonresident tuition and fees (2002–03); $5010 room and board; 52% average percent of need met; $4875 average financial aid amount received per undergraduate (2001–02).

Academics Columbus State University awards associate, bachelor's, and master's degrees and post-master's certificates. Challenging opportunities include advanced placement credit, freshman honors college, an honors program, independent study, and a senior project. Special programs include cooperative education, internships, summer session for credit, study-abroad, and Army ROTC. The faculty at Columbus State University has 218 full-time members, 73% with terminal degrees. The student-faculty ratio is 18:1.

Students of Columbus State University The student body totals 6,250, of whom 5,319 are undergraduates. 60.8% are women and 39.2% are men. Students come from 35 states and territories and 40 other countries. 93% are from Georgia. 1.7% are international students. 67% returned for their sophomore year.

Applying Columbus State University requires SAT I or ACT, a high school transcript, proof of immunization, and a minimum high school GPA of 2.5, and in some cases SAT II Subject Tests. Application deadline: 7/31; 5/1 priority date for financial aid. Early and deferred admission are possible.

COMMUNITY HOSPITAL OF ROANOKE VALLEY–COLLEGE OF HEALTH SCIENCES

Roanoke, VA

Urban setting ■ Private ■ Independent ■ Coed

Web site: www.chs.edu
Contact: Ms. Connie Cook, Admissions Representative, PO Box 13186, Roanoke, VA 24031-3186
Telephone: 540-985-8563 or toll-free 888-985-8483 **Fax:** 540-985-9773
E-mail: jmckeon@chs.edu

Getting in Last Year 303 applied; 35% were accepted; 77 enrolled (73%).

Financial Matters $5430 tuition and fees (2002–03); $2000 room only; 58% average percent of need met; $8457 average financial aid amount received per undergraduate (2001–02).

Academics College of Health Sciences awards associate and bachelor's degrees. Challenging opportunities include advanced placement credit, accelerated degree programs, and a senior project. Special programs include internships and summer session for credit. The most frequently chosen baccalaureate field is health professions and related sciences. The faculty at College of Health Sciences has 41 full-time members, 24% with terminal degrees. The student-faculty ratio is 11:1.

Students of College of Health Sciences The student body is made up of 697 undergraduates. 78.5% are women and 21.5% are men. Students come from 7 states and territories. 93% are from Virginia. 51% returned for their sophomore year.

Applying College of Health Sciences requires an essay, a high school transcript, and a minimum high school GPA of 2.0, and in some cases SAT I or ACT, ACT ASSET, an interview, recommendations, and volunteer experience. The school recommends SAT I. Application deadline: 7/31.

CONCEPTION SEMINARY COLLEGE
Conception, MO

Rural setting ■ Private ■ Independent Religious ■ Men Only

Web site: www.conceptionabbey.org
Contact: Mr. Keith Jiron, Director of Recruitment and Admissions, PO Box 502, Highway 136 & VV, 37174 State Highway VV, Conception, MO 64433
Telephone: 660-944-2886
E-mail: vocations@conception.edu

Getting in Last Year 17 applied; 100% were accepted; 17 enrolled (100%).

Financial Matters $9890 tuition and fees (2002–03); $5790 room and board; 91% average percent of need met; $8864 average financial aid amount received per undergraduate.

Academics Conception Seminary College awards bachelor's degrees. Challenging opportunities include advanced placement credit, double majors, independent study, and a senior project. Off-campus study is a special program. The most frequently chosen baccalaureate field is liberal arts/general studies. The faculty at Conception Seminary College has 20 full-time members, 85% with terminal degrees. The student-faculty ratio is 4:1.

Students of Conception Seminary College The student body is made up of 100 undergraduates. Students come from 18 states and territories and 5 other countries. 33% are from Missouri. 82% returned for their sophomore year.

Applying Conception Seminary College requires an essay, ACT, a high school transcript, 2 recommendations, church certificate, medical history, and a minimum high school GPA of 2.0. Application deadline: 7/31.

CONCORD COLLEGE
Athens, WV

Rural setting ■ Public ■ State-supported ■ Coed

Web site: www.concord.edu
Contact: Mr. Michael Curry, Vice President of Admissions and Financial Aid, 1000 Vermillion Street, Athens, WV 24712
Telephone: 304-384-5248 or toll-free 888-384-5249 **Fax:** 304-384-9044
E-mail: admissions@concord.edu

Getting in Last Year 2,299 applied; 56% were accepted; 603 enrolled (47%).

Financial Matters $2962 resident tuition and fees (2002–03); $6648 nonresident tuition and fees (2002–03); $4628 room and board; 79% average percent of need met; $6321 average financial aid amount received per undergraduate.

Academics Concord awards associate and bachelor's degrees. Challenging opportunities include advanced placement credit, accelerated degree programs, student-designed majors, an honors program, double majors, and independent study. Special programs include internships, summer session for credit, off-campus study, and study-abroad. The most frequently chosen baccalaureate fields are education, business/marketing, and liberal arts/general studies. The faculty at Concord has 102 full-time members, 60% with terminal degrees. The student-faculty ratio is 21:1.

Students of Concord The student body is made up of 3,015 undergraduates. 55.5% are women and 44.5% are men. Students come from 26 states and territories and 23 other countries. 85% are from West Virginia. 64% returned for their sophomore year.

Applying Concord requires SAT I or ACT, a high school transcript, and a minimum high school GPA of 2.0, and in some cases an essay and an interview. The school recommends ACT and an interview. Application deadline: rolling admissions, 1/15 for nonresidents; 4/15 priority date for financial aid. Early admission is possible.

CONCORDIA COLLEGE
Selma, AL

Small-town setting ■ Private ■ Independent Religious ■ Coed

Contact: Ms. Ruthie Orsborn, Director of Admissions, 1804 Green Street, PO Box 1329, Selma, AL 36701
Telephone: 334-874-7143 **Fax:** 334-874-3728

Getting in Last Year 210 enrolled.

Financial Matters $6174 tuition and fees (2002–03); $3600 room and board; 92% average percent of need met; $4410 average financial aid amount received per undergraduate (2001–02).

Academics Concordia College awards associate and bachelor's degrees. Summer session for credit is a special program. The faculty at Concordia College has 17 full-time members, 53% with terminal degrees. The student-faculty ratio is 20:1.

Students of Concordia College The student body is made up of 972 undergraduates. 76.7% are women and 23.3% are men. Students come from 7 states and territories and 5 other countries. 3.7% are international students. 95% returned for their sophomore year.

Applying Concordia College requires ACT, a high school transcript, and a minimum high school GPA of 2.0. Application deadline: 8/15; 4/15 priority date for financial aid. Deferred admission is possible.

CONCORDIA COLLEGE
Moorhead, MN

Suburban setting ■ Private ■ Independent Religious ■ Coed

Web site: www.concordiacollege.edu
Contact: Mr. Scott E. Ellingson, Director of Admissions, 901 8th Street South, Moorhead, MN 56562
Telephone: 218-299-3004 or toll-free 800-699-9897 **Fax:** 218-299-3947
E-mail: admissions@cord.edu

Getting in Last Year 2,383 applied; 87% were accepted; 748 enrolled (36%).

Financial Matters $15,635 tuition and fees (2002–03); $4310 room and board; 32% average percent of need met; $12,375 average financial aid amount received per undergraduate (2001–02).

Academics Concordia awards bachelor's degrees. Challenging opportunities include advanced placement credit, an honors program, double majors, independent study, and a senior project. Special programs include cooperative education, internships, summer session for credit, off-campus study, study-abroad, and Army and Air Force ROTC. The most frequently chosen baccalaureate fields are education, business/marketing, and foreign language/literature. The faculty at Concordia has 199 full-time members, 69% with terminal degrees. The student-faculty ratio is 15:1.

Students of Concordia The student body is made up of 2,775 undergraduates. 62.6% are women and 37.4% are men. Students come from 37 states and territories and 41 other countries. 66% are from Minnesota. 6.1% are international students. 81% returned for their sophomore year.

Applying Concordia requires SAT I or ACT, a high school transcript, and 2 recommendations. The school recommends ACT. Application deadline: rolling admissions. Early and deferred admission are possible.

CONCORDIA COLLEGE
Bronxville, NY

Suburban setting ■ Private ■ Independent Religious ■ Coed

Web site: www.concordia-ny.edu
Contact: Ms. Wendy Folwaczny, Director of Admission, 171 White Plains Road, Bronxville, NY 10708-1998
Telephone: 914-337-9300 ext. 2150 or toll-free 800-YES-COLLEGE **Fax:** 914-395-4636
E-mail: admission@concordia-ny.edu

Getting in Last Year 503 applied; 54% were accepted; 132 enrolled (49%).

Financial Matters $16,800 tuition and fees (2002–03); $7400 room and board.

Academics Concordia awards associate and bachelor's degrees. Challenging opportunities include advanced placement credit, accelerated degree programs, student-designed majors, an honors program, double majors, independent study, and a senior project. Special programs include internships, off-campus study, and study-abroad. The most frequently chosen baccalaureate fields are business/marketing, education, and liberal arts/general studies. The faculty at Concordia has 34 full-time members, 62% with terminal degrees. The student-faculty ratio is 11:1.

Students of Concordia The student body is made up of 662 undergraduates. 60.7% are women and 39.3% are men. Students come from 23 states and territories. 68% are from New York. 3% are international students. 72% returned for their sophomore year.

Applying Concordia requires SAT I or ACT, a high school transcript, and 1 recommendation, and in some cases an interview. The school recommends an essay and a minimum high school GPA of 2.5. Application deadline: 3/15. Early and deferred admission are possible.

CONCORDIA UNIVERSITY

Irvine, CA

Suburban setting ■ Private ■ Independent Religious ■ Coed

Web site: www.cui.edu
Contact: Mr. Paul Marquardt, Director of Undergraduate Admissions, 1530 Concordia West, Irvine, CA 92612-3299
Telephone: 949-854-8002 ext. 1118 or toll-free 800-229-1200
Fax: 949-854-6894
E-mail: admission@cui.edu

Getting in Last Year 878 applied; 28% were accepted; 249 enrolled (100%).

Financial Matters $17,300 tuition and fees (2002–03); $6110 room and board; 87% average percent of need met; $13,500 average financial aid amount received per undergraduate.

Academics Concordia at Irvine awards bachelor's and master's degrees and post-bachelor's certificates. Challenging opportunities include advanced placement credit, accelerated degree programs, student-designed majors, an honors program, double majors, and independent study. Special programs include internships and summer session for credit. The most frequently chosen baccalaureate fields are business/marketing, English, and social sciences and history. The faculty at Concordia at Irvine has 72 full-time members, 67% with terminal degrees. The student-faculty ratio is 14:1.

Students of Concordia at Irvine The student body totals 1,681, of whom 1,289 are undergraduates. 67.2% are women and 32.8% are men. Students come from 25 states and territories and 17 other countries. 85% are from California. 1.5% are international students. 80% returned for their sophomore year.

Applying Concordia at Irvine requires SAT I or ACT, a high school transcript, and 2 recommendations. The school recommends an interview and a minimum high school GPA of 2.8. Application deadline: rolling admissions; 4/30 for financial aid, with a 3/2 priority date. Deferred admission is possible.

CONCORDIA UNIVERSITY

River Forest, IL

Suburban setting ■ Private ■ Independent Religious ■ Coed

Web site: www.curf.edu
Contact: Dr. Evelyn Burdick, Vice President for Enrollment Services, 7400 Augusta Street, River Forest, IL 60305
Telephone: 708-209-3100 or toll-free 800-285-2668 **Fax:** 708-209-3473
E-mail: crfadmis@curf.edu

Getting in Last Year 981 applied; 25% were accepted; 242 enrolled (100%).

Financial Matters $16,900 tuition and fees (2002–03); $5100 room and board; 65% average percent of need met; $13,650 average financial aid amount received per undergraduate.

Academics Concordia awards bachelor's, master's, and doctoral degrees and post-bachelor's and post-master's certificates. Challenging opportunities include advanced placement credit, accelerated degree programs, an honors program, double majors, independent study, and a senior project. Special programs include internships, summer session for credit, off-campus study, and study-abroad. The most frequently chosen baccalaureate fields are education, business/marketing, and health professions and related sciences. The faculty at Concordia has 75 full-time members, 71% with terminal degrees. The student-faculty ratio is 11:1.

Students of Concordia The student body totals 1,802, of whom 1,285 are undergraduates. 68.2% are women and 31.8% are men. Students come from 40 states and territories and 4 other countries. 68% are from Illinois. 0.4% are international students.

Applying Concordia requires SAT I or ACT, a high school transcript, 1 recommendation, minimum ACT score of 20 or SAT I score of 930, and a minimum high school GPA of 2.0, and in some cases an essay and an interview. Application deadline: rolling admissions; 5/3 for financial aid, with a 4/1 priority date. Deferred admission is possible.

CONCORDIA UNIVERSITY

Ann Arbor, MI

Suburban setting ■ Private ■ Independent Religious ■ Coed

Web site: www.cuaa.edu
Contact: Ms. Sydney Wolf, Director of Admissions, 4090 Geddes Road, Ann Arbor, MI 48105
Telephone: 734-995-7322 ext. 7311 or toll-free 800-253-0680
Fax: 734-995-7455
E-mail: admissions@cuaa.edu

Getting in Last Year 306 applied; 87% were accepted; 97 enrolled (36%).

Financial Matters $16,650 tuition and fees (2002–03); $6600 room and board; 87% average percent of need met; $13,648 average financial aid amount received per undergraduate.

Academics Concordia awards associate, bachelor's, and master's degrees. Challenging opportunities include advanced placement credit, accelerated degree programs, student-designed majors, double majors, independent study, and a senior project. Special programs include internships, summer session for credit, off-campus study, study-abroad, and Army and Air Force ROTC. The most frequently chosen baccalaureate fields are business/marketing, education, and health professions and related sciences. The faculty at Concordia has 40 full-time members, 68% with terminal degrees. The student-faculty ratio is 10:1.

Students of Concordia The student body totals 552, of whom 516 are undergraduates. 54.3% are women and 45.7% are men. Students come from 22 states and territories and 3 other countries. 76% are from Michigan. 0.8% are international students. 77% returned for their sophomore year.

Applying Concordia requires SAT I or ACT, a high school transcript, and a minimum high school GPA of 2.5, and in some cases an essay and an interview. The school recommends ACT and 1 recommendation. Application deadline: rolling admissions; 5/1 priority date for financial aid. Deferred admission is possible.

CONCORDIA UNIVERSITY

St. Paul, MN

Urban setting ■ Private ■ Independent Religious ■ Coed

Web site: www.csp.edu
Contact: Ms. Rhonda Behm-Severeid, Director of Undergraduate Admissions, 275 Syndicate North, St. Paul, MN 55104-5494
Telephone: 651-641-8230 or toll-free 800-333-4705 **Fax:** 651-659-0207
E-mail: admiss@csp.edu

Getting in Last Year 754 applied; 53% were accepted; 175 enrolled (44%).

Financial Matters $17,326 tuition and fees (2002–03); $5530 room and board; 75% average percent of need met; $11,051 average financial aid amount received per undergraduate.

Academics Concordia-St. Paul awards associate, bachelor's, and master's degrees. Challenging opportunities include advanced placement credit, accelerated degree programs, student-designed majors, double majors, independent study, and a senior project. Special programs include cooperative education, internships, summer session for credit, off-campus study, study-abroad, and Army and Air Force ROTC. The most frequently chosen baccalaureate fields are business/marketing, education, and communications/communication technologies. The faculty at Concordia-St. Paul has 78 full-time members, 65% with terminal degrees. The student-faculty ratio is 10:1.

Students of Concordia-St. Paul The student body totals 1,921, of whom 1,677 are undergraduates. 61.5% are women and 38.5% are men. Students come from 40 states and territories and 4 other countries. 75% are from Minnesota. 0.4% are international students. 61% returned for their sophomore year.

Applying Concordia-St. Paul requires ACT, a high school transcript, and 2 recommendations, and in some cases an essay. The school recommends an interview and a minimum high school GPA of 2.0. Application deadline: 8/15. Early and deferred admission are possible.

CONCORDIA UNIVERSITY

Seward, NE

Small-town setting ■ Private ■ Independent Religious ■ Coed

Web site: www.cune.edu
Contact: Mr. Pete Kenow, Director of Admissions, 800 North Columbia Avenue, Seward, NE 68434-1599
Telephone: 402-643-7233 or toll-free 800-535-5494 **Fax:** 402-643-4073
E-mail: admiss@seward.ccsn.edu

Getting in Last Year 718 applied; 93% were accepted; 318 enrolled (47%).

Financial Matters $14,546 tuition and fees (2002–03); $4388 room and board; 94% average percent of need met; $13,280 average financial aid amount received per undergraduate.

Academics Concordia University awards bachelor's and master's degrees. Challenging opportunities include advanced placement credit, accelerated degree programs, an honors program, double majors, independent study, and a senior project. Special programs include cooperative education, internships, summer session for credit, off-campus study, study-abroad, and Army and Air Force ROTC. The faculty at Concordia University has 66 full-time members, 82% with terminal degrees. The student-faculty ratio is 14:1.

Students of Concordia University The student body totals 1,425, of whom 1,320 are undergraduates. 55.6% are women and 44.4% are men. Students come from 37 states and territories. 42% are from Nebraska. 80% returned for their sophomore year.

Applying Concordia University requires SAT I or ACT and a high school transcript, and in some cases recommendations. The school recommends an interview and a minimum high school GPA of 2.0. Application deadline: 8/1; 5/31 for financial aid, with a 3/1 priority date. Deferred admission is possible.

CONCORDIA UNIVERSITY

Portland, OR

Urban setting ■ Private ■ Independent Religious ■ Coed

Web site: www.cu-portland.edu

Contact: Dr. Neal F. McBride, Director of Admission, 2811 Northeast Holman, Portland, OR 97211-6099
Telephone: 503-493-6521 or toll-free 800-321-9371 **Fax:** 503-280-8531
E-mail: admissions@portland.edu

Getting in Last Year 573 applied; 71% were accepted; 124 enrolled (30%).

Financial Matters $16,900 tuition and fees (2002–03); $4400 room and board; $13,500 average financial aid amount received per undergraduate.

Academics Concordia Portland awards associate, bachelor's, and master's degrees and post-bachelor's and post-master's certificates. Challenging opportunities include advanced placement credit, accelerated degree programs, student-designed majors, double majors, and a senior project. Special programs include internships, summer session for credit, off-campus study, study-abroad, and Air Force ROTC. The most frequently chosen baccalaureate fields are liberal arts/general studies, business/marketing, and education. The faculty at Concordia Portland has 42 full-time members, 62% with terminal degrees. The student-faculty ratio is 18:1.

Students of Concordia Portland The student body totals 1,074, of whom 831 are undergraduates. 64.1% are women and 35.9% are men. Students come from 24 states and territories. 0.7% are international students. 60% returned for their sophomore year.

Applying Concordia Portland requires an essay, SAT I or ACT, a high school transcript, 1 recommendation, and a minimum high school GPA of 2.5, and in some cases an interview. The school recommends an interview. Application deadline: rolling admissions. Deferred admission is possible.

CONCORDIA UNIVERSITY

Montréal, QC Canada

Urban setting ■ Public ■ Coed

Web site: www.concordia.ca
Contact: Ms. Assunta Fargnoli, Assistant Registrar, Admissions Application Center, PO Box 2900, Montréal, QC H3G 2S2 Canada
Telephone: 514-848-2628 **Fax:** 514-848-8621
E-mail: admreg@alcor.concordia.ca

Getting in Last Year 16,196 applied; 63% were accepted.

Financial Matters $2595 resident tuition and fees (2002–03); $4785 nonresident tuition and fees (2002–03); $6500 room and board.

Academics Concordia awards bachelor's, master's, and doctoral degrees and post-bachelor's and post-master's certificates. Challenging opportunities include advanced placement credit, accelerated degree programs, student-designed majors, an honors program, double majors, independent study, and a senior project. Special programs include cooperative education, internships, summer session for credit, off-campus study, and study-abroad. The most frequently chosen baccalaureate fields are law/legal studies, business/marketing, and visual/performing arts. The faculty at Concordia has 769 full-time members, 100% with terminal degrees. The student-faculty ratio is 30:1.

Students of Concordia The student body totals 29,861, of whom 25,417 are undergraduates. 52.6% are women and 47.4% are men. Students come from 10 states and territories and 123 other countries. 76% returned for their sophomore year.

Applying Concordia requires a high school transcript and a minimum high school GPA of 2.76, and in some cases an essay, an interview, and 2 recommendations. Application deadline: 3/1; 3/31 for financial aid.

CONCORDIA UNIVERSITY AT AUSTIN

Austin, TX

Urban setting ■ Private ■ Independent Religious ■ Coed

Web site: www.concordia.edu
Contact: Mr. Jay Krause, Vice President for Enrollment Services, 3400 Interstate 35 North, Austin, TX 78705-2799
Telephone: 512-486-2000 ext. 1107 or toll-free 800-285-4252
Fax: 512-459-8517
E-mail: ctxadmis@crf.cuis.edu

Getting in Last Year 526 applied; 76% were accepted; 184 enrolled (46%).

Financial Matters $14,410 tuition and fees (2002–03); $6150 room and board; 81% average percent of need met; $10,370 average financial aid amount received per undergraduate (2001–02).

Academics Concordia awards associate, bachelor's, and master's degrees and post-bachelor's certificates. Challenging opportunities include advanced placement credit, accelerated degree programs, an honors program, double majors, independent study, and a senior project. Special programs include internships, summer session for credit, study-abroad, and Army and Air Force ROTC. The most frequently chosen baccalaureate fields are business/marketing, education, and psychology. The faculty at Concordia has 34 full-time members, 71% with terminal degrees. The student-faculty ratio is 16:1.

Students of Concordia The student body totals 1,076, of whom 978 are undergraduates. 55.9% are women and 44.1% are men. Students come from 26 states and territories. 94% are from Texas. 1.1% are international students. 55% returned for their sophomore year.

Applying Concordia requires SAT I or ACT, a high school transcript, and a minimum high school GPA of 2.5, and in some cases an interview and recommendations. Application deadline: rolling admissions; 7/1 for financial aid, with a 4/15 priority date. Early and deferred admission are possible.

CONCORDIA UNIVERSITY COLLEGE OF ALBERTA

Edmonton, AB Canada

Urban setting ■ Private ■ Independent Religious ■ Coed

Web site: www.concordia.ab.ca
Contact: Mr. Tony Norrad, Dean of Admissions and Financial Aid, 7128 Ada Boulevard, Edmonton, AB T5B 4E4 Canada
Telephone: 780-479-9224 or toll-free 800-479-5200 **Fax:** 780-474-1933
E-mail: admits@concordia.ab.ca

Getting in Last Year 1,264 applied; 41% were accepted.

Financial Matters $5349 tuition and fees (2002–03); $5168 room and board.

Academics Concordia University College of Alberta awards bachelor's degrees and post-bachelor's certificates. Challenging opportunities include advanced placement credit, an honors program, double majors, independent study, and a senior project. Special programs include internships and study-abroad. The most frequently chosen baccalaureate fields are education, psychology, and biological/life sciences. The faculty at Concordia University College of Alberta has 59 full-time members. The student-faculty ratio is 18:1.

Students of Concordia University College of Alberta The student body is made up of 1,524 undergraduates. Students come from 7 states and territories and 15 other countries.

Applying Concordia University College of Alberta requires a high school transcript and a minimum high school GPA of 2.0, and in some cases an essay, an interview, and 2 recommendations. Application deadline: 6/30. Early admission is possible.

CONCORDIA UNIVERSITY WISCONSIN

Mequon, WI

Suburban setting ■ Private ■ Independent Religious ■ Coed

Web site: www.cuw.edu
Contact: Mr. Ken Gaschk, Director of Admissions, 12800 North Lake Shore Drive, Mequon, WI 53097
Telephone: 262-243-4305 ext. 4305 or toll-free 888-628-9472
Fax: 262-243-4351
E-mail: admissions@cuw.edu

Getting in Last Year 1,009 applied; 79% were accepted; 294 enrolled (37%).

Financial Matters $14,560 tuition and fees (2002–03); $5520 room and board; 80% average percent of need met; $11,938 average financial aid amount received per undergraduate (2001–02).

Academics CUW awards bachelor's and master's degrees. Challenging opportunities include advanced placement credit, accelerated degree programs, student-designed majors, an honors program, double majors, independent study, and a senior project. Special programs include internships, summer session for credit, off-campus study, and study-abroad. The most frequently chosen baccalaureate fields are business/marketing, health professions and related sciences, and interdisciplinary studies. The faculty at CUW has 93 full-time members, 60% with terminal degrees. The student-faculty ratio is 11:1.

Students of CUW The student body totals 4,904, of whom 3,975 are undergraduates. 64.6% are women and 35.4% are men. Students come from 41 states and territories and 21 other countries. 65% are from Wisconsin. 0.8% are international students. 75% returned for their sophomore year.

Applying CUW requires SAT I or ACT, a high school transcript, and a minimum high school GPA of 2.0, and in some cases an essay, 3 recommendations, and a minimum high school GPA of 3.0. The school recommends an interview. Application deadline: 8/15; 5/1 priority date for financial aid. Deferred admission is possible.

CONNECTICUT COLLEGE

New London, CT

Suburban setting ■ Private ■ Independent ■ Coed

Web site: www.connecticutcollege.edu
Contact: Ms. Martha Merrill, Dean of Admissions and Financial Aid, 270 Mohegan Avenue, New London, CT 06320-4196
Telephone: 860-439-2200 **Fax:** 860-439-4301
E-mail: admission@conncoll.edu

Getting in Last Year 3,915 applied; 35% were accepted; 499 enrolled (36%).

Financial Matters $35,625 comprehensive fee (2002–03); 100% average percent of need met; $23,349 average financial aid amount received per undergraduate.

Academics Connecticut awards bachelor's and master's degrees. Challenging opportunities include advanced placement credit, accelerated degree programs, student-designed majors, an honors program, double majors, independent study, and a senior project. Special programs include internships, summer session for credit, off-campus study, and study-abroad. The most frequently chosen

Connecticut College (continued)

baccalaureate fields are social sciences and history, biological/life sciences, and psychology. The faculty at Connecticut has 149 full-time members, 89% with terminal degrees. The student-faculty ratio is 11:1.

Students of Connecticut The student body totals 1,912, of whom 1,890 are undergraduates. 60.4% are women and 39.6% are men. Students come from 45 states and territories and 57 other countries. 19% are from Connecticut. 7.6% are international students. 93% returned for their sophomore year.

Applying Connecticut requires an essay, ACT or 3 SAT II Subject Tests (any 3), a high school transcript, 2 recommendations, and a minimum high school GPA of 2.0. The school recommends SAT I and an interview. Application deadline: 1/1; 1/15 for financial aid. Deferred admission is possible.

CONSERVATORY OF MUSIC OF PUERTO RICO

San Juan, PR

Urban setting ■ Commonwealth-supported ■ Coed

Contact: Ms. Sandra Rodriquiez, Marketing and Recruitment Officer, 350 Calle Rafael Lamar, San Juian, PR 00718

Telephone: 787-751-6180 ext. 285 **Fax:** 787-758-8268

E-mail: srodriquez@cmpr.gobierno.pr

Getting in Last Year 36 enrolled (100%).

Financial Matters 62% average percent of need met.

Academics CMPR awards bachelor's degrees. Challenging opportunities include advanced placement credit and a senior project. Special programs include cooperative education, summer session for credit, off-campus study, and Army ROTC. The faculty at CMPR has 36 full-time members, 6% with terminal degrees. The student-faculty ratio is 4:1.

Students of CMPR The student body is made up of 266 undergraduates. 30.8% are women and 69.2% are men. Students come from 1 state or territory. 2% are from Puerto Rico.

Applying CMPR requires SAT I, SAT II Subject Tests, a high school transcript, an interview, audition, music and theory examinations, and a minimum high school GPA of 2.0, and in some cases an essay and a minimum high school GPA of 2.50. Application deadline: 3/6; 5/30 priority date for financial aid. Early admission is possible.

CONVERSE COLLEGE

Spartanburg, SC

Urban setting ■ Private ■ Independent ■ Women Only

Web site: www.converse.edu

Contact: Mrs. Robbie Richard, Director of Undergraduate Admissions, 580 East Main Street, Spartanburg, SC 29302

Telephone: 864-596-9040 ext. 9746 or toll-free 800-766-1125
Fax: 864-596-9225

E-mail: admissions@converse.edu

Getting in Last Year 692 applied; 57% were accepted; 124 enrolled (31%).

Financial Matters $17,860 tuition and fees (2002–03); $5450 room and board; 88% average percent of need met; $15,053 average financial aid amount received per undergraduate.

Academics Converse awards bachelor's and master's degrees and post-master's certificates. Challenging opportunities include advanced placement credit, accelerated degree programs, an honors program, double majors, independent study, and a senior project. Special programs include internships, summer session for credit, off-campus study, study-abroad, and Army ROTC. The most frequently chosen baccalaureate fields are visual/performing arts, education, and business/marketing. The faculty at Converse has 72 full-time members, 93% with terminal degrees. The student-faculty ratio is 13:1.

Students of Converse The student body totals 1,577, of whom 687 are undergraduates. Students come from 20 states and territories and 7 other countries. 76% are from South Carolina. 1.3% are international students. 73% returned for their sophomore year.

Applying Converse requires an essay, SAT I or ACT, a high school transcript, and a minimum high school GPA of 2.00, and in some cases 1 recommendation. The school recommends an interview and a minimum high school GPA of 2.50. Application deadline: 3/1; 3/1 priority date for financial aid. Early and deferred admission are possible.

COOPER UNION FOR THE ADVANCEMENT OF SCIENCE AND ART

New York, NY

Urban setting ■ Private ■ Independent ■ Coed

Web site: www.cooper.edu

Contact: Mr. Richard Bory, Dean of Admissions and Records and Registrar, 30 Cooper Square, New York, NY 10003

Telephone: 212-353-4120 **Fax:** 212-353-4342

E-mail: admission@cooper.edu

Getting in Last Year 2,041 applied; 14% were accepted; 191 enrolled (66%).

Financial Matters $750 tuition and fees (2002–03); $11,400 room and board; 92% average percent of need met; $5578 average financial aid amount received per undergraduate (2001–02).

Academics Cooper Union awards bachelor's degrees (also offers master's program with enrollment generally made up of currently-enrolled students). Challenging opportunities include advanced placement credit, student-designed majors, an honors program, independent study, and a senior project. Special programs include internships, summer session for credit, off-campus study, and study-abroad. The faculty at Cooper Union has 56 full-time members, 75% with terminal degrees. The student-faculty ratio is 7:1.

Students of Cooper Union The student body totals 955, of whom 917 are undergraduates. 33.2% are women and 66.8% are men. Students come from 40 states and territories. 56% are from New York. 9.3% are international students. 92% returned for their sophomore year.

Applying Cooper Union requires SAT I or ACT, a high school transcript, and a minimum high school GPA of 2.0, and in some cases an essay, SAT II Subject Tests, 3 recommendations, and portfolio, home examination. The school recommends a minimum high school GPA of 3.0. Application deadline: 1/1; 4/15 priority date for financial aid. Early and deferred admission are possible.

CORCORAN COLLEGE OF ART AND DESIGN

Washington, DC

Urban setting ■ Private ■ Independent ■ Coed

Web site: www.corcoran.edu

Contact: Ms. Anne E. Bowman, Director of Enrollment Management, 500 17th Street, NW, Washington, DC 20006-4804

Telephone: 202-639-1814 or toll-free 888-CORCORAN (out-of-state)
Fax: 202-639-1830

E-mail: admofc@corcoran.org

Getting in Last Year 232 applied; 58% were accepted; 60 enrolled (45%).

Financial Matters $18,740 tuition and fees (2002–03); $7100 room and board; 53% average percent of need met; $15,917 average financial aid amount received per undergraduate (2001–02).

Academics Corcoran awards associate and bachelor's degrees. Challenging opportunities include advanced placement credit, independent study, and a senior project. Special programs include internships, summer session for credit, and off-campus study. The most frequently chosen baccalaureate field is visual/performing arts. The faculty at Corcoran has 35 full-time members, 60% with terminal degrees. The student-faculty ratio is 10:1.

Students of Corcoran The student body is made up of 404 undergraduates. 67.3% are women and 32.7% are men. Students come from 19 states and territories. 12% are from District of Columbia. 10.9% are international students. 100% returned for their sophomore year.

Applying Corcoran requires SAT I or ACT, a high school transcript, portfolio, and a minimum high school GPA of 2.5, and in some cases an essay, an interview, and 2 recommendations. The school recommends an essay, an interview, 2 recommendations, and a minimum high school GPA of 3.0. Application deadline: rolling admissions; 3/15 priority date for financial aid. Early and deferred admission are possible.

CORNELL COLLEGE

Mount Vernon, IA

Small-town setting ■ Private ■ Independent Religious ■ Coed

Web site: www.cornellcollege.edu

Contact: Mr. Jonathan Stroud, Dean of Admissions and Financial Assistance, 600 First Street West, Mount Vernon, IA 52314-1098

Telephone: 319-895-4477 or toll-free 800-747-1112 **Fax:** 319-895-4451

E-mail: admissions@cornellcollege.edu

Getting in Last Year 1,625 applied; 62% were accepted; 314 enrolled (31%).

Financial Matters $20,955 tuition and fees (2002–03); $5800 room and board; 88% average percent of need met; $18,795 average financial aid amount received per undergraduate.

Academics Cornell awards bachelor's degrees. Challenging opportunities include advanced placement credit, student-designed majors, double majors, independent study, and a senior project. Special programs include internships, off-campus study, and study-abroad. The most frequently chosen baccalaureate fields are social sciences and history, biological/life sciences, and education. The faculty at Cornell has 82 full-time members, 83% with terminal degrees. The student-faculty ratio is 11:1.

Students of Cornell The student body is made up of 1,001 undergraduates. 60.4% are women and 39.6% are men. Students come from 38 states and territories and 7 other countries. 32% are from Iowa. 0.9% are international students. 79% returned for their sophomore year.

Applying Cornell requires an essay, SAT I or ACT, a high school transcript, and 1 recommendation. The school recommends an interview and a minimum high school GPA of 2.80. Application deadline: 2/1; 3/1 priority date for financial aid. Deferred admission is possible.

CORNELL UNIVERSITY

Ithaca, NY

Small-town setting ■ Private ■ Independent ■ Coed

Web site: www.cornell.edu
Contact: Ms. Angela G. Jones, Director of Undergraduate Admissions, 410 Thurston Avenue, Ithaca, NY 14850
Telephone: 607-255-5241 **Fax:** 607-255-0659
E-mail: admissions@cornell.edu

Getting in Last Year 21,502 applied; 29% were accepted; 3,003 enrolled (49%).

Financial Matters $27,394 tuition and fees (2002–03); $8980 room and board; 100% average percent of need met; $23,017 average financial aid amount received per undergraduate.

Academics Cornell awards bachelor's, master's, doctoral, and first-professional degrees. Challenging opportunities include advanced placement credit, accelerated degree programs, student-designed majors, an honors program, double majors, independent study, and a senior project. Special programs include cooperative education, internships, summer session for credit, off-campus study, study-abroad, and Army, Navy and Air Force ROTC. The most frequently chosen baccalaureate fields are engineering/engineering technologies, agriculture, and business/marketing. The faculty at Cornell has 1,644 full-time members, 90% with terminal degrees. The student-faculty ratio is 9:1.

Students of Cornell The student body totals 19,575, of whom 13,725 are undergraduates. Students come from 62 states and territories and 78 other countries. 40% are from New York. 7.1% are international students. 93% returned for their sophomore year.

Applying Cornell requires an essay, SAT I or ACT, a high school transcript, and 1 recommendation, and in some cases SAT II Subject Tests, SAT II: Writing Test, and an interview. Application deadline: 1/1; 2/10 for financial aid. Early and deferred admission are possible.

CORNERSTONE UNIVERSITY

Grand Rapids, MI

Suburban setting ■ Private ■ Independent Religious ■ Coed

Web site: www.cornerstone.edu
Contact: Mr. Brent Rudin, Director of Admissions, 1001 East Beltline Avenue, NE, Grand Rapids, MI 49525
Telephone: 616-222-1426 or toll-free 800-787-9778 **Fax:** 616-222-1400
E-mail: admissions@cornerstone.edu

Getting in Last Year 977 applied; 79% were accepted; 349 enrolled (46%).

Financial Matters $13,770 tuition and fees (2002–03); $5218 room and board; 80% average percent of need met; $11,570 average financial aid amount received per undergraduate.

Academics Cornerstone University awards associate, bachelor's, master's, and first-professional degrees. Challenging opportunities include advanced placement credit, accelerated degree programs, double majors, and independent study. Special programs include internships, summer session for credit, off-campus study, and Army ROTC. The most frequently chosen baccalaureate fields are business/marketing, education, and English. The faculty at Cornerstone University has 73 full-time members, 55% with terminal degrees. The student-faculty ratio is 16:1.

Students of Cornerstone University The student body totals 2,450, of whom 2,110 are undergraduates. 61.4% are women and 38.6% are men. Students come from 31 states and territories and 1 other country. 80% are from Michigan. 0.9% are international students. 64% returned for their sophomore year.

Applying Cornerstone University requires an essay, SAT I or ACT, a high school transcript, 1 recommendation, and a minimum high school GPA of 2.25. The school recommends an interview. Application deadline: rolling admissions; 2/3 for financial aid. Deferred admission is possible.

CORNISH COLLEGE OF THE ARTS

Seattle, WA

Urban setting ■ Private ■ Independent ■ Coed

Web site: www.cornish.edu
Contact: Ms. Sharron Starling, Associate Director of Admissions, 710 East Roy Street, Seattle, WA 98102-4696
Telephone: 206-726-5017 or toll-free 800-726-ARTS **Fax:** 206-720-1011
E-mail: admissions@cornish.edu

Getting in Last Year 594 applied; 81% were accepted; 128 enrolled (27%).

Financial Matters $17,150 tuition and fees (2002–03); 51% average percent of need met; $10,240 average financial aid amount received per undergraduate (2001–02).

Academics Cornish awards bachelor's degrees. Challenging opportunities include advanced placement credit, independent study, and a senior project. Special programs include internships, summer session for credit, and study-abroad. The faculty at Cornish has 108 full-time members, 21% with terminal degrees. The student-faculty ratio is 9:1.

Students of Cornish The student body is made up of 665 undergraduates. 63.2% are women and 36.8% are men. Students come from 27 states and territories and 14 other countries. 60% are from Washington. 5.1% are international students.

Applying Cornish requires an essay, a high school transcript, portfolio or audition, and a minimum high school GPA of 2.0, and in some cases 2 recommendations. The school recommends SAT I or ACT, an interview, and 2 recommendations. Application deadline: 8/15; 2/15 priority date for financial aid. Deferred admission is possible.

COVENANT COLLEGE

Lookout Mountain, GA

Suburban setting ■ Private ■ Independent Religious ■ Coed

Web site: www.covenant.edu
Contact: Ms. Leda Goodman, Regional Director, 14049 Scenic Highway, Lookout Mountain, GA 30750
Telephone: 706-419-1644 or toll-free 888-451-2683 (in-state)
Fax: 706-820-0893
E-mail: admissions@covenant.edu

Getting in Last Year 544 applied; 96% were accepted; 233 enrolled (45%).

Financial Matters $18,230 tuition and fees (2002–03); $5260 room and board; 84% average percent of need met; $15,903 average financial aid amount received per undergraduate.

Academics Covenant awards associate, bachelor's, and master's degrees (master's degree in education only). Challenging opportunities include advanced placement credit, student-designed majors, double majors, independent study, and a senior project. Special programs include internships, summer session for credit, and off-campus study. The most frequently chosen baccalaureate fields are social sciences and history, education, and biological/life sciences. The faculty at Covenant has 56 full-time members, 79% with terminal degrees. The student-faculty ratio is 14:1.

Students of Covenant The student body totals 1,221, of whom 1,167 are undergraduates. 59.3% are women and 40.7% are men. Students come from 47 states and territories and 8 other countries. 24% are from Georgia. 1.1% are international students. 83% returned for their sophomore year.

Applying Covenant requires an essay, SAT I or ACT, a high school transcript, an interview, 2 recommendations, and a minimum high school GPA of 2.5. The school recommends ACT. Application deadline: rolling admissions; 3/31 priority date for financial aid. Early and deferred admission are possible.

CREIGHTON UNIVERSITY

Omaha, NE

Urban setting ■ Private ■ Independent Religious ■ Coed

Web site: www.creighton.edu
Contact: Mr. Don Bishop, Associate Vice President of Enrollment Management, 2500 California Plaza, Omaha, NE 68178-0001
Telephone: 402-280-2703 ext. 2162 or toll-free 800-282-5835
Fax: 402-280-2685
E-mail: admissions@creighton.edu

Getting in Last Year 2,605 applied; 90% were accepted; 802 enrolled (34%).

Financial Matters $18,882 tuition and fees (2002–03); $6438 room and board; 85% average percent of need met; $17,552 average financial aid amount received per undergraduate.

Academics Creighton awards associate, bachelor's, master's, doctoral, and first-professional degrees. Challenging opportunities include advanced placement credit, accelerated degree programs, an honors program, double majors, independent study, and a senior project. Special programs include internships, summer session for credit, off-campus study, study-abroad, and Army and Air Force ROTC. The most frequently chosen baccalaureate fields are health professions and related sciences, business/marketing, and biological/life sciences. The faculty at Creighton has 622 full-time members, 92% with terminal degrees. The student-faculty ratio is 14:1.

Students of Creighton The student body totals 6,327, of whom 3,607 are undergraduates. 59.8% are women and 40.2% are men. Students come from 41 states and territories and 64 other countries. 50% are from Nebraska. 1.9% are international students. 85% returned for their sophomore year.

Applying Creighton requires SAT I or ACT, a high school transcript, 1 recommendation, and a minimum high school GPA of 2.75. The school recommends an essay. Application deadline: 8/1; 5/15 priority date for financial aid. Deferred admission is possible.

CRICHTON COLLEGE

Memphis, TN

Urban setting ■ *Private* ■ *Independent* ■ *Coed*

Web site: www.crichton.edu

Contact: Mr. David Wilson, Director of Admissions, 255 North Highland, Memphis, TN 38111-1375

Telephone: 901-320-9797 ext. 1041 or toll-free 800-960-9777 **Fax:** 901-320-9791

E-mail: info@crichton.edu

Getting in Last Year 292 applied; 74% were accepted; 145 enrolled (67%).

Financial Matters $10,920 tuition and fees (2002–03); $4950 room and board; 47% average percent of need met; $6729 average financial aid amount received per undergraduate (2001–02).

Academics Crichton College awards bachelor's degrees and post-bachelor's certificates. Challenging opportunities include advanced placement credit, accelerated degree programs, student-designed majors, an honors program, double majors, independent study, and a senior project. Special programs include cooperative education, internships, summer session for credit, off-campus study, and study-abroad. The most frequently chosen baccalaureate fields are business/marketing, education, and liberal arts/general studies. The faculty at Crichton College has 41 full-time members, 56% with terminal degrees. The student-faculty ratio is 15:1.

Students of Crichton College The student body is made up of 1,028 undergraduates. 59.1% are women and 40.9% are men. Students come from 15 states and territories and 4 other countries. 85% are from Tennessee. 1.4% are international students. 45% returned for their sophomore year.

Applying Crichton College requires an essay, SAT I or ACT, a high school transcript, 3 recommendations, and a minimum high school GPA of 2.0. The school recommends an interview. Application deadline: 8/15; 3/31 priority date for financial aid. Deferred admission is possible.

CROSSROADS BIBLE COLLEGE

Indianapolis, IN

Urban setting ■ *Private* ■ *Independent Religious* ■ *Coed*

Web site: www.crossroads.edu

Contact: Ms. Bethanie Holdcroft, Director of Admissions, 601 North Shortridge Road, Indianapolis, IN 46219

Telephone: 371-352-8736 ext. 230 or toll-free 800-273-2224 **Fax:** 317-352-9145 ext.

Getting in Last Year 29 applied; 100% were accepted; 29 enrolled (100%).

Financial Matters $5320 tuition and fees (2002–03); 60% average percent of need met; $1100 average financial aid amount received per undergraduate (2001–02).

Academics Crossroads Bible College awards associate and bachelor's degrees. The faculty at Crossroads Bible College has 5 full-time members, 60% with terminal degrees.

Students of Crossroads Bible College The student body is made up of 204 undergraduates. 39.2% are women and 60.8% are men. 70% returned for their sophomore year.

Applying Application deadline: 5/31 priority date for financial aid.

CROSSROADS COLLEGE

Rochester, MN

Urban setting ■ *Private* ■ *Independent Religious* ■ *Coed*

Web site: www.crossroadscollege.edu

Contact: Mr. Michael Golembiesky, Director of Admissions, 920 Mayowood Road, SW, Rochester, MN 55902-2382

Telephone: 507-288-4563 ext. 313 or toll-free 800-456-7651 **Fax:** 507-288-9046

E-mail: admissions@crossroadscollege.edu

Getting in Last Year 65 applied; 100% were accepted; 27 enrolled (42%).

Financial Matters $7010 tuition and fees (2002–03); $1750 room only; 84% average percent of need met; $7326 average financial aid amount received per undergraduate (2001–02).

Academics Crossroads College awards associate and bachelor's degrees. Challenging opportunities include advanced placement credit, student-designed majors, double majors, independent study, and a senior project. Internships is a special program. The most frequently chosen baccalaureate field is liberal arts/general studies. The faculty at Crossroads College has 8 full-time members, 38% with terminal degrees. The student-faculty ratio is 10:1.

Students of Crossroads College The student body is made up of 110 undergraduates. 48.2% are women and 51.8% are men. Students come from 6 states and territories and 4 other countries. 72% are from Minnesota. 6.2% are international students. 61% returned for their sophomore year.

Applying Crossroads College requires an essay, SAT I or ACT, a high school transcript, and 3 recommendations, and in some cases an interview. Application deadline: 8/15; 4/1 priority date for financial aid. Deferred admission is possible.

CROWN COLLEGE

St. Bonifacius, MN

Suburban setting ■ *Private* ■ *Independent Religious* ■ *Coed*

Web site: www.crown.edu

Contact: Ms. Kimberely LaQuay, Application Coordinator/Office Systems Manager, 6425 County Road 30, St. Bonifacius, MN 55375-9001

Telephone: 952-446-4143 or toll-free 800-68-CROWN **Fax:** 952-446-4149

E-mail: info@crown.edu

Getting in Last Year 408 applied; 75% were accepted; 137 enrolled (45%).

Financial Matters $11,982 tuition and fees (2002–03); $4980 room and board; 47% average percent of need met; $10,286 average financial aid amount received per undergraduate.

Academics Crown College awards associate, bachelor's, and master's degrees. Challenging opportunities include advanced placement credit, an honors program, double majors, and independent study. Special programs include internships, summer session for credit, and study-abroad. The most frequently chosen baccalaureate fields are education, business/marketing, and computer/information sciences. The faculty at Crown College has 33 full-time members, 58% with terminal degrees. The student-faculty ratio is 14:1.

Students of Crown College The student body totals 912, of whom 898 are undergraduates. 56.6% are women and 43.4% are men. Students come from 33 states and territories. 64% are from Minnesota. 70% returned for their sophomore year.

Applying Crown College requires an essay, SAT I or ACT, a high school transcript, 2 recommendations, and a minimum high school GPA of 2.0, and in some cases an interview. Application deadline: rolling admissions; 4/1 priority date for financial aid. Early and deferred admission are possible.

THE CULINARY INSTITUTE OF AMERICA

Hyde Park, NY

Small-town setting ■ *Private* ■ *Independent* ■ *Coed*

Web site: www.ciachef.edu

Contact: Mr. Larry Lopez, Director of Admissions, 1946 Campus Drive, Hyde Park, NY 12538

Telephone: 845-451-1534 or toll-free 800-CULINARY **Fax:** 845-451-1068

E-mail: admissions@culinary.edu

Getting in Last Year 1,383 applied; 46% were accepted; 540 enrolled (85%).

Financial Matters $16,940 tuition and fees (2002–03); $6200 room and board; 50% average percent of need met; $8500 average financial aid amount received per undergraduate (2001–02).

Academics The CIA awards associate and bachelor's degrees. Special programs include cooperative education, internships, and off-campus study. The most frequently chosen baccalaureate field is personal/miscellaneous services. The faculty at The CIA has 117 full-time members. The student-faculty ratio is 18:1.

Students of The CIA The student body is made up of 2,294 undergraduates. Students come from 50 states and territories and 28 other countries. 27% are from New York. 5.3% are international students.

Applying The CIA requires an essay, a high school transcript, and 2 recommendations, and in some cases an interview and TOEFL and an Affidavit of Support. The school recommends SAT I or ACT. Application deadline: 1/15; 2/15 for financial aid. Deferred admission is possible.

CULVER-STOCKTON COLLEGE

Canton, MO

Rural setting ■ *Private* ■ *Independent Religious* ■ *Coed*

Web site: www.culver.edu

Contact: Mr. Ron Cronacher, Director of Enrollment Services, One College Hill, Canton, MO 63435-1299

Telephone: 800-537-1883 or toll-free 800-537-1883 (out-of-state) **Fax:** 217-231-6618

E-mail: enrollment@culver.edu

Getting in Last Year 943 applied; 77% were accepted; 224 enrolled (31%).

Financial Matters $11,800 tuition and fees (2002–03); $5200 room and board; 83% average percent of need met; $11,614 average financial aid amount received per undergraduate.

Academics Culver-Stockton awards bachelor's degrees. Challenging opportunities include advanced placement credit, student-designed majors, an honors program, double majors, independent study, and a senior project. Special programs include internships, summer session for credit, off-campus study, and study-abroad. The most frequently chosen baccalaureate fields are education, business/marketing, and health professions and related sciences. The faculty at Culver-Stockton has 58 full-time members, 81% with terminal degrees. The student-faculty ratio is 12:1.

Students of Culver-Stockton The student body is made up of 828 undergraduates. 57.1% are women and 42.9% are men. Students come from 28 states and territories and 8 other countries. 56% are from Missouri. 1.3% are international students. 64% returned for their sophomore year.

Applying Culver-Stockton requires SAT I or ACT, a high school transcript, and a minimum high school GPA of 2.0, and in some cases an interview. The school recommends an essay, an interview, and recommendations. Application deadline: 6/15 for financial aid. Deferred admission is possible.

CUMBERLAND COLLEGE

Williamsburg, KY

Rural setting ■ Private ■ Independent Religious ■ Coed

Web site: www.cumberlandcollege.edu
Contact: Mrs. Erica Harris, Director of Admissions, 6178 College Station Drive, Williamsburg, KY 40769
Telephone: 606-539-4201 or toll-free 800-343-1609 **Fax:** 606-539-4303
E-mail: admiss@cumberlandcollege.edu

Getting in Last Year 1,147 applied; 67% were accepted; 393 enrolled (51%).

Financial Matters $10,958 tuition and fees (2002–03); $4676 room and board; 90% average percent of need met; $11,750 average financial aid amount received per undergraduate.

Academics Cumberland awards associate, bachelor's, and master's degrees. Challenging opportunities include advanced placement credit, accelerated degree programs, student-designed majors, freshman honors college, an honors program, double majors, independent study, and a senior project. Special programs include cooperative education, internships, summer session for credit, study-abroad, and Army ROTC. The most frequently chosen baccalaureate fields are education, business/marketing, and psychology. The faculty at Cumberland has 90 full-time members, 64% with terminal degrees. The student-faculty ratio is 17:1.

Students of Cumberland The student body totals 1,743, of whom 1,588 are undergraduates. 53.4% are women and 46.6% are men. Students come from 36 states and territories and 18 other countries. 59% are from Kentucky. 1.8% are international students. 63% returned for their sophomore year.

Applying Cumberland requires an essay, SAT I or ACT, a high school transcript, 1 recommendation, and a minimum high school GPA of 2.0. The school recommends an interview. Application deadline: rolling admissions; 3/1 priority date for financial aid.

CUMBERLAND UNIVERSITY

Lebanon, TN

Small-town setting ■ Private ■ Independent ■ Coed

Web site: www.cumberland.edu
Contact: Ms. Amanda Cook, Director of Admissions, One Cumberland Square, Lebanon, TN 37087
Telephone: 615-444-2562 ext. 1232 or toll-free 800-467-0562 (out-of-state) **Fax:** 615-444-2569
E-mail: admissions@cumberland.edu

Getting in Last Year 475 applied; 73% were accepted; 188 enrolled (54%).

Financial Matters $11,660 tuition and fees (2002–03); $4290 room and board; 65% average percent of need met; $10,192 average financial aid amount received per undergraduate.

Academics Cumberland awards associate, bachelor's, and master's degrees. Challenging opportunities include advanced placement credit, accelerated degree programs, freshman honors college, an honors program, and double majors. Special programs include cooperative education, internships, summer session for credit, and Army ROTC. The most frequently chosen baccalaureate fields are education, business/marketing, and health professions and related sciences. The faculty at Cumberland has 84 full-time members, 62% with terminal degrees. The student-faculty ratio is 10:1.

Students of Cumberland The student body totals 1,463, of whom 912 are undergraduates. 51.2% are women and 48.8% are men. Students come from 20 states and territories. 79% are from Tennessee. 60% returned for their sophomore year.

Applying Cumberland requires SAT I or ACT and a high school transcript, and in some cases 3 recommendations. The school recommends a minimum high school GPA of 2.0. Application deadline: rolling admissions; 2/15 priority date for financial aid. Deferred admission is possible.

CURRY COLLEGE

Milton, MA

Suburban setting ■ Private ■ Independent ■ Coed

Web site: www.curry.edu
Contact: Ms. Karin Kiernan, Dean of Admission and Financial Aid, 1071 Blue Hill Avenue, Milton, MA 02186
Telephone: 617-333-2210 or toll-free 800-669-0686 **Fax:** 617-333-2114
E-mail: curryadm@curry.edu

Getting in Last Year 2,066 applied; 79% were accepted; 459 enrolled (28%).

Financial Matters $19,650 tuition and fees (2002–03); $7570 room and board; 68% average percent of need met; $14,250 average financial aid amount received per undergraduate (2001–02 estimated).

Academics Curry awards bachelor's and master's degrees. Challenging opportunities include advanced placement credit, accelerated degree programs, student-designed majors, an honors program, double majors, independent study, and a senior project. Special programs include cooperative education, internships, summer session for credit, off-campus study, study-abroad, and Army ROTC. The faculty at Curry has 83 full-time members, 47% with terminal degrees. The student-faculty ratio is 12:1.

Students of Curry The student body totals 2,399, of whom 2,287 are undergraduates. 50.2% are women and 49.8% are men. Students come from 31 states and territories and 12 other countries. 68% are from Massachusetts. 65% returned for their sophomore year.

Applying Curry requires an essay, a high school transcript, 1 recommendation, and a minimum high school GPA of 2.0, and in some cases SAT I or ACT, Wechsler Adult Intelligence Scale-Revised for PAL candidates, and an interview. The school recommends an interview. Application deadline: 4/1; 3/1 priority date for financial aid. Early and deferred admission are possible.

THE CURTIS INSTITUTE OF MUSIC

Philadelphia, PA

Urban setting ■ Private ■ Independent ■ Coed

Web site: www.curtis.edu
Contact: Mr. Christopher Hodges, Admissions Officer, 1726 Locust Street, Philadelphia, PA 19103-6107
Telephone: 215-893-5262 **Fax:** 215-893-7900

Getting in Last Year 787 applied; 5% were accepted.

Financial Matters $1425 tuition and fees (2002–03); 86% average percent of need met; $10,651 average financial aid amount received per undergraduate.

Academics Curtis awards bachelor's and master's degrees. Challenging opportunities include advanced placement credit and accelerated degree programs. Off-campus study is a special program. The faculty at Curtis has 80 members.

Students of Curtis The student body totals 160, of whom 144 are undergraduates. 54.9% are women and 45.1% are men. Students come from 24 states and territories and 22 other countries.

Applying Curtis requires an essay, SAT I, a high school transcript, recommendations, and audition. Application deadline: 1/15; 3/1 for financial aid. Early admission is possible.

DAEMEN COLLEGE

Amherst, NY

Suburban setting ■ Private ■ Independent ■ Coed

Web site: www.daemen.edu
Contact: Mr. Cecil Foster, Director of Admissions, 4380 Main Street, Amherst, NY 14226-3592
Telephone: 716-839-8225 or toll-free 800-462-7652 **Fax:** 716-839-8229
E-mail: admissions@daemen.edu

Getting in Last Year 1,755 applied; 74% were accepted; 316 enrolled (24%).

Financial Matters $14,270 tuition and fees (2002–03); $6700 room and board; 72% average percent of need met; $10,606 average financial aid amount received per undergraduate (2001–02).

Academics Daemen awards bachelor's, master's, and first-professional degrees and post-bachelor's and post-master's certificates. Challenging opportunities include advanced placement credit, student-designed majors, an honors program, double majors, independent study, and a senior project. Special programs include cooperative education, internships, summer session for credit, off-campus study, study-abroad, and Army ROTC. The most frequently chosen baccalaureate fields are health professions and related sciences, business/marketing, and education. The faculty at Daemen has 70 full-time members, 76% with terminal degrees. The student-faculty ratio is 16:1.

Students of Daemen The student body totals 2,027, of whom 1,887 are undergraduates. 77.1% are women and 22.9% are men. Students come from 22 states and territories and 10 other countries. 96% are from New York. 1.4% are international students. 68% returned for their sophomore year.

Applying Daemen requires SAT I or ACT, a high school transcript, and a minimum high school GPA of 2.0, and in some cases an essay, an interview, 3 recommendations, and portfolio for art program, supplemental application for physician's assistant program. Application deadline: rolling admissions. Early and deferred admission are possible.

DAKOTA STATE UNIVERSITY

Madison, SD

Rural setting ■ Public ■ State-supported ■ Coed

Web site: www.dsu.edu
Contact: Ms. Katy O'Hara, Admissions Secretary, 820 North Washington, Madison, SD 57042-1799
Telephone: 605-256-5139 or toll-free 888-DSU-9988 **Fax:** 605-256-5316
E-mail: yourfuture@dsu.edu

Dakota State University (continued)

Getting in Last Year 584 applied; 86% were accepted; 294 enrolled (58%).

Financial Matters $3774 resident tuition and fees (2002–03); $7857 nonresident tuition and fees (2002–03); $3130 room and board; $5297 average financial aid amount received per undergraduate (2001–02).

Academics Dakota State awards associate, bachelor's, and master's degrees. Challenging opportunities include advanced placement credit, an honors program, double majors, independent study, and a senior project. Special programs include cooperative education, internships, summer session for credit, off-campus study, study-abroad, and Air Force ROTC. The most frequently chosen baccalaureate fields are computer/information sciences, engineering/engineering technologies, and business/marketing. The faculty at Dakota State has 77 full-time members, 60% with terminal degrees. The student-faculty ratio is 23:1.

Students of Dakota State The student body totals 2,188, of whom 1,965 are undergraduates. 51.3% are women and 48.7% are men. Students come from 12 states and territories and 6 other countries. 84% are from South Dakota. 0.9% are international students. 70% returned for their sophomore year.

Applying Dakota State requires ACT, a high school transcript, and rank in upper two-thirds of high school class. Application deadline: rolling admissions; 3/1 priority date for financial aid. Early admission is possible.

DAKOTA WESLEYAN UNIVERSITY

Mitchell, SD

Small-town setting ■ Private ■ Independent Religious ■ Coed

Web site: www.dwu.edu
Contact: Ms. Laura Miller, Director of Admissions Operations and Outreach Programming, 1200 West University Avenue, Mitchell, SD 57301-4398
Telephone: 605-995-2650 or toll-free 800-333-8506 **Fax:** 605-995-2699
E-mail: admissions@dwu.edu

Getting in Last Year 468 applied; 84% were accepted; 148 enrolled (38%).

Financial Matters $12,662 tuition and fees (2002–03); $4166 room and board; 71% average percent of need met; $11,061 average financial aid amount received per undergraduate.

Academics DWU awards associate and bachelor's degrees. Challenging opportunities include advanced placement credit, student-designed majors, an honors program, double majors, independent study, and a senior project. Special programs include internships, summer session for credit, and study-abroad. The most frequently chosen baccalaureate fields are protective services/public administration, business/marketing, and education. The faculty at DWU has 42 full-time members, 62% with terminal degrees. The student-faculty ratio is 14:1.

Students of DWU The student body is made up of 717 undergraduates. 58.7% are women and 41.3% are men. Students come from 30 states and territories. 73% are from South Dakota. 0.4% are international students. 63% returned for their sophomore year.

Applying DWU requires SAT I or ACT and a high school transcript. The school recommends a minimum high school GPA of 2.0. Application deadline: 8/25; 4/1 priority date for financial aid.

DALHOUSIE UNIVERSITY

Halifax, NS Canada

Urban setting ■ Public ■ Coed

Web site: www.dal.ca
Contact: Ms. Susan Tanner, Associate Registrar of Admissions, Halifax, NS B3H 4R2 Canada
Telephone: 902-494-6572 **Fax:** 902-494-1630
E-mail: admissions@dal.ca

Getting in Last Year 4,570 applied; 73% were accepted.

Financial Matters $5320 tuition and fees (2002–03); $5600 room and board.

Academics Dal awards bachelor's, master's, doctoral, and first-professional degrees. Challenging opportunities include advanced placement credit, an honors program, double majors, and a senior project. Special programs include cooperative education, summer session for credit, off-campus study, and study-abroad. The faculty at Dal has 1,516 members. The student-faculty ratio is 12:1.

Students of Dal The student body totals 13,643, of whom 9,313 are undergraduates. 56.3% are women and 43.7% are men. Students come from 13 states and territories and 84 other countries. 80% returned for their sophomore year.

Applying Dal requires SAT I, a high school transcript, and a minimum high school GPA of 3.0, and in some cases an essay, an interview, 1 recommendation, and minimum 1100 comprehensive score on SAT I for U.S. applicants. Application deadline: 6/1. Deferred admission is possible.

DALLAS BAPTIST UNIVERSITY

Dallas, TX

Urban setting ■ Private ■ Independent Religious ■ Coed

Web site: www.dbu.edu
Contact: Dr. Duke Jones, Director of Admissions, 3000 Mountain Creek Parkway, Dallas, TX 75211-9299
Telephone: 214-333-5360 or toll-free 800-460-1328 **Fax:** 214-333-5447
E-mail: admiss@dbu.edu

Getting in Last Year 678 applied; 62% were accepted; 268 enrolled (64%).

Financial Matters $10,350 tuition and fees (2002–03); $4140 room and board; 87% average percent of need met; $9529 average financial aid amount received per undergraduate.

Academics DBU awards associate, bachelor's, and master's degrees and post-bachelor's certificates. Challenging opportunities include advanced placement credit, double majors, independent study, and a senior project. Special programs include internships, summer session for credit, off-campus study, study-abroad, and Army and Air Force ROTC. The most frequently chosen baccalaureate fields are business/marketing, liberal arts/general studies, and visual/performing arts. The faculty at DBU has 85 full-time members, 75% with terminal degrees. The student-faculty ratio is 18:1.

Students of DBU The student body totals 4,417, of whom 3,407 are undergraduates. 60.5% are women and 39.5% are men. Students come from 32 states and territories and 43 other countries. 93% are from Texas. 5.9% are international students.

Applying DBU requires an essay, SAT I or ACT, a high school transcript, and rank in upper 50% of high school class or 3.0 high school GPA, minimum ACT score of 20, combined SAT score of 950. The school recommends an interview and recommendations. Application deadline: rolling admissions; 3/15 priority date for financial aid.

DALLAS CHRISTIAN COLLEGE

Dallas, TX

Urban setting ■ Private ■ Independent Religious ■ Coed

Web site: www.dallas.edu
Contact: Mr. Marty McKee, Director of Admissions, 2700 Christian Parkway, Dallas, TX 75234-7299
Telephone: 972-241-3371 ext. 153 **Fax:** 972-241-8021
E-mail: dcc@dallas.edu

Getting in Last Year 77 applied; 44% were accepted; 34 enrolled (100%).

Financial Matters $6900 tuition and fees (2002–03); $4100 room and board; 34% average percent of need met; $4327 average financial aid amount received per undergraduate.

Academics DCC awards bachelor's degrees. Challenging opportunities include advanced placement credit, accelerated degree programs, double majors, independent study, and a senior project. Special programs include internships and summer session for credit. The most frequently chosen baccalaureate field is business/marketing. The faculty at DCC has 8 full-time members, 50% with terminal degrees. The student-faculty ratio is 13:1.

Students of DCC The student body is made up of 298 undergraduates. 48.7% are women and 51.3% are men. Students come from 19 states and territories and 2 other countries. 85% are from Texas. 1.4% are international students. 45% returned for their sophomore year.

Applying DCC requires SAT I or ACT, a high school transcript, and 2 recommendations, and in some cases an essay and an interview. Application deadline: rolling admissions; 4/15 priority date for financial aid. Deferred admission is possible.

DALTON STATE COLLEGE

Dalton, GA

Small-town setting ■ Public ■ State-supported ■ Coed

Web site: www.daltonstate.edu
Contact: Dr. Angela Harris, Assistant Director of Admissions, 213 North College Drive, Dalton, GA 30720-3797
Telephone: 706-272-4476 or toll-free 800-829-4436 **Fax:** 706-272-2530
E-mail: aharris@em.daltonstate.edu

Getting in Last Year 2,022 applied; 62% were accepted; 612 enrolled (49%).

Financial Matters $2124 resident tuition and fees (2002–03); $8154 nonresident tuition and fees (2002–03).

Academics Dalton awards associate and bachelor's degrees. Advanced placement credit is a challenging opportunity. Special programs include internships, summer session for credit, off-campus study, and study-abroad. The faculty at Dalton has 144 full-time members, 41% with terminal degrees. The student-faculty ratio is 25:1.

Students of Dalton The student body is made up of 3,647 undergraduates. 62.8% are women and 37.2% are men. Students come from 2 states and territories. 99% are from Georgia.

Applying Dalton requires a high school transcript, and in some cases SAT II Subject Tests and SAT I or ACT. Application deadline: rolling admissions; 7/1 priority date for financial aid. Early admission is possible.

DANA COLLEGE

Blair, NE

Small-town setting ■ Private ■ Independent Religious ■ Coed

Web site: www.dana.edu

Contact: Ms. Judy Mathiesen, Office Manager, 2848 College Drive, Blair, NE 68008-1099

Telephone: 402-426-7337 or toll-free 800-444-3262 **Fax:** 402-426-7386

E-mail: admissions@acad2.dana.edu

Getting in Last Year 591 applied; 95% were accepted; 140 enrolled (25%).

Financial Matters $14,750 tuition and fees (2002–03); $4676 room and board; 88% average percent of need met; $13,864 average financial aid amount received per undergraduate.

Academics Dana awards bachelor's degrees. Challenging opportunities include advanced placement credit, accelerated degree programs, student-designed majors, an honors program, double majors, independent study, and a senior project. Special programs include internships, summer session for credit, off-campus study, study-abroad, and Army and Air Force ROTC. The most frequently chosen baccalaureate fields are education, business/marketing, and protective services/public administration. The faculty at Dana has 40 full-time members, 58% with terminal degrees. The student-faculty ratio is 12:1.

Students of Dana The student body is made up of 580 undergraduates. 45.3% are women and 54.7% are men. Students come from 34 states and territories and 6 other countries. 58% are from Nebraska. 1% are international students. 66% returned for their sophomore year.

Applying Dana requires SAT I or ACT, a high school transcript, and a minimum high school GPA of 2.0, and in some cases an essay, an interview, and 1 recommendation. The school recommends ACT. Application deadline: rolling admissions; 3/15 priority date for financial aid. Deferred admission is possible.

DANIEL WEBSTER COLLEGE

Nashua, NH

Suburban setting ■ Private ■ Independent ■ Coed

Web site: www.dwc.edu

Contact: Mr. Sean J. Ryan, Director of Admissions, 20 University Drive, Nashua, NH 03063

Telephone: 603-577-6604 or toll-free 800-325-6876 **Fax:** 603-577-6001

E-mail: admissions@dwc.edu

Getting in Last Year 683 applied; 77% were accepted; 165 enrolled (32%).

Financial Matters $19,000 tuition and fees (2002–03); $7440 room and board; 74% average percent of need met; $13,680 average financial aid amount received per undergraduate.

Academics DWC awards associate and bachelor's degrees. Challenging opportunities include advanced placement credit, accelerated degree programs, double majors, and independent study. Special programs include internships, summer session for credit, off-campus study, study-abroad, and Army and Air Force ROTC. The most frequently chosen baccalaureate fields are business/marketing, trade and industry, and computer/information sciences. The faculty at DWC has 34 full-time members, 47% with terminal degrees. The student-faculty ratio is 13:1.

Students of DWC The student body is made up of 1,058 undergraduates. 25.9% are women and 74.1% are men. Students come from 24 states and territories and 17 other countries. 54% are from New Hampshire. 0.6% are international students. 56% returned for their sophomore year.

Applying DWC requires SAT I or ACT and a high school transcript. The school recommends an interview and 1 recommendation. Application deadline: rolling admissions; 3/1 priority date for financial aid. Early and deferred admission are possible.

DARTMOUTH COLLEGE

Hanover, NH

Rural setting ■ Private ■ Independent ■ Coed

Web site: www.dartmouth.edu

Contact: Mr. Karl M. Furstenberg, Dean of Admissions and Financial Aid, 6016 McNutt Hall, Hanover, NH 03755

Telephone: 603-646-2875

E-mail: admissions.office@dartmouth.edu

Getting in Last Year 9,719 applied; 23% were accepted.

Financial Matters $27,771 tuition and fees (2002–03); $8217 room and board; 100% average percent of need met; $25,549 average financial aid amount received per undergraduate (2001–02).

Academics Dartmouth awards bachelor's, master's, doctoral, and first-professional degrees. Challenging opportunities include advanced placement credit, student-designed majors, an honors program, double majors, independent study, and a senior project. Special programs include internships, summer session for credit, off-campus study, study-abroad, and Army ROTC. The most frequently chosen baccalaureate fields are social sciences and history, English, and biological/life sciences. The faculty at Dartmouth has 446 full-time members, 96% with terminal degrees. The student-faculty ratio is 9:1.

Students of Dartmouth The student body totals 5,495, of whom 4,118 are undergraduates. 48.6% are women and 51.4% are men. Students come from 52 states and territories and 64 other countries. 3% are from New Hampshire. 4.5% are international students. 97% returned for their sophomore year.

Applying Dartmouth requires an essay, SAT I and SAT II or ACT, a high school transcript, and 3 recommendations. The school recommends an interview. Application deadline: 1/1; 2/1 for financial aid. Early and deferred admission are possible.

DAVENPORT UNIVERSITY

Grand Rapids, MI

Urban setting ■ Private ■ Independent ■ Coed

Web site: www.davenport.edu

Contact: Lynnae Selberg, Executive Director of Enrollment, 415 East Fulton, Grand Rapids, MI 49503

Telephone: 616-451-3511 ext. 1213 or toll-free 800-632-9569

Getting in Last Year 452 applied; 65% were accepted; 262 enrolled (89%).

Financial Matters $9015 tuition and fees (2002–03); $7410 room and board.

Academics Davenport awards associate, bachelor's, and master's degrees. Challenging opportunities include advanced placement credit, accelerated degree programs, independent study, and a senior project. Special programs include cooperative education, internships, summer session for credit, and study-abroad. The most frequently chosen baccalaureate field is law/legal studies. The faculty at Davenport has 23 full-time members, 43% with terminal degrees. The student-faculty ratio is 20:1.

Students of Davenport The student body totals 2,216, of whom 2,077 are undergraduates. 63.6% are women and 36.4% are men. Students come from 4 states and territories and 27 other countries. 1.5% are international students. 51% returned for their sophomore year.

Applying Davenport requires a high school transcript. The school recommends an essay, ACT, and an interview. Application deadline: rolling admissions, 9/15 for nonresidents; 3/15 priority date for financial aid. Early and deferred admission are possible.

DAVENPORT UNIVERSITY

Kalamazoo, MI

Suburban setting ■ Private ■ Independent ■ Coed

Web site: www.davenport.edu

Contact: Ms. Gloria Stender, Admissions Director, 4123 West Main Street, Kalamazoo, MI 49006-2791

Telephone: 616-382-2835 ext. 3309 or toll-free 800-632-8928 **Fax:** 616-382-2661

Getting in Last Year 161 applied; 100% were accepted; 161 enrolled (100%).

Financial Matters $10,147 tuition and fees (2002–03).

Academics Davenport University awards associate and bachelor's degrees and post-bachelor's certificates. Independent study is a challenging opportunity. Special programs include cooperative education, internships, summer session for credit, off-campus study, and study-abroad. The most frequently chosen baccalaureate field is law/legal studies. The faculty at Davenport University has 24 full-time members, 17% with terminal degrees. The student-faculty ratio is 13:1.

Students of Davenport University The student body is made up of 1,063 undergraduates. 75.2% are women and 24.8% are men. Students come from 2 states and territories and 6 other countries. 99% are from Michigan. 0.2% are international students.

Applying Davenport University requires an essay and a high school transcript. Application deadline: rolling admissions; 2/21 priority date for financial aid. Early and deferred admission are possible.

DAVENPORT UNIVERSITY

Lansing, MI

Suburban setting ■ Private ■ Independent ■ Coed

Web site: www.davenport.edu

Contact: Mr. Tom Woods, Associate Dean of Enrollment, 220 East Kalamazoo, Lansing, MI 48933-2197

Telephone: 517-484-2600 ext. 288 or toll-free 800-686-1600 **Fax:** 517-484-9719

E-mail: laadmissions@davenport.edu

Getting in Last Year 270 enrolled.

Financial Matters $8656 tuition and fees (2002–03).

Academics Davenport University awards associate and bachelor's degrees. Challenging opportunities include advanced placement credit, accelerated degree

Davenport University (continued)

programs, student-designed majors, and independent study. Special programs include cooperative education, internships, summer session for credit, and Army ROTC. The faculty at Davenport University has 11 full-time members. The student-faculty ratio is 15:1.

Students of Davenport University The student body is made up of 1,209 undergraduates. 72.3% are women and 27.7% are men. Students come from 1 state or territory. 0.2% are international students. 43% returned for their sophomore year.

Applying Davenport University requires a high school transcript, and in some cases ACT. The school recommends an interview. Application deadline: 9/15; 3/15 priority date for financial aid. Early and deferred admission are possible.

DAVIDSON COLLEGE

Davidson, NC

Small-town setting ■ Private ■ Independent Religious ■ Coed

Web site: www.davidson.edu
Contact: Dr. Nancy J. Cable, Dean of Admission and Financial Aid, Box 7156, Davidson, NC 28035-7156
Telephone: 704-894-2230 or toll-free 800-768-0380 **Fax:** 704-894-2016
E-mail: admission@davidson.edu

Getting in Last Year 3,387 applied; 34% were accepted; 467 enrolled (40%).

Financial Matters $24,930 tuition and fees (2002–03); $7094 room and board; 100% average percent of need met; $16,108 average financial aid amount received per undergraduate (2001–02).

Academics Davidson awards bachelor's degrees. Challenging opportunities include advanced placement credit, student-designed majors, an honors program, double majors, independent study, and a senior project. Special programs include off-campus study, study-abroad, and Army and Air Force ROTC. The most frequently chosen baccalaureate fields are social sciences and history, English, and biological/life sciences. The faculty at Davidson has 159 full-time members, 97% with terminal degrees. The student-faculty ratio is 10:1.

Students of Davidson The student body is made up of 1,645 undergraduates. 50.2% are women and 49.8% are men. Students come from 46 states and territories and 28 other countries. 18% are from North Carolina. 3.3% are international students. 96% returned for their sophomore year.

Applying Davidson requires an essay, SAT I or ACT, a high school transcript, and 4 recommendations. The school recommends SAT II Subject Tests, SAT II: Writing Test, and an interview. Application deadline: 1/2; 2/15 priority date for financial aid. Early and deferred admission are possible.

DAVIS & ELKINS COLLEGE

Elkins, WV

Small-town setting ■ Private ■ Independent Religious ■ Coed

Web site: www.davisandelkins.edu
Contact: Mr. Matt Shiflett, Director of Admissions, 100 Campus Drive, Elkins, WV 26241-3996
Telephone: 304-637-1332 or toll-free 800-624-3157 **Fax:** 304-637-1800
E-mail: admis@dne.edu

Getting in Last Year 691 applied; 70% were accepted.

Financial Matters $14,120 tuition and fees (2002–03); $5620 room and board; 79% average percent of need met; $10,238 average financial aid amount received per undergraduate (2001–02).

Academics D&E College awards associate and bachelor's degrees. Challenging opportunities include advanced placement credit, accelerated degree programs, student-designed majors, an honors program, double majors, independent study, and a senior project. Special programs include cooperative education, internships, summer session for credit, and study-abroad. The faculty at D&E College has 46 full-time members, 65% with terminal degrees. The student-faculty ratio is 12:1.

Students of D&E College The student body is made up of 654 undergraduates. 60.7% are women and 39.3% are men. Students come from 20 states and territories. 55% are from West Virginia. 0.2% are international students. 64% returned for their sophomore year.

Applying D&E College requires SAT I or ACT, a high school transcript, and a minimum high school GPA of 2.0, and in some cases 2 recommendations. The school recommends an interview. Application deadline: rolling admissions. Early and deferred admission are possible.

DEACONESS COLLEGE OF NURSING

St. Louis, MO

Urban setting ■ Private ■ Proprietary ■ Coed, Primarily Women

Web site: www.deaconess.edu
Contact: Ms. Lisa Mancini, Dean of Enrollment and Student Services, 6150 Oakland Avenue, St. Louis, MO 63139-3215
Telephone: 314-768-3179 or toll-free 800-942-4310 **Fax:** 314-768-5673

Getting in Last Year 160 enrolled.

Financial Matters $9936 tuition and fees (2002–03); $5200 room and board; 60% average percent of need met; $7081 average financial aid amount received per undergraduate.

Academics Deaconess awards associate and bachelor's degrees. Advanced placement credit is a challenging opportunity. Special programs include summer session for credit, off-campus study, and Army ROTC. The most frequently chosen baccalaureate field is health professions and related sciences. The faculty at Deaconess has 11 full-time members, 100% with terminal degrees. The student-faculty ratio is 12:1.

Students of Deaconess The student body is made up of 324 undergraduates. 97.8% are women and 2.2% are men. Students come from 15 states and territories. 62% returned for their sophomore year.

Applying Deaconess requires an essay, ACT, and a high school transcript, and in some cases an interview and recommendations. The school recommends a minimum high school GPA of 2.5. Application deadline: rolling admissions; 4/1 priority date for financial aid. Deferred admission is possible.

DEFIANCE COLLEGE

Defiance, OH

Small-town setting ■ Private ■ Independent Religious ■ Coed

Web site: www.defiance.edu
Contact: Mr. Brad M. Harsha, Acting Director of Admissions, 701 North Clinton Street, Defiance, OH 43512-1610
Telephone: 419-783-2365 or toll-free 800-520-4632 ext. 2359 **Fax:** 419-783-2468
E-mail: admissions@defiance.edu

Getting in Last Year 649 applied; 78% were accepted; 178 enrolled (35%).

Financial Matters $16,735 tuition and fees (2002–03); $5070 room and board; 85% average percent of need met; $15,477 average financial aid amount received per undergraduate (2001–02).

Academics Defiance College awards associate, bachelor's, and master's degrees. Challenging opportunities include advanced placement credit, student-designed majors, an honors program, double majors, independent study, and a senior project. Special programs include cooperative education, internships, summer session for credit, off-campus study, and study-abroad. The most frequently chosen baccalaureate fields are business/marketing, education, and law/legal studies. The faculty at Defiance College has 41 full-time members, 59% with terminal degrees. The student-faculty ratio is 14:1.

Students of Defiance College The student body totals 998, of whom 894 are undergraduates. 55.6% are women and 44.4% are men. Students come from 12 states and territories and 3 other countries. 0.6% are international students. 69% returned for their sophomore year.

Applying Defiance College requires SAT I or ACT, a high school transcript, and a minimum high school GPA of 2.25, and in some cases an essay and an interview. The school recommends an interview and recommendations. Application deadline: 8/15; 3/1 priority date for financial aid. Early and deferred admission are possible.

DELAWARE STATE UNIVERSITY

Dover, DE

Small-town setting ■ Public ■ State-supported ■ Coed

Web site: www.dsc.edu
Contact: Mr. Jethro C. Williams, Director of Admissions, 1200 North Dupont Highway, Dover, DE 19901
Telephone: 302-857-6353 or toll-free 800-845-2544 **Fax:** 302-857-6352
E-mail: dadmiss@dsc.edu

Getting in Last Year 2,712 applied; 68% were accepted; 823 enrolled (45%).

Financial Matters $4216 resident tuition and fees (2002–03); $9012 nonresident tuition and fees (2002–03); $6178 room and board; 76% average percent of need met; $7691 average financial aid amount received per undergraduate.

Academics DSU awards bachelor's and master's degrees. Challenging opportunities include advanced placement credit, accelerated degree programs, student-designed majors, an honors program, double majors, independent study, and a senior project. Special programs include cooperative education, internships, summer session for credit, off-campus study, and Army and Air Force ROTC. The faculty at DSU has 174 full-time members, 78% with terminal degrees. The student-faculty ratio is 15:1.

Students of DSU The student body is made up of 3,149 undergraduates. 57.2% are women and 42.8% are men. Students come from 31 states and territories. 56% are from Delaware. 0.4% are international students. 68% returned for their sophomore year.

Applying DSU requires SAT I or ACT, a high school transcript, 2 recommendations, and a minimum high school GPA of 2.0. The school recommends an interview. Application deadline: 4/1; 3/1 priority date for financial aid. Early admission is possible.

DELAWARE VALLEY COLLEGE

Doylestown, PA

Suburban setting ■ *Private* ■ *Independent* ■ *Coed*

Web site: www.devalcol.edu

Contact: Mr. Stephen Zenko, Director of Admissions, 700 East Butler Avenue, Doylestown, PA 18901-2697

Telephone: 215-489-2211 ext. 2211 or toll-free 800-2DELVAL (in-state) **Fax:** 215-230-2968

E-mail: admitme@devalcol.edu

Getting in Last Year 1,273 applied; 83% were accepted; 408 enrolled (39%).

Financial Matters $18,430 tuition and fees (2002–03); $6870 room and board; 85% average percent of need met; $15,583 average financial aid amount received per undergraduate.

Academics Del Val awards associate, bachelor's, and master's degrees and post-bachelor's certificates. Challenging opportunities include advanced placement credit and an honors program. Special programs include cooperative education, internships, summer session for credit, and study-abroad. The most frequently chosen baccalaureate fields are agriculture, business/marketing, and protective services/public administration. The faculty at Del Val has 76 full-time members, 61% with terminal degrees. The student-faculty ratio is 14:1.

Students of Del Val The student body totals 1,995, of whom 1,925 are undergraduates. 51.7% are women and 48.3% are men. Students come from 19 states and territories. 71% are from Pennsylvania. 0.3% are international students. 66% returned for their sophomore year.

Applying Del Val requires SAT I or ACT, a high school transcript, and 1 recommendation. The school recommends an interview. Application deadline: rolling admissions; 4/1 priority date for financial aid. Early and deferred admission are possible.

DELTA STATE UNIVERSITY

Cleveland, MS

Small-town setting ■ *Public* ■ *State-supported* ■ *Coed*

Web site: www.deltastate.edu

Contact: Ms. Debbie Heslep, Director of Admissions, Highway 8 West, Cleveland, MS 38733

Telephone: 662-846-4018 or toll-free 800-468-6378 **Fax:** 662-846-4683

E-mail: dheslep@deltastate.edu

Getting in Last Year 1,536 applied; 24% were accepted; 358 enrolled (97%).

Financial Matters $3348 resident tuition and fees (2002–03); $7965 nonresident tuition and fees (2002–03); $3180 room and board.

Academics Delta State awards bachelor's, master's, and doctoral degrees and post-master's certificates. Challenging opportunities include advanced placement credit, an honors program, double majors, independent study, and a senior project. Special programs include cooperative education, internships, summer session for credit, and Air Force ROTC. The most frequently chosen baccalaureate fields are education, business/marketing, and protective services/public administration. The faculty at Delta State has 177 full-time members, 59% with terminal degrees. The student-faculty ratio is 14:1.

Students of Delta State The student body totals 3,826, of whom 3,219 are undergraduates. 60.8% are women and 39.2% are men. Students come from 23 states and territories. 92% are from Mississippi. 68% returned for their sophomore year.

Applying Delta State requires SAT I or ACT and a high school transcript, and in some cases interview for art, music majors. Application deadline: 8/1; 3/1 priority date for financial aid. Deferred admission is possible.

DENISON UNIVERSITY

Granville, OH

Small-town setting ■ *Private* ■ *Independent* ■ *Coed*

Web site: www.denison.edu

Contact: Mr. Perry Robinson, Director of Admissions, Box H, Granville, OH 43023

Telephone: 740-587-6276 or toll-free 800-DENISON

E-mail: admissions@denison.edu

Getting in Last Year 3,289 applied; 61% were accepted; 633 enrolled (31%).

Financial Matters $24,240 tuition and fees (2002–03); $6880 room and board; 99% average percent of need met; $21,560 average financial aid amount received per undergraduate.

Academics Denison awards bachelor's degrees. Challenging opportunities include advanced placement credit, student-designed majors, an honors program, double majors, independent study, and a senior project. Special programs include cooperative education, internships, off-campus study, study-abroad, and Army ROTC. The most frequently chosen baccalaureate fields are social sciences and history, communications/communication technologies, and biological/life sciences. The faculty at Denison has 183 full-time members, 97% with terminal degrees. The student-faculty ratio is 11:1.

Students of Denison The student body is made up of 2,096 undergraduates. 56% are women and 44% are men. Students come from 48 states and territories and 29 other countries. 45% are from Ohio. 5.1% are international students. 87% returned for their sophomore year.

Applying Denison requires an essay, SAT I or ACT, a high school transcript, and 2 recommendations. The school recommends SAT II Subject Tests and an interview. Application deadline: 2/1; 2/15 priority date for financial aid. Early and deferred admission are possible.

DEPAUL UNIVERSITY

Chicago, IL

Urban setting ■ *Private* ■ *Independent Religious* ■ *Coed*

Web site: www.depaul.edu

Contact: Carlene Klaas, Undergraduate Admissions, 1 East Jackson Boulevard, Suite 9100, Chicago, IL 60604

Telephone: 312-362-8300 or toll-free 800-4DE-PAUL (out-of-state)

E-mail: admitdpu@depaul.edu

Getting in Last Year 8,906 applied; 78% were accepted; 2,256 enrolled (33%).

Financial Matters $17,850 tuition and fees (2002–03); $7455 room and board; 74% average percent of need met; $14,106 average financial aid amount received per undergraduate.

Academics DePaul awards bachelor's, master's, doctoral, and first-professional degrees and post-bachelor's and post-master's certificates. Challenging opportunities include advanced placement credit, accelerated degree programs, freshman honors college, an honors program, double majors, independent study, and a senior project. Special programs include cooperative education, internships, summer session for credit, study-abroad, and Army ROTC. The most frequently chosen baccalaureate fields are business/marketing, liberal arts/general studies, and computer/information sciences. The faculty at DePaul has 785 full-time members. The student-faculty ratio is 19:1.

Students of DePaul The student body totals 24,227, of whom 15,343 are undergraduates. 54.2% are women and 45.8% are men. Students come from 50 states and territories and 44 other countries. 89% are from Illinois. 1.6% are international students. 85% returned for their sophomore year.

Applying DePaul requires SAT I or ACT, a high school transcript, 1 recommendation, and a minimum high school GPA of 2.0, and in some cases an interview, audition, and a minimum high school GPA of 3.0. The school recommends a minimum high school GPA of 3.0. Application deadline: rolling admissions; 4/1 for financial aid, with a 3/1 priority date. Early and deferred admission are possible.

DEPAUW UNIVERSITY

Greencastle, IN

Small-town setting ■ *Private* ■ *Independent Religious* ■ *Coed*

Web site: www.depauw.edu

Contact: Director of Admission, 101 East Seminary Street, Greencastle, IN 46135-0037

Telephone: 765-658-4006 or toll-free 800-447-2495 **Fax:** 765-658-4007

E-mail: admission@depauw.edu

Getting in Last Year 3,682 applied; 61% were accepted; 685 enrolled (30%).

Financial Matters $22,840 tuition and fees (2002–03); $6800 room and board; 99% average percent of need met; $20,223 average financial aid amount received per undergraduate.

Academics DePauw awards bachelor's degrees. Challenging opportunities include advanced placement credit, student-designed majors, an honors program, double majors, independent study, and a senior project. Special programs include internships, off-campus study, study-abroad, and Army and Air Force ROTC. The most frequently chosen baccalaureate fields are communications/communication technologies, English, and computer/information sciences. The faculty at DePauw has 195 full-time members, 93% with terminal degrees. The student-faculty ratio is 11:1.

Students of DePauw The student body is made up of 2,338 undergraduates. 55.7% are women and 44.3% are men. Students come from 42 states and territories and 15 other countries. 53% are from Indiana. 1.5% are international students. 92% returned for their sophomore year.

Applying DePauw requires an essay, SAT I or ACT, a high school transcript, and 1 recommendation. The school recommends an interview and a minimum high school GPA of 3.25. Application deadline: 2/1; 2/15 for financial aid. Early and deferred admission are possible.

DEREE COLLEGE

Aghia Paraskevi Greece

Urban setting ■ *Private* ■ *Independent* ■ *Coed*

Web site: www.acg.edu

Contact: Mr. Nick Jiavaras, Director of Enrollment Management, 6 Gravias Street, Aghia Paraskevi Greece

Deree College (continued)

Telephone: 301-210-600-9800 ext. 1322 **Fax:** 301-801-600-9811
E-mail: dereeadm@hol.gr

Getting in Last Year 1,121 applied; 86% were accepted; 596 enrolled (62%).

Financial Matters $3563 tuition and fees (2002–03).

Academics Deree awards associate and bachelor's degrees. Challenging opportunities include accelerated degree programs, double majors, independent study, and a senior project. Special programs include internships, summer session for credit, and study-abroad. The most frequently chosen baccalaureate fields are business/marketing, social sciences and history, and computer/information sciences. The faculty at Deree has 81 full-time members, 49% with terminal degrees. The student-faculty ratio is 21:1.

Students of Deree The student body is made up of 6,273 undergraduates. 62.3% are women and 37.7% are men. 80% returned for their sophomore year.

Applying Deree requires a high school transcript, an interview, 1 recommendation, and a minimum high school GPA of 2.0, and in some cases an essay and SAT I and SAT II or ACT. The school recommends medical certificate. Application deadline: 7/25; 1/15 for financial aid. Deferred admission is possible.

DESALES UNIVERSITY

Center Valley, PA

Suburban setting ■ Private ■ Independent Religious ■ Coed

Web site: www.desales.edu
Contact: Mr. Peter Rautzhan, Director of Admissions and Financial Aid, 2755 Station Avenue, Center Valley, PA 18034-9568
Telephone: 610-282-1100 ext. 1332 or toll-free 877-4DESALES (in-state), 800-228-5114 (out-of-state) **Fax:** 610-282-2254
E-mail: admiss@desales.edu

Getting in Last Year 1,488 applied; 68% were accepted; 463 enrolled (46%).

Financial Matters $17,340 tuition and fees (2002–03); $6520 room and board; 79% average percent of need met; $12,555 average financial aid amount received per undergraduate.

Academics Allentown College awards bachelor's and master's degrees and post-bachelor's and post-master's certificates (also offers adult program with significant enrollment not reflected in profile). Challenging opportunities include advanced placement credit, accelerated degree programs, an honors program, double majors, independent study, and a senior project. Special programs include internships, summer session for credit, off-campus study, study-abroad, and Army ROTC. The most frequently chosen baccalaureate fields are business/marketing, health professions and related sciences, and visual/performing arts. The faculty at Allentown College has 89 full-time members, 76% with terminal degrees. The student-faculty ratio is 17:1.

Students of Allentown College The student body totals 2,933, of whom 2,179 are undergraduates. 57.3% are women and 42.7% are men. Students come from 12 states and territories. 71% are from Pennsylvania. 0.1% are international students. 81% returned for their sophomore year.

Applying Allentown College requires SAT I or ACT, a high school transcript, and 2 recommendations. The school recommends an essay and an interview. Application deadline: 8/1; 2/1 priority date for financial aid. Early and deferred admission are possible.

DESIGN INSTITUTE OF SAN DIEGO

San Diego, CA

Urban setting ■ Private ■ Proprietary ■ Coed

Web site: www.disd.edu
Contact: Ms. Paula Parrish, Director of Admissions, 8555 Commerce Avenue, San Diego, CA 92121
Telephone: 619-566-1200 or toll-free 800-619-4337 (in-state), 800-619-4DESIGN (out-of-state) **Fax:** 858-566-2711
E-mail: admissions@disd.edu

Financial Matters $10,800 tuition and fees (2002–03).

Academics Design Institute of San Diego awards bachelor's degrees. A senior project is a challenging opportunity. Special programs include internships and study-abroad. The faculty at Design Institute of San Diego has 50 members.

Students of Design Institute of San Diego The student body is made up of 450 undergraduates. Students come from 10 states and territories and 15 other countries. 87% returned for their sophomore year.

Applying Design Institute of San Diego requires a high school transcript and a minimum high school GPA of 2.0. The school recommends an interview. Application deadline: rolling admissions.

DEVRY COLLEGE OF TECHNOLOGY

North Brunswick, NJ

Urban setting ■ Private ■ Proprietary ■ Coed

Web site: www.nj.devry.edu
Contact: Ms. Norma Houze, New Student Coordinator, 630 US Highway One, North Brunswick, NJ 08902-3362
Telephone: 732-435-4880 or toll-free 800-333-3879

Getting in Last Year 881 enrolled.

Financial Matters $9665 tuition and fees (2002–03); 47% average percent of need met; $7419 average financial aid amount received per undergraduate (2001–02).

Academics DeVry awards associate and bachelor's degrees. Challenging opportunities include advanced placement credit and a senior project. Summer session for credit is a special program. The most frequently chosen baccalaureate fields are communications/communication technologies and engineering/engineering technologies. The faculty at DeVry has 78 full-time members. The student-faculty ratio is 19:1.

Students of DeVry The student body is made up of 3,268 undergraduates. 21.3% are women and 78.7% are men. Students come from 19 states and territories and 23 other countries. 88% are from New Jersey. 1.3% are international students. 52% returned for their sophomore year.

Applying DeVry requires CPT, a high school transcript, an interview, and CPT. The school recommends SAT I or ACT. Application deadline: rolling admissions. Deferred admission is possible.

DEVRY INSTITUTE OF TECHNOLOGY

Long Island City, NY

Urban setting ■ Private ■ Proprietary ■ Coed

Web site: www.ny.devry.edu
Contact: Ms. Edith Bolanos, New Student Coordinator, 30-20 Thomson Avenue, Long Island City, NY 11101
Telephone: 718-472-2728 or toll-free 888-71-Devry (out-of-state) **Fax:** 718-269-4288

Getting in Last Year 717 enrolled.

Financial Matters $10,615 tuition and fees (2002–03); 50% average percent of need met; $9227 average financial aid amount received per undergraduate (2001–02).

Academics DeVry awards associate and bachelor's degrees. Challenging opportunities include advanced placement credit, accelerated degree programs, and a senior project. Special programs include cooperative education and summer session for credit. The most frequently chosen baccalaureate fields are engineering/engineering technologies and business/marketing. The faculty at DeVry has 60 full-time members. The student-faculty ratio is 16:1.

Students of DeVry The student body is made up of 2,052 undergraduates. 22.9% are women and 77.1% are men. Students come from 20 states and territories and 17 other countries. 95% are from New York. 3.4% are international students. 41% returned for their sophomore year.

Applying DeVry requires CPT, a high school transcript, an interview, and CPT. The school recommends SAT I or ACT. Application deadline: rolling admissions. Deferred admission is possible.

DEVRY UNIVERSITY

Phoenix, AZ

Urban setting ■ Private ■ Proprietary ■ Coed

Contact: Mr. Jerry Driskill, Director of Admissions, 2149 West Dunlap, Phoenix, AZ 85021-2995
Telephone: 602-870-9201 or toll-free 800-528-0250 (out-of-state) **Fax:** 602-331-1494
E-mail: webadmin@devry-phx.edu

Getting in Last Year 911 applied; 65% were accepted; 529 enrolled (89%).

Financial Matters $9555 tuition and fees (2002–03); 50% average percent of need met; $8069 average financial aid amount received per undergraduate (2001–02).

Academics DeVry awards associate and bachelor's degrees and post-bachelor's certificates. Challenging opportunities include advanced placement credit, accelerated degree programs, and a senior project. Special programs include cooperative education, summer session for credit, and Air Force ROTC. The most frequently chosen baccalaureate fields are computer/information sciences, business/marketing, and engineering/engineering technologies. The faculty at DeVry has 73 full-time members. The student-faculty ratio is 25:1.

Students of DeVry The student body totals 2,721, of whom 2,529 are undergraduates. 23% are women and 77% are men. Students come from 41 states and territories and 4 other countries. 71% are from Arizona. 0.6% are international students. 41% returned for their sophomore year.

Applying DeVry requires CPT, a high school transcript, an interview, and CPT. The school recommends SAT I or ACT. Application deadline: rolling admissions. Deferred admission is possible.

DEVRY UNIVERSITY

Fremont, CA

Suburban setting ■ Private ■ Proprietary ■ Coed

Web site: www.fre.devry.edu

Contact: Mr. Bruce Williams, New Student Coordinator, 6600 Dumbarton Circle, Fremont, CA 94555
Telephone: 510-574-1111 or toll-free 888-393-3879

Getting in Last Year 444 enrolled.

Financial Matters $10,615 tuition and fees (2002–03); 50% average percent of need met; $8956 average financial aid amount received per undergraduate (2001–02).

Academics DeVry awards associate and bachelor's degrees and post-bachelor's certificates. Challenging opportunities include advanced placement credit, accelerated degree programs, and a senior project. Special programs include cooperative education and summer session for credit. The most frequently chosen baccalaureate fields are business/marketing, engineering/engineering technologies, and computer/information sciences. The faculty at DeVry has 51 full-time members. The student-faculty ratio is 23:1.

Students of DeVry The student body totals 2,070, of whom 1,978 are undergraduates. 22.8% are women and 77.2% are men. Students come from 25 states and territories and 9 other countries. 97% are from California. 2% are international students. 60% returned for their sophomore year.

Applying DeVry requires CPT, a high school transcript, an interview, and CPT. The school recommends SAT I or ACT. Application deadline: rolling admissions. Deferred admission is possible.

DEVRY UNIVERSITY
Long Beach, CA

Urban setting ■ Private ■ Proprietary ■ Coed

Web site: www.lb.devry.edu
Contact: Ms. Lisa Flores, New Student Coordinator, 3880 Kilroy Airport, Long Beach, CA 90806
Telephone: 562-427-0861 or toll-free 800-597-0444 (out-of-state)
Fax: 562-997-5371

Getting in Last Year 506 enrolled.

Financial Matters $10,115 tuition and fees (2002–03); 44% average percent of need met; $7440 average financial aid amount received per undergraduate (2001–02).

Academics DeVry awards associate and bachelor's degrees and post-bachelor's certificates. Challenging opportunities include advanced placement credit, accelerated degree programs, and a senior project. Special programs include cooperative education and summer session for credit. The most frequently chosen baccalaureate fields are business/marketing, computer/information sciences, and engineering/engineering technologies. The faculty at DeVry has 40 full-time members. The student-faculty ratio is 18:1.

Students of DeVry The student body totals 2,629, of whom 2,385 are undergraduates. 26.9% are women and 73.1% are men. Students come from 23 states and territories and 11 other countries. 98% are from California. 1.7% are international students. 45% returned for their sophomore year.

Applying DeVry requires CPT, a high school transcript, an interview, and CPT. The school recommends SAT I or ACT. Application deadline: rolling admissions. Deferred admission is possible.

DEVRY UNIVERSITY
Pomona, CA

Urban setting ■ Private ■ Proprietary ■ Coed

Web site: www.pom.devry.edu
Contact: Ms. Melanie Guerra, New Student Coordinator, 901 Corporate Center Drive, Pomona, CA 91768-2642
Telephone: 909-622-8866 or toll-free 800-243-3660 **Fax:** 909-868-4165

Getting in Last Year 632 enrolled.

Financial Matters $10,115 tuition and fees (2002–03); 44% average percent of need met; $7521 average financial aid amount received per undergraduate (2001–02).

Academics DeVry awards associate and bachelor's degrees and post-bachelor's certificates. Challenging opportunities include advanced placement credit, accelerated degree programs, and a senior project. Special programs include cooperative education and summer session for credit. The most frequently chosen baccalaureate fields are business/marketing, computer/information sciences, and engineering/engineering technologies. The faculty at DeVry has 49 full-time members. The student-faculty ratio is 22:1.

Students of DeVry The student body totals 3,197, of whom 2,998 are undergraduates. 24.9% are women and 75.1% are men. Students come from 25 states and territories and 19 other countries. 98% are from California. 2.4% are international students. 49% returned for their sophomore year.

Applying DeVry requires CPT, a high school transcript, an interview, and CPT. The school recommends SAT I or ACT. Application deadline: rolling admissions. Deferred admission is possible.

DEVRY UNIVERSITY
West Hills, CA

Suburban setting ■ Private ■ Proprietary ■ Coed

Web site: www.wh.devry.edu
Contact: Ms. Denise Barba, Acting Director of Admissions, 22801 Roscoe Boulevard, West Hills, CA 91304
Telephone: 818-932-3001 **Fax:** 818-713-8118

Getting in Last Year 300 enrolled.

Financial Matters $10,115 tuition and fees (2002–03); 40% average percent of need met; $7405 average financial aid amount received per undergraduate (2001–02).

Academics DeVry University awards associate and bachelor's degrees and post-bachelor's certificates. Challenging opportunities include advanced placement credit, accelerated degree programs, and a senior project. Special programs include cooperative education and summer session for credit. The most frequently chosen baccalaureate field is business/marketing. The faculty at DeVry University has 19 full-time members. The student-faculty ratio is 15:1.

Students of DeVry University The student body totals 1,423, of whom 1,306 are undergraduates. 23.9% are women and 76.1% are men. Students come from 10 states and territories and 13 other countries. 97% are from California. 1.7% are international students. 56% returned for their sophomore year.

Applying DeVry University requires CPT, a high school transcript, an interview, and CPT. The school recommends SAT I or ACT. Application deadline: rolling admissions. Deferred admission is possible.

DEVRY UNIVERSITY
Colorado Springs, CO

Urban setting ■ Private ■ Proprietary ■ Coed

Web site: www.cs.devry.edu
Contact: Mr. Rick Rodman, Director of Admissions, 925 South Niagara Street, Denver, CO 80224
Telephone: 303-329-3340 ext. 7221

Getting in Last Year 145 applied; 80% were accepted; 102 enrolled (88%).

Financial Matters $10,115 tuition and fees (2002–03); 32% average percent of need met; $4467 average financial aid amount received per undergraduate (2001–02).

Academics DeVry awards associate and bachelor's degrees and post-bachelor's certificates. Challenging opportunities include advanced placement credit, accelerated degree programs, and a senior project. Special programs include cooperative education and summer session for credit. The faculty at DeVry has 11 full-time members. The student-faculty ratio is 5:1.

Students of DeVry The student body totals 230, of whom 221 are undergraduates. 26.2% are women and 73.8% are men. Students come from 12 states and territories and 1 other country. 94% are from Colorado. 0.5% are international students.

Applying DeVry requires CPT, a high school transcript, an interview, and CPT. The school recommends SAT I or ACT. Application deadline: rolling admissions. Deferred admission is possible.

DEVRY UNIVERSITY
Denver, CO

Private ■ Proprietary ■ Coed

Web site: www.den.devry.edu
Contact: Mr. Rick Rodman, 925 South Niagara Street, Denver, CO 80224
Telephone: 303-329-3340 **Fax:** - ext.

Getting in Last Year 329 applied; 66% were accepted; 205 enrolled (95%).

Financial Matters $10,115 tuition and fees (2002–03); 37% average percent of need met; $5040 average financial aid amount received per undergraduate (2001–02).

Academics DeVry awards associate and bachelor's degrees. Challenging opportunities include advanced placement credit, accelerated degree programs, and a senior project. Cooperative education is a special program. The faculty at DeVry has 19 full-time members. The student-faculty ratio is 7:1.

Students of DeVry The student body is made up of 460 undergraduates. 22.8% are women and 77.2% are men. Students come from 16 states and territories and 4 other countries. 86% are from Colorado. 1.5% are international students.

Applying DeVry requires a high school transcript, an interview, and CPT. The school recommends SAT I or ACT. Deferred admission is possible.

DEVRY UNIVERSITY
Miramar, FL

Private ■ Proprietary ■ Coed

Web site: www.devry.edu/miramar

DeVry University (continued)

Contact: Ms. Tammy Gardener, New Student Coordinator, 2300 Southwest 145th Avenue, Miramar, FL 33207-4150
Telephone: 954-499-9707 **Fax:** 954-499-9723
Getting in Last Year 732 applied; 61% were accepted; 285 enrolled (63%).
Academics DeVry University awards associate and bachelor's degrees. Challenging opportunities include advanced placement credit and accelerated degree programs. Cooperative education is a special program. The faculty at DeVry University has 12 full-time members. The student-faculty ratio is 20:1.
Students of DeVry University The student body is made up of 314 undergraduates. 19.7% are women and 80.3% are men. Students come from 9 states and territories and 5 other countries. 95% are from Florida. 2.9% are international students.
Applying DeVry University requires a high school transcript, an interview, and CPT.

DEVRY UNIVERSITY
Orlando, FL
Urban setting ■ *Private* ■ *Proprietary* ■ *Coed*
Web site: www.orl.devry.edu
Contact: Ms. Laura Dorsey, New Student Coordinator, 4000 Millenia Boulevard, Orlando, FL 32839
Telephone: 407-355-4833 or toll-free 866-fl-devry (in-state) **Fax:** 407-370-3198
Getting in Last Year 486 enrolled.
Financial Matters $10,115 tuition and fees (2002–03); 36% average percent of need met; $6175 average financial aid amount received per undergraduate (2001–02).
Academics DeVry University awards associate and bachelor's degrees and post-bachelor's certificates. Challenging opportunities include advanced placement credit, accelerated degree programs, and a senior project. Special programs include cooperative education and summer session for credit. The faculty at DeVry University has 43 full-time members. The student-faculty ratio is 18:1.
Students of DeVry University The student body totals 1,227, of whom 1,172 are undergraduates. 26.4% are women and 73.6% are men. Students come from 30 states and territories and 13 other countries. 88% are from Florida. 3.6% are international students. 43% returned for their sophomore year.
Applying DeVry University requires CPT, a high school transcript, an interview, and CPT. The school recommends SAT I and SAT II or ACT. Application deadline: rolling admissions. Deferred admission is possible.

DEVRY UNIVERSITY
Alpharetta, GA
Suburban setting ■ *Private* ■ *Proprietary* ■ *Coed*
Web site: www.devry.edu/alpharetta
Contact: Ms. Kristi Franklin, New Student Coordinator, 2555 Northwinds Parkway, Alpharetta, GA 30004
Telephone: 770-521-4900 **Fax:** 770-664-8824
Getting in Last Year 573 applied; 74% were accepted; 303 enrolled (71%).
Financial Matters $9555 tuition and fees (2002–03); 45% average percent of need met; $7054 average financial aid amount received per undergraduate (2001–02).
Academics DeVry awards associate and bachelor's degrees and post-bachelor's certificates. Challenging opportunities include advanced placement credit, accelerated degree programs, and a senior project. Special programs include cooperative education and summer session for credit. The most frequently chosen baccalaureate fields are business/marketing, computer/information sciences, and engineering/engineering technologies. The faculty at DeVry has 38 full-time members. The student-faculty ratio is 16:1.
Students of DeVry The student body totals 1,508, of whom 1,329 are undergraduates. 32.9% are women and 67.1% are men. Students come from 29 states and territories and 17 other countries. 85% are from Georgia. 3.2% are international students. 40% returned for their sophomore year.
Applying DeVry requires CPT, a high school transcript, an interview, and CPT. The school recommends SAT I or ACT. Application deadline: rolling admissions. Deferred admission is possible.

DEVRY UNIVERSITY
Decatur, GA
Suburban setting ■ *Private* ■ *Proprietary* ■ *Coed*
Web site: www.atl.devry.edu
Contact: Ms. Karen Krumenaker, New Student Coordinator, 250 North Arcadia Avenue, Decatur, GA 30030
Telephone: 404-292-2645 or toll-free 800-221-4771 (out-of-state)
E-mail: dwalters@admin.atl.devry.edu
Getting in Last Year 1,080 applied; 61% were accepted; 572 enrolled (87%).
Financial Matters $9555 tuition and fees (2002–03); 56% average percent of need met; $12,676 average financial aid amount received per undergraduate (2001–02).
Academics DeVry awards associate and bachelor's degrees and post-bachelor's certificates. Challenging opportunities include advanced placement credit, accelerated degree programs, and a senior project. Special programs include cooperative education and summer session for credit. The most frequently chosen baccalaureate fields are business/marketing, computer/information sciences, and engineering/engineering technologies. The faculty at DeVry has 63 full-time members. The student-faculty ratio is 19:1.
Students of DeVry The student body totals 2,950, of whom 2,596 are undergraduates. 39.6% are women and 60.4% are men. Students come from 32 states and territories and 2 other countries. 83% are from Georgia. 1.9% are international students. 43% returned for their sophomore year.
Applying DeVry requires CPT, a high school transcript, an interview, and CPT. The school recommends SAT I or ACT. Application deadline: rolling admissions. Deferred admission is possible.

DEVRY UNIVERSITY
Addison, IL
Suburban setting ■ *Private* ■ *Proprietary* ■ *Coed*
Web site: www.dpg.devry.edu
Contact: Ms. Jane Miritello, Assistant New Student Coordinator, 18624 W. Creek Drive, Tinley Park, IL 60477
Telephone: 708-342-3300 or toll-free 877-305-8184 (out-of-state) **Fax:** 708-342-3120
Getting in Last Year 860 applied; 70% were accepted; 597 enrolled (99%).
Financial Matters $9665 tuition and fees (2002–03); 55% average percent of need met; $8374 average financial aid amount received per undergraduate (2001–02).
Academics DeVry awards associate and bachelor's degrees. Challenging opportunities include advanced placement credit, accelerated degree programs, and a senior project. Special programs include cooperative education and summer session for credit. The most frequently chosen baccalaureate fields are business/marketing, computer/information sciences, and engineering/engineering technologies. The faculty at DeVry has 69 full-time members. The student-faculty ratio is 19:1.
Students of DeVry The student body is made up of 3,028 undergraduates. 23.2% are women and 76.8% are men. Students come from 30 states and territories and 23 other countries. 94% are from Illinois. 1.8% are international students. 46% returned for their sophomore year.
Applying DeVry requires CPT, a high school transcript, an interview, and CPT. The school recommends SAT I or ACT. Application deadline: rolling admissions. Deferred admission is possible.

DEVRY UNIVERSITY
Chicago, IL
Urban setting ■ *Private* ■ *Proprietary* ■ *Coed*
Web site: www.chi.devry.edu
Contact: Ms. Christine Hierl, Director of Admissions, 3300 North Campbell Avenue, Chicago, IL 60618-5994
Telephone: 773-929-6550 or toll-free 800-383-3879 (out-of-state) **Fax:** 773-929-8093
Getting in Last Year 691 enrolled.
Financial Matters $9665 tuition and fees (2002–03); 57% average percent of need met; $10,268 average financial aid amount received per undergraduate (2001–02).
Academics DeVry awards associate and bachelor's degrees. Challenging opportunities include advanced placement credit, accelerated degree programs, and a senior project. Special programs include cooperative education and summer session for credit. The most frequently chosen baccalaureate fields are computer/information sciences, business/marketing, and engineering/engineering technologies. The faculty at DeVry has 74 full-time members. The student-faculty ratio is 21:1.
Students of DeVry The student body is made up of 3,539 undergraduates. 35.2% are women and 64.8% are men. Students come from 23 states and territories and 26 other countries. 98% are from Illinois. 2% are international students. 45% returned for their sophomore year.
Applying DeVry requires CPT, a high school transcript, an interview, and CPT. The school recommends SAT I or ACT. Application deadline: rolling admissions. Deferred admission is possible.

DEVRY UNIVERSITY
Tinley Park, IL
Suburban setting ■ *Private* ■ *Proprietary* ■ *Coed*
Web site: www.tp.devry.edu
Contact: Ms. Kerrie Flynn, Assistant New Student Coordinator, 18624 W. Creek Drive, Tinley Park, IL 60477
Telephone: 708-342-3300 or toll-free 877-305-8184 (out-of-state)
Getting in Last Year 546 applied; 67% were accepted; 321 enrolled (87%).

Financial Matters $9665 tuition and fees (2002–03); 55% average percent of need met; $8382 average financial aid amount received per undergraduate (2001–02).

Academics DeVry University awards associate and bachelor's degrees and post-bachelor's certificates. Challenging opportunities include advanced placement credit, accelerated degree programs, and a senior project. Special programs include cooperative education and summer session for credit. The faculty at DeVry University has 36 full-time members. The student-faculty ratio is 17:1.

Students of DeVry University The student body totals 1,928, of whom 1,701 are undergraduates. 26.6% are women and 73.4% are men. Students come from 19 states and territories and 9 other countries. 92% are from Illinois. 0.8% are international students. 56% returned for their sophomore year.

Applying DeVry University requires CPT, a high school transcript, an interview, and CPT. The school recommends SAT I or ACT. Application deadline: rolling admissions. Deferred admission is possible.

DEVRY UNIVERSITY
Kansas City, MO

Urban setting ■ Private ■ Proprietary ■ Coed

Web site: www.kc.devry.edu

Contact: Ms. Anna Diamond, New Student Coordinator, 11224 Holmes Street, Kansas City, MO 64131

Telephone: 816-941-0430 or toll-free 800-821-3766 (out-of-state)

Getting in Last Year 631 applied; 71% were accepted; 395 enrolled (88%).

Financial Matters $9555 tuition and fees (2002–03); 44% average percent of need met; $7095 average financial aid amount received per undergraduate (2001–02).

Academics DeVry awards associate and bachelor's degrees and post-bachelor's certificates. Challenging opportunities include advanced placement credit, accelerated degree programs, and a senior project. Special programs include cooperative education and summer session for credit. The most frequently chosen baccalaureate fields are business/marketing, computer/information sciences, and engineering/engineering technologies. The faculty at DeVry has 69 full-time members. The student-faculty ratio is 18:1.

Students of DeVry The student body totals 2,590, of whom 2,374 are undergraduates. 24.4% are women and 75.6% are men. Students come from 28 states and territories and 8 other countries. 58% are from Missouri. 0.8% are international students. 46% returned for their sophomore year.

Applying DeVry requires CPT, a high school transcript, an interview, and CPT. The school recommends SAT I or ACT. Application deadline: rolling admissions. Deferred admission is possible.

DEVRY UNIVERSITY
Columbus, OH

Urban setting ■ Private ■ Proprietary ■ Coed

Web site: www.devrycols.edu

Contact: Ms. Shelia Brown, New Student Coordinator, 1350 Alum Creek Drive, Columbus, OH 43209-2705

Telephone: 614-253-1850 or toll-free 800-426-3916 (in-state), 800-426-3090 (out-of-state)

E-mail: admissions@devrycol5.edu

Getting in Last Year 942 enrolled.

Financial Matters $9555 tuition and fees (2002–03); 47% average percent of need met; $7409 average financial aid amount received per undergraduate (2001–02).

Academics DeVry awards associate and bachelor's degrees and post-bachelor's certificates. Challenging opportunities include advanced placement credit, accelerated degree programs, and a senior project. Special programs include cooperative education, summer session for credit, and Army ROTC. The most frequently chosen baccalaureate fields are computer/information sciences, business/marketing, and engineering/engineering technologies. The faculty at DeVry has 83 full-time members. The student-faculty ratio is 22:1.

Students of DeVry The student body totals 3,632, of whom 3,493 are undergraduates. 23.7% are women and 76.3% are men. Students come from 32 states and territories and 3 other countries. 88% are from Ohio. 0.9% are international students. 45% returned for their sophomore year.

Applying DeVry requires CPT, a high school transcript, an interview, and CPT. The school recommends SAT I or ACT. Application deadline: rolling admissions. Deferred admission is possible.

DEVRY UNIVERSITY
Fort Washington, PA

Private ■ Proprietary ■ Coed

Web site: www.devry.edu/fortwashington

Contact: Mr. Steve Cohen, Director of Admissions, 501 Office Center Drive, Suite 420, Fort Washington, PA 19034

Telephone: 215-591-5700 or toll-free 866-303-3879 (out-of-state)

Getting in Last Year 273 enrolled.

Academics DeVry University awards associate and bachelor's degrees and post-bachelor's certificates. Challenging opportunities include advanced placement credit, accelerated degree programs, and a senior project. Special programs include cooperative education and summer session for credit. The faculty at DeVry University has 9 full-time members. The student-faculty ratio is 11:1.

Students of DeVry University The student body totals 357, of whom 322 are undergraduates. 16.1% are women and 83.9% are men. Students come from 8 states and territories. 80% are from Pennsylvania.

Applying DeVry University requires CPT, a high school transcript, an interview, and CPT. The school recommends SAT I or ACT. Application deadline: rolling admissions. Deferred admission is possible.

DEVRY UNIVERSITY
Irving, TX

Suburban setting ■ Private ■ Proprietary ■ Coed

Web site: www.dal.devry.edu

Contact: Ms. Vicki Carroll, New Student Coordinator, 4000 Millenia Drive, Orlando, FL 32839

Telephone: 972-929-5777 or toll-free 800-443-3879 (in-state), 800-633-3879 (out-of-state)

Getting in Last Year 845 enrolled.

Financial Matters $9555 tuition and fees (2002–03); 41% average percent of need met; $6831 average financial aid amount received per undergraduate (2001–02).

Academics DeVry awards associate and bachelor's degrees and post-bachelor's certificates. Challenging opportunities include advanced placement credit, accelerated degree programs, and a senior project. Special programs include cooperative education and summer session for credit. The most frequently chosen baccalaureate fields are business/marketing, computer/information sciences, and engineering/engineering technologies. The faculty at DeVry has 77 full-time members. The student-faculty ratio is 16:1.

Students of DeVry The student body totals 3,163, of whom 2,984 are undergraduates. 27.7% are women and 72.3% are men. Students come from 39 states and territories and 5 other countries. 93% are from Texas. 1.6% are international students. 39% returned for their sophomore year.

Applying DeVry requires CPT, a high school transcript, an interview, and CPT. The school recommends SAT I or ACT. Application deadline: rolling admissions. Deferred admission is possible.

DEVRY UNIVERSITY
Arlington, VA

Private ■ Proprietary ■ Coed

Web site: www.crys.devry.edu

Contact: Mr. Todd Marshburn, Director of Enrollment Services, Century Building I, Suite 200, 2341 Jefferson Davis Highway, Arlington, VA 22202

Telephone: 866-338-7932

Getting in Last Year 299 enrolled.

Financial Matters $10,615 tuition and fees (2002–03); 28% average percent of need met; $3091 average financial aid amount received per undergraduate (2001–02).

Academics DeVry awards associate and bachelor's degrees and post-bachelor's certificates. Challenging opportunities include advanced placement credit, accelerated degree programs, and a senior project. Special programs include cooperative education and summer session for credit. The faculty at DeVry has 20 full-time members. The student-faculty ratio is 17:1.

Students of DeVry The student body totals 685, of whom 561 are undergraduates. 21.7% are women and 78.3% are men. Students come from 18 states and territories and 1 other country. 37% are from Virginia. 2.9% are international students.

Applying DeVry requires CPT, a high school transcript, an interview, and CPT. The school recommends SAT I or ACT. Application deadline: rolling admissions. Deferred admission is possible.

DEVRY UNIVERSITY
Federal Way, WA

Suburban setting ■ Private ■ Proprietary ■ Coed

Web site: www.sea.devry.edu

Contact: Ms. Latanya Kibby, Assistant New Student Coordinator, 3600 South 344th Way, Federal Way, WA 98001-2995

Telephone: 253-943-2800

Getting in Last Year 419 enrolled.

Financial Matters $10,615 tuition and fees (2002–03); 34% average percent of need met; $5091 average financial aid amount received per undergraduate (2001–02).

Academics DeVry awards associate and bachelor's degrees and post-bachelor's certificates. Challenging opportunities include advanced placement credit, accelerated degree programs, and a senior project. Special programs include

DeVry University (continued)

cooperative education and summer session for credit. The faculty at DeVry has 21 full-time members. The student-faculty ratio is 24:1.

Students of DeVry The student body totals 889, of whom 865 are undergraduates. 20.6% are women and 79.4% are men. Students come from 20 states and territories. 90% are from Washington. 0.5% are international students.

Applying DeVry requires CPT, a high school transcript, an interview, and CPT. The school recommends SAT I or ACT. Application deadline: rolling admissions. Deferred admission is possible.

DICKINSON COLLEGE

Carlisle, PA

Suburban setting ■ Private ■ Independent ■ Coed

Web site: www.dickinson.edu

Contact: Mr. Christopher Seth Allen, Director of Admissions, PO Box 1773, Carlisle, PA 17013-2896

Telephone: 717-245-1231 or toll-free 800-644-1773 **Fax:** 717-245-1442

E-mail: admit@dickinson.edu

Getting in Last Year 4,095 applied; 51% were accepted; 574 enrolled (27%).

Financial Matters $26,635 tuition and fees (2002–03); $6860 room and board; 98% average percent of need met; $22,147 average financial aid amount received per undergraduate.

Academics Dickinson awards bachelor's degrees. Challenging opportunities include advanced placement credit, accelerated degree programs, student-designed majors, double majors, independent study, and a senior project. Special programs include internships, summer session for credit, off-campus study, study-abroad, and Army ROTC. The most frequently chosen baccalaureate fields are social sciences and history, foreign language/literature, and English. The faculty at Dickinson has 162 full-time members, 96% with terminal degrees. The student-faculty ratio is 13:1.

Students of Dickinson The student body is made up of 2,261 undergraduates. 58.1% are women and 41.9% are men. Students come from 43 states and territories and 19 other countries. 39% are from Pennsylvania. 1.4% are international students. 89% returned for their sophomore year.

Applying Dickinson requires an essay, a high school transcript, and 2 recommendations. The school recommends SAT I and SAT II or ACT, an interview, and a minimum high school GPA of 3.0. Application deadline: 2/1; 2/1 priority date for financial aid. Deferred admission is possible.

DICKINSON STATE UNIVERSITY

Dickinson, ND

Small-town setting ■ Public ■ State-supported ■ Coed

Web site: www.dsu.nodak.edu

Contact: Ms. Deb Dazell, Director of Student Recruitment, Campus Box 169, Dickinson, ND 58601

Telephone: 701-483-2175 or toll-free 800-279-4295 **Fax:** 701-483-2409

E-mail: dsu.hawks@dsu.nodak.edu

Getting in Last Year 625 applied; 100% were accepted; 433 enrolled (69%).

Financial Matters $2798 resident tuition and fees (2002–03); $6475 nonresident tuition and fees (2002–03); $2050 room and board.

Academics Dickinson State University awards associate and bachelor's degrees. Challenging opportunities include advanced placement credit, accelerated degree programs, student-designed majors, an honors program, double majors, independent study, and a senior project. Special programs include cooperative education, internships, summer session for credit, off-campus study, and study-abroad. The most frequently chosen baccalaureate fields are education, business/marketing, and health professions and related sciences. The faculty at Dickinson State University has 73 full-time members, 56% with terminal degrees. The student-faculty ratio is 19:1.

Students of Dickinson State University The student body is made up of 2,326 undergraduates. 56.1% are women and 43.9% are men. Students come from 26 states and territories and 26 other countries. 72% are from North Dakota. 3.7% are international students. 56% returned for their sophomore year.

Applying Dickinson State University requires SAT I or ACT, a high school transcript, and medical history, proof of measles-rubella shot. Application deadline: rolling admissions; 4/15 priority date for financial aid. Early and deferred admission are possible.

DILLARD UNIVERSITY

New Orleans, LA

Urban setting ■ Private ■ Independent Religious ■ Coed

Contact: Ms. Linda Nash, Director of Admissions, 2601 Gentilly Boulevard, New Orleans, LA 70122

Telephone: 504-816-4670 ext. 4673 or toll-free 800-216-6637 (out-of-state) **Fax:** 504-286-4895

E-mail: admissions@dillard.edu

Getting in Last Year 2,847 applied; 70% were accepted; 626 enrolled (31%).

Financial Matters $10,359 tuition and fees (2002–03); $6156 room and board; 85% average percent of need met; $12,708 average financial aid amount received per undergraduate.

Academics Dillard awards bachelor's degrees. Challenging opportunities include advanced placement credit, an honors program, double majors, and a senior project. Special programs include cooperative education, internships, summer session for credit, study-abroad, and Army and Air Force ROTC. The most frequently chosen baccalaureate fields are health professions and related sciences, business/marketing, and biological/life sciences. The faculty at Dillard has 122 full-time members, 65% with terminal degrees. The student-faculty ratio is 14:1.

Students of Dillard The student body is made up of 2,225 undergraduates. 77.3% are women and 22.7% are men. Students come from 35 states and territories. 56% are from Louisiana. 0.6% are international students. 70% returned for their sophomore year.

Applying Dillard requires an essay, SAT I or ACT, a high school transcript, 2 recommendations, and a minimum high school GPA of 2.0. The school recommends SAT II Subject Tests and an interview. Application deadline: 7/1; 3/1 priority date for financial aid.

DOANE COLLEGE

Crete, NE

Small-town setting ■ Private ■ Independent Religious ■ Coed

Web site: www.doane.edu

Contact: Mr. Dan Kunzman, Dean of Admissions, 1014 Boswell Avenue, Crete, NE 68333-2430

Telephone: 402-826-8222 or toll-free 800-333-6263 **Fax:** 402-826-8600

E-mail: admissions@doane.edu

Getting in Last Year 1,043 applied; 86% were accepted; 275 enrolled (31%).

Financial Matters $14,280 tuition and fees (2002–03); $4300 room and board; 98% average percent of need met; $12,570 average financial aid amount received per undergraduate.

Academics Doane awards bachelor's and master's degrees (nontraditional undergraduate programs and graduate programs offered at Lincoln campus). Challenging opportunities include advanced placement credit, accelerated degree programs, student-designed majors, an honors program, double majors, independent study, and a senior project. Special programs include cooperative education, internships, summer session for credit, off-campus study, study-abroad, and Army and Air Force ROTC. The most frequently chosen baccalaureate fields are business/marketing, education, and social sciences and history. The faculty at Doane has 72 full-time members, 63% with terminal degrees. The student-faculty ratio is 12:1.

Students of Doane The student body is made up of 1,015 undergraduates. 50.7% are women and 49.3% are men. Students come from 23 states and territories and 7 other countries. 83% are from Nebraska. 0.9% are international students. 82% returned for their sophomore year.

Applying Doane requires SAT I or ACT, a high school transcript, and 2 recommendations, and in some cases an interview. The school recommends a minimum high school GPA of 2.0. Application deadline: rolling admissions; 3/1 priority date for financial aid. Early and deferred admission are possible.

DOMINICAN COLLEGE

Orangeburg, NY

Suburban setting ■ Private ■ Independent ■ Coed

Web site: www.dc.edu

Contact: Ms. Joyce Elbe, Director of Admissions, 470 Western Highway, Orangeburg, NY 10962-1210

Telephone: 845-359-7800 ext. 271 **Fax:** 845-365-3150

E-mail: admissions@dc.edu

Getting in Last Year 686 applied; 84% were accepted; 219 enrolled (38%).

Financial Matters $15,650 tuition and fees (2002–03); $7770 room and board; 61% average percent of need met; $10,914 average financial aid amount received per undergraduate.

Academics Dominican awards associate, bachelor's, and master's degrees. Challenging opportunities include advanced placement credit, accelerated degree programs, an honors program, independent study, and a senior project. Special programs include cooperative education, internships, and summer session for credit. The most frequently chosen baccalaureate fields are health professions and related sciences, business/marketing, and social sciences and history. The faculty at Dominican has 56 full-time members, 55% with terminal degrees. The student-faculty ratio is 12:1.

Students of Dominican The student body totals 1,624, of whom 1,515 are undergraduates. 68.1% are women and 31.9% are men. Students come from 16 states and territories. 80% are from New York. 68% returned for their sophomore year.

Applying Dominican requires SAT I or ACT, a high school transcript, and a minimum high school GPA of 2.0, and in some cases an interview. The school recommends 2 recommendations. Application deadline: rolling admissions; 2/15 priority date for financial aid. Deferred admission is possible.

DOMINICAN SCHOOL OF PHILOSOPHY AND THEOLOGY

Berkeley, CA

Urban setting ■ Private ■ Independent Religious ■ Coed

Web site: www.dspt.edu

Contact: Ms. Susan McGinnis Hardie, Director of Admissions, 2401 Ridge Road, Berkeley, CA 94709-1295

Telephone: 510-883-2073 **Fax:** 510-849-1372

E-mail: admissions@dspt.edu

Financial Matters $9050 tuition and fees (2002–03).

Academics DSPT awards bachelor's, master's, and first-professional degrees. Challenging opportunities include double majors and independent study. Special programs include off-campus study and study-abroad. The faculty at DSPT has 11 full-time members, 100% with terminal degrees. The student-faculty ratio is 5:1.

Students of DSPT The student body totals 121, of whom 11 are undergraduates. 18.2% are women and 81.8% are men. Students come from 9 states and territories and 5 other countries. 50% are from California. 75% returned for their sophomore year.

Applying Early and deferred admission are possible.

DOMINICAN UNIVERSITY

River Forest, IL

Suburban setting ■ Private ■ Independent Religious ■ Coed

Web site: www.dom.edu

Contact: Ms. Hildegarde Schmidt, Dean of Admissions and Financial Aid, 7900 West Division Street, River Forest, IL 60305-1099

Telephone: 708-524-6800 or toll-free 800-828-8475 **Fax:** 708-366-5360

E-mail: domadmis@email.dom.edu

Getting in Last Year 513 applied; 81% were accepted; 192 enrolled (46%).

Financial Matters $16,720 tuition and fees (2002–03); $5400 room and board; 83% average percent of need met; $11,208 average financial aid amount received per undergraduate (2001–02).

Academics Dominican awards bachelor's and master's degrees and post-master's certificates. Challenging opportunities include advanced placement credit, accelerated degree programs, student-designed majors, an honors program, double majors, independent study, and a senior project. Special programs include internships, summer session for credit, off-campus study, and study-abroad. The most frequently chosen baccalaureate fields are business/marketing, social sciences and history, and psychology. The faculty at Dominican has 89 full-time members, 89% with terminal degrees. The student-faculty ratio is 13:1.

Students of Dominican The student body totals 2,776, of whom 1,170 are undergraduates. 69% are women and 31% are men. Students come from 23 states and territories and 19 other countries. 91% are from Illinois. 2.1% are international students. 84% returned for their sophomore year.

Applying Dominican requires an essay, SAT I or ACT, a high school transcript, and a minimum high school GPA of 2.75, and in some cases an interview and 2 recommendations. The school recommends an interview and recommendations. Application deadline: rolling admissions; 6/1 priority date for financial aid. Deferred admission is possible.

DOMINICAN UNIVERSITY OF CALIFORNIA

San Rafael, CA

Suburban setting ■ Private ■ Independent Religious ■ Coed

Web site: www.dominican.edu

Contact: Mr. Art Criss, Director of Admissions, 50 Acacia Avenue, San Rafael, CA 94901-2298

Telephone: 415-257-1376 or toll-free 888-323-6763 **Fax:** 415-385-3214

E-mail: enroll@dominican.edu

Getting in Last Year 208 enrolled.

Financial Matters $20,670 tuition and fees (2002–03); $9400 room and board; 80% average percent of need met; $16,173 average financial aid amount received per undergraduate (2001–02).

Academics Dominican awards bachelor's and master's degrees and post-bachelor's certificates. Challenging opportunities include advanced placement credit, student-designed majors, an honors program, double majors, independent study, and a senior project. Special programs include internships, summer session for credit, off-campus study, and study-abroad. The most frequently chosen baccalaureate fields are health professions and related sciences, business/marketing, and liberal arts/general studies. The faculty at Dominican has 72 full-time members, 82% with terminal degrees. The student-faculty ratio is 10:1.

Students of Dominican The student body totals 1,653, of whom 996 are undergraduates. 74.9% are women and 25.1% are men. Students come from 14 states and territories and 20 other countries. 95% are from California. 4.1% are international students. 78% returned for their sophomore year.

Applying Dominican requires an essay, SAT I or ACT, a high school transcript, 1 recommendation, and a minimum high school GPA of 2.5, and in some cases an interview. The school recommends SAT II Subject Tests. Application deadline: rolling admissions. Early and deferred admission are possible.

DORDT COLLEGE

Sioux Center, IA

Small-town setting ■ Private ■ Independent Religious ■ Coed

Web site: www.dordt.edu

Contact: Mr. Quentin Van Essen, Executive Director of Admissions, 498 4th Avenue, NE, Sioux Center, IA 51250-1697

Telephone: 712-722-6080 or toll-free 800-343-6738 **Fax:** 712-722-1967

E-mail: admissions@dordt.edu

Getting in Last Year 740 applied; 93% were accepted; 278 enrolled (40%).

Financial Matters $14,880 tuition and fees (2002–03); $4160 room and board; 75% average percent of need met; $13,323 average financial aid amount received per undergraduate.

Academics Dordt awards associate, bachelor's, and master's degrees. Challenging opportunities include advanced placement credit, student-designed majors, double majors, independent study, and a senior project. Special programs include internships, off-campus study, and study-abroad. The most frequently chosen baccalaureate fields are education, business/marketing, and engineering/engineering technologies. The faculty at Dordt has 80 full-time members, 85% with terminal degrees. The student-faculty ratio is 15:1.

Students of Dordt The student body totals 1,404, of whom 1,347 are undergraduates. 54.6% are women and 45.4% are men. Students come from 36 states and territories and 12 other countries. 42% are from Iowa. 12% are international students. 87% returned for their sophomore year.

Applying Dordt requires SAT I or ACT, a high school transcript, minimum ACT composite score of 19 or combined SAT I score of 920, and a minimum high school GPA of 2.25, and in some cases an essay and an interview. Application deadline: 8/1; 4/1 priority date for financial aid. Deferred admission is possible.

DOWLING COLLEGE

Oakdale, NY

Suburban setting ■ Private ■ Independent ■ Coed

Web site: www.dowling.edu

Contact: Ms. Nancy Brewer, Director of Enrollment Services and Financial Aid, 150 Idle Hour Boulevard, Oakdale, NY 11769

Telephone: 631-244-3385 or toll-free 800-DOWLING **Fax:** 631-563-3827

E-mail: admissions@dowling.edu

Getting in Last Year 2,104 applied; 93% were accepted; 478 enrolled (24%).

Financial Matters $14,700 tuition and fees (2002–03); $4800 room only; 74% average percent of need met; $14,107 average financial aid amount received per undergraduate.

Academics Dowling awards bachelor's, master's, and doctoral degrees and post-master's certificates. Challenging opportunities include advanced placement credit, accelerated degree programs, student-designed majors, an honors program, double majors, and independent study. Special programs include cooperative education, internships, summer session for credit, off-campus study, and Army, Navy and Air Force ROTC. The most frequently chosen baccalaureate fields are education, computer/information sciences, and liberal arts/general studies. The faculty at Dowling has 120 full-time members, 76% with terminal degrees. The student-faculty ratio is 17:1.

Students of Dowling The student body totals 6,446, of whom 3,046 are undergraduates. 61.4% are women and 38.6% are men. Students come from 23 states and territories. 85% are from New York. 0.6% are international students. 69% returned for their sophomore year.

Applying Dowling requires a high school transcript. The school recommends SAT I or ACT and an interview. Application deadline: rolling admissions; 5/31 priority date for financial aid. Deferred admission is possible.

DRAKE UNIVERSITY

Des Moines, IA

Suburban setting ■ Private ■ Independent ■ Coed

Web site: www.drake.edu

Contact: Mr. Thomas F. Willoughby, Dean of Admission and Financial Aid, 2507 University Avenue, Des Moines, IA 50311

Telephone: 515-271-3181 or toll-free 800-44DRAKE ext. 3181 **Fax:** 515-271-2831

E-mail: admission@drake.edu

Getting in Last Year 2,543 applied; 86% were accepted; 776 enrolled (35%).

Drake University (continued)

Financial Matters $18,510 tuition and fees (2002–03); $5490 room and board; 88% average percent of need met; $15,701 average financial aid amount received per undergraduate.

Academics Drake awards bachelor's, master's, doctoral, and first-professional degrees. Challenging opportunities include advanced placement credit, accelerated degree programs, student-designed majors, an honors program, double majors, independent study, and a senior project. Special programs include cooperative education, internships, summer session for credit, off-campus study, study-abroad, and Army and Air Force ROTC. The most frequently chosen baccalaureate fields are business/marketing, communications/communication technologies, and education. The faculty at Drake has 244 full-time members, 93% with terminal degrees. The student-faculty ratio is 13:1.

Students of Drake The student body totals 5,092, of whom 3,603 are undergraduates. 60.1% are women and 39.9% are men. Students come from 43 states and territories and 47 other countries. 39% are from Iowa. 6.1% are international students. 81% returned for their sophomore year.

Applying Drake requires SAT I or ACT and a high school transcript, and in some cases PCAT for pharmacy transfers. The school recommends an essay and an interview. Application deadline: rolling admissions; 3/1 priority date for financial aid. Early and deferred admission are possible.

DREW UNIVERSITY

Madison, NJ

Suburban setting ■ *Private* ■ *Independent Religious* ■ *Coed*

Web site: www.drew.edu

Contact: Mr. Roberto Noya, Dean of Admissions and Financial Aid, 36 Madison Avenue, Madison, NJ 07940-1493

Telephone: 973-408-3739 **Fax:** 973-408-3068

E-mail: cadm@drew.edu

Getting in Last Year 2,587 applied; 72% were accepted; 399 enrolled (21%).

Financial Matters $26,346 tuition and fees (2002–03); $7288 room and board; 83% average percent of need met; $19,403 average financial aid amount received per undergraduate (2001–02).

Academics Drew awards bachelor's, master's, doctoral, and first-professional degrees and post-bachelor's certificates. Challenging opportunities include advanced placement credit, accelerated degree programs, student-designed majors, double majors, independent study, and a senior project. Special programs include internships, summer session for credit, off-campus study, study-abroad, and Army and Air Force ROTC. The most frequently chosen baccalaureate fields are social sciences and history, psychology, and biological/life sciences. The faculty at Drew has 121 full-time members, 97% with terminal degrees. The student-faculty ratio is 12:1.

Students of Drew The student body totals 2,487, of whom 1,558 are undergraduates. 60.5% are women and 39.5% are men. Students come from 39 states and territories and 10 other countries. 59% are from New Jersey. 1% are international students. 85% returned for their sophomore year.

Applying Drew requires an essay, SAT I or ACT, a high school transcript, and 1 recommendation. The school recommends SAT I and an interview. Application deadline: 2/15; 2/15 for financial aid. Early and deferred admission are possible.

DREXEL UNIVERSITY

Philadelphia, PA

Urban setting ■ *Private* ■ *Independent* ■ *Coed*

Web site: www.drexel.edu

Contact: Mr. David Eddy, Director of Undergraduate Admissions, 3141 Chestnut Street, Philadelphia, PA 19104-2875

Telephone: 215-895-2400 or toll-free 800-2-DREXEL **Fax:** 215-895-5939

E-mail: enroll@drexel.edu

Getting in Last Year 11,981 applied; 61% were accepted; 2,110 enrolled (29%).

Financial Matters $18,413 tuition and fees (2002–03); $9090 room and board; 78% average percent of need met; $9515 average financial aid amount received per undergraduate.

Academics Drexel awards associate, bachelor's, master's, doctoral, and first-professional degrees and post-bachelor's, post-master's, and first-professional certificates. Challenging opportunities include advanced placement credit, accelerated degree programs, freshman honors college, an honors program, double majors, independent study, and a senior project. Special programs include cooperative education, internships, summer session for credit, study-abroad, and Army, Navy and Air Force ROTC. The most frequently chosen baccalaureate fields are business/marketing, engineering/engineering technologies, and computer/information sciences. The faculty at Drexel has 499 full-time members, 80% with terminal degrees. The student-faculty ratio is 14:1.

Students of Drexel The student body totals 16,345, of whom 11,585 are undergraduates. 39.1% are women and 60.9% are men. Students come from 44 states and territories and 96 other countries. 64% are from Pennsylvania. 5.4% are international students. 86% returned for their sophomore year.

Applying Drexel requires SAT I or ACT, a high school transcript, and a minimum high school GPA of 2.0, and in some cases an essay. The school recommends SAT I, an interview, and 2 recommendations. Application deadline: 3/1; 2/15 for financial aid. Deferred admission is possible.

DRURY UNIVERSITY

Springfield, MO

Urban setting ■ *Private* ■ *Independent* ■ *Coed*

Web site: www.drury.edu

Contact: Mr. Chip Parker, Director of Admission, 900 North Benton, Bay Hall, Springfield, MO 65802

Telephone: 417-873-7205 or toll-free 800-922-2274 **Fax:** 417-866-3873

E-mail: druryad@drury.edu

Getting in Last Year 1,078 applied; 83% were accepted; 381 enrolled (42%).

Financial Matters $12,565 tuition and fees (2002–03); $4460 room and board; 83% average percent of need met; $7985 average financial aid amount received per undergraduate.

Academics Drury awards bachelor's and master's degrees (also offers evening program with significant enrollment not reflected in profile). Challenging opportunities include advanced placement credit, accelerated degree programs, student-designed majors, an honors program, double majors, independent study, and a senior project. Special programs include cooperative education, internships, summer session for credit, off-campus study, study-abroad, and Army ROTC. The most frequently chosen baccalaureate fields are business/marketing, biological/life sciences, and communications/communication technologies. The faculty at Drury has 116 full-time members, 92% with terminal degrees. The student-faculty ratio is 11:1.

Students of Drury The student body totals 1,805, of whom 1,494 are undergraduates. 56.3% are women and 43.7% are men. Students come from 35 states and territories and 50 other countries. 80% are from Missouri. 5.8% are international students. 81% returned for their sophomore year.

Applying Drury requires an essay, SAT I or ACT, a high school transcript, 1 recommendation, minimum ACT score of 21, and a minimum high school GPA of 2.7. The school recommends an interview. Application deadline: 3/15; 3/15 priority date for financial aid. Deferred admission is possible.

DUKE UNIVERSITY

Durham, NC

Suburban setting ■ *Private* ■ *Independent Religious* ■ *Coed*

Web site: www.duke.edu

Contact: Mr. Christoph Guttentag, Director of Admissions, 2138 Campus Drive, Durham, NC 27708

Telephone: 919-684-3214 **Fax:** 919-684-8941

E-mail: askduke@admiss.duke.edu

Getting in Last Year 15,060 applied; 25% were accepted; 1,636 enrolled (44%).

Financial Matters $27,844 tuition and fees (2002–03); $7921 room and board; 100% average percent of need met; $24,955 average financial aid amount received per undergraduate.

Academics Duke awards bachelor's, master's, doctoral, and first-professional degrees and post-master's certificates. Challenging opportunities include advanced placement credit, accelerated degree programs, student-designed majors, an honors program, independent study, and a senior project. Special programs include internships, summer session for credit, off-campus study, study-abroad, and Army and Air Force ROTC. The most frequently chosen baccalaureate fields are social sciences and history, biological/life sciences, and engineering/engineering technologies. The faculty at Duke has 2,372 full-time members, 97% with terminal degrees. The student-faculty ratio is 11:1.

Students of Duke The student body totals 12,488, of whom 6,206 are undergraduates. 48.6% are women and 51.4% are men. Students come from 52 states and territories and 84 other countries. 15% are from North Carolina. 4.3% are international students. 96% returned for their sophomore year.

Applying Duke requires an essay, SAT I or ACT, a high school transcript, and 3 recommendations, and in some cases SAT II Subject Tests and SAT II: Writing Test. The school recommends an interview, audition tape for applicants with outstanding dance, dramatic, or musical talent; slides of artwork, and a minimum high school GPA of 3.0. Application deadline: 1/2; 2/1 for financial aid. Early and deferred admission are possible.

DUQUESNE UNIVERSITY

Pittsburgh, PA

Urban setting ■ *Private* ■ *Independent Religious* ■ *Coed*

Web site: www.duq.edu

Contact: Office of Admissions, 600 Forbes Avenue, Pittsburgh, PA 15282-0201

Telephone: 412-396-5000 or toll-free 800-456-0590 **Fax:** 412-396-5644

E-mail: admissions@duq.edu

Getting in Last Year 3,879 applied; 91% were accepted; 1,431 enrolled (40%).

Financial Matters $18,527 tuition and fees (2002–03); $7170 room and board; 80% average percent of need met; $13,979 average financial aid amount received per undergraduate.

Academics Duquesne awards bachelor's, master's, doctoral, and first-professional degrees and post-bachelor's and post-master's certificates. Challenging opportunities include advanced placement credit, accelerated degree programs, student-designed majors, freshman honors college, an honors program, double majors, independent study, and a senior project. Special programs include internships, summer session for credit, off-campus study, study-abroad, and Army, Navy and Air Force ROTC. The most frequently chosen baccalaureate fields are business/marketing, health professions and related sciences, and education. The faculty at Duquesne has 388 full-time members. The student-faculty ratio is 15:1.

Students of Duquesne The student body totals 9,595, of whom 5,556 are undergraduates. 58.3% are women and 41.7% are men. Students come from 49 states and territories and 73 other countries. 81% are from Pennsylvania. 2.7% are international students. 85% returned for their sophomore year.

Applying Duquesne requires an essay, SAT I or ACT, a high school transcript, and 2 recommendations, and in some cases an interview. The school recommends a minimum high school GPA of 3.0. Application deadline: 7/1; 5/1 for financial aid. Early and deferred admission are possible.

D'YOUVILLE COLLEGE

Buffalo, NY

Urban setting ■ Private ■ Independent ■ Coed

Web site: www.dyc.edu
Contact: Mr. Ron Dannecker, Director of Admissions and Financial Aid, 320 Porter Avenue, Buffalo, NY 14201-1084
Telephone: 716-881-7600 or toll-free 800-777-3921 **Fax:** 716-881-7790
E-mail: admiss@dyc.edu

Getting in Last Year 820 applied; 89% were accepted; 135 enrolled (18%).

Financial Matters $13,336 tuition and fees (2002–03); $6560 room and board; 60% average percent of need met; $10,984 average financial aid amount received per undergraduate (2001–02).

Academics D'Youville awards bachelor's and master's degrees and post-bachelor's and post-master's certificates. Challenging opportunities include accelerated degree programs, double majors, and independent study. Special programs include internships, summer session for credit, off-campus study, study-abroad, and Army ROTC. The most frequently chosen baccalaureate fields are health professions and related sciences, business/marketing, and home economics/vocational home economics. The faculty at D'Youville has 105 full-time members, 61% with terminal degrees. The student-faculty ratio is 14:1.

Students of D'Youville The student body totals 2,464, of whom 908 are undergraduates. 73.3% are women and 26.7% are men. Students come from 23 states and territories and 28 other countries. 94% are from New York. 12.6% are international students. 70% returned for their sophomore year.

Applying D'Youville requires SAT I or ACT, a high school transcript, and a minimum high school GPA of 2.0, and in some cases an essay, an interview, recommendations, and a minimum high school GPA of 3.0. Application deadline: rolling admissions; 3/1 priority date for financial aid.

EARLHAM COLLEGE

Richmond, IN

Small-town setting ■ Private ■ Independent Religious ■ Coed

Web site: www.earlham.edu
Contact: Mr. Jeff Rickey, Dean of Admissions and Financial Aid, 801 National Road West, Richmond, IN 47374
Telephone: 765-983-1600 or toll-free 800-327-5426 **Fax:** 765-983-1560
E-mail: admission@earlham.edu

Getting in Last Year 1,269 applied; 78% were accepted; 282 enrolled (28%).

Financial Matters $23,424 tuition and fees (2002–03); $5280 room and board; 93% average percent of need met; $20,439 average financial aid amount received per undergraduate.

Academics Earlham awards bachelor's, master's, and first-professional degrees. Challenging opportunities include advanced placement credit, accelerated degree programs, student-designed majors, double majors, independent study, and a senior project. Special programs include internships, off-campus study, and study-abroad. The most frequently chosen baccalaureate fields are social sciences and history, psychology, and biological/life sciences. The faculty at Earlham has 92 full-time members, 98% with terminal degrees. The student-faculty ratio is 11:1.

Students of Earlham The student body totals 1,153, of whom 1,080 are undergraduates. 56.2% are women and 43.8% are men. Students come from 47 states and territories and 35 other countries. 32% are from Indiana. 5.3% are international students. 89% returned for their sophomore year.

Applying Earlham requires an essay, SAT I or ACT, a high school transcript, 2 recommendations, and a minimum high school GPA of 3.0. The school recommends SAT I and an interview. Application deadline: 2/15; 3/1 priority date for financial aid. Early and deferred admission are possible.

EAST CAROLINA UNIVERSITY

Greenville, NC

Urban setting ■ Public ■ State-supported ■ Coed

Web site: www.ecu.edu
Contact: Dr. Thomas E. Powell, Director of Admissions, East 5th Street, Whichard Building 106, Greenville, NC 27858-4353
Telephone: 252-328-6640 **Fax:** 252-328-6945
E-mail: admis@mail.ecu.edu

Getting in Last Year 11,333 applied; 77% were accepted; 3,580 enrolled (41%).

Financial Matters $2980 resident tuition and fees (2002–03); $12,636 nonresident tuition and fees (2002–03); $5090 room and board.

Academics ECU awards bachelor's, master's, doctoral, and first-professional degrees and post-master's certificates. Challenging opportunities include advanced placement credit, accelerated degree programs, student-designed majors, an honors program, double majors, independent study, and a senior project. Special programs include cooperative education, internships, summer session for credit, off-campus study, study-abroad, and Army and Air Force ROTC. The most frequently chosen baccalaureate fields are business/marketing, health professions and related sciences, and education. The faculty at ECU has 952 full-time members, 68% with terminal degrees. The student-faculty ratio is 18:1.

Students of ECU The student body totals 20,577, of whom 16,225 are undergraduates. 58% are women and 42% are men. Students come from 40 states and territories and 30 other countries. 85% are from North Carolina. 0.4% are international students. 78% returned for their sophomore year.

Applying ECU requires SAT I or ACT, a high school transcript, and a minimum high school GPA of 2.0. Application deadline: 3/15; 4/15 priority date for financial aid. Early and deferred admission are possible.

EAST CENTRAL UNIVERSITY

Ada, OK

Small-town setting ■ Public ■ State-supported ■ Coed

Web site: www.ecok.edu
Contact: Ms. Pamela Armstrong, Registrar, PMBJ8, 1100 East 14th Street, Ada, OK 74820-6999
Telephone: 580-332-8000 ext. 239 **Fax:** 580-310-5432
E-mail: parmstro@mailclerk.ecok.edu

Getting in Last Year 1,197 enrolled.

Financial Matters $2371 resident tuition and fees (2002–03); $3967 nonresident tuition and fees (2002–03); $2646 room and board; 64% average percent of need met; $7105 average financial aid amount received per undergraduate.

Academics East Central awards bachelor's and master's degrees. Challenging opportunities include advanced placement credit, accelerated degree programs, an honors program, double majors, and a senior project. Special programs include internships, summer session for credit, and off-campus study. The most frequently chosen baccalaureate field is law/legal studies. The student-faculty ratio is 19:1.

Students of East Central The student body totals 4,195, of whom 3,423 are undergraduates. 59.2% are women and 40.8% are men. Students come from 20 states and territories and 25 other countries. 97% are from Oklahoma. 2.6% are international students. 62% returned for their sophomore year.

Applying East Central requires SAT I or ACT and a high school transcript, and in some cases rank in upper 50% of high school class and a minimum high school GPA of 2.7. The school recommends ACT. Application deadline: 9/1; 3/1 priority date for financial aid. Early admission is possible.

EASTERN CONNECTICUT STATE UNIVERSITY

Willimantic, CT

Small-town setting ■ Public ■ State-supported ■ Coed

Web site: www.easternct.edu
Contact: Ms. Kimberly Crone, Director of Admissions and Enrollment Management, 83 Windham Street, Willimantic, CT 06336
Telephone: 860-465-5286 or toll-free 877-353-3278 **Fax:** 860-465-5544
E-mail: admissions@easternct.edu

Getting in Last Year 3,057 applied; 60% were accepted; 823 enrolled (45%).

Financial Matters $4713 resident tuition and fees (2002–03); $9885 nonresident tuition and fees (2002–03); $6317 room and board; 80% average percent of need met.

Academics ECSU awards associate, bachelor's, and master's degrees. Challenging opportunities include advanced placement credit, student-designed majors, freshman honors college, an honors program, double majors, independent study, and a senior project. Special programs include cooperative education, internships, summer session for credit, off-campus study, study-abroad, and Army and Air Force ROTC. The most frequently chosen baccalaureate fields are social sciences and history, trade and industry, and business/marketing. The faculty at ECSU has 178 full-time members, 89% with terminal degrees. The student-faculty ratio is 17:1.

Eastern Connecticut State University (continued)

Students of ECSU The student body totals 5,215, of whom 4,869 are undergraduates. 57.6% are women and 42.4% are men. Students come from 23 states and territories and 27 other countries. 92% are from Connecticut. 2.1% are international students. 74% returned for their sophomore year.

Applying ECSU requires SAT I or ACT and a high school transcript, and in some cases an interview. The school recommends an essay, recommendations, and rank in upper 50% of high school class. Application deadline: 5/1; 3/15 priority date for financial aid. Early and deferred admission are possible.

EASTERN ILLINOIS UNIVERSITY

Charleston, IL

Small-town setting ■ *Public* ■ *State-supported* ■ *Coed*

Web site: www.eiu.edu
Contact: Mr. Dale W. Wolf, Director of Admissions, 600 Lincoln Avenue, Charleston, IL 61920-3099
Telephone: 217-581-2223 or toll-free 800-252-5711 **Fax:** 217-581-7060
E-mail: admissns@eiu.edu

Getting in Last Year 7,544 applied; 78% were accepted; 2,003 enrolled (34%).

Financial Matters $4648 resident tuition and fees (2002–03); $11,155 nonresident tuition and fees (2002–03); $6000 room and board; 18% average percent of need met; $8472 average financial aid amount received per undergraduate.

Academics Eastern awards bachelor's and master's degrees. Challenging opportunities include advanced placement credit, an honors program, double majors, independent study, and a senior project. Special programs include internships, summer session for credit, study-abroad, and Army ROTC. The most frequently chosen baccalaureate fields are education, business/marketing, and English. The faculty at Eastern has 585 full-time members, 73% with terminal degrees. The student-faculty ratio is 16:1.

Students of Eastern The student body totals 11,163, of whom 9,528 are undergraduates. 57.4% are women and 42.6% are men. Students come from 35 states and territories and 36 other countries. 98% are from Illinois. 0.7% are international students.

Applying Eastern requires SAT I or ACT, a high school transcript, and audition for music program, and in some cases an essay and 3 recommendations. Application deadline: rolling admissions; 4/15 priority date for financial aid.

EASTERN KENTUCKY UNIVERSITY

Richmond, KY

Small-town setting ■ *Public* ■ *State-supported* ■ *Coed*

Web site: www.eku.edu
Contact: Stephen A. Byrn, Director of Admissions, SSB CPO 54, 521 Lancaster Avenue, Richmond, KY 40475-3102
Telephone: 859-622-2106 or toll-free 800-465-9191 (in-state) **Fax:** 859-622-8024
E-mail: admissions@eku.edu

Getting in Last Year 5,003 applied; 79% were accepted; 2,352 enrolled (60%).

Financial Matters $2928 resident tuition and fees (2002–03); $8040 nonresident tuition and fees (2002–03); $4146 room and board; 86% average percent of need met; $6048 average financial aid amount received per undergraduate.

Academics EKU awards associate, bachelor's, and master's degrees and post-bachelor's and post-master's certificates. Challenging opportunities include advanced placement credit, accelerated degree programs, student-designed majors, an honors program, double majors, independent study, and a senior project. Special programs include cooperative education, internships, summer session for credit, and Army and Air Force ROTC. The most frequently chosen baccalaureate fields are education, health professions and related sciences, and protective services/public administration. The faculty at EKU has 643 full-time members, 81% with terminal degrees. The student-faculty ratio is 17:1.

Students of EKU The student body totals 15,061, of whom 12,867 are undergraduates. 59.7% are women and 40.3% are men. Students come from 51 states and territories and 56 other countries. 95% are from Kentucky. 1.3% are international students. 64% returned for their sophomore year.

Applying EKU requires ACT, a high school transcript, and a minimum high school GPA of 2.0. Application deadline: rolling admissions; 4/1 priority date for financial aid. Deferred admission is possible.

EASTERN MENNONITE UNIVERSITY

Harrisonburg, VA

Small-town setting ■ *Private* ■ *Independent Religious* ■ *Coed*

Web site: www.emu.edu
Contact: Mr. Lawrence W. Miller, Director of Admissions, 1200 Park Road, Harrisonburg, VA 22802-2462
Telephone: 540-432-4118 or toll-free 800-368-2665 **Fax:** 540-432-4444
E-mail: admiss@emu.edu

Getting in Last Year 676 applied; 77% were accepted; 210 enrolled (40%).

Financial Matters $16,370 tuition and fees (2002–03); $5350 room and board; 85% average percent of need met; $13,140 average financial aid amount received per undergraduate.

Academics EMU awards associate, bachelor's, master's, and first-professional degrees and post-bachelor's certificates. Challenging opportunities include advanced placement credit, an honors program, double majors, independent study, and a senior project. Special programs include internships, summer session for credit, off-campus study, and study-abroad. The most frequently chosen baccalaureate fields are business/marketing, liberal arts/general studies, and education. The faculty at EMU has 98 full-time members, 72% with terminal degrees. The student-faculty ratio is 13:1.

Students of EMU The student body totals 1,352, of whom 996 are undergraduates. 59.9% are women and 40.1% are men. Students come from 32 states and territories and 20 other countries. 43% are from Virginia. 3.8% are international students. 76% returned for their sophomore year.

Applying EMU requires SAT I or ACT, a high school transcript, 1 recommendation, statement of commitment, and a minimum high school GPA of 2.2. The school recommends an interview. Application deadline: 8/1; 3/15 priority date for financial aid. Early and deferred admission are possible.

EASTERN MICHIGAN UNIVERSITY

Ypsilanti, MI

Suburban setting ■ *Public* ■ *State-supported* ■ *Coed*

Web site: www.emich.edu
Contact: Ms. Judy Benfield-Tatum, Director of Admissions, Ypsilanti, MI 48197
Telephone: 734-487-3060 or toll-free 800-GO TO EMU **Fax:** 734-487-6559
E-mail: admissions@emich.edu

Getting in Last Year 8,947 applied; 75% were accepted; 2,760 enrolled (41%).

Financial Matters $5027 resident tuition and fees (2002–03); $13,760 nonresident tuition and fees (2002–03); $5597 room and board; 55% average percent of need met; $10,495 average financial aid amount received per undergraduate (2001–02).

Academics EMU awards bachelor's, master's, and doctoral degrees and post-master's certificates. Challenging opportunities include advanced placement credit, accelerated degree programs, student-designed majors, an honors program, double majors, independent study, and a senior project. Special programs include cooperative education, internships, summer session for credit, study-abroad, and Army, Navy and Air Force ROTC. The most frequently chosen baccalaureate fields are education, business/marketing, and social sciences and history. The faculty at EMU has 760 full-time members, 76% with terminal degrees. The student-faculty ratio is 19:1.

Students of EMU The student body totals 24,195, of whom 18,757 are undergraduates. 60.5% are women and 39.5% are men. Students come from 44 states and territories and 74 other countries. 93% are from Michigan. 1.9% are international students. 71% returned for their sophomore year.

Applying EMU requires SAT I or ACT, a high school transcript, and a minimum high school GPA of 2.0, and in some cases an interview and 1 recommendation. The school recommends ACT. Application deadline: 6/30; 3/15 priority date for financial aid. Deferred admission is possible.

EASTERN NAZARENE COLLEGE

Quincy, MA

Suburban setting ■ *Private* ■ *Independent Religious* ■ *Coed*

Web site: www.enc.edu
Contact: Ms. Doris Webb, Vice President of Admissions and Financial Aid, 23 East Elm Avenue, Quincy, MA 02170
Telephone: 617-745-3732 or toll-free 800-88-ENC88 **Fax:** 617-745-3929
E-mail: admissions@enc.edu

Getting in Last Year 552 applied; 62% were accepted; 178 enrolled (52%).

Financial Matters $15,315 tuition and fees (2002–03); $5215 room and board; 69% average percent of need met; $10,394 average financial aid amount received per undergraduate (2000–01).

Academics ENC awards associate, bachelor's, and master's degrees. Challenging opportunities include advanced placement credit, accelerated degree programs, an honors program, double majors, independent study, and a senior project. Special programs include internships, summer session for credit, off-campus study, study-abroad, and Army ROTC. The most frequently chosen baccalaureate fields are business/marketing, biological/life sciences, and communications/communication technologies. The faculty at ENC has 44 full-time members, 75% with terminal degrees. The student-faculty ratio is 15:1.

Students of ENC The student body totals 1,228, of whom 1,075 are undergraduates. 59.5% are women and 40.5% are men. Students come from 32 states and territories and 18 other countries. 43% are from Massachusetts. 71% returned for their sophomore year.

Applying ENC requires an essay, SAT I or ACT, a high school transcript, an interview, 2 recommendations, and a minimum high school GPA of 2.3. Application deadline: rolling admissions; 2/28 priority date for financial aid. Early and deferred admission are possible.

EASTERN NEW MEXICO UNIVERSITY

Portales, NM

Rural setting ■ Public ■ State-supported ■ Coed

Web site: www.enmu.edu
Contact: Ms. Phyllis Seefeld, Interim Director, Station #7 ENMU, Portales, NM 88130
Telephone: 505-562-2178 or toll-free 800-367-3668 **Fax:** 505-562-2118
E-mail: phyllis.seefeld@enmu.edu

Getting in Last Year 2,195 applied; 70% were accepted; 533 enrolled (35%).

Financial Matters $2292 resident tuition and fees (2002–03); $7848 nonresident tuition and fees (2002–03); $4540 room and board; $5866 average financial aid amount received per undergraduate (2000–01 estimated).

Academics ENMU awards associate, bachelor's, and master's degrees. Challenging opportunities include advanced placement credit, accelerated degree programs, student-designed majors, an honors program, double majors, and a senior project. Special programs include cooperative education, internships, summer session for credit, and study-abroad. The most frequently chosen baccalaureate fields are education, business/marketing, and social sciences and history. The faculty at ENMU has 135 full-time members, 81% with terminal degrees. The student-faculty ratio is 17:1.

Students of ENMU The student body totals 3,607, of whom 3,000 are undergraduates. 57.9% are women and 42.1% are men. Students come from 40 states and territories and 18 other countries. 83% are from New Mexico. 0.9% are international students. 62% returned for their sophomore year.

Applying ENMU requires SAT I or ACT, a high school transcript, and a minimum high school GPA of 2.0. Application deadline: rolling admissions; 3/1 priority date for financial aid. Early and deferred admission are possible.

EASTERN OREGON UNIVERSITY

La Grande, OR

Rural setting ■ Public ■ State-supported ■ Coed

Web site: www.eou.edu
Contact: Ms. Christian Steinmetz, Director, Admissions, 1 University Boulevard, La Grande, OR 97850-2899
Telephone: 541-962-3393 or toll-free 800-452-3393 **Fax:** 541-962-3418
E-mail: admissions@eou.edu

Getting in Last Year 765 applied; 93% were accepted; 417 enrolled (59%).

Financial Matters $4305 resident tuition and fees (2002–03); $4305 nonresident tuition and fees (2002–03); $5775 room and board; 43% average percent of need met; $8163 average financial aid amount received per undergraduate.

Academics Eastern awards bachelor's and master's degrees and post-bachelor's certificates. Challenging opportunities include advanced placement credit, student-designed majors, an honors program, double majors, independent study, and a senior project. Special programs include cooperative education, internships, summer session for credit, off-campus study, study-abroad, and Army ROTC. The most frequently chosen baccalaureate fields are liberal arts/general studies, interdisciplinary studies, and business/marketing. The faculty at Eastern has 91 full-time members. The student-faculty ratio is 15:1.

Students of Eastern The student body totals 3,408, of whom 3,075 are undergraduates. 58.2% are women and 41.8% are men. 72% are from Oregon. 3.1% are international students. 65% returned for their sophomore year.

Applying Eastern requires SAT I or ACT, a high school transcript, and a minimum high school GPA of 3.0, and in some cases an essay and 2 recommendations. Application deadline: 9/27; 3/1 priority date for financial aid. Deferred admission is possible.

EASTERN UNIVERSITY

St. Davids, PA

Small-town setting ■ Private ■ Independent Religious ■ Coed

Web site: www.eastern.edu
Contact: Mr. David Urban, Director of Undergraduate Admissions, 1300 Eagle Road, St. Davids, PA 19087-3696
Telephone: 610-225-5005 or toll-free 800-452-0996 **Fax:** 610-341-1723
E-mail: ugadm@eastern.edu

Getting in Last Year 1,045 applied; 78% were accepted; 391 enrolled (48%).

Financial Matters $15,832 tuition and fees (2002–03); $6784 room and board; 78% average percent of need met; $11,404 average financial aid amount received per undergraduate (2001–02).

Academics Eastern awards associate, bachelor's, and master's degrees. Challenging opportunities include advanced placement credit, accelerated degree programs, student-designed majors, an honors program, independent study, and a senior project. Special programs include internships, summer session for credit, off-campus study, and Army and Air Force ROTC. The most frequently chosen baccalaureate fields are business/marketing, education, and health professions and related sciences. The student-faculty ratio is 13:1.

Students of Eastern The student body totals 3,128, of whom 2,054 are undergraduates. 64.7% are women and 35.3% are men. Students come from 38 states and territories and 26 other countries. 60% are from Pennsylvania. 1.4% are international students. 77% returned for their sophomore year.

Applying Eastern requires an essay, SAT I or ACT, a high school transcript, 1 recommendation, and a minimum high school GPA of 2.0. The school recommends an interview, 3 recommendations, and a minimum high school GPA of 3.0. Application deadline: rolling admissions; 3/1 priority date for financial aid. Early and deferred admission are possible.

EASTERN WASHINGTON UNIVERSITY

Cheney, WA

Small-town setting ■ Public ■ State-supported ■ Coed

Web site: www.ewu.edu
Contact: Ms. Michelle Whittingham, Director of Admissions, 526 Fifth Street, SUT 101, Cheney, WA 99004-2447
Telephone: 509-359-6582 or toll-free 888-740-1914 **Fax:** 509-359-6692
E-mail: admissions@mail.ewu.edu

Getting in Last Year 3,578 applied; 81% were accepted; 1,291 enrolled (45%).

Financial Matters $3582 resident tuition and fees (2002–03); $11,859 nonresident tuition and fees (2002–03); $5025 room and board; 42% average percent of need met; $13,749 average financial aid amount received per undergraduate (2001–02).

Academics Eastern awards bachelor's, master's, and doctoral degrees. Challenging opportunities include advanced placement credit, student-designed majors, an honors program, double majors, independent study, and a senior project. Special programs include cooperative education, internships, summer session for credit, off-campus study, study-abroad, and Army ROTC. The most frequently chosen baccalaureate fields are education, business/marketing, and social sciences and history. The faculty at Eastern has 356 full-time members, 61% with terminal degrees. The student-faculty ratio is 23:1.

Students of Eastern The student body totals 9,924, of whom 8,798 are undergraduates. 57.9% are women and 42.1% are men. Students come from 40 states and territories and 26 other countries. 91% are from Washington. 2.2% are international students. 81% returned for their sophomore year.

Applying Eastern requires SAT I or ACT, a high school transcript, and a minimum high school GPA of 2.0, and in some cases an essay, an interview, and recommendations. The school recommends a minimum high school GPA of 3.0. Application deadline: rolling admissions; 2/15 priority date for financial aid. Early and deferred admission are possible.

EAST STROUDSBURG UNIVERSITY OF PENNSYLVANIA

East Stroudsburg, PA

Small-town setting ■ Public ■ State-supported ■ Coed

Web site: www.esu.edu
Contact: Mr. Alan T. Chesterton, Director of Admissions, 200 Prospect Street, East Stroudsburg, PA 18301
Telephone: 570-422-3542 or toll-free 877-230-5547 **Fax:** 570-422-3933
E-mail: undergrads@po-box.esu.edu

Getting in Last Year 3,805 applied; 79% were accepted; 1,132 enrolled (38%).

Financial Matters $5502 resident tuition and fees (2002–03); $12,070 nonresident tuition and fees (2002–03); $4346 room and board; 90% average percent of need met; $5252 average financial aid amount received per undergraduate (2001–02).

Academics East Stroudsburg awards associate, bachelor's, and master's degrees. Challenging opportunities include advanced placement credit, student-designed majors, an honors program, double majors, independent study, and a senior project. Special programs include internships, summer session for credit, off-campus study, study-abroad, and Army and Air Force ROTC. The most frequently chosen baccalaureate fields are education, business/marketing, and biological/life sciences. The faculty at East Stroudsburg has 246 full-time members, 76% with terminal degrees. The student-faculty ratio is 19:1.

Students of East Stroudsburg The student body totals 6,270, of whom 5,150 are undergraduates. 57.2% are women and 42.8% are men. Students come from 21 states and territories and 24 other countries. 81% are from Pennsylvania. 0.7% are international students. 75% returned for their sophomore year.

Applying East Stroudsburg requires SAT I or ACT and a high school transcript. The school recommends 1 recommendation. Application deadline: 4/1; 3/1 for financial aid.

EAST TENNESSEE STATE UNIVERSITY

Johnson City, TN

Small-town setting ■ Public ■ State-supported ■ Coed

East Tennessee State University (continued)

Web site: www.etsu.edu
Contact: Mr. Mike Pitts, Director of Admissions, PO Box 70731, Johnson City, TN 37614-0734
Telephone: 423-439-4213 or toll-free 800-462-3878 **Fax:** 423-439-4630
E-mail: go2etsu@mail.etsu.edu

Getting in Last Year 3,532 applied; 83% were accepted; 1,514 enrolled (52%).

Financial Matters $3311 resident tuition and fees (2002–03); $10,269 nonresident tuition and fees (2002–03); $4390 room and board; 81% average percent of need met; $4585 average financial aid amount received per undergraduate (2001–02).

Academics ETSU awards associate, bachelor's, master's, doctoral, and first-professional degrees and post-bachelor's and post-master's certificates. Challenging opportunities include advanced placement credit, accelerated degree programs, freshman honors college, an honors program, double majors, independent study, and a senior project. Special programs include cooperative education, internships, summer session for credit, off-campus study, study-abroad, and Army ROTC. The most frequently chosen baccalaureate fields are business/marketing, health professions and related sciences, and protective services/public administration. The faculty at ETSU has 464 full-time members, 69% with terminal degrees. The student-faculty ratio is 18:1.

Students of ETSU The student body totals 11,365, of whom 9,336 are undergraduates. 57.4% are women and 42.6% are men. Students come from 43 states and territories and 46 other countries. 91% are from Tennessee. 0.9% are international students. 69% returned for their sophomore year.

Applying ETSU requires SAT I or ACT, a high school transcript, minimum High School GPA of 2.3 or minimum ACT score of 19, and a minimum high school GPA of 2.3. Application deadline: rolling admissions; 4/15 priority date for financial aid. Early admission is possible.

EAST TEXAS BAPTIST UNIVERSITY

Marshall, TX

Small-town setting ■ Private ■ Independent Religious ■ Coed

Web site: www.etbu.edu
Contact: Mr. Vince Blankenship, Dean of Admissions and Marketing, 1209 North Grove, Marshall, TX 75670-1498
Telephone: 903-923-2000 or toll-free 800-804-ETBU **Fax:** 903-938-1705
E-mail: admissions@etbu.edu

Getting in Last Year 714 applied; 74% were accepted; 342 enrolled (65%).

Financial Matters $9800 tuition and fees (2002–03); $3456 room and board; 87% average percent of need met; $8468 average financial aid amount received per undergraduate.

Academics ETBU awards associate and bachelor's degrees. Challenging opportunities include advanced placement credit, accelerated degree programs, an honors program, double majors, independent study, and a senior project. Special programs include internships, summer session for credit, off-campus study, and study-abroad. The most frequently chosen baccalaureate fields are education, business/marketing, and health professions and related sciences. The faculty at ETBU has 78 full-time members, 71% with terminal degrees. The student-faculty ratio is 15:1.

Students of ETBU The student body is made up of 1,496 undergraduates. 54% are women and 46% are men. Students come from 28 states and territories and 18 other countries. 88% are from Texas. 1.9% are international students. 65% returned for their sophomore year.

Applying ETBU requires an essay, ACT, a high school transcript, and a minimum high school GPA of 2.0, and in some cases an interview. Application deadline: rolling admissions; 6/1 priority date for financial aid. Deferred admission is possible.

EAST-WEST UNIVERSITY

Chicago, IL

Urban setting ■ Private ■ Independent ■ Coed

Web site: www.eastwest.edu
Contact: Mr. William Link, Director of Admissions, 819 South Wabash Avenue, Chicago, IL 60605-2103
Telephone: 312-939-0111 ext. 1830 **Fax:** 312-939-0083
E-mail: seeyou@eastwest.edu

Getting in Last Year 947 applied; 90% were accepted; 763 enrolled (90%).

Financial Matters $9735 tuition and fees (2002–03); 90% average percent of need met; $8720 average financial aid amount received per undergraduate (2001–02).

Academics East-West University awards associate and bachelor's degrees. Challenging opportunities include double majors, independent study, and a senior project. Special programs include internships and summer session for credit. The most frequently chosen baccalaureate fields are business/marketing, computer/information sciences, and social sciences and history. The faculty at East-West University has 14 full-time members, 71% with terminal degrees. The student-faculty ratio is 20:1.

Students of East-West University The student body is made up of 1,113 undergraduates. 64.8% are women and 35.2% are men. Students come from 1 state or territory and 10 other countries. 13.6% are international students. 80% returned for their sophomore year.

Applying East-West University requires an essay, a high school transcript, and an interview, and in some cases 1 recommendation. The school recommends ACT. Application deadline: rolling admissions; 6/30 priority date for financial aid.

ECKERD COLLEGE

St. Petersburg, FL

Suburban setting ■ Private ■ Independent Religious ■ Coed

Web site: www.eckerd.edu
Contact: Dr. Richard R. Hallin, Dean of Admissions, 4200 54th Avenue South, St. Petersburg, FL 33711
Telephone: 727-864-8331 or toll-free 800-456-9009 **Fax:** 727-866-2304
E-mail: admissions@eckerd.edu

Getting in Last Year 1,943 applied; 79% were accepted; 440 enrolled (29%).

Financial Matters $21,488 tuition and fees (2002–03); $5686 room and board; 85% average percent of need met; $17,500 average financial aid amount received per undergraduate.

Academics Eckerd awards bachelor's degrees. Challenging opportunities include advanced placement credit, accelerated degree programs, student-designed majors, an honors program, double majors, independent study, and a senior project. Special programs include cooperative education, internships, summer session for credit, off-campus study, study-abroad, and Army and Air Force ROTC. The most frequently chosen baccalaureate fields are biological/life sciences, business/marketing, and social sciences and history. The faculty at Eckerd has 97 full-time members, 92% with terminal degrees. The student-faculty ratio is 14:1.

Students of Eckerd The student body is made up of 1,608 undergraduates. 54.2% are women and 45.8% are men. Students come from 47 states and territories and 49 other countries. 31% are from Florida. 6.5% are international students. 77% returned for their sophomore year.

Applying Eckerd requires an essay, SAT I or ACT, a high school transcript, and 1 recommendation. The school recommends SAT II Subject Tests, SAT II: Writing Test, an interview, and a minimum high school GPA of 3.0. Application deadline: rolling admissions; 4/1 priority date for financial aid. Early and deferred admission are possible.

ÉCOLE DES HAUTES ÉTUDES COMMERCIALES DE MONTRÉAL

Montréal, QC Canada

Urban setting ■ Public ■ Coed

Web site: www.hec.ca
Contact: Ms. Lyne Héroux, Administrative Director of Bachelor Program, 3000 chemin de la Côte-Sainte-Catherine, Montréal, QC H3T 2A7
Telephone: 514-340-6139 **Fax:** 514-340-5640
E-mail: registraire.info@hec.ca

Getting in Last Year 2,467 applied; 52% were accepted; 1,001 enrolled (79%).

Financial Matters $2150 resident tuition and fees (2002–03); $4494 nonresident tuition and fees (2002–03); $3000 room only.

Academics HEC de Montréal awards bachelor's, master's, and doctoral degrees. Challenging opportunities include student-designed majors, an honors program, and independent study. Special programs include summer session for credit, off-campus study, and study-abroad. The most frequently chosen baccalaureate field is business/marketing. The faculty at HEC de Montréal has 220 full-time members, 69% with terminal degrees. The student-faculty ratio is 22:1.

Students of HEC de Montréal The student body totals 11,351, of whom 8,618 are undergraduates. 50% are women and 50% are men. Students come from 8 states and territories and 80 other countries. 99% are from Quebec. 84% returned for their sophomore year.

Applying HEC de Montréal requires a high school transcript, and in some cases cote de rendement collégial. Application deadline: 3/1, 3/1 for nonresidents. Deferred admission is possible.

ECOLE HÔTELIÈRE DE LAUSANNE

Lausanne Switzerland

Private ■ Independent ■ Coed

Web site: www.ehl.ch
Contact: Ms. Margaret Boule, Head of Admissions, Le Chalet-a-Gobet, Lausanne Switzerland
Telephone: 41-21 785 1111 ext. 1345 **Fax:** -41-21-785-1121 ext.

Getting in Last Year 310 applied; 55% were accepted.

Financial Matters $26,480 tuition and fees (2002–03); $15,400 room and board.

Academics Ecole Hôtelière de Lausanne awards bachelor's degrees. The faculty at Ecole Hôtelière de Lausanne has 90 full-time members. The student-faculty ratio is 15:1.

Students of Ecole Hôtelière de Lausanne The student body is made up of 1,400 undergraduates. 48% are women and 52% are men. 87% returned for their sophomore year.

EDGEWOOD COLLEGE

Madison, WI

Urban setting ■ *Private* ■ *Independent Religious* ■ *Coed*

Web site: www.edgewood.edu

Contact: Mr. Jim Krystofiak, Associate Director of Admissions, 1000 Edgewood College Drive, Madison, WI 53711-1997

Telephone: 608-663-2265 or toll-free 800-444-4861 **Fax:** 608-663-3291

E-mail: admissions@edgewood.edu

Getting in Last Year 390 applied; 79% were accepted; 271 enrolled (88%).

Financial Matters $14,200 tuition and fees (2002–03); $5100 room and board; 75% average percent of need met; $11,172 average financial aid amount received per undergraduate.

Academics Edgewood awards associate, bachelor's, and master's degrees. Challenging opportunities include advanced placement credit, independent study, and a senior project. Special programs include summer session for credit and off-campus study. The faculty at Edgewood has 86 full-time members, 76% with terminal degrees. The student-faculty ratio is 12:1.

Students of Edgewood The student body totals 2,264, of whom 1,731 are undergraduates. 73.4% are women and 26.6% are men. Students come from 16 states and territories and 22 other countries. 92% are from Wisconsin. 2.8% are international students. 75% returned for their sophomore year.

Applying Edgewood requires SAT I or ACT, a high school transcript, and a minimum high school GPA of 2.5, and in some cases an essay, an interview, and 2 recommendations. Application deadline: rolling admissions; 3/15 priority date for financial aid. Deferred admission is possible.

EDINBORO UNIVERSITY OF PENNSYLVANIA

Edinboro, PA

Small-town setting ■ *Public* ■ *State-supported* ■ *Coed*

Web site: www.edinboro.edu

Contact: Mr. Terrence Carlin, Assistant Vice President for Admissions, Biggers House, Edinboro, PA 16444

Telephone: 814-732-2761 or toll-free 888-846-2676 (in-state), 800-626-2203 (out-of-state) **Fax:** 814-732-2420

E-mail: eup_admissions@edinboro.edu

Getting in Last Year 3,856 applied; 76% were accepted; 1,423 enrolled (49%).

Financial Matters $7654 nonresident tuition and fees (2002–03); $4884 room and board; 85% average percent of need met; $5482 average financial aid amount received per undergraduate (2001–02).

Academics Edinboro awards associate, bachelor's, and master's degrees and post-bachelor's and post-master's certificates. Challenging opportunities include advanced placement credit, student-designed majors, freshman honors college, an honors program, double majors, independent study, and a senior project. Special programs include internships, summer session for credit, off-campus study, study-abroad, and Army ROTC. The most frequently chosen baccalaureate fields are education, visual/performing arts, and protective services/public administration. The faculty at Edinboro has 378 full-time members, 51% with terminal degrees. The student-faculty ratio is 18:1.

Students of Edinboro The student body totals 7,778, of whom 6,922 are undergraduates. 56.7% are women and 43.3% are men. Students come from 34 states and territories and 55 other countries. 89% are from Pennsylvania. 3.3% are international students. 75% returned for their sophomore year.

Applying Edinboro requires a high school transcript, and in some cases SAT I or ACT and an interview. The school recommends a minimum high school GPA of 2.0. Application deadline: rolling admissions; 3/15 priority date for financial aid. Deferred admission is possible.

ELIZABETH CITY STATE UNIVERSITY

Elizabeth City, NC

Small-town setting ■ *Public* ■ *State-supported* ■ *Coed*

Web site: www.ecsu.edu

Contact: Mr. Grady Deese, Director of Admissions, Campus Box 901, Elizabeth City, NC 27909-7806

Telephone: 252-335-3305 or toll-free 800-347-3278 **Fax:** 252-335-3537

E-mail: admissions@mail.ecsu.edu

Getting in Last Year 1,262 applied; 77% were accepted; 464 enrolled (48%).

Financial Matters $2592 resident tuition and fees (2002–03); $10,463 nonresident tuition and fees (2002–03); $4464 room and board.

Academics ECSU awards bachelor's and master's degrees. Challenging opportunities include advanced placement credit, an honors program, double majors, independent study, and a senior project. Special programs include internships, summer session for credit, off-campus study, and Army ROTC. The faculty at ECSU has 131 full-time members, 61% with terminal degrees. The student-faculty ratio is 15:1.

Students of ECSU The student body totals 2,150, of whom 2,133 are undergraduates. 63.6% are women and 36.4% are men. Students come from 23 states and territories and 8 other countries. 88% are from North Carolina. 0.4% are international students. 73% returned for their sophomore year.

Applying ECSU requires SAT I or ACT, a high school transcript, and a minimum high school GPA of 2.0. Application deadline: rolling admissions; 3/1 priority date for financial aid. Deferred admission is possible.

ELIZABETHTOWN COLLEGE

Elizabethtown, PA

Small-town setting ■ *Private* ■ *Independent Religious* ■ *Coed*

Web site: www.etown.edu

Contact: Mr. W. Kent Barnds, Dean of Admissions and Enrollment Management, One Alpha Drive, Elizabethtown, PA 17022

Telephone: 717-361-1400 **Fax:** 717-361-1365

E-mail: admissions@acad.etown.edu

Getting in Last Year 2,509 applied; 68% were accepted; 465 enrolled (27%).

Financial Matters $21,350 tuition and fees (2002–03); $6000 room and board; 87% average percent of need met; $15,897 average financial aid amount received per undergraduate.

Academics E-town awards associate, bachelor's, and master's degrees and post-bachelor's certificates. Challenging opportunities include advanced placement credit, an honors program, double majors, independent study, and a senior project. Special programs include cooperative education, internships, summer session for credit, off-campus study, and study-abroad. The most frequently chosen baccalaureate fields are business/marketing, education, and health professions and related sciences. The faculty at E-town has 112 full-time members, 83% with terminal degrees. The student-faculty ratio is 13:1.

Students of E-town The student body totals 1,901, of whom 1,891 are undergraduates. 64.3% are women and 35.7% are men. Students come from 28 states and territories and 32 other countries. 74% are from Pennsylvania. 3.4% are international students. 84% returned for their sophomore year.

Applying E-town requires an essay, SAT I or ACT, a high school transcript, 2 recommendations, and a minimum high school GPA of 2.0, and in some cases an interview. The school recommends an interview and a minimum high school GPA of 3.0. Application deadline: rolling admissions. Early and deferred admission are possible.

ELMHURST COLLEGE

Elmhurst, IL

Suburban setting ■ *Private* ■ *Independent Religious* ■ *Coed*

Web site: www.elmhurst.edu

Contact: Mr. Andrew B. Sison, Director of Admission, 190 Prospect Avenue, Elmhurst, IL 60126

Telephone: 630-617-3400 ext. 3068 or toll-free 800-697-1871 (out-of-state) **Fax:** 630-617-5501

E-mail: admit@elmhurst.edu

Getting in Last Year 1,170 applied; 76% were accepted; 310 enrolled (35%).

Financial Matters $17,500 tuition and fees (2002–03); $5796 room and board; 97% average percent of need met; $15,715 average financial aid amount received per undergraduate.

Academics Elmhurst awards bachelor's and master's degrees. Challenging opportunities include advanced placement credit, accelerated degree programs, an honors program, double majors, independent study, and a senior project. Special programs include cooperative education, internships, summer session for credit, off-campus study, study-abroad, and Army and Air Force ROTC. The most frequently chosen baccalaureate fields are business/marketing, education, and communications/communication technologies. The faculty at Elmhurst has 113 full-time members, 87% with terminal degrees. The student-faculty ratio is 13:1.

Students of Elmhurst The student body totals 2,490, of whom 2,340 are undergraduates. 65.5% are women and 34.5% are men. Students come from 26 states and territories and 29 other countries. 92% are from Illinois. 1.3% are international students. 86% returned for their sophomore year.

Applying Elmhurst requires SAT I or ACT and a high school transcript, and in some cases an essay, an interview, and recommendations. The school recommends an essay and an interview. Application deadline: 7/15; 4/15 priority date for financial aid. Deferred admission is possible.

ELMIRA COLLEGE

Elmira, NY

Small-town setting ■ *Private* ■ *Independent* ■ *Coed*

Web site: www.elmira.edu

Elmira College (continued)

Contact: Mr. William S. Neal, Dean of Admissions, Office of Admissions, Elmira, NY 14901
Telephone: 607-735-1724 or toll-free 800-935-6472 **Fax:** 607-735-1718
E-mail: admissions@elmira.edu

Getting in Last Year 1,786 applied; 74% were accepted; 347 enrolled (26%).

Financial Matters $24,560 tuition and fees (2002–03); $7850 room and board; 90% average percent of need met; $20,242 average financial aid amount received per undergraduate.

Academics Elmira awards bachelor's degrees. Challenging opportunities include advanced placement credit, accelerated degree programs, student-designed majors, and independent study. Special programs include internships, summer session for credit, off-campus study, study-abroad, and Army and Air Force ROTC. The most frequently chosen baccalaureate fields are education, psychology, and business/marketing. The faculty at Elmira has 80 full-time members, 100% with terminal degrees. The student-faculty ratio is 12:1.

Students of Elmira The student body is made up of 1,547 undergraduates. 71% are women and 29% are men. Students come from 35 states and territories and 18 other countries. 52% are from New York. 4.7% are international students. 79% returned for their sophomore year.

Applying Elmira requires an essay, SAT I or ACT, a high school transcript, 2 recommendations, and a minimum high school GPA of 2.0, and in some cases an interview. The school recommends an interview. Application deadline: 5/15; 2/1 priority date for financial aid. Early and deferred admission are possible.

ELMS COLLEGE

Chicopee, MA

Suburban setting ■ *Private* ■ *Independent Religious* ■ *Coed, Primarily Women*

Web site: www.elms.edu
Contact: Mr. Jason M. Brown, Director of Admissions, 291 Springfield Street, Chicopee, MA 01013-2839
Telephone: 413-592-3189 ext. 350 or toll-free 800-255-ELMS **Fax:** 413-594-2781
E-mail: admissions@elms.edu

Getting in Last Year 384 applied; 90% were accepted; 143 enrolled (41%).

Financial Matters $17,160 tuition and fees (2002–03); $6490 room and board; 81% average percent of need met; $14,907 average financial aid amount received per undergraduate.

Academics Elms College awards associate, bachelor's, and master's degrees and post-bachelor's certificates. Challenging opportunities include advanced placement credit, accelerated degree programs, student-designed majors, an honors program, double majors, and a senior project. Special programs include internships, summer session for credit, off-campus study, study-abroad, and Army and Air Force ROTC. The most frequently chosen baccalaureate fields are health professions and related sciences, social sciences and history, and psychology. The faculty at Elms College has 42 full-time members, 79% with terminal degrees. The student-faculty ratio is 12:1.

Students of Elms College The student body totals 839, of whom 685 are undergraduates. 81.2% are women and 18.8% are men. Students come from 10 states and territories. 85% are from Massachusetts. 0.2% are international students. 86% returned for their sophomore year.

Applying Elms College requires an essay, SAT I or ACT, a high school transcript, 2 recommendations, and a minimum high school GPA of 2.0. The school recommends SAT II Subject Tests and an interview. Application deadline: rolling admissions; 3/1 priority date for financial aid. Early and deferred admission are possible.

ELON UNIVERSITY

Elon, NC

Suburban setting ■ *Private* ■ *Independent Religious* ■ *Coed*

Web site: www.elon.edu
Contact: Ms. Staci Powell, Director of Admissions Records, 2700 Campus Box, Elon, NC 27244
Telephone: 336-278-3566 or toll-free 800-334-8448 **Fax:** 336-278-7699
E-mail: admissions@elon.edu

Getting in Last Year 6,504 applied; 50% were accepted; 1,196 enrolled (37%).

Financial Matters $15,505 tuition and fees (2002–03); $5090 room and board; 77% average percent of need met; $10,694 average financial aid amount received per undergraduate.

Academics Elon awards bachelor's, master's, and doctoral degrees. Challenging opportunities include advanced placement credit, accelerated degree programs, student-designed majors, an honors program, double majors, independent study, and a senior project. Special programs include internships, summer session for credit, off-campus study, study-abroad, and Army and Air Force ROTC. The most frequently chosen baccalaureate fields are business/marketing, communications/communication technologies, and education. The faculty at Elon has 235 full-time members, 84% with terminal degrees. The student-faculty ratio is 15:1.

Students of Elon The student body totals 4,434, of whom 4,272 are undergraduates. 61.4% are women and 38.6% are men. Students come from 48 states and territories and 41 other countries. 28% are from North Carolina. 1.4% are international students. 83% returned for their sophomore year.

Applying Elon requires an essay, SAT I or ACT, a high school transcript, 1 recommendation, and a minimum high school GPA of 2.5. Application deadline: rolling admissions; 2/15 priority date for financial aid. Early and deferred admission are possible.

EMBRY-RIDDLE AERONAUTICAL UNIVERSITY

Prescott, AZ

Small-town setting ■ *Private* ■ *Independent* ■ *Coed, Primarily Men*

Web site: www.embryriddle.edu
Contact: Bill Thompson, Director of Admissions, 3200 Willow Creek Road, Prescott, AZ 86301
Telephone: 928-777-6692 or toll-free 800-888-3728 **Fax:** 928-777-6606
E-mail: pradmit@erau.edu

Getting in Last Year 1,389 applied; 78% were accepted; 309 enrolled (29%).

Financial Matters $18,420 tuition and fees (2002–03); $5250 room and board; $11,025 average financial aid amount received per undergraduate (2001–02).

Academics Embry-Riddle awards bachelor's and master's degrees. Challenging opportunities include advanced placement credit, double majors, independent study, and a senior project. Special programs include cooperative education, internships, summer session for credit, study-abroad, and Army and Air Force ROTC. The most frequently chosen baccalaureate fields are trade and industry, engineering/engineering technologies, and computer/information sciences. The faculty at Embry-Riddle has 84 full-time members, 57% with terminal degrees. The student-faculty ratio is 17:1.

Students of Embry-Riddle The student body totals 1,702, of whom 1,671 are undergraduates. 15.3% are women and 84.7% are men. Students come from 52 states and territories and 31 other countries. 23% are from Arizona. 9.2% are international students. 77% returned for their sophomore year.

Applying Embry-Riddle requires SAT I or ACT, a high school transcript, and a minimum high school GPA of 2.0, and in some cases medical examination for flight students and a minimum high school GPA of 3.0. The school recommends an essay, an interview, and recommendations. Application deadline: rolling admissions; 6/30 for financial aid, with a 4/15 priority date. Early and deferred admission are possible.

EMBRY-RIDDLE AERONAUTICAL UNIVERSITY

Daytona Beach, FL

Urban setting ■ *Private* ■ *Independent* ■ *Coed, Primarily Men*

Web site: www.embryriddle.edu
Contact: Mr. Michael Novak, Director of Admissions, 600 South Clyde Morris Boulevard, Daytona Beach, FL 32114-3900
Telephone: 386-226-6112 or toll-free 800-862-2416 **Fax:** 386-226-7070
E-mail: admit@erau.edu

Getting in Last Year 2,858 applied; 78% were accepted; 875 enrolled (39%).

Financial Matters $18,400 tuition and fees (2002–03); $5760 room and board; $11,350 average financial aid amount received per undergraduate (2001–02).

Academics Embry-Riddle awards associate, bachelor's, and master's degrees. Challenging opportunities include advanced placement credit, double majors, and independent study. Special programs include cooperative education, internships, summer session for credit, study-abroad, and Army and Air Force ROTC. The most frequently chosen baccalaureate fields are trade and industry, education, and business/marketing. The faculty at Embry-Riddle has 203 full-time members, 62% with terminal degrees. The student-faculty ratio is 19:1.

Students of Embry-Riddle The student body totals 4,772, of whom 4,485 are undergraduates. 17.5% are women and 82.5% are men. Students come from 53 states and territories and 99 other countries. 31% are from Florida. 16.3% are international students. 79% returned for their sophomore year.

Applying Embry-Riddle requires SAT I, a high school transcript, and a minimum high school GPA of 2.0, and in some cases medical examination for flight students and a minimum high school GPA of 3.0. The school recommends an essay, an interview, and recommendations. Application deadline: 7/1; 6/30 for financial aid, with a 4/15 priority date. Early and deferred admission are possible.

EMBRY-RIDDLE AERONAUTICAL UNIVERSITY, EXTENDED CAMPUS

Daytona Beach, FL

Private ■ *Independent* ■ *Coed, Primarily Men*

Web site: www.embryriddle.edu
Contact: Mrs. Pam Thomas, Director of Admissions, Records and Registration, 600 South Clyde Morris Boulevard, Daytona Beach, FL 32114-3900

Telephone: 386-226-7610 or toll-free 800-862-2416 (out-of-state)
Fax: 386-226-6984
E-mail: ecinfo@erau.edu

Getting in Last Year 195 enrolled.

Financial Matters $17,850 tuition and fees (2002–03); $4901 average financial aid amount received per undergraduate (2001–02).

Academics Embry-Riddle awards associate, bachelor's, and master's degrees (programs offered at 100 military bases worldwide). Challenging opportunities include advanced placement credit and independent study. Special programs include cooperative education and off-campus study. The most frequently chosen baccalaureate fields are trade and industry and business/marketing. The faculty at Embry-Riddle has 101 full-time members, 44% with terminal degrees.

Students of Embry-Riddle The student body totals 9,173, of whom 6,813 are undergraduates. 11.8% are women and 88.2% are men. 2% are international students.

Applying Embry-Riddle requires (in some cases) an essay. Application deadline: rolling admissions; 6/30 for financial aid, with a 4/15 priority date. Deferred admission is possible.

EMERSON COLLEGE
Boston, MA

Urban setting ■ Private ■ Independent ■ Coed

Web site: www.emerson.edu
Contact: Ms. Sara Ramirez, Director of Admission, 120 Boylston Street, Boston, MA 02116-4624
Telephone: 617-824-8600 **Fax:** 617-824-8609
E-mail: admission@emerson.edu

Getting in Last Year 3,805 applied; 52% were accepted; 651 enrolled (33%).

Financial Matters $21,624 tuition and fees (2002–03); $9542 room and board; 64% average percent of need met; $12,543 average financial aid amount received per undergraduate (2001–02).

Academics Emerson awards bachelor's, master's, and doctoral degrees. Challenging opportunities include advanced placement credit, student-designed majors, an honors program, double majors, independent study, and a senior project. Special programs include internships, summer session for credit, off-campus study, and study-abroad. The most frequently chosen baccalaureate fields are communications/communication technologies, visual/performing arts, and English. The faculty at Emerson has 128 full-time members, 71% with terminal degrees. The student-faculty ratio is 15:1.

Students of Emerson The student body totals 4,529, of whom 3,518 are undergraduates. 61.9% are women and 38.1% are men. Students come from 51 states and territories and 61 other countries. 35% are from Massachusetts. 4.4% are international students. 84% returned for their sophomore year.

Applying Emerson requires an essay, SAT I or ACT, a high school transcript, and 2 recommendations, and in some cases an interview and audition, portfolio, or resume for performing arts applicants. Application deadline: 2/1; 3/1 priority date for financial aid. Early and deferred admission are possible.

EMMANUEL COLLEGE
Franklin Springs, GA

Rural setting ■ Private ■ Independent Religious ■ Coed

Web site: www.emmanuelcollege.edu
Contact: Mrs. Angie Thompson, Associate Director of Admissions, PO Box 129, 181 Spring Street, Franklin Springs, GA 30639-0129
Telephone: 706-245-7226 ext. 2872 or toll-free 800-860-8800 (in-state)
Fax: 706-245-4424
E-mail: admissions@eclions.net

Getting in Last Year 1,304 applied; 40% were accepted; 194 enrolled (37%).

Financial Matters $8792 tuition and fees (2002–03); $4072 room and board; 53% average percent of need met; $8948 average financial aid amount received per undergraduate (2001–02).

Academics Emmanuel awards associate and bachelor's degrees. Challenging opportunities include advanced placement credit, independent study, and a senior project. Special programs include internships and summer session for credit. The most frequently chosen baccalaureate fields are education, business/marketing, and psychology. The faculty at Emmanuel has 43 full-time members, 58% with terminal degrees. The student-faculty ratio is 15:1.

Students of Emmanuel The student body is made up of 768 undergraduates. 54.9% are women and 45.1% are men. Students come from 21 states and territories and 10 other countries. 77% are from Georgia. 1.2% are international students. 58% returned for their sophomore year.

Applying Emmanuel requires SAT I or ACT and a high school transcript. Application deadline: 8/1; 5/1 priority date for financial aid. Early and deferred admission are possible.

EMMANUEL COLLEGE
Boston, MA

Urban setting ■ Private ■ Independent Religious ■ Coed

Web site: www.emmanuel.edu
Contact: Ms. Sandra Robbins, Dean of Admissions, 400 The Fenway, Boston, MA 02115
Telephone: 617-735-9715 **Fax:** 617-735-9801
E-mail: enroll@emmanuel.edu

Getting in Last Year 1,463 applied; 70% were accepted; 322 enrolled (31%).

Financial Matters $18,100 tuition and fees (2002–03); $8000 room and board; 79% average percent of need met; $15,971 average financial aid amount received per undergraduate.

Academics Emmanuel awards bachelor's and master's degrees. Challenging opportunities include advanced placement credit, accelerated degree programs, student-designed majors, an honors program, double majors, independent study, and a senior project. Special programs include internships, summer session for credit, off-campus study, study-abroad, and Army ROTC. The most frequently chosen baccalaureate fields are business/marketing, health professions and related sciences, and English. The faculty at Emmanuel has 51 full-time members, 86% with terminal degrees. The student-faculty ratio is 14:1.

Students of Emmanuel The student body totals 1,632, of whom 1,459 are undergraduates. 80.6% are women and 19.4% are men. Students come from 30 states and territories and 33 other countries. 64% are from Massachusetts. 4% are international students. 79% returned for their sophomore year.

Applying Emmanuel requires an essay, SAT I or ACT, a high school transcript, 2 recommendations, and a minimum high school GPA of 2.0, and in some cases an interview. Application deadline: rolling admissions; 4/1 priority date for financial aid. Early and deferred admission are possible.

EMMAUS BIBLE COLLEGE
Dubuque, IA

Small-town setting ■ Private ■ Independent Religious ■ Coed

Web site: www.emmaus.edu
Contact: Mr. Steve Schimpf, Enrollment Services Manager, 2570 Asbury Road, Dubuque, IA 52001
Telephone: 563-588-8000 ext. 1310 or toll-free 800-397-2425
Fax: 563-557-0573
E-mail: admissions@emmaus.edu

Getting in Last Year 145 applied; 69% were accepted; 57 enrolled (57%).

Financial Matters $6326 tuition and fees (2002–03); $3480 room and board; 71% average percent of need met; $4200 average financial aid amount received per undergraduate (2001–02).

Academics Emmaus awards associate and bachelor's degrees. Challenging opportunities include advanced placement credit, double majors, independent study, and a senior project. Special programs include internships and off-campus study. The most frequently chosen baccalaureate field is education. The faculty at Emmaus has 15 full-time members, 33% with terminal degrees. The student-faculty ratio is 12:1.

Students of Emmaus The student body is made up of 294 undergraduates. 56.5% are women and 43.5% are men. Students come from 42 states and territories and 7 other countries. 28% are from Iowa. 5.9% are international students. 86% returned for their sophomore year.

Applying Emmaus requires an essay, SAT I or ACT, a high school transcript, and 3 recommendations. Application deadline: 8/1; 6/10 for financial aid. Deferred admission is possible.

EMORY & HENRY COLLEGE
Emory, VA

Rural setting ■ Private ■ Independent Religious ■ Coed

Web site: www.ehc.edu
Contact: Ms. Lise Keller, Dean of Admissions and Financial Aid, 30479 Armbrister Drive, PO Box 10, Emory, VA 24327
Telephone: 276-944-6133 or toll-free 800-848-5493 **Fax:** 276-944-6935
E-mail: ehadmiss@ehc.edu

Getting in Last Year 900 applied; 80% were accepted; 237 enrolled (33%).

Financial Matters $14,800 tuition and fees (2002–03); $5550 room and board; 77% average percent of need met; $11,913 average financial aid amount received per undergraduate.

Academics Emory & Henry awards bachelor's and master's degrees. Challenging opportunities include advanced placement credit, student-designed majors, an honors program, double majors, independent study, and a senior project. Special programs include internships, summer session for credit, off-campus study, and study-abroad. The most frequently chosen baccalaureate fields are business/marketing, social sciences and history, and interdisciplinary studies. The faculty at Emory & Henry has 64 full-time members, 84% with terminal degrees. The student-faculty ratio is 14:1.

Emory & Henry College (continued)

Students of Emory & Henry The student body totals 1,003, of whom 959 are undergraduates. 52.2% are women and 47.8% are men. Students come from 24 states and territories. 74% are from Virginia. 0.7% are international students. 70% returned for their sophomore year.

Applying Emory & Henry requires an essay, SAT I or ACT, and a high school transcript, and in some cases 2 recommendations. The school recommends an interview. Application deadline: rolling admissions; 8/1 for financial aid, with a 4/1 priority date. Early and deferred admission are possible.

EMORY UNIVERSITY

Atlanta, GA

Suburban setting ■ Private ■ Independent Religious ■ Coed

Web site: www.emory.edu
Contact: Mr. Daniel C. Walls, Dean of Admission, 200 Boisfeuillet Jones Center–Office of Admissions, Atlanta, GA 30322-1100
Telephone: 404-727-6036 or toll-free 800-727-6036
E-mail: admiss@unix.cc.emory.edu

Getting in Last Year 9,789 applied; 42% were accepted; 1,565 enrolled (38%).

Financial Matters $26,932 tuition and fees (2002–03); $8498 room and board; 100% average percent of need met; $24,084 average financial aid amount received per undergraduate.

Academics Emory awards bachelor's, master's, doctoral, and first-professional degrees (enrollment figures include Emory University, Oxford College; application data for main campus only). Challenging opportunities include advanced placement credit, accelerated degree programs, an honors program, double majors, and a senior project. Special programs include internships, summer session for credit, off-campus study, study-abroad, and Air Force ROTC. The most frequently chosen baccalaureate fields are social sciences and history, business/marketing, and biological/life sciences. The faculty at Emory has 2,320 full-time members, 100% with terminal degrees. The student-faculty ratio is 7:1.

Students of Emory The student body totals 11,617, of whom 6,302 are undergraduates. 56% are women and 44% are men. Students come from 52 states and territories and 64 other countries. 20% are from Georgia. 3.7% are international students. 94% returned for their sophomore year.

Applying Emory requires an essay, SAT I or ACT, a high school transcript, and 1 recommendation. The school recommends SAT II Subject Tests and a minimum high school GPA of 3.0. Application deadline: 1/15; 4/1 for financial aid, with a 2/15 priority date. Early and deferred admission are possible.

EMPORIA STATE UNIVERSITY

Emporia, KS

Small-town setting ■ Public ■ State-supported ■ Coed

Web site: www.emporia.edu
Contact: Ms. Susan Brinkman, Director of Admissions, 1200 Commercial Street, Emporia, KS 66801-5087
Telephone: 620-341-5465 or toll-free 877-GOTOESU (in-state), 877-468-6378 (out-of-state) **Fax:** 620-341-5599
E-mail: go2esu@emporia.edu

Getting in Last Year 1,367 applied; 71% were accepted; 803 enrolled (82%).

Financial Matters $2454 resident tuition and fees (2002–03); $7746 nonresident tuition and fees (2002–03); $4046 room and board; 79% average percent of need met; $5139 average financial aid amount received per undergraduate (2001–02).

Academics ESU awards bachelor's, master's, and doctoral degrees and post-master's certificates. Challenging opportunities include advanced placement credit, accelerated degree programs, an honors program, double majors, independent study, and a senior project. Special programs include internships, summer session for credit, off-campus study, and study-abroad. The most frequently chosen baccalaureate fields are education, business/marketing, and social sciences and history. The faculty at ESU has 246 full-time members, 82% with terminal degrees. The student-faculty ratio is 19:1.

Students of ESU The student body totals 6,005, of whom 4,393 are undergraduates. 60.5% are women and 39.5% are men. Students come from 41 states and territories and 55 other countries. 93% are from Kansas. 2.6% are international students. 69% returned for their sophomore year.

Applying ESU requires SAT I or ACT and a high school transcript. The school recommends a minimum high school GPA of 2.0. Application deadline: rolling admissions; 3/15 priority date for financial aid. Early and deferred admission are possible.

ENDICOTT COLLEGE

Beverly, MA

Suburban setting ■ Private ■ Independent ■ Coed

Web site: www.endicott.edu
Contact: Mr. Thomas J. Redman, Vice President of Admissions and Financial Aid, 376 Hale Street, Beverly, MA 01915
Telephone: 978-921-1000 or toll-free 800-325-1114 (out-of-state)
Fax: 978-232-2520
E-mail: admissio@endicott.edu

Getting in Last Year 2,245 applied; 57% were accepted; 484 enrolled (38%).

Financial Matters $16,460 tuition and fees (2002–03); $8364 room and board; 76% average percent of need met; $12,742 average financial aid amount received per undergraduate.

Academics Endicott awards associate, bachelor's, and master's degrees. Challenging opportunities include advanced placement credit, accelerated degree programs, student-designed majors, an honors program, independent study, and a senior project. Special programs include internships, summer session for credit, off-campus study, study-abroad, and Army ROTC. The most frequently chosen baccalaureate fields are business/marketing, visual/performing arts, and parks and recreation. The faculty at Endicott has 53 full-time members, 55% with terminal degrees. The student-faculty ratio is 15:1.

Students of Endicott The student body totals 2,208, of whom 1,574 are undergraduates. 65.7% are women and 34.3% are men. Students come from 30 states and territories and 22 other countries. 47% are from Massachusetts. 7.8% are international students. 67% returned for their sophomore year.

Applying Endicott requires an essay, SAT I or ACT, a high school transcript, and a minimum high school GPA of 2.5, and in some cases an interview. The school recommends an interview. Application deadline: rolling admissions; 3/15 priority date for financial aid. Deferred admission is possible.

ERSKINE COLLEGE

Due West, SC

Rural setting ■ Private ■ Independent Religious ■ Coed

Web site: www.erskine.edu
Contact: Mr. Bart Walker, Director of Admissions, PO Box 176, Due West, SC 29639
Telephone: 864-379-8830 or toll-free 800-241-8721 **Fax:** 864-379-8759
E-mail: admissions@erskine.edu

Getting in Last Year 848 applied; 69% were accepted; 165 enrolled (28%).

Financial Matters $16,715 tuition and fees (2002–03); $5506 room and board; 80% average percent of need met; $16,500 average financial aid amount received per undergraduate (2001–02).

Academics Erskine awards bachelor's, master's, doctoral, and first-professional degrees. Challenging opportunities include advanced placement credit, double majors, independent study, and a senior project. Special programs include internships, summer session for credit, off-campus study, and study-abroad. The most frequently chosen baccalaureate fields are education, business/marketing, and biological/life sciences. The faculty at Erskine has 40 full-time members, 98% with terminal degrees. The student-faculty ratio is 12:1.

Students of Erskine The student body totals 948, of whom 594 are undergraduates. 59.8% are women and 40.2% are men. Students come from 15 states and territories and 4 other countries. 77% are from South Carolina. 1.2% are international students. 82% returned for their sophomore year.

Applying Erskine requires SAT I or ACT, a high school transcript, and 1 recommendation, and in some cases an essay, SAT II Subject Tests, and an interview. The school recommends an interview. Application deadline: rolling admissions; 2/15 for financial aid.

ESCUELA DE ARTES PLASTICAS DE PUERTO RICO

San Juan, PR

Urban setting ■ Commonwealth-supported ■ Coed

Web site: www.eap.edu.pr
Contact: Milagros Lugo, Admission Assistant, PO Box 9021112, San Juan, PR 00902-1112
Telephone: 787-725-8120 ext. 250 **Fax:** 787-725-8111
E-mail: eap@coqui.net

Getting in Last Year 150 applied; 43% were accepted; 59 enrolled (92%).

Financial Matters $1794 tuition and fees (2002–03); 82% average percent of need met.

Academics EAP awards bachelor's degrees. A senior project is a challenging opportunity. Special programs include cooperative education and summer session for credit. The most frequently chosen baccalaureate fields are visual/performing arts and education. The faculty at EAP has 23 full-time members, 4% with terminal degrees. The student-faculty ratio is 9:1.

Students of EAP The student body is made up of 461 undergraduates. 38.6% are women and 61.4% are men. Students come from 1 state or territory. 80% returned for their sophomore year.

Applying EAP requires an essay, SAT I, a high school transcript, an interview, portfolio, and a minimum high school GPA of 2.0. Application deadline: 4/1; 7/11 priority date for financial aid.

EUGENE BIBLE COLLEGE

Eugene, OR

Suburban setting ■ Private ■ Independent Religious ■ Coed

Web site: www.ebc.edu
Contact: Mr. Trent Combs, Director of Admissions, 2155 Bailey Hill Road, Eugene, OR 97405
Telephone: 541-485-1780 ext. 135 or toll-free 800-322-2638 **Fax:** 541-343-5801
E-mail: admissions@ebc.edu

Getting in Last Year 120 applied; 64% were accepted; 77 enrolled (100%).

Financial Matters $6990 tuition and fees (2002–03); $3990 room and board; $6300 average financial aid amount received per undergraduate.

Academics EBC awards bachelor's degrees. Challenging opportunities include advanced placement credit, double majors, and independent study. Special programs include internships and summer session for credit. The most frequently chosen baccalaureate fields are psychology and interdisciplinary studies. The faculty at EBC has 14 full-time members, 36% with terminal degrees. The student-faculty ratio is 12:1.

Students of EBC The student body is made up of 174 undergraduates. 53.4% are women and 46.6% are men. Students come from 18 states and territories and 4 other countries. 51% are from Oregon. 2.4% are international students. 51% returned for their sophomore year.

Applying EBC requires an essay, SAT I or ACT, a high school transcript, 2 recommendations, and a minimum high school GPA of 2.0. Application deadline: 9/1; 9/1 for financial aid, with a 3/1 priority date.

EUGENE LANG COLLEGE, NEW SCHOOL UNIVERSITY

New York, NY

Urban setting ■ Private ■ Independent ■ Coed

Web site: www.lang.edu
Contact: Mr. Terence Peavy, Director of Admissions, 65 West 11th Street, New York, NY 10011-8601
Telephone: 212-229-5665 or toll-free 877-528-3321 **Fax:** 212-229-5166
E-mail: lang@newschool.edu

Getting in Last Year 696 applied; 67% were accepted; 173 enrolled (37%).

Financial Matters $22,990 tuition and fees (2002–03); $9896 room and board; 69% average percent of need met; $17,088 average financial aid amount received per undergraduate.

Academics Eugene Lang College awards bachelor's degrees. Challenging opportunities include advanced placement credit, accelerated degree programs, student-designed majors, independent study, and a senior project. Special programs include internships, summer session for credit, off-campus study, and study-abroad. The most frequently chosen baccalaureate field is liberal arts/general studies. The faculty at Eugene Lang College has 48 full-time members. The student-faculty ratio is 11:1.

Students of Eugene Lang College The student body is made up of 637 undergraduates. 67.7% are women and 32.3% are men. Students come from 26 states and territories and 11 other countries. 43% are from New York. 2.5% are international students. 73% returned for their sophomore year.

Applying Eugene Lang College requires an essay, SAT I, ACT, or 4 SAT II Subject Tests, a high school transcript, an interview, 2 recommendations, and a minimum high school GPA of 2.0. The school recommends a minimum high school GPA of 3.0. Application deadline: 2/1; 3/1 priority date for financial aid. Early and deferred admission are possible.

EUREKA COLLEGE

Eureka, IL

Small-town setting ■ Private ■ Independent Religious ■ Coed

Web site: www.eureka.edu
Contact: Mr. Richard R. Eber, Dean of Admissions and Financial Aid, 300 East College Avenue, Eureka, IL 61530-0128
Telephone: 309-467-6350 or toll-free 888-4-EUREKA **Fax:** 309-467-6576
E-mail: admissions@eureka.edu

Getting in Last Year 635 applied; 75% were accepted; 138 enrolled (29%).

Financial Matters $17,780 tuition and fees (2002–03); $5610 room and board; 90% average percent of need met; $13,802 average financial aid amount received per undergraduate.

Academics Eureka awards bachelor's degrees. Challenging opportunities include advanced placement credit, student-designed majors, an honors program, double majors, independent study, and a senior project. Special programs include cooperative education, internships, summer session for credit, and study-abroad. The most frequently chosen baccalaureate fields are business/marketing, education, and biological/life sciences. The faculty at Eureka has 42 full-time members, 83% with terminal degrees. The student-faculty ratio is 13:1.

Students of Eureka The student body is made up of 516 undergraduates. 55.6% are women and 44.4% are men. Students come from 15 states and territories and 2 other countries. 1.4% are international students. 67% returned for their sophomore year.

Applying Eureka requires SAT I or ACT, a high school transcript, 1 recommendation, and a minimum high school GPA of 2.0, and in some cases an essay and 3 recommendations. The school recommends an interview. Application deadline: rolling admissions; 4/1 priority date for financial aid. Deferred admission is possible.

EVANGEL UNIVERSITY

Springfield, MO

Urban setting ■ Private ■ Independent Religious ■ Coed

Web site: www.evangel.edu
Contact: Ms. Charity Waltner, Director of Admissions, 1111 North Glenstone, Springfield, MO 65802
Telephone: 417-865-2811 ext. 7262 or toll-free 800-382-6435 (in-state) **Fax:** 417-865-9599
E-mail: admissions@evangel.edu

Getting in Last Year 925 applied; 89% were accepted; 442 enrolled (54%).

Financial Matters $10,770 tuition and fees (2002–03); $4000 room and board; 58% average percent of need met; $7795 average financial aid amount received per undergraduate (2001–02).

Academics Evangel University awards associate, bachelor's, and master's degrees. Challenging opportunities include advanced placement credit, accelerated degree programs, double majors, and a senior project. Special programs include internships, summer session for credit, and Army ROTC. The most frequently chosen baccalaureate fields are education, business/marketing, and psychology. The faculty at Evangel University has 97 full-time members, 55% with terminal degrees. The student-faculty ratio is 18:1.

Students of Evangel University The student body totals 1,666, of whom 1,597 are undergraduates. 59.7% are women and 40.3% are men. Students come from 51 states and territories. 49% are from Missouri. 0.4% are international students. 72% returned for their sophomore year.

Applying Evangel University requires SAT I or ACT and a high school transcript. The school recommends a minimum high school GPA of 2.0. Application deadline: 8/1; 3/1 priority date for financial aid. Deferred admission is possible.

EVERGLADES COLLEGE

Ft. Lauderdale, FL

Urban setting ■ Private ■ Proprietary ■ Coed

Web site: www.evergladescollege.edu
Contact: Ms. Susan Ziegelhoffer, Vice President of Enrollment Management, Everglades College, 1500 NW 49th Street, #600, Fort Lauderdale, FL 33309
Telephone: 954-772-2655 or toll-free 954-772-2655 (in-state), 888-772-6077 (out-of-state) **Fax:** 954-772-2695
E-mail: admissions@evergladecollege.edu

Getting in Last Year 66 applied; 76% were accepted; 22 enrolled (44%).

Financial Matters $9300 tuition and fees (2002–03).

Academics Everglades College awards associate and bachelor's degrees. Challenging opportunities include accelerated degree programs and a senior project. Special programs include cooperative education and summer session for credit. The faculty at Everglades College has 4 full-time members. The student-faculty ratio is 15:1.

Students of Everglades College The student body is made up of 217 undergraduates.

Applying Everglades College requires a high school transcript, and in some cases SAT I, ACT, SAT I or ACT, and Otis-Lennon School Ability Test. Application deadline: 6/1 for financial aid.

THE EVERGREEN STATE COLLEGE

Olympia, WA

Small-town setting ■ Public ■ State-supported ■ Coed

Web site: www.evergreen.edu
Contact: Mr. Doug P. Scrima, Director of Admissions, 2700 Evergreen Parkway NW, Olympia, WA 98505
Telephone: 360-867-6170 **Fax:** 360-867-6576
E-mail: admissions@evergreen.edu

Getting in Last Year 1,399 applied; 94% were accepted; 492 enrolled (37%).

Financial Matters $3591 resident tuition and fees (2002–03); $12,414 nonresident tuition and fees (2002–03); $5610 room and board; 85% average percent of need met; $9175 average financial aid amount received per undergraduate (2001–02).

Academics Evergreen awards bachelor's and master's degrees. Challenging opportunities include advanced placement credit, accelerated degree programs, student-designed majors, double majors, and independent study. Special programs include cooperative education, internships, summer session for credit, off-campus

The Evergreen State College (continued)

study, and study-abroad. The most frequently chosen baccalaureate field is interdisciplinary studies. The faculty at Evergreen has 161 full-time members, 83% with terminal degrees. The student-faculty ratio is 22:1.

Students of Evergreen The student body totals 4,367, of whom 4,081 are undergraduates. 56.3% are women and 43.7% are men. Students come from 52 states and territories and 12 other countries. 77% are from Washington. 0.2% are international students. 69% returned for their sophomore year.

Applying Evergreen requires SAT I or ACT, a high school transcript, and a minimum high school GPA of 2.0, and in some cases an interview. The school recommends an essay. Application deadline: 3/1; 3/15 priority date for financial aid. Early admission is possible.

EXCELSIOR COLLEGE

Albany, NY

Urban setting ■ Private ■ Independent ■ Coed

Web site: www.excelsior.edu
Contact: Ms. Chari Leader, Vice President for Enrollment Management, 7 Columbia Circle, Albany, NY 12203-5159
Telephone: 518-464-8500 or toll-free 888-647-2388 **Fax:** 518-464-8777
E-mail: info@excelsior.edu

Academics Excelsior College awards associate, bachelor's, and master's degrees and post-bachelor's certificates (offers only external degree programs). Challenging opportunities include advanced placement credit, accelerated degree programs, student-designed majors, and independent study. The most frequently chosen baccalaureate fields are liberal arts/general studies, business/marketing, and health professions and related sciences.

Students of Excelsior College The student body totals 20,492, of whom 20,105 are undergraduates. 62.3% are women and 37.7% are men. Students come from 50 states and territories and 51 other countries. 13% are from New York. 1% are international students.

Applying Application deadline: rolling admissions; 7/1 priority date for financial aid.

FAIRFIELD UNIVERSITY

Fairfield, CT

Suburban setting ■ Private ■ Independent Religious ■ Coed

Web site: www.fairfield.edu
Contact: Ms. Judith M. Dobai, Director of Admission, 1073 North Benson Road, Fairfield, CT 06824-5195
Telephone: 203-254-4100 **Fax:** 203-254-4199
E-mail: admis@mail.fairfield.edu

Getting in Last Year 6,974 applied; 50% were accepted; 814 enrolled (24%).

Financial Matters $24,555 tuition and fees (2002–03); $8560 room and board; 77% average percent of need met; $17,013 average financial aid amount received per undergraduate.

Academics Fairfield awards bachelor's and master's degrees and post-master's certificates. Challenging opportunities include advanced placement credit, student-designed majors, an honors program, double majors, independent study, and a senior project. Special programs include internships, summer session for credit, and study-abroad. The most frequently chosen baccalaureate fields are business/marketing, trade and industry, and English. The faculty at Fairfield has 223 full-time members, 93% with terminal degrees. The student-faculty ratio is 13:1.

Students of Fairfield The student body totals 5,114, of whom 4,073 are undergraduates. 55.8% are women and 44.2% are men. Students come from 37 states and territories and 40 other countries. 24% are from Connecticut. 1.4% are international students. 90% returned for their sophomore year.

Applying Fairfield requires an essay, SAT I or ACT, a high school transcript, 1 recommendation, rank in upper 20% of high school class, and a minimum high school GPA of 3.0. The school recommends an interview. Application deadline: 2/1; 2/15 for financial aid. Early and deferred admission are possible.

FAIRLEIGH DICKINSON UNIVERSITY, COLLEGE AT FLORHAM

Madison, NJ

Suburban setting ■ Private ■ Independent ■ Coed

Web site: www.fdu.edu
Contact: Mr. Gary Hamme, Vice President for Enrollment Services, 285 Madison Avenue, M-MS1-03, Madison, NJ 07940
Telephone: 201-692-7304 or toll-free 800-338-8803 **Fax:** 973-443-8088
E-mail: globaleducation@fdu.edu

Getting in Last Year 2,717 applied; 74% were accepted; 632 enrolled (31%).

Financial Matters $19,074 tuition and fees (2002–03); $7904 room and board.

Academics FDU awards associate, bachelor's, and master's degrees and post-bachelor's and post-master's certificates. Challenging opportunities include advanced placement credit, accelerated degree programs, an honors program, double majors, independent study, and a senior project. Special programs include cooperative education, internships, summer session for credit, off-campus study, study-abroad, and Army and Air Force ROTC. The most frequently chosen baccalaureate fields are business/marketing, liberal arts/general studies, and psychology. The faculty at FDU has 111 full-time members. The student-faculty ratio is 17:1.

Students of FDU The student body totals 3,682, of whom 2,578 are undergraduates. 53.8% are women and 46.2% are men. Students come from 23 states and territories and 33 other countries. 85% are from New Jersey. 1.9% are international students. 78% returned for their sophomore year.

Applying FDU requires an essay, SAT I or ACT, and a high school transcript. The school recommends SAT II Subject Tests. Application deadline: 3/1; 3/15 priority date for financial aid. Early and deferred admission are possible.

FAIRLEIGH DICKINSON UNIVERSITY, METROPOLITAN CAMPUS

Teaneck, NJ

Suburban setting ■ Private ■ Independent ■ Coed

Web site: www.fdu.edu
Contact: Mr. Gary Hamme, Vice President of Enrollment Services, 1000 River Road, Teaneck, NJ 07666
Telephone: 201-692-7304 or toll-free 800-338-8803 **Fax:** 201-692-7319
E-mail: globaleducation@fdu.edu

Getting in Last Year 2,327 applied; 67% were accepted; 513 enrolled (33%).

Financial Matters $19,074 tuition and fees (2002–03); $7904 room and board.

Academics FDU awards associate, bachelor's, master's, and doctoral degrees and post-bachelor's and post-master's certificates. Challenging opportunities include advanced placement credit, accelerated degree programs, student-designed majors, an honors program, double majors, independent study, and a senior project. Special programs include cooperative education, internships, summer session for credit, off-campus study, study-abroad, and Army and Air Force ROTC. The most frequently chosen baccalaureate fields are business/marketing, liberal arts/general studies, and psychology. The faculty at FDU has 165 full-time members. The student-faculty ratio is 15:1.

Students of FDU The student body totals 6,686, of whom 4,587 are undergraduates. 57% are women and 43% are men. Students come from 23 states and territories and 53 other countries. 89% are from New Jersey. 9.4% are international students. 74% returned for their sophomore year.

Applying FDU requires SAT I or ACT, a high school transcript, and 2 recommendations. The school recommends SAT II: Writing Test. Application deadline: 3/1; 3/15 priority date for financial aid. Early and deferred admission are possible.

FAIRMONT STATE COLLEGE

Fairmont, WV

Small-town setting ■ Public ■ State-supported ■ Coed

Web site: www.fscwv.edu
Contact: Mr. Douglas Dobbins, Executive Director of Enrollment Services, 1201 Locust Avenue, Fairmont, WV 26554
Telephone: 304-367-4000 or toll-free 800-641-5678 **Fax:** 304-367-4789
E-mail: admit@mail.fscwv.edu

Getting in Last Year 2,057 applied; 97% were accepted; 1,254 enrolled (63%).

Financial Matters $2766 resident tuition and fees (2002–03); $6340 nonresident tuition and fees (2002–03); $4788 room and board; 65% average percent of need met; $4841 average financial aid amount received per undergraduate (2001–02).

Academics Fairmont State awards associate, bachelor's, and master's degrees. Challenging opportunities include advanced placement credit, accelerated degree programs, an honors program, double majors, and a senior project. Special programs include internships, summer session for credit, and Army ROTC. The faculty at Fairmont State has 281 full-time members, 34% with terminal degrees. The student-faculty ratio is 20:1.

Students of Fairmont State The student body is made up of 6,813 undergraduates. 56% are women and 44% are men. Students come from 22 states and territories and 23 other countries. 94% are from West Virginia. 1.2% are international students. 63% returned for their sophomore year.

Applying Fairmont State requires SAT I or ACT and a high school transcript. The school recommends a minimum high school GPA of 2.0. Application deadline: 6/15; 3/1 priority date for financial aid. Early admission is possible.

FAITH BAPTIST BIBLE COLLEGE AND THEOLOGICAL SEMINARY

Ankeny, IA

Small-town setting ■ Private ■ Independent Religious ■ Coed

Web site: www.faith.edu

Contact: Mrs. Sherie Bartlett, Admissions Office Secretary, 1900 NW 4th Street, Ankeny, IA 50021
Telephone: 515-964-0601 ext. 233 or toll-free 888-FAITH 4U **Fax:** 515-964-1638
E-mail: admissions@faith.edu

Getting in Last Year 271 applied; 77% were accepted; 120 enrolled (58%).

Financial Matters $9692 tuition and fees (2002–03); $3726 room and board; 60% average percent of need met; $7450 average financial aid amount received per undergraduate.

Academics FBBC&TS awards associate, bachelor's, master's, and first-professional degrees. Challenging opportunities include advanced placement credit, double majors, independent study, and a senior project. Special programs include internships and summer session for credit. The most frequently chosen baccalaureate fields are education and visual/performing arts. The faculty at FBBC&TS has 20 full-time members, 65% with terminal degrees. The student-faculty ratio is 18:1.

Students of FBBC&TS The student body totals 505, of whom 403 are undergraduates. 53.8% are women and 46.2% are men. Students come from 27 states and territories. 47% are from Iowa. 0.5% are international students. 76% returned for their sophomore year.

Applying FBBC&TS requires an essay, SAT I or ACT, a high school transcript, and 2 recommendations, and in some cases an interview. Application deadline: 8/1; 3/1 priority date for financial aid. Early and deferred admission are possible.

FARMINGDALE STATE UNIVERSITY OF NEW YORK

Farmingdale, NY

Small-town setting ■ Public ■ State-supported ■ Coed

Web site: www.farmingdale.edu
Contact: Mr. Jim Hall, Director of Admissions, Route 110, Farmingdale, NY 11735-1021
Telephone: 631-420-2457 or toll-free 877-4-FARMINGDALE **Fax:** 631-420-2633
E-mail: admissions@farmingdale.edu

Getting in Last Year 2,949 applied; 70% were accepted; 1,092 enrolled (53%).

Financial Matters $4240 resident tuition and fees (2002–03); $9140 nonresident tuition and fees (2002–03); $7250 room and board; 63% average percent of need met; $5127 average financial aid amount received per undergraduate (2000–01).

Academics Farmingdale State University of New York awards associate and bachelor's degrees. Challenging opportunities include advanced placement credit, double majors, and a senior project. Special programs include internships, summer session for credit, study-abroad, and Army and Air Force ROTC. The most frequently chosen baccalaureate fields are trade and industry, engineering/engineering technologies, and communications/communication technologies. The faculty at Farmingdale State University of New York has 166 full-time members, 46% with terminal degrees. The student-faculty ratio is 20:1.

Students of Farmingdale State University of New York The student body is made up of 5,449 undergraduates. 44% are women and 56% are men. Students come from 8 states and territories. 99% are from New York. 0.5% are international students. 74% returned for their sophomore year.

Applying Farmingdale State University of New York requires SAT I or ACT, a high school transcript, and a minimum high school GPA of 2.0, and in some cases portfolio. Application deadline: rolling admissions; 4/1 priority date for financial aid. Early admission is possible.

FASHION INSTITUTE OF TECHNOLOGY

New York, NY

Urban setting ■ Public ■ State and locally supported ■ Coed

Web site: www.fitnyc.edu
Contact: Ms. Dolores Lombardi, Director of Admissions, Seventh Avenue at 27th Street, New York, NY 10001-5992
Telephone: 212-217-7675 or toll-free 800-GOTOFIT (out-of-state) **Fax:** 212-217-7481
E-mail: fitinfo@fitsuny.edu

Getting in Last Year 3,244 applied; 47% were accepted; 967 enrolled (64%).

Financial Matters $3670 resident tuition and fees (2002–03); $8262 nonresident tuition and fees (2002–03); $6138 room and board; 75% average percent of need met; $6118 average financial aid amount received per undergraduate (2001–02).

Academics FIT awards associate, bachelor's, and master's degrees. Challenging opportunities include advanced placement credit, an honors program, and a senior project. Special programs include cooperative education, internships, summer session for credit, and study-abroad. The most frequently chosen baccalaureate fields are business/marketing, visual/performing arts, and engineering/engineering technologies. The faculty at FIT has 208 full-time members. The student-faculty ratio is 15:1.

Students of FIT The student body totals 10,855, of whom 10,758 are undergraduates. 82.2% are women and 17.8% are men. Students come from 53 states and territories and 89 other countries. 74% are from New York. 12.5% are international students. 73% returned for their sophomore year.

Applying FIT requires an essay, a high school transcript, and portfolio for art and design programs. The school recommends SAT I or ACT. Application deadline: 1/1; 3/1 priority date for financial aid. Deferred admission is possible.

FAULKNER UNIVERSITY

Montgomery, AL

Urban setting ■ Private ■ Independent Religious ■ Coed

Web site: www.faulkner.edu
Contact: Mr. Keith Mock, Director of Admissions, 5345 Atlanta Highway, Montgomery, AL 36109
Telephone: 334-386-7200 or toll-free 800-879-9816 **Fax:** 334-386-7137
E-mail: admissions@faulkner.edu

Getting in Last Year 538 applied; 73% were accepted; 291 enrolled (74%).

Financial Matters $9300 tuition and fees (2002–03); $4600 room and board; 62% average percent of need met; $7000 average financial aid amount received per undergraduate (2001–02).

Academics Faulkner awards associate, bachelor's, master's, and first-professional degrees. Challenging opportunities include advanced placement credit, accelerated degree programs, freshman honors college, an honors program, double majors, independent study, and a senior project. Special programs include internships, summer session for credit, off-campus study, and Army and Air Force ROTC. The most frequently chosen baccalaureate fields are business/marketing, law/legal studies, and education. The faculty at Faulkner has 62 full-time members, 68% with terminal degrees. The student-faculty ratio is 22:1.

Students of Faulkner The student body totals 2,613, of whom 2,280 are undergraduates. 62.3% are women and 37.7% are men. Students come from 20 states and territories and 3 other countries. 89% are from Alabama. 0.5% are international students. 48% returned for their sophomore year.

Applying Faulkner requires SAT I or ACT, a high school transcript, 2 recommendations, and a minimum high school GPA of 2.0. The school recommends an essay and an interview. Application deadline: rolling admissions; 5/1 priority date for financial aid. Early and deferred admission are possible.

FAYETTEVILLE STATE UNIVERSITY

Fayetteville, NC

Urban setting ■ Public ■ State-supported ■ Coed

Web site: www.uncfsu.edu
Contact: Mr. Charles Darlington, Director of Enrollment Management and Admissions, 1200 Murchison Road, Fayetteville, NC 28301
Telephone: 910-486-1371 or toll-free 800-222-2594

Getting in Last Year 1,910 applied; 86% were accepted; 750 enrolled (45%).

Financial Matters $2052 resident tuition and fees (2002–03); $10,967 nonresident tuition and fees (2002–03); $3820 room and board; 69% average percent of need met; $6690 average financial aid amount received per undergraduate (2001–02).

Academics Fayetteville State University awards associate, bachelor's, master's, and doctoral degrees. Challenging opportunities include accelerated degree programs, an honors program, double majors, independent study, and a senior project. Special programs include cooperative education, internships, summer session for credit, and Army and Air Force ROTC. The most frequently chosen baccalaureate fields are business/marketing, social sciences and history, and protective services/public administration. The faculty at Fayetteville State University has 204 full-time members, 70% with terminal degrees. The student-faculty ratio is 20:1.

Students of Fayetteville State University The student body totals 5,308, of whom 4,328 are undergraduates. 64.6% are women and 35.4% are men. Students come from 41 states and territories and 8 other countries. 89% are from North Carolina. 0.5% are international students. 70% returned for their sophomore year.

Applying Fayetteville State University requires SAT I or ACT and a high school transcript. Application deadline: rolling admissions; 3/1 for financial aid. Early and deferred admission are possible.

FELICIAN COLLEGE

Lodi, NJ

Suburban setting ■ Private ■ Independent Religious ■ Coed

Web site: www.felician.edu
Contact: College Admissions Office, 262 South Main Street, Lodi, NJ 07644
Telephone: 201-559-6131 **Fax:** 201-559-6188
E-mail: admissions@inet.felician.edu

Getting in Last Year 947 applied; 63% were accepted; 326 enrolled (55%).

Financial Matters $13,100 tuition and fees (2002–03); $6600 room and board; 75% average percent of need met; $11,130 average financial aid amount received per undergraduate (2001–02).

Academics Felician awards associate, bachelor's, and master's degrees and post-bachelor's and post-master's certificates. Challenging opportunities include advanced placement credit, accelerated degree programs, student-designed majors, an honors program, double majors, independent study, and a senior

Felician College (continued)

project. Special programs include internships, summer session for credit, and off-campus study. The most frequently chosen baccalaureate fields are education, English, and psychology. The faculty at Felician has 72 full-time members, 49% with terminal degrees. The student-faculty ratio is 15:1.

Students of Felician The student body totals 1,717, of whom 1,618 are undergraduates. 75.9% are women and 24.1% are men. Students come from 10 states and territories and 5 other countries. 95% are from New Jersey. 2.3% are international students. 92% returned for their sophomore year.

Applying Felician requires SAT I, a high school transcript, and a minimum high school GPA of 2.0, and in some cases an essay and an interview. Application deadline: rolling admissions. Deferred admission is possible.

FERRIS STATE UNIVERSITY

Big Rapids, MI

Small-town setting ■ Public ■ State-supported ■ Coed

Web site: www.ferris.edu
Contact: Dr. Craig Westmann, Director Admissions Records/Associate Dean of Enrollment Services, CSS201, Big Rapids, MI 49307-2742
Telephone: 231-591-2100 or toll-free 800-433-7747 **Fax:** 616-592-2978
E-mail: admissions@ferris.edu

Getting in Last Year 7,657 applied; 74% were accepted; 2,067 enrolled (36%).

Financial Matters $5852 resident tuition and fees (2002–03); $11,503 nonresident tuition and fees (2002–03); $5968 room and board; 80% average percent of need met; $7800 average financial aid amount received per undergraduate (2001–02).

Academics Ferris awards associate, bachelor's, master's, and first-professional degrees. Challenging opportunities include advanced placement credit, accelerated degree programs, freshman honors college, an honors program, double majors, and a senior project. Special programs include cooperative education, internships, summer session for credit, off-campus study, study-abroad, and Army ROTC. The most frequently chosen baccalaureate fields are business/marketing, health professions and related sciences, and engineering/engineering technologies. The faculty at Ferris has 490 full-time members. The student-faculty ratio is 16:1.

Students of Ferris The student body totals 11,074, of whom 10,176 are undergraduates. 46.4% are women and 53.6% are men. Students come from 42 states and territories and 54 other countries. 95% are from Michigan. 1.8% are international students. 59% returned for their sophomore year.

Applying Ferris requires SAT I or ACT, a high school transcript, and a minimum high school GPA of 2.25, and in some cases an interview. The school recommends an interview. Application deadline: 8/4; 3/15 priority date for financial aid. Deferred admission is possible.

FERRUM COLLEGE

Ferrum, VA

Rural setting ■ Private ■ Independent Religious ■ Coed

Web site: www.ferrum.edu
Contact: Ms. Gilda Q. Woods, Director of Admissions, Spilman-Daniel House, PO Box 1000, Ferrum, VA 24088-9001
Telephone: 540-365-4290 or toll-free 800-868-9797 **Fax:** 540-365-4266
E-mail: admissions@ferrum.edu

Getting in Last Year 1,109 applied; 72% were accepted; 295 enrolled (37%).

Financial Matters $14,390 tuition and fees (2002–03); $5600 room and board.

Academics Ferrum awards bachelor's degrees. Challenging opportunities include advanced placement credit, student-designed majors, double majors, independent study, and a senior project. Special programs include cooperative education, internships, summer session for credit, and study-abroad. The most frequently chosen baccalaureate fields are business/marketing, protective services/public administration, and biological/life sciences. The faculty at Ferrum has 65 full-time members, 66% with terminal degrees. The student-faculty ratio is 13:1.

Students of Ferrum The student body is made up of 951 undergraduates. 40.4% are women and 59.6% are men. Students come from 23 states and territories and 4 other countries. 83% are from Virginia. 0.7% are international students. 56% returned for their sophomore year.

Applying Ferrum requires SAT I or ACT and a high school transcript, and in some cases an interview. The school recommends an essay, an interview, 2 recommendations, and a minimum high school GPA of 2.0. Application deadline: rolling admissions; 4/1 priority date for financial aid. Early and deferred admission are possible.

FINLANDIA UNIVERSITY

Hancock, MI

Small-town setting ■ Private ■ Independent Religious ■ Coed

Web site: www.finlandia.edu
Contact: Mr. Ben Larson, Executive Director of Admissions, 601 Quincy Street, Hancock, MI 49930
Telephone: 906-487-7311 ext. 311 or toll-free 877-202-5491 **Fax:** 906-487-7383
E-mail: admissions@finlandia.edu

Getting in Last Year 224 applied; 57% were accepted; 126 enrolled (99%).

Financial Matters $12,600 tuition and fees (2002–03); $4680 room and board; 87% average percent of need met; $10,700 average financial aid amount received per undergraduate.

Academics Finlandia University awards associate and bachelor's degrees. Challenging opportunities include advanced placement credit, accelerated degree programs, independent study, and a senior project. Special programs include internships, summer session for credit, study-abroad, and Army and Air Force ROTC. The most frequently chosen baccalaureate fields are protective services/public administration, business/marketing, and liberal arts/general studies. The faculty at Finlandia University has 32 full-time members, 9% with terminal degrees. The student-faculty ratio is 11:1.

Students of Finlandia University The student body is made up of 503 undergraduates. 67.2% are women and 32.8% are men. Students come from 8 states and territories. 95% are from Michigan. 54% returned for their sophomore year.

Applying Finlandia University requires a high school transcript and a minimum high school GPA of 2.5, and in some cases an essay, an interview, and recommendations. The school recommends SAT I or ACT. Application deadline: 8/15; 2/15 priority date for financial aid. Early admission is possible.

FISK UNIVERSITY

Nashville, TN

Urban setting ■ Private ■ Independent Religious ■ Coed

Web site: www.fisk.edu
Contact: Director of Admissions, 1000 17th Avenue North, Nashville, TN 37208
Telephone: 615-329-8666 or toll-free 800-443-FISK
E-mail: admit@fisk.edu

Getting in Last Year 853 applied; 75% were accepted; 220 enrolled (35%).

Financial Matters $11,235 tuition and fees (2002–03); $5770 room and board; 50% average percent of need met; $13,000 average financial aid amount received per undergraduate.

Academics Fisk awards bachelor's and master's degrees. Challenging opportunities include advanced placement credit, student-designed majors, an honors program, double majors, independent study, and a senior project. Special programs include cooperative education, internships, off-campus study, study-abroad, and Army and Navy ROTC. The most frequently chosen baccalaureate fields are psychology, business/marketing, and English. The faculty at Fisk has 60 full-time members, 75% with terminal degrees. The student-faculty ratio is 12:1.

Students of Fisk The student body totals 811, of whom 792 are undergraduates. 69.4% are women and 30.6% are men. Students come from 32 states and territories and 7 other countries. 27% are from Tennessee. 4.6% are international students. 88% returned for their sophomore year.

Applying Fisk requires an essay, SAT I or ACT, a high school transcript, 2 recommendations, and a minimum high school GPA of 2.5. Application deadline: 1/15; 3/1 priority date for financial aid.

FITCHBURG STATE COLLEGE

Fitchburg, MA

Small-town setting ■ Public ■ State-supported ■ Coed

Web site: www.fsc.edu
Contact: Ms. Lynn A. Petrillo, Director of Admissions, 160 Pearl Street, Fitchburg, MA 01420-2697
Telephone: 978-665-3140 or toll-free 800-705-9692 **Fax:** 978-665-4540
E-mail: admissions@fsc.edu

Getting in Last Year 3,057 applied; 54% were accepted; 524 enrolled (32%).

Financial Matters $3688 resident tuition and fees (2002–03); $9768 nonresident tuition and fees (2002–03); $5172 room and board; 100% average percent of need met; $5219 average financial aid amount received per undergraduate.

Academics Fitchburg State awards bachelor's and master's degrees and post-master's certificates. Challenging opportunities include advanced placement credit, accelerated degree programs, student-designed majors, an honors program, double majors, independent study, and a senior project. Special programs include internships, summer session for credit, off-campus study, study-abroad, and Air Force ROTC. The most frequently chosen baccalaureate fields are education, business/marketing, and communications/communication technologies. The faculty at Fitchburg State has 183 full-time members, 87% with terminal degrees. The student-faculty ratio is 13:1.

Students of Fitchburg State The student body totals 4,924, of whom 3,342 are undergraduates. 57.6% are women and 42.4% are men. 95% are from Massachusetts. 1.1% are international students. 75% returned for their sophomore year.

Applying Fitchburg State requires an essay, SAT I or ACT, a high school transcript, and a minimum high school GPA of 3.0, and in some cases an interview. The school recommends recommendations. Application deadline: 4/1; 3/1 priority date for financial aid. Deferred admission is possible.

FIVE TOWNS COLLEGE

Dix Hills, NY

Suburban setting ■ Private ■ Independent ■ Coed

Web site: www.fivetowns.edu
Contact: Mr. Jerry Cohen, Dean of Enrollment, 305 North Service Road, Dix Hills, NY 11746-6055
Telephone: 631-424-7000 ext. 2121 **Fax:** 631-656-2172

Getting in Last Year 532 applied; 70% were accepted; 250 enrolled (67%).

Financial Matters $11,800 tuition and fees (2002–03); $8400 room and board; 60% average percent of need met; $5000 average financial aid amount received per undergraduate.

Academics Five Towns awards associate, bachelor's, and master's degrees. Challenging opportunities include advanced placement credit, independent study, and a senior project. Special programs include cooperative education, internships, summer session for credit, and off-campus study. The most frequently chosen baccalaureate field is visual/performing arts. The faculty at Five Towns has 61 full-time members, 34% with terminal degrees. The student-faculty ratio is 13:1.

Students of Five Towns The student body totals 1,143, of whom 1,067 are undergraduates. 36.9% are women and 63.1% are men. Students come from 10 states and territories and 7 other countries. 1.2% are international students. 74% returned for their sophomore year.

Applying Five Towns requires an essay, SAT I and SAT II or ACT, a high school transcript, recommendations, and a minimum high school GPA of 2.3, and in some cases an interview. Application deadline: rolling admissions; 4/30 priority date for financial aid. Early and deferred admission are possible.

FLAGLER COLLEGE

St. Augustine, FL

Small-town setting ■ Private ■ Independent ■ Coed

Web site: www.flagler.edu
Contact: Mr. Marc G. Williar, Director of Admissions, PO Box 1027, St. Augustine, FL 32085-1027
Telephone: 904-829-6481 ext. 220 or toll-free 800-304-4208
E-mail: admiss@flagler.edu

Getting in Last Year 1,994 applied; 30% were accepted; 479 enrolled (81%).

Financial Matters $6870 tuition and fees (2002–03); $4120 room and board; 74% average percent of need met; $6930 average financial aid amount received per undergraduate (2001–02).

Academics Flagler awards bachelor's degrees. Challenging opportunities include advanced placement credit, double majors, independent study, and a senior project. Special programs include internships, summer session for credit, off-campus study, and study-abroad. The most frequently chosen baccalaureate fields are business/marketing, education, and communications/communication technologies. The faculty at Flagler has 65 full-time members, 68% with terminal degrees. The student-faculty ratio is 21:1.

Students of Flagler The student body is made up of 1,973 undergraduates. 62.3% are women and 37.7% are men. Students come from 47 states and territories and 21 other countries. 66% are from Florida. 2.4% are international students. 68% returned for their sophomore year.

Applying Flagler requires an essay, SAT I or ACT, a high school transcript, and 1 recommendation. The school recommends an interview, rank in upper 50% of high school class, and a minimum high school GPA of 2.75. Application deadline: 3/1. Early and deferred admission are possible.

FLORIDA AGRICULTURAL AND MECHANICAL UNIVERSITY

Tallahassee, FL

Urban setting ■ Public ■ State-supported ■ Coed

Web site: www.famu.edu
Contact: Ms. Barbara R. Cox, Director of Admissions, Office of Admissions, Tallahassee, FL 32307
Telephone: 850-599-3796 **Fax:** 850-599-3069
E-mail: barbara.cox@famu.edu

Getting in Last Year 4,819 applied; 78% were accepted; 2,187 enrolled (58%).

Financial Matters $2794 resident tuition and fees (2002–03); $11,091 nonresident tuition and fees (2002–03); $4966 room and board; 59% average percent of need met; $7827 average financial aid amount received per undergraduate.

Academics FAMU awards associate, bachelor's, master's, doctoral, and first-professional degrees. Challenging opportunities include advanced placement credit, accelerated degree programs, an honors program, and a senior project. Special programs include cooperative education, internships, summer session for credit, off-campus study, and Army, Navy and Air Force ROTC. The most frequently chosen baccalaureate fields are business/marketing, health professions and related sciences, and education. The faculty at FAMU has 488 full-time members, 72% with terminal degrees.

Students of FAMU The student body totals 12,465, of whom 10,804 are undergraduates. 57.1% are women and 42.9% are men. Students come from 47 states and territories and 50 other countries. 80% are from Florida. 0.6% are international students. 80% returned for their sophomore year.

Applying FAMU requires SAT I or ACT, a high school transcript, and a minimum high school GPA of 2.0, and in some cases an essay and recommendations. The school recommends a minimum high school GPA of 3.0. Application deadline: 5/9; 6/30 for financial aid, with a 3/1 priority date. Early and deferred admission are possible.

FLORIDA ATLANTIC UNIVERSITY

Boca Raton, FL

Suburban setting ■ Public ■ State-supported ■ Coed

Web site: www.fau.edu
Contact: Coordinator, Freshmen Recruitment, 777 Glades Road, PO Box 3091, Boca Raton, FL 33431-0991
Telephone: 561-297-2458 or toll-free 800-299-4FAU **Fax:** 561-297-2758

Getting in Last Year 7,283 applied; 69% were accepted; 2,307 enrolled (46%).

Financial Matters $2786 resident tuition and fees (2002–03); $12,314 nonresident tuition and fees (2002–03); $7112 room and board; $2100 average financial aid amount received per undergraduate (2001–02).

Academics FAU awards associate, bachelor's, master's, and doctoral degrees. Challenging opportunities include advanced placement credit, accelerated degree programs, freshman honors college, an honors program, double majors, independent study, and a senior project. Special programs include cooperative education, internships, summer session for credit, off-campus study, study-abroad, and Army and Air Force ROTC. The most frequently chosen baccalaureate fields are business/marketing, education, and English. The faculty at FAU has 689 full-time members, 89% with terminal degrees. The student-faculty ratio is 15:1.

Students of FAU The student body totals 23,836, of whom 19,236 are undergraduates. 60.8% are women and 39.2% are men. Students come from 48 states and territories and 147 other countries. 94% are from Florida. 6% are international students. 69% returned for their sophomore year.

Applying FAU requires SAT I or ACT, a high school transcript, and a minimum high school GPA of 2.0, and in some cases 1 recommendation. Application deadline: 6/1; 3/1 priority date for financial aid. Early and deferred admission are possible.

FLORIDA COLLEGE

Temple Terrace, FL

Small-town setting ■ Private ■ Independent ■ Coed

Web site: www.floridacollege.edu
Contact: Mrs. Mari Smith, Assistant Director of Admissions, 119 North Glen Arven Avenue, Temple Terrace, FL 33617
Telephone: 813-988-5131 ext. 6716 or toll-free 800-326-7655 **Fax:** 813-899-6772
E-mail: admissions@floridacollege.edu

Getting in Last Year 423 applied; 204 enrolled.

Financial Matters $8580 tuition and fees (2002–03); $5060 room and board.

Academics Florida College awards associate and bachelor's degrees. Challenging opportunities include advanced placement credit and independent study. Army and Air Force ROTC is a special program. The most frequently chosen baccalaureate field is education. The faculty at Florida College has 29 full-time members, 34% with terminal degrees. The student-faculty ratio is 13:1.

Students of Florida College The student body is made up of 460 undergraduates. 50.2% are women and 49.8% are men. Students come from 35 states and territories. 30% are from Florida. 0.9% are international students. 89% returned for their sophomore year.

Applying Florida College requires SAT I or ACT, a high school transcript, recommendations, and a minimum high school GPA of 2.0, and in some cases an essay. Application deadline: 8/1; 8/1 for financial aid, with a 4/1 priority date.

FLORIDA GULF COAST UNIVERSITY

Fort Myers, FL

Suburban setting ■ Public ■ State-supported ■ Coed

Web site: www.fgcu.edu
Contact: Ms. Kathy Peterson, Director of Admissions, Interim, 10501 FGCU Boulevard South, Fort Myers, FL 33965-6565
Telephone: 239-590-7878 or toll-free 800-590-3428 **Fax:** 239-590-7894
E-mail: oar@fgcu.edu

Getting in Last Year 2,372 applied; 76% were accepted; 848 enrolled (47%).

Financial Matters $2699 resident tuition and fees (2002–03); $12,243 nonresident tuition and fees (2002–03); $7000 room and board; 77% average percent of need met; $6618 average financial aid amount received per undergraduate (2001–02).

Florida Gulf Coast University (continued)

Academics FGCU awards associate, bachelor's, and master's degrees. Challenging opportunities include advanced placement credit, accelerated degree programs, an honors program, double majors, independent study, and a senior project. Special programs include cooperative education, internships, summer session for credit, off-campus study, and study-abroad. The most frequently chosen baccalaureate fields are education, liberal arts/general studies, and protective services/public administration. The faculty at FGCU has 176 full-time members, 80% with terminal degrees. The student-faculty ratio is 15:1.

Students of FGCU The student body totals 4,799, of whom 4,113 are undergraduates. 63.3% are women and 36.7% are men. Students come from 28 states and territories and 18 other countries. 98% are from Florida. 0.9% are international students. 69% returned for their sophomore year.

Applying FGCU requires SAT I or ACT, a high school transcript, and a minimum high school GPA of 2.0, and in some cases an essay, an interview, and recommendations. Application deadline: 7/1. Early and deferred admission are possible.

FLORIDA INSTITUTE OF TECHNOLOGY

Melbourne, FL

Small-town setting ■ Private ■ Independent ■ Coed

Web site: www.fit.edu
Contact: Ms. Judith Marino, Director of Undergraduate Admissions, 150 West University Boulevard, Melbourne, FL 32901-6975
Telephone: 321-674-8030 or toll-free 800-888-4348 **Fax:** 321-723-9468
E-mail: admissions@fit.edu

Getting in Last Year 1,982 applied; 84% were accepted; 519 enrolled (31%).

Financial Matters $20,900 tuition and fees (2002–03); $5800 room and board; 85% average percent of need met; $17,050 average financial aid amount received per undergraduate.

Academics Florida Tech awards bachelor's, master's, and doctoral degrees and post-master's certificates. Challenging opportunities include advanced placement credit, accelerated degree programs, double majors, and a senior project. Special programs include cooperative education, internships, summer session for credit, study-abroad, and Army ROTC. The most frequently chosen baccalaureate fields are engineering/engineering technologies, biological/life sciences, and trade and industry. The faculty at Florida Tech has 192 full-time members, 88% with terminal degrees. The student-faculty ratio is 12:1.

Students of Florida Tech The student body totals 4,506, of whom 2,168 are undergraduates. 29.4% are women and 70.6% are men. Students come from 52 states and territories and 87 other countries. 56% are from Florida. 22.5% are international students. 77% returned for their sophomore year.

Applying Florida Tech requires SAT I or ACT, a high school transcript, and a minimum high school GPA of 2.5, and in some cases a minimum high school GPA of 3.0. The school recommends an essay, an interview, and a minimum high school GPA of 2.8. Application deadline: rolling admissions; 3/15 priority date for financial aid. Early and deferred admission are possible.

FLORIDA INTERNATIONAL UNIVERSITY

Miami, FL

Urban setting ■ Public ■ State-supported ■ Coed

Web site: www.fiu.edu
Contact: Ms. Carmen Brown, Director of Admissions, University Park, PC 140, 11200 SW 8 Street, PC140, Miami, FL 33199
Telephone: 305-348-3675 **Fax:** 305-348-3648
E-mail: admiss@fiu.edu

Getting in Last Year 11,307 applied; 64% were accepted; 2,890 enrolled (40%).

Financial Matters $2881 resident tuition and fees (2002–03); $12,347 nonresident tuition and fees (2002–03); $7180 room and board; 56% average percent of need met; $6351 average financial aid amount received per undergraduate (2001–02).

Academics FIU awards bachelor's, master's, doctoral, and first-professional degrees. Challenging opportunities include advanced placement credit, accelerated degree programs, freshman honors college, an honors program, double majors, independent study, and a senior project. Special programs include cooperative education, internships, summer session for credit, off-campus study, study-abroad, and Army and Air Force ROTC. The most frequently chosen baccalaureate fields are business/marketing, education, and health professions and related sciences. The faculty at FIU has 714 full-time members, 98% with terminal degrees. The student-faculty ratio is 17:1.

Students of FIU The student body totals 33,451, of whom 27,153 are undergraduates. 56.4% are women and 43.6% are men. Students come from 52 states and territories and 115 other countries. 94% are from Florida. 7.1% are international students. 88% returned for their sophomore year.

Applying FIU requires SAT I or ACT, a high school transcript, and a minimum high school GPA of 3.0, and in some cases 1 recommendation. Application deadline: rolling admissions; 3/1 priority date for financial aid. Early and deferred admission are possible.

FLORIDA METROPOLITAN UNIVERSITY–BRANDON CAMPUS

Tampa, FL

Urban setting ■ Private ■ Proprietary ■ Coed

Web site: www.fmu.edu
Contact: Mrs. Dee McKee, Director of Admissions, 3924 Coconut Palm Drive, Tampa, FL 33619
Telephone: 813-621-0041 ext. 45 **Fax:** 813-623-5769
E-mail: dpearson@cci.edu

Financial Matters $7998 tuition and fees (2002–03); 15% average percent of need met.

Academics FMU-Brandon awards associate, bachelor's, and master's degrees. Challenging opportunities include accelerated degree programs, an honors program, and double majors. Special programs include cooperative education, internships, and summer session for credit. The most frequently chosen baccalaureate fields are business/marketing, protective services/public administration, and computer/information sciences. The faculty at FMU-Brandon has 16 full-time members. The student-faculty ratio is 25:1.

Students of FMU-Brandon The student body totals 1,350, of whom 1,276 are undergraduates. Students come from 1 state or territory.

Applying FMU-Brandon requires CPAt, a high school transcript, an interview, and minimum CPAt score of 120. Application deadline: rolling admissions. Early and deferred admission are possible.

FLORIDA METROPOLITAN UNIVERSITY–FORT LAUDERDALE CAMPUS

Fort Lauderdale, FL

Suburban setting ■ Private ■ Proprietary ■ Coed

Web site: www.fmu.edu
Contact: Mr. Tony Wallace, Director of Admissions, 1040 Bayview Drive, Fort Lauderdale, FL 33304-2522
Telephone: 954-568-1600 or toll-free 800-468-0168 **Fax:** 954-568-2008

Financial Matters $7998 tuition and fees (2002–03).

Academics FMU-Fort Lauderdale Campus awards associate, bachelor's, and master's degrees. Challenging opportunities include advanced placement credit and accelerated degree programs. Special programs include internships and summer session for credit. The faculty at FMU-Fort Lauderdale Campus has 24 full-time members. The student-faculty ratio is 17:1.

Students of FMU-Fort Lauderdale Campus The student body totals 1,868, of whom 1,765 are undergraduates. 66.5% are women and 33.5% are men. Students come from 25 states and territories and 41 other countries. 0.2% are international students.

Applying FMU-Fort Lauderdale Campus requires an essay, CPAt, and a high school transcript, and in some cases recommendations. The school recommends SAT I or ACT and an interview. Application deadline: rolling admissions. Deferred admission is possible.

FLORIDA METROPOLITAN UNIVERSITY–JACKSONVILLE CAMPUS

Jacksonville, FL

Private ■ Proprietary ■ Coed

Web site: www.cci.edu
Contact: Ms. Donna Wilhelm, Admissions Director, 8226 Phillips Highway, Jacksonville, FL 32256
Telephone: 904-731-4949 or toll-free 888-741-4271 **Fax:** 904-731-0599 ext.

Financial Matters $8058 tuition and fees (2002–03).

Academics Florida Metropolitan University–Jacksonville Campus awards associate, bachelor's, and master's degrees. The faculty at Florida Metropolitan University–Jacksonville Campus has 7 full-time members, 43% with terminal degrees.

Students of Florida Metropolitan University–Jacksonville Campus The student body totals 954.

FLORIDA METROPOLITAN UNIVERSITY–MELBOURNE CAMPUS

Melbourne, FL

Small-town setting ■ Private ■ Proprietary ■ Coed

Web site: www.fmu.edu
Contact: Mr. Timothy Alexander, Director of Admissions, 2401 North Harbor City Boulevard, Melbourne, FL 32935-6657
Telephone: 321-253-2929 ext. 121

Getting in Last Year 339 applied; 68% were accepted.

Financial Matters $8322 tuition and fees (2002–03).

Academics FMU-Melbourne awards associate, bachelor's, and master's degrees. Challenging opportunities include advanced placement credit and accelerated degree programs. Special programs include internships and summer session for credit. The faculty at FMU-Melbourne has 16 full-time members, 25% with terminal degrees. The student-faculty ratio is 18:1.

Students of FMU-Melbourne The student body totals 880, of whom 818 are undergraduates. 62.8% are women and 37.2% are men. Students come from 1 state or territory and 3 other countries. 0.9% are international students. 68% returned for their sophomore year.

Applying FMU-Melbourne requires CPAt, a high school transcript, and an interview. Application deadline: rolling admissions. Deferred admission is possible.

FLORIDA METROPOLITAN UNIVERSITY–NORTH ORLANDO CAMPUS

Orlando, FL

Urban setting ■ *Private* ■ *Proprietary* ■ *Coed*

Web site: www.fmu.edu

Contact: Ms. Charlene Donnelly, Director of Admissions, 5421 Diplomat Circle, Orlando, FL 32810-5674

Telephone: 407-628-5870 ext. 108 or toll-free 800-628-5870

Getting in Last Year 2,123 applied; 68% were accepted; 69 enrolled (5%).

Financial Matters $7998 tuition and fees (2002–03); $8800 average financial aid amount received per undergraduate.

Academics FMU awards associate, bachelor's, and master's degrees. Challenging opportunities include advanced placement credit, double majors, independent study, and a senior project. Special programs include internships and summer session for credit. The faculty at FMU has 10 full-time members, 10% with terminal degrees. The student-faculty ratio is 15:1.

Students of FMU The student body totals 1,444, of whom 1,364 are undergraduates. 66.6% are women and 33.4% are men. 2.6% are international students.

Applying FMU requires a high school transcript. Application deadline: rolling admissions. Deferred admission is possible.

FLORIDA METROPOLITAN UNIVERSITY–PINELLAS CAMPUS

Clearwater, FL

Urban setting ■ *Private* ■ *Proprietary* ■ *Coed*

Web site: www.fmu.edu

Contact: Mr. Wayne Childers, Director of Admissions, 2471 McMullen Booth Road, Suite 200, Clearwater, FL 33759

Telephone: 727-725-2688 ext. 702 or toll-free 800-353-FMUS **Fax:** 727-796-3722

E-mail: wchilder@cci.edu

Getting in Last Year 622 applied; 70% were accepted.

Financial Matters $7998 tuition and fees (2002–03); 90% average percent of need met; $7250 average financial aid amount received per undergraduate.

Academics FMU-Pinellas awards associate, bachelor's, and master's degrees. Challenging opportunities include advanced placement credit, accelerated degree programs, an honors program, and double majors. Special programs include cooperative education, internships, and summer session for credit. The faculty at FMU-Pinellas has 13 full-time members, 23% with terminal degrees. The student-faculty ratio is 24:1.

Students of FMU-Pinellas The student body totals 1,201, of whom 1,057 are undergraduates. 70.6% are women and 29.4% are men. Students come from 11 states and territories. 94% are from Florida. 72% returned for their sophomore year.

Applying FMU-Pinellas requires CPAt, a high school transcript, and an interview. The school recommends SAT I or ACT and a minimum high school GPA of 2.0. Application deadline: rolling admissions. Early and deferred admission are possible.

FLORIDA METROPOLITAN UNIVERSITY–SOUTH ORLANDO CAMPUS

Orlando, FL

Private ■ *Proprietary* ■ *Coed*

Web site: www.fmu.edu

Contact: Ms. Annette Cloin, Director of Admissions, 2411 Sand Lake Road, Orlando, FL 32809

Telephone: 407-851-2525 ext. 111 or toll-free 407-851 ext. 2525 (in-state), 866-508 ext. 0007 (out-of-state) **Fax:** 407-851-1477

Getting in Last Year 205 applied; 45% were accepted; 72 enrolled (78%).

Financial Matters $8048 tuition and fees (2002–03); 90% average percent of need met; $8000 average financial aid amount received per undergraduate.

Academics Florida Metropolitan University–South Orlando Campus awards associate, bachelor's, and master's degrees. Challenging opportunities include accelerated degree programs and double majors. Special programs include cooperative education and internships. The faculty at Florida Metropolitan University–South Orlando Campus has 10 full-time members, 30% with terminal degrees. The student-faculty ratio is 20:1.

Students of Florida Metropolitan University–South Orlando Campus The student body totals 1,964, of whom 1,888 are undergraduates. 74% are women and 26% are men. 1.6% are international students.

Applying Florida Metropolitan University–South Orlando Campus requires a high school transcript and an interview. Application deadline: rolling admissions.

FLORIDA SOUTHERN COLLEGE

Lakeland, FL

Suburban setting ■ *Private* ■ *Independent Religious* ■ *Coed*

Web site: www.flsouthern.edu

Contact: Mr. Barry Conners, Director of Admissions, 111 Lake Hollingsworth Drive, Lakeland, FL 33801-5698

Telephone: 863-680-3909 or toll-free 800-274-4131 **Fax:** 863-680-4120

E-mail: fscadm@flsouthern.edu

Getting in Last Year 1,668 applied; 78% were accepted; 493 enrolled (38%).

Financial Matters $15,078 tuition and fees (2002–03); $5700 room and board; 61% average percent of need met; $13,648 average financial aid amount received per undergraduate.

Academics Florida Southern awards bachelor's and master's degrees. Challenging opportunities include advanced placement credit, an honors program, double majors, independent study, and a senior project. Special programs include internships, summer session for credit, off-campus study, study-abroad, and Army ROTC. The most frequently chosen baccalaureate fields are business/marketing, education, and health professions and related sciences. The faculty at Florida Southern has 109 full-time members, 83% with terminal degrees. The student-faculty ratio is 17:1.

Students of Florida Southern The student body totals 1,932, of whom 1,881 are undergraduates. 61.1% are women and 38.9% are men. Students come from 47 states and territories and 44 other countries. 77% are from Florida. 4.4% are international students. 72% returned for their sophomore year.

Applying Florida Southern requires an essay, SAT I or ACT, a high school transcript, 3 recommendations, and a minimum high school GPA of 2.0. The school recommends an interview and a minimum high school GPA of 3.0. Application deadline: 8/1 for financial aid, with a 4/1 priority date. Early and deferred admission are possible.

FLORIDA STATE UNIVERSITY

Tallahassee, FL

Suburban setting ■ *Public* ■ *State-supported* ■ *Coed*

Web site: www.fsu.edu

Contact: Office of Admissions, A2500 University Center, Tallahassee, FL 32306-2400

Telephone: 850-644-6200 **Fax:** 850-644-0197

E-mail: admissions@admin.fsu.edu

Getting in Last Year 21,046 applied; 70% were accepted; 6,378 enrolled (43%).

Financial Matters $2538 resident tuition and fees (2002–03); $12,082 nonresident tuition and fees (2002–03); $5628 room and board; 25% average percent of need met; $6529 average financial aid amount received per undergraduate.

Academics Florida State awards associate, bachelor's, master's, doctoral, and first-professional degrees and post-bachelor's and post-master's certificates. Challenging opportunities include advanced placement credit, accelerated degree programs, an honors program, double majors, independent study, and a senior project. Special programs include cooperative education, internships, summer session for credit, off-campus study, study-abroad, and Army, Navy and Air Force ROTC. The most frequently chosen baccalaureate fields are business/marketing, social sciences and history, and protective services/public administration. The faculty at Florida State has 1,124 full-time members, 91% with terminal degrees. The student-faculty ratio is 22:1.

Students of Florida State The student body totals 36,210, of whom 29,195 are undergraduates. 56.2% are women and 43.8% are men. Students come from 51 states and territories and 117 other countries. 86% are from Florida. 0.7% are international students. 85% returned for their sophomore year.

Applying Florida State requires SAT I or ACT and a high school transcript, and in some cases audition. The school recommends an essay and a minimum high school GPA of 3.0. Application deadline: 3/1; 2/15 priority date for financial aid. Early admission is possible.

FONTBONNE UNIVERSITY

St. Louis, MO

Suburban setting ■ *Private* ■ *Independent Religious* ■ *Coed*

Fontbonne University (continued)

Web site: www.fontbonne.edu
Contact: Ms. Peggy Musen, Associate Dean for Enrollment Management, 6800 Wydown Boulevard, St. Louis, MO 63105-3098
Telephone: 314-889-1400 **Fax:** 314-719-8021
E-mail: pmusen@fontbonne.edu

Getting in Last Year 474 applied; 81% were accepted; 190 enrolled (49%).

Financial Matters $13,714 tuition and fees (2002–03); $6535 room and board; 86% average percent of need met; $15,600 average financial aid amount received per undergraduate.

Academics Fontbonne University awards bachelor's and master's degrees and post-bachelor's certificates. Challenging opportunities include advanced placement credit, accelerated degree programs, student-designed majors, an honors program, double majors, independent study, and a senior project. Special programs include cooperative education, internships, summer session for credit, off-campus study, and Army ROTC. The most frequently chosen baccalaureate fields are business/marketing, education, and visual/performing arts. The faculty at Fontbonne University has 55 full-time members, 73% with terminal degrees. The student-faculty ratio is 12:1.

Students of Fontbonne University The student body totals 2,344, of whom 1,611 are undergraduates. 75.9% are women and 24.1% are men. Students come from 21 states and territories and 1 other country. 86% are from Missouri. 0.5% are international students. 75% returned for their sophomore year.

Applying Fontbonne University requires an essay, SAT I or ACT, a high school transcript, and a minimum high school GPA of 2.5. The school recommends an interview and 2 recommendations. Application deadline: 8/1; 4/30 priority date for financial aid. Early and deferred admission are possible.

FORDHAM UNIVERSITY

New York, NY

Urban setting ■ Private ■ Independent Religious ■ Coed

Web site: www.fordham.edu
Contact: Ms. Karen Pellegrino, Director of Admission, Theband Hall, 441 East Fordham Road, New York, NY 10458
Telephone: 718-817-4000 or toll-free 800-FORDHAM **Fax:** 718-367-9404
E-mail: enroll@fordham.edu

Getting in Last Year 11,380 applied; 57% were accepted; 1,728 enrolled (27%).

Financial Matters $23,540 tuition and fees (2002–03); $9460 room and board; 79% average percent of need met; $19,536 average financial aid amount received per undergraduate (2001–02).

Academics Fordham awards bachelor's, master's, doctoral, and first-professional degrees and post-master's certificates (branch locations: an 85-acre campus at Rose Hill and an 8-acre campus at Lincoln Center). Challenging opportunities include advanced placement credit, accelerated degree programs, student-designed majors, an honors program, double majors, independent study, and a senior project. Special programs include internships, summer session for credit, off-campus study, study-abroad, and Army, Navy and Air Force ROTC. The most frequently chosen baccalaureate fields are social sciences and history, business/marketing, and communications/communication technologies. The faculty at Fordham has 601 full-time members, 16% with terminal degrees. The student-faculty ratio is 11:1.

Students of Fordham The student body totals 14,318, of whom 7,228 are undergraduates. 59.4% are women and 40.6% are men. Students come from 53 states and territories and 40 other countries. 61% are from New York. 1.3% are international students. 89% returned for their sophomore year.

Applying Fordham requires an essay, SAT I or ACT, a high school transcript, and 1 recommendation, and in some cases an interview. The school recommends SAT II Subject Tests, an interview, and a minimum high school GPA of 3.0. Application deadline: 2/1; 2/1 priority date for financial aid. Early admission is possible.

FORT HAYS STATE UNIVERSITY

Hays, KS

Small-town setting ■ Public ■ State-supported ■ Coed

Web site: www.fhsu.edu
Contact: Ms. Christy Befort, Senior Administrative Assistant, Office of Admissions, 600 Park Street, Hays, KS 67601-4099
Telephone: 785-628-5830 or toll-free 800-628-FHSU **Fax:** 785-628-4187
E-mail: tigers@fhsu.edu

Getting in Last Year 1,468 applied; 93% were accepted; 850 enrolled (62%).

Financial Matters $2328 resident tuition and fees (2002–03); $7488 nonresident tuition and fees (2002–03); $4843 room and board; 75% average percent of need met; $5085 average financial aid amount received per undergraduate (2001–02).

Academics FHSU awards associate, bachelor's, and master's degrees. Challenging opportunities include advanced placement credit, student-designed majors, double majors, and a senior project. Special programs include internships, summer session for credit, off-campus study, and study-abroad. The most frequently chosen baccalaureate fields are education, business/marketing, and health professions and related sciences. The faculty at FHSU has 256 full-time members, 79% with terminal degrees. The student-faculty ratio is 17:1.

Students of FHSU The student body totals 6,392, of whom 5,570 are undergraduates. 54.9% are women and 45.1% are men. Students come from 48 states and territories and 15 other countries. 91% are from Kansas. 9.9% are international students. 65% returned for their sophomore year.

Applying FHSU requires SAT I or ACT and a high school transcript. Application deadline: rolling admissions; 3/15 priority date for financial aid.

FORT LEWIS COLLEGE

Durango, CO

Small-town setting ■ Public ■ State-supported ■ Coed

Web site: www.fortlewis.edu
Contact: Ms. Gretchen Foster, Director of Admissions, 1000 Rim Drive, Durango, CO 81301
Telephone: 970-247-7184 **Fax:** 970-247-7179
E-mail: admission@fortlewis.edu

Getting in Last Year 3,350 applied; 80% were accepted; 1,079 enrolled (40%).

Financial Matters $2632 resident tuition and fees (2002–03); $10,330 nonresident tuition and fees (2002–03); $5446 room and board; 78% average percent of need met; $7251 average financial aid amount received per undergraduate (2001–02).

Academics Fort Lewis awards bachelor's degrees. Challenging opportunities include advanced placement credit, accelerated degree programs, student-designed majors, an honors program, double majors, independent study, and a senior project. Special programs include cooperative education, internships, summer session for credit, off-campus study, and study-abroad. The most frequently chosen baccalaureate fields are business/marketing, social sciences and history, and interdisciplinary studies. The faculty at Fort Lewis has 172 full-time members, 81% with terminal degrees. The student-faculty ratio is 19:1.

Students of Fort Lewis The student body is made up of 4,347 undergraduates. 47.3% are women and 52.7% are men. Students come from 50 states and territories and 16 other countries. 66% are from Colorado. 1.2% are international students. 55% returned for their sophomore year.

Applying Fort Lewis requires SAT I or ACT, a high school transcript, and a minimum high school GPA of 2.0. The school recommends an essay, an interview, and recommendations. Application deadline: 8/1.

FORT VALLEY STATE UNIVERSITY

Fort Valley, GA

Small-town setting ■ Public ■ State-supported ■ Coed

Web site: www.fvsu.edu
Contact: Mrs. Debra McGhee, Dean of Admissions and Enrollment Management, 1005 State University Drive, Fort Valley, GA 31030
Telephone: 478-825-6307 or toll-free 800-248-7343 **Fax:** 478-825-6169
E-mail: admissap@mail.fusu.edu

Getting in Last Year 2,329 applied; 49% were accepted.

Financial Matters $3150 resident tuition and fees (2002–03); $8610 nonresident tuition and fees (2002–03); $4078 room and board; 89% average percent of need met; $7200 average financial aid amount received per undergraduate.

Academics Fort Valley State University awards associate, bachelor's, master's, doctoral, and first-professional degrees. Challenging opportunities include advanced placement credit, freshman honors college, an honors program, double majors, and a senior project. Special programs include cooperative education, internships, summer session for credit, off-campus study, study-abroad, and Army ROTC. The faculty at Fort Valley State University has 152 full-time members. The student-faculty ratio is 19:1.

Students of Fort Valley State University The student body totals 2,823. Students come from 28 states and territories and 9 other countries. 74% returned for their sophomore year.

Applying Fort Valley State University requires SAT I or ACT and a high school transcript. Application deadline: 8/1; 4/15 priority date for financial aid. Early and deferred admission are possible.

FRAMINGHAM STATE COLLEGE

Framingham, MA

Suburban setting ■ Public ■ State-supported ■ Coed

Web site: www.framingham.edu
Contact: Ms. Elizabeth J. Canella, Associate Dean of Admissions, P.O. Box 9101, Dwight Hall, Room 209, Framingham, MA 01701-9101
Telephone: 508-626-4500
E-mail: admiss@frc.mass.edu

Getting in Last Year 3,994 applied; 59% were accepted; 735 enrolled (31%).

Financial Matters $3334 resident tuition and fees (2002–03); $9414 nonresident tuition and fees (2002–03); $4650 room and board; 89% average percent of need met; $6558 average financial aid amount received per undergraduate (2001–02 estimated).

Academics Framingham State College awards bachelor's and master's degrees and post-bachelor's certificates. Challenging opportunities include advanced placement credit, an honors program, double majors, independent study, and a senior project. Special programs include internships, summer session for credit, off-campus study, study-abroad, and Army ROTC. The most frequently chosen baccalaureate fields are social sciences and history, business/marketing, and psychology. The faculty at Framingham State College has 161 full-time members, 80% with terminal degrees. The student-faculty ratio is 15:1.

Students of Framingham State College The student body totals 5,959, of whom 4,052 are undergraduates. 65.5% are women and 34.5% are men. 92% are from Massachusetts. 2.2% are international students. 73% returned for their sophomore year.

Applying Framingham State College requires SAT I or ACT and a high school transcript, and in some cases an essay and an interview. The school recommends an essay, recommendations, and a minimum high school GPA of 3.0. Application deadline: 2/15; 3/1 priority date for financial aid. Early and deferred admission are possible.

THE FRANCISCAN UNIVERSITY

Clinton, IA

Small-town setting ■ Private ■ Independent Religious ■ Coed

Web site: www.clare.edu

Contact: Ms. Waunita M. Sullivan, Director of Enrollment, 400 North Bluff Boulevard, PO Box 2967, Clinton, IA 52733-2967

Telephone: 563-242-4023 ext. 3401 or toll-free 800-242-4153 **Fax:** 563-243-6102

E-mail: admissns@clare.edu

Getting in Last Year 224 applied; 76% were accepted; 48 enrolled (28%).

Financial Matters $14,060 tuition and fees (2002–03); $5000 room and board; 81% average percent of need met; $10,654 average financial aid amount received per undergraduate.

Academics The Franciscan University awards associate and bachelor's degrees (offers some graduate classes). Challenging opportunities include advanced placement credit, student-designed majors, freshman honors college, an honors program, double majors, independent study, and a senior project. Special programs include internships, summer session for credit, and study-abroad. The most frequently chosen baccalaureate fields are education, business/marketing, and liberal arts/general studies. The faculty at The Franciscan University has 27 full-time members, 48% with terminal degrees. The student-faculty ratio is 12:1.

Students of The Franciscan University The student body totals 492, of whom 458 are undergraduates. 56.6% are women and 43.4% are men. Students come from 11 states and territories and 10 other countries. 60% are from Iowa. 3.5% are international students. 63% returned for their sophomore year.

Applying The Franciscan University requires SAT I or ACT and a high school transcript, and in some cases an interview and recommendations. The school recommends an interview and a minimum high school GPA of 2.0. Application deadline: 8/15; 8/1 for financial aid, with a 3/1 priority date. Early and deferred admission are possible.

FRANCISCAN UNIVERSITY OF STEUBENVILLE

Steubenville, OH

Suburban setting ■ Private ■ Independent Religious ■ Coed

Web site: www.franciscan.edu

Contact: Mrs. Margaret Weber, Director of Admissions, 1235 University Boulevard, Steubenville, OH 43952-1763

Telephone: 740-283-6226 or toll-free 800-783-6220 **Fax:** 740-284-5456

E-mail: admissions@franciscan.edu

Getting in Last Year 765 applied; 89% were accepted; 359 enrolled (53%).

Financial Matters $14,400 tuition and fees (2002–03); $5200 room and board; 75% average percent of need met; $8570 average financial aid amount received per undergraduate.

Academics Franciscan University of Steubenville awards associate, bachelor's, and master's degrees. Challenging opportunities include advanced placement credit, accelerated degree programs, an honors program, double majors, independent study, and a senior project. Special programs include internships, summer session for credit, and study-abroad. The most frequently chosen baccalaureate fields are business/marketing, education, and health professions and related sciences. The faculty at Franciscan University of Steubenville has 102 full-time members, 71% with terminal degrees. The student-faculty ratio is 14:1.

Students of Franciscan University of Steubenville The student body totals 2,253, of whom 1,799 are undergraduates. 60.4% are women and 39.6% are men. Students come from 52 states and territories and 24 other countries. 21% are from Ohio. 2.5% are international students. 82% returned for their sophomore year.

Applying Franciscan University of Steubenville requires an essay, SAT I or ACT, a high school transcript, recommendations, and a minimum high school GPA of 2.4. The school recommends an interview. Application deadline: 5/1; 4/15 priority date for financial aid. Early and deferred admission are possible.

FRANCIS MARION UNIVERSITY

Florence, SC

Rural setting ■ Public ■ State-supported ■ Coed

Web site: www.fmarion.edu

Contact: Ms. Drucilla P. Russell, Director of Admissions, PO Box 100547, Florence, SC 29501-0547

Telephone: 843-661-1231 or toll-free 800-368-7551 **Fax:** 843-661-4635

E-mail: admission@fmarion.edu

Getting in Last Year 1,939 applied; 76% were accepted; 740 enrolled (51%).

Financial Matters $4340 resident tuition and fees (2002–03); $8530 nonresident tuition and fees (2002–03); $4082 room and board.

Academics FMU awards bachelor's and master's degrees. Challenging opportunities include advanced placement credit, accelerated degree programs, an honors program, double majors, independent study, and a senior project. Special programs include cooperative education, internships, summer session for credit, off-campus study, study-abroad, and Army ROTC. The most frequently chosen baccalaureate fields are business/marketing, biological/life sciences, and social sciences and history. The faculty at FMU has 159 full-time members, 83% with terminal degrees. The student-faculty ratio is 15:1.

Students of FMU The student body totals 3,496, of whom 2,966 are undergraduates. 61.5% are women and 38.5% are men. Students come from 30 states and territories and 27 other countries. 94% are from South Carolina. 1.6% are international students. 67% returned for their sophomore year.

Applying FMU requires SAT I or ACT and a high school transcript. The school recommends recommendations. Application deadline: rolling admissions; 3/1 priority date for financial aid. Early and deferred admission are possible.

FRANKLIN AND MARSHALL COLLEGE

Lancaster, PA

Suburban setting ■ Private ■ Independent ■ Coed

Web site: www.fandm.edu

Contact: Ms. Penny Johnston, Director of Admissions, PO Box 3003, Lancaster, PA 17604-3003

Telephone: 717-291-3953 **Fax:** 717-291-4389

E-mail: admission@fandm.edu

Getting in Last Year 3,425 applied; 62% were accepted; 534 enrolled (25%).

Financial Matters $27,280 tuition and fees (2002–03); $6580 room and board; 98% average percent of need met; $19,479 average financial aid amount received per undergraduate.

Academics F&M awards bachelor's degrees. Challenging opportunities include advanced placement credit, accelerated degree programs, student-designed majors, an honors program, double majors, independent study, and a senior project. Special programs include internships, summer session for credit, off-campus study, and study-abroad. The most frequently chosen baccalaureate fields are social sciences and history, business/marketing, and interdisciplinary studies. The faculty at F&M has 162 full-time members, 98% with terminal degrees. The student-faculty ratio is 11:1.

Students of F&M The student body is made up of 1,926 undergraduates. 48.1% are women and 51.9% are men. Students come from 40 states and territories and 60 other countries. 35% are from Pennsylvania. 7% are international students. 87% returned for their sophomore year.

Applying F&M requires an essay, SAT II: Writing Test, SAT I and SAT II or ACT, a high school transcript, and 2 recommendations. The school recommends an interview. Application deadline: 2/1; 2/1 for financial aid. Early and deferred admission are possible.

FRANKLIN COLLEGE

Franklin, IN

Small-town setting ■ Private ■ Independent Religious ■ Coed

Web site: www.franklincollege.edu

Contact: Mr. Alan Hill, Vice President for Enrollment and Student Affairs, 501 East Monroe Street, Franklin, IN 46131-2598

Telephone: 317-738-8062 or toll-free 800-852-0232 **Fax:** 317-738-8274

E-mail: admissions@franklincollege.edu

Getting in Last Year 713 applied; 85% were accepted; 293 enrolled (48%).

Financial Matters $15,635 tuition and fees (2002–03); $5280 room and board; 90% average percent of need met; $12,302 average financial aid amount received per undergraduate (2001–02).

Academics Franklin awards bachelor's degrees. Challenging opportunities include advanced placement credit, double majors, independent study, and a senior project. Special programs include internships, summer session for credit, off-campus study, study-abroad, and Army ROTC. The most frequently chosen baccalaureate fields are education, social sciences and history, and communications/communication technologies. The faculty at Franklin has 59 full-time members, 90% with terminal degrees. The student-faculty ratio is 14:1.

Franklin College (continued)

Students of Franklin The student body is made up of 1,048 undergraduates. 55.5% are women and 44.5% are men. Students come from 21 states and territories and 5 other countries. 94% are from Indiana. 0.6% are international students. 72% returned for their sophomore year.

Applying Franklin requires an essay, SAT I or ACT, a high school transcript, and 1 recommendation. The school recommends an interview. Application deadline: 5/1; 3/1 priority date for financial aid. Deferred admission is possible.

FRANKLIN COLLEGE SWITZERLAND

Sorengo Switzerland

Suburban setting ■ Private ■ Independent ■ Coed

Web site: www.fc.edu

Contact: Ms. Karen Ballard, Director of Admissions, 91-31 Queens Boulevard, Suite 411, Elmhurst, NY 11373

Telephone: 212-772-2090

E-mail: info@fc.edu

Getting in Last Year 364 applied; 75% were accepted; 94 enrolled (34%).

Financial Matters $21,480 tuition and fees (2002–03); $8000 room and board.

Academics Franklin College Switzerland awards associate and bachelor's degrees. Challenging opportunities include advanced placement credit, accelerated degree programs, an honors program, double majors, independent study, and a senior project. Special programs include internships, summer session for credit, and study-abroad. The most frequently chosen baccalaureate fields are business/marketing, interdisciplinary studies, and social sciences and history. The faculty at Franklin College Switzerland has 19 full-time members, 74% with terminal degrees. The student-faculty ratio is 10:1.

Students of Franklin College Switzerland The student body is made up of 309 undergraduates. 57.6% are women and 42.4% are men. Students come from 25 states and territories and 50 other countries. 48% returned for their sophomore year.

Applying Franklin College Switzerland requires an essay, SAT I or ACT, a high school transcript, 3 recommendations, and a minimum high school GPA of 2.0. The school recommends SAT II Subject Tests, SAT II: Writing Test, and an interview. Application deadline: 3/15; 2/15 priority date for financial aid. Early and deferred admission are possible.

FRANKLIN PIERCE COLLEGE

Rindge, NH

Rural setting ■ Private ■ Independent ■ Coed

Web site: www.fpc.edu

Contact: Ms. Lucy C. Shonk, Dean of Admissions, 20 College Road, Franklin Pierce College, Rindge, NH 03461-0060

Telephone: 603-899-4050 or toll-free 800-437-0048 **Fax:** 603-899-4394

E-mail: admissions@fpc.edu

Getting in Last Year 3,570 applied; 78% were accepted; 505 enrolled (18%).

Financial Matters $20,525 tuition and fees (2002–03); $6930 room and board; 73% average percent of need met; $16,296 average financial aid amount received per undergraduate.

Academics Franklin Pierce awards associate, bachelor's, and master's degrees (profile does not reflect significant enrollment at 6 continuing education sites; master's degree is only offered at these sites). Challenging opportunities include advanced placement credit, student-designed majors, an honors program, double majors, independent study, and a senior project. Special programs include internships, summer session for credit, off-campus study, study-abroad, and Air Force ROTC. The most frequently chosen baccalaureate fields are protective services/public administration, business/marketing, and visual/performing arts. The faculty at Franklin Pierce has 61 full-time members, 69% with terminal degrees. The student-faculty ratio is 18:1.

Students of Franklin Pierce The student body is made up of 1,574 undergraduates. 49.1% are women and 50.9% are men. Students come from 32 states and territories and 18 other countries. 16% are from New Hampshire. 2.6% are international students. 68% returned for their sophomore year.

Applying Franklin Pierce requires an essay, SAT I or ACT, a high school transcript, and 1 recommendation. The school recommends an interview and a minimum high school GPA of 2.0. Application deadline: rolling admissions. Early and deferred admission are possible.

FRANKLIN UNIVERSITY

Columbus, OH

Urban setting ■ Private ■ Independent ■ Coed

Web site: www.franklin.edu

Contact: Mr. Wayne Miller, Assistant Vice President for Students, 201 South Grant Avenue, Columbus, OH 43215

Telephone: 614-797-4700 ext. 7500 or toll-free 877-341-6300 **Fax:** 614-224-8027

E-mail: info@franklin.edu

Getting in Last Year 251 applied; 100% were accepted; 71 enrolled (28%).

Financial Matters $7704 tuition and fees (2002–03).

Academics Franklin University awards associate, bachelor's, and master's degrees. Challenging opportunities include advanced placement credit, accelerated degree programs, student-designed majors, independent study, and a senior project. Special programs include cooperative education, internships, summer session for credit, off-campus study, study-abroad, and Army and Air Force ROTC. The most frequently chosen baccalaureate fields are business/marketing, computer/information sciences, and health professions and related sciences. The faculty at Franklin University has 36 full-time members, 39% with terminal degrees. The student-faculty ratio is 17:1.

Students of Franklin University The student body totals 5,808, of whom 4,863 are undergraduates. 54.2% are women and 45.8% are men. Students come from 40 states and territories and 69 other countries. 84% are from Ohio. 8.7% are international students.

Applying Application deadline: rolling admissions; 6/15 priority date for financial aid. Deferred admission is possible.

FREED-HARDEMAN UNIVERSITY

Henderson, TN

Small-town setting ■ Private ■ Independent Religious ■ Coed

Web site: www.fhu.edu

Contact: Mr. Jim Brown, Director of Admissions, 158 East Main Street, Henderson, TN 38340

Telephone: 731-989-6651 or toll-free 800-630-3480 **Fax:** 731-989-6047

E-mail: admissions@fhu.edu

Getting in Last Year 836 applied; 100% were accepted; 414 enrolled (50%).

Financial Matters $10,158 tuition and fees (2002–03); $5170 room and board; 74% average percent of need met; $11,220 average financial aid amount received per undergraduate.

Academics FHU awards bachelor's and master's degrees. Challenging opportunities include advanced placement credit, accelerated degree programs, student-designed majors, an honors program, double majors, independent study, and a senior project. Special programs include cooperative education, internships, summer session for credit, off-campus study, and study-abroad. The most frequently chosen baccalaureate fields are business/marketing, education, and biological/life sciences. The faculty at FHU has 94 full-time members, 76% with terminal degrees. The student-faculty ratio is 16:1.

Students of FHU The student body totals 1,927, of whom 1,444 are undergraduates. 53% are women and 47% are men. Students come from 35 states and territories and 22 other countries. 49% are from Tennessee. 2.5% are international students. 69% returned for their sophomore year.

Applying FHU requires ACT, a high school transcript, and a minimum high school GPA of 2.25, and in some cases an interview. The school recommends an essay and recommendations. Application deadline: rolling admissions; 4/1 priority date for financial aid. Early and deferred admission are possible.

FREE WILL BAPTIST BIBLE COLLEGE

Nashville, TN

Suburban setting ■ Private ■ Independent Religious ■ Coed

Web site: www.fwbbc.edu

Contact: Mr. Frederick Burch, Registrar, 3606 West End Avenue, Nashville, TN 37205

Telephone: 615-383-1340 ext. 5233 or toll-free 800-763-9222 **Fax:** 615-269-6028

Academics Free Will Baptist Bible College awards associate and bachelor's degrees. Challenging opportunities include advanced placement credit, student-designed majors, double majors, and a senior project. Special programs include internships, summer session for credit, and Army and Air Force ROTC. The faculty at Free Will Baptist Bible College has 20 full-time members. The student-faculty ratio is 9:1.

Students of Free Will Baptist Bible College The student body is made up of 317 undergraduates. Students come from 28 states and territories and 8 other countries. 36% are from Tennessee. 1.9% are international students. 57% returned for their sophomore year.

Applying Free Will Baptist Bible College requires an essay, ACT, a high school transcript, 3 recommendations, and medical history. Application deadline: rolling admissions; 4/15 priority date for financial aid. Early and deferred admission are possible.

FRESNO PACIFIC UNIVERSITY

Fresno, CA

Suburban setting ■ Private ■ Independent Religious ■ Coed

Web site: www.fresno.edu

Contact: Ms. Suzana Dobril, Associates Director of Admissions, 1717 South Chestnut Avenue, Fresno, CA 93702-4709
Telephone: 559-453-2039 or toll-free 800-660-6089 (in-state)
Fax: 559-453-2007
E-mail: ugadmis@fresno.edu

Getting in Last Year 484 applied; 80% were accepted; 209 enrolled (54%).

Financial Matters $16,416 tuition and fees (2002–03); $4630 room and board.

Academics Fresno Pacific awards associate, bachelor's, and master's degrees. Challenging opportunities include advanced placement credit, accelerated degree programs, student-designed majors, double majors, independent study, and a senior project. Special programs include cooperative education, internships, summer session for credit, off-campus study, and study-abroad. The most frequently chosen baccalaureate fields are business/marketing, education, and English. The faculty at Fresno Pacific has 71 full-time members, 58% with terminal degrees. The student-faculty ratio is 16:1.

Students of Fresno Pacific The student body totals 1,891, of whom 963 are undergraduates. 67.4% are women and 32.6% are men. Students come from 15 states and territories and 12 other countries. 97% are from California. 4.8% are international students. 82% returned for their sophomore year.

Applying Fresno Pacific requires an essay, SAT I or ACT, a high school transcript, and 1 recommendation, and in some cases an interview. Application deadline: rolling admissions; 3/2 priority date for financial aid. Early and deferred admission are possible.

FROSTBURG STATE UNIVERSITY

Frostburg, MD

Small-town setting ■ Public ■ State-supported ■ Coed

Web site: www.frostburg.edu
Contact: Ms. Trish Gregory, Associate Director for Admissions, 101 Braddock Road, Frostburg, MD 21532-1099
Telephone: 301-687-4201 **Fax:** 301-687-7074
E-mail: fsuadmissions@frostburg.edu

Getting in Last Year 3,765 applied; 70% were accepted; 1,002 enrolled (38%).

Financial Matters $4800 resident tuition and fees (2002–03); $10,896 nonresident tuition and fees (2002–03); $5424 room and board; 78% average percent of need met; $6602 average financial aid amount received per undergraduate.

Academics FSU awards bachelor's and master's degrees and post-bachelor's and post-master's certificates. Challenging opportunities include advanced placement credit, freshman honors college, an honors program, double majors, independent study, and a senior project. Special programs include internships, summer session for credit, off-campus study, and study-abroad. The most frequently chosen baccalaureate fields are business/marketing, education, and social sciences and history. The faculty at FSU has 248 full-time members, 80% with terminal degrees. The student-faculty ratio is 17:1.

Students of FSU The student body totals 5,457, of whom 4,544 are undergraduates. 52.4% are women and 47.6% are men. Students come from 23 states and territories and 20 other countries. 88% are from Maryland. 0.5% are international students. 70% returned for their sophomore year.

Applying FSU requires SAT I or ACT, a high school transcript, and a minimum high school GPA of 2.0, and in some cases an essay. The school recommends an interview and recommendations. Application deadline: rolling admissions; 3/1 priority date for financial aid. Early admission is possible.

FURMAN UNIVERSITY

Greenville, SC

Suburban setting ■ Private ■ Independent ■ Coed

Web site: www.furman.edu
Contact: Mr. David R. O'Cain, Director of Admissions, 3300 Poinsett Highway, Greenville, SC 29613
Telephone: 864-294-2034 **Fax:** 864-294-3127
E-mail: admissions@furman.edu

Getting in Last Year 3,866 applied; 58% were accepted; 739 enrolled (33%).

Financial Matters $21,264 tuition and fees (2002–03); $5664 room and board; 90% average percent of need met; $18,349 average financial aid amount received per undergraduate.

Academics Furman awards bachelor's and master's degrees and post-bachelor's certificates. Challenging opportunities include advanced placement credit, accelerated degree programs, student-designed majors, double majors, independent study, and a senior project. Special programs include internships, summer session for credit, study-abroad, and Army ROTC. The most frequently chosen baccalaureate fields are social sciences and history, interdisciplinary studies, and business/marketing. The faculty at Furman has 211 full-time members, 98% with terminal degrees. The student-faculty ratio is 11:1.

Students of Furman The student body totals 3,208, of whom 2,772 are undergraduates. 55.6% are women and 44.4% are men. Students come from 48 states and territories and 20 other countries. 32% are from South Carolina. 1% are international students. 92% returned for their sophomore year.

Applying Furman requires an essay, SAT I or ACT, and a high school transcript, and in some cases SAT II Subject Tests and SAT II: Writing Test. The school recommends 2 recommendations and a minimum high school GPA of 3.0. Application deadline: 1/15; 1/15 for financial aid. Early admission is possible.

GALLAUDET UNIVERSITY

Washington, DC

Urban setting ■ Private ■ Independent ■ Coed

Web site: www.gallaudet.edu
Contact: Ms. Deborah E. DeStefano, Director of Admissions, 800 Florida Avenue, NE, Washington, DC 20002-3625
Telephone: 202-651-5750 or toll-free 800-995-0550 (out-of-state)
Fax: 202-651-5774
E-mail: admissions@gallua.gallaudet.edu

Getting in Last Year 603 applied; 71% were accepted.

Financial Matters $9040 tuition and fees (2002–03); $7850 room and board; 80% average percent of need met; $12,626 average financial aid amount received per undergraduate.

Academics Gallaudet University awards bachelor's, master's, and doctoral degrees (all undergraduate programs open primarily to hearing-impaired). Challenging opportunities include advanced placement credit, accelerated degree programs, student-designed majors, an honors program, double majors, and independent study. Special programs include cooperative education, internships, summer session for credit, off-campus study, and study-abroad. The most frequently chosen baccalaureate fields are education, psychology, and protective services/public administration. The faculty at Gallaudet University has 218 full-time members, 79% with terminal degrees. The student-faculty ratio is 7:1.

Students of Gallaudet University The student body totals 1,664, of whom 1,190 are undergraduates. 1% are from District of Columbia. 11% are international students. 65% returned for their sophomore year.

Applying Gallaudet University requires an essay, SAT I or ACT, a high school transcript, 2 recommendations, and audiogram, and in some cases an interview. Application deadline: 8/1. Early and deferred admission are possible.

GANNON UNIVERSITY

Erie, PA

Urban setting ■ Private ■ Independent Religious ■ Coed

Web site: www.gannon.edu
Contact: Mr. Christopher Tremblay, Director of Admissions, University Square, Erie, PA 16541
Telephone: 814-871-7240 or toll-free 800-GANNONU **Fax:** 814-871-5803
E-mail: admissions@gannon.edu

Getting in Last Year 2,188 applied; 84% were accepted; 559 enrolled (30%).

Financial Matters $15,780 tuition and fees (2002–03); $5990 room and board; 80% average percent of need met; $13,500 average financial aid amount received per undergraduate.

Academics Gannon awards associate, bachelor's, master's, and doctoral degrees and post-bachelor's certificates. Challenging opportunities include advanced placement credit, accelerated degree programs, an honors program, double majors, independent study, and a senior project. Special programs include cooperative education, internships, summer session for credit, off-campus study, study-abroad, and Army ROTC. The most frequently chosen baccalaureate fields are health professions and related sciences, business/marketing, and education. The faculty at Gannon has 171 full-time members. The student-faculty ratio is 13:1.

Students of Gannon The student body totals 3,357, of whom 2,374 are undergraduates. 58% are women and 42% are men. Students come from 29 states and territories and 20 other countries. 81% are from Pennsylvania. 2.3% are international students. 80% returned for their sophomore year.

Applying Gannon requires SAT I or ACT, a high school transcript, counselor's recommendation, and a minimum high school GPA of 2.0, and in some cases an interview, 3 recommendations, and a minimum high school GPA of 3.0. The school recommends an essay. Application deadline: rolling admissions; 3/15 priority date for financial aid. Early and deferred admission are possible.

GARDNER-WEBB UNIVERSITY

Boiling Springs, NC

Small-town setting ■ Private ■ Independent Religious ■ Coed

Web site: www.gardner-webb.edu
Contact: Mr. Nathan Alexander, Director of Admissions and Enrollment Management, PO Box 817, Boiling Springs, NC 28017
Telephone: 704-406-4491 or toll-free 800-253-6472 **Fax:** 810-253-6477
E-mail: admissions@gardner-webb.edu

Getting in Last Year 1,805 applied; 76% were accepted; 398 enrolled (29%).

Financial Matters $13,400 tuition and fees (2002–03); $4980 room and board; 85% average percent of need met; $9921 average financial aid amount received per undergraduate (2001–02).

Gardner-Webb University (continued)

Academics Gardner-Webb awards associate, bachelor's, master's, doctoral, and first-professional degrees. Challenging opportunities include advanced placement credit, accelerated degree programs, an honors program, and a senior project. Special programs include internships, summer session for credit, off-campus study, study-abroad, and Air Force ROTC. The faculty at Gardner-Webb has 123 full-time members, 78% with terminal degrees. The student-faculty ratio is 17:1.

Students of Gardner-Webb The student body totals 3,821, of whom 2,648 are undergraduates. 64.7% are women and 35.3% are men. Students come from 36 states and territories and 34 other countries. 74% are from North Carolina. 80% returned for their sophomore year.

Applying Gardner-Webb requires an essay, SAT I or ACT, a high school transcript, and a minimum high school GPA of 2.4, and in some cases recommendations. Application deadline: rolling admissions. Early and deferred admission are possible.

GENEVA COLLEGE

Beaver Falls, PA

Small-town setting ■ Private ■ Independent Religious ■ Coed

Web site: www.geneva.edu
Contact: Mr. David Layton, Associate Vice President for Enrollment Services, 3200 College Avenue, Beaver Falls, PA 15010-3599
Telephone: 724-847-6500 or toll-free 800-847-8255 **Fax:** 724-847-6776
E-mail: admissions@geneva.edu

Getting in Last Year 1,058 applied; 78% were accepted.

Financial Matters $14,760 tuition and fees (2002–03); $6130 room and board; 80% average percent of need met; $12,759 average financial aid amount received per undergraduate.

Academics Geneva awards associate, bachelor's, and master's degrees. Challenging opportunities include advanced placement credit, accelerated degree programs, student-designed majors, an honors program, double majors, independent study, and a senior project. Special programs include cooperative education, internships, summer session for credit, off-campus study, study-abroad, and Army ROTC. The most frequently chosen baccalaureate fields are business/marketing, education, and engineering/engineering technologies. The faculty at Geneva has 74 full-time members, 72% with terminal degrees. The student-faculty ratio is 17:1.

Students of Geneva The student body totals 1,919, of whom 1,763 are undergraduates. 56.1% are women and 43.9% are men. Students come from 37 states and territories and 25 other countries. 74% are from Pennsylvania. 1.2% are international students. 80% returned for their sophomore year.

Applying Geneva requires an essay, SAT I or ACT, a high school transcript, recommendations, and a minimum high school GPA of 2.0, and in some cases an interview. The school recommends an interview and a minimum high school GPA of 3.0. Application deadline: rolling admissions; 3/15 priority date for financial aid. Early and deferred admission are possible.

GEORGE FOX UNIVERSITY

Newberg, OR

Small-town setting ■ Private ■ Independent Religious ■ Coed

Web site: www.georgefox.edu
Contact: Mr. Dale Seipp, Director of Admissions, 414 North Meridian, Newberg, OR 97132
Telephone: 503-554-2240 or toll-free 800-765-4369 **Fax:** 503-554-3110
E-mail: admissions@georgefox.edu

Getting in Last Year 876 applied; 93% were accepted; 319 enrolled (39%).

Financial Matters $18,875 tuition and fees (2002–03); $5945 room and board; 83% average percent of need met; $15,332 average financial aid amount received per undergraduate (2001–02).

Academics George Fox awards bachelor's, master's, doctoral, and first-professional degrees. Challenging opportunities include advanced placement credit, accelerated degree programs, student-designed majors, an honors program, double majors, independent study, and a senior project. Special programs include cooperative education, internships, off-campus study, study-abroad, and Air Force ROTC. The most frequently chosen baccalaureate fields are business/marketing, education, and interdisciplinary studies. The faculty at George Fox has 71 full-time members, 61% with terminal degrees. The student-faculty ratio is 15:1.

Students of George Fox The student body totals 2,748, of whom 1,621 are undergraduates. 59.7% are women and 40.3% are men. Students come from 25 states and territories and 16 other countries. 83% returned for their sophomore year.

Applying George Fox requires an essay, SAT I or ACT, a high school transcript, and 2 recommendations, and in some cases an interview. The school recommends an interview. Application deadline: 6/1; 2/1 priority date for financial aid. Early and deferred admission are possible.

GEORGE MASON UNIVERSITY

Fairfax, VA

Suburban setting ■ Public ■ State-supported ■ Coed

Web site: www.gmu.edu
Contact: Mr. Eddie Tallent, Director of Admissions, 4400 University Drive, MSN 3A4, Fairfax, VA 22030-4444
Telephone: 703-993-2398 **Fax:** 703-993-2392
E-mail: admissions@gmu.edu

Getting in Last Year 8,845 applied; 66% were accepted; 2,225 enrolled (38%).

Financial Matters $5158 resident tuition and fees (2002–03); $15,240 nonresident tuition and fees (2002–03); $5560 room and board; 72% average percent of need met; $6851 average financial aid amount received per undergraduate.

Academics George Mason awards bachelor's, master's, doctoral, and first-professional degrees and post-bachelor's certificates. Challenging opportunities include advanced placement credit, accelerated degree programs, student-designed majors, an honors program, double majors, independent study, and a senior project. Special programs include cooperative education, internships, summer session for credit, off-campus study, study-abroad, and Army and Air Force ROTC. The most frequently chosen baccalaureate fields are business/marketing, social sciences and history, and interdisciplinary studies. The faculty at George Mason has 915 full-time members, 91% with terminal degrees. The student-faculty ratio is 16:1.

Students of George Mason The student body totals 26,796, of whom 16,687 are undergraduates. 55.8% are women and 44.2% are men. Students come from 52 states and territories and 129 other countries. 95% are from Virginia. 4.4% are international students. 79% returned for their sophomore year.

Applying George Mason requires an essay, SAT I or ACT, a high school transcript, an interview, and a minimum high school GPA of 2.0. The school recommends SAT II Subject Tests, recommendations, and a minimum high school GPA of 3.0. Application deadline: 1/15; 3/1 priority date for financial aid. Early and deferred admission are possible.

GEORGETOWN COLLEGE

Georgetown, KY

Suburban setting ■ Private ■ Independent Religious ■ Coed

Web site: www.georgetowncollege.edu
Contact: Mr. Brian Taylor, Director of Admissions, 400 East College Street, Georgetown, KY 40324
Telephone: 502-863-8009 or toll-free 800-788-9985 **Fax:** 502-868-7733
E-mail: admissions@georgetowncollege.edu

Getting in Last Year 810 applied; 93% were accepted; 327 enrolled (43%).

Financial Matters $14,640 tuition and fees (2002–03); $5050 room and board; 83% average percent of need met; $14,518 average financial aid amount received per undergraduate.

Academics Georgetown awards bachelor's and master's degrees. Challenging opportunities include advanced placement credit, student-designed majors, an honors program, double majors, independent study, and a senior project. Special programs include cooperative education, internships, summer session for credit, off-campus study, study-abroad, and Army and Air Force ROTC. The most frequently chosen baccalaureate fields are psychology, business/marketing, and visual/performing arts. The faculty at Georgetown has 92 full-time members, 91% with terminal degrees. The student-faculty ratio is 12:1.

Students of Georgetown The student body totals 1,673, of whom 1,290 are undergraduates. 56.5% are women and 43.5% are men. Students come from 25 states and territories and 17 other countries. 82% are from Kentucky. 2.1% are international students. 79% returned for their sophomore year.

Applying Georgetown requires an essay, SAT I or ACT, a high school transcript, and a minimum high school GPA of 2.5, and in some cases an interview and recommendations. The school recommends ACT. Application deadline: 7/1; 2/15 priority date for financial aid. Deferred admission is possible.

GEORGETOWN UNIVERSITY

Washington, DC

Urban setting ■ Private ■ Independent Religious ■ Coed

Web site: www.georgetown.edu
Contact: Mr. Charles A. Deacon, Dean of Undergraduate Admissions, 37th and O Street, NW, Washington, DC 20057
Telephone: 202-687-3600 **Fax:** 202-687-6660

Getting in Last Year 15,536 applied; 21% were accepted; 1,497 enrolled (46%).

Financial Matters $26,853 tuition and fees (2002–03); $9682 room and board; 100% average percent of need met; $21,650 average financial aid amount received per undergraduate.

Academics Georgetown awards bachelor's, master's, doctoral, and first-professional degrees. Challenging opportunities include advanced placement credit, student-designed majors, an honors program, double majors, independent study, and a senior project. Special programs include internships, summer session for credit, off-campus study, study-abroad, and Army, Navy and Air Force ROTC. The most frequently chosen baccalaureate fields are social sciences and history, business/marketing, and English. The faculty at Georgetown has 639 full-time members, 94% with terminal degrees. The student-faculty ratio is 11:1.

Students of Georgetown The student body totals 12,856, of whom 6,332 are undergraduates. 53.3% are women and 46.7% are men. Students come from 52 states and territories and 82 other countries. 2% are from District of Columbia. 4.5% are international students. 98% returned for their sophomore year.

Applying Georgetown requires an essay, SAT I or ACT, a high school transcript, an interview, and 2 recommendations. The school recommends SAT II Subject Tests and SAT II: Writing Test. Application deadline: 1/10; 2/1 priority date for financial aid. Early and deferred admission are possible.

THE GEORGE WASHINGTON UNIVERSITY

Washington, DC

Urban setting ■ Private ■ Independent ■ Coed

Web site: www.gwu.edu
Contact: Dr. Kathryn M. Napper, Director of Admission, 2121 I Street, NW, Suite 201, Washington, DC 20052
Telephone: 202-994-6040 or toll-free 800-447-3765 **Fax:** 202-944-0325
E-mail: gwadm@gwu.edu

Getting in Last Year 16,910 applied; 40% were accepted; 2,292 enrolled (34%).

Financial Matters $27,820 tuition and fees (2002–03); $9110 room and board; 94% average percent of need met; $25,695 average financial aid amount received per undergraduate (2001–02).

Academics GW awards associate, bachelor's, master's, doctoral, and first-professional degrees and post-bachelor's and post-master's certificates. Challenging opportunities include advanced placement credit, accelerated degree programs, student-designed majors, an honors program, double majors, independent study, and a senior project. Special programs include cooperative education, internships, summer session for credit, off-campus study, study-abroad, and Army, Navy and Air Force ROTC. The most frequently chosen baccalaureate fields are social sciences and history, business/marketing, and psychology. The faculty at GW has 787 full-time members, 90% with terminal degrees. The student-faculty ratio is 14:1.

Students of GW The student body totals 23,019, of whom 10,328 are undergraduates. 56.5% are women and 43.5% are men. Students come from 55 states and territories and 101 other countries. 3% are from District of Columbia. 4.7% are international students. 92% returned for their sophomore year.

Applying GW requires an essay, SAT I or ACT, a high school transcript, and 2 recommendations, and in some cases SAT II Subject Tests. The school recommends SAT II: Writing Test and an interview. Application deadline: 1/15; 1/31 priority date for financial aid. Early and deferred admission are possible.

GEORGIA COLLEGE & STATE UNIVERSITY

Milledgeville, GA

Small-town setting ■ Public ■ State-supported ■ Coed

Web site: www.gcsu.edu
Contact: Ms. Maryllis Wolfgang, Director of Admissions, CPO Box 023, Milledgeville, GA 31061
Telephone: 478-445-2774 or toll-free 800-342-0471 (in-state) **Fax:** 478-445-1914
E-mail: info@gcsu.edu

Getting in Last Year 2,700 applied; 68% were accepted; 912 enrolled (50%).

Financial Matters $3138 resident tuition and fees (2002–03); $10,968 nonresident tuition and fees (2002–03); $5324 room and board.

Academics Georgia College & State University awards bachelor's and master's degrees and post-master's certificates. Challenging opportunities include advanced placement credit, accelerated degree programs, student-designed majors, freshman honors college, an honors program, double majors, independent study, and a senior project. Special programs include internships, summer session for credit, study-abroad, and Army ROTC. The most frequently chosen baccalaureate fields are business/marketing, education, and health professions and related sciences. The faculty at Georgia College & State University has 274 full-time members, 76% with terminal degrees. The student-faculty ratio is 14:1.

Students of Georgia College & State University The student body totals 5,513, of whom 4,444 are undergraduates. 60.6% are women and 39.4% are men. Students come from 25 states and territories and 47 other countries. 98% are from Georgia. 2.3% are international students. 72% returned for their sophomore year.

Applying Georgia College & State University requires an essay, SAT I or ACT, a high school transcript, proof of immunization, essay, and a minimum high school GPA of 2.22. The school recommends an interview. Application deadline: 7/15. Early and deferred admission are possible.

GEORGIA INSTITUTE OF TECHNOLOGY

Atlanta, GA

Urban setting ■ Public ■ State-supported ■ Coed

Web site: www.gatech.edu
Contact: Ms. Deborah Smith, Director of Admissions, 225 North Avenue, NW, Atlanta, GA 30332-0320
Telephone: 404-894-4154 **Fax:** 404-894-9511
E-mail: admissions@success.gatech.edu

Getting in Last Year 8,953 applied; 59% were accepted; 2,281 enrolled (43%).

Financial Matters $3616 resident tuition and fees (2002–03); $13,986 nonresident tuition and fees (2002–03); $5922 room and board; 67% average percent of need met; $7141 average financial aid amount received per undergraduate.

Academics Georgia Tech awards bachelor's, master's, and doctoral degrees. Challenging opportunities include advanced placement credit, accelerated degree programs, student-designed majors, an honors program, double majors, independent study, and a senior project. Special programs include cooperative education, internships, summer session for credit, off-campus study, study-abroad, and Army, Navy and Air Force ROTC. The most frequently chosen baccalaureate fields are engineering/engineering technologies, business/marketing, and computer/information sciences. The faculty at Georgia Tech has 775 full-time members, 95% with terminal degrees. The student-faculty ratio is 14:1.

Students of Georgia Tech The student body totals 16,481, of whom 11,456 are undergraduates. 28% are women and 72% are men. Students come from 52 states and territories and 127 other countries. 65% are from Georgia. 4.7% are international students. 90% returned for their sophomore year.

Applying Georgia Tech requires an essay, SAT I or ACT, and a high school transcript, and in some cases SAT II Subject Tests. The school recommends SAT I. Application deadline: 1/15; 3/1 priority date for financial aid. Early admission is possible.

GEORGIAN COURT COLLEGE

Lakewood, NJ

Suburban setting ■ Private ■ Independent Religious ■ Women Only

Web site: www.georgian.edu
Contact: Office of Admissions, 900 Lakewood Avenue, Lakewood, NJ 08701-2697
Telephone: 732-364-2200 or toll-free 800-458-8422 **Fax:** 732-364-4442
E-mail: admissions@georgian.edu

Getting in Last Year 477 applied; 79% were accepted; 178 enrolled (47%).

Financial Matters $14,855 tuition and fees (2002–03); $5600 room and board; 66% average percent of need met; $10,373 average financial aid amount received per undergraduate (2001–02).

Academics The Court awards bachelor's and master's degrees and post-bachelor's and post-master's certificates. Challenging opportunities include advanced placement credit, accelerated degree programs, an honors program, double majors, independent study, and a senior project. Special programs include internships, summer session for credit, off-campus study, and study-abroad. The most frequently chosen baccalaureate fields are psychology, business/marketing, and education. The faculty at The Court has 87 full-time members, 78% with terminal degrees. The student-faculty ratio is 15:1.

Students of The Court The student body totals 2,871, of whom 1,885 are undergraduates. Students come from 9 states and territories and 13 other countries. 99% are from New Jersey. 1.1% are international students. 75% returned for their sophomore year.

Applying The Court requires SAT I or ACT, a high school transcript, recommendations, and a minimum high school GPA of 2.0. The school recommends an essay and an interview. Application deadline: 8/1.

GEORGIA SOUTHERN UNIVERSITY

Statesboro, GA

Small-town setting ■ Public ■ State-supported ■ Coed

Web site: www.gasou.edu
Contact: Dr. Teresa Thompson, Director of Admissions, GSU PO Box 8024, Building #805, Forest Drive, Statesboro, GA 30460
Telephone: 912-681-5391 **Fax:** 912-486-7240
E-mail: admissions@gasou.edu

Getting in Last Year 8,181 applied; 55% were accepted; 2,609 enrolled (58%).

Financial Matters $2694 resident tuition and fees (2002–03); $8724 nonresident tuition and fees (2002–03); $4620 room and board; 73% average percent of need met; $6056 average financial aid amount received per undergraduate (2001–02).

Academics Georgia Southern awards bachelor's, master's, and doctoral degrees and post-master's certificates. Challenging opportunities include advanced placement credit, accelerated degree programs, an honors program, double majors, independent study, and a senior project. Special programs include cooperative education, internships, summer session for credit, off-campus study, study-abroad, and Army ROTC. The most frequently chosen baccalaureate fields

Georgia Southern University (continued)

are business/marketing, education, and parks and recreation. The faculty at Georgia Southern has 612 full-time members, 77% with terminal degrees. The student-faculty ratio is 19:1.

Students of Georgia Southern The student body totals 15,075, of whom 13,354 are undergraduates. 50.8% are women and 49.2% are men. Students come from 51 states and territories and 77 other countries. 96% are from Georgia. 1.3% are international students. 75% returned for their sophomore year.

Applying Georgia Southern requires SAT I or ACT, a high school transcript, proof of immunization, and a minimum high school GPA of 2.0, and in some cases SAT II: Writing Test. Application deadline: 8/1; 3/31 priority date for financial aid. Early and deferred admission are possible.

GEORGIA SOUTHWESTERN STATE UNIVERSITY

Americus, GA

Small-town setting ■ Public ■ State-supported ■ Coed

Web site: www.gsw.edu

Contact: Mr. Gary Fallis, Director of Admissions, 800 Wheatley Street, Americus, GA 31709-4693

Telephone: 229-928-1273 or toll-free 800-338-0082 **Fax:** 229-931-2983

E-mail: gswapps@canes.gsw.edu

Getting in Last Year 1,026 applied; 79% were accepted; 354 enrolled (44%).

Financial Matters $2578 resident tuition and fees (2002–03); $8608 nonresident tuition and fees (2002–03); $3926 room and board; 63% average percent of need met; $5954 average financial aid amount received per undergraduate (2001–02).

Academics GSW awards associate, bachelor's, and master's degrees and post-master's certificates. Challenging opportunities include advanced placement credit, freshman honors college, an honors program, double majors, and a senior project. Special programs include cooperative education, internships, summer session for credit, off-campus study, and study-abroad. The most frequently chosen baccalaureate fields are business/marketing, education, and psychology. The faculty at GSW has 110 full-time members, 75% with terminal degrees. The student-faculty ratio is 14:1.

Students of GSW The student body totals 2,508, of whom 2,101 are undergraduates. 64.4% are women and 35.6% are men. Students come from 20 states and territories and 32 other countries. 98% are from Georgia. 2% are international students. 71% returned for their sophomore year.

Applying GSW requires SAT I or ACT, a high school transcript, proof of immunization, and a minimum high school GPA of 2.0. The school recommends an interview. Application deadline: rolling admissions; 4/1 priority date for financial aid. Early admission is possible.

GEORGIA STATE UNIVERSITY

Atlanta, GA

Urban setting ■ Public ■ State-supported ■ Coed

Web site: www.gsu.edu

Contact: Mr. Rob Sheinkopf, Dean of Admissions and Acting Dean for Enrollment Services, PO Box 4009, Atlanta, GA 30302-4009

Telephone: 404-651-2365 **Fax:** 404-651-4811

Getting in Last Year 9,654 applied; 57% were accepted; 3,001 enrolled (54%).

Financial Matters $3472 resident tuition and fees (2002–03); $11,842 nonresident tuition and fees (2002–03); $4680 room only; 20% average percent of need met; $6062 average financial aid amount received per undergraduate (2001–02).

Academics Georgia State awards bachelor's, master's, doctoral, and first-professional degrees and post-master's certificates. Challenging opportunities include accelerated degree programs, student-designed majors, an honors program, double majors, and independent study. Special programs include cooperative education, internships, summer session for credit, off-campus study, and study-abroad. The most frequently chosen baccalaureate fields are business/marketing, social sciences and history, and computer/information sciences. The faculty at Georgia State has 998 full-time members, 85% with terminal degrees. The student-faculty ratio is 24:1.

Students of Georgia State The student body totals 27,502, of whom 19,681 are undergraduates. 61.1% are women and 38.9% are men. Students come from 49 states and territories and 96 other countries. 96% are from Georgia. 5.6% are international students. 80% returned for their sophomore year.

Applying Georgia State requires SAT I or ACT and a high school transcript, and in some cases SAT II Subject Tests and an interview. The school recommends an essay and a minimum high school GPA of 2.9. Application deadline: 4/1; 4/1 priority date for financial aid. Deferred admission is possible.

GETTYSBURG COLLEGE

Gettysburg, PA

Small-town setting ■ Private ■ Independent Religious ■ Coed

Web site: www.gettysburg.edu

Contact: Ms. Gail Sweezey, Director of Admissions, 300 North Washington Street, Gettysburg, PA 17325

Telephone: 717-337-6100 or toll-free 800-431-0803 **Fax:** 717-337-6145

E-mail: admiss@gettysburg.edu

Getting in Last Year 4,573 applied; 50% were accepted; 687 enrolled (30%).

Financial Matters $27,070 tuition and fees (2002–03); $6640 room and board; 100% average percent of need met; $22,415 average financial aid amount received per undergraduate.

Academics Gettysburg College awards bachelor's degrees. Challenging opportunities include advanced placement credit, student-designed majors, double majors, independent study, and a senior project. Special programs include internships, off-campus study, study-abroad, and Army ROTC. The most frequently chosen baccalaureate fields are social sciences and history, business/marketing, and English. The faculty at Gettysburg College has 180 full-time members, 92% with terminal degrees. The student-faculty ratio is 11:1.

Students of Gettysburg College The student body is made up of 2,377 undergraduates. 49.9% are women and 50.1% are men. Students come from 39 states and territories and 32 other countries. 28% are from Pennsylvania. 2% are international students. 88% returned for their sophomore year.

Applying Gettysburg College requires an essay, SAT I or ACT, a high school transcript, and 2 recommendations. The school recommends an interview and a minimum high school GPA of 3.0. Application deadline: 2/15; 3/15 for financial aid, with a 2/15 priority date. Early and deferred admission are possible.

GLENVILLE STATE COLLEGE

Glenville, WV

Rural setting ■ Public ■ State-supported ■ Coed

Web site: www.glenville.edu

Contact: Ms. Brenda McCartney, Associate Registrar, 200 High Street, Glenville, WV 26351-1200

Telephone: 304-462-4117 ext. 347 or toll-free 800-924-2010 (in-state) **Fax:** 304-462-8619

E-mail: visitor@glenville.edu

Getting in Last Year 1,241 applied; 100% were accepted; 501 enrolled (40%).

Financial Matters $2412 resident tuition and fees (2002–03); $6766 nonresident tuition and fees (2002–03); $4440 room and board; 80% average percent of need met; $6757 average financial aid amount received per undergraduate.

Academics Glenville awards associate and bachelor's degrees. Challenging opportunities include advanced placement credit, accelerated degree programs, student-designed majors, an honors program, and double majors. Special programs include cooperative education, internships, summer session for credit, and Army ROTC. The most frequently chosen baccalaureate fields are social sciences and history, business/marketing, and education. The faculty at Glenville has 65 full-time members, 32% with terminal degrees. The student-faculty ratio is 19:1.

Students of Glenville The student body is made up of 2,184 undergraduates. 58.4% are women and 41.6% are men. Students come from 14 states and territories. 94% are from West Virginia.

Applying Glenville requires SAT I or ACT, a high school transcript, completion of college-preparatory program, and a minimum high school GPA of 2.0. Application deadline: 8/1; 3/1 priority date for financial aid. Deferred admission is possible.

GLOBAL UNIVERSITY OF THE ASSEMBLIES OF GOD

Springfield, MO

Private ■ Independent Religious ■ Coed

Web site: www.globaluniversity.edu

Contact: Ms. Jessica Dorn, Director of US Enrollments, 1211 South Glenstone Avenue, Springfield, MO 65804

Telephone: 800-443-1083 or toll-free 800-443-1083

Financial Matters $2040 tuition and fees (2002–03).

Academics Global University of the Assemblies of God awards associate, bachelor's, and master's degrees (offers only external degree programs). Challenging opportunities include advanced placement credit, accelerated degree programs, an honors program, independent study, and a senior project. Special programs include cooperative education and internships. The faculty at Global University of the Assemblies of God has 52 full-time members, 23% with terminal degrees.

Students of Global University of the Assemblies of God The student body totals 6,547, of whom 6,252 are undergraduates. 34.9% are women and 65.1% are men. Students come from 50 states and territories and 123 other countries. 3% are from Missouri.

Applying Global University of the Assemblies of God requires a high school transcript, and in some cases 1 recommendation. The school recommends an essay. Application deadline: rolling admissions.

GLOBE INSTITUTE OF TECHNOLOGY
New York, NY
Private ■ Proprietary ■ Coed

Web site: www.globe.edu
Contact: Oleg Rabinovich, Director, 291 Broadway, New York, NY 10007
Telephone: 212-349-4330 ext. 104 or toll-free 877-394-5623 **Fax:** 212-227-5920
E-mail: admissions@globe.edu

Getting in Last Year 184 applied; 64% were accepted; 118 enrolled (100%).

Financial Matters $9070 tuition and fees (2002–03).

Academics Globe Institute of Technology awards associate and bachelor's degrees. Challenging opportunities include advanced placement credit, accelerated degree programs, and a senior project. Internships is a special program. The most frequently chosen baccalaureate field is computer/information sciences. The faculty at Globe Institute of Technology has 14 full-time members, 36% with terminal degrees. The student-faculty ratio is 18:1.

Students of Globe Institute of Technology The student body is made up of 558 undergraduates. 41.4% are women and 58.6% are men. Students come from 7 states and territories and 51 other countries. 89% are from New York. 16.3% are international students.

Applying Globe Institute of Technology requires an interview. The school recommends SAT I and ACT.

GODDARD COLLEGE
Plainfield, VT
Rural setting ■ Private ■ Independent ■ Coed

Web site: www.goddard.edu
Contact: Mr. Josh Castle, Admissions Counselor, 123 Pitkin Road, Plainfield, VT 05667-9432
Telephone: 802-454-8311 ext. 322 or toll-free 800-468-4888 ext. 307 **Fax:** 802-454-1029
E-mail: admissions@earth.goddard.edu

Getting in Last Year 1 applied; 1 enrolled.

Financial Matters $8302 tuition and fees (2002–03); $684 room and board; 42% average percent of need met; $5973 average financial aid amount received per undergraduate.

Academics Goddard awards bachelor's and master's degrees. Challenging opportunities include advanced placement credit, student-designed majors, double majors, independent study, and a senior project. Special programs include cooperative education, internships, and off-campus study. The most frequently chosen baccalaureate fields are interdisciplinary studies, education, and health professions and related sciences. The faculty at Goddard has 14 full-time members. The student-faculty ratio is 11:1.

Students of Goddard The student body totals 502, of whom 197 are undergraduates. 61.9% are women and 38.1% are men. Students come from 34 states and territories. 13% are from Vermont. 1% are international students. 57% returned for their sophomore year.

Applying Goddard requires an essay, a high school transcript, an interview, and 2 recommendations. The school recommends SAT I and SAT II or ACT. Application deadline: rolling admissions; 3/1 priority date for financial aid. Deferred admission is possible.

GOD'S BIBLE SCHOOL AND COLLEGE
Cincinnati, OH
Urban setting ■ Private ■ Independent Religious ■ Coed

Contact: Ms. Laura Ellison, Director of Admissions, 1810 Young Street, Cincinnati, OH 45210-1599
Telephone: 513-721-7944 ext. 204 or toll-free 800-486-4637 **Fax:** 513-721-3971
E-mail: admissions@gbs.edu

Getting in Last Year 77 applied; 74% were accepted.

Financial Matters $4380 tuition and fees (2002–03); $2900 room and board.

Academics God's Bible College awards associate and bachelor's degrees. Challenging opportunities include advanced placement credit and independent study. Special programs include internships and summer session for credit. The student-faculty ratio is 15:1.

Students of God's Bible College The student body is made up of 247 undergraduates. Students come from 24 states and territories and 12 other countries. 62% returned for their sophomore year.

Applying God's Bible College requires SAT I or ACT, a high school transcript, an interview, and 3 recommendations. Application deadline: rolling admissions.

GOLDEN GATE UNIVERSITY
San Francisco, CA
Urban setting ■ Private ■ Independent ■ Coed

Web site: www.ggu.edu
Contact: Ms. Cherron Hoppes, Director of Admission, 536 Mission Street, San Francisco, CA 94105-2968
Telephone: 415-442-7800 or toll-free 800-448-4968 **Fax:** 415-442-7807
E-mail: info@ggu.edu

Getting in Last Year 13 applied; 100% were accepted; 13 enrolled (100%).

Financial Matters $9600 tuition and fees (2002–03); 25% average percent of need met; $2931 average financial aid amount received per undergraduate (2001–02).

Academics Golden Gate awards associate, bachelor's, master's, doctoral, and first-professional degrees. Challenging opportunities include advanced placement credit and accelerated degree programs. Special programs include cooperative education, internships, summer session for credit, and off-campus study. The most frequently chosen baccalaureate fields are business/marketing, computer/information sciences, and psychology. The faculty at Golden Gate has 33 full-time members, 97% with terminal degrees. The student-faculty ratio is 17:1.

Students of Golden Gate The student body totals 4,415, of whom 871 are undergraduates. 56% are women and 44% are men. 95% are from California. 9.6% are international students. 80% returned for their sophomore year.

Applying Golden Gate requires a high school transcript and a minimum high school GPA of 2.0, and in some cases an interview and a minimum high school GPA of 3.2. The school recommends an essay and a minimum high school GPA of 3.0. Application deadline: 6/1. Deferred admission is possible.

GOLDEY-BEACOM COLLEGE
Wilmington, DE
Suburban setting ■ Private ■ Independent ■ Coed

Web site: www.gbc.edu
Contact: Mr. Kevin M. McIntyre, Dean of Admissions, 4701 Limestone Road, Wilmington, DE 19808-1999
Telephone: 302-998-8814 ext. 266 or toll-free 800-833-4877 **Fax:** 302-996-5408
E-mail: mcintyrk@goldey.gbc.edu

Getting in Last Year 684 applied; 84% were accepted.

Financial Matters $10,132 tuition and fees (2002–03); $3937 room only.

Academics G-BC awards associate, bachelor's, and master's degrees. Challenging opportunities include advanced placement credit, accelerated degree programs, and an honors program. Special programs include cooperative education, internships, summer session for credit, and study-abroad. The faculty at G-BC has 25 full-time members, 48% with terminal degrees. The student-faculty ratio is 28:1.

Students of G-BC The student body totals 1,400. Students come from 15 states and territories and 50 other countries. 50% are from Delaware. 70% returned for their sophomore year.

Applying G-BC requires SAT I, a high school transcript, and a minimum high school GPA of 2.0, and in some cases DTLS, DTMS, an interview, and 1 recommendation. Application deadline: rolling admissions; 4/1 priority date for financial aid. Early and deferred admission are possible.

GONZAGA UNIVERSITY
Spokane, WA
Urban setting ■ Private ■ Independent Religious ■ Coed

Web site: www.gonzaga.edu
Contact: Ms. Julie McCulloh, Acting Dean of Admission, 502 East Boone Avenue, Spokane, WA 99258-0102
Telephone: 509-323-6591 or toll-free 800-322-2584 ext. 6572 **Fax:** 509-323-5780
E-mail: admissions@gonzaga.edu

Getting in Last Year 3,339 applied; 76% were accepted; 907 enrolled (36%).

Financial Matters $19,550 tuition and fees (2002–03); $5740 room and board; 83% average percent of need met; $12,525 average financial aid amount received per undergraduate (2001–02).

Academics Gonzaga awards bachelor's, master's, doctoral, and first-professional degrees and post-master's certificates. Challenging opportunities include advanced placement credit, student-designed majors, an honors program, double majors, independent study, and a senior project. Special programs include internships, summer session for credit, off-campus study, study-abroad, and Army ROTC. The most frequently chosen baccalaureate fields are business/marketing, social sciences and history, and communications/communication technologies. The faculty at Gonzaga has 291 full-time members, 83% with terminal degrees. The student-faculty ratio is 13:1.

Students of Gonzaga The student body totals 5,529, of whom 3,814 are undergraduates. 54.5% are women and 45.5% are men. Students come from 41 states and territories and 36 other countries. 48% are from Washington. 1.5% are international students. 90% returned for their sophomore year.

Applying Gonzaga requires an essay, SAT I or ACT, a high school transcript, 1 recommendation, and a minimum high school GPA of 3.0. The school recommends an interview. Application deadline: 2/1; 2/1 priority date for financial aid. Early and deferred admission are possible.

GORDON COLLEGE

Wenham, MA

Small-town setting ■ Private ■ Independent Religious ■ Coed

Web site: www.gordon.edu
Contact: Mr. Silvio E. Vazquez, Dean of Admissions, 255 Grapevine Road, Wenham, MA 01984-1899
Telephone: 978-867-4218 or toll-free 800-343-1379 **Fax:** 978-867-4657
E-mail: admissions@hope.gordon.edu

Getting in Last Year 1,100 applied; 74% were accepted; 399 enrolled (49%).

Financial Matters $19,100 tuition and fees (2002–03); $5650 room and board; 77% average percent of need met; $13,922 average financial aid amount received per undergraduate.

Academics Gordon awards bachelor's and master's degrees. Challenging opportunities include advanced placement credit, student-designed majors, an honors program, double majors, independent study, and a senior project. Special programs include cooperative education, internships, off-campus study, study-abroad, and Army and Air Force ROTC. The most frequently chosen baccalaureate fields are education, social sciences and history, and English. The faculty at Gordon has 92 full-time members, 86% with terminal degrees. The student-faculty ratio is 15:1.

Students of Gordon The student body totals 1,701, of whom 1,631 are undergraduates. 66.3% are women and 33.7% are men. Students come from 46 states and territories and 25 other countries. 26% are from Massachusetts. 1.9% are international students. 88% returned for their sophomore year.

Applying Gordon requires an essay, SAT I or ACT, a high school transcript, an interview, 2 recommendations, and pastoral recommendation, statement of Christian faith. The school recommends a minimum high school GPA of 3.0. Application deadline: rolling admissions; 3/1 priority date for financial aid. Early and deferred admission are possible.

GOSHEN COLLEGE

Goshen, IN

Small-town setting ■ Private ■ Independent Religious ■ Coed

Web site: www.goshen.edu
Contact: Ms. Karen Lowe Raftus, Director of Admission, 1700 South Main Street, Goshen, IN 46526-4794
Telephone: 574-535-7535 or toll-free 800-348-7422 **Fax:** 574-535-7609
E-mail: admissions@goshen.edu

Getting in Last Year 759 applied; 45% were accepted; 136 enrolled (40%).

Financial Matters $15,000 tuition and fees (2002–03); $5450 room and board; 88% average percent of need met; $13,629 average financial aid amount received per undergraduate.

Academics Goshen awards bachelor's degrees. Challenging opportunities include advanced placement credit, accelerated degree programs, student-designed majors, freshman honors college, an honors program, double majors, independent study, and a senior project. Special programs include cooperative education, internships, summer session for credit, off-campus study, and study-abroad. The most frequently chosen baccalaureate fields are business/marketing, education, and health professions and related sciences. The faculty at Goshen has 73 full-time members, 59% with terminal degrees. The student-faculty ratio is 9:1.

Students of Goshen The student body is made up of 871 undergraduates. 62.6% are women and 37.4% are men. Students come from 36 states and territories and 27 other countries. 45% are from Indiana. 9.5% are international students. 77% returned for their sophomore year.

Applying Goshen requires SAT I or ACT, a high school transcript, an interview, 2 recommendations, rank in upper 50% of high school class, minimum SAT score of 920, ACT score of 19, and a minimum high school GPA of 2.0. The school recommends an essay. Application deadline: 8/15; 2/15 priority date for financial aid. Early and deferred admission are possible.

GOUCHER COLLEGE

Baltimore, MD

Suburban setting ■ Private ■ Independent ■ Coed

Web site: www.goucher.edu
Contact: Mr. Carlton E. Surbeck III, Director of Admissions, 1021 Dulaney Valley Road, Baltimore, MD 21204-2794
Telephone: 410-337-6100 or toll-free 800-468-2437 **Fax:** 410-337-6354
E-mail: admission@goucher.edu

Getting in Last Year 2,596 applied; 68% were accepted; 365 enrolled (21%).

Financial Matters $23,250 tuition and fees (2002–03); $7900 room and board; 81% average percent of need met; $16,661 average financial aid amount received per undergraduate (2001–02).

Academics Goucher awards bachelor's and master's degrees and post-bachelor's certificates. Challenging opportunities include advanced placement credit, student-designed majors, an honors program, double majors, independent study, and a senior project. Special programs include internships, off-campus study, and study-abroad. The most frequently chosen baccalaureate fields are psychology, visual/performing arts, and communications/communication technologies. The faculty at Goucher has 96 full-time members, 88% with terminal degrees. The student-faculty ratio is 10:1.

Students of Goucher The student body totals 2,102, of whom 1,270 are undergraduates. 70.1% are women and 29.9% are men. Students come from 43 states and territories and 21 other countries. 38% are from Maryland. 2% are international students. 83% returned for their sophomore year.

Applying Goucher requires an essay, SAT I or ACT, a high school transcript, 3 recommendations, and a minimum high school GPA of 2.0. The school recommends SAT II Subject Tests, SAT II: Writing Test, an interview, and a minimum high school GPA of 3.0. Application deadline: 2/1; 2/15 priority date for financial aid. Early and deferred admission are possible.

GOVERNORS STATE UNIVERSITY

University Park, IL

Suburban setting ■ Public ■ State-supported ■ Coed

Web site: www.govst.edu
Contact: Mr. Larry Polselli, Executive Director of Enrollment Services, One University Parkway, University Park, IL 60466
Telephone: 708-534-3148 **Fax:** 708-534-1640

Financial Matters $2920 resident tuition and fees (2002–03); $8120 nonresident tuition and fees (2002–03).

Academics Governors State University awards bachelor's and master's degrees. Challenging opportunities include advanced placement credit, student-designed majors, an honors program, independent study, and a senior project. Special programs include internships, summer session for credit, off-campus study, study-abroad, and Army and Air Force ROTC. The faculty at Governors State University has 175 full-time members, 77% with terminal degrees. The student-faculty ratio is 16:1.

Students of Governors State University The student body totals 5,855, of whom 2,980 are undergraduates. 69% are women and 31% are men. Students come from 9 states and territories and 21 other countries. 97% are from Illinois. 1.1% are international students.

Applying Application deadline: 5/1 priority date for financial aid. Deferred admission is possible.

GRACE BIBLE COLLEGE

Grand Rapids, MI

Suburban setting ■ Private ■ Independent Religious ■ Coed

Web site: www.gbcol.edu
Contact: Mr. Kevin Gilliam, Director of Enrollment, 1101 Aldon Street, SW, PO Box 910, Grand Rapids, MI 49509
Telephone: 616-538-2330 or toll-free 800-968-1887 **Fax:** 616-538-0599
E-mail: gbc@gbcol.edu

Getting in Last Year 212 applied; 30% were accepted; 31 enrolled (48%).

Financial Matters $8690 tuition and fees (2002–03); $5050 room and board; 68% average percent of need met; $6873 average financial aid amount received per undergraduate (2001–02).

Academics Grace awards associate and bachelor's degrees. Challenging opportunities include advanced placement credit and independent study. Special programs include internships and off-campus study. The most frequently chosen baccalaureate fields are education, visual/performing arts, and business/marketing. The faculty at Grace has 9 full-time members, 22% with terminal degrees. The student-faculty ratio is 11:1.

Students of Grace The student body is made up of 145 undergraduates. 44.1% are women and 55.9% are men. Students come from 16 states and territories and 2 other countries. 74% are from Michigan. 1.4% are international students. 83% returned for their sophomore year.

Applying Grace requires ACT, a high school transcript, and 2 recommendations, and in some cases an interview. The school recommends a minimum high school GPA of 2.5. Application deadline: 7/15; 2/15 priority date for financial aid. Early and deferred admission are possible.

GRACE COLLEGE

Winona Lake, IN

Small-town setting ■ Private ■ Independent Religious ■ Coed

Web site: www.grace.edu
Contact: Ms. Rebecca E. Gehrke, Admission Coordinator, 200 Seminary Drive, Winona Lake, IN 46590-1294
Telephone: 574-372-5100 ext. 6008 or toll-free 800-54-GRACE (in-state), 800-54 GRACE (out-of-state)
E-mail: enroll@grace.edu

Getting in Last Year 786 applied; 75% were accepted; 217 enrolled (37%).

Financial Matters $12,466 tuition and fees (2002–03); $5311 room and board; 85% average percent of need met; $11,521 average financial aid amount received per undergraduate.

Academics Grace awards associate, bachelor's, and master's degrees. Challenging opportunities include advanced placement credit, accelerated degree programs, double majors, independent study, and a senior project. Special programs include internships, summer session for credit, off-campus study, and study-abroad. The most frequently chosen baccalaureate fields are education, business/marketing, and psychology. The faculty at Grace has 42 full-time members, 67% with terminal degrees. The student-faculty ratio is 19:1.

Students of Grace The student body totals 1,033, of whom 968 are undergraduates. 59.4% are women and 40.6% are men. Students come from 35 states and territories and 8 other countries. 52% are from Indiana. 80% returned for their sophomore year.

Applying Grace requires SAT I or ACT, a high school transcript, 2 recommendations, and a minimum high school GPA of 2.3, and in some cases an interview. Application deadline: 8/1; 3/1 priority date for financial aid. Early and deferred admission are possible.

GRACELAND UNIVERSITY

Lamoni, IA

Small-town setting ■ Private ■ Independent Religious ■ Coed

Web site: www.graceland.edu

Contact: Mr. Brian Shantz, Dean of Admissions, 1 University Place, Lamoni, IA 50140

Telephone: 641-784-5110 or toll-free 866-GRACELAND (in-state), 800-472-235263 (out-of-state) **Fax:** 641-784-5480

E-mail: admissions@graceland.edu

Getting in Last Year 1,057 applied; 57% were accepted; 272 enrolled (45%).

Financial Matters $13,900 tuition and fees (2002–03); $4530 room and board; 85% average percent of need met; $13,203 average financial aid amount received per undergraduate.

Academics Graceland awards bachelor's and master's degrees and post-master's certificates. Challenging opportunities include advanced placement credit, accelerated degree programs, student-designed majors, an honors program, double majors, independent study, and a senior project. Special programs include cooperative education, internships, summer session for credit, off-campus study, and study-abroad. The most frequently chosen baccalaureate fields are health professions and related sciences, business/marketing, and education. The faculty at Graceland has 90 full-time members, 58% with terminal degrees. The student-faculty ratio is 16:1.

Students of Graceland The student body totals 2,297, of whom 2,066 are undergraduates. 68.1% are women and 31.9% are men. Students come from 49 states and territories and 26 other countries. 32% are from Iowa. 5% are international students. 75% returned for their sophomore year.

Applying Graceland requires SAT I or ACT, a high school transcript, and a minimum high school GPA of 2.0, and in some cases an essay, an interview, and 2 recommendations. The school recommends minimum SAT score of 960 or ACT score of 21. Application deadline: rolling admissions. Early and deferred admission are possible.

GRACE UNIVERSITY

Omaha, NE

Urban setting ■ Private ■ Independent Religious ■ Coed

Web site: www.graceuniversity.edu

Contact: Mrs. Terri L. Dingfield, Director of Admissions, 1311 South Ninth Street, Omaha, NE 68108

Telephone: 402-449-2831 or toll-free 800-383-1422 **Fax:** 402-341-9587

E-mail: admissions@graceuniversity.com

Getting in Last Year 320 applied; 45% were accepted; 94 enrolled (65%).

Financial Matters $9475 tuition and fees (2002–03); $4190 room and board; 54% average percent of need met; $6160 average financial aid amount received per undergraduate (2001–02).

Academics Grace awards associate, bachelor's, and master's degrees. Challenging opportunities include advanced placement credit, accelerated degree programs, student-designed majors, double majors, independent study, and a senior project. Special programs include cooperative education, internships, summer session for credit, off-campus study, study-abroad, and Army and Air Force ROTC. The most frequently chosen baccalaureate fields are business/marketing, social sciences and history, and liberal arts/general studies. The faculty at Grace has 19 full-time members, 68% with terminal degrees. The student-faculty ratio is 18:1.

Students of Grace The student body totals 507, of whom 431 are undergraduates. 53.1% are women and 46.9% are men. Students come from 29 states and territories. 77% are from Nebraska. 0.7% are international students. 68% returned for their sophomore year.

Applying Grace requires an essay, SAT I or ACT, a high school transcript, 3 recommendations, and a minimum high school GPA of 2.0, and in some cases an interview. The school recommends ACT. Application deadline: rolling admissions; 2/1 priority date for financial aid. Early and deferred admission are possible.

GRAMBLING STATE UNIVERSITY

Grambling, LA

Small-town setting ■ Public ■ State-supported ■ Coed

Web site: www.gram.edu

Contact: Ms. Norma Taylor, Director of Admissions, PO Drawer 1165, 100 Main Street, Grambling, LA 71245

Telephone: 318-274-6308

E-mail: bingamann@medgar.gram.edu

Getting in Last Year 3,111 applied; 57% were accepted.

Financial Matters $2716 resident tuition and fees (2002–03); $8066 nonresident tuition and fees (2002–03); $2936 room and board; 80% average percent of need met; $6800 average financial aid amount received per undergraduate.

Academics GSU awards associate, bachelor's, master's, and doctoral degrees. Challenging opportunities include advanced placement credit, an honors program, and a senior project. Special programs include cooperative education, internships, summer session for credit, off-campus study, study-abroad, and Army and Air Force ROTC. The most frequently chosen baccalaureate fields are protective services/public administration, business/marketing, and computer/information sciences. The faculty at GSU has 241 full-time members, 58% with terminal degrees. The student-faculty ratio is 18:1.

Students of GSU The student body totals 4,464, of whom 4,005 are undergraduates. Students come from 39 states and territories and 17 other countries. 60% are from Louisiana. 1.7% are international students.

Applying GSU requires SAT I or ACT and a high school transcript. Application deadline: 7/15; 6/1 for financial aid. Early and deferred admission are possible.

GRAND CANYON UNIVERSITY

Phoenix, AZ

Suburban setting ■ Private ■ Independent Religious ■ Coed

Web site: www.grand-canyon.edu

Contact: Mrs. April Chapman, Director of Admissions, 3300 West Camelback Road, PO Box 11097, Phoenix, AZ 86017-3030

Telephone: 602-589-2855 ext. 2811 or toll-free 800-800-9776 (in-state) **Fax:** 602-589-2580

E-mail: admiss@grand-canyon.edu

Getting in Last Year 823 applied; 69% were accepted; 371 enrolled (65%).

Financial Matters $13,750 tuition and fees (2002–03); $4800 room and board; 41% average percent of need met; $8405 average financial aid amount received per undergraduate (2000–01).

Academics Grand Canyon University awards bachelor's and master's degrees. Challenging opportunities include advanced placement credit, accelerated degree programs, freshman honors college, an honors program, double majors, independent study, and a senior project. Special programs include cooperative education, internships, summer session for credit, off-campus study, study-abroad, and Army and Air Force ROTC. The most frequently chosen baccalaureate fields are business/marketing, health professions and related sciences, and education. The faculty at Grand Canyon University has 97 full-time members, 58% with terminal degrees. The student-faculty ratio is 16:1.

Students of Grand Canyon University The student body totals 4,113, of whom 1,609 are undergraduates. 64.3% are women and 35.7% are men. Students come from 40 states and territories and 14 other countries. 81% are from Arizona. 2.5% are international students. 76% returned for their sophomore year.

Applying Grand Canyon University requires SAT I or ACT, a high school transcript, and a minimum high school GPA of 3.0, and in some cases an essay, an interview, and 3 recommendations. The school recommends a minimum high school GPA of 3.0. Application deadline: rolling admissions.

GRAND VALLEY STATE UNIVERSITY

Allendale, MI

Small-town setting ■ Public ■ State-supported ■ Coed

Web site: www.gvsu.edu

Contact: Ms. Jodi Chycinski, Director of Admissions, 1 Campus Drive, Allendale, MI 49401

Telephone: 616-331-2025 or toll-free 800-748-0246 **Fax:** 616-331-2000

E-mail: go2gvsu@gvsu.edu

Getting in Last Year 10,167 applied; 71% were accepted; 2,894 enrolled (40%).

Financial Matters $5056 resident tuition and fees (2002–03); $10,936 nonresident tuition and fees (2002–03); $5656 room and board; 92% average percent of need met; $6428 average financial aid amount received per undergraduate.

Academics GVSU awards bachelor's and master's degrees and post-bachelor's and post-master's certificates. Challenging opportunities include advanced placement credit, accelerated degree programs, freshman honors college, an honors program, double majors, independent study, and a senior project. Special

Grand Valley State University (continued)

programs include cooperative education, internships, summer session for credit, and study-abroad. The most frequently chosen baccalaureate fields are business/marketing, health professions and related sciences, and psychology. The faculty at GVSU has 763 full-time members, 68% with terminal degrees. The student-faculty ratio is 22:1.

Students of GVSU The student body totals 20,407, of whom 16,875 are undergraduates. 60.1% are women and 39.9% are men. Students come from 43 states and territories and 39 other countries. 96% are from Michigan. 0.6% are international students. 78% returned for their sophomore year.

Applying GVSU requires SAT I or ACT and a high school transcript, and in some cases an essay and an interview. Application deadline: 7/25; 2/15 priority date for financial aid.

GRAND VIEW COLLEGE

Des Moines, IA

Urban setting ■ Private ■ Independent Religious ■ Coed

Web site: www.gvc.edu

Contact: Ms. Diane Johnson Schaefer, Director of Admissions, 1200 Grandview Avenue, Des Moines, IA 50316-1599

Telephone: 515-263-2810 or toll-free 800-444-6083 **Fax:** 515-263-2974

E-mail: admiss@gvc.edu

Getting in Last Year 421 applied; 94% were accepted; 198 enrolled (50%).

Financial Matters $14,194 tuition and fees (2002–03); $4798 room and board; 79% average percent of need met; $12,192 average financial aid amount received per undergraduate.

Academics Grand View awards associate and bachelor's degrees and post-bachelor's certificates. Challenging opportunities include advanced placement credit, accelerated degree programs, student-designed majors, freshman honors college, an honors program, double majors, independent study, and a senior project. Special programs include cooperative education, internships, summer session for credit, off-campus study, study-abroad, and Army and Air Force ROTC. The most frequently chosen baccalaureate fields are health professions and related sciences, business/marketing, and education. The faculty at Grand View has 77 full-time members, 57% with terminal degrees. The student-faculty ratio is 15:1.

Students of Grand View The student body is made up of 1,546 undergraduates. 68.4% are women and 31.6% are men. Students come from 22 states and territories and 19 other countries. 95% are from Iowa. 1.6% are international students. 63% returned for their sophomore year.

Applying Grand View requires SAT I or ACT and a high school transcript. The school recommends a minimum high school GPA of 2.0. Application deadline: 8/15; 3/1 priority date for financial aid.

GRANTHAM UNIVERSITY

Slidell, LA

Small-town setting ■ Private ■ Proprietary ■ Coed, Primarily Men

Web site: www.grantham.edu

Contact: Admissions Office, 34641 Grantham Road, Slidell, LA 70460-6815

Telephone: 985-649-4191 or toll-free 800-955-2527 **Fax:** 985-649-4183

E-mail: admissions@grantham.edu

Financial Matters $2489 tuition and fees (2002–03).

Academics Grantham University awards associate and bachelor's degrees (offers only external degree programs). Challenging opportunities include advanced placement credit, accelerated degree programs, an honors program, and independent study. Cooperative education is a special program. The faculty at Grantham University has 9 full-time members.

Students of Grantham University The student body is made up of 2,500 undergraduates. Students come from 52 states and territories and 25 other countries.

Applying Application deadline: rolling admissions.

GRATZ COLLEGE

Melrose Park, PA

Suburban setting ■ Private ■ Independent Religious ■ Coed

Web site: www.gratzcollege.edu

Contact: Ms. Adena E. Johnston, Director of Admissions, 7605 Old York Road, Melrose Park, PA 19027

Telephone: 215-635-7300 ext. 140 or toll-free 800-475-4635 ext. 140 (out-of-state) **Fax:** 215-635-7320

E-mail: admissions@gratz.edu

Getting in Last Year 7 applied; 71% were accepted.

Financial Matters $8190 tuition and fees (2002–03); 100% average percent of need met; $2900 average financial aid amount received per undergraduate (2001–02).

Academics Gratz College awards bachelor's and master's degrees and post-master's certificates. Challenging opportunities include double majors and independent study. Special programs include internships, summer session for credit, and study-abroad. The faculty at Gratz College has 8 full-time members, 100% with terminal degrees. The student-faculty ratio is 12:1.

Students of Gratz College The student body totals 696, of whom 16 are undergraduates. 87.5% are women and 12.5% are men. Students come from 5 states and territories. 56% are from Pennsylvania. 100% returned for their sophomore year.

Applying Gratz College requires an essay, a high school transcript, and recommendations, and in some cases an interview. Application deadline: rolling admissions. Early and deferred admission are possible.

GREAT LAKES CHRISTIAN COLLEGE

Lansing, MI

Suburban setting ■ Private ■ Independent Religious ■ Coed

Web site: www.glcc.edu

Contact: Mr. Mike Klauka, Dean of Student Affairs, 6211 West Willow Highway, Lansing, MI 48917-1299

Telephone: 517-321-0242 ext. 221 or toll-free 800-YES-GLCC **Fax:** 517-321-5902

Financial Matters $8000 tuition and fees (2002–03); $4500 room and board.

Academics GLCC awards associate and bachelor's degrees. Challenging opportunities include advanced placement credit, double majors, independent study, and a senior project. Special programs include internships and off-campus study. The most frequently chosen baccalaureate fields are education and psychology. The faculty at GLCC has 10 full-time members, 70% with terminal degrees. The student-faculty ratio is 14:1.

Students of GLCC The student body is made up of 207 undergraduates. Students come from 8 states and territories and 3 other countries. 2.4% are international students. 99% returned for their sophomore year.

Applying GLCC requires an essay, SAT I and SAT II or ACT, a high school transcript, 3 recommendations, and a minimum high school GPA of 2.25. Application deadline: 8/1. Early and deferred admission are possible.

GREEN MOUNTAIN COLLEGE

Poultney, VT

Small-town setting ■ Private ■ Independent Religious ■ Coed

Web site: www.greenmtn.edu

Contact: Ms. Noka Garrapy, Assistant Dean of Admissions, One College Circle, Poultney, VT 05764

Telephone: 802-287-8000 ext. 8305 or toll-free 800-776-6675 (out-of-state) **Fax:** 802-287-8099

E-mail: admiss@greenmtn.edu

Getting in Last Year 718 applied; 80% were accepted; 182 enrolled (32%).

Financial Matters $19,350 tuition and fees (2002–03); $5980 room and board; 65% average percent of need met; $13,074 average financial aid amount received per undergraduate.

Academics Green Mountain awards bachelor's degrees. Challenging opportunities include advanced placement credit, accelerated degree programs, student-designed majors, an honors program, double majors, independent study, and a senior project. Special programs include cooperative education, internships, summer session for credit, off-campus study, and study-abroad. The most frequently chosen baccalaureate fields are education, business/marketing, and parks and recreation. The faculty at Green Mountain has 36 full-time members, 75% with terminal degrees. The student-faculty ratio is 14:1.

Students of Green Mountain The student body is made up of 661 undergraduates. 46.6% are women and 53.4% are men. Students come from 31 states and territories and 17 other countries. 10% are from Vermont. 4.7% are international students. 57% returned for their sophomore year.

Applying Green Mountain requires SAT I or ACT, a high school transcript, and 2 recommendations. The school recommends an interview and a minimum high school GPA of 2.4. Application deadline: rolling admissions. Deferred admission is possible.

GREENSBORO COLLEGE

Greensboro, NC

Urban setting ■ Private ■ Independent Religious ■ Coed

Web site: www.gborocollege.edu

Contact: Mr. Timothy L. Jackson, Director of Admissions, 815 West Market Street, Greensboro, NC 27401-1875

Telephone: 336-272-7102 ext. 211 or toll-free 800-346-8226 **Fax:** 336-378-0154

E-mail: admissions@gborocollege.edu

Getting in Last Year 806 applied; 77% were accepted; 242 enrolled (39%).

Financial Matters $14,650 tuition and fees (2002–03); $5760 room and board; 90% average percent of need met; $9501 average financial aid amount received per undergraduate.

Academics Greensboro awards bachelor's and master's degrees and post-bachelor's certificates. Challenging opportunities include advanced placement credit, accelerated degree programs, student-designed majors, freshman honors college, an honors program, double majors, independent study, and a senior project. Special programs include internships, summer session for credit, off-campus study, study-abroad, and Army and Air Force ROTC. The most frequently chosen baccalaureate fields are business/marketing, education, and parks and recreation. The faculty at Greensboro has 56 full-time members, 80% with terminal degrees. The student-faculty ratio is 14:1.

Students of Greensboro The student body totals 1,235, of whom 1,208 are undergraduates. 54.1% are women and 45.9% are men. Students come from 30 states and territories. 71% are from North Carolina. 1% are international students. 66% returned for their sophomore year.

Applying Greensboro requires an essay, SAT I or ACT, and a high school transcript, and in some cases an interview and 2 recommendations. The school recommends an interview. Application deadline: rolling admissions; 4/15 priority date for financial aid. Early and deferred admission are possible.

GREENVILLE COLLEGE

Greenville, IL

Small-town setting ■ *Private* ■ *Independent Religious* ■ *Coed*

Web site: www.greenville.edu
Contact: Dr. R. Pepper Dill, Dean of Admissions, 315 East College Avenue, Greenville, IL 62246
Telephone: 618-664-7100 or toll-free 800-248-2288 (in-state), 800-345-4440 (out-of-state) **Fax:** 618-664-9841
E-mail: admissions@greenville.edu

Getting in Last Year 523 applied; 95% were accepted; 244 enrolled (49%).

Financial Matters $14,520 tuition and fees (2002–03); $5400 room and board; 81% average percent of need met; $13,400 average financial aid amount received per undergraduate.

Academics GC awards bachelor's and master's degrees. Challenging opportunities include advanced placement credit, accelerated degree programs, student-designed majors, an honors program, double majors, independent study, and a senior project. Special programs include cooperative education, internships, summer session for credit, off-campus study, and study-abroad. The most frequently chosen baccalaureate fields are business/marketing, education, and biological/life sciences. The faculty at GC has 69 full-time members, 51% with terminal degrees. The student-faculty ratio is 15:1.

Students of GC The student body totals 1,239, of whom 1,206 are undergraduates. 51.2% are women and 48.8% are men. Students come from 40 states and territories and 11 other countries. 73% are from Illinois. 1.5% are international students. 67% returned for their sophomore year.

Applying GC requires an essay, SAT I or ACT, a high school transcript, 2 recommendations, agreement to code of conduct, and a minimum high school GPA of 2.25, and in some cases an interview. Application deadline: rolling admissions. Early and deferred admission are possible.

GRIGGS UNIVERSITY

Silver Spring, MD

Suburban setting ■ *Private* ■ *Independent Religious* ■ *Coed, Primarily Men*

Web site: www.griggs.edu
Contact: Ms. Eva Michel, Enrollment Officer, PO Box 4437, Silver Spring, MD 20914-4437
Telephone: 301-680-6593 or toll-free 800-782-4769 (in-state) **Fax:** 301-680-6577
E-mail: emichel@hsi.edu

Financial Matters $6400 tuition and fees (2002–03).

Academics Griggs University awards associate and bachelor's degrees (offers only external degree programs). Challenging opportunities include advanced placement credit, accelerated degree programs, double majors, independent study, and a senior project. Summer session for credit is a special program. The faculty at Griggs University has 40 members, 55% with terminal degrees.

Students of Griggs University The student body is made up of 396 undergraduates.

Applying Griggs University requires an essay, a high school transcript, and a minimum high school GPA of 2.0. Application deadline: rolling admissions. Early and deferred admission are possible.

GRINNELL COLLEGE

Grinnell, IA

Small-town setting ■ *Private* ■ *Independent* ■ *Coed*

Web site: www.grinnell.edu
Contact: Mr. James Sumner, Dean for Admission and Financial Aid, 1103 Park Street, Grinnell, IA 50112-1690
Telephone: 641-269-3600 or toll-free 800-247-0113 **Fax:** 641-269-4800
E-mail: askgrin@grinnell.edu

Getting in Last Year 2,067 applied; 65% were accepted; 368 enrolled (28%).

Financial Matters $23,530 tuition and fees (2002–03); $6330 room and board; 100% average percent of need met; $19,611 average financial aid amount received per undergraduate.

Academics Grinnell College awards bachelor's degrees. Challenging opportunities include advanced placement credit, accelerated degree programs, student-designed majors, double majors, and independent study. Special programs include internships, off-campus study, and study-abroad. The most frequently chosen baccalaureate fields are social sciences and history, biological/life sciences, and English. The faculty at Grinnell College has 137 full-time members, 96% with terminal degrees. The student-faculty ratio is 10:1.

Students of Grinnell College The student body is made up of 1,485 undergraduates. 55.3% are women and 44.7% are men. Students come from 52 states and territories and 52 other countries. 15% are from Iowa. 10.5% are international students. 92% returned for their sophomore year.

Applying Grinnell College requires an essay, SAT I or ACT, a high school transcript, and 3 recommendations. The school recommends an interview. Application deadline: 1/20; 2/1 for financial aid. Early and deferred admission are possible.

GROVE CITY COLLEGE

Grove City, PA

Small-town setting ■ *Private* ■ *Independent Religious* ■ *Coed*

Web site: www.gcc.edu
Contact: Mr. Jeffrey C. Mincey, Director of Admissions, 100 Campus Drive, Grove City, PA 16127-2104
Telephone: 724-458-2100 **Fax:** 724-458-3395
E-mail: admissions@gcc.edu

Getting in Last Year 2,001 applied; 47% were accepted; 580 enrolled (62%).

Financial Matters $8876 tuition and fees (2002–03); $4626 room and board; 60% average percent of need met; $5047 average financial aid amount received per undergraduate.

Academics Grove City awards bachelor's degrees. Challenging opportunities include advanced placement credit, student-designed majors, double majors, independent study, and a senior project. Special programs include internships, summer session for credit, study-abroad, and Army ROTC. The most frequently chosen baccalaureate fields are business/marketing, education, and biological/life sciences. The faculty at Grove City has 122 full-time members, 76% with terminal degrees. The student-faculty ratio is 19:1.

Students of Grove City The student body is made up of 2,288 undergraduates. 50.7% are women and 49.3% are men. Students come from 46 states and territories and 12 other countries. 54% are from Pennsylvania. 1% are international students. 90% returned for their sophomore year.

Applying Grove City requires an essay, SAT I or ACT, a high school transcript, and 2 recommendations. The school recommends an interview. Application deadline: 2/15; 4/15 for financial aid. Early and deferred admission are possible.

GUILFORD COLLEGE

Greensboro, NC

Suburban setting ■ *Private* ■ *Independent Religious* ■ *Coed*

Web site: www.guilford.edu
Contact: Mr. Randy Doss, Vice President of Enrollment, 5800 West Friendly Avenue, Greensboro, NC 27410
Telephone: 336-316-2100 or toll-free 800-992-7759 **Fax:** 336-316-2954
E-mail: admission@guilford.edu

Getting in Last Year 1,211 applied; 83% were accepted; 337 enrolled (34%).

Financial Matters $18,200 tuition and fees (2002–03); $5780 room and board; 90% average percent of need met; $15,200 average financial aid amount received per undergraduate.

Academics Guilford awards bachelor's degrees. Challenging opportunities include advanced placement credit, accelerated degree programs, student-designed majors, an honors program, double majors, independent study, and a senior project. Special programs include internships, summer session for credit, off-campus study, and study-abroad. The most frequently chosen baccalaureate fields are social sciences and history, business/marketing, and English. The faculty at Guilford has 74 full-time members, 80% with terminal degrees. The student-faculty ratio is 15:1.

Students of Guilford The student body is made up of 1,801 undergraduates. 58.4% are women and 41.6% are men. Students come from 45 states and territories and 21 other countries. 61% are from North Carolina. 1.9% are international students. 77% returned for their sophomore year.

Applying Guilford requires an essay, SAT I or ACT, a high school transcript, 2 recommendations, and a minimum high school GPA of 2.0. The school

Guilford College (continued)

recommends an interview and a minimum high school GPA of 3.0. Application deadline: 2/15; 3/1 priority date for financial aid. Early and deferred admission are possible.

GUSTAVUS ADOLPHUS COLLEGE

St. Peter, MN

Small-town setting ■ Private ■ Independent Religious ■ Coed

Web site: www.gustavus.edu

Contact: Mr. Mark H. Anderson, Dean of Admission, 800 West College Avenue, St. Peter, MN 56082-1498

Telephone: 507-933-7676 or toll-free 800-GUSTAVU(S) **Fax:** 507-933-7474

E-mail: admission@gac.edu

Getting in Last Year 2,203 applied; 77% were accepted; 662 enrolled (39%).

Financial Matters $20,450 tuition and fees (2002–03); $5170 room and board; 92% average percent of need met; $14,501 average financial aid amount received per undergraduate (2001–02).

Academics Gustavus awards bachelor's degrees. Challenging opportunities include advanced placement credit, accelerated degree programs, student-designed majors, an honors program, double majors, independent study, and a senior project. Special programs include cooperative education, internships, summer session for credit, off-campus study, study-abroad, and Army ROTC. The most frequently chosen baccalaureate fields are social sciences and history, business/marketing, and biological/life sciences. The faculty at Gustavus has 178 full-time members, 87% with terminal degrees. The student-faculty ratio is 13:1.

Students of Gustavus The student body is made up of 2,536 undergraduates. 58.4% are women and 41.6% are men. Students come from 42 states and territories and 17 other countries. 78% are from Minnesota. 1.4% are international students. 89% returned for their sophomore year.

Applying Gustavus requires an essay, SAT I or ACT, a high school transcript, and 2 recommendations. The school recommends an interview. Application deadline: 4/1; 2/15 priority date for financial aid. Early and deferred admission are possible.

GWYNEDD-MERCY COLLEGE

Gwynedd Valley, PA

Suburban setting ■ Private ■ Independent Religious ■ Coed

Web site: www.gmc.edu

Contact: Mr. Dennis Murphy, Vice President of Enrollment Management, 1325 Sumneytown Pike, Gwynedd Valley, PA 19437-0901

Telephone: 215-646-7300 ext. 588 or toll-free 800-DIAL-GMC (in-state)

E-mail: admissions@gmc.edu

Getting in Last Year 1,258 applied; 68% were accepted; 266 enrolled (31%).

Financial Matters $16,100 tuition and fees (2002–03); $7210 room and board; 82% average percent of need met; $13,236 average financial aid amount received per undergraduate.

Academics Gwynedd awards associate, bachelor's, and master's degrees and post-bachelor's and post-master's certificates. Challenging opportunities include advanced placement credit, accelerated degree programs, freshman honors college, an honors program, double majors, independent study, and a senior project. Special programs include cooperative education, internships, and summer session for credit. The most frequently chosen baccalaureate fields are health professions and related sciences, education, and business/marketing. The faculty at Gwynedd has 72 full-time members, 50% with terminal degrees. The student-faculty ratio is 19:1.

Students of Gwynedd The student body totals 2,429, of whom 2,112 are undergraduates. 76.5% are women and 23.5% are men. Students come from 12 states and territories and 49 other countries. 96% are from Pennsylvania. 2% are international students. 88% returned for their sophomore year.

Applying Gwynedd requires SAT I, a high school transcript, and 1 recommendation, and in some cases an interview. The school recommends an interview. Application deadline: rolling admissions; 3/15 priority date for financial aid. Early and deferred admission are possible.

HAMILTON COLLEGE

Clinton, NY

Rural setting ■ Private ■ Independent ■ Coed

Web site: www.hamilton.edu

Contact: Mr. Richard M. Fuller, Dean of Admission and Financial Aid, 198 College Hill Road, Clinton, NY 13323-1296

Telephone: 315-859-4421 or toll-free 800-843-2655 **Fax:** 315-859-4457

E-mail: admission@hamilton.edu

Getting in Last Year 4,565 applied; 35% were accepted; 491 enrolled (31%).

Financial Matters $28,760 tuition and fees (2002–03); $7040 room and board; 99% average percent of need met; $22,460 average financial aid amount received per undergraduate.

Academics Hamilton awards bachelor's degrees. Challenging opportunities include advanced placement credit, accelerated degree programs, student-designed majors, double majors, independent study, and a senior project. Special programs include internships, off-campus study, study-abroad, and Army and Air Force ROTC. The most frequently chosen baccalaureate fields are social sciences and history, psychology, and English. The faculty at Hamilton has 179 full-time members, 94% with terminal degrees. The student-faculty ratio is 10:1.

Students of Hamilton The student body is made up of 1,851 undergraduates. 51.9% are women and 48.1% are men. Students come from 43 states and territories and 25 other countries. 42% are from New York. 3.4% are international students. 92% returned for their sophomore year.

Applying Hamilton requires an essay, SAT I, SAT II or ACT, a high school transcript, 1 recommendation, and sample of expository prose. The school recommends an interview. Application deadline: 1/15; 2/1 priority date for financial aid. Early and deferred admission are possible.

HAMILTON TECHNICAL COLLEGE

Davenport, IA

Urban setting ■ Private ■ Proprietary ■ Coed

Web site: www.hamiltontechcollege.com

Contact: Mr. Chad Nelson, Admissions, 1011 East 53rd Street, Davenport, IA 52807

Telephone: 563-386-3570 **Fax:** 319-386-6756

Financial Matters $6300 tuition and fees (2002–03).

Academics Hamilton Technical College awards associate and bachelor's degrees. Accelerated degree programs are a challenging opportunity. The faculty at Hamilton Technical College has 18 members. The student-faculty ratio is 20:1.

Students of Hamilton Technical College The student body is made up of 420 undergraduates.

Applying Hamilton Technical College requires a high school transcript and an interview. Application deadline: rolling admissions; 6/30 priority date for financial aid. Deferred admission is possible.

HAMLINE UNIVERSITY

St. Paul, MN

Urban setting ■ Private ■ Independent Religious ■ Coed

Web site: www.hamline.edu

Contact: Mr. Steven Bjork, Director of Undergraduate Admission, 1536 Hewitt Avenue C1930, St. Paul, MN 55104-1284

Telephone: 651-523-2207 or toll-free 800-753-9753 **Fax:** 651-523-2458

E-mail: cla-admis@gw.hamline.edu

Getting in Last Year 1,619 applied; 79% were accepted; 417 enrolled (33%).

Financial Matters $19,213 tuition and fees (2002–03); $5971 room and board; 68% average percent of need met; $16,865 average financial aid amount received per undergraduate.

Academics Hamline awards bachelor's, master's, doctoral, and first-professional degrees and post-bachelor's, post-master's, and first-professional certificates. Challenging opportunities include advanced placement credit, student-designed majors, an honors program, double majors, independent study, and a senior project. Special programs include cooperative education, internships, summer session for credit, off-campus study, study-abroad, and Air Force ROTC. The most frequently chosen baccalaureate fields are social sciences and history, psychology, and business/marketing. The faculty at Hamline has 174 full-time members, 89% with terminal degrees. The student-faculty ratio is 13:1.

Students of Hamline The student body totals 4,479, of whom 1,918 are undergraduates. 63.5% are women and 36.5% are men. Students come from 35 states and territories and 32 other countries. 3.4% are international students. 81% returned for their sophomore year.

Applying Hamline requires an essay, SAT I or ACT, a high school transcript, and 2 recommendations. The school recommends an interview. Application deadline: rolling admissions; 5/1 priority date for financial aid. Early and deferred admission are possible.

HAMPDEN-SYDNEY COLLEGE

Hampden-Sydney, VA

Rural setting ■ Private ■ Independent Religious ■ Men Only

Web site: www.hsc.edu

Contact: Ms. Anita H. Garland, Dean of Admissions, PO Box 667, Hampden-Sydney, VA 23943-0667

Telephone: 434-223-6120 or toll-free 800-755-0733 **Fax:** 434-223-6346

E-mail: hsapp@hsc.edu

Getting in Last Year 925 applied; 77% were accepted; 328 enrolled (46%).

Financial Matters $19,893 tuition and fees (2002–03); $6722 room and board; 85% average percent of need met; $14,409 average financial aid amount received per undergraduate.

Academics Hampden-Sydney awards bachelor's degrees. Challenging opportunities include advanced placement credit, accelerated degree programs, an honors program, double majors, independent study, and a senior project. Special programs include internships, summer session for credit, off-campus study, study-abroad, and Army ROTC. The most frequently chosen baccalaureate fields are social sciences and history, biological/life sciences, and English. The faculty at Hampden-Sydney has 79 full-time members, 81% with terminal degrees. The student-faculty ratio is 10:1.

Students of Hampden-Sydney The student body is made up of 1,026 undergraduates. Students come from 33 states and territories. 63% are from Virginia. 0.1% are international students. 79% returned for their sophomore year.

Applying Hampden-Sydney requires an essay, SAT I or ACT, a high school transcript, 2 recommendations, and a minimum high school GPA of 2.0. The school recommends SAT II Subject Tests, SAT II: Writing Test, an interview, and a minimum high school GPA of 3.0. Application deadline: 3/1; 3/1 priority date for financial aid. Early admission is possible.

HAMPSHIRE COLLEGE

Amherst, MA

Rural setting ■ Private ■ Independent ■ Coed

Web site: www.hampshire.edu

Contact: Ms. Karen S. Parker, Director of Admissions, 839 West Street, Amherst, MA 01002

Telephone: 413-559-5471 or toll-free 877-937-4267 (out-of-state) **Fax:** 413-559-5631

E-mail: admissions@hampshire.edu

Getting in Last Year 2,094 applied; 51% were accepted; 304 enrolled (29%).

Financial Matters $27,870 tuition and fees (2002–03); $7294 room and board; 100% average percent of need met; $27,015 average financial aid amount received per undergraduate.

Academics Hampshire awards bachelor's degrees. Challenging opportunities include advanced placement credit, accelerated degree programs, student-designed majors, double majors, independent study, and a senior project. Special programs include internships, off-campus study, study-abroad, and Army ROTC. The faculty at Hampshire has 103 full-time members, 87% with terminal degrees. The student-faculty ratio is 11:1.

Students of Hampshire The student body is made up of 1,267 undergraduates. 57.8% are women and 42.2% are men. Students come from 46 states and territories and 25 other countries. 19% are from Massachusetts. 3% are international students. 77% returned for their sophomore year.

Applying Hampshire requires an essay, a high school transcript, and 2 recommendations. The school recommends an interview. Application deadline: 2/1; 2/1 priority date for financial aid. Early and deferred admission are possible.

HAMPTON UNIVERSITY

Hampton, VA

Urban setting ■ Private ■ Independent ■ Coed

Web site: www.hamptonu.edu

Contact: Ms. Angela Boyd, Director of Admissions, Hampton, VA 23668

Telephone: 757-727-5328 or toll-free 800-624-3328 **Fax:** 757-727-5095

E-mail: admit@hamptonu.edu

Getting in Last Year 5,696 applied; 62% were accepted; 1,050 enrolled (30%).

Financial Matters $12,252 tuition and fees (2002–03); $5828 room and board.

Academics Hampton awards associate, bachelor's, master's, doctoral, and first-professional degrees and post-master's certificates. Challenging opportunities include advanced placement credit, accelerated degree programs, an honors program, double majors, independent study, and a senior project. Special programs include cooperative education, internships, summer session for credit, off-campus study, study-abroad, and Army and Navy ROTC. The most frequently chosen baccalaureate fields are business/marketing, biological/life sciences, and psychology. The faculty at Hampton has 284 full-time members, 79% with terminal degrees. The student-faculty ratio is 16:1.

Students of Hampton The student body totals 5,790, of whom 4,979 are undergraduates. 61% are women and 39% are men. Students come from 37 states and territories. 31% are from Virginia. 0.5% are international students. 85% returned for their sophomore year.

Applying Hampton requires an essay, SAT I or ACT, a high school transcript, 1 recommendation, and a minimum high school GPA of 2.0. Application deadline: 3/1; 3/1 for financial aid. Early and deferred admission are possible.

HANNIBAL-LAGRANGE COLLEGE

Hannibal, MO

Small-town setting ■ Private ■ Independent Religious ■ Coed

Web site: www.hlg.edu

Contact: Mr. Raymond Carty, Dean of Enrollment Management, 2800 Palmyra Road, Hannibal, MO 63401-1999

Telephone: 573-221-3113 or toll-free 800-HLG-1119

E-mail: admissio@hlg.edu

Getting in Last Year 362 applied; 97% were accepted.

Financial Matters $9500 tuition and fees (2002–03); $3530 room and board; 50% average percent of need met; $5310 average financial aid amount received per undergraduate (2001–02).

Academics HLG awards associate and bachelor's degrees. Challenging opportunities include advanced placement credit, accelerated degree programs, student-designed majors, freshman honors college, an honors program, double majors, independent study, and a senior project. Special programs include cooperative education, internships, summer session for credit, and study-abroad. The most frequently chosen baccalaureate fields are education, business/marketing, and protective services/public administration. The faculty at HLG has 51 full-time members, 31% with terminal degrees. The student-faculty ratio is 13:1.

Students of HLG The student body is made up of 1,117 undergraduates. Students come from 24 states and territories and 8 other countries. 76% are from Missouri. 1.6% are international students. 71% returned for their sophomore year.

Applying HLG requires SAT I or ACT, a high school transcript, and 2 recommendations. Application deadline: 8/26. Early and deferred admission are possible.

HANOVER COLLEGE

Hanover, IN

Rural setting ■ Private ■ Independent Religious ■ Coed

Web site: www.hanover.edu

Contact: Mr. Kenneth Moyer, Dean of Admission, PO Box 108, Hanover, IN 47243-0108

Telephone: 812-866-7021 or toll-free 800-213-2178 **Fax:** 812-866-7098

E-mail: info@hanover.edu

Getting in Last Year 1,227 applied; 76% were accepted; 280 enrolled (30%).

Financial Matters $13,500 tuition and fees (2002–03); $5500 room and board; 91% average percent of need met; $12,050 average financial aid amount received per undergraduate.

Academics Hanover awards bachelor's degrees. Challenging opportunities include advanced placement credit, accelerated degree programs, double majors, independent study, and a senior project. Special programs include internships, off-campus study, and study-abroad. The most frequently chosen baccalaureate fields are business/marketing, social sciences and history, and education. The faculty at Hanover has 92 full-time members, 92% with terminal degrees. The student-faculty ratio is 11:1.

Students of Hanover The student body is made up of 1,050 undergraduates. 54.1% are women and 45.9% are men. Students come from 35 states and territories and 18 other countries. 70% are from Indiana. 3.6% are international students. 78% returned for their sophomore year.

Applying Hanover requires an essay, SAT I or ACT, a high school transcript, and 1 recommendation. The school recommends an interview. Application deadline: 3/1; 3/10 priority date for financial aid. Early and deferred admission are possible.

HARDING UNIVERSITY

Searcy, AR

Small-town setting ■ Private ■ Independent Religious ■ Coed

Web site: www.harding.edu

Contact: Mr. Mike Williams, Assistant Vice President of Admissions, Box 11255, Searcy, AR 72149-0001

Telephone: 501-279-4407 or toll-free 800-477-4407 **Fax:** 501-279-4865

E-mail: admissions@harding.edu

Getting in Last Year 1,712 applied; 78% were accepted; 1,039 enrolled (78%).

Financial Matters $9530 tuition and fees (2002–03); $4650 room and board; 64% average percent of need met; $8673 average financial aid amount received per undergraduate.

Academics Harding awards bachelor's and master's degrees. Challenging opportunities include advanced placement credit, accelerated degree programs, student-designed majors, freshman honors college, an honors program, double majors, and a senior project. Special programs include cooperative education, internships, summer session for credit, study-abroad, and Army ROTC. The most frequently chosen baccalaureate fields are business/marketing, education, and health professions and related sciences. The faculty at Harding has 201 full-time members, 67% with terminal degrees. The student-faculty ratio is 16:1.

Students of Harding The student body totals 5,095, of whom 4,089 are undergraduates. 54.6% are women and 45.4% are men. Students come from 50 states and territories and 45 other countries. 31% are from Arkansas. 5.9% are international students. 77% returned for their sophomore year.

Applying Harding requires SAT I or ACT, a high school transcript, an interview, and 2 recommendations. Application deadline: 7/1. Early and deferred admission are possible.

HARDIN-SIMMONS UNIVERSITY

Abilene, TX

Urban setting ■ Private ■ Independent Religious ■ Coed

Web site: www.hsutx.edu
Contact: Mr. Forrest McMillan, Director of Recruiting, Box 16050, Abilene, TX 79698-6050
Telephone: 915-670-1207 or toll-free 800-568-2692 **Fax:** 915-671-2115
E-mail: enroll.services@hsutx.edu

Getting in Last Year 1,139 applied; 52% were accepted; 444 enrolled (76%).

Financial Matters $11,245 tuition and fees (2002–03); $3515 room and board; 22% average percent of need met; $10,950 average financial aid amount received per undergraduate.

Academics Hardin-Simmons awards bachelor's, master's, and first-professional degrees. Challenging opportunities include advanced placement credit, accelerated degree programs, double majors, independent study, and a senior project. Special programs include internships, summer session for credit, off-campus study, and study-abroad. The most frequently chosen baccalaureate fields are education, business/marketing, and biological/life sciences. The faculty at Hardin-Simmons has 127 full-time members, 72% with terminal degrees. The student-faculty ratio is 14:1.

Students of Hardin-Simmons The student body totals 2,291, of whom 1,914 are undergraduates. 54% are women and 46% are men. Students come from 26 states and territories. 96% are from Texas. 0.2% are international students. 66% returned for their sophomore year.

Applying Hardin-Simmons requires SAT I or ACT, a high school transcript, and a minimum high school GPA of 2.0. Application deadline: rolling admissions; 3/15 priority date for financial aid. Early and deferred admission are possible.

HARRINGTON INSTITUTE OF INTERIOR DESIGN

Chicago, IL

Urban setting ■ Private ■ Proprietary ■ Coed, Primarily Women

Web site: www.interiordesign.edu
Contact: Ms. Wendi Franczyk, Director of Admissions, 410 South Michigan Avenue, Chicago, IL 60605-1496
Telephone: 877-939-4975 or toll-free 877-939-4975 **Fax:** 312-939-8005
E-mail: hiid@interiordesign.edu

Getting in Last Year 411 applied; 73% were accepted.

Financial Matters $12,175 tuition and fees (2002–03); 30% average percent of need met; $3500 average financial aid amount received per undergraduate.

Academics Harrington Institute of Interior Design awards associate and bachelor's degrees. Special programs include internships, off-campus study, and study-abroad. The most frequently chosen baccalaureate field is visual/performing arts. The faculty at Harrington Institute of Interior Design has 100 members. The student-faculty ratio is 15:1.

Students of Harrington Institute of Interior Design The student body is made up of 1,125 undergraduates.

Applying Harrington Institute of Interior Design requires a high school transcript and an interview. Application deadline: rolling admissions. Deferred admission is possible.

HARRIS-STOWE STATE COLLEGE

St. Louis, MO

Urban setting ■ Public ■ State-supported ■ Coed

Web site: www.hssc.edu
Contact: Ms. LaShanda Boone, Interim Director of Admissions, 3026 Laclede Avenue, St. Louis, MO 63103
Telephone: 314-340-3301 **Fax:** 314-340-3555
E-mail: admissions@hssc.edu

Getting in Last Year 1,322 enrolled.

Financial Matters $3040 resident tuition and fees (2002–03); $5834 nonresident tuition and fees (2002–03).

Academics Harris-Stowe State College awards bachelor's degrees. Challenging opportunities include advanced placement credit, student-designed majors, and a senior project. Special programs include cooperative education, internships, summer session for credit, off-campus study, and Air Force ROTC. The most frequently chosen baccalaureate fields are education, business/marketing, and protective services/public administration. The faculty at Harris-Stowe State College has 52 full-time members. The student-faculty ratio is 18:1.

Students of Harris-Stowe State College The student body is made up of 1,968 undergraduates. 66.3% are women and 33.7% are men. Students come from 5 states and territories and 21 other countries. 91% are from Missouri. 1.9% are international students. 60% returned for their sophomore year.

Applying Harris-Stowe State College requires SAT I or ACT, a high school transcript, and a minimum high school GPA of 2.0. Application deadline: rolling admissions; 4/1 priority date for financial aid. Early and deferred admission are possible.

HARTFORD COLLEGE FOR WOMEN

Hartford, CT

Suburban setting ■ Private ■ Independent ■ Women Only

Web site: www.hartford.edu/hcw
Contact: Ms. Annette Rogers, Admissions Director, 1265 Asylum Avenue, Hartford, CT 06105-2299
Telephone: 860-768-5646 or toll-free 888-GO-TO-HCW **Fax:** 860-768-5693
E-mail: arogers@mail.hartford.edu

Getting in Last Year 60 applied; 62% were accepted.

Financial Matters $21,550 tuition and fees (2002–03); $8518 room and board.

Academics Hartford College awards associate and bachelor's degrees (offers mainly evening and weekend programs). Challenging opportunities include advanced placement credit, accelerated degree programs, double majors, independent study, and a senior project. Special programs include internships, summer session for credit, and off-campus study. The most frequently chosen baccalaureate fields are law/legal studies and area/ethnic studies. The faculty at Hartford College has 6 full-time members. The student-faculty ratio is 7:1.

Students of Hartford College The student body is made up of 166 undergraduates. Students come from 2 states and territories and 1 other country. 99% are from Connecticut. 0.6% are international students.

Applying Hartford College requires an essay and an interview, and in some cases SAT I. The school recommends recommendations. Application deadline: rolling admissions. Deferred admission is possible.

HARTWICK COLLEGE

Oneonta, NY

Small-town setting ■ Private ■ Independent ■ Coed

Web site: www.hartwick.edu
Contact: Ms. Susan Dileno, Dean of Admissions, PO Box 4022, Oneonta, NY 13820-4022
Telephone: 607-431-4150 or toll-free 888-HARTWICK (out-of-state) **Fax:** 607-431-4102
E-mail: admissions@hartwick.edu

Getting in Last Year 1,853 applied; 89% were accepted; 370 enrolled (22%).

Financial Matters $27,015 tuition and fees (2002–03); $7050 room and board; 82% average percent of need met; $20,000 average financial aid amount received per undergraduate.

Academics Hartwick awards bachelor's degrees. Challenging opportunities include advanced placement credit, accelerated degree programs, student-designed majors, an honors program, double majors, independent study, and a senior project. Special programs include internships, off-campus study, study-abroad, and Army and Air Force ROTC. The most frequently chosen baccalaureate fields are social sciences and history, business/marketing, and visual/performing arts. The faculty at Hartwick has 108 full-time members, 78% with terminal degrees. The student-faculty ratio is 11:1.

Students of Hartwick The student body is made up of 1,397 undergraduates. 57.4% are women and 42.6% are men. Students come from 30 states and territories and 34 other countries. 64% are from New York. 4.1% are international students. 76% returned for their sophomore year.

Applying Hartwick requires an essay, a high school transcript, 2 recommendations, and audition for music program. The school recommends SAT I or ACT, an interview, and a minimum high school GPA of 3.0. Application deadline: 2/15; 2/1 for financial aid. Early and deferred admission are possible.

HARVARD UNIVERSITY

Cambridge, MA

Urban setting ■ Private ■ Independent ■ Coed

Web site: www.harvard.edu
Contact: Office of Admissions and Financial Aid, Byerly Hall, 8 Garden Street, Cambridge, MA 02138
Telephone: 617-495-1551
E-mail: college@harvard.edu

Getting in Last Year 19,609 applied; 11% were accepted; 1,637 enrolled (79%).

Financial Matters $27,448 tuition and fees (2002–03); $8502 room and board; 100% average percent of need met; $23,739 average financial aid amount received per undergraduate (2001–02).

Academics Harvard awards bachelor's, master's, doctoral, and first-professional degrees. Challenging opportunities include advanced placement credit, accelerated degree programs, student-designed majors, an honors program, double majors, independent study, and a senior project. Special programs include internships, summer session for credit, off-campus study, study-abroad, and Army and Air Force ROTC. The faculty at Harvard has 760 members, 100% with terminal degrees. The student-faculty ratio is 8:1.

Students of Harvard The student body totals 20,132, of whom 6,637 are undergraduates. 47.3% are women and 52.7% are men. Students come from 53 states and territories and 82 other countries. 7% are international students. 97% returned for their sophomore year.

Applying Harvard requires an essay, SAT II Subject Tests, SAT I or ACT, a high school transcript, an interview, and 2 recommendations. Application deadline: 1/1; 2/1 priority date for financial aid. Deferred admission is possible.

HARVEY MUDD COLLEGE

Claremont, CA

Suburban setting ■ Private ■ Independent ■ Coed

Web site: www.hmc.edu

Contact: Mr. Deren Finks, Vice President and Dean of Admissions and Financial Aid, 301 East 12th Street, Claremont, CA 91711

Telephone: 909-621-8011 **Fax:** 909-607-7046

E-mail: admission@hmc.edu

Getting in Last Year 1,669 applied; 37% were accepted; 187 enrolled (30%).

Financial Matters $27,037 tuition and fees (2002–03); $8971 room and board; 100% average percent of need met; $21,358 average financial aid amount received per undergraduate.

Academics Harvey Mudd awards bachelor's and master's degrees. Challenging opportunities include advanced placement credit, student-designed majors, double majors, and a senior project. Special programs include internships, off-campus study, study-abroad, and Army and Air Force ROTC. The most frequently chosen baccalaureate fields are engineering/engineering technologies, physical sciences, and computer/information sciences. The faculty at Harvey Mudd has 80 full-time members, 100% with terminal degrees. The student-faculty ratio is 9:1.

Students of Harvey Mudd The student body totals 702, of whom 699 are undergraduates. 33.2% are women and 66.8% are men. Students come from 48 states and territories and 11 other countries. 46% are from California. 2.7% are international students. 94% returned for their sophomore year.

Applying Harvey Mudd requires an essay, SAT I, SAT II: Writing Test, SAT II Subject Test in math, third SAT II Subject Test, a high school transcript, and 3 recommendations. The school recommends an interview. Application deadline: 1/15; 2/1 for financial aid. Deferred admission is possible.

HASKELL INDIAN NATIONS UNIVERSITY

Lawrence, KS

Suburban setting ■ Public ■ Federally supported ■ Coed

Web site: www.haskell.edu

Contact: Ms. Patty Grant, Recruitment Officer, 155 Indian Avenue, #5031, Lawrence, KS 66046

Telephone: 785-749-8437 ext. 437 **Fax:** 785-749-8429

Getting in Last Year 350 enrolled.

Financial Matters $210 resident tuition and fees (2002–03); $210 nonresident tuition and fees (2002–03); $70 room and board.

Academics Haskell awards associate and bachelor's degrees. Challenging opportunities include advanced placement credit, student-designed majors, and independent study. Special programs include internships, summer session for credit, off-campus study, and Air Force ROTC. The faculty at Haskell has 48 full-time members. The student-faculty ratio is 15:1.

Students of Haskell The student body is made up of 1,028 undergraduates. 47.1% are women and 52.9% are men. Students come from 37 states and territories.

Applying Haskell requires ACT, SAT I or ACT, a high school transcript, and a minimum high school GPA of 2.0, and in some cases 2 recommendations. Application deadline: 7/30.

HASTINGS COLLEGE

Hastings, NE

Small-town setting ■ Private ■ Independent Religious ■ Coed

Web site: www.hastings.edu

Contact: Ms. Mary Molliconi, Director of Admissions, 800 Turner Avenue, Hastings, NE 68901-7696

Telephone: 402-461-7320 or toll-free 800-532-7642 **Fax:** 402-461-7490

E-mail: admissions@hastings.edu

Getting in Last Year 1,173 applied; 85% were accepted; 276 enrolled (28%).

Financial Matters $14,554 tuition and fees (2002–03); $4398 room and board; 79% average percent of need met; $11,407 average financial aid amount received per undergraduate.

Academics Hastings awards bachelor's and master's degrees. Challenging opportunities include advanced placement credit, student-designed majors, double majors, independent study, and a senior project. Special programs include internships, summer session for credit, off-campus study, and study-abroad. The most frequently chosen baccalaureate fields are business/marketing, education, and communications/communication technologies. The faculty at Hastings has 74 full-time members, 74% with terminal degrees. The student-faculty ratio is 13:1.

Students of Hastings The student body totals 1,078, of whom 1,033 are undergraduates. 51.7% are women and 48.3% are men. Students come from 25 states and territories and 5 other countries. 76% are from Nebraska. 1% are international students. 76% returned for their sophomore year.

Applying Hastings requires SAT I or ACT, a high school transcript, counselor's recommendation, and a minimum high school GPA of 2.0, and in some cases an essay, an interview, and 2 recommendations. Application deadline: 8/1; 9/1 for financial aid, with a 5/1 priority date.

HAVERFORD COLLEGE

Haverford, PA

Suburban setting ■ Private ■ Independent ■ Coed

Web site: www.haverford.edu

Contact: Ms. Delsie Z. Phillips, Director of Admission, 370 Lancaster Avenue, Haverford, PA 19041-1392

Telephone: 610-896-1350 **Fax:** 610-896-1338

E-mail: admitme@haverford.edu

Getting in Last Year 2,598 applied; 32% were accepted; 311 enrolled (37%).

Financial Matters $27,260 tuition and fees (2002–03); $8590 room and board; 100% average percent of need met; $23,550 average financial aid amount received per undergraduate.

Academics Haverford awards bachelor's degrees. Challenging opportunities include advanced placement credit, accelerated degree programs, student-designed majors, double majors, independent study, and a senior project. Special programs include internships, off-campus study, and study-abroad. The most frequently chosen baccalaureate fields are social sciences and history, biological/life sciences, and English. The faculty at Haverford has 105 full-time members, 100% with terminal degrees. The student-faculty ratio is 8:1.

Students of Haverford The student body is made up of 1,105 undergraduates. Students come from 36 states and territories and 38 other countries. 19% are from Pennsylvania. 2.7% are international students. 96% returned for their sophomore year.

Applying Haverford requires SAT II Subject Tests, SAT II: Writing Test, SAT I or ACT, a high school transcript, and 2 recommendations. The school recommends an interview. Application deadline: 1/15; 1/31 for financial aid. Early and deferred admission are possible.

HAWAI'I PACIFIC UNIVERSITY

Honolulu, HI

Urban setting ■ Private ■ Independent ■ Coed

Web site: www.hpu.edu

Contact: Mr. Scott Stensrud, Associate Vice President Enrollment Management, 1164 Bishop Street, Honolulu, HI 96813-2785

Telephone: 808-544-0238 or toll-free 866-225-5478 (out-of-state) **Fax:** 808-544-1136

E-mail: admissions@hpu.edu

Getting in Last Year 2,839 applied; 76% were accepted; 592 enrolled (27%).

Financial Matters $9850 tuition and fees (2002–03); $8530 room and board; 78% average percent of need met; $10,713 average financial aid amount received per undergraduate.

Academics HPU awards associate, bachelor's, and master's degrees and post-bachelor's certificates. Challenging opportunities include advanced placement credit, accelerated degree programs, student-designed majors, freshman honors college, an honors program, double majors, independent study, and a senior project. Special programs include cooperative education, internships, summer session for credit, study-abroad, and Army and Air Force ROTC. The most frequently chosen baccalaureate fields are business/marketing, health professions and related sciences, and protective services/public administration. The faculty at HPU has 213 full-time members, 76% with terminal degrees. The student-faculty ratio is 17:1.

Students of HPU The student body totals 8,137, of whom 6,899 are undergraduates. 54.5% are women and 45.5% are men. Students come from 52 states and territories and 105 other countries. 77% are from Hawaii. 16.2% are international students. 71% returned for their sophomore year.

Applying HPU requires SAT I or ACT, a high school transcript, and a minimum high school GPA of 2.5, and in some cases SAT I or ACT and an interview. The school recommends an essay and 2 recommendations. Application deadline: rolling admissions; 3/1 priority date for financial aid. Early and deferred admission are possible.

HEIDELBERG COLLEGE

Tiffin, OH

Small-town setting ■ Private ■ Independent Religious ■ Coed

Web site: www.heidelberg.edu

Contact: Director of Admission, 310 East Market Street, Tiffin, OH 44883

Telephone: 419-448-2000 or toll-free 800-434-3352 **Fax:** 419-448-2334

Heidelberg College (continued)

E-mail: adminfo@heidelberg.edu

Getting in Last Year 1,590 applied; 82% were accepted; 280 enrolled (21%).

Financial Matters $13,146 tuition and fees (2002–03); $6034 room and board; 87% average percent of need met; $15,414 average financial aid amount received per undergraduate.

Academics Heidelberg awards bachelor's and master's degrees. Challenging opportunities include advanced placement credit, accelerated degree programs, an honors program, double majors, and a senior project. Special programs include internships, summer session for credit, off-campus study, study-abroad, and Army and Air Force ROTC. The most frequently chosen baccalaureate fields are business/marketing, education, and parks and recreation. The faculty at Heidelberg has 74 full-time members, 73% with terminal degrees. The student-faculty ratio is 13:1.

Students of Heidelberg The student body totals 1,468, of whom 1,264 are undergraduates. 54.8% are women and 45.2% are men. Students come from 25 states and territories and 7 other countries. 87% are from Ohio. 1.8% are international students. 79% returned for their sophomore year.

Applying Heidelberg requires SAT I or ACT, a high school transcript, and a minimum high school GPA of 2.4. The school recommends an interview and 1 recommendation. Application deadline: 8/1; 3/1 priority date for financial aid. Deferred admission is possible.

HELLENIC COLLEGE

Brookline, MA

Suburban setting ■ *Private* ■ *Independent Religious* ■ *Coed*

Web site: www.hchc.edu

Contact: Ms. Sonia Daly, Director of Admissions and Records, 50 Goddard Avenue, Brookline, MA 02445-7496

Telephone: 617-731-3500 ext. 1285 **Fax:** 617-850-1460

E-mail: admissions@hchc.edu

Getting in Last Year 46 applied; 59% were accepted; 17 enrolled (63%).

Financial Matters $10,275 tuition and fees (2002–03); $7800 room and board; $7700 average financial aid amount received per undergraduate (2001–02).

Academics Hellenic awards bachelor's and master's degrees. Challenging opportunities include advanced placement credit, double majors, independent study, and a senior project. Special programs include internships, summer session for credit, and off-campus study. The most frequently chosen baccalaureate field is liberal arts/general studies. The faculty at Hellenic has 8 full-time members. The student-faculty ratio is 7:1.

Students of Hellenic The student body totals 195, of whom 72 are undergraduates. 40.3% are women and 59.7% are men. Students come from 39 states and territories and 7 other countries. 13% are from Massachusetts. 23.6% are international students. 100% returned for their sophomore year.

Applying Hellenic requires an essay, SAT I or ACT, a high school transcript, an interview, recommendations, health certificate, and a minimum high school GPA of 2.0, and in some cases SAT II Subject Tests and SAT II: Writing Test. Application deadline: rolling admissions; 5/1 priority date for financial aid. Deferred admission is possible.

HENDERSON STATE UNIVERSITY

Arkadelphia, AR

Small-town setting ■ *Public* ■ *State-supported* ■ *Coed*

Web site: www.hsu.edu

Contact: Ms. Vikita Hardwrick, Director of University Relations/Admissions, 1100 Henderson Street, PO Box 7560, Arkadelphia, AR 71999-0001

Telephone: 870-230-5028 or toll-free 800-228-7333 **Fax:** 870-230-5066

E-mail: hardwrv@hsu.edu

Getting in Last Year 2,048 applied; 75% were accepted; 463 enrolled (30%).

Financial Matters $3252 resident tuition and fees (2002–03); $6204 nonresident tuition and fees (2002–03); $3936 room and board; 72% average percent of need met; $5482 average financial aid amount received per undergraduate (2000–01).

Academics Henderson awards associate, bachelor's, and master's degrees. Challenging opportunities include advanced placement credit and an honors program. Special programs include internships, summer session for credit, and off-campus study. The most frequently chosen baccalaureate fields are education, business/marketing, and social sciences and history. The faculty at Henderson has 160 full-time members, 67% with terminal degrees. The student-faculty ratio is 16:1.

Students of Henderson The student body totals 3,444, of whom 3,130 are undergraduates. 56.1% are women and 43.9% are men. Students come from 25 states and territories and 30 other countries. 90% are from Arkansas. 4.6% are international students. 64% returned for their sophomore year.

Applying Henderson requires SAT I or ACT and a high school transcript, and in some cases an essay and 3 recommendations. The school recommends ACT and a minimum high school GPA of 2.5. Application deadline: 7/15; 6/1 priority date for financial aid. Deferred admission is possible.

HENDRIX COLLEGE

Conway, AR

Suburban setting ■ *Private* ■ *Independent Religious* ■ *Coed*

Web site: www.hendrix.edu

Contact: Ms. Amy Anderson, Director of Admission, 1600 Washington Avenue, Conway, AR 72032

Telephone: 501-450-1362 or toll-free 800-277-9017 **Fax:** 501-450-3843

E-mail: adm@hendrix.edu

Getting in Last Year 1,071 applied; 83% were accepted; 317 enrolled (35%).

Financial Matters $14,900 tuition and fees (2002–03); $5090 room and board; 88% average percent of need met; $13,738 average financial aid amount received per undergraduate.

Academics Hendrix awards bachelor's and master's degrees. Challenging opportunities include advanced placement credit, student-designed majors, double majors, independent study, and a senior project. Special programs include internships, off-campus study, study-abroad, and Army ROTC. The most frequently chosen baccalaureate fields are social sciences and history, biological/life sciences, and psychology. The faculty at Hendrix has 81 full-time members, 99% with terminal degrees. The student-faculty ratio is 12:1.

Students of Hendrix The student body totals 1,093, of whom 1,082 are undergraduates. 55.4% are women and 44.6% are men. Students come from 32 states and territories. 66% are from Arkansas. 1% are international students. 84% returned for their sophomore year.

Applying Hendrix requires an essay, SAT I or ACT, and a high school transcript, and in some cases an interview. The school recommends 2 recommendations. Application deadline: rolling admissions; 2/15 priority date for financial aid. Deferred admission is possible.

HENRY COGSWELL COLLEGE

Everett, WA

Urban setting ■ *Private* ■ *Independent* ■ *Coed*

Web site: www.henrycogswell.edu

Contact: Mr. Paul Wells, Director of Admissions, 3002 Colby Avenue, Everett, WA 98201

Telephone: 425-258-3351 ext. 116 or toll-free 866-411-HCC1 **Fax:** 425-257-0405

E-mail: information@henrycogswell.edu

Getting in Last Year 44 applied; 82% were accepted; 17 enrolled (47%).

Financial Matters $13,080 tuition and fees (2002–03); 42% average percent of need met; $4746 average financial aid amount received per undergraduate (2001–02).

Academics Cogswell College awards bachelor's degrees. Challenging opportunities include advanced placement credit, accelerated degree programs, double majors, independent study, and a senior project. Special programs include cooperative education and summer session for credit. The most frequently chosen baccalaureate fields are engineering/engineering technologies, visual/performing arts, and computer/information sciences. The faculty at Cogswell College has 8 full-time members, 75% with terminal degrees. The student-faculty ratio is 17:1.

Students of Cogswell College The student body is made up of 249 undergraduates. 16.9% are women and 83.1% are men. Students come from 3 states and territories and 2 other countries. 0.8% are international students. 86% returned for their sophomore year.

Applying Cogswell College requires an essay, SAT I or ACT, and a high school transcript, and in some cases 3 recommendations and portfolio. The school recommends SAT I and an interview. Application deadline: rolling admissions. Deferred admission is possible.

HERITAGE BIBLE COLLEGE

Dunn, NC

Small-town setting ■ *Private* ■ *Independent Religious* ■ *Coed*

Web site: www.heritagebiblecollege.org

Contact: Dale Wallace, Admission, PO Box 1628, Dunn, NC 28335

Telephone: 910-892-3178 or toll-free 800-297-6351 (in-state) **Fax:** 910-892-1809

E-mail: generalinfo@heritagebiblecollege.com

Getting in Last Year 30 applied; 40% were accepted; 12 enrolled (100%).

Financial Matters $4200 tuition and fees (2002–03); $2440 room and board; $4330 average financial aid amount received per undergraduate.

Academics HBC awards associate and bachelor's degrees. Independent study is a challenging opportunity. Special programs include internships, summer session for credit, and off-campus study. The faculty at HBC has 3 full-time members, 67% with terminal degrees. The student-faculty ratio is 11:1.

Students of HBC The student body is made up of 78 undergraduates. 32.1% are women and 67.9% are men. Students come from 1 state or territory. 95% are from North Carolina. 62% returned for their sophomore year.

Applying HBC requires an essay, ACT ASSET, a high school transcript, and recommendations. Application deadline: rolling admissions; 4/30 priority date for financial aid.

HERITAGE CHRISTIAN UNIVERSITY

Florence, AL

Small-town setting ■ Private ■ Independent Religious ■ Coed, Primarily Men

Web site: www.hcu.edu

Contact: Mr. Jim Collins, Director of Enrollment Services, PO Box HCU, Florence, AL 35630-0050

Telephone: 256-766-6610 ext. 48 or toll-free 800-367-3565

Getting in Last Year 19 enrolled.

Financial Matters $6304 tuition and fees (2002–03); $1300 room only; 66% average percent of need met; $3569 average financial aid amount received per undergraduate.

Academics HCU awards associate, bachelor's, and master's degrees. Challenging opportunities include accelerated degree programs and independent study. Special programs include internships and summer session for credit. The faculty at HCU has 13 full-time members, 62% with terminal degrees. The student-faculty ratio is 9:1.

Students of HCU The student body totals 147, of whom 134 are undergraduates. 14.2% are women and 85.8% are men. Students come from 21 states and territories and 14 other countries. 46% are from Alabama. 11.4% are international students.

Applying HCU requires a high school transcript and 3 recommendations. The school recommends an interview. Application deadline: rolling admissions; 6/1 priority date for financial aid. Early and deferred admission are possible.

HIGH POINT UNIVERSITY

High Point, NC

Suburban setting ■ Private ■ Independent Religious ■ Coed

Web site: www.highpoint.edu

Contact: Mr. James L. Schlimmer, Dean of Enrollment Management, University Station 3188, 833 Montlieu Avenue, High Point, NC 27262-3598

Telephone: 336-841-9216 or toll-free 800-345-6993 **Fax:** 336-841-5123

E-mail: admiss@highpoint.edu

Getting in Last Year 1,617 applied; 87% were accepted; 465 enrolled (33%).

Financial Matters $14,710 tuition and fees (2002–03); $6610 room and board; 87% average percent of need met; $11,427 average financial aid amount received per undergraduate (2001–02).

Academics High Point awards bachelor's and master's degrees and post-bachelor's certificates. Challenging opportunities include advanced placement credit, accelerated degree programs, student-designed majors, an honors program, double majors, independent study, and a senior project. Special programs include cooperative education, internships, summer session for credit, off-campus study, study-abroad, and Army and Air Force ROTC. The most frequently chosen baccalaureate fields are business/marketing, computer/information sciences, and education. The faculty at High Point has 121 full-time members, 74% with terminal degrees. The student-faculty ratio is 16:1.

Students of High Point The student body totals 2,750, of whom 2,559 are undergraduates. 61.6% are women and 38.4% are men. Students come from 38 states and territories. 45% are from North Carolina. 3.7% are international students. 74% returned for their sophomore year.

Applying High Point requires SAT I or ACT, a high school transcript, 2 recommendations, and a minimum high school GPA of 2.0. The school recommends an essay, SAT II Subject Tests, SAT II: Writing Test, an interview, and a minimum high school GPA of 3.0. Application deadline: 8/15; 3/1 priority date for financial aid. Deferred admission is possible.

HILBERT COLLEGE

Hamburg, NY

Small-town setting ■ Private ■ Independent ■ Coed

Web site: www.hilbert.edu

Contact: Admissions Counselor, 5200 South Park Avenue, Hamburg, NY 14075-1597

Telephone: 716-649-7900 ext. 211 **Fax:** 716-649-0702

Getting in Last Year 303 applied; 88% were accepted; 117 enrolled (44%).

Financial Matters $13,100 tuition and fees (2002–03); $4905 room and board; 73% average percent of need met; $8410 average financial aid amount received per undergraduate (2001–02).

Academics Hilbert awards associate and bachelor's degrees. Challenging opportunities include advanced placement credit, an honors program, independent study, and a senior project. Special programs include cooperative education, internships, and summer session for credit. The most frequently chosen baccalaureate fields are protective services/public administration, business/marketing, and law/legal studies. The faculty at Hilbert has 36 full-time members, 61% with terminal degrees. The student-faculty ratio is 16:1.

Students of Hilbert The student body is made up of 964 undergraduates. 65.4% are women and 34.6% are men. Students come from 4 states and territories and 3 other countries. 100% are from New York. 0.3% are international students. 81% returned for their sophomore year.

Applying Hilbert requires a high school transcript, and in some cases an interview. The school recommends SAT I, ACT, SAT I or ACT, an interview, and recommendations. Application deadline: 9/1; 5/1 for financial aid, with a 3/1 priority date. Early and deferred admission are possible.

HILLSDALE COLLEGE

Hillsdale, MI

Small-town setting ■ Private ■ Independent ■ Coed

Web site: www.hillsdale.edu

Contact: Mr. Jeffrey S. Lantis, Director of Admissions, 33 East College Street, Hillsdale, MI 49242-1298

Telephone: 517-607-2327 ext. 2327 **Fax:** 517-607-2223

E-mail: admissions@hillsdale.edu

Getting in Last Year 1,070 applied; 82% were accepted; 422 enrolled (48%).

Financial Matters $15,300 tuition and fees (2002–03); $6086 room and board; 77% average percent of need met; $14,000 average financial aid amount received per undergraduate (2001–02).

Academics Hillsdale awards bachelor's degrees. Challenging opportunities include advanced placement credit, accelerated degree programs, an honors program, double majors, independent study, and a senior project. Special programs include internships, summer session for credit, and study-abroad. The most frequently chosen baccalaureate fields are business/marketing, social sciences and history, and education. The faculty at Hillsdale has 89 full-time members, 97% with terminal degrees. The student-faculty ratio is 11:1.

Students of Hillsdale The student body is made up of 1,220 undergraduates. 53.8% are women and 46.2% are men. Students come from 46 states and territories and 11 other countries. 48% are from Michigan. 87% returned for their sophomore year.

Applying Hillsdale requires an essay, SAT I or ACT, a high school transcript, 1 recommendation, and a minimum high school GPA of 3.15, and in some cases an interview. The school recommends SAT II Subject Tests, SAT II: Writing Test, an interview, and 2 recommendations. Application deadline: rolling admissions; 3/15 priority date for financial aid. Early and deferred admission are possible.

HILLSDALE FREE WILL BAPTIST COLLEGE

Moore, OK

Suburban setting ■ Private ■ Independent Religious ■ Coed

Web site: www.hc.edu

Contact: Ms. Sue Chaffin, Registrar/Assistant Director of Admissions, PO Box 7208, Moore, OK 73153-1208

Telephone: 405-912-9005 **Fax:** 405-912-9050

E-mail: hillsdale@hc.edu

Getting in Last Year 80 applied; 98% were accepted; 74 enrolled (95%).

Financial Matters $7340 tuition and fees (2002–03); $4140 room and board.

Academics Hillsdale awards associate, bachelor's, and master's degrees. Challenging opportunities include advanced placement credit, accelerated degree programs, double majors, independent study, and a senior project. Special programs include internships and summer session for credit. The most frequently chosen baccalaureate fields are business/marketing and interdisciplinary studies. The faculty at Hillsdale has 25 full-time members, 24% with terminal degrees. The student-faculty ratio is 14:1.

Students of Hillsdale The student body totals 290, of whom 282 are undergraduates. 41.5% are women and 58.5% are men. Students come from 15 states and territories and 13 other countries. 81% are from Oklahoma. 7.6% are international students. 42% returned for their sophomore year.

Applying Hillsdale requires an essay, SAT I or ACT, a high school transcript, 1 recommendation, and Biblical foundation statement, student conduct pledge; medical form required for some, and in some cases an interview and 1 recommendation. The school recommends 2 recommendations and a minimum high school GPA of 2.0. Application deadline: rolling admissions. Early and deferred admission are possible.

HIRAM COLLEGE

Hiram, OH

Rural setting ■ Private ■ Independent Religious ■ Coed

Web site: www.hiram.edu

Contact: Ms. Brenda Swihart Meyer, Director of Admission, Box 96, Hiram, OH 44234-0067

Telephone: 330-569-5169 or toll-free 800-362-5280 **Fax:** 330-569-5944

E-mail: admission@hiram.edu

Hiram College (continued)

Getting in Last Year 1,294 applied; 69% were accepted; 241 enrolled (27%).

Financial Matters $20,312 tuition and fees (2002–03); $6820 room and board; 89% average percent of need met; $20,675 average financial aid amount received per undergraduate.

Academics Hiram awards bachelor's degrees. Challenging opportunities include advanced placement credit, accelerated degree programs, student-designed majors, double majors, independent study, and a senior project. Special programs include internships, summer session for credit, off-campus study, and study-abroad. The most frequently chosen baccalaureate fields are business/marketing, biological/life sciences, and social sciences and history. The faculty at Hiram has 73 full-time members, 96% with terminal degrees. The student-faculty ratio is 11:1.

Students of Hiram The student body is made up of 1,134 undergraduates. 58.6% are women and 41.4% are men. Students come from 31 states and territories and 20 other countries. 76% are from Ohio. 3.3% are international students. 77% returned for their sophomore year.

Applying Hiram requires an essay, SAT I or ACT, a high school transcript, and 2 recommendations, and in some cases an interview. The school recommends an interview and 3 recommendations. Application deadline: 2/1; 2/15 priority date for financial aid. Early and deferred admission are possible.

HOBART AND WILLIAM SMITH COLLEGES

Geneva, NY

Small-town setting ■ *Private* ■ *Independent* ■ *Coed*

Web site: www.hws.edu

Contact: Ms. Mara O'Laughlin, Director of Admissions, 629 South Main Street, Geneva, NY 14456-3397

Telephone: 315-781-3472 or toll-free 800-245-0100 **Fax:** 315-781-5471

E-mail: admissions@hws.edu

Getting in Last Year 3,108 applied; 66% were accepted; 532 enrolled (26%).

Financial Matters $27,348 tuition and fees (2002–03); $7230 room and board; 94% average percent of need met; $22,482 average financial aid amount received per undergraduate.

Academics HWS awards bachelor's degrees. Challenging opportunities include advanced placement credit, accelerated degree programs, student-designed majors, an honors program, double majors, independent study, and a senior project. Special programs include internships, off-campus study, and study-abroad. The most frequently chosen baccalaureate fields are social sciences and history, English, and psychology. The faculty at HWS has 157 full-time members, 92% with terminal degrees. The student-faculty ratio is 11:1.

Students of HWS The student body is made up of 1,893 undergraduates. 54.6% are women and 45.4% are men. Students come from 38 states and territories and 18 other countries. 50% are from New York. 1.8% are international students. 85% returned for their sophomore year.

Applying HWS requires an essay, SAT I or ACT, a high school transcript, and 2 recommendations. The school recommends SAT II Subject Tests and an interview. Application deadline: 2/1; 3/15 for financial aid, with a 2/15 priority date. Early and deferred admission are possible.

HOFSTRA UNIVERSITY

Hempstead, NY

Suburban setting ■ *Private* ■ *Independent* ■ *Coed*

Web site: www.hofstra.edu

Contact: Ms. Gigi Lamens, Vice President for Enrollment Services, 100 Hofstra University, Hempstead, NY 11549

Telephone: 516-463-6700 or toll-free 800-HOFSTRA **Fax:** 516-560-7660

E-mail: hofstra@hofstra.edu

Getting in Last Year 11,741 applied; 72% were accepted; 1,790 enrolled (21%).

Financial Matters $16,542 tuition and fees (2002–03); $8450 room and board; 66% average percent of need met; $11,197 average financial aid amount received per undergraduate.

Academics Hofstra awards bachelor's, master's, doctoral, and first-professional degrees and post-bachelor's and post-master's certificates. Challenging opportunities include advanced placement credit, accelerated degree programs, student-designed majors, freshman honors college, an honors program, double majors, independent study, and a senior project. Special programs include internships, summer session for credit, study-abroad, and Army ROTC. The most frequently chosen baccalaureate fields are business/marketing, psychology, and communications/communication technologies. The faculty at Hofstra has 507 full-time members, 91% with terminal degrees. The student-faculty ratio is 15:1.

Students of Hofstra The student body totals 13,412, of whom 9,469 are undergraduates. 53.6% are women and 46.4% are men. Students come from 43 states and territories and 67 other countries. 78% are from New York. 2.4% are international students. 77% returned for their sophomore year.

Applying Hofstra requires a high school transcript and 1 recommendation, and in some cases SAT I or ACT and for international students, proof of degree and 16 years' study. The school recommends an essay and an interview. Application deadline: rolling admissions; 2/15 priority date for financial aid. Early and deferred admission are possible.

HOLLINS UNIVERSITY

Roanoke, VA

Suburban setting ■ *Private* ■ *Independent* ■ *Women Only*

Web site: www.hollins.edu

Contact: Ms. Celia McCormick, Dean of Admissions, PO Box 9707, Roanoke, VA 24020-1707

Telephone: 540-362-6401 or toll-free 800-456-9595 **Fax:** 540-362-6218

E-mail: huadm@hollins.edu

Getting in Last Year 762 applied; 72% were accepted; 202 enrolled (37%).

Financial Matters $18,450 tuition and fees (2002–03); $6875 room and board; 80% average percent of need met; $15,737 average financial aid amount received per undergraduate.

Academics Hollins awards bachelor's and master's degrees and post-master's certificates. Challenging opportunities include advanced placement credit, accelerated degree programs, student-designed majors, double majors, independent study, and a senior project. Special programs include internships, off-campus study, and study-abroad. The most frequently chosen baccalaureate fields are English, visual/performing arts, and social sciences and history. The faculty at Hollins has 75 full-time members, 96% with terminal degrees. The student-faculty ratio is 9:1.

Students of Hollins The student body totals 1,153, of whom 847 are undergraduates. Students come from 46 states and territories and 7 other countries. 52% are from Virginia. 2.8% are international students. 81% returned for their sophomore year.

Applying Hollins requires an essay, SAT I or ACT, a high school transcript, and 1 recommendation. The school recommends SAT II Subject Tests and an interview. Application deadline: 2/15; 2/15 for financial aid, with a 2/1 priority date. Deferred admission is possible.

HOLY APOSTLES COLLEGE AND SEMINARY

Cromwell, CT

Small-town setting ■ *Private* ■ *Independent Religious* ■ *Coed*

Web site: www.holyapostles.edu

Contact: Very Rev. Douglas Mosey, CSB, Director of Admissions, 33 Prospect Hill Road, Cromwell, CT 06416-2005

Telephone: 860-632-3010 or toll-free 800-330-7272 **Fax:** 860-632-3075

E-mail: admissions@holyapostles.edu

Financial Matters $8240 tuition and fees (2002–03); $6600 room and board.

Academics Holy Apostles awards associate, bachelor's, master's, and first-professional degrees and post-master's certificates. Accelerated degree programs are a challenging opportunity. Internships is a special program. The faculty at Holy Apostles has 13 full-time members, 77% with terminal degrees. The student-faculty ratio is 7:1.

Students of Holy Apostles The student body totals 203, of whom 32 are undergraduates. 25% are women and 75% are men. Students come from 10 states and territories. 17% are from Connecticut. 100% returned for their sophomore year.

Applying Holy Apostles requires a high school transcript and an interview, and in some cases recommendations. Application deadline: rolling admissions. Deferred admission is possible.

HOLY FAMILY UNIVERSITY

Philadelphia, PA

Suburban setting ■ *Private* ■ *Independent Religious* ■ *Coed*

Web site: www.holyfamily.edu

Contact: Ms. Lauren McDermott, Interim Director of Admissions, Grant and Frankford Avenues, Philadelphia, PA 19114-2094

Telephone: 215-637-3050 or toll-free 800-637-1191 **Fax:** 215-281-1022

E-mail: undergra@hfc.edu

Getting in Last Year 573 applied; 77% were accepted; 230 enrolled (52%).

Financial Matters $14,490 tuition and fees (2002–03).

Academics Holy Family awards associate, bachelor's, and master's degrees and post-bachelor's certificates. Challenging opportunities include advanced placement credit, accelerated degree programs, freshman honors college, an honors program, double majors, independent study, and a senior project. Special programs include cooperative education, internships, summer session for credit, and study-abroad. The most frequently chosen baccalaureate fields are education, business/marketing, and health professions and related sciences. The faculty at Holy Family has 87 full-time members, 64% with terminal degrees. The student-faculty ratio is 11:1.

Students of Holy Family The student body totals 2,670, of whom 1,782 are undergraduates. 74.4% are women and 25.6% are men. Students come from 7 states and territories and 3 other countries. 88% are from Pennsylvania. 0.3% are international students. 82% returned for their sophomore year.

Applying Holy Family requires an essay, SAT I or ACT, a high school transcript, and 1 recommendation. The school recommends an interview. Application deadline: rolling admissions; 3/1 priority date for financial aid. Deferred admission is possible.

HOLY NAMES COLLEGE

Oakland, CA

Urban setting ■ Private ■ Independent Religious ■ Coed, Primarily Women

Web site: www.hnc.edu

Contact: Mr. Jeffrey D. Miller, Vice President for Enrollment Management, 3500 Mountain Boulevard, Oakland, CA 94619-1699

Telephone: 510-436-1351 or toll-free 800-430-1321 **Fax:** 510-436-1325

E-mail: admissions@admin.hnc.edu

Getting in Last Year 216 applied; 69% were accepted; 66 enrolled (44%).

Financial Matters $18,270 tuition and fees (2002–03); $7600 room and board; 78% average percent of need met; $20,582 average financial aid amount received per undergraduate.

Academics HNC awards bachelor's and master's degrees and post-bachelor's certificates. Challenging opportunities include advanced placement credit, accelerated degree programs, student-designed majors, an honors program, double majors, independent study, and a senior project. Special programs include internships, summer session for credit, off-campus study, study-abroad, and Army and Air Force ROTC. The most frequently chosen baccalaureate fields are business/marketing, health professions and related sciences, and liberal arts/general studies. The faculty at HNC has 36 full-time members, 92% with terminal degrees. The student-faculty ratio is 12:1.

Students of HNC The student body is made up of 881 undergraduates. 46.5% are women and 53.5% are men. Students come from 13 states and territories and 8 other countries. 96% are from California. 3.2% are international students. 69% returned for their sophomore year.

Applying HNC requires an essay, SAT I or ACT, a high school transcript, and 1 recommendation, and in some cases an interview. Application deadline: 8/1; 3/2 priority date for financial aid. Deferred admission is possible.

HOLY TRINITY ORTHODOX SEMINARY

Jordanville, NY

Rural setting ■ Private ■ Independent Religious ■ Men Only

Web site: www.hts.edu

Contact: Fr. Vladimir Tsurikov, Assistant Dean, PO Box 36, Jordanville, NY 13361

Telephone: 315-858-0945 **Fax:** 315-858-0945

E-mail: info@hts.edu

Getting in Last Year 14 applied; 64% were accepted; 6 enrolled (67%).

Financial Matters $2000 tuition and fees (2002–03); $2000 room and board.

Academics Holy Trinity Orthodox Seminary awards bachelor's degrees. Challenging opportunities include accelerated degree programs and a senior project. The faculty at Holy Trinity Orthodox Seminary has 6 full-time members. The student-faculty ratio is 4:1.

Students of Holy Trinity Orthodox Seminary The student body is made up of 28 undergraduates. Students come from 6 states and territories and 8 other countries. 100% returned for their sophomore year.

Applying Holy Trinity Orthodox Seminary requires an essay, a high school transcript, recommendations, and special examination, proficiency in Russian, Eastern Orthodox baptism. The school recommends a minimum high school GPA of 3.0. Application deadline: 5/1.

HOOD COLLEGE

Frederick, MD

Suburban setting ■ Private ■ Independent ■ Coed

Web site: www.hood.edu

Contact: Dr. Susan Hallenbeck, Dean of Admissions, 401 Rosemont Avenue, Frederick, MD 21701

Telephone: 301-696-3400 or toll-free 800-922-1599 **Fax:** 301-696-3819

E-mail: admissions@hood.edu

Getting in Last Year 530 applied; 78% were accepted; 179 enrolled (43%).

Financial Matters $19,695 tuition and fees (2002–03); $7300 room and board; 89% average percent of need met; $16,619 average financial aid amount received per undergraduate.

Academics Hood awards bachelor's and master's degrees and post-bachelor's certificates (also offers adult program with significant enrollment not reflected in profile). Challenging opportunities include advanced placement credit, accelerated degree programs, student-designed majors, an honors program, double majors, independent study, and a senior project. Special programs include internships, summer session for credit, off-campus study, study-abroad, and Army ROTC. The most frequently chosen baccalaureate fields are biological/life sciences, education, and business/marketing. The faculty at Hood has 78 full-time members, 95% with terminal degrees. The student-faculty ratio is 9:1.

Students of Hood The student body totals 1,693, of whom 820 are undergraduates. 88.3% are women and 11.7% are men. Students come from 27 states and territories and 24 other countries. 76% are from Maryland. 5.5% are international students. 85% returned for their sophomore year.

Applying Hood requires an essay, SAT I or ACT, a high school transcript, and 2 recommendations. The school recommends SAT II Subject Tests, an interview, and a minimum high school GPA of 3.0. Application deadline: 2/1; 2/15 priority date for financial aid. Early and deferred admission are possible.

HOPE COLLEGE

Holland, MI

Small-town setting ■ Private ■ Independent Religious ■ Coed

Web site: www.hope.edu

Contact: Dr. James R. Bekkering, Vice President for Admissions, 69 East 10th Street, PO Box 9000, Holland, MI 49422-9000

Telephone: 616-395-7955 or toll-free 800-968-7850 **Fax:** 616-395-7130

E-mail: admissions@hope.edu

Getting in Last Year 1,885 applied; 90% were accepted; 725 enrolled (43%).

Financial Matters $18,268 tuition and fees (2002–03); $5688 room and board; 88% average percent of need met; $15,673 average financial aid amount received per undergraduate.

Academics Hope awards bachelor's degrees. Challenging opportunities include advanced placement credit, student-designed majors, double majors, and independent study. Special programs include internships, summer session for credit, off-campus study, and study-abroad. The most frequently chosen baccalaureate fields are business/marketing, English, and social sciences and history. The faculty at Hope has 200 full-time members, 84% with terminal degrees. The student-faculty ratio is 13:1.

Students of Hope The student body is made up of 3,035 undergraduates. 60.9% are women and 39.1% are men. Students come from 38 states and territories and 40 other countries. 77% are from Michigan. 1.5% are international students. 87% returned for their sophomore year.

Applying Hope requires an essay, SAT I or ACT, and a high school transcript, and in some cases 1 recommendation. The school recommends an interview. Application deadline: rolling admissions; 2/15 priority date for financial aid. Early and deferred admission are possible.

HOPE INTERNATIONAL UNIVERSITY

Fullerton, CA

Suburban setting ■ Private ■ Independent Religious ■ Coed

Web site: www.hiu.edu

Contact: Ms. Midge Madden, Office Manager, 2500 East Nutwood Avenue, Fullerton, CA 92831-3138

Telephone: 714-879-3901 ext. 2235 or toll-free 800-762-1294 **Fax:** 714-526-0231

E-mail: mfmadden@hiu.edu

Getting in Last Year 368 applied; 42% were accepted; 121 enrolled (78%).

Financial Matters $14,100 tuition and fees (2002–03); $5092 room and board; 58% average percent of need met; $9509 average financial aid amount received per undergraduate.

Academics Hope International University awards associate, bachelor's, and master's degrees. Challenging opportunities include advanced placement credit, accelerated degree programs, student-designed majors, an honors program, double majors, independent study, and a senior project. Special programs include internships, summer session for credit, and off-campus study. The faculty at Hope International University has 27 full-time members, 52% with terminal degrees. The student-faculty ratio is 15:1.

Students of Hope International University The student body totals 1,204, of whom 926 are undergraduates. 64.4% are women and 35.6% are men. Students come from 22 states and territories and 20 other countries. 66% are from California. 4% are international students. 63% returned for their sophomore year.

Applying Hope International University requires an essay, SAT I or ACT, a high school transcript, 2 recommendations, and a minimum high school GPA of 2.5, and in some cases an interview. Application deadline: 6/1; 3/2 priority date for financial aid. Early and deferred admission are possible.

HOUGHTON COLLEGE

Houghton, NY

Rural setting ■ Private ■ Independent Religious ■ Coed

Web site: www.houghton.edu

Contact: Mr. Bruce Campbell, Director of Admission, PO Box 128, Houghton, NY 14744

Telephone: 585-567-9353 or toll-free 800-777-2556 **Fax:** 585-567-9522

E-mail: admission@houghton.edu

Houghton College (continued)

Getting in Last Year 1,206 applied; 84% were accepted; 300 enrolled (30%).

Financial Matters $17,160 tuition and fees (2002–03); $5600 room and board; 73% average percent of need met; $13,908 average financial aid amount received per undergraduate.

Academics Houghton awards associate and bachelor's degrees. Challenging opportunities include advanced placement credit, an honors program, double majors, independent study, and a senior project. Special programs include internships, summer session for credit, off-campus study, study-abroad, and Army ROTC. The most frequently chosen baccalaureate fields are business/marketing, education, and visual/performing arts. The faculty at Houghton has 80 full-time members, 81% with terminal degrees. The student-faculty ratio is 14:1.

Students of Houghton The student body is made up of 1,394 undergraduates. 63.8% are women and 36.2% are men. Students come from 40 states and territories and 19 other countries. 61% are from New York. 4.1% are international students. 88% returned for their sophomore year.

Applying Houghton requires an essay, SAT I or ACT, a high school transcript, 1 recommendation, and pastoral recommendation. The school recommends an interview and a minimum high school GPA of 2.5. Application deadline: rolling admissions; 3/1 priority date for financial aid. Deferred admission is possible.

HOUSTON BAPTIST UNIVERSITY

Houston, TX

Urban setting ■ Private ■ Independent Religious ■ Coed

Web site: www.hbu.edu
Contact: Mr. David Melton, Director of Admissions, 7502 Fondren Road, Houston, TX 77074-3298
Telephone: 281-649-3211 ext. 3208 or toll-free 800-969-3210 **Fax:** 281-649-3217
E-mail: unadm@hbu.edu

Getting in Last Year 724 applied; 67% were accepted; 254 enrolled (52%).

Financial Matters $11,355 tuition and fees (2002–03); $4443 room and board; 60% average percent of need met; $9699 average financial aid amount received per undergraduate.

Academics Houston Baptist awards associate, bachelor's, and master's degrees. Challenging opportunities include advanced placement credit, an honors program, double majors, independent study, and a senior project. Special programs include internships, summer session for credit, study-abroad, and Army ROTC. The most frequently chosen baccalaureate fields are business/marketing, education, and health professions and related sciences. The faculty at Houston Baptist has 110 full-time members, 75% with terminal degrees. The student-faculty ratio is 16:1.

Students of Houston Baptist The student body totals 2,745, of whom 1,941 are undergraduates. 69.7% are women and 30.3% are men. Students come from 20 states and territories and 26 other countries. 98% are from Texas. 4.7% are international students. 80% returned for their sophomore year.

Applying Houston Baptist requires an essay, SAT I or ACT, a high school transcript, and 1 recommendation. The school recommends an interview. Application deadline: rolling admissions; 3/1 priority date for financial aid. Early and deferred admission are possible.

HOWARD PAYNE UNIVERSITY

Brownwood, TX

Small-town setting ■ Private ■ Independent Religious ■ Coed

Web site: www.hputx.edu
Contact: Ms. Cheryl Mangrum, Coordinator of Admission Services, HPU Station Box 828, 1000 Fisk Avenue, Brownwood, TX 76801
Telephone: 915-649-8027 or toll-free 800-880-4478 **Fax:** 915-649-8901
E-mail: enroll@hputx.edu

Getting in Last Year 895 applied; 65% were accepted; 353 enrolled (60%).

Financial Matters $10,500 tuition and fees (2002–03); $4007 room and board; 70% average percent of need met; $7000 average financial aid amount received per undergraduate.

Academics Howard Payne awards associate and bachelor's degrees. Challenging opportunities include advanced placement credit, an honors program, double majors, independent study, and a senior project. Special programs include internships, summer session for credit, and study-abroad. The most frequently chosen baccalaureate fields are education, business/marketing, and communications/communication technologies. The faculty at Howard Payne has 70 full-time members, 56% with terminal degrees. The student-faculty ratio is 13:1.

Students of Howard Payne The student body is made up of 1,412 undergraduates. 48.3% are women and 51.7% are men. Students come from 13 states and territories. 97% are from Texas. 58% returned for their sophomore year.

Applying Howard Payne requires SAT I or ACT, a high school transcript, and a minimum high school GPA of 3.0, and in some cases an interview and recommendations. Application deadline: rolling admissions; 3/15 priority date for financial aid. Early admission is possible.

HOWARD UNIVERSITY

Washington, DC

Urban setting ■ Private ■ Independent ■ Coed

Web site: www.howard.edu
Contact: Interim Director of Admissions, 2400 Sixth Street, NW, Washington, DC 20059-0002
Telephone: 202-806-2700 or toll-free 800-HOWARD-U **Fax:** 202-806-4462
E-mail: admissions@howard.edu

Getting in Last Year 7,488 applied; 56% were accepted; 1,368 enrolled (33%).

Financial Matters $9515 tuition and fees (2002–03); 43% average percent of need met; $8978 average financial aid amount received per undergraduate (2001–02).

Academics Howard awards bachelor's, master's, doctoral, and first-professional degrees and post-master's and first-professional certificates. Challenging opportunities include advanced placement credit, accelerated degree programs, student-designed majors, freshman honors college, an honors program, double majors, independent study, and a senior project. Special programs include cooperative education, internships, summer session for credit, off-campus study, study-abroad, and Army and Air Force ROTC. The most frequently chosen baccalaureate fields are health professions and related sciences, communications/communication technologies, and biological/life sciences. The faculty at Howard has 1,093 full-time members, 91% with terminal degrees. The student-faculty ratio is 8:1.

Students of Howard The student body totals 10,517, of whom 6,892 are undergraduates. 65.9% are women and 34.1% are men. Students come from 50 states and territories and 95 other countries. 12% are from District of Columbia. 10% are international students. 87% returned for their sophomore year.

Applying Howard requires SAT II: Writing Test, SAT I and SAT II or ACT, and a high school transcript, and in some cases 2 recommendations. Application deadline: 2/15; 2/15 priority date for financial aid. Early and deferred admission are possible.

HSI LAI UNIVERSITY

Rosemead, CA

Private ■ Independent ■ Coed

Web site: www.hlu.edu
Contact: Ms. Grace Hsiao, Registrar and Admissions Officer, 1409 North Walnut Avenue, Rosemead, CA 91770
Telephone: 626-571-8811 ext. 120 **Fax:** 626-571-1413 ext.

HUMBOLDT STATE UNIVERSITY

Arcata, CA

Rural setting ■ Public ■ State-supported ■ Coed

Web site: www.humboldt.edu
Contact: Ms. Rebecca Kalal, Assistant Director of Admissions, 1 Harpst Street, Arcata, CA 95521-8299
Telephone: 707-826-4402 **Fax:** 707-826-6194
E-mail: hsuinfo@humboldt.edu

Getting in Last Year 4,807 applied; 73% were accepted; 846 enrolled (24%).

Financial Matters $1892 resident tuition and fees (2002–03); $7796 nonresident tuition and fees (2002–03); $6690 room and board; 82% average percent of need met; $8430 average financial aid amount received per undergraduate.

Academics Humboldt awards bachelor's and master's degrees. Challenging opportunities include advanced placement credit, student-designed majors, an honors program, double majors, independent study, and a senior project. Special programs include cooperative education, internships, summer session for credit, off-campus study, and study-abroad. The most frequently chosen baccalaureate fields are interdisciplinary studies, trade and industry, and natural resources/environmental science. The faculty at Humboldt has 303 full-time members, 81% with terminal degrees. The student-faculty ratio is 17:1.

Students of Humboldt The student body totals 7,611, of whom 6,566 are undergraduates. 54.8% are women and 45.2% are men. Students come from 50 states and territories and 24 other countries. 96% are from California. 0.5% are international students. 76% returned for their sophomore year.

Applying Humboldt requires a high school transcript and a minimum high school GPA of 2.0, and in some cases SAT I or ACT. Application deadline: rolling admissions. Deferred admission is possible.

HUNTER COLLEGE OF THE CITY UNIVERSITY OF NEW YORK

New York, NY

Urban setting ■ Public ■ State and locally supported ■ Coed

Web site: www.hunter.cuny.edu
Contact: Office of Admissions, 695 Park Avenue, New York, NY 10021-5085
Telephone: 212-772-4490

Getting in Last Year 10,550 applied; 29% were accepted; 1,491 enrolled (49%).

Financial Matters $3365 resident tuition and fees (2002–03); $6965 nonresident tuition and fees (2002–03); $1890 room only; $4809 average financial aid amount received per undergraduate.

Academics Hunter College awards bachelor's and master's degrees and post-master's certificates. Challenging opportunities include advanced placement credit, student-designed majors, freshman honors college, an honors program, double majors, independent study, and a senior project. Special programs include internships, summer session for credit, off-campus study, and study-abroad. The faculty at Hunter College has 552 full-time members, 81% with terminal degrees. The student-faculty ratio is 18:1.

Students of Hunter College The student body totals 20,607, of whom 15,494 are undergraduates. 69.8% are women and 30.2% are men. Students come from 29 states and territories. 97% are from New York. 6.5% are international students. 80% returned for their sophomore year.

Applying Hunter College requires SAT I or ACT and a high school transcript. Application deadline: 1/15; 4/1 priority date for financial aid. Early admission is possible.

HUNTINGDON COLLEGE

Montgomery, AL

Suburban setting ■ Private ■ Independent Religious ■ Coed

Web site: www.huntingdon.edu
Contact: Mrs. Laura Duncan, Director of Admissions, 1500 East Fairview Avenue, Montgomery, AL 36106
Telephone: 334-833-4496 or toll-free 800-763-0313 **Fax:** 334-833-4347
E-mail: admiss@huntingdon.edu

Getting in Last Year 579 applied; 82% were accepted; 152 enrolled (32%).

Financial Matters $13,800 tuition and fees (2002–03); $5820 room and board; 83% average percent of need met; $10,686 average financial aid amount received per undergraduate.

Academics Huntingdon awards associate and bachelor's degrees. Challenging opportunities include advanced placement credit, accelerated degree programs, student-designed majors, an honors program, double majors, independent study, and a senior project. Special programs include cooperative education, internships, summer session for credit, off-campus study, study-abroad, and Army and Air Force ROTC. The most frequently chosen baccalaureate fields are business/marketing, parks and recreation, and visual/performing arts. The faculty at Huntingdon has 41 full-time members, 85% with terminal degrees. The student-faculty ratio is 12:1.

Students of Huntingdon The student body is made up of 615 undergraduates. 64.6% are women and 35.4% are men. Students come from 21 states and territories and 12 other countries. 81% are from Alabama. 3.6% are international students. 80% returned for their sophomore year.

Applying Huntingdon requires SAT I or ACT, a high school transcript, and a minimum high school GPA of 2.25, and in some cases an essay, an interview, and 2 recommendations. The school recommends 3 recommendations. Application deadline: rolling admissions; 4/15 priority date for financial aid. Early and deferred admission are possible.

HUNTINGTON COLLEGE

Huntington, IN

Small-town setting ■ Private ■ Independent Religious ■ Coed

Web site: www.huntington.edu
Contact: Mr. Jeff Berggren, Dean of Enrollment, 2303 College Avenue, Huntington, IN 46750-1299
Telephone: 260-356-6000 ext. 4016 or toll-free 800-642-6493 **Fax:** 260-356-9448
E-mail: admissions@huntington.edu

Getting in Last Year 713 applied; 98% were accepted; 240 enrolled (34%).

Financial Matters $15,920 tuition and fees (2002–03); $5680 room and board; 96% average percent of need met; $11,823 average financial aid amount received per undergraduate.

Academics Huntington awards bachelor's and master's degrees and post-bachelor's certificates. Challenging opportunities include advanced placement credit, accelerated degree programs, double majors, independent study, and a senior project. Special programs include internships, summer session for credit, off-campus study, and study-abroad. The most frequently chosen baccalaureate fields are education, business/marketing, and physical sciences. The faculty at Huntington has 56 full-time members, 80% with terminal degrees. The student-faculty ratio is 16:1.

Students of Huntington The student body totals 1,016, of whom 868 are undergraduates. 57.7% are women and 42.3% are men. Students come from 24 states and territories and 15 other countries. 65% are from Indiana. 2.3% are international students. 75% returned for their sophomore year.

Applying Huntington requires an essay, SAT I or ACT, a high school transcript, and a minimum high school GPA of 2.3. The school recommends an interview. Application deadline: 8/1; 3/1 priority date for financial aid. Deferred admission is possible.

HURON UNIVERSITY USA IN LONDON

London United Kingdom

Urban setting ■ Private ■ Independent ■ Coed

Web site: www.huron.ac.uk
Contact: Mr. Rob Atkinson, Director of Admissions, 58 Princes Gate-Exhibition Road, London SW7 2PG United Kingdom
Telephone: 207-584-9696 **Fax:** 44-2075899406
E-mail: admissions@huron.ac.uk

Getting in Last Year 80 applied; 63% were accepted; 27 enrolled (54%).

Financial Matters $12,300 tuition and fees (2002–03); $5000 room only.

Academics Huron University USA in London awards bachelor's and master's degrees. Challenging opportunities include advanced placement credit, accelerated degree programs, student-designed majors, an honors program, double majors, independent study, and a senior project. Special programs include cooperative education, internships, summer session for credit, off-campus study, and study-abroad. The faculty at Huron University USA in London has 20 full-time members, 100% with terminal degrees. The student-faculty ratio is 8:1.

Students of Huron University USA in London The student body totals 292, of whom 200 are undergraduates. 51% are women and 49% are men. Students come from 6 states and territories and 61 other countries.

Applying Huron University USA in London requires an essay, a high school transcript, 2 recommendations, and a minimum high school GPA of 2.0, and in some cases SAT I or ACT and an interview. The school recommends a minimum high school GPA of 2.5. Application deadline: 7/1.

HUSSON COLLEGE

Bangor, ME

Suburban setting ■ Private ■ Independent ■ Coed

Web site: www.husson.edu
Contact: Mrs. Jane Goodwin, Director of Admissions, One College Circle, Bangor, ME 04401-2999
Telephone: 207-941-7100 or toll-free 800-4-HUSSON **Fax:** 207-941-7935
E-mail: admit@husson.edu

Getting in Last Year 500 applied; 99% were accepted; 215 enrolled (43%).

Financial Matters $10,370 tuition and fees (2002–03); $5510 room and board; 78% average percent of need met; $9465 average financial aid amount received per undergraduate.

Academics Husson awards associate, bachelor's, and master's degrees and post-bachelor's and post-master's certificates. Challenging opportunities include advanced placement credit, student-designed majors, double majors, independent study, and a senior project. Special programs include cooperative education, internships, summer session for credit, and Army and Navy ROTC. The most frequently chosen baccalaureate fields are business/marketing, health professions and related sciences, and computer/information sciences. The faculty at Husson has 46 full-time members, 63% with terminal degrees. The student-faculty ratio is 19:1.

Students of Husson The student body totals 1,868, of whom 1,609 are undergraduates. 63% are women and 37% are men. Students come from 28 states and territories and 7 other countries. 85% are from Maine. 4.1% are international students. 68% returned for their sophomore year.

Applying Husson requires an essay, SAT I or ACT, a high school transcript, and 1 recommendation. The school recommends an interview. Application deadline: 9/1; 4/15 priority date for financial aid. Early and deferred admission are possible.

HUSTON-TILLOTSON COLLEGE

Austin, TX

Urban setting ■ Private ■ Independent Religious ■ Coed

Web site: www.htc.edu
Contact: Ms. Bronte D. Jones, Admission and Financial Aid Services, 900 Chicon Street, Austin, TX 78702
Telephone: 512-505-3027 **Fax:** 512-505-3192
E-mail: taglenn@htc.edu

Getting in Last Year 326 applied; 93% were accepted; 135 enrolled (45%).

Financial Matters $8236 tuition and fees (2002–03); $5027 room and board; $8471 average financial aid amount received per undergraduate.

Academics Huston-Tillotson awards bachelor's degrees and post-bachelor's certificates. Challenging opportunities include advanced placement credit, accelerated degree programs, and double majors. Special programs include cooperative education, internships, summer session for credit, and Army and Navy ROTC. The faculty at Huston-Tillotson has 36 full-time members, 61% with terminal degrees. The student-faculty ratio is 12:1.

Students of Huston-Tillotson The student body is made up of 573 undergraduates. 50.1% are women and 49.9% are men. Students come from 17 states and territories and 15 other countries. 95% are from Texas. 6.3% are international students. 49% returned for their sophomore year.

Huston-Tillotson College (continued)

Applying Huston-Tillotson requires an essay, SAT I and SAT II or ACT, a high school transcript, and a minimum high school GPA of 2.0, and in some cases an interview. Application deadline: 3/1; 3/15 priority date for financial aid.

IDAHO STATE UNIVERSITY

Pocatello, ID

Small-town setting ■ Public ■ State-supported ■ Coed

Web site: www.isu.edu
Contact: Mr. Nathan Peterson, Associate Director of Recruitment, Campus Box 8270, Pocatello, ID 83209
Telephone: 208-282-3277 **Fax:** 208-282-4231
E-mail: info@isu.edu

Getting in Last Year 3,769 applied; 87% were accepted; 1,948 enrolled (60%).

Financial Matters $3136 resident tuition and fees (2002–03); $9376 nonresident tuition and fees (2002–03); $4410 room and board; 80% average percent of need met; $7066 average financial aid amount received per undergraduate.

Academics ISU awards associate, bachelor's, master's, doctoral, and first-professional degrees and post-bachelor's and post-master's certificates. Challenging opportunities include advanced placement credit, student-designed majors, an honors program, double majors, and independent study. Special programs include internships, summer session for credit, off-campus study, study-abroad, and Army ROTC. The most frequently chosen baccalaureate fields are education, business/marketing, and health professions and related sciences. The faculty at ISU has 538 full-time members, 61% with terminal degrees. The student-faculty ratio is 17:1.

Students of ISU The student body totals 13,350, of whom 11,330 are undergraduates. 54.9% are women and 45.1% are men. Students come from 46 states and territories and 62 other countries. 96% are from Idaho. 1.6% are international students. 61% returned for their sophomore year.

Applying ISU requires SAT I or ACT, a high school transcript, and a minimum high school GPA of 2.0. Application deadline: 8/1. Early and deferred admission are possible.

ILLINOIS COLLEGE

Jacksonville, IL

Small-town setting ■ Private ■ Independent Religious ■ Coed

Web site: www.ic.edu
Contact: Mr. Rick Bystry, Associate Director of Admission, 1101 West College, Jacksonville, IL 62650
Telephone: 217-245-3030 or toll-free 866-464-5265 **Fax:** 217-245-3034
E-mail: admissions@ic.edu

Getting in Last Year 989 applied; 77% were accepted; 306 enrolled (40%).

Financial Matters $11,850 tuition and fees (2002–03); $5260 room and board; 98% average percent of need met; $12,508 average financial aid amount received per undergraduate.

Academics IC awards bachelor's degrees. Challenging opportunities include advanced placement credit, accelerated degree programs, double majors, independent study, and a senior project. Special programs include internships, summer session for credit, and study-abroad. The most frequently chosen baccalaureate fields are education, business/marketing, and social sciences and history. The faculty at IC has 66 full-time members, 85% with terminal degrees. The student-faculty ratio is 14:1.

Students of IC The student body is made up of 963 undergraduates. 55.7% are women and 44.3% are men. Students come from 12 states and territories and 6 other countries. 98% are from Illinois. 0.7% are international students. 75% returned for their sophomore year.

Applying IC requires SAT I or ACT, a high school transcript, and 1 recommendation, and in some cases an essay. The school recommends an essay, an interview, and a minimum high school GPA of 2.5. Application deadline: 8/15; 3/15 priority date for financial aid.

THE ILLINOIS INSTITUTE OF ART

Chicago, IL

Urban setting ■ Private ■ Proprietary ■ Coed

Web site: www.ilia.aii.edu
Contact: Ms. Janis Anton, Director of Admissions, 350 North Orleans, Chicago, IL 60654
Telephone: 312-280-3500 ext. 132 or toll-free 800-351-3450 **Fax:** 312-280-8562
E-mail: antonj@aii.edu

Getting in Last Year 535 applied; 93% were accepted.

Financial Matters $15,189 tuition and fees (2002–03).

Academics The Illinois Institute of Art awards associate and bachelor's degrees. Challenging opportunities include advanced placement credit, accelerated degree programs, independent study, and a senior project. Special programs include cooperative education, internships, summer session for credit, and off-campus study. The faculty at The Illinois Institute of Art has 160 members. The student-faculty ratio is 20:1.

Students of The Illinois Institute of Art The student body is made up of 1,950 undergraduates. Students come from 42 states and territories and 26 other countries. 70% are from Illinois. 70% returned for their sophomore year.

Applying The Illinois Institute of Art requires an essay, a high school transcript, and an interview, and in some cases recommendations and portfolio. The school recommends SAT I or ACT and a minimum high school GPA of 2.0. Application deadline: rolling admissions. Early and deferred admission are possible.

THE ILLINOIS INSTITUTE OF ART-SCHAUMBURG

Schaumburg, IL

Private ■ Proprietary ■ Coed

Web site: www.ilis.artinstitutes.edu
Contact: Mr. Sam Hinojosa, Director of Admissions, 1000 Plaza Drive, Schaumburg, IL 60173
Telephone: 847-619-3450 ext. 4506 or toll-free 800-314-3450 **Fax:** 847-619-3064 ext. 3064

Getting in Last Year 750 applied; 75% were accepted; 270 enrolled (48%).

Financial Matters $15,364 tuition and fees (2002–03); $5500 room only; 62% average percent of need met; $9350 average financial aid amount received per undergraduate.

Academics The Illinois Institute of Art-Schaumburg awards bachelor's degrees. Challenging opportunities include advanced placement credit, accelerated degree programs, student-designed majors, double majors, independent study, and a senior project. Special programs include internships, summer session for credit, and off-campus study. The faculty at The Illinois Institute of Art-Schaumburg has 27 full-time members, 22% with terminal degrees. The student-faculty ratio is 16:1.

Students of The Illinois Institute of Art-Schaumburg The student body is made up of 1,107 undergraduates. 45% are women and 55% are men. Students come from 10 states and territories and 8 other countries. 90% are from Illinois. 1.1% are international students. 8% returned for their sophomore year.

Applying The Illinois Institute of Art-Schaumburg requires an essay, a high school transcript, and a minimum high school GPA of 2.0, and in some cases an interview and recommendations. The school recommends SAT I or ACT and SAT I and SAT II or ACT. Application deadline: rolling admissions; 5/1 priority date for financial aid.

ILLINOIS INSTITUTE OF TECHNOLOGY

Chicago, IL

Urban setting ■ Private ■ Independent ■ Coed

Web site: www.iit.edu
Contact: Mr. Brent Benner, Director of Undergraduate Admission, 10 West 33rd Street PH101, Chicago, IL 60616-3793
Telephone: 312-567-3025 or toll-free 800-448-2329 (out-of-state) **Fax:** 312-567-6939
E-mail: admission@iit.edu

Getting in Last Year 2,309 applied; 67% were accepted; 365 enrolled (23%).

Financial Matters $19,756 tuition and fees (2002–03); $5944 room and board; 85% average percent of need met; $18,232 average financial aid amount received per undergraduate (2001–02).

Academics IIT awards bachelor's, master's, doctoral, and first-professional degrees and post-bachelor's certificates. Challenging opportunities include advanced placement credit, accelerated degree programs, double majors, independent study, and a senior project. Special programs include cooperative education, internships, summer session for credit, study-abroad, and Army, Navy and Air Force ROTC. The most frequently chosen baccalaureate fields are engineering/engineering technologies, architecture, and computer/information sciences. The faculty at IIT has 339 full-time members, 91% with terminal degrees. The student-faculty ratio is 12:1.

Students of IIT The student body totals 6,199, of whom 1,905 are undergraduates. 24.1% are women and 75.9% are men. Students come from 50 states and territories and 61 other countries. 54% are from Illinois. 17.6% are international students. 88% returned for their sophomore year.

Applying IIT requires an essay, SAT I or ACT, a high school transcript, 1 recommendation, and a minimum high school GPA of 3.0, and in some cases an essay and an interview. The school recommends SAT II Subject Tests. Application deadline: rolling admissions; 4/15 priority date for financial aid. Deferred admission is possible.

ILLINOIS STATE UNIVERSITY

Normal, IL

Urban setting ■ Public ■ State-supported ■ Coed

Web site: www.ilstu.edu

Contact: Mr. Steve Adams, Director of Admissions, Campus Box 2200, Normal, IL 61790-2200
Telephone: 309-438-2181 or toll-free 800-366-2478 (in-state)
Fax: 309-438-3932
E-mail: ugradadm@ilstu.edu

Getting in Last Year 9,070 applied; 81% were accepted; 3,108 enrolled (42%).

Financial Matters $5036 resident tuition and fees (2002–03); $9227 nonresident tuition and fees (2002–03); $5062 room and board; 80% average percent of need met; $7675 average financial aid amount received per undergraduate.

Academics Illinois State awards bachelor's, master's, and doctoral degrees and post-bachelor's and post-master's certificates. Challenging opportunities include advanced placement credit, accelerated degree programs, student-designed majors, an honors program, double majors, independent study, and a senior project. Special programs include cooperative education, internships, summer session for credit, off-campus study, study-abroad, and Army ROTC. The faculty at Illinois State has 847 full-time members, 83% with terminal degrees. The student-faculty ratio is 19:1.

Students of Illinois State The student body totals 21,183, of whom 18,353 are undergraduates. 58% are women and 42% are men. Students come from 47 states and territories and 86 other countries. 98% are from Illinois. 0.8% are international students. 80% returned for their sophomore year.

Applying Illinois State requires an essay, SAT I or ACT, and a high school transcript. The school recommends ACT. Application deadline: 3/1; 3/1 priority date for financial aid.

ILLINOIS WESLEYAN UNIVERSITY

Bloomington, IL

Suburban setting ■ Private ■ Independent ■ Coed

Web site: www.iwu.edu
Contact: Mr. James R. Ruoti, Dean of Admissions, PO Box 2900, Bloomington, IL 61702-2900
Telephone: 309-556-3031 or toll-free 800-332-2498 **Fax:** 309-556-3411
E-mail: iwuadmit@titan.iwu.edu

Getting in Last Year 3,112 applied; 48% were accepted; 566 enrolled (38%).

Financial Matters $23,036 tuition and fees (2002–03); $5550 room and board; 95% average percent of need met; $16,671 average financial aid amount received per undergraduate.

Academics IWU awards bachelor's degrees. Challenging opportunities include advanced placement credit, student-designed majors, an honors program, double majors, and independent study. Special programs include cooperative education, internships, summer session for credit, off-campus study, study-abroad, and Army ROTC. The most frequently chosen baccalaureate fields are business/marketing, social sciences and history, and visual/performing arts. The faculty at IWU has 162 full-time members, 94% with terminal degrees. The student-faculty ratio is 12:1.

Students of IWU The student body is made up of 2,107 undergraduates. 57% are women and 43% are men. Students come from 32 states and territories and 22 other countries. 89% are from Illinois. 2.1% are international students. 90% returned for their sophomore year.

Applying IWU requires an essay, SAT I or ACT, a high school transcript, and a minimum high school GPA of 2.0. The school recommends an interview, 3 recommendations, and a minimum high school GPA of 3.0. Application deadline: 3/1; 3/1 for financial aid. Early and deferred admission are possible.

IMMACULATA UNIVERSITY

Immaculata, PA

Suburban setting ■ Private ■ Independent Religious ■ Women Only

Web site: www.immaculata.edu
Contact: Ms. Roberta Nolan, Executive Director of Admission, PO Box 642, Immaculata, PA 19345-0642
Telephone: 610-647-4400 ext. 3015 or toll-free 877-428-6328
Fax: 610-640-0836
E-mail: admiss@immaculata.edu

Getting in Last Year 356 applied; 89% were accepted; 111 enrolled (35%).

Financial Matters $16,400 tuition and fees (2002–03); $7600 room and board; 47% average percent of need met; $14,800 average financial aid amount received per undergraduate.

Academics Immaculata awards associate, bachelor's, master's, and doctoral degrees. Challenging opportunities include advanced placement credit, accelerated degree programs, student-designed majors, freshman honors college, an honors program, double majors, independent study, and a senior project. Special programs include internships, summer session for credit, and study-abroad. The most frequently chosen baccalaureate fields are business/marketing, health professions and related sciences, and psychology. The faculty at Immaculata has 74 full-time members, 68% with terminal degrees. The student-faculty ratio is 13:1.

Students of Immaculata The student body totals 3,564, of whom 2,768 are undergraduates. Students come from 15 states and territories and 17 other countries. 83% are from Pennsylvania. 1.3% are international students. 81% returned for their sophomore year.

Applying Immaculata requires SAT I or ACT, a high school transcript, 1 recommendation, and a minimum high school GPA of 2.0. The school recommends an essay, an interview, and a minimum high school GPA of 3.0. Application deadline: 8/15; 4/15 for financial aid. Early and deferred admission are possible.

INDIANA INSTITUTE OF TECHNOLOGY

Fort Wayne, IN

Urban setting ■ Private ■ Independent ■ Coed

Web site: www.indtech.edu
Contact: Ms. Allison Carnahan, Director of Admissions, 1600 East Washington Boulevard, Fort Wayne, IN 46803
Telephone: 260-422-5561 ext. 2206 or toll-free 800-937-2448 (in-state), 888-666-TECH (out-of-state) **Fax:** 260-422-7696
E-mail: admissions@indtech.edu

Getting in Last Year 2,589 applied; 49% were accepted; 741 enrolled (59%).

Financial Matters $14,848 tuition and fees (2002–03); $5744 room and board; $9125 average financial aid amount received per undergraduate (2000–01 estimated).

Academics Indiana Tech awards associate, bachelor's, and master's degrees. Challenging opportunities include advanced placement credit, accelerated degree programs, student-designed majors, double majors, independent study, and a senior project. Special programs include internships and summer session for credit. The most frequently chosen baccalaureate fields are business/marketing, engineering/engineering technologies, and computer/information sciences. The faculty at Indiana Tech has 39 full-time members, 38% with terminal degrees. The student-faculty ratio is 22:1.

Students of Indiana Tech The student body totals 3,019, of whom 2,680 are undergraduates. 55.1% are women and 44.9% are men. Students come from 34 states and territories and 6 other countries. 84% are from Indiana. 1.2% are international students.

Applying Indiana Tech requires SAT I or ACT and a high school transcript. The school recommends an interview, 2 references, and a minimum high school GPA of 3.0. Application deadline: 3/1 priority date for financial aid. Early and deferred admission are possible.

INDIANA STATE UNIVERSITY

Terre Haute, IN

Suburban setting ■ Public ■ State-supported ■ Coed

Web site: web.indstate.edu
Contact: Mr. Ronald Brown, Director of Admissions, Tirey Hall 134, 217 North 7th Street, Terre Haute, IN 47809
Telephone: 812-237-2121 or toll-free 800-742-0891 **Fax:** 812-237-8023
E-mail: admisu@amber.indstate.edu

Getting in Last Year 5,542 applied; 83% were accepted; 2,140 enrolled (47%).

Financial Matters $4216 resident tuition and fees (2002–03); $10,376 nonresident tuition and fees (2002–03); $4998 room and board; 77% average percent of need met; $6532 average financial aid amount received per undergraduate.

Academics Indiana State awards associate, bachelor's, master's, doctoral, and first-professional degrees and post-bachelor's certificates. Challenging opportunities include advanced placement credit, accelerated degree programs, an honors program, double majors, independent study, and a senior project. Special programs include cooperative education, internships, summer session for credit, off-campus study, study-abroad, and Army and Air Force ROTC. The most frequently chosen baccalaureate fields are education, business/marketing, and social sciences and history. The faculty at Indiana State has 536 full-time members. The student-faculty ratio is 18:1.

Students of Indiana State The student body totals 11,714, of whom 9,997 are undergraduates. 51.9% are women and 48.1% are men. Students come from 46 states and territories and 45 other countries. 92% are from Indiana. 1.9% are international students. 71% returned for their sophomore year.

Applying Indiana State requires SAT I or ACT, a high school transcript, and a minimum high school GPA of 2.0, and in some cases an interview and recommendations. The school recommends an essay. Application deadline: 8/15; 3/1 priority date for financial aid. Deferred admission is possible.

INDIANA UNIVERSITY BLOOMINGTON

Bloomington, IN

Small-town setting ■ Public ■ State-supported ■ Coed

Web site: www.indiana.edu
Contact: Mr. Don Hossler, Vice Chancellor for Enrollment Services, 300 North Jordan Avenue, Bloomington, IN 47405-1106

Indiana University Bloomington (continued)

Telephone: 812-855-0661 or toll-free 812-855-0661 (in-state)
Fax: 812-855-5102
E-mail: iuadmit@indiana.edu

Getting in Last Year 21,264 applied; 81% were accepted; 7,080 enrolled (41%).

Financial Matters $5315 resident tuition and fees (2002–03); $15,926 nonresident tuition and fees (2002–03); $5676 room and board; 64% average percent of need met; $7080 average financial aid amount received per undergraduate.

Academics IU awards associate, bachelor's, master's, doctoral, and first-professional degrees and post-bachelor's certificates. Challenging opportunities include advanced placement credit, accelerated degree programs, student-designed majors, freshman honors college, an honors program, double majors, independent study, and a senior project. Special programs include cooperative education, internships, summer session for credit, off-campus study, study-abroad, and Army and Air Force ROTC. The most frequently chosen baccalaureate fields are business/marketing, education, and protective services/public administration. The faculty at IU has 1,690 full-time members, 77% with terminal degrees. The student-faculty ratio is 20:1.

Students of IU The student body totals 38,903, of whom 30,752 are undergraduates. 52.8% are women and 47.2% are men. Students come from 56 states and territories and 135 other countries. 72% are from Indiana. 4.1% are international students. 87% returned for their sophomore year.

Applying IU requires SAT I or ACT and a high school transcript. The school recommends an interview. Application deadline: 2/1; 3/1 priority date for financial aid. Deferred admission is possible.

INDIANA UNIVERSITY EAST

Richmond, IN

Small-town setting ■ Public ■ State-supported ■ Coed

Web site: www.indiana.edu
Contact: Ms. Susanna Tanner, Admissions Counselor, 2325 Chester Boulevard, WZ 116, Richmond, IN 47374-1289
Telephone: 765-973-8415 or toll-free 800-959-EAST **Fax:** 765-973-8288
E-mail: eaadmit@indiana.edu

Getting in Last Year 531 applied; 89% were accepted; 471 enrolled (100%).

Financial Matters $3789 resident tuition and fees (2002–03); $9511 nonresident tuition and fees (2002–03); 50% average percent of need met; $4786 average financial aid amount received per undergraduate.

Academics IU East awards associate and bachelor's degrees and post-bachelor's certificates. Challenging opportunities include advanced placement credit, double majors, independent study, and a senior project. Special programs include cooperative education, internships, summer session for credit, and off-campus study. The most frequently chosen baccalaureate fields are education, health professions and related sciences, and liberal arts/general studies. The faculty at IU East has 69 full-time members, 51% with terminal degrees. The student-faculty ratio is 14:1.

Students of IU East The student body totals 2,481, of whom 2,416 are undergraduates. 70.2% are women and 29.8% are men. Students come from 7 states and territories. 92% are from Indiana. 0.1% are international students. 56% returned for their sophomore year.

Applying IU East requires a high school transcript. The school recommends SAT I or ACT and a minimum high school GPA of 2.0. Application deadline: rolling admissions; 3/1 priority date for financial aid. Early and deferred admission are possible.

INDIANA UNIVERSITY KOKOMO

Kokomo, IN

Small-town setting ■ Public ■ State-supported ■ Coed

Web site: www.indiana.edu
Contact: Ms. Patty Young, Admissions Director, PO Box 9003, Kelley Student Center 230A, Kokomo, IN 46904-9003
Telephone: 765-455-9217 or toll-free 888-875-4485 **Fax:** 765-455-9537
E-mail: iuadmis@iuk.edu

Getting in Last Year 680 applied; 87% were accepted; 476 enrolled (81%).

Financial Matters $3824 resident tuition and fees (2002–03); $9546 nonresident tuition and fees (2002–03); 68% average percent of need met; $5128 average financial aid amount received per undergraduate.

Academics IUK awards associate, bachelor's, and master's degrees and post-bachelor's certificates. Challenging opportunities include advanced placement credit, freshman honors college, an honors program, and independent study. Special programs include internships, summer session for credit, study-abroad, and Army ROTC. The most frequently chosen baccalaureate fields are education, liberal arts/general studies, and business/marketing. The faculty at IUK has 74 full-time members, 65% with terminal degrees. The student-faculty ratio is 15:1.

Students of IUK The student body totals 2,772, of whom 2,557 are undergraduates. 70.6% are women and 29.4% are men. Students come from 3 states and territories. 99% are from Indiana. 0.3% are international students. 53% returned for their sophomore year.

Applying IUK requires SAT I or ACT and a high school transcript. Application deadline: 8/3; 3/1 priority date for financial aid. Early and deferred admission are possible.

INDIANA UNIVERSITY NORTHWEST

Gary, IN

Urban setting ■ Public ■ State-supported ■ Coed

Web site: www.indiana.edu
Contact: Dr. Linda B. Templeton, Director of Admissions, Hawthorne 100, 3400 Broadway, Gary, IN 46408-1197
Telephone: 219-980-6767 or toll-free 800-968-7486 **Fax:** 219-981-4219
E-mail: pkeshei@iun.edu

Getting in Last Year 1,392 applied; 72% were accepted; 813 enrolled (81%).

Financial Matters $3895 resident tuition and fees (2002–03); $9617 nonresident tuition and fees (2002–03); 66% average percent of need met; $5877 average financial aid amount received per undergraduate.

Academics IUN awards associate, bachelor's, and master's degrees and post-bachelor's certificates. Challenging opportunities include advanced placement credit, accelerated degree programs, student-designed majors, an honors program, double majors, independent study, and a senior project. Special programs include cooperative education, internships, summer session for credit, off-campus study, study-abroad, and Army ROTC. The most frequently chosen baccalaureate fields are business/marketing, liberal arts/general studies, and health professions and related sciences. The faculty at IUN has 168 full-time members, 48% with terminal degrees. The student-faculty ratio is 14:1.

Students of IUN The student body totals 4,893, of whom 4,322 are undergraduates. 70.4% are women and 29.6% are men. Students come from 6 states and territories. 99% are from Indiana. 0.1% are international students. 60% returned for their sophomore year.

Applying IUN requires SAT I or ACT, a high school transcript, and a minimum high school GPA of 2.0. Application deadline: 8/1. Early and deferred admission are possible.

INDIANA UNIVERSITY OF PENNSYLVANIA

Indiana, PA

Small-town setting ■ Public ■ State-supported ■ Coed

Web site: www.iup.edu
Contact: Dr. Harold Goldsmith, Interim Dean of Admissions, 1011 South Drive, Sutton Hall 117, Indiana, PA 15705
Telephone: 724-357-2230 or toll-free 800-442-6830
E-mail: admissions-inquiry@iup.edu

Getting in Last Year 8,005 applied; 54% were accepted; 2,732 enrolled (64%).

Financial Matters $5541 resident tuition and fees (2002–03); $12,109 nonresident tuition and fees (2002–03); $4524 room and board; 87% average percent of need met; $6669 average financial aid amount received per undergraduate (2001–02).

Academics IUP awards associate, bachelor's, master's, and doctoral degrees and post-bachelor's and post-master's certificates. Challenging opportunities include advanced placement credit, accelerated degree programs, freshman honors college, an honors program, double majors, independent study, and a senior project. Special programs include cooperative education, internships, summer session for credit, off-campus study, study-abroad, and Army ROTC. The most frequently chosen baccalaureate fields are education, business/marketing, and social sciences and history. The faculty at IUP has 636 full-time members, 93% with terminal degrees. The student-faculty ratio is 17:1.

Students of IUP The student body totals 13,671, of whom 11,834 are undergraduates. 55.9% are women and 44.1% are men. Students come from 39 states and territories and 56 other countries. 97% are from Pennsylvania. 2.2% are international students. 74% returned for their sophomore year.

Applying IUP requires SAT I or ACT and a high school transcript. The school recommends recommendations. Application deadline: rolling admissions; 4/15 for financial aid. Early and deferred admission are possible.

INDIANA UNIVERSITY–PURDUE UNIVERSITY FORT WAYNE

Fort Wayne, IN

Urban setting ■ Public ■ State-supported ■ Coed

Web site: www.ipfw.edu
Contact: Ms. Carol Isaacs, Director of Admissions, Admissions Office, 2101 East Coliseum Boulevard, Fort Wayne, IN 46805-1499
Telephone: 260-481-6812 or toll-free 800-324-4739 (in-state)
Fax: 260-481-6880
E-mail: ipfwadms@ipfw.edu

Getting in Last Year 2,471 applied; 97% were accepted; 1,732 enrolled (72%).

Financial Matters $3892 resident tuition and fees (2002–03); $8520 nonresident tuition and fees (2002–03); 72% average percent of need met; $4601 average financial aid amount received per undergraduate (2001–02).

Academics IPFW awards associate, bachelor's, and master's degrees and post-bachelor's certificates. Challenging opportunities include advanced placement credit, accelerated degree programs, student-designed majors, an honors program, double majors, independent study, and a senior project. Special programs include cooperative education, internships, summer session for credit, off-campus study, and study-abroad. The most frequently chosen baccalaureate fields are business/marketing, education, and liberal arts/general studies. The faculty at IPFW has 329 full-time members, 83% with terminal degrees. The student-faculty ratio is 19:1.

Students of IPFW The student body totals 11,757, of whom 10,880 are undergraduates. 57.8% are women and 42.2% are men. Students come from 39 states and territories and 66 other countries. 95% are from Indiana. 1.5% are international students. 61% returned for their sophomore year.

Applying IPFW requires SAT I or ACT and a high school transcript. The school recommends rank in upper 50% of high school class. Application deadline: 8/1; 3/10 priority date for financial aid. Early and deferred admission are possible.

INDIANA UNIVERSITY–PURDUE UNIVERSITY INDIANAPOLIS

Indianapolis, IN

Urban setting ■ Public ■ State-supported ■ Coed

Web site: www.indiana.edu

Contact: Michael Donahue, Director of Admissions, 425 N. University Boulevard, Cavanaugh Hall Room 129, Indianapolis, IN 46202-5143

Telephone: 317-274-4591 **Fax:** 317-278-1862

E-mail: apply@iupui.edu

Getting in Last Year 5,744 applied; 75% were accepted; 2,787 enrolled (65%).

Financial Matters $4715 resident tuition and fees (2002–03); $13,545 nonresident tuition and fees (2002–03); $2080 room only; 52% average percent of need met; $6139 average financial aid amount received per undergraduate.

Academics IUPUI awards associate, bachelor's, master's, doctoral, and first-professional degrees and post-bachelor's certificates. Challenging opportunities include advanced placement credit, an honors program, double majors, independent study, and a senior project. Special programs include cooperative education, internships, summer session for credit, off-campus study, study-abroad, and Army, Navy and Air Force ROTC. The most frequently chosen baccalaureate fields are health professions and related sciences, biological/life sciences, and liberal arts/general studies. The faculty at IUPUI has 1,909 full-time members, 84% with terminal degrees. The student-faculty ratio is 18:1.

Students of IUPUI The student body totals 29,025, of whom 21,060 are undergraduates. 59.5% are women and 40.5% are men. Students come from 40 states and territories. 98% are from Indiana. 1.7% are international students. 62% returned for their sophomore year.

Applying IUPUI requires SAT I or ACT and a high school transcript, and in some cases an interview. The school recommends SAT I and portfolio for art program. Application deadline: rolling admissions. Early and deferred admission are possible.

INDIANA UNIVERSITY SOUTH BEND

South Bend, IN

Suburban setting ■ Public ■ State-supported ■ Coed

Web site: www.iusb.edu

Contact: Jeff Johnston, Director of Recruitment/Admissions, 1700 Mishawaka Avenue, Administration Building, Room 169, PO Box 7111, South Bend, IN 46634-7111

Telephone: 219-237-4480 or toll-free 877-GO-2-IUSB **Fax:** 219-237-4834

E-mail: admissions@iusb.edu

Getting in Last Year 1,475 applied; 80% were accepted; 932 enrolled (79%).

Financial Matters $3930 resident tuition and fees (2002–03); $10,269 nonresident tuition and fees (2002–03); 59% average percent of need met; $4854 average financial aid amount received per undergraduate.

Academics IUSB awards associate, bachelor's, and master's degrees and post-bachelor's certificates. Challenging opportunities include accelerated degree programs, an honors program, and double majors. Special programs include internships, summer session for credit, off-campus study, study-abroad, and Army, Navy and Air Force ROTC. The most frequently chosen baccalaureate fields are education, business/marketing, and liberal arts/general studies. The faculty at IUSB has 260 full-time members, 62% with terminal degrees. The student-faculty ratio is 14:1.

Students of IUSB The student body totals 7,457, of whom 6,177 are undergraduates. 63.6% are women and 36.4% are men. Students come from 13 states and territories. 97% are from Indiana. 2.7% are international students. 64% returned for their sophomore year.

Applying IUSB requires SAT I or ACT, a high school transcript, and a minimum high school GPA of 2.0. Application deadline: 7/1; 3/1 priority date for financial aid. Deferred admission is possible.

INDIANA UNIVERSITY SOUTHEAST

New Albany, IN

Suburban setting ■ Public ■ State-supported ■ Coed

Web site: www.indiana.edu

Contact: Mr. David B. Campbell, Director of Admissions, University Center Building, Room 100, 4201 Grant Line Road, New Albany, IN 47150

Telephone: 812-941-2212 or toll-free 800-852-8835 (in-state)
Fax: 812-941-2595

E-mail: admissions@ius.edu

Getting in Last Year 1,256 applied; 89% were accepted; 903 enrolled (81%).

Financial Matters $3865 resident tuition and fees (2002–03); $9587 nonresident tuition and fees (2002–03); 62% average percent of need met; $5053 average financial aid amount received per undergraduate.

Academics IU Southeast awards associate, bachelor's, and master's degrees and post-bachelor's certificates. Challenging opportunities include advanced placement credit, accelerated degree programs, double majors, and independent study. Special programs include internships, summer session for credit, off-campus study, study-abroad, and Army and Air Force ROTC. The most frequently chosen baccalaureate fields are education, business/marketing, and law/legal studies. The faculty at IU Southeast has 182 full-time members, 72% with terminal degrees. The student-faculty ratio is 17:1.

Students of IU Southeast The student body totals 6,716, of whom 5,860 are undergraduates. 62.8% are women and 37.2% are men. Students come from 3 states and territories. 83% are from Indiana. 0.4% are international students. 64% returned for their sophomore year.

Applying IU Southeast requires SAT I or ACT and a high school transcript, and in some cases an interview. Application deadline: 7/15; 3/1 priority date for financial aid. Early and deferred admission are possible.

INDIANA WESLEYAN UNIVERSITY

Marion, IN

Small-town setting ■ Private ■ Independent Religious ■ Coed

Web site: www.indwes.edu

Contact: Ms. Gaytha Holloway, Director of Admissions, 4201 South Washington Street, Marion, IN 46953

Telephone: 765-677-2138 or toll-free 800-332-6901 **Fax:** 765-677-2333

E-mail: admissions@indwes.edu

Getting in Last Year 2,577 applied; 90% were accepted; 1,036 enrolled (45%).

Financial Matters $13,496 tuition and fees (2002–03); $5158 room and board.

Academics IWU awards associate, bachelor's, and master's degrees (also offers adult program with significant enrollment not reflected in profile). Challenging opportunities include advanced placement credit, accelerated degree programs, student-designed majors, freshman honors college, an honors program, double majors, independent study, and a senior project. Special programs include internships, summer session for credit, off-campus study, and study-abroad. The most frequently chosen baccalaureate fields are business/marketing, health professions and related sciences, and education. The faculty at IWU has 106 full-time members, 51% with terminal degrees. The student-faculty ratio is 17:1.

Students of IWU The student body totals 8,765, of whom 6,204 are undergraduates. 63.3% are women and 36.7% are men. Students come from 42 states and territories and 17 other countries. 80% are from Indiana. 0.8% are international students. 89% returned for their sophomore year.

Applying IWU requires an essay, SAT I or ACT, a high school transcript, 1 recommendation, and a minimum high school GPA of 2.0, and in some cases an interview. Application deadline: rolling admissions; 3/1 priority date for financial aid. Deferred admission is possible.

INSTITUTE OF PUBLIC ADMINISTRATION

Dublin Ireland

Private ■ Proprietary ■ Coed

Web site: www.ipa.ie

Contact: Dr. Denis O'Brien, Registrar, 57-61 Lansdowne Road, Dublin 4 Ireland

Telephone: 353-01240-3600 **Fax:** 353-01269-8644

Getting in Last Year 296 applied; 100% were accepted; 296 enrolled (100%).

Financial Matters $700 tuition and fees (2002–03).

Academics Institute of Public Administration awards bachelor's, master's, and doctoral degrees and post-bachelor's certificates. The most frequently chosen baccalaureate fields are protective services/public administration, business/marketing, and health professions and related sciences. The faculty at Institute of Public Administration has 6 full-time members, 50% with terminal degrees. The student-faculty ratio is 22:1.

Institute of Public Administration (continued)

Students of Institute of Public Administration The student body totals 1,550, of whom 1,320 are undergraduates.

Applying Application deadline: 9/27.

INSTITUTO TECNOLÓGICO Y DE ESTUDIOS SUPERIORES DE MONTERREY, CAMPUS MONTERREY

Monterrey Mexico

Urban setting ■ Private ■ Independent ■ Coed

Web site: www.sistema.itesm.mx

Contact: Lic. Carlos Ordoñez, International Student Advisor, Avenida Eugenio Garza Sada 2501 Sur Colonia Tecnnologico, Sucursal de Correos J, Monterrey Mexico

Getting in Last Year 2,636 applied; 69% were accepted.

Academics ITESM awards bachelor's, master's, and doctoral degrees. Challenging opportunities include an honors program and independent study. Special programs include cooperative education, internships, summer session for credit, off-campus study, and study-abroad. The most frequently chosen baccalaureate fields are business/marketing, engineering/engineering technologies, and trade and industry. The faculty at ITESM has 519 full-time members, 100% with terminal degrees.

Students of ITESM The student body totals 18,985, of whom 16,406 are undergraduates.

Applying ITESM requires SAT I and a high school transcript. The school recommends an essay. Application deadline: 3/21. Deferred admission is possible.

INTER AMERICAN UNIVERSITY OF PUERTO RICO, AGUADILLA CAMPUS

Aguadilla, PR

Small-town setting ■ Private ■ Independent ■ Coed

Web site: aguadilla.inter.edu

Contact: Ms. Doris Pérez, Director of Admissions, PO Box 20,000, Road 459 Interstate 463, Aguadilla, PR 00605

Telephone: 787-891-0925 ext. 2101 **Fax:** 787-882-3020

Getting in Last Year 1,394 applied; 69% were accepted; 906 enrolled (94%).

Financial Matters $3364 tuition and fees (2002–03).

Academics Inter American University of Puerto Rico, Aguadilla Campus awards associate and bachelor's degrees. Challenging opportunities include advanced placement credit, an honors program, double majors, independent study, and a senior project. Special programs include cooperative education, internships, summer session for credit, and Army ROTC. The most frequently chosen baccalaureate fields are business/marketing, education, and protective services/ public administration. The faculty at Inter American University of Puerto Rico, Aguadilla Campus has 74 full-time members, 22% with terminal degrees. The student-faculty ratio is 19:1.

Students of Inter American University of Puerto Rico, Aguadilla Campus The student body is made up of 4,123 undergraduates. 58.8% are women and 41.2% are men. Students come from 1 state or territory.

Applying Inter American University of Puerto Rico, Aguadilla Campus requires PAA, a high school transcript, and a minimum high school GPA of 2.00, and in some cases SAT I. Application deadline: rolling admissions. Early admission is possible.

INTER AMERICAN UNIVERSITY OF PUERTO RICO, BARRANQUITAS CAMPUS

Barranquitas, PR

Small-town setting ■ Private ■ Independent ■ Coed

Contact: Ms. Carmen L. Ortiz, Admission Director, Box 517, Barranquitas, PR 00794

Telephone: 787-857-3600 ext. 2011 or toll-free 787-857-3600 ext. 2011 (in-state) **Fax:** 787-857-2244

E-mail: clortiz@inter.edu

Getting in Last Year 550 applied; 100% were accepted.

Financial Matters $3720 tuition and fees (2002–03).

Academics IAU, Barranquitas awards associate and bachelor's degrees and post-bachelor's certificates. Challenging opportunities include advanced placement credit and a senior project. Special programs include summer session for credit, study-abroad, and Army ROTC. The most frequently chosen baccalaureate fields are education, business/marketing, and computer/information sciences. The faculty at IAU, Barranquitas has 35 full-time members.

Students of IAU, Barranquitas The student body is made up of 2,060 undergraduates. 65% are women and 35% are men. Students come from 1 state or territory. 76% returned for their sophomore year.

Applying IAU, Barranquitas requires SAT I or ACT, a high school transcript, and an interview. Application deadline: 5/15; 4/30 priority date for financial aid. Deferred admission is possible.

INTER AMERICAN UNIVERSITY OF PUERTO RICO, GUAYAMA CAMPUS

Guayama, PR

Small-town setting ■ Private ■ Independent ■ Coed

Web site: www.inter.edu

Contact: Mrs. Laura E. Ferrer, Director of Admissions, Interamerican University of Puerto Rico, Guayoma Campus, Call Box 10004 Attention: Laura Ferrer, Guayama, PR 00785

Telephone: 787-864-2222 ext. 220 or toll-free 787-864-2222 ext. 2243 (in-state) **Fax:** 787-866-4986

Getting in Last Year 771 enrolled (100%).

Financial Matters $1622 tuition and fees (2002–03); 13% average percent of need met; $2397 average financial aid amount received per undergraduate (2001–02 estimated).

Academics Inter American University of Puerto Rico, Guayama Campus awards associate and bachelor's degrees. Challenging opportunities include an honors program and independent study. Special programs include summer session for credit, off-campus study, and Army ROTC. The faculty at Inter American University of Puerto Rico, Guayama Campus has 44 full-time members, 16% with terminal degrees.

Students of Inter American University of Puerto Rico, Guayama Campus The student body is made up of 1,246 undergraduates.

Applying Inter American University of Puerto Rico, Guayama Campus requires SAT I, PAA, a high school transcript, and a minimum high school GPA of 2.00, and in some cases an essay and an interview. Application deadline: 8/1.

INTER AMERICAN UNIVERSITY OF PUERTO RICO, SAN GERMÁN CAMPUS

San Germán, PR

Small-town setting ■ Private ■ Independent ■ Coed

Web site: www.sg.inter.edu

Contact: Mrs. Mildred Camacho, Director of Admissions, PO Box 5100, San Germán, PR 00683-5008

Telephone: 787-264-1912 ext. 7283 **Fax:** 787-892-6350

E-mail: milcama@sg.inter.edu

Getting in Last Year 4,445 applied; 44% were accepted.

Financial Matters $4166 tuition and fees (2002–03); $2400 room and board; 36% average percent of need met; $1592 average financial aid amount received per undergraduate.

Academics Inter American University awards associate, bachelor's, master's, and doctoral degrees and post-bachelor's certificates. Challenging opportunities include advanced placement credit, accelerated degree programs, an honors program, double majors, independent study, and a senior project. Special programs include cooperative education, internships, summer session for credit, off-campus study, and Army, Navy and Air Force ROTC. The most frequently chosen baccalaureate fields are business/marketing, biological/life sciences, and education. The faculty at Inter American University has 128 full-time members, 44% with terminal degrees. The student-faculty ratio is 25:1.

Students of Inter American University The student body totals 5,972, of whom 5,012 are undergraduates. Students come from 15 states and territories. 99% are from Puerto Rico.

Applying Inter American University requires CEEB, a high school transcript, and medical history, and in some cases an interview and 1 recommendation. The school recommends an essay and a minimum high school GPA of 2.0. Application deadline: 5/13; 4/26 priority date for financial aid. Early admission is possible.

INTERNATIONAL ACADEMY OF DESIGN & TECHNOLOGY

Tampa, FL

Urban setting ■ Private ■ Proprietary ■ Coed

Web site: www.academy.edu

Contact: Mr. Brandon Barnhill, Vice President of Admissions and Marketing, 5225 Memorial Highway, Tampa, FL 33634-7350

Telephone: 813-880-8029 or toll-free 800-ACADEMY **Fax:** 813-881-0008

E-mail: leads@academy.edu

Getting in Last Year 667 applied; 62% were accepted.

Financial Matters $14,160 tuition and fees (2002–03); 48% average percent of need met.

Academics The Academy awards associate and bachelor's degrees. Challenging opportunities include advanced placement credit and accelerated degree programs. Special programs include internships, summer session for credit, and study-abroad. The most frequently chosen baccalaureate fields are visual/performing arts and computer/information sciences. The faculty at The Academy has 20 full-time members, 25% with terminal degrees. The student-faculty ratio is 14:1.

Students of The Academy The student body is made up of 2,043 undergraduates. Students come from 27 states and territories and 9 other countries. 78% are from Florida. 3% are international students. 62% returned for their sophomore year.

Applying The Academy requires an essay and an interview. The school recommends a minimum high school GPA of 2.0. Application deadline: rolling admissions. Early and deferred admission are possible.

INTERNATIONAL ACADEMY OF DESIGN & TECHNOLOGY

Chicago, IL

Urban setting ■ Private ■ Proprietary ■ Coed

Web site: www.iadtchicago.com
Contact: Ms. Dorothy Foley, Vice President of Student Management, One North State Street, Suite 400, Chicago, IL 60602
Telephone: 312-980-9200 or toll-free 877-ACADEMY (out-of-state)
Fax: 312-541-3929
E-mail: academy@iadtchicago.com

Getting in Last Year 963 applied; 58% were accepted; 559 enrolled (100%).

Financial Matters $13,038 tuition and fees (2002–03).

Academics International Academy awards associate and bachelor's degrees. Challenging opportunities include advanced placement credit, independent study, and a senior project. Special programs include internships, summer session for credit, and study-abroad. The most frequently chosen baccalaureate fields are visual/performing arts and business/marketing. The faculty at International Academy has 17 full-time members. The student-faculty ratio is 15:1.

Students of International Academy The student body is made up of 2,309 undergraduates. 65.1% are women and 34.9% are men. Students come from 28 states and territories and 10 other countries. 92% are from Illinois. 1% are international students. 70% returned for their sophomore year.

Applying International Academy requires a high school transcript and an interview, and in some cases GED. The school recommends an essay, SAT II: Writing Test, SAT I and SAT II or ACT, and a minimum high school GPA of 2.0. Application deadline: rolling admissions. Early admission is possible.

INTERNATIONAL COLLEGE

Naples, FL

Suburban setting ■ Private ■ Independent ■ Coed

Web site: www.internationalcollege.edu
Contact: Ms. Rita Lampus, Director of Admissions, 2655 Northbrooke Drive, Naples, FL 34119
Telephone: 239-513-1122 ext. 104 or toll-free 800-466-8017
E-mail: admit@internationalcollege.edu

Getting in Last Year 115 enrolled.

Financial Matters $8050 tuition and fees (2002–03); 49% average percent of need met; $7600 average financial aid amount received per undergraduate.

Academics International College awards associate, bachelor's, and master's degrees and post-bachelor's certificates. Challenging opportunities include advanced placement credit, accelerated degree programs, and double majors. Special programs include cooperative education, internships, and summer session for credit. The most frequently chosen baccalaureate fields are business/marketing, protective services/public administration, and law/legal studies. The faculty at International College has 48 full-time members, 67% with terminal degrees. The student-faculty ratio is 15:1.

Students of International College The student body totals 1,349, of whom 1,207 are undergraduates. 62.1% are women and 37.9% are men. 2% are international students.

Applying International College requires an essay, CPAt, a high school transcript, and an interview. The school recommends SAT I and ACT. Application deadline: rolling admissions. Deferred admission is possible.

INTERNATIONAL COLLEGE AND GRADUATE SCHOOL

Honolulu, HI

Private ■ Independent Religious ■ Coed

Web site: www.icgshawaii.org
Contact: Mr. Jon Rawlings, Director of Admissions, 20 Dowsett Avenue, Honolulu, HI 96817
Telephone: 808-595-4247 ext. 108 **Fax:** 808-595-4779
E-mail: icgs@hawaii.rr.com

Getting in Last Year 10 enrolled.

Financial Matters $5750 tuition and fees (2002–03); 97% average percent of need met.

Academics International College and Graduate School awards bachelor's, master's, and first-professional degrees. Challenging opportunities include advanced placement credit and independent study. Special programs include internships, summer session for credit, and study-abroad. The faculty at International College and Graduate School has 3 full-time members. The student-faculty ratio is 12:1.

Students of International College and Graduate School The student body totals 74, of whom 33 are undergraduates. 36.4% are women and 63.6% are men. Students come from 1 state or territory and 3 other countries.

Applying Application deadline: 6/1 for financial aid. Deferred admission is possible.

INTERNATIONAL COLLEGE OF THE CAYMAN ISLANDS

Newlands Cayman Islands

Rural setting ■ Private ■ Independent ■ Coed

Web site: cayman.com.ky/pub/icci
Contact: Ms. Dianne Levy, Admissions Representative, PO Box 136, Savannah Post Office, Newlands Cayman Islands
Telephone: 345-947-1100 ext. 301
E-mail: icci@candw.ky

Getting in Last Year 116 applied; 85% were accepted; 46 enrolled (46%).

Academics ICCI awards associate, bachelor's, and master's degrees. Challenging opportunities include advanced placement credit, accelerated degree programs, student-designed majors, double majors, and independent study. Special programs include internships, summer session for credit, off-campus study, and study-abroad. The most frequently chosen baccalaureate fields are business/marketing, liberal arts/general studies, and protective services/public administration. The faculty at ICCI has 6 full-time members, 50% with terminal degrees. The student-faculty ratio is 15:1.

Students of ICCI The student body totals 350, of whom 200 are undergraduates. 77.5% are women and 22.5% are men.

Applying ICCI requires an essay, SAT I or ACT, a high school transcript, 2 recommendations, rank in upper 50% of high school class, and a minimum high school GPA of 2.0, and in some cases an interview. Application deadline: 7/1, 5/1 for nonresidents; 8/15 for financial aid. Deferred admission is possible.

INTERNATIONAL TECHNOLOGICAL UNIVERSITY

Santa Clara, CA

Private ■ Independent ■ Coed

Web site: www.itu.edu
Contact: Chun Mou Peng, Director of Operations, 1650 Warbunton Avenue, Santa Clara, CA 95050
Telephone: 408-556-9027
E-mail: chunmou@itu.edu

Financial Matters $8750 tuition and fees (2002–03).

Academics International Technological University awards bachelor's and master's degrees and post-bachelor's certificates. Internships is a special program. The faculty at International Technological University has 5 full-time members, 60% with terminal degrees. The student-faculty ratio is 6:1.

Students of International Technological University The student body totals 160, of whom 40 are undergraduates. 55% are women and 45% are men. Students come from 4 states and territories. 15% are international students.

Applying Application deadline: 9/1.

INTERNATIONAL UNIVERSITY IN GENEVA

Geneva Switzerland

Private ■ Coed

Web site: www.iun.ch
Contact: Mrs. Martha Negaard-Muller, Admissions Offices, ICC 20, Route de Pre-Bois, Geneva Switzerland
Telephone: 41-227107110 **Fax:** 41-22710-7111
E-mail: info@iun.ch

Getting in Last Year 110 applied; 66% were accepted.

Financial Matters $22,200 tuition and fees (2002–03).

Academics International University in Geneva awards bachelor's and master's degrees. Challenging opportunities include advanced placement credit, accelerated degree programs, an honors program, double majors, and a senior project. Special programs include summer session for credit and study-abroad. The faculty at International University in Geneva has 10 full-time members, 60% with terminal degrees. The student-faculty ratio is 12:1.

Students of International University in Geneva The student body totals 310, of whom 185 are undergraduates. Students come from 8 states and territories and 43 other countries. 71.2% are international students.

Applying International University in Geneva requires an essay, a high school transcript, 2 recommendations, and a minimum high school GPA of 2.3, and in some cases TOEFL. Application deadline: rolling admissions. Deferred admission is possible.

IONA COLLEGE

New Rochelle, NY

Suburban setting ■ Private ■ Independent Religious ■ Coed

Web site: www.iona.edu

Contact: Mr. Thomas Weede, Director of Undergraduate Admissions, Admissions, 715 North Avenue, New Rochelle, NY 10801

Telephone: 914-633-2502 or toll-free 800-231-IONA (in-state), 914-633-2502 (out-of-state) **Fax:** 914-637-2778

E-mail: icad@iona.edu

Getting in Last Year 3,318 applied; 69% were accepted; 798 enrolled (35%).

Financial Matters $17,866 tuition and fees (2002–03); $9700 room and board; 28% average percent of need met; $12,416 average financial aid amount received per undergraduate.

Academics Iona awards bachelor's and master's degrees and post-bachelor's and post-master's certificates. Challenging opportunities include advanced placement credit, accelerated degree programs, an honors program, double majors, and a senior project. Special programs include internships, summer session for credit, off-campus study, study-abroad, and Army ROTC. The most frequently chosen baccalaureate fields are business/marketing, communications/communication technologies, and health professions and related sciences. The faculty at Iona has 173 full-time members, 83% with terminal degrees. The student-faculty ratio is 15:1.

Students of Iona The student body totals 4,449, of whom 3,464 are undergraduates. 51.6% are women and 48.4% are men. Students come from 36 states and territories and 7 other countries. 84% are from New York. 0.4% are international students. 76% returned for their sophomore year.

Applying Iona requires an essay, SAT I or ACT, and a high school transcript. The school recommends SAT II Subject Tests, SAT II: Writing Test, an interview, recommendations, and a minimum high school GPA of 2.5. Application deadline: 3/15. Early and deferred admission are possible.

IOWA STATE UNIVERSITY OF SCIENCE AND TECHNOLOGY

Ames, IA

Suburban setting ■ Public ■ State-supported ■ Coed

Web site: www.iastate.edu

Contact: Mr. Phil Caffrey, Associate Director for Freshman Admissions, 100 Alumni Hall, Ames, IA 50011-2010

Telephone: 515-294-5836 or toll-free 800-262-3810 **Fax:** 515-294-2592

E-mail: admissions@iastate.edu

Getting in Last Year 10,370 applied; 89% were accepted; 4,219 enrolled (46%).

Financial Matters $4110 resident tuition and fees (2002–03); $12,802 nonresident tuition and fees (2002–03); $5020 room and board; 100% average percent of need met; $6772 average financial aid amount received per undergraduate (2001–02).

Academics Iowa State awards bachelor's, master's, doctoral, and first-professional degrees and post-master's certificates. Challenging opportunities include advanced placement credit, accelerated degree programs, student-designed majors, freshman honors college, an honors program, double majors, independent study, and a senior project. Special programs include cooperative education, internships, summer session for credit, off-campus study, study-abroad, and Army, Navy and Air Force ROTC. The most frequently chosen baccalaureate fields are business/marketing, engineering/engineering technologies, and agriculture. The faculty at Iowa State has 1,399 full-time members, 92% with terminal degrees. The student-faculty ratio is 16:1.

Students of Iowa State The student body totals 27,898, of whom 22,999 are undergraduates. 44.3% are women and 55.7% are men. Students come from 54 states and territories and 113 other countries. 81% are from Iowa. 4.6% are international students. 84% returned for their sophomore year.

Applying Iowa State requires SAT I or ACT, a high school transcript, and rank in upper 50% of high school class. Application deadline: 8/1; 3/1 priority date for financial aid. Deferred admission is possible.

IOWA WESLEYAN COLLEGE

Mount Pleasant, IA

Small-town setting ■ Private ■ Independent Religious ■ Coed

Web site: www.iwc.edu

Contact: Mr. Cary A. Owens, Dean of Enrollment Management, 601 North Main Street, Mount Pleasant, IA 52641-1398

Telephone: 319-385-6230 or toll-free 800-582-2383 **Fax:** 319-385-6296

E-mail: admitrwl@iwc.edu

Getting in Last Year 680 applied; 53% were accepted; 106 enrolled (30%).

Financial Matters $14,280 tuition and fees (2002–03); $4460 room and board; 82% average percent of need met; $10,775 average financial aid amount received per undergraduate.

Academics Iowa Wesleyan awards bachelor's degrees. Challenging opportunities include advanced placement credit, student-designed majors, double majors, independent study, and a senior project. Special programs include internships, summer session for credit, off-campus study, and study-abroad. The faculty at Iowa Wesleyan has 44 full-time members, 50% with terminal degrees. The student-faculty ratio is 14:1.

Students of Iowa Wesleyan The student body is made up of 721 undergraduates. 59.5% are women and 40.5% are men. Students come from 22 states and territories and 7 other countries. 83% are from Iowa. 2.6% are international students. 55% returned for their sophomore year.

Applying Iowa Wesleyan requires SAT I or ACT, a high school transcript, and a minimum high school GPA of 2.0, and in some cases an essay and recommendations. The school recommends an interview. Application deadline: 8/15; 4/1 priority date for financial aid. Early and deferred admission are possible.

ITHACA COLLEGE

Ithaca, NY

Small-town setting ■ Private ■ Independent ■ Coed

Web site: www.ithaca.edu

Contact: Ms. Paula J. Mitchell, Director of Admission, 100 Job Hall, Ithaca, NY 14850-7020

Telephone: 607-274-3124 or toll-free 800-429-4274 **Fax:** 607-274-1900

E-mail: admission@ithaca.edu

Getting in Last Year 11,305 applied; 56% were accepted; 1,518 enrolled (24%).

Financial Matters $21,102 tuition and fees (2002–03); $8960 room and board; 87% average percent of need met; $19,830 average financial aid amount received per undergraduate.

Academics Ithaca College awards bachelor's and master's degrees. Challenging opportunities include advanced placement credit, accelerated degree programs, student-designed majors, freshman honors college, an honors program, double majors, independent study, and a senior project. Special programs include internships, summer session for credit, off-campus study, study-abroad, and Army and Air Force ROTC. The most frequently chosen baccalaureate fields are communications/communication technologies, visual/performing arts, and health professions and related sciences. The faculty at Ithaca College has 440 full-time members, 89% with terminal degrees. The student-faculty ratio is 12:1.

Students of Ithaca College The student body totals 6,431, of whom 6,190 are undergraduates. 56.9% are women and 43.1% are men. Students come from 48 states and territories and 72 other countries. 49% are from New York. 2.6% are international students. 87% returned for their sophomore year.

Applying Ithaca College requires an essay, SAT I or ACT, a high school transcript, and 1 recommendation, and in some cases audition. The school recommends an interview and a minimum high school GPA of 3.0. Application deadline: 3/1; 2/1 priority date for financial aid. Early and deferred admission are possible.

JACKSON STATE UNIVERSITY

Jackson, MS

Urban setting ■ Public ■ State-supported ■ Coed

Web site: www.jsums.edu

Contact: Mrs. Linda Rush, Admissions Counselor, PO Box 17330, 1400 John R. Lynch Street, Jackson, MS 39217

Telephone: 601-968-2911 or toll-free 800-682-5390 (in-state), 800-848-6817 (out-of-state)

E-mail: schatman@ccaix.jsums.edu

Getting in Last Year 8,100 applied; 38% were accepted; 1,064 enrolled (34%).

Financial Matters $3462 resident tuition and fees (2002–03); $7966 nonresident tuition and fees (2002–03); $4676 room and board.

Academics Jackson State awards bachelor's, master's, and doctoral degrees and post-master's certificates. Challenging opportunities include advanced placement credit, an honors program, and a senior project. Special programs include cooperative education, internships, summer session for credit, off-campus study, study-abroad, and Army ROTC. The most frequently chosen baccalaureate fields are business/marketing, education, and protective services/public administration. The faculty at Jackson State has 339 full-time members, 71% with terminal degrees. The student-faculty ratio is 18:1.

Students of Jackson State The student body totals 7,783, of whom 6,315 are undergraduates. 61.1% are women and 38.9% are men. Students come from 40 states and territories and 34 other countries. 79% are from Mississippi. 0.9% are international students. 58% returned for their sophomore year.

Applying Jackson State requires SAT I or ACT, a high school transcript, and a minimum high school GPA of 3.0, and in some cases 3 recommendations. Application deadline: 8/1; 4/15 priority date for financial aid. Early and deferred admission are possible.

JACKSONVILLE STATE UNIVERSITY

Jacksonville, AL

Small-town setting ■ Public ■ State-supported ■ Coed

Web site: www.jsu.edu

Contact: Ms. Martha Mitchell, Director of Admission, 700 Pelham Road North, Jacksonville, AL 36265
Telephone: 256-782-5363 or toll-free 800-231-5291 **Fax:** 256-782-5291
E-mail: lbedford@jsucc.jsu.edu

Getting in Last Year 2,600 applied; 43% were accepted; 1,109 enrolled (100%).

Financial Matters $3240 resident tuition and fees (2002–03); $6480 nonresident tuition and fees (2002–03); $3080 room and board.

Academics Jacksonville State University awards bachelor's and master's degrees. Challenging opportunities include advanced placement credit, accelerated degree programs, an honors program, double majors, and independent study. Special programs include cooperative education, internships, summer session for credit, and Army ROTC. The most frequently chosen baccalaureate fields are education, business/marketing, and protective services/public administration. The faculty at Jacksonville State University has 289 full-time members, 62% with terminal degrees. The student-faculty ratio is 20:1.

Students of Jacksonville State University The student body totals 8,930, of whom 7,324 are undergraduates. 57.8% are women and 42.2% are men. Students come from 36 states and territories. 84% are from Alabama. 0.7% are international students. 60% returned for their sophomore year.

Applying Jacksonville State University requires SAT I or ACT and a high school transcript. Application deadline: rolling admissions; 3/15 priority date for financial aid. Early and deferred admission are possible.

JACKSONVILLE UNIVERSITY

Jacksonville, FL

Suburban setting ■ *Private* ■ *Independent* ■ *Coed*

Web site: www.ju.edu
Contact: Mr. John P. Grundig, Director of Admissions, 2800 University Boulevard North, Jacksonville, FL 32211
Telephone: 904-256-7000 or toll-free 800-225-2027 **Fax:** 904-256-7012
E-mail: admissions@ju.edu

Getting in Last Year 1,553 applied; 73% were accepted; 399 enrolled (35%).

Financial Matters $16,780 tuition and fees (2002–03); $5900 room and board; 82% average percent of need met; $14,786 average financial aid amount received per undergraduate.

Academics JU awards bachelor's and master's degrees. Challenging opportunities include advanced placement credit, accelerated degree programs, student-designed majors, an honors program, double majors, independent study, and a senior project. Special programs include cooperative education, internships, summer session for credit, off-campus study, study-abroad, and Navy ROTC. The most frequently chosen baccalaureate fields are business/marketing, health professions and related sciences, and computer/information sciences. The faculty at JU has 116 full-time members, 74% with terminal degrees. The student-faculty ratio is 14:1.

Students of JU The student body totals 2,565, of whom 2,171 are undergraduates. 50.3% are women and 49.7% are men. Students come from 44 states and territories and 68 other countries. 60% are from Florida. 3.3% are international students. 74% returned for their sophomore year.

Applying JU requires an essay, SAT I or ACT, a high school transcript, and a minimum high school GPA of 2.0. The school recommends an interview and recommendations. Application deadline: rolling admissions; 1/15 priority date for financial aid. Early and deferred admission are possible.

JAMES MADISON UNIVERSITY

Harrisonburg, VA

Small-town setting ■ *Public* ■ *State-supported* ■ *Coed*

Web site: www.jmu.edu
Contact: Ms. Laika K. Tamny, Associate Director of Admissions, Office of Admission, Sonner Hall MSC 0101, Harrisonburg, VA 22807
Telephone: 540-568-5681 **Fax:** 540-568-3332
E-mail: gotojmu@jmu.edu

Getting in Last Year 15,639 applied; 58% were accepted; 3,283 enrolled (36%).

Financial Matters $4458 resident tuition and fees (2002–03); $11,642 nonresident tuition and fees (2002–03); $5794 room and board; 54% average percent of need met; $5754 average financial aid amount received per undergraduate.

Academics JMU awards bachelor's, master's, and doctoral degrees and post-master's certificates (also offers specialist in education degree). Challenging opportunities include advanced placement credit, accelerated degree programs, freshman honors college, an honors program, double majors, independent study, and a senior project. Special programs include internships, summer session for credit, study-abroad, and Army and Air Force ROTC. The most frequently chosen baccalaureate fields are business/marketing, social sciences and history, and computer/information sciences. The faculty at JMU has 704 full-time members, 84% with terminal degrees. The student-faculty ratio is 17:1.

Students of JMU The student body totals 15,965, of whom 14,828 are undergraduates. 58.8% are women and 41.2% are men. Students come from 49 states and territories and 53 other countries. 71% are from Virginia. 1.2% are international students. 90% returned for their sophomore year.

Applying JMU requires an essay, SAT I or ACT, and a high school transcript. The school recommends a minimum high school GPA of 3.0. Application deadline: 1/15; 3/1 priority date for financial aid. Deferred admission is possible.

JAMESTOWN COLLEGE

Jamestown, ND

Small-town setting ■ *Private* ■ *Independent Religious* ■ *Coed*

Web site: www.jc.edu
Contact: Ms. Judy Erickson, Director of Admissions, 6081 College Lane, Jamestown, ND 58405
Telephone: 701-252-3467 ext. 2548 or toll-free 800-336-2554 **Fax:** 701-253-4318
E-mail: admissions@jc.edu

Getting in Last Year 930 applied; 99% were accepted; 353 enrolled (38%).

Financial Matters $8350 tuition and fees (2002–03); $3550 room and board; 67% average percent of need met; $7828 average financial aid amount received per undergraduate.

Academics Jamestown College awards bachelor's degrees. Challenging opportunities include advanced placement credit, student-designed majors, an honors program, double majors, independent study, and a senior project. Special programs include cooperative education, internships, summer session for credit, off-campus study, and study-abroad. The most frequently chosen baccalaureate fields are education, business/marketing, and health professions and related sciences. The faculty at Jamestown College has 56 full-time members, 52% with terminal degrees. The student-faculty ratio is 17:1.

Students of Jamestown College The student body is made up of 1,185 undergraduates. 56.4% are women and 43.6% are men. Students come from 34 states and territories and 12 other countries. 62% are from North Dakota. 3.1% are international students. 69% returned for their sophomore year.

Applying Jamestown College requires a high school transcript, and in some cases SAT I or ACT, recommendations, and minimum ACT score of 18 or minimum SAT score of 860. The school recommends SAT I or ACT, minimum ACT score of 18 or minimum SAT score of 860, and a minimum high school GPA of 2.5. Application deadline: rolling admissions. Deferred admission is possible.

JEWISH HOSPITAL COLLEGE OF NURSING AND ALLIED HEALTH

St. Louis, MO

Urban setting ■ *Private* ■ *Independent* ■ *Coed, Primarily Women*

Web site: jhconah.edu
Contact: Ms. Christie Schneider, Chief Admissions Officer, 306 S. Kingshighway Boulevard, St. Louis, MO 63110
Telephone: 314-454-7538 or toll-free 800-832-9009 (in-state) **Fax:** 314-454-5239
E-mail: jhcollegeinguiry@bjc.org

Getting in Last Year 67 applied; 100% were accepted; 48 enrolled (72%).

Financial Matters $11,519 tuition and fees (2002–03); $2385 room only; $12,000 average financial aid amount received per undergraduate.

Academics Jewish Hospital College awards associate, bachelor's, and master's degrees and post-bachelor's and post-master's certificates. Challenging opportunities include advanced placement credit, double majors, and independent study. Special programs include summer session for credit and off-campus study. The most frequently chosen baccalaureate field is health professions and related sciences. The faculty at Jewish Hospital College has 33 full-time members, 30% with terminal degrees. The student-faculty ratio is 10:1.

Students of Jewish Hospital College The student body totals 640, of whom 563 are undergraduates. 87.9% are women and 12.1% are men. Students come from 7 states and territories. 60% are from Missouri. 86% returned for their sophomore year.

Applying Jewish Hospital College requires SAT I or ACT, a high school transcript, 2 recommendations, and a minimum high school GPA of 2.5, and in some cases SCAT and an interview. Application deadline: rolling admissions; 4/1 priority date for financial aid.

JEWISH THEOLOGICAL SEMINARY OF AMERICA

New York, NY

Urban setting ■ *Private* ■ *Independent Religious* ■ *Coed*

Web site: www.jtsa.edu
Contact: Ms. Reena Kamins, Assistant Director of Admissions, Room 614 Schiff, 3080 Broadway, New York, NY 10027-4649
Telephone: 212-678-8832 **Fax:** 212-678-8947
E-mail: rekamins@jtsa.edu

Getting in Last Year 135 applied; 53% were accepted; 51 enrolled (71%).

Financial Matters $10,600 tuition and fees (2002–03); $6860 room only; 75% average percent of need met.

Jewish Theological Seminary of America (continued)

Academics JTS awards bachelor's, master's, doctoral, and first-professional degrees (double bachelor's degree with Barnard College, Columbia University, joint bachelor's degree with Columbia University). Challenging opportunities include advanced placement credit, student-designed majors, freshman honors college, an honors program, double majors, and a senior project. Special programs include internships, summer session for credit, off-campus study, and study-abroad. The faculty at JTS has 115 members. The student-faculty ratio is 5:1.

Students of JTS The student body totals 612, of whom 194 are undergraduates. 59.3% are women and 40.7% are men. Students come from 21 states and territories and 3 other countries. 35% are from New York. 88% returned for their sophomore year.

Applying JTS requires an essay, SAT II: Writing Test, SAT I and SAT II or ACT, a high school transcript, and 2 recommendations. The school recommends an interview and a minimum high school GPA of 3.0. Application deadline: 2/15; 3/1 for financial aid. Early and deferred admission are possible.

JOHN BROWN UNIVERSITY

Siloam Springs, AR

Small-town setting ■ Private ■ Independent Religious ■ Coed

Web site: www.jbu.edu

Contact: Mrs. Karen Elliott, Admissions Systems Manager, 200 West University Street, Siloam Springs, AR 72761-2121

Telephone: 501-524-7454 or toll-free 877-JBU-INFO **Fax:** 501-524-4196

E-mail: jbuinfo@acc.jbu.edu

Getting in Last Year 620 applied; 82% were accepted; 304 enrolled (59%).

Financial Matters $13,024 tuition and fees (2002–03); $4798 room and board; 63% average percent of need met; $11,178 average financial aid amount received per undergraduate.

Academics JBU awards associate, bachelor's, and master's degrees. Challenging opportunities include advanced placement credit, freshman honors college, an honors program, double majors, independent study, and a senior project. Special programs include internships, study-abroad, and Army and Air Force ROTC. The most frequently chosen baccalaureate fields are education, communications/communication technologies, and business/marketing. The faculty at JBU has 78 full-time members, 67% with terminal degrees. The student-faculty ratio is 16:1.

Students of JBU The student body totals 1,708, of whom 1,560 are undergraduates. 57.3% are women and 42.7% are men. Students come from 44 states and territories and 37 other countries. 36% are from Arkansas. 8.2% are international students. 80% returned for their sophomore year.

Applying JBU requires an essay, SAT I or ACT, a high school transcript, 2 recommendations, and a minimum high school GPA of 2.5. The school recommends an interview. Application deadline: 3/1; 3/1 priority date for financial aid. Deferred admission is possible.

JOHN CABOT UNIVERSITY

Rome Italy

Private ■ Independent ■ Coed

Web site: www.johncabot.edu

Contact: Dr. Francesca R. Gleason, Director of Admissions, Via Della Lungara 233, Rome Italy

Telephone: 39-06 6819121 or toll-free 866-227-0112 (in-state) **Fax:** 39-06 6833738

E-mail: adminssions@johncabot.edu

Getting in Last Year 110 applied; 88% were accepted; 90 enrolled (93%).

Financial Matters $12,950 tuition and fees (2002–03); $7800 room only.

Academics John Cabot University awards associate and bachelor's degrees and post-bachelor's certificates. Challenging opportunities include advanced placement credit, freshman honors college, an honors program, double majors, independent study, and a senior project. Special programs include cooperative education, internships, summer session for credit, and study-abroad. The most frequently chosen baccalaureate fields are business/marketing, social sciences and history, and visual/performing arts. The faculty at John Cabot University has 11 full-time members. The student-faculty ratio is 12:1.

Students of John Cabot University The student body is made up of 406 undergraduates. 62% returned for their sophomore year.

Applying John Cabot University requires an essay, a high school transcript, and 2 recommendations, and in some cases SAT I or ACT. The school recommends an interview and a minimum high school GPA of 2.69. Application deadline: 7/15. Deferred admission is possible.

JOHN CARROLL UNIVERSITY

University Heights, OH

Suburban setting ■ Private ■ Independent Religious ■ Coed

Web site: www.jcu.edu

Contact: Mr. Thomas P. Fanning, Director of Admission, 20700 North Park Boulevard, University Heights, OH 44118

Telephone: 216-397-4294 **Fax:** 216-397-4981

E-mail: admission@jcu.edu

Getting in Last Year 2,764 applied; 86% were accepted.

Financial Matters $19,182 tuition and fees (2002–03); $6564 room and board; $14,104 average financial aid amount received per undergraduate (2000–01 estimated).

Academics John Carroll awards bachelor's and master's degrees. Challenging opportunities include advanced placement credit, accelerated degree programs, student-designed majors, an honors program, double majors, independent study, and a senior project. Special programs include cooperative education, internships, summer session for credit, off-campus study, study-abroad, and Army ROTC. The most frequently chosen baccalaureate fields are business/marketing, social sciences and history, and communications/communication technologies. The faculty at John Carroll has 250 full-time members. The student-faculty ratio is 14:1.

Students of John Carroll The student body totals 4,294, of whom 3,281 are undergraduates. Students come from 35 states and territories. 73% are from Ohio. 86% returned for their sophomore year.

Applying John Carroll requires SAT I or ACT, a high school transcript, and 1 recommendation, and in some cases an interview. The school recommends an essay and an interview. Application deadline: 2/1; 3/1 priority date for financial aid. Early and deferred admission are possible.

JOHN F. KENNEDY UNIVERSITY

Orinda, CA

Suburban setting ■ Private ■ Independent ■ Coed

Web site: www.jfku.edu

Contact: Ms. Ellena Bloedorn, Director of Admissions and Records, 12 Altarinda Road, Orinda, CA 94563-2603

Telephone: 925-258-2213 or toll-free 800-696-JFKU **Fax:** 925-254-6964

E-mail: proginfo@jfku.edu

Financial Matters $13,092 tuition and fees (2002–03); 60% average percent of need met; $7000 average financial aid amount received per undergraduate.

Academics JFKU awards bachelor's, master's, doctoral, and first-professional degrees and post-bachelor's and post-master's certificates. Challenging opportunities include advanced placement credit, student-designed majors, independent study, and a senior project. Special programs include summer session for credit and off-campus study. The most frequently chosen baccalaureate fields are liberal arts/general studies, business/marketing, and psychology. The faculty at JFKU has 36 full-time members, 67% with terminal degrees. The student-faculty ratio is 12:1.

Students of JFKU The student body totals 1,586, of whom 237 are undergraduates. 77.6% are women and 22.4% are men.

Applying Application deadline: 3/2 priority date for financial aid. Deferred admission is possible.

JOHN JAY COLLEGE OF CRIMINAL JUSTICE OF THE CITY UNIVERSITY OF NEW YORK

New York, NY

Urban setting ■ Public ■ State and locally supported ■ Coed

Web site: www.jjay.cuny.edu

Contact: Mr. Richard Saulnier, Acting Dean for Admissions and Registration, 445 West 59th Street, Room 4205, New York, NY 10019

Telephone: 212-237-8878 or toll-free 877-JOHNJAY

Getting in Last Year 3,144 applied; 73% were accepted; 4,038 enrolled (176%).

Financial Matters $3459 resident tuition and fees (2002–03); $7059 nonresident tuition and fees (2002–03); 70% average percent of need met; $5100 average financial aid amount received per undergraduate (2001–02).

Academics John Jay awards associate, bachelor's, and master's degrees. Challenging opportunities include advanced placement credit and an honors program. Special programs include cooperative education, internships, summer session for credit, off-campus study, and Navy and Air Force ROTC. The most frequently chosen baccalaureate field is law/legal studies. The faculty at John Jay has 285 full-time members. The student-faculty ratio is 20:1.

Students of John Jay The student body totals 11,209, of whom 10,202 are undergraduates. Students come from 10 states and territories and 12 other countries. 72% returned for their sophomore year.

Applying John Jay requires SAT I or ACT and a high school transcript. Application deadline: rolling admissions; 6/1 priority date for financial aid. Early and deferred admission are possible.

JOHNS HOPKINS UNIVERSITY

Baltimore, MD

Urban setting ■ Private ■ Independent ■ Coed

Web site: www.jhu.edu

Contact: Mr. John Latting, Director of Undergraduate Admissions, 140 Garland Hall, 3400 North Charles Street, Baltimore, MD 21218-2699
Telephone: 410-516-8341 **Fax:** 410-516-6025
E-mail: gotojhu@jhu.edu

Getting in Last Year 8,932 applied; 35% were accepted; 1,127 enrolled (36%).

Financial Matters $27,690 tuition and fees (2002–03); $8870 room and board; 95% average percent of need met; $25,210 average financial aid amount received per undergraduate.

Academics Johns Hopkins awards bachelor's, master's, doctoral, and first-professional degrees and post-bachelor's and post-master's certificates. Challenging opportunities include advanced placement credit, accelerated degree programs, student-designed majors, an honors program, double majors, independent study, and a senior project. Special programs include internships, summer session for credit, off-campus study, study-abroad, and Army and Air Force ROTC. The most frequently chosen baccalaureate fields are health professions and related sciences, engineering/engineering technologies, and social sciences and history. The student-faculty ratio is 8:1.

Students of Johns Hopkins The student body totals 6,029, of whom 4,112 are undergraduates. 41.7% are women and 58.3% are men. Students come from 54 states and territories and 129 other countries. 48% are from Maryland. 6.4% are international students. 96% returned for their sophomore year.

Applying Johns Hopkins requires an essay, SAT II: Writing Test, SAT I and SAT II or ACT, a high school transcript, and 1 recommendation. The school recommends an interview. Application deadline: 1/1; 2/15 for financial aid, with a 2/1 priority date. Early and deferred admission are possible.

JOHNSON & WALES UNIVERSITY
Denver, CO

Small-town setting ■ Private ■ Independent ■ Coed

Web site: www.jwu.edu
Contact: Mr. Dave McKlveen, Director of Admissions, 7150 Montview Boulevard, Denver, CO 80220
Telephone: 303-256-9300 or toll-free 877-598-3368 **Fax:** 303-256-9333
E-mail: admissions@jwu.edu

Getting in Last Year 2,079 applied; 23% were accepted.

Financial Matters $18,282 tuition and fees (2002–03); $7881 room and board; 72% average percent of need met; $12,258 average financial aid amount received per undergraduate.

Academics Johnson & Wales University awards associate and bachelor's degrees. Special programs include cooperative education, internships, and summer session for credit.

Students of Johnson & Wales University The student body is made up of 952 undergraduates. Students come from 45 states and territories and 4 other countries. 58% are from Colorado. 0.6% are international students.

Applying Johnson & Wales University requires a high school transcript, and in some cases SAT I or ACT and a minimum high school GPA of 3.0. The school recommends SAT I or ACT, an interview, and a minimum high school GPA of 2.0. Application deadline: rolling admissions. Deferred admission is possible.

JOHNSON & WALES UNIVERSITY
North Miami, FL

Suburban setting ■ Private ■ Independent ■ Coed

Web site: www.jwu.edu
Contact: Mr. Jeff Greenip, Director of Admissions, 1701 Northeast 127th Street, North Miami, FL 33181
Telephone: 305-892-7002 or toll-free 800-232-2433 **Fax:** 305-892-7020
E-mail: admissions@jwu.edu

Getting in Last Year 5,161 applied; 68% were accepted; 717 enrolled (20%).

Financial Matters $18,282 tuition and fees (2002–03); $5616 room only; 68% average percent of need met; $12,712 average financial aid amount received per undergraduate.

Academics J & W at North Miami awards associate and bachelor's degrees. Challenging opportunities include advanced placement credit, accelerated degree programs, an honors program, and independent study. Special programs include cooperative education, internships, summer session for credit, and study-abroad. The faculty at J & W at North Miami has 56 full-time members. The student-faculty ratio is 23:1.

Students of J & W at North Miami The student body is made up of 2,145 undergraduates. 53.8% are women and 46.2% are men. Students come from 36 states and territories and 5 other countries. 40% are from Florida. 7.3% are international students. 63% returned for their sophomore year.

Applying J & W at North Miami requires a high school transcript, and in some cases an essay, SAT I or ACT, an interview, and recommendations. The school recommends a minimum high school GPA of 2.0. Application deadline: rolling admissions. Early and deferred admission are possible.

JOHNSON & WALES UNIVERSITY
Providence, RI

Urban setting ■ Private ■ Independent ■ Coed

Web site: www.jwu.edu
Contact: Ms. Maureen Dumas, Dean of Admissions, 8 Abbott Park Place, Providence, RI 02903-3703
Telephone: 401-598-2310 or toll-free 800-342-5598 (out-of-state) **Fax:** 401-598-2948
E-mail: admissions@jwu.edu

Getting in Last Year 12,780 applied; 80% were accepted.

Financial Matters $15,192 tuition and fees (2002–03); $6366 room and board; 69% average percent of need met; $10,895 average financial aid amount received per undergraduate.

Academics J&W awards associate, bachelor's, master's, and doctoral degrees (branch locations: Charleston, SC; Denver, CO; North Miami, FL; Norfolk, VA; Gothenberg, Sweden). Challenging opportunities include advanced placement credit, accelerated degree programs, freshman honors college, an honors program, double majors, independent study, and a senior project. Special programs include cooperative education, internships, summer session for credit, and study-abroad. The faculty at J&W has 281 full-time members. The student-faculty ratio is 30:1.

Students of J&W The student body totals 9,630, of whom 9,019 are undergraduates. 50% are women and 50% are men. Students come from 50 states and territories and 92 other countries. 11% are from Rhode Island. 4.4% are international students. 68% returned for their sophomore year.

Applying J&W requires a high school transcript, and in some cases SAT I or ACT, 1 recommendation, and a minimum high school GPA of 3.0. The school recommends SAT I or ACT, an interview, and a minimum high school GPA of 2.0. Application deadline: rolling admissions. Early and deferred admission are possible.

JOHNSON & WALES UNIVERSITY
Charleston, SC

Urban setting ■ Private ■ Independent ■ Coed

Web site: www.jwu.edu
Contact: Mr. Brian Stanley, Director of Admissions, 701 East Bay Street, Charleston, SC 29403
Telephone: 843-727-3000 or toll-free 800-868-1522 **Fax:** 843-763-0318
E-mail: admissions@jwu.edu

Getting in Last Year 1,479 applied; 74% were accepted.

Financial Matters $17,816 tuition and fees (2002–03); $4629 room only; 67% average percent of need met; $10,632 average financial aid amount received per undergraduate.

Academics J&W at Charleston awards associate and bachelor's degrees. Challenging opportunities include advanced placement credit and accelerated degree programs. Special programs include cooperative education, internships, summer session for credit, off-campus study, and study-abroad. The faculty at J&W at Charleston has 45 full-time members, 9% with terminal degrees. The student-faculty ratio is 29:1.

Students of J&W at Charleston The student body is made up of 1,497 undergraduates. 45.8% are women and 54.2% are men. Students come from 44 states and territories and 5 other countries. 0.7% are international students. 72% returned for their sophomore year.

Applying J&W at Charleston requires a high school transcript, and in some cases SAT I or ACT and a minimum high school GPA of 2.0. The school recommends an essay, an interview, and recommendations. Application deadline: rolling admissions. Early and deferred admission are possible.

JOHNSON & WALES UNIVERSITY
Norfolk, VA

Urban setting ■ Private ■ Independent ■ Coed

Web site: www.jwu.edu
Contact: Ms. Amy Driscoll, Director of Admissions, 2428 Almeda Avenue, Suite 316, Norfolk, VA 23513
Telephone: 757-853-3508 ext. 275 or toll-free 800-277-2433 **Fax:** 757-857-4869
E-mail: admissions@jwu.edu

Getting in Last Year 741 applied; 68% were accepted.

Financial Matters $16,680 tuition and fees (2002–03); $6336 room and board; 67% average percent of need met; $10,866 average financial aid amount received per undergraduate.

Academics J&W at Norfolk awards associate and bachelor's degrees. Challenging opportunities include accelerated degree programs and an honors program. Special programs include cooperative education, internships, and summer session for credit. The faculty at J&W at Norfolk has 19 full-time members. The student-faculty ratio is 26:1.

Johnson & Wales University (continued)

Students of J&W at Norfolk The student body is made up of 709 undergraduates. 47.5% are women and 52.5% are men. Students come from 23 states and territories. 0.1% are international students.

Applying J&W at Norfolk requires a high school transcript, and in some cases SAT I or ACT and recommendations. The school recommends an essay, an interview, and a minimum high school GPA of 2.0. Application deadline: rolling admissions. Early and deferred admission are possible.

JOHNSON BIBLE COLLEGE

Knoxville, TN

Rural setting ■ Private ■ Independent Religious ■ Coed

Web site: www.jbc.edu

Contact: Mr. Tim Wingfield, Director of Admissions, 7900 Johnson Drive, Knoxville, TN 37998

Telephone: 865-251-2346 or toll-free 800-827-2122 **Fax:** 423-251-2336

E-mail: twingfield@jbc.edu

Getting in Last Year 198 applied; 91% were accepted; 180 enrolled (99%).

Financial Matters $5670 tuition and fees (2002–03); $3600 room and board; 36% average percent of need met; $2561 average financial aid amount received per undergraduate (2001–02).

Academics Johnson Bible College awards associate, bachelor's, and master's degrees. Challenging opportunities include advanced placement credit, accelerated degree programs, an honors program, double majors, and independent study. Special programs include cooperative education, internships, and summer session for credit. The most frequently chosen baccalaureate field is education. The faculty at Johnson Bible College has 24 full-time members, 54% with terminal degrees. The student-faculty ratio is 17:1.

Students of Johnson Bible College The student body totals 824, of whom 707 are undergraduates. 51.1% are women and 48.9% are men. Students come from 39 states and territories and 12 other countries. 27% are from Tennessee. 3.1% are international students. 75% returned for their sophomore year.

Applying Johnson Bible College requires an essay, SAT I or ACT, a high school transcript, and 3 recommendations, and in some cases ACT and an interview. Application deadline: 8/1. Deferred admission is possible.

JOHNSON C. SMITH UNIVERSITY

Charlotte, NC

Urban setting ■ Private ■ Independent ■ Coed

Web site: www.jcsu.edu

Contact: Mr. Jeffrey Smith, Director of Admissions, 100 Beatties Ford Road, Charlotte, NC 28216

Telephone: 704-378-1010 or toll-free 800-782-7303

Getting in Last Year 3,476 applied; 37% were accepted; 464 enrolled (36%).

Financial Matters $12,444 tuition and fees (2002–03); $4806 room and board; 100% average percent of need met; $6200 average financial aid amount received per undergraduate (2001–02).

Academics JCSU awards bachelor's degrees. Challenging opportunities include advanced placement credit, accelerated degree programs, freshman honors college, an honors program, double majors, independent study, and a senior project. Special programs include cooperative education, internships, summer session for credit, off-campus study, study-abroad, and Army and Air Force ROTC. The faculty at JCSU has 84 full-time members, 76% with terminal degrees. The student-faculty ratio is 16:1.

Students of JCSU The student body is made up of 1,537 undergraduates. 60.4% are women and 39.6% are men. Students come from 37 states and territories. 28% are from North Carolina. 69% returned for their sophomore year.

Applying JCSU requires SAT I and SAT II or ACT and a high school transcript, and in some cases recommendations. The school recommends an essay and an interview. Application deadline: 8/1. Early and deferred admission are possible.

JOHNSON STATE COLLEGE

Johnson, VT

Rural setting ■ Public ■ State-supported ■ Coed

Web site: www.johnsonstatecollege.edu

Contact: Ms. Kellie Rose, Assistant Director of Admissions, 337 College Hill, Johnson, VT 05656-9405

Telephone: 802-635-1219 or toll-free 800-635-2356 **Fax:** 802-635-1230

E-mail: jscapply@badger.jsc.vsc.edu

Getting in Last Year 970 applied; 86% were accepted; 235 enrolled (28%).

Financial Matters $5504 resident tuition and fees (2002–03); $11,716 nonresident tuition and fees (2002–03); $5782 room and board; 80% average percent of need met; $7835 average financial aid amount received per undergraduate (2001–02).

Academics Johnson State awards associate, bachelor's, and master's degrees. Challenging opportunities include advanced placement credit, accelerated degree programs, an honors program, double majors, independent study, and a senior project. Special programs include cooperative education, internships, summer session for credit, off-campus study, and Army ROTC. The faculty at Johnson State has 55 full-time members, 85% with terminal degrees. The student-faculty ratio is 16:1.

Students of Johnson State The student body totals 1,646, of whom 1,443 are undergraduates. 61.2% are women and 38.8% are men. Students come from 25 states and territories. 60% are from Vermont. 0.6% are international students. 61% returned for their sophomore year.

Applying Johnson State requires an essay, SAT I or ACT, a high school transcript, 1 recommendation, and a minimum high school GPA of 2.0. The school recommends an interview and a minimum high school GPA of 2.5. Application deadline: rolling admissions; 3/1 priority date for financial aid. Deferred admission is possible.

JOHN WESLEY COLLEGE

High Point, NC

Urban setting ■ Private ■ Independent Religious ■ Coed

Web site: www.johnwesley.edu

Contact: Mr. Greg Workman, Admissions Officer, 2314 North Centennial Street, High Point, NC 27265-3197

Telephone: 336-889-2262 ext. 127 **Fax:** 336-889-2261

E-mail: admissions@johnwesley.edu

Getting in Last Year 25 applied; 48% were accepted; 12 enrolled (100%).

Financial Matters $7080 tuition and fees (2002–03); $1990 room only; 52% average percent of need met; $8000 average financial aid amount received per undergraduate (2001–02).

Academics JWC awards associate and bachelor's degrees. Challenging opportunities include advanced placement credit and a senior project. Special programs include internships, summer session for credit, and off-campus study. The most frequently chosen baccalaureate fields are business/marketing, psychology, and education. The faculty at JWC has 11 full-time members, 55% with terminal degrees. The student-faculty ratio is 12:1.

Students of JWC The student body is made up of 152 undergraduates. 42.8% are women and 57.2% are men. Students come from 8 states and territories. 95% are from North Carolina. 80% returned for their sophomore year.

Applying JWC requires a high school transcript, an interview, and 2 recommendations. The school recommends SAT II: Writing Test, SAT I and SAT II or ACT, and a minimum high school GPA of 2.0. Application deadline: 8/1; 3/15 priority date for financial aid. Early and deferred admission are possible.

JONES COLLEGE

Jacksonville, FL

Urban setting ■ Private ■ Independent ■ Coed

Web site: www.jones.edu

Contact: Mr. Barry Durden, Director of Admissions, 5355 Arlington Expressway, Jacksonville, FL 32211

Telephone: 904-743-1122 ext. 115 **Fax:** 904-743-4446

E-mail: bdurden@jones.edu

Getting in Last Year 290 applied; 72% were accepted; 51 enrolled (24%).

Financial Matters $5490 tuition and fees (2002–03).

Academics Jones College awards associate and bachelor's degrees. Challenging opportunities include advanced placement credit, accelerated degree programs, student-designed majors, and double majors. Special programs include cooperative education, internships, and summer session for credit. The faculty at Jones College has 7 full-time members, 100% with terminal degrees. The student-faculty ratio is 14:1.

Students of Jones College The student body is made up of 641 undergraduates. 78.8% are women and 21.2% are men. Students come from 3 states and territories. 0.5% are international students. 68% returned for their sophomore year.

Applying Jones College requires a high school transcript and an interview. Application deadline: rolling admissions. Early and deferred admission are possible.

JONES INTERNATIONAL UNIVERSITY

Englewood, CO

Private ■ Independent ■ Coed

Web site: www.jonesinternational.edu

Contact: Ms. Candice Morrissey, Associate Director of Admissions, 9697 East Mineral Avenue, Englewood, CO 80112

Telephone: 303-784-8247 or toll-free 800-811-5663 **Fax:** 303-799-0966

E-mail: admissions@international.edu

Academics JIU awards bachelor's and master's degrees. Challenging opportunities include advanced placement credit, accelerated degree programs, student-designed majors, double majors, independent study, and a senior project. Summer session for credit is a special program. The faculty at JIU has 400 members. The student-faculty ratio is 12:1.

Students of JIU The student body totals 2,000, of whom 835 are undergraduates. 10% are from Colorado. 97% returned for their sophomore year.

Applying JIU requires an essay, a high school transcript, 3 recommendations, and a minimum high school GPA of 2.5, and in some cases SAT I or ACT. Application deadline: rolling admissions. Deferred admission is possible.

JUDSON COLLEGE
Marion, AL

Rural setting ■ Private ■ Independent Religious ■ Women Only

Web site: home.judson.edu
Contact: Mrs. Charlotte Clements, Director of Admissions, PO Box 120, Marion, AL 36756
Telephone: 334-683-5110 ext. 110 or toll-free 800-447-9472 **Fax:** 334-683-5158
E-mail: admissions@future.judson.edu

Getting in Last Year 310 applied; 81% were accepted; 93 enrolled (37%).

Financial Matters $8550 tuition and fees (2002–03); $5300 room and board; 89% average percent of need met; $10,078 average financial aid amount received per undergraduate.

Academics Judson awards bachelor's degrees. Challenging opportunities include advanced placement credit, accelerated degree programs, student-designed majors, an honors program, double majors, independent study, and a senior project. Special programs include internships, summer session for credit, off-campus study, study-abroad, and Army ROTC. The most frequently chosen baccalaureate fields are business/marketing, psychology, and biological/life sciences. The faculty at Judson has 27 full-time members, 70% with terminal degrees. The student-faculty ratio is 11:1.

Students of Judson The student body is made up of 363 undergraduates. Students come from 22 states and territories. 84% are from Alabama. 0.6% are international students. 58% returned for their sophomore year.

Applying Judson requires SAT I or ACT, a high school transcript, an interview, 2 recommendations, and a minimum high school GPA of 2.0. The school recommends an essay. Application deadline: rolling admissions; 3/1 priority date for financial aid. Early admission is possible.

JUDSON COLLEGE
Elgin, IL

Suburban setting ■ Private ■ Independent Religious ■ Coed

Web site: www.judsoncollege.edu
Contact: Mr. Billy Dean, Director of Admissions, 1151 North State Street, Elgin, IL 60123-1498
Telephone: 847-695-2500 ext. 2322 or toll-free 800-879-5376 **Fax:** 847-695-0216
E-mail: admission@judson-il.edu

Getting in Last Year 534 applied; 71% were accepted; 160 enrolled (42%).

Financial Matters $15,150 tuition and fees (2002–03); $5800 room and board; 40% average percent of need met; $15,439 average financial aid amount received per undergraduate (2001–02).

Academics Judson awards bachelor's and master's degrees. Challenging opportunities include advanced placement credit, accelerated degree programs, student-designed majors, an honors program, double majors, independent study, and a senior project. Special programs include internships, off-campus study, and study-abroad. The most frequently chosen baccalaureate fields are business/marketing, personal/miscellaneous services, and education. The faculty at Judson has 55 full-time members, 65% with terminal degrees. The student-faculty ratio is 15:1.

Students of Judson The student body totals 1,172, of whom 1,167 are undergraduates. 56.4% are women and 43.6% are men. Students come from 21 states and territories and 18 other countries. 70% are from Illinois. 3.8% are international students. 89% returned for their sophomore year.

Applying Judson requires an essay, SAT I or ACT, a high school transcript, and a minimum high school GPA of 2.0, and in some cases an interview and 2 recommendations. The school recommends ACT. Application deadline: rolling admissions. Early admission is possible.

THE JUILLIARD SCHOOL
New York, NY

Urban setting ■ Private ■ Independent ■ Coed

Web site: www.juilliard.edu
Contact: Ms. Mary K. Gray, Associate Dean for Admissions, 60 Lincoln Center Plaza, New York, NY 10023-6588
Telephone: 212-799-5000 ext. 527 **Fax:** 212-724-0263
E-mail: admissions@juilliard.edu

Getting in Last Year 1,806 applied; 8% were accepted; 113 enrolled (81%).

Financial Matters $19,700 tuition and fees (2002–03); $7850 room and board; 85% average percent of need met; $20,791 average financial aid amount received per undergraduate.

Academics Juilliard awards bachelor's, master's, and doctoral degrees and post-bachelor's and post-master's certificates. Challenging opportunities include accelerated degree programs, double majors, and a senior project. Special programs include off-campus study and study-abroad. The faculty at Juilliard has 120 full-time members. The student-faculty ratio is 4:1.

Students of Juilliard The student body totals 850, of whom 488 are undergraduates. 51.4% are women and 48.6% are men. 22% are from New York. 23.4% are international students. 95% returned for their sophomore year.

Applying Juilliard requires an essay, a high school transcript, and audition. Application deadline: 12/1; 3/1 for financial aid.

JUNIATA COLLEGE
Huntingdon, PA

Small-town setting ■ Private ■ Independent Religious ■ Coed

Web site: www.juniata.edu
Contact: Terry Bollman, Director of Admissions, 1700 Moore Street, Huntingdon, PA 16652
Telephone: 814-641-3424 or toll-free 877-JUNIATA **Fax:** 814-641-3100
E-mail: info@juniata.edu

Getting in Last Year 1,346 applied; 79% were accepted; 375 enrolled (35%).

Financial Matters $21,580 tuition and fees (2002–03); $5930 room and board; 89% average percent of need met; $17,936 average financial aid amount received per undergraduate.

Academics Juniata awards bachelor's degrees. Challenging opportunities include advanced placement credit, accelerated degree programs, student-designed majors, freshman honors college, an honors program, double majors, independent study, and a senior project. Special programs include internships, summer session for credit, off-campus study, and study-abroad. The most frequently chosen baccalaureate fields are biological/life sciences, social sciences and history, and business/marketing. The faculty at Juniata has 89 full-time members, 94% with terminal degrees. The student-faculty ratio is 13:1.

Students of Juniata The student body is made up of 1,345 undergraduates. 58.4% are women and 41.6% are men. Students come from 34 states and territories and 27 other countries. 76% are from Pennsylvania. 3.3% are international students. 90% returned for their sophomore year.

Applying Juniata requires an essay, SAT I or ACT, a high school transcript, 1 recommendation, and a minimum high school GPA of 3.0. The school recommends an interview. Application deadline: 3/15; 3/1 priority date for financial aid. Early and deferred admission are possible.

KALAMAZOO COLLEGE
Kalamazoo, MI

Suburban setting ■ Private ■ Independent Religious ■ Coed

Web site: www.kzoo.edu
Contact: Mrs. Linda Wirgau, Records Manager, Mandelle Hall, 1200 Academy Street, Kalamazoo, MI 49006-3295
Telephone: 616-337-7166 or toll-free 800-253-3602
E-mail: admission@kzoo.edu

Getting in Last Year 1,411 applied; 73% were accepted; 337 enrolled (33%).

Financial Matters $21,603 tuition and fees (2002–03); $6354 room and board; $19,000 average financial aid amount received per undergraduate.

Academics K-College awards bachelor's degrees. Challenging opportunities include advanced placement credit, double majors, independent study, and a senior project. Special programs include cooperative education, internships, off-campus study, study-abroad, and Army ROTC. The most frequently chosen baccalaureate fields are social sciences and history, English, and biological/life sciences. The faculty at K-College has 103 full-time members, 86% with terminal degrees. The student-faculty ratio is 12:1.

Students of K-College The student body is made up of 1,265 undergraduates. 54.5% are women and 45.5% are men. Students come from 36 states and territories and 14 other countries. 79% are from Michigan. 1.7% are international students. 88% returned for their sophomore year.

Applying K-College requires an essay, SAT I or ACT, a high school transcript, and 2 recommendations. The school recommends an interview and a minimum high school GPA of 3.0. Application deadline: 2/15; 2/15 priority date for financial aid. Deferred admission is possible.

KANSAS CITY ART INSTITUTE
Kansas City, MO

Urban setting ■ Private ■ Independent ■ Coed

Web site: www.kcai.edu
Contact: Mr. Gerald Valet, Director of Admission Technology, 4415 Warwick Boulevard, Kansas City, MO 64111-1874

Kansas City Art Institute (continued)

Telephone: 816-474-5224 or toll-free 800-522-5224 **Fax:** 816-802-3309
E-mail: admiss@kcai.edu

Getting in Last Year 519 applied; 83% were accepted; 113 enrolled (26%).

Financial Matters $20,310 tuition and fees (2002–03); $6540 room and board; 69% average percent of need met; $15,661 average financial aid amount received per undergraduate.

Academics KCAI awards bachelor's degrees. Challenging opportunities include advanced placement credit, double majors, independent study, and a senior project. Special programs include cooperative education, internships, summer session for credit, off-campus study, and study-abroad. The most frequently chosen baccalaureate field is visual/performing arts. The faculty at KCAI has 44 full-time members, 86% with terminal degrees. The student-faculty ratio is 9:1.

Students of KCAI The student body is made up of 548 undergraduates. 54.2% are women and 45.8% are men. Students come from 33 states and territories and 9 other countries. 39% are from Missouri. 2.2% are international students. 79% returned for their sophomore year.

Applying KCAI requires an essay, SAT I or ACT, a high school transcript, 2 recommendations, portfolio, statement of purpose, and a minimum high school GPA of 2.5. The school recommends an interview. Application deadline: rolling admissions; 3/1 priority date for financial aid. Deferred admission is possible.

KANSAS STATE UNIVERSITY

Manhattan, KS

Suburban setting ■ Public ■ State-supported ■ Coed

Web site: www.ksu.edu
Contact: Mr. Larry Moeder, Interim Director of Admissions, 119 Anderson Hall, Manhattan, KS 66506
Telephone: 785-532-6250 or toll-free 800-432-8270 (in-state) **Fax:** 785-532-6393
E-mail: kstate@ksu.edu

Getting in Last Year 8,212 applied; 58% were accepted; 3,537 enrolled (74%).

Financial Matters $3444 resident tuition and fees (2002–03); $10,704 nonresident tuition and fees (2002–03); $4500 room and board; 75% average percent of need met; $4882 average financial aid amount received per undergraduate (2001–02).

Academics K-State awards associate, bachelor's, master's, doctoral, and first-professional degrees. Challenging opportunities include advanced placement credit, accelerated degree programs, freshman honors college, an honors program, double majors, independent study, and a senior project. Special programs include cooperative education, internships, summer session for credit, off-campus study, study-abroad, and Army and Air Force ROTC. The most frequently chosen baccalaureate fields are business/marketing, agriculture, and engineering/engineering technologies. The faculty at K-State has 882 full-time members, 85% with terminal degrees. The student-faculty ratio is 20:1.

Students of K-State The student body totals 22,732, of whom 19,048 are undergraduates. 47.5% are women and 52.5% are men. Students come from 50 states and territories and 98 other countries. 90% are from Kansas. 1.1% are international students. 79% returned for their sophomore year.

Applying K-State requires SAT I or ACT, a high school transcript, and a minimum high school GPA of 2.0. The school recommends ACT. Application deadline: rolling admissions; 3/1 priority date for financial aid.

KEAN UNIVERSITY

Union, NJ

Urban setting ■ Public ■ State-supported ■ Coed

Web site: www.kean.edu
Contact: Mr. Audley Bridges, Director of Admissions, PO Box 411, Union, NJ 07083
Telephone: 908-737-7100
E-mail: admitme@kean.edu

Getting in Last Year 5,081 applied; 52% were accepted; 1,396 enrolled (53%).

Financial Matters $5840 resident tuition and fees (2002–03); $8000 nonresident tuition and fees (2002–03); $6520 room and board; 67% average percent of need met; $6836 average financial aid amount received per undergraduate (2001–02).

Academics Kean awards bachelor's and master's degrees and post-bachelor's and post-master's certificates. Challenging opportunities include advanced placement credit, accelerated degree programs, freshman honors college, an honors program, double majors, independent study, and a senior project. Special programs include cooperative education, internships, summer session for credit, off-campus study, study-abroad, and Army and Air Force ROTC. The most frequently chosen baccalaureate fields are business/marketing, education, and social sciences and history. The faculty at Kean has 372 full-time members, 88% with terminal degrees. The student-faculty ratio is 21:1.

Students of Kean The student body totals 12,779, of whom 9,970 are undergraduates. 64.3% are women and 35.7% are men. Students come from 16 states and territories and 72 other countries. 98% are from New Jersey. 3.5% are international students. 80% returned for their sophomore year.

Applying Kean requires an essay, SAT I or ACT, a high school transcript, and a minimum high school GPA of 2.0, and in some cases an interview. Application deadline: 5/31; 3/15 priority date for financial aid. Early admission is possible.

KEENE STATE COLLEGE

Keene, NH

Small-town setting ■ Public ■ State-supported ■ Coed

Web site: www.keene.edu
Contact: Ms. Margaret Richmond, Director of Admissions, 229 Main Street, Keene, NH 03435-2604
Telephone: 603-358-2273 or toll-free 800-572-1909 **Fax:** 603-358-2767
E-mail: admissions@keene.edu

Getting in Last Year 3,925 applied; 78% were accepted.

Financial Matters $6152 resident tuition and fees (2002–03); $11,812 nonresident tuition and fees (2002–03); $5430 room and board; 90% average percent of need met; $6967 average financial aid amount received per undergraduate (2001–02).

Academics KSC awards associate, bachelor's, and master's degrees and post-bachelor's and post-master's certificates. Challenging opportunities include advanced placement credit, student-designed majors, an honors program, double majors, and independent study. Special programs include cooperative education, internships, summer session for credit, off-campus study, study-abroad, and Air Force ROTC. The most frequently chosen baccalaureate fields are education, visual/performing arts, and engineering/engineering technologies. The faculty at KSC has 184 full-time members, 83% with terminal degrees. The student-faculty ratio is 17:1.

Students of KSC The student body totals 4,962, of whom 4,690 are undergraduates. 57.8% are women and 42.2% are men. Students come from 27 states and territories. 54% are from New Hampshire. 0.3% are international students. 77% returned for their sophomore year.

Applying KSC requires an essay, SAT I or ACT, a high school transcript, and 1 recommendation, and in some cases an interview. The school recommends SAT I and an interview. Application deadline: 4/1; 3/1 for financial aid. Deferred admission is possible.

KENDALL COLLEGE

Evanston, IL

Suburban setting ■ Private ■ Independent Religious ■ Coed

Web site: www.kendall.edu
Contact: Carl Goodmonson, Assistant Director of Admissions, 2408 Orrington Avenue, Evanston, IL 60201-2899
Telephone: 847-866-1300 ext. 1307 or toll-free 877-588-8860 (in-state) **Fax:** 847-448-2120
E-mail: admissions@kendall.edu

Getting in Last Year 474 applied; 72% were accepted.

Financial Matters $13,650 tuition and fees (2002–03); $6030 room and board; 82% average percent of need met; $15,136 average financial aid amount received per undergraduate.

Academics Kendall awards associate and bachelor's degrees. Challenging opportunities include advanced placement credit, accelerated degree programs, student-designed majors, independent study, and a senior project. Special programs include cooperative education, internships, summer session for credit, and study-abroad. The faculty at Kendall has 74 members, 41% with terminal degrees. The student-faculty ratio is 15:1.

Students of Kendall The student body is made up of 550 undergraduates. Students come from 18 states and territories and 13 other countries. 3.1% are international students.

Applying Kendall requires an essay, SAT I or ACT, a high school transcript, and minimum ACT score of 18, and in some cases an interview and recommendations. The school recommends an interview and a minimum high school GPA of 2.0. Application deadline: rolling admissions; 5/1 priority date for financial aid. Deferred admission is possible.

KENDALL COLLEGE OF ART AND DESIGN OF FERRIS STATE UNIVERSITY

Grand Rapids, MI

Urban setting ■ Private ■ Independent ■ Coed

Web site: www.kcad.edu
Contact: Ms. Sandra Britton, Director of Enrollment Management, 17 Fountain Street, NW, Grand Rapids, MI 49503-3002
Telephone: 616-451-2787 ext. 113 or toll-free 800-676-2787 **Fax:** 616-831-9689

Financial Matters 83% average percent of need met; $10,526 average financial aid amount received per undergraduate (2000–01 estimated).

Academics Kendall awards bachelor's and master's degrees. Challenging opportunities include advanced placement credit, independent study, and a senior project. Special programs include internships, summer session for credit, off-campus study, and study-abroad. The most frequently chosen baccalaureate fields are visual/performing arts and trade and industry. The faculty at Kendall has 41 full-time members, 71% with terminal degrees. The student-faculty ratio is 13:1.

Students of Kendall The student body totals 855, of whom 844 are undergraduates. 58.8% are women and 41.2% are men. Students come from 17 states and territories and 5 other countries. 94% are from Michigan. 1.4% are international students. 70% returned for their sophomore year.

Applying Kendall requires an essay, ACT, a high school transcript, portfolio, and a minimum high school GPA of 2.5. The school recommends an interview. Application deadline: rolling admissions; 2/15 priority date for financial aid. Early and deferred admission are possible.

KENNESAW STATE UNIVERSITY

Kennesaw, GA

Suburban setting ■ Public ■ State-supported ■ Coed

Web site: www.kennesaw.edu
Contact: Mr. Joe F. Head, Director of Admissions and Dean of Enrollment Services, 1000 Chastain Road, Campus Box 0115, Kennesaw, GA 30144
Telephone: 770-423-6300 **Fax:** 770-423-6541
E-mail: ksuadmit@kennesaw.edu

Getting in Last Year 3,461 applied; 80% were accepted; 2,166 enrolled (78%).

Financial Matters $2516 resident tuition and fees (2002–03); $8546 nonresident tuition and fees (2002–03); $3105 room only; 11% average percent of need met; $3956 average financial aid amount received per undergraduate.

Academics Kennesaw State awards bachelor's and master's degrees. Challenging opportunities include advanced placement credit, freshman honors college, an honors program, and a senior project. Special programs include cooperative education, internships, summer session for credit, off-campus study, study-abroad, and Army and Air Force ROTC. The most frequently chosen baccalaureate fields are business/marketing, education, and computer/information sciences. The faculty at Kennesaw State has 382 full-time members, 76% with terminal degrees. The student-faculty ratio is 27:1.

Students of Kennesaw State The student body totals 15,655, of whom 13,897 are undergraduates. 62.9% are women and 37.1% are men. 96% are from Georgia. 67% returned for their sophomore year.

Applying Kennesaw State requires SAT I or ACT, a high school transcript, proof of immunization, and a minimum high school GPA of 2.0, and in some cases SAT II Subject Tests. Application deadline: 7/18. Deferred admission is possible.

KENT STATE UNIVERSITY

Kent, OH

Small-town setting ■ Public ■ State-supported ■ Coed

Web site: www.kent.edu
Contact: Mr. Christopher Buttenschon, Assistant Director of Admissions, 161 Michael Schwartz Center, Kent, OH 44242-0001
Telephone: 330-672-2444 or toll-free 800-988-KENT **Fax:** 330-672-2499
E-mail: kentadm@admissions.kent.edu

Getting in Last Year 10,056 applied; 90% were accepted; 3,729 enrolled (41%).

Financial Matters $6374 resident tuition and fees (2002–03); $12,330 nonresident tuition and fees (2002–03); $5570 room and board; 68% average percent of need met; $6368 average financial aid amount received per undergraduate.

Academics Kent awards associate, bachelor's, master's, and doctoral degrees. Challenging opportunities include advanced placement credit, accelerated degree programs, student-designed majors, freshman honors college, an honors program, double majors, independent study, and a senior project. Special programs include cooperative education, internships, summer session for credit, off-campus study, study-abroad, and Army and Air Force ROTC. The most frequently chosen baccalaureate fields are business/marketing, education, and health professions and related sciences. The faculty at Kent has 801 full-time members, 81% with terminal degrees. The student-faculty ratio is 20:1.

Students of Kent The student body totals 23,504, of whom 18,813 are undergraduates. 59.3% are women and 40.7% are men. Students come from 46 states and territories and 24 other countries. 93% are from Ohio. 1% are international students. 72% returned for their sophomore year.

Applying Kent requires a high school transcript and a minimum high school GPA of 2.5, and in some cases SAT I or ACT. The school recommends SAT I or ACT. Application deadline: 5/1; 3/1 priority date for financial aid. Early admission is possible.

KENTUCKY CHRISTIAN COLLEGE

Grayson, KY

Rural setting ■ Private ■ Independent Religious ■ Coed

Web site: www.kcc.edu
Contact: Sandra Deakins, Director of Admissions, 100 Academic Parkway, Box 2021, Grayson, KY 41143-2205
Telephone: 606-474-3266 or toll-free 800-522-3181 **Fax:** 606-474-3155
E-mail: knights@email.kcc.edu

Getting in Last Year 339 applied; 73% were accepted; 149 enrolled (61%).

Financial Matters $8614 tuition and fees (2002–03); $4128 room and board; 56% average percent of need met; $6295 average financial aid amount received per undergraduate.

Academics KCC awards associate, bachelor's, and master's degrees. Challenging opportunities include advanced placement credit, accelerated degree programs, double majors, independent study, and a senior project. Special programs include cooperative education, internships, summer session for credit, and off-campus study. The most frequently chosen baccalaureate fields are education, business/marketing, and psychology. The faculty at KCC has 32 full-time members, 78% with terminal degrees. The student-faculty ratio is 14:1.

Students of KCC The student body totals 595, of whom 581 are undergraduates. 53.2% are women and 46.8% are men. Students come from 24 states and territories and 7 other countries. 34% are from Kentucky. 2.8% are international students. 68% returned for their sophomore year.

Applying KCC requires an essay, SAT I or ACT, a high school transcript, and 3 recommendations, and in some cases an interview. The school recommends a minimum high school GPA of 2.0. Application deadline: rolling admissions; 4/1 priority date for financial aid. Deferred admission is possible.

KENTUCKY MOUNTAIN BIBLE COLLEGE

Vancleve, KY

Rural setting ■ Private ■ Independent Religious ■ Coed

Web site: www.kmbc.edu
Contact: Mr. Dana Beland, Director of Recruiting, PO Box 10, 855 Route 41, Vancleve, KY 41385
Telephone: 606-693-5000 ext. 130 or toll-free 800-879-KMBC ext. 130 (in-state), 800-879-KMBC ext. 136 (out-of-state) **Fax:** 606-693-4884
E-mail: jnelson@kmbc.edu

Financial Matters $4180 tuition and fees (2002–03); $3000 room and board; 30% average percent of need met; $2000 average financial aid amount received per undergraduate.

Academics KMBC awards associate and bachelor's degrees. A senior project is a challenging opportunity. Internships is a special program. The faculty at KMBC has 9 full-time members, 22% with terminal degrees. The student-faculty ratio is 6:1.

Students of KMBC The student body is made up of 88 undergraduates. Students come from 17 states and territories. 29% are from Kentucky. 2.7% are international students. 64% returned for their sophomore year.

Applying KMBC requires an essay, SAT I or ACT, a high school transcript, recommendations, and a minimum high school GPA of 2.0. The school recommends an interview. Application deadline: rolling admissions; 4/1 priority date for financial aid. Deferred admission is possible.

KENTUCKY STATE UNIVERSITY

Frankfort, KY

Small-town setting ■ Public ■ State-related ■ Coed

Web site: www.kysu.edu
Contact: Mr. Vory Billaps, Director of Records, Registration, and Admission, 400 East Main Street, Frankfort, KY 40601-9957
Telephone: 502-597-6340 or toll-free 800-633-9415 (in-state), 800-325-1716 (out-of-state) **Fax:** 502-597-5814
E-mail: jburrell@gwmail.kysu.edu

Getting in Last Year 1,134 applied; 45% were accepted; 339 enrolled (66%).

Financial Matters $2846 resident tuition and fees (2002–03); $7748 nonresident tuition and fees (2002–03); $4214 room and board; 85% average percent of need met; $11,500 average financial aid amount received per undergraduate.

Academics KSU awards associate, bachelor's, and master's degrees. Challenging opportunities include advanced placement credit, accelerated degree programs, student-designed majors, an honors program, and independent study. Special programs include cooperative education, internships, summer session for credit, off-campus study, study-abroad, and Air Force ROTC. The faculty at KSU has 123 full-time members. The student-faculty ratio is 15:1.

Students of KSU The student body totals 2,254, of whom 2,129 are undergraduates. 56.3% are women and 43.7% are men. Students come from 35 states and territories and 27 other countries. 66% are from Kentucky. 74% returned for their sophomore year.

Applying KSU requires SAT I or ACT and a high school transcript, and in some cases an essay, an interview, 2 recommendations, and a minimum high school GPA of 3.0. The school recommends ACT and a minimum high school GPA of 2.0. Application deadline: rolling admissions; 5/31 for financial aid, with a 4/15 priority date. Early admission is possible.

KENTUCKY WESLEYAN COLLEGE

Owensboro, KY

Suburban setting ■ Private ■ Independent Religious ■ Coed

Kentucky Wesleyan College (continued)

Web site: www.kwc.edu
Contact: Mr. Ken Rasp, Dean of Admission, 3000 Frederica Street, PO Box 1039, Owensboro, KY 42302-1039
Telephone: 270-852-3120 or toll-free 800-999-0592 (in-state), 270-926-3111 (out-of-state) **Fax:** 270-926-3196
E-mail: admission@kwc.edu

Getting in Last Year 696 applied; 75% were accepted; 160 enrolled (31%).

Financial Matters $11,400 tuition and fees (2002–03); $5160 room and board; 85% average percent of need met; $10,676 average financial aid amount received per undergraduate.

Academics Kentucky Wesleyan awards bachelor's degrees. Challenging opportunities include advanced placement credit, student-designed majors, double majors, independent study, and a senior project. Special programs include internships, summer session for credit, off-campus study, and study-abroad. The most frequently chosen baccalaureate fields are business/marketing, communications/communication technologies, and education. The faculty at Kentucky Wesleyan has 39 full-time members, 85% with terminal degrees. The student-faculty ratio is 12:1.

Students of Kentucky Wesleyan The student body is made up of 636 undergraduates. 49.5% are women and 50.5% are men. Students come from 19 states and territories and 3 other countries. 75% are from Kentucky. 0.5% are international students. 77% returned for their sophomore year.

Applying Kentucky Wesleyan requires an essay, SAT I or ACT, and a high school transcript, and in some cases recommendations. The school recommends recommendations. Application deadline: 9/1; 3/15 priority date for financial aid. Early and deferred admission are possible.

KENYON COLLEGE

Gambier, OH

Rural setting ■ Private ■ Independent ■ Coed

Web site: www.kenyon.edu
Contact: Ms. M. Beverly Morse, Acting Dean of Admissions, Gambier, OH 43022-9623
Telephone: 740-427-5776 or toll-free 800-848-2468 **Fax:** 740-427-5770
E-mail: admissions@kenyon.edu

Getting in Last Year 2,838 applied; 52% were accepted; 440 enrolled (30%).

Financial Matters $28,710 tuition and fees (2002–03); $4690 room and board; 98% average percent of need met; $21,499 average financial aid amount received per undergraduate.

Academics Kenyon awards bachelor's degrees. Challenging opportunities include advanced placement credit, accelerated degree programs, student-designed majors, an honors program, double majors, independent study, and a senior project. Special programs include internships, off-campus study, and study-abroad. The most frequently chosen baccalaureate fields are social sciences and history, English, and visual/performing arts. The faculty at Kenyon has 144 full-time members, 96% with terminal degrees. The student-faculty ratio is 9:1.

Students of Kenyon The student body is made up of 1,576 undergraduates. 54% are women and 46% are men. 2.6% are international students. 92% returned for their sophomore year.

Applying Kenyon requires an essay, SAT I or ACT, a high school transcript, 1 recommendation, and a minimum high school GPA of 2.0. The school recommends an interview, 2 recommendations, and a minimum high school GPA of 3.0. Application deadline: 2/1; 2/15 priority date for financial aid. Early and deferred admission are possible.

KETTERING UNIVERSITY

Flint, MI

Suburban setting ■ Private ■ Independent ■ Coed

Web site: www.kettering.edu
Contact: Ms. Barbara Sosin, Interim Director of Admissions, 1700 West Third Avenue, Flint, MI 48504-4898
Telephone: 810-762-7865 or toll-free 800-955-4464 ext. 7865 (in-state), 800-955-4464 (out-of-state) **Fax:** 810-762-9837
E-mail: admissions@kettering.edu

Getting in Last Year 2,596 applied; 56% were accepted; 435 enrolled (30%).

Financial Matters $20,333 tuition and fees (2002–03); $4752 room and board; 46% average percent of need met; $13,078 average financial aid amount received per undergraduate (2001–02).

Academics Kettering/GMI awards bachelor's and master's degrees. Challenging opportunities include advanced placement credit, accelerated degree programs, double majors, independent study, and a senior project. Special programs include cooperative education, internships, and study-abroad. The most frequently chosen baccalaureate fields are engineering/engineering technologies, business/marketing, and computer/information sciences. The faculty at Kettering/GMI has 140 full-time members, 90% with terminal degrees. The student-faculty ratio is 9:1.

Students of Kettering/GMI The student body totals 3,166, of whom 2,487 are undergraduates. 17.3% are women and 82.7% are men. Students come from 48 states and territories and 15 other countries. 63% are from Michigan. 2.2% are international students. 87% returned for their sophomore year.

Applying Kettering/GMI requires SAT I or ACT and a high school transcript, and in some cases an essay. The school recommends SAT II Subject Tests, an interview, and a minimum high school GPA of 3.0. Application deadline: rolling admissions; 2/14 priority date for financial aid. Deferred admission is possible.

KEUKA COLLEGE

Keuka Park, NY

Rural setting ■ Private ■ Independent Religious ■ Coed

Web site: www.keuka.edu
Contact: Ms. Claudine Ninestine, Director of Admissions, Keuka Park, NY 14478-0098
Telephone: 315-279-5413 or toll-free 800-33-KEUKA **Fax:** 315-279-5386
E-mail: admissions@mail.keuka.edu

Getting in Last Year 685 applied; 79% were accepted; 198 enrolled (36%).

Financial Matters $15,140 tuition and fees (2002–03); $7300 room and board; 80% average percent of need met; $13,718 average financial aid amount received per undergraduate.

Academics Keuka awards bachelor's and master's degrees. Challenging opportunities include advanced placement credit, accelerated degree programs, student-designed majors, double majors, independent study, and a senior project. Special programs include cooperative education, internships, summer session for credit, off-campus study, and study-abroad. The most frequently chosen baccalaureate fields are health professions and related sciences, education, and business/marketing. The faculty at Keuka has 52 full-time members, 60% with terminal degrees. The student-faculty ratio is 15:1.

Students of Keuka The student body is made up of 1,124 undergraduates. 69.2% are women and 30.8% are men. Students come from 17 states and territories. 94% are from New York. 71% returned for their sophomore year.

Applying Keuka requires an essay, SAT I or ACT, a high school transcript, and recommendations, and in some cases an interview. The school recommends an interview and a minimum high school GPA of 2.75. Application deadline: rolling admissions; 3/15 priority date for financial aid. Early and deferred admission are possible.

KING COLLEGE

Bristol, TN

Suburban setting ■ Private ■ Independent Religious ■ Coed

Web site: www.king.edu
Contact: Mr. Micah Crews, Director of Admissions, 1350 King College Road, Bristol, TN 37620-2699
Telephone: 423-652-4773 or toll-free 800-362-0014 **Fax:** 423-652-4727
E-mail: admissions@king.edu

Getting in Last Year 694 applied; 60% were accepted; 135 enrolled (33%).

Financial Matters $15,034 tuition and fees (2002–03); $4960 room and board; 65% average percent of need met; $14,330 average financial aid amount received per undergraduate.

Academics King awards bachelor's and master's degrees. Challenging opportunities include advanced placement credit, accelerated degree programs, an honors program, double majors, independent study, and a senior project. Special programs include internships, summer session for credit, off-campus study, study-abroad, and Army ROTC. The most frequently chosen baccalaureate fields are business/marketing, liberal arts/general studies, and biological/life sciences. The faculty at King has 45 full-time members, 76% with terminal degrees. The student-faculty ratio is 11:1.

Students of King The student body totals 733, of whom 688 are undergraduates. 61.3% are women and 38.7% are men. Students come from 24 states and territories and 27 other countries. 58% are from Tennessee. 9% are international students. 77% returned for their sophomore year.

Applying King requires an essay, SAT I or ACT, a high school transcript, and a minimum high school GPA of 2.4, and in some cases an interview and recommendations. The school recommends an interview and recommendations. Application deadline: rolling admissions. Early and deferred admission are possible.

KING'S COLLEGE

Wilkes-Barre, PA

Suburban setting ■ Private ■ Independent Religious ■ Coed

Web site: www.kings.edu
Contact: Ms. Michelle Lawrence-Schmude, Director of Admissions, 133 North River Street, Wilkes-Barre, PA 18711-0801
Telephone: 570-208-5858 or toll-free 888-KINGSPA **Fax:** 570-208-5971
E-mail: admissions@kings.edu

Getting in Last Year 1,543 applied; 78% were accepted; 410 enrolled (34%).

Financial Matters $18,150 tuition and fees (2002–03); $7550 room and board; 53% average percent of need met; $13,626 average financial aid amount received per undergraduate.

Academics King's awards associate, bachelor's, and master's degrees. Challenging opportunities include advanced placement credit, accelerated degree programs, student-designed majors, an honors program, double majors, independent study, and a senior project. Special programs include internships, summer session for credit, off-campus study, study-abroad, and Army and Air Force ROTC. The most frequently chosen baccalaureate fields are business/marketing, education, and health professions and related sciences. The faculty at King's has 114 full-time members, 81% with terminal degrees. The student-faculty ratio is 13:1.

Students of King's The student body totals 2,188, of whom 2,039 are undergraduates. 52.7% are women and 47.3% are men. Students come from 22 states and territories and 6 other countries. 76% are from Pennsylvania. 0.5% are international students. 81% returned for their sophomore year.

Applying King's requires an essay, SAT I or ACT, and a high school transcript. The school recommends an interview and 2 recommendations. Application deadline: rolling admissions; 2/15 priority date for financial aid. Early and deferred admission are possible.

THE KING'S UNIVERSITY COLLEGE

Edmonton, AB Canada

Suburban setting ■ Private ■ Independent Religious ■ Coed

Web site: www.kingsu.ca

Contact: Mr. Glenn J. Keeler, Registrar/Director of Admissions, 9125-50 Street, Edmonton, AB T6B 2H3

Telephone: 780-465-8335 or toll-free 800-661-8582 **Fax:** 780-465-3534

E-mail: admissions@kingsu.ca

Getting in Last Year 518 applied; 85% were accepted; 155 enrolled (35%).

Financial Matters $6223 tuition and fees (2002–03); $5505 room and board.

Academics King's awards bachelor's degrees. Challenging opportunities include advanced placement credit, double majors, independent study, and a senior project. Special programs include internships, off-campus study, and study-abroad. The most frequently chosen baccalaureate fields are psychology, social sciences and history, and education. The faculty at King's has 39 full-time members, 85% with terminal degrees. The student-faculty ratio is 10:1.

Students of King's The student body is made up of 632 undergraduates. 56.5% are women and 43.5% are men. Students come from 9 states and territories and 25 other countries. 72% are from Alberta. 73% returned for their sophomore year.

Applying King's requires a high school transcript, 1 recommendation, and a minimum high school GPA of 2.0, and in some cases an essay and an interview. The school recommends SAT I and SAT II or ACT. Application deadline: rolling admissions; 3/31 for financial aid.

KNOX COLLEGE

Galesburg, IL

Small-town setting ■ Private ■ Independent ■ Coed

Web site: www.knox.edu

Contact: Mr. Paul Steenis, Director of Admissions, Box K-148, Galesburg, IL 61401

Telephone: 309-341-7100 or toll-free 800-678-KNOX **Fax:** 309-341-7070

E-mail: admission@knox.edu

Getting in Last Year 1,542 applied; 72% were accepted; 300 enrolled (27%).

Financial Matters $23,499 tuition and fees (2002–03); $5760 room and board; 99% average percent of need met; $20,356 average financial aid amount received per undergraduate.

Academics Knox awards bachelor's degrees. Challenging opportunities include advanced placement credit, student-designed majors, an honors program, double majors, independent study, and a senior project. Special programs include internships, off-campus study, and study-abroad. The most frequently chosen baccalaureate fields are social sciences and history, biological/life sciences, and English. The faculty at Knox has 90 full-time members, 93% with terminal degrees. The student-faculty ratio is 12:1.

Students of Knox The student body is made up of 1,121 undergraduates. 53.4% are women and 46.6% are men. Students come from 45 states and territories and 42 other countries. 56% are from Illinois. 7.9% are international students. 88% returned for their sophomore year.

Applying Knox requires an essay, SAT I or ACT, a high school transcript, and 2 recommendations. The school recommends an interview. Application deadline: 2/1; 3/1 priority date for financial aid. Early and deferred admission are possible.

KUTZTOWN UNIVERSITY OF PENNSYLVANIA

Kutztown, PA

Rural setting ■ Public ■ State-supported ■ Coed

Web site: www.kutztown.edu

Contact: Dr. William Stahler, Director of Admissions, 15200 Kutztown Road, Kutztown, PA 19530-0730

Telephone: 610-683-4060 ext. 4053 or toll-free 877-628-1915 **Fax:** 610-683-1375

E-mail: admission@kutztown.edu

Getting in Last Year 6,688 applied; 66% were accepted; 1,788 enrolled (41%).

Financial Matters $5477 resident tuition and fees (2002–03); $12,045 nonresident tuition and fees (2002–03); $4682 room and board; 72% average percent of need met; $5831 average financial aid amount received per undergraduate (2001–02).

Academics Kutztown University awards bachelor's and master's degrees. Challenging opportunities include advanced placement credit, accelerated degree programs, student-designed majors, an honors program, double majors, independent study, and a senior project. Special programs include internships, summer session for credit, off-campus study, study-abroad, and Army and Air Force ROTC. The most frequently chosen baccalaureate fields are education, business/marketing, and visual/performing arts. The faculty at Kutztown University has 358 full-time members, 77% with terminal degrees. The student-faculty ratio is 21:1.

Students of Kutztown University The student body totals 8,524, of whom 7,591 are undergraduates. 60.6% are women and 39.4% are men. Students come from 17 states and territories and 36 other countries. 92% are from Pennsylvania. 1% are international students. 74% returned for their sophomore year.

Applying Kutztown University requires SAT I or ACT, a high school transcript, and a minimum high school GPA of 2.0, and in some cases SAT II Subject Tests and audition required for music program; portfolio and/or art test required for art education, communication design, crafts, and fine arts programs. Application deadline: 3/1; 2/15 priority date for financial aid. Early and deferred admission are possible.

KWANTLEN UNIVERSITY COLLEGE

Surrey, BC Canada

Public ■ Coed

Web site: www.kwantlen.bc.ca

Contact: Ms. Jody Gordon, Registrar, 12666 - 72nd Avenue, Surrey, BC V3W 2M8 Canada

Telephone: 604-599-2018 or toll-free 604-599-2100 (in-state) **Fax:** 604-599-2068

E-mail: admissio@kwantlen.ca

Getting in Last Year 11,500 enrolled.

Financial Matters $1280 resident tuition and fees (2002–03).

Academics Kwantlen University College awards associate and bachelor's degrees. Challenging opportunities include advanced placement credit, accelerated degree programs, double majors, and independent study. Special programs include cooperative education, internships, summer session for credit, and study-abroad. The faculty at Kwantlen University College has 672 members. The student-faculty ratio is 35:1.

Students of Kwantlen University College The student body totals 24,000, of whom 13,600 are undergraduates. 54.9% are women and 45.1% are men.

Applying Kwantlen University College requires a high school transcript, and in some cases an essay, an interview, portfolio, external testing, certain levels of certification (i.e. - first aid), and a minimum high school GPA of 2.0. The school recommends a high school transcript. Application deadline: 6/30. Early admission is possible.

LABORATORY INSTITUTE OF MERCHANDISING

New York, NY

Urban setting ■ Private ■ Proprietary ■ Coed, Primarily Women

Web site: www.limcollege.edu

Contact: Ms. Karen Hamill Iglio, Director of Admissions, 12 East 53rd Street, New York, NY 10022

Telephone: 212-752-1530 ext. 213 or toll-free 800-677-1323 **Fax:** 212-421-4341

E-mail: admissions@limcollege.edu

Getting in Last Year 302 applied; 62% were accepted; 92 enrolled (49%).

Financial Matters $14,250 tuition and fees (2002–03); 87% average percent of need met; $11,500 average financial aid amount received per undergraduate.

Academics LIM awards associate and bachelor's degrees. Challenging opportunities include advanced placement credit and a senior project. Special programs include internships, summer session for credit, and study-abroad. The faculty at LIM has 9 full-time members, 11% with terminal degrees. The student-faculty ratio is 8:1.

Students of LIM The student body is made up of 405 undergraduates. 96.3% are women and 3.7% are men. Students come from 26 states and territories and 6 other countries. 51% are from New York. 1.7% are international students.

Applying LIM requires an essay, SAT I or ACT, a high school transcript, and an interview. The school recommends recommendations and a minimum high school GPA of 2.5. Application deadline: rolling admissions. Deferred admission is possible.

LAFAYETTE COLLEGE

Easton, PA

Suburban setting ■ Private ■ Independent Religious ■ Coed

Web site: www.lafayette.edu
Contact: Ms. Carol Rowlands, Director of Admissions, Easton, PA 18042-1798
Telephone: 610-330-5100 **Fax:** 610-330-5355
E-mail: admissions@lafayette.edu

Getting in Last Year 5,504 applied; 36% were accepted; 580 enrolled (29%).

Financial Matters $24,921 tuition and fees (2002–03); $7734 room and board; 94% average percent of need met; $20,609 average financial aid amount received per undergraduate.

Academics Lafayette awards bachelor's degrees. Challenging opportunities include advanced placement credit, accelerated degree programs, student-designed majors, and an honors program. Special programs include internships, summer session for credit, off-campus study, study-abroad, and Army ROTC. The faculty at Lafayette has 183 full-time members, 100% with terminal degrees. The student-faculty ratio is 11:1.

Students of Lafayette The student body is made up of 2,300 undergraduates. 49.2% are women and 50.8% are men. Students come from 40 states and territories and 38 other countries. 29% are from Pennsylvania. 4.9% are international students. 95% returned for their sophomore year.

Applying Lafayette requires an essay, SAT I, SAT II Subject Tests, a high school transcript, and 1 recommendation. The school recommends SAT II: Writing Test and an interview. Application deadline: 1/1; 2/1 for financial aid. Early and deferred admission are possible.

LAGRANGE COLLEGE

LaGrange, GA

Small-town setting ■ Private ■ Independent Religious ■ Coed

Web site: www.lagrange.edu
Contact: Mr. Andy Geeter, Director of Admission, 601 Broad Street, LaGrange, GA 30240-2999
Telephone: 706-880-8253 or toll-free 800-593-2885 **Fax:** 706-880-8010
E-mail: lgcadmis@langrange.edu

Getting in Last Year 570 applied; 81% were accepted; 235 enrolled (51%).

Financial Matters $13,226 tuition and fees (2002–03); $5494 room and board; 79% average percent of need met; $12,269 average financial aid amount received per undergraduate.

Academics LaGrange awards associate, bachelor's, and master's degrees. Challenging opportunities include advanced placement credit, double majors, independent study, and a senior project. Special programs include internships, summer session for credit, and study-abroad. The most frequently chosen baccalaureate fields are business/marketing, education, and computer/information sciences. The faculty at LaGrange has 63 full-time members, 79% with terminal degrees. The student-faculty ratio is 10:1.

Students of LaGrange The student body totals 1,016, of whom 967 are undergraduates. 63.5% are women and 36.5% are men. Students come from 17 states and territories and 12 other countries. 89% are from Georgia. 2.2% are international students. 74% returned for their sophomore year.

Applying LaGrange requires an essay, SAT I or ACT, a high school transcript, and a minimum high school GPA of 2.0, and in some cases an interview and 1 recommendation. Application deadline: 8/15; 3/1 for financial aid. Early and deferred admission are possible.

LAGUNA COLLEGE OF ART & DESIGN

Laguna Beach, CA

Small-town setting ■ Private ■ Independent ■ Coed

Web site: aiscnews.org
Contact: Mr. Anthony Padilla, Vice President of Enrollment, 2222 Laguna Canyon Road, Laguna Beach, CA 92651-1136
Telephone: 949-376-6000 ext. 232 or toll-free 800-255-0762 **Fax:** 949-376-6009
E-mail: admissions@lagunacollege.edu

Getting in Last Year 245 applied; 88% were accepted; 70 enrolled (33%).

Financial Matters $14,900 tuition and fees (2002–03); 70% average percent of need met.

Academics Laguna College of Art & Design awards bachelor's degrees. Challenging opportunities include advanced placement credit, independent study, and a senior project. Special programs include internships, summer session for credit, and off-campus study. The most frequently chosen baccalaureate field is visual/performing arts. The faculty at Laguna College of Art & Design has 10 full-time members. The student-faculty ratio is 10:1.

Students of Laguna College of Art & Design The student body is made up of 310 undergraduates. 46.8% are women and 53.2% are men. Students come from 32 states and territories. 58% are from California. 6.5% are international students. 88% returned for their sophomore year.

Applying Laguna College of Art & Design requires an essay, SAT I or ACT, a high school transcript, an interview, 1 recommendation, portfolio, and a minimum high school GPA of 3.0. The school recommends a minimum high school GPA of 3.5. Application deadline: 2/2. Deferred admission is possible.

LAKE ERIE COLLEGE

Painesville, OH

Small-town setting ■ Private ■ Independent ■ Coed

Web site: www.lec.edu
Contact: Ms. Alison Dewey, Director of Admissions, 391 West Washington Street, Painesville, OH 44077-3389
Telephone: 440-639-7883 or toll-free 800-916-0904 **Fax:** 440-352-3533
E-mail: lecadmit@lec.edu

Getting in Last Year 487 applied; 84% were accepted; 135 enrolled (33%).

Financial Matters $17,210 tuition and fees (2002–03); $5700 room and board; 85% average percent of need met.

Academics Lake Erie awards bachelor's and master's degrees. Challenging opportunities include advanced placement credit, accelerated degree programs, student-designed majors, double majors, independent study, and a senior project. Special programs include cooperative education, internships, summer session for credit, off-campus study, and study-abroad. The most frequently chosen baccalaureate fields are business/marketing, computer/information sciences, and agriculture. The faculty at Lake Erie has 36 full-time members, 78% with terminal degrees. The student-faculty ratio is 13:1.

Students of Lake Erie The student body totals 977, of whom 690 are undergraduates. 75.5% are women and 24.5% are men. Students come from 19 states and territories and 8 other countries. 85% are from Ohio. 2.5% are international students. 70% returned for their sophomore year.

Applying Lake Erie requires SAT I or ACT, a high school transcript, and a minimum high school GPA of 2.0. The school recommends an interview. Early admission is possible.

LAKE FOREST COLLEGE

Lake Forest, IL

Suburban setting ■ Private ■ Independent ■ Coed

Web site: www.lakeforest.edu
Contact: Mr. William G. Motzer Jr., Director of Admissions, 555 North Sheridan Road, Lake Forest, IL 60045-2399
Telephone: 847-735-5000 or toll-free 800-828-4751 **Fax:** 847-735-6271
E-mail: admissions@lakeforest.edu

Getting in Last Year 1,666 applied; 66% were accepted; 359 enrolled (33%).

Financial Matters $23,286 tuition and fees (2002–03); $5524 room and board; 100% average percent of need met; $20,020 average financial aid amount received per undergraduate.

Academics Lake Forest awards bachelor's and master's degrees. Challenging opportunities include advanced placement credit, accelerated degree programs, student-designed majors, freshman honors college, an honors program, double majors, independent study, and a senior project. Special programs include internships, summer session for credit, off-campus study, and study-abroad. The most frequently chosen baccalaureate fields are social sciences and history, business/marketing, and psychology. The faculty at Lake Forest has 87 full-time members, 97% with terminal degrees. The student-faculty ratio is 12:1.

Students of Lake Forest The student body totals 1,341, of whom 1,319 are undergraduates. 58.7% are women and 41.3% are men. Students come from 45 states and territories and 42 other countries. 48% are from Illinois. 8.3% are international students. 77% returned for their sophomore year.

Applying Lake Forest requires an essay, SAT I or ACT, a high school transcript, 2 recommendations, and graded paper. The school recommends an interview. Application deadline: 3/1; 3/1 priority date for financial aid. Early and deferred admission are possible.

LAKEHEAD UNIVERSITY

Thunder Bay, ON Canada

Suburban setting ■ Public ■ Coed

Web site: www.lakeheadu.ca
Contact: Ms. Sarena Knapik, Director, Admissions and Recruitment, 955 Oliver Road, Thunder Bay, ON P7B 5E1 Canada
Telephone: 807-343-8500 or toll-free 800-465-3959 (in-state) **Fax:** 807-343-8156
E-mail: admissions@lakeheadu.ca

Getting in Last Year 6,982 applied; 67% were accepted.

Financial Matters $4488 nonresident tuition and fees (2002–03); $5815 room and board.

Academics Lakehead awards bachelor's, master's, and doctoral degrees. Challenging opportunities include advanced placement credit, accelerated degree programs, student-designed majors, an honors program, double majors, independent study, and a senior project. Special programs include cooperative education and summer session for credit. The faculty at Lakehead has 242 full-time members, 80% with terminal degrees. The student-faculty ratio is 19:1.

Students of Lakehead The student body totals 6,525, of whom 6,130 are undergraduates. 58.4% are women and 41.6% are men. Students come from 13 states and territories and 52 other countries. 94% are from Ontario.

Applying Lakehead requires (in some cases) an essay, a high school transcript, and 3 recommendations. Application deadline: rolling admissions; 6/30 for financial aid. Early admission is possible.

LAKELAND COLLEGE

Sheboygan, WI

Rural setting ■ Private ■ Independent Religious ■ Coed

Web site: www.lakeland.edu

Contact: Mr. Leo Gavrilos, Director of Admissions, PO Box 359, Nash Visitors Center, Sheboygan, WI 53082-0359

Telephone: 920-565-1217 or toll-free 800-242-3347 (in-state)

E-mail: admissions@lakeland.edu

Getting in Last Year 569 applied; 77% were accepted; 160 enrolled (37%).

Financial Matters $13,835 tuition and fees (2002–03); $5358 room and board; 83% average percent of need met; $9976 average financial aid amount received per undergraduate.

Academics Lakeland awards bachelor's and master's degrees. Challenging opportunities include advanced placement credit, an honors program, independent study, and a senior project. Special programs include internships, summer session for credit, off-campus study, and study-abroad. The most frequently chosen baccalaureate fields are business/marketing, computer/information sciences, and education. The faculty at Lakeland has 48 full-time members, 65% with terminal degrees. The student-faculty ratio is 19:1.

Students of Lakeland The student body totals 3,586, of whom 3,254 are undergraduates. 60.4% are women and 39.6% are men. Students come from 41 states and territories and 37 other countries. 85% are from Wisconsin. 4.6% are international students. 59% returned for their sophomore year.

Applying Lakeland requires an essay, SAT I or ACT, a high school transcript, and a minimum high school GPA of 2.0, and in some cases an interview. The school recommends recommendations. Application deadline: 7/15; 7/1 for financial aid, with a 5/1 priority date. Deferred admission is possible.

LAKEVIEW COLLEGE OF NURSING

Danville, IL

Small-town setting ■ Private ■ Independent ■ Coed

Web site: www.lakeviewcol.edu

Contact: Kelly M. Holden, MS Ed, Registrar, 903 North Logan Avenue, Danville, IL 61832

Telephone: 217-443-5238 ext. 5385 or toll-free 217-443-5238 ext. 5454 (in-state), 217-443-5238 (out-of-state) **Fax:** 217-442-2279

E-mail: kholden@lakeviewcol.edu

Getting in Last Year 45 applied; 87% were accepted.

Financial Matters $8000 tuition and fees (2002–03); 58% average percent of need met; $3200 average financial aid amount received per undergraduate.

Academics LCON awards bachelor's degrees. Challenging opportunities include an honors program and independent study. Special programs include summer session for credit and off-campus study. The most frequently chosen baccalaureate field is health professions and related sciences. The faculty at LCON has 3 full-time members. The student-faculty ratio is 8:1.

Students of LCON The student body is made up of 83 undergraduates. 94% are women and 6% are men. Students come from 3 states and territories. 95% are from Illinois.

Applying Deferred admission is possible.

LAMAR UNIVERSITY

Beaumont, TX

Suburban setting ■ Public ■ State-supported ■ Coed

Web site: www.lamar.edu

Contact: Ms. Melissa Chesser, Director of Recruitment, PO Box 10009, Beaumont, TX 77710

Telephone: 409-880-8888 **Fax:** 409-880-8463

E-mail: admissions@hal.lamar.edu

Getting in Last Year 3,269 applied; 69% were accepted; 1,312 enrolled (58%).

Financial Matters $3076 resident tuition and fees (2002–03); $9616 nonresident tuition and fees (2002–03); $5010 room and board; 12% average percent of need met; $792 average financial aid amount received per undergraduate.

Academics Lamar awards associate, bachelor's, master's, and doctoral degrees. Challenging opportunities include advanced placement credit, accelerated degree programs, student-designed majors, an honors program, and a senior project. Special programs include cooperative education, internships, summer session for credit, off-campus study, and study-abroad. The faculty at Lamar has 360 full-time members, 66% with terminal degrees. The student-faculty ratio is 25:1.

Students of Lamar The student body totals 9,802, of whom 8,669 are undergraduates. 59.5% are women and 40.5% are men. Students come from 39 states and territories. 0.7% are international students. 67% returned for their sophomore year.

Applying Lamar requires SAT I or ACT and a high school transcript, and in some cases an essay and SAT II Subject Tests. Application deadline: 8/1; 4/1 priority date for financial aid. Early admission is possible.

LAMBUTH UNIVERSITY

Jackson, TN

Urban setting ■ Private ■ Independent Religious ■ Coed

Web site: www.lambuth.edu

Contact: Ms. Andrea Shumate, Associate Director of Admissions, 705 Lambuth Boulevard, Jackson, TN 38301

Telephone: 731-425-3324 or toll-free 800-526-2884 **Fax:** 731-425-3496

E-mail: admit@lambuth.edu

Getting in Last Year 768 applied; 71% were accepted; 196 enrolled (36%).

Financial Matters $10,500 tuition and fees (2002–03); $4930 room and board; 72% average percent of need met; $8107 average financial aid amount received per undergraduate (2000–01 estimated).

Academics Lambuth awards bachelor's degrees. Challenging opportunities include advanced placement credit, accelerated degree programs, student-designed majors, an honors program, double majors, independent study, and a senior project. Special programs include internships, summer session for credit, off-campus study, and study-abroad. The most frequently chosen baccalaureate fields are business/marketing, education, and social sciences and history. The faculty at Lambuth has 52 full-time members, 75% with terminal degrees. The student-faculty ratio is 14:1.

Students of Lambuth The student body is made up of 888 undergraduates. 56% are women and 44% are men. Students come from 24 states and territories and 20 other countries. 79% are from Tennessee. 2.7% are international students. 63% returned for their sophomore year.

Applying Lambuth requires an essay, SAT I or ACT, a high school transcript, and a minimum high school GPA of 2.0, and in some cases 3 recommendations. The school recommends an interview. Application deadline: rolling admissions; 2/15 priority date for financial aid. Early and deferred admission are possible.

LANCASTER BIBLE COLLEGE

Lancaster, PA

Suburban setting ■ Private ■ Independent Religious ■ Coed

Web site: www.lbc.edu

Contact: Mrs. Joanne M. Roper, Director of Admissions, 901 Eden Road, Lancaster, PA 17601-5036

Telephone: 717-560-8271 or toll-free 888-866-LBC-4-YOU **Fax:** 717-560-8213

E-mail: admissions@lbc.edu

Getting in Last Year 235 applied; 80% were accepted; 130 enrolled (70%).

Financial Matters $10,990 tuition and fees (2002–03); $5010 room and board; 67% average percent of need met; $7969 average financial aid amount received per undergraduate.

Academics LBC awards associate, bachelor's, and master's degrees and post-bachelor's certificates. Challenging opportunities include advanced placement credit, double majors, and independent study. Special programs include internships, summer session for credit, and study-abroad. The most frequently chosen baccalaureate field is education. The faculty at LBC has 29 full-time members, 72% with terminal degrees. The student-faculty ratio is 15:1.

Students of LBC The student body totals 888, of whom 757 are undergraduates. 55.2% are women and 44.8% are men. Students come from 25 states and territories and 8 other countries. 71% are from Pennsylvania. 1.7% are international students. 83% returned for their sophomore year.

Applying LBC requires an essay, SAT I or ACT, a high school transcript, 3 recommendations, and a minimum high school GPA of 2.0, and in some cases an interview. Application deadline: rolling admissions; 5/1 priority date for financial aid. Early and deferred admission are possible.

LANDER UNIVERSITY

Greenwood, SC

Small-town setting ■ Public ■ State-supported ■ Coed

Web site: www.lander.edu

Contact: Mr. Jeffrey A. Constant, Assistant Director of Admissions, 320 Stanley Avenue, Greenwood, SC 29649-2099

Telephone: 864-388-8307 or toll-free 888-452-6337 **Fax:** 864-388-8125

E-mail: admissions@lander.edu

Getting in Last Year 1,603 applied; 81% were accepted; 529 enrolled (41%).

Lander University (continued)

Financial Matters $4804 resident tuition and fees (2002–03); $9748 nonresident tuition and fees (2002–03); $4548 room and board; 68% average percent of need met; $5105 average financial aid amount received per undergraduate (2001–02).

Academics Lander awards bachelor's and master's degrees. Challenging opportunities include advanced placement credit, accelerated degree programs, student-designed majors, an honors program, double majors, independent study, and a senior project. Special programs include cooperative education, internships, summer session for credit, off-campus study, study-abroad, and Army ROTC. The most frequently chosen baccalaureate fields are business/marketing, education, and social sciences and history. The faculty at Lander has 136 full-time members. The student-faculty ratio is 16:1.

Students of Lander The student body totals 2,947, of whom 2,613 are undergraduates. 62.5% are women and 37.5% are men. Students come from 24 states and territories and 22 other countries. 97% are from South Carolina. 2.1% are international students. 67% returned for their sophomore year.

Applying Lander requires SAT I or ACT, a high school transcript, and 1 recommendation. The school recommends an interview. Application deadline: rolling admissions. Early and deferred admission are possible.

LANE COLLEGE

Jackson, TN

Suburban setting ■ *Private* ■ *Independent Religious* ■ *Coed*

Web site: www.lanecollege.edu

Contact: Ms. E. Brown, Director of Admissions, 545 Lane Avenue, Bray Administration Building 2nd Floor, Jackson, TN 38301-4598

Telephone: 901-426-7532 or toll-free 800-960-7533 **Fax:** 731-426-7559

E-mail: admissions@lanecollege.edu

Getting in Last Year 2,097 applied; 38% were accepted; 299 enrolled (38%).

Financial Matters $6570 tuition and fees (2002–03); $4080 room and board; 77% average percent of need met; $7852 average financial aid amount received per undergraduate.

Academics LC awards bachelor's degrees. Challenging opportunities include advanced placement credit, accelerated degree programs, an honors program, double majors, independent study, and a senior project. Special programs include cooperative education, internships, summer session for credit, off-campus study, and study-abroad. The most frequently chosen baccalaureate fields are business/marketing, protective services/public administration, and education. The faculty at LC has 45 full-time members, 71% with terminal degrees. The student-faculty ratio is 15:1.

Students of LC The student body is made up of 813 undergraduates. 50.7% are women and 49.3% are men. Students come from 26 states and territories. 59% are from Tennessee. 74% returned for their sophomore year.

Applying LC requires SAT I or ACT, a high school transcript, 2 recommendations, and a minimum high school GPA of 2.0. Application deadline: rolling admissions; 4/1 priority date for financial aid. Early admission is possible.

LANGSTON UNIVERSITY

Langston, OK

Rural setting ■ *Public* ■ *State-supported* ■ *Coed*

Web site: www.lunet.edu

Contact: Brent Russell, Assistant Director of Admission, Langston University, PO Box 728, Langston, OK 73120

Telephone: 405-466-2984 or toll-free 405-466-3428 **Fax:** 405-466-3391

Getting in Last Year 2,088 applied; 50% were accepted; 481 enrolled (47%).

Financial Matters $5469 nonresident tuition and fees (2002–03); $1680 room and board; 77% average percent of need met; $6391 average financial aid amount received per undergraduate.

Academics Langston University awards associate, bachelor's, and master's degrees. Challenging opportunities include advanced placement credit, accelerated degree programs, and an honors program. Special programs include cooperative education, internships, summer session for credit, and Army ROTC. The most frequently chosen baccalaureate fields are health professions and related sciences, education, and psychology. The student-faculty ratio is 30:1.

Students of Langston University The student body totals 3,008, of whom 2,898 are undergraduates. Students come from 37 states and territories and 8 other countries. 0.5% are international students.

Applying Langston University requires SAT I or ACT, a high school transcript, and a minimum high school GPA of 2.70, and in some cases recommendations. Application deadline: rolling admissions; 3/15 priority date for financial aid.

LA ROCHE COLLEGE

Pittsburgh, PA

Suburban setting ■ *Private* ■ *Independent Religious* ■ *Coed*

Web site: www.laroche.edu

Contact: Ms. Dayna R. McNally, Dean of Admissions and Enrollment Management, 9000 Babcock Boulevard, Pittsburgh, PA 15237-5898

Telephone: 412-536-1049 or toll-free 800-838-4LRC **Fax:** 412-536-1048

E-mail: admsns@laroche.edu

Getting in Last Year 637 applied; 77% were accepted; 295 enrolled (60%).

Financial Matters $13,190 tuition and fees (2002–03); $6474 room and board; 90% average percent of need met; $11,750 average financial aid amount received per undergraduate.

Academics La Roche awards associate, bachelor's, and master's degrees. Challenging opportunities include advanced placement credit, accelerated degree programs, freshman honors college, an honors program, double majors, independent study, and a senior project. Special programs include internships, summer session for credit, study-abroad, and Army and Air Force ROTC. The most frequently chosen baccalaureate fields are business/marketing, health professions and related sciences, and visual/performing arts. The faculty at La Roche has 66 full-time members, 80% with terminal degrees. The student-faculty ratio is 14:1.

Students of La Roche The student body totals 1,981, of whom 1,760 are undergraduates. 63% are women and 37% are men. Students come from 16 states and territories and 28 other countries. 95% are from Pennsylvania. 19.8% are international students. 83% returned for their sophomore year.

Applying La Roche requires SAT I or ACT, a high school transcript, recommendations, and a minimum high school GPA of 2.0. The school recommends an essay, an interview, and a minimum high school GPA of 3.0. Application deadline: rolling admissions; 5/1 for financial aid, with a 3/1 priority date. Early and deferred admission are possible.

LA SALLE UNIVERSITY

Philadelphia, PA

Urban setting ■ *Private* ■ *Independent Religious* ■ *Coed*

Web site: www.lasalle.edu

Contact: Mr. Robert G. Voss, Dean of Admission and Financial Aid, 1900 West Olney Avenue, Philadelphia, PA 19141-1199

Telephone: 215-951-1500 or toll-free 800-328-1910 **Fax:** 215-951-1656

E-mail: admiss@lasalle.edu

Getting in Last Year 4,261 applied; 74% were accepted; 866 enrolled (28%).

Financial Matters $21,420 tuition and fees (2002–03); $8350 room and board; 79% average percent of need met; $15,519 average financial aid amount received per undergraduate.

Academics La Salle awards associate, bachelor's, master's, and doctoral degrees. Challenging opportunities include advanced placement credit, accelerated degree programs, student-designed majors, freshman honors college, an honors program, double majors, independent study, and a senior project. Special programs include cooperative education, internships, summer session for credit, off-campus study, study-abroad, and Army and Air Force ROTC. The most frequently chosen baccalaureate fields are business/marketing, communications/communication technologies, and education. The faculty at La Salle has 197 full-time members, 81% with terminal degrees. The student-faculty ratio is 16:1.

Students of La Salle The student body totals 5,752, of whom 4,060 are undergraduates. 57.1% are women and 42.9% are men. Students come from 30 states and territories and 35 other countries. 1% are international students. 88% returned for their sophomore year.

Applying La Salle requires an essay, SAT I or ACT, a high school transcript, and 1 recommendation. The school recommends an interview. Application deadline: 4/1; 3/15 priority date for financial aid. Early and deferred admission are possible.

LASELL COLLEGE

Newton, MA

Suburban setting ■ *Private* ■ *Independent* ■ *Coed*

Web site: www.lasell.edu

Contact: Mr. James Tweed, Director of Admission, 1844 Commonwealth Avenue, Newton, MA 02466

Telephone: 617-243-2225 or toll-free 888-LASELL-4 **Fax:** 617-796-4343

E-mail: info@lasell.edu

Getting in Last Year 2,182 applied; 70% were accepted; 319 enrolled (21%).

Financial Matters $16,700 tuition and fees (2002–03); $8300 room and board; 75% average percent of need met; $15,613 average financial aid amount received per undergraduate.

Academics Lasell awards bachelor's and master's degrees. Challenging opportunities include advanced placement credit, student-designed majors, an honors program, double majors, independent study, and a senior project. Special programs include cooperative education, internships, and study-abroad. The faculty at Lasell has 44 full-time members, 34% with terminal degrees. The student-faculty ratio is 11:1.

Students of Lasell The student body totals 1,048, of whom 1,036 are undergraduates. 75% are women and 25% are men. Students come from 20 states and territories and 8 other countries. 66% are from Massachusetts. 3.7% are international students. 82% returned for their sophomore year.

Applying Lasell requires SAT I, a high school transcript, 1 recommendation, and a minimum high school GPA of 2.0. The school recommends an essay and an interview. Application deadline: rolling admissions; 3/1 priority date for financial aid. Deferred admission is possible.

LA SIERRA UNIVERSITY

Riverside, CA

Suburban setting ■ *Private* ■ *Independent Religious* ■ *Coed*

Web site: www.lasierra.edu

Contact: Dr. Tom Smith, Director of Admissions, 4700 Pierce Street, Riverside, CA 92515-8247

Telephone: 909-785-2176 or toll-free 800-874-5587 **Fax:** 909-785-2477

E-mail: ivy@lasierra.edu

Getting in Last Year 929 applied; 59% were accepted; 344 enrolled (63%).

Financial Matters $15,997 tuition and fees (2002–03); $4302 room and board.

Academics La Sierra awards bachelor's, master's, and doctoral degrees and post-bachelor's and post-master's certificates. Challenging opportunities include advanced placement credit, accelerated degree programs, student-designed majors, an honors program, double majors, independent study, and a senior project. Special programs include internships, summer session for credit, off-campus study, and study-abroad. The most frequently chosen baccalaureate fields are biological/life sciences, business/marketing, and health professions and related sciences. The faculty at La Sierra has 95 members. The student-faculty ratio is 16:1.

Students of La Sierra The student body totals 1,758, of whom 1,448 are undergraduates. 59.1% are women and 40.9% are men. Students come from 34 states and territories and 51 other countries. 83% are from California. 66% returned for their sophomore year.

Applying La Sierra requires SAT I or ACT, a high school transcript, 2 recommendations, and a minimum high school GPA of 2.5, and in some cases SAT II: Writing Test and an interview. Application deadline: rolling admissions; 3/2 priority date for financial aid.

LAURA AND ALVIN SIEGAL COLLEGE OF JUDAIC STUDIES

Beachwood, OH

Suburban setting ■ *Private* ■ *Independent* ■ *Coed*

Web site: www.siegalcollege.edu

Contact: Ms. Linda L. Rosen, Director of Student Services, 26500 Shaker Boulevard, Beachwood, OH 44122-7116

Telephone: 216-464-4050 ext. 101 or toll-free 888-336-2257 **Fax:** 216-464-5827

E-mail: admissions@siegalcollege.edu

Getting in Last Year 8 applied; 63% were accepted; 2 enrolled (40%).

Financial Matters $7225 tuition and fees (2002–03); $200 average financial aid amount received per undergraduate.

Academics Siegal College awards bachelor's and master's degrees. Challenging opportunities include double majors, independent study, and a senior project. Special programs include cooperative education, internships, summer session for credit, and off-campus study. The faculty at Siegal College has 12 full-time members, 92% with terminal degrees. The student-faculty ratio is 8:1.

Students of Siegal College The student body totals 129, of whom 17 are undergraduates. 94.1% are women and 5.9% are men. Students come from 1 state or territory and 1 other country. 17.6% are international students. 100% returned for their sophomore year.

Applying Siegal College requires an essay, a high school transcript, an interview, and 2 recommendations. Application deadline: rolling admissions. Deferred admission is possible.

LAURENTIAN UNIVERSITY

Sudbury, ON Canada

Suburban setting ■ *Private* ■ *Independent Religious* ■ *Coed*

Web site: www.laurentian.ca

Contact: Mr. Ron Smith, Registrar, Ramsey Lake Road, Sudbury, ON P3E 2C6 Canada

Telephone: 705-675-1151 ext. 3919 **Fax:** 705-675-4891

E-mail: admissions@nickel.laurentian.ca

Getting in Last Year 5,268 applied; 77% were accepted.

Financial Matters $4437 tuition and fees (2002–03); $4550 room and board.

Academics Laurentian awards bachelor's and master's degrees. Challenging opportunities include accelerated degree programs, an honors program, and a senior project. Special programs include cooperative education, summer session for credit, and off-campus study. The faculty at Laurentian has 286 full-time members. The student-faculty ratio is 20:1.

Students of Laurentian The student body totals 6,173, of whom 5,791 are undergraduates. Students come from 13 states and territories and 16 other countries.

Applying Laurentian requires a high school transcript, and in some cases an essay, an interview, and 2 recommendations. Application deadline: rolling admissions, 6/30 for nonresidents. Early admission is possible.

LAWRENCE TECHNOLOGICAL UNIVERSITY

Southfield, MI

Suburban setting ■ *Private* ■ *Independent* ■ *Coed*

Web site: www.ltu.edu

Contact: Ms. Jane Rohrback, Director of Admissions, 21000 West Ten Mile Road, Southfield, MI 48075

Telephone: 248-204-3180 or toll-free 800-225-5588 **Fax:** 248-204-3188

E-mail: admissions@ltu.edu

Getting in Last Year 1,208 applied; 84% were accepted; 422 enrolled (42%).

Financial Matters $13,290 tuition and fees (2002–03); $4840 room and board; 91% average percent of need met; $9149 average financial aid amount received per undergraduate.

Academics Lawrence Tech awards associate, bachelor's, and master's degrees. Challenging opportunities include advanced placement credit, double majors, independent study, and a senior project. Special programs include cooperative education, internships, summer session for credit, off-campus study, study-abroad, and Army and Air Force ROTC. The faculty at Lawrence Tech has 103 full-time members, 78% with terminal degrees. The student-faculty ratio is 13:1.

Students of Lawrence Tech The student body totals 4,054, of whom 2,806 are undergraduates. 25.9% are women and 74.1% are men. Students come from 11 states and territories. 99% are from Michigan. 1.3% are international students. 75% returned for their sophomore year.

Applying Lawrence Tech requires SAT I or ACT, a high school transcript, and a minimum high school GPA of 2.5, and in some cases an essay, an interview, and recommendations. The school recommends an essay. Application deadline: 8/15; 5/1 priority date for financial aid. Early and deferred admission are possible.

LAWRENCE UNIVERSITY

Appleton, WI

Small-town setting ■ *Private* ■ *Independent* ■ *Coed*

Web site: www.lawrence.edu

Contact: Mr. Michael Thorp, Director of Admissions, PO Box 599, Appleton, WI 54912-0599

Telephone: 920-832-6992 or toll-free 800-227-0982 **Fax:** 920-832-6782

E-mail: excel@lawrence.edu

Getting in Last Year 1,812 applied; 68% were accepted; 352 enrolled (28%).

Financial Matters $23,667 tuition and fees (2002–03); $5457 room and board; 100% average percent of need met; $20,275 average financial aid amount received per undergraduate.

Academics Lawrence awards bachelor's degrees. Challenging opportunities include advanced placement credit, student-designed majors, double majors, independent study, and a senior project. Special programs include internships, off-campus study, and study-abroad. The most frequently chosen baccalaureate fields are visual/performing arts, social sciences and history, and biological/life sciences. The faculty at Lawrence has 137 full-time members, 91% with terminal degrees. The student-faculty ratio is 11:1.

Students of Lawrence The student body is made up of 1,389 undergraduates. 52.5% are women and 47.5% are men. Students come from 49 states and territories and 45 other countries. 41% are from Wisconsin. 10.4% are international students. 87% returned for their sophomore year.

Applying Lawrence requires an essay, SAT I or ACT, a high school transcript, 2 recommendations, and audition for music program. The school recommends an interview and a minimum high school GPA of 3.0. Application deadline: 1/15; 3/15 priority date for financial aid. Early and deferred admission are possible.

LEBANON VALLEY COLLEGE

Annville, PA

Small-town setting ■ *Private* ■ *Independent Religious* ■ *Coed*

Web site: www.lvc.edu

Contact: William J. Brown, Jr., Dean of Admission and Financial Aid, 101 N. College Avenue, Annville, PA 17003-1400

Telephone: 717-867-6181 or toll-free 866-LVC-4ADM **Fax:** 717-867-6026

E-mail: admission@lvc.edu

Getting in Last Year 1,802 applied; 77% were accepted; 425 enrolled (31%).

Financial Matters $21,200 tuition and fees (2002–03); $6110 room and board; 84% average percent of need met; $16,144 average financial aid amount received per undergraduate.

Academics LVC awards associate, bachelor's, and master's degrees and post-bachelor's certificates (offers master of business administration degree on a part-time basis only). Challenging opportunities include advanced placement credit, student-designed majors, double majors, and independent study. Special programs include internships, summer session for credit, off-campus study,

Lebanon Valley College (continued)

study-abroad, and Army ROTC. The most frequently chosen baccalaureate fields are business/marketing, education, and social sciences and history. The faculty at LVC has 95 full-time members, 87% with terminal degrees. The student-faculty ratio is 14:1.

Students of LVC The student body totals 2,070, of whom 1,879 are undergraduates. 58.9% are women and 41.1% are men. Students come from 19 states and territories and 5 other countries. 78% are from Pennsylvania. 0.3% are international students. 81% returned for their sophomore year.

Applying LVC requires SAT I or ACT and a high school transcript, and in some cases an essay and audition for music majors; interview for physical therapy program. The school recommends SAT I, an interview, and 2 recommendations. Application deadline: rolling admissions; 3/1 priority date for financial aid.

LEES-MCRAE COLLEGE

Banner Elk, NC

Rural setting ■ Private ■ Independent Religious ■ Coed

Web site: www.lmc.edu

Contact: Mr. Brad Parrish, Assistant Dean of Students for Admissions, PO Box 128, Banner Elk, NC 28604-0128

Telephone: 828-898-3432 or toll-free 800-280-4562 **Fax:** 828-898-8707

E-mail: admissions@lmc.edu

Getting in Last Year 799 applied; 79% were accepted; 199 enrolled (32%).

Financial Matters $13,488 tuition and fees (2002–03); $5060 room and board; 91% average percent of need met; $9871 average financial aid amount received per undergraduate (2001–02).

Academics Lees–McRae awards bachelor's degrees. Challenging opportunities include advanced placement credit, student-designed majors, an honors program, double majors, independent study, and a senior project. Special programs include internships, summer session for credit, off-campus study, study-abroad, and Army ROTC. The most frequently chosen baccalaureate fields are education, business/marketing, and biological/life sciences. The faculty at Lees–McRae has 69 full-time members, 59% with terminal degrees. The student-faculty ratio is 14:1.

Students of Lees–McRae The student body is made up of 792 undergraduates. 56.9% are women and 43.1% are men. Students come from 31 states and territories and 20 other countries. 62% are from North Carolina. 4.6% are international students. 58% returned for their sophomore year.

Applying Lees–McRae requires SAT I or ACT, a high school transcript, and a minimum high school GPA of 2.0, and in some cases an interview and recommendations. The school recommends an essay. Application deadline: 8/15; 3/15 priority date for financial aid. Early and deferred admission are possible.

LEE UNIVERSITY

Cleveland, TN

Small-town setting ■ Private ■ Independent Religious ■ Coed

Web site: www.leeuniversity.edu

Contact: Admissions Coordinator, PO Box 3450, Cleveland, TN 37311

Telephone: 423-614-8500 or toll-free 800-533-9930 **Fax:** 423-614-8533

E-mail: admissions@leeuniversity.edu

Getting in Last Year 889 enrolled.

Financial Matters $8200 tuition and fees (2002–03); $4950 room and board; 57% average percent of need met; $7273 average financial aid amount received per undergraduate.

Academics Lee awards bachelor's and master's degrees. Challenging opportunities include advanced placement credit, an honors program, double majors, independent study, and a senior project. Special programs include internships, summer session for credit, and study-abroad. The most frequently chosen baccalaureate fields are education, business/marketing, and psychology. The faculty at Lee has 136 full-time members, 63% with terminal degrees. The student-faculty ratio is 18:1.

Students of Lee The student body totals 3,711, of whom 3,487 are undergraduates. 57% are women and 43% are men. Students come from 48 states and territories and 39 other countries. 37% are from Tennessee. 3.4% are international students. 72% returned for their sophomore year.

Applying Lee requires SAT I or ACT, a high school transcript, MMR immunization record, and a minimum high school GPA of 2.0, and in some cases 1 recommendation. The school recommends ACT and 3 recommendations. Application deadline: 9/1; 4/15 priority date for financial aid. Early and deferred admission are possible.

LEHIGH UNIVERSITY

Bethlehem, PA

Suburban setting ■ Private ■ Independent ■ Coed

Web site: www.lehigh.edu

Contact: Mr. J. Bruce Gardiner, Interim Dean of Admissions and Financial Aid, 27 Memorial Drive West, Bethlehem, PA 18015

Telephone: 610-758-3100 **Fax:** 610-758-4361

E-mail: admissions@lehigh.edu

Getting in Last Year 8,254 applied; 44% were accepted; 1,144 enrolled (31%).

Financial Matters $26,180 tuition and fees (2002–03); $7530 room and board; 99% average percent of need met; $22,072 average financial aid amount received per undergraduate.

Academics Lehigh awards bachelor's, master's, and doctoral degrees and post-master's certificates. Challenging opportunities include advanced placement credit, accelerated degree programs, an honors program, double majors, independent study, and a senior project. Special programs include cooperative education, internships, summer session for credit, off-campus study, study-abroad, and Army ROTC. The most frequently chosen baccalaureate fields are business/marketing, engineering/engineering technologies, and social sciences and history. The faculty at Lehigh has 406 full-time members, 99% with terminal degrees. The student-faculty ratio is 11:1.

Students of Lehigh The student body totals 6,686, of whom 4,706 are undergraduates. 40.1% are women and 59.9% are men. Students come from 52 states and territories and 46 other countries. 32% are from Pennsylvania. 2.9% are international students. 94% returned for their sophomore year.

Applying Lehigh requires SAT I or ACT, a high school transcript, 1 recommendation, and graded writing sample. The school recommends an essay, SAT II Subject Tests, and an interview. Application deadline: 1/1; 2/1 for financial aid. Early and deferred admission are possible.

LEHMAN COLLEGE OF THE CITY UNIVERSITY OF NEW YORK

Bronx, NY

Urban setting ■ Public ■ State and locally supported ■ Coed

Web site: www.lehman.cuny.edu

Contact: Mr. Roland Velez, Deputy Director of Undergraduate Admissions, 250 Bedford Park Boulevard West, Bronx, NY 10468

Telephone: 718-960-8731 or toll-free 877-Lehman1 (out-of-state) **Fax:** 718-960-8712

E-mail: cawic@cunyum.cunx.edu

Getting in Last Year 3,882 applied; 32% were accepted; 754 enrolled (60%).

Financial Matters $3310 resident tuition and fees (2002–03); $6910 nonresident tuition and fees (2002–03); 70% average percent of need met; $4750 average financial aid amount received per undergraduate (2001–02).

Academics Lehman awards bachelor's and master's degrees. Challenging opportunities include advanced placement credit, student-designed majors, freshman honors college, an honors program, double majors, independent study, and a senior project. Special programs include cooperative education, internships, summer session for credit, off-campus study, study-abroad, and Army ROTC. The most frequently chosen baccalaureate fields are social sciences and history, health professions and related sciences, and computer/information sciences. The faculty at Lehman has 292 full-time members, 100% with terminal degrees. The student-faculty ratio is 14:1.

Students of Lehman The student body totals 9,510, of whom 7,322 are undergraduates. 72.4% are women and 27.6% are men. Students come from 5 states and territories. 100% are from New York. 2.3% are international students. 69% returned for their sophomore year.

Applying Lehman requires SAT I or ACT, a high school transcript, and a minimum high school GPA of 3.0, and in some cases an essay, an interview, and recommendations. The school recommends SAT I and ACT. Application deadline: rolling admissions. Deferred admission is possible.

LE MOYNE COLLEGE

Syracuse, NY

Suburban setting ■ Private ■ Independent Religious ■ Coed

Web site: www.lemoyne.edu

Contact: Mr. Dennis J. Nicholson, Director of Admission, 1419 Salt Spring Road, Syracuse, NY 13214-1399

Telephone: 315-445-4300 or toll-free 800-333-4733 **Fax:** 315-445-4711

E-mail: admission@lemoyne.edu

Getting in Last Year 2,667 applied; 74% were accepted; 561 enrolled (28%).

Financial Matters $17,910 tuition and fees (2002–03); $7250 room and board; 81% average percent of need met; $14,019 average financial aid amount received per undergraduate (2001–02).

Academics Le Moyne awards bachelor's and master's degrees and post-bachelor's certificates. Challenging opportunities include advanced placement credit, accelerated degree programs, an honors program, double majors, independent study, and a senior project. Special programs include internships, summer session for credit, off-campus study, study-abroad, and Army and Air Force ROTC. The most frequently chosen baccalaureate fields are business/marketing, psychology, and social sciences and history. The faculty at Le Moyne has 146 full-time members, 91% with terminal degrees. The student-faculty ratio is 13:1.

Students of Le Moyne The student body totals 3,288, of whom 2,485 are undergraduates. 59.5% are women and 40.5% are men. Students come from 27 states and territories and 4 other countries. 94% are from New York. 0.5% are international students. 84% returned for their sophomore year.

Applying Le Moyne requires an essay, SAT I or ACT, a high school transcript, and 2 recommendations. The school recommends an interview. Application deadline: 3/1; 2/1 priority date for financial aid. Early and deferred admission are possible.

LENOIR-RHYNE COLLEGE

Hickory, NC

Small-town setting ■ Private ■ Independent Religious ■ Coed

Web site: www.lrc.edu

Contact: Mrs. Rachel Nichols, Dean of Admissions and Financial Aid, PO Box 7227, Hickory, NC 28603

Telephone: 828-328-7300 or toll-free 800-277-5721 **Fax:** 828-328-7378

E-mail: admission@lrc.edu

Getting in Last Year 1,441 applied; 80% were accepted; 319 enrolled (28%).

Financial Matters $14,994 tuition and fees (2002–03); $5300 room and board; 73% average percent of need met; $10,277 average financial aid amount received per undergraduate (2001–02).

Academics L-R awards bachelor's and master's degrees. Challenging opportunities include advanced placement credit, accelerated degree programs, student-designed majors, an honors program, double majors, independent study, and a senior project. Special programs include cooperative education, internships, summer session for credit, study-abroad, and Army ROTC. The most frequently chosen baccalaureate fields are business/marketing, education, and psychology. The faculty at L-R has 95 full-time members, 73% with terminal degrees. The student-faculty ratio is 11:1.

Students of L-R The student body totals 1,492, of whom 1,358 are undergraduates. 64% are women and 36% are men. Students come from 28 states and territories and 4 other countries. 74% are from North Carolina. 0.3% are international students. 77% returned for their sophomore year.

Applying L-R requires SAT I or ACT, a high school transcript, and a minimum high school GPA of 2.5. The school recommends an interview. Application deadline: rolling admissions; 3/1 priority date for financial aid. Deferred admission is possible.

LESLEY UNIVERSITY

Cambridge, MA

Urban setting ■ Private ■ Independent ■ Coed, Primarily Women

Web site: www.lesley.edu

Contact: Ms. Jane A. Raley, Director of Women's College Admissions, 29 Everett Street, Cambridge, MA 02138-2790

Telephone: 617-349-8800 or toll-free 800-999-1959 ext. 8800
Fax: 617-349-8810

E-mail: ugadm@mail.lesley.edu

Getting in Last Year 345 applied; 84% were accepted; 118 enrolled (41%).

Financial Matters $18,475 tuition and fees (2002–03); $8300 room and board; 93% average percent of need met; $16,079 average financial aid amount received per undergraduate.

Academics Lesley awards associate, bachelor's, master's, and doctoral degrees and post-bachelor's and post-master's certificates. Challenging opportunities include advanced placement credit, accelerated degree programs, freshman honors college, an honors program, double majors, and independent study. Special programs include internships, summer session for credit, off-campus study, and study-abroad. The most frequently chosen baccalaureate fields are education, liberal arts/general studies, and psychology. The faculty at Lesley has 30 full-time members, 77% with terminal degrees. The student-faculty ratio is 13:1.

Students of Lesley The student body totals 6,455, of whom 1,071 are undergraduates. 78.7% are women and 21.3% are men. Students come from 25 states and territories and 18 other countries. 52% are from Massachusetts. 5.5% are international students. 76% returned for their sophomore year.

Applying Lesley requires an essay, SAT I or ACT, a high school transcript, and 3 recommendations. The school recommends an interview. Application deadline: 3/15; 2/1 priority date for financial aid. Deferred admission is possible.

LESTER L. COX COLLEGE OF NURSING AND HEALTH SCIENCES

Springfield, MO

Urban setting ■ Private ■ Independent ■ Coed, Primarily Women

Web site: www.coxcollege.edu

Contact: Ms. Jennifer Plimmer, Admission Coordinator, 1423 North Jefferson, Springfield, MO 65802

Telephone: 417-269-3069 or toll-free 866-898-5355 (in-state)
Fax: 417-269-3581

E-mail: jplimme@coxcollege.edu

Getting in Last Year 300 applied; 51% were accepted; 58 enrolled (38%).

Financial Matters $6600 tuition and fees (2002–03); $1925 room only; $8500 average financial aid amount received per undergraduate.

Academics Lester L. Cox College of Nursing and Health Sciences awards associate and bachelor's degrees. Challenging opportunities include accelerated degree programs and a senior project. Summer session for credit is a special program. The most frequently chosen baccalaureate field is health professions and related sciences. The faculty at Lester L. Cox College of Nursing and Health Sciences has 16 full-time members, 6% with terminal degrees. The student-faculty ratio is 15:1.

Students of Lester L. Cox College of Nursing and Health Sciences The student body is made up of 445 undergraduates. 92.4% are women and 7.6% are men. Students come from 4 states and territories. 99% are from Missouri. 60% returned for their sophomore year.

Applying Lester L. Cox College of Nursing and Health Sciences requires ACT, a high school transcript, and a minimum high school GPA of 2.5. Application deadline: 2/1; 4/1 priority date for financial aid.

LETOURNEAU UNIVERSITY

Longview, TX

Suburban setting ■ Private ■ Independent Religious ■ Coed

Web site: www.letu.edu

Contact: Mr. James Townsend, Director of Admissions, PO Box 7001, 2100 South Mobberly Avenue, Longview, TX 75607

Telephone: 903-233-3400 or toll-free 800-759-8811 **Fax:** 903-233-3411

E-mail: admissions@letu.edu

Getting in Last Year 698 applied; 93% were accepted; 245 enrolled (38%).

Financial Matters $13,410 tuition and fees (2002–03); $5610 room and board; 72% average percent of need met; $10,256 average financial aid amount received per undergraduate (2001–02).

Academics LeTourneau awards associate, bachelor's, and master's degrees. Challenging opportunities include an honors program, double majors, and independent study. Special programs include cooperative education, internships, and study-abroad. The most frequently chosen baccalaureate fields are engineering/engineering technologies, business/marketing, and education. The faculty at LeTourneau has 62 full-time members, 73% with terminal degrees. The student-faculty ratio is 16:1.

Students of LeTourneau The student body totals 3,338, of whom 2,921 are undergraduates. 51.6% are women and 48.4% are men. 48% are from Texas. 1.3% are international students. 75% returned for their sophomore year.

Applying LeTourneau requires SAT I or ACT. Application deadline: 8/1; 2/15 priority date for financial aid. Deferred admission is possible.

LEWIS & CLARK COLLEGE

Portland, OR

Suburban setting ■ Private ■ Independent ■ Coed

Web site: www.lclark.edu

Contact: Mr. Michael Sexton, Dean of Admissions, 0615 SW Palatine Hill Road, Portland, OR 97219-7899

Telephone: 503-768-7040 or toll-free 800-444-4111 **Fax:** 503-768-7055

E-mail: admissions@lclark.edu

Getting in Last Year 3,223 applied; 68% were accepted; 504 enrolled (23%).

Financial Matters $23,730 tuition and fees (2002–03); $6630 room and board; 84% average percent of need met; $19,545 average financial aid amount received per undergraduate.

Academics L & C awards bachelor's, master's, and first-professional degrees and first-professional certificates. Challenging opportunities include advanced placement credit, accelerated degree programs, student-designed majors, an honors program, double majors, independent study, and a senior project. Special programs include internships, summer session for credit, off-campus study, and study-abroad. The most frequently chosen baccalaureate fields are social sciences and history, biological/life sciences, and visual/performing arts. The faculty at L & C has 191 full-time members, 91% with terminal degrees. The student-faculty ratio is 12:1.

Students of L & C The student body totals 3,051, of whom 1,763 are undergraduates. 59.7% are women and 40.3% are men. Students come from 44 states and territories and 44 other countries. 13% are from Oregon. 5.1% are international students. 82% returned for their sophomore year.

Applying L & C requires an essay, SAT I, ACT, or academic portfolio, a high school transcript, 2 recommendations, and a minimum high school GPA of 2.0, and in some cases 4 recommendations and portfolio applicants must submit samples of graded work. The school recommends an interview and a minimum high school GPA of 3.0. Application deadline: 2/1; 3/1 priority date for financial aid. Early and deferred admission are possible.

LEWIS-CLARK STATE COLLEGE

Lewiston, ID

Small-town setting ■ Public ■ State-supported ■ Coed

Web site: www.lcsc.edu
Contact: Ms. Tracy Waffle, Admissions Supervisor, 500 8th Avenue, Lewiston, ID 83501
Telephone: 208-792-2210 or toll-free 800-933-LCSC ext. 2210
Fax: 208-792-2876
E-mail: admissions@lcsc.edu

Getting in Last Year 1,023 applied; 59% were accepted; 377 enrolled (62%).

Financial Matters $2852 resident tuition and fees (2002–03); $8562 nonresident tuition and fees (2002–03); $3880 room and board; 54% average percent of need met; $5008 average financial aid amount received per undergraduate (2001–02).

Academics LCSC awards associate and bachelor's degrees. Challenging opportunities include advanced placement credit, accelerated degree programs, student-designed majors, double majors, independent study, and a senior project. Special programs include cooperative education, internships, summer session for credit, off-campus study, study-abroad, and Army, Navy and Air Force ROTC. The most frequently chosen baccalaureate fields are education, business/marketing, and protective services/public administration. The faculty at LCSC has 134 full-time members, 70% with terminal degrees. The student-faculty ratio is 16:1.

Students of LCSC The student body is made up of 3,117 undergraduates. 60.5% are women and 39.5% are men. Students come from 21 states and territories and 32 other countries. 86% are from Idaho. 2.7% are international students. 50% returned for their sophomore year.

Applying LCSC requires a high school transcript and a minimum high school GPA of 2.0, and in some cases an essay, SAT I or ACT, ACT COMPASS, and an interview. The school recommends ACT. Application deadline: rolling admissions; 3/1 priority date for financial aid. Deferred admission is possible.

LEWIS UNIVERSITY

Romeoville, IL

Small-town setting ■ Private ■ Independent Religious ■ Coed

Web site: www.lewisu.edu
Contact: Mr. Ryan Cockerill, Admission Counselor, Box 297, One University Parkway, Romeoville, IL 60446
Telephone: 815-838-0500 ext. 5237 or toll-free 800-897-9000
Fax: 815-836-5002
E-mail: admissions@lewisu.edu

Getting in Last Year 1,208 applied; 68% were accepted; 373 enrolled (46%).

Financial Matters $15,250 tuition and fees (2002–03); $7250 room and board; 80% average percent of need met; $13,422 average financial aid amount received per undergraduate.

Academics Lewis awards associate, bachelor's, and master's degrees and post-bachelor's certificates. Challenging opportunities include advanced placement credit, accelerated degree programs, student-designed majors, an honors program, double majors, independent study, and a senior project. Special programs include internships, summer session for credit, study-abroad, and Army and Air Force ROTC. The most frequently chosen baccalaureate fields are business/marketing, health professions and related sciences, and protective services/public administration. The faculty at Lewis has 141 full-time members. The student-faculty ratio is 15:1.

Students of Lewis The student body totals 4,347, of whom 3,194 are undergraduates. 55.8% are women and 44.2% are men. Students come from 24 states and territories and 31 other countries. 96% are from Illinois. 4.2% are international students. 77% returned for their sophomore year.

Applying Lewis requires SAT I or ACT, a high school transcript, and a minimum high school GPA of 2.0, and in some cases an interview. Application deadline: rolling admissions; 5/1 priority date for financial aid. Deferred admission is possible.

LIBERTY UNIVERSITY

Lynchburg, VA

Suburban setting ■ Private ■ Independent Religious ■ Coed

Web site: www.liberty.edu
Contact: Mr. David Hart, Director of Admissions, 1971 University Boulevard, Lynchburg, VA 24502
Telephone: 434-582-2866 or toll-free 800-543-5317 **Fax:** 800-542-2311
E-mail: admissions@liberty.edu

Getting in Last Year 5,734 applied; 28% were accepted; 1,568 enrolled (99%).

Financial Matters $10,340 tuition and fees (2002–03); $5100 room and board; 63% average percent of need met; $7815 average financial aid amount received per undergraduate.

Academics Liberty awards associate, bachelor's, master's, doctoral, and first-professional degrees (also offers external degree program with significant enrollment not reflected in profile). Challenging opportunities include advanced placement credit, accelerated degree programs, student-designed majors, an honors program, double majors, independent study, and a senior project. Special programs include internships, summer session for credit, and Army and Air Force ROTC. The most frequently chosen baccalaureate fields are business/marketing, psychology, and law/legal studies. The faculty at Liberty has 181 full-time members, 62% with terminal degrees. The student-faculty ratio is 24:1.

Students of Liberty The student body totals 7,709, of whom 6,448 are undergraduates. 50.8% are women and 49.2% are men. Students come from 52 states and territories and 52 other countries. 41% are from Virginia. 3% are international students.

Applying Liberty requires an essay, SAT I or ACT, and a high school transcript, and in some cases ACT, an interview, and 1 recommendation. The school recommends 1 recommendation and a minimum high school GPA of 2.0. Application deadline: 6/30; 3/1 priority date for financial aid. Early and deferred admission are possible.

LIFE PACIFIC COLLEGE

San Dimas, CA

Suburban setting ■ Private ■ Independent Religious ■ Coed

Web site: www.lifepacific.edu
Contact: Mrs. Linda Hibdon, Admissions Director, 1100 Covina Boulevard, San Dimas, CA 91773-3298
Telephone: 909-599-5433 ext. 314 or toll-free 877-886-5433 **Fax:** 909-706-3070
E-mail: adm@lifepacific.edu

Getting in Last Year 100 applied; 57% were accepted; 55 enrolled (96%).

Financial Matters $6700 tuition and fees (2002–03); $3600 room and board; 62% average percent of need met; $7046 average financial aid amount received per undergraduate (2001–02).

Academics LIFE awards associate and bachelor's degrees. Challenging opportunities include advanced placement credit and independent study. Special programs include cooperative education, internships, and summer session for credit. The faculty at LIFE has 16 full-time members, 19% with terminal degrees. The student-faculty ratio is 17:1.

Students of LIFE The student body is made up of 435 undergraduates. 48% are women and 52% are men. Students come from 32 states and territories. 59% are from California. 0.5% are international students. 67% returned for their sophomore year.

Applying LIFE requires an essay, SAT I or ACT, a high school transcript, 3 recommendations, Christian testimony, and a minimum high school GPA of 2.0. The school recommends SAT II: Writing Test. Application deadline: 7/1; 7/1 priority date for financial aid. Deferred admission is possible.

LIFE UNIVERSITY

Marietta, GA

Private ■ Independent ■ Coed

Web site: www.life.edu
Contact: Ms. Denise Gordon, Office of Admissions, 1269 Barclay Circle, Marietta, GA 30060-2903
Telephone: 770-426-2884 or toll-free 800-543-3202 (in-state) **Fax:** - ext.

Financial Matters $3120 resident tuition and fees (2002–03); $5664 nonresident tuition and fees (2002–03); 19% average percent of need met; $7000 average financial aid amount received per undergraduate.

Academics Life University awards associate, bachelor's, and first-professional degrees.

Applying Application deadline: 3/1 priority date for financial aid.

LIMESTONE COLLEGE

Gaffney, SC

Small-town setting ■ Private ■ Independent ■ Coed

Web site: www.limestone.edu
Contact: Ms. Debbie Borders, Office Manager of Admissions, Limestone College, 1115 College Drive, Gaffney, SC 29340-3799
Telephone: 864-488-4554 or toll-free 800-795-7151 ext. 554 **Fax:** 864-487-8706
E-mail: cphenicie@limestone.edu

Getting in Last Year 162 enrolled.

Financial Matters $11,500 tuition and fees (2002–03); $5400 room and board; 65% average percent of need met; $8007 average financial aid amount received per undergraduate (2001–02).

Academics Limestone awards associate and bachelor's degrees. Challenging opportunities include advanced placement credit, accelerated degree programs, student-designed majors, an honors program, double majors, independent study, and a senior project. Special programs include internships, summer session for credit, and Army ROTC. The most frequently chosen baccalaureate fields are business/marketing, computer/information sciences, and social sciences and history. The faculty at Limestone has 41 full-time members, 66% with terminal degrees. The student-faculty ratio is 11:1.

Students of Limestone The student body is made up of 548 undergraduates. 47.3% are women and 52.7% are men. Students come from 23 states and territories and 10 other countries. 63% are from South Carolina. 1.8% are international students. 50% returned for their sophomore year.

Applying Limestone requires SAT I or ACT, a high school transcript, and a minimum high school GPA of 2.0. The school recommends an interview and 2 recommendations. Application deadline: rolling admissions; 5/1 priority date for financial aid.

LINCOLN CHRISTIAN COLLEGE

Lincoln, IL

Small-town setting ■ Private ■ Independent Religious ■ Coed

Web site: www.lccs.edu
Contact: Mrs. Mary K. Davis, Assistant Director of Admissions, 100 Campus View Drive, Lincoln, IL 62656
Telephone: 217-732-3168 ext. 2251 or toll-free 888-522-5228
Fax: 217-732-4199
E-mail: coladmis@lccs.edu

Getting in Last Year 278 applied; 77% were accepted; 172 enrolled (81%).

Financial Matters $8340 tuition and fees (2002–03); $4380 room and board; 80% average percent of need met; $8000 average financial aid amount received per undergraduate.

Academics Lincoln Christian awards associate and bachelor's degrees. Challenging opportunities include advanced placement credit, an honors program, double majors, independent study, and a senior project. Special programs include internships, summer session for credit, and off-campus study. The faculty at Lincoln Christian has 29 full-time members, 55% with terminal degrees. The student-faculty ratio is 16:1.

Students of Lincoln Christian The student body is made up of 756 undergraduates. 50.8% are women and 49.2% are men. Students come from 27 states and territories and 6 other countries. 70% are from Illinois. 1% are international students. 71% returned for their sophomore year.

Applying Lincoln Christian requires an essay, SAT I or ACT, a high school transcript, and 3 recommendations, and in some cases an interview. Application deadline: rolling admissions. Deferred admission is possible.

LINCOLN MEMORIAL UNIVERSITY

Harrogate, TN

Small-town setting ■ Private ■ Independent ■ Coed

Web site: www.lmunet.edu
Contact: Mr. Conrad Daniels, Dean of Admissions and Recruitment, 6965 Cumberland Gap Parkway, Harrogate, TN 37752-1901
Telephone: 423-869-6280 or toll-free 800-325-0900 **Fax:** 423-869-6250
E-mail: admissions@inetlmu.lmunet.edu

Getting in Last Year 539 applied; 72% were accepted.

Financial Matters $11,760 tuition and fees (2002–03); $4380 room and board; 90% average percent of need met; $9800 average financial aid amount received per undergraduate (2001–02 estimated).

Academics LMU awards associate, bachelor's, and master's degrees. Challenging opportunities include advanced placement credit, accelerated degree programs, student-designed majors, an honors program, double majors, and independent study. Summer session for credit is a special program. The faculty at LMU has 87 full-time members, 60% with terminal degrees. The student-faculty ratio is 16:1.

Students of LMU The student body totals 2,201, of whom 973 are undergraduates. Students come from 30 states and territories and 15 other countries. 46% are from Tennessee. 4.9% are international students. 54% returned for their sophomore year.

Applying LMU requires SAT I or ACT, a high school transcript, and a minimum high school GPA of 2.3, and in some cases an essay. The school recommends an interview. Application deadline: rolling admissions; 4/1 priority date for financial aid.

LINCOLN UNIVERSITY

Oakland, CA

Urban setting ■ Private ■ Independent ■ Coed

Web site: www.lincolnuca.edu
Contact: Ms. Vivian Xu, Admissions Officer, 401 15th Street, Oakland, CA 94612-2801
Telephone: 415-221-1212 ext. 115 **Fax:** 510-628-8012

Financial Matters $6680 tuition and fees (2002–03).

Academics Lincoln awards bachelor's and master's degrees. Advanced placement credit is a challenging opportunity. Special programs include internships and summer session for credit. The faculty at Lincoln has 8 full-time members. The student-faculty ratio is 14:1.

Students of Lincoln The student body totals 177, of whom 129 are undergraduates. Students come from 1 state or territory and 37 other countries.

Applying Lincoln requires Michigan English Language Assessment Battery, a high school transcript, and a minimum high school GPA of 2.0, and in some cases an essay, an interview, and recommendations. Application deadline: 8/31. Deferred admission is possible.

LINCOLN UNIVERSITY

Lincoln University, PA

Rural setting ■ Public ■ State-related ■ Coed

Web site: www.lincoln.edu
Contact: Dr. Robert Laney Jr., Director of Admissions, PO Box 179, Lincoln University, PA 19352
Telephone: 610-932-8300 ext. 3206 or toll-free 800-790-0191
Fax: 610-932-1209
E-mail: admiss@lu.lincoln.edu

Getting in Last Year 3,707 applied; 49% were accepted; 478 enrolled (26%).

Financial Matters $5744 resident tuition and fees (2002–03); $8724 nonresident tuition and fees (2002–03); $5584 room and board; 85% average percent of need met; $11,000 average financial aid amount received per undergraduate.

Academics Lincoln awards bachelor's and master's degrees. Challenging opportunities include advanced placement credit, accelerated degree programs, student-designed majors, an honors program, double majors, independent study, and a senior project. Special programs include cooperative education, internships, summer session for credit, off-campus study, study-abroad, and Army and Air Force ROTC. The most frequently chosen baccalaureate fields are social sciences and history, business/marketing, and education. The faculty at Lincoln has 88 full-time members, 77% with terminal degrees. The student-faculty ratio is 17:1.

Students of Lincoln The student body totals 1,998, of whom 1,561 are undergraduates. 60.9% are women and 39.1% are men. Students come from 25 states and territories and 27 other countries. 51% are from Pennsylvania. 7.8% are international students. 64% returned for their sophomore year.

Applying Lincoln requires an essay, SAT I or ACT, a high school transcript, an interview, 2 recommendations, and a minimum high school GPA of 2.0. Application deadline: rolling admissions; 5/1 priority date for financial aid. Early and deferred admission are possible.

LINDENWOOD UNIVERSITY

St. Charles, MO

Suburban setting ■ Private ■ Independent Religious ■ Coed

Web site: www.lindenwood.edu
Contact: Mr. John Guffey, Dean of Admissions, 209 South Kingshighway, St. Charles, MO 63301-1695
Telephone: 636-949-4933 **Fax:** 636-949-4989

Getting in Last Year 2,271 applied; 47% were accepted; 674 enrolled (63%).

Financial Matters $11,650 tuition and fees (2002–03); $5600 room and board.

Academics Lindenwood awards bachelor's and master's degrees and post-master's certificates. Challenging opportunities include advanced placement credit, accelerated degree programs, student-designed majors, freshman honors college, an honors program, double majors, independent study, and a senior project. Special programs include cooperative education, internships, summer session for credit, off-campus study, study-abroad, and Army and Air Force ROTC. The most frequently chosen baccalaureate fields are business/marketing, education, and communications/communication technologies. The faculty at Lindenwood has 155 full-time members, 46% with terminal degrees. The student-faculty ratio is 17:1.

Students of Lindenwood The student body totals 6,937, of whom 4,446 are undergraduates. 54.5% are women and 45.5% are men. Students come from 47 states and territories and 63 other countries. 89% are from Missouri. 8.4% are international students. 89% returned for their sophomore year.

Applying Lindenwood requires SAT I or ACT, a high school transcript, minimum ACT score of 20 or minimum SAT score of 900, and a minimum high school GPA of 2.0, and in some cases an essay, an interview, and recommendations. Application deadline: rolling admissions; 3/15 priority date for financial aid. Early and deferred admission are possible.

LINDSEY WILSON COLLEGE

Columbia, KY

Rural setting ■ Private ■ Independent Religious ■ Coed

Web site: www.lindsey.edu
Contact: Mr. David Alls, Director of Admissions, 210 Lindsey Wilson Street, Columbia, KY 42728-1298
Telephone: 270-384-8100 ext. 8007 or toll-free 800-264-0138
Fax: 270-384-8200
E-mail: allsd@lindsey.edu

Getting in Last Year 1,335 applied; 57% were accepted; 436 enrolled (57%).

Financial Matters $12,098 tuition and fees (2002–03); $5274 room and board.

Academics Lindsey awards associate, bachelor's, and master's degrees. Challenging opportunities include advanced placement credit, accelerated degree

Lindsey Wilson College (continued)

programs, student-designed majors, double majors, independent study, and a senior project. Special programs include cooperative education, internships, summer session for credit, off-campus study, study-abroad, and Army ROTC. The most frequently chosen baccalaureate fields are education, biological/life sciences, and communications/communication technologies. The faculty at Lindsey has 59 full-time members, 64% with terminal degrees. The student-faculty ratio is 19:1.

Students of Lindsey The student body totals 1,588, of whom 1,451 are undergraduates. 64.2% are women and 35.8% are men. Students come from 28 states and territories and 18 other countries. 88% are from Kentucky. 3.7% are international students. 54% returned for their sophomore year.

Applying Lindsey requires a high school transcript, and in some cases SAT I, ACT, SAT I or ACT, and 3 recommendations. The school recommends an interview. Application deadline: rolling admissions; 4/1 priority date for financial aid.

LINFIELD COLLEGE

McMinnville, OR

Small-town setting ■ Private ■ Independent Religious ■ Coed

Web site: www.linfield.edu
Contact: Ms. Lisa Knodle-Bragiel, Director of Admissions, 900 SE Baker Street, McMinnville, OR 97128-6894
Telephone: 503-883-2489 or toll-free 800-640-2287 **Fax:** 503-883-2472
E-mail: admissions@linfield.edu

Getting in Last Year 1,651 applied; 80% were accepted; 431 enrolled (33%).

Financial Matters $20,310 tuition and fees (2002–03); $6553 room and board; 90% average percent of need met; $15,709 average financial aid amount received per undergraduate.

Academics Linfield awards bachelor's degrees. Challenging opportunities include advanced placement credit, accelerated degree programs, student-designed majors, an honors program, double majors, independent study, and a senior project. Special programs include cooperative education, internships, summer session for credit, off-campus study, study-abroad, and Army and Air Force ROTC. The most frequently chosen baccalaureate fields are business/marketing, education, and social sciences and history. The faculty at Linfield has 100 full-time members, 98% with terminal degrees. The student-faculty ratio is 12:1.

Students of Linfield The student body is made up of 1,599 undergraduates. 56% are women and 44% are men. Students come from 26 states and territories and 23 other countries. 54% are from Oregon. 2.5% are international students. 84% returned for their sophomore year.

Applying Linfield requires an essay, SAT I or ACT, a high school transcript, and 1 recommendation. The school recommends an interview. Application deadline: 2/15; 2/1 priority date for financial aid. Deferred admission is possible.

LIPSCOMB UNIVERSITY

Nashville, TN

Urban setting ■ Private ■ Independent Religious ■ Coed

Web site: www.lipscomb.edu
Contact: Mr. Scott Gilmer, Director of Admissions, 3901 Granny White Pike, Nashville, TN 37204-3951
Telephone: 615-269-1776 or toll-free 800-333-4358 **Fax:** 615-269-1804
E-mail: admissions@lipscomb.edu

Getting in Last Year 1,601 applied; 85% were accepted; 596 enrolled (44%).

Financial Matters $11,356 tuition and fees (2002–03); $5590 room and board; $12,000 average financial aid amount received per undergraduate.

Academics Lipscomb University awards bachelor's, master's, and first-professional degrees. Challenging opportunities include advanced placement credit, accelerated degree programs, an honors program, double majors, independent study, and a senior project. Special programs include internships, summer session for credit, study-abroad, and Army and Air Force ROTC. The faculty at Lipscomb University has 115 full-time members, 77% with terminal degrees. The student-faculty ratio is 16:1.

Students of Lipscomb University The student body totals 2,661, of whom 2,408 are undergraduates. 56.9% are women and 43.1% are men. Students come from 42 states and territories and 41 other countries. 62% are from Tennessee. 74% returned for their sophomore year.

Applying Lipscomb University requires SAT I or ACT, a high school transcript, 2 recommendations, and a minimum high school GPA of 2.25. The school recommends an essay and an interview. Application deadline: rolling admissions; 2/28 priority date for financial aid. Early admission is possible.

LOCK HAVEN UNIVERSITY OF PENNSYLVANIA

Lock Haven, PA

Small-town setting ■ Public ■ State-supported ■ Coed

Web site: www.lhup.edu
Contact: Mr. Steven Lee, Director of Admissions, Office of Admission, Akeley Hall, Lock Haven, PA 17745
Telephone: 570-893-2027 or toll-free 800-332-8900 (in-state), 800-233-8978 (out-of-state) **Fax:** 570-893-2201
E-mail: admissions@lhup.edu

Getting in Last Year 3,577 applied; 83% were accepted; 1,134 enrolled (38%).

Financial Matters $5656 resident tuition and fees (2002–03); $10,224 nonresident tuition and fees (2002–03); $4996 room and board; 78% average percent of need met; $6900 average financial aid amount received per undergraduate (2001–02 estimated).

Academics Lock Haven awards associate, bachelor's, and master's degrees. Challenging opportunities include advanced placement credit, accelerated degree programs, student-designed majors, an honors program, double majors, independent study, and a senior project. Special programs include cooperative education, internships, summer session for credit, off-campus study, study-abroad, and Army ROTC. The most frequently chosen baccalaureate fields are education, health professions and related sciences, and parks and recreation. The faculty at Lock Haven has 225 full-time members. The student-faculty ratio is 18:1.

Students of Lock Haven The student body totals 4,574, of whom 4,394 are undergraduates. 59.9% are women and 40.1% are men. Students come from 24 states and territories and 35 other countries. 92% are from Pennsylvania. 2.5% are international students. 74% returned for their sophomore year.

Applying Lock Haven requires SAT I or ACT, and in some cases an essay, a high school transcript, and recommendations. The school recommends a minimum high school GPA of 3.0. Application deadline: rolling admissions; 3/15 priority date for financial aid. Deferred admission is possible.

LOGAN UNIVERSITY-COLLEGE OF CHIROPRACTIC

Chesterfield, MO

Suburban setting ■ Private ■ Independent ■ Coed

Web site: www.logan.edu
Contact: Dr. Patrick Browne, Vice President of Enrollment, 1851 Schoettler Road, Chesterfield, MO 63006-1065
Telephone: 636-227-2100 ext. 149 or toll-free 800-533-9210
E-mail: loganadm@logan.edu

Financial Matters $3220 tuition and fees (2002–03); 100% average percent of need met.

Academics Logan awards bachelor's and first-professional degrees. Challenging opportunities include advanced placement credit and independent study. Internships is a special program. The most frequently chosen baccalaureate field is biological/life sciences. The faculty at Logan has 49 full-time members, 96% with terminal degrees. The student-faculty ratio is 12:1.

Students of Logan The student body totals 874, of whom 92 are undergraduates. 32.6% are women and 67.4% are men. Students come from 24 states and territories and 4 other countries. 30% are from Missouri. 2.2% are international students. 99% returned for their sophomore year.

Applying Application deadline: rolling admissions; 4/30 priority date for financial aid. Deferred admission is possible.

LOMA LINDA UNIVERSITY

Loma Linda, CA

Small-town setting ■ Private ■ Independent Religious ■ Coed

Web site: www.llu.edu
Contact: Admissions Office, Loma Linda, CA 92350
Telephone: 909-558-1000

Financial Matters $20,640 tuition and fees (2002–03); $2780 room only; $15,386 average financial aid amount received per undergraduate.

Academics LLU awards associate, bachelor's, master's, doctoral, and first-professional degrees and post-bachelor's and post-master's certificates. Independent study is a challenging opportunity. Special programs include internships and off-campus study. The faculty at LLU has 1,005 full-time members.

Students of LLU The student body totals 3,427, of whom 952 are undergraduates. 73.2% are women and 26.8% are men. Students come from 29 states and territories and 28 other countries. 77% are from California. 8.5% are international students.

Applying Application deadline: 3/2 priority date for financial aid.

LONG ISLAND UNIVERSITY, BRENTWOOD CAMPUS

Brentwood, NY

Suburban setting ■ Private ■ Independent ■ Coed

Web site: www.liu.edu
Contact: Mr. John P. Metcalfe, Director of Admissions, 100 Second Avenue, Brentwood, NY 11717
Telephone: 631-273-5112 ext. 26
E-mail: information@brentwood.liu.edu

Financial Matters $19,820 tuition and fees (2002–03).

Academics Long Island University, Brentwood Campus awards bachelor's and master's degrees and post-master's certificates. Challenging opportunities include advanced placement credit, an honors program, independent study, and a senior project. Special programs include internships and summer session for credit. The faculty at Long Island University, Brentwood Campus has 20 full-time members, 100% with terminal degrees. The student-faculty ratio is 7:1.

Students of Long Island University, Brentwood Campus The student body totals 966, of whom 62 are undergraduates. 64.5% are women and 35.5% are men. Students come from 1 state or territory. 99% are from New York.

LONG ISLAND UNIVERSITY, BROOKLYN CAMPUS

Brooklyn, NY

Urban setting ■ Private ■ Independent ■ Coed

Web site: www.liu.edu
Contact: Mr. Alan B. Chaves, Dean of Admissions, 1 University Plaza, Brooklyn, NY 11201
Telephone: 718-488-1011 or toll-free 800-LIU-PLAN (in-state) **Fax:** 718-797-2399
E-mail: admissions@brooklyn.liu.edu

Getting in Last Year 3,338 applied; 70% were accepted; 1,001 enrolled (43%).

Financial Matters $16,377 tuition and fees (2002–03); $6280 room and board; 55% average percent of need met; $14,125 average financial aid amount received per undergraduate.

Academics Brooklyn Campus awards associate, bachelor's, master's, doctoral, and first-professional degrees and post-bachelor's, post-master's, and first-professional certificates. Challenging opportunities include advanced placement credit, student-designed majors, an honors program, and double majors. Special programs include cooperative education, internships, and summer session for credit. The most frequently chosen baccalaureate fields are health professions and related sciences, business/marketing, and education. The faculty at Brooklyn Campus has 289 full-time members. The student-faculty ratio is 19:1.

Students of Brooklyn Campus The student body totals 8,057, of whom 5,399 are undergraduates. 72% are women and 28% are men. Students come from 37 states and territories and 15 other countries. 91% are from New York. 1.4% are international students. 49% returned for their sophomore year.

Applying Brooklyn Campus requires a high school transcript and a minimum high school GPA of 2.0, and in some cases SAT I or ACT, an interview, and 2 recommendations. The school recommends an essay. Application deadline: rolling admissions. Deferred admission is possible.

LONG ISLAND UNIVERSITY, C.W. POST CAMPUS

Brookville, NY

Suburban setting ■ Private ■ Independent ■ Coed

Web site: www.liu.edu
Contact: Ms. Jacqueline Reyes, Associate Director of Admissions, 720 Northern Boulevard, Brookville, NY 11548-1300
Telephone: 516-299-2900 or toll-free 800-LIU-PLAN **Fax:** 516-299-2137
E-mail: enroll@cwpost.liu.edu

Getting in Last Year 4,620 applied; 76% were accepted; 864 enrolled (25%).

Financial Matters $19,160 tuition and fees (2002–03); $7400 room and board; 75% average percent of need met; $8791 average financial aid amount received per undergraduate (2001–02).

Academics C.W. Post Campus awards associate, bachelor's, master's, and doctoral degrees. Challenging opportunities include advanced placement credit, accelerated degree programs, student-designed majors, an honors program, double majors, independent study, and a senior project. Special programs include cooperative education, internships, summer session for credit, off-campus study, study-abroad, and Army and Air Force ROTC. The most frequently chosen baccalaureate fields are education, visual/performing arts, and communications/communication technologies. The faculty at C.W. Post Campus has 292 full-time members. The student-faculty ratio is 15:1.

Students of C.W. Post Campus The student body totals 10,644, of whom 6,914 are undergraduates. 57% are women and 43% are men. Students come from 31 states and territories and 46 other countries. 89% are from New York. 1.9% are international students. 87% returned for their sophomore year.

Applying C.W. Post Campus requires SAT I or ACT, a high school transcript, and a minimum high school GPA of 2.5. The school recommends an essay, an interview, 2 recommendations, and a minimum high school GPA of 3.0. Application deadline: rolling admissions; 3/1 for financial aid. Deferred admission is possible.

LONG ISLAND UNIVERSITY, SOUTHAMPTON COLLEGE

Southampton, NY

Rural setting ■ Private ■ Independent ■ Coed

Web site: www.southampton.liu.edu
Contact: Ms. Rory Shaffer-Walsh, Director of Admissions, 239 Montauk Highway, Southampton, NY 11968-9822
Telephone: 631-287-8000 or toll-free 800-LIU PLAN ext. 2 **Fax:** 631-287-8130
E-mail: admissions@southampton.liu.edu

Getting in Last Year 1,470 applied; 62% were accepted; 265 enrolled (29%).

Financial Matters $19,230 tuition and fees (2002–03); $8430 room and board; $12,185 average financial aid amount received per undergraduate (2001–02 estimated).

Academics Southampton College awards bachelor's and master's degrees. Challenging opportunities include advanced placement credit, accelerated degree programs, student-designed majors, an honors program, double majors, independent study, and a senior project. Special programs include cooperative education, internships, summer session for credit, off-campus study, and study-abroad. The most frequently chosen baccalaureate fields are interdisciplinary studies, biological/life sciences, and liberal arts/general studies. The faculty at Southampton College has 64 full-time members, 70% with terminal degrees. The student-faculty ratio is 17:1.

Students of Southampton College The student body totals 3,289, of whom 3,021 are undergraduates. 56.9% are women and 43.1% are men. Students come from 49 states and territories and 19 other countries. 63% are from New York. 3.7% are international students. 58% returned for their sophomore year.

Applying Southampton College requires SAT I or ACT and a high school transcript. The school recommends an essay, an interview, 2 recommendations, and a minimum high school GPA of 2.5. Application deadline: rolling admissions. Deferred admission is possible.

LONG ISLAND UNIVERSITY, SOUTHAMPTON COLLEGE, FRIENDS WORLD PROGRAM

Southampton, NY

Rural setting ■ Private ■ Independent ■ Coed

Web site: www.southampton.liu.edu/fw
Contact: Ms. Emily O'Sullivan, Admissions Counselor, 239 Montauk Highway, Southampton, NY 11968
Telephone: 631-287-8329 or toll-free 631-287-8474 (in-state), 800-LIU PLAN (out-of-state) **Fax:** 631-287-6465
E-mail: fw@southampton.liu.edu

Getting in Last Year 83 applied; 90% were accepted; 37 enrolled (49%).

Financial Matters $19,070 tuition and fees (2002–03); $8600 room and board.

Academics Friends World awards bachelor's degrees. Challenging opportunities include advanced placement credit, student-designed majors, independent study, and a senior project. Special programs include internships, off-campus study, and study-abroad. The most frequently chosen baccalaureate field is interdisciplinary studies. The faculty at Friends World has 16 full-time members, 100% with terminal degrees. The student-faculty ratio is 9:1.

Students of Friends World The student body is made up of 188 undergraduates. 67% are women and 33% are men. Students come from 38 states and territories. 18% are from New York. 1.1% are international students. 53% returned for their sophomore year.

Applying Friends World requires an essay, a high school transcript, and an interview. The school recommends 2 recommendations and a minimum high school GPA of 3.0. Application deadline: rolling admissions. Early and deferred admission are possible.

LONGWOOD UNIVERSITY

Farmville, VA

Small-town setting ■ Public ■ State-supported ■ Coed

Web site: www.longwood.edu
Contact: Mr. Robert J. Chonko, Director of Admissions, 201 High Street, Farmville, VA 23909
Telephone: 434-395-2060 or toll-free 800-281-4677 **Fax:** 434-395-2332
E-mail: admit@longwood.edu

Getting in Last Year 3,223 applied; 67% were accepted; 880 enrolled (41%).

Financial Matters $4661 resident tuition and fees (2002–03); $10,587 nonresident tuition and fees (2002–03); $5070 room and board; 84% average percent of need met; $6893 average financial aid amount received per undergraduate.

Academics Longwood awards bachelor's and master's degrees. Challenging opportunities include advanced placement credit, accelerated degree programs, an honors program, double majors, independent study, and a senior project. Special programs include internships, summer session for credit, off-campus study, study-abroad, and Army ROTC. The most frequently chosen baccalaureate fields are education, business/marketing, and social sciences and history. The faculty at Longwood has 171 full-time members, 80% with terminal degrees. The student-faculty ratio is 20:1.

Students of Longwood The student body totals 4,178, of whom 3,640 are undergraduates. 66.3% are women and 33.7% are men. Students come from 25 states and territories and 11 other countries. 90% are from Virginia. 0.5% are international students. 83% returned for their sophomore year.

Longwood University (continued)

Applying Longwood requires an essay, SAT I or ACT, and a high school transcript, and in some cases SAT II Subject Tests, an interview, and recommendations. The school recommends a minimum high school GPA of 2.7. Application deadline: 3/1; 3/1 priority date for financial aid. Early and deferred admission are possible.

LORAS COLLEGE

Dubuque, IA

Suburban setting ■ *Private* ■ *Independent Religious* ■ *Coed*

Web site: www.loras.edu
Contact: Mr. Tim Hauber, Director of Admissions, 1450 Alta Vista, Dubuque, IA 52004-0178
Telephone: 563-588-7829 or toll-free 800-245-6727 **Fax:** 563-588-7119
E-mail: adms@loras.edu

Getting in Last Year 1,374 applied; 80% were accepted; 373 enrolled (34%).

Financial Matters $17,949 tuition and fees (2002–03); $5895 room and board; 87% average percent of need met; $16,812 average financial aid amount received per undergraduate.

Academics Loras awards associate, bachelor's, and master's degrees. Challenging opportunities include advanced placement credit, student-designed majors, an honors program, double majors, independent study, and a senior project. Special programs include cooperative education, internships, summer session for credit, off-campus study, and study-abroad. The most frequently chosen baccalaureate fields are business/marketing, education, and communications/communication technologies. The faculty at Loras has 118 full-time members, 84% with terminal degrees. The student-faculty ratio is 12:1.

Students of Loras The student body totals 1,736, of whom 1,614 are undergraduates. 51.2% are women and 48.8% are men. Students come from 28 states and territories and 7 other countries. 56% are from Iowa. 1.5% are international students. 76% returned for their sophomore year.

Applying Loras requires SAT I or ACT, a high school transcript, and a minimum high school GPA of 2.5, and in some cases an interview. The school recommends an essay and 1 recommendation. Application deadline: rolling admissions; 4/15 priority date for financial aid. Deferred admission is possible.

LOUISIANA COLLEGE

Pineville, LA

Small-town setting ■ *Private* ■ *Independent Religious* ■ *Coed*

Web site: www.lacollege.edu
Contact: Mrs. Mary Wagner, Director of Admissions, Box 560, Pineville, LA 71359-0001
Telephone: 318-487-7259 ext. 7301 or toll-free 800-487-1906
Fax: 318-487-7550
E-mail: admissions@lacollege.edu

Getting in Last Year 664 applied; 77% were accepted; 247 enrolled (48%).

Financial Matters $9050 tuition and fees (2002–03); $3486 room and board; 44% average percent of need met; $10,591 average financial aid amount received per undergraduate (2001–02).

Academics LC awards bachelor's degrees. Challenging opportunities include advanced placement credit, accelerated degree programs, student-designed majors, an honors program, double majors, independent study, and a senior project. Special programs include internships, summer session for credit, study-abroad, and Army ROTC. The most frequently chosen baccalaureate fields are health professions and related sciences, biological/life sciences, and business/marketing. The faculty at LC has 74 full-time members, 64% with terminal degrees. The student-faculty ratio is 16:1.

Students of LC The student body is made up of 1,161 undergraduates. 58.5% are women and 41.5% are men. Students come from 16 states and territories and 10 other countries. 93% are from Louisiana. 0.7% are international students. 60% returned for their sophomore year.

Applying LC requires SAT I or ACT, a high school transcript, and recommendations, and in some cases 3 recommendations, class rank, and a minimum high school GPA of 2.0. The school recommends an interview. Application deadline: 8/1; 3/31 priority date for financial aid. Early admission is possible.

LOUISIANA STATE UNIVERSITY AND AGRICULTURAL AND MECHANICAL COLLEGE

Baton Rouge, LA

Urban setting ■ *Public* ■ *State-supported* ■ *Coed*

Web site: www.lsu.edu
Contact: Cleve Brooks, Director of Admissions, 110 Thomas Boyd Hall, Baton Rouge, LA 70803
Telephone: 225-578-1175 **Fax:** 225-578-4433
E-mail: admissions@lsu.edu

Getting in Last Year 10,376 applied; 77% were accepted; 5,262 enrolled (66%).

Financial Matters $3536 resident tuition and fees (2002–03); $8836 nonresident tuition and fees (2002–03); $4968 room and board; 71% average percent of need met; $6354 average financial aid amount received per undergraduate (2001–02).

Academics LSU awards bachelor's, master's, doctoral, and first-professional degrees and post-master's certificates. Challenging opportunities include advanced placement credit, accelerated degree programs, student-designed majors, freshman honors college, an honors program, double majors, independent study, and a senior project. Special programs include cooperative education, internships, summer session for credit, off-campus study, study-abroad, and Army, Navy and Air Force ROTC. The most frequently chosen baccalaureate fields are business/marketing, engineering/engineering technologies, and education. The faculty at LSU has 1,302 full-time members, 80% with terminal degrees. The student-faculty ratio is 21:1.

Students of LSU The student body totals 32,228, of whom 26,660 are undergraduates. 53.1% are women and 46.9% are men. Students come from 51 states and territories and 98 other countries. 92% are from Louisiana. 2.3% are international students. 83% returned for their sophomore year.

Applying LSU requires SAT I or ACT, a high school transcript, minimum ACT score of 20 or SAT I score of 940, and a minimum high school GPA of 2.8, and in some cases an essay, SAT I and SAT II or ACT, an interview, and 3 recommendations. Application deadline: 4/15. Early admission is possible.

LOUISIANA STATE UNIVERSITY HEALTH SCIENCES CENTER

New Orleans, LA

Urban setting ■ *Public* ■ *State-supported* ■ *Coed*

Web site: www.lsumc.edu
Contact: Mr. Edmund A. Vidacovich, Registrar, 433 Bolivar Street, New Orleans, LA 70112-2223
Telephone: 504-568-4829

Financial Matters $3214 resident tuition and fees (2002–03); $5714 nonresident tuition and fees (2002–03); $2748 room only.

Academics LSUMC awards associate, bachelor's, master's, doctoral, and first-professional degrees. Challenging opportunities include advanced placement credit, independent study, and a senior project. Special programs include internships and summer session for credit. The most frequently chosen baccalaureate field is health professions and related sciences. The faculty at LSUMC has 3,000 members.

Students of LSUMC The student body totals 2,851, of whom 761 are undergraduates. Students come from 14 states and territories. 99% are from Louisiana. 0.4% are international students.

Applying Application deadline: 4/15 priority date for financial aid.

LOUISIANA STATE UNIVERSITY IN SHREVEPORT

Shreveport, LA

Urban setting ■ *Public* ■ *State-supported* ■ *Coed*

Web site: www.lsus.edu
Contact: Ms. Julie Wilkins, Assistant Director of Admissions and Records, One University Place, Shreveport, LA 71115-2399
Telephone: 318-797-5061 or toll-free 800-229-5957 (in-state)
Fax: 318-797-5286
E-mail: admissions@pilot.lsus.edu

Getting in Last Year 790 applied; 63% were accepted; 501 enrolled (100%).

Financial Matters $2818 resident tuition and fees (2002–03); $7148 nonresident tuition and fees (2002–03).

Academics LSUS awards bachelor's and master's degrees. Challenging opportunities include advanced placement credit, accelerated degree programs, student-designed majors, an honors program, double majors, independent study, and a senior project. Special programs include cooperative education, internships, summer session for credit, off-campus study, and Army ROTC. The most frequently chosen baccalaureate fields are business/marketing, education, and liberal arts/general studies. The faculty at LSUS has 161 full-time members, 70% with terminal degrees. The student-faculty ratio is 16:1.

Students of LSUS The student body totals 4,228, of whom 3,542 are undergraduates. 61.9% are women and 38.1% are men. Students come from 31 states and territories and 7 other countries. 98% are from Louisiana. 0.4% are international students. 58% returned for their sophomore year.

Applying LSUS requires a high school transcript and a minimum high school GPA of 2.0, and in some cases minimum ACT score of 17 for nonresidents. The school recommends SAT II Subject Tests, ACT, and SAT I or ACT. Application deadline: 8/1; 6/1 priority date for financial aid. Early and deferred admission are possible.

LOUISIANA TECH UNIVERSITY

Ruston, LA

Small-town setting ■ *Public* ■ *State-supported* ■ *Coed*

Web site: www.latech.edu

Contact: Mrs. Jan B. Albritton, Director of Admissions, PO Box 3178, Ruston, LA 71272
Telephone: 318-257-3036 or toll-free 800-528-3241 **Fax:** 318-257-2499
E-mail: bulldog@latech.edu

Getting in Last Year 3,607 applied; 92% were accepted; 2,060 enrolled (62%).

Financial Matters $3157 resident tuition and fees (2002–03); $8062 nonresident tuition and fees (2002–03); $3345 room and board; 65% average percent of need met; $5473 average financial aid amount received per undergraduate (2001–02).

Academics Louisiana Tech awards associate, bachelor's, master's, and doctoral degrees and first-professional certificates. Challenging opportunities include advanced placement credit, an honors program, double majors, independent study, and a senior project. Special programs include cooperative education, internships, summer session for credit, off-campus study, study-abroad, and Army and Navy ROTC. The most frequently chosen baccalaureate fields are business/marketing, engineering/engineering technologies, and liberal arts/general studies. The faculty at Louisiana Tech has 389 full-time members, 80% with terminal degrees. The student-faculty ratio is 23:1.

Students of Louisiana Tech The student body totals 11,257, of whom 9,375 are undergraduates. 48% are women and 52% are men. Students come from 49 states and territories and 51 other countries. 88% are from Louisiana. 1.8% are international students.

Applying Louisiana Tech requires SAT I or ACT, a high school transcript, and a minimum high school GPA of 2.2. The school recommends ACT. Application deadline: 7/31. Early admission is possible.

LOURDES COLLEGE

Sylvania, OH

Suburban setting ■ Private ■ Independent Religious ■ Coed

Web site: www.lourdes.edu
Contact: Office of Admissions, 6832 Convent Boulevard, Sylvania, OH 43560
Telephone: 419-885-5291 or toll-free 800-878-3210 ext. 1299 **Fax:** 419-882-3987
E-mail: lcadmits@lourdes.edu

Getting in Last Year 356 applied; 27% were accepted; 73 enrolled (76%).

Financial Matters $14,600 tuition and fees (2002–03); 81% average percent of need met; $12,527 average financial aid amount received per undergraduate.

Academics Lourdes awards associate and bachelor's degrees. Challenging opportunities include advanced placement credit, accelerated degree programs, student-designed majors, double majors, independent study, and a senior project. Special programs include cooperative education, internships, summer session for credit, study-abroad, and Army ROTC. The most frequently chosen baccalaureate fields are business/marketing, health professions and related sciences, and protective services/public administration. The faculty at Lourdes has 61 full-time members, 28% with terminal degrees. The student-faculty ratio is 14:1.

Students of Lourdes The student body totals 1,300, of whom 1,272 are undergraduates. 80.6% are women and 19.4% are men. Students come from 2 states and territories and 1 other country. 93% are from Ohio. 0.1% are international students. 56% returned for their sophomore year.

Applying Lourdes requires SAT I or ACT and a high school transcript, and in some cases an interview. Application deadline: rolling admissions. Early and deferred admission are possible.

LOYOLA COLLEGE IN MARYLAND

Baltimore, MD

Urban setting ■ Private ■ Independent Religious ■ Coed

Web site: www.loyola.edu
Contact: Mr. David Dukor-Jackson, Director of Undergraduate Admissions, 4501 North Charles Street, Baltimore, MD 21210
Telephone: 410-617-2015 or toll-free 800-221-9107 ext. 2252 (in-state) **Fax:** 410-617-2176

Getting in Last Year 6,368 applied; 61% were accepted; 901 enrolled (23%).

Financial Matters $24,910 tuition and fees (2002–03); $7670 room and board; 98% average percent of need met; $16,950 average financial aid amount received per undergraduate.

Academics Loyola awards bachelor's, master's, and doctoral degrees and post-master's certificates. Challenging opportunities include advanced placement credit, accelerated degree programs, an honors program, double majors, independent study, and a senior project. Special programs include internships, summer session for credit, off-campus study, study-abroad, and Army and Air Force ROTC. The most frequently chosen baccalaureate fields are business/marketing, social sciences and history, and communications/communication technologies. The faculty at Loyola has 272 full-time members, 86% with terminal degrees. The student-faculty ratio is 12:1.

Students of Loyola The student body totals 6,144, of whom 3,488 are undergraduates. 57.6% are women and 42.4% are men. Students come from 39 states and territories and 17 other countries. 21% are from Maryland. 0.4% are international students. 89% returned for their sophomore year.

Applying Loyola requires an essay, SAT I, and a high school transcript. The school recommends an interview. Application deadline: 1/15; 2/10 for financial aid. Early and deferred admission are possible.

LOYOLA MARYMOUNT UNIVERSITY

Los Angeles, CA

Suburban setting ■ Private ■ Independent Religious ■ Coed

Web site: www.lmu.edu
Contact: Mr. Matthew X. Fissinger, Director of Admissions, One LMU Drive, Los Angeles, CA 90045-2659
Telephone: 310-338-2750 or toll-free 800-LMU-INFO
E-mail: admissions@lmu.edu

Getting in Last Year 7,959 applied; 56% were accepted; 1,207 enrolled (27%).

Financial Matters $22,016 tuition and fees (2002–03); $6930 room and board; 80% average percent of need met; $19,970 average financial aid amount received per undergraduate (2001–02).

Academics LMU awards bachelor's, master's, and first-professional degrees and post-bachelor's certificates. Challenging opportunities include advanced placement credit, accelerated degree programs, student-designed majors, an honors program, double majors, and independent study. Special programs include cooperative education, internships, summer session for credit, study-abroad, and Army and Air Force ROTC. The most frequently chosen baccalaureate fields are business/marketing, visual/performing arts, and psychology. The faculty at LMU has 405 full-time members, 88% with terminal degrees. The student-faculty ratio is 13:1.

Students of LMU The student body totals 8,178, of whom 5,356 are undergraduates. 58.5% are women and 41.5% are men. Students come from 49 states and territories and 71 other countries. 78% are from California. 1.9% are international students. 87% returned for their sophomore year.

Applying LMU requires an essay, SAT I or ACT, a high school transcript, and 1 recommendation. The school recommends an interview. Application deadline: 2/1; 2/15 priority date for financial aid. Early and deferred admission are possible.

LOYOLA UNIVERSITY CHICAGO

Chicago, IL

Urban setting ■ Private ■ Independent Religious ■ Coed

Web site: www.luc.edu
Contact: Ms. April Hansen, Director of Admissions, 820 North Michigan Avenue, Suite 613, Chicago, IL 60611
Telephone: 773-508-3080 or toll-free 800-262-2373 **Fax:** 312-915-7216
E-mail: admission@luc.edu

Getting in Last Year 8,759 applied; 84% were accepted; 1,623 enrolled (22%).

Financial Matters $19,932 tuition and fees (2002–03); $7430 room and board; 89% average percent of need met; $20,087 average financial aid amount received per undergraduate.

Academics Loyola awards bachelor's, master's, doctoral, and first-professional degrees and post-bachelor's and post-master's certificates (also offers adult part-time program with significant enrollment not reflected in profile). Challenging opportunities include advanced placement credit, accelerated degree programs, an honors program, and double majors. Special programs include internships, summer session for credit, off-campus study, study-abroad, and Army and Navy ROTC. The most frequently chosen baccalaureate fields are business/marketing, social sciences and history, and psychology. The faculty at Loyola has 940 full-time members, 98% with terminal degrees. The student-faculty ratio is 13:1.

Students of Loyola The student body totals 13,061, of whom 7,533 are undergraduates. 65.7% are women and 34.3% are men. Students come from 50 states and territories and 60 other countries. 68% are from Illinois. 1.7% are international students. 85% returned for their sophomore year.

Applying Loyola requires an essay, SAT I or ACT, and a high school transcript. The school recommends an interview. Application deadline: 4/1; 3/1 priority date for financial aid. Deferred admission is possible.

LOYOLA UNIVERSITY NEW ORLEANS

New Orleans, LA

Urban setting ■ Private ■ Independent Religious ■ Coed

Web site: www.loyno.edu
Contact: Ms. Deborah C. Stieffel, Dean of Admission and Enrollment Management, 6363 Saint Charles Avenue, Box 18, New Orleans, LA 70118-6195
Telephone: 504-865-3240 or toll-free 800-4-LOYOLA **Fax:** 504-865-3383
E-mail: admit@loyno.edu

Getting in Last Year 3,603 applied; 68% were accepted; 871 enrolled (36%).

Financial Matters $19,212 tuition and fees (2002–03); $6908 room and board; 84% average percent of need met; $15,288 average financial aid amount received per undergraduate.

Loyola University New Orleans (continued)

Academics Loyola awards bachelor's, master's, and first-professional degrees and post-bachelor's certificates. Challenging opportunities include advanced placement credit, accelerated degree programs, student-designed majors, an honors program, double majors, independent study, and a senior project. Special programs include internships, summer session for credit, off-campus study, study-abroad, and Army, Navy and Air Force ROTC. The most frequently chosen baccalaureate fields are communications/communication technologies, business/marketing, and social sciences and history. The faculty at Loyola has 277 full-time members, 91% with terminal degrees. The student-faculty ratio is 13:1.

Students of Loyola The student body totals 5,562, of whom 3,772 are undergraduates. 63.7% are women and 36.3% are men. Students come from 51 states and territories and 42 other countries. 50% are from Louisiana. 3.6% are international students. 81% returned for their sophomore year.

Applying Loyola requires an essay, SAT I or ACT, a high school transcript, and 1 recommendation, and in some cases PAA and an interview. The school recommends an interview. Application deadline: 1/15; 2/15 priority date for financial aid. Early and deferred admission are possible.

LUBBOCK CHRISTIAN UNIVERSITY

Lubbock, TX

Suburban setting ■ Private ■ Independent Religious ■ Coed

Web site: www.lcu.edu
Contact: Ms. Shannon Anderson, Director of Admissions, 5601 19th Street, Lubbock, TX 79407
Telephone: 806-720-7154 or toll-free 800-933-7601 **Fax:** 806-720-7162
E-mail: admissions@lcu.edu

Getting in Last Year 748 applied; 71% were accepted; 292 enrolled (55%).

Financial Matters $10,992 tuition and fees (2002–03); $4160 room and board; 74% average percent of need met; $10,334 average financial aid amount received per undergraduate.

Academics LCU awards bachelor's and master's degrees. Challenging opportunities include advanced placement credit, accelerated degree programs, student-designed majors, an honors program, double majors, and a senior project. Special programs include internships, summer session for credit, study-abroad, and Army and Air Force ROTC. The faculty at LCU has 74 full-time members, 51% with terminal degrees. The student-faculty ratio is 16:1.

Students of LCU The student body totals 1,851, of whom 1,686 are undergraduates. 56.5% are women and 43.5% are men. Students come from 29 states and territories and 12 other countries. 88% are from Texas. 1% are international students. 69% returned for their sophomore year.

Applying LCU requires SAT I or ACT and a high school transcript. Application deadline: rolling admissions; 6/1 priority date for financial aid.

LUTHER COLLEGE

Decorah, IA

Small-town setting ■ Private ■ Independent Religious ■ Coed

Web site: www.luther.edu
Contact: Mr. Jon Lund, Vice President for Enrollment and Marketing, 700 College Drive, Decorah, IA 52101
Telephone: 563-387-1287 or toll-free 800-458-8437 **Fax:** 563-387-2159
E-mail: admissions@luther.edu

Getting in Last Year 1,953 applied; 78% were accepted; 609 enrolled (40%).

Financial Matters $20,310 tuition and fees (2002–03); $4040 room and board; 85% average percent of need met; $16,554 average financial aid amount received per undergraduate (2001–02).

Academics Luther awards bachelor's degrees. Challenging opportunities include advanced placement credit, student-designed majors, an honors program, double majors, independent study, and a senior project. Special programs include internships, summer session for credit, off-campus study, and study-abroad. The most frequently chosen baccalaureate fields are biological/life sciences, business/marketing, and education. The faculty at Luther has 175 full-time members, 81% with terminal degrees. The student-faculty ratio is 13:1.

Students of Luther The student body is made up of 2,572 undergraduates. 60.1% are women and 39.9% are men. Students come from 37 states and territories and 41 other countries. 36% are from Iowa. 5.8% are international students. 84% returned for their sophomore year.

Applying Luther requires an essay, SAT I or ACT, a high school transcript, and 1 recommendation. The school recommends an interview. Application deadline: 2/15 priority date for financial aid. Early and deferred admission are possible.

LUTHER RICE BIBLE COLLEGE AND SEMINARY

Lithonia, GA

Urban setting ■ Private ■ Independent Religious ■ Coed

Web site: www.lrs.edu
Contact: Dr. Bruce Kreutzer, Director of Admissions and Records, 3038 Evans Mill Road, Lithonia, GA 30038-2454
Telephone: 770-484-1204 ext. 242 or toll-free 800-442-1577
E-mail: lrs@lrs.edu

Getting in Last Year 72 applied; 100% were accepted; 33 enrolled (46%).

Financial Matters $3050 tuition and fees (2002–03).

Academics LRS awards bachelor's, master's, and doctoral degrees. Challenging opportunities include advanced placement credit and independent study. Special programs include cooperative education, internships, off-campus study, and study-abroad. The faculty at LRS has 10 full-time members, 80% with terminal degrees.

Students of LRS The student body totals 1,600, of whom 655 are undergraduates. 18.8% are women and 81.2% are men. Students come from 38 states and territories and 23 other countries. 0.8% are international students. 60% returned for their sophomore year.

Applying LRS requires Bible examination, a high school transcript, and recommendations. Application deadline: rolling admissions. Early admission is possible.

LYCOMING COLLEGE

Williamsport, PA

Small-town setting ■ Private ■ Independent Religious ■ Coed

Web site: www.lycoming.edu
Contact: Mr. James Spencer, Dean of Admissions and Financial Aid, 700 College Place, Williamsport, PA 17701
Telephone: 570-321-4026 or toll-free 800-345-3920 ext. 4026 **Fax:** 570-321-4317
E-mail: admissions@lycoming.edu

Getting in Last Year 1,553 applied; 79% were accepted; 373 enrolled (30%).

Financial Matters $20,432 tuition and fees (2002–03); $5624 room and board; 81% average percent of need met; $16,676 average financial aid amount received per undergraduate.

Academics Lycoming awards bachelor's degrees. Challenging opportunities include advanced placement credit, accelerated degree programs, student-designed majors, an honors program, double majors, independent study, and a senior project. Special programs include internships, summer session for credit, off-campus study, study-abroad, and Army ROTC. The most frequently chosen baccalaureate fields are business/marketing, biological/life sciences, and psychology. The faculty at Lycoming has 88 full-time members, 86% with terminal degrees. The student-faculty ratio is 13:1.

Students of Lycoming The student body is made up of 1,418 undergraduates. 54.1% are women and 45.9% are men. Students come from 21 states and territories. 77% are from Pennsylvania. 0.6% are international students. 81% returned for their sophomore year.

Applying Lycoming requires an essay, SAT I or ACT, a high school transcript, and 2 recommendations. The school recommends an interview and a minimum high school GPA of 2.3. Application deadline: 4/1; 4/15 priority date for financial aid. Early and deferred admission are possible.

LYMEACADEMY COLLEGE OF FINE ARTS

Old Lyme, CT

Small-town setting ■ Private ■ Independent ■ Coed

Web site: www.lymeacademy.edu
Contact: Ms. Deborah J. Stanley, Director of Admissions, 84 Lyme Street, Old Lyme, CT 06371
Telephone: 860-434-5232 ext. 118 **Fax:** 860-434-8725
E-mail: admissions@lymeacademy.edu

Getting in Last Year 31 applied; 58% were accepted; 12 enrolled (67%).

Financial Matters $14,100 tuition and fees (2002–03); 51% average percent of need met; $9356 average financial aid amount received per undergraduate.

Academics LymeAcademy College of Fine Arts awards bachelor's degrees. A senior project is a challenging opportunity. Special programs include summer session for credit and off-campus study. The most frequently chosen baccalaureate field is visual/performing arts. The faculty at LymeAcademy College of Fine Arts has 11 full-time members, 64% with terminal degrees. The student-faculty ratio is 10:1.

Students of LymeAcademy College of Fine Arts The student body is made up of 160 undergraduates. 66.3% are women and 33.7% are men. Students come from 18 states and territories and 1 other country. 80% are from Connecticut. 48% returned for their sophomore year.

Applying LymeAcademy College of Fine Arts requires an essay, SAT I, ACT, a high school transcript, 2 recommendations, and portfolio, and in some cases an interview. The school recommends an interview and a minimum high school GPA of 2.0. Application deadline: rolling admissions; 3/15 for financial aid, with a 2/15 priority date. Deferred admission is possible.

LYNCHBURG COLLEGE

Lynchburg, VA

Suburban setting ■ Private ■ Independent Religious ■ Coed

Web site: www.lynchburg.edu

Contact: Ms. Sharon Walters-Bower, Director of Admissions, 1501 Lakeside Drive, Lynchburg, VA 24501-3199

Telephone: 434-544-8300 or toll-free 800-426-8101 **Fax:** 804-544-8653

E-mail: admissions@lynchburg.edu

Getting in Last Year 2,072 applied; 83% were accepted; 440 enrolled (26%).

Financial Matters $20,165 tuition and fees (2002–03); $4600 room and board; 87% average percent of need met; $12,600 average financial aid amount received per undergraduate.

Academics LC awards bachelor's and master's degrees. Challenging opportunities include advanced placement credit, accelerated degree programs, an honors program, double majors, and a senior project. Special programs include internships, summer session for credit, and off-campus study. The most frequently chosen baccalaureate fields are business/marketing, education, and psychology. The faculty at LC has 107 full-time members, 84% with terminal degrees. The student-faculty ratio is 13:1.

Students of LC The student body totals 1,874, of whom 1,665 are undergraduates. 60.1% are women and 39.9% are men. Students come from 31 states and territories and 10 other countries. 57% are from Virginia. 0.9% are international students. 71% returned for their sophomore year.

Applying LC requires SAT I or ACT and a high school transcript. The school recommends an essay, SAT II Subject Tests, SAT II: Writing Test, an interview, and 2 recommendations. Application deadline: rolling admissions; 3/1 priority date for financial aid. Early and deferred admission are possible.

LYNDON STATE COLLEGE

Lyndonville, VT

Rural setting ■ Public ■ State-supported ■ Coed

Web site: www.lyndonstate.edu

Contact: Ms. Michelle McCaffrey, Director of Admissions, 1001 College Road, PO Box 919, Lyndonville, VT 05851

Telephone: 802-626-6413 or toll-free 800-225-1998 (in-state) **Fax:** 802-626-6335

E-mail: admissions@lyndonstate.edu

Getting in Last Year 757 applied; 97% were accepted; 313 enrolled (43%).

Financial Matters $5504 resident tuition and fees (2002–03); $11,716 nonresident tuition and fees (2002–03); $5782 room and board.

Academics LSC awards associate, bachelor's, and master's degrees. Challenging opportunities include advanced placement credit, accelerated degree programs, student-designed majors, an honors program, double majors, independent study, and a senior project. Special programs include cooperative education, internships, summer session for credit, study-abroad, and Air Force ROTC. The faculty at LSC has 57 full-time members, 95% with terminal degrees. The student-faculty ratio is 17:1.

Students of LSC The student body totals 1,315, of whom 1,280 are undergraduates. 52.9% are women and 47.1% are men. Students come from 20 states and territories and 9 other countries. 57% are from Vermont. 0.1% are international students. 57% returned for their sophomore year.

Applying LSC requires SAT I or ACT, a high school transcript, 1 recommendation, and a minimum high school GPA of 2.0, and in some cases a minimum high school GPA of 3.0. The school recommends an essay, an interview, and a minimum high school GPA of 3.0. Application deadline: rolling admissions; 2/12 priority date for financial aid. Early and deferred admission are possible.

LYNN UNIVERSITY

Boca Raton, FL

Suburban setting ■ Private ■ Independent ■ Coed

Web site: www.lynn.edu

Contact: Ms. Melanie Glines, Director of Admissions, 3601 North Military Trail, Boca Raton, FL 33431-5598

Telephone: 561-237-7900 or toll-free 800-888-LYNN ext. 1 (in-state), 800-544-8035 (out-of-state) **Fax:** 561-237-7100

E-mail: admission@lynn.edu

Getting in Last Year 2,714 applied; 75% were accepted; 498 enrolled (25%).

Financial Matters $21,750 tuition and fees (2002–03); $7650 room and board; 62% average percent of need met; $14,819 average financial aid amount received per undergraduate.

Academics Lynn awards bachelor's, master's, and doctoral degrees. Challenging opportunities include advanced placement credit, freshman honors college, an honors program, double majors, and a senior project. Special programs include cooperative education, internships, summer session for credit, study-abroad, and Air Force ROTC. The most frequently chosen baccalaureate fields are business/marketing, communications/communication technologies, and education. The faculty at Lynn has 68 full-time members, 62% with terminal degrees. The student-faculty ratio is 14:1.

Students of Lynn The student body totals 1,888, of whom 1,617 are undergraduates. 47.6% are women and 52.4% are men. Students come from 44 states and territories and 89 other countries. 55% are from Florida. 82% returned for their sophomore year.

Applying Lynn requires an essay, SAT I or ACT, a high school transcript, 1 recommendation, and a minimum high school GPA of 2.5. The school recommends an essay, an interview, and a minimum high school GPA of 3.0. Application deadline: rolling admissions; 3/1 priority date for financial aid. Early and deferred admission are possible.

LYON COLLEGE

Batesville, AR

Small-town setting ■ Private ■ Independent Religious ■ Coed

Web site: www.lyon.edu

Contact: Mr. Denny Bardos, Vice President for Enrollment Services, PO Box 2317, Batesville, AR 72503-2317

Telephone: 870-698-4250 or toll-free 800-423-2542 **Fax:** 870-793-1791

E-mail: admissions@lyon.edu

Getting in Last Year 409 applied; 74% were accepted; 113 enrolled (37%).

Financial Matters $11,940 tuition and fees (2002–03); $5380 room and board; 87% average percent of need met; $13,006 average financial aid amount received per undergraduate.

Academics Lyon awards bachelor's degrees. Challenging opportunities include advanced placement credit, accelerated degree programs, student-designed majors, double majors, independent study, and a senior project. Special programs include internships, summer session for credit, and study-abroad. The most frequently chosen baccalaureate fields are social sciences and history, psychology, and business/marketing. The faculty at Lyon has 43 full-time members, 86% with terminal degrees. The student-faculty ratio is 11:1.

Students of Lyon The student body is made up of 538 undergraduates. 53.5% are women and 46.5% are men. Students come from 20 states and territories and 18 other countries. 86% are from Arkansas. 6.2% are international students. 87% returned for their sophomore year.

Applying Lyon requires an essay, SAT I or ACT, and a high school transcript. The school recommends 2 recommendations and a minimum high school GPA of 2.5. Application deadline: rolling admissions; 3/15 priority date for financial aid. Early and deferred admission are possible.

MACALESTER COLLEGE

St. Paul, MN

Urban setting ■ Private ■ Independent Religious ■ Coed

Web site: www.macalester.edu

Contact: Mr. Lorne T. Robinson, Dean of Admissions and Financial Aid, 1600 Grand Avenue, St. Paul, MN 55105-1899

Telephone: 651-696-6357 or toll-free 800-231-7974 **Fax:** 651-696-6724

E-mail: admissions@macalester.edu

Getting in Last Year 3,713 applied; 44% were accepted; 441 enrolled (27%).

Financial Matters $23,772 tuition and fees (2002–03); $6516 room and board; 100% average percent of need met; $20,539 average financial aid amount received per undergraduate.

Academics Mac awards bachelor's degrees. Challenging opportunities include student-designed majors, an honors program, double majors, independent study, and a senior project. Special programs include internships, off-campus study, study-abroad, and Navy and Air Force ROTC. The most frequently chosen baccalaureate fields are social sciences and history, biological/life sciences, and psychology. The faculty at Mac has 150 full-time members, 93% with terminal degrees. The student-faculty ratio is 10:1.

Students of Mac The student body is made up of 1,840 undergraduates. 58.3% are women and 41.7% are men. Students come from 50 states and territories and 88 other countries. 27% are from Minnesota. 14.7% are international students. 91% returned for their sophomore year.

Applying Mac requires an essay, SAT I or ACT, a high school transcript, and 3 recommendations. The school recommends an interview. Application deadline: 1/15; 2/7 priority date for financial aid. Early and deferred admission are possible.

MACHZIKEI HADATH RABBINICAL COLLEGE

Brooklyn, NY

Private ■ Independent Religious ■ Men Only

Contact: Rabbi Abraham M. Lezerowitz, Director of Admissions, 5407 Sixteenth Avenue, Brooklyn, NY 11204-1805

Telephone: 718-854-8777

Financial Matters $5500 tuition and fees (2002–03); $1800 room and board.

Academics Study-abroad is a special program.

Machzikei Hadath Rabbinical College (continued)

Students of Machzikei Hadath Rabbinical College The student body totals 137. Students come from 4 states and territories.

Applying Machzikei Hadath Rabbinical College requires an interview. Application deadline: rolling admissions.

MACMURRAY COLLEGE

Jacksonville, IL

Small-town setting ■ Private ■ Independent Religious ■ Coed

Web site: www.mac.edu

Contact: Ms. Rhonda Cors, Dean of Enrollment, 447 East College Avenue, Jacksonville, IL 62650

Telephone: 217-479-7056 or toll-free 800-252-7485 (in-state) **Fax:** 217-291-0702

E-mail: admiss@mac.edu

Getting in Last Year 1,102 applied; 55% were accepted; 127 enrolled (21%).

Financial Matters $14,500 tuition and fees (2002–03); $5165 room and board; 73% average percent of need met; $11,433 average financial aid amount received per undergraduate.

Academics MacMurray awards associate and bachelor's degrees. Challenging opportunities include advanced placement credit, an honors program, double majors, independent study, and a senior project. Special programs include internships, summer session for credit, and off-campus study. The most frequently chosen baccalaureate fields are education, protective services/public administration, and psychology. The faculty at MacMurray has 46 full-time members, 72% with terminal degrees. The student-faculty ratio is 12:1.

Students of MacMurray The student body is made up of 633 undergraduates. 58.5% are women and 41.5% are men. Students come from 27 states and territories and 5 other countries. 85% are from Illinois. 1.6% are international students. 56% returned for their sophomore year.

Applying MacMurray requires SAT I or ACT and a high school transcript, and in some cases an essay, an interview, recommendations, and a minimum high school GPA of 2.5. Application deadline: rolling admissions; 5/31 priority date for financial aid. Early admission is possible.

MACON STATE COLLEGE

Macon, GA

Urban setting ■ Public ■ State-supported ■ Coed

Web site: www.maconstate.edu

Contact: Mr. Terrell Mitchell, Director of Admissions, 100 College Station Drive, Macon, GA 31206-5144

Telephone: 912-471-2800 ext. 2854 or toll-free 800-272-7619

Financial Matters $1490 resident tuition and fees (2002–03); $5486 nonresident tuition and fees (2002–03); 60% average percent of need met; $6580 average financial aid amount received per undergraduate (2001–02).

Academics Macon State College awards associate and bachelor's degrees. Challenging opportunities include advanced placement credit and an honors program. Special programs include cooperative education, internships, summer session for credit, and study-abroad. The faculty at Macon State College has 118 full-time members, 79% with terminal degrees. The student-faculty ratio is 20:1.

Students of Macon State College The student body is made up of 4,989 undergraduates. 64.8% are women and 35.2% are men. 0.1% are international students.

Applying Macon State College requires SAT I or ACT and a high school transcript. Application deadline: rolling admissions; 4/1 priority date for financial aid. Early admission is possible.

MADONNA UNIVERSITY

Livonia, MI

Suburban setting ■ Private ■ Independent Religious ■ Coed

Web site: www.madonna.edu

Contact: Mr. Frank J. Hribar, Director of Enrollment Management, 36600 Schoolcraft Road, Livonia, MI 48150-1173

Telephone: 734-432-5317 or toll-free 800-852-4951 **Fax:** 734-432-5393

E-mail: muinfo@smtp.munet.edu

Getting in Last Year 580 applied; 94% were accepted; 199 enrolled (37%).

Financial Matters $8350 tuition and fees (2002–03); $5252 room and board; 80% average percent of need met; $1800 average financial aid amount received per undergraduate (2001–02 estimated).

Academics Madonna University awards associate, bachelor's, and master's degrees. Challenging opportunities include advanced placement credit, accelerated degree programs, double majors, independent study, and a senior project. Special programs include cooperative education, internships, summer session for credit, off-campus study, and study-abroad. The most frequently chosen baccalaureate fields are health professions and related sciences, protective services/public administration, and business/marketing. The faculty at Madonna University has 99 full-time members, 64% with terminal degrees. The student-faculty ratio is 17:1.

Students of Madonna University The student body totals 3,808, of whom 2,963 are undergraduates. 77.4% are women and 22.6% are men. Students come from 9 states and territories and 28 other countries. 99% are from Michigan. 2.5% are international students. 74% returned for their sophomore year.

Applying Madonna University requires ACT, a high school transcript, and a minimum high school GPA of 2.75, and in some cases 2 recommendations. Application deadline: rolling admissions; 2/21 priority date for financial aid. Early and deferred admission are possible.

MAGDALEN COLLEGE

Warner, NH

Private ■ Independent Religious ■ Coed

Web site: www.magdalen.edu

Contact: Paul V. Sullivan, Director of Admissions, 511 Kearsarge Mountain Road, Warner, NH 03278

Telephone: 603-456-2656 ext. 11 or toll-free 877-498-1723 (out-of-state) **Fax:** 603-456-2660

E-mail: admissions@magdalen.edu

Getting in Last Year 47 applied; 91% were accepted; 28 enrolled (65%).

Financial Matters $8000 tuition and fees (2002–03); $5250 room and board; 90% average percent of need met; $6000 average financial aid amount received per undergraduate.

Academics Magdalen College awards associate and bachelor's degrees. A senior project is a challenging opportunity. Cooperative education is a special program. The most frequently chosen baccalaureate field is liberal arts/general studies. The faculty at Magdalen College has 6 full-time members, 133% with terminal degrees. The student-faculty ratio is 9:1.

Students of Magdalen College The student body is made up of 81 undergraduates. Students come from 17 states and territories and 1 other country. 8% are from New Hampshire. 6.2% are international students. 81% returned for their sophomore year.

Applying Magdalen College requires an essay, SAT I or ACT, a high school transcript, an interview, 2 recommendations, and medical examination form. Application deadline: 5/1. Early admission is possible.

MAGNOLIA BIBLE COLLEGE

Kosciusko, MS

Small-town setting ■ Private ■ Independent Religious ■ Coed, Primarily Men

Web site: www.magnolia.edu

Contact: Mr. Allen Coker, Director of Admissions, PO Box 1109, 822 South Huntington Street, Kosciusko, MS 39090

Telephone: 601-289-2896 or toll-free 800-748-8655 (in-state) **Fax:** 662-289-1850

E-mail: mbcadmissions@hotmail.com

Getting in Last Year 8 applied; 75% were accepted; 4 enrolled (67%).

Financial Matters $4590 tuition and fees (2002–03); $1120 room only; 46% average percent of need met; $4993 average financial aid amount received per undergraduate.

Academics MBC awards bachelor's degrees. Independent study is a challenging opportunity. Special programs include internships and summer session for credit. The faculty at MBC has 2 full-time members, 100% with terminal degrees. The student-faculty ratio is 7:1.

Students of MBC The student body is made up of 44 undergraduates. 22.7% are women and 77.3% are men. Students come from 2 states and territories. 95% are from Mississippi. 100% returned for their sophomore year.

Applying MBC requires an essay, a high school transcript, and 3 recommendations. The school recommends SAT I or ACT. Application deadline: 8/31; 8/1 priority date for financial aid.

MAHARISHI UNIVERSITY OF MANAGEMENT

Fairfield, IA

Small-town setting ■ Private ■ Independent ■ Coed

Web site: www.mum.edu

Contact: Mr. Brad Mylett, Director of Admissions, 1000 North 4th Street, Fairfield, IA 52557

Telephone: 641-472-1110 or toll-free 800-369-6480 **Fax:** 641-472-1179

E-mail: admissions@mum.edu

Getting in Last Year 80 applied; 68% were accepted; 37 enrolled (69%).

Financial Matters $24,050 tuition and fees (2002–03); $5200 room and board; 95% average percent of need met; $29,462 average financial aid amount received per undergraduate.

Academics M.U.M. awards associate, bachelor's, master's, and doctoral degrees. Challenging opportunities include advanced placement credit, student-designed majors, an honors program, double majors, independent study, and a senior project. Special programs include cooperative education, internships, and study-abroad. The most frequently chosen baccalaureate fields are visual/performing arts, business/marketing, and biological/life sciences. The faculty at M.U.M. has 50 full-time members, 72% with terminal degrees. The student-faculty ratio is 11:1.

Students of M.U.M. The student body totals 756, of whom 186 are undergraduates. 50.5% are women and 49.5% are men. Students come from 26 states and territories and 20 other countries. 52% are from Iowa. 23.1% are international students. 66% returned for their sophomore year.

Applying M.U.M. requires an essay, SAT I or ACT, a high school transcript, 2 recommendations, minimum SAT score of 950 or ACT score of 19, and a minimum high school GPA of 2.5. The school recommends an interview. Application deadline: 8/1; 4/15 priority date for financial aid. Early and deferred admission are possible.

MAINE COLLEGE OF ART

Portland, ME

Urban setting ■ Private ■ Independent ■ Coed

Web site: www.meca.edu

Contact: Kathryn Quin-Easter, Admissions Assistant, 97 Spring Street, Portland, ME 04101-3987

Telephone: 207-775-5157 ext. 226 or toll-free 800-639-4808 **Fax:** 207-772-5069

E-mail: admissions@meca.edu

Getting in Last Year 296 applied; 90% were accepted; 96 enrolled (36%).

Financial Matters $19,878 tuition and fees (2002–03); $7140 room and board; 57% average percent of need met; $11,979 average financial aid amount received per undergraduate.

Academics MECA awards bachelor's and master's degrees. Challenging opportunities include student-designed majors, double majors, independent study, and a senior project. Special programs include cooperative education, internships, off-campus study, and study-abroad. The most frequently chosen baccalaureate field is visual/performing arts. The faculty at MECA has 32 full-time members, 94% with terminal degrees. The student-faculty ratio is 10:1.

Students of MECA The student body totals 459, of whom 430 are undergraduates. 61.2% are women and 38.8% are men. 56% are from Maine. 0.7% are international students. 52% returned for their sophomore year.

Applying MECA requires an essay, SAT I or ACT, a high school transcript, 2 recommendations, and portfolio. The school recommends an interview and a minimum high school GPA of 2.0. Application deadline: rolling admissions; 3/1 priority date for financial aid. Early and deferred admission are possible.

MAINE MARITIME ACADEMY

Castine, ME

Small-town setting ■ Public ■ State-supported ■ Coed, Primarily Men

Web site: www.mainemaritime.edu

Contact: Jeffrey C. Wright, Director of Admissions, Castine, ME 04420

Telephone: 207-326-2215 or toll-free 800-464-6565 (in-state), 800-227-8465 (out-of-state) **Fax:** 207-326-2515

E-mail: admissions@bell.mma.edu

Getting in Last Year 465 applied; 78% were accepted; 146 enrolled (40%).

Financial Matters $5384 resident tuition and fees (2002–03); $9419 nonresident tuition and fees (2002–03); $5327 room and board; 81% average percent of need met; $8048 average financial aid amount received per undergraduate (2001–02).

Academics Maine Maritime awards associate, bachelor's, and master's degrees. Challenging opportunities include advanced placement credit and a senior project. Special programs include internships and Navy ROTC. The most frequently chosen baccalaureate fields are engineering/engineering technologies, trade and industry, and business/marketing. The faculty at Maine Maritime has 65 full-time members, 58% with terminal degrees. The student-faculty ratio is 12:1.

Students of Maine Maritime The student body totals 762, of whom 721 are undergraduates. 14.7% are women and 85.3% are men. Students come from 37 states and territories and 6 other countries. 52% are from Maine. 4.2% are international students. 75% returned for their sophomore year.

Applying Maine Maritime requires SAT I or ACT, a high school transcript, 1 recommendation, and physical examination. The school recommends an interview. Application deadline: 7/1; 4/15 priority date for financial aid. Early and deferred admission are possible.

MALASPINA UNIVERSITY-COLLEGE

Nanaimo, BC Canada

Public ■ Coed

Web site: www.mala.bc.ca

Contact: Mr. Fred Jarklin, Admissions Manager, 900 Fifth Street, Nanaimo, BC V9R 5S5 Canada

Telephone: 250-740-6356 ext. 6356 **Fax:** - ext.

Academics Malaspina University-College awards associate, bachelor's, and master's degrees and post-bachelor's certificates. The most frequently chosen baccalaureate fields are liberal arts/general studies, education, and area/ethnic studies. The faculty at Malaspina University-College has 404 full-time members. The student-faculty ratio is 17:1.

Students of Malaspina University-College The student body is made up of 6,422 undergraduates.

MALONE COLLEGE

Canton, OH

Suburban setting ■ Private ■ Independent Religious ■ Coed

Web site: www.malone.edu

Contact: Mr. John Chopka, Vice President of Enrollment Management, 515 25th Street, NW, Canton, OH 44709-3897

Telephone: 330-471-8145 or toll-free 800-521-1146 **Fax:** 330-471-8149

E-mail: admissions@malone.edu

Getting in Last Year 896 applied; 91% were accepted; 355 enrolled (44%).

Financial Matters $14,150 tuition and fees (2002–03); $5830 room and board; 82% average percent of need met; $11,397 average financial aid amount received per undergraduate.

Academics Malone awards bachelor's and master's degrees. Challenging opportunities include advanced placement credit, accelerated degree programs, student-designed majors, an honors program, double majors, independent study, and a senior project. Special programs include cooperative education, internships, summer session for credit, off-campus study, study-abroad, and Army and Air Force ROTC. The most frequently chosen baccalaureate fields are business/marketing, education, and health professions and related sciences. The faculty at Malone has 100 full-time members, 65% with terminal degrees. The student-faculty ratio is 14:1.

Students of Malone The student body totals 2,137, of whom 1,878 are undergraduates. 60.3% are women and 39.7% are men. Students come from 27 states and territories and 9 other countries. 90% are from Ohio. 0.7% are international students. 74% returned for their sophomore year.

Applying Malone requires an essay, SAT I or ACT, a high school transcript, and a minimum high school GPA of 2.5, and in some cases an interview. Application deadline: 7/1; 7/31 for financial aid, with a 3/1 priority date. Early and deferred admission are possible.

MANCHESTER COLLEGE

North Manchester, IN

Small-town setting ■ Private ■ Independent Religious ■ Coed

Web site: www.manchester.edu

Contact: Ms. Jolane Rohr, Director of Admissions, 604 East College Avenue, North Manchester, IN 46962-1225

Telephone: 260-982-5055 or toll-free 800-852-3648 **Fax:** 260-982-5239

E-mail: admitinfo@manchester.edu

Getting in Last Year 1,061 applied; 83% were accepted; 309 enrolled (35%).

Financial Matters $16,080 tuition and fees (2002–03); $6340 room and board; 95% average percent of need met; $15,435 average financial aid amount received per undergraduate.

Academics MC awards associate, bachelor's, and master's degrees. Challenging opportunities include advanced placement credit, student-designed majors, an honors program, double majors, independent study, and a senior project. Special programs include internships, summer session for credit, off-campus study, and study-abroad. The most frequently chosen baccalaureate fields are business/marketing, education, and communications/communication technologies. The faculty at MC has 67 full-time members, 79% with terminal degrees. The student-faculty ratio is 14:1.

Students of MC The student body totals 1,140, of whom 1,127 are undergraduates. 56.9% are women and 43.1% are men. Students come from 23 states and territories and 29 other countries. 88% are from Indiana. 6.5% are international students. 76% returned for their sophomore year.

Applying MC requires SAT I or ACT, a high school transcript, 1 recommendation, and rank in upper 50% of high school class, and in some cases an essay, an interview, and a minimum high school GPA of 3.0. The school recommends an interview and a minimum high school GPA of 2.3. Application deadline: rolling admissions. Deferred admission is possible.

MANHATTAN CHRISTIAN COLLEGE

Manhattan, KS

Small-town setting ■ Private ■ Independent Religious ■ Coed

Web site: www.mccks.edu

Contact: Mr. Scott Jenkins, Director of Admissions, 1415 Anderson, Manhattan, KS 66502-4081

Telephone: 785-539-3571 or toll-free 877-246-4622 **Fax:** 785-776-9251

E-mail: admit@mccks.edu

Manhattan Christian College (continued)

Getting in Last Year 99 applied; 71% were accepted; 70 enrolled (100%).

Financial Matters $7966 tuition and fees (2002–03); $3954 room and board.

Academics MCC awards associate and bachelor's degrees. Challenging opportunities include advanced placement credit, double majors, and independent study. Special programs include internships, summer session for credit, off-campus study, and Army and Air Force ROTC. The most frequently chosen baccalaureate field is business/marketing. The faculty at MCC has 8 full-time members, 38% with terminal degrees. The student-faculty ratio is 17:1.

Students of MCC The student body is made up of 362 undergraduates. 52.5% are women and 47.5% are men. Students come from 17 states and territories. 76% are from Kansas. 0.3% are international students. 63% returned for their sophomore year.

Applying MCC requires an essay, SAT I or ACT, a high school transcript, 3 recommendations, and a minimum high school GPA of 2.0, and in some cases an interview. Application deadline: 8/1; 3/15 priority date for financial aid.

MANHATTAN COLLEGE

Riverdale, NY

Urban setting ■ Private ■ Independent Religious ■ Coed

Web site: www.manhattan.edu
Contact: Mr. William J. Bisset Jr., Assistant Vice President for Enrollment Management, 4513 Manhattan College Parkway, Riverdale, NY 10471
Telephone: 718-862-7200 or toll-free 800-622-9235 (in-state)
Fax: 718-862-8019
E-mail: admit@manhattan.edu

Getting in Last Year 3,775 applied; 67% were accepted; 748 enrolled (30%).

Financial Matters $18,600 tuition and fees (2002–03); $7850 room and board; 60% average percent of need met; $12,454 average financial aid amount received per undergraduate.

Academics Manhattan awards bachelor's and master's degrees and post-master's certificates. Challenging opportunities include advanced placement credit, accelerated degree programs, an honors program, double majors, independent study, and a senior project. Special programs include cooperative education, internships, summer session for credit, off-campus study, study-abroad, and Army and Air Force ROTC. The most frequently chosen baccalaureate fields are business/marketing, engineering/engineering technologies, and education. The faculty at Manhattan has 162 full-time members, 93% with terminal degrees. The student-faculty ratio is 14:1.

Students of Manhattan The student body totals 3,208, of whom 2,809 are undergraduates. 49.3% are women and 50.7% are men. Students come from 42 states and territories and 27 other countries. 72% are from New York. 1.4% are international students. 83% returned for their sophomore year.

Applying Manhattan requires an essay, SAT I or ACT, a high school transcript, and 1 recommendation, and in some cases an interview. The school recommends an interview. Application deadline: 3/1; 3/1 priority date for financial aid. Early and deferred admission are possible.

MANHATTAN SCHOOL OF MUSIC

New York, NY

Urban setting ■ Private ■ Independent ■ Coed

Web site: www.msmnyc.edu
Contact: Mrs. Amy Anderson, Director of Admission, 120 Claremont Avenue, New York, NY 10027
Telephone: 212-749-2802 ext. 4449 **Fax:** 212-749-3025
E-mail: admission@msmnyc.edu

Getting in Last Year 738 applied; 37% were accepted; 99 enrolled (36%).

Financial Matters $22,750 tuition and fees (2002–03); $7300 room only; 48% average percent of need met; $12,921 average financial aid amount received per undergraduate (2001–02).

Academics MSM awards bachelor's, master's, and doctoral degrees and post-bachelor's and post-master's certificates. Challenging opportunities include advanced placement credit and a senior project. Off-campus study is a special program. The most frequently chosen baccalaureate field is visual/performing arts. The faculty at MSM has 82 full-time members, 17% with terminal degrees. The student-faculty ratio is 8:1.

Students of MSM The student body totals 876, of whom 409 are undergraduates. 52.1% are women and 47.9% are men. Students come from 34 states and territories and 26 other countries. 37% are from New York. 29.6% are international students. 79% returned for their sophomore year.

Applying MSM requires an essay, a high school transcript, 1 recommendation, audition, and a minimum high school GPA of 2.5. The school recommends SAT I or ACT, an interview, and a minimum high school GPA of 3.0. Application deadline: 12/2; 3/15 priority date for financial aid. Deferred admission is possible.

MANHATTANVILLE COLLEGE

Purchase, NY

Suburban setting ■ Private ■ Independent ■ Coed

Web site: www.mville.edu
Contact: Mr. Jose Flores, Director of Admissions, 2900 Purchase Street, Purchase, NY 10577
Telephone: 914-323-5124 or toll-free 800-328-4553 **Fax:** 914-694-1732
E-mail: admissions@mville.edu

Getting in Last Year 2,330 applied; 55% were accepted; 415 enrolled (32%).

Financial Matters $21,430 tuition and fees (2002–03); $8730 room and board; 90% average percent of need met; $17,432 average financial aid amount received per undergraduate (2001–02).

Academics Manhattanville awards bachelor's and master's degrees. Challenging opportunities include advanced placement credit, accelerated degree programs, student-designed majors, freshman honors college, an honors program, double majors, independent study, and a senior project. Special programs include internships, summer session for credit, off-campus study, and study-abroad. The most frequently chosen baccalaureate fields are business/marketing, social sciences and history, and visual/performing arts. The faculty at Manhattanville has 82 full-time members, 95% with terminal degrees. The student-faculty ratio is 12:1.

Students of Manhattanville The student body totals 2,568, of whom 1,618 are undergraduates. 68.1% are women and 31.9% are men. Students come from 33 states and territories and 49 other countries. 69% are from New York. 7.8% are international students. 72% returned for their sophomore year.

Applying Manhattanville requires an essay, SAT I or ACT, a high school transcript, 2 recommendations, and a minimum high school GPA of 2.0, and in some cases SAT I, SAT II Subject Tests, SAT II: Writing Test, ACT, and SAT I and SAT II or ACT. The school recommends an interview and a minimum high school GPA of 3.0. Application deadline: 3/1; 4/15 priority date for financial aid. Early and deferred admission are possible.

MANNES COLLEGE OF MUSIC, NEW SCHOOL UNIVERSITY

New York, NY

Urban setting ■ Private ■ Independent ■ Coed

Web site: www.mannes.edu
Contact: Ms. Allison Scola, Director of Enrollment, 150 West 85th Street, New York, NY 10024-4402
Telephone: 212-580-0210 ext. 247 or toll-free 800-292-3040 (out-of-state)
Fax: 212-580-1738
E-mail: mannasadmissions@newschool.edu

Getting in Last Year 355 applied; 32% were accepted; 46 enrolled (41%).

Financial Matters $21,200 tuition and fees (2002–03); $9896 room and board; 52% average percent of need met; $13,625 average financial aid amount received per undergraduate.

Academics Mannes awards bachelor's and master's degrees and post-master's certificates. Challenging opportunities include advanced placement credit, double majors, and a senior project. Summer session for credit is a special program. The most frequently chosen baccalaureate field is visual/performing arts. The faculty at Mannes has 6 full-time members. The student-faculty ratio is 4:1.

Students of Mannes The student body totals 355, of whom 172 are undergraduates. 60.5% are women and 39.5% are men. Students come from 17 states and territories and 14 other countries. 64% are from New York. 31.4% are international students. 75% returned for their sophomore year.

Applying Mannes requires a high school transcript, 1 recommendation, audition, and a minimum high school GPA of 2.5. Application deadline: 12/15; 3/1 priority date for financial aid. Deferred admission is possible.

MANSFIELD UNIVERSITY OF PENNSYLVANIA

Mansfield, PA

Small-town setting ■ Public ■ State-supported ■ Coed

Web site: www.mansfield.edu
Contact: Mr. Brian D. Barden, Director of Admissions, Alumni Hall, Mansfield, PA 16933
Telephone: 570-662-4813 or toll-free 800-577-6826 **Fax:** 570-662-4121
E-mail: admissions@mansfield.edu

Getting in Last Year 2,094 applied; 78% were accepted; 667 enrolled (41%).

Financial Matters $5674 resident tuition and fees (2002–03); $12,242 nonresident tuition and fees (2002–03); $5006 room and board.

Academics Mansfield University awards associate, bachelor's, and master's degrees and post-bachelor's certificates. Challenging opportunities include advanced placement credit, accelerated degree programs, student-designed majors, freshman honors college, an honors program, double majors, independent study, and a senior project. Special programs include internships, summer session for credit, off-campus study, and study-abroad. The most frequently chosen baccalaureate fields are protective services/public administration, business/marketing, and education. The faculty at Mansfield University has 155 full-time members, 66% with terminal degrees. The student-faculty ratio is 18:1.

Students of Mansfield University The student body totals 3,368, of whom 3,057 are undergraduates. 60.9% are women and 39.1% are men. Students come from 14 states and territories and 13 other countries. 78% are from Pennsylvania. 1.3% are international students. 67% returned for their sophomore year.

Applying Mansfield University requires SAT I or ACT and a high school transcript, and in some cases an interview. The school recommends an essay, recommendations, and a minimum high school GPA of 2.5. Application deadline: rolling admissions; 3/15 priority date for financial aid. Early and deferred admission are possible.

MARANATHA BAPTIST BIBLE COLLEGE

Watertown, WI

Small-town setting ■ Private ■ Independent Religious ■ Coed

Web site: www.mbbc.edu

Contact: Mr. James H. Harrison, Director of Admissions, 745 West Main Street, Watertown, WI 53094

Telephone: 920-206-2327 or toll-free 800-622-2947 **Fax:** 920-261-9109

E-mail: admissions@mbbc.edu

Getting in Last Year 308 applied; 70% were accepted; 186 enrolled (87%).

Financial Matters $6720 tuition and fees (2002–03); $4200 room and board; 19% average percent of need met; $2597 average financial aid amount received per undergraduate.

Academics Maranatha awards associate, bachelor's, and master's degrees. Challenging opportunities include accelerated degree programs, double majors, independent study, and a senior project. Special programs include internships, summer session for credit, off-campus study, and Air Force ROTC. The faculty at Maranatha has 67 full-time members. The student-faculty ratio is 16:1.

Students of Maranatha The student body totals 803, of whom 776 are undergraduates. Students come from 29 states and territories and 5 other countries. 34% are from Wisconsin. 1.2% are international students. 64% returned for their sophomore year.

Applying Maranatha requires an essay, a high school transcript, and 3 recommendations. The school recommends ACT. Application deadline: rolling admissions; 3/1 priority date for financial aid. Early and deferred admission are possible.

MARIAN COLLEGE

Indianapolis, IN

Urban setting ■ Private ■ Independent Religious ■ Coed

Web site: www.marian.edu

Contact: Ms. Karen Kist, Director of Admission, 3200 Cold Spring Road, Indianapolis, IN 46222-1997

Telephone: 317-955-6300 or toll-free 800-772-7264 (in-state)

Getting in Last Year 836 applied; 76% were accepted; 257 enrolled (40%).

Financial Matters $16,560 tuition and fees (2002–03); $5600 room and board; 85% average percent of need met; $14,322 average financial aid amount received per undergraduate.

Academics Marian awards associate, bachelor's, and master's degrees. Challenging opportunities include advanced placement credit, accelerated degree programs, an honors program, double majors, independent study, and a senior project. Special programs include cooperative education, internships, summer session for credit, off-campus study, study-abroad, and Army ROTC. The most frequently chosen baccalaureate fields are business/marketing, education, and health professions and related sciences. The faculty at Marian has 65 full-time members, 55% with terminal degrees. The student-faculty ratio is 12:1.

Students of Marian The student body totals 1,431, of whom 1,416 are undergraduates. 68.4% are women and 31.6% are men. Students come from 22 states and territories and 15 other countries. 93% are from Indiana. 2% are international students. 69% returned for their sophomore year.

Applying Marian requires SAT I or ACT, a high school transcript, and a minimum high school GPA of 2.00. Application deadline: 8/15; 3/1 priority date for financial aid. Early and deferred admission are possible.

MARIAN COLLEGE OF FOND DU LAC

Fond du Lac, WI

Small-town setting ■ Private ■ Independent Religious ■ Coed

Web site: www.mariancollege.edu

Contact: Stacey L. Akey, Dean of Admissions, 45 South National Avenue, Fond du Lac, WI 54935

Telephone: 920-923-7652 or toll-free 800-2-MARIAN ext. 7652 (in-state) **Fax:** 920-923-8755

E-mail: admit@mariancollege.edu

Getting in Last Year 767 applied; 83% were accepted; 246 enrolled (38%).

Financial Matters $14,195 tuition and fees (2002–03); $4800 room and board; 93% average percent of need met; $15,490 average financial aid amount received per undergraduate.

Academics Marian College awards bachelor's and master's degrees. Challenging opportunities include advanced placement credit, accelerated degree programs, student-designed majors, an honors program, double majors, independent study, and a senior project. Special programs include cooperative education, internships, summer session for credit, study-abroad, and Army ROTC. The most frequently chosen baccalaureate fields are business/marketing, health professions and related sciences, and education. The faculty at Marian College has 73 full-time members, 64% with terminal degrees. The student-faculty ratio is 14:1.

Students of Marian College The student body totals 2,672, of whom 1,745 are undergraduates. 70.6% are women and 29.4% are men. Students come from 25 states and territories and 11 other countries. 94% are from Wisconsin. 1.7% are international students.

Applying Marian College requires SAT I or ACT and a high school transcript, and in some cases an interview. The school recommends recommendations and a minimum high school GPA of 2.0. Application deadline: rolling admissions; 3/1 priority date for financial aid. Deferred admission is possible.

MARIETTA COLLEGE

Marietta, OH

Small-town setting ■ Private ■ Independent ■ Coed

Web site: www.marietta.edu

Contact: Ms. Marke Vickers, Director of Admission, 215 Fifth Street, Marietta, OH 45750-4000

Telephone: 740-376-4600 or toll-free 800-331-7896 **Fax:** 740-376-8888

E-mail: admit@marietta.edu

Getting in Last Year 1,056 applied; 94% were accepted; 268 enrolled (27%).

Financial Matters $20,112 tuition and fees (2002–03); $5774 room and board; 91% average percent of need met; $17,455 average financial aid amount received per undergraduate (2001–02).

Academics Marietta awards associate, bachelor's, and master's degrees. Challenging opportunities include advanced placement credit, accelerated degree programs, student-designed majors, an honors program, double majors, independent study, and a senior project. Special programs include internships, summer session for credit, off-campus study, and study-abroad. The most frequently chosen baccalaureate fields are business/marketing, education, and parks and recreation. The faculty at Marietta has 78 full-time members, 86% with terminal degrees. The student-faculty ratio is 12:1.

Students of Marietta The student body totals 1,208, of whom 1,112 are undergraduates. 49.7% are women and 50.3% are men. Students come from 37 states and territories and 11 other countries. 64% are from Ohio. 5.2% are international students. 76% returned for their sophomore year.

Applying Marietta requires an essay, SAT I or ACT, a high school transcript, 2 recommendations, and a minimum high school GPA of 2.0. The school recommends SAT II Subject Tests, an interview, and a minimum high school GPA of 3.0. Application deadline: 4/15; 3/1 priority date for financial aid. Early and deferred admission are possible.

MARIST COLLEGE

Poughkeepsie, NY

Small-town setting ■ Private ■ Independent ■ Coed

Web site: www.marist.edu

Contact: Mr. Jay Murray, Director of Admissions, 3399 North Road, Poughkeepsie, NY 12601-1387

Telephone: 845-575-3226 ext. 2190 or toll-free 800-436-5483

E-mail: admissions@marist.edu

Getting in Last Year 6,204 applied; 54% were accepted; 1,048 enrolled (31%).

Financial Matters $17,882 tuition and fees (2002–03); $8332 room and board; 77% average percent of need met; $10,569 average financial aid amount received per undergraduate.

Academics Marist awards bachelor's and master's degrees. Challenging opportunities include advanced placement credit, accelerated degree programs, an honors program, double majors, independent study, and a senior project. Special programs include cooperative education, internships, summer session for credit, off-campus study, and study-abroad. The most frequently chosen baccalaureate fields are communications/communication technologies, business/marketing, and protective services/public administration. The faculty at Marist has 182 full-time members, 80% with terminal degrees. The student-faculty ratio is 16:1.

Students of Marist The student body totals 5,866, of whom 4,866 are undergraduates. 58.3% are women and 41.7% are men. Students come from 37 states and territories and 19 other countries. 65% are from New York. 0.3% are international students. 88% returned for their sophomore year.

Applying Marist requires an essay, SAT I or ACT, a high school transcript, and 2 recommendations. Application deadline: 2/15; 2/15 priority date for financial aid. Early and deferred admission are possible.

MARLBORO COLLEGE

Marlboro, VT

Rural setting ■ *Private* ■ *Independent* ■ *Coed*

Web site: www.marlboro.edu

Contact: Ms. Julie E. Richardson, Vice President, Enrollment and Financial Aid, PO Box A, South Road, Marlboro, VT 05344-0300

Telephone: 802-258-9261 or toll-free 800-343-0049 **Fax:** 802-451-7555

E-mail: admissions@marlboro.edu

Getting in Last Year 229 applied; 85% were accepted; 78 enrolled (40%).

Financial Matters $19,660 tuition and fees (2002–03); $6750 room and board; 94% average percent of need met; $15,091 average financial aid amount received per undergraduate (2000–01).

Academics Marlboro awards bachelor's and master's degrees. Challenging opportunities include advanced placement credit, accelerated degree programs, student-designed majors, double majors, independent study, and a senior project. Special programs include internships, off-campus study, and study-abroad. The most frequently chosen baccalaureate fields are social sciences and history, visual/performing arts, and English. The faculty at Marlboro has 35 full-time members, 83% with terminal degrees. The student-faculty ratio is 8:1.

Students of Marlboro The student body is made up of 324 undergraduates. 59.6% are women and 40.4% are men. Students come from 36 states and territories. 11% are from Vermont. 0.6% are international students. 68% returned for their sophomore year.

Applying Marlboro requires an essay, SAT I or ACT, a high school transcript, an interview, 2 recommendations, and graded expository essay. The school recommends SAT II Subject Tests and a minimum high school GPA of 3.0. Application deadline: 3/1; 3/1 priority date for financial aid. Early and deferred admission are possible.

MARQUETTE UNIVERSITY

Milwaukee, WI

Urban setting ■ *Private* ■ *Independent Religious* ■ *Coed*

Web site: www.marquette.edu

Contact: Mr. Robert Blust, Dean of Undergraduate Admissions, PO Box 1881, Milwaukee, WI 53201-1881

Telephone: 414-288-7004 or toll-free 800-222-6544 **Fax:** 414-288-3764

E-mail: admissions@marquette.edu

Getting in Last Year 7,593 applied; 82% were accepted; 1,856 enrolled (30%).

Financial Matters $19,706 tuition and fees (2002–03); $6350 room and board; 89% average percent of need met; $16,400 average financial aid amount received per undergraduate.

Academics Marquette awards associate, bachelor's, master's, doctoral, and first-professional degrees and post-bachelor's and post-master's certificates. Challenging opportunities include advanced placement credit, an honors program, double majors, and a senior project. Special programs include cooperative education, internships, summer session for credit, off-campus study, study-abroad, and Army, Navy and Air Force ROTC. The most frequently chosen baccalaureate fields are business/marketing, communications/communication technologies, and engineering/engineering technologies. The faculty at Marquette has 617 full-time members, 81% with terminal degrees. The student-faculty ratio is 15:1.

Students of Marquette The student body totals 11,042, of whom 7,644 are undergraduates. 55.8% are women and 44.2% are men. Students come from 54 states and territories and 80 other countries. 47% are from Wisconsin. 2% are international students. 89% returned for their sophomore year.

Applying Marquette requires an essay, SAT I or ACT, a high school transcript, and a minimum high school GPA of 2.5, and in some cases SAT II Subject Tests, SAT II: Writing Test, and SAT I and SAT II or ACT. The school recommends SAT I, an interview, 1 recommendation, and a minimum high school GPA of 3.4. Application deadline: rolling admissions. Early and deferred admission are possible.

MARSHALL UNIVERSITY

Huntington, WV

Urban setting ■ *Public* ■ *State-supported* ■ *Coed*

Web site: www.marshall.edu

Contact: Mr. Craig S. Grooms, Admissions Director, 1 John Marshall Drive, Huntington, WV 25755

Telephone: 304-696-3160 or toll-free 800-642-3499 (in-state) **Fax:** 304-696-3135

E-mail: admissions@marshall.edu

Getting in Last Year 2,339 applied; 94% were accepted; 1,889 enrolled (86%).

Financial Matters $2984 resident tuition and fees (2002–03); $7986 nonresident tuition and fees (2002–03); $5298 room and board; 67% average percent of need met; $6304 average financial aid amount received per undergraduate.

Academics Marshall awards associate, bachelor's, master's, doctoral, and first-professional degrees and post-master's certificates. Challenging opportunities include advanced placement credit, accelerated degree programs, an honors program, double majors, independent study, and a senior project. Special programs include cooperative education, internships, summer session for credit, off-campus study, study-abroad, and Army ROTC. The most frequently chosen baccalaureate fields are business/marketing, education, and liberal arts/general studies. The faculty at Marshall has 457 full-time members, 77% with terminal degrees. The student-faculty ratio is 17:1.

Students of Marshall The student body totals 13,788, of whom 9,823 are undergraduates. 55.4% are women and 44.6% are men. Students come from 45 states and territories and 35 other countries. 83% are from West Virginia. 0.9% are international students. 75% returned for their sophomore year.

Applying Marshall requires SAT I or ACT, a high school transcript, and a minimum high school GPA of 2.0. Application deadline: rolling admissions; 3/1 priority date for financial aid. Early and deferred admission are possible.

MARS HILL COLLEGE

Mars Hill, NC

Small-town setting ■ *Private* ■ *Independent Religious* ■ *Coed*

Web site: www.mhc.edu

Contact: Mr. Ryan C. Holt, Dean of Enrollment Services, PO Box 370, Mars Hill, NC 28754

Telephone: 828-689-1201 or toll-free 866-MHC-4-YOU **Fax:** 828-689-1473

E-mail: admissions@mhc.edu

Getting in Last Year 1,006 applied; 85% were accepted.

Financial Matters $14,500 tuition and fees (2002–03); $5200 room and board; 79% average percent of need met; $12,736 average financial aid amount received per undergraduate.

Academics Mars Hill awards bachelor's degrees. Challenging opportunities include advanced placement credit, accelerated degree programs, student-designed majors, an honors program, double majors, independent study, and a senior project. Special programs include cooperative education, internships, summer session for credit, and study-abroad. The most frequently chosen baccalaureate fields are education, business/marketing, and social sciences and history. The faculty at Mars Hill has 81 full-time members. The student-faculty ratio is 14:1.

Students of Mars Hill The student body is made up of 1,275 undergraduates. Students come from 29 states and territories and 16 other countries. 67% are from North Carolina. 1.9% are international students. 73% returned for their sophomore year.

Applying Mars Hill requires SAT I or ACT, a high school transcript, and a minimum high school GPA of 2.0, and in some cases an interview. The school recommends a minimum high school GPA of 3.0. Application deadline: rolling admissions; 4/15 priority date for financial aid. Early and deferred admission are possible.

MARTIN LUTHER COLLEGE

New Ulm, MN

Small-town setting ■ *Private* ■ *Independent Religious* ■ *Coed*

Web site: www.mlc-wels.edu

Contact: Prof. Ronald B. Brutlag, Associate Director of Admissions, 1995 Luther Court, New Ulm, MN 56073

Telephone: 507-354-8221 ext. 280 **Fax:** 507-354-8225

E-mail: mlcadmit@mlc-wels.edu

Getting in Last Year 320 applied; 93% were accepted; 242 enrolled (81%).

Financial Matters $11,710 tuition and fees (2002–03); $1850 room and board; 70% average percent of need met; $6131 average financial aid amount received per undergraduate (2001–02).

Academics MLC awards bachelor's degrees. Challenging opportunities include advanced placement credit, double majors, and independent study. Special programs include internships and summer session for credit. The most frequently chosen baccalaureate field is education. The faculty at MLC has 85 full-time members, 42% with terminal degrees. The student-faculty ratio is 13:1.

Students of MLC The student body is made up of 1,063 undergraduates. 50% are women and 50% are men. Students come from 35 states and territories and 9 other countries. 27% are from Minnesota. 1.3% are international students. 83% returned for their sophomore year.

Applying MLC requires ACT, a high school transcript, recommendations, and a minimum high school GPA of 2.0. Application deadline: 4/15; 4/15 for financial aid. Deferred admission is possible.

MARTIN METHODIST COLLEGE

Pulaski, TN

Small-town setting ■ *Private* ■ *Independent Religious* ■ *Coed*

Web site: www.martinmethodist.edu

Contact: Tony Booker, Director of Admissions, 433 West Madison Street, Pulaski, TN 38478-2716

Telephone: 931-363-9804 or toll-free 800-467-1273 **Fax:** 931-363-9818

E-mail: admissions@martinmethodist.edu

Getting in Last Year 377 applied; 97% were accepted; 157 enrolled (43%).

Financial Matters $12,100 tuition and fees (2002–03); $3900 room and board; 82% average percent of need met; $5625 average financial aid amount received per undergraduate (2001–02).

Academics Martin awards bachelor's degrees. Challenging opportunities include advanced placement credit, student-designed majors, and a senior project. Summer session for credit is a special program. The most frequently chosen baccalaureate fields are business/marketing, psychology, and education. The faculty at Martin has 33 full-time members, 61% with terminal degrees. The student-faculty ratio is 17:1.

Students of Martin The student body is made up of 631 undergraduates. 61.3% are women and 38.7% are men. Students come from 25 states and territories and 13 other countries. 76% are from Tennessee. 16.3% are international students. 29% returned for their sophomore year.

Applying Martin requires SAT I or ACT, a high school transcript, and a minimum high school GPA of 2.0. The school recommends an essay and an interview. Application deadline: 8/30; 2/1 priority date for financial aid. Early and deferred admission are possible.

MARTIN UNIVERSITY

Indianapolis, IN

Urban setting ■ Private ■ Independent ■ Coed

Web site: www.martin.edu
Contact: Ms. Brenda Shaheed, Director of Enrollment Management, P.O.Box 18567, 2171 Avondale Place, Indianapolis, IN 46218-3867
Telephone: 317-543-3237 **Fax:** 317-543-4790

Getting in Last Year 146 applied; 55% were accepted.

Financial Matters $9750 tuition and fees (2002–03); 80% average percent of need met; $12,924 average financial aid amount received per undergraduate (2001–02).

Academics Martin University awards bachelor's and master's degrees. Challenging opportunities include advanced placement credit, accelerated degree programs, student-designed majors, an honors program, double majors, independent study, and a senior project. Special programs include internships, summer session for credit, and off-campus study. The faculty at Martin University has 32 full-time members. The student-faculty ratio is 20:1.

Students of Martin University The student body totals 615, of whom 543 are undergraduates. Students come from 1 state or territory and 6 other countries. 95% returned for their sophomore year.

Applying Martin University requires an essay, a high school transcript, an interview, and writing sample, and in some cases Wonderlic aptitude test, Wide Range Achievement Test. Application deadline: rolling admissions; 3/1 priority date for financial aid. Early and deferred admission are possible.

MARY BALDWIN COLLEGE

Staunton, VA

Small-town setting ■ Private ■ Independent Religious ■ Coed, Primarily Women

Web site: www.mbc.edu
Contact: Ms. Lisa Branson, Assistant Dean of Admissions and Financial Aid, Frederick and New Streets, Staunton, VA 24401
Telephone: 540-887-7019 ext. 7260 or toll-free 800-468-2262 **Fax:** 540-887-7279
E-mail: admit@mbc.edu

Getting in Last Year 1,292 applied; 78% were accepted; 226 enrolled (23%).

Financial Matters $17,690 tuition and fees (2002–03); $6450 room and board; 89% average percent of need met; $18,010 average financial aid amount received per undergraduate (2001–02).

Academics MBC awards bachelor's and master's degrees. Challenging opportunities include advanced placement credit, accelerated degree programs, student-designed majors, freshman honors college, an honors program, double majors, independent study, and a senior project. Special programs include internships, off-campus study, study-abroad, and Army, Navy and Air Force ROTC. The most frequently chosen baccalaureate fields are social sciences and history, business/marketing, and psychology. The faculty at MBC has 75 full-time members, 87% with terminal degrees. The student-faculty ratio is 11:1.

Students of MBC The student body totals 1,625, of whom 1,514 are undergraduates. 94.8% are women and 5.2% are men. Students come from 38 states and territories and 9 other countries. 75% are from Virginia. 1.7% are international students. 74% returned for their sophomore year.

Applying MBC requires SAT I or ACT, a high school transcript, 1 recommendation, and a minimum high school GPA of 2.0. The school recommends an interview. Application deadline: rolling admissions; 5/15 for financial aid. Early and deferred admission are possible.

MARYGROVE COLLEGE

Detroit, MI

Urban setting ■ Private ■ Independent Religious ■ Coed, Primarily Women

Web site: www.marygrove.edu
Contact: Mr. Fred A. Schebor, Dean of Admissions, Office of Admissions, Detroit, MI 48221-2599
Telephone: 313-927-1570 or toll-free 866-313-1297 **Fax:** 313-927-1345
E-mail: info@marygrove.edu

Getting in Last Year 256 applied; 25% were accepted; 40 enrolled (62%).

Financial Matters $11,250 tuition and fees (2002–03); $5600 room and board.

Academics Marygrove awards associate, bachelor's, and master's degrees and post-bachelor's certificates. Challenging opportunities include advanced placement credit, student-designed majors, double majors, and a senior project. Special programs include cooperative education, internships, summer session for credit, and off-campus study. The most frequently chosen baccalaureate fields are social sciences and history, business/marketing, and education. The faculty at Marygrove has 71 full-time members, 68% with terminal degrees. The student-faculty ratio is 15:1.

Students of Marygrove The student body totals 6,465, of whom 866 are undergraduates. 82.4% are women and 17.6% are men. Students come from 2 states and territories and 3 other countries. 99% are from Michigan. 0.9% are international students. 67% returned for their sophomore year.

Applying Marygrove requires ACT, a high school transcript, and a minimum high school GPA of 2.7, and in some cases an interview and recommendations. Application deadline: 8/15. Early and deferred admission are possible.

MARYLAND INSTITUTE COLLEGE OF ART

Baltimore, MD

Urban setting ■ Private ■ Independent ■ Coed

Web site: www.mica.edu
Contact: Mr. Hans Ever, Director of Undergraduate Admission, 1300 Mount Royal Avenue, Baltimore, MD 21217-4191
Telephone: 410-225-2222 **Fax:** 410-225-2337
E-mail: admissions@mica.edu

Getting in Last Year 1,917 applied; 43% were accepted; 279 enrolled (34%).

Financial Matters $22,080 tuition and fees (2002–03); $6880 room and board.

Academics MICA awards bachelor's and master's degrees and post-bachelor's certificates. Challenging opportunities include advanced placement credit, accelerated degree programs, student-designed majors, double majors, independent study, and a senior project. Special programs include internships, summer session for credit, off-campus study, study-abroad, and Army ROTC. The most frequently chosen baccalaureate fields are visual/performing arts and education. The faculty at MICA has 101 full-time members, 72% with terminal degrees. The student-faculty ratio is 10:1.

Students of MICA The student body totals 1,363, of whom 1,201 are undergraduates. 62.2% are women and 37.8% are men. Students come from 43 states and territories and 50 other countries. 24% are from Maryland. 4.8% are international students. 82% returned for their sophomore year.

Applying MICA requires an essay, a high school transcript, and art portfolio, and in some cases SAT I or ACT. The school recommends an interview and 3 recommendations. Application deadline: 1/15; 3/1 priority date for financial aid. Early and deferred admission are possible.

MARYMOUNT COLLEGE OF FORDHAM UNIVERSITY

Tarrytown, NY

Suburban setting ■ Private ■ Independent ■ Women Only

Web site: www.marymt.edu
Contact: Ms. Barbara Seyter, Director of Admissions, 100 Marymount Avenue, Tarrytown, NY 10591-3796
Telephone: 914-332-8295 or toll-free 800-724-4312 **Fax:** 914-332-7442
E-mail: admiss@mmc.marymt.edu

Getting in Last Year 1,445 applied; 82% were accepted; 260 enrolled (22%).

Financial Matters $17,210 tuition and fees (2002–03); $8695 room and board; 67% average percent of need met; $14,441 average financial aid amount received per undergraduate (2001–02).

Academics Marymount awards associate and bachelor's degrees. Challenging opportunities include advanced placement credit, student-designed majors, an honors program, double majors, independent study, and a senior project. Special programs include internships, summer session for credit, off-campus study, and study-abroad. The most frequently chosen baccalaureate fields are education, visual/performing arts, and business/marketing. The faculty at Marymount has 58 full-time members, 86% with terminal degrees. The student-faculty ratio is 12:1.

Students of Marymount The student body is made up of 1,061 undergraduates. Students come from 32 states and territories and 20 other countries. 79% are from New York. 3.9% are international students. 69% returned for their sophomore year.

Marymount College of Fordham University (continued)

Applying Marymount requires an essay, SAT I or ACT, a high school transcript, and a minimum high school GPA of 2.0. The school recommends an interview, 1 recommendation, and a minimum high school GPA of 3.0. Deferred admission is possible.

MARYMOUNT MANHATTAN COLLEGE

New York, NY

Urban setting ■ Private ■ Independent ■ Coed

Web site: marymount.mmm.edu
Contact: Mr. Thomas Friebel, Associate Vice President for Enrollment Services, 221 East 71st Street, New York, NY 10021
Telephone: 212-517-0430 or toll-free 800-MARYMOUNT (out-of-state)
Fax: 212-517-0448
E-mail: admissions@mmm.edu

Getting in Last Year 1,422 applied; 78% were accepted; 385 enrolled (35%).

Financial Matters $15,535 tuition and fees (2002–03); $8800 room only; 46% average percent of need met; $10,050 average financial aid amount received per undergraduate.

Academics Marymount Manhattan awards bachelor's degrees. Challenging opportunities include advanced placement credit, accelerated degree programs, an honors program, double majors, and independent study. Special programs include internships, summer session for credit, off-campus study, and study-abroad. The faculty at Marymount Manhattan has 87 full-time members, 85% with terminal degrees. The student-faculty ratio is 11:1.

Students of Marymount Manhattan The student body is made up of 2,323 undergraduates. 78.8% are women and 21.2% are men. Students come from 48 states and territories and 62 other countries. 65% are from New York. 5.1% are international students. 65% returned for their sophomore year.

Applying Marymount Manhattan requires SAT I or ACT, a high school transcript, 2 recommendations, and audition for dance and theater programs, and in some cases an interview. The school recommends an essay. Application deadline: rolling admissions; 3/15 priority date for financial aid. Deferred admission is possible.

MARYMOUNT UNIVERSITY

Arlington, VA

Suburban setting ■ Private ■ Independent Religious ■ Coed

Web site: www.marymount.edu
Contact: Mr. Mike Canfield, Associate Director of Undergraduate Admissions, 2807 North Glebe Road, Arlington, VA 22207-4299
Telephone: 703-284-1500 or toll-free 800-548-7638 **Fax:** 703-522-0349
E-mail: admissions@marymount.edu

Getting in Last Year 1,461 applied; 87% were accepted; 367 enrolled (29%).

Financial Matters $15,732 tuition and fees (2002–03); $6920 room and board; 75% average percent of need met; $12,623 average financial aid amount received per undergraduate.

Academics Marymount awards associate, bachelor's, and master's degrees and post-bachelor's and post-master's certificates. Challenging opportunities include advanced placement credit, student-designed majors, double majors, independent study, and a senior project. Special programs include internships, summer session for credit, off-campus study, study-abroad, and Army ROTC. The most frequently chosen baccalaureate fields are business/marketing, visual/performing arts, and social sciences and history. The faculty at Marymount has 128 full-time members, 84% with terminal degrees. The student-faculty ratio is 13:1.

Students of Marymount The student body totals 3,638, of whom 2,145 are undergraduates. 72.5% are women and 27.5% are men. Students come from 39 states and territories and 71 other countries. 56% are from Virginia. 11% are international students. 73% returned for their sophomore year.

Applying Marymount requires SAT I or ACT, a high school transcript, 1 recommendation, and a minimum high school GPA of 2.0. The school recommends an essay and an interview. Application deadline: rolling admissions. Early and deferred admission are possible.

MARYVILLE COLLEGE

Maryville, TN

Suburban setting ■ Private ■ Independent Religious ■ Coed

Web site: www.maryvillecollege.edu
Contact: Ms. Linda L. Moore, Administrative Assistant of Admissions, 502 East Lamar Alexander Parkway, Maryville, TN 37804-5907
Telephone: 865-981-8092 or toll-free 800-597-2687 **Fax:** 865-981-8005
E-mail: admissions@maryvillecollege.edu

Getting in Last Year 1,456 applied; 80% were accepted; 248 enrolled (21%).

Financial Matters $18,835 tuition and fees (2002–03); $5900 room and board; 88% average percent of need met; $17,427 average financial aid amount received per undergraduate.

Academics MC awards bachelor's degrees. Challenging opportunities include advanced placement credit, student-designed majors, an honors program, double majors, independent study, and a senior project. Special programs include internships, summer session for credit, off-campus study, and study-abroad. The most frequently chosen baccalaureate fields are business/marketing, education, and biological/life sciences. The faculty at MC has 68 full-time members, 93% with terminal degrees. The student-faculty ratio is 12:1.

Students of MC The student body is made up of 1,020 undergraduates. 58.9% are women and 41.1% are men. Students come from 22 states and territories and 22 other countries. 77% are from Tennessee. 2.7% are international students. 70% returned for their sophomore year.

Applying MC requires SAT I or ACT, a high school transcript, and a minimum high school GPA of 2.5, and in some cases an essay, an interview, and recommendations. The school recommends a minimum high school GPA of 3.0. Application deadline: 3/1; 3/1 priority date for financial aid. Early and deferred admission are possible.

MARYVILLE UNIVERSITY OF SAINT LOUIS

St. Louis, MO

Suburban setting ■ Private ■ Independent ■ Coed

Web site: www.maryville.edu
Contact: Ms. Lynn Jackson, Admissions Director, 13550 Conway Road, St. Louis, MO 63141-7299
Telephone: 314-529-9350 or toll-free 800-627-9855 **Fax:** 314-529-9927
E-mail: admissions@maryville.edu

Getting in Last Year 1,007 applied; 76% were accepted; 303 enrolled (40%).

Financial Matters $14,560 tuition and fees (2002–03); $6300 room and board; 59% average percent of need met; $8110 average financial aid amount received per undergraduate.

Academics Maryville awards bachelor's and master's degrees. Challenging opportunities include advanced placement credit, accelerated degree programs, student-designed majors, freshman honors college, an honors program, double majors, independent study, and a senior project. Special programs include cooperative education, internships, summer session for credit, off-campus study, study-abroad, and Army ROTC. The most frequently chosen baccalaureate field is law/legal studies. The faculty at Maryville has 87 full-time members, 89% with terminal degrees. The student-faculty ratio is 13:1.

Students of Maryville The student body totals 3,265, of whom 2,710 are undergraduates. 74.4% are women and 25.6% are men. Students come from 15 states and territories and 34 other countries. 92% are from Missouri. 3.4% are international students. 80% returned for their sophomore year.

Applying Maryville requires SAT I or ACT, a high school transcript, and a minimum high school GPA of 2.5, and in some cases an essay, an interview, recommendations, and audition, portfolio. Application deadline: 8/15; 4/1 priority date for financial aid. Early and deferred admission are possible.

MARY WASHINGTON COLLEGE

Fredericksburg, VA

Small-town setting ■ Public ■ State-supported ■ Coed

Web site: www.mwc.edu
Contact: Dr. Jenifer Blair, Dean of Undergraduate Admissions, 1301 College Avenue, Fredericksburg, VA 22401-5358
Telephone: 540-654-2000 or toll-free 800-468-5614
E-mail: admit@mwc.edu

Getting in Last Year 4,303 applied; 60% were accepted; 885 enrolled (35%).

Financial Matters $3670 resident tuition and fees (2002–03); $10,858 nonresident tuition and fees (2002–03); $5318 room and board; 56% average percent of need met; $5326 average financial aid amount received per undergraduate.

Academics Mary Washington awards bachelor's and master's degrees. Challenging opportunities include advanced placement credit, accelerated degree programs, student-designed majors, double majors, independent study, and a senior project. Special programs include cooperative education, internships, summer session for credit, and study-abroad. The most frequently chosen baccalaureate fields are social sciences and history, business/marketing, and liberal arts/general studies. The faculty at Mary Washington has 205 full-time members, 86% with terminal degrees. The student-faculty ratio is 17:1.

Students of Mary Washington The student body totals 4,835, of whom 4,275 are undergraduates. 67.8% are women and 32.2% are men. Students come from 46 states and territories and 14 other countries. 65% are from Virginia. 0.4% are international students. 87% returned for their sophomore year.

Applying Mary Washington requires an essay, SAT I or ACT, and a high school transcript. The school recommends SAT II Subject Tests. Application deadline: 2/1; 3/1 priority date for financial aid. Deferred admission is possible.

MARYWOOD UNIVERSITY

Scranton, PA

Suburban setting ■ Private ■ Independent Religious ■ Coed

Web site: www.marywood.edu

Contact: Mr. Robert W. Reese, Director of Admissions, 2300 Adams Avenue, Scranton, PA 18509-1598

Telephone: 570-348-6234 or toll-free 800-346-5014 **Fax:** 570-961-4763

E-mail: ugadm@ac.marywood.edu

Getting in Last Year 1,307 applied; 77% were accepted; 315 enrolled (31%).

Financial Matters $18,450 tuition and fees (2002–03); $7710 room and board; 82% average percent of need met; $17,000 average financial aid amount received per undergraduate.

Academics Marywood University awards associate, bachelor's, master's, and doctoral degrees and post-bachelor's and post-master's certificates. Challenging opportunities include advanced placement credit, accelerated degree programs, student-designed majors, an honors program, double majors, independent study, and a senior project. Special programs include internships, summer session for credit, off-campus study, study-abroad, and Army and Air Force ROTC. The most frequently chosen baccalaureate fields are education, business/marketing, and visual/performing arts. The faculty at Marywood University has 135 full-time members, 83% with terminal degrees. The student-faculty ratio is 12:1.

Students of Marywood University The student body totals 3,133, of whom 1,750 are undergraduates. 72.8% are women and 27.2% are men. Students come from 19 states and territories and 18 other countries. 79% are from Pennsylvania. 1.5% are international students. 81% returned for their sophomore year.

Applying Marywood University requires SAT I or ACT, a high school transcript, and 1 recommendation, and in some cases an essay and an interview. The school recommends an essay and an interview. Application deadline: rolling admissions. Early and deferred admission are possible.

MASSACHUSETTS COLLEGE OF ART

Boston, MA

Urban setting ■ Public ■ State-supported ■ Coed

Web site: www.massart.edu

Contact: Ms. Kay Ransdell, Dean of Admissions, 621 Huntington Avenue, Boston, MA 02115-5882

Telephone: 617-232-1555 ext. 235 **Fax:** 617-879-7250

E-mail: admissions@massart.edu

Getting in Last Year 1,114 applied; 44% were accepted; 218 enrolled (44%).

Financial Matters $4968 resident tuition and fees (2002–03); $14,178 nonresident tuition and fees (2002–03); $9800 room and board; 83% average percent of need met; $8440 average financial aid amount received per undergraduate (2001–02).

Academics MassArt awards bachelor's and master's degrees and post-bachelor's certificates. Challenging opportunities include student-designed majors, double majors, independent study, and a senior project. Special programs include internships, summer session for credit, off-campus study, and study-abroad. The most frequently chosen baccalaureate fields are visual/performing arts and education. The faculty at MassArt has 74 full-time members, 74% with terminal degrees. The student-faculty ratio is 13:1.

Students of MassArt The student body totals 2,120, of whom 1,984 are undergraduates. 66% are women and 34% are men. Students come from 51 states and territories and 58 other countries. 77% are from Massachusetts. 5.4% are international students. 86% returned for their sophomore year.

Applying MassArt requires an essay, SAT I or ACT, a high school transcript, portfolio, and a minimum high school GPA of 2.9. The school recommends recommendations. Application deadline: 2/15; 3/15 priority date for financial aid. Early and deferred admission are possible.

MASSACHUSETTS COLLEGE OF LIBERAL ARTS

North Adams, MA

Small-town setting ■ Public ■ State-supported ■ Coed

Web site: www.mcla.edu

Contact: Ms. Denise Richardello, Dean of Enrollment Management, 375 Church Street, North Adams, MA 01247-4100

Telephone: 413-662-5410 ext. 5416 or toll-free 800-292-6632 (in-state) **Fax:** 413-662-5179

E-mail: admissions@mcla.mass.edu

Getting in Last Year 284 applied; 100% were accepted; 277 enrolled (98%).

Financial Matters $4197 resident tuition and fees (2002–03); $13,142 nonresident tuition and fees (2002–03); $5462 room and board; 69% average percent of need met; $6322 average financial aid amount received per undergraduate.

Academics MCLA awards bachelor's and master's degrees and post-bachelor's certificates. Challenging opportunities include advanced placement credit, student-designed majors, an honors program, double majors, independent study, and a senior project. Special programs include internships, summer session for credit, off-campus study, and study-abroad. The most frequently chosen baccalaureate fields are social sciences and history, business/marketing, and English. The faculty at MCLA has 82 full-time members, 78% with terminal degrees. The student-faculty ratio is 13:1.

Students of MCLA The student body totals 1,613, of whom 1,401 are undergraduates. 58.7% are women and 41.3% are men. 83% are from Massachusetts. 0.7% are international students. 71% returned for their sophomore year.

Applying MCLA requires an essay, SAT I, a high school transcript, and a minimum high school GPA of 3.0, and in some cases an interview. The school recommends an interview and recommendations. Application deadline: rolling admissions; 4/1 priority date for financial aid. Deferred admission is possible.

MASSACHUSETTS COLLEGE OF PHARMACY AND HEALTH SCIENCES

Boston, MA

Urban setting ■ Private ■ Independent ■ Coed

Web site: www.mcp.edu

Contact: Mr. Jim Zarakas, Admissions Assistant, 179 Longwood Avenue, Boston, MA 02115

Telephone: 617-732-2846 or toll-free 617-732-2850 (in-state), 800-225-5506 (out-of-state) **Fax:** 617-732-2801

E-mail: admissions@mcp.edu

Getting in Last Year 548 applied; 76% were accepted; 244 enrolled (58%).

Financial Matters $18,550 tuition and fees (2002–03); $9580 room and board; 45% average percent of need met; $11,631 average financial aid amount received per undergraduate (2001–02).

Academics MCPHS awards associate, bachelor's, master's, doctoral, and first-professional degrees and first-professional certificates. Challenging opportunities include advanced placement credit, double majors, and independent study. Special programs include internships, summer session for credit, off-campus study, and Army and Air Force ROTC. The most frequently chosen baccalaureate fields are health professions and related sciences and physical sciences. The faculty at MCPHS has 124 full-time members, 99% with terminal degrees. The student-faculty ratio is 14:1.

Students of MCPHS The student body totals 2,130, of whom 1,114 are undergraduates. 71.1% are women and 28.9% are men. Students come from 32 states and territories. 69% are from Massachusetts. 0.9% are international students. 86% returned for their sophomore year.

Applying MCPHS requires an essay, SAT I or ACT, a high school transcript, and 2 recommendations, and in some cases an interview and 3 recommendations. The school recommends an interview. Application deadline: 2/1; 3/1 priority date for financial aid. Early and deferred admission are possible.

MASSACHUSETTS INSTITUTE OF TECHNOLOGY

Cambridge, MA

Urban setting ■ Private ■ Independent ■ Coed

Web site: web.mit.edu

Contact: Ms. Marilee Jones, Dean of Admissions, Room 3-108, 77 Massachusetts Avenue, Cambridge, MA 02139-4307

Telephone: 617-253-4791 **Fax:** 617-258-8304

Getting in Last Year 10,664 applied; 16% were accepted; 978 enrolled (57%).

Financial Matters $28,230 tuition and fees (2002–03); $7830 room and board; 100% average percent of need met; $22,983 average financial aid amount received per undergraduate (2001–02).

Academics MIT awards bachelor's, master's, and doctoral degrees. Challenging opportunities include advanced placement credit, accelerated degree programs, student-designed majors, and a senior project. Special programs include cooperative education, internships, summer session for credit, off-campus study, and Army, Navy and Air Force ROTC. The most frequently chosen baccalaureate fields are engineering/engineering technologies, computer/information sciences, and biological/life sciences. The faculty at MIT has 1,344 full-time members, 95% with terminal degrees. The student-faculty ratio is 6:1.

Students of MIT The student body totals 10,317, of whom 4,178 are undergraduates. 41.3% are women and 58.7% are men. Students come from 55 states and territories and 86 other countries. 9% are from Massachusetts. 8.2% are international students. 97% returned for their sophomore year.

Applying MIT requires an essay, SAT II Subject Tests, SAT I or ACT, a high school transcript, an interview, and 2 recommendations. The school recommends an interview. Application deadline: 1/1; 2/1 for financial aid. Deferred admission is possible.

MASSACHUSETTS MARITIME ACADEMY

Buzzards Bay, MA

Small-town setting ■ Public ■ State-supported ■ Coed, Primarily Men

Web site: www.maritime.edu

Massachusetts Maritime Academy (continued)

Contact: Roy Fulgueras, Director of Admissions, 101 Academy Drive, Buzzards Bay, MA 02532-1803
Telephone: 508-830-5031 or toll-free 800-544-3411 **Fax:** 508-830-5077
E-mail: admissions@mma.mass.edu

Getting in Last Year 808 applied; 60% were accepted; 224 enrolled (46%).

Financial Matters $3663 resident tuition and fees (2002–03); $14,143 nonresident tuition and fees (2002–03); $5500 room and board; 27% average percent of need met; $7007 average financial aid amount received per undergraduate.

Academics Mass Maritime awards bachelor's degrees and first-professional certificates. Challenging opportunities include advanced placement credit and double majors. Special programs include cooperative education, internships, summer session for credit, and Army and Navy ROTC. The faculty at Mass Maritime has 59 full-time members, 69% with terminal degrees. The student-faculty ratio is 12:1.

Students of Mass Maritime The student body is made up of 904 undergraduates. 13.4% are women and 86.6% are men. Students come from 24 states and territories and 4 other countries. 89% are from Massachusetts. 79% returned for their sophomore year.

Applying Mass Maritime requires an essay, SAT I or ACT, a high school transcript, an interview, 2 recommendations, and physical examination. The school recommends SAT I. Application deadline: rolling admissions; 4/30 priority date for financial aid. Deferred admission is possible.

THE MASTER'S COLLEGE AND SEMINARY

Santa Clarita, CA

Suburban setting ■ *Private* ■ *Independent Religious* ■ *Coed*

Web site: www.masters.edu
Contact: Mr. Yaphet Peterson, Director of Enrollment, 21726 Placerita Canyon Road, Santa Clarita, CA 91321-1200
Telephone: 661-259-3540 ext. 3365 or toll-free 800-568-6248
Fax: 661-288-1037
E-mail: enrollment@masters.edu

Getting in Last Year 429 applied; 84% were accepted; 204 enrolled (57%).

Financial Matters $16,620 tuition and fees (2002–03); $5780 room and board; 76% average percent of need met; $13,872 average financial aid amount received per undergraduate.

Academics Master's awards bachelor's, master's, and first-professional degrees. Challenging opportunities include advanced placement credit, accelerated degree programs, double majors, independent study, and a senior project. Special programs include cooperative education, internships, summer session for credit, and study-abroad. The most frequently chosen baccalaureate fields are business/marketing, education, and social sciences and history. The faculty at Master's has 69 full-time members, 65% with terminal degrees. The student-faculty ratio is 14:1.

Students of Master's The student body totals 1,503, of whom 1,129 are undergraduates. 51.4% are women and 48.6% are men. Students come from 42 states and territories and 19 other countries. 72% are from California. 3.8% are international students. 81% returned for their sophomore year.

Applying Master's requires an essay, SAT I or ACT, a high school transcript, an interview, 2 recommendations, and a minimum high school GPA of 2.75. Application deadline: 3/2; 3/2 priority date for financial aid. Early and deferred admission are possible.

MASTER'S COLLEGE AND SEMINARY

Toronto, ON Canada

Small-town setting ■ *Private* ■ *Independent Religious* ■ *Coed*

Web site: www.mcs.edu
Contact: Rev. Merv Anthony, Registrar, 3080 Yonge Street, Suite 3040, Toronto, ON Canada
Telephone: 705-748-9111 ext. 139 or toll-free 800-295-6368
E-mail: manthony@mcs.edu

Getting in Last Year 82 applied; 89% were accepted.

Financial Matters $5440 tuition and fees (2002–03); $4340 room and board.

Academics Master's College and Seminary awards bachelor's degrees. Challenging opportunities include accelerated degree programs and independent study. Special programs include internships, summer session for credit, off-campus study, and study-abroad. The faculty at Master's College and Seminary has 8 full-time members, 25% with terminal degrees. The student-faculty ratio is 19:1.

Students of Master's College and Seminary The student body is made up of 464 undergraduates. Students come from 8 states and territories and 5 other countries. 66% returned for their sophomore year.

Applying Master's College and Seminary requires an essay, a high school transcript, 3 recommendations, and medical history, Christian commitment, and in some cases an interview. The school recommends a minimum high school GPA of 2.0. Application deadline: 8/31. Deferred admission is possible.

MAYO SCHOOL OF HEALTH SCIENCES

Rochester, MN

Urban setting ■ *Private* ■ *Independent* ■ *Coed*

Web site: www.mayo.edu/mshs
Contact: Ms. Kate Ray, Enrollment and Student Services, 200 First Street, SW, Siebens Building, Room 1138, Rochester, MN 55901
Telephone: 507-266-4077 or toll-free 800-626-9041 **Fax:** 507-284-0656
E-mail: kray@mayo.edu

Financial Matters 75% average percent of need met; $7868 average financial aid amount received per undergraduate.

Academics Mayo School of Health Sciences awards associate, bachelor's, and master's degrees and post-bachelor's certificates. Challenging opportunities include independent study and a senior project. Special programs include cooperative education, internships, and off-campus study.

Students of Mayo School of Health Sciences The student body totals 1,354, of whom 281 are undergraduates. 82.6% are women and 17.4% are men. 99% returned for their sophomore year.

Applying Mayo School of Health Sciences requires SAT I and SAT II or ACT. Deferred admission is possible.

MAYVILLE STATE UNIVERSITY

Mayville, ND

Rural setting ■ *Public* ■ *State-supported* ■ *Coed*

Web site: www.mayvillestate.edu
Contact: Mr. Brian Larson, Director of Enrollment Services, 330 3rd Street, NE, Mayville, ND 58257-1299
Telephone: 701-788-4768 ext. 34768 or toll-free 800-437-4104
Fax: 701-788-4748
E-mail: admit@mail.masu.nodak.edu

Getting in Last Year 197 applied; 99% were accepted; 175 enrolled (90%).

Financial Matters $3533 resident tuition and fees (2002–03); $7210 nonresident tuition and fees (2002–03); $3138 room and board; 90% average percent of need met; $6008 average financial aid amount received per undergraduate (2001–02).

Academics Mayville State University awards associate and bachelor's degrees. Challenging opportunities include advanced placement credit, accelerated degree programs, student-designed majors, and double majors. Special programs include cooperative education, internships, summer session for credit, and Air Force ROTC. The most frequently chosen baccalaureate fields are education, business/marketing, and computer/information sciences. The faculty at Mayville State University has 36 full-time members, 47% with terminal degrees. The student-faculty ratio is 14:1.

Students of Mayville State University The student body is made up of 746 undergraduates. 55.9% are women and 44.1% are men. Students come from 17 states and territories and 4 other countries. 77% are from North Dakota. 3.1% are international students. 60% returned for their sophomore year.

Applying Mayville State University requires SAT I or ACT and a high school transcript. The school recommends an interview. Application deadline: rolling admissions; 3/15 priority date for financial aid. Deferred admission is possible.

MCDANIEL COLLEGE

Westminster, MD

Small-town setting ■ *Private* ■ *Independent* ■ *Coed*

Web site: www.mcdaniel.edu
Contact: Ms. M. Martha O'Connell, Dean of Admissions, 2 College Hill, Westminster, MD 21157-4390
Telephone: 410-857-2230 or toll-free 800-638-5005 **Fax:** 410-857-2757
E-mail: admissio@mcdaniel.edu

Getting in Last Year 2,271 applied; 72% were accepted; 441 enrolled (27%).

Financial Matters $22,110 tuition and fees (2002–03); $5280 room and board; 96% average percent of need met; $17,589 average financial aid amount received per undergraduate.

Academics McDaniel College awards bachelor's and master's degrees. Challenging opportunities include advanced placement credit, student-designed majors, an honors program, double majors, independent study, and a senior project. Special programs include internships, summer session for credit, off-campus study, study-abroad, and Army ROTC. The most frequently chosen baccalaureate fields are social sciences and history, business/marketing, and communications/communication technologies. The faculty at McDaniel College has 93 full-time members, 96% with terminal degrees. The student-faculty ratio is 12:1.

Students of McDaniel College The student body totals 3,374, of whom 1,695 are undergraduates. 58.3% are women and 41.7% are men. Students come from 27 states and territories and 16 other countries. 72% are from Maryland. 3.2% are international students. 86% returned for their sophomore year.

Applying McDaniel College requires an essay, SAT I or ACT, a high school transcript, and a minimum high school GPA of 2.5, and in some cases an interview.

The school recommends SAT II Subject Tests, an interview, and recommendations. Application deadline: 2/1; 3/1 priority date for financial aid. Early and deferred admission are possible.

MCGILL UNIVERSITY

Montréal, QC Canada

Urban setting ■ Private ■ Independent ■ Coed

Web site: www.mcgill.ca
Contact: Ms. Kim Bartlett, Acting Director of Admissions, 845 Sherbrooke Street West, Montreal, QC H3A 2T5 Canada
Telephone: 514-398-4462 **Fax:** 514-398-8939
E-mail: admissions@mcgill.ca

Getting in Last Year 16,952 applied; 55% were accepted; 4,438 enrolled (47%).

Financial Matters $2868 resident tuition and fees (2002–03); $5212 nonresident tuition and fees (2002–03); $7500 room and board.

Academics McGill awards bachelor's, master's, doctoral, and first-professional degrees and post-bachelor's certificates. Challenging opportunities include advanced placement credit, student-designed majors, an honors program, and double majors. Special programs include internships, summer session for credit, off-campus study, and study-abroad. The most frequently chosen baccalaureate fields are social sciences and history, biological/life sciences, and business/marketing. The faculty at McGill has 1,534 full-time members, 95% with terminal degrees. The student-faculty ratio is 15:1.

Students of McGill The student body totals 30,580, of whom 21,745 are undergraduates. 60.5% are women and 39.5% are men. Students come from 12 states and territories and 133 other countries. 74% are from Quebec.

Applying McGill requires SAT I and SAT II or ACT, a high school transcript, and a minimum high school GPA of 3.3, and in some cases recommendations and audition for music program, portfolio for architecture program. Application deadline: 1/15. Deferred admission is possible.

MCKENDREE COLLEGE

Lebanon, IL

Small-town setting ■ Private ■ Independent Religious ■ Coed

Web site: www.mckendree.edu
Contact: Mr. Mark Campbell, Vice President for Admissions and Financial Aid, 701 College Road, Lebanon, IL 62254
Telephone: 618-537-4481 ext. 6835 or toll-free 800-232-7228 ext. 6835 **Fax:** 618-537-6496
E-mail: mecampbell@mckendree.edu

Getting in Last Year 1,156 applied; 68% were accepted; 283 enrolled (36%).

Financial Matters $14,200 tuition and fees (2002–03); $5400 room and board; 82% average percent of need met; $11,368 average financial aid amount received per undergraduate.

Academics McKendree awards bachelor's degrees. Challenging opportunities include advanced placement credit, accelerated degree programs, student-designed majors, an honors program, double majors, independent study, and a senior project. Special programs include internships, summer session for credit, off-campus study, study-abroad, and Army and Air Force ROTC. The most frequently chosen baccalaureate fields are business/marketing, health professions and related sciences, and education. The faculty at McKendree has 69 full-time members, 84% with terminal degrees. The student-faculty ratio is 15:1.

Students of McKendree The student body is made up of 2,067 undergraduates. 60.6% are women and 39.4% are men. Students come from 15 states and territories and 12 other countries. 71% are from Illinois. 1.2% are international students. 78% returned for their sophomore year.

Applying McKendree requires SAT I or ACT, a high school transcript, 1 recommendation, and a minimum high school GPA of 2.5, and in some cases an essay and an interview. Application deadline: rolling admissions; 5/31 priority date for financial aid. Deferred admission is possible.

MCMASTER UNIVERSITY

Hamilton, ON Canada

Suburban setting ■ Public ■ Coed

Web site: www.mcmaster.ca
Contact: Mrs. Lynn Giordano, Associate Registrar, Admissions, 1280 Main Street West, Hamilton, ON L8S 4M2 Canada
Telephone: 905-525-9140 ext. 24034 **Fax:** 905-527-1105
E-mail: macadmit@mcmaster.ca

Getting in Last Year 24,642 applied; 72% were accepted; 3,814 enrolled (21%).

Academics McMaster awards bachelor's, master's, doctoral, and first-professional degrees. Challenging opportunities include accelerated degree programs, student-designed majors, an honors program, independent study, and a senior project. Special programs include cooperative education, internships, summer session for credit, off-campus study, and study-abroad. The faculty at McMaster has 1,237 full-time members.

Students of McMaster The student body totals 20,370, of whom 17,010 are undergraduates. 57.3% are women and 42.7% are men. Students come from 12 states and territories and 79 other countries.

Applying McMaster requires a high school transcript, and in some cases an essay and an interview. Application deadline: 7/15, 5/1 for nonresidents.

MCMURRY UNIVERSITY

Abilene, TX

Urban setting ■ Private ■ Independent Religious ■ Coed

Web site: www.mcm.edu
Contact: Ms. Amy Weyant, Director of Admissions, Box 947, Abilene, TX 79697
Telephone: 915-793-4705 or toll-free 800-477-0077 **Fax:** 915-793-4718
E-mail: admissions@mcm.edu

Getting in Last Year 911 applied; 70% were accepted; 326 enrolled (51%).

Financial Matters $12,018 tuition and fees (2002–03); $4650 room and board; 65% average percent of need met; $13,061 average financial aid amount received per undergraduate.

Academics McMurry awards bachelor's degrees. Challenging opportunities include advanced placement credit, accelerated degree programs, an honors program, double majors, independent study, and a senior project. Special programs include internships, summer session for credit, and study-abroad. The most frequently chosen baccalaureate fields are education, business/marketing, and social sciences and history. The faculty at McMurry has 76 full-time members, 74% with terminal degrees. The student-faculty ratio is 14:1.

Students of McMurry The student body is made up of 1,418 undergraduates. 51.3% are women and 48.7% are men. Students come from 14 states and territories and 7 other countries. 97% are from Texas. 0.8% are international students. 66% returned for their sophomore year.

Applying McMurry requires SAT I or ACT, a high school transcript, and a minimum high school GPA of 2.0, and in some cases an essay and 3 recommendations. Application deadline: 8/15; 3/15 priority date for financial aid. Deferred admission is possible.

MCNEESE STATE UNIVERSITY

Lake Charles, LA

Suburban setting ■ Public ■ State-supported ■ Coed

Web site: www.mcneese.edu
Contact: Ms. Tammie Pettis, Director of Admissions, PO Box 92495, Kaufman Hall, 4100 Ryan Street, Lake Charles, LA 70609-2495
Telephone: 337-475-5148 or toll-free 800-622-3352 **Fax:** 337-475-5189
E-mail: info@mail.mcneese.edu

Getting in Last Year 2,066 applied; 84% were accepted; 1,400 enrolled (80%).

Financial Matters $2545 resident tuition and fees (2002–03); $9256 nonresident tuition and fees (2002–03); $2170 room and board; 58% average percent of need met.

Academics MSU awards associate, bachelor's, and master's degrees and post-bachelor's and post-master's certificates. Challenging opportunities include advanced placement credit, accelerated degree programs, freshman honors college, an honors program, double majors, independent study, and a senior project. Special programs include cooperative education, internships, summer session for credit, off-campus study, and study-abroad. The most frequently chosen baccalaureate fields are education, business/marketing, and health professions and related sciences. The faculty at MSU has 283 full-time members, 67% with terminal degrees. The student-faculty ratio is 22:1.

Students of MSU The student body totals 8,029, of whom 7,010 are undergraduates. 58.3% are women and 41.7% are men. Students come from 34 states and territories and 36 other countries. 94% are from Louisiana. 1.1% are international students. 58% returned for their sophomore year.

Applying MSU requires SAT I or ACT and a high school transcript. Application deadline: rolling admissions; 5/1 priority date for financial aid. Early admission is possible.

MCPHERSON COLLEGE

McPherson, KS

Small-town setting ■ Private ■ Independent Religious ■ Coed

Web site: www.mcpherson.edu
Contact: Mr. Fred Schmidt, Dean of Enrollment, 1600 East Euclid, PO Box 1402, McPherson, KS 67460-1402
Telephone: 620-241-0731 ext. 1270 or toll-free 800-365-7402 **Fax:** 620-241-8443
E-mail: admiss@mcpherson.edu

Getting in Last Year 344 applied; 68% were accepted; 77 enrolled (33%).

Financial Matters $13,345 tuition and fees (2002–03); $5200 room and board; 86% average percent of need met; $14,357 average financial aid amount received per undergraduate.

McPherson College (continued)

Academics McPherson College awards associate and bachelor's degrees. Challenging opportunities include advanced placement credit, student-designed majors, double majors, independent study, and a senior project. Special programs include internships, summer session for credit, off-campus study, and study-abroad. The most frequently chosen baccalaureate fields are business/marketing, social sciences and history, and education. The faculty at McPherson College has 36 full-time members, 67% with terminal degrees. The student-faculty ratio is 10:1.

Students of McPherson College The student body is made up of 379 undergraduates. 44.1% are women and 55.9% are men. Students come from 30 states and territories. 52% are from Kansas. 0.6% are international students. 45% returned for their sophomore year.

Applying McPherson College requires SAT I or ACT, a high school transcript, and a minimum high school GPA of 2.0. The school recommends ACT. Application deadline: rolling admissions. Deferred admission is possible.

MEDAILLE COLLEGE

Buffalo, NY

Urban setting ■ Private ■ Independent ■ Coed

Web site: www.medaille.edu

Contact: Mrs. Jacqueline S. Matheny, Director of Enrollment Management, Medaille College, Office of Admissions, Buffalo, NY 14214

Telephone: 716-884-3281 ext. 203 or toll-free 800-292-1582 (in-state) **Fax:** 716-884-0291

E-mail: jmatheny@medaille.edu

Getting in Last Year 655 applied; 66% were accepted; 250 enrolled (58%).

Financial Matters $13,030 tuition and fees (2002–03); $5950 room and board; 60% average percent of need met; $10,000 average financial aid amount received per undergraduate (2001–02).

Academics Medaille awards associate, bachelor's, and master's degrees. Challenging opportunities include advanced placement credit, accelerated degree programs, student-designed majors, an honors program, double majors, independent study, and a senior project. Special programs include internships, summer session for credit, off-campus study, and Army ROTC. The most frequently chosen baccalaureate fields are education, business/marketing, and liberal arts/general studies. The faculty at Medaille has 63 full-time members, 60% with terminal degrees. The student-faculty ratio is 15:1.

Students of Medaille The student body totals 2,000, of whom 1,630 are undergraduates. 67.8% are women and 32.2% are men. Students come from 1 state or territory and 2 other countries. 11.3% are international students. 70% returned for their sophomore year.

Applying Medaille requires SAT I or ACT, a high school transcript, and an interview, and in some cases an essay and 2.5 high school GPA for veterinary technology and elementary teacher education majors. The school recommends an essay, SAT I, 1 recommendation, and a minimum high school GPA of 2.0. Application deadline: 8/1; 4/1 priority date for financial aid. Early and deferred admission are possible.

MEDCENTER ONE COLLEGE OF NURSING

Bismarck, ND

Small-town setting ■ Private ■ Independent ■ Coed, Primarily Women

Web site: www.medcenterone.com/nursing/nursing.htm

Contact: Ms. Mary Smith, Director of Student Services, 512 North 7th Street, Bismarck, ND 58501-4494

Telephone: 701-323-6271 **Fax:** 701-323-6967

Getting in Last Year 79 applied; 75% were accepted.

Financial Matters $3986 tuition and fees (2002–03); $900 room only; 94% average percent of need met; $6532 average financial aid amount received per undergraduate.

Academics Medcenter One College of Nursing awards bachelor's degrees. Challenging opportunities include an honors program and independent study. Internships is a special program. The most frequently chosen baccalaureate field is health professions and related sciences. The faculty at Medcenter One College of Nursing has 10 full-time members. The student-faculty ratio is 9:1.

Students of Medcenter One College of Nursing The student body is made up of 99 undergraduates. 93.9% are women and 6.1% are men. Students come from 5 states and territories. 92% are from North Dakota. 92% returned for their sophomore year.

Applying Medcenter One College of Nursing requires an essay, a high school transcript, an interview, and transcripts of all college-level work, and in some cases 2 recommendations. Application deadline: 5/1 priority date for financial aid.

MEDGAR EVERS COLLEGE OF THE CITY UNIVERSITY OF NEW YORK

Brooklyn, NY

Urban setting ■ Public ■ State and locally supported ■ Coed

Web site: www.mec.cuny.edu

Contact: Mr. Warren Heusner, Director of Admissions, 1665 Bedford Avenue, Brooklyn, NY 11225

Telephone: 718-270-6025 **Fax:** 718-270-6198

E-mail: enroll@mec.cuny.edu

Getting in Last Year 1,679 applied; 80% were accepted; 668 enrolled (50%).

Financial Matters $3430 resident tuition and fees (2002–03); $7030 nonresident tuition and fees (2002–03).

Academics Medgar Evers College of the City University of New York awards associate and bachelor's degrees. Challenging opportunities include advanced placement credit, an honors program, and independent study. Special programs include cooperative education, internships, summer session for credit, off-campus study, and study-abroad. The most frequently chosen baccalaureate fields are education, health professions and related sciences, and business/marketing. The faculty at Medgar Evers College of the City University of New York has 127 full-time members. The student-faculty ratio is 17:1.

Students of Medgar Evers College of the City University of New York The student body is made up of 4,873 undergraduates. 78.7% are women and 21.3% are men. Students come from 3 states and territories and 50 other countries. 99% are from New York. 4.8% are international students.

Applying Medgar Evers College of the City University of New York requires a high school transcript and GED. The school recommends SAT I and SAT II or ACT. Application deadline: rolling admissions. Deferred admission is possible.

MEDICAL COLLEGE OF GEORGIA

Augusta, GA

Urban setting ■ Public ■ State-supported ■ Coed

Web site: www.mcg.edu

Contact: Ms. Carol S. Nobles, Director of Student Recruitment and Admissions, AA-170 Administration-Kelly Building, Augusta, GA 30912

Telephone: 706-721-2725 **Fax:** 706-721-7279

E-mail: underadm@mail.mcg.edu

Getting in Last Year 901 applied; 52% were accepted.

Financial Matters $3356 resident tuition and fees (2002–03); $11,726 nonresident tuition and fees (2002–03); $2591 room only; 58% average percent of need met; $8407 average financial aid amount received per undergraduate.

Academics MCG awards bachelor's, master's, doctoral, and first-professional degrees and post-bachelor's certificates. Special programs include summer session for credit and off-campus study. The most frequently chosen baccalaureate field is health professions and related sciences. The faculty at MCG has 590 full-time members, 87% with terminal degrees.

Students of MCG The student body totals 2,001, of whom 717 are undergraduates. 86.9% are women and 13.1% are men. Students come from 15 states and territories. 89% are from Georgia.

Applying MCG requires (in some cases) SAT I or ACT. Application deadline: 3/31 priority date for financial aid.

MEDICAL UNIVERSITY OF SOUTH CAROLINA

Charleston, SC

Urban setting ■ Public ■ State-supported ■ Coed

Web site: www.musc.edu

Contact: Mr. James F. Menzel, Executive Director, Office of Enrollment Services, PO Box 250203, Charleston, SC 29425

Telephone: 843-792-5396 **Fax:** 843-792-3764

E-mail: oes-web@musc.edu

Getting in Last Year 3,800 applied; 22% were accepted.

Financial Matters $6732 resident tuition and fees (2002–03); $17,729 nonresident tuition and fees (2002–03); 46% average percent of need met; $7893 average financial aid amount received per undergraduate (2001–02).

Academics MUSC awards bachelor's, master's, doctoral, and first-professional degrees and post-bachelor's certificates. Challenging opportunities include advanced placement credit and independent study. Special programs include internships and off-campus study. The most frequently chosen baccalaureate field is health professions and related sciences. The faculty at MUSC has 1,067 full-time members, 85% with terminal degrees. The student-faculty ratio is 12:1.

Students of MUSC The student body totals 2,286, of whom 382 are undergraduates. 81.9% are women and 18.1% are men. Students come from 15 states and territories. 90% are from South Carolina. 86% returned for their sophomore year.

Applying MUSC requires (in some cases) SAT I or ACT. Application deadline: 3/15 priority date for financial aid. Deferred admission is possible.

MEMORIAL UNIVERSITY OF NEWFOUNDLAND

St. John's, NF Canada

Urban setting ■ Public ■ Coed

Web site: www.mun.ca

Contact: Ms. Phyllis McCann, Admissions Manager, Elizabeth Avenue, St. John's, NF A1C 5S7 Canada
Telephone: 709-737-3705
E-mail: sturecru@morgan.ucs.mun.ca

Getting in Last Year 2,981 applied; 76% were accepted.

Financial Matters $2900 nonresident tuition and fees (2002–03); $4006 room and board.

Academics MUN awards bachelor's, master's, and doctoral degrees and post-bachelor's certificates. Challenging opportunities include advanced placement credit, accelerated degree programs, an honors program, double majors, and a senior project. Special programs include cooperative education, internships, summer session for credit, off-campus study, and study-abroad. The most frequently chosen baccalaureate fields are education, business/marketing, and social sciences and history. The faculty at MUN has 834 full-time members. The student-faculty ratio is 12:1.

Students of MUN The student body totals 15,630, of whom 14,037 are undergraduates. 59.7% are women and 40.3% are men. Students come from 12 states and territories. 95% are from Newfoundland. 80% returned for their sophomore year.

Applying MUN requires a high school transcript, and in some cases an essay, an interview, 2 recommendations, and audition, portfolio. Application deadline: rolling admissions, 3/1 for nonresidents.

MEMPHIS COLLEGE OF ART

Memphis, TN

Urban setting ■ Private ■ Independent ■ Coed

Web site: www.mca.edu
Contact: Ms. Annette Moore, Director of Admission, 1930 Poplar Avenue, Memphis, TN 38104
Telephone: 901-272-5153 or toll-free 800-727-1088 **Fax:** 901-272-5158
E-mail: info@mca.edu

Getting in Last Year 207 applied; 75% were accepted; 69 enrolled (44%).

Financial Matters $13,800 tuition and fees (2002–03); $5200 room and board; 90% average percent of need met; $7000 average financial aid amount received per undergraduate.

Academics MCA awards bachelor's and master's degrees. Challenging opportunities include advanced placement credit, double majors, independent study, and a senior project. Special programs include internships, summer session for credit, and off-campus study. The faculty at MCA has 17 full-time members, 24% with terminal degrees. The student-faculty ratio is 11:1.

Students of MCA The student body totals 318, of whom 285 are undergraduates. 49.8% are women and 50.2% are men. Students come from 23 states and territories and 10 other countries. 50% are from Tennessee. 4.6% are international students. 46% returned for their sophomore year.

Applying MCA requires an essay, SAT I or ACT, a high school transcript, and portfolio. The school recommends an interview. Application deadline: rolling admissions; 4/1 priority date for financial aid. Early and deferred admission are possible.

MENLO COLLEGE

Atherton, CA

Small-town setting ■ Private ■ Independent ■ Coed

Web site: www.menlo.edu
Contact: Dr. Greg Smith, Dean of Admission and Financial Aid, 1000 El Camino Real, Atherton, CA 94027
Telephone: 650-543-3910 or toll-free 800-556-3656 **Fax:** 650-617-2395
E-mail: admissions@menlo.edu

Getting in Last Year 1,061 applied; 56% were accepted; 172 enrolled (29%).

Financial Matters $20,450 tuition and fees (2002–03); $8650 room and board; 75% average percent of need met; $12,202 average financial aid amount received per undergraduate.

Academics Menlo awards bachelor's degrees. Challenging opportunities include advanced placement credit, accelerated degree programs, student-designed majors, an honors program, double majors, independent study, and a senior project. Special programs include internships, summer session for credit, study-abroad, and Army and Air Force ROTC. The most frequently chosen baccalaureate fields are business/marketing, communications/communication technologies, and liberal arts/general studies. The faculty at Menlo has 25 full-time members, 60% with terminal degrees. The student-faculty ratio is 17:1.

Students of Menlo The student body is made up of 660 undergraduates. 36.5% are women and 63.5% are men. Students come from 24 states and territories and 34 other countries. 82% are from California. 12% are international students. 48% returned for their sophomore year.

Applying Menlo requires an essay, SAT I or ACT, a high school transcript, and 1 recommendation. The school recommends an interview and a minimum high school GPA of 3.0. Application deadline: rolling admissions; 3/2 priority date for financial aid. Deferred admission is possible.

MERCER UNIVERSITY

Macon, GA

Suburban setting ■ Private ■ Independent Religious ■ Coed

Web site: www.mercer.edu
Contact: Mr. Allen S. London, Associate Vice President for Freshman Admissions, 1400 Coleman Avenue, Macon, GA 31207-0003
Telephone: 478-301-2650 or toll-free 800-840-8577 **Fax:** 478-301-2828
E-mail: admissions@mercer.edu

Getting in Last Year 2,697 applied; 85% were accepted; 723 enrolled (32%).

Financial Matters $19,728 tuition and fees (2002–03); $6420 room and board; 86% average percent of need met; $19,833 average financial aid amount received per undergraduate.

Academics Mercer awards bachelor's, master's, doctoral, and first-professional degrees and post-bachelor's and post-master's certificates. Challenging opportunities include advanced placement credit, accelerated degree programs, student-designed majors, an honors program, double majors, independent study, and a senior project. Special programs include cooperative education, internships, summer session for credit, off-campus study, study-abroad, and Army ROTC. The most frequently chosen baccalaureate fields are business/marketing, education, and social sciences and history. The faculty at Mercer has 330 full-time members, 85% with terminal degrees. The student-faculty ratio is 14:1.

Students of Mercer The student body totals 7,325, of whom 4,673 are undergraduates. 67% are women and 33% are men. Students come from 30 states and territories and 35 other countries. 84% are from Georgia. 4% are international students. 75% returned for their sophomore year.

Applying Mercer requires SAT I or ACT, a high school transcript, and a minimum high school GPA of 2.8, and in some cases an interview, 2 recommendations, counselor's evaluation, and a minimum high school GPA of 3.0. The school recommends an interview and a minimum high school GPA of 3.0. Application deadline: 7/1; 4/1 priority date for financial aid. Early and deferred admission are possible.

MERCY COLLEGE

Dobbs Ferry, NY

Suburban setting ■ Private ■ Independent ■ Coed

Web site: www.mercy.edu
Contact: Mrs. Sharon Handelson, Director of Admissions and Recruitment, 555 Broadway, Dobbs Ferry, NY 10522-1189
Telephone: 800-Mercy-NY ext. 7499 or toll-free 800-MERCY-NY **Fax:** 914-674-7382
E-mail: admissions@mercy.edu

Getting in Last Year 2,708 applied.

Financial Matters $10,000 tuition and fees (2002–03); $8000 room and board.

Academics Mercy awards associate, bachelor's, and master's degrees. Challenging opportunities include advanced placement credit, accelerated degree programs, student-designed majors, an honors program, double majors, and independent study. Special programs include cooperative education, internships, summer session for credit, off-campus study, study-abroad, and Air Force ROTC. The faculty at Mercy has 238 full-time members. The student-faculty ratio is 17:1.

Students of Mercy The student body totals 9,752, of whom 6,833 are undergraduates. 70.8% are women and 29.2% are men. Students come from 6 states and territories and 49 other countries.

Applying Mercy requires a high school transcript and 1 recommendation. The school recommends SAT I and an interview. Application deadline: rolling admissions; 5/1 priority date for financial aid. Early and deferred admission are possible.

MERCYHURST COLLEGE

Erie, PA

Suburban setting ■ Private ■ Independent Religious ■ Coed

Web site: www.mercyhurst.edu
Contact: Mr. Robin Engel, Director of Undergraduate Admissions, 501 East 38th Street, Erie, PA 16546-0001
Telephone: 814-824-2573 or toll-free 800-825-1926 ext. 2202 **Fax:** 814-824-2071
E-mail: admissions@mercyhurst.edu

Getting in Last Year 2,306 applied; 78% were accepted; 1,092 enrolled (61%).

Financial Matters $15,870 tuition and fees (2002–03); $5979 room and board.

Academics Mercyhurst awards associate, bachelor's, and master's degrees and post-bachelor's certificates. Challenging opportunities include advanced placement credit, accelerated degree programs, student-designed majors, freshman honors college, an honors program, double majors, independent study, and a senior project. Special programs include cooperative education, internships, summer session for credit, off-campus study, study-abroad, and Army ROTC. The most frequently chosen baccalaureate fields are business/marketing, protective

Mercyhurst College (continued)

services/public administration, and health professions and related sciences. The faculty at Mercyhurst has 148 full-time members, 58% with terminal degrees. The student-faculty ratio is 17:1.

Students of Mercyhurst The student body totals 3,617, of whom 3,445 are undergraduates. 61.4% are women and 38.6% are men. Students come from 41 states and territories and 12 other countries. 55% are from Pennsylvania. 2.5% are international students. 80% returned for their sophomore year.

Applying Mercyhurst requires SAT I or ACT and a high school transcript, and in some cases an essay and an interview. The school recommends 2 recommendations. Application deadline: rolling admissions; 3/1 priority date for financial aid. Early and deferred admission are possible.

MEREDITH COLLEGE

Raleigh, NC

Urban setting ■ *Private* ■ *Independent* ■ *Women Only*

Web site: www.meredith.edu

Contact: Ms. Carol R. Kercheval, Director of Admissions, 3800 Hillsborough Street, Raleigh, NC 27607-5298

Telephone: 919-760-8581 or toll-free 800-MEREDITH **Fax:** 919-760-2348

E-mail: admissions@meredith.edu

Getting in Last Year 1,039 applied; 86% were accepted; 394 enrolled (44%).

Financial Matters $15,100 tuition and fees (2002–03); $4600 room and board; 79% average percent of need met; $12,594 average financial aid amount received per undergraduate.

Academics Meredith awards bachelor's and master's degrees and post-bachelor's certificates. Challenging opportunities include advanced placement credit, accelerated degree programs, student-designed majors, an honors program, double majors, independent study, and a senior project. Special programs include cooperative education, internships, summer session for credit, off-campus study, study-abroad, and Army and Air Force ROTC. The most frequently chosen baccalaureate fields are business/marketing, visual/performing arts, and psychology. The faculty at Meredith has 139 full-time members, 83% with terminal degrees. The student-faculty ratio is 10:1.

Students of Meredith The student body totals 2,328, of whom 2,175 are undergraduates. Students come from 26 states and territories and 14 other countries. 92% are from North Carolina. 0.7% are international students. 79% returned for their sophomore year.

Applying Meredith requires SAT I or ACT, a high school transcript, 2 recommendations, and a minimum high school GPA of 2.0, and in some cases an essay, SAT II Subject Tests, and an interview. Application deadline: 2/15; 2/1 priority date for financial aid. Early and deferred admission are possible.

MERRIMACK COLLEGE

North Andover, MA

Suburban setting ■ *Private* ■ *Independent Religious* ■ *Coed*

Web site: www.merrimack.edu

Contact: Mr. John Hamel, Director of Admissions, Austin Hall, A22, North Andover, MA 01845

Telephone: 978-837-5000 ext. 4476 **Fax:** 978-837-5133

E-mail: admission@merrimack.edu

Getting in Last Year 3,243 applied; 67% were accepted; 560 enrolled (26%).

Financial Matters $19,000 tuition and fees (2002–03); $8410 room and board; 70% average percent of need met; $14,700 average financial aid amount received per undergraduate.

Academics Merrimack awards associate, bachelor's, and master's degrees. Challenging opportunities include advanced placement credit, student-designed majors, an honors program, double majors, independent study, and a senior project. Special programs include cooperative education, internships, summer session for credit, off-campus study, study-abroad, and Air Force ROTC. The most frequently chosen baccalaureate fields are business/marketing, social sciences and history, and psychology. The faculty at Merrimack has 142 full-time members, 72% with terminal degrees. The student-faculty ratio is 13:1.

Students of Merrimack The student body totals 2,518, of whom 2,501 are undergraduates. 53.3% are women and 46.7% are men. Students come from 29 states and territories and 25 other countries. 72% are from Massachusetts. 1.2% are international students. 82% returned for their sophomore year.

Applying Merrimack requires an essay, SAT I or ACT, and a high school transcript, and in some cases an interview. The school recommends an interview, 1 recommendation, and a minimum high school GPA of 2.8. Application deadline: 2/15; 2/15 for financial aid. Early and deferred admission are possible.

MESA STATE COLLEGE

Grand Junction, CO

Small-town setting ■ *Public* ■ *State-supported* ■ *Coed*

Web site: www.mesastate.edu

Contact: Ms. Tyre Bush, Director of Admission, 1100 North Avenue, Grand Junction, CO 81501

Telephone: 970-248-1875 or toll-free 800-982-MESA **Fax:** 970-248-1973

E-mail: admissions@mesastate.edu

Getting in Last Year 2,361 applied; 92% were accepted; 1,112 enrolled (51%).

Financial Matters $2373 resident tuition and fees (2002–03); $7623 nonresident tuition and fees (2002–03); $6037 room and board; 56% average percent of need met; $5871 average financial aid amount received per undergraduate (2001–02).

Academics Mesa State awards associate, bachelor's, and master's degrees. Challenging opportunities include advanced placement credit, accelerated degree programs, student-designed majors, an honors program, double majors, and independent study. Special programs include cooperative education, internships, summer session for credit, off-campus study, and study-abroad. The most frequently chosen baccalaureate fields are business/marketing, social sciences and history, and biological/life sciences. The faculty at Mesa State has 209 full-time members, 67% with terminal degrees. The student-faculty ratio is 18:1.

Students of Mesa State The student body totals 5,560, of whom 5,463 are undergraduates. 57.3% are women and 42.7% are men. Students come from 46 states and territories. 91% are from Colorado. 0.8% are international students. 60% returned for their sophomore year.

Applying Mesa State requires SAT I or ACT, a high school transcript, and a minimum high school GPA of 2.0, and in some cases an interview and 1 recommendation. Application deadline: 8/15; 3/1 priority date for financial aid. Early and deferred admission are possible.

MESSENGER COLLEGE

Joplin, MO

Small-town setting ■ *Private* ■ *Independent Religious* ■ *Coed*

Contact: Ms. Gwen Minor, Vice President of Academic Affairs, 300 East 50th, PO Box 4050, Joplin, MO 64803

Telephone: 417-624-7070 ext. 102 or toll-free 800-385-8940 (in-state) **Fax:** 417-624-5070

E-mail: mc@pcg.org

Getting in Last Year 43 applied; 98% were accepted; 23 enrolled (55%).

Financial Matters $4870 tuition and fees (2002–03); $3100 room and board; 83% average percent of need met; $4175 average financial aid amount received per undergraduate (2001–02).

Academics Messenger College awards associate and bachelor's degrees. Challenging opportunities include an honors program, double majors, independent study, and a senior project. Special programs include cooperative education and internships. The most frequently chosen baccalaureate field is visual/performing arts. The faculty at Messenger College has 4 full-time members, 75% with terminal degrees.

Students of Messenger College The student body is made up of 100 undergraduates. 41% are women and 59% are men. Students come from 18 states and territories. 48% are from Missouri. 47% returned for their sophomore year.

Applying Messenger College requires an essay, SAT I or ACT, a high school transcript, 2 recommendations, and a minimum high school GPA of 2.0, and in some cases an interview. Application deadline: 9/1.

MESSIAH COLLEGE

Grantham, PA

Small-town setting ■ *Private* ■ *Independent Religious* ■ *Coed*

Web site: www.messiah.edu

Contact: Mr. William G. Strausbaugh, Dean for Enrollment Management, One College Avenue, PO Box 3005, Grantham, PA 17027

Telephone: 717-691-6000 or toll-free 800-233-4220 **Fax:** 717-796-5374

E-mail: admiss@messiah.edu

Getting in Last Year 2,300 applied; 77% were accepted; 764 enrolled (43%).

Financial Matters $18,136 tuition and fees (2002–03); $6130 room and board; 71% average percent of need met; $12,398 average financial aid amount received per undergraduate.

Academics Messiah College awards bachelor's degrees. Challenging opportunities include advanced placement credit, accelerated degree programs, student-designed majors, an honors program, double majors, independent study, and a senior project. Special programs include internships, summer session for credit, off-campus study, and study-abroad. The most frequently chosen baccalaureate fields are education, business/marketing, and home economics/vocational home economics. The faculty at Messiah College has 166 full-time members, 73% with terminal degrees. The student-faculty ratio is 13:1.

Students of Messiah College The student body is made up of 2,895 undergraduates. 61.7% are women and 38.3% are men. Students come from 38 states and territories and 34 other countries. 52% are from Pennsylvania. 2.4% are international students. 85% returned for their sophomore year.

Applying Messiah College requires an essay, a high school transcript, and 2 recommendations, and in some cases SAT I or ACT. The school recommends an interview and a minimum high school GPA of 3.0. Application deadline: rolling admissions; 4/1 priority date for financial aid. Early and deferred admission are possible.

METHODIST COLLEGE
Fayetteville, NC

Suburban setting ■ Private ■ Independent Religious ■ Coed

Web site: www.methodist.edu
Contact: Mr. Jamie Legg, Director of Admissions, 5400 Ramsey Street, Fayetteville, NC 28311
Telephone: 910-630-7027 or toll-free 800-488-7110 ext. 7027 **Fax:** 910-630-7285
E-mail: admissions@methodist.edu

Getting in Last Year 1,906 applied; 84% were accepted; 469 enrolled (29%).

Financial Matters $14,970 tuition and fees (2002–03); $5580 room and board; 71% average percent of need met; $16,586 average financial aid amount received per undergraduate (2001–02).

Academics Methodist awards associate, bachelor's, and master's degrees. Challenging opportunities include advanced placement credit, accelerated degree programs, an honors program, double majors, independent study, and a senior project. Special programs include cooperative education, internships, summer session for credit, study-abroad, and Army and Air Force ROTC. The most frequently chosen baccalaureate fields are business/marketing, social sciences and history, and parks and recreation. The faculty at Methodist has 100 full-time members, 64% with terminal degrees. The student-faculty ratio is 15:1.

Students of Methodist The student body totals 2,180, of whom 2,161 are undergraduates. 43.1% are women and 56.9% are men. Students come from 48 states and territories and 37 other countries. 52% are from North Carolina. 2.8% are international students. 68% returned for their sophomore year.

Applying Methodist requires SAT I or ACT and a high school transcript, and in some cases an essay, an interview, and 2 recommendations. The school recommends an interview and 2 recommendations. Application deadline: rolling admissions. Deferred admission is possible.

METROPOLITAN COLLEGE
Oklahoma City, OK

Private ■ Proprietary ■ Coed, Primarily Women

Web site: www.metropolitancollege.edu
Contact: Ms. Pamela Picken, Admissions Director, 1900 NW Expressway R-302, Oklahoma City, OK 73118
Telephone: 405-843-1000

Financial Matters $6718 tuition and fees (2002–03).

Academics Metropolitan College awards associate and bachelor's degrees. The faculty at Metropolitan College has 3 full-time members, 33% with terminal degrees.

Students of Metropolitan College The student body is made up of 140 undergraduates. 93.6% are women and 6.4% are men. 0.7% are international students.

Applying Metropolitan College requires Wonderlic, a high school transcript, and an interview.

METROPOLITAN COLLEGE
Tulsa, OK

Urban setting ■ Private ■ Proprietary ■ Coed, Primarily Women

Web site: www.metropolitancollege.edu
Contact: Ms. Toby Quoss, Admissions Director, 4528 South Sheridan Road, Suite 105, Tulsa, OK 74145-1011
Telephone: 918-627-9300 **Fax:** 918-627-2122 ext.

Getting in Last Year 62 applied; 94% were accepted; 30 enrolled (52%).

Financial Matters $6535 tuition and fees (2002–03); 99% average percent of need met.

Academics Metropolitan College awards associate and bachelor's degrees. Accelerated degree programs are a challenging opportunity. Internships is a special program. The faculty at Metropolitan College has 4 full-time members, 50% with terminal degrees. The student-faculty ratio is 15:1.

Students of Metropolitan College The student body is made up of 149 undergraduates. 94% are women and 6% are men. Students come from 3 states and territories. 99% are from Oklahoma. 70% returned for their sophomore year.

Applying Metropolitan College requires Wonderlic aptitude test, a high school transcript, and an interview.

METROPOLITAN COLLEGE OF COURT REPORTING
Albuquerque, NM

Urban setting ■ Private ■ Proprietary ■ Coed

Web site: www.metropolitancollege.edu
Contact: 1717 Louisiana Boulevard NE, Suite 207, Albuquerque, NM 87110-7027
Telephone: 505-888-3400 **Fax:** 505-254-3738 ext.

Getting in Last Year 60 applied; 80% were accepted.

Financial Matters $6534 tuition and fees (2002–03).

Academics The faculty at Metropolitan College of Court Reporting has 3 full-time members.

Students of Metropolitan College of Court Reporting The student body is made up of 147 undergraduates.

METROPOLITAN COLLEGE OF NEW YORK
New York, NY

Urban setting ■ Private ■ Independent ■ Coed, Primarily Women

Web site: www.metropolitan.edu
Contact: Ms. Sabrina Badal-Mohammed, Director of Admissions, 75 Varick Street, 12th Floor, New York, NY 10013
Telephone: 212-343-1234 ext. 2711 or toll-free 800-33-THINK ext. 5001 (in-state) **Fax:** 212-343-8470

Getting in Last Year 680 applied; 53% were accepted.

Financial Matters $15,120 tuition and fees (2002–03); $6337 average financial aid amount received per undergraduate (2000–01).

Academics Metropolitan College of New York awards associate, bachelor's, and master's degrees. Accelerated degree programs are a challenging opportunity. Special programs include cooperative education, internships, summer session for credit, and study-abroad. The most frequently chosen baccalaureate fields are home economics/vocational home economics and business/marketing. The faculty at Metropolitan College of New York has 29 full-time members. The student-faculty ratio is 20:1.

Students of Metropolitan College of New York The student body totals 1,665, of whom 1,380 are undergraduates. Students come from 5 states and territories. 98% are from New York. 70% returned for their sophomore year.

Applying Metropolitan College of New York requires an essay, TABE, a high school transcript, an interview, and 2 recommendations, and in some cases TABE and college entrance exam. The school recommends SAT I, SAT I or ACT, and a minimum high school GPA of 3.0. Application deadline: 8/15. Deferred admission is possible.

METROPOLITAN STATE COLLEGE OF DENVER
Denver, CO

Urban setting ■ Public ■ State-supported ■ Coed

Web site: www.mscd.edu
Contact: Ms. Miriam Tapia, Associate Director, PO Box 173362, Campus Box 16, Denver, CO 80217-3362
Telephone: 303-556-2615 **Fax:** 303-556-6345

Getting in Last Year 4,479 applied; 81% were accepted; 2,278 enrolled (63%).

Financial Matters $2479 resident tuition and fees (2002–03); $8677 nonresident tuition and fees (2002–03); $567 room only; 55% average percent of need met; $5809 average financial aid amount received per undergraduate (2001–02).

Academics The Met awards bachelor's degrees. Challenging opportunities include advanced placement credit, accelerated degree programs, student-designed majors, an honors program, double majors, independent study, and a senior project. Special programs include cooperative education, internships, summer session for credit, off-campus study, study-abroad, and Air Force ROTC. The most frequently chosen baccalaureate fields are business/marketing, social sciences and history, and protective services/public administration. The faculty at The Met has 393 full-time members, 75% with terminal degrees. The student-faculty ratio is 23:1.

Students of The Met The student body is made up of 19,413 undergraduates. 57.1% are women and 42.9% are men. Students come from 42 states and territories and 68 other countries. 98% are from Colorado. 1.2% are international students. 62% returned for their sophomore year.

Applying The Met requires a high school transcript, and in some cases an essay, SAT I or ACT, and recommendations. The school recommends a minimum high school GPA of 2.0. Application deadline: 8/12. Deferred admission is possible.

METROPOLITAN STATE UNIVERSITY
St. Paul, MN

Urban setting ■ Public ■ State-supported ■ Coed

Web site: www.metrostate.edu
Contact: Dr. Janice Harring Hendon, Director, 700 East 7th Street, St. Paul, MN 55106-5000
Telephone: 651-793-1303 **Fax:** 651-793-1310
E-mail: admissionsmetro@metrostate.edu

Getting in Last Year 113 enrolled (45%).

Metropolitan State University (continued)

Financial Matters $3358 resident tuition and fees (2002–03); $7152 nonresident tuition and fees (2002–03); 65% average percent of need met; $7500 average financial aid amount received per undergraduate.

Academics Metro State awards bachelor's and master's degrees (offers primarily part-time evening degree programs). Challenging opportunities include student-designed majors, double majors, independent study, and a senior project. Special programs include internships, summer session for credit, and off-campus study. The most frequently chosen baccalaureate fields are business/marketing, interdisciplinary studies, and protective services/public administration. The faculty at Metro State has 116 full-time members, 76% with terminal degrees. The student-faculty ratio is 12:1.

Students of Metro State The student body totals 6,419, of whom 5,990 are undergraduates. 60.1% are women and 39.9% are men. Students come from 16 states and territories and 53 other countries. 98% are from Minnesota. 2.2% are international students. 51% returned for their sophomore year.

Applying Metro State requires a high school transcript and a minimum high school GPA of 2.0, and in some cases SAT I or ACT. Application deadline: rolling admissions; 6/1 priority date for financial aid. Deferred admission is possible.

MIAMI INTERNATIONAL UNIVERSITY OF ART & DESIGN

Miami, FL

Urban setting ■ Private ■ Proprietary ■ Coed

Web site: www.ifac.edu

Contact: Ms. Elsia Suarez, Director of Admissions, 1501 Biscayne Boulevard, Suite 100, Miami, FL 33132-1418

Telephone: 305-373-4684 or toll-free 800-225-9023

Financial Matters $21,440 tuition and fees (2002–03); $5800 room only.

Academics IFAC awards associate, bachelor's, and master's degrees. Special programs include internships and summer session for credit. The faculty at IFAC has 93 members. The student-faculty ratio is 18:1.

Students of IFAC The student body totals 1,016, of whom 972 are undergraduates. Students come from 45 states and territories and 50 other countries.

Applying IFAC requires a high school transcript, an interview, 2 photographs, art portfolio, and a minimum high school GPA of 2.0. The school recommends an essay, SAT II: Writing Test, SAT I and SAT II or ACT, and 2 recommendations. Application deadline: rolling admissions. Deferred admission is possible.

MIAMI UNIVERSITY

Oxford, OH

Small-town setting ■ Public ■ State-related ■ Coed

Web site: www.muohio.edu

Contact: Mr. Michael E. Mills, Director of Undergraduate Admissions, 301 South Campus Avenue, Oxford, OH 45056

Telephone: 513-529-5040 **Fax:** 513-529-1550

E-mail: admission@muohio.edu

Getting in Last Year 12,204 applied; 77% were accepted; 3,549 enrolled (38%).

Financial Matters $7600 resident tuition and fees (2002–03); $16,324 nonresident tuition and fees (2002–03); $6240 room and board; 68% average percent of need met; $6997 average financial aid amount received per undergraduate.

Academics Miami University awards associate, bachelor's, master's, and doctoral degrees and post-master's certificates. Challenging opportunities include advanced placement credit, student-designed majors, an honors program, double majors, independent study, and a senior project. Special programs include cooperative education, internships, summer session for credit, off-campus study, study-abroad, and Army, Navy and Air Force ROTC. The most frequently chosen baccalaureate fields are business/marketing, education, and social sciences and history. The faculty at Miami University has 807 full-time members, 87% with terminal degrees. The student-faculty ratio is 17:1.

Students of Miami University The student body totals 16,730, of whom 15,384 are undergraduates. 54.4% are women and 45.6% are men. Students come from 49 states and territories and 70 other countries. 73% are from Ohio. 0.7% are international students. 90% returned for their sophomore year.

Applying Miami University requires SAT I or ACT and a high school transcript. The school recommends an essay and 1 recommendation. Application deadline: 1/31; 2/15 priority date for financial aid.

MICHIGAN STATE UNIVERSITY

East Lansing, MI

Suburban setting ■ Public ■ State-supported ■ Coed

Web site: www.msu.edu

Contact: Ms. Pamela Horne, Assistant to the Provost for Enrollment and Director of Admissions, 250 Administration Building, East Lansing, MI 48824

Telephone: 517-355-8332 **Fax:** 517-353-1647

E-mail: admis@msu.edu

Getting in Last Year 25,210 applied; 67% were accepted; 7,000 enrolled (41%).

Financial Matters $6101 resident tuition and fees (2002–03); $4932 room and board; 98% average percent of need met; $9355 average financial aid amount received per undergraduate.

Academics Michigan State awards bachelor's, master's, doctoral, and first-professional degrees. Challenging opportunities include advanced placement credit, accelerated degree programs, student-designed majors, freshman honors college, an honors program, double majors, independent study, and a senior project. Special programs include cooperative education, internships, summer session for credit, off-campus study, study-abroad, and Army and Air Force ROTC. The most frequently chosen baccalaureate fields are business/marketing, communications/communication technologies, and social sciences and history. The faculty at Michigan State has 2,349 full-time members, 95% with terminal degrees. The student-faculty ratio is 18:1.

Students of Michigan State The student body totals 44,937, of whom 35,197 are undergraduates. 53.3% are women and 46.7% are men. Students come from 54 states and territories and 100 other countries. 94% are from Michigan. 2.4% are international students. 89% returned for their sophomore year.

Applying Michigan State requires SAT I or ACT and a high school transcript. Application deadline: 6/30 for financial aid, with a 2/21 priority date. Deferred admission is possible.

MICHIGAN TECHNOLOGICAL UNIVERSITY

Houghton, MI

Small-town setting ■ Public ■ State-supported ■ Coed

Web site: www.mtu.edu

Contact: Ms. Nancy Rehling, Director of Undergraduate Admissions, 1400 Townsend Drive, Houghton, MI 49931-1295

Telephone: 906-487-2335 or toll-free 888-MTU-1885 **Fax:** 906-487-2125

E-mail: mtu4u@mtu.edu

Getting in Last Year 2,957 applied; 92% were accepted; 1,190 enrolled (44%).

Financial Matters $6455 resident tuition and fees (2002–03); $14,825 nonresident tuition and fees (2002–03); $5465 room and board; 81% average percent of need met; $7855 average financial aid amount received per undergraduate.

Academics Michigan Tech awards associate, bachelor's, master's, and doctoral degrees. Challenging opportunities include advanced placement credit, student-designed majors, double majors, and a senior project. Special programs include cooperative education, internships, summer session for credit, off-campus study, study-abroad, and Army and Air Force ROTC. The faculty at Michigan Tech has 377 full-time members, 88% with terminal degrees. The student-faculty ratio is 11:1.

Students of Michigan Tech The student body totals 6,625, of whom 5,915 are undergraduates. 24% are women and 76% are men. Students come from 41 states and territories and 80 other countries. 81% are from Michigan. 5.7% are international students. 82% returned for their sophomore year.

Applying Michigan Tech requires SAT I or ACT and a high school transcript. The school recommends an interview. Application deadline: rolling admissions; 2/21 priority date for financial aid. Deferred admission is possible.

MIDAMERICA NAZARENE UNIVERSITY

Olathe, KS

Suburban setting ■ Private ■ Independent Religious ■ Coed

Web site: www.mnu.edu

Contact: Mr. Mike Redwine, Vice President for Enrollment Development, 2030 East College Way, Olathe, KS 66062-1899

Telephone: 913-791-3380 ext. 481 or toll-free 800-800-8887 **Fax:** 913-791-3481

E-mail: admissions@mnu.edu

Getting in Last Year 651 applied; 46% were accepted; 291 enrolled (96%).

Financial Matters $12,280 tuition and fees (2002–03); $5614 room and board; 66% average percent of need met; $10,180 average financial aid amount received per undergraduate.

Academics MNU awards associate, bachelor's, and master's degrees. Challenging opportunities include advanced placement credit, accelerated degree programs, double majors, independent study, and a senior project. Special programs include internships, summer session for credit, off-campus study, study-abroad, and Army and Air Force ROTC. The most frequently chosen baccalaureate fields are business/marketing, education, and health professions and related sciences. The faculty at MNU has 73 full-time members, 47% with terminal degrees. The student-faculty ratio is 18:1.

Students of MNU The student body totals 1,825, of whom 1,372 are undergraduates. 52.4% are women and 47.6% are men. Students come from 38 states and territories and 5 other countries. 61% are from Kansas. 76% returned for their sophomore year.

Applying MNU requires SAT I or ACT, a high school transcript, 1 recommendation, and a minimum high school GPA of 2.0. Application deadline: 8/1; 3/1 priority date for financial aid. Early and deferred admission are possible.

MID-CONTINENT COLLEGE

Mayfield, KY

Small-town setting ■ Private ■ Independent Religious ■ Coed

Web site: www.midcontinent.edu
Contact: Mrs. Darla Zakowicz, Director of Enrollment and Retention Management, 99 Powell Road East, Mayfield, KY 42068
Telephone: 270-247-8521 ext. 311
E-mail: mcc@midcontinent.edu

Getting in Last Year 89 enrolled.

Financial Matters $9000 tuition and fees (2002–03); $4900 room and board; 55% average percent of need met; $5685 average financial aid amount received per undergraduate.

Academics Mid-Continent College awards bachelor's degrees. Challenging opportunities include advanced placement credit, accelerated degree programs, double majors, and independent study. Special programs include summer session for credit and study-abroad. The most frequently chosen baccalaureate fields are business/marketing, education, and psychology. The faculty at Mid-Continent College has 28 full-time members, 50% with terminal degrees. The student-faculty ratio is 14:1.

Students of Mid-Continent College The student body is made up of 583 undergraduates. 48.7% are women and 51.3% are men. Students come from 15 states and territories and 10 other countries. 79% are from Kentucky. 4% are international students. 58% returned for their sophomore year.

Applying Mid-Continent College requires an essay, SAT I or ACT, a high school transcript, 2 recommendations, and a minimum high school GPA of 2.0. The school recommends 1 recommendation and a minimum high school GPA of 2.0. Application deadline: rolling admissions; 3/15 priority date for financial aid. Early admission is possible.

MIDDLEBURY COLLEGE

Middlebury, VT

Small-town setting ■ Private ■ Independent ■ Coed

Web site: www.middlebury.edu
Contact: Mr. John Hanson, Director of Admissions, Emma Willard House, Middlebury, VT 05753-6002
Telephone: 802-443-3000 **Fax:** 802-443-2056
E-mail: admissions@middlebury.edu

Getting in Last Year 5,299 applied; 27% were accepted; 586 enrolled (41%).

Financial Matters $36,100 comprehensive fee (2002–03); 100% average percent of need met; $26,979 average financial aid amount received per undergraduate.

Academics Middlebury awards bachelor's, master's, and doctoral degrees. Challenging opportunities include advanced placement credit, accelerated degree programs, student-designed majors, an honors program, double majors, and independent study. Special programs include internships, summer session for credit, off-campus study, study-abroad, and Army ROTC. The most frequently chosen baccalaureate fields are social sciences and history, area/ethnic studies, and English. The faculty at Middlebury has 217 full-time members, 95% with terminal degrees. The student-faculty ratio is 11:1.

Students of Middlebury The student body is made up of 2,297 undergraduates. 50.6% are women and 49.4% are men. Students come from 52 states and territories and 71 other countries. 6% are from Vermont. 8.3% are international students. 97% returned for their sophomore year.

Applying Middlebury requires an essay, ACT or 3 SAT II Subject Tests (including SAT II: Writing Test and 1 quantitative SAT II Test), or 3 Advanced Placement Tests (including AP English and 1 quantitative AP Test), or 3 I.B. Subsidiary Tests (including I.B. Languages and 1 quantitative I.B. Test), a high school transcript, and 3 recommendations. The school recommends an interview. Application deadline: 12/15; 12/31 priority date for financial aid. Early and deferred admission are possible.

MIDDLE TENNESSEE STATE UNIVERSITY

Murfreesboro, TN

Urban setting ■ Public ■ State-supported ■ Coed

Web site: www.mtsu.edu
Contact: Ms. Lynn Palmer, Director of Admissions, 1301 East Main Street, MTSU-CAB 208, Murfreesboro, TN 37132
Telephone: 615-898-2111 or toll-free 800-331-MTSU (in-state), 800-433-MTSU (out-of-state) **Fax:** 615-898-5478
E-mail: admissions@mtsu.edu

Getting in Last Year 7,051 applied; 78% were accepted; 3,136 enrolled (57%).

Financial Matters $3442 resident tuition and fees (2002–03); $10,400 nonresident tuition and fees (2002–03); $4060 room and board; 80% average percent of need met; $5057 average financial aid amount received per undergraduate (2001–02).

Academics MTSU awards associate, bachelor's, master's, and doctoral degrees and post-master's certificates. Challenging opportunities include advanced placement credit, accelerated degree programs, student-designed majors, freshman honors college, an honors program, double majors, independent study, and a senior project. Special programs include cooperative education, internships, summer session for credit, off-campus study, study-abroad, and Army and Air Force ROTC. The most frequently chosen baccalaureate fields are business/marketing, interdisciplinary studies, and visual/performing arts. The faculty at MTSU has 704 full-time members, 88% with terminal degrees. The student-faculty ratio is 24:1.

Students of MTSU The student body totals 21,163, of whom 19,160 are undergraduates. 53.8% are women and 46.2% are men. 92% are from Tennessee. 68% returned for their sophomore year.

Applying MTSU requires SAT I or ACT, a high school transcript, and a minimum high school GPA of 2.8, and in some cases an essay. Application deadline: rolling admissions; 5/15 priority date for financial aid. Early and deferred admission are possible.

MIDLAND LUTHERAN COLLEGE

Fremont, NE

Small-town setting ■ Private ■ Independent Religious ■ Coed

Web site: www.mlc.edu
Contact: Ms. Stacy Poggendorf, Assistant Vice President for Admissions, Admissions Office, Fremont, NE 68025-4200
Telephone: 402-941-6508 or toll-free 800-642-8382 ext. 6501
Fax: 402-941-6513
E-mail: admissions@admin.mlc.edu

Getting in Last Year 937 applied; 86% were accepted; 261 enrolled (33%).

Financial Matters $15,400 tuition and fees (2002–03); $4310 room and board; 92% average percent of need met; $13,600 average financial aid amount received per undergraduate.

Academics Midland awards associate and bachelor's degrees. Challenging opportunities include advanced placement credit, accelerated degree programs, student-designed majors, an honors program, double majors, independent study, and a senior project. Special programs include cooperative education, internships, summer session for credit, off-campus study, and study-abroad. The most frequently chosen baccalaureate fields are business/marketing, education, and social sciences and history. The faculty at Midland has 57 full-time members, 58% with terminal degrees. The student-faculty ratio is 15:1.

Students of Midland The student body is made up of 946 undergraduates. 58.1% are women and 41.9% are men. Students come from 24 states and territories. 77% are from Nebraska. 0.4% are international students. 80% returned for their sophomore year.

Applying Midland requires SAT I or ACT and a high school transcript, and in some cases an interview. The school recommends an essay, recommendations, and a minimum high school GPA of 3.0. Application deadline: rolling admissions. Early admission is possible.

MIDWAY COLLEGE

Midway, KY

Small-town setting ■ Private ■ Independent Religious ■ Women Only

Web site: www.midway.edu
Contact: Mr. Jim Wombles, Vice President of Admissions, 512 East Stephens Street, Pinkerton Building, Midway, KY 40347-1120
Telephone: 859-846-5799 or toll-free 800-755-0031 **Fax:** 859-846-5823
E-mail: admissions@midway.edu

Getting in Last Year 369 applied; 74% were accepted; 108 enrolled (39%).

Financial Matters $10,950 tuition and fees (2002–03); $5540 room and board; 74% average percent of need met; $8973 average financial aid amount received per undergraduate.

Academics Midway College awards associate and bachelor's degrees. Challenging opportunities include advanced placement credit, an honors program, independent study, and a senior project. Special programs include internships, summer session for credit, off-campus study, study-abroad, and Army ROTC. The most frequently chosen baccalaureate fields are business/marketing, agriculture, and education. The faculty at Midway College has 35 full-time members, 57% with terminal degrees. The student-faculty ratio is 14:1.

Students of Midway College The student body is made up of 1,042 undergraduates. Students come from 28 states and territories and 5 other countries. 89% are from Kentucky. 0.7% are international students. 64% returned for their sophomore year.

Applying Midway College requires SAT I or ACT and a high school transcript, and in some cases an essay, an interview, and recommendations. The school recommends a minimum high school GPA of 2.2. Application deadline: rolling admissions; 3/15 priority date for financial aid. Early and deferred admission are possible.

MIDWESTERN STATE UNIVERSITY

Wichita Falls, TX

Urban setting ■ Public ■ State-supported ■ Coed

Web site: www.mwsu.edu

Contact: Barbara Merkle, Director of Admissions, 3410 Taft Boulevard, Wichita Falls, TX 76308

Telephone: 940-397-4334 or toll-free 800-842-1922 **Fax:** 940-397-4672

E-mail: admissions@mwsu.edu

Getting in Last Year 2,196 applied; 68% were accepted; 762 enrolled (51%).

Financial Matters $3064 resident tuition and fees (2002–03); $9604 nonresident tuition and fees (2002–03); $4434 room and board; 60% average percent of need met.

Academics MSU awards associate, bachelor's, and master's degrees. Challenging opportunities include advanced placement credit, accelerated degree programs, an honors program, and a senior project. Special programs include internships, summer session for credit, study-abroad, and Air Force ROTC. The most frequently chosen baccalaureate fields are business/marketing, health professions and related sciences, and interdisciplinary studies. The faculty at MSU has 200 full-time members, 65% with terminal degrees. The student-faculty ratio is 20:1.

Students of MSU The student body totals 6,218, of whom 5,515 are undergraduates. 56.2% are women and 43.8% are men. Students come from 44 states and territories and 45 other countries. 95% are from Texas. 5% are international students. 64% returned for their sophomore year.

Applying MSU requires SAT I or ACT and a high school transcript. Application deadline: 8/7; 6/1 priority date for financial aid. Early and deferred admission are possible.

MIDWESTERN UNIVERSITY, GLENDALE CAMPUS

Glendale, AZ

Private ■ Independent ■ Coed

Web site: www.midwestern.edu

Contact: Mr. James Walter, Director of Admissions, 19555 North 59th Avenue, Glendale, AZ 85308

Telephone: 623-572-3340 or toll-free 888-247-9277 (in-state), 888-247-9271 (out-of-state) **Fax:** 623-572-3229

E-mail: admissionaz@arizona.midwestern.edu

Financial Matters $13,947 tuition and fees (2002–03); $2600 room only; 100% average percent of need met; $25,000 average financial aid amount received per undergraduate.

Academics Midwestern University, Glendale Campus awards bachelor's, master's, and doctoral degrees and post-bachelor's certificates.

Students of Midwestern University, Glendale Campus The student body totals 1,117, of whom 45 are undergraduates.

Applying Application deadline: 4/15 for financial aid, with a 3/10 priority date.

MILES COLLEGE

Birmingham, AL

Small-town setting ■ Private ■ Independent Religious ■ Coed

Web site: www.miles.edu

Contact: Dr. Sherrel Price, Interim Director of Admissions and Recruitment, PO Box 3800, Birmingham, AL 35208

Telephone: 205-929-1657

Getting in Last Year 500 applied; 100% were accepted.

Financial Matters $5008 tuition and fees (2002–03); $3800 room and board; $6744 average financial aid amount received per undergraduate.

Academics Miles awards bachelor's degrees. Challenging opportunities include accelerated degree programs, an honors program, and a senior project. Special programs include cooperative education, internships, summer session for credit, off-campus study, and Army and Air Force ROTC. The faculty at Miles has 87 full-time members, 38% with terminal degrees. The student-faculty ratio is 21:1.

Students of Miles The student body is made up of 1,807 undergraduates. 57.9% are women and 42.1% are men. Students come from 21 states and territories. 0.1% are international students. 78% returned for their sophomore year.

Applying Miles requires SAT I or ACT and a high school transcript. The school recommends recommendations. Application deadline: rolling admissions; 4/1 priority date for financial aid.

MILLERSVILLE UNIVERSITY OF PENNSYLVANIA

Millersville, PA

Suburban setting ■ Public ■ State-supported ■ Coed

Web site: www.millersville.edu

Contact: Mr. Douglas Zander, Director of Admissions, PO Box 1002, Millersville, PA 17551-0302

Telephone: 717-872-3371 or toll-free 800-MU-ADMIT (out-of-state) **Fax:** 717-871-2147

E-mail: admissions@millersville.edu

Getting in Last Year 6,019 applied; 63% were accepted; 1,293 enrolled (34%).

Financial Matters $5547 resident tuition and fees (2002–03); $12,115 nonresident tuition and fees (2002–03); $5310 room and board; 88% average percent of need met; $5672 average financial aid amount received per undergraduate (2001–02).

Academics Millersville University awards associate, bachelor's, and master's degrees and post-bachelor's and post-master's certificates. Challenging opportunities include advanced placement credit, accelerated degree programs, an honors program, double majors, independent study, and a senior project. Special programs include cooperative education, internships, summer session for credit, off-campus study, study-abroad, and Army ROTC. The most frequently chosen baccalaureate fields are education, business/marketing, and social sciences and history. The faculty at Millersville University has 295 full-time members, 93% with terminal degrees. The student-faculty ratio is 18:1.

Students of Millersville University The student body totals 7,650, of whom 6,646 are undergraduates. 57.7% are women and 42.3% are men. Students come from 23 states and territories and 48 other countries. 96% are from Pennsylvania. 0.6% are international students. 81% returned for their sophomore year.

Applying Millersville University requires SAT I or ACT, a high school transcript, and a minimum high school GPA of 2.0, and in some cases recommendations. The school recommends recommendations. Application deadline: rolling admissions; 3/15 for financial aid. Early and deferred admission are possible.

MILLIGAN COLLEGE

Milligan College, TN

Suburban setting ■ Private ■ Independent Religious ■ Coed

Web site: www.milligan.edu

Contact: Mr. David Mee, Vice President for Enrollment Management, PO Box 210, Milligan College, TN 37682

Telephone: 423-461-8730 or toll-free 800-262-8337 (in-state) **Fax:** 423-461-8982

E-mail: admissions@milligan.edu

Getting in Last Year 617 applied; 88% were accepted; 165 enrolled (30%).

Financial Matters $14,390 tuition and fees (2002–03); $4370 room and board; 89% average percent of need met; $14,993 average financial aid amount received per undergraduate (2001–02).

Academics Milligan awards bachelor's and master's degrees. Challenging opportunities include advanced placement credit, double majors, independent study, and a senior project. Special programs include cooperative education, internships, summer session for credit, off-campus study, study-abroad, and Army ROTC. The most frequently chosen baccalaureate fields are business/marketing, education, and biological/life sciences. The faculty at Milligan has 66 full-time members, 70% with terminal degrees. The student-faculty ratio is 11:1.

Students of Milligan The student body totals 839, of whom 757 are undergraduates. 59.2% are women and 40.8% are men. Students come from 37 states and territories and 4 other countries. 43% are from Tennessee. 1.7% are international students. 73% returned for their sophomore year.

Applying Milligan requires an essay, SAT I or ACT, a high school transcript, 2 recommendations, and a minimum high school GPA of 2.0, and in some cases an interview. The school recommends a minimum high school GPA of 3.0. Application deadline: rolling admissions; 3/1 priority date for financial aid. Deferred admission is possible.

MILLIKIN UNIVERSITY

Decatur, IL

Suburban setting ■ Private ■ Independent Religious ■ Coed

Web site: www.millikin.edu

Contact: Ms. Patricia Knox, Dean of Admission, 1184 West Main Street, Decatur, IL 62522-2084

Telephone: 217-424-6210 or toll-free 800-373-7733 ext. # 5 **Fax:** 217-425-4669

E-mail: admis@mail.millikin.edu

Getting in Last Year 2,753 applied; 78% were accepted; 638 enrolled (30%).

Financial Matters $18,384 tuition and fees (2002–03); $6106 room and board; 89% average percent of need met; $15,641 average financial aid amount received per undergraduate.

Academics Millikin awards bachelor's and master's degrees. Challenging opportunities include advanced placement credit, student-designed majors, an honors program, double majors, independent study, and a senior project. Special programs include internships, summer session for credit, off-campus study, and study-abroad. The most frequently chosen baccalaureate fields are business/marketing, visual/performing arts, and education. The faculty at Millikin has 152 full-time members, 84% with terminal degrees. The student-faculty ratio is 13:1.

Students of Millikin The student body totals 2,496, of whom 2,468 are undergraduates. 56.2% are women and 43.8% are men. Students come from 33 states and territories and 12 other countries. 84% are from Illinois. 0.5% are international students. 79% returned for their sophomore year.

Applying Millikin requires SAT I or ACT, a high school transcript, 2 recommendations, and a minimum high school GPA of 2.0, and in some cases audition for school of music; portfolio review for art program. The school recommends an interview. Application deadline: rolling admissions; 6/1 for financial aid, with a 4/15 priority date. Deferred admission is possible.

MILLSAPS COLLEGE

Jackson, MS

Urban setting ■ Private ■ Independent Religious ■ Coed

Web site: www.millsaps.edu

Contact: Ms. Ann Hendrick, Dean of Admissions and Financial Aid, 1701 North State Street, Jackson, MS 39210-0001

Telephone: 601-974-1050 or toll-free 800-352-1050 **Fax:** 601-974-1059

E-mail: admissions@millsaps.edu

Getting in Last Year 913 applied; 87% were accepted; 251 enrolled (31%).

Financial Matters $17,362 tuition and fees (2002–03); $6364 room and board; 87% average percent of need met; $16,072 average financial aid amount received per undergraduate.

Academics Millsaps awards bachelor's and master's degrees. Challenging opportunities include advanced placement credit, an honors program, double majors, independent study, and a senior project. Special programs include cooperative education, internships, summer session for credit, off-campus study, study-abroad, and Army ROTC. The most frequently chosen baccalaureate fields are business/marketing, social sciences and history, and psychology. The faculty at Millsaps has 93 full-time members, 92% with terminal degrees. The student-faculty ratio is 13:1.

Students of Millsaps The student body totals 1,251, of whom 1,158 are undergraduates. 54.8% are women and 45.2% are men. Students come from 29 states and territories and 8 other countries. 50% are from Mississippi. 0.9% are international students. 83% returned for their sophomore year.

Applying Millsaps requires an essay, SAT I or ACT, a high school transcript, and a minimum high school GPA of 2.5. The school recommends an interview and recommendations. Application deadline: 2/1; 3/1 priority date for financial aid. Early and deferred admission are possible.

MILLS COLLEGE

Oakland, CA

Urban setting ■ Private ■ Independent ■ Women Only

Web site: www.mills.edu

Contact: Avis Hinkson, Dean of Admission, 5000 MacArthur Boulevard, Oakland, CA 94613-1301

Telephone: 510-430-2135 or toll-free 800-87-MILLS **Fax:** 510-430-3314

E-mail: admission@mills.edu

Getting in Last Year 498 applied; 74% were accepted; 113 enrolled (31%).

Financial Matters $22,128 tuition and fees (2002–03); $8500 room and board; 86% average percent of need met; $20,357 average financial aid amount received per undergraduate.

Academics Mills awards bachelor's, master's, and doctoral degrees and post-bachelor's certificates. Challenging opportunities include advanced placement credit, student-designed majors, double majors, independent study, and a senior project. Special programs include internships, off-campus study, and Army ROTC. The most frequently chosen baccalaureate fields are mathematics, visual/performing arts, and social sciences and history. The faculty at Mills has 87 full-time members, 80% with terminal degrees. The student-faculty ratio is 10:1.

Students of Mills The student body totals 1,176, of whom 742 are undergraduates. Students come from 36 states and territories. 75% are from California. 80% returned for their sophomore year.

Applying Mills requires SAT I or ACT, a high school transcript, 3 recommendations, and essay or graded paper. The school recommends SAT II Subject Tests and an interview. Application deadline: 2/1; 2/15 priority date for financial aid. Deferred admission is possible.

MILWAUKEE INSTITUTE OF ART AND DESIGN

Milwaukee, WI

Urban setting ■ Private ■ Independent ■ Coed

Web site: www.miad.edu

Contact: Mr. Mark Fetherston, Director of Admissions, 273 East Erie Street, Milwaukee, WI 53202

Telephone: 414-847-3259 or toll-free 888-749-MIAD **Fax:** 414-291-8077

E-mail: admissions@miad.edu

Getting in Last Year 336 applied; 84% were accepted; 141 enrolled (50%).

Financial Matters $20,030 tuition and fees (2002–03); $6538 room and board; 70% average percent of need met; $14,115 average financial aid amount received per undergraduate (2001–02).

Academics MIAD awards bachelor's degrees. Challenging opportunities include advanced placement credit, double majors, independent study, and a senior project. Special programs include cooperative education, internships, summer session for credit, off-campus study, and study-abroad. The most frequently chosen baccalaureate field is visual/performing arts. The faculty at MIAD has 36 full-time members, 81% with terminal degrees. The student-faculty ratio is 16:1.

Students of MIAD The student body is made up of 632 undergraduates. 51.3% are women and 48.7% are men. Students come from 16 states and territories and 5 other countries. 72% are from Wisconsin. 2.4% are international students. 73% returned for their sophomore year.

Applying MIAD requires an essay, a high school transcript, an interview, and portfolio, and in some cases recommendations. The school recommends SAT I or ACT and a minimum high school GPA of 2.0. Application deadline: rolling admissions; 3/1 for financial aid. Deferred admission is possible.

MILWAUKEE SCHOOL OF ENGINEERING

Milwaukee, WI

Urban setting ■ Private ■ Independent ■ Coed, Primarily Men

Web site: www.msoe.edu

Contact: Mr. Tim A. Valley, Dean of Enrollment Management, 1025 North Broadway, Milwaukee, WI 53202-3109

Telephone: 414-277-6763 or toll-free 800-332-6763 **Fax:** 414-277-7475

E-mail: explore@msoe.edu

Getting in Last Year 1,749 applied; 72% were accepted; 508 enrolled (40%).

Financial Matters $21,855 tuition and fees (2002–03); $5115 room and board; 70% average percent of need met; $15,348 average financial aid amount received per undergraduate (2001–02).

Academics MSOE awards bachelor's and master's degrees. Challenging opportunities include advanced placement credit, accelerated degree programs, double majors, independent study, and a senior project. Special programs include internships, summer session for credit, study-abroad, and Army, Navy and Air Force ROTC. The most frequently chosen baccalaureate fields are engineering/engineering technologies, business/marketing, and communications/communication technologies. The faculty at MSOE has 120 full-time members, 58% with terminal degrees. The student-faculty ratio is 11:1.

Students of MSOE The student body totals 2,586, of whom 2,272 are undergraduates. 15.6% are women and 84.4% are men. Students come from 31 states and territories and 19 other countries. 79% are from Wisconsin. 3.1% are international students. 77% returned for their sophomore year.

Applying MSOE requires SAT I or ACT, a high school transcript, and a minimum high school GPA of 2.5, and in some cases an essay and an interview. Application deadline: rolling admissions. Deferred admission is possible.

MINNEAPOLIS COLLEGE OF ART AND DESIGN

Minneapolis, MN

Urban setting ■ Private ■ Independent ■ Coed

Web site: www.mcad.edu

Contact: Mr. William Mullen, Director of Admissions, 2501 Stevens Avenue South, Minneapolis, MN 55404-4347

Telephone: 612-874-3762 or toll-free 800-874-6223

E-mail: admissions@mn.mcad.edu

Getting in Last Year 222 applied; 73% were accepted; 123 enrolled (75%).

Financial Matters $21,440 tuition and fees (2002–03); $5300 room and board; 89% average percent of need met; $12,761 average financial aid amount received per undergraduate.

Academics MCAD awards bachelor's and master's degrees and post-bachelor's certificates. Challenging opportunities include advanced placement credit, independent study, and a senior project. Special programs include cooperative education, internships, summer session for credit, off-campus study, and study-abroad. The most frequently chosen baccalaureate field is visual/performing arts. The faculty at MCAD has 36 full-time members, 53% with terminal degrees. The student-faculty ratio is 15:1.

Students of MCAD The student body totals 659, of whom 606 are undergraduates. 42.6% are women and 57.4% are men. Students come from 30 states and territories. 61% are from Minnesota. 76% returned for their sophomore year.

Applying MCAD requires an essay, SAT I or ACT, a high school transcript, an interview, and 1 recommendation, and in some cases portfolio. Application deadline: rolling admissions; 3/15 priority date for financial aid. Early and deferred admission are possible.

MINNESOTA STATE UNIVERSITY, MANKATO

Mankato, MN

Small-town setting ■ Public ■ State-supported ■ Coed

Web site: www.mnsu.edu

Contact: Mr. Walt Wolff, Director of Admissions, 122 Taylor Center, Mankato, MN 56001

Telephone: 507-389-6670 or toll-free 800-722-0544 **Fax:** 507-389-1511

E-mail: admissions@mnsu.edu

Minnesota State University, Mankato (continued)

Getting in Last Year 4,877 applied; 89% were accepted; 2,083 enrolled (48%).

Financial Matters $3981 resident tuition and fees (2002–03); $7691 nonresident tuition and fees (2002–03); $4018 room and board; 82% average percent of need met; $5992 average financial aid amount received per undergraduate.

Academics Mankato State awards associate, bachelor's, and master's degrees and post-master's certificates. Challenging opportunities include advanced placement credit, student-designed majors, an honors program, double majors, independent study, and a senior project. Special programs include internships, summer session for credit, off-campus study, study-abroad, and Army ROTC. The most frequently chosen baccalaureate fields are business/marketing, education, and protective services/public administration. The faculty at Mankato State has 452 full-time members, 81% with terminal degrees. The student-faculty ratio is 24:1.

Students of Mankato State The student body totals 13,795, of whom 12,087 are undergraduates. 52.1% are women and 47.9% are men. Students come from 40 states and territories and 71 other countries. 88% are from Minnesota. 4.2% are international students. 77% returned for their sophomore year.

Applying Mankato State requires ACT and a high school transcript, and in some cases an essay and 3 recommendations. Application deadline: rolling admissions; 3/15 priority date for financial aid. Early and deferred admission are possible.

MINNESOTA STATE UNIVERSITY, MOORHEAD

Moorhead, MN

Urban setting ■ Public ■ State-supported ■ Coed

Web site: www.mnstate.edu

Contact: Ms. Gina Monson, Director of Admissions, Owens Hall, Moorhead, MN 56563-0002

Telephone: 218-236-2161 or toll-free 800-593-7246 **Fax:** 218-236-2168

Financial Matters $3388 resident tuition and fees (2002–03); $6958 nonresident tuition and fees (2002–03); $3706 room and board; $4094 average financial aid amount received per undergraduate.

Academics Minnesota State University, Moorhead awards associate, bachelor's, and master's degrees and post-master's certificates. Challenging opportunities include advanced placement credit, student-designed majors, freshman honors college, an honors program, double majors, independent study, and a senior project. Special programs include internships, summer session for credit, off-campus study, study-abroad, and Army and Air Force ROTC. The most frequently chosen baccalaureate field is law/legal studies. The faculty at Minnesota State University, Moorhead has 299 full-time members. The student-faculty ratio is 18:1.

Students of Minnesota State University, Moorhead The student body totals 7,431, of whom 7,048 are undergraduates. 62.4% are women and 37.6% are men. Students come from 34 states and territories and 32 other countries. 62% are from Minnesota. 1.9% are international students. 68% returned for their sophomore year.

Applying Minnesota State University, Moorhead requires SAT I or ACT, PSAT, and a high school transcript. Application deadline: 8/7; 3/1 priority date for financial aid. Early and deferred admission are possible.

MINOT STATE UNIVERSITY

Minot, ND

Small-town setting ■ Public ■ State-supported ■ Coed

Web site: www.minotstateu.edu

Contact: Ms. Lauralee Moseanko, Admissions Specialist, 500 University Avenue West, Minot, ND 58707-0002

Telephone: 701-858-3346 or toll-free 800-777-0750 ext. 3350 **Fax:** 701-839-6933

E-mail: askmsu@misu.nodak.edu

Getting in Last Year 743 applied; 86% were accepted; 567 enrolled (89%).

Financial Matters $2806 resident tuition and fees (2002–03); $6720 nonresident tuition and fees (2002–03); $3162 room and board; 91% average percent of need met; $5217 average financial aid amount received per undergraduate.

Academics Minot State awards bachelor's and master's degrees and post-master's certificates. Challenging opportunities include advanced placement credit, accelerated degree programs, student-designed majors, an honors program, double majors, independent study, and a senior project. Special programs include cooperative education, internships, summer session for credit, and study-abroad. The most frequently chosen baccalaureate fields are business/marketing, education, and protective services/public administration. The faculty at Minot State has 164 full-time members, 50% with terminal degrees. The student-faculty ratio is 16:1.

Students of Minot State The student body totals 3,625, of whom 3,425 are undergraduates. 63.4% are women and 36.6% are men. Students come from 40 states and territories and 18 other countries. 89% are from North Dakota. 5.1% are international students. 62% returned for their sophomore year.

Applying Minot State requires SAT I or ACT and a high school transcript, and in some cases a minimum high school GPA of 2.75. Application deadline: rolling admissions; 4/15 priority date for financial aid. Deferred admission is possible.

MISSISSIPPI COLLEGE

Clinton, MS

Suburban setting ■ Private ■ Independent Religious ■ Coed

Web site: www.mc.edu

Contact: Mr. Chad Phillips, Director of Admissions, PO Box 4026, South Capitol Street, Clinton, MS 39058

Telephone: 601-925-3800 or toll-free 800-738-1236 **Fax:** 601-925-3804

E-mail: enrollment-services@mc.edu

Getting in Last Year 1,145 applied; 68% were accepted; 412 enrolled (53%).

Financial Matters $10,712 tuition and fees (2002–03); $4680 room and board; 76% average percent of need met; $12,602 average financial aid amount received per undergraduate (2001–02).

Academics MC awards bachelor's, master's, and first-professional degrees and post-bachelor's certificates. Challenging opportunities include advanced placement credit, freshman honors college, an honors program, double majors, independent study, and a senior project. Special programs include cooperative education, internships, summer session for credit, study-abroad, and Army ROTC. The most frequently chosen baccalaureate fields are business/marketing, education, and biological/life sciences. The faculty at MC has 155 full-time members, 73% with terminal degrees. The student-faculty ratio is 15:1.

Students of MC The student body totals 3,227, of whom 2,269 are undergraduates. 59.7% are women and 40.3% are men. Students come from 36 states and territories and 4 other countries. 84% are from Mississippi. 0.1% are international students. 79% returned for their sophomore year.

Applying MC requires an essay, SAT I or ACT, and a high school transcript. The school recommends an interview, 1 recommendation, and a minimum high school GPA of 2.0. Application deadline: rolling admissions; 3/1 priority date for financial aid. Early and deferred admission are possible.

MISSISSIPPI STATE UNIVERSITY

Mississippi State, MS

Small-town setting ■ Public ■ State-supported ■ Coed

Web site: www.msstate.edu

Contact: Ms. Diane D. Wolfe, Director of Admissions, PO Box 6305, Mississippi State, MS 39762

Telephone: 662-325-2224 **Fax:** 662-325-7360

E-mail: admit@admissions.msstate.edu

Getting in Last Year 5,000 applied; 74% were accepted; 1,759 enrolled (48%).

Financial Matters $3874 resident tuition and fees (2002–03); $8780 nonresident tuition and fees (2002–03); $6080 room and board; 72% average percent of need met; $7142 average financial aid amount received per undergraduate (2001–02).

Academics MSU awards bachelor's, master's, doctoral, and first-professional degrees and post-master's certificates. Challenging opportunities include advanced placement credit, accelerated degree programs, student-designed majors, freshman honors college, an honors program, double majors, independent study, and a senior project. Special programs include cooperative education, internships, summer session for credit, off-campus study, study-abroad, and Army and Air Force ROTC. The most frequently chosen baccalaureate fields are business/marketing, education, and engineering/engineering technologies. The faculty at MSU has 971 full-time members, 88% with terminal degrees. The student-faculty ratio is 16:1.

Students of MSU The student body totals 16,610, of whom 13,373 are undergraduates. 46.7% are women and 53.3% are men. Students come from 51 states and territories and 40 other countries. 80% are from Mississippi. 1.1% are international students. 80% returned for their sophomore year.

Applying MSU requires SAT I or ACT, a high school transcript, and a minimum high school GPA of 2.0, and in some cases Placement testing and counseling for entering students with academic deficiencies and recommendations. Application deadline: 5/1; 4/1 priority date for financial aid. Early and deferred admission are possible.

MISSISSIPPI VALLEY STATE UNIVERSITY

Itta Bena, MS

Small-town setting ■ Public ■ State-supported ■ Coed

Web site: www.mvsu.edu

Contact: Mr. Wilson Lee, Director of Admissions and Recruitment, 14000 Highway 82 West, Itta Bena, MS 38941-1400

Telephone: 662-254-3344 or toll-free 800-844-6885 (in-state) **Fax:** 662-254-7900

Getting in Last Year 3,783 applied; 19% were accepted; 270 enrolled (38%).

Financial Matters $3410 resident tuition and fees (2002–03); $7965 nonresident tuition and fees (2002–03); $3374 room and board; 80% average percent of need met; $7000 average financial aid amount received per undergraduate.

Academics Valley State awards bachelor's and master's degrees. Challenging opportunities include freshman honors college, an honors program, and a senior project. Special programs include cooperative education, internships, summer session for credit, and Army and Air Force ROTC. The most frequently chosen baccalaureate fields are protective services/public administration, education, and social sciences and history. The faculty at Valley State has 106 full-time members, 55% with terminal degrees. The student-faculty ratio is 23:1.

Students of Valley State The student body totals 3,501, of whom 3,014 are undergraduates. 69.6% are women and 30.4% are men. Students come from 21 states and territories. 94% are from Mississippi. 74% returned for their sophomore year.

Applying Valley State requires SAT I or ACT and a high school transcript. The school recommends an interview. Application deadline: rolling admissions; 4/1 priority date for financial aid. Deferred admission is possible.

MISSOURI SOUTHERN STATE COLLEGE

Joplin, MO

Small-town setting ■ Public ■ State-supported ■ Coed

Web site: www.mssc.edu

Contact: Mr. Derek Skaggs, Director of Enrollment Services, 3950 East Newman Road, Joplin, MO 64801-1595

Telephone: 417-625-9537 or toll-free 800-606-MSSC **Fax:** 417-659-4429

E-mail: admissions@mail.mssc.edu

Getting in Last Year 1,809 applied; 74% were accepted; 725 enrolled (54%).

Financial Matters $3886 resident tuition and fees (2002–03); $7606 nonresident tuition and fees (2002–03); $4000 room and board; 66% average percent of need met; $4682 average financial aid amount received per undergraduate.

Academics Missouri Southern State awards associate and bachelor's degrees. Challenging opportunities include advanced placement credit, accelerated degree programs, an honors program, double majors, independent study, and a senior project. Special programs include cooperative education, internships, summer session for credit, off-campus study, and study-abroad. The most frequently chosen baccalaureate fields are business/marketing, education, and protective services/public administration. The faculty at Missouri Southern State has 202 full-time members, 62% with terminal degrees. The student-faculty ratio is 18:1.

Students of Missouri Southern State The student body is made up of 5,782 undergraduates. 58.6% are women and 41.4% are men. Students come from 31 states and territories and 32 other countries. 87% are from Missouri. 2% are international students. 64% returned for their sophomore year.

Applying Missouri Southern State requires SAT I or ACT and a high school transcript, and in some cases ACT and Michigan Test of English Language Proficiency. Application deadline: 8/3; 2/15 priority date for financial aid. Deferred admission is possible.

MISSOURI TECH

St. Louis, MO

Suburban setting ■ Private ■ Proprietary ■ Coed, Primarily Men

Web site: www.motech.edu

Contact: Mr. Bob Honaker, Director of Admissions, 1167 Corporate Lake Drive, St. Louis, MO 63132

Telephone: 314-569-3600 ext. 363 or toll-free 800-960-8324 (out-of-state) **Fax:** 314-569-1167

Getting in Last Year 13 enrolled (100%).

Financial Matters $11,593 tuition and fees (2002–03); $3190 room only.

Academics Missouri Tech awards associate and bachelor's degrees. Challenging opportunities include advanced placement credit, accelerated degree programs, and a senior project. Special programs include internships and summer session for credit. The most frequently chosen baccalaureate field is engineering/engineering technologies. The faculty at Missouri Tech has 7 full-time members, 29% with terminal degrees. The student-faculty ratio is 10:1.

Students of Missouri Tech The student body is made up of 193 undergraduates. 10.9% are women and 89.1% are men. Students come from 4 states and territories and 8 other countries.

Applying Missouri Tech requires a high school transcript, and in some cases an interview and minimum ACT score of 20. The school recommends ACT. Application deadline: rolling admissions.

MISSOURI VALLEY COLLEGE

Marshall, MO

Small-town setting ■ Private ■ Independent Religious ■ Coed

Web site: www.moval.edu

Contact: Ms. Debbie Bultman, Admissions, 500 East College, Marshall, MO 65340-3197

Telephone: 660-831-4114 **Fax:** 660-831-4039

E-mail: admissions@moval.edu

Getting in Last Year 1,105 applied; 85% were accepted; 430 enrolled (46%).

Financial Matters $12,750 tuition and fees (2002–03); $5200 room and board; 80% average percent of need met; $12,141 average financial aid amount received per undergraduate.

Academics Missouri Valley awards associate and bachelor's degrees. Challenging opportunities include advanced placement credit, double majors, independent study, and a senior project. Special programs include cooperative education, internships, summer session for credit, and Army ROTC. The most frequently chosen baccalaureate fields are business/marketing, education, and protective services/public administration. The faculty at Missouri Valley has 68 full-time members, 38% with terminal degrees. The student-faculty ratio is 17:1.

Students of Missouri Valley The student body is made up of 1,600 undergraduates. 44.1% are women and 55.9% are men. Students come from 40 states and territories and 29 other countries. 66% are from Missouri. 5.8% are international students. 49% returned for their sophomore year.

Applying Missouri Valley requires SAT I or ACT and a high school transcript, and in some cases an essay, an interview, and 3 recommendations. The school recommends SAT II: Writing Test, an interview, and a minimum high school GPA of 2.0. Application deadline: rolling admissions; 9/15 for financial aid, with a 3/20 priority date. Early and deferred admission are possible.

MISSOURI WESTERN STATE COLLEGE

St. Joseph, MO

Suburban setting ■ Public ■ State-supported ■ Coed

Web site: www.mwsc.edu

Contact: Mr. Howard McCauley, Director of Admissions, 4525 Downs Drive, St. Joseph, MO 64507-2294

Telephone: 816-271-4267 or toll-free 800-662-7041 ext. 60 **Fax:** 816-271-5833

E-mail: admissn@mwsc.edu

Getting in Last Year 2,789 applied; 100% were accepted; 1,234 enrolled (44%).

Financial Matters $4064 resident tuition and fees (2002–03); $7370 nonresident tuition and fees (2002–03); $3804 room and board; 18% average percent of need met; $6677 average financial aid amount received per undergraduate (2001–02).

Academics MWSC awards associate and bachelor's degrees. Challenging opportunities include advanced placement credit, accelerated degree programs, freshman honors college, an honors program, double majors, and a senior project. Special programs include internships, summer session for credit, and Army ROTC. The most frequently chosen baccalaureate fields are business/marketing, protective services/public administration, and education. The faculty at MWSC has 186 full-time members, 75% with terminal degrees. The student-faculty ratio is 19:1.

Students of MWSC The student body is made up of 5,197 undergraduates. 60.9% are women and 39.1% are men. Students come from 33 states and territories and 7 other countries. 94% are from Missouri. 0.2% are international students. 56% returned for their sophomore year.

Applying MWSC requires ACT and a high school transcript. Application deadline: 7/30; 4/1 priority date for financial aid. Early admission is possible.

MITCHELL COLLEGE

New London, CT

Suburban setting ■ Private ■ Independent ■ Coed

Web site: www.mitchell.edu

Contact: Ms. Kathleen E. Neal, Director of Admissions, 437 Pequot Avenue, New London, CT 06320

Telephone: 800-443-2811 or toll-free 800-443-2811 **Fax:** 860-444-1209

E-mail: admissions@mitchell.edu

Getting in Last Year 1,158 applied; 58% were accepted; 191 enrolled (28%).

Financial Matters $17,230 tuition and fees (2002–03); $7875 room and board.

Academics Mitchell awards associate and bachelor's degrees. Challenging opportunities include advanced placement credit, double majors, and a senior project. Special programs include cooperative education, internships, and summer session for credit. The most frequently chosen baccalaureate field is social sciences and history. The faculty at Mitchell has 26 full-time members, 46% with terminal degrees. The student-faculty ratio is 12:1.

Students of Mitchell The student body is made up of 555 undergraduates. 51.7% are women and 48.3% are men. Students come from 22 states and territories and 5 other countries. 58% are from Connecticut. 1.8% are international students.

Applying Mitchell requires an essay, SAT I or ACT, a high school transcript, recommendations, and a minimum high school GPA of 2.0. The school recommends an interview. Application deadline: rolling admissions; 4/1 priority date for financial aid. Early and deferred admission are possible.

MOLLOY COLLEGE

Rockville Centre, NY

Suburban setting ■ Private ■ Independent ■ Coed

Molloy College (continued)

Contact: Ms. Marguerite Lane, Director of Admissions, 1000 Hempstead Avenue, PO Box 5002, Rockville Centre, NY 11571-5002
Telephone: 516-678-5000 or toll-free 888-4MOLLOY **Fax:** 516-256-2247
E-mail: admissions@molloy.edu

Getting in Last Year 661 applied; 77% were accepted; 244 enrolled (48%).

Financial Matters $14,610 tuition and fees (2002–03); 75% average percent of need met.

Academics Molloy College awards associate, bachelor's, and master's degrees and post-master's certificates. Challenging opportunities include advanced placement credit, student-designed majors, an honors program, and double majors. Special programs include cooperative education, internships, summer session for credit, study-abroad, and Army, Navy and Air Force ROTC. The faculty at Molloy College has 129 full-time members, 54% with terminal degrees. The student-faculty ratio is 11:1.

Students of Molloy College The student body totals 2,893, of whom 2,318 are undergraduates. 76.4% are women and 23.6% are men. Students come from 4 states and territories and 7 other countries. 0.7% are international students. 82% returned for their sophomore year.

Applying Molloy College requires an essay, SAT I or ACT, and a high school transcript, and in some cases 1 recommendation. The school recommends an interview. Application deadline: rolling admissions; 5/1 priority date for financial aid. Early and deferred admission are possible.

MONMOUTH COLLEGE

Monmouth, IL

Small-town setting ■ Private ■ Independent Religious ■ Coed

Web site: www.monm.edu
Contact: Vice President for Enrollment, 700 East Broadway, Monmouth, IL 61462-1998
Telephone: 309-457-2131 or toll-free 800-747-2687 **Fax:** 309-457-2141
E-mail: admit@monm.edu

Getting in Last Year 1,372 applied; 75% were accepted; 291 enrolled (28%).

Financial Matters $17,760 tuition and fees (2002–03); $4730 room and board; 94% average percent of need met; $15,376 average financial aid amount received per undergraduate (2001–02).

Academics Monmouth awards bachelor's degrees. Challenging opportunities include advanced placement credit, student-designed majors, an honors program, double majors, independent study, and a senior project. Special programs include internships, off-campus study, study-abroad, and Army ROTC. The most frequently chosen baccalaureate fields are business/marketing, education, and social sciences and history. The faculty at Monmouth has 68 full-time members, 84% with terminal degrees. The student-faculty ratio is 14:1.

Students of Monmouth The student body is made up of 1,089 undergraduates. 52.9% are women and 47.1% are men. Students come from 19 states and territories and 20 other countries. 93% are from Illinois. 2.2% are international students. 80% returned for their sophomore year.

Applying Monmouth requires SAT I or ACT and a high school transcript, and in some cases an essay and 2 recommendations. The school recommends an interview. Application deadline: rolling admissions; 4/15 priority date for financial aid. Deferred admission is possible.

MONMOUTH UNIVERSITY

West Long Branch, NJ

Suburban setting ■ Private ■ Independent ■ Coed

Web site: www.monmouth.edu
Contact: Ms. Deanna Campbell, Director of Admission Processing, 400 Cedar Avenue, West Long Branch, NJ 07764-1898
Telephone: 732-571-3456 or toll-free 800-543-9671 **Fax:** 732-263-5166
E-mail: admission@monmouth.edu

Getting in Last Year 5,201 applied; 74% were accepted; 950 enrolled (25%).

Financial Matters $17,900 tuition and fees (2002–03); $7240 room and board; 70% average percent of need met; $14,068 average financial aid amount received per undergraduate.

Academics Monmouth awards associate, bachelor's, and master's degrees and post-master's certificates. Challenging opportunities include advanced placement credit, accelerated degree programs, student-designed majors, an honors program, double majors, independent study, and a senior project. Special programs include cooperative education, internships, summer session for credit, study-abroad, and Air Force ROTC. The faculty at Monmouth has 229 full-time members, 72% with terminal degrees. The student-faculty ratio is 18:1.

Students of Monmouth The student body totals 6,035, of whom 4,323 are undergraduates. 58.4% are women and 41.6% are men. Students come from 26 states and territories. 93% are from New Jersey. 0.3% are international students. 71% returned for their sophomore year.

Applying Monmouth requires SAT I or ACT and a high school transcript. The school recommends an essay, an interview, and a minimum high school GPA of 2.25. Application deadline: 3/1. Early and deferred admission are possible.

MONTANA STATE UNIVERSITY–BILLINGS

Billings, MT

Urban setting ■ Public ■ State-supported ■ Coed

Web site: www.msubillings.edu
Contact: Ms. Shelly Beatty, Associate Director of Admissions, 1500 University Drive, Billings, MT 59101
Telephone: 406-657-2158 or toll-free 800-565-6782 **Fax:** 406-657-2302
E-mail: keverett@msubillings.edu

Getting in Last Year 1,052 applied; 99% were accepted; 787 enrolled (76%).

Financial Matters $3973 resident tuition and fees (2002–03); $10,555 nonresident tuition and fees (2002–03); $3430 room and board; 67% average percent of need met; $6804 average financial aid amount received per undergraduate (2001–02).

Academics MSU-Billings awards associate, bachelor's, and master's degrees and post-bachelor's and post-master's certificates. Challenging opportunities include advanced placement credit, accelerated degree programs, an honors program, double majors, independent study, and a senior project. Special programs include cooperative education, internships, summer session for credit, off-campus study, and study-abroad. The most frequently chosen baccalaureate fields are business/marketing, education, and liberal arts/general studies. The faculty at MSU-Billings has 148 full-time members, 72% with terminal degrees. The student-faculty ratio is 21:1.

Students of MSU-Billings The student body totals 4,407, of whom 3,949 are undergraduates. 63.4% are women and 36.6% are men. Students come from 37 states and territories and 16 other countries. 93% are from Montana. 0.6% are international students. 53% returned for their sophomore year.

Applying MSU-Billings requires SAT I or ACT, a high school transcript, and a minimum high school GPA of 2.5. Application deadline: 7/1; 3/1 priority date for financial aid. Early and deferred admission are possible.

MONTANA STATE UNIVERSITY–BOZEMAN

Bozeman, MT

Small-town setting ■ Public ■ State-supported ■ Coed

Web site: www.montana.edu
Contact: Ms. Ronda Russell, Director of New Student Services, PO Box 172190, Bozeman, MT 59717-2190
Telephone: 406-994-2452 or toll-free 888-MSU-CATS **Fax:** 406-994-1923
E-mail: admissions@montana.edu

Getting in Last Year 4,072 applied; 85% were accepted; 2,181 enrolled (63%).

Financial Matters $3807 resident tuition and fees (2002–03); $11,444 nonresident tuition and fees (2002–03); $5120 room and board; 73% average percent of need met; $7017 average financial aid amount received per undergraduate (2001–02).

Academics MSU-Bozeman awards bachelor's, master's, and doctoral degrees. Challenging opportunities include advanced placement credit, student-designed majors, an honors program, double majors, independent study, and a senior project. Special programs include internships, summer session for credit, off-campus study, study-abroad, and Army and Air Force ROTC. The most frequently chosen baccalaureate fields are engineering/engineering technologies, business/marketing, and biological/life sciences. The faculty at MSU-Bozeman has 561 full-time members, 82% with terminal degrees. The student-faculty ratio is 17:1.

Students of MSU-Bozeman The student body totals 11,921, of whom 10,676 are undergraduates. 46.1% are women and 53.9% are men. Students come from 50 states and territories and 60 other countries. 71% are from Montana. 1.2% are international students. 71% returned for their sophomore year.

Applying MSU-Bozeman requires SAT I or ACT, a high school transcript, and a minimum high school GPA of 2.5. Application deadline: rolling admissions; 3/1 priority date for financial aid. Early and deferred admission are possible.

MONTANA STATE UNIVERSITY–NORTHERN

Havre, MT

Small-town setting ■ Public ■ State-supported ■ Coed

Web site: www.msun.edu
Contact: Ms. Rosalie Spinler, Director of Admissions, PO Box 7751, Havre, MT 59501-7751
Telephone: 406-265-3704 or toll-free 800-662-6132 (in-state) **Fax:** 406-265-3777
E-mail: msunadmit@nmc1.nmclites.edu

Getting in Last Year 868 applied; 82% were accepted; 234 enrolled (33%).

Financial Matters $3608 resident tuition and fees (2002–03); $10,462 nonresident tuition and fees (2002–03); $4420 room and board; 70% average percent of need met; $8185 average financial aid amount received per undergraduate (2001–02).

Academics MSU-Northern awards associate, bachelor's, and master's degrees. Challenging opportunities include advanced placement credit, an honors program, double majors, and a senior project. Special programs include cooperative education, internships, and summer session for credit. The most frequently chosen baccalaureate fields are education, business/marketing, and trade and industry. The faculty at MSU-Northern has 73 full-time members. The student-faculty ratio is 15:1.

Students of MSU-Northern The student body totals 1,589, of whom 1,428 are undergraduates. 52.8% are women and 47.2% are men. Students come from 7 states and territories and 3 other countries. 99% are from Montana. 1.1% are international students. 65% returned for their sophomore year.

Applying MSU-Northern requires ACT and a high school transcript, and in some cases a minimum high school GPA of 2.0. Application deadline: rolling admissions; 3/1 priority date for financial aid. Early and deferred admission are possible.

MONTANA TECH OF THE UNIVERSITY OF MONTANA

Butte, MT

Small-town setting ■ Public ■ State-supported ■ Coed

Web site: www.mtech.edu
Contact: Tony Campeau, Associate Director of Admissions, 1300 West Park Street, Butte, MT 59701-8997
Telephone: 406-496-4178 ext. 4632 or toll-free 800-445-TECH ext. 1
Fax: 406-496-4170
E-mail: admissions@mtech.edu

Getting in Last Year 612 applied; 95% were accepted; 379 enrolled (65%).

Financial Matters $3944 resident tuition and fees (2002–03); $8228 nonresident tuition and fees (2002–03); $4740 room and board; 60% average percent of need met; $7000 average financial aid amount received per undergraduate.

Academics Montana Tech awards associate, bachelor's, and master's degrees and post-bachelor's certificates. Challenging opportunities include advanced placement credit, student-designed majors, double majors, independent study, and a senior project. Special programs include cooperative education, internships, and summer session for credit. The most frequently chosen baccalaureate fields are engineering/engineering technologies, business/marketing, and health professions and related sciences. The faculty at Montana Tech has 110 full-time members, 45% with terminal degrees. The student-faculty ratio is 16:1.

Students of Montana Tech The student body totals 2,161, of whom 2,065 are undergraduates. 44.4% are women and 55.6% are men. Students come from 34 states and territories and 13 other countries. 89% are from Montana. 2.1% are international students. 71% returned for their sophomore year.

Applying Montana Tech requires SAT I or ACT, a high school transcript, proof of immunization, and a minimum high school GPA of 2.5. Application deadline: rolling admissions; 3/1 priority date for financial aid. Early admission is possible.

MONTCLAIR STATE UNIVERSITY

Upper Montclair, NJ

Suburban setting ■ Public ■ State-supported ■ Coed

Web site: www.montclair.edu
Contact: Mr. Dennis Craig, Director of Admissions, One Normal Avenue, Upper Montclair, NJ 07043-1624
Telephone: 973-655-5116 or toll-free 800-331-9205 **Fax:** 973-893-5455
E-mail: undergraduate.admissions@montclair.edu

Getting in Last Year 7,615 applied; 53% were accepted; 1,554 enrolled (38%).

Financial Matters $5741 resident tuition and fees (2002–03); $8493 nonresident tuition and fees (2002–03); $6956 room and board; 85% average percent of need met; $8220 average financial aid amount received per undergraduate.

Academics Montclair State awards bachelor's, master's, and doctoral degrees and post-bachelor's and post-master's certificates. Challenging opportunities include advanced placement credit, accelerated degree programs, freshman honors college, an honors program, double majors, and independent study. Special programs include cooperative education, internships, summer session for credit, off-campus study, and study-abroad. The most frequently chosen baccalaureate fields are business/marketing, social sciences and history, and psychology. The faculty at Montclair State has 434 full-time members, 92% with terminal degrees. The student-faculty ratio is 18:1.

Students of Montclair State The student body totals 14,673, of whom 10,939 are undergraduates. 61.7% are women and 38.3% are men. Students come from 32 states and territories and 75 other countries. 98% are from New Jersey. 4.7% are international students. 85% returned for their sophomore year.

Applying Montclair State requires SAT I or ACT and a high school transcript, and in some cases an essay and an interview. Application deadline: 3/1; 3/1 priority date for financial aid. Deferred admission is possible.

MONTREAT COLLEGE

Montreat, NC

Small-town setting ■ Private ■ Independent Religious ■ Coed

Web site: www.montreat.edu
Contact: Ms. Anita Darby, Director of Admissions, PO Box 1267, 310 Gaither Circle, Montreat, NC 28757-1267
Telephone: 828-669-8012 ext. 3784 or toll-free 800-622-6968 (in-state)
Fax: 828-669-0120
E-mail: admissions@montreat.edu

Getting in Last Year 388 applied; 73% were accepted; 162 enrolled (57%).

Financial Matters $13,448 tuition and fees (2002–03); $4230 room and board; $10,495 average financial aid amount received per undergraduate (2001–02).

Academics Montreat College awards associate, bachelor's, and master's degrees. Challenging opportunities include advanced placement credit, accelerated degree programs, double majors, independent study, and a senior project. Special programs include cooperative education, internships, off-campus study, and study-abroad. The most frequently chosen baccalaureate fields are business/marketing, parks and recreation, and social sciences and history. The faculty at Montreat College has 35 full-time members, 63% with terminal degrees. The student-faculty ratio is 18:1.

Students of Montreat College The student body totals 1,070, of whom 930 are undergraduates. 60.8% are women and 39.2% are men. Students come from 30 states and territories and 9 other countries. 80% are from North Carolina. 1.1% are international students.

Applying Montreat College requires an essay, SAT I or ACT, a high school transcript, 1 recommendation, and a minimum high school GPA of 2.25, and in some cases an interview. Application deadline: 8/15; 3/15 priority date for financial aid. Early and deferred admission are possible.

MONTSERRAT COLLEGE OF ART

Beverly, MA

Suburban setting ■ Private ■ Independent ■ Coed

Web site: www.montserrat.edu
Contact: Mr. Stephen M. Negron, Director of Admissions, 23 Essex Street, PO Box 26, Beverly, MA 01915
Telephone: 978-921-4242 ext. 1153 or toll-free 800-836-0487
Fax: 978-921-4241
E-mail: admiss@montserrat.edu

Getting in Last Year 377 applied; 81% were accepted; 114 enrolled (37%).

Financial Matters $16,655 tuition and fees (2002–03); $4640 room only; 50% average percent of need met; $6527 average financial aid amount received per undergraduate.

Academics Montserrat awards bachelor's degrees. Challenging opportunities include advanced placement credit, student-designed majors, double majors, independent study, and a senior project. Special programs include internships, off-campus study, study-abroad, and Air Force ROTC. The most frequently chosen baccalaureate field is visual/performing arts. The faculty at Montserrat has 21 full-time members, 71% with terminal degrees. The student-faculty ratio is 11:1.

Students of Montserrat The student body is made up of 412 undergraduates. 60.2% are women and 39.8% are men. Students come from 20 states and territories and 12 other countries. 44% are from Massachusetts. 1% are international students. 71% returned for their sophomore year.

Applying Montserrat requires an essay, a high school transcript, 2 recommendations, portfolio, and a minimum high school GPA of 2.25, and in some cases SAT I or ACT. The school recommends an interview and a minimum high school GPA of 2.5. Application deadline: 8/1; 3/1 priority date for financial aid. Deferred admission is possible.

MOODY BIBLE INSTITUTE

Chicago, IL

Urban setting ■ Private ■ Independent Religious ■ Coed

Web site: www.moody.edu
Contact: Mrs. Marthe Campa, Application Coordinator, 820 North LaSalle Boulevard, Chicago, IL 60610
Telephone: 312-329-4266 or toll-free 800-967-4MBI **Fax:** 312-329-8987
E-mail: admissions@moody.edu

Getting in Last Year 1,330 applied; 50% were accepted; 408 enrolled (61%).

Financial Matters $1586 tuition and fees (2002–03); $6020 room and board; 25% average percent of need met.

Academics MBI awards bachelor's, master's, and first-professional degrees. Challenging opportunities include advanced placement credit, double majors, and independent study. Special programs include internships, summer session for credit, off-campus study, and study-abroad. The most frequently chosen baccalaureate fields are communications/communication technologies, trade and industry, and area/ethnic studies. The faculty at MBI has 84 full-time members, 87% with terminal degrees. The student-faculty ratio is 20:1.

Students of MBI The student body totals 1,737, of whom 1,418 are undergraduates. 43.2% are women and 56.8% are men. Students come from 48 states and territories and 41 other countries. 31% are from Illinois. 6.8% are international students. 95% returned for their sophomore year.

Moody Bible Institute (continued)

Applying MBI requires an essay, SAT I and SAT II or ACT, a high school transcript, 4 recommendations, Christian testimony, and a minimum high school GPA of 2.3, and in some cases an interview. Application deadline: 3/1. Early admission is possible.

MOORE COLLEGE OF ART AND DESIGN

Philadelphia, PA

Urban setting ■ Private ■ Independent ■ Women Only

Web site: www.moore.edu
Contact: Wendy Elliott Pyle, Director of Admissions, 20th and The Parkway, Philadelphia, PA 19103-1179
Telephone: 215-568-4515 ext. 1108 or toll-free 800-523-2025
Fax: 215-965-8544
E-mail: admiss@moore.edu

Getting in Last Year 383 applied; 85% were accepted; 89 enrolled (27%).

Financial Matters $18,139 tuition and fees (2002–03); $6870 room and board; 54% average percent of need met; $11,513 average financial aid amount received per undergraduate.

Academics Moore awards bachelor's degrees and post-bachelor's certificates. Challenging opportunities include advanced placement credit, accelerated degree programs, double majors, independent study, and a senior project. Special programs include internships, summer session for credit, and study-abroad. The most frequently chosen baccalaureate field is visual/performing arts. The faculty at Moore has 36 full-time members, 83% with terminal degrees. The student-faculty ratio is 8:1.

Students of Moore The student body totals 631, of whom 597 are undergraduates. Students come from 29 states and territories and 7 other countries. 58% are from Pennsylvania. 1.3% are international students. 87% returned for their sophomore year.

Applying Moore requires SAT I or ACT, a high school transcript, 1 recommendation, portfolio, and a minimum high school GPA of 2.5, and in some cases a minimum high school GPA of 3.0. The school recommends an essay and an interview. Application deadline: 8/15; 3/1 priority date for financial aid. Early and deferred admission are possible.

MORAVIAN COLLEGE

Bethlehem, PA

Suburban setting ■ Private ■ Independent Religious ■ Coed

Web site: www.moravian.edu
Contact: Mr. James P. Mackin, Director of Admission, 1200 Main Street, Bethlehem, PA 18018
Telephone: 610-861-1320 or toll-free 800-441-3191 **Fax:** 610-625-7930
E-mail: admissions@moravian.edu

Getting in Last Year 1,509 applied; 77% were accepted; 373 enrolled (32%).

Financial Matters $21,315 tuition and fees (2002–03); $6595 room and board; 79% average percent of need met; $15,894 average financial aid amount received per undergraduate.

Academics Moravian awards bachelor's, master's, and first-professional degrees and post-bachelor's certificates. Challenging opportunities include advanced placement credit, student-designed majors, an honors program, double majors, independent study, and a senior project. Special programs include internships, summer session for credit, off-campus study, study-abroad, and Army ROTC. The most frequently chosen baccalaureate fields are social sciences and history, business/marketing, and psychology. The faculty at Moravian has 97 full-time members, 77% with terminal degrees. The student-faculty ratio is 12:1.

Students of Moravian The student body totals 2,049, of whom 1,824 are undergraduates. 60.5% are women and 39.5% are men. Students come from 23 states and territories and 21 other countries. 61% are from Pennsylvania. 1.9% are international students. 81% returned for their sophomore year.

Applying Moravian requires an essay, SAT I or ACT, a high school transcript, 3 recommendations, and a minimum high school GPA of 2.5. The school recommends an interview. Application deadline: 3/1; 2/15 priority date for financial aid. Early and deferred admission are possible.

MOREHEAD STATE UNIVERSITY

Morehead, KY

Small-town setting ■ Public ■ State-supported ■ Coed

Web site: www.moreheadstate.edu
Contact: Mr. Joel Pace, Director of Admissions, Howell McDowell 301, Morehead, KY 40351
Telephone: 606-783-2000 or toll-free 800-585-6781 **Fax:** 606-783-5038
E-mail: admissions@morehead-st.edu

Getting in Last Year 5,122 applied; 72% were accepted; 1,546 enrolled (42%).

Financial Matters $2926 resident tuition and fees (2002–03); $7780 nonresident tuition and fees (2002–03); $4000 room and board; 92% average percent of need met; $6387 average financial aid amount received per undergraduate.

Academics MSU awards associate, bachelor's, and master's degrees and post-master's certificates. Challenging opportunities include advanced placement credit, accelerated degree programs, student-designed majors, an honors program, double majors, and independent study. Special programs include cooperative education, internships, summer session for credit, off-campus study, study-abroad, and Army ROTC. The most frequently chosen baccalaureate fields are education, business/marketing, and social sciences and history. The faculty at MSU has 353 full-time members, 64% with terminal degrees. The student-faculty ratio is 18:1.

Students of MSU The student body totals 9,390, of whom 7,705 are undergraduates. 60.1% are women and 39.9% are men. Students come from 40 states and territories and 27 other countries. 83% are from Kentucky. 0.8% are international students.

Applying MSU requires SAT I or ACT and a high school transcript, and in some cases recommendations. The school recommends ACT. Application deadline: rolling admissions; 3/15 priority date for financial aid. Early and deferred admission are possible.

MOREHOUSE COLLEGE

Atlanta, GA

Urban setting ■ Private ■ Independent ■ Men Only

Web site: www.morehouse.edu
Contact: Mr. Terrance Dixon, Associate Dean for Admissions and Recruitment, 830 Westview Drive, SW, Atlanta, GA 30314
Telephone: 404-215-2632 or toll-free 800-851-1254 **Fax:** 404-524-5635
E-mail: admissions@morehouse.edu

Getting in Last Year 2,394 applied; 64% were accepted; 662 enrolled (43%).

Financial Matters $13,618 tuition and fees (2002–03); $8172 room and board.

Academics Morehouse College awards bachelor's degrees. Challenging opportunities include advanced placement credit, an honors program, double majors, and a senior project. Special programs include cooperative education, internships, summer session for credit, off-campus study, study-abroad, and Army, Navy and Air Force ROTC. The most frequently chosen baccalaureate fields are business/marketing, foreign language/literature, and biological/life sciences. The faculty at Morehouse College has 158 full-time members, 81% with terminal degrees. The student-faculty ratio is 15:1.

Students of Morehouse College The student body is made up of 2,738 undergraduates. Students come from 45 states and territories and 18 other countries. 32% are from Georgia. 4.4% are international students. 85% returned for their sophomore year.

Applying Morehouse College requires an essay, SAT I or ACT, a high school transcript, recommendations, and a minimum high school GPA of 2.8. The school recommends an interview and a minimum high school GPA of 3.0. Application deadline: 2/15; 4/1 priority date for financial aid. Early and deferred admission are possible.

MORGAN STATE UNIVERSITY

Baltimore, MD

Urban setting ■ Public ■ State-supported ■ Coed

Web site: www.morgan.edu
Contact: Mr. Edwin T. Johnson, Director of Admissions and Recruitment, 1700 East Cold Spring Lane, Baltimore, MD 21251
Telephone: 443-885-3000 or toll-free 800-332-6674

Getting in Last Year 11,112 applied; 35% were accepted; 1,315 enrolled (34%).

Financial Matters $4698 resident tuition and fees (2002–03); $11,118 nonresident tuition and fees (2002–03); $6150 room and board; 97% average percent of need met.

Academics Morgan State awards bachelor's, master's, and doctoral degrees. Challenging opportunities include advanced placement credit, accelerated degree programs, an honors program, independent study, and a senior project. Special programs include cooperative education, internships, summer session for credit, off-campus study, and Army ROTC. The most frequently chosen baccalaureate fields are trade and industry, engineering/engineering technologies, and computer/information sciences. The faculty at Morgan State has 360 full-time members. The student-faculty ratio is 14:1.

Students of Morgan State The student body totals 7,112, of whom 6,543 are undergraduates. 57.1% are women and 42.9% are men. Students come from 47 states and territories and 30 other countries. 4.8% are international students. 76% returned for their sophomore year.

Applying Morgan State requires SAT I or ACT, a high school transcript, and a minimum high school GPA of 2.0, and in some cases an interview and 2 recommendations. The school recommends an essay. Application deadline: rolling admissions; 4/1 priority date for financial aid. Early and deferred admission are possible.

MORNINGSIDE COLLEGE

Sioux City, IA

Suburban setting ■ *Private* ■ *Independent Religious* ■ *Coed*

Web site: www.morningside.edu
Contact: Mr. Joel Weyand, Director of Admissions, 1501 Morningside Avenue, Sioux City, IA 51106
Telephone: 712-274-5111 or toll-free 800-831-0806 ext. 5111
Fax: 712-274-5101
E-mail: mscadm@morningside.edu

Getting in Last Year 1,130 applied; 73% were accepted; 247 enrolled (30%).

Financial Matters $15,460 tuition and fees (2002–03); $5120 room and board; 86% average percent of need met; $15,516 average financial aid amount received per undergraduate.

Academics Morningside awards bachelor's and master's degrees. Challenging opportunities include advanced placement credit, student-designed majors, an honors program, double majors, independent study, and a senior project. Special programs include internships, summer session for credit, off-campus study, and study-abroad. The most frequently chosen baccalaureate fields are business/marketing, education, and health professions and related sciences. The faculty at Morningside has 67 full-time members, 81% with terminal degrees. The student-faculty ratio is 10:1.

Students of Morningside The student body totals 1,040, of whom 915 are undergraduates. 56.9% are women and 43.1% are men. Students come from 23 states and territories and 3 other countries. 69% are from Iowa. 2.2% are international students. 63% returned for their sophomore year.

Applying Morningside requires SAT I or ACT, a high school transcript, and minimum SAT score of 930 or ACT score of 20 and rank in top 50% of high school class or achieved GPA of 2.5 or better, and in some cases 2 recommendations. The school recommends an interview. Application deadline: rolling admissions; 3/1 priority date for financial aid. Deferred admission is possible.

MORRIS COLLEGE

Sumter, SC

Small-town setting ■ *Private* ■ *Independent Religious* ■ *Coed*

Web site: www.morris.edu
Contact: Ms. Deborah Calhoun, Director of Admissions and Records, 100 West College Street, Sumter, SC 29150-3599
Telephone: 803-934-3225 or toll-free 866-853-1345 **Fax:** 803-773-8241

Getting in Last Year 1,210 applied; 92% were accepted; 290 enrolled (26%).

Financial Matters $6993 tuition and fees (2002–03); $3410 room and board; 85% average percent of need met; $10,400 average financial aid amount received per undergraduate.

Academics Morris awards bachelor's degrees. Challenging opportunities include advanced placement credit, accelerated degree programs, an honors program, and double majors. Special programs include cooperative education, internships, summer session for credit, and Army ROTC. The most frequently chosen baccalaureate fields are business/marketing, protective services/public administration, and social sciences and history. The faculty at Morris has 49 full-time members, 61% with terminal degrees. The student-faculty ratio is 19:1.

Students of Morris The student body is made up of 1,049 undergraduates. 62.9% are women and 37.1% are men. Students come from 20 states and territories. 87% are from South Carolina. 0.1% are international students. 50% returned for their sophomore year.

Applying Morris requires a high school transcript and medical examination, and in some cases SAT I or ACT. Application deadline: rolling admissions; 3/30 priority date for financial aid. Deferred admission is possible.

MOUNTAIN STATE UNIVERSITY

Beckley, WV

Small-town setting ■ *Private* ■ *Independent* ■ *Coed*

Web site: www.mountainstate.edu
Contact: Ms. Darlene Brown, Administrative Assistant for Enrollment Management, P.O. Box 9003, Beckley, WV 25802-9003
Telephone: 304-253-7351 ext. 1433 or toll-free 800-766-6067 ext. 1433
Fax: 304-253-5072
E-mail: gomsu@mountainstate.edu

Getting in Last Year 991 applied; 58% were accepted; 146 enrolled (26%).

Financial Matters $4560 tuition and fees (2002–03); $2501 room and board; 51% average percent of need met; $6000 average financial aid amount received per undergraduate.

Academics Mountain State University awards associate, bachelor's, and master's degrees. Challenging opportunities include advanced placement credit, accelerated degree programs, student-designed majors, double majors, independent study, and a senior project. Special programs include cooperative education, internships, and summer session for credit. The most frequently chosen baccalaureate fields are education, business/marketing, and interdisciplinary studies. The faculty at Mountain State University has 65 full-time members, 32% with terminal degrees. The student-faculty ratio is 21:1.

Students of Mountain State University The student body totals 3,275, of whom 2,990 are undergraduates. 65.4% are women and 34.6% are men. Students come from 43 states and territories and 32 other countries. 89% are from West Virginia. 5.1% are international students. 67% returned for their sophomore year.

Applying Mountain State University requires a high school transcript, and in some cases SAT I or ACT. Application deadline: rolling admissions. Early and deferred admission are possible.

MOUNT ALLISON UNIVERSITY

Sackville, NB Canada

Small-town setting ■ *Public* ■ *Coed*

Web site: www.mta.ca
Contact: Mr. Mark Bishop, Admissions Counselor, 65 York Street, Sackville, NB E4L 1E4 Canada
Telephone: 506-364-2269
E-mail: admissions@mta.ca

Getting in Last Year 2,080 applied; 725 enrolled.

Financial Matters $5164 resident tuition and fees (2002–03); $6340 room and board.

Academics Mt A awards bachelor's and master's degrees. Challenging opportunities include advanced placement credit, student-designed majors, an honors program, double majors, independent study, and a senior project. Special programs include internships, summer session for credit, off-campus study, and study-abroad. The faculty at Mt A has 124 full-time members. The student-faculty ratio is 18:1.

Students of Mt A The student body totals 2,558, of whom 2,552 are undergraduates. 60.9% are women and 39.1% are men. Students come from 13 states and territories and 39 other countries. 34% are from New Brunswick. 90% returned for their sophomore year.

Applying Mt A requires a high school transcript and a minimum high school GPA of 3.0, and in some cases an essay, SAT II: Writing Test, SAT I and SAT II or ACT, and an interview. The school recommends 2 recommendations. Application deadline: rolling admissions. Deferred admission is possible.

MOUNT ALOYSIUS COLLEGE

Cresson, PA

Rural setting ■ *Private* ■ *Independent Religious* ■ *Coed*

Web site: www.mtaloy.edu
Contact: Mr. Francis Crouse, Dean of Enrollment Management, 7373 Admiral Peary Highway, Cresson, PA 16630
Telephone: 814-886-6383 or toll-free 888-823-2220 **Fax:** 814-886-6441
E-mail: admissions@mtaloy.edu

Getting in Last Year 785 applied; 74% were accepted; 264 enrolled (46%).

Financial Matters $14,660 tuition and fees (2002–03); $5440 room and board; 83% average percent of need met; $9000 average financial aid amount received per undergraduate.

Academics The Mount awards associate, bachelor's, and master's degrees and post-bachelor's certificates. Challenging opportunities include advanced placement credit, accelerated degree programs, student-designed majors, an honors program, independent study, and a senior project. Special programs include internships and summer session for credit. The most frequently chosen baccalaureate fields are psychology, health professions and related sciences, and business/marketing. The faculty at The Mount has 60 full-time members, 25% with terminal degrees. The student-faculty ratio is 14:1.

Students of The Mount The student body totals 1,311, of whom 1,305 are undergraduates. 74.1% are women and 25.9% are men. Students come from 15 states and territories. 97% are from Pennsylvania. 0.1% are international students.

Applying The Mount requires SAT I or ACT, a high school transcript, and a minimum high school GPA of 2.5, and in some cases an essay, an interview, and 3 recommendations. The school recommends an interview. Application deadline: rolling admissions; 2/15 priority date for financial aid. Early and deferred admission are possible.

MOUNT CARMEL COLLEGE OF NURSING

Columbus, OH

Private ■ *Independent* ■ *Coed, Primarily Women*

Web site: www.mccn.edu
Contact: Ms. Merschel Menefield, Director of Admissions, 127 South Davis Avenue, Columbus, OH 43222
Telephone: 614-234-5800

Getting in Last Year 90 applied; 71% were accepted; 42 enrolled (66%).

Mount Carmel College of Nursing (continued)

Financial Matters $11,507 tuition and fees (2002–03); $4300 room and board; 70% average percent of need met; $9000 average financial aid amount received per undergraduate.

Academics Mount Carmel College of Nursing awards bachelor's degrees. The most frequently chosen baccalaureate field is health professions and related sciences. The faculty at Mount Carmel College of Nursing has 23 full-time members. The student-faculty ratio is 11:1.

Students of Mount Carmel College of Nursing The student body is made up of 424 undergraduates. 90.6% are women and 9.4% are men. 80% returned for their sophomore year.

MOUNT HOLYOKE COLLEGE

South Hadley, MA

Small-town setting ■ Private ■ Independent ■ Women Only

Web site: www.mtholyoke.edu
Contact: Ms. Diane Anci, Dean of Admission, 50 College Street, South Hadley, MA 01075
Telephone: 413-538-2023 **Fax:** 413-538-2409
E-mail: admission@mtholyoke.edu

Getting in Last Year 2,936 applied; 52% were accepted; 573 enrolled (38%).

Financial Matters $27,708 tuition and fees (2002–03); $8100 room and board; 100% average percent of need met; $25,500 average financial aid amount received per undergraduate.

Academics Mount Holyoke awards bachelor's and master's degrees and post-bachelor's certificates. Challenging opportunities include advanced placement credit, student-designed majors, an honors program, double majors, independent study, and a senior project. Special programs include internships, off-campus study, study-abroad, and Army and Air Force ROTC. The most frequently chosen baccalaureate fields are social sciences and history, psychology, and English. The faculty at Mount Holyoke has 206 full-time members, 95% with terminal degrees. The student-faculty ratio is 10:1.

Students of Mount Holyoke The student body totals 2,194, of whom 2,191 are undergraduates. Students come from 48 states and territories and 77 other countries. 36% are from Massachusetts. 15.5% are international students. 97% returned for their sophomore year.

Applying Mount Holyoke requires an essay, a high school transcript, and 2 recommendations, and in some cases SAT II Subject Tests and SAT II: Writing Test. The school recommends an interview. Application deadline: 1/15; 2/1 for financial aid. Early and deferred admission are possible.

MOUNT IDA COLLEGE

Newton Center, MA

Suburban setting ■ Private ■ Independent ■ Coed

Web site: www.mountida.edu
Contact: Ms. Nancy Lemelman, Director of Admissions, 777 Dedham Street, Newton, MA 02459
Telephone: 617-928-4500 ext. 4508
E-mail: admissions@mountida.edu

Getting in Last Year 2,161 applied; 22% were accepted; 403 enrolled (85%).

Financial Matters $16,296 tuition and fees (2002–03); $8950 room and board; 56% average percent of need met; $12,000 average financial aid amount received per undergraduate.

Academics Mount Ida awards associate and bachelor's degrees and post-bachelor's certificates. Challenging opportunities include accelerated degree programs, student-designed majors, freshman honors college, an honors program, and a senior project. Special programs include cooperative education, internships, and study-abroad. The faculty at Mount Ida has 61 full-time members. The student-faculty ratio is 15:1.

Students of Mount Ida The student body is made up of 1,250 undergraduates. Students come from 29 states and territories and 42 other countries. 0.6% are international students.

Applying Mount Ida requires SAT I or ACT, a high school transcript, and 2 recommendations. The school recommends an essay, an interview, and a minimum high school GPA of 2.0. Application deadline: rolling admissions; 5/1 priority date for financial aid. Deferred admission is possible.

MOUNT MARTY COLLEGE

Yankton, SD

Small-town setting ■ Private ■ Independent Religious ■ Coed

Web site: www.mtmc.edu
Contact: Ms. Brandi Tschumper, Director of Enrollment, 1105 West 8th Street, Yankton, SD 57078
Telephone: 605-668-1545 or toll-free 800-658-4552 **Fax:** 605-668-1607
E-mail: mmcadmit@mtmc.edu

Getting in Last Year 315 applied; 90% were accepted; 167 enrolled (59%).

Financial Matters $12,660 tuition and fees (2002–03); $4600 room and board; 80% average percent of need met; $12,118 average financial aid amount received per undergraduate.

Academics Mount Marty awards associate, bachelor's, and master's degrees. Challenging opportunities include advanced placement credit, accelerated degree programs, student-designed majors, an honors program, double majors, independent study, and a senior project. Special programs include cooperative education, internships, summer session for credit, off-campus study, and Army ROTC. The most frequently chosen baccalaureate fields are health professions and related sciences, business/marketing, and education. The faculty at Mount Marty has 42 full-time members, 40% with terminal degrees. The student-faculty ratio is 13:1.

Students of Mount Marty The student body totals 1,123, of whom 1,030 are undergraduates. 67.6% are women and 32.4% are men. Students come from 29 states and territories and 2 other countries. 78% are from South Dakota. 0.6% are international students. 74% returned for their sophomore year.

Applying Mount Marty requires ACT, a high school transcript, and a minimum high school GPA of 2.0, and in some cases recommendations. The school recommends an interview. Application deadline: rolling admissions; 3/1 priority date for financial aid. Early and deferred admission are possible.

MOUNT MARY COLLEGE

Milwaukee, WI

Suburban setting ■ Private ■ Independent Religious ■ Women Only

Web site: www.mtmary.edu
Contact: Ms. Amy Dobson, Director of Enrollment, 2900 North Menomonee River Parkway, Milwaukee, WI 53222-4597
Telephone: 414-258-4810 ext. 360 **Fax:** 414-256-1205
E-mail: admiss@mtmary.edu

Getting in Last Year 346 applied; 71% were accepted; 121 enrolled (49%).

Financial Matters $14,165 tuition and fees (2002–03); $4895 room and board; 72% average percent of need met; $11,037 average financial aid amount received per undergraduate.

Academics MMC awards bachelor's and master's degrees. Challenging opportunities include advanced placement credit, accelerated degree programs, student-designed majors, an honors program, double majors, independent study, and a senior project. Special programs include internships, summer session for credit, study-abroad, and Army ROTC. The most frequently chosen baccalaureate fields are health professions and related sciences, visual/performing arts, and business/marketing. The faculty at MMC has 68 full-time members, 59% with terminal degrees. The student-faculty ratio is 9:1.

Students of MMC The student body totals 1,401, of whom 1,223 are undergraduates. Students come from 8 states and territories and 6 other countries. 97% are from Wisconsin. 0.7% are international students. 66% returned for their sophomore year.

Applying MMC requires SAT I or ACT, a high school transcript, and a minimum high school GPA of 2.5, and in some cases an essay and 2 recommendations. The school recommends an interview. Application deadline: rolling admissions; 3/1 priority date for financial aid. Deferred admission is possible.

MOUNT MERCY COLLEGE

Cedar Rapids, IA

Suburban setting ■ Private ■ Independent Religious ■ Coed

Web site: www.mtmercy.edu
Contact: Ms. Margaret M. Jackson, Dean of Admission, 1330 Elmhurst Drive, NE, Cedar Rapids, IA 52402
Telephone: 319-368-6460 or toll-free 800-248-4504 **Fax:** 319-363-5270
E-mail: admission@mmc.mtmercy.edu

Getting in Last Year 471 applied; 84% were accepted; 163 enrolled (41%).

Financial Matters $15,300 tuition and fees (2002–03); $5074 room and board; 82% average percent of need met; $12,943 average financial aid amount received per undergraduate.

Academics Mount Mercy awards bachelor's degrees. Challenging opportunities include advanced placement credit, accelerated degree programs, student-designed majors, freshman honors college, an honors program, double majors, independent study, and a senior project. Special programs include internships, summer session for credit, and off-campus study. The most frequently chosen baccalaureate fields are education, health professions and related sciences, and protective services/public administration. The faculty at Mount Mercy has 68 full-time members, 72% with terminal degrees. The student-faculty ratio is 14:1.

Students of Mount Mercy The student body is made up of 1,434 undergraduates. 68% are women and 32% are men. Students come from 23 states and territories. 78% are from Iowa. 0.1% are international students. 80% returned for their sophomore year.

Applying Mount Mercy requires SAT I or ACT, a high school transcript, 1 recommendation, and a minimum high school GPA of 2.5, and in some cases an interview. The school recommends an essay and a minimum high school GPA of 3.0. Application deadline: 8/30; 3/1 priority date for financial aid. Early and deferred admission are possible.

MOUNT OLIVE COLLEGE

Mount Olive, NC

Small-town setting ■ Private ■ Independent Religious ■ Coed

Web site: www.mountolivecollege.edu
Contact: Mr. Tim Woodard, Director of Admissions, 634 Henderson Street, Mount Olive, NC 28365
Telephone: 919-658-2502 ext. 3009 or toll-free 800-653-0854 (in-state) **Fax:** 919-658-8934
E-mail: twppdard@moc.edu

Getting in Last Year 652 applied; 77% were accepted; 250 enrolled (50%).

Financial Matters $10,010 tuition and fees (2002–03); $4400 room and board; 68% average percent of need met; $6114 average financial aid amount received per undergraduate (2001–02).

Academics Mount Olive awards associate and bachelor's degrees. Challenging opportunities include advanced placement credit, accelerated degree programs, freshman honors college, an honors program, double majors, independent study, and a senior project. Special programs include cooperative education, internships, summer session for credit, and off-campus study. The most frequently chosen baccalaureate fields are business/marketing, protective services/public administration, and parks and recreation. The faculty at Mount Olive has 55 full-time members, 65% with terminal degrees. The student-faculty ratio is 18:1.

Students of Mount Olive The student body is made up of 2,208 undergraduates. 54.4% are women and 45.6% are men. Students come from 21 states and territories. 86% are from North Carolina. 54% returned for their sophomore year.

Applying Mount Olive requires SAT I or ACT, a high school transcript, and a minimum high school GPA of 2.0, and in some cases TOEFL for foreign students. The school recommends SAT I, an interview, and 2 recommendations. Application deadline: rolling admissions; 3/1 priority date for financial aid. Early and deferred admission are possible.

MOUNT SAINT MARY COLLEGE

Newburgh, NY

Suburban setting ■ Private ■ Independent ■ Coed

Web site: www.msmc.edu
Contact: Mr. J. Randall Ognibene, Director of Admissions, 330 Powell Avenue, Newburgh, NY 12550
Telephone: 845-569-3248 or toll-free 888-937-6762 **Fax:** 845-562-6762
E-mail: admissions@msmc.edu

Getting in Last Year 1,362 applied; 79% were accepted; 354 enrolled (33%).

Financial Matters $13,335 tuition and fees (2002–03); $6520 room and board; 63% average percent of need met; $9115 average financial aid amount received per undergraduate.

Academics Mount Saint Mary awards bachelor's and master's degrees. Challenging opportunities include advanced placement credit, accelerated degree programs, freshman honors college, an honors program, double majors, independent study, and a senior project. Special programs include cooperative education, internships, summer session for credit, off-campus study, study-abroad, and Army ROTC. The most frequently chosen baccalaureate fields are business/marketing, health professions and related sciences, and social sciences and history. The faculty at Mount Saint Mary has 62 full-time members, 81% with terminal degrees. The student-faculty ratio is 18:1.

Students of Mount Saint Mary The student body totals 2,541, of whom 2,039 are undergraduates. 71.4% are women and 28.6% are men. Students come from 14 states and territories. 86% are from New York. 70% returned for their sophomore year.

Applying Mount Saint Mary requires SAT I or ACT and a high school transcript, and in some cases an essay, an interview, and 3 recommendations. The school recommends an interview and 3 recommendations. Application deadline: rolling admissions; 2/15 priority date for financial aid. Deferred admission is possible.

MOUNT ST. MARY'S COLLEGE

Los Angeles, CA

Suburban setting ■ Private ■ Independent Religious ■ Coed, Primarily Women

Web site: www.msmc.la.edu
Contact: Mr. Dean Kilgour, Director of Admissions, 12001 Chalon Road, Los Angeles, CA 90049-1599
Telephone: 310-954-4252 or toll-free 800-999-9893
E-mail: admissions@msmc.la.edu

Getting in Last Year 819 applied; 89% were accepted; 336 enrolled (46%).

Financial Matters $19,674 tuition and fees (2002–03); $7832 room and board.

Academics Mount St. Mary's awards associate, bachelor's, and master's degrees and post-bachelor's certificates. Challenging opportunities include advanced placement credit, accelerated degree programs, student-designed majors, freshman honors college, an honors program, double majors, independent study, and a senior project. Special programs include internships, summer session for credit, off-campus study, and study-abroad. The faculty at Mount St. Mary's has 86 full-time members, 53% with terminal degrees. The student-faculty ratio is 17:1.

Students of Mount St. Mary's The student body totals 1,988, of whom 1,677 are undergraduates. 95.2% are women and 4.8% are men. Students come from 23 states and territories. 97% are from California. 85% returned for their sophomore year.

Applying Mount St. Mary's requires an essay, SAT I or ACT, a high school transcript, 1 recommendation, and a minimum high school GPA of 2.0. The school recommends SAT I, an interview, and a minimum high school GPA of 3.0. Application deadline: rolling admissions; 5/15 for financial aid, with a 3/2 priority date. Deferred admission is possible.

MOUNT SAINT MARY'S COLLEGE AND SEMINARY

Emmitsburg, MD

Rural setting ■ Private ■ Independent Religious ■ Coed

Web site: www.msmary.edu
Contact: Mr. Stephen Neitz, Executive Director of Admissions and Financial Aid, 16300 Old Emmitsburg Road, Emmitsburg, MD 21727
Telephone: 301-447-5214 or toll-free 800-448-4347 **Fax:** 301-447-5860
E-mail: admissions@msmary.edu

Getting in Last Year 1,816 applied; 87% were accepted; 400 enrolled (25%).

Financial Matters $19,700 tuition and fees (2002–03); $7300 room and board; 78% average percent of need met; $14,020 average financial aid amount received per undergraduate.

Academics The Mount awards bachelor's, master's, and first-professional degrees and post-bachelor's certificates. Challenging opportunities include advanced placement credit, accelerated degree programs, student-designed majors, an honors program, double majors, independent study, and a senior project. Special programs include internships, summer session for credit, off-campus study, study-abroad, and Army ROTC. The most frequently chosen baccalaureate fields are business/marketing, social sciences and history, and education. The faculty at The Mount has 90 full-time members, 89% with terminal degrees. The student-faculty ratio is 15:1.

Students of The Mount The student body totals 2,032, of whom 1,583 are undergraduates. 58% are women and 42% are men. Students come from 27 states and territories and 8 other countries. 61% are from Maryland. 0.7% are international students. 80% returned for their sophomore year.

Applying The Mount requires SAT I or ACT, a high school transcript, 1 recommendation, and a minimum high school GPA of 2.0. The school recommends an essay, an interview, and a minimum high school GPA of 3.0. Application deadline: rolling admissions; 2/15 for financial aid. Deferred admission is possible.

MOUNT SAINT VINCENT UNIVERSITY

Halifax, NS Canada

Suburban setting ■ Public ■ Coed, Primarily Women

Web site: www.msvu.ca
Contact: Ms. Tara Wigglesworth-Hines, Assistant Registrar/Admissions, 166 Bedford Highway, Halifax, NS B3M2J6 Canada
Telephone: 902-457-6117 **Fax:** 902-457-6498
E-mail: admissions@msvu.ca

Getting in Last Year 1,989 applied; 94% were accepted; 1,281 enrolled (68%).

Financial Matters $4737 nonresident tuition and fees (2002–03); $5650 room and board.

Academics The Mount awards bachelor's, master's, and first-professional degrees and post-bachelor's certificates. Challenging opportunities include advanced placement credit, accelerated degree programs, student-designed majors, an honors program, double majors, independent study, and a senior project. Special programs include cooperative education, internships, summer session for credit, off-campus study, and study-abroad. The most frequently chosen baccalaureate fields are education, business/marketing, and home economics/vocational home economics. The faculty at The Mount has 144 full-time members, 74% with terminal degrees. The student-faculty ratio is 15:1.

Students of The Mount The student body totals 4,147, of whom 2,962 are undergraduates. 81.7% are women and 18.3% are men. Students come from 13 states and territories and 41 other countries. 85% are from Nova Scotia. 70% returned for their sophomore year.

Applying The Mount requires a high school transcript and a minimum high school GPA of 2.0, and in some cases an essay, SAT I and SAT II or ACT, an interview, 2 recommendations, and a minimum high school GPA of 3.0. Application deadline: 3/14, 5/30 for nonresidents; 1/3 for financial aid. Deferred admission is possible.

MT. SIERRA COLLEGE

Monrovia, CA

Suburban setting ■ Private ■ Proprietary ■ Coed

Web site: www.mtsierra.edu

Contact: Mr. Fred Chyr, Director of Admissions, 101 East Huntington Drive, Monrovia, CA 91016

Telephone: 626-873-2100 ext. 213 or toll-free 888-828-8800. **Fax:** 626-359-5528

Getting in Last Year 380 applied; 73% were accepted; 279 enrolled (100%).

Financial Matters $9600 tuition and fees (2002–03); 85% average percent of need met.

Academics Mt. Sierra College awards bachelor's degrees. Challenging opportunities include accelerated degree programs, independent study, and a senior project. Special programs include internships and summer session for credit. The most frequently chosen baccalaureate fields are computer/information sciences and visual/performing arts. The faculty at Mt. Sierra College has 22 full-time members, 23% with terminal degrees. The student-faculty ratio is 15:1.

Students of Mt. Sierra College The student body is made up of 1,100 undergraduates. 30% are women and 70% are men. Students come from 7 states and territories. 95% are from California.

Applying Mt. Sierra College requires CPT, a high school transcript, and an interview, and in some cases an essay.

MOUNT UNION COLLEGE

Alliance, OH

Suburban setting ■ Private ■ Independent Religious ■ Coed

Web site: www.muc.edu

Contact: Mr. Vince Heslop, Director of Admissions, 1972 Clark Avenue, Alliance, OH 44601

Telephone: 330-823-2590 or toll-free 800-334-6682 (in-state), 800-992-6682 (out-of-state) **Fax:** 330-823-3487

E-mail: admissn@muc.edu

Getting in Last Year 1,919 applied; 78% were accepted; 586 enrolled (39%).

Financial Matters $17,150 tuition and fees (2002–03); $5070 room and board; 87% average percent of need met; $14,667 average financial aid amount received per undergraduate.

Academics Mount Union awards bachelor's degrees. Challenging opportunities include advanced placement credit, accelerated degree programs, student-designed majors, an honors program, double majors, independent study, and a senior project. Special programs include cooperative education, internships, summer session for credit, off-campus study, study-abroad, and Army and Air Force ROTC. The most frequently chosen baccalaureate fields are business/marketing, education, and parks and recreation. The faculty at Mount Union has 126 full-time members, 75% with terminal degrees. The student-faculty ratio is 14:1.

Students of Mount Union The student body is made up of 2,372 undergraduates. 56.8% are women and 43.2% are men. Students come from 23 states and territories and 14 other countries. 91% are from Ohio. 1.4% are international students. 74% returned for their sophomore year.

Applying Mount Union requires an essay, SAT I or ACT, a high school transcript, 1 recommendation, and a minimum high school GPA of 2.0. The school recommends an interview. Application deadline: rolling admissions. Early and deferred admission are possible.

MOUNT VERNON NAZARENE UNIVERSITY

Mount Vernon, OH

Small-town setting ■ Private ■ Independent Religious ■ Coed

Web site: www.mvnu.edu

Contact: Dr. Jeff Williamson, Interim Director of Admissions and Student Recruitment, 800 Martinsburg Road, Mount Vernon, OH 43050

Telephone: 740-392-6868 ext. 4510 or toll-free 866-462-6868 **Fax:** 740-393-0511

E-mail: admissions@mvnu.edu

Getting in Last Year 825 applied; 77% were accepted; 352 enrolled (56%).

Financial Matters $13,288 tuition and fees (2002–03); $4527 room and board; $8025 average financial aid amount received per undergraduate (2001–02).

Academics MVNU awards associate, bachelor's, and master's degrees. Challenging opportunities include advanced placement credit, freshman honors college, an honors program, double majors, independent study, and a senior project. Special programs include internships, summer session for credit, off-campus study, and study-abroad. The most frequently chosen baccalaureate fields are business/marketing, education, and social sciences and history. The faculty at MVNU has 72 full-time members, 64% with terminal degrees. The student-faculty ratio is 18:1.

Students of MVNU The student body totals 2,337, of whom 2,235 are undergraduates. 57.4% are women and 42.6% are men. Students come from 29 states and territories. 90% are from Ohio. 0.4% are international students. 77% returned for their sophomore year.

Applying MVNU requires an essay, SAT I or ACT, a high school transcript, 2 recommendations, and a minimum high school GPA of 2.5. The school recommends an interview. Application deadline: 5/31; 3/15 priority date for financial aid. Early and deferred admission are possible.

MUHLENBERG COLLEGE

Allentown, PA

Suburban setting ■ Private ■ Independent Religious ■ Coed

Web site: www.muhlenberg.edu

Contact: Mr. Christopher Hooker-Haring, Dean of Admissions, 2400 Chew Street, Allentown, PA 18104-5586

Telephone: 484-664-3245 **Fax:** 484-664-3234

E-mail: adm@muhlenberg.edu

Getting in Last Year 3,822 applied; 35% were accepted; 547 enrolled (41%).

Financial Matters $23,455 tuition and fees (2002–03); $6295 room and board; 96% average percent of need met; $16,023 average financial aid amount received per undergraduate.

Academics Muhlenberg awards bachelor's degrees. Challenging opportunities include advanced placement credit, accelerated degree programs, student-designed majors, an honors program, double majors, independent study, and a senior project. Special programs include internships, summer session for credit, off-campus study, study-abroad, and Army ROTC. The most frequently chosen baccalaureate fields are business/marketing, social sciences and history, and communications/communication technologies. The faculty at Muhlenberg has 145 full-time members, 86% with terminal degrees. The student-faculty ratio is 12:1.

Students of Muhlenberg The student body is made up of 2,470 undergraduates. 55.9% are women and 44.1% are men. Students come from 34 states and territories and 6 other countries. 34% are from Pennsylvania. 0.3% are international students. 93% returned for their sophomore year.

Applying Muhlenberg requires an essay, a high school transcript, and 2 recommendations, and in some cases SAT I or ACT and an interview. The school recommends an interview. Application deadline: 2/15; 2/15 for financial aid. Early and deferred admission are possible.

MULTNOMAH BIBLE COLLEGE AND BIBLICAL SEMINARY

Portland, OR

Urban setting ■ Private ■ Independent Religious ■ Coed

Web site: www.multnomah.edu

Contact: Ms. Nancy Gerecz, Admissions Assistant, 8435 Northeast Glisan Street, Portland, OR 97220-5898

Telephone: 503-255-0332 ext. 373 or toll-free 800-275-4672 **Fax:** 503-254-1268

E-mail: admiss@multnomah.edu

Getting in Last Year 190 applied; 88% were accepted; 88 enrolled (53%).

Financial Matters $10,070 tuition and fees (2002–03); $4450 room and board; 56% average percent of need met; $7403 average financial aid amount received per undergraduate.

Academics Multnomah awards bachelor's, master's, and first-professional degrees. Challenging opportunities include advanced placement credit and double majors. Special programs include internships and summer session for credit. The faculty at Multnomah has 22 full-time members, 55% with terminal degrees. The student-faculty ratio is 18:1.

Students of Multnomah The student body totals 827, of whom 582 are undergraduates. 43.8% are women and 56.2% are men. Students come from 34 states and territories. 47% are from Oregon. 0.9% are international students. 66% returned for their sophomore year.

Applying Multnomah requires an essay, SAT I or ACT, a high school transcript, 4 recommendations, and a minimum high school GPA of 2.5. Application deadline: 7/15; 3/1 priority date for financial aid. Deferred admission is possible.

MURRAY STATE UNIVERSITY

Murray, KY

Small-town setting ■ Public ■ State-supported ■ Coed

Web site: www.murraystate.edu

Contact: Mrs. Stacy Bell, Admission Clerk, PO Box 9, Murray, KY 42071-0009

Telephone: 270-762-3035 or toll-free 800-272-4678 **Fax:** 270-762-3050

E-mail: admissions@murraystate.edu

Getting in Last Year 2,740 applied; 88% were accepted; 1,493 enrolled (62%).

Financial Matters $3032 resident tuition and fees (2002–03); $8112 nonresident tuition and fees (2002–03); $4420 room and board; 90% average percent of need met; $4580 average financial aid amount received per undergraduate (2001–02).

Academics Murray State awards associate, bachelor's, and master's degrees and post-bachelor's and post-master's certificates. Challenging opportunities include advanced placement credit, accelerated degree programs, freshman honors college, an honors program, double majors, independent study, and a senior project. Special programs include cooperative education, internships, summer session for credit, off-campus study, study-abroad, and Army ROTC. The most frequently chosen baccalaureate fields are business/marketing, education, and communications/communication technologies. The faculty at Murray State has 390 full-time members, 78% with terminal degrees. The student-faculty ratio is 16:1.

Students of Murray State The student body totals 9,915, of whom 8,083 are undergraduates. 58.7% are women and 41.3% are men. Students come from 47 states and territories and 64 other countries. 74% are from Kentucky. 3.2% are international students. 78% returned for their sophomore year.

Applying Murray State requires ACT, a high school transcript, rank in top 50% of graduating class, and a minimum high school GPA of 3.0, and in some cases recommendations. The school recommends an interview. Application deadline: rolling admissions, 8/1 for nonresidents; 4/1 priority date for financial aid. Early and deferred admission are possible.

MUSICIANS INSTITUTE

Hollywood, CA

Private ■ Proprietary ■ Coed

Web site: www.mi.edu

Contact: Mr. Steve Lunn, Admissions Representative, 1655 North McCadden Place, Hollywood, CA 90028

Telephone: 323-462-1384 ext. 156 or toll-free 800-255-PLAY

Financial Matters $13,500 tuition and fees (2002–03); 40% average percent of need met; $6250 average financial aid amount received per undergraduate.

Academics Musicians Institute awards associate and bachelor's degrees.

Students of Musicians Institute The student body is made up of 650 undergraduates.

Applying Application deadline: rolling admissions.

MUSKINGUM COLLEGE

New Concord, OH

Small-town setting ■ Private ■ Independent Religious ■ Coed

Web site: www.muskingum.edu

Contact: Mrs. Beth DaLonzo, Director of Admission, 163 Stormont Street, New Concord, OH 43762

Telephone: 740-825-8137 or toll-free 800-752-6082 **Fax:** 740-826-8100

E-mail: adminfo@muskingum.edu

Getting in Last Year 1,773 applied; 79% were accepted; 450 enrolled (32%).

Financial Matters $14,075 tuition and fees (2002–03); $5600 room and board; 89% average percent of need met; $12,693 average financial aid amount received per undergraduate.

Academics Muskingum awards bachelor's and master's degrees. Challenging opportunities include advanced placement credit, accelerated degree programs, student-designed majors, double majors, independent study, and a senior project. Special programs include internships, summer session for credit, off-campus study, and study-abroad. The faculty at Muskingum has 93 full-time members, 84% with terminal degrees. The student-faculty ratio is 16:1.

Students of Muskingum The student body totals 2,049, of whom 1,686 are undergraduates. 49.5% are women and 50.5% are men. Students come from 26 states and territories and 19 other countries. 88% are from Ohio. 2.1% are international students.

Applying Muskingum requires SAT I or ACT, a high school transcript, 1 recommendation, and a minimum high school GPA of 2.0. The school recommends an essay, an interview, and a minimum high school GPA of 3.0. Application deadline: 6/1; 3/15 priority date for financial aid. Early and deferred admission are possible.

NAROPA UNIVERSITY

Boulder, CO

Urban setting ■ Private ■ Independent ■ Coed

Web site: www.naropa.edu

Contact: Ms. Sally Forester, Admissions Counselor, 2130 Arapahoe Avenue, Boulder, CO 80302

Telephone: 303-546-5285 or toll-free 800-772-0410 (out-of-state) **Fax:** 303-546-3583

E-mail: admissions@naropa.edu

Getting in Last Year 97 applied; 84% were accepted; 37 enrolled (46%).

Financial Matters $15,860 tuition and fees (2002–03); $8400 room and board; 82% average percent of need met; $19,818 average financial aid amount received per undergraduate.

Academics Naropa awards bachelor's and master's degrees and post-bachelor's and post-master's certificates. Challenging opportunities include advanced placement credit, student-designed majors, double majors, independent study, and a senior project. Special programs include cooperative education, internships, summer session for credit, and study-abroad. The most frequently chosen baccalaureate fields are psychology, visual/performing arts, and English. The faculty at Naropa has 31 full-time members, 48% with terminal degrees. The student-faculty ratio is 12:1.

Students of Naropa The student body totals 1,201, of whom 448 are undergraduates. 65% are women and 35% are men. Students come from 44 states and territories and 8 other countries. 31% are from Colorado. 4% are international students. 60% returned for their sophomore year.

Applying Naropa requires an essay, a high school transcript, an interview, and 2 recommendations. The school recommends SAT I and ACT. Application deadline: rolling admissions; 3/1 priority date for financial aid. Deferred admission is possible.

NATIONAL AMERICAN UNIVERSITY

Colorado Springs, CO

Suburban setting ■ Private ■ Proprietary ■ Coed

Web site: www.national.edu/col_springs.html

Contact: Ms. Wendy Ranzinger, Senior Representative, 5125 North Academy Boulevard, Colorado Springs, CO 80918

Telephone: 719-277-0588 or toll-free 888-471-4781 **Fax:** 719-277-0589

E-mail: nau@clsp.uswest.net

Financial Matters $10,400 tuition and fees (2002–03).

Academics NAU awards associate, bachelor's, and master's degrees. Challenging opportunities include accelerated degree programs and independent study. Special programs include internships, summer session for credit, and off-campus study. The faculty at NAU has 10 full-time members. The student-faculty ratio is 15:1.

Students of NAU The student body is made up of 200 undergraduates. Students come from 75 states and territories and 5 other countries.

Applying NAU requires a high school transcript and an interview, and in some cases ACT. Application deadline: rolling admissions; 3/1 priority date for financial aid. Deferred admission is possible.

NATIONAL AMERICAN UNIVERSITY

Denver, CO

Urban setting ■ Private ■ Proprietary ■ Coed

Web site: www.national.edu

Contact: Ms. Karen Walker, Senior Admissions Representative, 1325 South Colorado Blvd, Suite 100, Denver, CO 80222

Telephone: 303-758-6700 **Fax:** 303-758-6810

Financial Matters $7695 tuition and fees (2002–03).

Academics NAU, Denver awards associate, bachelor's, and master's degrees. Challenging opportunities include advanced placement credit, accelerated degree programs, double majors, independent study, and a senior project. Special programs include internships and summer session for credit. The faculty at NAU, Denver has 35 members. The student-faculty ratio is 10:1.

Students of NAU, Denver The student body is made up of 300 undergraduates. 60% returned for their sophomore year.

Applying NAU, Denver requires a high school transcript. The school recommends SAT I or ACT. Application deadline: rolling admissions. Early and deferred admission are possible.

NATIONAL AMERICAN UNIVERSITY

Albuquerque, NM

Suburban setting ■ Private ■ Proprietary ■ Coed

Web site: www.national.edu

Contact: Ms. Karina Elliott-Long, Executive Admissions Representative, 4775 Indian School, NE, Albuquerque, NM 87110

Telephone: 505-265-7517 or toll-free 800-843-8892 **Fax:** 505-265-7542

Getting in Last Year 105 applied; 100% were accepted.

Financial Matters $10,020 tuition and fees (2002–03).

Academics National American University awards associate and bachelor's degrees. Challenging opportunities include accelerated degree programs, double majors, and independent study. Special programs include cooperative education, internships, summer session for credit, and off-campus study. The most frequently chosen baccalaureate fields are business/marketing and computer/information sciences. The faculty at National American University has 56 members, 9% with terminal degrees. The student-faculty ratio is 12:1.

Students of National American University The student body is made up of 625 undergraduates. 49% are women and 51% are men. Students come from 1 state or territory and 4 other countries. 60% returned for their sophomore year.

Applying National American University requires a high school transcript. Application deadline: rolling admissions.

NATIONAL AMERICAN UNIVERSITY

Rapid City, SD

Urban setting ■ Private ■ Proprietary ■ Coed

Web site: www.national.edu

Contact: Mr. Tom Shea, Vice President of Enrollment Management, 321 Kansas City Street, Rapid City, SD 57701

Telephone: 605-394-4902 or toll-free 800-843-8892 **Fax:** 605-394-4871

E-mail: apply@server1.natcol-rcy.edu

Getting in Last Year 166 enrolled.

Financial Matters $10,155 tuition and fees (2002–03); $3585 room and board.

Academics National American University awards associate, bachelor's, and master's degrees. Challenging opportunities include advanced placement credit, accelerated degree programs, and independent study. Special programs include cooperative education, internships, summer session for credit, and Army ROTC.

Students of National American University The student body totals 749, of whom 714 are undergraduates. 48.3% are women and 51.7% are men. Students come from 25 states and territories. 79% are from South Dakota. 0.7% are international students.

Applying National American University requires a high school transcript. The school recommends ACT and an interview. Application deadline: rolling admissions. Early and deferred admission are possible.

NATIONAL AMERICAN UNIVERSITY–SIOUX FALLS BRANCH

Sioux Falls, SD

Urban setting ■ Private ■ Proprietary ■ Coed, Primarily Women

Contact: Ms. Lisa Houtsma, Director of Admissions, 2801 South Kiwanis Avenue, Suite 100, Sioux Falls, SD 57105

Telephone: 605-334-5430

E-mail: lhautsma@national.edu

Getting in Last Year 9 applied; 100% were accepted.

Financial Matters $7515 tuition and fees (2002–03).

Academics National American University–Sioux Falls Branch awards associate and bachelor's degrees. Challenging opportunities include advanced placement credit, accelerated degree programs, and double majors. Special programs include cooperative education, internships, and summer session for credit. The most frequently chosen baccalaureate fields are business/marketing, computer/information sciences, and law/legal studies. The faculty at National American University–Sioux Falls Branch has 35 members.

Students of National American University–Sioux Falls Branch The student body is made up of 350 undergraduates. Students come from 5 states and territories. 70% returned for their sophomore year.

Applying National American University–Sioux Falls Branch requires a high school transcript and an interview. Application deadline: rolling admissions. Deferred admission is possible.

NATIONAL COLLEGE OF MIDWIFERY

Taos, NM

Private ■ Independent ■ Women Only

Web site: www.midwiferycollege.org

Contact: Ms. Beth Enson, Registrar, 209 State Road 240, Taos, NM 87571

Telephone: 505-758-8914

Getting in Last Year 30 applied; 100% were accepted; 30 enrolled (100%).

Financial Matters $6000 tuition and fees (2002–03).

Academics National College of Midwifery awards associate, bachelor's, master's, and doctoral degrees. The faculty at National College of Midwifery has 31 full-time members, 87% with terminal degrees. The student-faculty ratio is 2:1.

Students of National College of Midwifery The student body totals 59, of whom 57 are undergraduates.

THE NATIONAL HISPANIC UNIVERSITY

San Jose, CA

Urban setting ■ Private ■ Independent ■ Coed

Web site: www.nhu.edu

Contact: Office of Admissions, 14271 Story Road, San Jose, CA 95127-3823

Telephone: 408-254-6900

Getting in Last Year 179 applied; 82% were accepted; 34 enrolled (23%).

Financial Matters $3200 tuition and fees (2002–03).

Academics NHU awards associate and bachelor's degrees and post-bachelor's certificates. Challenging opportunities include advanced placement credit, accelerated degree programs, and a senior project. Special programs include cooperative education, internships, summer session for credit, off-campus study, and study-abroad. The most frequently chosen baccalaureate fields are liberal arts/general studies, business/marketing, and computer/information sciences. The faculty at NHU has 17 full-time members, 100% with terminal degrees. The student-faculty ratio is 14:1.

Students of NHU The student body totals 469, of whom 293 are undergraduates. 45.1% are women and 54.9% are men. Students come from 4 states and territories and 6 other countries. 4.7% are international students. 86% returned for their sophomore year.

Applying NHU requires an essay, a high school transcript, an interview, recommendations, and a minimum high school GPA of 2.0. The school recommends SAT II: Writing Test and SAT I and SAT II or ACT. Application deadline: 8/15.

NATIONAL-LOUIS UNIVERSITY

Chicago, IL

Urban setting ■ Private ■ Independent ■ Coed

Web site: www.nl.edu

Contact: Ms. Pat Petillo, Director of Admissions, 122 South Michigan Avenue, Chicago, IL 60603

Telephone: 888-NLU-TODAY or toll-free 888-NLU-TODAY (in-state), 800-443-5522 (out-of-state)

Getting in Last Year 118 enrolled.

Financial Matters $15,651 tuition and fees (2002–03); $5913 room and board.

Academics NLU awards bachelor's, master's, and doctoral degrees and post-bachelor's and post-master's certificates. Challenging opportunities include advanced placement credit, accelerated degree programs, an honors program, independent study, and a senior project. Special programs include internships and summer session for credit. The most frequently chosen baccalaureate fields are business/marketing, interdisciplinary studies, and education. The faculty at NLU has 282 full-time members, 17% with terminal degrees. The student-faculty ratio is 19:1.

Students of NLU The student body totals 7,904, of whom 3,043 are undergraduates. 72.9% are women and 27.1% are men. Students come from 19 states and territories. 99% are from Illinois. 0.1% are international students. 100% returned for their sophomore year.

Applying NLU requires a high school transcript and a minimum high school GPA of 2.0, and in some cases SAT I or ACT and 2 recommendations. The school recommends an interview. Application deadline: rolling admissions. Deferred admission is possible.

NATIONAL UNIVERSITY

La Jolla, CA

Urban setting ■ Private ■ Independent ■ Coed

Web site: www.nu.edu

Contact: Ms. Nancy Rohland, Associate Regional Dean, San Diego, 11255 North Torrey Pines Road, La Jolla, CA 92037

Telephone: 858-541-7701 or toll-free 800-628-8648 **Fax:** 858-642-8710

E-mail: nrohland@nu.edu

Getting in Last Year 156 applied; 100% were accepted; 56 enrolled (36%).

Financial Matters $8025 tuition and fees (2002–03).

Academics National University awards associate, bachelor's, and master's degrees and post-bachelor's and post-master's certificates. Challenging opportunities include advanced placement credit, accelerated degree programs, double majors, independent study, and a senior project. Special programs include internships, summer session for credit, off-campus study, and Army and Air Force ROTC. The most frequently chosen baccalaureate fields are business/marketing, computer/information sciences, and psychology. The faculty at National University has 141 full-time members, 93% with terminal degrees. The student-faculty ratio is 16:1.

Students of National University The student body totals 17,865, of whom 4,776 are undergraduates. 57.4% are women and 42.6% are men. 1.4% are international students. 53% returned for their sophomore year.

Applying National University requires a high school transcript and an interview, and in some cases an essay. Application deadline: rolling admissions. Deferred admission is possible.

NAZARENE BIBLE COLLEGE

Colorado Springs, CO

Urban setting ■ Private ■ Independent Religious ■ Coed

Web site: www.nbc.edu

Contact: Dr. David Phillips, Director of Admissions/Public Relations, 1111 Academy Park Loop, Colorado Springs, CO 80910-3704

Telephone: 719-884-5031 or toll-free 800-873-3873 **Fax:** 719-884-5199

Getting in Last Year 240 applied; 48% were accepted; 36 enrolled (31%).

Financial Matters $6574 tuition and fees (2002–03).

Academics NBC awards associate and bachelor's degrees. Challenging opportunities include double majors and independent study. Special programs include internships and summer session for credit. The faculty at NBC has 11 full-time members, 100% with terminal degrees. The student-faculty ratio is 15:1.

Students of NBC The student body is made up of 531 undergraduates. 30.1% are women and 69.9% are men. Students come from 49 states and territories and 2 other countries. 14% are from Colorado. 1.1% are international students. 89% returned for their sophomore year.

Applying NBC requires an essay, a high school transcript, and 2 recommendations. Application deadline: 8/31. Deferred admission is possible.

NAZARETH COLLEGE OF ROCHESTER

Rochester, NY

Suburban setting ■ Private ■ Independent ■ Coed

Web site: www.naz.edu

Contact: Ms. Barbara Mattingly, Application Coordinator, 4245 East Avenue, Rochester, NY 14618-3790

Telephone: 585-389-2827 or toll-free 800-462-3944 (in-state) **Fax:** 585-389-2826

E-mail: admissions@naz.edu

Getting in Last Year 1,654 applied; 84% were accepted; 387 enrolled (28%).

Financial Matters $16,376 tuition and fees (2002–03); $6930 room and board; 82% average percent of need met; $14,097 average financial aid amount received per undergraduate.

Academics Nazareth College awards bachelor's and master's degrees and post-master's certificates. Challenging opportunities include advanced placement credit, an honors program, double majors, independent study, and a senior project. Special programs include cooperative education, internships, summer session for credit, off-campus study, study-abroad, and Army and Air Force ROTC. The most frequently chosen baccalaureate fields are education, health professions and related sciences, and business/marketing. The faculty at Nazareth College has 132 full-time members, 92% with terminal degrees. The student-faculty ratio is 13:1.

Students of Nazareth College The student body totals 3,146, of whom 1,969 are undergraduates. 74.7% are women and 25.3% are men. Students come from 23 states and territories. 94% are from New York. 0.4% are international students. 84% returned for their sophomore year.

Applying Nazareth College requires an essay, SAT I or ACT, a high school transcript, and 1 recommendation. The school recommends an interview and 2 recommendations. Application deadline: 2/15; 2/15 priority date for financial aid. Early and deferred admission are possible.

NEBRASKA CHRISTIAN COLLEGE

Norfolk, NE

Small-town setting ■ Private ■ Independent Religious ■ Coed

Web site: www.nechristian.edu

Contact: Mr. Jason Epperson, Associate Director of Admissions, 1800 Syracuse Avenue, Norfolk, NE 68701

Telephone: 402-378-5000 ext. 413 **Fax:** 402-379-5100

E-mail: admissions@nechristian.edu

Getting in Last Year 175 applied; 45% were accepted; 60 enrolled (76%).

Financial Matters $5440 tuition and fees (2002–03); $4260 room and board.

Academics Nebraska Christian College awards associate and bachelor's degrees. A senior project is a challenging opportunity. Special programs include internships and off-campus study. The faculty at Nebraska Christian College has 16 members, 19% with terminal degrees. The student-faculty ratio is 17:1.

Students of Nebraska Christian College The student body is made up of 167 undergraduates. 48.5% are women and 51.5% are men. Students come from 15 states and territories and 3 other countries. 51% are from Nebraska. 1.8% are international students. 63% returned for their sophomore year.

Applying Nebraska Christian College requires ACT, a high school transcript, and 2 recommendations, and in some cases an interview. Application deadline: rolling admissions; 6/1 priority date for financial aid.

NEBRASKA METHODIST COLLEGE

Omaha, NE

Urban setting ■ Private ■ Independent Religious ■ Coed

Web site: www.methodistcollege.edu

Contact: Ms. Deann Sterner, Director of Admissions, 8501 West Dodge Road, Omaha, NE 68114-3426

Telephone: 402-354-4922 or toll-free 800-335-5510 **Fax:** 402-354-8875

E-mail: dsterne@methodistcollege.edu

Getting in Last Year 54 applied; 83% were accepted; 32 enrolled (71%).

Financial Matters $9900 tuition and fees (2002–03); $1600 room only; 62% average percent of need met; $6021 average financial aid amount received per undergraduate (2001–02).

Academics Nebraska Methodist College awards associate, bachelor's, and master's degrees and post-master's certificates. Challenging opportunities include advanced placement credit, accelerated degree programs, and independent study. Special programs include internships, summer session for credit, and Army ROTC. The most frequently chosen baccalaureate field is health professions and related sciences. The faculty at Nebraska Methodist College has 31 full-time members, 42% with terminal degrees. The student-faculty ratio is 10:1.

Students of Nebraska Methodist College The student body totals 343, of whom 304 are undergraduates. 90.8% are women and 9.2% are men. Students come from 6 states and territories and 1 other country. 80% are from Nebraska. 0.3% are international students. 72% returned for their sophomore year.

Applying Nebraska Methodist College requires an essay, SAT I or ACT, a high school transcript, an interview, 3 recommendations, and a minimum high school GPA of 2.0. Application deadline: 4/1; 5/1 priority date for financial aid. Deferred admission is possible.

NEBRASKA WESLEYAN UNIVERSITY

Lincoln, NE

Suburban setting ■ Private ■ Independent Religious ■ Coed

Web site: www.nebrwesleyan.edu

Contact: Mr. Kendal E. Sieg, Assistant Vice President for Admissions, 5000 Saint Paul Avenue, Lincoln, NE 68504

Telephone: 402-465-2218 or toll-free 800-541-3818 **Fax:** 402-465-2179

E-mail: admissions@nebrwesleyan.edu

Getting in Last Year 1,030 applied; 93% were accepted; 336 enrolled (35%).

Financial Matters $15,645 tuition and fees (2002–03); $4446 room and board; 74% average percent of need met; $11,866 average financial aid amount received per undergraduate.

Academics NWU awards bachelor's and master's degrees. Challenging opportunities include advanced placement credit, double majors, independent study, and a senior project. Special programs include internships, summer session for credit, off-campus study, study-abroad, and Army and Air Force ROTC. The most frequently chosen baccalaureate fields are business/marketing, psychology, and parks and recreation. The faculty at NWU has 95 full-time members, 84% with terminal degrees. The student-faculty ratio is 14:1.

Students of NWU The student body totals 1,684, of whom 1,559 are undergraduates. 55.4% are women and 44.6% are men. Students come from 25 states and territories and 9 other countries. 94% are from Nebraska. 0.5% are international students. 84% returned for their sophomore year.

Applying NWU requires SAT I or ACT, a high school transcript, and a minimum high school GPA of 2.0, and in some cases an essay and resume of activities. The school recommends an interview. Application deadline: 5/1. Early and deferred admission are possible.

NER ISRAEL RABBINICAL COLLEGE

Baltimore, MD

Suburban setting ■ Private ■ Independent Religious ■ Men Only

Contact: Rabbi Berel Weisbord, Dean of Admissions, Mount Wilson Lane, Baltimore, MD 21208

Telephone: 410-484-7200

Getting in Last Year 134 applied; 50% were accepted; 63 enrolled (94%).

Financial Matters $6500 tuition and fees (2002–03); $6500 room and board.

Academics Ner Israel Rabbinical College awards bachelor's, master's, doctoral, and first-professional degrees. An honors program is a challenging opportunity. Special programs include summer session for credit and study-abroad. The faculty at Ner Israel Rabbinical College has 22 full-time members.

Students of Ner Israel Rabbinical College The student body totals 577, of whom 353 are undergraduates. Students come from 36 states and territories. 26% are from Maryland.

Applying Ner Israel Rabbinical College requires recommendations. The school recommends an interview. Application deadline: rolling admissions. Early and deferred admission are possible.

NEUMANN COLLEGE

Aston, PA

Suburban setting ■ Private ■ Independent Religious ■ Coed

Web site: www.neumann.edu

Contact: Mr. Scott Bogard, Director of Admissions, One Neumann Drive, Aston, PA 19014-1298

Telephone: 610-558-5612 or toll-free 800-963-8626 **Fax:** 610-558-5652

E-mail: neumann@neumann.edu

Getting in Last Year 1,207 applied; 70% were accepted; 382 enrolled (45%).

Financial Matters $15,650 tuition and fees (2002–03); $7260 room and board; $15,000 average financial aid amount received per undergraduate (2001–02).

Academics Neumann awards associate, bachelor's, and master's degrees. Challenging opportunities include advanced placement credit, accelerated degree programs, student-designed majors, freshman honors college, an honors program, double majors, and independent study. Special programs include cooperative education, internships, summer session for credit, off-campus study, study-

Neumann College (continued)

abroad, and Army ROTC. The most frequently chosen baccalaureate fields are liberal arts/general studies, business/marketing, and health professions and related sciences. The faculty at Neumann has 67 full-time members, 63% with terminal degrees. The student-faculty ratio is 17:1.

Students of Neumann The student body totals 2,221, of whom 1,853 are undergraduates. 64.2% are women and 35.8% are men. Students come from 18 states and territories and 5 other countries. 73% are from Pennsylvania. 0.4% are international students. 76% returned for their sophomore year.

Applying Neumann requires SAT I or ACT, a high school transcript, and a minimum high school GPA of 2.00. The school recommends an interview. Application deadline: rolling admissions. Early and deferred admission are possible.

NEWBERRY COLLEGE

Newberry, SC

Small-town setting ■ Private ■ Independent Religious ■ Coed

Web site: www.newberry.edu
Contact: Mr. Jonathan Reece, Director of Admissions, 2100 College Street, Smeltzer Hall, Newberry, SC 29108
Telephone: 803-321-5127 or toll-free 800-845-4955 ext. 5127
Fax: 803-321-5138
E-mail: admissions@newberry.edu

Getting in Last Year 1,046 applied; 71% were accepted; 250 enrolled (34%).

Financial Matters $16,100 tuition and fees (2002–03); $4588 room and board; 79% average percent of need met; $13,886 average financial aid amount received per undergraduate.

Academics Newberry awards bachelor's degrees. Challenging opportunities include advanced placement credit, student-designed majors, an honors program, double majors, independent study, and a senior project. Special programs include cooperative education, internships, summer session for credit, study-abroad, and Army ROTC. The most frequently chosen baccalaureate fields are education, business/marketing, and social sciences and history. The faculty at Newberry has 44 full-time members, 73% with terminal degrees. The student-faculty ratio is 12:1.

Students of Newberry The student body is made up of 748 undergraduates. 44.4% are women and 55.6% are men. Students come from 27 states and territories and 9 other countries. 88% are from South Carolina. 1.3% are international students. 66% returned for their sophomore year.

Applying Newberry requires SAT I or ACT, a high school transcript, and a minimum high school GPA of 2.0, and in some cases an essay. The school recommends an interview and 2 recommendations. Application deadline: rolling admissions; 3/15 priority date for financial aid. Early and deferred admission are possible.

NEWBURY COLLEGE

Brookline, MA

Suburban setting ■ Private ■ Independent ■ Coed

Web site: www.newbury.edu
Contact: Ms. Jacqueline Giordano, Dean of Admission, 129 Fisher Avenue, Brookline, MA 02445-5796
Telephone: 617-730-7007 or toll-free 800-NEWBURY **Fax:** 617-731-9618
E-mail: info@newbury.edu

Getting in Last Year 964 applied; 88% were accepted; 366 enrolled (43%).

Financial Matters $14,550 tuition and fees (2002–03); $7450 room and board.

Academics Newbury awards associate and bachelor's degrees. Challenging opportunities include advanced placement credit, accelerated degree programs, freshman honors college, an honors program, double majors, independent study, and a senior project. Special programs include cooperative education, internships, summer session for credit, off-campus study, and study-abroad. The most frequently chosen baccalaureate field is law/legal studies. The faculty at Newbury has 35 full-time members, 66% with terminal degrees. The student-faculty ratio is 15:1.

Students of Newbury The student body is made up of 1,472 undergraduates. 62.5% are women and 37.5% are men. Students come from 24 states and territories and 40 other countries. 70% are from Massachusetts. 7.6% are international students. 80% returned for their sophomore year.

Applying Newbury requires an essay, a high school transcript, and recommendations, and in some cases SAT I or ACT. The school recommends SAT I or ACT, an interview, and a minimum high school GPA of 2.0. Application deadline: rolling admissions. Early and deferred admission are possible.

NEW COLLEGE OF CALIFORNIA

San Francisco, CA

Urban setting ■ Private ■ Independent ■ Coed

Web site: www.newcollege.edu
Contact: Ms. Sarah Starpoli, Admissions Inquiry Office, 777 Valencia Street, San Francisco, CA 94110
Telephone: 415-437-3420 or toll-free 888-437-3460 **Fax:** 415-865-2636
E-mail: admissions@newcollege.edu

Financial Matters $10,220 tuition and fees (2002–03).

Academics New College awards bachelor's and master's degrees and first-professional certificates. Challenging opportunities include advanced placement credit, accelerated degree programs, student-designed majors, and a senior project. Special programs include cooperative education, internships, and study-abroad. The faculty at New College has 40 full-time members. The student-faculty ratio is 15:1.

Students of New College The student body totals 1,088, of whom 234 are undergraduates. 87% returned for their sophomore year.

Applying New College requires an essay and a high school transcript, and in some cases 2 recommendations. The school recommends an interview. Application deadline: rolling admissions. Deferred admission is possible.

NEW COLLEGE OF FLORIDA

Sarasota, FL

Suburban setting ■ Public ■ State-supported ■ Coed

Web site: www.ncf.edu
Contact: Mr. Joel Bauman, Dean of Admissions and Financial Aid, 5700 North Tamiami Trail, Sarasota, FL 34243-2197
Telephone: 941-359-4269 **Fax:** 941-359-4435
E-mail: admissions@ncf.edu

Getting in Last Year 494 applied; 65% were accepted; 160 enrolled (50%).

Financial Matters $3020 resident tuition and fees (2002–03); $13,810 nonresident tuition and fees (2002–03); $5394 room and board; 84% average percent of need met; $7669 average financial aid amount received per undergraduate (2001–02).

Academics New College of Florida awards bachelor's degrees. Challenging opportunities include accelerated degree programs, student-designed majors, an honors program, double majors, independent study, and a senior project. Special programs include internships, off-campus study, and study-abroad. The most frequently chosen baccalaureate field is liberal arts/general studies. The faculty at New College of Florida has 60 full-time members, 98% with terminal degrees. The student-faculty ratio is 11:1.

Students of New College of Florida The student body is made up of 650 undergraduates. 64.2% are women and 35.8% are men. Students come from 35 states and territories and 8 other countries. 74% are from Florida. 1.5% are international students. 81% returned for their sophomore year.

Applying New College of Florida requires an essay, SAT I or ACT, a high school transcript, and 2 recommendations, and in some cases an interview. The school recommends an interview, graded writing sample, and a minimum high school GPA of 3.0. Application deadline: 5/1. Early and deferred admission are possible.

NEW ENGLAND COLLEGE

Henniker, NH

Small-town setting ■ Private ■ Independent ■ Coed

Web site: www.nec.edu
Contact: Mr. Paul Miller, Director of Admission/Financial Aid, 26 Bridge Street, Henniker, NH 03242
Telephone: 603-428-2223 or toll-free 800-521-7642 (out-of-state)
Fax: 603-428-3155
E-mail: admission@nec.edu

Getting in Last Year 1,010 applied; 96% were accepted; 239 enrolled (25%).

Financial Matters $20,326 tuition and fees (2002–03); $7434 room and board; 76% average percent of need met; $23,601 average financial aid amount received per undergraduate.

Academics NEC awards associate, bachelor's, and master's degrees. Challenging opportunities include advanced placement credit, student-designed majors, an honors program, double majors, independent study, and a senior project. Special programs include cooperative education, internships, summer session for credit, off-campus study, study-abroad, and Army and Air Force ROTC. The most frequently chosen baccalaureate fields are business/marketing, social sciences and history, and psychology. The faculty at NEC has 53 full-time members, 55% with terminal degrees. The student-faculty ratio is 13:1.

Students of NEC The student body totals 962, of whom 836 are undergraduates. 52.2% are women and 47.8% are men. Students come from 27 states and territories and 16 other countries. 26% are from New Hampshire. 2.4% are international students. 71% returned for their sophomore year.

Applying NEC requires an essay, a high school transcript, and 1 recommendation. The school recommends an interview. Application deadline: rolling admissions; 4/1 priority date for financial aid. Deferred admission is possible.

NEW ENGLAND CONSERVATORY OF MUSIC

Boston, MA

Urban setting ■ Private ■ Independent ■ Coed

Web site: www.newenglandconservatory.edu
Contact: Mr. Tom Novak, Dean of Admissions, 290 Huntington Avenue, Boston, MA 02115-5000
Telephone: 617-585-1101 **Fax:** 617-585-1115
E-mail: admissions@newenglandconservatory.edu

Getting in Last Year 831 applied; 42% were accepted; 118 enrolled (33%).

Financial Matters $23,250 tuition and fees (2002–03); $9850 room and board; 70% average percent of need met; $17,358 average financial aid amount received per undergraduate.

Academics NEC awards bachelor's, master's, and doctoral degrees and post-bachelor's certificates. Challenging opportunities include advanced placement credit, independent study, and a senior project. Special programs include internships, summer session for credit, off-campus study, and study-abroad. The most frequently chosen baccalaureate field is visual/performing arts. The faculty at NEC has 88 full-time members. The student-faculty ratio is 4:1.

Students of NEC The student body totals 706, of whom 362 are undergraduates. 46.7% are women and 53.3% are men. Students come from 46 states and territories and 36 other countries. 23% are from Massachusetts. 17.3% are international students.

Applying NEC requires an essay, SAT I or ACT, a high school transcript, 2 recommendations, audition, and a minimum high school GPA of 2.75. Application deadline: 12/3; 2/2 priority date for financial aid. Deferred admission is possible.

NEW ENGLAND SCHOOL OF COMMUNICATIONS

Bangor, ME

Small-town setting ■ Private ■ Coed

Web site: www.nescom.edu
Contact: Ms. Louise G. Grant, Director of Admissions, 1 College Circle, Bangor, ME 04401
Telephone: 207-941-7176 ext. 1093 or toll-free 888-877-1876
Fax: 207-947-3987
E-mail: info@nescom.edu

Getting in Last Year 270 applied; 68% were accepted; 98 enrolled (54%).

Financial Matters $8980 tuition and fees (2002–03); $5390 room and board; 92% average percent of need met; $6320 average financial aid amount received per undergraduate (2001–02).

Academics New England School of Communications awards associate and bachelor's degrees. Challenging opportunities include advanced placement credit, student-designed majors, double majors, independent study, and a senior project. Special programs include internships and summer session for credit. The most frequently chosen baccalaureate field is communications/communication technologies. The faculty at New England School of Communications has 6 full-time members, 100% with terminal degrees. The student-faculty ratio is 15:1.

Students of New England School of Communications The student body is made up of 204 undergraduates. 29.9% are women and 70.1% are men. Students come from 7 states and territories. 84% are from Maine.

Applying New England School of Communications requires an essay, Wonderlic aptitude test, a high school transcript, an interview, 2 recommendations, and Wonderlic Scholastic Test. The school recommends SAT I or ACT. Application deadline: rolling admissions; 5/1 priority date for financial aid. Early and deferred admission are possible.

NEW HAMPSHIRE INSTITUTE OF ART

Manchester, NH

Private ■ Proprietary ■ Coed

Contact: Ms. Jane Langlois, Admissions Officer, 148 Concord Street, Manchester, NH 03104-4858
Telephone: 603-623-0313 ext. 576 or toll-free 866-241-4918 (in-state)
E-mail: lsullivan@nhia.edu

Financial Matters $8600 tuition and fees (2002–03).

Academics New Hampshire Institute of Art awards bachelor's degrees. A senior project is a challenging opportunity. Summer session for credit is a special program. The faculty at New Hampshire Institute of Art has 4 full-time members, 100% with terminal degrees. The student-faculty ratio is 12:1.

Students of New Hampshire Institute of Art The student body is made up of 87 undergraduates. 77% are women and 23% are men. Students come from 2 states and territories and 1 other country. 99% are from New Hampshire. 1.1% are international students.

Applying New Hampshire Institute of Art requires an essay, SAT I or ACT, a high school transcript, and portfolio. The school recommends an interview. Application deadline: 5/1 priority date for financial aid.

NEW JERSEY CITY UNIVERSITY

Jersey City, NJ

Urban setting ■ Public ■ State-supported ■ Coed

Web site: www.njcu.edu
Contact: Ms. Drusilla Blackman, Director of Admissions, 2039 Kennedy Boulevard, Jersey City, NJ 07305
Telephone: 201-200-3234 or toll-free 888-441-NJCU
E-mail: admissions@njcu.edu

Getting in Last Year 2,642 applied; 53% were accepted; 662 enrolled (48%).

Financial Matters $5556 resident tuition and fees (2002–03); $9509 nonresident tuition and fees (2002–03); $6198 room and board.

Academics NJCU awards bachelor's and master's degrees and post-master's certificates. Challenging opportunities include advanced placement credit, accelerated degree programs, an honors program, double majors, independent study, and a senior project. Special programs include cooperative education, internships, summer session for credit, off-campus study, study-abroad, and Army and Air Force ROTC. The most frequently chosen baccalaureate fields are business/marketing, social sciences and history, and protective services/public administration. The faculty at NJCU has 238 full-time members, 80% with terminal degrees. The student-faculty ratio is 15:1.

Students of NJCU The student body totals 9,099, of whom 6,187 are undergraduates. 60.6% are women and 39.4% are men. Students come from 10 states and territories. 96% are from New Jersey. 1.8% are international students.

Applying NJCU requires an essay, SAT I or ACT, a high school transcript, and a minimum high school GPA of 2.0, and in some cases an interview. The school recommends 1 recommendation. Application deadline: 4/1; 4/15 priority date for financial aid. Deferred admission is possible.

NEW JERSEY INSTITUTE OF TECHNOLOGY

Newark, NJ

Urban setting ■ Public ■ State-supported ■ Coed

Web site: www.njit.edu
Contact: Ms. Kathy Kelly, Director of Admissions, University Heights, Newark, NJ 07102-1982
Telephone: 973-596-3300 or toll-free 800-925-NJIT **Fax:** 973-596-3461
E-mail: admissions@njit.edu

Getting in Last Year 2,591 applied; 58% were accepted; 662 enrolled (44%).

Financial Matters $7906 resident tuition and fees (2002–03); $12,858 nonresident tuition and fees (2002–03); $7864 room and board; 90% average percent of need met; $5400 average financial aid amount received per undergraduate.

Academics NJIT awards bachelor's, master's, and doctoral degrees and post-bachelor's certificates. Challenging opportunities include advanced placement credit, accelerated degree programs, freshman honors college, an honors program, double majors, independent study, and a senior project. Special programs include cooperative education, internships, summer session for credit, off-campus study, study-abroad, and Air Force ROTC. The most frequently chosen baccalaureate fields are engineering/engineering technologies, computer/information sciences, and business/marketing. The faculty at NJIT has 409 full-time members, 100% with terminal degrees. The student-faculty ratio is 13:1.

Students of NJIT The student body totals 8,828, of whom 5,730 are undergraduates. 21.3% are women and 78.7% are men. Students come from 30 states and territories and 61 other countries. 96% are from New Jersey. 5.9% are international students. 80% returned for their sophomore year.

Applying NJIT requires SAT I or ACT and a high school transcript, and in some cases an essay, SAT II Subject Tests, and an interview. The school recommends 1 recommendation. Application deadline: 4/1; 5/15 for financial aid, with a 3/15 priority date. Early and deferred admission are possible.

NEWMAN UNIVERSITY

Wichita, KS

Urban setting ■ Private ■ Independent Religious ■ Coed

Web site: www.newmanu.edu
Contact: Mrs. Marla Sexson, Dean of Admissions, 3100 McCormick Avenue, Wichita, KS 67213
Telephone: 316-942-4291 ext. 144 or toll-free 877-NEWMANU ext. 144
Fax: 316-942-4483
E-mail: admissions@newmanu.edu

Getting in Last Year 442 applied; 100% were accepted; 133 enrolled (30%).

Financial Matters $12,040 tuition and fees (2002–03); $4590 room and board; 70% average percent of need met; $8364 average financial aid amount received per undergraduate (2001–02).

Academics Newman awards associate, bachelor's, and master's degrees. Challenging opportunities include advanced placement credit, accelerated degree programs, double majors, independent study, and a senior project. Special programs include cooperative education, internships, summer session for credit,

Newman University (continued)

off-campus study, and study-abroad. The faculty at Newman has 68 full-time members, 54% with terminal degrees. The student-faculty ratio is 14:1.

Students of Newman The student body totals 1,929, of whom 1,678 are undergraduates. 65.5% are women and 34.5% are men. Students come from 30 states and territories and 33 other countries. 87% are from Kansas. 4.3% are international students. 63% returned for their sophomore year.

Applying Newman requires SAT I or ACT, a high school transcript, and a minimum high school GPA of 2.0. The school recommends an interview. Application deadline: rolling admissions; 3/1 priority date for financial aid. Early and deferred admission are possible.

NEW MEXICO HIGHLANDS UNIVERSITY

Las Vegas, NM

Small-town setting ■ Public ■ State-supported ■ Coed

Web site: www.nmhu.edu
Contact: Ms. Betsy Yost, Interim Dean of Students, Box 9000, Las Vegas, NM 87701
Telephone: 505-454-3020 or toll-free 800-338-6648 **Fax:** 505-454-3311
E-mail: admission@venus.nmnu.edu

Getting in Last Year 1,133 applied; 80% were accepted; 222 enrolled (25%).

Financial Matters $2184 resident tuition and fees (2002–03); $9096 nonresident tuition and fees (2002–03); $5638 room and board; 29% average percent of need met; $3830 average financial aid amount received per undergraduate.

Academics Highlands awards associate, bachelor's, and master's degrees. Challenging opportunities include advanced placement credit, accelerated degree programs, an honors program, double majors, independent study, and a senior project. Special programs include cooperative education, internships, summer session for credit, and off-campus study. The most frequently chosen baccalaureate fields are business/marketing, education, and health professions and related sciences. The faculty at Highlands has 134 full-time members, 80% with terminal degrees.

Students of Highlands The student body totals 3,225, of whom 1,657 are undergraduates. 62.8% are women and 37.2% are men. Students come from 24 states and territories and 8 other countries. 92% are from New Mexico. 0.7% are international students. 56% returned for their sophomore year.

Applying Highlands requires ACT, a high school transcript, and a minimum high school GPA of 2.0, and in some cases an interview and 2 recommendations. Application deadline: rolling admissions; 3/1 priority date for financial aid. Early and deferred admission are possible.

NEW MEXICO INSTITUTE OF MINING AND TECHNOLOGY

Socorro, NM

Small-town setting ■ Public ■ State-supported ■ Coed

Web site: www.nmt.edu
Contact: Ms. Melissa Jaramillo-Fleming, Director of Admissions, 801 Leroy Place, Socorro, NM 87801
Telephone: 505-835-5424 or toll-free 800-428-TECH **Fax:** 505-835-5989
E-mail: admission@admin.nmt.edu

Getting in Last Year 482 applied; 63% were accepted; 277 enrolled (91%).

Financial Matters $2911 resident tuition and fees (2002–03); $9122 nonresident tuition and fees (2002–03); $4218 room and board; 90% average percent of need met; $7945 average financial aid amount received per undergraduate.

Academics New Mexico Tech awards associate, bachelor's, master's, and doctoral degrees. Challenging opportunities include advanced placement credit, accelerated degree programs, student-designed majors, double majors, independent study, and a senior project. Special programs include cooperative education, internships, and summer session for credit. The most frequently chosen baccalaureate fields are engineering/engineering technologies, physical sciences, and computer/information sciences. The faculty at New Mexico Tech has 120 full-time members, 99% with terminal degrees. The student-faculty ratio is 13:1.

Students of New Mexico Tech The student body totals 1,727, of whom 1,336 are undergraduates. 35.5% are women and 64.5% are men. Students come from 52 states and territories and 14 other countries. 84% are from New Mexico. 2.8% are international students. 74% returned for their sophomore year.

Applying New Mexico Tech requires SAT I or ACT, a high school transcript, and a minimum high school GPA of 2.5, and in some cases 2 recommendations. The school recommends an interview. Application deadline: 8/1; 6/1 priority date for financial aid. Deferred admission is possible.

NEW MEXICO STATE UNIVERSITY

Las Cruces, NM

Suburban setting ■ Public ■ State-supported ■ Coed

Web site: www.nmsu.edu
Contact: Ms. Angela Mora-Riley, Director of Admissions, Box 30001, MSC, Las Cruces, NM 88003-8001
Telephone: 505-646-3121 or toll-free 800-662-6678 **Fax:** 505-646-6330
E-mail: admssions@nmsu.edu

Getting in Last Year 5,706 applied; 81% were accepted; 2,049 enrolled (44%).

Financial Matters $3456 resident tuition and fees (2002–03); $11,076 nonresident tuition and fees (2002–03); $4422 room and board; 74% average percent of need met; $8207 average financial aid amount received per undergraduate.

Academics NMSU awards associate, bachelor's, master's, and doctoral degrees and post-master's certificates. Challenging opportunities include advanced placement credit, accelerated degree programs, student-designed majors, an honors program, double majors, independent study, and a senior project. Special programs include cooperative education, internships, summer session for credit, off-campus study, study-abroad, and Army and Air Force ROTC. The most frequently chosen baccalaureate fields are business/marketing, engineering/engineering technologies, and education. The faculty at NMSU has 669 full-time members, 84% with terminal degrees. The student-faculty ratio is 19:1.

Students of NMSU The student body totals 15,243, of whom 12,531 are undergraduates. 54.3% are women and 45.7% are men. Students come from 52 states and territories and 49 other countries. 82% are from New Mexico. 1% are international students. 73% returned for their sophomore year.

Applying NMSU requires SAT I or ACT, a high school transcript, and a minimum high school GPA of 2.0. Application deadline: 8/14; 3/1 priority date for financial aid. Early and deferred admission are possible.

NEW SCHOOL BACHELOR OF ARTS, NEW SCHOOL UNIVERSITY

New York, NY

Urban setting ■ Private ■ Independent ■ Coed

Web site: www.newschool.edu
Contact: Ms. Gerianne Brusati, Director of Educational Advising and Admissions, 66 West 12th Street, New York, NY 10011-8603
Telephone: 212-229-5630
E-mail: admissions@dialnsa.edu

Getting in Last Year 8 enrolled.

Financial Matters $15,418 tuition and fees (2002–03); $9896 room and board; 67% average percent of need met; $10,260 average financial aid amount received per undergraduate (2001–02).

Academics The New School awards bachelor's, master's, and doctoral degrees. Challenging opportunities include advanced placement credit, accelerated degree programs, student-designed majors, and independent study. Special programs include internships and summer session for credit. The most frequently chosen baccalaureate field is liberal arts/general studies.

Students of The New School The student body totals 1,292, of whom 573 are undergraduates. 64.4% are women and 35.6% are men. Students come from 19 states and territories and 23 other countries. 80% are from New York. 4.2% are international students.

Applying Application deadline: 3/1 priority date for financial aid. Deferred admission is possible.

NEWSCHOOL OF ARCHITECTURE & DESIGN

San Diego, CA

Urban setting ■ Private ■ Proprietary ■ Coed, Primarily Men

Web site: www.newschoolarch.edu
Contact: Ms. Lexi Rogers, Director of Admissions, 1249 F Street, San Diego, CA 92101-6634
Telephone: 619-235-4100 ext. 106 or toll-free 619-235-4100 ext. 106
E-mail: admissions@newschoolarch.edu

Getting in Last Year 2 applied; 100% were accepted; 2 enrolled (100%).

Financial Matters $17,514 tuition and fees (2002–03); 90% average percent of need met; $9700 average financial aid amount received per undergraduate (2000–01).

Academics Newschool of Architecture & Design awards associate, bachelor's, master's, and first-professional degrees. Challenging opportunities include advanced placement credit and a senior project. Special programs include cooperative education, internships, summer session for credit, off-campus study, and study-abroad. The faculty at Newschool of Architecture & Design has 7 full-time members, 29% with terminal degrees. The student-faculty ratio is 15:1.

Students of Newschool of Architecture & Design The student body totals 198, of whom 4 are undergraduates. 100% are men. Students come from 4 states and territories. 85% are from California.

Applying Newschool of Architecture & Design requires an essay, a high school transcript, an interview, and a minimum high school GPA of 2.5, and in some cases portfolio. The school recommends recommendations. Application deadline: 8/30, 8/30 for nonresidents.

NEW WORLD SCHOOL OF THE ARTS

Miami, FL

Urban setting ■ Public ■ State-supported ■ Coed

Web site: www.mdcc.edu/nwsa
Contact: Ms. Pamela Neumann, Recruitment and Admissions Coordinator, 300 NE Second Avenue, Miami, FL 33132
Telephone: 305-237-7007 **Fax:** 305-237-3794
E-mail: nwsaadm@mdcc.edu

Getting in Last Year 277 applied; 49% were accepted; 98 enrolled (72%).

Financial Matters $1583 resident tuition and fees (2002–03); $5529 nonresident tuition and fees (2002–03).

Academics NWSA awards associate and bachelor's degrees. Challenging opportunities include advanced placement credit, freshman honors college, an honors program, and a senior project. Special programs include cooperative education, internships, and summer session for credit. The most frequently chosen baccalaureate field is visual/performing arts. The faculty at NWSA has 20 full-time members, 75% with terminal degrees. The student-faculty ratio is 8:1.

Students of NWSA The student body is made up of 350 undergraduates. 80% returned for their sophomore year.

Applying NWSA requires an essay, a high school transcript, an interview, 2 recommendations, and audition. The school recommends SAT I or ACT.

NEW YORK INSTITUTE OF TECHNOLOGY

Old Westbury, NY

Suburban setting ■ Private ■ Independent ■ Coed

Web site: www.nyit.edu
Contact: Ms. Robbie de Leur, Director of Financial Aid, PO Box 8000, Old Westbury, NY 11568
Telephone: 516-686-7680 or toll-free 800-345-NYIT **Fax:** 516-686-7613
E-mail: admissions@nyit.edu

Getting in Last Year 3,568 applied; 72% were accepted; 864 enrolled (34%).

Financial Matters $15,950 tuition and fees (2002–03); $7680 room and board; $8323 average financial aid amount received per undergraduate (2001–02).

Academics NYIT awards associate, bachelor's, master's, and first-professional degrees and post-bachelor's and post-master's certificates. Challenging opportunities include advanced placement credit, accelerated degree programs, student-designed majors, an honors program, double majors, independent study, and a senior project. Special programs include cooperative education, internships, summer session for credit, off-campus study, study-abroad, and Army and Air Force ROTC. The most frequently chosen baccalaureate fields are business/marketing, health professions and related sciences, and architecture. The faculty at NYIT has 283 full-time members, 88% with terminal degrees. The student-faculty ratio is 16:1.

Students of NYIT The student body totals 9,155, of whom 5,472 are undergraduates. 37.6% are women and 62.4% are men. Students come from 27 states and territories and 85 other countries. 93% are from New York. 7.9% are international students. 67% returned for their sophomore year.

Applying NYIT requires an essay, SAT I or ACT, and a high school transcript, and in some cases an interview, recommendations, proof of volunteer or work experience required for physical therapy, physician assistant and occupational therapy programs; portfolio for fine arts programs, and a minimum high school GPA of X. Application deadline: rolling admissions; 2/1 priority date for financial aid. Deferred admission is possible.

NEW YORK SCHOOL OF INTERIOR DESIGN

New York, NY

Urban setting ■ Private ■ Independent ■ Coed

Web site: www.nysid.edu
Contact: Mr. Douglas Robbins, Admissions Associate, 170 East 70th Street, New York, NY 10021-5110
Telephone: 212-472-1500 ext. 204 or toll-free 800-336-9743 **Fax:** 212-472-1867
E-mail: admissions@nysid.edu

Getting in Last Year 97 applied; 46% were accepted; 33 enrolled (73%).

Financial Matters $18,070 tuition and fees (2002–03); 50% average percent of need met; $8500 average financial aid amount received per undergraduate.

Academics NYSID awards associate, bachelor's, and master's degrees. Challenging opportunities include advanced placement credit, independent study, and a senior project. Special programs include internships, summer session for credit, and study-abroad. The most frequently chosen baccalaureate field is visual/performing arts. The faculty at NYSID has 2 full-time members. The student-faculty ratio is 9:1.

Students of NYSID The student body totals 733, of whom 725 are undergraduates. 85.9% are women and 14.1% are men. Students come from 16 states and territories. 83% are from New York. 11.2% are international students. 50% returned for their sophomore year.

Applying NYSID requires an essay, SAT I or ACT, a high school transcript, 2 recommendations, portfolio, and a minimum high school GPA of 2.5, and in some cases an interview. The school recommends an interview. Application deadline: rolling admissions; 5/1 priority date for financial aid. Deferred admission is possible.

NEW YORK UNIVERSITY

New York, NY

Urban setting ■ Private ■ Independent ■ Coed

Web site: www.nyu.edu
Contact: Ms. Barbara Han, Associate Provost for Admissions and Financial Aid, 22 Washington Square North, New York, NY 10011
Telephone: 212-998-4500 **Fax:** 212-995-4902

Getting in Last Year 29,581 applied; 28% were accepted; 3,977 enrolled (48%).

Financial Matters $26,646 tuition and fees (2002–03); $10,430 room and board; 70% average percent of need met; $17,715 average financial aid amount received per undergraduate.

Academics NYU awards associate, bachelor's, master's, doctoral, and first-professional degrees and post-bachelor's, post-master's, and first-professional certificates. Challenging opportunities include advanced placement credit, accelerated degree programs, student-designed majors, freshman honors college, an honors program, double majors, independent study, and a senior project. Special programs include internships, summer session for credit, off-campus study, and study-abroad. The faculty at NYU has 1,823 full-time members. The student-faculty ratio is 11:1.

Students of NYU The student body totals 38,096, of whom 19,490 are undergraduates. 60.4% are women and 39.6% are men. Students come from 52 states and territories and 91 other countries. 49% are from New York. 4.2% are international students. 91% returned for their sophomore year.

Applying NYU requires an essay, SAT I or ACT, a high school transcript, 2 recommendations, and a minimum high school GPA of 3.0, and in some cases SAT II Subject Tests, an interview, and audition, portfolio. The school recommends SAT II Subject Tests and SAT II: Writing Test. Application deadline: 1/15; 2/15 priority date for financial aid. Deferred admission is possible.

NIAGARA UNIVERSITY

Niagara University, NY

Suburban setting ■ Private ■ Independent Religious ■ Coed

Web site: www.niagara.edu
Contact: Ms. Christine M. McDermott, Associate Director of Admissions, Office of Admissions, Niagara, NY 14109
Telephone: 716-286-8700 ext. 8715 or toll-free 800-462-2111 **Fax:** 716-286-8733
E-mail: admissions@niagara.edu

Getting in Last Year 2,703 applied; 83% were accepted; 737 enrolled (33%).

Financial Matters $16,550 tuition and fees (2002–03); $7300 room and board; 87% average percent of need met; $15,555 average financial aid amount received per undergraduate.

Academics NU awards associate, bachelor's, and master's degrees and post-master's certificates. Challenging opportunities include advanced placement credit, accelerated degree programs, freshman honors college, an honors program, double majors, and a senior project. Special programs include cooperative education, internships, summer session for credit, off-campus study, study-abroad, and Army ROTC. The most frequently chosen baccalaureate fields are business/marketing, education, and social sciences and history. The faculty at NU has 135 full-time members, 91% with terminal degrees. The student-faculty ratio is 16:1.

Students of NU The student body totals 3,446, of whom 2,635 are undergraduates. 60.2% are women and 39.8% are men. Students come from 31 states and territories and 16 other countries. 92% are from New York. 4.6% are international students. 81% returned for their sophomore year.

Applying NU requires SAT I or ACT and a high school transcript. The school recommends an interview, 3 recommendations, and a minimum high school GPA of 3.0. Application deadline: 8/1; 2/15 priority date for financial aid. Early and deferred admission are possible.

NICHOLLS STATE UNIVERSITY

Thibodaux, LA

Small-town setting ■ Public ■ State-supported ■ Coed

Web site: www.nicholls.edu
Contact: Mrs. Becky L. Durocher, Director of Admissions, PO Box 2004-NSU, Thibodaux, LA 70310
Telephone: 985-448-4507 or toll-free 877-NICHOLLS **Fax:** 985-448-4929
E-mail: nicholls@nicholls.edu

Getting in Last Year 2,467 applied; 99% were accepted; 1,499 enrolled (61%).

Nicholls State University (continued)

Financial Matters $2454 resident tuition and fees (2002–03); $7902 nonresident tuition and fees (2002–03); $3352 room and board; 45% average percent of need met; $2714 average financial aid amount received per undergraduate (2000–01).

Academics Nicholls awards associate, bachelor's, and master's degrees and post-master's certificates. Challenging opportunities include advanced placement credit, accelerated degree programs, an honors program, double majors, independent study, and a senior project. Special programs include cooperative education, internships, summer session for credit, off-campus study, and study-abroad. The most frequently chosen baccalaureate fields are education, business/marketing, and health professions and related sciences. The faculty at Nicholls has 268 full-time members, 56% with terminal degrees. The student-faculty ratio is 23:1.

Students of Nicholls The student body totals 7,314, of whom 6,561 are undergraduates. 63.1% are women and 36.9% are men. Students come from 31 states and territories and 28 other countries. 97% are from Louisiana. 0.9% are international students. 57% returned for their sophomore year.

Applying Nicholls requires a high school transcript, and in some cases ACT. The school recommends ACT. Application deadline: rolling admissions; 4/14 priority date for financial aid. Early and deferred admission are possible.

NICHOLS COLLEGE

Dudley, MA

Rural setting ■ Private ■ Independent ■ Coed

Web site: www.nichols.edu
Contact: Ms. Susan Montville, Admissions Assistant, P.O. Box 5000, Dudley, MA 01571
Telephone: 508-943-2055 or toll-free 800-470-3379 **Fax:** 508-943-9885
E-mail: admissions@nichols.edu

Getting in Last Year 920 applied; 85% were accepted; 276 enrolled (35%).

Financial Matters $18,050 tuition and fees (2002–03); $7810 room and board; 72% average percent of need met; $12,921 average financial aid amount received per undergraduate.

Academics Nichols awards associate, bachelor's, and master's degrees. Challenging opportunities include advanced placement credit, accelerated degree programs, double majors, and independent study. Special programs include cooperative education, internships, summer session for credit, study-abroad, and Army ROTC. The most frequently chosen baccalaureate fields are business/marketing, psychology, and English. The faculty at Nichols has 32 full-time members, 63% with terminal degrees. The student-faculty ratio is 18:1.

Students of Nichols The student body totals 1,905, of whom 1,569 are undergraduates. 44.6% are women and 55.4% are men. Students come from 20 states and territories and 4 other countries. 69% are from Massachusetts. 76% returned for their sophomore year.

Applying Nichols requires an essay, SAT I or ACT, a high school transcript, and 1 recommendation, and in some cases an interview. Application deadline: rolling admissions; 3/1 priority date for financial aid. Early and deferred admission are possible.

NIPISSING UNIVERSITY

North Bay, ON Canada

Suburban setting ■ Public ■ Coed

Web site: www.nipissingu.ca
Contact: Ms. Diane Huber, Manager of Liaison Services, 100 College Drive, Box 5002, North Bay, ON P1B 8L7 Canada
Telephone: 705-474-3461 ext. 4518 **Fax:** 705-495-1772
E-mail: liaison@nipissingu.ca

Getting in Last Year 2,002 applied; 76% were accepted; 563 enrolled (37%).

Financial Matters $4581 nonresident tuition and fees (2002–03); $3538 room only.

Academics Nipissing University awards bachelor's and master's degrees. Challenging opportunities include an honors program, double majors, independent study, and a senior project. Special programs include summer session for credit, off-campus study, and study-abroad. The faculty at Nipissing University has 107 full-time members, 66% with terminal degrees. The student-faculty ratio is 18:1.

Students of Nipissing University The student body totals 4,985, of whom 2,070 are undergraduates. 69.5% are women and 30.5% are men. Students come from 10 states and territories and 19 other countries. 82% returned for their sophomore year.

Applying Nipissing University requires a high school transcript. Application deadline: 6/1. Early admission is possible.

NORFOLK STATE UNIVERSITY

Norfolk, VA

Urban setting ■ Public ■ State-supported ■ Coed

Web site: www.nsu.edu
Contact: Ms. Michelle Marable, Director of Admissions, 700 Park Avenue, Norfolk, VA 23504
Telephone: 757-823-8396 **Fax:** 757-823-2078
E-mail: admissions@nsu.edu

Getting in Last Year 4,700 applied; 77% were accepted; 1,178 enrolled (32%).

Financial Matters $3296 resident tuition and fees (2002–03); $11,703 nonresident tuition and fees (2002–03); $5588 room and board; 78% average percent of need met; $4830 average financial aid amount received per undergraduate.

Academics Norfolk State University awards associate, bachelor's, master's, and doctoral degrees. Challenging opportunities include advanced placement credit, accelerated degree programs, student-designed majors, freshman honors college, an honors program, double majors, independent study, and a senior project. Special programs include cooperative education, internships, summer session for credit, off-campus study, study-abroad, and Army and Navy ROTC. The most frequently chosen baccalaureate fields are interdisciplinary studies, business/marketing, and social sciences and history. The faculty at Norfolk State University has 314 full-time members, 58% with terminal degrees. The student-faculty ratio is 16:1.

Students of Norfolk State University The student body totals 6,839, of whom 5,968 are undergraduates. 62.3% are women and 37.7% are men. Students come from 44 states and territories and 38 other countries. 69% are from Virginia. 0.8% are international students. 66% returned for their sophomore year.

Applying Norfolk State University requires SAT I or ACT, a high school transcript, and a minimum high school GPA of 2.3, and in some cases recommendations. Application deadline: 4/15 priority date for financial aid. Deferred admission is possible.

NORTH CAROLINA AGRICULTURAL AND TECHNICAL STATE UNIVERSITY

Greensboro, NC

Urban setting ■ Public ■ State-supported ■ Coed

Web site: www.ncat.edu
Contact: Mr. John Smith, Director of Admissions, 1601 East Market Street, Webb Hall, Greensboro, NC 27411
Telephone: 336-334-7946 or toll-free 800-443-8964 (in-state)
Fax: 336-334-7478

Getting in Last Year 5,636 applied; 81% were accepted; 2,043 enrolled (45%).

Financial Matters $2561 resident tuition and fees (2002–03); $11,482 nonresident tuition and fees (2002–03); $4768 room and board; 54% average percent of need met; $5238 average financial aid amount received per undergraduate (2001–02).

Academics North Carolina A&T awards bachelor's, master's, and doctoral degrees. Challenging opportunities include advanced placement credit, an honors program, and a senior project. Special programs include cooperative education, internships, summer session for credit, off-campus study, study-abroad, and Army and Air Force ROTC. The faculty at North Carolina A&T has 458 members. The student-faculty ratio is 17:1.

Students of North Carolina A&T The student body totals 9,115, of whom 7,982 are undergraduates. 51.7% are women and 48.3% are men. Students come from 42 states and territories. 80% are from North Carolina. 0.8% are international students. 75% returned for their sophomore year.

Applying North Carolina A&T requires a high school transcript and a minimum high school GPA of 2.0. The school recommends SAT I or ACT. Application deadline: 6/1; 3/15 priority date for financial aid. Early and deferred admission are possible.

NORTH CAROLINA CENTRAL UNIVERSITY

Durham, NC

Urban setting ■ Public ■ State-supported ■ Coed

Web site: www.nccu.edu
Contact: Ms. Jocelyn L. Foy, Undergraduate Director of Admissions, PO Box 19717, Durham, NC 27707
Telephone: 919-530-6298 or toll-free 877-667-7533 **Fax:** 919-530-7625
E-mail: athorpe@wpo.nccu.edu

Getting in Last Year 2,184 applied; 88% were accepted; 843 enrolled (44%).

Financial Matters $3032 resident tuition and fees (2002–03); $11,955 nonresident tuition and fees (2002–03); $4206 room and board; 72% average percent of need met; $6621 average financial aid amount received per undergraduate (2001–02).

Academics NCCU awards bachelor's, master's, and first-professional degrees. Challenging opportunities include advanced placement credit, an honors program, double majors, independent study, and a senior project. Special programs include cooperative education, internships, summer session for credit, off-campus study, study-abroad, and Army and Air Force ROTC. The most frequently chosen baccalaureate fields are business/marketing, social sciences and history, and education. The faculty at NCCU has 257 full-time members, 74% with terminal degrees. The student-faculty ratio is 13:1.

Students of NCCU The student body totals 6,519, of whom 4,762 are undergraduates. 64.7% are women and 35.3% are men. Students come from 32 states and territories and 20 other countries. 90% are from North Carolina. 0.9% are international students.

Applying NCCU requires SAT I or ACT and a high school transcript. The school recommends 3 recommendations. Application deadline: 7/1; 4/1 priority date for financial aid.

NORTH CAROLINA SCHOOL OF THE ARTS

Winston-Salem, NC

Urban setting ■ Public ■ State-supported ■ Coed

Web site: www.ncarts.edu

Contact: Ms. Sheeler Lawson, Director of Admissions, 1533 South Main Street, PO Box 12189, Winston-Salem, NC 27127-2188

Telephone: 336-770-3290 **Fax:** 336-770-3370

E-mail: admissions@ncarts.edu

Getting in Last Year 744 applied; 46% were accepted; 200 enrolled (59%).

Financial Matters $3450 resident tuition and fees (2002–03); $14,050 nonresident tuition and fees (2002–03); $5115 room and board; 78% average percent of need met; $8499 average financial aid amount received per undergraduate (2001–02).

Academics NCSA awards bachelor's and master's degrees. A senior project is a challenging opportunity. The most frequently chosen baccalaureate field is visual/performing arts. The faculty at NCSA has 135 full-time members. The student-faculty ratio is 8:1.

Students of NCSA The student body totals 817, of whom 738 are undergraduates. 40.8% are women and 59.2% are men. Students come from 44 states and territories. 48% are from North Carolina. 1.4% are international students. 74% returned for their sophomore year.

Applying NCSA requires SAT I or ACT, a high school transcript, 2 recommendations, and audition, and in some cases an essay and an interview. Application deadline: rolling admissions; 3/1 priority date for financial aid.

NORTH CAROLINA STATE UNIVERSITY

Raleigh, NC

Suburban setting ■ Public ■ State-supported ■ Coed

Web site: www.ncsu.edu

Contact: Dr. George R. Dixon, Vice Provost and Director of Admissions, Box 7103, 112 Peele Hall, Raleigh, NC 27695

Telephone: 919-515-2434

E-mail: undergrad_admissions@ncsu.edu

Getting in Last Year 12,133 applied; 59% were accepted; 3,732 enrolled (52%).

Financial Matters $3827 resident tuition and fees (2002–03); $15,111 nonresident tuition and fees (2002–03); $5796 room and board; 85% average percent of need met; $7321 average financial aid amount received per undergraduate.

Academics NC State awards associate, bachelor's, master's, doctoral, and first-professional degrees and first-professional certificates. Challenging opportunities include advanced placement credit, accelerated degree programs, student-designed majors, freshman honors college, an honors program, double majors, independent study, and a senior project. Special programs include cooperative education, internships, summer session for credit, off-campus study, study-abroad, and Army, Navy and Air Force ROTC. The most frequently chosen baccalaureate fields are engineering/engineering technologies, business/marketing, and biological/life sciences. The faculty at NC State has 1,604 full-time members, 91% with terminal degrees. The student-faculty ratio is 15:1.

Students of NC State The student body totals 29,940, of whom 22,780 are undergraduates. 42.2% are women and 57.8% are men. Students come from 51 states and territories and 65 other countries. 93% are from North Carolina. 0.9% are international students. 89% returned for their sophomore year.

Applying NC State requires SAT I or ACT and a high school transcript, and in some cases an interview and 1 recommendation. The school recommends an essay, SAT II Subject Tests, and a minimum high school GPA of 3.0. Application deadline: 2/1; 3/1 priority date for financial aid. Early and deferred admission are possible.

NORTH CAROLINA WESLEYAN COLLEGE

Rocky Mount, NC

Suburban setting ■ Private ■ Independent Religious ■ Coed

Web site: www.ncwc.edu

Contact: Cecelia Summers, Associate Director of Admissions, 3400 North Wesleyan Boulevard, Rocky Mount, NC 27804

Telephone: 800-488-6292 ext. 5202 or toll-free 800-488-6292 **Fax:** 252-985-5309

E-mail: adm@ncwc.edu

Getting in Last Year 852 applied; 62% were accepted; 160 enrolled (30%).

Financial Matters $9768 tuition and fees (2002–03); $5882 room and board; 85% average percent of need met; $9725 average financial aid amount received per undergraduate (2001–02).

Academics NC Wesleyan awards bachelor's degrees (also offers adult part-time degree program with significant enrollment not reflected in profile). Challenging opportunities include advanced placement credit, accelerated degree programs, an honors program, double majors, independent study, and a senior project. Special programs include cooperative education, internships, and summer session for credit. The most frequently chosen baccalaureate fields are business/marketing, computer/information sciences, and law/legal studies. The faculty at NC Wesleyan has 46 full-time members, 72% with terminal degrees. The student-faculty ratio is 16:1.

Students of NC Wesleyan The student body is made up of 756 undergraduates. 59.4% are women and 40.6% are men. Students come from 22 states and territories. 86% are from North Carolina. 57% returned for their sophomore year.

Applying NC Wesleyan requires SAT I or ACT and a high school transcript. The school recommends SAT I, an interview, 2 recommendations, and a minimum high school GPA of 2.0. Application deadline: 7/30.

NORTH CENTRAL COLLEGE

Naperville, IL

Suburban setting ■ Private ■ Independent Religious ■ Coed

Web site: www.noctrl.edu

Contact: Mr. Stephen Potts, Coordinator of Freshman Admission, 30 North Brainard Street, PO Box 3063, Naperville, IL 60566-7063

Telephone: 630-637-5815 or toll-free 800-411-1861 **Fax:** 630-637-5819

E-mail: ncadm@noctrl.edu

Getting in Last Year 1,504 applied; 74% were accepted; 364 enrolled (33%).

Financial Matters $18,402 tuition and fees (2002–03); $6045 room and board; 89% average percent of need met; $16,323 average financial aid amount received per undergraduate (2001–02).

Academics North Central awards bachelor's and master's degrees. Challenging opportunities include advanced placement credit, accelerated degree programs, student-designed majors, an honors program, double majors, independent study, and a senior project. Special programs include cooperative education, internships, summer session for credit, off-campus study, study-abroad, and Army and Air Force ROTC. The most frequently chosen baccalaureate fields are business/marketing, social sciences and history, and education. The faculty at North Central has 125 full-time members, 83% with terminal degrees. The student-faculty ratio is 14:1.

Students of North Central The student body totals 2,533, of whom 2,116 are undergraduates. 58.2% are women and 41.8% are men. Students come from 26 states and territories and 18 other countries. 91% are from Illinois. 1.7% are international students. 81% returned for their sophomore year.

Applying North Central requires SAT I or ACT, a high school transcript, and a minimum high school GPA of 2.0, and in some cases an interview. The school recommends an essay, ACT, and 1 recommendation. Application deadline: rolling admissions. Early and deferred admission are possible.

NORTHCENTRAL UNIVERSITY

Prescott, AZ

Private ■ Proprietary ■ Coed

Web site: www.ncu.edu

Contact: Poppy Keegan, Admissions Counselor, 505 West Whipple Street, Prescott, AZ 86301

Telephone: 888-327-2877 ext. 8072 or toll-free 888-327-2877 **Fax:** 928-541-7817

E-mail: enroll@ncu.edu

Getting in Last Year 2 enrolled.

Academics Northcentral University awards bachelor's, master's, and doctoral degrees (distance learning only). Challenging opportunities include advanced placement credit and accelerated degree programs. Summer session for credit is a special program. The faculty at Northcentral University has 9 full-time members, 89% with terminal degrees.

Students of Northcentral University The student body totals 696, of whom 87 are undergraduates. 37.9% are women and 62.1% are men. Students come from 28 states and territories. 15% are from Arizona.

Applying Application deadline: rolling admissions.

NORTH DAKOTA STATE UNIVERSITY

Fargo, ND

Urban setting ■ Public ■ State-supported ■ Coed

Web site: www.ndsu.edu

Contact: Dr. Kate Haugen, Director of Admission, PO Box 5454, Fargo, ND 58105-5454

Telephone: 701-231-8643 or toll-free 800-488-NDSU **Fax:** 701-231-8802

E-mail: ndsu.admission@ndsu.nodak.edu

Getting in Last Year 3,547 applied; 60% were accepted; 1,856 enrolled (87%).

North Dakota State University (continued)

Financial Matters $3998 nonresident tuition and fees (2002–03); $4175 room and board; 78% average percent of need met; $5210 average financial aid amount received per undergraduate (2001–02).

Academics NDSU awards bachelor's, master's, doctoral, and first-professional degrees. Challenging opportunities include advanced placement credit, student-designed majors, an honors program, double majors, independent study, and a senior project. Special programs include cooperative education, internships, summer session for credit, off-campus study, study-abroad, and Army and Air Force ROTC. The most frequently chosen baccalaureate fields are engineering/engineering technologies, business/marketing, and health professions and related sciences. The faculty at NDSU has 495 full-time members, 82% with terminal degrees. The student-faculty ratio is 18:1.

Students of NDSU The student body totals 11,146, of whom 9,874 are undergraduates. 43% are women and 57% are men. Students come from 44 states and territories and 54 other countries. 60% are from North Dakota. 1.1% are international students. 71% returned for their sophomore year.

Applying NDSU requires SAT I or ACT, a high school transcript, and a minimum high school GPA of 2.5. Application deadline: 8/15; 4/15 priority date for financial aid.

NORTHEASTERN ILLINOIS UNIVERSITY

Chicago, IL

Urban setting ■ Public ■ State-supported ■ Coed

Web site: www.neiu.edu
Contact: Ms. Kay D. Gulli, Administrative Assistant, 5500 North St. Louis Avenue, Chicago, IL 60625
Telephone: 773-442-4000 **Fax:** 773-794-6243
E-mail: admrec@neiu.edu

Getting in Last Year 2,473 applied; 77% were accepted; 1,059 enrolled (55%).

Financial Matters $3000 resident tuition and fees (2002–03); $8016 nonresident tuition and fees (2002–03); 67% average percent of need met; $5426 average financial aid amount received per undergraduate.

Academics Northeastern Illinois University awards bachelor's and master's degrees. Challenging opportunities include advanced placement credit, an honors program, double majors, independent study, and a senior project. Special programs include cooperative education, internships, summer session for credit, off-campus study, study-abroad, and Army and Air Force ROTC. The most frequently chosen baccalaureate fields are education, liberal arts/general studies, and business/marketing. The faculty at Northeastern Illinois University has 370 full-time members, 76% with terminal degrees. The student-faculty ratio is 17:1.

Students of Northeastern Illinois University The student body totals 11,409, of whom 8,674 are undergraduates. 62.4% are women and 37.6% are men. Students come from 18 states and territories and 45 other countries. 99% are from Illinois. 2.5% are international students. 72% returned for their sophomore year.

Applying Northeastern Illinois University requires ACT and a high school transcript. Application deadline: 7/1; 3/1 priority date for financial aid. Deferred admission is possible.

NORTHEASTERN STATE UNIVERSITY

Tahlequah, OK

Small-town setting ■ Public ■ State-supported ■ Coed

Web site: www.nsuok.edu
Contact: Mr. Todd Essary, Director of High School and College Relations, 601 North Grand, Tahlequah, OK 74464
Telephone: 918-456-5511 ext. 4675 or toll-free 800-722-9614 (in-state) **Fax:** 918-458-2342
E-mail: nsuadmis@nsuok.edu

Getting in Last Year 2,070 applied; 87% were accepted; 1,231 enrolled (69%).

Financial Matters $2375 resident tuition and fees (2002–03); $4931 nonresident tuition and fees (2002–03); $2960 room and board; 68% average percent of need met; $7200 average financial aid amount received per undergraduate (2001–02).

Academics NSU awards bachelor's, master's, and first-professional degrees. Challenging opportunities include advanced placement credit, an honors program, double majors, and a senior project. Special programs include internships, summer session for credit, and Army ROTC. The most frequently chosen baccalaureate fields are business/marketing, education, and protective services/public administration. The faculty at NSU has 446 members. The student-faculty ratio is 24:1.

Students of NSU The student body totals 8,985, of whom 7,777 are undergraduates. 58.9% are women and 41.1% are men. Students come from 31 states and territories and 40 other countries. 100% are from Oklahoma. 1.3% are international students. 60% returned for their sophomore year.

Applying NSU requires ACT and a high school transcript, and in some cases an interview and recommendations. Application deadline: 8/5; 4/1 priority date for financial aid.

NORTHEASTERN UNIVERSITY

Boston, MA

Urban setting ■ Private ■ Independent ■ Coed

Web site: www.northeastern.edu
Contact: Ronne A. Patrick, Director of Admissions, 150 Richards Hall, Boston, MA 02115
Telephone: 617-373-2200 **Fax:** 617-373-8780
E-mail: admissions@neu.edu

Getting in Last Year 17,037 applied; 61% were accepted; 2,974 enrolled (28%).

Financial Matters $24,467 tuition and fees (2002–03); $9660 room and board; 62% average percent of need met; $14,925 average financial aid amount received per undergraduate.

Academics Northeastern awards associate, bachelor's, master's, doctoral, and first-professional degrees and post-bachelor's and post-master's certificates. Challenging opportunities include advanced placement credit, accelerated degree programs, student-designed majors, an honors program, double majors, independent study, and a senior project. Special programs include cooperative education, internships, summer session for credit, off-campus study, study-abroad, and Army, Navy and Air Force ROTC. The most frequently chosen baccalaureate fields are business/marketing, health professions and related sciences, and engineering/engineering technologies. The faculty at Northeastern has 801 full-time members, 77% with terminal degrees. The student-faculty ratio is 16:1.

Students of Northeastern The student body totals 18,507, of whom 14,144 are undergraduates. 49.5% are women and 50.5% are men. Students come from 50 states and territories and 110 other countries. 37% are from Massachusetts. 6.7% are international students. 84% returned for their sophomore year.

Applying Northeastern requires an essay, SAT I or ACT, and a high school transcript, and in some cases an interview. The school recommends 2 recommendations and a minimum high school GPA of 2.0. Application deadline: 2/15; 2/15 priority date for financial aid. Early and deferred admission are possible.

NORTHERN ARIZONA UNIVERSITY

Flagstaff, AZ

Small-town setting ■ Public ■ State-supported ■ Coed

Web site: www.nau.edu
Contact: Ms. Pamela Van Wyck, Assistant Director, PO Box 4084, Flagstaff, AZ 86011
Telephone: 928-523-6008 or toll-free 888-MORE-NAU **Fax:** 928-523-6023
E-mail: undergraduate.admissions@nau.edu

Getting in Last Year 7,912 applied; 81% were accepted; 2,396 enrolled (37%).

Financial Matters $2585 resident tuition and fees (2002–03); $11,105 nonresident tuition and fees (2002–03); $5156 room and board; 79% average percent of need met; $8004 average financial aid amount received per undergraduate.

Academics NAU awards bachelor's, master's, and doctoral degrees. Challenging opportunities include advanced placement credit, accelerated degree programs, freshman honors college, an honors program, double majors, independent study, and a senior project. Special programs include cooperative education, internships, summer session for credit, off-campus study, study-abroad, and Army and Air Force ROTC. The most frequently chosen baccalaureate fields are education, business/marketing, and liberal arts/general studies. The faculty at NAU has 698 full-time members, 85% with terminal degrees. The student-faculty ratio is 17:1.

Students of NAU The student body totals 19,907, of whom 13,577 are undergraduates. 59.2% are women and 40.8% are men. Students come from 50 states and territories and 72 other countries. 78% are from Arizona. 1.8% are international students. 64% returned for their sophomore year.

Applying NAU requires a high school transcript, and in some cases an essay, SAT I or ACT, an interview, and recommendations. The school recommends a minimum high school GPA of 3.0. Application deadline: rolling admissions; 2/14 priority date for financial aid. Deferred admission is possible.

NORTHERN ILLINOIS UNIVERSITY

De Kalb, IL

Small-town setting ■ Public ■ State-supported ■ Coed

Web site: www.niu.edu
Contact: Dr. Robert Burk, Director of Admissions, De Kalb, IL 60115-2854
Telephone: 815-753-0446 or toll-free 800-892-3050 (in-state)
E-mail: admission-info@niu.edu

Getting in Last Year 14,785 applied; 64% were accepted; 3,040 enrolled (32%).

Financial Matters $4802 resident tuition and fees (2002–03); $8382 nonresident tuition and fees (2002–03); $5198 room and board; 82% average percent of need met; $8948 average financial aid amount received per undergraduate.

Academics Northern Illinois University awards bachelor's, master's, doctoral, and first-professional degrees. Challenging opportunities include advanced placement credit, accelerated degree programs, student-designed majors, an honors program, double majors, independent study, and a senior project. Special programs include cooperative education, internships, summer session for credit, off-campus study, study-abroad, and Army and Air Force ROTC. The most frequently chosen baccalaureate fields are business/marketing, education, and social sciences and history. The faculty at Northern Illinois University has 960 full-time members. The student-faculty ratio is 17:1.

Students of Northern Illinois University The student body totals 24,948, of whom 18,104 are undergraduates. 53.1% are women and 46.9% are men. Students come from 50 states and territories and 105 other countries. 97% are from Illinois. 1.3% are international students. 76% returned for their sophomore year.

Applying Northern Illinois University requires SAT I or ACT and a high school transcript. Application deadline: 8/1; 3/1 priority date for financial aid.

NORTHERN KENTUCKY UNIVERSITY

Highland Heights, KY

Suburban setting ■ Public ■ State-supported ■ Coed

Web site: www.nku.edu
Contact: Mr. Dave Merriss, Associate Director of Admissions, Administrative Center 400, Highland Heights, KY 41099-7010
Telephone: 606-572-5220 ext. 5154 or toll-free 800-637-9948 (out-of-state) **Fax:** 859-572-6665
E-mail: admitnku@nku.edu

Getting in Last Year 3,528 applied; 90% were accepted; 1,977 enrolled (62%).

Financial Matters $3216 resident tuition and fees (2002–03); $7464 nonresident tuition and fees (2002–03); $4492 room and board; 85% average percent of need met; $6834 average financial aid amount received per undergraduate (2001–02).

Academics NKU awards associate, bachelor's, master's, and first-professional degrees and post-master's certificates. Challenging opportunities include advanced placement credit, an honors program, double majors, independent study, and a senior project. Special programs include cooperative education, internships, summer session for credit, off-campus study, study-abroad, and Army and Air Force ROTC. The most frequently chosen baccalaureate fields are business/marketing, education, and social sciences and history. The faculty at NKU has 463 full-time members, 68% with terminal degrees. The student-faculty ratio is 17:1.

Students of NKU The student body totals 13,715, of whom 12,136 are undergraduates. 58.9% are women and 41.1% are men. Students come from 32 states and territories and 11 other countries. 77% are from Kentucky. 1.5% are international students. 72% returned for their sophomore year.

Applying NKU requires SAT I or ACT and a high school transcript. Application deadline: 8/1; 3/1 priority date for financial aid. Early and deferred admission are possible.

NORTHERN MICHIGAN UNIVERSITY

Marquette, MI

Small-town setting ■ Public ■ State-supported ■ Coed

Web site: www.nmu.edu
Contact: Ms. Gerri Daniels, Director of Admissions, 1401 Presque Isle Avenue, Marquette, MI 49855-5301
Telephone: 906-227-2650 or toll-free 800-682-9797 ext. 1 (in-state), 800-682-9797 (out-of-state) **Fax:** 906-227-1747
E-mail: admiss@nmu.edu

Getting in Last Year 4,421 applied; 86% were accepted; 1,706 enrolled (45%).

Financial Matters $4128 resident tuition and fees (2002–03); $7080 nonresident tuition and fees (2002–03); $5630 room and board; 82% average percent of need met; $7054 average financial aid amount received per undergraduate.

Academics NMU awards associate, bachelor's, and master's degrees and post-bachelor's and post-master's certificates. Challenging opportunities include advanced placement credit, accelerated degree programs, student-designed majors, an honors program, double majors, independent study, and a senior project. Special programs include internships, summer session for credit, off-campus study, study-abroad, and Army ROTC. The most frequently chosen baccalaureate fields are business/marketing, education, and health professions and related sciences. The faculty at NMU has 311 full-time members, 86% with terminal degrees. The student-faculty ratio is 21:1.

Students of NMU The student body totals 9,016, of whom 8,113 are undergraduates. 52.3% are women and 47.7% are men. 82% are from Michigan. 1.4% are international students. 69% returned for their sophomore year.

Applying NMU requires SAT I or ACT and a high school transcript, and in some cases a minimum high school GPA of 2.25. Application deadline: rolling admissions; 2/20 priority date for financial aid. Deferred admission is possible.

NORTHERN STATE UNIVERSITY

Aberdeen, SD

Small-town setting ■ Public ■ State-supported ■ Coed

Web site: www.northern.edu
Contact: Ms. Sara Hanson, Interim Director of Admissions-Campus, 1200 South Jay Street, Aberdeen, SD 57401
Telephone: 605-626-2544 or toll-free 800-678-5330 **Fax:** 605-626-2587
E-mail: admissions1@northern.edu

Getting in Last Year 902 applied; 92% were accepted; 411 enrolled (49%).

Financial Matters $3874 resident tuition and fees (2002–03); $8123 nonresident tuition and fees (2002–03); $3234 room and board; $4988 average financial aid amount received per undergraduate (2001–02).

Academics NSU awards associate, bachelor's, and master's degrees and post-bachelor's certificates. Challenging opportunities include advanced placement credit, accelerated degree programs, student-designed majors, an honors program, and a senior project. Special programs include cooperative education, internships, summer session for credit, off-campus study, and study-abroad. The most frequently chosen baccalaureate fields are education, business/marketing, and social sciences and history. The faculty at NSU has 110 full-time members, 77% with terminal degrees. The student-faculty ratio is 20:1.

Students of NSU The student body totals 3,020, of whom 2,740 are undergraduates. 58.7% are women and 41.3% are men. Students come from 31 states and territories and 10 other countries. 85% are from South Dakota. 65% returned for their sophomore year.

Applying NSU requires SAT I or ACT, a high school transcript, and a minimum high school GPA of X, and in some cases recommendations. Application deadline: 9/1; 3/1 priority date for financial aid. Early and deferred admission are possible.

NORTH GEORGIA COLLEGE & STATE UNIVERSITY

Dahlonega, GA

Small-town setting ■ Public ■ State-supported ■ Coed

Web site: www.ngcsu.edu
Contact: Robert J. LaVerriere, Director of Admissions and Recruitment, Admissions Center, 32 College Circle, Dahlonega, GA 30597
Telephone: 706-864-1800 or toll-free 800-498-9581 **Fax:** 706-864-1478
E-mail: admissions@ngcsu.edu

Getting in Last Year 2,100 applied; 57% were accepted; 640 enrolled (54%).

Financial Matters $2600 resident tuition and fees (2002–03); $8624 nonresident tuition and fees (2002–03); $4016 room and board.

Academics North Georgia awards associate, bachelor's, and master's degrees and post-bachelor's and post-master's certificates. Challenging opportunities include advanced placement credit, freshman honors college, an honors program, double majors, and a senior project. Special programs include cooperative education, internships, summer session for credit, study-abroad, and Army ROTC. The most frequently chosen baccalaureate fields are business/marketing, education, and protective services/public administration. The faculty at North Georgia has 194 full-time members, 71% with terminal degrees. The student-faculty ratio is 14:1.

Students of North Georgia The student body totals 4,178, of whom 3,681 are undergraduates. 63.1% are women and 36.9% are men. Students come from 32 states and territories and 42 other countries. 96% are from Georgia. 1.1% are international students. 77% returned for their sophomore year.

Applying North Georgia requires SAT I or ACT, a high school transcript, proof of immunization, and a minimum high school GPA of 2.0. Application deadline: 7/1. Early and deferred admission are possible.

NORTH GREENVILLE COLLEGE

Tigerville, SC

Rural setting ■ Private ■ Independent Religious ■ Coed

Web site: www.ngc.edu
Contact: Mr. Buddy Freeman, Executive Director of Admissions, PO Box 1872, Tigerville, SC 29688
Telephone: 864-977-7052 or toll-free 800-468-6642 ext. 7001 **Fax:** 864-977-7177
E-mail: bfreeman@ngc.edu

Getting in Last Year 831 applied; 87% were accepted; 415 enrolled (57%).

Financial Matters $8860 tuition and fees (2002–03); $5030 room and board.

Academics NGC awards associate and bachelor's degrees. Challenging opportunities include advanced placement credit, accelerated degree programs, student-designed majors, freshman honors college, an honors program, double majors, independent study, and a senior project. Special programs include internships, summer session for credit, and Army ROTC. The most frequently chosen baccalaureate fields are interdisciplinary studies, business/marketing, and education. The faculty at NGC has 71 full-time members, 59% with terminal degrees. The student-faculty ratio is 16:1.

Students of NGC The student body is made up of 1,486 undergraduates. 48.2% are women and 51.8% are men. Students come from 30 states and territories and 17 other countries. 81% are from South Carolina. 2.1% are international students. 65% returned for their sophomore year.

Applying NGC requires SAT I or ACT and a high school transcript, and in some cases CPT and an interview. The school recommends CPT and a minimum high school GPA of 2.0. Application deadline: 8/21; 6/30 priority date for financial aid. Early and deferred admission are possible.

NORTHLAND COLLEGE

Ashland, WI

Small-town setting ■ Private ■ Independent Religious ■ Coed

Web site: www.northland.edu
Contact: Mr. Eric Peterson, Director of Admission, 1411 Ellis Avenue, Ashland, WI 54806
Telephone: 715-682-1224 or toll-free 800-753-1840 (in-state), 800-753-1040 (out-of-state) **Fax:** 715-682-1258
E-mail: admit@northland.edu

Getting in Last Year 860 applied; 94% were accepted; 186 enrolled (23%).

Financial Matters $16,940 tuition and fees (2002–03); $4835 room and board; 82% average percent of need met; $15,203 average financial aid amount received per undergraduate.

Academics Northland awards bachelor's degrees. Challenging opportunities include advanced placement credit, accelerated degree programs, student-designed majors, an honors program, double majors, independent study, and a senior project. Special programs include cooperative education, internships, summer session for credit, off-campus study, and study-abroad. The most frequently chosen baccalaureate fields are education, natural resources/environmental science, and biological/life sciences. The faculty at Northland has 48 full-time members, 81% with terminal degrees. The student-faculty ratio is 14:1.

Students of Northland The student body is made up of 752 undergraduates. 54.9% are women and 45.1% are men. Students come from 46 states and territories and 13 other countries. 33% are from Wisconsin. 3.2% are international students. 72% returned for their sophomore year.

Applying Northland requires an essay, SAT I or ACT, a high school transcript, and 1 recommendation. The school recommends an interview and a minimum high school GPA of 2.0. Application deadline: 8/1; 4/15 priority date for financial aid. Early and deferred admission are possible.

NORTH PARK UNIVERSITY

Chicago, IL

Urban setting ■ Private ■ Independent Religious ■ Coed

Web site: www.northpark.edu
Contact: Office of Admissions, 3225 West Foster Avenue, Chicago, IL 60625-4895
Telephone: 773-244-5500 or toll-free 800-888-NPC8 **Fax:** 773-583-0858
E-mail: afao@northpark.edu

Getting in Last Year 1,068 applied; 74% were accepted; 320 enrolled (40%).

Financial Matters $18,710 tuition and fees (2002–03); $6520 room and board.

Academics North Park awards bachelor's, master's, doctoral, and first-professional degrees. Challenging opportunities include advanced placement credit, accelerated degree programs, student-designed majors, freshman honors college, an honors program, and a senior project. Special programs include internships, summer session for credit, off-campus study, and study-abroad. The most frequently chosen baccalaureate fields are education, biological/life sciences, and health professions and related sciences. The faculty at North Park has 88 full-time members, 81% with terminal degrees. The student-faculty ratio is 16:1.

Students of North Park The student body totals 2,181, of whom 1,573 are undergraduates. 61.8% are women and 38.2% are men. Students come from 38 states and territories and 32 other countries. 61% are from Illinois. 5% are international students. 70% returned for their sophomore year.

Applying North Park requires an essay, SAT I or ACT, a high school transcript, 1 recommendation, and a minimum high school GPA of 2.0, and in some cases an interview. The school recommends a minimum high school GPA of 3.0. Application deadline: rolling admissions; 5/1 priority date for financial aid. Early admission is possible.

NORTHWEST BIBLE COLLEGE

Edmonton, AB Canada

Urban setting ■ Private ■ Independent Religious ■ Coed

Web site: www.nwbc.ab.ca
Contact: Ingrid Thompson, Registrar, 11617-106 Avenue, Edmonton, AB T5H 0S1 Canada
Telephone: 780-452-0808 or toll-free 866-222-0808 (in-state)
E-mail: info@nwbc.ab.ca

Getting in Last Year 127 applied; 99% were accepted.

Financial Matters $4715 tuition and fees (2002–03).

Academics Northwest Bible College awards bachelor's degrees. Challenging opportunities include advanced placement credit and independent study. Internships is a special program. The faculty at Northwest Bible College has 10 full-time members, 90% with terminal degrees. The student-faculty ratio is 12:1.

Students of Northwest Bible College The student body is made up of 257 undergraduates. 48.6% are women and 51.4% are men. Students come from 10 states and territories and 6 other countries. 74% are from Alberta. 55% returned for their sophomore year.

Applying Northwest Bible College requires an essay, a high school transcript, and recommendations. Application deadline: 8/20; 5/30 priority date for financial aid.

NORTHWEST CHRISTIAN COLLEGE

Eugene, OR

Urban setting ■ Private ■ Independent Religious ■ Coed

Web site: www.nwcc.edu
Contact: Mr. Bill Stenberg, Director of Admissions, 828 East 11th Avenue, Eugene, OR 97401-3745
Telephone: 541-684-7209 or toll-free 877-463-6622 **Fax:** 541-684-7317
E-mail: admissions@nwcc.edu

Getting in Last Year 178 applied; 75% were accepted; 64 enrolled (48%).

Financial Matters $15,435 tuition and fees (2002–03); $5448 room and board.

Academics NCC awards associate, bachelor's, and master's degrees and post-bachelor's certificates. Challenging opportunities include advanced placement credit, accelerated degree programs, double majors, independent study, and a senior project. Special programs include cooperative education, internships, summer session for credit, off-campus study, study-abroad, and Army ROTC. The most frequently chosen baccalaureate fields are business/marketing, education, and psychology. The faculty at NCC has 23 full-time members, 65% with terminal degrees. The student-faculty ratio is 13:1.

Students of NCC The student body totals 515, of whom 412 are undergraduates. 60.4% are women and 39.6% are men. Students come from 14 states and territories. 92% are from Oregon. 49% returned for their sophomore year.

Applying NCC requires an essay, SAT I or ACT, a high school transcript, 2 recommendations, and a minimum high school GPA of 2.5, and in some cases SAT II Subject Tests. The school recommends an interview. Application deadline: rolling admissions. Deferred admission is possible.

NORTHWEST COLLEGE

Kirkland, WA

Suburban setting ■ Private ■ Independent Religious ■ Coed

Web site: www.nwcollege.edu
Contact: Ms. Rose-Mary K. Smith, Director of Admissions, PO Box 579, Kirkland, WA 98083-0579
Telephone: 425-822-8266 or toll-free 800-669-3781 **Fax:** 425-889-5224
E-mail: admissions@ncag.edu

Getting in Last Year 308 applied; 90% were accepted; 166 enrolled (60%).

Financial Matters $12,858 tuition and fees (2002–03); $5996 room and board; 69% average percent of need met; $10,207 average financial aid amount received per undergraduate.

Academics NC awards associate, bachelor's, and master's degrees. Challenging opportunities include advanced placement credit, accelerated degree programs, student-designed majors, double majors, independent study, and a senior project. Special programs include cooperative education, internships, summer session for credit, study-abroad, and Army ROTC. The faculty at NC has 46 full-time members, 52% with terminal degrees. The student-faculty ratio is 18:1.

Students of NC The student body totals 1,120, of whom 1,082 are undergraduates. 60.6% are women and 39.4% are men. Students come from 30 states and territories. 82% are from Washington. 3% are international students. 65% returned for their sophomore year.

Applying NC requires an essay, SAT I or ACT, a high school transcript, 2 recommendations, and a minimum high school GPA of 2.3, and in some cases an interview. Application deadline: 8/1; 3/1 priority date for financial aid. Deferred admission is possible.

NORTHWEST COLLEGE OF ART

Poulsbo, WA

Small-town setting ■ Private ■ Proprietary ■ Coed

Web site: www.nca.edu
Contact: Mr. Craig Freeman, President, 16464 State Highway 305, Poulsbo, WA 98370
Telephone: 360-779-9993 or toll-free 800-769-ARTS **Fax:** 360-779-9933
E-mail: kimatnca@silverlink.net

Financial Matters $11,900 tuition and fees (2002–03).

Academics NCA awards bachelor's degrees. Challenging opportunities include double majors and a senior project. Special programs include internships and summer session for credit. The faculty at NCA has 2 full-time members.

Students of NCA The student body is made up of 118 undergraduates.

Applying NCA requires an essay, a high school transcript, an interview, 3 recommendations, portfolio, and a minimum high school GPA of 2.0. Application deadline: 6/1; 5/1 for financial aid. Deferred admission is possible.

NORTHWESTERN COLLEGE

Orange City, IA

Rural setting ■ Private ■ Independent Religious ■ Coed

Web site: www.nwciowa.edu

Contact: Mr. Ronald K. DeJong, Director of Admissions, 101 College Lane, Orange City, IA 51041-1996

Telephone: 712-737-7130 or toll-free 800-747-4757 **Fax:** 712-707-7164

E-mail: markb@nwciowa.edu

Getting in Last Year 1,150 applied; 83% were accepted; 347 enrolled (36%).

Financial Matters $14,290 tuition and fees (2002–03); $4130 room and board; 81% average percent of need met; $11,634 average financial aid amount received per undergraduate.

Academics Northwestern awards associate and bachelor's degrees. Challenging opportunities include advanced placement credit, accelerated degree programs, student-designed majors, freshman honors college, an honors program, double majors, independent study, and a senior project. Special programs include cooperative education, internships, summer session for credit, off-campus study, and study-abroad. The most frequently chosen baccalaureate fields are business/marketing, education, and biological/life sciences. The faculty at Northwestern has 73 full-time members, 85% with terminal degrees. The student-faculty ratio is 16:1.

Students of Northwestern The student body is made up of 1,313 undergraduates. 61.2% are women and 38.8% are men. Students come from 30 states and territories and 12 other countries. 57% are from Iowa. 2.4% are international students. 76% returned for their sophomore year.

Applying Northwestern requires an essay, SAT I or ACT, a high school transcript, 1 recommendation, and a minimum high school GPA of 2.0. The school recommends an interview and a minimum high school GPA of 2.5. Application deadline: rolling admissions; 4/1 priority date for financial aid. Deferred admission is possible.

NORTHWESTERN COLLEGE

St. Paul, MN

Suburban setting ■ Private ■ Independent Religious ■ Coed

Web site: www.nwc.edu

Contact: Mr. Kenneth K. Faffler, Director of Recruitment, 3003 Snelling Avenue North, Nazareth Hall, Room 229, St. Paul, MN 55113-1598

Telephone: 651-631-5209 or toll-free 800-827-6827 **Fax:** 651-631-5680

E-mail: admissions@nwc.edu

Getting in Last Year 890 applied; 91% were accepted; 470 enrolled (58%).

Financial Matters $16,500 tuition and fees (2002–03); $5330 room and board; 78% average percent of need met; $13,183 average financial aid amount received per undergraduate (2001–02).

Academics Northwestern awards associate and bachelor's degrees. Challenging opportunities include advanced placement credit, an honors program, double majors, independent study, and a senior project. Special programs include internships, summer session for credit, off-campus study, study-abroad, and Army and Air Force ROTC. The most frequently chosen baccalaureate fields are education, business/marketing, and social sciences and history. The faculty at Northwestern has 78 full-time members, 67% with terminal degrees. The student-faculty ratio is 15:1.

Students of Northwestern The student body is made up of 2,448 undergraduates. 61.6% are women and 38.4% are men. Students come from 34 states and territories. 61% are from Minnesota. 0.3% are international students. 78% returned for their sophomore year.

Applying Northwestern requires an essay, SAT I or ACT, a high school transcript, 2 recommendations, lifestyle agreement, statement of Christian faith, and a minimum high school GPA of 2.0, and in some cases an interview. The school recommends an interview and a minimum high school GPA of 3.0. Application deadline: 8/1; 7/1 for financial aid, with a 3/1 priority date. Early and deferred admission are possible.

NORTHWESTERN OKLAHOMA STATE UNIVERSITY

Alva, OK

Small-town setting ■ Public ■ State-supported ■ Coed

Web site: www.nwosu.edu

Contact: Mrs. Shirley Murrow, Registrar, 709 Oklahoma Boulevard, Alva, OK 73717-2799

Telephone: 580-327-8550 **Fax:** 580-327-8699

E-mail: smmurrow@nwosu.edu

Getting in Last Year 447 applied; 96% were accepted; 302 enrolled (71%).

Financial Matters $2323 resident tuition and fees (2002–03); $5476 nonresident tuition and fees (2002–03); $2600 room and board; 96% average percent of need met; $3780 average financial aid amount received per undergraduate (2001–02).

Academics NWOSU awards bachelor's and master's degrees and post-bachelor's and post-master's certificates. Challenging opportunities include advanced placement credit, double majors, independent study, and a senior project. Special programs include internships, summer session for credit, off-campus study, and study-abroad. The most frequently chosen baccalaureate fields are business/marketing, education, and protective services/public administration. The faculty at NWOSU has 73 full-time members, 59% with terminal degrees. The student-faculty ratio is 16:1.

Students of NWOSU The student body totals 2,013, of whom 1,776 are undergraduates. 57% are women and 43% are men. Students come from 28 states and territories and 25 other countries. 84% are from Oklahoma. 1.7% are international students. 64% returned for their sophomore year.

Applying NWOSU requires SAT I or ACT and a high school transcript, and in some cases an essay, 3 recommendations, and a minimum high school GPA of 2.0. Application deadline: rolling admissions; 3/1 priority date for financial aid. Early admission is possible.

NORTHWESTERN POLYTECHNIC UNIVERSITY

Fremont, CA

Urban setting ■ Private ■ Independent ■ Coed

Web site: www.npu.edu

Contact: Mr. Jack Xie, Director of Admission, 117 Fourier Avenue, Fremont, CA 94539

Telephone: 510-657-5913 **Fax:** 510-657-8975

E-mail: admission@npu.edu

Getting in Last Year 7 enrolled.

Financial Matters $6030 tuition and fees (2002–03); $2800 room only.

Academics NPU awards bachelor's, master's, and doctoral degrees. Challenging opportunities include advanced placement credit and a senior project. Special programs include internships and summer session for credit. The faculty at NPU has 8 full-time members, 63% with terminal degrees. The student-faculty ratio is 15:1.

Students of NPU The student body totals 591, of whom 190 are undergraduates. 36.3% are women and 63.7% are men. Students come from 20 states and territories and 13 other countries. 95% are from California. 85% returned for their sophomore year.

Applying NPU requires a high school transcript and a minimum high school GPA of 2.0, and in some cases an essay. The school recommends an interview. Application deadline: 8/12.

NORTHWESTERN STATE UNIVERSITY OF LOUISIANA

Natchitoches, LA

Small-town setting ■ Public ■ State-supported ■ Coed

Web site: www.nsula.edu

Contact: Ms. Jana Lucky, Director of Recruiting and Admissions, Roy Hall, Room 209, Natchitoches, LA 71497

Telephone: 318-357-4503 or toll-free 800-426-3754 (in-state), 800-327-1903 (out-of-state) **Fax:** 318-357-4257

E-mail: admissions@alpha.nsula.edu

Getting in Last Year 3,805 applied; 100% were accepted; 2,003 enrolled (53%).

Financial Matters $2645 resident tuition and fees (2002–03); $8519 nonresident tuition and fees (2002–03); $3266 room and board; $5306 average financial aid amount received per undergraduate.

Academics Northwestern awards associate, bachelor's, master's, and doctoral degrees and post-master's certificates. Challenging opportunities include advanced placement credit, accelerated degree programs, student-designed majors, freshman honors college, an honors program, double majors, and a senior project. Special programs include internships, summer session for credit, off-campus study, study-abroad, and Army ROTC. The faculty at Northwestern has 252 full-time members, 54% with terminal degrees. The student-faculty ratio is 30:1.

Students of Northwestern The student body totals 10,159, of whom 9,087 are undergraduates. 64% are women and 36% are men. Students come from 38 states and territories and 23 other countries. 94% are from Louisiana. 0.5% are international students. 67% returned for their sophomore year.

Applying Northwestern requires a high school transcript. The school recommends SAT I or ACT. Application deadline: rolling admissions. Early admission is possible.

NORTHWESTERN UNIVERSITY

Evanston, IL

Suburban setting ■ Private ■ Independent ■ Coed

Web site: www.northwestern.edu

Contact: Ms. Carol Lunkenheimer, Dean of Undergraduate Admission, PO Box 3060, Evanston, IL 60204-3060

Telephone: 847-491-7271

E-mail: ug-admission@northwestern.edu

Getting in Last Year 14,283 applied; 33% were accepted; 2,005 enrolled (43%).

Northwestern University (continued)

Financial Matters $27,228 tuition and fees (2002–03); $8446 room and board; 100% average percent of need met; $23,382 average financial aid amount received per undergraduate.

Academics Northwestern awards bachelor's, master's, doctoral, and first-professional degrees and post-master's certificates. Challenging opportunities include advanced placement credit, accelerated degree programs, student-designed majors, an honors program, double majors, independent study, and a senior project. Special programs include cooperative education, internships, summer session for credit, study-abroad, and Army, Navy and Air Force ROTC. The most frequently chosen baccalaureate fields are social sciences and history, engineering/engineering technologies, and communications/communication technologies. The faculty at Northwestern has 922 full-time members, 100% with terminal degrees. The student-faculty ratio is 7:1.

Students of Northwestern The student body totals 16,032, of whom 7,946 are undergraduates. 52.6% are women and 47.4% are men. Students come from 51 states and territories and 46 other countries. 26% are from Illinois. 4.7% are international students. 96% returned for their sophomore year.

Applying Northwestern requires an essay, SAT I or ACT, a high school transcript, and 1 recommendation, and in some cases SAT II Subject Tests, SAT II: Writing Test, and audition for music program. The school recommends SAT II Subject Tests and SAT II: Writing Test. Application deadline: 1/1; 2/1 priority date for financial aid. Early and deferred admission are possible.

NORTHWEST MISSOURI STATE UNIVERSITY

Maryville, MO

Small-town setting ■ Public ■ State-supported ■ Coed

Web site: www.nwmissouri.edu

Contact: Ms. Deb Powers, Associate Director of Admission, Office of Admissions, 800 University Drive, Maryville, MO 64468

Telephone: 660-562-1146 or toll-free 800-633-1175 **Fax:** 660-562-1121

E-mail: admissions@acad.nwmissouri.edu

Getting in Last Year 2,764 applied; 87% were accepted; 1,198 enrolled (50%).

Financial Matters $4110 resident tuition and fees (2002–03); $7012 nonresident tuition and fees (2002–03); $4556 room and board; 82% average percent of need met; $6047 average financial aid amount received per undergraduate (2001–02).

Academics Northwest awards bachelor's and master's degrees. Challenging opportunities include advanced placement credit, accelerated degree programs, double majors, independent study, and a senior project. Special programs include internships, summer session for credit, off-campus study, study-abroad, and Army ROTC. The most frequently chosen baccalaureate fields are education, business/marketing, and computer/information sciences. The faculty at Northwest has 243 full-time members, 70% with terminal degrees. The student-faculty ratio is 24:1.

Students of Northwest The student body totals 6,514, of whom 5,601 are undergraduates. 56.5% are women and 43.5% are men. Students come from 30 states and territories and 11 other countries. 64% are from Missouri. 2.8% are international students. 72% returned for their sophomore year.

Applying Northwest requires SAT I or ACT, a high school transcript, and a minimum high school GPA of 2.0, and in some cases an interview. Application deadline: rolling admissions; 3/1 priority date for financial aid. Deferred admission is possible.

NORTHWEST NAZARENE UNIVERSITY

Nampa, ID

Small-town setting ■ Private ■ Independent Religious ■ Coed

Web site: www.nnu.edu

Contact: Ms. Dianna Gibney, Director of Admissions, 623 Holly Street, Nampa, ID 83686

Telephone: 208-467-8000 or toll-free 877-NNU-4YOU **Fax:** 208-467-8645

E-mail: admissions@nnu.edu

Financial Matters $15,060 tuition and fees (2002–03); $4285 room and board; 77% average percent of need met; $11,942 average financial aid amount received per undergraduate.

Academics Northwest Nazarene University awards bachelor's and master's degrees. Challenging opportunities include advanced placement credit, accelerated degree programs, student-designed majors, freshman honors college, an honors program, independent study, and a senior project. Special programs include cooperative education, internships, summer session for credit, off-campus study, study-abroad, and Army ROTC. The faculty at Northwest Nazarene University has 88 full-time members, 69% with terminal degrees. The student-faculty ratio is 13:1.

Students of Northwest Nazarene University The student body totals 1,470, of whom 1,153 are undergraduates. 56.9% are women and 43.1% are men. Students come from 22 states and territories. 44% are from Idaho. 0.4% are international students. 72% returned for their sophomore year.

Applying Northwest Nazarene University requires ACT, a high school transcript, 2 recommendations, and a minimum high school GPA of 2.5, and in some cases an interview. Application deadline: 8/8; 3/1 priority date for financial aid. Early and deferred admission are possible.

NORTHWOOD UNIVERSITY

Midland, MI

Small-town setting ■ Private ■ Independent ■ Coed

Web site: www.northwood.edu

Contact: Mr. Daniel F. Toland, Director of Admission, 4000 Whiting Drive, Midland, MI 48640

Telephone: 989-837-4273 or toll-free 800-457-7878 **Fax:** 989-837-4490

E-mail: admissions@northwood.edu

Getting in Last Year 1,452 applied; 86% were accepted; 489 enrolled (39%).

Financial Matters $13,461 tuition and fees (2002–03); $6006 room and board; 64% average percent of need met; $10,556 average financial aid amount received per undergraduate.

Academics Northwood awards associate, bachelor's, and master's degrees. Challenging opportunities include advanced placement credit, accelerated degree programs, an honors program, double majors, and independent study. Special programs include cooperative education, internships, summer session for credit, off-campus study, and study-abroad. The most frequently chosen baccalaureate fields are business/marketing and computer/information sciences. The faculty at Northwood has 43 full-time members, 21% with terminal degrees. The student-faculty ratio is 34:1.

Students of Northwood The student body totals 3,627, of whom 3,361 are undergraduates. 46.6% are women and 53.4% are men. Students come from 33 states and territories and 23 other countries. 87% are from Michigan. 11% are international students. 78% returned for their sophomore year.

Applying Northwood requires SAT I or ACT and a high school transcript. The school recommends an essay, an interview, 1 recommendation, and a minimum high school GPA of 2.0. Application deadline: rolling admissions. Early and deferred admission are possible.

NORTHWOOD UNIVERSITY, FLORIDA CAMPUS

West Palm Beach, FL

Suburban setting ■ Private ■ Independent ■ Coed

Web site: www.northwood.edu

Contact: Mr. John M. Letvinchuck, Director of Admissions, 2600 North Military Trail, West Palm Beach, FL 33409-2911

Telephone: 561-478-5500 or toll-free 800-458-8325 **Fax:** 561-640-3328

E-mail: fladmit@northwood.edu

Getting in Last Year 662 applied; 67% were accepted; 136 enrolled (31%).

Financial Matters $13,995 tuition and fees (2002–03); $7045 room and board; 68% average percent of need met; $12,153 average financial aid amount received per undergraduate.

Academics Northwood University awards associate and bachelor's degrees. Challenging opportunities include advanced placement credit, accelerated degree programs, an honors program, double majors, and independent study. Special programs include cooperative education, internships, summer session for credit, and study-abroad. The most frequently chosen baccalaureate fields are business/marketing and computer/information sciences. The faculty at Northwood University has 15 full-time members, 33% with terminal degrees. The student-faculty ratio is 24:1.

Students of Northwood University The student body is made up of 938 undergraduates. 48.4% are women and 51.6% are men. Students come from 30 states and territories and 42 other countries. 66% are from Florida. 24.9% are international students. 66% returned for their sophomore year.

Applying Northwood University requires SAT I or ACT and a high school transcript. The school recommends an essay, an interview, 1 recommendation, and a minimum high school GPA of 2.0. Application deadline: rolling admissions; 4/15 priority date for financial aid. Early and deferred admission are possible.

NORTHWOOD UNIVERSITY, TEXAS CAMPUS

Cedar Hill, TX

Small-town setting ■ Private ■ Independent ■ Coed

Web site: www.northwood.edu

Contact: Mr. James R. Hickerson, Director of Admissions, 1114 West FM 1382, Cedar Hill, TX 75104

Telephone: 972-293-5400 or toll-free 800-927-9663 **Fax:** 972-291-3824

E-mail: txadmit@northwood.edu

Getting in Last Year 871 applied; 65% were accepted; 218 enrolled (39%).

Financial Matters $13,995 tuition and fees (2002–03); $6140 room and board; 69% average percent of need met; $11,334 average financial aid amount received per undergraduate.

Academics Northwood University, Texas Campus awards associate and bachelor's degrees. Challenging opportunities include advanced placement credit, accelerated degree programs, an honors program, double majors, and independent study. Special programs include internships, summer session for credit, off-campus study, and study-abroad. The most frequently chosen baccalaureate fields are business/marketing and computer/information sciences. The faculty at Northwood University, Texas Campus has 21 full-time members, 24% with terminal degrees. The student-faculty ratio is 27:1.

Students of Northwood University, Texas Campus The student body is made up of 1,179 undergraduates. 59% are women and 41% are men. Students come from 17 states and territories and 25 other countries. 89% are from Texas. 6.9% are international students. 68% returned for their sophomore year.

Applying Northwood University, Texas Campus requires SAT I or ACT and a high school transcript. The school recommends an essay, an interview, 1 recommendation, and a minimum high school GPA of 2.0. Application deadline: rolling admissions. Early and deferred admission are possible.

NORWICH UNIVERSITY

Northfield, VT

Small-town setting ■ Private ■ Independent ■ Coed

Web site: www.norwich.edu
Contact: Ms. Karen McGrath, Dean of Enrollment Management, 27 I.D. White Avenue, Northfield, VT 05663
Telephone: 802-485-2013 or toll-free 800-468-6679 **Fax:** 802-485-2032
E-mail: nuadm@norwich.edu

Getting in Last Year 1,472 applied; 91% were accepted.

Financial Matters $18,209 tuition and fees (2002–03); $6722 room and board.

Academics Norwich awards bachelor's and master's degrees. Challenging opportunities include advanced placement credit, double majors, independent study, and a senior project. Special programs include cooperative education, internships, summer session for credit, study-abroad, and Army, Navy and Air Force ROTC. The most frequently chosen baccalaureate fields are liberal arts/general studies, protective services/public administration, and social sciences and history. The faculty at Norwich has 139 full-time members, 75% with terminal degrees. The student-faculty ratio is 14:1.

Students of Norwich The student body totals 2,707, of whom 2,129 are undergraduates. Students come from 41 states and territories and 10 other countries. 26% are from Vermont. 71% returned for their sophomore year.

Applying Norwich requires SAT I or ACT and a high school transcript, and in some cases an essay and portfolio. The school recommends an essay, SAT II Subject Tests, an interview, 2 recommendations, and a minimum high school GPA of 2.0. Application deadline: rolling admissions; 3/1 priority date for financial aid. Early and deferred admission are possible.

NOTRE DAME COLLEGE

South Euclid, OH

Suburban setting ■ Private ■ Independent Religious ■ Coed

Web site: www.ndc.edu
Contact: Karen Poelkiz, Vice President for Recruitment, 4545 College Road, South Euclid, OH 44121-4293
Telephone: 216-381-1680 ext. 5239 or toll-free 800-NDC-1680
Fax: 216-381-3802
E-mail: admissions@ndc.edu

Getting in Last Year 187 applied; 78% were accepted.

Financial Matters $16,002 tuition and fees (2002–03); $5906 room and board; 97% average percent of need met; $15,336 average financial aid amount received per undergraduate (2001–02).

Academics Notre Dame College awards associate, bachelor's, and master's degrees. Challenging opportunities include advanced placement credit, accelerated degree programs, student-designed majors, double majors, independent study, and a senior project. Special programs include cooperative education, internships, summer session for credit, off-campus study, and study-abroad. The most frequently chosen baccalaureate fields are education, business/marketing, and computer/information sciences. The faculty at Notre Dame College has 26 full-time members, 69% with terminal degrees. The student-faculty ratio is 12:1.

Students of Notre Dame College The student body totals 925, of whom 767 are undergraduates. Students come from 8 states and territories and 15 other countries. 90% are from Ohio. 0.9% are international students. 62% returned for their sophomore year.

Applying Notre Dame College requires an essay, SAT I or ACT, a high school transcript, an interview, and a minimum high school GPA of 2.0. The school recommends an interview and a minimum high school GPA of 2.5. Application deadline: rolling admissions. Deferred admission is possible.

NOTRE DAME DE NAMUR UNIVERSITY

Belmont, CA

Suburban setting ■ Private ■ Independent Religious ■ Coed

Web site: www.ndnu.edu
Contact: Ms. Melissa Garcia, Assistant Director for Undergraduate Admission, 1500 Ralston Avenue, Belmont, CA 94002-1997
Telephone: 650-508-3532 or toll-free 800-263-0545 **Fax:** 650-508-3765
E-mail: admiss@ndnu.edu

Getting in Last Year 441 applied; 82% were accepted; 98 enrolled (27%).

Financial Matters $19,390 tuition and fees (2002–03); $8982 room and board.

Academics Notre Dame de Namur University awards bachelor's and master's degrees. Challenging opportunities include advanced placement credit, accelerated degree programs, double majors, and independent study. Special programs include cooperative education, internships, summer session for credit, off-campus study, study-abroad, and Air Force ROTC. The faculty at Notre Dame de Namur University has 51 full-time members, 98% with terminal degrees. The student-faculty ratio is 13:1.

Students of Notre Dame de Namur University The student body totals 1,799, of whom 987 are undergraduates. 69.9% are women and 30.1% are men. Students come from 24 states and territories and 17 other countries. 90% are from California. 5.7% are international students. 74% returned for their sophomore year.

Applying Notre Dame de Namur University requires an essay, SAT I or ACT, a high school transcript, and 1 recommendation, and in some cases an interview. Application deadline: rolling admissions; 3/2 priority date for financial aid. Deferred admission is possible.

NOVA SCOTIA COLLEGE OF ART AND DESIGN

Halifax, NS Canada

Urban setting ■ Public ■ Coed

Web site: www.nscad.ns.ca
Contact: Mr. Terry Bailey, Coordinator of Admissions, Off Campus and Recruitment, 5163 Duke Street, Halifax, NS B3J 3J6 Canada
Telephone: 902-494-8129 **Fax:** 902-425-2987
E-mail: admiss@nscad.ns.ca

Getting in Last Year 216 enrolled.

Financial Matters $4845 nonresident tuition and fees (2002–03).

Academics NSCAD awards bachelor's and master's degrees. Challenging opportunities include student-designed majors, an honors program, double majors, independent study, and a senior project. Special programs include cooperative education, internships, summer session for credit, off-campus study, and study-abroad. The most frequently chosen baccalaureate field is visual/performing arts. The faculty at NSCAD has 42 full-time members. The student-faculty ratio is 11:1.

Students of NSCAD The student body totals 911, of whom 842 are undergraduates. 68.8% are women and 31.2% are men. Students come from 12 states and territories and 26 other countries.

Applying NSCAD requires an essay, a high school transcript, and portfolio, and in some cases an interview and 2 recommendations. The school recommends a minimum high school GPA of 3.0. Application deadline: 5/15. Deferred admission is possible.

NOVA SOUTHEASTERN UNIVERSITY

Fort Lauderdale, FL

Suburban setting ■ Private ■ Independent ■ Coed

Web site: www.nova.edu
Contact: Ms. Zeida Roderiguez, Assistant Director of Undergraduate Admissions, 3301 College Avenue, Ft. Lauderdale, FL 33314
Telephone: 954-262-8017 or toll-free 800-541-6682 ext. 8000

Getting in Last Year 817 applied; 73% were accepted; 298 enrolled (50%).

Financial Matters $13,880 tuition and fees (2002–03); $6484 room and board; 56% average percent of need met; $14,635 average financial aid amount received per undergraduate.

Academics Nova Southeastern awards bachelor's, master's, doctoral, and first-professional degrees and first-professional certificates. Challenging opportunities include advanced placement credit, accelerated degree programs, and a senior project. Special programs include cooperative education, internships, summer session for credit, and study-abroad. The most frequently chosen baccalaureate fields are business/marketing, education, and health professions and related sciences. The faculty at Nova Southeastern has 503 full-time members. The student-faculty ratio is 14:1.

Students of Nova Southeastern The student body totals 21,619, of whom 4,700 are undergraduates. 74.4% are women and 25.6% are men. 10.2% are international students. 75% returned for their sophomore year.

Applying Nova Southeastern requires SAT I or ACT and a high school transcript. The school recommends an interview, recommendations, and a minimum high

Nova Southeastern University (continued)

school GPA of 2.5. Application deadline: rolling admissions; 4/15 priority date for financial aid. Early and deferred admission are possible.

NYACK COLLEGE

Nyack, NY

Suburban setting ■ Private ■ Independent Religious ■ Coed

Web site: www.nyackcollege.edu
Contact: Mr. Miguel Sanchez, Director of Admissions, 1 South Boulevard, Nyack, NY 10960-3698
Telephone: 845-358-1710 ext. 350 or toll-free 800-33-NYACK
Fax: 845-353-1297
E-mail: enroll@nyack.edu

Getting in Last Year 944 applied; 63% were accepted; 316 enrolled (53%).

Financial Matters $13,790 tuition and fees (2002–03); $6600 room and board; 54% average percent of need met; $12,614 average financial aid amount received per undergraduate (2001–02).

Academics Nyack awards associate, bachelor's, master's, and first-professional degrees. Challenging opportunities include advanced placement credit, accelerated degree programs, an honors program, double majors, independent study, and a senior project. Special programs include internships, summer session for credit, off-campus study, and study-abroad. The most frequently chosen baccalaureate fields are business/marketing, liberal arts/general studies, and education. The faculty at Nyack has 83 full-time members, 63% with terminal degrees. The student-faculty ratio is 17:1.

Students of Nyack The student body totals 2,618, of whom 1,990 are undergraduates. 59.1% are women and 40.9% are men. Students come from 41 states and territories and 43 other countries. 64% are from New York. 4.3% are international students. 64% returned for their sophomore year.

Applying Nyack requires an essay, a high school transcript, and 2 recommendations, and in some cases SAT I or ACT, an interview, and Evidence of faith commitment. Application deadline: rolling admissions; 3/1 priority date for financial aid. Early and deferred admission are possible.

OAK HILLS CHRISTIAN COLLEGE

Bemidji, MN

Rural setting ■ Private ■ Independent Religious ■ Coed

Web site: www.oakhills.edu
Contact: Mr. Dan Hovestol, Admissions Director, 1600 Oak Hills Road, SW, Bemidji, MN 56601-8832
Telephone: 218-751-8670 ext. 220 or toll-free 888-751-8670 ext. 285
Fax: 218-751-8825
E-mail: admissions@oakhills.edu

Getting in Last Year 49 applied; 80% were accepted.

Financial Matters $10,055 tuition and fees (2002–03); $3580 room and board; 66% average percent of need met; $8481 average financial aid amount received per undergraduate (2001–02).

Academics Oak Hills awards associate and bachelor's degrees. Challenging opportunities include advanced placement credit, an honors program, double majors, independent study, and a senior project. Special programs include internships and off-campus study. The faculty at Oak Hills has 8 full-time members, 38% with terminal degrees. The student-faculty ratio is 13:1.

Students of Oak Hills The student body is made up of 147 undergraduates. Students come from 15 states and territories. 75% are from Minnesota. 58% returned for their sophomore year.

Applying Oak Hills requires an essay, ACT, a high school transcript, and 2 recommendations, and in some cases a minimum high school GPA of 2.0. Application deadline: rolling admissions. Deferred admission is possible.

OAKLAND CITY UNIVERSITY

Oakland City, IN

Rural setting ■ Private ■ Independent Religious ■ Coed

Web site: www.oak.edu
Contact: Mr. Buddy Harris, Director of Admissions, 143 North Lucretia Street, Oakland City, IN 47660-1099
Telephone: 812-749-1222 or toll-free 800-737-5125

Getting in Last Year 382 applied; 100% were accepted; 329 enrolled (86%).

Financial Matters $11,808 tuition and fees (2002–03); $4330 room and board; 90% average percent of need met.

Academics OCU awards associate, bachelor's, master's, doctoral, and first-professional degrees. Challenging opportunities include advanced placement credit and accelerated degree programs. Summer session for credit is a special program. The most frequently chosen baccalaureate fields are education, business/marketing, and liberal arts/general studies. The faculty at OCU has 36 full-time members, 67% with terminal degrees. The student-faculty ratio is 15:1.

Students of OCU The student body totals 1,897, of whom 1,610 are undergraduates. 52.2% are women and 47.8% are men. Students come from 5 states and territories. 77% are from Indiana. 91% returned for their sophomore year.

Applying OCU requires an essay, SAT I or ACT, a high school transcript, 1 recommendation, and a minimum high school GPA of 2.0. The school recommends an interview. Application deadline: rolling admissions; 3/10 priority date for financial aid. Early and deferred admission are possible.

OAKLAND UNIVERSITY

Rochester, MI

Suburban setting ■ Public ■ State-supported ■ Coed

Web site: www.oakland.edu
Contact: Mr. Robert E. Johnson, Vice Provost for Enrollment Management, 101 North Foundation Hall, Rochester, MI 48309-4401
Telephone: 248-370-3360 or toll-free 800-OAK-UNIV **Fax:** 248-370-4462
E-mail: ouinfo@oakland.edu

Getting in Last Year 5,733 applied; 78% were accepted; 1,868 enrolled (42%).

Financial Matters $5031 resident tuition and fees (2002–03); $11,826 nonresident tuition and fees (2002–03); $5252 room and board; 90% average percent of need met; $5866 average financial aid amount received per undergraduate (2001–02 estimated).

Academics Oakland awards bachelor's, master's, and doctoral degrees and post-bachelor's and post-master's certificates. Challenging opportunities include advanced placement credit, accelerated degree programs, student-designed majors, an honors program, double majors, independent study, and a senior project. Special programs include cooperative education, internships, summer session for credit, off-campus study, study-abroad, and Air Force ROTC. The most frequently chosen baccalaureate fields are business/marketing, education, and health professions and related sciences. The faculty at Oakland has 452 full-time members. The student-faculty ratio is 21:1.

Students of Oakland The student body totals 16,059, of whom 12,634 are undergraduates. 62.6% are women and 37.4% are men. Students come from 40 states and territories and 49 other countries. 99% are from Michigan. 0.8% are international students. 74% returned for their sophomore year.

Applying Oakland requires ACT, a high school transcript, and a minimum high school GPA of 2.5, and in some cases an interview, recommendations, audition, and a minimum high school GPA of 3.0. Application deadline: rolling admissions. Deferred admission is possible.

OAKWOOD COLLEGE

Huntsville, AL

Private ■ Independent Religious ■ Coed

Web site: www.oakwood.edu
Contact: Mr. Fred Pullins, Director of Enrollment Management, 7000 Adventist Boulevard, NW, Huntsville, AL 35896
Telephone: 256-726-7354 or toll-free 800-358-3978 (in-state)
Fax: 256-726-7154
E-mail: admission@oakwood.edu

Getting in Last Year 847 applied; 55% were accepted; 399 enrolled (86%).

Financial Matters $10,194 tuition and fees (2002–03); $5852 room and board; 77% average percent of need met; $6500 average financial aid amount received per undergraduate (2001–02 estimated).

Academics Oakwood College awards associate and bachelor's degrees. Challenging opportunities include advanced placement credit, an honors program, double majors, and a senior project. Special programs include internships, off-campus study, and study-abroad. The most frequently chosen baccalaureate fields are business/marketing, biological/life sciences, and education. The faculty at Oakwood College has 101 full-time members, 57% with terminal degrees. The student-faculty ratio is 14:1.

Students of Oakwood College The student body is made up of 1,778 undergraduates. 56.5% are women and 43.5% are men. Students come from 39 states and territories and 22 other countries. 32% are from Alabama. 10.6% are international students. 70% returned for their sophomore year.

Applying Oakwood College requires SAT I or ACT, a high school transcript, and recommendations. Application deadline: rolling admissions; 3/31 priority date for financial aid. Deferred admission is possible.

OBERLIN COLLEGE

Oberlin, OH

Small-town setting ■ Private ■ Independent ■ Coed

Web site: www.oberlin.edu
Contact: Ms. Debra Chermonte, Dean of Admissions and Financial Aid, Admissions Office, Carnegie Building, Oberlin, OH 44074-1090
Telephone: 440-775-8411 or toll-free 800-622-OBIE **Fax:** 440-775-6905
E-mail: college.admissions@oberlin.edu

Getting in Last Year 5,934 applied; 33% were accepted; 746 enrolled (38%).

Financial Matters $28,050 tuition and fees (2002–03); $7830 room and board; 100% average percent of need met; $23,099 average financial aid amount received per undergraduate.

Academics Oberlin awards bachelor's and master's degrees and post-bachelor's certificates. Challenging opportunities include advanced placement credit, student-designed majors, an honors program, double majors, independent study, and a senior project. Special programs include internships, off-campus study, and study-abroad. The most frequently chosen baccalaureate fields are visual/performing arts, social sciences and history, and biological/life sciences. The faculty at Oberlin has 272 full-time members, 94% with terminal degrees. The student-faculty ratio is 10:1.

Students of Oberlin The student body totals 2,861, of whom 2,848 are undergraduates. 55.2% are women and 44.8% are men. Students come from 54 states and territories and 28 other countries. 11% are from Ohio. 6.2% are international students. 90% returned for their sophomore year.

Applying Oberlin requires an essay, SAT I or ACT, a high school transcript, and 2 recommendations, and in some cases an interview. The school recommends SAT II Subject Tests. Application deadline: 1/15; 2/15 priority date for financial aid. Early and deferred admission are possible.

OCCIDENTAL COLLEGE

Los Angeles, CA

Urban setting ■ Private ■ Independent ■ Coed

Web site: www.oxy.edu
Contact: Mr. Vince Cuseo, Director of Admission, 1600 Campus Road, Los Angeles, CA 90041
Telephone: 323-259-2700 or toll-free 800-825-5262 **Fax:** 323-341-4875
E-mail: admission@oxy.edu

Getting in Last Year 4,174 applied; 43% were accepted; 447 enrolled (25%).

Financial Matters $26,448 tuition and fees (2002–03); $7448 room and board; 94% average percent of need met; $26,883 average financial aid amount received per undergraduate.

Academics OXY awards bachelor's and master's degrees. Challenging opportunities include advanced placement credit, accelerated degree programs, student-designed majors, an honors program, double majors, independent study, and a senior project. Special programs include internships, summer session for credit, off-campus study, study-abroad, and Army, Navy and Air Force ROTC. The most frequently chosen baccalaureate field is visual/performing arts. The faculty at OXY has 142 full-time members, 93% with terminal degrees. The student-faculty ratio is 12:1.

Students of OXY The student body totals 1,832, of whom 1,808 are undergraduates. 57.7% are women and 42.3% are men. Students come from 43 states and territories and 27 other countries. 68% are from California. 92% returned for their sophomore year.

Applying OXY requires an essay, SAT I or ACT, a high school transcript, and 2 recommendations. The school recommends SAT II Subject Tests, SAT II: Writing Test, and an interview. Application deadline: 1/15; 2/1 priority date for financial aid. Early and deferred admission are possible.

OGLETHORPE UNIVERSITY

Atlanta, GA

Suburban setting ■ Private ■ Independent ■ Coed

Web site: www.oglethorpe.edu
Contact: Mr. Dennis T. Matthews, Associate Dean for Enrollment Management, 4484 Peachtree Road, NE, Atlanta, GA 30319
Telephone: 404-364-8307 or toll-free 800-428-4484 **Fax:** 404-364-8500
E-mail: admission@oglethorpe.edu

Getting in Last Year 602 applied; 90% were accepted; 183 enrolled (34%).

Financial Matters $19,440 tuition and fees (2002–03); $6360 room and board; 86% average percent of need met; $15,650 average financial aid amount received per undergraduate.

Academics Oglethorpe awards bachelor's and master's degrees. Challenging opportunities include advanced placement credit, accelerated degree programs, student-designed majors, an honors program, double majors, independent study, and a senior project. Special programs include cooperative education, internships, summer session for credit, off-campus study, and study-abroad. The faculty at Oglethorpe has 55 full-time members, 93% with terminal degrees. The student-faculty ratio is 12:1.

Students of Oglethorpe The student body totals 1,115, of whom 1,037 are undergraduates. 66.3% are women and 33.7% are men. Students come from 37 states and territories and 31 other countries. 56% are from Georgia. 5.9% are international students. 81% returned for their sophomore year.

Applying Oglethorpe requires an essay, SAT I or ACT, a high school transcript, and 1 recommendation, and in some cases an interview. The school recommends an interview and a minimum high school GPA of 2.5. Application deadline: rolling admissions; 3/1 priority date for financial aid. Deferred admission is possible.

OHIO DOMINICAN UNIVERSITY

Columbus, OH

Urban setting ■ Private ■ Independent Religious ■ Coed

Web site: www.ohiodominican.edu
Contact: Ms. Vicki Thompson-Campbell, Director of Admissions, 1216 Sunbury Road, Columbus, OH 43219-2099
Telephone: 614-251-4500 or toll-free 800-854-2670 **Fax:** 614-251-0156
E-mail: admissions@ohiodominican.edu

Getting in Last Year 1,116 applied; 64% were accepted; 265 enrolled (37%).

Financial Matters $16,200 tuition and fees (2002–03); $5370 room and board; 92% average percent of need met; $12,467 average financial aid amount received per undergraduate.

Academics ODU awards associate, bachelor's, and master's degrees. Challenging opportunities include advanced placement credit, student-designed majors, an honors program, independent study, and a senior project. Special programs include internships, summer session for credit, off-campus study, study-abroad, and Army ROTC. The most frequently chosen baccalaureate fields are business/marketing, education, and social sciences and history. The faculty at ODU has 62 full-time members, 87% with terminal degrees. The student-faculty ratio is 15:1.

Students of ODU The student body totals 2,317, of whom 2,250 are undergraduates. 70.9% are women and 29.1% are men. Students come from 18 states and territories and 13 other countries. 99% are from Ohio. 1.4% are international students. 68% returned for their sophomore year.

Applying ODU requires an essay, a high school transcript, an interview, and a minimum high school GPA of 2.0, and in some cases SAT I and SAT II or ACT and recommendations. Application deadline: rolling admissions; 4/1 priority date for financial aid. Deferred admission is possible.

OHIO NORTHERN UNIVERSITY

Ada, OH

Small-town setting ■ Private ■ Independent Religious ■ Coed

Web site: www.onu.edu
Contact: Ms. Karen Condeni, Vice President of Admissions and Financial Aid, 525 South Main, Ada, OH 45810-1599
Telephone: 419-772-2260 or toll-free 888-408-4ONU **Fax:** 419-772-2313
E-mail: admissions-ug@onu.edu

Getting in Last Year 2,469 applied; 89% were accepted; 533 enrolled (24%).

Financial Matters $23,310 tuition and fees (2002–03); $5805 room and board; 91% average percent of need met; $19,711 average financial aid amount received per undergraduate.

Academics Ohio Northern awards bachelor's and first-professional degrees. Challenging opportunities include advanced placement credit, an honors program, double majors, independent study, and a senior project. Special programs include cooperative education, internships, summer session for credit, off-campus study, study-abroad, and Army and Air Force ROTC. The most frequently chosen baccalaureate fields are engineering/engineering technologies, business/marketing, and health professions and related sciences. The faculty at Ohio Northern has 197 full-time members, 78% with terminal degrees. The student-faculty ratio is 13:1.

Students of Ohio Northern The student body totals 3,430, of whom 2,281 are undergraduates. 47% are women and 53% are men. Students come from 42 states and territories. 87% are from Ohio. 0.6% are international students. 82% returned for their sophomore year.

Applying Ohio Northern requires SAT I or ACT and a high school transcript, and in some cases 2 recommendations. The school recommends an essay, an interview, and a minimum high school GPA of 2.5. Application deadline: 8/15; 6/1 for financial aid, with a 4/15 priority date. Early and deferred admission are possible.

THE OHIO STATE UNIVERSITY

Columbus, OH

Urban setting ■ Public ■ State-supported ■ Coed

Web site: www.osu.edu
Contact: Dr. Mabel G. Freeman, Director of Undergraduate Admissions and Vice President for First-Year Experience, 3rd Floor, Lincoln Tower, 1800 Cannon Drive, Columbus, OH 43210
Telephone: 614-292-3974 **Fax:** 614-292-4818
E-mail: askabuckeye@osu.edu

Getting in Last Year 19,563 applied; 74% were accepted; 5,982 enrolled (42%).

Financial Matters $5664 resident tuition and fees (2002–03); $15,087 nonresident tuition and fees (2002–03); $6291 room and board; 75% average percent of need met; $8211 average financial aid amount received per undergraduate.

Academics Ohio State awards bachelor's, master's, doctoral, and first-professional degrees and post-master's certificates. Challenging opportunities include advanced placement credit, accelerated degree programs, student-designed majors, freshman honors college, an honors program, double majors, independent study, and a senior project. Special programs include cooperative education, internships,

The Ohio State University (continued)

summer session for credit, off-campus study, study-abroad, and Army and Air Force ROTC. The most frequently chosen baccalaureate fields are business/marketing, social sciences and history, and home economics/vocational home economics. The faculty at Ohio State has 2,710 full-time members, 99% with terminal degrees. The student-faculty ratio is 14:1.

Students of Ohio State The student body totals 49,676, of whom 36,855 are undergraduates. 47.6% are women and 52.4% are men. Students come from 53 states and territories and 89 other countries. 89% are from Ohio. 4.2% are international students. 86% returned for their sophomore year.

Applying Ohio State requires SAT I or ACT and a high school transcript. Application deadline: 2/15; 2/15 priority date for financial aid.

THE OHIO STATE UNIVERSITY AT LIMA

Lima, OH

Small-town setting ■ *Public* ■ *State-supported* ■ *Coed*

Web site: www.ohio-state.edu

Contact: Ms. Marissa Christoff Snyder, Admissions Counselor, 4240 Campus Drive, Lima, OH 45804

Telephone: 419-995-8220

E-mail: admissions@lima.ohio-state.edu

Getting in Last Year 548 applied; 96% were accepted; 389 enrolled (74%).

Financial Matters $3927 resident tuition and fees (2002–03); $13,350 nonresident tuition and fees (2002–03).

Academics OSU-Lima awards associate and bachelor's degrees (also offers some graduate courses). Challenging opportunities include advanced placement credit, accelerated degree programs, an honors program, and a senior project. Special programs include summer session for credit and Army, Navy and Air Force ROTC. The faculty at OSU-Lima has 56 full-time members. The student-faculty ratio is 13:1.

Students of OSU-Lima The student body totals 1,412, of whom 1,293 are undergraduates. 57.4% are women and 42.6% are men. Students come from 1 state or territory and 1 other country. 63% returned for their sophomore year.

Applying OSU-Lima requires ACT and a high school transcript. Application deadline: 7/1. Early admission is possible.

OHIO UNIVERSITY

Athens, OH

Small-town setting ■ *Public* ■ *State-supported* ■ *Coed*

Web site: www.ohio.edu

Contact: Mr. N. Kip Howard Jr., Director of Admissions, Athens, OH 45701-2979

Telephone: 740-593-4100

E-mail: admissions.freshmen@ohiou.edu

Getting in Last Year 13,195 applied; 75% were accepted; 3,700 enrolled (37%).

Financial Matters $6336 resident tuition and fees (2002–03); $13,818 nonresident tuition and fees (2002–03); $6777 room and board; 68% average percent of need met; $6581 average financial aid amount received per undergraduate.

Academics Ohio awards associate, bachelor's, master's, doctoral, and first-professional degrees. Challenging opportunities include advanced placement credit, accelerated degree programs, student-designed majors, an honors program, double majors, independent study, and a senior project. Special programs include cooperative education, internships, summer session for credit, off-campus study, study-abroad, and Army and Air Force ROTC. The most frequently chosen baccalaureate fields are communications/communication technologies, business/marketing, and education. The faculty at Ohio has 846 full-time members, 88% with terminal degrees. The student-faculty ratio is 20:1.

Students of Ohio The student body totals 20,528, of whom 17,343 are undergraduates. 54.9% are women and 45.1% are men. Students come from 52 states and territories and 52 other countries. 91% are from Ohio. 2.2% are international students. 85% returned for their sophomore year.

Applying Ohio requires SAT I or ACT and a high school transcript, and in some cases an essay and an interview. The school recommends 2 recommendations. Application deadline: 2/1; 3/15 priority date for financial aid. Early and deferred admission are possible.

OHIO UNIVERSITY–CHILLICOTHE

Chillicothe, OH

Small-town setting ■ *Public* ■ *State-supported* ■ *Coed*

Web site: www.ohio.edu/chillicothe

Contact: Mr. Richard R. Whitney, Director of Student Services, 571 West Fifth Street, Chillicothe, OH 45601

Telephone: 740-774-7200 ext. 242 or toll-free 877-462-6824 (in-state)
Fax: 740-774-7295

Financial Matters $3564 resident tuition and fees (2002–03); $9150 nonresident tuition and fees (2002–03); 59% average percent of need met; $6435 average financial aid amount received per undergraduate.

Academics Ohio University–Chillicothe awards associate, bachelor's, and master's degrees (offers first 2 years of most bachelor's degree programs available at the main campus in Athens; also offers several bachelor's degree programs that can be completed at this campus and several programs exclusive to this campus; also offers some graduate programs). Challenging opportunities include advanced placement credit, accelerated degree programs, student-designed majors, double majors, and independent study. Special programs include internships, summer session for credit, and Army and Air Force ROTC. The faculty at Ohio University–Chillicothe has 41 full-time members.

Students of Ohio University–Chillicothe The student body totals 1,999, of whom 1,816 are undergraduates. Students come from 2 states and territories. 55% returned for their sophomore year.

Applying Ohio University–Chillicothe requires SAT I or ACT and a high school transcript. Application deadline: 9/1; 3/15 priority date for financial aid. Early admission is possible.

OHIO UNIVERSITY–LANCASTER

Lancaster, OH

Small-town setting ■ *Public* ■ *State-supported* ■ *Coed*

Web site: www.ohiou.edu/lancaster

Contact: Mr. Nathan Thomas, Admissions Officer, 1570 Granville Pike, Lancaster, OH 43130-1097

Telephone: 740-654-6711 ext. 215 or toll-free 888-446-4468 ext. 215
Fax: 740-687-9497

E-mail: fox@ohio.edu

Getting in Last Year 486 applied; 100% were accepted; 308 enrolled (63%).

Financial Matters $4095 resident tuition and fees (2002–03); $9150 nonresident tuition and fees (2002–03); 62% average percent of need met; $6073 average financial aid amount received per undergraduate.

Academics Ohio University–Lancaster awards associate, bachelor's, and master's degrees. Challenging opportunities include advanced placement credit, accelerated degree programs, student-designed majors, double majors, and independent study. Special programs include internships, summer session for credit, and Army and Air Force ROTC. The most frequently chosen baccalaureate fields are education, communications/communication technologies, and business/marketing. The faculty at Ohio University–Lancaster has 31 full-time members, 71% with terminal degrees. The student-faculty ratio is 30:1.

Students of Ohio University–Lancaster The student body totals 1,744, of whom 1,617 are undergraduates. 67% are women and 33% are men. Students come from 12 states and territories and 1 other country. 0.2% are international students.

Applying Ohio University–Lancaster requires SAT I or ACT and a high school transcript. The school recommends an interview. Application deadline: rolling admissions; 3/15 priority date for financial aid. Early and deferred admission are possible.

OHIO UNIVERSITY–SOUTHERN CAMPUS

Ironton, OH

Small-town setting ■ *Public* ■ *State-supported* ■ *Coed*

Web site: www.ohiou.edu

Contact: Dr. Kim K. Lawson, Coordinator of Admissions, 1804 Liberty Avenue, Ironton, OH 45638

Telephone: 740-533-4612 or toll-free 800-626-0513 **Fax:** 740-593-0560

Getting in Last Year 552 applied; 100% were accepted; 348 enrolled (63%).

Financial Matters $3282 resident tuition and fees (2002–03); $4272 nonresident tuition and fees (2002–03); 62% average percent of need met; $6718 average financial aid amount received per undergraduate.

Academics Ohio University–Southern Campus awards associate, bachelor's, and master's degrees. Student-designed majors are a challenging opportunity. Summer session for credit is a special program. The faculty at Ohio University–Southern Campus has 10 full-time members.

Students of Ohio University–Southern Campus The student body totals 1,746, of whom 1,630 are undergraduates. 63.3% are women and 36.7% are men. Students come from 4 states and territories. 86% are from Ohio. 0.1% are international students.

Applying Ohio University–Southern Campus recommends SAT I or ACT. Application deadline: rolling admissions; 4/1 priority date for financial aid. Early and deferred admission are possible.

OHIO UNIVERSITY–ZANESVILLE

Zanesville, OH

Rural setting ■ *Public* ■ *State-supported* ■ *Coed*

Web site: www.zanesville.ohiou.edu

Contact: Mrs. Karen Ragsdale, Student Services Secretary, 1425 Newark Road, Zanesville, OH 43701-2695
Telephone: 740-588-1440 **Fax:** 740-453-6161

Getting in Last Year 521 applied; 100% were accepted; 348 enrolled (67%).

Financial Matters $3564 resident tuition and fees (2002–03); $9150 nonresident tuition and fees (2002–03); 65% average percent of need met; $6145 average financial aid amount received per undergraduate.

Academics OUZ awards associate, bachelor's, and master's degrees (offers first 2 years of most bachelor's degree programs available at the main campus in Athens; also offers several bachelor's degree programs that can be completed at this campus; also offers some graduate courses). Challenging opportunities include advanced placement credit and student-designed majors. Special programs include summer session for credit and off-campus study. The faculty at OUZ has 28 full-time members, 64% with terminal degrees. The student-faculty ratio is 23:1.

Students of OUZ The student body totals 1,635, of whom 1,506 are undergraduates. 72% are women and 28% are men. Students come from 4 states and territories. 99% are from Ohio. 64% returned for their sophomore year.

Applying OUZ requires a high school transcript, and in some cases SAT I or ACT and nursing examination. Application deadline: rolling admissions; 4/1 priority date for financial aid. Early and deferred admission are possible.

OHIO VALLEY COLLEGE

Vienna, WV

Small-town setting ■ *Private* ■ *Independent Religious* ■ *Coed*

Web site: www.ovc.edu
Contact: Ms. Sharon Woomer, Admissions Office Manager, 1 Campus View Drive, Vienna, WV 26105
Telephone: 304-865-6200 or toll-free 877-446-8668 ext. 6200 (out-of-state) **Fax:** 304-865-6001
E-mail: admissions@ovc.edu

Getting in Last Year 363 applied; 71% were accepted; 103 enrolled (40%).

Financial Matters $9960 tuition and fees (2002–03); $4840 room and board; 76% average percent of need met; $9353 average financial aid amount received per undergraduate.

Academics OVC awards associate and bachelor's degrees. Challenging opportunities include advanced placement credit, an honors program, double majors, and a senior project. Special programs include internships, summer session for credit, study-abroad, and Air Force ROTC. The most frequently chosen baccalaureate fields are business/marketing, education, and psychology. The faculty at OVC has 19 full-time members, 42% with terminal degrees. The student-faculty ratio is 15:1.

Students of OVC The student body is made up of 526 undergraduates. 54.6% are women and 45.4% are men. Students come from 23 states and territories and 17 other countries. 43% are from West Virginia. 6.8% are international students. 65% returned for their sophomore year.

Applying OVC requires SAT I or ACT and a high school transcript, and in some cases an essay and an interview. The school recommends recommendations. Application deadline: rolling admissions; 2/15 priority date for financial aid. Early and deferred admission are possible.

OHIO WESLEYAN UNIVERSITY

Delaware, OH

Small-town setting ■ *Private* ■ *Independent Religious* ■ *Coed*

Web site: web.owu.edu
Contact: Ms. Carol Wheatley, Director of Admission, 61 South Sandusky Street, Delaware, OH 43015
Telephone: 740-368-3020 or toll-free 800-922-8953 **Fax:** 740-368-3314
E-mail: owuadmit@owu.edu

Getting in Last Year 2,212 applied; 80% were accepted; 546 enrolled (31%).

Financial Matters $24,200 tuition and fees (2002–03); $7010 room and board; 88% average percent of need met; $20,866 average financial aid amount received per undergraduate.

Academics Ohio Wesleyan awards bachelor's degrees. Challenging opportunities include advanced placement credit, student-designed majors, freshman honors college, an honors program, double majors, independent study, and a senior project. Special programs include internships, summer session for credit, off-campus study, study-abroad, and Army ROTC. The most frequently chosen baccalaureate fields are social sciences and history, business/marketing, and biological/life sciences. The faculty at Ohio Wesleyan has 130 full-time members, 100% with terminal degrees. The student-faculty ratio is 13:1.

Students of Ohio Wesleyan The student body is made up of 1,935 undergraduates. 53.7% are women and 46.3% are men. Students come from 44 states and territories and 47 other countries. 60% are from Ohio. 11.1% are international students. 79% returned for their sophomore year.

Applying Ohio Wesleyan requires an essay, SAT I or ACT, a high school transcript, and 1 recommendation. The school recommends SAT II Subject Tests, an interview, 2 recommendations, and a minimum high school GPA of 2.5. Application deadline: 3/15; 3/15 priority date for financial aid. Early and deferred admission are possible.

OKANAGAN UNIVERSITY COLLEGE

Kelowna, BC Canada

Public ■ *Coed*

Web site: www.ouc.bc.ca
Contact: Ms. Lynn Graham, Manager of Admissions, 1000 K. L. O. Road, Kelowna, BC V1Y 4X8 Canada
Telephone: 250-862-5417 ext. 4213 or toll-free 888-733-6533 (in-state) **Fax:** 250-862-5466

Getting in Last Year 3,231 applied; 62% were accepted; 1,541 enrolled (77%).

Academics Okanagan University College awards associate and bachelor's degrees. Challenging opportunities include advanced placement credit, an honors program, double majors, independent study, and a senior project. Special programs include cooperative education, summer session for credit, and study-abroad. The most frequently chosen baccalaureate fields are liberal arts/general studies, health professions and related sciences, and business/marketing. The faculty at Okanagan University College has 361 full-time members, 32% with terminal degrees. The student-faculty ratio is 14:1.

Students of Okanagan University College The student body is made up of 7,140 undergraduates. 60.2% are women and 39.8% are men. Students come from 42 states and territories and 21 other countries. 99% are from British Columbia. 2% are international students. 57% returned for their sophomore year.

Applying Okanagan University College requires (in some cases) an essay, a high school transcript, an interview, and a minimum high school GPA of 2.0. Application deadline: rolling admissions.

OKLAHOMA BAPTIST UNIVERSITY

Shawnee, OK

Small-town setting ■ *Private* ■ *Independent Religious* ■ *Coed*

Web site: www.okbu.edu
Contact: Mr. Michael Cappo, Dean of Admissions, Box 61174, Shawnee, OK 74804
Telephone: 405-878-2033 or toll-free 800-654-3285 **Fax:** 405-878-2046
E-mail: admissions@mail.okbu.edu

Getting in Last Year 958 applied; 86% were accepted; 435 enrolled (53%).

Financial Matters $11,040 tuition and fees (2002–03); $3750 room and board; 70% average percent of need met; $11,142 average financial aid amount received per undergraduate.

Academics OBU awards bachelor's and master's degrees. Challenging opportunities include advanced placement credit, student-designed majors, an honors program, double majors, independent study, and a senior project. Special programs include cooperative education, internships, summer session for credit, off-campus study, study-abroad, and Air Force ROTC. The most frequently chosen baccalaureate fields are education, health professions and related sciences, and business/marketing. The faculty at OBU has 119 members. The student-faculty ratio is 15:1.

Students of OBU The student body totals 1,933, of whom 1,911 are undergraduates. 56.4% are women and 43.6% are men. Students come from 42 states and territories and 19 other countries. 61% are from Oklahoma. 74% returned for their sophomore year.

Applying OBU requires SAT I or ACT, a high school transcript, and a minimum high school GPA of 2.5, and in some cases an essay, an interview, and recommendations. Application deadline: 8/1; 3/1 priority date for financial aid. Early and deferred admission are possible.

OKLAHOMA CHRISTIAN UNIVERSITY

Oklahoma City, OK

Suburban setting ■ *Private* ■ *Independent Religious* ■ *Coed*

Web site: www.oc.edu
Contact: Ms. Rita Forrester, Director of Admissions, Box 11000, Oklahoma City, OK 73136-1100
Telephone: 405-425-5050 or toll-free 800-877-5010 (in-state) **Fax:** 405-425-5208
E-mail: info@oc.edu

Getting in Last Year 1,168 applied; 36% were accepted; 426 enrolled (101%).

Financial Matters $12,700 tuition and fees (2002–03); $4500 room and board; 50% average percent of need met; $11,048 average financial aid amount received per undergraduate.

Academics Oklahoma Christian awards bachelor's and master's degrees. Challenging opportunities include advanced placement credit, accelerated degree programs, an honors program, double majors, and a senior project. Special programs include internships, summer session for credit, off-campus study, study-abroad, and Army and Air Force ROTC. The most frequently chosen

Oklahoma Christian University (continued)

baccalaureate fields are business/marketing, education, and biological/life sciences. The faculty at Oklahoma Christian has 108 full-time members, 65% with terminal degrees. The student-faculty ratio is 13:1.

Students of Oklahoma Christian The student body totals 1,718, of whom 1,599 are undergraduates. 51.3% are women and 48.7% are men. Students come from 59 states and territories. 45% are from Oklahoma. 67% returned for their sophomore year.

Applying Oklahoma Christian requires SAT I or ACT and a high school transcript. Application deadline: rolling admissions; 8/31 for financial aid, with a 3/15 priority date. Early and deferred admission are possible.

OKLAHOMA CITY UNIVERSITY

Oklahoma City, OK

Urban setting ■ Private ■ Independent Religious ■ Coed

Web site: www.okcu.edu

Contact: Ms. Shery Boyles, Director of Admissions, 2501 North Blackwelder, Oklahoma City, OK 73106-1402

Telephone: 405-521-5050 or toll-free 800-633-7242 **Fax:** 405-521-5916

E-mail: uadmissions@okcu.edu

Getting in Last Year 891 applied; 67% were accepted; 258 enrolled (43%).

Financial Matters $12,000 tuition and fees (2002–03); $5200 room and board; $8796 average financial aid amount received per undergraduate (2001–02).

Academics OCU awards bachelor's, master's, and first-professional degrees. Challenging opportunities include advanced placement credit, accelerated degree programs, student-designed majors, an honors program, double majors, independent study, and a senior project. Special programs include cooperative education, internships, summer session for credit, off-campus study, study-abroad, and Army and Air Force ROTC. The most frequently chosen baccalaureate fields are liberal arts/general studies, visual/performing arts, and business/marketing. The faculty at OCU has 173 full-time members, 72% with terminal degrees. The student-faculty ratio is 14:1.

Students of OCU The student body totals 3,529, of whom 1,710 are undergraduates. 59.9% are women and 40.1% are men. Students come from 49 states and territories and 75 other countries. 32% are from Oklahoma. 22% are international students. 70% returned for their sophomore year.

Applying OCU requires SAT I or ACT, a high school transcript, and a minimum high school GPA of 2.5, and in some cases an interview and audition for music and dance programs. Application deadline: 8/22; 3/1 priority date for financial aid. Deferred admission is possible.

OKLAHOMA PANHANDLE STATE UNIVERSITY

Goodwell, OK

Rural setting ■ Public ■ State-supported ■ Coed

Web site: www.opsu.edu

Contact: Mr. Vic Shrock, Registrar and Director of Admissions, PO Box 430, 323 Eagle Boulevard, Goodwell, OK 73939-0430

Telephone: 580-349-1376 or toll-free 800-664-6778 **Fax:** 580-349-2302

E-mail: opsu@opsu.edu

Getting in Last Year 222 enrolled.

Financial Matters $2172 resident tuition and fees (2002–03); $3588 nonresident tuition and fees (2002–03); $2810 room and board; 70% average percent of need met; $9200 average financial aid amount received per undergraduate.

Academics OPSU awards associate and bachelor's degrees. Challenging opportunities include advanced placement credit, accelerated degree programs, double majors, and a senior project. Special programs include cooperative education, internships, and summer session for credit. The most frequently chosen baccalaureate fields are agriculture, business/marketing, and education. The faculty at OPSU has 53 full-time members, 38% with terminal degrees. The student-faculty ratio is 22:1.

Students of OPSU The student body is made up of 1,226 undergraduates. 53.1% are women and 46.9% are men. Students come from 36 states and territories and 26 other countries. 48% are from Oklahoma. 5% are international students. 50% returned for their sophomore year.

Applying OPSU requires SAT I or ACT and a high school transcript. Application deadline: rolling admissions; 1/1 priority date for financial aid.

OKLAHOMA STATE UNIVERSITY

Stillwater, OK

Small-town setting ■ Public ■ State-supported ■ Coed

Web site: www.okstate.edu

Contact: Ms. Paulette Cundiff, Coordinator of Admissions Processing, 324 Student Union, Stillwater, OK 74078

Telephone: 405-744-6858 or toll-free 800-233-5019 (in-state), 800-852-1255 (out-of-state) **Fax:** 405-744-5285

E-mail: admit@okstate.edu

Getting in Last Year 5,639 applied; 92% were accepted; 3,265 enrolled (63%).

Financial Matters $3025 resident tuition and fees (2002–03); $8079 nonresident tuition and fees (2002–03); $5150 room and board; 82% average percent of need met; $7550 average financial aid amount received per undergraduate (2001–02).

Academics OSU awards bachelor's, master's, doctoral, and first-professional degrees. Challenging opportunities include advanced placement credit, accelerated degree programs, student-designed majors, freshman honors college, an honors program, double majors, independent study, and a senior project. Special programs include cooperative education, internships, summer session for credit, off-campus study, study-abroad, and Army and Air Force ROTC. The most frequently chosen baccalaureate fields are business/marketing, engineering/engineering technologies, and agriculture. The faculty at OSU has 964 full-time members, 91% with terminal degrees. The student-faculty ratio is 19:1.

Students of OSU The student body totals 22,992, of whom 18,043 are undergraduates. 48.5% are women and 51.5% are men. Students come from 50 states and territories and 122 other countries. 88% are from Oklahoma. 4.6% are international students. 82% returned for their sophomore year.

Applying OSU requires SAT I or ACT, a high school transcript, class rank, and a minimum high school GPA of 3.0, and in some cases an interview. The school recommends ACT. Application deadline: rolling admissions. Early admission is possible.

OKLAHOMA WESLEYAN UNIVERSITY

Bartlesville, OK

Small-town setting ■ Private ■ Independent Religious ■ Coed

Web site: www.okwu.edu

Contact: Mr. Jim Weidman, Director of Enrollment Services, 2201 Silver Lake Road, Bartlesville, OK 74006-6299

Telephone: 800-468-6292 or toll-free 800-468-6292 (in-state) **Fax:** 918-335-6229

E-mail: admissions@okwu.edu

Getting in Last Year 427 applied; 60% were accepted.

Financial Matters $10,400 tuition and fees (2002–03); $4100 room and board; 58% average percent of need met; $6466 average financial aid amount received per undergraduate (2001–02).

Academics Oklahoma Wesleyan University awards associate, bachelor's, and master's degrees. Challenging opportunities include advanced placement credit, student-designed majors, independent study, and a senior project. Special programs include cooperative education, internships, summer session for credit, and off-campus study. The faculty at Oklahoma Wesleyan University has 37 members. The student-faculty ratio is 14:1.

Students of Oklahoma Wesleyan University The student body is made up of 675 undergraduates. Students come from 26 states and territories and 8 other countries. 54% are from Oklahoma. 70% returned for their sophomore year.

Applying Oklahoma Wesleyan University requires SAT I or ACT, a high school transcript, recommendations, and minimum ACT of 18 or SAT 860. The school recommends a minimum high school GPA of 2.0. Application deadline: rolling admissions; 3/31 priority date for financial aid. Early and deferred admission are possible.

OLD DOMINION UNIVERSITY

Norfolk, VA

Urban setting ■ Public ■ State-supported ■ Coed

Web site: www.odu.edu

Contact: Ms. Alice McAdory, (Acting) Director of Admissions, 108 Rollins Hall, Norfolk, VA 23529-0050

Telephone: 757-683-3685 or toll-free 800-348-7926 **Fax:** 757-683-3255

E-mail: admit@odu.edu

Getting in Last Year 6,472 applied; 70% were accepted; 1,754 enrolled (39%).

Financial Matters $4264 resident tuition and fees (2002–03); $13,294 nonresident tuition and fees (2002–03); $5498 room and board; 71% average percent of need met; $6916 average financial aid amount received per undergraduate.

Academics ODU awards bachelor's, master's, and doctoral degrees and post-master's certificates. Challenging opportunities include advanced placement credit, accelerated degree programs, student-designed majors, freshman honors college, an honors program, double majors, independent study, and a senior project. Special programs include cooperative education, internships, summer session for credit, off-campus study, study-abroad, and Army and Navy ROTC. The most frequently chosen baccalaureate fields are health professions and related sciences, business/marketing, and engineering/engineering technologies. The faculty at ODU has 592 full-time members, 84% with terminal degrees. The student-faculty ratio is 16:1.

Students of ODU The student body totals 20,105, of whom 13,578 are undergraduates. 57.2% are women and 42.8% are men. Students come from 41 states and territories and 93 other countries. 92% are from Virginia. 3% are international students. 77% returned for their sophomore year.

Applying ODU requires an essay, SAT I or ACT, a high school transcript, and a minimum high school GPA of 2.5, and in some cases an interview. The school recommends 1 recommendation. Application deadline: 3/15; 3/15 for financial aid, with a 2/15 priority date. Early and deferred admission are possible.

OLIVET COLLEGE

Olivet, MI

Small-town setting ■ Private ■ Independent Religious ■ Coed

Web site: www.olivetcollege.edu

Contact: Mr. Kevin Leonard, Director of Admissions, 320 South Main Street, Olivet, MI 49076

Telephone: 616-749-7635 or toll-free 800-456-7189 **Fax:** 269-749-6617

E-mail: bmcconnell@olivetcollege.edu

Getting in Last Year 750 applied; 65% were accepted; 309 enrolled (63%).

Financial Matters $14,752 tuition and fees (2002–03); $4702 room and board; 81% average percent of need met; $12,560 average financial aid amount received per undergraduate (2001–02).

Academics Olivet awards bachelor's and master's degrees. Challenging opportunities include advanced placement credit, accelerated degree programs, student-designed majors, an honors program, double majors, independent study, and a senior project. Special programs include cooperative education, internships, summer session for credit, and study-abroad. The most frequently chosen baccalaureate fields are education, biological/life sciences, and business/marketing. The faculty at Olivet has 46 full-time members. The student-faculty ratio is 15:1.

Students of Olivet The student body totals 941, of whom 912 are undergraduates. 45.6% are women and 54.4% are men. Students come from 19 states and territories. 78% are from Michigan. 5% are international students. 95% returned for their sophomore year.

Applying Olivet requires a high school transcript, and in some cases an essay, SAT I or ACT, an interview, and recommendations. The school recommends a minimum high school GPA of 2.6. Application deadline: rolling admissions. Deferred admission is possible.

OLIVET NAZARENE UNIVERSITY

Bourbonnais, IL

Small-town setting ■ Private ■ Independent Religious ■ Coed

Web site: www.olivet.edu

Contact: Ms. Mary Cary, Applicant Coordinator, One University Avenue, Bourbonnais, IL 60914

Telephone: 800-648-1463 ext. 5200 or toll-free 800-648-1463 **Fax:** 815-935-4998

E-mail: admissions@olivet.edu

Getting in Last Year 1,568 applied; 81% were accepted; 563 enrolled (45%).

Financial Matters $14,220 tuition and fees (2002–03); $5240 room and board; 83% average percent of need met; $12,470 average financial aid amount received per undergraduate (2001–02).

Academics Olivet awards bachelor's and master's degrees. Challenging opportunities include advanced placement credit, double majors, independent study, and a senior project. Special programs include internships, summer session for credit, study-abroad, and Army ROTC. The most frequently chosen baccalaureate fields are education, health professions and related sciences, and business/marketing. The faculty at Olivet has 86 full-time members, 60% with terminal degrees. The student-faculty ratio is 20:1.

Students of Olivet The student body totals 3,863, of whom 2,229 are undergraduates. 57.7% are women and 42.3% are men. Students come from 41 states and territories and 15 other countries. 49% are from Illinois. 1% are international students. 68% returned for their sophomore year.

Applying Olivet requires ACT, a high school transcript, 2 recommendations, and a minimum high school GPA of 2.0. The school recommends an essay and an interview. Application deadline: rolling admissions; 3/1 priority date for financial aid. Deferred admission is possible.

O'MORE COLLEGE OF DESIGN

Franklin, TN

Small-town setting ■ Private ■ Independent ■ Coed, Primarily Women

Web site: www.omorecollege.edu

Contact: Mr. Chris Lee, Director of Enrollment Management, 423 South Margin Street, Franklin, TN 37064-2816

Telephone: 615-794-4254 ext. 32 **Fax:** 615-790-1662

Getting in Last Year 90 applied; 72% were accepted.

Financial Matters $11,090 tuition and fees (2002–03).

Academics O'More College of Design awards bachelor's degrees. Challenging opportunities include advanced placement credit, double majors, independent study, and a senior project. Special programs include cooperative education, internships, and summer session for credit. The faculty at O'More College of Design has 7 full-time members. The student-faculty ratio is 3:1.

Students of O'More College of Design The student body is made up of 110 undergraduates. 89.1% are women and 10.9% are men. Students come from 18 states and territories. 1.8% are international students. 85% returned for their sophomore year.

Applying O'More College of Design requires SAT I or ACT, a high school transcript, and a minimum high school GPA of 2.5, and in some cases an essay, an interview, and portfolio. Application deadline: 8/1; 5/1 priority date for financial aid. Deferred admission is possible.

ORAL ROBERTS UNIVERSITY

Tulsa, OK

Urban setting ■ Private ■ Independent Religious ■ Coed

Web site: www.oru.edu

Contact: Chris Miller, Director of Undergraduate Admissions, 7777 South Lewis Avenue, Tulsa, OK 74171-0001

Telephone: 918-495-6518 or toll-free 800-678-8876 **Fax:** 918-495-6222

E-mail: admissions@oru.edu

Getting in Last Year 1,303 applied; 72% were accepted; 582 enrolled (62%).

Financial Matters $12,980 tuition and fees (2002–03); $5570 room and board; 90% average percent of need met; $12,448 average financial aid amount received per undergraduate (2001–02).

Academics ORU awards bachelor's, master's, doctoral, and first-professional degrees. Challenging opportunities include advanced placement credit, student-designed majors, freshman honors college, an honors program, double majors, independent study, and a senior project. Special programs include internships, summer session for credit, off-campus study, study-abroad, and Air Force ROTC. The most frequently chosen baccalaureate fields are business/marketing, communications/communication technologies, and education. The faculty at ORU has 207 full-time members, 56% with terminal degrees. The student-faculty ratio is 16:1.

Students of ORU The student body totals 3,542, of whom 3,041 are undergraduates. 58.6% are women and 41.4% are men. Students come from 63 states and territories and 41 other countries. 36% are from Oklahoma. 3.3% are international students. 78% returned for their sophomore year.

Applying ORU requires an essay, SAT I or ACT, a high school transcript, 1 recommendation, proof of immunization, and a minimum high school GPA of 2.0, and in some cases an interview. Application deadline: rolling admissions; 3/15 priority date for financial aid. Early and deferred admission are possible.

OREGON COLLEGE OF ART & CRAFT

Portland, OR

Urban setting ■ Private ■ Independent ■ Coed

Web site: www.ocac.edu

Contact: Mr. Barry Beach, Director of Admissions, 8245 Southwest Barnes Road, Portland, OR 97225

Telephone: 503-297-5544 or toll-free 800-390-0632 **Fax:** 503-297-9651

E-mail: admissions@ocac.edu

Getting in Last Year 13 applied; 100% were accepted; 4 enrolled (31%).

Financial Matters $14,150 tuition and fees (2002–03); 65% average percent of need met; $11,500 average financial aid amount received per undergraduate (2001–02).

Academics OCAC awards bachelor's degrees and post-bachelor's certificates. Challenging opportunities include advanced placement credit, double majors, independent study, and a senior project. Special programs include internships and off-campus study. The most frequently chosen baccalaureate field is visual/performing arts. The faculty at OCAC has 8 full-time members, 88% with terminal degrees. The student-faculty ratio is 8:1.

Students of OCAC The student body totals 116, of whom 109 are undergraduates. 74.3% are women and 25.7% are men. Students come from 21 states and territories. 49% are from Oregon. 0.9% are international students. 95% returned for their sophomore year.

Applying OCAC requires an essay, a high school transcript, an interview, 2 recommendations, portfolio, and a minimum high school GPA of 2.5. Application deadline: rolling admissions; 3/1 priority date for financial aid. Deferred admission is possible.

OREGON INSTITUTE OF TECHNOLOGY

Klamath Falls, OR

Small-town setting ■ Public ■ State-supported ■ Coed

Web site: www.oit.edu

Contact: Mr. Palmer Muntz, Director of Admissions, 3201 Campus Drive, Klamath Falls, OR 97601-8801

Telephone: 541-885-1150 or toll-free 800-422-2017 (in-state), 800-343-6653 (out-of-state) **Fax:** 541-885-1115

Oregon Institute of Technology (continued)

E-mail: oit@oit.edu

Getting in Last Year 822 applied; 80% were accepted; 361 enrolled (55%).

Financial Matters $3672 resident tuition and fees (2002–03); $12,630 nonresident tuition and fees (2002–03); $5515 room and board; 48% average percent of need met; $6354 average financial aid amount received per undergraduate.

Academics OIT awards associate and bachelor's degrees. Challenging opportunities include advanced placement credit, double majors, and a senior project. Special programs include cooperative education, internships, summer session for credit, off-campus study, and study-abroad. The most frequently chosen baccalaureate fields are engineering/engineering technologies, health professions and related sciences, and business/marketing. The faculty at OIT has 123 full-time members, 37% with terminal degrees. The student-faculty ratio is 14:1.

Students of OIT The student body totals 3,139, of whom 3,136 are undergraduates. 45.3% are women and 54.7% are men. Students come from 34 states and territories and 11 other countries. 86% are from Oregon. 0.8% are international students. 73% returned for their sophomore year.

Applying OIT requires SAT I or ACT, a high school transcript, and a minimum high school GPA of 2.5, and in some cases recommendations. Application deadline: 6/1; 3/1 priority date for financial aid. Deferred admission is possible.

OREGON STATE UNIVERSITY

Corvallis, OR

Small-town setting ■ Public ■ State-supported ■ Coed

Web site: oregonstate.edu
Contact: Ms. Michele Sandlin, Director of Admissions, Corvallis, OR 97331
Telephone: 541-737-4411 or toll-free 800-291-4192 (in-state)
E-mail: osuadmit@orst.edu

Getting in Last Year 5,811 applied; 75% were accepted; 3,058 enrolled (70%).

Financial Matters $4014 resident tuition and fees (2002–03); $14,898 nonresident tuition and fees (2002–03); $5976 room and board.

Academics OSU awards bachelor's, master's, doctoral, and first-professional degrees. Challenging opportunities include advanced placement credit, student-designed majors, freshman honors college, an honors program, double majors, and a senior project. Special programs include cooperative education, internships, summer session for credit, off-campus study, study-abroad, and Army and Air Force ROTC. The most frequently chosen baccalaureate fields are engineering/engineering technologies, business/marketing, and agriculture. The faculty at OSU has 634 full-time members, 63% with terminal degrees. The student-faculty ratio is 21:1.

Students of OSU The student body totals 18,789, of whom 15,413 are undergraduates. 46.9% are women and 53.1% are men. Students come from 50 states and territories and 90 other countries. 88% are from Oregon. 2% are international students. 80% returned for their sophomore year.

Applying OSU requires SAT I or ACT, a high school transcript, and a minimum high school GPA of 3.0, and in some cases SAT II Subject Tests. Application deadline: 3/1; 5/1 for financial aid. Early and deferred admission are possible.

OTIS COLLEGE OF ART AND DESIGN

Los Angeles, CA

Urban setting ■ Private ■ Independent ■ Coed

Web site: www.otis.edu
Contact: Mr. Marc D. Meredith, Dean of Admissions, 9045 Lincoln Boulevard, Los Angeles, CA 90045-9785
Telephone: 310-665-6820 or toll-free 800-527-OTIS **Fax:** 310-665-6821
E-mail: otisinfo@otis.edu

Getting in Last Year 581 applied; 65% were accepted; 143 enrolled (38%).

Financial Matters $22,892 tuition and fees (2002–03); 51% average percent of need met; $13,042 average financial aid amount received per undergraduate (2001–02).

Academics Otis awards bachelor's and master's degrees. Challenging opportunities include advanced placement credit, freshman honors college, an honors program, independent study, and a senior project. Special programs include cooperative education, internships, summer session for credit, off-campus study, and study-abroad. The most frequently chosen baccalaureate field is visual/performing arts. The faculty at Otis has 32 full-time members, 22% with terminal degrees. The student-faculty ratio is 12:1.

Students of Otis The student body totals 1,001, of whom 960 are undergraduates. 64% are women and 36% are men. 80% are from California. 12.2% are international students. 24% returned for their sophomore year.

Applying Otis requires an essay, SAT I or ACT, a high school transcript, portfolio, and a minimum high school GPA of 2.5. The school recommends an interview and 1 recommendation. Application deadline: rolling admissions; 2/15 priority date for financial aid. Early admission is possible.

OTTAWA UNIVERSITY

Ottawa, KS

Small-town setting ■ Private ■ Independent Religious ■ Coed

Web site: www.ottawa.edu
Contact: Mr. Ryan Ficken, Director of Admissions, 1001 South Cedar #17, Ottawa, KS 66067-3399
Telephone: 785-242-5200 ext. 1051 or toll-free 800-755-5200
Fax: 785-242-7429
E-mail: admiss@ottawa.edu

Getting in Last Year 516 applied; 94% were accepted; 144 enrolled (30%).

Financial Matters $12,450 tuition and fees (2002–03); $5300 room and board.

Academics OU awards bachelor's degrees (also offers adult, international and on-line education programs with significant enrollment not reflected in profile). Challenging opportunities include advanced placement credit, student-designed majors, double majors, independent study, and a senior project. Special programs include internships and summer session for credit. The faculty at OU has 15 full-time members, 73% with terminal degrees. The student-faculty ratio is 14:1.

Students of OU The student body is made up of 511 undergraduates. 43.8% are women and 56.2% are men. Students come from 25 states and territories and 4 other countries. 67% are from Kansas. 4.1% are international students. 54% returned for their sophomore year.

Applying OU requires SAT I or ACT, a high school transcript, and a minimum high school GPA of 2.5, and in some cases an essay. The school recommends an interview and 2 recommendations. Application deadline: rolling admissions; 3/15 priority date for financial aid.

OTTERBEIN COLLEGE

Westerville, OH

Suburban setting ■ Private ■ Independent Religious ■ Coed

Web site: www.otterbein.edu
Contact: Dr. Cass Johnson, Director of Admissions, One Otterbein College, Westerville, OH 43081-9924
Telephone: 614-823-1500 or toll-free 800-488-8144 **Fax:** 614-823-1200
E-mail: uotterb@otterbein.edu

Getting in Last Year 2,185 applied; 81% were accepted; 550 enrolled (31%).

Financial Matters $18,993 tuition and fees (2002–03); $5727 room and board.

Academics Otterbein awards bachelor's and master's degrees. Challenging opportunities include advanced placement credit, student-designed majors, an honors program, double majors, and a senior project. Special programs include internships, summer session for credit, off-campus study, study-abroad, and Army and Air Force ROTC. The most frequently chosen baccalaureate fields are business/marketing, education, and health professions and related sciences. The faculty at Otterbein has 144 full-time members, 92% with terminal degrees. The student-faculty ratio is 13:1.

Students of Otterbein The student body totals 3,064, of whom 2,622 are undergraduates. 66.1% are women and 33.9% are men. Students come from 34 states and territories. 92% are from Ohio. 90% returned for their sophomore year.

Applying Otterbein requires SAT I or ACT and a high school transcript. The school recommends an interview and a minimum high school GPA of 2.5. Application deadline: 3/1; 4/1 priority date for financial aid. Deferred admission is possible.

OUACHITA BAPTIST UNIVERSITY

Arkadelphia, AR

Small-town setting ■ Private ■ Independent Religious ■ Coed

Web site: www.obu.edu
Contact: Mrs. Rebecca Jones, Director of Admissions Counseling, 410 Ouachita Street, Arkadelphia, AR 71998-0001
Telephone: 870-245-5110 or toll-free 800-342-5628 (in-state)
Fax: 870-245-5500
E-mail: jonesj@obu.edu

Getting in Last Year 962 applied; 84% were accepted; 396 enrolled (49%).

Financial Matters $12,800 tuition and fees (2002–03); $4600 room and board; 97% average percent of need met; $12,033 average financial aid amount received per undergraduate (2001–02).

Academics Ouachita awards associate and bachelor's degrees. Challenging opportunities include advanced placement credit, accelerated degree programs, an honors program, double majors, and a senior project. Special programs include cooperative education, internships, summer session for credit, off-campus study, study-abroad, and Army ROTC. The most frequently chosen baccalaureate fields are education, business/marketing, and communications/communication technologies. The faculty at Ouachita has 117 full-time members, 81% with terminal degrees. The student-faculty ratio is 13:1.

Students of Ouachita The student body is made up of 1,653 undergraduates. 53% are women and 47% are men. Students come from 36 states and territories and 59 other countries. 53% are from Arkansas. 3.9% are international students. 74% returned for their sophomore year.

Applying Ouachita requires SAT I or ACT, a high school transcript, and a minimum high school GPA of 2.5. The school recommends an interview. Application deadline: 8/15; 6/1 for financial aid, with a 2/15 priority date. Early and deferred admission are possible.

OUR LADY OF HOLY CROSS COLLEGE

New Orleans, LA

Suburban setting ■ *Private* ■ *Independent Religious* ■ *Coed*

Web site: www.olhcc.edu
Contact: Ms. Kristine Hatfield Kopecky, Vice President for Student Affairs and Admissions, 4123 Woodland Drive, New Orleans, LA 70131-7399
Telephone: 504-394-7744 ext. 185 or toll-free 800-259-7744 ext. 175
Fax: 504-391-2421

Getting in Last Year 320 applied; 97% were accepted; 141 enrolled (46%).

Financial Matters $6900 tuition and fees (2002–03); 50% average percent of need met; $4584 average financial aid amount received per undergraduate (2001–02).

Academics OLHCC awards associate, bachelor's, and master's degrees and post-bachelor's certificates. Challenging opportunities include advanced placement credit, double majors, independent study, and a senior project. Special programs include cooperative education, internships, summer session for credit, off-campus study, study-abroad, and Army and Air Force ROTC. The most frequently chosen baccalaureate fields are health professions and related sciences, education, and business/marketing. The faculty at OLHCC has 35 full-time members, 63% with terminal degrees. The student-faculty ratio is 19:1.

Students of OLHCC The student body totals 1,390, of whom 1,268 are undergraduates. 77.8% are women and 22.2% are men. Students come from 4 states and territories and 3 other countries. 96% are from Louisiana. 0.6% are international students. 64% returned for their sophomore year.

Applying OLHCC requires SAT I or ACT and a high school transcript. The school recommends ACT and a minimum high school GPA of 2.0. Application deadline: rolling admissions; 4/15 priority date for financial aid. Deferred admission is possible.

OUR LADY OF THE LAKE COLLEGE

Baton Rouge, LA

Suburban setting ■ *Private* ■ *Independent Religious* ■ *Coed, Primarily Women*

Web site: www.ololcollege.edu
Contact: Mr. Mark Wetmore, Director of Admissions, 7434 Perkins Road, Baton Rouge, LA 70808
Telephone: 225-768-1718 or toll-free 877-242-3509
E-mail: admission@ololcollege.edu

Getting in Last Year 241 applied; 91% were accepted; 151 enrolled (69%).

Academics Our Lady of the Lake College awards associate and bachelor's degrees. Advanced placement credit is a challenging opportunity. Special programs include summer session for credit, off-campus study, and Army and Air Force ROTC. The faculty at Our Lady of the Lake College has 62 full-time members, 71% with terminal degrees. The student-faculty ratio is 17:1.

Students of Our Lady of the Lake College The student body is made up of 1,421 undergraduates. 85.7% are women and 14.3% are men. Students come from 3 states and territories. 99% are from Louisiana. 62% returned for their sophomore year.

Applying Our Lady of the Lake College requires ACT, ACT ASSET, a high school transcript, and a minimum high school GPA of 2.0. Application deadline: rolling admissions; 4/15 priority date for financial aid.

OUR LADY OF THE LAKE UNIVERSITY OF SAN ANTONIO

San Antonio, TX

Urban setting ■ *Private* ■ *Independent Religious* ■ *Coed*

Web site: www.ollusa.edu
Contact: Mr. Michael Boatner, Acting Director of Admissions, 411 Southwest 24th Street, San Antonio, TX 78207-4689
Telephone: 210-434-6711 ext. 314 or toll-free 800-436-6558 **Fax:** 210-431-4036
E-mail: admission@lake.ollusa.edu

Getting in Last Year 2,074 applied; 57% were accepted; 333 enrolled (28%).

Financial Matters $13,782 tuition and fees (2002–03); $4862 room and board; 87% average percent of need met; $12,944 average financial aid amount received per undergraduate (2001–02).

Academics The Lake awards bachelor's, master's, and doctoral degrees. Challenging opportunities include advanced placement credit, double majors, and a senior project. Special programs include internships, summer session for credit, off-campus study, and Army and Air Force ROTC. The most frequently chosen baccalaureate fields are business/marketing, psychology, and liberal arts/general studies. The faculty at The Lake has 128 full-time members, 70% with terminal degrees. The student-faculty ratio is 14:1.

Students of The Lake The student body totals 3,395, of whom 2,247 are undergraduates. 76.4% are women and 23.6% are men. Students come from 28 states and territories and 17 other countries. 99% are from Texas. 1% are international students. 68% returned for their sophomore year.

Applying The Lake requires SAT I or ACT and a high school transcript, and in some cases an interview. Application deadline: rolling admissions. Deferred admission is possible.

OZARK CHRISTIAN COLLEGE

Joplin, MO

Suburban setting ■ *Private* ■ *Independent Religious* ■ *Coed*

Web site: www.occ.edu
Contact: Mr. Troy B. Nelson, Executive Director of Admissions, 1111 North Main Street, Joplin, MO 64801-4804
Telephone: 417-624-2518 ext. 2006 or toll-free 800-299-4622
Fax: 417-624-0090
E-mail: occadmin@occ.edu

Getting in Last Year 332 applied; 100% were accepted.

Financial Matters $5795 tuition and fees (2002–03); $3830 room and board.

Academics OCC awards associate and bachelor's degrees. Challenging opportunities include double majors and a senior project. Special programs include internships and summer session for credit. The faculty at OCC has 30 full-time members, 17% with terminal degrees. The student-faculty ratio is 19:1.

Students of OCC The student body is made up of 799 undergraduates. 48.2% are women and 51.8% are men. Students come from 33 states and territories and 13 other countries. 43% are from Missouri. 1.6% are international students. 70% returned for their sophomore year.

Applying OCC requires an essay, SAT I or ACT, a high school transcript, and 4 recommendations, and in some cases an interview. Application deadline: 3/5; 4/1 for financial aid.

PACE UNIVERSITY

New York, NY

Private ■ *Independent* ■ *Coed*

Web site: www.pace.edu
Contact: Ms. Joanna Broda, Director of Admission, NY and Westchester, One Pace Plaza, New York, NY 10038
Telephone: 212-346-1323 or toll-free 800-874-7223 **Fax:** 212-346-1040
E-mail: infoctr@pace.edu

Getting in Last Year 7,644 applied; 79% were accepted; 1,539 enrolled (25%).

Financial Matters $18,180 tuition and fees (2002–03); $7590 room and board; 67% average percent of need met; $11,948 average financial aid amount received per undergraduate.

Academics Pace U awards associate, bachelor's, master's, doctoral, and first-professional degrees and post-bachelor's and post-master's certificates. Challenging opportunities include advanced placement credit, accelerated degree programs, freshman honors college, an honors program, double majors, independent study, and a senior project. Special programs include cooperative education, internships, summer session for credit, study-abroad, and Air Force ROTC. The most frequently chosen baccalaureate fields are business/marketing, computer/information sciences, and health professions and related sciences. The faculty at Pace U has 438 full-time members, 87% with terminal degrees. The student-faculty ratio is 16:1.

Students of Pace U The student body totals 14,095, of whom 9,149 are undergraduates. 60.2% are women and 39.8% are men. Students come from 38 states and territories and 19 other countries. 83% are from New York. 4.7% are international students. 76% returned for their sophomore year.

Applying Pace U requires SAT I or ACT and a high school transcript. The school recommends an essay, an interview, 2 recommendations, and a minimum high school GPA of 3.0. Application deadline: rolling admissions. Deferred admission is possible.

PACIFIC LUTHERAN UNIVERSITY

Tacoma, WA

Suburban setting ■ *Private* ■ *Independent Religious* ■ *Coed*

Web site: www.plu.edu
Contact: Office of Admissions, Tacoma, WA 98447
Telephone: 253-535-7151 or toll-free 800-274-6758 **Fax:** 253-536-5136
E-mail: admissions@plu.edu

Getting in Last Year 1,926 applied; 81% were accepted; 626 enrolled (40%).

Financial Matters $18,500 tuition and fees (2002–03); $5870 room and board; 89% average percent of need met; $16,411 average financial aid amount received per undergraduate.

Academics PLU awards bachelor's and master's degrees and post-bachelor's and post-master's certificates. Challenging opportunities include advanced placement credit, accelerated degree programs, student-designed majors, an honors

Pacific Lutheran University (continued)

program, double majors, independent study, and a senior project. Special programs include cooperative education, internships, summer session for credit, study-abroad, and Army ROTC. The most frequently chosen baccalaureate fields are business/marketing, education, and social sciences and history. The faculty at PLU has 221 full-time members, 95% with terminal degrees. The student-faculty ratio is 13:1.

Students of PLU The student body totals 3,385, of whom 3,133 are undergraduates. 62.8% are women and 37.2% are men. Students come from 42 states and territories and 23 other countries. 74% are from Washington. 6.8% are international students. 82% returned for their sophomore year.

Applying PLU requires an essay, SAT I or ACT, a high school transcript, 1 recommendation, and a minimum high school GPA of 2.5, and in some cases an interview. Application deadline: rolling admissions; 3/1 priority date for financial aid. Early and deferred admission are possible.

PACIFIC NORTHWEST COLLEGE OF ART

Portland, OR

Urban setting ■ Private ■ Independent ■ Coed

Web site: www.pnca.edu

Contact: Ms. Rebecca Haas, Director of Admissions, 1241 NW Johnson Street, Portland, OR 97209

Telephone: 503-821-8972 **Fax:** 503-821-8972

E-mail: admissions@pnca.edu

Getting in Last Year 55 applied; 82% were accepted.

Financial Matters $13,767 tuition and fees (2002–03); 72% average percent of need met; $6240 average financial aid amount received per undergraduate (2001–02).

Academics PNCA awards bachelor's degrees. Challenging opportunities include advanced placement credit, student-designed majors, independent study, and a senior project. Special programs include cooperative education, internships, summer session for credit, off-campus study, and study-abroad. The most frequently chosen baccalaureate field is visual/performing arts. The faculty at PNCA has 14 full-time members, 86% with terminal degrees. The student-faculty ratio is 9:1.

Students of PNCA The student body is made up of 298 undergraduates. Students come from 20 states and territories and 4 other countries. 80% are from Oregon. 2% are international students. 60% returned for their sophomore year.

Applying PNCA requires an essay, a high school transcript, 1 recommendation, portfolio of artwork, and a minimum high school GPA of 2.5. The school recommends an interview. Application deadline: rolling admissions; 3/11 priority date for financial aid. Deferred admission is possible.

PACIFIC OAKS COLLEGE

Pasadena, CA

Small-town setting ■ Private ■ Independent ■ Coed

Web site: www.pacificoaks.edu

Contact: Ms. Marsha Franker, Director of Admissions, Admissions Office, Pacific Oaks College, 5 Westmoreland Place, Pasadena, CA 91103

Telephone: 626-397-1349 or toll-free 800-684-0900 **Fax:** 626-685-2531

E-mail: admissions@pacificoaks.edu

Getting in Last Year 225 applied; 88% were accepted.

Financial Matters $17,310 tuition and fees (2002–03).

Academics PO awards bachelor's and master's degrees and post-bachelor's and post-master's certificates. Independent study is a challenging opportunity. Special programs include internships, summer session for credit, and off-campus study. The most frequently chosen baccalaureate field is social sciences and history. The faculty at PO has 29 full-time members, 59% with terminal degrees. The student-faculty ratio is 9:1.

Students of PO The student body totals 880, of whom 261 are undergraduates. 91.6% are women and 8.4% are men. Students come from 34 states and territories. 81% are from California. 0.4% are international students.

Applying Deferred admission is possible.

PACIFIC STATES UNIVERSITY

Los Angeles, CA

Urban setting ■ Private ■ Independent ■ Coed, Primarily Men

Web site: www.psuca.edu

Contact: Ms. Marina Miller, Assistant Director of Admissions, 1516 South Western Avenue, Los Angeles, CA 90006

Telephone: 323-731-2383 or toll-free 888-200-0383

E-mail: admission@psuca.edu

Getting in Last Year 30 enrolled.

Financial Matters $8880 tuition and fees (2002–03).

Academics PSU awards bachelor's and master's degrees. Challenging opportunities include accelerated degree programs, student-designed majors, and independent study. Special programs include summer session for credit and study-abroad. The most frequently chosen baccalaureate fields are business/marketing and computer/information sciences. The faculty at PSU has 4 full-time members, 100% with terminal degrees. The student-faculty ratio is 20:1.

Students of PSU The student body totals 127, of whom 64 are undergraduates. 9.4% are women and 90.6% are men. 90% are from California. 76% returned for their sophomore year.

Applying PSU requires an essay, a high school transcript, and a minimum high school GPA of 2.5. Application deadline: 9/21. Early and deferred admission are possible.

PACIFIC UNION COLLEGE

Angwin, CA

Rural setting ■ Private ■ Independent Religious ■ Coed

Web site: www.puc.edu

Contact: Mr. Sean Kootsey, Director of Enrollment Services, Enrollment Services, One Angwin Avenue, Angwin, CA 94508

Telephone: 707-965-6425 or toll-free 800-862-7080 **Fax:** 707-965-6432

E-mail: enroll@puc.edu

Getting in Last Year 1,157 applied; 36% were accepted; 393 enrolled (94%).

Financial Matters $16,575 tuition and fees (2002–03); $4806 room and board; 73% average percent of need met; $11,252 average financial aid amount received per undergraduate.

Academics PUC awards associate, bachelor's, and master's degrees. Challenging opportunities include advanced placement credit, accelerated degree programs, student-designed majors, freshman honors college, an honors program, double majors, independent study, and a senior project. Special programs include cooperative education, internships, summer session for credit, off-campus study, and study-abroad. The most frequently chosen baccalaureate fields are health professions and related sciences, business/marketing, and biological/life sciences. The faculty at PUC has 104 full-time members, 44% with terminal degrees. The student-faculty ratio is 12:1.

Students of PUC The student body totals 1,488, of whom 1,485 are undergraduates. 54.7% are women and 45.3% are men. Students come from 45 states and territories and 20 other countries. 81% are from California. 6.3% are international students.

Applying PUC requires SAT I and SAT II or ACT, a high school transcript, 3 recommendations, and a minimum high school GPA of 2.3. Application deadline: rolling admissions; 3/2 priority date for financial aid. Deferred admission is possible.

PACIFIC UNIVERSITY

Forest Grove, OR

Small-town setting ■ Private ■ Independent ■ Coed

Web site: www.pacificu.edu

Contact: Mr. Ian Symmonds, Executive Director of Admissions, 2043 College Way, Forest Grove, OR 97116-1797

Telephone: 503-352-2218 or toll-free 877-722-8648 **Fax:** 503-352-2975

E-mail: admissions@pacificu.edu

Getting in Last Year 1,166 applied; 87% were accepted; 275 enrolled (27%).

Financial Matters $19,292 tuition and fees (2002–03); $5379 room and board; 89% average percent of need met; $16,555 average financial aid amount received per undergraduate.

Academics Pacific awards bachelor's, master's, doctoral, and first-professional degrees. Challenging opportunities include advanced placement credit, accelerated degree programs, an honors program, double majors, independent study, and a senior project. Special programs include internships, summer session for credit, off-campus study, study-abroad, and Army and Air Force ROTC. The most frequently chosen baccalaureate fields are business/marketing, biological/life sciences, and physical sciences. The faculty at Pacific has 87 full-time members, 86% with terminal degrees. The student-faculty ratio is 11:1.

Students of Pacific The student body totals 2,414, of whom 1,173 are undergraduates. 60% are women and 40% are men. Students come from 35 states and territories and 6 other countries. 45% are from Oregon. 0.5% are international students. 78% returned for their sophomore year.

Applying Pacific requires an essay, SAT I or ACT, a high school transcript, 1 recommendation, and a minimum high school GPA of 3.0. The school recommends an interview. Application deadline: 8/15; 2/15 priority date for financial aid. Deferred admission is possible.

PAIER COLLEGE OF ART, INC.

Hamden, CT

Suburban setting ■ Private ■ Proprietary ■ Coed

Web site: www.paiercollegeofart.edu

Contact: Ms. Lynn Pascale, Secretary to Admissions, 20 Gorham Avenue, Hamden, CT 06514-3902
Telephone: 203-287-3031 **Fax:** 203-287-3021
E-mail: info@paierart.com

Getting in Last Year 108 applied; 84% were accepted; 68 enrolled (75%).

Financial Matters $11,200 tuition and fees (2002–03); 62% average percent of need met; $6717 average financial aid amount received per undergraduate (1999–2000).

Academics Paier awards associate and bachelor's degrees. Challenging opportunities include advanced placement credit, independent study, and a senior project. Summer session for credit is a special program. The most frequently chosen baccalaureate field is visual/performing arts. The faculty at Paier has 9 full-time members, 11% with terminal degrees. The student-faculty ratio is 7:1.

Students of Paier The student body is made up of 281 undergraduates. 55.5% are women and 44.5% are men. Students come from 4 states and territories and 1 other country. 99% are from Connecticut. 78% returned for their sophomore year.

Applying Paier requires SAT I or ACT, a high school transcript, an interview, 2 recommendations, portfolio, and a minimum high school GPA of 2.0. The school recommends an essay. Application deadline: rolling admissions; 4/15 priority date for financial aid. Deferred admission is possible.

PAINE COLLEGE

Augusta, GA

Urban setting ■ Private ■ Independent Religious ■ Coed

Web site: www.paine.edu
Contact: Mr. Joseph Tinsley, Director of Admissions, 1235 15th Street, Augusta, GA 30901-3182
Telephone: 706-821-8320 or toll-free 800-476-7703 **Fax:** 706-821-8691
E-mail: tinsleyj@mail.paine.edu

Getting in Last Year 2,542 applied; 29% were accepted; 202 enrolled (27%).

Financial Matters $8640 tuition and fees (2002–03); $3752 room and board; $185 average financial aid amount received per undergraduate (2000–01 estimated).

Academics Paine awards bachelor's degrees. Challenging opportunities include advanced placement credit, accelerated degree programs, an honors program, independent study, and a senior project. Special programs include cooperative education, internships, summer session for credit, off-campus study, study-abroad, and Army ROTC. The most frequently chosen baccalaureate fields are social sciences and history, business/marketing, and psychology. The faculty at Paine has 72 full-time members, 54% with terminal degrees. The student-faculty ratio is 11:1.

Students of Paine The student body is made up of 880 undergraduates. 71.6% are women and 28.4% are men. Students come from 32 states and territories and 5 other countries. 82% are from Georgia. 0.6% are international students. 66% returned for their sophomore year.

Applying Paine requires an essay, SAT I or ACT, a high school transcript, medical history, and a minimum high school GPA of 2.0. The school recommends 2 recommendations. Application deadline: 8/1; 3/1 priority date for financial aid. Early and deferred admission are possible.

PALM BEACH ATLANTIC UNIVERSITY

West Palm Beach, FL

Urban setting ■ Private ■ Independent Religious ■ Coed

Web site: www.pba.edu
Contact: Mr. Buck James, Vice President of Enrollment Services, PO Box 24708, West Palm Beach, FL 33416-4708
Telephone: 561-803-2100 or toll-free 800-238-3998 **Fax:** 561-803-2115
E-mail: admit@pba.edu

Getting in Last Year 1,547 applied; 53% were accepted; 433 enrolled (53%).

Financial Matters $13,950 tuition and fees (2002–03); $5655 room and board; 72% average percent of need met; $12,236 average financial aid amount received per undergraduate.

Academics PBA awards associate, bachelor's, master's, and first-professional degrees. Challenging opportunities include advanced placement credit, accelerated degree programs, freshman honors college, an honors program, double majors, independent study, and a senior project. Special programs include cooperative education, internships, summer session for credit, and study-abroad. The most frequently chosen baccalaureate fields are business/marketing, education, and psychology. The faculty at PBA has 118 full-time members, 73% with terminal degrees. The student-faculty ratio is 16:1.

Students of PBA The student body totals 2,784, of whom 2,323 are undergraduates. 63.5% are women and 36.5% are men. Students come from 43 states and territories. 77% are from Florida. 4.7% are international students. 66% returned for their sophomore year.

Applying PBA requires an essay, SAT I or ACT, a high school transcript, 2 recommendations, and a minimum high school GPA of 2.0. The school recommends an interview and a minimum high school GPA of 3.0. Application deadline: rolling admissions; 4/1 priority date for financial aid. Early and deferred admission are possible.

PALMER COLLEGE OF CHIROPRACTIC

Davenport, IA

Urban setting ■ Private ■ Independent ■ Coed

Web site: www.palmer.edu
Contact: Dr. David Anderson, Director of Admissions, 1000 Brady Street, Davenport, IA 52803-5287
Telephone: 563-884-5656 or toll-free 800-722-3648 **Fax:** 563-884-5414
E-mail: pcadmit@palmer.edu

Getting in Last Year 20 applied; 90% were accepted.

Financial Matters $18,945 tuition and fees (2002–03).

Academics PCC awards associate, bachelor's, master's, and first-professional degrees. Special programs include internships and summer session for credit. The most frequently chosen baccalaureate field is health professions and related sciences. The faculty at PCC has 87 full-time members. The student-faculty ratio is 20:1.

Students of PCC The student body totals 1,798, of whom 41 are undergraduates. 75.6% are women and 24.4% are men. Students come from 19 states and territories and 3 other countries. 61% are from Iowa. 9.8% are international students. 94% returned for their sophomore year.

Applying PCC requires a high school transcript, minimum 2.0 in math, sciences, and English courses, and a minimum high school GPA of 2.0, and in some cases an essay and an interview. Application deadline: rolling admissions. Deferred admission is possible.

PARK UNIVERSITY

Parkville, MO

Suburban setting ■ Private ■ Independent ■ Coed

Web site: www.park.edu
Contact: Office of Admissions, 8700 NW River Park Drive, Campus Box 1, Parkville, MO 64152
Telephone: 816-584-6215 or toll-free 800-745-7275 **Fax:** 816-741-4462
E-mail: admissions@mail.park.edu

Getting in Last Year 424 applied; 72% were accepted; 159 enrolled (52%).

Financial Matters $5152 tuition and fees (2002–03); $5180 room and board; 66% average percent of need met; $4753 average financial aid amount received per undergraduate.

Academics Park awards associate, bachelor's, and master's degrees. Challenging opportunities include advanced placement credit, student-designed majors, an honors program, double majors, independent study, and a senior project. Special programs include internships, summer session for credit, off-campus study, and Army ROTC. The most frequently chosen baccalaureate fields are business/marketing, psychology, and protective services/public administration. The faculty at Park has 57 full-time members, 56% with terminal degrees. The student-faculty ratio is 14:1.

Students of Park The student body totals 10,123, of whom 9,870 are undergraduates. 50.3% are women and 49.7% are men. Students come from 47 states and territories and 90 other countries. 23% are from Missouri. 2.1% are international students. 73% returned for their sophomore year.

Applying Park requires SAT I or ACT, a high school transcript, and a minimum high school GPA of 2.0, and in some cases an interview and 2 recommendations. The school recommends an essay. Application deadline: 8/1; 4/1 priority date for financial aid. Early and deferred admission are possible.

PARSONS SCHOOL OF DESIGN, NEW SCHOOL UNIVERSITY

New York, NY

Urban setting ■ Private ■ Independent ■ Coed

Web site: www.parsons.edu
Contact: Ms. Heather Ward, Director of Admissions, 66 Fifth Avenue, New York, NY 10011-8878
Telephone: 212-229-8910 or toll-free 877-528-3321 **Fax:** 212-229-5166
E-mail: customer@newschool.edu

Getting in Last Year 1,532 applied; 44% were accepted; 348 enrolled (51%).

Financial Matters $24,475 tuition and fees (2002–03); $9896 room and board; 56% average percent of need met; $13,156 average financial aid amount received per undergraduate.

Academics Parsons awards associate, bachelor's, and master's degrees. Challenging opportunities include advanced placement credit, accelerated degree programs, student-designed majors, an honors program, independent study, and a senior project. Special programs include cooperative education, internships, summer session for credit, off-campus study, and study-abroad. The most

Parsons School of Design, New School University (continued)

frequently chosen baccalaureate fields are visual/performing arts and architecture. The faculty at Parsons has 51 full-time members. The student-faculty ratio is 5:1.

Students of Parsons The student body totals 2,958, of whom 2,499 are undergraduates. 75.2% are women and 24.8% are men. Students come from 42 states and territories and 64 other countries. 51% are from New York. 29.3% are international students. 80% returned for their sophomore year.

Applying Parsons requires SAT I or ACT, a high school transcript, portfolio, home examination, and a minimum high school GPA of 2.0, and in some cases an essay and an interview. The school recommends a minimum high school GPA of 3.0. Application deadline: rolling admissions; 3/1 priority date for financial aid. Early admission is possible.

PATTEN COLLEGE

Oakland, CA

Urban setting ■ Private ■ Independent Religious ■ Coed

Web site: www.patten.edu

Contact: Ms. Inez Bailey, Director of Admissions, 2433 Coolidge Avenue, Oakland, CA 94601

Telephone: 510-261-8500 ext. 765 **Fax:** 510-534-4344

Getting in Last Year 67 applied; 58% were accepted; 10 enrolled (26%).

Financial Matters $9120 tuition and fees (2002–03); $5800 room and board.

Academics Patten awards associate, bachelor's, and master's degrees and post-bachelor's certificates. Challenging opportunities include advanced placement credit, accelerated degree programs, an honors program, and double majors. Special programs include internships and summer session for credit. The most frequently chosen baccalaureate fields are business/marketing and liberal arts/general studies. The faculty at Patten has 16 full-time members. The student-faculty ratio is 14:1.

Students of Patten The student body totals 559, of whom 446 are undergraduates. 39.9% are women and 60.1% are men. Students come from 12 states and territories. 95% are from California. 65% returned for their sophomore year.

Applying Patten requires an essay, SAT I or ACT, a high school transcript, 2 recommendations, and a minimum high school GPA of 2.5. The school recommends an interview. Application deadline: 7/31; 5/31 priority date for financial aid. Early and deferred admission are possible.

PAUL QUINN COLLEGE

Dallas, TX

Suburban setting ■ Private ■ Independent Religious ■ Coed

Web site: www.pqc.edu

Contact: Mr. Don Robinson, Director of Admissions, 3837 Simpson-Stuart Road, Dallas, TX 75241-4331

Telephone: 214-302-3520 or toll-free 800-237-2648 **Fax:** 214-302-3520

Getting in Last Year 800 applied; 72% were accepted.

Financial Matters $4980 tuition and fees (2002–03); $3800 room and board; 98% average percent of need met; $8752 average financial aid amount received per undergraduate.

Academics PQC awards bachelor's degrees. Challenging opportunities include advanced placement credit, accelerated degree programs, an honors program, and a senior project. Special programs include cooperative education, internships, summer session for credit, and off-campus study. The faculty at PQC has 88 full-time members.

Students of PQC The student body totals 868. Students come from 9 states and territories. 49% returned for their sophomore year.

Applying PQC requires SAT I or ACT, a high school transcript, and a minimum high school GPA of 2.0, and in some cases an interview and recommendations. Application deadline: 6/1; 4/1 priority date for financial aid.

PAUL SMITH'S COLLEGE OF ARTS AND SCIENCES

Paul Smiths, NY

Rural setting ■ Private ■ Independent ■ Coed

Web site: www.paulsmiths.edu

Contact: Ms. June Peoples, Vice President for Enrollment Management, PO Box 265, Paul Smiths, NY 12970-0265

Telephone: 518-327-6227 ext. 6230 or toll-free 800-421-2605 **Fax:** 518-327-6016

Getting in Last Year 1,173 applied; 80% were accepted; 330 enrolled (35%).

Financial Matters $14,900 tuition and fees (2002–03); $6160 room and board.

Academics Paul Smith's awards associate and bachelor's degrees. Challenging opportunities include advanced placement credit, student-designed majors, an honors program, double majors, and a senior project. Special programs include cooperative education, internships, summer session for credit, and study-abroad. The most frequently chosen baccalaureate fields are natural resources/environmental science, personal/miscellaneous services, and business/marketing. The faculty at Paul Smith's has 64 full-time members. The student-faculty ratio is 13:1.

Students of Paul Smith's The student body is made up of 817 undergraduates. 30.4% are women and 69.6% are men. Students come from 29 states and territories and 11 other countries. 60% are from New York. 1.1% are international students. 63% returned for their sophomore year.

Applying Paul Smith's requires an essay, SAT I or ACT, a high school transcript, and 1 recommendation, and in some cases an interview. Application deadline: rolling admissions; 3/3 priority date for financial aid. Early and deferred admission are possible.

PEABODY CONSERVATORY OF MUSIC OF THE JOHNS HOPKINS UNIVERSITY

Baltimore, MD

Urban setting ■ Private ■ Independent ■ Coed

Web site: www.peabody.jhu.edu

Contact: Mr. David Lane, Director of Admissions, 1 East Mount Vernon Place, Baltimore, MD 21202-2397

Telephone: 410-659-8110 or toll-free 800-368-2521 (out-of-state)

Getting in Last Year 638 applied; 57% were accepted; 89 enrolled (25%).

Financial Matters $25,025 tuition and fees (2002–03); $8800 room and board; 73% average percent of need met; $16,552 average financial aid amount received per undergraduate (2001–02).

Academics Peabody Conservatory awards bachelor's, master's, and doctoral degrees. Challenging opportunities include advanced placement credit, accelerated degree programs, an honors program, double majors, and independent study. Special programs include internships and off-campus study. The most frequently chosen baccalaureate field is visual/performing arts. The faculty at Peabody Conservatory has 165 members, 21% with terminal degrees. The student-faculty ratio is 4:1.

Students of Peabody Conservatory The student body totals 707, of whom 360 are undergraduates. 47.2% are women and 52.8% are men. Students come from 38 states and territories and 9 other countries. 29% are from Maryland. 13.2% are international students. 98% returned for their sophomore year.

Applying Peabody Conservatory requires a high school transcript, an interview, 3 recommendations, and audition, and in some cases an essay and SAT I or ACT. Application deadline: 12/15; 3/1 priority date for financial aid.

PEACE COLLEGE

Raleigh, NC

Urban setting ■ Private ■ Independent Religious ■ Women Only

Web site: www.peace.edu

Contact: Ms. Christie Mabry, Director of Admissions, 15 East Peace Street, Raleigh, NC 27604-1194

Telephone: 919-508-2222 or toll-free 800-PEACE-47 **Fax:** 919-508-2306

E-mail: chill@peace.edu

Getting in Last Year 449 applied; 87% were accepted; 173 enrolled (44%).

Financial Matters $12,450 tuition and fees (2002–03); $5650 room and board; 72% average percent of need met; $8569 average financial aid amount received per undergraduate.

Academics Peace College awards associate and bachelor's degrees. Challenging opportunities include advanced placement credit, freshman honors college, an honors program, double majors, independent study, and a senior project. Special programs include internships, off-campus study, study-abroad, and Army, Navy and Air Force ROTC. The most frequently chosen baccalaureate fields are business/marketing, psychology, and English. The faculty at Peace College has 40 full-time members, 75% with terminal degrees. The student-faculty ratio is 14:1.

Students of Peace College The student body is made up of 634 undergraduates. 37% are from North Carolina. 0.5% are international students. 71% returned for their sophomore year.

Applying Peace College requires an essay, SAT I or ACT, a high school transcript, 2 recommendations, and a minimum high school GPA of 2.0. The school recommends an interview. Application deadline: rolling admissions. Early and deferred admission are possible.

PEIRCE COLLEGE

Philadelphia, PA

Urban setting ■ Private ■ Independent ■ Coed, Primarily Women

Web site: www.peirce.edu

Contact: Mr. Steve W. Bird, College Representative, 1420 Pine Street, Philadelphia, PA 19102

Telephone: 215-670-9375 or toll-free 877-670-9190 ext. 9214 **Fax:** 215-893-4347

E-mail: info@peirce.edu

Getting in Last Year 201 applied; 91% were accepted; 117 enrolled (64%).

Financial Matters $11,200 tuition and fees (2002–03); 45% average percent of need met; $3500 average financial aid amount received per undergraduate (2001–02).

Academics Peirce awards associate and bachelor's degrees and post-bachelor's certificates. Challenging opportunities include advanced placement credit, accelerated degree programs, double majors, independent study, and a senior project. Special programs include cooperative education, internships, summer session for credit, and off-campus study. The most frequently chosen baccalaureate fields are law/legal studies, business/marketing, and computer/ information sciences. The faculty at Peirce has 30 full-time members, 33% with terminal degrees. The student-faculty ratio is 16:1.

Students of Peirce The student body is made up of 1,720 undergraduates. 71.9% are women and 28.1% are men. Students come from 30 states and territories and 24 other countries. 83% are from Pennsylvania. 2.2% are international students. 70% returned for their sophomore year.

Applying Peirce requires a high school transcript. Application deadline: rolling admissions; 4/15 priority date for financial aid.

PENNSYLVANIA COLLEGE OF ART & DESIGN

Lancaster, PA

Urban setting ■ Private ■ Independent ■ Coed

Web site: www.psad.org

Contact: Ms. Wendy Sweigart, Director of Admissions, Admissions Office, PO Box 59, Lancaster, PA 17608-0059

Telephone: 717-396-7833 ext. 19 **Fax:** 717-396-1339

E-mail: admissions@pcad.edu

Getting in Last Year 199 applied.

Financial Matters $11,500 tuition and fees (2002–03).

Academics PCA&D awards bachelor's degrees. Challenging opportunities include advanced placement credit and a senior project. Special programs include cooperative education and internships. The most frequently chosen baccalaureate field is visual/performing arts. The faculty at PCA&D has 10 full-time members, 70% with terminal degrees. The student-faculty ratio is 11:1.

Students of PCA&D The student body is made up of 217 undergraduates.

Applying PCA&D requires an essay, a high school transcript, an interview, and portfolio, and in some cases 2 recommendations. The school recommends 2 recommendations and a minimum high school GPA of 2.0. Application deadline: 5/1; 5/1 priority date for financial aid. Deferred admission is possible.

PENNSYLVANIA COLLEGE OF TECHNOLOGY

Williamsport, PA

Small-town setting ■ Public ■ State-related ■ Coed

Web site: www.pct.edu

Contact: Mr. Chester D. Schuman, Director of Admissions, One College Avenue, DIF #119, Williamsport, PA 17701

Telephone: 570-327-4761 or toll-free 800-367-9222 (in-state) **Fax:** 570-321-5551

E-mail: cschuman@pct.edu

Getting in Last Year 4,776 applied; 90% were accepted; 1,678 enrolled (39%).

Financial Matters $9540 resident tuition and fees (2002–03); $11,730 nonresident tuition and fees (2002–03); $5942 room and board.

Academics Penn College awards associate and bachelor's degrees. Challenging opportunities include advanced placement credit, student-designed majors, double majors, independent study, and a senior project. Special programs include cooperative education, internships, summer session for credit, off-campus study, and Army ROTC. The most frequently chosen baccalaureate field is law/legal studies. The faculty at Penn College has 250 full-time members. The student-faculty ratio is 18:1.

Students of Penn College The student body is made up of 5,963 undergraduates. 34.5% are women and 65.5% are men. Students come from 32 states and territories and 16 other countries. 93% are from Pennsylvania. 0.6% are international students.

Applying Penn College requires a high school transcript, and in some cases SAT I. Application deadline: rolling admissions; 4/1 priority date for financial aid. Early and deferred admission are possible.

THE PENNSYLVANIA STATE UNIVERSITY ABINGTON COLLEGE

Abington, PA

Small-town setting ■ Public ■ State-related ■ Coed

Web site: www.abington.psu.edu

Contact: Undergraduate Admissions Office, 1600 Woodland Road, Abington, PA 19001

Telephone: 814-865-5471 **Fax:** 215-881-7317

E-mail: abingtonadmissions@psu.edu

Getting in Last Year 2,753 applied; 77% were accepted; 769 enrolled (36%).

Financial Matters $8238 resident tuition and fees (2002–03); $12,596 nonresident tuition and fees (2002–03); 68% average percent of need met; $7711 average financial aid amount received per undergraduate (2001–02).

Academics Penn State Abington-Ogontz awards associate and bachelor's degrees. Challenging opportunities include advanced placement credit, accelerated degree programs, student-designed majors, an honors program, double majors, and independent study. Special programs include cooperative education, internships, summer session for credit, study-abroad, and Army and Air Force ROTC. The most frequently chosen baccalaureate fields are protective services/public administration, business/marketing, and liberal arts/general studies. The faculty at Penn State Abington-Ogontz has 105 full-time members, 57% with terminal degrees. The student-faculty ratio is 20:1.

Students of Penn State Abington-Ogontz The student body totals 3,319, of whom 3,316 are undergraduates. 51.5% are women and 48.5% are men. 96% are from Pennsylvania. 0.4% are international students. 75% returned for their sophomore year.

Applying Penn State Abington-Ogontz requires SAT I or ACT and a high school transcript. Application deadline: rolling admissions. Early and deferred admission are possible.

THE PENNSYLVANIA STATE UNIVERSITY ALTOONA COLLEGE

Altoona, PA

Suburban setting ■ Public ■ State-related ■ Coed

Web site: www.aa.psu.edu

Contact: Mr. Richard Shaffer, Director of Admissions and Enrollment Services, E108 Smith Building, 3000 Ivyside Park, Altoona, PA 16601-3760

Telephone: 814-949-5466 or toll-free 800-848-9843 **Fax:** 814-949-5564

E-mail: aaadmit@psu.edu

Getting in Last Year 4,386 applied; 80% were accepted; 1,356 enrolled (39%).

Financial Matters $8248 resident tuition and fees (2002–03); $12,606 nonresident tuition and fees (2002–03); $5660 room and board; 73% average percent of need met; $9909 average financial aid amount received per undergraduate (2001–02).

Academics Penn State Altoona awards associate and bachelor's degrees. Challenging opportunities include advanced placement credit, accelerated degree programs, student-designed majors, an honors program, double majors, and independent study. Special programs include cooperative education, internships, summer session for credit, study-abroad, and Army ROTC. The most frequently chosen baccalaureate fields are business/marketing, engineering/engineering technologies, and protective services/public administration. The faculty at Penn State Altoona has 126 full-time members, 70% with terminal degrees. The student-faculty ratio is 21:1.

Students of Penn State Altoona The student body totals 3,885, of whom 3,877 are undergraduates. 49.4% are women and 50.6% are men. 87% are from Pennsylvania. 1% are international students. 84% returned for their sophomore year.

Applying Penn State Altoona requires SAT I or ACT and a high school transcript. Application deadline: rolling admissions. Early and deferred admission are possible.

THE PENNSYLVANIA STATE UNIVERSITY AT ERIE, THE BEHREND COLLEGE

Erie, PA

Suburban setting ■ Public ■ State-related ■ Coed

Web site: www.pserie.psu.edu

Contact: Undergraduate Admissions Office, 5091 Station Road, Erie, PA 16563

Telephone: 814-865-5471 or toll-free 866-374-3378 **Fax:** 814-898-6044

E-mail: behrend.admissions@psu.edu

Getting in Last Year 3,132 applied; 76% were accepted; 877 enrolled (37%).

Financial Matters $8382 resident tuition and fees (2002–03); $15,740 nonresident tuition and fees (2002–03); $5660 room and board; 75% average percent of need met; $9959 average financial aid amount received per undergraduate (2001–02).

Academics Penn State Erie awards associate, bachelor's, and master's degrees. Challenging opportunities include advanced placement credit, accelerated degree programs, an honors program, double majors, independent study, and a senior project. Special programs include cooperative education, internships, summer session for credit, study-abroad, and Army ROTC. The most frequently chosen baccalaureate fields are business/marketing, engineering/engineering technologies, and psychology. The faculty at Penn State Erie has 195 full-time members, 58% with terminal degrees. The student-faculty ratio is 16:1.

Students of Penn State Erie The student body totals 3,710, of whom 3,586 are undergraduates. 35.4% are women and 64.6% are men. 92% are from Pennsylvania. 1.3% are international students. 85% returned for their sophomore year.

Applying Penn State Erie requires SAT I or ACT and a high school transcript. Application deadline: rolling admissions. Early and deferred admission are possible.

THE PENNSYLVANIA STATE UNIVERSITY BERKS CAMPUS OF THE BERKS–LEHIGH VALLEY COLLEGE

Reading, PA

Suburban setting ■ Public ■ State-related ■ Coed

Web site: www.bk.psu.edu
Contact: Ms. Jennifer Peters, Admissions Counselor, PO Box 7009, 14 Perkins Student Center, Reading, PA 19610-6009
Telephone: 610-396-6066 **Fax:** 610-396-6077
E-mail: admissionsbk@psu.edu

Getting in Last Year 2,457 applied; 81% were accepted; 828 enrolled (42%).

Financial Matters $8248 resident tuition and fees (2002–03); $12,606 nonresident tuition and fees (2002–03); $5660 room and board; 71% average percent of need met; $8918 average financial aid amount received per undergraduate (2001–02).

Academics Penn State Berks awards associate and bachelor's degrees. Challenging opportunities include advanced placement credit, accelerated degree programs, an honors program, and independent study. Special programs include internships, summer session for credit, and study-abroad. The most frequently chosen baccalaureate fields are business/marketing, engineering/engineering technologies, and computer/information sciences. The faculty at Penn State Berks has 88 full-time members, 68% with terminal degrees. The student-faculty ratio is 19:1.

Students of Penn State Berks The student body totals 2,471, of whom 2,443 are undergraduates. 39.3% are women and 60.7% are men. 93% are from Pennsylvania. 0.6% are international students. 79% returned for their sophomore year.

Applying Penn State Berks requires SAT I or ACT and a high school transcript. Application deadline: rolling admissions. Early and deferred admission are possible.

THE PENNSYLVANIA STATE UNIVERSITY HARRISBURG CAMPUS OF THE CAPITAL COLLEGE

Middletown, PA

Small-town setting ■ Public ■ State-related ■ Coed

Web site: www.hbg.psu.edu
Contact: Undergraduate Admissions Office, 777 West Harrisburg Pike, Middletown, PA 17057-4898
Telephone: 814-865-5471 or toll-free 800-222-2056 **Fax:** 717-948-6325
E-mail: hbgadmit@psu.edu

Getting in Last Year 237 applied; 13% were accepted; 18 enrolled (58%).

Financial Matters $8362 resident tuition and fees (2002–03); $15,720 nonresident tuition and fees (2002–03); $6950 room and board; 81% average percent of need met; $11,055 average financial aid amount received per undergraduate (2001–02).

Academics Penn State Harrisburg awards associate, bachelor's, master's, and doctoral degrees and post-bachelor's certificates. Challenging opportunities include advanced placement credit, accelerated degree programs, an honors program, double majors, independent study, and a senior project. Special programs include cooperative education, internships, summer session for credit, study-abroad, and Army ROTC. The most frequently chosen baccalaureate fields are business/marketing, engineering/engineering technologies, and education. The faculty at Penn State Harrisburg has 156 full-time members, 85% with terminal degrees. The student-faculty ratio is 10:1.

Students of Penn State Harrisburg The student body totals 3,258, of whom 1,710 are undergraduates. 49.5% are women and 50.5% are men. 96% are from Pennsylvania. 1% are international students.

Applying Penn State Harrisburg requires SAT I or ACT and a high school transcript. Application deadline: rolling admissions. Early and deferred admission are possible.

THE PENNSYLVANIA STATE UNIVERSITY LEHIGH VALLEY CAMPUS OF THE BERKS-LEHIGH VALLEY COLLEGE

Fogelsville, PA

Small-town setting ■ Public ■ State-related ■ Coed

Web site: www.an.psu.edu
Contact: Admissions Coordinator, 8380 Mohr Lane, Academic Building, Fogelsville, PA 18051-9999
Telephone: 610-821-6577 **Fax:** 610-285-5220
E-mail: admissionlv@psu.edu

Getting in Last Year 730 applied; 75% were accepted; 191 enrolled (35%).

Financial Matters $8130 resident tuition and fees (2002–03); $12,380 nonresident tuition and fees (2002–03); 73% average percent of need met; $8243 average financial aid amount received per undergraduate (2001–02).

Academics Penn State Lehigh Valley awards associate and bachelor's degrees. Challenging opportunities include advanced placement credit, accelerated degree programs, an honors program, and independent study. Special programs include internships, summer session for credit, and study-abroad. The most frequently chosen baccalaureate fields are business/marketing and psychology. The faculty at Penn State Lehigh Valley has 30 full-time members, 63% with terminal degrees. The student-faculty ratio is 14:1.

Students of Penn State Lehigh Valley The student body totals 734, of whom 706 are undergraduates. 36.4% are women and 63.6% are men. 97% are from Pennsylvania. 0.8% are international students. 74% returned for their sophomore year.

Applying Penn State Lehigh Valley requires SAT I or ACT and a high school transcript. Application deadline: rolling admissions. Early and deferred admission are possible.

THE PENNSYLVANIA STATE UNIVERSITY SCHUYLKILL CAMPUS OF THE CAPITAL COLLEGE

Schuylkill Haven, PA

Small-town setting ■ Public ■ State-related ■ Coed

Web site: www.sl.psu.edu
Contact: Undergraduate Admissions Office, 200 University Drive, Schuylkill Haven, PA 17972-2208
Telephone: 814-865-5471 **Fax:** 570-385-3672
E-mail: sl-admissions@psu.edu

Getting in Last Year 713 applied; 87% were accepted; 309 enrolled (50%).

Financial Matters $8110 resident tuition and fees (2002–03); $12,360 nonresident tuition and fees (2002–03); $5664 room and board; 75% average percent of need met; $9802 average financial aid amount received per undergraduate (2001–02).

Academics Penn State Schuylkill awards associate and bachelor's degrees (bachelor's degree programs completed at the Harrisburg campus). Challenging opportunities include advanced placement credit, accelerated degree programs, double majors, and independent study. Special programs include cooperative education, internships, summer session for credit, and study-abroad. The most frequently chosen baccalaureate fields are protective services/public administration, business/marketing, and psychology. The faculty at Penn State Schuylkill has 51 full-time members, 67% with terminal degrees. The student-faculty ratio is 15:1.

Students of Penn State Schuylkill The student body totals 1,101, of whom 1,062 are undergraduates. 58.8% are women and 41.2% are men. 89% are from Pennsylvania. 0.1% are international students. 85% returned for their sophomore year.

Applying Penn State Schuylkill requires SAT I or ACT and a high school transcript. Application deadline: rolling admissions. Early and deferred admission are possible.

THE PENNSYLVANIA STATE UNIVERSITY UNIVERSITY PARK CAMPUS

University Park, PA

Small-town setting ■ Public ■ State-related ■ Coed

Web site: www.psu.edu
Contact: Undergraduate Admissions Office, 201 Shields Building, University Park, PA 16802
Telephone: 814-865-5471 **Fax:** 814-863-7590
E-mail: admissions@psu.edu

Getting in Last Year 27,604 applied; 57% were accepted; 5,929 enrolled (38%).

Financial Matters $8382 resident tuition and fees (2002–03); $17,610 nonresident tuition and fees (2002–03); $5560 room and board; 75% average percent of need met; $10,954 average financial aid amount received per undergraduate (2001–02).

Academics Penn State awards associate, bachelor's, master's, and doctoral degrees and post-bachelor's certificates. Challenging opportunities include advanced placement credit, accelerated degree programs, student-designed majors, freshman honors college, an honors program, double majors, independent study, and a senior project. Special programs include cooperative education, internships, summer session for credit, study-abroad, and Army, Navy and Air Force ROTC. The most frequently chosen baccalaureate fields are business/marketing, engineering/engineering technologies, and education. The faculty at Penn State has 2,143 full-time members, 77% with terminal degrees. The student-faculty ratio is 17:1.

Students of Penn State The student body totals 41,445, of whom 34,829 are undergraduates. 46.5% are women and 53.5% are men. Students come from 54 states and territories. 76% are from Pennsylvania. 2% are international students. 92% returned for their sophomore year.

Applying Penn State requires SAT I or ACT, a high school transcript, and a minimum high school GPA of 2.0, and in some cases an interview and 1 recommendation. The school recommends an essay. Application deadline: rolling admissions. Early and deferred admission are possible.

PEPPERDINE UNIVERSITY

Malibu, CA

Small-town setting ■ Private ■ Independent Religious ■ Coed

Web site: www.pepperdine.edu
Contact: Mr. Paul A. Long, Dean of Admission and Enrollment Management, 24255 Pacific Coast Highway, Malibu, CA 90263-4392
Telephone: 310-506-4392 **Fax:** 310-506-4861
E-mail: admission-seaver@pepperdine.edu

Getting in Last Year 5,503 applied; 37% were accepted; 802 enrolled (39%).

Financial Matters $26,370 tuition and fees (2002–03); $7930 room and board; 89% average percent of need met; $22,611 average financial aid amount received per undergraduate (2001–02).

Academics Pepperdine awards bachelor's, master's, doctoral, and first-professional degrees. Challenging opportunities include advanced placement credit, accelerated degree programs, student-designed majors, an honors program, double majors, independent study, and a senior project. Special programs include internships, summer session for credit, study-abroad, and Army, Navy and Air Force ROTC. The most frequently chosen baccalaureate fields are communications/communication technologies, business/marketing, and social sciences and history. The faculty at Pepperdine has 366 full-time members, 97% with terminal degrees. The student-faculty ratio is 12:1.

Students of Pepperdine The student body totals 7,791, of whom 3,153 are undergraduates. 56.1% are women and 43.9% are men. Students come from 51 states and territories and 70 other countries. 52% are from California. 6.7% are international students. 87% returned for their sophomore year.

Applying Pepperdine requires an essay, SAT I or ACT, a high school transcript, and 2 recommendations. The school recommends an interview. Application deadline: 1/15; 2/15 priority date for financial aid.

PERU STATE COLLEGE

Peru, NE

Rural setting ■ Public ■ State-supported ■ Coed

Web site: www.peru.edu
Contact: Ms. Janelle Moran, Director of Recruitment and Admissions, PO Box 10, Peru, NE 68421
Telephone: 402-872-2221 or toll-free 800-742-4412 (in-state)
Fax: 402-872-2296
E-mail: jmoran@oakmail.peru.edu

Getting in Last Year 504 applied; 62% were accepted; 178 enrolled (57%).

Financial Matters $2902 resident tuition and fees (2002–03); $5189 nonresident tuition and fees (2002–03); $4010 room and board.

Academics PSC awards bachelor's and master's degrees. Challenging opportunities include advanced placement credit, freshman honors college, an honors program, and a senior project. Special programs include cooperative education, internships, summer session for credit, and off-campus study. The faculty at PSC has 41 full-time members, 73% with terminal degrees. The student-faculty ratio is 16:1.

Students of PSC The student body totals 1,687, of whom 1,482 are undergraduates. 57.6% are women and 42.4% are men. Students come from 27 states and territories and 3 other countries. 90% are from Nebraska. 0.7% are international students. 53% returned for their sophomore year.

Applying PSC requires a high school transcript, and in some cases SAT I or ACT, recommendations, and a minimum high school GPA of 2.0. Application deadline: rolling admissions; 3/1 priority date for financial aid. Early and deferred admission are possible.

PFEIFFER UNIVERSITY

Misenheimer, NC

Rural setting ■ Private ■ Independent Religious ■ Coed

Web site: www.pfeiffer.edu
Contact: Ms. Jennifer Bouchard, Admissions Counselor, PO Box 960, Highway 52 North, Misenheimer, NC 28109
Telephone: 704-463-1360 ext. 2066 or toll-free 800-338-2060
Fax: 704-463-1363
E-mail: admiss@pfeiffer.edu

Getting in Last Year 621 applied; 72% were accepted; 168 enrolled (37%).

Financial Matters $12,780 tuition and fees (2002–03); $5120 room and board; 84% average percent of need met; $9859 average financial aid amount received per undergraduate (2001–02).

Academics Pfeiffer awards bachelor's and master's degrees. Challenging opportunities include advanced placement credit, accelerated degree programs, an honors program, double majors, cooperative education, independent study, and a senior project. Special programs include cooperative education, internships, summer session for credit, study-abroad, and Army ROTC. The most frequently chosen baccalaureate fields are business/marketing, protective services/public administration, and education. The faculty at Pfeiffer has 63 full-time members, 70% with terminal degrees. The student-faculty ratio is 13:1.

Students of Pfeiffer The student body totals 1,892, of whom 1,142 are undergraduates. 59.2% are women and 40.8% are men. Students come from 27 states and territories and 14 other countries. 3% are international students. 68% returned for their sophomore year.

Applying Pfeiffer requires SAT I or ACT and a high school transcript, and in some cases 2 recommendations. The school recommends an interview and a minimum high school GPA of 2.0. Application deadline: rolling admissions; 3/15 priority date for financial aid. Early and deferred admission are possible.

PHILADELPHIA BIBLICAL UNIVERSITY

Langhorne, PA

Suburban setting ■ Private ■ Independent Religious ■ Coed

Web site: www.pbu.edu
Contact: Ms. Lisa Fuller, Director of Admissions, 200 Manor Avenue, Langhorne, PA 19047
Telephone: 215-702-4550 or toll-free 800-366-0049 (out-of-state)
Fax: 215-752-4248
E-mail: admissions@pbu.edu

Getting in Last Year 508 applied; 66% were accepted; 179 enrolled (53%).

Financial Matters $11,985 tuition and fees (2002–03); $5405 room and board; 61% average percent of need met; $8330 average financial aid amount received per undergraduate.

Academics Philadelphia Biblical University awards associate, bachelor's, master's, and first-professional degrees. Challenging opportunities include advanced placement credit, accelerated degree programs, an honors program, double majors, independent study, and a senior project. Special programs include internships, summer session for credit, off-campus study, study-abroad, and Air Force ROTC. The most frequently chosen baccalaureate fields are education, protective services/public administration, and visual/performing arts. The faculty at Philadelphia Biblical University has 55 full-time members, 56% with terminal degrees. The student-faculty ratio is 15:1.

Students of Philadelphia Biblical University The student body totals 1,425, of whom 1,058 are undergraduates. 54.8% are women and 45.2% are men. Students come from 39 states and territories and 32 other countries. 48% are from Pennsylvania. 3.1% are international students. 72% returned for their sophomore year.

Applying Philadelphia Biblical University requires an essay, SAT I or ACT, a high school transcript, and 1 recommendation, and in some cases an interview and a minimum high school GPA of 2.0. The school recommends an interview and a minimum high school GPA of 3.0. Application deadline: rolling admissions. Early and deferred admission are possible.

PHILADELPHIA UNIVERSITY

Philadelphia, PA

Suburban setting ■ Private ■ Independent ■ Coed

Web site: www.philau.edu
Contact: Ms. Christine Greb, Director of Admissions, School House Lane and Henry Avenue, Philadelphia, PA 19144-5497
Telephone: 215-951-2800 **Fax:** 215-951-2907
E-mail: admissions@philau.edu

Getting in Last Year 3,577 applied; 69% were accepted; 620 enrolled (25%).

Financial Matters $18,804 tuition and fees (2002–03); $7370 room and board; 68% average percent of need met; $13,519 average financial aid amount received per undergraduate.

Academics Philadelphia University awards associate, bachelor's, and master's degrees. Challenging opportunities include advanced placement credit, accelerated degree programs, freshman honors college, an honors program, independent study, and a senior project. Special programs include cooperative education, internships, summer session for credit, off-campus study, and study-abroad. The most frequently chosen baccalaureate fields are business/marketing, visual/performing arts, and architecture. The faculty at Philadelphia University has 99 full-time members, 73% with terminal degrees. The student-faculty ratio is 13:1.

Students of Philadelphia University The student body totals 3,154, of whom 2,692 are undergraduates. 66.8% are women and 33.2% are men. Students come from 42 states and territories and 28 other countries. 58% are from Pennsylvania. 2.7% are international students. 69% returned for their sophomore year.

Applying Philadelphia University requires SAT I or ACT and a high school transcript. The school recommends an essay, an interview, and 2 recommendations. Application deadline: rolling admissions; 4/15 for financial aid. Deferred admission is possible.

PIEDMONT BAPTIST COLLEGE

Winston-Salem, NC

Urban setting ■ *Private* ■ *Independent Religious* ■ *Coed*

Web site: www.pbc.edu
Contact: Troy Crain, Assistant Director of Admissions, 716 Franklin Street, Winston-Salem, NC 27101-5197
Telephone: 336-725-8344 ext. 2327 or toll-free 800-937-5097
Fax: 336-725-5522
E-mail: admissions@pbc.edu

Getting in Last Year 73 applied; 79% were accepted.

Financial Matters $7820 tuition and fees (2002–03); $4300 room and board.

Academics Piedmont awards associate, bachelor's, and master's degrees. Advanced placement credit is a challenging opportunity. Special programs include internships, summer session for credit, and study-abroad. The faculty at Piedmont has 20 full-time members, 25% with terminal degrees. The student-faculty ratio is 11:1.

Students of Piedmont The student body totals 273, of whom 261 are undergraduates. 54% are from North Carolina. 1.1% are international students. 68% returned for their sophomore year.

Applying Piedmont requires an essay, ACT, a high school transcript, 2 recommendations, and medical history, proof of immunization. The school recommends an interview and a minimum high school GPA of 2.0. Application deadline: rolling admissions; 8/31 for financial aid, with a 6/1 priority date. Early and deferred admission are possible.

PIEDMONT COLLEGE

Demorest, GA

Rural setting ■ *Private* ■ *Independent Religious* ■ *Coed*

Web site: www.piedmont.edu
Contact: Ms. Jem Clement, Dean of Students, PO Box 10, Demorest, GA 30535-0010
Telephone: 706-776-0103 ext. 1188 or toll-free 800-277-7020
Fax: 706-776-6635
E-mail: clement@piedmont.edu

Getting in Last Year 385 applied; 68% were accepted; 142 enrolled (55%).

Financial Matters $12,500 tuition and fees (2002–03); $4400 room and board; 75% average percent of need met; $8362 average financial aid amount received per undergraduate (2001–02).

Academics Piedmont awards bachelor's and master's degrees and post-master's certificates. Challenging opportunities include advanced placement credit, accelerated degree programs, student-designed majors, an honors program, double majors, independent study, and a senior project. Special programs include cooperative education, internships, summer session for credit, off-campus study, and study-abroad. The most frequently chosen baccalaureate fields are education, business/marketing, and social sciences and history. The faculty at Piedmont has 92 full-time members, 84% with terminal degrees. The student-faculty ratio is 15:1.

Students of Piedmont The student body totals 1,998, of whom 910 are undergraduates. 62.1% are women and 37.9% are men. Students come from 11 states and territories. 96% are from Georgia. 0.1% are international students. 75% returned for their sophomore year.

Applying Piedmont requires SAT I or ACT, a high school transcript, and a minimum high school GPA of 2.0, and in some cases an interview. The school recommends an essay. Application deadline: rolling admissions; 5/1 priority date for financial aid. Early and deferred admission are possible.

PIKEVILLE COLLEGE

Pikeville, KY

Small-town setting ■ *Private* ■ *Independent Religious* ■ *Coed*

Web site: www.pc.edu
Contact: Ms. Missy McCoy, Director of Admissions, 147 Sycamore Street, Pikeville, KY 41501
Telephone: 606-218-5251 or toll-free 866-232-7700 **Fax:** 606-218-5255
E-mail: wewantyou@pc.edu

Getting in Last Year 517 applied; 100% were accepted; 228 enrolled (44%).

Financial Matters $9000 tuition and fees (2002–03); $4600 room and board; 66% average percent of need met; $10,108 average financial aid amount received per undergraduate.

Academics Pikeville College awards associate, bachelor's, and first-professional degrees. Challenging opportunities include advanced placement credit, double majors, independent study, and a senior project. Special programs include internships, summer session for credit, off-campus study, and study-abroad. The most frequently chosen baccalaureate fields are business/marketing, biological/life sciences, and education. The faculty at Pikeville College has 67 full-time members, 39% with terminal degrees. The student-faculty ratio is 12:1.

Students of Pikeville College The student body totals 1,201, of whom 957 are undergraduates. 60.3% are women and 39.7% are men. Students come from 26 states and territories. 81% are from Kentucky. 0.2% are international students. 61% returned for their sophomore year.

Applying Pikeville College requires SAT I or ACT and a high school transcript. The school recommends an interview. Application deadline: 8/20; 8/20 for financial aid, with a 3/15 priority date. Early and deferred admission are possible.

PILLSBURY BAPTIST BIBLE COLLEGE

Owatonna, MN

Small-town setting ■ *Private* ■ *Independent Religious* ■ *Coed*

Web site: www.pillsbury.edu
Contact: Mr. Gene Young, Director of Admissions, 315 South Grove Avenue, Owatonna, MN 55060-3097
Telephone: 507-451-2710 ext. 279 or toll-free 800-747-4557 **Fax:** 507-451-6459
E-mail: ppbc@pillsbury.edu

Getting in Last Year 116 applied; 62% were accepted; 49 enrolled (68%).

Financial Matters $7680 tuition and fees (2002–03); $3440 room and board.

Academics Pillsbury awards associate and bachelor's degrees. Challenging opportunities include advanced placement credit, accelerated degree programs, double majors, independent study, and a senior project. Special programs include internships and summer session for credit. The most frequently chosen baccalaureate fields are business/marketing, education, and visual/performing arts. The faculty at Pillsbury has 15 full-time members, 7% with terminal degrees. The student-faculty ratio is 10:1.

Students of Pillsbury The student body is made up of 206 undergraduates. 52.9% are women and 47.1% are men. Students come from 28 states and territories and 2 other countries. 46% are from Minnesota. 1.5% are international students. 67% returned for their sophomore year.

Applying Pillsbury requires an essay, a high school transcript, 2 recommendations, and 2 photographs. The school recommends an interview. Application deadline: 8/20. Deferred admission is possible.

PINE MANOR COLLEGE

Chestnut Hill, MA

Suburban setting ■ *Private* ■ *Independent* ■ *Women Only*

Web site: www.pmc.edu
Contact: Mr. Bill Nichols, Dean of Admissions, 400 Heath Street, Chestnut Hill, MA 02167-2332
Telephone: 617-731-7104 or toll-free 800-762-1357 **Fax:** 617-731-7199
E-mail: admission@pmc.edu

Getting in Last Year 471 applied; 75% were accepted; 155 enrolled (44%).

Financial Matters $12,964 tuition and fees (2002–03); $8120 room and board; 80% average percent of need met; $13,839 average financial aid amount received per undergraduate.

Academics PMC awards associate and bachelor's degrees. Challenging opportunities include advanced placement credit, student-designed majors, an honors program, double majors, independent study, and a senior project. Special programs include internships, summer session for credit, off-campus study, and study-abroad. The most frequently chosen baccalaureate fields are business/marketing, education, and biological/life sciences. The faculty at PMC has 30 full-time members, 80% with terminal degrees. The student-faculty ratio is 9:1.

Students of PMC The student body is made up of 455 undergraduates. Students come from 27 states and territories and 27 other countries. 76% are from Massachusetts. 10.3% are international students. 60% returned for their sophomore year.

Applying PMC requires an essay, SAT I or ACT, a high school transcript, and 1 recommendation. The school recommends an interview and a minimum high school GPA of 2.0. Application deadline: rolling admissions; 3/1 priority date for financial aid. Deferred admission is possible.

PITTSBURG STATE UNIVERSITY

Pittsburg, KS

Small-town setting ■ *Public* ■ *State-supported* ■ *Coed*

Web site: www.pittstate.edu
Contact: Ms. Ange Peterson, Director of Admission and Retention, 1701 South Broadway, Pittsburg, KS 66762
Telephone: 620-235-4251 or toll-free 800-854-7488 ext. 1 **Fax:** 316-235-6003
E-mail: psuadmit@pittstate.edu

Getting in Last Year 1,580 applied; 56% were accepted.

Financial Matters $2534 resident tuition and fees (2002–03); $7946 nonresident tuition and fees (2002–03); $2003 room and board; 84% average percent of need met; $6439 average financial aid amount received per undergraduate.

Academics Pitt State awards associate, bachelor's, and master's degrees. Challenging opportunities include advanced placement credit, student-designed majors, freshman honors college, an honors program, double majors, independent study, and a senior project. Special programs include cooperative education, internships, summer session for credit, off-campus study, study-abroad, and Army ROTC. The faculty at Pitt State has 269 members. The student-faculty ratio is 23:1.

Students of Pitt State The student body totals 6,751, of whom 5,483 are undergraduates. 49.2% are women and 50.8% are men. Students come from 50 states and territories and 46 other countries. 79% are from Kansas. 3.6% are international students. 87% returned for their sophomore year.

Applying Pitt State requires ACT and a high school transcript, and in some cases a minimum high school GPA of 2.0. Application deadline: rolling admissions; 3/1 priority date for financial aid. Early and deferred admission are possible.

PITZER COLLEGE

Claremont, CA

Suburban setting ■ Private ■ Independent ■ Coed

Web site: www.pitzer.edu

Contact: Dr. Arnaldo Rodriguez, Vice President for Admission and Financial Aid, 1050 North Mills Avenue, Claremont, CA 91711-6101

Telephone: 909-621-8129 or toll-free 800-748-9371 **Fax:** 909-621-8770

E-mail: admission@pitzer.edu

Getting in Last Year 2,323 applied; 56% were accepted; 235 enrolled (18%).

Financial Matters $28,256 tuition and fees (2002–03); $7370 room and board; 100% average percent of need met; $25,947 average financial aid amount received per undergraduate.

Academics Pitzer awards bachelor's degrees. Challenging opportunities include advanced placement credit, student-designed majors, an honors program, double majors, independent study, and a senior project. Special programs include cooperative education, internships, off-campus study, and study-abroad. The most frequently chosen baccalaureate fields are social sciences and history, psychology, and visual/performing arts. The faculty at Pitzer has 61 full-time members, 97% with terminal degrees. The student-faculty ratio is 12:1.

Students of Pitzer The student body is made up of 954 undergraduates. 61.7% are women and 38.3% are men. Students come from 42 states and territories and 14 other countries. 55% are from California. 2.5% are international students. 82% returned for their sophomore year.

Applying Pitzer requires an essay, SAT I or ACT, a high school transcript, and 3 recommendations. The school recommends SAT II Subject Tests, SAT II: Writing Test, and an interview. Application deadline: 1/15; 2/1 for financial aid. Early and deferred admission are possible.

PLATTSBURGH STATE UNIVERSITY OF NEW YORK

Plattsburgh, NY

Small-town setting ■ Public ■ State-supported ■ Coed

Web site: www.plattsburgh.edu

Contact: Mr. Richard Higgins, Director of Admissions, 101 Broad Street, Plattsburgh, NY 12901-2681

Telephone: 518-564-2040 or toll-free 888-673-0012 (in-state) **Fax:** 518-564-2045

E-mail: admissions@plattsburgh.edu

Getting in Last Year 5,138 applied; 60% were accepted; 1,013 enrolled (33%).

Financial Matters $4229 resident tuition and fees (2002–03); $9129 nonresident tuition and fees (2002–03); $5920 room and board; 92% average percent of need met; $7718 average financial aid amount received per undergraduate (2001–02).

Academics Plattsburgh State University awards bachelor's and master's degrees and post-master's certificates. Challenging opportunities include advanced placement credit, accelerated degree programs, student-designed majors, an honors program, double majors, independent study, and a senior project. Special programs include cooperative education, internships, summer session for credit, off-campus study, and study-abroad. The most frequently chosen baccalaureate fields are education, business/marketing, and social sciences and history. The faculty at Plattsburgh State University has 252 full-time members, 82% with terminal degrees. The student-faculty ratio is 18:1.

Students of Plattsburgh State University The student body totals 6,238, of whom 5,459 are undergraduates. 57.9% are women and 42.1% are men. Students come from 27 states and territories and 55 other countries. 97% are from New York. 7.3% are international students. 79% returned for their sophomore year.

Applying Plattsburgh State University requires SAT I or ACT, a high school transcript, and a minimum high school GPA of 2.5. The school recommends an essay, an interview, recommendations, and a minimum high school GPA of 3.4. Application deadline: rolling admissions, 8/1 for nonresidents. Early and deferred admission are possible.

PLYMOUTH STATE COLLEGE

Plymouth, NH

Small-town setting ■ Public ■ State-supported ■ Coed

Web site: www.plymouth.edu

Contact: Mr. Eugene Fahey, Senior Associate Director of Admission, 17 High Street, MSC #52, Plymouth, NH 03264-1595

Telephone: 800-842-6900 or toll-free 800-842-6900 **Fax:** 603-535-2714

E-mail: pscadmit@mail.plymouth.edu

Getting in Last Year 3,573 applied; 77% were accepted; 947 enrolled (34%).

Financial Matters $5856 resident tuition and fees (2002–03); $11,516 nonresident tuition and fees (2002–03); $5768 room and board; 77% average percent of need met; $7677 average financial aid amount received per undergraduate.

Academics Plymouth State College awards bachelor's and master's degrees and post-bachelor's and post-master's certificates. Challenging opportunities include advanced placement credit, accelerated degree programs, student-designed majors, an honors program, double majors, independent study, and a senior project. Special programs include internships, summer session for credit, off-campus study, study-abroad, and Army and Air Force ROTC. The most frequently chosen baccalaureate fields are education, business/marketing, and visual/performing arts. The faculty at Plymouth State College has 170 full-time members, 88% with terminal degrees. The student-faculty ratio is 17:1.

Students of Plymouth State College The student body totals 4,629, of whom 3,790 are undergraduates. 51.2% are women and 48.8% are men. Students come from 29 states and territories and 11 other countries. 55% are from New Hampshire. 0.3% are international students. 73% returned for their sophomore year.

Applying Plymouth State College requires an essay, SAT I or ACT, a high school transcript, and 2 recommendations, and in some cases an interview. The school recommends a minimum high school GPA of 2.0. Application deadline: 4/1; 3/1 priority date for financial aid. Deferred admission is possible.

POINT LOMA NAZARENE UNIVERSITY

San Diego, CA

Suburban setting ■ Private ■ Independent Religious ■ Coed

Web site: www.ptloma.edu

Contact: Mr. Scott Shoemaker, Dean of Enrollment, 3900 Lomaland Drive, San Diego, CA 92106

Telephone: 619-849-2273 or toll-free 800-733-7770 **Fax:** 619-849-2601

E-mail: admissions@ptloma.edu

Getting in Last Year 1,404 applied; 73% were accepted; 540 enrolled (53%).

Financial Matters $16,260 tuition and fees (2002–03); $6380 room and board; 71% average percent of need met; $11,509 average financial aid amount received per undergraduate (2001–02).

Academics PLNU awards bachelor's and master's degrees and post-bachelor's and post-master's certificates. Challenging opportunities include advanced placement credit, double majors, and a senior project. Special programs include internships, summer session for credit, off-campus study, study-abroad, and Army, Navy and Air Force ROTC. The most frequently chosen baccalaureate fields are business/marketing, liberal arts/general studies, and health professions and related sciences. The faculty at PLNU has 129 full-time members, 73% with terminal degrees. The student-faculty ratio is 16:1.

Students of PLNU The student body totals 2,998, of whom 2,390 are undergraduates. 59.2% are women and 40.8% are men. Students come from 41 states and territories and 16 other countries. 78% are from California. 1% are international students. 79% returned for their sophomore year.

Applying PLNU requires an essay, SAT I or ACT, a high school transcript, 2 recommendations, and a minimum high school GPA of 2.8, and in some cases an interview. The school recommends SAT I. Application deadline: 3/1; 3/15 priority date for financial aid. Deferred admission is possible.

POINT PARK COLLEGE

Pittsburgh, PA

Urban setting ■ Private ■ Independent ■ Coed

Web site: www.ppc.edu

Contact: Ms. Joell Minford, Director of Admissions, Point Park College, 201 Wood Street, Pittsburgh, PA 15222

Telephone: 412-392-3422 or toll-free 800-321-0129 **Fax:** 412-391-1980

E-mail: enroll@ppc.edu

Getting in Last Year 1,651 applied; 79% were accepted; 364 enrolled (28%).

Financial Matters $14,348 tuition and fees (2002–03); $6098 room and board; 75% average percent of need met; $11,728 average financial aid amount received per undergraduate.

Academics Point Park awards associate, bachelor's, and master's degrees and post-bachelor's and post-master's certificates. Challenging opportunities include advanced placement credit, accelerated degree programs, student-designed majors, an honors program, double majors, independent study, and a senior project. Special programs include internships, summer session for credit, off-campus study, and Army and Air Force ROTC. The most frequently chosen baccalaureate fields are business/marketing, engineering/engineering technologies, and visual/performing arts. The faculty at Point Park has 79 full-time members, 49% with terminal degrees. The student-faculty ratio is 13:1.

Point Park College (continued)

Students of Point Park The student body totals 3,132, of whom 2,743 are undergraduates. 56.7% are women and 43.3% are men. Students come from 44 states and territories and 32 other countries. 87% are from Pennsylvania. 1.3% are international students. 68% returned for their sophomore year.

Applying Point Park requires SAT I or ACT and a high school transcript, and in some cases an interview, 2 recommendations, and audition. The school recommends an essay and a minimum high school GPA of 2.0. Application deadline: rolling admissions; 5/1 priority date for financial aid. Early and deferred admission are possible.

POLYTECHNIC UNIVERSITY, BROOKLYN CAMPUS

Brooklyn, NY

Urban setting ■ *Private* ■ *Independent* ■ *Coed*

Web site: www.poly.edu
Contact: Jonathan D. Wexlar, Dean of Undergraduate Admissions, Six Metrotech Center, Brooklyn, NY 11201-2990
Telephone: 718-260-3100 or toll-free 800-POLYTECH **Fax:** 718-260-3446
E-mail: admitme@poly.edu

Getting in Last Year 1,553 applied; 77% were accepted; 412 enrolled (34%).

Financial Matters $24,480 tuition and fees (2002–03); $8000 room and board; 84% average percent of need met; $18,578 average financial aid amount received per undergraduate (2001–02).

Academics Polytechnic awards bachelor's, master's, and doctoral degrees. Challenging opportunities include advanced placement credit, accelerated degree programs, an honors program, double majors, and a senior project. Special programs include cooperative education, internships, summer session for credit, and Air Force ROTC. The most frequently chosen baccalaureate fields are engineering/engineering technologies, computer/information sciences, and liberal arts/general studies. The faculty at Polytechnic has 160 full-time members, 89% with terminal degrees. The student-faculty ratio is 12:1.

Students of Polytechnic The student body totals 3,032, of whom 1,685 are undergraduates. 19.5% are women and 80.5% are men. Students come from 14 states and territories and 6 other countries. 97% are from New York. 6.7% are international students. 81% returned for their sophomore year.

Applying Polytechnic requires an essay, SAT I or ACT, a high school transcript, and 2 recommendations. The school recommends SAT II Subject Tests, SAT II: Writing Test, and an interview. Application deadline: rolling admissions. Deferred admission is possible.

POMONA COLLEGE

Claremont, CA

Suburban setting ■ *Private* ■ *Independent* ■ *Coed*

Web site: www.pomona.edu
Contact: Mr. Bruce Poch, Vice President and Dean of Admissions, 333 North College Way, Claremont, CA 91711
Telephone: 909-621-8134 **Fax:** 909-621-8952
E-mail: admissions@pomona.edu

Getting in Last Year 4,230 applied; 23% were accepted; 374 enrolled (39%).

Financial Matters $26,020 tuition and fees (2002–03); $9600 room and board; 100% average percent of need met; $25,900 average financial aid amount received per undergraduate.

Academics Pomona awards bachelor's degrees. Challenging opportunities include advanced placement credit, student-designed majors, double majors, independent study, and a senior project. Special programs include internships, off-campus study, and study-abroad. The faculty at Pomona has 161 full-time members, 96% with terminal degrees. The student-faculty ratio is 9:1.

Students of Pomona The student body is made up of 1,551 undergraduates. 50.3% are women and 49.7% are men. Students come from 48 states and territories and 27 other countries. 34% are from California. 1.8% are international students. 98% returned for their sophomore year.

Applying Pomona requires an essay, SAT I and SAT II or ACT, 3 SAT II Subject Tests (including SAT II: Writing Test), a high school transcript, and 2 recommendations. The school recommends an interview, portfolio or tapes for art and performing arts programs, and a minimum high school GPA of 3.0. Application deadline: 1/2; 2/1 for financial aid. Early and deferred admission are possible.

PONTIFICAL CATHOLIC UNIVERSITY OF PUERTO RICO

Ponce, PR

Urban setting ■ *Private* ■ *Independent Religious* ■ *Coed*

Web site: www.pucpr.edu
Contact: Sra. Ana O. Bonilla, Director of Admissions, 2250 Avenida Las Americas, Ponce, PR 00717-0777
Telephone: 787-841-2000 ext. 1004 or toll-free 800-981-5040
Fax: 787-840-4295
E-mail: admissions@pucpr.edu

Getting in Last Year 1,348 applied; 87% were accepted; 1,104 enrolled (94%).

Financial Matters $4458 tuition and fees (2002–03); $2840 room and board; 71% average percent of need met.

Academics PCUPR-La Catolica awards associate, bachelor's, master's, doctoral, and first-professional degrees (branch locations: Arecibo, Guayana, Mayagüez). Challenging opportunities include advanced placement credit, an honors program, double majors, and independent study. Special programs include cooperative education, summer session for credit, off-campus study, and Army ROTC. The most frequently chosen baccalaureate fields are business/marketing, education, and health professions and related sciences. The faculty at PCUPR-La Catolica has 236 full-time members. The student-faculty ratio is 33:1.

Students of PCUPR-La Catolica The student body totals 7,150, of whom 5,350 are undergraduates. 65.1% are women and 34.9% are men. Students come from 1 state or territory.

Applying PCUPR-La Catolica requires SAT I, a high school transcript, and a minimum high school GPA of 2.0, and in some cases an essay, an interview, 1 recommendation, and a minimum high school GPA of 3.0. Application deadline: 3/15; 5/14 priority date for financial aid. Early and deferred admission are possible.

PONTIFICAL COLLEGE JOSEPHINUM

Columbus, OH

Suburban setting ■ *Private* ■ *Independent Religious* ■ *Coed, Primarily Men*

Web site: www.pcj.edu
Contact: Arminda Crawford, Secretary for Admissions, 7625 North High Street, Columbus, OH 43235-1498
Telephone: 614-985-2241 or toll-free 888-252-5812 **Fax:** 614-885-2307
E-mail: acrawford@pcj.edu

Getting in Last Year 14 applied; 64% were accepted; 9 enrolled (100%).

Financial Matters $9740 tuition and fees (2002–03); $5660 room and board; 86% average percent of need met; $13,560 average financial aid amount received per undergraduate.

Academics Josephinum awards bachelor's, master's, and first-professional degrees. Challenging opportunities include advanced placement credit, an honors program, double majors, and a senior project. Special programs include internships and off-campus study. The most frequently chosen baccalaureate field is area/ethnic studies. The faculty at Josephinum has 10 full-time members. The student-faculty ratio is 4:1.

Students of Josephinum The student body totals 130, of whom 69 are undergraduates. Students come from 16 states and territories. 60% are from Ohio. 2.9% are international students. 50% returned for their sophomore year.

Applying Josephinum requires an essay, a high school transcript, and 3 recommendations. The school recommends SAT I and SAT II or ACT and an interview. Application deadline: rolling admissions; 9/2 priority date for financial aid. Deferred admission is possible.

PORTLAND STATE UNIVERSITY

Portland, OR

Urban setting ■ *Public* ■ *State-supported* ■ *Coed*

Web site: www.pdx.edu
Contact: Ms. Agnes A. Hoffman, Director of Admissions and Records, PO Box 751, Portland, OR 97207-0751
Telephone: 503-725-3511 or toll-free 800-547-8887 **Fax:** 503-725-5525
E-mail: admissions@pdx.edu

Getting in Last Year 3,147 applied; 84% were accepted; 1,467 enrolled (55%).

Financial Matters $3885 resident tuition and fees (2002–03); $13,266 nonresident tuition and fees (2002–03); $7725 room and board; 67% average percent of need met; $7484 average financial aid amount received per undergraduate (2001–02).

Academics PSU awards bachelor's, master's, and doctoral degrees and post-bachelor's certificates. Challenging opportunities include advanced placement credit, accelerated degree programs, student-designed majors, an honors program, double majors, independent study, and a senior project. Special programs include cooperative education, internships, summer session for credit, off-campus study, study-abroad, and Army and Air Force ROTC. The most frequently chosen baccalaureate fields are social sciences and history, business/marketing, and psychology. The faculty at PSU has 641 full-time members, 80% with terminal degrees. The student-faculty ratio is 19:1.

Students of PSU The student body totals 21,841, of whom 15,808 are undergraduates. 54.4% are women and 45.6% are men. Students come from 51 states and territories and 81 other countries. 90% are from Oregon. 3.6% are international students. 69% returned for their sophomore year.

Applying PSU requires SAT I or ACT, a high school transcript, and a minimum high school GPA of 2.5. Application deadline: rolling admissions. Early and deferred admission are possible.

POTOMAC COLLEGE

Washington, DC

Urban setting ■ Private ■ Proprietary ■ Coed

Web site: www.potomac.edu

Contact: Ms. Florence Tate, President, 4000 Chesapeake Street, NW, Washington, DC 20016

Telephone: 202-686-0876 ext. 203 or toll-free 888-686-0876 **Fax:** 202-686-0818

E-mail: cdresser@potomac.edu

Getting in Last Year 167 applied; 77% were accepted.

Financial Matters $11,160 tuition and fees (2002–03).

Academics Potomac College awards bachelor's degrees. Challenging opportunities include advanced placement credit, accelerated degree programs, double majors, independent study, and a senior project. Special programs include internships and summer session for credit. The most frequently chosen baccalaureate fields are business/marketing and computer/information sciences. The faculty at Potomac College has 14 full-time members, 36% with terminal degrees. The student-faculty ratio is 11:1.

Students of Potomac College The student body is made up of 511 undergraduates. 57.1% are women and 42.9% are men. Students come from 4 states and territories. 8% are from District of Columbia. 76% returned for their sophomore year.

Applying Potomac College requires a high school transcript, an interview, and 4 years post high school work experience; minimum employment of 20 hours per week. Application deadline: rolling admissions.

PRACTICAL BIBLE COLLEGE

Bible School Park, NY

Suburban setting ■ Private ■ Independent Religious ■ Coed

Web site: www.practical.edu

Contact: Mr. Brian J. Murphy, Director of Admissions, PO Box 601, Bible School Park, NY 13737-0601

Telephone: 607-729-1581 ext. 406 or toll-free 800-331-4137 ext. 406
Fax: 607-729-2962

E-mail: admissions@practical.edu

Getting in Last Year 98 applied; 53% were accepted.

Financial Matters $8150 tuition and fees (2002–03); $4420 room and board; 37% average percent of need met; $5120 average financial aid amount received per undergraduate (2001–02).

Academics Practical awards associate and bachelor's degrees. Challenging opportunities include advanced placement credit, independent study, and a senior project. Special programs include cooperative education, internships, and summer session for credit. The faculty at Practical has 7 full-time members, 57% with terminal degrees. The student-faculty ratio is 17:1.

Students of Practical The student body is made up of 293 undergraduates. 50.2% are women and 49.8% are men. Students come from 13 states and territories and 4 other countries. 77% are from New York. 2% are international students. 84% returned for their sophomore year.

Applying Practical requires SAT I or ACT, a high school transcript, 2 recommendations, and references, and in some cases an essay. The school recommends ACT, an interview, and a minimum high school GPA of 2.0. Application deadline: rolling admissions; 7/15 priority date for financial aid. Deferred admission is possible.

PRAIRIE BIBLE COLLEGE

Three Hills, AB Canada

Small-town setting ■ Private ■ Independent Religious ■ Coed

Web site: www.pbi.edu

Contact: Mr. Vance Neudorf, Director of Enrollment, 319 Fifth Avenue North, PO Box 4000, Three Hills, AB T0M 2N0

Telephone: 403-443-5511 ext. 3033 or toll-free 800-661-2425
Fax: 403-443-5540

E-mail: vance.neudorf@pbi.ab.ca

Getting in Last Year 248 applied; 96% were accepted; 179 enrolled (75%).

Financial Matters $5846 tuition and fees (2002–03); $3430 room and board.

Academics Prairie awards bachelor's degrees. Challenging opportunities include advanced placement credit, accelerated degree programs, and a senior project. Special programs include internships and study-abroad. The faculty at Prairie has 31 full-time members, 35% with terminal degrees. The student-faculty ratio is 12:1.

Students of Prairie The student body is made up of 457 undergraduates. 40.3% are women and 59.7% are men. 43% returned for their sophomore year.

Applying Prairie requires an essay, a high school transcript, and 2 recommendations, and in some cases a minimum high school GPA of 3.0. The school recommends a minimum high school GPA of 2.0. Application deadline: 8/15.

PRAIRIE VIEW A&M UNIVERSITY

Prairie View, TX

Small-town setting ■ Public ■ State-supported ■ Coed

Web site: www.pvamu.edu

Contact: Ms. Mary Gooch, Director of Admissions, PO Box 3089, Prairie View, TX 77446-0188

Telephone: 936-857-2626 **Fax:** 936-857-2699

E-mail: mary_gooch@pvamu.edu

Getting in Last Year 2,643 applied; 97% were accepted; 1,298 enrolled (51%).

Financial Matters $3232 resident tuition and fees (2002–03); $9772 nonresident tuition and fees (2002–03); $6461 room and board; 75% average percent of need met; $6920 average financial aid amount received per undergraduate (2001–02).

Academics Prairie View A&M awards bachelor's, master's, and doctoral degrees. Challenging opportunities include advanced placement credit, accelerated degree programs, an honors program, double majors, independent study, and a senior project. Special programs include cooperative education, internships, summer session for credit, and Army and Navy ROTC. The most frequently chosen baccalaureate fields are business/marketing, health professions and related sciences, and engineering/engineering technologies. The faculty at Prairie View A&M has 306 full-time members, 75% with terminal degrees. The student-faculty ratio is 18:1.

Students of Prairie View A&M The student body totals 7,255, of whom 5,754 are undergraduates. 56.3% are women and 43.7% are men. Students come from 44 states and territories and 39 other countries. 95% are from Texas. 1.4% are international students. 70% returned for their sophomore year.

Applying Prairie View A&M requires SAT I or ACT, a high school transcript, recommendations, and a minimum high school GPA of 2.5. Application deadline: 7/1; 4/1 priority date for financial aid. Deferred admission is possible.

PRATT INSTITUTE

Brooklyn, NY

Urban setting ■ Private ■ Independent ■ Coed

Web site: www.pratt.edu

Contact: Mr. Micah Moody, Visit Coordinator, DeKalb Hall, 200 Willoughby Avenue, Brooklyn, NY 11205-3899

Telephone: 718-636-3669 ext. 3779 or toll-free 800-331-0834 (out-of-state)
Fax: 718-636-3670

E-mail: admissions@pratt.edu

Getting in Last Year 3,640 applied; 42% were accepted; 715 enrolled (47%).

Financial Matters $24,148 tuition and fees (2002–03); $8186 room and board; 56% average percent of need met; $13,705 average financial aid amount received per undergraduate.

Academics Pratt awards associate, bachelor's, master's, and first-professional degrees. Challenging opportunities include advanced placement credit, independent study, and a senior project. Special programs include internships, summer session for credit, off-campus study, study-abroad, and Army ROTC. The most frequently chosen baccalaureate fields are architecture, education, and visual/performing arts. The faculty at Pratt has 111 full-time members, 74% with terminal degrees. The student-faculty ratio is 11:1.

Students of Pratt The student body totals 4,439, of whom 3,124 are undergraduates. 54.3% are women and 45.7% are men. Students come from 41 states and territories and 70 other countries. 11.3% are international students. 90% returned for their sophomore year.

Applying Pratt requires an essay, SAT I or ACT, a high school transcript, and 1 recommendation, and in some cases SAT II Subject Tests, SAT II: Writing Test, an interview, and portfolio. The school recommends a minimum high school GPA of 3.2. Application deadline: 2/1; 2/1 priority date for financial aid.

PRESBYTERIAN COLLEGE

Clinton, SC

Small-town setting ■ Private ■ Independent Religious ■ Coed

Web site: www.presby.edu

Contact: Mr. Richard Dana Paul, Vice President of Enrollment and Dean of Admissions, South Broad Street, Clinton, SC 29325

Telephone: 864-833-8229 or toll-free 800-476-7272 **Fax:** 864-833-8481

E-mail: rdpaul@admin.presby.edu

Getting in Last Year 1,034 applied; 79% were accepted; 319 enrolled (39%).

Financial Matters $19,144 tuition and fees (2002–03); $5508 room and board; 88% average percent of need met; $19,081 average financial aid amount received per undergraduate.

Academics Presbyterian College awards bachelor's degrees. Challenging opportunities include advanced placement credit, freshman honors college, an honors program, double majors, independent study, and a senior project. Special programs include internships, summer session for credit, off-campus study, study-abroad, and Army ROTC. The most frequently chosen baccalaureate fields

Presbyterian College (continued)

are business/marketing, biological/life sciences, and psychology. The faculty at Presbyterian College has 80 full-time members, 89% with terminal degrees. The student-faculty ratio is 13:1.

Students of Presbyterian College The student body is made up of 1,217 undergraduates. 54.5% are women and 45.5% are men. Students come from 27 states and territories. 62% are from South Carolina. 86% returned for their sophomore year.

Applying Presbyterian College requires an essay, SAT I or ACT, a high school transcript, and 1 recommendation. The school recommends an interview. Application deadline: 4/1; 3/1 priority date for financial aid. Deferred admission is possible.

PRESCOTT COLLEGE

Prescott, AZ

Small-town setting ■ Private ■ Independent ■ Coed

Web site: www.prescott.edu
Contact: Ms. Shari Sterling, Director of Admissions, 220 Grove Avenue, Prescott, AZ 86301-2990
Telephone: 928-778-2090 ext. 2101 or toll-free 800-628-6364
Fax: 928-776-5242
E-mail: admissions@prescott.edu

Getting in Last Year 129 applied; 69% were accepted; 44 enrolled (49%).

Financial Matters $15,140 tuition and fees (2002–03); 69% average percent of need met; $4542 average financial aid amount received per undergraduate (2001–02).

Academics Prescott College awards bachelor's and master's degrees. Challenging opportunities include advanced placement credit, student-designed majors, double majors, independent study, and a senior project. Special programs include internships, summer session for credit, and off-campus study. The most frequently chosen baccalaureate fields are education, parks and recreation, and protective services/public administration. The faculty at Prescott College has 45 full-time members, 44% with terminal degrees. The student-faculty ratio is 12:1.

Students of Prescott College The student body totals 1,031, of whom 834 are undergraduates. 58.5% are women and 41.5% are men. Students come from 44 states and territories and 1 other country. 15% are from Arizona. 0.4% are international students. 55% returned for their sophomore year.

Applying Prescott College requires an essay, a high school transcript, and 2 recommendations, and in some cases an interview. Application deadline: 2/1. Deferred admission is possible.

PRESENTATION COLLEGE

Aberdeen, SD

Small-town setting ■ Private ■ Independent Religious ■ Coed

Web site: www.presentation.edu
Contact: Mr. Joddy Meidinger, Director of Admissions, 1500 North Main Street, Aberdeen, SD 57401-1299
Telephone: 605-229-8493 ext. 492 or toll-free 800-437-6060
E-mail: admit@presentation.edu

Getting in Last Year 108 applied; 100% were accepted.

Financial Matters $9025 tuition and fees (2002–03); $4150 room and board; 97% average percent of need met; $8574 average financial aid amount received per undergraduate (2001–02).

Academics Presentation College awards associate and bachelor's degrees. Challenging opportunities include advanced placement credit, accelerated degree programs, double majors, and a senior project. Special programs include cooperative education, internships, and summer session for credit. The most frequently chosen baccalaureate fields are health professions and related sciences, business/marketing, and protective services/public administration. The faculty at Presentation College has 26 full-time members, 19% with terminal degrees. The student-faculty ratio is 12:1.

Students of Presentation College The student body is made up of 594 undergraduates. 87.4% are women and 12.6% are men. Students come from 1 state or territory. 73% are from South Dakota. 0.2% are international students.

Applying Presentation College requires ACT ASSET and a high school transcript, and in some cases ACT and a minimum high school GPA of 2.0. The school recommends ACT. Application deadline: rolling admissions; 4/1 for financial aid.

PRINCETON UNIVERSITY

Princeton, NJ

Suburban setting ■ Private ■ Independent ■ Coed

Web site: www.princeton.edu
Contact: Mr. Fred A. Hargadon, Dean of Admission, PO Box 430, Princeton, NJ 08544
Telephone: 609-258-3062 **Fax:** 609-258-6743

Getting in Last Year 14,521 applied; 11% were accepted; 1,164 enrolled (73%).

Financial Matters $27,230 tuition and fees (2002–03); $7842 room and board; 100% average percent of need met; $23,289 average financial aid amount received per undergraduate (2001–02).

Academics Princeton awards bachelor's, master's, and doctoral degrees. Challenging opportunities include advanced placement credit, accelerated degree programs, student-designed majors, an honors program, independent study, and a senior project. Special programs include cooperative education, internships, off-campus study, study-abroad, and Army and Air Force ROTC. The most frequently chosen baccalaureate fields are social sciences and history, engineering/engineering technologies, and biological/life sciences. The faculty at Princeton has 818 full-time members, 92% with terminal degrees. The student-faculty ratio is 5:1.

Students of Princeton The student body totals 6,790, of whom 4,779 are undergraduates. 48.3% are women and 51.7% are men. Students come from 54 states and territories and 65 other countries. 14% are from New Jersey. 7.5% are international students. 97% returned for their sophomore year.

Applying Princeton requires an essay, SAT II Subject Tests, SAT I or ACT, a high school transcript, and 3 recommendations. The school recommends an interview. Application deadline: 1/1; 2/1 priority date for financial aid. Early and deferred admission are possible.

PRINCIPIA COLLEGE

Elsah, IL

Rural setting ■ Private ■ Independent Religious ■ Coed

Web site: www.prin.edu/college
Contact: Mrs. Martha Green Quirk, Dean of Admissions, One Maybeck Place, Elsah, IL 62028-9799
Telephone: 618-374-5180 or toll-free 800-277-4648 Ext. 2802
Fax: 618-374-4000
E-mail: collegeadmissions@prin.edu

Getting in Last Year 274 applied; 83% were accepted; 114 enrolled (50%).

Financial Matters $17,670 tuition and fees (2002–03); $6195 room and board; 90% average percent of need met; $15,269 average financial aid amount received per undergraduate (2001–02).

Academics Prin awards bachelor's degrees. Challenging opportunities include advanced placement credit, accelerated degree programs, student-designed majors, an honors program, double majors, independent study, and a senior project. Special programs include internships and study-abroad. The most frequently chosen baccalaureate fields are social sciences and history, visual/performing arts, and biological/life sciences. The faculty at Prin has 52 full-time members, 62% with terminal degrees. The student-faculty ratio is 9:1.

Students of Prin The student body is made up of 538 undergraduates. 53.9% are women and 46.1% are men. Students come from 29 states and territories and 20 other countries. 9% are from Illinois. 12.3% are international students. 86% returned for their sophomore year.

Applying Prin requires an essay, SAT I or ACT, a high school transcript, 4 recommendations, Christian Science commitment, and a minimum high school GPA of 2.0, and in some cases an interview. The school recommends an interview. Application deadline: 3/1. Deferred admission is possible.

PROVIDENCE COLLEGE

Providence, RI

Suburban setting ■ Private ■ Independent Religious ■ Coed

Web site: www.providence.edu
Contact: Mr. Christopher Lydon, Dean of Enrollment Management, River Avenue and Eaton Street, Providence, RI 02918
Telephone: 401-865-2535 or toll-free 800-721-6444 **Fax:** 401-865-2826
E-mail: pcadmiss@providence.edu

Getting in Last Year 7,354 applied; 49% were accepted; 878 enrolled (24%).

Financial Matters $20,860 tuition and fees (2002–03); $8120 room and board; 83% average percent of need met; $14,582 average financial aid amount received per undergraduate.

Academics PC awards associate, bachelor's, and master's degrees. Challenging opportunities include advanced placement credit, student-designed majors, an honors program, double majors, independent study, and a senior project. Special programs include cooperative education, internships, summer session for credit, study-abroad, and Army ROTC. The most frequently chosen baccalaureate fields are business/marketing, social sciences and history, and education. The faculty at PC has 249 full-time members, 88% with terminal degrees. The student-faculty ratio is 14:1.

Students of PC The student body totals 5,275, of whom 4,371 are undergraduates. 58.4% are women and 41.6% are men. Students come from 47 states and territories and 15 other countries. 25% are from Rhode Island. 0.7% are international students. 92% returned for their sophomore year.

Applying PC requires an essay, SAT I or ACT, a high school transcript, and 2 recommendations. The school recommends SAT II Subject Tests, SAT II: Writing Test, and an interview. Application deadline: 1/15; 2/1 for financial aid. Early and deferred admission are possible.

PROVIDENCE COLLEGE AND THEOLOGICAL SEMINARY

Otterburne, MB Canada

Rural setting ■ Private ■ Independent Religious ■ Coed

Web site: www.prov.ca

Contact: Mr. Mark Little, Dean of Admissions and Records, General Delivery, Otterburne, MB R0A 1G0 Canada

Telephone: 204-433-7488 ext. 249 or toll-free 800-668-7768 **Fax:** 204-433-7158

E-mail: info@prov.ca

Financial Matters $5176 tuition and fees (2002–03); $3700 room and board.

Academics Providence College and Theological Seminary awards bachelor's, master's, and doctoral degrees. Challenging opportunities include accelerated degree programs, freshman honors college, double majors, and independent study. Internships is a special program. The most frequently chosen baccalaureate fields are liberal arts/general studies, social sciences and history, and education. The faculty at Providence College and Theological Seminary has 18 full-time members, 100% with terminal degrees. The student-faculty ratio is 19:1.

Students of Providence College and Theological Seminary The student body totals 884, of whom 407 are undergraduates. 50.4% are women and 49.6% are men. Students come from 16 states and territories and 17 other countries. 70% are from Manitoba. 70% returned for their sophomore year.

Applying Providence College and Theological Seminary requires a high school transcript and 4 recommendations. The school recommends SAT I or ACT. Application deadline: rolling admissions. Deferred admission is possible.

PURCHASE COLLEGE, STATE UNIVERSITY OF NEW YORK

Purchase, NY

Small-town setting ■ Public ■ State-supported ■ Coed

Web site: www.purchase.edu

Contact: Ms. Betsy Immergut, Director of Admissions, 735 Anderson Hill Road, Purchase, NY 10577-1400

Telephone: 914-251-6300 **Fax:** 914-251-6314

E-mail: admissn@purchase.edu

Getting in Last Year 7,102 applied; 37% were accepted; 689 enrolled (26%).

Financial Matters $4200 resident tuition and fees (2002–03); $9100 nonresident tuition and fees (2002–03); $6500 room and board; 69% average percent of need met; $7235 average financial aid amount received per undergraduate.

Academics Purchase awards bachelor's and master's degrees and post-master's certificates. Challenging opportunities include advanced placement credit, student-designed majors, double majors, independent study, and a senior project. Special programs include internships, summer session for credit, off-campus study, and study-abroad. The most frequently chosen baccalaureate fields are visual/performing arts, liberal arts/general studies, and social sciences and history. The faculty at Purchase has 136 full-time members. The student-faculty ratio is 17:1.

Students of Purchase The student body totals 4,063, of whom 3,920 are undergraduates. 56.1% are women and 43.9% are men. Students come from 46 states and territories and 30 other countries. 85% are from New York. 2.9% are international students. 77% returned for their sophomore year.

Applying Purchase requires SAT I, a high school transcript, and a minimum high school GPA of 3.0, and in some cases an essay, an interview, 1 recommendation, and audition, portfolio. Application deadline: rolling admissions; 3/15 priority date for financial aid. Early and deferred admission are possible.

PURDUE UNIVERSITY

West Lafayette, IN

Suburban setting ■ Public ■ State-supported ■ Coed

Web site: www.purdue.edu

Contact: Director of Admissions, 475 Stadium Mall Drive, Schleman Hall, West Lafayette, IN 47907-2050

Telephone: 765-494-4600

E-mail: admissions@purdue.edu

Getting in Last Year 22,872 applied; 76% were accepted; 6,265 enrolled (36%).

Financial Matters $5580 resident tuition and fees (2002–03); $16,260 nonresident tuition and fees (2002–03); $6340 room and board; 90% average percent of need met; $7387 average financial aid amount received per undergraduate.

Academics Purdue awards associate, bachelor's, master's, doctoral, and first-professional degrees. Challenging opportunities include advanced placement credit, freshman honors college, an honors program, double majors, independent study, and a senior project. Special programs include cooperative education, internships, summer session for credit, study-abroad, and Army, Navy and Air Force ROTC. The most frequently chosen baccalaureate fields are engineering/engineering technologies, business/marketing, and education. The faculty at Purdue has 1,869 full-time members, 99% with terminal degrees. The student-faculty ratio is 16:1.

Students of Purdue The student body totals 38,546, of whom 30,908 are undergraduates. 41.5% are women and 58.5% are men. Students come from 52 states and territories and 120 other countries. 76% are from Indiana. 6.5% are international students. 89% returned for their sophomore year.

Applying Purdue requires SAT I or ACT and a high school transcript. Application deadline: rolling admissions; 3/1 priority date for financial aid. Early and deferred admission are possible.

PURDUE UNIVERSITY CALUMET

Hammond, IN

Urban setting ■ Public ■ State-supported ■ Coed

Web site: www.calumet.purdue.edu

Contact: Mr. Paul McGuinness, Director of Admissions, 173rd and Woodmar Avenue, Hammond, IN 46323-2094

Telephone: 219-989-2213 or toll-free 800-447-8738 (in-state)

E-mail: adms@calumet.purdue.edu

Getting in Last Year 1,941 applied; 88% were accepted; 1,579 enrolled (93%).

Financial Matters $4111 resident tuition and fees (2002–03); $8836 nonresident tuition and fees (2002–03); 34% average percent of need met; $4638 average financial aid amount received per undergraduate.

Academics Purdue Cal awards associate, bachelor's, and master's degrees and post-bachelor's certificates. Challenging opportunities include advanced placement credit and an honors program. Special programs include cooperative education, internships, summer session for credit, and Army ROTC. The faculty at Purdue Cal has 267 full-time members, 99% with terminal degrees. The student-faculty ratio is 21:1.

Students of Purdue Cal The student body totals 8,863, of whom 7,920 are undergraduates. 55.8% are women and 44.2% are men. 0.8% are international students. 100% returned for their sophomore year.

Applying Purdue Cal requires a high school transcript, and in some cases SAT I or ACT. Application deadline: rolling admissions; 3/1 priority date for financial aid. Early admission is possible.

PURDUE UNIVERSITY NORTH CENTRAL

Westville, IN

Rural setting ■ Public ■ State-supported ■ Coed

Web site: www.purduenc.edu

Contact: Ms. Cathy Buckman, Director of Admissions, 1401 South U.S. Highway 421, Westville, IN 46391

Telephone: 219-785-5458 or toll-free 800-872-1231 (in-state)

E-mail: cbuckman@purduenc.edu

Getting in Last Year 1,089 applied; 91% were accepted; 692 enrolled (70%).

Financial Matters $3590 resident tuition and fees (2002–03); $8015 nonresident tuition and fees (2002–03); 80% average percent of need met; $4893 average financial aid amount received per undergraduate.

Academics Purdue University North Central awards associate, bachelor's, and master's degrees. Challenging opportunities include advanced placement credit, student-designed majors, an honors program, and double majors. Special programs include cooperative education, internships, summer session for credit, and study-abroad. The most frequently chosen baccalaureate fields are liberal arts/general studies, education, and trade and industry. The faculty at Purdue University North Central has 96 full-time members, 58% with terminal degrees. The student-faculty ratio is 18:1.

Students of Purdue University North Central The student body totals 3,658, of whom 3,636 are undergraduates. 59.2% are women and 40.8% are men. Students come from 5 states and territories. 99% are from Indiana. 0.1% are international students. 54% returned for their sophomore year.

Applying Purdue University North Central requires a high school transcript, and in some cases an essay, SAT I or ACT, an interview, and a minimum high school GPA of 2.0. The school recommends SAT I and ACT. Application deadline: 8/6; 3/1 priority date for financial aid. Early admission is possible.

QUEENS COLLEGE OF THE CITY UNIVERSITY OF NEW YORK

Flushing, NY

Urban setting ■ Public ■ State and locally supported ■ Coed

Web site: www.qc.edu

Contact: Undergraduate Admissions Office, Undergraduate Admissions, Kiely Hall 217, 65-30 Kissena Boulevard, Flushing, NY 11367

Telephone: 718-997-5600 **Fax:** 718-997-5617

E-mail: admissions@qc.edu

Queens College of the City University of New York (continued)

Getting in Last Year 6,280 applied; 41% were accepted; 1,233 enrolled (48%).

Financial Matters $3561 resident tuition and fees (2002–03); $7161 nonresident tuition and fees (2002–03); 90% average percent of need met; $5000 average financial aid amount received per undergraduate (2001–02).

Academics Queens College awards bachelor's and master's degrees. Challenging opportunities include advanced placement credit, accelerated degree programs, student-designed majors, freshman honors college, an honors program, double majors, independent study, and a senior project. Special programs include cooperative education, internships, summer session for credit, off-campus study, study-abroad, and Army and Navy ROTC. The most frequently chosen baccalaureate fields are social sciences and history, business/marketing, and psychology. The faculty at Queens College has 548 full-time members, 93% with terminal degrees. The student-faculty ratio is 23:1.

Students of Queens College The student body totals 16,604, of whom 12,012 are undergraduates. 62.9% are women and 37.1% are men. Students come from 18 states and territories and 118 other countries. 99% are from New York. 4.9% are international students. 85% returned for their sophomore year.

Applying Queens College requires SAT I, a high school transcript, and a minimum high school GPA of 3.0, and in some cases SAT II Subject Tests and 2 recommendations. The school recommends SAT II Subject Tests. Application deadline: 1/1; 3/1 priority date for financial aid. Deferred admission is possible.

QUEEN'S UNIVERSITY AT KINGSTON

Kingston, ON Canada

Urban setting ■ Public ■ Coed

Web site: www.queensu.ca
Contact: Mr. Nicholas Snider, Manager of Student Recruitment, Richardson Hall, Kingston, ON K7L 3N6 Canada
Telephone: 613-533-2217 **Fax:** 613-533-6810
E-mail: admissn@post.queensu.ca

Getting in Last Year 26,586 applied; 48% were accepted.

Financial Matters $4828 nonresident tuition and fees (2002–03); $7793 room and board.

Academics Queen's awards bachelor's, master's, and doctoral degrees. Challenging opportunities include accelerated degree programs, student-designed majors, an honors program, and double majors. Special programs include cooperative education, internships, summer session for credit, and study-abroad. The faculty at Queen's has 984 members. The student-faculty ratio is 12:1.

Students of Queen's The student body totals 18,616, of whom 15,252 are undergraduates. Students come from 13 states and territories and 76 other countries. 89% are from Ontario.

Applying Queen's requires SAT I, a high school transcript, and a minimum high school GPA of 2.0, and in some cases an essay, SAT II Subject Tests, an interview, and 1 recommendation. Application deadline: 2/28. Deferred admission is possible.

QUEENS UNIVERSITY OF CHARLOTTE

Charlotte, NC

Suburban setting ■ Private ■ Independent Religious ■ Coed

Web site: www.queens.edu
Contact: Mr. William Lee, Director of Admissions, 1900 Selwyn Avenue, Charlotte, NC 28274
Telephone: 704-337-2212 or toll-free 800-849-0202 **Fax:** 704-337-2403
E-mail: admissions@queens.edu

Getting in Last Year 600 applied; 79% were accepted; 195 enrolled (41%).

Financial Matters $12,290 tuition and fees (2002–03); $6010 room and board; 77% average percent of need met; $9713 average financial aid amount received per undergraduate (2001–02).

Academics Queens awards bachelor's and master's degrees and post-bachelor's certificates. Challenging opportunities include advanced placement credit, an honors program, double majors, independent study, and a senior project. Special programs include internships, summer session for credit, off-campus study, study-abroad, and Army and Air Force ROTC. The most frequently chosen baccalaureate fields are business/marketing, communications/communication technologies, and health professions and related sciences. The faculty at Queens has 63 full-time members, 83% with terminal degrees. The student-faculty ratio is 13:1.

Students of Queens The student body totals 1,753, of whom 1,205 are undergraduates. 76.3% are women and 23.7% are men. Students come from 32 states and territories and 21 other countries. 67% are from North Carolina. 4.4% are international students. 77% returned for their sophomore year.

Applying Queens requires an essay, SAT I or ACT, a high school transcript, 2 recommendations, and a minimum high school GPA of 2.0. The school recommends an interview. Application deadline: rolling admissions. Deferred admission is possible.

QUINCY UNIVERSITY

Quincy, IL

Small-town setting ■ Private ■ Independent Religious ■ Coed

Web site: www.quincy.edu
Contact: Mr. Kevin A. Brown, Director of Admissions, 1800 College Avenue, Quincy, IL 62301-2699
Telephone: 217-222-8020 ext. 5215 or toll-free 800-688-4295
E-mail: admissions@quincy.edu

Getting in Last Year 1,034 applied; 97% were accepted; 231 enrolled (23%).

Financial Matters $16,360 tuition and fees (2002–03); $5320 room and board; 93% average percent of need met; $14,444 average financial aid amount received per undergraduate (2001–02).

Academics Quincy University awards associate, bachelor's, and master's degrees. Challenging opportunities include advanced placement credit, accelerated degree programs, student-designed majors, an honors program, double majors, independent study, and a senior project. Special programs include internships, summer session for credit, and study-abroad. The most frequently chosen baccalaureate fields are business/marketing, education, and protective services/public administration. The faculty at Quincy University has 58 full-time members, 86% with terminal degrees. The student-faculty ratio is 14:1.

Students of Quincy University The student body totals 1,192, of whom 1,057 are undergraduates. 55.2% are women and 44.8% are men. Students come from 2 states and territories and 10 other countries. 75% are from Illinois. 1% are international students. 74% returned for their sophomore year.

Applying Quincy University requires SAT I or ACT and a high school transcript. The school recommends an interview and a minimum high school GPA of 2.0. Application deadline: rolling admissions; 4/15 priority date for financial aid. Early and deferred admission are possible.

QUINNIPIAC UNIVERSITY

Hamden, CT

Suburban setting ■ Private ■ Independent ■ Coed

Web site: www.quinnipiac.edu
Contact: Ms. Joan Isaac Mohr, Vice President and Dean of Admissions, 275 Mount Carmel Avenue, Hamden, CT 06518-1940
Telephone: 203-582-8600 or toll-free 800-462-1944 (out-of-state) **Fax:** 203-582-8906
E-mail: admissions@quinnipiac.edu

Getting in Last Year 7,468 applied; 74% were accepted; 1,353 enrolled (25%).

Financial Matters $19,890 tuition and fees (2002–03); $8980 room and board; 68% average percent of need met; $12,555 average financial aid amount received per undergraduate.

Academics Quinnipiac awards bachelor's, master's, and first-professional degrees and post-bachelor's certificates. Challenging opportunities include advanced placement credit, student-designed majors, an honors program, double majors, independent study, and a senior project. Special programs include internships, summer session for credit, study-abroad, and Army and Air Force ROTC. The most frequently chosen baccalaureate fields are health professions and related sciences, business/marketing, and liberal arts/general studies. The faculty at Quinnipiac has 265 full-time members, 79% with terminal degrees. The student-faculty ratio is 16:1.

Students of Quinnipiac The student body totals 6,951, of whom 5,317 are undergraduates. 62.5% are women and 37.5% are men. Students come from 27 states and territories and 18 other countries. 28% are from Connecticut. 0.4% are international students. 83% returned for their sophomore year.

Applying Quinnipiac requires an essay, SAT I or ACT, a high school transcript, and 1 recommendation, and in some cases a minimum high school GPA of 3.0. The school recommends an interview and a minimum high school GPA of 2.5. Application deadline: 2/15; 3/1 priority date for financial aid. Early and deferred admission are possible.

RABBINICAL COLLEGE BETH SHRAGA

Monsey, NY

Small-town setting ■ Private ■ Independent Religious ■ Men Only

Contact: Rabbi Schiff, Director of Admissions, 28 Saddle River Road, Monsey, NY 10952-3035
Telephone: 914-356-1980

Financial Matters $6200 tuition and fees (2002–03); $3300 room and board.

Students of Rabbinical College Beth Shraga The student body totals 30.

RADFORD UNIVERSITY

Radford, VA

Small-town setting ■ Public ■ State-supported ■ Coed

Web site: www.radford.edu

Contact: Dr. David Kraus, Director of Admissions and Records, PO Box 6903, RU Station, Radford, VA 24142
Telephone: 540-831-5371 or toll-free 800-890-4265 **Fax:** 540-831-5038
E-mail: ruadmiss@runet.edu

Getting in Last Year 6,278 applied; 75% were accepted; 1,820 enrolled (39%).

Financial Matters $3344 resident tuition and fees (2002–03); $9792 nonresident tuition and fees (2002–03); $5442 room and board; 80% average percent of need met; $7404 average financial aid amount received per undergraduate.

Academics RU awards bachelor's and master's degrees and post-master's certificates. Challenging opportunities include advanced placement credit, accelerated degree programs, student-designed majors, an honors program, double majors, independent study, and a senior project. Special programs include internships, summer session for credit, off-campus study, study-abroad, and Army and Navy ROTC. The most frequently chosen baccalaureate fields are business/marketing, interdisciplinary studies, and protective services/public administration. The faculty at RU has 355 full-time members. The student-faculty ratio is 19:1.

Students of RU The student body totals 9,242, of whom 8,200 are undergraduates. 58.5% are women and 41.5% are men. Students come from 45 states and territories and 65 other countries. 88% are from Virginia. 1% are international students. 79% returned for their sophomore year.

Applying RU requires SAT I or ACT, a high school transcript, and a minimum high school GPA of 2.0, and in some cases an essay. The school recommends an interview and 1 recommendation. Application deadline: 5/1; 3/1 priority date for financial aid. Early admission is possible.

RAMAPO COLLEGE OF NEW JERSEY

Mahwah, NJ

Suburban setting ■ Public ■ State-supported ■ Coed

Web site: www.ramapo.edu
Contact: Mr. Peter Goetz, Director of Recruitment and Retention, Office of Admissions, 505 Ramapo Valley Road, Mahwah, NJ 07430-1680
Telephone: 201-684-7307 ext. 7307 or toll-free 800-9RAMAPO (in-state) **Fax:** 201-684-7964
E-mail: admissions@ramapo.edu

Getting in Last Year 3,785 applied; 43% were accepted; 687 enrolled (42%).

Financial Matters $6775 resident tuition and fees (2002–03); $10,677 nonresident tuition and fees (2002–03); $7722 room and board; 86% average percent of need met; $8966 average financial aid amount received per undergraduate (2001–02).

Academics Ramapo awards bachelor's and master's degrees. Challenging opportunities include advanced placement credit, accelerated degree programs, student-designed majors, freshman honors college, an honors program, double majors, independent study, and a senior project. Special programs include cooperative education, internships, summer session for credit, off-campus study, study-abroad, and Air Force ROTC. The most frequently chosen baccalaureate fields are business/marketing, communications/communication technologies, and psychology. The faculty at Ramapo has 168 full-time members, 95% with terminal degrees. The student-faculty ratio is 17:1.

Students of Ramapo The student body totals 5,494, of whom 5,143 are undergraduates. 60.8% are women and 39.2% are men. Students come from 18 states and territories and 67 other countries. 88% are from New Jersey. 3.8% are international students. 85% returned for their sophomore year.

Applying Ramapo requires an essay, SAT I, and a high school transcript, and in some cases ACT. The school recommends an interview and a minimum high school GPA of 3.0. Application deadline: 2/15; 3/1 priority date for financial aid. Early and deferred admission are possible.

RANDOLPH-MACON COLLEGE

Ashland, VA

Suburban setting ■ Private ■ Independent Religious ■ Coed

Web site: www.rmc.edu
Contact: Mr. John C. Conkright, Dean of Admissions and Financial Aid, PO Box 5005, Ashland, VA 23005-5505
Telephone: 804-752-7305 or toll-free 800-888-1762 **Fax:** 804-752-4707
E-mail: admissions@rmc.edu

Getting in Last Year 1,689 applied; 78% were accepted; 377 enrolled (29%).

Financial Matters $20,045 tuition and fees (2002–03); $5715 room and board; 85% average percent of need met; $14,858 average financial aid amount received per undergraduate.

Academics Randolph-Macon awards bachelor's degrees. Challenging opportunities include advanced placement credit, accelerated degree programs, an honors program, double majors, independent study, and a senior project. Special programs include internships, summer session for credit, off-campus study, study-abroad, and Army ROTC. The most frequently chosen baccalaureate fields are business/marketing, social sciences and history, and interdisciplinary studies. The faculty at Randolph-Macon has 88 full-time members, 93% with terminal degrees. The student-faculty ratio is 11:1.

Students of Randolph-Macon The student body is made up of 1,154 undergraduates. 50.3% are women and 49.7% are men. Students come from 30 states and territories. 65% are from Virginia. 0.9% are international students. 78% returned for their sophomore year.

Applying Randolph-Macon requires an essay, SAT I or ACT, a high school transcript, and 1 recommendation. The school recommends SAT II Subject Tests, SAT II: Writing Test, and an interview. Application deadline: 3/1; 2/1 priority date for financial aid. Early and deferred admission are possible.

RANDOLPH-MACON WOMAN'S COLLEGE

Lynchburg, VA

Suburban setting ■ Private ■ Independent Religious ■ Women Only

Web site: www.rmwc.edu
Contact: Pat LeDonne, Director of Admissions, 2500 Rivermont Avenue, Lynchburg, VA 24503-1526
Telephone: 434-947-8100 or toll-free 800-745-7692 **Fax:** 434-947-8996
E-mail: admissions@rmwc.edu

Getting in Last Year 723 applied; 85% were accepted; 206 enrolled (33%).

Financial Matters $19,280 tuition and fees (2002–03); $7560 room and board; 90% average percent of need met; $18,381 average financial aid amount received per undergraduate.

Academics R-MWC awards bachelor's degrees. Challenging opportunities include advanced placement credit, accelerated degree programs, student-designed majors, an honors program, double majors, independent study, and a senior project. Special programs include internships, off-campus study, and study-abroad. The most frequently chosen baccalaureate fields are social sciences and history, biological/life sciences, and English. The faculty at R-MWC has 77 full-time members, 90% with terminal degrees. The student-faculty ratio is 9:1.

Students of R-MWC The student body is made up of 764 undergraduates. Students come from 43 states and territories and 47 other countries. 45% are from Virginia. 11.9% are international students. 76% returned for their sophomore year.

Applying R-MWC requires an essay, SAT I or ACT, a high school transcript, and 2 recommendations. The school recommends an interview. Application deadline: 3/1; 3/1 priority date for financial aid. Early and deferred admission are possible.

REED COLLEGE

Portland, OR

Suburban setting ■ Private ■ Independent ■ Coed

Web site: www.reed.edu
Contact: Mr. Paul Marthers, Dean of Admission, 3203 Southeast Woodstock Boulevard, Portland, OR 97202-8199
Telephone: 503-777-7511 or toll-free 800-547-4750 (out-of-state) **Fax:** 503-777-7553
E-mail: admission@reed.edu

Getting in Last Year 1,847 applied; 55% were accepted; 314 enrolled (31%).

Financial Matters $27,560 tuition and fees (2002–03); $7380 room and board; 100% average percent of need met; $21,254 average financial aid amount received per undergraduate.

Academics Reed awards bachelor's and master's degrees. Challenging opportunities include advanced placement credit, accelerated degree programs, student-designed majors, double majors, independent study, and a senior project. Special programs include off-campus study, study-abroad, and Army ROTC. The most frequently chosen baccalaureate fields are social sciences and history, psychology, and biological/life sciences. The faculty at Reed has 118 full-time members, 87% with terminal degrees. The student-faculty ratio is 10:1.

Students of Reed The student body totals 1,389, of whom 1,363 are undergraduates. 53.7% are women and 46.3% are men. Students come from 49 states and territories and 38 other countries. 21% are from Oregon. 3.8% are international students. 87% returned for their sophomore year.

Applying Reed requires an essay, SAT I or ACT, a high school transcript, and 2 recommendations. The school recommends SAT II Subject Tests, SAT II: Writing Test, an interview, and a minimum high school GPA of 3.0. Application deadline: 1/15; 2/1 for financial aid, with a 1/15 priority date. Early and deferred admission are possible.

REFORMED BIBLE COLLEGE

Grand Rapids, MI

Suburban setting ■ Private ■ Independent Religious ■ Coed

Web site: www.reformed.edu
Contact: Ms. Jeanine Kopaska Broek, Assistant Director of Admissions, 3333 East Beltline North East, Grand Rapids, MI 49525
Telephone: 616-222-3000 ext. 695 or toll-free 800-511-3749 **Fax:** 616-222-3045
E-mail: admissions@reformed.edu

Getting in Last Year 87 applied; 70% were accepted; 61 enrolled (100%).

Reformed Bible College (continued)

Financial Matters $9536 tuition and fees (2002–03); $4900 room and board; 53% average percent of need met; $8519 average financial aid amount received per undergraduate.

Academics RBC awards associate and bachelor's degrees and post-bachelor's certificates. Challenging opportunities include advanced placement credit, double majors, and independent study. Special programs include cooperative education, internships, summer session for credit, off-campus study, and study-abroad. The faculty at RBC has 14 full-time members, 36% with terminal degrees. The student-faculty ratio is 16:1.

Students of RBC The student body is made up of 278 undergraduates. 52.9% are women and 47.1% are men. Students come from 16 states and territories and 12 other countries. 92% are from Michigan. 9.3% are international students.

Applying RBC requires an essay, SAT I or ACT, a high school transcript, an interview, 2 recommendations, and a minimum high school GPA of 2.5. Application deadline: rolling admissions; 2/15 priority date for financial aid. Deferred admission is possible.

REGIS COLLEGE

Weston, MA

Small-town setting ■ Private ■ Independent Religious ■ Women Only

Web site: www.regiscollege.edu
Contact: Ms. Judith Pearson, Dean of Admission and Financial Aid, 235 Wellesley Street, Weston, MA 02493
Telephone: 781-768-7100 or toll-free 866-438-7344 **Fax:** 781-768-7071
E-mail: admission@regiscollege.edu

Getting in Last Year 574 applied; 84% were accepted; 137 enrolled (28%).

Financial Matters $19,000 tuition and fees (2002–03); $8675 room and board; 82% average percent of need met; $18,143 average financial aid amount received per undergraduate.

Academics Regis awards associate, bachelor's, and master's degrees and post-master's certificates. Challenging opportunities include advanced placement credit, student-designed majors, an honors program, double majors, independent study, and a senior project. Special programs include internships, summer session for credit, off-campus study, study-abroad, and Army ROTC. The most frequently chosen baccalaureate fields are social sciences and history, health professions and related sciences, and communications/communication technologies. The faculty at Regis has 50 full-time members, 84% with terminal degrees. The student-faculty ratio is 12:1.

Students of Regis The student body totals 1,045, of whom 773 are undergraduates. Students come from 21 states and territories and 7 other countries. 86% are from Massachusetts. 1.9% are international students. 73% returned for their sophomore year.

Applying Regis requires an essay, SAT I or ACT, a high school transcript, 2 recommendations, and a minimum high school GPA of 2.5, and in some cases an interview. The school recommends SAT II Subject Tests, an interview, rank in upper 50% of high school class, and a minimum high school GPA of 3.0. Application deadline: rolling admissions; 3/1 priority date for financial aid. Deferred admission is possible.

REGIS UNIVERSITY

Denver, CO

Suburban setting ■ Private ■ Independent Religious ■ Coed

Web site: www.regis.edu
Contact: Mr. Vic Davolt, Director of Admissions, 3333 Regis Boulevard, Denver, CO 80221-1099
Telephone: 303-458-4905 or toll-free 800-388-2366 ext. 4900 **Fax:** 303-964-5534
E-mail: regisadm@regis.edu

Getting in Last Year 1,528 applied; 83% were accepted; 391 enrolled (31%).

Financial Matters $19,550 tuition and fees (2002–03); $7500 room and board; 84% average percent of need met; $17,315 average financial aid amount received per undergraduate.

Academics Regis University awards bachelor's and master's degrees. Challenging opportunities include advanced placement credit, accelerated degree programs, student-designed majors, freshman honors college, an honors program, double majors, independent study, and a senior project. Special programs include cooperative education, internships, summer session for credit, off-campus study, study-abroad, and Army and Air Force ROTC. The faculty at Regis University has 176 full-time members, 95% with terminal degrees. The student-faculty ratio is 14:1.

Students of Regis University The student body totals 11,460, of whom 6,028 are undergraduates. 60.7% are women and 39.3% are men. Students come from 40 states and territories and 11 other countries. 57% are from Colorado. 0.8% are international students. 79% returned for their sophomore year.

Applying Regis University requires an essay, SAT I or ACT, a high school transcript, 1 recommendation, and a minimum high school GPA of 2.5, and in some cases an interview and 2 recommendations. The school recommends SAT II Subject Tests. Application deadline: rolling admissions; 3/5 priority date for financial aid.

REINHARDT COLLEGE

Waleska, GA

Rural setting ■ Private ■ Independent Religious ■ Coed

Web site: www.reinhardt.edu
Contact: Ms. Kathryn Smith, Director of Admissions, 7300 Reinhardt College Circle, Waleska, GA 30183-0128
Telephone: 770-720-5526 or toll-free 87-REINHARDT **Fax:** 770-720-5602
E-mail: admissions@mail.reinhardt.edu

Getting in Last Year 539 applied; 76% were accepted; 372 enrolled (91%).

Financial Matters $9840 tuition and fees (2002–03); $5380 room and board; $6500 average financial aid amount received per undergraduate.

Academics Reinhardt College awards associate and bachelor's degrees. Challenging opportunities include advanced placement credit, an honors program, double majors, and independent study. Special programs include cooperative education, internships, summer session for credit, and study-abroad. The most frequently chosen baccalaureate fields are business/marketing, education, and communications/communication technologies. The faculty at Reinhardt College has 49 full-time members, 61% with terminal degrees. The student-faculty ratio is 15:1.

Students of Reinhardt College The student body is made up of 1,118 undergraduates. 58.6% are women and 41.4% are men. Students come from 14 states and territories. 97% are from Georgia. 0.9% are international students.

Applying Reinhardt College requires SAT I or ACT, a high school transcript, and a minimum high school GPA of 2.0. The school recommends an essay and an interview. Application deadline: rolling admissions. Early and deferred admission are possible.

REMINGTON COLLEGE–COLORADO SPRINGS CAMPUS

Colorado Springs, CO

Private ■ Proprietary ■ Coed

Web site: www.remingtoncollege.edu
Contact: Mr. Scott Prester, Director of Recruitment, 6050 Erin Park Drive, #250, Colorado Springs, CO 80918
Telephone: 769-532-1234 ext. 225 **Fax:** 719-264-1234 ext.

Getting in Last Year 71 applied; 100% were accepted; 71 enrolled (100%).

Financial Matters $13,920 tuition and fees (2002–03).

Academics Remington College–Colorado Springs Campus awards associate and bachelor's degrees. The faculty at Remington College–Colorado Springs Campus has 7 full-time members, 29% with terminal degrees. The student-faculty ratio is 17:1.

Students of Remington College–Colorado Springs Campus The student body is made up of 282 undergraduates.

RENSSELAER POLYTECHNIC INSTITUTE

Troy, NY

Suburban setting ■ Private ■ Independent ■ Coed

Web site: www.rpi.edu
Contact: Ms. Teresa Duffy, Dean of Enrollment Management, 110 8th Street, Troy, NY 12180-3590
Telephone: 518-276-6216 or toll-free 800-448-6562 **Fax:** 518-276-4072
E-mail: admissions@rpi.edu

Getting in Last Year 5,480 applied; 70% were accepted; 1,049 enrolled (27%).

Financial Matters $27,170 tuition and fees (2002–03); $8902 room and board; 90% average percent of need met; $22,791 average financial aid amount received per undergraduate.

Academics Rensselaer awards bachelor's, master's, and doctoral degrees. Challenging opportunities include advanced placement credit, accelerated degree programs, student-designed majors, double majors, independent study, and a senior project. Special programs include cooperative education, internships, summer session for credit, off-campus study, study-abroad, and Army, Navy and Air Force ROTC. The most frequently chosen baccalaureate fields are engineering/engineering technologies, business/marketing, and computer/information sciences. The faculty at Rensselaer has 384 full-time members, 94% with terminal degrees. The student-faculty ratio is 17:1.

Students of Rensselaer The student body totals 7,687, of whom 5,139 are undergraduates. 24.6% are women and 75.4% are men. Students come from 51 states and territories and 37 other countries. 53% are from New York. 4.1% are international students. 91% returned for their sophomore year.

Applying Rensselaer requires an essay, SAT I or ACT, a high school transcript, and 1 recommendation, and in some cases SAT II Subject Tests and portfolio for architecture and electronic arts programs. Application deadline: 1/1; 2/15 priority date for financial aid. Early and deferred admission are possible.

RESEARCH COLLEGE OF NURSING

Kansas City, MO

Urban setting ■ Private ■ Independent ■ Coed, Primarily Women

Web site: www.researchcollege.edu
Contact: Ms. Marisa Ferrara, Rockhurst College Admission Office, 1100 Rockhurst Road, Kansas City, MO 64110
Telephone: 816-501-4100 ext. 4654 or toll-free 800-842-6776
Fax: 816-501-4588
E-mail: mendenhall@vax2.rockhurst.edu

Getting in Last Year 92 applied; 74% were accepted; 20 enrolled (29%).

Financial Matters $16,430 tuition and fees (2002–03); $5450 room and board; 60% average percent of need met; $10,300 average financial aid amount received per undergraduate (2001–02).

Academics Research College of Nursing awards bachelor's and master's degrees (bachelor's degree offered jointly with Rockhurst College). Challenging opportunities include advanced placement credit, accelerated degree programs, an honors program, double majors, and independent study. Special programs include summer session for credit, study-abroad, and Army ROTC. The most frequently chosen baccalaureate field is health professions and related sciences. The faculty at Research College of Nursing has 25 full-time members. The student-faculty ratio is 7:1.

Students of Research College of Nursing The student body totals 203, of whom 176 are undergraduates. 92% are women and 8% are men. Students come from 7 states and territories.

Applying Research College of Nursing requires SAT I or ACT, a high school transcript, and 1 recommendation. The school recommends an interview, minimum ACT score of 20, and a minimum high school GPA of 2.8. Application deadline: 6/30; 3/15 priority date for financial aid. Deferred admission is possible.

RHODE ISLAND COLLEGE

Providence, RI

Suburban setting ■ Public ■ State-supported ■ Coed

Web site: www.ric.edu
Contact: Dr. Holly L. Shadoian, Director of Admissions, 600 Mount Pleasant Avenue, Providence, RI 02908-1924
Telephone: 401-456-8234 or toll-free 800-669-5760 **Fax:** 401-456-8817
E-mail: admissions@ric.edu

Getting in Last Year 2,901 applied; 72% were accepted; 962 enrolled (46%).

Financial Matters $3761 resident tuition and fees (2002–03); $9525 nonresident tuition and fees (2002–03); $6136 room and board.

Academics Rhode Island College awards bachelor's, master's, and doctoral degrees and post-master's certificates. Challenging opportunities include advanced placement credit, student-designed majors, freshman honors college, an honors program, double majors, independent study, and a senior project. Special programs include internships, summer session for credit, off-campus study, study-abroad, and Army ROTC. The most frequently chosen baccalaureate fields are education, psychology, and health professions and related sciences. The faculty at Rhode Island College has 306 full-time members, 85% with terminal degrees. The student-faculty ratio is 14:1.

Students of Rhode Island College The student body totals 8,758, of whom 7,098 are undergraduates. 67.2% are women and 32.8% are men. Students come from 10 states and territories. 92% are from Rhode Island. 74% returned for their sophomore year.

Applying Rhode Island College requires an essay, SAT I, a high school transcript, and recommendations, and in some cases an interview. Application deadline: 5/1; 3/1 priority date for financial aid. Early and deferred admission are possible.

RHODE ISLAND SCHOOL OF DESIGN

Providence, RI

Urban setting ■ Private ■ Independent ■ Coed

Web site: www.risd.edu
Contact: Mr. Edward Newhall, Director of Admissions, 2 College Street, Providence, RI 02905-2791
Telephone: 401-454-6300 or toll-free 800-364-RISD **Fax:** 401-454-6309
E-mail: admissions@risd.edu

Getting in Last Year 2,524 applied; 32% were accepted; 392 enrolled (49%).

Financial Matters $24,765 tuition and fees (2002–03); $7049 room and board; 69% average percent of need met; $15,100 average financial aid amount received per undergraduate.

Academics RISD awards bachelor's, master's, and first-professional degrees. Challenging opportunities include advanced placement credit, independent study, and a senior project. Special programs include internships, off-campus study, and study-abroad. The most frequently chosen baccalaureate fields are visual/performing arts and architecture. The faculty at RISD has 145 full-time members. The student-faculty ratio is 11:1.

Students of RISD The student body totals 2,204, of whom 1,882 are undergraduates. Students come from 51 states and territories and 53 other countries. 6% are from Rhode Island. 11.8% are international students. 96% returned for their sophomore year.

Applying RISD requires an essay, SAT I or ACT, a high school transcript, and portfolio, drawing assignments. The school recommends 3 recommendations. Application deadline: 2/15; 2/15 priority date for financial aid. Early and deferred admission are possible.

RHODES COLLEGE

Memphis, TN

Suburban setting ■ Private ■ Independent Religious ■ Coed

Web site: www.rhodes.edu
Contact: Mr. David J. Wottle, Dean of Admissions and Financial Aid, 2000 North Parkway, Memphis, TN 38112
Telephone: 901-843-3700 or toll-free 800-844-5969 (out-of-state)
Fax: 901-843-3631
E-mail: adminfo@rhodes.edu

Getting in Last Year 2,345 applied; 70% were accepted; 439 enrolled (27%).

Financial Matters $21,566 tuition and fees (2002–03); $6136 room and board; 84% average percent of need met; $16,054 average financial aid amount received per undergraduate.

Academics Rhodes awards bachelor's and master's degrees (master's degree in accounting only). Challenging opportunities include advanced placement credit, accelerated degree programs, student-designed majors, an honors program, double majors, independent study, and a senior project. Special programs include internships, off-campus study, study-abroad, and Army and Air Force ROTC. The most frequently chosen baccalaureate fields are social sciences and history, business/marketing, and biological/life sciences. The faculty at Rhodes has 129 full-time members, 90% with terminal degrees. The student-faculty ratio is 11:1.

Students of Rhodes The student body totals 1,553, of whom 1,541 are undergraduates. 56.4% are women and 43.6% are men. Students come from 43 states and territories and 13 other countries. 29% are from Tennessee. 1.5% are international students. 89% returned for their sophomore year.

Applying Rhodes requires an essay, SAT I or ACT, a high school transcript, and 2 recommendations. The school recommends an interview. Application deadline: 2/1; 3/1 priority date for financial aid. Early and deferred admission are possible.

RICE UNIVERSITY

Houston, TX

Urban setting ■ Private ■ Independent ■ Coed

Web site: www.rice.edu
Contact: Ms. Julie M. Browning, Dean for Undergraduate Enrollment, Office of Admission, PO Box 1892, MS 17, Houston, TX 77251-1892
Telephone: 713-348-RICE or toll-free 800-527-OWLS

Getting in Last Year 7,079 applied; 24% were accepted; 700 enrolled (42%).

Financial Matters $17,526 tuition and fees (2002–03); $7480 room and board; 100% average percent of need met; $15,498 average financial aid amount received per undergraduate.

Academics Rice awards bachelor's, master's, and doctoral degrees. Challenging opportunities include advanced placement credit, accelerated degree programs, student-designed majors, an honors program, double majors, independent study, and a senior project. Special programs include internships, summer session for credit, off-campus study, study-abroad, and Army and Navy ROTC. The most frequently chosen baccalaureate fields are social sciences and history, engineering/engineering technologies, and biological/life sciences. The faculty at Rice has 503 full-time members, 96% with terminal degrees. The student-faculty ratio is 5:1.

Students of Rice The student body totals 4,785, of whom 2,787 are undergraduates. 46.9% are women and 53.1% are men. Students come from 54 states and territories and 25 other countries. 54% are from Texas. 3.1% are international students. 96% returned for their sophomore year.

Applying Rice requires an essay, SAT II Subject Tests, SAT II: Writing Test, SAT I or ACT, a high school transcript, and 2 recommendations. The school recommends an interview. Application deadline: 1/2; 3/1 priority date for financial aid. Early and deferred admission are possible.

THE RICHARD STOCKTON COLLEGE OF NEW JERSEY

Pomona, NJ

Suburban setting ■ Public ■ State-supported ■ Coed

Web site: www.stockton.edu
Contact: Mr. Salvatore Catalfamo, Dean of Enrollment Management, PO Box 195, Pomona, NJ 08240-0195
Telephone: 609-652-4261 **Fax:** 609-748-5541
E-mail: admissions@stockton.edu

Getting in Last Year 3,384 applied; 45% were accepted; 803 enrolled (52%).

The Richard Stockton College of New Jersey (continued)

Financial Matters $4352 resident tuition and fees (2002–03); $7040 nonresident tuition and fees (2002–03); $6290 room and board; 78% average percent of need met; $9542 average financial aid amount received per undergraduate.

Academics Stockton awards bachelor's and master's degrees. Challenging opportunities include advanced placement credit, accelerated degree programs, student-designed majors, freshman honors college, an honors program, independent study, and a senior project. Special programs include internships, summer session for credit, off-campus study, study-abroad, and Army ROTC. The most frequently chosen baccalaureate fields are social sciences and history, business/marketing, and biological/life sciences. The faculty at Stockton has 202 full-time members, 97% with terminal degrees. The student-faculty ratio is 19:1.

Students of Stockton The student body totals 6,538, of whom 6,261 are undergraduates. 58.5% are women and 41.5% are men. Students come from 23 states and territories and 24 other countries. 98% are from New Jersey. 0.8% are international students. 84% returned for their sophomore year.

Applying Stockton requires an essay, SAT I or ACT, a high school transcript, and a minimum high school GPA of 2.0. The school recommends recommendations and a minimum high school GPA of 3.0. Application deadline: 5/1; 3/1 priority date for financial aid. Early admission is possible.

RICHMOND, THE AMERICAN INTERNATIONAL UNIVERSITY IN LONDON

Richmond United Kingdom

Urban setting ■ Private ■ Independent ■ Coed

Web site: www.richmond.ac.uk
Contact: Mr. Brian E. Davis, Director of United States Admissions, 343 Congress Street, Suite 3100, Boston, MA 02210-1214
Telephone: 617-450-5617 **Fax:** 617-450-5601
E-mail: us_admissions@richmond.ac.uk

Getting in Last Year 1,874 applied; 44% were accepted; 170 enrolled (21%).

Financial Matters $15,550 tuition and fees (2002–03); $8567 room and board.

Academics Richmond College awards associate, bachelor's, and master's degrees and post-bachelor's certificates. Challenging opportunities include advanced placement credit, an honors program, independent study, and a senior project. Special programs include internships, summer session for credit, and study-abroad. The most frequently chosen baccalaureate fields are business/marketing, social sciences and history, and communications/communication technologies. The faculty at Richmond College has 39 full-time members. The student-faculty ratio is 12:1.

Students of Richmond College The student body totals 933, of whom 911 are undergraduates. 56.8% are women and 43.2% are men. Students come from 40 states and territories and 104 other countries. 73% returned for their sophomore year.

Applying Richmond College requires an essay, SAT I or ACT, a high school transcript, 1 recommendation, and a minimum high school GPA of 2.5. Application deadline: 8/1. Deferred admission is possible.

RIDER UNIVERSITY

Lawrenceville, NJ

Suburban setting ■ Private ■ Independent ■ Coed

Web site: www.rider.edu
Contact: Ms. Laurie Marie Kennedy, Director of Admissions, 2083 Lawrenceville Road, Lawrenceville, NJ 08648-3099
Telephone: 609-896-5177 or toll-free 800-257-9026 **Fax:** 609-895-6645
E-mail: admissions@rider.edu

Getting in Last Year 4,091 applied; 82% were accepted; 964 enrolled (29%).

Financial Matters $19,700 tuition and fees (2002–03); $7950 room and board; 83% average percent of need met; $17,189 average financial aid amount received per undergraduate.

Academics Rider awards associate, bachelor's, and master's degrees and post-master's certificates. Challenging opportunities include advanced placement credit, an honors program, double majors, independent study, and a senior project. Special programs include cooperative education, internships, summer session for credit, study-abroad, and Army ROTC. The most frequently chosen baccalaureate fields are business/marketing, education, and communications/communication technologies. The faculty at Rider has 229 full-time members, 93% with terminal degrees. The student-faculty ratio is 12:1.

Students of Rider The student body totals 5,469, of whom 4,284 are undergraduates. 59.1% are women and 40.9% are men. Students come from 35 states and territories and 12 other countries. 79% are from New Jersey. 2.5% are international students. 77% returned for their sophomore year.

Applying Rider requires an essay, SAT I or ACT, a high school transcript, and a minimum high school GPA of 2.0, and in some cases an interview. The school recommends an interview and 2 recommendations. Application deadline: rolling admissions; 3/1 priority date for financial aid. Early and deferred admission are possible.

RINGLING SCHOOL OF ART AND DESIGN

Sarasota, FL

Urban setting ■ Private ■ Independent ■ Coed

Web site: www.rsad.edu
Contact: Mr. James Dean, Dean of Admissions, 2700 North Tamiami Trail, Sarasota, FL 34234
Telephone: 937-351-5100 ext. 7525 or toll-free 800-255-7695
Fax: 937-359-7517
E-mail: admissions@rsad.edu

Getting in Last Year 701 applied; 44% were accepted; 202 enrolled (65%).

Financial Matters $17,420 tuition and fees (2002–03); $8544 room and board; 38% average percent of need met; $8547 average financial aid amount received per undergraduate.

Academics Ringling School awards bachelor's degrees. Challenging opportunities include advanced placement credit, independent study, and a senior project. Special programs include internships, off-campus study, and study-abroad. The most frequently chosen baccalaureate field is visual/performing arts. The faculty at Ringling School has 54 full-time members, 44% with terminal degrees. The student-faculty ratio is 14:1.

Students of Ringling School The student body is made up of 1,015 undergraduates. 46.5% are women and 53.5% are men. Students come from 45 states and territories and 32 other countries. 55% are from Florida. 6.6% are international students. 73% returned for their sophomore year.

Applying Ringling School requires an essay, a high school transcript, 2 recommendations, portfolio, resume, and a minimum high school GPA of 2.0. The school recommends SAT I and SAT II or ACT and an interview. Application deadline: rolling admissions; 3/1 priority date for financial aid. Deferred admission is possible.

RIPON COLLEGE

Ripon, WI

Small-town setting ■ Private ■ Independent ■ Coed

Web site: www.ripon.edu
Contact: Mr. Scott J. Goplin, Vice President and Dean of Admission and Financial Aid, 300 Seward Street, PO Box 248, Ripon, WI 54971
Telephone: 920-748-8185 or toll-free 800-947-4766 **Fax:** 920-748-8335
E-mail: adminfo@ripon.edu

Getting in Last Year 934 applied; 84% were accepted; 250 enrolled (32%).

Financial Matters $19,500 tuition and fees (2002–03); $4820 room and board; 82% average percent of need met; $18,573 average financial aid amount received per undergraduate.

Academics Ripon awards bachelor's degrees. Challenging opportunities include advanced placement credit, accelerated degree programs, student-designed majors, double majors, and a senior project. Special programs include internships, off-campus study, study-abroad, and Army ROTC. The most frequently chosen baccalaureate fields are trade and industry, English, and education. The faculty at Ripon has 47 full-time members, 96% with terminal degrees. The student-faculty ratio is 15:1.

Students of Ripon The student body is made up of 987 undergraduates. 52.9% are women and 47.1% are men. Students come from 36 states and territories and 14 other countries. 68% are from Wisconsin. 1.9% are international students. 88% returned for their sophomore year.

Applying Ripon requires SAT I or ACT, a high school transcript, 1 recommendation, and a minimum high school GPA of 2.0. The school recommends an essay and an interview. Application deadline: rolling admissions; 3/1 priority date for financial aid. Deferred admission is possible.

RIVIER COLLEGE

Nashua, NH

Suburban setting ■ Private ■ Independent Religious ■ Coed

Web site: www.rivier.edu
Contact: Mr. David Boisvert, (Director of Undergraduate Admissions) Executive Assistant to President for Enrollment Management, 420 Main Street, Nashua, NH 03060
Telephone: 603-897-8502 or toll-free 800-44RIVIER **Fax:** 603-891-1799
E-mail: rivadmit@rivier.edu

Getting in Last Year 899 applied; 80% were accepted; 186 enrolled (26%).

Financial Matters $18,355 tuition and fees (2002–03); $6916 room and board; 75% average percent of need met; $11,932 average financial aid amount received per undergraduate.

Academics Rivier awards associate, bachelor's, and master's degrees and post-bachelor's and post-master's certificates. Challenging opportunities include advanced placement credit, accelerated degree programs, an honors program, double majors, independent study, and a senior project. Special programs include internships, off-campus study, and Air Force ROTC. The most frequently chosen baccalaureate field is law/legal studies. The faculty at Rivier has 80 full-time members. The student-faculty ratio is 18:1.

Students of Rivier The student body totals 2,331, of whom 1,489 are undergraduates. 81.5% are women and 18.5% are men. Students come from 10 states and territories and 6 other countries. 68% are from New Hampshire. 1.1% are international students. 78% returned for their sophomore year.

Applying Rivier requires an essay, SAT I or ACT, a high school transcript, and 1 recommendation, and in some cases nursing examination, an interview, and portfolio for art program. The school recommends an interview and a minimum high school GPA of 2.3. Application deadline: rolling admissions; 2/1 priority date for financial aid. Deferred admission is possible.

ROANOKE BIBLE COLLEGE

Elizabeth City, NC

Small-town setting ■ Private ■ Independent Religious ■ Coed

Web site: www.roanokebible.edu

Contact: Mrs. Julie Fields, Director of Admissions and Financial Aid, 715 North Poindexter Street, Elizabeth City, NC 27909-4054

Telephone: 252-334-2019 or toll-free 800-RBC-8980 **Fax:** 252-334-2071

E-mail: admissions@roanokebible.edu

Getting in Last Year 136 applied; 44% were accepted; 57 enrolled (95%).

Financial Matters $6424 tuition and fees (2002–03); $4842 room and board; 65% average percent of need met; $5600 average financial aid amount received per undergraduate (2001–02).

Academics Roanoke awards associate and bachelor's degrees. Advanced placement credit is a challenging opportunity. Internships is a special program. The faculty at Roanoke has 10 full-time members, 30% with terminal degrees. The student-faculty ratio is 13:1.

Students of Roanoke The student body is made up of 187 undergraduates. 43.3% are women and 56.7% are men. Students come from 12 states and territories and 1 other country. 39% are from North Carolina. 0.5% are international students. 54% returned for their sophomore year.

Applying Roanoke requires an essay, SAT I or ACT, a high school transcript, and reference from church, and in some cases an interview. Application deadline: 8/1; 3/15 priority date for financial aid. Early and deferred admission are possible.

ROANOKE COLLEGE

Salem, VA

Suburban setting ■ Private ■ Independent Religious ■ Coed

Web site: www.roanoke.edu

Contact: Mr. Michael C. Maxey, Vice President of Admissions, 221 College Lane, Salem, VA 24153

Telephone: 540-375-2270 or toll-free 800-388-2276 **Fax:** 540-375-2267

E-mail: admissions@roanoke.edu

Getting in Last Year 2,767 applied; 72% were accepted; 461 enrolled (23%).

Financial Matters $19,716 tuition and fees (2002–03); $6338 room and board; 91% average percent of need met; $17,370 average financial aid amount received per undergraduate.

Academics Roanoke awards bachelor's degrees. Challenging opportunities include advanced placement credit, accelerated degree programs, an honors program, double majors, independent study, and a senior project. Special programs include internships, summer session for credit, off-campus study, and study-abroad. The most frequently chosen baccalaureate fields are social sciences and history, business/marketing, and English. The faculty at Roanoke has 118 full-time members, 91% with terminal degrees. The student-faculty ratio is 14:1.

Students of Roanoke The student body is made up of 1,822 undergraduates. 60.8% are women and 39.2% are men. Students come from 40 states and territories and 17 other countries. 59% are from Virginia. 1.1% are international students. 79% returned for their sophomore year.

Applying Roanoke requires SAT I or ACT and a high school transcript. The school recommends an essay, an interview, and 3 recommendations. Application deadline: 3/1; 3/1 priority date for financial aid. Early and deferred admission are possible.

ROBERT MORRIS COLLEGE

Chicago, IL

Urban setting ■ Private ■ Independent ■ Coed

Web site: www.robertmorris.edu

Contact: Candace Goodwin, Senior Vice President for Enrollment, 401 South State Street, Chicago, IL 60605

Telephone: 312-935-6600 or toll-free 800-225-1520 **Fax:** 312-935-6819

E-mail: enroll@robertmorris.edu

Getting in Last Year 2,604 applied; 76% were accepted; 1,190 enrolled (60%).

Financial Matters $12,750 tuition and fees (2002–03); 56% average percent of need met; $10,032 average financial aid amount received per undergraduate.

Academics RMC awards associate and bachelor's degrees. Challenging opportunities include advanced placement credit, accelerated degree programs, an honors program, and a senior project. Special programs include cooperative education, internships, summer session for credit, and study-abroad. The most frequently chosen baccalaureate fields are business/marketing, computer/information sciences, and visual/performing arts. The faculty at RMC has 123 full-time members, 22% with terminal degrees. The student-faculty ratio is 15:1.

Students of RMC The student body is made up of 5,231 undergraduates. 68% are women and 32% are men. Students come from 10 states and territories and 15 other countries. 99% are from Illinois. 0.5% are international students. 68% returned for their sophomore year.

Applying RMC requires a high school transcript, an interview, and a minimum high school GPA of 2.0. Application deadline: rolling admissions. Deferred admission is possible.

ROBERT MORRIS UNIVERSITY

Moon Township, PA

Suburban setting ■ Private ■ Independent ■ Coed

Web site: www.rmu.edu

Contact: Ms. Marianne L. Budziszewski, Dean of Enrollment Services, Enrollment Services Department, 881 Narrows Run Road, Moon Township, PA 15108-1189

Telephone: 412-262-8412 or toll-free 800-762-0097 **Fax:** 412-299-2425

E-mail: enrollmentoffice@rmu.edu

Getting in Last Year 2,127 applied; 78% were accepted; 487 enrolled (29%).

Financial Matters $12,720 tuition and fees (2002–03); $6752 room and board; 44% average percent of need met; $8254 average financial aid amount received per undergraduate.

Academics Robert Morris awards bachelor's, master's, and doctoral degrees and post-bachelor's certificates. Challenging opportunities include advanced placement credit, accelerated degree programs, an honors program, double majors, independent study, and a senior project. Special programs include cooperative education, internships, summer session for credit, off-campus study, study-abroad, and Army and Air Force ROTC. The most frequently chosen baccalaureate fields are business/marketing, computer/information sciences, and communications/communication technologies. The faculty at Robert Morris has 122 full-time members, 81% with terminal degrees. The student-faculty ratio is 19:1.

Students of Robert Morris The student body totals 4,726, of whom 3,747 are undergraduates. 49.2% are women and 50.8% are men. Students come from 27 states and territories and 21 other countries. 92% are from Pennsylvania. 1.7% are international students. 74% returned for their sophomore year.

Applying Robert Morris requires SAT I or ACT, a high school transcript, and a minimum high school GPA of 2.5, and in some cases an interview. The school recommends an interview, recommendations, and a minimum high school GPA of 3.0. Application deadline: 7/1; 5/1 priority date for financial aid. Deferred admission is possible.

ROBERTS WESLEYAN COLLEGE

Rochester, NY

Suburban setting ■ Private ■ Independent Religious ■ Coed

Web site: www.roberts.edu

Contact: Ms. Linda Kurtz, Dean of Admissions, 2301 Westside Drive, Rochester, NY 14624

Telephone: 585-594-6400 or toll-free 800-777-4RWC **Fax:** 585-594-6371

E-mail: admissions@roberts.edu

Getting in Last Year 708 applied; 82% were accepted; 250 enrolled (43%).

Financial Matters $15,774 tuition and fees (2002–03); $5746 room and board; 81% average percent of need met; $13,271 average financial aid amount received per undergraduate (2001–02).

Academics Roberts Wesleyan awards associate, bachelor's, and master's degrees. Challenging opportunities include advanced placement credit, freshman honors college, an honors program, double majors, independent study, and a senior project. Special programs include cooperative education, internships, summer session for credit, off-campus study, study-abroad, and Army and Air Force ROTC. The most frequently chosen baccalaureate fields are business/marketing, education, and health professions and related sciences. The faculty at Roberts Wesleyan has 84 full-time members, 63% with terminal degrees. The student-faculty ratio is 14:1.

Students of Roberts Wesleyan The student body totals 1,835, of whom 1,266 are undergraduates. 67.3% are women and 32.7% are men. Students come from 21 states and territories and 18 other countries. 88% are from New York. 4.3% are international students. 81% returned for their sophomore year.

Applying Roberts Wesleyan requires an essay, SAT I or ACT, a high school transcript, and 2 recommendations. The school recommends an interview and a minimum high school GPA of 2.5. Application deadline: 2/1; 3/15 priority date for financial aid. Early and deferred admission are possible.

ROCHESTER COLLEGE

Rochester Hills, MI

Suburban setting ■ Private ■ Independent Religious ■ Coed

Web site: www.rc.edu
Contact: Mr. Larry Norman, Vice President for Enrollment Management, 800 West Avon Road, Rochester Hills, MI 48307-2764
Telephone: 248-218-2032 or toll-free 800-521-6010 **Fax:** 248-218-2005
E-mail: admissions@rc.edu

Getting in Last Year 385 applied; 42% were accepted; 119 enrolled (73%).

Financial Matters $11,035 tuition and fees (2002–03); $5624 room and board; 78% average percent of need met; $9838 average financial aid amount received per undergraduate.

Academics Rochester College awards associate and bachelor's degrees. Challenging opportunities include advanced placement credit, accelerated degree programs, double majors, and independent study. Special programs include internships, summer session for credit, off-campus study, and study-abroad. The most frequently chosen baccalaureate fields are business/marketing, education, and psychology. The faculty at Rochester College has 37 full-time members, 65% with terminal degrees. The student-faculty ratio is 13:1.

Students of Rochester College The student body is made up of 932 undergraduates. 61.1% are women and 38.9% are men. Students come from 18 states and territories and 15 other countries. 87% are from Michigan. 3% are international students. 69% returned for their sophomore year.

Applying Rochester College requires SAT I or ACT and a high school transcript, and in some cases an interview. The school recommends an essay, 1 recommendation, and a minimum high school GPA of 2.25. Application deadline: rolling admissions; 4/1 priority date for financial aid. Early and deferred admission are possible.

ROCHESTER INSTITUTE OF TECHNOLOGY

Rochester, NY

Suburban setting ■ Private ■ Independent ■ Coed

Web site: www.rit.edu
Contact: Dr. Daniel Shelley, Director of Undergraduate Admissions, 60 Lomb Memorial Drive, Rochester, NY 14623-5604
Telephone: 585-475-6631 **Fax:** 585-475-7424
E-mail: admissions@rit.edu

Getting in Last Year 8,697 applied; 69% were accepted; 2,342 enrolled (39%).

Financial Matters $19,815 tuition and fees (2002–03); $7527 room and board; 90% average percent of need met; $15,250 average financial aid amount received per undergraduate (2001–02).

Academics RIT awards associate, bachelor's, master's, and doctoral degrees and post-bachelor's and post-master's certificates. Challenging opportunities include advanced placement credit, accelerated degree programs, student-designed majors, an honors program, independent study, and a senior project. Special programs include cooperative education, internships, summer session for credit, off-campus study, study-abroad, and Army and Air Force ROTC. The most frequently chosen baccalaureate fields are engineering/engineering technologies, visual/performing arts, and computer/information sciences. The faculty at RIT has 684 full-time members, 80% with terminal degrees. The student-faculty ratio is 13:1.

Students of RIT The student body totals 14,634, of whom 12,279 are undergraduates. 30.9% are women and 69.1% are men. Students come from 50 states and territories and 85 other countries. 55% are from New York. 4.8% are international students. 87% returned for their sophomore year.

Applying RIT requires an essay, SAT I or ACT, and a high school transcript, and in some cases portfolio. The school recommends an interview, 1 recommendation, and a minimum high school GPA of 3.0. Application deadline: 3/15; 3/1 priority date for financial aid. Early and deferred admission are possible.

ROCKFORD COLLEGE

Rockford, IL

Suburban setting ■ Private ■ Independent ■ Coed

Web site: www.rockford.edu
Contact: Mr. William Laffey, Director of Admission, Nelson Hall, Rockford, IL 61108-2393
Telephone: 815-226-4050 ext. 3330 or toll-free 800-892-2984 **Fax:** 815-226-2822
E-mail: admission@rockford.edu

Getting in Last Year 654 applied; 59% were accepted; 131 enrolled (34%).

Financial Matters $18,320 tuition and fees (2002–03); $5930 room and board; 99% average percent of need met.

Academics RC awards bachelor's and master's degrees. Challenging opportunities include advanced placement credit, student-designed majors, an honors program, double majors, and a senior project. Special programs include internships, summer session for credit, off-campus study, study-abroad, and Army ROTC. The faculty at RC has 75 full-time members, 68% with terminal degrees. The student-faculty ratio is 10:1.

Students of RC The student body totals 1,280, of whom 976 are undergraduates. 62.5% are women and 37.5% are men. Students come from 8 states and territories and 10 other countries. 96% are from Illinois. 2.7% are international students. 55% returned for their sophomore year.

Applying RC requires SAT I or ACT and a high school transcript, and in some cases an essay, 2 recommendations, and a minimum high school GPA of 2.5. The school recommends an interview, campus visit, and a minimum high school GPA of 2.5. Application deadline: rolling admissions; 4/15 priority date for financial aid. Early and deferred admission are possible.

ROCKHURST UNIVERSITY

Kansas City, MO

Urban setting ■ Private ■ Independent Religious ■ Coed

Web site: www.rockhurst.edu
Contact: Mr. Lane Ramey, Director of Freshman Admissions, 1100 Rockhurst Road, Kansas City, MO 64110-2561
Telephone: 816-501-4100 or toll-free 800-842-6776 **Fax:** 816-501-4142
E-mail: admission@rockhurst.edu

Getting in Last Year 1,032 applied; 83% were accepted; 214 enrolled (25%).

Financial Matters $16,380 tuition and fees (2002–03); $5200 room and board; 79% average percent of need met; $14,306 average financial aid amount received per undergraduate.

Academics Rockhurst awards bachelor's and master's degrees and post-bachelor's certificates. Challenging opportunities include advanced placement credit, accelerated degree programs, freshman honors college, an honors program, double majors, independent study, and a senior project. Special programs include cooperative education, internships, summer session for credit, off-campus study, study-abroad, and Army ROTC. The most frequently chosen baccalaureate fields are business/marketing, health professions and related sciences, and psychology. The faculty at Rockhurst has 131 full-time members, 80% with terminal degrees. The student-faculty ratio is 10:1.

Students of Rockhurst The student body totals 2,870, of whom 2,020 are undergraduates. 56.2% are women and 43.8% are men. Students come from 26 states and territories and 13 other countries. 72% are from Missouri. 2.5% are international students. 79% returned for their sophomore year.

Applying Rockhurst requires SAT I or ACT, a high school transcript, 1 recommendation, and a minimum high school GPA of 2.0, and in some cases an essay and an interview. Application deadline: 6/30; 3/1 priority date for financial aid. Deferred admission is possible.

ROCKY MOUNTAIN COLLEGE

Billings, MT

Urban setting ■ Private ■ Independent Religious ■ Coed

Web site: www.rocky.edu
Contact: Ms. LynAnn Henderson, Director of Admissions, 1511 Poly Drive, Billings, MT 59102
Telephone: 406-657-1026 or toll-free 800-877-6259 **Fax:** 406-259-9751
E-mail: admissions@rocky.edu

Getting in Last Year 575 applied; 82% were accepted; 160 enrolled (34%).

Financial Matters $13,465 tuition and fees (2002–03); $4800 room and board; 70% average percent of need met; $9919 average financial aid amount received per undergraduate.

Academics Rocky awards associate and bachelor's degrees. Challenging opportunities include advanced placement credit, accelerated degree programs, student-designed majors, an honors program, double majors, independent study, and a senior project. Special programs include cooperative education, internships, summer session for credit, and study-abroad. The most frequently chosen baccalaureate fields are business/marketing, education, and health professions and related sciences. The faculty at Rocky has 44 full-time members, 70% with terminal degrees. The student-faculty ratio is 13:1.

Students of Rocky The student body is made up of 807 undergraduates. 52.8% are women and 47.2% are men. Students come from 39 states and territories and 20 other countries. 72% are from Montana. 5% are international students. 67% returned for their sophomore year.

Applying Rocky requires SAT I or ACT, a high school transcript, and a minimum high school GPA of 2.5, and in some cases an essay and an interview. The school recommends ACT and 2 recommendations. Application deadline: rolling admissions. Early and deferred admission are possible.

ROCKY MOUNTAIN COLLEGE

Calgary, AB Canada

Suburban setting ■ Private ■ Independent Religious ■ Coed

Web site: www.rockymountaincollege.ca

Contact: Mr. Randy Young, 4039 Brentwood Road, NW, Calgary, AB T2L 1L1 Canada
Telephone: 403-284-5100 ext. 222
E-mail: rockymc@rockymountaincollege.ca

Getting in Last Year 169 applied; 96% were accepted.

Financial Matters $6220 tuition and fees (2002–03).

Academics Rocky Mountain College awards bachelor's degrees. Challenging opportunities include advanced placement credit and a senior project. Special programs include internships and summer session for credit. The faculty at Rocky Mountain College has 14 full-time members, 14% with terminal degrees.

Students of Rocky Mountain College The student body is made up of 342 undergraduates. Students come from 6 states and territories and 2 other countries. 62% returned for their sophomore year.

Applying Rocky Mountain College requires an essay, a high school transcript, and 2 recommendations, and in some cases an interview. Application deadline: rolling admissions. Deferred admission is possible.

ROCKY MOUNTAIN COLLEGE OF ART & DESIGN

Denver, CO

Urban setting ■ Private ■ Proprietary ■ Coed

Web site: www.rmcad.edu
Contact: Ms. Sandy Sprock, Director of Admissions, 6875 East Evans Avenue, Denver, CO 80224-2329
Telephone: 303-753-6046 or toll-free 800-888-ARTS **Fax:** 303-759-4970
E-mail: admit@rmcad.edu

Getting in Last Year 140 applied; 92% were accepted; 54 enrolled (42%).

Financial Matters $12,426 tuition and fees (2002–03); $3110 room only; 55% average percent of need met; $3033 average financial aid amount received per undergraduate (2001–02).

Academics Rocky Mountain College of Art & Design awards bachelor's degrees. Challenging opportunities include advanced placement credit, accelerated degree programs, double majors, independent study, and a senior project. Special programs include cooperative education, internships, summer session for credit, and study-abroad. The most frequently chosen baccalaureate field is visual/performing arts. The faculty at Rocky Mountain College of Art & Design has 18 full-time members, 89% with terminal degrees. The student-faculty ratio is 12:1.

Students of Rocky Mountain College of Art & Design The student body is made up of 503 undergraduates. 54.9% are women and 45.1% are men. Students come from 36 states and territories and 4 other countries. 76% are from Colorado. 1.1% are international students.

Applying Rocky Mountain College of Art & Design requires an essay, a high school transcript, an interview, 1 recommendation, portfolio, and a minimum high school GPA of 2.0, and in some cases SAT I and SAT II or ACT. Application deadline: rolling admissions; 3/15 priority date for financial aid. Deferred admission is possible.

ROGERS STATE UNIVERSITY

Claremore, OK

Small-town setting ■ Public ■ State-supported ■ Coed

Web site: www.rsu.edu
Contact: Ms. Becky Noah, Director of Enrollment Management, Roger's State University, Office of Admissions, 1701 West Will Rogers Boulevard, Claremore, OK 74017
Telephone: 918-343-7545 or toll-free 800-256-7511 **Fax:** 918-343-7595
E-mail: shunter@rsu.edu

Getting in Last Year 1,001 applied; 89% were accepted; 763 enrolled (86%).

Financial Matters $1839 resident tuition and fees (2002–03); $4233 nonresident tuition and fees (2002–03); $3321 room only; 76% average percent of need met.

Academics Rogers State University awards associate and bachelor's degrees. Challenging opportunities include advanced placement credit, double majors, independent study, and a senior project. Special programs include cooperative education, internships, summer session for credit, off-campus study, and Air Force ROTC. The faculty at Rogers State University has 88 full-time members, 52% with terminal degrees. The student-faculty ratio is 19:1.

Students of Rogers State University The student body is made up of 3,300 undergraduates. 62.9% are women and 37.1% are men. 97% are from Oklahoma. 51% returned for their sophomore year.

Applying Rogers State University requires a high school transcript, and in some cases ACT, ACT COMPASS (for students over 21), and a minimum high school GPA of 2.7. Application deadline: rolling admissions.

ROGER WILLIAMS UNIVERSITY

Bristol, RI

Small-town setting ■ Private ■ Independent ■ Coed

Web site: www.rwu.edu
Contact: Ms. Julie H. Cairns, Director of Freshman Admission, 1 Old Ferry Road, Bristol, RI 02809
Telephone: 401-254-3500 or toll-free 800-458-7144 (out-of-state)
Fax: 401-254-3557
E-mail: admit@rwu.edu

Getting in Last Year 4,793 applied; 84% were accepted; 981 enrolled (24%).

Financial Matters $20,110 tuition and fees (2002–03); $8930 room and board; 86% average percent of need met; $14,500 average financial aid amount received per undergraduate.

Academics RWU awards associate, bachelor's, master's, and first-professional degrees. Challenging opportunities include advanced placement credit, student-designed majors, freshman honors college, an honors program, double majors, independent study, and a senior project. Special programs include cooperative education, internships, summer session for credit, study-abroad, and Army ROTC. The most frequently chosen baccalaureate fields are business/marketing, engineering/engineering technologies, and architecture. The faculty at RWU has 144 full-time members, 83% with terminal degrees. The student-faculty ratio is 16:1.

Students of RWU The student body totals 4,851, of whom 4,127 are undergraduates. 50.8% are women and 49.2% are men. Students come from 27 states and territories and 34 other countries. 15% are from Rhode Island. 1.6% are international students. 81% returned for their sophomore year.

Applying RWU requires an essay, SAT I or ACT, a high school transcript, recommendations, and a minimum high school GPA of 2.0. The school recommends an interview and 2.0 recommendations. Application deadline: rolling admissions; 2/1 for financial aid. Deferred admission is possible.

ROLLINS COLLEGE

Winter Park, FL

Suburban setting ■ Private ■ Independent ■ Coed

Web site: www.rollins.edu
Contact: Mr. David Erdmann, Dean of Admission and Enrollment, 1000 Holt Avenue, Bpx 2720, Winter Park, FL 32789-4499
Telephone: 407-646-2161 **Fax:** 407-646-1502
E-mail: admission@rollins.edu

Getting in Last Year 2,307 applied; 63% were accepted; 467 enrolled (32%).

Financial Matters $24,958 tuition and fees (2002–03); $7652 room and board; 91% average percent of need met; $26,716 average financial aid amount received per undergraduate.

Academics Rollins awards bachelor's and master's degrees. Challenging opportunities include advanced placement credit, accelerated degree programs, student-designed majors, an honors program, double majors, independent study, and a senior project. Special programs include internships, off-campus study, and study-abroad. The most frequently chosen baccalaureate fields are social sciences and history, visual/performing arts, and psychology. The faculty at Rollins has 177 full-time members, 81% with terminal degrees. The student-faculty ratio is 11:1.

Students of Rollins The student body totals 2,505, of whom 1,723 are undergraduates. 59.6% are women and 40.4% are men. Students come from 44 states and territories and 31 other countries. 52% are from Florida. 3.9% are international students. 84% returned for their sophomore year.

Applying Rollins requires an essay, SAT I or ACT, a high school transcript, and 1 recommendation. The school recommends SAT II Subject Tests and an interview. Application deadline: 2/15; 2/15 priority date for financial aid. Early and deferred admission are possible.

ROOSEVELT UNIVERSITY

Chicago, IL

Urban setting ■ Private ■ Independent ■ Coed

Web site: www.roosevelt.edu
Contact: Mr. Brian Lynch, Director of Admission, 430 South Michigan Avenue, Room 576, Chicago, IL 60605-1394
Telephone: 312-341-2101 or toll-free 877-APPLYRU **Fax:** 312-341-3523
E-mail: applyru@roosevelt.edu

Getting in Last Year 935 applied; 67% were accepted; 286 enrolled (45%).

Financial Matters $14,660 tuition and fees (2002–03); $6500 room and board; 75% average percent of need met; $11,395 average financial aid amount received per undergraduate.

Academics Roosevelt awards bachelor's, master's, and doctoral degrees. Challenging opportunities include advanced placement credit, accelerated degree programs, student-designed majors, an honors program, double majors, independent study, and a senior project. Special programs include internships, summer session for credit, and off-campus study. The most frequently chosen baccalaureate fields are business/marketing, social sciences and history, and psychology. The faculty at Roosevelt has 210 full-time members. The student-faculty ratio is 11:1.

Students of Roosevelt The student body totals 7,321, of whom 4,307 are undergraduates. 66.9% are women and 33.1% are men. Students come from 24

Roosevelt University (continued)

states and territories and 70 other countries. 96% are from Illinois. 3.4% are international students. 63% returned for their sophomore year.

Applying Roosevelt requires an essay, SAT I or ACT, a high school transcript, audition for music and theater programs, and a minimum high school GPA of 2.0, and in some cases an interview and recommendations. Application deadline: 9/1; 4/1 priority date for financial aid. Deferred admission is possible.

ROSE-HULMAN INSTITUTE OF TECHNOLOGY

Terre Haute, IN

Rural setting ■ Private ■ Independent ■ Coed, Primarily Men

Web site: www.rose-hulman.edu

Contact: Mr. Charles G. Howard, Dean of Admissions/Vice President, 5500 Wabash Avenue, Terre Haute, IN 47803-3920

Telephone: 812-877-8213 or toll-free 800-552-0725 (in-state), 800-248-7448 (out-of-state) **Fax:** 812-877-8941

E-mail: admis.ofc@rose-hulman.edu

Getting in Last Year 3,207 applied; 65% were accepted; 451 enrolled (22%).

Financial Matters $23,425 tuition and fees (2002–03); $6348 room and board; 60% average percent of need met; $14,471 average financial aid amount received per undergraduate (2001–02).

Academics Rose-Hulman awards bachelor's and master's degrees. Challenging opportunities include advanced placement credit, accelerated degree programs, an honors program, double majors, independent study, and a senior project. Special programs include cooperative education, summer session for credit, off-campus study, study-abroad, and Army and Air Force ROTC. The most frequently chosen baccalaureate fields are engineering/engineering technologies, computer/information sciences, and physical sciences. The faculty at Rose-Hulman has 126 full-time members, 98% with terminal degrees. The student-faculty ratio is 13:1.

Students of Rose-Hulman The student body totals 1,804, of whom 1,642 are undergraduates. 18.1% are women and 81.9% are men. Students come from 48 states and territories and 9 other countries. 49% are from Indiana. 0.9% are international students. 93% returned for their sophomore year.

Applying Rose-Hulman requires SAT I or ACT, a high school transcript, and 1 recommendation. The school recommends an essay and an interview. Application deadline: 3/1; 3/1 priority date for financial aid. Deferred admission is possible.

ROSEMONT COLLEGE

Rosemont, PA

Suburban setting ■ Private ■ Independent Religious ■ Women Only

Web site: www.rosemont.edu

Contact: Ms. Rennie H. Andrews, Dean of Admissions, 1400 Montgomery Avenue, Rosemont, PA 19010

Telephone: 610-527-0200 ext. 2952 or toll-free 800-331-0708 **Fax:** 610-520-4399

E-mail: admissions@rosemont.edu

Getting in Last Year 234 applied; 77% were accepted; 76 enrolled (42%).

Financial Matters $17,600 tuition and fees (2002–03); $7700 room and board; 93% average percent of need met; $17,939 average financial aid amount received per undergraduate.

Academics Rosemont College awards bachelor's and master's degrees and post-bachelor's certificates. Challenging opportunities include advanced placement credit, accelerated degree programs, student-designed majors, an honors program, double majors, independent study, and a senior project. Special programs include internships, summer session for credit, off-campus study, study-abroad, and Army ROTC. The most frequently chosen baccalaureate fields are psychology, social sciences and history, and business/marketing. The faculty at Rosemont College has 35 full-time members, 91% with terminal degrees. The student-faculty ratio is 8:1.

Students of Rosemont College The student body totals 1,066, of whom 732 are undergraduates. Students come from 17 states and territories. 69% are from Pennsylvania. 1.8% are international students. 72% returned for their sophomore year.

Applying Rosemont College requires an essay, SAT I or ACT, a high school transcript, and 2 recommendations. The school recommends an interview and a minimum high school GPA of 3.0. Application deadline: rolling admissions; 3/1 priority date for financial aid. Early and deferred admission are possible.

ROWAN UNIVERSITY

Glassboro, NJ

Small-town setting ■ Public ■ State-supported ■ Coed

Web site: www.rowan.edu

Contact: Mr. Marvin G. Sills, Director of Admissions, 201 Mullica Hill Road, Glassboro, NJ 08028

Telephone: 856-256-4200 or toll-free 800-447-1165 (in-state) **Fax:** 856-256-4430

E-mail: admissions@rowan.edu

Getting in Last Year 6,881 applied; 44% were accepted; 1,266 enrolled (41%).

Financial Matters $6658 resident tuition and fees (2002–03); $11,608 nonresident tuition and fees (2002–03); $6846 room and board; 91% average percent of need met; $6447 average financial aid amount received per undergraduate (2001–02).

Academics Rowan awards bachelor's, master's, and doctoral degrees. Challenging opportunities include advanced placement credit, an honors program, double majors, independent study, and a senior project. Special programs include internships, summer session for credit, study-abroad, and Army ROTC. The most frequently chosen baccalaureate fields are education, communications/communication technologies, and business/marketing. The faculty at Rowan has 371 full-time members, 77% with terminal degrees. The student-faculty ratio is 14:1.

Students of Rowan The student body totals 9,685, of whom 8,324 are undergraduates. 58% are women and 42% are men. Students come from 16 states and territories. 98% are from New Jersey. 87% returned for their sophomore year.

Applying Rowan requires an essay, SAT I or ACT, a high school transcript, 1 recommendation, and a minimum high school GPA of 2.0, and in some cases an interview. The school recommends SAT I and a minimum high school GPA of 3.0. Application deadline: 3/15. Deferred admission is possible.

ROYAL ROADS UNIVERSITY

Victoria, BC Canada

Suburban setting ■ Public ■ Coed

Web site: www.royalroads.ca

Contact: Ms. Ann Nightingale, Registrar and Director, Learner Services, Office of Learner Services and Registrar, 2005 Sooke Road, Victoria, BC V9B 5Y2 Canada

Telephone: 250-391-2552 or toll-free 800-788-8028

E-mail: rruregistrar@royalroads.ca

Financial Matters $4110 nonresident tuition and fees (2002–03).

Academics RRU awards bachelor's and master's degrees. Challenging opportunities include advanced placement credit, accelerated degree programs, and a senior project. Special programs include summer session for credit and off-campus study. The most frequently chosen baccalaureate fields are business/marketing and natural resources/environmental science. The faculty at RRU has 15 full-time members, 100% with terminal degrees. The student-faculty ratio is 23:1.

Students of RRU The student body totals 2,984, of whom 410 are undergraduates. 43.7% are women and 56.3% are men. Students come from 10 states and territories and 3 other countries. 85% are from British Columbia. 0.7% are international students.

RUSH UNIVERSITY

Chicago, IL

Urban setting ■ Private ■ Independent ■ Coed

Web site: www.rushu.rush.edu

Contact: Ms. Hicela Castruita Woods, Director of College Admission Services, 600 S. Paulina - Suite 440, College Admissions Services, Chicago, IL 60612-3878

Telephone: 312-942-7100 **Fax:** 312-942-2219

E-mail: rush_admissions@rush.edu

Getting in Last Year 154 applied; 54% were accepted.

Financial Matters $14,880 tuition and fees (2002–03); $7250 room only; 100% average percent of need met.

Academics Rush awards bachelor's, master's, doctoral, and first-professional degrees and post-master's certificates. Accelerated degree programs are a challenging opportunity. The most frequently chosen baccalaureate field is biological/life sciences. The faculty at Rush has 796 full-time members. The student-faculty ratio is 8:1.

Students of Rush The student body totals 1,232, of whom 133 are undergraduates. 92.5% are women and 7.5% are men. Students come from 14 states and territories and 4 other countries. 94% are from Illinois. 1.5% are international students.

Applying Application deadline: 4/1 for financial aid, with a 3/1 priority date.

RUSSELL SAGE COLLEGE

Troy, NY

Urban setting ■ Private ■ Independent ■ Women Only

Web site: www.sage.edu/html/rsc/welcome.html

Contact: Ms. Beth Robertson, Senior Associate Director of Admissions, 45 Ferry Street, Troy, NY 12180

Telephone: 518-244-2217 or toll-free 888-VERY-SAGE (in-state), 888-VERY SAGE (out-of-state) **Fax:** 518-244-6880

E-mail: rscadm@sage.edu

Getting in Last Year 367 applied; 57% were accepted; 97 enrolled (47%).

Financial Matters $18,820 tuition and fees (2002–03); $6526 room and board.

Academics Russell Sage awards bachelor's degrees. Challenging opportunities include advanced placement credit, accelerated degree programs, student-designed majors, freshman honors college, an honors program, double majors, independent study, and a senior project. Special programs include cooperative education, internships, summer session for credit, off-campus study, study-abroad, and Army and Air Force ROTC. The most frequently chosen baccalaureate fields are health professions and related sciences, education, and biological/life sciences. The faculty at Russell Sage has 56 full-time members, 68% with terminal degrees. The student-faculty ratio is 11:1.

Students of Russell Sage The student body is made up of 787 undergraduates. Students come from 15 states and territories and 2 other countries. 91% are from New York. 0.3% are international students. 88% returned for their sophomore year.

Applying Russell Sage requires an essay, SAT I or ACT, a high school transcript, 2 recommendations, and a minimum high school GPA of 2.0. The school recommends an interview. Application deadline: 8/1; 3/1 priority date for financial aid. Early and deferred admission are possible.

RUST COLLEGE

Holly Springs, MS

Rural setting ■ Private ■ Independent Religious ■ Coed

Web site: www.rustcollege.edu
Contact: Mr. Johnny McDonald, Director of Enrollment Services, 150 Rust Avenue, Holly Springs, MS 38635-2328
Telephone: 601-252-8000 ext. 4065 or toll-free 888-886-8492 ext. 4065 **Fax:** 662-252-8895
E-mail: admissions@rustcollege.edu

Getting in Last Year 3,400 applied; 49% were accepted; 201 enrolled (12%).

Financial Matters $5735 tuition and fees (2002–03); $2600 room and board; 69% average percent of need met; $5886 average financial aid amount received per undergraduate.

Academics Rust awards associate and bachelor's degrees. Challenging opportunities include accelerated degree programs, an honors program, independent study, and a senior project. Special programs include cooperative education, internships, summer session for credit, study-abroad, and Army ROTC. The most frequently chosen baccalaureate fields are business/marketing, biological/life sciences, and communications/communication technologies. The faculty at Rust has 43 full-time members, 47% with terminal degrees. The student-faculty ratio is 19:1.

Students of Rust The student body is made up of 943 undergraduates. 66.9% are women and 33.1% are men. Students come from 22 states and territories and 7 other countries. 69% are from Mississippi. 6.9% are international students. 48% returned for their sophomore year.

Applying Rust requires ACT, a high school transcript, 3 recommendations, and a minimum high school GPA of 2.0, and in some cases an essay. Application deadline: 7/15; 4/1 priority date for financial aid. Deferred admission is possible.

RUTGERS, THE STATE UNIVERSITY OF NEW JERSEY, CAMDEN

Camden, NJ

Public ■ State-supported ■ Coed

Web site: www.rutgers.edu
Contact: Ms. Diane Williams Harris, Associate Director of University Undergraduate Admissions, 65 Davidson Road, Piscataway, NJ 08854-8097
Telephone: 732-932-4636 **Fax:** 856-225-6498

Getting in Last Year 6,430 applied; 54% were accepted; 455 enrolled (13%).

Financial Matters $7126 resident tuition and fees (2002–03); $13,102 nonresident tuition and fees (2002–03); $7106 room and board; 91% average percent of need met; $8903 average financial aid amount received per undergraduate.

Academics Rutgers, The State University of New Jersey, Camden awards bachelor's, master's, and first-professional degrees. Challenging opportunities include advanced placement credit, accelerated degree programs, student-designed majors, freshman honors college, an honors program, double majors, independent study, and a senior project. Special programs include cooperative education, summer session for credit, study-abroad, and Army and Air Force ROTC. The most frequently chosen baccalaureate fields are business/marketing, psychology, and social sciences and history. The faculty at Rutgers, The State University of New Jersey, Camden has 222 full-time members, 99% with terminal degrees. The student-faculty ratio is 11:1.

Students of Rutgers, The State University of New Jersey, Camden The student body totals 5,248, of whom 3,800 are undergraduates. 59.4% are women and 40.6% are men. 96% are from New Jersey. 1.1% are international students.

Applying Rutgers, The State University of New Jersey, Camden requires SAT I or ACT and a high school transcript, and in some cases SAT II Subject Tests. Application deadline: rolling admissions; 3/15 priority date for financial aid. Early admission is possible.

RUTGERS, THE STATE UNIVERSITY OF NEW JERSEY, NEWARK

Newark, NJ

Public ■ State-supported ■ Coed

Web site: www.rutgers.edu
Contact: Ms. Diane William Harris, Associate Director of University Undergraduate Admissions, 65 Davidson Road, Piscataway, NJ 08854-8097
Telephone: 732-932-4636 **Fax:** 973-353-1440

Getting in Last Year 9,168 applied; 50% were accepted; 1,019 enrolled (22%).

Financial Matters $7007 resident tuition and fees (2002–03); $12,983 nonresident tuition and fees (2002–03); $7570 room and board; 83% average percent of need met; $9019 average financial aid amount received per undergraduate.

Academics Rutgers, The State University of New Jersey, Newark awards bachelor's, master's, doctoral, and first-professional degrees. Challenging opportunities include advanced placement credit, accelerated degree programs, student-designed majors, freshman honors college, an honors program, double majors, independent study, and a senior project. Special programs include internships, summer session for credit, off-campus study, study-abroad, and Army and Air Force ROTC. The most frequently chosen baccalaureate fields are business/marketing, health professions and related sciences, and protective services/public administration. The faculty at Rutgers, The State University of New Jersey, Newark has 382 full-time members, 99% with terminal degrees. The student-faculty ratio is 12:1.

Students of Rutgers, The State University of New Jersey, Newark The student body totals 10,346, of whom 6,706 are undergraduates. 57.9% are women and 42.1% are men. 91% are from New Jersey. 3.9% are international students.

Applying Rutgers, The State University of New Jersey, Newark requires SAT I or ACT and a high school transcript, and in some cases SAT II Subject Tests. Application deadline: rolling admissions; 3/15 priority date for financial aid. Early admission is possible.

RUTGERS, THE STATE UNIVERSITY OF NEW JERSEY, NEW BRUNSWICK

New Brunswick, NJ

Public ■ State-supported ■ Coed

Web site: www.rutgers.edu
Contact: Ms. Diane Williams Harris, Associate Director of University Undergraduate Admissions, 65 Davidson Road, Piscataway, NJ 08854-8097
Telephone: 732-932-4636 **Fax:** 732-445-0237

Getting in Last Year 26,678 applied; 55% were accepted; 5,086 enrolled (34%).

Financial Matters $7308 resident tuition and fees (2002–03); $13,284 nonresident tuition and fees (2002–03); $6970 room and board; 86% average percent of need met; $9952 average financial aid amount received per undergraduate.

Academics Rutgers, The State University of New Jersey, New Brunswick awards bachelor's, master's, doctoral, and first-professional degrees. Challenging opportunities include advanced placement credit, accelerated degree programs, student-designed majors, an honors program, double majors, independent study, and a senior project. Special programs include cooperative education, study-abroad, and Army and Air Force ROTC. The most frequently chosen baccalaureate fields are social sciences and history, psychology, and biological/life sciences. The faculty at Rutgers, The State University of New Jersey, New Brunswick has 1,522 full-time members, 99% with terminal degrees. The student-faculty ratio is 14:1.

Students of Rutgers, The State University of New Jersey, New Brunswick The student body totals 35,886, of whom 28,070 are undergraduates. 52.8% are women and 47.2% are men. 92% are from New Jersey. 2.7% are international students.

Applying Rutgers, The State University of New Jersey, New Brunswick requires SAT I or ACT and a high school transcript, and in some cases SAT II: Writing Test. Application deadline: rolling admissions; 3/15 priority date for financial aid. Early admission is possible.

RYERSON UNIVERSITY

Toronto, ON Canada

Urban setting ■ Public ■ Coed

Web site: www.ryerson.ca
Contact: Office of Admissions, 350 Victoria Street, Toronto, ON M5B 2K3 Canada
Telephone: 416-979-5036 **Fax:** 416-979-5221
E-mail: inquire@ryerson.ca

Getting in Last Year 4,068 enrolled.

Financial Matters $4691 resident tuition and fees (2002–03); $6807 room and board.

Academics Ryerson awards bachelor's and master's degrees. Challenging opportunities include advanced placement credit, an honors program, double majors, and a senior project. Special programs include cooperative education, internships, summer session for credit, off-campus study, and study-abroad. The faculty at Ryerson has 528 full-time members.

Ryerson University (continued)

Students of Ryerson The student body totals 24,437, of whom 24,041 are undergraduates. 55.8% are women and 44.2% are men.

Applying Ryerson requires a high school transcript, and in some cases an essay, an interview, recommendations, and portfolio, audition, entrance examination. Application deadline: 1/15 for financial aid.

SACRED HEART MAJOR SEMINARY

Detroit, MI

Urban setting ■ *Private* ■ *Independent Religious* ■ *Coed*

Contact: Fr. Patrick Halfpenny, Vice Rector, 2701 Chicago Boulevard, Detroit, MI 48206

Telephone: 313-883-8552

Getting in Last Year 2 applied; 100% were accepted.

Financial Matters $7429 tuition and fees (2002–03); $4914 room and board; 67% average percent of need met; $3000 average financial aid amount received per undergraduate.

Academics Sacred Heart Major Seminary awards associate, bachelor's, master's, and first-professional degrees. Challenging opportunities include advanced placement credit, independent study, and a senior project. Off-campus study is a special program. The most frequently chosen baccalaureate field is liberal arts/general studies. The faculty at Sacred Heart Major Seminary has 14 full-time members, 100% with terminal degrees. The student-faculty ratio is 9:1.

Students of Sacred Heart Major Seminary The student body totals 387, of whom 260 are undergraduates. Students come from 5 states and territories. 72% are from Michigan. 2.4% are international students. 100% returned for their sophomore year.

Applying Sacred Heart Major Seminary requires an essay, SAT I or ACT, a high school transcript, an interview, 1 recommendation, and a minimum high school GPA of 2.0. Application deadline: 7/31. Deferred admission is possible.

SACRED HEART UNIVERSITY

Fairfield, CT

Suburban setting ■ *Private* ■ *Independent Religious* ■ *Coed*

Web site: www.sacredheart.edu

Contact: Ms. Karen N. Guastelle, Dean of Undergraduate Admissions, 5151 Park Avenue, Fairfield, CT 06825-1000

Telephone: 203-371-7880 **Fax:** 203-365-7607

E-mail: enroll@sacredheart.edu

Getting in Last Year 4,642 applied; 69% were accepted; 797 enrolled (25%).

Financial Matters $19,260 tuition and fees (2002–03); $8430 room and board; 71% average percent of need met; $12,614 average financial aid amount received per undergraduate.

Academics Sacred Heart University awards associate, bachelor's, and master's degrees and post-bachelor's and post-master's certificates (also offers part-time program with significant enrollment not reflected in profile). Challenging opportunities include advanced placement credit, accelerated degree programs, student-designed majors, an honors program, double majors, independent study, and a senior project. Special programs include cooperative education, internships, summer session for credit, off-campus study, study-abroad, and Army ROTC. The most frequently chosen baccalaureate fields are business/marketing, psychology, and biological/life sciences. The faculty at Sacred Heart University has 160 full-time members, 76% with terminal degrees. The student-faculty ratio is 13:1.

Students of Sacred Heart University The student body totals 6,028, of whom 4,207 are undergraduates. 61.9% are women and 38.1% are men. Students come from 25 states and territories and 20 other countries. 39% are from Connecticut. 1.1% are international students. 81% returned for their sophomore year.

Applying Sacred Heart University requires an essay, SAT I or ACT, a high school transcript, 1 recommendation, and a minimum high school GPA of 3.0. The school recommends an interview and a minimum high school GPA of 3.2. Application deadline: rolling admissions; 2/15 priority date for financial aid. Early and deferred admission are possible.

SAGE COLLEGE OF ALBANY

Albany, NY

Urban setting ■ *Private* ■ *Independent* ■ *Coed*

Web site: www.sage.edu/SCA

Contact: Mr. Rob Janeski, Director of Admission, 140 New Scotland Avenue, Albany, NY 12208

Telephone: 518-292-1730 or toll-free 888-VERY-SAGE **Fax:** 518-292-1912

E-mail: scaadm@sage.edu

Getting in Last Year 367 applied; 57% were accepted; 121 enrolled (58%).

Financial Matters $14,320 tuition and fees (2002–03); $6626 room and board.

Academics Sage College of Albany awards associate and bachelor's degrees. Challenging opportunities include advanced placement credit, student-designed majors, freshman honors college, an honors program, and independent study. Special programs include cooperative education, internships, summer session for credit, and off-campus study. The most frequently chosen baccalaureate fields are business/marketing, psychology, and protective services/public administration. The faculty at Sage College of Albany has 37 full-time members, 57% with terminal degrees. The student-faculty ratio is 11:1.

Students of Sage College of Albany The student body is made up of 1,097 undergraduates. 71.9% are women and 28.1% are men. Students come from 11 states and territories and 1 other country. 99% are from New York. 0.1% are international students. 65% returned for their sophomore year.

Applying Sage College of Albany requires SAT I or ACT, a high school transcript, 1 recommendation, and portfolio for fine arts program. The school recommends an essay and an interview. Application deadline: 8/1; 3/1 priority date for financial aid. Deferred admission is possible.

SAGINAW VALLEY STATE UNIVERSITY

University Center, MI

Rural setting ■ *Public* ■ *State-supported* ■ *Coed*

Web site: www.svsu.edu

Contact: Mr. James P. Dwyer, Director of Admissions, 7400 Bay Road, University Center, MI 48710-0001

Telephone: 989-964-4200 or toll-free 800-968-9500 **Fax:** 517-790-0180

E-mail: admissions@svsu.edu

Getting in Last Year 3,219 applied; 88% were accepted; 1,162 enrolled (41%).

Financial Matters $4940 resident tuition and fees (2002–03); $9846 nonresident tuition and fees (2002–03); $5485 room and board; 90% average percent of need met; $5382 average financial aid amount received per undergraduate.

Academics SVSU awards bachelor's and master's degrees and post-master's certificates. Challenging opportunities include advanced placement credit, accelerated degree programs, student-designed majors, an honors program, double majors, independent study, and a senior project. Special programs include cooperative education, internships, summer session for credit, and study-abroad. The most frequently chosen baccalaureate fields are education, protective services/public administration, and business/marketing. The faculty at SVSU has 233 full-time members, 78% with terminal degrees. The student-faculty ratio is 29:1.

Students of SVSU The student body totals 9,189, of whom 7,506 are undergraduates. 60.3% are women and 39.7% are men. Students come from 15 states and territories and 50 other countries. 38% are from Michigan. 3.3% are international students. 65% returned for their sophomore year.

Applying SVSU requires SAT I or ACT and a high school transcript. The school recommends a minimum high school GPA of 2.5. Application deadline: rolling admissions; 2/14 priority date for financial aid. Deferred admission is possible.

ST. AMBROSE UNIVERSITY

Davenport, IA

Urban setting ■ *Private* ■ *Independent Religious* ■ *Coed*

Web site: www.sau.edu

Contact: Ms. Meg Higgins, Director of Admissions, 518 West Locust Street, Davenport, IA 52803-2898

Telephone: 563-333-6300 ext. 6311 or toll-free 800-383-2627 **Fax:** 563-333-6297

E-mail: higginsmegf@sau.edu

Getting in Last Year 1,150 applied; 85% were accepted; 393 enrolled (40%).

Financial Matters $15,750 tuition and fees (2002–03); $5560 room and board; 49% average percent of need met; $12,696 average financial aid amount received per undergraduate.

Academics St. Ambrose awards bachelor's, master's, and doctoral degrees and post-bachelor's and post-master's certificates. Challenging opportunities include advanced placement credit, accelerated degree programs, student-designed majors, double majors, independent study, and a senior project. Special programs include cooperative education, internships, summer session for credit, off-campus study, and study-abroad. The most frequently chosen baccalaureate fields are business/marketing, education, and psychology. The faculty at St. Ambrose has 149 full-time members, 75% with terminal degrees. The student-faculty ratio is 17:1.

Students of St. Ambrose The student body totals 3,500, of whom 2,454 are undergraduates. 58.7% are women and 41.3% are men. Students come from 23 states and territories and 15 other countries. 63% are from Iowa. 0.7% are international students. 80% returned for their sophomore year.

Applying St. Ambrose requires SAT I or ACT, a high school transcript, minimum ACT score of 20 or rank in top 50% of high school class, and a minimum high school GPA of 2.5, and in some cases an interview and recommendations. The school recommends ACT and an interview. Application deadline: rolling admissions; 3/15 priority date for financial aid. Deferred admission is possible.

ST. ANDREWS PRESBYTERIAN COLLEGE

Laurinburg, NC

Small-town setting ■ Private ■ Independent Religious ■ Coed

Web site: www.sapc.edu
Contact: Rev. Glenn Batten, Dean for Student Affairs and Enrollment, 1700 Dogwood Mile, Laurinburg, NC 28352
Telephone: 910-277-5555 or toll-free 800-763-0198 **Fax:** 910-277-5087
E-mail: admission@sapc.edu

Getting in Last Year 459 applied; 89% were accepted; 119 enrolled (29%).

Financial Matters $14,760 tuition and fees (2002–03); $5410 room and board; 76% average percent of need met; $11,633 average financial aid amount received per undergraduate (2001–02).

Academics St. Andrews awards bachelor's degrees. Challenging opportunities include advanced placement credit, accelerated degree programs, student-designed majors, an honors program, double majors, independent study, and a senior project. Special programs include internships, summer session for credit, and study-abroad. The most frequently chosen baccalaureate fields are business/marketing, computer/information sciences, and social sciences and history. The faculty at St. Andrews has 33 full-time members, 70% with terminal degrees. The student-faculty ratio is 10:1.

Students of St. Andrews The student body is made up of 613 undergraduates. 62.3% are women and 37.7% are men. Students come from 34 states and territories and 13 other countries. 55% are from North Carolina. 4.1% are international students. 40% returned for their sophomore year.

Applying St. Andrews requires SAT I or ACT, a high school transcript, and 1 recommendation, and in some cases an essay and an interview. The school recommends a minimum high school GPA of 2.0. Application deadline: rolling admissions. Early and deferred admission are possible.

SAINT ANSELM COLLEGE

Manchester, NH

Suburban setting ■ Private ■ Independent Religious ■ Coed

Web site: www.anselm.edu
Contact: Ms. Nancy Davis Griffin, Director of Admissions, 100 Saint Anselm Drive, Manchester, NH 03102-1310
Telephone: 603-641-7500 or toll-free 888-4ANSELM **Fax:** 603-641-7550
E-mail: admissions@anselm.edu

Getting in Last Year 2,907 applied; 73% were accepted; 572 enrolled (27%).

Financial Matters $21,140 tuition and fees (2002–03); $7700 room and board; 89% average percent of need met; $21,933 average financial aid amount received per undergraduate.

Academics Saint Anselm awards bachelor's degrees. Challenging opportunities include advanced placement credit, an honors program, independent study, and a senior project. Special programs include internships, summer session for credit, off-campus study, study-abroad, and Army and Air Force ROTC. The most frequently chosen baccalaureate fields are social sciences and history, business/marketing, and psychology. The faculty at Saint Anselm has 120 full-time members, 93% with terminal degrees. The student-faculty ratio is 14:1.

Students of Saint Anselm The student body is made up of 1,956 undergraduates. 56.6% are women and 43.4% are men. Students come from 28 states and territories and 15 other countries. 23% are from New Hampshire. 1.3% are international students. 80% returned for their sophomore year.

Applying Saint Anselm requires an essay, SAT I or ACT, a high school transcript, 2 recommendations, and a minimum high school GPA of 2.0, and in some cases TOEFL. The school recommends an interview. Application deadline: rolling admissions; 3/1 priority date for financial aid. Early and deferred admission are possible.

SAINT ANTHONY COLLEGE OF NURSING

Rockford, IL

Urban setting ■ Private ■ Independent Religious ■ Coed, Primarily Women

Web site: www.sacn.edu
Contact: Ms. Nancy Sanders, Director of Student Services, 5658 East State Street, Rockford, IL 61108-2468
Telephone: 815-395-5100 **Fax:** 815-395-2275
E-mail: cheryldelgado@sacn.edu

Financial Matters $12,593 tuition and fees (2002–03); 50% average percent of need met; $6800 average financial aid amount received per undergraduate.

Academics SACN awards bachelor's degrees. Challenging opportunities include advanced placement credit, accelerated degree programs, and independent study. Special programs include internships, summer session for credit, and off-campus study. The most frequently chosen baccalaureate field is health professions and related sciences. The faculty at SACN has 10 full-time members, 10% with terminal degrees. The student-faculty ratio is 6:1.

Students of SACN The student body is made up of 91 undergraduates. 94.5% are women and 5.5% are men. Students come from 2 states and territories. 95% are from Illinois.

Applying Application deadline: 5/1 priority date for financial aid. Deferred admission is possible.

ST. AUGUSTINE COLLEGE

Chicago, IL

Urban setting ■ Private ■ Independent ■ Coed

Web site: www.staugustinecollege.edu
Contact: Ms. Soledad Ruiz, Director of Admissions, 1345 West Argyle Street, Chicago, IL 60604-3501
Telephone: 773-878-8756 ext. 243
E-mail: info@staugustinecollege.edu

Getting in Last Year 555 applied; 100% were accepted; 555 enrolled (100%).

Financial Matters $7000 tuition and fees (2002–03); $13,490 average financial aid amount received per undergraduate.

Academics St. Augustine College awards associate and bachelor's degrees (bilingual Spanish/English degree programs). Independent study is a challenging opportunity. Special programs include cooperative education, internships, and summer session for credit. The most frequently chosen baccalaureate field is social sciences and history. The faculty at St. Augustine College has 26 full-time members, 19% with terminal degrees. The student-faculty ratio is 13:1.

Students of St. Augustine College The student body is made up of 1,769 undergraduates. 78.3% are women and 21.7% are men. Students come from 1 state or territory. 68% returned for their sophomore year.

Applying Application deadline: rolling admissions. Deferred admission is possible.

SAINT AUGUSTINE'S COLLEGE

Raleigh, NC

Urban setting ■ Private ■ Independent Religious ■ Coed

Web site: www.st-aug.edu
Contact: Mr. Tim Chapman, Director of Admissions, 1315 Oakwood Avenue, Raleigh, NC 27610-2298
Telephone: 919-516-4011 or toll-free 800-948-1126 **Fax:** 919-516-5805
E-mail: admissions@es.st-aug.edu

Getting in Last Year 1,287 applied; 66% were accepted; 449 enrolled (53%).

Financial Matters $8280 tuition and fees (2002–03); $4960 room and board; 69% average percent of need met; $11,387 average financial aid amount received per undergraduate.

Academics Saint Aug's awards bachelor's degrees. Challenging opportunities include accelerated degree programs, an honors program, double majors, independent study, and a senior project. Special programs include cooperative education, internships, summer session for credit, off-campus study, and Army and Air Force ROTC. The most frequently chosen baccalaureate fields are business/marketing, computer/information sciences, and social sciences and history. The faculty at Saint Aug's has 76 full-time members, 66% with terminal degrees. The student-faculty ratio is 16:1.

Students of Saint Aug's The student body is made up of 1,502 undergraduates. 52.5% are women and 47.5% are men. Students come from 32 states and territories and 22 other countries. 7.1% are international students. 58% returned for their sophomore year.

Applying Saint Aug's requires an essay, SAT I or ACT, a high school transcript, 3 recommendations, and medical history. The school recommends a minimum high school GPA of 2.0. Application deadline: 7/1; 4/15 priority date for financial aid. Deferred admission is possible.

ST. BONAVENTURE UNIVERSITY

St. Bonaventure, NY

Small-town setting ■ Private ■ Independent Religious ■ Coed

Web site: www.sbu.edu
Contact: Mr. James M. DiRisio, Director of Admissions, PO Box D, St. Bonaventure, NY 14778
Telephone: 716-375-2400 or toll-free 800-462-5050 **Fax:** 716-375-4005
E-mail: admissions@sbu.edu

Getting in Last Year 1,704 applied; 88% were accepted; 586 enrolled (39%).

Financial Matters $16,845 tuition and fees (2002–03); $6280 room and board; 87% average percent of need met; $14,448 average financial aid amount received per undergraduate.

Academics St. Bonaventure awards bachelor's and master's degrees and post-bachelor's and post-master's certificates. Challenging opportunities include advanced placement credit, student-designed majors, freshman honors college, an honors program, double majors, independent study, and a senior project. Special programs include internships, summer session for credit, off-campus study, study-abroad, and Army ROTC. The most frequently chosen baccalaureate fields are business/marketing, education, and communications/communication technolo-

St. Bonaventure University (continued)

gies. The faculty at St. Bonaventure has 152 full-time members, 82% with terminal degrees. The student-faculty ratio is 15:1.

Students of St. Bonaventure The student body totals 2,719, of whom 2,229 are undergraduates. 53.7% are women and 46.3% are men. Students come from 35 states and territories and 9 other countries. 79% are from New York. 1.4% are international students. 85% returned for their sophomore year.

Applying St. Bonaventure requires SAT I or ACT, a high school transcript, and 1 recommendation, and in some cases an essay. The school recommends an essay, an interview, 3 recommendations, and a minimum high school GPA of 3.0. Application deadline: 4/15; 2/1 priority date for financial aid. Early and deferred admission are possible.

ST. CHARLES BORROMEO SEMINARY, OVERBROOK

Wynnewood, PA

Suburban setting ■ Private ■ Independent Religious ■ Men Only

Web site: www.scs.edu

Contact: Rev. Joseph Prior, Chief Academic Officer, 100 East Wynnewood Road, Wynnewood, PA 19096

Telephone: 610-785-6271 ext. 271

E-mail: vicerectorscs@adphila.org

Getting in Last Year 8 applied; 100% were accepted; 8 enrolled (100%).

Financial Matters $9150 tuition and fees (2002–03); $6260 room and board.

Academics St. Charles Seminary awards bachelor's, master's, and first-professional degrees (also offers co-ed part-time programs). Challenging opportunities include advanced placement credit, accelerated degree programs, and independent study. Summer session for credit is a special program. The faculty at St. Charles Seminary has 14 full-time members, 50% with terminal degrees. The student-faculty ratio is 8:1.

Students of St. Charles Seminary The student body totals 428, of whom 266 are undergraduates. Students come from 6 states and territories and 2 other countries. 64% are from Pennsylvania. 4.8% are international students. 100% returned for their sophomore year.

Applying St. Charles Seminary requires an essay, a high school transcript, an interview, 3 recommendations, and sponsorship by diocese or religious community. The school recommends SAT I or ACT. Application deadline: 7/15; 4/15 priority date for financial aid. Deferred admission is possible.

ST. CLOUD STATE UNIVERSITY

St. Cloud, MN

Suburban setting ■ Public ■ State-supported ■ Coed

Web site: www.stcloudstate.edu

Contact: Ms. Debbie Tamte-Horan, Director of Admissions, 115 AS Building, 720 4th Avenue South, St. Cloud, MN 56301-4498

Telephone: 320-255-2286 or toll-free 877-654-7278 **Fax:** 320-255-2243

E-mail: scsu4u@stcloudstate.edu

Getting in Last Year 5,733 applied; 76% were accepted; 2,449 enrolled (56%).

Financial Matters $3998 resident tuition and fees (2002–03); $8049 nonresident tuition and fees (2002–03); $3788 room and board; 96% average percent of need met; $5911 average financial aid amount received per undergraduate.

Academics SCSU awards associate, bachelor's, and master's degrees and post-bachelor's and first-professional certificates. Challenging opportunities include advanced placement credit, accelerated degree programs, student-designed majors, an honors program, double majors, independent study, and a senior project. Special programs include internships, summer session for credit, off-campus study, study-abroad, and Army ROTC. The most frequently chosen baccalaureate fields are social sciences and history, business/marketing, and communications/communication technologies. The faculty at SCSU has 659 full-time members. The student-faculty ratio is 19:1.

Students of SCSU The student body totals 15,719, of whom 14,513 are undergraduates. 54.5% are women and 45.5% are men. Students come from 50 states and territories and 84 other countries. 86% are from Minnesota. 5.1% are international students. 71% returned for their sophomore year.

Applying SCSU requires ACT and a high school transcript, and in some cases recommendations. Application deadline: 5/1 priority date for financial aid. Early and deferred admission are possible.

ST. EDWARD'S UNIVERSITY

Austin, TX

Urban setting ■ Private ■ Independent Religious ■ Coed

Web site: www.stedwards.edu

Contact: Ms. Tracy Manier, Director of Admission, 3001 South Congress Avenue, Austin, TX 78704-6489

Telephone: 512-448-8602 or toll-free 800-555-0164 **Fax:** 512-464-8877

E-mail: seu.admit@admin.stedwards.edu

Getting in Last Year 1,511 applied; 70% were accepted; 464 enrolled (44%).

Financial Matters $13,620 tuition and fees (2002–03); $5960 room and board; 69% average percent of need met; $10,873 average financial aid amount received per undergraduate.

Academics St. Edward's awards bachelor's and master's degrees and post-bachelor's certificates. Challenging opportunities include advanced placement credit, an honors program, double majors, and a senior project. Special programs include internships, summer session for credit, study-abroad, and Army and Air Force ROTC. The most frequently chosen baccalaureate fields are liberal arts/general studies, business/marketing, and social sciences and history. The faculty at St. Edward's has 125 full-time members, 78% with terminal degrees. The student-faculty ratio is 15:1.

Students of St. Edward's The student body totals 4,267, of whom 3,402 are undergraduates. 55.9% are women and 44.1% are men. Students come from 31 states and territories and 35 other countries. 96% are from Texas. 2.6% are international students. 78% returned for their sophomore year.

Applying St. Edward's requires an essay, SAT I or ACT, and a high school transcript. The school recommends an interview and recommendations. Application deadline: 7/1. Deferred admission is possible.

ST. FRANCIS COLLEGE

Brooklyn Heights, NY

Urban setting ■ Private ■ Independent Religious ■ Coed

Web site: www.stfranciscollege.edu

Contact: Br. George Larkin, OSF, Dean of Admissions, 180 Remsen Street, Brooklyn Heights, NY 11201-4398

Telephone: 718-489-5200 **Fax:** 718-522-1274

Getting in Last Year 1,510 applied; 87% were accepted; 478 enrolled (36%).

Financial Matters $10,180 tuition and fees (2002–03); 68% average percent of need met; $6940 average financial aid amount received per undergraduate (2001–02).

Academics St. Francis awards associate and bachelor's degrees. Challenging opportunities include advanced placement credit, accelerated degree programs, an honors program, double majors, independent study, and a senior project. Special programs include internships, summer session for credit, study-abroad, and Army and Air Force ROTC. The faculty at St. Francis has 65 full-time members, 80% with terminal degrees. The student-faculty ratio is 18:1.

Students of St. Francis The student body is made up of 2,512 undergraduates. 59.3% are women and 40.7% are men. Students come from 8 states and territories and 46 other countries. 99% are from New York. 13.9% are international students. 76% returned for their sophomore year.

Applying St. Francis requires an essay, SAT I or ACT, a high school transcript, and 1 recommendation, and in some cases an interview. The school recommends an interview. Application deadline: rolling admissions; 2/15 priority date for financial aid. Deferred admission is possible.

SAINT FRANCIS MEDICAL CENTER COLLEGE OF NURSING

Peoria, IL

Urban setting ■ Private ■ Independent Religious ■ Coed, Primarily Women

Web site: www.sfmccon.edu

Contact: Mrs. Janice Farquharson, Director of Admissions and Registrar, 511 Greenleaf Street, Peoria, IL 61603-3783

Telephone: 309-624-8980 **Fax:** 309-624-8973

E-mail: janice.farquharson@osfhealthcare.org

Getting in Last Year 50 applied; 100% were accepted.

Financial Matters $9512 tuition and fees (2002–03); $1680 room only; 86% average percent of need met; $9543 average financial aid amount received per undergraduate (2001–02).

Academics Saint Francis College of Nursing awards bachelor's and master's degrees. Challenging opportunities include advanced placement credit and independent study. Summer session for credit is a special program. The most frequently chosen baccalaureate field is health professions and related sciences. The faculty at Saint Francis College of Nursing has 19 full-time members, 26% with terminal degrees. The student-faculty ratio is 8:1.

Students of Saint Francis College of Nursing The student body totals 181, of whom 154 are undergraduates. 92.9% are women and 7.1% are men. Students come from 1 state or territory. 100% returned for their sophomore year.

Applying Application deadline: 3/1 priority date for financial aid. Deferred admission is possible.

SAINT FRANCIS UNIVERSITY

Loretto, PA

Rural setting ■ Private ■ Independent Religious ■ Coed

Web site: www.francis.edu

Contact: Mr. Evan E. Lipp, Dean for Enrollment Management, PO Box 600, Loretto, PA 15940-0600
Telephone: 814-472-3000 or toll-free 800-342-5732 **Fax:** 814-472-3335
E-mail: admission@sfcpa.edu

Getting in Last Year 1,172 applied; 83% were accepted; 281 enrolled (29%).

Financial Matters $18,024 tuition and fees (2002–03); $7346 room and board; 82% average percent of need met; $15,810 average financial aid amount received per undergraduate.

Academics Saint Francis awards associate, bachelor's, and master's degrees. Challenging opportunities include advanced placement credit, accelerated degree programs, student-designed majors, freshman honors college, an honors program, double majors, and a senior project. Special programs include internships, summer session for credit, off-campus study, study-abroad, and Army ROTC. The faculty at Saint Francis has 87 full-time members, 71% with terminal degrees. The student-faculty ratio is 11:1.

Students of Saint Francis The student body totals 2,003, of whom 1,470 are undergraduates. 61.6% are women and 38.4% are men. Students come from 27 states and territories and 16 other countries. 78% are from Pennsylvania. 2.9% are international students. 75% returned for their sophomore year.

Applying Saint Francis requires SAT I or ACT, a high school transcript, and 1 recommendation, and in some cases an interview and 3 recommendations. The school recommends an essay and an interview. Application deadline: rolling admissions. Deferred admission is possible.

ST. FRANCIS XAVIER UNIVERSITY

Antigonish, NS Canada

Small-town setting ■ Private ■ Independent Religious ■ Coed

Web site: www.stfx.ca
Contact: Ms. Janice Lukeman, Admissions Officer, PO Box 5000, Antigonish, NS B2G 2L1
Telephone: 902-867-2219 or toll-free 877-867 ext. 7839 (in-state) **Fax:** 902-867-2329
E-mail: admit@stfx.ca

Getting in Last Year 2,281 applied; 42% were accepted.

Financial Matters $5334 tuition and fees (2002–03); $5885 room and board.

Academics St FX awards bachelor's and master's degrees. Challenging opportunities include advanced placement credit, accelerated degree programs, student-designed majors, an honors program, double majors, independent study, and a senior project. Special programs include cooperative education, internships, summer session for credit, off-campus study, and study-abroad. The most frequently chosen baccalaureate fields are education, biological/life sciences, and business/marketing. The faculty at St FX has 222 full-time members, 75% with terminal degrees. The student-faculty ratio is 16:1.

Students of St FX The student body totals 4,969, of whom 4,495 are undergraduates. 61.9% are women and 38.1% are men. Students come from 12 states and territories and 25 other countries. 59% are from Nova Scotia. 88% returned for their sophomore year.

Applying St FX requires a high school transcript, and in some cases SAT II: Writing Test and SAT I or ACT. The school recommends SAT II Subject Tests, SAT II: Writing Test, and SAT I or ACT. Application deadline: rolling admissions.

ST. GREGORY'S UNIVERSITY

Shawnee, OK

Small-town setting ■ Private ■ Independent Religious ■ Coed

Web site: www.sgc.edu
Contact: Mr. Dan Rutledge, Director of Admissions, 1900 West MacArthur Drive, Shawnee, OK 74804
Telephone: 405-878-5447 or toll-free 888-STGREGS **Fax:** 405-878-5198
E-mail: admissions@sgc.edu

Getting in Last Year 281 applied; 86% were accepted; 162 enrolled (67%).

Financial Matters $9880 tuition and fees (2002–03); $4646 room and board; 59% average percent of need met; $8037 average financial aid amount received per undergraduate (2001–02).

Academics St. Gregory's University awards associate and bachelor's degrees. Challenging opportunities include advanced placement credit, student-designed majors, an honors program, double majors, independent study, and a senior project. Special programs include internships, summer session for credit, off-campus study, study-abroad, and Army, Navy and Air Force ROTC. The most frequently chosen baccalaureate fields are business/marketing, social sciences and history, and health professions and related sciences. The faculty at St. Gregory's University has 35 full-time members, 37% with terminal degrees. The student-faculty ratio is 17:1.

Students of St. Gregory's University The student body is made up of 793 undergraduates. 51.5% are women and 48.5% are men. Students come from 20 states and territories and 17 other countries. 91% are from Oklahoma. 10.2% are international students. 63% returned for their sophomore year.

Applying St. Gregory's University requires SAT I or ACT, a high school transcript, and a minimum high school GPA of 2.0, and in some cases an essay, an interview, and recommendations. Application deadline: rolling admissions. Deferred admission is possible.

ST. JOHN FISHER COLLEGE

Rochester, NY

Suburban setting ■ Private ■ Independent Religious ■ Coed

Web site: www.sjfc.edu
Contact: Mrs. Stacy A. Ledermann, Director of Freshmen Admissions, 3690 East Avenue, Rochester, NY 14618
Telephone: 585-385-8064 or toll-free 800-444-4640 **Fax:** 585-385-8386
E-mail: admissions@sjfc.edu

Getting in Last Year 1,934 applied; 75% were accepted; 498 enrolled (34%).

Financial Matters $16,550 tuition and fees (2002–03); $7050 room and board; 83% average percent of need met; $12,237 average financial aid amount received per undergraduate (2001–02).

Academics St. John Fisher awards bachelor's and master's degrees. Challenging opportunities include advanced placement credit, accelerated degree programs, student-designed majors, an honors program, double majors, independent study, and a senior project. Special programs include internships, summer session for credit, off-campus study, study-abroad, and Army, Navy and Air Force ROTC. The most frequently chosen baccalaureate fields are business/marketing, social sciences and history, and psychology. The faculty at St. John Fisher has 120 full-time members, 88% with terminal degrees. The student-faculty ratio is 13:1.

Students of St. John Fisher The student body totals 3,072, of whom 2,430 are undergraduates. 58.7% are women and 41.3% are men. Students come from 8 states and territories. 98% are from New York. 0.2% are international students. 82% returned for their sophomore year.

Applying St. John Fisher requires SAT I or ACT, a high school transcript, 1 recommendation, and a minimum high school GPA of 2.0. The school recommends an interview. Application deadline: rolling admissions; 2/15 priority date for financial aid. Early and deferred admission are possible.

ST. JOHN'S COLLEGE

Springfield, IL

Urban setting ■ Private ■ Independent Religious ■ Coed, Primarily Women

Web site: www.st-johns.org/education/schools/nursing
Contact: Ms. Beth Beasley, Student Development Officer, 421 North Ninth Street, Springfield, IL 62702-5317
Telephone: 217-525-5628 ext. 45468 **Fax:** 217-757-6870
E-mail: college@st-johns.org

Getting in Last Year 40 applied; 100% were accepted.

Financial Matters $9118 tuition and fees (2002–03); 80% average percent of need met; $8927 average financial aid amount received per undergraduate.

Academics St. John's College awards bachelor's degrees. The most frequently chosen baccalaureate field is health professions and related sciences. The faculty at St. John's College has 14 full-time members, 7% with terminal degrees. The student-faculty ratio is 4:1.

Students of St. John's College The student body is made up of 66 undergraduates. 97% are women and 3% are men. Students come from 2 states and territories and 1 other country. 99% are from Illinois. 1.5% are international students.

Applying Application deadline: 5/31 priority date for financial aid.

ST. JOHN'S COLLEGE

Annapolis, MD

Small-town setting ■ Private ■ Independent ■ Coed

Web site: www.sjca.edu
Contact: Mr. John Christensen, Director of Admissions, PO Box 2800, 60 College Avenue, Annapolis, MD 21404
Telephone: 410-626-2522 or toll-free 800-727-9238 **Fax:** 410-269-7916
E-mail: admissions@sjca.edu

Getting in Last Year 450 applied; 71% were accepted; 124 enrolled (39%).

Financial Matters $27,410 tuition and fees (2002–03); $6970 room and board; 90% average percent of need met; $22,262 average financial aid amount received per undergraduate.

Academics St. John's awards bachelor's and master's degrees. A senior project is a challenging opportunity. Special programs include internships and off-campus study. The most frequently chosen baccalaureate field is liberal arts/general studies. The faculty at St. John's has 72 full-time members, 72% with terminal degrees. The student-faculty ratio is 8:1.

Students of St. John's The student body totals 549, of whom 465 are undergraduates. 44.7% are women and 55.3% are men. Students come from 52 states and territories and 10 other countries. 13% are from Maryland. 2.6% are international students. 81% returned for their sophomore year.

St. John's College (continued)

Applying St. John's requires an essay, a high school transcript, and 2 recommendations, and in some cases SAT I or ACT. The school recommends SAT I or ACT and an interview. Application deadline: rolling admissions; 2/15 priority date for financial aid. Early and deferred admission are possible.

ST. JOHN'S COLLEGE

Santa Fe, NM

Small-town setting ■ Private ■ Independent ■ Coed

Web site: www.sjcsf.edu
Contact: Mr. Larry Clendenin, Director of Admissions, 1160 Camino Cruz Blanca, Santa Fe, NM 87501
Telephone: 505-984-6060 or toll-free 800-331-5232 **Fax:** 505-984-6162
E-mail: admissions@mail.sjcsf.edu

Getting in Last Year 358 applied; 80% were accepted; 114 enrolled (40%).

Financial Matters $27,410 tuition and fees (2002–03); $6970 room and board; 91% average percent of need met; $20,424 average financial aid amount received per undergraduate.

Academics St. John's awards bachelor's and master's degrees. A senior project is a challenging opportunity. Special programs include summer session for credit and off-campus study. The faculty at St. John's has 69 full-time members, 83% with terminal degrees. The student-faculty ratio is 8:1.

Students of St. John's The student body totals 531, of whom 444 are undergraduates. 44.4% are women and 55.6% are men. Students come from 43 states and territories and 6 other countries. 14% are from New Mexico. 1.8% are international students. 73% returned for their sophomore year.

Applying St. John's requires an essay, a high school transcript, and 2 recommendations, and in some cases SAT I or ACT and an interview. The school recommends an interview and 3 recommendations. Application deadline: rolling admissions; 2/15 priority date for financial aid. Early and deferred admission are possible.

SAINT JOHN'S UNIVERSITY

Collegeville, MN

Rural setting ■ Private ■ Independent Religious ■ Coed, Primarily Men

Web site: www.csbsju.edu
Contact: Ms. Renee Miller, Director of Admission, PO Box 7155, Collegeville, MN 56321-7155
Telephone: 320-363-2196 or toll-free 800-24JOHNS **Fax:** 320-363-3206
E-mail: admissions@csbsju.edu

Getting in Last Year 1,101 applied; 87% were accepted; 468 enrolled (49%).

Financial Matters $19,226 tuition and fees (2002–03); $5554 room and board; 88% average percent of need met; $16,895 average financial aid amount received per undergraduate.

Academics St. John's awards bachelor's, master's, and first-professional degrees (coordinate with College of Saint Benedict for women). Challenging opportunities include advanced placement credit, accelerated degree programs, student-designed majors, an honors program, double majors, independent study, and a senior project. Special programs include internships, off-campus study, study-abroad, and Army ROTC. The most frequently chosen baccalaureate fields are business/marketing, social sciences and history, and English. The faculty at St. John's has 148 full-time members, 97% with terminal degrees. The student-faculty ratio is 13:1.

Students of St. John's The student body totals 2,046, of whom 1,897 are undergraduates. 100% are men. Students come from 30 states and territories and 27 other countries. 86% are from Minnesota. 3% are international students. 92% returned for their sophomore year.

Applying St. John's requires an essay, SAT I or ACT, a high school transcript, and 1 recommendation. The school recommends an interview and a minimum high school GPA of 3.0. Application deadline: rolling admissions; 3/15 priority date for financial aid. Early and deferred admission are possible.

ST. JOHN'S UNIVERSITY

Jamaica, NY

Urban setting ■ Private ■ Independent Religious ■ Coed

Web site: www.stjohns.edu
Contact: Mr. Matthew Whelan, Director, Office of Admission, 8000 Utopia Parkway, Jamaica, NY 11439
Telephone: 718-990-2000 or toll-free 888-9STJOHNS (in-state), 888-9ST JOHNS (out-of-state) **Fax:** 718-990-1677
E-mail: admissions@stjohns.edu

Getting in Last Year 12,274 applied; 75% were accepted; 2,976 enrolled (32%).

Financial Matters $18,330 tuition and fees (2002–03); $9700 room and board; 74% average percent of need met; $13,386 average financial aid amount received per undergraduate (2001–02).

Academics St. John's awards associate, bachelor's, master's, doctoral, and first-professional degrees and post-bachelor's and post-master's certificates. Challenging opportunities include advanced placement credit, accelerated degree programs, an honors program, double majors, independent study, and a senior project. Special programs include internships, summer session for credit, off-campus study, study-abroad, and Army ROTC. The most frequently chosen baccalaureate fields are business/marketing, health professions and related sciences, and education. The faculty at St. John's has 551 full-time members, 89% with terminal degrees. The student-faculty ratio is 19:1.

Students of St. John's The student body totals 19,288, of whom 14,708 are undergraduates. 57.6% are women and 42.4% are men. Students come from 45 states and territories and 98 other countries. 91% are from New York. 3.4% are international students. 80% returned for their sophomore year.

Applying St. John's requires an essay, SAT I or ACT, a high school transcript, and recommendations. Application deadline: rolling admissions; 2/1 priority date for financial aid. Deferred admission is possible.

SAINT JOSEPH COLLEGE

West Hartford, CT

Suburban setting ■ Private ■ Independent Religious ■ Women Only

Web site: www.sjc.edu
Contact: Ms. Mary Yuskis, Director of Admissions, 1678 Asylum Avenue, West Hartford, CT 06117
Telephone: 860-231-5216 **Fax:** 860-233-5695
E-mail: admissions@mercy.sjc.edu

Getting in Last Year 669 applied; 76% were accepted; 201 enrolled (40%).

Financial Matters $19,610 tuition and fees (2002–03); $8210 room and board; 63% average percent of need met; $18,304 average financial aid amount received per undergraduate.

Academics SJC awards bachelor's and master's degrees. Challenging opportunities include advanced placement credit, accelerated degree programs, student-designed majors, an honors program, double majors, and a senior project. Special programs include internships, summer session for credit, off-campus study, and study-abroad. The most frequently chosen baccalaureate fields are health professions and related sciences, social sciences and history, and education. The faculty at SJC has 75 full-time members, 81% with terminal degrees. The student-faculty ratio is 11:1.

Students of SJC The student body totals 1,778, of whom 1,169 are undergraduates. Students come from 10 states and territories. 77% are from Connecticut. 72% returned for their sophomore year.

Applying SJC requires an essay, SAT I or ACT, a high school transcript, 1 recommendation, and a minimum high school GPA of 2.5. The school recommends an interview. Application deadline: 5/1; 3/15 priority date for financial aid. Early and deferred admission are possible.

SAINT JOSEPH'S COLLEGE

Rensselaer, IN

Small-town setting ■ Private ■ Independent Religious ■ Coed

Web site: www.saintjoe.edu
Contact: Mr. Frank P. Bevec, Director of Admissions, Assistant Vice President for Enrollment Management, PO Box 815, Rensselaer, IN 47978-0850
Telephone: 219-866-6170 or toll-free 800-447-8781 (out-of-state)
Fax: 219-866-6122
E-mail: admissions@saintjoe.edu

Getting in Last Year 971 applied; 77% were accepted; 247 enrolled (33%).

Financial Matters $17,060 tuition and fees (2002–03); $5880 room and board; 85% average percent of need met; $12,500 average financial aid amount received per undergraduate (2001–02).

Academics Saint Joseph's awards associate, bachelor's, and master's degrees. Challenging opportunities include advanced placement credit, accelerated degree programs, student-designed majors, an honors program, double majors, independent study, and a senior project. Special programs include internships, summer session for credit, and study-abroad. The most frequently chosen baccalaureate fields are business/marketing, education, and social sciences and history. The faculty at Saint Joseph's has 54 full-time members, 83% with terminal degrees. The student-faculty ratio is 15:1.

Students of Saint Joseph's The student body totals 974, of whom 972 are undergraduates. 57.7% are women and 42.3% are men. Students come from 22 states and territories. 72% are from Indiana. 0.2% are international students. 69% returned for their sophomore year.

Applying Saint Joseph's requires SAT I or ACT, a high school transcript, and a minimum high school GPA of 2.0, and in some cases an interview. The school recommends an essay and recommendations. Application deadline: rolling admissions; 3/1 priority date for financial aid. Early and deferred admission are possible.

ST. JOSEPH'S COLLEGE, NEW YORK

Brooklyn, NY

Urban setting ■ *Private* ■ *Independent* ■ *Coed*

Web site: www.sjcny.edu
Contact: Ms. Theresa LaRocca-Meyer, Director of Admissions, 245 Clinton Avenue, Brooklyn, NY 11205-3688
Telephone: 718-636-6868
E-mail: asinfob@sjcny.edu

Getting in Last Year 509 applied; 70% were accepted; 126 enrolled (35%).

Financial Matters $10,400 tuition and fees (2002–03); 85% average percent of need met; $9500 average financial aid amount received per undergraduate.

Academics St. Joseph's awards bachelor's and master's degrees. Challenging opportunities include advanced placement credit, an honors program, and a senior project. Special programs include internships and summer session for credit. The most frequently chosen baccalaureate fields are health professions and related sciences, education, and business/marketing. The faculty at St. Joseph's has 52 full-time members, 69% with terminal degrees. The student-faculty ratio is 16:1.

Students of St. Joseph's The student body totals 1,198, of whom 1,120 are undergraduates. 79.5% are women and 20.5% are men. Students come from 1 state or territory. 99% are from New York. 0.6% are international students. 86% returned for their sophomore year.

Applying St. Joseph's requires SAT I or ACT, a high school transcript, and a minimum high school GPA of 3.0, and in some cases an interview. The school recommends an essay and 2 recommendations. Application deadline: 8/15; 2/25 priority date for financial aid. Early and deferred admission are possible.

SAINT JOSEPH'S COLLEGE OF MAINE

Standish, ME

Small-town setting ■ *Private* ■ *Independent Religious* ■ *Coed*

Web site: www.sjcme.edu
Contact: Dr. Alexander Popovics, Vice President for Enrollment and Dean of Admission and Financial Aid, 278 Whites Bridge Road, Standish, ME 04084-5263
Telephone: 207-893-7746 ext. 7741 or toll-free 800-338-7057
Fax: 207-893-7862
E-mail: admissions@sjcme.edu

Getting in Last Year 1,129 applied; 82% were accepted; 290 enrolled (31%).

Financial Matters $16,740 tuition and fees (2002–03); $6980 room and board; 81% average percent of need met; $13,886 average financial aid amount received per undergraduate.

Academics Saint Joseph's awards bachelor's and master's degrees (profile does not include enrollment in distance learning master's program). Challenging opportunities include advanced placement credit, freshman honors college, an honors program, double majors, independent study, and a senior project. Special programs include cooperative education, internships, summer session for credit, off-campus study, study-abroad, and Army ROTC. The most frequently chosen baccalaureate fields are liberal arts/general studies, health professions and related sciences, and education. The faculty at Saint Joseph's has 59 full-time members, 97% with terminal degrees. The student-faculty ratio is 13:1.

Students of Saint Joseph's The student body is made up of 975 undergraduates. 66.6% are women and 33.4% are men. Students come from 15 states and territories and 1 other country. 66% are from Maine. 0.1% are international students. 70% returned for their sophomore year.

Applying Saint Joseph's requires an essay, SAT I or ACT, a high school transcript, 1 recommendation, and a minimum high school GPA of 2.0. The school recommends an interview. Application deadline: rolling admissions; 3/1 priority date for financial aid. Deferred admission is possible.

ST. JOSEPH'S COLLEGE, SUFFOLK CAMPUS

Patchogue, NY

Small-town setting ■ *Private* ■ *Independent* ■ *Coed*

Web site: www.sjcny.edu
Contact: Mrs. Marion E. Salgado, Director of Admissions, 155 West Roe Boulevard, Patchogue, NY 11772
Telephone: 631-447-3219 or toll-free 866-AT ST JOE (in-state)
Fax: 631-447-1734
E-mail: admissions_patchogue@sjcny.edu

Getting in Last Year 968 applied; 73% were accepted; 409 enrolled (58%).

Financial Matters $10,675 tuition and fees (2002–03); 47% average percent of need met; $7400 average financial aid amount received per undergraduate.

Academics St. Joseph's College, Suffolk Campus awards bachelor's and master's degrees (master's degree in education only). Challenging opportunities include advanced placement credit and a senior project. Special programs include summer session for credit, off-campus study, and Army and Air Force ROTC. The most frequently chosen baccalaureate fields are education, business/marketing, and health professions and related sciences. The faculty at St. Joseph's College, Suffolk Campus has 95 full-time members, 62% with terminal degrees. The student-faculty ratio is 15:1.

Students of St. Joseph's College, Suffolk Campus The student body totals 3,653, of whom 3,521 are undergraduates. 76.9% are women and 23.1% are men. Students come from 4 states and territories. 100% are from New York. 0.1% are international students. 98% returned for their sophomore year.

Applying St. Joseph's College, Suffolk Campus requires SAT I or ACT, a high school transcript, and a minimum high school GPA of 3.0, and in some cases 2 recommendations. The school recommends an essay and an interview. Application deadline: rolling admissions; 2/25 priority date for financial aid. Early and deferred admission are possible.

SAINT JOSEPH SEMINARY COLLEGE

Saint Benedict, LA

Rural setting ■ *Private* ■ *Independent Religious* ■ *Coed, Primarily Men*

Web site: www.sjasc.edu
Contact: Br. Bernard Boudreaux, OSB, Academic Assistant, 75376 River Road, St. Benedict, LA 70457
Telephone: 985-867-2248
E-mail: asec@sjasc.edu

Getting in Last Year 9 enrolled.

Financial Matters $8900 tuition and fees (2002–03); $5700 room and board; 100% average percent of need met; $12,386 average financial aid amount received per undergraduate (2001–02).

Academics Saint Joseph Seminary College awards bachelor's degrees. Advanced placement credit is a challenging opportunity. The faculty at Saint Joseph Seminary College has 15 full-time members, 40% with terminal degrees. The student-faculty ratio is 4:1.

Students of Saint Joseph Seminary College The student body is made up of 166 undergraduates. 28.3% are women and 71.7% are men. Students come from 8 states and territories. 89% are from Louisiana. 85% returned for their sophomore year.

Applying Saint Joseph Seminary College requires ACT, a high school transcript, an interview, recommendations, and a minimum high school GPA of 2.0. Application deadline: rolling admissions; 3/15 priority date for financial aid. Early and deferred admission are possible.

SAINT JOSEPH'S UNIVERSITY

Philadelphia, PA

Suburban setting ■ *Private* ■ *Independent Religious* ■ *Coed*

Web site: www.sju.edu
Contact: Mr. David Conway, Assistant Vice President of Enrollment Management, 5600 City Avenue, Philadelphia, PA 19131-1395
Telephone: 610-660-1300 or toll-free 888-BEAHAWK (in-state)
Fax: 610-660-1314
E-mail: admi@sju.edu

Getting in Last Year 7,051 applied; 55% were accepted; 1,056 enrolled (27%).

Financial Matters $22,545 tuition and fees (2002–03); $9040 room and board; 80% average percent of need met; $11,300 average financial aid amount received per undergraduate (2001–02).

Academics St. Joseph's awards associate, bachelor's, master's, and doctoral degrees and post-master's certificates. Challenging opportunities include advanced placement credit, student-designed majors, an honors program, double majors, independent study, and a senior project. Special programs include cooperative education, internships, summer session for credit, off-campus study, study-abroad, and Army and Air Force ROTC. The most frequently chosen baccalaureate fields are business/marketing, social sciences and history, and education. The faculty at St. Joseph's has 240 full-time members, 91% with terminal degrees. The student-faculty ratio is 14:1.

Students of St. Joseph's The student body totals 7,315, of whom 4,584 are undergraduates. 52.9% are women and 47.1% are men. 50% are from Pennsylvania. 1.2% are international students. 86% returned for their sophomore year.

Applying St. Joseph's requires an essay, SAT I or ACT, a high school transcript, and 1 recommendation. The school recommends a minimum high school GPA of 3.0. Application deadline: 2/15 priority date for financial aid. Deferred admission is possible.

ST. LAWRENCE UNIVERSITY

Canton, NY

Small-town setting ■ *Private* ■ *Independent* ■ *Coed*

Web site: www.stlawu.edu
Contact: Ms. Terry Cowdrey, Dean of Admissions and Financial Aid, Payson Hall, Canton, NY 13617-1455
Telephone: 315-229-5261 or toll-free 800-285-1856 **Fax:** 315-229-5818

St. Lawrence University (continued)

E-mail: admissions@stlawu.edu

Getting in Last Year 2,867 applied; 58% were accepted; 619 enrolled (37%).

Financial Matters $26,480 tuition and fees (2002–03); $7755 room and board; 91% average percent of need met; $25,373 average financial aid amount received per undergraduate.

Academics St. Lawrence awards bachelor's and master's degrees and post-master's certificates. Challenging opportunities include advanced placement credit, student-designed majors, double majors, independent study, and a senior project. Special programs include internships, summer session for credit, off-campus study, study-abroad, and Army and Air Force ROTC. The most frequently chosen baccalaureate fields are social sciences and history, biological/life sciences, and psychology. The faculty at St. Lawrence has 165 full-time members, 99% with terminal degrees. The student-faculty ratio is 12:1.

Students of St. Lawrence The student body totals 2,293, of whom 2,150 are undergraduates. 53% are women and 47% are men. Students come from 40 states and territories and 20 other countries. 54% are from New York. 3.9% are international students. 84% returned for their sophomore year.

Applying St. Lawrence requires an essay, SAT I or ACT, a high school transcript, and 2 recommendations. The school recommends SAT II Subject Tests, an interview, and a minimum high school GPA of 2.0. Application deadline: 2/15; 2/15 priority date for financial aid. Deferred admission is possible.

SAINT LEO UNIVERSITY

Saint Leo, FL

Rural setting ■ Private ■ Independent Religious ■ Coed

Web site: www.saintleo.edu

Contact: Mr. Gary Bracken, Vice President for Enrollment, MC 2008, PO Box 6665, Saint Leo, FL 33574-6665

Telephone: 352-588-8283 or toll-free 800-334-5532 **Fax:** 352-588-8257

E-mail: admission@saintleo.edu

Getting in Last Year 1,334 applied; 68% were accepted; 286 enrolled (31%).

Financial Matters $13,170 tuition and fees (2002–03); $6834 room and board; 88% average percent of need met; $17,695 average financial aid amount received per undergraduate.

Academics Saint Leo awards associate, bachelor's, and master's degrees. Challenging opportunities include advanced placement credit, an honors program, double majors, independent study, and a senior project. Special programs include internships, summer session for credit, study-abroad, and Army and Air Force ROTC. The most frequently chosen baccalaureate fields are education, business/marketing, and social sciences and history. The faculty at Saint Leo has 55 full-time members, 85% with terminal degrees. The student-faculty ratio is 15:1.

Students of Saint Leo The student body totals 1,346, of whom 1,004 are undergraduates. 56.8% are women and 43.2% are men. Students come from 35 states and territories and 35 other countries. 78% are from Florida. 5% are international students. 70% returned for their sophomore year.

Applying Saint Leo requires an essay, SAT I or ACT, a high school transcript, 1 recommendation, and a minimum high school GPA of 2.3, and in some cases an interview. The school recommends an interview and a minimum high school GPA of 3.0. Application deadline: 8/15; 3/1 priority date for financial aid. Early and deferred admission are possible.

ST. LOUIS CHRISTIAN COLLEGE

Florissant, MO

Suburban setting ■ Private ■ Independent Religious ■ Coed

Web site: www.slcc4ministry.edu

Contact: Mr. Richard Fordyce, Registrar, 1360 Grandview Drive, Florissant, MO 63033-6499

Telephone: 314-837-6777 ext. 1500 or toll-free 800-887-SLCC
Fax: 314-837-8291

E-mail: questions@slcc4ministry.edu

Getting in Last Year 55 applied; 76% were accepted; 29 enrolled (69%).

Financial Matters $5910 tuition and fees (2002–03); $3380 room and board; 66% average percent of need met; $6332 average financial aid amount received per undergraduate.

Academics SLCC awards associate and bachelor's degrees. Challenging opportunities include advanced placement credit, accelerated degree programs, and a senior project. Internships is a special program. The faculty at SLCC has 11 full-time members, 27% with terminal degrees. The student-faculty ratio is 12:1.

Students of SLCC The student body is made up of 232 undergraduates. 42.2% are women and 57.8% are men. Students come from 11 states and territories and 3 other countries. 63% are from Missouri. 3% are international students. 76% returned for their sophomore year.

Applying SLCC requires an essay, ACT, a high school transcript, and 2 recommendations, and in some cases an interview. The school recommends a minimum high school GPA of 2.0. Application deadline: 8/15; 5/1 priority date for financial aid. Early admission is possible.

ST. LOUIS COLLEGE OF PHARMACY

St. Louis, MO

Urban setting ■ Private ■ Independent ■ Coed

Web site: www.stlcop.edu

Contact: Ms. Patty Kulage, Admissions and Financial Aid Coordinator, 4588 Parkview Place, St. Louis, MO 63110-1088

Telephone: 314-367-8700 ext. 1065 or toll-free 800-278-5267 (in-state)
Fax: 314-367-2784

E-mail: pkulage@stlcop.edu

Getting in Last Year 493 applied; 65% were accepted; 203 enrolled (63%).

Financial Matters $15,485 tuition and fees (2002–03); $6000 room and board; 31% average percent of need met; $11,324 average financial aid amount received per undergraduate (2000–01 estimated).

Academics St. Louis College of Pharmacy awards bachelor's, master's, and first-professional degrees (bachelor of science degree program in pharmaceutical studies cannot be applied to directly; students have the option to transfer in after their second year in the PharmD program. Bachelor's degree candidates are not eligible to take the pharmacist's licensing examination). Advanced placement credit is a challenging opportunity. Special programs include internships, summer session for credit, and Army and Air Force ROTC. The most frequently chosen baccalaureate field is health professions and related sciences. The faculty at St. Louis College of Pharmacy has 64 full-time members, 100% with terminal degrees. The student-faculty ratio is 12:1.

Students of St. Louis College of Pharmacy The student body totals 900, of whom 825 are undergraduates. 64.4% are women and 35.6% are men. Students come from 24 states and territories and 3 other countries. 50% are from Missouri. 0.4% are international students. 89% returned for their sophomore year.

Applying St. Louis College of Pharmacy requires an essay, SAT I or ACT, a high school transcript, recommendations, and a minimum high school GPA of 3.0, and in some cases an interview. Application deadline: rolling admissions; 11/15 for financial aid, with a 4/1 priority date.

SAINT LOUIS UNIVERSITY

St. Louis, MO

Urban setting ■ Private ■ Independent Religious ■ Coed

Web site: www.slu.edu

Contact: Ms. Shani Lenore, Director, 221 North Grand Boulevard, St. Louis, MO 63103-2097

Telephone: 314-977-3415 or toll-free 800-758-3678 (out-of-state)
Fax: 314-977-7136

E-mail: admitme@slu.edu

Getting in Last Year 5,992 applied; 72% were accepted; 1,539 enrolled (36%).

Financial Matters $21,008 tuition and fees (2002–03); $7310 room and board; 71% average percent of need met; $20,707 average financial aid amount received per undergraduate.

Academics SLU awards associate, bachelor's, master's, doctoral, and first-professional degrees and post-bachelor's and post-master's certificates. Challenging opportunities include advanced placement credit, accelerated degree programs, student-designed majors, an honors program, double majors, independent study, and a senior project. Special programs include cooperative education, internships, summer session for credit, off-campus study, study-abroad, and Army and Air Force ROTC. The most frequently chosen baccalaureate fields are business/marketing, health professions and related sciences, and communications/communication technologies. The faculty at SLU has 591 full-time members, 91% with terminal degrees. The student-faculty ratio is 12:1.

Students of SLU The student body totals 11,272, of whom 7,178 are undergraduates. 53.9% are women and 46.1% are men. Students come from 52 states and territories and 73 other countries. 53% are from Missouri. 2.7% are international students. 86% returned for their sophomore year.

Applying SLU requires an essay, SAT I or ACT, a high school transcript, and secondary school report form. The school recommends an interview, 2 recommendations, and a minimum high school GPA of 2.5. Application deadline: 8/1; 3/1 priority date for financial aid. Deferred admission is possible.

SAINT LUKE'S COLLEGE

Kansas City, MO

Urban setting ■ Private ■ Independent Religious ■ Coed, Primarily Women

Web site: www.saint-lukes.org

Contact: Ms. Marsha Thomas, Director of Admissions, 4426 Wornall Road, Kansas City, MO 64111

Telephone: 816-932-2073

E-mail: slc-admissions@saint-lukes.org

Financial Matters $9510 tuition and fees (2002–03); 75% average percent of need met; $6500 average financial aid amount received per undergraduate.

Academics Saint Luke's College awards bachelor's degrees. Special programs include cooperative education and summer session for credit. The most frequently chosen baccalaureate field is health professions and related sciences. The faculty at Saint Luke's College has 17 full-time members, 6% with terminal degrees. The student-faculty ratio is 7:1.

Students of Saint Luke's College The student body is made up of 129 undergraduates. 95.3% are women and 4.7% are men.

SAINT MARTIN'S COLLEGE

Lacey, WA

Suburban setting ■ Private ■ Independent Religious ■ Coed

Web site: www.stmartin.edu

Contact: Mr. Todd Abbott, Director of Admission, 5300 Pacific Avenue, SE, Lacey, WA 98503

Telephone: 360-438-4590 or toll-free 800-368-8803 **Fax:** 360-412-6189

E-mail: admissions@stmartin.edu

Getting in Last Year 380 applied; 92% were accepted; 131 enrolled (37%).

Financial Matters $16,860 tuition and fees (2002–03); $5098 room and board; 84% average percent of need met; $14,659 average financial aid amount received per undergraduate.

Academics St. Martin's awards associate, bachelor's, and master's degrees. Challenging opportunities include advanced placement credit, accelerated degree programs, double majors, independent study, and a senior project. Special programs include cooperative education, internships, summer session for credit, off-campus study, study-abroad, and Army ROTC. The most frequently chosen baccalaureate fields are business/marketing, psychology, and social sciences and history. The faculty at St. Martin's has 55 full-time members, 87% with terminal degrees. The student-faculty ratio is 14:1.

Students of St. Martin's The student body totals 1,547, of whom 1,121 are undergraduates. 55.9% are women and 44.1% are men. Students come from 19 states and territories and 13 other countries. 93% are from Washington. 4.7% are international students. 72% returned for their sophomore year.

Applying St. Martin's requires an essay, SAT I or ACT, a high school transcript, 1 recommendation, and a minimum high school GPA of 2.5, and in some cases an interview. Application deadline: 8/1; 3/1 priority date for financial aid.

SAINT MARY COLLEGE

Leavenworth, KS

Small-town setting ■ Private ■ Independent Religious ■ Coed

Web site: www.smcks.edu

Contact: Ms. Judy Wiedower, Director of Admissions and Financial Aid, 4100 South Fourth Street, Leavenworth, KS 66048

Telephone: 913-682-5151 ext. 6118 or toll-free 800-752-7043 (out-of-state) **Fax:** 913-758-6140

E-mail: admiss@hub.smcks.edu

Getting in Last Year 538 applied; 57% were accepted; 71 enrolled (23%).

Financial Matters $13,128 tuition and fees (2002–03); $5122 room and board.

Academics Saint Mary awards associate, bachelor's, and master's degrees. Challenging opportunities include advanced placement credit, student-designed majors, an honors program, double majors, independent study, and a senior project. Special programs include cooperative education, internships, summer session for credit, off-campus study, study-abroad, and Army ROTC. The most frequently chosen baccalaureate fields are engineering/engineering technologies, communications/communication technologies, and psychology. The faculty at Saint Mary has 36 full-time members, 50% with terminal degrees. The student-faculty ratio is 12:1.

Students of Saint Mary The student body totals 891, of whom 543 are undergraduates. 58.6% are women and 41.4% are men. Students come from 20 states and territories and 3 other countries. 74% are from Kansas. 0.9% are international students. 64% returned for their sophomore year.

Applying Saint Mary requires SAT I or ACT, a high school transcript, 1 recommendation, and a minimum high school GPA of 2.5. The school recommends an interview. Application deadline: rolling admissions.

SAINT MARY-OF-THE-WOODS COLLEGE

Saint Mary-of-the-Woods, IN

Rural setting ■ Private ■ Independent Religious ■ Women Only

Web site: www.smwc.edu

Contact: Ms. Jessica Day, Director, Guerin Hall, Saint Mary-of-the-Woods, IN 47876

Telephone: 812-535-5229 or toll-free 800-926-SMWC **Fax:** 812-535-4900

E-mail: smwcadms@smwc.edu

Getting in Last Year 258 applied; 79% were accepted; 185 enrolled (91%).

Financial Matters $16,370 tuition and fees (2002–03); $6009 room and board.

Academics The Woods awards associate, bachelor's, and master's degrees and post-master's certificates (also offers external degree program with significant enrollment reflected in profile). Challenging opportunities include advanced placement credit, accelerated degree programs, student-designed majors, double majors, independent study, and a senior project. Special programs include internships, summer session for credit, off-campus study, study-abroad, and Army and Air Force ROTC. The most frequently chosen baccalaureate fields are education, business/marketing, and liberal arts/general studies. The faculty at The Woods has 60 full-time members, 72% with terminal degrees. The student-faculty ratio is 12:1.

Students of The Woods The student body totals 1,612, of whom 1,495 are undergraduates. Students come from 24 states and territories. 70% are from Indiana. 0.3% are international students. 68% returned for their sophomore year.

Applying The Woods requires 1 recommendation and a minimum high school GPA of 2.0, and in some cases an essay, SAT I or ACT, a high school transcript, and an interview. Application deadline: 8/15. Early and deferred admission are possible.

SAINT MARY'S COLLEGE

Notre Dame, IN

Suburban setting ■ Private ■ Independent Religious ■ Women Only

Web site: www.saintmarys.edu

Contact: Ms. Mary Pat Nolan, Director of Admission, Notre Dame, IN 46556

Telephone: 574-284-4587 or toll-free 800-551-7621 (in-state), 574-284-4716 (out-of-state)

E-mail: admission@saintmarys.edu

Getting in Last Year 997 applied; 82% were accepted; 376 enrolled (46%).

Financial Matters $20,550 tuition and fees (2002–03); $6942 room and board; 86% average percent of need met; $16,507 average financial aid amount received per undergraduate.

Academics Saint Mary's awards bachelor's degrees. Challenging opportunities include advanced placement credit, accelerated degree programs, student-designed majors, double majors, independent study, and a senior project. Special programs include cooperative education, internships, summer session for credit, off-campus study, study-abroad, and Army, Navy and Air Force ROTC. The most frequently chosen baccalaureate fields are business/marketing, education, and social sciences and history. The faculty at Saint Mary's has 114 full-time members, 93% with terminal degrees. The student-faculty ratio is 11:1.

Students of Saint Mary's The student body is made up of 1,492 undergraduates. Students come from 46 states and territories and 8 other countries. 26% are from Indiana. 0.8% are international students. 82% returned for their sophomore year.

Applying Saint Mary's requires an essay, SAT I and SAT II or ACT, a high school transcript, and 1 recommendation. The school recommends an interview. Application deadline: 3/1; 3/1 priority date for financial aid. Early and deferred admission are possible.

SAINT MARY'S COLLEGE OF MADONNA UNIVERSITY

Orchard Lake, MI

Suburban setting ■ Private ■ Independent Religious ■ Coed

Web site: www.stmarys.avemaria.edu

Contact: Mr. Jim Bass, Director of Enrollment, 3535 Indian Trail, Orchard Lake, MI 48324-1623

Telephone: 248-683-0523 or toll-free 877-252-3131 (in-state) **Fax:** 248-683-1756

E-mail: admissions@stmarys.avemaria.edu

Getting in Last Year 129 applied; 74% were accepted; 40 enrolled (42%).

Financial Matters $8088 tuition and fees (2002–03); $5640 room and board; $6770 average financial aid amount received per undergraduate.

Academics Saint Mary's awards bachelor's degrees. Challenging opportunities include advanced placement credit, accelerated degree programs, double majors, independent study, and a senior project. Special programs include cooperative education, internships, off-campus study, and study-abroad. The most frequently chosen baccalaureate fields are biological/life sciences, communications/communication technologies, and business/marketing. The faculty at Saint Mary's has 25 full-time members, 72% with terminal degrees. The student-faculty ratio is 12:1.

Students of Saint Mary's The student body totals 628, of whom 459 are undergraduates. 44% are women and 56% are men. Students come from 9 states and territories and 12 other countries. 98% are from Michigan. 31% are international students. 56% returned for their sophomore year.

Applying Saint Mary's requires an essay, SAT I or ACT, a high school transcript, minimum ACT score of 19 or SAT I score of 900, and a minimum high school GPA of 2.5, and in some cases an interview. The school recommends 2 recommendations. Application deadline: rolling admissions; 4/30 for financial aid, with a 2/21 priority date. Early admission is possible.

SAINT MARY'S COLLEGE OF CALIFORNIA

Moraga, CA

Suburban setting ■ *Private* ■ *Independent Religious* ■ *Coed*

Web site: www.stmarys-ca.edu

Contact: Ms. Dorothy Benjamin, Dean of Admissions, PO Box 4800, Moraga, CA 94556-4800

Telephone: 925-631-4224 or toll-free 800-800-4SMC **Fax:** 925-376-7193

E-mail: smcadmit@stmarys-ca.edu

Getting in Last Year 3,021 applied; 85% were accepted.

Financial Matters $20,885 tuition and fees (2002–03); $8550 room and board; 82% average percent of need met; $20,096 average financial aid amount received per undergraduate.

Academics Saint Mary's awards bachelor's, master's, and doctoral degrees. Challenging opportunities include advanced placement credit, student-designed majors, an honors program, double majors, independent study, and a senior project. Special programs include internships, off-campus study, study-abroad, and Army and Air Force ROTC. The most frequently chosen baccalaureate fields are business/marketing, psychology, and social sciences and history. The faculty at Saint Mary's has 193 full-time members, 95% with terminal degrees. The student-faculty ratio is 13:1.

Students of Saint Mary's The student body totals 4,442, of whom 2,572 are undergraduates. Students come from 26 states and territories and 29 other countries. 83% are from California. 3.1% are international students. 82% returned for their sophomore year.

Applying Saint Mary's requires an essay, SAT I or ACT, a high school transcript, 1 recommendation, and a minimum high school GPA of 2.0, and in some cases an interview and a minimum high school GPA of 3.0. The school recommends a minimum high school GPA of 3.0. Application deadline: 2/1; 3/2 for financial aid. Deferred admission is possible.

ST. MARY'S COLLEGE OF MARYLAND

St. Mary's City, MD

Rural setting ■ *Public* ■ *State-supported* ■ *Coed*

Web site: www.smcm.edu

Contact: Mr. Richard J. Edgar, Director of Admissions, 18952 East Fisher Road, St. Mary's City, MD 20686-3001

Telephone: 240-895-5000 or toll-free 800-492-7181 **Fax:** 240-895-5001

E-mail: admissions@smcm.edu

Getting in Last Year 1,884 applied; 59% were accepted; 426 enrolled (38%).

Financial Matters $8082 resident tuition and fees (2002–03); $13,417 nonresident tuition and fees (2002–03); $6613 room and board; 61% average percent of need met; $6695 average financial aid amount received per undergraduate.

Academics St. Mary's awards bachelor's degrees. Challenging opportunities include advanced placement credit, student-designed majors, freshman honors college, an honors program, double majors, independent study, and a senior project. Special programs include cooperative education, internships, summer session for credit, off-campus study, and study-abroad. The most frequently chosen baccalaureate fields are social sciences and history, biological/life sciences, and psychology. The faculty at St. Mary's has 118 full-time members, 97% with terminal degrees. The student-faculty ratio is 12:1.

Students of St. Mary's The student body is made up of 1,823 undergraduates. 60% are women and 40% are men. Students come from 38 states and territories and 25 other countries. 85% are from Maryland. 0.5% are international students. 87% returned for their sophomore year.

Applying St. Mary's requires an essay, SAT I or ACT, a high school transcript, and a minimum high school GPA of 2.0. The school recommends an interview and 2 recommendations. Application deadline: 1/15; 3/1 for financial aid. Early admission is possible.

SAINT MARY'S UNIVERSITY

Halifax, NS Canada

Urban setting ■ *Public* ■ *Coed*

Web site: www.stmarys.ca

Contact: Mr. Greg Ferguson, Director of Admissions, Halifax, NS B3H 3C3 Canada

Telephone: 902-420-5415 **Fax:** 902-496-8100

E-mail: jim.dunn@stmarys.ca

Getting in Last Year 2,175 enrolled.

Financial Matters $4807 nonresident tuition and fees (2002–03); $5581 room and board.

Academics Saint Mary's awards bachelor's, master's, and doctoral degrees. Challenging opportunities include accelerated degree programs, student-designed majors, an honors program, double majors, independent study, and a senior project. Special programs include cooperative education, internships, summer session for credit, off-campus study, and study-abroad. The most frequently chosen baccalaureate fields are psychology, social sciences and history, and English. The faculty at Saint Mary's has 211 full-time members, 95% with terminal degrees. The student-faculty ratio is 24:1.

Students of Saint Mary's The student body totals 7,904, of whom 7,422 are undergraduates. 53.3% are women and 46.7% are men. Students come from 12 states and territories and 55 other countries. 88% are from Nova Scotia.

Applying Saint Mary's requires a high school transcript and a minimum high school GPA of 2.0, and in some cases an interview. Application deadline: 7/1; 6/30 priority date for financial aid.

SAINT MARY'S UNIVERSITY OF MINNESOTA

Winona, MN

Small-town setting ■ *Private* ■ *Independent Religious* ■ *Coed*

Web site: www.smumn.edu

Contact: Mr. Anthony M. Piscitiello, Vice President for Admission, 700 Terrace Heights, Winona, MN 55987-1399

Telephone: 507-457-1700 or toll-free 800-635-5987 **Fax:** 507-457-1722

E-mail: admissions@smumn.edu

Getting in Last Year 1,122 applied; 79% were accepted; 396 enrolled (45%).

Financial Matters $15,695 tuition and fees (2002–03); $4920 room and board.

Academics Saint Mary's awards bachelor's, master's, and doctoral degrees and post-bachelor's and post-master's certificates. Challenging opportunities include advanced placement credit, accelerated degree programs, student-designed majors, an honors program, double majors, independent study, and a senior project. Special programs include internships, summer session for credit, off-campus study, and study-abroad. The most frequently chosen baccalaureate fields are business/marketing, communications/communication technologies, and social sciences and history. The faculty at Saint Mary's has 107 full-time members, 75% with terminal degrees. The student-faculty ratio is 12:1.

Students of Saint Mary's The student body totals 5,065, of whom 1,654 are undergraduates. 52.5% are women and 47.5% are men. Students come from 25 states and territories and 21 other countries. 69% are from Minnesota. 2.4% are international students. 77% returned for their sophomore year.

Applying Saint Mary's requires an essay, SAT I or ACT, a high school transcript, and a minimum high school GPA of 2.5, and in some cases an interview. The school recommends 2 recommendations. Application deadline: 5/1; 3/15 priority date for financial aid. Early and deferred admission are possible.

ST. MARY'S UNIVERSITY OF SAN ANTONIO

San Antonio, TX

Urban setting ■ *Private* ■ *Independent Religious* ■ *Coed*

Web site: www.stmarytx.edu

Contact: Mr. Richard Castillo, Director of Admissions, 1 Camino Santa Maria, San Antonio, TX 78228-8503

Telephone: 210-436-3126 or toll-free 800-FOR-STMU **Fax:** 210-431-6742

E-mail: uadm@stmarytx.edu

Getting in Last Year 1,664 applied; 85% were accepted; 667 enrolled (47%).

Financial Matters $15,227 tuition and fees (2002–03); $6246 room and board; 55% average percent of need met; $12,207 average financial aid amount received per undergraduate.

Academics St. Mary's University awards bachelor's, master's, doctoral, and first-professional degrees. Challenging opportunities include advanced placement credit, an honors program, double majors, independent study, and a senior project. Special programs include cooperative education, internships, summer session for credit, off-campus study, study-abroad, and Army ROTC. The most frequently chosen baccalaureate fields are business/marketing, social sciences and history, and biological/life sciences. The faculty at St. Mary's University has 185 full-time members, 87% with terminal degrees. The student-faculty ratio is 15:1.

Students of St. Mary's University The student body totals 4,243, of whom 2,725 are undergraduates. 59.2% are women and 40.8% are men. Students come from 35 states and territories and 50 other countries. 96% are from Texas. 3.9% are international students. 79% returned for their sophomore year.

Applying St. Mary's University requires an essay, SAT I or ACT, and a high school transcript, and in some cases recommendations. The school recommends an interview. Application deadline: rolling admissions. Early and deferred admission are possible.

SAINT MICHAEL'S COLLEGE

Colchester, VT

Small-town setting ■ *Private* ■ *Independent Religious* ■ *Coed*

Web site: www.smcvt.edu

Contact: Ms. Jacqueline Murphy, Director of Admission, One Winooski Park, Colchester, VT 05439

Telephone: 802-654-3000 or toll-free 800-762-8000 **Fax:** 802-654-2906

E-mail: admission@smcvt.edu

Getting in Last Year 2,552 applied; 68% were accepted; 527 enrolled (30%).

Financial Matters $21,200 tuition and fees (2002–03); $7255 room and board; 90% average percent of need met; $17,145 average financial aid amount received per undergraduate.

Academics Saint Michael's awards bachelor's and master's degrees and post-bachelor's and post-master's certificates. Challenging opportunities include advanced placement credit, student-designed majors, an honors program, double majors, independent study, and a senior project. Special programs include internships, summer session for credit, off-campus study, study-abroad, and Army and Air Force ROTC. The most frequently chosen baccalaureate fields are business/marketing, social sciences and history, and psychology. The faculty at Saint Michael's has 144 full-time members, 83% with terminal degrees. The student-faculty ratio is 13:1.

Students of Saint Michael's The student body totals 2,637, of whom 2,040 are undergraduates. 55.5% are women and 44.5% are men. Students come from 28 states and territories and 17 other countries. 25% are from Vermont. 2.3% are international students. 89% returned for their sophomore year.

Applying Saint Michael's requires an essay, SAT I or ACT, and a high school transcript. The school recommends an interview, recommendations, and a minimum high school GPA of 3.0. Application deadline: 2/1; 3/15 priority date for financial aid. Deferred admission is possible.

ST. NORBERT COLLEGE

De Pere, WI

Suburban setting ■ Private ■ Independent Religious ■ Coed

Web site: www.snc.edu

Contact: Mr. Daniel L. Meyer, Dean of Admission and Enrollment Management, 100 Grant Street, De Pere, WI 54115-2099

Telephone: 920-403-3005 or toll-free 800-236-4878 **Fax:** 920-403-4072

E-mail: admit@snc.edu

Getting in Last Year 1,714 applied; 83% were accepted; 499 enrolled (35%).

Financial Matters $19,084 tuition and fees (2002–03); $5440 room and board; 88% average percent of need met; $14,718 average financial aid amount received per undergraduate.

Academics St. Norbert awards bachelor's and master's degrees. Challenging opportunities include advanced placement credit, student-designed majors, an honors program, double majors, independent study, and a senior project. Special programs include cooperative education, internships, summer session for credit, off-campus study, study-abroad, and Army ROTC. The most frequently chosen baccalaureate fields are business/marketing, social sciences and history, and communications/communication technologies. The faculty at St. Norbert has 122 full-time members, 92% with terminal degrees.

Students of St. Norbert The student body totals 2,133, of whom 2,072 are undergraduates. 57.4% are women and 42.6% are men. Students come from 26 states and territories and 27 other countries. 71% are from Wisconsin. 2.2% are international students. 82% returned for their sophomore year.

Applying St. Norbert requires an essay, SAT I or ACT, a high school transcript, and 1 recommendation. The school recommends an interview. Application deadline: rolling admissions; 3/1 priority date for financial aid. Deferred admission is possible.

ST. OLAF COLLEGE

Northfield, MN

Small-town setting ■ Private ■ Independent Religious ■ Coed

Web site: www.stolaf.edu

Contact: Jeff McLaughlin, Director of Admissions, 1520 St. Olaf Avenue, Northfield, MN 55057

Telephone: 507-646-3025 or toll-free 800-800-3025 **Fax:** 507-646-3832

E-mail: admiss@stolaf.edu

Getting in Last Year 2,624 applied; 73% were accepted; 779 enrolled (41%).

Financial Matters $22,200 tuition and fees (2002–03); $4750 room and board; 100% average percent of need met; $16,873 average financial aid amount received per undergraduate.

Academics St. Olaf awards bachelor's degrees. Challenging opportunities include advanced placement credit, student-designed majors, double majors, independent study, and a senior project. Special programs include internships, summer session for credit, off-campus study, and study-abroad. The most frequently chosen baccalaureate fields are social sciences and history, biological/life sciences, and visual/performing arts. The faculty at St. Olaf has 192 full-time members, 89% with terminal degrees. The student-faculty ratio is 13:1.

Students of St. Olaf The student body is made up of 3,041 undergraduates. 59.1% are women and 40.9% are men. Students come from 49 states and territories and 27 other countries. 53% are from Minnesota. 1.3% are international students. 93% returned for their sophomore year.

Applying St. Olaf requires an essay, SAT I or ACT, a high school transcript, and 2 recommendations. The school recommends an interview. Application deadline: rolling admissions; 2/15 priority date for financial aid. Deferred admission is possible.

SAINT PAUL UNIVERSITY

Ottawa, ON Canada

Urban setting ■ Public ■ Coed

Web site: ustpaul.ca

Contact: Claudette Dubé-Socqué, Registrar, 223 Main Street, Ottawa, ON K1S 1C4 Canada

Telephone: 613-236-1393 ext. 2238 **Fax:** 613-782-3014

Academics Saint Paul University awards bachelor's, master's, and doctoral degrees. An honors program is a challenging opportunity. Summer session for credit is a special program. The most frequently chosen baccalaureate field is communications/communication technologies. The faculty at Saint Paul University has 64 full-time members.

Students of Saint Paul University The student body totals 757, of whom 445 are undergraduates. 63.6% are women and 36.4% are men. Students come from 15 states and territories and 40 other countries.

Applying Saint Paul University requires a high school transcript. The school recommends SAT I. Application deadline: 8/15. Deferred admission is possible.

SAINT PETER'S COLLEGE

Jersey City, NJ

Urban setting ■ Private ■ Independent Religious ■ Coed

Web site: www.spc.edu

Contact: Stephanie Decker, Director of Recruitment, 2627 Kennedy Blvd., Jersey City, NJ 07306

Telephone: 201-915-9213 or toll-free 888-SPC-9933 **Fax:** 201-432-5860

E-mail: admissions@spcvxa.spc.edu

Getting in Last Year 2,041 applied; 67% were accepted; 462 enrolled (34%).

Financial Matters $17,358 tuition and fees (2002–03); $7340 room and board; 78% average percent of need met; $14,583 average financial aid amount received per undergraduate (2001–02).

Academics SPC awards associate, bachelor's, and master's degrees. Challenging opportunities include advanced placement credit, accelerated degree programs, student-designed majors, an honors program, double majors, independent study, and a senior project. Special programs include cooperative education, internships, summer session for credit, off-campus study, study-abroad, and Army and Air Force ROTC. The most frequently chosen baccalaureate fields are business/marketing, computer/information sciences, and social sciences and history. The faculty at SPC has 110 full-time members, 77% with terminal degrees. The student-faculty ratio is 15:1.

Students of SPC The student body totals 3,054, of whom 2,389 are undergraduates. 56% are women and 44% are men. Students come from 28 states and territories and 9 other countries. 87% are from New Jersey. 1.9% are international students. 69% returned for their sophomore year.

Applying SPC requires an essay, SAT I or ACT, a high school transcript, 2 recommendations, and a minimum high school GPA of 2.0, and in some cases an interview. The school recommends an interview. Application deadline: rolling admissions; 4/15 priority date for financial aid. Early and deferred admission are possible.

ST. THOMAS AQUINAS COLLEGE

Sparkill, NY

Suburban setting ■ Private ■ Independent ■ Coed

Web site: www.stac.edu

Contact: Mr. John Edel, Dean of Enrollment Management, 125 Route 340, Sparkill, NY 10976

Telephone: 845-398-4100 or toll-free 800-999-STAC

Getting in Last Year 1,080 applied; 75% were accepted; 306 enrolled (38%).

Financial Matters $14,100 tuition and fees (2002–03); $7980 room and board.

Academics St. Thomas Aquinas College awards associate, bachelor's, and master's degrees and post-bachelor's and post-master's certificates. Challenging opportunities include advanced placement credit, accelerated degree programs, freshman honors college, an honors program, and a senior project. Special programs include internships, summer session for credit, off-campus study, and Air Force ROTC. The faculty at St. Thomas Aquinas College has 65 full-time members, 89% with terminal degrees. The student-faculty ratio is 17:1.

Students of St. Thomas Aquinas College The student body totals 2,140, of whom 1,944 are undergraduates. 55.3% are women and 44.7% are men. Students come from 17 states and territories and 10 other countries. 63% are from New York. 2.2% are international students. 74% returned for their sophomore year.

Applying St. Thomas Aquinas College requires SAT I or ACT, a high school transcript, and a minimum high school GPA of 2.0, and in some cases 3 recommendations. The school recommends an essay and an interview. Application deadline: rolling admissions; 2/15 priority date for financial aid. Early and deferred admission are possible.

ST. THOMAS UNIVERSITY

Miami, FL

Suburban setting ■ Private ■ Independent Religious ■ Coed

Web site: www.stu.edu
Contact: Mr. Andre Lightbourne, Associate Director of Admissions, 1540 Northwest 32nd Avenue, Miami, FL 33054-6459
Telephone: 305-628-6546 or toll-free 800-367-9006 (in-state), 800-367-9010 (out-of-state) **Fax:** 305-628-6591
E-mail: signup@stu.edu

Getting in Last Year 767 applied; 55% were accepted; 167 enrolled (39%).

Financial Matters $15,450 tuition and fees (2002–03); $5040 room and board.

Academics STU awards bachelor's, master's, and first-professional degrees and post-bachelor's and post-master's certificates. Challenging opportunities include advanced placement credit, freshman honors college, an honors program, double majors, independent study, and a senior project. Special programs include summer session for credit and Army and Air Force ROTC. The most frequently chosen baccalaureate fields are business/marketing, protective services/public administration, and communications/communication technologies. The faculty at STU has 91 full-time members. The student-faculty ratio is 14:1.

Students of STU The student body totals 2,365, of whom 1,205 are undergraduates. 60.9% are women and 39.1% are men. Students come from 25 states and territories and 58 other countries. 97% are from Florida. 14.7% are international students. 71% returned for their sophomore year.

Applying STU requires SAT I and SAT II or ACT, a high school transcript, and a minimum high school GPA of 2.0. The school recommends an essay, SAT I and SAT II or ACT, an interview, and 1 recommendation. Application deadline: rolling admissions; 4/1 priority date for financial aid. Early and deferred admission are possible.

ST. THOMAS UNIVERSITY

Fredericton, NB Canada

Small-town setting ■ Private ■ Independent Religious ■ Coed

Web site: www.stu.ca
Contact: Ms. Kathryn Monti, Director of Admissions, Admissions and Welcome Building, Fredericton, NB E3B 5G3
Telephone: 506-452-0603 **Fax:** 506-452-0617
E-mail: admissions@stthomasu.ca

Getting in Last Year 2,758 applied; 57% were accepted; 976 enrolled (62%).

Financial Matters $3622 tuition and fees (2002–03); $4650 room and board.

Academics STU awards bachelor's degrees and post-bachelor's certificates. Challenging opportunities include accelerated degree programs, student-designed majors, an honors program, double majors, independent study, and a senior project. Special programs include cooperative education, internships, summer session for credit, and off-campus study. The most frequently chosen baccalaureate fields are liberal arts/general studies, social sciences and history, and health professions and related sciences. The faculty at STU has 110 full-time members, 74% with terminal degrees. The student-faculty ratio is 25:1.

Students of STU The student body totals 3,110, of whom 3,028 are undergraduates. 67.4% are women and 32.6% are men. Students come from 9 states and territories and 26 other countries. 75% are from New Brunswick.

Applying STU requires a high school transcript and a minimum high school GPA of 2.5, and in some cases an essay, SAT I, SAT II Subject Tests, SAT II: Writing Test, an interview, and recommendations. The school recommends a minimum high school GPA of 3.0. Application deadline: 7/31. Deferred admission is possible.

SAINT VINCENT COLLEGE

Latrobe, PA

Suburban setting ■ Private ■ Independent Religious ■ Coed

Web site: www.stvincent.edu
Contact: Mr. David A. Collins, Assistant Vice President of Admission and Financial Aid, 300 Fraser Purchase Road, Latrobe, PA 15650
Telephone: 724-532-5089 or toll-free 800-782-5549 **Fax:** 724-532-5069
E-mail: admission@stvincent.edu

Getting in Last Year 1,005 applied; 84% were accepted; 320 enrolled (38%).

Financial Matters $18,430 tuition and fees (2002–03); $5784 room and board; 86% average percent of need met; $15,143 average financial aid amount received per undergraduate.

Academics Saint Vincent awards bachelor's and master's degrees. Challenging opportunities include advanced placement credit, accelerated degree programs, an honors program, independent study, and a senior project. Special programs include cooperative education, internships, summer session for credit, off-campus study, study-abroad, and Air Force ROTC. The most frequently chosen baccalaureate fields are business/marketing, social sciences and history, and psychology. The faculty at Saint Vincent has 75 full-time members, 84% with terminal degrees. The student-faculty ratio is 14:1.

Students of Saint Vincent The student body totals 1,413, of whom 1,371 are undergraduates. 50.5% are women and 49.5% are men. Students come from 25 states and territories and 20 other countries. 84% are from Pennsylvania. 2% are international students. 85% returned for their sophomore year.

Applying Saint Vincent requires an essay, SAT I or ACT, a high school transcript, and a minimum high school GPA of 2.5, and in some cases an interview. The school recommends an interview, 3 recommendations, and a minimum high school GPA of 3.2. Application deadline: 5/1; 5/1 for financial aid, with a 3/1 priority date. Early and deferred admission are possible.

SAINT XAVIER UNIVERSITY

Chicago, IL

Urban setting ■ Private ■ Independent Religious ■ Coed

Web site: www.sxu.edu
Contact: Elizabeth A. Gierach, Director of Enrollment Services, 3700 West 103rd Street, Chicago, IL 60655-3105
Telephone: 773-298-3063 or toll-free 800-462-9288 **Fax:** 773-298-3076
E-mail: admissions@sxu.edu

Getting in Last Year 1,702 applied; 70% were accepted; 380 enrolled (32%).

Financial Matters $15,930 tuition and fees (2002–03); $6233 room and board; 84% average percent of need met; $13,849 average financial aid amount received per undergraduate.

Academics Saint Xavier awards bachelor's and master's degrees and post-bachelor's and post-master's certificates. Challenging opportunities include advanced placement credit, accelerated degree programs, student-designed majors, an honors program, double majors, independent study, and a senior project. Special programs include cooperative education, internships, summer session for credit, study-abroad, and Air Force ROTC. The most frequently chosen baccalaureate fields are health professions and related sciences, business/marketing, and education. The faculty at Saint Xavier has 151 full-time members, 83% with terminal degrees. The student-faculty ratio is 15:1.

Students of Saint Xavier The student body totals 5,278, of whom 2,958 are undergraduates. 72.3% are women and 27.7% are men. Students come from 19 states and territories and 5 other countries. 97% are from Illinois. 0.4% are international students. 81% returned for their sophomore year.

Applying Saint Xavier requires SAT I or ACT and a high school transcript, and in some cases an interview. The school recommends an essay, an interview, and a minimum high school GPA of 2.5. Application deadline: rolling admissions; 3/1 priority date for financial aid. Deferred admission is possible.

SALEM COLLEGE

Winston-Salem, NC

Urban setting ■ Private ■ Independent Religious ■ Women Only

Web site: www.salem.edu
Contact: Ms. Joyce K. Jackson, Registrar/Director of Institutional Research, PO Box 10548, Shober House, Winston-Salem, NC 27108
Telephone: 336-721-2618 or toll-free 800-327-2536 **Fax:** 336-724-7102
E-mail: admissions@salem.edu

Getting in Last Year 411 applied; 76% were accepted; 148 enrolled (48%).

Financial Matters $14,995 tuition and fees (2002–03); $8870 room and board; $12,300 average financial aid amount received per undergraduate.

Academics Salem awards bachelor's and master's degrees (only students 23 or over are eligible to enroll part-time; men may attend evening program only). Challenging opportunities include advanced placement credit, student-designed majors, an honors program, double majors, independent study, and a senior project. Special programs include internships, summer session for credit, off-campus study, study-abroad, and Army ROTC. The most frequently chosen baccalaureate fields are social sciences and history, English, and business/marketing. The faculty at Salem has 45 full-time members, 91% with terminal degrees. The student-faculty ratio is 13:1.

Students of Salem The student body totals 1,027, of whom 873 are undergraduates. Students come from 24 states and territories and 16 other countries. 52% are from North Carolina. 3.7% are international students. 79% returned for their sophomore year.

Applying Salem requires an essay, SAT I or ACT, a high school transcript, and 2 recommendations. The school recommends an interview. Application deadline: rolling admissions; 3/1 priority date for financial aid. Early and deferred admission are possible.

SALEM INTERNATIONAL UNIVERSITY

Salem, WV

Rural setting ■ Private ■ Independent ■ Coed

Web site: www.salemiu.edu
Contact: Director of Admissions, PO Box 500, Salem, WV 26426-0500
Telephone: 304-782-5336 ext. 336 or toll-free 800-283-4562
E-mail: admiss_new@salemiu.edu

Getting in Last Year 251 applied; 99% were accepted; 51 enrolled (20%).

Financial Matters $14,050 tuition and fees (2002–03); $4632 room and board; 89% average percent of need met; $15,213 average financial aid amount received per undergraduate.

Academics Salem International University awards associate, bachelor's, and master's degrees. Challenging opportunities include advanced placement credit, accelerated degree programs, double majors, independent study, and a senior project. Special programs include internships, off-campus study, and study-abroad. The most frequently chosen baccalaureate fields are biological/life sciences, education, and business/marketing. The faculty at Salem International University has 33 full-time members, 70% with terminal degrees. The student-faculty ratio is 14:1.

Students of Salem International University The student body totals 568, of whom 443 are undergraduates. 47% are women and 53% are men. Students come from 33 states and territories and 17 other countries. 44% are from West Virginia. 39.2% are international students. 68% returned for their sophomore year.

Applying Salem International University requires SAT I or ACT, a high school transcript, and a minimum high school GPA of 2.00, and in some cases an interview. The school recommends an essay and an interview. Application deadline: rolling admissions. Deferred admission is possible.

SALEM STATE COLLEGE

Salem, MA

Small-town setting ■ Public ■ State-supported ■ Coed

Web site: www.salemstate.edu

Contact: Mr. Nate Bryant, Director of Admissions, Admissions Office, 352 Lafayette Street, Salem, MA 01970

Telephone: 978-542-6200

Getting in Last Year 4,099 applied; 72% were accepted.

Financial Matters $3988 resident tuition and fees (2002–03); $10,128 nonresident tuition and fees (2002–03); $5428 room and board; 68% average percent of need met; $5714 average financial aid amount received per undergraduate (2001–02).

Academics Salem State College awards bachelor's and master's degrees and post-master's certificates. Challenging opportunities include advanced placement credit, student-designed majors, an honors program, double majors, independent study, and a senior project. Special programs include internships, summer session for credit, off-campus study, and study-abroad. The most frequently chosen baccalaureate fields are business/marketing, protective services/public administration, and education. The faculty at Salem State College has 277 full-time members, 68% with terminal degrees. The student-faculty ratio is 16:1.

Students of Salem State College The student body totals 8,793, of whom 6,404 are undergraduates. Students come from 18 states and territories. 4.4% are international students. 70% returned for their sophomore year.

Applying Salem State College requires SAT I or ACT, a high school transcript, recommendations, and a minimum high school GPA of 2.9, and in some cases an interview. The school recommends an essay. Application deadline: rolling admissions; 4/1 priority date for financial aid. Early admission is possible.

SALISBURY UNIVERSITY

Salisbury, MD

Small-town setting ■ Public ■ State-supported ■ Coed

Web site: www.salisbury.edu

Contact: Mrs. Jane H. Dané, Dean of Admissions, Admissions House, 1101 Camden Avenue, Salisbury, MD 21801

Telephone: 410-543-6161 or toll-free 888-543-0148 **Fax:** 410-546-6016

E-mail: admissions@salisbury.edu

Getting in Last Year 5,298 applied; 50% were accepted; 900 enrolled (34%).

Financial Matters $6214 resident tuition and fees (2002–03); $11,978 nonresident tuition and fees (2002–03); $6356 room and board; 66% average percent of need met; $5654 average financial aid amount received per undergraduate (2001–02).

Academics Salisbury University awards bachelor's and master's degrees. Challenging opportunities include advanced placement credit, student-designed majors, an honors program, double majors, independent study, and a senior project. Special programs include internships, summer session for credit, off-campus study, study-abroad, and Army ROTC. The most frequently chosen baccalaureate fields are business/marketing, education, and communications/communication technologies. The faculty at Salisbury University has 298 full-time members, 80% with terminal degrees. The student-faculty ratio is 17:1.

Students of Salisbury University The student body totals 6,851, of whom 6,206 are undergraduates. 56.9% are women and 43.1% are men. Students come from 31 states and territories and 32 other countries. 82% are from Maryland. 0.8% are international students. 83% returned for their sophomore year.

Applying Salisbury University requires SAT I or ACT, a high school transcript, and a minimum high school GPA of 2.0. Application deadline: 1/15; 2/1 priority date for financial aid. Early admission is possible.

SALVE REGINA UNIVERSITY

Newport, RI

Suburban setting ■ Private ■ Independent Religious ■ Coed

Web site: www.salve.edu

Contact: Colleen Emerson, Director of Admissions, 100 Ochre Point Avenue, Newport, RI 02840-4192

Telephone: 401-341-2109 or toll-free 888-GO SALVE **Fax:** 401-848-2823

E-mail: sruadmis@salve.edu

Getting in Last Year 3,564 applied; 59% were accepted; 526 enrolled (25%).

Financial Matters $19,410 tuition and fees (2002–03); $8400 room and board; 72% average percent of need met; $14,533 average financial aid amount received per undergraduate.

Academics Salve Regina awards associate, bachelor's, master's, and doctoral degrees and post-master's certificates. Challenging opportunities include advanced placement credit, accelerated degree programs, freshman honors college, an honors program, double majors, independent study, and a senior project. Special programs include internships, summer session for credit, study-abroad, and Army ROTC. The most frequently chosen baccalaureate fields are education, business/marketing, and protective services/public administration. The faculty at Salve Regina has 105 full-time members, 69% with terminal degrees. The student-faculty ratio is 13:1.

Students of Salve Regina The student body totals 2,283, of whom 1,916 are undergraduates. 69.5% are women and 30.5% are men. Students come from 40 states and territories and 10 other countries. 19% are from Rhode Island. 1.5% are international students. 77% returned for their sophomore year.

Applying Salve Regina requires an essay, SAT I or ACT, a high school transcript, and 2 recommendations, and in some cases an interview. The school recommends a minimum high school GPA of 2.5. Application deadline: 3/1; 3/1 priority date for financial aid. Deferred admission is possible.

SAMFORD UNIVERSITY

Birmingham, AL

Suburban setting ■ Private ■ Independent Religious ■ Coed

Web site: www.samford.edu

Contact: Dr. Phil Kimrey, Dean of Admissions and Financial Aid, 800 Lakeshore Drive, Samford Hall, Birmingham, AL 35229-0002

Telephone: 205-726-3673 or toll-free 800-888-7218 **Fax:** 205-726-2171

E-mail: seberry@samford.edu

Getting in Last Year 1,954 applied; 89% were accepted; 662 enrolled (38%).

Financial Matters $12,294 tuition and fees (2002–03); $4994 room and board; 72% average percent of need met; $9708 average financial aid amount received per undergraduate.

Academics Samford awards associate, bachelor's, master's, doctoral, and first-professional degrees and post-master's certificates. Challenging opportunities include advanced placement credit, accelerated degree programs, an honors program, double majors, and a senior project. Special programs include cooperative education, internships, summer session for credit, off-campus study, study-abroad, and Army and Air Force ROTC. The most frequently chosen baccalaureate fields are business/marketing, education, and social sciences and history. The faculty at Samford has 256 full-time members, 80% with terminal degrees. The student-faculty ratio is 13:1.

Students of Samford The student body totals 4,366, of whom 2,853 are undergraduates. 63.3% are women and 36.7% are men. Students come from 42 states and territories and 23 other countries. 48% are from Alabama. 0.4% are international students. 84% returned for their sophomore year.

Applying Samford requires an essay, SAT I or ACT, a high school transcript, and 1 recommendation. The school recommends an interview. Application deadline: 8/15; 3/1 priority date for financial aid. Early and deferred admission are possible.

SAM HOUSTON STATE UNIVERSITY

Huntsville, TX

Small-town setting ■ Public ■ State-supported ■ Coed

Web site: www.shsu.edu

Contact: Ms. Joey Chandler, Director of Admissions and Recruitment, PO Box 2418, Huntsville, TX 77341

Telephone: 936-294-1828 **Fax:** 936-294-3758

Getting in Last Year 5,777 applied; 70% were accepted; 1,673 enrolled (42%).

Financial Matters $3382 resident tuition and fees (2002–03); $9922 nonresident tuition and fees (2002–03); $4090 room and board; $5520 average financial aid amount received per undergraduate.

Academics Sam Houston State awards bachelor's, master's, and doctoral degrees. Challenging opportunities include advanced placement credit, accelerated degree programs, an honors program, double majors, independent study, and a senior project. Special programs include cooperative education, internships, summer session for credit, and Army ROTC. The most frequently chosen baccalaureate fields are business/marketing, protective services/public administration, and

Sam Houston State University (continued)

interdisciplinary studies. The faculty at Sam Houston State has 390 full-time members, 79% with terminal degrees. The student-faculty ratio is 21:1.

Students of Sam Houston State The student body totals 13,091, of whom 11,222 are undergraduates. 57.3% are women and 42.7% are men. Students come from 43 states and territories and 45 other countries. 98% are from Texas. 0.7% are international students. 67% returned for their sophomore year.

Applying Sam Houston State requires SAT I or ACT, a high school transcript, and a minimum high school GPA of 2.0. Application deadline: rolling admissions; 5/31 for financial aid, with a 3/31 priority date. Early admission is possible.

SAMUEL MERRITT COLLEGE

Oakland, CA

Urban setting ■ Private ■ Independent ■ Coed, Primarily Women

Web site: www.samuelmerritt.edu

Contact: Ms. Anne Seed, Director of Admissions, 570 Hawthorne Avenue, Oakland, CA 94609

Telephone: 510-869-6610 or toll-free 800-607-MERRITT **Fax:** 510-869-6525

E-mail: admission@samuelmerritt.edu

Getting in Last Year 56 applied; 59% were accepted; 10 enrolled (30%).

Financial Matters $19,814 tuition and fees (2002–03); $3780 room only; 82% average percent of need met; $22,000 average financial aid amount received per undergraduate (2001–02).

Academics Samuel Merritt College awards bachelor's and master's degrees (bachelor's degree offered jointly with Saint Mary's College of California). Challenging opportunities include advanced placement credit, double majors, independent study, and a senior project. Special programs include internships, summer session for credit, off-campus study, study-abroad, and Army, Navy and Air Force ROTC. The most frequently chosen baccalaureate field is health professions and related sciences. The student-faculty ratio is 7:1.

Students of Samuel Merritt College The student body totals 867, of whom 256 are undergraduates. 91.4% are women and 8.6% are men. Students come from 2 states and territories. 99% are from California. 100% returned for their sophomore year.

Applying Samuel Merritt College requires an essay, SAT I or ACT, a high school transcript, 1 recommendation, and a minimum high school GPA of 2.5, and in some cases an interview. Application deadline: 3/1; 3/2 priority date for financial aid. Deferred admission is possible.

SAN DIEGO STATE UNIVERSITY

San Diego, CA

Urban setting ■ Public ■ State-supported ■ Coed

Web site: www.sdsu.edu

Contact: Prospective Student Center, 5500 Campanile Drive, San Diego, CA 92182-7455

Telephone: 619-594-6886 **Fax:** 619-594-1250

E-mail: admissions@sdsu.edu

Getting in Last Year 29,217 applied; 54% were accepted; 4,107 enrolled (26%).

Financial Matters $2014 resident tuition and fees (2002–03); $10,474 nonresident tuition and fees (2002–03); $8307 room and board; 88% average percent of need met; $8000 average financial aid amount received per undergraduate.

Academics SDSU awards bachelor's, master's, and doctoral degrees and post-bachelor's and post-master's certificates. Challenging opportunities include advanced placement credit, student-designed majors, an honors program, double majors, independent study, and a senior project. Special programs include internships, summer session for credit, off-campus study, study-abroad, and Army, Navy and Air Force ROTC. The most frequently chosen baccalaureate fields are business/marketing, social sciences and history, and liberal arts/general studies. The faculty at SDSU has 1,050 full-time members, 90% with terminal degrees. The student-faculty ratio is 19:1.

Students of SDSU The student body totals 34,304, of whom 27,846 are undergraduates. 57.6% are women and 42.4% are men. Students come from 50 states and territories and 125 other countries. 97% are from California. 3% are international students. 75% returned for their sophomore year.

Applying SDSU requires SAT I or ACT, a high school transcript, and a minimum high school GPA of 2.0. Application deadline: 11/30.

SAN FRANCISCO ART INSTITUTE

San Francisco, CA

Urban setting ■ Private ■ Independent ■ Coed

Web site: www.sfai.edu

Contact: Mark Takiguchi, Director of Admissions, 800 Chestnut Street, San Francisco, CA 94133

Telephone: 415-749-4500 or toll-free 800-345-SFAI

E-mail: admissions@sfai.edu

Getting in Last Year 248 applied; 87% were accepted; 51 enrolled (24%).

Financial Matters $22,176 tuition and fees (2002–03).

Academics SFAI awards bachelor's and master's degrees and post-bachelor's certificates. Challenging opportunities include advanced placement credit, accelerated degree programs, double majors, independent study, and a senior project. Special programs include internships, summer session for credit, off-campus study, and study-abroad. The most frequently chosen baccalaureate field is visual/performing arts. The faculty at SFAI has 34 full-time members. The student-faculty ratio is 8:1.

Students of SFAI The student body totals 674, of whom 466 are undergraduates. 54.1% are women and 45.9% are men. Students come from 24 states and territories and 18 other countries. 67% are from California. 9.4% are international students. 62% returned for their sophomore year.

Applying SFAI requires an essay, SAT I or ACT, a high school transcript, and portfolio. The school recommends an interview. Application deadline: 8/27. Deferred admission is possible.

SAN FRANCISCO CONSERVATORY OF MUSIC

San Francisco, CA

Urban setting ■ Private ■ Independent ■ Coed

Web site: www.sfcm.edu

Contact: Ms. Susan Dean, Director of Admissions, 1201 Ortega Street, San Francisco, CA 94122-4411

Telephone: 415-759-3431 **Fax:** 415-759-3499

E-mail: admit@sfcm.edu

Getting in Last Year 116 applied; 63% were accepted.

Financial Matters $22,280 tuition and fees (2002–03); 85% average percent of need met; $18,584 average financial aid amount received per undergraduate.

Academics SFCM awards bachelor's and master's degrees. Challenging opportunities include advanced placement credit and independent study. The most frequently chosen baccalaureate field is visual/performing arts. The faculty at SFCM has 24 full-time members, 54% with terminal degrees. The student-faculty ratio is 6:1.

Students of SFCM The student body totals 287, of whom 158 are undergraduates. Students come from 28 states and territories and 16 other countries. 51% are from California. 19.9% are international students. 86% returned for their sophomore year.

Applying SFCM requires SAT I or ACT, a high school transcript, 2 recommendations, and audition. The school recommends SAT I. Application deadline: 2/1; 3/1 priority date for financial aid. Early admission is possible.

SAN FRANCISCO STATE UNIVERSITY

San Francisco, CA

Urban setting ■ Public ■ State-supported ■ Coed

Web site: www.sfsu.edu

Contact: Ms. Patricia Wade, Admissions Officer, 1600 Holloway Avenue, San Francisco, CA 94132

Telephone: 415-338-2037 **Fax:** 415-338-7196

E-mail: ugadmit@sfsu.edu

Getting in Last Year 14,531 applied; 66% were accepted; 2,328 enrolled (24%).

Financial Matters $1826 resident tuition and fees (2002–03); $8594 nonresident tuition and fees (2002–03); $6930 room and board; 70% average percent of need met; $8202 average financial aid amount received per undergraduate.

Academics SF State awards bachelor's, master's, and doctoral degrees. Challenging opportunities include advanced placement credit, accelerated degree programs, student-designed majors, an honors program, double majors, independent study, and a senior project. Special programs include cooperative education, internships, summer session for credit, off-campus study, and study-abroad. The faculty at SF State has 887 full-time members, 71% with terminal degrees. The student-faculty ratio is 20:1.

Students of SF State The student body totals 28,378, of whom 20,828 are undergraduates. 58.6% are women and 41.4% are men. Students come from 48 states and territories and 113 other countries. 99% are from California. 6.5% are international students. 75% returned for their sophomore year.

Applying SF State requires a high school transcript, and in some cases SAT I or ACT. Application deadline: rolling admissions.

SAN JOSE CHRISTIAN COLLEGE

San Jose, CA

Urban setting ■ Private ■ Independent Religious ■ Coed

Web site: www.sjchristian.edu

Contact: Mr. Rob Jones, Director of Admissions, 790 South 12th Street, San Jose, CA 95112

Telephone: 408-278-4330 or toll-free 800-355-7522 **Fax:** 408-293-9299

E-mail: admissions@sjchristian.edu

Getting in Last Year 96 applied; 45% were accepted.

Financial Matters $11,436 tuition and fees (2002–03); $5475 room and board; $6244 average financial aid amount received per undergraduate (2000–01).

Academics SJCC awards associate and bachelor's degrees. Challenging opportunities include advanced placement credit, accelerated degree programs, double majors, and a senior project. Special programs include cooperative education, internships, and summer session for credit. The most frequently chosen baccalaureate fields are protective services/public administration and education. The faculty at SJCC has 12 full-time members, 58% with terminal degrees. The student-faculty ratio is 12:1.

Students of SJCC The student body is made up of 328 undergraduates. 42.4% are women and 57.6% are men. Students come from 9 states and territories. 96% are from California. 6.7% are international students. 62% returned for their sophomore year.

Applying SJCC requires an essay, SAT I or ACT, a high school transcript, 2 recommendations, letter of introduction, and a minimum high school GPA of 2.0. Application deadline: 8/1; 6/1 priority date for financial aid. Deferred admission is possible.

SAN JOSE STATE UNIVERSITY

San Jose, CA

Urban setting ■ Public ■ State-supported ■ Coed

Web site: www.sjsu.edu
Contact: Mr. John Loera, Director of Admissions, One Washington Square, San Jose, CA 95192-0001
Telephone: 408-283-7500 **Fax:** 408-924-2050
E-mail: contact@sjsu.edu

Getting in Last Year 13,453 applied; 72% were accepted; 2,720 enrolled (28%).

Financial Matters $2059 resident tuition and fees (2002–03); $7963 nonresident tuition and fees (2002–03); $7583 room and board; 78% average percent of need met; $7562 average financial aid amount received per undergraduate.

Academics SJSU awards bachelor's and master's degrees. Challenging opportunities include advanced placement credit, accelerated degree programs, student-designed majors, an honors program, double majors, independent study, and a senior project. Special programs include cooperative education, internships, summer session for credit, off-campus study, study-abroad, and Army and Air Force ROTC. The faculty at SJSU has 812 full-time members. The student-faculty ratio is 16:1.

Students of SJSU The student body totals 28,955, of whom 22,784 are undergraduates. 50.6% are women and 49.4% are men. Students come from 43 states and territories and 104 other countries. 20% are from California. 3.7% are international students.

Applying SJSU requires a high school transcript, and in some cases SAT I or ACT. Application deadline: 11/30; 3/2 priority date for financial aid.

SANTA CLARA UNIVERSITY

Santa Clara, CA

Suburban setting ■ Private ■ Independent Religious ■ Coed

Web site: www.scu.edu
Contact: Ms. Sandra Hayes, Dean of Undergraduate Admissions, 500 El Camino Real, Santa Clara, CA 95053
Telephone: 408-554-4700 **Fax:** 408-554-5255
E-mail: ugadmissions@scu.edu

Getting in Last Year 5,842 applied; 70% were accepted; 1,122 enrolled (28%).

Financial Matters $24,185 tuition and fees (2002–03); $8904 room and board; 81% average percent of need met; $14,718 average financial aid amount received per undergraduate (2001–02).

Academics Santa Clara awards bachelor's, master's, doctoral, and first-professional degrees and post-bachelor's, post-master's, and first-professional certificates. Challenging opportunities include advanced placement credit, student-designed majors, an honors program, double majors, independent study, and a senior project. Special programs include cooperative education, internships, summer session for credit, study-abroad, and Army and Air Force ROTC. The most frequently chosen baccalaureate fields are business/marketing, social sciences and history, and engineering/engineering technologies. The faculty at Santa Clara has 411 full-time members, 92% with terminal degrees. The student-faculty ratio is 12:1.

Students of Santa Clara The student body totals 7,811, of whom 4,394 are undergraduates. 54.8% are women and 45.2% are men. Students come from 33 states and territories and 31 other countries. 66% are from California. 2.8% are international students. 92% returned for their sophomore year.

Applying Santa Clara requires an essay, SAT I or ACT, a high school transcript, and 1 recommendation. The school recommends an interview. Application deadline: 1/15; 2/1 priority date for financial aid. Deferred admission is possible.

SARAH LAWRENCE COLLEGE

Bronxville, NY

Suburban setting ■ Private ■ Independent ■ Coed

Web site: www.sarahlawrence.edu
Contact: Ms. Thyra L. Briggs, Dean of Admission, 1 Mead Way, Bronxville, NY 10708-5999
Telephone: 914-395-2510 or toll-free 800-888-2858 **Fax:** 914-395-2515
E-mail: slcadmit@slc.edu

Getting in Last Year 2,667 applied; 40% were accepted; 323 enrolled (30%).

Financial Matters $29,360 tuition and fees (2002–03); $10,010 room and board; 94% average percent of need met; $26,289 average financial aid amount received per undergraduate.

Academics Sarah Lawrence awards bachelor's and master's degrees. Challenging opportunities include advanced placement credit, student-designed majors, and independent study. Special programs include internships, off-campus study, and study-abroad. The most frequently chosen baccalaureate field is liberal arts/general studies. The faculty at Sarah Lawrence has 180 full-time members. The student-faculty ratio is 6:1.

Students of Sarah Lawrence The student body totals 1,556, of whom 1,226 are undergraduates. 74% are women and 26% are men. Students come from 46 states and territories and 27 other countries. 16% are from New York. 2.3% are international students. 94% returned for their sophomore year.

Applying Sarah Lawrence requires an essay, SAT I, ACT, or any 3 SAT II Subject Tests, a high school transcript, and 3 recommendations. The school recommends an interview and a minimum high school GPA of 3.0. Application deadline: 1/15; 2/1 for financial aid. Early and deferred admission are possible.

SAVANNAH COLLEGE OF ART AND DESIGN

Savannah, GA

Urban setting ■ Private ■ Independent ■ Coed

Web site: www.scad.edu
Contact: Ms. Pamela Poetter, Vice President for Admission, 342 Bull Street, PO Box 3146, Savannah, GA 31402-3146
Telephone: 912-525-5100 or toll-free 800-869-7223 **Fax:** 912-525-5983
E-mail: admission@scad.edu

Getting in Last Year 3,471 applied; 83% were accepted; 1,061 enrolled (37%).

Financial Matters $17,955 tuition and fees (2002–03); $7620 room and board; 50% average percent of need met; $8206 average financial aid amount received per undergraduate.

Academics SCAD awards bachelor's and master's degrees. Challenging opportunities include advanced placement credit, double majors, independent study, and a senior project. Special programs include internships, summer session for credit, off-campus study, and study-abroad. The most frequently chosen baccalaureate fields are visual/performing arts and architecture. The faculty at SCAD has 270 full-time members, 77% with terminal degrees. The student-faculty ratio is 19:1.

Students of SCAD The student body totals 5,792, of whom 5,055 are undergraduates. 48.1% are women and 51.9% are men. Students come from 54 states and territories and 74 other countries. 19% are from Georgia. 6.7% are international students. 81% returned for their sophomore year.

Applying SCAD requires SAT I or ACT, a high school transcript, and 3 recommendations. The school recommends an interview. Application deadline: rolling admissions; 4/1 priority date for financial aid. Early admission is possible.

SAVANNAH STATE UNIVERSITY

Savannah, GA

Suburban setting ■ Public ■ State-supported ■ Coed

Web site: www.savstate.edu
Contact: Mrs. Gwendolyn J. Moore, Associate Director of Admissions, PO Box 20209, Savannah, GA 31404
Telephone: 912-356-2181 or toll-free 800-788-0478 **Fax:** 912-356-2566

Getting in Last Year 2,500 applied; 27% were accepted.

Financial Matters $2628 resident tuition and fees (2002–03); $8658 nonresident tuition and fees (2002–03); $4386 room and board; 75% average percent of need met; $3200 average financial aid amount received per undergraduate (2001–02).

Academics Savannah State awards bachelor's and master's degrees. Challenging opportunities include advanced placement credit, accelerated degree programs, and a senior project. Special programs include cooperative education, internships, summer session for credit, off-campus study, and Army and Navy ROTC. The faculty at Savannah State has 115 full-time members, 79% with terminal degrees. The student-faculty ratio is 16:1.

Students of Savannah State The student body totals 2,360, of whom 2,259 are undergraduates. Students come from 28 states and territories and 18 other countries. 83% are from Georgia. 68% returned for their sophomore year.

Applying Savannah State requires SAT I or ACT, a high school transcript, and a minimum high school GPA of 2.0, and in some cases SAT II Subject Tests. The

Savannah State University (continued)

school recommends SAT I. Application deadline: 6/1; 5/1 priority date for financial aid. Early and deferred admission are possible.

SCHILLER INTERNATIONAL UNIVERSITY

Dunedin, FL

Suburban setting ■ Private ■ Independent ■ Coed

Web site: www.schiller.edu
Contact: Ms. Kamala Dontamsetti, Associate Director of Admissions, 453 Edgewater Drive, Dunedin, FL 34698-7532
Telephone: 727-736-5082 ext. 240 or toll-free 800-336-4133 **Fax:** 727-734-0359
E-mail: admissions@schiller.edu

Getting in Last Year 20 enrolled.

Financial Matters $13,560 tuition and fees (2002–03); $5700 room and board.

Academics SIU awards associate, bachelor's, and master's degrees. Challenging opportunities include advanced placement credit, accelerated degree programs, and student-designed majors. Special programs include internships, summer session for credit, and study-abroad. The faculty at SIU has 4 full-time members.

Students of SIU The student body totals 177, of whom 108 are undergraduates. 39.8% are women and 60.2% are men. 22% returned for their sophomore year.

Applying SIU requires an essay and a high school transcript. The school recommends a minimum high school GPA of 2.0. Application deadline: rolling admissions. Deferred admission is possible.

SCHILLER INTERNATIONAL UNIVERSITY

Paris France

Urban setting ■ Private ■ Independent ■ Coed

Web site: www.schiller.edu
Contact: Ms. Kamala Dontamsetti, Associate Director of Admissions, 32 Boulevard de Vaugirard, Paris France
Telephone: 727-736-5082 ext. 240

Getting in Last Year 4 enrolled.

Financial Matters $14,560 tuition and fees (2002–03).

Academics SIU awards associate, bachelor's, and master's degrees. Challenging opportunities include advanced placement credit, accelerated degree programs, and student-designed majors. Special programs include internships, summer session for credit, and study-abroad.

Students of SIU The student body totals 100, of whom 57 are undergraduates. 42.1% are women and 57.9% are men.

Applying SIU requires an essay and a high school transcript. The school recommends a minimum high school GPA of 2.0. Application deadline: rolling admissions; 6/1 for financial aid, with a 4/1 priority date. Deferred admission is possible.

SCHILLER INTERNATIONAL UNIVERSITY

Heidelberg Germany

Urban setting ■ Private ■ Independent ■ Coed

Web site: www.schiller.edu
Contact: Ms. Kamala Dontamasetti, Associate Director of Admissions, Bergstrasse 106, Heidelberg Germany
Telephone: 727-736-5082 ext. 240
E-mail: siu_hd@compuserve.com

Getting in Last Year 43 enrolled.

Financial Matters $14,560 tuition and fees (2002–03); $7200 room and board.

Academics SIU awards associate, bachelor's, and master's degrees. Challenging opportunities include advanced placement credit, accelerated degree programs, and student-designed majors. Special programs include summer session for credit and study-abroad. The faculty at SIU has 9 full-time members.

Students of SIU The student body totals 215, of whom 163 are undergraduates. 45.4% are women and 54.6% are men.

Applying SIU requires an essay and a high school transcript. The school recommends a minimum high school GPA of 2.0. Application deadline: rolling admissions; 6/1 for financial aid, with a 4/1 priority date. Deferred admission is possible.

SCHILLER INTERNATIONAL UNIVERSITY

Madrid Spain

Urban setting ■ Private ■ Independent ■ Coed

Web site: www.schiller.edu
Contact: Ms. Kamala Dontamsetti, Associate Director of Admissions, San Bernardo 97-99, Edif. Colomina, Madrid Spain
Telephone: 727-736-5082 ext. 240

Getting in Last Year 22 enrolled.

Financial Matters $14,560 tuition and fees (2002–03).

Academics SIU awards associate, bachelor's, and master's degrees. Challenging opportunities include advanced placement credit, accelerated degree programs, and student-designed majors. Special programs include internships, summer session for credit, and study-abroad. The faculty at SIU has 6 full-time members.

Students of SIU The student body totals 214, of whom 173 are undergraduates. 37.6% are women and 62.4% are men.

Applying SIU requires an essay and a high school transcript. The school recommends a minimum high school GPA of 2.0. Application deadline: rolling admissions; 4/15 for financial aid. Deferred admission is possible.

SCHILLER INTERNATIONAL UNIVERSITY

London United Kingdom

Urban setting ■ Private ■ Independent ■ Coed

Web site: www.schiller.edu
Contact: Ms. Susan Russeff, Associate Director of Admissions, 453 Edgewater Drive, Dunedin, FL 34698
Telephone: 727-736-5082 ext. 239 or toll-free 800-336-4133 ext. 234 (out-of-state) **Fax:** 727-734-0359
E-mail: admissions@schiller.edu

Financial Matters $14,560 tuition and fees (2002–03); $7200 room and board.

Academics SIU awards associate, bachelor's, and master's degrees. Challenging opportunities include advanced placement credit, accelerated degree programs, student-designed majors, double majors, and independent study. Special programs include internships, summer session for credit, and study-abroad.

Students of SIU The student body totals 392, of whom 283 are undergraduates.

Applying SIU requires an essay and a high school transcript. The school recommends a minimum high school GPA of 2.0. Application deadline: rolling admissions; 4/15 priority date for financial aid. Deferred admission is possible.

SCHILLER INTERNATIONAL UNIVERSITY, AMERICAN COLLEGE OF SWITZERLAND

Leysin Switzerland

Small-town setting ■ Private ■ Independent ■ Coed

Web site: www.schiller.edu
Contact: United States Admissions Representative (ACS), 453 Edgewater Drive, Dunedin, FL 34698
Telephone: Toll-free 800-336-4133 (out-of-state) **Fax:** 813-734-0359

Getting in Last Year 10 enrolled.

Financial Matters $22,000 tuition and fees (2002–03); $16,400 room and board.

Academics ACS awards associate, bachelor's, and master's degrees. Challenging opportunities include advanced placement credit, accelerated degree programs, and student-designed majors. Special programs include internships, summer session for credit, and study-abroad. The faculty at ACS has 5 full-time members.

Students of ACS The student body totals 83, of whom 66 are undergraduates. 50% are women and 50% are men. Students come from 7 states and territories and 25 other countries. 75% returned for their sophomore year.

Applying ACS requires an essay, a high school transcript, 1 recommendation, and a minimum high school GPA of 2.0. Application deadline: rolling admissions. Deferred admission is possible.

SCHOOL OF THE ART INSTITUTE OF CHICAGO

Chicago, IL

Urban setting ■ Private ■ Independent ■ Coed

Web site: www.artic.edu/saic
Contact: Kendra E. Dane, Executive Director of Admissions and Marketing, 37 South Wabash, Chicago, IL 60603
Telephone: 312-899-5219 or toll-free 800-232-SAIC
E-mail: admiss@artic.edu

Getting in Last Year 1,121 applied; 77% were accepted; 292 enrolled (34%).

Financial Matters $22,500 tuition and fees (2002–03); $6825 room only.

Academics SAIC awards bachelor's and master's degrees. Challenging opportunities include advanced placement credit, student-designed majors, double majors, independent study, and a senior project. Special programs include cooperative education, internships, summer session for credit, off-campus study, and study-abroad. The faculty at SAIC has 123 full-time members, 89% with terminal degrees. The student-faculty ratio is 13:1.

Students of SAIC The student body totals 2,698, of whom 2,147 are undergraduates. 66.7% are women and 33.3% are men. Students come from 50 states and territories and 41 other countries. 23% are from Illinois. 13.7% are international students. 79% returned for their sophomore year.

Applying SAIC requires an essay, SAT I or ACT, a high school transcript, 1 recommendation, and portfolio. The school recommends an interview. Application deadline: 8/15; 3/15 priority date for financial aid. Deferred admission is possible.

SCHOOL OF THE MUSEUM OF FINE ARTS

Boston, MA

Urban setting ■ Private ■ Independent ■ Coed

Web site: www.smfa.edu
Contact: Mr. John A. Williamson, Director of Enrollment and Student Services, 230 The Fenway, Boston, MA 02115
Telephone: 617-369-3626 or toll-free 800-643-6078 (in-state)
Fax: 617-369-3679
E-mail: admissions@smfa.edu

Financial Matters $20,103 tuition and fees (2002–03); $9800 room and board; 47% average percent of need met; $16,532 average financial aid amount received per undergraduate.

Academics Museum School awards bachelor's and master's degrees and post-bachelor's certificates. Challenging opportunities include student-designed majors, double majors, and independent study. Special programs include internships, summer session for credit, off-campus study, study-abroad, and Army, Navy and Air Force ROTC. The most frequently chosen baccalaureate field is visual/performing arts. The faculty at Museum School has 57 full-time members.

Students of Museum School The student body is made up of 1,085 undergraduates. Students come from 33 states and territories and 30 other countries. 60% are from Massachusetts.

Applying Museum School requires an essay, a high school transcript, and portfolio, and in some cases SAT I or ACT and an interview. Application deadline: 3/1; 3/15 priority date for financial aid. Deferred admission is possible.

SCHOOL OF VISUAL ARTS

New York, NY

Urban setting ■ Private ■ Proprietary ■ Coed

Web site: www.schoolofvisualarts.edu
Contact: Mr. Richard M. Longo, Executive Director of Admissions, 209 East 23rd Street, New York, NY 10010
Telephone: 212-592-2100 ext. 2182 or toll-free 800-436-4204
Fax: 212-592-2116
E-mail: admissions@adm.schoolofvisualarts.edu

Getting in Last Year 1,876 applied; 69% were accepted; 464 enrolled (36%).

Financial Matters $17,830 tuition and fees (2002–03); $8000 room only; 50% average percent of need met; $10,753 average financial aid amount received per undergraduate (2001–02).

Academics SVA awards bachelor's and master's degrees. Challenging opportunities include double majors, independent study, and a senior project. Special programs include internships, summer session for credit, and study-abroad. The most frequently chosen baccalaureate field is visual/performing arts. The faculty at SVA has 148 full-time members, 32% with terminal degrees. The student-faculty ratio is 8:1.

Students of SVA The student body totals 5,243, of whom 4,867 are undergraduates. 54.5% are women and 45.5% are men. Students come from 45 states and territories and 19 other countries. 62% are from New York. 11.6% are international students. 86% returned for their sophomore year.

Applying SVA requires an essay, SAT I or ACT, a high school transcript, portfolio, and a minimum high school GPA of 2.3, and in some cases 1 recommendation. The school recommends an interview. Application deadline: rolling admissions; 2/1 priority date for financial aid. Deferred admission is possible.

SCHREINER UNIVERSITY

Kerrville, TX

Small-town setting ■ Private ■ Independent Religious ■ Coed

Web site: www.schreiner.edu
Contact: Ms. Peg Layton, Dean of Admission and Financial Aid, 2100 Memorial Boulevard, Kerrville, TX 78028
Telephone: 830-792-7277 or toll-free 800-343-4919 **Fax:** 830-792-7226
E-mail: admissions@schreiner.edu

Getting in Last Year 583 applied; 67% were accepted; 178 enrolled (45%).

Financial Matters $13,002 tuition and fees (2002–03); $6654 room and board; 69% average percent of need met; $12,528 average financial aid amount received per undergraduate (2001–02).

Academics Schreiner awards associate, bachelor's, and master's degrees and post-bachelor's certificates. Challenging opportunities include advanced placement credit, accelerated degree programs, student-designed majors, freshman honors college, an honors program, double majors, independent study, and a senior project. Special programs include cooperative education, internships, summer session for credit, and study-abroad. The most frequently chosen baccalaureate fields are business/marketing, parks and recreation, and psychology. The faculty at Schreiner has 50 full-time members, 64% with terminal degrees. The student-faculty ratio is 13:1.

Students of Schreiner The student body totals 780, of whom 739 are undergraduates. 58.3% are women and 41.7% are men. Students come from 8 states and territories. 98% are from Texas. 0.6% are international students. 66% returned for their sophomore year.

Applying Schreiner requires SAT I or ACT and a high school transcript, and in some cases an essay and 1 recommendation. The school recommends an essay, an interview, and a minimum high school GPA of 2.0. Application deadline: 8/1; 4/1 priority date for financial aid. Deferred admission is possible.

SCRIPPS COLLEGE

Claremont, CA

Suburban setting ■ Private ■ Independent ■ Women Only

Web site: www.scrippscollege.edu
Contact: Ms. Patricia F. Goldsmith, Dean of Admission and Financial Aid, 1030 Columbia Avenue, Claremont, CA 91711-3948
Telephone: 909-621-8149 or toll-free 800-770-1333 **Fax:** 909-607-7508
E-mail: admission@scrippscollege.edu

Getting in Last Year 1,371 applied; 58% were accepted; 201 enrolled (25%).

Financial Matters $25,700 tuition and fees (2002–03); $8300 room and board; 100% average percent of need met; $23,802 average financial aid amount received per undergraduate.

Academics Scripps awards bachelor's degrees and post-bachelor's certificates. Challenging opportunities include advanced placement credit, accelerated degree programs, student-designed majors, an honors program, double majors, independent study, and a senior project. Special programs include internships, off-campus study, study-abroad, and Army and Air Force ROTC. The most frequently chosen baccalaureate fields are social sciences and history, visual/performing arts, and biological/life sciences. The faculty at Scripps has 59 full-time members, 97% with terminal degrees. The student-faculty ratio is 12:1.

Students of Scripps The student body totals 816, of whom 798 are undergraduates. Students come from 45 states and territories and 16 other countries. 48% are from California. 2.3% are international students. 77% returned for their sophomore year.

Applying Scripps requires an essay, SAT I or ACT, a high school transcript, 3 recommendations, and graded writing sample. The school recommends an interview and a minimum high school GPA of 3.0. Application deadline: 2/1; 2/1 priority date for financial aid. Deferred admission is possible.

SEATTLE PACIFIC UNIVERSITY

Seattle, WA

Urban setting ■ Private ■ Independent Religious ■ Coed

Web site: www.spu.edu
Contact: Mrs. Jennifer Feddern Kenney, Director of Admissions, 3307 Third Avenue West, Seattle, WA 98119-1997
Telephone: 206-281-2517 or toll-free 800-366-3344 **Fax:** 206-281-2669
E-mail: admissions@spu.edu

Getting in Last Year 1,564 applied; 96% were accepted; 603 enrolled (40%).

Financial Matters $17,682 tuition and fees (2002–03); $6660 room and board; 79% average percent of need met; $14,140 average financial aid amount received per undergraduate.

Academics SPU awards bachelor's, master's, and doctoral degrees and post-master's certificates. Challenging opportunities include advanced placement credit, student-designed majors, an honors program, double majors, independent study, and a senior project. Special programs include cooperative education, internships, summer session for credit, off-campus study, study-abroad, and Army, Navy and Air Force ROTC. The most frequently chosen baccalaureate fields are business/marketing, social sciences and history, and health professions and related sciences. The faculty at SPU has 174 full-time members, 89% with terminal degrees. The student-faculty ratio is 16:1.

Students of SPU The student body totals 3,684, of whom 2,818 are undergraduates. 65.7% are women and 34.3% are men. Students come from 39 states and territories and 34 other countries. 65% are from Washington. 1.6% are international students. 80% returned for their sophomore year.

Applying SPU requires an essay, SAT I or ACT, a high school transcript, 2 recommendations, and a minimum high school GPA of 2.5. The school recommends SAT I. Application deadline: 6/1; 3/1 priority date for financial aid. Early and deferred admission are possible.

SEATTLE UNIVERSITY

Seattle, WA

Urban setting ■ Private ■ Independent Religious ■ Coed

Web site: www.seattleu.edu
Contact: Mr. Michael K. McKeon, Dean of Admissions, 900 Broadway, Seattle, WA 98122-4340
Telephone: 206-296-2000 or toll-free 800-542-0833 (in-state), 800-426-7123 (out-of-state) **Fax:** 206-296-5656

Seattle University (continued)

E-mail: admissions@seattleu.edu

Getting in Last Year 2,951 applied; 82% were accepted; 679 enrolled (28%).

Financial Matters $18,855 tuition and fees (2002–03); $7902 room and board; 90% average percent of need met; $18,926 average financial aid amount received per undergraduate.

Academics Seattle U awards bachelor's, master's, doctoral, and first-professional degrees and post-bachelor's and post-master's certificates. Challenging opportunities include advanced placement credit, accelerated degree programs, student-designed majors, freshman honors college, an honors program, double majors, independent study, and a senior project. Special programs include internships, summer session for credit, off-campus study, study-abroad, and Army and Air Force ROTC. The most frequently chosen baccalaureate fields are business/marketing, health professions and related sciences, and engineering/engineering technologies. The faculty at Seattle U has 335 full-time members, 87% with terminal degrees. The student-faculty ratio is 14:1.

Students of Seattle U The student body totals 6,337, of whom 3,561 are undergraduates. 61.3% are women and 38.7% are men. Students come from 54 states and territories and 69 other countries. 68% are from Washington. 9.2% are international students. 83% returned for their sophomore year.

Applying Seattle U requires an essay, SAT I or ACT, a high school transcript, 2 recommendations, and a minimum high school GPA of 2.5. Application deadline: 7/1; 2/1 priority date for financial aid. Early and deferred admission are possible.

SETON HALL UNIVERSITY

South Orange, NJ

Suburban setting ■ *Private* ■ *Independent Religious* ■ *Coed*

Web site: www.shu.edu

Contact: Ms. Alyssa McCloud, Acting Director of Admissions, Enrollment Services, Bayley Hall, South Orange, NJ 07079-2697

Telephone: 973-275-2576 or toll-free 800-THE HALL (out-of-state) **Fax:** 973-275-2040

E-mail: thehall@shu.edu

Getting in Last Year 5,575 applied; 85% were accepted; 1,164 enrolled (25%).

Financial Matters $20,830 tuition and fees (2002–03); $9268 room and board; 52% average percent of need met; $12,416 average financial aid amount received per undergraduate (2001–02).

Academics Seton Hall awards bachelor's, master's, doctoral, and first-professional degrees and post-master's certificates. Challenging opportunities include advanced placement credit, accelerated degree programs, an honors program, double majors, independent study, and a senior project. Special programs include cooperative education, internships, summer session for credit, study-abroad, and Army and Air Force ROTC. The most frequently chosen baccalaureate fields are business/marketing, protective services/public administration, and communications/communication technologies. The faculty at Seton Hall has 393 full-time members, 91% with terminal degrees. The student-faculty ratio is 14:1.

Students of Seton Hall The student body totals 9,596, of whom 5,080 are undergraduates. 52.4% are women and 47.6% are men. Students come from 41 states and territories and 54 other countries. 79% are from New Jersey. 2.2% are international students. 79% returned for their sophomore year.

Applying Seton Hall requires an essay, SAT I or ACT, a high school transcript, and counselor report, and in some cases an interview and a minimum high school GPA of 3.0. The school recommends an interview, recommendations, and a minimum high school GPA of 3.0. Application deadline: 3/1. Deferred admission is possible.

SETON HILL UNIVERSITY

Greensburg, PA

Small-town setting ■ *Private* ■ *Independent Religious* ■ *Coed*

Web site: www.setonhill.edu

Contact: Ms. Mary Kay Cooper, Director of Admissions, Seton Hill Drive, Greensburg, PA 15601

Telephone: 724-838-4255 or toll-free 800-826-6234 **Fax:** 724-830-1294

E-mail: admit@setonhill.edu

Getting in Last Year 912 applied; 83% were accepted; 215 enrolled (28%).

Financial Matters $17,370 tuition and fees (2002–03); $5900 room and board; 85% average percent of need met; $15,500 average financial aid amount received per undergraduate.

Academics Seton Hill awards bachelor's and master's degrees and post-bachelor's and post-master's certificates. Challenging opportunities include advanced placement credit, accelerated degree programs, student-designed majors, an honors program, double majors, independent study, and a senior project. Special programs include internships, summer session for credit, off-campus study, study-abroad, and Army ROTC. The most frequently chosen baccalaureate fields are business/marketing, health professions and related sciences, and psychology. The faculty at Seton Hill has 61 full-time members, 82% with terminal degrees. The student-faculty ratio is 13:1.

Students of Seton Hill The student body totals 1,564, of whom 1,188 are undergraduates. 78.5% are women and 21.5% are men. Students come from 23 states and territories and 9 other countries. 85% are from Pennsylvania. 1.9% are international students. 71% returned for their sophomore year.

Applying Seton Hill requires a high school transcript, portfolio for art program, audition for music and theater programs, separate application process required for physician assistant program, and a minimum high school GPA of 2.0. The school recommends an essay, SAT I or ACT, an interview, and recommendations. Application deadline: rolling admissions. Early and deferred admission are possible.

SHASTA BIBLE COLLEGE

Redding, CA

Small-town setting ■ *Private* ■ *Independent Religious* ■ *Coed*

Web site: www.shasta.edu

Contact: Ms. Dawn Rodriguez, Registrar, 2980 Hartnell Avenue, Redding, CA 96002

Telephone: 530-221-4275 or toll-free 800-800-45BC (in-state), 800-800-6929 (out-of-state) **Fax:** 530-221-6929

E-mail: ggunn@shasta.edu

Getting in Last Year 43 enrolled.

Financial Matters $5870 tuition and fees (2002–03); $1575 room only; 63% average percent of need met; $3684 average financial aid amount received per undergraduate.

Academics Shasta Bible College awards associate, bachelor's, and master's degrees. Challenging opportunities include double majors, independent study, and a senior project. The most frequently chosen baccalaureate field is education. The faculty at Shasta Bible College has 6 full-time members, 100% with terminal degrees. The student-faculty ratio is 11:1.

Students of Shasta Bible College The student body totals 178, of whom 84 are undergraduates. 35.7% are women and 64.3% are men. Students come from 5 states and territories and 1 other country. 97% are from California. 3.6% are international students. 90% returned for their sophomore year.

Applying Shasta Bible College requires an essay, a high school transcript, and 4 recommendations.

SHAWNEE STATE UNIVERSITY

Portsmouth, OH

Small-town setting ■ *Public* ■ *State-supported* ■ *Coed*

Web site: www.shawnee.edu

Contact: Mr. Bob Trusz, Director of Admission, 940 Second Street, Commons Building, Portsmouth, OH 45662

Telephone: 740-351-3610 ext. 610 or toll-free 800-959-2SSU **Fax:** 740-351-3111

E-mail: to_ssu@shawnee.edu

Getting in Last Year 2,478 applied; 100% were accepted; 730 enrolled (29%).

Financial Matters $4869 resident tuition and fees (2002–03); $7965 nonresident tuition and fees (2002–03); $5421 room and board; 70% average percent of need met; $3972 average financial aid amount received per undergraduate (1999–2000 estimated).

Academics Shawnee State awards associate and bachelor's degrees. Challenging opportunities include advanced placement credit, an honors program, double majors, independent study, and a senior project. Special programs include internships, summer session for credit, off-campus study, and study-abroad. The most frequently chosen baccalaureate fields are social sciences and history, business/marketing, and liberal arts/general studies. The faculty at Shawnee State has 121 full-time members, 49% with terminal degrees. The student-faculty ratio is 18:1.

Students of Shawnee State The student body is made up of 3,606 undergraduates. 61.6% are women and 38.4% are men. Students come from 10 states and territories and 9 other countries. 91% are from Ohio. 0.4% are international students. 56% returned for their sophomore year.

Applying Shawnee State requires a high school transcript, and in some cases an interview and recommendations. The school recommends ACT. Application deadline: rolling admissions; 4/1 priority date for financial aid. Deferred admission is possible.

SHAW UNIVERSITY

Raleigh, NC

Urban setting ■ *Private* ■ *Independent Religious* ■ *Coed*

Web site: www.shawuniversity.edu

Contact: Mr. Paul Vandergrift, Director of Admissions and Recruitment, 118 East South Street, Raleigh, NC 27601-2399

Telephone: 919-546-8275 or toll-free 800-214-6683 **Fax:** 919-546-8271

E-mail: paulv@shawu.edu

Getting in Last Year 3,471 applied; 57% were accepted; 564 enrolled (28%).

Financial Matters $8898 tuition and fees (2002–03); $5488 room and board; $7634 average financial aid amount received per undergraduate (2001–02).

Academics Shaw University awards associate, bachelor's, master's, and first-professional degrees. Challenging opportunities include advanced placement credit, accelerated degree programs, student-designed majors, an honors program, double majors, independent study, and a senior project. Special programs include internships, summer session for credit, off-campus study, study-abroad, and Army and Air Force ROTC. The most frequently chosen baccalaureate fields are business/marketing, protective services/public administration, and social sciences and history. The faculty at Shaw University has 85 full-time members, 68% with terminal degrees. The student-faculty ratio is 15:1.

Students of Shaw University The student body totals 2,683, of whom 2,535 are undergraduates. 62.2% are women and 37.8% are men. Students come from 33 states and territories and 10 other countries. 75% are from North Carolina. 3.3% are international students. 60% returned for their sophomore year.

Applying Shaw University requires an essay, SAT I or ACT, a high school transcript, and a minimum high school GPA of 2.0. Application deadline: 7/30; 3/1 priority date for financial aid. Early and deferred admission are possible.

SHELDON JACKSON COLLEGE

Sitka, AK

Small-town setting ■ Private ■ Independent Religious ■ Coed

Web site: www.sj-alaska.edu
Contact: Ms. Louise Driver, Director of Admissions, 801 Lincoln Street, Sitka, AK 99835
Telephone: 907-747-5208 or toll-free 800-478-4556 **Fax:** 907-747-6366
E-mail: ldriver@sj-alaska.edu

Getting in Last Year 242 applied; 66% were accepted.

Financial Matters $9650 tuition and fees (2002–03); $6920 room and board; 60% average percent of need met; $7300 average financial aid amount received per undergraduate (2001–02).

Academics Sheldon Jackson awards associate and bachelor's degrees. Challenging opportunities include advanced placement credit, student-designed majors, double majors, independent study, and a senior project. Internships is a special program. The faculty at Sheldon Jackson has 20 full-time members, 55% with terminal degrees. The student-faculty ratio is 14:1.

Students of Sheldon Jackson The student body is made up of 271 undergraduates. Students come from 26 states and territories. 58% are from Alaska. 60% returned for their sophomore year.

Applying Sheldon Jackson requires a high school transcript. The school recommends an essay and a minimum high school GPA of 2.0. Application deadline: rolling admissions; 5/1 for financial aid. Deferred admission is possible.

SHENANDOAH UNIVERSITY

Winchester, VA

Small-town setting ■ Private ■ Independent Religious ■ Coed

Web site: www.su.edu
Contact: Mr. David Anthony, Dean of Admissions, 1460 University Drive, Winchester, VA 22601-5195
Telephone: 540-665-4581 or toll-free 800-432-2266 **Fax:** 540-665-4627
E-mail: admit@su.edu

Getting in Last Year 1,312 applied; 80% were accepted; 326 enrolled (31%).

Financial Matters $17,510 tuition and fees (2002–03); $6600 room and board; 84% average percent of need met; $12,107 average financial aid amount received per undergraduate.

Academics Shenandoah awards associate, bachelor's, master's, doctoral, and first-professional degrees and post-bachelor's and post-master's certificates. Challenging opportunities include advanced placement credit, accelerated degree programs, double majors, independent study, and a senior project. Special programs include internships, summer session for credit, off-campus study, and study-abroad. The most frequently chosen baccalaureate fields are visual/performing arts, education, and health professions and related sciences. The faculty at Shenandoah has 167 full-time members, 78% with terminal degrees. The student-faculty ratio is 10:1.

Students of Shenandoah The student body totals 2,583, of whom 1,391 are undergraduates. 55.9% are women and 44.1% are men. Students come from 37 states and territories and 22 other countries. 63% are from Virginia. 4.7% are international students. 68% returned for their sophomore year.

Applying Shenandoah requires SAT I or ACT and a high school transcript, and in some cases an interview and audition. The school recommends a minimum high school GPA of 2.0. Application deadline: rolling admissions; 3/1 priority date for financial aid. Deferred admission is possible.

SHEPHERD COLLEGE

Shepherdstown, WV

Small-town setting ■ Public ■ State-supported ■ Coed

Web site: www.shepherd.edu
Contact: Mr. Karl L. Wolf, Director of Admissions, PO Box 3210, Shepherdstown, WV 25443-3210
Telephone: 304-876-5212 or toll-free 800-344-5231 **Fax:** 304-876-5165
E-mail: admoff@shepherd.edu

Getting in Last Year 1,615 applied; 91% were accepted; 774 enrolled (52%).

Financial Matters $6982 nonresident tuition and fees (2002–03); $4738 room and board; 71% average percent of need met; $7435 average financial aid amount received per undergraduate.

Academics Shepherd awards associate and bachelor's degrees. Challenging opportunities include advanced placement credit, accelerated degree programs, an honors program, double majors, and a senior project. Special programs include cooperative education, internships, and summer session for credit. The most frequently chosen baccalaureate fields are education, liberal arts/general studies, and business/marketing. The faculty at Shepherd has 107 full-time members, 80% with terminal degrees. The student-faculty ratio is 18:1.

Students of Shepherd The student body is made up of 4,676 undergraduates. 58.4% are women and 41.6% are men. Students come from 50 states and territories and 23 other countries. 66% are from West Virginia. 1.1% are international students. 69% returned for their sophomore year.

Applying Shepherd requires SAT I or ACT, a high school transcript, and a minimum high school GPA of 2.5. The school recommends an essay, an interview, 3 recommendations, and a minimum high school GPA of 3.0. Application deadline: 2/1; 3/1 priority date for financial aid. Early and deferred admission are possible.

SHIMER COLLEGE

Waukegan, IL

Suburban setting ■ Private ■ Independent ■ Coed

Web site: www.shimer.edu
Contact: Mr. Bill Paterson, Associate Director of Admissions, PO Box 500, Waukegan, IL 60079-0500
Telephone: 847-249-7175 or toll-free 800-215-7173 **Fax:** 847-249-8798
E-mail: admissions@shimer.edu

Getting in Last Year 47 applied; 94% were accepted; 23 enrolled (52%).

Financial Matters $16,050 tuition and fees (2002–03); $2530 room and board.

Academics Shimer awards bachelor's degrees and post-bachelor's certificates. Challenging opportunities include student-designed majors, double majors, independent study, and a senior project. Special programs include cooperative education, internships, summer session for credit, off-campus study, and study-abroad. The faculty at Shimer has 13 full-time members, 85% with terminal degrees. The student-faculty ratio is 10:1.

Students of Shimer The student body totals 136, of whom 115 are undergraduates. 43.5% are women and 56.5% are men. Students come from 12 states and territories and 3 other countries. 70% are from Illinois. 3.5% are international students. 66% returned for their sophomore year.

Applying Shimer requires an essay, a high school transcript, an interview, and 1 recommendation, and in some cases SAT I or ACT. The school recommends SAT I or ACT. Application deadline: 8/30. Early and deferred admission are possible.

SHIPPENSBURG UNIVERSITY OF PENNSYLVANIA

Shippensburg, PA

Rural setting ■ Public ■ State-supported ■ Coed

Web site: www.ship.edu
Contact: Mr. Joseph Cretella, Dean of Undergraduate and Graduate Admissions, 1871 Old Main Drive, Shippensburg, PA 17257-2299
Telephone: 717-477-1231 or toll-free 800-822-8028 (in-state) **Fax:** 717-477-4016
E-mail: admiss@ship.edu

Getting in Last Year 5,769 applied; 69% were accepted; 1,509 enrolled (38%).

Financial Matters $5502 resident tuition and fees (2002–03); $12,070 nonresident tuition and fees (2002–03); $4864 room and board; 79% average percent of need met; $5863 average financial aid amount received per undergraduate.

Academics Ship awards bachelor's and master's degrees and post-master's certificates. Challenging opportunities include advanced placement credit, accelerated degree programs, an honors program, double majors, independent study, and a senior project. Special programs include cooperative education, internships, summer session for credit, off-campus study, study-abroad, and Army ROTC. The most frequently chosen baccalaureate fields are business/marketing, education, and protective services/public administration. The faculty at Ship has 302 full-time members, 88% with terminal degrees. The student-faculty ratio is 19:1.

Students of Ship The student body totals 7,412, of whom 6,413 are undergraduates. 54.4% are women and 45.6% are men. Students come from 23 states and territories and 33 other countries. 94% are from Pennsylvania. 0.6% are international students. 80% returned for their sophomore year.

Shippensburg University of Pennsylvania (continued)

Applying Ship requires SAT I or ACT and a high school transcript. The school recommends recommendations. Application deadline: rolling admissions. Early and deferred admission are possible.

SHORTER COLLEGE

Rome, GA

Small-town setting ■ Private ■ Independent Religious ■ Coed

Web site: www.shorter.edu

Contact: Ms. Wendy Sutton, Director of Admissions, 315 Shorter Avenue, Rome, GA 30165

Telephone: 706-233-7342 or toll-free 800-868-6980 **Fax:** 706-236-7224

E-mail: admissions@shorter.edu

Getting in Last Year 580 applied; 83% were accepted; 218 enrolled (45%).

Financial Matters $10,640 tuition and fees (2002–03); $5565 room and board; 70% average percent of need met; $9416 average financial aid amount received per undergraduate.

Academics Shorter awards associate and bachelor's degrees. Challenging opportunities include advanced placement credit, student-designed majors, an honors program, double majors, independent study, and a senior project. Special programs include internships, summer session for credit, off-campus study, and study-abroad. The most frequently chosen baccalaureate fields are education, biological/life sciences, and business/marketing. The faculty at Shorter has 65 full-time members, 72% with terminal degrees. The student-faculty ratio is 11:1.

Students of Shorter The student body is made up of 925 undergraduates. 65.9% are women and 34.1% are men. Students come from 18 states and territories and 18 other countries. 89% are from Georgia. 3.5% are international students. 68% returned for their sophomore year.

Applying Shorter requires an essay, SAT I or ACT, and a high school transcript, and in some cases an interview and audition for music and theater programs. The school recommends an interview, 1 recommendation, and a minimum high school GPA of 2.0. Application deadline: 8/25. Early and deferred admission are possible.

SIENA COLLEGE

Loudonville, NY

Suburban setting ■ Private ■ Independent Religious ■ Coed

Web site: www.siena.edu

Contact: Mr. Edward Jones, Director of Admissions, 515 Loudon Road, Loudonville, NY 12211-1462

Telephone: 518-783-2423 or toll-free 888-AT-SIENA **Fax:** 518-783-2436

E-mail: admit@siena.edu

Getting in Last Year 3,945 applied; 58% were accepted; 678 enrolled (30%).

Financial Matters $16,945 tuition and fees (2002–03); $7010 room and board; 80% average percent of need met; $11,754 average financial aid amount received per undergraduate (2001–02).

Academics Siena awards bachelor's degrees. Challenging opportunities include advanced placement credit, accelerated degree programs, an honors program, double majors, independent study, and a senior project. Special programs include internships, summer session for credit, off-campus study, study-abroad, and Army and Air Force ROTC. The most frequently chosen baccalaureate fields are business/marketing, social sciences and history, and psychology. The faculty at Siena has 166 full-time members, 86% with terminal degrees. The student-faculty ratio is 14:1.

Students of Siena The student body is made up of 3,405 undergraduates. 56.5% are women and 43.5% are men. Students come from 27 states and territories. 80% are from New York. 0.3% are international students. 88% returned for their sophomore year.

Applying Siena requires an essay, SAT I or ACT, a high school transcript, and 1 recommendation, and in some cases an interview. Application deadline: 3/1; 2/1 priority date for financial aid. Early and deferred admission are possible.

SIENA HEIGHTS UNIVERSITY

Adrian, MI

Small-town setting ■ Private ■ Independent Religious ■ Coed

Web site: www.sienahts.edu

Contact: Mr. Kevin Kucera, Dean of Admissions and Enrollment Services, 1247 East Siena Heights Drive, Adrian, MI 49221-1796

Telephone: 517-264-7180 or toll-free 800-521-0009 **Fax:** 517-264-7745

E-mail: admissions@sienahts.edu

Getting in Last Year 870 applied; 72% were accepted.

Financial Matters $13,630 tuition and fees (2002–03); $5130 room and board; 66% average percent of need met; $12,200 average financial aid amount received per undergraduate.

Academics Siena awards associate, bachelor's, and master's degrees. Challenging opportunities include advanced placement credit, accelerated degree programs, student-designed majors, double majors, independent study, and a senior project. Special programs include cooperative education, internships, summer session for credit, off-campus study, and study-abroad. The faculty at Siena has 65 full-time members, 72% with terminal degrees. The student-faculty ratio is 14:1.

Students of Siena The student body totals 2,024, of whom 1,810 are undergraduates. Students come from 8 states and territories.

Applying Siena requires SAT I or ACT and a high school transcript, and in some cases an essay, an interview, and recommendations. The school recommends an interview and a minimum high school GPA of 2.3. Application deadline: rolling admissions; 3/15 priority date for financial aid. Deferred admission is possible.

SIERRA NEVADA COLLEGE

Incline Village, NV

Small-town setting ■ Private ■ Independent ■ Coed

Web site: www.sierranevada.edu

Contact: Mr. Brett Schraeder, Dean of Enrollment, 999 Tahoe Boulevard, David Hall II, Incline Village, NV 89451

Telephone: 775-831-7799 ext. 4047 or toll-free 800-332-8666 ext. 4046 (out-of-state) **Fax:** 775-831-1347

E-mail: admissions@sierranevada.edu

Getting in Last Year 265 applied; 85% were accepted; 92 enrolled (41%).

Financial Matters $18,810 tuition and fees (2002–03); $6580 room and board; 60% average percent of need met; $14,000 average financial aid amount received per undergraduate (2001–02).

Academics SNC awards bachelor's degrees and post-bachelor's certificates. Challenging opportunities include advanced placement credit, accelerated degree programs, an honors program, double majors, independent study, and a senior project. Special programs include cooperative education, internships, summer session for credit, study-abroad, and Army ROTC. The faculty at SNC has 21 full-time members, 71% with terminal degrees. The student-faculty ratio is 8:1.

Students of SNC The student body is made up of 295 undergraduates. 47.1% are women and 52.9% are men. Students come from 33 states and territories and 6 other countries. 30% are from Nevada. 3.4% are international students. 54% returned for their sophomore year.

Applying SNC requires an essay, SAT I and SAT II or ACT, a high school transcript, and a minimum high school GPA of 2.0, and in some cases recommendations and school report form for high school seniors. The school recommends an interview. Application deadline: rolling admissions; 6/1 priority date for financial aid. Early and deferred admission are possible.

SILVER LAKE COLLEGE

Manitowoc, WI

Rural setting ■ Private ■ Independent Religious ■ Coed

Web site: www.sl.edu

Contact: Ms. Janis Algozine, Vice President, Dean of Students, 2406 South Alverno Road, Manitowoc, WI

Telephone: 920-684-5955 ext. 175 or toll-free 800-236-4752 ext. 175 (in-state) **Fax:** 920-684-7082

E-mail: admslc@silver.sl.edu

Getting in Last Year 86 applied; 47% were accepted; 35 enrolled (88%).

Financial Matters $13,650 tuition and fees (2002–03); $3800 room only; 68% average percent of need met; $6443 average financial aid amount received per undergraduate (2001–02).

Academics SLC awards associate, bachelor's, and master's degrees and post-bachelor's certificates. Challenging opportunities include advanced placement credit, accelerated degree programs, student-designed majors, double majors, independent study, and a senior project. Special programs include cooperative education, internships, and summer session for credit. The most frequently chosen baccalaureate fields are business/marketing, education, and engineering/engineering technologies. The faculty at SLC has 44 full-time members, 50% with terminal degrees. The student-faculty ratio is 8:1.

Students of SLC The student body totals 1,146, of whom 733 are undergraduates. 69.2% are women and 30.8% are men. Students come from 3 states and territories and 1 other country. 98% are from Wisconsin. 0.2% are international students. 66% returned for their sophomore year.

Applying SLC requires SAT I or ACT, a high school transcript, and a minimum high school GPA of 2.0, and in some cases an interview and audition. Application deadline: 8/31; 6/1 for financial aid, with a 4/15 priority date. Early and deferred admission are possible.

SIMMONS COLLEGE

Boston, MA

Urban setting ■ Private ■ Independent ■ Women Only

Web site: www.simmons.edu

Contact: Ms. Jennifer O'Loughlin Hieber, Director of Undergraduate Admissions, 300 The Fenway, Boston, MA 02115

Telephone: 617-521-2048 or toll-free 800-345-8468 (out-of-state)
Fax: 617-521-3190
E-mail: ugadm@simmons.edu

Getting in Last Year 1,704 applied; 68% were accepted; 258 enrolled (22%).

Financial Matters $22,668 tuition and fees (2002–03); $9100 room and board; 95% average percent of need met; $15,695 average financial aid amount received per undergraduate.

Academics Simmons awards bachelor's, master's, and doctoral degrees and post-bachelor's and post-master's certificates. Challenging opportunities include advanced placement credit, accelerated degree programs, student-designed majors, freshman honors college, an honors program, double majors, independent study, and a senior project. Special programs include internships, summer session for credit, off-campus study, study-abroad, and Army, Navy and Air Force ROTC. The most frequently chosen baccalaureate fields are health professions and related sciences, social sciences and history, and communications/communication technologies. The faculty at Simmons has 175 full-time members, 65% with terminal degrees. The student-faculty ratio is 12:1.

Students of Simmons The student body totals 3,315, of whom 1,224 are undergraduates. Students come from 38 states and territories and 26 other countries. 57% are from Massachusetts. 4.5% are international students. 83% returned for their sophomore year.

Applying Simmons requires an essay, SAT I or ACT, a high school transcript, and 2 recommendations. The school recommends an interview and a minimum high school GPA of 3.0. Application deadline: 2/2; 2/1 priority date for financial aid. Early and deferred admission are possible.

SIMON FRASER UNIVERSITY

Burnaby, BC Canada

Suburban setting ■ *Public* ■ *Coed*

Web site: www.sfu.ca
Contact: Mr. Nick Heath, Director of Admissions, 8888 University Drive, Burnaby, BC V5A 1S6 Canada
Telephone: 604-291-3224 **Fax:** 604-291-4969
E-mail: undergraduate-admissions@sfu.ca

Getting in Last Year 2,692 enrolled (49%).

Financial Matters $3091 nonresident tuition and fees (2002–03); $2628 room only.

Academics SFU awards bachelor's, master's, and doctoral degrees and post-bachelor's and post-master's certificates. Challenging opportunities include advanced placement credit, student-designed majors, an honors program, double majors, independent study, and a senior project. Special programs include cooperative education, summer session for credit, off-campus study, and study-abroad. The faculty at SFU has 685 members, 88% with terminal degrees. The student-faculty ratio is 23:1.

Students of SFU The student body totals 21,624, of whom 18,188 are undergraduates. 55.9% are women and 44.1% are men. Students come from 11 states and territories and 78 other countries. 94% are from British Columbia. 83% returned for their sophomore year.

Applying SFU requires SAT I or ACT, a high school transcript, and a minimum high school GPA of 3.2, and in some cases an essay, an interview, and recommendations. Application deadline: 4/30; 11/15 for financial aid, with a 7/1 priority date. Early admission is possible.

SIMON'S ROCK COLLEGE OF BARD

Great Barrington, MA

Rural setting ■ *Private* ■ *Independent* ■ *Coed*

Web site: www.simons-rock.edu
Contact: Ms. Mary King Austin, Director of Admissions, 84 Alford Road, Great Barrington, MA 01230-9702
Telephone: 413-528-7317 or toll-free 800-235-7186 **Fax:** 413-528-7334
E-mail: admit@simons-rock.edu

Getting in Last Year 480 applied; 50% were accepted; 154 enrolled (64%).

Financial Matters $27,180 tuition and fees (2002–03); $7160 room and board; 70% average percent of need met; $15,763 average financial aid amount received per undergraduate.

Academics Simon's Rock awards associate and bachelor's degrees. Challenging opportunities include student-designed majors, double majors, independent study, and a senior project. Special programs include internships, off-campus study, and study-abroad. The most frequently chosen baccalaureate fields are visual/performing arts, English, and social sciences and history. The faculty at Simon's Rock has 35 full-time members, 91% with terminal degrees. The student-faculty ratio is 9:1.

Students of Simon's Rock The student body is made up of 409 undergraduates. 58.9% are women and 41.1% are men. Students come from 42 states and territories and 5 other countries. 20% are from Massachusetts. 1.5% are international students. 81% returned for their sophomore year.

Applying Simon's Rock requires an essay, SAT I, PSAT, a high school transcript, an interview, 2 recommendations, parent application, and a minimum high school GPA of 2.0. The school recommends ACT and a minimum high school GPA of 3.0. Application deadline: 6/15. Early and deferred admission are possible.

SIMPSON COLLEGE

Indianola, IA

Small-town setting ■ *Private* ■ *Independent Religious* ■ *Coed*

Web site: www.simpson.edu
Contact: Ms. Deborah Tierney, Vice President for Enrollment, 701 North C Street, Indianola, IA 50125
Telephone: 515-961-1624 or toll-free 800-362-2454 **Fax:** 515-961-1870
E-mail: admiss@simpson.edu

Getting in Last Year 1,177 applied; 85% were accepted; 381 enrolled (38%).

Financial Matters $16,649 tuition and fees (2002–03); $5561 room and board; 88% average percent of need met; $17,200 average financial aid amount received per undergraduate.

Academics Simpson awards bachelor's degrees and post-bachelor's certificates. Challenging opportunities include advanced placement credit, accelerated degree programs, student-designed majors, freshman honors college, an honors program, double majors, independent study, and a senior project. Special programs include cooperative education, internships, summer session for credit, off-campus study, and study-abroad. The most frequently chosen baccalaureate fields are business/marketing, communications/communication technologies, and education. The faculty at Simpson has 84 full-time members, 87% with terminal degrees. The student-faculty ratio is 14:1.

Students of Simpson The student body is made up of 1,845 undergraduates. 59.3% are women and 40.7% are men. Students come from 26 states and territories and 13 other countries. 90% are from Iowa. 1.7% are international students. 82% returned for their sophomore year.

Applying Simpson requires SAT I or ACT, a high school transcript, and 1 recommendation. The school recommends an interview and rank in upper 50% of high school class. Application deadline: 8/15. Early and deferred admission are possible.

SIMPSON COLLEGE AND GRADUATE SCHOOL

Redding, CA

Suburban setting ■ *Private* ■ *Independent Religious* ■ *Coed*

Web site: www.simpsonca.edu
Contact: Mrs. Beth Spencer, Director of Enrollment Support, 2211 College View Drive, Redding, CA 96003
Telephone: 530-226-4606 ext. 2602 or toll-free 800-598-2493
Fax: 530-226-4861
E-mail: admissions@simpsonca.edu

Getting in Last Year 766 applied; 66% were accepted; 205 enrolled (41%).

Financial Matters $13,680 tuition and fees (2002–03); $5520 room and board; 84% average percent of need met; $10,815 average financial aid amount received per undergraduate.

Academics Simpson awards associate, bachelor's, and master's degrees. Challenging opportunities include advanced placement credit, accelerated degree programs, student-designed majors, an honors program, double majors, independent study, and a senior project. Special programs include internships, summer session for credit, off-campus study, and study-abroad. The most frequently chosen baccalaureate fields are liberal arts/general studies, business/marketing, and psychology. The faculty at Simpson has 40 full-time members, 63% with terminal degrees. The student-faculty ratio is 23:1.

Students of Simpson The student body totals 1,265, of whom 1,031 are undergraduates. 63.7% are women and 36.3% are men. Students come from 30 states and territories and 8 other countries. 76% are from California. 0.7% are international students. 72% returned for their sophomore year.

Applying Simpson requires an essay, SAT I or ACT, a high school transcript, 2 recommendations, Christian commitment, and a minimum high school GPA of 2.0, and in some cases an interview. Application deadline: rolling admissions; 3/2 priority date for financial aid. Deferred admission is possible.

SI TANKA HURON UNIVERSITY

Huron, SD

Small-town setting ■ *Private* ■ *Proprietary* ■ *Coed*

Web site: www.huron.edu
Contact: Mr. Tyler Fisher, Director of Admissions, 333 9th Street Southwest, Huron, SD 57350
Telephone: 605-352-8721 ext. 41 or toll-free 800-710-7159 **Fax:** 605-352-7421
E-mail: admissions@huron.edu

Getting in Last Year 622 applied; 39% were accepted; 175 enrolled (72%).

Si Tanka Huron University (continued)

Financial Matters $8700 tuition and fees (2002–03); $2950 room and board; 75% average percent of need met; $5250 average financial aid amount received per undergraduate (2001–02).

Academics Si Tanka Huron University awards associate and bachelor's degrees. Challenging opportunities include advanced placement credit, accelerated degree programs, freshman honors college, an honors program, double majors, independent study, and a senior project. Special programs include cooperative education and summer session for credit. The most frequently chosen baccalaureate field is law/legal studies. The faculty at Si Tanka Huron University has 18 full-time members. The student-faculty ratio is 12:1.

Students of Si Tanka Huron University The student body is made up of 528 undergraduates. 44.9% are women and 55.1% are men. Students come from 27 states and territories. 62% are from South Dakota. 41% returned for their sophomore year.

Applying Si Tanka Huron University requires a high school transcript, applicants for athletic scholarship programs must meet approved ACT requirement, and a minimum high school GPA of 2.0. The school recommends SAT I or ACT and an interview. Application deadline: rolling admissions. Early and deferred admission are possible.

SKIDMORE COLLEGE

Saratoga Springs, NY

Small-town setting ■ Private ■ Independent ■ Coed

Web site: www.skidmore.edu
Contact: Ms. Mary Lou W. Bates, Director of Admissions, 815 North Broadway, Saratoga Springs, NY 12866-1632
Telephone: 518-580-5570 or toll-free 800-867-6007 **Fax:** 518-580-5584
E-mail: admissions@skidmore.edu

Getting in Last Year 5,606 applied; 46% were accepted; 636 enrolled (25%).

Financial Matters $27,980 tuition and fees (2002–03); $7835 room and board; 98% average percent of need met; $23,148 average financial aid amount received per undergraduate.

Academics Skidmore awards bachelor's and master's degrees. Challenging opportunities include advanced placement credit, accelerated degree programs, student-designed majors, an honors program, double majors, independent study, and a senior project. Special programs include internships, summer session for credit, off-campus study, study-abroad, and Army and Air Force ROTC. The most frequently chosen baccalaureate fields are social sciences and history, business/marketing, and visual/performing arts. The faculty at Skidmore has 192 full-time members, 84% with terminal degrees. The student-faculty ratio is 11:1.

Students of Skidmore The student body totals 2,557, of whom 2,506 are undergraduates. 60.4% are women and 39.6% are men. Students come from 44 states and territories and 27 other countries. 29% are from New York. 1.1% are international students. 93% returned for their sophomore year.

Applying Skidmore requires an essay, SAT I or ACT, a high school transcript, and 2 recommendations. The school recommends an interview. Application deadline: 1/15; 1/15 for financial aid. Early and deferred admission are possible.

SLIPPERY ROCK UNIVERSITY OF PENNSYLVANIA

Slippery Rock, PA

Rural setting ■ Public ■ State-supported ■ Coed

Web site: www.sru.edu
Contact: Mr. James Barrett, Director of Undergraduate Admissions, 104 Maltby Center, Slippery Rock, PA 16057
Telephone: 724-738-2015 ext. 4984 or toll-free 800-SRU-9111 **Fax:** 724-738-2913
E-mail: asktherock@sru.edu

Getting in Last Year 3,859 applied; 78% were accepted; 1,437 enrolled (48%).

Financial Matters $5548 resident tuition and fees (2002–03); $12,116 nonresident tuition and fees (2002–03); $4400 room and board; 89% average percent of need met; $6162 average financial aid amount received per undergraduate.

Academics Slippery Rock awards bachelor's, master's, and doctoral degrees and post-bachelor's and post-master's certificates. Challenging opportunities include advanced placement credit, accelerated degree programs, an honors program, double majors, independent study, and a senior project. Special programs include internships, summer session for credit, off-campus study, study-abroad, and Army ROTC. The most frequently chosen baccalaureate fields are education, parks and recreation, and business/marketing. The faculty at Slippery Rock has 361 full-time members, 78% with terminal degrees. The student-faculty ratio is 18:1.

Students of Slippery Rock The student body totals 7,530, of whom 6,814 are undergraduates. 57.3% are women and 42.7% are men. Students come from 27 states and territories and 55 other countries. 96% are from Pennsylvania. 2.9% are international students. 71% returned for their sophomore year.

Applying Slippery Rock requires SAT I or ACT and a high school transcript, and in some cases an essay and an interview. The school recommends an essay and an interview. Application deadline: 5/1 priority date for financial aid. Early and deferred admission are possible.

SMITH COLLEGE

Northampton, MA

Urban setting ■ Private ■ Independent ■ Women Only

Web site: www.smith.edu
Contact: Ms. Audrey Y. Smith, Director of Admissions, 7 College Lane, Northampton, MA 01063
Telephone: 413-585-2500 **Fax:** 413-585-2527
E-mail: admission@smith.edu

Getting in Last Year 3,047 applied; 53% were accepted; 679 enrolled (42%).

Financial Matters $25,986 tuition and fees (2002–03); $8950 room and board; 100% average percent of need met; $25,647 average financial aid amount received per undergraduate.

Academics Smith awards bachelor's, master's, and doctoral degrees and post-bachelor's and post-master's certificates. Challenging opportunities include advanced placement credit, accelerated degree programs, student-designed majors, double majors, independent study, and a senior project. Special programs include internships, off-campus study, study-abroad, and Army and Air Force ROTC. The most frequently chosen baccalaureate fields are social sciences and history, biological/life sciences, and visual/performing arts. The faculty at Smith has 287 full-time members, 95% with terminal degrees. The student-faculty ratio is 9:1.

Students of Smith The student body totals 3,121, of whom 2,647 are undergraduates. Students come from 53 states and territories and 62 other countries. 24% are from Massachusetts. 6.5% are international students. 91% returned for their sophomore year.

Applying Smith requires an essay, SAT I or ACT, a high school transcript, and 3 recommendations. The school recommends SAT II Subject Tests, SAT II: Writing Test, and an interview. Application deadline: 1/15; 2/1 for financial aid. Early and deferred admission are possible.

SONOMA STATE UNIVERSITY

Rohnert Park, CA

Small-town setting ■ Public ■ State-supported ■ Coed

Web site: www.sonoma.edu
Contact: Mr. Gustavo Flores, Interim Director of Admissions, 1801 East Cotati Avenue, Rohnert Park, CA 94928
Telephone: 707-664-2074 **Fax:** 707-664-2060
E-mail: csumentor@sonoma.edu

Getting in Last Year 5,821 applied; 75% were accepted; 1,236 enrolled (28%).

Financial Matters $2226 resident tuition and fees (2002–03); $10,404 nonresident tuition and fees (2002–03); $7294 room and board; 57% average percent of need met; $8411 average financial aid amount received per undergraduate.

Academics SSU awards bachelor's and master's degrees. Challenging opportunities include advanced placement credit, accelerated degree programs, student-designed majors, an honors program, double majors, independent study, and a senior project. Special programs include cooperative education, internships, summer session for credit, off-campus study, study-abroad, and Army and Air Force ROTC. The most frequently chosen baccalaureate fields are business/marketing, social sciences and history, and liberal arts/general studies. The faculty at SSU has 246 full-time members, 100% with terminal degrees.

Students of SSU The student body totals 8,162, of whom 6,700 are undergraduates. 63.7% are women and 36.3% are men. Students come from 38 states and territories and 37 other countries. 98% are from California. 1.5% are international students. 78% returned for their sophomore year.

Applying SSU requires SAT I or ACT and a high school transcript. Application deadline: 12/31; 1/31 priority date for financial aid. Early admission is possible.

SOUTH CAROLINA STATE UNIVERSITY

Orangeburg, SC

Small-town setting ■ Public ■ State-supported ■ Coed

Web site: www.scsu.edu
Contact: Ms. Lillian Adderson, Director of Admissions, 300 College Street Northeast, Orangeburg, SC 29117-0001
Telephone: 803-536-8408 or toll-free 800-260-5956 **Fax:** 803-536-8990
E-mail: admissions@scsu.edu

Getting in Last Year 2,346 applied; 53% were accepted; 716 enrolled (58%).

Financial Matters $4556 resident tuition and fees (2002–03); $8820 nonresident tuition and fees (2002–03); $4145 room and board; 56% average percent of need met.

Academics SC State awards bachelor's, master's, and doctoral degrees and post-bachelor's and post-master's certificates. Challenging opportunities include advanced placement credit, an honors program, independent study, and a senior project. Special programs include cooperative education, internships, summer session for credit, off-campus study, study-abroad, and Army and Air Force ROTC. The most frequently chosen baccalaureate fields are business/marketing, education, and home economics/vocational home economics. The faculty at SC State has 190 full-time members, 87% with terminal degrees. The student-faculty ratio is 17:1.

Students of SC State The student body totals 4,568, of whom 3,553 are undergraduates. 58.1% are women and 41.9% are men. Students come from 36 states and territories. 0.1% are international students. 80% returned for their sophomore year.

Applying SC State requires SAT I or ACT, a high school transcript, and a minimum high school GPA of 2.0. The school recommends SAT II Subject Tests. Application deadline: 7/31; 5/1 priority date for financial aid. Deferred admission is possible.

SOUTH DAKOTA SCHOOL OF MINES AND TECHNOLOGY

Rapid City, SD

Suburban setting ■ *Public* ■ *State-supported* ■ *Coed*

Web site: www.sdsmt.edu

Contact: Mr. Joseph Mueller, Director of Admissions, 501 East Saint Joseph, Rapid City, SD 57701-3995

Telephone: 605-394-2414 ext. 1266 or toll-free 800-544-8162 ext. 2414
Fax: 605-394-1268

E-mail: admissions@sdsmt.edu

Getting in Last Year 885 applied; 98% were accepted; 446 enrolled (51%).

Financial Matters $4092 resident tuition and fees (2002–03); $8342 nonresident tuition and fees (2002–03); $3484 room and board; 82% average percent of need met; $6067 average financial aid amount received per undergraduate (2001–02).

Academics SDSM&T awards associate, bachelor's, master's, and doctoral degrees. Challenging opportunities include advanced placement credit, double majors, independent study, and a senior project. Special programs include cooperative education, internships, summer session for credit, study-abroad, and Army ROTC. The faculty at SDSM&T has 101 full-time members, 80% with terminal degrees. The student-faculty ratio is 16:1.

Students of SDSM&T The student body totals 2,447, of whom 2,094 are undergraduates. 31.8% are women and 68.2% are men. Students come from 34 states and territories and 8 other countries. 74% are from South Dakota. 1.3% are international students.

Applying SDSM&T requires SAT I or ACT and a high school transcript, and in some cases ACT. The school recommends a minimum high school GPA of 2.6. Application deadline: rolling admissions; 3/15 priority date for financial aid.

SOUTH DAKOTA STATE UNIVERSITY

Brookings, SD

Small-town setting ■ *Public* ■ *State-supported* ■ *Coed*

Web site: www.sdstate.edu

Contact: Ms. Michelle Kuebler, Assistant Director of Admissions, PO Box 2201, Brookings, SD 57007

Telephone: 605-688-4121 or toll-free 800-952-3541 **Fax:** 605-688-6891

E-mail: sdsu_admissions@sdstate.edu

Getting in Last Year 3,343 applied; 94% were accepted.

Financial Matters $4088 resident tuition and fees (2002–03); $8621 nonresident tuition and fees (2002–03); $3208 room and board; 85% average percent of need met; $6912 average financial aid amount received per undergraduate.

Academics SDSU awards associate, bachelor's, master's, doctoral, and first-professional degrees. Challenging opportunities include advanced placement credit, accelerated degree programs, freshman honors college, an honors program, double majors, independent study, and a senior project. Special programs include cooperative education, internships, summer session for credit, off-campus study, study-abroad, and Army and Air Force ROTC. The most frequently chosen baccalaureate fields are health professions and related sciences, agriculture, and engineering/engineering technologies. The faculty at SDSU has 486 full-time members, 75% with terminal degrees. The student-faculty ratio is 18:1.

Students of SDSU The student body totals 9,952, of whom 8,445 are undergraduates. Students come from 39 states and territories and 19 other countries. 74% are from South Dakota.

Applying SDSU requires ACT, a high school transcript, minimum ACT score of 18, and a minimum high school GPA of 2.6. Application deadline: rolling admissions; 3/7 priority date for financial aid. Deferred admission is possible.

SOUTHEASTERN BAPTIST COLLEGE

Laurel, MS

Small-town setting ■ *Private* ■ *Independent Religious* ■ *Coed*

Contact: Mrs. Emma Bond, Director of Admissions, 4229 Highway 15 North, Laurel, MS 39440-1096

Telephone: 601-426-6346

Getting in Last Year 19 applied; 100% were accepted.

Academics Southeastern awards associate and bachelor's degrees. Advanced placement credit is a challenging opportunity. Summer session for credit is a special program. The faculty at Southeastern has 9 full-time members, 22% with terminal degrees.

Students of Southeastern The student body is made up of 104 undergraduates. 50% returned for their sophomore year.

Applying Southeastern requires a high school transcript and 2 recommendations, and in some cases an interview. The school recommends ACT. Application deadline: rolling admissions. Early and deferred admission are possible.

SOUTHEASTERN BAPTIST THEOLOGICAL SEMINARY

Wake Forest, NC

Small-town setting ■ *Private* ■ *Independent Religious* ■ *Coed*

Web site: www.sebts.edu

Contact: Mr. Jerry Yandell, Director of Admissions, PO Box 1889, Wake Forest, NC 27588

Telephone: 919-761-2280 or toll-free 800-284-6317

E-mail: admissions@sebts.edu

Getting in Last Year 46 enrolled.

Academics Southeastern Seminary awards associate, bachelor's, master's, doctoral, and first-professional degrees. A senior project is a challenging opportunity. Special programs include internships and summer session for credit. The faculty at Southeastern Seminary has 59 full-time members, 90% with terminal degrees.

Students of Southeastern Seminary The student body totals 1,979, of whom 452 are undergraduates. 24.6% are women and 75.4% are men. Students come from 27 states and territories and 14 other countries. 60% are from North Carolina. 5.3% are international students.

Applying Southeastern Seminary requires an essay, a high school transcript, and 3 recommendations, and in some cases an interview. The school recommends SAT I and SAT II or ACT. Application deadline: 7/20.

SOUTHEASTERN BIBLE COLLEGE

Birmingham, AL

Suburban setting ■ *Private* ■ *Independent Religious* ■ *Coed*

Web site: www.sebc.edu

Contact: Mr. Adam McClendon, Admissions Director, 3001 Highway 280 East, Birmingham, AL 35243

Telephone: 205-970-9209 or toll-free 800-749-8878 (in-state)
Fax: 205-970-9207

E-mail: amcclendon@sebc.edu

Getting in Last Year 62 enrolled.

Financial Matters $6600 tuition and fees (2002–03); $3540 room and board; 60% average percent of need met; $6457 average financial aid amount received per undergraduate.

Academics Southeastern Bible College awards associate and bachelor's degrees. Challenging opportunities include advanced placement credit and a senior project. Special programs include internships and summer session for credit. The most frequently chosen baccalaureate fields are education and liberal arts/general studies. The faculty at Southeastern Bible College has 12 full-time members, 83% with terminal degrees. The student-faculty ratio is 13:1.

Students of Southeastern Bible College The student body is made up of 202 undergraduates. 35.1% are women and 64.9% are men. Students come from 15 states and territories. 1% are international students. 62% returned for their sophomore year.

Applying Southeastern Bible College requires an essay, SAT I or ACT, a high school transcript, 3 recommendations, and a minimum high school GPA of 2.0, and in some cases an interview. Application deadline: rolling admissions; 5/1 priority date for financial aid. Deferred admission is possible.

SOUTHEASTERN COLLEGE OF THE ASSEMBLIES OF GOD

Lakeland, FL

Small-town setting ■ *Private* ■ *Independent Religious* ■ *Coed*

Web site: www.secollege.edu

Contact: Mr. Omar Rashed, Director of Admission, 1000 Longfellow Boulevard, Lakeland, FL 33801-6099

Telephone: 863-667-5000 or toll-free 800-500-8760 **Fax:** 863-667-5200

E-mail: admission@secollege.edu

Getting in Last Year 280 enrolled.

Financial Matters $8312 tuition and fees (2002–03); $4606 room and board; 64% average percent of need met; $6286 average financial aid amount received per undergraduate (2001–02).

Southeastern College of the Assemblies of God (continued)

Academics Southeastern College awards bachelor's degrees. Advanced placement credit is a challenging opportunity. Special programs include internships, summer session for credit, and Army and Air Force ROTC. The faculty at Southeastern College has 44 full-time members. The student-faculty ratio is 23:1.

Students of Southeastern College The student body is made up of 1,458 undergraduates. 54.4% are women and 45.6% are men. Students come from 43 states and territories. 47% are from Florida. 0.5% are international students. 66% returned for their sophomore year.

Applying Southeastern College requires SAT I or ACT, a high school transcript, and 2 recommendations, and in some cases an essay and an interview. Application deadline: 8/1; 4/1 priority date for financial aid. Early and deferred admission are possible.

SOUTHEASTERN LOUISIANA UNIVERSITY

Hammond, LA

Small-town setting ■ Public ■ State-supported ■ Coed

Web site: www.selu.edu
Contact: Ms. Pat Duplessis, University Admissions Analyst, SLU 10752, North Campus-Basic Studies, Hammond, LA 70402
Telephone: 985-549-2066 or toll-free 800-222-7358 **Fax:** 985-549-5632
E-mail: jmercante@selu.edu

Getting in Last Year 3,480 applied; 91% were accepted; 2,556 enrolled (81%).

Financial Matters $2618 resident tuition and fees (2002–03); $7946 nonresident tuition and fees (2002–03); $3720 room and board; $4803 average financial aid amount received per undergraduate (2001–02).

Academics SLU awards associate, bachelor's, and master's degrees. Challenging opportunities include advanced placement credit, an honors program, double majors, independent study, and a senior project. Special programs include internships, summer session for credit, off-campus study, study-abroad, and Army ROTC. The most frequently chosen baccalaureate fields are business/marketing, education, and protective services/public administration. The faculty at SLU has 477 full-time members, 57% with terminal degrees. The student-faculty ratio is 26:1.

Students of SLU The student body totals 15,205, of whom 13,398 are undergraduates. 62.1% are women and 37.9% are men. Students come from 39 states and territories and 41 other countries. 98% are from Louisiana. 0.8% are international students. 66% returned for their sophomore year.

Applying SLU requires ACT, a high school transcript, and proof of immunization, and in some cases a minimum high school GPA of 2.0. Application deadline: 7/15; 5/1 priority date for financial aid. Early and deferred admission are possible.

SOUTHEASTERN OKLAHOMA STATE UNIVERSITY

Durant, OK

Small-town setting ■ Public ■ State-supported ■ Coed

Web site: www.sosu.edu
Contact: Mr. Kyle Stafford, Director of Admissions and Enrollment Services, 1405 North 4th Avenue PMB 4225, Durant, OK 74701-0609
Telephone: 580-745-2060 or toll-free 800-435-1327 ext. 2060 **Fax:** 580-745-7502
E-mail: admissions@sosu.edu

Getting in Last Year 1,021 applied; 68% were accepted; 593 enrolled (85%).

Financial Matters $2264 resident tuition and fees (2002–03); $5011 nonresident tuition and fees (2002–03); $2312 room and board; 66% average percent of need met; $3111 average financial aid amount received per undergraduate (2001–02).

Academics SOSU awards bachelor's and master's degrees and post-master's certificates. Challenging opportunities include advanced placement credit, accelerated degree programs, an honors program, double majors, independent study, and a senior project. Special programs include internships, summer session for credit, and off-campus study. The most frequently chosen baccalaureate fields are business/marketing, education, and engineering/engineering technologies. The faculty at SOSU has 155 full-time members, 66% with terminal degrees. The student-faculty ratio is 19:1.

Students of SOSU The student body totals 4,033, of whom 3,637 are undergraduates. 53% are women and 47% are men. Students come from 34 states and territories and 25 other countries. 78% are from Oklahoma. 1.8% are international students. 52% returned for their sophomore year.

Applying SOSU requires a high school transcript, and in some cases SAT II Subject Tests, ACT, and an interview. Application deadline: rolling admissions; 3/1 priority date for financial aid.

SOUTHEASTERN UNIVERSITY

Washington, DC

Urban setting ■ Private ■ Independent ■ Coed

Web site: www.seu.edu
Contact: Admissions Office, 501 I Street, SW, Washington, DC 20024-2788
Telephone: 202-265-5343 ext. 211 **Fax:** 202-488-8162
E-mail: jackf@admin.seu.edu

Getting in Last Year 375 applied; 43% were accepted.

Financial Matters $9165 tuition and fees (2002–03).

Academics Southeastern University awards associate, bachelor's, and master's degrees. Challenging opportunities include advanced placement credit, accelerated degree programs, an honors program, double majors, and independent study. Special programs include cooperative education, internships, summer session for credit, and study-abroad. The most frequently chosen baccalaureate fields are computer/information sciences, liberal arts/general studies, and protective services/public administration. The faculty at Southeastern University has 13 full-time members, 62% with terminal degrees. The student-faculty ratio is 11:1.

Students of Southeastern University The student body totals 989, of whom 598 are undergraduates. Students come from 7 states and territories and 40 other countries. 75% are from District of Columbia. 11% are international students. 45% returned for their sophomore year.

Applying Southeastern University requires a high school transcript. The school recommends an essay, SAT I or ACT, and an interview. Application deadline: rolling admissions. Deferred admission is possible.

SOUTHEAST MISSOURI STATE UNIVERSITY

Cape Girardeau, MO

Small-town setting ■ Public ■ State-supported ■ Coed

Web site: www.semo.edu
Contact: Ms. Deborah Below, Director of Admissions, MS 3550, Cape Girardeau, MO 63701
Telephone: 573-651-2590 **Fax:** 573-651-5936
E-mail: admissions@semo.edu

Getting in Last Year 3,441 applied; 53% were accepted; 1,566 enrolled (86%).

Financial Matters $4035 resident tuition and fees (2002–03); $7110 nonresident tuition and fees (2002–03); $4938 room and board; 81% average percent of need met; $5506 average financial aid amount received per undergraduate (2001–02).

Academics Southeast awards associate, bachelor's, and master's degrees. Challenging opportunities include advanced placement credit, student-designed majors, an honors program, double majors, independent study, and a senior project. Special programs include cooperative education, internships, summer session for credit, study-abroad, and Air Force ROTC. The most frequently chosen baccalaureate fields are education, business/marketing, and protective services/ public administration. The faculty at Southeast has 388 full-time members, 86% with terminal degrees. The student-faculty ratio is 18:1.

Students of Southeast The student body totals 9,534, of whom 8,351 are undergraduates. 58.8% are women and 41.2% are men. Students come from 37 states and territories and 35 other countries. 87% are from Missouri. 2.2% are international students. 70% returned for their sophomore year.

Applying Southeast requires SAT I or ACT, a high school transcript, and a minimum high school GPA of 2.0. Application deadline: 8/1. Deferred admission is possible.

SOUTHERN ADVENTIST UNIVERSITY

Collegedale, TN

Small-town setting ■ Private ■ Independent Religious ■ Coed

Web site: www.southern.edu
Contact: Mr. Marc Grundy, Director of Admissions and Recruitment, PO Box 370, Collegedale, TN 37315-0370
Telephone: 423-238-2843 or toll-free 800-768-8437 **Fax:** 423-238-3005
E-mail: admissions@southern.edu

Getting in Last Year 1,293 applied; 76% were accepted; 485 enrolled (49%).

Financial Matters $12,220 tuition and fees (2002–03); $4110 room and board; 64% average percent of need met; $9121 average financial aid amount received per undergraduate.

Academics Southern awards associate, bachelor's, and master's degrees. Challenging opportunities include advanced placement credit, an honors program, double majors, independent study, and a senior project. Special programs include internships, summer session for credit, and study-abroad. The most frequently chosen baccalaureate fields are business/marketing, health professions and related sciences, and education. The faculty at Southern has 118 full-time members, 63% with terminal degrees. The student-faculty ratio is 16:1.

Students of Southern The student body totals 2,290, of whom 2,199 are undergraduates. 54.2% are women and 45.8% are men. Students come from 48 states and territories and 55 other countries. 30% are from Tennessee. 4.4% are international students. 67% returned for their sophomore year.

Applying Southern requires SAT I or ACT, a high school transcript, 2 recommendations, and a minimum high school GPA of 2.0, and in some cases an essay. The school recommends an interview. Application deadline: rolling admissions; 3/31 priority date for financial aid. Early and deferred admission are possible.

SOUTHERN ARKANSAS UNIVERSITY–MAGNOLIA

Magnolia, AR

Small-town setting ■ Public ■ State-supported ■ Coed

Web site: www.saumag.edu
Contact: Ms. Sarah Jennings, Dean of Enrollment Services, PO Box 9382, Magnolia, AR 71754-9382
Telephone: 870-235-4040 **Fax:** 870-235-5005
E-mail: addanne@saumag.edu

Getting in Last Year 1,166 applied; 99% were accepted; 566 enrolled (49%).

Financial Matters $3064 resident tuition and fees (2002–03); $4552 nonresident tuition and fees (2002–03); $3220 room and board; 100% average percent of need met; $6011 average financial aid amount received per undergraduate.

Academics SAU-M awards associate, bachelor's, and master's degrees. Challenging opportunities include advanced placement credit, accelerated degree programs, double majors, independent study, and a senior project. Special programs include internships, summer session for credit, and study-abroad. The most frequently chosen baccalaureate fields are business/marketing, education, and agriculture. The faculty at SAU-M has 126 full-time members, 61% with terminal degrees. The student-faculty ratio is 19:1.

Students of SAU-M The student body totals 3,013, of whom 2,855 are undergraduates. 56.3% are women and 43.7% are men. Students come from 24 states and territories and 33 other countries. 79% are from Arkansas. 4.4% are international students. 67% returned for their sophomore year.

Applying SAU-M requires ACT and a high school transcript, and in some cases an interview. Application deadline: 8/28; 7/1 priority date for financial aid. Early and deferred admission are possible.

SOUTHERN CALIFORNIA INSTITUTE OF ARCHITECTURE

Los Angeles, CA

Urban setting ■ Private ■ Independent ■ Coed

Web site: www.sciarc.edu
Contact: Ms. Wenona Colinco, Director of Admissions, Freight Yard, 960 East 3rd Street, Los Angeles, CA 90013
Telephone: 213-613-2200 ext. 321 or toll-free 800-774-7242 **Fax:** 213-613-2260
E-mail: admissions@sciarc.edu

Getting in Last Year 23 enrolled.

Financial Matters $17,476 tuition and fees (2002–03); 25% average percent of need met; $9500 average financial aid amount received per undergraduate.

Academics SCI-Arc awards bachelor's, master's, and first-professional degrees. Challenging opportunities include advanced placement credit and a senior project. Special programs include cooperative education, internships, summer session for credit, and study-abroad. The most frequently chosen baccalaureate field is architecture. The faculty at SCI-Arc has 89 members. The student-faculty ratio is 15:1.

Students of SCI-Arc The student body totals 468, of whom 194 are undergraduates. 30.9% are women and 69.1% are men. Students come from 35 states and territories and 17 other countries. 36.1% are international students. 40% returned for their sophomore year.

Applying SCI-Arc requires an essay, SAT I or ACT, a high school transcript, 3 recommendations, portfolio, and a minimum high school GPA of 2.0. The school recommends an interview. Application deadline: rolling admissions; 3/3 priority date for financial aid. Deferred admission is possible.

SOUTHERN CHRISTIAN UNIVERSITY

Montgomery, AL

Urban setting ■ Private ■ Independent Religious ■ Coed

Web site: www.southernchristian.edu
Contact: Mr. Rick Johnson, Director of Enrollment Management, 1200 Taylor Road, Montgomery, AL 36117
Telephone: 334-387-3877 ext. 213 or toll-free 800-351-4040 ext. 213
E-mail: admissions@southernchristian.edu

Financial Matters $8960 tuition and fees (2002–03); 85% average percent of need met; $8500 average financial aid amount received per undergraduate.

Academics SCU awards bachelor's, master's, doctoral, and first-professional degrees. Challenging opportunities include advanced placement credit, accelerated degree programs, and double majors. Special programs include internships and summer session for credit. The faculty at SCU has 31 full-time members, 100% with terminal degrees. The student-faculty ratio is 10:1.

Students of SCU The student body totals 525, of whom 268 are undergraduates. 42.2% are women and 57.8% are men. Students come from 48 states and territories. 25% are from Alabama. 85% returned for their sophomore year.

Applying SCU requires SAT I or ACT, a high school transcript, and a minimum high school GPA of 2.0. Application deadline: rolling admissions.

SOUTHERN CONNECTICUT STATE UNIVERSITY

New Haven, CT

Urban setting ■ Public ■ State-supported ■ Coed

Web site: www.southernct.edu
Contact: Ms. Paula Kennedy, Associate Director of Admissions, Admissions House, New Haven, CT 06515-1202
Telephone: 203-392-5651 **Fax:** 203-392-5727

Getting in Last Year 4,708 applied; 64% were accepted; 1,308 enrolled (43%).

Financial Matters $4444 resident tuition and fees (2002–03); $10,646 nonresident tuition and fees (2002–03); $6537 room and board; 79% average percent of need met; $6056 average financial aid amount received per undergraduate (2001–02).

Academics SCSU awards bachelor's and master's degrees and post-master's certificates. Challenging opportunities include advanced placement credit, accelerated degree programs, student-designed majors, freshman honors college, an honors program, double majors, independent study, and a senior project. Special programs include cooperative education, internships, summer session for credit, off-campus study, study-abroad, and Army and Air Force ROTC. The most frequently chosen baccalaureate fields are psychology, social sciences and history, and education. The faculty at SCSU has 407 full-time members, 89% with terminal degrees. The student-faculty ratio is 16:1.

Students of SCSU The student body totals 12,219, of whom 8,291 are undergraduates. 60% are women and 40% are men. Students come from 26 states and territories and 36 other countries. 95% are from Connecticut. 1.3% are international students. 74% returned for their sophomore year.

Applying SCSU requires an essay, SAT I, and a high school transcript. The school recommends recommendations. Application deadline: 7/1; 4/14 priority date for financial aid. Deferred admission is possible.

SOUTHERN ILLINOIS UNIVERSITY CARBONDALE

Carbondale, IL

Small-town setting ■ Public ■ State-supported ■ Coed

Web site: www.siuc.edu
Contact: Ms. Anne DeLuca, Assistant Vice Chancellor, Student Affairs and Enrollment Management and Director of Admissions, Mail Code 4701, Carbondale, IL 62901-4701
Telephone: 618-453-2908 **Fax:** 618-453-3250
E-mail: admrec@siu.edu

Getting in Last Year 8,073 applied; 78% were accepted; 2,532 enrolled (40%).

Financial Matters $4865 resident tuition and fees (2002–03); $8525 nonresident tuition and fees (2002–03); $4610 room and board; 96% average percent of need met; $7892 average financial aid amount received per undergraduate (2001–02).

Academics SIUC awards associate, bachelor's, master's, doctoral, and first-professional degrees and post-bachelor's, post-master's, and first-professional certificates. Challenging opportunities include advanced placement credit, accelerated degree programs, an honors program, double majors, independent study, and a senior project. Special programs include cooperative education, internships, summer session for credit, off-campus study, study-abroad, and Army and Air Force ROTC. The most frequently chosen baccalaureate fields are education, engineering/engineering technologies, and business/marketing. The faculty at SIUC has 894 full-time members, 76% with terminal degrees. The student-faculty ratio is 17:1.

Students of SIUC The student body totals 21,873, of whom 16,863 are undergraduates. 43.7% are women and 56.3% are men. Students come from 52 states and territories and 117 other countries. 85% are from Illinois. 3.4% are international students. 67% returned for their sophomore year.

Applying SIUC requires SAT I or ACT and a high school transcript. Application deadline: rolling admissions; 4/1 priority date for financial aid. Deferred admission is possible.

SOUTHERN ILLINOIS UNIVERSITY EDWARDSVILLE

Edwardsville, IL

Suburban setting ■ Public ■ State-supported ■ Coed

Web site: www.siue.edu
Contact: Mr. Boyd Bradshaw, Acting Vice Chancellor for Enrollment Management, Edwardsville, IL 62026-0001
Telephone: 618-650-3705 or toll-free 800-447-SIUE **Fax:** 618-650-5013
E-mail: admis@siue.edu

Getting in Last Year 4,263 applied; 79% were accepted; 1,655 enrolled (49%).

Financial Matters $3573 resident tuition and fees (2002–03); $6423 nonresident tuition and fees (2002–03); $5016 room and board; 81% average percent of need met; $7500 average financial aid amount received per undergraduate (2001–02).

Academics SIUE awards bachelor's, master's, and first-professional degrees and post-bachelor's, post-master's, and first-professional certificates. Challenging opportunities include advanced placement credit, accelerated degree programs, student-designed majors, an honors program, double majors, independent study, and a senior project. Special programs include cooperative education, internships,

Southern Illinois University Edwardsville (continued)

summer session for credit, off-campus study, study-abroad, and Army and Air Force ROTC. The most frequently chosen baccalaureate fields are business/marketing, education, and social sciences and history. The faculty at SIUE has 494 full-time members, 83% with terminal degrees. The student-faculty ratio is 17:1.

Students of SIUE The student body totals 12,708, of whom 10,014 are undergraduates. 56.4% are women and 43.6% are men. Students come from 47 states and territories and 62 other countries. 90% are from Illinois. 1.4% are international students. 72% returned for their sophomore year.

Applying SIUE requires SAT I or ACT and a high school transcript. Application deadline: 5/31; 2/15 priority date for financial aid. Early and deferred admission are possible.

SOUTHERN METHODIST COLLEGE

Orangeburg, SC

Private ■ Independent Religious ■ Coed

Web site: www.southernmethodistcollege.org

Contact: Mr. Glenn Blank, Director of Admissions, PO Box 1027, 541 Broughton Street, Orangeburg, SC 29116-1027

Telephone: 803-534-7826

Getting in Last Year 3 enrolled.

Financial Matters $4700 tuition and fees (2002–03); $4200 room and board.

Academics Southern Methodist College awards associate and bachelor's degrees. Double majors are a challenging opportunity. Internships is a special program. The faculty at Southern Methodist College has 8 full-time members, 50% with terminal degrees. The student-faculty ratio is 8:1.

Students of Southern Methodist College The student body is made up of 92 undergraduates. 51.1% are women and 48.9% are men. Students come from 4 states and territories and 3 other countries. 93% are from South Carolina. 8.7% are international students.

Applying Southern Methodist College requires an essay, a high school transcript, an interview, 3 recommendations, and health certificate. The school recommends SAT I and ACT. Application deadline: 7/15. Early admission is possible.

SOUTHERN METHODIST UNIVERSITY

Dallas, TX

Suburban setting ■ Private ■ Independent Religious ■ Coed

Web site: www. smu.edu

Contact: Mr. Ron W. Moss, Director of Admission and Enrollment Management, PO Box 750181, Dallas, TX 75275-0181

Telephone: 214-768-2058 or toll-free 800-323-0672 **Fax:** 214-768-0103

E-mail: enrol_serv@mail.smu.edu

Getting in Last Year 6,152 applied; 66% were accepted; 1,380 enrolled (34%).

Financial Matters $21,942 tuition and fees (2002–03); $7954 room and board; 91% average percent of need met; $20,885 average financial aid amount received per undergraduate.

Academics SMU awards bachelor's, master's, doctoral, and first-professional degrees and post-bachelor's certificates. Challenging opportunities include advanced placement credit, accelerated degree programs, student-designed majors, an honors program, double majors, and independent study. Special programs include internships, summer session for credit, study-abroad, and Army and Air Force ROTC. The most frequently chosen baccalaureate fields are business/marketing, trade and industry, and communications/communication technologies. The faculty at SMU has 535 full-time members, 84% with terminal degrees. The student-faculty ratio is 12:1.

Students of SMU The student body totals 10,955, of whom 6,210 are undergraduates. 54.2% are women and 45.8% are men. Students come from 48 states and territories and 54 other countries. 64% are from Texas. 4.7% are international students. 86% returned for their sophomore year.

Applying SMU requires an essay, SAT I or ACT, a high school transcript, and 1 recommendation, and in some cases SAT II Subject Tests. Application deadline: 1/15; 2/1 priority date for financial aid. Early and deferred admission are possible.

SOUTHERN NAZARENE UNIVERSITY

Bethany, OK

Suburban setting ■ Private ■ Independent Religious ■ Coed

Contact: Mr. Larry Hess, Director of Admissions, 6729 Northwest 39th Expressway, Bethany, OK 73008

Telephone: 405-491-6324 or toll-free 800-648-9899 **Fax:** 405-491-6320

E-mail: admiss@snu.edu

Getting in Last Year 739 applied; 42% were accepted; 310 enrolled (100%).

Financial Matters $11,216 tuition and fees (2002–03); $4767 room and board.

Academics SNU awards associate, bachelor's, and master's degrees. Challenging opportunities include advanced placement credit, accelerated degree programs, student-designed majors, an honors program, double majors, and a senior project. Special programs include internships, summer session for credit, off-campus study, study-abroad, and Army and Air Force ROTC. The most frequently chosen baccalaureate fields are business/marketing, social sciences and history, and health professions and related sciences. The faculty at SNU has 73 full-time members, 82% with terminal degrees. The student-faculty ratio is 21:1.

Students of SNU The student body totals 2,120, of whom 1,780 are undergraduates. 53.8% are women and 46.2% are men. Students come from 32 states and territories and 17 other countries. 53% are from Oklahoma. 1.1% are international students. 77% returned for their sophomore year.

Applying SNU requires SAT I or ACT and a high school transcript. The school recommends an interview. Application deadline: 8/15; 3/1 priority date for financial aid. Deferred admission is possible.

SOUTHERN NEW HAMPSHIRE UNIVERSITY

Manchester, NH

Suburban setting ■ Private ■ Independent ■ Coed

Web site: www.snhu.edu

Contact: Mr. Steve Soba, Director of Admission, 2500 North River Road, Belknap Hall, Manchester, NH 03106-1045

Telephone: 603-645-9611 ext. 9633 or toll-free 800-642-4968 **Fax:** 603-645-9693

E-mail: admission@snhu.edu

Getting in Last Year 2,255 applied; 80% were accepted; 806 enrolled (45%).

Financial Matters $17,656 tuition and fees (2002–03); $7340 room and board.

Academics Southern New Hampshire University awards associate, bachelor's, master's, and doctoral degrees and post-bachelor's certificates. Challenging opportunities include advanced placement credit, accelerated degree programs, an honors program, double majors, independent study, and a senior project. Special programs include cooperative education, internships, summer session for credit, off-campus study, study-abroad, and Army and Air Force ROTC. The faculty at Southern New Hampshire University has 110 full-time members, 68% with terminal degrees. The student-faculty ratio is 18:1.

Students of Southern New Hampshire University The student body totals 5,611, of whom 3,907 are undergraduates. 54.5% are women and 45.5% are men. Students come from 23 states and territories and 60 other countries. 49% are from New Hampshire. 4.8% are international students. 75% returned for their sophomore year.

Applying Southern New Hampshire University requires an essay, SAT I or ACT, a high school transcript, recommendations, 1 letter of recommendation from guidance counselor, and a minimum high school GPA of 2.0. The school recommends an interview. Application deadline: rolling admissions; 3/15 priority date for financial aid. Deferred admission is possible.

SOUTHERN OREGON UNIVERSITY

Ashland, OR

Small-town setting ■ Public ■ State-supported ■ Coed

Web site: www.sou.edu

Contact: Ms. Mara A. Affre, Director of Admissions, 1250 Siskiyou Boulevard, Ashland, OR 97520

Telephone: 541-552-6411 or toll-free 800-482-7672 (in-state) **Fax:** 541-552-6614

E-mail: admissions@sou.edu

Getting in Last Year 2,169 applied; 85% were accepted; 883 enrolled (48%).

Financial Matters $3687 resident tuition and fees (2002–03); $11,526 nonresident tuition and fees (2002–03); $5665 room and board; 67% average percent of need met; $6942 average financial aid amount received per undergraduate (2001–02).

Academics Southern Oregon awards bachelor's and master's degrees and post-bachelor's certificates. Challenging opportunities include advanced placement credit, accelerated degree programs, student-designed majors, freshman honors college, an honors program, double majors, independent study, and a senior project. Special programs include cooperative education, internships, summer session for credit, off-campus study, and study-abroad. The most frequently chosen baccalaureate fields are business/marketing, social sciences and history, and communications/communication technologies. The faculty at Southern Oregon has 189 full-time members, 83% with terminal degrees. The student-faculty ratio is 19:1.

Students of Southern Oregon The student body totals 5,478, of whom 4,917 are undergraduates. 56.7% are women and 43.3% are men. Students come from 45 states and territories and 33 other countries. 80% are from Oregon. 2.3% are international students. 67% returned for their sophomore year.

Applying Southern Oregon requires SAT I or ACT, a high school transcript, and 2.75 high school GPA or minimum SAT score of 1010, and in some cases SAT II Subject Tests. Application deadline: rolling admissions. Early and deferred admission are possible.

SOUTHERN POLYTECHNIC STATE UNIVERSITY

Marietta, GA

Suburban setting ■ Public ■ State-supported ■ Coed

Web site: www.spsu.edu
Contact: Ms. Virginia A. Head, Director of Admissions, 1100 South Marietta Parkway, Marietta, GA 30060-2896
Telephone: 770-528-7281 or toll-free 800-635-3204 **Fax:** 770-528-7292
E-mail: admissions@spsu.edu

Getting in Last Year 918 applied; 65% were accepted; 397 enrolled (66%).

Financial Matters $2452 resident tuition and fees (2002–03); $8482 nonresident tuition and fees (2002–03); $4806 room and board; 78% average percent of need met; $4463 average financial aid amount received per undergraduate (2001–02).

Academics Southern Poly awards associate, bachelor's, and master's degrees and post-bachelor's certificates. Challenging opportunities include advanced placement credit, double majors, independent study, and a senior project. Special programs include cooperative education, internships, summer session for credit, study-abroad, and Army, Navy and Air Force ROTC. The most frequently chosen baccalaureate fields are engineering/engineering technologies, computer/information sciences, and business/marketing. The faculty at Southern Poly has 136 full-time members, 57% with terminal degrees. The student-faculty ratio is 20:1.

Students of Southern Poly The student body totals 3,683, of whom 3,084 are undergraduates. 17.2% are women and 82.8% are men. Students come from 40 states and territories. 96% are from Georgia. 5.5% are international students. 60% returned for their sophomore year.

Applying Southern Poly requires SAT I or ACT, a high school transcript, proof of immunization, and a minimum high school GPA of 2.0, and in some cases SAT II Subject Tests. Application deadline: 8/1; 3/15 priority date for financial aid. Early admission is possible.

SOUTHERN UNIVERSITY AND AGRICULTURAL AND MECHANICAL COLLEGE

Baton Rouge, LA

Suburban setting ■ Public ■ State-supported ■ Coed

Web site: www.subr.edu
Contact: Ms. Velva Thomas, Director of Admissions, PO Box 9901, Baton Rouge, LA 70813
Telephone: 225-771-2430 or toll-free 800-256-1531 **Fax:** 225-771-2500
E-mail: admit@subr.edu

Getting in Last Year 3,626 applied; 54% were accepted; 1,191 enrolled (60%).

Financial Matters $2702 resident tuition and fees (2002–03); $8494 nonresident tuition and fees (2002–03); $4306 room and board; 65% average percent of need met; $7098 average financial aid amount received per undergraduate.

Academics Southern University at Baton Rouge awards associate, bachelor's, master's, and doctoral degrees. Challenging opportunities include advanced placement credit, an honors program, and a senior project. Special programs include cooperative education, internships, summer session for credit, off-campus study, study-abroad, and Army, Navy and Air Force ROTC. The most frequently chosen baccalaureate fields are education, health professions and related sciences, and business/marketing. The faculty at Southern University at Baton Rouge has 422 full-time members, 68% with terminal degrees. The student-faculty ratio is 16:1.

Students of Southern University at Baton Rouge The student body totals 8,572, of whom 7,352 are undergraduates. 59.4% are women and 40.6% are men. Students come from 40 states and territories and 35 other countries. 86% are from Louisiana. 0.7% are international students. 60% returned for their sophomore year.

Applying Southern University at Baton Rouge requires SAT I or ACT, a high school transcript, and a minimum high school GPA of 2.2. Application deadline: 7/1; 5/31 priority date for financial aid. Early admission is possible.

SOUTHERN UTAH UNIVERSITY

Cedar City, UT

Small-town setting ■ Public ■ State-supported ■ Coed

Web site: www.suu.edu
Contact: Mr. Dale S. Orton, Director of Admissions, 351 West Center Street, Cedar City, UT 84720
Telephone: 801-586-7740 **Fax:** 435-865-8223
E-mail: adminfo@suu.edu

Getting in Last Year 1,398 applied; 81% were accepted; 739 enrolled (65%).

Financial Matters $2350 resident tuition and fees (2002–03); $7344 nonresident tuition and fees (2002–03); $5224 room and board; 79% average percent of need met; $4463 average financial aid amount received per undergraduate (2001–02).

Academics SUU awards associate, bachelor's, and master's degrees. Challenging opportunities include advanced placement credit, an honors program, double majors, independent study, and a senior project. Special programs include cooperative education, internships, summer session for credit, and Army ROTC. The most frequently chosen baccalaureate fields are education, business/marketing, and communications/communication technologies. The faculty at SUU has 221 full-time members, 64% with terminal degrees. The student-faculty ratio is 21:1.

Students of SUU The student body totals 5,881, of whom 5,680 are undergraduates. 56.4% are women and 43.6% are men. Students come from 40 states and territories and 14 other countries. 85% are from Utah. 1.3% are international students. 63% returned for their sophomore year.

Applying SUU requires SAT I or ACT, a high school transcript, and a minimum high school GPA of 2.0. The school recommends ACT. Application deadline: 7/1. Early and deferred admission are possible.

SOUTHERN VERMONT COLLEGE

Bennington, VT

Small-town setting ■ Private ■ Independent ■ Coed

Web site: www.svc.edu
Contact: Ms. Elizabeth Gatti, Director of Admissions, 982 Mansion Drive, Bennington, VT 05201
Telephone: 802-447-6304 or toll-free 800-378-2782 (in-state)
Fax: 802-447-4695
E-mail: admis@svc.edu

Getting in Last Year 351 applied; 63% were accepted.

Financial Matters $11,695 tuition and fees (2002–03); $5990 room and board; 85% average percent of need met; $12,580 average financial aid amount received per undergraduate.

Academics SVC awards associate and bachelor's degrees. Challenging opportunities include advanced placement credit, accelerated degree programs, student-designed majors, an honors program, double majors, independent study, and a senior project. Special programs include cooperative education, internships, summer session for credit, and study-abroad. The faculty at SVC has 16 full-time members, 25% with terminal degrees. The student-faculty ratio is 11:1.

Students of SVC The student body is made up of 448 undergraduates. 63.6% are women and 36.4% are men. Students come from 26 states and territories and 5 other countries. 34% are from Vermont. 1.3% are international students. 64% returned for their sophomore year.

Applying SVC requires an essay, SAT I or ACT, a high school transcript, and 2 recommendations, and in some cases an interview. The school recommends an interview and a minimum high school GPA of 2.0. Application deadline: rolling admissions; 5/1 priority date for financial aid. Early and deferred admission are possible.

SOUTHERN VIRGINIA UNIVERSITY

Buena Vista, VA

Small-town setting ■ Private ■ Independent Religious ■ Coed

Web site: www.southernvirginia.edu
Contact: Mr. Tony Caputo, Dean of Admissions, One University Hill Drive, Buena Vista, VA 24416
Telephone: 540-261-2756 or toll-free 800-229-8420
E-mail: admissions@southernvirginia.edu

Getting in Last Year 1,052 applied; 29% were accepted.

Financial Matters $13,500 tuition and fees (2002–03); $5000 room and board.

Academics Southern Virginia awards bachelor's degrees. A senior project is a challenging opportunity. Special programs include cooperative education, summer session for credit, and Army ROTC. The faculty at Southern Virginia has 35 full-time members. The student-faculty ratio is 15:1.

Students of Southern Virginia The student body is made up of 490 undergraduates. 60% are women and 40% are men. 25% are from Virginia.

Applying Southern Virginia requires SAT I or ACT, a high school transcript, and ecclesiastical endorsement. The school recommends a minimum high school GPA of 2.5. Application deadline: 7/31; 4/15 priority date for financial aid.

SOUTHERN WESLEYAN UNIVERSITY

Central, SC

Small-town setting ■ Private ■ Independent Religious ■ Coed

Web site: www.swu.edu
Contact: Mrs. Joy Bryant, Director of Admissions, PO Box 1020, 907 Wesleyan Drive, Central, SC 29630-1020
Telephone: 864-644-5550 or toll-free 800-289-1292 **Fax:** 864-644-5972
E-mail: admissions@swu.edu

Getting in Last Year 284 applied; 69% were accepted; 113 enrolled (57%).

Financial Matters $13,450 tuition and fees (2002–03); $4700 room and board; 58% average percent of need met; $7452 average financial aid amount received per undergraduate.

Academics SWU awards associate, bachelor's, and master's degrees. Challenging opportunities include advanced placement credit, accelerated degree programs, student-designed majors, freshman honors college, an honors program, double

Southern Wesleyan University (continued)

majors, independent study, and a senior project. Special programs include cooperative education, internships, summer session for credit, off-campus study, study-abroad, and Army and Air Force ROTC. The most frequently chosen baccalaureate fields are business/marketing, education, and psychology. The faculty at SWU has 49 full-time members, 73% with terminal degrees. The student-faculty ratio is 12:1.

Students of SWU The student body totals 2,301, of whom 2,024 are undergraduates. 63.3% are women and 36.7% are men. Students come from 15 states and territories and 8 other countries. 88% are from South Carolina. 0.5% are international students. 75% returned for their sophomore year.

Applying SWU requires SAT I or ACT, a high school transcript, 2 recommendations, lifestyle statement, and a minimum high school GPA of 2.0, and in some cases an interview. Application deadline: 8/10; 3/31 priority date for financial aid. Early and deferred admission are possible.

SOUTH UNIVERSITY

Montgomery, AL

Urban setting ■ Private ■ Proprietary ■ Coed, Primarily Women

Web site: www.southuniversity.edu

Contact: Ms. Anna Pearson, Director of Admissions, 5355 Vaughn Road, Montgomery, AL 36116-1120

Telephone: 334-395-8800 **Fax:** 334-395-8800

Getting in Last Year 61 applied; 75% were accepted; 29 enrolled (63%).

Financial Matters $9585 tuition and fees (2002–03).

Academics South awards associate and bachelor's degrees. Double majors are a challenging opportunity. Special programs include internships and summer session for credit. The faculty at South has 9 full-time members, 22% with terminal degrees. The student-faculty ratio is 11:1.

Students of South The student body is made up of 272 undergraduates. 78.7% are women and 21.3% are men. Students come from 1 state or territory.

Applying South requires CPT, a high school transcript, and an interview, and in some cases SAT I or ACT and 3 recommendations.

SOUTHWEST BAPTIST UNIVERSITY

Bolivar, MO

Small-town setting ■ Private ■ Independent Religious ■ Coed

Web site: www.sbuniv.edu

Contact: Mr. Rob Harris, Director of Admissions, 1600 University Avenue, Bolivar, MO 65613-2597

Telephone: 417-328-1809 or toll-free 800-526-5859 **Fax:** 417-328-1514

E-mail: rharris@sbuniv.edu

Getting in Last Year 853 applied; 89% were accepted; 463 enrolled (61%).

Financial Matters $10,932 tuition and fees (2002–03); $3230 room and board; 71% average percent of need met; $9613 average financial aid amount received per undergraduate.

Academics SBU awards associate, bachelor's, and master's degrees. Challenging opportunities include advanced placement credit, accelerated degree programs, an honors program, double majors, independent study, and a senior project. Special programs include cooperative education, internships, summer session for credit, study-abroad, and Army ROTC. The most frequently chosen baccalaureate fields are education, psychology, and health professions and related sciences. The faculty at SBU has 104 full-time members, 61% with terminal degrees. The student-faculty ratio is 21:1.

Students of SBU The student body totals 3,534, of whom 2,663 are undergraduates. 67.1% are women and 32.9% are men. Students come from 40 states and territories and 11 other countries. 49% are from Missouri. 0.7% are international students. 70% returned for their sophomore year.

Applying SBU requires SAT I or ACT and a high school transcript. The school recommends an interview. Application deadline: rolling admissions; 3/15 priority date for financial aid.

SOUTHWESTERN ASSEMBLIES OF GOD UNIVERSITY

Waxahachie, TX

Small-town setting ■ Private ■ Independent Religious ■ Coed

Web site: www.sagu.edu

Contact: Mr. Pat Thompson, Admissions Counselor, 1200 Sycamore Street, Waxahachie, TX 75165-2397

Telephone: 972-937-4010 or toll-free 888-937-7248 **Fax:** 972-923-0006

E-mail: info@sagu.edu

Getting in Last Year 1,676 applied; 34% were accepted.

Financial Matters $8648 tuition and fees (2002–03); $4470 room and board; 64% average percent of need met; $6728 average financial aid amount received per undergraduate (2000–01).

Academics SAGU awards associate, bachelor's, and master's degrees. Challenging opportunities include advanced placement credit, double majors, and independent study. Special programs include internships, summer session for credit, and Air Force ROTC. The most frequently chosen baccalaureate fields are education, liberal arts/general studies, and business/marketing. The faculty at SAGU has 65 full-time members, 51% with terminal degrees. The student-faculty ratio is 20:1.

Students of SAGU The student body totals 1,676, of whom 1,527 are undergraduates. Students come from 42 states and territories. 65% are from Texas. 0.8% are international students. 61% returned for their sophomore year.

Applying SAGU requires an essay, SAT I or ACT, a high school transcript, 2 recommendations, and medical history, evidence of approved Christian character. Application deadline: rolling admissions; 7/1 for financial aid, with a 3/1 priority date. Early and deferred admission are possible.

SOUTHWESTERN CHRISTIAN COLLEGE

Terrell, TX

Small-town setting ■ Private ■ Independent Religious ■ Coed

Web site: www.swcc.edu

Contact: Admissions Department, Box 10, 200 Bowser Street, Terrell, TX 75160

Telephone: 214-524-3341

Getting in Last Year 389 applied; 90% were accepted.

Financial Matters $5186 tuition and fees (2002–03); $3290 room and board.

Academics Southwestern Christian College awards associate and bachelor's degrees. The faculty at Southwestern Christian College has 10 full-time members.

Students of Southwestern Christian College The student body totals 186. Students come from 26 states and territories and 5 other countries. 92% returned for their sophomore year.

Applying Southwestern Christian College requires a high school transcript and 1 recommendation. The school recommends SAT I or ACT. Application deadline: 7/15; 6/1 priority date for financial aid. Early and deferred admission are possible.

SOUTHWESTERN COLLEGE

Winfield, KS

Small-town setting ■ Private ■ Independent Religious ■ Coed

Web site: www.sckans.edu

Contact: Mr. Todd Moore, Director of Admission, 100 College Street, Winfield, KS 67156

Telephone: 620-229-6236 or toll-free 800-846-1543 **Fax:** 620-229-6344

E-mail: scadmit@sckans.edu

Getting in Last Year 353 applied; 75% were accepted; 106 enrolled (40%).

Financial Matters $13,922 tuition and fees (2002–03); $4736 room and board; 88% average percent of need met; $12,576 average financial aid amount received per undergraduate (2001–02).

Academics Southwestern awards bachelor's and master's degrees. Challenging opportunities include advanced placement credit, student-designed majors, an honors program, double majors, independent study, and a senior project. Special programs include internships, summer session for credit, off-campus study, and study-abroad. The most frequently chosen baccalaureate fields are business/marketing, health professions and related sciences, and computer/information sciences. The faculty at Southwestern has 54 full-time members, 56% with terminal degrees. The student-faculty ratio is 13:1.

Students of Southwestern The student body totals 1,298, of whom 1,137 are undergraduates. 48.5% are women and 51.5% are men. Students come from 22 states and territories and 9 other countries. 85% are from Kansas. 2.8% are international students. 64% returned for their sophomore year.

Applying Southwestern requires an essay, SAT I or ACT, a high school transcript, and a minimum high school GPA of 2.25, and in some cases an interview. Application deadline: 8/15; 8/1 for financial aid, with a 7/1 priority date. Deferred admission is possible.

SOUTHWESTERN OKLAHOMA STATE UNIVERSITY

Weatherford, OK

Small-town setting ■ Public ■ State-supported ■ Coed

Web site: www.swosu.edu

Contact: Ms. Connie Phillips, Admission Counselor, 100 Campus Drive, Weatherford, OK 73096

Telephone: 580-774-3009 **Fax:** 580-774-3795

E-mail: phillic@swosu.edu

Getting in Last Year 1,395 applied; 94% were accepted; 912 enrolled (70%).

Financial Matters $2448 resident tuition and fees (2002–03); $5601 nonresident tuition and fees (2002–03); $2680 room and board; 87% average percent of need met; $3377 average financial aid amount received per undergraduate.

Academics Southwestern awards bachelor's, master's, and first-professional degrees. Challenging opportunities include advanced placement credit, accelerated degree programs, student-designed majors, double majors, independent study, and a senior project. Special programs include cooperative education, internships, summer session for credit, and off-campus study. The most frequently chosen baccalaureate fields are business/marketing, health professions and related sciences, and education. The faculty at Southwestern has 195 full-time members, 64% with terminal degrees. The student-faculty ratio is 20:1.

Students of Southwestern The student body totals 4,652, of whom 4,015 are undergraduates. 55.9% are women and 44.1% are men. Students come from 32 states and territories and 32 other countries. 90% are from Oklahoma. 2.6% are international students. 65% returned for their sophomore year.

Applying Southwestern requires ACT, a high school transcript, and a minimum high school GPA of 2.0. Application deadline: 3/1 for financial aid. Deferred admission is possible.

SOUTHWESTERN UNIVERSITY

Georgetown, TX

Suburban setting ■ Private ■ Independent Religious ■ Coed

Web site: www.southwestern.edu

Contact: Mr. John W. Lind, Vice President for Enrollment Management, 1001 East University Avenue, Georgetown, TX 78626

Telephone: 512-863-1200 or toll-free 800-252-3166 **Fax:** 512-863-9601

E-mail: admission@southwestern.edu

Getting in Last Year 1,572 applied; 61% were accepted; 342 enrolled (36%).

Financial Matters $17,570 tuition and fees (2002–03); $6240 room and board; 98% average percent of need met; $15,038 average financial aid amount received per undergraduate.

Academics SU awards bachelor's degrees. Challenging opportunities include advanced placement credit, accelerated degree programs, student-designed majors, freshman honors college, an honors program, double majors, independent study, and a senior project. Special programs include internships, summer session for credit, off-campus study, and study-abroad. The faculty at SU has 107 full-time members, 93% with terminal degrees. The student-faculty ratio is 11:1.

Students of SU The student body is made up of 1,266 undergraduates. 58.7% are women and 41.3% are men. Students come from 35 states and territories. 91% are from Texas. 0.1% are international students. 88% returned for their sophomore year.

Applying SU requires an essay, SAT I or ACT, a high school transcript, and 1 recommendation, and in some cases an interview. The school recommends an interview. Application deadline: 2/15; 3/1 for financial aid. Early and deferred admission are possible.

SOUTHWEST MISSOURI STATE UNIVERSITY

Springfield, MO

Suburban setting ■ Public ■ State-supported ■ Coed

Web site: www.smsu.edu

Contact: Ms. Jill Duncan, Associate Director of Admissions, 901 South National, Springfield, MO 65804-0094

Telephone: 417-836-5517 or toll-free 800-492-7900 **Fax:** 417-836-6334

E-mail: smsuinfo@smsu.edu

Getting in Last Year 6,892 applied; 80% were accepted; 2,761 enrolled (50%).

Financial Matters $4708 resident tuition and fees (2002–03); $8548 nonresident tuition and fees (2002–03); $4850 room and board; 63% average percent of need met; $7253 average financial aid amount received per undergraduate (2001–02).

Academics SMSU awards bachelor's and master's degrees and post-bachelor's certificates. Challenging opportunities include advanced placement credit, accelerated degree programs, student-designed majors, freshman honors college, an honors program, double majors, independent study, and a senior project. Special programs include cooperative education, internships, summer session for credit, off-campus study, study-abroad, and Army ROTC. The most frequently chosen baccalaureate fields are business/marketing, education, and communications/communication technologies. The faculty at SMSU has 731 full-time members, 79% with terminal degrees. The student-faculty ratio is 18:1.

Students of SMSU The student body totals 18,718, of whom 15,448 are undergraduates. 55.3% are women and 44.7% are men. Students come from 49 states and territories and 91 other countries. 92% are from Missouri. 2.2% are international students. 73% returned for their sophomore year.

Applying SMSU requires SAT I or ACT and a high school transcript, and in some cases an essay and an interview. The school recommends ACT. Application deadline: 8/2; 3/30 priority date for financial aid.

SOUTHWEST STATE UNIVERSITY

Marshall, MN

Small-town setting ■ Public ■ State-supported ■ Coed

Web site: www.southwest.msus.edu

Contact: Richard Shearer, Director of Enrollment Services, 1501 State Street, Marshall, MN 56258-1598

Telephone: 507-537-6286 or toll-free 800-642-0684 **Fax:** 507-537-7154

E-mail: shearerr@southwest.msus.edu

Getting in Last Year 1,232 enrolled.

Financial Matters $4091 resident tuition and fees (2002–03); $4091 nonresident tuition and fees (2002–03); $4248 room and board; 83% average percent of need met; $5810 average financial aid amount received per undergraduate.

Academics SSU awards associate, bachelor's, and master's degrees. Challenging opportunities include advanced placement credit, accelerated degree programs, student-designed majors, freshman honors college, an honors program, double majors, independent study, and a senior project. Special programs include internships, summer session for credit, off-campus study, and study-abroad. The faculty at SSU has 122 full-time members, 70% with terminal degrees. The student-faculty ratio is 18:1.

Students of SSU The student body totals 5,636, of whom 5,167 are undergraduates. 59.9% are women and 40.1% are men. Students come from 27 states and territories and 29 other countries. 88% are from Minnesota. 2.5% are international students. 86% returned for their sophomore year.

Applying SSU requires an essay, SAT I or ACT, a high school transcript, and an interview. The school recommends SAT I and SAT II or ACT. Application deadline: rolling admissions; 4/1 priority date for financial aid. Early and deferred admission are possible.

SOUTHWEST TEXAS STATE UNIVERSITY

San Marcos, TX

Small-town setting ■ Public ■ State-supported ■ Coed

Web site: www.swt.edu

Contact: Mrs. Christie Kangas, Director of Admissions, Admissions and Visitors Center, San Marcos, TX 78666

Telephone: 512-245-2364 ext. 2803 **Fax:** 512-245-8044

E-mail: admissions@swt.edu

Getting in Last Year 10,269 applied; 56% were accepted; 2,731 enrolled (47%).

Financial Matters $3750 resident tuition and fees (2002–03); $10,290 nonresident tuition and fees (2002–03); $5524 room and board; 72% average percent of need met; $7384 average financial aid amount received per undergraduate (2001–02).

Academics SWT awards bachelor's, master's, and doctoral degrees and post-bachelor's certificates. Challenging opportunities include advanced placement credit, accelerated degree programs, an honors program, double majors, independent study, and a senior project. Special programs include internships, summer session for credit, off-campus study, study-abroad, and Army and Air Force ROTC. The most frequently chosen baccalaureate fields are business/marketing, interdisciplinary studies, and social sciences and history. The faculty at SWT has 684 full-time members, 78% with terminal degrees. The student-faculty ratio is 26:1.

Students of SWT The student body totals 25,055, of whom 21,119 are undergraduates. 55.5% are women and 44.5% are men. Students come from 44 states and territories and 57 other countries. 99% are from Texas. 0.9% are international students. 74% returned for their sophomore year.

Applying SWT requires an essay, SAT I or ACT, and a high school transcript, and in some cases an interview. Application deadline: 7/1; 4/1 priority date for financial aid. Early and deferred admission are possible.

SPALDING UNIVERSITY

Louisville, KY

Urban setting ■ Private ■ Independent Religious ■ Coed

Web site: www.spalding.edu

Contact: Ms. Kathleen C. Hodapp, Director of Admission, 851 South Fourth Street, Louisville, KY 40203-2188

Telephone: 502-585-7111 ext. 2226 or toll-free 800-896-8941 ext. 2111 **Fax:** 502-992-2148

E-mail: admissions@spalding.edu

Getting in Last Year 373 applied; 74% were accepted; 118 enrolled (43%).

Financial Matters $12,946 tuition and fees (2002–03); $1620 room and board; 75% average percent of need met; $11,500 average financial aid amount received per undergraduate.

Academics Spalding awards associate, bachelor's, master's, and doctoral degrees. Challenging opportunities include advanced placement credit, accelerated degree programs, double majors, independent study, and a senior project. Special programs include internships, summer session for credit, off-campus study, study-abroad, and Army and Air Force ROTC. The faculty at Spalding has 82 full-time members, 78% with terminal degrees. The student-faculty ratio is 12:1.

Students of Spalding The student body totals 1,702, of whom 964 are undergraduates. 76.2% are women and 23.8% are men. Students come from 8 states and territories and 27 other countries. 87% are from Kentucky. 10.5% are international students. 74% returned for their sophomore year.

Applying Spalding requires SAT I or ACT, a high school transcript, and a minimum high school GPA of 2.0. The school recommends an interview and a minimum high school GPA of 3.0. Application deadline: 8/1; 3/1 priority date for financial aid. Early and deferred admission are possible.

SPELMAN COLLEGE

Atlanta, GA

Urban setting ■ Private ■ Independent ■ Women Only

Web site: www.spelman.edu
Contact: Ms. Theodora Riley, Director of Admissions and Orientation Services, 350 Spelman Lane, SW, Atlanta, GA 30314-4399
Telephone: 404-681-3643 ext. 2585 or toll-free 800-982-2411 (out-of-state) **Fax:** 404-215-7788
E-mail: admiss@spelman.edu

Getting in Last Year 3,751 applied; 44% were accepted.

Financial Matters $12,675 tuition and fees (2002–03); $7300 room and board; $3250 average financial aid amount received per undergraduate (2001–02 estimated).

Academics Spelman awards bachelor's degrees. Challenging opportunities include advanced placement credit, student-designed majors, an honors program, double majors, independent study, and a senior project. Special programs include internships, off-campus study, study-abroad, and Army and Air Force ROTC. The most frequently chosen baccalaureate fields are social sciences and history, psychology, and English. The faculty at Spelman has 155 full-time members, 81% with terminal degrees. The student-faculty ratio is 12:1.

Students of Spelman The student body is made up of 2,121 undergraduates. Students come from 41 states and territories and 15 other countries. 30% are from Georgia. 1.7% are international students. 91% returned for their sophomore year.

Applying Spelman requires an essay, SAT I or ACT, a high school transcript, 2 recommendations, and a minimum high school GPA of 2.0, and in some cases an interview. Application deadline: 2/1; 3/15 priority date for financial aid. Early and deferred admission are possible.

SPRING ARBOR UNIVERSITY

Spring Arbor, MI

Small-town setting ■ Private ■ Independent Religious ■ Coed

Web site: www.arbor.edu
Contact: Mr. Jim Weidman, Director of Admissions, 106 East Main Street, Spring Arbor, MI 49283-9799
Telephone: 517-750-1200 ext. 1475 or toll-free 800-968-0011 **Fax:** 517-750-6620
E-mail: shellya@admin.arbor.edu

Getting in Last Year 793 applied; 87% were accepted; 304 enrolled (44%).

Financial Matters $14,016 tuition and fees (2002–03); $5080 room and board; 80% average percent of need met; $11,293 average financial aid amount received per undergraduate.

Academics Spring Arbor awards associate, bachelor's, and master's degrees. Challenging opportunities include advanced placement credit, accelerated degree programs, student-designed majors, an honors program, double majors, independent study, and a senior project. Special programs include internships, summer session for credit, and off-campus study. The most frequently chosen baccalaureate fields are business/marketing, home economics/vocational home economics, and health professions and related sciences. The faculty at Spring Arbor has 68 full-time members, 62% with terminal degrees. The student-faculty ratio is 16:1.

Students of Spring Arbor The student body totals 3,124, of whom 2,441 are undergraduates. 69.8% are women and 30.2% are men. 87% are from Michigan. 1.2% are international students. 83% returned for their sophomore year.

Applying Spring Arbor requires SAT I or ACT and a high school transcript, and in some cases recommendations. The school recommends an essay, an interview, and guidance counselor's evaluation form. Application deadline: rolling admissions; 2/15 priority date for financial aid. Early and deferred admission are possible.

SPRINGFIELD COLLEGE

Springfield, MA

Suburban setting ■ Private ■ Independent ■ Coed

Web site: www.spfldcol.edu
Contact: Ms. Mary N. DeAngelo, Director of Undergraduate Admissions, 263 Alden Street, Box M, Springfield, MA 01109
Telephone: 413-748-3136 or toll-free 800-343-1257 (out-of-state) **Fax:** 413-748-3694
E-mail: admissions@spfldcol.edu

Getting in Last Year 2,196 applied; 73% were accepted; 586 enrolled (37%).

Financial Matters $18,690 tuition and fees (2002–03); $6740 room and board; 81% average percent of need met; $14,600 average financial aid amount received per undergraduate.

Academics Springfield College awards bachelor's, master's, and doctoral degrees and post-master's certificates. Challenging opportunities include advanced placement credit, accelerated degree programs, double majors, and independent study. Special programs include cooperative education, internships, summer session for credit, off-campus study, study-abroad, and Army and Air Force ROTC. The most frequently chosen baccalaureate fields are education, health professions and related sciences, and business/marketing. The faculty at Springfield College has 210 full-time members. The student-faculty ratio is 12:1.

Students of Springfield College The student body totals 3,130, of whom 2,207 are undergraduates. 47.5% are women and 52.5% are men. Students come from 37 states and territories. 0.8% are international students. 83% returned for their sophomore year.

Applying Springfield College requires an essay, SAT I or ACT, a high school transcript, and 1 recommendation, and in some cases portfolio. The school recommends an interview. Application deadline: 4/1; 3/15 priority date for financial aid. Early and deferred admission are possible.

SPRING HILL COLLEGE

Mobile, AL

Suburban setting ■ Private ■ Independent Religious ■ Coed

Web site: www.shc.edu
Contact: Ms. Florence W. Hines, Dean of Enrollment Management, 4000 Dauphin Street, Mobile, AL 36608-1791
Telephone: 251-380-3030 or toll-free 800-SHC-6704 **Fax:** 251-460-2186
E-mail: admit@shc.edu

Getting in Last Year 988 applied; 81% were accepted; 288 enrolled (36%).

Financial Matters $18,092 tuition and fees (2002–03); $6540 room and board; 85% average percent of need met; $16,254 average financial aid amount received per undergraduate.

Academics Spring Hill awards associate, bachelor's, and master's degrees and post-bachelor's certificates. Challenging opportunities include advanced placement credit, accelerated degree programs, student-designed majors, an honors program, double majors, independent study, and a senior project. Special programs include internships, summer session for credit, off-campus study, study-abroad, and Army and Air Force ROTC. The most frequently chosen baccalaureate fields are communications/communication technologies, business/marketing, and biological/life sciences. The faculty at Spring Hill has 69 full-time members, 91% with terminal degrees. The student-faculty ratio is 14:1.

Students of Spring Hill The student body totals 1,467, of whom 1,221 are undergraduates. 64.5% are women and 35.5% are men. Students come from 37 states and territories and 8 other countries. 52% are from Alabama. 1.2% are international students. 82% returned for their sophomore year.

Applying Spring Hill requires an essay, SAT I or ACT, a high school transcript, and 1 recommendation. The school recommends an interview and a minimum high school GPA of 2.5. Application deadline: 7/1. Early and deferred admission are possible.

STANFORD UNIVERSITY

Stanford, CA

Suburban setting ■ Private ■ Independent ■ Coed

Web site: www.stanford.edu
Contact: Ms. Robin G. Mamlet, Dean of Undergraduate Admissions and Financial Aid, Old Union 232, 520 Lasuen Mall, Stanford, CA 94305
Telephone: 650-723-2091 **Fax:** 650-723-6050
E-mail: undergrad.admissions@forsythe.stanford.edu

Getting in Last Year 18,599 applied; 13% were accepted; 1,636 enrolled (69%).

Financial Matters $27,204 tuition and fees (2002–03); $8680 room and board; 100% average percent of need met; $24,648 average financial aid amount received per undergraduate (2001–02).

Academics Stanford awards bachelor's, master's, doctoral, and first-professional degrees. Challenging opportunities include advanced placement credit, student-designed majors, an honors program, double majors, independent study, and a senior project. Special programs include internships, summer session for credit, off-campus study, study-abroad, and Army, Navy and Air Force ROTC. The most frequently chosen baccalaureate fields are social sciences and history, engineering/engineering technologies, and interdisciplinary studies. The faculty at Stanford has 1,687 full-time members, 99% with terminal degrees. The student-faculty ratio is 7:1.

Students of Stanford The student body totals 18,297, of whom 7,360 are undergraduates. 51% are women and 49% are men. Students come from 52 states and territories and 62 other countries. 50% are from California. 5.3% are international students. 98% returned for their sophomore year.

Applying Stanford requires an essay, SAT I or ACT, a high school transcript, and 2 recommendations. The school recommends SAT II Subject Tests and SAT II: Writing Test. Application deadline: 12/15; 2/1 priority date for financial aid. Deferred admission is possible.

STATE UNIVERSITY OF NEW YORK AT ALBANY

Albany, NY

Suburban setting ■ Public ■ State-supported ■ Coed

Web site: www.albany.edu
Contact: Mr. Robert Andrea, Director of Undergraduate Admissions, 1400 Washington Avenue, University Administration Building 101, Albany, NY 12222
Telephone: 518-442-5435 or toll-free 800-293-7869 (in-state)
E-mail: ugadmissions@albany.edu

Getting in Last Year 17,667 applied; 56% were accepted; 2,276 enrolled (23%).

Financial Matters $4820 resident tuition and fees (2002–03); $9720 nonresident tuition and fees (2002–03); $7052 room and board; 71% average percent of need met; $7739 average financial aid amount received per undergraduate.

Academics University at Albany awards bachelor's, master's, and doctoral degrees and post-master's certificates. Challenging opportunities include advanced placement credit, student-designed majors, freshman honors college, an honors program, double majors, independent study, and a senior project. Special programs include internships, summer session for credit, off-campus study, study-abroad, and Army and Air Force ROTC. The most frequently chosen baccalaureate fields are mathematics, protective services/public administration, and health professions and related sciences. The faculty at University at Albany has 610 full-time members, 91% with terminal degrees. The student-faculty ratio is 21:1.

Students of University at Albany The student body totals 17,426, of whom 11,953 are undergraduates. 50% are women and 50% are men. Students come from 38 states and territories and 36 other countries. 95% are from New York. 1.7% are international students. 83% returned for their sophomore year.

Applying University at Albany requires SAT I or ACT and a high school transcript, and in some cases portfolio, audition. The school recommends an essay and recommendations. Application deadline: 3/1; 3/15 priority date for financial aid. Early and deferred admission are possible.

STATE UNIVERSITY OF NEW YORK AT BINGHAMTON

Binghamton, NY

Suburban setting ■ *Public* ■ *State-supported* ■ *Coed*

Web site: www.binghamton.edu
Contact: Ms. Cheryl S. Brown, Director of Admissions, PO Box 6001, Binghamton, NY 13902-6001
Telephone: 607-777-2000 **Fax:** 607-777-4445
E-mail: admit@binghamton.edu

Getting in Last Year 18,315 applied; 42% were accepted; 2,077 enrolled (27%).

Financial Matters $4717 resident tuition and fees (2002–03); $9617 nonresident tuition and fees (2002–03); $6412 room and board; 80% average percent of need met; $9136 average financial aid amount received per undergraduate.

Academics Binghamton University awards bachelor's, master's, and doctoral degrees and post-master's certificates. Challenging opportunities include advanced placement credit, accelerated degree programs, student-designed majors, an honors program, double majors, independent study, and a senior project. Special programs include internships, summer session for credit, off-campus study, and Air Force ROTC. The most frequently chosen baccalaureate fields are social sciences and history, business/marketing, and psychology. The faculty at Binghamton University has 493 full-time members, 94% with terminal degrees. The student-faculty ratio is 19:1.

Students of Binghamton University The student body totals 13,099, of whom 10,328 are undergraduates. 52.2% are women and 47.8% are men. Students come from 35 states and territories and 51 other countries. 95% are from New York. 2.8% are international students. 91% returned for their sophomore year.

Applying Binghamton University requires an essay, SAT I or ACT, and a high school transcript, and in some cases 1 recommendation and portfolio, audition. Application deadline: rolling admissions; 3/1 priority date for financial aid. Early and deferred admission are possible.

STATE UNIVERSITY OF NEW YORK AT NEW PALTZ

New Paltz, NY

Small-town setting ■ *Public* ■ *State-supported* ■ *Coed*

Web site: www.newpaltz.edu
Contact: Ms. Kimberly A. Lavoie, Director of Freshmen and International Admissions, 75 South Manheim Boulevard, Suite 1, New Paltz, NY 12561-2499
Telephone: 845-257-3200 or toll-free 888-639-7589 (in-state) **Fax:** 845-257-3209
E-mail: admissions@newpaltz.edu

Getting in Last Year 10,372 applied; 40% were accepted; 938 enrolled (23%).

Financial Matters $4000 resident tuition and fees (2002–03); $8900 nonresident tuition and fees (2002–03); $5600 room and board; 75% average percent of need met; $7000 average financial aid amount received per undergraduate (2001–02).

Academics SUNY New Paltz awards bachelor's and master's degrees and post-master's certificates. Challenging opportunities include advanced placement credit, an honors program, double majors, independent study, and a senior project. Special programs include internships, summer session for credit, off-campus study, and study-abroad. The most frequently chosen baccalaureate fields are education, social sciences and history, and business/marketing. The faculty at SUNY New Paltz has 296 full-time members, 87% with terminal degrees. The student-faculty ratio is 17:1.

Students of SUNY New Paltz The student body totals 8,019, of whom 6,187 are undergraduates. 64.1% are women and 35.9% are men. Students come from 25 states and territories and 30 other countries. 95% are from New York. 2.5% are international students. 83% returned for their sophomore year.

Applying SUNY New Paltz requires SAT I or ACT, a high school transcript, and portfolio for art program, audition for music and theater programs, and in some cases an essay, an interview, and recommendations. The school recommends a minimum high school GPA of 3.0. Application deadline: 3/30; 3/1 priority date for financial aid. Early and deferred admission are possible.

STATE UNIVERSITY OF NEW YORK AT OSWEGO

Oswego, NY

Small-town setting ■ *Public* ■ *State-supported* ■ *Coed*

Web site: www.oswego.edu
Contact: Dr. Joseph F. Grant Jr., Vice President for Student Affairs and Enrollment, 7060 State Route 104, Oswego, NY 13126
Telephone: 315-312-2250 **Fax:** 315-312-3260
E-mail: admiss@oswego.edu

Getting in Last Year 7,594 applied; 57% were accepted; 1,358 enrolled (31%).

Financial Matters $4184 resident tuition and fees (2002–03); $9084 nonresident tuition and fees (2002–03); $7194 room and board; 89% average percent of need met; $7802 average financial aid amount received per undergraduate.

Academics Oswego State University awards bachelor's and master's degrees and post-master's certificates. Challenging opportunities include advanced placement credit, accelerated degree programs, student-designed majors, freshman honors college, an honors program, double majors, independent study, and a senior project. Special programs include cooperative education, internships, summer session for credit, off-campus study, study-abroad, and Army ROTC. The most frequently chosen baccalaureate fields are education, business/marketing, and communications/communication technologies. The faculty at Oswego State University has 310 full-time members, 76% with terminal degrees. The student-faculty ratio is 20:1.

Students of Oswego State University The student body totals 8,716, of whom 7,337 are undergraduates. 54.1% are women and 45.9% are men. Students come from 34 states and territories and 18 other countries. 98% are from New York. 0.6% are international students. 75% returned for their sophomore year.

Applying Oswego State University requires SAT I or ACT and a high school transcript, and in some cases recommendations. The school recommends an essay and an interview. Application deadline: rolling admissions; 4/1 priority date for financial aid. Early and deferred admission are possible.

STATE UNIVERSITY OF NEW YORK COLLEGE AT BROCKPORT

Brockport, NY

Small-town setting ■ *Public* ■ *State-supported* ■ *Coed*

Web site: www.brockport.edu
Contact: Mr. Bernard S. Valento, Associate Director of Undergraduate Admissions, 350 New Campus Drive, Brockport, NY 14420-2997
Telephone: 585-395-5059 ext. 5059 **Fax:** 585-395-5452
E-mail: admit@brockport.edu

Getting in Last Year 7,350 applied; 51% were accepted; 983 enrolled (26%).

Financial Matters $4271 resident tuition and fees (2002–03); $9171 nonresident tuition and fees (2002–03); $6520 room and board; 85% average percent of need met; $7228 average financial aid amount received per undergraduate (2001–02).

Academics SUNY Brockport awards bachelor's and master's degrees and post-bachelor's certificates. Challenging opportunities include advanced placement credit, accelerated degree programs, student-designed majors, freshman honors college, an honors program, double majors, independent study, and a senior project. Special programs include cooperative education, internships, summer session for credit, off-campus study, study-abroad, and Army and Air Force ROTC. The most frequently chosen baccalaureate fields are business/marketing, protective services/public administration, and health professions and related sciences. The faculty at SUNY Brockport has 313 full-time members, 68% with terminal degrees. The student-faculty ratio is 18:1.

Students of SUNY Brockport The student body totals 8,862, of whom 6,959 are undergraduates. 57.3% are women and 42.7% are men. Students come from 35 states and territories and 21 other countries. 98% are from New York. 0.8% are international students. 76% returned for their sophomore year.

Applying SUNY Brockport requires SAT I or ACT and a high school transcript, and in some cases an essay, an interview, and recommendations. The school recommends recommendations and a minimum high school GPA of 2.5. Application deadline: rolling admissions; 3/15 priority date for financial aid. Deferred admission is possible.

STATE UNIVERSITY OF NEW YORK COLLEGE AT BUFFALO

Buffalo, NY

Urban setting ■ Public ■ State-supported ■ Coed

Web site: www.buffalostate.edu

Contact: Ms. Lesa Loritts, Director of Admissions, 1300 Elmwood Avenue, Buffalo, NY 14222-1095

Telephone: 716-878-5519 **Fax:** 716-878-6100

E-mail: admissio@buffalostate.edu

Getting in Last Year 7,852 applied; 54% were accepted; 1,322 enrolled (31%).

Financial Matters $4109 resident tuition and fees (2002–03); $9009 nonresident tuition and fees (2002–03); $5640 room and board; 62% average percent of need met; $3037 average financial aid amount received per undergraduate (2001–02).

Academics Buffalo State College awards bachelor's and master's degrees and post-master's certificates. Challenging opportunities include advanced placement credit, freshman honors college, an honors program, double majors, independent study, and a senior project. Special programs include cooperative education, internships, summer session for credit, off-campus study, study-abroad, and Army ROTC. The most frequently chosen baccalaureate fields are education, business/marketing, and social sciences and history. The faculty at Buffalo State College has 411 full-time members. The student-faculty ratio is 16:1.

Students of Buffalo State College The student body totals 11,803, of whom 9,495 are undergraduates. 59.6% are women and 40.4% are men. Students come from 4 states and territories and 8 other countries. 99% are from New York. 0.5% are international students. 77% returned for their sophomore year.

Applying Buffalo State College requires SAT I or ACT, a high school transcript, and a minimum high school GPA of 3.0, and in some cases an essay, an interview, and recommendations. Application deadline: rolling admissions. Early and deferred admission are possible.

STATE UNIVERSITY OF NEW YORK COLLEGE AT CORTLAND

Cortland, NY

Small-town setting ■ Public ■ State-supported ■ Coed

Web site: www.cortland.edu

Contact: Mr. Gradon Avery, Director of Admission, PO Box 2000, Cortland, NY 13045

Telephone: 607-753-4711 **Fax:** 607-753-5998

E-mail: admssn_info@snycorva.cortland.edu

Getting in Last Year 9,278 applied; 46% were accepted; 1,049 enrolled (25%).

Financial Matters $4265 resident tuition and fees (2002–03); $9165 nonresident tuition and fees (2002–03); $6700 room and board; 77% average percent of need met; $7880 average financial aid amount received per undergraduate (2001–02).

Academics SUNY Cortland awards bachelor's and master's degrees and post-bachelor's and post-master's certificates. Challenging opportunities include advanced placement credit, student-designed majors, an honors program, double majors, independent study, and a senior project. Special programs include cooperative education, internships, summer session for credit, off-campus study, study-abroad, and Army and Air Force ROTC. The most frequently chosen baccalaureate fields are health professions and related sciences, education, and social sciences and history. The faculty at SUNY Cortland has 272 full-time members, 79% with terminal degrees. The student-faculty ratio is 15:1.

Students of SUNY Cortland The student body totals 7,472, of whom 5,781 are undergraduates. 59.5% are women and 40.5% are men. 98% are from New York. 0.1% are international students.

Applying SUNY Cortland requires an essay, SAT I or ACT, a high school transcript, 1 recommendation, and a minimum high school GPA of 2.3. The school recommends an interview, 3 recommendations, and a minimum high school GPA of 3.0. Application deadline: 4/1 for financial aid. Early and deferred admission are possible.

STATE UNIVERSITY OF NEW YORK COLLEGE AT FREDONIA

Fredonia, NY

Small-town setting ■ Public ■ State-supported ■ Coed

Web site: www.fredonia.edu

Contact: Mr. Daniel Tramuta, Director of Admissions, Fredonia, NY 14063-1136

Telephone: 716-673-3251 or toll-free 800-252-1212 **Fax:** 716-673-3249

E-mail: admissions.office@fredonia.edu

Getting in Last Year 6,178 applied; 53% were accepted; 1,060 enrolled (33%).

Financial Matters $4375 resident tuition and fees (2002–03); $9275 nonresident tuition and fees (2002–03); $5800 room and board; 77% average percent of need met; $6481 average financial aid amount received per undergraduate.

Academics SUNY College at Fredonia awards bachelor's and master's degrees. Challenging opportunities include advanced placement credit, accelerated degree programs, student-designed majors, an honors program, double majors, independent study, and a senior project. Special programs include internships, summer session for credit, off-campus study, and study-abroad. The most frequently chosen baccalaureate fields are education, business/marketing, and communications/communication technologies. The faculty at SUNY College at Fredonia has 254 full-time members, 84% with terminal degrees. The student-faculty ratio is 18:1.

Students of SUNY College at Fredonia The student body totals 5,301, of whom 4,900 are undergraduates. 58.3% are women and 41.7% are men. Students come from 27 states and territories and 9 other countries. 98% are from New York. 0.6% are international students. 81% returned for their sophomore year.

Applying SUNY College at Fredonia requires SAT I or ACT, a high school transcript, and a minimum high school GPA of 2.5, and in some cases an essay, an interview, and audition for music and theater programs, portfolio for art and media arts program. The school recommends recommendations. Application deadline: rolling admissions; 2/1 priority date for financial aid. Early and deferred admission are possible.

STATE UNIVERSITY OF NEW YORK COLLEGE AT GENESEO

Geneseo, NY

Small-town setting ■ Public ■ State-supported ■ Coed

Web site: www.geneseo.edu

Contact: Kris Shay, Associate Director of Admissions, 1 College Circle, Geneseo, NY 14454-1401

Telephone: 585-245-5571 or toll-free 866-245-5211 **Fax:** 585-245-5550

E-mail: admissions@geneseo.edu

Getting in Last Year 8,535 applied; 49% were accepted; 1,149 enrolled (27%).

Financial Matters $4440 resident tuition and fees (2002–03); $9340 nonresident tuition and fees (2002–03); $5940 room and board; 90% average percent of need met; $7873 average financial aid amount received per undergraduate.

Academics Geneseo College awards bachelor's and master's degrees. Challenging opportunities include advanced placement credit, an honors program, double majors, independent study, and a senior project. Special programs include internships, summer session for credit, off-campus study, study-abroad, and Army and Air Force ROTC. The most frequently chosen baccalaureate fields are education, social sciences and history, and business/marketing. The faculty at Geneseo College has 252 full-time members, 85% with terminal degrees. The student-faculty ratio is 19:1.

Students of Geneseo College The student body totals 5,668, of whom 5,387 are undergraduates. 64.5% are women and 35.5% are men. Students come from 20 states and territories and 23 other countries. 99% are from New York. 1.5% are international students. 91% returned for their sophomore year.

Applying Geneseo College requires an essay, SAT I or ACT, and a high school transcript. The school recommends an interview and recommendations. Application deadline: 1/15; 2/15 priority date for financial aid. Early and deferred admission are possible.

STATE UNIVERSITY OF NEW YORK COLLEGE AT OLD WESTBURY

Old Westbury, NY

Suburban setting ■ Public ■ State-supported ■ Coed

Web site: www.oldwestbury.edu

Contact: Ms. Mary Marquez Bell, Vice President, PO Box 307, Old Westbury, NY 11568

Telephone: 516-876-3073 **Fax:** 516-876-3307

Getting in Last Year 2,970 applied; 52% were accepted.

Financial Matters $3985 resident tuition and fees (2002–03); $8885 nonresident tuition and fees (2002–03); $5837 room and board; 57% average percent of need met; $6429 average financial aid amount received per undergraduate.

Academics SUNY/Old Westbury awards bachelor's degrees. Challenging opportunities include advanced placement credit, double majors, independent study, and a senior project. Special programs include internships, summer session for credit, off-campus study, study-abroad, and Army and Air Force ROTC. The most frequently chosen baccalaureate fields are business/marketing, education, and social sciences and history. The faculty at SUNY/Old Westbury has 119 full-time members. The student-faculty ratio is 20:1.

Students of SUNY/Old Westbury The student body is made up of 3,142 undergraduates. 59.9% are women and 40.1% are men. Students come from 12 states and territories and 25 other countries. 86% are from New York. 1.6% are international students. 70% returned for their sophomore year.

Applying SUNY/Old Westbury requires SAT I or ACT and a high school transcript, and in some cases an essay, an interview, and 2 recommendations. Application deadline: rolling admissions; 4/17 priority date for financial aid. Early and deferred admission are possible.

STATE UNIVERSITY OF NEW YORK COLLEGE AT ONEONTA

Oneonta, NY

Small-town setting ■ Public ■ State-supported ■ Coed

Web site: www.oneonta.edu

Contact: Ms. Karen A. Brown, Director of Admissions, Alumni Hall 116, Oneonta, NY 13820-4015

Telephone: 607-436-2524 or toll-free 800-SUNY-123 **Fax:** 607-436-3074

E-mail: admissions@oneonta.edu

Getting in Last Year 10,304 applied; 47% were accepted; 1,087 enrolled (22%).

Financial Matters $4306 resident tuition and fees (2002–03); $9206 nonresident tuition and fees (2002–03); $6158 room and board; 66% average percent of need met; $7766 average financial aid amount received per undergraduate (2001–02).

Academics Oneonta awards bachelor's and master's degrees and post-master's certificates. Challenging opportunities include advanced placement credit, an honors program, double majors, and independent study. Special programs include internships, summer session for credit, off-campus study, and study-abroad. The most frequently chosen baccalaureate fields are education, business/marketing, and home economics/vocational home economics. The faculty at Oneonta has 245 full-time members, 76% with terminal degrees. The student-faculty ratio is 18:1.

Students of Oneonta The student body totals 5,728, of whom 5,477 are undergraduates. 59.6% are women and 40.4% are men. Students come from 18 states and territories and 19 other countries. 98% are from New York. 1.2% are international students. 72% returned for their sophomore year.

Applying Oneonta requires an essay, SAT I or ACT, and a high school transcript. The school recommends 3 recommendations and a minimum high school GPA of 3.0. Application deadline: rolling admissions; 3/15 priority date for financial aid. Early and deferred admission are possible.

STATE UNIVERSITY OF NEW YORK COLLEGE AT POTSDAM

Potsdam, NY

Small-town setting ■ Public ■ State-supported ■ Coed

Web site: www.potsdam.edu

Contact: Mr. Thomas Nesbitt, Director of Admissions, 44 Pierrepont Avenue, Potsdam, NY 13676

Telephone: 315-267-4872 or toll-free 877-POTSDAM **Fax:** 315-267-2163

E-mail: admissions@potsdam.edu

Getting in Last Year 3,609 applied; 69% were accepted; 743 enrolled (30%).

Financial Matters $4215 resident tuition and fees (2002–03); $9115 nonresident tuition and fees (2002–03); $6620 room and board; 89% average percent of need met; $9998 average financial aid amount received per undergraduate.

Academics SUNY Potsdam awards bachelor's and master's degrees. Challenging opportunities include advanced placement credit, student-designed majors, an honors program, double majors, independent study, and a senior project. Special programs include internships, summer session for credit, off-campus study, study-abroad, and Army and Air Force ROTC. The most frequently chosen baccalaureate fields are social sciences and history, psychology, and education. The faculty at SUNY Potsdam has 235 full-time members, 91% with terminal degrees. The student-faculty ratio is 18:1.

Students of SUNY Potsdam The student body totals 4,444, of whom 3,561 are undergraduates. 60.4% are women and 39.6% are men. Students come from 21 states and territories and 11 other countries. 97% are from New York. 1.9% are international students. 75% returned for their sophomore year.

Applying SUNY Potsdam requires SAT I or ACT, a high school transcript, and a minimum high school GPA of 3.0, and in some cases an essay and audition for music program. The school recommends an interview. Application deadline: rolling admissions. Early and deferred admission are possible.

STATE UNIVERSITY OF NEW YORK COLLEGE OF AGRICULTURE AND TECHNOLOGY AT COBLESKILL

Cobleskill, NY

Rural setting ■ Public ■ State-supported ■ Coed

Web site: www.cobleskill.edu

Contact: Mr. Clayton Smith, Director of Admissions, Office of Admissions, Cobleskill, NY 12043

Telephone: 518-255-5525 or toll-free 800-295-8988 **Fax:** 518-255-6769

E-mail: admissions@cobleskill.edu

Getting in Last Year 2,966 applied; 92% were accepted; 991 enrolled (36%).

Financial Matters $4261 resident tuition and fees (2002–03); $9161 nonresident tuition and fees (2002–03); $6600 room and board; 78% average percent of need met; $4792 average financial aid amount received per undergraduate (2001–02).

Academics SUNY Cobleskill awards associate and bachelor's degrees. Challenging opportunities include advanced placement credit, freshman honors college, and an honors program. Special programs include internships, summer session for credit, off-campus study, and study-abroad. The most frequently chosen baccalaureate fields are agriculture and computer/information sciences. The faculty at SUNY Cobleskill has 107 full-time members, 30% with terminal degrees. The student-faculty ratio is 19:1.

Students of SUNY Cobleskill The student body is made up of 2,443 undergraduates. 46.7% are women and 53.3% are men. Students come from 16 states and territories and 8 other countries. 92% are from New York. 2.3% are international students. 80% returned for their sophomore year.

Applying SUNY Cobleskill requires a high school transcript and a minimum high school GPA of 2.0, and in some cases SAT I or ACT and an interview. The school recommends SAT I or ACT. Application deadline: rolling admissions; 3/15 for financial aid. Early and deferred admission are possible.

STATE UNIVERSITY OF NEW YORK COLLEGE OF ENVIRONMENTAL SCIENCE AND FORESTRY

Syracuse, NY

Urban setting ■ Public ■ State-supported ■ Coed

Web site: www.esf.edu

Contact: Ms. Susan Sanford, Director of Admissions, 1 Forestry Drive, Syracuse, NY 13210-2779

Telephone: 315-470-6600 or toll-free 800-777-7373 **Fax:** 315-470-6933

E-mail: esfinfo@esf.edu

Getting in Last Year 770 applied; 58% were accepted; 198 enrolled (45%).

Financial Matters $3826 resident tuition and fees (2002–03); $8726 nonresident tuition and fees (2002–03); $9040 room and board; 79% average percent of need met; $7434 average financial aid amount received per undergraduate.

Academics ESF awards associate, bachelor's, master's, and doctoral degrees. Challenging opportunities include advanced placement credit, accelerated degree programs, freshman honors college, an honors program, double majors, independent study, and a senior project. Special programs include cooperative education, internships, off-campus study, study-abroad, and Army and Air Force ROTC. The most frequently chosen baccalaureate fields are biological/life sciences, natural resources/environmental science, and architecture. The faculty at ESF has 118 full-time members, 90% with terminal degrees. The student-faculty ratio is 10:1.

Students of ESF The student body totals 1,909, of whom 1,312 are undergraduates. 41.2% are women and 58.8% are men. Students come from 23 states and territories and 3 other countries. 90% are from New York. 0.6% are international students. 81% returned for their sophomore year.

Applying ESF requires an essay, SAT I or ACT, a high school transcript, inventory of courses-in-progress form, and a minimum high school GPA of 3.3. The school recommends an interview and 3 recommendations. Application deadline: rolling admissions; 3/1 priority date for financial aid. Early and deferred admission are possible.

STATE UNIVERSITY OF NEW YORK EMPIRE STATE COLLEGE

Saratoga Springs, NY

Small-town setting ■ Public ■ State-supported ■ Coed

Web site: www.esc.edu

Contact: Ms. Jennifer Riley, Assistant Director of Admissions, One Union Avenue, Saratoga Springs, NY 12866

Telephone: 518-587-2100 ext. 214 or toll-free 800-847-3000 (out-of-state) **Fax:** 518-580-0105

E-mail: admissions@esc.edu

Getting in Last Year 704 enrolled.

Financial Matters $3555 resident tuition and fees (2002–03); $8455 nonresident tuition and fees (2002–03).

Academics Empire State College awards associate, bachelor's, and master's degrees (branch locations at 7 regional centers with 38 auxiliary units). Challenging opportunities include advanced placement credit, student-designed majors, and independent study. Special programs include cooperative education, off-campus study, and study-abroad. The most frequently chosen baccalaureate fields are business/marketing, protective services/public administration, and interdisciplinary studies. The faculty at Empire State College has 350 members. The student-faculty ratio is 30:1.

Students of Empire State College The student body totals 8,395, of whom 8,060 are undergraduates. 55.1% are women and 44.9% are men. Students come from 13 states and territories and 25 other countries. 99% are from New York. 4.6% are international students. 35% returned for their sophomore year.

Applying Empire State College requires an essay, and in some cases an interview. Application deadline: rolling admissions. Early admission is possible.

STATE UNIVERSITY OF NEW YORK HEALTH SCIENCE CENTER AT BROOKLYN

Brooklyn, NY

Urban setting ■ Public ■ State-supported ■ Coed

State University of New York Health Science Center at Brooklyn (continued)

Web site: www.downstate.edu
Contact: Mr. Tom Sabia, Assistant Dean of Admissions, 450 Clarkson Avenue, Box 60, Brooklyn, NY 11203
Telephone: 718-270-2446 **Fax:** 718-270-7592

Financial Matters $4030 resident tuition and fees (2002–03); $8930 nonresident tuition and fees (2002–03); $10,206 room and board.

Academics State University of New York Health Science Center at Brooklyn awards bachelor's, master's, doctoral, and first-professional degrees and post-bachelor's and post-master's certificates. Challenging opportunities include advanced placement credit, accelerated degree programs, and independent study. Special programs include internships, summer session for credit, and off-campus study. The most frequently chosen baccalaureate field is health professions and related sciences.

Students of State University of New York Health Science Center at Brooklyn The student body totals 1,430, of whom 262 are undergraduates. 84% are women and 16% are men. 99% are from New York. 0.4% are international students.

Applying State University of New York Health Science Center at Brooklyn recommends SAT I. Application deadline: 2/15 for financial aid.

STATE UNIVERSITY OF NEW YORK INSTITUTE OF TECHNOLOGY AT UTICA/ROME

Utica, NY

Suburban setting ■ Public ■ State-supported ■ Coed

Web site: www.sunyit.edu
Contact: Ms. Marybeth Lyons, Director of Admissions, PO Box 3050, Utica, NY 13504-3050
Telephone: 315-792-7500 or toll-free 800-SUNYTEC **Fax:** 315-792-7837
E-mail: admissions@sunyit.edu

Financial Matters $4418 resident tuition and fees (2002–03); $9318 nonresident tuition and fees (2002–03); $6560 room and board; 81% average percent of need met; $7672 average financial aid amount received per undergraduate (2001–02).

Academics SUNY Utica/Rome awards bachelor's and master's degrees and post-master's certificates. Challenging opportunities include advanced placement credit, accelerated degree programs, double majors, independent study, and a senior project. Special programs include internships, summer session for credit, and Army and Air Force ROTC. The most frequently chosen baccalaureate fields are business/marketing, engineering/engineering technologies, and computer/information sciences. The faculty at SUNY Utica/Rome has 85 full-time members. The student-faculty ratio is 19:1.

Students of SUNY Utica/Rome The student body totals 2,628, of whom 1,974 are undergraduates. 49.9% are women and 50.1% are men. Students come from 10 states and territories and 14 other countries. 99% are from New York. 2.1% are international students.

Applying Deferred admission is possible.

STATE UNIVERSITY OF NEW YORK MARITIME COLLEGE

Throggs Neck, NY

Suburban setting ■ Public ■ State-supported ■ Coed, Primarily Men

Web site: www.sunymaritime.edu
Contact: Ms. Deirdre Whitman, Vice President of Enrollment and Campus Life, 6 Pennyfield Avenue, Throggs Neck, NY 10465-4198
Telephone: 718-409-7220 ext. 7222 or toll-free 800-654-1874 (in-state), 800-642-1874 (out-of-state) **Fax:** 718-409-7465
E-mail: admissions@sunymaritime.edu

Getting in Last Year 818 applied; 82% were accepted; 238 enrolled (35%).

Financial Matters $4900 resident tuition and fees (2002–03); $9800 nonresident tuition and fees (2002–03); $6500 room and board.

Academics Maritime College awards associate, bachelor's, and master's degrees. Challenging opportunities include advanced placement credit, student-designed majors, independent study, and a senior project. Special programs include cooperative education, internships, summer session for credit, study-abroad, and Navy and Air Force ROTC. The most frequently chosen baccalaureate fields are engineering/engineering technologies, business/marketing, and natural resources/environmental science. The faculty at Maritime College has 58 full-time members, 53% with terminal degrees. The student-faculty ratio is 8:1.

Students of Maritime College The student body totals 856, of whom 713 are undergraduates. 10.1% are women and 89.9% are men. Students come from 15 states and territories and 28 other countries. 71% are from New York. 3.1% are international students. 87% returned for their sophomore year.

Applying Maritime College requires SAT I or ACT, a high school transcript, medical history, and a minimum high school GPA of 2.5. The school recommends an essay, SAT II Subject Tests, an interview, and 1 recommendation. Application deadline: rolling admissions. Early and deferred admission are possible.

STATE UNIVERSITY OF NEW YORK UPSTATE MEDICAL UNIVERSITY

Syracuse, NY

Urban setting ■ Public ■ State-supported ■ Coed

Web site: www.upstate.edu
Contact: Ms. Donna L. Vavonese, Associate Director of Admissions, Weiskotten Hall, 766 Irving Avenue, Syracuse, NY 13210
Telephone: 315-464-4570 or toll-free 800-736-2171 **Fax:** 315-464-8867
E-mail: stuadmis@upstate.edu

Financial Matters $3875 resident tuition and fees (2002–03); $8775 nonresident tuition and fees (2002–03); $7225 room and board.

Academics State University of New York Upstate Medical University awards bachelor's, master's, doctoral, and first-professional degrees. Advanced placement credit is a challenging opportunity. Special programs include internships, summer session for credit, and off-campus study. The most frequently chosen baccalaureate field is health professions and related sciences. The faculty at State University of New York Upstate Medical University has 480 full-time members. The student-faculty ratio is 10:1.

Students of State University of New York Upstate Medical University The student body totals 1,136, of whom 262 are undergraduates. Students come from 4 states and territories and 2 other countries. 98% are from New York. 1.2% are international students. 95% returned for their sophomore year.

Applying Application deadline: 4/1 for financial aid, with a 3/1 priority date. Early and deferred admission are possible.

STATE UNIVERSITY OF WEST GEORGIA

Carrollton, GA

Small-town setting ■ Public ■ State-supported ■ Coed

Web site: www.westga.edu
Contact: Dr. Robert Johnson, Director of Admissions, 1600 Maple Street, Carrollton, GA 30118
Telephone: 770-836-6416 **Fax:** 770-836-4659
E-mail: rjohnson@westga.edu

Getting in Last Year 4,451 applied; 64% were accepted; 1,689 enrolled (60%).

Financial Matters $2558 resident tuition and fees (2002–03); $8588 nonresident tuition and fees (2002–03); $4244 room and board; 71% average percent of need met; $6425 average financial aid amount received per undergraduate.

Academics West Georgia awards bachelor's, master's, and doctoral degrees and post-master's certificates. Challenging opportunities include advanced placement credit, accelerated degree programs, an honors program, double majors, independent study, and a senior project. Special programs include cooperative education, internships, summer session for credit, off-campus study, study-abroad, and Army ROTC. The most frequently chosen baccalaureate fields are business/marketing, education, and social sciences and history. The faculty at West Georgia has 344 full-time members, 82% with terminal degrees. The student-faculty ratio is 23:1.

Students of West Georgia The student body totals 9,673, of whom 7,661 are undergraduates. 60.2% are women and 39.8% are men. Students come from 39 states and territories and 31 other countries. 96% are from Georgia. 0.9% are international students. 70% returned for their sophomore year.

Applying West Georgia requires SAT I or ACT, a high school transcript, and proof of immunization, and in some cases an interview and 2 recommendations. Application deadline: 7/31; 4/1 priority date for financial aid. Early and deferred admission are possible.

STEINBACH BIBLE COLLEGE

Steinbach, MB Canada

Small-town setting ■ Private ■ Independent Religious ■ Coed

Web site: www.SBCollege.mb.ca
Contact: Dr. Terry Hiebert, Registrar, PO Box 1420, Steinbach, MB R0A 2A0 Canada
Telephone: 204-326-6451 ext. 230
E-mail: info@sbcollege.mb.ca

Getting in Last Year 54 applied; 83% were accepted.

Financial Matters $4000 tuition and fees (2002–03); $3700 room and board.

Academics SBC awards bachelor's degrees. The faculty at SBC has 6 full-time members, 33% with terminal degrees. The student-faculty ratio is 11:1.

Students of SBC The student body is made up of 102 undergraduates. 52% are women and 48% are men.

STEPHEN F. AUSTIN STATE UNIVERSITY

Nacogdoches, TX

Small-town setting ■ Public ■ State-supported ■ Coed

Web site: www.sfasu.edu

Contact: Ms. Beth Smith, Assistant Director of Admissions, SFA Box 13051, Nacogdoches, TX 75962
Telephone: 936-468-2504 or toll-free 800-731-2902 **Fax:** 936-468-3849
E-mail: admissions@sfasu.edu

Getting in Last Year 5,836 applied; 76% were accepted; 1,983 enrolled (44%).

Financial Matters $2486 resident tuition and fees (2002–03); $7718 nonresident tuition and fees (2002–03); $4546 room and board; 74% average percent of need met; $7038 average financial aid amount received per undergraduate (2001–02).

Academics SFA awards bachelor's, master's, and doctoral degrees. Challenging opportunities include advanced placement credit, accelerated degree programs, student-designed majors, freshman honors college, an honors program, double majors, and independent study. Special programs include internships, summer session for credit, off-campus study, study-abroad, and Army ROTC. The most frequently chosen baccalaureate fields are business/marketing, interdisciplinary studies, and health professions and related sciences. The faculty at SFA has 416 full-time members, 75% with terminal degrees. The student-faculty ratio is 21:1.

Students of SFA The student body totals 11,356, of whom 9,783 are undergraduates. 58% are women and 42% are men. Students come from 35 states and territories and 49 other countries. 98% are from Texas. 0.5% are international students. 60% returned for their sophomore year.

Applying SFA requires SAT I or ACT and a high school transcript. Application deadline: rolling admissions; 4/15 for financial aid, with a 4/1 priority date.

STEPHENS COLLEGE

Columbia, MO

Urban setting ■ Private ■ Independent ■ Women Only

Web site: www.stephens.edu

Contact: Ms. Amy Shaver, Director of Admissions, Box 2121, Columbia, MO 65215-0002
Telephone: 573-876-7207 or toll-free 800-876-7207 **Fax:** 573-876-7237
E-mail: apply@stephens.edu

Getting in Last Year 331 applied; 84% were accepted; 126 enrolled (45%).

Financial Matters $16,175 tuition and fees (2002–03); $5690 room and board; 89% average percent of need met; $17,694 average financial aid amount received per undergraduate.

Academics Stephens awards associate, bachelor's, and master's degrees. Challenging opportunities include advanced placement credit, accelerated degree programs, student-designed majors, freshman honors college, an honors program, double majors, independent study, and a senior project. Special programs include cooperative education, internships, off-campus study, study-abroad, and Army and Air Force ROTC. The most frequently chosen baccalaureate fields are visual/performing arts, business/marketing, and education. The faculty at Stephens has 51 full-time members, 88% with terminal degrees. The student-faculty ratio is 10:1.

Students of Stephens The student body totals 669, of whom 618 are undergraduates. Students come from 41 states and territories and 3 other countries. 48% are from Missouri. 3% are international students. 68% returned for their sophomore year.

Applying Stephens requires an essay, SAT I or ACT, a high school transcript, 1 recommendation, and a minimum high school GPA of 2.5. The school recommends an interview. Application deadline: 7/31; 3/15 priority date for financial aid. Early and deferred admission are possible.

STERLING COLLEGE

Sterling, KS

Small-town setting ■ Private ■ Independent Religious ■ Coed

Web site: www.sterling.edu

Contact: Mr. Chris Burlew, Vice President for Enrollment Services, PO Box 98, Administration Building, 125 West Cooper, Sterling, KS 67579-0098
Telephone: 620-278-4364 ext. 364 or toll-free 800-346-1017 **Fax:** 620-278-4416
E-mail: admissions@sterling.edu

Getting in Last Year 359 applied; 57% were accepted; 106 enrolled (52%).

Financial Matters $13,120 tuition and fees (2002–03); $5240 room and board; 83% average percent of need met; $12,143 average financial aid amount received per undergraduate.

Academics Sterling College awards bachelor's degrees. Challenging opportunities include advanced placement credit, student-designed majors, an honors program, double majors, independent study, and a senior project. Special programs include internships, off-campus study, and study-abroad. The most frequently chosen baccalaureate fields are education, business/marketing, and biological/life sciences. The faculty at Sterling College has 33 full-time members, 52% with terminal degrees. The student-faculty ratio is 11:1.

Students of Sterling College The student body is made up of 461 undergraduates. 52.3% are women and 47.7% are men. Students come from 28 states and territories and 14 other countries. 64% are from Kansas. 2% are international students. 65% returned for their sophomore year.

Applying Sterling College requires SAT I or ACT, a high school transcript, and a minimum high school GPA of 2.2, and in some cases 2 recommendations. The school recommends an essay. Application deadline: rolling admissions; 3/15 priority date for financial aid. Deferred admission is possible.

STERLING COLLEGE

Craftsbury Common, VT

Rural setting ■ Private ■ Independent ■ Coed

Web site: www.sterlingcollege.edu

Contact: John Zaber, Director of Admissions, PO Box 72, Craftsbury Common, VT 05827
Telephone: 802-586-7711 ext. 35 or toll-free 800-648-3591 **Fax:** 802-586-2596
E-mail: admissions@sterlingcollege.edu

Getting in Last Year 69 applied; 70% were accepted; 27 enrolled (56%).

Financial Matters $14,750 tuition and fees (2002–03); $5670 room and board; 78% average percent of need met; $11,411 average financial aid amount received per undergraduate.

Academics Sterling awards associate and bachelor's degrees. Challenging opportunities include student-designed majors, an honors program, independent study, and a senior project. Special programs include internships, summer session for credit, off-campus study, and study-abroad. The most frequently chosen baccalaureate field is natural resources/environmental science. The faculty at Sterling has 10 full-time members, 30% with terminal degrees. The student-faculty ratio is 10:1.

Students of Sterling The student body is made up of 103 undergraduates. 38.8% are women and 61.2% are men. Students come from 20 states and territories. 22% are from Vermont. 83% returned for their sophomore year.

Applying Sterling requires an essay, a high school transcript, an interview, and 3 recommendations. The school recommends a minimum high school GPA of 2.0. Application deadline: rolling admissions. Early and deferred admission are possible.

STETSON UNIVERSITY

DeLand, FL

Small-town setting ■ Private ■ Independent ■ Coed

Web site: www.stetson.edu

Contact: Ms. Deborah Thompson, Vice President for Admissions, Unit 8378, Griffith Hall, DeLand, FL 32723
Telephone: 386-822-7100 or toll-free 800-688-0101 **Fax:** 386-822-8832
E-mail: admissions@stetson.edu

Getting in Last Year 1,919 applied; 80% were accepted; 544 enrolled (35%).

Financial Matters $20,975 tuition and fees (2002–03); $6650 room and board; 84% average percent of need met; $18,791 average financial aid amount received per undergraduate.

Academics Stetson awards bachelor's, master's, and first-professional degrees and post-master's certificates. Challenging opportunities include advanced placement credit, accelerated degree programs, student-designed majors, an honors program, double majors, independent study, and a senior project. Special programs include internships, summer session for credit, off-campus study, study-abroad, and Army ROTC. The most frequently chosen baccalaureate fields are business/marketing, social sciences and history, and parks and recreation. The faculty at Stetson has 195 full-time members, 90% with terminal degrees. The student-faculty ratio is 11:1.

Students of Stetson The student body totals 3,318, of whom 2,142 are undergraduates. 58% are women and 42% are men. Students come from 45 states and territories and 43 other countries. 77% are from Florida. 3% are international students. 77% returned for their sophomore year.

Applying Stetson requires an essay, SAT I or ACT, a high school transcript, and recommendations. The school recommends an interview. Application deadline: 3/1; 4/15 priority date for financial aid. Early admission is possible.

STEVENS INSTITUTE OF TECHNOLOGY

Hoboken, NJ

Urban setting ■ Private ■ Independent ■ Coed

Web site: www.stevens.edu

Contact: Mr. Daniel Gallagher, Dean of University Admissions, 1 Castle Point on Hudson, Hoboken, NJ 07030
Telephone: 201-216-5197 or toll-free 800-458-5323 **Fax:** 201-216-8348
E-mail: admissions@stevens-tech.edu

Getting in Last Year 2,049 applied; 50% were accepted; 390 enrolled (38%).

Financial Matters $24,750 tuition and fees (2002–03); $8100 room and board; 87% average percent of need met; $20,837 average financial aid amount received per undergraduate.

Academics Stevens awards bachelor's, master's, and doctoral degrees and post-bachelor's certificates. Challenging opportunities include advanced placement credit, accelerated degree programs, an honors program, double majors,

Stevens Institute of Technology (continued)

independent study, and a senior project. Special programs include cooperative education, internships, summer session for credit, off-campus study, study-abroad, and Army and Air Force ROTC. The most frequently chosen baccalaureate fields are engineering/engineering technologies, computer/information sciences, and business/marketing. The faculty at Stevens has 171 full-time members, 94% with terminal degrees. The student-faculty ratio is 9:1.

Students of Stevens The student body totals 4,597, of whom 1,755 are undergraduates. 25.2% are women and 74.8% are men. Students come from 40 states and territories and 68 other countries. 65% are from New Jersey. 7.2% are international students. 89% returned for their sophomore year.

Applying Stevens requires SAT I or ACT, a high school transcript, and an interview, and in some cases SAT II Subject Tests, SAT II: Writing Test, and SAT I and SAT II or ACT. The school recommends an essay, SAT II Subject Tests, SAT II: Writing Test, and recommendations. Application deadline: 2/15; 2/15 priority date for financial aid. Early and deferred admission are possible.

STONEHILL COLLEGE

Easton, MA

Suburban setting ■ Private ■ Independent Religious ■ Coed

Web site: www.stonehill.edu
Contact: Mr. Brian P. Murphy, Dean of Admissions and Enrollment, 320 Washington Street, Easton, MA 02357-5610
Telephone: 508-565-1373 **Fax:** 508-565-1545
E-mail: admissions@stonehill.edu

Getting in Last Year 5,331 applied; 42% were accepted; 566 enrolled (25%).

Financial Matters $19,908 tuition and fees (2002–03); $9172 room and board; 80% average percent of need met; $13,923 average financial aid amount received per undergraduate.

Academics Stonehill awards bachelor's and master's degrees. Challenging opportunities include advanced placement credit, student-designed majors, an honors program, double majors, independent study, and a senior project. Special programs include internships, summer session for credit, off-campus study, study-abroad, and Army ROTC. The most frequently chosen baccalaureate fields are business/marketing, social sciences and history, and education. The faculty at Stonehill has 125 full-time members, 82% with terminal degrees. The student-faculty ratio is 15:1.

Students of Stonehill The student body totals 2,617, of whom 2,602 are undergraduates. 59.9% are women and 40.1% are men. Students come from 31 states and territories and 5 other countries. 61% are from Massachusetts. 0.7% are international students. 90% returned for their sophomore year.

Applying Stonehill requires an essay, SAT I or ACT, a high school transcript, and 2 recommendations, and in some cases an interview. The school recommends campus visit. Application deadline: 1/15; 2/1 priority date for financial aid. Early and deferred admission are possible.

STONY BROOK UNIVERSITY, STATE UNIVERSITY OF NEW YORK

Stony Brook, NY

Small-town setting ■ Public ■ State-supported ■ Coed

Web site: www.stonybrook.edu
Contact: Ms. Judith Burke-Berhanan, Acting Director of Admissions and Enrollment Planning, Nicolls Road, Stony Brook, NY 11794
Telephone: 631-632-6868 or toll-free 800-872-7869 (out-of-state) **Fax:** 631-632-9898
E-mail: ugadmissions@notes.cc.sunysb.edu

Getting in Last Year 16,849 applied; 54% were accepted; 2,415 enrolled (27%).

Financial Matters $4358 resident tuition and fees (2002–03); $9258 nonresident tuition and fees (2002–03); $6974 room and board; 72% average percent of need met; $7579 average financial aid amount received per undergraduate (2001–02).

Academics Stony Brook awards bachelor's, master's, doctoral, and first-professional degrees and post-bachelor's, post-master's, and first-professional certificates. Challenging opportunities include advanced placement credit, student-designed majors, freshman honors college, an honors program, double majors, independent study, and a senior project. Special programs include internships, summer session for credit, off-campus study, and study-abroad. The most frequently chosen baccalaureate fields are social sciences and history, psychology, and biological/life sciences. The faculty at Stony Brook has 871 full-time members, 95% with terminal degrees. The student-faculty ratio is 18:1.

Students of Stony Brook The student body totals 21,989, of whom 14,224 are undergraduates. 48.2% are women and 51.8% are men. Students come from 39 states and territories and 62 other countries. 98% are from New York. 4.3% are international students. 85% returned for their sophomore year.

Applying Stony Brook requires an essay, SAT I or ACT, a high school transcript, and a minimum high school GPA of 3.0, and in some cases audition. The school recommends SAT II Subject Tests, an interview, and 2 recommendations. Application deadline: 3/1 priority date for financial aid. Deferred admission is possible.

STRATFORD UNIVERSITY

Falls Church, VA

Private ■ Proprietary ■ Coed

Web site: www.stratford.edu
Contact: Ms. Denise Baxter, Director of High School Program, 7777 Leesburg Pike, Falls Church, VA 22043
Telephone: 703-821-8570 or toll-free 800-444-0804 **Fax:** 703-734-5339
E-mail: dbaxter@stratford.edu

Getting in Last Year 557 enrolled.

Financial Matters $15,000 tuition and fees (2002–03).

Academics Stratford University awards associate, bachelor's, and master's degrees. Challenging opportunities include advanced placement credit, accelerated degree programs, and a senior project. Special programs include cooperative education and internships. The faculty at Stratford University has 17 full-time members, 29% with terminal degrees. The student-faculty ratio is 20:1.

Students of Stratford University The student body totals 720, of whom 689 are undergraduates. Students come from 9 states and territories. 64% are from Virginia. 0.8% are international students.

Applying Stratford University requires CPAt, a high school transcript, an interview, and a minimum high school GPA of 2.0. The school recommends SAT I. Application deadline: 7/30.

STRAYER UNIVERSITY

Washington, DC

Urban setting ■ Private ■ Proprietary ■ Coed

Web site: www.strayer.edu
Contact: Regional Director, 1025 Fifteenth Street, NW, Washington, DC 20005
Telephone: 888-378-7293 or toll-free 888-4-STRAYER **Fax:** 202-289-1831
E-mail: info40@strayer.edu

Getting in Last Year 1,490 enrolled (72%).

Financial Matters $8928 tuition and fees (2002–03).

Academics Strayer awards associate, bachelor's, and master's degrees and post-bachelor's certificates. Challenging opportunities include advanced placement credit, accelerated degree programs, double majors, and a senior project. Special programs include cooperative education, internships, summer session for credit, and off-campus study. The most frequently chosen baccalaureate fields are computer/information sciences, business/marketing, and social sciences and history. The faculty at Strayer has 137 full-time members, 34% with terminal degrees. The student-faculty ratio is 20:1.

Students of Strayer The student body totals 16,451, of whom 13,402 are undergraduates. 57.6% are women and 42.4% are men. Students come from 26 states and territories and 124 other countries. 95% are from District of Columbia. 5.1% are international students.

Applying Strayer requires a high school transcript, and in some cases 1 recommendation. The school recommends an essay, SAT I, an interview, and 1 recommendation. Application deadline: rolling admissions. Early and deferred admission are possible.

SUFFOLK UNIVERSITY

Boston, MA

Urban setting ■ Private ■ Independent ■ Coed

Web site: www.suffolk.edu
Contact: Mr. Walter Caffey, Dean of Enrollment, 8 Ashburton Place, Boston, MA 02108
Telephone: 617-573-8460 or toll-free 800-6-SUFFOLK **Fax:** 617-742-4291
E-mail: admission@suffolk.edu

Getting in Last Year 3,466 applied; 84% were accepted; 792 enrolled (27%).

Financial Matters $17,690 tuition and fees (2002–03); $10,290 room and board; 73% average percent of need met; $12,645 average financial aid amount received per undergraduate.

Academics Suffolk awards associate, bachelor's, master's, doctoral, and first-professional degrees and post-bachelor's, post-master's, and first-professional certificates (doctoral degree in law). Challenging opportunities include advanced placement credit, accelerated degree programs, freshman honors college, an honors program, double majors, independent study, and a senior project. Special programs include cooperative education, internships, summer session for credit, off-campus study, study-abroad, and Army ROTC. The most frequently chosen baccalaureate fields are business/marketing, social sciences and history, and communications/communication technologies. The faculty at Suffolk has 242 full-time members, 92% with terminal degrees. The student-faculty ratio is 12:1.

Students of Suffolk The student body totals 5,941, of whom 3,962 are undergraduates. 58.9% are women and 41.1% are men. Students come from 33 states and territories and 100 other countries. 86% are from Massachusetts. 13.6% are international students. 77% returned for their sophomore year.

Applying Suffolk requires an essay, SAT I or ACT, a high school transcript, and 2 recommendations, and in some cases an interview. The school recommends a minimum high school GPA of 2.5. Application deadline: rolling admissions; 3/1 priority date for financial aid. Deferred admission is possible.

SULLIVAN UNIVERSITY

Louisville, KY

Suburban setting ■ Private ■ Proprietary ■ Coed

Web site: www.sullivan.edu
Contact: Mr. Greg Cawthon, Director of Admissions, 3101 Bardstown Road, Louisville, KY 40205
Telephone: 502-456-6505 ext. 370 or toll-free 800-844-1354 **Fax:** 502-456-0040
E-mail: admissions@sullivan.edu

Getting in Last Year 890 enrolled.

Financial Matters $11,695 tuition and fees (2002–03); $3555 room only.

Academics Sullivan awards associate, bachelor's, and master's degrees. Challenging opportunities include advanced placement credit, accelerated degree programs, double majors, and independent study. Special programs include cooperative education, summer session for credit, and Army ROTC. The faculty at Sullivan has 67 full-time members, 13% with terminal degrees. The student-faculty ratio is 19:1.

Students of Sullivan The student body totals 4,720, of whom 4,443 are undergraduates. 64.2% are women and 35.8% are men. Students come from 22 states and territories and 11 other countries. 87% are from Kentucky. 0.7% are international students. 60% returned for their sophomore year.

Applying Sullivan requires ACT or CPAt, a high school transcript, and an interview. The school recommends ACT. Application deadline: rolling admissions.

SUL ROSS STATE UNIVERSITY

Alpine, TX

Small-town setting ■ Public ■ State-supported ■ Coed

Web site: www.sulross.edu
Contact: Dr. Nadine Jenkins, Vice President for Enrollment Management and Student Services, Box C-2, Alpine, TX 79832
Telephone: 915-837-8050 or toll-free 888-722-7778 **Fax:** 915-837-8431
E-mail: rcullins@sulross.edu

Getting in Last Year 1,021 applied; 73% were accepted; 323 enrolled (43%).

Financial Matters $3032 resident tuition and fees (2002–03); $9572 nonresident tuition and fees (2002–03); $3850 room and board.

Academics SRSU awards associate, bachelor's, and master's degrees. Challenging opportunities include advanced placement credit, an honors program, and a senior project. Special programs include internships and summer session for credit. The most frequently chosen baccalaureate fields are education, agriculture, and business/marketing. The faculty at SRSU has 88 full-time members, 72% with terminal degrees. The student-faculty ratio is 13:1.

Students of SRSU The student body totals 1,954, of whom 1,402 are undergraduates. 48.4% are women and 51.6% are men. Students come from 12 states and territories and 2 other countries. 98% are from Texas. 0.5% are international students. 50% returned for their sophomore year.

Applying SRSU requires SAT I or ACT and a high school transcript. The school recommends an interview. Application deadline: rolling admissions. Deferred admission is possible.

SUSQUEHANNA UNIVERSITY

Selinsgrove, PA

Small-town setting ■ Private ■ Independent Religious ■ Coed

Web site: www.susqu.edu
Contact: Mr. Chris Markle, Director of Admissions, 514 University Avenue, Selinsgrove, PA 17870-1040
Telephone: 570-372-4260 or toll-free 800-326-9672 **Fax:** 570-372-2722
E-mail: suadmiss@susqu.edu

Getting in Last Year 2,411 applied; 63% were accepted; 504 enrolled (33%).

Financial Matters $22,240 tuition and fees (2002–03); $6260 room and board; $15,535 average financial aid amount received per undergraduate (2000–01 estimated).

Academics Susquehanna awards bachelor's degrees (also offers associate degree through evening program to local students). Challenging opportunities include advanced placement credit, accelerated degree programs, student-designed majors, an honors program, double majors, independent study, and a senior project. Special programs include internships, summer session for credit, off-campus study, study-abroad, and Army ROTC. The most frequently chosen baccalaureate fields are business/marketing, communications/communication technologies, and education. The faculty at Susquehanna has 112 full-time members, 88% with terminal degrees. The student-faculty ratio is 14:1.

Students of Susquehanna The student body is made up of 1,995 undergraduates. 57.9% are women and 42.1% are men. Students come from 24 states and territories and 16 other countries. 64% are from Pennsylvania. 0.8% are international students. 90% returned for their sophomore year.

Applying Susquehanna requires an essay, a high school transcript, 1 recommendation, and a minimum high school GPA of 2.5, and in some cases SAT I or ACT and writing portfolio, auditions for music programs. The school recommends SAT II Subject Tests, SAT II: Writing Test, an interview, and a minimum high school GPA of 3.0. Application deadline: 3/1; 3/1 priority date for financial aid. Early and deferred admission are possible.

SWARTHMORE COLLEGE

Swarthmore, PA

Suburban setting ■ Private ■ Independent ■ Coed

Web site: www.swarthmore.edu
Contact: Office of Admissions, 500 College Avenue, Swarthmore, PA 19081-1397
Telephone: 610-328-8300 or toll-free 800-667-3110 **Fax:** 610-328-8580
E-mail: admissions@swarthmore.edu

Getting in Last Year 3,886 applied; 24% were accepted; 371 enrolled (40%).

Financial Matters $27,562 tuition and fees (2002–03); $8530 room and board; 100% average percent of need met; $25,032 average financial aid amount received per undergraduate.

Academics Swarthmore awards bachelor's degrees. Challenging opportunities include advanced placement credit, student-designed majors, an honors program, double majors, independent study, and a senior project. Special programs include internships, off-campus study, study-abroad, and Army and Air Force ROTC. The most frequently chosen baccalaureate fields are social sciences and history, biological/life sciences, and English. The faculty at Swarthmore has 167 full-time members, 99% with terminal degrees. The student-faculty ratio is 8:1.

Students of Swarthmore The student body is made up of 1,479 undergraduates. 52.2% are women and 47.8% are men. Students come from 50 states and territories and 43 other countries. 18% are from Pennsylvania. 5.8% are international students. 95% returned for their sophomore year.

Applying Swarthmore requires an essay, SAT II Subject Tests, SAT II: Writing Test, SAT I or ACT, a high school transcript, and 2 recommendations, and in some cases SAT II Subject Test in math. The school recommends an interview. Application deadline: 1/1; 2/15 priority date for financial aid. Early and deferred admission are possible.

SWEET BRIAR COLLEGE

Sweet Briar, VA

Rural setting ■ Private ■ Independent ■ Women Only

Web site: www.sbc.edu
Contact: Ms. Margaret Williams Blount, Director of Admissions, PO Box B, Sweet Briar, VA 24595
Telephone: 434-381-6142 or toll-free 800-381-6142 **Fax:** 434-381-6152
E-mail: admissions@sbc.edu

Getting in Last Year 420 applied; 86% were accepted; 151 enrolled (42%).

Financial Matters $18,910 tuition and fees (2002–03); $7660 room and board; 92% average percent of need met; $16,690 average financial aid amount received per undergraduate (2001–02).

Academics Sweet Briar awards bachelor's degrees. Challenging opportunities include advanced placement credit, accelerated degree programs, student-designed majors, an honors program, double majors, independent study, and a senior project. Special programs include internships, summer session for credit, off-campus study, and study-abroad. The most frequently chosen baccalaureate fields are social sciences and history, mathematics, and psychology. The faculty at Sweet Briar has 70 full-time members, 94% with terminal degrees. The student-faculty ratio is 8:1.

Students of Sweet Briar The student body is made up of 688 undergraduates. Students come from 45 states and territories and 11 other countries. 44% are from Virginia. 2.3% are international students. 82% returned for their sophomore year.

Applying Sweet Briar requires an essay, SAT I or ACT, a high school transcript, and 2 recommendations, and in some cases an interview and portfolio with courses taken, list of texts covered, essay about homeschooling, campus visit, interview for homeschooled applicants. The school recommends SAT II Subject Tests. Application deadline: 2/1; 3/1 priority date for financial aid. Early and deferred admission are possible.

SYRACUSE UNIVERSITY

Syracuse, NY

Urban setting ■ Private ■ Independent ■ Coed

Web site: www.syracuse.edu

Syracuse University (continued)

Contact: Office of Admissions, 201 Tolley Administration Building, Syracuse, NY 13244-1100
Telephone: 315-443-3611
E-mail: orange@syr.edu

Getting in Last Year 13,644 applied; 69% were accepted; 2,916 enrolled (31%).

Financial Matters $23,424 tuition and fees (2002–03); $9510 room and board; 80% average percent of need met; $18,000 average financial aid amount received per undergraduate.

Academics SU awards bachelor's, master's, doctoral, and first-professional degrees and post-master's certificates. Challenging opportunities include advanced placement credit, accelerated degree programs, student-designed majors, an honors program, double majors, independent study, and a senior project. Special programs include cooperative education, internships, summer session for credit, off-campus study, study-abroad, and Army and Air Force ROTC. The most frequently chosen baccalaureate fields are communications/communication technologies, business/marketing, and social sciences and history. The faculty at SU has 859 full-time members, 87% with terminal degrees. The student-faculty ratio is 12:1.

Students of SU The student body totals 14,830, of whom 10,936 are undergraduates. 55.9% are women and 44.1% are men. Students come from 52 states and territories and 61 other countries. 44% are from New York. 3.1% are international students. 92% returned for their sophomore year.

Applying SU requires an essay, SAT I or ACT, a high school transcript, and 2 recommendations, and in some cases audition for drama and music programs, portfolio for art and architecture programs. The school recommends an interview. Application deadline: 1/1; 2/1 priority date for financial aid. Early and deferred admission are possible.

TABOR COLLEGE

Hillsboro, KS

Small-town setting ■ Private ■ Independent Religious ■ Coed

Web site: www.tabor.edu
Contact: Ms. Cara Marrs, Director of Admissions, 400 South Jefferson, Hillsboro, KS 67063
Telephone: 620-947-3121 ext. 1727 or toll-free 800-822-6799
Fax: 620-947-2607
E-mail: admissions@tabor.edu

Getting in Last Year 335 applied; 59% were accepted; 108 enrolled (55%).

Financial Matters $13,634 tuition and fees (2002–03); $4900 room and board; 87% average percent of need met; $13,955 average financial aid amount received per undergraduate.

Academics Tabor awards associate, bachelor's, and master's degrees. Challenging opportunities include advanced placement credit, accelerated degree programs, student-designed majors, an honors program, double majors, independent study, and a senior project. Special programs include cooperative education, internships, summer session for credit, off-campus study, and study-abroad. The most frequently chosen baccalaureate fields are business/marketing, education, and biological/life sciences. The faculty at Tabor has 29 full-time members, 66% with terminal degrees. The student-faculty ratio is 12:1.

Students of Tabor The student body totals 575, of whom 557 are undergraduates. 51.9% are women and 48.1% are men. Students come from 27 states and territories and 4 other countries. 70% are from Kansas. 1.1% are international students. 69% returned for their sophomore year.

Applying Tabor requires an essay, SAT I or ACT, a high school transcript, 2 recommendations, ACT-18, and a minimum high school GPA of 2.0. The school recommends an interview and a minimum high school GPA of 3.0. Application deadline: 8/1; 8/15 for financial aid, with a 3/1 priority date. Deferred admission is possible.

TALLADEGA COLLEGE

Talladega, AL

Small-town setting ■ Private ■ Independent ■ Coed

Web site: www.talladega.edu
Contact: Mr. Johnny Byrd, Enrollment Manager, 627 West Battle Street, Talladega, AL 35160
Telephone: 256-761-6235 or toll-free 800-762-2468 (in-state), 800-633-2440 (out-of-state) **Fax:** 256-362-2268
E-mail: be21long@talladega.edu

Getting in Last Year 1,655 applied; 70% were accepted; 191 enrolled (17%).

Financial Matters $6752 tuition and fees (2002–03); $3395 room and board; 98% average percent of need met; $5900 average financial aid amount received per undergraduate (2001–02).

Academics TC awards bachelor's degrees. Challenging opportunities include double majors, independent study, and a senior project. Special programs include cooperative education, internships, off-campus study, and Army ROTC. The most frequently chosen baccalaureate fields are biological/life sciences, social sciences and history, and psychology. The faculty at TC has 42 full-time members. The student-faculty ratio is 13:1.

Students of TC The student body is made up of 540 undergraduates. 64.1% are women and 35.9% are men. Students come from 26 states and territories. 57% are from Alabama. 72% returned for their sophomore year.

Applying TC requires an essay, SAT I or ACT, a high school transcript, 1 recommendation, and a minimum high school GPA of 2.0. Application deadline: 4/1; 6/30 for financial aid, with a 5/1 priority date. Deferred admission is possible.

TALMUDICAL YESHIVA OF PHILADELPHIA

Philadelphia, PA

Urban setting ■ Private ■ Independent Religious ■ Men Only

Contact: Rabbi Shmuel Kamenetsky, Co-Dean, 6063 Drexel Road, Philadelphia, PA 19131-1296
Telephone: 215-473-1212

Getting in Last Year 45 applied; 78% were accepted; 34 enrolled (97%).

Financial Matters $5600 tuition and fees (2002–03); $5000 room and board; 100% average percent of need met; $4870 average financial aid amount received per undergraduate.

Academics TYP awards bachelor's degrees (also offers some graduate courses). An honors program is a challenging opportunity. Special programs include internships and study-abroad. The faculty at TYP has 3 full-time members. The student-faculty ratio is 23:1.

Students of TYP The student body is made up of 85 undergraduates. Students come from 11 states and territories and 4 other countries. 15% are from Pennsylvania. 12.9% are international students. 87% returned for their sophomore year.

Applying TYP requires a high school transcript, an interview, 1 recommendation, and oral examination. Application deadline: 7/15. Early and deferred admission are possible.

TALMUDIC COLLEGE OF FLORIDA

Miami Beach, FL

Private ■ Independent Religious ■ Men Only

Web site: www.talmudicu.edu
Contact: Rabbi Ira Hill, Admissions Director, 1910 Alton Road, Miami Beach, FL 33139
Telephone: 305-534-7050 or toll-free 888-825-6834 **Fax:** 305-534-8444
E-mail: ryhill@talmudicu.edu

Getting in Last Year 20 applied; 75% were accepted; 15 enrolled (100%).

Financial Matters $7250 tuition and fees (2002–03); $5000 room and board; 57% average percent of need met; $7125 average financial aid amount received per undergraduate.

Academics Talmudic College of Florida awards bachelor's, master's, and doctoral degrees. Challenging opportunities include an honors program and independent study. Special programs include summer session for credit and study-abroad. The faculty at Talmudic College of Florida has 8 full-time members, 75% with terminal degrees. The student-faculty ratio is 12:1.

Students of Talmudic College of Florida The student body totals 66, of whom 50 are undergraduates. Students come from 8 states and territories and 7 other countries. 10% are from Florida. 24% are international students.

Applying Talmudic College of Florida requires an interview. The school recommends an essay and 1 recommendation. Application deadline: 9/5. Early and deferred admission are possible.

TARLETON STATE UNIVERSITY

Stephenville, TX

Small-town setting ■ Public ■ State-supported ■ Coed

Web site: www.tarleton.edu
Contact: Ms. Denise Siler, Director of Admissions, Box T-0030, Tarleton Station, Stephenville, TX 76402
Telephone: 254-968-9125 or toll-free 800-687-4878 **Fax:** 254-968-9951

Getting in Last Year 1,901 applied; 83% were accepted; 1,161 enrolled (74%).

Financial Matters $3444 resident tuition and fees (2002–03); $8676 nonresident tuition and fees (2002–03); $4896 room and board; 61% average percent of need met; $6323 average financial aid amount received per undergraduate.

Academics Tarleton awards bachelor's and master's degrees. Challenging opportunities include advanced placement credit, accelerated degree programs, an honors program, double majors, and a senior project. Special programs include cooperative education, internships, summer session for credit, off-campus study, study-abroad, and Army ROTC. The most frequently chosen baccalaureate fields are business/marketing, agriculture, and interdisciplinary studies. The faculty at Tarleton has 308 full-time members, 64% with terminal degrees. The student-faculty ratio is 18:1.

Students of Tarleton The student body totals 8,320, of whom 6,970 are undergraduates. 55% are women and 45% are men. Students come from 50 states and territories and 24 other countries. 96% are from Texas. 0.6% are international students. 61% returned for their sophomore year.

Applying Tarleton requires SAT I or ACT and a high school transcript, and in some cases an interview. Application deadline: 8/1; 6/1 priority date for financial aid. Early and deferred admission are possible.

TAYLOR UNIVERSITY

Upland, IN

Rural setting ■ Private ■ Independent Religious ■ Coed

Web site: www.tayloru.edu

Contact: Mr. Stephen R. Mortland, Director of Admissions, 236 West Reade Avenue, Upland, IN 46989-1001

Telephone: 765-998-5134 or toll-free 800-882-3456 **Fax:** 765-998-4925

E-mail: admissions_u@tayloru.edu

Getting in Last Year 1,325 applied; 78% were accepted; 457 enrolled (44%).

Financial Matters $17,490 tuition and fees (2002–03); $5130 room and board; 81% average percent of need met; $12,425 average financial aid amount received per undergraduate.

Academics Taylor awards associate and bachelor's degrees. Challenging opportunities include advanced placement credit, student-designed majors, an honors program, double majors, independent study, and a senior project. Special programs include cooperative education, internships, summer session for credit, off-campus study, and study-abroad. The most frequently chosen baccalaureate fields are education, business/marketing, and computer/information sciences. The faculty at Taylor has 118 full-time members, 79% with terminal degrees. The student-faculty ratio is 15:1.

Students of Taylor The student body is made up of 1,869 undergraduates. 52.4% are women and 47.6% are men. Students come from 47 states and territories and 25 other countries. 31% are from Indiana. 1.7% are international students. 89% returned for their sophomore year.

Applying Taylor requires an essay, SAT I or ACT, a high school transcript, an interview, and 2 recommendations. The school recommends a minimum high school GPA of 2.8. Application deadline: 2/15; 3/10 for financial aid. Deferred admission is possible.

TAYLOR UNIVERSITY, FORT WAYNE CAMPUS

Fort Wayne, IN

Suburban setting ■ Private ■ Independent Religious ■ Coed

Web site: www.tayloru.edu/fw

Contact: Mr. Leo Gonot, Director of Admissions, 1025 West Rudisill Boulevard, Fort Wayne, IN 46807-2197

Telephone: 219-744-8689 or toll-free 800-233-3922 **Fax:** 219-744-8660

E-mail: admissions_f@tayloru.edu

Getting in Last Year 455 applied; 85% were accepted; 142 enrolled (37%).

Financial Matters $14,990 tuition and fees (2002–03); $4620 room and board; 88% average percent of need met; $14,469 average financial aid amount received per undergraduate (2001–02).

Academics Taylor Fort Wayne awards associate, bachelor's, and master's degrees. Challenging opportunities include advanced placement credit, accelerated degree programs, student-designed majors, double majors, independent study, and a senior project. Special programs include cooperative education, internships, summer session for credit, off-campus study, and study-abroad. The most frequently chosen baccalaureate fields are communications/communication technologies, psychology, and law/legal studies. The faculty at Taylor Fort Wayne has 30 full-time members, 53% with terminal degrees. The student-faculty ratio is 14:1.

Students of Taylor Fort Wayne The student body is made up of 633 undergraduates. 63.2% are women and 36.8% are men. Students come from 26 states and territories and 2 other countries. 75% are from Indiana. 0.6% are international students. 76% returned for their sophomore year.

Applying Taylor Fort Wayne requires an essay, SAT I or ACT, a high school transcript, 2 recommendations, and a minimum high school GPA of 2.0. The school recommends an interview and a minimum high school GPA of 3.0. Application deadline: rolling admissions; 3/10 priority date for financial aid. Deferred admission is possible.

TEIKYO POST UNIVERSITY

Waterbury, CT

Suburban setting ■ Private ■ Independent ■ Coed

Web site: teikyopost.edu

Contact: Mr. William Johnson, Senior Assistant Director of Admissions, PO Box 2540, Waterbury, CT 06723

Telephone: 203-596-4520 or toll-free 800-345-2562 **Fax:** 203-756-5810

E-mail: tpuadmiss@teikyopost.edu

Getting in Last Year 1,109 applied; 36% were accepted; 245 enrolled (62%).

Financial Matters $16,500 tuition and fees (2002–03); $6800 room and board; 75% average percent of need met; $12,000 average financial aid amount received per undergraduate.

Academics TPU awards associate and bachelor's degrees and post-bachelor's certificates. Challenging opportunities include advanced placement credit, accelerated degree programs, double majors, independent study, and a senior project. Special programs include cooperative education, internships, summer session for credit, and study-abroad. The most frequently chosen baccalaureate fields are business/marketing, liberal arts/general studies, and psychology. The faculty at TPU has 29 full-time members, 72% with terminal degrees. The student-faculty ratio is 11:1.

Students of TPU The student body is made up of 1,378 undergraduates. 63.1% are women and 36.9% are men. Students come from 15 states and territories and 20 other countries. 83% are from Connecticut. 2.8% are international students. 78% returned for their sophomore year.

Applying TPU requires a high school transcript and 1 recommendation. The school recommends an essay, SAT I or ACT, and an interview. Application deadline: rolling admissions; 3/15 priority date for financial aid. Deferred admission is possible.

TEMPLE UNIVERSITY

Philadelphia, PA

Urban setting ■ Public ■ State-related ■ Coed

Web site: www.temple.edu

Contact: Dr. Timm Rinehart, Acting Director of Admissions, 1801 North Broad Street, Philadelphia, PA 19122-6096

Telephone: 215-204-8556 or toll-free 888-340-2222 **Fax:** 215-204-5694

E-mail: tuadm@vm.temple.edu

Getting in Last Year 15,316 applied; 78% were accepted; 3,496 enrolled (29%).

Financial Matters $8062 resident tuition and fees (2002–03); $14,316 nonresident tuition and fees (2002–03); $7112 room and board; 86% average percent of need met; $10,715 average financial aid amount received per undergraduate (2001–02).

Academics Temple awards associate, bachelor's, master's, doctoral, and first-professional degrees and post-master's and first-professional certificates. Challenging opportunities include advanced placement credit, student-designed majors, an honors program, double majors, independent study, and a senior project. Special programs include cooperative education, internships, summer session for credit, off-campus study, study-abroad, and Army, Navy and Air Force ROTC. The most frequently chosen baccalaureate fields are business/marketing, education, and communications/communication technologies. The faculty at Temple has 1,222 full-time members, 83% with terminal degrees. The student-faculty ratio is 18:1.

Students of Temple The student body totals 32,351, of whom 21,429 are undergraduates. 58% are women and 42% are men. Students come from 49 states and territories and 130 other countries. 75% are from Pennsylvania. 3.5% are international students. 78% returned for their sophomore year.

Applying Temple requires SAT I or ACT, a high school transcript, and a minimum high school GPA of 2.0, and in some cases an interview, recommendations, and portfolio, audition. The school recommends an essay. Application deadline: 4/1; 3/1 priority date for financial aid. Early and deferred admission are possible.

TENNESSEE STATE UNIVERSITY

Nashville, TN

Urban setting ■ Public ■ State-supported ■ Coed

Web site: www.tnstate.edu

Contact: Ms. Vernella Smith, Admissions Coordinator, 3500 John A Merritt Boulevard, Nashville, TN 37209-1561

Telephone: 615-963-5104 **Fax:** 615-963-5108

E-mail: jcade@tnstate.edu

Getting in Last Year 6,772 applied; 46% were accepted; 1,304 enrolled (42%).

Financial Matters $3297 resident tuition and fees (2002–03); $10,255 nonresident tuition and fees (2002–03); $3600 room and board; 76% average percent of need met; $3864 average financial aid amount received per undergraduate (2001–02).

Academics TSU awards associate, bachelor's, master's, and doctoral degrees. Challenging opportunities include accelerated degree programs, freshman honors college, an honors program, independent study, and a senior project. Special programs include cooperative education, internships, summer session for credit, off-campus study, and Army, Navy and Air Force ROTC. The most frequently chosen baccalaureate fields are health professions and related sciences, education, and liberal arts/general studies. The faculty at TSU has 360 full-time members, 79% with terminal degrees. The student-faculty ratio is 25:1.

Students of TSU The student body totals 8,881, of whom 7,239 are undergraduates. 62.4% are women and 37.6% are men. Students come from 45 states and territories. 58% are from Tennessee. 1.1% are international students. 76% returned for their sophomore year.

Tennessee State University (continued)

Applying TSU requires SAT I or ACT and a high school transcript, and in some cases 3 recommendations. Application deadline: 8/1; 4/1 priority date for financial aid.

TENNESSEE TECHNOLOGICAL UNIVERSITY

Cookeville, TN

Small-town setting ■ Public ■ State-supported ■ Coed

Web site: www.tntech.edu
Contact: Mr. Robert L. Hodum, Assistant Director of Admissions, TTU Box 5006, Cookeville, TN 38505
Telephone: 931-372-3888 ext. 3636 or toll-free 800-255-8881
Fax: 931-372-6250
E-mail: admissions@tntech.edu

Getting in Last Year 3,294 applied; 79% were accepted; 1,398 enrolled (53%).

Financial Matters $3288 resident tuition and fees (2002–03); $10,246 nonresident tuition and fees (2002–03); $4798 room and board; 75% average percent of need met; $3693 average financial aid amount received per undergraduate.

Academics Tennessee Tech awards bachelor's, master's, and doctoral degrees. Challenging opportunities include advanced placement credit, accelerated degree programs, an honors program, double majors, independent study, and a senior project. Special programs include cooperative education, internships, summer session for credit, off-campus study, study-abroad, and Army and Air Force ROTC. The most frequently chosen baccalaureate fields are business/marketing, engineering/engineering technologies, and education. The faculty at Tennessee Tech has 371 full-time members, 78% with terminal degrees. The student-faculty ratio is 18:1.

Students of Tennessee Tech The student body totals 8,890, of whom 7,251 are undergraduates. 45.7% are women and 54.3% are men. Students come from 38 states and territories and 53 other countries. 95% are from Tennessee. 0.9% are international students. 71% returned for their sophomore year.

Applying Tennessee Tech requires SAT I or ACT, a high school transcript, and 2.35 high school GPA or ACT composite score of 19. The school recommends ACT and an interview. Application deadline: rolling admissions; 3/15 priority date for financial aid. Early and deferred admission are possible.

TENNESSEE TEMPLE UNIVERSITY

Chattanooga, TN

Urban setting ■ Private ■ Independent Religious ■ Coed

Contact: Mr. Mark Mathews, Director of Enrollment Services, 1815 Union Avenue, Chattanooga, TN 37404-3587
Telephone: 423-493-4371 or toll-free 800-553-4050 **Fax:** 423-492-4308
E-mail: ttuinfo@tntemple.edu

Getting in Last Year 274 applied; 99% were accepted; 126 enrolled (47%).

Financial Matters $6730 tuition and fees (2002–03); $5400 room and board; 75% average percent of need met; $8425 average financial aid amount received per undergraduate.

Academics Tennessee Temple awards associate, bachelor's, and master's degrees. Challenging opportunities include advanced placement credit, an honors program, double majors, independent study, and a senior project. Special programs include cooperative education, internships, and summer session for credit. The most frequently chosen baccalaureate fields are education, business/marketing, and psychology. The faculty at Tennessee Temple has 37 full-time members, 43% with terminal degrees. The student-faculty ratio is 15:1.

Students of Tennessee Temple The student body totals 606, of whom 582 are undergraduates. 48.6% are women and 51.4% are men. Students come from 40 states and territories and 1 other country. 31% are from Tennessee. 3.4% are international students. 64% returned for their sophomore year.

Applying Tennessee Temple requires SAT I or ACT, a high school transcript, an interview, 3 recommendations, and a minimum high school GPA of 2.0, and in some cases an essay. Application deadline: 8/20; 5/15 for financial aid, with a 4/15 priority date. Deferred admission is possible.

TENNESSEE WESLEYAN COLLEGE

Athens, TN

Small-town setting ■ Private ■ Independent Religious ■ Coed

Web site: www.twcnet.edu
Contact: Mrs. Ruthie Cawood, Director of Admission, PO Box 40, Athens, TN 37371-0040
Telephone: 423-746-5287 or toll-free 800-PICK-TWC **Fax:** 423-745-9335

Getting in Last Year 560 applied; 81% were accepted.

Financial Matters $10,240 tuition and fees (2002–03); $4380 room and board; 71% average percent of need met; $7980 average financial aid amount received per undergraduate (2001–02).

Academics TWC awards bachelor's degrees (all information given is for both main and branch campuses). Challenging opportunities include advanced placement credit, accelerated degree programs, student-designed majors, freshman honors college, an honors program, double majors, and independent study. Special programs include cooperative education, internships, summer session for credit, off-campus study, and study-abroad. The most frequently chosen baccalaureate fields are business/marketing, psychology, and parks and recreation. The faculty at TWC has 43 full-time members, 72% with terminal degrees. The student-faculty ratio is 17:1.

Students of TWC The student body is made up of 803 undergraduates. Students come from 15 states and territories and 11 other countries. 92% are from Tennessee. 0.4% are international students. 65% returned for their sophomore year.

Applying TWC requires SAT I or ACT, a high school transcript, 1 recommendation, and a minimum high school GPA of 2.25, and in some cases an interview. The school recommends an essay. Application deadline: rolling admissions; 5/1 for financial aid, with a 2/28 priority date. Early and deferred admission are possible.

TEXAS A&M INTERNATIONAL UNIVERSITY

Laredo, TX

Urban setting ■ Public ■ State-supported ■ Coed

Web site: www.tamiu.edu
Contact: Ms. Veronica Gonzalez, Director of Enrollment Management and School Relations, 5201 University Boulevard, Laredo, TX 78041-1900
Telephone: 956-326-2270 or toll-free 888-489-2648 **Fax:** 956-326-2199
E-mail: enroll@tamiu.edu

Getting in Last Year 1,010 applied; 72% were accepted; 456 enrolled (62%).

Financial Matters $2869 resident tuition and fees (2002–03); $9139 nonresident tuition and fees (2002–03); $3210 room only; 96% average percent of need met; $7986 average financial aid amount received per undergraduate (2001–02).

Academics TAMIU awards bachelor's and master's degrees. Challenging opportunities include advanced placement credit, an honors program, and a senior project. Special programs include internships, summer session for credit, and study-abroad. The most frequently chosen baccalaureate fields are business/marketing, education, and health professions and related sciences. The faculty at TAMIU has 228 members, 62% with terminal degrees. The student-faculty ratio is 14:1.

Students of TAMIU The student body totals 3,753, of whom 2,933 are undergraduates. 64.7% are women and 35.3% are men. Students come from 30 states and territories and 9 other countries. 99% are from Texas. 3% are international students. 66% returned for their sophomore year.

Applying TAMIU requires SAT I or ACT and a high school transcript. Application deadline: 7/1; 3/15 priority date for financial aid. Early and deferred admission are possible.

TEXAS A&M UNIVERSITY

College Station, TX

Suburban setting ■ Public ■ State-supported ■ Coed

Web site: www.tamu.edu
Contact: Dr. Frank Ashley, Director of Admissions, 217 John J. Koldus Building, College Station, TX 77843-1265
Telephone: 979-845-3741 **Fax:** 979-845-8737
E-mail: admissions@tamu.edu

Getting in Last Year 17,284 applied; 68% were accepted; 6,949 enrolled (59%).

Financial Matters $4748 resident tuition and fees (2002–03); $11,288 nonresident tuition and fees (2002–03); $6030 room and board; 82% average percent of need met; $6664 average financial aid amount received per undergraduate.

Academics Texas A&M awards bachelor's, master's, doctoral, and first-professional degrees and post-bachelor's certificates. Challenging opportunities include advanced placement credit, accelerated degree programs, an honors program, double majors, independent study, and a senior project. Special programs include cooperative education, internships, summer session for credit, off-campus study, study-abroad, and Army, Navy and Air Force ROTC. The most frequently chosen baccalaureate fields are business/marketing, engineering/engineering technologies, and agriculture. The faculty at Texas A&M has 1,917 full-time members, 91% with terminal degrees. The student-faculty ratio is 21:1.

Students of Texas A&M The student body totals 45,083, of whom 36,775 are undergraduates. 49% are women and 51% are men. Students come from 52 states and territories and 111 other countries. 97% are from Texas. 1.3% are international students. 88% returned for their sophomore year.

Applying Texas A&M requires an essay, SAT I or ACT, and a high school transcript. Application deadline: 2/1.

TEXAS A&M UNIVERSITY AT GALVESTON

Galveston, TX

Suburban setting ■ Public ■ State-supported ■ Coed

Web site: www.tamug.edu
Contact: Sarah Wilson, Assistant Director of Admissions and Records, PO Box 1675, Galveston, TX 77553-1675
Telephone: 409-740-4448 or toll-free 87—SEAAGGIE **Fax:** 409-740-4731
E-mail: seaaggie@tamug.edu

Getting in Last Year 1,151 applied; 84% were accepted; 416 enrolled (43%).

Financial Matters $3465 resident tuition and fees (2002–03); $10,005 nonresident tuition and fees (2002–03); $4692 room and board; 74% average percent of need met; $6161 average financial aid amount received per undergraduate (1999–2000).

Academics Texas A&M Galveston awards bachelor's and master's degrees. Challenging opportunities include advanced placement credit, accelerated degree programs, double majors, independent study, and a senior project. Special programs include cooperative education, internships, summer session for credit, study-abroad, and Navy ROTC. The most frequently chosen baccalaureate fields are biological/life sciences, business/marketing, and engineering/engineering technologies. The faculty at Texas A&M Galveston has 83 full-time members, 73% with terminal degrees. The student-faculty ratio is 16:1.

Students of Texas A&M Galveston The student body totals 1,556, of whom 1,517 are undergraduates. 47.5% are women and 52.5% are men. Students come from 50 states and territories and 10 other countries. 78% are from Texas. 0.5% are international students. 70% returned for their sophomore year.

Applying Texas A&M Galveston requires an essay, SAT I or ACT, TASP, and a high school transcript, and in some cases an interview. The school recommends an essay, SAT II Subject Tests, SAT II: Writing Test, and recommendations. Application deadline: rolling admissions. Early and deferred admission are possible.

TEXAS A&M UNIVERSITY–COMMERCE

Commerce, TX

Small-town setting ■ Public ■ State-supported ■ Coed

Web site: www.tamu-commerce.edu
Contact: Mr. Randy McDonald, Director of Admissions, PO Box 3011, Commerce, TX 75429
Telephone: 903-886-5103 or toll-free 800-331-3878 **Fax:** 903-886-5888
E-mail: admissions@tamu-commerce.edu

Getting in Last Year 2,565 applied; 54% were accepted.

Financial Matters $3988 resident tuition and fees (2002–03); $10,528 nonresident tuition and fees (2002–03); $4786 room and board; 77% average percent of need met; $6758 average financial aid amount received per undergraduate.

Academics TAMU-C awards bachelor's, master's, and doctoral degrees. Challenging opportunities include advanced placement credit, an honors program, double majors, independent study, and a senior project. Special programs include cooperative education, internships, summer session for credit, off-campus study, and study-abroad. The most frequently chosen baccalaureate fields are business/marketing, interdisciplinary studies, and social sciences and history. The faculty at TAMU-C has 283 full-time members. The student-faculty ratio is 17:1.

Students of TAMU-C The student body totals 8,487, of whom 4,815 are undergraduates. 58.9% are women and 41.1% are men. Students come from 27 states and territories and 31 other countries. 98% are from Texas. 1.2% are international students. 65% returned for their sophomore year.

Applying TAMU-C requires SAT I or ACT and a high school transcript. Application deadline: 8/1; 5/1 priority date for financial aid. Early admission is possible.

TEXAS A&M UNIVERSITY–CORPUS CHRISTI

Corpus Christi, TX

Suburban setting ■ Public ■ State-supported ■ Coed

Web site: www.tamucc.edu
Contact: Ms. Margaret Dechant, Director of Admissions, 6300 Ocean Drive, Corpus Christi, TX 78412-5503
Telephone: 361-825-2414 or toll-free 800-482-6822 **Fax:** 361-825-5887
E-mail: judith.perales@mail.tamucc.edu

Getting in Last Year 3,114 applied; 85% were accepted; 1,001 enrolled (38%).

Financial Matters 76% average percent of need met; $6320 average financial aid amount received per undergraduate.

Academics Texas A&M-Corpus Christi awards bachelor's, master's, and doctoral degrees and post-bachelor's certificates. Challenging opportunities include advanced placement credit, double majors, independent study, and a senior project. Special programs include cooperative education, internships, summer session for credit, off-campus study, and Army ROTC. The most frequently chosen baccalaureate fields are business/marketing, interdisciplinary studies, and health professions and related sciences. The faculty at Texas A&M-Corpus Christi has 141 full-time members. The student-faculty ratio is 16:1.

Students of Texas A&M-Corpus Christi The student body totals 7,607, of whom 6,098 are undergraduates. 60.4% are women and 39.6% are men. Students come from 37 states and territories and 23 other countries. 98% are from Texas. 0.7% are international students. 71% returned for their sophomore year.

Applying Texas A&M-Corpus Christi requires SAT I or ACT, a high school transcript, and a minimum high school GPA of 2.0. Application deadline: 7/1; 4/1 priority date for financial aid.

TEXAS A&M UNIVERSITY–KINGSVILLE

Kingsville, TX

Small-town setting ■ Public ■ State-supported ■ Coed

Web site: www.tamuk.edu
Contact: Ms. Laura Knippers, Director of Admissions, Campus Box 105, Kingsville, TX 78363
Telephone: 361-593-2811 or toll-free 800-687-6000 **Fax:** 361-593-2195

Getting in Last Year 2,105 applied; 99% were accepted; 910 enrolled (43%).

Financial Matters $2982 resident tuition and fees (2002–03); $9192 nonresident tuition and fees (2002–03); $3966 room and board; 89% average percent of need met; $6500 average financial aid amount received per undergraduate.

Academics TAMUK awards bachelor's, master's, and doctoral degrees and post-bachelor's and post-master's certificates. Challenging opportunities include advanced placement credit, accelerated degree programs, an honors program, double majors, and a senior project. Special programs include cooperative education, internships, summer session for credit, study-abroad, and Army ROTC. The most frequently chosen baccalaureate fields are engineering/engineering technologies, business/marketing, and interdisciplinary studies. The faculty at TAMUK has 276 full-time members, 70% with terminal degrees. The student-faculty ratio is 15:1.

Students of TAMUK The student body totals 6,559, of whom 5,287 are undergraduates. 49.4% are women and 50.6% are men. Students come from 37 states and territories and 58 other countries. 98% are from Texas. 1.2% are international students. 61% returned for their sophomore year.

Applying TAMUK requires a high school transcript, and in some cases SAT I or ACT and an interview. The school recommends a minimum high school GPA of 2.0. Application deadline: rolling admissions. Early and deferred admission are possible.

TEXAS A&M UNIVERSITY SYSTEM HEALTH SCIENCE CENTER

Bryan, TX

Urban setting ■ Public ■ State-supported ■ Coed

Web site: tamushsc.tamu.edu
Contact: Dr. Jack L. Long, Director of Admissions and Records, PO Box 660677, 3302 Gaston Avenue, Dallas, TX 75266-0677
Telephone: 214-828-8230 **Fax:** 214-874-4567

Financial Matters $5130 resident tuition and fees (2002–03); $12,130 nonresident tuition and fees (2002–03).

Academics Texas A&M University System Health Science Center awards bachelor's, master's, doctoral, and first-professional degrees and post-master's and first-professional certificates (profile only includes information for the Baylor College of Dentistry). The most frequently chosen baccalaureate field is health professions and related sciences. The faculty at Texas A&M University System Health Science Center has 137 full-time members.

Students of Texas A&M University System Health Science Center The student body totals 539, of whom 60 are undergraduates. Students come from 4 states and territories. 97% are from Texas.

TEXAS A&M UNIVERSITY–TEXARKANA

Texarkana, TX

Small-town setting ■ Public ■ State-supported ■ Coed

Web site: www.tamut.edu
Contact: Mrs. Patricia E. Black, Director of Admissions and Registrar, PO Box 5518, Texarkana, TX 75505-5518
Telephone: 903-223-3068 **Fax:** 903-223-3140
E-mail: admissions@tamut.edu

Financial Matters $2004 resident tuition and fees (2002–03); $7236 nonresident tuition and fees (2002–03).

Academics Texas A&M University–Texarkana awards bachelor's and master's degrees. Challenging opportunities include advanced placement credit, student-designed majors, and independent study. Special programs include internships and summer session for credit. The most frequently chosen baccalaureate fields are interdisciplinary studies, business/marketing, and liberal arts/general studies. The faculty at Texas A&M University–Texarkana has 91 members, 70% with terminal degrees. The student-faculty ratio is 15:1.

Students of Texas A&M University–Texarkana The student body totals 1,385, of whom 889 are undergraduates. 71.3% are women and 28.7% are men. Students come from 7 states and territories. 70% are from Texas.

Applying Texas A&M University–Texarkana requires TASP. Application deadline: 5/1 priority date for financial aid.

TEXAS CHRISTIAN UNIVERSITY

Fort Worth, TX

Suburban setting ■ *Private* ■ *Independent Religious* ■ *Coed*

Web site: www.tcu.edu
Contact: Mr. Ray Brown, Dean of Admissions, TCU Box 297013, Fort Worth, TX 76129-0002
Telephone: 817-257-7490 or toll-free 800-828-3764 **Fax:** 817-257-7268
E-mail: frogmail@tcu.edu

Getting in Last Year 6,137 applied; 71% were accepted; 1,451 enrolled (33%).

Financial Matters $16,340 tuition and fees (2002–03); $5302 room and board; 70% average percent of need met; $12,268 average financial aid amount received per undergraduate.

Academics TCU awards bachelor's, master's, doctoral, and first-professional degrees and post-bachelor's and first-professional certificates. Challenging opportunities include advanced placement credit, an honors program, double majors, independent study, and a senior project. Special programs include internships, summer session for credit, study-abroad, and Army and Air Force ROTC. The most frequently chosen baccalaureate fields are business/marketing, communications/communication technologies, and education. The faculty at TCU has 415 full-time members, 90% with terminal degrees. The student-faculty ratio is 15:1.

Students of TCU The student body totals 8,074, of whom 6,851 are undergraduates. 58.4% are women and 41.6% are men. Students come from 50 states and territories and 75 other countries. 77% are from Texas. 4.1% are international students. 82% returned for their sophomore year.

Applying TCU requires an essay, SAT I or ACT, a high school transcript, 2 recommendations, and a minimum high school GPA of 2.0. The school recommends an interview and a minimum high school GPA of 3.0. Application deadline: 2/15; 5/1 priority date for financial aid. Deferred admission is possible.

TEXAS COLLEGE

Tyler, TX

Private ■ *Independent Religious* ■ *Coed*

Web site: www.texascollege.edu
Contact: Ms. Teresa Galinda, Enrollment Services Clerk, PO Box 4500, 2404 North Grand Avenue, Tyler, TX 75702
Telephone: 903-593-8311 ext. 2297 or toll-free 800-306-6299 (out-of-state) **Fax:** 903-596-0001
E-mail: admissions@texascollege.edu

Getting in Last Year 182 enrolled.

Financial Matters $8830 tuition and fees (2002–03); $5820 room and board.

Academics Texas College awards bachelor's degrees. A senior project is a challenging opportunity. Special programs include internships and summer session for credit. The most frequently chosen baccalaureate fields are biological/life sciences, social sciences and history, and parks and recreation. The faculty at Texas College has 30 full-time members, 57% with terminal degrees. The student-faculty ratio is 10:1.

Students of Texas College The student body is made up of 617 undergraduates. 63.7% are women and 36.3% are men.

Applying Texas College requires a high school transcript. The school recommends SAT I and SAT II or ACT. Application deadline: rolling admissions; 4/15 priority date for financial aid.

TEXAS LUTHERAN UNIVERSITY

Seguin, TX

Suburban setting ■ *Private* ■ *Independent Religious* ■ *Coed*

Web site: www.tlu.edu
Contact: Mr. E. Norman Jones, Vice President for Enrollment Services, 1000 West Court Street, Seguin, TX 78155-5999
Telephone: 830-372-8050 or toll-free 800-771-8521 **Fax:** 830-372-8096
E-mail: admissions@tlu.edu

Getting in Last Year 1,060 applied; 79% were accepted; 371 enrolled (44%).

Financial Matters $14,550 tuition and fees (2002–03); $4442 room and board; 91% average percent of need met; $13,991 average financial aid amount received per undergraduate (2001–02).

Academics TLU awards bachelor's degrees. Challenging opportunities include advanced placement credit, an honors program, double majors, independent study, and a senior project. Special programs include internships, summer session for credit, study-abroad, and Army and Air Force ROTC. The most frequently chosen baccalaureate fields are business/marketing, biological/life sciences, and parks and recreation. The faculty at TLU has 69 full-time members, 80% with terminal degrees. The student-faculty ratio is 15:1.

Students of TLU The student body is made up of 1,368 undergraduates. 52% are women and 48% are men. Students come from 24 states and territories and 10 other countries. 97% are from Texas. 2.2% are international students. 78% returned for their sophomore year.

Applying TLU requires an essay, SAT I or ACT, a high school transcript, and recommendations, and in some cases an interview, 2 recommendations, and a minimum high school GPA of 2.0. Application deadline: rolling admissions; 4/1 priority date for financial aid. Deferred admission is possible.

TEXAS SOUTHERN UNIVERSITY

Houston, TX

Urban setting ■ *Public* ■ *State-supported* ■ *Coed*

Web site: www.tsu.edu
Contact: Mrs. Joyce Waddell, Director of Admissions, 3100 Cleburne Street, Houston, TX 77004-4598
Telephone: 713-313-7472

Getting in Last Year 5,601 applied; 35% were accepted; 1,789 enrolled (90%).

Financial Matters $2298 resident tuition and fees (2002–03); $7530 nonresident tuition and fees (2002–03); $3322 room and board.

Academics Texas Southern awards bachelor's, master's, doctoral, and first-professional degrees. Challenging opportunities include accelerated degree programs, an honors program, and a senior project. Special programs include cooperative education, internships, summer session for credit, and Army and Navy ROTC. The most frequently chosen baccalaureate fields are business/marketing, protective services/public administration, and health professions and related sciences. The faculty at Texas Southern has 277 full-time members, 75% with terminal degrees. The student-faculty ratio is 22:1.

Students of Texas Southern The student body totals 9,739, of whom 7,811 are undergraduates. 56.4% are women and 43.6% are men. Students come from 48 states and territories and 56 other countries. 90% are from Texas. 4.3% are international students. 62% returned for their sophomore year.

Applying Texas Southern requires SAT I or ACT and a high school transcript. Application deadline: 8/10.

TEXAS TECH UNIVERSITY

Lubbock, TX

Urban setting ■ *Public* ■ *State-supported* ■ *Coed*

Web site: www.ttu.edu
Contact: Ms. Marlene Hernandez, Associate Director, Admissions and School Relations, Box 45005, Lubbock, TX 79409-5005
Telephone: 806-742-1480 **Fax:** 806-742-0980
E-mail: admissions@ttu.edu

Getting in Last Year 13,101 applied; 69% were accepted; 4,531 enrolled (50%).

Financial Matters $3867 resident tuition and fees (2002–03); $10,407 nonresident tuition and fees (2002–03); $5497 room and board; 52% average percent of need met; $5710 average financial aid amount received per undergraduate (2001–02).

Academics Texas Tech awards bachelor's, master's, doctoral, and first-professional degrees. Challenging opportunities include advanced placement credit, accelerated degree programs, student-designed majors, freshman honors college, an honors program, double majors, independent study, and a senior project. Special programs include cooperative education, internships, summer session for credit, off-campus study, study-abroad, and Army and Air Force ROTC. The most frequently chosen baccalaureate fields are business/marketing, engineering/engineering technologies, and communications/communication technologies. The faculty at Texas Tech has 977 full-time members, 93% with terminal degrees. The student-faculty ratio is 20:1.

Students of Texas Tech The student body totals 27,569, of whom 22,768 are undergraduates. 45.5% are women and 54.5% are men. Students come from 49 states and territories and 87 other countries. 95% are from Texas. 0.8% are international students. 81% returned for their sophomore year.

Applying Texas Tech requires SAT I or ACT, a high school transcript, and a minimum high school GPA of 2.0, and in some cases an essay. Application deadline: rolling admissions; 5/1 priority date for financial aid. Early and deferred admission are possible.

TEXAS WESLEYAN UNIVERSITY

Fort Worth, TX

Urban setting ■ *Private* ■ *Independent Religious* ■ *Coed*

Web site: www.txwesleyan.edu
Contact: Ms. Stephanie Lewis-Boatner, Director of Freshman Admissions, 1201 Wesleyan Street, Fort Worth, TX 76105-1536
Telephone: 817-531-4422 or toll-free 800-580-8980 (in-state) **Fax:** 817-531-7515
E-mail: freshman@txwesleyan.edu

Getting in Last Year 602 applied; 83% were accepted; 146 enrolled (29%).

Financial Matters $10,730 tuition and fees (2002–03); $4310 room and board.

Academics Texas Wesleyan awards bachelor's, master's, and first-professional degrees. Challenging opportunities include advanced placement credit and a senior project. Special programs include internships, summer session for credit, study-abroad, and Army and Air Force ROTC. The most frequently chosen baccalaureate fields are business/marketing, education, and psychology. The faculty at Texas Wesleyan has 110 full-time members, 83% with terminal degrees. The student-faculty ratio is 15:1.

Students of Texas Wesleyan The student body totals 2,813, of whom 1,623 are undergraduates. 61.1% are women and 38.9% are men. Students come from 16 states and territories. 96% are from Texas. 0.9% are international students. 100% returned for their sophomore year.

Applying Texas Wesleyan requires an essay, SAT I or ACT, a high school transcript, and a minimum high school GPA of 2.5, and in some cases an interview. Application deadline: rolling admissions. Deferred admission is possible.

TEXAS WOMAN'S UNIVERSITY

Denton, TX

Suburban setting ■ Public ■ State-supported ■ Coed, Primarily Women

Web site: www.twu.edu

Contact: Ms. Teresa Mauk, Director of Admissions, PO Box 425589, Denton, TX 76204-5589

Telephone: 940-898-3040 or toll-free 888-948-9984 **Fax:** 940-898-3081

E-mail: admissions@twu.edu

Getting in Last Year 1,510 applied; 76% were accepted; 529 enrolled (46%).

Financial Matters $3272 resident tuition and fees (2002–03); $9812 nonresident tuition and fees (2002–03); $4683 room and board; 98% average percent of need met; $8214 average financial aid amount received per undergraduate (2001–02).

Academics TWU awards bachelor's, master's, and doctoral degrees and post-master's certificates. Challenging opportunities include advanced placement credit, accelerated degree programs, an honors program, double majors, independent study, and a senior project. Special programs include cooperative education, internships, summer session for credit, and off-campus study. The most frequently chosen baccalaureate fields are health professions and related sciences, interdisciplinary studies, and home economics/vocational home economics. The faculty at TWU has 376 full-time members. The student-faculty ratio is 16:1.

Students of TWU The student body totals 8,694, of whom 4,817 are undergraduates. 94.8% are women and 5.2% are men. Students come from 21 states and territories and 42 other countries. 99% are from Texas. 2.2% are international students. 67% returned for their sophomore year.

Applying TWU requires SAT I or ACT, a high school transcript, and a minimum high school GPA of 2.0. Application deadline: 7/15; 4/1 priority date for financial aid. Early and deferred admission are possible.

THIEL COLLEGE

Greenville, PA

Rural setting ■ Private ■ Independent Religious ■ Coed

Web site: www.thiel.edu

Contact: Mr. Mark Thompson, Director of Admissions, 75 College Avenue, Greenville, PA 16125-2181

Telephone: 724-589-2176 or toll-free 800-24THIEL **Fax:** 724-589-2013

E-mail: admission@thiel.edu

Getting in Last Year 1,537 applied; 81% were accepted; 404 enrolled (32%).

Financial Matters $13,428 tuition and fees (2002–03); $6454 room and board; 80% average percent of need met; $14,214 average financial aid amount received per undergraduate.

Academics Thiel awards associate and bachelor's degrees. Challenging opportunities include advanced placement credit, freshman honors college, an honors program, double majors, and a senior project. Special programs include cooperative education, internships, summer session for credit, off-campus study, and study-abroad. The most frequently chosen baccalaureate fields are business/marketing, social sciences and history, and health professions and related sciences. The faculty at Thiel has 61 full-time members, 70% with terminal degrees. The student-faculty ratio is 15:1.

Students of Thiel The student body is made up of 1,279 undergraduates. 48.9% are women and 51.1% are men. Students come from 19 states and territories and 13 other countries. 74% are from Pennsylvania. 3.6% are international students. 72% returned for their sophomore year.

Applying Thiel requires SAT I or ACT, a high school transcript, and a minimum high school GPA of 2.0, and in some cases an essay, an interview, and recommendations. The school recommends an essay, an interview, and recommendations. Application deadline: 8/15. Deferred admission is possible.

THOMAS AQUINAS COLLEGE

Santa Paula, CA

Rural setting ■ Private ■ Independent Religious ■ Coed

Web site: www.thomasaquinas.edu

Contact: Mr. Thomas J. Susanka Jr., Director of Admissions, 10000 North Ojai Road, Santa Paula, CA 93060-9980

Telephone: 805-525-4417 ext. 361 or toll-free 800-634-9797 **Fax:** 805-525-9342

E-mail: admissions@thomasaquinas.edu

Getting in Last Year 185 applied; 82% were accepted; 102 enrolled (68%).

Financial Matters $16,200 tuition and fees (2002–03); $4800 room and board; 100% average percent of need met; $13,480 average financial aid amount received per undergraduate.

Academics TAC awards bachelor's degrees. A senior project is a challenging opportunity. The most frequently chosen baccalaureate field is liberal arts/general studies. The faculty at TAC has 30 full-time members, 73% with terminal degrees. The student-faculty ratio is 10:1.

Students of TAC The student body is made up of 330 undergraduates. 50.6% are women and 49.4% are men. Students come from 38 states and territories and 5 other countries. 52% are from California. 10.6% are international students. 88% returned for their sophomore year.

Applying TAC requires an essay, SAT I or ACT, a high school transcript, and 3 recommendations, and in some cases an interview. The school recommends a minimum high school GPA of 2.0. Application deadline: rolling admissions. Early and deferred admission are possible.

THOMAS COLLEGE

Waterville, ME

Small-town setting ■ Private ■ Independent ■ Coed

Web site: www.thomas.edu

Contact: Mr. Robert Callahan, Vice President, Enrollment Management, 180 West River Road, Waterville, ME 04901

Telephone: 207-859-1101 or toll-free 800-339-7001 **Fax:** 207-859-1114

E-mail: admiss@thomas.edu

Getting in Last Year 428 applied; 93% were accepted; 189 enrolled (48%).

Financial Matters $13,890 tuition and fees (2002–03); $6070 room and board; 85% average percent of need met; $11,575 average financial aid amount received per undergraduate.

Academics Thomas awards associate, bachelor's, and master's degrees. Advanced placement credit is a challenging opportunity. Special programs include cooperative education, internships, summer session for credit, off-campus study, and study-abroad. The most frequently chosen baccalaureate fields are business/marketing, parks and recreation, and computer/information sciences. The faculty at Thomas has 22 full-time members, 55% with terminal degrees. The student-faculty ratio is 12:1.

Students of Thomas The student body totals 819, of whom 671 are undergraduates. 53.2% are women and 46.8% are men. Students come from 13 states and territories and 2 other countries. 91% are from Maine. 0.2% are international students. 63% returned for their sophomore year.

Applying Thomas requires an essay, SAT I or ACT, a high school transcript, and 1 recommendation. The school recommends an interview, rank in upper 50% of high school class, and a minimum high school GPA of 2.0. Application deadline: rolling admissions; 2/15 priority date for financial aid. Deferred admission is possible.

THOMAS EDISON STATE COLLEGE

Trenton, NJ

Urban setting ■ Public ■ State-supported ■ Coed

Web site: www.tesc.edu

Contact: Mr. Gordon Holly, Director of Admissions Services, 101 West State Street, Trenton, NJ 08608-1176

Telephone: 888-442-8372 or toll-free 888-442-8372 **Fax:** 609-984-8447

E-mail: info@tesc.edu

Academics Thomas Edison awards associate, bachelor's, and master's degrees (offers only distance learning degree programs). Challenging opportunities include advanced placement credit, double majors, and independent study. Summer session for credit is a special program. The most frequently chosen baccalaureate fields are liberal arts/general studies, physical sciences, and business/marketing.

Students of Thomas Edison The student body totals 9,225, of whom 9,012 are undergraduates. 48.3% are women and 51.7% are men. Students come from 54 states and territories and 84 other countries. 56% are from New Jersey. 3.1% are international students.

Applying Thomas Edison requires age 21 or over and a high school graduate.

THOMAS JEFFERSON UNIVERSITY

Philadelphia, PA

Urban setting ■ Private ■ Independent ■ Coed

Web site: www.jefferson.edu

Contact: Assistant Director of Admissions, Edison Building, Suite 1610, 130 South Ninth Street, Philadelphia, PA 19107

Telephone: 215-503-8890 or toll-free 877-533-3247 **Fax:** 215-503-7241

E-mail: chpadmissions@mail.tju.edu

Getting in Last Year 1,036 applied; 31% were accepted.

Financial Matters $18,614 tuition and fees (2002–03); $8440 room and board.

Thomas Jefferson University (continued)

Academics TJU awards bachelor's and master's degrees and post-bachelor's certificates. Advanced placement credit is a challenging opportunity. Special programs include study-abroad and Air Force ROTC. The faculty at TJU has 48 full-time members, 52% with terminal degrees. The student-faculty ratio is 9:1.

Students of TJU The student body totals 2,272, of whom 791 are undergraduates. 81.2% are women and 18.8% are men. Students come from 13 states and territories. 63% are from Pennsylvania.

Applying TJU recommends SAT I or ACT. Deferred admission is possible.

THOMAS MORE COLLEGE

Crestview Hills, KY

Suburban setting ■ Private ■ Independent Religious ■ Coed

Web site: www.thomasmore.edu

Contact: Mr. Robert A. McDermott, Director of Enrollment Management, 333 Thomas More Parkway, Crestview Hills, KY 41017-3495

Telephone: 606-344-3332 or toll-free 800-825-4557 **Fax:** 859-344-3444

E-mail: robert.mcdermott@thomasmore.edu

Getting in Last Year 1,356 applied; 69% were accepted.

Financial Matters $14,600 tuition and fees (2002–03); $5300 room and board; 90% average percent of need met; $10,671 average financial aid amount received per undergraduate (2001–02).

Academics Thomas More awards associate, bachelor's, and master's degrees. Challenging opportunities include advanced placement credit, accelerated degree programs, student-designed majors, an honors program, double majors, independent study, and a senior project. Special programs include cooperative education, internships, summer session for credit, off-campus study, study-abroad, and Army and Air Force ROTC. The most frequently chosen baccalaureate fields are business/marketing, biological/life sciences, and health professions and related sciences. The faculty at Thomas More has 74 full-time members, 69% with terminal degrees. The student-faculty ratio is 13:1.

Students of Thomas More The student body totals 1,402, of whom 1,300 are undergraduates. 52.1% are women and 47.9% are men. Students come from 13 states and territories. 65% are from Kentucky. 0.8% are international students. 63% returned for their sophomore year.

Applying Thomas More requires SAT I or ACT, a high school transcript, rank in top 50%, admissions committee may consider those not meeting criteria, and a minimum high school GPA of 2.0, and in some cases an essay and 2 recommendations. The school recommends an interview. Application deadline: 8/15; 3/15 priority date for financial aid. Deferred admission is possible.

THOMAS MORE COLLEGE OF LIBERAL ARTS

Merrimack, NH

Small-town setting ■ Private ■ Independent Religious ■ Coed

Web site: www.thomasmorecollege.edu

Contact: Ms. Catherine M. Alcarez, Director of Admissions, 6 Manchester Street, Merrimack, NH 03054-4818

Telephone: 800-880-8308 or toll-free 800-880-8308 **Fax:** 603-880-9280

E-mail: admissions@thomasmorecollege.edu

Getting in Last Year 44 applied; 100% were accepted; 20 enrolled (45%).

Financial Matters $10,450 tuition and fees (2002–03); $7700 room and board; 80% average percent of need met; $9198 average financial aid amount received per undergraduate.

Academics Thomas More College awards bachelor's degrees. Challenging opportunities include independent study and a senior project. Study-abroad is a special program. The most frequently chosen baccalaureate fields are social sciences and history, English, and biological/life sciences. The faculty at Thomas More College has 5 full-time members, 100% with terminal degrees. The student-faculty ratio is 13:1.

Students of Thomas More College The student body is made up of 77 undergraduates. 48.1% are women and 51.9% are men. Students come from 21 states and territories. 19% are from New Hampshire. 85% returned for their sophomore year.

Applying Thomas More College requires an essay, SAT I or ACT, a high school transcript, and 2 recommendations, and in some cases an interview. Application deadline: rolling admissions. Early and deferred admission are possible.

THOMAS UNIVERSITY

Thomasville, GA

Small-town setting ■ Private ■ Independent ■ Coed

Web site: www.thomasu.edu

Contact: Darla M. Glass, Director of Student Affairs, 1501 Millpond Road, Thomasville, GA 31792-7499

Telephone: 229-226-1621 ext. 122 or toll-free 800-538-9784 **Fax:** 229-227-1653

Getting in Last Year 91 applied; 100% were accepted; 73 enrolled (80%).

Financial Matters $8390 tuition and fees (2002–03); $2400 room only; 67% average percent of need met; $5372 average financial aid amount received per undergraduate (2001–02).

Academics Thomas University awards associate, bachelor's, and master's degrees and post-bachelor's certificates. Challenging opportunities include advanced placement credit, accelerated degree programs, double majors, independent study, and a senior project. Special programs include cooperative education, internships, summer session for credit, and study-abroad. The most frequently chosen baccalaureate fields are health professions and related sciences, protective services/public administration, and business/marketing. The faculty at Thomas University has 38 full-time members, 61% with terminal degrees. The student-faculty ratio is 10:1.

Students of Thomas University The student body totals 734, of whom 653 are undergraduates. 69.7% are women and 30.3% are men. Students come from 4 states and territories and 23 other countries. 92% are from Georgia. 5.7% are international students. 59% returned for their sophomore year.

Applying Thomas University requires MAPS, a high school transcript, and a minimum high school GPA of 2.0. The school recommends SAT I or ACT. Application deadline: rolling admissions. Early and deferred admission are possible.

TIFFIN UNIVERSITY

Tiffin, OH

Small-town setting ■ Private ■ Independent ■ Coed

Web site: www.tiffin.edu

Contact: Mr. Darby Roggow, Director of Admissions, 155 Miami Street, Tiffin, OH 44883-2161

Telephone: 419-448-3425 or toll-free 800-968-6446 **Fax:** 419-443-5006

E-mail: admiss@tiffin.edu

Getting in Last Year 1,424 applied; 73% were accepted; 265 enrolled (25%).

Financial Matters $12,850 tuition and fees (2002–03); $5750 room and board; 69% average percent of need met; $9770 average financial aid amount received per undergraduate.

Academics Tiffin awards associate, bachelor's, and master's degrees. Challenging opportunities include advanced placement credit, accelerated degree programs, double majors, independent study, and a senior project. Special programs include internships, summer session for credit, study-abroad, and Army and Air Force ROTC. The most frequently chosen baccalaureate fields are business/marketing, protective services/public administration, and liberal arts/general studies. The faculty at Tiffin has 42 full-time members, 83% with terminal degrees. The student-faculty ratio is 10:1.

Students of Tiffin The student body totals 1,533, of whom 1,204 are undergraduates. 56% are women and 44% are men. Students come from 22 states and territories and 19 other countries. 91% are from Ohio. 2.4% are international students. 61% returned for their sophomore year.

Applying Tiffin requires an essay, SAT I or ACT, and a high school transcript, and in some cases an interview and recommendations. The school recommends an interview and a minimum high school GPA of 2.50. Application deadline: rolling admissions; 3/31 priority date for financial aid. Deferred admission is possible.

TOCCOA FALLS COLLEGE

Toccoa Falls, GA

Small-town setting ■ Private ■ Independent Religious ■ Coed

Web site: www.toccoafalls.edu

Contact: Mr. Tommy Campbell, Director of Admissions, Office of Admissions, PO Box 899, Toccoa Falls, GA 30598-1000

Telephone: 706-886-6831 ext. 5380 or toll-free 800-868-3257 **Fax:** 706-282-6012

E-mail: admissions@toccoafalls.edu

Getting in Last Year 646 applied; 69% were accepted; 821 enrolled (185%).

Financial Matters $9900 tuition and fees (2002–03); $4300 room and board; 71% average percent of need met; $7671 average financial aid amount received per undergraduate (2001–02).

Academics Toccoa Falls awards associate and bachelor's degrees. Challenging opportunities include advanced placement credit, accelerated degree programs, double majors, independent study, and a senior project. Special programs include internships and summer session for credit. The most frequently chosen baccalaureate fields are psychology, education, and communications/ communication technologies. The faculty at Toccoa Falls has 54 full-time members. The student-faculty ratio is 12:1.

Students of Toccoa Falls The student body is made up of 821 undergraduates. Students come from 48 states and territories. 39% are from Georgia. 68% returned for their sophomore year.

Applying Toccoa Falls requires an essay, SAT I or ACT, a high school transcript, 1 recommendation, and a minimum high school GPA of 2.0, and in some cases an interview. Application deadline: rolling admissions. Early and deferred admission are possible.

TOURO COLLEGE

New York, NY

Urban setting ■ Private ■ Independent ■ Coed

Web site: www.touro.edu
Contact: Mr. Andre Baron, Director of Admissions, 27-33 West 23rd Street, New York, NY 10010
Telephone: 212-463-0400 ext. 665

Getting in Last Year 3,942 applied; 69% were accepted; 3,389 enrolled (125%).

Financial Matters $10,400 tuition and fees (2002–03); $4700 room and board.

Academics Touro College awards associate, bachelor's, master's, doctoral, and first-professional degrees and post-master's certificates. Challenging opportunities include advanced placement credit, accelerated degree programs, student-designed majors, an honors program, double majors, and independent study. Special programs include internships, summer session for credit, and study-abroad. The most frequently chosen baccalaureate fields are business/marketing, health professions and related sciences, and liberal arts/general studies. The faculty at Touro College has 264 full-time members. The student-faculty ratio is 16:1.

Students of Touro College The student body totals 11,447, of whom 7,393 are undergraduates. 69.6% are women and 30.4% are men. Students come from 33 states and territories and 30 other countries. 90% are from New York.

Applying Touro College requires a high school transcript, and in some cases an interview and 2 recommendations. The school recommends an essay, SAT I or ACT, and 1 recommendation. Application deadline: rolling admissions; 5/15 priority date for financial aid. Early and deferred admission are possible.

TOURO UNIVERSITY INTERNATIONAL

Cypress, CA

Private ■ Independent ■ Coed

Web site: www.tourou.edu
Contact: Wei Ren, Registrar, 5336 Plaza Drive, 3rd Floor, Cypress, CA 90630
Telephone: 714-816-0366 **Fax:** 714-827-7407
E-mail: registration@tourou.edu

Getting in Last Year 109 applied; 73% were accepted; 80 enrolled (100%).

Financial Matters $7200 tuition and fees (2002–03).

Academics Touro University International awards bachelor's, master's, and doctoral degrees and post-bachelor's certificates (offers only online degree programs). Special programs include summer session for credit and off-campus study. The most frequently chosen baccalaureate fields are business/marketing and health professions and related sciences. The faculty at Touro University International has 61 full-time members, 100% with terminal degrees. The student-faculty ratio is 18:1.

Students of Touro University International The student body totals 3,082, of whom 1,190 are undergraduates. 31.8% are women and 68.2% are men. Students come from 50 states and territories and 15 other countries. 10% are from California. 85% returned for their sophomore year.

Applying Touro University International requires a high school transcript and a minimum high school GPA of 3.0, and in some cases an essay. The school recommends an interview. Application deadline: rolling admissions.

TOWSON UNIVERSITY

Towson, MD

Suburban setting ■ Public ■ State-supported ■ Coed

Web site: www.towson.edu
Contact: Ms. Louise Shulack, Director of Admissions, 8000 York Road, Towson, MD 21252
Telephone: 410-704-3687 or toll-free 888-4TOWSON **Fax:** 410-830-3030
E-mail: admissions@towson.edu

Getting in Last Year 10,824 applied; 58% were accepted; 2,191 enrolled (35%).

Financial Matters $5281 resident tuition and fees (2002–03); $12,633 nonresident tuition and fees (2002–03); $6378 room and board; 81% average percent of need met; $8109 average financial aid amount received per undergraduate.

Academics Towson awards bachelor's, master's, and doctoral degrees and post-bachelor's and post-master's certificates. Challenging opportunities include advanced placement credit, student-designed majors, freshman honors college, an honors program, double majors, and independent study. Special programs include cooperative education, internships, summer session for credit, off-campus study, study-abroad, and Army ROTC. The most frequently chosen baccalaureate fields are business/marketing, communications/communication technologies, and education. The faculty at Towson has 585 full-time members, 77% with terminal degrees. The student-faculty ratio is 19:1.

Students of Towson The student body totals 17,481, of whom 14,296 are undergraduates. 60.5% are women and 39.5% are men. Students come from 46 states and territories and 90 other countries. 81% are from Maryland. 2.4% are international students. 82% returned for their sophomore year.

Applying Towson requires SAT I or ACT and a high school transcript, and in some cases an interview. The school recommends an essay, an interview, recommendations, and a minimum high school GPA of 2.75. Application deadline: 5/1; 3/1 priority date for financial aid. Early and deferred admission are possible.

TRANSYLVANIA UNIVERSITY

Lexington, KY

Urban setting ■ Private ■ Independent Religious ■ Coed

Web site: www.transy.edu
Contact: Ms. Sarah Coen, Director of Admissions, 300 North Broadway, Lexington, KY 40508-1797
Telephone: 859-233-8242 or toll-free 800-872-6798 **Fax:** 859-233-8797
E-mail: admissions@transy.edu

Getting in Last Year 1,179 applied; 87% were accepted; 327 enrolled (32%).

Financial Matters $16,790 tuition and fees (2002–03); $5940 room and board; 88% average percent of need met; $14,175 average financial aid amount received per undergraduate.

Academics Transylvania awards bachelor's degrees. Challenging opportunities include advanced placement credit, student-designed majors, double majors, and independent study. Special programs include internships, summer session for credit, off-campus study, study-abroad, and Army and Air Force ROTC. The most frequently chosen baccalaureate fields are business/marketing, biological/life sciences, and psychology. The faculty at Transylvania has 78 full-time members, 91% with terminal degrees. The student-faculty ratio is 13:1.

Students of Transylvania The student body is made up of 1,109 undergraduates. 57.7% are women and 42.3% are men. Students come from 30 states and territories and 2 other countries. 80% are from Kentucky. 0.3% are international students. 80% returned for their sophomore year.

Applying Transylvania requires an essay, SAT I or ACT, a high school transcript, 2 recommendations, and a minimum high school GPA of 2.75, and in some cases an interview. The school recommends an interview. Application deadline: 2/1; 3/1 priority date for financial aid. Early and deferred admission are possible.

TRENT UNIVERSITY

Peterborough, ON Canada

Suburban setting ■ Public ■ Coed

Web site: www.trentu.ca
Contact: Mrs. Carol Murray, Admissions Officer, Office of the Registrar, Peterborough, ON K9J 7B8 Canada
Telephone: 705-748-1215 **Fax:** 705-748-1629
E-mail: leaders@trentu.ca

Getting in Last Year 1,781 enrolled.

Academics Trent awards bachelor's, master's, and doctoral degrees. Challenging opportunities include advanced placement credit, accelerated degree programs, student-designed majors, an honors program, double majors, and a senior project. Special programs include summer session for credit, off-campus study, and study-abroad. The faculty at Trent has 236 full-time members, 87% with terminal degrees. The student-faculty ratio is 21:1.

Students of Trent The student body totals 6,347, of whom 6,140 are undergraduates. 66.9% are women and 33.1% are men. Students come from 21 states and territories and 106 other countries. 86% returned for their sophomore year.

Applying Trent requires a high school transcript and a minimum high school GPA of 2.8, and in some cases an essay, SAT I or ACT, an interview, and recommendations. Application deadline: 6/1. Deferred admission is possible.

TREVECCA NAZARENE UNIVERSITY

Nashville, TN

Urban setting ■ Private ■ Independent Religious ■ Coed

Web site: www.trevecca.edu
Contact: Ms. Patricia D. Cook, Director of Admissions, 333 Murfreesboro Road, Nashville, TN 37210-2834
Telephone: 615-248-1320 or toll-free 888-210-4TNU **Fax:** 615-248-7406
E-mail: admissions_und@trevecca.edu

Getting in Last Year 535 applied; 82% were accepted; 200 enrolled (46%).

Financial Matters $11,390 tuition and fees (2002–03); $5150 room and board; 43% average percent of need met; $10,449 average financial aid amount received per undergraduate (2001–02).

Academics Trevecca awards associate, bachelor's, master's, and doctoral degrees and post-master's certificates. Challenging opportunities include advanced placement credit, double majors, and a senior project. Special programs include internships, summer session for credit, and Army ROTC. The most frequently chosen baccalaureate fields are business/marketing, education, and biological/life sciences. The faculty at Trevecca has 74 full-time members, 68% with terminal degrees. The student-faculty ratio is 16:1.

Trevecca Nazarene University (continued)

Students of Trevecca The student body totals 1,878, of whom 1,185 are undergraduates. 58.9% are women and 41.1% are men. Students come from 34 states and territories and 13 other countries. 64% are from Tennessee. 1.6% are international students. 58% returned for their sophomore year.

Applying Trevecca requires SAT I or ACT, a high school transcript, medical history and immunization records, and a minimum high school GPA of 2.5. The school recommends recommendations. Application deadline: rolling admissions; 3/1 priority date for financial aid. Early and deferred admission are possible.

TRINITY BAPTIST COLLEGE

Jacksonville, FL

Urban setting ■ Private ■ Independent Religious ■ Coed

Web site: www.tbc.edu
Contact: Mr. Larry Appleby, Administrative Dean, 800 Hammond Boulevard, Jacksonville, FL 32221
Telephone: 904-596-2538 or toll-free 800-786-2206 (out-of-state)
Fax: 904-596-2531
E-mail: trinity@tbc.edu

Getting in Last Year 205 applied; 68% were accepted; 111 enrolled (79%).

Financial Matters $4650 tuition and fees (2002–03); $3500 room and board; 55% average percent of need met; $4458 average financial aid amount received per undergraduate (2001–02 estimated).

Academics Trinity awards associate and bachelor's degrees. Challenging opportunities include advanced placement credit, accelerated degree programs, and independent study. Special programs include internships and summer session for credit. The most frequently chosen baccalaureate field is education. The faculty at Trinity has 12 full-time members, 75% with terminal degrees. The student-faculty ratio is 10:1.

Students of Trinity The student body is made up of 391 undergraduates. 49.1% are women and 50.9% are men. Students come from 24 states and territories and 4 other countries. 65% are from Florida. 1.8% are international students.

Applying Trinity requires an essay, SAT I or ACT, a high school transcript, 3 recommendations, and a minimum high school GPA of 2.0. Application deadline: rolling admissions; 4/15 for financial aid.

TRINITY BIBLE COLLEGE

Ellendale, ND

Rural setting ■ Private ■ Independent Religious ■ Coed

Web site: www.trinitybiblecollege.edu
Contact: Rev. Steve Tvedt, Vice President of College Relations, 50 South Sixth Avenue, Ellendale, ND 58436
Telephone: 701-349-3621 ext. 2045 or toll-free 888-TBC-2DAY
Fax: 701-349-5443
E-mail: admissions@trinitybiblecollege.edu

Getting in Last Year 214 applied; 51% were accepted; 59 enrolled (54%).

Financial Matters $9258 tuition and fees (2002–03); $3990 room and board.

Academics TBC awards associate and bachelor's degrees. Challenging opportunities include advanced placement credit, accelerated degree programs, and double majors. Special programs include internships and summer session for credit. The most frequently chosen baccalaureate field is education. The student-faculty ratio is 11:1.

Students of TBC The student body is made up of 287 undergraduates. 53.3% are women and 46.7% are men. Students come from 30 states and territories. 34% are from North Dakota. 67% returned for their sophomore year.

Applying TBC requires an essay, ACT, a high school transcript, 2 recommendations, health form, evidence of Christian conversion, and a minimum high school GPA of 2.0, and in some cases SAT I and an interview. Application deadline: rolling admissions; 9/1 for financial aid, with a 3/1 priority date. Deferred admission is possible.

TRINITY CHRISTIAN COLLEGE

Palos Heights, IL

Suburban setting ■ Private ■ Independent Religious ■ Coed

Web site: www.trnty.edu
Contact: Mr. Pete Hamstra, Dean of Admissions, 6601 West College Drive, Palos Heights, IL 60463
Telephone: 708-239-4709 or toll-free 800-748-0085 **Fax:** 708-239-4826
E-mail: admissions@trnty.edu

Getting in Last Year 538 applied; 91% were accepted; 216 enrolled (44%).

Financial Matters $14,640 tuition and fees (2002–03); $5700 room and board; 67% average percent of need met; $9875 average financial aid amount received per undergraduate (2001–02).

Academics Trinity Christian College awards bachelor's degrees. Challenging opportunities include advanced placement credit, an honors program, double majors, independent study, and a senior project. Special programs include cooperative education, internships, off-campus study, and study-abroad. The most frequently chosen baccalaureate fields are business/marketing, education, and health professions and related sciences. The faculty at Trinity Christian College has 56 full-time members, 61% with terminal degrees. The student-faculty ratio is 13:1.

Students of Trinity Christian College The student body is made up of 1,135 undergraduates. 62% are women and 38% are men. Students come from 36 states and territories and 11 other countries. 58% are from Illinois. 1.9% are international students. 76% returned for their sophomore year.

Applying Trinity Christian College requires an essay, SAT I or ACT, a high school transcript, an interview, and a minimum high school GPA of 2.0, and in some cases 1 recommendation. Application deadline: rolling admissions. Deferred admission is possible.

TRINITY COLLEGE

Hartford, CT

Urban setting ■ Private ■ Independent ■ Coed

Web site: www.trincoll.edu
Contact: Mr. Larry Dow, Dean of Admissions and Financial Aid, 300 Summit Street, Hartford, CT 06106-3100
Telephone: 860-297-2180 **Fax:** 860-297-2287
E-mail: admissions.office@trincoll.edu

Getting in Last Year 5,417 applied; 36% were accepted; 550 enrolled (28%).

Financial Matters $28,602 tuition and fees (2002–03); $7380 room and board; 100% average percent of need met; $22,505 average financial aid amount received per undergraduate (2001–02).

Academics Trinity College awards bachelor's and master's degrees. Challenging opportunities include advanced placement credit, accelerated degree programs, student-designed majors, an honors program, double majors, independent study, and a senior project. Special programs include internships, summer session for credit, off-campus study, study-abroad, and Army ROTC. The most frequently chosen baccalaureate fields are social sciences and history, area/ethnic studies, and English. The faculty at Trinity College has 198 full-time members, 89% with terminal degrees. The student-faculty ratio is 9:1.

Students of Trinity College The student body totals 2,298, of whom 2,098 are undergraduates. 51.5% are women and 48.5% are men. Students come from 46 states and territories and 35 other countries. 22% are from Connecticut. 2.3% are international students. 91% returned for their sophomore year.

Applying Trinity College requires an essay, ACT or SAT I and SAT II Writing Test or SAT II Writing Test and two additional SAT II subject tests, a high school transcript, and 3 recommendations. The school recommends an interview. Application deadline: 1/15; 3/1 for financial aid, with a 2/1 priority date. Early and deferred admission are possible.

TRINITY COLLEGE

Washington, DC

Urban setting ■ Private ■ Independent Religious ■ Women Only

Web site: www.trinitydc.edu
Contact: Ms. Wendy Kares, Director of Admissions, 125 Michigan Avenue, NE, Washington, DC 20017-1094
Telephone: 202-884-9400 or toll-free 800-IWANTTC **Fax:** 202-884-9403
E-mail: admissions@trinitydc.edu

Getting in Last Year 373 applied; 74% were accepted; 174 enrolled (63%).

Financial Matters $15,600 tuition and fees (2002–03); $6970 room and board; 77% average percent of need met; $16,313 average financial aid amount received per undergraduate (2001–02).

Academics Trinity awards bachelor's and master's degrees and post-bachelor's certificates. Challenging opportunities include advanced placement credit, accelerated degree programs, student-designed majors, an honors program, double majors, independent study, and a senior project. Special programs include cooperative education, internships, summer session for credit, off-campus study, study-abroad, and Army ROTC. The most frequently chosen baccalaureate fields are psychology, business/marketing, and social sciences and history. The faculty at Trinity has 52 full-time members, 94% with terminal degrees. The student-faculty ratio is 11:1.

Students of Trinity The student body totals 1,645, of whom 1,050 are undergraduates. Students come from 17 states and territories. 51% are from District of Columbia. 2.9% are international students. 58% returned for their sophomore year.

Applying Trinity requires an essay, a high school transcript, 1 recommendation, and a minimum high school GPA of 2.0. The school recommends SAT I or ACT and an interview. Application deadline: 2/1; 2/1 priority date for financial aid. Deferred admission is possible.

TRINITY COLLEGE OF FLORIDA

New Port Richey, FL

Small-town setting ■ Private ■ Independent Religious ■ Coed

Web site: www.trinitycollege.edu

Contact: Mr. Kevin Bonsignore, Assistant Director Enrollment, 2430 Welbilt Boulevard, New Port Richey, FL 34655

Telephone: 727-376-6911 ext. 1105 or toll-free 888-776-4999 **Fax:** 727-376-0781

E-mail: admissions@trinitycollege.edu

Getting in Last Year 150 applied; 27% were accepted; 26 enrolled (63%).

Financial Matters $6830 tuition and fees (2002–03); $3350 room and board.

Academics Trinity awards associate and bachelor's degrees. Challenging opportunities include advanced placement credit, double majors, independent study, and a senior project. Special programs include internships and summer session for credit. The faculty at Trinity has 5 full-time members, 60% with terminal degrees. The student-faculty ratio is 16:1.

Students of Trinity The student body is made up of 172 undergraduates. 45.3% are women and 54.7% are men. Students come from 9 states and territories and 4 other countries. 92% are from Florida. 3.5% are international students. 50% returned for their sophomore year.

Applying Trinity requires an essay, SAT I or ACT, a high school transcript, an interview, and 3 recommendations. The school recommends a minimum high school GPA of 2.75. Application deadline: rolling admissions; 3/1 priority date for financial aid. Early and deferred admission are possible.

TRINITY COLLEGE OF NURSING AND HEALTH SCIENCES SCHOOLS

Moline, IL

Urban setting ■ Private ■ Independent ■ Coed, Primarily Women

Web site: www.trinitycollegeqc.edu

Contact: Ms. Barbara Kimpe, Admissions Representative, 2122 25th Avenue, Rock Island, IL 61201

Telephone: 309-779-7812 **Fax:** 309-779-7748

E-mail: con@trinityqc.com

Getting in Last Year 100 applied; 50% were accepted; 5 enrolled (10%).

Financial Matters $9100 tuition and fees (2002–03).

Academics Trinity College of Nursing and Health Sciences Schools awards associate and bachelor's degrees (general education requirements are taken off campus, usually at Black Hawk College, Eastern Iowa Community College District and Western Illinois University). Challenging opportunities include an honors program and independent study. Special programs include summer session for credit and off-campus study. The most frequently chosen baccalaureate field is health professions and related sciences. The faculty at Trinity College of Nursing and Health Sciences Schools has 12 full-time members. The student-faculty ratio is 10:1.

Students of Trinity College of Nursing and Health Sciences Schools The student body is made up of 108 undergraduates. 95.4% are women and 4.6% are men. Students come from 2 states and territories. 72% are from Illinois.

Applying Trinity College of Nursing and Health Sciences Schools requires SAT I or ACT, a high school transcript, and a minimum high school GPA of 2.5. Application deadline: 6/1.

TRINITY INTERNATIONAL UNIVERSITY

Deerfield, IL

Suburban setting ■ Private ■ Independent Religious ■ Coed

Web site: www.tiu.edu

Contact: Mr. Matt Yoder, Director of Undergraduate Admissions, 2065 Half Day Road, Peterson Wing, McClennan Building, Deerfield, IL 60015-1284

Telephone: 847-317-7000 or toll-free 800-822-3225 (out-of-state) **Fax:** 847-317-8097

E-mail: tcdadm@tiu.edu

Getting in Last Year 455 applied; 84% were accepted; 257 enrolled (67%).

Financial Matters $16,350 tuition and fees (2002–03); $5510 room and board; 58% average percent of need met; $12,955 average financial aid amount received per undergraduate.

Academics Trinity awards bachelor's, master's, doctoral, and first-professional degrees. Challenging opportunities include advanced placement credit, an honors program, double majors, independent study, and a senior project. Special programs include internships, off-campus study, and study-abroad. The most frequently chosen baccalaureate fields are education, communications/communication technologies, and business/marketing. The faculty at Trinity has 40 full-time members, 60% with terminal degrees. The student-faculty ratio is 16:1.

Students of Trinity The student body totals 2,078, of whom 1,162 are undergraduates. 58.2% are women and 41.8% are men. Students come from 29 states and territories and 6 other countries. 62% are from Illinois. 1.2% are international students. 88% returned for their sophomore year.

Applying Trinity requires an essay, SAT I or ACT, a high school transcript, 1 recommendation, and a minimum high school GPA of 2.5, and in some cases an interview. The school recommends a minimum high school GPA of 3.0. Application deadline: rolling admissions; 4/1 priority date for financial aid. Early and deferred admission are possible.

TRINITY LUTHERAN COLLEGE

Issaquah, WA

Suburban setting ■ Private ■ Independent Religious ■ Coed

Web site: www.tlc.edu

Contact: Ms. Sigrid Olsen, Director of Admission, 4221 228th Avenue, SE, Issaquah, WA 98029-9299

Telephone: 425-961-5516 or toll-free 800-843-5659 **Fax:** 425-392-0404

E-mail: admission@tlc.edu

Getting in Last Year 50 applied; 70% were accepted; 19 enrolled (54%).

Financial Matters $9590 tuition and fees (2002–03); $5350 room and board.

Academics Trinity Lutheran College awards associate and bachelor's degrees and post-bachelor's certificates. Challenging opportunities include advanced placement credit, double majors, independent study, and a senior project. Special programs include internships, off-campus study, and study-abroad. The faculty at Trinity Lutheran College has 10 full-time members, 40% with terminal degrees. The student-faculty ratio is 9:1.

Students of Trinity Lutheran College The student body is made up of 156 undergraduates. 64.1% are women and 35.9% are men. Students come from 13 states and territories and 6 other countries. 57% are from Washington. 88% returned for their sophomore year.

Applying Trinity Lutheran College requires SAT I or ACT, a high school transcript, 2 recommendations, and a minimum high school GPA of 2.0, and in some cases an interview. Application deadline: 9/15; 3/1 priority date for financial aid. Early and deferred admission are possible.

TRINITY UNIVERSITY

San Antonio, TX

Urban setting ■ Private ■ Independent Religious ■ Coed

Web site: www.trinity.edu

Contact: Mr. Christopher Ellertson, Dean of Admissions and Financial Aid, 715 Stadium Drive, San Antonio, TX 78212-7200

Telephone: 210-999-7207 or toll-free 800-TRINITY **Fax:** 210-999-8164

E-mail: admissions@trinity.edu

Getting in Last Year 3,108 applied; 69% were accepted; 674 enrolled (31%).

Financial Matters $17,364 tuition and fees (2002–03); $7040 room and board; 86% average percent of need met; $14,518 average financial aid amount received per undergraduate.

Academics Trinity awards bachelor's and master's degrees. Challenging opportunities include advanced placement credit, accelerated degree programs, an honors program, double majors, independent study, and a senior project. Special programs include internships, summer session for credit, study-abroad, and Air Force ROTC. The most frequently chosen baccalaureate fields are business/marketing, social sciences and history, and English. The faculty at Trinity has 211 full-time members, 98% with terminal degrees. The student-faculty ratio is 11:1.

Students of Trinity The student body totals 2,621, of whom 2,406 are undergraduates. 51.9% are women and 48.1% are men. Students come from 51 states and territories and 18 other countries. 70% are from Texas. 1.4% are international students. 86% returned for their sophomore year.

Applying Trinity requires an essay, a high school transcript, and 2 recommendations. The school recommends SAT I or ACT and an interview. Application deadline: 2/1; 2/1 priority date for financial aid. Deferred admission is possible.

TRINITY WESTERN UNIVERSITY

Langley, BC Canada

Suburban setting ■ Private ■ Independent Religious ■ Coed

Web site: www.twu.ca

Contact: Mr. Jeff Suderman, Director of Undergraduate Admissions, 7600 Glover Road, Langley, BC V2Y 1Y1 Canada

Telephone: 604-888-7511 ext. 3004 or toll-free 888-468-6898 **Fax:** 604-513-2064

E-mail: admissions@twu.ca

Getting in Last Year 1,759 applied; 77% were accepted.

Financial Matters $11,960 tuition and fees (2002–03); $6820 room and board.

Academics TWU awards bachelor's and master's degrees. Challenging opportunities include advanced placement credit, an honors program, double majors, independent study, and a senior project. Special programs include cooperative education, internships, summer session for credit, off-campus study, and study-abroad. The faculty at TWU has 77 full-time members, 90% with terminal degrees. The student-faculty ratio is 18:1.

Trinity Western University (continued)

Students of TWU The student body totals 3,250, of whom 2,750 are undergraduates. Students come from 10 states and territories and 29 other countries. 67% are from British Columbia. 80% returned for their sophomore year.

Applying TWU requires an essay, a high school transcript, 2 recommendations, community standards document, and a minimum high school GPA of 2.5, and in some cases SAT I or ACT and an interview. Application deadline: 6/15; 2/28 priority date for financial aid. Deferred admission is possible.

TRI-STATE UNIVERSITY

Angola, IN

Small-town setting ■ *Private* ■ *Independent* ■ *Coed*

Web site: www.tristate.edu
Contact: Ms. Sara Yarian, Admissions Officer, 1 University Avenue, Angola, IN 46703-1764
Telephone: 260-665-4365 or toll-free 800-347-4TSU **Fax:** 260-665-4578
E-mail: admit@tristate.edu

Getting in Last Year 1,352 applied; 74% were accepted; 286 enrolled (29%).

Financial Matters $16,910 tuition and fees (2002–03); $5250 room and board; 85% average percent of need met; $11,128 average financial aid amount received per undergraduate.

Academics Tri-State awards associate, bachelor's, and master's degrees. Challenging opportunities include advanced placement credit, double majors, and a senior project. Special programs include cooperative education, internships, summer session for credit, and study-abroad. The most frequently chosen baccalaureate fields are engineering/engineering technologies, business/marketing, and education. The faculty at Tri-State has 64 full-time members, 63% with terminal degrees. The student-faculty ratio is 15:1.

Students of Tri-State The student body is made up of 1,267 undergraduates. 36% are women and 64% are men. Students come from 22 states and territories and 20 other countries. 60% are from Indiana. 2.8% are international students. 68% returned for their sophomore year.

Applying Tri-State requires SAT I or ACT, a high school transcript, and a minimum high school GPA of 2.0. The school recommends an interview and recommendations. Application deadline: 6/1; 3/1 priority date for financial aid.

TROY STATE UNIVERSITY

Troy, AL

Small-town setting ■ *Public* ■ *State-supported* ■ *Coed*

Web site: www.troyst.edu
Contact: Mr. Buddy Starling, Dean of Enrollment Management, Adams Administration Building, Room 134, Troy, AL 36082
Telephone: 334-670-3243 or toll-free 800-551-9716 (in-state)
Fax: 334-670-3733
E-mail: bstar@trojan.troyst.edu

Getting in Last Year 3,089 applied; 75% were accepted; 987 enrolled (43%).

Financial Matters $3532 resident tuition and fees (2002–03); $6752 nonresident tuition and fees (2002–03); $4684 room and board; 58% average percent of need met; $9000 average financial aid amount received per undergraduate.

Academics Troy State awards associate, bachelor's, and master's degrees and post-master's certificates. Challenging opportunities include advanced placement credit, accelerated degree programs, student-designed majors, an honors program, double majors, independent study, and a senior project. Special programs include internships, summer session for credit, and Army and Air Force ROTC. The most frequently chosen baccalaureate fields are business/marketing, education, and protective services/public administration. The faculty at Troy State has 218 full-time members, 61% with terminal degrees. The student-faculty ratio is 20:1.

Students of Troy State The student body totals 7,500, of whom 4,687 are undergraduates. 58.2% are women and 41.8% are men. Students come from 49 states and territories and 55 other countries. 4.9% are international students. 72% returned for their sophomore year.

Applying Troy State requires SAT I or ACT and a high school transcript. The school recommends an interview. Application deadline: rolling admissions; 5/1 priority date for financial aid. Deferred admission is possible.

TROY STATE UNIVERSITY DOTHAN

Dothan, AL

Small-town setting ■ *Public* ■ *State-supported* ■ *Coed*

Web site: www.tsud.edu
Contact: Mr. Bob Willis, Director of Enrollment Services, 500 University Drive, PO Box 8368, Dothan, AL 36303
Telephone: 334-983-6556 ext. 205 **Fax:** 334-983-6322
E-mail: bwillis@tsud.edu

Getting in Last Year 112 applied; 69% were accepted; 71 enrolled (92%).

Financial Matters $3532 resident tuition and fees (2002–03); $6752 nonresident tuition and fees (2002–03); 63% average percent of need met; $7500 average financial aid amount received per undergraduate.

Academics TSUD awards associate, bachelor's, and master's degrees and post-master's certificates. Challenging opportunities include advanced placement credit, double majors, and independent study. Special programs include cooperative education, internships, and summer session for credit. The most frequently chosen baccalaureate fields are business/marketing, education, and computer/information sciences. The faculty at TSUD has 59 full-time members, 80% with terminal degrees. The student-faculty ratio is 15:1.

Students of TSUD The student body totals 1,891, of whom 1,538 are undergraduates. 64.7% are women and 35.3% are men. Students come from 5 states and territories. 91% are from Alabama. 46% returned for their sophomore year.

Applying TSUD requires a high school transcript and a minimum high school GPA of 2.0, and in some cases SAT I or ACT. The school recommends a minimum high school GPA of 3.0. Application deadline: rolling admissions. Deferred admission is possible.

TROY STATE UNIVERSITY MONTGOMERY

Montgomery, AL

Urban setting ■ *Public* ■ *State-supported* ■ *Coed*

Web site: www.tsum.edu
Contact: Mr. Larry Hawkins, Director of Enrollment Management, PO Drawer 4419, Montgomery, AL 36103-4419
Telephone: 334-241-9506 or toll-free 800-355-TSUM
E-mail: admit@tsum.edu

Getting in Last Year 451 applied; 100% were accepted; 248 enrolled (55%).

Financial Matters $3290 resident tuition and fees (2002–03); $6510 nonresident tuition and fees (2002–03); 60% average percent of need met; $5000 average financial aid amount received per undergraduate (2001–02).

Academics TSUM awards associate, bachelor's, and master's degrees and post-master's certificates. Challenging opportunities include advanced placement credit, accelerated degree programs, student-designed majors, an honors program, double majors, and independent study. Special programs include summer session for credit and Army and Air Force ROTC. The most frequently chosen baccalaureate fields are business/marketing, psychology, and social sciences and history. The faculty at TSUM has 36 full-time members, 97% with terminal degrees. The student-faculty ratio is 20:1.

Students of TSUM The student body totals 3,295, of whom 2,831 are undergraduates. 65.9% are women and 34.1% are men. Students come from 45 states and territories. 99% are from Alabama.

Applying TSUM requires SAT I, a high school transcript, and a minimum high school GPA of 2.0. The school recommends ACT. Application deadline: rolling admissions; 5/1 priority date for financial aid. Early and deferred admission are possible.

TRUMAN STATE UNIVERSITY

Kirksville, MO

Small-town setting ■ *Public* ■ *State-supported* ■ *Coed*

Web site: www.truman.edu
Contact: Mr. Brad Chambers, Co-Director of Admissions, 205 McClain Hall, Kirksville, MO 63501-4221
Telephone: 660-785-4114 or toll-free 800-892-7792 (in-state)
Fax: 660-785-7456
E-mail: admissions@truman.edu

Getting in Last Year 5,132 applied; 79% were accepted; 1,448 enrolled (36%).

Financial Matters $4200 resident tuition and fees (2002–03); $7600 nonresident tuition and fees (2002–03); $4928 room and board; 84% average percent of need met; $5263 average financial aid amount received per undergraduate (2001–02).

Academics Truman awards bachelor's and master's degrees. Challenging opportunities include advanced placement credit, accelerated degree programs, an honors program, double majors, and a senior project. Special programs include internships, summer session for credit, off-campus study, study-abroad, and Army ROTC. The most frequently chosen baccalaureate fields are business/marketing, biological/life sciences, and English. The faculty at Truman has 366 full-time members, 84% with terminal degrees. The student-faculty ratio is 15:1.

Students of Truman The student body totals 5,867, of whom 5,636 are undergraduates. 58.6% are women and 41.4% are men. Students come from 38 states and territories and 49 other countries. 76% are from Missouri. 4.1% are international students.

Applying Truman requires an essay, SAT I or ACT, and a high school transcript. The school recommends ACT, an interview, and a minimum high school GPA of 3.0. Application deadline: 3/1; 4/1 priority date for financial aid. Early and deferred admission are possible.

TUFTS UNIVERSITY
Medford, MA

Suburban setting ■ Private ■ Independent ■ Coed

Web site: www.tufts.edu
Contact: Mr. David D. Cuttino, Dean of Undergraduate Admissions, Bendetson Hall, Medford, MA 02155
Telephone: 617-627-3170 **Fax:** 617-627-3860
E-mail: admissions.inquiry@ase.tufts.edu

Getting in Last Year 14,308 applied; 27% were accepted; 1,276 enrolled (33%).

Financial Matters $28,155 tuition and fees (2002–03); $8310 room and board; 100% average percent of need met; $22,334 average financial aid amount received per undergraduate.

Academics Tufts awards bachelor's, master's, doctoral, and first-professional degrees and post-master's certificates. Challenging opportunities include advanced placement credit, student-designed majors, an honors program, double majors, independent study, and a senior project. Special programs include internships, summer session for credit, off-campus study, study-abroad, and Army, Navy and Air Force ROTC. The most frequently chosen baccalaureate fields are social sciences and history, engineering/engineering technologies, and visual/performing arts. The faculty at Tufts has 716 full-time members. The student-faculty ratio is 9:1.

Students of Tufts The student body totals 9,432, of whom 4,910 are undergraduates. 55.4% are women and 44.6% are men. Students come from 51 states and territories and 65 other countries. 24% are from Massachusetts. 6.8% are international students. 96% returned for their sophomore year.

Applying Tufts requires an essay, SAT I and SAT II or ACT, a high school transcript, and 1 recommendation, and in some cases SAT II: Writing Test. The school recommends an interview. Application deadline: 1/1; 2/15 priority date for financial aid. Early and deferred admission are possible.

TULANE UNIVERSITY
New Orleans, LA

Urban setting ■ Private ■ Independent ■ Coed

Web site: www.tulane.edu
Contact: Ms. Jane Armstrong, Acting Vice President of Enrollment Management, 6823 St Charles Avenue, New Orleans, LA 70118-5669
Telephone: 504-865-5731 or toll-free 800-873-9283 **Fax:** 504-862-8715
E-mail: undergrad.admission@tulane.edu

Getting in Last Year 12,985 applied; 56% were accepted; 1,540 enrolled (21%).

Financial Matters $28,310 tuition and fees (2002–03); $7394 room and board; 94% average percent of need met; $22,948 average financial aid amount received per undergraduate (1999–2000).

Academics Tulane awards associate, bachelor's, master's, doctoral, and first-professional degrees and post-bachelor's certificates. Challenging opportunities include advanced placement credit, accelerated degree programs, student-designed majors, freshman honors college, an honors program, double majors, independent study, and a senior project. Special programs include cooperative education, internships, summer session for credit, off-campus study, study-abroad, and Army, Navy and Air Force ROTC. The most frequently chosen baccalaureate fields are business/marketing, social sciences and history, and engineering/engineering technologies. The faculty at Tulane has 518 full-time members, 88% with terminal degrees. The student-faculty ratio is 10:1.

Students of Tulane The student body totals 12,759, of whom 7,701 are undergraduates. 53.2% are women and 46.8% are men. Students come from 59 states and territories and 108 other countries. 34% are from Louisiana. 2.7% are international students. 83% returned for their sophomore year.

Applying Tulane requires an essay, SAT I or ACT, a high school transcript, and 1 recommendation, and in some cases SAT II Subject Tests. The school recommends SAT II Subject Tests. Application deadline: 1/15; 2/1 for financial aid, with a 1/15 priority date. Early and deferred admission are possible.

TUSCULUM COLLEGE
Greeneville, TN

Small-town setting ■ Private ■ Independent Religious ■ Coed

Web site: www.tusculum.edu
Contact: Mr. George Wolf, Director of Admissions, PO Box 5047, Greeneville, TN 37743-9997
Telephone: 423-636-7300 ext. 611 or toll-free 800-729-0256 **Fax:** 423-638-7166
E-mail: admissions@tusculum.edu

Getting in Last Year 1,381 applied; 76% were accepted; 289 enrolled (28%).

Financial Matters $13,700 tuition and fees (2002–03); $5290 room and board; 72% average percent of need met; $8128 average financial aid amount received per undergraduate (2001–02).

Academics Tusculum awards bachelor's and master's degrees. Challenging opportunities include advanced placement credit, student-designed majors, double majors, independent study, and a senior project. Special programs include internships, summer session for credit, and study-abroad. The most frequently chosen baccalaureate fields are business/marketing, education, and physical sciences. The faculty at Tusculum has 68 full-time members, 56% with terminal degrees. The student-faculty ratio is 15:1.

Students of Tusculum The student body totals 1,886, of whom 1,696 are undergraduates. 52.8% are women and 47.2% are men. Students come from 33 states and territories and 12 other countries. 82% are from Tennessee. 1.9% are international students. 68% returned for their sophomore year.

Applying Tusculum requires an essay, SAT I or ACT, a high school transcript, recommendations, and a minimum high school GPA of 2.0. The school recommends an interview. Application deadline: rolling admissions; 2/1 priority date for financial aid. Early and deferred admission are possible.

TUSKEGEE UNIVERSITY
Tuskegee, AL

Small-town setting ■ Private ■ Independent ■ Coed

Web site: www.tusk.edu
Contact: Ms. Iolantha E. Spencer, Admissions, 102 Old Administration Building, Tuskegee, AL 36088
Telephone: 334-727-8500 or toll-free 800-622-6531

Getting in Last Year 1,902 applied; 81% were accepted; 747 enrolled (49%).

Financial Matters $10,784 tuition and fees (2002–03); $5680 room and board; 85% average percent of need met; $13,666 average financial aid amount received per undergraduate (2001–02).

Academics Tuskegee awards bachelor's, master's, doctoral, and first-professional degrees. Challenging opportunities include an honors program and a senior project. Special programs include cooperative education, internships, summer session for credit, off-campus study, and Army and Air Force ROTC. The most frequently chosen baccalaureate fields are business/marketing, engineering/engineering technologies, and social sciences and history. The faculty at Tuskegee has 218 full-time members, 71% with terminal degrees. The student-faculty ratio is 13:1.

Students of Tuskegee The student body totals 3,001, of whom 2,608 are undergraduates. 57.1% are women and 42.9% are men. Students come from 45 states and territories. 43% are from Alabama. 1% are international students. 74% returned for their sophomore year.

Applying Tuskegee requires SAT I or ACT, a high school transcript, and a minimum high school GPA of 2.0. Application deadline: 4/15; 3/31 priority date for financial aid. Early admission is possible.

TYNDALE COLLEGE & SEMINARY
Toronto, ON Canada

Urban setting ■ Private ■ Independent Religious ■ Coed

Web site: www.tyndale-canada.edu
Contact: Ms. Kathleen Steadman, Assistant Registrar, 25 Ballyconnor Court, Toronto, ON M2M 4B3 Canada
Telephone: 416-226-6620 ext. 6738 or toll-free 800-663-6052 (in-state)
E-mail: enroll@tyndale.ca

Getting in Last Year 326 applied; 63% were accepted.

Financial Matters $6450 tuition and fees (2002–03); $3995 room and board.

Academics Tyndale College & Seminary awards bachelor's, master's, and first-professional degrees. Challenging opportunities include accelerated degree programs, an honors program, and a senior project. Special programs include summer session for credit and off-campus study. The faculty at Tyndale College & Seminary has 14 full-time members, 100% with terminal degrees. The student-faculty ratio is 10:1.

Students of Tyndale College & Seminary The student body totals 1,195, of whom 470 are undergraduates. Students come from 7 states and territories and 12 other countries. 49% returned for their sophomore year.

Applying Tyndale College & Seminary requires an essay, a high school transcript, 2 recommendations, and all post-secondary transcripts, and in some cases an interview. Application deadline: 8/15; 5/1 priority date for financial aid. Deferred admission is possible.

UNION COLLEGE
Barbourville, KY

Small-town setting ■ Private ■ Independent Religious ■ Coed

Web site: www.unionky.edu
Contact: Mr. Andre Washington, Dean of Admission and Financial Aid, 310 College Street, Barbourville, KY 40906
Telephone: 606-546-1220 or toll-free 800-489-8646 **Fax:** 606-546-1667
E-mail: enroll@unionky.edu

Getting in Last Year 594 applied; 51% were accepted; 138 enrolled (45%).

Financial Matters $12,480 tuition and fees (2002–03); $4250 room and board; 77% average percent of need met; $11,294 average financial aid amount received per undergraduate.

Union College (continued)

Academics Union awards bachelor's and master's degrees. Challenging opportunities include advanced placement credit, accelerated degree programs, student-designed majors, double majors, and a senior project. Special programs include cooperative education, internships, summer session for credit, off-campus study, and study-abroad. The most frequently chosen baccalaureate fields are education, business/marketing, and social sciences and history. The faculty at Union has 49 full-time members, 69% with terminal degrees. The student-faculty ratio is 10:1.

Students of Union The student body totals 939, of whom 618 are undergraduates. 50.8% are women and 49.2% are men. Students come from 24 states and territories and 7 other countries. 76% are from Kentucky. 4.5% are international students. 56% returned for their sophomore year.

Applying Union requires SAT I or ACT, a high school transcript, and a minimum high school GPA of 2.0, and in some cases an essay and recommendations. The school recommends an interview. Application deadline: 8/1; 3/15 priority date for financial aid. Early and deferred admission are possible.

UNION COLLEGE

Lincoln, NE

Suburban setting ■ Private ■ Independent Religious ■ Coed

Web site: www.ucollege.edu

Contact: Huda McClelland, Director of Admissions, 3800 South 48th Street, Lincoln, NE 68506-4300

Telephone: 402-486-2504 or toll-free 800-228-4600 (out-of-state) **Fax:** 402-486-2895

E-mail: ucenrol@ucollege.edu

Getting in Last Year 458 applied; 55% were accepted; 184 enrolled (72%).

Financial Matters $12,280 tuition and fees (2002–03); $3484 room and board; 44% average percent of need met; $8376 average financial aid amount received per undergraduate.

Academics Union awards associate and bachelor's degrees. Challenging opportunities include advanced placement credit, accelerated degree programs, student-designed majors, an honors program, double majors, independent study, and a senior project. Special programs include cooperative education, internships, summer session for credit, off-campus study, and study-abroad. The most frequently chosen baccalaureate fields are health professions and related sciences, education, and business/marketing. The faculty at Union has 49 full-time members, 45% with terminal degrees. The student-faculty ratio is 14:1.

Students of Union The student body is made up of 951 undergraduates. 57.3% are women and 42.7% are men. Students come from 41 states and territories and 34 other countries. 23% are from Nebraska. 13.5% are international students. 69% returned for their sophomore year.

Applying Union requires ACT, a high school transcript, 3 recommendations, and a minimum high school GPA of 2.5, and in some cases an interview. The school recommends an essay. Application deadline: rolling admissions; 5/1 priority date for financial aid.

UNION COLLEGE

Schenectady, NY

Suburban setting ■ Private ■ Independent ■ Coed

Web site: www.union.edu

Contact: Mr. Daniel Lundquist, Vice President for Admissions and Financial Aid, Grant Hall, Schenectady, NY 12308

Telephone: 518-388-6112 or toll-free 888-843-6688 (in-state) **Fax:** 518-388-6986

E-mail: admissions@union.edu

Getting in Last Year 3,828 applied; 45% were accepted; 573 enrolled (33%).

Financial Matters $27,514 tuition and fees (2002–03); $6738 room and board; 97% average percent of need met; $22,750 average financial aid amount received per undergraduate (2001–02).

Academics Union College awards bachelor's and master's degrees. Challenging opportunities include advanced placement credit, accelerated degree programs, student-designed majors, an honors program, double majors, independent study, and a senior project. Special programs include cooperative education, internships, summer session for credit, off-campus study, study-abroad, and Army, Navy and Air Force ROTC. The most frequently chosen baccalaureate fields are social sciences and history, business/marketing, and engineering/engineering technologies. The faculty at Union College has 208 full-time members, 94% with terminal degrees. The student-faculty ratio is 11:1.

Students of Union College The student body totals 2,512, of whom 2,147 are undergraduates. 46.6% are women and 53.4% are men. Students come from 34 states and territories and 21 other countries. 46% are from New York. 2.2% are international students. 92% returned for their sophomore year.

Applying Union College requires an essay, SAT I, ACT, or 3 SAT II Subject Tests (including SAT II: Writing Test), a high school transcript, and 2 recommendations. The school recommends an interview. Application deadline: 1/15; 2/1 priority date for financial aid. Early and deferred admission are possible.

UNION INSTITUTE & UNIVERSITY

Cincinnati, OH

Urban setting ■ Private ■ Independent ■ Coed

Web site: www.tui.edu

Contact: Ms. Lisa Schrenger, Director, Admissions, 36 College Street, Montpelier, VT 05602

Telephone: 800-486-3116 or toll-free 800-486-3116

E-mail: admissions@tui.edu

Financial Matters $7291 tuition and fees (2002–03); 70% average percent of need met; $8000 average financial aid amount received per undergraduate (2000–01).

Academics Union awards bachelor's, master's, and doctoral degrees and post-master's certificates. Challenging opportunities include advanced placement credit, accelerated degree programs, student-designed majors, double majors, independent study, and a senior project. Summer session for credit is a special program. The most frequently chosen baccalaureate fields are protective services/public administration, education, and business/marketing. The faculty at Union has 110 full-time members, 92% with terminal degrees. The student-faculty ratio is 16:1.

Students of Union The student body totals 2,801, of whom 1,153 are undergraduates. 68.6% are women and 31.4% are men. Students come from 42 states and territories and 8 other countries. 76% are from Ohio. 1.1% are international students. 62% returned for their sophomore year.

Applying Union requires an essay, a high school transcript, an interview, and 2 recommendations. Application deadline: 10/1; 4/15 priority date for financial aid. Deferred admission is possible.

UNION UNIVERSITY

Jackson, TN

Small-town setting ■ Private ■ Independent Religious ■ Coed

Web site: www.uu.edu

Contact: Mr. Robbie Graves, Director of Enrollment Services, 1050 Union University Drive, Jackson, TN 38305-3697

Telephone: 731-661-5008 or toll-free 800-33-UNION **Fax:** 731-661-5017

E-mail: info@uu.edu

Getting in Last Year 1,011 applied; 88% were accepted; 427 enrolled (48%).

Financial Matters $13,700 tuition and fees (2002–03); $4300 room and board.

Academics Union awards associate, bachelor's, master's, and doctoral degrees and post-master's certificates. Challenging opportunities include advanced placement credit, accelerated degree programs, an honors program, double majors, independent study, and a senior project. Special programs include cooperative education, internships, summer session for credit, off-campus study, and study-abroad. The most frequently chosen baccalaureate fields are business/marketing, health professions and related sciences, and education. The faculty at Union has 146 full-time members, 79% with terminal degrees. The student-faculty ratio is 12:1.

Students of Union The student body totals 2,575, of whom 1,935 are undergraduates. 58.1% are women and 41.9% are men. Students come from 43 states and territories and 27 other countries. 70% are from Tennessee. 2% are international students. 93% returned for their sophomore year.

Applying Union requires SAT I or ACT, a high school transcript, and a minimum high school GPA of 2.5, and in some cases recommendations. The school recommends an essay and an interview. Application deadline: rolling admissions; 1/15 priority date for financial aid. Early and deferred admission are possible.

UNITED STATES AIR FORCE ACADEMY

USAF Academy, CO

Suburban setting ■ Public ■ Federally supported ■ Coed, Primarily Men

Web site: www.usafa.edu/rr

Contact: Mr. Rolland Stoneman, Associate Director of Admissions/Selections, HQ USAFA/RR 2304 Cadet Drive, Suite 200, USAF Academy, CO 80840-5025

Telephone: 719-333-2520 or toll-free 800-443-9266 **Fax:** 719-333-3012

E-mail: rr_webmail@usafa.af.mil

Getting in Last Year 9,041 applied; 17% were accepted; 1,207 enrolled (79%).

Academics USAFA awards bachelor's degrees. Challenging opportunities include advanced placement credit, student-designed majors, double majors, independent study, and a senior project. Special programs include internships, summer session for credit, off-campus study, and study-abroad. The most frequently chosen baccalaureate fields are engineering/engineering technologies, social sciences and history, and business/marketing. The faculty at USAFA has 531 full-time members, 57% with terminal degrees. The student-faculty ratio is 8:1.

Students of USAFA The student body is made up of 4,219 undergraduates. Students come from 54 states and territories and 22 other countries. 5% are from Colorado. 0.9% are international students. 90% returned for their sophomore year.

Applying USAFA requires an essay, SAT I or ACT, a high school transcript, an interview, authorized nomination, and a minimum high school GPA of 2.0. Application deadline: 1/31.

UNITED STATES COAST GUARD ACADEMY

New London, CT

Suburban setting ■ Public ■ Federally supported ■ Coed

Web site: www.cga.edu

Contact: Capt. Susan D. Bibeau, Director of Admissions, 31 Mohegan Avenue, New London, CT 06320-4195

Telephone: 860-444-8500 or toll-free 800-883-8724 **Fax:** 860-701-6700

E-mail: admissions@cga.uscg.mil

Getting in Last Year 4,911 applied; 8% were accepted; 291 enrolled (76%).

Academics USCGA awards bachelor's degrees. Challenging opportunities include an honors program, double majors, independent study, and a senior project. Special programs include cooperative education, internships, summer session for credit, and off-campus study. The most frequently chosen baccalaureate fields are engineering/engineering technologies, social sciences and history, and law/legal studies.

Students of USCGA The student body is made up of 985 undergraduates. 27.8% are women and 72.2% are men. Students come from 49 states and territories. 6% are from Connecticut. 1.8% are international students. 84% returned for their sophomore year.

Applying USCGA requires an essay, SAT I or ACT, a high school transcript, and 3 recommendations. The school recommends an interview. Application deadline: 12/15.

UNITED STATES INTERNATIONAL UNIVERSITY

Nairobi Kenya

Urban setting ■ Private ■ Independent ■ Coed

Web site: www.usiu.ac.ke

Contact: Ms. Susan Topham, Associate Director of Admissions, 10455 Pomerado Road, San Diego, CA 92131-1799

Telephone: 619-635-4772 **Fax:** 619-635-4739

E-mail: admission@usiu.edu

Getting in Last Year 694 applied; 66% were accepted; 359 enrolled (78%).

Financial Matters $235,056 tuition and fees (2002–03); $174,020 room and board.

Academics USIU awards bachelor's and master's degrees. Challenging opportunities include advanced placement credit, accelerated degree programs, and a senior project. Special programs include internships, summer session for credit, and study-abroad. The faculty at USIU has 50 full-time members, 48% with terminal degrees. The student-faculty ratio is 30:1.

Students of USIU The student body totals 2,614, of whom 2,246 are undergraduates. 51.6% are women and 48.4% are men. 91% returned for their sophomore year.

Applying USIU requires an essay, a high school transcript, 1 recommendation, and a minimum high school GPA of 2.0, and in some cases SAT I or ACT. The school recommends an interview and a minimum high school GPA of 3.0. Application deadline: rolling admissions. Deferred admission is possible.

UNITED STATES MERCHANT MARINE ACADEMY

Kings Point, NY

Suburban setting ■ Public ■ Federally supported ■ Coed

Web site: www.usmma.edu

Contact: Capt. James M. Skinner, Director of Admissions, 300 Steamboat Road, Wiley Hall, Kings Point, NY 11024-1699

Telephone: 516-773-5391 or toll-free 866-546-4778 (out-of-state) **Fax:** 516-773-5390

E-mail: admissions@usmma.edu

Getting in Last Year 1,558 applied; 18% were accepted; 282 enrolled (100%).

Academics United States Merchant Marine Academy awards bachelor's degrees. Challenging opportunities include an honors program and a senior project. Internships is a special program. The most frequently chosen baccalaureate field is engineering/engineering technologies. The faculty at United States Merchant Marine Academy has 80 full-time members. The student-faculty ratio is 12:1.

Students of United States Merchant Marine Academy The student body is made up of 943 undergraduates. 11.2% are women and 88.8% are men. Students come from 53 states and territories and 4 other countries. 14% are from New York. 92% returned for their sophomore year.

Applying United States Merchant Marine Academy requires an essay, SAT I or ACT, a high school transcript, and 3 recommendations. The school recommends an interview. Application deadline: 3/1.

UNITED STATES MILITARY ACADEMY

West Point, NY

Small-town setting ■ Public ■ Federally supported ■ Coed, Primarily Men

Web site: www.usma.edu

Contact: Col. Michael C. Jones, Director of Admissions, Building 606, West Point, NY 10996

Telephone: 845-938-4041

E-mail: 8dad@sunams.usma.army.mil

Getting in Last Year 10,844 applied; 11% were accepted.

Academics West Point awards bachelor's degrees. Challenging opportunities include advanced placement credit and double majors. Special programs include summer session for credit and off-campus study. The most frequently chosen baccalaureate fields are engineering/engineering technologies, social sciences and history, and physical sciences. The faculty at West Point has 588 full-time members, 56% with terminal degrees. The student-faculty ratio is 7:1.

Students of West Point The student body is made up of 4,394 undergraduates. Students come from 53 states and territories and 18 other countries. 8% are from New York. 0.7% are international students. 92% returned for their sophomore year.

Applying West Point requires an essay, SAT I or ACT, a high school transcript, 4 recommendations, and medical examination, authorized nomination. The school recommends an interview. Application deadline: 3/21.

UNITED STATES NAVAL ACADEMY

Annapolis, MD

Small-town setting ■ Public ■ Federally supported ■ Coed, Primarily Men

Web site: www.usna.edu

Contact: Col. David A. Vetter, Dean of Admissions, 117 Decatur Road, Annapolis, MD 21402-5000

Telephone: 410-293-4361 **Fax:** 410-293-4348

E-mail: webmail@gwmail.usna.edu

Getting in Last Year 12,331 applied; 12% were accepted; 1,155 enrolled (79%).

Academics Naval Academy awards bachelor's degrees. Challenging opportunities include advanced placement credit, an honors program, double majors, and independent study. Summer session for credit is a special program. The most frequently chosen baccalaureate fields are social sciences and history, engineering/engineering technologies, and physical sciences. The faculty at Naval Academy has 560 full-time members, 60% with terminal degrees. The student-faculty ratio is 7:1.

Students of Naval Academy The student body is made up of 4,309 undergraduates. Students come from 54 states and territories and 17 other countries. 4% are from Maryland. 0.8% are international students. 96% returned for their sophomore year.

Applying Naval Academy requires an essay, SAT I or ACT, a high school transcript, an interview, 2 recommendations, authorized nomination, and a minimum high school GPA of 2.0. Application deadline: 2/15.

UNITY COLLEGE

Unity, ME

Rural setting ■ Private ■ Independent ■ Coed

Web site: www.unity.edu

Contact: Ms. Kay Fiedler, Director of Admissions, PO Box 532, Unity, ME 04988-0532

Telephone: 800-624-1024 **Fax:** 207-948-6277

Getting in Last Year 506 applied; 81% were accepted; 138 enrolled (33%).

Financial Matters $14,250 tuition and fees (2002–03); $5500 room and board; 82% average percent of need met; $11,565 average financial aid amount received per undergraduate.

Academics Unity awards associate and bachelor's degrees. Challenging opportunities include advanced placement credit, accelerated degree programs, student-designed majors, an honors program, independent study, and a senior project. Special programs include cooperative education, internships, summer session for credit, off-campus study, and Army ROTC. The most frequently chosen baccalaureate fields are natural resources/environmental science, parks and recreation, and liberal arts/general studies. The faculty at Unity has 36 full-time members, 64% with terminal degrees. The student-faculty ratio is 12:1.

Students of Unity The student body is made up of 484 undergraduates. 31.4% are women and 68.6% are men. Students come from 21 states and territories and 2 other countries. 38% are from Maine. 0.4% are international students. 98% returned for their sophomore year.

Applying Unity requires an essay, a high school transcript, and 2 recommendations, and in some cases an interview. The school recommends SAT I or ACT, an interview, and a minimum high school GPA of 2.0. Application deadline: rolling admissions. Early and deferred admission are possible.

UNIVERSIDAD ADVENTISTA DE LAS ANTILLAS

Mayagüez, PR

Rural setting ■ Private ■ Independent Religious ■ Coed

Web site: www.uaa.edu

Contact: Prof. Hèctor Acosta, Recruiter, Oficina de Admisiones, PO Box 118, Mayaguez, PR 00681-0118

Telephone: 787-834-9595 ext. 2208 **Fax:** 787-834-9597

E-mail: admissions@uaa.edu

Getting in Last Year 528 applied; 83% were accepted; 185 enrolled (42%).

Financial Matters $4080 tuition and fees (2002–03); $2500 room and board; 70% average percent of need met.

Academics UAA awards associate, bachelor's, and master's degrees. Challenging opportunities include advanced placement credit, double majors, and a senior project. Special programs include cooperative education, internships, and summer session for credit. The most frequently chosen baccalaureate fields are health professions and related sciences, business/marketing, and biological/life sciences. The faculty at UAA has 42 full-time members, 24% with terminal degrees. The student-faculty ratio is 13:1.

Students of UAA The student body totals 811, of whom 785 are undergraduates. 60.3% are women and 39.7% are men. Students come from 10 states and territories and 22 other countries. 76% are from Puerto Rico. 2.7% are international students. 72% returned for their sophomore year.

Applying UAA requires a high school transcript, recommendations, and a minimum high school GPA of 2.0, and in some cases an interview. The school recommends SAT I or ACT and PAA. Early admission is possible.

UNIVERSITÉ DE SHERBROOKE

Sherbrooke, QC Canada

Urban setting ■ Private ■ Independent ■ Coed

Web site: www.usherbrooke.ca

Contact: Ms. Lisa Bedard, Admissions Officer, 2500, Boulevard de l'Université, Sherbrooke, QC J1K 2R1 Canada

Telephone: 819-821-7687 or toll-free 800-267-UDES (in-state)

E-mail: information@usherbrooke.ca

Getting in Last Year 7,820 applied; 73% were accepted.

Financial Matters $1914 resident tuition and fees (2002–03); $4258 nonresident tuition and fees (2002–03); $3384 room and board.

Academics Sherbrooke awards bachelor's, master's, doctoral, and first-professional degrees. Challenging opportunities include accelerated degree programs and student-designed majors. Special programs include cooperative education, internships, summer session for credit, off-campus study, and study-abroad. The faculty at Sherbrooke has 1,014 full-time members.

Students of Sherbrooke The student body totals 12,300, of whom 9,500 are undergraduates. Students come from 3 states and territories and 62 other countries.

Applying Sherbrooke requires a high school transcript, and in some cases an interview and recommendations. Application deadline: 3/1; 3/31 for financial aid. Early admission is possible.

UNIVERSITÉ DU QUÉBEC À TROIS-RIVIÈRES

Trois-Rivières, QC Canada

Urban setting ■ Public ■ Coed

Web site: www.uqtr.ca

Contact: Mrs. Suzanne Camirand, Admissions Officer, 3351 blvd des Forges, Case post 500, Trois-Rivières, QC G9A 5H7 Canada

Telephone: 819-376-5045 or toll-free 800-365-0922 **Fax:** 819-376-5210

E-mail: registraire@uqtr.uquebec.ca

Academics UQTR awards bachelor's, master's, and doctoral degrees. Accelerated degree programs are a challenging opportunity. Special programs include summer session for credit and off-campus study. The faculty at UQTR has 317 full-time members.

Students of UQTR The student body totals 9,618, of whom 8,301 are undergraduates.

Applying UQTR requires Diploma of Collegiate Studies (and transcript) or equivalent, and in some cases an interview. Application deadline: 3/1.

UNIVERSITÉ DU QUÉBEC, ÉCOLE DE TECHNOLOGIE SUPÉRIEURE

Montréal, QC Canada

Urban setting ■ Public ■ Coed, Primarily Men

Web site: www.uquebec.ca

Contact: Mme. Francine Gamache, Registraire, 1100, rue Notre Dame Ouest, Montréal, QC H3C 1K3 Canada

Telephone: 514-396-8885

E-mail: admission@ets.mtl.ca

Getting in Last Year 1,541 applied; 88% were accepted; 816 enrolled (60%).

Academics ETS awards bachelor's, master's, and doctoral degrees. Challenging opportunities include accelerated degree programs and a senior project. Special programs include cooperative education, summer session for credit, and off-campus study. The faculty at ETS has 119 full-time members.

Students of ETS The student body totals 4,262, of whom 3,854 are undergraduates. 10.5% are women and 89.5% are men.

Applying ETS requires Diploma of Collegiate Studies (and transcript) or equivalent. Application deadline: 3/1; 3/1 priority date for financial aid.

UNIVERSITÉ DU QUÉBEC EN OUTAOUAIS

Hull, QC Canada

Small-town setting ■ Public ■ Coed

Web site: www.uqo.ca

Contact: Ms. Line Blais, Admissions Officer, C.P. 1250, Station "B", 101, rue Saint-Jean-Bosco, bureau B-0150, Hull, QC J8X 3X7 Canada

Telephone: 819-595-3900 ext. 1841 **Fax:** 819-773-1835

E-mail: line.blais@uqo.ca

Academics UQAH awards bachelor's, master's, and doctoral degrees. Accelerated degree programs are a challenging opportunity. Special programs include internships, summer session for credit, off-campus study, and study-abroad.

Students of UQAH The student body totals 5,000. 90% returned for their sophomore year.

Applying UQAH requires a high school transcript and Diploma of Collegiate Studies (and transcript) or equivalent, and in some cases an interview. Application deadline: 3/1.

UNIVERSITÉ LAVAL

Québec, QC Canada

Urban setting ■ Private ■ Independent ■ Coed

Web site: www.ulaval.ca

Contact: Mrs. Claire Sormany, Director of Information and Promotion, Universitè Laval, Quèbec, QC G1K 7P4 Canada

Telephone: 877-785-2825 or toll-free 877-785-2825 **Fax:** 418-656-5216

E-mail: sg@sg.ulaval.ca

Getting in Last Year 19,443 applied; 79% were accepted.

Financial Matters $2651 resident tuition and fees (2002–03); $4841 nonresident tuition and fees (2002–03); $8000 room and board.

Academics Université Laval awards associate, bachelor's, master's, doctoral, and first-professional degrees and post-bachelor's and first-professional certificates. Challenging opportunities include accelerated degree programs, student-designed majors, an honors program, and a senior project. Special programs include cooperative education, internships, summer session for credit, off-campus study, and study-abroad. The most frequently chosen baccalaureate fields are business/marketing, engineering/engineering technologies, and foreign language/literature.

Students of Université Laval The student body totals 36,123, of whom 28,429 are undergraduates. 59% are women and 41% are men. Students come from 12 states and territories and 70 other countries. 98% are from Quebec. 83% returned for their sophomore year.

Applying Université Laval requires a high school transcript and general knowledge of French language, and in some cases an essay and an interview. Application deadline: 3/1.

UNIVERSITY AT BUFFALO, THE STATE UNIVERSITY OF NEW YORK

Buffalo, NY

Suburban setting ■ Public ■ State-supported ■ Coed

Web site: www.buffalo.edu

Contact: Ms. Patricia Armstrong, Director of Admissions, Capen Hall, Room 15, North Campus, Buffalo, NY 14260-1660

Telephone: 716-645-6900 or toll-free 888-UB-ADMIT **Fax:** 716-645-6411

E-mail: ub-admissions@buffalo.edu

Getting in Last Year 16,057 applied; 61% were accepted; 3,047 enrolled (31%).

Financial Matters $4850 resident tuition and fees (2002–03); $9750 nonresident tuition and fees (2002–03); $6512 room and board; 69% average percent of need met; $7525 average financial aid amount received per undergraduate.

Academics UB awards associate, bachelor's, master's, doctoral, and first-professional degrees and post-master's and first-professional certificates. Challenging opportunities include advanced placement credit, accelerated degree programs, student-designed majors, freshman honors college, an honors program, double majors, independent study, and a senior project. Special programs include internships, summer session for credit, off-campus study, study-abroad, and Army ROTC. The most frequently chosen baccalaureate fields are business/marketing, social sciences and history, and engineering/engineering technologies. The faculty at UB has 1,248 full-time members, 97% with terminal degrees. The student-faculty ratio is 14:1.

Students of UB The student body totals 26,168, of whom 17,054 are undergraduates. 45.3% are women and 54.7% are men. Students come from 40 states and territories and 83 other countries. 98% are from New York. 5.3% are international students. 85% returned for their sophomore year.

Applying UB requires SAT I or ACT and a high school transcript, and in some cases recommendations and portfolio, audition. Application deadline: rolling admissions; 3/1 priority date for financial aid. Early admission is possible.

UNIVERSITY COLLEGE OF THE CARIBOO

Kamloops, BC Canada

Small-town setting ■ Public ■ Coed

Web site: www.cariboo.bc.ca

Contact: Mr. Josh Keller, Director, Public Relations and Student Recruitment, PO Box 3010, 900 McGill Road, Kamloops, BC V2C 5N3 Canada

Telephone: 250-828-5008 or toll-free 250-828-5071 **Fax:** 250-828-5159

E-mail: jkeller@cariboo.bc.ca

Getting in Last Year 2,210 applied; 57% were accepted.

Financial Matters $2900 nonresident tuition and fees (2002–03); $2600 room only.

Academics University College of the Cariboo awards associate and bachelor's degrees and post-bachelor's certificates. Challenging opportunities include advanced placement credit, an honors program, double majors, independent study, and a senior project. Special programs include cooperative education, internships, summer session for credit, off-campus study, and study-abroad. The most frequently chosen baccalaureate fields are liberal arts/general studies, business/marketing, and protective services/public administration. The faculty at University College of the Cariboo has 419 full-time members, 35% with terminal degrees. The student-faculty ratio is 13:1.

Students of University College of the Cariboo The student body totals 8,400, of whom 4,830 are undergraduates. 61.1% are women and 38.9% are men. Students come from 10 states and territories and 45 other countries. 93% are from British Columbia.

Applying University College of the Cariboo requires a high school transcript, and in some cases an interview and recommendations. Application deadline: 3/1.

UNIVERSITY OF ADVANCING TECHNOLOGY

Tempe, AZ

Urban setting ■ Private ■ Proprietary ■ Coed

Web site: www.uat.edu

Contact: Mr. Dominic Pistillo, President, 2625 West Baseline Road, Tempe, AZ 85283-1042

Telephone: 602-383-8228 or toll-free 602-383-8228 (in-state), 800-658-5744 (out-of-state) **Fax:** 602-383-8222

E-mail: admissions@uact.edu

Financial Matters $10,199 tuition and fees (2002–03).

Academics UAT awards associate, bachelor's, and master's degrees. Accelerated degree programs are a challenging opportunity. The faculty at UAT has 41 full-time members. The student-faculty ratio is 15:1.

Students of UAT The student body totals 726, of whom 710 are undergraduates. 1.5% are international students.

Applying UAT requires SAT I or ACT, a high school transcript, and an interview, and in some cases Wonderlic aptitude test and a minimum high school GPA of 2.5. The school recommends an essay. Application deadline: rolling admissions. Early admission is possible.

THE UNIVERSITY OF AKRON

Akron, OH

Urban setting ■ Public ■ State-supported ■ Coed

Web site: www.uakron.edu

Contact: Ms. Diane Raybuck, Director of Admissions, 381 Buchtel Common, Akron, OH 44325-2001

Telephone: 330-972-6425 or toll-free 800-655-4884 **Fax:** 330-972-7676

E-mail: admissions@uakron.edu

Getting in Last Year 7,945 applied; 85% were accepted; 3,668 enrolled (55%).

Financial Matters $5798 resident tuition and fees (2002–03); $12,612 nonresident tuition and fees (2002–03); $5959 room and board; 51% average percent of need met; $5969 average financial aid amount received per undergraduate.

Academics Akron awards associate, bachelor's, master's, doctoral, and first-professional degrees. Challenging opportunities include advanced placement credit, accelerated degree programs, student-designed majors, an honors program, double majors, independent study, and a senior project. Special programs include cooperative education, internships, summer session for credit, study-abroad, and Army and Air Force ROTC. The most frequently chosen baccalaureate fields are protective services/public administration, business/marketing, and education. The faculty at Akron has 779 full-time members, 82% with terminal degrees. The student-faculty ratio is 17:1.

Students of Akron The student body totals 24,348, of whom 20,182 are undergraduates. 54.9% are women and 45.1% are men. Students come from 32 states and territories and 70 other countries. 98% are from Ohio. 0.8% are international students. 67% returned for their sophomore year.

Applying Akron requires SAT I or ACT and a high school transcript, and in some cases an essay, an interview, and 3 recommendations. Application deadline: 8/15; 3/1 priority date for financial aid. Early and deferred admission are possible.

THE UNIVERSITY OF ALABAMA

Tuscaloosa, AL

Suburban setting ■ Public ■ State-supported ■ Coed

Web site: www.ua.edu

Contact: Dr. Lisa B. Harris, Assistant Vice President for Undergraduate Admissions and Financial Aid, Box 870132, Tuscaloosa, AL 35487-0132

Telephone: 205-348-5666 or toll-free 800-933-BAMA **Fax:** 205-348-9046

E-mail: admissions@ua.edu

Getting in Last Year 7,322 applied; 85% were accepted; 2,654 enrolled (43%).

Financial Matters $3556 resident tuition and fees (2002–03); $9624 nonresident tuition and fees (2002–03); $4232 room and board; 72% average percent of need met; $7622 average financial aid amount received per undergraduate (2001–02).

Academics Alabama awards bachelor's, master's, doctoral, and first-professional degrees and post-master's certificates. Challenging opportunities include advanced placement credit, accelerated degree programs, student-designed majors, freshman honors college, an honors program, double majors, independent study, and a senior project. Special programs include cooperative education, internships, summer session for credit, off-campus study, study-abroad, and Army and Air Force ROTC. The most frequently chosen baccalaureate fields are business/marketing, communications/communication technologies, and education. The faculty at Alabama has 885 full-time members, 92% with terminal degrees. The student-faculty ratio is 18:1.

Students of Alabama The student body totals 19,584, of whom 15,441 are undergraduates. 53.3% are women and 46.7% are men. Students come from 52 states and territories and 81 other countries. 80% are from Alabama. 1.4% are international students. 82% returned for their sophomore year.

Applying Alabama requires SAT I or ACT, a high school transcript, and a minimum high school GPA of 2.0, and in some cases an interview. Application deadline: 7/1; 3/1 priority date for financial aid. Early and deferred admission are possible.

THE UNIVERSITY OF ALABAMA AT BIRMINGHAM

Birmingham, AL

Urban setting ■ Public ■ State-supported ■ Coed

Web site: www.uab.edu

Contact: Ms. Chenise Ryan, Director of Undergraduate Admissions, Office of Undergraduate Admissions, 260 HUC, 1530 3rd Avenue south, Birmingham, AL 35294-1150

Telephone: 205-934-8221 or toll-free 800-421-8743 (in-state) **Fax:** 205-975-7114

E-mail: UndergradAdmit@uab.edu

Getting in Last Year 3,532 applied; 91% were accepted; 1,471 enrolled (46%).

Financial Matters $3880 resident tuition and fees (2002–03); $7810 nonresident tuition and fees (2002–03); $2588 room only; 45% average percent of need met; $8582 average financial aid amount received per undergraduate.

Academics UAB awards bachelor's, master's, doctoral, and first-professional degrees and post-bachelor's and post-master's certificates. Challenging opportunities include advanced placement credit, student-designed majors, an honors program, double majors, independent study, and a senior project. Special programs include cooperative education, internships, summer session for credit, off-campus study, study-abroad, and Army and Air Force ROTC. The most frequently chosen baccalaureate fields are business/marketing, health professions and related sciences, and education. The faculty at UAB has 756 full-time members, 88% with terminal degrees. The student-faculty ratio is 18:1.

Students of UAB The student body totals 15,579, of whom 10,501 are undergraduates. 59.5% are women and 40.5% are men. Students come from 40 states and territories and 77 other countries. 95% are from Alabama. 3.4% are international students. 72% returned for their sophomore year.

Applying UAB requires SAT I or ACT, a high school transcript, and a minimum high school GPA of 2.0. Application deadline: 7/1; 4/1 priority date for financial aid. Early and deferred admission are possible.

THE UNIVERSITY OF ALABAMA IN HUNTSVILLE

Huntsville, AL

Suburban setting ■ Public ■ State-supported ■ Coed

Web site: www.uah.edu

The University of Alabama in Huntsville (continued)

Contact: Ms. Sabrina Williams, Associate Director of Admissions, 301 Sparkman Drive, Huntsville, AL 35899
Telephone: 256-824-6070 or toll-free 800-UAH-CALL **Fax:** 256-824-6073
E-mail: admitme@email.uah.edu

Getting in Last Year 1,537 applied; 91% were accepted; 628 enrolled (45%).

Financial Matters $3764 resident tuition and fees (2002–03); $7940 nonresident tuition and fees (2002–03); $4700 room and board; 54% average percent of need met; $5702 average financial aid amount received per undergraduate.

Academics UAH awards bachelor's, master's, and doctoral degrees and post-bachelor's and post-master's certificates. Challenging opportunities include advanced placement credit, accelerated degree programs, an honors program, double majors, independent study, and a senior project. Special programs include cooperative education, internships, summer session for credit, off-campus study, and Army ROTC. The most frequently chosen baccalaureate fields are engineering/engineering technologies, business/marketing, and health professions and related sciences. The faculty at UAH has 275 full-time members, 91% with terminal degrees. The student-faculty ratio is 15:1.

Students of UAH The student body totals 7,045, of whom 5,598 are undergraduates. 49.9% are women and 50.1% are men. Students come from 49 states and territories and 85 other countries. 87% are from Alabama. 3.7% are international students. 71% returned for their sophomore year.

Applying UAH requires SAT I or ACT and a high school transcript. Application deadline: 8/15; 7/31 for financial aid, with a 4/1 priority date. Early and deferred admission are possible.

UNIVERSITY OF ALASKA ANCHORAGE

Anchorage, AK

Urban setting ■ Public ■ State-supported ■ Coed

Web site: www.uaa.alaska.edu
Contact: Ms. Cecile Mitchell, Director of Enrollment Services, Administration Building, Room 176, Anchorage, AK 99508-8060
Telephone: 907-786-1558 **Fax:** 907-786-4888

Getting in Last Year 2,001 applied; 87% were accepted; 1,327 enrolled (76%).

Financial Matters $3329 resident tuition and fees (2002–03); $8549 nonresident tuition and fees (2002–03); $6030 room and board; 92% average percent of need met; $7614 average financial aid amount received per undergraduate (2001–02).

Academics UAA awards associate, bachelor's, and master's degrees. Challenging opportunities include advanced placement credit, student-designed majors, an honors program, double majors, independent study, and a senior project. Special programs include cooperative education, internships, summer session for credit, off-campus study, study-abroad, and Air Force ROTC. The most frequently chosen baccalaureate fields are business/marketing, education, and protective services/ public administration. The faculty at UAA has 487 full-time members, 64% with terminal degrees. The student-faculty ratio is 18:1.

Students of UAA The student body totals 15,843, of whom 15,091 are undergraduates. 61.2% are women and 38.8% are men. Students come from 50 states and territories and 41 other countries. 95% are from Alaska. 2.6% are international students. 68% returned for their sophomore year.

Applying UAA requires a minimum high school GPA of 2.0, and in some cases SAT I or ACT, ACT ASSET, and a high school transcript. Application deadline: 8/1; 8/1 for financial aid, with a 4/1 priority date. Deferred admission is possible.

UNIVERSITY OF ALASKA FAIRBANKS

Fairbanks, AK

Small-town setting ■ Public ■ State-supported ■ Coed

Web site: www.uaf.edu
Contact: Ms. Nancy Dix, Director, Admissions, PO Box 757480, Fairbanks, AK 99775-7480
Telephone: 907-474-7500 or toll-free 800-478-1823 **Fax:** 907-474-5379
E-mail: fyapply@uaf.edu

Getting in Last Year 1,721 applied; 85% were accepted; 942 enrolled (64%).

Financial Matters $3595 resident tuition and fees (2002–03); $8815 nonresident tuition and fees (2002–03); $4950 room and board; 68% average percent of need met; $8082 average financial aid amount received per undergraduate.

Academics UAF awards associate, bachelor's, master's, and doctoral degrees. Challenging opportunities include advanced placement credit, accelerated degree programs, student-designed majors, an honors program, double majors, independent study, and a senior project. Special programs include cooperative education, internships, summer session for credit, off-campus study, study-abroad, and Army ROTC. The most frequently chosen baccalaureate fields are business/marketing, social sciences and history, and engineering/engineering technologies. The faculty at UAF has 426 full-time members. The student-faculty ratio is 10:1.

Students of UAF The student body totals 7,661, of whom 6,727 are undergraduates. 58.3% are women and 41.7% are men. Students come from 52 states and territories and 26 other countries. 85% are from Alaska. 1.7% are international students. 62% returned for their sophomore year.

Applying UAF requires SAT I or ACT, a high school transcript, and a minimum high school GPA of 2.0. Application deadline: 8/1; 7/1 priority date for financial aid. Early and deferred admission are possible.

UNIVERSITY OF ALASKA SOUTHEAST

Juneau, AK

Small-town setting ■ Public ■ State-supported ■ Coed

Web site: www.uas.alaska.edu
Contact: Mr. Greg Wagner, Director of Admissions, 11120 Glacier Highway, Juneau, AK 99801
Telephone: 907-465-6239 or toll-free 877-465-4827 **Fax:** 907-465-6365
E-mail: jyuas@acadi.alaska.edu

Getting in Last Year 504 applied; 54% were accepted; 168 enrolled (61%).

Financial Matters $2835 resident tuition and fees (2002–03); $8055 nonresident tuition and fees (2002–03); $5400 room and board; 64% average percent of need met; $6082 average financial aid amount received per undergraduate.

Academics UAS awards associate, bachelor's, and master's degrees. Challenging opportunities include advanced placement credit, student-designed majors, independent study, and a senior project. Special programs include cooperative education, internships, summer session for credit, off-campus study, and study-abroad. The faculty at UAS has 91 full-time members, 2% with terminal degrees. The student-faculty ratio is 12:1.

Students of UAS The student body totals 3,470, of whom 3,338 are undergraduates. 63.3% are women and 36.7% are men. Students come from 39 states and territories and 6 other countries. 85% are from Alaska. 1.6% are international students. 62% returned for their sophomore year.

Applying UAS requires SAT I or ACT, a high school transcript, and a minimum high school GPA of 2.0, and in some cases an essay. Application deadline: rolling admissions; 6/1 priority date for financial aid. Early and deferred admission are possible.

UNIVERSITY OF ALBERTA

Edmonton, AB Canada

Urban setting ■ Public ■ Coed

Web site: www.ualberta.ca
Contact: Ms. Carole Byrne, Associate Registrar/Director of Admissions, 201 Administration Building, Edmonton, AB T6G 2M7 Canada
Telephone: 780-492-3113 **Fax:** 780-492-7172
E-mail: registrar@ualberta.ca

Getting in Last Year 14,252 applied; 43% were accepted; 3,793 enrolled (62%).

Financial Matters $4943 nonresident tuition and fees (2002–03); $3828 room and board.

Academics U of A awards bachelor's, master's, doctoral, and first-professional degrees. Challenging opportunities include advanced placement credit, an honors program, double majors, and a senior project. Special programs include cooperative education, internships, summer session for credit, off-campus study, and study-abroad. The most frequently chosen baccalaureate fields are education, health professions and related sciences, and business/marketing. The faculty at U of A has 1,456 members. The student-faculty ratio is 14:1.

Students of U of A The student body totals 33,946, of whom 28,717 are undergraduates. 56.7% are women and 43.3% are men. Students come from 13 states and territories and 110 other countries. 86% are from Alberta.

Applying U of A requires a high school transcript, and in some cases an essay, an interview, and recommendations. The school recommends SAT I, SAT II Subject Tests, and a minimum high school GPA of 2.0. Application deadline: 5/1. Deferred admission is possible.

THE UNIVERSITY OF ARIZONA

Tucson, AZ

Urban setting ■ Public ■ State-supported ■ Coed

Web site: www.arizona.edu
Contact: Ms. Lori Goldman, Director of Admissions, PO Box 210011, Tucson, AZ 85721-0040
Telephone: 520-621-3237 **Fax:** 520-621-9799
E-mail: appinfo@arizona.edu

Getting in Last Year 19,832 applied; 86% were accepted; 5,808 enrolled (34%).

Financial Matters $2593 resident tuition and fees (2002–03); $11,113 nonresident tuition and fees (2002–03); $6568 room and board; $9502 average financial aid amount received per undergraduate (2001–02).

Academics UA awards bachelor's, master's, doctoral, and first-professional degrees and post-bachelor's certificates. Challenging opportunities include advanced placement credit, freshman honors college, an honors program, double majors, independent study, and a senior project. Special programs include internships, summer session for credit, study-abroad, and Army, Navy and Air

Force ROTC. The most frequently chosen baccalaureate fields are business/marketing, social sciences and history, and biological/life sciences. The faculty at UA has 1,375 full-time members, 98% with terminal degrees. The student-faculty ratio is 19:1.

Students of UA The student body totals 36,847, of whom 28,278 are undergraduates. 52.7% are women and 47.3% are men. Students come from 55 states and territories and 130 other countries. 70% are from Arizona. 3.9% are international students.

Applying UA requires SAT I or ACT and a high school transcript, and in some cases an interview, recommendations, and a minimum high school GPA of 3.0. Application deadline: 4/1; 3/1 priority date for financial aid. Early admission is possible.

UNIVERSITY OF ARKANSAS

Fayetteville, AR

Suburban setting ■ Public ■ State-supported ■ Coed

Web site: www.uark.edu

Contact: Mr. Clark Adams, Assistant Director of Admissions, 200 Silas H. Hunt Hall, Fayetteville, AR 72701-1201

Telephone: 479-575-7724 or toll-free 800-377-5346 (in-state), 800-377-8632 (out-of-state) **Fax:** 479-575-7515

E-mail: uofa@uark.edu

Getting in Last Year 5,025 applied; 86% were accepted; 2,251 enrolled (52%).

Financial Matters $4456 resident tuition and fees (2002–03); $10,828 nonresident tuition and fees (2002–03); $4810 room and board; 75% average percent of need met; $8052 average financial aid amount received per undergraduate.

Academics Arkansas awards bachelor's, master's, doctoral, and first-professional degrees. Challenging opportunities include advanced placement credit, accelerated degree programs, freshman honors college, an honors program, double majors, independent study, and a senior project. Special programs include cooperative education, internships, summer session for credit, study-abroad, and Army and Air Force ROTC. The most frequently chosen baccalaureate fields are business/marketing, engineering/engineering technologies, and education. The faculty at Arkansas has 791 full-time members. The student-faculty ratio is 17:1.

Students of Arkansas The student body totals 15,995, of whom 12,889 are undergraduates. 48.8% are women and 51.2% are men. Students come from 50 states and territories and 107 other countries. 89% are from Arkansas. 2.7% are international students. 82% returned for their sophomore year.

Applying Arkansas requires SAT I or ACT and a high school transcript, and in some cases recommendations. The school recommends an essay, 1 recommendation, and a minimum high school GPA of 3.0. Application deadline: 8/15. Early and deferred admission are possible.

UNIVERSITY OF ARKANSAS AT FORT SMITH

Fort Smith, AR

Suburban setting ■ Public ■ State and locally supported ■ Coed

Web site: www.uafortsmith.edu

Contact: Mr. Scott McDonald, Director of Admissions and School Relations, 5210 Grand Avenue, PO Box 3649, Fort Smith, AR 72913-3649

Telephone: 501-788-7125 or toll-free 888-512-5466 **Fax:** 479-788-7016

E-mail: information@uafortsmith.edu

Getting in Last Year 2,033 applied; 100% were accepted; 1,314 enrolled (65%).

Financial Matters $2100 resident tuition and fees (2002–03); $6480 nonresident tuition and fees (2002–03).

Academics University of Arkansas at Fort Smith awards associate and bachelor's degrees. Challenging opportunities include advanced placement credit, accelerated degree programs, and an honors program. Special programs include cooperative education, internships, summer session for credit, off-campus study, and Air Force ROTC. The faculty at University of Arkansas at Fort Smith has 158 full-time members, 20% with terminal degrees. The student-faculty ratio is 20:1.

Students of University of Arkansas at Fort Smith The student body is made up of 6,183 undergraduates. 58.5% are women and 41.5% are men. Students come from 21 states and territories and 4 other countries. 88% are from Arkansas. 0.2% are international students. 55% returned for their sophomore year.

Applying University of Arkansas at Fort Smith requires a high school transcript, and in some cases ACT and ACT ASSET, ACT COMPASS. The school recommends ACT and ACT ASSET, ACT COMPASS. Application deadline: rolling admissions. Early and deferred admission are possible.

UNIVERSITY OF ARKANSAS AT LITTLE ROCK

Little Rock, AR

Urban setting ■ Public ■ State-supported ■ Coed

Web site: www.ualr.edu

Contact: John Noah, Director of Admissions, 2801 South University Avenue, Little Rock, AR 72204-1099

Telephone: 501-569-3127 or toll-free 800-482-8892 (in-state) **Fax:** 501-569-8915

Getting in Last Year 2,320 applied; 96% were accepted; 853 enrolled (38%).

Financial Matters $4210 resident tuition and fees (2002–03); $9827 nonresident tuition and fees (2002–03); $2700 room only; $7190 average financial aid amount received per undergraduate (2001–02).

Academics UALR awards associate, bachelor's, master's, doctoral, and first-professional degrees and post-master's certificates. Challenging opportunities include advanced placement credit, accelerated degree programs, student-designed majors, freshman honors college, an honors program, independent study, and a senior project. Special programs include cooperative education, internships, summer session for credit, off-campus study, study-abroad, and Army ROTC. The most frequently chosen baccalaureate fields are business/marketing, liberal arts/general studies, and protective services/public administration. The faculty at UALR has 438 full-time members, 78% with terminal degrees. The student-faculty ratio is 11:1.

Students of UALR The student body totals 11,488, of whom 9,258 are undergraduates. 61.9% are women and 38.1% are men. Students come from 45 states and territories and 43 other countries. 96% are from Arkansas. 2.4% are international students. 64% returned for their sophomore year.

Applying UALR requires SAT I or ACT, a high school transcript, proof of immunization, and a minimum high school GPA of 2.5. Application deadline: rolling admissions; 3/1 priority date for financial aid. Early and deferred admission are possible.

UNIVERSITY OF ARKANSAS AT MONTICELLO

Monticello, AR

Small-town setting ■ Public ■ State-supported ■ Coed

Web site: www.uamont.edu

Contact: Ms. Mary Whiting, Director of Admissions, PO Box 3600, Monticello, AR 71656

Telephone: 870-460-1026 or toll-free 800-844-1826 (in-state) **Fax:** 870-460-1321

E-mail: admissions@uamont.edu

Getting in Last Year 1,208 applied; 73% were accepted; 547 enrolled (62%).

Financial Matters $3175 resident tuition and fees (2002–03); $6415 nonresident tuition and fees (2002–03); $3100 room and board.

Academics UAM awards associate, bachelor's, and master's degrees and post-bachelor's certificates. Challenging opportunities include advanced placement credit, accelerated degree programs, freshman honors college, and independent study. Special programs include summer session for credit and off-campus study. The most frequently chosen baccalaureate fields are business/marketing, education, and agriculture. The faculty at UAM has 119 full-time members, 55% with terminal degrees. The student-faculty ratio is 18:1.

Students of UAM The student body totals 2,482, of whom 2,316 are undergraduates. 57.6% are women and 42.4% are men. Students come from 20 states and territories and 2 other countries. 91% are from Arkansas. 0.2% are international students. 54% returned for their sophomore year.

Applying UAM requires SAT I or ACT, a high school transcript, and proof of immunization. The school recommends ACT. Application deadline: 8/1. Early and deferred admission are possible.

UNIVERSITY OF ARKANSAS FOR MEDICAL SCIENCES

Little Rock, AR

Urban setting ■ Public ■ State-supported ■ Coed

Web site: www.uams.edu

Contact: Ms. Mona Stiles, Admissions Officer, 4301 West Markham-Slot 601, Little Rock, AR 72205-7199

Telephone: 501-686-5730

Financial Matters $3144 resident tuition and fees (2002–03); $1530 room only; 65% average percent of need met; $3000 average financial aid amount received per undergraduate.

Academics UAMS awards associate, bachelor's, master's, doctoral, and first-professional degrees (bachelor's degree is upper-level). Army ROTC is a special program. The most frequently chosen baccalaureate field is health professions and related sciences.

Students of UAMS The student body totals 2,016, of whom 683 are undergraduates. 85.5% are women and 14.5% are men.

UNIVERSITY OF BALTIMORE

Baltimore, MD

Urban setting ■ Public ■ State-supported ■ Coed

Web site: www.ubalt.edu

Contact: Mrs. Julia Pitman, Director of Admissions, 1420 North Charles St., Baltimore, MD 21201-5779

University of Baltimore (continued)

Telephone: 410-837-4777 or toll-free 877-APPLYUB (in-state)
Fax: 410-837-4793
E-mail: admissions@ubalt.edu

Getting in Last Year 960 applied; 85% were accepted.

Financial Matters $5190 resident tuition and fees (2002–03); $14,398 nonresident tuition and fees (2002–03); $11,210 average financial aid amount received per undergraduate.

Academics UB awards bachelor's, master's, doctoral, and first-professional degrees and post-bachelor's and post-master's certificates. Challenging opportunities include advanced placement credit, accelerated degree programs, student-designed majors, an honors program, independent study, and a senior project. Special programs include cooperative education, internships, summer session for credit, off-campus study, and Army ROTC. The most frequently chosen baccalaureate field is law/legal studies. The faculty at UB has 162 full-time members, 88% with terminal degrees. The student-faculty ratio is 14:1.

Students of UB The student body totals 4,792, of whom 2,008 are undergraduates. 62.4% are women and 37.6% are men. Students come from 12 states and territories and 54 other countries. 93% are from Maryland. 3.7% are international students.

Applying Application deadline: 4/1 priority date for financial aid.

UNIVERSITY OF BRIDGEPORT

Bridgeport, CT

Urban setting ■ Private ■ Independent ■ Coed

Web site: www.bridgeport.edu
Contact: Joseph Marrone, Director of Undergraduate Admissions, 126 Park Avenue, Bridgeport, CT 06604
Telephone: 203-576-4552 or toll-free 800-EXCEL-UB (in-state), 800-243-9496 (out-of-state) **Fax:** 203-576-4941
E-mail: admit@bridgeport.edu

Getting in Last Year 1,500 applied; 87% were accepted; 249 enrolled (19%).

Financial Matters $16,466 tuition and fees (2002–03); $7760 room and board; 75% average percent of need met.

Academics UB awards associate, bachelor's, master's, doctoral, and first-professional degrees and post-master's certificates. Challenging opportunities include advanced placement credit, accelerated degree programs, student-designed majors, an honors program, double majors, independent study, and a senior project. Special programs include cooperative education, internships, summer session for credit, off-campus study, and Army ROTC. The most frequently chosen baccalaureate fields are business/marketing, interdisciplinary studies, and engineering/engineering technologies. The faculty at UB has 86 full-time members, 91% with terminal degrees. The student-faculty ratio is 12:1.

Students of UB The student body totals 3,173, of whom 1,100 are undergraduates. 58% are women and 42% are men. Students come from 37 states and territories and 65 other countries. 61% are from Connecticut. 26.8% are international students. 75% returned for their sophomore year.

Applying UB requires an essay, SAT I or ACT, a high school transcript, and a minimum high school GPA of 2.0, and in some cases SAT II Subject Tests, an interview, and portfolio, audition. The school recommends an interview and 1 recommendation. Application deadline: 4/1; 4/15 priority date for financial aid. Early and deferred admission are possible.

THE UNIVERSITY OF BRITISH COLUMBIA

Vancouver, BC Canada

Urban setting ■ Public ■ Coed

Web site: www.welcome.ubc.ca
Contact: International Student Recruitment and Reception, 1874 East Mall, Vancouver, BC V6T 1Z1 Canada
Telephone: 604-822-8999 or toll-free 877-292-1422 (in-state)
Fax: 604-822-9888
E-mail: international.reception@ubc.ca

Getting in Last Year 18,646 applied; 49% were accepted; 4,953 enrolled (54%).

Financial Matters $2941 nonresident tuition and fees (2002–03); $5500 room and board.

Academics UBC awards bachelor's, master's, doctoral, and first-professional degrees and post-bachelor's certificates. Challenging opportunities include advanced placement credit, student-designed majors, freshman honors college, an honors program, double majors, and a senior project. Special programs include cooperative education, internships, summer session for credit, off-campus study, study-abroad, and Army and Air Force ROTC. The most frequently chosen baccalaureate fields are education, health professions and related sciences, and biological/life sciences. The faculty at UBC has 1,883 full-time members, 98% with terminal degrees. The student-faculty ratio is 15:1.

Students of UBC The student body totals 38,634, of whom 28,030 are undergraduates. 56.3% are women and 43.7% are men. Students come from 12 states and territories and 90 other countries. 90% are from British Columbia.

Applying UBC requires a high school transcript and a minimum high school GPA of 2.6, and in some cases an essay and recommendations. The school recommends SAT I or ACT. Application deadline: 3/31; 9/15 for financial aid, with a 4/15 priority date. Early admission is possible.

UNIVERSITY OF CALGARY

Calgary, AB Canada

Urban setting ■ Public ■ Coed

Web site: www.ucalgary.ca
Contact: Mr. Kevin Paul, Director of Enrollment Services, Office of Admissions, Calgary, AB T2N 1N4 Canada
Telephone: 403-220-6645 **Fax:** 403-220-0762
E-mail: applinfo@ucalgary.ca

Getting in Last Year 6,223 applied; 68% were accepted.

Academics U of C awards bachelor's, master's, and doctoral degrees. Challenging opportunities include advanced placement credit, an honors program, and double majors. Special programs include cooperative education, internships, summer session for credit, and study-abroad. The most frequently chosen baccalaureate field is law/legal studies. The faculty at U of C has 1,541 full-time members. The student-faculty ratio is 13:1.

Students of U of C The student body totals 26,945, of whom 22,879 are undergraduates. 55.3% are women and 44.7% are men. Students come from 12 states and territories and 80 other countries.

Applying U of C requires a high school transcript, and in some cases SAT I, SAT II Subject Tests, and SAT II: Writing Test. Application deadline: 6/1; 6/15 for financial aid. Early admission is possible.

UNIVERSITY OF CALIFORNIA, BERKELEY

Berkeley, CA

Urban setting ■ Public ■ State-supported ■ Coed

Web site: www.berkeley.edu
Contact: Pre-Admission Advising, Office of Undergraduate Admission and Relations With Schools, Berkeley, CA 94720-1500
Telephone: 510-642-3175 **Fax:** 510-642-7333
E-mail: ouars@uclink.berkeley.edu

Getting in Last Year 36,099 applied; 25% were accepted; 3,653 enrolled (41%).

Financial Matters $4200 resident tuition and fees (2002–03); $15,702 nonresident tuition and fees (2002–03); $10,608 room and board; 90% average percent of need met; $11,952 average financial aid amount received per undergraduate.

Academics Cal awards bachelor's, master's, doctoral, and first-professional degrees. Challenging opportunities include advanced placement credit, accelerated degree programs, student-designed majors, an honors program, double majors, independent study, and a senior project. Special programs include internships, summer session for credit, off-campus study, study-abroad, and Army, Navy and Air Force ROTC. The most frequently chosen baccalaureate fields are social sciences and history, biological/life sciences, and engineering/engineering technologies. The faculty at Cal has 1,442 full-time members, 98% with terminal degrees. The student-faculty ratio is 17:1.

Students of Cal The student body totals 33,145, of whom 23,835 are undergraduates. 53.9% are women and 46.1% are men. Students come from 53 states and territories and 100 other countries. 89% are from California. 3.3% are international students. 95% returned for their sophomore year.

Applying Cal requires an essay, SAT II Subject Tests, SAT II: Writing Test, SAT I or ACT, a high school transcript, and minimum 2.8 GPA for California residents; 3.4 for all others. Application deadline: 11/30; 3/2 priority date for financial aid.

UNIVERSITY OF CALIFORNIA, DAVIS

Davis, CA

Suburban setting ■ Public ■ State-supported ■ Coed

Web site: www.ucdavis.edu
Contact: Dr. Gary Tudor, Director of Undergraduate Admissions, Undergraduate Admission and Outreach Services, 175 Mrak Hall, Davis, CA 95616
Telephone: 530-752-2971 **Fax:** 530-752-1280
E-mail: thinkucd@ucdavis.edu

Getting in Last Year 28,794 applied; 63% were accepted; 4,672 enrolled (26%).

Financial Matters $4629 resident tuition and fees (2002–03); $15,808 nonresident tuition and fees (2002–03); $8522 room and board; 77% average percent of need met; $8623 average financial aid amount received per undergraduate.

Academics UC Davis awards bachelor's, master's, doctoral, and first-professional degrees and post-bachelor's certificates. Challenging opportunities include advanced placement credit, student-designed majors, freshman honors college, an honors program, double majors, independent study, and a senior project. Special programs include internships, summer session for credit, study-abroad, and Army and Air Force ROTC. The most frequently chosen baccalaureate fields are social sciences and history, biological/life sciences, and engineering/engineering technologies. The faculty at UC Davis has 1,620 full-time members, 98% with terminal degrees. The student-faculty ratio is 19:1.

Students of UC Davis The student body totals 28,269, of whom 22,661 are undergraduates. 56.2% are women and 43.8% are men. Students come from 49 states and territories and 113 other countries. 96% are from California. 1.6% are international students. 99% returned for their sophomore year.

Applying UC Davis requires an essay, SAT II: Writing Test, SAT I and SAT II or ACT, and a high school transcript. Application deadline: 11/30.

UNIVERSITY OF CALIFORNIA, IRVINE

Irvine, CA

Suburban setting ■ *Public* ■ *State-supported* ■ *Coed*

Web site: www.uci.edu

Contact: Dr. Juan Francisco Lara, Acting Director of Admissions, 204 Administration, Irvine, CA 92697-1075

Telephone: 949-824-6701

Getting in Last Year 30,433 applied; 57% were accepted; 4,027 enrolled (23%).

Financial Matters $4739 resident tuition and fees (2002–03); $17,118 nonresident tuition and fees (2002–03); $7422 room and board; 81% average percent of need met; $10,021 average financial aid amount received per undergraduate.

Academics UCI awards bachelor's, master's, doctoral, and first-professional degrees. Challenging opportunities include advanced placement credit, an honors program, double majors, independent study, and a senior project. Special programs include cooperative education, internships, summer session for credit, off-campus study, study-abroad, and Army and Air Force ROTC. The faculty at UCI has 845 full-time members, 98% with terminal degrees. The student-faculty ratio is 18:1.

Students of UCI The student body totals 23,779, of whom 19,179 are undergraduates. 51.6% are women and 48.4% are men. Students come from 45 states and territories and 41 other countries. 98% are from California. 2.7% are international students. 91% returned for their sophomore year.

Applying UCI requires an essay, SAT II: Writing Test, SAT I and SAT II or ACT, a high school transcript, and a minimum high school GPA of 2.0. Application deadline: 11/30; 3/2 priority date for financial aid.

UNIVERSITY OF CALIFORNIA, LOS ANGELES

Los Angeles, CA

Urban setting ■ *Public* ■ *State-supported* ■ *Coed*

Web site: www.ucla.edu

Contact: Mr. Vu T. Tran, Director of Undergraduate Admissions, 405 Hilgard Avenue, Box 951436, Los Angeles, CA 90095-1436

Telephone: 310-825-3101

E-mail: ugadm@saonet.ucla.edu

Getting in Last Year 43,443 applied; 24% were accepted; 4,257 enrolled (41%).

Financial Matters $4378 resident tuition and fees (2002–03); $16,757 nonresident tuition and fees (2002–03); $9480 room and board; 82% average percent of need met; $10,634 average financial aid amount received per undergraduate.

Academics UCLA awards bachelor's, master's, doctoral, and first-professional degrees. Challenging opportunities include advanced placement credit, student-designed majors, freshman honors college, an honors program, double majors, independent study, and a senior project. Special programs include internships, summer session for credit, off-campus study, study-abroad, and Army, Navy and Air Force ROTC. The most frequently chosen baccalaureate fields are social sciences and history, psychology, and biological/life sciences. The faculty at UCLA has 1,855 full-time members, 98% with terminal degrees. The student-faculty ratio is 17:1.

Students of UCLA The student body totals 37,599, of whom 24,899 are undergraduates. 55.6% are women and 44.4% are men. Students come from 49 states and territories and 66 other countries. 96% are from California. 2.8% are international students. 97% returned for their sophomore year.

Applying UCLA requires an essay, SAT II: Writing Test, SAT I or ACT, SAT II Subject Test in math, third SAT II Subject Test, and a high school transcript. Application deadline: 11/30; 3/2 priority date for financial aid.

UNIVERSITY OF CALIFORNIA, RIVERSIDE

Riverside, CA

Urban setting ■ *Public* ■ *State-supported* ■ *Coed*

Web site: www.ucr.edu

Contact: Ms. Laurie Nelson, Director of Undergraduate Admission, 1138 Hinderaker Hall, Riverside, CA 92521

Telephone: 909-787-3411 **Fax:** 909-787-6344

E-mail: discover@pop.ucr.edu

Getting in Last Year 22,975 applied; 86% were accepted; 3,563 enrolled (18%).

Financial Matters $4421 resident tuition and fees (2002–03); $16,196 nonresident tuition and fees (2002–03); $8232 room and board; 82% average percent of need met; $9274 average financial aid amount received per undergraduate (2001–02).

Academics UCR awards bachelor's, master's, and doctoral degrees. Challenging opportunities include advanced placement credit, accelerated degree programs, student-designed majors, freshman honors college, an honors program, double majors, independent study, and a senior project. Special programs include cooperative education, internships, summer session for credit, off-campus study, study-abroad, and Army and Air Force ROTC. The most frequently chosen baccalaureate fields are business/marketing, social sciences and history, and biological/life sciences. The faculty at UCR has 647 full-time members, 98% with terminal degrees. The student-faculty ratio is 19:1.

Students of UCR The student body totals 15,934, of whom 14,124 are undergraduates. 53.9% are women and 46.1% are men. Students come from 35 states and territories and 22 other countries. 99% are from California. 1.8% are international students. 84% returned for their sophomore year.

Applying UCR requires an essay, SAT II Subject Tests, SAT II: Writing Test, SAT I or ACT, a high school transcript, and a minimum high school GPA of 2.82. Application deadline: 11/30; 3/2 priority date for financial aid. Early admission is possible.

UNIVERSITY OF CALIFORNIA, SAN DIEGO

La Jolla, CA

Suburban setting ■ *Public* ■ *State-supported* ■ *Coed*

Web site: www.ucsd.edu

Contact: Mr. Nathan Evans, Associate Director of Admissions and Relations with Schools, 9500 Gilman Drive, 0021, La Jolla, CA 92093-0021

Telephone: 858-534-4831

E-mail: admissionsinfo@ucsd.edu

Getting in Last Year 41,354 applied; 41% were accepted; 4,242 enrolled (25%).

Financial Matters $4493 resident tuition and fees (2002–03); $20,452 nonresident tuition and fees (2002–03); $8066 room and board; 97% average percent of need met; $10,407 average financial aid amount received per undergraduate (2001–02 estimated).

Academics UCSD awards bachelor's, master's, doctoral, and first-professional degrees. Challenging opportunities include advanced placement credit, accelerated degree programs, student-designed majors, freshman honors college, an honors program, double majors, independent study, and a senior project. Special programs include cooperative education, internships, summer session for credit, off-campus study, study-abroad, and Army and Navy ROTC. The faculty at UCSD has 917 full-time members, 98% with terminal degrees. The student-faculty ratio is 19:1.

Students of UCSD The student body totals 23,548, of whom 19,087 are undergraduates. 51.9% are women and 48.1% are men. 97% are from California. 93% returned for their sophomore year.

Applying UCSD requires an essay, SAT I or ACT, 3 SAT II Subject Tests (including SAT II: Writing Test), a high school transcript, and a minimum high school GPA of 2.8, and in some cases a minimum high school GPA of 3.4. Application deadline: 11/30; 3/2 priority date for financial aid.

UNIVERSITY OF CALIFORNIA, SANTA BARBARA

Santa Barbara, CA

Suburban setting ■ *Public* ■ *State-supported* ■ *Coed*

Web site: www.ucsb.edu

Contact: Ms. Christine Van Gieson, Director of Admissions/Outreach Services, 1234 Cheadle Hall, Santa Barbara, CA 93106-2014

Telephone: 805-893-2485 **Fax:** 805-893-2676

E-mail: appinfo@sa.ucsb.edu

Getting in Last Year 34,703 applied; 51% were accepted; 3,839 enrolled (22%).

Financial Matters $3853 resident tuition and fees (2002–03); $15,862 nonresident tuition and fees (2002–03); $8680 room and board; 87% average percent of need met; $8851 average financial aid amount received per undergraduate (2001–02).

Academics UCSB awards bachelor's, master's, and doctoral degrees. Challenging opportunities include advanced placement credit, accelerated degree programs, student-designed majors, an honors program, double majors, independent study, and a senior project. Special programs include cooperative education, internships, summer session for credit, off-campus study, study-abroad, and Army ROTC. The most frequently chosen baccalaureate fields are social sciences and history, business/marketing, and biological/life sciences. The faculty at UCSB has 835 full-time members. The student-faculty ratio is 19:1.

Students of UCSB The student body totals 20,559, of whom 17,714 are undergraduates. 53.9% are women and 46.1% are men. Students come from 41 states and territories and 110 other countries. 95% are from California. 1.3% are international students. 91% returned for their sophomore year.

Applying UCSB requires an essay, SAT II Subject Tests, SAT II: Writing Test, SAT I or ACT, and a high school transcript, and in some cases an interview. Application deadline: 11/30; 3/2 priority date for financial aid.

UNIVERSITY OF CALIFORNIA, SANTA CRUZ

Santa Cruz, CA

Small-town setting ■ Public ■ State-supported ■ Coed

Web site: www.ucsc.edu
Contact: Mr. Kevin M. Browne, Executive Director of Admissions and University Registrar, Admissions Office, Cook House, Santa Cruz, CA 95064
Telephone: 831-459-5779 **Fax:** 831-459-4452
E-mail: admissions@ucsc.edu

Getting in Last Year 20,616 applied; 80% were accepted; 3,221 enrolled (19%).

Financial Matters $4300 resident tuition and fees (2002–03); $16,679 nonresident tuition and fees (2002–03); $9355 room and board; 90% average percent of need met; $11,124 average financial aid amount received per undergraduate.

Academics UCSC awards bachelor's, master's, and doctoral degrees. Challenging opportunities include advanced placement credit, student-designed majors, freshman honors college, an honors program, double majors, independent study, and a senior project. Special programs include cooperative education, internships, summer session for credit, off-campus study, study-abroad, and Army, Navy and Air Force ROTC. The most frequently chosen baccalaureate fields are biological/life sciences, visual/performing arts, and psychology. The faculty at UCSC has 485 full-time members. The student-faculty ratio is 19:1.

Students of UCSC The student body totals 14,139, of whom 12,881 are undergraduates. 56.2% are women and 43.8% are men. 94% are from California. 1.1% are international students. 87% returned for their sophomore year.

Applying UCSC requires an essay, SAT I or ACT, and a high school transcript. Application deadline: 11/30; 3/2 priority date for financial aid.

UNIVERSITY OF CENTRAL ARKANSAS

Conway, AR

Small-town setting ■ Public ■ State-supported ■ Coed

Web site: www.uca.edu
Contact: Ms. Penny Hatfield, Director of Admissions, 201 Donaghey Avenue, Conway, AR 72035-0001
Telephone: 501-450-5145 or toll-free 800-243-8245 (in-state) **Fax:** 501-450-5228
E-mail: admissons@mail.uca.edu

Getting in Last Year 3,622 applied; 83% were accepted; 1,787 enrolled (59%).

Financial Matters $3990 resident tuition and fees (2002–03); $7302 nonresident tuition and fees (2002–03); $3600 room and board.

Academics UCA awards associate, bachelor's, master's, and doctoral degrees and post-bachelor's and post-master's certificates. Challenging opportunities include advanced placement credit, accelerated degree programs, freshman honors college, an honors program, double majors, independent study, and a senior project. Special programs include cooperative education, internships, summer session for credit, study-abroad, and Army ROTC. The most frequently chosen baccalaureate fields are business/marketing, health professions and related sciences, and education. The faculty at UCA has 390 full-time members, 71% with terminal degrees. The student-faculty ratio is 18:1.

Students of UCA The student body totals 8,553, of whom 7,663 are undergraduates. 59.4% are women and 40.6% are men. Students come from 36 states and territories and 53 other countries. 92% are from Arkansas. 2.5% are international students. 66% returned for their sophomore year.

Applying UCA requires SAT I or ACT and a high school transcript, and in some cases a minimum high school GPA of 2.75. Application deadline: rolling admissions; 2/15 priority date for financial aid. Early and deferred admission are possible.

UNIVERSITY OF CENTRAL FLORIDA

Orlando, FL

Suburban setting ■ Public ■ State-supported ■ Coed

Web site: www.ucf.edu
Contact: Undergraduate Admissions Office, PO Box 160111, Orlando, FL 32816
Telephone: 407-823-2000 **Fax:** 407-823-5625
E-mail: admission@mail.ucf.edu

Getting in Last Year 19,307 applied; 62% were accepted; 5,621 enrolled (47%).

Financial Matters $2820 resident tuition and fees (2002–03); $12,229 nonresident tuition and fees (2002–03); $6212 room and board; 77% average percent of need met; $7109 average financial aid amount received per undergraduate.

Academics UCF awards associate, bachelor's, master's, and doctoral degrees and post-bachelor's certificates. Challenging opportunities include advanced placement credit, accelerated degree programs, student-designed majors, freshman honors college, an honors program, double majors, independent study, and a senior project. Special programs include cooperative education, internships, summer session for credit, off-campus study, study-abroad, and Army and Air Force ROTC. The most frequently chosen baccalaureate fields are business/marketing, education, and health professions and related sciences. The faculty at UCF has 1,093 full-time members, 78% with terminal degrees. The student-faculty ratio is 24:1.

Students of UCF The student body totals 38,598, of whom 32,044 are undergraduates. 54.9% are women and 45.1% are men. Students come from 52 states and territories and 105 other countries. 94% are from Florida. 1.2% are international students. 79% returned for their sophomore year.

Applying UCF requires SAT I or ACT, a high school transcript, and a minimum high school GPA of 2.0. The school recommends an essay. Application deadline: 5/1; 6/30 for financial aid, with a 3/1 priority date. Early admission is possible.

UNIVERSITY OF CENTRAL OKLAHOMA

Edmond, OK

Suburban setting ■ Public ■ State-supported ■ Coed

Web site: www.ucok.edu
Contact: Ms. Linda Lofton, Director, Admissions and Records Processing, Office of Enrollment Services, 100 North University Drive, Box 151, Edmond, OK 73034
Telephone: 405-974-2338 ext. 2338 or toll-free 800-254-4215 (in-state) **Fax:** 405-341-4964
E-mail: admituco@ucok.edu

Getting in Last Year 6,701 applied; 96% were accepted; 2,045 enrolled (32%).

Financial Matters $2210 resident tuition and fees (2002–03); $5203 nonresident tuition and fees (2002–03); $3600 room and board; 75% average percent of need met; $5000 average financial aid amount received per undergraduate (2001–02).

Academics UCO awards bachelor's and master's degrees. Challenging opportunities include advanced placement credit, accelerated degree programs, an honors program, double majors, independent study, and a senior project. Special programs include internships, summer session for credit, and Army ROTC. The most frequently chosen baccalaureate fields are business/marketing, education, and law/legal studies. The faculty at UCO has 377 full-time members, 76% with terminal degrees. The student-faculty ratio is 20:1.

Students of UCO The student body totals 14,099, of whom 11,790 are undergraduates. 57.2% are women and 42.8% are men. Students come from 38 states and territories and 108 other countries. 98% are from Oklahoma. 10% are international students. 57% returned for their sophomore year.

Applying UCO requires SAT I or ACT, a high school transcript, rank in upper 50% of high school class, and a minimum high school GPA of 2.7. Application deadline: rolling admissions. Deferred admission is possible.

UNIVERSITY OF CHARLESTON

Charleston, WV

Urban setting ■ Private ■ Independent ■ Coed

Web site: www.uchaswv.edu
Contact: Ms. Kim Scranage, Director of Admissions, 2300 MacCorkle Avenue, SE, Charleston, WV 25304
Telephone: 304-357-4800 or toll-free 800-995-GOUC **Fax:** 304-357-4781
E-mail: admissions@ucwv.edu

Getting in Last Year 1,438 applied; 69% were accepted; 165 enrolled (17%).

Financial Matters $16,500 tuition and fees (2002–03); $4850 room and board; 82% average percent of need met; $13,794 average financial aid amount received per undergraduate.

Academics UC awards associate, bachelor's, and master's degrees. Challenging opportunities include advanced placement credit, accelerated degree programs, student-designed majors, double majors, independent study, and a senior project. Special programs include internships, summer session for credit, study-abroad, and Army ROTC. The most frequently chosen baccalaureate fields are health professions and related sciences, business/marketing, and parks and recreation. The faculty at UC has 68 full-time members, 57% with terminal degrees. The student-faculty ratio is 15:1.

Students of UC The student body totals 1,004, of whom 955 are undergraduates. 69.6% are women and 30.4% are men. Students come from 27 states and territories and 26 other countries. 86% are from West Virginia. 5.2% are international students. 66% returned for their sophomore year.

Applying UC requires SAT I or ACT, a high school transcript, and a minimum high school GPA of 2.25. The school recommends an essay and recommendations. Application deadline: rolling admissions; 3/1 priority date for financial aid. Early and deferred admission are possible.

UNIVERSITY OF CHICAGO

Chicago, IL

Urban setting ■ Private ■ Independent ■ Coed

Web site: www.uchicago.edu
Contact: Mr. Theodore O'Neill, Dean of Admissions, 1116 East 59th Street, Chicago, IL 60637-1513
Telephone: 773-702-8650 **Fax:** 773-702-4199

Getting in Last Year 8,162 applied; 42% were accepted; 1,081 enrolled (32%).

Financial Matters $27,825 tuition and fees (2002–03); $8728 room and board.

Academics Chicago awards bachelor's, master's, doctoral, and first-professional degrees. Challenging opportunities include advanced placement credit, accelerated degree programs, student-designed majors, double majors, independent study, and a senior project. Special programs include internships, summer session for credit, off-campus study, study-abroad, and Army and Air Force ROTC. The most frequently chosen baccalaureate fields are social sciences and history, biological/life sciences, and English. The faculty at Chicago has 1,595 full-time members. The student-faculty ratio is 4:1.

Students of Chicago The student body totals 12,576, of whom 4,075 are undergraduates. 50.5% are women and 49.5% are men. Students come from 52 states and territories and 49 other countries. 22% are from Illinois. 7% are international students. 95% returned for their sophomore year.

Applying Chicago requires an essay, SAT I or ACT, a high school transcript, and 3 recommendations. The school recommends an interview. Application deadline: 1/1; 2/1 priority date for financial aid. Early and deferred admission are possible.

UNIVERSITY OF CINCINNATI

Cincinnati, OH

Urban setting ■ Public ■ State-supported ■ Coed

Web site: www.uc.edu

Contact: Terry Davis, Director of Admissions, 2624 Clifton Avenue, Cincinnati, OH 45221

Telephone: 513-556-1100 **Fax:** 513-556-1105

E-mail: admissions@uc.edu

Getting in Last Year 9,899 applied; 88% were accepted; 3,943 enrolled (45%).

Financial Matters $6936 resident tuition and fees (2002–03); $17,310 nonresident tuition and fees (2002–03); $6774 room and board; 60% average percent of need met; $7125 average financial aid amount received per undergraduate.

Academics UC awards associate, bachelor's, master's, doctoral, and first-professional degrees and post-bachelor's certificates. Challenging opportunities include advanced placement credit, accelerated degree programs, an honors program, double majors, and independent study. Special programs include cooperative education, internships, summer session for credit, off-campus study, study-abroad, and Army and Air Force ROTC. The most frequently chosen baccalaureate fields are business/marketing, engineering/engineering technologies, and social sciences and history. The faculty at UC has 1,333 full-time members, 58% with terminal degrees. The student-faculty ratio is 18:1.

Students of UC The student body totals 26,552, of whom 19,204 are undergraduates. 48.8% are women and 51.2% are men. Students come from 46 states and territories and 50 other countries. 93% are from Ohio. 1% are international students. 70% returned for their sophomore year.

Applying UC requires SAT I or ACT and a high school transcript, and in some cases 2 recommendations and audition. The school recommends ACT and an interview. Application deadline: rolling admissions.

UNIVERSITY OF COLORADO AT BOULDER

Boulder, CO

Suburban setting ■ Public ■ State-supported ■ Coed

Web site: www.colorado.edu

Contact: Mr. Kevin MacLennan, Associate Director, 552 UCB, Boulder, CO 80309-0552

Telephone: 303-492-1394 **Fax:** 303-492-7115

E-mail: apply@colorado.edu

Getting in Last Year 19,152 applied; 80% were accepted; 5,467 enrolled (36%).

Financial Matters $3575 resident tuition and fees (2002–03); $18,919 nonresident tuition and fees (2002–03); $6272 room and board; 75% average percent of need met; $9434 average financial aid amount received per undergraduate (2001–02).

Academics CU-Boulder awards bachelor's, master's, doctoral, and first-professional degrees. Challenging opportunities include advanced placement credit, accelerated degree programs, student-designed majors, freshman honors college, an honors program, double majors, independent study, and a senior project. Special programs include cooperative education, internships, summer session for credit, off-campus study, study-abroad, and Army, Navy and Air Force ROTC. The most frequently chosen baccalaureate fields are social sciences and history, business/marketing, and communications/communication technologies. The faculty at CU-Boulder has 1,225 full-time members, 85% with terminal degrees. The student-faculty ratio is 16:1.

Students of CU-Boulder The student body totals 30,983, of whom 25,158 are undergraduates. 47.2% are women and 52.8% are men. Students come from 53 states and territories and 100 other countries. 67% are from Colorado. 1.4% are international students. 82% returned for their sophomore year.

Applying CU-Boulder requires an essay, SAT I or ACT, a high school transcript, and a minimum high school GPA of 2.0, and in some cases audition for music program. The school recommends recommendations and a minimum high school GPA of 3.0. Application deadline: 1/15; 4/1 priority date for financial aid. Deferred admission is possible.

UNIVERSITY OF COLORADO AT COLORADO SPRINGS

Colorado Springs, CO

Suburban setting ■ Public ■ State-supported ■ Coed

Web site: www.uccs.edu

Contact: Mr. James Tidwell, Assistant Admissions Director, PO Box 7150, Colorado Springs, CO 80933-7150

Telephone: 719-262-3383 or toll-free 800-990-8227 ext. 3383 **Fax:** 719-262-3116

E-mail: admrec@uccs.edu

Getting in Last Year 2,551 applied; 74% were accepted; 726 enrolled (38%).

Financial Matters $4082 resident tuition and fees (2002–03); $17,306 nonresident tuition and fees (2002–03); $5893 room and board; 59% average percent of need met; $6875 average financial aid amount received per undergraduate.

Academics CU-Colorado Springs awards bachelor's, master's, and doctoral degrees. Challenging opportunities include advanced placement credit, accelerated degree programs, double majors, independent study, and a senior project. Special programs include cooperative education, internships, summer session for credit, and Army ROTC. The most frequently chosen baccalaureate fields are business/marketing, social sciences and history, and psychology. The faculty at CU-Colorado Springs has 265 full-time members, 87% with terminal degrees. The student-faculty ratio is 16:1.

Students of CU-Colorado Springs The student body totals 7,407, of whom 5,649 are undergraduates. 61.1% are women and 38.9% are men. Students come from 44 states and territories and 26 other countries. 93% are from Colorado. 63% returned for their sophomore year.

Applying CU-Colorado Springs requires SAT I or ACT and a high school transcript. Application deadline: 7/1; 4/1 priority date for financial aid. Deferred admission is possible.

UNIVERSITY OF COLORADO AT DENVER

Denver, CO

Urban setting ■ Public ■ State-supported ■ Coed

Web site: www.cudenver.edu

Contact: Ms. Barbara Edwards, Director of Admissions, PO Box 173364, Cmapus Box 167, Denver, CO 80217

Telephone: 303-556-3287 **Fax:** 303-556-4838

Getting in Last Year 1,778 applied; 70% were accepted.

Financial Matters $3240 resident tuition and fees (2002–03); $13,814 nonresident tuition and fees (2002–03); 70% average percent of need met; $6628 average financial aid amount received per undergraduate (2001–02).

Academics UCD awards bachelor's, master's, and doctoral degrees. Challenging opportunities include advanced placement credit, accelerated degree programs, student-designed majors, an honors program, double majors, independent study, and a senior project. Special programs include cooperative education, internships, summer session for credit, off-campus study, study-abroad, and Army and Air Force ROTC. The most frequently chosen baccalaureate fields are business/marketing, social sciences and history, and psychology. The faculty at UCD has 482 full-time members, 83% with terminal degrees. The student-faculty ratio is 14:1.

Students of UCD 78% returned for their sophomore year.

Applying UCD requires SAT I or ACT, a high school transcript, and a minimum high school GPA of 2.5. Application deadline: 7/22; 3/31 priority date for financial aid. Deferred admission is possible.

UNIVERSITY OF COLORADO HEALTH SCIENCES CENTER

Denver, CO

Urban setting ■ Public ■ State-supported ■ Coed

Web site: www.uchsc.edu

Contact: Dr. Lynn Mason, Director of Admissions, A-054, 4200 East 9th Avenue, Denver, CO 80262

Telephone: 303-315-7676 **Fax:** 303-315-3358

Getting in Last Year 793 applied; 35% were accepted.

Financial Matters $5392 resident tuition and fees (2002–03); $18,253 nonresident tuition and fees (2002–03); $14,685 average financial aid amount received per undergraduate (2001–02).

Academics UCHSC awards bachelor's, master's, doctoral, and first-professional degrees and post-master's and first-professional certificates. Advanced placement credit is a challenging opportunity. Special programs include internships and summer session for credit. The most frequently chosen baccalaureate field is health professions and related sciences. The faculty at UCHSC has 1,700 members.

Students of UCHSC The student body totals 2,323, of whom 430 are undergraduates. 84.7% are women and 15.3% are men. 90% are from Colorado. 99% returned for their sophomore year.

Applying UCHSC requires an essay, and in some cases an interview.

UNIVERSITY OF CONNECTICUT

Storrs, CT

Rural setting ■ Public ■ State-supported ■ Coed

Web site: www.uconn.edu
Contact: Mr. Brian Usher, Associate Director of Admissions, 2131 Hillside Road, Unit 3088, Storrs, CT 06269-3088
Telephone: 860-486-3137 **Fax:** 860-486-1476
E-mail: beahusky@uconnvm.uconn.edu

Getting in Last Year 13,760 applied; 62% were accepted; 3,186 enrolled (37%).

Financial Matters $6154 resident tuition and fees (2002–03); $15,849 nonresident tuition and fees (2002–03); $6542 room and board; 79% average percent of need met; $8313 average financial aid amount received per undergraduate.

Academics UCONN awards associate, bachelor's, master's, doctoral, and first-professional degrees and post-bachelor's and post-master's certificates. Challenging opportunities include advanced placement credit, accelerated degree programs, student-designed majors, an honors program, double majors, independent study, and a senior project. Special programs include cooperative education, internships, summer session for credit, off-campus study, study-abroad, and Army and Air Force ROTC. The most frequently chosen baccalaureate fields are business/marketing, social sciences and history, and liberal arts/general studies. The faculty at UCONN has 886 full-time members, 95% with terminal degrees. The student-faculty ratio is 17:1.

Students of UCONN The student body totals 21,427, of whom 14,716 are undergraduates. 52.4% are women and 47.6% are men. Students come from 49 states and territories and 59 other countries. 77% are from Connecticut. 1% are international students. 88% returned for their sophomore year.

Applying UCONN requires an essay, SAT I or ACT, and a high school transcript. The school recommends 1 recommendation. Application deadline: 3/1; 3/1 priority date for financial aid. Early and deferred admission are possible.

UNIVERSITY OF DALLAS

Irving, TX

Suburban setting ■ Private ■ Independent Religious ■ Coed

Web site: www.udallas.edu
Contact: Mr. Curt Eley, Dean of Enrollment Management, 1845 East Northgate Drive, Irving, TX 75062-4799
Telephone: 972-721-5266 or toll-free 800-628-6999 **Fax:** 972-721-5017
E-mail: ugadmis@mailadmin.udallas.edu

Getting in Last Year 1,183 applied; 90% were accepted; 308 enrolled (29%).

Financial Matters $17,024 tuition and fees (2002–03); $6304 room and board; 77% average percent of need met; $14,409 average financial aid amount received per undergraduate (2001–02).

Academics UD awards bachelor's, master's, and doctoral degrees. Challenging opportunities include advanced placement credit, accelerated degree programs, student-designed majors, double majors, independent study, and a senior project. Special programs include internships, summer session for credit, off-campus study, study-abroad, and Army and Air Force ROTC. The most frequently chosen baccalaureate fields are social sciences and history, biological/life sciences, and English. The faculty at UD has 130 full-time members, 90% with terminal degrees. The student-faculty ratio is 11:1.

Students of UD The student body totals 3,170, of whom 1,218 are undergraduates. 56.2% are women and 43.8% are men. Students come from 50 states and territories and 18 other countries. 59% are from Texas. 1.9% are international students. 78% returned for their sophomore year.

Applying UD requires an essay, SAT I or ACT, a high school transcript, and 1 recommendation, and in some cases an interview. The school recommends an interview. Application deadline: 8/1; 3/1 priority date for financial aid. Early and deferred admission are possible.

UNIVERSITY OF DAYTON

Dayton, OH

Suburban setting ■ Private ■ Independent Religious ■ Coed

Web site: www.udayton.edu
Contact: Mr. Robert F. Durkle, Director of Admission, 300 College Park, Dayton, OH 45469-1300
Telephone: 937-229-4411 or toll-free 800-837-7433 **Fax:** 937-229-4729
E-mail: admission@udayton.edu

Getting in Last Year 7,496 applied; 84% were accepted; 1,666 enrolled (26%).

Financial Matters $18,000 tuition and fees (2002–03); $5600 room and board; 79% average percent of need met; $9410 average financial aid amount received per undergraduate (2001–02).

Academics UD awards bachelor's, master's, doctoral, and first-professional degrees. Challenging opportunities include advanced placement credit, accelerated degree programs, an honors program, double majors, independent study, and a senior project. Special programs include cooperative education, internships, summer session for credit, off-campus study, study-abroad, and Army and Air Force ROTC. The most frequently chosen baccalaureate fields are business/marketing, engineering/engineering technologies, and education. The faculty at UD has 407 full-time members, 95% with terminal degrees. The student-faculty ratio is 15:1.

Students of UD The student body totals 10,126, of whom 7,085 are undergraduates. 50.1% are women and 49.9% are men. Students come from 48 states and territories and 29 other countries. 67% are from Ohio. 0.7% are international students. 89% returned for their sophomore year.

Applying UD requires SAT I or ACT, a high school transcript, and 1 recommendation, and in some cases audition required for music, music therapy, music education programs. The school recommends an essay and an interview. Application deadline: 3/31 priority date for financial aid. Deferred admission is possible.

UNIVERSITY OF DELAWARE

Newark, DE

Small-town setting ■ Public ■ State-related ■ Coed

Web site: www.udel.edu
Contact: Mr. Lou Hirsh, Deputy Director of Admissions, 116 Hullihen Hall, Newark, DE 19716
Telephone: 302-831-8123 **Fax:** 302-831-6905
E-mail: admissions@udel.edu

Getting in Last Year 20,365 applied; 48% were accepted; 3,349 enrolled (35%).

Financial Matters $5640 resident tuition and fees (2002–03); $15,170 nonresident tuition and fees (2002–03); $5822 room and board; 82% average percent of need met; $9750 average financial aid amount received per undergraduate.

Academics Delaware awards associate, bachelor's, master's, and doctoral degrees (enrollment data for undergraduate students does not include non-degree-seeking students). Challenging opportunities include advanced placement credit, accelerated degree programs, student-designed majors, an honors program, double majors, independent study, and a senior project. Special programs include cooperative education, internships, summer session for credit, study-abroad, and Army and Air Force ROTC. The most frequently chosen baccalaureate fields are business/marketing, social sciences and history, and education. The faculty at Delaware has 1,119 full-time members, 85% with terminal degrees. The student-faculty ratio is 12:1.

Students of Delaware The student body totals 20,676, of whom 17,486 are undergraduates. 58.5% are women and 41.5% are men. Students come from 52 states and territories and 100 other countries. 41% are from Delaware. 1.1% are international students. 88% returned for their sophomore year.

Applying Delaware requires an essay, SAT I or ACT, a high school transcript, and 1 recommendation. The school recommends SAT II Subject Tests and SAT II: Writing Test. Application deadline: 2/15; 2/1 priority date for financial aid. Deferred admission is possible.

UNIVERSITY OF DENVER

Denver, CO

Suburban setting ■ Private ■ Independent ■ Coed

Web site: www.du.edu
Contact: Ms. Colleen Hillmeyer, Director of New Student Programs, University Park, Denver, CO 80208
Telephone: 303-871-2782 or toll-free 800-525-9495 (out-of-state) **Fax:** 303-871-3301
E-mail: admission@du.edu

Getting in Last Year 4,305 applied; 87% were accepted; 1,021 enrolled (27%).

Financial Matters $23,259 tuition and fees (2002–03); $6987 room and board; 89% average percent of need met; $19,074 average financial aid amount received per undergraduate (2001–02).

Academics DU awards bachelor's, master's, doctoral, and first-professional degrees. Challenging opportunities include advanced placement credit, accelerated degree programs, student-designed majors, freshman honors college, an honors program, double majors, independent study, and a senior project. Special programs include cooperative education, internships, summer session for credit, study-abroad, and Army and Air Force ROTC. The most frequently chosen baccalaureate fields are business/marketing, communications/communication technologies, and social sciences and history. The faculty at DU has 425 full-time members, 88% with terminal degrees. The student-faculty ratio is 9:1.

Students of DU The student body totals 9,229, of whom 4,257 are undergraduates. 55.7% are women and 44.3% are men. Students come from 52 states and territories and 54 other countries. 50% are from Colorado. 4.7% are international students. 86% returned for their sophomore year.

Applying DU requires an essay, SAT I or ACT, a high school transcript, and 2 recommendations, and in some cases a minimum high school GPA of 2.0. The school recommends an interview and a minimum high school GPA of 2.7. Application deadline: 2/1; 2/15 priority date for financial aid. Early and deferred admission are possible.

UNIVERSITY OF DUBUQUE

Dubuque, IA

Suburban setting ■ *Private* ■ *Independent Religious* ■ *Coed*

Web site: www.dbq.edu
Contact: Mr. Jesse James, Director of Admissions and Records, 2000 University Avenue, Dubuque, IA 52001-5099
Telephone: 563-589-3214 or toll-free 800-722-5583 (in-state)
Fax: 563-589-3690
E-mail: admssns@dbq.edu

Getting in Last Year 625 applied; 78% were accepted; 277 enrolled (57%).

Financial Matters $15,700 tuition and fees (2002–03); $5220 room and board; 84% average percent of need met; $15,355 average financial aid amount received per undergraduate.

Academics UD awards bachelor's, master's, and first-professional degrees. Challenging opportunities include advanced placement credit, accelerated degree programs, student-designed majors, double majors, independent study, and a senior project. Special programs include internships, summer session for credit, off-campus study, study-abroad, and Army ROTC. The most frequently chosen baccalaureate fields are business/marketing, education, and computer/information sciences. The faculty at UD has 45 full-time members, 62% with terminal degrees. The student-faculty ratio is 14:1.

Students of UD The student body totals 1,120, of whom 843 are undergraduates. 34.8% are women and 65.2% are men. Students come from 30 states and territories. 52% are from Iowa. 0.6% are international students. 75% returned for their sophomore year.

Applying UD requires an essay, SAT I or ACT, a high school transcript, 2 recommendations, and a minimum high school GPA of 2.0. The school recommends an interview. Application deadline: rolling admissions.

UNIVERSITY OF EVANSVILLE

Evansville, IN

Suburban setting ■ *Private* ■ *Independent Religious* ■ *Coed*

Web site: www.evansville.edu
Contact: Dr. Tom Bear, Dean of Admission, 1800 Lincoln Avenue, Evansville, IN 47722-0002
Telephone: 812-479-2468 or toll-free 800-423-8633 (out-of-state)
Fax: 812-474-4076
E-mail: admission@evansville.edu

Getting in Last Year 1,883 applied; 85% were accepted; 603 enrolled (38%).

Financial Matters $18,230 tuition and fees (2002–03); $5420 room and board; 90% average percent of need met; $16,197 average financial aid amount received per undergraduate.

Academics UE awards associate, bachelor's, and master's degrees. Challenging opportunities include advanced placement credit, accelerated degree programs, student-designed majors, freshman honors college, an honors program, double majors, independent study, and a senior project. Special programs include cooperative education, internships, summer session for credit, and study-abroad. The most frequently chosen baccalaureate fields are education, business/marketing, and health professions and related sciences. The faculty at UE has 166 full-time members, 86% with terminal degrees. The student-faculty ratio is 13:1.

Students of UE The student body totals 2,668, of whom 2,600 are undergraduates. 60.3% are women and 39.7% are men. Students come from 47 states and territories and 44 other countries. 66% are from Indiana. 5.5% are international students. 81% returned for their sophomore year.

Applying UE requires an essay, SAT I or ACT, a high school transcript, 1 recommendation, and a minimum high school GPA of 2.0, and in some cases an interview. The school recommends an interview and a minimum high school GPA of 3.0. Application deadline: 2/15; 3/1 priority date for financial aid. Early and deferred admission are possible.

THE UNIVERSITY OF FINDLAY

Findlay, OH

Small-town setting ■ *Private* ■ *Independent Religious* ■ *Coed*

Web site: www.findlay.edu
Contact: Mr. Michael Momany, Executive Director of Enrollment Services, 1000 North Main Street, Findlay, OH 45840-3653
Telephone: 419-434-4732 or toll-free 800-548-0932 **Fax:** 419-434-4898
E-mail: admissions@findlay.edu

Getting in Last Year 2,723 applied; 71% were accepted; 910 enrolled (47%).

Financial Matters $18,724 tuition and fees (2002–03); $6792 room and board; 84% average percent of need met; $13,850 average financial aid amount received per undergraduate.

Academics Findlay awards associate, bachelor's, and master's degrees. Challenging opportunities include advanced placement credit, accelerated degree programs, student-designed majors, an honors program, double majors, independent study, and a senior project. Special programs include cooperative education, internships, summer session for credit, off-campus study, study-abroad, and Army and Air Force ROTC. The most frequently chosen baccalaureate fields are health professions and related sciences, business/marketing, and education. The faculty at Findlay has 160 full-time members, 51% with terminal degrees. The student-faculty ratio is 19:1.

Students of Findlay The student body totals 4,591, of whom 3,384 are undergraduates. 56.1% are women and 43.9% are men. Students come from 45 states and territories and 34 other countries. 87% are from Ohio. 2% are international students. 72% returned for their sophomore year.

Applying Findlay requires SAT I or ACT, a high school transcript, and a minimum high school GPA of 2.3, and in some cases an essay, an interview, and recommendations. Application deadline: 6/1. Deferred admission is possible.

UNIVERSITY OF FLORIDA

Gainesville, FL

Suburban setting ■ *Public* ■ *State-supported* ■ *Coed*

Web site: www.ufl.edu
Contact: Office of Admissions, PO Box 114000, Gainesville, FL 32611-4000
Telephone: 352-392-1365
E-mail: freshmen@ufl.edu

Getting in Last Year 20,119 applied; 58% were accepted; 6,536 enrolled (56%).

Financial Matters $2581 resident tuition and fees (2002–03); $12,046 nonresident tuition and fees (2002–03); $5640 room and board; 85% average percent of need met; $9082 average financial aid amount received per undergraduate (2001–02).

Academics UF awards bachelor's, master's, doctoral, and first-professional degrees. Challenging opportunities include advanced placement credit, accelerated degree programs, student-designed majors, an honors program, double majors, independent study, and a senior project. Special programs include cooperative education, internships, summer session for credit, off-campus study, study-abroad, and Army, Navy and Air Force ROTC. The most frequently chosen baccalaureate fields are business/marketing, engineering/engineering technologies, and trade and industry. The faculty at UF has 1,686 full-time members, 94% with terminal degrees. The student-faculty ratio is 21:1.

Students of UF The student body totals 47,373, of whom 34,031 are undergraduates. 53.1% are women and 46.9% are men. Students come from 52 states and territories and 114 other countries. 95% are from Florida. 0.9% are international students. 92% returned for their sophomore year.

Applying UF requires SAT I or ACT and a high school transcript. Application deadline: 1/13; 3/15 priority date for financial aid. Early admission is possible.

UNIVERSITY OF GEORGIA

Athens, GA

Suburban setting ■ *Public* ■ *State-supported* ■ *Coed*

Web site: www.uga.edu
Contact: Mr. J. Robert Spatig, Associate Director of Admissions, Athens, GA 30602
Telephone: 706-542-3000 **Fax:** 706-542-1466
E-mail: undergrad@admissions.uga.edu

Getting in Last Year 12,786 applied; 65% were accepted; 4,295 enrolled (51%).

Financial Matters $3616 resident tuition and fees (2002–03); $12,986 nonresident tuition and fees (2002–03); $5748 room and board; 75% average percent of need met; $6874 average financial aid amount received per undergraduate.

Academics UGA awards associate, bachelor's, master's, doctoral, and first-professional degrees. Challenging opportunities include advanced placement credit, accelerated degree programs, student-designed majors, an honors program, double majors, independent study, and a senior project. Special programs include cooperative education, internships, summer session for credit, off-campus study, study-abroad, and Army and Air Force ROTC. The most frequently chosen baccalaureate fields are business/marketing, education, and social sciences and history. The faculty at UGA has 1,709 full-time members, 94% with terminal degrees. The student-faculty ratio is 13:1.

Students of UGA The student body totals 32,941, of whom 24,983 are undergraduates. 56.1% are women and 43.9% are men. 91% are from Georgia. 0.8% are international students. 90% returned for their sophomore year.

Applying UGA requires SAT I or ACT and a high school transcript. The school recommends an essay. Application deadline: 2/1; 3/1 priority date for financial aid. Early and deferred admission are possible.

UNIVERSITY OF GREAT FALLS

Great Falls, MT

Urban setting ■ *Private* ■ *Independent Religious* ■ *Coed*

Web site: www.ugf.edu
Contact: Ms. Cathy Day, Director of Admissions and Enrollment Management, 1301 20th Street South, Great Falls, MT 59405
Telephone: 406-791-5200 or toll-free 800-856-9544 **Fax:** 406-791-5209
E-mail: enroll@ugf.edu

University of Great Falls (continued)

Getting in Last Year 196 applied; 96% were accepted; 82 enrolled (44%).

Financial Matters $10,960 tuition and fees (2002–03); $5100 room and board; 74% average percent of need met; $8973 average financial aid amount received per undergraduate.

Academics UGF awards associate, bachelor's, and master's degrees. Challenging opportunities include advanced placement credit, double majors, independent study, and a senior project. Special programs include cooperative education, internships, and summer session for credit. The most frequently chosen baccalaureate fields are education, protective services/public administration, and business/marketing. The faculty at UGF has 40 full-time members, 55% with terminal degrees. The student-faculty ratio is 9:1.

Students of UGF The student body totals 816, of whom 717 are undergraduates. 72.8% are women and 27.2% are men. Students come from 16 states and territories and 5 other countries. 95% are from Montana. 2.3% are international students. 54% returned for their sophomore year.

Applying UGF requires a high school transcript. The school recommends SAT I and SAT II or ACT and an interview. Application deadline: 8/1. Early and deferred admission are possible.

UNIVERSITY OF GUELPH

Guelph, ON Canada

Urban setting ■ *Public* ■ *Coed*

Web site: www.uoguelph.ca
Contact: Mr. Hugh Clark, Admissions Coordinator, L-3 University Centre, Guelph, ON N1G 2W1 Canada
Telephone: 519-824-4120 ext. 6066
E-mail: usinfo@registrar.uoguelph.ca

Getting in Last Year 17,991 applied; 79% were accepted; 3,075 enrolled (22%).

Financial Matters $4826 resident tuition and fees (2002–03); $6290 room and board.

Academics University of Guelph awards bachelor's, master's, doctoral, and first-professional degrees. Challenging opportunities include advanced placement credit, accelerated degree programs, student-designed majors, freshman honors college, an honors program, double majors, independent study, and a senior project. Special programs include cooperative education, summer session for credit, and study-abroad. The most frequently chosen baccalaureate fields are biological/life sciences, social sciences and history, and liberal arts/general studies. The faculty at University of Guelph has 692 full-time members. The student-faculty ratio is 22:1.

Students of University of Guelph The student body totals 16,811, of whom 14,126 are undergraduates. 63.1% are women and 36.9% are men. Students come from 12 states and territories and 85 other countries. 94% returned for their sophomore year.

Applying University of Guelph requires a high school transcript, and in some cases an essay and SAT I or ACT. The school recommends recommendations and a minimum high school GPA of 3.0. Application deadline: 4/1; 7/1 priority date for financial aid. Early admission is possible.

UNIVERSITY OF HARTFORD

West Hartford, CT

Suburban setting ■ *Private* ■ *Independent* ■ *Coed*

Web site: www.hartford.edu
Contact: Mr. Richard Zeiser, Dean of Admissions, 200 Bloomfield Avenue, West Hartford, CT 06117-1599
Telephone: 860-768-4296 or toll-free 800-947-4303 **Fax:** 860-768-4961
E-mail: admission@hartford.edu

Getting in Last Year 10,145 applied; 69% were accepted; 1,349 enrolled (19%).

Financial Matters $21,550 tuition and fees (2002–03); $8316 room and board; 79% average percent of need met; $17,368 average financial aid amount received per undergraduate (2001–02).

Academics U of H awards associate, bachelor's, master's, and doctoral degrees. Challenging opportunities include advanced placement credit, student-designed majors, an honors program, double majors, and independent study. Special programs include cooperative education, internships, summer session for credit, off-campus study, study-abroad, and Army and Air Force ROTC. The most frequently chosen baccalaureate fields are visual/performing arts, health professions and related sciences, and engineering/engineering technologies. The faculty at U of H has 328 full-time members, 79% with terminal degrees. The student-faculty ratio is 12:1.

Students of U of H The student body totals 6,998, of whom 5,542 are undergraduates. 52.2% are women and 47.8% are men. Students come from 47 states and territories and 69 other countries. 39% are from Connecticut. 3% are international students. 71% returned for their sophomore year.

Applying U of H requires SAT I or ACT and a high school transcript. The school recommends an essay, an interview, and 2 recommendations. Application deadline: rolling admissions; 2/1 priority date for financial aid. Early and deferred admission are possible.

UNIVERSITY OF HAWAII AT HILO

Hilo, HI

Small-town setting ■ *Public* ■ *State-supported* ■ *Coed*

Web site: www.uhh.hawaii.edu
Contact: Mr. James Cromwell, UH Student Services Specialist III/Director of Admissions, 200 West Kawili Street, Hilo, HI 96720-4091
Telephone: 808-974-7414 or toll-free 808-974-7414 (in-state), 800-897-4456 (out-of-state)
E-mail: uhhao@hawaii.edu

Getting in Last Year 1,572 applied; 59% were accepted; 443 enrolled (48%).

Financial Matters $1658 resident tuition and fees (2002–03); $7274 nonresident tuition and fees (2002–03); $4839 room and board; 76% average percent of need met; $6372 average financial aid amount received per undergraduate (2000–01).

Academics UH Hilo awards bachelor's and master's degrees. Challenging opportunities include advanced placement credit, student-designed majors, an honors program, double majors, independent study, and a senior project. Special programs include internships, summer session for credit, off-campus study, and study-abroad. The most frequently chosen baccalaureate fields are social sciences and history, physical sciences, and psychology. The faculty at UH Hilo has 169 full-time members, 74% with terminal degrees. The student-faculty ratio is 13:1.

Students of UH Hilo The student body totals 3,040, of whom 2,904 are undergraduates. 60.1% are women and 39.9% are men. Students come from 48 states and territories and 40 other countries. 79% are from Hawaii. 11.8% are international students. 58% returned for their sophomore year.

Applying UH Hilo requires SAT I or ACT and a high school transcript, and in some cases recommendations. The school recommends a minimum high school GPA of 3.0. Application deadline: 7/1; 3/1 priority date for financial aid. Deferred admission is possible.

UNIVERSITY OF HAWAII AT MANOA

Honolulu, HI

Urban setting ■ *Public* ■ *State-supported* ■ *Coed*

Web site: www.uhm.hawaii.edu
Contact: Ms. Janice Heu, Interim Director of Admissions and Records, 2600 Campus Road, Room 001, Honolulu, HI 96822
Telephone: 808-956-8975 or toll-free 800-823-9771 **Fax:** 808-956-4148
E-mail: ar-info@hawaii.edu

Getting in Last Year 4,915 applied; 73% were accepted; 1,877 enrolled (52%).

Financial Matters $3349 resident tuition and fees (2002–03); $9829 nonresident tuition and fees (2002–03); $5359 room and board; 76% average percent of need met; $5947 average financial aid amount received per undergraduate (2001–02).

Academics UHM awards bachelor's, master's, doctoral, and first-professional degrees and post-bachelor's certificates. Challenging opportunities include advanced placement credit, accelerated degree programs, student-designed majors, an honors program, double majors, independent study, and a senior project. Special programs include cooperative education, internships, summer session for credit, off-campus study, study-abroad, and Army and Air Force ROTC. The most frequently chosen baccalaureate fields are business/marketing, social sciences and history, and education. The faculty at UHM has 1,092 full-time members, 83% with terminal degrees. The student-faculty ratio is 13:1.

Students of UHM The student body totals 18,696, of whom 12,820 are undergraduates. 55.8% are women and 44.2% are men. 88% are from Hawaii. 6.1% are international students. 79% returned for their sophomore year.

Applying UHM requires SAT I or ACT, a high school transcript, minimum SAT I score of 510 for verbal and math sections, and a minimum high school GPA of 2.8. Application deadline: 6/1; 3/15 priority date for financial aid.

UNIVERSITY OF HAWAII–WEST OAHU

Pearl City, HI

Small-town setting ■ *Public* ■ *State-supported* ■ *Coed*

Contact: Jean M. Osumi, Dean of Student Services, 96-043 Ala Ike, Pearl City, HI 96782
Telephone: 808-453-4700 **Fax:** 805-453-6076
E-mail: jeano@uhwo.hawaii.edu

Getting in Last Year 528 applied; 81% were accepted.

Financial Matters $2050 resident tuition and fees (2002–03); $7186 nonresident tuition and fees (2002–03); $3960 average financial aid amount received per undergraduate (2001–02).

Academics UH-West Oahu awards bachelor's degrees. A senior project is a challenging opportunity. Special programs include internships, summer session for credit, off-campus study, and Army ROTC. The faculty at UH-West Oahu has 23 full-time members, 100% with terminal degrees. The student-faculty ratio is 13:1.

Students of UH-West Oahu The student body is made up of 834 undergraduates. 70.4% are women and 29.6% are men. Students come from 16 states and territories. 92% are from Hawaii. 60% returned for their sophomore year.

Applying Application deadline: 5/1 priority date for financial aid.

UNIVERSITY OF HOUSTON

Houston, TX

Urban setting ■ Public ■ State-supported ■ Coed

Web site: www.uh.edu

Contact: Mr. Jose Cantu, Co-Assistant Director of Student Outreach Services, Room 122, Ezekiel Cullen Building, Houston, TX 77204-2023

Telephone: 713-743-9617 **Fax:** 713-743-9633

E-mail: admissions@uh.edu

Getting in Last Year 8,175 applied; 78% were accepted; 3,457 enrolled (54%).

Financial Matters $3348 resident tuition and fees (2002–03); $9888 nonresident tuition and fees (2002–03); $5694 room and board; 80% average percent of need met; $11,340 average financial aid amount received per undergraduate.

Academics UH awards bachelor's, master's, doctoral, and first-professional degrees. Challenging opportunities include advanced placement credit, accelerated degree programs, freshman honors college, an honors program, double majors, independent study, and a senior project. Special programs include cooperative education, internships, summer session for credit, off-campus study, study-abroad, and Army and Navy ROTC. The most frequently chosen baccalaureate fields are business/marketing, psychology, and engineering/engineering technologies. The faculty at UH has 1,052 full-time members, 85% with terminal degrees. The student-faculty ratio is 21:1.

Students of UH The student body totals 34,443, of whom 26,283 are undergraduates. 52.3% are women and 47.7% are men. Students come from 52 states and territories and 130 other countries. 98% are from Texas. 4.3% are international students. 78% returned for their sophomore year.

Applying UH requires SAT I or ACT, a high school transcript, and a minimum high school GPA of 2.0. The school recommends SAT II Subject Tests and recommendations. Application deadline: 5/1; 4/1 priority date for financial aid. Early and deferred admission are possible.

UNIVERSITY OF HOUSTON–CLEAR LAKE

Houston, TX

Suburban setting ■ Public ■ State-supported ■ Coed

Web site: www.cl.uh.edu

Contact: Ms. Rose Sklar, Director of Enrollment Services, 2700 Bay Area Boulevard, Box 13, Houston, TX 77058-1098

Telephone: 281-283-2533 **Fax:** 281-283-2530

E-mail: admissions@cl.uh.edu

Getting in Last Year 1,256 applied; 99% were accepted.

Financial Matters $3568 resident tuition and fees (2002–03); $8800 nonresident tuition and fees (2002–03); 34% average percent of need met; $4150 average financial aid amount received per undergraduate (2001–02).

Academics UH-Clear Lake awards bachelor's and master's degrees. Challenging opportunities include accelerated degree programs, student-designed majors, double majors, independent study, and a senior project. Special programs include cooperative education, internships, and summer session for credit. The most frequently chosen baccalaureate fields are business/marketing, interdisciplinary studies, and computer/information sciences. The faculty at UH-Clear Lake has 227 full-time members. The student-faculty ratio is 16:1.

Students of UH-Clear Lake The student body totals 7,753, of whom 4,017 are undergraduates. 63.6% are women and 36.4% are men. 100% are from Texas. 3.1% are international students.

Applying Application deadline: 5/1 priority date for financial aid. Deferred admission is possible.

UNIVERSITY OF HOUSTON–DOWNTOWN

Houston, TX

Urban setting ■ Public ■ State-supported ■ Coed

Web site: www.uhd.edu

Contact: Ms. Penny Cureton, Executive Director of Enrollment Management, One Main Street, Houston, TX 77002

Telephone: 713-221-8522 **Fax:** 713-221-8157

E-mail: uhdadmit@dt.uh.edu

Getting in Last Year 1,761 applied; 100% were accepted; 1,099 enrolled (62%).

Financial Matters $2684 resident tuition and fees (2002–03); $7544 nonresident tuition and fees (2002–03); 74% average percent of need met; $6250 average financial aid amount received per undergraduate.

Academics UH-Downtown awards bachelor's and master's degrees. Challenging opportunities include advanced placement credit, accelerated degree programs, double majors, and independent study. Special programs include cooperative education, internships, summer session for credit, and Army ROTC. The most frequently chosen baccalaureate fields are business/marketing, liberal arts/general studies, and protective services/public administration. The faculty at UH-Downtown has 244 full-time members, 79% with terminal degrees. The student-faculty ratio is 19:1.

Students of UH-Downtown The student body totals 10,528, of whom 10,423 are undergraduates. 59.7% are women and 40.3% are men. Students come from 17 states and territories and 76 other countries. 99% are from Texas. 4% are international students.

Applying UH-Downtown requires a high school transcript. Application deadline: 8/1; 4/1 priority date for financial aid. Deferred admission is possible.

UNIVERSITY OF HOUSTON–VICTORIA

Victoria, TX

Small-town setting ■ Public ■ State-supported ■ Coed

Web site: www.uhv.edu

Contact: Mr. Richard Phillips, Director of Enrollment Management, 3007 North Ben Wilson, Victoria, TX 77901-4450

Telephone: 361-570-4110 or toll-free 877-940-4848 **Fax:** 361-570-4114

E-mail: urbanom@jade.vic.uh.edu

Financial Matters $2388 resident tuition and fees (2002–03); $7404 nonresident tuition and fees (2002–03); 61% average percent of need met; $6328 average financial aid amount received per undergraduate (2001–02).

Academics University of Houston–Victoria awards bachelor's and master's degrees. Challenging opportunities include double majors and independent study. Special programs include internships, summer session for credit, off-campus study, and study-abroad. The most frequently chosen baccalaureate fields are interdisciplinary studies, business/marketing, and computer/information sciences. The faculty at University of Houston–Victoria has 67 full-time members, 96% with terminal degrees. The student-faculty ratio is 16:1.

Students of University of Houston–Victoria The student body totals 2,183, of whom 1,014 are undergraduates. 71.1% are women and 28.9% are men. Students come from 1 state or territory. 1% are international students.

Applying Application deadline: 4/15 priority date for financial aid.

UNIVERSITY OF IDAHO

Moscow, ID

Small-town setting ■ Public ■ State-supported ■ Coed

Web site: www.its.uidaho.edu/uihome

Contact: Mr. Dan Davenport, Director of Admissions, Admissions Office, PO Box 444264, Moscow, ID 83844-4264

Telephone: 208-885-6326 or toll-free 888-884-3246 (out-of-state) **Fax:** 208-885-9119

E-mail: admappl@uidaho.edu

Getting in Last Year 3,936 applied; 82% were accepted; 1,697 enrolled (53%).

Financial Matters $3044 resident tuition and fees (2002–03); $9764 nonresident tuition and fees (2002–03); $4680 room and board; 80% average percent of need met; $8072 average financial aid amount received per undergraduate (2001–02).

Academics Idaho awards bachelor's, master's, doctoral, and first-professional degrees and post-master's certificates. Challenging opportunities include advanced placement credit, accelerated degree programs, student-designed majors, an honors program, double majors, independent study, and a senior project. Special programs include cooperative education, internships, summer session for credit, off-campus study, study-abroad, and Army, Navy and Air Force ROTC. The most frequently chosen baccalaureate fields are education, business/marketing, and engineering/engineering technologies. The faculty at Idaho has 570 full-time members, 82% with terminal degrees. The student-faculty ratio is 19:1.

Students of Idaho The student body totals 12,419, of whom 9,368 are undergraduates. 45.6% are women and 54.4% are men. Students come from 58 states and territories and 25 other countries. 81% are from Idaho. 2.4% are international students. 80% returned for their sophomore year.

Applying Idaho requires SAT I or ACT, a high school transcript, and a minimum high school GPA of 2.2, and in some cases an essay. The school recommends SAT I. Application deadline: 8/1; 2/15 priority date for financial aid. Deferred admission is possible.

UNIVERSITY OF ILLINOIS AT CHICAGO

Chicago, IL

Urban setting ■ Public ■ State-supported ■ Coed

Web site: www.uic.edu

Contact: Mr. Rob Sheinkopf, Executive Director of Admissions, Box 5220, Chicago, IL 60680-5220

Telephone: 312-996-4350 **Fax:** 312-413-7628

E-mail: uic.admit@uic.edu

Getting in Last Year 11,727 applied; 63% were accepted; 3,015 enrolled (41%).

University of Illinois at Chicago (continued)

Financial Matters $6442 resident tuition and fees (2002–03); $13,770 nonresident tuition and fees (2002–03); $6428 room and board; 86% average percent of need met; $11,900 average financial aid amount received per undergraduate (2001–02).

Academics UIC awards bachelor's, master's, doctoral, and first-professional degrees and first-professional certificates. Challenging opportunities include advanced placement credit, accelerated degree programs, student-designed majors, an honors program, double majors, independent study, and a senior project. Special programs include cooperative education, internships, summer session for credit, off-campus study, study-abroad, and Army, Navy and Air Force ROTC. The most frequently chosen baccalaureate fields are business/marketing, psychology, and engineering/engineering technologies. The faculty at UIC has 1,233 full-time members, 83% with terminal degrees. The student-faculty ratio is 15:1.

Students of UIC The student body totals 26,138, of whom 16,543 are undergraduates. 55% are women and 45% are men. Students come from 52 states and territories and 100 other countries. 97% are from Illinois. 1.5% are international students. 79% returned for their sophomore year.

Applying UIC requires SAT I or ACT and a high school transcript, and in some cases an essay and an interview. Application deadline: 4/1; 3/1 priority date for financial aid.

UNIVERSITY OF ILLINOIS AT SPRINGFIELD

Springfield, IL

Suburban setting ■ Public ■ State-supported ■ Coed

Web site: www.uis.edu

Contact: Office of Enrollment Services, 1 University Plaza, Springfield, IL 62703-5404

Telephone: 217-206-6626 or toll-free 888-977-4847 **Fax:** 217-206-6620

Getting in Last Year 427 applied; 23% were accepted; 97 enrolled (100%).

Financial Matters $4009 resident tuition and fees (2002–03); $10,579 nonresident tuition and fees (2002–03); $6370 room and board; 71% average percent of need met; $7501 average financial aid amount received per undergraduate (2001–02).

Academics UIS awards bachelor's, master's, and doctoral degrees. Challenging opportunities include student-designed majors and a senior project. Special programs include cooperative education, internships, summer session for credit, and off-campus study. The most frequently chosen baccalaureate fields are business/marketing, psychology, and communications/communication technologies. The faculty at UIS has 170 full-time members. The student-faculty ratio is 15:1.

Students of UIS The student body totals 4,451, of whom 2,445 are undergraduates. 61.8% are women and 38.2% are men. Students come from 18 states and territories and 33 other countries. 98% are from Illinois. 1.3% are international students.

Applying UIS recommends an essay, a high school transcript, and an interview. Application deadline: 11/15 for financial aid, with a 4/1 priority date. Deferred admission is possible.

UNIVERSITY OF ILLINOIS AT URBANA–CHAMPAIGN

Champaign, IL

Small-town setting ■ Public ■ State-supported ■ Coed

Web site: www.uiuc.edu

Contact: Mr. Abel Montoya, Assistant Director of Admissions, 901 West Illinois, Urbana, IL 61801

Telephone: 217-333-0302

E-mail: admissions@oar.uiuc.edu

Getting in Last Year 21,484 applied; 60% were accepted; 6,366 enrolled (49%).

Financial Matters $5748 resident tuition and fees (2002–03); $15,798 nonresident tuition and fees (2002–03); $6360 room and board; 87% average percent of need met; $9263 average financial aid amount received per undergraduate.

Academics Illinois awards bachelor's, master's, doctoral, and first-professional degrees. Challenging opportunities include advanced placement credit, accelerated degree programs, student-designed majors, an honors program, double majors, and a senior project. Special programs include cooperative education, internships, summer session for credit, off-campus study, study-abroad, and Army and Air Force ROTC. The most frequently chosen baccalaureate fields are business/marketing, engineering/engineering technologies, and social sciences and history. The faculty at Illinois has 2,206 full-time members, 91% with terminal degrees. The student-faculty ratio is 13:1.

Students of Illinois The student body totals 39,999, of whom 28,947 are undergraduates. 47.6% are women and 52.4% are men. Students come from 49 states and territories and 69 other countries. 89% are from Illinois. 2.6% are international students. 93% returned for their sophomore year.

Applying Illinois requires an essay, SAT I or ACT, and a high school transcript, and in some cases audition, statement of professional interest. Application deadline: 1/1; 3/15 priority date for financial aid. Deferred admission is possible.

UNIVERSITY OF INDIANAPOLIS

Indianapolis, IN

Suburban setting ■ Private ■ Independent Religious ■ Coed

Web site: www.uindy.edu

Contact: Mr. Ronald W. Wilks, Director of Admissions, 1400 East Hanna Avenue, Indianapolis, IN 46227-3697

Telephone: 317-788-3216 or toll-free 800-232-8634 ext. 3216
Fax: 317-778-3300

E-mail: admissions@uindy.edu

Getting in Last Year 2,194 applied; 80% were accepted; 600 enrolled (34%).

Financial Matters $15,820 tuition and fees (2002–03); $5660 room and board; 81% average percent of need met; $13,688 average financial aid amount received per undergraduate (2001–02).

Academics U of I awards associate, bachelor's, master's, and doctoral degrees. Challenging opportunities include advanced placement credit, accelerated degree programs, student-designed majors, an honors program, double majors, independent study, and a senior project. Special programs include cooperative education, internships, summer session for credit, off-campus study, study-abroad, and Army ROTC. The most frequently chosen baccalaureate fields are business/marketing, education, and psychology. The faculty at U of I has 160 full-time members, 75% with terminal degrees. The student-faculty ratio is 14:1.

Students of U of I The student body totals 3,776, of whom 2,868 are undergraduates. 66.6% are women and 33.4% are men. Students come from 31 states and territories and 55 other countries. 92% are from Indiana. 4.6% are international students. 80% returned for their sophomore year.

Applying U of I requires SAT I or ACT, a high school transcript, and a minimum high school GPA of 2.0, and in some cases an interview. Application deadline: rolling admissions; 3/1 priority date for financial aid. Deferred admission is possible.

THE UNIVERSITY OF IOWA

Iowa City, IA

Small-town setting ■ Public ■ State-supported ■ Coed

Web site: www.uiowa.edu

Contact: Mr. Michael Barron, Director of Admissions, 107 Calvin Hall, Iowa City, IA 52242

Telephone: 319-335-3847 or toll-free 800-553-4692 **Fax:** 319-335-1535

E-mail: admissions@uiowa.edu

Getting in Last Year 13,079 applied; 84% were accepted; 4,184 enrolled (38%).

Financial Matters $4191 resident tuition and fees (2002–03); $13,833 nonresident tuition and fees (2002–03); $5440 room and board; 88% average percent of need met; $6806 average financial aid amount received per undergraduate (2001–02).

Academics Iowa awards bachelor's, master's, doctoral, and first-professional degrees. Challenging opportunities include advanced placement credit, accelerated degree programs, student-designed majors, an honors program, double majors, independent study, and a senior project. Special programs include cooperative education, internships, summer session for credit, off-campus study, study-abroad, and Army and Air Force ROTC. The most frequently chosen baccalaureate fields are business/marketing, social sciences and history, and communications/communication technologies. The faculty at Iowa has 1,595 full-time members, 96% with terminal degrees. The student-faculty ratio is 15:1.

Students of Iowa The student body totals 29,697, of whom 20,487 are undergraduates. 54.8% are women and 45.2% are men. Students come from 52 states and territories and 72 other countries. 67% are from Iowa. 1.2% are international students. 82% returned for their sophomore year.

Applying Iowa requires SAT I or ACT, a high school transcript, and rank in top 50% for residents, rank in top 30% for nonresidents. Application deadline: 4/1. Early and deferred admission are possible.

UNIVERSITY OF JUDAISM

Bel Air, CA

Suburban setting ■ Private ■ Independent Religious ■ Coed

Web site: www.uj.edu

Contact: Ms. Shoshana Kapnek, Assistant Director of Undergraduate Admissions, 15600 Mulholland Drive, Bel Air, CA 90077

Telephone: 310-476-9777 ext. 299 or toll-free 888-853-6763 **Fax:** 310-471-3657

E-mail: admissions@uj.edu

Getting in Last Year 87 applied; 79% were accepted.

Financial Matters $16,590 tuition and fees (2002–03); $9120 room and board; 100% average percent of need met; $19,214 average financial aid amount received per undergraduate.

Academics UJ awards bachelor's and master's degrees. Challenging opportunities include advanced placement credit, accelerated degree programs, student-designed majors, an honors program, independent study, and a senior project. Special programs include internships, off-campus study, and study-abroad. The most frequently chosen baccalaureate fields are area/ethnic studies, English, and psychology. The faculty at UJ has 19 full-time members, 84% with terminal degrees. The student-faculty ratio is 6:1.

Students of UJ The student body totals 336, of whom 135 are undergraduates. Students come from 22 states and territories and 4 other countries. 69% are from California. 5.9% are international students. 58% returned for their sophomore year.

Applying UJ requires an essay, SAT I or ACT, a high school transcript, and 2 recommendations, and in some cases an interview. The school recommends an interview and a minimum high school GPA of 3.2. Application deadline: 1/31; 3/2 priority date for financial aid. Early and deferred admission are possible.

UNIVERSITY OF KANSAS

Lawrence, KS

Suburban setting ■ Public ■ State-supported ■ Coed

Web site: www.ku.edu
Contact: Ms. Lisa Pinamonti, Interim Director of Admissions and Scholarships, KU Visitor Center, 1502 Iowa Street, Lawrence, KS 66045-7576
Telephone: 785-864-3911 or toll-free 888-686-7323 (in-state)
Fax: 785-864-5006
E-mail: adm@ku.edu

Getting in Last Year 9,573 applied; 67% were accepted; 4,074 enrolled (63%).

Financial Matters $3484 resident tuition and fees (2002–03); $10,687 nonresident tuition and fees (2002–03); $4642 room and board; 76% average percent of need met; $6173 average financial aid amount received per undergraduate (2001–02).

Academics KU awards bachelor's, master's, doctoral, and first-professional degrees and post-master's and first-professional certificates (University of Kansas is a single institution with academic programs and facilities at two primary locations: Lawrence and Kansas City. Undergraduate, graduate, and professional education are the principal missions of the Lawrence campus, with medicine and related professional education the focus of the Kansas City campus). Challenging opportunities include advanced placement credit, accelerated degree programs, an honors program, double majors, independent study, and a senior project. Special programs include cooperative education, internships, summer session for credit, study-abroad, and Army, Navy and Air Force ROTC. The most frequently chosen baccalaureate fields are business/marketing, social sciences and history, and English. The faculty at KU has 1,194 full-time members, 92% with terminal degrees. The student-faculty ratio is 19:1.

Students of KU The student body totals 28,196, of whom 20,605 are undergraduates. 52.4% are women and 47.6% are men. Students come from 53 states and territories and 118 other countries. 76% are from Kansas. 3.3% are international students. 80% returned for their sophomore year.

Applying KU requires SAT I or ACT, a high school transcript, Kansas Board of Regents admissions criteria with GPA of 2.0/2.5; top third of high school class; minimum ACT score of 24 or minimum SAT score of 1090, and a minimum high school GPA of 2.0, and in some cases a minimum high school GPA of 2.5. Application deadline: 4/1; 3/1 priority date for financial aid. Deferred admission is possible.

UNIVERSITY OF KENTUCKY

Lexington, KY

Urban setting ■ Public ■ State-supported ■ Coed

Web site: www.uky.edu
Contact: Ms. Michelle Nordin, Associate Director of Admissions, 100 W.D. Funkhouser Building, Lexington, KY 40506-0054
Telephone: 859-257-2000 or toll-free 800-432-0967 (in-state)
E-mail: admissio@uky.edu

Getting in Last Year 8,449 applied; 82% were accepted.

Financial Matters $3975 resident tuition and fees (2002–03); $10,527 nonresident tuition and fees (2002–03); $4050 room and board; 86% average percent of need met; $8106 average financial aid amount received per undergraduate (2001–02).

Academics UK awards bachelor's, master's, doctoral, and first-professional degrees and post-master's certificates. Challenging opportunities include advanced placement credit, accelerated degree programs, student-designed majors, an honors program, double majors, and independent study. Special programs include cooperative education, internships, summer session for credit, off-campus study, study-abroad, and Army and Air Force ROTC. The most frequently chosen baccalaureate fields are business/marketing, health professions and related sciences, and education. The faculty at UK has 1,231 full-time members, 95% with terminal degrees. The student-faculty ratio is 17:1.

Students of UK The student body totals 25,741, of whom 17,878 are undergraduates. Students come from 53 states and territories and 123 other countries. 88% are from Kentucky. 1.6% are international students. 77% returned for their sophomore year.

Applying UK requires SAT I or ACT, a high school transcript, and a minimum high school GPA of 2.0. Application deadline: 2/15; 2/15 priority date for financial aid. Early admission is possible.

UNIVERSITY OF KING'S COLLEGE

Halifax, NS Canada

Urban setting ■ Public ■ Coed

Web site: www.ukings.ns.ca
Contact: Karl Turner, Admissions Officer, Registrar's Office, Halifax, NS B3H 2A1 Canada
Telephone: 902-422-1271 ext. 193 **Fax:** 902-423-3357
E-mail: admissions@ukings.ns.ca

Getting in Last Year 963 applied; 65% were accepted; 294 enrolled (47%).

Financial Matters $5547 resident tuition and fees (2002–03); $5547 nonresident tuition and fees (2002–03); $5840 room and board.

Academics King's awards bachelor's degrees. Challenging opportunities include advanced placement credit, accelerated degree programs, student-designed majors, an honors program, double majors, independent study, and a senior project. Special programs include cooperative education, internships, summer session for credit, off-campus study, and study-abroad. The faculty at King's has 46 full-time members, 76% with terminal degrees.

Students of King's The student body is made up of 961 undergraduates. 57.6% are women and 42.4% are men. Students come from 11 states and territories and 8 other countries. 45% are from Nova Scotia. 56% returned for their sophomore year.

Applying King's requires a high school transcript and a minimum high school GPA of 3.0, and in some cases an essay, SAT I, recommendations, and writing sample. Application deadline: 3/1.

UNIVERSITY OF LA VERNE

La Verne, CA

Suburban setting ■ Private ■ Independent ■ Coed

Web site: www.ulv.edu
Contact: Ms. Lisa Meyer, Dean of Admissions, 1950 Third Street, La Verne, CA 91750-4443
Telephone: 800-876-4858 or toll-free 800-876-4858 **Fax:** 909-392-2714
E-mail: admissions@ulv.edu

Getting in Last Year 1,261 applied; 61% were accepted; 296 enrolled (39%).

Financial Matters $19,500 tuition and fees (2002–03); $7360 room and board; 83% average percent of need met; $19,477 average financial aid amount received per undergraduate.

Academics ULV awards associate, bachelor's, master's, doctoral, and first-professional degrees and post-bachelor's and post-master's certificates (also offers continuing education program with significant enrollment not reflected in profile). Challenging opportunities include advanced placement credit, accelerated degree programs, student-designed majors, freshman honors college, an honors program, double majors, independent study, and a senior project. Special programs include internships, summer session for credit, off-campus study, and study-abroad. The most frequently chosen baccalaureate fields are business/marketing, social sciences and history, and liberal arts/general studies. The faculty at ULV has 109 full-time members, 81% with terminal degrees. The student-faculty ratio is 11:1.

Students of ULV The student body totals 3,583, of whom 1,439 are undergraduates. 61.8% are women and 38.2% are men. Students come from 26 states and territories and 14 other countries. 95% are from California. 1.6% are international students. 82% returned for their sophomore year.

Applying ULV requires an essay, SAT I or ACT, a high school transcript, and 2 recommendations. The school recommends an interview. Application deadline: 2/1; 3/2 priority date for financial aid. Deferred admission is possible.

THE UNIVERSITY OF LETHBRIDGE

Lethbridge, AB Canada

Urban setting ■ Public ■ Coed

Web site: www.uleth.ca
Contact: Mr. Peter Haney, Assistant Registrar, 4401 University Drive, Lethbridge, AB T1K 3M4 Canada
Telephone: 403-382-7134 or toll-free 403-320-5700 **Fax:** 403-329-5159
E-mail: inquiries@uleth.ca

Getting in Last Year 1,832 applied; 56% were accepted.

Financial Matters $4152 nonresident tuition and fees (2002–03); $5000 room and board.

Academics U of L awards bachelor's, master's, and doctoral degrees. Challenging opportunities include accelerated degree programs, student-designed majors, double majors, independent study, and a senior project. Special programs include cooperative education, internships, summer session for credit, off-campus study, and study-abroad. The most frequently chosen baccalaureate fields are business/marketing, liberal arts/general studies, and visual/performing arts. The faculty at U of L has 313 full-time members, 72% with terminal degrees. The student-faculty ratio is 20:1.

The University of Lethbridge (continued)

Students of U of L The student body totals 7,139, of whom 6,822 are undergraduates. 57.7% are women and 42.3% are men. Students come from 10 states and territories and 49 other countries. 85% are from Alberta. 72% returned for their sophomore year.

Applying U of L requires a high school transcript and a minimum high school GPA of 2.0, and in some cases SAT II: Writing Test, SAT I and SAT II or ACT, an interview, recommendations, and a minimum high school GPA of 3.0. Application deadline: 8/26. Early and deferred admission are possible.

UNIVERSITY OF LOUISIANA AT LAFAYETTE

Lafayette, LA

Urban setting ■ Public ■ State-supported ■ Coed

Web site: www.louisiana.edu
Contact: Mr. Dan Rosenfield, Dean of Enrollment Management, PO Drawer 41210, Lafayette, LA 70504
Telephone: 337-482-6553 or toll-free 800-752-6553 (in-state) **Fax:** 337-482-6195
E-mail: dan@louisiana.edu

Getting in Last Year 4,302 applied; 85% were accepted; 2,469 enrolled (67%).

Financial Matters $2440 resident tuition and fees (2002–03); $8620 nonresident tuition and fees (2002–03); $2896 room and board; 90% average percent of need met; $4500 average financial aid amount received per undergraduate (2001–02).

Academics University of Louisiana at Lafayette awards bachelor's, master's, and doctoral degrees and post-master's certificates. Challenging opportunities include advanced placement credit, an honors program, double majors, independent study, and a senior project. Special programs include cooperative education, internships, summer session for credit, study-abroad, and Army ROTC. The most frequently chosen baccalaureate fields are business/marketing, liberal arts/general studies, and education. The faculty at University of Louisiana at Lafayette has 433 full-time members, 75% with terminal degrees. The student-faculty ratio is 23:1.

Students of University of Louisiana at Lafayette The student body totals 16,006, of whom 14,341 are undergraduates. 57.7% are women and 42.3% are men. Students come from 44 states and territories and 85 other countries. 97% are from Louisiana. 1.8% are international students. 72% returned for their sophomore year.

Applying University of Louisiana at Lafayette requires SAT I or ACT, a high school transcript, and a minimum high school GPA of 2.0. Application deadline: rolling admissions; 5/1 priority date for financial aid. Early and deferred admission are possible.

UNIVERSITY OF LOUISVILLE

Louisville, KY

Urban setting ■ Public ■ State-supported ■ Coed

Web site: www.louisville.edu
Contact: Ms. Jenny Sawyer, Executive Director for Admissions, 2211 South Brook, Louisville, KY 40292
Telephone: 502-852-6531 or toll-free 502-852-6531 (in-state), 800-334-8635 (out-of-state) **Fax:** 502-852-4776
E-mail: admitme@gwise.louisville.edu

Getting in Last Year 5,306 applied; 77% were accepted; 2,308 enrolled (57%).

Financial Matters $4082 resident tuition and fees (2002–03); $11,162 nonresident tuition and fees (2002–03); $3872 room and board; 68% average percent of need met; $7062 average financial aid amount received per undergraduate (2001–02).

Academics U of L awards associate, bachelor's, master's, doctoral, and first-professional degrees and post-bachelor's and post-master's certificates. Challenging opportunities include advanced placement credit, accelerated degree programs, student-designed majors, an honors program, double majors, independent study, and a senior project. Special programs include cooperative education, internships, summer session for credit, off-campus study, study-abroad, and Army and Air Force ROTC. The most frequently chosen baccalaureate fields are business/marketing, engineering/engineering technologies, and social sciences and history. The faculty at U of L has 726 full-time members, 92% with terminal degrees. The student-faculty ratio is 13:1.

Students of U of L The student body totals 20,416, of whom 14,458 are undergraduates. 53.1% are women and 46.9% are men. Students come from 50 states and territories and 67 other countries. 89% are from Kentucky. 1.4% are international students. 72% returned for their sophomore year.

Applying U of L requires SAT I or ACT, a high school transcript, and a minimum high school GPA of 2.50. Application deadline: rolling admissions; 3/15 priority date for financial aid. Early and deferred admission are possible.

UNIVERSITY OF MAINE

Orono, ME

Small-town setting ■ Public ■ State-supported ■ Coed

Web site: www.umaine.edu
Contact: Mr. Jonathan H. Henry, Director, 5713 Chadbourne Hall, Orono, ME 04469-5713
Telephone: 207-581-1561 or toll-free 877-486-2364 **Fax:** 207-581-1213
E-mail: um-admit@maine.edu

Getting in Last Year 5,249 applied; 79% were accepted; 1,744 enrolled (42%).

Financial Matters $5480 resident tuition and fees (2002–03); $13,550 nonresident tuition and fees (2002–03); $5922 room and board; 79% average percent of need met; $7829 average financial aid amount received per undergraduate.

Academics UMaine awards bachelor's, master's, and doctoral degrees and post-bachelor's and post-master's certificates. Challenging opportunities include advanced placement credit, student-designed majors, freshman honors college, an honors program, double majors, independent study, and a senior project. Special programs include cooperative education, internships, summer session for credit, off-campus study, study-abroad, and Army and Navy ROTC. The most frequently chosen baccalaureate fields are engineering/engineering technologies, education, and business/marketing. The faculty at UMaine has 509 full-time members, 86% with terminal degrees. The student-faculty ratio is 15:1.

Students of UMaine The student body totals 11,135, of whom 8,817 are undergraduates. 51.7% are women and 48.3% are men. Students come from 49 states and territories and 47 other countries. 86% are from Maine. 2% are international students. 79% returned for their sophomore year.

Applying UMaine requires an essay, SAT I or ACT, a high school transcript, and 1 recommendation. Application deadline: rolling admissions; 3/1 priority date for financial aid. Early and deferred admission are possible.

THE UNIVERSITY OF MAINE AT AUGUSTA

Augusta, ME

Small-town setting ■ Public ■ State-supported ■ Coed

Web site: www.uma.maine.edu
Contact: Ms. Sheri Cranston-Fraser, Interim Director of Admissions and Advising, 46 University Drive, Robinson Hall, Augusta, ME 04330
Telephone: 207-621-3185 or toll-free 800-696-6000 ext. 3185 (in-state) **Fax:** 207-621-3116
E-mail: umaar@maine.maine.edu

Getting in Last Year 2,491 applied; 52% were accepted; 627 enrolled (49%).

Financial Matters $4290 resident tuition and fees (2002–03); $9180 nonresident tuition and fees (2002–03); 69% average percent of need met; $6976 average financial aid amount received per undergraduate.

Academics UMA awards associate and bachelor's degrees and post-bachelor's certificates (also offers some graduate courses and continuing education programs with significant enrollment not reflected in profile). Challenging opportunities include advanced placement credit, student-designed majors, an honors program, double majors, independent study, and a senior project. Special programs include cooperative education, internships, summer session for credit, off-campus study, and study-abroad. The most frequently chosen baccalaureate fields are health professions and related sciences, business/marketing, and social sciences and history. The faculty at UMA has 95 full-time members, 39% with terminal degrees. The student-faculty ratio is 20:1.

Students of UMA The student body is made up of 5,722 undergraduates. 74.6% are women and 25.4% are men. Students come from 30 states and territories. 98% are from Maine. 0.1% are international students.

Applying UMA requires a high school transcript, and in some cases SAT I, an interview, and music audition. The school recommends SAT I. Application deadline: rolling admissions; 3/1 priority date for financial aid. Early and deferred admission are possible.

UNIVERSITY OF MAINE AT FARMINGTON

Farmington, ME

Small-town setting ■ Public ■ State-supported ■ Coed

Web site: www.umf.maine.edu
Contact: Mr. James G. Collins, Associate Director of Admissions, 246 Main Street, Farmington, ME 04938-1994
Telephone: 207-778-7050 **Fax:** 207-778-8182
E-mail: umfadmit@maine.edu

Getting in Last Year 1,410 applied; 71% were accepted; 460 enrolled (46%).

Financial Matters $4482 resident tuition and fees (2002–03); $10,242 nonresident tuition and fees (2002–03); $5064 room and board; 86% average percent of need met; $7816 average financial aid amount received per undergraduate (2001–02).

Academics UMF awards bachelor's degrees. Challenging opportunities include advanced placement credit, accelerated degree programs, student-designed majors, an honors program, double majors, independent study, and a senior project. Special programs include internships, summer session for credit, off-campus study, and study-abroad. The most frequently chosen baccalaureate fields are education, interdisciplinary studies, and psychology. The faculty at UMF has 120 full-time members, 83% with terminal degrees. The student-faculty ratio is 16:1.

Students of UMF The student body is made up of 2,395 undergraduates. 66.9% are women and 33.1% are men. Students come from 25 states and territories and 16 other countries. 77% are from Maine. 1.1% are international students. 74% returned for their sophomore year.

Applying UMF requires an essay, a high school transcript, 1 recommendation, and a minimum high school GPA of 2.0. The school recommends SAT I or ACT and an interview. Application deadline: 3/1 priority date for financial aid. Early and deferred admission are possible.

UNIVERSITY OF MAINE AT FORT KENT

Fort Kent, ME

Rural setting ■ *Public* ■ *State-supported* ■ *Coed*

Web site: www.umfk.maine.edu

Contact: Mr. Melik Peter Khoury, Director of Admissions, 23 University Drive, Fort Kent, ME 04743

Telephone: 207-834-7600 ext. 608 or toll-free 888-TRY-UMFK **Fax:** 207-834-7609

E-mail: umfkadm@maine.maine.edu

Getting in Last Year 292 applied; 91% were accepted; 144 enrolled (54%).

Financial Matters $3824 resident tuition and fees (2002–03); $8714 nonresident tuition and fees (2002–03); $4436 room and board; 87% average percent of need met; $5003 average financial aid amount received per undergraduate (2001–02).

Academics UMFK awards associate and bachelor's degrees. Challenging opportunities include advanced placement credit, student-designed majors, an honors program, double majors, independent study, and a senior project. Special programs include internships and summer session for credit. The faculty at UMFK has 35 full-time members, 69% with terminal degrees. The student-faculty ratio is 15:1.

Students of UMFK The student body is made up of 827 undergraduates. 62.2% are women and 37.8% are men. Students come from 16 states and territories and 9 other countries. 67% are from Maine. 1.3% are international students. 81% returned for their sophomore year.

Applying UMFK requires an essay and a high school transcript, and in some cases an interview. The school recommends SAT I and SAT II or ACT and recommendations. Application deadline: rolling admissions; 3/15 priority date for financial aid. Early and deferred admission are possible.

UNIVERSITY OF MAINE AT MACHIAS

Machias, ME

Rural setting ■ *Public* ■ *State-supported* ■ *Coed*

Web site: www.umm.maine.edu

Contact: Mr. David Baldwin, Director of Admissions, 9 O'Brien Avenue, Machias, ME 04654

Telephone: 207-255-1318 or toll-free 888-GOTOUMM **Fax:** 207-255-1363

E-mail: ummadmissions@maine.edu

Getting in Last Year 478 applied; 83% were accepted; 154 enrolled (39%).

Financial Matters $4390 resident tuition and fees (2002–03); $9700 nonresident tuition and fees (2002–03); $4880 room and board; 83% average percent of need met; $8182 average financial aid amount received per undergraduate.

Academics UMM awards associate and bachelor's degrees. Challenging opportunities include advanced placement credit, student-designed majors, an honors program, double majors, independent study, and a senior project. Special programs include cooperative education, internships, summer session for credit, off-campus study, and study-abroad. The most frequently chosen baccalaureate fields are health professions and related sciences, business/marketing, and biological/life sciences. The faculty at UMM has 35 full-time members, 74% with terminal degrees. The student-faculty ratio is 15:1.

Students of UMM The student body is made up of 1,068 undergraduates. 71.4% are women and 28.6% are men. Students come from 24 states and territories and 19 other countries. 77% are from Maine. 6.6% are international students. 71% returned for their sophomore year.

Applying UMM requires an essay, a high school transcript, and 1 recommendation, and in some cases SAT I or ACT and a minimum high school GPA of 2.0. The school recommends an interview and 2 recommendations. Application deadline: rolling admissions; 3/1 priority date for financial aid. Early and deferred admission are possible.

UNIVERSITY OF MAINE AT PRESQUE ISLE

Presque Isle, ME

Small-town setting ■ *Public* ■ *State-supported* ■ *Coed*

Web site: www.umpi.maine.edu

Contact: Mr. Brian Manter, Director of Admissions, 181 Main Street, Presque Isle, ME 04769

Telephone: 207-768-9536 **Fax:** 207-768-9777

E-mail: adventure@umpi.maine.edu

Getting in Last Year 532 applied; 86% were accepted; 243 enrolled (53%).

Financial Matters $3850 resident tuition and fees (2002–03); $9010 nonresident tuition and fees (2002–03); $4494 room and board; 87% average percent of need met; $6730 average financial aid amount received per undergraduate.

Academics UMPI awards associate and bachelor's degrees. Challenging opportunities include advanced placement credit, accelerated degree programs, student-designed majors, an honors program, double majors, independent study, and a senior project. Special programs include internships, summer session for credit, off-campus study, and study-abroad. The most frequently chosen baccalaureate fields are liberal arts/general studies, education, and interdisciplinary studies. The faculty at UMPI has 60 full-time members, 77% with terminal degrees. The student-faculty ratio is 14:1.

Students of UMPI The student body is made up of 1,560 undergraduates. 65.1% are women and 34.9% are men. Students come from 20 states and territories and 6 other countries. 97% are from Maine. 14.5% are international students. 64% returned for their sophomore year.

Applying UMPI requires an essay, a high school transcript, and a minimum high school GPA of 2.0, and in some cases an interview and 1 recommendation. The school recommends SAT I or ACT. Application deadline: rolling admissions; 4/1 priority date for financial aid. Early and deferred admission are possible.

UNIVERSITY OF MANITOBA

Winnipeg, MB Canada

Suburban setting ■ *Public* ■ *Coed*

Web site: www.umanitoba.ca

Contact: Mr. Peter Dueck, Director of Enrollment Services, Winnipeg, MB R3T 2N2 Canada

Telephone: 204-474-6382

Getting in Last Year 7,356 enrolled.

Financial Matters $3132 nonresident tuition and fees (2002–03); $4520 room and board.

Academics University of Manitoba awards bachelor's, master's, and doctoral degrees. An honors program is a challenging opportunity. Special programs include internships, summer session for credit, off-campus study, and Army and Air Force ROTC. The faculty at University of Manitoba has 1,073 members.

Students of University of Manitoba The student body totals 24,981, of whom 21,724 are undergraduates. 57.6% are women and 42.4% are men.

Applying University of Manitoba requires a high school transcript. Application deadline: 7/1; 6/30 priority date for financial aid.

UNIVERSITY OF MARY

Bismarck, ND

Suburban setting ■ *Private* ■ *Independent Religious* ■ *Coed*

Web site: www.umary.edu

Contact: Dr. Dave Hebinger, Vice President for Enrollment Services, 7500 University Drive, Bismarck, ND 58504-9652

Telephone: 701-255-7500 ext. 8190 or toll-free 800-288-6279 **Fax:** 701-255-7687

E-mail: marauder@umary.edu

Getting in Last Year 943 applied; 94% were accepted; 402 enrolled (45%).

Financial Matters $9400 tuition and fees (2002–03); $3735 room and board.

Academics Mary awards associate, bachelor's, and master's degrees. Challenging opportunities include advanced placement credit, accelerated degree programs, double majors, independent study, and a senior project. Special programs include cooperative education, internships, summer session for credit, off-campus study, and study-abroad. The most frequently chosen baccalaureate fields are business/marketing, health professions and related sciences, and education. The faculty at Mary has 89 full-time members, 38% with terminal degrees. The student-faculty ratio is 16:1.

Students of Mary The student body totals 2,546, of whom 2,100 are undergraduates. 60.1% are women and 39.9% are men. Students come from 25 states and territories and 15 other countries. 72% are from North Dakota. 1.6% are international students. 72% returned for their sophomore year.

Applying Mary requires ACT, SAT I and SAT II or ACT, a high school transcript, and 1 recommendation, and in some cases an essay and an interview. The school recommends 2.5 GPA. Application deadline: rolling admissions; 5/1 priority date for financial aid. Early and deferred admission are possible.

UNIVERSITY OF MARY HARDIN-BAYLOR

Belton, TX

Small-town setting ■ *Private* ■ *Independent Religious* ■ *Coed*

Web site: www.umhb.edu

Contact: Ms. Valerie Hampton, Admissions Clerk, UMHB Station Box 8004, 900 College Street, Belton, TX 76513-2599

Telephone: 254-295-4520 or toll-free 800-727-8642 **Fax:** 254-295-5049

E-mail: admission@umhb.edu

Getting in Last Year 747 applied; 92% were accepted; 473 enrolled (69%).

University of Mary Hardin-Baylor (continued)

Financial Matters $10,640 tuition and fees (2002–03); $4210 room and board; 75% average percent of need met; $8026 average financial aid amount received per undergraduate.

Academics UMHB awards bachelor's and master's degrees. Challenging opportunities include advanced placement credit, accelerated degree programs, an honors program, double majors, independent study, and a senior project. Special programs include internships, summer session for credit, and Air Force ROTC. The most frequently chosen baccalaureate fields are education, business/marketing, and liberal arts/general studies. The faculty at UMHB has 120 full-time members, 68% with terminal degrees. The student-faculty ratio is 16:1.

Students of UMHB The student body totals 2,664, of whom 2,486 are undergraduates. 64.6% are women and 35.4% are men. Students come from 27 states and territories and 10 other countries. 98% are from Texas. 0.6% are international students. 62% returned for their sophomore year.

Applying UMHB requires SAT I or ACT and a high school transcript, and in some cases an interview. Application deadline: rolling admissions; 4/1 priority date for financial aid. Early and deferred admission are possible.

UNIVERSITY OF MARYLAND, BALTIMORE COUNTY

Baltimore, MD

Suburban setting ■ Public ■ State-supported ■ Coed

Web site: www.umbc.edu

Contact: Ms. Yvette Mozie-Ross, Director of Admissions, 1000 Hilltop Circle, Baltimore, MD 21250-5398

Telephone: 410-455-3799 or toll-free 800-UMBC-4U2 (in-state), 800-862-2402 (out-of-state) **Fax:** 410-455-1094

E-mail: admissions@umbc.edu

Getting in Last Year 5,211 applied; 63% were accepted; 1,347 enrolled (41%).

Financial Matters $6362 resident tuition and fees (2002–03); $12,546 nonresident tuition and fees (2002–03); $6780 room and board; 61% average percent of need met; $6212 average financial aid amount received per undergraduate (2001–02).

Academics UMBC awards bachelor's, master's, and doctoral degrees and post-bachelor's certificates. Challenging opportunities include advanced placement credit, student-designed majors, freshman honors college, an honors program, double majors, independent study, and a senior project. Special programs include cooperative education, internships, summer session for credit, off-campus study, study-abroad, and Army and Air Force ROTC. The most frequently chosen baccalaureate fields are computer/information sciences, social sciences and history, and visual/performing arts. The faculty at UMBC has 471 full-time members, 86% with terminal degrees. The student-faculty ratio is 17:1.

Students of UMBC The student body totals 11,711, of whom 9,549 are undergraduates. 48.3% are women and 51.7% are men. Students come from 46 states and territories and 106 other countries. 92% are from Maryland. 5% are international students. 82% returned for their sophomore year.

Applying UMBC requires an essay, SAT I or ACT, a high school transcript, and a minimum high school GPA of 2.0. The school recommends 2 recommendations. Application deadline: 2/1; 3/1 priority date for financial aid. Early and deferred admission are possible.

UNIVERSITY OF MARYLAND, COLLEGE PARK

College Park, MD

Suburban setting ■ Public ■ State-supported ■ Coed

Web site: www.maryland.edu

Contact: Ms. Barbara Gill, Director of Undergraduate Admissions, Mitchell Building, College Park, MD 20742-5235

Telephone: 301-314-8385 or toll-free 800-422-5867 **Fax:** 301-314-9693

E-mail: um-admit@uga.umd.edu

Getting in Last Year 23,117 applied; 43% were accepted; 3,912 enrolled (39%).

Financial Matters $5670 resident tuition and fees (2002–03); $14,434 nonresident tuition and fees (2002–03); $7241 room and board; 72% average percent of need met; $8051 average financial aid amount received per undergraduate (2001–02).

Academics University of Maryland, College Park awards bachelor's, master's, doctoral, and first-professional degrees and post-bachelor's and post-master's certificates. Challenging opportunities include advanced placement credit, accelerated degree programs, student-designed majors, an honors program, double majors, independent study, and a senior project. Special programs include cooperative education, internships, summer session for credit, off-campus study, study-abroad, and Army, Navy and Air Force ROTC. The most frequently chosen baccalaureate fields are business/marketing, social sciences and history, and biological/life sciences. The faculty at University of Maryland, College Park has 1,621 full-time members, 91% with terminal degrees. The student-faculty ratio is 13:1.

Students of University of Maryland, College Park The student body totals 34,740, of whom 25,179 are undergraduates. 49.1% are women and 50.9% are men. Students come from 54 states and territories and 155 other countries. 75% are from Maryland. 2.7% are international students. 91% returned for their sophomore year.

Applying University of Maryland, College Park requires an essay, SAT I or ACT, a high school transcript, and 1 recommendation, and in some cases an interview. The school recommends 2 recommendations and resume of activities, auditions. Application deadline: 1/20; 2/15 priority date for financial aid. Early admission is possible.

UNIVERSITY OF MARYLAND EASTERN SHORE

Princess Anne, MD

Rural setting ■ Public ■ State-supported ■ Coed

Web site: www.umes.edu

Contact: Ms. Cheryll Collier-Mills, Director of Admissions and Recruitment, Princess Anne, MD 21853-1299

Telephone: 410-651-8410 **Fax:** 410-651-7922

E-mail: umesadmissions@mail.umes.edu

Getting in Last Year 1,905 applied; 66% were accepted.

Financial Matters $4537 resident tuition and fees (2002–03); $9188 nonresident tuition and fees (2002–03); $5380 room and board; 70% average percent of need met; $10,150 average financial aid amount received per undergraduate.

Academics UMES awards bachelor's, master's, and doctoral degrees. Challenging opportunities include advanced placement credit, accelerated degree programs, student-designed majors, an honors program, and a senior project. Special programs include cooperative education, internships, summer session for credit, and off-campus study. The faculty at UMES has 215 full-time members. The student-faculty ratio is 20:1.

Students of UMES The student body totals 3,426, of whom 3,134 are undergraduates. 58.2% are women and 41.8% are men. Students come from 30 states and territories and 50 other countries. 72% are from Maryland. 10.8% are international students. 74% returned for their sophomore year.

Applying UMES requires an essay, SAT I or ACT, a high school transcript, 2 recommendations, and a minimum high school GPA of 2.5. The school recommends an interview. Application deadline: 7/15; 2/1 priority date for financial aid. Early and deferred admission are possible.

UNIVERSITY OF MARYLAND UNIVERSITY COLLEGE

Adelphi, MD

Suburban setting ■ Public ■ State-supported ■ Coed

Web site: www.umuc.edu

Contact: Ms. Anne Rahill, Technical Director, Admissions, 3501 University Boulevard, East, Adelphi, MD 20783

Telephone: 301-985-7000 or toll-free 800-888-8682 (in-state) **Fax:** 301-985-7364

E-mail: umucinfo@nova.umuc.edu

Getting in Last Year 970 applied; 100% were accepted; 376 enrolled (39%).

Financial Matters $5064 resident tuition and fees (2002–03); $9336 nonresident tuition and fees (2002–03); 29% average percent of need met; $1631 average financial aid amount received per undergraduate (2001–02).

Academics UMUC awards associate, bachelor's, master's, and doctoral degrees and post-bachelor's certificates (offers primarily part-time evening and weekend degree programs at more than 30 off-campus locations in Maryland and the Washington, DC area, and more than 180 military communities in Europe and Asia with military enrollment not reflected in this profile; associate of arts program available to military students only). Challenging opportunities include advanced placement credit, accelerated degree programs, and double majors. Special programs include cooperative education, summer session for credit, and off-campus study. The most frequently chosen baccalaureate field is interdisciplinary studies. The faculty at UMUC has 76 full-time members, 84% with terminal degrees. The student-faculty ratio is 19:1.

Students of UMUC The student body totals 24,030, of whom 16,990 are undergraduates. 57.8% are women and 42.2% are men. Students come from 54 states and territories and 41 other countries. 75% are from Maryland. 1.9% are international students.

Applying UMUC requires a high school transcript. Application deadline: rolling admissions; 6/1 priority date for financial aid. Deferred admission is possible.

UNIVERSITY OF MASSACHUSETTS AMHERST

Amherst, MA

Small-town setting ■ Public ■ State-supported ■ Coed

Web site: www.umass.edu

Contact: Mr. Joseph Marshall, Assistant Dean for Enrollment Services, 37 Mather Drive, Amherst, MA 01003-9291

Telephone: 413-545-0222 **Fax:** 413-545-4312

E-mail: mail@admissions.umass.edu

Getting in Last Year 20,449 applied; 58% were accepted; 3,460 enrolled (29%).

Financial Matters $6482 resident tuition and fees (2002–03); $14,705 nonresident tuition and fees (2002–03); $5630 room and board; 87% average percent of need met; $8439 average financial aid amount received per undergraduate (2001–02).

Academics UMass Amherst awards associate, bachelor's, master's, and doctoral degrees and post-master's certificates. Challenging opportunities include advanced placement credit, student-designed majors, freshman honors college, an honors program, double majors, independent study, and a senior project. Special programs include cooperative education, internships, summer session for credit, off-campus study, study-abroad, and Army and Air Force ROTC. The most frequently chosen baccalaureate fields are business/marketing, social sciences and history, and communications/communication technologies. The faculty at UMass Amherst has 1,063 full-time members, 94% with terminal degrees. The student-faculty ratio is 19:1.

Students of UMass Amherst The student body totals 24,062, of whom 18,606 are undergraduates. 50.9% are women and 49.1% are men. Students come from 52 states and territories and 114 other countries. 82% are from Massachusetts. 1.7% are international students. 84% returned for their sophomore year.

Applying UMass Amherst requires an essay, SAT I or ACT, and a high school transcript. The school recommends recommendations and a minimum high school GPA of 3.0. Application deadline: 1/15; 3/1 priority date for financial aid.

UNIVERSITY OF MASSACHUSETTS BOSTON

Boston, MA

Urban setting ■ *Public* ■ *State-supported* ■ *Coed*

Web site: www.umb.edu

Contact: Office of Admissions Information Service, 100 Morrissey Boulevard, Boston, MA 02125-3393

Telephone: 617-287-6100 **Fax:** 617-287-5999

E-mail: undergrad@umb.edu

Getting in Last Year 2,704 applied; 55% were accepted; 578 enrolled (39%).

Financial Matters $5222 resident tuition and fees (2002–03); $13,266 nonresident tuition and fees (2002–03); 68% average percent of need met; $7327 average financial aid amount received per undergraduate.

Academics UMass Boston awards bachelor's, master's, and doctoral degrees and post-bachelor's and post-master's certificates. Challenging opportunities include advanced placement credit, accelerated degree programs, student-designed majors, freshman honors college, an honors program, double majors, independent study, and a senior project. Special programs include cooperative education, internships, summer session for credit, off-campus study, and study-abroad. The most frequently chosen baccalaureate field is law/legal studies. The faculty at UMass Boston has 427 full-time members, 100% with terminal degrees. The student-faculty ratio is 15:1.

Students of UMass Boston The student body totals 12,719, of whom 10,071 are undergraduates. 56.9% are women and 43.1% are men. Students come from 38 states and territories and 97 other countries. 96% are from Massachusetts. 5.8% are international students. 69% returned for their sophomore year.

Applying UMass Boston requires SAT I or ACT, a high school transcript, and a minimum high school GPA of 2.75, and in some cases an essay, an interview, and recommendations. The school recommends an essay. Application deadline: rolling admissions; 3/1 priority date for financial aid. Deferred admission is possible.

UNIVERSITY OF MASSACHUSETTS DARTMOUTH

North Dartmouth, MA

Suburban setting ■ *Public* ■ *State-supported* ■ *Coed*

Web site: www.umassd.edu

Contact: Mr. Steven Briggs, Director of Admissions, 285 Old Westport Road, North Dartmouth, MA 02747-2300

Telephone: 508-999-8606 **Fax:** 508-999-8755

E-mail: admissions@umassd.edu

Getting in Last Year 6,039 applied; 70% were accepted; 1,674 enrolled (40%).

Financial Matters $5164 resident tuition and fees (2002–03); $13,664 nonresident tuition and fees (2002–03); $6526 room and board; 88% average percent of need met; $6859 average financial aid amount received per undergraduate (2001–02).

Academics U Mass Dartmouth awards bachelor's, master's, and doctoral degrees and post-bachelor's and post-master's certificates. Challenging opportunities include advanced placement credit, student-designed majors, an honors program, double majors, independent study, and a senior project. Special programs include cooperative education, internships, summer session for credit, off-campus study, study-abroad, and Army ROTC. The most frequently chosen baccalaureate fields are business/marketing, social sciences and history, and visual/performing arts. The faculty at U Mass Dartmouth has 321 full-time members. The student-faculty ratio is 16:1.

Students of U Mass Dartmouth The student body totals 8,122, of whom 7,309 are undergraduates. 52.4% are women and 47.6% are men. Students come from 30 states and territories and 33 other countries. 93% are from Massachusetts. 1.3% are international students. 80% returned for their sophomore year.

Applying U Mass Dartmouth requires an essay, SAT I or ACT, a high school transcript, and a minimum high school GPA of 2.0. The school recommends recommendations and a minimum high school GPA of 3.0. Application deadline: rolling admissions; 3/1 priority date for financial aid. Early and deferred admission are possible.

UNIVERSITY OF MASSACHUSETTS LOWELL

Lowell, MA

Urban setting ■ *Public* ■ *State-supported* ■ *Coed*

Web site: www.uml.edu

Contact: Ms. Lisa Johnson, Assistant Vice Chancellor of Enrollment Management, 883 Broadway Street, Room 110, Lowell, MA 01854-5104

Telephone: 978-934-3944 or toll-free 800-410-4607 **Fax:** 978-934-3086

E-mail: admissions@uml.edu

Getting in Last Year 3,583 applied; 63% were accepted; 1,020 enrolled (45%).

Financial Matters $5213 resident tuition and fees (2002–03); $12,326 nonresident tuition and fees (2002–03); $5464 room and board; 96% average percent of need met; $6728 average financial aid amount received per undergraduate (2001–02).

Academics UMass Lowell awards associate, bachelor's, master's, and doctoral degrees. Challenging opportunities include advanced placement credit, accelerated degree programs, an honors program, and double majors. Special programs include cooperative education, internships, summer session for credit, off-campus study, study-abroad, and Air Force ROTC. The most frequently chosen baccalaureate fields are business/marketing, engineering/engineering technologies, and protective services/public administration. The faculty at UMass Lowell has 399 full-time members. The student-faculty ratio is 15:1.

Students of UMass Lowell The student body totals 12,086, of whom 9,334 are undergraduates. 40.4% are women and 59.6% are men. Students come from 34 states and territories and 73 other countries. 89% are from Massachusetts. 2.6% are international students. 74% returned for their sophomore year.

Applying UMass Lowell requires an essay, SAT I or ACT, a high school transcript, 1 recommendation, and a minimum high school GPA of 3.0, and in some cases an interview. Application deadline: rolling admissions; 3/1 priority date for financial aid. Deferred admission is possible.

THE UNIVERSITY OF MEMPHIS

Memphis, TN

Urban setting ■ *Public* ■ *State-supported* ■ *Coed*

Web site: www.memphis.edu

Contact: Mr. David Wallace, Director of Admissions, Memphis, TN 38152

Telephone: 901-678-2101 **Fax:** 901-678-3053

E-mail: dwallace@memphis.edu

Getting in Last Year 4,439 applied; 70% were accepted.

Financial Matters $3792 resident tuition and fees (2002–03); $10,946 nonresident tuition and fees (2002–03); $4380 room and board; 77% average percent of need met; $3578 average financial aid amount received per undergraduate (2001–02).

Academics The University of Memphis awards bachelor's, master's, doctoral, and first-professional degrees and post-bachelor's, post-master's, and first-professional certificates. Challenging opportunities include advanced placement credit, accelerated degree programs, student-designed majors, an honors program, double majors, independent study, and a senior project. Special programs include cooperative education, internships, summer session for credit, study-abroad, and Army, Navy and Air Force ROTC. The most frequently chosen baccalaureate fields are business/marketing, interdisciplinary studies, and visual/performing arts. The faculty at The University of Memphis has 846 full-time members, 68% with terminal degrees. The student-faculty ratio is 13:1.

Students of The University of Memphis The student body totals 19,797, of whom 15,025 are undergraduates. 58.8% are women and 41.2% are men. Students come from 44 states and territories and 94 other countries. 92% are from Tennessee. 2% are international students. 72% returned for their sophomore year.

Applying The University of Memphis requires SAT I or ACT and a high school transcript, and in some cases an interview, 2 recommendations, and a minimum high school GPA of 2.0. Application deadline: 8/1; 3/1 priority date for financial aid. Early admission is possible.

UNIVERSITY OF MIAMI

Coral Gables, FL

Suburban setting ■ *Private* ■ *Independent* ■ *Coed*

Web site: www.miami.edu

Contact: Mr. Edward M. Gillis, Associate Dean of Enrollment and Director of Admission, PO Box 248025, Ashe Building Room 132, 1252 Memorial Drive, Coral Gables, FL 33146-4616

Telephone: 305-284-4323 **Fax:** 305-284-2507

E-mail: admission@miami.edu

Getting in Last Year 15,909 applied; 44% were accepted; 2,059 enrolled (30%).

Financial Matters $24,810 tuition and fees (2002–03); $8062 room and board; 84% average percent of need met; $22,399 average financial aid amount received per undergraduate.

University of Miami (continued)

Academics UM awards bachelor's, master's, doctoral, and first-professional degrees and post-bachelor's and post-master's certificates. Challenging opportunities include advanced placement credit, accelerated degree programs, student-designed majors, an honors program, double majors, independent study, and a senior project. Special programs include internships, summer session for credit, study-abroad, and Army and Air Force ROTC. The most frequently chosen baccalaureate fields are business/marketing, visual/performing arts, and engineering/engineering technologies. The faculty at UM has 837 full-time members, 87% with terminal degrees. The student-faculty ratio is 13:1.

Students of UM The student body totals 14,978, of whom 9,794 are undergraduates. 56.9% are women and 43.1% are men. Students come from 54 states and territories and 102 other countries. 56% are from Florida. 7.2% are international students. 82% returned for their sophomore year.

Applying UM requires an essay, SAT I or ACT, a high school transcript, 1 recommendation, and counselor evaluation form, and in some cases SAT II Subject Tests and an interview. The school recommends a minimum high school GPA of 3.0. Application deadline: 2/1; 2/15 priority date for financial aid. Early and deferred admission are possible.

UNIVERSITY OF MICHIGAN

Ann Arbor, MI

Suburban setting ■ *Public* ■ *State-supported* ■ *Coed*

Web site: www.umich.edu
Contact: Mr. Ted Spencer, Director of Undergraduate Admissions, 1220 Student Activities Building, 515 East Jefferson, Ann Arbor, MI 48109-1316
Telephone: 734-764-7433 **Fax:** 734-936-0740
E-mail: ugadmiss@umich.edu

Getting in Last Year 25,108 applied; 49% were accepted; 5,187 enrolled (42%).

Financial Matters $7277 resident tuition and fees (2002–03); $23,501 nonresident tuition and fees (2002–03); $6366 room and board; 90% average percent of need met; $10,022 average financial aid amount received per undergraduate (2001–02).

Academics Michigan awards bachelor's, master's, doctoral, and first-professional degrees and post-master's certificates. Challenging opportunities include advanced placement credit, accelerated degree programs, student-designed majors, an honors program, double majors, independent study, and a senior project. Special programs include cooperative education, internships, summer session for credit, off-campus study, study-abroad, and Army and Air Force ROTC. The most frequently chosen baccalaureate fields are engineering/engineering technologies, social sciences and history, and psychology. The faculty at Michigan has 2,176 full-time members, 91% with terminal degrees. The student-faculty ratio is 15:1.

Students of Michigan The student body totals 38,972, of whom 24,472 are undergraduates. 51.1% are women and 48.9% are men. Students come from 54 states and territories and 87 other countries. 69% are from Michigan. 4.4% are international students. 95% returned for their sophomore year.

Applying Michigan requires an essay, SAT I or ACT, and a high school transcript, and in some cases SAT II Subject Tests, SAT II: Writing Test, an interview, and recommendations. Application deadline: 2/1; 2/15 priority date for financial aid. Deferred admission is possible.

UNIVERSITY OF MICHIGAN–DEARBORN

Dearborn, MI

Suburban setting ■ *Public* ■ *State-supported* ■ *Coed*

Web site: www.umd.umich.edu
Contact: Mr. David Placey, Director of Admissions, 4901 Evergreen Road, Dearborn, MI 48128-1491
Telephone: 313-593-5100 **Fax:** 313-436-9167
E-mail: admissions@umd.umich.edu

Getting in Last Year 2,553 applied; 67% were accepted; 815 enrolled (47%).

Financial Matters $5332 resident tuition and fees (2002–03); $12,893 nonresident tuition and fees (2002–03); 32% average percent of need met; $7252 average financial aid amount received per undergraduate (2001–02).

Academics UM-D awards bachelor's and master's degrees and post-bachelor's certificates. Challenging opportunities include accelerated degree programs, student-designed majors, an honors program, double majors, independent study, and a senior project. Special programs include cooperative education, internships, summer session for credit, off-campus study, study-abroad, and Army, Navy and Air Force ROTC. The most frequently chosen baccalaureate fields are business/marketing, education, and engineering/engineering technologies. The faculty at UM-D has 261 full-time members, 88% with terminal degrees. The student-faculty ratio is 17:1.

Students of UM-D The student body totals 8,725, of whom 6,556 are undergraduates. 54% are women and 46% are men. Students come from 25 states and territories and 22 other countries. 97% are from Michigan. 2% are international students. 86% returned for their sophomore year.

Applying UM-D requires SAT I or ACT, a high school transcript, and a minimum high school GPA of 3.0, and in some cases an interview. The school recommends ACT. Application deadline: rolling admissions. Deferred admission is possible.

UNIVERSITY OF MICHIGAN–FLINT

Flint, MI

Urban setting ■ *Public* ■ *State-supported* ■ *Coed*

Web site: www.flint.umich.edu
Contact: Dr. Virginia R. Allen, Vice Chancellor for Student Services and Enrollment, 303 East Kearsley Street, Flint, MI 48502-1950
Telephone: 810-762-3434 or toll-free 800-742-5363 (in-state)
Fax: 810-762-3272
E-mail: admissions@list.flint.umich.edu

Getting in Last Year 1,357 applied; 79% were accepted; 527 enrolled (49%).

Financial Matters $4752 resident tuition and fees (2002–03); $9246 nonresident tuition and fees (2002–03); $6562 average financial aid amount received per undergraduate.

Academics UM-Flint awards bachelor's, master's, and first-professional degrees and post-bachelor's certificates. Challenging opportunities include advanced placement credit, student-designed majors, an honors program, double majors, independent study, and a senior project. Special programs include cooperative education, internships, summer session for credit, and study-abroad. The most frequently chosen baccalaureate fields are education, business/marketing, and health professions and related sciences. The faculty at UM-Flint has 209 full-time members, 72% with terminal degrees. The student-faculty ratio is 16:1.

Students of UM-Flint The student body totals 6,434, of whom 5,877 are undergraduates. 64.2% are women and 35.8% are men. Students come from 21 states and territories and 3 other countries. 99% are from Michigan. 0.4% are international students. 70% returned for their sophomore year.

Applying UM-Flint requires a high school transcript. The school recommends an essay and SAT I or ACT. Application deadline: 9/2; 2/21 priority date for financial aid. Deferred admission is possible.

UNIVERSITY OF MINNESOTA, CROOKSTON

Crookston, MN

Rural setting ■ *Public* ■ *State-supported* ■ *Coed*

Web site: www.crk.umn.edu
Contact: Mr. Russell L. Kreager, Director of Admissions, 2900 University Avenue, 170 Owen Hall, Crookston, MN 56716-5001
Telephone: 218-281-8569 or toll-free 800-862-6466 **Fax:** 218-281-8575
E-mail: info@mail.crk.umn.edu

Getting in Last Year 551 applied; 81% were accepted; 276 enrolled (61%).

Financial Matters $6422 resident tuition and fees (2002–03); $6422 nonresident tuition and fees (2002–03); $4464 room and board; 87% average percent of need met; $8069 average financial aid amount received per undergraduate (2001–02).

Academics UMC awards associate and bachelor's degrees. Challenging opportunities include advanced placement credit, double majors, and independent study. Special programs include internships, summer session for credit, study-abroad, and Air Force ROTC. The most frequently chosen baccalaureate fields are agriculture, business/marketing, and computer/information sciences. The faculty at UMC has 55 full-time members, 45% with terminal degrees. The student-faculty ratio is 15:1.

Students of UMC The student body is made up of 2,387 undergraduates. 55% are women and 45% are men. Students come from 21 states and territories and 18 other countries. 72% are from Minnesota. 2.8% are international students. 65% returned for their sophomore year.

Applying UMC requires ACT and a high school transcript. Application deadline: 7/15; 3/31 priority date for financial aid. Deferred admission is possible.

UNIVERSITY OF MINNESOTA, DULUTH

Duluth, MN

Suburban setting ■ *Public* ■ *State-supported* ■ *Coed*

Web site: www.d.umn.edu
Contact: Ms. Beth Esselstrom, Director of Admissions, 23 Solon Campus Center, 1117 University Drive, Duluth, MN 55812-3000
Telephone: 218-726-7171 or toll-free 800-232-1339 **Fax:** 218-726-7040
E-mail: umdadmis@d.umn.edu

Getting in Last Year 6,208 applied; 77% were accepted; 2,051 enrolled (43%).

Financial Matters $6467 resident tuition and fees (2002–03); $16,727 nonresident tuition and fees (2002–03); $4960 room and board; 74% average percent of need met; $7371 average financial aid amount received per undergraduate.

Academics UMD awards bachelor's, master's, and first-professional degrees. Challenging opportunities include advanced placement credit, student-designed majors, an honors program, double majors, independent study, and a senior project. Special programs include internships, summer session for credit, off-campus study, study-abroad, and Air Force ROTC. The most frequently chosen baccalaureate fields are business/marketing, education, and social sciences and history. The faculty at UMD has 363 full-time members, 77% with terminal degrees. The student-faculty ratio is 20:1.

Students of UMD The student body totals 9,815, of whom 9,144 are undergraduates. 51% are women and 49% are men. Students come from 36 states and territories and 32 other countries. 88% are from Minnesota. 2.3% are international students. 78% returned for their sophomore year.

Applying UMD requires SAT I or ACT and a high school transcript. Application deadline: 2/1; 3/1 priority date for financial aid.

UNIVERSITY OF MINNESOTA, MORRIS

Morris, MN

Small-town setting ■ Public ■ State-supported ■ Coed

Web site: www.mrs.umn.edu

Contact: Mr. Scott K. Hagg, Director of Admissions, 600 East 4th Street, Morris, MN 56267-2199

Telephone: 320-539-6035 or toll-free 800-992-8863 **Fax:** 320-589-1673

E-mail: admissions@mrs.umn.edu

Getting in Last Year 1,297 applied; 82% were accepted; 477 enrolled (45%).

Financial Matters $7259 resident tuition and fees (2002–03); $4680 room and board; 81% average percent of need met; $9754 average financial aid amount received per undergraduate.

Academics UMM awards bachelor's degrees. Challenging opportunities include advanced placement credit, accelerated degree programs, student-designed majors, freshman honors college, an honors program, double majors, and a senior project. Special programs include internships, summer session for credit, off-campus study, and study-abroad. The most frequently chosen baccalaureate fields are social sciences and history, English, and biological/life sciences. The faculty at UMM has 120 full-time members. The student-faculty ratio is 14:1.

Students of UMM The student body is made up of 1,910 undergraduates. 60.4% are women and 39.6% are men. Students come from 31 states and territories and 13 other countries. 85% are from Minnesota. 1.1% are international students. 84% returned for their sophomore year.

Applying UMM requires an essay, SAT I or ACT, and a high school transcript, and in some cases an interview. The school recommends a minimum high school GPA of 3.0. Application deadline: 3/15; 3/1 priority date for financial aid. Early and deferred admission are possible.

UNIVERSITY OF MINNESOTA, TWIN CITIES CAMPUS

Minneapolis, MN

Urban setting ■ Public ■ State-supported ■ Coed

Web site: www.umn.edu/tc

Contact: Ms. Patricia Jones Whyte, Associate Director of Admissions, 240 Williamson Hall, Minneapolis, MN 55455-0115

Telephone: 612-625-2008 or toll-free 800-752-1000 **Fax:** 612-626-1693

E-mail: admissions@tc.umn.edu

Getting in Last Year 14,724 applied; 74% were accepted; 5,188 enrolled (47%).

Financial Matters $6280 resident tuition and fees (2002–03); $16,854 nonresident tuition and fees (2002–03); $5696 room and board; 79% average percent of need met; $8496 average financial aid amount received per undergraduate.

Academics U of M-Twin Cities Campus awards bachelor's, master's, doctoral, and first-professional degrees and post-bachelor's and post-master's certificates. Challenging opportunities include advanced placement credit, accelerated degree programs, student-designed majors, freshman honors college, an honors program, double majors, independent study, and a senior project. Special programs include cooperative education, internships, summer session for credit, off-campus study, study-abroad, and Army, Navy and Air Force ROTC. The most frequently chosen baccalaureate fields are social sciences and history, engineering/engineering technologies, and business/marketing. The faculty at U of M-Twin Cities Campus has 2,711 full-time members, 96% with terminal degrees. The student-faculty ratio is 15:1.

Students of U of M-Twin Cities Campus The student body totals 48,677, of whom 32,457 are undergraduates. 52.9% are women and 47.1% are men. Students come from 55 states and territories and 85 other countries. 74% are from Minnesota. 2.1% are international students. 82% returned for their sophomore year.

Applying U of M-Twin Cities Campus requires SAT I or ACT and a high school transcript. The school recommends a minimum high school GPA of 2.0. Application deadline: rolling admissions; 1/15 priority date for financial aid. Early and deferred admission are possible.

UNIVERSITY OF MISSISSIPPI

University, MS

Small-town setting ■ Public ■ State-supported ■ Coed

Web site: www.olemiss.edu

Contact: Mr. Beckett Howorth, Director of Admissions, 145 Martindale Student Services Center, University, MS 38677

Telephone: 662-915-7226 or toll-free 800-653-6477 (in-state) **Fax:** 662-915-5869

E-mail: admissions@olemiss.edu

Getting in Last Year 6,601 applied; 80% were accepted; 2,196 enrolled (42%).

Financial Matters $3916 resident tuition and fees (2002–03); $8826 nonresident tuition and fees (2002–03); $5200 room and board; 76% average percent of need met; $7374 average financial aid amount received per undergraduate (2001–02).

Academics Ole Miss awards bachelor's, master's, doctoral, and first-professional degrees. Challenging opportunities include advanced placement credit, accelerated degree programs, freshman honors college, an honors program, double majors, independent study, and a senior project. Special programs include internships, summer session for credit, study-abroad, and Army and Air Force ROTC. The student-faculty ratio is 19:1.

Students of Ole Miss The student body totals 13,135, of whom 10,661 are undergraduates. Students come from 47 states and territories and 39 other countries. 69% are from Mississippi. 0.9% are international students.

Applying Ole Miss requires a high school transcript and a minimum high school GPA of 2.0. The school recommends SAT I or ACT. Application deadline: 7/20; 3/15 priority date for financial aid. Early admission is possible.

UNIVERSITY OF MISSISSIPPI MEDICAL CENTER

Jackson, MS

Urban setting ■ Public ■ State-supported ■ Coed

Web site: umc.edu

Contact: Ms. Barbara Westerfield, Director of Student Records and Registrar, 2500 North State Street, Jackson, MS 39216-4505

Telephone: 601-984-1080 **Fax:** 601-984-1079

Financial Matters $2850 resident tuition and fees (2002–03); $6090 nonresident tuition and fees (2002–03); $1890 room only; 47% average percent of need met; $6300 average financial aid amount received per undergraduate (2001–02).

Academics UMC awards bachelor's, master's, doctoral, and first-professional degrees. Special programs include internships and study-abroad. The most frequently chosen baccalaureate field is health professions and related sciences. The faculty at UMC has 605 full-time members, 86% with terminal degrees. The student-faculty ratio is 2:1.

Students of UMC The student body totals 1,673, of whom 426 are undergraduates. 80.3% are women and 19.7% are men. Students come from 1 state or territory.

Applying Application deadline: 4/1 priority date for financial aid.

UNIVERSITY OF MISSOURI–COLUMBIA

Columbia, MO

Small-town setting ■ Public ■ State-supported ■ Coed

Web site: www.missouri.edu

Contact: Ms. Georgeanne Porter, Director of Admissions, 230 Jesse Hall, Columbia, MO 65211

Telephone: 573-882-7786 or toll-free 800-225-6075 (in-state) **Fax:** 573-882-7887

E-mail: mu4u@missouri.edu

Getting in Last Year 10,215 applied; 88% were accepted; 4,439 enrolled (49%).

Financial Matters $5552 resident tuition and fees (2002–03); $14,705 nonresident tuition and fees (2002–03); $5374 room and board; 87% average percent of need met; $7544 average financial aid amount received per undergraduate.

Academics MU awards bachelor's, master's, doctoral, and first-professional degrees and post-master's certificates. Challenging opportunities include advanced placement credit, accelerated degree programs, student-designed majors, freshman honors college, an honors program, double majors, independent study, and a senior project. Special programs include cooperative education, internships, summer session for credit, off-campus study, study-abroad, and Army, Navy and Air Force ROTC. The most frequently chosen baccalaureate fields are business/marketing, communications/communication technologies, and engineering/engineering technologies. The faculty at MU has 1,680 full-time members, 87% with terminal degrees. The student-faculty ratio is 18:1.

Students of MU The student body totals 26,124, of whom 19,698 are undergraduates. 51.8% are women and 48.2% are men. Students come from 51 states and territories and 88 other countries. 88% are from Missouri. 1.3% are international students. 85% returned for their sophomore year.

Applying MU requires ACT, a high school transcript, and specific high school curriculum. Application deadline: rolling admissions; 3/1 priority date for financial aid. Deferred admission is possible.

UNIVERSITY OF MISSOURI–KANSAS CITY

Kansas City, MO

Urban setting ■ Public ■ State-supported ■ Coed

Web site: www.umkc.edu

Contact: Ms. Jennifer DeHaemers, Director of Admissions, Office of Admissions, 5100 Rockhill Road, Kansas City, MO 64110-2499

University of Missouri–Kansas City (continued)

Telephone: 816-235-1111 or toll-free 800-775-8652 (out-of-state)
Fax: 816-235-5544
E-mail: admit@umkc.edu

Getting in Last Year 2,480 applied; 78% were accepted; 763 enrolled (39%).

Financial Matters $4932 resident tuition and fees (2002–03); $14,083 nonresident tuition and fees (2002–03); $5235 room and board; 65% average percent of need met; $10,778 average financial aid amount received per undergraduate.

Academics UMKC awards bachelor's, master's, doctoral, and first-professional degrees and first-professional certificates. Challenging opportunities include advanced placement credit, accelerated degree programs, student-designed majors, an honors program, and a senior project. Special programs include cooperative education, internships, summer session for credit, off-campus study, study-abroad, and Army ROTC. The most frequently chosen baccalaureate fields are liberal arts/general studies, business/marketing, and education. The faculty at UMKC has 524 full-time members, 85% with terminal degrees. The student-faculty ratio is 9:1.

Students of UMKC The student body totals 13,881, of whom 8,870 are undergraduates. 59.5% are women and 40.5% are men. Students come from 45 states and territories and 105 other countries. 81% are from Missouri. 4.5% are international students. 72% returned for their sophomore year.

Applying UMKC requires ACT and a high school transcript. Application deadline: rolling admissions; 3/1 priority date for financial aid. Deferred admission is possible.

UNIVERSITY OF MISSOURI–ROLLA

Rolla, MO

Small-town setting ■ Public ■ State-supported ■ Coed

Web site: www.umr.edu
Contact: Ms. Lynn Stichnote, Director of Admissions, 106 Parker Hall, Rolla, MO 65409
Telephone: 573-341-4164 or toll-free 800-522-0938 **Fax:** 573-341-4082
E-mail: umrolla@umr.edu

Getting in Last Year 1,977 applied; 92% were accepted; 795 enrolled (44%).

Financial Matters $5650 resident tuition and fees (2002–03); $14,695 nonresident tuition and fees (2002–03); $5230 room and board; 87% average percent of need met; $8203 average financial aid amount received per undergraduate (2001–02).

Academics UMR awards bachelor's, master's, and doctoral degrees. Challenging opportunities include advanced placement credit, accelerated degree programs, freshman honors college, an honors program, double majors, independent study, and a senior project. Special programs include cooperative education, internships, summer session for credit, off-campus study, study-abroad, and Army and Air Force ROTC. The most frequently chosen baccalaureate fields are engineering/engineering technologies, computer/information sciences, and physical sciences. The faculty at UMR has 311 full-time members, 89% with terminal degrees. The student-faculty ratio is 14:1.

Students of UMR The student body totals 5,240, of whom 3,849 are undergraduates. 22.9% are women and 77.1% are men. Students come from 47 states and territories and 38 other countries. 78% are from Missouri. 3.2% are international students. 83% returned for their sophomore year.

Applying UMR requires SAT I or ACT and a high school transcript. Application deadline: 7/1; 3/1 priority date for financial aid. Early and deferred admission are possible.

UNIVERSITY OF MISSOURI–ST. LOUIS

St. Louis, MO

Suburban setting ■ Public ■ State-supported ■ Coed

Web site: www.umsl.edu
Contact: Ms. Melissa Hattman, Director of Admissions, 351 Millennuim Student Center, 8001 National Bridge Road, St. Louis, MO 63121-4499
Telephone: 314-516-5460 or toll-free 888-GO2-UMSL (in-state)
Fax: 314-516-5310
E-mail: mhattman@umsl.edu

Getting in Last Year 2,204 applied; 45% were accepted; 519 enrolled (52%).

Financial Matters $4566 resident tuition and fees (2002–03); $11,888 nonresident tuition and fees (2002–03); $5400 room and board; 50% average percent of need met; $6680 average financial aid amount received per undergraduate.

Academics UM-St. Louis awards bachelor's, master's, doctoral, and first-professional degrees and post-bachelor's certificates. Challenging opportunities include advanced placement credit, accelerated degree programs, student-designed majors, freshman honors college, an honors program, double majors, independent study, and a senior project. Special programs include cooperative education, internships, summer session for credit, off-campus study, study-abroad, and Army and Air Force ROTC. The most frequently chosen baccalaureate fields are business/marketing, education, and social sciences and history. The faculty at UM-St. Louis has 299 full-time members, 96% with terminal degrees. The student-faculty ratio is 19:1.

Students of UM-St. Louis The student body totals 15,658, of whom 12,715 are undergraduates. 60.3% are women and 39.7% are men. Students come from 38 states and territories and 61 other countries. 96% are from Missouri. 2.6% are international students. 61% returned for their sophomore year.

Applying UM-St. Louis requires SAT I or ACT and a high school transcript. Application deadline: rolling admissions; 4/1 priority date for financial aid. Early and deferred admission are possible.

UNIVERSITY OF MOBILE

Mobile, AL

Suburban setting ■ Private ■ Independent Religious ■ Coed

Web site: www.umobile.edu
Contact: Mr. Brian Boyle, Director of Admissions, PO Box 13220, Mobile, AL 36663-0220
Telephone: 251-442-2287 or toll-free 800-946-7267 **Fax:** 251-442-2498
E-mail: adminfo@umobile.edu

Getting in Last Year 477 applied; 100% were accepted; 220 enrolled (46%).

Financial Matters $9010 tuition and fees (2002–03); $5000 room and board; 54% average percent of need met; $7000 average financial aid amount received per undergraduate.

Academics UM awards associate, bachelor's, and master's degrees. Challenging opportunities include advanced placement credit, accelerated degree programs, an honors program, double majors, independent study, and a senior project. Special programs include internships, summer session for credit, and Army and Air Force ROTC. The most frequently chosen baccalaureate fields are education, interdisciplinary studies, and health professions and related sciences. The faculty at UM has 87 full-time members, 61% with terminal degrees. The student-faculty ratio is 17:1.

Students of UM The student body totals 2,003, of whom 1,802 are undergraduates. 68% are women and 32% are men. Students come from 24 states and territories and 15 other countries. 0.8% are international students.

Applying UM requires SAT I or ACT, a high school transcript, and a minimum high school GPA of 2.0, and in some cases an interview. Application deadline: rolling admissions; 3/31 priority date for financial aid. Early and deferred admission are possible.

THE UNIVERSITY OF MONTANA–MISSOULA

Missoula, MT

Urban setting ■ Public ■ State-supported ■ Coed

Web site: www.umt.edu
Contact: Office of New Student Services, Missoula, MT 59812-0002
Telephone: 406-243-6266 or toll-free 800-462-8636 **Fax:** 406-243-5711
E-mail: admiss@selway.umt.edu

Getting in Last Year 3,987 applied; 96% were accepted; 2,183 enrolled (57%).

Financial Matters $3988 resident tuition and fees (2002–03); $10,771 nonresident tuition and fees (2002–03); $5090 room and board; 81% average percent of need met; $7596 average financial aid amount received per undergraduate (2001–02).

Academics U of M awards associate, bachelor's, master's, doctoral, and first-professional degrees and post-master's certificates. Challenging opportunities include advanced placement credit, freshman honors college, an honors program, double majors, independent study, and a senior project. Special programs include cooperative education, internships, summer session for credit, off-campus study, study-abroad, and Army ROTC. The most frequently chosen baccalaureate fields are business/marketing, social sciences and history, and English. The faculty at U of M has 487 full-time members, 83% with terminal degrees. The student-faculty ratio is 19:1.

Students of U of M The student body totals 13,026, of whom 11,152 are undergraduates. 52.9% are women and 47.1% are men. Students come from 52 states and territories and 61 other countries. 74% are from Montana. 1.6% are international students. 69% returned for their sophomore year.

Applying U of M requires SAT I or ACT, a high school transcript, and a minimum high school GPA of 2.5, and in some cases ACT ASSET or ACT COMPASS. Application deadline: 7/1; 3/1 priority date for financial aid. Early and deferred admission are possible.

THE UNIVERSITY OF MONTANA–WESTERN

Dillon, MT

Small-town setting ■ Public ■ State-supported ■ Coed

Web site: www.umwestern.edu
Contact: Ms. Arlene Williams, Director of Admissions, 710 South Atlantic, Dillon, MT 59725
Telephone: 406-683-7331 or toll-free 866-869-6668 **Fax:** 406-683-7493
E-mail: admissions@umwestern.edu

Getting in Last Year 321 applied; 100% were accepted; 199 enrolled (62%).

Financial Matters $3265 resident tuition and fees (2002–03); $10,600 nonresident tuition and fees (2002–03); $4060 room and board; 16% average percent of need met; $2549 average financial aid amount received per undergraduate.

Academics The University of Montana–Western awards associate and bachelor's degrees. Challenging opportunities include advanced placement credit, accelerated degree programs, student-designed majors, an honors program, double majors, independent study, and a senior project. Special programs include cooperative education, internships, and summer session for credit. The most frequently chosen baccalaureate fields are education, business/marketing, and natural resources/environmental science. The faculty at The University of Montana–Western has 48 full-time members, 73% with terminal degrees. The student-faculty ratio is 19:1.

Students of The University of Montana–Western The student body totals 1,142, of whom 1,063 are undergraduates. 58.3% are women and 41.7% are men. Students come from 19 states and territories and 4 other countries. 86% are from Montana. 0.6% are international students.

Applying The University of Montana–Western requires SAT I or ACT, a high school transcript, and a minimum high school GPA of 2.5. Application deadline: 7/1; 3/1 priority date for financial aid. Early and deferred admission are possible.

UNIVERSITY OF MONTEVALLO

Montevallo, AL

Small-town setting ■ Public ■ State-supported ■ Coed

Web site: www.montevallo.edu
Contact: Mr. William C. Cannon, Director of Admissions, Station 6030, Montevallo, AL 35115-6030
Telephone: 205-665-6030 or toll-free 800-292-4349 **Fax:** 205-665-6032
E-mail: admissions@montevallo.edu

Getting in Last Year 1,329 applied; 74% were accepted; 507 enrolled (52%).

Financial Matters $4334 resident tuition and fees (2002–03); $8384 nonresident tuition and fees (2002–03); $3638 room and board; 77% average percent of need met; $6650 average financial aid amount received per undergraduate (2001–02).

Academics UM awards bachelor's and master's degrees and post-master's certificates. Challenging opportunities include advanced placement credit, accelerated degree programs, an honors program, double majors, independent study, and a senior project. Special programs include internships, summer session for credit, study-abroad, and Army and Air Force ROTC. The most frequently chosen baccalaureate fields are business/marketing, education, and social sciences and history. The faculty at UM has 132 full-time members, 77% with terminal degrees. The student-faculty ratio is 16:1.

Students of UM The student body totals 2,935, of whom 2,513 are undergraduates. 67.6% are women and 32.4% are men. Students come from 17 states and territories and 22 other countries. 97% are from Alabama. 1.7% are international students. 71% returned for their sophomore year.

Applying UM requires SAT I or ACT, a high school transcript, and a minimum high school GPA of 2.0. The school recommends ACT and an interview. Application deadline: 8/1; 4/15 priority date for financial aid. Early and deferred admission are possible.

UNIVERSITY OF NEBRASKA AT KEARNEY

Kearney, NE

Small-town setting ■ Public ■ State-supported ■ Coed

Web site: www.unk.edu
Contact: Mr. John Kundel, Director of Admissions, 905 West 25th Street, Kearney, NE 68849-0001
Telephone: 308-865-8702 or toll-free 800-532-7639 **Fax:** 308-865-8987
E-mail: admissionsug@unk.edu

Getting in Last Year 2,599 applied; 88% were accepted; 1,138 enrolled (50%).

Financial Matters $3383 resident tuition and fees (2002–03); $6218 nonresident tuition and fees (2002–03); $4156 room and board; 80% average percent of need met; $5417 average financial aid amount received per undergraduate (2001–02).

Academics UNK awards bachelor's and master's degrees. Challenging opportunities include advanced placement credit, an honors program, double majors, independent study, and a senior project. Special programs include cooperative education, internships, summer session for credit, off-campus study, and study-abroad. The most frequently chosen baccalaureate fields are business/marketing, education, and protective services/public administration. The faculty at UNK has 307 full-time members, 72% with terminal degrees. The student-faculty ratio is 16:1.

Students of UNK The student body totals 6,395, of whom 5,366 are undergraduates. 54.8% are women and 45.2% are men. Students come from 38 states and territories and 46 other countries. 94% are from Nebraska. 5.4% are international students. 80% returned for their sophomore year.

Applying UNK requires SAT I or ACT and a high school transcript, and in some cases 3 recommendations. The school recommends ACT. Application deadline: 8/1; 3/1 priority date for financial aid.

UNIVERSITY OF NEBRASKA AT OMAHA

Omaha, NE

Urban setting ■ Public ■ State-supported ■ Coed

Web site: www.unomaha.edu
Contact: Ms. Jolene Adams, Associate Director of Admissions, 6001 Dodge Street, Omaha, NE 68182
Telephone: 402-554-2416 or toll-free 800-858-8648 (in-state)
Fax: 402-554-3472

Getting in Last Year 4,094 applied; 86% were accepted; 1,723 enrolled (49%).

Financial Matters $3552 resident tuition and fees (2002–03); $9500 nonresident tuition and fees (2002–03); $4517 room and board.

Academics UNO awards bachelor's, master's, and doctoral degrees and post-bachelor's and post-master's certificates. Challenging opportunities include advanced placement credit, student-designed majors, an honors program, double majors, and a senior project. Special programs include cooperative education, internships, summer session for credit, off-campus study, study-abroad, and Army and Air Force ROTC. The most frequently chosen baccalaureate fields are business/marketing, education, and protective services/public administration. The faculty at UNO has 462 full-time members, 82% with terminal degrees. The student-faculty ratio is 18:1.

Students of UNO The student body totals 14,451, of whom 11,333 are undergraduates. 53.2% are women and 46.8% are men. Students come from 48 states and territories and 83 other countries. 92% are from Nebraska. 2.8% are international students. 72% returned for their sophomore year.

Applying UNO requires SAT I or ACT, a high school transcript, and minimum ACT score of 20 or rank in upper 50% of high school class. Application deadline: 8/1; 3/1 priority date for financial aid. Deferred admission is possible.

UNIVERSITY OF NEBRASKA–LINCOLN

Lincoln, NE

Urban setting ■ Public ■ State-supported ■ Coed

Web site: www.unl.edu
Contact: Mr. Alan Cerveny, Dean of Admissions, 1410 Q Street, Lincoln, NE 68588-0417
Telephone: 402-472-2030 or toll-free 800-742-8800 **Fax:** 402-472-0670
E-mail: nuhusker@unl.edu

Getting in Last Year 7,631 applied; 90% were accepted; 3,653 enrolled (53%).

Financial Matters $4125 resident tuition and fees (2002–03); $10,718 nonresident tuition and fees (2002–03); $4875 room and board; 84% average percent of need met; $6334 average financial aid amount received per undergraduate.

Academics UNL awards associate, bachelor's, master's, doctoral, and first-professional degrees and post-master's certificates. Challenging opportunities include advanced placement credit, accelerated degree programs, student-designed majors, an honors program, double majors, and independent study. Special programs include cooperative education, internships, summer session for credit, off-campus study, study-abroad, and Army, Navy and Air Force ROTC. The most frequently chosen baccalaureate fields are business/marketing, engineering/engineering technologies, and communications/communication technologies. The faculty at UNL has 1,057 full-time members, 93% with terminal degrees. The student-faculty ratio is 19:1.

Students of UNL The student body totals 22,988, of whom 18,118 are undergraduates. 47.7% are women and 52.3% are men. Students come from 52 states and territories and 101 other countries. 86% are from Nebraska. 3.1% are international students. 80% returned for their sophomore year.

Applying UNL requires SAT I or ACT and a high school transcript, and in some cases rank in upper 50% of high school class. Application deadline: 6/30.

UNIVERSITY OF NEBRASKA MEDICAL CENTER

Omaha, NE

Urban setting ■ Public ■ State-supported ■ Coed

Web site: www.unmc.edu
Contact: Crystal Oldham, Administrative Technician, 984230 Nebraska Medical Center, Omaha, NE 68198-4230
Telephone: 402-559-6468 or toll-free 800-626-8431 ext. 6468
Fax: 402-559-6796
E-mail: thorton@unmc.edu

Getting in Last Year 2,884 applied; 33% were accepted.

Financial Matters $4497 resident tuition and fees (2002–03); $12,680 nonresident tuition and fees (2002–03); 59% average percent of need met.

Academics UNMC awards bachelor's, master's, doctoral, and first-professional degrees and post-bachelor's, post-master's, and first-professional certificates. An honors program is a challenging opportunity. Special programs include internships, summer session for credit, off-campus study, and Army and Air Force ROTC. The most frequently chosen baccalaureate field is health professions and related sciences. The faculty at UNMC has 677 full-time members.

University of Nebraska Medical Center (continued)

Students of UNMC The student body totals 2,724, of whom 663 are undergraduates. 92% are women and 8% are men. Students come from 12 states and territories. 91% are from Nebraska. 0.2% are international students. 98% returned for their sophomore year.

Applying Application deadline: 2/1 priority date for financial aid.

UNIVERSITY OF NEVADA, LAS VEGAS

Las Vegas, NV

Urban setting ■ *Public* ■ *State-supported* ■ *Coed*

Web site: www.unlv.edu

Contact: Ms. Kristi Rodriguez, Assistant Director for Undergraduate Recruitment, 4505 Maryland Parkway, Box 451021, Las Vegas, NV 89154

Telephone: 702-895-4678 **Fax:** 702-895-1200

E-mail: gounlv@ccmail.nevada.edu

Getting in Last Year 5,538 applied; 82% were accepted; 2,529 enrolled (56%).

Financial Matters $2556 resident tuition and fees (2002–03); $10,341 nonresident tuition and fees (2002–03); $6140 room and board; 75% average percent of need met; $6889 average financial aid amount received per undergraduate.

Academics UNLV awards bachelor's, master's, doctoral, and first-professional degrees and post-bachelor's and post-master's certificates. Challenging opportunities include advanced placement credit, student-designed majors, an honors program, double majors, independent study, and a senior project. Special programs include cooperative education, internships, summer session for credit, off-campus study, and study-abroad. The most frequently chosen baccalaureate fields are business/marketing, education, and health professions and related sciences. The faculty at UNLV has 755 full-time members, 89% with terminal degrees. The student-faculty ratio is 19:1.

Students of UNLV The student body totals 24,679, of whom 19,761 are undergraduates. 55.5% are women and 44.5% are men. Students come from 51 states and territories and 84 other countries. 79% are from Nevada. 4.5% are international students. 72% returned for their sophomore year.

Applying UNLV requires a high school transcript and a minimum high school GPA of 2.5, and in some cases SAT I or ACT and 2 recommendations. The school recommends SAT I or ACT. Application deadline: 5/1; 2/1 priority date for financial aid. Deferred admission is possible.

UNIVERSITY OF NEVADA, RENO

Reno, NV

Urban setting ■ *Public* ■ *State-supported* ■ *Coed*

Web site: www.unr.edu

Contact: Dr. Melissa N. Choroszy, Associate Dean of Records and Enrollment Services, Mail Stop 120, Reno, NV 89557

Telephone: 775-784-6865 **Fax:** 775-784-4283

E-mail: asknevada@unr.edu

Getting in Last Year 4,144 applied; 90% were accepted; 2,107 enrolled (56%).

Financial Matters $2622 resident tuition and fees (2002–03); $10,072 nonresident tuition and fees (2002–03); $6580 room and board; 59% average percent of need met; $6288 average financial aid amount received per undergraduate (2001–02).

Academics Nevada awards bachelor's, master's, doctoral, and first-professional degrees and post-bachelor's and post-master's certificates. Challenging opportunities include advanced placement credit, an honors program, double majors, independent study, and a senior project. Special programs include internships, summer session for credit, off-campus study, study-abroad, and Army ROTC. The most frequently chosen baccalaureate fields are education, business/marketing, and health professions and related sciences. The faculty at Nevada has 652 full-time members, 87% with terminal degrees. The student-faculty ratio is 17:1.

Students of Nevada The student body totals 15,093, of whom 11,752 are undergraduates. 55.3% are women and 44.7% are men. Students come from 53 states and territories and 78 other countries. 82% are from Nevada. 3.2% are international students. 77% returned for their sophomore year.

Applying Nevada requires SAT I or ACT, a high school transcript, and a minimum high school GPA of 2.5. Application deadline: rolling admissions. Deferred admission is possible.

UNIVERSITY OF NEW BRUNSWICK FREDERICTON

Fredericton, NB Canada

Urban setting ■ *Public* ■ *Coed*

Web site: www.unb.ca

Contact: Ms. Shirley Carroll, Assistant Registrar/Admissions, PO Box 4400, Sir Howard Douglas Hall, Fredericton, NB E3B 5Z8 Canada

Telephone: 506-453-4865 **Fax:** 506-453-5016

E-mail: unbfacts@unb.ca

Getting in Last Year 2,858 applied; 76% were accepted.

Financial Matters $4265 tuition and fees (2002–03).

Academics UNB awards bachelor's, master's, and doctoral degrees. Challenging opportunities include advanced placement credit, accelerated degree programs, student-designed majors, an honors program, double majors, independent study, and a senior project. Special programs include cooperative education, internships, summer session for credit, off-campus study, and study-abroad. The faculty at UNB has 500 full-time members. The student-faculty ratio is 15:1.

Students of UNB The student body totals 9,047, of whom 7,975 are undergraduates. 51.9% are women and 48.1% are men. Students come from 12 states and territories and 65 other countries. 75% returned for their sophomore year.

Applying UNB requires a high school transcript, and in some cases an essay, SAT I, an interview, and 1 recommendation. Application deadline: rolling admissions, rolling admissions for nonresidents. Early and deferred admission are possible.

UNIVERSITY OF NEW BRUNSWICK SAINT JOHN

Saint John, NB Canada

Urban setting ■ *Public* ■ *Coed*

Web site: www.unb.ca

Contact: Ms. Sue Ellis Loparco, Admissions Officer, PO Box 5050, Tucker Park Road, Saint John, NB E2L 4L5

Telephone: 506-648-5674 or toll-free 800-743-4333 (in-state), 800-743-5691 (out-of-state) **Fax:** 506-648-5691

E-mail: apply@unbsj.ca

Getting in Last Year 2,600 applied; 85% were accepted.

Financial Matters $4440 resident tuition and fees (2002–03).

Academics UNB Saint John awards bachelor's, master's, and doctoral degrees and post-bachelor's certificates. Challenging opportunities include advanced placement credit, accelerated degree programs, student-designed majors, an honors program, double majors, independent study, and a senior project. Special programs include cooperative education, internships, summer session for credit, off-campus study, and study-abroad. The most frequently chosen baccalaureate fields are business/marketing, psychology, and biological/life sciences. The faculty at UNB Saint John has 128 full-time members. The student-faculty ratio is 10:1.

Students of UNB Saint John The student body totals 2,791, of whom 2,740 are undergraduates. 62.2% are women and 37.8% are men. Students come from 8 states and territories and 45 other countries. 94% are from New Brunswick. 85% returned for their sophomore year.

Applying UNB Saint John requires SAT I and a high school transcript, and in some cases recommendations. Application deadline: rolling admissions, 3/31 for nonresidents. Early and deferred admission are possible.

UNIVERSITY OF NEW ENGLAND

Biddeford, ME

Small-town setting ■ *Private* ■ *Independent* ■ *Coed*

Web site: www.une.edu

Contact: Mr. Robert Pecchia, Director of Admissions, Hills Beach Road, Biddeford, ME 04005-9526

Telephone: 207-283-0170 ext. 2240 or toll-free 800-477-4UNE

E-mail: admissions@une.edu

Getting in Last Year 1,264 applied; 89% were accepted; 305 enrolled (27%).

Financial Matters $18,430 tuition and fees (2002–03); $7100 room and board; 74% average percent of need met; $13,705 average financial aid amount received per undergraduate.

Academics UNE awards associate, bachelor's, master's, and first-professional degrees and post-bachelor's and post-master's certificates. Challenging opportunities include advanced placement credit, accelerated degree programs, student-designed majors, an honors program, double majors, independent study, and a senior project. Special programs include cooperative education, internships, summer session for credit, off-campus study, study-abroad, and Army ROTC. The most frequently chosen baccalaureate fields are health professions and related sciences, business/marketing, and biological/life sciences. The faculty at UNE has 142 full-time members. The student-faculty ratio is 16:1.

Students of UNE The student body totals 3,097, of whom 1,550 are undergraduates. 73% are women and 27% are men. Students come from 34 states and territories and 2 other countries. 53% are from Maine. 0.7% are international students.

Applying UNE requires SAT I or ACT and a high school transcript, and in some cases an interview. The school recommends an interview. Application deadline: rolling admissions; 5/1 priority date for financial aid. Early and deferred admission are possible.

UNIVERSITY OF NEW HAMPSHIRE

Durham, NH

Small-town setting ■ *Public* ■ *State-supported* ■ *Coed*

Web site: www.unh.edu

Contact: Mr. Gary Cilley, Acting Co-Director of Admissions, Grant House, 4 Garrison Avenue, Durham, NH 03824
Telephone: 603-862-1360 **Fax:** 603-862-0077

Getting in Last Year 10,376 applied; 77% were accepted; 2,709 enrolled (34%).

Financial Matters $8130 resident tuition and fees (2002–03); $17,830 nonresident tuition and fees (2002–03); $5882 room and board; 80% average percent of need met; $13,429 average financial aid amount received per undergraduate.

Academics UNH awards associate, bachelor's, master's, and doctoral degrees and post-master's certificates. Challenging opportunities include advanced placement credit, accelerated degree programs, student-designed majors, an honors program, double majors, independent study, and a senior project. Special programs include internships, summer session for credit, off-campus study, study-abroad, and Army and Air Force ROTC. The most frequently chosen baccalaureate fields are business/marketing, health professions and related sciences, and social sciences and history. The faculty at UNH has 596 full-time members, 90% with terminal degrees. The student-faculty ratio is 14:1.

Students of UNH The student body totals 14,248, of whom 11,496 are undergraduates. 56.8% are women and 43.2% are men. Students come from 45 states and territories and 28 other countries. 57% are from New Hampshire. 0.7% are international students. 85% returned for their sophomore year.

Applying UNH requires an essay, SAT I or ACT, a high school transcript, and 1 recommendation. The school recommends a minimum high school GPA of 3.0. Application deadline: 2/1; 3/1 priority date for financial aid. Deferred admission is possible.

UNIVERSITY OF NEW HAVEN

West Haven, CT

Suburban setting ■ *Private* ■ *Independent* ■ *Coed*

Web site: www.newhaven.edu
Contact: Ms. Jane C. Sangeloty, Director of Undergraduate Admissions, Bayer Hall, 300 Orange Avenue, West Haven, CT 06516
Telephone: 203-932-7319 or toll-free 800-DIAL-UNH **Fax:** 203-931-6093
E-mail: adminfo@newhaven.edu

Getting in Last Year 2,917 applied; 71% were accepted; 599 enrolled (29%).

Financial Matters $19,357 tuition and fees (2002–03); $7960 room and board; 75% average percent of need met; $12,884 average financial aid amount received per undergraduate (2001–02).

Academics UNH awards associate, bachelor's, and master's degrees and post-bachelor's certificates. Challenging opportunities include advanced placement credit, accelerated degree programs, student-designed majors, an honors program, double majors, independent study, and a senior project. Special programs include cooperative education, internships, summer session for credit, and Navy ROTC. The most frequently chosen baccalaureate fields are protective services/public administration, business/marketing, and engineering/engineering technologies. The faculty at UNH has 175 full-time members, 90% with terminal degrees. The student-faculty ratio is 11:1.

Students of UNH The student body totals 4,329, of whom 2,546 are undergraduates. 43.8% are women and 56.2% are men. Students come from 29 states and territories and 52 other countries. 66% are from Connecticut. 5.1% are international students. 73% returned for their sophomore year.

Applying UNH requires an essay, SAT I or ACT, and a high school transcript. The school recommends SAT I, an interview, and a minimum high school GPA of 2.75. Application deadline: rolling admissions; 3/1 priority date for financial aid. Deferred admission is possible.

UNIVERSITY OF NEW MEXICO

Albuquerque, NM

Urban setting ■ *Public* ■ *State-supported* ■ *Coed*

Web site: www.unm.edu
Contact: Ms. Robin Ryan, Associate Director of Admissions, Office of Admissions, Student Service Center Room 140, MS C06 3720, I University of New Mexico, Albuquerque, NM 87131-0001
Telephone: 505-277-2446 or toll-free 800-CALLUNM (in-state) **Fax:** 505-277-6686
E-mail: apply@unm.edu

Getting in Last Year 6,232 applied; 77% were accepted; 2,821 enrolled (59%).

Financial Matters $3169 resident tuition and fees (2002–03); $11,436 nonresident tuition and fees (2002–03); $5300 room and board; 75% average percent of need met; $7829 average financial aid amount received per undergraduate (2001–02).

Academics UNM awards associate, bachelor's, master's, doctoral, and first-professional degrees and post-master's certificates. Challenging opportunities include advanced placement credit, accelerated degree programs, student-designed majors, an honors program, double majors, independent study, and a senior project. Special programs include internships, summer session for credit, off-campus study, study-abroad, and Army and Air Force ROTC. The most frequently chosen baccalaureate fields are business/marketing, education, and health professions and related sciences. The faculty at UNM has 872 full-time members, 89% with terminal degrees. The student-faculty ratio is 16:1.

Students of UNM The student body totals 24,593, of whom 17,166 are undergraduates. 56.9% are women and 43.1% are men. Students come from 51 states and territories and 90 other countries. 81% are from New Mexico. 0.8% are international students. 73% returned for their sophomore year.

Applying UNM requires SAT I or ACT, a high school transcript, and a minimum high school GPA of 2.25, and in some cases an essay, SAT II Subject Tests, SAT II: Writing Test, and recommendations. Application deadline: 6/15; 3/1 priority date for financial aid. Early and deferred admission are possible.

UNIVERSITY OF NEW ORLEANS

New Orleans, LA

Urban setting ■ *Public* ■ *State-supported* ■ *Coed*

Web site: www.uno.edu
Contact: Ms. Roslyn S. Sheley, Director of Admissions, Lake Front, New Orleans, LA 70148
Telephone: 504-280-7013 or toll-free 800-256-5866 (out-of-state) **Fax:** 504-280-5522
E-mail: admission@uno.edu

Getting in Last Year 5,011 applied; 66% were accepted; 1,974 enrolled (59%).

Financial Matters $3026 resident tuition and fees (2002–03); $10,070 nonresident tuition and fees (2002–03); $3888 room only; 63% average percent of need met; $4493 average financial aid amount received per undergraduate (2001–02).

Academics UNO awards bachelor's, master's, and doctoral degrees and post-bachelor's certificates. Challenging opportunities include advanced placement credit, student-designed majors, an honors program, double majors, independent study, and a senior project. Special programs include cooperative education, internships, summer session for credit, off-campus study, study-abroad, and Army, Navy and Air Force ROTC. The most frequently chosen baccalaureate fields are business/marketing, liberal arts/general studies, and education. The faculty at UNO has 480 full-time members, 72% with terminal degrees. The student-faculty ratio is 25:1.

Students of UNO The student body totals 17,320, of whom 13,189 are undergraduates. 56.9% are women and 43.1% are men. Students come from 50 states and territories and 72 other countries. 95% are from Louisiana. 2.7% are international students. 64% returned for their sophomore year.

Applying UNO requires SAT I or ACT and a high school transcript, and in some cases an essay, an interview, 3 recommendations, 2.0 high school GPA on high school core program, and a minimum high school GPA of 2.0. Application deadline: rolling admissions; 5/15 priority date for financial aid. Early and deferred admission are possible.

UNIVERSITY OF NORTH ALABAMA

Florence, AL

Urban setting ■ *Public* ■ *State-supported* ■ *Coed*

Web site: www.una.edu
Contact: Mrs. Kim O. Mauldin, Director of Admissions, Office of Admissions, Box 5011, Florence, AL 35632-0001
Telephone: 256-765-4680 or toll-free 800-TALKUNA **Fax:** 256-765-4329
E-mail: admissions@una.edu

Getting in Last Year 1,590 applied; 80% were accepted; 741 enrolled (59%).

Financial Matters $3820 resident tuition and fees (2002–03); $7300 nonresident tuition and fees (2002–03); $4034 room and board; $3945 average financial aid amount received per undergraduate (2001–02).

Academics UNA awards bachelor's and master's degrees and post-master's certificates. Challenging opportunities include advanced placement credit, accelerated degree programs, double majors, independent study, and a senior project. Special programs include cooperative education, internships, summer session for credit, and Army ROTC. The most frequently chosen baccalaureate fields are business/marketing, education, and social sciences and history. The faculty at UNA has 200 full-time members, 71% with terminal degrees. The student-faculty ratio is 22:1.

Students of UNA The student body totals 5,416, of whom 4,826 are undergraduates. 58.7% are women and 41.3% are men. Students come from 35 states and territories and 42 other countries. 77% are from Alabama. 3.5% are international students. 65% returned for their sophomore year.

Applying UNA requires SAT I or ACT and a high school transcript. Application deadline: rolling admissions. Early and deferred admission are possible.

THE UNIVERSITY OF NORTH CAROLINA AT ASHEVILLE

Asheville, NC

Suburban setting ■ *Public* ■ *State-supported* ■ *Coed*

Web site: www.unca.edu

The University of North Carolina at Asheville (continued)

Contact: Mr. Scot Schaeffer, Director of Admissions and Financial Aid, 117 Lipinsky Hall, CPO 2210, One University Heights, Asheville, NC 28804-8510
Telephone: 828-251-6481 or toll-free 800-531-9842 **Fax:** 828-251-6482
E-mail: admissions@unca.edu

Getting in Last Year 1,937 applied; 67% were accepted; 428 enrolled (33%).

Financial Matters $2957 resident tuition and fees (2002–03); $11,362 nonresident tuition and fees (2002–03); $4650 room and board; 84% average percent of need met; $6951 average financial aid amount received per undergraduate (2001–02).

Academics UNC Asheville awards bachelor's and master's degrees and post-bachelor's certificates. Challenging opportunities include advanced placement credit, student-designed majors, an honors program, double majors, independent study, and a senior project. Special programs include internships, summer session for credit, off-campus study, and study-abroad. The most frequently chosen baccalaureate fields are psychology, business/marketing, and social sciences and history. The faculty at UNC Asheville has 179 full-time members, 85% with terminal degrees. The student-faculty ratio is 14:1.

Students of UNC Asheville The student body totals 3,391, of whom 3,351 are undergraduates. 57.4% are women and 42.6% are men. Students come from 38 states and territories and 18 other countries. 89% are from North Carolina. 0.8% are international students. 80% returned for their sophomore year.

Applying UNC Asheville requires SAT I or ACT and a high school transcript, and in some cases an interview. The school recommends an essay and a minimum high school GPA of 3.0. Application deadline: 3/15; 3/1 priority date for financial aid. Deferred admission is possible.

THE UNIVERSITY OF NORTH CAROLINA AT CHAPEL HILL

Chapel Hill, NC

Suburban setting ■ Public ■ State-supported ■ Coed

Web site: www.unc.edu
Contact: Mr. Jerome A. Lucido, Vice Provost and Director of Undergraduate Admissions, Office of Undergraduate Admissions, Jackson Hall 153A, Campus Box 2200, Chapel Hill, NC 27599-2200
Telephone: 919-966-3621 **Fax:** 919-962-3045
E-mail: uadm@email.unc.edu

Getting in Last Year 17,141 applied; 35% were accepted; 3,460 enrolled (57%).

Financial Matters $3856 resident tuition and fees (2002–03); $15,140 nonresident tuition and fees (2002–03); $5805 room and board; 100% average percent of need met; $7824 average financial aid amount received per undergraduate (2001–02).

Academics UNC Chapel Hill awards bachelor's, master's, doctoral, and first-professional degrees and post-master's certificates. Challenging opportunities include advanced placement credit, student-designed majors, freshman honors college, an honors program, double majors, and independent study. Special programs include internships, summer session for credit, off-campus study, study-abroad, and Army, Navy and Air Force ROTC. The most frequently chosen baccalaureate fields are communications/communication technologies, social sciences and history, and business/marketing. The faculty at UNC Chapel Hill has 1,356 full-time members, 83% with terminal degrees. The student-faculty ratio is 14:1.

Students of UNC Chapel Hill The student body totals 26,028, of whom 15,961 are undergraduates. 59.6% are women and 40.4% are men. Students come from 52 states and territories and 100 other countries. 82% are from North Carolina. 1.2% are international students. 95% returned for their sophomore year.

Applying UNC Chapel Hill requires an essay, SAT I or ACT, a high school transcript, 1 recommendation, and counselor's statement. Application deadline: 1/15; 3/1 priority date for financial aid. Deferred admission is possible.

THE UNIVERSITY OF NORTH CAROLINA AT CHARLOTTE

Charlotte, NC

Suburban setting ■ Public ■ State-supported ■ Coed

Web site: www.uncc.edu
Contact: Mr. Craig Fulton, Director of Admissions, 9201 University City Boulevard, New Admissions Building, 1st Floor, Charlotte, NC 28223-0001
Telephone: 704-687-2213 **Fax:** 704-687-6483
E-mail: unccadm@email.uncc.edu

Getting in Last Year 8,112 applied; 70% were accepted; 2,430 enrolled (43%).

Financial Matters $2948 resident tuition and fees (2002–03); $12,507 nonresident tuition and fees (2002–03); $4856 room and board; 79% average percent of need met; $7758 average financial aid amount received per undergraduate.

Academics UNC Charlotte awards bachelor's, master's, and doctoral degrees and post-master's certificates. Challenging opportunities include advanced placement credit, freshman honors college, an honors program, double majors, and a senior project. Special programs include cooperative education, internships, summer session for credit, off-campus study, study-abroad, and Army and Air Force ROTC. The most frequently chosen baccalaureate fields are business/marketing, social sciences and history, and engineering/engineering technologies. The faculty at UNC Charlotte has 727 full-time members, 87% with terminal degrees. The student-faculty ratio is 16:1.

Students of UNC Charlotte The student body totals 18,916, of whom 15,364 are undergraduates. 53.6% are women and 46.4% are men. Students come from 51 states and territories and 79 other countries. 91% are from North Carolina. 2.3% are international students. 78% returned for their sophomore year.

Applying UNC Charlotte requires SAT I or ACT, a high school transcript, 1 recommendation, medical history, and a minimum high school GPA of 2.0, and in some cases an interview. Application deadline: 7/1; 4/1 priority date for financial aid. Early and deferred admission are possible.

THE UNIVERSITY OF NORTH CAROLINA AT GREENSBORO

Greensboro, NC

Urban setting ■ Public ■ State-supported ■ Coed

Web site: www.uncg.edu
Contact: Associate Director of Admissions, 1000 Spring Garden Street, Greensboro, NC 27412-5001
Telephone: 336-334-5243 **Fax:** 336-334-4180
E-mail: undergrad_admissions@uncg.edu

Getting in Last Year 7,065 applied; 76% were accepted; 2,099 enrolled (39%).

Financial Matters $3006 resident tuition and fees (2002–03); $13,380 nonresident tuition and fees (2002–03); $4656 room and board; 86% average percent of need met; $9002 average financial aid amount received per undergraduate.

Academics UNCG awards bachelor's, master's, and doctoral degrees. Challenging opportunities include advanced placement credit, accelerated degree programs, student-designed majors, freshman honors college, an honors program, double majors, independent study, and a senior project. Special programs include internships, summer session for credit, off-campus study, study-abroad, and Army and Air Force ROTC. The most frequently chosen baccalaureate fields are business/marketing, health professions and related sciences, and education. The faculty at UNCG has 666 full-time members, 83% with terminal degrees. The student-faculty ratio is 15:1.

Students of UNCG The student body totals 13,918, of whom 10,751 are undergraduates. 67.4% are women and 32.6% are men. Students come from 41 states and territories and 55 other countries. 91% are from North Carolina. 1.2% are international students. 75% returned for their sophomore year.

Applying UNCG requires SAT I or ACT, a high school transcript, and a minimum high school GPA of 2.0. The school recommends SAT II Subject Tests. Application deadline: 8/1; 3/1 priority date for financial aid. Early admission is possible.

THE UNIVERSITY OF NORTH CAROLINA AT PEMBROKE

Pembroke, NC

Rural setting ■ Public ■ State-supported ■ Coed

Web site: www.uncp.edu
Contact: John McMillian, Associate Director of Admissions, PO Box 1510, Pembroke, NC 28372-1510
Telephone: 910-521-6262 or toll-free 800-949-UNCP (in-state), 800-949-uncp (out-of-state) **Fax:** 910-521-6497

Getting in Last Year 1,422 applied; 51% were accepted; 722 enrolled (100%).

Financial Matters $2365 resident tuition and fees (2002–03); $11,284 nonresident tuition and fees (2002–03); $4150 room and board; 77% average percent of need met; $5956 average financial aid amount received per undergraduate.

Academics UNC Pembroke awards bachelor's and master's degrees. Challenging opportunities include advanced placement credit, accelerated degree programs, an honors program, double majors, independent study, and a senior project. Special programs include cooperative education, internships, summer session for credit, off-campus study, and Army and Air Force ROTC. The most frequently chosen baccalaureate fields are business/marketing, protective services/public administration, and social sciences and history. The faculty at UNC Pembroke has 180 full-time members, 72% with terminal degrees. The student-faculty ratio is 17:1.

Students of UNC Pembroke The student body totals 4,432, of whom 3,951 are undergraduates. 63.4% are women and 36.6% are men. Students come from 30 states and territories and 19 other countries. 94% are from North Carolina. 0.7% are international students. 69% returned for their sophomore year.

Applying UNC Pembroke requires SAT I or ACT and a high school transcript, and in some cases an interview and recommendations. The school recommends an essay and a minimum high school GPA of 2.0. Application deadline: rolling admissions; 3/15 priority date for financial aid. Early and deferred admission are possible.

THE UNIVERSITY OF NORTH CAROLINA AT WILMINGTON

Wilmington, NC

Urban setting ■ Public ■ State-supported ■ Coed

Web site: www.uncwil.edu
Contact: Dr. Roxie Shabazz, Assistant Vice Chancellor for Admissions, 601 South College Road, Wilmington, NC 28403-3297
Telephone: 910-962-4198 or toll-free 800-228-5571 (out-of-state)
Fax: 910-962-3038
E-mail: admissions@uncwil.edu

Getting in Last Year 7,188 applied; 55% were accepted; 1,640 enrolled (41%).

Financial Matters $3074 resident tuition and fees (2002–03); $12,193 nonresident tuition and fees (2002–03); $5378 room and board; 88% average percent of need met; $6254 average financial aid amount received per undergraduate.

Academics UNCW awards bachelor's, master's, and doctoral degrees. Challenging opportunities include advanced placement credit, accelerated degree programs, freshman honors college, an honors program, double majors, independent study, and a senior project. Special programs include cooperative education, internships, summer session for credit, and study-abroad. The most frequently chosen baccalaureate fields are business/marketing, education, and English. The faculty at UNCW has 434 full-time members, 86% with terminal degrees. The student-faculty ratio is 16:1.

Students of UNCW The student body totals 10,729, of whom 9,803 are undergraduates. 60.1% are women and 39.9% are men. Students come from 47 states and territories and 36 other countries. 86% are from North Carolina. 0.6% are international students. 82% returned for their sophomore year.

Applying UNCW requires an essay, SAT I or ACT, a high school transcript, and a minimum high school GPA of 2.2. Application deadline: 2/1; 3/1 priority date for financial aid.

UNIVERSITY OF NORTH DAKOTA

Grand Forks, ND

Small-town setting ■ Public ■ State-supported ■ Coed

Web site: www.und.edu
Contact: Ms. Heidi Kippenhan, Director of Admissions, Box 8382, Grand Forks, ND 58202
Telephone: 701-777-3821 or toll-free 800-CALL UND **Fax:** 701-777-2696
E-mail: enrolser@sage.und.nodak.edu

Getting in Last Year 3,628 applied; 72% were accepted; 2,020 enrolled (77%).

Financial Matters $4370 resident tuition and fees (2002–03); $9302 nonresident tuition and fees (2002–03); $3987 room and board; 89% average percent of need met; $9107 average financial aid amount received per undergraduate.

Academics UND awards bachelor's, master's, doctoral, and first-professional degrees and post-master's certificates. Challenging opportunities include advanced placement credit, accelerated degree programs, student-designed majors, an honors program, double majors, independent study, and a senior project. Special programs include cooperative education, internships, summer session for credit, off-campus study, study-abroad, and Army and Air Force ROTC. The most frequently chosen baccalaureate fields are business/marketing, health professions and related sciences, and trade and industry. The faculty at UND has 466 full-time members. The student-faculty ratio is 18:1.

Students of UND The student body totals 12,423, of whom 10,277 are undergraduates. 47.1% are women and 52.9% are men. Students come from 54 states and territories and 45 other countries. 58% are from North Dakota. 2.4% are international students. 12% returned for their sophomore year.

Applying UND requires SAT I or ACT and a high school transcript. The school recommends ACT and a minimum high school GPA of 2.25. Application deadline: 7/1; 4/15 priority date for financial aid. Deferred admission is possible.

UNIVERSITY OF NORTHERN BRITISH COLUMBIA

Prince George, BC Canada

Public ■ Coed

Web site: www.unbc.ca
Contact: Ms. Darlene Poehlmann, Assistant Registrar, 3333 University Way, Prince George, BC V2N 4Z9 Canada
Telephone: 250-960-6345 **Fax:** 250-960-5791 ext.

Getting in Last Year 1,902 applied; 55% were accepted; 442 enrolled (43%).

Academics University of Northern British Columbia awards bachelor's, master's, doctoral, and first-professional degrees and post-bachelor's certificates. The faculty at University of Northern British Columbia has 143 full-time members, 87% with terminal degrees. The student-faculty ratio is 17:1.

Students of University of Northern British Columbia The student body totals 3,630, of whom 3,260 are undergraduates. 56.9% are women and 43.1% are men. 71% returned for their sophomore year.

Applying Application deadline: 4/1 priority date for financial aid.

UNIVERSITY OF NORTHERN COLORADO

Greeley, CO

Suburban setting ■ Public ■ State-supported ■ Coed

Web site: www.unco.edu
Contact: Mr. Gary O. Gullickson, Director of Admissions, Campus Box 10, Carter Hall 3006, Greeley, CO 80639
Telephone: 970-351-2881 or toll-free 888-700-4UNC (in-state)
Fax: 970-351-2984
E-mail: unc@mail.unco.edu

Getting in Last Year 6,961 applied; 72% were accepted; 1,983 enrolled (40%).

Financial Matters $2984 resident tuition and fees (2002–03); $11,278 nonresident tuition and fees (2002–03); $5560 room and board; 83% average percent of need met; $7356 average financial aid amount received per undergraduate (2001–02).

Academics UNC awards bachelor's, master's, and doctoral degrees. Challenging opportunities include advanced placement credit, student-designed majors, an honors program, double majors, independent study, and a senior project. Special programs include cooperative education, internships, summer session for credit, off-campus study, study-abroad, and Army and Air Force ROTC. The most frequently chosen baccalaureate fields are social sciences and history, business/marketing, and communications/communication technologies. The faculty at UNC has 439 full-time members, 78% with terminal degrees. The student-faculty ratio is 20:1.

Students of UNC The student body totals 12,434, of whom 10,211 are undergraduates. 61% are women and 39% are men. Students come from 49 states and territories. 95% are from Colorado. 0.4% are international students. 70% returned for their sophomore year.

Applying UNC requires SAT I or ACT, a high school transcript, and a minimum high school GPA of 2.9, and in some cases an interview. Application deadline: rolling admissions; 3/1 priority date for financial aid. Deferred admission is possible.

UNIVERSITY OF NORTHERN IOWA

Cedar Falls, IA

Small-town setting ■ Public ■ State-supported ■ Coed

Web site: www.uni.edu
Contact: Mr. Clark Elmer, Director of Enrollment Management and Admissions, 120 Gilchrist Hall, Cedar Falls, IA 50614-0018
Telephone: 319-273-2281 or toll-free 800-772-2037 **Fax:** 319-273-2885
E-mail: admissions@uni.edu

Getting in Last Year 4,446 applied; 80% were accepted; 1,858 enrolled (52%).

Financial Matters $4117 resident tuition and fees (2002–03); $10,425 nonresident tuition and fees (2002–03); $4640 room and board; 74% average percent of need met; $6222 average financial aid amount received per undergraduate.

Academics UNI awards bachelor's, master's, and doctoral degrees. Challenging opportunities include advanced placement credit, accelerated degree programs, student-designed majors, an honors program, double majors, independent study, and a senior project. Special programs include cooperative education, internships, summer session for credit, off-campus study, study-abroad, and Army ROTC. The most frequently chosen baccalaureate fields are education, business/marketing, and social sciences and history. The faculty at UNI has 678 full-time members, 79% with terminal degrees. The student-faculty ratio is 16:1.

Students of UNI The student body totals 14,167, of whom 12,397 are undergraduates. 57.6% are women and 42.4% are men. Students come from 42 states and territories and 72 other countries. 95% are from Iowa. 1.7% are international students. 84% returned for their sophomore year.

Applying UNI requires SAT I or ACT and a high school transcript, and in some cases an interview. Application deadline: 8/15. Deferred admission is possible.

UNIVERSITY OF NORTH FLORIDA

Jacksonville, FL

Urban setting ■ Public ■ State-supported ■ Coed

Web site: www.unf.edu
Contact: Ms. Sherry David, Director of Admissions, 4567 St. Johns Bluff Road South, Jacksonville, FL 32224
Telephone: 904-620-2624 **Fax:** 904-620-2014
E-mail: osprey@unf.edu

Getting in Last Year 7,188 applied; 70% were accepted; 1,937 enrolled (38%).

Financial Matters $2757 resident tuition and fees (2002–03); $11,749 nonresident tuition and fees (2002–03); $5486 room and board; 72% average percent of need met; $2253 average financial aid amount received per undergraduate.

Academics UNF awards associate, bachelor's, master's, and doctoral degrees and post-bachelor's and post-master's certificates (doctoral degree in education only). Challenging opportunities include advanced placement credit, accelerated degree programs, freshman honors college, an honors program, double majors, independent study, and a senior project. Special programs include cooperative education, internships, summer session for credit, off-campus study, study-abroad, and Navy ROTC. The most frequently chosen baccalaureate fields are

University of North Florida (continued)

business/marketing, health professions and related sciences, and education. The faculty at UNF has 383 full-time members, 96% with terminal degrees. The student-faculty ratio is 22:1.

Students of UNF The student body totals 13,470, of whom 11,618 are undergraduates. 57.9% are women and 42.1% are men. Students come from 46 states and territories and 66 other countries. 95% are from Florida. 1% are international students. 76% returned for their sophomore year.

Applying UNF requires SAT I or ACT, a high school transcript, and a minimum high school GPA of 2.0, and in some cases an essay and recommendations. The school recommends a minimum high school GPA of 3.0. Application deadline: 7/2; 4/1 priority date for financial aid. Early and deferred admission are possible.

UNIVERSITY OF NORTH TEXAS

Denton, TX

Urban setting ■ Public ■ State-supported ■ Coed

Web site: www.unt.edu
Contact: Ms. Janet Trepka, Coordinator or New Student Mentoring Programs and Vice President of Student Development, Box 311277, Denton, TX 76203-9988
Telephone: 940-565-3190 or toll-free 800-868-8211 (in-state) **Fax:** 940-565-2408
E-mail: undergrad@unt.edu

Getting in Last Year 8,003 applied; 70% were accepted; 3,029 enrolled (54%).

Financial Matters $3217 resident tuition and fees (2002–03); $8449 nonresident tuition and fees (2002–03); $4598 room and board; 69% average percent of need met; $6050 average financial aid amount received per undergraduate.

Academics UNT awards bachelor's, master's, and doctoral degrees and post-bachelor's certificates. Challenging opportunities include advanced placement credit, accelerated degree programs, freshman honors college, an honors program, double majors, and a senior project. Special programs include cooperative education, internships, summer session for credit, study-abroad, and Army and Navy ROTC. The most frequently chosen baccalaureate fields are business/marketing, interdisciplinary studies, and visual/performing arts. The faculty at UNT has 799 full-time members, 80% with terminal degrees. The student-faculty ratio is 17:1.

Students of UNT The student body totals 30,183, of whom 22,618 are undergraduates. 54.9% are women and 45.1% are men. Students come from 49 states and territories and 115 other countries. 96% are from Texas. 2.9% are international students. 69% returned for their sophomore year.

Applying UNT requires SAT I or ACT and a high school transcript, and in some cases an essay, an interview, and 3 recommendations. Application deadline: 6/15; 6/1 priority date for financial aid. Early and deferred admission are possible.

UNIVERSITY OF NOTRE DAME

Notre Dame, IN

Suburban setting ■ Private ■ Independent Religious ■ Coed

Web site: www.nd.edu
Contact: Mr. Daniel J. Saracino, Assistant Provost for Enrollment, 220 Main Building, Notre Dame, IN 46556-5612
Telephone: 574-631-7505 **Fax:** 574-631-8865
E-mail: admissions.admissio.1@nd.edu

Getting in Last Year 9,744 applied; 34% were accepted; 1,946 enrolled (58%).

Financial Matters $25,852 tuition and fees (2002–03); $6510 room and board; 100% average percent of need met; $23,432 average financial aid amount received per undergraduate.

Academics Notre Dame awards bachelor's, master's, doctoral, and first-professional degrees. Challenging opportunities include advanced placement credit, accelerated degree programs, student-designed majors, an honors program, double majors, independent study, and a senior project. Special programs include cooperative education, internships, summer session for credit, off-campus study, study-abroad, and Army, Navy and Air Force ROTC. The most frequently chosen baccalaureate fields are business/marketing, social sciences and history, and health professions and related sciences. The faculty at Notre Dame has 763 full-time members, 98% with terminal degrees.

Students of Notre Dame The student body totals 11,311, of whom 8,261 are undergraduates. 46.7% are women and 53.3% are men. Students come from 54 states and territories and 68 other countries. 12% are from Indiana. 3.2% are international students.

Applying Notre Dame requires an essay, SAT I or ACT, a high school transcript, and 1 recommendation. Application deadline: 1/9; 2/15 for financial aid. Deferred admission is possible.

UNIVERSITY OF OKLAHOMA

Norman, OK

Suburban setting ■ Public ■ State-supported ■ Coed

Web site: www.ou.edu
Contact: Karen Renfroe, Executive Director of Recruitment Services, 1000 Asp Avenue, Norman, OK 73019
Telephone: 405-325-2151 or toll-free 800-234-6868 **Fax:** 405-325-7124
E-mail: admrec@ou.edu

Getting in Last Year 7,248 applied; 89% were accepted; 3,833 enrolled (60%).

Financial Matters $2929 resident tuition and fees (2002–03); $8077 nonresident tuition and fees (2002–03); $5030 room and board; 88% average percent of need met; $7635 average financial aid amount received per undergraduate (2001–02).

Academics OU awards bachelor's, master's, doctoral, and first-professional degrees and post-master's certificates. Challenging opportunities include advanced placement credit, accelerated degree programs, student-designed majors, freshman honors college, an honors program, double majors, independent study, and a senior project. Special programs include cooperative education, internships, summer session for credit, off-campus study, study-abroad, and Army and Air Force ROTC. The most frequently chosen baccalaureate fields are business/marketing, social sciences and history, and engineering/engineering technologies. The faculty at OU has 963 full-time members, 88% with terminal degrees. The student-faculty ratio is 21:1.

Students of OU The student body totals 23,799, of whom 19,570 are undergraduates. 49% are women and 51% are men. Students come from 50 states and territories and 79 other countries. 81% are from Oklahoma. 2.8% are international students. 83% returned for their sophomore year.

Applying OU requires SAT I or ACT, a high school transcript, and a minimum high school GPA of 3.0, and in some cases an essay. Application deadline: 6/1.

UNIVERSITY OF OKLAHOMA HEALTH SCIENCES CENTER

Oklahoma City, OK

Urban setting ■ Public ■ State-supported ■ Coed

Web site: www.ouhsc.edu
Contact: Ms. Leslie Wilbourn, Director of Admissions and Records, BSE-200, PO Box 26901, 941 S. L. Young Boulevard, Oklahoma City, OK 73190
Telephone: 405-271-2359 ext. 48902 **Fax:** 405-271-2480
E-mail: admissions@ouhsc.edu

Getting in Last Year 648 applied; 52% were accepted.

Financial Matters $2330 resident tuition and fees (2002–03); $6692 nonresident tuition and fees (2002–03).

Academics OU Health Sciences Center awards bachelor's, master's, doctoral, and first-professional degrees and post-bachelor's, post-master's, and first-professional certificates. Challenging opportunities include advanced placement credit and an honors program. Special programs include internships, summer session for credit, and Army and Air Force ROTC. The most frequently chosen baccalaureate field is health professions and related sciences. The faculty at OU Health Sciences Center has 227 full-time members, 95% with terminal degrees.

Students of OU Health Sciences Center The student body totals 2,935, of whom 621 are undergraduates. 89.5% are women and 10.5% are men. Students come from 18 states and territories and 4 other countries. 91% are from Oklahoma. 1.6% are international students.

Applying Deferred admission is possible.

UNIVERSITY OF OREGON

Eugene, OR

Urban setting ■ Public ■ State-supported ■ Coed

Web site: www.uoregon.edu
Contact: Ms. Martha Pitts, Director of Admissions, Eugene, OR 97403
Telephone: 541-346-3201 or toll-free 800-232-3825 (in-state) **Fax:** 541-346-5815
E-mail: uoadmit@oregon.uoregon.edu

Getting in Last Year 9,889 applied; 86% were accepted; 3,317 enrolled (39%).

Financial Matters $4230 resident tuition and fees (2002–03); $15,219 nonresident tuition and fees (2002–03); $6252 room and board; 77% average percent of need met; $7825 average financial aid amount received per undergraduate.

Academics UO awards bachelor's, master's, doctoral, and first-professional degrees. Challenging opportunities include advanced placement credit, accelerated degree programs, student-designed majors, freshman honors college, an honors program, double majors, independent study, and a senior project. Special programs include internships, summer session for credit, off-campus study, study-abroad, and Army and Air Force ROTC. The most frequently chosen baccalaureate fields are social sciences and history, business/marketing, and communications/communication technologies. The faculty at UO has 795 full-time members, 98% with terminal degrees. The student-faculty ratio is 18:1.

Students of UO The student body totals 19,997, of whom 16,041 are undergraduates. 53.7% are women and 46.3% are men. Students come from 54 states and territories and 78 other countries. 74% are from Oregon. 5.4% are international students. 82% returned for their sophomore year.

Applying UO requires SAT I or ACT, a high school transcript, and a minimum high school GPA of 3.0, and in some cases an essay and 2 recommendations. Application deadline: 1/15; 3/1 priority date for financial aid. Early admission is possible.

UNIVERSITY OF OTTAWA

Ottawa, ON Canada

Urban setting ■ Public ■ Coed

Web site: www.uottawa.ca
Contact: Ms. Michéle Dextras, Manager, Admissions, 550 Cumberland Street, PO Box 450, Station A, Ottawa, ON K1N 6N5 Canada
Telephone: 613-562-5800 ext. 1593
E-mail: admissio@uottawa.ca

Getting in Last Year 19,056 applied; 20% were accepted.

Financial Matters $4438 nonresident tuition and fees (2002–03); $5242 room and board.

Academics University of Ottawa awards bachelor's, master's, and doctoral degrees. Challenging opportunities include advanced placement credit, accelerated degree programs, student-designed majors, an honors program, double majors, and a senior project. Special programs include cooperative education, internships, summer session for credit, off-campus study, and study-abroad. The faculty at University of Ottawa has 847 full-time members. The student-faculty ratio is 18:1.

Students of University of Ottawa The student body totals 27,445, of whom 23,651 are undergraduates. 59.7% are women and 40.3% are men. Students come from 13 states and territories and 62 other countries. 81% are from Ontario.

Applying University of Ottawa requires a high school transcript and a minimum high school GPA of 3.0, and in some cases an interview. Application deadline: 4/30; 1/31 for financial aid. Early admission is possible.

UNIVERSITY OF PENNSYLVANIA

Philadelphia, PA

Urban setting ■ Private ■ Independent ■ Coed

Web site: www.upenn.edu
Contact: Mr. Willis J. Stetson Jr., Dean of Admissions, 1 College Hall, Levy Park, Philadelphia, PA 19104
Telephone: 215-898-7507

Getting in Last Year 18,784 applied; 21% were accepted; 2,426 enrolled (61%).

Financial Matters $27,988 tuition and fees (2002–03); $8224 room and board; 100% average percent of need met; $23,875 average financial aid amount received per undergraduate (2001–02).

Academics Penn awards associate, bachelor's, master's, doctoral, and first-professional degrees and post-bachelor's, post-master's, and first-professional certificates (also offers evening program with significant enrollment not reflected in profile). Challenging opportunities include advanced placement credit, accelerated degree programs, student-designed majors, an honors program, double majors, independent study, and a senior project. Special programs include internships, summer session for credit, off-campus study, study-abroad, and Army, Navy and Air Force ROTC. The most frequently chosen baccalaureate fields are social sciences and history, business/marketing, and engineering/engineering technologies. The faculty at Penn has 1,344 full-time members, 100% with terminal degrees. The student-faculty ratio is 6:1.

Students of Penn The student body totals 20,295, of whom 9,742 are undergraduates. 48.7% are women and 51.3% are men. Students come from 54 states and territories and 100 other countries. 19% are from Pennsylvania. 9.2% are international students. 96% returned for their sophomore year.

Applying Penn requires an essay, SAT II: Writing Test, SAT I and SAT II or ACT, a high school transcript, and 2 recommendations. Application deadline: 1/1; 2/15 priority date for financial aid. Early and deferred admission are possible.

UNIVERSITY OF PHOENIX-ATLANTA CAMPUS

Atlanta, GA

Urban setting ■ Private ■ Proprietary ■ Coed

Web site: www.phoenix.edu
Contact: Ms. Beth Barilla, Director of Admissions, 4615 East Elwood Street, Mail Stop 10-0030, Phoenix, AZ 85040-1958
Telephone: 480-317-6000 or toll-free 800-228-7240 **Fax:** 480-594-1758
E-mail: beth.barilla@apollogrp.edu

Financial Matters $8970 tuition and fees (2002–03).

Academics University of Phoenix-Atlanta Campus awards associate, bachelor's, master's, and doctoral degrees and post-bachelor's and post-master's certificates (courses conducted at 121 campuses and learning centers in 25 states). Challenging opportunities include advanced placement credit, accelerated degree programs, independent study, and a senior project. The faculty at University of Phoenix-Atlanta Campus has 3 full-time members, 33% with terminal degrees. The student-faculty ratio is 16:1.

Students of University of Phoenix-Atlanta Campus The student body totals 585, of whom 366 are undergraduates. 61.5% are women and 38.5% are men. 1.9% are international students.

Applying University of Phoenix-Atlanta Campus requires 1 recommendation and 2 years of work experience, 23 years of age. Application deadline: rolling admissions. Deferred admission is possible.

UNIVERSITY OF PHOENIX–BOSTON CAMPUS

Braintree, MA

Private ■ Proprietary ■ Coed

Web site: www.phoenix.edu
Contact: Ms. Beth Barilla, Director of Admissions, 4615 East Elwood Street, Mail Stop 10-0030, Phoenix, AZ 85040-1958
Telephone: 480-317-6000 or toll-free 800-228-7240 **Fax:** 480-594-1758
E-mail: beth.barilla@apollogrp.edu

Getting in Last Year 31 enrolled.

Financial Matters $10,800 tuition and fees (2002–03).

Academics University of Phoenix–Boston Campus awards associate, bachelor's, master's, and doctoral degrees and post-bachelor's and post-master's certificates (courses conducted at 121 campuses and learning centers in 25 states). Challenging opportunities include advanced placement credit, accelerated degree programs, independent study, and a senior project. The faculty at University of Phoenix–Boston Campus has 3 full-time members, 67% with terminal degrees. The student-faculty ratio is 8:1.

Students of University of Phoenix–Boston Campus The student body totals 310, of whom 203 are undergraduates. 54.7% are women and 45.3% are men.

Applying University of Phoenix–Boston Campus requires an essay and 2 years of work experience, 23 years of age. Application deadline: rolling admissions. Deferred admission is possible.

UNIVERSITY OF PHOENIX-CHICAGO CAMPUS

Schaumburg, IL

Private ■ Proprietary ■ Coed

Web site: www.phoenix.edu
Contact: Ms. Beth Barilla, Director of Admissions, 4615 East Elwood Street, Mail Stop 10-0030, Phoenix, AZ 85040-1958
Telephone: 480-317-6000 or toll-free 800-228-7240 **Fax:** 480-594-1758

Getting in Last Year 16 enrolled.

Financial Matters $9540 tuition and fees (2002–03).

Academics University of Phoenix-Chicago Campus awards associate, bachelor's, master's, and doctoral degrees and post-bachelor's and post-master's certificates (courses conducted at 121 campuses and learning centers in 25 states). Challenging opportunities include advanced placement credit, accelerated degree programs, and independent study. The faculty at University of Phoenix-Chicago Campus has 2 full-time members, 50% with terminal degrees.

Students of University of Phoenix-Chicago Campus The student body totals 119, of whom 92 are undergraduates. 44.6% are women and 55.4% are men.

Applying University of Phoenix-Chicago Campus requires 1 recommendation and 2 years of work experience, 23 years of age. Application deadline: rolling admissions. Deferred admission is possible.

UNIVERSITY OF PHOENIX–COLORADO CAMPUS

Lone Tree, CO

Urban setting ■ Private ■ Proprietary ■ Coed

Web site: www.phoenix.edu
Contact: Ms. Beth Barilla, Director of Admissions, 4615 East Elwood Street, Mail Stop 10-0030, Phoenix, AZ 85040-1958
Telephone: 480-317-6000 or toll-free 800-228-7240 **Fax:** 480-594-1758
E-mail: beth.barilla@apollogrp.edu

Getting in Last Year 5 enrolled (100%).

Financial Matters $8250 tuition and fees (2002–03).

Academics University of Phoenix–Colorado Campus awards associate, bachelor's, master's, and doctoral degrees and post-bachelor's and post-master's certificates (courses conducted at 121 campuses and learning centers in 25 states). Challenging opportunities include advanced placement credit, accelerated degree programs, independent study, and a senior project. The most frequently chosen baccalaureate fields are business/marketing and health professions and related sciences. The faculty at University of Phoenix–Colorado Campus has 5 full-time members, 20% with terminal degrees. The student-faculty ratio is 13:1.

Students of University of Phoenix–Colorado Campus The student body totals 2,783, of whom 1,775 are undergraduates. 52.5% are women and 47.5% are men. 1.4% are international students.

Applying University of Phoenix–Colorado Campus requires 1 recommendation and 2 years of work experience, 23 years of age. Application deadline: rolling admissions. Deferred admission is possible.

UNIVERSITY OF PHOENIX–DALLAS CAMPUS

Dallas, TX

Urban setting ■ *Private* ■ *Proprietary* ■ *Coed*

Web site: www.phoenix.edu
Contact: Ms. Beth Barilla, Director of Admissions, 4615 East Elwood Street, Mail Stop 10-0030, Phoenix, AZ 85040-1958
Telephone: 480-317-6000 or toll-free 800-228-7240 **Fax:** 480-594-1758
E-mail: beth.barilla@apollogrp.edu

Getting in Last Year 2 enrolled (100%).

Financial Matters $8820 tuition and fees (2002–03).

Academics University of Phoenix–Dallas Campus awards associate, bachelor's, master's, and doctoral degrees and post-bachelor's and post-master's certificates (courses conducted at 121 campuses and learning centers in 25 states). Challenging opportunities include advanced placement credit, accelerated degree programs, and independent study. The faculty at University of Phoenix–Dallas Campus has 1 full-time members, 100% with terminal degrees. The student-faculty ratio is 18:1.

Students of University of Phoenix–Dallas Campus The student body totals 1,449, of whom 1,063 are undergraduates. 59.9% are women and 40.1% are men. 16.4% are international students.

Applying University of Phoenix–Dallas Campus requires 1 recommendation and 2 years of work experience, 23 years of age. Application deadline: rolling admissions.

UNIVERSITY OF PHOENIX–FORT LAUDERDALE CAMPUS

Fort Lauderdale, FL

Urban setting ■ *Private* ■ *Proprietary* ■ *Coed*

Web site: www.phoenix.edu
Contact: Ms. Beth Barilla, Director of Admissions, 4615 East Elwood Street, Mail Stop 10-0030, Phoenix, AZ 85040-1958
Telephone: 480-317-6000 or toll-free 800-228-7240 **Fax:** 480-594-1758
E-mail: beth.barilla@apollogrp.edu

Financial Matters $8340 tuition and fees (2002–03).

Academics University of Phoenix–Fort Lauderdale Campus awards associate, bachelor's, master's, and doctoral degrees and post-bachelor's and post-master's certificates (courses conducted at 121 campuses and learning centers in 25 states). Challenging opportunities include advanced placement credit, accelerated degree programs, independent study, and a senior project. The most frequently chosen baccalaureate field is business/marketing. The faculty at University of Phoenix–Fort Lauderdale Campus has 5 full-time members, 20% with terminal degrees. The student-faculty ratio is 13:1.

Students of University of Phoenix–Fort Lauderdale Campus The student body totals 1,805, of whom 1,276 are undergraduates. 64.5% are women and 35.5% are men. 12.9% are international students.

Applying University of Phoenix–Fort Lauderdale Campus requires 1 recommendation and 2 years of work experience, 23 years of age. Application deadline: rolling admissions. Deferred admission is possible.

UNIVERSITY OF PHOENIX–HAWAII CAMPUS

Honolulu, HI

Urban setting ■ *Private* ■ *Proprietary* ■ *Coed*

Web site: www.phoenix.edu
Contact: Ms. Beth Barilla, Director of Admissions, 4615 East Elwood Street, Mail Stop 10-0030, Phoenix, AZ 85040-1958
Telephone: 480-317-6300 or toll-free 800-228-7240 (out-of-state) **Fax:** 480-594-1758
E-mail: beth.barilla@apollogrp.edu

Financial Matters $9600 tuition and fees (2002–03).

Academics University of Phoenix–Hawaii Campus awards associate, bachelor's, master's, and doctoral degrees and post-bachelor's and post-master's certificates (courses conducted at 121 campuses and learning centers in 25 states). Challenging opportunities include advanced placement credit, accelerated degree programs, independent study, and a senior project. The most frequently chosen baccalaureate fields are business/marketing and health professions and related sciences. The faculty at University of Phoenix–Hawaii Campus has 2 full-time members, 50% with terminal degrees. The student-faculty ratio is 10:1.

Students of University of Phoenix–Hawaii Campus The student body totals 1,264, of whom 781 are undergraduates. 60.2% are women and 39.8% are men.

Applying University of Phoenix–Hawaii Campus requires 1 recommendation and 2 years of work experience, 23 years of age. Application deadline: rolling admissions. Deferred admission is possible.

UNIVERSITY OF PHOENIX–HOUSTON CAMPUS

Houston, TX

Urban setting ■ *Private* ■ *Proprietary* ■ *Coed*

Web site: www.phoenix.edu
Contact: Ms. Beth Barilla, Director of Admissions, 4615 East Elwood Street, Mail Stop 10-0030, Phoenix, AZ 85040-1958
Telephone: 480-317-6000 or toll-free 800-228-7240 **Fax:** 480-594-1758
E-mail: beth.barilla@apollogrp.edu

Getting in Last Year 1 enrolled (100%).

Financial Matters $8820 tuition and fees (2002–03).

Academics University of Phoenix–Houston Campus awards associate, bachelor's, master's, and doctoral degrees and post-bachelor's and post-master's certificates (courses conducted at 121 campuses and learning centers in 25 states). Challenging opportunities include advanced placement credit, accelerated degree programs, independent study, and a senior project. The faculty at University of Phoenix–Houston Campus has 2 full-time members. The student-faculty ratio is 18:1.

Students of University of Phoenix–Houston Campus The student body totals 1,841, of whom 1,281 are undergraduates. 63.2% are women and 36.8% are men. 20% are international students.

Applying University of Phoenix–Houston Campus requires 1 recommendation and 2 years of work experience, 23 years of age. Application deadline: rolling admissions. Deferred admission is possible.

UNIVERSITY OF PHOENIX-IDAHO CAMPUS

Meridian, ID

Urban setting ■ *Private* ■ *Proprietary* ■ *Coed*

Web site: www.phoenix.edu
Contact: Ms. Beth Barilla, Director of Admissions, 4615 East Elwood Street, Mail Stop 10-0030, Phoenix, AZ 85040-1958
Telephone: 480-317-6000 or toll-free 800-228-7240 **Fax:** 480-574-1758
E-mail: beth.barilla@apollogrp.edu

Financial Matters $8640 tuition and fees (2002–03).

Academics University of Phoenix-Idaho Campus awards associate, bachelor's, master's, and doctoral degrees and post-bachelor's and post-master's certificates (courses conducted at 121 campuses and learning centers in 25 states). Challenging opportunities include advanced placement credit, accelerated degree programs, independent study, and a senior project. The faculty at University of Phoenix-Idaho Campus has 14 members. The student-faculty ratio is 14:1.

Students of University of Phoenix-Idaho Campus The student body totals 261, of whom 210 are undergraduates. 40% are women and 60% are men.

Applying University of Phoenix-Idaho Campus requires 1 recommendation and 2 years of work experience, 23 years of age. Deferred admission is possible.

UNIVERSITY OF PHOENIX–JACKSONVILLE CAMPUS

Jacksonville, FL

Urban setting ■ *Private* ■ *Proprietary* ■ *Coed*

Web site: www.phoenix.edu
Contact: Ms. Beth Barilla, Director of Admissions, 4615 East Elwood Street, Mail Stop 10-0030, Phoenix, AZ 85040-1958
Telephone: 480-317-6000 or toll-free 800-228-7240 **Fax:** 480-594-1758
E-mail: beth.barilla@apollogrp.edu

Getting in Last Year 2 enrolled (100%).

Financial Matters $8430 tuition and fees (2002–03).

Academics University of Phoenix–Jacksonville Campus awards associate, bachelor's, master's, and doctoral degrees and post-bachelor's and post-master's certificates (courses conducted at 121 campuses and learning centers in 25 states). Challenging opportunities include advanced placement credit, accelerated degree programs, independent study, and a senior project. The most frequently chosen baccalaureate fields are business/marketing and health professions and related sciences. The faculty at University of Phoenix–Jacksonville Campus has 4 full-time members, 75% with terminal degrees. The student-faculty ratio is 14:1.

Students of University of Phoenix–Jacksonville Campus The student body totals 1,590, of whom 1,160 are undergraduates. 57.8% are women and 42.2% are men. 8.2% are international students.

Applying University of Phoenix–Jacksonville Campus requires 1 recommendation and 2 years of work experience, 23 years of age. Application deadline: rolling admissions. Deferred admission is possible.

UNIVERSITY OF PHOENIX-KANSAS CITY CAMPUS

Kansas City, MO

Private ■ *Proprietary* ■ *Coed*

Web site: www.phoenix.edu
Contact: Ms. Beth Barilla, Director of Admissions, 4615 East Elwood Street, Mail Stop 10-0030, Phoenix, AZ 85040-1958

Telephone: 480-317-6000 or toll-free 800-228-7240 **Fax:** 480-594-1758
E-mail: beth.barilla@apollogrp.edu

Getting in Last Year 20 enrolled (91%).

Financial Matters $9600 tuition and fees (2002–03).

Academics University of Phoenix-Kansas City Campus awards associate, bachelor's, master's, and doctoral degrees and post-bachelor's and post-master's certificates (courses conducted at 121 campuses and learning centers in 25 states). Challenging opportunities include advanced placement credit, accelerated degree programs, independent study, and a senior project. The faculty at University of Phoenix-Kansas City Campus has 3 full-time members.

Students of University of Phoenix-Kansas City Campus The student body totals 260, of whom 178 are undergraduates. 55.1% are women and 44.9% are men.

Applying University of Phoenix-Kansas City Campus requires 1 recommendation and 2 years of work experience, 23 years of age. Application deadline: rolling admissions. Deferred admission is possible.

UNIVERSITY OF PHOENIX–LOUISIANA CAMPUS

Metairie, LA

Urban setting ■ *Private* ■ *Proprietary* ■ *Coed*

Web site: www.phoenix.edu
Contact: Ms. Beth Barilla, Director of Admissions, 4615 East Elwood Street, Mail Stop 10-0030, Phoenix, AZ 85040-1958
Telephone: 480-317-6000 or toll-free 800-228-7240 **Fax:** 480-594-1758
E-mail: beth.barilla@apollogrp.edu

Getting in Last Year 4 enrolled (4%).

Financial Matters $7710 tuition and fees (2002–03).

Academics University of Phoenix–Louisiana Campus awards associate, bachelor's, master's, and doctoral degrees and post-bachelor's and post-master's certificates (courses conducted at 121 campuses and learning centers in 25 states). Challenging opportunities include advanced placement credit, accelerated degree programs, independent study, and a senior project. The most frequently chosen baccalaureate fields are business/marketing and health professions and related sciences. The faculty at University of Phoenix–Louisiana Campus has 4 full-time members, 50% with terminal degrees. The student-faculty ratio is 14:1.

Students of University of Phoenix–Louisiana Campus The student body totals 1,893, of whom 1,377 are undergraduates. 62.8% are women and 37.2% are men. 4.1% are international students.

Applying University of Phoenix–Louisiana Campus requires 1 recommendation and 2 years of work experience, 23 years of age. Application deadline: rolling admissions. Deferred admission is possible.

UNIVERSITY OF PHOENIX–MARYLAND CAMPUS

Columbia, MD

Urban setting ■ *Private* ■ *Proprietary* ■ *Coed*

Web site: www.phoenix.edu
Contact: Ms. Beth Barilla, Director of Admissions, 4615 East Elwood Street, Mail Stop 10-0030, Phoenix, AZ 85040-1958
Telephone: 480-317-6000 or toll-free 800-228-7240 **Fax:** 480-894-1758
E-mail: beth.barilla@apollogrp.edu

Financial Matters $9600 tuition and fees (2002–03).

Academics University of Phoenix–Maryland Campus awards associate, bachelor's, master's, and doctoral degrees and post-bachelor's and post-master's certificates (courses conducted at 121 campuses and learning centers in 25 states). Challenging opportunities include advanced placement credit, accelerated degree programs, independent study, and a senior project. The most frequently chosen baccalaureate field is business/marketing. The faculty at University of Phoenix–Maryland Campus has 3 full-time members. The student-faculty ratio is 13:1.

Students of University of Phoenix–Maryland Campus The student body totals 1,544, of whom 1,118 are undergraduates. 8.5% are international students.

Applying University of Phoenix–Maryland Campus requires 1 recommendation and 2 years of work experience, 23 years of age. Application deadline: rolling admissions. Deferred admission is possible.

UNIVERSITY OF PHOENIX–METRO DETROIT CAMPUS

Troy, MI

Urban setting ■ *Private* ■ *Proprietary* ■ *Coed*

Web site: www.phoenix.edu
Contact: Ms. Beth Barilla, Director of Admissions, 4615 East Elwood Street, Mail Stop 10-0030, Phoenix, AZ 85040-1958
Telephone: 480-317-6000 or toll-free 800-834-2438 **Fax:** 480-594-1758
E-mail: beth.barilla@apollogrp.edu

Getting in Last Year 1 enrolled (100%).

Financial Matters $9540 tuition and fees (2002–03).

Academics University of Phoenix–Metro Detroit Campus awards associate, bachelor's, master's, and doctoral degrees and post-bachelor's and post-master's certificates (courses conducted at 121 campuses and learning centers in 25 states). Challenging opportunities include advanced placement credit, accelerated degree programs, independent study, and a senior project. The most frequently chosen baccalaureate fields are business/marketing, computer/information sciences, and health professions and related sciences. The faculty at University of Phoenix–Metro Detroit Campus has 6 full-time members, 33% with terminal degrees. The student-faculty ratio is 11:1.

Students of University of Phoenix–Metro Detroit Campus The student body totals 3,318, of whom 2,511 are undergraduates. 65.8% are women and 34.2% are men. 2.2% are international students.

Applying University of Phoenix–Metro Detroit Campus requires 1 recommendation and 2 years of work experience, 23 years of age. Application deadline: rolling admissions. Deferred admission is possible.

UNIVERSITY OF PHOENIX–NEVADA CAMPUS

Las Vegas, NV

Urban setting ■ *Private* ■ *Proprietary* ■ *Coed*

Web site: www.phoenix.edu
Contact: Ms. Beth Barilla, Director of Admissions, 4615 East Elwood Street, Mail Stop 10-0030, Phoenix, AZ 85040-1958
Telephone: 480-317-6000 or toll-free 800-228-7240 **Fax:** 480-594-1758
E-mail: beth.barilla@apollogrp.edu

Getting in Last Year 1 enrolled (1%).

Financial Matters $8520 tuition and fees (2002–03).

Academics University of Phoenix–Nevada Campus awards associate, bachelor's, master's, and doctoral degrees and post-bachelor's and post-master's certificates (courses conducted at 121 campuses and learning centers in 25 states). Challenging opportunities include advanced placement credit, accelerated degree programs, independent study, and a senior project. The most frequently chosen baccalaureate field is business/marketing. The faculty at University of Phoenix–Nevada Campus has 5 full-time members, 20% with terminal degrees. The student-faculty ratio is 16:1.

Students of University of Phoenix–Nevada Campus The student body totals 3,042, of whom 1,976 are undergraduates. 5.5% are international students.

Applying University of Phoenix–Nevada Campus requires 1 recommendation and 2 years of work experience, 23 years of age. Application deadline: rolling admissions. Deferred admission is possible.

UNIVERSITY OF PHOENIX–NEW MEXICO CAMPUS

Albuquerque, NM

Urban setting ■ *Private* ■ *Proprietary* ■ *Coed*

Web site: www.phoenix.edu
Contact: Ms. Beth Barilla, Director of Admissions, 4615 East Elwood Street, Mail Stop 10-0030, Phoenix, AZ 85040-1958
Telephone: 480-317-6000 or toll-free 800-228-7240 **Fax:** 480-594-1758
E-mail: beth.barilla@apollogrp.edu

Financial Matters $8190 tuition and fees (2002–03).

Academics University of Phoenix–New Mexico Campus awards associate, bachelor's, master's, and doctoral degrees and post-bachelor's and post-master's certificates (courses conducted at 121 campuses and learning centers in 25 states). Challenging opportunities include advanced placement credit, accelerated degree programs, independent study, and a senior project. The most frequently chosen baccalaureate fields are business/marketing, health professions and related sciences, and computer/information sciences. The faculty at University of Phoenix–New Mexico Campus has 6 full-time members, 50% with terminal degrees. The student-faculty ratio is 14:1.

Students of University of Phoenix–New Mexico Campus The student body totals 3,445, of whom 2,666 are undergraduates. 57.1% are women and 42.9% are men. 4.4% are international students.

Applying University of Phoenix–New Mexico Campus requires 1 recommendation and 2 years of work experience, 23 years of age. Application deadline: rolling admissions. Deferred admission is possible.

UNIVERSITY OF PHOENIX–NORTHERN CALIFORNIA CAMPUS

Pleasanton, CA

Urban setting ■ *Private* ■ *Proprietary* ■ *Coed*

Web site: www.phoenix.edu
Contact: Ms. Beth Barilla, Director of Admissions, 4615 East Elwood Street, Mail Stop 10-0030, Phoenix, AZ 85040-1958
Telephone: 480-317-6000 or toll-free 877-4-STUDENT **Fax:** 480-594-1758
E-mail: beth.barilla@apollogrp.edu

Getting in Last Year 3 enrolled (100%).

Financial Matters $11,670 tuition and fees (2002–03).

Academics University of Phoenix–Northern California Campus awards associate, bachelor's, master's, and doctoral degrees and post-bachelor's and post-master's certificates (courses conducted at 121 campuses and learning centers in 25

University of Phoenix–Northern California Campus (continued)

states). Challenging opportunities include advanced placement credit, accelerated degree programs, independent study, and a senior project. The most frequently chosen baccalaureate fields are business/marketing and health professions and related sciences. The faculty at University of Phoenix–Northern California Campus has 7 full-time members, 29% with terminal degrees. The student-faculty ratio is 11:1.

Students of University of Phoenix–Northern California Campus The student body totals 5,513, of whom 4,233 are undergraduates. 57.8% are women and 42.2% are men. 6.3% are international students.

Applying University of Phoenix–Northern California Campus requires 1 recommendation and 2 years of work experience, 23 years of age. Application deadline: rolling admissions. Deferred admission is possible.

UNIVERSITY OF PHOENIX–OHIO CAMPUS

Independence, OH

Urban setting ■ Private ■ Proprietary ■ Coed

Web site: www.phoenix.edu
Contact: Ms. Beth Barilla, Director of Admissions, 4615 East Elwood Street, Mail Stop 10-0030, Phoenix, AZ 85040-1958
Telephone: 480-317-6000 **Fax:** 480-594-1758
E-mail: beth.barilla@apollogrp.edu

Financial Matters $11,250 tuition and fees (2002–03).

Academics University of Phoenix–Ohio Campus awards associate, bachelor's, master's, and doctoral degrees and post-bachelor's and post-master's certificates (courses conducted at 121 campuses and learning centers in 25 states). Challenging opportunities include advanced placement credit, accelerated degree programs, independent study, and a senior project. The faculty at University of Phoenix–Ohio Campus has 2 full-time members, 50% with terminal degrees. The student-faculty ratio is 13:1.

Students of University of Phoenix–Ohio Campus The student body totals 740, of whom 480 are undergraduates. 56.7% are women and 43.3% are men. 0.8% are international students.

Applying University of Phoenix–Ohio Campus requires 1 recommendation and 2 years of work experience, 23 years of age. Application deadline: rolling admissions. Deferred admission is possible.

UNIVERSITY OF PHOENIX–OKLAHOMA CITY CAMPUS

Oklahoma City, OK

Urban setting ■ Private ■ Proprietary ■ Coed

Web site: www.phoenix.edu
Contact: Ms. Beth Barilla, Director of Admissions, 4615 East Elwood Street, Mail Stop 10-0030, Phoenix, AZ 85040-1958
Telephone: 480-317-6000 or toll-free 800-228-7240 **Fax:** 480-594-1758
E-mail: beth.barilla@apollogrp.edu

Financial Matters $8250 tuition and fees (2002–03).

Academics University of Phoenix–Oklahoma City Campus awards associate, bachelor's, master's, and doctoral degrees and post-bachelor's and post-master's certificates (courses conducted at 121 campuses and learning centers in 25 states). Challenging opportunities include advanced placement credit, accelerated degree programs, independent study, and a senior project. The most frequently chosen baccalaureate field is business/marketing. The faculty at University of Phoenix–Oklahoma City Campus has 3 full-time members, 33% with terminal degrees. The student-faculty ratio is 14:1.

Students of University of Phoenix–Oklahoma City Campus The student body totals 874, of whom 683 are undergraduates. 48.3% are women and 51.7% are men. 1% are international students.

Applying University of Phoenix–Oklahoma City Campus requires 1 recommendation and 2 years of work experience, 23 years of age. Application deadline: rolling admissions. Deferred admission is possible.

UNIVERSITY OF PHOENIX ONLINE CAMPUS

Phoenix, AZ

Private ■ Proprietary ■ Coed

Web site: www.uoponline.com
Contact: Ms. Beth Barilla, Director of Admissions, 4615 East Elwood Street, Mail Stop 10-0030, Phoenix, AZ 85040-1958
Telephone: 480-317-6000 or toll-free 800-776-4867 (in-state), 800-228-7240 (out-of-state)
E-mail: beth.barilla@apollogrp.edu

Getting in Last Year 2,811 enrolled.

Financial Matters $12,660 tuition and fees (2002–03).

Academics UOP awards associate, bachelor's, master's, and doctoral degrees and post-bachelor's and post-master's certificates (courses conducted at 121 campuses and learning centers in 25 states). Challenging opportunities include advanced placement credit, accelerated degree programs, independent study, and a senior project. The faculty at UOP has 8 full-time members, 63% with terminal degrees.

Students of UOP The student body totals 48,118, of whom 30,702 are undergraduates. 53.9% are women and 46.1% are men.

Applying UOP requires 1 recommendation and 2 years of work experience, 23 years of age. Application deadline: rolling admissions. Deferred admission is possible.

UNIVERSITY OF PHOENIX–OREGON CAMPUS

Portland, OR

Urban setting ■ Private ■ Proprietary ■ Coed

Web site: www.phoenix.edu
Contact: Ms. Beth Barilla, Director of Admissions, 4615 East Elwood Street, Mail Stop 10-0030, Phoenix, AZ 85040-1958
Telephone: 480-317*6000 or toll-free 800-228-7240 **Fax:** 480-594-1758
E-mail: beth.barilla@apollogrp.edu

Financial Matters $9150 tuition and fees (2002–03).

Academics University of Phoenix–Oregon Campus awards associate, bachelor's, master's, and doctoral degrees and post-bachelor's and post-master's certificates (courses conducted at 121 campuses and learning centers in 25 states). Challenging opportunities include advanced placement credit, accelerated degree programs, independent study, and a senior project. The most frequently chosen baccalaureate field is business/marketing. The faculty at University of Phoenix–Oregon Campus has 4 full-time members, 50% with terminal degrees. The student-faculty ratio is 12:1.

Students of University of Phoenix–Oregon Campus The student body totals 1,536, of whom 1,235 are undergraduates. 41% are women and 59% are men. 1.9% are international students.

Applying University of Phoenix–Oregon Campus requires 1 recommendation and 2 years of work experience, 23 years of age. Application deadline: rolling admissions. Deferred admission is possible.

UNIVERSITY OF PHOENIX–ORLANDO CAMPUS

Maitland, FL

Urban setting ■ Private ■ Proprietary ■ Coed

Web site: www.phoenix.edu
Contact: Ms. Beth Barilla, Director of Admissions, 4615 East Elwood Street, Mail Stop 10-0030, Phoenix, AZ 85040-1958
Telephone: 480-317-6000 or toll-free 800-228-7240 **Fax:** 480-594-1758
E-mail: beth.barilla@apollogrp.edu

Getting in Last Year 1 enrolled (100%).

Financial Matters $8430 tuition and fees (2002–03).

Academics University of Phoenix–Orlando Campus awards associate, bachelor's, master's, and doctoral degrees and post-bachelor's and post-master's certificates (courses conducted at 121 campuses and learning centers in 25 states). Challenging opportunities include advanced placement credit, accelerated degree programs, and independent study. The most frequently chosen baccalaureate fields are business/marketing and health professions and related sciences. The faculty at University of Phoenix–Orlando Campus has 5 full-time members, 40% with terminal degrees. The student-faculty ratio is 13:1.

Students of University of Phoenix–Orlando Campus The student body totals 1,395, of whom 962 are undergraduates. 55.2% are women and 44.8% are men. 13.9% are international students.

Applying University of Phoenix–Orlando Campus requires 2 years of work experience, 23 years of age and a minimum high school GPA of 1. Application deadline: rolling admissions. Deferred admission is possible.

UNIVERSITY OF PHOENIX–PHILADELPHIA CAMPUS

Wayne, PA

Urban setting ■ Private ■ Proprietary ■ Coed

Web site: www.phoenix.edu
Contact: Ms. Beth Barilla, Director of Admissions, 4615 East Elwood Street, Mail Stop 10-0030, Phoenix, AZ 85040-1958
Telephone: 480-317-6000 or toll-free 800-228-7240 **Fax:** 480-594-1758
E-mail: beth.barilla@apollogrp.edu

Financial Matters $10,800 tuition and fees (2002–03).

Academics University of Phoenix–Philadelphia Campus awards associate, bachelor's, master's, and doctoral degrees and post-bachelor's and post-master's certificates (courses conducted at 121 campuses and learning centers in 25 states). Challenging opportunities include advanced placement credit, accelerated degree programs, independent study, and a senior project. The most frequently chosen baccalaureate field is business/marketing. The faculty at University of Phoenix–Philadelphia Campus has 4 full-time members, 25% with terminal degrees. The student-faculty ratio is 13:1.

Students of University of Phoenix–Philadelphia Campus The student body totals 1,179, of whom 783 are undergraduates. 50.7% are women and 49.3% are men. 4.6% are international students.

Applying University of Phoenix–Philadelphia Campus requires 1 recommendation and 2 years of work experience, 23 years of age. Application deadline: rolling admissions. Deferred admission is possible.

UNIVERSITY OF PHOENIX–PHOENIX CAMPUS

Phoenix, AZ

Urban setting ■ Private ■ Proprietary ■ Coed

Web site: www.phoenix.edu
Contact: Ms. Beth Barilla, Director of Admissions, 4615 East Elwood Street, Mail Stop 10-0030, Phoenix, AZ 85040-1958
Telephone: 480-317-6000 or toll-free 800-776-4867 (in-state), 800-228-7240 (out-of-state) **Fax:** 480-894-1758
E-mail: beth.barilla@apollogrp.edu

Getting in Last Year 7 enrolled (100%).

Financial Matters $8400 tuition and fees (2002–03).

Academics UOP awards associate, bachelor's, master's, and doctoral degrees and post-bachelor's and post-master's certificates (courses conducted at 121 campuses and learning centers in 25 states). Challenging opportunities include advanced placement credit, accelerated degree programs, independent study, and a senior project. The most frequently chosen baccalaureate fields are business/marketing, health professions and related sciences, and computer/information sciences. The faculty at UOP has 6 full-time members, 50% with terminal degrees. The student-faculty ratio is 14:1.

Students of UOP The student body totals 8,112, of whom 4,684 are undergraduates. 53.7% are women and 46.3% are men. 2.6% are international students.

Applying UOP requires 1 recommendation and 2 years of work experience, 23 years of age. Application deadline: rolling admissions. Deferred admission is possible.

UNIVERSITY OF PHOENIX–PITTSBURGH CAMPUS

Pittsburgh, PA

Urban setting ■ Private ■ Proprietary ■ Coed

Web site: www.phoenix.edu
Contact: Ms. Beth Barilla, Director of Admissions, 4615 East Elwood Street, Mail Stop 10-0030, Phoenix, AZ 85040-1958
Telephone: 480-317-6000 or toll-free 800-228-7240 **Fax:** 480-594-1758
E-mail: beth.barilla@apollogrp.edu

Getting in Last Year 1 enrolled (5%).

Financial Matters $10,800 tuition and fees (2002–03).

Academics University of Phoenix–Pittsburgh Campus awards associate, bachelor's, master's, and doctoral degrees and post-bachelor's and post-master's certificates (courses conducted at 121 campuses and learning centers in 25 states). Challenging opportunities include accelerated degree programs, independent study, and a senior project. Cooperative education is a special program. The faculty at University of Phoenix–Pittsburgh Campus has 4 full-time members, 25% with terminal degrees. The student-faculty ratio is 10:1.

Students of University of Phoenix–Pittsburgh Campus The student body totals 364, of whom 207 are undergraduates. 41.5% are women and 58.5% are men. 3.4% are international students.

Applying University of Phoenix–Pittsburgh Campus requires 1 recommendation and 2 years of work experience, 23 years of age. Application deadline: rolling admissions. Deferred admission is possible.

UNIVERSITY OF PHOENIX–PUERTO RICO CAMPUS

Guaynabo, PR

Urban setting ■ Private ■ Proprietary ■ Coed

Web site: www.phoenix.edu
Contact: Ms. Beth Barilla, Director of Admissions, 4615 East Elwood Street, Mail Stop 10-0030, Phoenix, AZ 85040-1958
Telephone: 480-317-6000 or toll-free 800-228-7240 **Fax:** 480-594-1758
E-mail: beth.barilla@apollogrp.edu

Getting in Last Year 2 enrolled (100%).

Financial Matters $4950 tuition and fees (2002–03).

Academics University of Phoenix–Puerto Rico Campus awards associate, bachelor's, master's, and doctoral degrees and post-bachelor's and post-master's certificates (courses conducted at 121 campuses and learning centers in 25 states). Challenging opportunities include advanced placement credit, accelerated degree programs, independent study, and a senior project. The most frequently chosen baccalaureate field is business/marketing. The faculty at University of Phoenix–Puerto Rico Campus has 4 full-time members, 75% with terminal degrees. The student-faculty ratio is 13:1.

Students of University of Phoenix–Puerto Rico Campus The student body totals 2,016, of whom 356 are undergraduates. 56.2% are women and 43.8% are men.

Applying University of Phoenix–Puerto Rico Campus requires 1 recommendation and 2 years of work experience, 23 years of age. Application deadline: rolling admissions. Deferred admission is possible.

UNIVERSITY OF PHOENIX–SACRAMENTO CAMPUS

Sacramento, CA

Urban setting ■ Private ■ Proprietary ■ Coed

Web site: www.phoenix.edu
Contact: Ms. Beth Barilla, Director of Admissions, 4615 East Elwood Street, Mail Stop 10-0030, Phoenix, AZ 85040-1958
Telephone: 480-317-6000 or toll-free 800-266-2107 **Fax:** 480-594-1758
E-mail: beth.barilla@apollo.grp.edu

Getting in Last Year 2 enrolled (2%).

Financial Matters $10,950 tuition and fees (2002–03).

Academics University of Phoenix–Sacramento Campus awards associate, bachelor's, master's, and doctoral degrees and post-bachelor's and post-master's certificates (courses conducted at 121 campuses and learning centers in 25 states). Challenging opportunities include advanced placement credit, accelerated degree programs, independent study, and a senior project. The most frequently chosen baccalaureate fields are business/marketing and health professions and related sciences. The faculty at University of Phoenix–Sacramento Campus has 7 full-time members, 29% with terminal degrees. The student-faculty ratio is 12:1.

Students of University of Phoenix–Sacramento Campus The student body totals 3,468, of whom 2,606 are undergraduates. 57.1% are women and 42.9% are men. 2.3% are international students.

Applying University of Phoenix–Sacramento Campus requires 1 recommendation and 2 years of work experience, 23 years of age. Application deadline: rolling admissions. Deferred admission is possible.

UNIVERSITY OF PHOENIX–ST. LOUIS CAMPUS

St. Louis, MO

Urban setting ■ Private ■ Proprietary ■ Coed

Web site: www.phoenix.edu
Contact: Ms. Beth Barilla, Director of Admissions, 4615 East Elwood Street, Mail Stop 10-0030, Phoenix, AZ 85040-1958
Telephone: 480-317-6000 or toll-free 888-326-7737 (in-state), 800-228-7240 (out-of-state) **Fax:** 480-594-1758
E-mail: beth.barilla@apollogrp.edu

Financial Matters $10,080 tuition and fees (2002–03).

Academics University of Phoenix–St. Louis Campus awards associate, bachelor's, master's, and doctoral degrees and post-bachelor's and post-master's certificates (courses conducted at 121 campuses and learning centers in 25 states). Challenging opportunities include advanced placement credit, accelerated degree programs, independent study, and a senior project. The faculty at University of Phoenix–St. Louis Campus has 2 full-time members, 50% with terminal degrees. The student-faculty ratio is 10:1.

Students of University of Phoenix–St. Louis Campus The student body totals 447, of whom 328 are undergraduates. 59.5% are women and 40.5% are men. 0.6% are international students.

Applying University of Phoenix–St. Louis Campus requires 1 recommendation and 2 years of work experience, 23 years of age. Application deadline: rolling admissions. Deferred admission is possible.

UNIVERSITY OF PHOENIX–SAN DIEGO CAMPUS

San Diego, CA

Urban setting ■ Private ■ Proprietary ■ Coed

Web site: www.phoenix.edu
Contact: Ms. Beth Barilla, Director of Admissions, 4615 East Elwood Street, Mail Stop 10-0030, Phoenix, AZ 85040-1958
Telephone: 480-317-6000 or toll-free 888-UOP-INFO **Fax:** 480-594-1758
E-mail: beth.barilla@apollogrp.edu

Financial Matters $10,200 tuition and fees (2002–03).

Academics University of Phoenix–San Diego Campus awards associate, bachelor's, master's, and doctoral degrees and post-bachelor's and post-master's certificates (courses conducted at 121 campuses and learning centers in 25 states). Challenging opportunities include advanced placement credit, accelerated degree programs, independent study, and a senior project. The most frequently chosen baccalaureate fields are business/marketing and health professions and related sciences. The faculty at University of Phoenix–San Diego Campus has 8 full-time members, 38% with terminal degrees. The student-faculty ratio is 14:1.

Students of University of Phoenix–San Diego Campus The student body totals 4,244, of whom 3,202 are undergraduates. 49.5% are women and 50.5% are men. 3.6% are international students.

University of Phoenix–San Diego Campus (continued)

Applying University of Phoenix–San Diego Campus requires 1 recommendation and 2 years of work experience, 23 years of age. Application deadline: rolling admissions. Deferred admission is possible.

UNIVERSITY OF PHOENIX–SOUTHERN ARIZONA CAMPUS

Tucson, AZ

Urban setting ■ *Private* ■ *Proprietary* ■ *Coed*

Web site: www.phoenix.edu
Contact: Ms. Beth Barilla, Director of Admissions, 4615 East Elwood Street, Mail Stop 10-0030, Phoenix, AZ 85040-1958
Telephone: 480-317-6000 or toll-free 800-228-7240 **Fax:** 480-594-1756
E-mail: beth.barilla@apollogrp.edu

Getting in Last Year 3 enrolled (2%).

Financial Matters $8100 tuition and fees (2002–03).

Academics University of Phoenix–Southern Arizona Campus awards associate, bachelor's, master's, and doctoral degrees and post-bachelor's and post-master's certificates (courses conducted at 121 campuses and learning centers in 25 states). Challenging opportunities include advanced placement credit, accelerated degree programs, independent study, and a senior project. The most frequently chosen baccalaureate fields are business/marketing, health professions and related sciences, and computer/information sciences. The faculty at University of Phoenix–Southern Arizona Campus has 7 full-time members, 29% with terminal degrees. The student-faculty ratio is 15:1.

Students of University of Phoenix–Southern Arizona Campus The student body totals 3,165, of whom 1,999 are undergraduates. 54.7% are women and 45.3% are men. 4.3% are international students.

Applying University of Phoenix–Southern Arizona Campus requires 1 recommendation and 2 years of work experience, 23 years of age. Application deadline: rolling admissions. Deferred admission is possible.

UNIVERSITY OF PHOENIX–SOUTHERN CALIFORNIA CAMPUS

Fountain Valley, CA

Urban setting ■ *Private* ■ *Proprietary* ■ *Coed*

Web site: www.phoenix.edu
Contact: Ms. Beth Barilla, Director of Admissions, 4615 East Elwood Street, Mail Stop 10-0030, Phoenix, AZ 85040-1958
Telephone: 480-317-6000 or toll-free 800-228-7240
E-mail: beth.barilla@apollogrp.edu

Getting in Last Year 5 enrolled (1%).

Financial Matters $11,100 tuition and fees (2002–03).

Academics University of Phoenix–Southern California Campus awards associate, bachelor's, master's, and doctoral degrees and post-bachelor's and post-master's certificates (courses conducted at 121 campuses and learning centers in 25 states). Challenging opportunities include advanced placement credit, accelerated degree programs, independent study, and a senior project. The most frequently chosen baccalaureate fields are business/marketing and health professions and related sciences. The faculty at University of Phoenix–Southern California Campus has 6 full-time members, 50% with terminal degrees. The student-faculty ratio is 14:1.

Students of University of Phoenix–Southern California Campus The student body totals 12,161, of whom 9,627 are undergraduates. 3.8% are international students.

Applying University of Phoenix–Southern California Campus requires 1 recommendation and 2 years of work experience, 23 years of age. Application deadline: rolling admissions. Deferred admission is possible.

UNIVERSITY OF PHOENIX–SOUTHERN COLORADO CAMPUS

Colorado Springs, CO

Urban setting ■ *Private* ■ *Proprietary* ■ *Coed*

Web site: www.phoenix.edu
Contact: Ms. Beth Barilla, Director of Admissions, 4615 East Elwood Street, Mail Stop 10-0030, Phoenix, AZ 85040-1958
Telephone: 480-317-6000 or toll-free 800-228-7240 **Fax:** 480-894-1758
E-mail: beth.barilla@apollogrp.edu

Financial Matters $8250 tuition and fees (2002–03).

Academics University of Phoenix–Southern Colorado Campus awards associate, bachelor's, master's, and doctoral degrees and post-bachelor's and post-master's certificates (courses conducted at 121 campuses and learning centers in 25 states). Challenging opportunities include advanced placement credit, accelerated degree programs, independent study, and a senior project. The faculty at University of Phoenix–Southern Colorado Campus has 5 full-time members, 40% with terminal degrees. The student-faculty ratio is 12:1.

Students of University of Phoenix–Southern Colorado Campus The student body totals 1,256, of whom 852 are undergraduates. 45.8% are women and 54.2% are men. 3.3% are international students.

Applying University of Phoenix–Southern Colorado Campus requires 1 recommendation and 2 years of work experience, 23 years of age. Application deadline: rolling admissions. Deferred admission is possible.

UNIVERSITY OF PHOENIX–TAMPA CAMPUS

Tampa, FL

Private ■ *Proprietary* ■ *Coed*

Web site: www.phoenix.edu
Contact: Ms. Beth Barilla, Director of Admissions, 4615 East Elwood Street, Mail Stop 10-0030, Phoenix, AZ 85040-1958
Telephone: 480-317-6000 or toll-free 800-228-7240 **Fax:** 480-594-1758
E-mail: beth.barilla@apollogrp.edu

Getting in Last Year 1 enrolled (100%).

Financial Matters $8100 tuition and fees (2002–03).

Academics University of Phoenix–Tampa Campus awards associate, bachelor's, master's, and doctoral degrees and post-bachelor's and post-master's certificates (courses conducted at 121 campuses and learning centers in 25 states). Challenging opportunities include advanced placement credit, accelerated degree programs, independent study, and a senior project. The most frequently chosen baccalaureate fields are business/marketing and health professions and related sciences. The faculty at University of Phoenix–Tampa Campus has 6 full-time members, 33% with terminal degrees. The student-faculty ratio is 12:1.

Students of University of Phoenix–Tampa Campus The student body totals 1,702, of whom 1,127 are undergraduates. 52.6% are women and 47.4% are men. 5.3% are international students.

Applying University of Phoenix–Tampa Campus requires 2 years of work experience, 23 years of age and a minimum high school GPA of 1. Application deadline: rolling admissions. Deferred admission is possible.

UNIVERSITY OF PHOENIX–TULSA CAMPUS

Tulsa, OK

Urban setting ■ *Private* ■ *Proprietary* ■ *Coed*

Web site: www.phoenix.edu
Contact: Ms. Beth Barilla, Director of Admissions, 4615 East Elwood Street, Mail Stop 10-0030, Phoenix, AZ 85040-1958
Telephone: 480-317-6000 or toll-free 800-228-7240 **Fax:** 480-594-1758
E-mail: beth.barilla@apollogrp.edu

Getting in Last Year 3 enrolled (15%).

Financial Matters $8250 tuition and fees (2002–03).

Academics University of Phoenix–Tulsa Campus awards associate, bachelor's, master's, and doctoral degrees and post-bachelor's and post-master's certificates (courses conducted at 121 campuses and learning centers in 25 states). Challenging opportunities include advanced placement credit, accelerated degree programs, independent study, and a senior project. The most frequently chosen baccalaureate field is business/marketing. The faculty at University of Phoenix–Tulsa Campus has 3 full-time members, 33% with terminal degrees. The student-faculty ratio is 14:1.

Students of University of Phoenix–Tulsa Campus The student body totals 912, of whom 705 are undergraduates. 51.5% are women and 48.5% are men. 21.7% are international students.

Applying University of Phoenix–Tulsa Campus requires 1 recommendation and 2 years of work experience, 23 years of age. Application deadline: rolling admissions. Deferred admission is possible.

UNIVERSITY OF PHOENIX–UTAH CAMPUS

Salt Lake City, UT

Urban setting ■ *Private* ■ *Proprietary* ■ *Coed*

Web site: www.phoenix.edu
Contact: Ms. Beth Barilla, Director of Admissions, 4615 East Elwood Street, Mail Stop 10-0030, Phoenix, AZ 85040-1958
Telephone: 480-317-6000 or toll-free 800-224-2844 **Fax:** 480-594-1758
E-mail: beth.barilla@apollogrp.edu

Getting in Last Year 1 enrolled (1%).

Financial Matters $8640 tuition and fees (2002–03); $3948 average financial aid amount received per undergraduate (2001–02).

Academics University of Phoenix–Utah Campus awards associate, bachelor's, master's, and doctoral degrees and post-bachelor's and post-master's certificates (courses conducted at 121 campuses and learning centers in 25 states). Challenging opportunities include advanced placement credit, accelerated degree programs, independent study, and a senior project. The most frequently chosen baccalaureate fields are business/marketing and health professions and related sciences. The faculty at University of Phoenix–Utah Campus has 7 full-time members, 29% with terminal degrees. The student-faculty ratio is 13:1.

Students of University of Phoenix–Utah Campus The student body totals 3,168, of whom 1,978 are undergraduates. 38.7% are women and 61.3% are men. 2.5% are international students.

Applying University of Phoenix–Utah Campus requires 1 recommendation and 2 years of work experience, 23 years of age. Application deadline: rolling admissions. Deferred admission is possible.

UNIVERSITY OF PHOENIX-VANCOUVER CAMPUS

Burnaby, BC Canada

Urban setting ■ Private ■ Proprietary ■ Coed

Web site: www.phoenix.edu
Contact: Ms. Beth Barilla, Director of Admissions, 4615 East Elwood Street, Mail Stop 10-0030, Phoenix, AZ 85040-1958
Telephone: 480-317-6000 **Fax:** 480-594-1758
E-mail: beth.barilla@apollogrp.edu

Financial Matters $10,800 tuition and fees (2002–03).

Academics University of Phoenix-Vancouver Campus awards associate, bachelor's, master's, and doctoral degrees and post-bachelor's and post-master's certificates (courses conducted at 121 campuses and learning centers in 25 states). Challenging opportunities include advanced placement credit, accelerated degree programs, independent study, and a senior project. The most frequently chosen baccalaureate field is business/marketing. The faculty at University of Phoenix-Vancouver Campus has 1 full-time members. The student-faculty ratio is 13:1.

Students of University of Phoenix-Vancouver Campus The student body totals 364, of whom 121 are undergraduates. 54.5% are women and 45.5% are men.

Applying University of Phoenix-Vancouver Campus requires 2 years of work experience, 23 years of age. Application deadline: rolling admissions. Deferred admission is possible.

UNIVERSITY OF PHOENIX–WASHINGTON CAMPUS

Seattle, WA

Private ■ Proprietary ■ Coed

Web site: www.phoenix.edu
Contact: Ms. Beth Barilla, Director of Admissions, 4615 East Elwood Street, Mail Stop 10-0030, Phoenix, AZ 85040-1958
Telephone: 480-317-6000 or toll-free 800-228-7240 **Fax:** 480-894-1758
E-mail: beth.barilla@apollogrp.edu

Financial Matters $9450 tuition and fees (2002–03).

Academics University of Phoenix–Washington Campus awards associate, bachelor's, master's, and doctoral degrees and post-bachelor's and post-master's certificates (courses conducted at 121 campuses and learning centers in 25 states). Challenging opportunities include advanced placement credit, accelerated degree programs, independent study, and a senior project. The most frequently chosen baccalaureate field is business/marketing. The faculty at University of Phoenix–Washington Campus has 4 full-time members, 25% with terminal degrees. The student-faculty ratio is 13:1.

Students of University of Phoenix–Washington Campus The student body totals 1,826, of whom 1,363 are undergraduates. 1.5% are international students.

Applying University of Phoenix–Washington Campus requires 2 years of work experience, 23 years of age and a minimum high school GPA of 1. Application deadline: rolling admissions. Deferred admission is possible.

UNIVERSITY OF PHOENIX–WEST MICHIGAN CAMPUS

Grand Rapids, MI

Urban setting ■ Private ■ Proprietary ■ Coed

Web site: www.phoenix.edu
Contact: Ms. Beth Barilla, Director of Admissions, 4615 East Elwood Street, Mail Stop 10-0030, Phoenix, AZ 85040-1958
Telephone: 480-317-6000 or toll-free 800-228-7240
E-mail: beth.barilla@apollogrp.edu

Getting in Last Year 1 enrolled (100%).

Financial Matters $9210 tuition and fees (2002–03).

Academics University of Phoenix–West Michigan Campus awards associate, bachelor's, master's, and doctoral degrees and post-bachelor's and post-master's certificates (courses conducted at 121 campuses and learning centers in 25 states). Challenging opportunities include advanced placement credit, accelerated degree programs, independent study, and a senior project. The most frequently chosen baccalaureate field is business/marketing. The faculty at University of Phoenix–West Michigan Campus has 5 full-time members, 20% with terminal degrees. The student-faculty ratio is 11:1.

Students of University of Phoenix–West Michigan Campus The student body totals 786, of whom 572 are undergraduates. 50.9% are women and 49.1% are men. 0.5% are international students.

Applying University of Phoenix–West Michigan Campus requires 1 recommendation and 2 years of work experience, 23 years of age. Application deadline: rolling admissions. Deferred admission is possible.

UNIVERSITY OF PHOENIX-WISCONSIN CAMPUS

Brookfield, WI

Urban setting ■ Private ■ Proprietary ■ Coed

Web site: www.phoenix.edu
Contact: Ms. Beth Barilla, Director of Admissions, 4615 East Elwood Street, Mail Stop 10-0030, Phoenix, AZ 85040-1958
Telephone: 480-317-6000 or toll-free 800-228-7240
E-mail: beth.barilla@apollogrp.edu

Getting in Last Year 1 enrolled (4%).

Financial Matters $9210 tuition and fees (2002–03).

Academics University of Phoenix-Wisconsin Campus awards associate, bachelor's, master's, and doctoral degrees and post-bachelor's and post-master's certificates (courses conducted at 121 campuses and learning centers in 25 states). Challenging opportunities include advanced placement credit, accelerated degree programs, independent study, and a senior project. The faculty at University of Phoenix-Wisconsin Campus has 50 members, 18% with terminal degrees. The student-faculty ratio is 13:1.

Students of University of Phoenix-Wisconsin Campus The student body totals 533, of whom 376 are undergraduates. 50.8% are women and 49.2% are men. 4.8% are international students.

Applying University of Phoenix-Wisconsin Campus requires 1 recommendation and 2 years of work experience, 23 years of age. Application deadline: rolling admissions. Deferred admission is possible.

UNIVERSITY OF PITTSBURGH

Pittsburgh, PA

Urban setting ■ Public ■ State-related ■ Coed

Web site: www.pitt.edu
Contact: Dr. Betsy A. Porter, Director of Office of Admissions and Financial Aid, 4227 Fifth Avenue, First Floor, Alumni Hall, Pittsburgh, PA 15213
Telephone: 412-624-7488 **Fax:** 412-648-8815
E-mail: oafa@pitt.edu

Getting in Last Year 15,888 applied; 55% were accepted; 3,169 enrolled (36%).

Financial Matters $8528 resident tuition and fees (2002–03); $17,336 nonresident tuition and fees (2002–03); $6470 room and board; 86% average percent of need met; $10,798 average financial aid amount received per undergraduate.

Academics Pitt awards bachelor's, master's, doctoral, and first-professional degrees and post-bachelor's and post-master's certificates. Challenging opportunities include advanced placement credit, student-designed majors, freshman honors college, an honors program, double majors, independent study, and a senior project. Special programs include cooperative education, internships, summer session for credit, off-campus study, study-abroad, and Army, Navy and Air Force ROTC. The most frequently chosen baccalaureate fields are social sciences and history, business/marketing, and English. The faculty at Pitt has 1,285 full-time members, 92% with terminal degrees. The student-faculty ratio is 17:1.

Students of Pitt The student body totals 27,190, of whom 17,910 are undergraduates. 52.5% are women and 47.5% are men. Students come from 53 states and territories and 53 other countries. 86% are from Pennsylvania. 0.9% are international students. 88% returned for their sophomore year.

Applying Pitt requires SAT I or ACT and a high school transcript. The school recommends an essay, SAT I, an interview, and recommendations. Application deadline: rolling admissions; 3/1 priority date for financial aid. Early and deferred admission are possible.

UNIVERSITY OF PITTSBURGH AT BRADFORD

Bradford, PA

Small-town setting ■ Public ■ State-related ■ Coed

Web site: www.upb.pitt.edu
Contact: Janet Shade, Administrative Secretary, 300 Campus Drive, Bradford, PA 16701
Telephone: 814-362-7555 or toll-free 800-872-1787
E-mail: admissions@upb.pitt.edu

Getting in Last Year 644 applied; 92% were accepted; 299 enrolled (50%).

Financial Matters $8452 resident tuition and fees (2002–03); $17,260 nonresident tuition and fees (2002–03); $5470 room and board.

Academics Pitt-Bradford awards associate and bachelor's degrees. Challenging opportunities include advanced placement credit, accelerated degree programs, double majors, independent study, and a senior project. Special programs include

University of Pittsburgh at Bradford (continued)

internships, summer session for credit, off-campus study, and Army ROTC. The most frequently chosen baccalaureate fields are social sciences and history, business/marketing, and psychology. The faculty at Pitt-Bradford has 70 full-time members, 70% with terminal degrees. The student-faculty ratio is 13:1.

Students of Pitt-Bradford The student body is made up of 1,352 undergraduates. 61.8% are women and 38.2% are men. Students come from 17 states and territories and 2 other countries. 87% are from Pennsylvania. 0.4% are international students. 70% returned for their sophomore year.

Applying Pitt-Bradford requires SAT I or ACT, a high school transcript, and a minimum high school GPA of 2.0, and in some cases a minimum high school GPA of 3.0. The school recommends an essay, an interview, and recommendations. Application deadline: rolling admissions; 3/1 priority date for financial aid. Deferred admission is possible.

UNIVERSITY OF PITTSBURGH AT GREENSBURG

Greensburg, PA

Small-town setting ■ Public ■ State-related ■ Coed

Web site: www.pitt.edu/~upg

Contact: Mrs. Brandi S. Darr, Director of Admissions and Financial Aid, 1150 Mount Pleasant Road, Greensburg, PA 15601-5860

Telephone: 724-836-9880 **Fax:** 724-836-7160

E-mail: upgadmit@pitt.edu

Getting in Last Year 1,291 applied; 67% were accepted; 498 enrolled (57%).

Financial Matters $8468 resident tuition and fees (2002–03); $17,276 nonresident tuition and fees (2002–03); $6330 room and board; 70% average percent of need met; $12,000 average financial aid amount received per undergraduate (2001–02).

Academics Pitt-Greensburg awards bachelor's degrees. Challenging opportunities include advanced placement credit, accelerated degree programs, student-designed majors, double majors, independent study, and a senior project. Special programs include internships, summer session for credit, off-campus study, study-abroad, and Army and Air Force ROTC. The most frequently chosen baccalaureate fields are psychology, business/marketing, and social sciences and history. The faculty at Pitt-Greensburg has 72 full-time members, 88% with terminal degrees. The student-faculty ratio is 20:1.

Students of Pitt-Greensburg The student body is made up of 1,888 undergraduates. 56.2% are women and 43.8% are men. Students come from 10 states and territories and 1 other country. 98% are from Pennsylvania. 0.1% are international students. 75% returned for their sophomore year.

Applying Pitt-Greensburg requires SAT I or ACT, a high school transcript, and a minimum high school GPA of 2.5, and in some cases recommendations. The school recommends an essay and an interview. Application deadline: 8/1; 3/1 priority date for financial aid. Early and deferred admission are possible.

UNIVERSITY OF PITTSBURGH AT JOHNSTOWN

Johnstown, PA

Suburban setting ■ Public ■ State-related ■ Coed

Web site: info.pitt.edu/~upjweb

Contact: Mr. James F. Gyure, Director of Admissions, 157 Blackington Hall, 450 Schoolhouse Road, Johnstown, PA 15904-2990

Telephone: 814-269-7050 or toll-free 800-765-4875 **Fax:** 814-269-7044

E-mail: upjadmit@pitt.edu

Getting in Last Year 2,721 applied; 84% were accepted; 837 enrolled (37%).

Financial Matters $8480 resident tuition and fees (2002–03); $17,288 nonresident tuition and fees (2002–03); $5570 room and board; 60% average percent of need met; $7072 average financial aid amount received per undergraduate.

Academics Pitt-Johnstown awards associate and bachelor's degrees. Challenging opportunities include advanced placement credit, accelerated degree programs, student-designed majors, double majors, independent study, and a senior project. Special programs include cooperative education, internships, summer session for credit, off-campus study, and study-abroad. The most frequently chosen baccalaureate fields are education, business/marketing, and social sciences and history. The faculty at Pitt-Johnstown has 136 full-time members, 64% with terminal degrees. The student-faculty ratio is 19:1.

Students of Pitt-Johnstown The student body is made up of 3,122 undergraduates. 52.6% are women and 47.4% are men. Students come from 11 states and territories. 99% are from Pennsylvania. 77% returned for their sophomore year.

Applying Pitt-Johnstown requires an essay, SAT I or ACT, a high school transcript, and a minimum high school GPA of 2.0, and in some cases an interview. Application deadline: rolling admissions; 4/1 priority date for financial aid. Early and deferred admission are possible.

UNIVERSITY OF PORTLAND

Portland, OR

Suburban setting ■ Private ■ Independent Religious ■ Coed

Web site: www.up.edu

Contact: Mr. James C. Lyons, Dean of Admissions, 5000 North Willamette Boulevard, Portland, OR 97203-5798

Telephone: 503-943-7147 or toll-free 888-627-5601 (out-of-state)
Fax: 503-943-7315

E-mail: admissio@up.edu

Getting in Last Year 2,571 applied; 80% were accepted; 734 enrolled (36%).

Financial Matters $20,740 tuition and fees (2002–03); $6250 room and board; 89% average percent of need met; $18,209 average financial aid amount received per undergraduate.

Academics U of P awards bachelor's and master's degrees and post-master's certificates. Challenging opportunities include advanced placement credit, an honors program, double majors, independent study, and a senior project. Special programs include internships, summer session for credit, off-campus study, study-abroad, and Army and Air Force ROTC. The most frequently chosen baccalaureate fields are business/marketing, engineering/engineering technologies, and health professions and related sciences. The faculty at U of P has 170 full-time members, 94% with terminal degrees. The student-faculty ratio is 13:1.

Students of U of P The student body totals 3,234, of whom 2,691 are undergraduates. 59.2% are women and 40.8% are men. Students come from 42 states and territories and 19 other countries. 45% are from Oregon. 2.4% are international students. 84% returned for their sophomore year.

Applying U of P requires an essay, SAT I or ACT, a high school transcript, and 1 recommendation. Application deadline: 6/1; 3/1 priority date for financial aid. Deferred admission is possible.

UNIVERSITY OF PRINCE EDWARD ISLAND

Charlottetown, PE Canada

Small-town setting ■ Public ■ Coed

Web site: www.upei.ca

Contact: Mr. Paul Cantelo, Liaison Officer, 550 University Avenue, Charlottetown, PE C1A 4P3 Canada

Telephone: 902-628-4353 **Fax:** 902-566-0795

E-mail: registrar@upei.ca

Getting in Last Year 2,134 applied; 56% were accepted.

Financial Matters $8257 resident tuition and fees (2002–03); $5896 room and board.

Academics UPEI awards bachelor's, master's, doctoral, and first-professional degrees. Challenging opportunities include an honors program, double majors, and a senior project. Summer session for credit is a special program. The faculty at UPEI has 205 full-time members. The student-faculty ratio is 15:1.

Students of UPEI The student body totals 3,599, of whom 3,030 are undergraduates. 64.2% are women and 35.8% are men. Students come from 12 states and territories and 28 other countries. 69% returned for their sophomore year.

Applying UPEI requires a high school transcript and a minimum high school GPA of 2.0, and in some cases 3 recommendations. Application deadline: 8/15, 4/1 for nonresidents. Early admission is possible.

UNIVERSITY OF PUERTO RICO AT ARECIBO

Arecibo, PR

Urban setting ■ Commonwealth-supported ■ Coed

Web site: upra.upr.clu.edu

Contact: Mrs. Delma Barrios, Director of Admissions, PO Box 4010, Arecibo, PR 00614-4010

Telephone: 787-878-2830 ext. 3023

Getting in Last Year 4,213 applied; 31% were accepted; 1,023 enrolled (79%).

Academics Arecibo Technological University College awards associate and bachelor's degrees. Challenging opportunities include advanced placement credit, an honors program, and a senior project. Special programs include summer session for credit and Army ROTC. The faculty at Arecibo Technological University College has 234 full-time members, 100% with terminal degrees. The student-faculty ratio is 17:1.

Students of Arecibo Technological University College The student body is made up of 4,617 undergraduates. 71.1% are women and 28.9% are men. Students come from 1 state or territory. 89% returned for their sophomore year.

Applying Arecibo Technological University College requires SAT II Subject Tests, PAA or SAT I, CEEB, and a high school transcript. Application deadline: 12/8; 6/2 for financial aid, with a 5/16 priority date.

UNIVERSITY OF PUERTO RICO AT HUMACAO

Humacao, PR

Suburban setting ■ Commonwealth-supported ■ Coed

Web site: cuhwww.upr.clu.edu

Contact: Mrs. Inara Ferrer, Director of Admissions, CUH Station 100 Road 908, Humacao, PR 00791-4300

Telephone: 787-850-9301 **Fax:** 787-850-9428
E-mail: i_ferrer@cuhac.upr.clu.edu

Getting in Last Year 2,137 applied; 48% were accepted; 883 enrolled (86%).

Financial Matters $1245 resident tuition and fees (2002–03); 50% average percent of need met; $3929 average financial aid amount received per undergraduate (2001–02).

Academics University of Puerto Rico at Humacao awards associate and bachelor's degrees. Challenging opportunities include freshman honors college, an honors program, and a senior project. Special programs include internships, summer session for credit, off-campus study, and Army ROTC. The most frequently chosen baccalaureate fields are business/marketing, education, and biological/life sciences. The faculty at University of Puerto Rico at Humacao has 258 full-time members, 40% with terminal degrees. The student-faculty ratio is 15:1.

Students of University of Puerto Rico at Humacao The student body is made up of 4,507 undergraduates. 71.1% are women and 28.9% are men. Students come from 3 states and territories. 100% are from Puerto Rico. 87% returned for their sophomore year.

Applying University of Puerto Rico at Humacao requires CEEB for Puerto Rican applicants, PAA and 3 achievement tests, a high school transcript, and a minimum high school GPA of 2.0, and in some cases SAT I and SAT II Subject Tests. Application deadline: 11/15; 6/30 for financial aid. Deferred admission is possible.

UNIVERSITY OF PUERTO RICO AT PONCE

Ponce, PR

Urban setting ■ Commonwealth-supported ■ Coed

Contact: Mr. William Rodriguez Mercado, Admissions Officer, PO Box 7186, Ponce, PR 00732-7186
Telephone: 787-844-8181 ext. 2530 **Fax:** 787-842-3875

Getting in Last Year 1,366 applied; 54% were accepted; 683 enrolled (93%).

Financial Matters 40% average percent of need met.

Academics UPR-Ponce awards associate and bachelor's degrees. Challenging opportunities include advanced placement credit, accelerated degree programs, freshman honors college, an honors program, and a senior project. Special programs include internships, summer session for credit, and Army ROTC. The most frequently chosen baccalaureate fields are business/marketing, education, and health professions and related sciences. The faculty at UPR-Ponce has 149 full-time members, 14% with terminal degrees. The student-faculty ratio is 19:1.

Students of UPR-Ponce The student body is made up of 3,837 undergraduates. 66.9% are women and 33.1% are men. Students come from 1 state or territory. 18% returned for their sophomore year.

Applying UPR-Ponce requires SAT I, PAA, and a high school transcript. Application deadline: 11/15; 6/30 for financial aid, with a 5/29 priority date. Early admission is possible.

UNIVERSITY OF PUERTO RICO AT UTUADO

Utuado, PR

Small-town setting ■ Commonwealth-supported ■ Coed

Web site: upr-utuado.upr.clu.edu
Contact: Mrs. Maria V. Robles Serrano, Admissions Officer, PO Box 2500, Utuado, PR 00641-2500
Telephone: 787-894-2828 ext. 2240 **Fax:** 787-894-2877

Getting in Last Year 778 applied; 80% were accepted; 585 enrolled (95%).

Financial Matters $1315 resident tuition and fees (2002–03); $2470 nonresident tuition and fees (2002–03).

Academics CORMO awards associate and bachelor's degrees. An honors program is a challenging opportunity. Special programs include cooperative education and summer session for credit. The faculty at CORMO has 79 full-time members, 100% with terminal degrees. The student-faculty ratio is 17:1.

Students of CORMO The student body is made up of 1,766 undergraduates. 60% are women and 40% are men. Students come from 1 state or territory.

Applying CORMO requires SAT I and SAT II or ACT and PAA. Application deadline: rolling admissions; 6/15 for financial aid, with a 5/31 priority date. Early and deferred admission are possible.

UNIVERSITY OF PUERTO RICO, CAYEY UNIVERSITY COLLEGE

Cayey, PR

Urban setting ■ Commonwealth-supported ■ Coed

Web site: www.upr.clu.edu
Contact: Mr. Wilfredo Lopez, Admissions Officer, Avenue Antonio R. Barcelo, Cayey, PR 00736
Telephone: 787-738-2161 ext. 2208 **Fax:** 787-738-5633

Getting in Last Year 1,194 applied; 81% were accepted; 887 enrolled (91%).

Financial Matters $4200 average financial aid amount received per undergraduate (2000–01 estimated).

Academics CUC awards associate and bachelor's degrees. Challenging opportunities include advanced placement credit, accelerated degree programs, and an honors program. Special programs include summer session for credit, off-campus study, study-abroad, and Army ROTC. The most frequently chosen baccalaureate fields are biological/life sciences, business/marketing, and education. The faculty at CUC has 176 full-time members, 47% with terminal degrees. The student-faculty ratio is 18:1.

Students of CUC The student body is made up of 4,128 undergraduates. 71% are women and 29% are men. Students come from 1 state or territory. 89% returned for their sophomore year.

Applying CUC requires CEEB, a high school transcript, and a minimum high school GPA of 2.0, and in some cases SAT I. Application deadline: 12/1; 3/31 priority date for financial aid. Early admission is possible.

UNIVERSITY OF PUERTO RICO, MEDICAL SCIENCES CAMPUS

San Juan, PR

Urban setting ■ Commonwealth-supported ■ Coed, Primarily Women

Web site: www.rcm.upr.edu
Contact: Mrs. Rosa Vèlez, Acting Director of Admission Office, P.O. Box 365067, San Juan, PR 00936-5067
Telephone: 787-758-2525 ext. 5211
E-mail: rvelez@rcm.upr.edu

Financial Matters $1620 resident tuition and fees (2002–03); 68% average percent of need met; $4535 average financial aid amount received per undergraduate (2001–02).

Academics MSC-UPR awards associate, bachelor's, master's, doctoral, and first-professional degrees and post-bachelor's and first-professional certificates (bachelor's degree is upper-level). A senior project is a challenging opportunity. Special programs include internships, summer session for credit, and off-campus study. The most frequently chosen baccalaureate field is health professions and related sciences. The faculty at MSC-UPR has 557 full-time members.

Students of MSC-UPR The student body totals 2,457, of whom 678 are undergraduates. 87.3% are women and 12.7% are men. Students come from 1 state or territory.

Applying MSC-UPR requires SAT I, and in some cases PCAT, MCAT, DAT, ASPHAT, GRE, PAEG. Application deadline: 5/15 for financial aid.

UNIVERSITY OF PUERTO RICO, RÍO PIEDRAS

San Juan, PR

Urban setting ■ Commonwealth-supported ■ Coed

Web site: www.rrp.upr.edu
Contact: Mrs. Cruz B. Valentín, Director of Admissions, PO Box 21907, San Juan, PR 00931-1907
Telephone: 787-764-0000 ext. 5666 **Fax:** 787-764-3680 ext. 5352

Getting in Last Year 6,043 applied; 66% were accepted; 3,109 enrolled (78%).

Financial Matters $1383 resident tuition and fees (2002–03); $3063 nonresident tuition and fees (2002–03); $4940 room and board.

Academics University of Puerto Rico, Río Piedras awards bachelor's, master's, doctoral, and first-professional degrees and post-bachelor's and post-master's certificates. Challenging opportunities include advanced placement credit, accelerated degree programs, and an honors program. Special programs include summer session for credit, study-abroad, and Army and Air Force ROTC. The most frequently chosen baccalaureate fields are business/marketing, education, and biological/life sciences. The faculty at University of Puerto Rico, Río Piedras has 1,420 full-time members, 49% with terminal degrees. The student-faculty ratio is 22:1.

Students of University of Puerto Rico, Río Piedras The student body totals 21,666, of whom 17,746 are undergraduates. 66.7% are women and 33.3% are men. Students come from 4 states and territories and 9 other countries. 99% are from Puerto Rico. 0.2% are international students.

Applying University of Puerto Rico, Río Piedras requires SAT I, SAT II Subject Tests, CEEB, a high school transcript, and a minimum high school GPA of 2.0, and in some cases an interview. Application deadline: 2/15.

UNIVERSITY OF PUGET SOUND

Tacoma, WA

Suburban setting ■ Private ■ Independent ■ Coed

Web site: www.ups.edu
Contact: Dr. George H. Mills Jr., Vice President for Enrollment, 1500 North Warner Street, Tacoma, WA 98416-1062
Telephone: 253-879-3211 or toll-free 800-396-7191 **Fax:** 253-879-3993
E-mail: admission@ups.edu

Getting in Last Year 4,154 applied; 72% were accepted; 666 enrolled (22%).

University of Puget Sound (continued)

Financial Matters $23,945 tuition and fees (2002–03); $6140 room and board; 88% average percent of need met; $18,963 average financial aid amount received per undergraduate.

Academics Puget Sound awards bachelor's, master's, and doctoral degrees and post-master's certificates. Challenging opportunities include advanced placement credit, student-designed majors, an honors program, double majors, independent study, and a senior project. Special programs include cooperative education, internships, summer session for credit, study-abroad, and Army ROTC. The most frequently chosen baccalaureate fields are social sciences and history, business/marketing, and English. The faculty at Puget Sound has 218 full-time members, 85% with terminal degrees. The student-faculty ratio is 11:1.

Students of Puget Sound The student body totals 2,846, of whom 2,604 are undergraduates. 59.9% are women and 40.1% are men. Students come from 47 states and territories and 16 other countries. 31% are from Washington. 1.2% are international students. 84% returned for their sophomore year.

Applying Puget Sound requires an essay, SAT I or ACT, a high school transcript, and 2 recommendations. The school recommends an interview and a minimum high school GPA of 3.0. Application deadline: 5/1; 2/1 for financial aid. Early and deferred admission are possible.

UNIVERSITY OF REDLANDS

Redlands, CA

Small-town setting ■ Private ■ Independent ■ Coed

Web site: www.redlands.edu

Contact: Mr. Paul Driscoll, Dean of Admissions, PO Box 3080, Redlands, CA 92373-0999

Telephone: 909-335-4074 or toll-free 800-455-5064 **Fax:** 909-335-4089

E-mail: admissions@redlands.edu

Getting in Last Year 2,499 applied; 76% were accepted; 602 enrolled (32%).

Financial Matters $22,750 tuition and fees (2002–03); $8114 room and board; 91% average percent of need met; $22,020 average financial aid amount received per undergraduate.

Academics Redlands awards bachelor's and master's degrees and post-bachelor's and post-master's certificates. Challenging opportunities include advanced placement credit, student-designed majors, freshman honors college, an honors program, double majors, independent study, and a senior project. Special programs include internships, off-campus study, and study-abroad. The most frequently chosen baccalaureate fields are liberal arts/general studies, social sciences and history, and business/marketing. The faculty at Redlands has 144 full-time members, 84% with terminal degrees. The student-faculty ratio is 13:1.

Students of Redlands The student body totals 2,180, of whom 2,088 are undergraduates. 59.9% are women and 40.1% are men. Students come from 41 states and territories and 10 other countries. 74% are from California. 1.9% are international students. 81% returned for their sophomore year.

Applying Redlands requires an essay, SAT I or ACT, a high school transcript, and 2 recommendations. The school recommends an interview. Application deadline: 12/15; 2/15 priority date for financial aid. Deferred admission is possible.

UNIVERSITY OF REGINA

Regina, SK Canada

Urban setting ■ Public ■ Coed

Web site: www.uregina.ca

Contact: Mr. Clarence Gray, Assistant Registrar/Admissions and Awards, 3737 Wascana Parkway, Regina, SK S4S 0A2 Canada

Telephone: 306-585-4591

E-mail: admissions.office@uregina.ca

Financial Matters $4183 nonresident tuition and fees (2002–03); $4924 room and board.

Academics U of R awards bachelor's, master's, and doctoral degrees. Challenging opportunities include advanced placement credit, student-designed majors, an honors program, and a senior project. Special programs include cooperative education, internships, summer session for credit, and off-campus study. The faculty at U of R has 388 full-time members, 70% with terminal degrees. The student-faculty ratio is 26:1.

Students of U of R The student body totals 11,779, of whom 10,818 are undergraduates. Students come from 12 states and territories and 57 other countries.

Applying U of R requires a high school transcript and a minimum high school GPA of 2.5, and in some cases an essay, CELT, Michigan Test of English Language Proficiency, an interview, and recommendations. Application deadline: 7/1, 4/1 for nonresidents. Early and deferred admission are possible.

UNIVERSITY OF RHODE ISLAND

Kingston, RI

Small-town setting ■ Public ■ State-supported ■ Coed

Web site: www.uri.edu

Contact: Ms. Catherine Zeiser, Assistant Dean of Admissions, 8 Ranger Road, Suite 1, Kingston, RI 02881-2020

Telephone: 401-874-7100 **Fax:** 401-874-5523

E-mail: uriadmit@uri.edu

Getting in Last Year 11,072 applied; 69% were accepted; 2,360 enrolled (31%).

Financial Matters $5854 resident tuition and fees (2002–03); $15,324 nonresident tuition and fees (2002–03); $7402 room and board; 68% average percent of need met; $8965 average financial aid amount received per undergraduate.

Academics Rhode Island awards bachelor's, master's, doctoral, and first-professional degrees and post-bachelor's certificates. Challenging opportunities include advanced placement credit, accelerated degree programs, student-designed majors, an honors program, double majors, independent study, and a senior project. Special programs include cooperative education, internships, summer session for credit, off-campus study, study-abroad, and Army ROTC. The most frequently chosen baccalaureate fields are business/marketing, health professions and related sciences, and communications/communication technologies. The faculty at Rhode Island has 626 full-time members, 91% with terminal degrees. The student-faculty ratio is 18:1.

Students of Rhode Island The student body totals 14,180, of whom 10,784 are undergraduates. 56% are women and 44% are men. Students come from 38 states and territories and 47 other countries. 62% are from Rhode Island. 0.3% are international students. 79% returned for their sophomore year.

Applying Rhode Island requires SAT I or ACT and a high school transcript, and in some cases a minimum high school GPA of 3.0. The school recommends an interview, recommendations, and a minimum high school GPA of 3.0. Application deadline: 3/1; 3/1 priority date for financial aid. Early admission is possible.

UNIVERSITY OF RICHMOND

University of Richmond, VA

Suburban setting ■ Private ■ Independent ■ Coed

Web site: www.richmond.edu

Contact: Ms. Pamela Spence, Dean of Admission, 28 Westhampton Way, University of Richmond, VA 23173

Telephone: 804-289-8640 or toll-free 800-700-1662 **Fax:** 804-287-6003

E-mail: admissions@richmond.edu

Getting in Last Year 5,895 applied; 41% were accepted; 776 enrolled (32%).

Financial Matters $23,730 tuition and fees (2002–03); $4940 room and board; 96% average percent of need met; $17,657 average financial aid amount received per undergraduate.

Academics University of Richmond awards associate, bachelor's, master's, and first-professional degrees and post-bachelor's certificates. Challenging opportunities include advanced placement credit, accelerated degree programs, student-designed majors, an honors program, double majors, independent study, and a senior project. Special programs include cooperative education, internships, summer session for credit, off-campus study, study-abroad, and Army ROTC. The most frequently chosen baccalaureate fields are business/marketing, social sciences and history, and biological/life sciences. The faculty at University of Richmond has 274 full-time members, 88% with terminal degrees. The student-faculty ratio is 10:1.

Students of University of Richmond The student body totals 3,774, of whom 2,998 are undergraduates. 52.8% are women and 47.2% are men. Students come from 48 states and territories and 77 other countries. 17% are from Virginia. 4.2% are international students. 89% returned for their sophomore year.

Applying University of Richmond requires an essay, SAT II: Writing Test, SAT I and SAT II or ACT, SAT II Subject Test in math, a high school transcript, 1 recommendation, signed character statement, and a minimum high school GPA of 2.0. Application deadline: 1/15; 2/25 for financial aid. Early and deferred admission are possible.

UNIVERSITY OF RIO GRANDE

Rio Grande, OH

Rural setting ■ Private ■ Independent ■ Coed

Web site: www.rio.edu

Contact: Mr. Mark F. Abell, Executive Director of Admissions, PO Box 500, Rio Grande, OH 45674

Telephone: 740-245-5353 ext. 7206 or toll-free 800-288-2746 (in-state), 800-282-7204 (out-of-state) **Fax:** 740-245-7260

E-mail: mabell@urgrgcc.edu

Getting in Last Year 597 applied; 100% were accepted; 343 enrolled (57%).

Financial Matters $9678 resident tuition and fees (2002–03); $10,446 nonresident tuition and fees (2002–03); $5442 room and board; 65% average percent of need met; $7406 average financial aid amount received per undergraduate (2001–02).

Academics Rio Grande awards associate, bachelor's, and master's degrees. Challenging opportunities include advanced placement credit, accelerated degree programs, student-designed majors, freshman honors college, an honors program, independent study, and a senior project. Special programs include cooperative education, internships, summer session for credit, and Army ROTC. The most frequently chosen baccalaureate fields are education, business/marketing, and communications/communication technologies. The faculty at Rio Grande has 85 full-time members, 53% with terminal degrees. The student-faculty ratio is 18:1.

Students of Rio Grande The student body totals 2,076, of whom 1,932 are undergraduates. 59% are women and 41% are men. Students come from 11 states and territories and 15 other countries. 95% are from Ohio. 60% returned for their sophomore year.

Applying Rio Grande requires ACT, a high school transcript, and medical history. Application deadline: rolling admissions.

UNIVERSITY OF ROCHESTER

Rochester, NY

Suburban setting ■ Private ■ Independent ■ Coed

Web site: www.rochester.edu

Contact: Mr. Jamie Hobba, Director of Admissions, PO Box 270251, Rochester, NY 14627-0251

Telephone: 585-275-3221 or toll-free 888-822-2256 **Fax:** 585-461-4595

E-mail: admit@admissions.rochester.edu

Getting in Last Year 10,080 applied; 50% were accepted.

Financial Matters $26,077 tuition and fees (2002–03); $8924 room and board; 100% average percent of need met; $21,803 average financial aid amount received per undergraduate.

Academics University of Rochester awards bachelor's, master's, doctoral, and first-professional degrees. Challenging opportunities include advanced placement credit, student-designed majors, double majors, and independent study. Special programs include internships, summer session for credit, off-campus study, study-abroad, and Army and Air Force ROTC. The most frequently chosen baccalaureate field is law/legal studies. The student-faculty ratio is 12:1.

Students of University of Rochester The student body totals 8,335, of whom 4,440 are undergraduates. Students come from 52 states and territories and 45 other countries. 93% returned for their sophomore year.

Applying University of Rochester requires an essay, SAT I or ACT, a high school transcript, and 1 recommendation, and in some cases audition, portfolio. The school recommends SAT II Subject Tests and 2 recommendations. Application deadline: 1/15; 2/1 priority date for financial aid. Early and deferred admission are possible.

UNIVERSITY OF ST. FRANCIS

Joliet, IL

Suburban setting ■ Private ■ Independent Religious ■ Coed

Web site: www.stfrancis.edu

Contact: Ms. Michelle Mega, Assistant Director On-Campus Admissions, 500 North Wilcox Street, Joliet, IL 60435-6188

Telephone: 815-740-3385 or toll-free 800-735-3500 **Fax:** 815-740-5032

E-mail: admissions@stfrancis.edu

Getting in Last Year 664 applied; 69% were accepted; 148 enrolled (32%).

Financial Matters $16,030 tuition and fees (2002–03); $5800 room and board; 81% average percent of need met; $14,279 average financial aid amount received per undergraduate.

Academics USF awards bachelor's and master's degrees and post-bachelor's certificates. Challenging opportunities include advanced placement credit, accelerated degree programs, student-designed majors, double majors, independent study, and a senior project. Special programs include internships, summer session for credit, off-campus study, and study-abroad. The most frequently chosen baccalaureate fields are health professions and related sciences, education, and communications/communication technologies. The faculty at USF has 74 full-time members, 55% with terminal degrees. The student-faculty ratio is 10:1.

Students of USF The student body totals 2,079, of whom 1,362 are undergraduates. 67.7% are women and 32.3% are men. Students come from 9 states and territories. 97% are from Illinois. 0.3% are international students. 76% returned for their sophomore year.

Applying USF requires SAT I or ACT, a high school transcript, and a minimum high school GPA of 2.5, and in some cases an essay, an interview, and 2 recommendations. Application deadline: 9/1; 5/1 priority date for financial aid. Deferred admission is possible.

UNIVERSITY OF SAINT FRANCIS

Fort Wayne, IN

Suburban setting ■ Private ■ Independent Religious ■ Coed

Web site: www.sf.edu

Contact: Mr. Ron Schumacher, Vice President for Enrollment Management, 2701 Spring Street, Fort Wayne, IN 46808

Telephone: 260-434-3279 or toll-free 800-729-4732

E-mail: admiss@sfc.edu

Getting in Last Year 722 applied; 75% were accepted; 269 enrolled (50%).

Financial Matters $14,560 tuition and fees (2002–03); $5240 room and board; 76% average percent of need met; $10,901 average financial aid amount received per undergraduate (2001–02).

Academics University of Saint Francis awards associate, bachelor's, and master's degrees and post-bachelor's certificates. Challenging opportunities include advanced placement credit, freshman honors college, an honors program, double majors, independent study, and a senior project. Special programs include cooperative education, internships, summer session for credit, and study-abroad. The most frequently chosen baccalaureate fields are health professions and related sciences, education, and business/marketing. The faculty at University of Saint Francis has 106 full-time members, 45% with terminal degrees. The student-faculty ratio is 11:1.

Students of University of Saint Francis The student body totals 1,709, of whom 1,515 are undergraduates. 68.4% are women and 31.6% are men. Students come from 10 states and territories and 15 other countries. 92% are from Indiana. 78% returned for their sophomore year.

Applying University of Saint Francis requires a high school transcript, and in some cases an interview and recommendations. The school recommends an essay, SAT I or ACT, and a minimum high school GPA of 2.0. Application deadline: rolling admissions; 3/1 priority date for financial aid. Deferred admission is possible.

UNIVERSITY OF ST. THOMAS

St. Paul, MN

Urban setting ■ Private ■ Independent Religious ■ Coed

Web site: www.stthomas.edu

Contact: Ms. Marla Friederichs, Associate Vice President of Enrollment Management, Mail #32F-1, 2115 Summit Avenue, St. Paul, MN 55105-1096

Telephone: 651-962-6150 or toll-free 800-328-6819 ext. 26150 **Fax:** 651-962-6160

E-mail: admissions@stthomas.edu

Getting in Last Year 3,094 applied; 87% were accepted; 1,104 enrolled (41%).

Financial Matters $19,468 tuition and fees (2002–03); $6129 room and board; 85% average percent of need met; $15,313 average financial aid amount received per undergraduate.

Academics St. Thomas awards bachelor's, master's, doctoral, and first-professional degrees and post-bachelor's and post-master's certificates. Challenging opportunities include advanced placement credit, student-designed majors, an honors program, double majors, independent study, and a senior project. Special programs include internships, summer session for credit, off-campus study, study-abroad, and Army, Navy and Air Force ROTC. The most frequently chosen baccalaureate fields are business/marketing, communications/communication technologies, and social sciences and history. The faculty at St. Thomas has 399 full-time members, 87% with terminal degrees. The student-faculty ratio is 14:1.

Students of St. Thomas The student body totals 11,321, of whom 5,429 are undergraduates. 51.8% are women and 48.2% are men. 83% are from Minnesota. 0.9% are international students. 84% returned for their sophomore year.

Applying St. Thomas requires an essay, SAT I or ACT, and a high school transcript. The school recommends ACT, an interview, and recommendations. Application deadline: rolling admissions; 4/1 priority date for financial aid. Deferred admission is possible.

UNIVERSITY OF ST. THOMAS

Houston, TX

Urban setting ■ Private ■ Independent Religious ■ Coed

Web site: www.stthom.edu

Contact: Mr. Eduardo Prieto, Dean of Admissions, 3800 Montrose Boulevard, Houston, TX 77006-4696

Telephone: 713-525-3500 or toll-free 800-856-8565 **Fax:** 713-525-3558

E-mail: admissions@stthom.edu

Getting in Last Year 823 applied; 81% were accepted; 284 enrolled (43%).

Financial Matters $13,912 tuition and fees (2002–03); $6070 room and board; 72% average percent of need met; $11,832 average financial aid amount received per undergraduate.

Academics St. Thomas awards bachelor's, master's, doctoral, and first-professional degrees. Challenging opportunities include advanced placement credit, accelerated degree programs, an honors program, double majors, independent study, and a senior project. Special programs include cooperative education, internships, summer session for credit, off-campus study, study-abroad, and Army ROTC. The most frequently chosen baccalaureate fields are business/marketing, liberal arts/general studies, and education. The faculty at St. Thomas has 117 full-time members, 87% with terminal degrees. The student-faculty ratio is 14:1.

Students of St. Thomas The student body totals 5,154, of whom 1,933 are undergraduates. 62.2% are women and 37.8% are men. Students come from 22 states and territories and 34 other countries. 97% are from Texas. 3.2% are international students. 76% returned for their sophomore year.

University of St. Thomas (continued)

Applying St. Thomas requires SAT I or ACT, a high school transcript, and a minimum high school GPA of 2.25, and in some cases an essay and an interview. Application deadline: rolling admissions; 3/1 priority date for financial aid. Deferred admission is possible.

UNIVERSITY OF SAN DIEGO

San Diego, CA

Urban setting ■ Private ■ Independent Religious ■ Coed

Web site: www.sandiego.edu
Contact: Mr. Stephen Pultz, Director of Admission, 5998 Alcala Park, San Diego, CA 92110
Telephone: 619-260-4506 or toll-free 800-248-4873 **Fax:** 619-260-6836
E-mail: admissions@sandiego.edu

Getting in Last Year 6,815 applied; 53% were accepted; 1,051 enrolled (29%).

Financial Matters $21,988 tuition and fees (2002–03); $9130 room and board; 96% average percent of need met; $19,700 average financial aid amount received per undergraduate (2001–02).

Academics USD awards bachelor's, master's, doctoral, and first-professional degrees and post-bachelor's, post-master's, and first-professional certificates. Challenging opportunities include advanced placement credit, an honors program, double majors, independent study, and a senior project. Special programs include internships, summer session for credit, study-abroad, and Army, Navy and Air Force ROTC. The most frequently chosen baccalaureate fields are business/marketing, social sciences and history, and communications/communication technologies. The faculty at USD has 328 full-time members, 96% with terminal degrees. The student-faculty ratio is 15:1.

Students of USD The student body totals 7,126, of whom 4,837 are undergraduates. 60.8% are women and 39.2% are men. Students come from 50 states and territories and 67 other countries. 61% are from California. 2.6% are international students. 88% returned for their sophomore year.

Applying USD requires an essay, SAT I or ACT, a high school transcript, and 1 recommendation. The school recommends SAT II: Writing Test. Application deadline: 1/5; 2/20 priority date for financial aid. Early admission is possible.

UNIVERSITY OF SAN FRANCISCO

San Francisco, CA

Urban setting ■ Private ■ Independent Religious ■ Coed

Web site: www.usfca.edu
Contact: Mr. Michael Hughes, Associate Director, 2130 Fulton Street, San Francisco, CA 94117-1080
Telephone: 415-422-6563 or toll-free 800-CALL USF (out-of-state)
Fax: 415-422-2217
E-mail: admissions@usfca.edu

Getting in Last Year 3,590 applied; 82% were accepted; 843 enrolled (28%).

Financial Matters $21,780 tuition and fees (2002–03); $9080 room and board; 69% average percent of need met; $15,590 average financial aid amount received per undergraduate (2001–02).

Academics USF awards bachelor's, master's, doctoral, and first-professional degrees and post-master's certificates. Challenging opportunities include advanced placement credit, student-designed majors, an honors program, double majors, and a senior project. Special programs include cooperative education, internships, summer session for credit, off-campus study, study-abroad, and Army and Air Force ROTC. The most frequently chosen baccalaureate fields are business/marketing, health professions and related sciences, and interdisciplinary studies. The faculty at USF has 326 full-time members, 94% with terminal degrees. The student-faculty ratio is 16:1.

Students of USF The student body totals 8,194, of whom 4,695 are undergraduates. 63.4% are women and 36.6% are men. Students come from 51 states and territories and 70 other countries. 77% are from California. 7.8% are international students. 82% returned for their sophomore year.

Applying USF requires an essay, SAT I or ACT, a high school transcript, 1 recommendation, and a minimum high school GPA of 2.8, and in some cases an interview. The school recommends a minimum high school GPA of 3.0. Application deadline: 2/1; 2/15 priority date for financial aid. Deferred admission is possible.

UNIVERSITY OF SASKATCHEWAN

Saskatoon, SK Canada

Urban setting ■ Public ■ Coed

Web site: www.usask.ca
Contact: Director of Admissions, Recruitment and Admissions, 105 Administration Place, Saskatoon, SK S7N 5A2
Telephone: 306-966-6718 **Fax:** 306-966-2115
E-mail: admissions@usask.ca

Getting in Last Year 6,437 applied; 86% were accepted; 3,177 enrolled (58%).

Academics University of Saskatchewan awards bachelor's, master's, doctoral, and first-professional degrees. Challenging opportunities include advanced placement credit, accelerated degree programs, an honors program, double majors, independent study, and a senior project. Special programs include cooperative education, internships, summer session for credit, off-campus study, and study-abroad. The most frequently chosen baccalaureate fields are law/legal studies, health professions and related sciences, and education. The faculty at University of Saskatchewan has 983 full-time members, 71% with terminal degrees.

Students of University of Saskatchewan The student body totals 10,955, of whom 9,211 are undergraduates. 57.4% are women and 42.6% are men.

Applying University of Saskatchewan requires a high school transcript, and in some cases an essay and an interview. Application deadline: 5/15; 4/1 for financial aid. Early admission is possible.

UNIVERSITY OF SCIENCE AND ARTS OF OKLAHOMA

Chickasha, OK

Small-town setting ■ Public ■ State-supported ■ Coed

Web site: www.usao.edu
Contact: Mr. Joseph Evans, Registrar and Director of Admissions and Records, 1727 West Alabama, Chickasha, OK 73018-5322
Telephone: 405-574-1204 or toll-free 800-933-8726 ext. 1204
Fax: 405-574-1220
E-mail: jwevans@usao.edu

Getting in Last Year 471 applied; 82% were accepted; 289 enrolled (75%).

Financial Matters $2308 resident tuition and fees (2002–03); $5404 nonresident tuition and fees (2002–03); $2790 room and board; 82% average percent of need met; $6231 average financial aid amount received per undergraduate.

Academics USAO awards bachelor's degrees. Challenging opportunities include advanced placement credit, accelerated degree programs, student-designed majors, double majors, independent study, and a senior project. Special programs include internships, summer session for credit, and off-campus study. The most frequently chosen baccalaureate fields are business/marketing, education, and social sciences and history. The faculty at USAO has 53 full-time members, 87% with terminal degrees. The student-faculty ratio is 19:1.

Students of USAO The student body is made up of 1,490 undergraduates. 64.3% are women and 35.7% are men. 96% are from Oklahoma. 2.2% are international students. 59% returned for their sophomore year.

Applying USAO requires SAT I or ACT and a high school transcript. The school recommends a minimum high school GPA of 2.7. Application deadline: 9/3; 3/15 priority date for financial aid. Early and deferred admission are possible.

THE UNIVERSITY OF SCRANTON

Scranton, PA

Urban setting ■ Private ■ Independent Religious ■ Coed

Web site: www.scranton.edu
Contact: Mr. Joseph Roback, Director of Admissions, 800 Linden Street, Scranton, PA 18510
Telephone: 570-941-7540 or toll-free 888-SCRANTON **Fax:** 570-941-4370
E-mail: admissions@uofs.edu

Getting in Last Year 5,121 applied; 70% were accepted; 980 enrolled (27%).

Financial Matters $20,448 tuition and fees (2002–03); $8770 room and board; 74% average percent of need met; $14,346 average financial aid amount received per undergraduate.

Academics Scranton awards associate, bachelor's, and master's degrees and post-bachelor's and post-master's certificates. Challenging opportunities include advanced placement credit, student-designed majors, freshman honors college, an honors program, double majors, independent study, and a senior project. Special programs include internships, summer session for credit, off-campus study, study-abroad, and Army and Air Force ROTC. The most frequently chosen baccalaureate fields are business/marketing, health professions and related sciences, and education. The faculty at Scranton has 243 full-time members, 85% with terminal degrees. The student-faculty ratio is 13:1.

Students of Scranton The student body totals 4,728, of whom 4,060 are undergraduates. 57.6% are women and 42.4% are men. Students come from 30 states and territories and 12 other countries. 52% are from Pennsylvania. 0.5% are international students. 90% returned for their sophomore year.

Applying Scranton requires SAT I or ACT and a high school transcript, and in some cases an interview and 2 recommendations. The school recommends an essay. Application deadline: 3/1; 2/15 priority date for financial aid. Early and deferred admission are possible.

UNIVERSITY OF SIOUX FALLS

Sioux Falls, SD

Suburban setting ■ Private ■ Independent Religious ■ Coed

Web site: www.usiouxfalls.edu

Contact: Ms. Laura A. Olson, Assistant Director of Admissions, 1101 West 22nd Street, Sioux Falls, SD 57105
Telephone: 605-331-6700 or toll-free 800-888-1047 **Fax:** 605-331-6615
E-mail: admissions@usiouxfalls.edu

Getting in Last Year 706 applied; 94% were accepted; 209 enrolled (31%).

Financial Matters $13,400 tuition and fees (2002–03); $3900 room and board.

Academics USF awards associate, bachelor's, master's, and doctoral degrees. Challenging opportunities include advanced placement credit, accelerated degree programs, student-designed majors, an honors program, double majors, independent study, and a senior project. Special programs include cooperative education, internships, summer session for credit, off-campus study, and study-abroad. The most frequently chosen baccalaureate fields are business/marketing, education, and psychology. The faculty at USF has 47 full-time members, 72% with terminal degrees. The student-faculty ratio is 17:1.

Students of USF The student body totals 1,405, of whom 1,186 are undergraduates. 55.9% are women and 44.1% are men. Students come from 22 states and territories and 6 other countries. 67% are from South Dakota. 0.8% are international students. 66% returned for their sophomore year.

Applying USF requires SAT I and SAT II or ACT and a high school transcript, and in some cases an interview and 2 recommendations. The school recommends an essay and a minimum high school GPA of 2.0. Application deadline: rolling admissions; 3/1 priority date for financial aid. Early and deferred admission are possible.

UNIVERSITY OF SOUTH ALABAMA

Mobile, AL

Suburban setting ■ Public ■ State-supported ■ Coed

Web site: www.southalabama.edu
Contact: Ms. Melissa Jones, Director, 307 University Boulevard, Mobile, AL 36688-0002
Telephone: 251-460-6141 or toll-free 800-872-5247

Getting in Last Year 2,512 applied; 93% were accepted; 1,389 enrolled (60%).

Financial Matters $3410 resident tuition and fees (2002–03); $6500 nonresident tuition and fees (2002–03); $3910 room and board; 45% average percent of need met; $5702 average financial aid amount received per undergraduate (2001–02).

Academics USA awards bachelor's, master's, doctoral, and first-professional degrees and post-bachelor's and post-master's certificates. Challenging opportunities include advanced placement credit, accelerated degree programs, student-designed majors, freshman honors college, double majors, independent study, and a senior project. Special programs include cooperative education, internships, summer session for credit, study-abroad, and Army and Air Force ROTC. The most frequently chosen baccalaureate fields are education, business/marketing, and health professions and related sciences. The faculty at USA has 438 full-time members. The student-faculty ratio is 17:1.

Students of USA The student body totals 12,323, of whom 9,723 are undergraduates. 59.1% are women and 40.9% are men. Students come from 41 states and territories and 99 other countries. 78% are from Alabama. 5.1% are international students. 71% returned for their sophomore year.

Applying USA requires SAT I or ACT and a high school transcript. The school recommends a minimum high school GPA of 2.0. Application deadline: 8/10. Early admission is possible.

UNIVERSITY OF SOUTH CAROLINA

Columbia, SC

Urban setting ■ Public ■ State-supported ■ Coed

Web site: www.sc.edu
Contact: Ms. Terry L. Davis, Director of Undergraduate Admissions, Columbia, SC 29208
Telephone: 803-777-7700 or toll-free 800-868-5872 (in-state)
Fax: 803-777-0101
E-mail: admissions-ugrad@sc.edu

Getting in Last Year 12,016 applied; 70% were accepted; 3,561 enrolled (42%).

Financial Matters $4984 resident tuition and fees (2002–03); $13,104 nonresident tuition and fees (2002–03); $5064 room and board; 91% average percent of need met; $8263 average financial aid amount received per undergraduate (2001–02).

Academics Carolina awards associate, bachelor's, master's, doctoral, and first-professional degrees and post-bachelor's and post-master's certificates. Challenging opportunities include advanced placement credit, accelerated degree programs, student-designed majors, freshman honors college, an honors program, double majors, independent study, and a senior project. Special programs include cooperative education, internships, summer session for credit, study-abroad, and Army and Air Force ROTC. The most frequently chosen baccalaureate fields are business/marketing, social sciences and history, and psychology. The faculty at Carolina has 1,015 full-time members, 89% with terminal degrees. The student-faculty ratio is 17:1.

Students of Carolina The student body totals 25,140, of whom 16,567 are undergraduates. 54.1% are women and 45.9% are men. Students come from 52 states and territories and 75 other countries. 87% are from South Carolina. 1.6% are international students. 81% returned for their sophomore year.

Applying Carolina requires SAT I or ACT and a high school transcript. Application deadline: 5/15; 4/1 priority date for financial aid.

UNIVERSITY OF SOUTH CAROLINA AIKEN

Aiken, SC

Suburban setting ■ Public ■ State-supported ■ Coed

Web site: www.usca.edu
Contact: Mr. Andrew Hendrix, Director of Admissions, 471 University Parkway, Aiken, SC 29801-6309
Telephone: 803-648-6851 ext. 3366 or toll-free 888-WOW-USCA
Fax: 803-641-3727
E-mail: admit@usca.edu

Getting in Last Year 1,231 applied; 58% were accepted; 497 enrolled (69%).

Financial Matters $4424 resident tuition and fees (2002–03); $9134 nonresident tuition and fees (2002–03); $4060 room and board.

Academics USC-Aiken awards associate, bachelor's, and master's degrees. Challenging opportunities include advanced placement credit, accelerated degree programs, student-designed majors, an honors program, double majors, independent study, and a senior project. Special programs include cooperative education, internships, summer session for credit, off-campus study, and study-abroad. The most frequently chosen baccalaureate fields are business/marketing, education, and health professions and related sciences. The faculty at USC-Aiken has 130 full-time members. The student-faculty ratio is 15:1.

Students of USC-Aiken The student body totals 3,416, of whom 3,279 are undergraduates. 67% are women and 33% are men. Students come from 34 states and territories and 23 other countries. 87% are from South Carolina. 1.5% are international students. 70% returned for their sophomore year.

Applying USC-Aiken requires SAT I or ACT and a high school transcript. The school recommends an essay, an interview, and recommendations. Application deadline: 8/1; 3/15 priority date for financial aid. Early and deferred admission are possible.

UNIVERSITY OF SOUTH CAROLINA SPARTANBURG

Spartanburg, SC

Urban setting ■ Public ■ State-supported ■ Coed

Web site: www.uscs.edu
Contact: Ms. Donette Stewart, Director of Admissions, 800 University Way, Spartanburg, SC 29303
Telephone: 864-503-5280 or toll-free 800-277-8727 **Fax:** 864-503-5727
E-mail: dstawart@uscs.edu

Getting in Last Year 1,566 applied; 62% were accepted; 687 enrolled (71%).

Financial Matters $4788 resident tuition and fees (2002–03); $9680 nonresident tuition and fees (2002–03); $4700 room and board; 26% average percent of need met; $5405 average financial aid amount received per undergraduate (2001–02).

Academics USC Spartanburg awards associate, bachelor's, and master's degrees. Challenging opportunities include advanced placement credit, accelerated degree programs, student-designed majors, double majors, independent study, and a senior project. Special programs include cooperative education, internships, summer session for credit, off-campus study, study-abroad, and Army ROTC. The most frequently chosen baccalaureate fields are education, business/marketing, and health professions and related sciences. The faculty at USC Spartanburg has 174 full-time members, 77% with terminal degrees. The student-faculty ratio is 18:1.

Students of USC Spartanburg The student body totals 4,362, of whom 4,249 are undergraduates. 64.8% are women and 35.2% are men. Students come from 34 states and territories and 33 other countries. 95% are from South Carolina. 2.2% are international students. 61% returned for their sophomore year.

Applying USC Spartanburg requires SAT I or ACT and a minimum high school GPA of 2.0. Application deadline: 3/1 priority date for financial aid. Deferred admission is possible.

THE UNIVERSITY OF SOUTH DAKOTA

Vermillion, SD

Small-town setting ■ Public ■ State-supported ■ Coed

Web site: www.usd.edu
Contact: Ms. Paula Tacke, Director of Admissions, 414 East Clark Street, Vermillion, SD 57069
Telephone: 605-677-5434 or toll-free 877-269-6837 **Fax:** 605-677-6753
E-mail: admiss@usd.edu

Getting in Last Year 2,539 applied; 86% were accepted; 1,109 enrolled (51%).

Financial Matters $3872 resident tuition and fees (2002–03); $8122 nonresident tuition and fees (2002–03); $3278 room and board; 85% average percent of need met; $6565 average financial aid amount received per undergraduate (2001–02).

The University of South Dakota (continued)

Academics USD awards associate, bachelor's, master's, doctoral, and first-professional degrees and post-bachelor's and post-master's certificates. Challenging opportunities include advanced placement credit, an honors program, double majors, independent study, and a senior project. Special programs include internships, summer session for credit, off-campus study, study-abroad, and Army ROTC. The most frequently chosen baccalaureate fields are business/marketing, education, and health professions and related sciences. The faculty at USD has 283 full-time members, 80% with terminal degrees. The student-faculty ratio is 14:1.

Students of USD The student body totals 8,873, of whom 5,769 are undergraduates. 61.1% are women and 38.9% are men. Students come from 40 states and territories and 57 other countries. 77% are from South Dakota. 1.3% are international students. 74% returned for their sophomore year.

Applying USD requires SAT I or ACT and a high school transcript, and in some cases recommendations. The school recommends a minimum high school GPA of 2.6. Application deadline: rolling admissions; 3/15 priority date for financial aid. Early and deferred admission are possible.

UNIVERSITY OF SOUTHERN CALIFORNIA

Los Angeles, CA

Urban setting ■ Private ■ Independent ■ Coed

Web site: www.usc.edu

Contact: Ms. Laurel Baker-Tew, Director of Admission, University Park Campus, Los Angeles, CA 90089

Telephone: 213-740-1111 **Fax:** 213-740-6364

E-mail: admitusc@usc.edu

Getting in Last Year 28,362 applied; 30% were accepted; 2,766 enrolled (32%).

Financial Matters $26,954 tuition and fees (2002–03); $8512 room and board; 99% average percent of need met; $23,961 average financial aid amount received per undergraduate (2000–01).

Academics USC awards bachelor's, master's, doctoral, and first-professional degrees and post-bachelor's, post-master's, and first-professional certificates. Challenging opportunities include advanced placement credit, accelerated degree programs, student-designed majors, freshman honors college, an honors program, double majors, independent study, and a senior project. Special programs include cooperative education, internships, summer session for credit, off-campus study, study-abroad, and Army, Navy and Air Force ROTC. The most frequently chosen baccalaureate fields are business/marketing, social sciences and history, and visual/performing arts. The faculty at USC has 1,406 full-time members, 86% with terminal degrees. The student-faculty ratio is 10:1.

Students of USC The student body totals 30,682, of whom 16,145 are undergraduates. 50.1% are women and 49.9% are men. Students come from 52 states and territories and 100 other countries. 69% are from California. 7.4% are international students. 94% returned for their sophomore year.

Applying USC requires an essay, SAT I or ACT, and a high school transcript, and in some cases SAT II Subject Tests and recommendations. The school recommends an interview and recommendations. Application deadline: 1/10; 1/22 priority date for financial aid.

UNIVERSITY OF SOUTHERN INDIANA

Evansville, IN

Suburban setting ■ Public ■ State-supported ■ Coed

Web site: www.usi.edu

Contact: Mr. Eric Otto, Director of Admission, 8600 University Boulevard, Evansville, IN 47712-3590

Telephone: 812-464-1765 or toll-free 800-467-1965 **Fax:** 812-465-7154

E-mail: enroll@usi.edu

Getting in Last Year 4,258 applied; 94% were accepted; 2,032 enrolled (51%).

Financial Matters $3525 resident tuition and fees (2002–03); $8423 nonresident tuition and fees (2002–03); $4940 room and board; 42% average percent of need met; $5658 average financial aid amount received per undergraduate.

Academics USI awards associate, bachelor's, and master's degrees and post-bachelor's certificates. Challenging opportunities include advanced placement credit, an honors program, double majors, independent study, and a senior project. Special programs include cooperative education, internships, summer session for credit, study-abroad, and Army ROTC. The most frequently chosen baccalaureate fields are business/marketing, education, and health professions and related sciences. The faculty at USI has 283 full-time members, 64% with terminal degrees. The student-faculty ratio is 18:1.

Students of USI The student body totals 9,675, of whom 8,998 are undergraduates. 60.2% are women and 39.8% are men. Students come from 32 states and territories and 33 other countries. 90% are from Indiana. 0.5% are international students. 62% returned for their sophomore year.

Applying USI requires SAT I or ACT and a high school transcript, and in some cases an interview. The school recommends an essay and a minimum high school GPA of 2.0. Application deadline: 8/15; 3/1 for financial aid.

UNIVERSITY OF SOUTHERN MAINE

Portland, ME

Suburban setting ■ Public ■ State-supported ■ Coed

Web site: www.usm.maine.edu

Contact: Mr. Jon Barker, Assistant Director, 37 College Avenue, Gorham, ME 04038

Telephone: 207-780-5724 or toll-free 800-800-4USM ext. 5670 **Fax:** 207-780-5640

E-mail: usmadm@usm.maine.edu

Getting in Last Year 3,664 applied; 75% were accepted; 1,016 enrolled (37%).

Financial Matters $4861 resident tuition and fees (2002–03); $12,031 nonresident tuition and fees (2002–03); $6328 room and board; 84% average percent of need met; $8494 average financial aid amount received per undergraduate.

Academics USM awards associate, bachelor's, master's, doctoral, and first-professional degrees and post-master's certificates. Challenging opportunities include advanced placement credit, student-designed majors, an honors program, double majors, independent study, and a senior project. Special programs include cooperative education, internships, summer session for credit, off-campus study, study-abroad, and Army and Air Force ROTC. The most frequently chosen baccalaureate fields are social sciences and history, business/marketing, and health professions and related sciences. The faculty at USM has 440 full-time members, 68% with terminal degrees. The student-faculty ratio is 13:1.

Students of USM The student body totals 11,382, of whom 9,017 are undergraduates. 60.7% are women and 39.3% are men. Students come from 27 states and territories. 87% are from Maine. 69% returned for their sophomore year.

Applying USM requires an essay, SAT I or ACT, and a high school transcript, and in some cases an interview and auditions for music majors. The school recommends an interview, 1 recommendation, and a minimum high school GPA of 2.8. Application deadline: 2/1; 2/15 priority date for financial aid. Early and deferred admission are possible.

UNIVERSITY OF SOUTHERN MISSISSIPPI

Hattiesburg, MS

Suburban setting ■ Public ■ State-supported ■ Coed

Web site: www.usm.edu

Contact: Dr. Homer Wesley, Dean of Admissions, Box 5166, Hattiesburg, MS 39406-5166

Telephone: 601-266-5000 **Fax:** 601-266-5148

E-mail: admissions@usm.edu

Getting in Last Year 4,921 applied; 62% were accepted; 1,600 enrolled (53%).

Financial Matters $3874 resident tuition and fees (2002–03); $8752 nonresident tuition and fees (2002–03); $4450 room and board; 84% average percent of need met; $5805 average financial aid amount received per undergraduate.

Academics University of Southern Mississippi awards bachelor's, master's, and doctoral degrees. Challenging opportunities include advanced placement credit, accelerated degree programs, an honors program, double majors, and a senior project. Special programs include cooperative education, summer session for credit, off-campus study, study-abroad, and Army and Air Force ROTC. The most frequently chosen baccalaureate fields are business/marketing, education, and health professions and related sciences. The faculty at University of Southern Mississippi has 614 full-time members, 73% with terminal degrees. The student-faculty ratio is 20:1.

Students of University of Southern Mississippi The student body totals 15,267, of whom 12,612 are undergraduates. 60.6% are women and 39.4% are men. Students come from 50 states and territories and 61 other countries. 90% are from Mississippi. 1% are international students. 73% returned for their sophomore year.

Applying University of Southern Mississippi requires SAT I or ACT, a high school transcript, and a minimum high school GPA of 2.0, and in some cases an interview. Application deadline: rolling admissions; 3/15 priority date for financial aid. Early and deferred admission are possible.

UNIVERSITY OF SOUTH FLORIDA

Tampa, FL

Urban setting ■ Public ■ State-supported ■ Coed

Web site: www.usf.edu

Contact: Mr. Dewey Holleman, Director of Admissions, 4202 East Fowler Avenue, SVC 1036, Tampa, FL 33620-9951

Telephone: 813-974-3350 or toll-free 877-USF-BULLS **Fax:** 813-974-9689

E-mail: bullseye@admin.usf.edu

Getting in Last Year 13,535 applied; 62% were accepted; 4,345 enrolled (52%).

Financial Matters $2734 resident tuition and fees (2002–03); $12,278 nonresident tuition and fees (2002–03); $6110 room and board; 17% average percent of need met; $8211 average financial aid amount received per undergraduate.

Academics USF awards associate, bachelor's, master's, doctoral, and first-professional degrees and post-bachelor's certificates. Challenging opportunities include advanced placement credit, accelerated degree programs, student-designed majors, freshman honors college, an honors program, double majors, independent study, and a senior project. Special programs include cooperative education, internships, summer session for credit, off-campus study, study-abroad, and Army, Navy and Air Force ROTC. The most frequently chosen baccalaureate fields are business/marketing, education, and social sciences and history. The faculty at USF has 1,535 full-time members. The student-faculty ratio is 17:1.

Students of USF The student body totals 38,854, of whom 29,986 are undergraduates. 59.4% are women and 40.6% are men. Students come from 52 states and territories and 120 other countries. 95% are from Florida. 1.3% are international students.

Applying USF requires SAT I or ACT, a high school transcript, and a minimum high school GPA of 2.0, and in some cases recommendations. Application deadline: 6/1; 3/1 priority date for financial aid. Early admission is possible.

THE UNIVERSITY OF TAMPA

Tampa, FL

Urban setting ■ *Private* ■ *Independent* ■ *Coed*

Web site: www.ut.edu

Contact: Ms. Barbara P. Strickler, Vice President for Enrollment, 401 West Kennedy Boulevard, Tampa, FL 33606-1480

Telephone: 813-253-6211 or toll-free 888-646-2438 (in-state), 888-MINARET (out-of-state) **Fax:** 813-258-7398

E-mail: admissions@ut.edu

Getting in Last Year 4,169 applied; 68% were accepted; 989 enrolled (35%).

Financial Matters $17,032 tuition and fees (2002–03); $6132 room and board; 85% average percent of need met; $14,099 average financial aid amount received per undergraduate.

Academics UT awards associate, bachelor's, and master's degrees. Challenging opportunities include advanced placement credit, student-designed majors, an honors program, double majors, independent study, and a senior project. Special programs include cooperative education, internships, summer session for credit, off-campus study, study-abroad, and Army and Air Force ROTC. The most frequently chosen baccalaureate fields are business/marketing, social sciences and history, and education. The faculty at UT has 164 full-time members, 87% with terminal degrees. The student-faculty ratio is 17:1.

Students of UT The student body totals 4,265, of whom 3,730 are undergraduates. 63.3% are women and 36.7% are men. Students come from 50 states and territories and 78 other countries. 51% are from Florida. 4.7% are international students. 76% returned for their sophomore year.

Applying UT requires an essay, SAT I or ACT, a high school transcript, 1 recommendation, and a minimum high school GPA of 2.0. The school recommends an interview. Application deadline: rolling admissions. Early and deferred admission are possible.

THE UNIVERSITY OF TENNESSEE

Knoxville, TN

Urban setting ■ *Public* ■ *State-supported* ■ *Coed*

Web site: www.tennessee.edu

Contact: Mr. Marshall Rose, Acting Director of Admissions, 320 Student Services Building, Knoxville, TN 37996-0230

Telephone: 865-974-2184 or toll-free 800-221-8657 (in-state) **Fax:** 865-974-6341

E-mail: admissions@tennessee.edu

Getting in Last Year 9,724 applied; 58% were accepted; 3,682 enrolled (65%).

Financial Matters $3476 resident tuition and fees (2002–03); $11,828 nonresident tuition and fees (2002–03); $4912 room and board; 68% average percent of need met; $6943 average financial aid amount received per undergraduate.

Academics The University of Tennessee awards bachelor's, master's, doctoral, and first-professional degrees. Challenging opportunities include advanced placement credit, accelerated degree programs, student-designed majors, an honors program, double majors, independent study, and a senior project. Special programs include cooperative education, internships, summer session for credit, off-campus study, study-abroad, and Army and Air Force ROTC. The most frequently chosen baccalaureate fields are business/marketing, social sciences and history, and engineering/engineering technologies. The faculty at The University of Tennessee has 1,398 full-time members, 84% with terminal degrees. The student-faculty ratio is 18:1.

Students of The University of Tennessee The student body totals 27,971, of whom 19,956 are undergraduates. 51.3% are women and 48.7% are men. Students come from 50 states and territories and 101 other countries. 86% are from Tennessee. 1.6% are international students. 78% returned for their sophomore year.

Applying The University of Tennessee requires an essay, SAT I or ACT, a high school transcript, specific high school units, and a minimum high school GPA of 2.0. Application deadline: 2/1. Early and deferred admission are possible.

THE UNIVERSITY OF TENNESSEE AT CHATTANOOGA

Chattanooga, TN

Urban setting ■ *Public* ■ *State-supported* ■ *Coed*

Web site: www.utc.edu

Contact: Mr. Yancy Freeman, Director of Student Recruitment, 131 Hooper Hall, Chattanooga, TN 37403

Telephone: 423-755-4597 or toll-free 800-UTC-MOCS (in-state) **Fax:** 423-425-4157

E-mail: yancy-freeman@utc.edu

Getting in Last Year 2,686 applied; 55% were accepted; 1,201 enrolled (82%).

Financial Matters $3550 resident tuition and fees (2002–03); $10,570 nonresident tuition and fees (2002–03); $2800 room only; 80% average percent of need met; $8240 average financial aid amount received per undergraduate.

Academics UTC awards bachelor's and master's degrees and post-bachelor's and post-master's certificates. Challenging opportunities include advanced placement credit, an honors program, double majors, independent study, and a senior project. Special programs include cooperative education, internships, summer session for credit, off-campus study, and study-abroad. The most frequently chosen baccalaureate fields are business/marketing, education, and psychology. The faculty at UTC has 348 full-time members, 84% with terminal degrees. The student-faculty ratio is 16:1.

Students of UTC The student body totals 8,524, of whom 7,133 are undergraduates. 57.4% are women and 42.6% are men. Students come from 41 states and territories and 49 other countries. 92% are from Tennessee. 1.1% are international students. 74% returned for their sophomore year.

Applying UTC requires SAT I or ACT, a high school transcript, and 1 recommendation. The school recommends an essay. Application deadline: rolling admissions. Deferred admission is possible.

THE UNIVERSITY OF TENNESSEE AT MARTIN

Martin, TN

Small-town setting ■ *Public* ■ *State-supported* ■ *Coed*

Web site: www.utm.edu

Contact: Ms. Judy Rayburn, Director of Admission, 200 Hall-Moody Administration Building, Martin, TN 38238

Telephone: 901-587-7032 or toll-free 800-829-8861 **Fax:** 731-587-7029

E-mail: jrayburn@utm.edu

Getting in Last Year 2,324 applied; 55% were accepted; 1,086 enrolled (84%).

Financial Matters $3849 resident tuition and fees (2002–03); $11,033 nonresident tuition and fees (2002–03); $4480 room and board; 76% average percent of need met; $7001 average financial aid amount received per undergraduate.

Academics UT Martin awards bachelor's and master's degrees. Challenging opportunities include advanced placement credit, accelerated degree programs, student-designed majors, an honors program, double majors, independent study, and a senior project. Special programs include cooperative education, internships, summer session for credit, off-campus study, study-abroad, and Army ROTC. The most frequently chosen baccalaureate fields are business/marketing, interdisciplinary studies, and agriculture. The faculty at UT Martin has 243 full-time members, 69% with terminal degrees. The student-faculty ratio is 18:1.

Students of UT Martin The student body totals 5,714, of whom 5,300 are undergraduates. 57% are women and 43% are men. Students come from 35 states and territories and 30 other countries. 94% are from Tennessee. 2.9% are international students. 66% returned for their sophomore year.

Applying UT Martin requires SAT I or ACT, a high school transcript, and a minimum high school GPA of 2.25. Application deadline: rolling admissions; 3/1 priority date for financial aid. Deferred admission is possible.

THE UNIVERSITY OF TEXAS AT ARLINGTON

Arlington, TX

Urban setting ■ *Public* ■ *State-supported* ■ *Coed*

Web site: www.uta.edu

Contact: Dr. Hans Gatterdam, Director of Admissions, PO Box 19111, 701 South Nedderman Drive, Room 110, Davis Hall, Arlington, TX 76019-0088

Telephone: 817-272-6287 **Fax:** 817-272-3435

E-mail: admissions@uta.edu

Getting in Last Year 4,791 applied; 90% were accepted; 2,007 enrolled (47%).

Financial Matters $4128 resident tuition and fees (2002–03); $10,668 nonresident tuition and fees (2002–03); $4607 room and board; 83% average percent of need met; $7831 average financial aid amount received per undergraduate.

Academics UTA awards bachelor's, master's, and doctoral degrees and post-bachelor's and post-master's certificates. Challenging opportunities include advanced placement credit, student-designed majors, freshman honors college, an honors program, double majors, independent study, and a senior project. Special programs include cooperative education, internships, summer session for credit, study-abroad, and Army and Air Force ROTC. The most frequently chosen baccalaureate fields are business/marketing, engineering/engineering technologies,

The University of Texas at Arlington (continued)

and health professions and related sciences. The faculty at UTA has 678 full-time members. The student-faculty ratio is 23:1.

Students of UTA The student body totals 23,821, of whom 17,650 are undergraduates. 53.3% are women and 46.7% are men. Students come from 47 states and territories and 92 other countries. 98% are from Texas. 5.1% are international students. 69% returned for their sophomore year.

Applying UTA requires SAT I or ACT, a high school transcript, and class rank. Application deadline: rolling admissions; 6/1 priority date for financial aid. Early and deferred admission are possible.

THE UNIVERSITY OF TEXAS AT AUSTIN

Austin, TX

Urban setting ■ Public ■ State-supported ■ Coed

Web site: www.utexas.edu
Contact: Freshman Admissions Center, John Hargis Hall, Campus Mail Code D0700, Austin, TX 78712-1111
Telephone: 512-475-7440 **Fax:** 512-475-7475

Getting in Last Year 22,179 applied; 61% were accepted; 7,935 enrolled (59%).

Financial Matters $3950 resident tuition and fees (2002–03); $10,490 nonresident tuition and fees (2002–03); $5975 room and board; 94% average percent of need met; $7470 average financial aid amount received per undergraduate (2001–02).

Academics UT Austin awards bachelor's, master's, doctoral, and first-professional degrees. Challenging opportunities include advanced placement credit, accelerated degree programs, student-designed majors, an honors program, double majors, independent study, and a senior project. Special programs include cooperative education, internships, summer session for credit, study-abroad, and Army, Navy and Air Force ROTC. The most frequently chosen baccalaureate fields are social sciences and history, business/marketing, and communications/communication technologies. The faculty at UT Austin has 2,476 full-time members. The student-faculty ratio is 19:1.

Students of UT Austin The student body totals 52,261, of whom 39,661 are undergraduates. 50.6% are women and 49.4% are men. Students come from 54 states and territories and 126 other countries. 95% are from Texas. 3.5% are international students. 92% returned for their sophomore year.

Applying UT Austin requires SAT I or ACT and a high school transcript, and in some cases an essay. Application deadline: 2/1. Deferred admission is possible.

THE UNIVERSITY OF TEXAS AT BROWNSVILLE

Brownsville, TX

Urban setting ■ Public ■ State-supported ■ Coed

Web site: www.utb.edu
Contact: Carlo Tamayo, New Student Relations Coordinator, 80 Fort Brown, Brownsville, TX 78520-4991
Telephone: 956-544-8860 or toll-free 800-850-0160 (in-state) **Fax:** 956-983-7810
E-mail: cata01@utb.edu

Getting in Last Year 1,901 applied; 100% were accepted; 1,413 enrolled (74%).

Financial Matters $2121 resident tuition and fees (2002–03); $7401 nonresident tuition and fees (2002–03); 9% average percent of need met; $3071 average financial aid amount received per undergraduate.

Academics UTB awards associate, bachelor's, and master's degrees. Challenging opportunities include advanced placement credit, double majors, independent study, and a senior project. Special programs include cooperative education, internships, and summer session for credit. The most frequently chosen baccalaureate fields are business/marketing, foreign language/literature, and liberal arts/general studies. The faculty at UTB has 289 full-time members, 50% with terminal degrees. The student-faculty ratio is 17:1.

Students of UTB The student body totals 9,973, of whom 9,198 are undergraduates. 60.7% are women and 39.3% are men. 0.4% are international students.

Applying UTB requires TASP and a high school transcript. Application deadline: 4/1 priority date for financial aid. Early admission is possible.

THE UNIVERSITY OF TEXAS AT DALLAS

Richardson, TX

Suburban setting ■ Public ■ State-supported ■ Coed

Web site: www.utdallas.edu
Contact: Mr. Barry Samsula, Director of Enrollment Services, PO Box 830688 Mail Station MC11, Richardson, TX 75083-0688
Telephone: 972-883-2270 or toll-free 800-889-2443 **Fax:** 972-883-2599
E-mail: admissions-status@utdallas.edu

Getting in Last Year 4,086 applied; 53% were accepted; 913 enrolled (42%).

Financial Matters $4775 resident tuition and fees (2002–03); $11,315 nonresident tuition and fees (2002–03); $6032 room and board; 69% average percent of need met; $9376 average financial aid amount received per undergraduate.

Academics U.T. Dallas awards bachelor's, master's, and doctoral degrees. Challenging opportunities include advanced placement credit, accelerated degree programs, student-designed majors, freshman honors college, an honors program, double majors, independent study, and a senior project. Special programs include cooperative education, internships, summer session for credit, study-abroad, and Army and Air Force ROTC. The most frequently chosen baccalaureate fields are business/marketing, computer/information sciences, and interdisciplinary studies. The faculty at U.T. Dallas has 390 full-time members, 98% with terminal degrees. The student-faculty ratio is 20:1.

Students of U.T. Dallas The student body totals 13,228, of whom 7,961 are undergraduates. 49.3% are women and 50.7% are men. Students come from 43 states and territories and 137 other countries. 97% are from Texas. 5% are international students. 78% returned for their sophomore year.

Applying U.T. Dallas requires an essay, SAT I or ACT, and a high school transcript, and in some cases TASP and an interview. The school recommends SAT II: Writing Test and 3 recommendations. Application deadline: 8/1; 3/12 priority date for financial aid. Deferred admission is possible.

THE UNIVERSITY OF TEXAS AT EL PASO

El Paso, TX

Urban setting ■ Public ■ State-supported ■ Coed

Web site: www.utep.edu
Contact: Ms. Diana Guerrero, Director of Admissions, 500 West University Avenue, El Paso, TX 79968-0001
Telephone: 915-747-5588 **Fax:** 915-747-5848
E-mail: admission@utep.edu

Getting in Last Year 3,724 applied; 94% were accepted; 2,370 enrolled (68%).

Financial Matters $2796 resident tuition and fees (2002–03); $8028 nonresident tuition and fees (2002–03); $4255 room and board; 83% average percent of need met; $7761 average financial aid amount received per undergraduate.

Academics UT El Paso awards bachelor's, master's, and doctoral degrees. Challenging opportunities include advanced placement credit, accelerated degree programs, an honors program, and independent study. Special programs include cooperative education, internships, summer session for credit, off-campus study, and Army and Air Force ROTC. The most frequently chosen baccalaureate fields are interdisciplinary studies, business/marketing, and engineering/engineering technologies. The faculty at UT El Paso has 593 full-time members. The student-faculty ratio is 20:1.

Students of UT El Paso The student body totals 17,232, of whom 14,384 are undergraduates. 54.7% are women and 45.3% are men. Students come from 47 states and territories and 67 other countries. 97% are from Texas. 11.3% are international students. 68% returned for their sophomore year.

Applying UT El Paso requires a high school transcript, and in some cases SAT I or ACT and PAA. Application deadline: 7/31; 3/15 priority date for financial aid. Deferred admission is possible.

THE UNIVERSITY OF TEXAS AT SAN ANTONIO

San Antonio, TX

Suburban setting ■ Public ■ State-supported ■ Coed

Web site: www.utsa.edu
Contact: Mr. John Wallace, Interim Director, 6900 North Loop 1604 West, San Antonio, TX 78249
Telephone: 210-458-4530 or toll-free 800-669-0916 (in-state), 800-669-0919 (out-of-state)
E-mail: prospects@utsa.edu

Getting in Last Year 5,519 applied; 99% were accepted; 2,294 enrolled (42%).

Financial Matters $3920 resident tuition and fees (2002–03); $10,460 nonresident tuition and fees (2002–03); $7656 room and board.

Academics UTSA awards bachelor's, master's, and doctoral degrees. Challenging opportunities include advanced placement credit, accelerated degree programs, freshman honors college, an honors program, and independent study. Special programs include cooperative education, internships, summer session for credit, study-abroad, and Army and Air Force ROTC. The most frequently chosen baccalaureate fields are business/marketing, interdisciplinary studies, and biological/life sciences. The faculty at UTSA has 461 full-time members, 87% with terminal degrees. The student-faculty ratio is 24:1.

Students of UTSA The student body totals 19,883, of whom 17,425 are undergraduates. 54.9% are women and 45.1% are men. Students come from 52 states and territories and 83 other countries. 98% are from Texas. 1.7% are international students. 64% returned for their sophomore year.

Applying UTSA requires SAT I or ACT and a high school transcript. Application deadline: 7/1; 3/31 priority date for financial aid.

THE UNIVERSITY OF TEXAS AT TYLER

Tyler, TX

Urban setting ■ Public ■ State-supported ■ Coed

Web site: www.uttyler.edu
Contact: Mr. Jim Hutto, Dean of Enrollment Management, 3900 University Boulevard, Tyler, TX 75799-0001
Telephone: 903-566-7195 or toll-free 800-UTTYLER (in-state) **Fax:** 903-566-7068
E-mail: admissions@uttyler.edu

Getting in Last Year 1,168 applied; 54% were accepted; 297 enrolled (47%).

Financial Matters $3062 resident tuition and fees (2002–03); $9392 nonresident tuition and fees (2002–03); $3267 room only; 100% average percent of need met; $1575 average financial aid amount received per undergraduate.

Academics UTT awards bachelor's and master's degrees. Challenging opportunities include advanced placement credit, student-designed majors, an honors program, double majors, independent study, and a senior project. Special programs include cooperative education, internships, summer session for credit, and study-abroad. The most frequently chosen baccalaureate fields are health professions and related sciences, interdisciplinary studies, and business/marketing. The faculty at UTT has 165 full-time members, 78% with terminal degrees. The student-faculty ratio is 14:1.

Students of UTT The student body totals 4,241, of whom 3,026 are undergraduates. 62.4% are women and 37.6% are men. Students come from 23 states and territories and 43 other countries. 99% are from Texas. 1.5% are international students. 58% returned for their sophomore year.

Applying UTT requires SAT I or ACT and a high school transcript, and in some cases TASP. Application deadline: 4/1 priority date for financial aid. Deferred admission is possible.

THE UNIVERSITY OF TEXAS HEALTH SCIENCE CENTER AT HOUSTON

Houston, TX

Urban setting ■ Public ■ State-supported ■ Coed

Web site: www.uth.tmc.edu
Contact: Mr. Robert L. Jenkins, Associate Registrar, 7000 Fannin, PO Box 20036, Houston, TX 77225-0036
Telephone: 713-500-3361 **Fax:** 713-500-3356
E-mail: registrar@uth.tmc.edu

Financial Matters $4076 resident tuition and fees (2002–03); $13,886 nonresident tuition and fees (2002–03); 95% average percent of need met; $14,074 average financial aid amount received per undergraduate (2001–02).

Academics The University of Texas Health Science Center at Houston awards bachelor's, master's, doctoral, and first-professional degrees and post-master's certificates. Challenging opportunities include accelerated degree programs, double majors, and independent study. Special programs include internships and Army ROTC. The most frequently chosen baccalaureate field is health professions and related sciences. The faculty at The University of Texas Health Science Center at Houston has 867 full-time members.

Students of The University of Texas Health Science Center at Houston The student body totals 3,335, of whom 359 are undergraduates. 90.3% are women and 9.7% are men. 0.8% are international students.

THE UNIVERSITY OF TEXAS MEDICAL BRANCH

Galveston, TX

Small-town setting ■ Public ■ State-supported ■ Coed

Web site: www.utmb.edu
Contact: Ms. Vicki L. Brewer, Registrar, 301 University Boulevard, Galveston, TX 77555-1305
Telephone: 409-772-1215 **Fax:** 409-772-5056
E-mail: student.admissions@utmb.edu

Getting in Last Year 523 applied; 64% were accepted.

Academics UTMB awards bachelor's, master's, doctoral, and first-professional degrees. Challenging opportunities include advanced placement credit and independent study. Special programs include internships and summer session for credit. The most frequently chosen baccalaureate field is health professions and related sciences. The faculty at UTMB has 81 full-time members. The student-faculty ratio is 7:1.

Students of UTMB The student body totals 2,005, of whom 557 are undergraduates. 85.5% are women and 14.5% are men. Students come from 3 states and territories and 5 other countries. 100% are from Texas. 1.1% are international students.

THE UNIVERSITY OF TEXAS OF THE PERMIAN BASIN

Odessa, TX

Urban setting ■ Public ■ State-supported ■ Coed

Web site: www.utpb.edu
Contact: Ms. Vicki Gomez, Assistant Vice President for Enrollment Management, Director of Admissions, 4901 East University, Odessa, TX 79762-0001
Telephone: 915-552-2605 or toll-free 866-552-UTPB **Fax:** 915-552-3605
E-mail: admissions@utpb.edu

Getting in Last Year 453 applied; 88% were accepted; 226 enrolled (57%).

Financial Matters $3398 resident tuition and fees (2002–03); $8630 nonresident tuition and fees (2002–03); $4004 room and board; 79% average percent of need met; $7444 average financial aid amount received per undergraduate (2001–02).

Academics UTPB awards bachelor's and master's degrees. Challenging opportunities include advanced placement credit, accelerated degree programs, double majors, independent study, and a senior project. Special programs include internships and summer session for credit. The most frequently chosen baccalaureate fields are social sciences and history, business/marketing, and foreign language/literature. The faculty at UTPB has 103 full-time members, 84% with terminal degrees. The student-faculty ratio is 18:1.

Students of UTPB The student body totals 2,695, of whom 2,012 are undergraduates. 64.7% are women and 35.3% are men. Students come from 13 states and territories. 98% are from Texas. 0.3% are international students. 59% returned for their sophomore year.

Applying UTPB requires SAT I or ACT and a high school transcript, and in some cases an interview and recommendations. Application deadline: 8/15; 5/1 priority date for financial aid. Deferred admission is possible.

THE UNIVERSITY OF TEXAS–PAN AMERICAN

Edinburg, TX

Rural setting ■ Public ■ State-supported ■ Coed

Web site: www.panam.edu
Contact: Mr. David Zuniga, Director of Admissions, Office of Admissions and Records, 1201 West University Drive, Edinburg, TX 78541
Telephone: 956-381-2201 **Fax:** 956-381-2212
E-mail: admissions@panam.edu

Getting in Last Year 5,728 applied; 72% were accepted; 1,975 enrolled (48%).

Financial Matters $2719 resident tuition and fees (2002–03); $8989 nonresident tuition and fees (2002–03); $4333 room and board; 77% average percent of need met; $6915 average financial aid amount received per undergraduate (2001–02).

Academics UT-Pan American awards bachelor's, master's, and doctoral degrees and post-bachelor's and post-master's certificates. Challenging opportunities include an honors program, double majors, and independent study. Special programs include cooperative education, internships, summer session for credit, study-abroad, and Army ROTC. The most frequently chosen baccalaureate fields are interdisciplinary studies, business/marketing, and health professions and related sciences. The faculty at UT-Pan American has 460 full-time members. The student-faculty ratio is 22:1.

Students of UT-Pan American The student body totals 14,392, of whom 12,509 are undergraduates. 58.3% are women and 41.7% are men. Students come from 41 states and territories and 10 other countries. 99% are from Texas. 1.8% are international students. 61% returned for their sophomore year.

Applying UT-Pan American requires SAT I or ACT and a high school transcript, and in some cases an interview. The school recommends ACT. Application deadline: 7/10; 2/28 priority date for financial aid. Early admission is possible.

THE UNIVERSITY OF THE ARTS

Philadelphia, PA

Urban setting ■ Private ■ Independent ■ Coed

Web site: www.uarts.edu
Contact: Barbara Elliott, Director of Admissions, 320 South Broad Street, Philadelphia, PA 19102-4944
Telephone: 215-717-6030 or toll-free 800-616-ARTS **Fax:** 215-717-6045
E-mail: admissions@uarts.edu

Getting in Last Year 2,007 applied; 47% were accepted; 444 enrolled (47%).

Financial Matters $20,480 tuition and fees (2002–03); $5300 room only; 65% average percent of need met; $16,500 average financial aid amount received per undergraduate.

Academics UArts awards bachelor's and master's degrees and post-bachelor's certificates. Challenging opportunities include advanced placement credit, double majors, independent study, and a senior project. Special programs include internships, off-campus study, and study-abroad. The most frequently chosen baccalaureate fields are visual/performing arts, interdisciplinary studies, and communications/communication technologies. The faculty at UArts has 109 full-time members, 50% with terminal degrees. The student-faculty ratio is 10:1.

Students of UArts The student body totals 2,091, of whom 1,923 are undergraduates. 56% are women and 44% are men. Students come from 41 states and territories and 40 other countries. 39% are from Pennsylvania. 2.4% are international students. 80% returned for their sophomore year.

Applying UArts requires an essay, SAT I or ACT, a high school transcript, 1 recommendation, portfolio or audition, and a minimum high school GPA of 2.0,

The University of the Arts (continued)

and in some cases an interview. The school recommends an interview. Application deadline: rolling admissions; 3/1 priority date for financial aid. Early and deferred admission are possible.

UNIVERSITY OF THE DISTRICT OF COLUMBIA

Washington, DC

Urban setting ■ Public ■ District-supported ■ Coed

Web site: www.udc.edu

Contact: Mr. LaHugh Bankston, Registrar, 4200 Connecticut Avenue NW, Building 39 - A-Level, Washington, DC 20008

Telephone: 202-274-6200 **Fax:** 202-274-5553

Getting in Last Year 1,988 applied; 89% were accepted; 1,223 enrolled (69%).

Financial Matters $2070 resident tuition and fees (2002–03); $4710 nonresident tuition and fees (2002–03); 71% average percent of need met; $5927 average financial aid amount received per undergraduate (2001–02).

Academics UDC awards associate, bachelor's, and master's degrees. Challenging opportunities include accelerated degree programs and an honors program. Special programs include cooperative education, internships, summer session for credit, off-campus study, and Army and Air Force ROTC. The most frequently chosen baccalaureate fields are computer/information sciences, education, and biological/life sciences. The faculty at UDC has 233 full-time members, 60% with terminal degrees. The student-faculty ratio is 13:1.

Students of UDC The student body totals 5,470, of whom 5,184 are undergraduates. 62.9% are women and 37.1% are men. Students come from 54 states and territories and 125 other countries. 88% are from District of Columbia. 7.9% are international students.

Applying UDC requires a high school transcript, and in some cases GED. The school recommends SAT I. Application deadline: 8/1; 3/15 priority date for financial aid. Deferred admission is possible.

UNIVERSITY OF THE INCARNATE WORD

San Antonio, TX

Urban setting ■ Private ■ Independent Religious ■ Coed

Web site: www.uiw.edu

Contact: Ms. Andrea Cyterski, Director of Admissions, Box 285, San Antonio, TX 78209-6397

Telephone: 210-829-6005 or toll-free 800-749-WORD **Fax:** 210-829-3921

E-mail: admis@universe.uiwtx.edu

Getting in Last Year 1,350 applied; 33% were accepted; 412 enrolled (94%).

Financial Matters $13,498 tuition and fees (2002–03); $5250 room and board; 84% average percent of need met; $14,427 average financial aid amount received per undergraduate.

Academics UIW awards bachelor's, master's, and doctoral degrees. Challenging opportunities include advanced placement credit, accelerated degree programs, double majors, independent study, and a senior project. Special programs include internships, summer session for credit, off-campus study, study-abroad, and Army and Air Force ROTC. The most frequently chosen baccalaureate fields are business/marketing, health professions and related sciences, and liberal arts/general studies. The faculty at UIW has 131 full-time members, 79% with terminal degrees. The student-faculty ratio is 14:1.

Students of UIW The student body totals 4,264, of whom 3,522 are undergraduates. 65.9% are women and 34.1% are men. Students come from 27 states and territories and 28 other countries. 98% are from Texas. 8.3% are international students. 70% returned for their sophomore year.

Applying UIW requires SAT I or ACT and a high school transcript, and in some cases an essay and an interview. The school recommends an interview, 1 recommendation, and a minimum high school GPA of 2.0. Application deadline: rolling admissions; 4/1 priority date for financial aid. Early and deferred admission are possible.

UNIVERSITY OF THE OZARKS

Clarksville, AR

Small-town setting ■ Private ■ Independent Religious ■ Coed

Web site: www.ozarks.edu

Contact: Mr. James D. Decker, Director of Admissions, 415 North College Avenue, Clarksville, AR 72830-2880

Telephone: 479-979-1421 or toll-free 800-264-8636 **Fax:** 479-979-1355

E-mail: admiss@ozarks.edu

Getting in Last Year 548 applied; 85% were accepted; 203 enrolled (44%).

Financial Matters $10,576 tuition and fees (2002–03); $4480 room and board; 68% average percent of need met; $12,667 average financial aid amount received per undergraduate.

Academics U of O awards bachelor's degrees. Challenging opportunities include advanced placement credit, double majors, independent study, and a senior project. Special programs include cooperative education, internships, summer session for credit, off-campus study, and study-abroad. The most frequently chosen baccalaureate fields are business/marketing, communications/communication technologies, and education. The faculty at U of O has 43 full-time members, 86% with terminal degrees. The student-faculty ratio is 14:1.

Students of U of O The student body is made up of 703 undergraduates. 55% are women and 45% are men. Students come from 22 states and territories and 15 other countries. 59% are from Arkansas. 16.8% are international students. 65% returned for their sophomore year.

Applying U of O requires SAT I or ACT and a minimum high school GPA of 2.0, and in some cases an essay, a high school transcript, an interview, and recommendations. Application deadline: rolling admissions; 2/15 priority date for financial aid. Deferred admission is possible.

UNIVERSITY OF THE PACIFIC

Stockton, CA

Suburban setting ■ Private ■ Independent ■ Coed

Web site: www.uop.edu

Contact: Mr. Marc McGee, Director of Admissions, 3601 Pacific Avenue, Stockton, CA 95211-0197

Telephone: 209-946-2211 or toll-free 800-959-2867 **Fax:** 209-946-2413

E-mail: admissions@uop.edu

Getting in Last Year 3,736 applied; 71% were accepted; 700 enrolled (26%).

Financial Matters $22,555 tuition and fees (2002–03); $7198 room and board; $21,837 average financial aid amount received per undergraduate.

Academics UOP awards bachelor's, master's, doctoral, and first-professional degrees. Challenging opportunities include advanced placement credit, accelerated degree programs, student-designed majors, an honors program, double majors, independent study, and a senior project. Special programs include cooperative education, internships, summer session for credit, and study-abroad. The most frequently chosen baccalaureate fields are business/marketing, social sciences and history, and biological/life sciences. The faculty at UOP has 378 full-time members, 91% with terminal degrees. The student-faculty ratio is 13:1.

Students of UOP The student body totals 5,886, of whom 3,233 are undergraduates. 58.2% are women and 41.8% are men. Students come from 37 states and territories and 14 other countries. 89% are from California. 2.8% are international students. 87% returned for their sophomore year.

Applying UOP requires an essay, SAT I or ACT, a high school transcript, 1 recommendation, and a minimum high school GPA of 2.5, and in some cases audition for music program. The school recommends an interview and a minimum high school GPA of 3.0. Application deadline: 1/15; 2/15 priority date for financial aid.

UNIVERSITY OF THE SACRED HEART

San Juan, PR

Urban setting ■ Private ■ Independent Religious ■ Coed

Web site: www.sagrado.edu

Contact: Mr. Luis Laborde, Director of Admissions, Admissions Office, PO Box 12383, San Juan, PR 00914-0383

Telephone: 787-728-1515 ext. 3237

Getting in Last Year 2,273 applied; 87% were accepted; 938 enrolled (48%).

Financial Matters $5030 tuition and fees (2002–03); $1800 room only.

Academics University of the Sacred Heart awards associate, bachelor's, and master's degrees. Challenging opportunities include advanced placement credit, accelerated degree programs, an honors program, and a senior project. Special programs include cooperative education, internships, summer session for credit, and study-abroad. The most frequently chosen baccalaureate fields are business/marketing, communications/communication technologies, and psychology. The faculty at University of the Sacred Heart has 134 full-time members, 31% with terminal degrees. The student-faculty ratio is 20:1.

Students of University of the Sacred Heart The student body totals 5,229, of whom 4,631 are undergraduates. 64.9% are women and 35.1% are men. Students come from 1 state or territory. 95% are from Puerto Rico. 77% returned for their sophomore year.

Applying University of the Sacred Heart requires PAA, CEEB, a high school transcript, 1 recommendation, and a minimum high school GPA of 2.5. Application deadline: 6/30; 5/30 priority date for financial aid. Early admission is possible.

UNIVERSITY OF THE SCIENCES IN PHILADELPHIA

Philadelphia, PA

Urban setting ■ Private ■ Independent ■ Coed

Web site: www.usip.edu

Contact: Mr. Louis L. Hegyes, Director of Admission, 600 South 43rd Street, Philadelphia, PA 19104-4495

Telephone: 215-596-8810 or toll-free 888-996-8747 (in-state) **Fax:** 215-596-8821

E-mail: admit@usip.edu

Getting in Last Year 2,080 applied; 79% were accepted; 361 enrolled (22%).

Financial Matters $19,338 tuition and fees (2002–03); $7949 room and board.

Academics USP awards bachelor's, master's, doctoral, and first-professional degrees. Challenging opportunities include advanced placement credit, an honors program, double majors, and a senior project. Special programs include cooperative education, internships, summer session for credit, off-campus study, and Army and Air Force ROTC. The most frequently chosen baccalaureate fields are health professions and related sciences, biological/life sciences, and physical sciences. The faculty at USP has 152 full-time members, 76% with terminal degrees. The student-faculty ratio is 11:1.

Students of USP The student body totals 2,516, of whom 1,240 are undergraduates. 69.4% are women and 30.6% are men. Students come from 27 states and territories and 13 other countries. 51% are from Pennsylvania. 1.7% are international students. 87% returned for their sophomore year.

Applying USP requires SAT I or ACT and a high school transcript. The school recommends SAT I and a minimum high school GPA of 3.0. Application deadline: rolling admissions; 3/15 priority date for financial aid. Deferred admission is possible.

UNIVERSITY OF THE SOUTH

Sewanee, TN

Small-town setting ■ Private ■ Independent Religious ■ Coed

Web site: www.sewanee.edu
Contact: Mr. David Lesesne, Dean of Admission, 735 University Avenue, Sewanee, TN 37383
Telephone: 931-598-1238 or toll-free 800-522-2234 **Fax:** 931-598-3248
E-mail: admiss@sewanee.edu

Getting in Last Year 1,669 applied; 71% were accepted; 367 enrolled (31%).

Financial Matters $22,570 tuition and fees (2002–03); $6290 room and board; 100% average percent of need met; $21,067 average financial aid amount received per undergraduate (2001–02).

Academics Sewanee awards bachelor's, master's, doctoral, and first-professional degrees and first-professional certificates. Challenging opportunities include advanced placement credit, student-designed majors, double majors, independent study, and a senior project. Special programs include internships, summer session for credit, and study-abroad. The most frequently chosen baccalaureate fields are social sciences and history, English, and visual/performing arts. The faculty at Sewanee has 124 full-time members, 97% with terminal degrees. The student-faculty ratio is 10:1.

Students of Sewanee The student body totals 1,449, of whom 1,340 are undergraduates. 53.3% are women and 46.7% are men. Students come from 44 states and territories. 24% are from Tennessee. 1.9% are international students. 85% returned for their sophomore year.

Applying Sewanee requires an essay, SAT I or ACT, a high school transcript, and 2 recommendations. The school recommends SAT II Subject Tests and an interview. Application deadline: 2/1; 3/1 priority date for financial aid. Early and deferred admission are possible.

UNIVERSITY OF THE VIRGIN ISLANDS

Charlotte Amalie, VI

Small-town setting ■ Public ■ Territory-supported ■ Coed

Web site: www.uvi.edu
Contact: Ms. Carolyn Cook, Director of Admissions & New Student Services, No. 2 John Brewers Bay, St. Thomas, VI 00802
Telephone: 340-693-1224 **Fax:** 340-693-1155
E-mail: admissions@uvi.edu

Getting in Last Year 631 enrolled.

Financial Matters $2860 resident tuition and fees (2002–03); $8320 nonresident tuition and fees (2002–03); $5830 room and board; 45% average percent of need met; $4000 average financial aid amount received per undergraduate (2001–02).

Academics UVI awards associate, bachelor's, and master's degrees. Challenging opportunities include advanced placement credit, independent study, and a senior project. Special programs include internships, summer session for credit, and off-campus study. The most frequently chosen baccalaureate fields are business/marketing, education, and health professions and related sciences. The faculty at UVI has 107 full-time members, 63% with terminal degrees. The student-faculty ratio is 9:1.

Students of UVI The student body totals 2,524, of whom 2,244 are undergraduates. 76.8% are women and 23.2% are men. Students come from 29 states and territories and 10 other countries. 97% are from Virgin Islands. 5.6% are international students.

Applying UVI requires an essay, SAT I or ACT, a high school transcript, and 2 recommendations. Application deadline: 4/30; 3/1 priority date for financial aid. Early and deferred admission are possible.

UNIVERSITY OF TOLEDO

Toledo, OH

Suburban setting ■ Public ■ State-supported ■ Coed

Web site: www.utoledo.edu
Contact: Ms. Nancy Hintz, Assistant Director, 2801 West Bancroft, Toledo, OH 43606-3398
Telephone: 419-530-5728 or toll-free 800-5TOLEDO (in-state)
Fax: 419-530-5872
E-mail: enroll@utnet.utoledo.edu

Getting in Last Year 9,248 applied; 97% were accepted; 3,895 enrolled (43%).

Financial Matters $5849 resident tuition and fees (2002–03); $14,302 nonresident tuition and fees (2002–03); $6511 room and board; 34% average percent of need met; $5539 average financial aid amount received per undergraduate.

Academics UT awards associate, bachelor's, master's, doctoral, and first-professional degrees and post-bachelor's and post-master's certificates. Challenging opportunities include advanced placement credit, student-designed majors, an honors program, double majors, independent study, and a senior project. Special programs include cooperative education, internships, summer session for credit, off-campus study, study-abroad, and Army and Air Force ROTC. The most frequently chosen baccalaureate fields are education, business/marketing, and engineering/engineering technologies. The faculty at UT has 687 full-time members, 79% with terminal degrees. The student-faculty ratio is 18:1.

Students of UT The student body totals 20,889, of whom 17,563 are undergraduates. 51.1% are women and 48.9% are men. Students come from 42 states and territories and 82 other countries. 91% are from Ohio. 2.3% are international students. 72% returned for their sophomore year.

Applying UT requires a high school transcript, and in some cases SAT I or ACT and a minimum high school GPA of 2.0. Application deadline: rolling admissions; 3/15 priority date for financial aid. Deferred admission is possible.

UNIVERSITY OF TORONTO

Toronto, ON Canada

Urban setting ■ Public ■ Coed

Web site: www.utoronto.ca
Contact: Admissions and Awards, Toronto, ON M5S 1A1 Canada
Telephone: 416-978-2190 **Fax:** 416-978-7022
E-mail: ask@adm.utoronto.ca

Getting in Last Year 54,474 applied; 60% were accepted; 13,027 enrolled (40%).

Financial Matters $3275 nonresident tuition and fees (2002–03); $4059 room and board.

Academics U of T awards bachelor's, master's, doctoral, and first-professional degrees. Double majors are a challenging opportunity. Special programs include cooperative education, summer session for credit, off-campus study, and study-abroad. The faculty at U of T has 2,699 full-time members. The student-faculty ratio is 15:1.

Students of U of T The student body totals 55,891, of whom 40,341 are undergraduates. 56.5% are women and 43.5% are men. Students come from 12 states and territories and 126 other countries. 97% are from Ontario. 94% returned for their sophomore year.

Applying U of T requires a high school transcript, and in some cases SAT I, SAT II Subject Tests, and an interview. Application deadline: 3/1. Deferred admission is possible.

UNIVERSITY OF TULSA

Tulsa, OK

Urban setting ■ Private ■ Independent Religious ■ Coed

Web site: www.utulsa.edu
Contact: Mr. John C. Corso, Associate Vice President for Administration/Dean of Admission, 600 South College Avenue, Tulsa, OK 74104
Telephone: 918-631-2307 or toll-free 800-331-3050 **Fax:** 918-631-5003
E-mail: admission@utulsa.edu

Getting in Last Year 2,077 applied; 73% were accepted; 552 enrolled (36%).

Financial Matters $14,990 tuition and fees (2002–03); $5088 room and board; 91% average percent of need met; $13,737 average financial aid amount received per undergraduate.

Academics TU awards bachelor's, master's, doctoral, and first-professional degrees and first-professional certificates. Challenging opportunities include advanced placement credit, accelerated degree programs, student-designed majors, an honors program, double majors, independent study, and a senior project. Special programs include internships, summer session for credit, study-abroad, and Air Force ROTC. The most frequently chosen baccalaureate fields are business/marketing, engineering/engineering technologies, and visual/

University of Tulsa (continued)

performing arts. The faculty at TU has 297 full-time members, 96% with terminal degrees. The student-faculty ratio is 11:1.

Students of TU The student body totals 4,049, of whom 2,691 are undergraduates. 52.2% are women and 47.8% are men. Students come from 38 states and territories and 56 other countries. 76% are from Oklahoma. 10.8% are international students. 77% returned for their sophomore year.

Applying TU requires SAT I or ACT, a high school transcript, and 1 recommendation. The school recommends an essay, an interview, and a minimum high school GPA of 3.0. Application deadline: 4/1 priority date for financial aid. Early and deferred admission are possible.

UNIVERSITY OF UTAH

Salt Lake City, UT

Urban setting ■ *Public* ■ *State-supported* ■ *Coed*

Web site: www.utah.edu

Contact: Ms. Suzanne Espinoza, Director of High School Services, 250 South Student Services Building, 201 South, 460 E Room 205, Salt Lake City, UT 84112

Telephone: 801-581-8761 or toll-free 800-444-8638 **Fax:** 801-585-7864

Getting in Last Year 5,802 applied; 90% were accepted; 2,600 enrolled (50%).

Financial Matters $3324 resident tuition and fees (2002–03); $10,182 nonresident tuition and fees (2002–03); $5036 room and board; 69% average percent of need met; $6310 average financial aid amount received per undergraduate.

Academics U of U awards bachelor's, master's, doctoral, and first-professional degrees and post-bachelor's and post-master's certificates. Challenging opportunities include advanced placement credit, accelerated degree programs, student-designed majors, an honors program, double majors, independent study, and a senior project. Special programs include cooperative education, internships, summer session for credit, off-campus study, study-abroad, and Army, Navy and Air Force ROTC. The most frequently chosen baccalaureate fields are business/marketing, social sciences and history, and health professions and related sciences. The faculty at U of U has 1,042 full-time members, 77% with terminal degrees. The student-faculty ratio is 25:1.

Students of U of U The student body totals 28,369, of whom 22,648 are undergraduates. 44.4% are women and 55.6% are men. Students come from 54 states and territories and 106 other countries. 93% are from Utah. 2.8% are international students. 75% returned for their sophomore year.

Applying U of U requires SAT I or ACT, a high school transcript, and a minimum high school GPA of 2.0. The school recommends ACT and a minimum high school GPA of 3.0. Application deadline: 5/1; 3/15 priority date for financial aid. Early and deferred admission are possible.

UNIVERSITY OF VERMONT

Burlington, VT

Suburban setting ■ *Public* ■ *State-supported* ■ *Coed*

Web site: www.uvm.edu

Contact: Mr. Donald M. Honeman, Director of Admissions, Office of Admissions, 194 South Prospect Street, Burlington, VT 05401-3596

Telephone: 802-656-3370 **Fax:** 802-656-8611

E-mail: admissions@uvm.edu

Getting in Last Year 9,776 applied; 71% were accepted; 1,841 enrolled (26%).

Financial Matters $8994 resident tuition and fees (2002–03); $21,484 nonresident tuition and fees (2002–03); $6378 room and board; 90% average percent of need met; $12,867 average financial aid amount received per undergraduate (2001–02).

Academics UVM awards associate, bachelor's, master's, doctoral, and first-professional degrees and post-bachelor's and post-master's certificates. Challenging opportunities include advanced placement credit, student-designed majors, an honors program, double majors, independent study, and a senior project. Special programs include cooperative education, internships, summer session for credit, off-campus study, study-abroad, and Army ROTC. The most frequently chosen baccalaureate fields are social sciences and history, business/marketing, and natural resources/environmental science. The faculty at UVM has 548 full-time members, 85% with terminal degrees. The student-faculty ratio is 14:1.

Students of UVM The student body totals 10,314, of whom 8,792 are undergraduates. 55.9% are women and 44.1% are men. Students come from 51 states and territories and 30 other countries. 39% are from Vermont. 0.9% are international students. 82% returned for their sophomore year.

Applying UVM requires an essay, SAT I or ACT, a high school transcript, and 1 recommendation. The school recommends an interview and 2 recommendations. Application deadline: 1/15. Deferred admission is possible.

UNIVERSITY OF VICTORIA

Victoria, BC Canada

Suburban setting ■ *Public* ■ *Coed*

Web site: www.uvic.ca

Contact: Mr. Bruno Rocca, Admission Services Office, PO Box 3025, Victoria, BC V8W 3P2

Telephone: 250-721-8121 ext. 8109 **Fax:** 250-721-6225

E-mail: admit@uvic.ca

Getting in Last Year 7,055 applied; 51% were accepted; 1,806 enrolled (50%).

Financial Matters $6234 resident tuition and fees (2002–03); $6234 nonresident tuition and fees (2002–03); $10,760 room and board.

Academics UVIC awards bachelor's, master's, doctoral, and first-professional degrees. Challenging opportunities include advanced placement credit, an honors program, double majors, independent study, and a senior project. Special programs include cooperative education, internships, summer session for credit, off-campus study, and study-abroad. The faculty at UVIC has 583 full-time members. The student-faculty ratio is 27:1.

Students of UVIC The student body totals 18,062, of whom 15,756 are undergraduates. 60% are women and 40% are men. Students come from 11 states and territories and 71 other countries. 87% are from British Columbia.

Applying UVIC requires a high school transcript and a minimum high school GPA of 2.5, and in some cases an essay, an interview, audition, portfolio, and a minimum high school GPA of 3.0. Application deadline: 4/30; 6/30 priority date for financial aid. Early and deferred admission are possible.

UNIVERSITY OF VIRGINIA

Charlottesville, VA

Suburban setting ■ *Public* ■ *State-supported* ■ *Coed*

Web site: www.virginia.edu

Contact: Mr. John A. Blackburn, Dean of Admission, PO Box 400160, Charlottesville, VA 22904-4160

Telephone: 434-982-3200 **Fax:** 434-924-3587

E-mail: undergrad-admission@virginia.edu

Getting in Last Year 14,320 applied; 39% were accepted; 2,999 enrolled (54%).

Financial Matters $4780 resident tuition and fees (2002–03); $19,990 nonresident tuition and fees (2002–03); $5231 room and board; 92% average percent of need met; $11,462 average financial aid amount received per undergraduate.

Academics UVA awards bachelor's, master's, doctoral, and first-professional degrees and post-master's certificates. Challenging opportunities include advanced placement credit, accelerated degree programs, student-designed majors, an honors program, double majors, independent study, and a senior project. Special programs include cooperative education, internships, summer session for credit, study-abroad, and Army, Navy and Air Force ROTC. The most frequently chosen baccalaureate fields are social sciences and history, engineering/engineering technologies, and business/marketing. The faculty at UVA has 1,099 full-time members, 92% with terminal degrees. The student-faculty ratio is 16:1.

Students of UVA The student body totals 23,144, of whom 13,805 are undergraduates. 54% are women and 46% are men. Students come from 52 states and territories and 97 other countries. 72% are from Virginia. 4.3% are international students. 96% returned for their sophomore year.

Applying UVA requires an essay, SAT II Subject Tests, SAT II: Writing Test, SAT I or ACT, a high school transcript, and 1 recommendation. Application deadline: 1/2; 3/1 priority date for financial aid. Deferred admission is possible.

THE UNIVERSITY OF VIRGINIA'S COLLEGE AT WISE

Wise, VA

Small-town setting ■ *Public* ■ *State-supported* ■ *Coed*

Web site: www.uvawise.edu

Contact: Mr. Russell Necessary, Director of Admissions and Financial Aid, 1 College Avenue, Wise, VA 24293

Telephone: 276-328-0322 or toll-free 888-282-9324 **Fax:** 540-328-0251

E-mail: admissions@uvawise.edu

Getting in Last Year 937 applied; 79% were accepted; 346 enrolled (47%).

Financial Matters $4040 resident tuition and fees (2002–03); $11,800 nonresident tuition and fees (2002–03); $5401 room and board; 95% average percent of need met; $5043 average financial aid amount received per undergraduate (2001–02).

Academics The University of Virginia's College at Wise awards bachelor's degrees and post-bachelor's certificates. Challenging opportunities include advanced placement credit, accelerated degree programs, student-designed majors, an honors program, double majors, independent study, and a senior project. Special programs include cooperative education, internships, summer session for credit, and study-abroad. The most frequently chosen baccalaureate fields are social sciences and history, business/marketing, and psychology. The faculty at The University of Virginia's College at Wise has 67 full-time members, 72% with terminal degrees. The student-faculty ratio is 17:1.

Students of The University of Virginia's College at Wise The student body is made up of 1,632 undergraduates. 55.4% are women and 44.6% are men. Students come from 11 states and territories and 10 other countries. 94% are from Virginia. 1.1% are international students. 74% returned for their sophomore year.

Applying The University of Virginia's College at Wise requires SAT I or ACT, a high school transcript, and a minimum high school GPA of 2.3, and in some cases an interview. The school recommends 2 recommendations. Application deadline: 8/1; 4/1 priority date for financial aid. Early admission is possible.

UNIVERSITY OF WASHINGTON

Seattle, WA

Urban setting ■ Public ■ State-supported ■ Coed

Web site: www.washington.edu
Contact: Mr. Wilbur W. Washburn, IV, Assistant Vice President for Enrollment Services, Box 355852, Seattle, WA 98195-5852
Telephone: 206-543-9686

Getting in Last Year 15,950 applied; 68% were accepted; 4,771 enrolled (44%).

Financial Matters $4636 resident tuition and fees (2002–03); $15,337 nonresident tuition and fees (2002–03); $6570 room and board; 88% average percent of need met; $9784 average financial aid amount received per undergraduate.

Academics UW awards bachelor's, master's, doctoral, and first-professional degrees. Challenging opportunities include advanced placement credit, accelerated degree programs, student-designed majors, an honors program, double majors, independent study, and a senior project. Special programs include cooperative education, internships, summer session for credit, study-abroad, and Army, Navy and Air Force ROTC. The most frequently chosen baccalaureate fields are social sciences and history, business/marketing, and biological/life sciences. The faculty at UW has 2,764 full-time members, 94% with terminal degrees. The student-faculty ratio is 11:1.

Students of UW The student body totals 39,246, of whom 28,362 are undergraduates. 51.7% are women and 48.3% are men. Students come from 52 states and territories and 59 other countries. 85% are from Washington. 3.3% are international students. 90% returned for their sophomore year.

Applying UW requires an essay, SAT I or ACT, a high school transcript, and a minimum high school GPA of 2.0. Application deadline: 1/15; 2/28 priority date for financial aid. Early admission is possible.

UNIVERSITY OF WATERLOO

Waterloo, ON Canada

Suburban setting ■ Public ■ Coed

Web site: www.uwaterloo.ca
Contact: Mr. P. Burroughs, Director of Admissions, 200 University Avenue West, Waterloo, ON N2L 3G1 Canada
Telephone: 519-888-4567 ext. 3777 **Fax:** 519-746-8088 ext. 3777

Getting in Last Year 27,545 applied; 62% were accepted.

Financial Matters $4623 nonresident tuition and fees (2002–03); $6445 room and board.

Academics University of Waterloo awards bachelor's, master's, doctoral, and first-professional degrees. Challenging opportunities include accelerated degree programs, student-designed majors, an honors program, double majors, independent study, and a senior project. Special programs include cooperative education, internships, summer session for credit, off-campus study, and study-abroad. The most frequently chosen baccalaureate fields are engineering/engineering technologies, computer/information sciences, and social sciences and history. The faculty at University of Waterloo has 788 full-time members. The student-faculty ratio is 16:1.

Students of University of Waterloo The student body totals 22,640, of whom 20,424 are undergraduates. 48.2% are women and 51.8% are men. Students come from 12 states and territories. 85% returned for their sophomore year.

Applying University of Waterloo requires a high school transcript, and in some cases an essay, SAT II Subject Tests, SAT I or ACT, an interview, recommendations, and a minimum high school GPA of 3.0. Application deadline: 7/1 priority date for financial aid. Early admission is possible.

THE UNIVERSITY OF WEST ALABAMA

Livingston, AL

Small-town setting ■ Public ■ State-supported ■ Coed

Web site: www.uwa.edu
Contact: Mr. Richard Hester, Vice President for Student Affairs, Station 4, Livingston, AL 35470
Telephone: 205-652-3400 ext. 3578 or toll-free 800-621-7742 (in-state), 800-621-8044 (out-of-state) **Fax:** 205-652-3522
E-mail: rhester@uwa.edu

Getting in Last Year 690 applied; 40% were accepted; 275 enrolled (100%).

Financial Matters $3498 resident tuition and fees (2002–03); $6558 nonresident tuition and fees (2002–03); $2958 room and board; $7793 average financial aid amount received per undergraduate (2001–02).

Academics The University of West Alabama awards associate, bachelor's, and master's degrees. Challenging opportunities include advanced placement credit, accelerated degree programs, an honors program, and double majors. Special programs include internships, summer session for credit, off-campus study, and Army and Air Force ROTC. The most frequently chosen baccalaureate fields are education, business/marketing, and biological/life sciences. The faculty at The University of West Alabama has 82 full-time members, 57% with terminal degrees. The student-faculty ratio is 20:1.

Students of The University of West Alabama The student body totals 2,002, of whom 1,621 are undergraduates. 54.3% are women and 45.7% are men. Students come from 19 states and territories and 9 other countries. 84% are from Alabama. 1.9% are international students. 80% returned for their sophomore year.

Applying The University of West Alabama requires SAT I or ACT, a high school transcript, and a minimum high school GPA of 2.0. Application deadline: rolling admissions; 4/1 priority date for financial aid. Early and deferred admission are possible.

THE UNIVERSITY OF WESTERN ONTARIO

London, ON Canada

Suburban setting ■ Public ■ Coed

Web site: www.uwo.ca
Contact: Ms. Lori Gribbon, Manager, Admissions, London, ON N6A 5B8 Canada
Telephone: 519-661-2116 **Fax:** 519-661-3710
E-mail: reg-admissions@uwo.ca

Getting in Last Year 36,435 applied; 16% were accepted.

Financial Matters $5000 nonresident tuition and fees (2002–03); $5780 room and board.

Academics Western awards bachelor's, master's, doctoral, and first-professional degrees. Challenging opportunities include student-designed majors, an honors program, double majors, and a senior project. Special programs include cooperative education, internships, summer session for credit, off-campus study, and study-abroad. The faculty at Western has 1,164 full-time members. The student-faculty ratio is 18:1.

Students of Western The student body totals 24,425, of whom 21,370 are undergraduates. 54.3% are women and 45.7% are men. Students come from 12 states and territories. 93% returned for their sophomore year.

Applying Western requires a high school transcript and a minimum high school GPA of 3.0, and in some cases SAT I. Application deadline: 6/1, 5/15 for nonresidents. Deferred admission is possible.

UNIVERSITY OF WEST FLORIDA

Pensacola, FL

Suburban setting ■ Public ■ State-supported ■ Coed

Web site: uwf.edu
Contact: Mr. Richard M. Hulett, Director of Admissions, 11000 University Parkway, Pensacola, FL 32514-5750
Telephone: 850-474-2230 or toll-free 800-263-1074
E-mail: admissions@uwf.edu

Getting in Last Year 2,569 applied; 78% were accepted; 933 enrolled (47%).

Financial Matters $2639 resident tuition and fees (2002–03); $11,277 nonresident tuition and fees (2002–03); $6000 room and board.

Academics UWF awards associate, bachelor's, master's, and doctoral degrees. Challenging opportunities include advanced placement credit, an honors program, independent study, and a senior project. Special programs include cooperative education, internships, summer session for credit, off-campus study, study-abroad, and Army and Air Force ROTC. The most frequently chosen baccalaureate fields are business/marketing, education, and communications/communication technologies. The faculty at UWF has 245 full-time members, 80% with terminal degrees. The student-faculty ratio is 20:1.

Students of UWF The student body totals 9,185, of whom 7,595 are undergraduates. 58.4% are women and 41.6% are men. Students come from 50 states and territories and 82 other countries. 89% are from Florida. 1.3% are international students. 73% returned for their sophomore year.

Applying UWF requires SAT I or ACT, a high school transcript, and a minimum high school GPA of 2.0. Application deadline: 6/30. Early and deferred admission are possible.

UNIVERSITY OF WEST LOS ANGELES

Inglewood, CA

Suburban setting ■ Private ■ Independent ■ Coed

Web site: www.uwla.edu
Contact: Ms. Yvonne Alwag, Admissions Counselor, School of Paralegal Studies, 1155 West Arbor Vitae Street, Inglewood, CA 90301-2902
Telephone: 310-342-5287 **Fax:** 310-342-5296
E-mail: aalwag@uwla.edu

Financial Matters $7410 tuition and fees (2002–03); 60% average percent of need met; $8150 average financial aid amount received per undergraduate (2001–02).

Academics UWLA awards bachelor's and first-professional degrees. Challenging opportunities include independent study and a senior project. Internships is a

University of West Los Angeles (continued)

special program. The most frequently chosen baccalaureate field is law/legal studies. The faculty at UWLA has 1 full-time members, 100% with terminal degrees. The student-faculty ratio is 10:1.

Students of UWLA The student body totals 358, of whom 64 are undergraduates. 71.9% are women and 28.1% are men. Students come from 1 state or territory.

Applying Deferred admission is possible.

UNIVERSITY OF WINDSOR

Windsor, ON Canada

Urban setting ■ Public ■ Coed

Web site: www.uwindsor.ca

Contact: Ms. Charlene Yates, Assistant Registrar, Office of the Registrar, 401 Sunset Avenue, Windsor, ON N9B 3P4 Canada

Telephone: 519-253-3000 ext. 3332 or toll-free 800-864-2860 (in-state) **Fax:** 519-971-3653

E-mail: registr@uwindsor.ca

Getting in Last Year 12,073 applied; 91% were accepted; 2,855 enrolled (26%).

Academics Windsor awards bachelor's, master's, doctoral, and first-professional degrees. Challenging opportunities include advanced placement credit, accelerated degree programs, student-designed majors, an honors program, double majors, and a senior project. Special programs include cooperative education, internships, summer session for credit, off-campus study, and study-abroad. The most frequently chosen baccalaureate fields are education, business/marketing, and social sciences and history. The faculty at Windsor has 489 full-time members. The student-faculty ratio is 22:1.

Students of Windsor The student body totals 14,254, of whom 11,917 are undergraduates. 52.8% are women and 47.2% are men. Students come from 25 states and territories and 86 other countries. 76% returned for their sophomore year.

Applying Windsor requires a high school transcript and a minimum high school GPA of 2.7, and in some cases an essay, SAT I, SAT I and SAT II or ACT, an interview, 1 recommendation, and a minimum high school GPA of 3.3. Application deadline: rolling admissions, 7/1 for nonresidents; 6/15 for financial aid. Early admission is possible.

UNIVERSITY OF WISCONSIN–EAU CLAIRE

Eau Claire, WI

Urban setting ■ Public ■ State-supported ■ Coed

Web site: www.uwec.edu

Contact: Mr. Robert Lopez, Executive Director of Enrollment Management and Director of Admissions, PO Box 4004, Eau Claire, WI 54702-4004

Telephone: 715-836-5415 **Fax:** 715-836-2409

E-mail: admissions@uwec.edu

Getting in Last Year 6,777 applied; 68% were accepted; 2,053 enrolled (44%).

Financial Matters $3722 resident tuition and fees (2002–03); $13,768 nonresident tuition and fees (2002–03); $3910 room and board; 81% average percent of need met; $5830 average financial aid amount received per undergraduate (2001–02).

Academics UWEC awards associate, bachelor's, and master's degrees and post-bachelor's, post-master's, and first-professional certificates. Challenging opportunities include advanced placement credit, an honors program, double majors, independent study, and a senior project. Special programs include cooperative education, internships, summer session for credit, off-campus study, and study-abroad. The most frequently chosen baccalaureate fields are business/marketing, education, and health professions and related sciences. The faculty at UWEC has 418 full-time members, 85% with terminal degrees. The student-faculty ratio is 21:1.

Students of UWEC The student body totals 10,861, of whom 10,364 are undergraduates. 60.2% are women and 39.8% are men. Students come from 22 states and territories and 47 other countries. 78% are from Wisconsin. 1.1% are international students. 78% returned for their sophomore year.

Applying UWEC requires SAT I or ACT, a high school transcript, and rank in upper 50% of high school class. Application deadline: rolling admissions; 4/15 priority date for financial aid. Early admission is possible.

UNIVERSITY OF WISCONSIN–GREEN BAY

Green Bay, WI

Suburban setting ■ Public ■ State-supported ■ Coed

Web site: www.uwgb.edu

Contact: Ms. Pam Harvey-Jacobs, Interim Director of Admissions, 2420 Nicolet Drive, Green Bay, WI 54311-7001

Telephone: 920-465-2111 or toll-free 888-367-8942 (out-of-state) **Fax:** 920-465-5754

E-mail: admissions@uwgb.edu

Getting in Last Year 2,598 applied; 76% were accepted; 901 enrolled (45%).

Financial Matters $4023 resident tuition and fees (2002–03); $14,069 nonresident tuition and fees (2002–03); $3700 room and board; 83% average percent of need met; $6666 average financial aid amount received per undergraduate.

Academics UW-Green Bay awards associate, bachelor's, and master's degrees and post-bachelor's certificates. Challenging opportunities include advanced placement credit, accelerated degree programs, student-designed majors, double majors, independent study, and a senior project. Special programs include cooperative education, internships, summer session for credit, off-campus study, study-abroad, and Army ROTC. The most frequently chosen baccalaureate fields are business/marketing, interdisciplinary studies, and biological/life sciences. The faculty at UW-Green Bay has 173 full-time members, 85% with terminal degrees. The student-faculty ratio is 23:1.

Students of UW-Green Bay The student body totals 5,255, of whom 5,101 are undergraduates. 66.2% are women and 33.8% are men. Students come from 25 states and territories and 31 other countries. 96% are from Wisconsin. 1.1% are international students. 74% returned for their sophomore year.

Applying UW-Green Bay requires an essay, SAT I or ACT, a high school transcript, and rank in upper 45% of high school class, minimum ACT score of 17, and in some cases an interview and recommendations. The school recommends a minimum high school GPA of 2.25. Application deadline: 2/1; 4/15 priority date for financial aid. Deferred admission is possible.

UNIVERSITY OF WISCONSIN–LA CROSSE

La Crosse, WI

Suburban setting ■ Public ■ State-supported ■ Coed

Web site: www.uwlax.edu

Contact: Mr. Tim Lewis, Director of Admissions, 1725 State Street, LaCrosse, WI 54601

Telephone: 608-785-8939 **Fax:** 608-785-8940

E-mail: admissions@uwlax.edu

Getting in Last Year 5,027 applied; 65% were accepted; 1,562 enrolled (48%).

Financial Matters $3804 resident tuition and fees (2002–03); $13,850 nonresident tuition and fees (2002–03); $3800 room and board; 92% average percent of need met; $5658 average financial aid amount received per undergraduate (2001–02).

Academics UW-La Crosse awards associate, bachelor's, and master's degrees. Challenging opportunities include advanced placement credit, freshman honors college, an honors program, and double majors. Special programs include internships, summer session for credit, off-campus study, study-abroad, and Army ROTC. The most frequently chosen baccalaureate fields are business/marketing, parks and recreation, and social sciences and history. The faculty at UW-La Crosse has 375 full-time members, 77% with terminal degrees. The student-faculty ratio is 21:1.

Students of UW-La Crosse The student body totals 8,770, of whom 8,158 are undergraduates. 59.4% are women and 40.6% are men. Students come from 33 states and territories and 43 other countries. 83% are from Wisconsin. 0.5% are international students. 85% returned for their sophomore year.

Applying UW-La Crosse requires SAT I or ACT and a high school transcript, and in some cases an interview. The school recommends an essay. Application deadline: rolling admissions; 3/15 priority date for financial aid. Early and deferred admission are possible.

UNIVERSITY OF WISCONSIN–MADISON

Madison, WI

Urban setting ■ Public ■ State-supported ■ Coed

Web site: www.wisc.edu

Contact: Mr. Keith White, Associate Director of Admission, 716 Langdon Street, Madison, WI 53706-1481

Telephone: 608-262-3961 **Fax:** 608-262-7706

E-mail: on.wisconsin@mail.admin.wisc.edu

Getting in Last Year 19,249 applied; 71% were accepted; 5,514 enrolled (40%).

Financial Matters $4470 resident tuition and fees (2002–03); $18,390 nonresident tuition and fees (2002–03); $5940 room and board; $8722 average financial aid amount received per undergraduate (2001–02).

Academics Wisconsin awards bachelor's, master's, doctoral, and first-professional degrees and post-bachelor's and post-master's certificates. Challenging opportunities include advanced placement credit, student-designed majors, freshman honors college, an honors program, double majors, independent study, and a senior project. Special programs include cooperative education, internships, summer session for credit, study-abroad, and Army ROTC. The faculty at Wisconsin has 2,219 full-time members, 99% with terminal degrees. The student-faculty ratio is 14:1.

Students of Wisconsin The student body totals 41,515, of whom 29,708 are undergraduates. 53.4% are women and 46.6% are men. Students come from 52 states and territories and 116 other countries. 61% are from Wisconsin. 3.2% are international students. 96% returned for their sophomore year.

Applying Wisconsin requires an essay, SAT I or ACT, and a high school transcript, and in some cases SAT II Subject Tests. The school recommends SAT II Subject Tests. Application deadline: 2/1. Early and deferred admission are possible.

UNIVERSITY OF WISCONSIN–MILWAUKEE

Milwaukee, WI

Urban setting ■ Public ■ State-supported ■ Coed

Web site: www.uwm.edu
Contact: Ms. Jan Ford, Director, Recruitment and Outreach, PO Box 749, Milwaukee, WI 53201
Telephone: 414-229-4397 **Fax:** 414-229-6940
E-mail: uwmlook@des.uwm.edu

Getting in Last Year 8,412 applied; 78% were accepted; 3,277 enrolled (50%).

Financial Matters $4356 resident tuition and fees (2002–03); $17,108 nonresident tuition and fees (2002–03); $4400 room and board; 74% average percent of need met; $6669 average financial aid amount received per undergraduate (1999–2000).

Academics UWM awards bachelor's, master's, and doctoral degrees and post-master's certificates. Challenging opportunities include advanced placement credit, accelerated degree programs, student-designed majors, an honors program, double majors, and independent study. Special programs include cooperative education, internships, summer session for credit, off-campus study, and study-abroad. The most frequently chosen baccalaureate fields are business/marketing, education, and health professions and related sciences.

Students of UWM The student body totals 24,587, of whom 20,259 are undergraduates. 55.4% are women and 44.6% are men. Students come from 53 states and territories. 98% are from Wisconsin. 0.9% are international students. 76% returned for their sophomore year.

Applying UWM requires SAT I or ACT, ACT for state residents, and a high school transcript. The school recommends ACT. Application deadline: 8/1; 3/1 priority date for financial aid. Deferred admission is possible.

UNIVERSITY OF WISCONSIN–OSHKOSH

Oshkosh, WI

Suburban setting ■ Public ■ State-supported ■ Coed

Web site: www.uwosh.edu
Contact: Mr. Richard Hillman, Associate Director of Admissions, 800 Algoma Boulevard, Oshkosh, WI 54901
Telephone: 920-424-0202 **Fax:** 920-424-1098
E-mail: oshadmuw@uwosh.edu

Getting in Last Year 4,270 applied; 57% were accepted; 1,805 enrolled (74%).

Financial Matters $3460 resident tuition and fees (2002–03); $13,565 nonresident tuition and fees (2002–03); $3970 room and board; 55% average percent of need met; $5000 average financial aid amount received per undergraduate.

Academics UW Oshkosh awards associate, bachelor's, and master's degrees. Challenging opportunities include advanced placement credit, accelerated degree programs, student-designed majors, an honors program, double majors, independent study, and a senior project. Special programs include cooperative education, internships, summer session for credit, study-abroad, and Army ROTC. The most frequently chosen baccalaureate fields are business/marketing, education, and protective services/public administration. The faculty at UW Oshkosh has 420 full-time members, 99% with terminal degrees. The student-faculty ratio is 20:1.

Students of UW Oshkosh The student body totals 11,211, of whom 9,749 are undergraduates. 59.3% are women and 40.7% are men. Students come from 30 states and territories and 32 other countries. 98% are from Wisconsin. 0.8% are international students. 71% returned for their sophomore year.

Applying UW Oshkosh requires SAT I or ACT for nonresidents, ACT for state residents, a high school transcript, and rank in upper 50% of high school class or ACT composite score of 23 or above. The school recommends an essay. Application deadline: 8/1; 3/15 priority date for financial aid. Deferred admission is possible.

UNIVERSITY OF WISCONSIN–PARKSIDE

Kenosha, WI

Suburban setting ■ Public ■ State-supported ■ Coed

Web site: www.uwp.edu
Contact: Mr. Matthew Jensen, Director of Admissions, PO Box 2000, 900 Wood Road, Kenosha, WI 53141-2000
Telephone: 262-595-2757 or toll-free 877-633-3897 (in-state)
Fax: 262-595-2008
E-mail: matthew.jensen@uwp.edu

Getting in Last Year 1,523 applied; 91% were accepted; 831 enrolled (60%).

Financial Matters $3532 resident tuition and fees (2002–03); $13,578 nonresident tuition and fees (2002–03); $5056 room and board; 78% average percent of need met; $5953 average financial aid amount received per undergraduate.

Academics University of Wisconsin–Parkside awards bachelor's and master's degrees. Challenging opportunities include advanced placement credit, accelerated degree programs, double majors, independent study, and a senior project. Special programs include internships, summer session for credit, off-campus study, and Army ROTC. The most frequently chosen baccalaureate fields are business/marketing, social sciences and history, and communications/communication technologies. The faculty at University of Wisconsin–Parkside has 185 full-time members, 77% with terminal degrees. The student-faculty ratio is 21:1.

Students of University of Wisconsin–Parkside The student body totals 4,972, of whom 4,815 are undergraduates. 57.8% are women and 42.2% are men. Students come from 21 states and territories and 21 other countries. 91% are from Wisconsin. 1.5% are international students. 61% returned for their sophomore year.

Applying University of Wisconsin–Parkside requires a high school transcript and minimum of 17 high school units distributed as specified in the UW-Parkside catalog, and in some cases SAT I or ACT. Application deadline: 8/1; 4/1 priority date for financial aid. Deferred admission is possible.

UNIVERSITY OF WISCONSIN–PLATTEVILLE

Platteville, WI

Small-town setting ■ Public ■ State-supported ■ Coed

Web site: www.uwplatt.edu
Contact: Dr. Richard Schumacher, Dean of Admissions and Enrollment Management, 1 University Plaza, Platteville, WI 53818-3099
Telephone: 608-342-1125 or toll-free 800-362-5515 (in-state)
Fax: 608-342-1122
E-mail: admit@uwplatt.edu

Getting in Last Year 2,530 applied; 87% were accepted; 1,119 enrolled (51%).

Financial Matters $3723 resident tuition and fees (2002–03); $13,769 nonresident tuition and fees (2002–03); $3978 room and board; 85% average percent of need met; $4836 average financial aid amount received per undergraduate (2001–02).

Academics UW Platteville awards associate, bachelor's, and master's degrees. Challenging opportunities include advanced placement credit, student-designed majors, an honors program, double majors, independent study, and a senior project. Special programs include cooperative education, internships, summer session for credit, off-campus study, and study-abroad. The most frequently chosen baccalaureate fields are engineering/engineering technologies, business/marketing, and agriculture. The faculty at UW Platteville has 244 full-time members, 75% with terminal degrees. The student-faculty ratio is 22:1.

Students of UW Platteville The student body totals 6,017, of whom 5,506 are undergraduates. 39% are women and 61% are men. Students come from 34 states and territories and 47 other countries. 89% are from Wisconsin. 0.7% are international students. 60% returned for their sophomore year.

Applying UW Platteville requires SAT I or ACT and a high school transcript, and in some cases recommendations. The school recommends ACT. Application deadline: rolling admissions; 3/15 priority date for financial aid.

UNIVERSITY OF WISCONSIN–RIVER FALLS

River Falls, WI

Suburban setting ■ Public ■ State-supported ■ Coed

Web site: www.uwrf.edu
Contact: Mr. Alan Tuchtenhagen, Director of Admissions, 410 South Third Street, 112 South Hall, River Falls, WI 54022-5001
Telephone: 715-425-3500 **Fax:** 715-425-0676
E-mail: admit@uwrf.edu

Getting in Last Year 2,786 applied; 76% were accepted; 1,052 enrolled (50%).

Financial Matters $3876 resident tuition and fees (2002–03); $13,922 nonresident tuition and fees (2002–03); $3806 room and board; 77% average percent of need met; $4429 average financial aid amount received per undergraduate (1999–2000).

Academics UW River Falls awards bachelor's and master's degrees. Challenging opportunities include advanced placement credit, accelerated degree programs, student-designed majors, an honors program, double majors, independent study, and a senior project. Special programs include cooperative education, internships, summer session for credit, off-campus study, and study-abroad. The faculty at UW River Falls has 214 full-time members. The student-faculty ratio is 19:1.

Students of UW River Falls The student body totals 5,670, of whom 5,285 are undergraduates. 61.1% are women and 38.9% are men. Students come from 26 states and territories and 12 other countries. 52% are from Wisconsin. 1% are international students. 68% returned for their sophomore year.

Applying UW River Falls requires ACT and a high school transcript. The school recommends rank in upper 40% of high school class. Application deadline: rolling admissions; 3/15 priority date for financial aid. Deferred admission is possible.

UNIVERSITY OF WISCONSIN–STEVENS POINT

Stevens Point, WI

Small-town setting ■ Public ■ State-supported ■ Coed

Web site: www.uwsp.edu
Contact: Ms. Catherine Glennon, Director of Admissions, 2100 Main Street, Stevens Point, WI 54481
Telephone: 715-346-2441 **Fax:** 715-346-3296
E-mail: admiss@uwsp.edu

University of Wisconsin–Stevens Point (continued)

Getting in Last Year 4,450 applied; 72% were accepted; 1,457 enrolled (46%).

Financial Matters $3631 resident tuition and fees (2002–03); $13,677 nonresident tuition and fees (2002–03); $3816 room and board; 89% average percent of need met; $5817 average financial aid amount received per undergraduate (2001–02).

Academics UWSP awards associate, bachelor's, and master's degrees. Challenging opportunities include advanced placement credit, accelerated degree programs, student-designed majors, double majors, and independent study. Special programs include cooperative education, internships, summer session for credit, off-campus study, study-abroad, and Army ROTC. The most frequently chosen baccalaureate fields are natural resources/environmental science, business/marketing, and biological/life sciences. The faculty at UWSP has 367 full-time members, 83% with terminal degrees. The student-faculty ratio is 20:1.

Students of UWSP The student body totals 8,954, of whom 8,466 are undergraduates. 55.5% are women and 44.5% are men. Students come from 28 states and territories and 26 other countries. 94% are from Wisconsin. 1.9% are international students. 78% returned for their sophomore year.

Applying UWSP requires SAT I or ACT and a high school transcript. The school recommends campus visit. Application deadline: rolling admissions; 6/15 priority date for financial aid. Deferred admission is possible.

UNIVERSITY OF WISCONSIN–STOUT

Menomonie, WI

Small-town setting ■ Public ■ State-supported ■ Coed

Web site: www.uwstout.edu

Contact: Ms. Cynthia Jenkins, Director of Admissions, Menomonie, WI 54751

Telephone: 715-232-2639 or toll-free 800-HI-STOUT (in-state)
Fax: 715-232-1667

E-mail: admissions@uwstout.edu

Getting in Last Year 3,383 applied; 70% were accepted; 1,308 enrolled (55%).

Financial Matters $3757 resident tuition and fees (2002–03); $13,803 nonresident tuition and fees (2002–03); $3830 room and board; 85% average percent of need met; $6197 average financial aid amount received per undergraduate.

Academics UW Stout awards bachelor's and master's degrees and post-master's certificates. Challenging opportunities include advanced placement credit, accelerated degree programs, an honors program, double majors, independent study, and a senior project. Special programs include cooperative education, internships, summer session for credit, off-campus study, and study-abroad. The most frequently chosen baccalaureate fields are business/marketing, education, and engineering/engineering technologies. The faculty at UW Stout has 294 full-time members, 72% with terminal degrees. The student-faculty ratio is 19:1.

Students of UW Stout The student body totals 7,902, of whom 7,316 are undergraduates. 47.9% are women and 52.1% are men. Students come from 30 states and territories and 30 other countries. 71% are from Wisconsin. 0.4% are international students. 75% returned for their sophomore year.

Applying UW Stout requires SAT I or ACT and a high school transcript, and in some cases a minimum high school GPA of 2.75. Application deadline: rolling admissions; 4/1 priority date for financial aid.

UNIVERSITY OF WISCONSIN–SUPERIOR

Superior, WI

Small-town setting ■ Public ■ State-supported ■ Coed

Web site: www.uwsuper.edu

Contact: Ms. Lorraine Washa, Student Application Contact, Belknap and Catlin, PO Box 2000, Superior, WI 54880-4500

Telephone: 715-394-8230 or toll-free 715-394-8230 (in-state)
Fax: 715-394-8407

E-mail: admissions@uwsuper.edu

Getting in Last Year 747 applied; 76% were accepted; 313 enrolled (55%).

Financial Matters $3928 resident tuition and fees (2002–03); $13,974 nonresident tuition and fees (2002–03); $3962 room and board; $8020 average financial aid amount received per undergraduate.

Academics UW-Superior awards associate, bachelor's, master's, and first-professional degrees and post-bachelor's certificates. Challenging opportunities include advanced placement credit, student-designed majors, freshman honors college, an honors program, double majors, independent study, and a senior project. Special programs include cooperative education, internships, summer session for credit, off-campus study, study-abroad, and Air Force ROTC. The most frequently chosen baccalaureate fields are business/marketing, education, and social sciences and history. The faculty at UW-Superior has 101 full-time members, 84% with terminal degrees. The student-faculty ratio is 17:1.

Students of UW-Superior The student body totals 2,887, of whom 2,513 are undergraduates. 59.3% are women and 40.7% are men. Students come from 17 states and territories and 32 other countries. 55% are from Wisconsin. 5.7% are international students. 65% returned for their sophomore year.

Applying UW-Superior requires SAT I or ACT and a high school transcript, and in some cases recommendations and a minimum high school GPA of 2.6. The school recommends ACT and an interview. Application deadline: 4/1; 5/15 for financial aid, with a 4/15 priority date. Early and deferred admission are possible.

UNIVERSITY OF WISCONSIN–WHITEWATER

Whitewater, WI

Small-town setting ■ Public ■ State-supported ■ Coed

Web site: www.uww.edu

Contact: Dr. Tori A. McGuire, Executive Director of Admissions, 800 West Main Street, Whitewater, WI 53190-1790

Telephone: 262-472-1440 ext. 1512 **Fax:** 262-472-1515

E-mail: uwwadmit@mail.uww.edu

Getting in Last Year 5,239 applied; 74% were accepted; 2,035 enrolled (52%).

Financial Matters $4006 resident tuition and fees (2002–03); $14,414 nonresident tuition and fees (2002–03); $3570 room and board; 76% average percent of need met; $6411 average financial aid amount received per undergraduate.

Academics UW-Whitewater awards associate, bachelor's, and master's degrees. Challenging opportunities include advanced placement credit, accelerated degree programs, student-designed majors, an honors program, double majors, independent study, and a senior project. Special programs include cooperative education, internships, summer session for credit, study-abroad, and Army and Air Force ROTC. The most frequently chosen baccalaureate fields are business/marketing, education, and communications/communication technologies. The faculty at UW-Whitewater has 392 full-time members, 75% with terminal degrees. The student-faculty ratio is 20:1.

Students of UW-Whitewater The student body totals 10,796, of whom 9,513 are undergraduates. 53.8% are women and 46.2% are men. Students come from 29 states and territories and 37 other countries. 93% are from Wisconsin. 0.6% are international students. 75% returned for their sophomore year.

Applying UW-Whitewater requires a high school transcript, and in some cases SAT I or ACT and recommendations. The school recommends SAT I or ACT. Application deadline: rolling admissions; 3/15 priority date for financial aid. Early and deferred admission are possible.

UNIVERSITY OF WYOMING

Laramie, WY

Small-town setting ■ Public ■ State-supported ■ Coed

Web site: www.uwyo.edu

Contact: Ms. Sara Axelson, Associate Vice President Enrollment and Director of Admissions, Box 3435, Laramie, WY 82071

Telephone: 307-766-5160 or toll-free 800-342-5996 **Fax:** 307-766-4042

E-mail: why-wyo@uwyo.edu

Getting in Last Year 2,954 applied; 95% were accepted; 1,471 enrolled (52%).

Financial Matters $2997 resident tuition and fees (2002–03); $8661 nonresident tuition and fees (2002–03); $5120 room and board; 75% average percent of need met; $7467 average financial aid amount received per undergraduate (2001–02).

Academics UW awards bachelor's, master's, doctoral, and first-professional degrees and post-master's certificates. Challenging opportunities include advanced placement credit, accelerated degree programs, student-designed majors, an honors program, double majors, independent study, and a senior project. Special programs include internships, summer session for credit, off-campus study, study-abroad, and Army and Air Force ROTC. The most frequently chosen baccalaureate fields are education, business/marketing, and engineering/engineering technologies. The faculty at UW has 612 full-time members, 87% with terminal degrees. The student-faculty ratio is 15:1.

Students of UW The student body totals 12,745, of whom 9,250 are undergraduates. 53.1% are women and 46.9% are men. Students come from 52 states and territories and 48 other countries. 74% are from Wyoming. 1.1% are international students. 78% returned for their sophomore year.

Applying UW requires a high school transcript and a minimum high school GPA of 2.75, and in some cases SAT I or ACT and a minimum high school GPA of 3.0. The school recommends an interview. Application deadline: 8/10; 2/1 priority date for financial aid. Deferred admission is possible.

UNIVERSITY SYSTEM COLLEGE FOR LIFELONG LEARNING

Concord, NH

Rural setting ■ Public ■ State and locally supported ■ Coed

Web site: www.cll.edu

Contact: Ms. Teresa McDonnell, Associate Dean of Learner Services, 125 North State Street, Concord, NH 03301

Telephone: 603-228-3000 ext. 308 or toll-free 800-582-7248 ext. 313 (in-state)
Fax: 603-229-0964

E-mail: n_dumont@unhf.unh.edu

Financial Matters $4518 resident tuition and fees (2002–03); $4998 nonresident tuition and fees (2002–03).

Academics College for Lifelong Learning awards associate and bachelor's degrees and post-bachelor's certificates (offers primarily part-time degree programs; courses offered at 50 locations in New Hampshire). Challenging opportunities include advanced placement credit, accelerated degree programs, student-designed majors, double majors, independent study, and a senior project. Special programs include cooperative education, internships, summer session for credit, and off-campus study. The faculty at College for Lifelong Learning has 458 members, 22% with terminal degrees. The student-faculty ratio is 10:1.

Students of College for Lifelong Learning The student body totals 1,823, of whom 1,766 are undergraduates. 79.1% are women and 20.9% are men. 0.1% are international students.

Applying Application deadline: rolling admissions.

UPPER IOWA UNIVERSITY

Fayette, IA

Rural setting ■ Private ■ Independent ■ Coed

Web site: www.uiu.edu
Contact: Ms. Linda Hoopes, Director of Admissions, Box 1859, 605 Washington Street, Fayette, IA 52142-1857
Telephone: 563-425-5281 ext. 5279 or toll-free 800-553-4150 ext. 2
Fax: 563-425-5277
E-mail: admission@uiu.edu

Getting in Last Year 500 applied; 68% were accepted; 106 enrolled (31%).

Financial Matters $14,056 tuition and fees (2002–03); $4782 room and board; $6000 average financial aid amount received per undergraduate (2000–01 estimated).

Academics Upper Iowa awards associate, bachelor's, and master's degrees (also offers continuing education program with significant enrollment not reflected in profile). Challenging opportunities include advanced placement credit, accelerated degree programs, student-designed majors, double majors, independent study, and a senior project. Special programs include internships, summer session for credit, and study-abroad. The faculty at Upper Iowa has 57 full-time members, 63% with terminal degrees. The student-faculty ratio is 14:1.

Students of Upper Iowa The student body totals 870, of whom 630 are undergraduates. 35.7% are women and 64.3% are men. Students come from 25 states and territories and 7 other countries. 58% are from Iowa. 6.8% are international students. 3% returned for their sophomore year.

Applying Upper Iowa requires SAT I or ACT, a high school transcript, and a minimum high school GPA of 2.0, and in some cases an essay, an interview, and recommendations. Application deadline: rolling admissions; 6/1 priority date for financial aid. Early and deferred admission are possible.

URBANA UNIVERSITY

Urbana, OH

Small-town setting ■ Private ■ Independent Religious ■ Coed

Web site: www.urbana.edu
Contact: Ms. Melissa Tolle, Associate Director of Admissions, 579 College Way, Urbana, OH 93078
Telephone: 937-484-1356 or toll-free 800-787-2262 ext. 1356 (in-state)
Fax: 937-484-1389
E-mail: admiss@urbana.edu

Getting in Last Year 520 applied; 57% were accepted; 159 enrolled (54%).

Financial Matters $12,820 tuition and fees (2002–03); $5140 room and board; 62% average percent of need met; $11,636 average financial aid amount received per undergraduate.

Academics Urbana awards associate, bachelor's, and master's degrees. Challenging opportunities include advanced placement credit, accelerated degree programs, student-designed majors, an honors program, double majors, independent study, and a senior project. Special programs include cooperative education, internships, summer session for credit, and off-campus study. The most frequently chosen baccalaureate fields are business/marketing, education, and communications/communication technologies. The faculty at Urbana has 50 full-time members, 56% with terminal degrees. The student-faculty ratio is 16:1.

Students of Urbana The student body totals 1,411, of whom 1,338 are undergraduates. 56.4% are women and 43.6% are men. Students come from 11 states and territories and 2 other countries. 99% are from Ohio. 0.3% are international students. 76% returned for their sophomore year.

Applying Urbana requires an essay, SAT I or ACT, a high school transcript, and a minimum high school GPA of 2.0, and in some cases an interview and 2 recommendations. The school recommends an interview. Application deadline: rolling admissions; 4/1 priority date for financial aid. Deferred admission is possible.

URSINUS COLLEGE

Collegeville, PA

Suburban setting ■ Private ■ Independent Religious ■ Coed

Web site: www.ursinus.edu
Contact: Mr. Paul M. Cramer, Director of Admissions, Box 1000, Main Street, Collegeville, PA 19426
Telephone: 610-409-3200 **Fax:** 610-409-3662
E-mail: admissions@ursinus.edu

Getting in Last Year 1,562 applied; 78% were accepted.

Financial Matters $26,200 tuition and fees (2002–03); $6600 room and board; 90% average percent of need met; $21,981 average financial aid amount received per undergraduate.

Academics Ursinus awards bachelor's degrees. Challenging opportunities include advanced placement credit, student-designed majors, an honors program, double majors, independent study, and a senior project. Special programs include internships, off-campus study, and study-abroad. The faculty at Ursinus has 97 full-time members, 87% with terminal degrees. The student-faculty ratio is 11:1.

Students of Ursinus The student body is made up of 1,340 undergraduates. 57% are women and 43% are men. Students come from 25 states and territories and 19 other countries. 72% are from Pennsylvania. 3.4% are international students. 94% returned for their sophomore year.

Applying Ursinus requires an essay, SAT I or ACT, a high school transcript, 2 recommendations, and a graded paper. The school recommends SAT II Subject Tests and an interview. Application deadline: 2/15; 2/15 priority date for financial aid. Early and deferred admission are possible.

URSULINE COLLEGE

Pepper Pike, OH

Suburban setting ■ Private ■ Independent Religious ■ Women Only

Web site: www.ursuline.edu
Contact: Ms. Sarah Carr, Director of Admissions, 2550 Lander Road, Pepper Pike, OH 44124
Telephone: 440-449-4203 or toll-free 888-URSULINE **Fax:** 440-684-6138
E-mail: admission@ursuline.edu

Getting in Last Year 290 applied; 67% were accepted; 96 enrolled (49%).

Financial Matters $15,900 tuition and fees (2002–03); $5030 room and board; $13,976 average financial aid amount received per undergraduate.

Academics Ursuline awards bachelor's and master's degrees (applications from men are also accepted). Challenging opportunities include advanced placement credit, accelerated degree programs, double majors, independent study, and a senior project. Special programs include cooperative education, internships, summer session for credit, and off-campus study. The most frequently chosen baccalaureate fields are health professions and related sciences, business/marketing, and psychology. The faculty at Ursuline has 62 full-time members, 65% with terminal degrees. The student-faculty ratio is 9:1.

Students of Ursuline The student body totals 1,319, of whom 1,008 are undergraduates. Students come from 8 states and territories and 7 other countries. 98% are from Ohio. 0.9% are international students. 64% returned for their sophomore year.

Applying Ursuline requires SAT I or ACT and a high school transcript. The school recommends an essay, an interview, recommendations, and a minimum high school GPA of 2.0. Application deadline: rolling admissions; 3/15 priority date for financial aid. Deferred admission is possible.

UTAH STATE UNIVERSITY

Logan, UT

Urban setting ■ Public ■ State-supported ■ Coed

Web site: www.usu.edu
Contact: Dr. Eric Olsen, Director, Recruitment and Enrollment Services, 0160 Old Main Hill, Logan, UT 84322-0160
Telephone: 435-797-1129 or toll-free 800-488-8108 **Fax:** 435-797-3708
E-mail: admit@cc.usu.edu

Getting in Last Year 5,689 applied; 89% were accepted; 2,663 enrolled (53%).

Financial Matters $2898 resident tuition and fees (2002–03); $8199 nonresident tuition and fees (2002–03); $4180 room and board; 59% average percent of need met; $4830 average financial aid amount received per undergraduate (2001–02).

Academics USU awards associate, bachelor's, master's, and doctoral degrees. Challenging opportunities include advanced placement credit, accelerated degree programs, student-designed majors, freshman honors college, an honors program, double majors, independent study, and a senior project. Special programs include cooperative education, internships, summer session for credit, off-campus study, study-abroad, and Army and Air Force ROTC. The most frequently chosen baccalaureate fields are business/marketing, education, and home economics/vocational home economics. The faculty at USU has 719 full-time members, 87% with terminal degrees. The student-faculty ratio is 26:1.

Students of USU The student body totals 22,848, of whom 19,736 are undergraduates. 51.6% are women and 48.4% are men. Students come from 52 states and territories and 55 other countries. 70% are from Utah. 2.5% are international students.

Utah State University (continued)

Applying USU requires SAT I or ACT and a high school transcript. The school recommends ACT and a minimum high school GPA of 2.75. Early and deferred admission are possible.

UTICA COLLEGE

Utica, NY

Suburban setting ■ Private ■ Independent ■ Coed

Web site: www.utica.edu

Contact: Mr. Patrick Quinn, Vice President for Enrollment Management, 160 Burrstone Road, Utica, NY 13502

Telephone: 315-792-3006 or toll-free 800-782-8884 **Fax:** 315-792-3003

E-mail: admiss@utica.edu

Getting in Last Year 2,007 applied; 79% were accepted; 455 enrolled (29%).

Financial Matters $19,118 tuition and fees (2002–03); $7580 room and board.

Academics Utica College awards bachelor's and master's degrees. Challenging opportunities include advanced placement credit, accelerated degree programs, freshman honors college, an honors program, double majors, independent study, and a senior project. Special programs include cooperative education, internships, summer session for credit, off-campus study, study-abroad, and Army and Air Force ROTC. The most frequently chosen baccalaureate fields are health professions and related sciences, business/marketing, and protective services/ public administration. The faculty at Utica College has 102 full-time members, 94% with terminal degrees. The student-faculty ratio is 17:1.

Students of Utica College The student body totals 2,392, of whom 2,177 are undergraduates. 57.5% are women and 42.5% are men. Students come from 28 states and territories and 20 other countries. 92% are from New York. 2.2% are international students. 68% returned for their sophomore year.

Applying Utica College requires an essay, a high school transcript, and a minimum high school GPA of 2.0, and in some cases a minimum high school GPA of 3.0. The school recommends SAT I or ACT, an interview, and recommendations. Application deadline: rolling admissions; 2/15 priority date for financial aid.

VALDOSTA STATE UNIVERSITY

Valdosta, GA

Small-town setting ■ Public ■ State-supported ■ Coed

Web site: www.valdosta.edu

Contact: Mr. Walter Peacock, Director of Admissions, 1500 North Patterson Street, Valdosta, GA 31698

Telephone: 229-333-5791 or toll-free 800-618-1878 ext. 1 **Fax:** 229-333-5482

E-mail: admissions@valdosta.edu

Getting in Last Year 4,844 applied; 71% were accepted; 1,584 enrolled (46%).

Financial Matters $2634 resident tuition and fees (2002–03); $8664 nonresident tuition and fees (2002–03); $4680 room and board; 86% average percent of need met; $7050 average financial aid amount received per undergraduate (2001–02).

Academics Valdosta State awards associate, bachelor's, master's, and doctoral degrees. Challenging opportunities include advanced placement credit, accelerated degree programs, freshman honors college, and an honors program. Special programs include cooperative education, internships, summer session for credit, off-campus study, study-abroad, and Air Force ROTC. The most frequently chosen baccalaureate fields are education, social sciences and history, and health professions and related sciences. The faculty at Valdosta State has 468 full-time members, 74% with terminal degrees. The student-faculty ratio is 16:1.

Students of Valdosta State The student body totals 9,919, of whom 8,419 are undergraduates. 60.5% are women and 39.5% are men. Students come from 48 states and territories and 53 other countries. 93% are from Georgia. 1.7% are international students. 68% returned for their sophomore year.

Applying Valdosta State requires SAT I or ACT, a high school transcript, proof of immunization, and a minimum high school GPA of 2.0. Application deadline: 8/1; 5/1 priority date for financial aid. Early and deferred admission are possible.

VALLEY CITY STATE UNIVERSITY

Valley City, ND

Small-town setting ■ Public ■ State-supported ■ Coed

Web site: www.vcsu.edu

Contact: Mr. Monte Johnson, Director of Admissions, 101 College Street Southwest, Valley City, ND 58072

Telephone: 701-845-7101 ext. 37297 or toll-free 800-532-8641 ext. 37101 **Fax:** 701-845-7299

E-mail: enrollment_services@mail.vcsu.nodak.edu

Getting in Last Year 290 applied; 94% were accepted; 162 enrolled (59%).

Financial Matters $2202 resident tuition and fees (2002–03); $5879 nonresident tuition and fees (2002–03); $3130 room and board; 93% average percent of need met; $6043 average financial aid amount received per undergraduate (2001–02).

Academics VCSU awards bachelor's degrees. Challenging opportunities include student-designed majors, double majors, and a senior project. Special programs include cooperative education, internships, summer session for credit, and off-campus study. The most frequently chosen baccalaureate fields are education, business/marketing, and liberal arts/general studies. The faculty at VCSU has 61 full-time members, 39% with terminal degrees. The student-faculty ratio is 12:1.

Students of VCSU The student body is made up of 1,022 undergraduates. 54.8% are women and 45.2% are men. Students come from 27 states and territories and 8 other countries. 75% are from North Dakota. 4.6% are international students. 57% returned for their sophomore year.

Applying VCSU requires SAT I or ACT and a high school transcript. Application deadline: rolling admissions; 3/15 priority date for financial aid. Early and deferred admission are possible.

VALLEY FORGE CHRISTIAN COLLEGE

Phoenixville, PA

Small-town setting ■ Private ■ Independent Religious ■ Coed

Web site: www.vfcc.edu

Contact: Rev. William Chenco, Director of Admissions, 1401 Charlestown Road, Phoenixville, PA 19460

Telephone: 610-935-0450 ext. 1430 or toll-free 800-432-8322 **Fax:** 610-935-9353

E-mail: admissions@vfcc.edu

Getting in Last Year 341 applied; 48% were accepted.

Financial Matters $8872 tuition and fees (2002–03); $4780 room and board; 62% average percent of need met; $6877 average financial aid amount received per undergraduate (2001–02).

Academics VFCC awards associate and bachelor's degrees. Challenging opportunities include advanced placement credit, double majors, and independent study. Special programs include internships and summer session for credit. The most frequently chosen baccalaureate field is education. The faculty at VFCC has 28 full-time members, 29% with terminal degrees. The student-faculty ratio is 19:1.

Students of VFCC The student body is made up of 722 undergraduates. 49.9% are women and 50.1% are men. Students come from 23 states and territories and 2 other countries. 60% are from Pennsylvania. 0.6% are international students.

Applying VFCC requires SAT I or ACT, a high school transcript, and 2 recommendations, and in some cases an interview. The school recommends an essay. Application deadline: 8/15; 5/1 priority date for financial aid. Early and deferred admission are possible.

VALPARAISO UNIVERSITY

Valparaiso, IN

Small-town setting ■ Private ■ Independent Religious ■ Coed

Web site: www.valpo.edu

Contact: Ms. Karen Foust, Director of Admissions, Kretzmann Hall, 1700 Chapel Drive, Valparaiso, IN 46383-6493

Telephone: 219-464-5011 or toll-free 888-GO-VALPO (out-of-state) **Fax:** 219-464-6898

E-mail: undergrad.admissions@valpo.edu

Getting in Last Year 3,117 applied; 91% were accepted; 717 enrolled (25%).

Financial Matters $19,632 tuition and fees (2002–03); $5130 room and board; 94% average percent of need met; $16,448 average financial aid amount received per undergraduate.

Academics Valpo awards associate, bachelor's, master's, and first-professional degrees and post-bachelor's and post-master's certificates. Challenging opportunities include advanced placement credit, accelerated degree programs, student-designed majors, freshman honors college, an honors program, double majors, independent study, and a senior project. Special programs include cooperative education, internships, summer session for credit, off-campus study, study-abroad, and Air Force ROTC. The most frequently chosen baccalaureate fields are business/marketing, education, and engineering/engineering technologies. The faculty at Valpo has 225 full-time members, 87% with terminal degrees. The student-faculty ratio is 13:1.

Students of Valpo The student body totals 3,661, of whom 2,910 are undergraduates. 53% are women and 47% are men. Students come from 49 states and territories and 37 other countries. 34% are from Indiana. 2.5% are international students. 86% returned for their sophomore year.

Applying Valpo requires SAT I or ACT and a high school transcript, and in some cases an interview. The school recommends an essay and 2 recommendations. Application deadline: 8/15; 3/1 priority date for financial aid. Deferred admission is possible.

VANDERBILT UNIVERSITY

Nashville, TN

Urban setting ■ Private ■ Independent ■ Coed

Web site: www.vanderbilt.edu
Contact: Mr. Bill Shain, Dean of Undergraduate Admissions, Nashville, TN 37240-1001
Telephone: 615-322-2561 or toll-free 800-288-0432 **Fax:** 615-343-7765
E-mail: admissions@vanderbilt.edu

Getting in Last Year 9,836 applied; 46% were accepted; 1,579 enrolled (35%).

Financial Matters $27,087 tuition and fees (2002–03); $9060 room and board; 99% average percent of need met; $27,981 average financial aid amount received per undergraduate.

Academics Vanderbilt awards bachelor's, master's, doctoral, and first-professional degrees. Challenging opportunities include advanced placement credit, accelerated degree programs, student-designed majors, an honors program, double majors, independent study, and a senior project. Special programs include cooperative education, internships, summer session for credit, off-campus study, study-abroad, and Army, Navy and Air Force ROTC. The most frequently chosen baccalaureate fields are social sciences and history, engineering/engineering technologies, and biological/life sciences. The faculty at Vanderbilt has 690 full-time members, 97% with terminal degrees. The student-faculty ratio is 9:1.

Students of Vanderbilt The student body totals 10,712, of whom 6,146 are undergraduates. 51.8% are women and 48.2% are men. Students come from 54 states and territories and 36 other countries. 20% are from Tennessee. 2.1% are international students. 94% returned for their sophomore year.

Applying Vanderbilt requires an essay, SAT I or ACT, a high school transcript, and 2 recommendations. The school recommends SAT II Subject Tests and SAT II: Writing Test. Application deadline: 1/3; 2/1 priority date for financial aid. Early and deferred admission are possible.

VANDERCOOK COLLEGE OF MUSIC

Chicago, IL

Urban setting ■ *Private* ■ *Independent* ■ *Coed*

Web site: www.vandercook.edu
Contact: Mr. James Malley, Director of Undergraduate Admission, 3140 South Federal Street, Chicago, IL 60616
Telephone: 800-448-2655 ext. 241 or toll-free 800-448-2655 ext. 230 **Fax:** 312-225-5211
E-mail: admissions@vandercook.edu

Getting in Last Year 36 applied; 81% were accepted; 24 enrolled (83%).

Financial Matters $14,490 tuition and fees (2002–03); $5945 room and board; $7983 average financial aid amount received per undergraduate (2001–02 estimated).

Academics VCM awards bachelor's and master's degrees. Challenging opportunities include advanced placement credit, independent study, and a senior project. Internships is a special program. The most frequently chosen baccalaureate field is education. The faculty at VCM has 7 full-time members, 14% with terminal degrees. The student-faculty ratio is 7:1.

Students of VCM The student body totals 214, of whom 132 are undergraduates. 39.4% are women and 60.6% are men. Students come from 9 states and territories and 2 other countries. 71% are from Illinois. 2.3% are international students. 85% returned for their sophomore year.

Applying VCM requires an essay, SAT I or ACT, a high school transcript, an interview, 3 recommendations, and audition, and in some cases a minimum high school GPA of 3.0. The school recommends a minimum high school GPA of 3.0. Application deadline: 5/1; 6/7 for financial aid. Deferred admission is possible.

VANGUARD UNIVERSITY OF SOUTHERN CALIFORNIA

Costa Mesa, CA

Suburban setting ■ *Private* ■ *Independent Religious* ■ *Coed*

Web site: www.vanguard.edu
Contact: Ms. Jessica Mireles, Director of Admissions, 55 Fair Drive, Costa Mesa, CA 92626
Telephone: 714-556-3610 ext. 327 or toll-free 800-722-6279 **Fax:** 714-966-5471
E-mail: admissions@vanguard.edu

Getting in Last Year 798 applied; 79% were accepted; 322 enrolled (51%).

Financial Matters $15,308 tuition and fees (2002–03); $5458 room and board; 76% average percent of need met; $12,651 average financial aid amount received per undergraduate.

Academics VU awards bachelor's and master's degrees. Challenging opportunities include advanced placement credit, accelerated degree programs, double majors, independent study, and a senior project. Special programs include internships, summer session for credit, off-campus study, study-abroad, and Air Force ROTC. The most frequently chosen baccalaureate fields are business/marketing, psychology, and education. The faculty at VU has 71 full-time members, 65% with terminal degrees. The student-faculty ratio is 16:1.

Students of VU The student body totals 1,540, of whom 1,227 are undergraduates. 60.7% are women and 39.3% are men. Students come from 40 states and territories and 10 other countries. 79% are from California. 0.8% are international students. 74% returned for their sophomore year.

Applying VU requires an essay, SAT I or ACT, a high school transcript, 1 recommendation, and a minimum high school GPA of 2.8, and in some cases an interview. Application deadline: rolling admissions; 3/2 for financial aid. Deferred admission is possible.

VASSAR COLLEGE

Poughkeepsie, NY

Suburban setting ■ *Private* ■ *Independent* ■ *Coed*

Web site: www.vassar.edu
Contact: Dr. David M. Borus, Dean of Admission and Financial Aid, 124 Raymond Avenue, Poughkeepsie, NY 12604
Telephone: 845-437-7300 or toll-free 800-827-7270 **Fax:** 914-437-7063
E-mail: admissions@vassar.edu

Getting in Last Year 5,733 applied; 31% were accepted; 632 enrolled (36%).

Financial Matters $27,960 tuition and fees (2002–03); $7340 room and board; 100% average percent of need met; $23,655 average financial aid amount received per undergraduate.

Academics Vassar awards bachelor's and master's degrees. Challenging opportunities include advanced placement credit, student-designed majors, double majors, independent study, and a senior project. Special programs include cooperative education, internships, off-campus study, and study-abroad. The most frequently chosen baccalaureate fields are social sciences and history, visual/performing arts, and English. The faculty at Vassar has 258 full-time members, 98% with terminal degrees. The student-faculty ratio is 9:1.

Students of Vassar The student body is made up of 2,472 undergraduates. 61% are women and 39% are men. Students come from 52 states and territories and 44 other countries. 29% are from New York. 4.5% are international students. 94% returned for their sophomore year.

Applying Vassar requires an essay, SAT I and SAT II or ACT, a high school transcript, and 2 recommendations. The school recommends an interview. Application deadline: 1/1; 2/1 for financial aid. Deferred admission is possible.

VENNARD COLLEGE

University Park, IA

Private ■ *Independent Religious* ■ *Coed*

Web site: www.vennard.edu
Contact: Randy Ozan, Director of Admissions, PO Box 29, University Park, IA 52595
Telephone: 641-673-8391 ext. 218 or toll-free 800-686-8391 **Fax:** 641-673-8365

Getting in Last Year 51 applied; 47% were accepted.

Financial Matters 60% average percent of need met; $7000 average financial aid amount received per undergraduate.

Academics Vennard awards associate and bachelor's degrees. Challenging opportunities include advanced placement credit, student-designed majors, double majors, and independent study. Special programs include cooperative education, internships, summer session for credit, and off-campus study. The faculty at Vennard has 6 full-time members, 33% with terminal degrees. The student-faculty ratio is 11:1.

Students of Vennard The student body is made up of 114 undergraduates. Students come from 19 states and territories and 2 other countries. 45% are from Iowa. 1.8% are international students.

Applying Vennard requires an essay, a high school transcript, 3 recommendations, and a minimum high school GPA of 2.5, and in some cases SAT I and SAT II or ACT. The school recommends SAT I or ACT. Application deadline: 4/1 priority date for financial aid. Early admission is possible.

VERMONT TECHNICAL COLLEGE

Randolph Center, VT

Rural setting ■ *Public* ■ *State-supported* ■ *Coed*

Web site: www.vtc.edu
Contact: Ms. Rosemary W. Distel, Director of Admissions, PO Box 500, Randolph Center, VT 05061
Telephone: 802-728-1245 or toll-free 800-442-VTC1 **Fax:** 802-728-1390
E-mail: admissions@vtc.edu

Getting in Last Year 751 applied; 67% were accepted; 258 enrolled (51%).

Financial Matters $6488 resident tuition and fees (2002–03); $12,208 nonresident tuition and fees (2002–03); $5782 room and board; 78% average percent of need met; $9200 average financial aid amount received per undergraduate (2001–02).

Academics Vermont Tech awards associate and bachelor's degrees. Challenging opportunities include advanced placement credit, accelerated degree programs, an honors program, double majors, independent study, and a senior project. Special programs include cooperative education, internships, summer session for credit, and Army ROTC. The most frequently chosen baccalaureate fields are architecture and engineering/engineering technologies. The faculty at Vermont Tech has 73 full-time members, 29% with terminal degrees. The student-faculty ratio is 11:1.

Vermont Technical College (continued)

Students of Vermont Tech The student body is made up of 1,256 undergraduates. 32.2% are women and 67.8% are men. Students come from 12 states and territories and 4 other countries. 84% are from Vermont. 0.6% are international students. 65% returned for their sophomore year.

Applying Vermont Tech requires a high school transcript, and in some cases an essay, SAT I, SAT I or ACT, nursing examination, an interview, and recommendations. The school recommends SAT I or ACT, an interview, recommendations, and a minimum high school GPA of 3.0. Application deadline: rolling admissions; 3/1 priority date for financial aid.

VILLA JULIE COLLEGE

Stevenson, MD

Suburban setting ■ Private ■ Independent ■ Coed

Web site: www.vjc.edu

Contact: Mr. Mark Hergan, Dean of Admissions, 125 Greenspring Valley Road, Stevenson, MD 21153

Telephone: 410-486-7001 or toll-free 877-468-6852 (in-state), 877-468-3852 (out-of-state) **Fax:** 410-602-6600

E-mail: admissions@vjc.edu

Getting in Last Year 1,493 applied; 83% were accepted; 490 enrolled (40%).

Financial Matters $12,798 tuition and fees (2002–03); $4450 room only; 41% average percent of need met; $17,560 average financial aid amount received per undergraduate.

Academics VJC awards associate, bachelor's, and master's degrees. Challenging opportunities include advanced placement credit, accelerated degree programs, student-designed majors, freshman honors college, an honors program, double majors, independent study, and a senior project. Special programs include cooperative education, internships, summer session for credit, off-campus study, and Army ROTC. The most frequently chosen baccalaureate fields are computer/information sciences, health professions and related sciences, and interdisciplinary studies. The faculty at VJC has 80 full-time members, 63% with terminal degrees. The student-faculty ratio is 12:1.

Students of VJC The student body totals 2,500, of whom 2,437 are undergraduates. 73.9% are women and 26.1% are men. Students come from 11 states and territories and 5 other countries. 97% are from Maryland. 0.2% are international students. 76% returned for their sophomore year.

Applying VJC requires an essay, SAT I or ACT, a high school transcript, an interview, and 2 recommendations. The school recommends a minimum high school GPA of 3.0. Application deadline: 7/15; 3/1 priority date for financial aid. Early and deferred admission are possible.

VILLANOVA UNIVERSITY

Villanova, PA

Suburban setting ■ Private ■ Independent Religious ■ Coed

Web site: www.villanova.edu

Contact: Mr. Michael M. Gaynor, Director of University Admission, 800 Lancaster Avenue, Villanova, PA 19085-1672

Telephone: 610-519-4000 or toll-free 610-519-4000 **Fax:** 610-519-6450

E-mail: gotovu@villanova.edu

Getting in Last Year 10,896 applied; 47% were accepted; 1,584 enrolled (31%).

Financial Matters $24,090 tuition and fees (2002–03); $8330 room and board; 76% average percent of need met; $17,641 average financial aid amount received per undergraduate.

Academics Villanova awards associate, bachelor's, master's, doctoral, and first-professional degrees. Challenging opportunities include advanced placement credit, accelerated degree programs, an honors program, double majors, independent study, and a senior project. Special programs include internships, summer session for credit, off-campus study, study-abroad, and Army, Navy and Air Force ROTC. The most frequently chosen baccalaureate fields are business/marketing, social sciences and history, and engineering/engineering technologies. The faculty at Villanova has 511 full-time members, 89% with terminal degrees. The student-faculty ratio is 13:1.

Students of Villanova The student body totals 10,489, of whom 7,375 are undergraduates. 50.5% are women and 49.5% are men. Students come from 49 states and territories and 29 other countries. 34% are from Pennsylvania. 2.3% are international students. 94% returned for their sophomore year.

Applying Villanova requires an essay, SAT I or ACT, a high school transcript, and activities resume. Application deadline: 1/7; 2/14 priority date for financial aid. Early and deferred admission are possible.

VIRGINIA COLLEGE AT BIRMINGHAM

Birmingham, AL

Urban setting ■ Private ■ Proprietary ■ Coed

Web site: www.vc.edu

Contact: Ms. Bibbie J. McLaughlin, Director of Admissions, 65 Bagby Drive, PO Box 19249, Birmingham, AL 35209

Telephone: 205-802-1200 ext. 1207 **Fax:** 205-802-7045

E-mail: bibbie@vc.edu

Getting in Last Year 600 applied; 86% were accepted; 515 enrolled (100%).

Financial Matters $10,100 tuition and fees (2002–03); $7500 average financial aid amount received per undergraduate.

Academics Virginia College at Birmingham awards associate and bachelor's degrees. The faculty at Virginia College at Birmingham has 138 full-time members. The student-faculty ratio is 14:1.

Students of Virginia College at Birmingham The student body is made up of 2,407 undergraduates. 65.6% are women and 34.4% are men. Students come from 7 states and territories. 70% returned for their sophomore year.

Applying Virginia College at Birmingham requires CPAt and a high school transcript. Application deadline: rolling admissions.

VIRGINIA COMMONWEALTH UNIVERSITY

Richmond, VA

Urban setting ■ Public ■ State-supported ■ Coed

Web site: www.vcu.edu

Contact: Counseling Staff, 821 West Franklin Street, Box 842526, Richmond, VA 23284-2526

Telephone: 804-828-1222 or toll-free 800-841-3638 **Fax:** 804-828-1899

E-mail: vcuinfo@vcu.edu

Getting in Last Year 8,540 applied; 73% were accepted; 3,048 enrolled (49%).

Financial Matters $4218 resident tuition and fees (2002–03); $15,188 nonresident tuition and fees (2002–03); $5750 room and board; 54% average percent of need met; $6457 average financial aid amount received per undergraduate (2001–02).

Academics VCU awards bachelor's, master's, doctoral, and first-professional degrees and post-bachelor's and post-master's certificates. Challenging opportunities include advanced placement credit, accelerated degree programs, student-designed majors, an honors program, double majors, independent study, and a senior project. Special programs include cooperative education, internships, summer session for credit, off-campus study, study-abroad, and Army ROTC. The most frequently chosen baccalaureate fields are visual/performing arts, business/marketing, and health professions and related sciences. The faculty at VCU has 1,078 full-time members. The student-faculty ratio is 13:1.

Students of VCU The student body totals 26,009, of whom 18,069 are undergraduates. 57.9% are women and 42.1% are men. Students come from 45 states and territories and 71 other countries. 94% are from Virginia. 1.3% are international students. 77% returned for their sophomore year.

Applying VCU requires SAT I or ACT and a high school transcript, and in some cases an interview, 2 recommendations, and a minimum high school GPA of 3.0. The school recommends an essay and a minimum high school GPA of 2.5. Application deadline: 2/1; 4/1 priority date for financial aid. Early and deferred admission are possible.

VIRGINIA INTERMONT COLLEGE

Bristol, VA

Small-town setting ■ Private ■ Independent Religious ■ Coed

Web site: www.vic.edu

Contact: Mr. Everett Honaker, Vice President for Enrollment Management, 1013 Moore Street, Campus Box D-460, Bristol, VA 24201

Telephone: 540-645-7857 or toll-free 800-451-1842 **Fax:** 540-466-7855

E-mail: viadmit@vic.edu

Getting in Last Year 722 applied; 50% were accepted.

Financial Matters $13,220 tuition and fees (2002–03); $5470 room and board; 56% average percent of need met; $11,747 average financial aid amount received per undergraduate.

Academics VI awards associate and bachelor's degrees. Challenging opportunities include advanced placement credit, double majors, independent study, and a senior project. Special programs include internships, summer session for credit, off-campus study, and study-abroad. The most frequently chosen baccalaureate fields are business/marketing, education, and visual/performing arts. The faculty at VI has 58 full-time members, 48% with terminal degrees. The student-faculty ratio is 15:1.

Students of VI The student body is made up of 1,045 undergraduates. Students come from 29 states and territories and 9 other countries. 54% are from Virginia. 1.1% are international students. 50% returned for their sophomore year.

Applying VI requires SAT I or ACT, a high school transcript, and a minimum high school GPA of 2.0, and in some cases an essay. The school recommends an interview. Application deadline: rolling admissions. Early and deferred admission are possible.

VIRGINIA MILITARY INSTITUTE

Lexington, VA

Small-town setting ■ Public ■ State-supported ■ Coed, Primarily Men

Web site: www.vmi.edu
Contact: Lt. Col. Tom Mortenson, Associate Director of Admissions, 309 Letcher Avenue, Lexington, VA 24450
Telephone: 540-464-7211 or toll-free 800-767-4207 **Fax:** 540-464-7746
E-mail: admissions@vmi.edu

Getting in Last Year 1,479 applied; 55% were accepted; 359 enrolled (44%).

Financial Matters $5582 resident tuition and fees (2002–03); $17,402 nonresident tuition and fees (2002–03); $5055 room and board; 92% average percent of need met; $12,369 average financial aid amount received per undergraduate.

Academics VMI awards bachelor's degrees. Challenging opportunities include advanced placement credit, accelerated degree programs, an honors program, double majors, independent study, and a senior project. Special programs include internships, summer session for credit, study-abroad, and Army, Navy and Air Force ROTC. The faculty at VMI has 102 full-time members, 95% with terminal degrees. The student-faculty ratio is 11:1.

Students of VMI The student body is made up of 1,299 undergraduates. 5.9% are women and 94.1% are men. Students come from 44 states and territories and 19 other countries. 51% are from Virginia. 3% are international students. 86% returned for their sophomore year.

Applying VMI requires SAT I or ACT and a high school transcript. The school recommends an essay, an interview, and 2 recommendations. Application deadline: 3/1; 3/1 priority date for financial aid. Early admission is possible.

VIRGINIA POLYTECHNIC INSTITUTE AND STATE UNIVERSITY

Blacksburg, VA

Small-town setting ■ Public ■ State-supported ■ Coed

Web site: www.vt.edu
Contact: Ms. Mildred Johnson, Associate Director for Freshmen Admissions, 201 Burruss Hall, Blacksburg, VA 24061
Telephone: 540-231-6267 **Fax:** 540-231-3242
E-mail: vtadmiss@vt.edu

Getting in Last Year 17,800 applied; 65% were accepted; 5,778 enrolled (50%).

Financial Matters $4336 resident tuition and fees (2002–03); $13,952 nonresident tuition and fees (2002–03); $4070 room and board; 64% average percent of need met; $7044 average financial aid amount received per undergraduate.

Academics Virginia Tech awards associate, bachelor's, master's, doctoral, and first-professional degrees. Challenging opportunities include advanced placement credit, accelerated degree programs, an honors program, double majors, independent study, and a senior project. Special programs include cooperative education, internships, summer session for credit, study-abroad, and Army, Navy and Air Force ROTC. The faculty at Virginia Tech has 1,242 full-time members. The student-faculty ratio is 15:1.

Students of Virginia Tech The student body totals 27,662, of whom 21,468 are undergraduates. 40.7% are women and 59.3% are men. Students come from 52 states and territories and 104 other countries. 71% are from Virginia. 3% are international students. 90% returned for their sophomore year.

Applying Virginia Tech requires SAT I or ACT, a high school transcript, and a minimum high school GPA of 2.0. The school recommends a minimum high school GPA of 3.3. Application deadline: 1/15; 3/11 priority date for financial aid. Early and deferred admission are possible.

VIRGINIA STATE UNIVERSITY

Petersburg, VA

Suburban setting ■ Public ■ State-supported ■ Coed

Web site: www.vsu.edu
Contact: Mrs. Irene Logan, Director of Admissions (Interim), PO Box 9018, Petersburg, VA 23806-2096
Telephone: 804-524-5902 or toll-free 800-871-7611
E-mail: lwinn@vsu.edu

Getting in Last Year 3,780 applied; 66% were accepted; 1,133 enrolled (46%).

Financial Matters $3804 resident tuition and fees (2002–03); $10,398 nonresident tuition and fees (2002–03); $5694 room and board; 75% average percent of need met; $7975 average financial aid amount received per undergraduate.

Academics VSU awards bachelor's, master's, and doctoral degrees and post-master's certificates. Challenging opportunities include advanced placement credit, student-designed majors, an honors program, double majors, independent study, and a senior project. Special programs include cooperative education, internships, summer session for credit, and Army ROTC. The most frequently chosen baccalaureate fields are business/marketing, social sciences and history, and interdisciplinary studies. The faculty at VSU has 207 full-time members, 80% with terminal degrees. The student-faculty ratio is 18:1.

Students of VSU The student body totals 4,974, of whom 4,144 are undergraduates. 56.6% are women and 43.4% are men. Students come from 27 states and territories. 65% are from Virginia. 72% returned for their sophomore year.

Applying VSU requires SAT I or ACT, a high school transcript, 2 recommendations, and a minimum high school GPA of 2.2. Application deadline: 5/1; 5/1 for financial aid, with a 3/31 priority date.

VIRGINIA UNION UNIVERSITY

Richmond, VA

Urban setting ■ Private ■ Independent Religious ■ Coed

Web site: www.vuu.edu
Contact: Mr. Gil Powell, Director of Admissions, 1500 North Lombardy Street, Richmond, VA 23220-1170
Telephone: 804-257-5881 or toll-free 800-368-3227 (out-of-state)

Getting in Last Year 2,991 applied; 68% were accepted; 443 enrolled (22%).

Financial Matters $11,400 tuition and fees (2002–03); $4932 room and board; 77% average percent of need met; $7075 average financial aid amount received per undergraduate.

Academics VUU awards bachelor's, master's, doctoral, and first-professional degrees. Challenging opportunities include advanced placement credit and an honors program. Special programs include cooperative education, internships, summer session for credit, off-campus study, and Army ROTC. The most frequently chosen baccalaureate fields are business/marketing, social sciences and history, and education. The faculty at VUU has 84 full-time members, 44% with terminal degrees. The student-faculty ratio is 15:1.

Students of VUU The student body totals 1,622, of whom 1,260 are undergraduates. 59.7% are women and 40.3% are men. Students come from 21 states and territories. 0.5% are international students. 70% returned for their sophomore year.

Applying VUU requires SAT I or ACT and a high school transcript. The school recommends an essay and 3 recommendations. Application deadline: rolling admissions; 5/1 priority date for financial aid. Early and deferred admission are possible.

VIRGINIA WESLEYAN COLLEGE

Norfolk, VA

Urban setting ■ Private ■ Independent Religious ■ Coed

Web site: www.vwc.edu
Contact: Mr. Richard T. Hinshaw, Vice President for Enrollment Management, Dean of Admissions, 1584 Wesleyan Drive, Norfolk, VA 23502-5599
Telephone: 757-455-3208 or toll-free 800-737-8684 **Fax:** 757-461-5238
E-mail: admissions@vwc.edu

Getting in Last Year 977 applied; 79% were accepted; 290 enrolled (37%).

Financial Matters $18,000 tuition and fees (2002–03); $5950 room and board; 83% average percent of need met; $16,366 average financial aid amount received per undergraduate (2001–02).

Academics Virginia Wesleyan awards bachelor's degrees. Challenging opportunities include advanced placement credit, student-designed majors, freshman honors college, an honors program, double majors, independent study, and a senior project. Special programs include internships, summer session for credit, off-campus study, study-abroad, and Army ROTC. The most frequently chosen baccalaureate fields are business/marketing, social sciences and history, and interdisciplinary studies. The faculty at Virginia Wesleyan has 74 full-time members, 85% with terminal degrees. The student-faculty ratio is 13:1.

Students of Virginia Wesleyan The student body is made up of 1,396 undergraduates. 67.7% are women and 32.3% are men. Students come from 31 states and territories. 80% are from Virginia. 0.6% are international students.

Applying Virginia Wesleyan requires an essay, SAT I or ACT, a high school transcript, and a minimum high school GPA of 2.0. The school recommends an interview and a minimum high school GPA of 2.5. Application deadline: rolling admissions. Early and deferred admission are possible.

VITERBO UNIVERSITY

La Crosse, WI

Urban setting ■ Private ■ Independent Religious ■ Coed

Web site: www.viterbo.edu
Contact: Admission Counselor, 815 South 9th Street, LaCrosse, WI 54601
Telephone: 608-796-3010 ext. 3010 or toll-free 800-VIT-ERBO ext. 3010 **Fax:** 608-796-3020
E-mail: admission@viterbo.edu

Getting in Last Year 1,507 applied; 80% were accepted; 325 enrolled (27%).

Financial Matters $14,300 tuition and fees (2002–03); $4910 room and board; 85% average percent of need met; $11,826 average financial aid amount received per undergraduate (2001–02).

Viterbo University (continued)

Academics Viterbo awards bachelor's and master's degrees. Challenging opportunities include advanced placement credit, accelerated degree programs, student-designed majors, double majors, independent study, and a senior project. Special programs include cooperative education, internships, summer session for credit, off-campus study, study-abroad, and Army ROTC. The most frequently chosen baccalaureate fields are health professions and related sciences, business/marketing, and education. The faculty at Viterbo has 108 full-time members, 52% with terminal degrees. The student-faculty ratio is 12:1.

Students of Viterbo The student body totals 2,331, of whom 1,778 are undergraduates. 74.6% are women and 25.4% are men. Students come from 21 states and territories and 11 other countries. 78% are from Wisconsin. 1% are international students. 71% returned for their sophomore year.

Applying Viterbo requires ACT, a high school transcript, audition for theater and music; portfolio for art, and a minimum high school GPA of 2.0, and in some cases an essay, an interview, and 1 recommendation. Application deadline: rolling admissions; 3/15 priority date for financial aid.

VOORHEES COLLEGE

Denmark, SC

Rural setting ■ Private ■ Independent Religious ■ Coed

Web site: www.voorhees.edu
Contact: Mr. Benjamin O. Watson, Assistant Director, Admission and Recruitment, Halmi Hall, PO Box 678, Denmark, SC 29042
Telephone: 803-703-7124 or toll-free 800-446-6250 **Fax:** 803-793-1117
E-mail: bwatson@voorhees.edu

Getting in Last Year 2,624 applied; 41% were accepted; 156 enrolled (15%).

Financial Matters $6630 tuition and fees (2002–03); $3516 room and board; 53% average percent of need met; $7701 average financial aid amount received per undergraduate.

Academics Voorhees College awards bachelor's degrees. Challenging opportunities include advanced placement credit, an honors program, double majors, and a senior project. Special programs include cooperative education, internships, summer session for credit, and Army ROTC. The faculty at Voorhees College has 37 full-time members, 43% with terminal degrees. The student-faculty ratio is 20:1.

Students of Voorhees College The student body is made up of 745 undergraduates. 63.5% are women and 36.5% are men. Students come from 18 states and territories and 5 other countries. 0.8% are international students. 58% returned for their sophomore year.

Applying Voorhees College requires SAT I or ACT, a high school transcript, and a minimum high school GPA of 2.0, and in some cases a high school transcript and an interview. The school recommends a minimum high school GPA of 2.0. Application deadline: rolling admissions; 4/15 priority date for financial aid. Deferred admission is possible.

WABASH COLLEGE

Crawfordsville, IN

Small-town setting ■ Private ■ Independent ■ Men Only

Web site: www.wabash.edu
Contact: Mr. Steve Klein, Director of Admissions, PO Box 362, Crawfordsville, IN 47933-0352
Telephone: 765-361-6225 or toll-free 800-345-5385 **Fax:** 765-361-6437
E-mail: admissions@wabash.edu

Getting in Last Year 1,287 applied; 50% were accepted; 270 enrolled (42%).

Financial Matters $20,205 tuition and fees (2002–03); $6397 room and board; 100% average percent of need met; $18,585 average financial aid amount received per undergraduate (2001–02).

Academics Wabash awards bachelor's degrees. Challenging opportunities include advanced placement credit, accelerated degree programs, double majors, independent study, and a senior project. Special programs include cooperative education, internships, off-campus study, study-abroad, and Army ROTC. The most frequently chosen baccalaureate fields are social sciences and history, English, and biological/life sciences. The faculty at Wabash has 82 full-time members, 96% with terminal degrees. The student-faculty ratio is 11:1.

Students of Wabash The student body is made up of 912 undergraduates. Students come from 36 states and territories and 13 other countries. 74% are from Indiana. 3.3% are international students. 86% returned for their sophomore year.

Applying Wabash requires an essay, SAT I or ACT, a high school transcript, 1 recommendation, and a minimum high school GPA of 2.0. The school recommends an interview and a minimum high school GPA of 3.0. Application deadline: 3/15; 3/1 for financial aid, with a 2/15 priority date. Early and deferred admission are possible.

WAGNER COLLEGE

Staten Island, NY

Urban setting ■ Private ■ Independent ■ Coed

Web site: www.wagner.edu
Contact: Mr. Angelo Araimo, Dean of Admissions, One Campus Road, Staten Island, NY 10301
Telephone: 718-390-3411 ext. 3412 or toll-free 800-221-1010 (out-of-state) **Fax:** 718-390-3105
E-mail: admissions@wagner.edu

Getting in Last Year 2,419 applied; 67% were accepted; 516 enrolled (32%).

Financial Matters $21,500 tuition and fees (2002–03); $7000 room and board; 76% average percent of need met; $14,245 average financial aid amount received per undergraduate.

Academics Wagner awards bachelor's and master's degrees. Challenging opportunities include advanced placement credit, accelerated degree programs, student-designed majors, an honors program, double majors, and a senior project. Special programs include internships, summer session for credit, off-campus study, study-abroad, and Army and Air Force ROTC. The most frequently chosen baccalaureate fields are business/marketing, biological/life sciences, and education. The faculty at Wagner has 95 full-time members, 79% with terminal degrees. The student-faculty ratio is 16:1.

Students of Wagner The student body totals 2,180, of whom 1,810 are undergraduates. 59.1% are women and 40.9% are men. Students come from 38 states and territories and 14 other countries. 52% are from New York. 1.5% are international students. 84% returned for their sophomore year.

Applying Wagner requires an essay, SAT I or ACT, a high school transcript, 2 recommendations, and a minimum high school GPA of 2.7, and in some cases SAT II Subject Tests and an interview. The school recommends SAT II Subject Tests, SAT II: Writing Test, an interview, and a minimum high school GPA of 3.0. Application deadline: 2/15; 2/15 priority date for financial aid. Early and deferred admission are possible.

WAKE FOREST UNIVERSITY

Winston-Salem, NC

Suburban setting ■ Private ■ Independent Religious ■ Coed

Web site: www.wfu.edu
Contact: Ms. Martha Allman, Director of Admissions, PO Box 7305, Winston-Salem, NC 27109
Telephone: 336-758-5201
E-mail: admissions@wfu.edu

Getting in Last Year 5,995 applied; 41% were accepted; 1,004 enrolled (41%).

Financial Matters $24,750 tuition and fees (2002–03); $7190 room and board; 90% average percent of need met; $19,394 average financial aid amount received per undergraduate (2001–02).

Academics Wake Forest awards bachelor's, master's, doctoral, and first-professional degrees. Challenging opportunities include advanced placement credit, accelerated degree programs, an honors program, double majors, independent study, and a senior project. Special programs include internships, summer session for credit, off-campus study, study-abroad, and Army ROTC. The most frequently chosen baccalaureate fields are social sciences and history, business/marketing, and communications/communication technologies. The faculty at Wake Forest has 439 full-time members, 89% with terminal degrees. The student-faculty ratio is 10:1.

Students of Wake Forest The student body totals 6,425, of whom 4,045 are undergraduates. 51.1% are women and 48.9% are men. Students come from 50 states and territories and 26 other countries. 26% are from North Carolina. 93% returned for their sophomore year.

Applying Wake Forest requires an essay, SAT I, a high school transcript, and 1 recommendation. The school recommends SAT II Subject Tests. Application deadline: 1/15; 3/1 priority date for financial aid. Early and deferred admission are possible.

WALDORF COLLEGE

Forest City, IA

Small-town setting ■ Private ■ Independent Religious ■ Coed

Web site: www.waldorf.edu
Contact: Mr. Steve Hall, Assistant Dean of Admission, 106 South 6th Street, Forest City, IA 50436
Telephone: 641-585-8119 or toll-free 800-292-1903 **Fax:** 641-585-8125
E-mail: admissions@waldorf.edu

Getting in Last Year 652 applied; 69% were accepted.

Financial Matters $14,661 tuition and fees (2002–03); $4200 room and board; 85% average percent of need met; $15,565 average financial aid amount received per undergraduate.

Academics Waldorf awards associate and bachelor's degrees. Challenging opportunities include advanced placement credit, accelerated degree programs, freshman honors college, an honors program, and double majors. Special programs include cooperative education, internships, summer session for credit, and study-abroad. The faculty at Waldorf has 36 full-time members, 44% with terminal degrees. The student-faculty ratio is 13:1.

Students of Waldorf The student body is made up of 547 undergraduates. 46.3% are women and 53.7% are men. 67% are from Iowa. 6.2% are international students. 75% returned for their sophomore year.

Applying Waldorf requires SAT I or ACT, a high school transcript, and 1 recommendation, and in some cases an interview. The school recommends a minimum high school GPA of 2.0. Application deadline: rolling admissions; 3/1 priority date for financial aid. Early admission is possible.

WALLA WALLA COLLEGE

College Place, WA

Small-town setting ■ Private ■ Independent Religious ■ Coed

Web site: www.wwc.edu

Contact: Mr. Dallas Weis, Director of Admissions, 204 South College Avenue, College Place, WA 99324

Telephone: 509-527-2327 or toll-free 800-541-8900 **Fax:** 509-527-2397

E-mail: info@wwc.edu

Getting in Last Year 457 applied; 86% were accepted; 344 enrolled (88%).

Financial Matters $16,944 tuition and fees (2002–03); $4605 room and board; 82% average percent of need met; $13,641 average financial aid amount received per undergraduate (2001–02).

Academics WWC awards associate, bachelor's, and master's degrees. Challenging opportunities include advanced placement credit, freshman honors college, an honors program, double majors, independent study, and a senior project. Special programs include cooperative education, internships, summer session for credit, and study-abroad. The most frequently chosen baccalaureate fields are engineering/engineering technologies, health professions and related sciences, and business/marketing. The faculty at WWC has 116 full-time members, 62% with terminal degrees. The student-faculty ratio is 11:1.

Students of WWC The student body totals 1,865, of whom 1,610 are undergraduates. 49.3% are women and 50.7% are men. Students come from 45 states and territories. 39% are from Washington. 0.8% are international students. 100% returned for their sophomore year.

Applying WWC requires SAT I or ACT, a high school transcript, 3 recommendations, and a minimum high school GPA of 2.0. The school recommends ACT. Application deadline: rolling admissions. Deferred admission is possible.

WALSH COLLEGE OF ACCOUNTANCY AND BUSINESS ADMINISTRATION

Troy, MI

Suburban setting ■ Private ■ Independent ■ Coed

Web site: www.walshcollege.edu

Contact: Ms. Karen Mahaffy, Director of Admissions, 3838 Livernois Road, PO Box 7006, Troy, MI 48007-7006

Telephone: 248-823-1610 or toll-free 800-925-7401 (in-state) **Fax:** 248-524-2520

E-mail: admissions@walshcollege.edu

Getting in Last Year 316 applied; 78% were accepted.

Financial Matters $7100 tuition and fees (2002–03); 44% average percent of need met; $10,937 average financial aid amount received per undergraduate.

Academics Walsh College awards bachelor's and master's degrees. Challenging opportunities include advanced placement credit, double majors, and independent study. Special programs include internships, summer session for credit, and off-campus study. The most frequently chosen baccalaureate field is business/marketing. The faculty at Walsh College has 16 full-time members, 50% with terminal degrees. The student-faculty ratio is 20:1.

Students of Walsh College The student body totals 3,216, of whom 1,098 are undergraduates. 61.2% are women and 38.8% are men. Students come from 1 state or territory. 1.5% are international students.

Applying Deferred admission is possible.

WALSH UNIVERSITY

North Canton, OH

Small-town setting ■ Private ■ Independent Religious ■ Coed

Web site: www.walsh.edu

Contact: Mr. Brett Freshour, Dean of Enrollment Management, 2020 Easton Street, NW, North Canton, OH 44720-3396

Telephone: 330-490-7171 or toll-free 800-362-9846 (in-state), 800-362-8846 (out-of-state) **Fax:** 330-490-7165

E-mail: admissions@walsh.edu

Getting in Last Year 920 applied; 79% were accepted; 302 enrolled (41%).

Financial Matters $13,870 tuition and fees (2002–03); $8270 room and board; 86% average percent of need met; $9778 average financial aid amount received per undergraduate.

Academics Walsh awards associate, bachelor's, and master's degrees. Challenging opportunities include advanced placement credit, accelerated degree programs, student-designed majors, freshman honors college, an honors program, double majors, and a senior project. Special programs include internships, summer session for credit, and off-campus study. The most frequently chosen baccalaureate fields are business/marketing, education, and health professions and related sciences. The faculty at Walsh has 67 full-time members, 72% with terminal degrees. The student-faculty ratio is 15:1.

Students of Walsh The student body totals 1,648, of whom 1,480 are undergraduates. 58.1% are women and 41.9% are men. Students come from 14 states and territories and 12 other countries. 98% are from Ohio. 1.2% are international students.

Applying Walsh requires SAT I or ACT, a high school transcript, and a minimum high school GPA of 2.1, and in some cases an essay, 2 recommendations, and a minimum high school GPA of 3.0. The school recommends an interview. Application deadline: rolling admissions. Early and deferred admission are possible.

WARNER PACIFIC COLLEGE

Portland, OR

Urban setting ■ Private ■ Independent Religious ■ Coed

Web site: www.warnerpacific.edu

Contact: Dr. Jack P. Powell, Dean of Enrollment Management, 2219 Southeast 68th Avenue, Portland, OR 97215

Telephone: 503-517-1020 or toll-free 800-582-7885 (in-state), 800-804-1510 (out-of-state) **Fax:** 503-517-1352

E-mail: admiss@warnerpacific.edu

Getting in Last Year 235 applied; 59% were accepted; 74 enrolled (54%).

Financial Matters $15,950 tuition and fees (2002–03); $4930 room and board; 64% average percent of need met; $11,151 average financial aid amount received per undergraduate.

Academics Warner Pacific awards associate, bachelor's, and master's degrees and post-bachelor's certificates. Challenging opportunities include advanced placement credit, student-designed majors, an honors program, double majors, independent study, and a senior project. Special programs include cooperative education, internships, summer session for credit, off-campus study, study-abroad, and Army and Air Force ROTC. The most frequently chosen baccalaureate fields are education, business/marketing, and social sciences and history. The faculty at Warner Pacific has 41 full-time members. The student-faculty ratio is 14:1.

Students of Warner Pacific The student body totals 593, of whom 587 are undergraduates. 61.8% are women and 38.2% are men. Students come from 16 states and territories and 5 other countries. 74% are from Oregon. 1.2% are international students. 76% returned for their sophomore year.

Applying Warner Pacific requires an essay, SAT I or ACT, a high school transcript, 2 recommendations, and a minimum high school GPA of 2.5, and in some cases an interview. The school recommends SAT II Subject Tests, SAT II: Writing Test, an interview, and a minimum high school GPA of 3.0. Application deadline: rolling admissions.

WARNER SOUTHERN COLLEGE

Lake Wales, FL

Rural setting ■ Private ■ Independent Religious ■ Coed

Web site: www.warner.edu

Contact: Mr. Jason Roe, Director of Admissions, Warner Southern Center, 13895 US 27, Lake Wales, FL 33859

Telephone: 863-638-7212 ext. 7213 or toll-free 800-949-7248 (in-state) **Fax:** 863-638-1472

E-mail: admissions@warner.edu

Getting in Last Year 289 applied; 71% were accepted; 121 enrolled (59%).

Financial Matters $10,540 tuition and fees (2002–03); $5060 room and board; $10,091 average financial aid amount received per undergraduate (2001–02).

Academics Warner Southern awards associate, bachelor's, and master's degrees. Challenging opportunities include advanced placement credit, accelerated degree programs, double majors, independent study, and a senior project. Special programs include internships and summer session for credit. The most frequently chosen baccalaureate fields are business/marketing, education, and psychology. The faculty at Warner Southern has 44 full-time members, 43% with terminal degrees. The student-faculty ratio is 16:1.

Students of Warner Southern The student body totals 1,132, of whom 1,087 are undergraduates. 57.7% are women and 42.3% are men. Students come from 28 states and territories and 16 other countries. 90% are from Florida. 2.7% are international students. 80% returned for their sophomore year.

Applying Warner Southern requires SAT I or ACT, a high school transcript, 1 recommendation, and a minimum high school GPA of 2.25, and in some cases an

Warner Southern College (continued)

interview. The school recommends an essay. Application deadline: rolling admissions; 10/1 for financial aid, with a 5/15 priority date. Deferred admission is possible.

WARREN WILSON COLLEGE

Asheville, NC

Small-town setting ■ Private ■ Independent Religious ■ Coed

Web site: www.warren-wilson.edu
Contact: Mr. Richard Blomgren, Dean of Admission, PO Box 9000, Asheville, NC 28815-9000
Telephone: 828-771-2073 or toll-free 800-934-3536 **Fax:** 828-298-1440
E-mail: admit@warren-wilson.edu

Getting in Last Year 644 applied; 78% were accepted; 193 enrolled (39%).

Financial Matters $16,098 tuition and fees (2002–03); $4994 room and board; 75% average percent of need met; $12,374 average financial aid amount received per undergraduate.

Academics Warren Wilson awards bachelor's and master's degrees. Challenging opportunities include advanced placement credit, student-designed majors, an honors program, double majors, independent study, and a senior project. Special programs include cooperative education, internships, off-campus study, and study-abroad. The most frequently chosen baccalaureate fields are social sciences and history, natural resources/environmental science, and English. The faculty at Warren Wilson has 59 full-time members. The student-faculty ratio is 10:1.

Students of Warren Wilson The student body totals 828, of whom 769 are undergraduates. 63.1% are women and 36.9% are men. Students come from 38 states and territories and 23 other countries. 31% are from North Carolina. 5% are international students. 67% returned for their sophomore year.

Applying Warren Wilson requires an essay, SAT I or ACT, a high school transcript, 2 recommendations, and a minimum high school GPA of 2.5. The school recommends an interview. Application deadline: 3/15; 4/1 priority date for financial aid. Early and deferred admission are possible.

WARTBURG COLLEGE

Waverly, IA

Small-town setting ■ Private ■ Independent Religious ■ Coed

Web site: www.wartburg.edu
Contact: Doug Bowman, Dean of Admissions/Financial Aid, 100 Wartburg Boulevard, PO Box 1003, Waverly, IA 50677-0903
Telephone: 319-352-8264 or toll-free 800-772-2085 **Fax:** 319-352-8579
E-mail: admissions@wartburg.edu

Getting in Last Year 1,713 applied; 84% were accepted; 513 enrolled (36%).

Financial Matters $17,530 tuition and fees (2002–03); $4900 room and board; 95% average percent of need met; $16,135 average financial aid amount received per undergraduate.

Academics Wartburg awards bachelor's degrees. Challenging opportunities include advanced placement credit, accelerated degree programs, student-designed majors, double majors, independent study, and a senior project. Special programs include internships, summer session for credit, off-campus study, and study-abroad. The most frequently chosen baccalaureate fields are business/marketing, education, and biological/life sciences. The faculty at Wartburg has 101 full-time members, 79% with terminal degrees. The student-faculty ratio is 14:1.

Students of Wartburg The student body is made up of 1,695 undergraduates. 56.2% are women and 43.8% are men. Students come from 29 states and territories and 32 other countries. 80% are from Iowa. 3.7% are international students. 75% returned for their sophomore year.

Applying Wartburg requires SAT I or ACT, a high school transcript, and a minimum high school GPA of 2.0, and in some cases an interview. The school recommends recommendations and secondary school report. Application deadline: 3/1 priority date for financial aid. Deferred admission is possible.

WASHINGTON & JEFFERSON COLLEGE

Washington, PA

Small-town setting ■ Private ■ Independent ■ Coed

Web site: www.washjeff.edu
Contact: Mr. Alton E. Newell, Dean of Enrollment, 60 South Lincoln Street, Washington, PA 15301
Telephone: 724-223-6025 or toll-free 888-WANDJAY **Fax:** 724-223-6534
E-mail: admission@washjeff.edu

Getting in Last Year 1,874 applied; 51% were accepted; 331 enrolled (34%).

Financial Matters $21,658 tuition and fees (2002–03); $5992 room and board; 74% average percent of need met; $15,229 average financial aid amount received per undergraduate.

Academics W & J awards associate and bachelor's degrees. Challenging opportunities include advanced placement credit, accelerated degree programs, student-designed majors, an honors program, double majors, independent study, and a senior project. Special programs include internships, summer session for credit, study-abroad, and Army and Air Force ROTC. The most frequently chosen baccalaureate fields are business/marketing, social sciences and history, and psychology. The faculty at W & J has 89 full-time members, 100% with terminal degrees. The student-faculty ratio is 12:1.

Students of W & J The student body is made up of 1,209 undergraduates. 48.1% are women and 51.9% are men. Students come from 33 states and territories and 7 other countries. 80% are from Pennsylvania. 0.9% are international students. 82% returned for their sophomore year.

Applying W & J requires an essay, SAT I or ACT, and a high school transcript. The school recommends an interview and 1 recommendation. Application deadline: 3/1; 2/15 priority date for financial aid. Early and deferred admission are possible.

WASHINGTON AND LEE UNIVERSITY

Lexington, VA

Small-town setting ■ Private ■ Independent ■ Coed

Web site: www.wlu.edu
Contact: Mr. William M. Hartog, Dean of Admissions and Financial Aid, Lexington, VA 24450-0303
Telephone: 540-463-8710 **Fax:** 540-463-8062
E-mail: admissions@wlu.edu

Getting in Last Year 3,188 applied; 31% were accepted; 458 enrolled (46%).

Financial Matters $21,175 tuition and fees (2002–03); $5913 room and board; 99% average percent of need met; $16,928 average financial aid amount received per undergraduate (2001–02).

Academics W & L awards bachelor's and first-professional degrees. Challenging opportunities include advanced placement credit, accelerated degree programs, student-designed majors, an honors program, double majors, independent study, and a senior project. Special programs include internships, off-campus study, study-abroad, and Army ROTC. The faculty at W & L has 191 full-time members. The student-faculty ratio is 11:1.

Students of W & L The student body totals 2,130, of whom 1,750 are undergraduates. 46.5% are women and 53.5% are men. Students come from 47 states and territories and 38 other countries. 14% are from Virginia. 4% are international students. 94% returned for their sophomore year.

Applying W & L requires an essay, SAT I or ACT, 3 unrelated SAT II Subject Tests (including SAT II: Writing Test), a high school transcript, and 3 recommendations. The school recommends an interview. Application deadline: 1/15; 2/1 priority date for financial aid. Deferred admission is possible.

WASHINGTON BIBLE COLLEGE

Lanham, MD

Suburban setting ■ Private ■ Independent Religious ■ Coed

Web site: www.bible.edu
Contact: Barbara Fox, Director of Enrollment Management, 6511 Princess Garden Parkway, Lanham, MD 20706
Telephone: 301-552-1400 ext. 213 or toll-free 800-787-0256 ext. 212 **Fax:** 301-552-2775
E-mail: admissions@bible.edu

Getting in Last Year 167 applied; 65% were accepted.

Financial Matters $8205 tuition and fees (2002–03); $5000 room and board.

Academics WBC awards associate and bachelor's degrees. Challenging opportunities include advanced placement credit, accelerated degree programs, double majors, and a senior project. Special programs include cooperative education, internships, summer session for credit, and off-campus study. The faculty at WBC has 14 full-time members, 14% with terminal degrees. The student-faculty ratio is 13:1.

Students of WBC The student body is made up of 331 undergraduates. 47.1% are women and 52.9% are men. Students come from 14 states and territories and 9 other countries. 76% are from Maryland. 2.5% are international students. 70% returned for their sophomore year.

Applying WBC requires an essay, SAT I or ACT, a high school transcript, 2 recommendations, and Christian testimony, and in some cases an interview. Application deadline: rolling admissions; 6/1 priority date for financial aid. Early and deferred admission are possible.

WASHINGTON COLLEGE

Chestertown, MD

Small-town setting ■ Private ■ Independent ■ Coed

Web site: www.washcoll.edu
Contact: Mr. Kevin Coveney, Vice President for Admissions, 300 Washington Avenue, Chestertown, MD 21620-1197
Telephone: 410-778-7700 or toll-free 800-422-1782
E-mail: admissions_office@washcoll.edu

Getting in Last Year 2,032 applied; 64% were accepted; 368 enrolled (28%).

Financial Matters $23,300 tuition and fees (2002–03); $5740 room and board; 88% average percent of need met; $18,409 average financial aid amount received per undergraduate (2001–02).

Academics WC awards bachelor's and master's degrees. Challenging opportunities include advanced placement credit, student-designed majors, double majors, independent study, and a senior project. Special programs include cooperative education, internships, off-campus study, and study-abroad. The most frequently chosen baccalaureate fields are social sciences and history, biological/life sciences, and psychology. The faculty at WC has 80 full-time members, 89% with terminal degrees. The student-faculty ratio is 12:1.

Students of WC The student body totals 1,358, of whom 1,302 are undergraduates. 62.3% are women and 37.7% are men. Students come from 36 states and territories and 40 other countries. 56% are from Maryland. 5.4% are international students. 82% returned for their sophomore year.

Applying WC requires an essay, SAT I or ACT, a high school transcript, and 1 recommendation, and in some cases an interview. The school recommends an interview. Application deadline: 2/15; 2/15 priority date for financial aid. Early and deferred admission are possible.

WASHINGTON STATE UNIVERSITY

Pullman, WA

Rural setting ■ Public ■ State-supported ■ Coed

Web site: www.wsu.edu

Contact: Ms. Wendy Peterson, Director of Admissions, Pullman, WA 99164

Telephone: 509-335-5586 or toll-free 888-468-6978 **Fax:** 509-335-7468

E-mail: ir@wsu.edu

Getting in Last Year 8,989 applied; 77% were accepted; 2,803 enrolled (41%).

Financial Matters $5268 resident tuition and fees (2002–03); $13,018 nonresident tuition and fees (2002–03); $5882 room and board; 98% average percent of need met; $8874 average financial aid amount received per undergraduate (2001–02).

Academics WSU awards bachelor's, master's, doctoral, and first-professional degrees and post-bachelor's certificates. Challenging opportunities include advanced placement credit, an honors program, double majors, and a senior project. Special programs include cooperative education, internships, summer session for credit, off-campus study, study-abroad, and Army, Navy and Air Force ROTC. The most frequently chosen baccalaureate fields are business/marketing, social sciences and history, and communications/communication technologies. The faculty at WSU has 1,082 full-time members, 87% with terminal degrees. The student-faculty ratio is 17:1.

Students of WSU The student body totals 21,881, of whom 18,025 are undergraduates. 52.6% are women and 47.4% are men. Students come from 43 states and territories and 42 other countries. 98% are from Washington. 3.4% are international students. 83% returned for their sophomore year.

Applying WSU requires an essay, SAT I or ACT, a high school transcript, and a minimum high school GPA of 2.0, and in some cases 3 recommendations. Application deadline: 3/1 priority date for financial aid. Early admission is possible.

WASHINGTON UNIVERSITY IN ST. LOUIS

St. Louis, MO

Suburban setting ■ Private ■ Independent ■ Coed

Web site: www.wustl.edu

Contact: Ms. Nanette Tarbouni, Director of Admissions, Campus Box 1089, One Brookings Drive, St. Louis, MO 63130-4899

Telephone: 314-935-6000 or toll-free 800-638-0700 **Fax:** 314-935-4290

E-mail: admissions@wustl.edu

Getting in Last Year 19,514 applied; 24% were accepted; 1,342 enrolled (29%).

Financial Matters $27,619 tuition and fees (2002–03); $8678 room and board; 100% average percent of need met; $22,979 average financial aid amount received per undergraduate.

Academics Washington awards bachelor's, master's, doctoral, and first-professional degrees and post-bachelor's certificates. Challenging opportunities include advanced placement credit, accelerated degree programs, student-designed majors, double majors, and independent study. Special programs include cooperative education, internships, summer session for credit, off-campus study, study-abroad, and Army and Air Force ROTC. The most frequently chosen baccalaureate fields are engineering/engineering technologies, business/marketing, and social sciences and history. The faculty at Washington has 811 full-time members, 99% with terminal degrees. The student-faculty ratio is 7:1.

Students of Washington The student body totals 12,767, of whom 7,219 are undergraduates. 53% are women and 47% are men. Students come from 52 states and territories and 104 other countries. 11% are from Missouri. 4.6% are international students. 96% returned for their sophomore year.

Applying Washington requires an essay, SAT I or ACT, a high school transcript, and 2 recommendations. The school recommends portfolio for art and architecture programs and a minimum high school GPA of 3.0. Application deadline: 1/15; 2/15 for financial aid. Early and deferred admission are possible.

WATKINS COLLEGE OF ART AND DESIGN

Nashville, TN

Urban setting ■ Private ■ Independent ■ Coed

Web site: www.watkins.edu

Contact: Mr. Ted Gray, Director of Admissions, 2298 Metro Center Boulevard, Nashville, TN 37228

Telephone: 615-383-4848 **Fax:** 615-383-4849

E-mail: tgray@watkins.edu

Getting in Last Year 82 applied; 73% were accepted; 39 enrolled (65%).

Financial Matters $8860 tuition and fees (2002–03); 60% average percent of need met; $8000 average financial aid amount received per undergraduate (2001–02).

Academics Watkins College of Art and Design awards associate and bachelor's degrees and post-bachelor's certificates. Challenging opportunities include double majors and a senior project. Special programs include cooperative education, internships, and summer session for credit. The most frequently chosen baccalaureate field is visual/performing arts. The faculty at Watkins College of Art and Design has 13 full-time members, 46% with terminal degrees.

Students of Watkins College of Art and Design The student body is made up of 365 undergraduates. 64.1% are women and 35.9% are men. Students come from 10 states and territories and 3 other countries. 60% are from Tennessee. 1.1% are international students. 62% returned for their sophomore year.

Applying Watkins College of Art and Design requires an essay, SAT I or ACT, a high school transcript, recommendations, and a minimum high school GPA of 2.5, and in some cases an interview and statement of good standing from prior institution(s), portfolio. The school recommends an interview. Application deadline: 4/1; 4/1 priority date for financial aid. Deferred admission is possible.

WAYLAND BAPTIST UNIVERSITY

Plainview, TX

Small-town setting ■ Private ■ Independent Religious ■ Coed

Web site: www.wbu.edu

Contact: Mr. Shawn Thomas, Director of Student Admissions, 1900 West 7th Street, CMB #712, Plainview, TX 79072

Telephone: 806-291-3508 or toll-free 800-588-1928

E-mail: admityou@mail.wbu.edu

Getting in Last Year 264 applied; 98% were accepted; 190 enrolled (73%).

Financial Matters $8450 tuition and fees (2002–03); $3354 room and board; 75% average percent of need met; $9208 average financial aid amount received per undergraduate.

Academics Wayland awards associate, bachelor's, and master's degrees (branch locations: Anchorage, AK; Amarillo, TX; Luke Airforce Base, AZ; Glorieta, NM; Aiea, HI; Lubbock, TX; San Antonio, TX; Wichita Falls, TX). Challenging opportunities include advanced placement credit, accelerated degree programs, an honors program, double majors, and a senior project. Special programs include internships, summer session for credit, and Army and Air Force ROTC. The most frequently chosen baccalaureate fields are education, business/marketing, and biological/life sciences. The faculty at Wayland has 61 full-time members, 69% with terminal degrees. The student-faculty ratio is 12:1.

Students of Wayland The student body totals 1,000, of whom 943 are undergraduates. 58.9% are women and 41.1% are men. Students come from 17 states and territories and 8 other countries. 87% are from Texas. 1% are international students. 58% returned for their sophomore year.

Applying Wayland requires SAT I or ACT and a high school transcript. The school recommends ACT and an interview. Application deadline: rolling admissions; 5/1 priority date for financial aid.

WAYNESBURG COLLEGE

Waynesburg, PA

Small-town setting ■ Private ■ Independent Religious ■ Coed

Web site: www.waynesburg.edu

Contact: Ms. Robin L. King, Dean of Admissions, 51 West College Street, Waynesburg, PA 15070

Telephone: 724-852-3333 or toll-free 800-225-7393 **Fax:** 724-627-8124

E-mail: admissions@waynesburg.edu

Getting in Last Year 1,251 applied; 79% were accepted; 306 enrolled (31%).

Financial Matters $13,200 tuition and fees (2002–03); $5050 room and board; 83% average percent of need met; $11,120 average financial aid amount received per undergraduate (2001–02).

Academics Waynesburg awards associate, bachelor's, and master's degrees. Challenging opportunities include advanced placement credit, accelerated degree programs, an honors program, double majors, independent study, and a senior project. Special programs include internships, study-abroad, and Army ROTC. The most frequently chosen baccalaureate fields are health professions and related sciences, business/marketing, and protective services/public administration. The faculty at Waynesburg has 65 full-time members, 71% with terminal degrees. The student-faculty ratio is 16:1.

Waynesburg College (continued)

Students of Waynesburg The student body totals 1,714, of whom 1,442 are undergraduates. 54.6% are women and 45.4% are men. Students come from 16 states and territories and 5 other countries. 82% are from Pennsylvania. 0.4% are international students. 72% returned for their sophomore year.

Applying Waynesburg requires SAT I or ACT, a high school transcript, and a minimum high school GPA of 2.0, and in some cases an essay and recommendations. The school recommends an interview and a minimum high school GPA of 3.0. Application deadline: rolling admissions; 3/15 priority date for financial aid. Early admission is possible.

WAYNE STATE COLLEGE

Wayne, NE

Small-town setting ■ Public ■ State-supported ■ Coed

Web site: www.wsc.edu
Contact: R. Lincoln Morris, Director of Admissions, 1111 Main Street, Wayne, NE 68787
Telephone: 402-375-7234 or toll-free 800-228-9972 (in-state) **Fax:** 402-375-7204
E-mail: admit1@wsc.edu

Getting in Last Year 1,253 applied; 71% were accepted; 607 enrolled (69%).

Financial Matters $3014 resident tuition and fees (2002–03); $5301 nonresident tuition and fees (2002–03); $3760 room and board; 41% average percent of need met; $2996 average financial aid amount received per undergraduate.

Academics WSC awards bachelor's and master's degrees and post-master's certificates. Challenging opportunities include student-designed majors, an honors program, double majors, independent study, and a senior project. Special programs include cooperative education, internships, summer session for credit, off-campus study, and Army ROTC. The most frequently chosen baccalaureate fields are business/marketing, education, and psychology. The faculty at WSC has 126 full-time members, 79% with terminal degrees. The student-faculty ratio is 18:1.

Students of WSC The student body totals 3,220, of whom 2,743 are undergraduates. 57.7% are women and 42.3% are men. Students come from 25 states and territories and 22 other countries. 85% are from Nebraska. 1% are international students. 72% returned for their sophomore year.

Applying WSC requires a high school transcript. The school recommends SAT I or ACT. Application deadline: rolling admissions; 6/1 priority date for financial aid. Deferred admission is possible.

WAYNE STATE UNIVERSITY

Detroit, MI

Urban setting ■ Public ■ State-supported ■ Coed

Web site: www.wayne.edu
Contact: Ms. Susan Swieg, Director of University Admissions, 3E HNJ, Detroit, MI 48202
Telephone: 313-577-3581 **Fax:** 313-577-7536
E-mail: admissions@wayne.edu

Getting in Last Year 6,939 applied; 69% were accepted.

Financial Matters $4723 resident tuition and fees (2002–03); $10,201 nonresident tuition and fees (2002–03); $6100 room and board; 60% average percent of need met; $6488 average financial aid amount received per undergraduate (2001–02).

Academics Wayne State awards bachelor's, master's, doctoral, and first-professional degrees and post-bachelor's and post-master's certificates. Challenging opportunities include advanced placement credit, accelerated degree programs, student-designed majors, an honors program, double majors, independent study, and a senior project. Special programs include cooperative education, internships, summer session for credit, off-campus study, study-abroad, and Air Force ROTC. The most frequently chosen baccalaureate fields are business/marketing, health professions and related sciences, and education. The faculty at Wayne State has 896 full-time members. The student-faculty ratio is 11:1.

Students of Wayne State The student body totals 31,167, of whom 18,408 are undergraduates. 60.2% are women and 39.8% are men. Students come from 39 states and territories and 100 other countries. 99% are from Michigan. 7.1% are international students.

Applying Wayne State requires SAT I or ACT, a high school transcript, and a minimum high school GPA of 2.0, and in some cases an interview, recommendations, and portfolio. Application deadline: 8/1; 3/1 priority date for financial aid.

WEBBER INTERNATIONAL UNIVERSITY

Babson Park, FL

Small-town setting ■ Private ■ Independent ■ Coed

Web site: www.webber.edu
Contact: Ms. Jacquie Guiley, Counselor, 1201 Scenic Highway, South, Babson Park, FL 33827
Telephone: 863-638-2910 or toll-free 800-741-1844 **Fax:** 863-638-1591
E-mail: admissions@webber.edu

Getting in Last Year 377 applied; 40% were accepted; 142 enrolled (93%).

Financial Matters $11,330 tuition and fees (2002–03); $4020 room and board; 66% average percent of need met; $10,639 average financial aid amount received per undergraduate.

Academics Webber awards associate, bachelor's, and master's degrees. Challenging opportunities include advanced placement credit, accelerated degree programs, and double majors. Special programs include cooperative education, internships, summer session for credit, and study-abroad. The most frequently chosen baccalaureate fields are business/marketing, parks and recreation, and law/legal studies. The faculty at Webber has 16 full-time members, 50% with terminal degrees. The student-faculty ratio is 22:1.

Students of Webber The student body totals 582, of whom 521 are undergraduates. 40.5% are women and 59.5% are men. Students come from 18 states and territories and 36 other countries. 96% are from Florida. 18.6% are international students. 58% returned for their sophomore year.

Applying Webber requires an essay, SAT I or ACT, a high school transcript, recommendations, and a minimum high school GPA of 2.0, and in some cases SAT I and SAT II or ACT. The school recommends an interview. Application deadline: 8/1, 8/1 for nonresidents; 8/1 for financial aid, with a 5/1 priority date.

WEBB INSTITUTE

Glen Cove, NY

Suburban setting ■ Private ■ Independent ■ Coed

Web site: www.webb-institute.edu
Contact: Mr. William G. Murray, Executive Director of Student Administrative Services, Crescent Beach Road, Glen Cove, NY 11542-1398
Telephone: 516-671-2213 **Fax:** 516-674-9838
E-mail: admissions@webb-institute.edu

Getting in Last Year 85 applied; 42% were accepted; 17 enrolled (47%).

Financial Matters $0 tuition and fees (2002–03); $6250 room and board; 20% average percent of need met; $800 average financial aid amount received per undergraduate (2001–02).

Academics Webb awards bachelor's degrees. Challenging opportunities include double majors, independent study, and a senior project. Special programs include cooperative education, internships, and off-campus study. The most frequently chosen baccalaureate field is engineering/engineering technologies. The faculty at Webb has 8 full-time members, 38% with terminal degrees. The student-faculty ratio is 7:1.

Students of Webb The student body is made up of 67 undergraduates. 19.4% are women and 80.6% are men. Students come from 21 states and territories. 22% are from New York. 90% returned for their sophomore year.

Applying Webb requires SAT I, SAT II: Writing Test, SAT II Subject Tests in math and either physics or chemistry, a high school transcript, an interview, 2 recommendations, proof of U.S. citizenship, and a minimum high school GPA of 3.5. Application deadline: 2/15; 7/1 priority date for financial aid.

WEBER STATE UNIVERSITY

Ogden, UT

Urban setting ■ Public ■ State-supported ■ Coed

Web site: weber.edu
Contact: John Allred, Admissions Advisor, 1137 University Circle, 3750 Harrison Boulevard, Ogden, UT 84408-1137
Telephone: 801-626-6050 or toll-free 800-634-6568 (in-state), 800-848-7770 (out-of-state) **Fax:** 801-626-6744
E-mail: admissions@weber.edu

Getting in Last Year 5,663 applied; 100% were accepted; 2,807 enrolled (50%).

Financial Matters $2426 resident tuition and fees (2002–03); $7292 nonresident tuition and fees (2002–03); $5160 room and board; 87% average percent of need met; $5300 average financial aid amount received per undergraduate (2001–02).

Academics Weber State awards associate, bachelor's, and master's degrees and post-bachelor's certificates. Challenging opportunities include advanced placement credit, accelerated degree programs, student-designed majors, freshman honors college, an honors program, double majors, independent study, and a senior project. Special programs include cooperative education, internships, summer session for credit, off-campus study, study-abroad, and Army, Navy and Air Force ROTC. The most frequently chosen baccalaureate fields are business/marketing, education, and health professions and related sciences. The faculty at Weber State has 450 full-time members, 90% with terminal degrees. The student-faculty ratio is 23:1.

Students of Weber State The student body totals 18,059, of whom 17,794 are undergraduates. 51.6% are women and 48.4% are men. Students come from 52 states and territories and 47 other countries. 94% are from Utah. 1.3% are international students. 69% returned for their sophomore year.

Applying Weber State requires SAT I or ACT and a high school transcript. Application deadline: 8/23; 3/1 priority date for financial aid. Early and deferred admission are possible.

WEBSTER UNIVERSITY

St. Louis, MO

Suburban setting ■ *Private* ■ *Independent* ■ *Coed*

Web site: www.webster.edu
Contact: Mr. Andrew Laue, Associate Director of Undergraduate Admission, 470 East Lockwood Avenue, St. Louis, MO 63119-3194
Telephone: 314-961-2660 ext. 7712 or toll-free 800-75-ENROL
Fax: 314-968-7115
E-mail: admit@webster.edu

Getting in Last Year 1,118 applied; 58% were accepted; 393 enrolled (61%).

Financial Matters $14,600 tuition and fees (2002–03); $6120 room and board; $15,236 average financial aid amount received per undergraduate.

Academics Webster awards bachelor's, master's, and doctoral degrees. Challenging opportunities include advanced placement credit, accelerated degree programs, student-designed majors, double majors, independent study, and a senior project. Special programs include cooperative education, internships, summer session for credit, off-campus study, study-abroad, and Army and Air Force ROTC. The most frequently chosen baccalaureate fields are business/marketing, computer/information sciences, and communications/communication technologies. The faculty at Webster has 146 full-time members, 81% with terminal degrees. The student-faculty ratio is 13:1.

Students of Webster The student body totals 6,890, of whom 3,458 are undergraduates. 62.3% are women and 37.7% are men. Students come from 48 states and territories and 104 other countries. 72% are from Missouri. 3.7% are international students. 79% returned for their sophomore year.

Applying Webster requires SAT I or ACT, a high school transcript, 1 recommendation, and a minimum high school GPA of 2.5, and in some cases audition. The school recommends an essay, an interview, and a minimum high school GPA of 3.0. Application deadline: 7/1; 4/1 priority date for financial aid. Early and deferred admission are possible.

WELLESLEY COLLEGE

Wellesley, MA

Suburban setting ■ *Private* ■ *Independent* ■ *Women Only*

Web site: www.wellesley.edu
Contact: Ms. Janet Lavin Rapelye, Dean of Admission, 106 Central Street, Green Hall 240, Wellesley, MA 02481-8203
Telephone: 781-283-2270 **Fax:** 781-283-3678
E-mail: admission@wellesley.edu

Getting in Last Year 2,877 applied; 47% were accepted; 593 enrolled (44%).

Financial Matters $26,702 tuition and fees (2002–03); $8242 room and board; 100% average percent of need met; $22,614 average financial aid amount received per undergraduate.

Academics Wellesley awards bachelor's degrees (double bachelor's degree with Massachusetts Institute of Technology). Challenging opportunities include advanced placement credit, student-designed majors, double majors, independent study, and a senior project. Special programs include internships, summer session for credit, off-campus study, study-abroad, and Army and Air Force ROTC. The most frequently chosen baccalaureate fields are social sciences and history, psychology, and English. The faculty at Wellesley has 217 full-time members, 96% with terminal degrees. The student-faculty ratio is 9:1.

Students of Wellesley The student body is made up of 2,300 undergraduates. Students come from 52 states and territories and 54 other countries. 17% are from Massachusetts. 6.9% are international students. 96% returned for their sophomore year.

Applying Wellesley requires an essay, SAT II Subject Tests, SAT I and SAT II or ACT, a high school transcript, and 3 recommendations, and in some cases an interview. The school recommends an interview. Application deadline: 1/15; 1/15 priority date for financial aid. Early and deferred admission are possible.

WELLS COLLEGE

Aurora, NY

Rural setting ■ *Private* ■ *Independent* ■ *Women Only*

Web site: www.wells.edu
Contact: Ms. Susan Raith Sloan, Director of Admissions, 170 Main Street, Aurora, NY 13026
Telephone: 315-364-3264 or toll-free 800-952-9355 **Fax:** 315-364-3227
E-mail: admissions@wells.edu

Getting in Last Year 404 applied; 86% were accepted; 109 enrolled (31%).

Financial Matters $13,750 tuition and fees (2002–03); $6450 room and board; 90% average percent of need met; $13,131 average financial aid amount received per undergraduate (2001–02).

Academics Wells awards bachelor's degrees. Challenging opportunities include advanced placement credit, accelerated degree programs, student-designed majors, double majors, independent study, and a senior project. Special programs include internships, off-campus study, study-abroad, and Air Force ROTC. The most frequently chosen baccalaureate fields are social sciences and history, psychology, and visual/performing arts. The faculty at Wells has 40 full-time members, 98% with terminal degrees. The student-faculty ratio is 7:1.

Students of Wells The student body is made up of 437 undergraduates. Students come from 32 states and territories and 8 other countries. 73% are from New York. 2.4% are international students. 69% returned for their sophomore year.

Applying Wells requires an essay, SAT I or ACT, a high school transcript, and 2 recommendations. The school recommends an interview. Application deadline: 3/1; 2/15 priority date for financial aid. Early and deferred admission are possible.

WENTWORTH INSTITUTE OF TECHNOLOGY

Boston, MA

Urban setting ■ *Private* ■ *Independent* ■ *Coed*

Web site: www.wit.edu
Contact: Ms. Keiko S. Broomhead, Director of Admissions, 550 Huntington Avenue, Boston, MA 02115-5998
Telephone: 617-989-4009 or toll-free 800-556-0610 **Fax:** 617-989-4010
E-mail: admissions@wit.edu

Getting in Last Year 3,623 applied; 70% were accepted; 1,064 enrolled (42%).

Financial Matters $14,300 tuition and fees (2002–03); $7800 room and board; 65% average percent of need met; $8146 average financial aid amount received per undergraduate (2000–01).

Academics Wentworth awards associate and bachelor's degrees. Challenging opportunities include advanced placement credit, accelerated degree programs, freshman honors college, and a senior project. Special programs include cooperative education, internships, summer session for credit, off-campus study, study-abroad, and Army and Air Force ROTC. The most frequently chosen baccalaureate fields are engineering/engineering technologies, computer/information sciences, and visual/performing arts. The faculty at Wentworth has 115 full-time members. The student-faculty ratio is 24:1.

Students of Wentworth The student body is made up of 3,273 undergraduates. 18.5% are women and 81.5% are men. 6.3% are international students.

Applying Wentworth requires SAT I or ACT and a high school transcript. The school recommends an essay, an interview, recommendations, and a minimum high school GPA of 2.0. Application deadline: rolling admissions; 3/1 priority date for financial aid. Deferred admission is possible.

WESLEYAN COLLEGE

Macon, GA

Suburban setting ■ *Private* ■ *Independent Religious* ■ *Women Only*

Web site: www.wesleyancollege.edu
Contact: Ms. Betsy Anderberg, Administrative Assistant to Vice President for Enrollment, 4760 Forsyth Road, Macon, GA 31210-4462
Telephone: 478-757-5206 or toll-free 800-447-6610 **Fax:** 478-757-4030
E-mail: admissions@wesleyancollege.edu

Getting in Last Year 449 applied; 72% were accepted; 163 enrolled (50%).

Financial Matters $9800 tuition and fees (2002–03); $7250 room and board; 87% average percent of need met; $11,409 average financial aid amount received per undergraduate.

Academics Wesleyan awards bachelor's and master's degrees. Challenging opportunities include advanced placement credit, student-designed majors, an honors program, double majors, independent study, and a senior project. Special programs include cooperative education, internships, summer session for credit, off-campus study, and study-abroad. The most frequently chosen baccalaureate fields are psychology, business/marketing, and communications/communication technologies. The faculty at Wesleyan has 48 full-time members, 92% with terminal degrees. The student-faculty ratio is 11:1.

Students of Wesleyan The student body totals 733, of whom 679 are undergraduates. Students come from 25 states and territories and 30 other countries. 81% are from Georgia. 16.3% are international students. 73% returned for their sophomore year.

Applying Wesleyan requires an essay, SAT I or ACT, a high school transcript, and 1 recommendation. The school recommends an interview and 2 recommendations. Application deadline: 6/1. Early and deferred admission are possible.

WESLEYAN UNIVERSITY

Middletown, CT

Small-town setting ■ *Private* ■ *Independent* ■ *Coed*

Web site: www.wesleyan.edu
Contact: Ms. Nancy Hargrave Meislahn, Dean of Admission and Financial Aid, Stewart M Reid House, 70 Wyllys Avenue, Middletown, CT 06459-0265
Telephone: 860-685-3000 **Fax:** 860-685-3001

Wesleyan University (continued)

E-mail: admissions@wesleyan.edu

Getting in Last Year 6,474 applied; 28% were accepted; 717 enrolled (39%).

Financial Matters $28,320 tuition and fees (2002–03); $7610 room and board; 100% average percent of need met; $24,532 average financial aid amount received per undergraduate (2001–02).

Academics Wesleyan awards bachelor's, master's, and doctoral degrees and post-master's certificates. Challenging opportunities include advanced placement credit, accelerated degree programs, student-designed majors, an honors program, double majors, independent study, and a senior project. Special programs include internships, summer session for credit, off-campus study, study-abroad, and Air Force ROTC. The most frequently chosen baccalaureate fields are social sciences and history, visual/performing arts, and area/ethnic studies. The faculty at Wesleyan has 311 full-time members, 95% with terminal degrees. The student-faculty ratio is 9:1.

Students of Wesleyan The student body totals 3,192, of whom 2,733 are undergraduates. 51.8% are women and 48.2% are men. Students come from 51 states and territories and 47 other countries. 10% are from Connecticut. 5.7% are international students. 95% returned for their sophomore year.

Applying Wesleyan requires an essay, SAT I and SAT II or ACT, a high school transcript, and 3 recommendations. The school recommends an interview. Application deadline: 1/1; 2/1 for financial aid. Early and deferred admission are possible.

WESLEY COLLEGE

Dover, DE

Small-town setting ■ Private ■ Independent Religious ■ Coed

Web site: www.wesley.edu
Contact: Mr. Art Jacobs, Director of Admissions, 120 North State Street, Dover, DE 19901-3875
Telephone: 302-736-2400 or toll-free 800-937-5398 ext. 2400 (out-of-state)
Fax: 302-736-2301
E-mail: admissions@wesley.edu

Getting in Last Year 1,700 applied; 72% were accepted; 551 enrolled (45%).

Financial Matters $13,123 tuition and fees (2002–03); $5810 room and board; 99% average percent of need met.

Academics Wesley awards associate, bachelor's, and master's degrees and post-bachelor's certificates. Challenging opportunities include advanced placement credit, accelerated degree programs, double majors, independent study, and a senior project. Special programs include internships, summer session for credit, study-abroad, and Army ROTC. The most frequently chosen baccalaureate fields are business/marketing, education, and psychology. The faculty at Wesley has 59 full-time members, 80% with terminal degrees. The student-faculty ratio is 17:1.

Students of Wesley The student body totals 2,254, of whom 2,121 are undergraduates. 59.7% are women and 40.3% are men. Students come from 17 states and territories and 12 other countries. 39% are from Delaware. 1.1% are international students. 58% returned for their sophomore year.

Applying Wesley requires an essay, SAT I or ACT, a high school transcript, 1 recommendation, and a minimum high school GPA of 2.2. The school recommends an interview. Application deadline: rolling admissions; 4/15 priority date for financial aid. Early and deferred admission are possible.

WEST CHESTER UNIVERSITY OF PENNSYLVANIA

West Chester, PA

Suburban setting ■ Public ■ State-supported ■ Coed

Web site: www.wcupa.edu
Contact: Ms. Marsha Haug, Director of Admissions, Messikomer Hall, Rosedale Avenue, West Chester, PA 19383
Telephone: 610-436-3411 or toll-free 877-315-2165 (in-state)
Fax: 610-436-2907
E-mail: ugadmiss@wcupa.edu

Getting in Last Year 9,100 applied; 50% were accepted; 1,773 enrolled (39%).

Financial Matters $4923 resident tuition and fees (2002–03); $11,491 nonresident tuition and fees (2002–03); $5146 room and board; $5686 average financial aid amount received per undergraduate.

Academics West Chester University awards associate, bachelor's, and master's degrees. Challenging opportunities include advanced placement credit, student-designed majors, an honors program, double majors, independent study, and a senior project. Special programs include internships, summer session for credit, off-campus study, study-abroad, and Army and Air Force ROTC. The most frequently chosen baccalaureate fields are education, business/marketing, and English. The faculty at West Chester University has 589 full-time members, 77% with terminal degrees. The student-faculty ratio is 18:1.

Students of West Chester University The student body totals 12,584, of whom 10,467 are undergraduates. 60.7% are women and 39.3% are men. Students come from 30 states and territories. 89% are from Pennsylvania. 83% returned for their sophomore year.

Applying West Chester University requires an essay, SAT I or ACT, a high school transcript, and a minimum high school GPA of 2.0, and in some cases an interview, recommendations, and a minimum high school GPA of 3.0. The school recommends a minimum high school GPA of 3.0. Application deadline: rolling admissions; 3/1 priority date for financial aid. Early and deferred admission are possible.

WESTERN BAPTIST COLLEGE

Salem, OR

Suburban setting ■ Private ■ Independent Religious ■ Coed

Web site: www.wbc.edu
Contact: Mr. Marty Ziesemer, Director of Admissions, 5000 Deer Park Drive, SE, Salem, OR 97301-9392
Telephone: 503-375-7115 or toll-free 800-845-3005 (out-of-state)
E-mail: admissions@wbc.edu

Getting in Last Year 554 applied; 79% were accepted; 144 enrolled (33%).

Financial Matters $15,175 tuition and fees (2002–03); $5400 room and board; 68% average percent of need met; $12,087 average financial aid amount received per undergraduate.

Academics Western awards associate and bachelor's degrees. Challenging opportunities include advanced placement credit, accelerated degree programs, freshman honors college, an honors program, double majors, independent study, and a senior project. Special programs include internships, summer session for credit, off-campus study, study-abroad, and Army and Air Force ROTC. The most frequently chosen baccalaureate fields are business/marketing, education, and home economics/vocational home economics. The faculty at Western has 34 full-time members, 41% with terminal degrees. The student-faculty ratio is 15:1.

Students of Western The student body is made up of 729 undergraduates. 62.3% are women and 37.7% are men. Students come from 24 states and territories and 7 other countries. 67% are from Oregon. 1% are international students. 78% returned for their sophomore year.

Applying Western requires an essay, SAT I or ACT, a high school transcript, 3 recommendations, and a minimum high school GPA of 2.5. Application deadline: 8/1; 2/15 priority date for financial aid. Early admission is possible.

WESTERN CAROLINA UNIVERSITY

Cullowhee, NC

Rural setting ■ Public ■ State-supported ■ Coed

Web site: www.wcu.edu
Contact: Mr. Philip Cauley, Director of Admissions, Cullowhee, NC 28723
Telephone: 828-227-7317 or toll-free 877-WCU4YOU **Fax:** 828-277-7319
E-mail: admiss@email.wcu.edu

Getting in Last Year 4,121 applied; 72% were accepted; 1,224 enrolled (41%).

Financial Matters $2610 resident tuition and fees (2002–03); $11,525 nonresident tuition and fees (2002–03); $3596 room and board; 60% average percent of need met; $5970 average financial aid amount received per undergraduate.

Academics Western Carolina awards bachelor's, master's, and doctoral degrees and post-master's certificates. Challenging opportunities include advanced placement credit, accelerated degree programs, student-designed majors, an honors program, double majors, independent study, and a senior project. Special programs include cooperative education, internships, summer session for credit, and study-abroad. The most frequently chosen baccalaureate fields are business/marketing, education, and health professions and related sciences. The faculty at Western Carolina has 323 full-time members, 78% with terminal degrees. The student-faculty ratio is 16:1.

Students of Western Carolina The student body totals 7,033, of whom 5,665 are undergraduates. 51.4% are women and 48.6% are men. Students come from 35 states and territories and 31 other countries. 92% are from North Carolina. 2.1% are international students. 69% returned for their sophomore year.

Applying Western Carolina requires SAT I, a high school transcript, and a minimum high school GPA of 2.5. Application deadline: 8/1; 3/31 priority date for financial aid. Early admission is possible.

WESTERN CONNECTICUT STATE UNIVERSITY

Danbury, CT

Urban setting ■ Public ■ State-supported ■ Coed

Web site: www.wcsu.edu
Contact: Mr. William Hawkins, Enrollment Management Officer, 181 White Street, Danbury, CT 06810
Telephone: 203-837-9000 or toll-free 877-837-9278

Getting in Last Year 3,131 applied; 61% were accepted; 818 enrolled (43%).

Financial Matters $4455 resident tuition and fees (2002–03); $10,674 nonresident tuition and fees (2002–03); $6224 room and board; 63% average percent of need met; $6314 average financial aid amount received per undergraduate (2001–02).

Academics Western awards associate, bachelor's, and master's degrees. Challenging opportunities include advanced placement credit, accelerated degree programs, student-designed majors, an honors program, double majors, independent study, and a senior project. Special programs include cooperative education, internships, summer session for credit, off-campus study, study-abroad, and Army and Air Force ROTC. The most frequently chosen baccalaureate fields are business/marketing, protective services/public administration, and education. The faculty at Western has 188 full-time members, 83% with terminal degrees. The student-faculty ratio is 17:1.

Students of Western The student body totals 6,050, of whom 5,274 are undergraduates. 55.2% are women and 44.8% are men. Students come from 25 states and territories and 19 other countries. 88% are from Connecticut. 2.2% are international students. 71% returned for their sophomore year.

Applying Western requires SAT I or ACT and a high school transcript. The school recommends an essay, an interview, and recommendations. Application deadline: 5/1; 4/15 for financial aid, with a 3/15 priority date. Early and deferred admission are possible.

WESTERN GOVERNORS UNIVERSITY

Salt Lake City, UT

Private ■ Independent ■ Coed

Web site: www.wgu.edu
Contact: Ms. Wendy Gregory, Admissions Manager, 2040 East Murray Holladay Road, Suite 106, Salt Lake City, UT 84117
Telephone: 801-274-3280 ext. 315 or toll-free 877-435-7948 **Fax:** 801-274-3305
E-mail: info@wgu.edu

Financial Matters $4030 tuition and fees (2002–03); 100% average percent of need met; $2719 average financial aid amount received per undergraduate.

Academics Western Governors University awards associate, bachelor's, and master's degrees and post-bachelor's and post-master's certificates. Challenging opportunities include accelerated degree programs, double majors, independent study, and a senior project. The faculty at Western Governors University has 18 full-time members, 78% with terminal degrees. The student-faculty ratio is 46:1.

Students of Western Governors University The student body totals 1,128, of whom 576 are undergraduates. 53.8% are women and 46.2% are men. Students come from 37 states and territories.

WESTERN ILLINOIS UNIVERSITY

Macomb, IL

Small-town setting ■ Public ■ State-supported ■ Coed

Web site: www.wiu.edu
Contact: Ms. Karen Helmers, Director of Admissions, 1 University Circle, 115 Sherman Hall, Macomb, IL 61455-1390
Telephone: 309-298-3157 or toll-free 877-742-5948 **Fax:** 309-298-3111
E-mail: kl-helmers@wiu.edu

Getting in Last Year 9,682 applied; 64% were accepted; 1,939 enrolled (31%).

Financial Matters $4846 resident tuition and fees (2002–03); $8311 nonresident tuition and fees (2002–03); $5062 room and board; 71% average percent of need met; $7220 average financial aid amount received per undergraduate.

Academics WIU awards bachelor's and master's degrees and post-bachelor's certificates. Challenging opportunities include advanced placement credit, student-designed majors, freshman honors college, an honors program, double majors, independent study, and a senior project. Special programs include internships, summer session for credit, off-campus study, study-abroad, and Army ROTC. The most frequently chosen baccalaureate fields are education, protective services/public administration, and liberal arts/general studies. The faculty at WIU has 613 full-time members, 67% with terminal degrees. The student-faculty ratio is 17:1.

Students of WIU The student body totals 13,461, of whom 11,033 are undergraduates. 50.2% are women and 49.8% are men. Students come from 42 states and territories and 54 other countries. 94% are from Illinois. 1.6% are international students. 75% returned for their sophomore year.

Applying WIU requires SAT I or ACT and a high school transcript. Application deadline: 8/1; 2/15 priority date for financial aid. Deferred admission is possible.

WESTERN INTERNATIONAL UNIVERSITY

Phoenix, AZ

Urban setting ■ Private ■ Proprietary ■ Coed

Web site: www.wintu.edu
Contact: Ms. Jo Arney, Director of Student Services, 9215 North Black Canyon Highway, Phoenix, AZ 85021
Telephone: 602-943-2311 ext. 139

Getting in Last Year 132 enrolled.

Financial Matters $8320 tuition and fees (2002–03).

Academics WIU awards associate, bachelor's, and master's degrees. Challenging opportunities include advanced placement credit, accelerated degree programs, an honors program, double majors, independent study, and a senior project. Special programs include summer session for credit and study-abroad. The faculty at WIU has 243 members. The student-faculty ratio is 10:1.

Students of WIU The student body totals 3,751, of whom 2,856 are undergraduates. 55.7% are women and 44.3% are men. 1.5% are international students.

Applying WIU requires a high school transcript, an interview, and a minimum high school GPA of 2.5, and in some cases 3 recommendations. The school recommends 3 recommendations. Application deadline: rolling admissions. Deferred admission is possible.

WESTERN KENTUCKY UNIVERSITY

Bowling Green, KY

Suburban setting ■ Public ■ State-supported ■ Coed

Web site: www.wku.edu
Contact: Dr. Dean R. Kaliler, Director of Admissions and Academic Services, Potter Hall 117, 1 Big Red Way, Bowling Green, KY 42101-3576
Telephone: 270-745-2551 or toll-free 800-495-8463 (in-state)
Fax: 270-745-6133
E-mail: admission@wku.edu

Getting in Last Year 5,730 applied; 88% were accepted; 3,072 enrolled (61%).

Financial Matters $3120 resident tuition and fees (2002–03); $7992 nonresident tuition and fees (2002–03); $3786 room and board; 38% average percent of need met; $5700 average financial aid amount received per undergraduate (2001–02).

Academics WKU awards associate, bachelor's, and master's degrees and first-professional certificates. Challenging opportunities include advanced placement credit, accelerated degree programs, student-designed majors, an honors program, double majors, and a senior project. Special programs include cooperative education, internships, summer session for credit, study-abroad, and Army and Air Force ROTC. The most frequently chosen baccalaureate fields are business/marketing, education, and social sciences and history. The faculty at WKU has 620 full-time members, 67% with terminal degrees. The student-faculty ratio is 19:1.

Students of WKU The student body totals 17,818, of whom 15,234 are undergraduates. 58.9% are women and 41.1% are men. Students come from 46 states and territories and 60 other countries. 83% are from Kentucky. 0.6% are international students. 75% returned for their sophomore year.

Applying WKU requires SAT I or ACT, a high school transcript, and a minimum high school GPA of 2.5. Application deadline: 8/1, 6/1 for nonresidents; 4/1 priority date for financial aid.

WESTERN MICHIGAN UNIVERSITY

Kalamazoo, MI

Urban setting ■ Public ■ State-supported ■ Coed

Web site: www.wmich.edu
Contact: Mr. John Fraire, Dean, Office of Admissions and Orientation, 1903 West Michigan Avenue, Kalamazoo, MI 49008
Telephone: 269-387-2000 or toll-free 800-400-4968 (in-state)
Fax: 269-387-2096
E-mail: ask-wmu@wmich.edu

Getting in Last Year 15,832 applied; 80% were accepted; 4,474 enrolled (35%).

Financial Matters $4924 resident tuition and fees (2002–03); $11,609 nonresident tuition and fees (2002–03); $6128 room and board; 69% average percent of need met; $7006 average financial aid amount received per undergraduate.

Academics WMU awards bachelor's, master's, and doctoral degrees and post-master's certificates. Challenging opportunities include advanced placement credit, accelerated degree programs, student-designed majors, freshman honors college, an honors program, double majors, independent study, and a senior project. Special programs include cooperative education, internships, summer session for credit, off-campus study, study-abroad, and Army ROTC. The most frequently chosen baccalaureate fields are business/marketing, education, and engineering/engineering technologies. The faculty at WMU has 985 full-time members, 87% with terminal degrees. The student-faculty ratio is 16:1.

Students of WMU The student body totals 29,732, of whom 23,643 are undergraduates. 51.5% are women and 48.5% are men. Students come from 52 states and territories and 102 other countries. 93% are from Michigan. 3.8% are international students. 77% returned for their sophomore year.

Applying WMU requires SAT I or ACT and a high school transcript, and in some cases an interview. Application deadline: rolling admissions. Early and deferred admission are possible.

WESTERN NEW ENGLAND COLLEGE

Springfield, MA

Suburban setting ■ Private ■ Independent ■ Coed

Web site: www.wnec.edu
Contact: Dr. Charles R. Pollock, Vice President of Enrollment Management, 1215 Wilbraham Road, Springfield, MA 01119-2654
Telephone: 413-782-1321 or toll-free 800-325-1122 ext. 1321
Fax: 413-782-1777
E-mail: ugradmis@wnec.edu

Getting in Last Year 4,180 applied; 73% were accepted; 778 enrolled (25%).

Financial Matters $17,754 tuition and fees (2002–03); $7688 room and board; 72% average percent of need met; $12,001 average financial aid amount received per undergraduate.

Academics WNEC awards associate, bachelor's, master's, and first-professional degrees. Challenging opportunities include advanced placement credit, student-designed majors, an honors program, double majors, independent study, and a senior project. Special programs include internships, summer session for credit, off-campus study, study-abroad, and Army and Air Force ROTC. The most frequently chosen baccalaureate fields are protective services/public administration, business/marketing, and engineering/engineering technologies. The faculty at WNEC has 154 full-time members, 88% with terminal degrees. The student-faculty ratio is 17:1.

Students of WNEC The student body totals 4,461, of whom 3,151 are undergraduates. 37% are women and 63% are men. Students come from 27 states and territories and 11 other countries. 43% are from Massachusetts. 0.7% are international students. 74% returned for their sophomore year.

Applying WNEC requires SAT I or ACT, a high school transcript, 1 recommendation, and a minimum high school GPA of 2.2. The school recommends an essay and an interview. Application deadline: rolling admissions.

WESTERN NEW MEXICO UNIVERSITY

Silver City, NM

Rural setting ■ Public ■ State-supported ■ Coed

Web site: www.wnmu.edu
Contact: Mr. Michael Alecksen, Director of Admissions, College Avenue, Silver City, NM 88062-0680
Telephone: 505-538-6106 or toll-free 800-872-WNMU (in-state)
Fax: 505-538-6155

Financial Matters $2289 resident tuition and fees (2002–03); $7433 nonresident tuition and fees (2002–03); 83% average percent of need met; $5230 average financial aid amount received per undergraduate (2001–02).

Academics WNMU awards associate, bachelor's, and master's degrees. Challenging opportunities include advanced placement credit, accelerated degree programs, student-designed majors, and a senior project. Special programs include cooperative education, internships, and summer session for credit. The faculty at WNMU has 90 full-time members. The student-faculty ratio is 17:1.

Students of WNMU The student body totals 3,074, of whom 2,555 are undergraduates. Students come from 33 states and territories and 6 other countries. 52% returned for their sophomore year.

Applying WNMU requires ACT COMPASS and a high school transcript. The school recommends ACT. Application deadline: 8/1; 4/1 priority date for financial aid. Early and deferred admission are possible.

WESTERN OREGON UNIVERSITY

Monmouth, OR

Rural setting ■ Public ■ State-supported ■ Coed

Web site: www.wou.edu
Contact: Mr. Rob Kvidt, Director of Admissions, 345 North Monmouth Avenue, Monmouth, OR 97361
Telephone: 503-838-8211 or toll-free 877-877-1593 **Fax:** 503-838-8067
E-mail: wolfgram@wou.edu

Getting in Last Year 1,541 applied; 93% were accepted; 790 enrolled (55%).

Financial Matters $3720 resident tuition and fees (2002–03); $11,772 nonresident tuition and fees (2002–03); $5724 room and board; 71% average percent of need met; $6278 average financial aid amount received per undergraduate.

Academics Western Oregon University awards associate, bachelor's, and master's degrees. Challenging opportunities include advanced placement credit, student-designed majors, freshman honors college, an honors program, double majors, independent study, and a senior project. Special programs include internships, summer session for credit, off-campus study, study-abroad, and Army and Air Force ROTC. The most frequently chosen baccalaureate fields are business/marketing, psychology, and protective services/public administration. The faculty at Western Oregon University has 178 full-time members, 83% with terminal degrees. The student-faculty ratio is 20:1.

Students of Western Oregon University The student body totals 5,030, of whom 4,463 are undergraduates. 58.1% are women and 41.9% are men. Students come from 29 states and territories and 15 other countries. 91% are from Oregon. 1.7% are international students. 69% returned for their sophomore year.

Applying Western Oregon University requires SAT I or ACT, a high school transcript, and a minimum high school GPA of 2.75. The school recommends SAT I and SAT II or ACT. Application deadline: rolling admissions; 3/1 priority date for financial aid. Deferred admission is possible.

WESTERN STATE COLLEGE OF COLORADO

Gunnison, CO

Small-town setting ■ Public ■ State-supported ■ Coed

Web site: www.western.edu
Contact: Mr. Timothy L. Albers, Director of Admissions, Western State College of Colorado, 6 Admission Office, 600 North Adams, Gunnison, CO 81231
Telephone: 970-943-2119 or toll-free 800-876-5309 **Fax:** 970-943-2212
E-mail: discover@western.edu

Getting in Last Year 1,985 applied; 81% were accepted; 609 enrolled (38%).

Financial Matters $2479 resident tuition and fees (2002–03); $9043 nonresident tuition and fees (2002–03); $5680 room and board; 55% average percent of need met; $8800 average financial aid amount received per undergraduate.

Academics Western State College awards bachelor's degrees. Challenging opportunities include advanced placement credit, accelerated degree programs, student-designed majors, an honors program, double majors, and a senior project. Special programs include cooperative education, internships, summer session for credit, off-campus study, and study-abroad. The most frequently chosen baccalaureate fields are business/marketing, social sciences and history, and parks and recreation. The faculty at Western State College has 97 full-time members, 82% with terminal degrees. The student-faculty ratio is 20:1.

Students of Western State College The student body is made up of 2,320 undergraduates. 42.1% are women and 57.9% are men. Students come from 50 states and territories and 11 other countries. 72% are from Colorado. 53% returned for their sophomore year.

Applying Western State College requires SAT I or ACT and a high school transcript, and in some cases an essay, an interview, and 2 recommendations. The school recommends a minimum high school GPA of 2.5. Application deadline: rolling admissions; 4/1 priority date for financial aid. Deferred admission is possible.

WESTERN WASHINGTON UNIVERSITY

Bellingham, WA

Small-town setting ■ Public ■ State-supported ■ Coed

Web site: www.wwu.edu
Contact: Ms. Karen Copetas, Director of Admissions, 516 High Street, Bellingham, WA 98225-9009
Telephone: 360-650-3440 ext. 3440 **Fax:** 360-650-7369
E-mail: admit@cc.wwu.edu

Getting in Last Year 7,464 applied; 74% were accepted; 2,240 enrolled (40%).

Financial Matters $3702 resident tuition and fees (2002–03); $11,901 nonresident tuition and fees (2002–03); $5648 room and board; 87% average percent of need met; $7854 average financial aid amount received per undergraduate.

Academics Western awards bachelor's and master's degrees and post-bachelor's certificates. Challenging opportunities include advanced placement credit, accelerated degree programs, student-designed majors, an honors program, double majors, independent study, and a senior project. Special programs include cooperative education, internships, summer session for credit, off-campus study, and study-abroad. The most frequently chosen baccalaureate fields are business/marketing, education, and social sciences and history. The faculty at Western has 455 full-time members, 86% with terminal degrees. The student-faculty ratio is 20:1.

Students of Western The student body totals 12,409, of whom 11,647 are undergraduates. 55.8% are women and 44.2% are men. Students come from 47 states and territories and 41 other countries. 92% are from Washington. 1.1% are international students. 79% returned for their sophomore year.

Applying Western requires SAT I or ACT, TOEFL for international applicants, a high school transcript, and a minimum high school GPA of 2.5. The school recommends an essay. Application deadline: 3/1; 2/15 priority date for financial aid.

WESTFIELD STATE COLLEGE

Westfield, MA

Small-town setting ■ Public ■ State-supported ■ Coed

Web site: www.wsc.ma.edu
Contact: Ms. Emily Wilson, Assistant Director of Admissions, 333 Western Avenue, Westfield, MA 01086
Telephone: 413-572-5218 or toll-free 800-322-8401 (in-state)
Fax: 413-572-0520
E-mail: admission@wsc.mass.edu

Getting in Last Year 3,858 applied; 64% were accepted; 922 enrolled (37%).

Financial Matters $3755 resident tuition and fees (2002–03); $9835 nonresident tuition and fees (2002–03); $4762 room and board; 79% average percent of need met; $4561 average financial aid amount received per undergraduate (2001–02).

Academics Westfield State awards bachelor's and master's degrees and post-bachelor's and post-master's certificates. Challenging opportunities include advanced placement credit, student-designed majors, an honors program, double majors, independent study, and a senior project. Special programs include cooperative education, internships, summer session for credit, off-campus study, study-abroad, and Army and Air Force ROTC. The most frequently chosen baccalaureate fields are protective services/public administration, education, and business/marketing. The faculty at Westfield State has 159 full-time members, 82% with terminal degrees. The student-faculty ratio is 18:1.

Students of Westfield State The student body totals 5,188, of whom 4,415 are undergraduates. 55.6% are women and 44.4% are men. Students come from 13 states and territories. 93% are from Massachusetts. 0.1% are international students. 74% returned for their sophomore year.

Applying Westfield State requires SAT I or ACT and a high school transcript. The school recommends SAT I and recommendations. Application deadline: 3/1; 3/1 priority date for financial aid. Deferred admission is possible.

WEST LIBERTY STATE COLLEGE
West Liberty, WV

Rural setting ■ Public ■ State-supported ■ Coed

Web site: www.wlsc.edu
Contact: Ms. Stephanie North, Admissions Counselor, PO Box 295, West Liberty, WV 26074
Telephone: 304-336-8078 or toll-free 800-732-6204 ext. 8076
Fax: 304-336-8403
E-mail: wladmsn1@whsc.edu

Getting in Last Year 1,201 applied; 98% were accepted; 486 enrolled (41%).

Financial Matters $2748 resident tuition and fees (2002–03); $7098 nonresident tuition and fees (2002–03); $4180 room and board; 77% average percent of need met; $5592 average financial aid amount received per undergraduate.

Academics West Liberty awards associate and bachelor's degrees. Challenging opportunities include advanced placement credit, accelerated degree programs, student-designed majors, an honors program, double majors, independent study, and a senior project. Special programs include internships, summer session for credit, and off-campus study. The most frequently chosen baccalaureate fields are education, business/marketing, and protective services/public administration. The faculty at West Liberty has 111 full-time members, 43% with terminal degrees. The student-faculty ratio is 19:1.

Students of West Liberty The student body totals 2,589, of whom 2,566 are undergraduates. 55.4% are women and 44.6% are men. Students come from 22 states and territories and 9 other countries. 72% are from West Virginia. 0.7% are international students. 68% returned for their sophomore year.

Applying West Liberty requires SAT I or ACT, a high school transcript, and a minimum high school GPA of 2.0. The school recommends an interview. Application deadline: 3/1 priority date for financial aid.

WESTMINSTER CHOIR COLLEGE OF RIDER UNIVERSITY
Princeton, NJ

Small-town setting ■ Private ■ Independent ■ Coed

Web site: westminster.rider.edu
Contact: Elizabeth S. Rush, Assistant Director of Admissions, 101 Walnut Lane, Princeton, NJ 08540-3899
Telephone: 609-921-7144 ext. 8221 or toll-free 800-96-CHOIR
Fax: 609-921-2538
E-mail: wccadmission@rider.edu

Getting in Last Year 193 applied; 67% were accepted; 80 enrolled (62%).

Financial Matters $19,480 tuition and fees (2002–03); $7890 room and board; 75% average percent of need met; $15,424 average financial aid amount received per undergraduate.

Academics Westminster awards bachelor's and master's degrees. Challenging opportunities include advanced placement credit, an honors program, double majors, independent study, and a senior project. Special programs include internships, summer session for credit, and off-campus study. The most frequently chosen baccalaureate field is visual/performing arts. The faculty at Westminster has 35 full-time members. The student-faculty ratio is 7:1.

Students of Westminster The student body totals 446, of whom 340 are undergraduates. 59.7% are women and 40.3% are men. Students come from 40 states and territories. 36% are from New Jersey. 84% returned for their sophomore year.

Applying Westminster requires an essay, SAT I or ACT, a high school transcript, 2 recommendations, and audition, music examination. The school recommends an interview and a minimum high school GPA of 2.5. Application deadline: rolling admissions; 3/1 priority date for financial aid. Deferred admission is possible.

WESTMINSTER COLLEGE
Fulton, MO

Small-town setting ■ Private ■ Independent Religious ■ Coed

Web site: www.westminster-mo.edu
Contact: Dr. Patrick Kirby, Dean of Enrollment Services, 501 Westminster Avenue, Fulton, MO 65251-1299
Telephone: 573-592-5251 or toll-free 800-475-3361 **Fax:** 573-592-5255
E-mail: admissions@jaynet.wcmo.edu

Getting in Last Year 941 applied; 66% were accepted; 208 enrolled (33%).

Financial Matters $16,370 tuition and fees (2002–03); $5430 room and board; 93% average percent of need met; $14,906 average financial aid amount received per undergraduate.

Academics Westminster awards bachelor's degrees. Challenging opportunities include advanced placement credit, student-designed majors, an honors program, double majors, independent study, and a senior project. Special programs include cooperative education, internships, summer session for credit, off-campus study, study-abroad, and Army and Air Force ROTC. The most frequently chosen baccalaureate fields are social sciences and history, education, and psychology. The faculty at Westminster has 56 full-time members, 86% with terminal degrees. The student-faculty ratio is 12:1.

Students of Westminster The student body is made up of 789 undergraduates. 44.7% are women and 55.3% are men. Students come from 28 states and territories and 15 other countries. 73% are from Missouri. 5.3% are international students. 80% returned for their sophomore year.

Applying Westminster requires SAT I or ACT, a high school transcript, and 1 recommendation, and in some cases an interview. The school recommends an essay. Application deadline: rolling admissions; 2/28 priority date for financial aid. Early and deferred admission are possible.

WESTMINSTER COLLEGE
New Wilmington, PA

Small-town setting ■ Private ■ Independent Religious ■ Coed

Web site: www.westminster.edu
Contact: Mr. Doug Swartz, Director of Admissions, 319 South Market Street, New Wilmington, PA 16172-0001
Telephone: 724-946-7100 or toll-free 800-942-8033 (in-state)
Fax: 724-946-7171
E-mail: swartzdl@westminster.edu

Getting in Last Year 1,191 applied; 78% were accepted; 352 enrolled (38%).

Financial Matters $18,960 tuition and fees (2002–03); $5590 room and board; 92% average percent of need met; $16,605 average financial aid amount received per undergraduate.

Academics Westminster awards bachelor's and master's degrees. Challenging opportunities include advanced placement credit, student-designed majors, an honors program, double majors, and independent study. Special programs include internships, summer session for credit, off-campus study, study-abroad, and Army ROTC. The most frequently chosen baccalaureate fields are education, business/marketing, and social sciences and history. The faculty at Westminster has 99 full-time members, 82% with terminal degrees. The student-faculty ratio is 13:1.

Students of Westminster The student body totals 1,576, of whom 1,440 are undergraduates. 61.2% are women and 38.8% are men. Students come from 22 states and territories. 78% are from Pennsylvania. 89% returned for their sophomore year.

Applying Westminster requires an essay, SAT I or ACT, a high school transcript, 2 recommendations, and a minimum high school GPA of 2.0. The school recommends an interview and a minimum high school GPA of 3.0. Application deadline: 5/1; 5/1 priority date for financial aid. Deferred admission is possible.

WESTMINSTER COLLEGE
Salt Lake City, UT

Suburban setting ■ Private ■ Independent ■ Coed

Web site: www.westminstercollege.edu
Contact: Mr. Philip J. Alletto, Vice President of Student Development and Enrollment Management, 1840 South 1300 East, Salt Lake City, UT 84105-3697
Telephone: 801-832-2200 or toll-free 800-748-4753 **Fax:** 801-484-3252
E-mail: admispub@westminstercollege.edu

Getting in Last Year 775 applied; 87% were accepted; 302 enrolled (45%).

Financial Matters $15,990 tuition and fees (2002–03); $4820 room and board; 87% average percent of need met; $13,573 average financial aid amount received per undergraduate.

Academics Westminster College awards bachelor's and master's degrees and post-bachelor's certificates. Challenging opportunities include advanced placement credit, accelerated degree programs, student-designed majors, an honors program, independent study, and a senior project. Special programs include

Westminster College (continued)

cooperative education, internships, summer session for credit, and Army, Navy and Air Force ROTC. The most frequently chosen baccalaureate fields are business/marketing, health professions and related sciences, and education. The faculty at Westminster College has 112 full-time members, 89% with terminal degrees. The student-faculty ratio is 11:1.

Students of Westminster College The student body totals 2,353, of whom 1,915 are undergraduates. 57.4% are women and 42.6% are men. Students come from 30 states and territories and 19 other countries. 92% are from Utah. 1.7% are international students. 77% returned for their sophomore year.

Applying Westminster College requires SAT I or ACT, a high school transcript, and a minimum high school GPA of 2.5. The school recommends an essay, an interview, 1 recommendation, and a minimum high school GPA of 3.0. Application deadline: rolling admissions. Early and deferred admission are possible.

WESTMONT COLLEGE

Santa Barbara, CA

Suburban setting ■ Private ■ Independent Religious ■ Coed

Web site: www.westmont.edu

Contact: Mrs. Joyce Luy, Director of Admissions, 955 La Paz Road, Santa Barbara, CA 93108

Telephone: 805-565-6200 ext. 6005 or toll-free 800-777-9011 **Fax:** 805-565-6234

E-mail: admissions@westmont.edu

Getting in Last Year 1,530 applied; 65% were accepted; 333 enrolled (34%).

Financial Matters $23,536 tuition and fees (2002–03); $7922 room and board; 72% average percent of need met; $16,324 average financial aid amount received per undergraduate.

Academics Westmont awards bachelor's degrees and post-bachelor's certificates. Challenging opportunities include advanced placement credit, accelerated degree programs, student-designed majors, an honors program, double majors, independent study, and a senior project. Special programs include cooperative education, internships, summer session for credit, off-campus study, study-abroad, and Army and Air Force ROTC. The most frequently chosen baccalaureate fields are social sciences and history, communications/communication technologies, and biological/life sciences. The faculty at Westmont has 83 full-time members, 88% with terminal degrees. The student-faculty ratio is 13:1.

Students of Westmont The student body is made up of 1,323 undergraduates. 65.5% are women and 34.5% are men. Students come from 41 states and territories. 66% are from California. 0.5% are international students. 85% returned for their sophomore year.

Applying Westmont requires an essay, SAT I or ACT, a high school transcript, and recommendations, and in some cases an interview. The school recommends an interview and a minimum high school GPA of 3.0. Application deadline: 2/15; 3/1 priority date for financial aid.

WEST SUBURBAN COLLEGE OF NURSING

Oak Park, IL

Suburban setting ■ Private ■ Independent ■ Coed, Primarily Women

Web site: www.wscn.edu

Contact: Ms. Cindy Valdez, Director of Admission and Records/Registrar, 3 Erie Court, Oak Park, IL 60302

Telephone: 708-763-6530 **Fax:** 708-763-1531

Getting in Last Year 40 applied; 35% were accepted; 10 enrolled (71%).

Financial Matters $16,999 tuition and fees (2002–03); $5100 room and board.

Academics West Suburban College of Nursing awards bachelor's degrees. Challenging opportunities include advanced placement credit, accelerated degree programs, and independent study. Summer session for credit is a special program. The most frequently chosen baccalaureate field is health professions and related sciences. The faculty at West Suburban College of Nursing has 10 full-time members, 30% with terminal degrees. The student-faculty ratio is 14:1.

Students of West Suburban College of Nursing The student body is made up of 105 undergraduates. 97.1% are women and 2.9% are men. Students come from 8 states and territories. 92% are from Illinois.

Applying Application deadline: rolling admissions. Deferred admission is possible.

WEST TEXAS A&M UNIVERSITY

Canyon, TX

Small-town setting ■ Public ■ State-supported ■ Coed

Web site: www.wtamu.edu

Contact: Ms. Lila Vars, Director of Admissions, WT Box 60907, Canyon, TX 79016-0001

Telephone: 806-651-2020 or toll-free 800-99-WTAMU (in-state), 800-99-WTMAU (out-of-state) **Fax:** 806-651-5268

E-mail: lvars@mail.wtamu.edu

Getting in Last Year 1,673 applied; 70% were accepted; 825 enrolled (71%).

Financial Matters $2420 resident tuition and fees (2002–03); $7652 nonresident tuition and fees (2002–03); $4215 room and board; 68% average percent of need met; $5770 average financial aid amount received per undergraduate.

Academics WTAMU awards bachelor's and master's degrees. Challenging opportunities include advanced placement credit, student-designed majors, an honors program, double majors, independent study, and a senior project. Special programs include cooperative education, internships, and summer session for credit. The most frequently chosen baccalaureate fields are business/marketing, interdisciplinary studies, and health professions and related sciences. The faculty at WTAMU has 225 full-time members, 72% with terminal degrees. The student-faculty ratio is 23:1.

Students of WTAMU The student body totals 6,781, of whom 5,410 are undergraduates. 54.9% are women and 45.1% are men. Students come from 32 states and territories and 28 other countries. 92% are from Texas. 1.8% are international students. 66% returned for their sophomore year.

Applying WTAMU requires SAT I or ACT, a high school transcript, and class rank. Application deadline: rolling admissions; 5/1 priority date for financial aid.

WEST VIRGINIA STATE COLLEGE

Institute, WV

Suburban setting ■ Public ■ State-supported ■ Coed

Web site: www.wvsc.edu

Contact: Ms. Alice Ruhnke, Director of Admissions, Campus Box 197, PO Box 1000, Ferrell Hall, Room 106, Institute, WV 25112-1000

Telephone: 304-766-3221 or toll-free 800-987-2112 **Fax:** 304-766-4158

E-mail: ruhnkeam@mail.wvsc.edu

Getting in Last Year 732 enrolled.

Financial Matters $2754 resident tuition and fees (2002–03); $6334 nonresident tuition and fees (2002–03); $4400 room and board.

Academics WVSC awards associate and bachelor's degrees. Challenging opportunities include advanced placement credit and accelerated degree programs. Special programs include cooperative education, internships, summer session for credit, and Army ROTC. The faculty at WVSC has 149 full-time members, 50% with terminal degrees. The student-faculty ratio is 23:1.

Students of WVSC The student body is made up of 4,992 undergraduates. 60.2% are women and 39.8% are men. Students come from 34 states and territories. 97% are from West Virginia.

Applying WVSC requires SAT I or ACT and a high school transcript. Application deadline: 8/11; 6/15 for financial aid, with a 4/1 priority date. Early admission is possible.

WEST VIRGINIA UNIVERSITY

Morgantown, WV

Small-town setting ■ Public ■ State-supported ■ Coed

Web site: www.wvu.edu

Contact: Ms. Kim Guynn, Admissions Supervisor, Box 6009, Morgantown, WV 26506-6009

Telephone: 304-293-2124 ext. 1560 or toll-free 800-344-9881 **Fax:** 304-293-3080

E-mail: wvuadmissions@arc.wvu.edu

Getting in Last Year 9,147 applied; 94% were accepted; 3,978 enrolled (46%).

Financial Matters $3240 resident tuition and fees (2002–03); $9710 nonresident tuition and fees (2002–03); $5572 room and board; 88% average percent of need met; $7125 average financial aid amount received per undergraduate.

Academics WVU awards bachelor's, master's, doctoral, and first-professional degrees. Challenging opportunities include advanced placement credit, accelerated degree programs, student-designed majors, an honors program, double majors, independent study, and a senior project. Special programs include internships, summer session for credit, off-campus study, study-abroad, and Army and Air Force ROTC. The most frequently chosen baccalaureate fields are business/marketing, engineering/engineering technologies, and liberal arts/general studies. The faculty at WVU has 796 full-time members, 83% with terminal degrees. The student-faculty ratio is 19:1.

Students of WVU The student body totals 23,492, of whom 16,692 are undergraduates. 46.4% are women and 53.6% are men. Students come from 53 states and territories and 61 other countries. 62% are from West Virginia. 1.9% are international students. 76% returned for their sophomore year.

Applying WVU requires SAT I or ACT, a high school transcript, and a minimum high school GPA of 2.0, and in some cases an essay and a minimum high school GPA of 2.25. Application deadline: 8/1; 3/1 for financial aid, with a 2/15 priority date. Early and deferred admission are possible.

WEST VIRGINIA UNIVERSITY INSTITUTE OF TECHNOLOGY

Montgomery, WV

Small-town setting ■ Public ■ State-supported ■ Coed

Web site: www.wvutech.edu
Contact: Ms. Lisa Graham, Director of Admissions, Box 10, Old Main, Montgomery, WV 25136
Telephone: 304-442-3167 or toll-free 888-554-8324 **Fax:** 304-442-3097
E-mail: admissions@wvutech.edu

Getting in Last Year 1,191 applied; 74% were accepted; 417 enrolled (47%).

Financial Matters $3322 resident tuition and fees (2002–03); $7972 nonresident tuition and fees (2002–03); $4682 room and board; 90% average percent of need met; $6536 average financial aid amount received per undergraduate.

Academics West Virginia Tech awards associate, bachelor's, and master's degrees. Challenging opportunities include advanced placement credit, accelerated degree programs, student-designed majors, and a senior project. Special programs include cooperative education, internships, summer session for credit, and Army ROTC. The most frequently chosen baccalaureate fields are engineering/engineering technologies, business/marketing, and liberal arts/general studies. The faculty at West Virginia Tech has 119 full-time members, 47% with terminal degrees. The student-faculty ratio is 17:1.

Students of West Virginia Tech The student body totals 2,468, of whom 2,435 are undergraduates. 39.9% are women and 60.1% are men. Students come from 26 states and territories and 23 other countries. 94% are from West Virginia. 3.7% are international students. 60% returned for their sophomore year.

Applying West Virginia Tech requires SAT I or ACT and a high school transcript, and in some cases a minimum high school GPA of 2.0. Application deadline: rolling admissions; 4/1 priority date for financial aid. Early admission is possible.

WEST VIRGINIA WESLEYAN COLLEGE

Buckhannon, WV

Small-town setting ■ Private ■ Independent Religious ■ Coed

Web site: www.wvwc.edu
Contact: Mr. Robert N. Skinner II, Director of Admission, 59 College Avenue, Buckhannon, WV 26201
Telephone: 304-473-8510 or toll-free 800-722-9933 (out-of-state)
Fax: 304-473-8108
E-mail: admissions@wvwc.edu

Getting in Last Year 1,362 applied; 83% were accepted; 502 enrolled (44%).

Financial Matters $19,300 tuition and fees (2002–03); $4820 room and board; 96% average percent of need met; $19,384 average financial aid amount received per undergraduate (2001–02).

Academics Wesleyan awards bachelor's and master's degrees. Challenging opportunities include advanced placement credit, student-designed majors, an honors program, double majors, independent study, and a senior project. Special programs include internships, summer session for credit, off-campus study, and study-abroad. The most frequently chosen baccalaureate fields are engineering/engineering technologies, communications/communication technologies, and social sciences and history. The faculty at Wesleyan has 85 full-time members, 75% with terminal degrees. The student-faculty ratio is 15:1.

Students of Wesleyan The student body totals 1,597, of whom 1,563 are undergraduates. 55% are women and 45% are men. 53% are from West Virginia. 3.1% are international students. 74% returned for their sophomore year.

Applying Wesleyan requires SAT I or ACT and a high school transcript. The school recommends an essay, an interview, and recommendations. Application deadline: 8/1; 2/15 priority date for financial aid. Deferred admission is possible.

WHEATON COLLEGE

Wheaton, IL

Suburban setting ■ Private ■ Independent Religious ■ Coed

Web site: www.wheaton.edu
Contact: Ms. Shawn Leftwich, Director of Admissions, 501 College Avenue, Wheaton, IL 60187-5593
Telephone: 630-752-5011 or toll-free 800-222-2419 (out-of-state)
Fax: 630-752-5285
E-mail: admissions@wheaton.edu

Getting in Last Year 1,968 applied; 54% were accepted; 569 enrolled (53%).

Financial Matters $17,320 tuition and fees (2002–03); $5738 room and board; 85% average percent of need met; $14,830 average financial aid amount received per undergraduate.

Academics Wheaton awards bachelor's, master's, and doctoral degrees and post-bachelor's certificates. Challenging opportunities include advanced placement credit, student-designed majors, double majors, independent study, and a senior project. Special programs include internships, summer session for credit, off-campus study, study-abroad, and Army and Air Force ROTC. The most frequently chosen baccalaureate fields are English, trade and industry, and education. The faculty at Wheaton has 183 full-time members, 95% with terminal degrees. The student-faculty ratio is 11:1.

Students of Wheaton The student body totals 2,872, of whom 2,395 are undergraduates. 50.9% are women and 49.1% are men. Students come from 51 states and territories and 19 other countries. 23% are from Illinois. 1.1% are international students. 92% returned for their sophomore year.

Applying Wheaton requires an essay, SAT I or ACT, a high school transcript, and 2 recommendations. The school recommends SAT II: Writing Test, SAT II Subject Test in French, German, Latin, Spanish or Hebrew, and an interview. Application deadline: 1/15; 2/15 priority date for financial aid. Deferred admission is possible.

WHEATON COLLEGE

Norton, MA

Small-town setting ■ Private ■ Independent ■ Coed

Web site: www.wheatoncollege.edu
Contact: Ms. Lynne M. Stack, Director of Admission, East Main Street, Norton, MA 02766
Telephone: 508-286-8251 or toll-free 800-394-6003 **Fax:** 508-286-8271
E-mail: admission@wheatoncollege.edu

Getting in Last Year 3,534 applied; 44% were accepted; 411 enrolled (27%).

Financial Matters $27,330 tuition and fees (2002–03); $7260 room and board; 97% average percent of need met; $20,390 average financial aid amount received per undergraduate.

Academics Wheaton awards bachelor's degrees. Challenging opportunities include advanced placement credit, accelerated degree programs, student-designed majors, an honors program, double majors, independent study, and a senior project. Special programs include internships, off-campus study, study-abroad, and Army ROTC. The most frequently chosen baccalaureate fields are social sciences and history, psychology, and English. The faculty at Wheaton has 122 full-time members, 97% with terminal degrees. The student-faculty ratio is 11:1.

Students of Wheaton The student body is made up of 1,521 undergraduates. 63.8% are women and 36.2% are men. Students come from 43 states and territories and 26 other countries. 33% are from Massachusetts. 2.3% are international students. 80% returned for their sophomore year.

Applying Wheaton requires an essay, a high school transcript, and 2 recommendations. The school recommends an interview. Application deadline: 1/15; 1/15 for financial aid. Early and deferred admission are possible.

WHEELING JESUIT UNIVERSITY

Wheeling, WV

Suburban setting ■ Private ■ Independent Religious ■ Coed

Web site: www.wju.edu
Contact: Mr. Thomas M. Pie, Director of Admissions, 316 Washington Avenue, Wheeling, WV 26003-6295
Telephone: 304-243-2359 or toll-free 800-624-6992 **Fax:** 304-243-2397
E-mail: admiss@wju.edu

Getting in Last Year 1,007 applied; 83% were accepted; 295 enrolled (35%).

Financial Matters $18,100 tuition and fees (2002–03); $5610 room and board; 91% average percent of need met; $15,155 average financial aid amount received per undergraduate.

Academics Wheeling awards bachelor's and master's degrees. Challenging opportunities include advanced placement credit, student-designed majors, an honors program, and a senior project. Special programs include cooperative education, internships, summer session for credit, and off-campus study. The most frequently chosen baccalaureate fields are biological/life sciences, health professions and related sciences, and liberal arts/general studies. The faculty at Wheeling has 83 full-time members, 86% with terminal degrees. The student-faculty ratio is 12:1.

Students of Wheeling The student body totals 1,703, of whom 1,318 are undergraduates. 61% are women and 39% are men. Students come from 32 states and territories and 28 other countries. 33% are from West Virginia. 3.7% are international students. 70% returned for their sophomore year.

Applying Wheeling requires SAT I or ACT, a high school transcript, and a minimum high school GPA of 2.2, and in some cases an interview, recommendations, and a minimum high school GPA of 3.0. The school recommends an interview and recommendations. Application deadline: rolling admissions; 3/1 priority date for financial aid. Early and deferred admission are possible.

WHEELOCK COLLEGE

Boston, MA

Urban setting ■ Private ■ Independent ■ Coed, Primarily Women

Web site: www.wheelock.edu
Contact: Ms. Lynne E. Harding, Dean of Admissions, 200 The Riverway, Boston, MA 02215
Telephone: 617-879-2204 or toll-free 800-734-5212 (out-of-state)
Fax: 617-566-4453
E-mail: undergrad@wheelock.edu

Getting in Last Year 513 applied; 79% were accepted; 137 enrolled (34%).

Financial Matters $18,925 tuition and fees (2002–03); $7690 room and board; 76% average percent of need met; $14,176 average financial aid amount received per undergraduate.

Wheelock College (continued)

Academics Wheelock awards bachelor's and master's degrees. Challenging opportunities include advanced placement credit, an honors program, double majors, independent study, and a senior project. Special programs include internships, off-campus study, and study-abroad. The most frequently chosen baccalaureate fields are education, health professions and related sciences, and protective services/public administration. The faculty at Wheelock has 57 full-time members, 84% with terminal degrees. The student-faculty ratio is 11:1.

Students of Wheelock The student body totals 967, of whom 592 are undergraduates. 93.9% are women and 6.1% are men. Students come from 20 states and territories. 42% are from Massachusetts. 0.7% are international students. 82% returned for their sophomore year.

Applying Wheelock requires an essay, SAT I or ACT, a high school transcript, and 2 recommendations. The school recommends an interview and a minimum high school GPA of 2.0. Application deadline: 3/1; 3/1 priority date for financial aid. Deferred admission is possible.

WHITMAN COLLEGE

Walla Walla, WA

Small-town setting ■ Private ■ Independent ■ Coed

Web site: www.whitman.edu
Contact: Mr. John Bogley, Dean of Admission and Financial Aid, 345 Boyer Avenue, Walla Walla, WA 99362-2083
Telephone: 509-527-5176 or toll-free 877-462-9448 **Fax:** 509-527-4967
E-mail: admission@whitman.edu

Getting in Last Year 2,411 applied; 50% were accepted; 379 enrolled (31%).

Financial Matters $24,274 tuition and fees (2002–03); $6550 room and board; 94% average percent of need met; $17,950 average financial aid amount received per undergraduate.

Academics Whitman awards bachelor's degrees. Challenging opportunities include advanced placement credit, student-designed majors, an honors program, double majors, independent study, and a senior project. Special programs include internships, off-campus study, and study-abroad. The most frequently chosen baccalaureate fields are social sciences and history, visual/performing arts, and biological/life sciences. The faculty at Whitman has 113 full-time members, 93% with terminal degrees. The student-faculty ratio is 10:1.

Students of Whitman The student body is made up of 1,454 undergraduates. 57.5% are women and 42.5% are men. Students come from 48 states and territories and 23 other countries. 44% are from Washington. 2% are international students. 94% returned for their sophomore year.

Applying Whitman requires an essay, SAT I or ACT, a high school transcript, and 1 recommendation. The school recommends SAT II: Writing Test and an interview. Application deadline: 1/15; 11/15 priority date for financial aid. Deferred admission is possible.

WHITTIER COLLEGE

Whittier, CA

Suburban setting ■ Private ■ Independent ■ Coed

Web site: www.whittier.edu
Contact: Ms. Urmi Kar, Dean of Enrollment, PO Box 634, Whittier, CA 90608-0634
Telephone: 562-907-4238 **Fax:** 562-907-4870
E-mail: admission@whittier.edu

Getting in Last Year 1,511 applied; 80% were accepted; 348 enrolled (29%).

Financial Matters $22,178 tuition and fees (2002–03); $7366 room and board; 100% average percent of need met; $24,660 average financial aid amount received per undergraduate.

Academics Whittier awards bachelor's, master's, and first-professional degrees. Challenging opportunities include advanced placement credit, accelerated degree programs, student-designed majors, double majors, independent study, and a senior project. Special programs include internships, summer session for credit, off-campus study, study-abroad, and Army and Air Force ROTC. The faculty at Whittier has 96 full-time members, 96% with terminal degrees. The student-faculty ratio is 13:1.

Students of Whittier The student body totals 2,170, of whom 1,263 are undergraduates. 57.8% are women and 42.2% are men. Students come from 33 states and territories and 20 other countries. 73% are from California. 4.3% are international students. 74% returned for their sophomore year.

Applying Whittier requires an essay, SAT I or ACT, a high school transcript, 2 recommendations, and a minimum high school GPA of 2.0, and in some cases a minimum high school GPA of 3.5. The school recommends SAT II Subject Tests, an interview, and a minimum high school GPA of 2.5. Application deadline: rolling admissions; 3/1 priority date for financial aid. Deferred admission is possible.

WHITWORTH COLLEGE

Spokane, WA

Suburban setting ■ Private ■ Independent Religious ■ Coed

Web site: www.whitworth.edu
Contact: Admissions Office, 300 West, Hawthorne Road, Spokane, WA 99251
Telephone: 800-533-4668 or toll-free 800-533-4668 (out-of-state)
Fax: 509-777-3758
E-mail: admission@whitworth.edu

Getting in Last Year 1,816 applied; 73% were accepted; 453 enrolled (34%).

Financial Matters $18,798 tuition and fees (2002–03); $6050 room and board; 85% average percent of need met; $16,510 average financial aid amount received per undergraduate.

Academics Whitworth awards bachelor's and master's degrees. Challenging opportunities include advanced placement credit, student-designed majors, double majors, independent study, and a senior project. Special programs include cooperative education, internships, summer session for credit, off-campus study, study-abroad, and Army ROTC. The student-faculty ratio is 13:1.

Students of Whitworth The student body totals 2,193, of whom 1,971 are undergraduates. 59.3% are women and 40.7% are men. Students come from 31 states and territories and 25 other countries. 62% are from Washington. 2.6% are international students. 86% returned for their sophomore year.

Applying Whitworth requires an essay, SAT I or ACT, a high school transcript, and recommendations, and in some cases an interview. Application deadline: 3/1; 3/1 priority date for financial aid. Early and deferred admission are possible.

WICHITA STATE UNIVERSITY

Wichita, KS

Urban setting ■ Public ■ State-supported ■ Coed

Web site: www.wichita.edu
Contact: Ms. Christine Schneikart-Luebbe, Director of Admissions, 1845 North Fairmount, Wichita, KS 67260
Telephone: 316-978-3085 or toll-free 800-362-2594 **Fax:** 316-978-3174
E-mail: admissions@wichita.edu

Getting in Last Year 3,971 applied; 62% were accepted; 1,303 enrolled (53%).

Financial Matters $3055 resident tuition and fees (2002–03); $9832 nonresident tuition and fees (2002–03); $4420 room and board; 59% average percent of need met; $5516 average financial aid amount received per undergraduate (2001–02).

Academics WSU awards associate, bachelor's, master's, and doctoral degrees and post-bachelor's and post-master's certificates. Challenging opportunities include advanced placement credit, accelerated degree programs, student-designed majors, freshman honors college, an honors program, double majors, independent study, and a senior project. Special programs include cooperative education, internships, summer session for credit, off-campus study, and study-abroad. The most frequently chosen baccalaureate fields are business/marketing, education, and health professions and related sciences. The faculty at WSU has 480 full-time members, 71% with terminal degrees. The student-faculty ratio is 17:1.

Students of WSU The student body totals 15,534, of whom 11,940 are undergraduates. 56.6% are women and 43.4% are men. Students come from 49 states and territories and 82 other countries. 97% are from Kansas. 5.7% are international students. 67% returned for their sophomore year.

Applying WSU requires a high school transcript, and in some cases ACT and a minimum high school GPA of 2.0. Application deadline: 3/15 priority date for financial aid. Deferred admission is possible.

WIDENER UNIVERSITY

Chester, PA

Suburban setting ■ Private ■ Independent ■ Coed

Web site: www.widener.edu
Contact: Mr. Michael Hendricks, Dean of Admissions, One University Place, Chester, PA 19013
Telephone: 610-499-4126 or toll-free 888-WIDENER (in-state)
Fax: 610-499-4676
E-mail: admissions.office@widener.edu

Getting in Last Year 3,008 applied; 74% were accepted; 715 enrolled (32%).

Financial Matters $20,450 tuition and fees (2002–03); $8050 room and board; 90% average percent of need met; $18,481 average financial aid amount received per undergraduate.

Academics Widener awards bachelor's, master's, doctoral, and first-professional degrees. Challenging opportunities include advanced placement credit, accelerated degree programs, student-designed majors, an honors program, double majors, independent study, and a senior project. Special programs include cooperative education, internships, summer session for credit, off-campus study, study-abroad, and Army and Air Force ROTC. The most frequently chosen baccalaureate fields are business/marketing, health professions and related sciences, and protective services/public administration. The faculty at Widener has 221 full-time members, 85% with terminal degrees. The student-faculty ratio is 12:1.

Students of Widener The student body totals 5,828, of whom 2,407 are undergraduates. 45.9% are women and 54.1% are men. Students come from 33 states and territories and 35 other countries. 55% are from Pennsylvania. 1.8% are international students. 85% returned for their sophomore year.

Applying Widener requires an essay, SAT I or ACT, a high school transcript, an interview, and recommendations, and in some cases a minimum high school GPA of 2.5. The school recommends SAT II Subject Tests and a minimum high school GPA of 3.0. Application deadline: rolling admissions; 2/15 priority date for financial aid. Early and deferred admission are possible.

WILBERFORCE UNIVERSITY

Wilberforce, OH

Rural setting ■ *Private* ■ *Independent Religious* ■ *Coed*

Web site: www.wilberforce.edu

Contact: Mr. Kenneth C. Christmon, Director of Admissions, PO Box 1001, Wilberforce, OH 45384-1001

Telephone: 937-708-5789 or toll-free 800-367-8568 **Fax:** 937-376-4751

E-mail: kchristm@wilberforce.edu

Getting in Last Year 2,028 applied; 28% were accepted; 212 enrolled (37%).

Financial Matters $10,780 tuition and fees (2002–03); $5320 room and board.

Academics Wilberforce University awards bachelor's degrees. Challenging opportunities include advanced placement credit, freshman honors college, and an honors program. Special programs include cooperative education, off-campus study, study-abroad, and Army and Air Force ROTC. The faculty at Wilberforce University has 52 full-time members. The student-faculty ratio is 14:1.

Students of Wilberforce University The student body is made up of 1,190 undergraduates. 60.3% are women and 39.7% are men. Students come from 34 states and territories and 8 other countries. 46% are from Ohio. 1.4% are international students.

Applying Wilberforce University requires an essay, SAT I or ACT, a high school transcript, 2 recommendations, and a minimum high school GPA of 2.0. The school recommends an interview. Application deadline: 7/1; 6/1 for financial aid, with a 4/30 priority date. Early and deferred admission are possible.

WILEY COLLEGE

Marshall, TX

Small-town setting ■ *Private* ■ *Independent Religious* ■ *Coed*

Web site: www.wileyc.edu

Contact: Ms. Lalita Estes, Director of Admissions, 711 Wiley Avenue, Marshall, TX 75670

Telephone: 903-927-3356 or toll-free 800-658-6889

E-mail: vvalentine@wileyc.edu

Getting in Last Year 725 applied; 44% were accepted; 165 enrolled (52%).

Financial Matters $5960 tuition and fees (2002–03); $3824 room and board; 65% average percent of need met; $8500 average financial aid amount received per undergraduate.

Academics Wiley awards associate and bachelor's degrees. Challenging opportunities include student-designed majors and a senior project. Special programs include summer session for credit, off-campus study, and study-abroad. The most frequently chosen baccalaureate fields are business/marketing, biological/life sciences, and education. The faculty at Wiley has 50 full-time members, 62% with terminal degrees. The student-faculty ratio is 8:1.

Students of Wiley The student body is made up of 666 undergraduates. 55.6% are women and 44.4% are men. Students come from 16 states and territories and 7 other countries. 65% are from Texas. 7.5% are international students. 100% returned for their sophomore year.

Applying Wiley requires a high school transcript and 1 recommendation. The school recommends SAT I or ACT. Application deadline: 8/1; 6/1 priority date for financial aid. Early and deferred admission are possible.

WILKES UNIVERSITY

Wilkes-Barre, PA

Urban setting ■ *Private* ■ *Independent* ■ *Coed*

Web site: www.wilkes.edu

Contact: Mr. Michael Frantz, Dean, Enrollment, PO Box 111, Wilkes-Barre, PA 18766

Telephone: 570-408-4400 or toll-free 800-945-5378 ext. 4400
Fax: 570-408-4904

E-mail: admissions@wilkes.edu

Getting in Last Year 1,938 applied; 83% were accepted; 484 enrolled (30%).

Financial Matters $18,860 tuition and fees (2002–03); $8092 room and board; 82% average percent of need met; $14,793 average financial aid amount received per undergraduate.

Academics Wilkes awards bachelor's, master's, and first-professional degrees. Challenging opportunities include advanced placement credit, accelerated degree programs, student-designed majors, an honors program, double majors, independent study, and a senior project. Special programs include cooperative education, internships, summer session for credit, study-abroad, and Army and Air Force ROTC. The most frequently chosen baccalaureate fields are liberal arts/general studies, business/marketing, and psychology. The faculty at Wilkes has 116 full-time members, 81% with terminal degrees. The student-faculty ratio is 13:1.

Students of Wilkes The student body totals 3,954, of whom 1,916 are undergraduates. 49.1% are women and 50.9% are men. Students come from 22 states and territories and 6 other countries. 84% are from Pennsylvania. 0.5% are international students. 75% returned for their sophomore year.

Applying Wilkes requires SAT I or ACT and a high school transcript, and in some cases recommendations. The school recommends an interview. Application deadline: rolling admissions. Early and deferred admission are possible.

WILLAMETTE UNIVERSITY

Salem, OR

Urban setting ■ *Private* ■ *Independent Religious* ■ *Coed*

Web site: www.willamette.edu

Contact: Dr. Robin Brown, Vice President for Enrollment, 900 State Street, Salem, OR 97301-3931

Telephone: 503-370-6303 or toll-free 877-542-2787 **Fax:** 503-375-5363

E-mail: undergrad-admission@willamette.edu

Getting in Last Year 1,640 applied; 83% were accepted; 353 enrolled (26%).

Financial Matters $24,172 tuition and fees (2002–03); $6400 room and board; 93% average percent of need met; $21,886 average financial aid amount received per undergraduate.

Academics Willamette awards bachelor's, master's, and first-professional degrees and post-bachelor's and first-professional certificates. Challenging opportunities include advanced placement credit, accelerated degree programs, student-designed majors, double majors, independent study, and a senior project. Special programs include cooperative education, internships, off-campus study, study-abroad, and Air Force ROTC. The most frequently chosen baccalaureate fields are social sciences and history, foreign language/literature, and biological/life sciences. The faculty at Willamette has 187 full-time members, 91% with terminal degrees. The student-faculty ratio is 10:1.

Students of Willamette The student body totals 2,420, of whom 1,750 are undergraduates. 53.9% are women and 46.1% are men. Students come from 37 states and territories and 12 other countries. 46% are from Oregon. 1.1% are international students. 87% returned for their sophomore year.

Applying Willamette requires an essay, SAT I or ACT, a high school transcript, 1 recommendation, and a minimum high school GPA of 2.0, and in some cases an interview. The school recommends an interview. Application deadline: 2/1; 2/1 priority date for financial aid. Early and deferred admission are possible.

WILLIAM CAREY COLLEGE

Hattiesburg, MS

Small-town setting ■ *Private* ■ *Independent Religious* ■ *Coed*

Web site: www.wmcarey.edu

Contact: Mr. David Armstrong, Director of Admissions, 498 Tuscan Avenue, Hattiesburg, MS 39401-5499

Telephone: 601-318-6051 ext. 103 or toll-free 800-962-5991 (in-state), 601-318-6765 (out-of-state)

E-mail: admissions@wmcarey.edu

Getting in Last Year 232 applied; 59% were accepted; 130 enrolled (94%).

Financial Matters $7665 tuition and fees (2002–03); $3285 room and board; 75% average percent of need met; $8000 average financial aid amount received per undergraduate.

Academics Carey awards bachelor's and master's degrees. Challenging opportunities include advanced placement credit, accelerated degree programs, an honors program, double majors, independent study, and a senior project. Special programs include internships, summer session for credit, off-campus study, and Army and Air Force ROTC. The most frequently chosen baccalaureate fields are education, health professions and related sciences, and psychology. The faculty at Carey has 101 full-time members, 62% with terminal degrees. The student-faculty ratio is 15:1.

Students of Carey The student body totals 2,301, of whom 1,560 are undergraduates. 68% are women and 32% are men. Students come from 15 states and territories and 9 other countries. 79% are from Mississippi. 1.8% are international students. 64% returned for their sophomore year.

Applying Carey requires SAT I or ACT and a high school transcript, and in some cases recommendations. The school recommends a minimum high school GPA of 2.0. Application deadline: rolling admissions; 3/1 priority date for financial aid. Early and deferred admission are possible.

WILLIAM JEWELL COLLEGE

Liberty, MO

Small-town setting ■ Private ■ Independent Religious ■ Coed

Web site: www.jewell.edu
Contact: Mr. Chad Jolly, Dean of Enrollment Development, 500 College Hill, Liberty, MO 64068
Telephone: 816-781-7700 or toll-free 800-753-7009 **Fax:** 816-415-5027
E-mail: admission@william.jewell.edu

Getting in Last Year 811 applied; 96% were accepted; 345 enrolled (44%).

Financial Matters $15,400 tuition and fees (2002–03); $4550 room and board; $11,899 average financial aid amount received per undergraduate.

Academics William Jewell awards bachelor's degrees (also offers evening program with significant enrollment not reflected in profile). Challenging opportunities include advanced placement credit, student-designed majors, an honors program, double majors, independent study, and a senior project. Special programs include cooperative education, internships, summer session for credit, and study-abroad. The most frequently chosen baccalaureate fields are business/marketing, education, and psychology. The faculty at William Jewell has 75 full-time members, 85% with terminal degrees. The student-faculty ratio is 12:1.

Students of William Jewell The student body is made up of 1,168 undergraduates. 57.9% are women and 42.1% are men. Students come from 32 states and territories and 12 other countries. 97% are from Missouri. 1.8% are international students. 75% returned for their sophomore year.

Applying William Jewell requires SAT I or ACT, a high school transcript, and a minimum high school GPA of 2.0. The school recommends an essay, an interview, 2 recommendations, and a minimum high school GPA of 2.5. Application deadline: rolling admissions; 3/1 priority date for financial aid. Deferred admission is possible.

WILLIAM PATERSON UNIVERSITY OF NEW JERSEY

Wayne, NJ

Suburban setting ■ Public ■ State-supported ■ Coed

Web site: www.wpunj.edu
Contact: Mr. Jonathan McCoy, Director of Admissions, 300 Pompton Road, Wayne, NJ 07470
Telephone: 973-720-2906 or toll-free 877-WPU-EXCEL (in-state) **Fax:** 973-720-2910
E-mail: admissions@wpunj.edu

Getting in Last Year 5,490 applied; 64% were accepted; 1,396 enrolled (40%).

Financial Matters $6400 resident tuition and fees (2002–03); $10,200 nonresident tuition and fees (2002–03); $7030 room and board; 85% average percent of need met; $7983 average financial aid amount received per undergraduate.

Academics William Paterson University awards bachelor's and master's degrees and post-bachelor's and post-master's certificates. Challenging opportunities include advanced placement credit, accelerated degree programs, an honors program, double majors, independent study, and a senior project. Special programs include internships, summer session for credit, off-campus study, and study-abroad. The most frequently chosen baccalaureate fields are social sciences and history, business/marketing, and communications/communication technologies. The faculty at William Paterson University has 359 full-time members, 90% with terminal degrees. The student-faculty ratio is 12:1.

Students of William Paterson University The student body totals 10,924, of whom 9,198 are undergraduates. 59% are women and 41% are men. Students come from 39 states and territories and 55 other countries. 98% are from New Jersey. 1.3% are international students. 81% returned for their sophomore year.

Applying William Paterson University requires an essay, SAT I or ACT, and a high school transcript, and in some cases an interview and recommendations. The school recommends a minimum high school GPA of 2.5. Application deadline: 5/1; 4/1 priority date for financial aid. Deferred admission is possible.

WILLIAM PENN UNIVERSITY

Oskaloosa, IA

Rural setting ■ Private ■ Independent Religious ■ Coed

Web site: www.wmpenn.edu
Contact: Mrs. Mary Boyd, Director of Admissions, 201 Trueblood Avenue, Oskaloosa, IA 52577-1799
Telephone: 641-673-1012 or toll-free 800-779-7366 **Fax:** 641-673-2113
E-mail: admissions@wmpenn.edu

Getting in Last Year 781 applied; 62% were accepted; 230 enrolled (48%).

Financial Matters $13,654 tuition and fees (2002–03); $4430 room and board.

Academics William Penn awards associate and bachelor's degrees. Challenging opportunities include advanced placement credit, student-designed majors, double majors, independent study, and a senior project. Special programs include cooperative education, internships, summer session for credit, and study-abroad. The most frequently chosen baccalaureate fields are business/marketing, education, and psychology. The faculty at William Penn has 35 full-time members, 49% with terminal degrees. The student-faculty ratio is 14:1.

Students of William Penn The student body is made up of 1,499 undergraduates. 47.6% are women and 52.4% are men. Students come from 41 states and territories and 10 other countries. 72% are from Iowa. 1.1% are international students. 55% returned for their sophomore year.

Applying William Penn requires SAT I or ACT, a high school transcript, and a minimum high school GPA of 2.0, and in some cases an essay, an interview, and recommendations. Application deadline: 4/15 priority date for financial aid. Deferred admission is possible.

WILLIAMS BAPTIST COLLEGE

Walnut Ridge, AR

Rural setting ■ Private ■ Independent Religious ■ Coed

Web site: wbcoll.edu
Contact: Ms. Angela Flippo, Vice President for Enrollment, PO Box 3665, Walnut Ridge, AR 72476
Telephone: 870-886-6741 ext. 4117 or toll-free 800-722-4434 **Fax:** 870-886-3924
E-mail: admissions@wbcoll.edu

Getting in Last Year 412 applied; 69% were accepted; 111 enrolled (39%).

Financial Matters $7650 tuition and fees (2002–03); $3600 room and board; 73% average percent of need met; $8435 average financial aid amount received per undergraduate (2001–02).

Academics Williams awards associate and bachelor's degrees. Challenging opportunities include advanced placement credit, student-designed majors, an honors program, double majors, independent study, and a senior project. Special programs include internships, summer session for credit, off-campus study, study-abroad, and Army ROTC. The most frequently chosen baccalaureate fields are education, psychology, and business/marketing. The faculty at Williams has 27 full-time members, 52% with terminal degrees. The student-faculty ratio is 13:1.

Students of Williams The student body is made up of 616 undergraduates. 56.7% are women and 43.3% are men. Students come from 13 states and territories and 5 other countries. 80% are from Arkansas. 2% are international students. 61% returned for their sophomore year.

Applying Williams requires SAT I or ACT, a high school transcript, and a minimum high school GPA of 2.5. The school recommends an essay and an interview. Application deadline: rolling admissions.

WILLIAMS COLLEGE

Williamstown, MA

Small-town setting ■ Private ■ Independent ■ Coed

Web site: www.williams.edu
Contact: Mr. Richard L. Nesbitt, Director of Admission, 988 Main Street, Williamstown, MA 01267
Telephone: 413-597-2211 **Fax:** 413-597-4052
E-mail: admission@williams.edu

Getting in Last Year 4,921 applied; 23% were accepted; 537 enrolled (48%).

Financial Matters $26,520 tuition and fees (2002–03); $7230 room and board; 100% average percent of need met; $24,390 average financial aid amount received per undergraduate.

Academics Williams awards bachelor's and master's degrees. Challenging opportunities include advanced placement credit, accelerated degree programs, student-designed majors, an honors program, double majors, independent study, and a senior project. Special programs include internships, off-campus study, and study-abroad. The most frequently chosen baccalaureate fields are social sciences and history, psychology, and English. The faculty at Williams has 243 full-time members, 96% with terminal degrees. The student-faculty ratio is 8:1.

Students of Williams The student body totals 2,033, of whom 1,985 are undergraduates. 49.4% are women and 50.6% are men. Students come from 51 states and territories and 32 other countries. 20% are from Massachusetts. 5.7% are international students. 97% returned for their sophomore year.

Applying Williams requires an essay, SAT I and SAT II or ACT, a high school transcript, and 2 recommendations. Application deadline: 1/1; 2/1 for financial aid. Early and deferred admission are possible.

WILLIAMSON CHRISTIAN COLLEGE

Franklin, TN

Private ■ Independent Religious ■ Coed

Web site: www.williamsoncc.edu
Contact: Steven T. Smith, Registrar/Director or Admissions, 200 Seaboard Lane, Franklin, TN 37067
Telephone: 615-771-7821 **Fax:** 615-771-7810
E-mail: info@williamsoncc.edu

Getting in Last Year 19 applied; 79% were accepted; 1 enrolled (7%).

Financial Matters $4770 tuition and fees (2002–03); 30% average percent of need met; $3000 average financial aid amount received per undergraduate.

Academics Williamson Christian College awards associate and bachelor's degrees. Challenging opportunities include accelerated degree programs, double majors, and independent study. Internships is a special program. The faculty at Williamson Christian College has 4 full-time members, 100% with terminal degrees. The student-faculty ratio is 8:1.

Students of Williamson Christian College The student body is made up of 52 undergraduates. 42.3% are women and 57.7% are men. Students come from 1 state or territory and 1 other country. 1.9% are international students.

Applying Williamson Christian College requires a high school transcript and an interview. Application deadline: 9/1. Early admission is possible.

WILLIAM WOODS UNIVERSITY

Fulton, MO

Small-town setting ■ Private ■ Independent Religious ■ Coed

Web site: www.williamwoods.edu

Contact: Ms. Laura Archuleta, Executive Director of Enrollment Services, One University Avenue, Fulton, MO 65251

Telephone: 573-592-4221 or toll-free 800-995-3159 ext. 4221 **Fax:** 573-592-1146

E-mail: admissions@williamwoods.edu

Getting in Last Year 534 applied; 94% were accepted; 247 enrolled (49%).

Financial Matters $14,040 tuition and fees (2002–03); $5700 room and board; 79% average percent of need met; $14,162 average financial aid amount received per undergraduate.

Academics William Woods awards associate, bachelor's, and master's degrees. Challenging opportunities include advanced placement credit, accelerated degree programs, student-designed majors, an honors program, double majors, independent study, and a senior project. Special programs include internships, summer session for credit, off-campus study, study-abroad, and Army, Navy and Air Force ROTC. The most frequently chosen baccalaureate fields are business/marketing, computer/information sciences, and visual/performing arts. The faculty at William Woods has 43 full-time members, 63% with terminal degrees. The student-faculty ratio is 13:1.

Students of William Woods The student body totals 1,813, of whom 912 are undergraduates. 72.9% are women and 27.1% are men. Students come from 38 states and territories and 11 other countries. 78% are from Missouri. 4.2% are international students.

Applying William Woods requires SAT I or ACT and a high school transcript, and in some cases an essay and 2 recommendations. The school recommends an interview. Application deadline: rolling admissions; 3/1 priority date for financial aid. Early and deferred admission are possible.

WILMINGTON COLLEGE

New Castle, DE

Suburban setting ■ Private ■ Independent ■ Coed

Web site: www.wilmcoll.edu

Contact: Mr. Christopher Ferguson, Director of Admissions, 320 DuPont Highway, New Castle, DE 19720-6491

Telephone: 302-328-9407 or toll-free 877-967-5464 **Fax:** 302-328-5902

E-mail: inquire@wilmcoll.edu

Getting in Last Year 548 applied; 99% were accepted; 334 enrolled (62%).

Financial Matters $6740 tuition and fees (2002–03); 72% average percent of need met; $5136 average financial aid amount received per undergraduate (2001–02).

Academics Wilmington College awards associate, bachelor's, master's, and doctoral degrees and post-bachelor's and post-master's certificates. Challenging opportunities include accelerated degree programs, double majors, and independent study. Special programs include cooperative education, internships, summer session for credit, and Army and Air Force ROTC. The faculty at Wilmington College has 47 full-time members. The student-faculty ratio is 18:1.

Students of Wilmington College The student body totals 7,277, of whom 4,399 are undergraduates. 53.4% are women and 46.6% are men. Students come from 7 states and territories and 8 other countries. 85% returned for their sophomore year.

Applying Wilmington College requires a high school transcript. The school recommends SAT I or ACT, an interview, and recommendations. Application deadline: rolling admissions. Early and deferred admission are possible.

WILMINGTON COLLEGE

Wilmington, OH

Small-town setting ■ Private ■ Independent Religious ■ Coed

Web site: www.wilmington.edu

Contact: Ms. Tina Garland, Interim Director of Admission and Financial Aid, Pyle Center Box 1325, 251 Ludovic Street, Wilmington, OH 45177

Telephone: 937-382-6661 ext. 260 or toll-free 800-341-9318 ext. 260 **Fax:** 937-382-7077

E-mail: admission@wilmington.edu

Getting in Last Year 988 applied; 83% were accepted; 339 enrolled (41%).

Financial Matters $16,514 tuition and fees (2002–03); $6240 room and board; 91% average percent of need met; $15,091 average financial aid amount received per undergraduate (2001–02).

Academics Wilmington College awards bachelor's and master's degrees. Challenging opportunities include advanced placement credit, student-designed majors, an honors program, double majors, independent study, and a senior project. Special programs include internships, summer session for credit, off-campus study, and study-abroad. The most frequently chosen baccalaureate fields are business/marketing, education, and agriculture. The faculty at Wilmington College has 65 full-time members, 69% with terminal degrees. The student-faculty ratio is 16:1.

Students of Wilmington College The student body totals 1,262, of whom 1,231 are undergraduates. 55.6% are women and 44.4% are men. Students come from 15 states and territories and 6 other countries. 95% are from Ohio. 0.6% are international students. 93% returned for their sophomore year.

Applying Wilmington College requires SAT I or ACT and a high school transcript. The school recommends an interview, 1 recommendation, and a minimum high school GPA of 2.5. Application deadline: rolling admissions; 6/1 for financial aid, with a 3/1 priority date. Deferred admission is possible.

WILSON COLLEGE

Chambersburg, PA

Small-town setting ■ Private ■ Independent Religious ■ Women Only

Web site: www.wilson.edu

Contact: Deborah Arthur, Admissions Administrator, 1015 Philadelphia Avenue, Chambersburg, PA 17201

Telephone: 717-262-2002 or toll-free 800-421-8402 **Fax:** 717-262-2546

E-mail: admissions@wilson.edu

Getting in Last Year 213 applied; 68% were accepted; 68 enrolled (47%).

Financial Matters $15,630 tuition and fees (2002–03); $6790 room and board; 83% average percent of need met; $15,159 average financial aid amount received per undergraduate.

Academics Wilson awards associate and bachelor's degrees. Challenging opportunities include advanced placement credit, student-designed majors, double majors, independent study, and a senior project. Special programs include cooperative education, internships, summer session for credit, off-campus study, study-abroad, and Army ROTC. The most frequently chosen baccalaureate fields are business/marketing, biological/life sciences, and agriculture. The faculty at Wilson has 37 full-time members, 86% with terminal degrees. The student-faculty ratio is 9:1.

Students of Wilson The student body is made up of 738 undergraduates. Students come from 19 states and territories and 11 other countries. 71% are from Pennsylvania. 5.5% are international students. 72% returned for their sophomore year.

Applying Wilson requires an essay, SAT I or ACT, a high school transcript, and recommendations. The school recommends an interview and a minimum high school GPA of 2.7. Application deadline: rolling admissions; 4/30 priority date for financial aid. Early and deferred admission are possible.

WINGATE UNIVERSITY

Wingate, NC

Small-town setting ■ Private ■ Independent Religious ■ Coed

Web site: www.wingate.edu

Contact: Mr. Walter P. Crutchfield III, Dean of Admissions, PO Box 159, Wingate, NC 28174

Telephone: 704-233-8000 or toll-free 800-755-5550 **Fax:** 704-233-8110

E-mail: admit@wingate.edu

Getting in Last Year 1,210 applied; 79% were accepted; 374 enrolled (39%).

Financial Matters $14,550 tuition and fees (2002–03); $5460 room and board; 56% average percent of need met; $10,818 average financial aid amount received per undergraduate.

Academics Wingate awards bachelor's and master's degrees. Challenging opportunities include advanced placement credit, accelerated degree programs, an honors program, double majors, independent study, and a senior project. Special programs include internships, summer session for credit, off-campus study, study-abroad, and Army and Air Force ROTC. The most frequently chosen baccalaureate fields are business/marketing, liberal arts/general studies, and parks and recreation. The faculty at Wingate has 83 full-time members, 90% with terminal degrees. The student-faculty ratio is 13:1.

Students of Wingate The student body totals 1,433, of whom 1,328 are undergraduates. 54.7% are women and 45.3% are men. Students come from 35 states and territories and 17 other countries. 51% are from North Carolina. 2.8% are international students. 72% returned for their sophomore year.

Wingate University (continued)

Applying Wingate requires SAT I or ACT, a high school transcript, and a minimum high school GPA of 2.0, and in some cases an interview and recommendations. The school recommends an essay and a minimum high school GPA of 3.0. Application deadline: rolling admissions; 5/1 priority date for financial aid. Early and deferred admission are possible.

WINONA STATE UNIVERSITY

Winona, MN

Small-town setting ■ Public ■ State-supported ■ Coed

Web site: www.winona.edu
Contact: Mr. Douglas Schacke, Director of Admissions, PO Box 5838, Winona, MN 55987
Telephone: 507-457-5100 or toll-free 800-DIAL WSU **Fax:** 507-457-5620
E-mail: admissions@winona.edu

Getting in Last Year 4,248 applied; 82% were accepted.

Financial Matters $4165 resident tuition and fees (2002–03); $8045 nonresident tuition and fees (2002–03); $4140 room and board; 65% average percent of need met; $5406 average financial aid amount received per undergraduate (2001–02).

Academics Winona State awards associate, bachelor's, and master's degrees and post-master's certificates. Challenging opportunities include advanced placement credit, accelerated degree programs, student-designed majors, an honors program, double majors, independent study, and a senior project. Special programs include internships, summer session for credit, off-campus study, study-abroad, and Army ROTC. The most frequently chosen baccalaureate field is law/legal studies. The faculty at Winona State has 315 full-time members, 69% with terminal degrees. The student-faculty ratio is 19:1.

Students of Winona State The student body totals 7,760, of whom 7,130 are undergraduates. 63.8% are women and 36.2% are men. Students come from 39 states and territories and 55 other countries. 60% are from Minnesota. 4.1% are international students. 75% returned for their sophomore year.

Applying Winona State requires SAT I or ACT, a high school transcript, and class rank, and in some cases an essay, an interview, and recommendations. Application deadline: rolling admissions. Early and deferred admission are possible.

WINSTON-SALEM BIBLE COLLEGE

Winston-Salem, NC

Private ■ Independent Religious ■ Coed

Web site: www.wsbc.edu
Contact: Admissions Office, 4117 Northampton Drive, PO Box 777, Winston-Salem, NC 27102-0777
Telephone: 336-744-0900 **Fax:** 336-744-0901 ext.

Financial Matters $4200 tuition and fees (2002–03).

Academics Winston-Salem Bible College awards associate and bachelor's degrees.

Students of Winston-Salem Bible College The student body is made up of 40 undergraduates.

WINSTON-SALEM STATE UNIVERSITY

Winston-Salem, NC

Urban setting ■ Public ■ State-supported ■ Coed

Web site: www.wssu.edu
Contact: Ms. Patrice B. Mitchell, Director of Admissions, 601 Martin Luther King Jr Drive, Winston-Salem, NC 27110-0003
Telephone: 336-750-2070 or toll-free 800-257-4052 **Fax:** 336-750-2079
E-mail: admissions@wssu.edu

Getting in Last Year 2,213 applied; 76% were accepted; 687 enrolled (41%).

Financial Matters $2326 resident tuition and fees (2002–03); $10,197 nonresident tuition and fees (2002–03); $4272 room and board; 80% average percent of need met; $3925 average financial aid amount received per undergraduate (2001–02).

Academics Winston-Salem State awards bachelor's and master's degrees. Challenging opportunities include advanced placement credit, accelerated degree programs, freshman honors college, an honors program, double majors, independent study, and a senior project. Special programs include cooperative education, internships, summer session for credit, and Army and Air Force ROTC. The most frequently chosen baccalaureate fields are health professions and related sciences, business/marketing, and social sciences and history. The faculty at Winston-Salem State has 190 full-time members, 66% with terminal degrees. The student-faculty ratio is 12:1.

Students of Winston-Salem State The student body totals 3,495, of whom 3,396 are undergraduates. 69.1% are women and 30.9% are men. Students come from 30 states and territories. 92% are from North Carolina. 73% returned for their sophomore year.

Applying Winston-Salem State requires SAT I or ACT and a high school transcript. The school recommends 1 recommendation. Application deadline: rolling admissions; 4/1 for financial aid, with a 3/1 priority date. Early and deferred admission are possible.

WINTHROP UNIVERSITY

Rock Hill, SC

Suburban setting ■ Public ■ State-supported ■ Coed

Web site: www.winthrop.edu
Contact: Ms. Deborah Barber, Director of Admissions, Stewart House, Rock Hill, SC 29733
Telephone: 803-323-2191 or toll-free 800-763-0230 **Fax:** 803-323-2137
E-mail: admissions@winthrop.edu

Getting in Last Year 3,600 applied; 72% were accepted; 1,086 enrolled (42%).

Financial Matters $5600 resident tuition and fees (2002–03); $10,310 nonresident tuition and fees (2002–03); $4470 room and board; 70% average percent of need met; $7092 average financial aid amount received per undergraduate.

Academics Winthrop awards bachelor's and master's degrees and post-bachelor's certificates. Challenging opportunities include advanced placement credit, an honors program, double majors, and independent study. Special programs include cooperative education, internships, summer session for credit, off-campus study, and study-abroad. The most frequently chosen baccalaureate fields are business/marketing, education, and visual/performing arts. The faculty at Winthrop has 262 full-time members, 81% with terminal degrees. The student-faculty ratio is 17:1.

Students of Winthrop The student body totals 6,459, of whom 5,053 are undergraduates. 69.8% are women and 30.2% are men. Students come from 41 states and territories and 30 other countries. 88% are from South Carolina. 2% are international students. 75% returned for their sophomore year.

Applying Winthrop requires SAT I or ACT, a high school transcript, and 1 recommendation. The school recommends an essay. Application deadline: 6/1; 3/1 priority date for financial aid. Deferred admission is possible.

WISCONSIN LUTHERAN COLLEGE

Milwaukee, WI

Suburban setting ■ Private ■ Independent Religious ■ Coed

Web site: www.wlc.edu
Contact: Mr. Craig Swiontek, Director of Admissions, 8800 West Bluemound Road, Milwaukee, WI 53226-9942
Telephone: 414-443-8713 or toll-free 888-WIS LUTH **Fax:** 414-443-8514
E-mail: admissions@wlc.edu

Getting in Last Year 419 applied; 79% were accepted; 160 enrolled (49%).

Financial Matters $15,096 tuition and fees (2002–03); $5320 room and board; 88% average percent of need met; $13,268 average financial aid amount received per undergraduate.

Academics Wisconsin Lutheran awards bachelor's degrees. Challenging opportunities include advanced placement credit, student-designed majors, double majors, independent study, and a senior project. Special programs include internships, summer session for credit, study-abroad, and Army, Navy and Air Force ROTC. The most frequently chosen baccalaureate fields are communications/communication technologies, visual/performing arts, and education. The faculty at Wisconsin Lutheran has 48 full-time members, 65% with terminal degrees. The student-faculty ratio is 11:1.

Students of Wisconsin Lutheran The student body is made up of 669 undergraduates. 60.5% are women and 39.5% are men. Students come from 27 states and territories and 4 other countries. 81% are from Wisconsin. 0.9% are international students. 79% returned for their sophomore year.

Applying Wisconsin Lutheran requires SAT I or ACT, a high school transcript, 1 recommendation, minimum ACT score of 21, and a minimum high school GPA of 2.70, and in some cases an interview.

WITTENBERG UNIVERSITY

Springfield, OH

Suburban setting ■ Private ■ Independent Religious ■ Coed

Web site: www.wittenberg.edu
Contact: Mr. Kenneth G. Benne, Dean of Admissions and Financial Aid, PO Box 720, Springfield, OH 45501-0720
Telephone: 937-327-6314 ext. 6366 or toll-free 800-677-7558 ext. 6314 **Fax:** 937-327-6379
E-mail: admission@wittenberg.edu

Getting in Last Year 2,524 applied; 85% were accepted; 652 enrolled (30%).

Financial Matters $23,760 tuition and fees (2002–03); $6066 room and board; 91% average percent of need met; $21,286 average financial aid amount received per undergraduate.

Academics Wittenberg University awards bachelor's and master's degrees. Challenging opportunities include advanced placement credit, accelerated degree programs, student-designed majors, freshman honors college, an honors program, double majors, independent study, and a senior project. Special programs include cooperative education, internships, summer session for credit, off-campus study, study-abroad, and Army and Air Force ROTC. The faculty at Wittenberg University has 138 full-time members, 86% with terminal degrees. The student-faculty ratio is 14:1.

Students of Wittenberg University The student body totals 2,346, of whom 2,320 are undergraduates. 56.5% are women and 43.5% are men. Students come from 46 states and territories and 32 other countries. 57% are from Ohio. 2.5% are international students. 85% returned for their sophomore year.

Applying Wittenberg University requires an essay, SAT I or ACT, a high school transcript, and 1 recommendation, and in some cases an interview. The school recommends SAT II Subject Tests and an interview. Application deadline: 3/15; 3/15 for financial aid, with a 2/15 priority date. Early and deferred admission are possible.

WOFFORD COLLEGE

Spartanburg, SC

Urban setting ■ Private ■ Independent Religious ■ Coed

Web site: www.wofford.edu

Contact: Mr. Brand Stille, Director of Admissions, 429 North Church Street, Spartanburg, SC 29303-3663

Telephone: 864-597-4130 **Fax:** 864-597-4147

E-mail: admissions@wofford.edu

Getting in Last Year 1,349 applied; 78% were accepted; 297 enrolled (28%).

Financial Matters $19,415 tuition and fees (2002–03); $5780 room and board; 89% average percent of need met; $15,796 average financial aid amount received per undergraduate.

Academics Wofford awards bachelor's degrees. Challenging opportunities include advanced placement credit, accelerated degree programs, student-designed majors, double majors, independent study, and a senior project. Special programs include internships, summer session for credit, off-campus study, study-abroad, and Army ROTC. The most frequently chosen baccalaureate fields are business/marketing, social sciences and history, and biological/life sciences. The faculty at Wofford has 80 full-time members, 91% with terminal degrees. The student-faculty ratio is 12:1.

Students of Wofford The student body is made up of 1,085 undergraduates. 50.8% are women and 49.2% are men. Students come from 35 states and territories and 2 other countries. 65% are from South Carolina. 0.2% are international students. 90% returned for their sophomore year.

Applying Wofford requires an essay, SAT I or ACT, and a high school transcript. The school recommends SAT II: Writing Test, an interview, and 2 recommendations. Application deadline: 2/1; 3/15 priority date for financial aid. Early and deferred admission are possible.

WOODBURY UNIVERSITY

Burbank, CA

Suburban setting ■ Private ■ Independent ■ Coed

Web site: www.woodbury.edu

Contact: Mr. Don St. Clair, Vice President of Enrollment Planning, 7500 Glenoaks Boulvard, Burbank, CA 91510-7846

Telephone: 818-767-0888 or toll-free 800-784-WOOD **Fax:** 818-767-7520

E-mail: info@woodbury.edu

Getting in Last Year 330 applied; 79% were accepted; 118 enrolled (45%).

Financial Matters $19,900 tuition and fees (2002–03); $6874 room and board; 85% average percent of need met; $19,750 average financial aid amount received per undergraduate (2001–02).

Academics Woodbury awards bachelor's and master's degrees. Challenging opportunities include advanced placement credit, accelerated degree programs, double majors, independent study, and a senior project. Special programs include internships, summer session for credit, and study-abroad. The most frequently chosen baccalaureate fields are business/marketing, architecture, and computer/information sciences. The faculty at Woodbury has 41 full-time members, 85% with terminal degrees. The student-faculty ratio is 18:1.

Students of Woodbury The student body totals 1,404, of whom 1,189 are undergraduates. 56.4% are women and 43.6% are men. 7.4% are international students. 75% returned for their sophomore year.

Applying Woodbury requires an essay, SAT I or ACT, a high school transcript, 2 recommendations, and a minimum high school GPA of 2.0, and in some cases portfolio. The school recommends an interview and a minimum high school GPA of 3.0. Application deadline: rolling admissions. Deferred admission is possible.

WORCESTER POLYTECHNIC INSTITUTE

Worcester, MA

Suburban setting ■ Private ■ Independent ■ Coed

Web site: www.wpi.edu

Contact: Ms. Kristin Tichenor, Director of Admissions, 100 Institute Road, Worcester, MA 01609-2280

Telephone: 508-831-5286 **Fax:** 508-831-5875

E-mail: admissions@wpi.edu

Getting in Last Year 3,191 applied; 76% were accepted; 714 enrolled (29%).

Financial Matters $26,360 tuition and fees (2002–03); $8430 room and board; 91% average percent of need met; $19,334 average financial aid amount received per undergraduate.

Academics WPI awards bachelor's, master's, and doctoral degrees and post-bachelor's and post-master's certificates. Challenging opportunities include advanced placement credit, accelerated degree programs, student-designed majors, double majors, independent study, and a senior project. Special programs include cooperative education, summer session for credit, off-campus study, study-abroad, and Army, Navy and Air Force ROTC. The most frequently chosen baccalaureate fields are engineering/engineering technologies, computer/information sciences, and biological/life sciences. The faculty at WPI has 237 full-time members, 97% with terminal degrees. The student-faculty ratio is 13:1.

Students of WPI The student body totals 3,802, of whom 2,767 are undergraduates. 22.9% are women and 77.1% are men. Students come from 45 states and territories and 36 other countries. 50% are from Massachusetts. 4.8% are international students. 92% returned for their sophomore year.

Applying WPI requires an essay, SAT I and SAT II or ACT, a high school transcript, and 1 recommendation. The school recommends an interview. Application deadline: 2/1; 3/1 priority date for financial aid. Early and deferred admission are possible.

WORCESTER STATE COLLEGE

Worcester, MA

Urban setting ■ Public ■ State-supported ■ Coed

Web site: www.worcester.edu

Contact: Mr. Alan Kines, Director of Admissions, 486 Chandler Street, Administration Building, Room 204, Worcester, MA 01602-2597

Telephone: 508-929-8758 or toll-free 866-WSC-CALL **Fax:** 508-929-8183

E-mail: admissions@worcester.edu

Getting in Last Year 2,834 applied; 51% were accepted; 494 enrolled (34%).

Financial Matters $3273 resident tuition and fees (2002–03); $9353 nonresident tuition and fees (2002–03); $5452 room and board; $3980 average financial aid amount received per undergraduate (2001–02).

Academics WSC awards bachelor's and master's degrees. Challenging opportunities include advanced placement credit, accelerated degree programs, an honors program, double majors, and independent study. Special programs include internships, summer session for credit, off-campus study, study-abroad, and Army, Navy and Air Force ROTC. The most frequently chosen baccalaureate fields are health professions and related sciences, business/marketing, and psychology. The faculty at WSC has 166 full-time members, 71% with terminal degrees. The student-faculty ratio is 17:1.

Students of WSC The student body totals 5,532, of whom 4,833 are undergraduates. 61.5% are women and 38.5% are men. Students come from 20 states and territories and 84 other countries. 97% are from Massachusetts. 3% are international students. 74% returned for their sophomore year.

Applying WSC requires a high school transcript and a minimum high school GPA of 3.0, and in some cases SAT I or ACT. Application deadline: 6/1; 3/1 priority date for financial aid. Early and deferred admission are possible.

WORLD COLLEGE

Virginia Beach, VA

Suburban setting ■ Private ■ Proprietary ■ Coed

Web site: www.worldcollege.net

Contact: Mr. Michael Smith, Director of Operations and Registrar, 5193 Shore Drive, Suite 105, Virginia Beach, VA 23455

Telephone: 757-464-4600 or toll-free 800-696-7532 **Fax:** 757-464-3687

E-mail: instruct@cie-wc.edu

Academics World College awards bachelor's degrees (offers only external degree programs). Challenging opportunities include accelerated degree programs and a senior project. The most frequently chosen baccalaureate field is education. The faculty at World College has 6 full-time members.

Students of World College The student body is made up of 355 undergraduates. Students come from 50 states and territories and 25 other countries.

Applying World College requires a high school transcript. Application deadline: rolling admissions. Early admission is possible.

WRIGHT STATE UNIVERSITY

Dayton, OH

Suburban setting ■ Public ■ State-supported ■ Coed

Web site: www.wright.edu

Wright State University (continued)

Contact: Ms. Cathy Davis, Director of Undergraduate Admissions, 3640 Colonel Glenn Highway, Dayton, OH 45435
Telephone: 937-775-5700 or toll-free 800-247-1770 **Fax:** 937-775-5795
E-mail: admissions@wright.edu

Getting in Last Year 4,390 applied; 92% were accepted; 2,356 enrolled (58%).

Financial Matters $5361 resident tuition and fees (2002–03); $10,524 nonresident tuition and fees (2002–03); $5772 room and board; $7857 average financial aid amount received per undergraduate.

Academics Wright State awards associate, bachelor's, master's, doctoral, and first-professional degrees and post-bachelor's certificates. Challenging opportunities include advanced placement credit, student-designed majors, and an honors program. Special programs include cooperative education, internships, summer session for credit, off-campus study, study-abroad, and Army and Air Force ROTC. The most frequently chosen baccalaureate fields are business/marketing, education, and communications/communication technologies. The faculty at Wright State has 512 full-time members. The student-faculty ratio is 20:1.

Students of Wright State The student body totals 16,517, of whom 12,531 are undergraduates. 57.1% are women and 42.9% are men. Students come from 49 states and territories and 69 other countries. 97% are from Ohio. 1.1% are international students. 73% returned for their sophomore year.

Applying Wright State requires SAT I or ACT and a high school transcript. The school recommends a minimum high school GPA of 2.0. Application deadline: rolling admissions; 2/15 priority date for financial aid. Early and deferred admission are possible.

XAVIER UNIVERSITY

Cincinnati, OH

Suburban setting ■ Private ■ Independent Religious ■ Coed

Web site: www.xu.edu
Contact: Mr. Marc Camille, Dean of Admission, 3800 Victory Parkway, Cincinnati, OH 45207-5311
Telephone: 513-745-3301 or toll-free 800-344-4698 **Fax:** 513-745-4319
E-mail: xuadmit@xu.edu

Getting in Last Year 3,514 applied; 83% were accepted; 757 enrolled (26%).

Financial Matters $18,020 tuition and fees (2002–03); $7600 room and board; 77% average percent of need met; $12,947 average financial aid amount received per undergraduate.

Academics Xavier awards associate, bachelor's, master's, and doctoral degrees and post-bachelor's and post-master's certificates. Challenging opportunities include advanced placement credit, an honors program, double majors, independent study, and a senior project. Special programs include cooperative education, internships, summer session for credit, off-campus study, study-abroad, and Army and Air Force ROTC. The most frequently chosen baccalaureate fields are business/marketing, liberal arts/general studies, and communications/communication technologies. The faculty at Xavier has 268 full-time members, 81% with terminal degrees. The student-faculty ratio is 13:1.

Students of Xavier The student body totals 6,573, of whom 3,942 are undergraduates. 58.1% are women and 41.9% are men. Students come from 46 states and territories and 51 other countries. 66% are from Ohio. 2.6% are international students. 88% returned for their sophomore year.

Applying Xavier requires an essay, SAT I or ACT, a high school transcript, and 1 recommendation. The school recommends an interview. Application deadline: 2/1; 2/15 priority date for financial aid. Early and deferred admission are possible.

XAVIER UNIVERSITY OF LOUISIANA

New Orleans, LA

Urban setting ■ Private ■ Independent Religious ■ Coed

Web site: www.xula.edu
Contact: Mr. Winston Brown, Dean of Admissions, 1 Drexel Drive, New Orleans, LA 70125
Telephone: 504-483-7388 **Fax:** 504-485-7941
E-mail: apply@xula.edu

Getting in Last Year 3,862 applied; 87% were accepted; 976 enrolled (29%).

Financial Matters $10,900 tuition and fees (2002–03); $6000 room and board; 12% average percent of need met; $9159 average financial aid amount received per undergraduate.

Academics Xavier awards bachelor's, master's, and first-professional degrees and post-master's certificates. Challenging opportunities include advanced placement credit, accelerated degree programs, freshman honors college, an honors program, double majors, and a senior project. Special programs include cooperative education, internships, summer session for credit, off-campus study, study-abroad, and Army, Navy and Air Force ROTC. The most frequently chosen baccalaureate fields are biological/life sciences, physical sciences, and psychology. The faculty at Xavier has 226 full-time members, 91% with terminal degrees. The student-faculty ratio is 16:1.

Students of Xavier The student body totals 3,994, of whom 3,184 are undergraduates. 74.2% are women and 25.8% are men. Students come from 48 states and territories and 27 other countries. 48% are from Louisiana. 1.5% are international students. 73% returned for their sophomore year.

Applying Xavier requires SAT I or ACT, a high school transcript, 1 recommendation, and a minimum high school GPA of 2.0, and in some cases an interview. Application deadline: 3/1; 1/1 priority date for financial aid.

YALE UNIVERSITY

New Haven, CT

Urban setting ■ Private ■ Independent ■ Coed

Web site: www.yale.edu
Contact: Admissions Director, PO Box 208234, New Haven, CT 06520-8324
Telephone: 203-432-9300 **Fax:** 203-432-9392
E-mail: undergraduate.admissions@yale.edu

Getting in Last Year 15,466 applied; 8% were accepted; 1,300 enrolled (100%).

Financial Matters $27,130 tuition and fees (2002–03); $8240 room and board; 100% average percent of need met; $25,501 average financial aid amount received per undergraduate.

Academics Yale awards bachelor's, master's, doctoral, and first-professional degrees and post-master's certificates. Challenging opportunities include advanced placement credit, accelerated degree programs, student-designed majors, an honors program, double majors, independent study, and a senior project. Special programs include summer session for credit, study-abroad, and Army and Air Force ROTC. The most frequently chosen baccalaureate fields are social sciences and history, biological/life sciences, and English. The faculty at Yale has 994 full-time members, 89% with terminal degrees. The student-faculty ratio is 7:1.

Students of Yale The student body totals 11,378, of whom 5,339 are undergraduates. 49.8% are women and 50.2% are men. Students come from 55 states and territories and 74 other countries. 10% are from Connecticut. 7.9% are international students. 98% returned for their sophomore year.

Applying Yale requires an essay, SAT I and SAT II or ACT, a high school transcript, and 3 recommendations. The school recommends an interview. Application deadline: 12/31; 3/1 priority date for financial aid. Early and deferred admission are possible.

YORK COLLEGE

York, NE

Small-town setting ■ Private ■ Independent Religious ■ Coed

Web site: www.york.edu
Contact: Ms. Kristin Mathews, Associate Director of Admissions, 1125 East 8th Street, York, NE 68467-2699
Telephone: 402-363-5629 or toll-free 800-950-9675 **Fax:** 402-363-5623
E-mail: enroll@york.edu

Getting in Last Year 353 applied; 68% were accepted; 123 enrolled (51%).

Financial Matters $11,100 tuition and fees (2002–03); $3400 room and board; 80% average percent of need met.

Academics York awards associate and bachelor's degrees. Challenging opportunities include advanced placement credit, an honors program, double majors, independent study, and a senior project. Special programs include cooperative education, internships, summer session for credit, study-abroad, and Army, Navy and Air Force ROTC. The most frequently chosen baccalaureate fields are education, business/marketing, and psychology. The faculty at York has 24 full-time members, 46% with terminal degrees. The student-faculty ratio is 12:1.

Students of York The student body is made up of 462 undergraduates. 52.8% are women and 47.2% are men. Students come from 32 states and territories. 28% are from Nebraska. 0.6% are international students. 84% returned for their sophomore year.

Applying York requires SAT I or ACT, a high school transcript, and 2 recommendations, and in some cases a minimum high school GPA of 2.0. The school recommends a minimum high school GPA of 2.0. Application deadline: rolling admissions; 4/30 priority date for financial aid. Early and deferred admission are possible.

YORK COLLEGE OF PENNSYLVANIA

York, PA

Suburban setting ■ Private ■ Independent ■ Coed

Web site: www.ycp.edu
Contact: Mrs. Nancy L. Spataro, Director of Admissions, York, PA 17405-7199
Telephone: 717-849-1600 or toll-free 800-455-8018 **Fax:** 717-849-1607
E-mail: admissions@ycp.edu

Getting in Last Year 3,993 applied; 72% were accepted; 944 enrolled (33%).

Financial Matters $8000 tuition and fees (2002–03); $5570 room and board; 68% average percent of need met; $6625 average financial aid amount received per undergraduate.

Academics York awards associate, bachelor's, and master's degrees. Challenging opportunities include advanced placement credit, accelerated degree programs, student-designed majors, and a senior project. Special programs include internships, summer session for credit, and study-abroad. The most frequently chosen baccalaureate fields are business/marketing, health professions and related sciences, and education. The faculty at York has 141 full-time members, 78% with terminal degrees. The student-faculty ratio is 15:1.

Students of York The student body totals 5,463, of whom 5,259 are undergraduates. 60% are women and 40% are men. Students come from 32 states and territories and 35 other countries. 55% are from Pennsylvania. 1% are international students. 82% returned for their sophomore year.

Applying York requires an essay, SAT I or ACT, and a high school transcript, and in some cases an interview. The school recommends 1 recommendation. Application deadline: rolling admissions; 3/1 priority date for financial aid. Early and deferred admission are possible.

YORK COLLEGE OF THE CITY UNIVERSITY OF NEW YORK

Jamaica, NY

Urban setting ■ Public ■ State and locally supported ■ Coed

Web site: www.york.cuny.edu

Contact: Ms. Sally Nelson, Director of Admissions, 94-20 Guy R. Brewer Boulevard, Jamaica, NY 11451

Telephone: 718-262-2165 **Fax:** 718-262-2601

Getting in Last Year 2,389 applied; 31% were accepted; 594 enrolled (80%).

Financial Matters $3442 resident tuition and fees (2002–03); $7042 nonresident tuition and fees (2002–03).

Academics York awards bachelor's degrees. Challenging opportunities include advanced placement credit, an honors program, double majors, and independent study. Special programs include cooperative education, internships, summer session for credit, off-campus study, and Army and Air Force ROTC. The most frequently chosen baccalaureate fields are psychology, business/marketing, and education. The faculty at York has 166 full-time members, 73% with terminal degrees. The student-faculty ratio is 15:1.

Students of York The student body is made up of 5,748 undergraduates. 71.2% are women and 28.8% are men. Students come from 4 states and territories and 100 other countries. 7% are international students. 88% returned for their sophomore year.

Applying York requires SAT I or ACT, a high school transcript, and a minimum high school GPA of 2.0, and in some cases a minimum high school GPA of 2.5. The school recommends a minimum high school GPA of 3.0. Application deadline: rolling admissions. Deferred admission is possible.

YORK UNIVERSITY

Toronto, ON Canada

Urban setting ■ Public ■ Coed

Web site: www.yorku.ca

Contact: Vanessa Grafi, International Recruitment Officer, 140 Atkinson Building, Toronto, ON M3J 1P3 Canada

Telephone: 416-736-5825 **Fax:** 416-650-8195

E-mail: intlenq@yorku.ca

Getting in Last Year 35,394 applied; 31% were accepted.

Financial Matters $4876 nonresident tuition and fees (2002–03); $5696 room and board.

Academics York awards bachelor's, master's, doctoral, and first-professional degrees and post-bachelor's and post-master's certificates. Challenging opportunities include advanced placement credit, accelerated degree programs, student-designed majors, an honors program, double majors, independent study, and a senior project. Special programs include internships, summer session for credit, off-campus study, and study-abroad. The faculty at York has 1,226 full-time members.

Students of York The student body totals 46,974, of whom 43,635 are undergraduates. 60.1% are women and 39.9% are men. 97% are from Ontario.

Applying York requires SAT I or ACT, a high school transcript, audition/evaluation for fine arts program, supplemental applications for business and environmental studies, and a minimum high school GPA of 3.0, and in some cases an essay, an interview, and 1 recommendation. Application deadline: 4/1. Early and deferred admission are possible.

YOUNGSTOWN STATE UNIVERSITY

Youngstown, OH

Urban setting ■ Public ■ State-supported ■ Coed

Web site: www.ysu.edu

Contact: Ms. Sue Davis, Director of Undergraduate Admissions, One University Plaza, Youngstown, OH 44555-0001

Telephone: 330-941-2000 or toll-free 877-468-6978 (in-state), 877-466-6978 (out-of-state) **Fax:** 330-941-3674

E-mail: enroll@ysu.edu

Getting in Last Year 4,210 applied; 100% were accepted; 2,172 enrolled (52%).

Financial Matters $4996 resident tuition and fees (2002–03); $9748 nonresident tuition and fees (2002–03); $5320 room and board.

Academics YSU awards associate, bachelor's, master's, and doctoral degrees and post-bachelor's certificates. Challenging opportunities include advanced placement credit, accelerated degree programs, student-designed majors, an honors program, double majors, and a senior project. Special programs include cooperative education, internships, summer session for credit, off-campus study, study-abroad, and Army and Air Force ROTC. The most frequently chosen baccalaureate fields are education, business/marketing, and protective services/public administration. The faculty at YSU has 402 full-time members, 84% with terminal degrees. The student-faculty ratio is 18:1.

Students of YSU The student body totals 12,698, of whom 11,375 are undergraduates. 54.4% are women and 45.6% are men. Students come from 37 states and territories and 51 other countries. 91% are from Ohio. 0.8% are international students. 71% returned for their sophomore year.

Applying YSU requires SAT I or ACT and a high school transcript, and in some cases an interview. Application deadline: 8/15; 2/15 priority date for financial aid. Early and deferred admission are possible.

NOTES

NOTES

NOTES

NOTES

NOTES

THOMSON
PETERSON'S